Contents

Literature of the Middle Ages and the Renaissance

Literature of the Seventeenth and Eighteenth Centuries

Literature of the Nineteenth Century

Turn-of-the-Century Literature

Modernist Literature

Contemporary Literature

Preface

"Books continue each other," Virginia Woolf reminds us in *A Room of One's Own*, advising her readers to consider contemporary fiction by women "as if it were the last volume in a fairly long series. . . ." She was recommending that her audience contemplate the connections between the Restoration iconoclast Aphra Behn, the eighteenth-century lyricist Anne Finch, and the four great novelists of the nineteenth century—Jane Austen, Charlotte Brontë, Emily Brontë, and George Eliot. By implication, moreover, Woolf was also arguing that such American writers as Harriet Beecher Stowe and Emily Dickinson, Sarah Orne Jewett and Zora Neale Hurston, ought to be included in the tradition she was subtly defining. Yet sound as it is, her advice has been difficult to follow, for even now—half a century after she wrote *A Room of One's Own*—no single anthology has represented the exuberant variety yet strong continuity of the literature that English-speaking women have produced between the fourteenth century and the present. In the *Norton Anthology of Literature by Women*, we are attempting to do just that.

By gathering in a single volume a range of literary works in which women writers have expressed their sometimes problematic, sometimes triumphant relationship to culture and society, our collection seeks to recover a long and often neglected literary history. Although this history cannot be adequately defined by the categories and chronology customarily used to organize "mainstream" literature, its contours document Woolf's thesis that women's "books continue each other." Complementing and supplementing the standard Norton anthologies of English and American literature, *NALW* should help readers for the first time to appreciate fully the female literary tradition which, for several centuries, has coexisted with, revised, and influenced male literary models. Designed to serve as a "core-curriculum" text for the many courses in literature by women that have been developed over the past ten years, this collection includes examples of women's work in every genre and period; it thus carries on the tradition of a "course in a book" pioneered by the other Norton anthologies of British and American literature which have proved so consistently useful.

Like all historically oriented Norton anthologies, our volume provides a broad chronological overview of every aspect of its subject—an overview, that is, of both the evolution and the revolutions of women's literature (and women's images of women) in England, America, Canada, Australia, and other English-speaking countries. Ranging from the fourteenth century, when women's writings were first preserved, through the seventeenth century, when women first began to publish their writings, to the rich vitality of the present, our table of contents includes distinguished selections from the works of such figures as Anne Bradstreet, Anne Finch, Mary Wollstonecraft, Jane Austen, Mary Shelley, Elizabeth Barrett Browning, Margaret Fuller, Harriet Beecher Stowe, the Brontës, George Eliot, Emily Dickinson, Christina Rossetti, Kate Chopin, Olive Schreiner, Charlotte Perkins Gilman, Edith Wharton, Willa Cather, Gertrude Stein, Virginia Woolf, H.D., Katherine Mansfield, Zora Neale Hurston, Doris Lessing, Flannery O'Connor, Adrienne Rich, Toni Morrison, Sylvia Plath, and Margaret Atwood, as well as samples of the works of many others. In a number of cases, moreover, the writings of both well-known and comparatively little-known authors are here made accessible to the general reader for the first time. (Our texts by Jane Lead, for instance, have heretofore only been available in rare book rooms; some of our selections by Cavendish, Finch, Edgeworth, Barrett Browning, Rossetti, and Eliot have never been reprinted in widely available popular editions; our texts by Lorraine Hansberry, Ruth Stone, and Margaret Drabble include work that has never before been published in book form.)

Perhaps it will be helpful to explain our principles of selection and organization. To begin with, we believe that, though conventional literary periodization does not suit women's literary history, women's history does have significant phases of its own. Thus, we have omitted references to the usual literary "ages" (i.e., Augustan, Romantic, Victorian) and instead organized our authors by birthdate into six eras, which our "period introductions" attempt to discuss in a way that will reveal the historical and thematic coherence of the material within each section: 1) Literature of the Middle Ages and the Renaissance; 2) Literature of the Seventeenth and Eighteenth Centuries; 3) Literature of the Nineteenth Century; 4) Turn-of-the-Century Literature; 5) Modernist Literature; 6) Contemporary Literature. In addition, because we believe that what historians have begun to call "female culture" expresses itself across both generic and national boundaries, our anthology integrates generically diverse texts—poems, stories, essays, memoirs, plays, novels, and letters—produced in and about geographically various contexts—England, the United States, Canada, New Zealand, Africa, and Australia; all these texts, of course, have in common the fact that they were originally composed in English.

Less widely known figures such as Phillis Wheatley, Mary Elizabeth Coleridge, Alice Meynell, Alice Dunbar-Nelson, and Radclyffe Hall we have tried to represent by what we consider their most teachable and typical work; we have tried also, wherever possible, to place the writings of these women in their relevant sociocultural contexts by including important documents by feminist polemicists—Margaret Fuller, Sojourner Truth, Elizabeth Cady Stanton, and Lorraine Hansberry. We are particularly glad that we have been able to recover works by comparatively neglected women artists—Jane Lead, Rebecca Cox Jackson, Elizabeth Drew Stoddard, Charlotte Mew, Anzia Yezierska, Mourning Dove, and Anna Wickham. Finally, we have sought to reprint texts by writers from as many English-speaking countries as possible, including selections by H. H. Richardson, Katharine Susannah Prichard, and Judith Wright (Australia); Dorothy Livesay, Alice Munro, P. K. Page, Margaret Laurence, and Margaret Atwood (Canada); Nadine Gordimer (South Africa); Lady Augusta Gregory and Edna O'Brien (Ireland); Kamala Das (India); and Ama Ata Aidoo (Ghana). Together, these texts not only emphasize the vitality of women's literary history, they also allow us to trace a number of traditions within that history—the black, the regional, the lesbian, the working-class, and the native-American traditions—as well as to document the many ways in which women poets and fiction writers have confronted female experiences of creation and procreation, marriage and maternity, adolescence and aging, desire and death.

Of course, no anthology can pretend to completeness. Editors inevitably find themselves unable to keep up with the rapid evolution of new literary movements and traditions. In addition, permissions problems sometimes lead to the exclusion of important texts, and space restrictions often require similar exclusions. Thus we regret that we have been unable to represent such increasingly self-aware movements as those currently being pioneered by Chicanas and Italian-American women. Similarly, we are sorry that we could not obtain permission to reprint works by the modernist poet/critic Laura (Riding) Jackson and by the contemporary British playwright Caryl Churchill. Finally, however, we regret that even in this compendious volume, we have not had room to include texts by countless women writers whose achievements we much admire. We are convinced, however, that the texts we have included in *NALW* will, at the very least, suggest the contours of the canon into which readers will be able to assimilate the works of many other women authors, both those who are writing now and those who have written in the past. In addition, whatever the subject, form, or provenance of *NALW*'s texts, we believe that throughout this anthology we have reprinted works whose historical, intellectual, or aesthetic significance seems to us clearly to merit their inclusion.

At the same time, because we wish to celebrate the continuing tradition Woolf implicitly defined in *A Room of One's Own*, we have allotted a special amount of space in this book to the notable literary achievements of the figures we listed earlier. We reprint a rich range of poems by Bradstreet and Dickinson, Barrett Browning and H. D., as well as long stories or novellas by, for example, Cather and Lessing. We have, furthermore, included, in their entirety, Charlotte Brontë's *Jane Eyre*, Kate Chopin's *The Awakening*, and Toni Morrison's *The Bluest Eye*, not only because they are three novels frequently taught in women's literature courses but also because their plots, themes, and images have been especially important in delineating the distinctively female literary tradition that our anthology charts. In addition, because one of these novels is about Victorian England, another about turn-of-the-century America, and the third about contemporary black culture, we feel that among them they indicate the varied historical roots as well as the thematic range of women's literary heritage. Finally, because these novels draw on modes and materials with which many women writers have characteristically worked—each is a form of *Bildungsroman*, and focuses on problems of gender—each novel summarizes influential earlier traditions and at the same time forecasts crucial later developments in those traditions.

Because it was impossible to reprint novels by all the major nineteenth- and twentieth-century women writers of prose fiction, for some figures—Jane Austen, George Eliot, and Virginia Woolf—we have selected important but sometimes difficult-to-obtain shorter works, works which significantly illuminate the relationship between these artists and the female literary culture within which they knew they were writing. Thus we have represented Jane Austen by *Love and Freindship*, a witty early story that casts interesting light upon her later major novels while also illustrating both the sentimental education accorded Regency ladies and the parodic stance by which some women resisted that education. Similarly, we have represented George Eliot and Virginia Woolf by essays and stories that illuminate their longer works while also documenting the self-consciousness with which these writers situated themselves and their texts in specifically female and often feminist contexts. George Eliot's *The Lifted Veil* reveals a new aspect of this versatile artist, namely her awareness and dramatic use of what the literary critic Ellen Moers has called "female Gothic," while Eliot's *Brother and Sister* sonnet sequence glosses the ambivalent sibling relationship that is central to *The Mill on the Floss*. In the case of Virginia Woolf, we have included, along with some of her major critical and specifically feminist statements, autobiographical and fictional works which demonstrate her own persistent participation in the literary tradition which she herself defined.

Adopting editorial procedures that have proved helpful in other Norton anthologies, we have in every case used what seemed to us the most accurate texts. In some instances, in order to make a work more easily accessible to the reader, we have modernized spelling and Americanized punctuation; otherwise, the spelling and punctuation of our texts is that of their authors or—as in the case of, say, Charlotte and Emily Brontë or Emily Dickinson—their editors. After every selection, we have indicated the date of first periodical or book publication (and, when appropriate, the date of a revised reprinting) on the right; whenever the facts are available, we have also indicated the date of composition on the left. Difficult allusions, foreign phrases, unfamiliar idioms, and arcane words have been glossed in annotations at the bottom of the page. Whenever we found it necessary to present a text only in part, we have indicated internal cuts by three asterisks, and prefaced the title of the work by the word "from." If we have supplied our own title for an excerpt, that title is enclosed in square brackets. A selected bibliography in standard Norton format has been provided at the end of the volume in order to encourage and expedite further reading and research by students.

In addition, we have tried to compose headnotes and period introductions that are as lucid and informative as possible, providing necessary historical and biographical background without interposing our own critical interpretations between the reader and the text. Following our usual collaborative procedures, each of the two editors drafted approximately half the headnotes, then exchanged and helped revise the drafts of the other editor. Two period introductions—those on Literature of the Middle Ages and the Renaissance and on Contemporary Literature—were written entirely in collaboration, while the other four were composed individually, then exchanged and revised: Susan Gubar drafted the introductions to Literature of the Seventeenth and Eighteenth Centuries and Turn-of-the-Century Literature; Sandra Gilbert drafted the introductions to Literature of the Nineteenth Century and Modernist Literature.

In conclusion, we should note that much of the scholarly apparatus we have assembled, many of the texts we have included, and a good deal of the material we have incorporated into headnotes and period introductions would not have been available to us were it not for the work that feminist critics and scholars in women's studies have produced over the past fifteen years. We began these prefatory remarks with a reference to Virginia Woolf's pioneering essay on women and fiction; we want to acknowledge now our deep intellectual indebtedness to the hundreds of teachers all over the world who have recently responded to Woolf's impassioned explanation that "we think back through our mothers if we are women" by laboring to recover the female literary inheritance that we have attempted to reconstitute here. We have included a separate list of acknowledgements in which we thank the many teachers, critics, and scholars who prepared detailed critiques of our material or offered special textual suggestions, but their ideas—like our own—seem to us to be part of a larger and ongoing collective enterprise on the part of countless researchers to whom we must all be profoundly grateful.

We want also to express our gratitude to a number of research and secretarial assistants, institutions, colleagues, friends, and relatives whose aid facilitated our work on this project. Specifically, we thank Vivienne Thompson, Catherine Thompson, and Huma Ibrahim for their library work, Susan Leonardi for her crucial bibliographical assistance, and Rachel Teplow for her consistent attention to countless editorial details. We thank, too, Reba Amerson, Anne Cabello, Kristi Hover, Gary Konas, and Janet Turner for secretarial assistance, and Tufts University, Indiana University, and the University of California, Davis, for financial support. In addition, we wish to thank a number of colleagues and friends—notably Edwin Barber, Mary Burgan, Gina Campbell, Joyce Gilbert, Donald Gray, Kenneth Gros Louis, Leonard Gubar, Carolyn Heilbrun, Nancy K. Palmquist, Charlotte Sheedy, Elaine Showalter, Barry Wade, Nancy Wechsler and Mary Jo Weaver —for advice and assistance with many matters. Sandra Gilbert wishes to thank, as well, the members of her class at Williams College, English 219, during the fall of 1984; Susan Gubar wishes to thank Indiana University's Institute for Advanced Study. And we are grateful to members of our families—Elliot, Roger, Katherine, and Susanna Gilbert, and Edward, Molly, and Simone Gubar—for frequent acts of kindness and even of critical or secretarial assistance, as well as for what at times seemed almost superhuman tolerance and grace under pressure.

Finally, though, our greatest debt is to three co-workers who in some sense helped author this book. The scholarly diligence of Roger Gilbert, not only a family member but also a graduate student at Yale University, helped produce scrupulous and detailed annotations. The wise counsel of M. H. Abrams, Class of 1916 Professor of English at Cornell University and Norton's advisor on English texts, helped shape a strong table of contents along with historically balanced period introductions. The enthusiastic support, editorial expertise, and intellectual vitality of John Benedict, our editor at Norton, quite simply transformed a utopian project into a concrete reality. With his unflagging assistance, we have tried to fashion a book that will define the ways in which the female imagination has struggled to articulate visions and revisions of a literature energized by female consciousness, impelled by female creativity, and empowered by female community.

Acknowledgments

Among our many advisors and friends, the following were of special help in providing critiques of particular periods or of the anthology as a whole, or assisting in preparing texts and editorial matter: Elizabeth Abel (University of California, Berkeley), Jerry C. Beasley (University of Delaware), Ann Beltran (Indiana University), Dorothy Berkson (Lewis and Clark College), Frank Bidart (Wellesley College), Elyse Blankley (University of California, Davis), Sylvia Bowerbank (McMaster University), Claire Brooke, Lisa Browar (Vassar College), Lawrence Buell (Oberlin College), Carolyn Burke (University of California, Santa Cruz), Carol Christ (University of California, Berkeley), Barbara Christian (University of California, Berkeley), Keith Christiansen (The Metropolitan Museum of Art) Bonnie Costello (Boston University), Carmen Cramer (Southwestern Louisiana University), Philip Daghlian (Indiana University), Brenda Daly (University of Minnesota), Joanne Feit Diehl (University of California, Davis), Mary C. Erler (Fordham University), Stuart Friebert (Oberlin College), Susan Stanford Friedman (University of Wisconsin, Madison), Judith Kegan Gardiner (University of Illinois, Chicago Circle), Blanche Gelfant (Dartmouth College), Albert Gelpi (Stanford University), Barbara Gelpi (Stanford University), Barbara Godard (York University), Gayle Greene (Scripps College), Ron Hafft (Indiana University), Helen Hoy (Lethbridge University, Alberta), Gloria Hull (University of Delaware), Rhynette Hurd (Memphis State University), Kay Isenman, Marean Jordan (University of California, Davis), Barbara Johnson (Harvard University), Luke Johnson (Indiana University), Sydney Janet Kaplan (University of Washington), Philip Kelley (Wedgestone Press), Cynthia Kinnard (Indiana University) Joan Lidoff (University of Texas, Austin), Joanna Lipking (Northwestern University), Lawrence Lipking (Northwestern University), Marlene Longenecker (Ohio State University), Dolores Gros Louis (Indiana University), Nan Bauer Maglin (Manhattan Community College), Ann Mandel, Jane Marcus (University of Texas, Austin), Francis O. Mattson (Rare Book Room, New York Public Library), Nora McGuinnis (University of California, Davis), Elizabeth Meese (University of Alabama), Ann

Messenger (Simon Fraser University, British Columbia), Diane Middlebrook (Stanford University), Adalaide Morris (University of Iowa), Carolyn Naylor (University of Santa Clara), Mary Nyquist (University of Toronto), Nadine Ollman (Drew University), Tillie Olsen, Alicia Ostriker (Rutgers University), Dolores Palomo (University of Washington), Ruth Perry (Massachusetts Institute of Technology), John Pope-Hennessy (The Metropolitan Museum of Art), Marjorie Pryse (University of Tennessee), Jarold Ramsey (University of Rochester), Tey Diana Rebolledo (University of Nevada, Reno), Maureen Reddy (University of Minnesota), Dolores Rosenblum (Indiana University), Samuel Schuman (Guilford College), Lloyd Schwartz (University of Massachusetts, Boston), Anthony Shipps (Indiana University), Merrill Skaggs (Drew University), Catherine Smith (Bucknell University), Murray Sperber (Indiana University), Ann Stanford (California State University), Erlene Stetson (Indiana University), Catharine Stimpson (Rutgers University), Jennifer Sutherland, Martha Vicinus (University of Michigan), Alan Williamson (University of California, Davis), Sandra Zagarell (Oberlin College).

The Norton Anthology
of Literature by Women

Literature of the Middle Ages and the Renaissance

The years that historians define as the Old English period, the Middle Ages, and the Renaissance constitute a time of important literary activity. From the first half of the eighth century, when scholars speculate that the great Anglo-Saxon epic called *Beowulf* was composed, to 1386–1400, when Geoffrey Chaucer wrote his *Canterbury Tales*, to 1603, when Shakespeare's *Hamlet* was first printed in London, these ages produced a number of classics. Besides *Beowulf*, the Old English era saw the composition of major poems like the *Wanderer* and the *Seafarer*. In the Middle Ages, besides the *Canterbury Tales*, artists created courtly romances such as *Sir Gawain and the Green Knight* (1374–1400), dream-visions such as *Piers Plowman* (c. 1372–1389), and religious dramas, including *The Second Shepherd's Play* (c. 1425) and *Everyman* (after 1485). Finally, the Renaissance years that fostered Shakespeare's astounding creativity also developed the talents of such poets as Edmund Spenser (*The Faerie Queene*, 1590, 1596, 1609), Christopher Marlowe (*Doctor Faustus*, 1604, 1616), Sir Philip Sidney (*Arcadia*, 1590, 1593), Thomas Wyatt, and Ben Jonson. It is significant, however, that all the writers who flourished in these periods were men. When we turn to the literary history of women in these nine hundred years, we find no texts in the Old English period that have been definitively identified as composed by women, hardly any works by medieval women, and very few indeed by Renaissance women.

The five female writers whose works we include here seem significantly representative of the types of women whose words have been preserved. A religious recluse, an eccentric preacher, a queen, the aristocratic sister of a famous poet, and the bohemian wife of a court musician, these early literary ladies lived lives which suggest that only women affiliated with the church or the court could take themselves seriously enough, and be taken seriously enough, to produce accounts of their experiences. What were their female contemporaries doing? No doubt some of them also wrote, but for the most part their works were evidently not thought worth saving, have been handed down to us anonymously, or have not yet been discovered in the attics, abbeys, and libraries where they may still be stored. It is likely, though, that most women did not write, first, because few had access to either the education or the social authority that would facilitate such activity, and second, because, mostly confined to the home—whether farm, castle, or convent—and constrained by cultural definitions of femininity, most had neither the experience of public life nor the expectation of an audience that would foster creativity.

No wonder, then, that our five authors were spiritually or socially exceptional: Julian of Norwich was a solitary visionary, Margery Kempe was impelled by inner voices to rebel against social conventions, Elizabeth I was England's most powerful and learned queen, Mary Sidney Herbert was the extraordinarily well educated and wealthy patroness of many Elizabethan intellectuals, and some scholars speculate that Amelia Lanier may actually have been the flirtatiously independent "Dark Lady" of Shakespeare's sonnets. Atypical in both education and intellectual authority, these women responded to spiritual movements and historical events from which most of their female counterparts were excluded.

Those events included a series of major political upheavals, a set of drastic social changes, and a dramatic succession of cultural transformations. In the years before Julian and Margery were born in the fourteenth century, English history had been shaped through the fifth-century invasion of the country by the Germanic tribes of the Angles, the Saxons, and the Jutes, as well as the eleventh-century conquest of the island by French (Norman) invaders. The Anglo-Saxon language in which the heroic saga *Beowulf* is written had metamorphosed, because of the Norman conquest, into a range of French-influenced dialects called Middle English, dialects in which such major works as *Sir Gawain and the Green Knight*, *Piers Plowman*, and *The Canterbury Tales* were composed. As English evolved, moreover, it became an ever more viable alternative to the Latin that had long been used by chroniclers, theologians, and poets to signify the seriousness of their work. In particular, it became a language in which women like Julian and Margery, who would probably never have studied Latin, could record their visions and lives.

But the lives that these women recorded must also have been determined by the shift from an essentially tribal Anglo-Saxon culture to a hierarchical society organized around a so-called feudal system in which serfs (peasants) swore loyalty to vassals (knights and landowners), who, in turn, pledged their allegiance to great lords, as well as by the slow disintegration of that system with the rise to power of a literate, mercantile, town-dwelling middle class. In addition, the lives of Julian and Margery must have been marked by the cultural centrality of the Roman Catholic Church, which increasingly dominated English life and letters after the seventh-century conversion of the Anglo Saxons to Christianity. Both women, after all, were associated with the church, and it is known that Margery was a member of the growing middle class. Julian's mystical revelations, moreover, were part of a long medieval tradition of spiritual meditations, while Margery's individualistic preachings reflect a tumultuous moment in church history, a moment when a number of revolutionary monastic orders arose throughout Europe, demanding spiritual reform.

Even more than Julian and Margery, however, Elizabeth I, Mary Sidney Herbert, and Amelia Lanier were involved in crucial political, social, and cultural events. Indeed, Elizabeth not only was shaped by such events, she shaped them. By the time Elizabeth came to the throne, the Middle English of Julian and Margery had developed into something much closer to modern English, and, as England was unified by Elizabeth's rule, the divergent dialects of the Middle Ages began to be consolidated into a single national language, laying the groundwork for the emergence of a national literature. Before Elizabeth's accession, moreover, the country, earlier divided by the fifteenth-century War of the Roses (which set the great houses of York and Lancaster against each other in a battle for the throne), had begun to be unified by two Tudor monarchs, Henry VII and Henry VIII. The most charismatic of the Tudor rulers, Elizabeth completed the transformation of what had been a comparatively fragmented feudal society into a centralized nation-state dominated by a single royal court. It was this court which facilitated literary production throughout the English Renaissance, and, not insignificantly therefore, both Mary Sidney Herbert and Amelia Lanier were members of courtly circles: their respective places are made clear by the fact that Lanier dedicated her poems to Herbert while Herbert dedicated hers to Elizabeth.

But these three women were not just associated with the centralized authority of the court, they were also learned ladies who had the rare good fortune to be educated in the fashion recommended by the new movement called humanism—that is, they had studied the classics and had been trained in the intricacies of Renaissance rhetoric and logic. Elaborately paradoxical, stylistically ornate, and ingeniously allusive, their verse embodies the humanist passion for polemical skill and classical knowledge that was imported to England from Italy during the sixteenth century by such thinkers as Sir Thomas More, the English author of *Utopia* (1516), and Desiderius Erasmus, the Dutch-born author of *In Praise of Folly* (1510). The lives of these women also coincided with the secularization of culture brought about by humanism's renewal of interest in the pre-Christian classics of Greece and Rome, by the increasing substitution of the vernacular for churchly Latin, by the growing literacy of the non-Latin-speaking middle class, by the new nationalism of the aristocracy, and by the Reformation's questioning of papal power. As the English church separated itself from, on the one hand, the Rome-dominated international hierarchy of Roman Catholicism and from, on the other hand, the German and Swiss Protestantism established by Luther and Calvin, it developed a distinctive national identity, with the English monarch replacing the pope as a central earthly symbol of sacred authority. Not surprisingly, this phenomenon, along with the rise of modern English and the dramatic strength of the queen, contributed to an extraordinary cultural vitality that expressed itself in the exuberant energy of Elizabethan literature, an energy that manifests itself in the words and works of both Herbert and Lanier.

Nevertheless, although their writings are infused with the energy of the age, it must be noted that not even these exceptional women were able to produce anything in the least comparable to the ambitious masterpieces created by their male contemporaries. While their lives and letters were no less shaped by prevailing aesthetic and intellectual movements than Julian's and Margery's had been, they were clearly not able to compose the number of elaborate sonnet-sequences, popular comedies and tragedies, or elegant romances and allegorical epics that male poets, dramatists, and prose stylists circulated in manuscripts, staged in the theatre, and published to critical acclaim. Just as important, the scarcity of women writers in both the Middle Ages and the Renaissance means that none of the authors we are studying here can be said to have belonged to literary communities comparable to the loosely organized groups of male writers who supported and encouraged the works of artists like Marlowe,

Shakespeare, and Jonson. That, in order to represent the earliest writings of English women, we have had to conflate three periods into one is simply the most dramatic sign of women's literary marginality in the years from 700 to 1600. Perhaps further evidence of their aesthetic dilemma is manifested in the themes and dreams recorded by those women who did manage to write. For while the works of Julian, Margery, Elizabeth, Mary Sidney Herbert, and Amelia Lanier mirror the varying spirits of their ages, they are also—no matter when they were written—distinctively and consistently concerned with the problems creativity posed for women, and they may therefore seem idiosyncratic when set against the texts of male contemporaries. Haunted by the images of women that men had constructed for them, these writers created a tradition which seeks either to redefine or to resign itself to male preconceptions about femininity. Specifically, in the years from the 1370s, when Julian began to describe her revelation of divine love in the *Book of Showings*, to the 1590s, when Mary Sidney Herbert undertook to translate the Psalms into English, women had to confront the misogyny of male theologians who sought to censure and silence them, as well as an ideal of courtly love that glamorized and glorified them in ways that were sometimes problematic.

MEDIEVAL AND RENAISSANCE IMAGES OF WOMEN

"By God," exclaimed Chaucer's Wife of Bath in a famous passage from *The Canterbury Tales*, "If wommen hadden writen stories / As clerkes han within hir oratories, / They wolde han writen of men more wikkednesse / Than al the merk of Adam may redresse." Afflicted by the book of "wikked wives" from which her fifth husband persistently read to her every evening, this lively female character was responding to the tradition of misogyny that extended from early church fathers like Saints Paul and Jerome to later theologians like Augustine and Tertullian; it was, indeed, a tradition that would reach beyond her author's lifetime into the antifemale diatribes of the *Malleus Maleficarum* ("Hammer of Witches," 1486), a fifteenth-century German handbook for witch hunters, into the portrait of the dissembling seductress Duessa in Edmund Spenser's *The Faerie Queene*, and into the punitive subjugation of Kate in William Shakespeare's *The Taming of the Shrew* (1594). While it is clear that no book of "wikked wives" will ever stifle Chaucer's exuberant Wife, such texts may well have inhibited her real-life contemporaries. Though, as we have seen, the two periods were in many ways very different, in the Middle Ages and the Renaissance alike even the most talented literary women were constrained by cultural strictures which implied that any intellectual ambition might mean they were evil. Worse still, such would-be writers had to struggle against gender definitions suggesting that femaleness itself was an intrinsically debased and secondary condition.

Defining woman's essential nature, Tertullian, the third-century philosopher of asceticism, proclaimed that she is a "temple built over a sewer." About women's history and particularly the culpability of Eve, the first woman, whose rebellious eating of forbidden fruit led to the fall of all humanity, the thirteenth-century writer Jacques de Vitry declared: "Between Adam and God in Paradise there was but one woman and she had no rest until she had succeeded in banishing her husband from the garden of delights and in condemning

Christ to the torment of the cross." About woman's biological character, the views of the first-century Roman philosopher Pliny persisted: "Contact with [menstrual fluid] turns new wine sour, crops touched by it become barren . . . the edge of steel and the gleam of ivory are dulled, hives of bees die, even bronze and iron are at once seized by rust, and a horrible smell fills the air." Nor were such views unique to the Judaeo-Christian tradition out of which these three thinkers wrote. The Anglo-Saxon culture which predated Christianity in England was oblivious of or hostile to women. Indeed, one of the few lyrics from this period which scholars have tentatively attributed to a woman—a piece called *The Wife's Lament* (c. 900)—begins with an impassioned complaint: "I make this song sadly about myself, / about my life. I a woman say / I've been unhappy since I grew up" (translation by Willis Barnstone and Elene Kolb). In *Beowulf*, the age's major epic, moreover, women are objects of exchange, servants to men, monsters, or mothers of monsters. Similarly, the Greek philosopher Aristotle had argued in the fourth century B.C. that woman is a "deformity of nature." That pre-Christian definition, combining with the Bible's excoriation of Eve, informed the work of such major medieval thinkers as Saint Augustine and Saint Thomas Aquinas, both of whom believed that women were physically and spiritually inferior to men.

But if Eve, the primordial female, was both secondary (created from Adam's rib) and destructive (a temptress who condemned humanity to death and degradation), she did have a positive counterpart: the mother of Christ, the Virgin Mary, who redeemed the world with the fruit of her womb. It might seem, then, that even though ambitious women were oppressed by what we now call "negative role models," they could gain strength from the sacred example of Mary. From the twelfth century to about the fifteenth, Mariolatry—the cult of the Virgin—swept Europe. As one historian has observed, "her miracles were on every lip," and "provided the stock themes for miracle plays," the festival dramas in which modern English theater had its origins. Indeed, in England, worship of the Blessed Mother seems often to have taken precedence over devotion to the Father and the Son, so much so that some scholars have seen the adoration of Mary as a lingering remnant of primitive religions which worshipped the Great Goddess. Whatever its origins, Mariolatry gave rise in sermons, songs, plays, and poems to celebrations of the female body and soul which directly controverted contemporary monastic misogyny, works in which even the sin of Eve was justified because it resulted in the sanctity of Mary, mother of the Redeemer of that sin.

A popular Middle English lyric summarized this potentially feminist theory of what has been called the *Fortunate Fall*, the idea that the calamity brought about by Eve's rebellion led to the redemption promised by Mary's sacred maternity:

> Ne hadde the appil take ben
> The appil taken ben,
> Ne hadde never our lady
> A ben hevene's quene
> Blessed be the time
> That appil take was
> Therefore we moun singen
> "Deo Gracias!"

Other poems, moreover, celebrated the paradox of Mary's maidenly mother-hood. The lyric that begins "I sing of a maiden / That is makelees" (matchless), for instance, affirms that "moder and maiden / Was nevere noon but she: / Wel may swich a lady / Godes moder be." Such texts implied that, far from being man's inferior, woman, made in Mary's image, might be his superior. As one medieval theologian argued:

> Woman is to be preferred to man, to wit in material: Adam made from clay and Eve from side of Adam; in place: Adam made outside paradise and Eve w'in; in conception: a woman conceived God which a man did not do; in apparition: Christ appeared to a woman after the Resurrection, to wit the Magdalene; in exaltation: a woman is exalted above the choirs of angels, to wit the Blessed Mary. St. Bernadine even declares thus: "It is a great grace to be a woman: more women are saved than men."

What is most noteworthy here is that Mary's grace sanctifies all women, even an ostensibly fallen one such as Christ's disciple the reformed prostitute Mary Magdalene. Thus, though Mary herself may have been unique—"alone of all her sex," as the title of Marina Warner's recent study of Mariolatry has it—even ordinary women are not to be excluded from the queendom of heaven that she rules.

The implications of such a vindication of the female were far-reaching. First, they put in question the presuppositions of antifemale clerics and instigated a dialogue between misogynists like the author of the sardonic French *Quinze Joies de Mariage* ("The Fifteen Joys of Marriage") and defenders of women like the Chaucer of *The Legend of Good Women*, a long poem praising female virtue. Second, they even transformed some of the philosophical foundations of Western literature. From Plato on, the European world view had been based on what A. O. Lovejoy called "The Great Chain of Being," a hierarchy of the created world which extended from God down through man to woman and then to animals, plants, and stones. With the ascendancy of Mary, however, came a seemingly subversive revision of this system of stratification. For some late medieval writers, it was a mortal woman, a blessed beloved such as Dante's Beatrice or Petrarch's Laura, who mediated between God and the writer in just the way that the immortal Mary mediated between God and man. Influenced by Mariolatry, these artists were also working out of a tradition of courtly love which functioned as a secular counterpoint to the cult of our Lady. As early as the twelfth century, lyricists called troubadours in France and Minnesingers in Germany had begun to praise the elegance and excellence of aristocratic ladies, to whom they swore fealty and dedicated their art. Their poems set a fashion which spread rapidly from the courts of France, Germany, and Italy to the English court and thence to the great castles of aristocrats in all these nations. Works like Gottfried Von Strassbourg's *Tristan*, Guillaume de Loris's *Roman de la Rose* ("The Romance of the Rose") Part I, Petrarch's sonnets to Laura, and Dante's *La Vita Nuova* ("The New Life") marked the culmination of this tradition, which for the first time identified secular desire with spiritual love, the creation of poetry with the consecration of prayer. In *Tristan*, the Cave of Love is a sacred place; in *La Vita Nuova*, Beatrice is an earthly angel; in the *Roman de la Rose*, the rose, representative of the beloved lady, is an emblem of heavenly perfection. For all these poets, and for the knights who followed the fashion they set, love was—in the phrase of the noted medieval historian Eileen Power—"feudalized," for "the lover served his lady as humbly as the vassal served his lord."

Even during the Renaissance, when medieval feudalism had begun to disintegrate, the conventions of courtly love persisted in literature, if not in life. Sir Philip Sidney's prose narrative *Arcadia*, for instance, recounts the romances of knights and ladies in a pastoral realm where the art of love represents an aesthetic ideal, while his sonnet sequence *Astrophel and Stella* (1582) explores the poet-lover's feelings for his mistress on the assumption that such passionate emotions toward a beloved woman were the most appropriate subject for lyric poetry. Influenced by the highly stylized modes and elaborately romantic themes of "Petrarchanism," a literary movement that began in Italy with Petrarch and was brought to England by Sir Thomas Wyatt, Sidney was only one of the many major Renaissance poets who produced such sonnet cycles meditating on the rapture and torment of man's love for woman. Others included Spenser (*Amoretti*, 1595), Samuel Daniel (*Delia*, 1592), and Shakespeare (*Sonnets*, 1609). In the same years when these writers were composing their celebratory sonnets, moreover, Edmund Spenser's *The Faerie Queene* offered images of pure and powerful heroines such as Una, Gloriana, and Britomart.

Ennobling and empowering as the rhetoric of Mariolatry, the rhymes of courtly love, the sonnets of Petrarchanism, and the allegorical figures of Spenser might seem to have been for women, however, they still retained traces of the very misogyny they would appear to have replaced. About Mary, after all, one lyric declared "moder and maiden / Was nevere noon but she": no earthly woman could achieve such paradoxical grandeur. As for courtly love, it too posed problems. Highly stylized and abstract, the poet's or knight's service to the lady was often merely lip-service, even in literary works that praised her powers. Functioning as muse or mistress, the blessed damsel was really no more than an object, albeit an object of worship. For the most part, she herself was granted no subjectivity, nor was she portrayed as engaging in the kinds of heroic deeds that redeemed her lover.

Worse still, embedded in even the most chivalric texts are images of women as monsters and witches: any beautiful lady, these romances hint, may be a sorceress. In the medieval tale of *Sir Gawain and the Green Knight*, for instance, the hero is tested by a temptress whose wiles threaten his destruction and whose charms force him to confront his own mortality. Similarly, the medieval *Tristan* documents Tristan's death at the hands of a false Isolde even while it dramatizes the joys of the Cave of Love, and Sir Thomas Malory's fifteenth-century Arthurian cycle preserves the gestures of chivalry but also traces the way the disintegration of the Round Table is brought about by Queen Guinevere's faithlessness. Witches and bad ladies abound in medieval literature, and they are almost always associated with female sexuality, assertion, and creativity. No wonder, then, that Chaucer has his sexy, assertive, and creative Wife of Bath revise and reverse this association by telling the story of a knight who is tricked into wedding and bedding an aged crone and rewarded for relinquishing his authority to her when she transforms herself into a beautiful lady.

If Chaucer's *Wife of Bath's Tale* parodies the courtly romance to reveal its underlying misogyny, the Wife of Bath herself is a character out of another genre, which dwelt more frankly on the defects of women: the *fabliau*. In fact, this genre makes explicit the misogyny implicit in the courtly romance. Realistic and comic, *fabliaux* were folk tales addressed to a bourgeois audience. Their plots generally turned on the machinations of cuckolding wives and cunning maids, while the resolutions they recommended for men who wanted to tame such shrews ranged from public humiliation to wife-beating. At the same time, as Chaucer himself suggests in his *envoi* to the *Clerk's Tale*, about a famously submissive heroine called Patient Griselda, some writers implied, perhaps ironically and perhaps not, that woman could avoid Griselda's hardships only by taking "the high / And overpowering hand against the male." Enormously popular throughout the Middle Ages, *fabliaux* formed the basis of a number of Chaucer's narratives, including *The Miller's Tale* and *The Nun's Priest's Tale*, the first a story of a faithless young wife and the second a tale of a henpecked rooster. Good-humored though they are—in each case the storyteller clearly feels as much sympathy for the wife as for the husband—these tales deflate romantic ideals of love by depicting the female as fleshly, shrewd, earth-bound.

In the same way that medieval genres which seemed to praise women covertly implied critiques of femininity and were accompanied by franker treatments of the battle of the sexes in the *fabliau*, Renaissance epics, lyrics, and dramas castigated as well as celebrated key female figures. These writings suggest that below the surface of even the most honorific language there may frequently be a secret hostility to women. Such heroines of *The Faerie Queene* as Una and Gloriana are shadowed, after all, by the sinister witch appropriately named Duessa, whose lovely façade cracks open to reveal the horror of "her neather parts, the shame of all her kind" as well as, "at her rompe," a "foxes taile, with dong all fowly dight" (decked). To be sure, *The Faerie Queene's* heroes are often balanced by sinister or villainous male figures, but the evil of those characters is never so specifically associated with sexuality. Similarly, while Shakespeare used idealizing rhetoric to praise both Mr. W. H., who was the "onlie begetter" of his famous sonnet cycle, and the "Dark Lady" to whom he also pledged erotic devotion in the cycle, he subverted that rhetoric only when he turned his attention to his mistress's femaleness. In particular, Sonnet 130 ("My mistress's eyes are nothing like the sun") ostensibly praises his beloved, but concedes that her breast are "dun," her hair is "black wires," and her breath "reeks," while implying that such realistic descriptions should also be applied to many other women who are "belied with false compare"—that is, falsely and foolishly flattered by the metaphoric excesses of poetry.

Finally, for every Shakespeare heroine who is as ingenious and imaginative as Viola in *Twelfth Night* (1601) or as vigorously dutiful as Cordelia in *King Lear* (1606), there is a ferocious figure like Lady Macbeth in *Macbeth* (1606) and Goneril and Regan in *King Lear*. Of course, Shakespeare's dramas also offer countless examples of villainous male characters like Iago in *Othello* (1603) or Edmund in *King Lear*. But, again, the evil of such men is not usually identified with warped or excessive sexuality. By contrast, women such as Lady Macbeth, Goneril, and Regan are marked by monstrous female ambition or grotesque erotic energy. Lady Macbeth's perversity is manifested at one point by her plea "Come, unsex me here," and at another by her admission that, if she had sworn to do so, she would have "plucked" her nipple from her child's "boneless gums / And dashed [its] brains out." Similarly, the voracious lust for power and the sexual insatiability of Goneril and Regan are dramatized not only through their treatment of their aged father but also in their erotic intrigues with the bastard Edmund. Indeed, when in his madness the dispossessed King Lear proclaims that "Down from the waist" even dainty ladies are "Centaurs / Though women all above: / But to the girdle do the Gods inherit, / Beneath is all the fiend's . . . ," his apparently insane misogyny seems ultimately sane in light of his two older daughters' viciousness. What clarifies the assumptions about the proper relations between the sexes that these plays dramatized, moreover, is the fact that even attractively autonomous characters like Viola in *Twelfth Night* and Rosalind in *As You Like It* (1600) must ultimately be stripped of their independence to acquiesce in a husband's power. All's well that ends well, Shakespeare declared, but to "end well" a woman must, like Viola, become her lord's "mistress and his fancy's queen."

MEDIEVAL AND RENAISSANCE WOMEN'S LIVES

Did Shakespeare's plays reflect the reality of Renaissance women's lives? Did courtly romances mirror the lives of aristocratic medieval ladies, and did *fabliaux* tell the truth about ordinary women in the Middle Ages? By all accounts, both Renaissance and medieval texts did and did not record real facts about female experience.

Women's Lives in the Middle Ages

Because feudal society was organized for war, it was essentially a masculine world in which great landlords preserved the integrity of their estates through the rule of primogeniture (the right of the eldest son to inherit property). As the historian Doris Stenton has explained, women generally passed from father to husband, with the age of marital consent for girls usually defined as twelve. Canon law (that is, church law) permitted and sometimes even encouraged wife-beating, while secular as well as religious legal tradition forbade divorce and, except under special circumstances, female ownership of property. Still, although women could not serve as judges, on juries, or in government councils, a widow could obtain some degree of power, for she usually received a third part of her husband's estate, and in 1215 King John promised such widows a measure of freedom from royal authority: they were no longer forced to remarry (as they had been before that year) according to the king's wishes. Yet their daughters continued to be wed at early ages to ensure the integrity of important estates, and even grown women could be summarily married off, against their own wishes, unless they could purchase from their feudal lords the right to choose their own husbands.

A number of great ladies did, however, have the power of patronage, a power to elevate poets and knights through financial as well as personal encouragement. From the eleventh century on, aristocratic women commissioned illuminated manuscripts for their own uses. Because they were themselves untutored in Latin and because they were often the primary tutors of the next generation, such women had, by the end of the Middle Ages, been influential in promoting vernacular translations of Latin religious works. As daughters, wives, and mothers, medieval ladies also helped guard their lords' manors, regularly organizing almsgiving, household budgets, clothing, and food for large families and retinues of servants, and even, when their men were away, supervising farm affairs, lawsuits, and other estate business.

When a family like the Pastons in Norfolk rose by acquiring large land holdings, their sons were sent to Eton and Oxford and sometimes educated to enter the Inns of Court, while their daughters remained at home. Yet, as the Paston Letters—an extraordinary set of late medieval documents—reveal, these fifteenth-century wives and daughters actively concerned themselves with the legal, educational, and moral welfare of their husbands and brothers. Similarly, the wives of middle-class English farmers were responsible for looking after their husbands' stock, making butter and cheese, helping in the fields, and producing cloth for the family from the wool of their own sheep. From the evidence of manorial court records, it is also clear that many widows independently farmed the holdings of their deceased husbands and engaged in litigation on their own behalf. Moreover, country women brewed and sold ale at a profit, while bourgeois and working-class women in towns and cities earned considerable sums of money from two other major home industries—textiles (spinning and weaving) and food production (brewing and baking); wives and so-called *femes soles* (widows and unmarried women) also sometimes worked as leather sellers, wool merchants, shopkeepers, chandlers, shoemakers, bookbinders, and goldsmiths. Significantly, in 1469 the Crown awarded an annual salary of ten pounds to the first known English midwife, Margaret Cobbe, and in 1470 she attended the labor of Queen Elizabeth (1437–1483), wife of Edward IV (1442–1483). In addition, documents before 1200 listing needle artists refer almost exclusively to women: men's names appeared only after 1200, and began to dominate the lists only after production came to be centered in London. In the early Middle Ages, women were often active members of craft guilds (the counterpart of modern trade unions), but, as the era progressed, female workers were less frequently admitted as full members of these organizations.

To be sure, whether the working-class girl was apprenticed at an early age as a child laborer or the aristocratic daughter was given by her father in a marriage that was essentially a business contract, the lives of both were shaped by a male-controlled socioeconomic system. In addition, their lives were shadowed by the perils of childbearing that began early and ended late, by a high infant mortality rate, and by the never-ending cares of a household that had to be sustained and maintained at great physical cost to the woman. Worse still, the peace of both was frequently threatened by the virulent phenomenon of witch-hunting, an activity which became increasingly ferocious between the fourteenth and the seventeenth centuries. The ratio of women to men accused of witchcraft ranged from twenty to one in some parts of Europe to one hundred to one in other areas. Like the Jew, the witch was blamed for social ills which, in the fourteenth century, included the Black Death (the plague) and the Hundred Years' War between England and France. Like the heretic, she was believed to worship strange gods, whose ways would undermine the authority of the established church. In this era, the *Malleus Maleficarum*, mentioned earlier, functioned with great efficiency as a handbook for witch-hunters: the scholars

Barbara Ehrenreich and Deirdre English have estimated that the total number of women tortured and executed during the period may have climbed into the millions.

It is hardly surprising, therefore, that a significant group of young women took refuge in the church. Some simply turned to prayer or meditation, but others entered convents, where they could educate themselves and tutor the daughters of wealthy families, where they were safe from harrassment, and where their administrative as well as intellectual abilities were given scope. Medieval nunneries were usually poorer as well as smaller in number and in population than monasteries. Their official business, especially record-keeping, was frequently carried on by male chaplains who were better educated than their female counterparts. Yet these institutions did serve as sanctuaries for the unmarried daughters of the nobility and even of the middle class. A Benedictine nun like the German writer Hroswitha could pursue a serious literary career within the convent, producing hymns, Latin plays, and saints' lives. Moreover, although by the fifteenth century the nunneries of England were being faulted for worldly frivolity, and although most had never in any case been as powerful as the monasteries, a few had long been bastions of wealth. "If the Abbot of Glastonbury would marry the Abbess of Shaftesbury," observed one wit, "their heir would have more land than the King of England." While to most convents such a statement would not apply, even the poorest medieval nunneries clearly functioned as communities of women, providing their inhabitants with an autonomy unmatched in the secular world.

Like most medieval women's lives, the lives of nuns are only partially reflected in the images of women that can be drawn from most medieval texts. The ladies to whom troubadours and other courtly poets swore fealty, for instance, did have the power of patronage, but that power was translated in works like *La Vita Nuova*, the *Roman de la Rose*, and *Gawain and the Green Knight* into images of the beloved woman not as a financial investor but as a muse. Similarly, as we have seen, many bourgeois women were as enterprising and inventive as Chaucer's Wife of Bath, but their creative industry was reflected in *The Canterbury Tales'* characterization of a Wife whose business is not, say, brewing but matrimony. Finally, a number of nuns did, like Chaucer's Prioress, achieve significant independence in the convent, but few were either as elegant or as frivolous as Chaucer's portrait of that figure might suggest; indeed, most, far from possessing such emblems of conspicuous consumption as the Prioress's well-fed lapdog and her expensive jewelry, were obliged to support themselves as "educators" who functioned more as high-class babysitters than as real teachers. Thus, even though literary works did summarize some key contemporary visions of women, social historians must inevitably draw more information from guild records and legal documents than they do from courtly romances and *fabliaux*. As we shall suggest, Renaissance scholars must depend on similar sources to supplement the images they find in plays, prose romances, and sonnet cycles.

Women's Lives in the Renaissance

During the Renaissance, women in England continued to be defined as either *femes sole* (unmarried or widowed women) or *femes covert* ("covered" or married women). Some of those who belonged to the first of these groups might have—as they had had in the Middle Ages—considerable freedom. Aristocratic widows could manage their own property, choose second, third, or fourth husbands, and handle marriage settlements for themselves. Middle-class widows could establish businesses, join guilds, enter into foreign trade, and even, in some cases, sue or be sued. Similarly, some of those who belonged to the second group were also surprisingly independent. Although as *femes covert* they had practically no legal rights, they were often entrusted by their husbands with major responsibilities. As in the Middle Ages, aristocratic wives supervised great estates, including large landholdings, and frequently functioned almost as the business partners of the men to whom they were married. Similarly, middle-class wives—like medieval bourgeoises—often shared in their husbands' mercantile enterprises or oversaw home industries (spinning, weaving, silkmaking, bookbinding, brewing) that could be quite remunerative.

In fact, the only Renaissance women who may be said to have been entirely without legal, economic, or social power of any kind were young unmarried women, especially girls from wealthy families, who might bring large financial settlements to their future husbands. These girls were frequently pressured or forced by their parents to enter into marriages of convenience in order to consolidate important estates. Worse still, if they had any property of their own, they were sometimes subject to abduction by unscrupulous adventurers who would hold them as prisoners until they agreed to marry (and surrender their property). That this problem was no small matter is suggested by the fact that statutes to protect "ladies, gentlewomen, and other women sole" from such treatment were passed in 1453, 1557, and 1597; in that last year, as one historian reports, "maids . . . and widows with property were still being abducted and defiled or forced into marriage."

Of course, as in the Middle Ages, *all* women were enjoined to be submissive and modest in their relations to men. The Renaissance scholar Pearl Hogrefe observes that "Tudor women would have been models of chaste, passive obedience if they had only followed the advice given them in much didactic literature of the sixteenth century." But then, as the same writer also remarks, in this era as in so many others, there was a notable difference between the "ideal" woman and the real woman. Indeed, visiting England in 1592, Frederick, duke of Wirtemberg, wittily declared that "England is a paradise for women, a prison for servants, and a hell or purgatory for horses—for the females have great liberty and are almost like masters." Though ultimately his remark must be considered hyperbolical, he and a few other contemporaries—most notably the Protestant reformer John Knox, author of *The First Blast of the Trumpet against the Monstrous Regiment* [*Government*] *of Women* (1558)—thought the British Isles had "unnaturally" succumbed to the rule of women because England and Scotland were governed by queens like Mary Tudor, Mary Stuart, and Elizabeth I, and because a few great ladies had considerable power in courtly circles.

Nevertheless, the average woman very likely did not feel that she lived in a "paradise." It is true that after 1500 a surprising number of aristocratic women began, for the first time, to receive the same kind of education in the classics that their brothers did; the unprecedented training in Greek and Latin that marked the upbringing of women like Elizabeth I and Mary Sidney Herbert was a strong positive consequence of the humanist Sir Thomas More's idea that both sexes were "equally suited for the knowledge of learning by which reason is cultivated." But most girls, even the very well born, received very little education. In addition, although many middle-class women did undertake to carry on their own businesses, historians have demonstrated that in the years between 1485 and 1500 the numbers of such women declined drastically. Evidently the rise of an increasingly ambitious group of male entrepreneurs institutionalized and professionalized work that had previously gone on somewhat informally, so that Renaissance men tended to take over guilds and industries where medieval women had earlier dominated or at least participated on an equal basis.

It should finally be noted that the "power" wielded by *femes covert* who joined with their husbands in the supervision of estates or businesses was completely dependent on the good will of the husbands. If a husband was brutal, oppressive, or merely indifferent, his wife had no legal recourse because she had no rights of her own. Thus, though plays like Shakespeare's *The Taming of the Shrew* or his *Twelfth Night* may subtly misrepresent the "reality" of most women's lives—the first exaggerating the Renaissance ideology of male dominance and the second glamorizing a portrait of female independence followed by an even more romantic vision of female surrender—both contain at least a modicum of truth. Because marriage was a woman's principal goal and the role of wife her primary role, she must always—unless she was a unique exception like Elizabeth, the "virgin" queen—define herself in relation to men. Given such a self-definition, however, it would be hard indeed for her to gain the intellectual authority required for writing serious works. Not surprisingly, then, even the most learned ladies assumed what were generally secondary positions in relation to literary tradition: talented though they might have been, they often became translators (of male texts) and patronesses (of male artists). As we shall see, moreover, such original writings as they did produce tended to be as decorously submissive and as modestly "minor" as women themselves were supposed to be, perhaps because any female artist who flouted convention was sharply censured: when Lady Mary Wroth's long but unfinished prose romance *The Countess of Montgomery's Urania* appeared in 1621, it was greeted by a chorus of protest because, as the critic Barbara Lewalski has pointed out, it included disguised references to "scandals and personages of the Jacobean court." Understandably distressed, Lady Mary failed to publish a continuation of the work, which has only recently been discovered. Her decision dramatizes at least one of the more obvious ways in which a female literary career could be discouraged or deformed.

FIRST VOICES: MEDIEVAL AND RENAISSANCE WOMEN WRITERS

Despite the sense of secondariness that had been instilled in so many medieval and Renaissance women, a yearning for a female community, together with a corollary vision of female power, informed much of the literature by women in this period. Such a yearning, for instance, characterized the work of perhaps the most prominent early European feminist, the fifteenth-century writer Christine de Pisan, whose *La Cité des Dames (The City of Ladies)* offered an unprecedented dream-vision of a female utopia in which what Renaissance thinkers called "Women Worthies"—great women from all ages and nations—were gathered to prove the worthiness of women.

Participating in an early version of the French debate over femininity that was termed the *"Querelle des Femmes"* (quarrel about women), Christine assumed equality with male thinkers to contest Jean de Meun's misogynistic continuation of Guillaume de Loris's *Roman de la Rose*, a satire on women's wiles in which Jean scathingly repudiated the courtly humility toward the female Rose that was cultivated by his predecessor, Guillaume. Besides producing her fervent affirmation not just of the rights but also of the achievements of women, the widowed Christine wrote a number of other books and became, as a French scholar has noted, the first female "man of letters" to support herself (along with three children) by her pen. Yet significantly, like the writing of so many medieval and Renaissance women, her major feminist treatise was out of print from the sixteenth century to the twentieth; in France, the book remains unavailable except at the *Bibliothèque National*, while in the United States it has only just been reissued in translation. Nevertheless, despite such neglect, *The City of Ladies* summarized a vision of female power that would also be recorded in various ways by mystics like Julian of Norwich and Margery Kempe and by secular gentlewomen like Mary Sidney Herbert and Amelia Lanier.

As compared to the career of Christine de Pisan, what was striking about the literary lives of these Englishwomen was their protected quality, as well as their apparently greater docility. Whether they were cloistered like Julian of Norwich, well off like Margery Kempe, richly married like Mary Sidney Herbert, or precariously attached to the court like Amelia Lanier, these women were not in any modern sense "men of letters." On the contrary, several of them—notably Queen Elizabeth and Mary Sidney Herbert, countess of Pembroke—were themselves important literary patronesses. Among their wealthy contemporaries, moreover, were many other literary ladies, like Elizabeth Cary, Viscountess Falkland (author of *The Tragedy of Mariam, the Fair Queen of Jewry*, 1613, as well as unpublished works on Saint Mary Magdalene and the Virgin Mary), Lucy Harrington Russell, countess of Bedford (possibly author of a number of lost works), and Lady Mary Wroth (author of the sonnet sequence *Pamphilia to Amphilanthus*, 1621, which was appended to her *Urania*), most of whom also contributed to the production of poetry by financing such male artists as Thomas Nashe, Ben Jonson, and John Donne. Although they wielded some power as patronesses, these English women of letters were almost always economically dependent on church or state. (An exception was Isabella Whitney, fl. 1567–1573, a middle-class Londoner who produced a number of devotional and secular verses in her lifetime.) Thus, unlike the independent bourgeoise Christine de Pisan, they seem for the most part to articulate conventional pieties, as if to prove their loyalty to the system that supported them. Yet a passion not unlike Christine's frequently disrupted their careful decorum. Julian redefined Christ as a mother; Kempe revised the rules of marriage to liberate herself from her husband; Herbert compared Queen Elizabeth to God; Lanier justified the ways of Eve to man. As for Queen Elizabeth herself, she provided a paradigm of female regality for all her contemporaries, and in her own verse, sparse though it was, she vaunted and flaunted her power, threatening to "poll" the "tops" (cut off the heads) of those who vexed her.

To be sure, however, all these women were extraordinary and extraordinarily fortunate—a point they themselves generally understood, for most of their female contemporaries had neither a medieval flowering nor a Renaissance. If Shakespeare was the common man transformed into Western culture's most uncommon genius, he had no woman counterpart drawn, as he was, from the intellectually ambitious, aspiring middle class. In 1928, Virginia Woolf told us why. Had Shakespeare had a "wonderfully gifted sister," she explained in *A Room of One's Own,* the girl would have been given no education; her parents would have forced her to do dull domestic chores and tried to make her marry young; she would have run away to London, only to be seduced and abandoned· by a predatory theatrical entrepreneur; finally, she would have died a suicide, though "the birds that sang in the hedge were not more musical than she was [and] she had the quickest fancy, a gift like her brother's for the tune of words." But for the first sixteen hundred years after Christ was born to Mary, Queen of Heaven, the tune of words was not fostered in women. Given the fact that for the female imagination the so-called Dark Ages persisted well beyond the male-defined Renaissance, it is impressive enough that a small but talented set of writers implicitly chose to declare, with Amelia Lanier, that "Our Mother Eve, who tasted of the tree . . . was simply good" and therefore to dream, as Lanier did, that women might "have our liberty again."

JULIAN OF NORWICH
1342–?

"Because I am a woman should I therefore believe that I ought not to tell you about the goodness of God since I saw at the time that it is his will that it be known?" Specifically what Julian of Norwich saw were sixteen "showings" or direct experiences of God's goodness, which she described in a powerful spiritual meditation. While she considered herself "a woman, unlettered, feeble and frail," this first English woman of letters drew her authority from "the showing of Him who is Sovereign Teacher" and was thereby empowered to record her mystical visions in a prose remarkable for its brilliant transformations of images drawn from everyday experiences.

Dame Julian's revelations occurred in two days of her thirtieth year, during a near-fatal illness when she experienced pity for Christ's suffering. After receiving last rites, she perceived a "sudden change" that was accompanied by the series of visions of Christ which comprise the substance of her book. A recluse or anchoress in St. Julian's Church, Norwich, Dame Julian most probably underwent a rite of enclosure, which resembled a burial service for the soul that sought to die to the world in order to live more fully with Christ. In a cell attached to the church, probably with a maidservant, an anchoress like Julian could dedicate herself to solitary meditation and silent prayer. Little else is known about her, although she clearly had some renown as a pious woman, for she was visited by Margery Kempe, another visionary, who sought spiritual advice and counsel. Modesty, ignorance of Latin, or literal illiteracy may have caused Dame Julian to consider herself "unlettered"; however, she drew on biblical imagery and on a range of books that included the works of Richard Rolle, *The Cloud of Unknowing,* and the *Ancren Riwle,* all popular religious texts in her time.

Two records of her revelations exist, either written by her or dictated to an amanuensis: a shorter account, which is thought to have been written first and which vividly presents the sixteen revelations, and a longer version, in which she records the growth in her understanding of the revelations over a period of some twenty years. The survival of a number of manuscripts may indicate the popularity of Julian's work, although after the Reformation it ceased to attract readers. The text modernized here by Edmund Colledge and James Walsh is from the longer version. In the context of Thomas Aquinas's assertion of the inferiority of women in his *Summa Theologica* (1265–1277), Dame Julian's description of the maternity of God may seem startling. Yet, as Caroline Walker Bynum has shown in *Jesus as Mother*, the image of "mother Jesus" flowered in twelfth-century works by Anselm of Canterbury and Bernard of Clairvaux. Throughout *A Book of Showings* (sometimes called *A Revelation of Divine Love*), Dame Julian associated her "bodily" and "ghostly" visions of Christ with the "words [which] formed in my understanding." In the following excerpt, she implies that the incarnation has a unique meaning for women, who can affirm their spirituality and creativity through imagery of conception, birth, and nurturance.

From A Book of Showings

[*God the Mother*]

From THE FIFTY-NINTH CHAPTER

* * *

As truly as God is our Father, so truly is God our Mother, and he revealed that in everything, and especially in these sweet words where he says. I am he;[1] that is to say: I am he, the power and goodness of fatherhood; I am he, the wisdom and the lovingness of motherhood; I am he, the light and the grace which is all blessed love; I am he, the Trinity;[2] I am he, the unity; I am he, the great supreme goodness of every kind of thing; I am he who makes you to love; I am he who makes you to long; I am he, the endless fulfilling of all true desires. For where the soul is highest, noblest, most honourable, still it is lowest, meekest and mildest.

And from this foundation in substance we have all the powers of our sensuality by the gift of nature, and by the help and the furthering of mercy and grace, without which we cannot profit. Our great Father, almighty God, who is being, knows us and loved us before time began. Out of this knowledge, in his most wonderful deep love, by the prescient eternal counsel of all the blessed Trinity he wanted the second person to become our Mother, our brother and our saviour. From this it follows that as truly as God is our Father, so truly is God our Mother. Our Father wills, our Mother works, our good Lord the Holy Spirit

---

1. In a series of visions in the previous chapters, Christ showed himself to Julian and spoke words which she then interprets in the later chapters.
2. The first person of the Trinity is God, the sec-ond person is Jesus Christ, and the third is the Holy Spirit; all three, however, may bear the name God.

confirms. And therefore it is our part to love our God in whom we have our being, reverently thanking and praising him for our creation, mightily praying to our Mother for mercy and pity, and to our Lord the Holy Spirit for help and grace. For in these three is all our life: nature, mercy and grace, of which we have mildness, patience and pity, and hatred of sin and wickedness; for the virtues must of themselves hate sin and wickedness.

And so Jesus is our true Mother in nature by our first creation, and he is our true Mother in grace by his taking our created nature. All the lovely works and all the sweet loving offices of beloved motherhood are appropriated to the second person, for in him we have this godly will, whole and safe forever, both in nature and in grace, from his own goodness proper to him.

I understand three ways of contemplating motherhood in God. The first is the foundation of our nature's creation; the second is his taking of our nature, where the motherhood of grace begins; the third is the motherhood at work. And in that, by the same grace, everything is penetrated, in length and in breadth, in height and in depth without end; and it is all one love.

THE SIXTIETH CHAPTER

But now I should say a little more about this penetration, as I understood our Lord to mean: How we are brought back by the motherhood of mercy and grace into our natural place, in which we were created by the motherhood of love, a mother's love which never leaves us.

Our Mother in nature, our Mother in grace, because he wanted altogether to become our Mother in all things, made the foundation of his work most humbly and most mildly in the maiden's womb. And he revealed that in the first revelation, when he brought that meek maiden before the eye of my understanding in the simple stature which she had when she conceived; that is to say that our great God, the supreme wisdom of all things, arrayed and prepared himself in this humble place, all ready in our poor flesh, himself to do the service and the office of motherhood in everything. The mother's service is nearest, readiest and surest: nearest because it is most natural, readiest because it is most loving, and surest because it is truest. No one ever might or could perform this office fully, except only him. We know that all our mothers bear us for pain and for death. O, what is that? But our true Mother Jesus, he alone bears us for joy and for endless life, blessed may he be. So he carries us within him in love and travail, until the full time when he wanted to suffer the sharpest thorns and cruel pains that ever were or will be, and at the last he died. And when he had finished, and had borne us so for bliss, still all this could not satisfy his wonderful love. And he revealed this in these great surpassing words of love. If I could suffer more, I would suffer more.[3] He could not die any more, but he did not want to cease working; therefore he must needs nourish us, for the precious love of motherhood has made him our debtor.

The mother can give her child to suck of her milk, but our precious Mother Jesus can feed us with himself, and does, most courteously and most tenderly, with the blessed sacrament,[4] which is the precious food of true life; and with all the sweet sacraments he sustains us most mercifully and graciously, and so he meant in these blessed words, where he said: I am he whom Holy Church preaches and teaches to you.[5] That is to say: All the health and the life of the sacraments, all the power and the grace of my word, all the goodness which is ordained in Holy Church for you, I am he.

The mother can lay her child tenderly to her breast, but our tender Mother Jesus can lead us easily into his blessed breast through his sweet open side, and show us there a part of the godhead and of the joys of heaven, with inner certainty of endless bliss. And that he revealed in the tenth revelation,[6] giving us the same understanding in these sweet words which he says: See, how I love you, looking into his blessed side, rejoicing.

This fair lovely word "mother" is so sweet and so kind in itself that it cannot truly be said of anyone or to anyone except of him and to him who is the true Mother of life and of all things. To the property of motherhood belong nature, love, wisdom and knowledge, and this is God. For though it may be so that our bodily bringing to birth is only little, humble and simple in comparison with our spiritual bringing to birth, still it is he who does it in the creatures by whom it is done. The kind, loving mother who knows and sees the need of her child guards it very tenderly, as the nature and condition of motherhood will have. And always as the child grows in age and in stature, she acts differently, but she does not change her love. And when it is even older, she allows it to be chastised to destroy its faults, so as to make the child receive virtues and grace. This work, with everything which is lovely and good, our Lord performs in those by whom it is done.[7] So he is our Mother in nature by the operation of grace in the lower part, for love of the higher part. And he wants us to know it, for he wants to have all our love attached to him; and in this I saw that every debt which we owe by God's command to fatherhood and motherhood is fulfilled in truly loving God, which blessed love Christ works in us. And this was revealed in everything, and especially in the great bounteous words when he says: I am he whom you love.[8]

---

3. In the ninth revelation, Christ spoke these words to Julian.
4. The bread and wine consumed during the Catholic mass, which represent the body and blood of Christ.
5. In the twelfth revelation.

6. In the tenth revelation Christ showed Julian a wound in his side, through which she saw "his blessed heart riven in two."
7. I.e., in disciplining her child the mother acts as an agent of God's will.
8. In the twelfth revelation.

THE SIXTY-FIRST CHAPTER

And in our spiritual bringing to birth he uses more tenderness, without any comparison, in protecting us. By so much as our soul is more precious in his sight, he kindles our understanding, he prepares our ways, he eases our conscience, he comforts our soul, he illumines our heart and gives us partial knowledge and love of his blessed divinity, with gracious memory of his sweet humanity and his blessed Passion,[9] with courteous wonder over his great surpassing goodness, and makes us to love everything which he loves for love of him, and to be well satisfied with him and with all his works. And when we fall, quickly he raises us up with his loving embrace and his gracious touch. And when we are strengthened by his sweet working, then we willingly choose him by his grace, that we shall be his servants and his lovers, constantly and forever.

And yet after this he allows some of us to fall more heavily and more grievously than ever we did before, as it seems to us. And then we who are not all wise think that everything which we have undertaken was all nothing. But it is not so, for we need to fall, and we need to see it; for if we did not fall, we should not know how feeble and how wretched we are in ourselves, nor, too, should we know so completely the wonderful love of our Creator.

For we shall truly see in heaven without end that we have sinned grievously in this life; and notwithstanding this, we shall truly see that we were never hurt in his love, nor were we ever of less value in his sight. And by the experience of this falling we shall have a great and marvellous knowledge of love in God without end; for enduring and marvellous is that love which cannot and will not be broken because of offences.

And this was one profitable understanding; another is the humility and meekness which we shall obtain by the sight of our fall, for by that we shall be raised high in heaven, to which raising we might never have come without that meekness. And therefore we need to see it; and if we do not see it, though we fell, that would not profit us. And commonly we first fall and then see it; and both are from the mercy of God.

The mother may sometimes suffer[1] the child to fall and to be distressed in various ways, for its own benefit, but she can never suffer any kind of peril to come to her child, because of her love. And though our earthly mother may suffer her child to perish, our heavenly Mother Jesus may never suffer us who are his children to perish, for he is almighty, all wisdom and all love, and so is none but he, blessed may he be.

But often when our falling and our wretchedness are shown to us, we

9. The crucifixion, in which Christ sacrificed his   1. Allow.
own life as payment for humanity's sins.

are so much afraid and so greatly ashamed of ourselves that we scarcely know where we can put ourselves. But then our courteous Mother does not wish us to flee away, for nothing would be less pleasing to him; but he then wants us to behave like a child. For when it is distressed and frightened, it runs quickly to its mother; and if it can do no more, it calls to the mother for help with all its might. So he wants us to act as a meek child, saying: My kind Mother, my gracious Mother, my beloved Mother, have mercy on me. I have made myself filthy and unlike you, and I may not and cannot make it right except with your help and grace.

And if we do not then feel ourselves eased, let us at once be sure that he is behaving as a wise Mother. For if he sees that it is profitable to us to mourn and to weep, with compassion and pity he suffers that until the right time has come, out of his love. And then he wants us to show a child's characteristics, which always naturally trusts in its mother's love in well-being and in woe. And he wants us to commit ourselves fervently to the faith of Holy Church, and find there our beloved Mother in consolation and true understanding, with all the company of the blessed. For one single person may often be broken, as it seems to him, but the entire body of Holy Church was never broken, nor ever will be without end. And therefore it is a certain thing, and good and gracious to will, meekly and fervently, to be fastened and united to our mother Holy Church, who is Christ Jesus. For the flood of mercy which is his dear blood and precious water is plentiful to make us fair and clean. The blessed wounds of our saviour are open and rejoice to heal us. The sweet gracious hands of our Mother are ready and diligent about us; for he in all this work exercises the true office of a kind nurse, who has nothing else to do but attend to the safety of her child.

It is his office to save us, it is his glory to do it, and it is his will that we know it; for he wants us to love him sweetly and trust in him meekly and greatly. And he revealed this in these gracious words: I protect you very safely.[2]

1393?

2. In Chapter Thirty-seven after the thirteenth revelation.

MARGERY KEMPE

1373?–?

When Margery Kempe visited Julian of Norwich, the aging anchoress and author of *A Book of Showings*, she sought "good counsel" about her own divine revelations. The forty-year-old Kempe had decided, after almost twenty years of marriage and fourteen children, that she was meant to be married not to her husband but to Christ. While Dame Julian confirmed Kempe's grace, the anchoress also warned her visitor about "the language of the world, for the more despite, shame and reproof that ye have in the world," Julian explained, "the more is your merit in the sight of God." What Julian seemed to understand in her "holy dalliance" with Margery Kempe was the vulnerability of a "sister" whose spirituality took a quite different form from her own, for Margery Kempe dramatically enacted her religious enthusiasm in the world. Indeed, dressed all in white, wearing a ring (engraved "Jesus Christ is my love"), frequently called to fast or weep, Margery Kempe traveled throughout England and went on pilgrimages to Jerusalem, Rome, Germany, and in the Baltic. Not dedicated to the vow of silence, she reproved even the highest church officials for what she considered their moral lapses and preached to people wherever she found them. Whether her audience threatened to burn her at the stake as a heretic or promised to follow what they deemed her saintly tales and exhortations, Margery Kempe exhibited notable courage, inventiveness, and zeal, or so it seems in the major source we have of her life, *The Book of Margery Kempe*.

The same feisty energy that characterized Margery Kempe's life must have impelled her to write the first extant autobiography in the vernacular. *The Book of Margery Kempe* was narrated to several scribes, who recorded what Kempe remembered about her adventures as a spiritual teacher. Kempe did not focus on her youth in Lynn, where she was raised by a prosperous mayor named John Burnham, or her marriage in 1393 to John Kempe, a tax collector, brewer, and miller by turns. Instead, she began when she was twenty-one, pregnant, and in the midst of a disabling spiritual struggle which she placed in the context of her visions of Christ on the one hand and her marital responsibilities on the other. Kempe's eventual marriage to Christ, which she attained by bargaining with her husband for freedom from sexual relations, evidently involved a sexualized relation with God not uncommon in the mystical tradition. While some scholars have diagnosed Kempe as hysterical, others have compared her brash vitality to the irreverence of Chaucer's candid Wife of Bath or her spiritual ecstasy to the intensity of Saint Bridget of Sweden, who also claimed to have visions of being present at Christ's birth.

As the self-defined "creature" of her Creator, Kempe recorded both mystical revelations and homely anecdotes. Invariably she defended herself against the injunction, based on the teachings of Saint Paul, that "no woman should preach," by explaining "I preach not sin; I come into no pulpit. I use but communication and good words, and that I will do while I live." Unlike Dame Julian, who meditated exclusively on the growth of her spiritual understanding, Margery Kempe produced a lively, realistic narrative as well as an illuminating document of fifteenth-century society.

A modernization of *The Book of Margery Kempe* was not printed until 1936, when it was produced by W. Butler-Bowden, and we are indebted to him in the selections which follow. A critical edition of the original manuscript was published in 1940 by S. B. Meech and H. E. Allen.

From The Book of Margery Kempe[1]

[*On Female Celibacy*]

CHAPTER 3. HER VISION OF PARADISE. SHE DESIRES TO LIVE APART FROM
HER HUSBAND. DOES PENANCE AND WEARS A HAIRCLOTH.[2]

On a night, as this creature[3] lay in her bed with her husband, she heard a sound of melody so sweet and delectable, that she thought she had been in Paradise, and therewith she started out of her bed and said:—

"Alas, that ever I did sin! It is full merry in Heaven."

This melody was so sweet that it surpassed all melody that ever might be heard in this world, without any comparison, and caused her, when she heard any mirth or melody afterwards, to have full plenteous and abundant tears of high devotion, with great sobbings and sighings after the bliss of Heaven, not dreading the shames and the spites of this wretched world. Ever after this inspiration, she had in her mind the mirth and the melody that was in Heaven, so much, that she could not well restrain herself from speaking thereof, for wherever she was in any company she would say oftentimes:—"It is full merry in Heaven.".

And they that knew her behaviour beforetime, and now heard her speaking so much of the bliss of Heaven, said to her:—

"Why speak ye so of the mirth that is in Heaven? Ye know it not, and ye have not been there, any more than we." And were wroth with her, for she would not hear nor speak of worldly things as they did, and as she did beforetime.

And after this time she had never desired to commune fleshly with her husband, for the debt of matrimony was so abominable to her that she would rather, she thought, have eaten or drunk the ooze and the muck in the gutter than consent to any fleshly communing, save only for obedience.

So she said to her husband:—"I may not deny you my body, but the love of my heart and my affections are withdrawn from all earthly creatures, and set only in God."

He would have his will and she obeyed, with great weeping and sorrowing that she might not live chaste. And oftentimes this creature counselled her husband to live chaste, and said that they often, she knew well, had displeased God by their inordinate love, and the great delectation they each had in using the other, and now it was good that they should, by the common will and consent of them both, punish and

---

1. The first two chapters of this third-person spiritual autobiography recount Margery's worldly desires and ambitions, prior to her Christian renunciation of the world.
2. A garment made from an extremely rough and uncomfortable fabric containing horsehair, worn by penitents as punishment for their sins.
3. I.e., Margery, who refers to herself in the third person.

chastise themselves wilfully by abstaining from the lust of their bodies. Her husband said it was good to do so, but he might not yet. He would when God willed. And so he used her as he had done before. He would not spare her. And ever she prayed to God that she might live chaste; and three or four years after, when it pleased Our Lord, he made a vow of chastity, as shall be written afterwards, by leave of Jesus.

And also, after this creature heard this heavenly melody, she did great bodily penance. She was shriven sometimes twice or thrice on a day, and specially of that sin she so long had (hid), concealed and covered, as is written in the beginning of the book.[4]

She gave herself up to great fasting and great watching; she rose at two or three of the clock, and went to church, and was there at her prayers unto the time of noon and also all the afternoon. Then she was slandered and reproved by many people, because she kept so strict a life. She got a hair-cloth from a kiln, such as men dry malt on, and laid it in her kirtle[5] as secretly and privily as she might, so that her husband should not espy it. Nor did he, and she lay by him every night in his bed and wore the hair-cloth every day, and bore children in the time.

Then she had three years of great labour with temptations which she bore as meekly as she could, thanking Our Lord for all His gifts, and was as merry when she was reproved, scorned and japed for Our Lord's love, and much more merry than she was beforetime in the worship of the world. For she knew right well she had sinned greatly against God and was worthy of more shame and sorrow than any man could cause her, and despite[6] of the world was the right way Heavenwards, since Christ Himself had chosen that way. All His apostles, martyrs, confessors and virgins, and all that ever came to Heaven, passed by the way of tribulation, and she, desiring nothing so much as Heaven, then was glad in her conscience when she believed that she was entering the way that would lead her to the place she most desired.

And this creature had contrition and great compunction with plenteous tears and many boisterous sobbings for her sins and for her unkindness against her Maker. She repented from her childhood for unkindness, as Our Lord would put it in her mind, full many a time. Then, beholding her own wickedness, she could but sorrow and weep and ever pray for mercy and forgiveness. Her weeping was so plenteous and continuing, that many people thought she could weep and leave off, as she liked. And therefore many men said she was a false hypocrite, and wept before the world for succour and worldly goods. Then full many forsook her that loved her before while she was in the world, and would not know her. And ever, she thanked God for all, desiring nothing but mercy and forgiveness of sin.

4. In Chapter 1 we learned that Margery had not made a practice of going to confession.

5. Skirt.

6. Contempt or defiance.

CHAPTER 4. HER TEMPTATION TO ADULTERY WITH A MAN, WHO, WHEN
SHE CONSENTS, REJECTS HER.

The first two years when this creature was thus drawn to Our Lord,
she had great quiet in spirit from any temptations. She could well endure to fast, and it did not trouble her. She hated the joys of the world.
She felt no rebellion in her flesh. She was so strong, as she thought, that
she dreaded no devil in Hell, as she did such great bodily penance. She
thought that she loved God more than He did her. She was smitten
with the deadly wound of vainglory, and felt it not, for she many times
desired that the crucifix should loosen His hands from the Cross, and
embrace her in token of love. Our Merciful Lord Jesus Christ, seeing
this creature's presumption, sent her, as is written before, three years of
great temptations, one of the hardest of which I purpose to write as an
example to those who come after, so that they should not trust in
themselves, or have joy in themselves, as she had. For, no dread, our
ghostly enemy sleepeth not, but he full busily searcheth our complex-
ions and dispositions and where he findeth us most frail, there, by Our
Lord's sufferance, he layeth his snare, which no man may escape by his
own power.

So he laid before this woman the snare of lechery, when she believed
that all fleshly lust had wholly been quenched in her. And so for a long
time she was tempted with the sin of lechery, for aught that she could
do. Yet she was often shriven, she wore her hair-cloth, and did great
bodily penance and wept many a bitter tear, and prayed full often to
Our Lord that He should preserve her and keep her, so that she should
not fall into temptation, for she thought she would rather be dead than
consent thereto. All this time she had no lust to commune with her
husband; but it was very painful and horrible unto her.

In the second year of her temptation, it so fell that a man whom she
loved well, said unto her on St. Margaret's[7] Eve before evensong that,
for anything, he would lie by her and have his lust of his body, and she
should not withstand him, for if he did not have his will that time, he
said he would anyhow have it another time; she should not choose. And
he did it to see what she would do, but she thought that he had meant it
in full earnest at that time, and said but little thereto. So they parted
then and both went to hear evensong, for her church was that of Saint
Margaret. This woman was so laboured with the man's words that she
could not hear her evensong, nor say her Paternoster,[8] or think any
other good thought, but was more troubled than ever she was before.

The devil put into her mind that God had forsaken her, or else she
would not be so tempted. She believed the devil's persuasion, and
began to consent because she could think no good thought. Therefore

---

7. A queen of Scotland in the eleventh century,   8. Latin version of the Lord's Prayer.
known for her pious and ascetic way of life.

thought she that God had forsaken her, and when evensong was done, she went to the man aforesaid, so that he could have his lust, as she thought he had desired, but he made such simulation[9] that she could not know his intent, and so they parted asunder for that night. This creature was so laboured and vexed all that night, that she never knew what she might do. She lay by her husband, and to commune with him was so abominable to her that she could not endure it, and yet it was lawful unto her, in lawful time, if she would. But ever she was laboured with the other man, to sin with him inasmuch as he had spoken to her. At last, through the importunity of temptation, and lack of discretion, she was overcome and consented in her mind, and went to the man to know if he would then consent to her, and he said he never would, for all the gold in this world; he would rather be hewn as small as flesh for the pot.

She went away all shamed and confused in herself at seeing his stability and her own instability. Then thought she of the grace that God had given her before; how she had had two years of great quiet in her soul, repenting of her sin with many bitter tears of compunction, and a perfect will never again to turn to her sin, but rather to die. Now she saw how she had consented in her will to do sin, and then fell she half into despair. She thought she must have been in Hell for the sorrow she felt. She thought she was worthy of no mercy, for her consent was so wilfully done, nor ever worthy to do Him service, because she was so false to Him. Nevertheless she was shriven many times and often, and did whatever penance her confessor would enjoin her to do, and was governed by the rules of the Church. That grace, God gave his creature, blessed may He be, but He withdrew not her temptation, but rather increased it, as she thought.

Therefore she thought He had forsaken her, and dared not trust to His mercy, but was afflicted with horrible temptations to lechery and despair all the next year following. But Our Lord, of His mercy, as she said herself, gave her each day for the most part two hours of sorrow for her sins, with many bitter tears. Afterwards, she was laboured with temptation to despair as she was before, and was as far from feelings of grace, as they that never felt any, and that she could not bear, and so she gave way to despair. But for the time that she felt grace, her labours were so wonderful that she could evil fare[1] with them, but ever mourned and sorrowed as though God had forsaken her.

CHAPTER 11. ON THE WAY BACK FROM YORK, SHE AND HER HUSBAND
ARGUE AS TO THEIR CARNAL RELATIONSHIP TO EACH OTHER.

It befell on a Friday on Midsummer Eve in right hot weather, as this creature was coming from York-ward carrying a bottle with beer in her

9. Unclear; he feigned indifference, or gave her   1. Endure, resist.
conflicting signs of his desire.

hand, and her husband a cake in his bosom, that he asked his wife this question:—

"Margery, if there came a man with a sword, who would strike off my head, unless I should commune naturally with you as I have done before, tell me on your conscience—for ye say ye will not lie—whether ye would suffer my head to be smitten off, or whether ye would suffer me to meddle with you again, as I did at one time?"

"Alas, sir," said she, "why raise this matter, when we have been chaste these eight weeks?"

"For I will know the truth of your heart."

And then she said with great sorrow:—"Forsooth, I would rather see you being slain, than that we should turn again to our uncleanness."

And he replied:—"Ye are no good wife."

She then asked her husband what was the cause that he had not meddled with her for eight weeks, since she lay with him every night in his bed. He said he was made so afraid when he would have touched her, that he dare do no more.

"Now, good sir, amend your ways, and ask God's mercy, for I told you nearly three years ago that ye[2] should be slain suddenly, and now is this the third year, and so I hope I shall have my desire. Good sir, I pray you grant me what I ask, and I will pray for you that ye shall be saved through the mercy of Our Lord Jesus Christ, and ye shall have more reward in Heaven than if ye wore a hair-cloth or a habergeon.[3] I pray you, suffer me to make a vow of chastity at what bishop's hand God wills."

"Nay," he said, "that I will not grant you, for now may I use you without deadly sin, and then might I not do so."

Then she said to him:—"If it be the will of the Holy Ghost to fulfil what I have said, I pray God that ye may consent thereto; and if it be not the will of the Holy Ghost, I pray God ye never consent to it."

Then they went forth towards Bridlington in right hot weather, the creature having great sorrow and dread for her chastity. As they came by a cross, her husband sat down under the cross, calling his wife to him and saying these words unto her:—"Margery, grant me my desire, and I shall grant you your desire. My first desire is that we shall lie together in bed as we have done before; the second, that ye shall pay my debts, ere ye go to Jerusalem; and the third, that ye shall eat and drink with me on the Friday as ye were wont to do."[4]

"Nay, sir," said she, "to break the Friday, I will never grant you whilst I live."

---

2. According to one editor, "ye" should be read as "your lust"; but her emphasis on his salvation suggests it is a literal death as well. Christ gave her this prophecy in Chapter 9 while she was praying.

3. A coat of armor sometimes worn for penance.

4. Friday is a traditional day of fasting in the Catholic church.

"Well," said he, "then I shall meddle with you again."

She prayed him that he would give her leave to say her prayers, and he granted it kindly. Then she knelt down beside a cross in the field and prayed in this manner, with a great abundance of tears:—

"Lord God, Thou knowest all things. Thou knowest what sorrow I have had to be chaste in my body to Thee all these three years, and now might I have my will, and dare not for love of Thee. For if I should break that manner of fasting which Thou commandest me to keep on the Friday, without meat or drink, I should now have my desire. But, Blessed Lord, Thou knowest that I will not contravene Thy will, and much now is my sorrow unless I find comfort in Thee. Now, Blessed Jesus, make Thy will known to me unworthy, that I may follow it thereafter and fulfil it with all my might."

Then Our Lord Jesus Christ with great sweetness, spoke to her, commanding her to go again to her husband, and pray him to grant her what she desired, "And he shall have what he desireth. For, my dearworthy daughter, this was the cause that I bade thee fast, so that thou shouldst the sooner obtain and get thy desire, and now it is granted to thee. I will no longer that thou fast. Therefore I bid thee in the Name of Jesus, eat and drink as thy husband doth."

Then this creature thanked Our Lord Jesus Christ for His grace and goodness, and rose up and went to her husband, saying to him:—

"Sir, if it please you, ye shall grant me my desire, and ye shall have your desire. Grant me that ye will not come into my bed, and I grant you to requite your debts ere I go to Jerusalem. Make my body free to God so that ye never make challenge to me, by asking any debt of matrimony. After this day, whilst ye live, I will eat and drink on the Friday at your bidding."

Then said her husband:—"As free may your body be to God, as it hath been to me."

This creature thanked God, greatly rejoicing that she had her desire, praying her husband that they should say three Paternosters in worship of the Trinity for the great grace that He had granted them. And so they did, kneeling under a cross, and afterwards they ate and drank together in great gladness of spirit. This was on a Friday on Midsummer's Eve. Then went they forth Bridlingtonward and also to many other countries and spoke with God's servants, both anchorites[5] and recluses, and many others of Our Lord's lovers, with many worthy clerks, doctors of divinity and bachelors also, in divers places. And this creature, to many of them, shewed her feelings and her contemplations, as she was commanded to do, to find out if any deceit were in her feelings.

1436

5. Religiously motivated recluses.

QUEEN ELIZABETH I
1533–1603

By 1558, when Elizabeth Tudor ascended the throne at the age of twenty-five, she was proficient in Greek and Latin as well as French, Italian, Spanish, and German. Her translations, speeches, and poems illustrate her political genius and her rhetorical ingenuity. She needed both of these assets, for she faced personal, political, and religious opposition to her rule. As the daughter of Henry VIII and Anne Boleyn, she had been declared illegitimate by Pope Clement VII, who refused to sanction her father's remarriage, and, even after her supremacy had been established, she confronted public reservations about her unmarried state. As monarch, she was caught in the middle: she had to deal with a Protestant Parliament, papal objection to her legitimacy, and constant threat of war from the Catholic powers, Spain and France. As the head of the church established by her father, Elizabeth presided over an institution which, in its structure, doctrines, and rituals, was effectively Roman Catholic; Henry had simply replaced the pope as the supreme ruler of the church in England. Elizabeth was opposed on the one hand by Catholics, who resented Henry's rejection of papal supremacy, and on the other hand by Puritan Protestants, who believed that the church had not been sufficiently "purified" of its Roman Catholic elements. Neither Protestant nor Catholic, Elizabeth, to insure peace in England, followed a *via media*, a middle course, which eventually prevailed and became Anglicanism.

Most historians agree that, paradoxically enough, Queen Elizabeth achieved complete sovereignty only after a papal condemnation of 1570 excommunicated her and released her subjects from their allegiance to her rule. Public opinion consolidated against her Catholic rival, Mary Queen of Scots, and in favor of Elizabeth, who quickly became the symbol of English nationalism. When, in 1588, she commanded land forces and supervised naval raids against a papal-financed Spanish fleet (the famous Armada) that was planning to invade Britain, she defeated the last pretender to the throne, Philip II of Spain. Her resulting popularity was enhanced by the diplomatic course she maintained in strengthening the Anglican church to resist the influence of both the Catholics and the Puritans. During the prolific literary age that was named for her forty-five-year-long reign, she was celebrated in many poems and plays as a uniquely English embodiment of the female power associated with such biblical and mythological heroines as Judith, Esther, Diana, and Minerva. In her own writing, moreover, she revealed the same witty intelligence that distinguishes so much Elizabethan literature.

The Doubt of Future Foes[1]

> The doubt of future foes exiles my present joy,
> And wit[2] me warns to shun such snares as threaten
> mine annoy;

---

1. "The poem concerns Elizabeth's Roman Catholic cousin, Mary Stuart, Queen of Scotland, who in 1568 sought refuge in England from her rebellious subjects. Mary was the focus of several Roman Catholic conspiracies to place her on the English throne in place of Elizabeth. 'Doubt': fear" [Barbara Lewalski's note].

2. Intelligence.

For falsehood now doth flow, and subjects' faith
   doth ebb,
Which should not be if reason ruled or wisdom
   weaved the web.
But clouds of joys untried do cloak aspiring minds,   5
Which turn to rain of late repent by changéd course
   of winds.
The top of hope supposed the root upreared shall be,[3]
And fruitless all their grafted guile, as shortly ye shall see.
The dazzled eyes with pride, which great ambition blinds,
Shall be unsealed by worthy wights[4] whose foresight
   falsehood finds.   10
The daughter of debate that discord aye[5] doth sow
Shall reap no gain where former rule still peace hath
   taught to know.
No foreign banished wight shall anchor in this port;
Our realm brooks not seditious sects, let them
   elsewhere resort.
My rusty sword through rest shall first his edge employ   15
To poll their tops[6] that seek such change or gape for
   future joy.

1570   1589

On Monsieur's Departure[7]

I grieve and dare not show my discontent,
I love and yet am forced to seem to hate,
I do, yet dare not say I ever meant,[8]
I seem stark mute but inwardly do prate.[9]
   I am and not, I freeze and yet am burned,   5
   Since from myself another self I turned.

My care is like my shadow in the sun,
Follows me flying, flies when I pursue it,
Stands and lies by me, doth what I have done.
His too familiar care doth make me rue it.   10
   No means I find to rid him from my breast,
   Till by the end of things[1] it be suppressed.

Some gentler passion slide into my mind,
For I am soft and made of melting snow;

---

3. I.e., her enemies' unfounded hopes concentrate on the "top" or outcome of their schemes, while Elizabeth defeats them by pulling up their "roots." In the next line "grafted" continues the botanical metaphor; her enemies have unsuccessfully tried to "graft" their plans onto roots that will not support them.
4. Men. "Falsehood": treachery.
5. Always. "Discord" is the object of "sow."

6. To prune or crop the tops of trees, with an obvious suggestion of beheading.
7. "Monsieur" has been identified as either the French duke of Anjou, with whom Elizabeth had negotiated marriage, or the earl of Essex, one of her favorite courtiers.
8. I.e., meant to do.
9. Babble.
1. The Day of Judgment.

Or be more cruel, love, and so be kind.   15
Let me or float or sink, be high or low.
   Or let me live with some more sweet content,
   Or die and so forget what love ere meant.

1600   1823

Speech to the Troops at Tilbury[2]

My loving people,

We have been persuaded by some that are careful of[3] our safety, to
take heed how we commit our selves to armed multitudes, for fear of
treachery; but I assure you I do not desire to live to distrust my faithful
and loving people. Let tyrants fear, I have always so behaved myself
that, under God, I have placed my chiefest strength and safeguard in
the loyal hearts and good-will of my subjects; and therefore I am come
amongst you, as you see, at this time, not for my recreation and disport,
but being resolved, in the midst and heat of the battle, to live or die
amongst you all; to lay down for my God, and for my kingdom, and my
people, my honour and my blood, even in the dust. I know I have the
body but of a weak and feeble woman; but I have the heart and stomach
of a king, and of a king of England too, and think foul scorn that Parma
or Spain, or any prince of Europe, should dare to invade the borders of
my realm; to which rather than any dishonour shall grow by me, I myself will take up arms, I myself will be your general, judge, and rewarder
of every one of your virtues in the field. I know already, for your for-
wardness you have deserved rewards and crowns;[4] and We do assure
you in the word of a prince, they shall be duly paid you. In the mean
time, my lieutenant general shall be in my stead, than whom never
prince commanded a more noble or worthy subject; not doubting but
by your obedience to my general, by your concord in the camp, and
your valour in the field, we shall shortly have a famous victory over
those enemies of my God, of my kingdom, and of my people.

1588   1752

---

2. Delivered by Elizabeth to land forces that had
assembled at Tilbury in anticipation of the landing of the Spanish Armada, a fleet of warships
sent by Philip II to invade England. In fact the
Armada was defeated at sea, and so never
reached England; but Elizabeth's courage in
personally leading her troops was not therefore
diminished.
3. Anxious for.
4. An English monetary unit; also possibly honorary titles.

MARY SIDNEY HERBERT, COUNTESS
OF PEMBROKE
1561–1621

Mary Sidney Herbert is probably best known today as the sister of the poet Sir Philip Sidney and one of the sixteenth century's great patronesses of learning. But besides facilitating the work of others, she was herself a translator and poet of considerable skill. Amelia Lanier, dedicating her verse narrative of "the passion of Christ" to Herbert, self-deprecatingly admitted "many books she writes that are more rare," while other literary figures such as Edmund Spenser, John Donne, and Ben Jonson praised what Spenser called the "heavenly gifts and graces of her mind."

The fifth of seven children, Mary Sidney Herbert was born at Tickenhill Palace in Worcestershire, into an aristocratic family. Her father was the godson of Henry VIII and a close friend of Edward VI. Her mother was a lady in waiting to Queen Elizabeth, a post Mary herself was to fill between 1575 and 1577. Exceptionally well educated for her time—she knew Latin as well as French and Italian—she was always particularly close to her older brother Philip, with whom she shared a passion for literature. Married in 1577 to Henry Herbert, the earl of Pembroke, she settled with him at Wilton House, near Salisbury, one of the most majestic of England's stately homes, and in 1580, when Philip Sidney was temporarily exiled from Elizabeth's court, the poet made a number of long visits to her there. "In her time," remembered the seventeenth-century diarist John Aubrey, "Wilton House was like a college, there were so many learned and ingenious persons." It is likely that Sir Philip Sidney wrote portions of his *Arcadia* and wrote or revised his *Apology for Poetry* when he was in residence. In addition—to name only a few other members of the Wilton House circle—the poet Samuel Daniel was employed as a tutor for the countess's sons, and the chemist Adrian Gilbert, half-brother of Sir Walter Raleigh, had a laboratory in the house.

After Sir Philip Sidney was killed fighting in the Netherlands in 1586, his sister devoted herself to editing and publishing his poems. During the nineties, she also began working on translations of her own. Her most enduring accomplishment, however, was a continuation of the English version of the Psalms that her brother had begun before his death. Fascinating in its metrical variety and stanzaic inventiveness, the 150-psalm sequence—first published in its entirety in 1823—is a virtual compendium of Elizabethan verse strategies. Mary Sidney Herbert's renderings start with Psalm 44, and her style is brilliantly complex, as *To the Thrice-Sacred Queen Elizabeth* (her dedication of the psalms to the queen, included here) suggests. Whether she wrote many other original poems is not known, for a number of manuscripts may have been lost in a fire that destroyed the Wilton House library in 1647, twenty-six years after the countess's death. But even as it stands, Mary Sidney Herbert's achievement in translation and versification justifies Amelia Lanier's description of her as "a Lady whom Minerva [the goddess of wisdom] chose / To live with her in height of all respect."

To the Thrice-Sacred Queen Elizabeth[1]

1

Even now that care[2] which on thy crown attends
And with thy happy[3] greatness daily grows
Tells me, thrice-sacred Queen, my muse[4] offends,
And of respect to thee the line out goes.[5]
One instant will or willing can she lose[6]   5
I say not reading, but receiving rhymes,
On whom in chief dependeth to dispose[7]
What Europe acts in these most active times?

2

Yet dare I so, as humbleness may dare,
Cherish some hope they shall acceptance find;   10
Now weighing less thy state, lighter thy care,
But knowing more thy grace, abler thy mind.
What heavenly powers thee highest throne assigned,
Assigned thee goodness suiting that degree,[8]
And by thy strength thy burthen so designed,[9]   15
To others toil is exercise to thee.

3

Cares though still great, cannot be greatest still,
Business must ebb, though leisure never flow;
Then these the posts[1] of duty and goodwill
Shall press to offer what their senders[2] owe,   20
Which once in two, now in one subject go,
The poorer left, the richer[3] rest away,
Who better might (O might, ah word of woe)
Have given for me what I for him defray.[4]

4

How can I name whom sighing signs extend,[5]   25
And not unstop my tears' eternal spring?
But he did warp, I weaved this web to end;[6]
The stuff[7] not ours, our work no curious thing,

1. This poem was written to accompany a translation of the Psalms of David, begun by Herbert's brother Sir Philip Sidney and completed by Herbert after his death. Sidney was exiled from Elizabeth's court when he incurred her disfavor by counseling against a marriage with the duke of Anjou.
2. Burden.
3. Fortunate.
4. The poet's personal goddess of inspiration. In Greek myth, the muses were nine goddesses of art and inspiration, thought to be the daughters of memory.
5. I.e., the meter is broken.
6. I.e., Will she, or can she willingly, lose one instant. . . ?
7. Arrange, settle.
8. I.e., degree.

9. I.e., those powers designated your responsibilities according to your strength.
1. The poems, presumably as delivered to Elizabeth by postal couriers.
2. I.e., Herbert and the late Sidney. "Press": eagerly advance.
3. Sidney. "Rest" may here be a variation of "wrested," seized and pulled (by death).
4. Pay (metaphorically, present a tribute).
5. I.e., how can I name him (Sidney) to whom sighs, the signs of grief, are extended. . . ?
6. In clothmaking, to lay down the first set of threads (the warp), which is then intersected by another set (the woof). Herbert is referring to the fact that Sidney only began the Psalms, which she completed.
7. Raw material (i.e., the Hebrew Bible). "Curious": accomplished, ingenious.

Wherein yet well we thought the Psalmist King[8]
How English denizened, though Hebrew born,   30
Would to thy music undispleaséd sing,
Oft having worse, without repining worn;

5

And I the cloth in both our names present,
A livery robe[9] to be bestowed by thee;
Small parcel of the undischargéd rent,   35
From which no pains nor payments can us free.
And yet enough to cause our neighbors see
We will[1] our best, though scanted in our will;
And those nigh fields where sown they favors be
Unwealthy do, not else unworthy till.[2]   40

6

For in our work what bring we but thine own?
What English is, by many names is thine,
There humble laurels[3] in thy shadows grown
To garland others would themselves repine.[4]
Thy breast the cabinet,[5] thy seat the shrine,   45
Where muses hang their vowéd memories;
Where wit,[6] where art, where all that is divine
Conceivéd best, and best defended lies.

7

Which if men did not (as they do) confess,[7]
And wronging[8] worlds would otherwise consent,   50
Yet here who minds so meet a patroness[9]
For authors' state or writings' argument?[1]
A King should only to a Queen be sent;
God's lovéd choice unto his chosen love;
Devotion[2] to devotion's president;   55
What all applaud, to her whom none reprove.

8

And who sees ought, but sees[3] how justly square
His haughty ditties to thy glorious days?

---

8. David. "English denizened": naturalized as
an English subject. I.e., if David were an English
subject, he would willingly serve you, since he
had served under a worse ruler (the tyrant Saul)
without complaining.
9. Courtly dress. "Bestowed": housed, stored.
1. Desire to do. "Scanted": limited, or possibly
presumed to be inadequate (perhaps a reference
to Elizabeth's anger at Sidney).
2. I.e., we till the fields of your favor without
shows of wealth (as in costly gifts), but otherwise
worthily.
3. Leaves used to crown the heads of great poets.
4. I.e., the laurels themselves would complain at
being worn by others, since all English art ultimately stems from Elizabeth.

5. Small room. "Seat": place of abode and of rul-
ership.
6. Intelligence. "Conceived": understood.
7. I.e., if men did not agree that Elizabeth is the
author of all English works.
8. Doing a great wrong. "Consent": agree in
opinion.
9. I.e., who in England can remember so fitting a
supporter. . . ?
1. Plot or meaning; "state": financial condition.
2. Worship or prayer; the second usage is closer
to piety, devoutness. "President": one who presides, leads (as queen, Elizabeth was the head of
the church of England).
3. I.e., who sees anything, who does not see. . . ?
"Square" is a verb meaning "correspond," "fit."

How well beseeming[4] thee his triumphs are?
His hope, his zeal, his prayer, plaint, and praise,   60
Needless thy person[5] to their height to raise;
Less need to bend them down to thy degree;
These holy garments[6] each good soul assays,
Some sorting all, all sort[7] to none but thee.

9

For even thy rule is painted[8] in his reign;   65
Both clear in right; both nigh[9] by wrong oppressed;
And each at length (man crossing God in vain)
Possessed of place, and each in peace possessed.
Proud Philistines did interrupt his rest,
The foes of heaven no less have been thy foes;   70
He with great conquest, thou with greater blessed;
Thou sure to win, and he secure to lose.[1]

10

Thus hand in hand with him thy glories walk;
But who can trace them where alone they go?
Of thee who hemispheres on honor talk,[2]   75
And lands and seas thy trophies[3] jointly show.
The very winds did on thy party blow,
And rocks in arms thy foemen eft[4] defy.
But soft, my muse, thy pitch[5] is earthly love;
Forbear this heaven where only eagles fly.   80

11

Kings on a Queen enforced their states to lay;[6]
Mainlands for empire[7] waiting on an isle;
Men drawn by worth a woman to obey;
One moving all, herself unmoved the while;
Truth's restitution, vanity exile,   85
Wealth sprung of want, war held without annoy,[8]
Let subject be of some inspired style,
Till then the object of her subjects' joy.

---

4. Matching, resembling. "Triumphs": both victories and triumphal songs.
5. Self.
6. I.e., the psalms. "Assays": tries on.
7. A play on "sort": (1) going through, (2) are appropriate.
8. Represented, figured.
9. Almost; "oppressed" is probably closer to "defeated" than in its modern meaning. Both Elizabeth and David reigned during times of war; their enemies, the Spanish and the Philistines, were perceived as enemies of the true religion.
1. I.e., facing overwhelming odds against winning.
2. I.e., talk of your honor.
3. Victories. In 1588 England defeated the

Spanish Armada, with the aid of the weather.
4. Probably a misprint for "oft." "Rocks": an allusion to David's killing of the Philistine Goliath with a single stone; here they represent cannonballs. The rocks defy or challenge the foemen.
5. In music, a tone or level of dynamics. Here, the subject of the muse's song. Herbert feels she is not qualified to write of war, traditionally a male subject.
6. I.e., kings forced to place their states under Elizabeth's rule; Herbert is somewhat exaggerating Elizabeth's gains in power.
7. Government. "Waiting on": obeying; also courting.
8. Vexation.

12

Thy utmost[9] can but offer to her sight
Her handmaids' task, which most her will endears;[1]   90
And pray unto thy pains life from that light
Which lively light some, court and kingdom cheers,[2]
What[3] wish she may (far past her living peers
And rival still to Judah's faithful king)[4]
In more than he and more triumphant years,[5]   95
Sing what God doth, and do what men may sing.

1599   1962

9. I.e., Herbert's muse's greatest effort.
1. I.e., simple tokens of loyalty are more endearing to the queen than great works.
2. I.e., that lively light (Elizabeth) which is cheered by court and kingdom. The meaning of

"some" here is not clear; it may be a misprint.
3. Who (i.e., court and kingdom).
4. David; "Judah" is another name for Israel.
5. I.e., in a longer and more triumphant reign.

AMELIA LANIER
1570?–1640?

Known in her own day as a woman "of distinguished . . . learning," Amelia Lanier spent much of her career at court during the reigns of Elizabeth I, James I, and Charles I. Though her origins are obscure—even her parentage is uncertain—it is known that she was married to a royal musician, Alphonso Lanier, and that she bore him a son, Henry, who entered the king's service as a flutist. After her husband's death in 1613, she appears to have been involved with his relatives in various legal squabbles over his estate. Otherwise her history is shadowy, although the historian A. L. Rowse has recently argued that she may well have been the "Dark Lady" of Shakespeare's sonnets, the independent and impetuous mistress to whom the great playwright claimed he was hopelessly enthralled.

Whatever the truth about this poet's life, her verse is striking and accomplished, so much so that Rowse uses its radicalism as a basis for his assertion about her role in Shakespeare's poetry. In particular, her retelling of the biblical story of the "fall" functions as a kind of pioneering vindication of the rights of "Our Mother Eve," who, declares Lanier, gave Adam "What she held most dear"—the apple of knowledge—because she was "simply good." In fact, insists Lanier, Eve's primordial female act of "betrayal" was performed in unconscious innocence, while men are more culpable because they consciously betrayed Jesus Christ to his crucifixion: "If one weak woman simply did offend, / This sin of yours hath no excuse, nor end." Significantly, in sketching out such a feminist version of two of Western culture's major legends, Lanier outlined a pattern of revisionary mythmaking that was to be followed by many female descendants who may never even have read her work.

From Salve Deus Rex Judaeorum

[*Eve's Apology in Defense of Women*]

Now Pontius Pilate is to judge the cause[1]
Of faultless Jesus, who before him stands,
Who neither hath offended prince, nor laws,
Although he now be brought in woeful bands.
"O noble governor, make thou yet a pause,   5
Do not in innocent blood imbrue[2] thy hands;
  But hear the words of thy most worthy wife,[3]
  Who sends to thee, to beg her Saviour's life.

"Let barbarous cruelty far depart from thee,
And in true justice take affliction's part;   10
Open thine eyes, that thou the truth mayest see.
Do not the thing that goes against thy heart,
Condemn not him that must thy Saviour be;
But view his holy life, his good desert.
  Let not us women glory in men's fall.[4]   15
  Who had power given to overrule us all.

"Till now your indiscretion sets us free,
And makes our former fault[5] much less appear;
Our mother Eve, who tasted of the tree,
Giving to Adam what she held most dear,   20
Was simply good, and had no power to see;[6]
The after-coming harm did not appear:
  The subtle serpent that our sex betrayed
  Before our fall so sure a plot had laid

"That undiscerning ignorance perceived   25
No guile or craft that was by him intended;
For had she known of what we were bereaved,[7]
To his request she had not condescended.
But she, poor soul, by cunning was deceived;
No hurt therein her harmless heart intended: 30
  For she alleged[8] God's word, which he denies,
  That they should die, but even as gods be wise.

---

1. Case; Pontius Pilate was the Roman official who authorized Christ's execution.
2. Stain.
3. According to Matthew, Pilate's wife wrote a letter to her husband telling him of a dream she had, which warned against harming Jesus.
4. The fall of both Adam and Christ (perhaps also Pilate).
5. Eve's tempting of Adam in Eden.
6. According to the Book of Genesis, Eve, the first woman, enticed her husband Adam at the behest of the serpent to eat of an apple from the forbidden Tree of Knowledge. As punishment God banished Adam and Eve from the Garden of Eden and brought death into the world.
7. Deprived, specifically of immortal life.
8. Cited, repeated. The referent of "he" is unclear; it may be either the serpent or Adam. In any case, Eve seems aware that the consequences of her act are mortality, but prefers godlike wisdom to immortal ignorance.

"But surely Adam cannot be excused;
Her fault though great, yet he was most to blame.
What weakness offered, strength might have refused;   35
Being lord of all, the greater was his shame;
Although the serpent's craft had her abused,
God's holy word ought all his actions frame;[9]
    For he was lord and king of all the earth,
    Before poor Eve had either life or breath,   40

"Who being framed[1] by God's eternal hand
The perfectest man that ever breathed on earth,
And from God's mouth received that strait[2] command,
The breach whereof he knew was present death;
Yea, having power to rule both sea and land,   45
Yet with one apple won to lose that breath[3]
    Which God had breathéd in his beauteous face,
    Bringing us all in danger and disgrace;

"And then to lay the fault on patience's back,
That we (poor women) must endure it all;   50
We know right well he did discretion lack,
Being not persuaded thereunto at all.
If Eve did err, it was for knowledge sake;
The fruit being fair persuaded him to fall.
    No subtle serpent's falsehood did betray him;   55
    If he would eat it, who had power to stay[4] him?

"Not Eve, whose fault was only too much love,
Which made her give this present to her dear,
That what she tasted he likewise might prove,[5]
Whereby his knowledge might become more clear;   60
He never sought her weakness to reprove
With those sharp words which he of God did hear;
    Yet men will boast of knowledge, which he took
    From Eve's fair hand, as from a learned book.

"If any evil did in her remain,   65
Being made of him,[6] he was the ground of all.
If one of many worlds[7] could lay a stain
Upon our sex, and work so great a fall
To wretched man by Satan's subtle train,[8]
What will so foul a fault amongst you all?[9]   70

---

9. Enclose, determine.
1. Here, made or fashioned.
2. Strict.
3. I.e., the breath of immortal life.
4. Prevent.
5. Experience.
6. In Genesis, Eve was formed from Adam's rib.

7. One woman out of many. "Worlds" probably is meant to suggest great quantities.
8. Satan's serpentine arguments to Eve. Later tradition identified Satan with the serpent; Genesis makes no such connection.
9. Implicitly, how great a stigma will your crime cast upon your sex?

Her weakness did the serpent's words obey,
But you in malice God's dear son betray,

"Whom, if unjustly you condemn to die,
Her sin was small to what you do commit.
All mortal sins[1] that do for vengeance cry   75
Are not to be compared unto it;
If many worlds would altogether try
By all their sins the wrath of God to get,
    This sin of yours surmounts them all as far
    As doth the sun another little star.[2]   80

"Then let us have our liberty again,
And challenge[3] to yourselves no sovereignty.
You came not in the world without our pain,
Make that a bar[4] against your cruelty;
Your fault being greater, why should you disdain   85
Our being your equals, free from tyranny?
    If one weak woman simply did offend,
    This sin of yours hath no excuse nor end,

"To which, poor souls, we never gave consent.
Witness, thy wife, O Pilate, speaks for all,   90
Who did but dream, and yet a message sent
That thou shouldest have nothing to do at all
With that just man;[6] which, if thy heart relent,
Why wilt thou be a reprobate with Saul[7]
    To seek the death of him that is so good,   95
    For thy soul's health to shed his dearest blood?"

1611

---

1. Sins punishable by eternal damnation.
2. It was then assumed, on the Ptolemaic model, that the sun actually was larger than the stars.
3. Claim.
4. Check, prevention.

5. Purpose.
6. Christ.
7. King of Israel who went mad periodically; "reprobate": morally unprincipled person.

Literature of the Seventeenth and Eighteenth Centuries

In her fantasy, *Orlando* (1928), Virginia Woolf told the story of a writer, representing English literary history, who was born male during the Renaissance and started life as an Elizabethan, but turned into a woman in the second half of the seventeenth century. Her protagonist's sex change dramatizes a major event in the history of English letters, namely, the entrance of women into the literary marketplace. Not insignificantly, a number of women began to write and publish just when the production of literature became commercialized, when the patron started to give way to the printer, and the small courtly audience began to give way to a large reading public. For the first time, too, many of these women were not exceptionally privileged by virtue of their aristocratic rank or religious calling; some, indeed, were ordinary middle-class women.

What in *A Room of One's Own* Woolf considers "a change" of "greater importance than the Crusades or the Wars of the Roses"—the moment when the middle-class woman began to write—took place during an era of transition that is usually associated with the emergence of the modern world. Such vocations as law, medicine, science, journalism, and politics became professionalized in ways that would have been unimaginable before. On both sides of the Atlantic, the religious disputes of the seventeenth century gave way to the commercial growth of the eighteenth century: the Church of England was supplemented as a central cultural institution by the Bank of England, and the early Puritan settlers, pilgrims searching for an earthly paradise, were succeeded by American citizens determined to establish their economic independence. The religious, intellectual, and social movements that accompanied this transformation—Puritanism, empiricism, and urbanization—had a paradoxical and complex impact on women's lives, on the one hand overtly excluding women or further subjecting them to male regulation, and on the other hand implicitly providing precedents for questioning the conventional authorities who had defined women as the second sex. While, as many historians have argued, women's contribution to production decreased when the English and American economies shifted from agriculture to manufacturing and commerce, the spread of education and the expansion of middle-class professions helped make possible the emergence of productive, publishing literary women, who began to form a unique tradition of their own.

English Revolution and Consolidation

English political history in the seventeenth century, which has been characterized as "a history of hurts," included two revolutions within fifty years, two kings deposed and one killed, and an Anglican church which was consolidated, overthrown, and rebuilt. Civil strife was a direct result of religious disputes dating back to the Reformation, when the Church of England separated from the Catholic church, for radical reformers continued to believe that the church had to "purify" itself further of Catholic rites and creeds. Attacking the church, which was the official church of England, such Puritans fought for civic and religious freedom from the authority of the Bishops and the authoritarianism of the Stuart kings, James I (1603–1625) and Charles I (1625–1649). They were therefore viewed as rebels by both moderate Protestants and Catholics. But a crisis ensued when the Stuart monarchs aligned themselves with Rome, levied high taxes, and attempted to assert, as James I did, that "kings are not only God's lieutenants on earth, but even by God himself they are called gods." Many moderate Protestants in Parliament, elected representatives of men of property, united with the reformers against the crown. By 1642, the struggle between Parliament and king—Puritans and Royalists, country and court—culminated in armed conflict. The execution of King Charles I in 1649 and the succession of Oliver Cromwell, the leader of the parliamentary army and Lord Protector of England (1653–1658), hastened the rise to power of the middle class, led to the persecution of such supposedly tradition-bound groups as Anglicans and Catholics, and—perhaps most importantly—effectively ended the divine right of the king.

Before, during, and after the English Civil War, many Parliamentarians and Royalists feared the chaos associated with a growing number of radical Protestant sects. Such anxious citizens as Samuel Pepys and John Evelyn recorded the confusion of the times in their diaries. Pepys, for example, described a royalist uncle condemned in the Tower of London while another uncle served as a captain in the parliamentary militia, and Evelyn protested against an anarchistic mechanic preaching "feculent stuff" from a church pulpit. Nevertheless, the political upheavals of the seventeenth century had a liberating impact on the lives of many women, for the Puritan Revolution created a crisis in which women on both sides were charged with new, unforeseen responsibilites. Royalists like Margaret Cavendish, duchess of Newcastle, and Charlotte Stanley, countess of Derby, defended their homes against parliamentary armies or traveled back and forth between England and France in their husbands' behalf. Similarly, Puritans like Lucy Hutchinson and Quakers like Margaret Fell recorded their efforts to help their families survive quickly shifting political circumstances. Still, their virtual exclusion from political institutions meant that their role was confined mainly to personal influence in a time when revolutionary instability was followed first by conservative reaction and then by compromise.

Internal disputes among Parliamentarians, fear of fanaticism and the mob, desire for stability, and dislike of military rule resulted in the Restoration of the Stuart monarchy of Charles II (1660–1685). Whereas Catholic families and royalist bishops had been persecuted under Cromwell, Puritans were excluded from positions of civil and religious authority during the reign of Charles II. In stark contrast to the Puritans, who had closed the theaters and instituted fines against swearing, drinking, and dancing, aristocratic courtiers in the Restoration quickly became infamous for the sexual freedom that was reflected in the comedies now performed regularly on the reopened stage, not only by actors, but, for the first time, by actresses too. In spite of the courtly decadence associated with, for instance, Charles II's actress-mistress Nell Gwyn, however, the king had to conform to the policies of a Parliament which worked to strengthen England's trading and agricultural industries, for the balance of power had already begun to shift from the court to the city, from the king to the two-party system: the Tories, associated with a conservative aristocracy, and the Whigs, identified with the growing commercial class. When the restored Stuart monarchs again asserted their autonomy, as well as their sympathy with Roman Catholicism, popular sentiment led to the so-called Glorious Revolution of 1689. Charles II's successor, James II (1685–1688), was forced to relinquish the crown to his Protestant daughter and her husband, a nonviolent change in government that promised an end to a century of violent upheaval and the beginning of a stable equilibrium. John Dryden expressed the relieved optimism of the next generation when, in his *Secular Masque* (1700), he exclaimed, " 'Tis well an old age is out, / And time to begin a new."

As divisive as these civil and religious disorders undoubtedly were, they had, by the middle of the eighteenth century, given way to a secularized, parliamentary government. Church and state had been effectively separated, and an Act of Toleration (1689) freed Dissenters (Protestants outside the Church of England) from religious persecution. Parliament also joined Scotland with England and established the stability of royal succession. Religious toleration and governmental continuity were matched by freedom of the press and free trade. With Parliament now controlling taxation and foreign policy, England became the wealthiest world power. Throughout the eighteenth century, the authority of government continued to shift from the court to the Parliament and the ministerial cabinet, an institution that took shape during the reign of Anne (1702–1714) and became dominant during Sir Robert Walpole's long ministry (1721–1742), in part because the three King Georges (1712–1820) were less than charismatic leaders. By midcentury, when the last Stuart heir was defeated in his effort to restore a more orthodox monarchy, mercantile interests provided the impetus for a series of wars against France, which led to England's acquisition of an empire reaching from India to Gibraltar to Canada. Paradoxically, however, the very principles of religious toleration, civic autonomy, and vigorous mercantile development that infused eighteenth-century English growth would lead in America to a revolt against English rule.

The New World

The Puritans began to leave England before the Civil War. From 1629 to 1640, thousands, mostly from the middle classes, emigrated to New England in the hope of finding a place free from the religious persecution and economic harassment they associated with the Old World. After an arduous, three-month voyage across the Atlantic, the emigrants embarked upon what the colonist Samuel Danforth described as "an errand into the wilderness." They were strengthened to face the threats of illness, privation, wild animals, and homesickness by the conviction that, like the tribe of Moses in search of the promised land, they had received a divine covenant, which would enable them to build a holy "city on the hill" in the New World. Puritan leaders in the Massachusetts Bay Colony like John Winthrop and Cotton Mather saw America as an ideal location for a "new Zion," a theocracy in which God's will could be carried out without interference from Anglican bishops or English monarchs.

Whether the impetus for settlement was predominantly religious, as in Pennsylvania, where the Quakers sought refuge, or financial, as in Virginia, with its profitable tobacco crop, many later colonists saw the New World as an inspiring, if sometimes bewildering, opportunity for development. Yet the eastern edge of the American continent was also being populated by prisoners sent by their jailors, convicts transported by their judges, indentured servants, and slaves sold to Southern planters by English, French, Portuguese, and Spanish traders. By the 1770s and 1780s, seventy thousand African slaves were landed annually, half of them carried in British ships. Chained into overcrowded and filthy quarters, thousands of Africans died of smallpox, dysentery, insanity, and suicidal mutinies throughout the eighteenth century. Meanwhile, the number of colonists grew from 111,000 in 1670 to 1,600,000 by 1760. During the second half of the century, they were joined by additional Dutch, French Protestant, and German settlers. Together, the colonists appropriated the lands of native American Indians, who were forced either to migrate or fight.

Economic impediments, brought about by parliamentary acts, led the colonists toward the independence movement. England's policy of taxation without representation fueled American resentment, and political resistance to George III reached new heights in a skeptical generation that no longer espoused the Puritanism of the pioneers: Benjamin Franklin, for example, began his publishing career by writing the *Silence Dogood Papers* (1722), a satire on Cotton Mather's *Essays to Do Good* (1710). If America was still viewed as "the most perfect society now existing in the world," as it was by the French settler Jean de Crèvecoeur in 1782, it was precisely because it was free of the religious fervor prevalent in Europe, for "zeal in Europe is confined . . . a grain of powder enclosed; here it burns away in the open air, and consumes without effect." Essayists and philosophers based their arguments for separation from England on the national identity of America, as did poets like Philip Freneau and Hugh Henry Brackenridge when they delivered a collaborative *Poem on the Rising Glory of America* at the 1771 Princeton commencement. When attempts of king and Parliament to control the political and economic life of the American colonies finally led to the revolution of 1776, that insurrection was also justified by English-born men like Tom Paine and Joseph Priestley, who supported the inalienable rights of ordinary citizens as opposed to the tyrannies of kings, states, and churches. Their ideal had informed the English Civil War, and it would profoundly affect not only the lives but the letters of women on both sides of the Atlantic.

Puritanism

Puritanism, which shaped English history and American identity throughout the seventeenth century, dramatically endowed the inner life of the self and the historical development of the state with divine significance. Early English and colonial Puritans believed that, after Adam's fall, God had offered a Covenant of Grace through Christ to certain elect souls. Because God was thought to visit his grace directly on each of these individuals, the Puritans minimized the rule of church ritual and liturgy, and instead emphasized each individual's need to study the self, the world, and the Bible so as to attain spiritual certitude and moral rectitude. Advocating what the historian Christopher Hill has called "a doctrine of spiritual equality" ("one good man was as good as another, and better than a bad peer or bishop or king"), the Puritans in England posed the challenge of individual conscience to civil and religious institutions, for the "Witness of the Indwelling Spirit" was a better spiritual authority than the Anglican church, which had not yet "purified" itself "to recover," in the phrase of William Bradford, first governor of Plymouth, "primitive order, liberty, and beauty."

Besides raising the individual's conscience above the dictates of the church, the doctrine of predestination meant that "though none are Sav'd that wickednesse imbrace, / Yet none are Damn'd that have Inherent Grace," or so it was interpreted by the colonial poet Edward Taylor in his *God's Determinations Touching His Elect* (c. 1690). Puritans could not earn grace through good works; however, English preachers like Thomas Taylor explained that "we teach that only doers shall be saved, and by their doing though not for their doing." In the cosmic drama of salvation that they witnessed in their private and public lives, therefore, Puritan poets and preachers were motivated by a high sense of moral purpose that paradoxically infused not only their struggle to wean the soul away from earthly desire, but also their effort to serve the community through productive labor. If Puritanism thereby fostered self-education and spiritual introspection, it also contributed, as a number of sociologists have pointed out, to the rise of capitalism.

Before and after the Civil War in England, the Puritans were stereotyped as sternly self-absorbed fanatics, opposed to the frivolity and idolatry of the arts. Both English and colonial writers did, in fact, express their distrust of the imagination, in much the same strain as Cotton Mather when, in 1726, he warned ministry students to "beware of a boundless and sickly appetite for the reading of the poems which now the rickety nation swarms withal." Yet the aim of Puritanism was not to obliterate imaginative literature, but to turn it toward the search for evidences of God's grace. During the Civil War, pulpit oratory and political pamphleteering resulted in a simpler, more functional prose style. Not only the bawdy satires of Ben Jonson and the melodramatic tragedies of John Webster, but the elaborately paradoxical poems of Richard Crashaw and John Donne were succeeded by introspective, spiritual meditations on biblical themes. The publication of the King James version of the Bible in 1611 had already made that book more widely read than ever before. Second only in popularity during this period was John Bunyan's *The Pilgrim's Progress* (1678), a prose allegory written while Bunyan was in jail for his religious beliefs. Just as

Bunyan in England stressed the virtues of faith and industry, American Puritans like John Winthrop and Cotton Mather traced the New World's mission in terms of God's covenant with man. A similar confidence that history develops according to a providential plan characterizes the highly popular Indian captivity narrative authored by Mary Rowlandson, who witnessed her own and her children's injuries and escapes as divine signs of God's grand design.

In its emphasis on the importance of each soul, its association of atheism with illiteracy, and its concomitant commitment to the education of the laity, Puritanism allowed a number of women to explore and articulate the authority of their spiritual experiences. Although, as the historian Sheila Rowbotham has argued, Puritan culture reenforced the power of the father as the head of the family, it defined the wife as her husband's partner: her soul was equal to his in the sight of God. The emphasis on conscience, not only in Puritanism but also in other dissenting Protestant sects, meant that women were sometimes allowed to preach, as Jane Holmes, Anne Wentworth, and Margaret Fox did in the seventeenth century and as Ann Lee, Joanna Southcott, and Betty Gray did in the eighteenth century. Significantly, the Protestant mystic Jane Lead prophesied a female savior, a "woman clothed with the sun," while the Quaker Margaret Fell argued that Christ was the same in men and women, who could both speak of and for him. In addition, implicitly granting authority to the female conscience as well as to the male, the self-consciousness of Puritanism made possible Anne Bradstreet's meditative poetry.

Nevertheless, like most Puritan women, Bradstreet was forbidden to participate publicly in the interpretation of Scripture and excluded from the governing boards that ruled over civic and religious issues. Both English literary history and American social history provide evidence that, as potentially liberating as Puritanism could be for women, it was embedded in a patriarchal ideology that was hostile to women. The clash between the midwife-preacher Anne Hutchinson and the Puritan theocracy of Boston demonstrates just how threatening a woman preacher could seem, for Mistress Hutchinson was attacked by civil and religious authorities after she had attracted as many as sixty people to her discussions of the "indwelling Christ." Found guilty of heresy, she was excommunicated by the church and banished from the colony. Subsequent lecturers in Boston described an infant Hutchinson had miscarried in prison as a "monstrous birth" that "embodied her spiritual errors" and as "the work of the devil," an apelike being with horns and claws. Like that of Bradstreet's sister, who was also excommunicated for her preaching, the case of Anne Hutchinson highlights the misogyny that informed the Salem witchcraft trials. Nineteen people and two dogs were hanged for witchcraft in those trials, and few people appear to have had the audacity of Sarah Good, who, when convicted during one such trial, cried out on the scaffold to the Reverend Nicholas Noye, "You are a liar. I am no more a witch than you are a wizard, and if you take away my life God will give you blood to drink."

In England, the two-edged implications of Puritan thought were probably best expressed by John Milton, who composed the age's principal hymn to matrimonial love in his epic poem *Paradise Lost* (1667). In the garden of Eden, Adam and Eve express pleasure at finding the mutuality of their desire for each other, for sexuality is the "perpetual fountain of domestic sweets" and Adam's higher reason is said to complement Eve's greater sensitivity. Drawing on Puritan arguments for freedom of choice in marriage and on the idea of the wife as a helpmate, Milton argued in a number of tracts that wives could sue for divorce from husbands and that "unchastity" was worse in men than in women. Yet in *Paradise Lost*, Milton portrayed an Eve created out of and for Adam. Following the biblical story, moreover, he allotted culpability for the Fall to a woman who disobeys not only God's commandment but Milton's description of her proper place: "He for God only, she for God in him." Eve's fascination with Satan leads to man's Fall and humankind's punishment: expulsion from paradise, mortality, and labor. Just as important, Eve's alliance with Satan is prefigured in the poem by the thralldom of the allegorical figure Sin, who also serves Satan and brings death into the world. To be sure, in the moral scheme of Milton's epic Sin signifies a great deal more than maternity. But because she is the only mother in the work, it seems crucial that she foreshadows the painful maternity which is God's punishment of Eve by embodying a nauseated sense of female generativity, for Sin breeds innumerable hellhounds, animals that emerge from and return to her womb, where they bark and howl unseen. Milton's Puritan radicalism—his defense of regicide, republicanism, and freedom of the press—did not extend to women, as Mary Astell would point out when she wondered why a man so concerned about freedom did not "cry up liberty to poor female slaves." Images of women in *Paradise Lost* would haunt women writers from Mary Wollstonecraft to Charlotte Brontë and Virginia Woolf. As the scholar Hilda L. Smith has argued, however, the Puritan protest against tyranny that Milton articulated may have contributed to the rise of feminism, because in that protest women could witness their exclusion from even the most radical movement of their time.

Science and Rationalism

Perhaps, as some historians have suggested, it was precisely the civic and religious upheavals of the seventeenth century that gave rise to the belief that no single creed could be accepted over all the others. In any case, the tolerant pluralism that characterized eighteenth-century intellectual history was in part the result of direct challenges to traditional religion, challenges associated with the rise of mathematics, physics, and anatomy. The telescope, which furnished evidence of a Copernican universe, and the microscope, which provided proof of the corpuscular composition of the blood and thereby added the final support to Harvey's theory of circulation, were both invented in the seventeenth century, as were such instruments as the barometer and the thermometer. At the beginning of the century, Francis Bacon (1561–1626) emphasized the need to liberate knowledge from blind acceptance of Greek and medieval philosophies by testing authority against experience. Already in Bacon's time, poets and theologians like John Donne worried that the "new philosophy calls all in doubt; / The element of fire is quite put out," for the world seemed "all in pieces, all coherence gone." By the Restoration, however, science had become fashionable in court, and the Royal Society, a scientific institute, was founded with the motto *Nullius in verba*, meaning "on the word of no one."

Although advances like Robert Boyle's substitution of chemistry for medieval alchemy were viewed by many as a direct assault on religion, the scientists' investigations of physical experience were not unrelated to the Puritans' spiritual examination of personal experience. By the turn of the century, moreover, a number of empiricists sought to affirm the principles of a new faith based upon the "laws" of nature that Sir Isaac Newton (1642–1727) had discovered by applying mathematics to physics. The result was Deism, a philosophy that viewed nature as a well-ordered mechanism in which God functioned only as a divine mechanic. Rejecting the need for supernatural revelation in general and for Christian doctrine in particular, the Deists assumed that logic and observation would allow them to deduce the intelligibility and coherence of the universe. Just as the philosopher John Locke (1632–1704) explained with confidence that "the works of nature in every part of them sufficiently evidence a Deity," Alexander Pope proclaimed in his *Essay on Man* (1733–1734), "All are but parts of one stupendous whole: / Whose body Nature is, and God the soul."

Both the new science and Deism exerted a profound effect on eighteenth-century literature. Gone were the baroque rhetorical flourishes of "false wit," replaced by what Jonathan Swift hailed as a "clear, masculine, and smooth" style. Inspiration was derided by English satirists as "enthusiasm," which was associated with the madness of the Puritans in particular and the Whigs in general, for some of the most prominent writers of this period were conservatives whose satire attempted to right the wrongs of an age descending into crass commercialism and individualism. Modeling their work on the poetry produced by Virgil and Horace in the Rome of Augustus, these Augustan or neoclassical writers assumed that, if nature had its laws, then poetry probably did too. While literary critics began to enumerate the rules that regulated various genres, poets like Dryden and Pope assumed that the classics best articulated general truths about the nature of man, so that "Homer and Nature were," in fact, "the same." They chose the heroic couplet—two rhymed lines composed in iambic pentameter—for a discursive, public poetry that was as didactic as the new science was utilitarian.

While many of the satirists were pessimistic about the depravity of humanity and society, Pope's optimism in his *Essay on Man*—"Whatever IS, is RIGHT"—resembled the cheerful argument of the Whig philosopher Anthony Ashley Cooper, third earl of Shaftesbury: because human nature is as well constructed as physical nature, Shaftesbury reasoned, an innate benevolence governs man's moral instincts. The cult of feeling that would develop out of this idea was associated with the sympathetic tears that heroes and heroines alike shed from the 1720s on in sentimental comedies on the English stage. Paradoxically, however, Deism also contributed to the formation of what the title of a book by Tom Paine called *The Age of Reason* (1795): not only did Paine's book begin with the assertion that all institutions of faith have tyrannized over humankind, it also went on to attack the Bible, contrasting a corrupt Solomon, with his seven hundred wives and three hundred concubines, to an enlightened Benjamin Franklin, whose "mind was ever young, [whose] temper ever serene; science, that never grows gray, was always his mistress." The new secularism doubtless molded Benjamin Franklin and Thomas Jefferson, both of whom played important roles in the American version of the Royal Society. Indeed, Franklin's experiments in electricity reflected the sanguine practicality of his famous *Almanac* (1732–1757) and *Autobiography* (1791), just as Jefferson's rejection of "superstition" in his *The Life and Morals of Jesus of Nazareth* represented the same confidence in a well-regulated universe that inspired him to construct a government that would "govern least."

By the middle of the eighteenth century, the new empiricism had contributed to a general decline in traditional religion, which was only further accelerated in England by the complacency of the church. On both sides of the Atlantic, the 1740s saw religious revivals that were clearly a reaction against the weakening of traditional faith. In England, John Wesley began to preach salvation through Christ to large middle- and working-class crowds in open air meetings. Although his followers, known as Methodists, were initially ridiculed as illiterate fanatics, the spiritual fervor of this movement had after a time a major impact within the church, inspiring the growth of evangelicalism. In America, the first Great Awakening was led, in part, by the eminent American preacher Jonathan Edwards, and it too gave rise to a great number of what Edwards himself called "surprising conversions."

That Edwards was eventually forced to resign from his church by his own congregation, however, illustrates the changing religious temper of the times. The inductive method, respect for each individual's experience, and belief in the innate benevolence of the creator undermined the influences of Edwards' sovereign and arbitrary God. For all the severity of his sermon *Sinners in the Hands of an Angry God* (1741), moreover, Edwards himself wrote a scientific essay, *Of Insects*, early in life, read John Locke at Yale University, and ended his career by returning to the mystical pantheism of his youth. Similarly, Wesley, who preached forty thousand sermons and traveled many thousands of miles on horseback, tried to keep his followers within the Church of England and maintained a lively, observant *Journal* that was published posthumously. In other words, even those thinkers who opposed the secularization of culture demonstrated the new fascination with documentation which developed in proliferating diaries, biographies, travelogues, histories, natural histories, and encyclopedias.

Not a few women lamented the fact that men "refuse to let us know / What sacred Science doth impart." Yet, from Margaret Cavendish's scientific investigations to Sarah Frye Egerton's poem in praise of Robert Boyle and Mary Wortley Montagu's pioneering advocacy of innoculation, literary women were involved in the scientific revolution of their time. As with Puritanism, the impact of the new science on women's history was complex. On the one hand, as the scholar Carolyn Merchant has shown, Bacon's view that nature had to be "hounded in her wanderings"—that the scientist should "torture nature's secrets from her"—paralleled the widespread torture of witches in the early seventeenth century and reduced men's sense of responsibility to an earth no longer viewed as a nurturing mother. On the other hand, the materialistic philosophers associated with this revolution called into question the divine right of patriarchal authority. In his *Leviathan* (1651), Thomas Hobbes described the state of nature as a matriarchy in which "every woman that bears children, becomes both a mother and a lord." Although Hobbes argued that the predatory precultural state is bestial and must be replaced by the consent of men to the authority of a powerful king, his theory nevertheless undermined the idea of the father's natural ownership of the child, as did John Locke's direct attack on the "absolute arbitrary dominion of the father."

Just as important, Locke's psychological model of the mind as a *tabula rasa* (blank tablet) implied that all knowledge is the result of sensuous experience. Besides opening up the discourse of rights and responsibilities, then, Locke paved a way to the realism that would allow many eighteenth-century women to record in letters and journals the private experiences that had shaped their development. Similarly, both the cult of sentimentality fostered by Deist benevolence and the religious revivals of the 1740s quickly became associated with women, who had, since Milton's time, been identified with an emotional receptivity thought to complement male rationalism: it is hardly insignificant that John Wesley, the founder of Methodism, was said to have acquired his new doctrines from his mother's preachings and that the tearful heroine of Samuel Richardson's *Pamela* (1740), a best seller both in England and America, embodied the middle-class virtues of industry, moral integrity, and upward mobility. Yet the rise of the novel, which was so important to women's history, was dependent not only on the new empiricism and the cult of sentimentality, but also on the formation of a middle-class reading public, a development which reflected the extraordinary growth of capitalism in the late eighteenth century.

Urbanization

As England moved from a predominantly rural economy of local farmers and yeomen to an industrial economy of large landholders and national markets, it became what the novelist Daniel Defoe (1659–1731) called "the most flourishing and opulent country in the world." After the founding of the Bank of England (1694) and the world's first stock exchange (1689) made possible vast investments both in England and in the colonies, inventions like Newcomen's steam pump (1712), Kemp's flying shuttle (1733), Hargreaves's spinning jenny (1764), Arkwright's water frame (1764), and Cartwright's power loom (1785–1787) began to transform the woolen industry, which manufactured England's most stable export. In addition, large landowners began consolidating open fields previously cultivated by tenant farmers, and this process (called *enclosure*) permitted techniques of farming to be applied on a more productive scale, although it also turned many independent smallholders into agricultural laborers. Coalmining and ironmongering grew, sustained by Watt's new steam engine (1769), so that the midland cities began to expand. With the shift of population to industrial towns, the English working class began to face the exploitative conditions that would give rise at the end of the century to trade unionism.

London remained the center of what was now the first of the industrialized countries. After the Great Fire of 1666 destroyed many sections of the city, the capital was rebuilt on a larger scale, and the architect Sir Christopher Wren established his reputation with St. Paul's Church while the painter William Hogarth gained renown with his portrayals of London street scenes. Celia Fienne's *Journey through England on Side Saddle in the Time of William and Mary* (1702) described the hazardous road conditions outside London in the late seventeenth century, but by the middle of the eighteenth century turnpikes and macadamized roads connected the capital to the rest of Great Britain, as did canals, which gave the country the most efficient system of transport it had known. A falling death rate after 1740 and a rising birth rate caused the population to grow steadily in the last decades of the eighteenth century. A similar growth spurt in America created three cities—Boston, New York, and Philadelphia—that were larger than any English towns other than London.

The growth of these urban centers throughout the eighteenth century was reflected in the cosmopolitan wit of much writing which focused on topical social and political issues. The first daily newspapers—for instance, *The Daily Courant* (1702) in England and the *News-Letter* (1704) in Boston—as well as periodicals like *The Spectator*, *The Gentleman's Magazine*, and *The American Magazine*, published reviews, stories, social instruction, and moral essays for the literati, who populated coffeehouses on both sides of the Atlantic. In addition, by the second decade of the eighteenth century there were already more than seventy printing and publishing shops in London. Although the Augustan wits leveled much of their satire against the mediocrity they associated with commercial writing, the literary marketplace had been transformed. "Writing," as Defoe explained in 1725, had "become a very considerable branch of the English commerce," a view corroborated by the fact that he sold eighty thousand copies of *The True-Born Englishman*.

Pope was the first major English poet to support himself through the sales of his books, and his most influential successor, Dr. Samuel Johnson, the son of a Lichfield bookseller, was the first major author to establish his reputation through scholarship (his *Dictionary*, 1755), criticism (his *Lives of the Poets*, 1779–1781), and conversational genius (preserved in James Boswell's *Life*, 1791). With the proliferation of publishing houses in America, moreover, American writers were less dependent on English acceptance than they had been at the beginning of the century. But the threat to neoclassical standards posed by the commercialization of literature and the emergence of subscription sales and circulating libraries is probably best gauged by the growing popularity of a new form which was appropriately called the novel. Both Daniel Defoe, a journalist-turned-novelist who wrote about an entrepreneurial adventurer in *Robinson Crusoe* (1719), and Samuel Richardson, a printer-turned-novelist who wrote about an industrious servant girl in *Pamela*, articulated the bourgeois values of the large reading public who bought unprecedented numbers of their books.

Perhaps no other change had a greater impact on literary women than the demise of the older, more closed patronage system for the support of authors, and this change was instantaneous. After Charles II licensed two theatrical companies, women dramatists from Aphra Behn to Susannah Centlivre, Mary Pix, and Catherine Trotter began producing and publishing their own plays. Behn's *Oroonoko* (1688), sometimes considered the first English novel, marks the beginning of the prose fiction produced by popular women writers such as Mary Manley and Eliza Haywood, the last of whom also marketed a periodical called *The Female Spectator*. Novelists, in particular, began to realize that literature was one of the few lucrative professions open to women, and economic need quickly became a defense for publication. As Sarah Fielding explained in the preface to *David Simple* (1744), "Perhaps the best excuse that can be made for a woman's venturing to write at all, is that which really produced this book;

distress in her circumstances: which she could not so well remove by any other means in her power." While the poets Anne Bradstreet, Katherine Philips, and Phillis Wheatley depended on male relatives and friends to publish their books, historians like Catharine Macaulay and essayists like Elizabeth Montagu increasingly negotiated with booksellers and printers themselves. Eventually the philanthropist Hannah More and the novelists Charlotte Smith and Susanna Rowson helped support their families by publishing numerous books on manners and morals. In addition, the predominantly middle-class women who frequented the circulating libraries provided such writers with an audience interested in the private lives of wives and daughters. Women participated vigorously in almost all of the major literary movements and genres in the eighteenth century, frequently supporting themselves in the process; however, their contributions remained distinctive, no doubt because of the myths and realities that differentiated the female experience from the male in this period.

IMAGES OF WOMEN

Literary ladies, no less than other women, had to confront the misogynist images of women still prevalent in their culture, for popular writers like Joseph Swetnam continued to castigate women during the seventeenth century in phrases that harked back to medieval times: "Eagles eat not men till they are dead but women devour them alive, for a woman will pick thy pocket and empty thy purse, laugh in thy face and cut thy throat, they are ungrateful, perjured, full of fraud, flouting and deceit, unconstant, waspish, toyish, light, sullen, proud, discourteous, and cruel" (*The Arraignment of Lewd, Idle, Forward and Unconstant Women*, 1615). During the period before the English Civil War, there were many portraits of conniving, ambitious ladies like those attacked by the likes of Swetnam, but there were also patronesses and mistresses idealized in courtly poetry. Yet even in the many erotic and romantic verses of seventeenth-century lyricists, the visions of women that such works recorded were often projections of, on the one hand, male anxieties and, on the other hand, male desire. To be sure, great poems like John Donne's 1633 *The Ecstasy*, *A Valediction: Forbidding Mourning*, and *The Relic* acknowledged female subjectivity and even argued that in their love the poet and his mistress transcended gender: "Difference of sex no more we knew," wrote Donne in *The Relic*, "than our guardian angels do." Yet even Donne, for instance in such a work as *Elegy XIX: To His Mistress Going to Bed* (1669), tended to make an object out of woman, possessively defining his beloved as "my America! my new-found-land, / My kingdom; safeliest when with one man manned." Moreover, if Donne celebrated his conquest of his mistress in terms of the laying of the land, in such sardonic pieces as *Song: Go and Catch a Falling Star* and *Woman's Constancy*, both 1633, he argued that "nowhere / Lives a woman true, and fair."

In this regard, his attitudes were typical of those held by many of his contemporaries, who not only reproached women for inconstancy but also blamed them for unnatural eroticism. Ben Jonson's scathing *To Fine Lady Would-Be* (1616), for example, savagely excoriates a court lady for loving to make love but refusing to bear children, noting that "the world reputes you barren; but I know / Your 'pothecary, and his drug says no." Accusing her of using medicinal arts either to abort babies or prevent conception, Jonson concludes, "Write, then on thy womb, / Of the not born, yet buried, here's the tomb." But if poets like Donne and Jonson reproached women for inconstancy or wanton sexuality, such poets as Andrew Marvell and Robert Herrick and even Jonson himself censured women for clinging to virginity. Poems urging women to yield them-selves to their lovers were so ubiquitous in the period as to constitute a literary tradition of their own. Based on the so-called *carpe diem* (seize the day) theme, such verses urged the beloved to yield to the importunities of her lover before it was too late. Jonson's *Come, My Celia* (1606) argues that the lovers should "prove, / While we can, the sports of love" because "Time will not be ours for-ever; / He at length our good will sever"; Andrew Marvell's *To His Coy Mis-tress* (1681) explains that, if his mistress does not yield herself, "worms shall try that long preserved virginity"; and Robert Herrick's *To the Virgins, to Make Much of Time* notoriously advises young girls to "Gather ye rosebuds while ye may, / Old time is still a-flying."

A number of Restoration and early-eighteenth-century literary works also protested against chastity in women, but less through erotic lyricism than through the negative image of the gossiping shrew, the affected devout, or the proud prude. As satire gained literary prominence, however, more artists drew on the classical writer Juvenal's *Sixth Satire* to bemoan the demise of female fi-delity, modesty, and purity, and to express their horror of female sexuality. "Let the porter, and the groom, / Things designed for dirty slaves; / Drudge in fair Aurelia's womb, / To get supplies for age and graves," John Wilmot, second earl of Rochester, exclaimed in *A Song* (1691), as if to illustrate the satirists' equation of the womb with the tomb. From John Oldham's *A Satire upon a Woman, Who by Her Falsehood and Scorn Was the Death of His Friend* (1678) to Jonathan Swift's *Strephon and Chloe* (1731) and *A Beautiful Young Nymph Going to Bed* (1734), misogynist poems portrayed women as adulter-ous wantons, syphilitic prostitutes, and flirtatious coquettes: Oldham, who cursed his female subject as "Vil'st of that viler sex, who damn'd us all!", was just as scatological in his depiction of women as Swift, who stripped away the make-up, clothing, perfume, and wigs that adorned women in order to reveal that "Caelia, Caelia, Caelia shits!" Frequently using mock-pastoral conven-tions to uncover the filthy physicality of the contaminating whore who lurks behind the idealized shepherdess, the satirists projected on the female figure their horror at materialistic acquisition, pride, and hypocrisy, a perversion of values that would eventually result in the death of culture. But if female incon-stancy and physicality implied deceitfulness and death, they also meant, in Pope's famous line, that " 'Most women have no characters at all.' " It is hardly surprising, in the context established by his *Epistle to a Lady* (1735), that the only female model Pope could imagine was described as a "contradiction," "a softer man."

As the century progressed, more and more thinkers came to counsel women, in the words of Lord Lyttleton, "Seek to be good, but aim not to be great: / A woman's noblest station is retreat: / Her fairest virtues fly from public sight, / Domestic worth, that shuns too strong a light." As satire gave way to sentiment, moreover, popular pamphlets, conduct books, sermons, and essays analyzed the proper duties of wives and daughters with the more genteel condescension of

Lord Chesterfield, explaining that "women are but children of a larger growth. . . ." Middle-class women, now increasingly confined to the domestic sphere, were told by essayists like Richard Steele that all they have "to do in this world, is contained within the duties of a daughter, a sister, a wife, and a mother." As the literature about domestic conduct proliferated, it applied the ideal of politeness implicit in Augustan literature to women, who were now expected to be modest and decorous: as the naturalist-poet Erasmus Darwin explained, "The Muses are young ladies; we expect to see them dressed."

Such literature also began to contribute to the sentimentality implicit in Shaftesbury's Deism, creating a middle-class cult of weeping and delicacy in women praised for their emotional sensitivity as well as their purity and passivity. Sentimental fiction, as the critic Katharine Rogers has pointed out, featured moral ideals of gentleness and refined feelings that were considered feminine. By the time Richardson published *Pamela* and *Clarissa* (1747–1748), the bourgeoisie had associated its moral superiority with the image of an angelic, chaste woman who was engaged in a struggle for supremacy with a predatory, masculine nobility. To be sure, comic novelists like Henry Fielding continued to criticize Richardson's heroines as conniving upstarts, while pornographers like John Cleland continued to focus on the exotic pleasures provided by whores. But in countless popular novels imitating Richardson's astonishingly successful fiction, women were transformed from demonic sinners into domestic saints.

Clearly both eighteenth-century satires on female vice and celebrations of feminine virture were informed by medieval portraits of a destructive Eve and a redemptive Mary. More striking, however, was the emergence of a new image of woman, a satiric portrait of the female artist which constituted a reaction against the growing visibility of literary women. The late-seventeenth- and eighteenth-century attacks on literary ladies are important not only because they demonstrate why many women were unable to write or publish, but also because they explain why those who did write and publish frequently felt it necessary to apologize or justify their efforts. As the scholar Wendy Martin has explained, Puritan scorn for so-called scribbling women is aptly illustrated by Thomas Parker's 1650 condemnation of his sister: "Your printing of a book beyond the custom of your sex," Parker wrote in a public letter, "doth rankly smell." Similarly, as the literary historian Myra Reynolds has shown, both the plays and the poetry produced in England after the Restoration attacked women writers, readers, and speakers, who were only represented as mangling the language they wrote, read, or regurgitated. From a learned lady named "Bisarre" in George Farquahar's *The Inconstant* (1703) to Sophronia and Lady Wrangle in Colly Cibber's *The Refusal* (1721), female erudition was satirized as affectation. But feminine addiction to romantic literature was also attacked: Biddy Tipkins in Steele's *The Tender Husband* (1705), who would rather be called "Elismonda" or "Deidania," inhabits a hodge-podge world of shepherds, knights, and groves: she is a type of the "female Quixote" Charlotte Lennox would popularize in 1752, whose descendants were George Colman's Polly Honeycomb (1760) and Richard Sheridan's Lydia Languish (1775).

Just as the American Puritan John Winthrop had bemoaned the lot of a woman who had "fallen into a sad infirmity, the loss of her understanding, and reason, which had been growing upon her diverse years, by occasion of her giving herself wholly to reading and writing, and written many books" (1645), the Augustan satirists implied that reading and writing would derange weaker female minds. In *Three Hours after Marriage* (1717), Pope, Swift, and Arbuthnot directly satirized the poet Anne Finch as Phoebe Clinket, a prototypical female dunce who proves the point Pope had made earlier in *The Rape of the Lock* (1714), that "the poetic and the hysteric fit" are near allied in the female. A loose lady novelist is the prize in a contest between hack writers in one of Pope's early versions of *The Dunciad* (1728) while a monstrous Goddess of Criticism represents the self-indulgence of modern literature in Swift's *Tale of a Tub* (1704) and a nursing Goddess of Dullness is the deity of the hacks in the last book of *The Dunciad* (1743). Toward the end of the century, when Dr. Johnson compared a woman preacher to a dancing dog, or when he condemned portrait-painting as improper in women because "public practice of any art . . . and staring in men's faces, is very indelicate in a female," he was assuming that creativity and femininity were contradictory terms.

WOMEN'S LIVES

If the literary woman suffered from being considered an anomaly, all women in this period were burdened by the judgments prescribed by judicial authorities. In 1632 the author of *The Laws' Resolution of Women's Rights* succinctly explained that women "have nothing to do in constituting laws, of consenting to them, in interpreting of laws, or in hearing them interpreted . . . and yet they stand strictly tied to men's establishments, little or nothing excused by ignorance." Within the legal system throughout the seventeenth and eighteenth centuries, women were held to different standards of behavior than men and were punished more severely for departing from those standards. For example, mothers of stillborn babies could be charged with infanticide (if they could not produce witnesses to prove the child born dead) until 1803. So-called "scolding women" were punished with the "brank" (an iron framework caging the head) or the "ducking stool" (a chair with straps which was let down into a river) until 1809. As late as 1770 Parliament passed a statute declaring that "all women of whatever age, rank, profession, or degree, whether virgin maid or widow, that shall from and after such Act impose upon, seduce, and betray into matrimony any of His Majesty's subjects by means of scent, paints, cosmetics, washes, artificial teeth, false hair, Spanish wool, iron stays, hoops, high-heeled shoes, or bolstered hips, shall incur the penalty of the law now in force against witchcraft and like misdemeanours, and that the marriage upon conviction shall stand null and void."

The misogyny implicit in such a statute also informed laws unrelated to criminality. Although an unmarried woman could own property and a widow was entitled to a portion of her deceased husband's estate, a married woman throughout this period could neither own property nor make a will, "for the husband is entitled to the fruits of his wife's labour." By virtue of the judicial concept of the *feme covert* ("covered" woman), the woman's legal existence was suspended by marriage: she was theoretically incorporated into the person of her husband, under whose protection she carried on all her activities. With no right to divorce, no rights with respect to her own children, she also had no rights over her own body, for English husbands could imprison wives in their houses until 1891. While in America the concept of civil marriage resulted in a slightly more tolerant attitude toward divorce, and the patriarchal rule of primogeniture (the right of the oldest son to inherit the estate) was more erratic, legal conditions were almost as difficult for women.

Although women clearly labored under legal disadvantages, both men and women in this period gained greater freedom in choosing a marriage partner. To be sure, in wealthy families marriage was often still settled through treaties, and a number of women were forced either to marry against their wishes or to wait many years for their fathers' consent. But many women were allowed to follow the dictates of their affection in choosing husbands. Both married and single aristocrats, like the duchess of Marlborough, intimate friend of Queen Anne, and Lady Hester Stanhope, niece of the prime minister William Pitt, exercised considerable political influence and lived luxurious, even adventurous, lives. But middle- and working-class single women, wives, and widows lost many of their previously important economic roles. For the middle class, in particular, the assumption that husbands should support their wives gave rise to an ideology of female idleness, a belief that wives were symbols of their husbands' status by virtue of their leisure.

Many historians agree that working-class women lost much of their economic independence during the period when England and America moved from agricultural to industrial production. The specialization that accompanied industrialization meant that a number of home industries previously open to women (spinning, baking, preserving, sewing, farming, and brewing) steadily decreased. In the country, yeoman's wives tended to withdraw from agricultural labor, and in the city journeymen's wives were less involved in their husbands' trades. Though women continued to work as brewsters and spinsters, they were beginning to be excluded from many other industries by the separation of the workplace from the home.

In America, of course, the lady on a Southern plantation or the wife of a Massachusetts fisherman would be expected to help carry on her husband's business. When exploration and Indian wars resulted in labor shortages, moreover, women worked in craftsmaking, innkeeping, and shopkeeping. In southern England, too, women continued to specialize in dairy and poultry work. But with the enclosures of the second half of the eighteenth century, as Sir Frederick Eden remarked in 1797, "the acquisition of the necessities of life required by a labourer's family, rests entirely in the husband." Working-class women could, of course, always become servants, yet even Dr. Johnson could not give Boswell a satisfactory reason why "women servants . . . have much lower wages than men servants" although "our female house servants work much harder than the male." When, toward the end of the eighteenth century, women began working in the developing mills and factories, they generally earned only two-thirds of a man's pay.

Perhaps there is no better example of how professionalization excluded women than the struggle between midwives and physicians. In the sixteenth century, church examiners certified midwives; in the seventeenth century, greater emphasis was placed on medical knowledge, and examiners were frequently members of the College of Physicians. Two writers defended the autonomy of midwives: Mrs. Jane Sharp, in *The Midwives' Book* (1671), attempted to provide women with the anatomical information men received in universities, and Elizabeth Cellier, in A *Scheme for the Foundation of a Royal Hospital*, proposed a corporation that would establish standards for midwives. Yet, castigated as witches or incompetents, midwives were replaced throughout the eighteenth century by male physicians, both in lying-in hospitals and in middle-class homes. Using new instruments like the forceps, placing women in beds instead of on birthing stools, doctors, who worked under covers to protect women's modesty, were reminded in textbooks that "Degorges, one of the best obstetricians of his time, was blind." Yet despite their best efforts, infant mortality rates remained quite high throughout the period. None of Queen Anne's seventeen offspring survived her. Only about one child in four born in London survived in the early part of the eighteenth century. One baby died out of every fifteen born at the British Lying-In Hospital between 1749 and 1759.

That midwives were excluded from the medical education which would have insured their professional survival illustrates widespread acceptance of Lord Halifax's view that "there is inequality in the sexes, and that for the better economy of the world, the men, who were to be the lawgivers, had the larger share of reason bestowed upon them." Frequently reprinted in England and advertised extensively in colonial newspapers, Halifax's *The Lady's New Year's Gift; or, Advice to a Daughter* (1688) was far more typical than, say, Defoe's advocacy of equalizing the educational opportunities of the sexes (*Essay on Projects*, 1697). Even within the increasingly popular boarding schools for middle-class girls in Defoe's time, a "liberal education" consisted mainly of embroidery, modeling in wax, painting on glass, and musical accomplishments, although some girls' schools did put on plays and teach cooking skills. Between 1698 and 1715, more than one hundred charity schools were established in London and Westminster, but most of the girls who attended were trained there for domestic service. There was, of course, no formal higher education for women of any class. Like Oxford and Cambridge, Harvard (1636), Yale (1701), and Princeton (1746) were closed to women.

As the anonymous author of *An Essay in Defense of the Female Sex* (1696) explained, "We are taught only our mother tongue, or perhaps French," while "the other sex by means of a more extensive education to the knowledge of the Roman and Greek languages, have a vaster field for the imaginations to rove in, and their capacities thereby enlarged." Yet with classical imitation, allusion, and translation playing a major role in neoclassical literature, a knowledge of Greek and Latin was virtually a prerequisite for poetic authorship. When an exceptional woman like Elizabeth Elstob was encouraged by her family to become an Anglo-Saxon scholar, her publications did not save her from pecuniary difficulties after she lost that support: following her brother's death, the author of *Rudiments of Grammar for the Anglo-Saxon Tongue* (1715) was forced to become first a poorly paid teacher and then a dependent governess. Furthermore, such a learned woman was constantly cautioned, in the words of the moralist Dr. Gregory, to "keep [her learning] a profound secret, especially from the men, who generally look with a jealous and malignant eye on a woman of great parts or a cultivated understanding" (A *Father's Legacy to His Daughters*, 1774). Still, in spite of such discouragement, by the 1760s in London a small circle of aristocratic ladies, imitating the salons of French hostesses, became renowned for learning and grace. Elizabeth Montagu, Elizabeth Carter, and Frances Boscawen were called "bluestockings," a phrase that the historian Doris Stenton traces back to the informality of their conversational gatherings, which gentlemen could attend "even in their blue stockings."

WOMEN'S NEW PROFESSION OF LETTERS

Although it subjected them to ridicule and censure, writing was one of the few professions open to middle-class women, one they could pursue in their homes with financial success. Some women—by virtue of their leisure—were able to follow Joseph Addison's advice that they should "apply themselves to letters," for "they have more spare time on their hands, and lead a more sedentary life" than men. Yet, constantly reminded of their inadequacies, not a few shared the views of the poet Mary Oxlie, who meditated anxiously on the impediments to female creativity posed by women's lack of education and their domestic preoccupations, and by the resentment such confinement necessarily breeds:

> Perfection in a woman's work is rare;
> From an untroubled mind should verses flow;
> My discontents make mine too muddy show;
> And hoarse encumbrances of household care,
> Where these remain the Muses ne'er repair.

Because "all heroic actions, public employments, powerful governments and eloquent pleadings are denied our sex in this age," Margaret Cavendish believed that her own "restless" ambition caused her "to run upon every subject." Women who refused to submit to the distraction or the notoriety she suffered understandably wrote only in private and in forms considered "trivial," like Dorothy Osborne, whose observant, witty letters in the 1650s were meant only for her lover, William Temple. If women agreed to publication, it was often—as with Katherine Philips—"with the same reluctancy as I would cut off a limb to save my life," and frequently they published anonymously.

A few women writers, especially if protected by anonymity or rank, directly questioned male assumptions about female inferiority. The nameless author of a poem in praise of the poet Sarah Egerton, for example, declared in 1706, "No more let haughty man with fierce disdain, / Despise the product of a female brain." Later in the century, Mary Wortley Montagu explained her conviction, after reading *Gulliver's Travels*, that "if there was a commonwealth of rational horses (as Doctor Swift has supposed), it would be an established maxim among them that a mare could not be taught to pace." Later still, in a poem published in *The Gentleman's Magazine* (1771) to which the scholar Roger Gilbert has called attention, an anonymous literary lady complained of "Mr. Pope's characters of women": "By custom doom'd to folly, sloth, and ease, / No wonder Pope such female triflers sees; / But, would the satirist confess the truth, / Nothing so like as male and female youth." But more frequently women's opinions were like those of the poet Anne Finch, who contrasted the "happy . . . race of men" with the sadness of female "ciphers," to lament the fact that "since the Fall (by our seducement wrought) / Ours is the greater loss as ours the greater fault."

Finally, conservative writers like Mrs. Chapone, Mrs. Trimmer, and Mrs. Barbauld accepted the view that their own literary success was an aberration: Hannah More advised girls to "aspire only to those virtues that are *peculiar to your sex*; follow your natural modesty, and think it your greatest commendation not to be talked of one way or another."

Yet even Hannah More changed her mind as the eighteenth century progressed, writing in 1799 that women's potential is unknown, for their minds have been as "stunted and cramped" as the "crippled" feet of Chinese women. In an age that equated reason with virtue, it was a protest against female miseducation that motivated and shaped a new form of writing. Proposals to reform women's morals and manners were, to be sure, based on the earlier arguments of Anna von Schurman, whose *The Learned Maid; or, Whether a Maid May Be a Scholar* was translated into English in 1659, and Bathsua Pell (Mrs. Makin), who published an essay to revive the *Ancient Education of Gentlewomen* in 1673. From Mary Astell to Lady Mary Wortley Montagu and Catharine Macaulay, the foundation was laid for the radical vindication of women's rights that Mary Wollstonecraft published in 1792. In the crucible of revolutionary idealism associated with the French and the American revolutions, Wollstonecraft made the connection between the ideals of fraternity and those of sorority, much as Abigail Adams, wife of John Adams, did in letters that admonished her husband to "remember the ladies," for they were "determined to foment a rebellion" and refused to be "bound by any laws in which we have no voice, or representation" (1776).

Like the polemicists, female poets both participated in and diverged from the literary conventions and genres established by their male contemporaries. Aphra Behn used the sexual license of the Restoration to satirize male impotence rather than female debauchery, while Anne Finch, who composed in all the conventional Augustan forms (song, satire, fable, tragedy), resisted the closure of the heroic couplet in her verse, and rejected the prevailing political didacticism for a more personal observation of nature. Katherine Philips's poems on the pleasures of female friendship are no less marked by her gender than Lady Chudleigh's bitter attack on marriage in *To the Ladies*. In a quite different mode, Anne Bradstreet placed her Puritan spiritual meditations in a domestic and maternal context, and Phillis Wheatley presented her decidedly pious poems in terms of her experience as a slave. Although American women in this period did not produce as many polemical tracts against female miseducation as did their English contemporaries, on both sides of the Atlantic women poets used and subverted the literary traditions they inherited from an overwhelmingly male-dominated literary history.

Though the classical forms and subjects of eighteenth-century verse were not always suited to an exploration of women's lives, the quickly proliferating prose narratives of this period were ideal for such a project. At the end of the seventeenth and the beginning of the eighteenth century, prose narratives like Behn's *Oroonoko*, Manley's *The Adventures of Rivella* (1714), and Haywood's *Love in Excess* (1719–1720) combined romantic intrigue with adventure plots and achieved instant success; *Love in Excess*, for example, became the most popular novel in England besides *Robinson Crusoe*. Later nonfictional prose included moralizing tracts, conduct books, and personal essays along with collections of letters; the letters of aristocrats like Lady Russell and Mrs. Delaunay, for instance, were as popular as Mrs. Hester Thrale's account of Dr. Johnson's life. The writers in this last group elevated social and literary gossip into a suitable subject of analysis, and, as the critic Ian Watt has explained, it was only a small step from such minute accounts of authentic experience to the production of what purported to be such an account. In addition, the realistic mode allowed female authors to record the domestic experiences of women, who were doubtless also encouraged to write in this mode by the fact that the conventional identification of the speaking subject as a male in poetry did not hold true in eighteenth-century fiction.

In other words, the significance of the female narrators invented by Defoe (in *Moll Flanders*, 1722, or *Roxana*, 1724) and Richardson (in *Pamela* or *Clarissa*) would not have been lost on women writers. Richardson, who presented his novels as collections of letters, and Defoe, who presented his as autobiographies, were fictionalizing genres already popular with women readers and writers. Richardson, in particular, involved a circle of female friends in his subtle analyses of emotional reactions, going so far as to send a copy of *Pamela* to a friend's daughters with interleaved pages for their corrections. Empowered by the extraordinary popularity of these books, especially with women readers, women writers began to produce their own heroines in novels of manners and Gothic romances. With the publication of commercially successful novels like Fanny Burney's *Evelina* (1778), Susanna Rowson's *Charlotte Temple* (1791), and Ann Radcliffe's *The Mysteries of Udolpho* (1794), the female imagination had found the forms and the themes that would sustain it for another, even more productive century.

As Virginia Woolf understood, the seventeenth century inaugurated a new age of female creativity. Literary women like Sarah Egerton were determined to reject the strictures of male contemporaries and to keep on writing: "My daring pen will bolder sallies make," she declared, "And like myself, an unchecked freedom take." No wonder, then, that by Queen Anne's reign Woolf's artistic heroine, Orlando, "was apt to think of poetry when she should have been thinking of taffeta." Although "there was something in the sneer of Mr. Pope, in the condescension of Mr. Addison . . . which took away her relish for the society of wits," Orlando creates a salon and discovers the pleasures of writing as a woman.

ANNE BRADSTREET
1612–1672

When she arrived in America in 1630, Anne Bradstreet later remembered, "I found a new world and new manners, at which my heart rose. But," she added, "after I was convinced it was the way of God, I submitted to it and joined to the church at Boston." Combining a rebellious spirit with the scrupulousness of conscience fostered by the Puritan community to which she belonged, her statement reveals both the independence and the integrity that characterized this woman whose *The Tenth Muse, Lately Sprung Up in America* was to become the first collection of verse produced in the New World and, according to contemporary booksellers, one of the "most vendible"—that is, one of the most saleable—volumes in seventeenth-century London. Born in England, Bradstreet was raised in luxurious surroundings on the estates of the earl of Lincoln, where her father, Thomas Dudley, managed the nobleman's property. Both her parents were well born and well bred; she herself was educated by private tutors and was evidently quite early given access to the earl's extensive library. In 1628, at the age of sixteen, she married Simon Bradstreet, a cultivated Cambridge graduate nine years her senior, who had also worked as the earl's steward. Her life in England would seem to have been one of easy elegance so that she might well, in that year, have looked forward to a comfortable and civilized future.

Besides being humane and genteel, however, the Dudley family were devout Puritans, for whom life's trials symbolized God's intention to educate the soul. As a child of six or seven, Bradstreet recalled in a memoir, "I began to make conscience of my ways," confessing that "as I grew up to be about 14 or 15, I found my heart more carnal, and sitting loose from God." Just before her marriage, she therefore continued, "the Lord laid His hand sore upon me and smote me with the smallpox." Even before her arrival in Puritan New England, then, she felt she had experienced considerable "affliction," and she had learned to see the world as a text in which the divine will was inscribed. Still, nothing in her English girlhood could have entirely prepared this disciplined young woman for the hardships of the wilderness outpost to which the whole Dudley family, including the recently married Bradstreets, journeyed in 1630, when Anne was eighteen. Like the other Massachusetts colonists, they had come to escape the political and religious persecutions to which Puritans were subject in the old country, and though they were of higher rank than most—indeed, both Bradstreet's father and her husband were to become governors of Massachusetts—they had to confront the same rigors that troubled all the settlers: famine and fever, severe winters and scorching summers, a savage coast and a mysterious new land that stretched, it must have seemed, indefinitely off to the west.

For the Dudleys and the Bradstreets, as for the other colonists, there was only one way to survive such difficulties with sanity and with what the Puritans called "grace": one clung to God and to the Bible that was his word; one ceaselessly examined experience to interpret its theological message; and one redefined life as a passionate pilgrimage to a better life after death. Inevitably, however, in defending themselves with such religious intensity against the dangers of the New World, the settlers became fiercely doctrinaire, and their righteously reiterated dogmas had some especially problematic implications for women. By God's will, the Puritans felt, woman was created as man's helpmate and subordinate; thus a good wife must be submissive and self-abnegating, renouncing what would seem to be egotistical ambitions and desires for intellectual self-advancement or self-fulfillment. Indeed, such desires were often seen as potentially dangerous. In 1645, John Winthrop, then the governor of the colony, wrote sorrowfully about "a godly young woman," who had gone mad by "giving herself wholly to reading and writing, and written many books." Less than a decade earlier, moreover, in 1637 and 1638, Winthrop's election as governor had facilitated the trial, imprisonment, and banishment of the unorthodox Anne Hutchinson, who was accused of "traducing the ministers and their ministry" by preaching her own interpretations of Puritan theology.

Given such strictures against female ambition, it is no wonder that, so far as biographers can tell, Anne Bradstreet never attempted to publish her poetry in her own lifetime. Rather, in 1650 her brother-in-law, John Woodbridge, arranged without her knowledge (or so he claimed) to have *The Tenth Muse* printed in London. When he did so he wrote a careful foreword, explaining that her verse was "the work of a woman, honoured and esteemed where she lives, for . . . her exact diligence in her place, and discreet managing of her family occasions, and . . . these poems are but the fruit of some few hours, curtailed from her sleep and other refreshments." And in fact, at this point, Bradstreet was the diligent mother of a growing family—she eventually had eight children —as well as the devoted wife of an increasingly prosperous settler. The poems collected in *The Tenth Muse*, moreover, betray little overt rebellion against such a lot, although, largely written before she was thirty, they do show considerable learning and literary ambition. Bradstreet had obviously studied the works of Sir Walter Raleigh and Sir Philip Sidney with care, and she was deeply influenced by Joshua Sylvester's translation of Guillaume du Bartas's *La Septmaine du Creation*, a compendious poem which appeared in English as *The Divine Weeks and Works* and which, in Bradstreet's own words, was marked by a mastery of "natural philosophy . . . grave divinity . . . high astronomy . . . anatomy . . . music and state policy." But, perhaps precisely because their composition had been so consciously scholarly and their author was so decorous, poems like *The Humours, The Ages of Man*, and *The Four Monarchies* read like studiously versified notes rather than personal utterances.

Even in the 1650 edition of *The Tenth Muse*, though, we can discern, if not a rebellion against woman's domestic "place," a rising of the heart against female intellectual subordination. *The Prologue*, for instance, claims to be the product of a "foolish, broken, blemished Muse," a talent "made . . . irreparable" by nature, for "men can do best, and women know it well." But at the same time, the poet allows herself a flash of anger. "I am obnoxious to each carping tongue / Who says my hand a needle better fits," she observes, adding that "if what I do prove well, it won't advance, / They'll say it's stolen, or else it was by chance." The modesty of the poem's conclusion, in which Bradstreet renounces what would be an artist's natural desire to be crowned with the laurel or bay wreath of Apollo that traditionally announced a poet's success ("Give thyme or parsley wreath, I ask no bays"), can be seen as sardonic. Similarly, her fine elegy *In Honour of That High and Mighty Princess Queen Elizabeth of Happy Memory* may seem at first like a conventional celebration of royalty, full of rhetorical flourishes and elegant compliments. But again, a vein of feminist anger embedded in the work surfaces when the poet declares, "Nay masculines, you have thus taxed us long, / But she, though dead, will vindicate our wrong. / Let such as say our sex is void of reason, / Know 'tis a slander now but once was treason." Clearly this diligent wife and mother knew her own worth, and in the "few hours, curtailed from her sleep and other refreshment" when she ostensibly wrote her poems, she confronted her role as domestic helpmate with a sharp wit.

Ultimately, however, Bradstreet's situation as wife and mother was to prove not an obstacle to creativity but an inspiration, for the poems and prose meditations she wrote after the 1650 publication of *The Tenth Muse* depended heavily on images and metaphors drawn from her life as a woman. Her verses to her husband and children, her *Meditations Divine and Moral*, and her famous *Upon the Burning of Our House* all show the ways in which, as she matured into "Mistress Anne Bradstreet," a powerful matron and patroness of the Massachusetts Bay Colony, the domestic and the theological merged and glowed in her mind, even God himself coming to be seen (in the *Meditations*) as a nursing mother or a "prudent mother" so that the converse of such a proposition might also be true: the nursing mother or the "prudent mother" might be considered analogous to God.

Anne Bradstreet died in 1672, after decades of intermittent "affliction" which she sought, in characteristic Puritan fashion, to transform into a divine education, and the second edition of *The Tenth Muse*, containing numerous corrections and additions to the 1650 volume, was not published until six years later. As time went by, her reputation declined, so that by the nineteenth century, critics of American literature were defining her achievement as "a pitiful indication of the literary poverty of the days and land in which it was popular." Still, over the years, poets from the seventeenth-century writer Edward Taylor to the twentieth-century artists Conrad Aiken and John Berryman have rendered her respect in their various ways, with Berryman's *Homage to Mistress Anne Bradstreet* constituting a major acknowledgment of her genius. For after all, as Adrienne Rich has argued, "to have written . . . the first good poems in America, while rearing eight children, lying frequently sick, keeping house at the edge of the wilderness, was to have managed a poet's range and extension within confines as severe as any American poet has confronted."

The Prologue

1

To sing of wars, of captains, and of kings,
Of cities founded, commonwealths begun,
For my mean[1] pen are too superior things:
Or how they all or each their dates have run,[2]
Let poets and historians set these forth;   5
My obscure lines shall not so dim their worth.

2

But when my wondering eyes and envious heart
Great Bartas'[3] sugared lines do but read o'er,
Fool I do grudge the Muses did not part
'Twixt him and me that overfluent store;[4]   10

---

1. Humble, lowly.
2. I.e., how their sequences of events fell.
3. Guillaume du Bartas (1544–1590), author of *The Divine Weeks*, an epic poem on Christian

history.
4. I.e., I foolishly regret that the Muses (Greek goddesses of art and inspiration) did not equally divide their overflowing wealth between us both.

A Bartas can do what a Bartas will,
But simple I according to my skill.[5]

3

From schoolboy's tongue no rhetoric[6] we expect,
Nor yet a sweet consort[7] from broken strings,
Nor perfect beauty where's a main defect: 15
My foolish, broken, blemished Muse so sings,
And this to mend, alas, no art is able,
'Cause nature made it so irreparable.

4

Nor can I, like that fluent sweet-tongued Greek,
Who lisped at first,[8] in future times speak plain.   20
By art he gladly found what he did seek,
A full requital of his striving pain.
Art can do much, but this maxim's most sure:
A weak or wounded brain admits no cure.

5

I am obnoxious to each carping[9] tongue   25
Who says my hand a needle better fits;
A poet's pen all scorn I should thus wrong,[1]
For such despite they cast on female wits;[2]
If what I do prove[3] well, it won't advance,
They'll say it's stolen, or else it was by chance.   30

6

But sure the antique[4] Greeks were far more mild,
Else of our sex why feignéd they those nine,[5]
And poesy made Calliope's own child?[6]
So 'mongst the rest they placed the arts divine.
But this weak knot they[7] will full soon untie: 35
The Greeks did nought but play the fools and lie.[8]

7

Let Greeks be Greeks, and women what they are,
Men have precedency and still excel.
It is but vain unjustly[9] to wage war;
Men can do best, and women know it well.   40
Preeminence in all and each is yours;
Yet grant some small acknowledgement of ours.

8

And oh ye highflown quills[1] that soar the skies,
And ever with your prey still catch your praise,

5. I.e., a simple person like me can only do what she has the ability to do; "will": desires.
6. Highflown or literary language.
7. Harmony, as in music.
8. Demosthenes (c. 383–322 B.C.), a Greek orator who overcame a speech defect by placing pebbles in his mouth and addressing the sea.
9. Complaining; "obnoxious": vulnerable, exposed to.
1. I.e., all scornfully say "I should thus" abuse.
2. Intelligence; "despite": contempt.

3. Turn out; "advance": be recognized, praised.
4. Ancient.
5. I.e., why did they invent the Muses?
6. Calliope is the Muse of epic poetry.
7. I.e., "they": the speaker's critics; "knot": argument.
8. This line anticipates what the critics will say.
9. On false premises.
1. Pens made from birds' feathers; by association, poets; "prey": metaphorically, the poets' works.

If e'er you deign[2] these lowly lines your eyes,   45
Give thyme or parsley wreath, I ask no bays;[3]
This mean and unrefinéd ore of mine
Will make your glistering gold but more to shine.

1650

In Honour of That High and Mighty Princess Queen Elizabeth[4] of Happy Memory

The Proem[5]

Although, great Queen, thou now in silence lie   5
Yet thy loud herald[6] Fame doth to the sky
Thy wondrous worth proclaim in every clime,
And so hath vowed while there is world or time.
So great's thy glory and thine excellence,
The sound thereof rapts[7] every human sense,   10
That men account it no impiety
To say thou wert a fleshly deity.
Thousands bring offerings (though out of date)
Thy world of honours to accumulate;
'Mongst hundred hecatombs[8] of roaring verse,   15
Mine bleating stands before thy royal hearse.[9]
Thou never didst nor canst thou now disdain
T'accept the tribute of a loyal brain.
Thy clemency did erst[1] esteem as much
The acclamations of the poor as rich,   20
Which makes me deem my rudeness is no wrong,
Though I resound thy praises 'mongst the throng.

The Poem

No Phoenix[2] pen, nor Spenser's poetry,
No Speed's nor Camden's learned history,   25
Eliza's works, wars, praise, can e'er compact;[3]
The world's the theatre where she did act.

---

2. Condescend to give.
3. Laurel leaves, used to crown the heads of great poets.
4. Elizabeth Tudor (1533–1603, queen of England 1558–1603).
5. Brief introductory verse.
6. Royal crier or messenger.
7. Holds the complete attention of.
8. Honorary tributes (literally, sacrificial slaughter of animals).
9. Frame placed over a coffin or tomb for holding epitaphs.

1. Formerly, at one time; "clemency": leniency.
2. A mythical bird that immolates itself and is then reborn from its own ashes. Bradstreet associates the bird with both the immortality of both great poetry and Elizabeth's name. "No": neither.
3. Condense, summarize; the allusions are to Edmund Spenser (1552–1599), major English poet; John Speed (1542–1629), English historian and mapmaker; and William Camden (1551–1623), English historian.

No memories nor volumes can contain
The 'leven Olympiads of her happy reign,[4]
Who was so good, so just, so learn'd, so wise,   30
From all the kings on earth she won the prize.
Nor say I more than duly is her due,
Millions will testify that this is true.
She hath wiped off th' aspersion of her sex,[5]
That women wisdom lack to play the rex.[6]   35
Spain's monarch says not so, nor yet his host;[6]
She taught them better manners, to their cost.
The Salic law[7] in force now had not been,
If France had ever hoped for such a queen.
But can you, doctors,[8] now this point dispute.   40
She's argument enough to make you mute.
Since first the Sun did run his ne'er run race,
And earth had, once a year, a new old face,
Since time was time, and unmanly man,
Come show me such a phoenix if you can.   45
Was ever people better ruled than hers?
Was ever land more happy freed from stirs[9]
Did ever wealth in England more abound?
Her victories in foreign coasts resound;
Ships more invincible than Spain's, her foe,   50
She wracked,[1] she sacked, she sunk his Armado;
Her stately troops advanced to Lisbon's wall,[2]
Don Anthony in's right there to install.
She frankly helped Frank's brave distresséd king;
The states united now her fame do sing.   55
She their protectrix[3] was; they well do know
Unto our dread virago, what they owe,
Her nobles sacrificed their noble blood,
Nor men nor coin she spared to do them good.
The rude untaméd Irish she did quell;   60
Before her picture the proud Tyrone[4] fell.
Had ever prince such counsellors as she?

---

4. An Olympiad is the four-year period between Olympic games in ancient Greece; thus Elizabeth reigned for forty-four years.
5. Latin, "king."
6. Army. Philip II (1527–1598) was king of Spain, Portugal, the Netherlands; under his rule the Spanish Armada, a fleet of warships, attempted to invade England and was defeated in 1588.
7. Law forbidding women to inherit land, used in France and Spain to prevent the ascension of female monarchs.
8. Scholars.
9. Conflicts, wars.
1. Destroyed; "sacked": looted.

2. The references are: first, to Philip II's unsuccessful rival for the throne of Portugal, supported by England and France (Lisbon is the capitol city of Portugal); then, to Henri IV, who assumed the throne of France in 1589, and was aided generously with money and arms by Elizabeth in fighting the Catholic rebels backed by Spain; and finally, to the British colonies that later became the United States.
3. Female protector; "virago": a strong, courageous woman.
4. Nobleman who led the Irish rebellion against English rule, assisted by the Spanish; defeated at Kinsale.

Herself Minerva[5] caused them so to be.
Such captains and such soldiers never seen,
As were the subjects of our Pallas[6] queen.   65
Her seamen though all straits the world did round;
Terra incognita[7] might know the sound.
Her Drake came laden home with Spanish gold;[8]
Her Essex took Cadiz, their Herculean hold.
But time would fail me, so my tongue would too,   70
To tell of half she did, or she could do.
Semiramis[9] to her is but obscure,
More infamy than fame she did procure.
She build her glory but on Babel's walls,[1]
World's wonder for a while, but yet it falls.   75
Fierce Tomris[2] (Cyrus' headsman) Scythians' queen,
Had put her harness off, had she but seen
Our Amazon in th' Camp of Tilbury,[3]
Judging all valour and all majesty
Within that princess to have residence,   80
And prostrate yielded to her excellence,
Dido,[4] first foundress of proud Carthage walls
(Who living consummates her funerals),
A great Eliza, but compared with ours,
How vanisheth her glory, wealth, and powers.   85
Profuse, proud Cleopatra,[5] whose wrong name,
Instead of glory, proved her country's shame,
Of her what worth in stories to be seen,
But that she was a rich Egyptain queen.
Zenobya,[6] potent empress of the East,   90
And of all these without compare the best,
Whom none but great Aurelius[7] could quell;
Yet for our Queen is no fit parallel.
She was a phoenix queen, so shall she be,
Her ashes not revived, more phoenix she.   95
Her personal perfections, who would tell

5. Roman name for the Greek goddess of wisdom, Athena, protectress of the city of Athens.
6. Another name for Athena.
7. Latin, "unknown land."
8. The references are to Sir Francis Drake (1540–1596), English admiral and explorer, and to Robert Devereux, second earl of Essex (1566–1601), English soldier and statesman. Cádiz is a city in southern Spain; "Herculean," from Hercules, a Greek hero: strong, mighty.
9. Legendary Assyrian queen, noted for her wisdom and beauty.
1. According to the Book of Genesis, a great tower was built in the ancient city of Babylon, which God destroyed in anger because it revealed humanity's desire to rival his creations.
2. Queen of Scythia, an ancient region of Asia, who executed Cyrus, founder of the Persian Empire.
3. Site of Elizabeth's famous speech to her troops (see above); "Amazon": member of a mythical race of women possessed of great strength and courage.
4. Queen of Carthage, an ancient city in North Africa, whose abandonment by her lover Aeneas and subsequent self-immolation on her own funeral pyre are recounted in Virgil's epic *The Aeneid*.
5. (69–30 B.C.), queen of Egypt and mistress of Roman statesmen Julius Caesar and Mark Antony; her name means "glory to the father" (or "fatherland").
6. Queen of Palmyra (267–272 A.D.), an ancient city in Syria.
7. Marcus Aurelius, emperor of Rome (161–180 A.D.).

Must dip his pen in th' Heleconian well,[8]
Which I may not; my pride doth but aspire
To read what others write and so admire.
Now say, have women worth? or have they none?   100
Or had they some, but with our Queen is't gone?
Nay masculines, you have thus taxed[9] us long,
But she, though dead, will vindicate our wrong.
Let such as say our sex is void of reason
Know 'tis a slander now but once was treason.   105
But happy England which had such a queen;
Yea happy, happy, had those days still been.
But happiness lies in the higher sphere,
Then wonder not Eliza moves not here.
Full fraught with honour, riches and with days   110
She set, she set, like Titan in his rays.
No more shall rise or set so glorious sun
Until the heaven's great revolution,[1]
If then new things their old forms shall retain,
Eliza shall rule Albion[2] once again.   115

Her Epitaph

Here sleeps the queen, this is the royal bed
Of th' damask rose,[3] sprung from the white and red,
Whose sweet perfume fills the all-filling air.
This rose is withered, once so lovely fair.   120
On neither tree did grow such rose before,
The greater was our gain, our loss the more.

Another

Here lies the pride of queens, pattern of kings,
So blaze[4] it, Fame, here's feathers for thy wings.   125
Here lies the envied, yet unparalleled prince,
Whose living virtues speak (though dead long since).
If many worlds, as that fantastic framed,[5]
In every one be her great glory famed.

1650

8. Well found on Helicon, mountain of poetic inspiration in Greek myth.
9. Accused.
1. The Day of Judgment.
2. Britain.
3. A fragrant red rose, symbolic of the Tudors' union of the warring houses of York and Lancaster; "white and red" were the colors of the two houses in the War of the Roses.

4. Blazon, proclaim.
5. I.e., as that visionary or demented person theorized; this may be a reference to the Polish astronomer Nicolaus Copernicus (1473–1543), who challenged the Ptolemaic model of the universe, which placed the earth at the center, by asserting that the earth revolved around the sun along with the other planets.

The Author to Her Book[6]

Thou ill-formed offspring of my feeble brain,
Who after birth didst by my side remain,
Till snatched from thence by friends, less wise than true,
Who thee abroad, exposed to public view,   5
Made thee in rags, halting to th' press to trudge,
Where errors were not lessened (all may judge).
At thy return my blushing was not small,
My rambling brat (in print) should mother call,
I cast thee by as one unfit for light,   10
Thy visage was so irksome in my sight;
Yet being mine own, at length affection would
Thy blemishes amend, if so I could:
I washed thy face, but more defects I saw,
And rubbing off a spot still made a flaw.   15
I stretched thy joints to make thee even feet,[7]
Yet still thou run'st more hobbling than is meet;[8]
In better dress to trim thee was my mind,
But nought save homespun cloth i' th' house I find.
In this array 'mongst vulgars[9] may'st thou roam.   20
In critic's hands beware thou dost not come,
And take thy way where yet thou art not known
If for thy father asked, say thou hadst none;
And for thy mother, she alas is poor,
Which caused her thus to send thee out of door.   25

                                                          1678

A Letter to Her Husband, Absent upon Public Employment

My head, my heart, mine eyes, my life, nay, more,
My joy, my magazine[1] of earthly store,
If two be one, as surely thou and I,
How stayest thou there, whilst I at Ipswich[2] lie?
So many steps, head from the heart to sever,   5
If but a neck, soon should we be together.
I, like the Earth this season, mourn in black,
My Sun is gone so far in's zodiac,[3]

---

6. Bradstreet's volume of poems *The Tenth Muse* was published in 1650 without her knowledge; this poem was probably written while she was preparing a revised second edition for publication.
7. I.e., metrical feet; thus, to smooth out the meter of the lines.

8. Appropriate, decorous.
9. Common people.
1. Warehouse.
2. Town in Massachusetts, north of Boston.
3. The path of the sun and planets through the heavens; "My Sun": her husband.

Whom whilst I'joyed, nor storms, nor frost I felt,
His warmth such frigid colds did cause to melt.   10
My chilled limbs now numbed lie forlorn:
Return, return, sweet Sol, from Capricorn;[4]
In this dead time, alas, what can I more
Than view those fruits which through thy heat I bore?
Which sweet contentment yield me for a space,   15
True living pictures of their father's face.
O strange effect! now thou art southward gone,
I weary grow the tedious day so long;
But when thou northward to me shalt return,
I wish my Sun may never set, but burn   20
Within the Cancer[5] of my glowing breast,
The welcome house of him my dearest guest.
Where ever, ever stay, and go not thence,
Till nature's sad decree shall call thee hence;
Flesh of thy flesh, bone of thy bone,   25
I here, thou there, yet both but one.

                                                                   1678

To Her Father with Some Verses

Most truly honoured, and as truly dear,
If worth in me or ought I do appear,
Who can of right better demand the same
Than may your worthy self from whom it came?   5
The principal[6] might yield a greater sum,
Yet handled ill, amounts but to this crumb;
My stock's so small I know not how to pay,
My bond remains in force unto this day:[7]
Yet for part payment take this simple mite,[8]   10
Where nothing's to be had, kings loose their right.
Such is my debt I may not say forgive,
But as I can, I'll pay it while I live;
Such is my bond, none can discharge but I,
Yet paying is not paid until I die.   15

                                                                   1678

---

4. Capricorn, the tenth sign of the zodiac, rises
in winter; "Sol": the sun.
5. Cancer, the fourth sign of the zodiac, rises in
summer.

6. Sum of money that accrues interest.
7. I.e., I am still indebted to you.
8. Small contribution that is all one can afford.

For Deliverance from a Fever

When sorrows had begirt me round,
And pains within and out,
When in my flesh no part was found,[9]
Then didst Thou rid me out.[1]   5
My burning flesh in sweat did boil,
My aching head did break,
From side to side for ease I toil,
So faint I could not speak.
Beclouded was my soul with fear   10
Of Thy displeasure sore,
Nor could I read my evidence
Which oft I read before.
"Hide not Thy face from me!" I cried,
"From burnings keep my soul.   15
Thou know'st my heart, and hast me tried;
I on Thy mercies roll."
"O heal my soul," Thou know'st I said,
"Though flesh consume to nought,
What though in dust it shall be laid,   20
To glory t' shall be brought."
Thou heard'st, Thy rod Thou didst remove
And spared my body frail,
Thou show'st to me Thy tender love,
My heart no more might quail   25
O, praises to my mighty God,
Praise to my Lord, I say,
Who hath redeemed my soul from pit,[2]
Praises to Him for aye.[3]

1867

From Meditations Divine and Moral

6

The finest bread hath the least bran, the purest honey the least wax, and the sincerest Christian the least self-love.

8

Downy beds make drowsy persons, but hard lodging keeps the eyes open; a prosperous state makes a secure Christian, but adversity makes him consider.

9

Sweet words are like honey: a little may refresh, but too much gluts the stomach.

9. I.e., no healthy part.
1. Rid me of illness; "Thou": God.

2. Hell.
3. Ever.

10

Diverse children have their different natures: some are like flesh[4] which nothing but salt will keep from putrefaction, some again like tender fruits that are best preserved with sugar. Those parents are wise that can fit their nurture according to their nature.

12

Authority without wisdom is like a heavy axe without an edge: fitter to bruise than polish.

16

That house which is not often swept makes the cleanly inhabitant soon loathe it, and that heart which is not continually purifying itself is no fit temple for the spirit of God to dwell in.

19

Corn,[5] till it have passed through the mill and been ground to powder, is not fit for bread. God so deals with his servants: he grinds them with grief and pain till they turn to dust, and then are they fit manchet[6] for his mansion.

38

Some children are hardly weaned; although the teat be rubbed with wormwood[7] or mustard, they will either wipe it off, or else suck down sweet and bitter together. So is it with some Christians: let God embitter all the sweets of this life, that so they might feed upon more substantial food, yet they are so childishly sottish[8] that they are still hugging and sucking these empty breasts that God is forced to hedge up their way with thorns or lay affliction on their loins that so they might shake hands with the world, before it bid them farewell.

39

A prudent mother will not clothe her little child with a long and cumbersome garment; she easily forsees what events it is like to produce, at the best, but falls and bruises or perhaps somewhat worse. Much more will the all-wise God proportion His dispensations according to the stature and strength of the person He bestows them on. Large endowments of honour, wealth, or a healthful body would quite overthrow some weak Christian; therefore God cuts their garments short to keep them in such a trim that they might run the ways of His commandment.

1867

Here Follows Some Verses upon the Burning of Our House July 10th, 1666. Copied out of a Loose Paper

In silent night when rest I took   5
For sorrow near I did not look

---

4. Meat.
5. Grain.
6. White bread made from the finest flour.

7. A bitter extract placed on a mother's breast ("teat") to wean her child from breast-feeding.
8. Both drunken and addicted to drink.

I wakened was with thund'ring noise
And piteous shrieks of dreadful voice.
That fearful sound of "Fire!" and "Fire!"
Let no man know is my desire.   10
I, starting up, the light did spy,
And to my God my heart did cry
To strengthen me in my distress
And not to leave me succorless.[9]
Then, coming out, beheld a space[1]   15
The flame consume my dwelling place.
And when I could no longer look,
I blest His name that gave and took,
That laid my goods now in the dust.
Yea, so it was, and so 'twas just.   20
It was His own, it was not mine,
Far be it that I should repine;[2]
He might of all justly bereft[3]
But yet sufficient for us left.
When by the ruins oft I passed   25
My sorrowing eyes aside did cast,
And here and there the places spy
Where oft I sat and long did lie:
Here stood that trunk, and there that chest,
There lay that store I counted best.   30
My pleasant things in ashes lie,
And them behold no more shall I.
Under thy roof no guest shall sit,
Nor at thy table eat a bit.
No pleasant tale shall e'er be told,   35
Nor things recounted done of old.
No candle e'er shall shine in thee,
Nor bridegroom's voice e'er heard shall be.
In silence ever shall thou lie,
Adieu, Adieu, all's vanity.   40
Then straight I 'gin my heart to chide,
And did thy wealth on earth abide?
Didst fix thy hope on mold'ring dust?
The arm of flesh didst make thy trust?
Raise up thy thoughts above the sky   45
That dunghill mists away may fly.
Thou hast an house on high erect,
Framed by that mighty Architect,
With glory richly furnishéd,
Stands permanent though this be fled.   50
It's purchaséd and paid for too
By Him who hath enough to do.

9. Helpless.
1. For a short period of time.
2. Complain.

3. I.e., he might have taken everything from us
with good cause.

A price so vast as is unknown
Yet by His gift is made thine own;
There's wealth enough, I need no more,   55
Farewell, my pelf,[4] farewell my store.
The world no longer let me love,
My hope and treasure lies above.

1867

4. Money, usually falsely gained.

MARGARET CAVENDISH, DUCHESS OF NEWCASTLE
1623–1674

"What a vision of loneliness and riot the thought of Margaret Cavendish brings to mind!" exclaimed Virginia Woolf in 1928. The author of "philosophical fancies" and scientific speculations, poems and plays, the woman who so bemused Woolf was born Margaret Lucas to an aristocratic Essex family where "all the brothers were valiant, and all the sisters virtuous," and although many at court disliked her for her shyness and eccentricity, she became a maid of honor to the Queen. In 1645 she married William Cavendish, duke of Newcastle, a Royalist soldier with whom she lived on the Continent in poverty and exile during Cromwell's reign. After the Restoration, the couple returned to their English estate, where the childless duchess pursued her literary career with diligence. But although she published numerous books in her lifetime— including *Poems and Fancies* (1653), *Nature's Pictures Drawn by Fancie's Pencil* (1656), and *Plays Written by Lady Marchioness of Newcastle* (1667)— most of Cavendish's contemporaries regarded her as a freak because of the oddity of her writings and the peculiarity of her dress. At a time when it was considered bold for women to produce even the tamest of compositions, "the crazy duchess" tried to combine metaphysical poetry with scientific speculation, philosophical meditation with fanciful fantasizing. No wonder, then, that Dorothy Osborne, a seventeenth-century letter-writer, believed "the poor woman is a little distracted, she could never have been so ridiculous else as to venture at writing books and in verse too."

Despite her undoubted strangeness, however, the duchess at her best produced some witty verse as well as some lively and thoughtful prose. Though her work was never as strong as the poetry of her American contemporary Anne Bradstreet, her imagery, like Bradstreet's, often drew upon the realities of female life—fashion, cooking, housekeeping. In addition, her speculations on the meaning of femininity—in particular those dramatized in *Female Orations*— were unusually sophisticated in their acknowledgment of the complex problems posed by woman's cultural situation.

Female Orations

I

Ladies, gentlewomen, and other inferior women, but not less worthy: I have been industrious to assemble you together, and wish I were so fortunate as to persuade you to make frequent assemblies, associations, and combinations amongst our sex, that we may unite in prudent counsels, to make ourselves as free, happy, and famous as men; whereas now we live and die as if we were produced from beasts, rather than from men; for men are happy, and we women are miserable; they possess all the ease, rest, pleasure, wealth, power, and fame; whereas women are restless with labour, easeless with pain, melancholy for want of pleasures, helpless for want of power, and die in oblivion, for want of fame. Nevertheless, men are so unconscionable and cruel against us that they endeavour to bar us of all sorts of liberty, and will not suffer us freely to associate amongst our own sex; but would fain bury us in their houses or beds, as in a grave. The truth is, we live like bats or owls, labour like beasts, and die like worms.

II

Ladies, gentlewomen, and other inferior women: The lady that spoke to you hath spoken wisely and eloquently, in expressing our unhappiness; but she hath not declared a remedy, or showed us a way to come out of our miseries; but, if she could or would be our guide, to lead us out of the labyrinth men have put us into, we should not only praise and admire her, but adore and worship her as our goddess: but alas! men, that are not only our tyrants but our devils, keep us in the hell of subjection, from whence I cannot perceive any redemption or getting out; we may complain and bewail our condition, yet that will not free us; we may murmur and rail against men, yet they regard not what we say. In short, our words to men are as empty sounds; our sighs, as puffs of winds; and our tears, as fruitless showers; and our power is so inconsiderable, that men laugh at our weakness.

III

Ladies, gentlewomen, and other inferior women: The former orations were exclamations against men, repining at their condition and mourning for our own; but we have no reason to speak against men, who are our admirers and lovers; they are our protectors, defenders, and maintainers; they admire our beauties, and love our persons; they protect us from injuries, defend us from dangers, are industrious for our subsistence, and provide for our children; they swim great voyages by sea, travel long journeys by land, to get us rarities and curiosities; they dig to the center of the earth for gold for us; they dive to the bottom of the sea for jewels for us: they build to the skies houses for us: they hunt, fowl, fish, plant, and reap for food for us. All which, we could not do ourselves; and yet we complain of men, as if they were our enemies, whenas[1] we could not possibly live without them, which shows we are as ungrateful as inconstant. But we have more reason to murmur against Nature, than against men, who hath made men more ingenious, witty,[2] and wise than women; more strong, industrious, and laborious than women; for women are witless and strengthless, and unprofitable creatures, did they not bear children. Wherefore, let us love men, praise men, and pray for men; for without men, we should be the most miserable creatures that Nature hath made or could make.

IV

Noble ladies, gentlewomen, and other inferior women: The former oratoress says we are witless and strengthless; if so, it is that we neglect the one and make no use of the other, for strength is increased by exercise, and wit is lost for want of conversation. But to show men we are not so weak and foolish as the former oratoress doth express us to be, let us hawk, hunt, race, and do the like exercises that men have; and let us converse in camps,[3] courts, and cities; in schools, colleges, and courts of judicature; in taverns, brothels, and gaming houses; all of which will make our strength and wit known, both to men and to our own selves, for we are as ignorant of ourselves as men are of us. And how should we know ourselves, when we never made a trial of ourselves? Or how should men know us, when they never put us to the proof?[4] Wherefore my advice is, we should imitate men; so will our bodies and minds appear more masculine, and our power will increase by our actions.

V

Noble, honorable, and virtuous women: The former oration was to persuade us to change the custom of our sex, which is a strange and unwise persuasion, since we cannot change the nature of our sex, nor make ourselves men; and to have female bodies, and yet to act masculine parts, will be very preposterous and unnatural. In truth, we shall make ourselves like the defects of Nature, and be hermaphroditical,[5] neither perfect women, nor perfect men, but corrupt and imperfect creatures. Wherefore let me persuade you, since we cannot alter the nature of our persons, not to alter the course of our lives; but to rule so our lives and behaviours that we be acceptable and pleasing to God and men; which is, to be modest, chaste, temperate, humble, patient, and pious; also, be houswifely, cleanly, and of few words. All which will gain us praise from men and blessing from Heaven; love in this world and glory in the next.

VI

Worthy women: The former oratoress's oration endeavoured to persuade us that it would not only be a reproach and disgrace, but unnatu-

---

1. For the reason that.
2. Imaginative.
3. I.e., military camps.
4. Test.

5. Male and female within one body (from the name in Greek legend of the child born to the god Hermes and the goddess Aphrodite).

ral, for women in their actions and behaviour to imitate men: we may as well say it will be a reproach, disgrace, and unnatural to imitate the gods, which imitation we are commanded both by the gods and their ministers; and shall we neglect the imitation of men, which is more easy and natural than the imitation of the gods? For how can terrestrial creatures imitate celestial deities? Yet one terrestrial may imitate another, although in different sorts of creatures. Wherefore, since all terrestrial imitations ought to ascend to the better and not to descend to the worse, women ought to imitate men, as being a degree in nature more perfect than they themselves; and all masculine women ought to be as much praised as effeminate men to be dispraised; for the one advances to perfection, the other sinks to imperfection; that so, by our industry, we may come, at last, to equal men, both in perfection and power.

VII

Noble ladies, honourable gentlewomen, and worthy female-commoners: The former oratoress's speech was to persuade us out of ourselves and to be that which Nature never intended us to be, to wit, masculine. But why should we desire to be masculine, since our own sex and condition is far the better? For if men have more courage, they have more danger; and if men have more strength, they have more labour than women have; if men are more eloquent in speech, women are more harmonious in voice; if men be more active, women are more graceful; if men have more liberty, women have more safety; for we never fight duels nor battles; nor do we go long travels or dangerous voyages; we labor not in building nor digging in mines, quarries, or pits, for metal, stone, or coals; neither do we waste or shorten our lives with university or scholastical studies, questions, and disputes; we burn not our faces with smiths' forges or chemists'[6] furnaces; and hundreds of other actions which men are employed in; for they would not only fade the fresh beauty, spoil the lovely features, and decay the youth of women, causing them to appear old, when they are young; but would break their small limbs, and destroy their tender lives. Wherefore women have no reason to complain against Nature or the god of Nature, for although the gifts are not the same as they have given to men, yet those gifts they have given to women are much better; for we women are much more favoured by Nature than men, in giving us such beauties, features, shapes, graceful demeanor, and such insinuating and enticing attractives, that men are forced to admire us, love us, and be desirous of us; insomuch that rather than not have and enjoy us, they will deliver to our disposals their power, persons, and lives, enslaving themselves to our will and pleasures; also, we are their saints, whom

---

6. Alchemists'.

they adore and worship; and what can we desire more than to be men's tyrants, destinies, and goddesses?

1662

JANE LEAD
1624–1704

A mystic and spiritual autobiographer, the visionary writer Jane Lead was born Jane Ward in Norfolk and educated "like other girls" until at the age of fifteen she heard a miraculous voice speaking to her amid Christmas festivities and resolved to lead a devotional life. When she was twenty-one, she married William Lead, a distant relative six years her senior, to whom she bore four daughters. After his death when she was forty-six, she renewed her commitment to mystical theology and to what she called "Spiritual Virginity." At around this time, moreover, she had the striking vision excerpted here of a female figure whom the critic Catherine Smith regards as "Lead's revision of Sophia, the Virgin Wisdom of God in esoteric theology and apocalyptic tradition."

Already a student of the works of the radical German theologian Jacob Boehme (1575–1624), Lead now became even more passionately mystical, and in 1674 she moved into the household of Dr. John Pordage, the leader of one of the many nonconformist congregations that were springing up in England at around this time. In 1681, after Pordage's death, she began to publish her own spiritual writings, and in 1694, with the assistance of a young disciple, Dr. Francis Lee, she founded the Philadelphia Society, a nonconformist group (like the Diggers and the Ranters) based on Boehme's teachings. Her books include *The Heavenly Cloud Now Breaking* (1681), *The Enochian Walks With God* (1694), and, perhaps most important, the four-volume *A Fountain of Gardens, Watered by the Rivers of Divine Pleasure* (1696–1701). Although her works are primarily religious and she was not consciously a feminist, her writing was consistently energized by images of the magical woman within the soul who, she believed, would bring redemption to male and female spirits alike, and her metaphors of rebirth are distinctively feminine.

From A Fountain of Gardens[1]

[The First Vision]

The first vision that appeared to me was in the month of April, 1670. which was on this wise—

Being my lot at that time to visit a friend in a solitary country place, where I had great advantage of retirement, often frequenting lonely

---

1. The full title is A *Fountain of Gardens, Watered by the Rivers of Divine Pleasure, and Springing Up in All the Variety of Spiritual* *Plants; Blown Up by the Pure Breath into a Paradise.*

walks in a grove or wood, contemplating the happy state of the angelical world and how desirous I was to have my conversation there, my thoughts were much exercised upon Solomon's choice, which was to find out the noble stone of divine Wisdom;[2] for by acquainting myself with her, all desirable good in spiritual things would meet upon me. The report and fame that Solomon gave of Wisdom did much excite me to seek her favour and friendship; demurring in myself from whence she was descended, still questioning whether she was a distinct being from the Deity or no? Which while in this debate within my mind, there came upon me an overshadowing bright cloud, and in the midst of it the figure of a woman, most richly adorned with transparent gold, her hair hanging down, and her face as the terrible crystal for brightness, but her countenance was sweet and mild. At which sight I was somewhat amazed, but immediately this voice came, saying, "Behold, I am God's eternal Virgin Wisdom, whom thou hast been inquiring after; I am to unseal the treasures of God's deep wisdom unto thee, and will be as Rebecca was unto Jacob, a true natural mother;[3] for out of my womb thou shalt be brought forth after the manner of a spirit, conceived and born again; this thou shalt know by a new motion of life, stirring and giving a restlessness, till wisdom be born within the inward parts of thy soul. Now consider of my saying till I return to thee again."

This vision took great impression on me, yet I kept it for the present hid, but it operated so much upon me, as indeed I was incapable to converse with any mortals; which was taken notice of, that some extraordinary thing had happened, for the which I begged my friend's excuse and desired that she would give me the liberty to be much alone, and to walk in the silent woods, where I might contemplate what had so lately happened. Now after three days, sitting under a tree, the same figure in greater glory did appear, with a crown upon her head, full of majesty, saying, "Behold me as thy mother, and know thou art to enter into covenant[4] to obey the new creation laws, that shall be revealed unto thee." Then did she hold out a golden book, with three seals[5] upon it, saying, "Herein lieth hidden the deep wonders of Jehovah's wisdom, which hath been sealed up, that none could or ever shall break up, but such as of her virgin offspring shall appear to be, who will her laws receive and keep, as they shall spring daily in the new heart and mind." This appearance and words was wonderfully sweet and refreshing in my soul; at which I bowed and prostrated at her feet, promising to be obedient to all her laws. So the vision shut up for that time.

---

2. The biblical king Solomon, noted for his wisdom, is here associated with the legendary philosopher's stone, which was reputed to change base metals into gold.

3. Rebecca, the mother of Jacob and his older brother Esau, helped Jacob bargain for the birthright his dying father, Isaac, had promised to Esau (Genesis 25–27).

4. Solemn agreement; here alluding to God's covenant with the Israelites (Genesis 6:18).

5. Three is a mystical number—as in the Holy Trinity.

Pondering this in my heart with great comfort, that this daystar[6] had visited me from on high, I returned to London to my own habitation, retiring myself from all my acquaintance, saving one person that was highly illuminated, who encouraged me still to wait upon this vision, for he was acquainted with somewhat of this kind. So after six days the vision appeared again, with a train of virgin spirits, and with an angelical host; and called to me to come and see the virgin queen, with her first-born children; asking me whether I was willing to be joined amongst this virgin company? At which I replied, "All willing to offer up myself most free." Then immediately I was encompassed about with this heavenly host, and made a spirit of light. Then these words from the Virgin proceeded, saying, "I shall now cease to appear in a visible figure unto thee, but I will not fail to transfigure myself in thy mind and there open the spring of Wisdom and understanding, that so thou mayst come to know the only True God, in and by the formation of Christ, the anointed prophet in thee; that shall reveal great and wonderful things unto thee, that are to be made known and public in its time and day. Therefore be watchful, and to thy mother Wisdom's counsel give good heed, and thou shalt greatly prosper, and succeed the prophets and apostles to perfect what was left behind, for completing as to Christ the fullness of God's great mystery: so go on, and nothing fear or doubt; for I thy glass[7] for divine seeing shall evermore stand before thee." Then my spirit replied, "According to thy word let all this be fulfilled." And so this glory withdrew; but an inward glory did my heart fill, for a burning love to all of those heavenly beings did kindle within my heart vehemently.

[The Second Vision]

In the Month of August

The mind of Wisdom thus opened itself in me, as I waited in my spirit upon her; she did show me what key would open the great mystery, which lay deeply hid in myself. It was wrought and carved out of such pure gold as had passed though many fires; many keys I had tried, but could not turn in this secret enclosed lock, but still it shut upon me, though I thought I had that key which was compounded of such metals as would have made its entrance, as love, faith, patience, humility,[8] which with strong supplication and prayer I presented, as the key of the work. All which was too short to reach it. Whereupon I was put to a loss altogether to seek how this gate should be opened, having compassed the Holy City,[9] and waited and tried every way, where I might find passage, circling from one path to another, from prayer to prayer, and from faith to faith; so that in good earnest I began to consider I had not

6. I.e., morning star.   8. Several of the cardinal virtues.
7. Telescope.   9. I.e., the New Jerusalem of Revelations.

found this wonderful key, for want[1] of which I might run out in waste all my days, and grope as in the dark, yet never find the door which opens into my true shepherd's fold.[2] Whereupon being cast into a deep astonishing silence and stillness, the word of Wisdom thus opened itself unto me: "Oh, thou deep searching spirit, marvel not thou hast been so long frustrated, for as to thy present state and dispensation, thou couldst never reach me to all eternity, for my birth in thee lies deeper than thy present gift of faith and prayer can open; thou hast with many others been in a great mistake. But in as much thou ownest and bewailest thy unskillfulness, I will make known to thee what key will turn this great wheel of my Wisdom, so as it may move and manifest itself in thee through all thy properties,[3] if thou canst bid up to the price of it. For understand that it is compounded of all pure gold, subsisting in a burning furnace of many fires. And although this wonderful key is of Wisdom's carving out, and her free gift, yet, O thou seeking spirit, she will cost thee very dear, if ever thou obtainest her. Yet she goeth about seeking such as are worthy of her, and will show herself within the walls of the mind, and meet them in every thought that waits for her laws and counsel, and brings a kingdom which will be well worth thy selling all for. But the great thing," saith Wisdom, "now is to discipline and make thy spirit a cunning artist, to give it knowledge of what matter in number, weight, and measure this pure key is made up of, which is all pure deity in the number THREE, which is weighty indeed, being one exceeding weighty glory, fitting in the circle of the heavens within man's heart, measuring with the line of his power, the temple and inward court, with the worshippers therein. This is Wisdom's key, which will make our hands drop with sweet-smelling myrrh[4] upon the handles of her lock." Which while I was opening her privy[5] door with this key, my soul failed within me, and I retained no strength; my sun of reason and the moon of my outward sense were folded up and withdrew. I knew nothing by myself, as to those working properties from nature and creature,[6] and the wheel of the motion standing still, another moved from a central fire;[7] so that I felt myself transmuted into one pure flame. Then came that word to me, "This is no other than the gate of my eternal deep; canst thou subsist in this fiery region, which is Wisdom's mansion, where she meets with holy abstracted spirits, and gives forth a fiery law, which if thereunto thou canst give heed, so as to come up to her requirings, then no secret shall be withheld from thee." Thus far

---

1. Lack.
2. Pen for sheep (here used in a religious sense).
3. I.e., personal qualities.
4. An aromatic resin, one of the gifts of the Magi to the Christ child (Matthew 2:11).
5. Private.

6. I.e., she knew nothing of her natural human functions.
7. I.e., the wheel of ordinary motion stopping, another wheel (i.e., the wheel of Wisdom) moved from a central fire.

am I admitted to come into the entrance of her house, where I must stop till I hear further from her.

Now as I was attending to obtain a fresh visit, being entered into this first mansion[8] of her house, to hear and learn further, she said on this wise, that I was greatly beloved, and she would be my mother, and so should I own her and call her, who would now be to me as Rebecca was to Jacob, to contrive and put me in a way how I should obtain the birthright blessing. For if I would apply myself to her doctrine, and draw my life's food from no other breast, I should then know the recovery of a lost kingdom; at which salutation I was dissolved and melted, the fervent heat of this love strongly impulsing me to a resolve for to obey her in all things.

When pure oil from Wisdom's vessel stopping, it opened again not till October the 20th in the morning watch; then heard I her voice thus, "Sequester and draw out of thy animal sensitive life[9] that is too gross: I cannot appear till that disappear. There must be spirit with spirit, light with light." No sooner had I this caution, but I felt power which suspended the active busy mind, which for a time was expired into silence. "Know then," said the same voice, "thou shalt supplant thy brother Esau, who according to the figure, is a cunning hunter in the out-birth[1] and field of nature. While he with his subtlety seeking it abroad in the wild properties of the external region, I will now help thee to it near at hand, even in thy own enclosed ground. There the true scapegoat[2] feeds, of which I will make savoury meat, such as God thy Father loves." Hearing this salutation from my late known mother, I was deadly ravished in the spirit, in the light of the Lord, and feared to return to the dark house of my outward senses again; which opened a spring of intercession in me, that as one of the friends of the bridegroom I might hear his voice still,[3] which indeed was so pleasant and sweet as I could well have admitted of a dissolution of my elementary being, rather than this conference should not still be maintained with this renowned pearl of wisdom. But I have learned to observe her time and seasons; I witness her opening as in the twinkling of an eye, a pure bright, subtle, swift spirit, a working motion, a circling fire, a penetrating oil.

1697–1701

8. I.e., room.
9. I.e., life of the senses.
1. Progeny, something brought forth.
2. In Leviticus 16, the scapegoat is heaped with the sins of the people and sent into the wilderness while the goat of the Lord is offered as a sacrifice; but Lead may also be thinking of Christ as "the true scapegoat."
3. In Matthew 9:15, Jesus compares himself to a bridegroom: "Can the children of the bridechamber mourn, as long as the bridegroom is with them?"

KATHERINE PHILIPS
1631–1664

Known in her own day as "The Matchless Orinda," Katherine Philips was the daughter of John Fowler, a London merchant. In 1647 she married James Philips, a wealthy Puritan some years her senior, who shared many of her interests and supported her literary career with enthusiasm. At Cardigan Priory, their Welsh home, the pair saw themselves as the center of an intellectual circle called the Society of Friendship, in which each member was given a playfully neoclassical pseudonym. Katherine herself, for instance, became "Orinda" and James became "Antenor," while Katherine's friend Anne Owen, viscountess of Dungannon, was the original of the "Excellent Lucasia" to whom a number of "Orinda's" pieces on friendship are dedicated.

Though few of Philips's poems were published in her lifetime, she did have several translations of Corneille's plays performed to great acclaim, and her verses, circulated privately, received much praise from such contemporary poets and intellectuals as Abraham Cowley, Jeremy Taylor, and John Dryden. The mother of two children, one of whom died in infancy, she clearly had a "room of her own" in which to write and leisure for friendship as well as literary activity. That her most loving poems are addressed to female friends suggests the bonds that were beginning to develop between seventeenth-century intellectual women, who felt that they had found "all the world" in each other rather than in romanticized heroes. Nevertheless, "The Matchless Orinda" was admired by male as well as female readers. When she died of smallpox at the early age of thirty-three, countless tributes appeared, eulogizing her. Though some of her work was conventionally pious or sentimental, her first collection of plays and poems, posthumously printed, was extraordinarily popular; as the poet Anne Killigrew somewhat enviously remarked, "every laurel to her laurel bowed"—that is, every respected poet praised her artistry.

To My Excellent Lucasia, on Our Friendship

I did not live until this time
    Crowned my felicity,
When I could say without a crime,[1]
    I am not thine, but thee.

This carcass breathed, and walked, and slept,
    So that the world believed
There was a soul the motions kept;[2]
    But they were all deceived.

1. I.e., lying.   2. I.e., that controlled the body's movements.

For as a watch by art[3] is wound
    To motion, such was mine:
But never had Orinda[4] found
    A soul till she found thine;

Which now inspires,[5] cures and supplies,
    And guides my darkened breast:
For thou art all that I can prize,
    My joy, my life, my rest.

No bridegroom's nor crown-conqueror's[6] mirth
    To mine compared can be:
They have but pieces of the earth,
    I've all the world in thee.

Then let our flames still light and shine,
    And no false fear control,
As innocent as our design,[7]
    Immortal as our soul.

1667

3. Artificial means, skill.
4. Philips herself.
5. Fills with air.

6. One who has become a monarch by force.
7. Intention.

MARY ROWLANDSON
(c. 1636–c. 1678)

At dawn on February 10, 1676, Mary Rowlandson, her six-year-old daughter, and her two older children were captured by a tribe of New England Indians. Both Rowlandson and the six-year-old were wounded, and they were separated from the older children. Though a number of people, including Rowlandson's sister, were killed in the raid, her husband—a minister—survived because he was away from home. During a three-month imprisonment that followed, Rowlandson lived with the members of the Algonquin squaw Weetamoo's household, migrating with them into southwestern New Hampshire, visiting, when possible, with her son, Joseph, and her daughter, Mary, coping with cold by reading a Bible that was given to her and with hunger by knitting or sewing in exchange for pancakes and bear meat. Her resiliency and survival skills seem to have surprised even herself: before the Indian raid she had believed that she would "choose rather to be killed by them than taken alive." But, she explains in a narrative that has since become a classic of frontier literature, "when it came to the trial my mind changed; their glittering weapons so daunted my spirit, that I chose rather to go along with those (as I may say) ravenous beasts, than that moment to end my days."

The raid on her house had been part of a year-long series of attacks on colonial outposts led by Metacomet, or "Philip," as the white settlers called him. Mary Rowlandson was understandably irate, if not racist, about the "merciless heathen" who taunted her and tormented her children. Yet even her account implies that the Indians were themselves starving and uprooted. In fact, what became known as "King Philip's War" was a futile effort on the part of the Indians to reclaim the homeland they had lost to Puritans like the Rowlandsons. By May 2, 1676, Rowlandson was thankful that the Indian community assented to the ransom her husband offered for her, that several of its representatives provided a hood and scarf for her journey, and that during her captivity "not one of them ever offered me the least abuse of unchastity to me, in word or action." Documenting, as it does, her shifting attitudes toward Indian culture, her capacity for endurance, and the Puritan rhetorical tradition, Mary Rowlandson's Indian captivity narrative, which she wrote for her surviving children, has been exceptionally popular, going through more than thirty editions after it was published in 1682.

From A Narrative of the Captivity and Restoration of Mrs. Mary Rowlandson

The Third Remove[1]

The morning being come, they prepared to go on their way. One of the Indians got up upon a horse, and they set me up behind him, with my poor sick babe in my lap. A very wearisome and tedious day I had of it; what with my own wound, and my child's being so exceeding sick, and in a lamentable condition with her wound. It may be easily judged what a poor feeble condition we were in, there being not the least crumb of refreshing that came within either of our mouths from Wednesday night to Saturday night, except only a little cold water. This day in the afternoon, about an hour by sun, we came to the place where they intended, *viz.* an Indian town, called Wenimesset, northward of Quabaug. When we were come, Oh the number of pagans (now merciless enemies) that there came about me, that I may say as David, "I had fainted, unless I had believed, etc" (Psalm 27:13). The next day was the sabbath. I then remembered how careless I had been of God's holy time; how many sabbaths I had lost and misspent, and how evilly I had walked in God's sight; which lay so close unto my spirit, that it was easy for me see how righteous it was with God to cut off the thread of my life and cast me out of His presence for ever. Yet the Lord still showed mercy to me, and upheld me; and as He wounded me with one hand, so he healed me with the other. This day there came to me one

---

1. I.e., departure. From February 12 to 27 Rowlandson and her captors stayed at an Indian village on the Ware River, near New Braintree.

Robert Pepper (a man belonging to Roxbury) who was taken in Captain Beers's fight, and had been now a considerable time with the Indians; and up with them almost as far as Albany, to see king Philip, as he told me, and was now very lately come into these parts.[2] Hearing, I say, that I was in this Indian town, he obtained leave to come and see me. He told me he himself was wounded in the leg at Captain Beer's fight; and was not able some time to go, but as they carried him, and as he took oaken leaves and laid to his wound, and through the blessing of God he was able to travel again. Then I took oaken leaves and laid to my side, and with the blessing of God it cured me also; yet before the cure was wrought, I may say, as it is in Psalm 38:5-6 "My wounds stink and are corrupt, I am troubled, I am bowed down greatly, I go mourning all the day long." I sat much alone with a poor wounded child in my lap, which moaned night and day, having nothing to revive the body, or cheer the spirits of her, but instead of that, sometimes one Indian would come and tell me one hour that "your master will knock your child in the head," and then a second, and then a third, "your master will quickly knock your child in the head."

This was the comfort I had from them, miserable comforters are ye all, as he[3] said. Thus nine days I sat upon my knees, with my babe in my lap, till my flesh was raw again; my child being even ready to depart this sorrowful world, they bade me carry it out to another wigwam (I suppose because they would not be troubled with such spectacles) whither I went with a very heavy heart, and down I sat with the picture of death in my lap. About two hours in the night, my sweet babe like a lamb departed this life on Feb. 18, 1675.[4] It being about six years, and five months old. It was nine days from the first wounding, in this miserable condition, without any refreshing of one nature or other, except a little cold water. I cannot but take notice how at another time I could not bear to be in the room where any dead person was, but now the case is changed; I must and could lie down by my dead babe, side by side all the night after. I have thought since of the wonderful goodness of God to me in preserving me in the use of my reason and senses in that distressed time, that I did not use wicked and violent means to end my own miserable life. In the morning, when they understood that my child was dead they sent for me home to my master's wigwam (by my master in this writing, must be understood Quanopin,[5] who was a Sagamore, and married King Philip's wife's sister; not that he first took me, but I was sold to him by another Narraganset Indian, who took me when first I came out of the garrison). I went to take up my dead child in my arms to

---

2. Captain Beers battled to rescue the garrison of Northfield, Massachusetts, September 4, 1675.

3. I.e., Job: "I have heard many such things: miserable comforters are ye all" (Job 16:2).

4. Using the present Gregorian calendar, 1676.

5. Quanopin was Weetamoo's husband; Rowlandson became her servant. "Sagamore": subordinate chief among Algonquin Indians.

carry it with me, but they bid me let it alone; there was no resisting, but go I must and leave it. When I had been at my master's wigwam, I took the first opportunity I could get to go look after my dead child. When I came I asked them what they had done with it; then they told me it was upon the hill. Then they went and showed me where it was, where I saw the ground was newly digged, and there they told me they had buried it. There I left that child in the wilderness, and must commit it, and myself also in this wilderness-condition, to Him who is above all. God having taken away this dear child, I went to see my daughter Mary, who was at this same Indian town, at a wigwam not very far off, though we had little liberty or opportunity to see one another. She was about ten years old, and taken from the door at first by a Praying Ind. and afterward sold for a gun. When I came in sight, she would fall aweeping; at which they were provoked, and would not let me come near her, but bade me be gone; which was a heart-cutting word to me. I had one child dead, another in the wilderness, I knew not where, the third they would not let me come near to: "Me (as he said) have ye bereaved of my Children, Joseph is not, and Simeon is not, and ye will take Benjamin also, all these things are against me."[6] I could not sit still in this condition, but kept walking from one place to another. And as I was going along, my heart was even overwhelmed with the thoughts of my condition, and that I should have children, and a nation which I knew not, ruled over them. Whereupon I earnestly entreated the Lord, that He would consider my low estate, and show me a token for good, and if it were His blessed will, some sign and hope of some relief. And indeed quickly the Lord answered, in some measure, my poor prayers; for as I was going up and down mourning and lamenting my condition, my son came to me, and asked me how I did. I had not seen him before, since the destruction of the town, and I knew not where he was, till I was informed by himself, that he was amongst a smaller parcel of Indians, whose place was about six miles off. With tears in his eyes, he asked me whether his sister Sarah was dead; and told me he had seen his sister Mary; and prayed me, that I would not be troubled in reference to himself. The occasion of his coming to see me at this time, was this: there was, as I said, about six miles from us, a small plantation of Indians, where it seems he had been during his captivity; and at this time, there were some forces of the Ind. gathered out of our company, and some also from them (among whom was my son's master) to go to assault and burn Medfield.[7] In this time of the absence of his master, his dame brought him to see me. I took this to be some gracious answer to my earnest and unfeigned desire. The next day, *viz.* to this, the Indians returned from Medfield, all the company, for those that belonged to the

6. The lament of Jacob (Genesis 42:36).   took place on February 21.
7. This attack on Medfield, Massachussetts,

other small company, came through the town that now we were at. But before they came to us, Oh! the outrageous roaring and hooping that there was. They began their din about a mile before they came to us. By their noise and hooping they signified how many they had destroyed (which was at that time twenty three.) Those that were with us at home were gathered together as soon as they heard the hooping, and every time that the other went over their number, these at home gave a shout, that the very earth rung again. And thus they continued till those that had been upon the expedition were come up to the Sagamore's wigwam; then, Oh, the hideous insulting and triumphing that there was over some Englishmen's scalps that they had taken (as their manner is) and brought with them. I cannot but take notice of the wonderful mercy of God to me in those afflictions, in sending me a Bible. One of the Indians that came from Medfield fight, had brought some plunder, came to me, and asked me, if I would have a Bible, he had got one in his basket. I was glad of it, and asked him, whether he thought the Indians would let me read? He answered, yes. So I took the Bible, and in that melancholy time, it came into my mind to read first the 28th chapter of Deuteronomy,[8] which I did, and when I had read it, my dark heart wrought on this manner: that there was no mercy for me, that the blessings were gone, and the curses come in their room, and that I had lost my opportunity. But the Lord helped me still to go on reading till I came to Chap. 30, the seven first verses, where I found, there was mercy promised again, if we would return to Him by repentance;[9] and though we were scattered from one end of the earth to the other, yet the Lord would gather us together, and turn all those curses upon our enemies. I do not desire to live to forget this Scripture, and what comfort it was to me.

Now the Ind. began to talk of removing from this place, some one way, and some another. There were now besides myself nine English captives in this place (all of them children, except one woman). I got an opportunity to go and take my leave of them. They being to go one way, and I another, I asked them whether they were earnest with God for deliverance. They told me they did as they were able, and it was some comfort to me, that the Lord stirred up children to look to Him. The woman, *viz.* goodwife[1] Joslin, told me she should never see me again, and that she could find in her heart to run away. I wished her not to run away by any means, for we were near thirty miles from any English town, and she very big with child, and had but one week to reckon, and another child in her arms, two years old, and bad rivers there were

---

8. This chapter concerns God's blessings and curses on those who obey and disobey Him.
9. "That then the Lord thy God will turn thy capitivity, and have compassion upon thee, and will return and gather thee from all the nations. . . ." (Deuteronomy 30:3).
1. I.e., mistress of the house.

to go over, and we were feeble, with our poor and coarse entertainment. I had my Bible with me, I pulled it out, and asked her whether she would read. We opened the Bible and lighted on Psalm 27, in which Psalm we especially took notice of that, *ver. ult.*, "Wait on the Lord, Be of good courage, and he shall strengthen thine Heart, wait I say on the Lord."[2]

1682

2. Verse 14.

APHRA BEHN
1640–1689

Spy and playwright, traveler and wit, Aphra Behn was England's first professional woman writer. In an age when many women of letters were intellectual aristocrats like Anne Finch, countess of Winchilsea, and Margaret Cavendish, duchess of Newcastle, wealthy ladies who claimed to write only for pleasure and "fame" among their friends, Behn was a middle-class widow who frankly wrote for money and public acclaim. Of uncertain parentage, she seems in around 1663 to have traveled with a foster family to Surinam in the West Indies, where her adventures are said by some biographers to have included an involvement in a slave rebellion and a visit to a tribe of Indians who had never before seen Europeans. Returning to England in 1664, she was briefly married to a Mr. Behn, about whom little is known except that he was a London merchant of Dutch ancestry, who very likely died in the terrible plague of 1665.

In 1666, widowed and casting about for some means of support, Mrs. Behn entered the intelligence service of King Charles II, though as she later acknowledged, such "public toils of state affairs" were "unusual with my sex, or in my years." Assigned to work as a spy in Antwerp, she carried out her mission "remarkably well," according to Angeline Goreau, the author of a recent biography, but the king's agents never paid her properly for her labors, so that she ended up spending some time in 1668 in a London debtors' prison. Apparently it was the trauma of this last experience that decided her upon what was, for a woman, an unprecedented step: writing for money. By 1670, Aphra Behn's first play, *The Forced Marriage*, was successfully produced on the London stage.

From 1670 on, Behn's groundbreaking literary career was characterized by remarkable productivity. She had always been a literary young woman, a fluent diarist, and an enthusiastic reader of French romances. Now, as she became a professional playwright, she moved from writing somewhat derivative tragicomedies to producing farces in the style of such contemporaries as the comic dramatist William Wycherley. Altogether, during her years in the theater she wrote and published some fourteen plays, including *The Rover* (1677), *Sir Patient Fancy* (1678), *The Roundheads* (1681), and *The City Heiress* (1682).

At the same time, inquiring "What has poor woman done that she must be / Debarred from . . . . sacred poetry?" and demanding freedom to assert what society defined as " my masculine part, the poet in me," Behn was composing and publishing a series of briskly witty verses, some marked by an erotic honesty that scandalized many of her readers. For although the Restoration circles in which she traveled permitted extraordinary license to male artists like Behn's libertine friend and patron the poet John Wilmot, earl of Rochester, the same circles expected women to remain decently silent about their own desires. As her poem *The Disappointment* suggests, however, Behn did not maintain such a silence, so that even a supporter like the writer Anne Finch was later to concede that "a little too loosely she writ."

In Aphra Behn's later years, the London theaters on which she had depended for her livelihood suffered a number of reverses, and her income from playwriting was severely reduced. Enterprising as ever, she turned her talents in yet another direction, writing and publishing a set of pioneering prose fictions —*Love Letters between a Nobleman and His Sister* (1684–1686), *The Fair Jilt* (1688), *Agnes de Castro* (1688), and most notably, *Oroonoko* (1688). Loosely based on "real life," with the revolutionary *Oroonoko* supposedly recounting Behn's early experiences in Surinam and including a passionate protest against the institution of slavery, these literary novelties were to play a part in the development of a new form, the novel, in which, as some critics have suggested, women of letters were at last to find a genre of their own. Though she died in pain and poverty within a year of the publication of *Oroonoko*, and though her reputation was to be obscured or defaced for centuries after her death, Aphra Behn had once again broken new ground. It is no wonder, then, that several centuries later, Virginia Woolf paid special tribute to her memory. "All women together ought to let flowers fall upon the tomb of Aphra Behn," declared the author of *A Room of One's Own*, "for it was she who earned them the right to speak their minds."

The Willing Mistress[1]

Amyntas led me to a grove,
   Where all the trees did shade us;
The sun itself, though it had strove,
   It could not have betrayed us.[2]
The place secured from human eyes   5
   No other fear allows
But when the winds that gently rise
   Do kiss the yielding boughs.

Down there we sat upon the moss,
   And did begin to play   10

1. This song appears in Behn's play *The Dutch Lover*, where it is sung by a maidservant to her   mistress.
2. I.e., revealed us to others.

A thousand amorous tricks,[3] to pass
   The heat of all the day.
A many kisses did he give
   And I returned the same,
Which made me willing to receive   15
   That which I dare not name.

His charming eyes no aid required
   To tell their softening tale;
On her that was already fired,[4]
   'Twas easy to prevail.   20
He did but kiss and clasp me round,
   Whilst those his thoughts expressed:
And laid me gently on the ground;
   Ah who can guess the rest?

                         1673

Love Armed[5]

Love in fantastic triumph[6] sat
Whilst bleeding hearts around him flowed,
For whom fresh[7] pains he did create
And strange tyrannic power he showed.

From thy bright eyes he took the fires   5
Which round about in sport he hurled,
But 'twas from mine he took desires
Enough t'undo the amorous world.[8]

From me he took his sighs and tears,
From thee his pride and cruelty;   10
From me his languishments and fears.
And every killing dart[9] from thee.

Thus thou and I the God have armed
And set him up a deity;
But my poor heart alone is harmed,   15
Whilst thine the victor is, and free.

                         1676

---

3. Games, amusements.
4. I.e., made warm with desire.
5. A song in Behn's play *Abdelazer; or, The Moor's Revenge.* "Love" in this poem is Cupid, often depicted during the Renaissance as a cruel and arbitrary god (see, for example, the Maske of Cupid in Spenser's *The Faerie Queene*, Book III, canto xii).
6. In a splendid procession.
7. New.
8. To drown the world's lovers in the sufferings of desire.
9. Cupid's darts.

The Disappointment[1]

One day the amorous Lysander,
By an impatient passion swayed,[2]
Surprised fair Cloris, that lovéd maid,
Who could defend herself no longer.
All things did with his love conspire;[3]   5
The gilded planet of the day,
In his gay chariot drawn by fire,
Was now descending to the sea,
And left no light to guide the world
But what from Cloris' brighter eyes was hurled.   10

In a lone thicket made for love,
Silent as yielding maid's consent,
She with a charming languishment,
Permits his force, yet gently strove;[4]
Her hands his bosom softly meet,   15
But not to put him back designed,
Rather to draw 'em on inclined:
Whilst he lay trembling at her feet,
Resistance 'tis in vain to show:
She wants[5] the power to say—*Ah! what d'ye do?*   20

Her bright eyes sweet and yet severe,
Where love and shame confusedly strive,
Fresh vigor to Lysander give;
And breathing faintly in his ear,
She cried—*Cease, cease—your vain desire,*   25
Or I'll call out—what would you do?
My dearer honor[6] *even to you*
I cannot, must not give—Retire,[7]
Or take this life, whose chiefest part
I gave you with the conquest of my heart.   30

But he as much unused to fear,
As he was capable of love,
The blessed minutes to improve[8]
Kisses her mouth, her neck, her hair;
Each touch her new desire alarms;   35
His burning, trembling hand he pressed
Upon her swelling snowy breast,
While she lay panting in his arms.

---

1. Based on a French poem entitled *Une Impuissance*, i.e., an impotence.
2. By desire moved.
3. I.e., the outside world seemed to encourage his love; "gilded planet": the sun.
4. Struggles.
5. Lacks.
6. Virginity.
7. Leave.
8. Make more pleasurable.

All her unguarded beauties lie
The spoils and trophies of the enemy.   40

And now without respect or fear
He seeks the object of his vows
(His love no modesty allows)
By swift degrees advancing—where
His daring hand that altar[9] seized,   45
Where gods of love do sacrifice:
That awful throne, that paradise
Where rage is calmed, and anger pleased;
That fountain where delight still flows,
And gives the universal world respose.   50

Her balmy lips encountering his,
Their bodies, as their souls, are joined;
Where both in transports unconfined
Extend themselves upon the moss.
Cloris half dead and breathless lay;   55
Her soft eyes cast a humid light
Such as divides the day and night;
Or falling stars, whose fires decay:
And now no signs of life she shows,
But what in short-breathed sighs returns and goes.   60

He saw how at her length she lay;
He saw her rising bosom bare;
Her loose thin robes, through which appear
A shape designed for love and play;
Abandoned by her pride and shame   65
She does her softest joys dispense,
Offering her virgin innocence
A victim to love's sacred flame;
While the o'er-ravished shepherd lies
Unable to perform the sacrifice.   70

Ready to taste a thousand joys,
The too transported hapless swain[1]
Found the vast pleasure turned to pain;
Pleasure which too much love destroys:
The willing garments[2] by he laid,   75
And heaven all opened to his view.
Mad to possess, himself he threw
On the defenceless lovely maid.
But oh what envying god conspires
To snatch his power, yet leave him the desire!   80

9. I.e., her genitalia.   2. I.e., hers.
1. Unfortunate lover.

Nature's support (without whose aid
She can no human being give)
Itself now wants the art[3] to live;
Faintness its slackened nerves invade:
In vain th'enragéd youth essayed   85
To call its fleeting vigor back;
No motion 'twill from motion take;
Excess of love his love betrayed:
In vain he toils, in vain commands:
The insensible fell weeping in his hand.   90

In this so amorous cruel strife,
Where love and fate were too severe,
The poor Lysander in despair
Renounced his reason with his life:
Now all the brisk and active fire   95
That should the nobler part[4] inflame
Served to increase his rage and shame,
And left no spark for new desire:
Not all her naked charms could move
Or calm that rage that had debauched[5] his love.   100

Cloris returning from the trance
Which love and soft desire had bred,
Her timorous hand she gently laid
(Or guided by design or chance)
Upon that fabulous Priapus,[6]
That potent god, as poets feign:[7]   105
But never did young shepherdess,
Gathering the fern upon the plain,
More nimbly[8] draw her fingers back,
Finding beneath the verdant leaves a snake,   110

Than Cloris her fair hand withdrew,
Finding that god of her desires
Disarmed of all his awful fires,
And cold as flowers bathed in the morning dew.
Who can the nymph's confusion guess?
The blood forsook the hinder place,[9]   115
And strewed with blushes all her face,
Which both disdain and shame expressed:
And from Lysander's arms she fled,
Leaving him fainting on the gloomy bed.   120

---

3. Lacks the ability.
4. His reason, but also his impotent phallus.
5. Dissipated, rendered impotent.
6. I.e., his erect penis (from Priapus, Greek god

of procreation).
7. Claim, but also pretend falsely.
8. Quickly; "verdant": green.
9. Her genitals; "strewed": scattered, covered.

Like lightning through the grove she hies,
Or Daphne from the Delphic god;[1]
No print upon the grassy road
She leaves, to instruct pursuing eyes.
The wind that wantoned[2] in her hair   125
And with her ruffled garments played,
Discovered[3] in the flying maid
All that the gods e'er made, if fair.
So Venus, when her love was slain,[4]
With fear and haste flew o'er the fatal plain.   130

The nymph's resentments none but I
Can well imagine or condole:
But none can guess Lysander's soul,
But those who swayed[5] his destiny.
His silent griefs swell up to storms,   135
And not one god his fury spares;
He cursed his birth, his fate, his stars;
But more the shepherdess's charms,
Whose soft bewitching influence
Had damned him to the hell of impotence.   140

1680

On Her Loving Two Equally

I

How strong does my passion flow,
Divided equally twixt[6] two?
Damon had ne'er subdued my heart
Had not Alexis took his part;
Nor could Alexis powerful prove,[7]   5
Without my Damon's aid, to gain my love.

II

When my Alexis present is,
Then I for Damon sigh and mourn;
But when Alexis I do miss,
Damon gains nothing but my scorn.   10
But if it chance they both are by,[8]
For both alike I languish, sigh, and die.

1. In Greek myth, Daphne is a nymph who
escapes the god Apollo's lecherous pursuit by
turning herself into a laurel tree.
2. Played wildly, frolicked.
3. Uncovered, displayed.
4. Venus is the Roman name for Aphrodite, the
Greek goddess of love. Her lover Adonis was
slain by a boar.
5. Here, deflected, turned from its proper
course; compare line 2. "Those" refers to the
gods.
6. Between.
7. Show himself.
8. Near.

III

Cure then, thou mighty wingéd god,[9]
This restless fever in my blood;
One golden-pointed dart[1] take back: 15
But which, O Cupid, wilt thou take?
If Damon's, all my hopes are crossed;[2]
Or that of my Alexis, I am lost.

                                                                  1684

To the Fair Clarinda, Who Made Love to Me, Imagined More than Woman[3]

Fair lovely maid, or if that title be
Too weak, too feminine for nobler thee,
Permit a name that more approaches truth:
And let me call thee lovely charming youth.
This last will justify my soft complaint,[4]   5
While that may serve to lessen my constraint;
And without blushes I the youth pursue,
When so much beauteous woman is in view.
Against thy charms we struggle but in vain;
With thy deluding form thou givest us pain,
While the bright nymph betrays us to the swain.[5]   10
In pity to our sex sure thou wert sent,
That we might love, and yet be innocent:[6]
For sure no crime[7] with thee we can commit;
Or if we should—thy form excuses it.
For who that gathers fairest flowers believes   15
A snake lies hid beneath the fragrant leaves.

Thou beauteous wonder of a different kind,
Soft Cloris with the dear Alexis joined;
Whene'er the manly part of thee would plead[8]
Thou tempts us with the image of the maid,   20
While we the noblest passions[9] do extend
The love to Hermes, Aphrodite[1] the friend.

                                                                  1688

---

9. Cupid.
1. According to myth, Cupid shot darts of lead and of gold at the hearts of lovers, corresponding to false and true love respectively.
2. Blocked, ruined.
3. I.e., as a hermaphrodite, a union of male and female in one body.
4. Declaration of love. "This last": the title of youth (male); "that": the title of maid (female).
5. A nymph is a mythic female spirit; a swain is a male shepherd, also more generally a lover. I.e.,

her feminine beauty induces us to surrender to her masculine aggressiveness.
6. I.e., virginal.
7. Sexual transgression.
8. I.e., beg for sexual favors.
9. Love and friendship, sharply distinguished in the eighteenth century.
1. The Greek messenger god and the Greek goddess of love, joined together as the androgynous being called Hermaphrodite; "friend": i.e. friendship.

LADY MARY CHUDLEIGH
(1656–1710)

In the preface to her *Poems on Several Occasions* (1703), Lady Mary Chudleigh explained that readers would discover in her verse "a picture of my mind, my sentiments all laid open to their view." *To the Ladies* suggests that she was unhappily married to Sir George Chudleigh, of Ashton, Devon. But as the critic Joanna Lipking has argued, the poem's technical expertise also places it in a highly stylized genre, whose poetic conventions Chudleigh may be expertly following. Little is known about her personal life except that she suffered over her children dying young. Yet Lady Mary also reveals her strikingly feminist sentiments in *The Female Advocate; or, A Plea for the Just Liberty of the Tender Sex and Particularly of Married Women* (1701) and *The Ladies' Defence; or, "The Bride-Woman's Counselor" Answered* (1701). These books—the former in prose and the latter in verse—respond to a minister, John Sprint, whose sermon *The Bride-Woman's Counselor* (1700) argued that a wife's whole duty was to love, honor, and obey her husband. Indignant that women are "Debarred from knowledge, banished from the schools, / And with the utmost industry bred fools," Lady Mary scorns the "mean low trivial cares of life," asserting that women must "read and think, and think and read again, / And on our minds bestow the utmost pain."

To the Ladies

Wife and servant are the same,
But only differ in the name:
For when that fatal knot is tied,
Which nothing, nothing can divide:
When she the word *obey* has said,   5
And man by law supreme has made,
Then all that's kind is laid aside,
And nothing left but state[1] and pride:
Fierce as an Eastern prince he grows,
And all his innate rigor shows: 10
Then but to look, to laugh, or speak,
Will the nuptial contract break.
Like mutes she signs alone must make,
And never any freedom take:
But still be governed by a nod,   15
And fear her husband as her God:
Him still must serve, him still obey,
And nothing act, and nothing say,

---

1. Pomp; "kind": natural.

> But what her haughty lord thinks fit,
> Who with the power, has all the wit.[2]   20
> Then shun, oh! shun that wretched state,
> And all the fawning flatt'rers hate:
> Value your selves, and men despise,
> You must be proud, if you'll be wise.

1703

2. Intelligence.

ANNE KILLIGREW
1660–1685

The author of a small but skillful body of verse, Anne Killigrew is best known today as the subject of John Dryden's famous elegy *To the Pious Memory of the Accomplished Young Lady Mrs. Anne Killigrew* (1686). Born in London shortly before the Restoration, she was the daughter of Dr. Henry Killigrew, chaplain to the duke of York and himself a dramatist whose genius, Dryden declared, had been "transfused into [her] blood." Because of her father's position, she was raised in an atmosphere where female talent was encouraged; she frequented court circles; and she became maid of honor to Mary Modena, duchess of York. But though, when Killigrew died of smallpox at the age of twenty-five, Dryden defined her as a modern equivalent of the famous Greek woman poet Sappho, her literary career cannot have been quite as successful as his ceremonial eulogy suggested. Certainly her plaintive *Upon the Saying That My Verses Were Made by Another* implies a literary anxiety comparable to the fear expressed by Anne Bradstreet when she wrote in her *Prologue* that "if what I do prove well, it won't advance / They'll say it's stol'n, or else it was by chance." The hazards of female authorship were not insignificant, even in an age when women intellectuals were beginning to gain some strength.

Upon the Saying That My Verses Were Made by Another

> Next heaven,[1] my vows to thee, O sacred Muse!
> I offered up, nor didst thou them refuse.
>
> O queen of verse, said I, if thou'lt inspire,
> And warm my soul with thy poetic fire,
> No love of gold shall share with thee my heart,
> Or yet ambition in my breast have part,
> More rich, more noble I will ever hold   5
> The Muse's laurel,[2] than a crown of gold.

1. I.e., next to heaven. "Muse": goddess of poetry and inspiration.

2. Leaves of a tree traditionally used to crown famous poets.

An undivided sacrifice I'll lay
Upon thine altar, soul and body pay;
Thou shalt my pleasure, my employment be,
My all I'll make a holocaust[3] to thee.   10

   The deity that ever does attend
Prayers so sincere, to mine did condescend.[4]
I writ, and the judicious praised my pen:
Could any doubt ensuing glory then?
What pleasing raptures filled my ravished sense,   15
How strong, how sweet, fame, was thy influence!
And thine, false hope, that to my flattered sight
Did'st glories represent so near and bright!
By thee deceived, methought each verdant[5] tree
Apollo's transformed Daphne[6] seemed to be;   20
And every fresher branch, and every bough,
Appeared as garlands to empale[7] my brow.
The learn'd in love say, thus the winged boy[8]
Does first approach, dressed up in welcome joy;
At first he to the cheated[9] lover's sight   25
Nought represents but rapture and delight,
Alluring hopes, soft fears, which stronger bind
Their hearts, than when they more assurance find.

   Emboldened thus, to fame I did commit,
By some few hands,[1] my most unlucky wit.   30
But ah, the sad effects that from it came!
What ought t'have brought me honour, brought me shame!
Like Aesop's painted jay,[2] I seemed to all,
Adorned in plumes, I not my own could call:
Rifled like her, each one my feathers tore,   35
And, as they thought, unto the owner bore.
My laurels thus another's brow adorned,
My numbers[3] they admired, but me they scorned:
Another's brow, that had so rich a store
Of sacred wreaths that circled it before;   40
While mine quite lost (like a small stream that ran
Into a vast and boundless ocean,)
Was swallowed up with what it joined, and drowned.
And that abyss yet no accession[4] found.

---

3. Burnt offering.
4. Assent, "attend": hear.
5. Green.
6. Nymph who transformed herself into a tree in order to escape the lecherous pursuit of Apollo, the sun god in Greek myth.
7. Surround.
8. Cupid, the Greek god of love.

9. Deceived.
1. I.e., those who helped to publish her work. "Wit": imagination.
2. In one of Aesop's fables, a jay adorns himself in a peacock's feathers, and is angrily attacked by the other birds.
3. Meter.
4. Addition.

Orinda[5] (Albion's and her sex's grace)   45
Owed not her glory to a beauteous face;
It was her radiant soul that shone within,
Which struck a luster through her outward skin;
That did her lips and cheeks with roses dye,
Advanced[6] her height, and sparkled in her eye.   50
Nor did her sex at all obstruct her fame,
But higher 'mong the stars it fixed her name;
What she did write, not only all allowed,[7]
But every laurel to her laurel bowed!

The envious age, only to me alone,   55
Will not allow[8] what I do write, my own;
But let them rage, and 'gainst a maid conspire,
So deathless numbers from my tuneful lyre[9]
Do ever flow; so, Phoebus,[1] I by thee
Divinely inspired and possessed may be,   60
I willingly accept Cassandra's fate,[2]
To speak the truth, although believed too late.

1686

5. Orinda is Katherine Philips (see above); Albion is England.
6. Increased.
7. Acknowledged.
8. Consider.
9. A Greek musical instrument like a small harp.

1. Apollo, Greek god of the sun and poetry.
2. Cassandra was a Greek prophetess who foretold the coming of the Greeks to Troy; in anger at being spurned by her, Apollo brought it to pass that no one believed her predictions.

ANNE FINCH, COUNTESS OF WINCHILSEA
1661–1720

The very first poem in Anne Finch's 1713 collection of verse—the only volume she published in her lifetime—outlines her gloomy vision of the literary woman's situation. Accomplished artist though she was, Finch had every reason to feel bitterness, for she had long been, in the words of the critic Cora Kaplan, "a prime butt for anti-'bluestocking' jokes on the stage and in verse." Even her sometime friend Alexander Pope, for instance, had caricatured her in a play called *Three Hours after Marriage* (coauthored with John Gay and John Arbuthnot) as a mad poetess named "Phoebe Clinket," and as late as 1954 Sylvia Plath, herself destined to become one of the twentieth century's major literary women, was amused by that character's "high flown and very funny ambitions to write poetry." Nor is there any evidence that Plath, who played the part of Phoebe Clinket in a Cambridge University production of Pope's comedy, ever read the verse written by Anne Finch herself.

Yet this woman who feared she would be thought "a presumptuous creature" was a perceptive and productive poet. Her work was admired by many in her own day, and after her death discriminating readers from William Words-worth to Virginia Woolf continued to celebrate her talent. The daughter of Sir William Kingsmill and Anne Hazlewood, both members of wealthy upper-class families, she was raised in aristocratic circles. Carefully nurtured and well edu-cated, she went to court in 1683 as a Maid of Honor—an attendant—to Mary Modena, duchess of York, a position in which she may well have known Anne Killigrew, who was also one of the duchess's ladies in waiting. Apparently the young Anne Kingsmill was charming and beautiful; when Heneage Finch, also a royal attendant—a Gentleman of the Bedchamber—met her in those years, he courted her vigorously. The couple wed in 1684, and their marriage was a happy one, as many of Finch's poems—for instance, her *Letter to Dafnis*—testify.

When the former duke of York, now King James II, was exiled in the late 1680s and replaced as king by William of Orange, the Finches remained stub-bornly loyal to their former patron and his wife. Swept out of court, they lived in comparative poverty among their relatives, in a kind of political exile of their own. In 1690, however, Heneage Finch's distant cousin the earl of Winchilsea died unexpectedly, and the former Gentleman of the Bedchamber inherited both his title and his luxurious estate at Eastwell; here the couple settled into a life of comfortable retirement, with Anne, now countess of Winchilsea, writing many poems in praise of rural pleasures. A work like her *Nocturnal Reverie*, for instance, with its accurate and detailed descriptions of nighttime meadows and groves, reveals how attentively she observed the pastoral world she loved so much and explains why William Wordsworth, the great Romantic poet of na-ture, was to remark in 1815 that this poem contained almost the only "new image[s] of external nature" produced between Milton's *Paradise Lost* and Thomson's *The Seasons*.

For Anne Finch, however, the serenity of the countryside around Eastwell was more than an emblem of nature's beauty; it symbolized escape from a soci-ety where "all's confused"—and where the role of a literary woman was partic-ularly confusing. Even during her days in the service of Mary Modena, this imaginative woman had written poetry. But, perhaps mindful of Anne Killi-grew's fate, she had refused to publish it, explaining later that "I was not so far abandoned by my prudence as, out of mistaken vanity, to let any attempts of mine in poetry show themselves while I lived in such a public place as the court, where every one would have made their remarks upon a versifying Maid of Honor, and far the greater number with prejudice, if not contempt." Living and writing at Eastwell, though, she became the center of a circle of intellectual friends not unlike the group that had gathered around Katherine Philips a few decades earlier, and her poems were read in manuscript by many of these peo-ple. But while the reputation she thus achieved brought a good deal of admira-tion, it also brought from some quarters exactly the "prejudice, if not contempt," that she had earlier feared. No wonder, then, that in many of her verses she meditated with some bitterness on woman's lot. "How are we fallen, fallen by mistaken rules?" she asked in her *Introduction*, wondering, as Mary Wollstonecraft was also to wonder, if women are "education's more than na-ture's fools." Moreover, just as Anne Bradstreet had mused nostalgically on the reign of Queen Elizabeth, when it was "treason" to consider the female sex "void of reason," Finch dreamed of an age when women were not "fallen" and wished to be told "fables of women that excelled of old"—stories of exemplary biblical heroines like Miriam and Deborah, for instance.

Perhaps because her sense of woman's "fall" was so keen, Finch was often a prey to melancholy as well as bitterness. Some of her most famous works brood on the state of depression and anxiety that her contemporaries called "the spleen," and others, like *Ardelia to Melancholy*, try to combat such feelings. To Virginia Woolf, meditating in *A Room of One's Own* on this poet's career, it seemed "a thousand pities that [her mind] should have been forced to [such] anger and bitterness," yet sympathetic readers can see now that even "spleen" became an important source of inspiration for Finch. In addition, we can see that her "spleen" was at least partly justified. Even today, more than two hundred and fifty years after her death, there is no complete edition of her poetic works; the most recent collection, edited in 1903 by Myra Reynolds, omits an important group of manuscripts that Reynolds did not know about.

The Introduction

Did I my lines intend for public view,
How many censures[1] would their faults pursue,
Some would, because such words they do affect,
Cry they're insipid, empty, uncorrect.
And many have attained, dull and untaught,   5
The name of wit[2] only by finding fault.
True judges might condemn their want[3] of wit,
And all might say they're by a woman writ.
Alas! a woman that attempts the pen
Such an intruder on the rights of men,   10
Such a presumptuous creature is esteemed,
The fault can by no virtue be redeemed.
They tell us we mistake our sex and way;
Good breeding, fashion, dancing, dressing, play
Are the accomplishments we should desire;   15
To write, or read, or think, or to enquire
Would cloud our beauty, and exhaust our time,
And interrupt the conquests of our prime;[4]
Whilst the dull manage of a servile house[5]
Is held by some our utmost art, and use.   20
    Sure 'twas not ever thus, nor are we told
Fables,[6] of women that excelled of old;
To whom, by the diffusive[7] hand of Heaven
Some share of wit and poetry was given.

---

1. Severe criticisms.
2. Intelligence, learning.
3. Lack.
4. Maturity; the "conquests" are amorous.

5. A house full of servants.
6. Falsehoods.
7. Scattering.

On that glad day on which the Ark[8] returned,   25
The holy pledge for which the land had mourned,
The joyful tribes attend it on the way,
The Levites do the sacred charge[9] convey,
Whilst various instruments before it play;
Here holy virgins in the concert join,   30
The louder notes to soften and refine,
And with alternate verse complete the hymn divine.[1]
Lo! the young poet, after God's own heart,
By Him inspired, and taught the Muses' art,[2]
Returned from conquest, a bright chorus meets,   35
That sing his slain ten thousand in the streets.
In such loud numbers they his acts declare,
Proclaim the wonders of his early war,
That Saul upon the vast applause does frown,
And feels its mighty thunder shake the crown.   40
What, can the threatened judgment now prolong?[3]
Half of the kingdom[4] is already gone;
The fairest half, whose influence guides the rest,
Have David's empire o'er their hearts confessed.

   A woman here leads fainting Israel on,[5]   45
She fights, she wins, she triumphs with a song,
Devout, majestic, for the subject fit,
And far above her arms exalts her wit,
Then to the peaceful, shady palm withdraws,
And rules the rescued nation with her laws.   50
How are we fallen, fallen by mistaken rules?
And education's, more than nature's fools,
Debarred from all improvements of the mind,
And to be dull, expected and designed;[6]
And if some one would soar above the rest,   55
With warmer fancy[7] and ambition pressed,
So strong th'opposing faction still appears.
The hopes to thrive can ne'er outweigh the fears.
Be cautioned then my Muse, and still retired;[8]
Nor be despised, aiming to be admired;   60
Conscious of wants, still with contracted wing,

8. The Ark of the Covenant, a chest containing the Ten Commandments engraved on stone tablets, was carried by the Hebrews during their desert wanderings; the Ark was carried into Jerusalem by the priests of the Levites amid great celebration (I Chronicles, 15).
9. I.e., the Ark.
1. I.e., the virgins' voices alternate with the men's in song.
2. Greek goddesses of art and inspiration; all artists were said to have their own personal muse. The "young poet" is David, a young Israelite musician and warrior, who slew the giant Goli-

ath and defeated the Philistine army, earning the love of his people and the jealousy of Saul, king of Israel (1 Samuel, 17–18).
3. Be prolonged; Saul's doom had been foreshadowed;
4. I.e., the women.
5. Deborah, an Israelite judge, led her people in battle and wrote a song celebrating their victory (Judges 4–5).
6. Designated, required.
7. More intense desire.
8. Withdrawn, restrained.

To some few friends and to thy sorrows sing;
For groves of laurel[9] thou wert never meant;
Be dark enough thy shades, and be thou there content.

1689?   1903

A Letter to Daphnis,[1] April 2, 1685

This to the crown and blessing of my life,
The much loved husband of a happy wife,
To him whose constant passion found the art[2]
To win a stubborn and ungrateful heart;
And to the world by tenderest proof discovers[3]   5
They err, who say that husbands can't be lovers.
With such return of passion, as is due,
Daphnis I love, Daphnis my thoughts pursue,
Daphnis, my hopes, my joys, are bounded all in you:
Even I, for Daphnis, and my promise[4] sake,   10
What I in women censure,[5] undertake.
But this from love, not vanity, proceeds;
You know who writes; and I who 'tis that reads.
Judge not my passion by my want of skill,
Many love well, though they express it ill;   15
And I your censure could with pleasure bear,
Would you but soon return, and speak it here.

1685   1903

Friendship between Ephelia and Ardelia[6]

Eph. What friendship is, Ardelia, show.
Ard. 'Tis to love, as I love you.
Eph. This account, so short (though kind)
         Suits not my inquiring mind.
         Therefore farther now repeat: 5
         What is friendship when complete?[7]
Ard. 'Tis to share all joy and grief;
         'Tis to lend all due relief
         From the tongue, the heart, the hand;
         'Tis to mortgage house and land;   10
         For a friend be sold a slave;

---

9. Tree whose leaves were used to crown
famous poets.
1. Finch's neoclassical name for her husband,
Heneage Finch.
2. Skill.

3. Reveals.
4. I.e., her wedding vows.
5. Criticize, namely servility, devotion.
6. Finch's neoclassical penname.
7. Perfect.

>   'Tis to die upon a grave,
>   If a friend therein do lie.
> *Eph.*   This indeed, though carried high,
>   This, though more than e'er was done   15
>   Underneath the rolling sun,
>   This has all been said before.
>   Can Ardelia say no more?
> *Ard.*   Words indeed no more can show: 20
>   But 'tis to love, as I love you.

1713

The Circuit of Apollo[8]

Apollo as lately a circuit he made
Through the lands of the muses when Kent[9] he surveyed
And saw there that poets were not very common,
But most that pretended[1] to verse were the women,
Resolved to encourage the few that he found,   5
And she that writ best with a wreath[2] should be crowned.
A summons sent out was obeyed but by four,
When Phoebus,[3] afflicted to meet with no more,
And standing where sadly he now might descry
From the banks of the Stoure the desolate Wye,[4]   10
He lamented for Behn o'er[5] that place of her birth,
And said amongst femens[6] was not on the earth
Her superior in fancy,[7] in language, or wit,
Yet owned that a little too loosely[8] she writ,
Since the art of the muse is to stir up soft thoughts,   15
Yet to make all hearts beat without blushes or faults.

But now to proceed, and their merits to know
Before he on any the bays[9] would bestow,
He ordered them each in their several[1] way
To show him their papers, to sing or to say   20
Whate'er they thought best, their pretensions might prove,
When Alinda began, with a song upon love.
So easy the verse, yet composed with such art,
That not one expression fell short of the heart.
Apollo himself did their influence obey;   25

---

8. I.e., the circular journey or tour of the Greek god of the sun and of poetry.
9. Greek goddesses of art and inspiration; "Kent": county in England where Finch lived.
1. Claimed to be poets.
2. Of laurel.
3. Another name for Apollo; "afflicted": pained, saddened.
4. The Stour and the Wye are two rivers that flow through Kent.
5. Aphra Behn, English poet (see above).
6. Women.
7. Imagination.
8. With too much sexual explicitness.
9. Leaves of the laurel.
1. Individual, distinct.

He catched up his lyre,[2] and a part he would play,
Declaring no harmony else could be found
Fit to wait upon[3] words of so moving a sound.
The wreath he reached out, to have placed on her head,
If Laura not quickly a paper had read,   30
Wherein she Orinda has praiséd so high,
He owned it had reached him while yet in the sky,
That he thought with himself when it first struck his ear,
Whoe'er could write that ought the laurel to wear.
Betwixt them he stood in a musing suspense,   35
Till Valeria withdrew him a little from thence,
And told him as soon as she'd got him aside
Her works by no other but him should be tried;[4]
Which so often he read, and with still new delight,
That judgement 'twas thought would not pass till 'twas night;   40
Yet at length he restored them, but told her withal[5]
If she kept it still close, he'd the talent recall.
Ardelia[6] came last as expecting least praise,
Who writ for her pleasure and not for the bays,
But yet, as occasion or fancy should sway,   45
Would sometimes endeavour to pass a dull day
In composing a song, or a scene of a play
Not seeking for fame, which so little does last
That ere we can taste it the pleasure is past.
But Apollo replied, though so careless[7] she seemed,   50
Yet the bays, if her share, would be highly esteemed.

And now he was going to make an oration,
Had thrown by one lock with a delicate fashion,
Upon the left foot most genteelly did stand,
Had drawn back the other and waved his white hand,   55
When calling to mind how the prize, although given
By Paris[8] to her who was fairest in heaven,
Had pulled on the rash, inconsiderate boy
The fall of his house, with the ruin of Troy;
Since in wit or in beauty it never was heard   60
One female could yield to have another preferred,
He changed his design, and divided his praise,
And said that they all had a right to the bays,

2. A Greek instrument like a small harp; "part":
piece.
3. Accompany.
4. Judged.
5. Nevertheless.
6. Finch's neoclassical penname; "Orinda"
(l.31) is Katherine Philips, and the other names
in the poem may also refer to women Finch
knew.
7. Indifferent.

8. A young Trojan shepherd, he was asked to
decide which of the three goddesses Hera,
Aphrodite, and Athena was the most beautiful,
by awarding one of them a golden apple. Paris
chose Aphrodite, and in return she helped him
to abduct the beautiful Greek woman Helen,
thereby instigating the Trojan War, and ultimately bringing about the fall of his city and dynasty ("house").

And that 'twere injustice one brow to adorn
With a wreath which so fitly by each might be worn;   65
Then smiled to himself, and applauded his art,[9]
Who thus nicely[1] has acted so subtle a part
Four women to wheedle, but found 'em too many,
For who would please all can never please any.
In vain then he thought it, there longer to stay,   70
But told them he now must go drive on the day,[2]
Yet the case to Parnassus[3] should soon be referred,
And there in a council of muses be heard,
Who of their own sex best the title might try,
Since no man upon earth, nor Himself in the sky   75
Would be so imprudent, so dull, or so blind,
To lose three parts in four amongst womankind.

1702?   1903

The Answer

[to Pope's *Impromptu*][4]

Disarmed with so genteel an air,
   The contest I give o'er;
Yet, Alexander, have a care,
   And shock the sex[5] no more.
We rule the world our life's whole race,[6]   5
   Men but assume[7] that right;
First slaves to every tempting face,
   Then martyrs to our spite.
You of one Orpheus[8] sure have read,
   Who would like you have writ   10
Had he in London town been bred,
   And polished too his wit;
But he poor soul thought all was well,

---

9. Skill.
1. Cleverly, prudently.
2. In Greek myth, Apollo drove the chariot which pulled the sun across the sky.
3. The mountain where the shades of great poets reside.
4. A short poem by Alexander Pope addressed to Finch, with the subtitle "Occasioned by four satirical verses on women wits in *The Rape of the Lock*." The lines from Pope's great mock-epic slyly suggest that some women "scribble plays" as a manifestation of the same disorder that causes others to "take physic" (medicine), and that female discontent expresses itself alternately in "the hysteric or poetic fit." Finch, a friend of Pope's, evidently took issue with this, as might be expected, and seems to have argued with him in person on the issue of female poetic talent. Pope responded with his brief *Impromptu* (improvisation), in which he flattered Finch by claiming that all the examples of female poets she cites pale beside her own accomplishments. *The Answer* is Finch's correspondingly deferential reply.
5. I.e., the female sex.
6. Length.
7. Claim without truly possessing.
8. Mythical Greek poet whose wife, Eurydice, was forced to remain behind in the underworld when he looked back at her as they were leaving, against the instruction of Hades, god of the dead. Orpheus's singing had the power to charm wild animals; he was torn to pieces by a band of frenzied women called Maenads ("resenting heroines").

And great should be his fame,
When he had left his wife in hell,   15
And birds and beasts could tame.
Yet venturing then with scoffing rhymes
The women to incense,
Resenting heroines of those times
Soon punished his offense.   20
And as the Hebrus[9] rolled his skull
And harp besmeared with blood,
They clashing as the waves grew full
Still harmonized the flood.
But you our follies gently[1] treat,   25
And spin so fine the thread,
You need not fear his awkward fate,
The lock won't cost the head.[2]
Our admiration you command
For all that's gone before;   30
What next we look for at your hand
Can only raise it more.
Yet sooth[3] the ladies I advise
(As me too pride has wrought),[4]
We're born to wit, but to be wise   35
By admonitions taught.

1734–1741   1903

The Spleen[5]

A *Pindaric Poem*[6]

What art thou, Spleen, which ev'ry thing dost ape.[7]
Thou Proteus[8] to abused mankind;
Who never yet thy real cause could find,
Or fix thee to remain in one continued[9] shape
Still varying thy perplexing form,   5
Now a Dead Sea[1] thou'lt represent,
A calm of stupid discontent,
Then, dashing on the rocks, wilt rage into a storm.
Trembling sometimes thou dost appear,
Dissolved into a panic fear;   10

9. River into which Orpheus's dismembered body was cast.
1. Genteelly, wittily.
2. A reference to *The Rape of the Lock*, in which a lock of hair is stolen from Belinda, the heroine.
3. Truly.
4. Made (wise).
5. One of the four humors, a bodily fluid thought to cause depression or melancholy.

6. A poetic form derived from the Greek poet Pindar, consisting of several units called strophes, generally addressed to some spiritual or material object; also called an ode.
7. Imitate.
8. Mythological sea creature capable of changing shape at will.
9. Constant, unchanging.
1. A salt lake in the Middle East, lacking tidal movement.

On sleep intruding dost thy shadows spread,
Thy gloomy terrors round the silent bed,
And crowd with boding[2] dreams the melancholy head;
Or, when the midnight hour is told,[3]
And drooping lids thou still dost waking hold,   15
Thy fond delusions cheat[4] the eyes:
Before them antic[5] spectres dance,
Unusual fires their pointed heads advance,
And airy phantoms rise.
Such was the monstrous vision seen,   20
When Brutus (now beneath his cares oppressed,
And all Rome's fortunes rolling on his breast,
Before Philippi's latest field,
Before his fate did to Octavius lead)
Was vanquished by the spleen.[6]   25

Falsely the mortal part[7] we blame
Of our depressed and pond'rous frame,[8]
Which, till the first degrading sin[9]
Let thee, its dull attendant, in,
Still with the other[1] did comply,   30
Nor clogged the active soul, disposed[2] to fly,
And range[3] the mansions of its native sky.
Nor, whilst in his own heaven he dwelt,
Whilst man his Paradise possessed,
His fertile garden in the fragrant east,   35
And all united odours smelt,
No arméd sweets,[4] until thy reign,
Could shock the sense, or in the face
A flushed unhandsome colour place.
Now the jonquil[5] o'ercomes the feeble brain;   40
We faint beneath the aromatic pain,
Till some offensive scent thy pow'rs appease,
And pleasure we resign[6] for short, and nauseous ease.

In ev'ry one thou dost possess
New are thy motions,[7] and thy dress: 45
Now in some grove a list'ning friend
Thy false suggestions must attend,[8]
Thy whispered griefs, thy fancied[9] sorrows hear,

2. Foreboding, menacing.
3. Tolled, as by a bell.
4. Deceive.
5. Fantastic, clownlike.
6. In Shakespeare's *Julius Caesar*, the Roman leader Brutus is visited by the ghost of Caesar, whom he has assassinated, on the eve of his battle at Philippi with Octavius, the rival claimant to the Roman crown.
7. The flesh.
8. The body.

9. Adam's eating of the apple in Eden (Genesis 3); "attendant": accompaniment.
1. I.e., the soul.
2. Accustomed, desiring.
3. Travel through.
4. Painfully sweet fragrances.
5. A fragrant yellow and white flower.
6. Give up.
7. Effects.
8. Listen to.
9. Imagined.

Breathed in a sigh, and witnessed[1] by a tear;
    Whilst in the light and vulgar[2] crowd,   50
    Thy slaves, more clamorous and loud,
By laughters unprovoked,[3] thy influence too confess.
In the imperious wife thou vapours[4] art,
    Which from o'er-heated passions rise
    In clouds to the attractive brain,[5]   55
    Until descending thence again,
Through the o'er-cast, and show'ring eyes,
    Upon her husband's softened heart,
    He the disputed point must yield,
Something resign of the contested field:[6]   60
Till lordly man, born to imperial sway,[7]
Compounds[8] for peace, to make that right away,
And woman, armed with Spleen, does servilely obey.

    The fool, to imitate the wits,[9]
    Complains of thy pretended fits,[1]   65
    And dullness, born with him, would lay[2]
    Upon thy accidental[3] sway;
    Because, sometimes, thou dost presume
    Into the ablest heads to come:
    That, often, men of thoughts refined,   70
    Impatient of unequal sense,
Such slow returns, where they so much dispense,[4]
Retiring from the crowd, are to thy shades inclined.
    O'er me alas! thou dost too much prevail:
    I feel thy force, whilst I against thee rail;[5]   75
I feel my verse decay, and my cramped numbers[6] fail.
Through thy black jaundice,[7] I all objects see,
    As dark, and terrible as thee,
My lines decried, and my employment[8] thought
An useless folly, or presumptuous fault: 80
    Whilst in the Muses' paths I stray,
    Whilst in their groves, and by their secret springs
My hand delights to trace unusual things,
And deviates from the known, and common way;
    Nor will in fading silks compose[9]   85

1. Confirmed, validated.
2. Frivolous and common.
3. Without cause.
4. Brief attacks of faintness and dizziness to which eighteenth-century women were thought extremely susceptible.
5. I.e., the brain attracts vapors from the more bodily "passions" or emotions.
6. The passage describes a wife's hypocritical use of tears to win an argument with her husband.
7. Power.
8. Makes a concession; "that": peace.

9. Intelligent, educated people.
1. I.e., falsely complains of fits of spleen.
2. Blame; "dullness": stupidity.
3. Not innate, but circumstantial.
4. I.e., impatient at receiving so little intellectual stimulation when they provide so much.
5. Complain bitterly.
6. Bad meter.
7. I.e., discoloration of the tissues caused by accumulation of bile; usually yellow, but spleen is black bile.
8. I.e., as a poet.
9. Embroider, thought to be a woman's pastime.

Faintly th' inimitable rose,
Fill up an ill-drawn bird, or paint on glass
The sov'reign's blurred and undistinguished face,
The threat'ning angel, and the speaking ass.[1]

Patron thou art to ev'ry gross abuse,[2]   90
        The sullen husband's feigned excuse,
When the ill humour[3] with his wife he spends,
And bears recruited wit and spirits to his friends.
        The son of Bacchus[4] pleads thy pow'r,
        As to the glass he still repairs,[5]   95
        Pretends but to remove thy cares,
Snatch from thy shades one gay and smiling hour,
And drown thy kingdom in a purple show'r.
When the coquette,[6] whom ev'ry fool admires,
        Would in variety be fair,   100
        And, changing hastily the scene
        From light, impertinent, and vain,
        Assumes a soft, a melancholy air,
        And of her eyes rebates[7] the wand'ring fires,
        The careless posture, and the head reclined,   105
        The thoughtful, and composéd[8] face,
        Proclaiming the withdrawn, the absent mind,
        Allows the fop[9] more liberty to gaze,
        Who gently for the tender cause enquires:
The cause, indeed, is a defect in sense,   110
Yet is the Spleen alleged[1] and still the dull pretence.
        But these are thy fantastic[2] harms,
        The tricks of thy pernicious stage,
        Which do the weaker sort engage;
Worse are the dire effects of thy more pow'rful charms.   115
        By thee religion, all we know,
        That should enlighten here below,
        Is veiled in darkness, and perplexed
        With anxious doubts, with endless scruples[3] vexed,
And some restraint implied from each perverted text.[4]   120
        Whilst touch not, taste not, what is freely giv'n,
Is but thy niggard[5] voice, disgracing bounteous heav'n.
        From speech restrained, by thy deceits abused,
        To deserts banished, or in cells reclused

---

1. Women's "artistic" activities: coloring or painting Biblical scenes on glass (the speaking ass appears in Deuteronomy).
2. Blatant wrongdoing.
3. Spleen; "spends": consumes, exhausts; "humour": i.e., spleen; "recruited": replenished.
4. I.e., the drunkard: Bacchus was the Greek god of wine and revelry; "son": one who follows Bacchus's example.
5. Turns, resorts.

6. Flirtatious woman.
7. Removes.
8. Calm.
9. Vain, fashionable young man.
1. Blamed; "sense": intelligence.
2. Outward, theatrical.
3. Hesitations of conscience.
4. I.e., prohibitions inferred from distorted readings of the Bible.
5. Miserly.

Mistaken vot'ries[6] to the Powers Divine,   125
Whilst they a purer sacrifice design,[7]
Do but the Spleen obey, and worship at thy shrine.
  In vain to chase thee ev'ry art we try,
    In vain all remedies apply,
    In vain the Indian leaf infuse,   130
    Or the parched eastern berry[8] bruise;
Some pass, in vain, those bounds, and nobler liquors use.
    Now harmony, in vain, we bring,
    Inspire the flute and touch the string.
    From harmony no help is had;   135
Music but soothes thee, if too sweetly sad,
And if too light, but turns thee gaily mad.
      Though the physician's greatest gains,
      Although his growing wealth he sees
      Daily increased by ladies' fees,   140
  Yet dost thou baffle all his studious pains.
    Not skilful Lower[9] thy source could find,
Or, through the well-dissected body trace
The secret, the mysterious ways,
By which thou dost surprise, and prey upon the mind.   145
    Though in the search, too deep for human thought,
      With unsuccessful toil he wrought,[1]
Till thinking thee to've catched, himself by thee caught,
    Retained thy pris'ner, thy acknowledged slave,
And sank beneath thy chain to a lamented grave.   150

1702?   1713

To the Nightingale

Exert thy voice, sweet harbinger[2] of spring!
  This moment is thy time to sing,
  This moment I attend[3] to praise,
And set my numbers to thy lays.[4]
  Free as thine shall be my song;   5
  As thy music, short, or long.
Poets, wild as thee, were born,
  Pleasing best when unconfined,
  When to please is least designed,
Soothing but their cares to rest;[5]   10

---

6. Persons bound by religious vows.
7. Intend.
8. Coffee; "Indian leaf": tea.
9. Richard Lower (1631–1691), famous British physiologist who studied the human nervous system.

1. Worked.
2. Forerunner.
3. Devote.
4. Songs; "numbers": i.e., verses.
5. I.e., they intend only to soothe their own cares, not to please others.

Cares do still their thoughts molest,
  And still th'unhappy poet's breast,
Like thine, when best he sings, is placed against a thorn.
She begins. Let all be still!
  Muse, thy promise now fulfill!   15
Sweet, oh! sweet, still sweeter yet
Can thy words such accents fit,[6]
Canst thou syllables refine,
Melt a sense that shall retain
Still some spirit of the brain,[7]   20
Till with sounds like these it join.
  'Twill not be! then change thy note;
  Let division[8] shake thy throat.
Hark! Division now she tries;
Yet as far the muse outflies.   25
  Cease then, prithee, cease thy tune;
  Trifler[9] wilt thou sing till June?
Till thy business all lies waste,
And the time of building's past!
  Thus we poets that have speech,   30
Unlike what thy forests teach,
  If a fluent vein[1] be shown
  That's transcendent[2] to our own,
Criticize, reform, or preach,
Or censure what we cannot reach.   35

1702?   1713

A Nocturnal Reverie

In such a night, when every louder wind
Is to its distant cavern safe confined;
And only gentle Zephyr[3] fans his wings,
And lonely Philomel,[4] still waking, sings;
Or from some tree, famed for the owl's delight,   5
She, hollowing[5] clear, directs the wanderer right:
In such a night, when passing clouds give place,[6]
Or thinly veil the heavens' mysterious face;
When in some river, overhung with green,
The waving moon and trembling leaves are seen;   10
When freshened grass now bears itself upright,

6. I.e., can the muse's poetry match the bird's music?
7. The speaker asks her muse for a more musical strain of poetry that will still have an intellectual content; i.e., will not be mere sound. The metaphor is of refining or melting base ore into purer metals.
8. A musical term, defining a series of rapid decorative runs or variations on a melody.

9. Frivolous person.
1. Stream, metaphorically of song or poetry.
2. Superior.
3. The west wind.
4. A woman who was changed into a nightingale, according to Ovid and Greek myth.
5. Sounding.
6. Disappear.

And makes cool banks to pleasing rest invite,
Whence springs the woodbind, and the bramble-rose,
And where the sleepy cowslip sheltered grows;
Whilst now a paler hue the foxglove takes,   15
Yet checkers still with red the dusky brakes;[7]
When scattered glow-worms, but in twilight fine,[8]
Show trivial beauties watch their hour to shine;
Whilst Salisbury[9] stands the test of every light,
In perfect charm and perfect virtue bright: 20
When odours, which declined repelling day,
Through temperate air uninterrupted stray;
When darkened groves their softest shadows wear,
And falling waters we distinctly hear;
When through the gloom more venerable shows   25
Some ancient fabric,[1] awful in repose,
While sunburnt hills their swarthy[2] looks conceal,
And swelling haycocks[3] thicken up the vale:
When the loosed horse now, as his pasture leads,
Comes slowly grazing through th'adjoining meads.[4]   30
Whose stealing pace and lengthened shade we fear,
Till torn up forage[5] in his teeth we hear:
When nibbling sheep at large pursue their food,
And unmolested kine[6] rechew the cud;
When curlews cry beneath the village-walls,   35
And to her straggling brood the partridge calls;
Their shortlived jubilee the creatures keep,
Which but endures, whilst tyrant-man does sleep;
When a sedate content the spirit feels,
And no fierce light disturbs, whilst it reveals;   40
But silent musings urge the mind to seek
Something, too high for syllables to speak;
Till the free soul to a composedness charmed,
Finding the elements[7] of rage disarmed,
O'er all below a solemn quiet grown,   45
Joys in th'inferior world,[8] and thinks it like her own:
In such a night let me abroad remain,
Till morning breaks, and all's confused again;
Our cares, our toils, our clamours are renewed,
Or pleasures, seldom reached, again pursued.   50

                                                             1713

7. Thickets.
8. Clear; i.e., the glow-worms demonstrate that small beauties must choose their moment to be seen.
9. Either a reference to Salisbury Plain, in Wiltshire, England, or, as some commentators have suggested, an allusion to Finch's friend Anne Tafton, countess of Salisbury.
1. Artifact; perhaps a reference to the Druidic ruin Stonehenge, located on Salisbury Plain.

"Awful": awesome.
2. Dark, esp. of skin.
3. Conical mounds of hay.
4. Meadows.
5. Grass eaten by animals.
6. Cattle.
7. Earth, air and water; i.e., the weather.
8. The material world, thought to be lower than the spiritual world.

MARY ASTELL
1666–1731

In her preface to a collection of Lady Mary Wortley Montagu's Turkish Embassy letters (1724), Mary Astell compared them favorably to the travel literature composed by men, and encouraged women readers to "be pleased that a *woman* triumphs." The mutual esteem of these two learned friends, evidenced not only by Astell's pride in Lady Mary's epistolary triumphs but also by Lady Mary's financial support of Astell's writing career, epitomizes the ideal that had earlier impelled Astell to write A *Serious Proposal to the Ladies* (1692), her project to establish a retreat in which women could educate themselves even as they pursued the "blessings" of friendship. Clearly Astell's description of this intellectual community of women was a response to the frequent attacks on the vanity of female wishes in Restoration literature: while a number of satiric poems and plays criticized flirtatiousness and dilettantism as inherently female, Astell believed that religious and philosophic training could correct such feminine failings.

Astell's proposal therefore begins by arguing that women have been debarred from advantages, which they are later reproached for not having, and inculcated with vices, for which they are then upbraided. Uncompromising as she was in this claim, Astell accepted the legal, vocational, and economic subordination of women. Although she was quite conservative in subsequent essays on the inalterable subjugation of wives to husbands, in her proposal she could insist, by emphasizing the moral benefits of what amounts to a Protestant convent, on women's natural equality with men. Thus, as Katharine M. Rogers has argued in *Feminism in Eighteenth-Century England*, "Astell was able to combine acceptance of the external status quo with radical questioning of the alleged natural superiority on which men based their prerogatives." She was able to do this, also, because she limited her claims to single women. Significantly, Astell herself remained single, and, in A *Serious Proposal to the Ladies*, which went through several editions, she attempted to provide a feasible alternative to marriage for other women.

From A Serious Proposal to the Ladies

[A *Religious Retirement*]

Now as to the proposal, it is to erect a monastery, or if you will (to avoid giving offence to the scrupulous and injudicious, by names which though innocent in themselves, have been abused by superstitious practices),[1] we will call it a religious retirement, and such as shall have a double aspect, being not only a retreat from the world for those who desire that advantage, but likewise, an institution and previous disci-

---

1. Monks had acquired a reputation among English anti-Papists for dabbling in the supernatural.

pline, to fit us to do the greatest good in it; such an institution as this (if I do not mightily deceive my self) would be the most probable method to amend the present, and improve the future age. * * *

You are therefore ladies, invited into a place, where you shall suffer no other confinement, but to be kept out of the road of sin: * * * Happy retreat! which will be the introducing you into such a paradise as your mother Eve forfeited,[2] where you shall feast on pleasures, that do not, like those of the world, disappoint your expectations, pall your appetites, and by the disgust they give you put you on the fruitless search after new delights, which when obtained are as empty as the former; but such as will make you truly happy now, and prepare you to be perfectly so hereafter. Here are no serpents to deceive you, whilst you entertain your selves in these delicious gardens. No provocations will be given in this amicable society, but to love and to good works, which will afford such an entertaining employment, that you'll have as little inclination as leisure to pursue those follies, which in the time of your ignorance passed with you under the name of love, although there is not in nature two more different things, than true love and that brutish passion, which pretends to ape it. Here will be no rivalling but for the love of God, no ambition but to procure his favour, to which nothing will more effectually recommend you, than a great and dear affection to each other. * * *

One great end of this institution shall be, to expel that cloud of ignorance which custom has involved us in, to furnish our minds with a stock of solid and useful knowledge, that the souls of women may no longer be the only unadorned and neglected things. It is not intended that our religious should waste their time, and trouble their heads about such unconcerning matters, as the vogue of the world has turn'd up for learning, the impertinency of which has been excellently exposed by an ingenious pen,[3] but busy themselves in a serious enquiry after necessary and perfective truths, something which it concerns them to know, and which tends to their real interest and perfection, and what that is the excellent author just now mentioned will sufficiently inform them. Such a course of study will neither be too troublesome nor out of the reach of a female virtuoso;[4] for it is not intended she should spend her hours in learning words but things, and therefore no more languages than are necessary to acquaint her with useful authors. Nor need she trouble her self in turning over a great number of books, but take care to understand and digest a few well chosen and good ones. Let her but obtain right ideas, and be truly acquainted with the nature of those ob-

---

2. Eve was cast out of the Garden of Eden with Adam when she ate an apple from the tree of knowledge (Genesis 3:6).

3. "Mr. Nor. *Conduct of Hum. Life*." [Astell's note].
4. I.e., one interested in the pursuit of knowledge.

jects that present themselves to her mind, and then no matter whether or no she be able to tell what fanciful people have said about them: And thoroughly to understand Christianity as professed by the Church of England,[5] will be sufficient to confirm her in the truth, though she have not a catalogue of those particular errors which oppose it. Indeed a learned education of the women will appear so unfashionable, that I began to startle at the singularity of the proposition, but was extremely pleased when I found a late ingenious author (whose book I met with since the writing of this) agree with me in my opinion.[6] For speaking of the repute that learning was in about 150 years ago, "It was so very modish," says he "that the fair sex seemed to believe that Greek and Latin added to their charms: and Plato and Aristotle untranslated, were frequent ornaments of their closets. One would think by the effects, that it was a proper way of educating them, since there are no accounts in history of so many great women in any one age, as are to be found between the years 15 and 1600."

For since God has given women as well as men intelligent souls, why should they be forbidden to improve them? Since he has not denied us the faculty of thinking, why should we not (at least in gratitude to him) employ our thoughts on himself their noblest object, and not unworthily bestow them on trifles and gaities and secular affairs? Being[7] the soul was created for the contemplation of truth as well as for the fruition of good, is it not as cruel and unjust to exclude women from the knowledge of the one as from the enjoyment of the other? Especially since the will is blind, and cannot choose but by the direction of the understanding; or to speak more properly, since the soul always wills according as she understands, so that if she understands amiss, she wills amiss. And as exercise enlarges and exalts any faculty, so through want of using it becomes cramp and lessened; if therefore we make little or no use of our understandings, we shall shortly have none to use; and the more contracted and unemployed the deliberating and directive power is, the more liable is the elective to unworthy and mischievous choices. What is it but the want[8] of an ingenious education, that renders the generality of feminine conversations so insipid and foolish and their solitude so insupportable? Learning is therefore necessary to render them more agreeable and useful in company, and to furnish them with becoming entertainments when alone, that so they may not be driven to those miserable shifts,[9] which too many make use of to put off their time, that precious talent that never lies on the hands of a judicious

---

5. The Church of England set itself against the doctrines and ceremonies of the Catholic Church.
6. Astell's note cites William Wotton's *Reflections upon Ancient and Modern Learning*, 1694.
7. I.e., given that.
8. Lack.
9. Tricks, here evidently referring to women's traditional leisure activities, such as music, embroidery, etc.

person. And since our happiness in the next world, depends so far on those dispositions which we carry along with us out of this, that without a right habitude and temper of mind we are not capable of felicity; and seeing our beatitude consists in the contemplation of the divine truth and beauty, as well as in the fruition of his goodness, can ignorance be a fit preparative for Heaven? Is't likely that she whose understanding has been busied about nothing but froth and trifles, should be capable of delighting her self in noble and sublime truths? Let such therefore as deny us the improvement of our intellectuals, either take up his[1] Paradox, who said that women have no souls, which at a time when the most contend to have them allowed to brutes, would be as unphilosophical as it is unmannerly, or else let them permit us to cultivate and improve them. There is a sort of learning indeed which is worse than the greatest ignorance: A woman may study plays and romances all her days, and be a great deal more knowing but never a jot the wiser. Such a knowledge as this serves only to instruct and put her forward in the practice of the greatest follies, yet how can they justly blame her who forbid, or at least won't afford opportunity of better? A rational mind will be employed, it will never be satisfied in doing nothing, and if you neglect to furnish it with good materials, 'tis like to take up with such as come to hand.

We pretend not that women should teach in the church, or usurp authority where it is not allowed them; permit us only to understand our own duty, and not be forced to take it upon trust from others; to be at least so far learned, as to be able to form in our minds a true idea of Christianity, it being so very necessary to fence us against the danger of these last and perilous days, in which deceivers a part of whose character is to lead captive silly women, need not creep into houses since they have authority to proclaim their errors on the housetop. And let us also acquire a true practical knowledge, such as will convince us of the absolute necessity of holy living as well as of right believing, and that no heresy is more dangerous than that of an ungodly and wicked life. And since the French tongue is understood by most ladies, methinks they may much better improve it by the study of philosophy (as I hear the French ladies do) Descartes, Malebranche[2] and others, than by reading idle novels and romances. 'Tis strange we shou'd be so forward to imitate their fashions and fopperies, and have no regard to what really deserves our imitation. And why shall it not be thought as genteel to understand French philosophy, as to be accoutred in a French mode? Let therefore the famous Madam D'acier, Scudery, &c, and our own incomparable Orinda, excite the emulation of the English ladies.[3]

1. Perhaps Mohammed, who was commonly thought to have claimed in the Koran that women lacked souls.

2. René Descartes and Nicholas de Malebranche, well-known seventeenth-century philosophers.

3. Anne Lefebvre D'Acier (1654–1720), French classical scholar who translated the *Iliad* and *Odyssey*; Magdeleine de Scudéry (1607–1701), French poet and novelist; Katherine Philips (1631–1664), English poet known as "the Matchless Orinda."

The ladies, I'm sure, have no reason to dislike this proposal, but I know not how the men will resent it to have their enclosure broke down, and women invited to taste of that tree of knowledge they have so long unjustly monopolized. But they must excuse me, if I be as partial to my own sex as they are to theirs, and think women as capable of learning as men are, and that it becomes them as well. For I cannot imagine wherein the hurt lies, if instead of doing mischief to one another, by an uncharitable and vain conversation, women be enabled to inform and instruct those of their own sex at least; the holy ghost having left it on record, that Priscilla as well as her husband, catechized the eloquent Apollos and the great Apostle found no fault with her.[4] It will therefore be very proper for our ladies to spend part of their time in this retirement, in adorning their minds with useful knowledge.

1694

4. In Acts 18:2, an eloquent preacher named Apollos who knows only the teachings of John the Baptist is educated in Christianity by Priscilla and her husband Aquilas, two followers of the Apostle Paul.

LADY MARY WORTLEY MONTAGU
1689–1762

At twenty-one years of age, Lady Mary Pierrepont sent her translation of the *Enchiridion of Epictetus* to her mentor, Bishop Burnet, with a letter in which she explained, "My sex is usually forbid studies of this nature, and folly reckoned so much our proper sphere, that we are sooner pardoned any excesses of that, than the least pretensions to reading or good sense." Although she knew that "there is hardly a character in the world more despicable, or more liable to universal ridicule than that of a learned woman," through her witty conversation and the letters and poems she circulated to friends the woman who became Lady Mary Wortley Montagu went on to attain a reputation for learning that gained her staunch friends and merciless foes. Writing in the age of great epistolary productions, Lady Mary fashioned her letters into a fascinating record of women's customs and conduct both in England and abroad. The explicit sexual themes she addressed in her poems made her vulnerable to scandalous rumors, but she was also hailed by contemporaries as a "she meteor" or "the female traveler."

Almost every major event in Mary Wortley Montagu's life was recorded in letters to her sister, her husband, and her daughter. It was a life of privilege and publicity. Her father was a wealthy Whig peer, Evelyn Pierrepont, who became earl of Kingston in 1690 and duke of Kingston in 1713; her mother, the Honorable Mary Fielding, died when Lady Mary Pierrepont was five years old. The education she pursued in her father's library was stimulated by her uncle and Bishop Burnet, and by two close friends, Mary Astell and Anne Montagu. After Anne's death in 1709, her brother continued this correspondence. When it turned into a courtship, which Lady Mary's father opposed, Edward Wortley Montagu and Lady Mary eloped in 1712. Edward Wortley Montagu was made ambassador to Constantinople in 1716, and for two years Lady Mary sent letters home describing her journeys and adventures in Turkey. On her return to England, she helped to popularize smallpox inoculation by having her own two children inoculated: a 1724 article in *The Plaindealer* viewed her education of an antagonistic medical profession as proof "that England has owed to women the greatest blessings she has been distinguished by."

Throughout her adult life, Lady Mary was active at the center of London's cultural coteries: she helped advance the career of her cousin, the dramatist and novelist Henry Fielding; she maintained friendships with Joseph Addison and Richard Steele, the author-editors of the influential periodical *The Spectator*; in 1717 she received Alexander Pope's *Eloisa to Abelard*, which was addressed to her as to a close friend, and in 1735 she withstood Pope's furious attack on her as a slovenly "Sappho" in *Epistle II: To a Lady*. After a bitter political feud with Pope and the marriage of her daughter in 1739, she fell in love with Francesco Algarotti, a young writer she followed to Italy. She never established a lasting relationship with him, but she remained separated from her husband, returning to England only after his death in 1761 for the remaining year of her own life. A year after her death, the Turkish Embassy letters consolidated her literary reputation; she had prepared them for publication herself, keeping copies of those she mailed and deleting the more personal passages. Forty years later, her other correspondences began to appear in print, and today they total almost nine hundred letters. A number of her poems—*Town Eclogues* and *Court Poems*—appeared in a pirated volume in 1716, a portion of which was reprinted in 1747. In 1837, Lord Wharncliffe produced an edition of her *Letters and Works*.

To the Countess of Bute, Lady Montagu's Daughter.

[*On Her Granddaughter*]   Jan. 28, N.S.[1] (1753)

Dear Child,—You have given me a great deal of satisfaction by your account of your eldest daughter. I am particularly pleased to hear she is a good arithmetician; it is the best proof of understanding: the knowledge of numbers is one of the chief distinctions between us and the brutes.[2] If there is anything in blood, you may reasonably expect your children should be endowed with an uncommon share of good sense. Mr. Wortley's family and mine have both produced some of the greatest men that have been born in England: I mean Admiral Sandwich, and my grandfather, who was distinguished by the name of Wise William. I have heard Lord Bute's father mentioned as an extraordinary genius, though he had not many opportunities of showing it; and his uncle, the present Duke of Argyll, has one of the best heads I ever knew.

1. "New style" date.   2. Beasts.

I will therefore speak to you as supposing Lady Mary[3] not only capable, but desirous of learning: in that case by all means let her be indulged in it. You will tell me I did not make it a part of your education: your prospect was very different from hers. As you had no defect either in mind or person to hinder, and much in your circumstances to attract, the highest offers it seemed your business to learn how to live in the world, as it is hers to know how to be easy[4] but of it. It is the common error of builders and parents to follow some plan they think beautiful (and perhaps is so), without considering that nothing is beautiful that is misplaced. Hence we see so many edifices raised that the raisers can never inhabit, being too large for their fortunes. Vistas[5] are laid open over barren heaths, and apartments contrived for a coolness very agreeable in Italy, but killing in the north of Britain: thus every woman endeavours to breed her daughter a fine lady, qualifying her for a station in which she will never appear, and at the same time incapacitating her for that retirement[6] to which she is destined. Learning, if she has a real taste for it, will not only make her contented, but happy in it. No entertainment is so cheap as reading, nor any pleasure so lasting. She will not want new fashions, nor regret the loss of expensive diversions, or variety of company, if she can be amused with an author in her closet.[7] To render this amusement extensive, she should be permitted to learn the languages. I have heard it lamented that boys lose so many years in mere learning of words: this is no objection to a girl, whose time is not so precious: she cannot advance herself in any profession, and has therefore more hours to spare: and as you say her memory is good, she will be very agreeably employed this way.

There are two cautions to be given on this subject: first, not to think herself learned when she can read Latin, or even Greek. Languages are more properly to be called vehicles of learning than learning itself, as may be observed in many schoolmasters, who, though perhaps critics in grammar are the most ignorant fellows upon earth. True knowledge consists in knowing things, not words. I would wish her no further a linguist than to enable her to read books in their originals that are often corrupted, and always injured by translations. Two hours' application every morning will bring this about much sooner than you can imagine and she will have leisure enough besides to run over the English poetry, which is a more important part of a woman's education than it is generally supposed. Many a young damsel has been ruined by a fine copy of verses, which she would have laughed at if she had known it had been stolen from Mr. Waller.[8] I remember when I was a girl, I saved one of

---

3. Montagu's granddaughter.
4. At ease, contented. "The world": high society. Apparently Montagu did not consider her granddaughter to be "marriageable."
5. A passage between trees or buildings opening onto a distant prospect.
6. I.e., life of solitude.
7. Bedroom.
8. Edmund Waller (1606–1687), English poet.

my companions from destruction who communicated to me an epistle she was quite charmed with. As she had a natural good taste, she observed the lines were not so smooth as Prior's or Pope's[9] but had more thought and spirit than any of theirs. She was wonderfully delighted with such a demonstration of her lover's sense and passion, and not a little pleased with her own charms, that had force enough to inspire such elegancies. In the midst of this triumph I showed her that they were taken from Randolph's poems[1] and the unfortunate transcriber was dismissed with the scorn he deserved. To say truth, the poor plagiary[2] was very unlucky to fall into my hands; that author being no longer in fashion, would have escaped any one of less universal reading than myself. You should encourage your daughter to talk over with you what she reads; and, as you are very capable of distinguishing, take care she does not mistake pert folly for wit[3] and humour, or rhyme for poetry, which are the common errors of young people, and have a train of ill consequences.

The second caution to be given her (and which is most absolutely necessary) is to conceal whatever learning she attains, with as much solicitude as she would hide crookedness or lameness; the parade[4] of it can only serve to draw on her the envy, and consequently the most inveterate hatred, of all he and she fools, which will certainly be at least three parts in four of all her acquaintance. The use of knowledge in our sex, besides the amusement of solitude, is to moderate the passions, and learn to be contented with a small expense which are the certain effects of a studious life; and it may be preferable even to that fame which men have engrossed[5] to themselves, and will not suffer us to share. You will tell me I have not observed this rule myself: but you are mistaken: it is only inevitable accident that has given me any reputation that way. I have always carefully avoided it and ever thought it a misfortune.

The explanation of this paragraph would occasion a long digression, which I will not trouble you with it being my present design only to say what I think useful for the instruction of my granddaughter, which I have much at heart. If she has the same inclination (I should say passion) for learning that I was born with history, geography, and philosophy will furnish her with materials to pass away cheerfully a longer life than is allotted to mortals. I believe there are few heads capable of making Sir I. Newton's[6] calculations, but the result of them is not difficult to be understood by a moderate capacity. Do not fear this should make her affect the character of Lady ———— or Lady ————, or Mrs.

9. Matthew Prior (1664–1721), English diplomat and poet; Alexander Pope (1688–1744), English poet.
1. Thomas Randolph (1605–1635); his *Poems* was published in 1638.
2. Plagiarist.

3. Intelligence.
4. Proud display.
5. Appropriated.
6. English scientist, founder of modern physics (1642–1727).

———. Those women are ridiculous, not because they have learning but because they have it not. One thinks herself a complete historian after reading Echard's Roman History; another a profound philosopher, having got by heart some of Pope's unintelligible essays; and a third an able divine, on the strength of Whitefield's sermons:[7] thus you hear them screaming politics and controversy. It is a saying of Thucydides, ignorance is bold, and knowledge reserved.[8] Indeed, it is impossible to be far advanced in it without being more humbled by a conviction of human ignorance, than elated by learning. At the same time I recommend books, I neither exclude work nor drawing. I think it as scandalous for a woman not to know how to use a needle, as for a man not to know how to use a sword. I was once extreme fond of my pencil,[9] and it was a great mortification to me when my father turned off my master, having made a considerable progress for a short time I learnt. My overeagerness in the pursuit of it had brought a weakness on my eyes, that made it necessary to leave it off; and all the advantage I got was the improvement of my hand.[1] I see, by hers, that practice will make her a ready writer: she may attain it by serving you for a secretary, when your health or affairs make it troublesome to you to write yourself: and custom will make it an agreeable amusement to her. She cannot have too many for that station of life which will probably be her fate. The ultimate end of your education was to make you a good wife (and I have the comfort to hear that you are one): hers ought to be, to make her happy in a virgin state. I will not say it is happier; but it is undoubtedly safer than any marriage. In a lottery, where there are (at the lowest computation) ten thousand blanks to a prize it is the most prudent choice not to venture.

I have always been so thoroughly persuaded of this truth, that, notwithstanding the flattering views I had for you (as I never intended you a sacrifice to my vanity), I thought I owed you the justice to lay before you all the hazards attending matrimony: you may recollect I did so in the strongest manner. Perhaps you may have more success in the instructing your daughter: she has so much company at home, she will not need seeking it abroad, and will more readily take the notions you think fit to give her. As you were alone in my family, it would have been thought a great cruelty to suffer[2] you no companions of your own age, especially having so many near relations, and I do not wonder their opinions influenced yours. I was not sorry to see you not determined on a single life, knowing it was not your father's intention, and contented

7. George Whitefield (1714–1770), famous Methodist preacher who published many of his sermons. "Divine": theologian. Lawrence Echard (1670–1730) wrote *The Roman History* (1695–1698); Pope wrote several essays in verse.

8. Greek historian of the fifth century B.C.; Montagu is paraphrasing a line from his *Peloponnesian War*.
9. A fine brush for artwork.
1. Handwriting.
2. Allow.

myself with endeavouring to make your home so easy that you might
not be in haste to leave it.

I am afraid you will think this a very long and insignificant letter. I
hope the kindness of the design will excuse it, being willing to give you
every proof in my power that I am

> Your most affectionate mother.

1753   1763

Epistle from Mrs. Yonge to Her Husband[3]

Think not this paper comes with vain pretense
To move your pity, or to mourn th' offense.
Too well I know that hard obdurate heart;
No softening mercy there will take my part,
Nor can a woman's arguments prevail.   5
When even your patron's wise example fails.[4]
But this last privilege I still retain;
Th' oppressed and injured always may complain.
    Too, too severely laws of honor bind
The weak submissive sex of womankind.   10
If sighs have gained or force compelled our hand,
Deceived by art,[5] or urged by stern command,
Whatever motive binds the fatal tie,
The judging world expects our constancy.
    Just heaven! (for sure in heaven does justice reign,   15
Though tricks below that sacred name profane)
To you appealing I submit my cause,
Nor fear a judgment from impartial laws.
All bargains but conditional[6] are made;
The purchase void, the creditor unpaid,   20
Defrauded servants are from service free;
A wounded slave regains his liberty.
For wives ill used[7] no remedy remains,
To daily racks condemned, and to eternal chains.
    From whence is this unjust distinction grown?   25
Are we not formed with passions like your own?
Nature with equal fire our souls endued,[8]

---

3. We gratefully acknowledge the permission of
Lawrence Lipking to use information contained
in his notes to this poem in *The Norton Anthology of English Literature*. In this epistle, or
verse-letter, Montagu assumes the role of Mary
Yonge, a woman who, having separated from
her adulterous husband, William, herself took a
lover and was then publicly disgraced by the divorce proceedings which her husband instigated.
Intimate details of her relationship with her lover

were revealed during the trial, and the court
awarded Mr. Yonge his wife's dowry and the
greater part of her fortune.
4. Sir Robert Walpole, a powerful friend of
Yonge's at court, who was said to tolerate his
own wife's infidelity.
5. Artifice.
6. Only conditionally.
7. Poorly treated.
8. Endowed.

Our minds as haughty, and as warm our blood;
O'er the wide world your pleasures you pursue,
The change is justified by something new;   30
But we must sigh in silence—and be true.
Our sex's weakness you expose and blame
(Of every prattling fop the common theme),
Yet from this weakness you suppose is due
Sublimer virtue than your Cato[9] knew.   35
Had heaven designed us trials so severe,
It would have formed our tempers then to bear.[1]
    And I have borne (oh what have I not borne!)
The pang of jealousy, the insults of scorn.
Wearied at length, I from your sight remove,   40
And place my future hopes in secret love.
In the gay bloom of glowing youth retired,
I quit[2] the woman's joy to be admired,
With that small pension your hard heart allows,
Renounce your fortune, and release your vows.   45
To custom (though unjust) so much is due;
I hide my frailty from the public view.
My conscience clear, yet sensible of shame,
My life I hazard, to preserve my fame.
And I prefer this low inglorious state   50
To vile dependence on the thing I hate—
But you pursue me to this last retreat.
Dragged into light, my tender crime is shown
And every circumstance of fondness known.
Beneath the shelter of the law you stand,   55
And urge my ruin with a cruel hand,
While to my fault thus rigidly severe,
Tamely submissive to the man you fear.[3]
    This wretched outcast, this abandoned wife,
Has yet this joy to sweeten shameful life: 60
By your mean[4] conduct, infamously loose,
You are at once my accuser and excuse.
Let me be damned by the censorious prude
(Stupidly dull, or spiritually lewd),
My hapless case will surely pity find   65
From every just and reasonable mind.
When to the final sentence I submit,
The lips condemn me, but their souls acquit.
    No more my husband, to your pleasures go,
The sweets of your recovered freedom know.   70
Go: court the brittle friendship of the great;

9. A Roman statesman known for his self-disci-   2. Gave up.
pline.   3. I.e., Walpole.
1. I.e., capable of bearing such trials; "tempers"   4. Immoral (i.e., adulterous); "mean": low.
characters.

Smile at his board[5] or at his levee wait;
And when dismissed, to madam's toilet fly,[6]
More than her chambermaids, or glasses, lie,
Tell her how young she looks, how heavenly fair,   75
Admire the lilies and the roses there.
Your high ambition may be gratified,
Some cousin of her own be made your bride,
And you the father of a glorious race
Endowed with Ch——l's strength and Low——r's face[7]   80

1724   1977

5. Dining table; "levee": morning reception of visitors.
6. It was fashionable for upper-class women to receive visitors during the last stages of dressing (their "toilet"). "Glasses": mirrors.

7. General Churchill was rumored to have had an affair with Lady Walpole; Antony Lowther was a notorious lady's man. Montague insinuates that Yonge's next wife may be untrue as his first.

CHARLOTTE SMITH
1749–1806

Describing herself in *Beachy Head* (1807) as "an early worshipper at Nature's shrine," the poet-novelist Charlotte Smith was an important precursor of such Romantic poets as William Wordsworth and Samuel Taylor Coleridge, as well as a significant ancestress of the Victorian poet Elizabeth Barrett Browning. Though she has been largely forgotten until quite recently, Smith's productivity was extraordinary: even while bearing and rearing ten children, she wrote and published more than twenty novels and books of verse, many of which were exceptionally popular and influential; her *Elegiac Sonnets and Other Essays* (1784) had gone through eleven editions by 1851.

At sixteen, after a comfortable childhood at Bignor Park in Sussex, Charlotte Turner married Benjamin Smith, the extravagant son of a London merchant. Though the marriage was evidently a happy one, Benjamin was eventually sent to debtors' prison, where his wife stayed with him during his incarceration. Finally, therefore, despite her responsibilities for the care of her growing children, Charlotte Smith undertook to write and publish both poetry and prose fiction in the hope of solving the family's financial problems. Her many novels included the Gothic works *Emmeline, the Orphan of the Castle* (1788) and *The Old Manor House* (1793), as well as the more doctrinaire, political works *Desmond* (1792) and *The Young Philosopher* (1798), both of which show the influence of the philosopher Jean Jacques Rousseau and an enthusiastic sympathy with the ideals that motivated the French Revolution of 1789.

Smith's sonnet *Pressed by the Moon, Mute Arbitress of Tides* reveals a Romantic tendency toward self-analysis, even self-dramatization, that is quite consistent with the spirit of many of her novels. Her witty and genial *Thirty-eight* is perhaps more surprising, however, coming as it does from an artist whose lifelong struggle for financial survival must often have seemed to be "doomed" by intransigent circumstances. Yet if Smith's life was a hard one and her literary reputation obscured for many years, she did survive, at least through the effect her proto-Romantic modes and moods had upon disparate but unquestionably major descendants like Wordsworth, Coleridge, and Barrett Browning.

Pressed by the Moon, Mute Arbitress of Tides

Written in the churchyard at Middleton in Sussex

Pressed by the moon, mute arbitress of tides,
   While the loud equinox[1] its power combines,
   The sea no more its swelling surge confines,
But o'er the shrinking land sublimely rides.
The wild blast, rising from the western cave,   5
   Drives the huge billows from their heaving bed,
   Tears from their grassy tombs the village dead,
And breaks the silent sabbath[2] of the grave!
With shells and seaweed mingled, on the shore
   Lo! their bones whiten in the frequent wave;   10
   But vain to them the winds and waters rave;
They hear the warring elements no more:
While I am doomed—by life's long storm oppressed,
To gaze with envy on their gloomy rest.

1786

Thirty-eight

Addressed to Mrs. H——y

In early youth's unclouded scene,
The brilliant morning of eighteen,
With health and sprightly joy elate
   We gazed on life's enchanting spring,
   Nor thought how quickly time would bring   5
The mournful period[3]——Thirty-eight.

Then the starch maid or matron sage,
Already of that sober age,
We viewed with mingled scorn and hate,
   In whose sharp words or sharper face   10
   With thoughtless mirth we loved to trace
The sad effects of——Thirty-eight.

1. I.e., equinoctial (powerful) wind.   3. I.e., occasion.
2. I.e., rest.

Till saddening, sickening at the view,
We learned to dread what time might do;
And then preferred[4] a prayer to fate   15
    To end our days ere that arrived,
    When (power and pleasure long survived)
We met neglect and——Thirty-eight.

But time, in spite of wishes, flies,
And fate our simple prayer denies,   20
And bids us death's own hour await:
    The auburn locks are mixed with grey,
    The transient roses fade away,
But reason comes at——Thirty-eight.

Her voice the anguish contradicts   25
That dying vanity inflicts;
Her hand new pleasures can create.
    For us she opens to the view
    Prospects less bright—but far more true,
And bids us smile at——Thirty-eight.   30

No more shall scandal's breath destroy
The social converse we enjoy
With bard or critic tête à tête;[5]
    O'er youth's bright blooms her blights shall pour,
    But spare the improving friendly hour   35
That science[6] gives to——Thirty-eight.

Stripped of their gaudy hues by truth,
We view the glitt'ring toys of youth,
And blush to think how poor the bait
    For which to public scenes we ran   40
    And scorned of sober sense the plan
Which gives content at——Thirty-eight.

Though time's inexorable sway
Has torn the myrtle bands away,
For other wreaths 'tis not too late;[7]   45
    The amaranth's purple glow survives,
    And still Minerva's olive lives
On the calm brow of——Thirty-eight.

With eye more steady we engage
To contemplate approaching age,   50

4. Offered.
5. In privacy.
6. I.e., knowledge.
7. The myrtle was sacred to Venus, goddess of

love; the amaranth was a legendary flower that
never faded; the olive was sacred to Minerva,
Roman goddess of wisdom.

And life more justly estimate.
  With firmer souls and stronger powers,
  With reason, faith, and friendship ours,
  We'll not regret the stealing hours
That lead from Thirty——even to Forty-eight.   55

1786

FANNY BURNEY
1752–1840

At fifteen years of age, with her twelve-year-old sister Susan sobbing by her
side, Fanny Burney burned all of her early writing because her stepmother felt
that a reputation for scribbling would harm the girl's marriage prospects and
because she herself was early impressed "with ideas that fastened degradation to
this class of composition" then, as now, called the novel. Soon after, however,
she began to keep a secret journal addressed to "A Certain Miss Nobody," because "to Nobody can I be wholly unreserved." While she would eventually
write her diary for the members of her family, her early determination to counterpoint decorous public submission with private literary assertion was to play a
crucial role in her life.

The third of six children, Frances Burney was eight years old when the family moved from King's Lynn to London, and ten years old when she lost her
mother, Esther (Sleepe) Burney. She became greatly attached to her father, the
historian of music Dr. Charles Burney, and to his friend Samuel ("Daddy")
Crisp, the recipient of many of her early confidences. Although she was said to
be shy and had only received a few months of formal schooling, through her
gregarious father she met a number of artists and intellectuals. Her first and
most important novel, *Evelina* (1778), explored the social development of a
heroine who proves herself worthy of her well-born suitor. Published anonymously when Burney was twenty-six, this epistolary fiction was an instant success. When its author's identity became known, first to her family and then to
the public, it won Burney such prominent friends as the essayist and lexicogra-
pher Samuel Johnson, his companion Mrs. Thrale, the painter Sir Joshua
Reynolds, the playwright Richard Sheridan, and the philosopher Edmund
Burke, all of whom appear in the *Diary*. With the encouragement of these supporters, her father, and her "Daddy" Crisp, Burney next published *Cecilia; or,
Memoirs of an Heiress* (1782). While not as popular as *Evelina*, it also analyzed
the social and economic problems of women. In both of these novels, Burney
self-consciously tried to raise the status of the novel by combining verisimilitude
with instruction. In the process, she helped establish a new genre, the novel of
manners. Indeed, she conveyed the manners and morals of polite society with a
relish for the ridiculous and a respect for the conventional that explain why Jane
Austen found both the theme and the title of *Pride and Prejudice* in the concluding chapter of *Cecilia*.

In spite of enthusiastic reviews, Burney felt she had exhausted her subject with *Cecilia* and, again with the encouragement of her father, she accepted a place at court in 1786. Although the position of Second Keeper of the Robes to Queen Charlotte secured her a salary of two hundred pounds a year, it involved such official duties as mixing the queen's snuff and attending to her dressing, even as it placed Burney under the grating supervision of the First Keeper of the Robes, a Mrs. Schwellenberg. In 1791 Burney was allowed to retire with a pension of one hundred pounds, and two years later, at the age of forty-one, she married a penniless French exile, General Alexandre D'Arblay. She continued to publish, first *Brief Revelations Relative to the Emigrant French Clergy* (1793), and later *Camilla; or, Female Difficulties* (1796) and *The Wanderer* (1814). From 1802 to 1812, she lived with her husband and their son in France, where she received the title of countess from Louis XVIII. After fleeing to Brussels during Napoleon's Hundred Days, she returned with her family to London. She remained in retirement after her husband's death in 1818, editing her father's memoirs (1832). Three years after her death, her niece, Charlotte Frances Barrett, began issuing the *Diary and Letters*, but the *Early Diary* was not published until 1889. Our selection from the *Diary and Letters of Madame d'Arblay* (7 volumes) demonstrates Burney's ear for dialogue and her eye for social detail.

From The Diary and Letters of Madame D'Arblay

Letter from Miss F. Burney to Mrs. Phillips[1] [*Authoress of "Evelina"*]

I thank you most heartily for your two sweet letters, my ever dearest Susy, and equally for the kindness they contain and the kindness they accept. And, as I have a frank[2] and a subject, I will leave my *bothers*, and write you and my dear brother Molesworth a little account of a *rout* I have just been at, at the house of Mr. Paradise.[3]

You will wonder, perhaps, in this time of hurry, why I went thither; but when I tell you Pacchierotti[4] was there, you will not think it surprising.

There was a crowd of company; Charlotte and I went together; my father came afterwards. Mrs. Paradise received us very graciously, and led me immediately up to Miss Thrale, who was sitting by the Pac.[5] The Miss Kirwans, you may be sure, were not far off, and so I did pretty well. There was nobody else I knew but Dr. Solander, Mr. Coxe, the traveller, Sir Sampson and Lady Gideon (Streatham acquaintances), Mr. Sastres, and Count Zenobia, a noble Venetian, whom I have often met lately at Mrs. Thrale's.

---

1. Susan Burney Phillips, the author's sister.
2. An envelope marked or signed by an official so that it can be mailed without postage.
3. An acquaintance in polite society. "Rout":
   wild party.
4. A well-known operatic singer.
5. I.e., Pacchierotti.

We were very late, for we had waited cruelly for the coach, and Pac. had sung a song out of *Artaxerxes*, composed for a tenor, which we lost, to my infinite regret.[6] Afterwards he sang "Dolce speme," set by Bertoni, less elegantly than by Sacchini, but more expressively for the words. He sang it delightfully. It was but the second time I have heard him in a room since his return to England.

After this he went into another room, to try if it would be cooler; and Mrs. Paradise, leaning over the Kirwans and Charlotte, who hardly got a seat all night for the crowd, said she begged to speak to me. I squeezed my great person out, and she then said,

"Miss Burney, Lady Say and Sele[7] desires the honour of being introduced to you."

Her ladyship stood by her side. She seems pretty near fifty—at least turned forty; her head was full of feathers, flowers, jewels, and geegaws, and as high as Lady Archer's; her dress was trimmed with beads, silver, persian sashes, and all sort of fine fancies; her face is thin and fiery, and her whole manner spoke a lady all alive.

"Miss Burney," cried she, with great quickness, and a look all curiosity, "I am very happy to see you; I have longed to see you a great while; I have read your performance,[8] and I am quite delighted with it. I think it's the most elegant novel I ever read in my life. Such a style! I am quite surprised at it. I can't think where you got so much invention!"

You may believe this was a reception not to make me very loquacious. I did not know which way to turn my head.

"I must introduce you," continued her ladyship, "to my sister; she'll be quite delighted to see you. She has written a novel herself; so you are sister authoresses. A most elegant thing it is, I assure you; almost as pretty as yours, only not quite so elegant. She has written two novels, only one is not so pretty as the other. But I shall insist upon your seeing them. One is in letters, like yours, only yours is prettiest; it's called the *Mausoleum of Julia!*"

What unfeeling things, thought I, are *my* sisters! I'm sure I never heard them go about thus praising *me*!

Mrs. Paradise then again came forward, and taking my hand, led me up to her ladyship's sister, Lady Hawke, saying aloud, and with a courteous smirk, "Miss Burney, ma'am, authoress of *Evelina*."

"Yes," cried my friend, Lady Say and Sele, who followed me close, "it's the authoress of *Evelina*; so you are sister authoresses!"

Lady Hawke arose and curtsied. She is much younger than her sister, and rather pretty; extremely languishing, delicate, and pathetic;[9] ap-

6. I.e., they arrived too late to hear it.
7. A title, not a name; her husband is the Baron Say and Sele.
8. Burney's first published novel, *Evelina*.
9. I.e., arousing sympathy, tenderness.

parently accustomed to be reckoned the genius of her family, and well contented to be looked upon as a creature dropped from the clouds.

I was then seated between their ladyships, and Lady S. and S., drawing as near to me as possible, said,

"Well, and so you wrote this pretty book!—and pray did your papa know of it?"

"No, ma'am; not till some months after the publication."

"So I've heard; it's surprising! I can't think how you invented it!—there's a vast deal of invention in it! And you've got so much humour, too! Now my sister has no humour—hers is all sentiment. You can't think how I was entertained with that old grandmother and her son!"

I suppose she meant Tom Branghton for the son.

"How much pleasure you must have had in writing it; had not you?"

"Y—e—s, ma'am."

"So has my sister; she's never without a pen in her hand; she can't help writing for her life. When Lord Hawke is travelling about with her, she keeps writing all the way."

"Yes," said Lady Hawke; "I really can't help writing. One has great pleasure in writing the things; has not one, Miss Burney?"

"Y—e—s, ma'am."

"But your novel," cried Lady Say and Sele, "is in such a style!—so elegant! I am vastly glad you made it end happily. I hate a novel that don't end happy."

"Yes," said Lady Hawke, with a languid smile, "I was vastly glad when she married Lord Orville. I was sadly afraid it would not have been."

"My sister intends," said Lady Say and Sele, "to print her *Mausoleum*, just for her own friends and acquaintants."

"Yes," said Lady Hawke, "I have never printed yet."

"I saw Lady Hawke's name," quoth I to my first friend, "ascribed to the play of *Variety*."[1]

"Did you indeed?" cried Lady Say, in an ecstasy. "Sister! do you know Miss Burney saw your name in the newspapers, about the play!"

"Did she?" said Lady Hawke, smiling complacently. "But I really did not write it; I never wrote a play in my life."

"Well," cried Lady Say, "but do repeat that sweet part that I am so fond of—you know what I mean; Miss Burney *must* hear it,—out of your novel, you know!"

Lady H.—No, I can't; I have forgot it.

Lady S.—Oh no! I am sure you have not; I insist upon it.

Lady H.—But I know you can repeat it yourself; you have so fine a memory; I am sure you can repeat it.

---

1. I.e., a play by the name of *Variety*, anonymously produced at Drury Lane. The author was actually Richard Griffith.

Lady S.—Oh, but I should not do it justice! that's all,—I should not do it justice!

Lady Hawke then bent forward, and repeated—" 'If, when he made the declaration of his love, the sensibility[2] that beamed in his eyes was felt in his heart, what pleasing sensations and soft alarms might not that tender avowal awaken!' "

"And from what, ma'am," cried I, astonished, and imagining I had mistaken them, "is this taken?"

"From my sister's novel!" answered the delighted Lady Say and Sele, expecting my raptures to be equal to her own; "it's in the *Mausoleum*,—did not you know that? Well, I can't think how you can write these sweet novels! And it's all just like that part. Lord Hawke himself says it's all poetry. For my part, I'm sure I never could write so. I suppose, Miss Burney, you are producing another,—a'n't you?"

"No, ma'am."

"Oh, I daresay you are. I daresay you are writing one at this very minute!"

Mrs. Paradise now came up to me again, followed by a square man, middle-aged, and humdrum, who, I found, was Lord Say and Sele, afterwards from the Kirwans; for though they introduced him to me, I was so confounded by their vehemence and their manners, that I did not hear his name.

"Miss Burney," said Mrs. P., presenting me to him, "authoress of *Evelina*."

"Yes," cried Lady Say and Sele, starting up, "'tis the authoress of *Evelina*!"

"Of what?" cried he.

"Of *Evelina*. You'd never think it,—she looks so young, to have so much invention, and such an elegant style! Well, I could write a play, I think, but I'm sure I could never write a novel."

"Oh yes, you could, if you would try," said Lady Hawke.

"Oh no, I could not," answered she; "I could not get a style—that's the thing—I could not tell how to get a style! and a novel's nothing without a style, you know!"

"Why no," said Lady Hawke; "that's true. But then you write such charming letters, you know!"

"Letters!" repeated Lady S. and S., simpering; "do you think so? Do you know I wrote a long letter to Mrs. Ray just before I came here, this very afternoon,—quite a long letter! I did, I assure you!"

Here Mrs. Paradise came forward with another gentleman, younger, slimmer, and smarter, and saying to me, "Sir Gregory Page Turner," said to him, "Miss Burney, authoress of *Evelina*."

2. Sensitivity, emotion.

At which Lady Say and Sele, in fresh transport, again arose, and rapturously again repeated—"Yes, she's authoress of *Evelina!* Have you read it?"

"No; is it to be had?"[3]

"Oh dear, yes! it's been printed these two years! You'd never think it! But it's the most elegant novel I ever read in my life. Writ in such a style!"

"Certainly," said he, very civilly; "I have every inducement to get it. Pray where is it to be had? everywhere, I suppose?"

"Oh, nowhere, I hope!" cried I, wishing at that moment it had been never in human ken.[4]

My *square* friend, Lord Say and Sele, then putting his head forward, said, very solemnly, "I'll purchase it!"

His lady then mentioned to me a hundred novels that I had never heard of, asking my opinion of them, and whether I knew the authors; Lady Hawke only occasionally and languidly joining in the discourse: and then Lady S. and S., suddenly arising, begged me not to move, for she should be back again in a minute, and flew to the next room.

I took, however, the first opportunity of Lady Hawke's casting down her eyes, and reclining her delicate head, to make away from this terrible set; and, just as I was got by the piano-forte, where I hoped Pacchierotti would soon present himself, Mrs. Paradise again came to me, and said,

"Miss Burney, Lady Say and Sele wishes vastly to cultivate your acquaintance, and begs to know if she may have the honour of your company to an assembly at her house next Friday?—and I will do myself the pleasure to call for you, if you will give me leave."

"Her ladyship does me much honour, but I am unfortunately engaged," was my answer, with as much promptness as I could command. F.B.

1782

3. For sale.   4. Knowing.

PHILLIS WHEATLEY
c. 1753–1784

Just enough is known about Phillis Wheatley's life to suggest the extent of her poetic talent, for she developed it against great odds. The time and place of Wheatley's birth are as unknown as her African name, but she probably came from what is now called Senegal or Gambia. Purchased directly off a slave ship in Boston by a wealthy tailor, John Wheatley, in 1761, she was losing her first teeth, and so she was believed to be about seven years of age. Because of her pre-cocity, the girl, who became Mrs. Susannah Wheatley's personal servant, was treated beneficently by the standards of the time. She learned English in sixteen months, and soon studied Latin, as well as the Bible and English poetry by Alexander Pope and Thomas Gray. She began writing religious verse when she was thirteen, and she could not have been more than seventeen years old when she published her first poem, an elegy on the death of the English evangelical preacher George Whitehead. In 1773, in poor health, she was sent to England with the Wheatleys' son, and there her only book, *Poems on Various Subjects, Religious and Moral*, was published. After she returned to Boston to witness first Mrs. and then Mr. Wheatley's death, she was freed and married John Peters, a freedman who seems later to have been imprisoned for debt. Two of her three children died, and eventually Wheatley worked in a dilapidated lodging house to support herself and the third child, who died soon after she did.

Even the scanty information we have about Wheatley's career implies that she lived the life of a prodigy. Whether praised as an exemplary figure or scrutinized as a strange aberration, she was famous for her wit in conversation, her modesty, and her social poise. Certainly, her poems are decorous and pious in their stylistic use of conventional neoclassical couplets and in their thematic focus on spiritual salvation achieved through Christ. She was the guest of the countess of Huntington in London and met General George Washington after publishing a poem about him in the April 1776 issue of the *Philadelphia Magazine*. The volume of verse the countess of Huntington helped publish contains a foreword attesting to Wheatley's talents and signed by eighteen prominent Massachusetts men, including John Hancock. Yet none of these testimonials saved her from the obscurity and destitution of her life after slavery. *Poems on Various Subjects* was published in America in 1786. But Wheatley's fame as the first black American woman poet was not established until Margaretta M. Odell published a *Memoir* in her 1834 edition of the *Poems*.

On Being Brought from Africa to America

'Twas mercy brought me from my pagan land,
Taught my benighted[1] soul to understand
That there's a God, that there's a Saviour too:
Once I redemption neither sought nor knew.
Some view that sable[2] race with scornful eye: 5
"Their colour is a diabolic dye."
Remember, Christians, Negroes black as Cain[3]
May be refined[4] and join the angelic strain.

1773

1. Unenlightened.
2. Black.
3. After Cain murdered his brother Abel, God "marked" him so that his crime would be

known. This has sometimes been interpreted as the story of the origin of the Negro.
4. Purified; "strain": race.

To the Right Honourable William, Earl of Dartmouth, His Majesty's Principal Secretary of State for North America, Etc.[5]

Hail, happy day, when, smiling like the morn,
Fair Freedom rose New England to adorn:
The northern clime[6] beneath her genial ray,
Dartmouth, congratulates thy blissful sway:[7]
Elate with hope her race no longer mourns,   5
Each soul expands, each grateful bosom burns,
While in thine hand with pleasure we behold
The silken reins, and Freedom's charms unfold.
Long lost to realms beneath the northern skies
She shines supreme, while hated Faction dies: 10
Soon as appeared the goddess[8] long desired,
Sick at the view, she[9] languished and expired;
Thus from the splendors of the morning light
The owl in sadness seeks the caves of night.

No more, America, in mournful strain[1]   15
Of wrongs, and grievance unredressed complain,
No longer shalt thou dread the iron chain
Which wanton Tyranny with lawless hand
Had made, and with it meant to enslave the land.

Should you, my lord, while you peruse my song,   20
Wonder from whence my love of Freedom sprung,
Whence flow these wishes for the common good,
By feeling hearts alone best understood,
I, young in life, by seeming cruel fate,
Was snatched from Afric's fancied happy seat:[2]   25
What pangs excruciating must molest,
What sorrows labour in my parents' breast?
Steeled was that soul and by no misery moved
That from a father seized his babe beloved:
Such, such my case. And can I then but pray   30
Others may never feel tyrannic sway?

For favours past, great Sir, our thanks are due,
And thee we ask thy favors to renew,
Since[3] in thy power, as in thy will before,

5. Lord Dartmouth was appointed secretary in charge of the American colonies in August 1772, replacing the stern Lord Hillsborough. American sympathizers in England were hopeful that Dartmouth would prove to be more amenable to the colonies' grievances.
6. Region.
7. Reign, leadership.
8. I.e., Freedom.

9. I.e., Faction (internal conflict).
1. Eloquent burst of language or melody.
2. Place of abode; "fancied": imagined.
3. The words "it is" have been omitted. The line draws a distinction between Dartmouth's powerless state of sympathy for the colonies before his appointment, and his new-found ability to help them.

To soothe the griefs which thou didst once deplore.   35
May heavenly grace the sacred sanction give
To all thy works, and thou forever live
Not only on the wings of fleeting Fame,
Though praise immortal crowns the patriot's[4] name,
But to conduct to heaven's refulgent fane,[5]   40
May fiery coursers[6] sweep the ethereal plain,
And bear thee upwards to that blessed abode,
Where, like the prophet,[7] thou shalt find thy God.

1773

4. I.e., Dartmouth's.
5. Shining temple.
6. Swift horses; "ethereal": airy.

7. The prophet Elijah was borne up into heaven on a chariot of fire (2 Kings 2:11).

MARY WOLLSTONECRAFT
1759–1797

"It is time to effect a revolution in female manners—time to restore to them their lost dignity—and make them, as part of the human species, labour by reforming themselves, to reform the world": Mary Wollstonecraft's fervent radicalism extended from a critique of private property and political oppression to a protest against the subjection of women. Her most famous book, A *Vindication of the Rights of Woman* (1792), is a justification of women's rights and an attack against the wrongs inflicted on women, in which this author claims that women's manners have been corrupted by a culture that exalts feminine inferiority. Vanity, triviality, duplicity, and selfishness are the secondary characteristics of a creature, called female, who has been constructed to suit society. It is in this context that A *Vindication of the Rights of Woman* presents the first fully elaborated feminist criticism of misogynist images of women in literature, as well as the first sustained argument for female political, economic, and legal equality. To be sure, a number of polemical tracts on the injustice of women's situation preceded Wollstonecraft's, with Catharine Macaulay's *Letters on Education*, which Wollstonecraft reviewed, published only two years earlier. But Wollstonecraft's impassioned plea against the miseducation of women constituted a groundbreaking demonstration of how the very protection offered women confines them to the vices and virtues of an inferior class and thereby inhibits both women and men from establishing their common humanity.

Wollstonecraft's own education seems to have been acquired in spite of the impoverishment and instability of her family, but the energy of her revolt against injustice was very much shaped by her struggle for independence from that family. The woman who would dedicate her philosophical inquiries to a protest against arbitrary tyranny found political impetus in the personal injustices she both witnessed and experienced. The second of five children, Wollstonecraft suffered from the brutality of her father and the submissiveness of her mother. Although Edward John Wollstonecraft inherited a fortune from his father, a weaver, he lost it in a succession of farming failures that led to drunken physical abuse of his wife. Wollstonecraft tried to protect her mother, sleeping on the landing outside her mother's room on more than one occasion; however, she was regarded or regarded herself as second to her older brother in her mother's affections. As the family moved from London to Yorkshire to Wales, and back to London, Wollstonecraft suffered from the financial constraints that eventually led her father to use up most of the money settled on his daughters. To relieve him from debt and to extricate herself from his intolerable rule, she left home in 1778, at the age of nineteen, earning her living as a companion to a widow in Bath. Later, she would pursue her independence by opening a school and by becoming a governess. The school failed and the mother of her charges discharged her, but Wollstonecraft pursued her education, teaching herself both French and German, even as she sustained and was sustained by a succession of friendships.

In contrast to the violence she identified with her parents' marriage, friendships provided the bonds of affection in Wollstonecraft's life. At the age of eleven, in Beverley, for example, she wrote vivid letters to her best friend, Jane Arden, whom she would see again in Bath. She met her most cherished friend, Fanny Blood, in 1774, and their relationship flourished when, two years later, Wollstonecraft's father brought the family to Walworth. Two years older than Wollstonecraft, Fanny Blood lived in almost as difficult a home, with an improvident father and a patient mother who took in sewing to eke out a living for the family. When, in 1782, her mother died, Wollstonecraft, then twenty-three, joined the Blood family, where she sewed with Mrs. Blood and Fanny from sunrise to sunset.

During this same period, the two friends joined forces to rescue one of Wollstonecraft's younger sisters from a marriage she found intolerable: after giving birth to a child, Eliza Wollstonecraft Bishop suffered a severe emotional breakdown; Fanny Blood moved Eliza's belongings, while Mary Wollstonecraft removed Eliza from her husband and child. Whether the friends' audacious plan was heartless and foolhardy (the child died later that year) or redemptive and courageous (divorce was difficult for women to obtain), it illustrates Wollstonecraft's rebellious independence and her identification with women's suffering. Both traits are evident in her continued commitment to Fanny Blood. When, in 1785, Fanny Blood was pregnant in a foreign country, Wollstonecraft undertook the arduous voyage to Lisbon to be with her friend for the delivery. The despondency she experienced after the subsequent death of Fanny would haunt her for the rest of her life, although she continued to give financial support to her friend's relatives, as well as to her own.

It was not until Wollstonecraft arrived in London in 1787 that she identified her ambitions with the profession of writing. Earlier, at her girls' school in Newington Green, she had benefited from the intellectual companionship of Richard Price, a famous liberal author of the period, and she had written *Thoughts on the Education of Daughters* on her return from Portugal. But under the auspices of Joseph Johnson, the mainstay of publishing associated with the revolutionary movements in France and America, she earned her living by writing essays for his *Analytic Review* and by translating Jacques Necker's *Of the Importance of Religious Opinions* (1788) and Christian Salzmann's *Elements of Morality* (1790). The appearances of her first novel, *Mary*, *a Fiction*, her children's book, *Original Stories*, and her no longer extant anthology, *The Female Reader*, in 1788 and 1789 were followed in 1790 by the instantaneous success of her *Vindication of the Rights of Man*. Wollstonecraft had clearly profited from the intellectual stimulation of Johnson's circle of acquaintances, men like the mystic poet William Blake, who illustrated the second edition of *Original Stories*, the physician Dr. George Fordyce, a Fellow of The Royal Society, the revolutionary theorist Tom Paine, and the Romantic painter Henry Fuseli.

Although later readers of *A Vindication of the Rights of Man* have faulted the book as disorganized, and although it was obscured by the subsequent popularity of Tom Paine's *The Rights of Man* (1791–1792), it was the first rebuttal of Edmund Burke's *Reflections on the Revolution in France* (1790). Wollstonecraft responded to Burke's eloquent attack on the French Revolution and his conservative idealization of England by defending the radical principles of her friend Richard Price and by analyzing the exploitation of the working class and the disproportionate privileges of the propertied class in England. Her next work, *A Vindication of the Rights of Woman*, can be read as a sequel to *A Vindication of the Rights of Man*, an extension of her enthusiastic response to the French Revolution. Written in six weeks, it was dedicated to the revolutionary French statesman Talleyrand in order to argue that the goals of liberty, equality, and fraternity would be undermined by the exclusion of women and their rights from programs for social reform. By the time she published her second *Vindication*, Wollstonecraft had joined the ranks of such professional literary women as Fanny Burney and Hannah More. Indeed, she had exceeded them, for the philosophic breadth of her writing established links between radicalism, Romanticism, and feminism that would be of lasting importance.

Throughout her career, Wollstonecraft confronted the discrepancy between her revolutionary theories and the material realities they sought to address and redress. Nowhere is this more evident than in the tension between the ideal of male-female friendship in her polemical writing and the torment of romantic thralldom she suffered in her life. In spite of her growing reputation, after she had analyzed the destructiveness of romance in her second *Vindication*, Wollstonecraft left England when it became clear that she could not join the household of Fuseli, the married man she had begun to love. Escaping to France in order to witness the Revolution at first hand, she fell in love with an American, Gilbert Imlay, and was registered as his wife, to gain the protection of American citizenship. Yet she refused the legal claim of marriage. Imlay had been an officer in the American revolutionary army and had published a book about the Kentucky wilderness, but he was engaged in shady political and financial intrigues about which Wollstonecraft knew little or nothing. When she was abandoned by him in Paris under dangerous circumstances—with her baby daughter, Fanny, during the Reign of Terror—she wrote numerous letters lamenting his want of feeling. When she returned to London from a trip through the Scandinavian countries which he had arranged for her, she discovered his infidelity and tried to kill herself by throwing herself off Putney Bridge into the Thames. Astonishingly, however, she never stopped writing during this period, publishing *A Historical and Moral View of the Origins and Progress of the French Revolution* in 1794, the same year she gave birth to her daughter, and

Letters Written during a Short Residence in Sweden, Norway, and Denmark in
1796, less than a year after her suicide attempt. Indeed, this book was constructed out of letters to Imlay which were returned at her request.

The next year Wollstonecraft went to visit William Godwin. The already
established philosopher and novelist had met her earlier at Johnson's, but now
Godwin was looking for a lifelong companion. Their ideas and careers meshed,
and, in spite of their principles, they decided to legalize the relationship when
Wollstonecraft became pregnant for the second time. Tragically, however,
their marriage lasted less than a year: Wollstonecraft died at thirty-six years of
age of puerperal fever, eleven days after she gave birth to Mary Wollstonecraft
Godwin. The physicians, who may have caused blood poisoning in their efforts
to remove the placenta, were hampered by the primitive state of medicine in
this period. They could counteract the painful effects of Wollstonecraft's infection only with wine, of her lactation only with puppies brought in to draw the
milk from her breasts. She had been unable to complete her last project, a novel
entitled *Maria; or, The Wrongs of Women*.

The gruesome irony of Wollstonecraft's personal tragedies when viewed
from the perspective of her pioneering principles is also apparent in the use
made of Godwin's laudatory *Memoirs of the Author of "A Vindication of the
Rights of Woman"* (1789) and his edition of her *Posthumous Works*, in which
he reprinted her love letters to Imlay. The scandal that resulted caused Wollstonecraft to be castigated as an "hyena in petticoats" and a "philosophical
wanton." It also effectively erased her philosophic achievement for more than a
century. Yet women from George Eliot to Ruth Benedict continued to be fascinated by Wollstonecraft's life. The personal suffering which she dramatized in
her novels, and the visionary reforms for which she called in her political writing, are twin aspects of what she saw as the injustice of a social system that defined women as male property. While in *A Vindication of the Rights of
Woman* she condemned Milton, Pope, Chesterfield, and Rousseau for promulgating pernicious images of women, she was equally contemptuous of the
reading habits of women, whose addiction to romance seemed to her to propa-
gate only ignorance and further dependency. In all these respects, Wollstonecraft became a foremother, not only for her biological daughter Mary
Wollstonecraft Godwin Shelley, who read her parents' books while sitting by
her mother's grave, but also for literary women from Margaret Fuller and Florence Nightingale to Charlotte Perkins Gilman, Olive Schreiner, Virginia
Woolf, and Adrienne Rich, all of whom have extended the tradition of feminist
polemic she established.

From A Vindication of the Rights of Woman[1]

Introduction

After considering the historic page, and viewing the living world with
anxious solicitude, the most melancholy emotions of sorrowful indig-

1. The text is from the second revised edition of   (1975). The editors gratefully acknowledge Ms.
1792, as edited by Carol H. Poston from the   Poston's permission to make use of the informa-
Norton Critical Edition of *A Vindication*   tion in her annotations.

nation have depressed my spirits, and I have sighed when obliged to confess, that either nature has made a great difference between man and man, or that the civilization which has hitherto taken place in the world has been very partial. I have turned over various books written on the subject of education, and patiently observed the conduct of parents and the management of schools; but what has been the result?—a profound conviction that the neglected education of my fellow-creatures is the grand source of the misery I deplore; and that women, in particular, are rendered weak and wretched by a variety of concurring causes, originating from one hasty conclusion. The conduct and manners of women, in fact, evidently prove that their minds are not in a healthy state; for, like the flowers which are planted in too rich a soil, strength and usefulness are sacrificed to beauty; and the flaunting leaves, after having pleased a fastidious eye, fade, disregarded on the stalk, long before the season when they ought to have arrived at maturity.—One cause of this barren blooming I attribute to a false system of education, gathered from the books written on this subject by men who, considering females rather as women than human creatures, have been more anxious to make them alluring mistresses than affectionate wives and rational mothers; and the understanding of the sex has been so bubbled[2] by this specious homage, that the civilized women of the present century, with a few exceptions, are only anxious to inspire love, when they ought to cherish a nobler ambition, and by their abilities and virtues exact respect.

In a treatise, therefore, on female rights and manners, the works which have been particularly written for their improvement must not be overlooked; especially when it is asserted, in direct terms, that the minds of women are enfeebled by false refinement; that the books of instruction, written by men of genius, have had the same tendency as more frivolous productions; and that, in the true style of Mahometanism, they are treated as a kind of subordinate beings,[3] and not as a part of the human species, when improveable reason is allowed to be the dignified distinction which raises men above the brute creation, and puts a natural sceptre in a feeble hand.

Yet, because I am a woman, I would not lead my readers to suppose that I mean violently to agitate the contested question respecting the equality or inferiority of the sex; but as the subject lies in my way, and I cannot pass it over without subjecting the main tendency of my reasoning to misconstruction, I shall stop a moment to deliver, in a few words, my opinion.—In the government of the physical world it is observable that the female in point of strength is, in general, inferior to the

---

2. Deceived by "bubbles," i.e., insubstantial fictions.
3. Europeans commonly though mistakenly assumed that the Koran, the sacred text of the Mohammedans, teaches that women have no souls.

male. This is the law of nature; and it does not appear to be suspended or abrogated in favour of women. A degree of physical superiority cannot, therefore, be denied—and it is a noble prerogative! But not content with this natural pre-eminence, men endeavour to sink us still lower, merely to render us alluring objects for a moment; and women, intoxicated by the adoration which men, under the influence of their senses, pay them, do not seek to obtain a durable interest in their hearts, or to become the friends of the fellow creatures who find amusement in their society.

I am aware of an obvious inference:—from every quarter have I heard exclamations against masculine women; but where are they to be found? If by this appellation men mean to inveigh against their ardour in hunting, shooting, and gaming, I shall most cordially join in the cry; but if it be against the imitation of manly virtues, or, more properly speaking, the attainment of those talents and virtues, the exercise of which ennobles the human character, and which raise females in the scale of animal being, when they are comprehensively termed mankind;—all those who view them with a philosophic eye must, I should think, wish with me, that they may every day grow more and more masculine.

This discussion naturally divides the subject. I shall first consider women in the grand light of human creatures, who, in common with men, are placed on this earth to unfold their faculties; and afterwards I shall more particularly point out their peculiar designation.

I wish also to steer clear of an error which many respectable writers have fallen into; for the instruction which has hitherto been addressed to women, has rather been applicable to *ladies*, if the little indirect advice, that is scattered through Sandford and Merton,[4] be excepted; but, addressing my sex in a firmer tone, I pay particular attention to those in the middle class, because they appear to be in the most natural state.[5] Perhaps the seeds of false-refinement, immorality, and vanity, have ever been shed by the great. Weak, artificial beings, raised above the common wants and affections of their race, in a premature unnatural manner, undermine the very foundation of virtue, and spread corruption through the whole mass of society! As a class of mankind they have the strongest claim to pity; the education of the rich tends to render them vain and helpless, and the unfolding mind is not strengthened by the practice of those duties which dignify the human character.—They only live to amuse themselves, and by the same law which in nature in-

---

4. The popular children's story *The History of Sandford and Merton*, by Thomas Day, was published in three volumes (1786–1789). The tutor in it frequently cites the moral superiority of Harry Sandford, son of a poor farmer, over Tommy Merton, the son of a rich family.

5. The middle class is here considered more "natural" than the rich because uncorrupted by titles, property, and wealth.

variably produces certain effects, they soon only afford barren amusement.

But as I purpose taking a separate view of the different ranks of society, and of the moral character of women, in each, this hint is, for the present, sufficient; and I have only alluded to the subject, because it appears to me to be the very essence of an introduction to give a cursory account of the contents of the work it introduces.

My own sex, I hope, will excuse me, if I treat them like rational creatures, instead of flattering their *fascinating* graces, and viewing them as if they were in a state of perpetual childhood, unable to stand alone. I earnestly wish to point out in what true dignity and human happiness consists—I wish to persuade women to endeavour to acquire strength, both of mind and body, and to convince them that the soft phrases, susceptibility of heart, delicacy of sentiment, and refinement of taste, are almost synonymous with epithets of weakness, and that those beings who are only the objects of pity and that kind of love, which has been termed its sister, will soon become objects of contempt.

Dismissing then those pretty feminine phrases, which the men condescendingly use to soften our slavish dependence, and despising that weak elegancy of mind, exquisite sensibility, and sweet docility of manners, supposed to be the sexual characteristics of the weaker vessel, I wish to shew that elegance is inferior to virtue, that the first object of laudable ambition is to obtain a character as a human being, regardless of the distinction of sex; and that secondary views should be brought to this simple touchstone.

This is a rough sketch of my plan; and should I express my conviction with the energetic emotions that I feel whenever I think of the subject, the dictates of experience and reflection will be felt by some of my readers. Animated by this important object, I shall disdain to cull[6] my phrases or polish my style;—I aim at being useful, and sincerity will render me unaffected; for, wishing rather to persuade by the force of my arguments, than dazzle by the elegance of my language, I shall not waste my time in rounding periods,[7] or in fabricating the turgid bombast of artificial feelings, which, coming from the head, never reach the heart.—I shall be employed about things, not words!—and, anxious to render my sex more respectable members of society, I shall try to avoid that flowery diction which has slided from essays into novels, and from novels into familiar letters and conversation.

These pretty superlatives, dropping glibly from the tongue, vitiate the taste, and create a kind of sickly delicacy that turns away from simple unadorned truth, and a deluge of false sentiments and overstretched

6. Be selective in.
7. I.e., in rounding out elaborate sentences. A "period" is a formal sentence made up of balanced clauses.

feelings, stifling the natural emotions of the heart, render the domestic pleasures insipid, that ought to sweeten the exercise of those severe duties, which educate a rational and immortal being for a nobler field of action.

The education of women has, of late, been more attended to than formerly; yet they are still reckoned a frivolous sex, and ridiculed or pitied by the writers who endeavour by satire or instruction to improve them. It is acknowledged that they spend many of the first years of their lives in acquiring a smattering of accomplishments; meanwhile strength of body and mind are sacrificed to libertine notions of beauty, to the desire of establishing themselves,—the only way women can rise in the world,—by marriage. And this desire making mere animals of them, when they marry they act as such children may be expected to act:—they dress; they paint, and nickname God's creatures.[8]—Surely these weak beings are only fit for a seraglio!—Can they be expected to govern a family with judgment, or take care of the poor babes whom they bring into the world?

If then it can be fairly deduced from the present conduct of the sex, from the prevalent fondness for pleasure which takes place of ambition and those nobler passions that open and enlarge the soul; that the instruction which women have hitherto received has only tended, with the constitution of civil society, to render them insignificant objects of desire—mere propagators of fools!—if it can be proved that in aiming to accomplish them, without cultivating their understandings, they are taken out of their sphere of duties, and made ridiculous and useless when the short-lived bloom of beauty is over,[9] I presume that *rational* men will excuse me for endeavouring to persuade them to become more masculine and respectable.

Indeed the word masculine is only a bugbear:[1] there is little reason to fear that women will acquire too much courage or fortitude; for their apparent inferiority with respect to bodily strength, must render them, in some degree, dependent on men in the various relations of life, but why should it be increased by prejudices that give a sex to virtue, and confound simple truths with sensual reveries?

Women are, in fact, so much degraded by mistaken notions of female excellence, that I do not mean to add a paradox when I assert, that this artificial weakness produces a propensity to tyrannize, and gives

---

8. Hamlet accuses Ophelia of "female" faults: "You jig, you amble, and you lisp; you nickname God's creatures and make your wantonness your ignorance" (*Hamlet* III.i.150). "Seraglio": harem, the women's quarters in a Moslem palace.

9. "A lively writer, I cannot recollect his name, asks what business women turned of forty have to do in the world?" [Wollstonecraft's note]. In her edition of the *Vindication*, Poston suggests that the passage may be from Fanny Burney's *Evelina* (1778), a novel in which a licentious lord exclaims, "I don't know what the devil a woman lives for after thirty; she is only in other folks' way."

1. A fictive object of dread.

birth to cunning, the natural opponent of strength, which leads them to play off those contemptible infantine airs that undermine esteem even whilst they excite desire. Let men become more chaste and modest, and if women do not grow wiser in the same ratio, it will be clear that they have weaker understandings. It seems scarcely necessary to say, that I now speak of the sex in general. Many individuals have more sense than their male relatives; and, as nothing preponderates where there is a constant struggle for an equilibrium, without it has[2] naturally more gravity, some women govern their husbands without degrading themselves, because intellect will always govern.

From *Chapter II*

THE PREVAILING OPINION OF A SEXUAL CHARACTER DISCUSSED

To account for, and excuse the tyranny of man, many ingenious arguments have been brought forward to prove, that the two sexes, in the acquirement of virtue, ought to aim at attaining a very different character: or, to speak explicitly, women are not allowed to have sufficient strength of mind to acquire what really deserves the name of virtue. Yet it should seem, allowing them to have souls, that there is but one way appointed by Providence to lead *mankind* to either virtue or happiness.

If then women are not a swarm of ephemeron[3] triflers, why should they be kept in ignorance under the specious name of innocence? Men complain, and with reason, of the follies and caprices of our sex, when they do not keenly satirize our headstrong passions and groveling vices.—Behold, I should answer, the natural effect of ignorance! The mind will ever be unstable that has only prejudices to rest on, and the current will run with destructive fury when there are no barriers to break its force. Women are told from their infancy, and taught by the example of their mothers, that a little knowledge of human weakness, justly termed cunning, softness of temper, *outward* obedience, and a scrupulous attention to a puerile kind of propriety, will obtain for them the protection of man; and should they be beautiful, every thing else is needless, for, at least, twenty years of their lives.

Thus Milton describes our first frail mother; though when he tells us that women are formed for softness and sweet attractive grace,[4] I cannot comprehend his meaning, unless, in the true Mahometan strain, he meant to deprive us of souls and insinuate that we were beings only designed by sweet attractive grace, and docile blind obedience, to gratify

---

2. I.e., "unless it has. . . ."
3. A flying insect that lives only one day.
4. Milton, *Paradise Lost* IV.297–99: "For contemplation he and valor form'd, / For softness she and sweet attractive grace; / He for God only, she for God in him."

the senses of man when he can no longer soar on the wing of contemplation.

How grossly do they insult us who thus advise us only to render ourselves gentle, domestic brutes![5] For instance, the winning softness so warmly, and frequently, recommended, that governs by obeying. What childish expressions, and how insignificant is the being—can it be an immortal one? who will condescend to govern by such sinister methods! "Certainly," says Lord Bacon, "man is of kin to the beasts by his body; and if he be not of kin to God by his spirit, he is a base and ignoble creature!"[6] Men, indeed, appear to me to act in a very unphilosophical manner when they try to secure the good conduct of women by attempting to keep them always in a state of childhood. Rousseau was more consistent when he wished to stop the progress of reason in both sexes, for if men eat of the tree of knowledge, women will come in for a taste[7] but, from the imperfect cultivation which their understandings now receive, they only attain a knowledge of evil.

Children, I grant, should be innocent; but when the epithet is applied to men, or women, it is but a civil[8] term for weakness. For if it be allowed that women were destined by Providence to acquire human virtues, and by the exercise of their understandings, that stability of character which is the firmest ground to rest our future hopes upon, they must be permitted to turn to the fountain of light, and not forced to shape their course by the twinkling of a mere satellite.[9] Milton, I grant, was of a very different opinion; for he only bends to the indefeasible right of beauty, though it would be difficult to render two passages which I now mean to contrast, consistent. But into similar inconsistencies are great men often led by their senses.

> To whom thus Eve with *perfect beauty* adorned.
> My Author and Disposer, what thou bidst
> *Unargued* I obey; So God ordains;
> God is thy *law, thou mine*:—to know no more
> Is Woman's *happiest* knowledge and her *praise*.[1]

These are exactly the arguments that I have used to children; but I have added, your reason is now gaining strength, and, till it arrives at some degree of maturity, you must look up to me for advice—then you ought to *think*, and only rely on God.

---

5. Purely physical beings, lacking reason and intelligence.
6. Francis Bacon, essay *Of Atheism* (1597).
7. Jean-Jacques Rousseau (1712–1778), who advocated intuition and instinct over rationality. Rousseau's views on the education of women, alluded to throughout Wollstonecraft's treatise, are set forth in his work *Émile* (1762), especially in Book V, *Sophy; or, Woman*.
8. Polite, euphemistic.
9. Any body that orbits a larger body.
1. *Paradise Lost* IV.634–38 (Wollstonecraft's italics).

Yet in the following lines Milton seems to coincide with me; when he makes Adam thus expostulate with his Maker.

> Hast thou not made me here thy substitute,
> And these inferior far beneath me set?
> Among *unequals* what society
> Can sort, what harmony or true delight?
> Which must be mutual, in proportion due
> Giv'n and *received*; but in *disparity*
> The one intense, the other still remiss
> Cannot well suit with either, but soon prove
> Tedious alike: of *fellowship* I speak
> Such as I seek, fit to participate
> All rational delight—[2]

In treating, therefore, of the manners of women, let us, disregarding sensual arguments, trace what we should endeavour to make them in order to co-operate, if the expression be not too bold, with the supreme Being.

By individual education, I mean, for the sense of the word is not precisely defined, such an attention to a child as will slowly sharpen the senses, form the temper,[3] regulate the passions as they begin to ferment, and set the understanding to work before the body arrives at maturity; so that the man may only have to proceed, not to begin, the important task of learning to think and reason.

To prevent any misconstruction, I must add, that I do not believe that a private education can work the wonders which some sanguine writers have attributed to it. Men and women must be educated, in a great degree, by the opinions and manners of the society they live in. In every age there has been a stream of popular opinion that has carried all before it, and given a family character, as it were, to the century. It may then fairly be inferred, that, till society be differently constituted, much cannot be expected from education. It is, however, sufficient for my present purpose to assert, that, whatever effect circumstances have on the abilities, every being may become virtuous by the exercise of its own reason; for if but one being was created with vicious inclinations, that is positively bad, what can save us from atheism? or if we worship a god, is not that god a devil?

Consequently, the most perfect education, in my opinion, is such an exercise of the understanding as is best calculated to strengthen the body and form the heart. Or, in other words, to enable the individual to attain such habits of virtue as will render it independent. In fact, it is a farce to call any being virtuous whose virtues do not result from the ex-

2. *Paradise Lost* VII.381–92 (Wollstonecraft's italics).   3. Temperament, character.

ercise of its own reason. This was Rousseau's opinion respecting men: I extend it to women, and confidently assert that they have been drawn out of their sphere by false refinement, and not by an endeavour to acquire masculine qualities. Still the regal homage which they receive is so intoxicating, that till the manners of the times are changed, and formed on more reasonable principles, it may be impossible to convince them that the illegitimate power, which they obtain, by degrading themselves, is a curse, and that they must return to nature and equality, if they wish to secure the placid satisfaction that unsophisticated affections impart. But for this epoch we must wait—wait, perhaps, till kings and nobles, enlightened by reason, and, preferring the real dignity of man to childish state[4] throw off their gaudy hereditary trappings: and if then women do not resign the arbitrary power of beauty—they will prove that they have *less* mind than man.

I may be accused of arrogance; still I must declare what I firmly believe, that all the writers who have written on the subject of female education and manners from Rousseau to Dr. Gregory,[5] have contributed to render women more artificial, weak characters, than they would otherwise have been, and, consequently, more useless members of society. I might have expressed this conviction in a lower key; but I am afraid it would have been the whine of affectation, and not the faithful expression of my feelings, of the clear result, which experience and reflection have led me to draw. When I come to that division of the subject, I shall advert to the passages that I more particularly disapprove of, in the works of the authors I have just alluded to; but it is first necessary to observe, that my objection extends to the whole purport of those books, which tend, in my opinion, to degrade one half of the human species, and render women pleasing at the expense of every solid virtue.

Though, to reason on Rousseau's ground, if man did attain a degree of perfection of mind when his body arrived at maturity, it might be proper, in order to make a man and his wife *one*, that she should rely entirely on his understanding: and the graceful ivy, clasping the oak that supported it, would form a whole in which strength and beauty would be equally conspicuous. But, alas! husbands, as well as their helpmates, are often only overgrown children: nay, thanks to early debauchery, scarcely men in their outward form—and if the blind lead the blind, one need not come from heaven to tell us the consequence.

Many are the causes that, in the present corrupt state of society, contribute to enslave women by cramping their understandings and sharpening their senses. One, perhaps, that silently does more mischief than all the rest, is their disregard of order.

4. Pomp, rich display.
5. Dr. John Gregory (1724–1773), author of a popular book on the education of women, *A Father's Legacy to His Daughters* (1774).

To do every thing in an orderly manner, is a most important precept, which women, who, generally speaking, receive only a disorderly kind of education, seldom attend to with that degree of exactness that men, who from their infancy are broken into method, observe. This negligent kind of guess-work, for what other epithet can be used to point out the random exertions of a sort of instinctive common sense, never brought to the test of reason? prevents their generalizing matters of fact—so they do today, what they did yesterday, merely because they did it yesterday.

This contempt of the understanding in early life has more baneful consequences than is commonly supposed; for the little knowledge which women of strong minds attain, is, from various circumstances, of a more desultory kind than the knowledge of men, and it is acquired more by sheer observations on real life, than from comparing what has been individually observed with the results of experience generalized by speculation. Led by their dependent situation and domestic employments more into society, what they learn is rather by snatches; and as learning is with them, in general, only a secondary thing, they do not pursue any one branch with that persevering ardour necessary to give vigour to the faculties, and clearness to the judgment. In the present state of society, a little learning is required to support the character of a gentleman; and boys are obliged to submit to a few years of discipline. But in the education of women, the cultivation of the understanding is always subordinate to the acquirement of some corporeal accomplishment: even while enervated by confinement and false notions of modesty, the body is prevented from attaining that grace and beauty which relaxed half-formed limbs never exhibit. Besides, in youth their faculties are not brought forward by emulation; and having no serious scientific study, if they have natural sagacity it is turned too soon on life and manners. They dwell on effects, and modifications, without tracing them back to causes; and complicated rules to adjust behaviour are a weak substitute for simple principles.

As a proof that education gives this appearance of weakness to females, we may instance the example of military men, who are, like them, sent into the world before their minds have been stored with knowledge or fortified by principles. The consequences are similar; soldiers acquire a little superficial knowledge, snatched from the muddy current of conversation, and, from continually mixing with society, they gain, what is termed a knowledge of the world; and this acquaintance with manners and customs has frequently been confounded with a knowledge of the human heart. But can the crude fruit of casual observation, never brought to the test of judgment, formed by comparing speculation and experience, deserve such a distinction? Soldiers, as well as women, practice the minor virtues with punctilious politeness.

Where is then the sexual difference, when the education has been the same? All the difference that I can discern, arises from the superior advantage of liberty, which enables the former to see more of life.

* * *

Probably the prevailing opinion, that woman was created for man, may have taken its rise from Moses's poetical story;[6] yet, as very few, it is presumed, who have bestowed any serious thought on the subject, ever supposed that Eve was, literally speaking, one of Adam's ribs, the deduction must be allowed to fall to the ground; or, only be so far admitted as it proves that man, from the remotest antiquity, found it convenient to exert his strength to subjugate his companion, and his invention to shew that she ought to have her neck bent under the yoke, because the whole creation was only created for his convenience or pleasure.

Let it not be concluded that I wish to invert the order of things; I have already granted, that, from the constitution of their bodies, men seem to be designed by Providence to attain a greater degree of virtue.[7] I speak collectively of the whole sex; but I see not the shadow of a reason to conclude that their virtues should differ in respect to their nature. In fact, how can they, if virtue has only one eternal standard? I must therefore, if I reason consequentially, as strenuously maintain that they have the same simple direction, as that there is a God.

It follows then that cunning should not be opposed to wisdom, little cares to great exertions, or insipid softness, varnished over with the name of gentleness, to that fortitude which grand views alone can inspire.

I shall be told that woman would then lose many of her peculiar graces, and the opinion of a well known poet might be quoted to refute my unqualified assertion. For Pope has said, in the name of the whole male sex,

> Yet ne'er so sure our passion to create,
> As when she touched the brink of all we hate.[8]

In what light this sally places men and women, I shall leave to the judicious to determine: meanwhile I shall content myself with observing, that I cannot discover why, unless they are mortal, females should always be degraded by being made subservient to love or lust.

To speak disrespectfully of love is, I know, high treason against sen-

---

6. The story of Eve's creation from one of the ribs of Adam (Genesis 2:21–22). Until the nineteenth century, Moses was believed to have written the first five books of the Bible.

7. I.e., men have more passions and less conti-

nence than women, and must therefore exercise greater restraint.

8. Alexander Pope, *Moral Essays II, Of the Characters of Women*, lines 51–52.

timent and fine feelings; but I wish to speak the simple language of truth, and rather to address the head than the heart. To endeavour to reason love out of the world, would be to out Quixote Cervantes,[9] and equally offend against common sense; but an endeavour to restrain this tumultuous passion, and to prove that it should not be allowed to dethrone superior powers, or to usurp the sceptre which the understanding should ever coolly wield, appears less wild.

Youth is the season for love in both sexes; but in those days of thoughtless enjoyment provision should be made for the more important years of life, when reflection takes place of sensation. But Rousseau, and most of the male writers who have followed his steps, have warmly inculcated that the whole tendency of female education ought to be directed to one point:—to render them pleasing.

Let me reason with the supporters of this opinion who have any knowledge of human nature, do they imagine that marriage can eradicate the habitude of life? The woman who has only been taught to please will soon find that her charms are oblique sun-beams, and that they cannot have much effect on her husband's heart when they are seen every day, when the summer is passed and gone. Will she then have sufficient native energy to look into herself for comfort, and cultivate her dormant faculties? or, is it not more rational to expect that she will try to please other men; and, in the emotions raised by the expectation of new conquests, endeavour to forget the mortification her love or pride has received? When the husband ceases to be a lover—and the time will inevitably come, her desire of pleasing will then grow languid, or become a spring of bitterness; and love, perhaps, the most evanescent of all passions, gives place to jealousy or vanity.

I now speak of women who are restrained by principle or prejudice; such women, though they would shrink from an intrigue[1] with real abhorrence, yet, nevertheless, wish to be convinced by the homage of gallantry that they are cruelly neglected by their husbands; or, days and weeks are spent in dreaming of the happiness enjoyed by congenial souls till their health is undermined and their spirits broken by discontent. How then can the great art of pleasing be such a necessary study? It is only useful to a mistress; the chaste wife, and serious mother, should only consider her power to please as the polish of her virtues, and the affection of her husband as one of the comforts that render her task less difficult and her life happier.—But, whether she be loved or neglected, her first wish should be to make herself respectable[2] and not to rely for all her happiness on a being subject to like infirmities with herself.

---

9. I.e., to outdo the hero of Cervantes's *Don Quixote* (1605) in trying to rid the world of evil.

1. An extramarital affair.
2. I.e., morally worthy of respect.

The worthy Dr. Gregory fell into a similar error. I respect his heart; but entirely disapprove of his celebrated *Legacy to His Daughters*.

He advises them to cultivate a fondness for dress, because a fondness for dress, he asserts, is natural to them. I am unable to comprehend what either he or Rousseau mean, when they frequently use this indefinite term.[3] If they told us that in a pre-existent state the soul was fond of dress, and brought this inclination with it into a new body, I should listen to them with a half smile, as I often do when I hear a rant about innate elegance.—But if he only meant to say that the exercise of the faculties will produce this fondness—I deny it—It is not natural, but arises, like false ambition in men, from a love of power.

Dr. Gregory goes much further; he actually recommends dissimulation, and advises an innocent girl to give the lie to her feelings, and not dance with spirit, when gaiety of heart would make her feel eloquent without making her gestures immodest. In the name of truth and common sense, why should not one woman acknowledge that she can take more exercise than another? or, in other words, that she has a sound constitution; and why, to damp innocent vivacity, is she darkly to be told that men will draw conclusions which she little thinks of?[4]—Let the libertine draw what inference he pleases; but, I hope, that no sensible mother will restrain the natural frankness of youth by instilling such indecent cautions. Out of the abundance of the heart the mouth speaketh;[5] and a wiser than Solomon hath said, that the heart should be made clean,[6] and not trivial ceremonies observed, which it is not very difficult to fulfill with scrupulous exactness when vice reigns in the heart.

Women ought to endeavour to purify their heart; but can they do so when their uncultivated understandings make them entirely dependent on their senses for employment and amusement, when no noble pursuit sets them above the little vanities of the day, or enables them to curb the wild emotions that agitate a reed over which every passing breeze has power? To gain the affections of a virtuous man is affectation necessary? Nature has given woman a weaker frame[7] than man; but, to ensure her husband's affections, must a wife, who by the exercise of her mind and body whilst she was discharging the duties of a daughter, wife, and mother, has allowed her constitution to retain its natural strength, and her nerves a healthy tone, is she, I say, to condescend to use art[8] and feign a sickly delicacy in order to secure her hus-

---

3. I.e., the term "natural."

4. Gregory, in A *Father's Legacy to His Daughters*, writes: "I would have you to dance with spirit; but never allow yourselves to be so far transported with mirth, as to forget the delicacy of your sex.—Many a girl dancing in the gaiety and innocence of her heart, is thought to discover [reveal] a spirit she little dreams of."

5. Matthew 12:34.

6. Psalm 24 (attributed to David, the "wiser than Solomon"), 3–4: "Who shall ascend into the hill of the Lord? or who shall stand in his holy place? He that hath clean hands, and a pure heart. . . ."

7. Body.

8. Artifice, deceit.

band's affection? Weakness may excite tenderness, and gratify the arrogant pride of man; but the lordly caresses of a protector will not gratify a noble mind that pants for, and deserves to be respected. Fondness is a poor substitute for friendship!

In a seraglio,[9] I grant, that all these arts are necessary; the epicure must have his palate tickled, or he will sink into apathy, but have women so little ambition as to be satisfied with such a condition? Can they supinely dream life away in the lap of pleasure, or the languor of weariness, rather than assert their claim to pursue reasonable pleasures and render themselves conspicuous by practising the virtues which dignify mankind? Surely she has not an immortal soul who can loiter life away merely employed to adorn her person, that she may amuse the languid hours, and soften the cares of a fellow-creature who is willing to be enlivened by her smiles and tricks, when the serious business of life is over.

Besides, the woman who strengthens her body and exercises her mind will, by managing her family and practising various virtues, become the friend, and not the humble dependent of her husband; and if she, by possessing such substantial qualities, merit his regard, she will not find it necessary to conceal her affection, nor to pretend to an unnatural coldness of constitution to excite her husband's passions. In fact, if we revert to history, we shall find that the women who have distinguished themselves have neither been the most beautiful nor the most gentle[1] of their sex.

Nature, or, to speak with strict propriety, God, has made all things right; but man has sought him out many inventions to mar the work. I now allude to that part of Dr. Gregory's treatise, where he advises a wife never to let her husband know the extent of her sensibility or affection. Voluptuous precaution, and as ineffectual as absurd.—Love, from its very nature, must be transitory. To seek for a secret that would render it constant, would be as wild a search as for the philosopher's stone, or the grand panacea[2] and the discovery would be equally useless, or rather pernicious to mankind. The most holy band of society is friendship. It has been well said, by a shrewd satirist, "that rare as true love is, true friendship is still rarer."[3]

This is an obvious truth, and the cause not lying deep, will not elude a slight glance of inquiry.

Love, the common passion,[4] in which chance and sensation take place of choice and reason, is, in some degree, felt by the mass of man-

---

9. A harem. An "epicure" in this sense is a person devoted to sensual pleasure, here the sultan catered to sexually by his harem.
1. Genteel, refined.
2. A medicine reputed to cure all illness. "Phi-

losopher's stone": substance which alchemists believed could transform base matter into gold.
3. Maxim 473 de de La Rochefoucauld (1613–1680), great French epigrammist.
4. Emotion.

kind; for it is not necessary to speak, at present, of the emotions that rise above or sink below love. This passion, naturally increased by suspense and difficulties, draws the mind out of its accustomed state, and exalts the affections; but the security of marriage, allowing the fever of love to subside, a healthy temperature is thought insipid, only by those who have not sufficient intellect to substitute the calm tenderness of friendship, the confidence of respect instead of blind admiration, and the sensual emotions of fondness.

This is, must be, the course of nature.—Friendship or indifference inevitably succeeds love.—And this constitution seems perfectly to harmonize with the system of government which prevails in the moral world. Passions are spurs to action, and open the mind; but they sink into mere appetites, become a personal and momentary gratification, when the object is gained, and the satisfied mind rests in enjoyment. The man who had some virtue whilst he was struggling for a crown, often becomes a voluptuous tyrant when it graces his brow; and, when the lover is not lost in the husband, the dotard, a prey to childish caprices, and fond jealousies, neglects the serious duties of life, and the caresses which should excite confidence in his children are lavished on the overgrown child, his wife.

In order to fulfill the duties of life, and to be able to pursue with vigour the various employments which form the moral character, a master and mistress of a family ought not to continue to love each other with passion. I mean to say, that they ought not to indulge those emotions which disturb the order of society, and engross the thoughts that should be otherwise employed. The mind that has never been engrossed by one object wants[5] vigour—if it can long be so, it is weak.

A mistaken education, a narrow, uncultivated mind, and many sexual prejudices, tend to make women more constant than men; but, for the present, I shall not touch on this branch of the subject. I will go still further, and advance, without dreaming of a paradox, that an unhappy marriage is often very advantageous to a family, and that the neglected wife is, in general, the best mother.[6] And this would almost always be the consequence if the female mind were more enlarged: for, it seems to be the common dispensation of Providence, that what we gain in present enjoyment should be deducted from the treasure of life, experience; and that when we are gathering the flowers of the day and revelling in pleasure, the solid fruit of toil and wisdom should not be caught at the same time. The way lies before us, we must turn to the right or left; and he who will pass life away in bounding from one pleasure to

5. Lacks.
6. Wollstonecraft sounds somewhat more cynical about married love here than she really is; she simply means that a woman not completely preoccupied with her husband has more time and energy for her children.

another, must not complain if he acquire neither wisdom nor respectability of character.

Supposing, for a moment, that the soul is not immortal, and that man was only created for the present scene,—I think we should have reason to complain that love, infantine fondness, ever grew insipid and palled upon the sense. Let us eat, drink, and love, for tomorrow we die, would be, in fact, the language of reason, the morality of life; and who but a fool would part with a reality for a fleeting shadow? But, if awed by observing the improbable[7] powers of the mind, we disdain to confine our wishes or thoughts to such a comparatively mean field of action; that only appears grand and important, as it is connected with a boundless prospect and sublime hopes, what necessity is there for falsehood in conduct, and why must the sacred majesty of truth be violated to detain a deceitful good that saps the very foundation of virtue? Why must the female mind be tainted by coquetish arts to gratify the sensualist, and prevent love from subsiding into friendship, or compassionate tenderness, when there are not qualities on which friendship can be built? Let the honest heart shew itself, and *reason* teach passion to submit to necessity; or, let the dignified, pursuit of virtue and knowledge raise the mind above those emotions which rather imbitter than sweeten the cup of life, when they are not restrained within due bounds.

I do not mean to allude to the romantic passion,[8] which is the concomitant of genius.—Who can clip its wing? But that grand passion not proportioned to the puny enjoyments of life, is only true to the sentiment, and feeds on itself. The passions which have been celebrated for their durability have always been unfortunate. They have acquired strength by absence and constitutional melancholy.—The fancy[9] has hovered round a form of beauty dimly seen—but familiarity might have turned admiration into disgust; or, at least, into indifference, and allowed the imagination leisure to start fresh game. With perfect propriety, according to this view of things, does Rousseau make the mistress of his soul, Eloisa, love St. Preux when life was fading before her;[1] but this is no proof of the immortality of the passion.

Of the same complexion is Dr. Gregory's advice respecting delicacy of sentiment, which he advises a woman not to acquire, if she have determined to marry. This determination, however, perfectly consistent with his former advice, he calls *indelicate*, and earnestly persuades his

---

7. Poston suggests that this is a misprint in the second edition for "improvable," i.e., unknowable.

8. I.e., the indefinite longings and ambitions characteristic of the poetry of this period, and associated with the notion of the "sublime."

9. The imagination.

1. In Rousseau's novel *Julie; ou, La Nouvelle Héloïse* (1761), Julie reveals on her deathbed to her husband Wolmar that her real, passionate love is for her former lover St. Preux. Julie or "Eloisa" was thought to represent a woman with whom Rousseau was in love at the time.

daughters to conceal it, though it may govern their conduct;—as if it were indelicate to have the common appetites of human nature.

Noble morality! and consistent with the cautious prudence of a little soul that cannot extend its views beyond the present minute division of existence. If all the faculties of woman's mind are only to be cultivated as they respect her dependence on man; if, when a husband be obtained, she have arrived at her goal, and meanly proud rests satisfied with such a paltry crown, let her grovel contentedly, scarcely raised by her employments above the animal kingdom; but, if, struggling for the prize of her high calling, she look beyond the present scene, let her cultivate her understanding without stopping to consider what character the husband may have whom she is destined to marry. Let her only determine, without being too anxious about present happiness, to acquire the qualities that ennoble a rational being, and a rough inelegant husband may shock her taste without destroying her peace of mind. She will not model her soul to suit the frailties of her companion, but to bear with them: his character may be a trial, but not an impediment to virtue.

If Dr. Gregory confined his remark to romantic expectations of constant love and congenial feelings, he should have recollected that experience will banish what advice can never make us cease to wish for, when the imagination is kept alive at the expense of reason.

I own it frequently happens that women who have fostered a romantic unnatural delicacy of feeling, waste their[2] lives in *imagining* how happy they should have been with a husband who could love them with a fervid increasing affection every day, and all day. But they might as well pine married as single—and would not be a jot more unhappy with a bad husband than longing for a good one. That a proper education; or, to speak with more precision, a well stored mind, would enable a woman to support a single life with dignity, I grant; but that she should avoid cultivating her taste, lest her husband should occasionally shock it, is quitting a substance for a shadow. To say the truth, I do not know of what use is an improved taste, if the individual be not rendered more independent of the casualties of life; if new sources of enjoyment, only dependent on the solitary operations of the mind, are not opened. People of taste, married or single, without distinction, will ever be disgusted by various things that touch not less observing minds. On this conclusion the argument must not be allowed to hinge; but in the whole sum of enjoyment is taste to be denominated a blessing?

The question is, whether it procures most pain or pleasure? The answer will decide the propriety of Dr. Gregory's advice, and shew how absurd and tyrannic it is thus to lay down a system of slavery; or to at-

---

2. "For example, the herd of Novelists" [Wollstonecraft's note]. Wollstonecraft is referring both to women who base their expectations in love on the distortions of sentimental novels, and to women who indulge their fantasies by writing such novels.

tempt to educate moral beings by any other rules than those deduced from pure reason, which apply to the whole species.

Gentleness of manners, forbearance and long-suffering, are such amiable Godlike qualities, that in sublime poetic strains the Deity has been invested with them; and perhaps, no representation of his goodness so strongly fastens on the human affections as those that represent him abundant in mercy and willing to pardon. Gentleness, considered in this point of view, bears on its front all the characteristics of grandeur, combined with the winning graces of condescension; but what a different aspect it assumes when it is the submissive demeanour of dependence, the support of weakness that loves, because it wants protection, and is forbearing, because it must silently endure injuries; smiling under the lash at which it dare not snarl. Abject as this picture appears, it is the portrait of an accomplished woman, according to the received opinion of female excellence, separated by specious reasoners from human excellence. Or, they[3] kindly restore the rib, and make one moral being a man and woman; not forgetting to give her all the "submissive charms."[4]

How women are to exist in that state where there is to be neither marrying nor giving in marriage,[5] we are not told. For though moralists have agreed that the tenor of life seems to prove that *man* is prepared by various circumstances for a future state, they constantly concur in advising *woman* only to provide for the present. Gentleness, docility, and a spaniel-like affection are, on this ground, consistently recommended as the cardinal virtues of the sex; and, disregarding the arbitrary economy of nature, one writer has declared that it is masculine for a woman to be melancholy.[6] She was created to be the toy of man, his rattle, and it must jingle in his ears whenever, dismissing reason, he chooses to be amused.

To recommend gentleness, indeed, on a broad basis is strictly philosophical. A frail being should labour to be gentle. But when forbearance confounds right and wrong, it ceases to be a virtue; and, however convenient it may be found in a companion—that companion will ever be considered as an inferior, and only inspire a vapid tenderness, which easily degenerates into contempt. Still, if advice could really make a being gentle, whose natural disposition admitted not of such a fine polish, something towards the advancement of order would be attained; but if, as might quickly be demonstrated, only affectation be produced

---

3. "*Vide* [see] Rousseau and Swedenborg" [Wollstonecraft's note]. Rousseau asserted that a married couple formed a single unit. Emmanuel Swedenborg (1688–1772), Swedish theologian, believed that in heaven, husband and wife are united in a single body.

4. *Paradise Lost* IV.497–99: "he in delight / Both of her Beauty and submissive charms / Smiled with superior love."

5. "For in the resurrection they neither marry, nor are given in marriage, but are as the angels in heaven" (Matthew 22:30).

6. Perhaps a reference to Edmund Burke's *Inquiry* into the sublime, where he associates melancholy with the nonfeminine.

by this indiscriminate counsel, which throws a stumbling-block in the way of gradual improvement, and true melioration of temper, the sex is not much benefited by sacrificing solid virtues to the attainment of superficial graces, though for a few years they may procure the individuals regal sway.

As a philosopher, I read with indignation the plausible epithets which men use to soften their insults, and, as a moralist, I ask what is meant by such heterogeneous associations, as fair defects, amiable weaknesses, &c.?[7] If there be but one criterion of morals, but one archetype for man, women appear to be suspended by destiny, according to the vulgar tale of Mahomet's coffin,[8] they have neither the unerring instinct of brutes, nor are allowed to fix the eye of reason on a perfect model. They were made to be loved, and must not aim at respect, lest they should be hunted out of society as masculine.

But to view the subject in another point of view. Do passive indolent women make the best wives? Confining our discussion to the present moment of existence, let us see how such weak creatures perform their part? Do the women who, by the attainment of a few superficial accomplishments, have strengthened the prevailing prejudice, merely contribute to the happiness of their husbands? Do they display their charms merely to amuse them? And have women, who have early imbibed notions of passive obedience, sufficient character to manage a family or educate children? So far from it, that, after surveying the history of woman, I cannot help, agreeing with the severest satirist, considering the sex as the weakest as well as the most oppressed half of the species. What does history disclose but marks of inferiority, and how few women have emancipated themselves from the galling yoke of sovereign man?—So few, that the exceptions remind me of an ingenious conjecture respecting Newton: that he was probably a being of a superior order, accidentally caged in a human body.[9] Following the same train of thinking, I have been led to imagine that the few extraordinary women who have rushed in eccentrical directions out of the orbit prescribed to their sex, were *male* spirits, confined by mistake in female frames. But if it be not philosophical to think of sex when the soul is mentioned, the inferiority must depend on the organs; or the heavenly fire, which is to ferment the clay, is not given in equal portions.

But avoiding, as I have hitherto done, any direct comparison of the two sexes collectively, or frankly acknowledging the inferiority of woman, according to the present appearance of things, I shall only in-

---

7. *Paradise Lost* X.891–92: "This fair defect / Of nature"; and Pope, *Moral Essays* II.44: "Fine by defect, and delicately weak."
8. According to "vulgar" [popular] legend, Mohammed's coffin hovers magically inside his tomb.

9. Isaac Newton (1642–1727), great English scientist who founded modern physics. Wollstonecraft may be recalling Pope's *Essay on Man* II:31–34: "Superior beings . . . / Admired such wisdom in an earthly shape, / And showed a Newton as we show an ape."

sist that men have increased that inferiority till women are almost sunk below the standard of rational creatures. Let their faculties have room to unfold, and their virtues to gain strength, and then determine where the whole sex must stand in the intellectual scale. Yet let it be remembered, that for a small number of distinguished women I do not ask a place.

* * *

From *Chapter XIII*

SOME INSTANCES OF THE FOLLY WHICH THE IGNORANCE OF WOMEN
GENERATES; WITH CONCLUDING REFLECTIONS ON THE MORAL
IMPROVEMENT THAT A REVOLUTION IN FEMALE MANNERS MIGHT
NATURALLY BE EXPECTED TO PRODUCE

Another instance of that feminine weakness of character, often produced by a confined education, is a romantic twist of the mind, which has been very properly termed *sentimental*.

Women subjected by ignorance to their sensations, and only taught to look for happiness in love, refine[1] on sensual feelings, and adopt metaphysical notions respecting that passion, which lead them shamefully to neglect the duties of life, and frequently in the midst of these sublime refinements they plump into actual vice.

These are the women who are amused by the reveries of the stupid novelists, who, knowing little of human nature, work up stale tales, and describe meretricious scenes, all retailed in a sentimental jargon, which equally tend to corrupt the taste, and draw the heart aside from its daily duties. I do not mention the understanding, because never having been exercised, its slumbering energies rest inactive, like the lurking particles of fire which are supposed universally to pervade matter.[2]

Females, in fact, denied all political privileges, and not allowed, as married women, excepting in criminal cases, a civil existence, have their attention naturally drawn from the interest of the whole community to that of the minute parts, though the private duty of any member of society must be very imperfectly performed when not connected with the general good. The mighty business of female life is to please, and restrained from entering into more important concerns by political and civil oppression, sentiments become events, and reflection deepens what it should, and would have effaced, if the understanding had been allowed to take a wider range.

But, confined to trifling employments, they naturally imbibe opinions which the only kind of reading calculated to interest an innocent

1. Intensify, heighten.
2. Popular belief held that all matter was made

up of four elements in varying proportions: air, earth, fire, and water.

frivolous mind, inspires. Unable to grasp any thing great, is it surprising that they find the reading of history a very dry task, and disquisitions addressed to the understanding intolerably tedious, and almost unintelligible? Thus are they necessarily dependent on the novelist for amusement. Yet, when I exclaim against novels, I mean when contrasted with those works which exercise the understanding and regulate the imagination.—For any kind of reading I think better than leaving a blank still a blank, because the mind must receive a degree of enlargement and obtain a little strength by a slight exertion of its thinking powers; besides, even the productions that are only addressed to the imagination, raise the reader a little above the gross gratification of appetites, to which the mind has not given a shade of delicacy.

This observation is the result of experience; for I have known several notable women, and one in particular, who was a very good woman— as good as such a narrow mind would allow her to be, who took care that her daughters (three in number) should never see a novel. As she was a woman of fortune and fashion, they had various masters to attend them, and a sort of menial governess to watch their footsteps. From their masters they learned how tables, chairs. &c. were called in French and Italian; but as the few books thrown in their way were far above their capacities, or devotional, they neither acquired ideas nor sentiments, and passed their time, when not compelled to repeat *words*, in dressing, quarrelling with each other, or conversing with their maids by stealth, till they were brought into company as marriageable.

Their mother, a widow, was busy in the meantime in keeping up her connections, as she termed a numerous acquaintance, lest her girls should want a proper introduction into the great world. And these young ladies, with minds vulgar in every sense of the word, and spoiled tempers, entered life puffed up with notions of their own consequence, and looking down with contempt on those who could not vie with them in dress and parade.

With respect to love, nature, or their nurses, had taken care to teach them the physical meaning of the word; and, as they had few topics of conversation, and fewer refinements of sentiment, they expressed their gross[3] wishes not in very delicate phrases, when they spoke freely, talking of matrimony.

Could these girls have been injured by the perusal of novels? I almost forgot a shade[4] in the character of one of them; she affected a simplicity bordering on folly, and with a simper would utter the most immodest remarks and questions, the full meaning of which she had learned whilst secluded from the world, and afraid to speak in her mother's presence, who governed with a high hand: they were all educated, as she

---

3. Unrefined, blatant.   4. Mark, flaw.

prided herself, in a most exemplary manner; and read their chapters and psalms before breakfast, never touching a silly novel.

This is only one instance; but I recollect many other women who, not led by degrees to proper studies, and not permitted to choose for themselves, have indeed been overgrown children; or have obtained, by mixing in the world, a little of what is termed common sense: that is, a distinct manner of seeing common occurrences, as they stand detached: but what deserves the name of intellect, the power of gaining general or abstract ideas, or even intermediate ones, was out of the question. Their minds were quiescent, and when they were not roused by sensible objects and employments of that kind, they were low-spirited, would cry, or go to sleep.

When, therefore, I advise my sex not to read such flimsy works, it is to induce them to read something superiour; for I coincide in opinion with a sagacious man, who, having a daughter and niece under his care, pursued a very different plan with each.

The niece, who had considerable abilities, had, before she was left to his guardianship, been indulged in desultory reading. Her he endeavoured to lead, and did lead to history and moral essays; but his daughter, whom a fond weak mother had indulged, and who consequently was averse to every thing like application, he allowed to read novels: and used to justify his conduct by saying, that if she ever attained a relish for reading them, he should have some foundation to work upon; and that erroneous opinions were better than none at all.

In fact the female mind has been so totally neglected, that knowledge was only to be acquired from this muddy source, till from reading novels some women of superiour talents learned to despise them.

The best method, I believe, that can be adopted to correct a fondness for novels is to ridicule them: not indiscriminately, for then it would have little effect; but, if a judicious person, with some turn for humour, would read several to a young girl, and point out both by tones, and apt comparisons with pathetic[5] incidents and heroic characters in history how foolishly and ridiculously they caricatured human nature, just opinions might be substituted instead of romantic sentiments.

In one respect, however, the majority of both sexes resemble, and equally show a want of taste and modesty. Ignorant women, forced to be chaste to preserve their reputation, allow their imagination to revel in the unnatural and meretricious scenes sketched by the novel writers of the day, slighting as insipid the sober dignity and matron graces of history[6] whilst men carry the same vitiated taste into life, and fly for

---

5. Stirring.
6. "I am not now alluding to that superiority of mind which leads to the creation of ideal beauty, when he, surveyed with a penetrating eye, appears a tragicomedy, in which little can be seen to satisfy the heart without the help of fancy" [Wollstonecraft's note]. "He" refers to the superior person, presumably an artist or poet.

amusement to the wanton, from the unsophisticated charms of virtue, and the grave respectability of sense.

Besides, the reading of novels makes women, and particularly ladies of fashion, very fond of using strong expressions and superlatives in conversation; and, though the dissipated artificial life which they lead prevents their cherishing any strong legitimate passion, the language of passion in affected tones slips for ever from their glib tongues, and every trifle produces those phosphoric bursts which only mimic in the dark the flame of passion.

1742

Literature of the Nineteenth Century

"There can be no question that the present epoch is initiating an empire of the higher reason, of arts, affections, aspirations; and for that epoch the genius of woman has been reserved," declared Thomas Wentworth Higginson in 1859. The editor of the *Atlantic Monthly* and the sometime mentor of the American poet Emily Dickinson, Higginson was neither alone nor eccentric in holding such a belief. For both in England and America the nineteenth century saw unprecedented changes in the conditions of women's lives, as well as the formation, for the first time, of a powerful female literary tradition. Battling for the vote, demanding the right to own property and retain custody of their children after divorce, entering institutions of higher education, studying to be physicians and nurses, lawyers and journalists, forming trade unions, establishing businesses, and writing best sellers, women both at home and abroad had become so dramatically visible that by the end of the century the so-called Woman Question—the issue of just what woman's "place" ought to be in a proper society—had begun to obsess a startling range of thinkers. That for three quarters of a century, one woman—Queen Victoria—had occupied a place of extraordinary international significance may have added to the intensity with which such matters were discussed, for, though she was no feminist, the increasingly bulky figure of the queen loomed ever larger as the age progressed.

The nineteenth century was in any case an era of remarkable, even shocking cultural transformation. In London for Victoria's 1897 Diamond Jubilee, sixty years after she had ascended the throne in 1837, the American writer Mark Twain mused that though "British history is two thousand years old . . . in a good many ways the world has moved farther ahead since the Queen was born than it moved in all the rest of the two thousand put together." His observation applied with special force to the "moves ahead" experienced or imagined for the first time by women. Yet those particular changes were inextricably related to more general changes. As the feminist historian Ray Strachey wrote in *The Cause* (1928), her account of the British struggle for female emancipation, "The true history of the Woman's Movement is the whole history of the nineteenth century; nothing which occurred in those years could be irrelevant to the great social change which was going on and nothing was without its share of influence upon it." No doubt she was referring to exactly the kinds of sociocultural shifts Twain himself was contemplating: revolutionary upheaval, industrialization, imperialist expansion, political reform, and the so-called disappearance of God.

Revolutionary Ideologies

The eighteenth century had ended with two revolutions that radically redefined Western politics. The American Revolution (1776) revised the relationship between the Old World and the New. The French Revolution (1789), at least partly influenced by recent events in North America, brought the threat of such changes dramatically, and in the end bloodily, home to Europe. Together, the two revolutions reminded both the ruling class and the intellectual class whom the French called the "third estate" that old hierarchies were inexorably disintegrating. Both the middle class (rising merchants and professionals) and the proletariat (the peasant and working classes) were no longer willing to acquiesce in a system that taxed or oppressed them while denying them the power to make significant decisions about their own futures. Though the American Revolution has been seen by some commentators as upper-middle-class or even aristocratic in its origins while the French Revolution seems to many historians to represent a more genuine rising of "the people," both events have in common an ideology based for the first time on a passionately articulated vision of what Enlightenment thinkers from the French Jean Jacques Rousseau to the American Tom Paine called "the Rights of Man."

To men of letters, such a vision was profoundly inspiring, so that they greeted, in William Blake's phrases, the "stiff shudderings" that "shook the heavenly thrones" of European tradition with outbursts of enthusiasm. Blake himself acclaimed the passing of the old order and the coming of the new, while William Wordsworth, describing the hopes for social metamorphosis that had been aroused in the early days of the uprising in France, recalled that "bliss was it in that dawn to be alive/But to be young was very heaven." Though these and other writers were later to be in various degrees disillusioned by the failures of both revolutions to live up to the great expectations they had elicited, the common ideology that both events dramatized was, as we shall see, to be profoundly influential throughout the nineteenth century and up to our own day, not only on middle-of-the-road political movements like the one that led to the first Reform Act of 1832 but on more radical movements like chartism, abolitionism, and women's suffrage.

Industrialization and Its Implications

What equally, and just as urgently, impelled these movements, however, was a very different kind of revolution: the so-called Industrial Revolution. As early as the mid-eighteenth century, methods of manufacturing had begun to become more technologically sophisticated, especially in England and particularly in the production of textiles, one of the country's major industries. By the 1760s, the invention of the steam engine and the spinning jenny had pointed the way to an age when the work of spinning and weaving would go on in large centralized factories rather than individual cottages and when such work would require ever larger amounts of coal to fire the engines that drove increasingly complex machines. At the same time, the English Enclosure Acts of the mid-eighteenth century had transformed communally worked lands into private agricultural businesses, forcing many small farmers to migrate to urban centers, where they joined the new class of industrial laborers required by the burgeoning factory system, while the opening of textile mills, paper factories, and other industries had begun to create a similar working class in America.

The striking metamorphoses of both England and America (but, again, especially England) from essentially agrarian nations to modern states commanding all the resources of power looms, printing presses, railroads, steamships, and telegraphs fostered a virtual religion of progress which was exhilarating to many, not least to a number of writers. In 1833, for instance, William Wordsworth, the sometime celebrant of pastoral nature, wrote a sonnet praising the wonders of *Steamboats, Viaducts, and Railways*, while in *Locksley Hall* (1842) Alfred, Lord Tennyson created a speaker who glorified the achievements of "men the workers, ever reaping something new." Similarly, some decades later, Walt Whitman in America wrote a paean *To a Locomotive in Winter* (1876), in which he exulted in the great engine as a "type of the modern—emblem of motion and power," and his reclusive contemporary Emily Dickinson admitted to similar feelings about what was then called "the iron horse," confiding that "I like to see it lap the Miles" (c. 1862). In articulating such sentiments, moreover, these writers were simply expressing a prevailing cultural attitude.

Soon enough, however, the industrial "progress" such poems celebrated began to reveal its darker side. Quite early in the nineteenth century, sensitive observers had become aware of the dreadful conditions under which many of their contemporaries lived and worked. In the first decade of the new age, William Blake had prophetically inveighed against "dark Satanic Mills," the products of an unbridled rationalism that he saw threatening to disfigure "England's green and pleasant Land." The meaning of such mills, however, was more forcefully brought home to those who labored in them for what were practically starvation wages as well as to those whose traditional employments as handloom weavers, spinners, dyers, and other craftsworkers were annihilated by their technology. In the teens, a number of workers, both those who were exploited by the new system and those who were dispossessed by it, tried sporadically to unite, in some cases actually attempting to destroy the machines that were oppressing them, in others holding mass meetings to demand reform. But their efforts were unsuccessful. The policy known as "laissez faire" (let it be), advocated by many contemporary thinkers, held that socioeconomic factors should and would adjust themselves without governmental intervention so that all would turn out for the best in the end, and conservative governments in both England and America were committed to that policy. In 1812, England's House of Lords passed a bill requiring the death penalty for anyone who destroyed the apparatus used in the stocking industry, and in 1819 British troops charged a huge but peaceful crowd that had gathered at St. Peter's Fields, Manchester, to press for reform, killing nine and injuring hundreds of others.

By the 1840s, the situation in England, particularly in the industrial north, was appalling: in the slums of Manchester and Liverpool, hungry families were packed into filthy hovels; five-year-old children and pregnant women worked like mules for fifteen-hour days, dragging loads of coal in the mines outside Nottingham; London seamstresses toiled for eighteen hours at a time during the height of the four-month social "season" and starved for the rest of the year; for workers who inhaled the polluted air of badly ventilated mills and factories the death rate from tuberculosis was double the national average; and protective tariffs known as the "Corn Laws" kept foreign grain from entering the country so that the price of the bread made from English wheat could be inflated to exorbitant levels.

Friedrich Engels's radical *Condition of the Working Class in England* (1845) meticulously documented many of these problems, but even an "establishment" politician like Benjamin Disraeli raised his voice in dismay, arguing in the subtitle of his 1845 novel *Sybil* that there were really "Two Nations" in England—the rich and the poor. For of course what made the situation of the workers even more poignant was the fact that their labor had contributed to the steady rise of a newly rich group of capitalist entrepreneurs—tradesmen and factory owners, stockbrokers and professional managers—who were anything but hungry. Prosperous and often piously smug, it was this comfortable middle class which set the tone of nineteenth-century society in both England and America, decorously imitating what they believed to be the manners of the aristocracy, furnishing their parlors with ornate *bric-à-brac*, dressing their women in expensively complicated costumes—and, more often than not, ignoring or scorning the sufferings of the poor.

If conditions for the workers in the United States were not quite so extreme as they were in England, that was because the possibility of westward migration often acted as a kind of escape valve. Nevertheless, even as it created a newly wealthy middle class in centers like Boston and New York, industrialization took its toll in Britain's former colony, particularly in the factory towns of New England, where workers in the textile and paper industries, among others—frequently young girls from poor rural families or recent refugees from the great Irish potato famine—labored from sunup to sundown for meager wages. Not surprisingly, then, many writers on both sides of the Atlantic indited passionate protests against the abuses fostered by the new technology and by the capitalist system that sponsored it, decrying the powerlessness and pain of the poor as well as the insensitivity and materialism of the rich. As early as 1819, Percy Bysshe Shelley had responded to the massacre at St. Peter's Fields with a hortatory song to the *Men of England*, in which he demanded, "Wherefore plough / For the lords who lay ye low?" As time passed and conditions deteriorated further, other writers took up the theme, if not quite so radically. Novels like Charles Dickens's *Bleak House* (1853), along with Elizabeth Gaskell's *Mary Barton* (1848) and Charlotte Brontë's *Shirley* (1849), incisively portrayed both the wretchedness and the rebellion of the laboring classes, and tales like Herman Melville's *The Paradise of Bachelors and the Tartarus of Maids* (1855) set the comfortably "heavenly" lives of the wealthy—in this case a group of bachelors dwelling in London's Inns of Court—against the metaphorically infernal existence of New England factory girls.

Imperialism and Reform

If both a religion of progress and a reaction against technology's discontents were contradictory consequences of the Industrial Revolution, a third was even more problematic. Creating a need for fresh markets as well as a demand for raw materials that could not be supplied at home, the new age of the machine inevitably led to that definitive expansion of the British Empire into "underdeveloped" parts of the globe which was called imperialism. Africa, Egypt, India —all previously colonized, to be sure—now became crucially interdependent segments of a new international organism, administered in London, Cairo, Calcutta, and elsewhere by a class of bureaucrats who felt it was, in the words of the late-nineteenth-century writer Rudyard Kipling, "the white man's burden" to bring civilization to supposedly barbaric natives. Even those who had expressed doubts about the efficacy of nineteenth-century progress often pledged allegiance to this enterprise; as the speaker of Tennyson's *Locksley Hall* declared, "Better fifty years of Europe / Than a cycle of Cathay."

At the same time, the only recently "United" States, themselves former colonies, were engaging in similar efforts of expansion and colonization. Following the eighteenth-century English philosopher George Berkeley's dictum that "Westward the course of Empire takes its way," Americans of European descent set out to conquer the wild frontiers of the New World they saw as their own, in the process exterminating or subordinating countless native-American tribes. Furthermore, to acquire laborers to work the vast cotton and tobacco plantations they had established in the South, American settlers purchased black slaves from traders who ruthlessly raided the coast of West Africa to steal human "raw materials" in a grim apotheosis of the imperialist impulse. By 1800, such activity had of course been going on for more than a century, and though in 1808 slave trading had been officially discontinued by both England and the United States, the practice continued unabated: traders often "dumped" their manacled cargo (sometimes as many as five hundred to seven hundred and fifty men and women) overboard if a patrol ship were sighted. By 1830, scholars estimate that there were approximately two million "assimilated" slaves—Africans who had learned to speak English and to do plantation work—in the United States; by 1860, when the Civil War began, there were almost four million, and in a number of southern states, such as Virginia and North Carolina, the "major cash crop," as the historian Eleanor Flexner has remarked, "was not cotton, or tobacco—but slaves," for black laborers were bred like cattle in order to reproduce more laborers, and young women in particular were prized for their "generating qualities."

Given the predatory impulses on which the imperialist imperatives of expansion and exploitation were based, it was probably inevitable that they should have triggered wars and uprisings in Europe, North America, and elsewhere. These ranged from struggles between competing imperial powers (like the Crimean War of 1850–1853, in which England and France attempted to wrest control of portions of the disintegrating Ottoman Empire from Russia) to wars of colonial conquest (like the so-called Indian wars in the American West) and native insurrections (like the sporadic mutinies in nineteenth-century British India and the continuing battle for home rule in colonial Ireland). But perhaps the most dramatic of these conflicts was the American Civil War (1861–1865), which combined elements of several different kinds of struggles, representing at the same time a war of liberation for the enslaved blacks and a conflict of economic interests between two quasi-imperial powers, the industrial North and the agrarian South.

Not surprisingly, the Civil War was preceded and accompanied by a reiteration of the ideology of human rights that was earlier associated with the American and French Revolutions, an ideology that was rapidly to become crucial to leaders of liberation movements in colonized countries around the world and to the founders of the British and American women's suffrage movements. Expressing their horror at what Melville called "man's foulest crime"—Negro slavery—white writers of both sexes on both sides of the Atlantic, from Henry David Thoreau and John Stuart Mill to Walt Whitman, from Harriet Beecher Stowe and Louisa May Alcott to Elizabeth Barrett Browning, argued for human dignity, freedom, and self-determination, while a new generation of black writers and speakers, including Frederick Douglass, Sojourner Truth, Linda Brent, Harriet E. Wilson, and Frances E. W. Harper, arose in the United States to testify from personal experience about the iniquity of slavery. Their commitment to justice was finally rewarded when, after a tragic and bloody five-year struggle, the Union defeated the Confederacy, and the Congress of the newly re-United States enacted the Thirteenth Amendment to the Constitution, which permanently outlawed slavery, thereby freeing all slaves and, within a few years, leading to the Fifteenth Amendment, which enfranchised all black men.

Dramatic as it was, however, the widespread protest of intellectuals against slavery and the major constitutional amendments to which it led were symptomatic of quieter protests that were also based on the ideology of human rights and that fostered important, if less sweeping, political reforms throughout the nineteenth century. Chief among these were the moves in England to extend the vote to middle- and working-class men and to repeal the Corn Laws. In 1832, the first Reform Bill was passed, enfranchising all men owning property worth ten pounds or more in annual rent; in 1867, after much agitation from a working-class party known as the Chartists (because they proposed a "People's Charter" allowing for universal suffrage), a second Reform Bill was enacted, which in effect extended the right to vote to all English men; and in 1846 the Corn Laws were repealed, reducing tariffs on imported grain and alleviating the inflationary conditions that had made the lives of the poor not only harsh but hungry.

The Disappearance of God

The agitations and anxieties that surrounded such vast social changes soon took their toll on the spiritual serenity of those bred in an old order that was rapidly giving way to a new one. As factories darkened the landscape of England and battles of "brother against brother" raged in the valleys of America, it no longer seemed possible to share the philosophical confidence in the destined progress of humanity that had marked the thinking of the eighteenth century. Indeed, despite the proclamations of some nineteenth-century optimists that, as one of Robert Browning's characters observes, "the best is yet to be," and the insistence of others that social and industrial advances sped humanity ever closer to what Tennyson called the "one far-off divine event, / To which the whole creation moves," to many thinkers it no longer seemed possible to believe in God or in the divine at all. Writing in *The Scholar Gypsy* (1853) about "this strange disease of modern life," Matthew Arnold warned of "the infection of our mental strife," and in *Dover Beach* (1867) he described the "melancholy, long, withdrawing roar" of "the Sea of Faith." He was responding to what the critic J.

Hillis Miller has called the "disappearance of God" from the intellectual horizon of many contemporary thinkers.

There were, it is true, a number of figures who tried desperately to revive and revise old creeds, including American Transcendentalists like Emerson and Thoreau, who substituted a belief in the luminous beneficence of Nature for more orthodox faiths, and British conservatives like John Henry, Cardinal Newman, who argued for the redemptive powers of a return to Roman Catholic traditions. But many poets were haunted by a nightmarish refrain like that of Arthur Hugh Clough's *Dipsychus* (1865)—"Ting, ting, there is no God; ting, ting— / Dong, there is no God; dong . . . ."—and they were convinced that the supposed piety of their more conventional middle-class countrymen was merely hypocritical, even mercenary in its motives. What intensified the skepticism of such thinkers was precisely the industrial "progress" of which so many nineteenth-century citizens were proud. For more often than not such advances issued in social and scientific research that subverted the very foundations of traditional faith. The "condition of the working class" as described by Engels, after all, had inexorably led to the *Communist Manifesto* (1847), coauthored by Engels and Karl Marx, a document that severely questioned what had once seemed to be the almost divine rights of rulers and property owners. Similarly, the empirical impulses that fostered the invention of steamships and railways led just as inexorably to the discoveries of Charles Darwin, whose *Origin of Species* (1859) definitively supplanted the old idea of a seven-day divine creation of Adam and Eve with the new and unnerving concept of human evolution from lower organisms. Looking at a world in which a man seemed no "higher" than an animal, and men treated each other (as well as women and children) like animals, it is no wonder that Tennyson had an anxious vision of "Nature red in tooth and claw." Though the Victorian Poet Laureate (official national poet) himself recovered from his moment of doubt, many of his contemporaries could not free themselves from such pessimism and skepticism. Thus the changes that Mark Twain observed—the "move[s] ahead" the world had made in Queen Victoria's lifetime—were both radical and radically unsettling.

WOMAN'S SPHERE

For women, though the nineteenth century's startling changes often triggered considerable unease, such shifts were always significant and frequently beneficial. In 1800, however, eight years after the publication of Mary Wollstonecraft's *A Vindication of the Rights of Woman* (1792), nothing could have seemed more unlikely than the possibility that for this "epoch the genius of woman has been reserved." Indeed, despite the new conceptions of human rights dramatized by the American and French Revolutions and the arguments for women's rights eloquently advanced by Wollstonecraft and earlier by writers such as Hannah More and Anne Finch, almost all women were still confined by law and custom in a secondary, private "sphere." Worse still, even some of the most liberal thinkers of the age helped formulate a concept of a "woman's sphere" that was in its way no less oppressive than the misogyny of medieval monks and the antifeminism of Augustan wits.

The Ideology of Femininity

Ironically enough, in the middle of the eighteenth century the French philosopher Jean Jacques Rousseau, whose demands for human liberty had been influential upon a number of movements for political reform, forcefully articulated some of the most restrictive tenets of what can be called the nineteenth century's ideology of femininity, declaring in *Émile* (1762) that "the whole education of women ought to be relative to men. To please them, to be useful to them, to make themselves loved and honored by them, to educate them when young, to care for them when grown, to counsel them, to console them, and to make life sweet and agreeable to them—these are the duties of women at all times, and what should be taught them from their infancy." The ideal women he thus envisioned—a pure, submissive, decorous, and even angelic creature —was only one particularly notable representative of a standard against which every middle- and upper-class woman's conduct was measured, and other writers, female as well as male, elaborated upon the virtues of such an ideal.

In 1844, for instance, the selflessness of the model woman was discussed by the English writer Mrs. Sarah Ellis, who admonished readers of her conduct books (volumes of advice on manners and morals) that " 'what shall I do to gratify myself—to be admired—or to vary the tenor of my existence?' are not the questions which a woman of right feelings asks on first waking to the avocations of the day. Much more congenial to the highest attributes of woman's character are inquiries such as these: 'How shall I endeavor through this day to turn the time, the health and the means permitted me to enjoy to the best account?' " In 1854, in a long and very popular poem about femininity with the telling title *The Angel in the House*, Coventry Patmore described such selflessness more extravagantly, casting it in terms that suggest self-sacrifice, even self-immolation:

> Man must be pleased; but him to please
> Is woman's pleasure; down the gulf
> Of his condoled necessities
> She casts her best, she flings herself. . . .

In fact, for many writers, such a self-sacrificing and angelic woman became the paradigm of renunciatory Christian love. Working out of a tradition that went back at least as far as the German poet-novelist Goethe, whose Faust (in *Faust*, 1808/1832) is redeemed by the "Eternal Feminine" (*das Ewige Weibliche*) which draws man's mind to "higher" things, such thinkers employed a rhetoric drawn from religion to characterize the good mother as a kind of Madonna and the dutiful maiden as a virginal angel. Significantly, as the critic Nina Auerbach has observed, it was only in the nineteenth century that painters began regularly portraying angels as female; perhaps even more significantly, as Auerbach has also noted, the Victorian cult of the "angel in the house" can be associated with the "disappearance of God" we discussed earlier, with its theological imagery arising in part from a displacement of traditional metaphors for the sacred onto the secular figure of the woman.

Where some writers characterized the feminine ideal through a vocabulary drawn from religion, others used a rhetoric of chivalry. If for such thinkers the model woman was not an "angel," she was at least a "queen." John Ruskin's *Of Queens' Gardens* (1865), with its assertion that woman's "great function is Praise; she enters into no contest but infallibly judges the crown of contest," implicitly alludes to medieval jousts and tournaments to characterize the regal lady whose "intellect is not for invention or creation" but who "rules" man's home so that it is "the place of Peace." Just a few years later the American writer Louisa May Alcott would argue in similar terms in *Little Women* (1869) that "a woman's happiest kingdom is home."

Whether a selfless angel or a serene queen, the model woman was often seen by both British and American ideologists of femininity as delicate, frail, ethereal. To certify her spirituality and refinement, she must look and act like a fragile creature. Instructions as to how a young girl, or even an older woman, was to manage such a task often ranged from the ridiculous to the bizarre. Marriageable maidens on both sides of the Atlantic drank vinegar to cultivate an "interesting" pallor, tight-laced themselves into narrow corsets so as to achieve an uncannily slender waist (18 inches was the ideal), and practiced the "art" of fainting to remind beaux of their delicacy. More problematic still, many medical men and laymen believed that a "good"—that is, a well-bred middle- or upper-class—woman was essentially passionless: if men were beasts ruled by sexual desire, their pure wives and daughters knew nothing of such matters. To be sure, as the historian Peter Gay has lately documented, a number of nineteenth-century women both experienced and expressed erotic pleasure. Nevertheless, in public it was generally agreed that on her wedding night, the angelic virgin should in one way or another behave as Queen Victoria was said to have: close her eyes "and think of England." As for childbirth, the details of confinement and delivery constituted a darkly secret knowledge that was to be confined only to those who had already delivered; and even for such initiates they were "functions" not to be "dwelt upon" at any length, certainly not in public.

At its most extreme, this nineteenth-century ideal of the frail, even sickly female ultimately led to a glorification of the dead or dying woman. The most fruitful subject for literature, announced the American romancer Edgar Allan Poe in 1846, is "the death . . . of a beautiful woman," and four years later, in *The Blessed Damozel* (1850), the English poet Dante Gabriel Rossetti offered a postmortem vision of a seductive angel-lady leaning over the golden walls of heaven and yearning toward her earthly lover. But if dead women were fascinating, dying girl-children were even more enthralling: the extravagantly sentimental death scenes of Charles Dickens's "Little Nell" (in *The Old Curiosity Shop*, 1840) and Harriet Beecher Stowe's "Little Eva" (in *Uncle Tom's Cabin*, 1851) are only two examples of brilliantly morbid melodramas which center on such figures. What these episodes seem to do, however, is to bring to the surface an extraordinary imperative that underlay much of the nineteenth-century ideology of femininity: in one way or another, woman must be "killed" into passivity in order for her to acquiesce in what Rousseau and others considered her duty of self-abnegation "relative to men."

But what of women who refused to be passive, or, just as problematic, were forced by circumstance into "unwomanly" activity? For nineteenth-century ideologists of femininity, these fell into two categories: subordinate working-class women and insubordinate middle- or upper-class ladies. About the first category, most ideologists had comparatively little to say: although the working-class woman could never be a lady—and indeed the verbal distinction between "woman" and "lady" was a crucial one—at her best she could reflect the lady's virtues. If she was neither angelically delicate nor gracefully regal, she could still mimic the characteristics of such figures by making herself into a kind of proletarian Madonna who submerged her own interests in those of husband and children, as Rousseau had advised the more educated woman to do. Were she single, however, her situation was far more perilous, for whether she worked on a farm or in a factory, as a kitchen helper or a parlormaid, moralists feared that she was constantly in danger of becoming a "fallen woman," a prostitute. Dante Gabriel Rossetti's 1870 poem *Jenny* brilliantly articulated the horror felt by a representative middle-class speaker at the "poor flower" of "lazy laughing, languid Jenny, / Fond of a kiss and fond of a guinea," a golden-haired whore whose favors he himself has just enjoyed. If the idealized lady was in some sense "sick"—fragile, pale, ethereal—her fallen contemporary was figuratively sickening: her "beauty goads / A man tonight to think of toads!" Indeed, even the virtue of the lady is finally put in question by Jenny's troublesome vice. Though the young prostitute is "like a rose shut in a book / In which pure women may not look," the speaker confesses his secret belief that she and her respectable counterpart are really sisters under the skin: "Of the same lump (it has been said) / For honour and dishonour made, / Two sister vessels."

The anxious notion that the angel and the whore might be counterparts was a crucial one. Rossetti implicitly conceded that Jenny and others of her class may have been forced to "fall" by poverty or ignorance, but what of those who "fell" by their own free will? More particularly, what of those who fell not merely by demanding the sexual liberty that the Victorian double standard gave to men and forbade to women but by asserting just those emotional and intellectual needs which Rousseau thought should be sacrificed to the claims of husbands, fathers, and sons? As if to warn against such female insubordination, nineteenth-century novelists and poets, in both England and America, frequently counterpointed glowing portraits of angelic ladies with fearful depictions of demonic madwomen and murderesses, or, less extravagantly but just as censoriously, biting portrayals of scheming sorceresses, social-climbers, and female intellectuals.

Thackeray's delineation of the ambitious Becky Sharp in *Vanity Fair* (1848) was a fairly typical (if unusually successful) example of the way in which a number of nineteenth-century writers perceived a sharp-witted woman's refusal to be selfless as ultimately pernicious. Paralleling the figure of Amelia Sedley, an almost maddeningly angelic heroine (at whom Thackeray also pokes fun), Becky is an apparently realistic character, embedded in the scrupulously observed minutiae of Victorian society. Yet her shrewd charm cracks open when Thackeray sardonically reminds his readers that he hasn't "showed the monster's [i.e. Becky's] hideous tail above water." More explicitly fantastic portraits of unladylike ladies counterpointed pictures of ethereal maidens to make similar points in other novels. The passionate self-will of Zenobia, for instance, the dark heroine of Hawthorne's *Blithedale Romance* (1852), is unfavorably compared to the spiritual self-abnegation of her half-sister Priscilla, and the first of these women is punished with a hideous death by drowning when she fails to accept her sometime lover's dictum that "woman is a monster . . . without man as her acknowledged principal." Similarly, Charles Dickens's fallen aristocrat Lady Dedlock, is contrasted to her illegitimate but virtuous daughter, Esther Summerson, and horribly murdered in *Bleak House* (1853); the reader is clearly meant to understand that her punishment appropriately fits her early crime of sexual indulgence. Fictions by women were also haunted by such double images of female self-assertion and self-abnegation: Charlotte Brontë's Bertha Mason Rochester, the madwoman in *Jane Eyre* (1847), is the counterpart of the novel's decorous heroine, Jane, and Elizabeth Barrett Browning's Lady Waldemar, the villainness of *Aurora Leigh* (1857), is set against the poem's noble protagonist, Aurora. For both sexes, these sometimes stereotypical figures originated in an ideology of femininity that stipulated the moral possibilities of "woman's sphere" by defining conflicting extremes: angel and monster, virgin and whore.

The Reality of Female Life

Were Victorian wives and daughters in fact angels and queens, monsters and madwoman? A reading of the literature of the period would at first suggest that such sentimental or melodramatic figures were to be found in every other British and American drawing room. Yet although a few women no doubt tried to replicate some of these fictional prototypes in their own lives, it is unlikely that many succeeded, given the intransigent facts of their social, economic, and cultural status. Qualified, to be sure, by class and (in the United States) race, the female situation in England and America continued to be as problematic as ever for most of the century.

Despite her ostensible power to rule, even the most queenly or angelic married lady had in fact few legal rights. On her marriage, as her ancestresses had from the Middle Ages on, she still became what the eighteenth-century English jurist Sir William Blackstone, echoing earlier legal commentators, described as a *feme covert* (a "covered" woman). "By marriage," Blackstone declared in a magisterial passage that was repeatedly cited throughout the nineteenth century, "the very being or legal existence of a woman is suspended, or at least it is incorporated or consolidated into that of the husband, under whose wing, protection, and cover she performs everything, and she is therefore called in our law a feme covert." Such an obliteration of legal reality, or "civil death," as it was sometimes termed, was also the lot of American married women, for the traditions of English common law were long the foundations of colonial jurisprudence.

Practically speaking, the consequences of such a definition of the wife's status were drastic indeed. In the year 1800 and long into the century that followed, a married woman could not own property, even what she herself might have brought to the marriage or inherited after she was wed. Furthermore, her husband could, and sometimes did, will his estate—including what had been her own inheritance—away from her. Finally, if he died intestate (without having made a will), her rights in the property they might have jointly accumulated were minimal; Eleanor Flexner has reported that in New York State, for instance, a widow was allowed nothing but the family Bible and a few other books, some cattle and household goods, and, no matter how many children she had, "one table, six chairs, six knives and forks, six tea-cups and saucers, one sugar dish, one milk-pot, one tea-pot, and six spoons." In addition, a husband's power over his wife's property extended to power over her earnings, such as they were.

As for a woman's children, her husband had sole rights in their guardianship if the couple were separated for any reason, including his moral turpitude. Nor was it easy for wives to escape even the worst husbands: until past the middle of the nineteenth century, divorce was virtually unobtainable in both England and America, except by extraordinary legislative or parliamentary decrees (almost all of which were enacted at the behest of husbands), and a woman did not even have an inalienable entitlement to her own physical liberty; as Ray Strachey points out, in England "the right of a man to imprison his wife in his own house was not questioned till 1891." Finally, the married woman's moral as well as legal obliteration was signaled by the fact that until fairly late in the nineteenth century she could neither sue nor be sued: her husband was held responsible for all her acts and debts as if she were minor, defective, or mentally ill.

In addition to legal denials and constraints, severe restrictions were imposed upon women by education and social custom. On the face of it, Rousseau's prescription that a girl be taught to subordinate her interests to men's should not necessarily entail the relegation of young women to virtual ignorance. To converse intelligently with gentlemen, after all, it might seem that a girl would have to be taught history, mathematics, classics—all subjects her brothers had studied and of which presumably they might like to speak. In practice, though, middle- and upper-class female education meant a minimal training in modern languages, a study of drawing or water-coloring, embroidery, and music, and a strict training in "propriety," which, wrote the influential educator Hannah More in 1799, "is to a woman what the great Roman critic says action is to an orator: it is the first, the second, the third requisite."

As for more serious subjects, such fields as classics or mathematics were considered absolutely improper for women, though a few, like Elizabeth Barrett Browning and George Eliot, were privileged to study them on their own. Rather, to complete the lady's training and render her figure "elegant," she was often strapped to a "backboard"—an iron collar fastened to a board and fixed over the shoulders—for many hours every day, while her less aristocratic but almost equally genteel middle-class sister might be obliged to spend many tedious hours embroidering homiletic samplers and reading aloud from the Bible. How a spirited upper-class girl responded to such an education is made clear in Barrett Browning's *Aurora Leigh*, where the poet-heroine describes the "cage-bird life" for which her aristocratic English aunt educated her. Similarly, the reaction of a lively middle-class girl to the lugubrious education in "propriety" offered by a charitable boarding school is dramatized in the great Lowood episode of Charlotte Brontë's *Jane Eyre*, in which pedagogical humiliations that the Brontë sisters themselves had to endure are vividly and movingly recounted.

Where law and education restricted many possibilities of intellectual development for nineteenth-century ladies, custom closed off almost all the rest. The very doctrine of woman's "sphere," for instance, implied that there was an almost unbridgeable gulf between the public world of politics and business, ruled by men, and the domestic world of the household, ostensibly "ruled" but, more accurately, inhabited by women. "Man for the field and woman for the hearth,/Man for the sword and for the needle she;/Man with the head and woman with the heart,/Man to command and woman to obey," intones a solidly old-fashioned king in Tennyson's *The Princess* (1847), and his precepts aptly summarize the guidelines by which middle- and upper-class married women lived: a lady could not go out alone, especially not in the city and certainly not at night; her days were to be spent supervising her servants, doing needlework, and making or receiving visits; her mind was to be occupied largely with fashion and society and perhaps to some small extent with charitable projects.

To be sure, she did have to bear children, and she often bore a great many. Despite efforts by a few radical physicians on both sides of the Atlantic to educate the public about birth control, contraceptive methods were still primitive as well as obscure in the nineteenth century, so that, if in theory a lady was an angel, she was often in practice transformed by multiple pregnancies into a "poor animal," as Jane Austen pityingly described one young female relative. Once her children were born, however, and if they survived—for infant mortality rates remained high throughout the century—they were handed over to nurses and governesses who did the major work of raising them, depriving the lady of at least one meaningful function she might have had. As the Industrial Revolution progressed and more newly wealthy entrepreneurial families rose into the middle and upper classes, moreover, the division of woman's sphere from man's became increasingly sharp. With more money to pay more servants, the lady's household duties virtually disappeared, and with man's work —once done in or near the home and shared by wives on farms or in family trades—now located in offices and factories, the two spheres were geographically as well as socially separated.

No wonder, then, that Florence Nightingale complained in 1852 that "women's life is spent in pastime, men's in business," adding bitterly:

> A married woman's life consists in superintending what she does not know how to do. . . . [She] is to direct the servants, who are to provide conveniences and luxuries not thought of formerly. She has never learnt, and does not know how, but she must take care to provide them. She must superintend the nurse, and the governess of her children, though she knows nothing and has learnt nothing of the nurse's work. And the governess . . . what is she to do? *She* must direct the characters of her pupils. How is she fit for it? . . . Over her, so little prepared, the mother so little prepared is to preside.

Nightingale's mention of the "little prepared" governess reminds us that it was not only married upper- and middle-class women who suffered from the constraints of law, education, and custom: the situation of the unmarried woman of "gentle" birth was equally difficult, if not more so. She could only comparatively rarely, and in unusual circumstances, inherit property. Most fortunes in England (and America as well) devolved upon eldest sons, and in England great estates were frequently "entailed" upon the male line, so that in the absence of sons some distant male relative would inherit a man's property—precisely the situation which triggers the comic action of Jane Austen's *Pride and Prejudice* (1813). Under the circumstances, it is not surprising that most women would prefer the subjugation of matrimony to the uncertainties of spinsterhood, not surprising that mothers struggled, often desperately, to further their daughters' chances on the "marriage market." No matter how gentle her birth, a portion-less young woman who did not wed was frequently obliged to live as a maiden aunt on the good will of male relations or married sisters, or she survived on a meager income as what Jane Austen sardonically called a "ridiculous old maid, the proper sport of boys and girls."

Worse still, if she had neither charitable relations nor a modest income of her own, such a woman was generally obliged to turn to the only genteel careers open to her: in England, governessing, and in England and America, school-teaching. Ill-paid, badly trained, and overworked, both governesses and school-teachers often lived lives of quiet desperation, dreaming of matrimonial rescue. The governess's lot was especially difficult because, while the schoolteacher at least had some authority in her classroom, the governess, living with a single family, was continually subject to the whims of her employers, who often in-sisted that in addition to her instructional tasks, she care for infants, do much of the family sewing, and perform countless other miscellaneous chores. What made the governess's situation even more problematic was the fact that she fre-quently suffered from an anxiety that one recent social historian has termed "status incongruence": since she was herself of "good birth," she felt equal and akin to the family in which she lived, yet she was, after all, as much a servant as any kitchen maid. A contemporary observer commented that though "the Governess is a class rapidly on the increase" because such employment is "the only recourse left to young girls in the highest ranks of society who are forced to earn their living," the sorrowful practitioner of that profession "may be known at a glance from her plain and quiet style of dress" and because "on her face [there] is a fixed sad look of despair."

One reason why the governess represented a class "on the increase" was the phenomenon of so-called "redundant women" in Victorian England. Histo-rians speculate that the emigration of large numbers of single men to America and to the Commonwealth colonies had left nineteeth-century England with a disproportionate mass of single women: according to the Victorian social critic H. R. Greg, thirty out of every one hundred British women were unmarried in 1851, and twelve were widows; altogether, he estimated that 1,148,000 women in England and Wales were, as he put it, "unnaturally" single. The problem of such female "redundancy" was endlessly discussed in newspapers and maga-zines, but according to contemporary statistics at least 25,000 of these hapless "old maids" mournfully resolved their difficulties by becoming governesses.

Much as they may have deviated from the nineteenth-century ideology of femininity, however, the real lives of nineteenth-century upper- and middle-class women did not swerve quite so radically from literary stereotypes as did the lives of their working-class sisters. Whether married or single, working-class women were usually expected, indeed obliged, to labor in both the private and the public spheres. Before the Industrial Revolution, such women had lived hard enough lives—spinning, sewing, cooking, and sharing farm work with their husbands, fathers, or brothers—but after 1800 their situation became even more difficult, in both England and America. Because women were often willing to work for lower wages and longer hours than men, factories in both countries depended heavily on female labor, a fact which aroused considerable male resentment. As the historian Sheila Rowbotham observes, "One of the frequent complaints in the early stages of the Industrial Revolution was that although women and children could find work, the men could not." Whether a husband was employed or unemployed, however, the working-class wife was still his property—and his servant. After long hours of factory work, she still had her domestic duties to do; in addition, if her children were not old enough to go into factories themselves, she had to arrange for their care. Nursing mothers often rushed home during factory breaks to breast-feed their infants, but many, inevitably, weaned their babies as early as they could, feeding them what Rowbotham describes as "watered-down, often infected cow's milk," a formula which accounts, at least in part, for the high infant mortality rate among the working classes.

Women who labored in dressmaking or in the mines struggled with equally harsh conditions. Young seamstresses often worked virtually around the clock during the London season, crowded into dark, ill-ventilated rooms that one contemporary witness described as "worse than in the worst-conducted factories," adding that "the dressmakers themselves state their belief that 'no man could sustain the labor which is imposed on these young and delicate women.'" As for women in the mines, their situation, according to a Mines Commission report (1842), was if anything, more extreme: even in the advanced stages of pregnancy, they "always did the lifting or heavy part of the work, and neither they nor the children [who labored alongside them] were treated like human beings." Testified one woman worker: "I have a belt round my waist and a chain passing between my legs and go on my hands and feet [pulling loads of coal]. . . . I have drawn till I have had the skin off me; the belt and chain is worse when we are in the family way."

Though the working conditions of female domestic servants (of whom there were 750,000 in England alone in 1851) were not so extreme, such conditions too were arduous, marked by low pay, long hours, and little leisure time— usually only one half-day per week. Worse still, of course, were the living and working conditions of black slaves in America. Bred like cattle in order to produce crops of new workers, subject to sexual exploitation and harrassment by their white masters, frequently separated from husbands and children, forced to perform endless hours of unpaid labor in cotton fields and plantation houses, these women were no doubt the most oppressed of all nineteenth-century female workers. Paradoxically, however, such diverse writers as the black memoirist Linda Brent and the white novelist Harriet Beecher Stowe frequently see these women—forced to be single and to sustain families against overwhelming odds—as repositories of strength, even as heroic figures. And indeed, the career of the legendary Harriet Tubman, a former slave who became a "conductor" on the Underground Railroad which funneled Southern blacks to freedom in the North, more than supported such a view. Called "Moses" by her contemporaries, Tubman undertook some nineteen journeys into slave territory and liberated at least three hundred people.

Along with black heroines like Brent's grandmother, Stowe's Eliza, and Harriet Tubman, the only women workers who might seem to have achieved a rough equality with men and some control over their own lives were the pioneer women who labored to settle the American West. These women did work together with their husbands, as agricultural women traditionally had in England, and while they were frequently exhausted by the hardships they encountered, they could at least in some sense reap the rewards of their labor. The French writer Alexis de Tocqueville described one such woman with admiration, praising her energetic offspring as "true children of the wilderness" and noting that "she does not regret what [their upbringing has] cost her." But the American suffrage leader Anna Howard Shaw was less celebratory in her recollection of her own mother's first encounter with the primitive cabin in the backwoods of Michigan where her father (who remained in Massachusetts to work in a textile mill) sent his family: "Something within her seemed to give way and she sank upon the floor. She could not realize . . . that this was really the place father had prepared for us, that here he expected us to live."

If the married lady had no rights, the working-class woman had none either. The wages she earned were, of course, her husband's money, and she had no reciprocal claim on his earnings, nor did she have the right to leave or divorce him. On the contrary; as Ray Strachey reminds us, "If a man was displeased with the way his wife worked for him—or with any other aspect of her conduct —he had a perfect right to beat her with a stick, provided it was not thicker than his own thumb." Moreover, if the lady's education was a training in submissive "propriety," the working-class woman's education—if she had any at all—was a training in industrious submission. In England, parish or "ragged" schools, charitable institutions for poor children, taught girls sewing, knitting, and other household skills, along with just enough reading to enable them to study the Bible; at one such institution, children over five worked from 5 A.M. to 6 P.M. at a "manufactory" and then attended school. Similarly, in America poor girls were expected to sew and knit while their brothers studied arithmetic and other subjects. Moreover, for many girls in both countries—but especially in England—a job as a domestic "apprentice" took the place of formal schooling altogether. Theoretically, such children were being trained to be good servants, but in fact most were simply exploited as household "slaveys," expected at the ages of seven or eight to do a full day's work in the kitchen or the laundry. As for the young black girls who were slaves in America, they generally received no education at all but worked alongside their parents in the cottonfields and cookhouses of the South.

Considering how few attractive vocational or personal alternatives working-class women had in the nineteenth century, it is surprising that more did not "fall," like Rossetti's "languid Jenny," into a life of prostitution. As it was, however, a number did, on both sides of the Atlantic. In the middle of the century, some contemporary observers estimated that there were approximately 50,000 "streetwalkers" in London alone, and proportionally similar numbers may have been concentrated in other urban centers like Edinburgh, New York, Chicago, and New Orleans. The "unskilled daughters of the unskilled classes," as one historian has defined them, these were mostly young women who turned to what was called "the life" when they could not support themselves as seamstresses and domestics, or in the hope—futile, as they usually discovered—of earning extra luxuries and mimicking the glittering fashions of upper-class ladies. Many rapidly contracted syphilis and other venereal diseases; some married and retired or established businesses, including brothels, of their own; few achieved even the small comforts Rossetti characterizes his Jenny as possessing, and fewer still looked as stylish as the heroine of Thomas Hardy's sardonic *The Ruined Maid* (1866), who boasts to a roughly clad country cousin with chapped hands and a sunburnt face that *she* is elegantly dressed and fair-complexioned because she is "ruined."

In fact, tattered and ill, most prostitutes were seen not only as diseased but as a source of disease, and, worse still, every working-class woman was defined as potentially a prostitute. In England in 1864, 1866, and 1869 Parliament passed what were known as the "Contagious Diseases Acts," legislation which empowered the police in certain districts to arrest any working-class woman on suspicion of prostitution and subject her to enforced gynecological examinations. If a woman refused such an examination, it was generally assumed she was guilty in any case; if she acquiesced in the examination, that too proved her culpability. (Men who might have been the customers of such women were not subject to similar treatment, though they too, of course, might be considered responsible for the spread of venereal disease.) Enforcing a double standard of morality which humiliated women while encouraging male sexual exploitation, the Contagious Diseases Acts may finally summarize the problematic reality that shadowed the nineteenth century's ideology of femininity. In particular, an anxiety about the female body led, on the one hand, to fantasies about the upper-class woman's rare spirituality, and, on the other hand, to imaginings of the working-class woman's corrosive sexuality.

WOMAN'S REVOLUTION

Throughout the history of Western culture there had always, of course, been a notable dissonance between what we have here been calling the ideology of femininity and what we have just defined as the reality of women's lives. During the nineteenth century, however, this discrepancy between fiction and fact became so striking that it created precisely the revolution to which Higginson was alluding when he claimed in 1859 that "now Cinderella [is thinking] of putting on her royal robes." Historians have speculated that the egalitarian ideologies with which the era began, along with the impulses toward political reform that accompanied such ideologies, were essential to the battle for women's rights and votes that marked this century. Similarly, the demands of women for higher education and their eagerness to enter trades and professions were fostered by those radical ideas about the world, while the large-scale social changes impelled by the Industrial Revolution forced many working-class women out of the home and into the factory, at the same time making a number of middle- and upper-class women unpleasantly aware of just how unproductive a "lady's" leisure was. Finally, the rebelliousness of even the most religious women was implicitly encouraged by the newly antihierarchical thinking associated with what the so-called disappearance of God.

Rights and Votes

It is not surprising that women, and some men as well, should early have understood the feminist implications of the intellectual assumptions that underlay the French Revolution and also, to some extent, the American war for independence. As early as 1819, the Chartists who assembled at the disastrous St. Peter's Fields meeting near Manchester to demand government attention to their plight included not only a number of working-class women but also some men who supported their right to join in political protests. By the early 1830s, French socialist and utopian thinkers had begun to proselytize in England for causes that included "the emancipation of women." Among the middle classes, too, similar ideas were stirring: in 1831, the *Westminster Review* published an anonymous article advocating female suffrage, and in 1832 a Member of Parliament actually presented a petition to the House of Commons, asking that "every unmarried female possessing the necessary pecuniary qualification . . . be allowed to vote."

At the same time, even the most apparently privileged aristocratic women had begun to become aware of the disadvantages of their sex, and as Ray Strachey observes, one of them actually brought about "the first legislative attempt to improve the position of women in England": Lady Caroline Norton, a dashing and witty London hostess, was divorced by her husband and denied custody of her children in 1836; in despair, she wrote a series of fierce pamphlets, including *The Natural Right of a Mother to the Custody of Her Child*. . . . (1837), which finally resulted in Parliament's passage of the Infants' Custody Act of 1839. This bill was, as Strachey remarks, "a timid and hesitating measure," but nevertheless it represented a legal landmark because it actually conceded some rights to women, who had hitherto had none.

In the United States, however, it was the antislavery movement that most dramatically inaugurated a feminist groundswell. Beginning in the 1830s, countless American women were intensely active in the struggle to emancipate the blacks in the South. Their participation ranged from work in the Underground Railroad, which helped escaping slaves to find their way to freedom, to membership in the first National Female Anti-Slavery Society, founded in 1837. Among the most prominent speakers for the abolitionist cause were the Grimké sisters, Sarah and Angelina, who early saw a connection between their own political powerlessness and the subjugation of slaves. If women were not allowed to speak in the public sphere, they argued, how could they bear witness to what they knew was just? "I surrender not our claim to equality," declared Sarah Grimké in 1838, emphasizing her belief that *"whatsoever it is morally right for a man to do, it is morally right for a woman to do."* In a sardonic poem entitled *The Times That Try Men's Souls*, her contemporary and co-worker Maria Weston Chapman surfaced the protofeminist beliefs that informed such a statement: women, she exclaimed with mock horror, have

> . . . taken a notion to speak for themselves,
> And are wielding the tongue and the pen;

They've mounted the rostrum; the termagent elves,
And—oh horrid!—are talking to men!

Some few years after Chapman wrote these lines, the dilemma of both American and English women who wanted to speak for the rights of slaves was powerfully dramatized by an event that occurred in London. A group of American women were denied the right to be seated as delegates to an 1840 World Anti-Slavery Convention. Nothing could have more effectively clarified the disparity between the male abolitionists' transatlantic rhetoric of liberation and the reality of their misogyny, a misogyny that seemed to their female colleagues a shocking shadow of more general social feelings about women. Eight years later, in 1848, two of the would-be delegates to the London Anti-Slavery Convention—Lucretia Mott and Elizabeth Cady Stanton—were among five women who called a meeting of their own at Seneca Falls, in New York State. The resulting Woman's Rights Convention revised the American Declaration of Independence in order to support the proposition that sometimes "in the course of human events it becomes necessary for one portion of the family of man to assume among the people of the earth a position different from that they have hitherto occupied."

Many other English and American figures were among the nineteenth-century women who contributed to the feminist effort. In the United States, for instance, Margaret Fuller published her impassioned and influential *Woman in the Nineteenth Century* in 1845, while Lucy Stone began a brilliant career as what Eleanor Flexner calls a lecturer "on behalf of the oppressed," declaring: "I expect to plead not for the slave only, but for suffering humanity everywhere. ESPECIALLY DO I MEAN TO LABOR FOR THE ELEVATION OF MY SEX." By 1851, Susan B. Anthony had joined Stone, Mott, and Stanton as one of the leaders of the suffrage movement; Sojourner Truth had risen in Akron, Ohio, to speak for the rights of black women; Frances E. W. Harper had begun to write eloquent poetry demanding the liberation of slaves and women; and countless other American women, black and white, of all ages and classes, had become converts to "the cause." Their work was slow and arduous. They wrote pamphlets, made speeches, carried petitions from house to house in villages, towns, and cities throughout the nation, testified before legislative bodies that were frequently amused or hostile, and marched in demonstrations. Their struggle—the longest single political battle in American history—did not gain them the vote nationally for more than three quarters of a century. Yet they did make progress in achieving some rights for women. By 1860, Married Women's Property Acts had been passed in fourteen states, including Massachusetts, New York, and Illinois, while a few states and territories (for instance, Wyoming and Utah in 1870, Colorado in 1893, and Idaho in 1896) gradually extended voting rights to women.

The United States movement had a specific transatlantic impact through a story about the first Worcester (Massachusetts) Women's Rights convention written in 1851 for the *Westminster Review* by Harriet Taylor, a young Englishwoman, who described the proceedings and stated the case for women's rights. In the same year, Taylor married the philosopher John Stuart Mill, a figure whose intensely feminist *The Subjection of Women*, written in 1861 and published in 1869, was to formulate arguments for female equality that would become central to the British women's movement. The book's ideas, insisted Mill, were "acquired mainly through [his wife's] teaching," and, though some critics have disputed this claim, it is at least clear that the couple had an egalitarian relationship which was essential in shaping Mill's thought, and that Taylor had lucidly summarized some important American feminist concepts.

Even before Mill had started to draft his feminist treatise, however, a number of Englishwomen had begun to organize committees for women's rights roughly comparable to the groups working in America. Foremost among these early pioneers was Barbara Leigh Smith, later Barbara Bodichon: in 1855 she undertook to circulate petitions in support of a Married Women's Property Act; in 1857 she was instrumental in founding a feminist paper called *The Englishwoman's Journal*; and in 1865, at a meeting of a Kensington Ladies' Discussion Society, she adopted a strong position in favor of women's suffrage, a position that led to the formation of England's first Women's Suffrage Committee. In 1866, a year after John Stuart Mill had been elected to Parliament, this group presented him with several petitions, containing thousands of signatures in support of votes for women, which allowed him to bring about the first parliamentary debate on women's suffrage, an action he himself defined as "by far the most important public service" he performed during his membership in the House of Commons.

Still, despite the energy and enthusiasm of Bodichon, Mill, and others, the progress of the woman's "revolution" was as slow in England as in America. The first Married Women's Property Act was defeated in 1856, and Parliament passed a far more conservative Marriage and Divorce Law in 1857, an act that served to defuse demands for the much-needed property bill. Similarly, the Contagious Diseases Acts of the 1860s, legislation which, as we noted, allowed the harrassment of countless working-class women, were stubbornly defended by the government for several decades. Finally, despite a brilliant speech by Mill, the 1866 bill for women's suffrage received comparatively few votes. It was not until 1882 that a serious and effective Married Women's Property Act was passed in England and not until 1886 that the Contagious Diseases Acts were formally repealed, after a long and vigorous campaign led by Josephine Butler. As for suffrage, by the seventies and eighties the battle in England had barely been joined, and, like their American sisters, Englishwomen would have to wait for the vote until after World War I.

Education, Trades, and Professions

Though feminist political and legal advances came only gradually and sporadically, nineteenth-century women did make extraordinary progress in other ways. The philosophy of human rights that shaped so many of the suffrage and abolition movements' assumptions proved an equally crucial influence on theories about women's education. In the United States, such thinkers as Emma Willard, Frances Wright, and Catherine Beecher, each in her own way, insisted on demanding serious training for girls, and in 1833 what is now Oberlin College became the first institution to admit young women "coeds." Perhaps an even more important milestone in the history of women's fight for learning was the founding of Mount Holyoke in 1837. Mary Lyon, the school's principal, was determined to teach her students such varied (and heretofore masculine) subjects as rhetoric and logic, human physiology and "intellectual philosophy," astronomy and chemistry. A number of interested observers in New England and elsewhere were impressed, for the establishment of Mount Holyoke was followed by the opening of Vassar in 1865, of Smith and Wellesley in 1875, of the "Harvard Annex" (Radcliffe) in 1879, and of Bryn Mawr in 1885.

During these years, similar struggles for educational opportunities were being waged by women in England. In the 1840s, Christian Socialists concerned about the condition of governesses founded a Governesses' Benevolent Institution designed to provide annuities for "ladies in temporary distress," but they discovered they could hardly meet the needs of all those who applied for assistance. Reasoning that if such women "could teach better they could command higher salaries," the founders of the Benevolent Institution initiated a series of "Lectures to Ladies," which by 1848 had evolved into Queens College for Women in London, a kind of adult education school that offered basic courses in literature, science, and philosophy.

In addition, just as American feminists fought for admission to Harvard and managed to establish Radcliffe as the "Harvard Annex," so British feminists laid siege to the great universities of Cambridge and Oxford. Their leader in this struggle was Emily Davies, who worked for years to arrange the admission of women, first to London University, and then to Cambridge. Though she did not achieve her goal in London, she triumphed when in 1870 Girton College for Women, now part of Cambridge University, was established. A year later, moreover, Anne Jemima Clough, another pioneering educator, was instrumental in founding what is now Newnham College, Cambridge. Finally, in the seventies and eighties, two more women's colleges—Somerville and Lady Margaret Hall—were established at Oxford. By 1884, women were allowed to study at both major British universities—although, they were still, for many years, denied the right to earn formal degrees.

A natural consequence of women's entrance into higher education was an intensification of female interest in joining the professions. Perhaps the most dramatic struggle here was the fight of a few courageous young women to enter medical schools and begin work as practicing physicians. Again, it was an American who led this battle: despite much opposition, Elizabeth Blackwell gained admission to Geneva College as a medical student and graduated at the head of her class in 1849. Journeying to Europe for further training, she met and was influenced by the young Florence Nightingale, and later she returned to England, where she supported the long but ultimately successful struggles of two English women, Elizabeth Garrett and Sophia Jex-Blake, to gain medical degrees of their own.

Of course, such accomplishments as medical degrees and university study were largely the prerogative of upper- and middle-class women. But working-class women, too, began to fight for their rights and to unite in newly vital ways during the nineteenth century, for the philosophy of human rights preached by Chartists in England and similar reformers in America influenced all classes. In Lowell, Massachusetts, textile workers edited and published a widely known magazine, *The Lowell Offering*, and, even more important, organized a Female Labor Reform Association which served as a model for a number of comparable groups that sprang up in other New England mill towns. Although working-class women were not quite so active in England, similar organizations were also established there throughout the century. In the thirties, as Sheila Rowbotham notes, Female Reform Societies and Female Political Unions supported the protests of male workers, while in 1874 Emma Paterson formed the Women's Protective and Provident League and the National Union of Working Women to encourage female trade unionism. The passion for justice of these activist women on both sides of the Atlantic, like the feminist principles of their middle- and upper-class sisters, was aptly expressed by what Eleanor Flexner explains was "a parody on an old song, *I Can't Be a Nun,* "which striking factory girls in Lowell, Massachusetts, sang as they marched through the town in 1836:

> Oh, I cannot be a slave,
> I will not be a slave,
> For I'm so fond of liberty
> That I cannot be a slave.

A GOLDEN AGE OF WOMEN'S LITERATURE

It is no coincidence that this century of feminist revolution was a kind of golden age of women's literature. In the nineteenth century, after a female—and, more particularly, a feminist—tradition had earlier begun to establish itself in the words and works of women like Bradstreet, Finch, and Wollstonecraft, the female imagination first achieved a full flowering. Significantly, the women Woolf defined as "the four great novelists"—Jane Austen, Charlotte and Emily Brontë, and George Eliot—were all nineteenth-century artists, and artists very much of their time. Similarly, the era produced such major poets as Emily Dickinson, Elizabeth Barrett Browning, and Christina Rossetti. In addition, the century fostered the work of a range of political or quasi-political figures—Margaret Fuller, Harriet Beecher Stowe, Frances E. W. Harper, and Florence Nightingale—as well as the art of novelists like Maria Edgeworth and Elizabeth Gaskell, whose achievements appear "minor" only when they are set against the extraordinary accomplishments of the Brontës, Austen, and Eliot. Clearly, the spirit of the age that motivated such activists as Mott and Stanton, Bodichon and Blackwell, also inspired the imaginings of their literary sisters. Indeed, as their texts suggest, nineteenth-century women writers were as haunted as were American and English suffragists by the discrepancy between ideology and reality, a discrepancy that frequently forced these artists to tell tales of pain even while it fueled their fantasies of freedom. Still, though the writings of nineteenth-century women in England and America often drew, implicitly or explicitly, on precisely the impulses that energized the contemporary women's movement, the nature of those writings cannot be completely understood in isolation from the literary achievements of nineteenth-century men.

Male and Female Traditions

As in earlier eras, women writers in the nineteenth century worked both with and against the grain of male aesthetic assumptions and practices. There were no great women Romantic poets contemporary with Wordsworth and Coleridge, Shelley, Byron, and Keats, for instance, yet a few women artists did write poetry that can clearly be identified as Romantic in its praise of the unspoiled beauty of wild landscapes, its commitment to the power of the imagination, and its philosophy of what the critic M. H. Abrams, following Thomas Carlyle, has called "Natural Supernaturalism." The poet-novelist Charlotte Smith, for instance, published a long meditation on nature as well as a series of *Elegiac Sonnets* (1784), which may almost be said to have pioneered in the formation of the Romantic aesthetic, while the poet Mary Tighe (1772–1810) produced a Spenserian narrative entitled *Cupid and Psyche* (1805) which is known to have significantly influenced John Keats's famous *Ode to Psyche* (1820).

At the same time, it is plain that a number of the ideas formulated by the male Romantics (and earlier by Smith and Tighe), as well as some recurrent Romantic themes and images, had considerable impact on the nineteenth-century female contemporaries and descendants of writers like Wordsworth and Byron. Obviously, the writings of such relatives of poets as Dorothy Wordsworth (William Wordsworth's sister) and Mary Shelley (Percy Shelley's wife) would reveal these influences: Dorothy Wordsworth's journals are marked by (and in fact influenced) exactly the steady, detailed, and reverent observations of nature that characterize her brother's *Lyrical Ballads* (1798) and *The Prelude* (1850), while Mary Shelley's tales and novels, especially *Frankenstein* (1818), exhibit just the concern with issues of liberty and authority, will and imagination, that works of her husband's like *Prometheus Unbound* (1820) and *The Triumph of Life* (1824) dramatize. Yet even a fiction writer like Jane Austen, famous for preferring "sense" to "sensibility" (as her novel entitled *Sense and Sensibility*, 1811, demonstrates), had to confront questions about the world that were raised by the Romantics: in her early, parodic *Northanger Abbey* (composed before 1803), for instance, she comically yet seriously considered the implications for women of the Gothic romance that obsessed many of her contemporaries, as well as the cult of the picturesque that so influenced the Romantics, while in her late *Persuasion* (1818) she meditated on just the relationships between individual desire and social authority that also interested her male contemporaries.

Paradoxically, however, it is in the work of midcentury novelists like Charlotte and Emily Brontë that we can find the most vivid traces of Romanticism as it was defined by male poets like Byron, Shelley, and their precursor William Blake. Jane Eyre's impassioned plea for social and spiritual liberty is, after all, both a Byronic assertion of the claims of the self and a Shelleyan demand for social transformation, while the characterization of Jane's darkly brooding lover, Edward Rochester, clearly draws upon the traits of such haunting Byronic heroes as Manfred and Childe Harold. In fact, the Byronic hero—a dashing yet Satanic rebel who seized the imagination of readers throughout Europe in the first decades of the nineteenth century—provided a model of simultaneously tempting and terrifying masculinity for many women writers, including, besides Charlotte Brontë, Charlotte's sister Emily. Heathcliff, the mysteriously demonic foundling whose vengeful passions trigger the plot of *Wuthering Heights* (1847), clearly derives much of his power from that Romantic paradigm even while his hellish energies recall the subversive intensity of earlier, quasi-mythic figures like William Blake's Orc and Los.

At the same time, however, the Byronic hero also provided a pattern for a new kind of character: a Byronic *heroine*. Charlotte Brontë's rebellious Jane Eyre and Emily Brontë's fierce Catherine Earnshaw are each in her own way revisions of this brooding outcast who rejects any cultural commandments that fail to meet the needs of his or her own soul. Similarly, Elizabeth Barrett Browning's Aurora Leigh, at least at the moment when she refuses to acquiesce in Romney's demand that she abnegate her own ambition in order to become his helpmate, argues with defiant passion for the authority of her own desire, while Emily Dickinson, in a number of her most intensely rebellious poems, assumes a posture of Byronic alienation from God and man alike. Considering that most of these women artists were confronting exactly the dissonance between ideology and reality that their feminist-activist contemporaries were, it is not surprising that they should have adopted such a revolutionary stance. What is impressive, however, is the inventiveness with which they transformed a male figure into a female (and implicitly feminist) model.

But of course Byronic Romanticism was only a single strain in the literary chorus nineteenth-century women writers heard on both sides of the Atlantic. In the United States, that strain, modified by the writings of the Victorian sage Thomas Carlyle and by the ideas of German Romantic philosophers, modulated into the concept of "self-reliance," which was central to Transcendentalists like Emerson and Thoreau, a concept which Margaret Fuller turned to feminist purposes in the brilliant polemics of *The Great Lawsuit*, later published as *Woman in the Nineteenth Century*. In England, the questioning of authority that had marked the texts of all the British Romantics evolved into a Victorian skepticism about received theology and a commitment to the common life, a commitment to serious public service in the complex world of the "here and now" that often virtually replaced traditional religious faith not only in the writings of men like Tennyson, Browning, and Carlyle himself but also in the works of women like George Eliot and Elizabeth Barrett Browning. In other words, throughout the century the male and female literary traditions in England and America continued to be both intertwined and interdependent.

Yet those traditions could not be identical, despite the connections that we can trace between them. For one thing, although a number of literary women did manage to achieve not only greatness but fame in the course of the age, most continued to experience precisely the anxieties about literary authority that had been expressed by precursors like Anne Bradstreet and Anne Finch. That artists like Charlotte and Emily Brontë and Marian Evans had to publish their works under male pseudonyms (respectively, Currer and Ellis Bell and George Eliot) is one indication that such anxieties persisted. That poets like Elizabeth Barrett Browning, Emily Dickinson, and Christina Rossetti had, in various degrees, to withdraw from the public world is another indication that the old anxieties lingered: Barrett Browning confined herself to a sickroom for more than a decade; Dickinson not only imprisoned herself in her "Father's house" (as she put it) but refused to publish; and Rossetti, at least metaphorically, immured herself in the convent of her own soul.

Finally, that a number of these writers, both novelists and poets, frequently had to follow Byronic assertions of ambition with qualifying avowals of renunciation—a phenomenon we can see in the works of women from Jane Austen to Emily Dickinson, from Charlotte Brontë to Christina Rossetti—is yet another sign of continuing anxiety. If a "lady" was supposed to be an angel in the house, after all, how could she allow herself to make the kinds of self-confident claims for her own creativity that empowered her male contemporaries? "I think I shall be among the English Poets after my death," John Keats had written in 1818, but his American descendant, Emily Dickinson—who may have felt equal certainty—had to be more careful in her self-definitions: calling herself "the slightest in the House," she remarked ironically that "they shut me up in Prose. . . . Because they liked me 'still.' " Similarly, Christina Rossetti reminded herself in *The Lowest Room* that it was best to be "last," and George Eliot defined Dorothea Brooke, the protagonist of *Middlemarch* (1872) and perhaps this novelist's favorite heroine, as "the foundress of nothing."

Nevertheless, even while expressing and enacting such striking conflicts, these women did continue to write, and, as we have already observed, they created what was in some sense a golden age of the female imagination. How did they do it? Clearly, they were energized by the unprecedented fact that they *did* have some female precursors as well as a growing number of highly visible female contemporaries.

For novelists from Austen and the Brontës to Stowe, Eliot, and Alcott, there was a newly viable—and popular—genre in which they could work, a genre that had been developed by such eighteenth-century precursors as Fanny Burney and Anne Radcliffe, and that was in their own century to be exploited with great commercial success by best-selling writers like (in England) the sensational novelists Mary Elizabeth Braddon (1837–1915) and Rhoda Broughton (1849–1920), and (in America) the sentimental novelists Susan Warner (1819–1885) and Maria Cummins (1827–1866). That a sensational work like Braddon's *Lady Audley's Secret* (1862) was often scorned by elite male critics as merely a "thriller" and that a sentimental work like Cummins' *The Wide, Wide World* (1851) was frequently dismissed as little more than a tearjerker could not disguise from readers of both sexes the fact that women like the authors of these novels had finally become key presences in a literary marketplace that had hitherto been primarily dominated by male writers and editors. Nathaniel Hawthorne's complaint in 1855 that his art was being threatened by a "damned mob of scribbling women" represents the reaction of many men of letters to this new female commercial power, but—despite George Eliot's diatribe *Silly Novels by Lady Novelists*—many women of letters must have been encouraged rather than disturbed by such power.

Similarly, poets like Barrett Browning, Rossetti, and Dickinson must have been heartened by the examples of such well-known women poets as Felicia Hemans (1793–1835), L.E.L. (Letitia Elizabeth Landon, 1802–1838), and many more. That some of these artists, like such popular novelists as Braddon and Warner, were scorned as effusive and sentimental (the American Lydia Sigourney, for instance, was labeled "The Sweet Singer of Hartford") does not mean that their presence was not in some sense a strengthening one for poets like Barrett Browning and Rossetti (both of whom wrote elegies on the death of L.E.L.) and even for an artist like Dickinson (who frequently attempted to "rewrite" in her own style the hearts-and-flowers verses of women poets whose works she read in the *Springfield Gazette*). In addition, of course, ambitious writers like Dickinson and Rossetti were profoundly inspired by the powerful example of Barrett Browning, a poet whose work, unlike that of Sigourney and L.E.L., was so widely admired in the nineteenth century that she was very seriously considered for the position of English Poet Laureate after William Wordsworth died in 1850.

Besides the existence of significant precursors and contemporaries, however, the revolutionary social changes to which Mark Twain was referring when he remarked that the world had been transformed in the seventy-five years of Queen Victoria's reign affected women writers at least as strongly as they affected male artists. Some of these women—for instance the legendary speaker Sojourner Truth, the escaped slave Linda Brent, and the feminist orator Elizabeth Cady Stanton—were of course integrally involved in the various public movements that brought about these changes. But even those women who lived less overtly political lives saw that the tumult of the age required a record, and Elizabeth Barrett Browning provided one in her verse-novel *Aurora Leigh* just as George Eliot offered one in *Middlemarch*, Rebecca Cox Jackson in her journal, Harriet Beecher Stowe in *Uncle Tom's Cabin*, Harriet Wilson in *Our Nig*, Florence Nightingale in *Cassandra*, and Rebecca Harding Davis in *Life in the Iron-Mills*. Working in all the forms in which their aesthetic brothers worked—the novel, the essay, the long poem, the sonnet, the lyric—these diverse artists wrote their way out of the female "sphere" to which they had been confined.

As their texts will show, such nineteenth-century women writers were often only covertly subversive, producing decorous surfaces that erupted to reveal indecorous, even Byronic, passions for liberty, as if many had decided to follow a dictum like Emily Dickinson's to "tell all the truth / But tell it slant." Yet their power was irrepressible. With Elizabeth Barrett Browning's poet-heroine Aurora Leigh, each would have asserted that "every creature, female as the male, / Stands single in responsible act and thought," and, also with Aurora, each would have insisted that "I too have my vocation,—work to do. . . . Most serious work, most necessary work / As any of the economists." Significantly, it was Barrett Browning herself who once lamented that she looked "everywhere for [poetic] grandmothers, and found none." But after she and the other female artists of her century had made their enduring contributions to our culture, no aspiring young woman writer would ever have to level such a complaint again. At least in literature, what Thomas Wentworth Higginson called an "epoch" reserved for "the genius of woman" had finally begun—an era that certainly did not exclude the contributions of men but at last also, definitively, included women's achievements.

MARIA EDGEWORTH
1767–1849

Maria Edgeworth was born at Black Bourton, Oxfordshire, the second of the twenty-one children of Richard Lovell Edgeworth, a brilliant, if eccentric, inventor and educator of Anglo-Irish descent. Her mother, Anna Maria Elers, was apparently the least loved of his wives, and, after her death in 1773, Maria Edgeworth grew up under the care of three successive stepmothers. After attending one school at Derby and another in London, she accompanied her father and her current stepmother to Ireland in 1782. On the family estate, Edgeworthstown, he completed her education first through his lessons, then by involving her in local politics, and finally by collaborating with her on *Practical Education* (1798), a book that demonstrates his interest in the pedagogic theories of the French philosopher Jean Jacques Rousseau. Maria Edgeworth had already begun to teach her younger siblings and, at her father's request, to translate works of the conservative moralist Madame de Genlis.

When the publication of Genlis's *Adèlaide and Théodore* was canceled because of the subsequent appearance of another English version, her father's friend, Thomas Day, wrote a congratulatory letter, for, as Maria Edgeworth explained later, he was nearly of the opinion "that the extent of a woman's erudition should consist in her knowing her simple letters, without their mischievous combinations." Her first signed work, *Letters for Literary Ladies* (1795), appropriately begins with an exchange of letters between a liberal father and his conservative friend on the subject of female authorship. Although these figures, modeled on Edgeworth and Day, contend over the propriety of women writing, they agree that women are meant to be wives and mothers, two roles Maria Edgeworth would extol in her fiction and avoid in her life. The second and third sections of *Letters for Literary Ladies* are characteristic of Maria Edgeworth's later writing: in *Letters of Julia and Caroline*, she contrasts the sense and sensibility of two heroines, one rational and the other self-destructively sentimental; in *An Essay on the Noble Science of Self-Justification*, Edgeworth satirizes feminine manipulation and hypocrisy to teach the importance of honesty and humility. Just as these early efforts repeat her father's opinions in fictional forms, her later work would gloss his social theories. Under the close supervision of her father, who "corrected" her manuscripts, she produced financially successful moral tales and children's stories which contemporary reviewers praised for their instructiveness.

During the same period in which she was writing *Letters for Literary Ladies*, Edgeworth entertained her family with specimens of the speech of their Irish steward. An early dramatic monologue grew into her most famous novel, *Castle Rackrent* (1800), a humorous but telling critique of exploitative Irish landlords recounted by a shrewdly observant family retainer. Her realism in portraying Irish customs and speech was unprecedented. It also shaped a later novel like *The Absentee* (1812), which criticized absentee Irish gentry ashamed of their origins. By the end of her life, when she helped relieve sufferers during the Irish potato famine of 1847, Edgeworth had become an honorary member of the Royal Irish Academy. Her contribution to Irish literature led Sir Walter Scott to explain that he hoped to attain for his country—Scotland—"the rich humour, pathetic tenderness, and admirable taste" she had "so fortunately achieved for Ireland."

Edgeworth had begun writing, she explained, "to please my father," and "to please him I continued." Although she traveled several times to London, France, and Switzerland, where, on one occasion, she rejected a marriage proposal, she focused in her novels on the conventions of the domestic life she led. With the publication of *Belinda* (1801) and *Ormond* (1817), Edgeworth extended the tradition first established in Fanny Burney's novel of manners and later perfected in Jane Austen's comic fiction. Like Austen, Edgeworth wrote in the common sitting room; in fact, she sat at a desk on which her father inscribed his view that, "in these works which were chiefly written to please me," his daughter had "improved and amused her own mind, and gratified her heart, which I do believe is better than her head." After his death, she completed only one novel and his *Memoirs of Richard Lovell Edgeworth, Esq.* (1820): without his presence she seemed to lack a motive for writing. But for the youthful Jane Austen, Maria Edgeworth, like Fanny Burney, had succeeded in securing the status of the novel by producing works "in which the greatest powers of the mind are displayed, in which the most thorough knowledge of human nature, the happiest delineation of its varieties, the liveliest effusions of wit and humour, are conveyed to the world in the best-chosen language."

From Letters to Literary Ladies[1]

[*An Attack on Literary Ladies*]

Women of literature are much more numerous of late than they were a few years ago. They make a class in society, they fill the public eye, and have acquired a degree of consequence and an appropriate character. The esteem of private friends, and the admiration of the public for their talents, are circumstances highly flattering to their vanity, and as such I will allow[2] them to be substantial pleasures. I am also ready to acknowledge that a taste for literature adds much to the happiness of life, and that women may enjoy to a certain degree this happiness as well as men. But with literary women this silent happiness seems at best but a subordinate consideration; it is not by the treasures they possess, but by those which they have an opportunity of displaying, that they estimate their wealth. To obtain public applause, they are betrayed too often into a miserable ostentation of their learning. Coxe tells us, that certain Russian ladies split their pearls, in order to make a greater display of finery.

1. The first selection is written from the point of view of Thomas Day, a family friend, while the second is supposedly Edgeworth's father's perspective.
2. Admit.

The pleasure of being admired for wit[3] or erudition I cannot exactly measure in a female mind; but state it to be as delightful as you can imagine it to be, there are evils attendant upon it, which, in the estimation of a prudent father, may overbalance the good. The intoxicating effect of wit upon the brain has been well remarked by a poet, who was a friend to the fair sex, and too many ridiculous, and too many disgusting, examples confirm the truth of the observation. The deference that is paid to genius sometimes makes the fair sex forget, that genius will be respected only when united with discretion. Those who have acquired fame, fancy that they can afford to sacrifice reputation. I will suppose, however, that their heads shall be strong enough to bear inebriating admiration; and that their conduct shall be essentially irreproachable, yet they will show in their manners and conversation that contempt of inferior minds, and that neglect of common forms and customs, which will provoke the indignation of fools, and which cannot escape the censure of the wise. Even whilst we are secure of their innocence, we dislike that daring spirit in the female sex, which delights to oppose the common opinions of society, and from apparent trifles we draw unfavourable omens, which experience too often confirms. * * *

Men of literature, if we may trust to the bitter expressions of anguish in their writings, and in their private letters, feel acutely all the stings of envy. Women, who have more susceptibility of temper, and less strength of mind, and who, from the delicate nature of their reputation, are more exposed to attack, are also less able to endure it. Malignant critics, when they cannot attack an author's peace in his writings, frequently scrutinize his private life; and every personal anecdote is published without regard to truth or propriety. How will the delicacy of the female character endure this treatment? how will her friends bear to see her pursued even in domestic retirement,[4] if she should be wise enough to make that retirement her choice? how will they like to see premature memoirs and spurious collections of familiar letters published by needy booksellers or designing enemies? Yet to all these things men of letters are subject; and such must literary ladies expect, if they attain to any degree of eminence.—Judging, then, from the experience of our sex, I may pronounce envy to be one of the evils which women of uncommon genius have to dread. "Censure," says a celebrated writer, "is a tax which every man must pay to the public, who seeks to be eminent." Women must expect to pay it doubly.

Your daughter, perhaps, shall be above scandal. She shall despise the idle whisper, and the common tattle of her sex; her soul shall be raised above the ignorant and the frivolous; she shall have a relish for higher conversation, and a taste for higher society. But where is she to find, or

3. Intelligence.   4. I.e., privacy.

how is she to obtain this society? You make her incapable of friendship with her own sex. Where is she to look for friends, for companions, for equals? Amongst men? Amongst what class of men? Not amongst men of business, or men of gallantry, but amongst men of literature.

Learned men have usually chosen for their wives, or for their companions, women who were rather below than above the standard of mediocrity: this seems to me natural and reasonable. Such men, probably, feel their own incapacity for the daily business of life, their ignorance of the world, their slovenly habits, and neglect of domestic affairs. They do not want wives who have precisely their own defects; they rather desire to find such as shall, by the opposite habits and virtues, supply[5] their deficiencies. I do not see why two books should marry, any more than two estates. Some few exceptions might be quoted against Stuart's observations. I have just seen, under the article "A Literary Wife," in D'Israeli's Curiosities of Literature, an account of Francis Phidelphus, a great scholar in the fifteenth century, who was so desirous of acquiring the Greek language in perfection, that he travelled to Constantinople in search of a *Grecian wife*: the lady proved a scold. "But to do justice to the name of Theodora," as this author adds, "she has been honourably mentioned in the French Academy of Sciences." I hope this proved an adequate compensation to her husband for his domestic broils.

Happy Madame Dacier![6] you found a husband suited to your taste! You and Monsieur Dacier, if D'Alembert tells the story rightly, once cooked a dish in concert, by a receipt,[7] which you found in Apicius, and you both sat down and ate of your learned ragout till you were both like to die.

Were I sure, my dear friend, that every literary lady would be equally fortunate in finding in a husband a man who would sympathise in her tastes, I should diminish my formidable catalogue of evils. But alas! Monsieur Dacier is no more! "and we shall never live to see his fellow." Literary ladies will, I am afraid, be losers in love as well as in friendship, by their superiority.—Cupid is a timid, playful child, and is frightened at the helmet of Minerva.[8] It has been observed, that gentlemen are not apt to admire a prodigious quantity of learning and masculine acquirements in the fair sex—we usually consider a certain degree of weakness, both of mind and body, as friendly to female grace. I am not absolutely of this opinion, yet I do not see the advantage of supernatural force, either of body or mind, to female excellence. Hercules-Spinster found his strength rather an incumbrance than an advantage.[9]

---

5. Fill, make up.
6. Anne Dacier (1654–1720) was a French classical scholar married to André Dacier, also a classicist; Jean Le Rond D'Alembert was an eighteenth-century French writer who helped to edit the *Encyclopedia*; Apicius was a famous Roman epicure.
7. Recipe. "Ragout": a stew.
8. Cupid is the Greek god of love; Minerva is the goddess of wisdom.
9. The Greek hero Hercules was forced to dress as a woman and perform female tasks.

Superiority of mind must be united with great temper and generosity, to be tolerated by those who are forced to submit to its influence. I have seen witty and learned ladies, who did not seem to think it at all incumbent upon them to sacrifice any thing to the sense of propriety. On the contrary, they seemed to take both pride and pleasure in showing the utmost stretch of their strength, regardless of the consequences, panting only for victory. Upon such occasions, when the adversary has been a husband or a father, I must acknowledge that I have felt sensations, which few ladies can easily believe they excite. Airs and graces I can bear as well as another—but airs without graces, no man thinks himself bound to bear—and learned airs least of all. Ladies of high rank, in the Court of Parnassus,[1] are apt, sometimes, to claim precedency out of their own dominions, which creates much confusion, and generally ends in their being affronted. That knowledge of the world, which keeps people in their proper places, they will never learn from the Muses.[2]

Molière has pointed out with all the force of comic ridicule, in the Femmes Savantes,[3] that a lady who aspires to the sublime delights of philosophy and poetry, must forego the simple pleasures, and will despise the duties of domestic life. I should not expect that my house affairs would be with haste dispatched by a Desdemona,[4] weeping over some unvarnished tale, or petrified with some history of horrors, at the very time when she should be ordering dinner, or paying the butcher's bill—I should have the less hope of rousing her attention to my culinary concerns and domestic grievances, because I should probably incur her contempt for hinting at these sublunary[5] matters, and her indignation for supposing that she ought to be employed in such degrading occupations. I have heard that if these sublime geniuses are wakened from their reveries by the *appulse*[6] of external circumstances, they start and exhibit all the perturbation and amazement of *cataleptic*[7] patients.

[A *Defense of Literary Ladies*]

* * * I acknowledge with regret that women who have been but half instructed, who have seen only superficially the relations of moral and political ideas, who have obtained but an imperfect knowledge of the human heart, and who have conducted themselves so as to disgrace their talents and their sex: these are conspicuous and melancholy examples, which are cited oftener with malice than with pity. But I appeal to

1. Mythic mountain where the shades of great poets gather.
2. Greek goddesses of art and inspiration.
3. *The Learned Women*, a farce by Molière (1622–1673). The play satirizes the pretensions to knowledge of science, art, and grammar on the part of a group of women.
4. A character in Shakespeare's tragedy *Othello*

who reacts with great sympathy to stories of suffering and hardship.
5. Earthly (literally: beneath the moon).
6. Near approach.
7. Having muscular rigidity, where the parts of the body remain fixed in the positions they are put into.

examples amongst our contemporaries, to which every man of literature will immediately advert to prove, that where the female understanding has been properly cultivated, women have not only obtained
admiration by their useful abilities, but respect by their exemplary conduct.

I apprehend that many of the errors into which women of literature
have fallen, may have arisen from an improper choice of books: those
who read chiefly works of imagination, receive from them false ideas of
life and of the human heart. Many of these productions I shall keep as I
would deadly poison from my child; I should rather endeavour to turn
her attention to science than to romance,[8] and to give her early that
taste for truth and utility, which when once implanted can scarcely be
eradicated. There is a wide difference between innocence and ignorance; ignorant women may have minds the most debased and perverted, whilst the most cultivated understanding may be united with the
most perfect innocence and simplicity.

Even if literature were of no other use to the fair sex than to supply
them with employment, I should think the time dedicated to the cultivation of their minds well bestowed: they are surely better occupied
when they are reading or writing than when coquetting or gaming, losing their fortunes or their characters. You despise the writings of
women—you think that they might have made a better use of the pen
than to write plays, and poetry, and romances. Considering that the pen
was to women a new instrument, I think they have made at least as good
a use of it as learned men did of the needle some centuries ago, when
they set themselves to determine how many spirits could stand upon its
point,[9] and were ready to tear one another to pieces in the discussion of
this sublime question. Let the sexes mutually forgive each other their
follies, or what is much better, let them combine their talents for their
general advantage.—You say that the experiments we have made do
not encourage us to proceed, that the increased care and pains which
have been of late years bestowed upon female education, have produced no adequate returns; but you in the same breath allow that
amongst your contemporaries whom you prudently forbear to mention,
there are some instances of great talents applied to useful purposes. Did
you expect that the fruits of good cultivation should appear before the
seed was sown?—You triumphantly enumerate the disadvantages to
which women, from the laws and customs of society, are liable—they
cannot converse freely with men of wit, science, and learning, nor even
with the artist, or artificers;[1] they are excluded from academies, public
libraries, &c. Even our politeness prevents us, you say, from ever

---

8. I.e., imaginative fiction.
9. A notorious subject of debate among medieval scholastics. More commonly phrased: How

many angels can dance on the head of a pin?
1. Craftsmen.

speaking plain truth and sense to the fair sex—every assistance that foreign or domestic ingenuity can invent to encourage literary studies, is, as you boast, almost exclusively ours: and after pointing out all these causes for the inferiority of women in knowledge, you ask for a list of the inventions and discoveries of those who, by your own statement of the question, have not been allowed opportunities for observation. With the insulting injustice of an Egyptian task-master, you demand the work, and deny the necessary materials.[2]

I admit, that with respect to the opportunities of acquiring knowledge, institution and manners, are, as you have stated, much in favour of our sex; but your argument concerning *time* appears to me to be unfounded.—Women who do not love dissipation must have more time for the cultivation of their understandings than men can have, if you compute the whole of life—whilst the knowledge of the learned languages[3] continues to form an indispensable part of a gentleman's education, many years of childhood and youth must be devoted to their attainment.—During these studies, the general cultivation of the understanding is in some degree retarded. All the intellectual powers are cramped, except the memory, which is sufficiently exercised, but which is overloaded with words, and with words that are not always understood.—The genius of living and of dead languages differs so much, that the pains which are taken to write elegant Latin frequently spoil the English style.—Girls usually write much better than boys; they think and express their thoughts clearly at an age when young men can scarcely write an easy letter upon any common occasion. Women do not read the good authors of antiquity as school-books, but they can have excellent translations of most of them when they are capable of tasting the beauties of composition.—I know that it is supposed we cannot judge of the classics by translations, and I am sensible that much of the merit of the originals may be lost; but I think the difference in pleasure is more than overbalanced to women by the *time* that is saved, and by the labour and misapplication of abilities which is spared. If they do not acquire a classical taste, neither do they imbibe classic prejudices, nor are they early disgusted with literature by pedagogues, lexicons, grammars, and all the melancholy apparatus of learning.—Women begin to taste the pleasures of reading, and the best authors in the English language are their amusement just at the age when young men disgusted by their studies begin to be ashamed of alluding to literature amongst their companions. Travelling, lounging, field sports, gaming, and what is called pleasure in various shapes, usually fill the interval between quitting the university and settling for life.—When

2. In Exodus 5, the Egyptians order their slaves,   3. I.e., Greek and Latin.
the Israelites, to make bricks without straw.

this period is past, business, the necessity of pursuing a profession, the ambition to shine in parliament, or to rise in public life, occupy a large portion of their lives.—In many professions the understanding is but partially cultivated; and general literature must be neglected by those who are occupied in earning bread or amassing riches for their family: —men of genius are often heard to complain, that in the pursuit of a profession they are obliged to contract their inquiries and concentrate their powers.—Statesmen lament that they must often pursue the *expedient* even when they discern that it is not *the right*; and men of letters who earn their bread by their writings, inveigh bitterly against the tyranny of booksellers who degrade them to the state of "literary artisans."—"Literary artisans" is the comprehensive term under which a celebrated philosopher[4] classes all those who cultivate only particular talents or powers of the mind, and who suffer[5] their other faculties to lose all strength and vigour for want of exercise. The other sex have no such constraint upon their understandings; neither the necessity of earning their bread, nor the ambition to shine in public affairs, hurry or prejudice their minds; in domestic life they have leisure to be wise.

Far from being ashamed that so little has been done by female abilities in science and useful literature, I am surprised that so much has been affected. On natural history, on criticism, on moral philosophy, on education, they have written with elegance, eloquence, precision, and ingenuity. Your complaint that women do not turn their attention to useful literature, is surely ill timed: if they merely increased the number of books in circulation, you might declaim against them with success; but when they add to the general fund of useful and entertaining knowledge, you cannot with any show of justice prohibit their labours: there can be no danger that the market should ever be overstocked with produce of intrinsic worth.

1795

4. Professor Dugald Stewart—*History of the Philosophy of the Human Mind* [Edgeworth's note].
5. Allow.

DOROTHY WORDSWORTH
1771–1855

Through times of personal crisis, she "preserved me still a Poet," wrote William Wordsworth about his younger sister, Dorothy, in Book XI of *The Prelude*. Earlier, in *Tintern Abbey*, his great meditation on the redemptive powers of nature, he was more explicit. Addressing Dorothy as his "dearest Friend," he told her that "in thy voice I catch / The language of my former heart, and read /

My former pleasures in the shooting lights / Of thy wild eyes." Though she was hardly as childlike as that last quotation implies, the woman who elicited such praise was in fact her brother's "dearest Friend" for most of his life. Born in 1771, the only girl among five Wordsworth children, Dorothy Wordsworth was twenty-one months William's junior. After their mother's death when Dorothy was quite young, the girl was raised by various relatives and saw her brothers only occasionally. But in 1795, when she was twenty-four, William came into a legacy which enabled the two to settle together permanently, first in a cottage in Dorsetshire, then at Grasmere, in the English Lake Country Wordsworth was to celebrate throughout his poetic career.

At Alfoxden, in Dorsetshire, Dorothy began the journals on which her own reputation chiefly rests today, and she began them because, as she noted, "I shall give William Pleasure" by undertaking such a task. For many readers, then—as for Dorothy herself—the principal virtue of these works inheres in the source material they provided for the writer's brother, along with the William Wordsworth biography they record. As the critic Helen Darbishire once observed, they are important documents that show us "the life of a great poet." At the same time, however, Dorothy's diaries are extraordinarily compelling in and of themselves.

Vividly observed, often passionately frank, these journals are written with a hasty energy that perfectly captures the kaleidoscope of the Wordsworths' rural yet literary world. Though outwardly serene, that world was full of variety and vitality, as Dorothy continually demonstrates. Daily life alternated domesticity with adventure: Dorothy baked pies, broiled beefsteaks, and climbed craggy hillsides in rainy weather. William brooded on new poems, and Dorothy soothed his headaches, then wandered along country roads where she met a host of beggars, tinkers, and other itinerants who would provide him with subjects for more poems and her with further observations. Throughout the *Journals*, her narration of such matters is unfailingly brisk yet extraordinarily meticulous. On parting with her brother, for instance, she noted that "after a flood of tears my heart was easier," then demonstrated her recovery with keen observations of wildflowers and of "a blind man driving a very large beautiful Bull and a cow." Nor did she ever yield to excessive sentimentality, even about her adored William: she could not, for example, resist recording an episode in a meadow when the poet "took a sheep for me, and then me for a sheep."

On the day William Wordsworth married Mary Hutchinson in October 1802, his sister was so distraught—as her journal entry, included here, reveals —that she could not attend the wedding. Yet after the couple returned to Grasmere, Dorothy went on living with them, and there is every indication that the family was harmonious. Not only did Dorothy continue to "preserve" her brother as a poet, she became a fond nurse to his children, for whom she wrote some accomplished verses. As these works suggest, and as the piece entitled *Peaceful Our Valley* also indicates, she may well have had considerable poetic ability of her own. Why she did not produce more poetry than she did is thus a troublesome question, for, as her *Journals* reveal, she was never merely her brother's literary handmaiden, though critics have often defined her that way. Perhaps, as Virginia Woolf was to speculate in A *Room of One's Own*, she turned her talents to prose because "the poetry" is most often "denied outlet"

in women. In any case, she continued writing her lively and scrupulously detailed journals until 1828. In 1835, she suffered a serious collapse, which physicians now suspect was caused by hardening of arteries in the brain, and she
lingered on in what M. H. Abrams has called a kind of "half-life" for another
twenty years; for most of that time she was devotedly nursed by the brother to
whom her own devotion had once been so important.

From The Grasmere Journals

May 14 1800 [*Wednesday*]. Wm and John set off into Yorkshire
after dinner at ½ past 2 o'clock, cold pork in their pockets.[1] I left them
at the turning of the Low-wood bay under the trees. My heart was so
full that I could hardly speak to W. when I gave him a farewell kiss. I
sate a long time upon a stone at the margin of the lake, and after a flood
of tears my heart was easier. The lake looked to me I knew not why dull
and melancholy, and the weltering on the shores seemed a heavy
sound. I walked as long as I could amongst the stones of the shore. The
wood rich in flowers. A beautiful yellow, palish yellow flower, that
looked thick round and double, and smelt very sweet—I supposed it
was a ranunculus—Crowfoot, the grassy-leaved Rabbit-toothed white
flower, strawberries, geranium—scentless violet, anemones two kinds,
orchises, primroses. The heckberry very beautiful, the crab coming out
as a low shrub. Met a blind man, driving a very large beautiful Bull and
a cow—he walked with two sticks. Came home by Clappersgate. The
valley very green, many sweet views up to Rydale head when I could
juggle away the fine houses,[2] but they disturbed me even more than
when I have been happier. One beautiful view of the Bridge, without
Sir Michael's.[3] Sat down very often, though it was cold. I resolved to
write a journal of the time till W. and J. return, and I set about keeping
my resolve because I will not quarrel with myself, and because I shall
give Wm Pleasure by it when he comes home again. At Rydale a
woman of the village, stout and well dressed, begged a halfpenny—she
had never she said done it before, but these hard times——Arrived at
home with a bad headache, set some slips of privett.[4] The evening cold,
had a fire—my face now flame-coloured. It is nine o'clock. I shall soon
go to bed. A young woman begged at the door—she had come from
Manchester on Sunday morn with two shillings and a slip of paper
which she supposed a Bank note—it was a cheat. She had buried her
husband and three children within a year and a half—all in one grave

1. The poet William Wordsworth and his
younger brother John were on the way to visit
Mary Hutchinson, whom William would marry
two years later.

2. I.e., keep them out of view.
3. Sir Michael le Fleming's estate, Rydal Hall.
4. I.e., arranged cuttings from a privet, a kind of
shrub.

—burying very dear—paupers all put in one place—20 shillings paid for as much ground as will bury a man—a stone to be put over it or the right will be lost—11/6 each time the ground is opened. Oh! that I had a letter from William!

* * *

Friday 27th November 1801. Snow upon the ground thinly scattered. It snowed after we got up and then the sun shone and it was very warm though frosty—now the sun shines sweetly. A woman came who was travelling with her husband—he had been wounded and was going with her to live at Whitehaven. She had been at Ambleside the night before, offered 4d[5] at the Cock for a bed—they sent her to one Harrison's where she and her husband had slept upon the hearth and bought a pennyworth of chips for a fire. Her husband was gone before very lame—"Aye" says she "I was once an officer's wife I, as you see me now. My first husband married me at Appleby. I had 18£ a year for teaching a school and because I had no fortune his father turned him out of doors. I have been in the West Indies. I lost the use of this finger just before he died he came to me and said he must bid farewell to his dear children and me. I had a muslin gown on like yours—I seized hold of his coat as he went from me and slipped the joint of my finger. He was shot directly. I came to London and married this man. He was clerk to Judge Chambray, *that man*, that man that's going on the Road now. If he, Judge Chambray, had been at Kendal he would [have] given us a guinea or two and made nought of it, for he is very generous." Before dinner we set forward to walk intending to return to dinner. But as we had got as far as Rydale Wm thought he would go on to Mr Luff's. We accompanied him under Loughrigg, and parted near the stepping stones. * * *

Tuesday 22nd [December 1801]. Still thaw. I washed my head. Wm and I went to Rydale for letters. The road was covered with dirty snow, rough and rather slippery. We had a melancholy letter from C.,[6] for he had been very ill, though he was better when he wrote. We walked home almost without speaking. Wm composed a few lines of the Pedlar. We talked about Lamb's Tragedy[7] as we went down the White Moss. We stopped a long time in going to watch a little bird with a salmon coloured breast—a white cross or T upon its wings, and a brownish back with faint stripes. It was pecking the scattered Dung upon the road. It began to peck at the distance of 4 yards from us and advanced nearer and nearer till it came within the length of Wm's stick without any apparent fear of us. As we came up the White Moss we met an old man, who I saw was a beggar by his two bags hanging over

---

5. Fourpence.
6. Samuel Taylor Coleridge (1772–1834), poet

and friend of the Wordsworths.
7. *John Woodvil* (1802), by Charles Lamb.

his shoulder, but from a half laziness, half indifference and a wanting to *try* him if he would speak I let him pass. He said nothing, and my heart smote me. I turned back and said You are begging? "Ay," says he. I gave him a halfpenny. William, judging from his appearance joined in, I suppose you were a sailor? "Ay," he replied, "I have been 57 years at sea, 12 of them on board a man-of-war[8] under Sir Hugh Palmer." Why have you not a pension? "I have no pension, but I could have got into Greenwich hospital but all my officers are dead." He was 75 years of age, had a freshish colour in his cheeks, grey hair, a decent hat with a binding round the edge, the hat worn brown and glossy, his shoes were small thin shoes low in the quarters, pretty good. They had belonged to a gentleman. His coat was blue, frock shaped coming over his thighs, it had been joined up at the seams behind with paler blue to let it out, and there were three Bell-shaped patches of darker blue behind where the buttons had been. His breeches were either of fustian or grey cloth, with strings hanging down, whole and tight; he had a checked shirt on, and a small coloured handkerchief tied round his neck. His bags were hung over each shoulder and lay on each side of him, below his breast. One was brownish and of coarse stuff, the other was white with meal[9] on the outside, and his blue waist-coat was whitened with meal. In the coarse bag I guessed he put his scraps of meat etc. He walked with a slender stick decently stout, but his legs bowed outwards. We overtook old Fleming[1] at Rydale, leading his little Dutchmanlike grandchild along the slippery road. The same pace seemed to be natural to them both, the old man and the little child, and they went hand in hand, the grandfather cautious, yet looking proud of his charge. * * *

Tuesday 29th [*December 1801*]. A fine morning. A thin fog upon the hills which soon disappeared. The sun shone. Wilkinson went with us to the top of the hill. We turned out of the road at the 2nd mile stone and passed a pretty cluster of houses at the foot of St. John's Vale. The houses were among tall trees partly of Scotch fir, and some naked forest trees. We crossed a Bridge just below these houses and the river winded sweetly along the meadows. Our road soon led us along the sides of dreary bare hills, but we had a glorious prospect to the left of Saddle-back, half way covered with snow and underneath the comfortable white houses and the village of Threlkeld. These houses and the village want trees about them. Skiddaw was behind us and dear Coleridge's desert[2] home——As we ascended the hills it grew very cold and slippery. Luckily the wind was at our backs and helped us on. A sharp hail shower gathered at the head of Matterdale and the view upwards was very grand—the wild cottages seen through the hurrying hail shower. The wind drove and eddied about and about and the hills looked large

8. A warship.   1. Thomas Fleming, an innkeeper at Rydale.
9. Flour.   2. Deserted.

and swelling through the storm. We thought of Coleridge. O the bonny nooks and windings and curlings of the Beck down at the bottom of the steep green mossy Banks. * * *

Sunday 31st January 1809. William had slept very ill—he was tired and had a bad headache. We walked round the two lakes. Grasmere was very soft and Rydale was extremely beautiful from the pasture side. Nab Scar was just topped by a cloud which cutting it off as high as it could be cut off made the mountain look uncommonly lofty. We sate down a long time in different places. I always love to walk that way because it is the way I first came to Rydale and Grasmere, and because our dear Coleridge did also. When I came with Wm 6½ years ago it was just at sunset. There was a rich yellow light on the waters and the Islands were reflected there. Today it was grave and soft but not perfectly calm. William says it was much such a day as when Coleridge came with him. The sun shone out before we reached Grasmere. We sate by the road-side at the foot of the Lake close to Mary's dear name which she had cut herself upon the stone. William cut at it with his knife to make it plainer. We amused ourselves for a long time in watching the Breezes some as if they came from the bottom of the lake spread in a circle, brushing along the surface of the water, and growing more delicate, as it were thinner and of a *paler* colour till they died away. Others spread out like a peacock's tail, and some went right forward this way and that in all directions. The lake was still where these breezes were not, but they made it all alive. I found a strawberry blossom in a rock. The little slender flower had more courage than the green leaves, for *they* were but half expanded and half grown, but the blossom was spread full out. I uprooted it rashly, and I felt as if I had been committing an outrage, so I planted it again. It will have but a stormy life of it, but let it live if it can. * * * Mr Simpson drank tea with us. We payed our rent to Benson. William's head bad after Mr S. was gone. I petted him on the carpet and began a letter to Sara.

* * *

Sunday 14th February 1802. * * * After dinner a little before sunset I walked out. About 20 yards above glowworm Rock I met a Carman, a Highlander I suppose, with 4 carts, the first 3 belonging to himself, the last evidently to a man and his family who had joined company with him and who I guessed to be Potters. The carman was cheering his horses and talking to a little lass about 10 years of age who seemed to make him her companion. She ran to the Wall and took up a large stone to support the wheel of one of his carts and ran on before with it in her arms to be ready for him. She was a beautiful creature and there was something uncommonly impressive in the lightness and joyousness of her manner. Her business seemed to be all pleasure—pleasure in her own motions—and the man looked at her as if he too was pleased and spoke to her in the same tone in which he spoke to his horses. There was a wildness in her whole figure, not the wildness of a Mountain lass but a *Road* lass, a traveller from her Birth, who had wanted neither food nor clothes. Her Mother followed the last cart with a lovely child, perhaps about a year old, at her Back and a good-looking girl about 15 years old walked beside her. All the children were like the mother. She had a very fresh complexion, but she was blown with fagging[3] up the hill with the steepness of the hill and the Bairn that she carried. Her husband was helping the horse to drag the cart up by pushing it with his Shoulder. I got tea when I reached home and read German till about 9 o'clock. Then Molly went away and I wrote to Coleridge. Went to bed at about 12 o'clock. I slept in Wm's bed, and I slept badly, for my thoughts were full of William.

Thursday [*4th*] *March 1802.* Before we had quite finished Breakfast Calvert's man brought the horses for Wm.[4] We had a deal to do to shave—pens to make—poems to put in order for writing, to settle the dress pack up etc. The man came before the pens were made and he was obliged to leave me with only two. Since he has left me (at ½ past 11) it is now 2 I have been putting the Drawers into order, laid by his clothes which we had thrown here and there and everywhere, filed two months' newspapers and got my dinner 2 boiled eggs and 2 apple tarts. I have set Molly on to clear the garden a little, and I myself have helped. I transplanted some snowdrops—The Bees are busy—Wm has a nice bright day. It was hard frost in the night. The Robins are singing sweetly. Now for my walk. I *will* be busy, I *will* look well and be well when he comes back to me. O the Darling! Here is one of his bitten apples! I can hardly find in my heart to throw it into the fire. I must wash myself, then off—I walked round the two Lakes crossed the stepping stones at Rydale Foot. Sate down where we always sit. I was full of thoughts about my darling. Blessings on him. I came home at the foot of our own hill under Loughrigg. They are making sad ravages in the woods. Benson's Wood is going and the wood above the River. The wind has blown down a [?small] fir tree on the Rock that terminates John's path—I suppose the wind of Wednesday night. I read German after my return till tea time. After tea I worked and read the LB, enchanted with the Idiot Boy.[5] Wrote to Wm then went to Bed. It snowed when I went to Bed.

* * *

Thursday [*18th March 1802*]. A very fine morning. The sun shone but it was far colder than yesterday. I felt myself weak, and William

---

3. I.e., tired with struggling. "Bairn": baby.
4. In preparation for an expedition to Keswick, to meet Coleridge.
5. *Lyrical Ballads*, the book of poems which

Wordsworth and Coleridge published together in 1798. *The Idiot Boy* was one of William's contributions.

charged me not to go to Mrs Lloyd's. I seemed indeed, to myself unfit for it but when he was gone[6] I thought I would get the visit over if I could—So I ate a Beef-steak thinking it would strengthen me so it did, and I went off. I had a very pleasant walk. Rydale vale was full of life and motion. The wind blew briskly and the lake was covered all over with Bright silver waves that were there each the twinkling of an eye, then others rose up and took their place as fast as they went away. The Rocks glittered in the sunshine, the crows and the ravens were busy, and the thrushes and little Birds sang. I went through the fields, and sate ½ an hour afraid to pass a Cow. The Cow looked at me and I looked at the Cow and whenever I stirred the Cow gave over eating. I was not very much tired when I reached Lloyds, I walked in the garden. Charles is all for agriculture. Mrs L. in her kindest way. A parcel came in from Birmingham, with Lamb's play for us and for C. They came with me as far as Rydale. As we came along Ambleside vale in the twilight—it was a grave evening—there was something in the air that compelled me to serious thought. The hills were large, closed in by the sky. It was nearly dark when I parted from the Lloyds that is, night was come on and the moon came out from behind a mountain mass of Black clouds—O the unutterable darkness of the sky and the earth below the moon! and the glorious brightness of the moon itself! There was a vivid sparkling streak of light at this end of Rydale water but the rest was very dark and Loughrigg fell and Silver How were white and bright as if they were covered with hoar frost. The moon retired again and appeared and disappeared several times before I reached home. Once there was no moonlight to be seen but upon the Island house and the promontory of the Island where it stands, "That needs must be a holy place"[7] etc. etc. I had many very exquisite feelings and when I saw this lowly Building in the waters among the Dark and lofty hills, with that bright soft light upon it, it made me more than half a poet. I was tired when I reached home. I could not sit down to reading and tried to write verses but alas! I gave up expecting William and went soon to bed. Fletcher's carts came home late.

* * *

Thursday 15th April 1802. It was a threatening misty morning—but mild. We set off after dinner from Eusemere. * * * When we were in the woods beyond Gowbarrow park we saw a few daffodils[8] close to the water side. We fancied that the lake had floated the seeds ashore and that the little colony had so sprung up. But as we went along there were more and yet more and at last under the boughs of the trees, we saw that there was a long belt of them along the shore, about the breadth of a

6. To Keswick.
7. Source unknown; possibly from an early version of Coleridge's *Kubla Khan*.
8. Two years later William wrote a poem about

the daffodils, *I Wandered Lonely as a Cloud*, which appears to rely heavily on Dorothy's prose description.

country turnpike road. I never saw daffodils so beautiful they grew among the mossy stones about and about them, some rested their heads upon these stones as on a pillow for weariness and the rest tossed and reeled and danced and seemed as if they verily laughed with the wind that blew upon them over the lake, they looked so gay ever glancing ever changing. This wind blew directly over the lake to them. There was here and there a little knot and a few stragglers a few yards higher up but they were so few as not to disturb the simplicity and unity and life of that one busy highway. We rested again and again. The Bays were stormy, and we heard the waves at different distances and in the middle of the water like the sea.

* * *

Thursday 29th, April 1802. A beautiful morning. The sun shone and all was pleasant. * * * We * * * went to John's Grove, sate a while at first. Afterwards William lay, and I lay in the trench under the fence— he with his eyes shut and listening to the waterfalls and the Birds. There was no one waterfall above another—it was a sound of waters in the air —the voice of the air. William heard me breathing and rustling now and then but we both lay still, and unseen by one another. He thought that it would be as sweet thus to lie so in the grave, to hear the *peaceful* sounds of the earth and just to know that our dear friends were near. The Lake was still. There was a Boat out. Silver How reflected with delicate purple and yellowish hues as I have seen Spar. Lambs on the island and running races together by the half dozen in the round field near us. The copses green*ish*, hawthorn green.—Came home to dinner then went to Mr. Simpson. We rested a long time under a wall. Sheep and lambs were in the field—cottages smoking. As I lay down on the grass, I observed the glittering silver line on the ridges of the Backs of the sheep, owing to their situation respecting the Sun—which made them look beautiful but with something of strangeness, like animals of another kind—as if belonging to a more splendid world. * * *

[*Sept. 24, 1802*]. Mary first met us in the avenue. She looked so fat and well that we were made very happy by the sight of her. Then came Sara, and last of all Joanna.[9] Tom was forking corn standing upon the corn cart. We dressed ourselves immediately and got tea—the garden looked gay with asters and sweet peas. I looked at everything with tranquility and happiness—was ill on Saturday and on Sunday and continued to be during most of the time of our stay. Jack and George came on Friday Evening 1st October. On Saturday 2nd we rode to Hackness, William Jack George and Sara single, I behind Tom. On Sunday 3rd Mary and Sara were busy packing. On Monday 4th October 1802, my

9. The occasion is the marriage of William and Mary. All Mary's sisters and brothers were present, but only three attended the wedding, apparently because Dorothy was overwrought.

Brother William was married to Mary Hutchinson. I slept a good deal of the night and rose fresh and well in the morning. At a little after 8 o'clock I saw them go down the avenue towards the Church. William had parted from me upstairs. I gave him the wedding ring—with how deep a blessing! I took it from my forefinger where I had worn it the whole of the night before—he slipped it again onto my finger and blessed me fervently. When they were absent my dear little Sara prepared the breakfast. I kept myself as quiet as I could, but when I saw the two men running up the walk, coming to tell us it was over, I could stand it no longer and threw myself on the bed where I lay in stillness, neither hearing or seeing anything, till Sara came upstairs to me and said "They are coming" This forced me from the bed where I lay and I moved I knew not how straight forward, faster than my strength could carry me till I met my beloved William and fell upon his bosom. He and John Hutchinson led me to the house and there I stayed to welcome my dear Mary. As soon as we had breakfasted we departed.[1] It rained when we set off. Poor Mary was much agitated when she parted from her Brothers and Sisters and her home. Nothing particular occurred till we reached Kirby. We had sunshine and showers, pleasant talk, love and cheerfulness. * * * It rained very hard when we reached Windermere. We sate in the rain at Wilcock's to change horses, and arrived at Grasmere at about 6 o'clock on Wednesday Evening, the 6th of October 1802. Molly was overjoyed to see us, for my part I cannot describe what I felt, and our dear Mary's feelings would I dare say not be easy to speak of. We went by candle light into the garden and were astonished at the growth of the Brooms, Portugal Laurels, etc. etc. etc. The next day, Thursday, we unpacked the Boxes. On Friday 8th we baked Bread, and Mary and I walked, first upon the Hill side, and then in John's Grove, then in view of Rydale, the first walk that I had taken with my Sister.

* * *

1800–1803   1971

Peaceful Our Valley, Fair and Green

Peaceful our valley, fair and green;
    And beautiful the cottages
Each in its nook, its sheltered hold,
    Or underneath its tuft of trees.

Many and beautiful they are;   5
    But there is one that I love best,

---

1. Dorothy traveled back to Grasmere Cottage with William and Mary.

A lowly roof in truth it is,
   A brother of the rest.

Yet when I sit on rock or hill
   Down-looking on the valley fair,   10
That cottage with its grove of trees
   Summons my heart; it settles there.

Others there are whose small domain
   Of fertile fields with hedgerows green
Might more seduce the traveller's mind   15
   To wish that there his home had been.

Such wish be his! I blame him not,
   My fancies they, perchance, are wild;
I love that house because it is
   The very mountain's child.   20

Fields hath it of its own, green fields;
   But they are craggy, steep, and bare;
Their fence is of the mountain stone,
   And moss and lichen flourish there.

And when the storm comes from the North   25
   It lingers near that pastoral spot,
And piping through the mossy walls,
   It seems delighted with its lot.

And let it take its own delight,
   And let it range the pastures bare   30
Until it reach that grove of trees
   —It may not enter there!

A green unfading grove it is,
   Skirted with many a lesser tree,
Hazel and holly, beech and oak,   35
   A fair and flourishing company!

Precious the shelter of those trees!
   They screen the cottage that I love;
The sunshine pierces to the roof
   And the tall pine trees tower above.   40

When first I saw that dear abode
   It was a lovely winter's day:
After a night of perilous storm
   The West wind ruled with gentle sway;

A day so mild, it might have been   45
   The first day of the gladsome spring;
The robins warbled; and I heard
   One solitary throstle sing:

A stranger in the neighborhood,
   All faces then to me unknown,   50
I left my sole companion-friend
   To wander out alone.

Lured by a little winding path,
   I quitted soon the public road,
A smooth and tempting path it was   55
   By sheep and shepherds trod.

Eastward, toward the mighty hills
   This pathway led me on,
Until I reached a lofty Rock
   With velvet moss o'ergrown.   60

With russet Oak and tufts of Fern
   Its top was richly garlanded;
Its sides adorned with Eglantine
   Bedropped with hips of glossy red.

There too in many a sheltered chink   65
   The foxglove's broad leaves flourished fair,
And silver birch whose purple twigs
   Bend to the softest breathing air.

Beneath that rock my course I stayed
   And, looking to its summit high,   70
"Thou wear'st," said I, "a splendid garb,
   Here winter keeps his revelry.

"I've been a dweller on the plains,
   Have sighed when summer days were gone;
No more I'll sigh; for winter here   75
   Hath gladsome gardens of his own.

"What need of flowers? The splendid moss
   Is gayer than an April mead;
More rich its hues of various green,
   Orange and gold and glowing red."   80

—Beside that gay and lovely rock
   There came with merry voice

A foaming streamlet glancing by,
  It seemed to say "Rejoice!"

My youthful wishes all fulfilled   85
  Wishes matured by thoughtful choice,
I stood an Inmate[2] of this vale,
  How could I but rejoice?

1892

2. Inhabitant.

JANE AUSTEN
1775–1817

In 1816, writing to her nephew about his fiction and her own, Jane Austen asked, "What should I do with your strong, manly spirited sketches, full of variety and glow?—How could I possibly join them on to the little bit (two inches wide) of ivory on which I work with so fine a brush, as produces little effect after much labor?" This modest deprecation of her miniature art recalls the discreet figure Virginia Woolf evokes in *A Room of One's Own*, an Austen who sits writing in the common sitting room, readying herself for inevitable interruptions by providing herself with a blotter under which she can hide her manuscript. Yet by the time Austen was corresponding with J. Edward Austen at her desk in the common sitting room, she had already published four of the six novels that would gain her immediate and lasting acclaim. *Northanger Abbey* (1818), *Sense and Sensibility* (1811), *Pride and Prejudice* (1813), *Mansfield Park* (1814), *Emma* (1816), and *Persuasion* (1818) are unprecedented achievements which inaugurate the great novelistic tradition that continues in the work of Mary Shelley, the Brontës, George Eliot, and Virginia Woolf herself.

    Although Austen did not publish until she was thirty-six years old, she had two periods of literary productivity, first in her father's rectory when she was in her teens and early twenties, and second at Chawton, during the last decade of her life. Though shrouded in obscurity, the biographical background of her achievement has always been considered singularly uneventful. The daughter of George Austen, a rector and schoolteacher, and Cassandra (Leigh) Austen, the niece of the master of Balliol College, Oxford, Jane Austen was the seventh of eight children. Five of her six brothers married, and their children participated in the lively correspondence Austen maintained throughout her life. But her most intimate companion and correspondent was her older sister, Cassandra, a painter who was also, according to Austen, "the finest comic writer of the present age." Although Jane, beginning at six, and Cassandra, at nine, were sent away briefly to three different schools, they received most of their education at home from their father. When Mr. Austen discontinued his school, the two sisters shared a sitting room which included Jane's piano and notebooks and

Cassandra's drawing implements. From this period, 1787–1793, date such precocious juvenilia as *Love and Freindship* (Austen's youthful spelling) and *The Beautiful Cassandra*. Four years later, Austen also drafted *First Impressions* (1797), which was the original version of *Pride and Prejudice*, *Elinor and Marianne* (begun in 1797), the original of *Sense and Sensibility*, and *Northanger Abbey* (begun in 1797 and completed in 1803 but not published in her lifetime). Whether performing in home theatricals or circulating her manuscripts, Austen found in her immediate family her first and most enthusiastic audience. And Austen's characters would be drawn almost entirely from her family's class, the country gentry that distinguished itself from both the growing commercial class and the wealthier aristocracy.

In 1801, Mr. Austen gave his Steventon living (his Church office and the revenue attached to it) over to his eldest son, and moved with his wife and daughters to Bath. Either before or directly after leaving Steventon—the evidence is contradictory and unclear—Austen may have been in love with a young man who died, exactly the experience Cassandra had apparently endured in 1797. In any case, the subsequent death of her father in 1805 left her mother with an inadequate income of two hundred and ten pounds a year which was subsequently raised by her brothers to the barely adequate sum of four hundred and fifty pounds. After a short stay in Southampton, Mrs. Austen and her daughters settled down in a cottage on Edward Austen's estate. In what must have been confining circumstances at Chawton—living with her mother, Cassandra, an unmarried friend, and, occasionally, her brother James's daughter—Austen began revising and publishing her novels in rapid succession. Although she published anonymously, the immediate success of her fiction led to the identification of its author. Yet Austen managed to maintain a life of obscurity that Cassandra abetted after her sister's death by burning many of her letters. A year of an undetermined illness ended Austen's life when she was forty-two years of age. She was mourned by many relatives, but by none more grievously than her sister, who wrote, "She was the sun of my life, the gilder of every pleasure, the soother of every sorrow, I had not a thought concealed from her, and it is as if I had lost a part of myself."

Modesty and a desire for anonymity characterize Austen's most famous pronouncements, whether she is describing her subject ("three or four families in a country village") or defining herself ("the most unlearned and uninformed female who ever dared to be an authoress"). Yet she was well read in the eighteenth-century and Romantic classics of Richardson, Fielding, Pope, Goldsmith, Hume, Johnson, Scott, Cowper, and Byron. She was also an avid reader of books by her female contemporaries, especially Fanny Burney, Mary Brunton, Ann Radcliffe, and Maria Edgeworth. Indeed, in works like *Love and Freindship*, *Volume the First*, and *Northanger Abbey*, she began to define herself as a writer by self-consciously satirizing not only the female tradition in literature but also its effects on the growth and development of the female imagination: focusing either on the sentimental romance and the epistolary form or the Gothic novel, Austen comically criticized the overvaluation of love, the miseducation of women, the subterfuges of the marriage market, the rivalry among women for male approval, the female cult of weakness and dependency, the discrepancy between women's private sphere and public (male) history.

Precisely these themes, moreover, would inform her major novels.

From *Sense and Sensibility* to *Persuasion*, Austen delineated the lot of upper-middle-class girls who can escape the constraints of family life only by marrying. Just as the Dashwood sisters of *Sense and Sensibility* watch the family's fortune going to their half-brother, the Bennet daughters realize that their father's property has been entailed to a male cousin in *Pride and Prejudice*, Fanny Price in *Mansfield Park* is a poor dependent, and Anne Elliot of *Persuasion* is resigned to an impoverished spinsterhood. Even Austen's peremptory Emma, the heroine "whom no one but myself will much like," must learn to respect the ethical and economic authority of the well-named Mr. Knightley. Given the financial, social, and political power of men, Austen implies, female survival depends on gaining male approval and protection. As each heroine learns to distinguish among several apparently eligible suitors, Austen satirizes the bombastic self-importance of clergymen, the autocratic pride of aristocrats, the crudity of the *nouveau riche*, and, always, the flightiness of girls who delude themselves into thinking they are the masters of their own or anyone else's fate. Beneath the bright, sparkling tone of the narrator's voice, then, Austen's "two inches of ivory" become, in Dorothy Van Ghent's phrase, "a lady's fan," which is "in substance an elephant's tusk; it is a savagely probing instrument as well as a masterpiece of refinement." And Austen seems supremely confident about the scope and subject of her comedy. When, after the publication of *Emma*, the prince regent transmitted a message to her that she could "dedicate any future book to H.R.H." and his librarian suggested that it be "an historical romance illustrative of the august House of Cobourg," Austen explained, "I could not sit down seriously to write a serious romance under any motive than to save my life; and if it were indispensable for me to keep it up and never relax into laughing at myself or at any other, I am sure I should be hung before I finished the first chapter. I must keep to my own style and go on in my own way."

The limits Austen set for her art are exactly the limits she perceived as imposed on female experience. By analyzing the manners and morals of women whose lives were confined to the common sitting room, with exuberant hilarity in the juvenilia and a more ironic wit in the mature fiction, Austen provides a subtle portrayal of female values, a precise examination of female grief and joy. While a few readers, most famously Mark Twain and Ralph Waldo Emerson, took her own assessment at face value and faulted her fiction for its limitations, most have followed the example of such dissimilar artists as Scott, Macaulay, Tennyson, Trollope, Kipling, and Woolf in placing Austen's accomplishment next to Shakespeare's. For Woolf, Austen is ultimately "a mistress of much deeper emotion than appears upon the surface. She stimulates us to provide what is not there. What she offers is, apparently, a trifle, yet is composed of something that expands in the reader's mind and endows with the enduring form of life scenes which are outwardly trivial." Austen is, therefore, "the most perfect artist among women."

Love and Freindship

A NOVEL IN A SERIES OF LETTERS[1]

"Deceived in Freindship & Betrayed in Love"

Letter the First. From Isabel to Laura

How often, in answer to my repeated intreaties that you would give
my Daughter a regular detail of the Misfortunes and Adventures of
your Life, have you said "No, my freind never will I comply with your
request till I may be no longer in Danger of again experiencing such
dreadful ones." Surely that time is now at hand. You are this Day 55. If
a woman may ever be said to be in safety from the determined Perseverance of disagreable Lovers and the cruel Persecutions of obstinate Fathers, surely it must be at such a time of Life.

                                                                    Isabel

Letter 2d. Laura to Isabel

Altho' I cannot agree with you in supposing that I shall never again
be exposed to Misfortunes as unmerited as those I have already experienced, yet to avoid the imputation of Obstinacy or ill-nature, I will gratify the curiosity of your daughter; and may the fortitude with which I
have suffered the many Afflictions of my past Life, prove to her a useful
Lesson for the support of those which may befall her in her own.

                                                                    Laura

Letter 3d. Laura to Marianne

As the Daughter of my most intimate friend I think you entitled to
that knowledge of my unhappy Story, which your Mother has so often
solicited me to give you.

My Father was a native of Ireland & an inhabitant of Wales; My
Mother was the natural Daughter of a Scotch Peer by an italian
Opera-girl[2]—I was born in Spain & received my Education at a Con-
vent in France.

When I had reached my eighteenth Year I was recalled by my Parents to my paternal roof in Wales. Our mansion was situated in one of
the most romantic parts of the Vale of Uske. Tho' my Charms are now

---

1. The epistolary novel (i.e., a novel cast as a
series of letters) was a popular form in the eighteenth century, the most famous example being
Richardson's *Clarissa*; Austen is satirizing this
extremely sentimental genre. Following R. W.

Chapman, we have retained Austen's idiosyncratic spelling and capitalization throughout this
text.
2. Dancer in the ballet which was then a regular
part of all operas; thought to be of loose morals.

considerably softened and somewhat impaired by the Misfortunes I have undergone, I was once beautiful. But lovely as I was the Graces of my Person were the least of my Perfections. Of every accomplishment accustomary to my sex, I was Mistress. When in the Convent, my progress had always exceeded my instructions, my Acquirements had been wonderfull for my Age, and I had shortly surpassed my Masters.

In my Mind, every Virtue that could adorn it was centered; it was the Rendezvous of every good Quality & of every noble sentiment.

A sensibility[3] too tremblingly alive to every affliction of my Freinds, my Acquaintance and particularly to every affliction of my own, was my only fault, if a fault it could be called. Alas! how altered now! Tho' indeed my own misfortunes do not make less impression on me than they ever did, yet now I never feel for those of an other. My accomplishments too, begin to fade—I can neither sing so well nor Dance so gracefully as I once did and I have entirely forgot the *Minuet Dela Cour*[4]

Adeiu
Laura

Letter 4th. Laura to Marianne

Our neighbourhood was small, for it consisted only of your mother. She may probably have already told you that being left by her Parents in indigent Circumstances she had retired into Wales on eoconomical motives. There it was, our freindship first commenced. Isabel was then one and twenty—Tho' pleasing both in her Person and Manners (between ourselves) she never possessed the hundredth part of my Beauty or Accomplishments. Isabel had seen the World. She had passed 2 Years at one of the first Boarding schools in London; had spent a fortnight in Bath & had supped one night in Southampton.[5]

"Beware my Laura (she would often say) Beware of the insipid Vanities and idle Dissipations of the Metropolis of England; Beware of the unmeaning Luxuries of Bath & of the Stinking fish of Southampton."

"Alas! (exclaimed I) how am I to avoid those evils I shall never be exposed to? What probability is there of my ever tasting the Dissipations of London, the Luxuries of Bath or the stinking Fish of Southampton? I who am doomed to waste my Days of Youth & Beauty in an humble Cottage in the Vale of Uske."

---

3. A strong capacity for emotional response, highly valued especially by upper-class women.
4. Minuet of the court, an elegant French dance popular at the time.

5. Bath is an English resort famous for its mineral springs; Southampton is an English port city.

Ah! little did I then think I was ordained so soon to quit that humble Cottage for the Deceitfull Pleasures of the World.

adeiu
Laura

Letter 5th. Laura to Marianne

One Evening in December as my Father, my Mother and myself, were arranged in social converse round our Fireside, we were on a sudden, greatly astonished, by hearing a violent knocking on the outward Door of our rustic Cot.[6]

My Father started—"What noise is that," (said he.) "It sounds like a loud rapping at the Door"—(replied my Mother.) "it does indeed." (cried I.) "I am of your opinion; (said my Father) it certainly does appear to proceed from some uncommon violence exerted against our unoffending Door." "Yes (exclaimed I) I cannot help thinking it must be somebody who knocks for Admittance."

"That is another point (replied he;) We must not pretend to determine on what motive the person may knock—tho' that someone *does* rap at the Door, I am partly convinced."

Here, a 2d tremendous rap interrupted my Father in his speech and somewhat alarmed my Mother and me.

"Had we not better go and see who it is,? (said she) the Servants are out." "I think we had." (replied I.) "Certainly, (added my Father) by all means." "Shall we go now?" (said my Mother.) "The sooner the better." (answered he). "Oh! let no time be lost." (cried I.)

A third more violent Rap than ever again assaulted our ears. "I am certain there is somebody knocking at the Door." (said my Mother.) "I think there must," (replied my Father) "I fancy the Servants are returned; (said I) I think I hear Mary going to the Door." "I'm glad of it (cried my Father) for I long to know who it is."

I was right in my Conjecture; for Mary instantly entering the Room, informed us that a young Gentleman & his Servant were at the Door, who had lossed their way, were very cold and begged leave to warm themselves by our fire.

"Wont you admit them?" (said I) "You have no objection, my Dear?" (said my Father.) "None in the World." (replied my Mother.)

Mary, without waiting for any further commands immediately left the room and quickly returned introducing the most beauteous and amiable Youth, I had ever beheld. The servant, She kept to herself.

My natural Sensibility had already been greatly affected by the sufferings of the unfortunate Stranger and no sooner did I first behold him,

6. Cottage.

than I felt that on him the happiness or Misery of my future Life must depend.

adeiu
Laura

Letter 6th. Laura to Marianne

The noble Youth informed us that his name was Lindsay—for particular reasons however I shall conceal it under that of Talbot. He told us that he was the son of an English Baronet,[7] that his Mother had been many years no more and that he had a Sister of the middle size. "My Father (he continued) is a mean and mercenary wretch—it is only to such particular freinds as this Dear Party that I would thus betray his failings. Your Virtues my amiable Polydore (addressing himself to my father) yours Dear Claudia and yours my Charming Laura call on me to repose in you, my Confidence." We bowed. "My Father, seduced by the false glare of Fortune and the Deluding Pomp of Title, insisted on my giving my hand to Lady Dorothea. No never exclaimed I. Lady Dorothea is lovely and Engaging; I prefer no woman to her; but know Sir, that I scorn to marry her in compliance with your wishes. No! Never shall it be said that I obliged my Father."

We all admired the noble Manliness of his reply. He continued.

"Sir Edward was surprized; he had perhaps little expected to meet with so spirited an opposition to his will. 'Where Edward in the name of wonder (said he) did you pick up this unmeaning Gibberish? You have been studying Novels I suspect.' I scorned to answer: it would have been beneath my Dignity. I mounted my Horse and followed by my faithful William set forwards for my Aunts."

"My Father's house is situated in Bedfordshire my Aunt's in Middlesex, and tho' I flatter myself with being a tolerable proficienz in Geography, I know not how it happened, but I found myself entering this beautiful Vale which I find is in South Wales, when I had expected to have reached my Aunts.

"After having wandered some time on the Banks of the Uske without knowing which way to go, I began to lament my cruel Destiny in the bitterest and most pathetic Manner. It was now perfectly dark, not a single Star was there to direct my steps, and I know not what might have befallen me had I not at length discerned thro' the solemn Gloom that surrounded me a distant Light, which as I approached it, I discovered to be the chearfull Blaze of your fire. Impelled by the combination of Misfortunes under which I laboured, namely Fear, Cold and Hunger I hesitated not to ask admittance which at length I have gained; and now my Adorable Laura (continued he taking my Hand) when may I hope

---

7. One of the less prestigious British titles.

to receive that reward of all the painfull sufferings I have undergone during the course of my Attachment to you, to which I have ever aspired? Oh! when will you reward me with Yourself?"

"This instant, Dear and Amiable Edward." (replied I.). We were immediately united by my Father, who tho' he had never taken orders had been bred to the Church.

adeiu
Laura

Letter 7th. Laura to Marianne

We remained but a few Days after our Marriage, in the Vale of Uske. After taking an affecting Farewell of my father, my Mother and my Isabel, I accompanied Edward to his Aunt's in Middlesex. Philippa received us both with every expression of affectionate Love. My arrival was indeed a most agreable surprize to her as she had not only been totally ignorant of my Marriage with her Nephew, but had never even had the slightest idea of there being such a person in the World.

Augusta, the sister of Edward was on a visit to her when we arrived. I found her exactly what her Brother had described her to be—of the middle size. She received me with equal surprize though not with equal Cordiality, as Philippa. There was a Disagreable Coldness and Forbidding Reserve in her reception of me which was equally Distressing and Unexpected. None of that interesting Sensibility or amiable Simpathy in her Manners and Address to me which should have Distinguished our introduction to each other. Her Language was neither warm, nor affectionate, her expressions of regard were neither animated nor cordial; her arms were not opened to receive me to her Heart, tho' my own were extended to press her to mine.

A short Conversation between Augusta and her Brother, which I accidentally overheard encreased my Dislike to her, and convinced me that her Heart was no more formed for the soft ties of Love than for the endearing intercourse of Freindship.

"But do you think that my Father will ever be reconciled to this imprudent connection?" (said Augusta.)

"Augusta (replied the noble Youth) I thought you had a better opinion of me, than to imagine I would so abjectly degrade myself as to consider my Father's Concurrence in any of my Affairs, either of Consequence or concern to me. Tell me Augusta tell me with sincerity; did you ever know me consult his inclinations or follow his Advice in the least trifling Particular since the age of fifteen?"

"Edward (replied she) you are surely too diffident in your own praise. Since you were fifteen only!—My Dear Brother since you were five years old, I entirely acquit you of ever having willingly contributed to the Satisfaction of your Father. But still I am not without apprehensions of your being shortly obliged to degrade yourself in your own eyes by seeking a Support for your Wife in the Generosity of Sir Edward."

"Never, never Augusta will I so demean myself. (said Edward). Support! What Support will Laura want which she can receive from him?"

"Only those very insignificant ones of Victuals and Drink." (answered she.)

"Victuals and Drink! (replied my Husband in a most nobly contemtuous Manner) and dost thou then imagine that there is no other support for an exalted Mind (such as is my Laura's) than the mean and indelicate employment of Eating and Drinking?"

"None that I know of, so efficacious." (returned Augusta).

"And did you then never feel the pleasing Pangs of Love, Augusta? (replied my Edward). Does it appear impossible to your vile and corrupted Palate, to exist on Love? Can you not conceive the Luxury of living in every Distress that Poverty can inflict, with the object of your tenderest Affection?"

"You are too ridiculous (said Augusta) to argue with; perhaps however you may in time be convinced that. . . ."

Here I was prevented from hearing the remainder of her Speech, by the Appearance of a very Handsome Young Woman, who was ushered into the Room at the Door of which I had been listening. On hearing her announced by the Name of "Lady Dorothea", I instantly quitted my Post and followed her into the Parlour, for I well remembered that she was the Lady, proposed as a Wife for my Edward by the Cruel and Unrelenting Baronet.

Altho' Lady Dorothea's visit was nominally to Philippa and Augusta, yet I have some reason to imagine that (acquainted with the Marriage and arrival of Edward) to see me was a principal motive to it.

I soon perceived that tho' lovely and Elegant in her Person and tho' Easy and Polite in her Address, she was of that inferior order of Beings with regard to Delicate feeling, tender Sentiments, and refined Sensibility, of which Augusta was one.

She staid but half an hour and neither in the Course of her Visit, confided to me any of her Secret thoughts, nor requested me to confide in her, any of mine. You will easily imagine therefore my Dear Marianne that I could not feel any ardent Affection or very sincere Attachment for Lady Dorothea.

Adeiu
Laura

Letter 8th. Laura to Marianne, in continuation

Lady Dorothea had not left us long before another visitor as unexpected a one as her Ladyship, was announced. It was Sir Edward, who informed by Augusta of her Brother's marriage, came doubtless to reproach him for having dared to unite himself to me without his Knowledge. But Edward foreseeing his Design, approached him with heroic fortitude as soon as he entered the Room, and addressed him in the following Manner.

"Sir Edward, I know the motive of your Journey here—You come with the base Design of reproaching me for having entered into an indissoluble engagement with my Laura without your Consent—But Sir, I glory in the Act—. It is my greatest boast that I have incurred the Displeasure of my Father!"

So saying, he took my hand and whilst Sir Edward, Philippa, and Augusta were doubtless reflecting with Admiration on his undaunted Bravery, led me from the Parlour to his Father's Carriage, which yet remained at the Door and in which we were instantly conveyed from the pursuit of Sir Edward.

The Postilions[8] had at first received orders only to take the London road; as soon as we had sufficiently reflected However, we ordered them to Drive to M——, the seat of Edward's most particular freind, which was but a few miles distant.

At M——. we arrived in a few hours; and on sending in our names were immediately admitted to Sophia, the Wife of Edward's freind. After having been deprived during the course of 3 weeks of a real freind (for such I term your Mother) imagine my transports[9] at beholding one, most truly worthy of the Name. Sophia was rather above the middle size; most elegantly formed. A soft Languor spread over her lovely features, but increased their Beauty.—It was the Charectaristic of her Mind—. She was all Sensibility and Feeling. We flew into each others arms & after having exchanged vows of mutual Freindship for the rest of our Lives, instantly unfolded to each other the most inward Secrets of our Hearts—. We were interrupted in this Delightfull Employment by the entrance of Augustus, (Edward's freind) who was just returned from a solitary ramble.

Never did I see such an affecting Scene as was the meeting of Edward & Augustus.

"My Life! my Soul!" (exclaimed the former) "My Adorable Angel!" (replied the latter) as they flew into each other's arms. It was too pathetic for the feelings of Sophia and myself—We fainted Alternately on a Sofa.

Adeiu
Laura

Letter the 9th. From the Same to the Same

Towards the close of the Day we received the following Letter from Philippa.

8. Riders who guide the horses drawing a coach.   9. Joy.

"Sir Edward is greatly incensed by your abrupt departure; he has taken back Augusta with him to Bedfordshire. Much as I wish to enjoy again your charming society, I cannot determine to snatch you from that, of such dear & deserving Freinds—When your Visit to them is terminated, I trust you will return to the arms of your"

"Philippa."

We returned a suitable answer to this affectionate Note & after thanking her for her kind invitation assured her that we would certainly avail ourselves of it, whenever we might have no other place to go to. Tho' certainly nothing could to any reasonable Being, have appeared more satisfactory, than so gratefull a reply to her invitation, yet I know not how it was, but she was certainly capricious enough to be displeased with our behaviour and in a few weeks after, either to revenge our Conduct, or releive her own solitude, married a young and illiterate Fortune-hunter. This imprudent Step (tho' we were sensible that it would probably deprive us of that fortune which Philippa had ever taught us to expect) could not on our own accounts, excite from our exalted Minds a single sigh; yet fearfull lest it might prove a source of endless misery to the deluded Bride, our trembling Sensibility was greatly affected when we were first informed of the Event. The affectionate Entreaties of Augustus and Sophia that we would for ever consider their House as our Home, easily prevailed on us to determine never more to leave them—. In the Society of my Edward & this Amiable Pair, I passed the happiest moments of my Life: Our time was most delightfully spent, in mutual Protestations of Freindship, and in vows of unalterable Love, in which we were secure from being interrupted, by intruding & disagreable Visitors, as Augustus & Sophia had on their first Entrance in the Neighbourhood, taken due care to inform the surrounding Families, that as their Happiness centered wholly in themselves, they wished for no other society. But alas! my Dear Marianne such Happiness as I then enjoyed was too perfect to be lasting. A most severe & unexpected Blow at once destroyed every Sensation of Pleasure. Convinced as you must be from what I have already told you concerning Augustus & Sophia, that there never were a happier Couple, I need not I imagine inform you that their union had been contrary to the inclinations of their Cruel & Mercenary Parents; who had vainly endeavoured with obstinate Perseverance to force them into a Marriage with those whom they had ever abhorred, but with an Heroic Fortitude worthy to be related & Admired, they had both, constantly refused to submit to such despotic Power.

After having so nobly disentangled themselves from the Shackles of Parental Authority, by a Clandestine Marriage, they were determined never to forfeit the good opinion they had gained in the World, in so doing, by accepting any proposals of reconciliation that might be of-

fered them by their Fathers—to this farther tryal of their noble inde-
pendance however they never were exposed.

They had been married but a few months when our visit to them
commenced during which time they had been amply supported by a
considerable sum of Money which Augustus had gracefully purloined
from his Unworthy father's Escritoire,[1] a few days before his union with
Sophia.

By our arrival their Expences were considerably encreased tho' their
means for supplying them were then nearly exhausted. But they, Exalted Creatures! scorned to reflect a moment on their pecuniary Distresses & would have blushed at the idea of paying their Debts.—Alas!
what was their Reward for such disinterested Behaviour. The beautifull
Augustus was arrested and we were all undone. Such perfidious
Treachery in the merciless perpetrators of the Deed will shock your
gentle nature Dearest Marianne as much as it then affected the Delicate Sensibility of Edward, Sophia, your Laura, & of Augustus himself.
To compleat such unparalelled Barbarity we were informed that an
Execution[2] in the House would shortly take place. Ah! what could we
do but what we did! We sighed & fainted on the Sofa.

Adeiu
Laura

Letter 10th. Laura in continuation

When we were somewhat recovered from the overpowering Effusions of our Grief, Edward desired that we would consider what was the
most prudent step to be taken in our unhappy situation while he repaired to his imprisoned freind to lament over his misfortunes. We
promised that we would, & he set forwards on his Journey to Town.
During his Absence we faithfully complied with his Desire & after the
most mature Deliberation, at length agreed that the best thing we could
do was to leave the House; of which we every moment expected the
Officers of Justice to take possession. We waited therefore with the
greatest impatience, for the return of Edward in order to impart to him
the result of our Deliberations—. But no Edward appeared—. In vain
did we count the tedious Moments of his Absence—in vain did we
weep—in vain even did we sigh—no Edward returned—. This was too
cruel, too unexpected a Blow to our Gentle Sensibility—. we could not
support it—we could only faint—. At length collecting all the Resolution I was Mistress of, I arose & after packing up some necessary Apparel for Sophia & myself, I dragged her to a Carriage I had ordered &
instantly we set out for London. As the Habitation of Augustus was
within twelve miles of Town, it was not long e'er we arrived there, & no

---

1. A writing desk.   2. Legal siezure of property to pay bad debts.

sooner had we entered Holbourn than letting down one of the Front
Glasses I enquired of every decent-looking Person that we passed "If
they had seen my Edward"?

But as we drove too rapidly to allow them to answer my repeated
Enquiries, I gained little, or indeed, no information concerning him.
"Where am I to Drive?" said the Postilion. "To Newgate[3] Gentle
Youth (replied I), to see Augustus." "Oh! no, no, (exclaimed Sophia) I
cannot go to Newgate; I shall not be able to support the sight of my
Augustus in so cruel a confinement—my feelings are sufficiently
shocked by the *recital*, of his Distress, but to behold it will overpower
my Sensibility." As I perfectly agreed with her in the Justice of her
Sentiments the Postilion was instantly directed to return into the Country. You may perhaps have been somewhat surprised my Dearest Marianne, that in the Distress I then endured, destitute of any Support, &
unprovided with any Habitation, I should never once have remembered my Father & Mother or my paternal Cottage in the Vale of Uske.
To account for this seeming forgetfullness I must inform you of a trifling Circumstance concerning them which I have as yet never mentioned—. The death of my Parents a few weeks after my Departure, is
the circumstance I allude to. By their decease I became the lawfull In-
heritress of their House & Fortune. But alas! the House had never been
their own & their Fortune had only been an Annuity[4] on their own
Lives. Such is the Depravity of the World! To your Mother I should
have returned with Pleasure, should have been happy to have introduced to her, my Charming Sophia & should have with Chearfullness
have passed the remainder of my Life in their dear Society in the Vale
of Uske, had not one obstacle to the execution of so agreable a Scheme,
intervened; which was the Marriage & Removal of your Mother to a
Distant part of Ireland.

Adeiu

Laura

Letter 11th. Laura in continuation

"I have a Relation in Scotland (said Sophia to me as we left London)
who I am certain would not hesitate in receiving me." "Shall I order
the Boy to drive there?" said I—but instantly recollecting myself, exclaimed "Alas I fear it will be too long a Journey for the Horses." Unwilling however to act only from my own inadequate Knowledge of the
Strength & Abilities of Horses, I consulted the Postilion, who was entirely of my Opinion concerning the Affair. We therefore determined
to change Horses at the next Town & to travel Post[5] the remainder of

---

3. A well-known British prison.   5. In relays, changing horses at intervals.
4. A sum of money paid annually for life.

the Journey.—. When we arrived at the last Inn we were to stop at, which was but a few miles from the House of Sophia's Relation, unwilling to intrude our Society on him unexpected & unthought of, we wrote a very elegant & well-penned Note to him containing an Account of our Destitute & melancholy Situation, and of our intention to spend some months with him in Scotland. As soon as we had dispatched this letter, we immediately prepared to follow it in person & were stepping into the Carriage for that Purpose when our Attention was attracted by the Entrance of a coroneted Coach & 4[6] into the Innyard. A Gentleman considerably advanced in years, descended from it—. At his first Appearance my Sensibility was wonderfully affected & e'er I had gazed at him a 2d time, an instinctive Sympathy whispered to my Heart, that he was my Grandfather.

Convinced that I could not be mistaken in my conjecture I instantly sprang from the Carriage I had just entered, & following the Venerable Stranger into the Room he had been shewn to, I threw myself on my knees before him & besought him to acknowledge me as his Grand Child.—He started, & after having attentively examined my features, raised me from the Ground & throwing his Grand-fatherly arms around my neck, exclaimed, "Acknowledge thee! Yes dear resemblance of my Laurina & my Laurina's Daughter, sweet image of my Claudia & my Claudia's Mother, I do acknowledge thee as the Daughter of the one & the Grandaughter of the other." While he was thus tenderly embracing me, Sophia astonished at my precipitate Departure, entered the Room in search of me—. No sooner had she caught the eye of the venerable Peer, than he exclaimed with every mark of Astonishment—"Another Grandaughter! Yes, yes, I see you are the Daughter of my Laurina's eldest Girl; Your resemblance to the beauteous Matilda sufficiently proclaims it." "Oh.!" replied Sophia, "when I first beheld you the instinct of Nature whispered me that we were in some degree related—But whether Grandfathers, or Grandmothers, I could not pretend to determine." He folded her in his arms, and whilst they were tenderly embracing, the Door of the Apartment opened and a most beautifull Young Man appeared. On perceiving him Lord St. Clair started and retreating back a few paces, with uplifted Hands, said, "Another Grandchild! What an unexpected Happiness is this! to discover in the space of 3 minutes, as many of my Descendants! This, I am certain is Philander[7] the son of my Laurina's 3d Girl the amiable Bertha; there wants now but the presence of Gustavus to compleat the Union of my Laurina's Grand-Children."

"And here he is; (said a Gracefull Youth who that instant entered the room) here is the Gustavus you desire to see. I am the son of Agatha

---

6. A fancy coach drawn by four horses.   7. Traditional name for a lover or flirt.

your Laurina's 4th & Youngest Daughter." "I see you are indeed; re-plied Lord St. Clair—But tell me (continued he looking fearfully to-wards the Door) tell me, have I any other Grand-Children in the House." "None my Lord." "Then I will provide for you all without further delay—Here are 4 Banknotes of 50£ each—Take them & re-member I have done the Duty of a Grandfather—." He instantly left the Room & immediately afterwards the House.

Adeiu

Laura

Letter the 12th. Laura in continuation

You may imagine how greatly we were surprised by the sudden de-parture of Lord St. Clair. "Ignoble Grand-sire!" exclaimed Sophia. "Unworthy Grandfather!" said I, & instantly fainted in each other's arms. How long we remained in this situation I know not; but when we recovered we found ourselves alone, without either Gustavus, Phil-ander or the Bank-notes. As we were deploring our unhappy fate, the Door of the Apartment opened & "Macdonald" was announced. He was Sophia's cousin. The haste with which he came to our relief so soon after the receipt of our Note, spoke so greatly in his favour that I hesitated not to pronounce him at first sight, a tender & Simpathetic Freind. Alas! he little deserved the name—for though he told us that he was much concerned at our Misfortunes, yet by his own account it ap-peared that the perusal of them, had neither drawn from him a single sigh, nor induced him to bestow one curse on our vindictive Stars.—. He told Sophia that his Daughter depended on her returning with him to Macdonald-Hall, & that as his Cousin's freind he should be happy to see me there also. To Macdonald-Hall, therefore, we went, and were received with great kindness by Janetta the daughter of Macdonald, & the Mistress of the Mansion. Janetta was then only fifteen; naturally well disposed, endowed with a susceptible Heart, and a simpathetic Disposition, she might, had these amiable Qualities been properly en-couraged, have been an ornament to human Nature; but unfortunately her Father possessed not a soul sufficiently exalted to admire so promis-ing a Disposition, and had endeavoured by every means in his power to prevent its encreasing with her Years. He had actually so far extin-guished the natural noble Sensibility of her Heart, as to prevail on her to accept an offer from a young man of his Recommendation. They were to be married in a few months, and Graham, was in the House when we arrived. We soon saw through his Character.—. He was just such a Man as one might have expected to be the choice of Macdonald. They said he was Sensible, well-informed, and Agreable; we did not pretend to Judge of such trifles, but as we were convinced he had no soul, that he had never read the *Sorrows of Werter*,[8] & that his Hair bore not the slightest resemblance to Auburn, we were certain that Janetta could feel no affection for him, or at least that she ought to feel none. The very circumstance of his being her father's choice too, was so much in his disfavour, that had he been deserving her, in every other respect yet *that* of itself ought to have been a sufficient reason in the Eyes of Janetta for rejecting him. These considerations we were determined to represent to her in their proper light & doubted not of meeting with the desired success from one naturally so well disposed, whose errors in the Affair had only arisen from a want of proper confidence in her own opinion, & a suitable contempt of her father's. We found her indeed all that our warmest wishes could have hoped for; we had no difficulty to convince her that it was impossible she could love Graham, or that it was her duty to disobey her Father; the only thing at which she rather seemed to hesitate was our assertion that she must be attached to some other Person. For some time, she persevered in declaring that she knew no other young Man for whom she had the smallest Affection; but upon explaining the impossibility of such a thing she said that she believed she *did like* Captain M'Kenzie better than any one she knew besides. This confession satisfied us and after having enumerated the good Qualities of M'Kenzie & assured her that she was violently in love with him, we desired to know whether he had ever in any wise declared his Affection to her.

"So far from having ever declared it, I have no reason to imagine that he has ever felt any for me." said Janetta. "That he certainly adores you (replied Sophia) there can be no doubt—. The Attachment must be reciprocal—. Did he never gaze on you with Admiration—tenderly press your hand—drop an involuntary tear—& leave the room abruptly?" "Never (replied She) that I remember—he has always left the room indeed when his visit has been ended, but has never gone away particularly abruptly or without making a bow". "Indeed my Love (said I) you must be mistaken—: for it is absolutely impossible that he should ever have left you but with Confusion, Despair, & Precipitation[9]—. Consider but for a moment Janetta, & you must be convinced how absurd it is to suppose that he could ever make a Bow, or behave like any other Person." Having settled this Point to our satisfaction, the next we took into consideration was, to determine in what manner we should inform M'Kenzie of the favourable Opinion Janetta entertained of him.—. We at length agreed to acquaint him with it by an anonymous Letter which Sophia drew up in the following Manner.

8. *The Sorrows of Young Werther* a novel by Johann Wolfgang von Goethe (1749–1832), records the brief and stormy life of a passionate young man.
9. I.e., tears.

"Oh! happy Lover of the beautifull Janetta, oh! enviable Possessor of *her* Heart whose hand is destined to another, why do you thus delay a confession of your Attachment to the amiable Object of it? Oh! consider that a few weeks will at once put an end to every flattering Hope that you may now entertain, by uniting the unfortunate Victim of her father's Cruelty to the execrable & detested Graham."

"Alas! why do you thus so cruelly connive at the projected Misery of her & of yourself by delaying to communicate that scheme which had doubtless long possessed your imagination? A secret Union will at once secure the felicity of both."

The amiable M'Kenzie, whose modesty as he afterwards assured us had been the only reason of his having so long concealed the violence of his affection for Janetta, on receiving this Billet[1] flew on the wings of Love to Macdonald-Hall, and so powerfully pleaded his Attachment to her who inspired it, that after a few more private interviews, Sophia & I experienced the Satisfaction of seeing them depart for Gretna-Green, which they chose for the celebration of their Nuptials, in preference to any other place although it was at a considerable distance from Macdonald-Hall.

Adeiu
Laura

Letter the 13th. Laura in Continuation

They had been gone nearly a couple of Hours, before either Macdonald or Graham had entertained any suspicion of the affair—. And they might not even then have suspected it, but for the following little Accident. Sophia happening one Day to open a private Drawer in Macdonald's Library with one of her own keys, discovered that it was the Place where he kept his Papers of consequence & amongst them some bank notes of considerable amount. This discovery she imparted to me; and having agreed together that it would be a proper treatment of so vile a Wretch as Macdonald to deprive him of money, perhaps dishonestly gained, it was determined that the next time we should either of us happen to go that way, we would take one or more of the Bank notes from the drawer. This well-meant Plan we had often successfully put in Execution; but alas! on the very day of Janetta's Escape, as Sophia was majestically removing the 5th Bank-note from the Drawer to her own purse, she was suddenly most impertinently interrupted in her employment by the entrance of Macdonald himself, in a most abrupt & precipitate Manner. Sophia (who though naturally all winning sweetness could when occasions demanded it call forth the

1. Note.

Dignity of her Sex) instantly put on a most forbiding look, & darting an angry frown on the undaunted Culprit, demanded in a haughty tone of voice "Wherefore her retirement[2] was thus insolently broken in on?" The unblushing Macdonald, without even endeavouring to exculpate himself from the crime he was charged with, meanly endeavoured to reproach Sophia with ignobly defrauding him of his Money. The dignity of Sophia was wounded; "Wretch (exclaimed she, hastily replacing the Bank-note in the Drawer) how darest thou to accuse me of an Act, of which the bare idea makes me blush?" The base wretch was still unconvinced & continued to upbraid the justly-offended Sophia in such opprobrious Language, that at length he so greatly provoked the gentle sweetness of her Nature, as to induce her to revenge herself on him by informing him of Janetta's Elopement, and of the active Part we had both taken in the Affair. At this period of their Quarrel I entered the Library and was as you may imagine equally offended as Sophia at the ill-grounded Accusations of the malevolent and contemptible Macdonald. "Base Miscreant (cried I) how canst thou thus undauntedly endeavour to sully the spotless reputation of such bright Excellence? Why dost thou not suspect *my* innocence as soon?" "Be satisfied Madam (replied he) I *do* suspect it, & therefore must desire that you will both leave this House in less than half an hour."

"We shall go willingly; (answered Sophia) our hearts have long detested thee, & nothing but our freindship for thy Daughter could have induced us to remain so long beneath thy roof."

"Your Freindship for my Daughter has indeed been most powerfully exerted by throwing her into the arms of an unprincipled Fortune-hunter." (replied he)

"Yes, (exclaimed I) amidst every misfortune, it will afford us some consolation to reflect that by this one act of Freindship to Janetta, we have amply discharged every obligation that we have received from her father."

"It must indeed be a most gratefull reflection, to your exalted minds." (said he.)

As soon as we had packed up our wardrobe & valuables, we left Macdonald Hall, & after having walked about a mile & a half we sate down by the side of a clear limpid stream to refresh our exhausted limbs. The place was suited to meditation.—.A Grove of full-grown Elms sheltered us from the East—. A Bed of full-grown Nettles from the West—. Before us ran the murmuring brook & behind us ran the turn-pike road. We were in a mood for contemplation & in a Disposition to enjoy so beautifull a spot. A mutual Silence which had for some time reigned between us, was at length broke by my exclaiming—

2. Privacy, solitude.

"What a lovely Scene! Alas why are not Edward & Augustus here to enjoy its Beauties with us?"

"Ah! my beloved Laura (cried Sophia) for pity's sake forbear recalling to my remembrance the unhappy situation of my imprisoned Husband. Alas, what would I not give to learn the fate of my Augustus! to know if he is still in Newgate, or if he is yet hung. But never shall I be able so far to conquer my tender sensibility as to enquire after him. Oh! do not I beseech you ever let me again hear you repeat his beloved name—. It affects me too deeply—. I cannot bear to hear him mentioned, it wounds my feelings."

"Excuse me my Sophia for having thus unwillingly offended you—" replied I—and then changing the conversation, desired her to admire the Noble Grandeur of the Elms which Sheltered us from the Eastern Zephyr.[3] "Alas! my Laura (returned she) avoid so melancholy a subject, I intreat you.—Do not again wound my Sensibility by Observations on those elms. They remind me of Augustus—. He was like them, tall, magestic—he possessed that noble grandeur which you admire in them."

I was silent, fearfull lest I might any more unwillingly distress her by fixing on any other subject of conversation which might again remind her of Augustus.

"Why do you not speak my Laura?" (said she after a short pause) "I cannot support this silence—you must not leave me to my own reflections; they ever recur to Augustus."

"What a beautifull Sky! (said I) How charmingly is the azure varied by those delicate streaks of white!"

"Oh! my Laura (replied she hastily withdrawing her Eyes from a momentary glance at the sky) do not thus distress me by calling my Attention to an object which so cruelly reminds me of my Augustus's blue sattin Waist-coat striped with white! In pity to your unhappy freind avoid a subject so distressing." What could I do? The feelings of Sophia were at that time so exquisite, & the tenderness she felt for Augustus so poignant that I had not the power to start any other topic, justly fearing that it might in some unforseen manner again awaken all her sensibility by directing her thoughts to her Husband.—Yet to be silent would be cruel; She had intreated me to talk.

From this Dilemma I was most fortunately releived by an accident truly apropos; it was the lucky overturning of a Gentleman's Phaeton,[4] on the road which ran murmuring behind us. It was a most fortunate Accident as it diverted the Attention of Sophia from the melancholy reflections which she had been before indulging. We instantly quitted our seats & ran to the rescue of those who but a few moments before

---

3. Gentle breeze.   4. A light, open carriage.

had been in so elevated a situation as a fashionably high Phaeton, but who were now laid low and sprawling in the Dust—. "What an ample subject for reflection on the uncertain Enjoyments of this World, would not that Phaeton & the Life of Cardinal Wolsey[5] afford a thinking Mind!" said I to Sophia as we were hastening to the field of Action.

She had not time to answer me for every thought was now engaged by the horrid Spectacle before us. Two Gentlemen most elegantly attired but weltering in their blood was what first struck our Eyes—we approached—they were Edward & Augustus—Yes dearest Marianne they were our Husbands. Sophia shreiked & fainted on the Ground—I screamed and instantly ran mad—. We remained thus mutually deprived of our Senses some minutes, & on regaining them were deprived of them again—. For an Hour & a Quarter did we continue in this unfortunate Situation—Sophia fainting every moment & I running Mad as often. At length a Groan from the hapless Edward (who alone retained any share of Life) restored us to ourselves—. Had we indeed before imagined that either of them lived, we should have been more sparing of our Greif—but as we had supposed when we first beheld them that they were no more, we knew that nothing could remain to be done but what we were about—. No sooner therefore did we hear my Edward's groan than postponing our Lamentations for the present, we hastily ran to the Dear Youth and kneeling on each side of him implored him not to die—. "Laura (said He fixing his now languid Eyes on me) I fear I have been overturned."

I was overjoyed to find him yet sensible—.

"Oh! tell me Edward (said I) tell me I beseech you before you die, what has befallen you since that unhappy Day in which Augustus was arrested & we were separated—"

"I will" (said he) and instantly fetching a Deep sigh, expired—. Sophia immediately sunk again into a swoon—. *My* Greif was more audible, My voice faltered, My Eyes assumed a vacant Stare, My face became as pale as Death, and my Senses were considerably impaired—.

"Talk not to me of Phaetons (said I, raving in a frantic, incoherent manner)—Give me a violin—. I'll play to him & sooth him in his melancholy Hours—Beware ye gentle Nymphs of Cupid's Thunderbolts, avoid the piercing Shafts of Jupiter[6]—Look at that Grove of Firs—I see a Leg of Mutton—They told me Edward was not Dead; but they deceived me—they took him for a Cucumber—" Thus I continued

---

5. Thomas Wolsey (c. 1475–1530), British cardinal who fell from power as a result of a quarrel with Henry VIII.
6. Cupid is the god of love in Greek mythology, traditionally armed with arrows, while Jupiter is the sovereign god who brandishes thunderbolts; Laura has confused the two. "Nymphs" are mythical female spirits, but the word may also refer to young girls in general.

wildly exclaiming on my Edward's death—. For two Hours did I rave thus madly and should not then have left off, as I was not in the least fatigued, had not Sophia who was just recovered from her swoon, intreated me to consider that Night was now approaching and that the Damps began to fall. "And whither shall we go (said I) to shelter us from either"? "To that white Cottage." (replied she pointing to a neat building which rose up amidst the Grove of Elms & which I had not before observed—) I agreed & we instantly walked to it—we knocked at the door—it was opened by an old Woman; on being requested to afford us a Night's Lodging, she informed us that her House was but small, that she had only two Bed-rooms, but that However we should be wellcome to one of them. We were satisfied & followed the good Woman into the House where we were greatly cheered by the sight of a comfortable fire—. She was a Widow & had only one Daughter, who was then just Seventeen—One of the best of ages; but alas! she was very plain & her name was Bridget. . . . . . Nothing therefore could be expected from her—she could not be supposed to posses either exalted Ideas, Delicate Feelings or refined Sensibilities—She was nothing more than a mere good-tempered, civil & obliging Young Woman; as such we could scarcely dislike her—she was only an Object of Contempt—.

Adeiu

Laura

Letter the 14th. Laura in continuation

Arm yourself my amiable Young Freind with all the philosophy you are Mistress of; summon up all the fortitude you possess, for Alas! in the perusal of the following Pages your sensibility will be most severely tried. Ah! what were the Misfortunes I had before experienced & which I have already related to you, to the one I am now going to inform you of. The Death of my Father, my Mother, and my Husband though almost more than my gentle Nature could support, were trifles in comparison to the misfortune I am now proceeding to relate. The morning after our arrival at the Cottage, Sophia complained of a violent pain in her delicate limbs, accompanied with a disagreable Head-ake. She attributed it to a cold caught by her continued faintings in the open Air as the Dew was falling the Evening before. This I feared was but too probably the case; since how could it be otherwise accounted for that I should have escaped the same indisposition, but by supposing that the bodily Exertions I had undergone in my repeated fits of frenzy, had so effectually circulated & warmed my Blood as to make me proof against the chilling Damps of Night, whereas, Sophia lying totally inactive on the Ground must have been exposed to all their Severity. I was most seriously alarmed by her illness which trifling as it may appear to you, a certain instinctive Sensibility whispered me, would in the End be fatal to her.

Alas! my fears were but too fully justified; she grew gradually worse & I daily became more alarmed for her.—At length she was obliged to confine herself solely to the Bed allotted us by our worthy Landlady—. Her disorder turned to a galloping Consumption[7] & in a few Days carried her off. Amidst all my Lamentations for her (& violent you may suppose they were) I yet received some consolation in the reflection of my having paid every Attention to her, that could be offered, in her illness. I had wept over her every Day—had bathed her sweet face with my tears & had pressed her fair Hands continually in mine—. "My beloved Laura (said she to me a few Hours before she died) take warning from my unhappy End & avoid the imprudent conduct which has occasioned it . . beware of fainting-fits . . Though at the time they may be refreshing & Agreable yet beleive me they will in the end, if too often repeated & at improper seasons, prove destructive to your Constitution . . . . . My fate will teach you this . . I die a Martyr to my greif for the loss of Augustus . . . . One fatal swoon has cost me my Life . . . . Beware of swoons Dear Laura . . . A frenzy fit is not one quarter so pernicious; it is an exercise to the Body & if not too violent, is I dare say conducive to Health in its consequences—Run mad as often as you chuse; but do not faint—".

These were the last words she ever adressed to me . . . It was her dieing Advice to her afflicted Laura, who has ever most faithfully adhered to it.

After having attended my lamented freind to her Early Grave, I immediately (tho' late at night) left the detested Village in which she died, & near which had expired my Husband & Augustus. I had not walked many yards from it before I was overtaken by a Stage-Coach, in which I instantly took a place, determined to proceed in it to Edinburgh, where I hoped to find some kind pitying Freind who would receive and comfort me in my Afflictions.

It was so dark when I entered the Coach that I could not distinguish the Number of my Fellow-travellers; I could only perceive that they were Many. Regardless however of any thing concerning them, I gave myself up to my own sad Reflections. A general Silence prevailed—A Silence, which was by nothing interrupted but by the loud & repeated snores of one of the Party.

"What an illiterate villain must that Man be! (thought I to myself) What a total Want of delicate refinement must he have who can thus shock our senses by such a brutal Noise! He must I am certain be capable of every bad Action! There is no crime too black for such a Charac-

7. Tuberculosis.

ter!" Thus reasoned I within myself, & doubtless such were the reflections of my fellow travellers.

At length, returning Day enabled me to behold the unprincipled Scoundrel who had so violently disturbed my feelings. It was Sir Edward the father of my Deceased Husband. By his side, sate Augusta, & on the same seat with me were your Mother & Lady Dorothea. Imagine my Surprise at finding myself thus seated amongst my old Acquaintance. Great as was my astonishment, it was yet increased, when on look out of Windows, I beheld the Husband of Philippa, with Philippa by his side, on the Coach-box, & when on looking behind, I beheld, Philander & Gustavus in the Basket.[8] "Oh! Heavens, (exclaimed I) is it possible that I should so unexpectedly be surrounded by my nearest Relations and Connections"? These words roused the rest of the Party, and every eye was directed to the corner in which I sat. "Oh! my Isabel (continued I throwing myself across Lady Dorothea into her arms) receive once more to your Bosom the unfortunate Laura. Alas! when we last parted in the Vale of Usk, I was happy in being united to the best of Edwards; I had then a Father and a Mother, & had never known misfortunes—But now deprived of every freind but you—"

"What! (interrupted Augusta) is my Brother dead then? Tell us I intreat you what is become of him?" "Yes, cold & insensible Nymph, (replied I) that luckless Swain[9] your Brother, is no more, & you may now glory in being the Heiress of Sir Edward's fortune."

Although I had always despised her from the Day I had overheard her conversation with my Edward, yet in civility I complied with hers & Sir Edward's intreaties that I would inform them of the whole melancholy Affair. They were greatly shocked—Even the obdurate Heart of Sir Edward & the insensible one of Augusta, were touched with Sorrow, by the unhappy tale. At the request of your Mother I related to them every other misfortune which had befallen me since we parted. Of the imprisonment of Augustus & the absence of Edward—of our arrival in Scotland—of our unexpected Meeting with our Grandfather and our cousins—of our visit to Macdonald-Hall—of the singular Service we there performed towards Janetta—of her Fathers ingratitude for it . . . . . of his inhuman Behaviour, unaccountable suspicions, & barbarous treatment of us, in obliging us to leave the House . . . . . of our Lamentations on the loss of Edward & Augustus & finally of the melancholy Death of my beloved Companion.

Pity & Surprise were strongly depictured in your Mother's Countenance, during the whole of my narration, but I am sorry to say, that to the eternal reproach of her Sensibility, the latter infinitely predomi-

8. The rear compartment of a coach.

9. "Nymph" and "swain" are terms derived from pastoral poetry designating female and male lovers.

nated. Nay, faultless as my Conduct had certainly been during the whole Course of my late Misfortunes & Adventures, she pretended to find fault with my Behaviour in many of the situations in which I had been placed. As I was sensible myself, that I had always behaved in a manner which reflected Honour on my Feelings & Refinement, I paid little attention to what she said, & desired her to satisfy my Curiosity by informing me how she came there, instead of wounding my spotless reputation with unjustifiable Reproaches. As soon as she had complyed with my wishes in this particular & had given me an accurate detail of every thing that had befallen her since our separation (the particulars of which if you are not already acquainted with, your Mother will give you) I applied to Augusta for the same information respecting herself, Sir Edward & Lady Dorothea.

She told me that having a considerable taste for the Beauties of Nature, her curiosity to behold the delightful scenes it exhibited in that part of the World had been so much raised by Gilpin's Tour to the Highlands,[1] that she had prevailed on her Father to undertake a Tour of Scotland & had persuaded Lady Dorothea to accompany them. That they had arrived at Edinburgh a few days before & from thence had made daily Excursions into the Country around in the Stage Coach they were then in, from one of which Excursions they were at that time returning. My next enquiries were concerning Philippa & her Husband, the latter of whom I learned having spent all her fortune, had recourse for subsistance to the talent in which, he had always most excelled, namely, Driving, & that having sold every thing which belonged to them except their Coach, had converted it into a Stage,[2] & in order to be removed from any of his former Acquaintance, had driven it to Edinburgh from whence he went to Sterling every other Day; That Philippa still retaining her affection for her ungratefull Husband, had followed him to Scotland & generally accompanied him in his little Excursions to Sterling. "It has only been to throw a little money into their Pockets (continued Augusta) that my Father has always travelled in their Coach to veiw the beauties of the Country since our arrival in Scotland—for it would certainly have been much more agreable to us, to visit the Highlands in a Postchaise[3] than merely to travel from Edinburgh to Sterling & from Sterling to Edinburgh every other Day in a crouded & uncomfortable Stage." I perfectly agreed with her in her sentiments on the Affair, & secretly blamed Sir Edward for thus sacrificing his Daughter's pleasure for the sake of a ridiculous old Woman whose folly in marrying so young a Man ought to be punished. His Be-

1. William Gilpin (1724–1804) was a British clergyman who wrote a number of works on landscapes, and helped to begin the eighteenth-century cult of the "picturesque."

2. A coach that carries passengers for money.

3. A closed carriage that transports mail and passengers.

haviour however was entirely of a piece with his general Character; for what could be expected from a Man who possessed not the smallest atom of Sensibility, who scarcely knew the meaning of Simpathy, & who actually snored—.

Adeiu

Laura

Letter the 15th. Laura in continuation

When we arrived at the town where we were to Breakfast, I was determined to speak with Philander & Gustavus, & to that purpose as soon as I left the Carriage, I went to the Basket & tenderly enquired after their Health, expressing my fears of the uneasiness of their Situation. At first they seemed rather confused at my Appearance dreading no doubt that I might call them to account for the money which our Grandfather had left me & which they had unjustly deprived me of, but finding that I mentioned nothing of the Matter, they desired me to step into the Basket as we might there converse with greater case. Accordingly I entered & whilst the rest of the party were devouring Green tea & buttered toast, we feasted ourselves in a more refined & Sentimental Manner by a confidential Conversation. I informed them of every thing which had befallen me during the course of my Life, and at my request they related to me every incident of theirs.

"We are the sons as you already know, of the two youngest Daughters which Lord St. Clair had by Laurina an italian opera girl. Our mothers could neither of them exactly ascertain who were our fathers; though it is generally believed that Philander, is the son of one Philip Jones a Bricklayer and that my father was Gregory Staves a Staymaker of Edinburgh. This is however of little consequence, for as our Mothers were certainly never married to either of them, it reflects no Dishonour on our Blood which is of a most ancient & unpolluted kind. Bertha (the Mother of Philander) & Agatha (my own Mother) always lived together. They were neither of them very rich; their united fortunes had originally amounted to nine thousand Pounds, but as they had always lived upon the principal of it, when we were fifteen it was diminished to nine Hundred. This nine Hundred, they always kept in a Drawer in one of the Tables which stood in our common sitting Parlour, for the Convenience of having it always at Hand. Whether it was from this circumstance, of its being easily taken, or from a wish of being indepandant, or from an excess of Sensibility (for which we were always remarkable) I cannot now determine, but certain it is that when we had reached our 15th year, we took the Nine Hundred Pounds & ran away. Having obtained this prize we were determined to manage it with eoconomy & not to spend it either with folly or Extravagance. To this purpose we therefore divided it into nine parcels, one of which we devoted to Victuals, the 2d to Drink, the 3d to Housekeeping, the 4th to Carriages, the 5th to Horses, the 6th to Servants, the 7th to Amusements, the 8th to Cloathes & the 9th to Silver Buckles. Having thus arranged our Expences for two Months (for we expected to make the nine Hundred Pounds last as long) we hastened to London & had the good luck to spend it in 7 weeks & a Day which was 6 Days sooner than we had intended. As soon as we had thus happily disencumbered ourselves from the weight of so much Money, we began to think of returning to our Mothers, but accidentally hearing that they were both starved to death, we gave over the design & determined to engage ourselves to some strolling Company of Players, as we had always a turn for the Stage. Accordingly we offered our services to one & were accepted; our Company was indeed rather small, as it consisted only of the Manager his wife & ourselves, but there were fewer to pay and the only inconvenience attending it was the Scarcity of Plays which for want of People to fill the Characters, we could perform.—. We did not mind trifles however—. One of our most admired Performances was *Macbeth*, in which we were truly great. The Manager always played *Banquo* himself, his Wife my *Lady Macbeth*. I did the *Three Witches* & Philander acted *all the rest*. To say the truth this tragedy was not only the Best, but the only Play we ever performed; & after having acted it all over England, and Wales, we came to Scotland to exhibit it over the remainder of Great Britain. We happened to be quartered in that very Town, where you came and met your Grandfather—. We were in the Inn-yard when his Carriage entered & perceiving by the Arms to whom it belonged, & knowing that Lord St. Clair was our Grandfather, we agreed to endeavour to get something from him by discovering the Relationship—. You know how well it succeeded—. Having obtained the two Hundred Pounds, we instantly left the Town, leaving our Manager & his wife to act *Macbeth* by themselves, & took the road to Sterling, where we spent our little fortune with great *eclat*.[4] We are now returning to Edinburgh to get some preferment[5] in the Acting way; & such my Dear Cousin is our History."

I thanked the amiable Youth for his entertaining Narration, & after expressing my Wishes for their Welfare & Happiness, left them in their little Habitation & returned to my other Freinds who impatiently expected me.

My Adventures are now drawing to a close my dearest Marianne; at least for the present.

When we arrived at Edinburgh Sir Edward told me that as the Widow of his Son, he desired I would accept from his Hands of four

---

4. Flamboyance, conspicuousness.   5. Employment.

Hundred a year. I graciously promised that I would, but could not help observing that the unsimpathetic Baronet offered it more on account of my being the Widow of Edward than in being the refined & Amiable Laura.

I took up my Residence in a romantic Village in the Highlands of Scotland, where I have ever since continued, & where I can uninterrupted by unmeaning Visits, indulge in a melancholy solitude, my unceasing Lamentations for the Death of my Father, my Mother, my Husband & my Freind.

Augusta has been for several Years united to Graham the Man of all others most suited to her; she became acquainted with him during her stay in Scotland.

Sir Edward in hopes of gaining an Heir to his Title & Estate, at the same time married Lady Dorothea—. His wishes have been answered.

Philander & Gustavus, after having raised their reputation by their Performances in the Theatrical Line at Edinburgh, removed to Covent Garden,[6] where they still Exhibit under the assumed names of *Lewis* & *Quick*.

Philippa has long paid the Debt of Nature, Her Husband however still continues to drive the Stage-Coach from Edinburgh to Sterling:—

Adeiu my Dearest Marianne

Laura

Finis

June 13th 1790   1922

6. A theater in London.

REBECCA COX JACKSON
1795–1871

In a moving account of her self-education, the Shaker visionary and preacher Rebecca Jackson remembered a moment when her shame at her own illiteracy "pierced my soul like a sword" so that she "could not keep from crying." But then, she explained, "these words were spoken in my heart, 'Be faithful, and the time shall come when you can write.' " Not long after that, she added, an inner voice reminded her that God, "who learned the first man to read . . . can learn you," and in fact, apparently quite miraculously, she started that very day to read the Bible. Some years later, moreover, she began to write the striking spiritual autobiography excerpted here, and she continued composing this memoir on and off throughout her religious career.

Jackson was a free black woman. She was born just outside Philadelphia and for many years worked as a seamstress, a job which brought her some financial independence. Her husband, Samuel S. Jackson, lived with her, her older brother Joseph Cox, and her brother's children in a comfortable house in Philadelphia. Jackson renounced the security of this life, however, after being profoundly transformed by a powerful experience of religious "awakening" that seized her during a thunderstorm in July 1830. Suddenly feeling herself to be an instrument of divine authority, she chose—like such earlier women as the fourteenth-century visionary Margery Kempe or the seventeenth-century mystic Jane Lead—to leave her husband, her home, and her family for a career of spiritual commitment. After having achieved considerable success as an itinerant preacher whose "gift," according to a contemporary witness, "was to travel some and speak to the people," she joined the radical sect known as the Shakers, a group of Protestant believers who advocated the Motherhood as well as the Fatherhood of God and who seemed to her, with their austere dress and communal ways, to be "living to live forever." Throughout these years, moreover, she lived and journeyed through the countryside with a younger woman disciple named Rebecca Perot; known as "the two Rebeccas," the women were evidently both inseparable and inspiring.

Around 1843, Jackson undertook to write her memoirs, including a series of dreams and visions. Although these remained unpublished until the historian Jean McMahon Humez edited them in 1981, Shaker scholars transcribed and preserved them during the nineteenth century. In their dramatizations of violence as well as in their magical meditations on domesticity, such passages as "The Dream of Slaughter," "The Dream of the Cakes," and "The Dream of Washing Quilts" suggest the intensity with which an apparently unschooled woman could enrich her inner life with imagery drawn from "ordinary" reality. Moreover, in the simultaneous sense of peril and resistance that these dreams convey, as well as in their sometimes haunted consciousness of racial difference, Jackson's memoirs imply that even for a supposedly "free" black woman nineteenth-century America was hardly an unthreatening place. As another nineteenth-century black woman preacher, Amanda Smith, remarked, "Some people would understand the quintessence of sanctifying grace if they could be black about twenty-four hours."

Gifts of Power

A *Dream of Slaughter*

In a night or two after I had this dream,[1] I also dreamed I was in a house, entered in at the south door. I heard a footstep quick behind me and looked at the east window and saw a man coming. I run upstairs, told the child's nurse a robber was in the house. She fled. I went to the east window, then to the west, to jump out. I found in so doing I should kill myself, so I sat down on a chair by the west window with my face to the north. He came up and came right to me. He took a lance and laid

---

1. She has just recounted a dream in which, by   carnal pleasures and to follow God.
her own interpretation, she has learned to resist

my nose open and then he cut my head on the right side, from the back to the front above my nose, and pulled the skin down over that side. Then he cut the left, did the same way, and pulled the skin down. The skin and blood covered me like a veil from my head to my lap. All my body was covered with blood. Then he took a long knife and cut my chest open in the form of the cross and took all my bowels out and laid them on the floor by my right side, and then went in search of all the rest of the family. This was a family that I sewed in. When the lance was going through my nose it felt like a feather was going over my nose. I sat in silent prayer all the time saying these words in my mind, "Lord Jesus, receive my spirit."

After I found he was gone I thought I would make my escape before he returned. I was afraid if he found me alive he would want to treat me more cruel. But a voice above my head told me to sit still, as though I was dead, for that was the only thing that would save me. And this was the way I sat all the time he was amangling my body—as though I was dead. So in a moment after those words were spoken to me, he came in and came to me as if he was agoing to do something else to me, and I was afraid. I thought I would implore his mercy to save my life, but the same voice spoke to me and said, "He can show no mercy." And in the same moment, the same voice from above spoke to him and asked, "What is your occupation?" (and also the man that was with him). He said the man rid[2] the entrails but he opened the heart. And He commanded him not to touch me again. And they both fled from before me by the power of that voice. And then I found what it was that keep me alive. He had not as yet taken out my heart, but my entrails were laying all this time by my right side on the floor.

And then I awoke and my dream troubled me. I was so faint when I woke I could not get up for sometime. And when I did I cried, "I shall die! I shall die!" Samuel said, "What is the matter?" "Oh my dream! My dream!" And I was all in a tremble. And these words were spoken to me, "Thy life is hid in Christ. Thy life is hid in Christ. Thy life is hid in Christ." Three times these words were spoken to me. And I was strengthened and my soul filled with the love of God. And I began to walk the floor back and forth apraising the Lord as though nothing had been.

* * *

The Dream of the Cakes

A dream. I thought I was going to bake some cakes. A sister come in that belonged to the Covenant. I said, "I am glad you have come!" "Why?" "Because I am going to bake some cakes." I sat down on a low

---

2. Removed.

stool before the griddle. It laid on two bricks, the fire under it. It stood in the northeast corner of the room on the floor. The fireplace was on the west side of the room. However, I greased the griddle, put on a little batter, about a tablespoonful. It run all over the griddle, a beautiful brown on both sides, though I did not turn it. And in a moment the people ate it all up—they were all white.[3] I did not see them before I saw them eating my cake. I knowed not where they came from—I looked at the sister. "Did you see that? Well, I will try it again."

I poured on another. It run all over, under, and into the fire. They ate it out of the fire and off of the griddle. And the people increased as the cake enlarged. I put on the third. It run all over the griddle, on the fire, under it, on the ashes, under it, and spread about one yard around. The people ate it off the griddle, off the fire, from under it, off the ashes, under the ashes. They ate it all, except a little piece about one inch in length, a half inch in width. This little piece lay before my right foot in the ashes. It was all I seen. I picked it up and said, "Let us taste it. They ate it so good." I broke it and put the piece in my mouth. It was the sweetest I ever tasted. I gave her the other, said, "Here, taste. No wonder they ate it up!"

So the people increased at the baking of the third cake to a large multitude. I don't think I put on more than a spoonful each time—it is my manner in baking any kind of batter cakes to try the griddle with batter enough to make a cake the size of a half a dollar, so that if it sticks, then there is not much batter wasted.

And I woke in the morning. I told my dream. My dreams became a burden to my family. I shall only mention a few of them in this writing in order to show how it pleased God in His wisdom to lead a poor unlearned ignorant woman, without the aid of mortal.

The Dream of Washing Quilts

A dream. I was washing. I was squatting down, washing three bed quilts and singing as I was awashing. And this same sister[4] came to the south door and said, "What are you adoing here?" "I am awashing." "Ain't you afraid to be here?" "No." "Why, you are in great danger."

I then looked and saw I was in a place walled all around with stone. The place was four square. I was in the center of it. There was no window in it, only one door. That was in the southwest corner, opened in. The south door she stood in, which brought her behind me, rather to my left. My face was east. Under me was a pool of water. This walled place was full of water like a bowl. Nobody could get to me. There were

3. According to one editor, this dream reflects the fact that Jackson's early congregations were largely white.

4. Jackson reveals later that this "sister" (the same who appeared in the previous dream) is jealous of her influence over the Covenant Meeting.

three pieces of boards about one yard in length. They were all one size. On one of them I sat. On the one at my right side sat a tub. In it was two quilts, which I had washed in this pool, though I knowed not I was in such a dangerous place till she spoke. Yet I did not feel to move till I had done my washing. So I sat still singing until I was done.

Then I picked up my tub with my three clean quilts in, put the tub on my head, came out with great ease and went eastward, came into a street ran north and south. I then stopped, turned around to see where I had come from, found I was standing by a gate as though I had come through it, saw a bridge alongside the gate. This bridge was over a stream of water. I could not tell whether I had come through this gate or over the bridge.

While I stood here awonder, I looked up, saw the gate post on the south side had a steeple on it, and on the top of the steeple was a gold ball. As I looked from the top to where I stood, I found a little white cord hanging right by my right hand. I caught hold of it, made a squat, then leaped into the air, placed my right foot on the ball, with my left foot swinging in the air. I was above all earthly things. I saw three cities, one in the east, one in the south, one in the west. These cities were clean and beautiful. Then I leaped down with as great ease as I ascended.

Then I heard this same sister speak behind me. "What are you doing here?" "Why, I have been on that pinnacle." She doubted. I caught hold of the cord and leaped upon it again. This I done three times—I had done it twice before she came. I then went through the gate and along this stream of water until I headed it. This was the same way I had come with my clean quilts in the tub upon my head, but I did not see this water nor this gate nor this bridge until I got into the street that ran north and south. This street which I came in from the washing ran east and west. Now as I returned the same way, it brought me westward, and when I headed this stream, I went south—but when I found myself at that gate, I had no tub nor quilts.

So now I went south. After I got far in the south, I looked up to the heavens, saw three pictures all of one size and of one appearance, very majestic, long, and beautiful, of the male order. They were some distance apart. They faced the north. Each one was on a black cloud. And there was three heavy claps of thunder. Each clap came out of each cloud. I found I had traveled a long distance—no house nor shelter near, as far as my eyes could see, and I saw a heavy thunderstorm rising. I wondered what I should do. It was said, "Turn back." I turned, and when I turned in the same road that I came—for I never turned out of the road in all my journey—being turned on my right (that is, on my right hand side off the road, east), I saw a beautiful white cottage into which I was told to enter, which I did. And when I found myself in so beautiful a house, sheltered from the storm, I was filled with joy and rejoicing. And it was said to me, "This is yours."

Then I heard this sister holler behind the cottage, "What are you adoing here?" "Why, I live here." "You live here?" "Yes, I live here." "Why, how can you live here? Nobody lives here." "Why, this is my cottage, and I am as happy as a lord." "Why, the sun never rises here." "The sun never rises here?" As I made this reply I advanced to the door which I came in at, which was in the south side of the cottage. (She was on the north side which made her behind the cottage—I only heard her voice.) And when I went out and looked in the west, I saw the fourth picture, like the three I saw in the south—same size, same height in the heavens—and it faced the east and it was on a black cloud. And as I kept repeating, "The sun never rises here? No? Why, yonder she is arising —arising now!" "Well, she has only rose to you."

The sun, while I looked in the faces of the pictures, rose from behind the picture as though it came out of the cloud. And it rose out on the south side of this fourth picture, bearing her course toward these three pictures in the south, out of which came three claps of heavy thunder. The thunder out of the three black clouds behind the three pictures in the south, the sun out of the black cloud behind the fourth picture in the west. Then I waked.

1843–1845   1981

MARY SHELLEY
1797–1851

Mary Wollstonecraft Godwin Shelley, wrote her friend Leigh Hunt in his *Blue Stocking Revels* (1837), was "four-famed—for her parents, her lord, / And the poor lone impossible monster abhorred." Amiably sardonic though it is, this couplet tersely summarizes some of the major facts of this author's remarkable career. The daughter of the feminist theoretician Mary Wollstonecraft (famous for her *Vindication of the Rights of Woman*, 1792) and the rationalist philosopher William Godwin (equally well known for his *Enquiry Concerning Political Justice*, 1793), she eloped with the Romantic poet Percy Bysshe Shelley when she was only seventeen, and when she was merely nineteen she wrote *Frankenstein*, perhaps the most memorable and influential science fiction fantasy ever published in English.

Putting aside the intellectual achievements of her mother and father, Mary Shelley's existence was marked from the first by emotional extremes. Though her parents were radically opposed to marriage (Godwin had called it "the worst of all laws" and Wollstonecraft had defined it as "legalized prostitution"), they had somewhat embarrassedly wed not only in order to legitimize the birth of their child but also with every expectation of a peaceful life together. But Wollstonecraft died of puerperal fever just after giving birth to her daughter Mary, and Godwin, left in charge of his motherless infant as well as Wollstonecraft's illegitimate daughter, Fanny Imlay, was plunged into gloom. Nor did conditions substantially improve after Mary's father remarried, when she was four. His new wife, the widowed Mary Jane Clairmont, had two children of her own, Charles and Jane, to whom she was inevitably partial, so that Mary soon began to feel like a rebellious Cinderella. Idolizing her scholarly but distant father, she grew up headstrong and literary, educating herself through voracious reading, scorning her stepmother, and making long brooding pilgrimages to her mother's grave.

Sent to live with family friends in Scotland when she was fifteen, Mary spent a good deal of time "scribbling." On her return to London in 1814, when she was nearly seventeen, she was immediately struck by a young friend of her father's, the poet Percy Bysshe Shelley, who appears to have been equally struck by her. Injudiciously married at the age of nineteen to the sixteen-year-old Harriet Westbrook, Shelley was now twenty-two, the scion of an aristocratic family, who had glamorously repudiated his heritage in order to devote himself to art and ideas. In a few years, however, he had wearied of the comparatively ordinary wife who had already borne him one child and was about to give birth to another; clearly he was ready for amorous redemption. A disciple of Godwin's, Shelley had also long venerated the by now mythical Mary Wollstonecraft, and no doubt Mary Godwin's physical charm—she was evidently a coolly attractive girl—together with her imaginative power and her fascinating heritage enthralled him as rapidly as his poetic charisma enchanted her. Within a month, the pair had confessed their feelings to each other, appropriately enough at Wollstonecraft's grave, and fled to the Continent together, bringing Mary's stepsister Jane—who had now renamed herself "Claire"—Clairmont with them; Mary was already pregnant with their first child.

It is an understatement to say that Mary's years with Shelley were hectic ones. Almost from the beginning, they were tragic. At the age of seventeen, she gave birth to her first child, a premature daughter who died in two weeks. Her journal entries from this period are hauntingly evocative. Indeed, as the feminist critic Ellen Moers has pointed out, their preoccupation with death and resurrection prefigures some of the central concerns of *Frankenstein*. "Dream that my little baby came to life again," she wrote on Sunday, March 19, 1815; "that it had been only cold, and that we rubbed it before the fire, and it lived." An imaginative, theatrical girl, Mary Shelley was being gradually transformed into a woman subject to genuine terrors. In 1816, both Fanny Imlay and Harriet Shelley committed suicide. Now Shelley was able to wed Mary, but to his distress he was never considered respectable enough to be given custody of his two children by Harriet. Married at last, the young couple wandered between England, Switzerland, and Italy, often impoverished and always beset by importunate friends and relatives. At the same time, many of their relationships were richly rewarding: Keats, Byron, Leigh Hunt, Thomas Love Peacock, James Hogg, Edward Trelawney, and many other notable Romantics enlivened their social circle, and their growing intellectual as well as emotional dependence on each other seems also to have helped them endure many difficulties.

Though such difficulties must often have appeared unremitting, then, the Shelleys did have respites of relative calm. It was during one of these periods that Mary began the composition of *Frankenstein*. Summering in Geneva, she, Shelley, their six-month-old son William, and Claire occupied a small house near Lord Byron's grander Villa Diodati; Claire was embroiled in a fitful affair with Byron, and Shelley, too, had become close to the aristocratic poet, who was already celebrated, even notorious, for both his work and his womanizing. One night, Mary later recalled, the group, which also included Byron's eccentric young Italian physician, William Polidori, were regaling each other with tales of the supernatural in the villa's candlelit salon when Byron suddenly declared, "We will each write a ghost story." Mary was at first frustratingly empty of inspiration, but after brooding for a few days, she had a terrifying nightmare about a "pale student of unhallowed arts" who employed a "powerful engine" to awaken "the hideous phantasm of a man." Almost at once she understood that this horrifying dream might be the basis of "my ghost story— my tiresome, unlucky ghost story!" for she longed to "contrive [a tale] which would frighten my reader as I myself had been frightened that night!"

Frightening *Frankenstein* certainly is, but, as readers from 1818 to the present have generally realized, it is considerably more than that. Subtitled *The Modern Prometheus* and prefaced with an epigraph from Milton's *Paradise Lost* in which the fallen Adam reproaches God for having abandoned him, the novel openly meditates on large issues of responsibility and desire, science and sinfulness. Far more covertly, it re-imagines Aeschylus's overreachingly ambitious Prometheus (whom Shelley himself was later to vindicate in his great verse drama *Prometheus Unbound*) and Milton's arrogantly vengeful Satan to consider questions about woman's anatomy and destiny that had always concerned Mary's own mother. For in "giving life" to a monster assembled from parts of corpses dug up in a nearby graveyard, the novel's protagonist, Victor Frankenstein, not only usurps the creative function of God, he enacts the maternal role of a woman; while, in experiencing himself as a lonely outcast, barred from education and inheritance, the book's nameless monster represents in exaggerated form some of the feelings a nineteenth-century daughter might well have had about her own place in a society where she had only the most minimal rights. Although such interpretations did not occur to the tale's earliest critics, most knew at once that they were encountering a work that was almost inexplicably resonant, and Mary Shelley herself, years later, was driven to contemplate the vexing question of "how I, then a young girl, came to think of and to dilate upon so very hideous an idea." The answer, as a number of recent writers have suggested, lay at least partly in the way early traumas of loss and sexuality, maternity and death had become intertwined in her life.

After the popular success of *Frankenstein* such traumas unfortunately continued unabated. In the fall of 1817, six months before the publication of her novel, Mary had given birth to a daughter, Clara Everina; in the fall of 1818, six months after the book's appearance, the child died of dysentery in Venice. A year and a half later, in June 1819, the Shelleys' three-year-old son William succumbed to a similar malady in Rome. Mary, in particular, was devastated, and to distract herself she began a novel, *Mathilda*, which was unpublished in her lifetime but which served "to quell my wretchedness temporarily." Even more therapeutic was the birth of her son Percy Florence in November of the same year. He was the only one among her children to survive, and though he grew up to be a comparatively ordinary man—unworthy, as some thought, of the Godwin-Wollstonecraft-Shelley heritage—he soon became his mother's only consolation. For, two and a half years later, in the summer of 1822, Shelley himself, along with his friend Edward Williams, drowned in the bay of Lerici when the poet's boat, the *Ariel*, was overturned.

Shortly before the catastrophe, Mary herself had suffered a miscarriage; overwrought and exhausted, she had parted with her husband coldly before he embarked on his fateful voyage—a failing for which she was never to forgive herself. But in any case this last blow was almost overwhelmingly heavy. A journal entry she wrote shortly after Shelley's death hardly seems to overstate the intensity of the dramas through which she had lived in the eight years since her elopement:

> I am now on the eve of completing my five & twentieth year—how drearily young for one so lost as I! How young in years for one lives ages each day in sorrow—think you that these moments are counted in my life as in other people's?—oh no! . . . what I have suffered . . . will write years on my brow & intrench them in my heart.

Despite such a sense of enduring pain, Mary was to live some thirty more years after Shelley's death, and in those years she remained consistently productive, publishing a number of tales, five more novels—*Valperga* (1823), *The Last Man* (1826), *Perkin Warbeck* (1830), *Lodore* (1835), and *Falkner* (1837)—essays, travel sketches, and a series of biographies, as well as a set of useful and perceptive notes to her husband's poems. Vigorously inventive, her prose continued to enthrall many readers, though only *The Last Man* begins to compare with *Frankenstein* in force and originality. Significantly, that novel, like her brief tale *The Mortal Immortal*, expressed her anguished sense of having survived what seemed to be the deaths of almost everyone around her. And indeed she had, for not only were her husband and three of her children gone but so were Shelley's friend Keats, who had died in Rome not long before Shelley himself drowned, and the couple's friend Byron, who died at Missolonghi in 1824, where he had gone to fight for the cause of Greek independence, as well as her father, who died in 1836, and her half-sister Fanny Imlay, who had committed suicide in 1816.

Yet Mary herself stubbornly survived, writing, raising her son Percy, recovering from smallpox, and refusing to remarry, with the proud explanation that she wanted the name "Mary Shelley" to be engraved on her tombstone. Always conscious of her maternal inheritance, she once declared: "If I have never written to vindicate the rights of women, I have ever befriended women when oppressed. At every risk I have befriended and supported victims to the social system." But she need not have struggled to justify herself, for with her imaginative energy she had accomplished at least as much as her mother had.

The Mortal Immortal

A *Tale*

July 16, 1833.—This is a memorable anniversary for me; on it I complete my three hundred and twenty-third year!

The Wandering Jew?[1]—certainly not. More than eighteen centuries have passed over his head. In comparison with him, I am a very young immortal.

Am I, then, immortal? This is a question which I have asked myself, by day and night, for now three hundred and three years, and yet cannot answer it. I detected a gray hair amidst my brown locks this very day—that surely signifies decay. Yet it may have remained concealed there for three hundred years—for some persons have become entirely white-headed before twenty years of age.

I will tell my story, and my reader shall judge for me. I will tell my story, and so contrive to pass some few hours of a long eternity, become so wearisome to me. For ever! Can it be? to live for ever! I have heard of enchantments, in which the victims were plunged into a deep sleep, to wake, after a hundred years, as fresh as ever: I have heard of the Seven Sleepers[2]—thus to be immortal would not be so burthensome: but, oh! the weight of never-ending time—the tedious passage of the still-succeeding hours! How happy was the fabled Nourjahad!—But to my task.

All the world has heard of Cornelius Agrippa.[3] His memory is as immortal as his arts have made me. All the world has also heard of his scholar, who, unawares, raised the foul fiend during his master's absence, and was destroyed by him. The report, true or false, of this accident, was attended with many inconveniences to the renowned philosopher. All his scholars at once deserted him—his servants disappeared. He had no one near him to put coals on his ever-burning fires while he slept, or to attend to the changeful colours of his medicines while he studied. Experiment after experiment failed, because one pair of hands was insufficient to complete them: the dark spirits laughed at him for not being able to retain a single mortal in his service.

I was then very young—very poor—and very much in love. I had been for about a year the pupil of Cornelius, though I was absent when this accident took place. On my return, my friends implored me not to return to the alchymist's abode. I trembled as I listened to the dire tale they told; I required no second warning; and when Cornelius came and

---

1. According to medieval legend, a Jew was condemned by Christ to wander through the world until Christ's second coming.
2. A legend about seven youths of Ephesus who slept in a cave for 187 years to escape persecution.
3. Heinrich Cornelius Agrippa von Nettesheim (1486–1535), German occult philosopher and alchemist.

offered me a purse of gold if I would remain under his roof, I felt as if Satan himself tempted me. My teeth chattered—my hair stood on end:—I ran off as fast as my trembling knees would permit.

My failing steps were directed whither for two years they had every evening been attracted,—a gently bubbling spring of pure living waters, beside which lingered a dark-haired girl, whose beaming eyes were fixed on the path I was accustomed each night to tread. I cannot remember the hour when I did not love Bertha; we had been neighbours and playmates from infancy—her parents, like mine, were of humble life, yet respectable—our attachment had been a source of pleasure to them. In an evil hour, a malignant fever carried off both her father and mother, and Bertha became an orphan. She would have found a home beneath my paternal roof, but, unfortunately, the old lady of the near castle, rich, childless, and solitary, declared her intention to adopt her. Henceforth Bertha was clad in silk—inhabited a marble palace—and was looked on as being highly favoured by fortune. But in her new situation among her new associates, Bertha remained true to the friend of her humbler days; she often visited the cottage of my father, and when forbidden to go thither, she would stray towards the neighbouring wood, and meet me beside its shady fountain.

She often declared that she owed no duty to her new protectress equal in sanctity to that which bound us. Yet still I was too poor to marry, and she grew weary of being tormented on my account. She had a haughty but an impatient spirit, and grew angry at the obstacles that prevented our union. We met now after an absence, and she had been sorely beset while I was away; she complained bitterly, and almost reproached me for being poor. I replied hastily,—

"I am honest, if I am poor!—were I not, I might soon become rich!"

This exclamation produced a thousand questions. I feared to shock her by owning[4] the truth, but she drew it from me; and then, casting a look of disdain on me, she said—

"You pretend to love, and you fear to face the Devil for my sake!"

I protested that I had only dreaded to offend her;—while she dwelt on the magnitude of the reward that I should receive. Thus encouraged—shamed by her—led on by love and hope, laughing at my late fears, with quick steps and a light heart, I returned to accept the offers of the alchymist, and was instantly installed in my office.

A year passed away. I became possessed of no insignificant sum of money. Custom had banished my fears. In spite of the most painful vigilance, I had never detected the trace of a cloven foot;[5] nor was the studious silence of our abode ever disturbed by demoniac howls. I still

---

4. Admitting.
5. A feature thought to be possessed by the devil and his servants.

continued my stolen interviews with Bertha, and Hope dawned on me
—Hope—but not perfect joy; for Bertha fancied that love and security
were enemies, and her pleasure was to divide them in my bosom.
Though true of heart, she was somewhat of a coquette in manner; and I
was jealous as a Turk. She slighted me in a thousand ways, yet would
never acknowledge herself to be in the wrong. She would drive me mad
with anger, and then force me to beg her pardon. Sometimes she fancied that I was not sufficiently submissive, and then she had some story
of a rival, favoured by her protectress. She was surrounded by silk-clad
youths—the rich and gay—What chance had the sad-robed scholar of
Cornelius compared with these?

On one occasion, the philosopher made such large demands upon
my time, that I was unable to meet her as I was wont. He was engaged
in some mighty work, and I was forced to remain, day and night, feeding his furnaces and watching his chemical preparations. Bertha waited
for me in vain at the fountain. Her haughty spirit fired at this neglect;
and when at last I stole out during the few short minutes allotted to me
for slumber, and hoped to be consoled by her, she received me with
disdain, dismissed me in scorn, and vowed that any man should possess
her hand rather than he who could not be in two places at once for her
sake. She would be revenged!—And truly she was. In my dingy retreat
I heard that she had been hunting, attended by Albert Hoffer. Albert
Hoffer was favoured by her protectress, and the three passed in cavalcade before my smoky window. Methought that they mentioned my
name—it was followed by a laugh of derision, as her dark eyes glanced
contemptuously towards my abode.

Jealousy, with all its venom, and all its misery, entered my breast.
Now I shed a torrent of tears, to think that I should never call her mine;
and, anon,[6] I imprecated a thousand curses on her inconstancy. Yet,
still I must stir the fires of the alchymist, still attend on the changes of
his unintelligible medicines.

Cornelius had watched for three days and nights, nor closed his eyes.
The progress of his alembics[7] was slower than he expected: in spite of
his anxiety, sleep weighed upon his eyelids. Again and again he threw
off drowsiness with more than human energy; again and again it stole
away his senses. He eyed his crucibles wistfully. "Not ready yet," he
murmured; "will another night pass before the work is accomplished?
Winzy,[8] you are vigilant—you are faithful—you have slept, my boy—
you slept last night. Look at that glass vessel. The liquid it contains is of
a soft rose-colour: the moment it begins to change its hue, awaken me
—till then I may close my eyes. First, it will turn white, and then emit

6. Shortly afterwards.   8. The name of the narrator.
7. Apparatus used for distilling fluids.

golden flashes; but wait not till then; when the rose-colour fades, rouse me." I scarcely heard the last words, muttered, as they were, in sleep. Even then he did not quite yield to nature. "Winzy, my boy," he again said, "do not touch the vessel—do not put it to your lips; it is a philter[9] —a philter to cure love; you would not cease to love your Bertha—beware to drink!"

And he slept. His venerable head sunk on his breast, and I scarce heard his regular breathing. For a few minutes I watched the vessel— the rosy hue of the liquid remained unchanged. Then my thoughts wandered—they visited the fountain, and dwelt on a thousand charming scenes never to be renewed—never! Serpents and adders were in my heart as the word "Never!" half formed itself on my lips. False girl! —false and cruel! Never more would she smile on me as that evening she smiled on Albert. Worthless, detested woman! I would not remain unrevenged—she should see Albert expire at her feet—she should die beneath my vengeance. She had smiled in disdain and triumph—she knew my wretchedness and her power. Yet what power had she?—the power of exciting my hate—my utter scorn—my—oh, all but indifference! Could I attain that—could I regard her with careless eyes, transferring my rejected love to one fairer and more true, that were indeed a victory!

A bright flash darted before my eyes. I had forgotten the medicine of the adept;[1] I gazed on it with wonder: flashes of admirable beauty, more bright than those which the diamond emits when the sun's rays are on it, glanced from the surface of the liquid; an odour the most fragrant and grateful stole over my sense; the vessel seemed one globe of living radiance, lovely to the eye, and most inviting to the taste. The first thought, instinctively inspired by the grosser sense, was, I will—I must drink. I raised the vessel to my lips. "It will cure me of love—of torture!" Already I had quaffed half of the most delicious liquor ever tasted by the palate of man, when the philosopher stirred. I started—I dropped the glass—the fluid flamed and glanced along the floor, while I felt Cornelius's grip at my throat, as he shrieked aloud, "Wretch! you have destroyed the labour of my life!"

The philosopher was totally unaware that I had drunk any portion of his drug. His idea was, and I gave a tacit assent to it, that I had raised the vessel from curiosity, and that, frighted at its brightness, and the flashes of intense light it gave forth, I had let it fall. I never undeceived him. The fire of the medicine was quenched—the fragrance died away—he grew calm, as a philosopher should under the heaviest trials, and dismissed me to rest.

---

9. A potion or charm; "would not": do not wish to.

1. Alchemist who has learned the secrets of his art.

I will not attempt to describe the sleep of glory and bliss which bathed
my soul in paradise during the remaining hours of that memorable
night. Words would be faint and shallow types[2] of my enjoyment, or of
the gladness that possessed my bosom when I woke. I trod air—my
thoughts were in heaven. Earth appeared heaven, and my inheritance
upon it was to be one trance of delight. "This it is to be cured of love," I
thought; "I will see Bertha this day, and she will find her lover cold and
regardless; too happy to be disdainful, yet how utterly indifferent to
her!"

The hours danced away. The philosopher, secure that he had once
succeeded, and believing that he might again, began to concoct the
same medicine once more. He was shut up with his books and drugs,
and I had a holiday. I dressed myself with care; I looked in an old but
polished shield, which served me for a mirror; methought my good
looks had wonderfully improved. I hurried beyond the precincts of the
town, joy in my soul, the beauty of heaven and earth around me. I
turned my steps towards the castle—I could look on its lofty turrets with
lightness of heart, for I was cured of love. My Bertha saw me afar off, as
I came up the avenue. I know not what sudden impulse animated her
bosom, but at the sight, she sprung with a light fawn-like bound down
the marble steps, and was hastening towards me. But I had been perceived by another person. The old high-born hag, who called herself
her protectress, and was her tyrant, had seen me, also; she hobbled,
panting, up the terrace; a page, as ugly as herself, held up her train, and
fanned her as she hurried along, and stopped my fair girl with a "How,
now, my bold mistress? whither so fast? Back to your cage—hawks are
abroad!"

Bertha clasped her hands—her eyes were still bent on my approaching figure. I saw the contest. How I abhorred the old crone who
checked the kind impulses of my Bertha's softening heart. Hitherto,
respect for her rank had caused me to avoid the lady of the castle; now I
disdained such trivial considerations. I was cured of love, and lifted
above all human fears; I hastened forwards, and soon reached the terrace. How lovely Bertha looked! her eyes flashing fire, her cheeks
glowing with impatience and anger, she was a thousand times more
graceful and charming than ever—I no longer loved—Oh! no, I
adored—worshipped—idolized her!

She had that morning been persecuted, with more than usual vehemence, to consent to an immediate marriage with my rival. She was
reproached with the encouragement that she had shown him—she was
threatened with being turned out of doors with disgrace and shame.
Her proud spirit rose in arms at the threat; but when she remembered

2. Signs, symbols.

the scorn that she had heaped upon me, and how, perhaps, she had thus lost one whom she now regarded as her only friend, she wept with remorse and rage. At that moment I appeared. "O, Winzy!" she exclaimed, "take me to your mother's cot;[3] swiftly let me leave the detested luxuries and wretchedness of this noble dwelling—take me to poverty and happiness."

I clasped her in my arms with transport. The old lady was speechless with fury, and broke forth into invective only when we were far on our road to my natal cottage. My mother received the fair fugitive, escaped from a gilt cage to nature and liberty, with tenderness and joy; my father, who loved her, welcomed her heartily; it was a day of rejoicing, which did not need the addition of the celestial potion of the alchymist to steep me in delight.

Soon after this eventful day, I became the husband of Bertha. I ceased to be the scholar of Cornelius, but I continued his friend. I always felt grateful to him for having, unawares, procured me that delicious draught of a divine elixir, which, instead of curing me of love (sad cure! solitary and joyless remedy for evils which seem blessings to the memory), had inspired me with courage and resolution, thus winning for me an inestimable treasure in my Bertha.

I often called to mind that period of trance-like inebriation with wonder. The drink of Cornelius had not fulfilled the task for which he affirmed that it had been prepared, but its effects were more potent and blissful than words can express. They had faded by degrees, yet they lingered long—and painted life in hues of splendour. Bertha often wondered at my lightness of heart and unaccustomed gaiety; for, before, I had been rather serious, or even sad, in my disposition. She loved me the better for my cheerful temper, and our days were winged by joy.

Five years afterwards I was suddenly summoned to the bedside of the dying Cornelius. He had sent for me in haste, conjuring my instant presence. I found him stretched on his pallet,[4] enfeebled even to death; all of life that yet remained animated his piercing eyes, and they were fixed on a glass vessel, full of a roseate liquid.

"Behold," he said, in a broken and inward voice, "the vanity of human wishes! a second time my hopes are about to be crowned, a second time they are destroyed. Look at that liquor—you remember five years ago I had prepared the same, with the same success;—then, as now, my thirsting lips expected to taste the immortal elixir—you dashed it from me! and at present it is too late."

He spoke with difficulty, and fell back on his pillow. I could not help saying,—

"How, revered master, can a cure for love restore you to life?"

3. Cottage.   4. Thin mattress.

A faint smile gleamed across his face as I listened earnestly to his scarcely intelligible answer.

"A cure for love and for all things—the Elixir of Immortality. Ah! if now I might drink, I should live for ever!"

As he spoke, a golden flash gleamed from the fluid; a well-remembered fragrance stole over the air; he raised himself, all weak as he was —strength seemed miraculously to re-enter his frame—he stretched forth his hand—a loud explosion startled me—a ray of fire shot up from the elixir, and the glass vessel which contained it was shivered to atoms! I turned my eyes towards the philosopher; he had fallen back—his eyes were glassy—his features rigid—he was dead!

But I lived, and was to live for ever! So said the unfortunate alchymist, and for a few days I believed his words. I remembered the glorious drunkenness that had followed my stolen draught. I reflected on the change I had felt in my frame—in my soul. The bounding elasticity of the one—the buoyant lightness of the other. I surveyed myself in a mirror, and could perceive no change in my features during the space of the five years which had elapsed. I remembered the radiant hues and grateful scent of that delicious beverage—worthy the gift it was capable of bestowing—I was, then, IMMORTAL!

A few days after I laughed at my credulity. The old proverb, that "a prophet is least regarded in his own country," was true with respect to me and my defunct master. I loved him as a man—I respected him as a sage—but I derided the notion that he could command the powers of darkness, and laughed at the superstitious fears with which he was regarded by the vulgar.[5] He was a wise philosopher, but had no acquaintance with any spirits but those clad in flesh and blood. His science was simply human; and human science, I soon persuaded myself, could never conquer nature's laws so far as to imprison the soul for ever within its carnal habitation. Cornelius had brewed a soul-refreshing drink—more inebriating than wine—sweeter and more fragrant than any fruit: it possessed probably strong medicinal powers, imparting gladness to the heart and vigor to the limbs; but its effects would wear out; already were they diminished in my frame. I was a lucky fellow to have quaffed health and joyous spirits, and perhaps long life, at my master's hands; but my good fortune ended there: longevity was far different from immortality.

I continued to entertain this belief for many years. Sometimes a thought stole across me—Was the alchymist indeed deceived? But my habitual credence was, that I should meet the fate of all the children of Adam[6] at my appointed time—a little late, but still at a natural age. Yet

5. Common, uneducated people.
6. According to Genesis 3, the first man, whose eating of the apple in Eden brought death into the world.

it was certain that I retained a wonderfully youthful look. I was laughed at for my vanity in consulting the mirror so often, but I consulted it in vain—my brow was untrenched[7]—my cheeks—my eyes—my whole person continued as untarnished as in my twentieth year.

I was troubled. I looked at the faded beauty of Bertha—I seemed more like her son. By degrees our neighbours began to make similar observations, and I found at last that I went by the name of the Scholar bewitched. Bertha herself grew uneasy. She became jealous and peevish, and at length she began to question me. We had no children; we were all in all to each other; and though, as she grew older, her vivacious spirit became a little allied to ill-temper, and her beauty sadly diminished, I cherished her in my heart as the mistress I had idolized, the wife I had sought and won with such perfect love.

At last our situation became intolerable: Bertha was fifty—I twenty years of age. I had, in very shame, in some measure adopted the habits of a more advanced age; I no longer mingled in the dance among the young and gay, but my heart bounded along with them while I restrained my feet; and a sorry figure I cut among the Nestors[8] of our village. But before the time I mention, things were altered—we were universally shunned; we were—at least, I was—reported to have kept up an iniquitous acquaintance with some of my former master's supposed friends. Poor Bertha was pitied, but deserted. I was regarded with horror and detestation.

What was to be done? we sat by our winter fire—poverty had made itself felt, for none would buy the produce of my farm; and often I had been forced to journey twenty miles, to some place where I was not known, to dispose of our property. It is true we had saved something for an evil day—that day was come.

We sat by our lone fireside—the old-hearted youth and his antiquated wife. Again Bertha insisted on knowing the truth; she recapitulated all she had ever heard said about me, and added her own observations. She conjured me to cast off the spell; she described how much more comely gray hairs were than my chestnut locks; she descanted[9] on the reverence and respect due to age—how preferable to the slight regard paid to mere children: could I imagine that the despicable gifts of youth and good looks outweighed disgrace, hatred, and scorn? Nay, in the end I should be burnt as a dealer in the black art, while she, to whom I had not deigned to communicate any portion of my good fortune, might be stoned as my accomplice. At length she insinuated that I must share my secret with her, and bestow on her like benefits to those I myself enjoyed, or she would denounce me—and then she burst into tears.

7. Unwrinkled.   9. Discoursed.
8. Old man in Homer's *Iliad*.

Thus beset, methought it was the best way to tell the truth. I revealed it as tenderly as I could, and spoke only of a *very long life*, not of immortality—which representation, indeed, coincided best with my own ideas. When I ended, I rose and said,

"And now, my Bertha, will you denounce the lover of your youth? —You will not, I know. But it is too hard, my poor wife, that you should suffer from my ill-luck and the accursed arts of Cornelius. I will leave you—you have wealth enough, and friends will return in my absence. I will go; young as I seem, and strong as I am, I can work and gain my bread among strangers, unsuspected and unknown. I loved you in youth; God is my witness that I would not desert you in age, but that your safety and happiness require it."

I took my cap and moved towards the door; in a moment Bertha's arms were round my neck, and her lips were pressed to mine. "No, my husband, my Winzy," she said, "you shall not go alone—take me with you; we will remove from this place, and, as you say, among strangers we shall be unsuspected and safe. I am not so very old as quite to shame you, my Winzy; and I dare say the charm will soon wear off, and, with the blessing of God, you will become more elderly-looking, as is fitting; you shall not leave me."

I returned the good soul's embrace heartily. "I will not, my Bertha; but for your sake I had not thought of such a thing.[1] I will be your true, faithful husband while you are spared to me, and do my duty by you to the last."

The next day we prepared secretly for our emigration. We were obliged to make great pecuniary sacrifices—it could not be helped. We realised a sum sufficient, at least, to maintain us while Bertha lived; and, without saying adieu to any one, quitted our native country to take refuge in a remote part of western France.

It was a cruel thing to transport poor Bertha from her native village, and the friends of her youth, to a new country, new language, new customs. The strange secret of my destiny rendered this removal immaterial to me; but I compassionated her deeply, and was glad to perceive that she found compensation for her misfortunes in a variety of little ridiculous circumstances. Away from all tell-tale chroniclers, she sought to decrease the apparent disparity of our ages by a thousand feminine arts—rouge, youthful dress, and assumed juvenility of manner. I could not be angry—Did not I myself wear a mask? Why quarrel with hers, because it was less successful? I grieved deeply when I remembered that this was my Bertha, whom I had loved so fondly, and won with such transport—the dark-eyed, dark-haired girl, with smiles of enchanting archness and a step like a fawn—this mincing, simpering, jealous

1. I.e., I thought of it only for your sake.

old woman. I should have revered her gray locks and withered cheeks; but thus!—It was my work, I knew; but I did not the less deplore this type of human weakness.

Her jealousy never slept. Her chief occupation was to discover that, in spite of outward appearances, I was myself growing old. I verily believe that the poor soul loved me truly in her heart, but never had woman so tormenting a mode of displaying fondness. She would discern wrinkles in my face and decrepitude in my walk, while I bounded along in youthful vigour, the youngest looking of twenty youths. I never dared address another woman: on one occasion, fancying that the belle of the village regarded me with favouring eyes, she bought me a gray wig. Her constant discourse among her acquaintants was, that though I looked so young, there was ruin at work within my frame; and she affirmed that the worst symptom about me was my apparent health. My youth was a disease, she said, and I ought at all times to prepare, if not for a sudden and awful death, at least to awake some morning white-headed, and bowed down with all the marks of advanced years. I let her talk—I often joined in her conjectures. Her warnings chimed in with my never-ceasing speculations concerning my state, and I took an earnest, though painful, interest in listening to all that her quick wit and excited imagination could say on the subject.

Why dwell on these minute circumstances? We lived on for many long years. Bertha became bed-rid and paralytic: I nursed her as a mother might a child. She grew peevish, and still harped upon one string—of how long I should survive her. It has ever been a source of consolation to me, that I performed my duty scrupulously towards her. She had been mine in youth, she was mine in age, and at last, when I heaped the sod over her corpse, I wept to feel that I had lost all that really bound me to humanity.

Since then how many have been my cares and woes, how few and empty my enjoyments! I pause here in my history—I will pursue it no further. A sailor without rudder or compass, tossed on a stormy sea—a traveller lost on a wide-spread heath, without landmark or star to guide him—such have I been: more lost, more hopeless than either. A nearing ship, a gleam from some far cot, may save them; but I have no beacon except the hope of death.

Death! mysterious, ill-visaged friend of weak humanity! Why alone of all mortals have you cast me from your sheltering fold?[2] O, for the peace of the grave! the deep silence of the iron-bound tomb! that thought would cease to work in my brain, and my heart beat no more with emotions varied only by new forms of sadness!

---

2. An enclosure for sheep. Christ is traditionally represented as a shepherd; here Shelley places Death in that protective role.

Am I immortal? I return to my first question. In the first place, is it
not more probable that the beverage of the alchymist was fraught rather
with longevity than eternal life? Such is my hope. And then be it remembered, that I only drank *half* of the potion prepared by him. Was
not the whole necessary to complete the charm? To have drained half
the Elixir of Immortality is but to be half immortal—my Forever is thus
truncated and null.

But again, who shall number the years of the half of eternity? I often
try to imagine by what rule the infinite may be divided. Sometimes I
fancy age advancing upon me. One gray hair I have found. Fool! do I
lament? Yes, the fear of age and death often creeps coldly into my
heart; and the more I live, the more I dread death, even while I abhor
life. Such an enigma is man—born to perish—when he wars, as I do,
against the established laws of his nature.

But for this anomaly of feeling surely I might die: the medicine of the
alchymist would not be proof[3] against fire—sword—and the strangling
waters. I have gazed upon the blue depths of many a placid lake, and
the tumultuous rushing of many a mighty river, and have said, peace
inhabits those waters; yet I have turned my steps away, to live yet another day. I have asked myself, whether suicide would be a crime in one
to whom thus only the portals of the other world could be opened. I
have done all, except presenting myself as a soldier or duellist, an object
of destruction to my—no, *not* my fellow-mortals, and therefore I have
shrunk away. They are not my fellows. The inextinguishable power of
life in my frame, and their ephemeral existence, place us wide as the
poles asunder. I could not raise a hand against the meanest[4] or the most
powerful among them.

Thus I have lived on for many a year—alone, and weary of myself
—desirous of death, yet never dying—a mortal immortal. Neither ambition nor avarice can enter my mind, and the ardent love that gnaws at
my heart, never to be returned—never to find an equal on which to
expend itself—lives there only to torment me.

This very day I conceived a design by which I may end all—without
self-slaughter, without making another man a Cain[5]—an expedition,
which mortal frame can never survive, even endued with the youth and
strength that inhabits mine. Thus I shall put my immortality to the test,
and rest for ever—or return, the wonder and benefactor of the human
species.

Before I go, a miserable vanity has caused me to pen these pages. I
would not die, and leave no name behind. Three centuries have passed
since I quaffed the fatal beverage: another year shall not elapse before,

---

3. Safe, protected.
4. Lowest.
5. I.e., a murderer. In Genesis 4, Cain, the son
of Adam and Eve, murders his brother Abel and
is cast out into the world. "Endued": endowed.

encountering gigantic dangers—warring with the powers of frost in their home—beset by famine, toil, and tempest—I yield this body, too tenacious a cage for a soul which thirsts for freedom, to the destructive elements of air and water—or, if I survive, my name shall be recorded as one of the most famous among the sons of men; and, my task achieved, I shall adopt more resolute means; and, by scattering and annihilating the atoms that compose my frame, set at liberty the life imprisoned within, and so cruelly prevented from soaring from this dim earth to a sphere more congenial to its immortal essence.

1833   1834

SOJOURNER TRUTH
c. 1797–1883

Our understanding of both the life and the art of Sojourner Truth is limited, for this woman, who by all accounts became a brilliant speechmaker, exemplifies an oral tradition only partially preserved. Born into slavery in Hurley, Ulster County, New York, she was called Isabella, and, after she fled to freedom in 1827, she took the last name of the family that protected her. Isabella Van Wagener had already witnessed the sale of two of her four surviving children when she settled as a domestic servant with her youngest son and daughter in New York City in or around 1829. There she worked with the evangelical preacher Elijah Pierson, who encouraged her efforts to convert prostitutes, and Robert Matthew, whose communal household, "Zion Hill," in Sing Sing, New York, was her home for two years. In 1843, mystical visions and voices gave her the new name "Sojourner Truth." So christened, she sojourned alone to speak the truth on tours that would make her famous throughout the United States.

Her religious zeal was linked to abolitionist goals when, at a communal farm in Northampton, Massachusetts, in that first winter of her travels, she came into contact with George W. Benson, brother-in-law of the newspaper editor William Lloyd Garrison. Subsequently hailed by abolitionist leaders, she toured Ohio, Indiana, Missouri, and Kansas throughout the 1850s, singing gospel songs, engaging large crowds with her speeches, and selling the *Narrative of Sojourner Truth* (1850), an autobiographical account transcribed and edited by Olive Gilbert. Illiterate all of her life, speaking an English accented with her original language, Dutch, Sojourner Truth was effective even with hostile audiences. In an essay in the April 1863 issue of the *Atlantic Monthly*, Harriet Beecher Stowe described the subtle power of this "sibyl" who had found enough charity to declare, "Lord, Lord, I can love *even de white folk!*" During the postwar period, encouraged by Elizabeth Cady Stanton, Sojourner Truth began speaking for the cause of women's suffrage, but she never relinquished her spiritual and racial themes. Her later call for a "Negro State" met with no success; however, she continued to lecture and sing in many Eastern and Midwestern states until, nearly a century old, she retired to Battle Creek, Michigan, where she died.

As one of the most effective female orators of her time, Sojourner Truth spoke for oppressed people with humor and courage that are evident, too, in the story of her response to allegations that she was a man: she was said to have bared her breast at a women's rights convention. Although we are dependent on the records of her white friends, in her speeches Sojourner Truth emerges, as the scholar Sterling Stuckey has observed, with the vitality of a great Blues singer who sustains the most essential values of her people.

We are indebted to Miriam Schneir for her modernization of Truth's speeches in *Feminism: The Essential Historical Writings* (1972); the speeches were originally recorded in Elizabeth Cady Stanton *et al.*, *The History of Woman Suffrage* (1881–1886).

Ain't I a Woman?

Well, children, where there is so much racket there must be something out of kilter. I think that 'twixt the negroes of the South and the women at the North, all talking about rights, the white men will be in a fix pretty soon. But what's all this here talking about?

That man over there says that women need to be helped into carriages, and lifted over ditches, and to have the best place everywhere. Nobody ever helps me into carriages, or over mud-puddles, or gives me any best place! And ain't I a woman? Look at me! Look at my arm! I have ploughed and planted, and gathered into barns, and no man could head me! And ain't I a woman? I could work as much and eat as much as a man—when I could get it—and bear the lash as well! And ain't I a woman? I have borne thirteen children, and seen them most all sold off to slavery, and when I cried out with my mother's grief, none but Jesus heard me! And ain't I a woman?

Then they talk about this thing in the head; what's this they call it? [Intellect, someone whispers.] That's it, honey. What's that got to do with women's rights or negro's rights? If my cup won't hold but a pint, and yours holds a quart, wouldn't you be mean not to let me have my little half-measure full?

Then that little man in black there, he says women can't have as much rights as men, 'cause Christ wasn't a woman! Where did your Christ come from? Where did your Christ come from? From God and a woman! Man had nothing to do with Him.

If the first woman God ever made was strong enough to turn the world upside down all alone, these women together ought to be able to turn it back, and get it right side up again! And now they is asking to do it, the men better let them.

Obliged to you for hearing me, and now old Sojourner ain't got nothing more to say.

1851   1881–1886

What Time of Night It Is

Is it not good for me to come and draw forth a spirit,[1] to see what kind of spirit people are of? I see that some of you have got the spirit of a goose, and some have got the spirit of a snake. I feel at home here. I come to you, citizens of New York, as I suppose you ought to be. I am a citizen of the state of New York; I was born in it, and I was a slave in the state of New York; and now I am a good citizen of this state. I was born here, and I can tell you I feel at home here. I've been lookin' round and watchin' things, and I know a little mite[2] 'bout Woman's Rights, too. I come forth to speak 'bout Woman's Rights, and want to throw in my little mite, to keep the scales a-movin'. I know that it feels a kind o' hissin' and ticklin' like to see a colored woman get up and tell you about things, and Woman's Rights. We have all been thrown down so low that nobody thought we'd ever get up again; but we have been long enough trodden now; we will come up again, and now I am here.

I was a-thinkin', when I see women contendin' for their rights, I was a-thinkin' what a difference there is now, and what there was in old times. I have only a few minutes to speak; but in the old times the kings of the earth would[n't] hear a woman. There was a king in the Scriptures;[3] and then it was the kings of the earth would kill a woman if she come into their presence; but Queen Esther come forth, for she was oppressed, and felt there was a great wrong, and she said I will die or I will bring my complaint before the king. Should the king of the United States be greater, or more crueler, or more harder? But the king, he raised up his sceptre and said: "Thy request shall be granted unto thee —to the half of my kingdom will I grant it to thee!" Then he said he would hang Haman on the gallows he had made up high. But that is not what women come forward to contend. The women want their rights as Esther. She only wanted to explain her rights. And he was so liberal that he said, "the half of my kingdom shall be granted to thee," and he did not wait for her to ask, he was so liberal with her.

Now, women do not ask half of a kingdom, but their rights, and they don't get 'em. When she comes to demand 'em, don't you hear how sons hiss their mothers like snakes because they ask for their rights; and can they ask for anything less? The king ordered Haman to be hung on the gallows which he prepared to hang others; but I do not want any man to be killed, but I am sorry to see them so short-minded. But we'll have our rights; see if we don't; and you can't stop us from them; see if you can. You may hiss as much as you like, but it is comin'. Women don't get half as much rights as they ought to; we want more, and we

---

1. An energetic response.
2. Bit.
3. Probably a reference to Solomon, king of Israel, who heard the complaints of his subjects. Esther was a Jewish queen of Persia who saved her people from massacre.

will have it. Jesus says: "What I say to one, I say to all—watch!" I'm a-watchin'. God says: "Honor your father and your mother."[4] Sons and daughters ought to behave themselves before their mothers, but they do not. I can see them a-laughin', and pointin' at their mothers up here on the stage. They hiss when an aged woman comes forth. If they'd been brought up proper they'd have known better than hissin' like snakes and geese. I'm 'round watchin' these things, and I wanted to come up and say these few things to you, and I'm glad of the hearin' you give me. I wanted to tell you a mite about Woman's Rights, and so I came out and said so. I am sittin' among you to watch; and every once and awhile I will come out and tell you what time of night it is.

1853   1881–1886

Keeping the Thing Going while Things Are Stirring

My friends, I am rejoiced that you are glad, but I don't know how you will feel when I get through. I come from another field—the country of the slave. They have got their liberty—so much good luck to have slavery partly destroyed; not entirely. I want it root and branch destroyed. Then we will all be free indeed. I feel that if I have to answer for the deeds done in my body just as much as a man, I have a right to have just as much as a man. There is a great stir about colored men getting their rights,[5] but not a word about the colored women; and if colored men get their rights, and not colored women theirs, you see the colored men will be masters over the women, and it will be just as bad as it was before. So I am for keeping the thing going while things are stirring; because if we wait till it is still, it will take a great while to get it going again. White women are a great deal smarter, and know more than colored women, while colored women do not know scarcely anything. They go out washing, which is about as high as a colored woman gets, and their men go about idle, strutting up and down; and when the women come home, they[6] ask for their money and take it all, and then scold because there is no food. I want you to consider on that, chil'n. I call you chil'n; you are somebody's chil'n, and I am old enough to be mother of all that is here. I want women to have their rights. In the courts women have no right, no voice; nobody speaks for them. I wish woman to have her voice there among the pettifoggers.[7] If it is not a fit place for women, it is unfit for men to be there.

I am above eighty years old; it is about time for me to be going. I have

4. One of the Ten Commandments issued by God to Moses.
5. The 14th Amendment was proposed in 1866 and ratified in 1868; the 15th Amendment was proposed in 1869 and ratified in 1870.
6. I.e., the men.
7. Unscrupulous lawyers.

been forty years a slave and forty years free, and would be here forty years more to have equal rights for all. I suppose I am kept here because something remains for me to do; I suppose I am yet to help to break the chain. I have done a great deal of work; as much as a man, but did not get so much pay. I used to work in the field and bind grain, keeping up with the cradler;[8] but men doing no more, got twice as much pay; so with the German women. They work in the field and do as much work, but do not get the pay. We do as much, we eat as much, we want as much. I suppose I am about the only colored woman that goes about to speak for the rights of the colored women. I want to keep the thing stirring, now that the ice is cracked. What we want is a little money. You men know that you get as much again as women when you write, or for what you do. When we get our rights we shall not have to come to you for money, for then we shall have money enough in our own pockets; and may be you will ask us for money. But help us now until we get it. It is a good consolation to know that when we have got this battle once fought we shall not be coming to you any more. You have been having our rights so long, that you think, like a slave-holder, that you own us. I know that it is hard for one who has held the reins for so long to give up; it cuts like a knife. It will feel all the better when it closes up again. I have been in Washington about three years, seeing about these colored people. Now colored men have the right to vote. There ought to be equal rights now more than ever, since colored people have got their freedom. I am going to talk several times while I am here; so now I will do a little singing. I have not heard any singing since I came here.

1867   1881–1886

8. A worker who reaps grain and lays it flat.

ELIZABETH BARRETT BROWNING
1806–1861

Elizabeth Barrett Browning is probably best known today for her romance with Robert Browning. Her *Sonnets from the Portuguese,* a series of love poems dedicated to him, are still popular, while the dramatic elopement of the two writers has been the subject of many books and at least one play, *The Barretts of Wimpole Street* (1930) by Rudolf Besier. Yet in her own era this prolific, scholarly, and highly political poet was considered a major author rather than a romance heroine. Older and more famous than the husband whose reputation has since eclipsed hers, she was seriously mentioned for the post of Poet Laureate when Wordsworth died in 1850. Admired by such diverse figures as William Makepeace Thackeray and Harriet Martineau, Edgar Allan Poe and Harriet Beecher Stowe, Alfred, Lord Tennyson and Margaret Fuller, she was an accomplished student and translator of Greek, the center of a lively circle of English expatriates in mid-nineteenth-century Florence, a passionate abolitionist, a powerful supporter of the movement for Italian unification, and a strong feminist. Indeed, nothing could be more misleading than the twentieth-century image of "Mrs. Browning" as a swooning Victorian invalid, languishing on a sofa, smelling salts in one hand and sentimental verses in the other.

Born on a pleasant estate at Durham in Herefordshire, Elizabeth Barrett was the oldest of eleven children. Her father, Edward Moulton Barrett, owned extensive plantations in Jamaica, from which the family fortune derived, though Elizabeth herself was later to be troubled by the link with slavery such holdings represented. Strong-willed and autocratic, he dominated the household, and Elizabeth's submissive mother, Mary Barrett, was evidently an appropriate wife for him: she was "one of those women," the poet later wrote, who "in . . . bowing themselves make a mark, a plait, within—a sign of suffering." Yet Elizabeth clearly loved and admired her; after Mrs. Barrett's death in 1828, she indicated in letters and journals that, like her heroine Aurora Leigh, she "felt a mother-want about the world."

A precocious child, Barrett Browning started to write poetry early. According to some reports, she composed verses at the age of four, and when she was fourteen her father—whose patriarchal sternness did not prevent him from taking pride in his oldest child's accomplishments—had her "epic," *The Battle of Marathon*, privately printed. At the age of sixteen, she wrote a long philosophical poem, *An Essay on Mind*, and around this time she began studying Greek, with special attention to the Greek Christian poets. Her life was not entirely carefree, however. In 1821 she suffered what was defined as a "nervous collapse"; her general health had, in any case, always been precarious. Quite early, therefore, like so many other nineteenth-century invalids, she began using what she called "muriate of morphine . . . in a combination with ether" to ease both physical pain and mental distress. For much of her adult life, especially her years of confinement in the famous house at 50 Wimpole Street from which Browning rescued her, she seems to have been virtually dependent on such drugs.

Despite these problems, Barrett Browning's earliest years at Wimpole Street were by no means bleak. After some financial losses, the family had moved there in 1838, just as Elizabeth was beginning to establish a considerable literary reputation with her first books, a translation of Aeschylus's *Prometheus Bound* (1833) and a collection of her own verse, *The Seraphim* (1838). After her mother's death, she and her father had become particularly close—she was evidently always a special favorite of his—and she was also devoted to her brothers and sisters, especially her brother Edward ("Bro"), the sibling closest to her in age. In addition, she had formed friendships with a number of notable literary figures, including the essayist Mary Russell Mitford, the dramatist Richard Horne, and the man of letters John Kenyon. Her health continued to be poor, however, and in 1840 she was advised by doctors to vacation in Cornwall, where the climate was supposed to be good for invalids. She persuaded her father that "Bro" should accompany her there, and, in what may well have been the major catastrophe of her life, the young man was drowned that year in a sailing accident off Torquay. Earlier in the year, her brother Samuel had also died, and the loss of "Bro," coming so soon after another fatality, dealt her a terrible blow. Plunged into "hopeless grief," feeling herself to be "dead before death," and "living on the outside of my life," she retired into the notorious sickroom at Wimpole Street, from which she was not to emerge for another five years.

Still, although she was ill and in mourning, Barrett Browning continued her indefatigable correspondence and her vigorous composition. In 1844 she published a two-volume collection of her poems, with an American edition that had an introduction by Edgar Allan Poe. Friends visited her, she maintained a lively interest in London's literary world, and she continued her study of Greek; her *Account of the Greek Christian Poets* appeared serially in the *Athenaeum*, a major British periodical, in 1842. Finally, in 1845, she received a surprising letter from an admirer, Robert Browning, a little-known but increasingly well-regarded poet whose veneration of her work was to change her life. "I do . . . love these books with all my heart—and I love you too," he wrote, imploring her for the privilege of a meeting. At their first encounter, and thereafter, the two poets discovered many mutual affinities; within a year and a half of Browning's first letter to Elizabeth Barrett, they eloped to the Continent together.

Six years younger than his wife-to-be, Browning was a struggling experimental writer when the pair met. Because he was extraordinarily intellectual, his work was often considered "obscure," but in an effort to surmount such judgments he had been trying to write popular dramas, a labor that no doubt influenced his later mastery of the dramatic monologue and that must also have left its mark on his wife's work, perhaps enhancing her interest in capturing the theatrical intensity of immediate events. Because Elizabeth Barrett was far more established than Robert Browning at the time of their first meeting, however, it is just as likely that her stylistic inventiveness influenced *his* writing. Certainly, even in his first letter to her, he expressed his respect for her work, defining himself "as a loyal fellow-craftsman." Their flight from the dark house at Wimpole Street to the sunnier streets of France and Italy was obviously romantic: Edward Moulton Barrett had long refused to allow any of his children to marry, so the couple had to wed furtively in a London church, with only Elizabeth's maid and a cousin of Robert's as witnesses. But what was ultimately more crucial than the crisis of their love was the seriousness of their aesthetic as well as emotional engagement with each other and the psychological support that the poet formerly known as Elizabeth Barrett was to derive from that many-leveled relationship.

That she did derive such support from Browning is made clear by the intensity of the verse she wrote in the fifteen years of her marriage, years when the couple lived primarily in Florence at the house called Casa Guidi, which she memorialized in *Casa Guidi Windows*, her brilliant meditation on the successes and setbacks of the Italian nationalist movement. Traveling through France, where Elizabeth insisted on meeting and doing homage to the novelist George Sand—about whom she had already written several sonnets—the Brownings came to Italy, the land that was to become a significant second home for both. Here the two began to write what were obviously ambitious and major works. Elizabeth, for instance, produced her *Poems* of 1850, which included such fierce political statements as *The Runaway Slave at Pilgrim's Point*.

Shortly thereafter, she published *Sonnets from the Portuguese*, a sequence that adapted the usually male-oriented genre of the sonnet cycle to female requirements, telling the story of a love affair from a woman's, instead of a man's, point of view. Then, in 1851, she produced *Casa Guidi Windows*, and in 1856 her "epic-novel," *Aurora Leigh*, appeared. Finally, in 1860, she published *Poems before Congress*, a collection of frankly political manifestos dedicated to the cause of Italian unification; and in 1862, the year after her death from complications of bronchitis, her *Last Poems* were assembled by her husband. To the end, she had been vital and productive.

Aesthetically energized, Barrett Browning had also been socially and intellectually refreshed by her new life. In Florence she made many friends, including the American writers Harriet Beecher Stowe and Margaret Fuller as well as the increasingly eccentric English poet Walter Savage Landor, and she developed new interests, including—along with the Italian "cause"—the popular spiritualist movement. Most important, in Florence in 1849, after several miscarriages, she gave birth to a son, Robert Wiedeman Barrett-Browning, called "Pennini" (or "Pen" for short). Like marriage, maternity seemed only to enhance her creative imagination. Her "own young Florentine" with "brave blue English eyes" appears as a redemptive figure at the conclusion of *Casa Guidi Windows*, and again, thinly disguised, as a sacramental child in *Aurora Leigh*. Gracing poems and romping in parlors, he seems to have been a muse rather than an encumbrance for his forty-three-year-old mother.

If her own real child functioned as a herald of art as well as reality for Barrett Browning, however, that is because, especially during her Italian years, she had evolved a passionate aesthetic of reality. In *Aurora Leigh*, her heroine, a poet like herself, articulates this creed, and following such beliefs, Barrett Browning wrote with commitment about the problem of slavery in the United States, an issue she dramatized in *The Runaway Slave at Pilgrim's Point*, and about the pain of impoverished children in England, a matter she had already begun to treat in the early polemics of *The Cry of the Children*, and that she later took up in *A Song for the Ragged Schools of London*. More elaborately, she recorded not only her aesthetic of reality but also her protofeminist philosophy in the book-length verse-novel *Aurora Leigh*, where she attacked the degrading education most nineteenth-century women received and defended their right to intellectual self-determination. Attempting a range of forms and meters— the sonnet and the verse drama, the ballad and the blank verse epic—she constantly tested herself against the highest standards of male-defined poetic genres, as if to declare, with her Aurora, "I too have my vocation—work to do . . . most serious work."

A True Dream

(Dreamed at Sidmouth[1] 1833)

> I had not an evil end in view,
>   Though I trod the evil way;

---

1. An English seaside town.

And why I practised the magic art,
    My dream it did not say.

I unsealed the vial mystical,   5
    I outpoured the liquid thing,
And while the smoke came wreathing out,
    I stood unshuddering.

The smoke came wreathing, wreathing out,
    All mute, and dark, and slow,   10
Till its cloud was stained with a fleshly hue,
    And a fleshly form 'gan show.

Then paused the smoke—the fleshly form
    Looked steadfast in mine ee,[2]
His beard was black as a thundercloud,   15
    But I trembled not to see.[3]

I unsealed the vial mystical,
    I outpoured the liquid thing,
And while the smoke came wreathing out,
    I stood unshuddering.   20

The smoke came wreathing, wreathing out,
    All mute, and dark, and slow,
Till its cloud was stained with a fleshly hue,
    And a fleshly form 'gan show.

Then paused the smoke—but the mortal form   25
    A garment swart[4] did veil,
I looked on it with fixéd heart,
    Yea—not a pulse did fail!

I unsealed the vial mystical,
    I outpoured the liquid thing,   30
And while the smoke came wreathing out,
    I stood unshuddering.

The smoke came wreathing, wreathing out,
    And now it was faster and lighter,
And it bore on its folds the rainbow's hues,   35
    Heaven could not show them brighter.

Then paused the smoke, the rainbow's hues
    Did a childish face express—

2. Archaic form of "eye"; Barrett Browning is   3. I.e., did not tremble to see him.
evoking both the language and form of old Eng-   4. Black or dark-colored.
lish ballads like "Sir Patrick Spens" here.

The rose in the cheek, the blue in the eyne,
　　The yellow in the tress.   40

The fair young child shook back her hair,
　　And round me her arms did wreathe,
Her lips were hard and cold as stone,
　　They sucked away my breath.

I cast her off as she clung to me,   45
　　With hate and shuddering;
I brake the vials, and foresware
　　The curse, curséd thing.

Anon[5] outspake a brother of mine—
　　"Upon the pavement, see,   50
Besprent[6] with noisome poison slime,
　　Those twining serpents three."

Anon outspake my wildered[7] heart
　　As I saw the serpent train—
I have called up three existences   55
　　I cannot quench again.

"Alas! with unholy company,
　　My lifetime they will scathe;
They will hiss in the storm, and on sunny days
　　Will gleam and thwart my path."   60

Outspake that pitying brother of mine—
　　"Now nay, my sister, nay,
I will pour on them oil of vitriol,[8]
　　And burn their lives away."

"Now nay, my brother, torture not,   65
　　Now hold thine hand, and spare."
He poured on them oil of vitriol,
　　And did not heed my prayer.

I saw the drops of torture fall;
　　I heard the shriekings rise,   70
While the serpents writhed in agony
　　Beneath my dreaming eyes.

And while they shrieked, and while they writhed,
　　And inward and outward wound,

---

5. Then, shortly after.　　　　　　　　　7. Bewildered.
6. Sprinkled; "noisome": repulsive.　　　8. A caustic chemical substance.

They waxéd larger, and their wail   75
    Assumed a human sound.

And glared their eyes, and their slimy scales
    Were roundly and redly bright,
Most like the lidless sun,[9] what time
Through the mist he meets your sight.   80

And larger and larger they waxéd still,
    And longer still and longer;
And they shrieked in their pain, "Come, come to us,
    We are stronger, we are stronger."

Upon the ground I laid mine head,   85
    And heard the wailing sound;
I did not wail, I did not writhe—
    I laid me on the ground.

And larger and larger they waxéd still
    And longer still and longer;
And they shrieked in their pangs, "Come, come to us,
    We are stronger, we are stronger."

Then up I raised my burning brow,
    My quiv'ring arms on high;
I spake in prayer, and I named aloud   95
    The name of sanctity.

And as in my anguish I prayed and named
    Aloud the holy name,
The impious mocking serpent voice
    Did echo back the same.   100

And larger and larger they waxéd still,
    And stronger still and longer!
And they shrieked in their pangs, "Come, come to us,
    We are stronger, we are stronger."

Then out from among them arose a form   105
    In shroud of death indued[1]—
I fled from him with wings of wind,
    With whirlwinds he pursued.

                    . . .

I stood by a chamber door, and thought
    Within its gloom to hide;   110

9. The sun is compared to an eye with no lid.   1. I.e., "wrapped" or "covered."
"What time": when.

I locked the door, and the while forgot
　　That I stood on the outer side.

And the knell of mine heart was wildly tolled
　　While I graspéd still the key;
For I felt beside me the icy breath,   115
　　And knew that *that* was *he*.

I heard these words, "Who'er doth *taste*,
　　Will *drink* the magic bowl;
So her body may do my mission here
　　Companioned by her soul."   120

Mine hand was cold as the key it held,
　　Mine heart had an iron weight;
I saw a gleam, I heard a sound—
　　The clock was striking eight.

1833   1913

Grief

I tell you, hopeless grief is passionless;
That only men incredulous of despair,
Half-taught in anguish, through the midnight air
Beat upward to God's throne in loud access[2]
Of shrieking and reproach. Full desertness,   5
In souls as countries, lieth silent-bare
Under the blanching, vertical eye-glare
Of the absolute heavens. Deep-hearted man, express
Grief for thy dead in silence like to death—
Most like a monumental statue set   10
In everlasting watch and moveless woe
Till itself crumble to the dust beneath.
Touch it; the marble eyelids are not wet:
If it could weep, it could arise and go.

1844

To George Sand[3]

A *Desire*

Thou large-brained woman and large-hearted man,
Self-called George Sand! whose soul, amid the lions[4]
Of thy tumultuous senses, moans defiance

2. Outburst.
3. French female novelist (1804–1876) whose novels and style of life were considered immoral by some.
4. In the ancient Roman "circus" or arena slaves were pitted against lions for the amusement of spectators.

And answers roar for roar, as spirits can:
I would some mild miraculous thunder ran   5
Above the applauded circus, in appliance
Of thine own nobler nature's strength and science,
Drawing two pinions,[5] white as wings of swan,
From thy strong shoulders, to amaze the place
With holier light! that thou to woman's claim   10
And man's, mightst join beside the angel's grace
Of a pure genius sanctified from blame,
Till child and maiden pressed to thine embrace
To kiss upon thy lips a stainless fame.[6]

1844

To George Sand

A Recognition

True genius, but true woman! dost deny
The woman's nature with a manly scorn,
And break away the gauds[7] and armlets worn
By weaker women in captivity?
Ah, vain denial! that revolted cry   5
Is sobbed in by a woman's voice forlorn,—
Thy woman's hair, my sister, all unshorn
Floats back dishevelled strength in agony,
Disproving thy man's name: and while before
The world thou burnest in a poet-fire,   10
We[8] see thy woman-heart beat evermore
Through the large flame. Beat purer, heart, and higher,
Till God unsex thee on the heavenly shore
Where unincarnate spirits purely aspire!

1844

The Cry of the Children[1]

'Φευ Φευ. τι προσδερκεσθε μ'ὁμμασιν, τεκνα;'[2]
— Medea

I

Do ye hear the children weeping, O my brothers,
   Ere the sorrow comes with years?

---

5. Wings.
6. I.e., a fame unstained by immorality.
7. Ornaments, here representing womanly things Sand has rejected, such as a woman's name and the role of a wife.
8. I.e., chiefly Barrett Browning herself, perhaps along with a select few who see Sand's true nature.

1. This poem was inspired by a contemporary government report on the employment of children in mines and factories, one of the major social issues in England at the time.
2. "Do you hear the cry, do you hear the children's cry?" (Euripides, Medea, line 1271).

They are leaning their young heads against their mothers,
    And *that* cannot stop their tears.
The young lambs are bleating in the meadows,   5
    The young birds are chirping in the nest,
The young fawns are playing with the shadows,
    The young flowers are blowing[3] toward the west—
But the young, young children, O my brothers,
    They are weeping bitterly!   10
They are weeping in the playtime of the others,
    In the country of the free.

II

Do you question the young children in the sorrow
    Why their tears are falling so?
The old man may weep for his tomorrow   15
    Which is lost in long ago;
The old tree is leafless in the forest,
    The old year is ending in the frost,
The old wound, if stricken, is the sorest,
    The old hope is hardest to be lost: 20
But the young, young children, O my brothers,
    Do you ask them why they stand
Weeping sore before the bosoms of their mothers,
    In our happy fatherland?

III

They look up with their pale and sunken faces,   25
    And their looks are sad to see,
For the man's hoary[4] anguish draws and presses
    Down the cheeks of infancy;
"Your old earth," they say, "is very dreary,
    Our young feet," they say, "are very weak;   30
Few paces have we taken, yet are weary—
    Our grave-rest is very far to seek:
Ask the aged why they weep, and not the children,
    For the outside earth is cold,
And we young ones stand without, in our bewildering,   35
    And the graves are for the old.

IV

"True," say the children, "it may happen
    That we die before our time:
Little Alice died last year, her grave is shapen
    Like a snowball, in the rime.[5]   40
We looked into the pit prepared to take her:
    Was no room for any work in the close clay!
From the sleep wherein she lieth none will wake her,
    Crying, 'Get up, little Alice! it is day.'
If you listen by that grave, in sun and shower,   45

---

3. Blooming.   5. Frost.
4. White-haired.

With your ear down, little Alice never cries;
Could we see her face, be sure we should not know her,
    For the smile has time for growing in her eyes:
And merry go her moments, lulled and stilled in
    The shroud by the kirk-chime.[6]   50
It is good when it happens," say the children,
    "That we die before our time."

V

Alas, alas, the children! they are seeking
    Death in life, as best to have:
They are binding up[7] their hearts away from breaking,   55
    With a cerement from the grave.
Go out, children, from the mine and from the city,
    Sing out, children, as the little thrushes do;
Pluck your handfuls of the meadow-cowslips pretty.
    Laugh aloud, to feel your fingers let them through!   60
But they answer, "Are your cowslips of the meadows
    Like our weeds anear the mine?
Leave us quiet in the dark of the coal-shadows,
    From your pleasures fair and fine!

VI

"For oh," say the children, "we are weary,   65
    And we cannot run or leap;
If we cared for any meadows, it were merely
    To drop down in them and sleep.
Our knees tremble sorely in the stooping,
    We fall upon our faces, trying to go;   70
And, underneath our heavy eyelids drooping
    The reddest flower would look as pale as snow.
For, all day, we drag our burden tiring
    Through the coal-dark, underground;
Or, all day, we drive the wheels of iron   75
    In the factories, round and round.

VII

"For all day the wheels are droning, turning;
    Their wind comes in our faces,
Till our hearts turn, our heads with pulses burning,
    And the walls turn in their places: 80
Turns the sky in the high window, blank and reeling,
    Turns the long light that drops adown the wall,
Turn the black flies that crawl along the ceiling:
    All are turning, all the day, and we with all.
And all day the iron wheels are droning,   85
    And sometimes we could pray,
'O ye wheels' (breaking out in a mad moaning),
    "Stop! be silent for today!' "

6. Church bell.
7. Wrapping in order to strengthen, reinforce; "cerement": shroud for the dead.

VIII

Ay, be silent! Let them hear each other breathing
    For a moment, mouth to mouth!   90
Let them touch each other's hands, in a fresh wreathing
    Of their tender human youth!
Let them feel that this cold metallic motion
    Is not all the life God fashions or reveals:
Let them prove[8] their living souls against the notion   95
    That they live in you, or under you, O wheels!
Still, all day, the iron wheels go onward,
    Grinding life down from its mark;
And the children's souls, which God is calling sunward,
    Spin on blindly in the dark.   100

IX

Now tell the poor young children, O my brothers,
    To look up to Him and pray;
So the blessèd One who blesseth all the others,
    Will bless them another day.
They answer, "Who is God that He should hear us,   105
    While the rushing of the iron wheels is stirred?
When we sob aloud, the human creatures near us
    Pass by, hearing not, or answer not a word.
And *we* hear not (for the wheels in their resounding)
    Strangers speaking at the door: 110
Is it likely God, with angels singing round Him,
    Hears our weeping any more?

X

"Two words, indeed, of praying we remember,
    And at midnight's hour of harm.
'Our Father,'[9] looking upward in the chamber,   115
    We say softly for a charm.
We know no other words except 'Our Father,'
    And we think that, in some pause of angels' song,
God may pluck them with the silence sweet to gather,
    And hold both within his right hand which is strong.   120
'Our Father!' If He heard us, He would surely
    (For they call Him good and mild)
Answer, smiling down the steep world very purely,
    'Come and rest with me, my child.'

XI

"But, no!" say the children, weeping faster,   125
    "He is speechless as a stone:
And they tell us, of His image is the master[1]
    Who commands us to work on.
Go to!" say the children,—"up in Heaven,
    Dark, wheel-like, turning clouds are all we find.   130

8. Test.
9. The first words of the Lord's Prayer.

1. Even the cruel taskmaster of the children was made in God's image.

Do not mock us; grief has made us unbelieving:
　　We look up for God, but tears have made us blind."
Do you hear the children weeping and disproving,
　　O my brothers, what ye preach?
For God's possible is taught by his world's loving,   135
　　And the children doubt of each.

XII

And well may the children weep before you!
　　They are weary ere they run;
They have never seen the sunshine, nor the glory
　　Which is brighter than the sun.   140
They know the grief of man, without its wisdom;
　　They sink in man's despair, without its calm;
Are slaves, without the liberty in Christdom,
　　Are martyrs, by the pang without the palm:[2]
Are worn as if with age, yet unretrievingly   145
　　The harvest of its memories cannot reap,—
Are orphans of the earthly love and heavenly.
　　Let them weep! let them weep!

XIII

They look up with their pale and sunken faces,
　　And their look is dread to see,   150
For they mind[3] you of their angels in high places,
　　With eyes turned on Deity.
"How long," they say, "how long, O cruel nation,
　　Will you stand, to move the world, on a child's heart,—
Stifle down with a mailéd heel its palpitation,   155
　　And tread onward to your throne amid the mart?[4]
Our blood splashes upward, O goldheaper,
　　And your purple[5] shows your path!
But the child's sob in the silence curses deeper
　　Than the strong man in his wrath."

1844

The Runaway Slave at Pilgrim's Point[1]

I

I stand on the mark beside the shore
　　Of the first white pilgrim's bended knee,
Where exile turned to ancestor,[2]
　　And God was thanked for liberty.

---

2. Symbol of triumph; thus, martyrs by their suffering only, not by their redemption.
3. Remind.
4. Market.
5. I.e., the blood left in their trail after trampling the children.

1. The point at Plymouth Rock, Massachusetts, where the Puritans, fleeing persecution in England, first landed their ships in the seventeenth century.
2. I.e., where the pilgrims, exiled from one nation, became ancestors to a new one.

I have run through the night, my skin is as dark,   5
I bend my knee down on this mark:
   I look on the sky and the sea.

II

O pilgrim-souls, I speak to you!
   I see you come proud and slow
From the land of the spirits pale as dew   10
   And round me and round me ye go.
O pilgrims, I have gasped and run
All night long from the whips of one
   Who in your names works sin and woe!

III

And thus I thought that I would come   15
   And kneel here where ye knelt before,
And feel your souls around me hum
   In undertone to the ocean's roar;
And lift my black face, my black hand,
Here, in your names, to curse this land   20
   Ye blessed in freedom's, evermore.

IV

I am black, I am black,
   And yet God made me, they say:
But if He did so, smiling back
   He must have cast his work away   25
Under the feet of his white creatures,
With a look of scorn, that the dusky features
   Might be trodden again to clay.

V

And yet He has made dark things
   To be glad and merry as light: 30
There's a little dark bird sits and sings,
   There's a dark stream ripples out of sight,
And the dark[3] frogs chant in the safe morass,
And the sweetest stars are made to pass
   O'er the face of the darkest night.   35

VI

But *we* who are dark, we are dark!
   Ah God, we have no stars!
About our souls in care and cark[4]
   Our blackness shuts like prison-bars:
The poor souls crouch so far behind   40
That never a comfort can they find
   By reaching through the prison-bars.

VII

Indeed we live beneath the sky,
   That great smooth Hand of God stretched out

3. Swamp.   4. Distress.

On all his children fatherly,   45
　　To save them from the dread and doubt
Which would be if, from this low place,
All opened straight up to his face
　　Into the grand eternity.

VIII

And still God's sunshine and his frost,   50
　　They make us hot, they make us cold,
As if we were not black and lost;
　　And the beasts and birds, in wood and fold,
Do fear and take us for very men:
Could the whippoorwill or the cat of the glen   55
　　Look into my eyes and be bold?

IX

I am black, I am black!
　　But, once, I laughed in girlish glee,
For one of my color stood in the track
　　Where the drivers drove, and looked at me,   60
And tender and full was the look he gave—
Could a slave look *so* at another slave?—
　　I look at the sky and the sea.

X

And from that hour our spirits grew
　　As free as if unsold, unbought: 65
Oh, strong enough, since we were two,
　　To conquer the world, we thought.
The drivers drove us day by day;
We did not mind, we went one way,
And no better a freedom sought.   70

XI

In the sunny ground between the canes,[5]
　　He said "I love you" as he passed;
When the shingle-roof rang sharp with the rains,
　　I heard how he vowed it fast:
While others shook he smiled in the hut,   75
As he carved me a bowl of the cocoanut
　　Through the roar of the hurricanes.

XII

I sang his name instead of a song,
　　Over and over I sang his name,
Upward and downward I drew it along   80
　　My various notes,—the same, the same!
I sang it low, that the slave-girls near
Might never guess, from aught they could hear,
　　It was only a name—a name.

5. Sugar canes; the two worked on a sugar plantation.

XIII

I look on the sky and the sea.   85
　　We were two to love and two to pray:
Yes, two, O God, who cried to Thee,
　　Though nothing didst Thou say!
Coldly Thou sat'st behind the sun:
And now I cry who am but one,   90
　　Thou wilt not speak today.

XIV

We were black, we were black,
　　We had no claim to love and bliss,
What marvel if each went to wrack?
　　They wrung my cold hands out of his,   95
They dragged him—where? I crawled to touch
His blood's mark in the dust . . . not much,
　　Ye pilgrim-souls, though plain as *this*![6]

XV

Wrong, followed by a deeper wrong!
　　Mere grief's too good for such as I: 100
So the white men brought the shame ere long
　　To strangle the sob of my agony.
They would not leave me for my dull
Wet eyes!—it was too merciful
　　To let me weep pure tears and die.   105

XVI

I am black, I am black!
　　I wore a child upon my breast,
An amulet that hung too slack,
　　And, in my unrest, could not rest:
Thus we went moaning, child and mother,   110
One to another, one to another,
　　Until all ended for the best.

XVII

For hark! I will tell you low, low,
　　I am black, you see,—
And the babe who lay on my bosom so,   115
　　Was far too white, too white for me;
As white as the ladies who scorned to pray
Beside me at church but yesterday,
　　Though my tears had washed a place for my knee.

XVIII

My own, own child! I could not bear   120
　　To look in his face, it was so white;
I covered him up with a kerchief there,
　　I covered his face in close and tight:

---

6. The "mark beside the shore" where the speaker stands.

And he moaned and struggled, as well might be,
For the white child wanted his liberty—   125
   Ha, ha! he wanted the master-right.

XIX

He moaned and beat with his head and feet,
   His little feet that never grew;
He struck them out, as it was meet,
   Against my heart to break it through: 130
I might have sung and made him mild,
But I dared not sing to the white-faced child
   The only song I knew.

XX

I pulled the kerchief very close:
   He could not see the sun, I swear,   135
More, then, alive, than now he does
   From between the roots of the mango . . . where?
I know where. Close! A child and mother
Do wrong to look at one another
   When one is black and one is fair.   140

XXI

Why, in that single glance I had
   Of my child's face, . . . I tell you all,
I saw a look that made me mad!
   The *master's* look, that used to fall
On my soul like his lash . . . or worse!   145
And so, to save it from my curse,
   I twisted it round in my shawl.

XXII

And he moaned and trembled from foot to head,
   He shivered from head to foot;
Till after a time, he lay instead   150
   Too suddenly still and mute.
I felt, beside, a stiffening cold:
I dared to lift up just a fold,
   As in lifting a leaf of the mango-fruit.

XXII

But *my* fruit . . . ha, ha!—there, had been   155
   (I laugh to think on't at this hour!)
Your fine white angels (who have seen
   Nearest the secret of God's power)
And plucked my fruit to make them wine,
And sucked the soul of that child of mine   160
   As the hummingbird sucks the soul of the flower.

XXIV

Ha, ha, the trick of the angels white!
   They freed the white child's spirit so.
I said not a word, but day and night
   I carried the body to and fro,   165

And it lay on my heart like a stone, as chill.
—The sun may shine out as much as he will:
   I am cold, though it happened a month ago.

XXV

From the white man's house, and the black man's hut,
   I carried the little body on: 170
The forest's arms did round us shut,
   And silence through the trees did run:
They asked no question as I went,
They stood too high for astonishment,
   They could see God sit on his throne.   175

XXVI

My little body, kerchiefed fast,
   I bore it on through the forest, on;
And when I felt it was tired at last,
   I scooped a hole beneath the moon:
Through the forest-tops the angels far,   180
With a white sharp finger from every star,
   Did point and mock at what was done.

XXVII

Yet when it was all done aright,—
   Earth, 'twixt me and my baby, strewed,—
All, changed to black earth,—nothing white,—   185
   A dark child in the dark!—ensued
Some comfort, and my heart grew young;
I sate down smiling there and sung
   The song I learnt in my maidenhood.

XXVIII

And thus we two were reconciled,   190
   The white child and black mother, thus;
For as I sang it soft and wild,
   The same song, more melodious,
Rose from the grave whereon I sate:
It was the dead child singing that,   195
   To join the souls of both of us.

XXIX

I look on the sea and the sky.
   Where the pilgrims' ships first anchored lay
The free sun rideth gloriously,
   But the pilgrim ghosts have slid away   200
Through the earliest streaks of the morn:
My face is black, but it glares with a scorn
   Which they dare not meet by day.

XXX

Ha!—in their stead, their hunter sons!
   Ha, ha! they are on me—they hunt in a ring!   205
Keep off! I brave you all at once,
   I throw off your eyes like snakes that sting!

You have killed the black eagle at nest, I think:
Did you ever stand still in your triumph, and shrink
From the stroke of her wounded wing? 210

XXXI

(Man, drop that stone you dared to lift!—)
I wish you who stand there five abreast,
Each, for his own wife's joy and gift,
A little corpse as safely at rest
As mine in the mangoes! Yes, but *she* 215
May keep live babies on her knee,
And sing the song she likes the best.

XXXII

I am not mad: I am black.
I see you staring in my face—
I know you staring, shrinking back, 220
Ye are born of the Washington-race,[7]
And this land is the free America,
And this mark on my wrist—(I prove[8] what I say)
Ropes tied me up here to the flogging-place.

XXXIII

You think I shrieked then? Not a sound 225
I hung, as a gourd hangs in the sun;
I only cursed them all around
As softly as I might have done
My very own child: from these sands
Up to the mountains, lift your hands, 230
O slaves, and end what I begun!

XXXIV

Whips, curses; these must answer those!
For in this union you have set
Two kinds of men in adverse rows,
Each loathing each; and all forget 235
The seven wounds in Christ's body fair,
While He sees gaping everywhere
Our countless wounds that pay no debt.[9]

XXXV

Our wounds are different. Your white men
Are, after all, not gods indeed, 240
Nor able to make Christs again
Do good with bleeding. *We* who bleed
(Stand off!) we help not in our loss!
We are too heavy for our cross,
And fall and crush you and your seed. 245

XXXVI

I fall, I swoon![1] I look at the sky.

7. I.e., the race of George Washington.
8. Experience.
9. According to the Bible, Jesus Christ died on the cross in payment for the sins of humanity.
1. Possibly an echo of Shelley's *Ode to the West Wind*: "I fall upon the thorns of life! I bleed!"

The clouds are breaking on my brain;
I am floated along, as if I should die
   Of liberty's exquisite pain.
In the name of the white child waiting for me   250
In the death-dark where we may kiss and agree,
White men, I leave you all curse-free
   In my broken heart's disdain!

1850

Hiram Powers' "Greek Slave"[1]

They say ideal beauty cannot enter
The house of anguish. On the threshold stands
An alien image with enshackled hands,
Called the Greek Slave! as if the artist meant her
(That passionless perfection which he lent her,   5
Shadowed not darkened where the sill expands)[2]
To so confront man's crimes in different lands
With man's ideal sense. Pierce to the centre,
Art's fiery finger, and break up ere long
The serfdom of this world. Appeal, fair stone,   10
From God's pure heights of beauty against man's wrong!
Catch up in thy divine face, not alone
East griefs but west,[3] and strike and shame the strong,
By thunders of white silence, overthrown.

1850

From Sonnets from the Portuguese[3]

V

I lift my heavy heart up solemnly,
As once Electra[4] her sepulchral urn,
And, looking in thine eyes, I overturn
The ashes at thy feet. Behold and see
What a great heap of grief lay hid in me,   5
And how the red wild sparkles dimly burn

---

1. The work of an American sculptor who became a close friend of the Brownings while they were living in Florence.
2. I.e., where the threshold to the house of anguish begins; her beauty is not lessened by that threshold, only given a more somber cast.
3. The Greeks took slaves from Eastern countries; Browning may be thinking here of American slavery as a grief of the West.
3. All the sonnets in the sequence are addressed to Elizabeth's husband, Robert, himself a famous poet.
4. In Sophocles' play *Electra*, the heroine's brother Orestes disguises himself and presents his sister with a funeral urn which he claims contains her brother's ashes.

Through the ashen grayness. If thy foot in scorn
Could tread them out to darkness utterly,
It might be well perhaps. But if instead
Thou wait beside me for the wind to blow   10
The gray dust up, . . . those laurels[3] on thine head,
O my Belovéd, will not shield thee so,
That none of all the fires shall scorch and shred
The hair beneath. Stand farther off then! go.

XXII

When our two souls stand up erect and strong,
Face to face, silent, drawing nigh[1] and nigher,
Until the lengthening wings break into fire
At either curvéd point,—what bitter wrong
Can the earth do to us, that we should not long   5
Be here contented? Think. In mounting higher,
The angels would press on us and aspire
To drop some golden orb[2] of perfect song
Into our deep, dear silence. Let us stay
Rather on earth, Belovéd,—where the unfit   10
Contrarious moods of men recoil away
And isolate pure spirits, and permit
A place to stand and love in for a day,
With darkness and the death-hour rounding it.

XLIII

How do I love thee? Let me count the ways.
I love thee to the depth and breadth and height
My soul can reach, when feeling out of sight[3]
For the ends of Being and ideal Grace.
I love thee to the level of everyday's   5
Most quiet need, by sun and candlelight.
I love thee freely, as men strive for Right;
I love thee purely, as they turn from Praise.
I love thee with the passion put to use[4]
In my old griefs, and with my childhood's faith.   10
I love thee with a love I seemed to lose
With my lost saints,—I love thee with the breath,
Smiles, tears, of all my life!—and, if God choose,
I shall but love thee better after death.

1850

---

3. Leaves used to crown the heads of famous poets.
1. Near.
2. Ball or sphere. The image may recall the old notion of the "music of the spheres," created by the motions of stars and planets.
3. Limits.
4. I.e., a natural reserve of passion which had formerly been directed to grief, now transformed to love.

From Aurora Leigh

Book I[1] [Aurora's Parents]

* * * My mother was a Florentine,[2]
Whose rare blue eyes were shut from seeing me
When scarcely I was four years old, my life
A poor spark snatched up from a failing lamp
Which went out therefore. She was weak and frail;   5
She could not bear the joy of giving life,
The mother's rapture slew her. If her kiss
Had left a longer weight upon my lips
It might have steadied the uneasy breath,
And reconciled and fraternized my soul   10
With the new order.[3] As it was, indeed,
I felt a mother-want about the world,
And still went seeking, like a bleating lamb
Left out at night in shutting up the fold,[4]—
As restless as a nest-deserted bird   15
Grown chill through something being away, though what
It knows not. * * *

My father was an austere Englishman,
Who, after a dry lifetime spent at home
In college-learning, law, and parish talk,   20
Was flooded with a passion unaware,
His whole provisioned and complacent past
Drowned out from him that moment. As he stood
In Florence, where he had come to spend a month
And note the secret of Da Vinci's drains,[5]   25
He musing somewhat absently perhaps
Some English question . . . whether men should pay
The unpopular but necessary tax
With left or right hand—in the alien sun
In that great square of the Santissima[6]   30
There drifted past him (scarcely marked enough
To move his comfortable island scorn)
A train of priestly banners, cross and psalm,
The white-veiled rose-crowned maidens holding up
Tall tapers, weighty for such wrists, aslant   35

1. In Book I, the poet-to-be Aurora, born in
Italy of an Italian mother and an English father,
is orphaned early and brought to England, where
she is raised and educated by her father's sister,
an austere British lady. The first selection from
Book I covers her memories of her mother and
the second records some of her reactions to her
Victorian training in decorum.
2. Florence was a center of Renaissance art and

culture.
3. I.e., her motherless state, and her aunt's government.
4. An enclosure for sheep.
5. Leonardo da Vinci (1452–1519), artist, scientist, and engineer, devised a system of irriga-
tion for the plains of Lombardy.
6. The *piazza* or square before the thirteenth-
century Church of Santissima Annunziata.

To the blue luminous tremor of the air,
And letting drop the white wax as they went
To eat the bishop's wafer at the church;[7]
From which long trail of chanting priests and girls,
A face flashed like a cymbal on his face   40
And shook with silent clangor brain and heart,
Transfiguring him to music. Thus, even thus,
He too received his sacramental gift
With eucharistic[8] meanings; for he loved.

And thus beloved, she died. * * *   45
* * *Father, then, and child,
We lived among the mountains many years,
God's silence on the outside of the house,
And we who did not speak too loud within,
And old Assunta to make up the fire,   50
Crossing herself whene'er a sudden flame
Which lightened from the firewood, made alive
That picture of my mother on the wall.

The painter drew it after she was dead,
And when the face was finished, throat and hands,   55
Her cameriera[9] carried him, in hate
Of the English-fashioned shroud, the last brocade
She dressed in at the Pitti;[1] "he should paint
No sadder thing than that," she swore, "to wrong
Her poor signora." Therefore very strange   60
The effect was. I, a little child, would crouch
For hours upon the floor with knees drawn up,
And gaze across them, half in terror, half
In adoration, at the picture there,—
That swan-like supernatural white life   65
Just sailing upward from the red stiff silk
Which seemed to have no part in it nor power
To keep it from quite breaking out of bounds.
For hours I sat and stared. Assunta's awe
And my poor father's melancholy eyes   70
Still pointed that way. That way went my thoughts
When wandering beyond sight. And as I grew
In years, I mixed, confused, unconsciously,
Whatever I last read or heard or dreamed,
Abhorrent, admirable, beautiful,   75
Pathetical, or ghastly, or grotesque,
With still that face . . . which did not therefore change,

7. I.e., to receive holy communion, in which a
wafer and wine, thought to reincarnate the body
of Christ, are consumed, from the bishop.
8. Relating to holy communion.

9. Lady's maid.
1. The Pitti Palace in Florence, once occupied
by nobility.

But kept the mystic level of all forms,
Hates, fears, and admirations, was by turns
Ghost, fiend, and angel, fairy, witch, and sprite,   80
A dauntless Muse who eyes a dreadful Fate,
A loving Psyche who loses sight of Love,
A still Medusa[2] with mild milky brows
All curdled and all clothed upon with snakes
Whose slime falls fast as sweat will; or anon   85
Our Lady of the Passion, stabbed with swords[3]
Where the Babe sucked; or Lamia[4] in her first
Moonlighted pallor, ere she shrunk and blinked
And shuddering wriggled down to the unclean;
Or my own mother, leaving her last smile   90
In her last kiss upon the baby-mouth
My father pushed down on the bed for that,—
Or my dead mother, without smile or kiss,
Buried at Florence. * * *

*Book I [Aurora's Journey to England and Education
There by Her Father's Sister]*

I think I see my father's sister stand   95
Upon the hall-step of her country-house
To give me welcome. She stood straight and calm,
Her somewhat narrow forehead braided tight
As if for taming accidental thoughts
From possible pulses;[5] brown hair pricked with gray   100
By frigid use of life (she was not old,
Although my father's elder by a year),
A nose drawn sharply, yet in delicate lines;
A close mild mouth, a little soured about
The ends, through speaking unrequited loves   105
Or peradventure niggardly half-truths;[6]
Eyes of no color,—once they might have smiled,
But never, never have forgot themselves
In smiling; cheeks, in which was yet a rose
Of perished summers, like a rose in a book,   110
Kept more for ruth[7] than pleasure,—if past bloom,
Past fading also.
                    She had lived, we'll say,

---

2. A mythological female with snakes growing from her head. A Muse is a Greek goddess of art; the Fates are three sisters who decide the destiny of each human being. Psyche, according to Greek myth, was a beautiful maiden who was wooed by Cupid (Love) by night, until she attempted to catch sight of him, and he fled.
3. The virgin Mary, "stabbed" with grief by her son Jesus's crucifixion and suffering (the Passion).
4. In Keats' poem *Lamia*, a young man falls in love with a beautiful woman who is then revealed to be a serpent.
5. Actions, deeds.
6. Perhaps.
7. Pity.

A harmless life, she called a virtuous life,
A quiet life, which was not life at all   115
(But that, she had not lived enough to know),
Between the vicar and the county squires,
The lord-lieutenant looking down sometimes
From the empyrean[8] to assure their souls
Against chance vulgarisms, and, in the abyss,   120
The apothecary, looked on once a year
To prove their soundness of humility.
The poor-club[9] exercised her Christian gifts
Of knitting stockings, stitching petticoats,
Because we are of one flesh, after all,   125
And need one flannel (with a proper sense
Of difference in the quality)—and still
The book-club, guarded from your modern trick
Of shaking dangerous questions from the crease,[1]
Preserved her intellectual. She had lived   130
A sort of cage-bird life, born in a cage,
Accounting that to leap from perch to perch
Was act and joy enough for any bird.
Dear heaven, how silly are the things that live
In thickets, and eat berries!   135
                    I, alas,
A wild bird scarcely fledged, was brought to her cage,
And she was there to meet me. Very kind.
Bring the clean water, give out the fresh seed.
                    * * *
I broke the copious curls upon my head   140
In braids, because she liked smooth-ordered hair.
I left off saying my sweet Tuscan words[2]
Which still at any stirring of the heart
Came up to float across the English phrase
As lilies (*Bene* or *Che che*),[3] because   145
She liked my father's child to speak his tongue.
I learnt the collects and the catechism,
The creeds, from Athanasius back to Nice,
The Articles, the Tracts *against* the times
(By no means Buonaventure's *Prick of Love*),   150
And various popular synopses of
Inhuman doctrines never taught by John,[4]
Because she liked instructed piety.

8. The highest reaches of heaven.
9. Charitable organization.
1. I.e., of finding subversive ideas hidden in
books.
2. The dialect of Tuscany, the region of Italy
where Florence is located.
3. "Good" and "What's the matter?"
4. All the works in this list are strict religious

primers and treatises. "Tracts against the times"
is a humorous reference to *Tracts for the Times*
by Newman, Pusey, and Keble, which condemned church reform. Buonaventure's *Prick of
Love* is a religious work which prefers love to
reason. John, author of one of the Gospels, did
not concern himself with fine technical points of
theology.

I learnt my complement of classic French
(Kept pure of Balzac[5] and neologism)   155
And German also, since she liked a range
Of liberal education,—tongues, not books.
I learnt a little algebra, a little
Of the mathematics,—brushed with extreme flounce[6]
The circle of the sciences, because   160
She misliked women who are frivolous.
I learnt the royal genealogies
Of Oviedo, the internal laws
Of the Burmese empire,[7]—by how many feet
Mount Chimborazo outsoars Teneriffe,   165
What navigable river joins itself
To Lara, and what census of the year five
Was taken at Klagenfurt,—because she liked
A general insight into useful facts.
I learnt much music,—such as would have been   170
As quite impossible in Johnson's day[8]
As still it might be wished—fine sleights of hand
And unimagined fingering, shuffling off
The hearer's soul through hurricanes of notes
To a noisy Tophet;[9] and I drew . . . costumes   175
From French engravings, nereids[1] neatly draped
(With smirks of simmering godship): I washed in
Landscapes from nature (rather say, washed out).
I danced the polka and Cellarius,[2]
Spun glass, stuffed birds, and modelled flowers in wax,   180
Because she liked accomplishments in girls.
I read a score of books on womanhood
To prove, if women do not think at all,
They may teach thinking (to a maiden aunt
Or else the author),—books that boldly assert   185
Their right of comprehending husband's talk
When not too deep, and even of answering
With pretty "may it please you," or "so it is,"—
Their rapid insight and fine aptitude,
Particular worth and general missionariness,[3]   190
As long as they keep quiet by the fire
And never say "no" when the world says "ay,"
For that is fatal,—their angelic reach[4]

5. Honoré de Balzac (1799–1850) wrote many popular novels dealing with the corruption of Parisian society. "Neologism": new doctrines.
6. Abruptness, impatience.
7. Oviedo is a city in Spain; Burma is an Asian country. All the facts mentioned in this passage are noteworthy only for being esoteric, unrelated to Aurora's real concerns.
8. Samuel Johnson (1709–1784), famous critic and poet.
9. A hellish place.
1. Sea nymphs, mermaids.
2. Probably a dance.
3. I.e., desire to convert others to virtue.
4. Coventry Patmore's popular book-length poem *The Angel in the House* (1854) celebrated the ideals of domestic virtue.

Of virtue, chiefly used to sit and darn,
And fatten household sinners,—their, in brief,   195
Potential faculty in everything
Of abdicating power in it: she owned
She liked a woman to be womanly,
And English women, she thanked God and sighed
(Some people always sigh in thanking God),   200
Were models to the universe. And last
I learnt cross-stitch, because she did not like
To see me wear the night with empty hands
A-doing nothing. So, my shepherdess
Was something after all (the pastoral[5] saints   205
Be praised for't), leaning lovelorn with pink eyes
To match her shoes, when I mistook the silks;
Her head uncrushed by that round weight of hat
So strangely similar to the tortoise shell
Which slew the tragic poet.[6]   210
                                    By the way,
The works of women are symbolical.
We sew, sew, prick our fingers, dull our sight,
Producing what? A pair of slippers, sir,
To put on when you're weary—or a stool   215
To stumble over and vex you . . . "curse that stool!"
Or else at best, a cushion, where you lean
And sleep, and dream of something we are not
But would be for your sake. Alas, alas!
This hurts most, this—that, after all, we are paid   220
The worth of our work, perhaps.
                            In looking down
Those years of education (to return)
I wonder if Brinvilliers[7] suffered more
In the water-torture . . . flood succeeding flood   225
To drench the incapable throat and split the veins . . .
Than I did. Certain of your feebler souls
Go out[8] in such a process; many pine
To a sick, inodorous light; my own endured:
I had relations in the Unseen, and drew   230
The elemental nutriment and heat
From nature, as earth feels the sun at nights,
Or as a babe sucks surely in the dark.
I kept the life thrust on me, on the outside
Of the inner life with all its ample room   235

5. Pertaining to shepherdry. Saints and other religious leaders are often compared to shepherds.
6. The Greek tragedian Aeschylus was reputedly killed when an eagle dropped a tortoise on
his head.
7. The Marquise de Brinvilliers was tortured by
being made to drink buckets of water, because
she allegedly murdered her husband's relatives
in order to win his fortune for herself and her
lover.
8. I.e., die.

For heart and lungs, for will and intellect,
Inviolable by conventions. God,
I thank thee for that grace of thine!

Book II [*Romney's Proposal of Marriage to Aurora and Her Refusal*][9]

    * * * "Then, must it be
Indeed farewell? And was I so far wrong   240
In hope and in illusion, when I took
The woman to be nobler than the man,
Yourself the noblest woman, in the use[1]
And comprehension of what love is,—love,
That generates the likeness of itself   245
Through all heroic duties? so far wrong,
In saying bluntly, venturing truth on love,
'Come, human creature, love and work with me,'—
Instead of 'Lady, thou art wondrous fair,
And, where the Graces[2] walk before, the Muse   250
Will follow at the lightning of their eyes,
And where the Muse walks, lovers need to creep:
Turn round and love me, or I die of love.' "

With quiet indignation I broke in.
"You misconceive the question like a man,   255
Who sees the woman as the complement
Of his sex merely. You forget too much
That every creature, female as the male,
Stands single in responsible act and thought
As also in birth and death. Whoever says   260
To a loyal woman, 'Love and work with me,'
Will get fair answers if the work and love,
Being good themselves, are good for her—the best
She was born for. Women of a softer mood,
Surprised by men when scarcely awake to life,   265
Will sometimes only hear the first word, love,
And catch up with it any kind of work,
Indifferent, so that dear love go with it.
I do not blame such women, though, for love,
They pick much oakum;[3] earth's fanatics make   270
Too frequently heaven's saints. But *me* your work
Is not the best for,—nor your love the best,

---

9. In this selection Aurora's cousin Romney Leigh, now the head of the family, has proposed to her, arguing that it would be better for her to join him in working for social welfare than to continue with her plan to become a poet, since he believes that women cannot write effective verse. She refuses, insisting upon her commitment to her chosen vocation.
1. Practice.
2. Greek goddesses of charm and beauty.
3. Loose hemp or fiber; i.e., condemned to hard labor.

Nor able to commend the kind of work
For love's sake merely. Ah, you force me, sir,
To be overbold in speaking of myself: 275
I too have my vocation,—work to do,
The heavens and earth have set me since I changed
My father's face for theirs, and, though your world
Were twice as wretched as you represent,
Most serious work, most necessary work   280
As any of the economists'.[4] Reform,
Make trade a Christian possibility,
And individual right no general wrong;
Wipe out earth's furrows of the Thine and Mine,
And leave one green for men to play at bowls,[5]   285
With innings for them all! . . . What then, indeed,
If mortals are not greater by the head
Than any of their prosperities? what then,
Unless the artist keep up open roads
Betwixt the seen and unseen,—bursting through   290
The best of your conventions with his best,
The speakable, imaginable best
God bids him speak, to prove what lies beyond
Both speech and imagination? A starved man
Exceeds a fat beast: we'll not barter, sir,   295
The beautiful for barley.—And, even so,
I hold you will not compass your poor ends
Of barley-feeding and material ease,
Without a poet's individualism
To work your universal. It takes a soul,   300
To move a body: it takes a high-souled man,
To move the masses, even to a cleaner stye:[6]
It takes the ideal, to blow a hair's-breadth off
The dust of the actual.—Ah, your Fouriers[7] failed,
Because not poets enough to understand   305
That life develops from within.—For me,
Perhaps I am not worthy, as you say,
Of work like this: perhaps a woman's soul
Aspires, and not creates: yet we aspire,
And yet I'll try out your perhapses, sir,   310
And if I fail . . . why, burn me up my straw
Like other false works—I'll not ask for grace;
Your scorn is better, cousin Romney. I
Who love my art, would never wish it lower
To suit my stature. I may love my art.   315
You'll grant that even a woman may love art,

4. The economists wished to reform British
trade; Aurora hopes to reform the British soul.
5. A form of outdoor bowling.
6. Enclosure for pigs.

7. Francois Fourier (1772–1837), French social theorist who wished to abolish trade and
commerce.

Seeing that to waste true love on anything
Is womanly, past question."

         * * *

Book V [*Aurora's Theories of Poetry*][8]

The critics say that epics have died out
With Agamemnon[9] and the goat-nursed gods;   320
I'll not believe it. I could never deem,
As Payne Knight[1] did (the mythic mountaineer
Who travelled higher than he was born to live,
And showed sometimes the goiter in his throat
Discoursing of an image seen through fog),   325
That Homer's heroes measured twelve feet high.
They were but men:—his Helen's[2] hair turned gray
Like any plain Miss Smith's who wears a front;[3]
And Hector's[4] infant whimpered at a plume
As yours last Friday at a turkey-cock.   330
All actual heroes are essential men,
And all men possible heroes: every age,
Heroic in proportions, double-faced,
Looks backward and before, expects a morn
And claims an epos.[5]   335
               Ay, but every age
Appears to souls who live in't (ask Carlyle)[6]
Most unheroic. Ours, for instance, ours:
The thinkers scout it, and the poets abound
Who scorn to touch it with a fingertip: 340
A pewter age[7]—mixed metal, silver-washed;
An age of scum, spooned off the richer past.
An age of patches for old gaberdines,
An age of mere transition, meaning nought
Except that what succeeds must shame it quite   345
If God please. That's wrong thinking, to my mind,
And wrong thoughts make poor poems.
                  Every age,
Through being beheld too close, is ill-discerned
By those who have not lived past it. We'll suppose   350

---

8. In this selection, Aurora, now a struggling poet living in London, formulates her artistic beliefs and goals, distinguishing her ideas about poetry from those of her contemporaries. In a sense, this aesthetic manifesto will prove to be the foundation of the success she achieves later in Barrett Browning's verse-novel.
9. Famous Greek king who led the war against Troy.
1. Richard Payne Knight (1750–1824), a classical scholar.
2. Helen of Troy, a renowned beauty whose abduction caused the Trojan War.
3. False hair.
4. Hector, whose courage and skill are depicted in Homer's *Iliad*, was a Trojan warrior and son of Priam.
5. Epic poem.
6. Thomas Carlyle (1795–1881), Scottish historian and essayist who celebrated the heroic ideal in such works as *Heroes and Hero-Worship* and *Past and Present*.
7. A metal alloy; in contrast to the Gold and Silver Ages.

Mount Athos[8] carved, as Alexander schemed,
To some colossal statue of a man.
The peasants, gathering brushwood in his ear,
Had guessed as little as the browsing goats
Of form or feature of humanity   355
Up there,—in fact, had travelled five miles off
Or ere the giant image broke on them,
Full human profile, nose and chin distinct,
Mouth, muttering rhythms of silence up the sky
And fed at evening with the blood of suns;   360
Grand torso,—hand, that flung perpetually
The largesse of a silver river down
To all the country pastures. 'Tis even thus
With times we live in,—evermore too great
To be apprehended near.
                              But poets should   365
Exert a double vision; should have eyes
To see near things as comprehensively
As if afar they took their point of sight,
And distant things as intimately deep   370
As if they touched them. Let us strive for this.
I do distrust the poet who discerns
No character or glory in his times,
And trundles back his soul five hundred years,
Past moat and drawbridge, into a castle-court,   375
To sing—oh, not of lizard or of toad
Alive i' the ditch there,—'t were excusable,
But of some black chief, half knight, half sheep-lifter,[9]
Some beauteous dame, half chattel and half queen,
As dead as must be, for the greater part,   380
The poems made on their chivalric bones;
And that's no wonder: death inherits death.

Nay, if there's room for poets in this world
A little overgrown (I think there is),
Their sole work is to represent the age,   385
Their age, not Charlemagne's,[1]—this live, throbbing age,
That brawls, cheats, maddens, calculates, aspires,
And spends more passion, more heroic heat,
Betwixt the mirrors of its drawing-rooms,
Than Roland[2] with his knights at Roncesvalles.   390
To flinch from modern varnish, coat or flounce,
Cry out for togas and the picturesque,
Is fatal,—foolish too. King Arthur's self

8. A mountain in northern Greece which Alex-   1. (724–818 A.D.), king of the Franks during the
ander the Great, the Greek general, desired to   chivalric period.
have carved into an enormous monument.   2. A knight and nephew of Charlemagne, killed
9. Thief of livestock. "Chattel": property.   in battle at Roncesvalles.

Was commonplace to Lady Guenever;
And Camelot to minstrels seemed as flat   395
As Fleet Street[3] to our poets. Never flinch,
But still, unscrupulously epic, catch
Upon the burning lava of a song
The full-veined, heaving, double-breasted Age:
That, when the next shall come, the men of that   400
May touch the impress[4] with reverent hand, and say
"Behold,—behold the paps[5] we all have sucked!
This bosom seems to beat still, or at least
It sets ours beating: this is living art,
Which thus presents and thus records true life."   405

1857

A Curse for a Nation[1]

Prologue

I heard an angel speak last night,
   And he said "Write!
Write a Nation's curse for me,
And send it over the Western Sea."

I faltered, taking up the word: 5
   "Not so, my lord!
If curses must be, choose another
To send thy curse against my brother.

"For I am bound by gratitude,
   By love and blood,   10
To brothers of mine across the sea,
Who stretch out kindly hands to me."

"Therefore," the voice said, "shalt thou write
   My curse tonight.
From the summits of love a curse is driven,   15
As lightning is from the tops of heaven."

"Not so," I answered. "Evermore
   My heart is sore
For my own land's sins: for little feet
Of children bleeding along the street: 20

3. A London street, headquarters for the press. "Camelot": legendary British seat of King Arthur and his knights.
4. The image is of a molten substance being molded by the present age, which leaves its "impress" in the metal.
5. Breasts.
1. The nation is the United States, then practicing slavery.

"For parked-up[2] honors that gainsay
   The right of way:
For almsgiving through a door that is
Not open enough for two friends to kiss:

"For love of freedom which abates   25
   Beyond the Straits:[3]
For patriot virtue starved to vice on
Self-praise, self-interest, and suspicion:

"For an oligarchic parliament,[4]
   And bribes well-meant.   30
What curse to another land assign,
When heavy-souled for the sins of mine?"

"Therefore," the voice said, "shalt thou write
   My curse tonight.
Because thou hast strength to see and hate   35
A foul thing done *within* thy gate."

"Not so," I answered once again.
   "To curse, choose men.
For I, a woman, have only known
How the heart melts and the tears run down."   40

"Therefore," the voice said, "shalt thou write
   My curse tonight.
Some women weep and curse, I say
(And no one marvels), night and day.

"And thou shalt take their part tonight,   45
   Weep and write.
A curse from the depths of womanhood
Is very salt, and bitter, and good."

So thus I wrote, and mourned indeed,
   What all may read.   50
And thus, as was enjoined on me,
I send it over the Western Sea.

The Curse

I

Because ye have broken your own chain
   With the strain
Of brave men climbing a Nation's height,   55

2. Gathered in one place.
3. The Straits of Gibraltar, which divide Europe from Africa, where England had extensive colo-nies and imperial interests.
4. I.e., a parliament controlled by an aristocratic elite.

Yet thence bear down with brand and thong
On souls of others,—for this wrong
   This is the curse.   Write.

Because yourselves are standing straight
   In the state   60
Of Freedom's foremost acolyte,
Yet keep calm footing all the time
On writhing bond-slaves,—for this crime
   This is the curse.   Write.

Because ye prosper in God's name,   65
   With a claim
To honor in the old world's sight,
Yet do the fiend's work perfectly
In strangling martyrs,—for this lie
   This is the curse.   Write.   70

II

Ye shall watch while kings conspire
Round the people's smouldering fire
   And, warm for your part,
Shall never dare—O shame!
To utter the thought into flame   75
   Which burns at your heart.
   This is the curse.   Write.

Ye shall watch while nations strive
With the bloodhounds, die or survive,
   Drop faint from their jaws,   80
Or throttle them backward to death;
And only under your breath
   Shall favour the cause.
   This is the curse.   Write.

Ye shall watch while strong men draw   85
The nets of feudal law
   To strangle the weak;
And, counting the sin for a sin,
Your soul shall be sadder within
   Than the word ye shall speak.   90
   This is the curse.   Write.

When good men are praying erect
That Christ may avenge his elect
   And deliver the earth,
The prayer in your ears, said low,   95
Shall sound like the tramp of a foe
   That's driving you forth.
   This is the curse.   Write.

When wise men give you their praise,
They shall pause in the heat of the phrase,   100
    As if carried too far.
When ye boast your own charters kept true,
Ye shall blush; for the thing which ye do
    Derides what ye are.
        This is the curse.   Write.   105

When fools cast taunts at your gate,
Your scorn ye shall somewhat abate
    As ye look o'er the wall;
For your conscience, tradition, and name
Explode with a deadlier blame   110
Than the worst of them all.
        This is the curse.   Write.

Go, wherever ill deeds shall be done,
Go, plant your flag in the sun
    Beside the ill-doers!   115
And recoil from clenching the curse
Of God's witnessing Universe
    With a curse of yours.
        THIS is the curse.   Write.

                                                          1860

Mother and Poet

Turin, after news from Gaeta, 1861[1]

I

Dead! One of them shot by the sea in the east,
    And one of them shot in the west by the sea.
Dead! both my boys! When you sit at the feast
    And are wanting a great song for Italy free,
        Let none look at *me*!   5

II

Yet I was a poetess only last year,
    And good at my art, for a woman, men said;
But *this* woman, *this*, who is agonized here,
    —The east sea and west sea rhyme on in her head
        For ever instead.   10

1. "The mother was Laura Savio of Turin, poet and patriot, whose two sons were killed at Ancona and Gaeta" [Browning's note]. At this time Italy was struggling to free itself from foreign rule and become a unified state.

III

What art can a woman be good at? Oh, vain!
 What art *is* she good at, but hurting her breast
With the milk-teeth of babes, and a smile at the pain?
 Ah boys, how you hurt! you were strong as you pressed,
 And I proud, by that test.   15

IV

What art's for a woman? To hold on her knees
 Both darlings! to feel all their arms round her throat,
Cling, strangle a little! to sew by degrees
 And 'broider the long-clothes and neat little coat;
 To dream and to doat.   20

V

To teach them . . . It stings there! I made them indeed
 Speak plain the word *country*. I taught them, no doubt,
That a country's a thing men should die for at need.
 I prated of liberty, rights, and about
 The tyrant cast out.   25

VI

And when their eyes flashed . . . O my beautiful eyes! . . .
 I exulted: nay, let them go forth at the wheels
Of the guns, and denied not. But then the surprise
 When one sits quite alone! Then one weeps, then one kneels!
 God, how the house feels!   30

VII

At first, happy news came, in gay letters moiled[2]
 With my kisses,—of camp-life and glory, and how
They both loved me; and, soon coming home to be spoiled
 In return would fan off every fly from my brow
 With their green laurel-bough.   35

VIII

Then was triumph at Turin: "Ancona was free!"
 And some one came out of the cheers in the street,
With a face pale as stone, to say something to me.
 My Guido was dead! I fell down at his feet,
 While they cheered in the street.   40

IX

I bore it; friends soothed me; my grief looked sublime
 As the ransom of Italy. One boy remained
To be leant on and walked with, recalling the time
 When the first grew immortal, while both of us strained
 To the height he had gained.   45

X

And letters still came, shorter, sadder, more strong,
 Writ now but in one hand, "I was not to faint,—
One loved me for two—would be with me ere long:

2. Smeared.

And *Viva l'Italia!*[3]—*he* died for, our saint,
  Who forbids our complaint."

XI

My Nanni would add, "he was safe, and aware
  Of a presence that turned off the balls,[4]—was imprest
It was Guido himself, who knew what I could bear,
  And how 't was impossible, quite dispossessed
  To live on for the rest."   55

XII

On which, without pause, up the telegraph line
  Swept smoothly the next news from Gaeta:—*Shot.*
Tell his mother. Ah, ah, "his,""their" mother,—not "mine,"
  No voice says "*My* mother" again to me. What!
  You think Guido forgot?   60

XIII

Are souls straight so happy that, dizzy with Heaven,
  They drop earth's affections, conceive not of woe?
I think not. Themselves were too lately forgiven
  Through THAT Love and Sorrow which reconciled so
  The Above and Below.[5]   65

XIV

O Christ of the five wounds, who look'dst through the dark
  To the face of thy mother! consider, I pray,
How we common mothers stand desolate, mark,
  Whose sons, not being Christs, die with eyes turned away,
  And no last word to say!   70

XV

Both boys dead? but that's out of nature. We all
  Have been patriots, yet each house must always keep one.
'Twere imbecile, hewing out roads to a wall;
  And, when Italy's made, for what end is it done   75
  If we have not a son?

XVI

Ah, ah, ah! when Gaeta's taken, what then?
  When the fair wicked queen sits no more at her sport
Of the fire-balls of death crashing souls out of men?
  When the guns of Cavalli with final retort
  Have cut the game short?   80

XVII

When Venice and Rome keep their new jubilee,
  When your flag takes all heaven for its white, green, and red,[6]
When *you* have your country from mountain to sea,
  When King Victor has Italy's crown on his head,   85
  (And *I* have my dead)—

---

3. "Long live Italy!"
4. Bullets.
5. I.e., the Love and Sorrow of Jesus Christ.

6. The colors of the new Italian flag, symbolizing national unity.

ate of Harvard, the Speaker of the Massachusetts House of Representatives, a Unitarian in religion and a Jeffersonian in politics. He taught his precocious first child Latin and English grammar at an early age, even as he encouraged direct discourse and discouraged stereotypically "feminine" hesitation, apology, or euphemism. This strenuous education produced a child prodigy who read Virgil, Ovid, and Horace at the age of seven, and who suffered terrifying nightmares and recurrent headaches for most of her life. Torn between her training as her father's "son" and her knowledge of her female self, Fuller felt that womanhood was "too straitly bounded" to give her scope, but she suffered feelings of inauthenticity when she "played" the part of the great man.

After a short stay at the Misses Prescott's School in Groton, Massachusetts, presumably designed to address this dilemma, Fuller continued her education at home in Cambridgeport until, after a move to Groton, her father died. To support the family, she taught at Bronson Alcott's experimental school in Boston and then at the Greene Street School in Providence. At both establishments she began to cultivate the friendships which would play a prominent role throughout her life. After more than one adolescent infatuation with female friends, she began her "Conversations," meetings or classes usually composed of an elite group of Bostonians who discussed such topics as ethics and Greek mythology. From 1839 to 1840, New England's version of the salon took place in Elizabeth Peabody's bookstore, where Fuller could draw on the connections she had already established in Cambridge intellectual society, which was composed of Transcendentalists like Frederick Henry Hedge, W. E. Channing, and James Freeman Clark. From 1840 to 1841, with the encouragement of Emerson, she edited the Transcendentalists' magazine, *The Dial*. In 1844, Horace Greeley, editor of the *New York Tribune*, hired her to write literary criticism and moved her to New York.

As the first self-supporting American woman journalist, the translator of Johann Peter Eckermann's *Conversations with Goethe* (1839), and the author of *Summer on the Lakes* (1844), Fuller undertook to mediate between American society and European culture, represented by such figures as the German poet-dramatist Goethe, the Romantic poet Lord Byron, and the French novelist George Sand. While her *Papers on Literature and Art*, published in 1846, consolidated her reputation, her fame today depends largely upon *Woman in the Nineteenth Century* (1845). Originally a *Dial* essay entitled *The Great Lawsuit* (1843), this feminist polemic applied to women Transcendentalist tenets regarding the sacred duty of self-development, but it also solved the problem of Fuller's own sense of self-division: "there is no wholly masculine man," she proclaimed, "no purely feminine women." Hortatory in tone, *Woman in the Nineteenth Century* resembles a sermon, insisting, as it does, that men and women alike must fulfill their potential for the greater spiritual good of both sexes. Although her prose is sometimes marred by strained rhetoric, the broadly based humanism Fuller stressed here was to inform the rest of her life as she widened her concerns from feminism to the politics of liberation.

Already, in New York, she had helped establish a "halfway house" for convicts and translated one of the earliest discussions of Karl Marx and Friedrich Engels to be offered in the United States. After she sailed for Europe as a foreign correspondent, she met Giuseppe Mazzini, the Italian patriot in exile, as well as two artists associated with sexual liberation, the French novelist George Sand and the exiled Polish writer Adam Mickiewicz. Eventually she settled in Italy, where she took Giovanni Angelo, marchese d'Ossoli, as her lover. Ten years her junior, he was instrumental in consolidating her commitment to the cause of Italian independence. Her son, Angelo Eugene, was born on September 5, 1849, and in November Fuller left him to rejoin Ossoli in Rome. There she witnessed and reported on the arrival of the Italian nationalist Giuseppe Garibaldi, the proclamation of the Roman Republic, and the intervention of the French on behalf of the pope. During the French siege, she took over an emergency hospital, but, when the Republic was overthrown in July, she fled with Ossoli and her child, first to Florence and then to America. It is unclear whether the two married before leaving Italy, although it is known that Fuller was working on a history of the Roman revolution at this time.

Just outside of New York's harbor, the ship bearing Fuller, Ossoli, and their child drove into a sandbar during a storm. The baby's body was washed ashore, but neither Margaret Fuller nor Ossoli was ever found. In spite of the fame Fuller had attained during her relatively short lifetime, the critic Bell Gale Chevigny has recently demonstrated how subsequent editors and biographers trivialized this woman of letters' image. Yet, as Chevigny also shows, Fuller continued to exert a profound influence on the growing American women's movement. In the words of the nineteenth-century suffragist Ednah Cheney, "Whatever she spoke of revealed a hidden meaning, and everything seemed to be put into true relation. . . . I was no longer the limitation of myself, but I felt that the whole wealth of the universe was open to me." Cheney understood, as did many of her contemporaries, that Fuller's famous presumption—her saying, for example, "I accept the universe"—could be misinterpreted as conceit, but what it truly signified was "consciousness of the illimitable ego, the divinity in the soul."

From Woman in the Nineteenth Century

[Prejudice against Women]

* * * Knowing that there exists in the minds of men a tone of feeling toward women as toward slaves, such as is expressed in the common phrase, "Tell that to women and children;" that the infinite soul[1] can only work through them in already ascertained limits; that the gift of reason, Man's highest prerogative, is allotted to them in much lower degree; that they must be kept from mischief and melancholy by being constantly engaged in active labor, which is to be furnished and directed by those better able to think, &c., &c.,—we need not multiply instances, for who can review the experience of last week without re-

---

1. A Transcendentalist concept probably derived from Emerson's "Over-Soul."

calling words which imply, whether in jest or earnest, these views, or views like these,—knowing this, can we wonder that many reformers think that measures are not likely to be taken in behalf of women, unless their wishes could be publicly represented by women?

"That can never be necessary," cry the other side. "All men are privately influenced by women; each has his wife, sister, or female friends, and is too much biased by these relations to fail of representing their interests; and, if this is not enough, let them propose and enforce their wishes with the pen. The beauty of home would be destroyed, the delicacy of the sex be violated, the dignity of halls of legislation degraded, by an attempt to introduce them there. Such duties are inconsistent with those of a mother;" and then we have ludicrous pictures of ladies in hysterics at the polls, and senate-chambers filled with cradles.

But if, in reply, we admit as truth that Woman seems destined by nature rather for the inner circle, we must add that the arrangements of civilized life have not been, as yet, such as to secure it to her. Her circle, if the duller, is not the quieter. If kept from "excitement," she is not from drudgery. Not only the Indian squaw carries the burdens of the camp, but the favorites of Louis XIV[2] accompany him in his journeys, and the washerwoman stands at her tub, and carries home her work at all seasons, and in all states of health. Those who think the physical circumstances of Woman would make a part in the affairs of national government unsuitable, are by no means those who think it impossible for negresses to endure field-work, even during pregnancy, or for sempstresses to go through their killing labors.

As to the use of the pen, there was quite as much opposition to Woman's possessing herself of that help to free agency as there is now to her seizing on the rostrum or the desk; and she is likely to draw, from a permission to plead her cause that way, opposite inferences to what might be wished by those who now grant it.

As to the possiblity of her filling with grace and dignity any such position, we should think those who had seen the great actresses, and heard the Quaker preachers of modern times, would not doubt that Woman can express publicly the fulness of thought and creation, without losing any of the peculiar beauty of her sex. What can pollute and tarnish is to act thus from any motive except that something needs to be said or done. Woman could take part in the processions, the songs, the dances of old religion; no one fancied her delicacy was impaired by appearing in public for such a cause.

As to her home, she is not likely to leave it more than she now does for balls, theatres, meetings for promoting missions, revival meetings, and others to which she flies, in hope of an animation for her existence

2. Women in favor at the court of the French king.

commensurate with what she sees enjoyed by men. Governors of ladies'-fairs[3] are no less engrossed by such a charge, than the governor of a state by his; presidents of Washingtonian societies no less away from home than presidents of conventions. If men look straitly to it, they will find that, unless their lives are domestic, those of the women will not be. A house is no home unless it contain food and fire for the mind as well as for the body. The female Greek, of our day, is as much in the street as the male to cry, "What news?"[4] We doubt not it was the same in Athens of old. The women, shut out from the market-place, made up for it at the religious festivals. For human beings are not so constituted that they can live without expansion. If they do not get it in one way, they must in another, or perish.

As to men's representing women fairly at present, while we hear from men who owe to their wives not only all that is comfortable or graceful, but all that is wise, in the arrangement of their lives, the frequent remark, "You cannot reason with a woman,"—when from those of delicacy, nobleness, and poetic culture, falls the contemptuous phrase "women and children," and that in no light sally of the hour, but in works intended to give a permanent statement of the best experiences,—when not one man, in the million, shall I say? no, not in the hundred million, can rise above the belief that Woman was made *for Man*,—when such traits as these are daily forced upon the attention, can we feel that Man will always do justice to the interests of Woman? Can we think that he takes a sufficiently discerning and religious view of her office and destiny *ever* to do her justice, except when prompted by sentiment,—accidentally or transiently, that is, for the sentiment will vary according to the relations in which he is placed? The lover, the poet, the artist, are likely to view her nobly. The father and the philosopher have some chance of liberality; the man of the world, the legislator for expediency, none.

Under these circumstances, without attaching importance, in themselves, to the changes demanded by the champions of Woman, we hail them as signs of the times. We would have every arbitrary barrier thrown down. We would have every path laid open to Woman as freely as to Man. Were this done, and a slight temporary fermentation allowed to subside, we should see crystallizations more pure and of more various beauty. We believe the divine energy would pervade nature to a degree unknown in the history of former ages, and that no discordant collision, but a ravishing harmony of the spheres,[5] would ensue.

Yet, then and only then will mankind be ripe for this, when inward

3. Bazaars organized by women.
4. Greek men were satirized for newsmongering, just as the Latin "quid nunc" became a term for male busybodies.

5. According to ancient astronomical belief, the motions of the planets created a music of order and perfection.

and outward freedom for Woman as much as for Man shall be acknowledged as *a right*, not yielded as a concession. As the friend of the Negro
assumes that one man cannot by right hold another in bondage, so
should the friend of Woman assume that Man cannot by right lay even
well-meant restrictions on Woman. If the Negro be a soul, if the
woman be a soul, apparelled in flesh, to one Master only are they accountable. There is but one law for souls, and, if there is to be an interpreter of it, he must come not as man, or son of man, but as son of God.

Were thought and feeling once so far elevated that Man should esteem himself the brother and friend, but nowise the lord and tutor, of
Woman,—were he really bound with her in equal worship,—arrangements as to function and employment would be of no consequence.
What Woman needs is not as a woman to act or rule, but as a nature to
grow, as an intellect to discern, as a soul to live freely and unimpeded,
to unfold such powers as were given her when we left our common
home. If fewer talents were given her, yet if allowed the free and full
employment of these, so that she may render back to the giver his own
with usury,[6] she will not complain; nay, I dare to say she will bless and
rejoice in her earthly birth-place, her earthly lot. Let us consider what
obstructions impede this good era, and what signs give reason to hope
that it draws near.

I was talking on this subject with Miranda,[7] a woman, who, if any in
the world could, might speak without heat and bitterness of the position
of her sex. Her father was a man who cherished no sentimental reverence for Woman, but a firm belief in the equality of the sexes. She was
his eldest child, and came to him at an age when he needed a companion. From the time she could speak and go alone, he addressed her not
as a plaything, but as a living mind. Among the few verses he ever wrote
was a copy addressed to this child, when the first locks were cut from
her head; and the reverence expressed on this occasion for that cherished head, he never belied. It was to him the temple of immortal intellect. He respected his child, however, too much to be an indulgent
parent. He called on her for clear judgment, for courage, for honor and
fidelity; in short, for such virtues as he knew. In so far as he possessed
the keys to the wonders of this universe, he allowed free use of them to
her, and, by the incentive of a high expectation, he forbade, so far as
possible, that she should let the privilege lie idle.

Thus this child was early led to feel herself a child of the spirit. She
took her place easily, not only in the world of organized being, but in
the world of mind. A dignified sense of self-dependence was given as all
her portion, and she found it a sure anchor. Herself securely anchored,

6. Interest.
7. "Miranda" reflects an idealized version of Fuller's own experiences and opinions.

her relations with others were established with equal security. She was fortunate in a total absence of those charms which might have drawn to her bewildering flatteries, and in a strong electric nature, which re-pelled those who did not belong to her, and attracted those who did. With men and women her relations were noble,—affectionate without passion, intellectual without coldness. The world was free to her, and she lived freely in it. Outward adversity came, and inward conflict; but that faith and self-respect had early been awakened which must always lead, at last, to an outward serenity and an inward peace.

Of Miranda I had always thought as an example, that the restraints upon the sex were insuperable only to those who think them so, or who noisily strive to break them. She had taken a course of her own, and no man stood in her way. Many of her acts had been unusual, but excited no uproar. Few helped, but none checked her; and the many men who knew her mind and her life, showed to her confidence as to a brother, gentleness as to a sister. And not only refined, but very coarse men ap-proved and aided one in whom they saw resolution and clearness of design. Her mind was often the leading one, always effective.

When I talked with her upon these matters, and had said very much what I have written, she smilingly replied: "And yet we must admit that I have been fortunate, and this should not be.[8] My good father's early trust gave the first bias, and the rest followed, of course. It is true that I have had less outward aid, in after years, than most women; but that is of little consequence. Religion was early awakened in my soul,—a sense that what the soul is capable to ask it must attain, and that, though I might be aided and instructed by others, I must depend on myself as the only constant friend. This self-dependence, which was honored in me, is deprecated as a fault in most women. They are taught to learn their rule from without, not to unfold it from within.

"This is the fault of Man, who is still vain, and wishes to be more important to Woman than, by right, he should be."

"Men have not shown this disposition toward you," I said.

"No; because the position I early was enabled to take was one of self-reliance.[9] And were all women as sure of their wants as I was, the result would be the same. But they are so overloaded with precepts by guardians, who think that nothing is so much to be dreaded for a woman as originality of thought or character, that their minds are im-peded by doubts till they lose their chance of fair, free proportions. The difficulty is to get them to the point from which they shall naturally de-velop self-respect, and learn self-help.

"Once I thought that men would help to forward this state of things

---

8. I.e., I would not be as I am without my good fortune.

9. Another Emersonian concept, expressing a faith in individualism.

more than I do now. I saw so many of them wretched in the connections[1] they had formed in weakness and vanity. They seemed so glad to
esteem women whenever they could.

" 'The soft arms of affection,' said one of the most discerning spirits,
'will not suffice for me, unless on them I see the steel bracelets of
strength.'

"But early I perceived that men never, in any extreme of despair,
wished to be women. On the contrary, they were ever ready to taunt
one another, at any sign of weakness, with,

Art thou not like the women, who,—

The passage ends various ways, according to the occasion and rhetoric
of the speaker. When they admired any woman, they were inclined to
speak of her as 'above her sex.' Silently I observed this, and feared it argued a rooted scepticism, which for ages had been fastening on the
heart, and which only an age of miracles could eradicate. Ever I have
been treated with great sincerity; and I look upon it as a signal instance
of this, that an intimate friend of the other sex said, in a fervent moment, that I 'deserved in some star to be a man.' He was much surprised
when I disclosed my view of my position and hopes, when I declared
my faith that the feminine side, the side of love, of beauty, of holiness,
was now to have its full chance, and that, if either were better, it was
better now to be a woman; for even the slightest achievement of good
was furthering an especial work of our time. He smiled incredulously.
'She makes the best she can of it,' thought he. 'Let Jews believe the
pride of Jewry, but I am of the better sort, and know better.'

"Another used as highest praise, in speaking of a character in literature, the words 'a manly woman.'

"So in the noble passage of Ben Jonson:[2]

> I meant the day-star should not brighter ride,
>   Nor shed like influence from its lucent seat;
> I meant she should be courteous, facile, sweet,
>   Free from that solemn vice of greatness, pride;
> I meant each softest virtue there should meet,
>   Fit in that softer bosom to abide,
> Only a learned and a *manly* soul
>   I purposed her, that should with even powers
> The rock, the spindle, and the shears control
>   Of destiny,[3] and spin her own free hours."

---

1. Marriages, relationships.
2. English poet (1572–1637).
3. The Fates spin out the thread of each person's destiny, cutting it when the time of death
arrives.

"Methinks," said I, "you are too fastidious in objecting to this. Jonson, in using the word 'manly,' only meant to heighten the picture of this, the true, the intelligent fate, with one of the deeper colors."

"And yet," said she, "so invariable is the use of this word where a heroic quality is to be described, and I feel so sure that persistence and courage are the most womanly no less than the most manly qualities, that I would exchange these words for others of a larger sense, at the risk of marring the fine tissue of the verse.[4] Read, 'A heavenward and instructed soul,' and I should be satisfied. Let it not be said, wherever there is energy or creative genius, 'She has a masculine mind.'"

[Muse and Minerva]

There are two aspects of Woman's nature, represented by the ancients as Muse and Minerva.[5] It is the former to which the writer in the Pathfinder[6] looks. It is the latter which Wordsworth has in mind, when he says,

> With a placid brow,
> Which woman ne'er should forfeit, keep thy vow.[7]

The especial genius of Woman I believe to be electrical[8] in movement, intuitive in function, spiritual in tendency. She excels not so easily in classification, or recreation,[9] as in an instinctive seizure of causes, and a simple breathing out of what she receives, that has the singleness of life, rather than the selecting and energizing of art.

More native is it to her to be the living model of the artist than to set apart from herself any one form in objective reality; more native to inspire and receive the poem, than to create it. In so far as soul is in her completely developed, all soul is the same; but in so far as it is modified in her as Woman, it flows, it breathes, it sings, rather than deposits soil, or finishes work; and that which is especially feminine flushes, in blossom, the face of earth, and pervades, like air and water, all this seeming solid globe, daily renewing and purifying its life. Such may be the especially feminine element spoken of as Femality. But it is no more the order of nature that it should be incarnated pure in any form, than that the masculine energy should exist unmingled with it in any form.

Male and female represent the two sides of the great radical dualism. But, in fact, they are perpetually passing into one another. Fluid

4. I.e., its prosody.
5. The muse, any of nine sister goddesses in Greek mythology, presides over learning and creative arts; Minerva is the ancient goddess of wisdom, known as Athena in Greek myth.
6. The *New York Pathfinder*, a periodical in existence at the time.
7. William Wordsworth, *Liberty: Sequel to the Preceding* (1835)
8. Quick and darting.
9. Careful analysis.

hardens to solid, solid rushes to fluid. There is no wholly masculine man, no purely feminine woman.

History jeers at the attempts of physiologists to bind great original laws by the forms which flow from them. They make a rule; they say from observation what can and cannot be. In vain! Nature provides exceptions to every rule. She sends women to battle, and sets Hercules spinning; she enables women to bear immense burdens, cold, and frost; she enables the man, who feels maternal love, to nourish his infant like a mother. Of late she plays still gayer pranks. Not only she deprives organizations, but organs, of a necessary end. She enables people to read with the top of the head, and see with the pit of the stomach. Presently she will make a female Newton, and a male Siren.[1]

Man partakes of the feminine in the Apollo,[2] Woman of the masculine as Minerva.

What I mean by the Muse is that unimpeded clearness of the intuitive powers, which a perfectly truthful adherence to every admonition of the higher instincts would bring to a finely organized human being. It may appear as prophecy or as poesy. It enabled Cassandra to foresee the results of actions passing round her; the Seeress to behold the true character of the person through the mask of his customary life.[3] (Sometimes she saw a feminine form behind the man, sometimes the reverse.) It enabled the daughter of Linnaeus to see the soul of the flower exhaling from the flower.[4] It gave a man, but a poet-man, the power of which he thus speaks: "Often in my contemplation of nature, radiant intimations, and as it were sheaves of light, appear before me as to the facts of cosmogony, in which my mind has, perhaps, taken especial part." He wisely adds, "but it is necessary with earnestness to verify the knowledge we gain by these flashes of light." And none should forget this. Sight must be verified by light before it can deserve the honors of piety and genius. Yet sight comes first, and of this sight of the world of causes, this approximation to the region of primitive motions, women I hold to be especially capable. Even without equal freedom with the other sex, they have already shown themselves so; and should these faculties have free play, I believe they will open new, deeper and purer sources of joyous inspiration than have as yet refreshed the earth.

Let us be wise, and not impede the soul. Let her work as she will. Let us have one creative energy, one incessant revelation. Let it take what

1. Sir Isaac Newton (1642–1727), major English scientist. "Siren": mythical female who lures sailors onto rocks through the enchanting power of her song.

2. The Greek god of the sun and of poetry.

3. Cassandra was a fabled Greek prophetess who foresaw the outcome of the Trojan War. "Seeress": female seer or clairvoyant.

4. "The daughter of Linnaeus [eighteenth-century botanist] states, that, while looking steadfastly at the red lily, she saw its spirit hovering above it, as a red flame. It is true, this, like many fair spirit-stories, may be explained away as an optical illusion, but its poetic beauty and meaning would, even then, make it valuable, as an illustration of the spiritual fact" [Fuller's note].

form it will, and let us not bind it by the past to man or woman, black or white. Jove sprang from Rhea, Pallas from Jove.[5] So let it be.

If it has been the tendency of these remarks to call Woman rather to the Minerva side,—if I, unlike the more generous writer, have spoken from society no less than the soul,—let it be pardoned! It is love that has caused this,—love for many incarcerated souls, that might be freed, could the idea of religious self-dependence be established in them, could the weakening habit of dependence on others be broken up.

Proclus[6] teaches that every life has, in its sphere, a totality or whole-ness of the animating powers of the other spheres; having only, as its own characteristic, a predominance of some one power. Thus Jupiter comprises, within himself, the other twelve powers, which stand thus: The first triad is *demiurgic* or *fabricative*, that is, Jupiter, Neptune, Vulcan; the second, *defensive*, Vesta, Minerva, Mars; the third, *vivific*, Ceres, Juno, Diana; and the fourth, Mercury, Venus, Apollo, *elevating and harmonic*. In the sphere of Jupiter, energy is predominant—with Venus, beauty; but each comprehends and apprehends all the others.

When the same community of life and consciousness of mind begin among men, humanity will have, positively and finally, subjugated its brute elements and Titanic childhood;[7] criticism will have perished; ar-bitrary limits and ignorant censure be impossible; all will have entered upon the liberty of law,[8] and the harmony of common growth.

Then Apollo will sing to his lyre what Vulcan forges on the anvil, and the Muse weave anew the tapestries of Minerva.

It is, therefore, only in the present crisis that the preference is given to Minerva. The power of continence must establish the legitimacy of freedom, the power of self-poise the perfection of motion.

Every relation, every gradation of nature is incalculably precious, but only to the soul which is poised upon itself, and to whom no loss, no change, can bring dull discord, for it is in harmony with the central soul.[9]

* * *

* * * Women must leave off asking [men] and being influenced by them, but retire within themselves, and explore the ground-work of life till they find their peculiar secret. Then, when they come forth again, renovated and baptized, they will know how to turn all dross[1] to gold, and will be rich and free though they live in a hut, tranquil if in a crowd. Then their sweet singing shall not be from passionate impulse, but the

---

5. Jove is Zeus, the king of the Greek gods, whose mother was Rhea. Pallas is Minerva, god-dess of wisdom, said to have been born from the head of Jove.
6. Proclus (412–485 A.D.), Greek philosopher and mystic.

7. The Titans were a race of giants who were succeeded by the gods in Greek myth.
8. Natural law or necessity.
9. Another reference to the Emersonian doc-trine of the "Over-Soul."
1. Waste materials found in metals.

lyrical overflow of a divine rapture, and a new music shall be evolved
from this many-chorded world.

Grant her, then, for a while, the armor and the javelin. Let her put
from her the press of other minds, and meditate in virgin loneliness.
The same idea shall reappear in due time as Muse, or Ceres,[2] the all-
kindly, patient Earth-Spirit.

[The Future of Women]

And now I have designated in outline, if not in fulness, the stream
which is ever flowing from the heights of my thought.

In the earlier tract[3] I was told I did not make my meaning sufficiently
clear. In this I have consequently tried to illustrate it in various ways,
and may have been guilty of much repetition. Yet, as I am anxious to
leave no room for doubt, I shall venture to retrace, once more, the
scope of my design in points, as was done in old-fashioned sermons.

Man is a being of two-fold relations, to nature beneath, and intelli-
gences above him. The earth is his school, if not his birth-place; God
his object; life and thought his means of interpreting nature, and aspiring to God.

Only a fraction of this purpose is accomplished in the life of any one
man. Its entire accomplishment is to be hoped only from the sum of the
lives of men, or Man considered as a whole.

As this whole has one soul and one body, any injury or obstruction to
a part, or to the meanest member, affects the whole. Man can never be
perfectly happy or virtuous, till all men are so.

To address[4] Man wisely, you must not forget that his life is partly
animal, subject to the same laws with Nature.

But you cannot address him wisely unless you consider him still
more as soul, and appreciate the conditions and destiny of soul.

The growth of Man is two-fold, masculine and feminine.

So far as these two methods can be distinguished, they are so as

Energy and Harmony;

Power and Beauty;

Intellect and Love;

or by some such rude classification; for we have not language primitive
and pure enough to express such ideas with precision.

These two sides are supposed to be expressed in Man and Woman,
that is, as the more and the less, for the faculties have not been given
pure to either, but only in preponderance. There are also exceptions in
great number, such as men of far more beauty than power, and the re-

2. Roman goddess of agriculture.   Dial (1843).
3. Her first version of this work, *The Great*   4. Consider.
Lawsuit, was criticized when it appeared in the

verse. But, as a general rule, it seems to have been the intention to give a preponderance on the one side, that is called masculine, and on the other, one that is called feminine.

There cannot be a doubt that, if these two developments were in perfect harmony, they would correspond to and fulfill one another, like hemispheres, or the tenor and bass in music.

But there is no perfect harmony in human nature; and the two parts answer one another only now and then; or, if there be a persistent consonance, it can only be traced at long intervals, instead of discoursing an obvious melody.

What is the cause of this?

Man, in the order of time, was developed first; as energy comes before harmony; power before beauty.

Woman was therefore under his care as an elder. He might have been her guardian and teacher.

But, as human nature goes not straightforward, but by excessive action and then reaction in an undulated course, he misunderstood and abused his advantages, and became her temporal master instead of her spiritual sire.

On himself came the punishment. He educated Woman more as a servant than a daughter, and found himself a king without a queen.

The children of this unequal union showed unequal natures, and, more and more, men seemed sons of the handmaid, rather than princess.

At last, there were so many Ishmaelites[5] that the rest grew frightened and indignant. They laid the blame on Hagar, and drove her forth into the wilderness.

But there were none the fewer Ishmaelites for that.

At last men became a little wiser, and saw that the infant Moses was, in every case, saved by the pure instincts of Woman's breast.[6] For, as too much adversity is better for the moral nature than too much prosperity, Woman, in this respect, dwindled less than Man, though in other respects still a child in leading-strings.[7]

So Man did her more and more justice, and grew more and more kind.

But yet—his habits and his will corrupted by the past—he did not clearly see that Woman was half himself; that her interests were identical with his; and that, by the law of their common being, he could never reach his true proportions while she remained in any wise shorn[8] of hers.

5. I.e., outcasts from society. "Hagar": Hebrew servant who bore an illegitimate son, Ishmael, to Abraham, and was driven into the desert by his wife Sarah.
6. Moses was found floating on the river Nile in a basket by the Pharoah's daughter, who rescued him.
7. Strings used to support a child who is learning to walk.
8. In any way deprived.

And so it has gone on to our day; both ideas developing, but more slowly than they would under a clearer recognition of truth and justice, which would have permitted the sexes their due influence on one another, and mutual improvement from more dignified relations.

Wherever there was pure love, the natural influences were, for the time, restored.

Wherever the poet or artist gave free course to his genius, he saw the truth, and expressed it in worthy forms, for these men especially share and need the feminine principle. The divine birds need to be brooded[9] into life and song by mothers.

Wherever religion (I mean the thirst for truth and good, not the love of sect and dogma) had its course, the original design was apprehended in its simplicity, and the dove presaged sweetly from Dodona's oak.[1]

I have aimed to show that no age was left entirely without a witness of the equality of the sexes in function, duty, and hope.

Also that, when there was unwillingness or ignorance, which prevented this being acted upon, women had not the less power for their want of light and noble freedom. But it was power which hurt alike them and those against whom they made use of the arms of the servile, —cunning, blandishment, and unreasonable emotion.

That now the time has come when a clearer vision and better action are possible—when Man and Woman may regard one another as brother and sister, the pillars of one porch, the priests of one worship.

I have believed and intimated that this hope would receive an ampler fruition, than ever before, in our own land.

And it will do so if this land carry out the principles from which sprang our national life.

I believe that, at present, women are the best helpers of one another.

Let them think; let them act; till they know what they need.

We only ask of men to remove arbitrary barriers. Some would like to do more. But I believe it needs that Woman show herself in her native dignity, to teach them how to aid her; their minds are so encumbered by tradition.

When Lord Edward Fitzgerald travelled with the Indians, his manly heart obliged him at once to take the packs from the squaws and carry them. But we do not read that the red men followed his example, though they are ready enough to carry the pack of the white woman, because she seems to them a superior being.

Let Woman appear in the mild majesty of Ceres, and rudest churls[2] will be willing to learn from her.

You ask, what use will she make of liberty, when she has so long been sustained and restrained?

9. Hatched.
1. An ancient Greek oracle at which doves spoke in human language.
2. Uneducated men.

I answer; in the first place, this will not be suddenly given. I read yesterday a debate of this year on the subject of enlarging women's rights over property. It was a leaf from the class-book that is preparing for the needed instruction. The men learned visibly as they spoke. The champions of Woman saw the fallacy of arguments on the opposite side, and were startled by their own convictions. With their wives at home, and the readers of the paper, it was the same. And so the stream flows on; thought urging action, and action leading to the evolution of still better thought.

But, were this freedom to come suddenly, I have no fear of the consequences. Individuals might commit excesses, but there is not only in the sex a reverence for decorums and limits inherited and enhanced from generation to generation, which many years of other life could not efface, but a native love, in Woman as Woman, of proportion, of "the simple art of not too much,"—a Greek moderation, which would create immediately a restraining party, the natural legislators and instructors of the rest, and would gradually establish such rules as are needed to guard, without impeding, life.

The Graces[3] would lead the choral dance, and teach the rest to regulate their steps to the measure of beauty.

But if you ask me what offices they may fill, I reply—any. I do not care what case you put; let them be sea-captains, if you will. I do not doubt there are women well fitted for such an office, and, if so, I should be as glad to see them in it, as to welcome the maid of Saragossa, or the maid of Missolonghi, or the Suliote heroine, or Emily Plater.[4]

I think women need, especially at this juncture, a much greater range of occupation than they have, to rouse their latent powers. A party of travellers lately visited a lonely hut on a mountain. There they found an old woman, who told them she and her husband had lived there forty years. "Why," they said, "did you choose so barren a spot?" She "did not know; *it was the man's notion.*"

And, during forty years, she had been content to act, without knowing why, upon "the man's notion." I would not have it so.

In families that I know, some little girls like to saw wood, others to use carpenters' tools. Where these tastes are indulged, cheerfulness and good-humor are promoted. Where they are forbidden, because "such things are not proper for girls," they grow sullen and mischievous.

Fourier[5] had observed these wants of women, as no one can fail to do

---

3. Three Greek goddesses responsible for life's gentle pleasures.
4. The Maid of Saragossa was Maria Austin, who fought against the French in Spain (1808); the Maid of Missolonghi, an unidentified Greek, fought during the Turkish sieges of 1822 or 1826; the Suliote heroine was probably Moscha, who led a band of women during the siege of Souli in Albania (1803); Emily Plater commanded a company in the Polish army fighting against Russia (1831).
5. François Fourier (1772–1837), French social theorist.

who watches the desires of little girls, or knows the ennui that haunts grown women, except where they make to themselves a serene little world by art of some kind. He, therefore, in proposing a great variety of employments, in manufactures or the care of plants and animals, allows for one third of women as likely to have a taste for masculine pursuits, one third of men for feminine.

Who does not observe the immediate glow and serenity that is diffused over the life of women, before restless or fretful, by engaging in gardening, building, or the lowest department of art? Here is something that is not routine, something that draws forth life towards the infinite.

I have no doubt, however, that a large proportion of women would give themselves to the same employments as now, because there are circumstances that must lead them. Mothers will delight to make the nest soft and warm. Nature would take care of that; no need to clip the wings of any bird that wants to soar and sing, or finds in itself the strength of pinion[6] for a migratory flight unusual to its kind. The difference would be that *all* need not be constrained to employments for which *some* are unfit.

I have urged upon the sex self-subsistence in its two forms of self-reliance and self-impulse, because I believe them to be the needed means of the present juncture.

I have urged on Woman independence of Man, not that I do not think the sexes mutually needed by one another, but because in Woman this fact has led to an excessive devotion, which has cooled love, degraded marriage, and prevented either sex from being what it should be to itself or the other.

I wish Woman to live, *first* for God's sake. Then she will not make an imperfect man her god, and thus sink to idolatry. Then she will not take what is not fit for her from a sense of weakness and poverty. Then, if she finds what she needs in Man embodied, she will know how to love, and be worthy of being loved.

By being more a soul, she will not be less Woman, for nature is perfected through spirit.

Now there is no woman, only an overgrown child.

That her hand may be given with dignity, she must be able to stand alone. I wish to see men and women capable of such relations as are depicted by Landor[7] in his Pericles and Aspasia, where grace is the natural garb of strength, and the affections are calm, because deep. The softness is that of a firm tissue, as when

> The gods approve
> The depth, but not the tumult of the soul,
> A fervent, not ungovernable love.

6. Wing.
7. Walter Savage Landor, English poet (1775–1864).

A profound thinker has said, "No married woman can represent the female world, for she belongs to her husband. The idea of Woman must be represented by a virgin."

But that is the very fault of marriage, and of the present relation between the sexes, that the woman *does* belong to the man, instead of forming a whole with him. Were it otherwise, there would be no such limitation to the thought.

Woman, self-centred, would never be absorbed by any relation; it would be only an experience to her as to man. It is a vulgar error that love, *a* love, to Woman is her whole existence; she also is born for Truth and Love in their universal energy. Would she but assume her inheritance, Mary would not be the only virgin mother. Not Manzoni alone would celebrate in his wife the virgin mind with the maternal wisdom and conjugal affections.[8] The soul is ever young, ever virgin.

And will not she soon appear?—the woman who shall vindicate their birthright for all women; who shall teach them what to claim, and how to use what they obtain? Shall not her name be for her era Victoria, for her country and life Virginia?[9] Yet predictions are rash; she herself must teach us to give her the fitting name.

1845

8. Alessandro Manzoni (1785–1873), Italian novelist and poet.
9. Victoria was then Queen of England; Virginia is a reference both to America, where Fuller sees woman's future lying, and to the virginity of soul she celebrates here.

ELIZABETH CLEGHORN GASKELL
1810–1865

Although she was born in London, the woman who gained fame as "Mrs. Gaskell" was destined to become one of the nineteenth century's foremost recorders of life in England's provinces during the height of the Industrial Revolution. Her father, William Stevenson, a sometime Unitarian minister, had come to the capital to take up a position as Keeper of the Records to the Treasury, but soon after his wife's death, when Elizabeth—the last of eight children—was still very young, he sent this youngest daughter to live with an aunt at Knutsford, the small rural town that inspired her later depictions of isolated, pastoral "Cranford." There, at the age of twenty-one, she married the Reverend William Gaskell, also a Unitarian minister, with whom she was to live happily for the rest of her life.

After their marriage, the Gaskells settled in the industrial city of Manchester, where the Reverend Gaskell had his church, and within a decade or so the couple were the parents of four children, whose upbringing constituted a full-time job for Mrs. Gaskell until 1845. In that year, her son William died, and, although she had another child within a year, she may have begun writing what was to be her first novel, *Mary Barton* (1848), to "divert her mind," as one biographer puts it, from the pain of her loss. Even before she started to take herself seriously as a potential novelist, however, Elizabeth Gaskell had clearly developed the observational skills that give her works such force. Manchester in the forties was a city in turmoil, with fiercely expanding factories dominating both the town and the lives of its enormous, increasingly impoverished population. In 1843, the historian-philosopher Thomas Carlyle published his *Past and Present*, a work that addressed itself in part to the crises afflicting such cities; in 1845, the German thinker Friedrich Engels, who was later to coauthor with Karl Marx *The Communist Manifesto* (1848), produced *The Condition of the Working Class in England in 1844*, which offered an extended analysis of the plight of Manchester's industrial laborers. Like these men—or perhaps even more than them—Mrs. Gaskell had countless opportunities to observe the misery that lay all around her. She had collaborated with her husband on the beginning of a series entitled *Sketches Among the Poor* in 1837; in addition, as the wife of a minister, she was frequently obliged to visit and console sufferers; as a nascent novelist, too, she had a keen sense of the drama that marked what Virginia Woolf was to call the "lives of the obscure."

Not surprisingly, then, *Mary Barton* constituted a memorable portrait of a series of those lives at the same time that it offered a detailed examination of the tensions between industrial leaders and industrial laborers that shadowed (and sometimes shattered) the public world of Manchester. In later novels, moreover—particularly *Ruth* (1853), the story of an unwed working-class mother, and *North and South* (1855), a tale that explicitly compared the industrialized north of England to the more agrarian south—Mrs. Gaskell continued to undertake fictional studies of what nineteenth-century writers called the "condition of England" question.

Set against Gaskell's other works, *Cranford* (1853) may at first appear to be little more than a nostalgic idyll of village life in the early Victorian period. Yet this writer's loving descriptions of the "elegant economy" practiced by her heroines of gentle birth but slender means are as incisive in their way as her more obviously analytical evocations of class conflict in Manchester. Begun as a series of sketches commissioned by Charles Dickens for *Household Words*, a weekly journal he founded in 1850, *Cranford* quickly evolved from a quietly comic memoir to a more searching (though still humorous) consideration of the relationship between old and new ways of life in a society that was rapidly changing. For though Miss Jenkyns and her friends appear to inhabit a timeless world of decorous customs and delicate china, their old-fashioned sphere seems increasingly like some fragile object that has been artificially preserved, and its tenuous elegance is continually threatened by forces from the "modern" industrial towns that come ever nearer. Disturbed by critics who argued that in *Mary Barton* she had been guilty of class prejudice, preferring the workers to their employers, Gaskell clearly set out in *Cranford* to show the trials of a vanishing genteel class even while she both celebrated and satirized the foibles of that class.

Considering the novelistic skills she displayed in books as diverse as *Mary Barton* and *Cranford*, it is not surprising that Mrs. Gaskell quickly became one of England's most successful writers and the friend of such notables as Charles

Dickens, Harriet Beecher Stowe, John Ruskin, and Florence Nightingale. But her most important literary relationship was with Charlotte Brontë, whom she met in 1850, when the author of *Jane Eyre* was at the height of her fame. Although the two women saw each other only a few times, they corresponded regularly, and Gaskell was increasingly moved by both Brontë's sufferings and her fortitude. "Such a life as Miss B's I never heard of before [it was] described . . . to me," she wrote in awe to one of her friends, shortly after learning about the hardships of the novelist's history from a mutual acquaintance. After Brontë's death in 1855, Gaskell explored the conditions of that existence more fully when the Reverend Patrick Brontë asked her to write a life of his daughter, and the work she produced, despite inaccuracies and omissions designed to spare the feelings of the family, is regarded as a classic of English biography.

Mrs. Gaskell's special ability to enter with sensitivity and sympathy into circumstances so different from her own constitutes yet another indication of the range of her literary talents. Some critics have considered those talents as distinctively "womanly" because of their delineation of "women's oddities" in a work like *Cranford*, but Gaskell's skills might just as easily be defined as distinctively humane in their combination of scrupulous observation and compassionate imagination. Given her novelistic energy, she must certainly have been planning more works when she died quite suddenly at "The Lawn," a country house she had just purchased as a retirement gift for her husband. She was buried in the town she had memorialized as "Cranford," an appropriate gesture because, as she once wrote to the critic John Ruskin, "Whenever I am ailing or ill, I take *Cranford* and—I was going to say, *enjoy* it! (but that would not be pretty!) laugh over it afresh!"

From Cranford[1]

Chapter I. Our Society

In the first place, Cranford is in possession of the Amazons;[2] all the holders of houses above a certain rent are women. If a married couple come to settle in the town, somehow the gentleman disappears; he is either fairly frightened to death by being the only man in the Cranford evening parties, or he is accounted for by being with his regiment, his ship, or closely engaged in business all the week in the great neighbouring commercial town of Drumble, distant only twenty miles on a railroad. In short, whatever does become of the gentlemen, they are not at Cranford. What could they do if they were there? The surgeon has his round of thirty miles, and sleeps at Cranford; but every man cannot be a surgeon. For keeping the trim gardens full of choice flowers without a weed to speck them; for frightening away little boys who look

---

1. These two opening chapters of *Cranford* were originally published in 1851 as a single self-contained episode entitled *Our Society at Cranford* in Charles Dickens' journal *House-*

hold Words.
2. A mythical race of giant women who live independently of men.

wistfully at the said flowers through the railings; for rushing out at the geese that occasionally venture in to the gardens if the gates are left open; for deciding all questions of literature and politics without troubling themselves with unnecessary reasons or arguments; for obtaining clear and correct knowledge of everybody's affairs in the parish; for keeping their neat maid-servants in admirable order; for kindness (somewhat dictatorial) to the poor, and real tender good offices to each other whenever they are in distress, the ladies of Cranford are quite sufficient. "A man," as one of them observed to me once, "is *so* in the way in the house." Although the ladies of Cranford know all each other's proceedings, they are exceedingly indifferent to each other's opinions. Indeed, as each has her own individuality, not to say eccentricity, pretty strongly developed, nothing is so easy as verbal retaliation; but, somehow, goodwill reigns among them to a considerable degree.

The Cranford ladies have only an occasional little quarrel, spirted out in a few peppery words and angry jerks of the head; just enough to prevent the even tenor of their lives from becoming too flat. Their dress is very independent of fashion; as they observe, "What does it signify how we dress here at Cranford, where everybody knows us?" And if they go from home, their reason is equally cogent, "What does it signify how we dress here, where nobody knows us?" The materials of their clothes are, in general, good and plain, and most of them are nearly as scrupulous as Miss Tyler, of cleanly memory; but I will answer for it, the last gigot,[3] the last tight and scanty petticoat in wear in England, was seen at Cranford—and seen without a smile.

I can testify to a magnificent family red silk umbrella, under which a gentle little spinster, left alone of many brothers and sisters, used to patter to church on rainy days. Have you any red silk umbrellas in London? We had a tradition of the first that had ever been seen in Cranford; and the little boys mobbed it, and called it "a stick in petticoats." It might have been the very red silk one I have described, held up by a strong father over a troop of little ones; the poor little lady—the survivor of all—could scarcely carry it.

Then there were rules and regulations for visiting and calls; and they were announced to any young people who might be staying in the town, with all the solemnity with which the old Manx laws were read once a year on the Tinwald Mount.[4]

"Our friends have sent to inquire how you are after your journey tonight, my dear" (fifteen miles in a gentleman's carriage); "they will give you some rest tomorrow, but the next day, I have no doubt, they will

---

3. A ballooning sleeve tightly gathered at the wrist.
4. Manx is the language of the Isle of Man, off Great Britain in the Irish Sea; the island's traditional legislature, known as the Tynwald, met for centuries in an open-air assembly once a year.

call; so be at liberty after twelve—from twelve to three are our calling hours."

Then, after they had called:

"It is the third day; I dare say your mamma has told you, my dear, never to let more than three days elapse between receiving a call and returning it; and also, that you are never to stay longer than a quarter of an hour."

"But am I to look at my watch? How am I to find out when a quarter of an hour has passed?"

"You must keep thinking about the time, my dear, and not allow yourself to forget it in conversation."

As everybody had this rule in their minds, whether they received or paid a call, of course no absorbing subject was ever spoken about. We kept ourselves to short sentences of small talk, and were punctual to our time.

I imagine that a few of the gentlefolks of Cranford were poor, and had some difficulty in making both ends meet; but they were like the Spartans,[5] and concealed their smart under a smiling face. We none of us spoke of money, because that subject savoured of commerce and trade, and though some might be poor, we were all aristocratic. The Cranfordians had that kindly *esprit de corps*[6] which made them overlook all deficiencies in success when some among them tried to conceal their poverty. When Mrs. Forrester, for instance, gave a party in her baby-house of a dwelling, and the little maiden disturbed the ladies on the sofa by a request that she might get the tea-tray out from underneath, every one took this novel proceeding as the most natural thing in the world, and talked on about household forms and ceremonies as if we all believed that our hostess had a regular servants' hall, second table, with housekeeper and steward, instead of the one little charity-school maiden,[7] whose short ruddy arms could never have been strong enough to carry the tray upstairs, if she had not been assisted in private by her mistress, who now sat in state,[8] pretending not to know what cakes were sent up, though she knew, and we knew, and she knew that we knew, and we knew that she knew that we knew, she had been busy all the morning making tea-bread and sponge-cakes.

There were one or two consequences arising from this general but unacknowledged poverty, and this very much acknowledged gentility, which were not amiss, and which might be introduced into many circles of society to their great improvement. For instance, the inhabitants of Cranford kept early hours, and clattered home in their pattens,[9] under

5. Citizens of a Greek city known for their austerity.
6. Group feeling.
7. A poor girl hired out by a public institution.
8. Regal pomp.
9. Wooden sandals.

the guidance of a lantern-bearer, about nine o'clock at night; and the whole town was abed and asleep by half-past ten. Moreover, it was considered "vulgar" (a tremendous word in Cranford) to give anything expensive, in the way of eatable or drinkable, at the evening entertainments. Wafer bread-and-butter and sponge-biscuits were all that the Honourable Mrs. Jamieson gave; and she was sister-in-law to the late Earl of Glenmire, although she did practise such "elegant economy."

"Elegant economy!" How naturally one falls back into the phraseology of Cranford! There, economy was always "elegant," and money-spending always "vulgar and ostentatious"; a sort of sour-grapeism which made us very peaceful and satisfied. I never shall forget the dismay felt when a certain Captain Brown came to live at Cranford, and openly spoke about his being poor—not in a whisper to an intimate friend, the doors and windows being previously closed, but in the public street! in a loud military voice! alleging his poverty as a reason for not taking a particular house. The ladies of Cranford were already rather moaning over the invasion of their territories by a man and a gentleman. He was a half-pay captain, and had obtained some situation on a neighbouring railroad, which had been vehemently petitioned against by the little town; and if, in addition to his masculine gender, and his connection with the obnoxious railroad, he was so brazen as to talk of being poor—why, then, indeed, he must be sent to Coventry.[1] Death was as true and as common as poverty; yet people never spoke about that, loud out in the streets. It was a word not to be mentioned to ears polite. We had tacitly agreed to ignore that any with whom we associated on terms of visiting equality could ever be prevented by poverty from doing anything that they wished. If we walked to or from a party, it was because the night was so fine, or the air so refreshing, not because sedan-chairs[2] were expensive. If we wore prints, instead of summer silks, it was because we preferred a washing material; and so on, till we blinded ourselves to the vulgar fact that we were, all of us, people of very moderate means. Of course, then, we did not know what to make of a man who could speak of poverty as if it was not a disgrace. Yet, somehow, Captain Brown made himself respected in Cranford, and was called upon, in spite of all resolutions to the contrary. I was surprised to hear his opinions quoted as authority at a visit which I paid to Cranford about a year after he had settled in the town. My own friends had been among the bitterest opponents of any proposal to visit the Captain and his daughters, only twelve months before; and now he was even admitted in the tabooed hours before twelve. True, it was to discover the cause of a smoking chimney, before the fire was lighted; but

1. Idiomatic for "ostracized."
2. A portable enclosed chair carried by two men.

still Captain Brown walked upstairs, nothing daunted, spoke in a voice too large for the room, and joked quite in the way of a tame man about the house. He had been blind to all the small slights, and omissions of trivial ceremonies, with which he had been received. He had been friendly, though the Cranford ladies had been cool; he had answered small sarcastic compliments in good faith; and with his manly frankness had overpowered all the shrinking which met him as a man who was not ashamed to be poor. And, at last, his excellent masculine common sense, and his facility in devising expedients to overcome domestic dilemmas, had gained him an extraordinary place as an authority among the Cranford ladies. He himself went on in his course, as unaware of his popularity as he had been of the reverse; and I am sure he was startled one day when he found his advice so highly esteemed as to make some counsel which he had given in jest to be taken in sober, serious earnest.

It was on this subject: An old lady had an Alderney cow, which she looked upon as a daughter. You could not pay the short quarter of an hour call without being told of the wonderful milk or wonderful intelligence of this animal. The whole town knew and kindly regarded Miss Betsy Barker's Alderney; therefore great was the sympathy and regret when, in an unguarded moment, the poor cow tumbled into a lime-pit.[3] She moaned so loudly that she was soon heard and rescued; but meanwhile the poor beast had lost most of her hair, and came out looking naked, cold, and miserable, in a bare skin. Everybody pitied the animal, though a few could not restrain their smiles at her droll appearance. Miss Betsy Barker absolutely cried with sorrow and dismay; and it was said she thought of trying a bath of oil. This remedy, perhaps, was recommended by some one of the number whose advice she asked; but the proposal, if ever it was made, was knocked on the head by Captain Brown's decided "Get her a flannel waistcoat and flannel drawers, ma'am, if you wish to keep her alive. But my advice is, kill the poor creature at once."

Miss Betsy Barker dried her eyes, and thanked the Captain heartily; she set to work, and by and by all the town turned out to see the Alderney meekly going to her pasture, clad in dark grey flannel. I have watched her myself many a time. Do you ever see cows dressed in grey flannel in London?

Captain Brown had taken a small house on the outskirts of the town, where he lived with his two daughters. He must have been upwards of sixty at the time of the first visit I paid to Cranford after I had left it as a residence. But he had a wiry, well-trained, elastic figure, a stiff military throw-back of his head, and a springing step, which made him appear much younger than he was. His eldest daughter looked almost as old as

3. A pit filled with lime, for disposing of waste.

himself, and betrayed the fact that his real was more than his apparent age. Miss Brown must have been forty; she had a sickly, pained, careworn expression on her face, and looked as if the gaiety of youth had long faded out of sight. Even when young she must have been plain and hard-featured. Miss Jessie Brown was ten years younger than her sister, and twenty shades prettier. Her face was round and dimpled. Miss Jenkyns once said, in a passion against Captain Brown (the cause of which I will tell you presently), "that she thought it was time for Miss Jessie to leave off her dimples, and not always to be trying to look like a child." It was true there was something childlike in her face; and there will be, I think, till she dies, though she should live to a hundred. Her eyes were large blue wondering eyes, looking straight at you; her nose was unformed and snub, and her lips were red and dewy; she wore her hair, too, in little rows of curls, which heightened this appearance. I do not know whether she was pretty or not; but I liked her face, and so did everybody, and I do not think she could help her dimples. She had something of her father's jauntiness of gait and manner; and any female observer might detect a slight difference in the attire of the two sisters —that of Miss Jessie being about two pounds per annum more expensive than Miss Brown's. Two pounds was a large sum in Captain Brown's annual disbursements.

Such was the impression made upon me by the Brown family when I first saw them all together in Cranford Church. The Captain I had met before—on the occasion of the smoky chimney, which he had cured by some simple alteration in the flue. In church, he held his double eyeglass[4] to his eyes during the Morning Hymn, and then lifted up his head erect and sang out loud and joyfully. He made the responses louder than the clerk—an old man with a piping feeble voice, who, I think, felt aggrieved at the Captain's sonorous bass, and quavered higher and higher in consequence.

On coming out of church, the brisk Captain paid the most gallant attention to his two daughters. He nodded and smiled to his acquaintances, but he shook hands with none until he had helped Miss Brown to unfurl her umbrella, had relieved her of her prayer-book, and had waited patiently till she, with trembling nervous hands, had taken up her gown to walk through the wet roads.

I wondered what the Cranford ladies did with Captain Brown at their parties. We had often rejoiced, in former days, that there was no gentleman to be attended to, and to find conversation for, at the card-parties. We had congratulated ourselves upon the snugness of the evenings; and, in our love for gentility, and distaste of mankind, we had almost persuaded ourselves that to be a man was to be "vulgar"; so that when I

---

4. An early form of spectacles.

found my friend and hostess, Miss Jenkyns, was going to have a party in my honour, and that Captain and the Miss Browns were invited, I wondered much what would be the course of the evening. Card-tables, with green baize tops, were set out by daylight, just as usual; it was the third week in November, so the evenings closed in about four. Candles, and clean packs of cards, were arranged on each table. The fire was made up; the neat maid-servant had received her last directions; and there we stood, dressed in our best, each with a candle-lighter in our hands, ready to dart at the candles as soon as the first knock came. Parties in Cranford were solemn festivities, making the ladies feel gravely elated as they sat together in their best dresses. As soon as three had arrived, we sat down to "Preference,"[5] I being the unlucky fourth. The next four comers were put down immediately to another table; and presently the tea-trays, which I had seen set out in the store-room as I passed in the morning, were placed each on the middle of a card-table. The china was delicate egg-shell; the old-fashioned silver glittered with polishing; but the eatables were of the slightest description. While the trays were yet on the tables, Captain and the Miss Browns came in: and I could see that, somehow or other, the Captain was a favourite with all the ladies present. Ruffled brows were smoothed, sharp voices lowered at his approach. Miss Brown looked ill, and depressed almost to gloom. Miss Jessie smiled as usual, and seemed nearly as popular as her father. He immediately and quietly assumed the man's place in the room; attended to every one's wants, lessened the pretty maid-servant's labour by waiting on empty cups and bread-and-butterless ladies; and yet did it all in so easy and dignified a manner, and so much as if it were a matter of course for the strong to attend to the weak, that he was a true man throughout. He played for threepenny points with as grave an interest as if they had been pounds; and yet, in all his attention to strangers, he had an eye on his suffering daughter—for suffering I was sure she was, though to many eyes she might only appear to be irritable. Miss Jessie could not play cards: but she talked to the sitters-out, who, before her coming, had been rather inclined to be cross. She sang, too, to an old cracked piano, which I think had been a spinet in its youth. Miss Jessie sang *Jock of Hazeldean* a little out of tune; but we were none of us musical, though Miss Jenkyns beat time, out of time, by way of appearing to be so.

It was very good of Miss Jenkyns to do this; for I had seen that, a little before, she had been a good deal annoyed by Miss Jessie Brown's unguarded admission (apropos of Shetland wool) that she had an uncle, her mother's brother, who was a shopkeeper in Edinburgh. Miss Jenkyns tried to drown this confession by a terrible cough—for the Hon-

5. A card game.

ourable Mrs. Jamieson was sitting at the card-table nearest Miss Jessie, and what would she say or think if she found out she was in the same room with a shopkeeper's niece! But Miss Jessie Brown (who had no tact, as we all agreed the next morning) *would* repeat the information, and assure Miss Pole she could easily get her the identical Shetland wool required, "through my uncle, who has the best assortment of Shetland goods of any one in Edinbro'." It was to take the taste of this out of our mouths, and the sound of this out of our ears, that Miss Jenkyns proposed music; so I say again, it was very good of her to beat time to the song.

When the trays re-appeared with biscuits and wine, punctually at a quarter to nine, there was conversation, comparing of cards, and talking over tricks; but by and by Captain Brown sported a bit of literature.

"Have you seen any numbers of *The Pickwick Papers*?"[6] said he. (They were then publishing in parts.) "Capital thing!"

Now Miss Jenkyns was daughter of a deceased rector of Cranford; and, on the strength of a number of manuscript sermons, and a pretty good library of divinity, considered herself literary, and looked upon any conversation about books as a challenge to her. So she answered and said, "Yes, she had seen them; indeed, she might say she had read them."

"And what do you think of them?" exclaimed Captain Brown. "Aren't they famously good?"

So urged Miss Jenkyns could not but speak.

"I must say, I don't think they are by any means equal to Dr. Johnson.[7] Still, perhaps, the author is young. Let him persevere, and who knows what he may become if he will take the great Doctor for his model?" This was evidently too much for Captain Brown to take placidly; and I saw the words on the tip of his tongue before Miss Jenkyns had finished her sentence.

"It is quite a different sort of thing, my dear madam," he began.

"I am quite aware of that," returned she. "And I make allowances, Captain Brown."

"Just allow me to read you a scene out of this month's number," pleaded he. "I had it only this morning, and I don't think the company can have read it yet."

"As you please," said she, settling herself with an air of resignation. He read the account of the "swarry" which Sam Weller gave at Bath.[8] Some of us laughed heartily. *I* did not dare, because I was staying in the

6. *The Posthumous Papers of the Pickwick Club*, a comic novel by Charles Dickens, originally published in serial form in 1836–37.
7. Samuel Johnson (1709–1784), British poet, critic, and essayist, upholder of high moral stan-

dards in literature.
8. Sam Weller is a comic manservant in *The Pickwick Papers*; Bath is a popular British resort; "swarry" is Weller's anglicization of "soirée," an elegant evening party.

house. Miss Jenkyns sat in patient gravity. When it was ended, she turned to me, and said with mild dignity:

"Fetch me *Rasselas*,[9] my dear, out of the book-room."

When I had brought it to her, she turned to Captain Brown.

"Now allow *me* to read you a scene, and then the present company can judge between your favourite, Mr. Boz,[1] and Dr. Johnson."

She read one of the conversations between Rasselas and Imlac, in a high-pitched, majestic voice: and when she had ended, she said: "I imagine I am now justified in my preference of Dr. Johnson as a writer of fiction." The Captain screwed his lips up, and drummed on the table, but he did not speak. She thought she would give him a finishing blow or two.

"I consider it vulgar, and below the dignity of literature, to publish in numbers."

"How was the *Rambler*[2] published, ma'am?" asked Captain Brown in a low voice, which I think Miss Jenkyns could not have heard.

"Dr. Johnson's style is a model for young beginners. My father recommended it to me when I began to write letters—I have formed my own style upon it; I recommend it to your favourite."

"I should be very sorry for him to exchange his style for any such pompous writing," said Captain Brown.

Miss Jenkyns felt this as a personal affront, in a way of which the Captain had not dreamed. Epistolary writing she and her friends considered as her *forte*. Many a copy of many a letter have I seen written and corrected on the slate, before she "seized the half-hour just previous to post-time to assure" her friends of this or of that; and Dr. Johnson was, as she said, her model in these compositions. She drew herself up with dignity, and only replied to Captain Brown's last remark by saying, with marked emphasis on every syllable: "I prefer Dr. Johnson to Mr. Boz."

It is said—I won't vouch for the fact—that Captain Brown was heard to say, *sotto voce*, "D——n Dr. Johnson!" If he did, he was penitent afterwards, as he showed by going to stand near Miss Jenkyns's armchair, and endeavouring to beguile her into conversation on some more pleasing subject. But she was inexorable. The next day she made the remark I have mentioned about Miss Jessie's dimples.

Chapter II. The Captain

It was impossible to live a month at Cranford and not know the daily habits of each resident; and long before my visit was ended I knew

---

9. Johnson's didactic romance *The History of Rasselas, Prince of Abissinia* (1759), in which characters engage in protracted moral debates.

1. Dickens's pseudonym in his early work.
2. A weekly paper put out by Johnson, consisting chiefly of his essays.

much concerning the whole Brown trio. There was nothing new to be discovered respecting their poverty; for they had spoken simply and openly about that from the very first. They made no mystery of the necessity for their being economical. All that remained to be discovered was the Captain's infinite kindness of heart, and the various modes in which, unconsciously to himself, he manifested it. Some little anecdotes were talked about for some time after they occurred. As we did not read much, and as all the ladies were pretty well suited with servants, there was a dearth of subjects for conversation. We therefore discussed the circumstance of the Captain taking a poor old woman's dinner out of her hands one very slippery Sunday. He had met her returning from the bakehouse as he came from church, and noticed her precarious footing; and, with the grave dignity with which he did everything, he relieved her of her burden, and steered along the street by her side, carrying her baked mutton and potatoes safely home. This was thought very eccentric; and it was rather expected that he would pay a round of calls, on the Monday morning, to explain and apologize to the Cranford sense of propriety: but he did no such thing: and then it was decided that he was ashamed, and was keeping out of sight. In a kindly pity for him, we began to say: "After all, the Sunday morning's occurrence showed great goodness of heart," and it was resolved that he should be comforted on his next appearance amongst us; but, lo! he came down upon us, untouched by any sense of shame, speaking loud and bass as ever, his head thrown back, his wig as jaunty and well-curled as usual, and we were obliged to conclude he had forgotten all about Sunday.

Miss Pole and Miss Jessie Brown had set up a kind of intimacy on the strength of the Shetland wool and the new knitting stitches; so it happened that when I went to visit Miss Pole I saw more of the Browns than I had done while staying with Miss Jenkyns, who had never got over what she called Captain Brown's disparaging remarks upon Dr. Johnson as a writer of light and agreeable fiction. I found that Miss Brown was seriously ill of some lingering, incurable complaint, the pain occasioned by which gave the uneasy expression to her face that I had taken for unmitigated crossness. Cross, too, she was at times, when the nervous irritability occasioned by her disease became past endurance. Miss Jessie bore with her at these times, even more patiently than she did with the bitter self-upbraidings by which they were invariably succeeded. Miss Brown used to accuse herself, not merely of hasty and irritable temper, but also of being the cause why her father and sister were obliged to pinch, in order to allow her the small luxuries which were necessaries in her condition. She would so fain have made sacrifices for them, and have lightened their cares, that the original generosity of her disposition added acerbity to her temper. All this was borne by Miss

Jessie and her father with more than placidity—with absolute tenderness. I forgave Miss Jessie her singing out of tune, and her juvenility of
dress, when I saw her at home. I came to perceive that Captain Brown's
dark Brutus wig[3] and padded coat (alas! too often threadbare) were
remnants of the military smartness of his youth, which he now wore
unconsciously. He was a man of infinite resources, gained in his barrack
experience. As he confessed, no one could black his boots to please him
except himself; but, indeed, he was not above saving the little maid-
servant's labours in every way—knowing, most likely, that his daughter's illness made the place a hard one.

He endeavoured to make peace with Miss Jenkyns soon after the
memorable dispute I have named, by a present of a wooden fire-shovel
(his own making), having heard her say how much the grating of an
iron one annoyed her. She received the present with cool gratitude, and
thanked him formally. When he was gone, she bade me put it away in
the lumber-room; feeling, probably, that no present from a man who
preferred Mr. Boz to Dr. Johnson could be less jarring than an iron
fire-shovel.

Such was the state of things when I left Cranford and went to
Drumble. I had, however, several correspondents, who kept me *au fait*[4]
as to the proceedings of the dear little town. There was Miss Pole, who
was becoming as much absorbed in crochet as she had been once in
knitting, and the burden of whose letter was something like: "But don't
you forget the white worsted at Flint's" of the old song; for at the end of
every sentence of news came a fresh direction as to some crochet commission which I was to execute for her. Miss Matilda Jenkyns (who did
not mind being called Miss Matty, when Miss Jenkyns was not by)
wrote nice, kind, rambling letters, now and then venturing into an
opinion of her own; but suddenly pulling herself up, and either begging
me not to name what she had said, as Deborah thought differently, and
she knew, or else putting in a postscript to the effect that, since writing
the above, she had been talking over the subject with Deborah, and was
quite convinced that, etc.—(here probably followed a recantation of
every opinion she had given in the letter). Then came Miss Jenkyns—
Debōrah as she liked Miss Matty to call her, her father having once said
that the Hebrew name ought to be so pronounced. I secretly think she
took the Hebrew prophetess for a model in character; and, indeed, she
was not unlike the stern prophetess in some ways, making allowance, of
course, for modern customs and difference in dress. Miss Jenkyns wore
a cravat, and a little bonnet like a jockey-cap, and altogether had the appearance of a strong-minded woman; although she would have de-

3. A wig arranged in the pseudo-Roman style
and favored during the Regency period; Marcus
Junius Brutus (85? B.C.–42 B.C.) was a Roman
general.
4. Informed; literally, "at the fact."

spised the modern idea of women being equal to men. Equal, indeed! she knew they were superior. But to return to her letters. Everything in them was stately and grand like herself. I have been looking them over (dear Miss Jenkyns, how I honoured her!) and I will give an extract, more especially because it relates to our friend Captain Brown:

"The honourable Mrs. Jamieson has only just quitted me; and, in the course of conversation, she communicated to me the intelligence that she had yesterday received a call from her revered husband's quondam[5] friend, Lord Mauleverer. You will not easily conjecture what brought his lordship within the precincts of our little town. It was to see Captain Brown, with whom, it appears, his lordship was acquainted in the plumed wars,[6] and who had the privilege of averting destruction from his lordship's head when some great peril was impending over it, off the misnomered Cape of Good Hope. You know our friend the Honourable Mrs. Jamieson's deficiency in the spirit of innocent curiosity, and you will therefore not be so much surprised when I tell you she was quite unable to disclose to me the exact nature of the peril in question. I was anxious, I confess, to ascertain in what manner Captain Brown, with his limited establishment, could receive so distinguished a guest; and I discovered that his lordship retired to rest, and, let us hope, to re-freshing slumbers, at the Angel Hotel; but shared the Brunonian[7] meals during the two days that he honoured Cranford with his august pres-ence. Mrs. Johnson, our civil butcher's wife, informs me that Miss Jes-sie purchased a leg of lamb; but, besides this, I can hear of no preparation whatever to give a suitable reception to so distinguished a visitor. Perhaps they entertained him with the feast of reason and the flow of soul; and to us, who are acquainted with Captain Brown's sad want[8] of relish for the pure wells of English undefiled, it may be matter for congratulation that he has had the opportunity of improving his taste by holding converse with an elegant and refined member of the British aristocracy. But from some mundane failings who is altogether free?"

Miss Pole and Miss Matty wrote to me by the same post. Such a piece of news as Lord Mauleverer's visit was not to be lost on the Cranford letter-writers: they made the most of it. Miss Matty humbly apologized for writing at the same time as her sister, who was so much more capable than she to describe the honour done to Cranford; but in spite of a little bad spelling, Miss Matty's account gave me the best idea of the commotion occasioned by his lordship's visit, after it had oc-curred; for, except the people at the "Angel," the Browns, Mrs. Jamie-son, and a little lad his lordship had sworn at for driving a dirty hoop

---

5. Former.   7. Latinate adjectival form of "Brown."
6. Wars against France under Napoleon.   8. Lack.

against the aristocratic legs, I could not hear of any one with whom his lordship had held conversation.

My next visit to Cranford was in the summer. There had been neither births, deaths, nor marriages since I was there last. Everybody lived in the same house, and wore pretty nearly the same well-preserved, old-fashioned clothes. The greatest event was, that Miss Jenkyns had purchased a new carpet for the drawing-room. Oh, the busy work Miss Matty and I had in chasing the sunbeams, as they fell in an afternoon right down on this carpet through the blindless window! We spread newspapers over the places and sat down to our book or our work; and, lo! in a quarter of an hour the sun had moved, and was blazing away on a fresh spot; and down again we went on our knees to alter the position of the newspapers. We were very busy, too, one whole morning, before Miss Jenkyns gave her party, in following her directions, and in cutting out and stitching together pieces of newspaper so as to form little paths to every chair set for the expected visitors, lest their shoes might dirty or defile the purity of the carpet. Do you make paper paths for every guest to walk upon in London?

Captain Brown and Miss Jenkyns were not very cordial to each other. The literary dispute, of which I had seen the beginning, was a "raw,"[9] the slightest touch on which made them wince. It was the only difference of opinion they had ever had; but that difference was enough. Miss Jenkyns could not refrain from talking *at* Captain Brown; and, though he did not reply, he drummed with his fingers, which action she felt and resented as very disparaging to Dr. Johnson. He was rather ostentatious in his preference of the writings of Mr. Boz; would walk through the streets so absorbed in them that he all but ran against Miss Jenkyns; and though his apologies were earnest and sincere, and though he did not, in fact, do more than startle her and himself, she owned to me she had rather he had knocked her down, if he had only been reading a higher style of literature. The poor, brave Captain! he looked older, and more worn, and his clothes were very threadbare. But he seemed as bright and cheerful as ever, unless he was asked about his daughter's health.

"She suffers a great deal, and she must suffer more: we do what we can to alleviate her pain—God's will be done!" He took off his hat at these last words. I found, from Miss Matty, that everything had been done, in fact. A medical man, of high repute in that country neighbourhood, had been sent for, and every injunction he had given was attended to, regardless of expense. Miss Matty was sure they denied themselves many things in order to make the invalid comfortable; but they never spoke about it; and as for Miss Jessie!—"I really think she's

9. Sore spot.

an angel," said poor Miss Matty, quite overcome. "To see her way of bearing with Miss Brown's crossness, and the bright face she puts on after she's been sitting up a whole night and scolded above half of it, is quite beautiful. Yet she looks as neat and as ready to welcome the Captain at breakfast-time as if she had been asleep in the Queen's bed all night. My dear! you could never laugh at her prim little curls or her pink bows again if you saw her as I have done." I could only feel very penitent, and greet Miss Jessie with double respect when I met her next. She looked faded and pinched; and her lips began to quiver, as if she was very weak, when she spoke of her sister. But she brightened, and sent back the tears that were glittering in her pretty eyes, as she said:

"But, to be sure, what a town Cranford is for kindness! I don't suppose any one has a better dinner than usual cooked but the best part of all comes in a little covered basin for my sister. The poor people will leave their earliest vegetables at our door for her. They speak short and gruff, as if they were ashamed of it: but I am sure it often goes to my heart to see their thoughtfulness." The tears now came back and overflowed; but after a minute or two she began to scold herself, and ended by going away the same cheerful Miss Jessie as ever.

"But why does not this Lord Mauleverer do something for the man who saved his life?" said I.

"Why, you see, unless Captain Brown has some reason for it, he never speaks about being poor; and he walked along by his lordship looking as happy and cheerful as a prince; and as they never called attention to their dinners by apologies, and as Miss Brown was better that day, and all seemed bright, I dare say his lordship never knew how much care there was in the background. He did send game in the winter pretty often, but now he is gone abroad."

I had often occasion to notice the use that was made of fragments and small opportunities in Cranford; the rose-leaves that were gathered ere they fell to make into a pot-pourri for someone who had no garden; the little bundles of lavender flowers sent to strew the drawers of some town-dweller, or to burn in the chamber of some invalid. Things that many would despise, and actions which it seemed scarcely worth while to perform, were all attended to in Cranford. Miss Jenkyns stuck an apple full of cloves, to be heated and smell pleasantly in Miss Brown's room; and as she put in each clove she uttered a Johnsonian sentence. Indeed, she never could think of the Browns without talking Johnson; and, as they were seldom absent from her thoughts just then, I heard many a rolling, three-piled sentence.[1]

Captain Brown called one day to thank Miss Jenkyns for many little kindnesses, which I did not know until then that she had rendered. He

---

1. Johnson was famous for his long, periodic sentences; "three-piled" refers to the number of clauses.

had suddenly become like an old man; his deep bass voice had a quavering in it, his eyes looked dim, and the lines on his face were deep. He did not—could not—speak cheerfully of his daughter's state, but he talked with manly, pious resignation, and not much. Twice over he said: "What Jessie has been to us, God only knows!" and after the second time, he got up hastily, shook hands all round without speaking, and left the room.

That afternoon we perceived little groups in the street, all listening with faces aghast to some tale or other. Miss Jenkyns wondered what could be the matter for some time before she took the undignified step of sending Jenny out to inquire.

Jenny came back with a white face of terror. "Oh, ma'am! Oh, Miss Jenkyns, ma'am! Captain Brown is killed by them nasty cruel railroads!" and she burst into tears. She, along with many others, had experienced the poor Captain's kindness.

"How?—where—where? Good God! Jenny, don't waste time in crying, but tell us something." Miss Matty rushed out into the street at once, and collared the man who was telling the tale.

"Come in—come to my sister at once, Miss Jenkyns, the rector's daughter. Oh, man, man! say it is not true," she cried, as she brought the affrighted carter, sleeking down his hair, into the drawing-room, where he stood with his wet boots on the new carpet, and no one regarded it.

"Please, mum, it is true. I seed it myself," and he shuddered at the recollection. "The Captain was a-reading some new book as he was deep in, a-waiting for the down train; and there was a little lass as wanted to come to its mammy, and gave its sister the slip, and came toddling across the line. And he looked up sudden, at the sound of the train coming, and seed the child, and he darted on the line and cotched it up, and his foot slipped, and the train came over him in no time. O Lord, Lord! Mum, it's quite true, and they've come over to tell his daughters. The child's safe, though, with only a bang on its shoulder as he threw it to its mammy. Poor Captain would be glad of that, mum, wouldn't he? God bless him!" The great rough carter puckered up his manly face, and turned away to hide his tears. I turned to Miss Jenkyns. She looked very ill, as if she were going to faint, and signed to me to open the window.

"Matilda, bring me my bonnet. I must go to those girls. God pardon me, if ever I have spoken contemptuously to the Captain!"

Miss Jenkyns arrayed herself to go out, telling Miss Matilda to give the man a glass of wine. While she was away, Miss Matty and I huddled over the fire, talking in a low and awestruck voice. I know we cried quietly all the time.

Miss Jenkyns came home in a silent mood, and we durst not ask her many questions. She told us that Miss Jessie had fainted, and that she and Miss Pole had had some difficulty in bringing her round; but that, as soon as she recovered, she begged one of them to go and sit with her sister.

"Mr. Hoggins says she cannot live many days, and she shall be spared this shock," said Miss Jessie, shivering with feelings to which she dared not give way.

"But how can you manage, my dear?" asked Miss Jenkyns; "you cannot bear up, she must see your tears."

"God will help me—I will not give way—she was asleep when the news came; she may be asleep yet. She would be so utterly miserable, not merely at my father's death, but to think of what would become of me; she is so good to me." She looked up earnestly in their faces with her soft true eyes, and Miss Pole told Miss Jenkyns afterwards she could hardly bear it, knowing, as she did, how Miss Brown treated her sister.

However, it was settled according to Miss Jessie's wish. Miss Brown was to be told her father had been summoned to take a short journey on railway business. They had managed it in some way—Miss Jenkyns could not exactly say how. Miss Pole was to stop with Miss Jessie. Mrs. Jamieson had sent to inquire. And this was all we heard that night; and a sorrowful night it was. The next day a full account of the fatal accident was in the county paper which Miss Jenkyns took in. Her eyes were very weak, she said, and she asked me to read it. When I came to the "gallant gentleman was deeply engaged in the perusal of a number of *Pickwick*, which he had just received," Miss Jenkyns shook her head long and solemnly, and then sighed out: "Poor, dear, infatuated man!"

The corpse was to be taken from the station to the parish church, there to be interred. Miss Jessie had set her heart on following it to the grave; and no dissuasives could alter her resolve. Her restraint upon herself made her almost obstinate; she resisted all Miss Pole's entreaties and Miss Jenkyns's advice. At last Miss Jenkyns gave up the point; and after a silence, which I feared portended some deep displeasure against Miss Jessie, Miss Jenkyns said she should accompany the latter to the funeral.

"It is not fit for you to go alone. It would be against both propriety and humanity were I to allow it."

Miss Jessie seemed as if she did not half like this arrangement; but her obstinacy, if she had any, had been exhausted in her determination to go to the interment. She longed, poor thing, I have no doubt, to cry alone over the grave of the dear father to whom she had been all in all, and to give way, for one little half-hour, uninterrupted by sympathy and unobserved by friendship. But it was not to be. That afternoon Miss Jenkyns sent out for a yard of black crape, and employed herself busily in trimming the little black silk bonnet I have spoken about. When it was finished she put it on, and looked at us for approbation—admiration she despised. I was full of sorrow, but, by one of those whimsical thoughts which come unbidden into our heads, in times of deepest grief, I no sooner saw the bonnet than I was reminded of a helmet; and in that hybrid bonnet, half helmet, half jockey-cap, did Miss Jenkyns attend Captain Brown's funeral, and, I believe, supported Miss Jessie with a tender, indulgent firmness which was invaluable, allowing her to weep her passionate fill before they left.

Miss Pole, Miss Matty, and I, meanwhile attended to Miss Brown: and hard work we found it to relieve her querulous and never-ending complaints. But if we were so weary and dispirited, what must Miss Jessie have been! Yet she came back almost calm, as if she had gained a new strength. She put off her mourning dress, and came in, looking pale and gentle, thanking us each with a soft long pressure of the hand. She could even smile—a faint, sweet, wintry smile—as if to reassure us of her power to endure; but her look made our eyes fill suddenly with tears, more than if she had cried outright.

It was settled that Miss Pole was to remain with her all the watching livelong night; and that Miss Matty and I were to return in the morning to relieve them, and give Miss Jessie the opportunity for a few hours of sleep. But when the morning came, Miss Jenkyns appeared at the breakfast-table, equipped in her helmet-bonnet, and ordered Miss Matty to stay at home, as she meant to go and help to nurse. She was evidently in a state of great friendly excitement, which she showed by eating her breakfast standing, and scolding the household all round.

No nursing—no energetic strong-minded woman could help Miss Brown now. There was that in the room as we entered which was stronger than us all, and made us shrink into solemn awestruck helplessness. Miss Brown was dying. We hardly knew her voice, it was so devoid of the complaining tone we had always associated with it. Miss Jessie told me afterwards that it, and her face too, were just what they had been formerly, when her mother's death left her the young anxious head of the family, of whom only Miss Jessie survived.

She was conscious of her sister's presence, though not, I think, of ours. We stood a little behind the curtain: Miss Jessie knelt with her face near her sister's, in order to catch the last soft awful whispers.

"Oh, Jessie! Jessie! How selfish I have been! God forgive me for letting you sacrifice yourself for me as you did! I have so loved you—and yet, I have thought only of myself. God forgive me!"

"Hush, love! hush!" said Miss Jessie, sobbing.

"And my father, my dear, dear father! I will not complain now, if God will give me strength to be patient. But, oh, Jessie! tell my father how I longed and yearned to see him at last, and to ask his forgiveness. He can never know now how I loved him—oh! if I might but tell him, before I die! What a life of sorrow his has been, and I have done so little to cheer him!"

A light came into Miss Jessie's face. "Would it comfort you, dearest, to think that he does know?—would it comfort you, love, to know that his cares, his sorrows"—Her voice quivered, but she steadied it into calmness—"Mary! he has gone before you to the place where the weary are at rest. He knows now how you loved him."

A strange look, which was not distress, came over Miss Brown's face. She did not speak for some time, but then we saw her lips form the words, rather than heard the sound—"Father, mother, Harry, Archy" —then, as if it were a new idea throwing a filmy shadow over her dark-ened mind—"But you will be alone, Jessie!"

Miss Jessie had been feeling this all during the silence, I think; for the tears rolled down her cheeks like rain, at these words, and she could not answer at first. Then she put her hands together tight, and lifted them up, and said—but not to us—"Though He slay me, yet will I trust in Him."[2]

In a few moments more Miss Brown lay calm and still—never to sorrow or murmur more.

After this second funeral, Miss Jenkyns insisted that Miss Jessie should come to stay with her rather than go back to the desolate house, which, in fact, we learned from Miss Jessie, must now be given up, as she had not wherewithal to maintain it. She had something above twenty pounds a year, besides the interest of the money for which the furniture would sell; but she could not live upon that: and so we talked over her qualifications for earning money.

"I can sew neatly," said she, "and I like nursing. I think, too, I could manage a house, if any one would try me as housekeeper; or I would go into a shop as saleswoman, if they would have patience with me at first."

Miss Jenkyns declared, in an angry voice, that she should do no such thing; and talked to herself about "some people having no idea of their rank as a captain's daughter," nearly an hour afterwards, when she brought Miss Jessie up a basin of delicately-made arrowroot,[3] and stood over her like a dragoon[4] until the last spoonful was finished: then she disappeared. Miss Jessie began to tell me some more of the plans which had suggested themselves to her, and insensibly fell into talking of the days that were past and gone, and interested me so much I neither knew nor heeded how time passed. We were both startled when Miss Jenkyns reappeared, and caught us crying. I was afraid lest she would be dis-

2. Job 13:15.   4. A mounted infantryman.
3. A kind of starchy pudding.

pleased, as she often said that crying hindered digestion, and I knew she wanted Miss Jessie to get strong; but, instead, she looked queer and excited, and fidgeted round us without saying anything. At last she spoke.

"I have been so much startled—no, I've not been at all startled—don't mind me, my dear Miss Jessie—I've been very much surprised—in fact, I've had a caller, whom you knew once, my dear Miss Jessie"—

Miss Jessie went very white, then flushed scarlet, and looked eagerly at Miss Jenkyns.

"A gentleman, my dear, who wants to know if you would see him."

"Is it?—it is not"—stammered out Miss Jessie—and got no farther.

"This is his card," said Miss Jenkyns, giving it to Miss Jessie; and while her head was bent over it, Miss Jenkyns went through a series of winks and odd faces to me, and formed her lips into a long sentence, of which, of course, I could not understand a word.

"May he come up?" asked Miss Jenkyns at last.

"Oh, yes! certainly!" said Miss Jessie, as much as to say, this is your house, you may show any visitor where you like. She took up some knitting of Miss Matty's and began to be very busy, though I could see how she trembled all over.

Miss Jenkyns rang the bell, and told the servant who answered it to show Major Gordon upstairs; and, presently, in walked a tall, fine, frank-looking man of forty or upwards. He shook hands with Miss Jessie; but he could not see her eyes, she kept them so fixed on the ground. Miss Jenkyns asked me if I would come and help her to tie up the preserves in the store-room; and though Miss Jessie plucked at my gown, and even looked up at me with begging eye, I durst not refuse to go where Miss Jenkyns asked. Instead of tying up preserves in the store-room, however, we went to talk in the dining-room; and there Miss Jenkyns told me what Major Gordon had told her; how he had served in the same regiment with Captain Brown, and had become acquainted with Miss Jessie, then a sweet-looking, blooming girl of eighteen; how the acquaintance had grown into love on his part, though it had been some years before he had spoken; how, on becoming possessed, through the will of an uncle, of a good estate in Scotland, he had offered and been refused, though with so much agitation and evident distress that he was sure she was not indifferent to him; and how he had discovered that the obstacle was the fell disease which was, even then, too surely threatening her sister. She had mentioned that the surgeons foretold intense suffering; and there was no one but herself to nurse her poor Mary, or cheer and comfort her father during the time of illness. They had had long discussions; and on her refusal to pledge herself to him as his wife when all should be over, he had grown angry, and broken off entirely, and gone abroad, believing that she was a cold-hearted person whom he would do well to forget. He had been travelling in the East, and was on his return home when, at Rome, he saw the account of Captain Brown's death in *Galignani*.[5]

Just then Miss Matty, who had been out all the morning, and had only lately returned to the house, burst in with a face of dismay and outraged propriety.

"Oh, goodness me!" she said. "Deborah, there's a gentleman sitting in the drawing-room with his arm round Miss Jessie's waist!" Miss Matty's eyes looked large with terror.

Miss Jenkyns snubbed her down in an instant.

"The most proper place in the world for his arm to be in. Go away, Matilda, and mind your own business." This from her sister, who had hitherto been a model of feminine decorum, was a blow for poor Miss Matty, and with a double shock she left the room.

The last time I ever saw poor Miss Jenkyns was many years after this. Mrs. Gordon had kept up a warm and affectionate intercourse with all at Cranford. Miss Jenkyns, Miss Matty, and Miss Pole had all been to visit her, and returned with wonderful accounts of her house, her husband, her dress, and her looks. For, with happiness, something of her early bloom returned; she had been a year or two younger than we had taken her for. Her eyes were always lovely, and, as Mrs. Gordon, her dimples were not out of place. At the time to which I have referred, when I last saw Miss Jenkyns, that lady was old and feeble, and had lost something of her strong mind. Little Flora Gordon was staying with the Misses Jenkyns, and when I came in she was reading aloud to Miss Jenkyns, who lay feeble and changed on the sofa. Flora put down the *Rambler* when I came in.

"Ah!" said Miss Jenkyns, "you find me changed, my dear. I can't see as I used to do. If Flora were not here to read to me, I hardly know how I should get through the day. Did you ever read the *Rambler*? It's a wonderful book—wonderful! and the most improving reading for Flora" (which I dare say it would have been, if she could have read half the words without spelling, and could have understood the meaning of a third), "better than that strange old book, with the queer name, poor Captain Brown was killed for reading—that book by Mr. Boz, you know—Old Poz; when I was a girl—but that's a long time ago—I acted Lucy in Old Poz." She babbled on long enough for Flora to get a good long spell at the *Christmas Carol*,[6] which Miss Matty had left on the table.

1851, 1853

5. A Roman newspaper.
6. Charles Dickens's *A Christmas Carol* (1843).

HARRIET BEECHER STOWE
1811–1896

Harriet Beecher Stowe is still one of the most popular of the women novelists who published best sellers in America during the mid-nineteenth century. 350,000 copies of *Uncle Tom's Cabin; or, Life among the Lowly* (1851–1852) were purchased during the first year of its printing, bringing its author ten thousand dollars in just the first three months. While the book, which sold more than a million pirated copies in England, earned Stowe friends like George Eliot and Charles Dickens, within three years it had given rise to some thirty anti–*Uncle Tom* novels by Southern sympathizers. As a protest against the Fugitive Slave Act, which denied runaway slaves sanctuary and made it criminal to assist them, Stowe's novel preached the evils of slavery to a nation shown to be in need of Christian humility. By now *Uncle Tom's Cabin* has transcended both the partisanship of Northern abolitionists, who used it for propaganda purposes during the Civil War, and the more recent critical reaction of Afro-American scholars, who have objected to the docility of "Uncle Tomism." Yet its controversial reception may have been responsible for obscuring the fact that Stowe published more than twenty-five other novels, essays, and stories.

To what familial influences can Stowe's prolific career be attributed? First, most biographers agree, Stowe's father, the eminent Congregational minister Lyman Beecher, was instrumental in instilling a sense of mission in his children: all nine of them were educated, according to his Calvinist values, for a life of public service as ministers or mothers, depending on their gender. Stowe received a theological education from her father, and all her life she struggled with despair over her inability to meet his spiritual standards, even as she sought to emulate the conversion-work she saw him effecting in his church in her childhood hometown of Litchfield, Connecticut, and in the Lane Theological Seminary in Cincinnati, Ohio, where the family moved in 1832 when he became president of Lane. Stowe's mother, Roxana (Foote) Beecher, exerted her influence more as an absence than a presence: dead by the time her seventh child reached the age of four, she was remembered and cherished as a pious, devoted mother. Stowe was also imbued with a sense of the moral power of women by her older sister, Catherine Beecher, who took over their mother's household duties in 1815. After Harriet graduated from Miss Sarah Pierce's school in Litchfield, she attended the female seminary established by Catherine in Hartford. There she learned the lesson Catherine Beecher taught throughout her prominent career, the doctrine that women in their traditional roles could transform and redeem American culture through their exemplary Christian benevolence.

If the Beecher inheritance sustained and shaped the ethical impulse informing Stowe's subsequent fiction, her marriage to Calvin Ellis Stowe in 1836 provided her with a financial impetus for writing. This professor of biblical literature at Lane shared her New England background, as well as her propensity for nervous depression and religious compunction. Never well paid, by 1844 he handed over the management of the family's finances to his wife, who discovered, to her relief, that she could lighten the load of what she considered "domestic slavery" by hiring a helper with the money she gained from publishing stories. In 1850, after six pregnancies and the death in infancy of her sixth baby, and with a seventh child on the way, Stowe moved with her husband to Maine, where he taught at Bowdoin College and where she experienced what she later called her "vision" of the death scene of Uncle Tom.

Her reading of abolitionist literature; the letters of her brother Charles, which recorded the voice of a sadistic Louisiana overseer he knew; the sermons of her other two brothers, Edward and Henry Ward, who denounced the Fugitive Slave Act from their pulpits; as well as the threat to one of her servants, who was claimed as a slave and managed to escape through the help of the family— all of these contributed to Stowe's growing reaction against slavery, as had the death of her six-month-old baby, which taught her, she later explained, "what a poor slave mother may feel when her child is torn from her." If Stowe's pattern of imagery in *Uncle Tom's Cabin* is any index, she was haunted by a feeling of maternal loss—the loss of her infant and the earlier death of her mother—that she brilliantly described as the byproduct of slavery. The faith in Christian humility she preached was associated with the spiritual agency of women, for her portraits of the submissive Tom, the angelic little Eva, and the maternal Quaker Rachel dramatized her attack on a slave system that divided mother and child. When *Uncle Tom's Cabin* was met by a storm of protests, she answered with *A Key to Uncle Tom's Cabin* (1853), documenting the horror of slavery she had fictionalized so effectively. After a triumphal European tour, recorded in *Sunny Memories of Foreign Lands* (1854), she wrote *Dread* (1856), a novel which depicts the disabling ethical effects of slavery on the white race.

Throughout her life, Stowe continued to support her family with writings that contributed to the formation of a national American literature. Turning to her native New England, she fashioned a regionalist perspective marked by respect for women's domestic sphere, a perspective that would later characterize the stories of Sarah Orne Jewett and Mary Wilkins Freeman. *The Minister's Wooing* (1859), *The Pearl of Orr's Island* (1862), *Oldtown Folks* (1869), and *Poganuc People* (1878) contain her finest portraits of New Englanders, dramatized through dialect, set in a somber physical landscape, and infused with a sometimes severe Calvinist spiritual atmosphere. *The Minister's Housekeeper*, which is reprinted here from *Sam Lawson's Oldtown Fireside Stories* (1872), is narrated by a lazy but lively village storyteller Stowe had created in *Oldtown Folks* for comic relief. In the Oldtown tales, as in her children's stories, housekeeping manuals, and journalism, she achieved remarkable popularity and diversity.

Stowe had purchased an orange plantation in Mandarin, Florida, to escape Hartford winters after Calvin Stowe retired, and to provide a rehabilitating occupation for her alcoholic son, Frederick William. She continued to support this son, her husband, and two unmarried daughters until her husband died in 1886. Suffering the signs of senility and depression, she spent the last ten years of her life in Hartford. Seven years after her death, the Stowe cabinet in the library of the Woman's Building at the World's Columbian Exposition in Chicago contained a complete set of her works in twenty volumes, forty-two translations of *Uncle Tom's Cabin*, and a bust of the author done by the successful Boston sculptor Anne Whitney. The display was a fitting tribute to Stowe's achievement.

The Minister's Housekeeper[1]

SCENE.—*The shady side of a blueberry-pasture.—Sam Lawson with the boys, picking blueberries.—Sam, loq.*

"Wal, you see, boys, 't was just here,—Parson Carryl's wife she died along in the forepart o' March: my cousin Huldy she undertook to keep house for him. The way on 't was, that Huldy she went to take care o' Mis' Carryl in the fust on 't, when she fust took sick. Huldy was a tailoress by trade; but then she was one o' these 'ere facultized[2] persons that has a gift for most anything, and that was how Mis' Carryl come to set sech store by her, that, when she was sick, nothin' would do for her but she must have Huldy round all the time: and the minister he said he'd make it good to her all the same, and she should n't lose nothin' by it. And so Huldy she stayed with Mis' Carryl full three months afore she died, and got to seein' to everything pretty much round the place.

"Wal, arter Mis' Carryl died, Parson Carryl he'd got so kind o' used to hevin' on her round, takin' care o' things, that he wanted her to stay along a spell; and so Huldy she stayed along a spell, and poured out his tea, and mended his close, and made pies and cakes, and cooked and washed and ironed, and kep' everything as neat as a pin. Huldy was a drefful chipper sort o' gal; and work sort o' rolled off from her like water off a duck's back. There wa'n't no gal in Sherburne that could put sich a sight o' work through as Huldy; and yet, Sunday mornin', she always come out in the singers' seat[3] like one o' these 'ere June roses, lookin' so fresh and smilin', and her voice was jest as clear and sweet as a meadow lark's—Lordy massy! I 'member how she used to sing some o' them 'ere places where the treble and counter used to go together:[4] her voice kind o' trembled a little, and it sort o' went through and through a feller! tuck him right where he lived!"

Here Sam leaned contemplatively back with his head in a clump of sweet-fern, and refreshed himself with a chew of young wintergreen. "This 'ere young wintergreen, boys, is jest like a feller's thoughts o' things that happened when he was young: it comes up jest so fresh and tender every year, the longest time you hev to live; and you can't help

1. This is part of a series of stories narrated by Sam Lawson, the village loafer in a New England town; "*loq.*": *loquitor*; i.e., Sam Speaker.
2. A hybrid word, apparently of Sam's invention, meaning "multi-talented."
3. The pew in a church where the choir sits.
4. High and low female parts in a choral work.

chawin' on 't though 't is sort o' stingin'. I don't never get over likin'
young wintergreen."

"But about Huldah, Sam?"

"Oh yes! about Huldy. Lordy massy! when a feller is Indianin'
round,[5] there 'ere pleasant summer days, a feller's thoughts gits like a
flock o' young partridges: they's up and down and everywhere; 'cause
one place is jest about as good as another, when they's all so kind o'
comfortable and nice. Wal, about Huldy,—as I was a-sayin'. She was
jest as handsome a gal to look at as a feller could have; and I think a nice,
well-behaved young gal in the singers' seat of a Sunday is a means o'
grace: it's sort o' drawin' to the unregenerate, you know. Why, boys, in
them days, I've walked ten miles over to Sherburne of a Sunday mornin', jest to play the bass-viol in the same singers' seat with Huldy. She
was very much respected, Huldy was; and, when she went out to tai-
lorin',[6] she was allers bespoke six months ahead, and sent for in waggins
up and down for ten miles round; for the young fellers was allers
'mazin' anxious to be sent after Huldy, and was quite free to offer to go
for her. Wal, after Mis' Carryl died, Huldy got to be sort o' housekeeper
at the minister's, and saw to everything, and did everything: so that
there wa'n't a pin out o' the way.

"But you know how 't is in parishes: there allers is women that thinks
the minister's affairs belongs to them, and they ought to have the rulin'
and guidin' of 'em; and, if a minister's wife dies, there's folks that allers
has their eyes open on providences,[7]—lookin' out who's to be the next
one.

"Now, there was Mis' Amaziah Pipperidge, a widder with snappin'
black eyes, and a hook nose,—kind o' like a hawk; and she was one o'
them up-and-down commandin' sort o' women, that feel that they have
a call to be seein' to everything that goes on in the parish, and 'specially
to the minister.

"Folks did say that Mis' Pipperidge sort o' sot her eye on the Parson
for herself: wal, now that 'ere might 'a' been, or it might not. Some folks
thought it was a very suitable connection. You see, she hed a good
property of her own, right nigh to the minister's lot, and was allers kind
o' active and busy; so, takin' one thing with another, I should n't
wonder if Mis' Pipperidge should a thought that Providence p'inted
that way. At any rate, she went up to Deakin[8] Blodgett's wife, and they
two sort o' put their heads together a-mournin' and condolin' about the
way things was likely to go on at the minister's now Mis' Carryl was
dead. Ye see, the parson's wife, she was one of them women who hed
their eyes everywhere and on everything. She was a little thin woman,

5. Loafing.
6. Hired herself out as a seamstress; "bespoke":
hired or engaged beforehand.

7. Opportunities, presumed to be "provided"
by God.
8. Deacon, a church administrator.

but tough as Inger rubber,[9] and smart as a steel trap; and there wa'n't a hen laid an egg, or cackled, but Mis' Carryl was right there to see about it; and she hed the garden made in the spring, and the medders mowed in summer, and the cider made, and the corn husked, and the apples got in the fall; and the doctor, he hed n't nothin' to do but jest sit stock-still a-meditatin' on Jerusalem and Jericho and them things that ministers think about. But Lordy massy! he did n't know nothin' about where anything he eat or drunk or wore come from or went to: his wife jest led him round in temporal things[1] and took care on him like a baby.

"Wal, to be sure, Mis' Carryl looked up to him in spirituals, and thought all the world on him; for there wa'n't a smarter minister nowhere round. Why, when he preached on decrees and election,[2] they used to come clear over from South Parish, and West Sherburne, and Oldtown to hear him; and there was sich a row o' waggins tied along by the meetin'-house that the stables was all full, and all the hitchin'-posts was full clean up to the tavern, so that folks said the doctor made the town look like a gineral trainin' day a Sunday.[3]

"He was gret on texts, the doctor was. When he hed a p'int to prove, he'd jest go through the Bible, and drive all the texts ahead o' him like a flock o' sheep; and then, if there was a text that seemed agin him, why, he'd come out with his Greek and Hebrew, and kind o' chase it round a spell, jest as ye see a feller chase a contrary bell-wether,[4] and make him jump the fence arter the rest. I tell you, there wa'n't no text in the Bible that could stand agin the doctor when his blood was up. The year arter the doctor was app'inted to preach the 'lection sermon in Boston, he made such a figger that the Brattle Street Church sent a committee right down to see if they could n't get him to Boston; and then the Sherburne folks, they up and raised his salary; ye see, there ain't nothin' wakes folks up like somebody else's wantin' what you've got. Wal, that fall they made him a Doctor o' Divinity at Cambridge College,[5] and so they sot more by him than ever. Wal, you see, the doctor, of course he felt kind o' lonesome and afflicted when Mis' Carryl was gone; but railly and truly, Huldy was so up to everything about house, that the doctor did n't miss nothin' in a temporal way. His shirt-bosoms was pleated finer than they ever was, and them ruffles round his wrists was kep' like the driven snow; and there wa'n't a brack[6] in his silk stockin's, and his shoe-buckles was kep' polished up, and his coats brushed, and then there wa'n't no bread and biscuit like Huldy's; and her butter was like solid lumps o' gold; and there were n't no pies to equal hers; and so

---

9. India rubber.
1. Worldly matters, as opposed to the eternal.
2. Divine choice in Puritan theology, the belief in predestination.
3. Day for training or parade by a volunteer mil-

itary company.
4. Leading sheep of a flock.
5. Harvard University in Cambridge, Massachusetts.
6. Flaw.

the doctor never felt the loss o' Mis' Carryl at table. Then there was Huldy allers oppisite to him, with her blue eyes and her cheeks like two fresh peaches. She was kind o' pleasant to look at; and the more the doctor looked at her the better he liked her; and so things seemed to be goin' on quite quiet and comfortable ef it had n't been that Mis' Pipperidge and Mis' Deakin Blodgett and Mis' Sawin got their heads together a-talkin' about things.

" 'Poor man,' says Mis' Pipperidge, 'what can that child that he's got there do towards takin' the care of all that place? It takes a mature woman,' she says, 'to tread in Mis' Carryl's shoes.'

" 'That it does,' said Mis' Blodgett; 'and, when things once get to runnin' downhill, there ain't no stoppin' on 'em,' says she.

"Then Mis' Sawin she took it up. (Ye see, Mis' Sawin used to go out to dressmakin', and was sort o' jealous, 'cause folks sot more by Huldy than they did by her.) 'Well,' says she, 'Huldy Peters is well enough at her trade. I never denied that, though I do say I never did believe in her way o' makin' buttonholes; and I must say, if 't was the dearest friend I hed, that I thought Huldy tryin' to fit Mis' Kittridge's plum-colored silk was a clear piece o' presumption; the silk was jist sp'iled, so 't wa'n't fit to come into the meetin'-house. I must say, Huldy 's a gal that's always too ventersome about takin' 'sponsibilities she don't know nothin' about.'

" 'Of course she don't,' said Mis' Deakin Blodgett. 'What does she know about all the lookin' and seein' to that there ought to be in guidin' the minister's house. Huldy 's well meanin', and she's good at her work, and good in the singers' seat; but Lordy massy! she hain't got no experience. Parson Carryl ought to have an experienced woman to keep house for him. There 's the spring house-cleanin' and the fall house-cleanin' to be seen to, and the things to be put away from the moths; and then the gettin' ready for the Association[7] and all the ministers' meetin's; and the makin' the soap and the candles, and settin' the hens and turkeys, watchin' the calves, and seein' after the hired men and the garden; and there that 'ere blessed man jist sets there at home as serene, and has nobody round but that 'ere gal, and don't even know how things must be a-runnin' to waste!'

"Wal, the upshot on 't was, they fussed and fuzzled and wuzzled[8] till they'd drinked up all the tea in the teapot; and then they went down and called on the parson, and wuzzled him all up talkin' about this, that, and t'other that wanted lookin' to, and that it was no way to leave everything to a young chit[9] like Huldy, and that he ought to be lookin' about for an experienced woman. The parson he thanked 'em kindly, and said he

7. Regional association of churches.
8. I.e., gossiped and worried.

9. Pert young woman.

believed their motives was good, but he did n't go no further. He did n't ask Mis' Pipperidge to come and stay there and help him, nor nothin' o' that kind; but he said he'd attend to matters himself. The fact was, the parson had got such a likin' for havin' Huldy round, that he couldn't think o' such a thing as swappin' her off for the Widder Pipperidge.

"But he thought to himself, 'Huldy is a good girl; but I ought n't to be a-leavin' everything to her,—it 's too hard on her. I ought to be in-structin' and guidin' and helpin' of her; 'cause 't ain't everybody could be expected to know and do what Mis' Carryl did;' and so at it he went; and Lordy massy! did n't Huldy hev a time on 't when the minister began to come out of his study, and want to tew round and see to things? Huldy, you see, thought all the world of the minister, and she was 'most afraid to laugh; but she told me she could n't, for the life of her, help it when his back was turned, for he wuzzled things up in the most singular way. But Huldy she 'd jest say, 'Yes, sir,' and get him off into his study, and go on her own way.

" 'Huldy,' says the minister one day, 'you ain't experienced out-doors; and, when you want to know anything, you must come to me.'

" 'Yes, sir,' says Huldy.

" 'Now, Huldy,' says the parson, 'you must be sure to save the tur-key-eggs, so that we can have a lot of turkeys for Thanksgiving.'

" 'Yes, sir,' says Huldy; and she opened the pantry-door, and showed him a nice dishful she'd been a-savin' up. Wal, the very next day the parson's hen-turkey was found killed up to old Jim Scrogg's barn. Folks said Scroggs killed it; though Scroggs he stood to it he did n't: at any rate, the Scroggses they made a meal on 't; and Huldy she felt bad about it, 'cause she'd set her heart on raisin' the turkeys; and says she, 'Oh, dear! I don't know what I shall do. I was just ready to set her.'[1]

" 'Do, Huldy?' says the parson. 'Why, there's the other turkey, out there by the door; and a fine bird, too, he is.'

"Sure enough, there was the old tom-turkey a-struttin' and a-sidlin' and a-quitterin', and a-floutin' his tail-feathers in the sun, like a lively young widower, all ready to begin life over ag'in.

" 'But,' says Huldy, 'you know *he* can't set on eggs.'

" 'He can't? I'd like to know why,' says the parson. 'He shall set on eggs, and hatch 'em too.'

" 'O doctor!' says Huldy, all in a tremble; 'cause, you know, she didn't want to contradict the minister, and she was afraid she should laugh,—'I never heard that a tom-turkey would set on eggs.'

" 'Why, they ought to,' said the parson, getting quite 'arnest; 'what else be they good for? you just bring out the eggs, now, and put 'em in the nest, and I 'll make him set on 'em.'

---

1. I.e., allow her to hatch her eggs by sitting on them.

"So Huldy she thought there were n't no way to convince him but to let him try: so she took the eggs out, and fixed 'em all nice in the nest; and then she come back and found old Tom a-skirmishin' with the parson pretty lively, I tell ye. Ye see, old Tom he didn't take the idee at all; and he flopped and gobbled, and fit the parson; and the parson's wig got round so that his cue[2] stuck straight out over his ear, but he'd got his blood up. Ye see, the old doctor was used to carryin' his p'ints o' doctrine; and he had n't fit the Arminians and Socinians[3] to be beat by a tom-turkey; so finally he made a dive, and ketched him by the neck in spite o' his floppin', and stroked him down, and put Huldy's apron round him.

" 'There, Huldy,' he says, quite red in the face, 'we've got him now;' and he *traveled* off to the barn with him as lively as a cricket.

"Huldy came behind jist chokin' with laugh, and afraid the minister would look round and see her.

" 'Now, Huldy, we'll crook his legs, and set him down,' says the parson, when they got him to the nest; 'you see he is getting quiet, and he'll set there all right.'

"And the parson he sot him down; and old Tom he sot there solemn enough, and held his head down all droopin', lookin' like a rail pious old cock, as long as the parson sot by him.

" 'There! you see how still he sets,' says the parson to Huldy.

"Huldy was 'most dyin' for fear she should laugh. 'I'm afraid he'll get up,' says she, 'when you do.'

" 'Oh no, he won't!' says the parson, quite confident. 'There, there,' says he, layin' his hands on him, as if pronouncin' a blessin'. But when the parson riz up, old Tom he riz up too, and began to march over the eggs.

" 'Stop, now!' says the parson. 'I'll make him get down ag'in: hand me that corn-basket; we'll put that over him.'

"So he crooked old Tom's legs, and got him down ag'in; and they put the corn-basket over him, and then they both stood and waited.

" 'That'll do the thing, Huldy,' said the Parson.

" 'I don't know about it,' says Huldy.

" 'Oh yes, it will, child! I understand,' says he.

"Just as he spoke, the basket riz right up and stood, and they could see old Tom's long legs.

" 'I'll make him stay down, confound him,' says the parson; for, ye see, parsons is men, like the rest on us, and the doctor had got his spunk up.

" 'You just hold him a minute, and I'll get something that'll make

2. I.e., queue—the braid of his wig.
3. Two religious sects that opposed parts of the Calvinist doctrine of religious faith.

him stay, I guess;' and out he went to the fence, and brought in a long, thin, flat stone, and laid it on old Tom's back.

"Old Tom he wilted down considerable under this, and looked railly as if he was goin' to give in. He stayed still there a good long spell, and the minister and Huldy left him there and come up to the house; but they had n't more than got in the door before they see Tom a-hippin' along, as high-steppin' as ever, sayin', 'Talk! talk! and quitter! quitter!' and struttin' and gobblin' as if he'd come through the Red Sea, and got the victory.[4]

" 'Oh, my eggs!' says Huldy. 'I'm afraid he's smashed 'em!'

"And sure enough, there they was, smashed flat enough under the stone.

" 'I'll have him killed,' said the parson: 'we won't have such a critter round.'

"But the parson he slep' on 't, and then did n't do it; he only come out next Sunday with a tiptop sermon on the "Riginal Cuss' that was pronounced on things in gineral, when Adam fell, [5] and showed how everything was allowed to go contrary ever since. There was pigweed, and pusley, and Canady thistles, cut-worms, and bag-worms, and canker-worms, to say nothin' of rattlesnakes. The doctor made it very impressive and sort o' improvin'; but Huldy she told me, goin' home, that she hardly could keep from laughin' two or three times in the sermon when she thought of old Tom a-standin' up with the corn-basket on his back.

"Wal, next week Huldy she jist borrowed the minister's horse and side-saddle, and rode over to South Parish to her Aunt Bascome's,— Widder Bascome's, you know, that lives there by the trout-brook,—and got a lot o' turkey-eggs o' her, and come back and set a hen on 'em, and said nothin'; and in good time there was as nice a lot o' turkey-chicks as ever ye see.

"Huldy never said a word to the minister about his experiment, and he never said a word to her; but he sort o' kep' more to his books, and didn't take it on him to advise so much.

"But not long arter he took it into his head that Huldy ought to have a pig to be a-fattin' with the buttermilk. Mis' Pipperidge set him up to it; and jist then old Tim Bigelow, out to Juniper Hill, told him if he'd call over he'd give him a little pig.

"So he sent for a man, and told him to build a pig-pen right out by the well, and have it all ready when he came home with his pig.

"Huldy she said she wished he might put a curb round the well out

---

4. Moses led the Israelites across the Red Sea and defeated the Egyptians, who pursued them (Exodus 14:19–31).

5. In Genesis Adam falls from grace by eating an apple from the Tree of Knowledge, thus bringing the curse of death and labor upon himself and his descendants (Genesis 3). "'Riginal Cuss": Original Curse or Sin.

there, because in the dark, sometimes, a body might stumble into it; and the parson he told him he might do that.

"Wal, old Aikin, the carpenter, he did n't come till most the middle of the arternoon; and then he sort o' idled, so that he did n't get up the well-curb till sundown; and then he went off and said he'd come and do the pig-pen next day.

"Wal, arter dark, Parson Carryl he driv into the yard, full chizel,[6] with his pig. He'd tied up his mouth to keep him from squealin'; and he see what he thought was the pig-pen,—he was rather near-sighted,— and so he ran and threw piggy over; and down he dropped into the water, and the minister put out his horse and pranced off into the house quite delighted.

" 'There, Huldy, I've got you a nice little pig.'

" 'Dear me!' says Huldy: 'where have you put him?'

" 'Why, out there in the pig-pen, to be sure.'

" 'Oh dear me!' says Huldy: 'that's the well-curb. There ain't no pig-pen built,' says she.

" 'Lordy massy!' says the parson: 'then I've thrown the pig in the well!'

"Wal, Huldy she worked and worked, and finally she fished piggy out in the bucket, but he was dead as a door-nail; and she got him out o' the way quietly, and did n't say much; and the parson he took to a great Hebrew book in his study; and says he, 'Huldy, I ain't much in temporals,' says he. Huldy says she kind o' felt her heart go out to him, he was so sort o' meek and helpless and larned; and says she, 'Wal, Parson Carryl, don't trouble your head no more about it; I'll see to things;' and sure enough, a week arter there was a nice pen, all ship-shape, and two little white pigs that Huldy bought with the money for the butter she sold at the store.

" 'Wal, Huldy,' said the parson, 'you are a most amazin' child: you don't say nothin,' but you do more than most folks.'

"Arter that the parson set sich store by Huldy that he come to her and asked her about everything, and it was amazin' how everything she put her hand to prospered. Huldy planted marigolds and larkspurs, pinks and carnations, all up and down the path to the front door, and trained up mornin'-glories and scarlet-runners round the windows. And she was always a-gettin' a root here, and a sprig there, and a seed from somebody else,—for Huldy was one o' them that has the gift, so that ef you jist give 'em the leastest sprig of anything they make a great bush out of it right away; so that in six months Huldy had roses and geraniums and lilies, sich as it would a took a gardener to raise. The parson he took no notice at fust; but when the yard was all ablaze with flowers

6. Full speed.

he used to come and stand in a kind o' maze[7] at the front door, and say, 'Beautiful, beautiful! Why, Huldy, I never see anything like it.' And then when her work was done arternoons, Huldy would sit with her sewin' in the porch, and sing and trill away till she'd draw the meadow larks and the bobolinks and the orioles to answer her, and the great big elm-tree overhead would get perfectly rackety with the birds; and the parson, settin' there in his study, would git to kind o' dreamin' about the angels, and golden harps, and the New Jerusalem;[8] but he would n't speak a word, 'cause Huldy she was jist like them wood-thrushes, she never could sing so well when she thought folks was hearin'. Folks noticed, about this time, that the parson's sermons got to be like Aaron's rod, that budded and blossomed;[9] there was things in 'em about flowers and birds, and more 'special about the music o' heaven. And Huldy she noticed, that ef there was a hymn run in her head while she was round a-workin' the minister was sure to give it out next Sunday. You see, Huldy was jist like a bee: she always sung when she was workin', and you could hear her trillin', now down in the corn-patch, while she was pickin' the corn; and now in the buttery, while she was workin' the butter; and now she'd go singin' down cellar, and then she'd be singin' up overhead, so that she seemed to fill a house chock full o' music.

"Huldy was so sort o' chipper and fair-spoken that she got the hired men all under her thumb: they come to her and took her orders jist as meek as so many calves; and she traded at the store, and kep' the accounts, and she hed her eyes everywhere, and tied up all the ends so tight that there wa'n't no gettin' round her. She would n't let nobody put nothin' off[1] on Parson Carryl, 'cause he was a minister. Huldy was allers up to anybody that wanted to make a hard bargain; and, afore he knew jist what he was about, she'd got the best end of it, and everybody said that Huldy was the most capable gal that they'd ever traded with.

"Wal, come to the meetin' of the Association, Mis' Deakin Blodgett and Mis' Pipperidge come callin' up to the Parson's, all in a stew, and offerin' their services to get the house ready; but the doctor he jist thanked 'em quite quiet, and turned 'em over to Huldy; and Huldy she told 'em that she'd got everything ready, and showed 'em her pantries, and her cakes and her pies and her puddin's, and took 'em all over the house; and they went peekin' and pokin', openin' cupboard doors, and lookin' into drawers; and they could n't find so much as a thread out o' the way, from garret to cellar, and so they went off quite discontented. Arter that the women set a new trouble a-brewin'. Then they begun to talk that it was a year now since Mis' Carryl died; and it railly was n't

---

7. State of amazement.
8. Holy city where redeemed souls abide.
9. In Exodus 4.14–16 the high priest Aaron's rod is caused to blossom by Moses as a sign of God's favor to the Hebrews.
1. Cheat.

proper such a young gal to be stayin' there, who everybody could see
was a-settin' her cap for the minister.

"Mis' Pipperidge said that, so long as she looked on Huldy as the
hired gal, she had n't thought much about it; but Huldy was railly takin'
on airs as an equal, and appearin' as mistress o' the house in a way that
would make talk if it went on. And Mis' Pipperidge she driv round up to
Deakin Abner Snow's, and down to Mis' Lijah Perry's, and asked them
if they was n't afraid that the way the parson and Huldy was a-goin' on
might make talk. And they said they had n't thought on't before, but
now, come to think on't, they was sure it would; and they all went and
talked with somebody else, and asked them if they did n't think it would
make talk. So come Sunday, between meetin's there wa'n't nothin' else
talked about; and Huldy saw folks a-noddin' and a-winkin', and a-look-
in' arter her, and she begun to feel drefful sort o' disagreeable. Finally
Mis' Sawin she says to her, 'My dear, did n't you never think folks
would talk about you and the minister?'

" 'No: why should they?' says Huldy, quite innocent.

" 'Wal, dear,' says she, 'I think it's a shame; but they say you're tryin'
to catch him, and that it's so bold and improper for you to be courtin' of
him right in his own house,—you know folks will talk,—I thought I'd
tell you 'cause I think so much of you,' says she.

"Huldy was a gal of spirit, and she despised the talk, but it made her
drefful uncomfortable; and when she got home at night she sat down in
the mornin'-glory porch, quite quiet, and did n't sing a word.

"The minister he had heard the same thing from one of his deakins
that day; and when he saw Huldy so kind o' silent, he says to her, 'Why
don't you sing, my child?'

"He hed a pleasant sort o' way with him, the minister had, and Huldy
had got a likin' to be with him, and it all come over her that perhaps she
ought to go away; and her throat kind o' filled up so she could n't hardly
speak; and, says she, 'I can't sing tonight.'

"Says he, 'You don't know how much good your singin' has done
me, nor how much good *you* have done me in all ways, Huldy. I wish I
knew how to show my gratitude.'

" 'O sir!' says Huldy, '*is* it improper for me to be here?'

" 'No dear,' says the minister, 'but ill-natured folks will talk; but there
is one way we can stop it, Huldy—if you will marry me. You'll make
me very happy, and I'll do all I can to make you happy. Will you?'

"Wal, Huldy never told me jist what she said to the minister,—gals
never does give you the particulars of them 'ere things jist as you'd like
'em,—only I know the upshot and the hull on't was, that Huldy she did
a consid'able lot o' clear starchin' and ironin' the next two days; and the
Friday o' next week the minister and she rode over together to Dr.
Lothrop's in Oldtown; and the doctor, he jist made 'em man and wife,

'spite of envy of the Jews,' as the hymn says. Wal, you'd better believe there was a-starin' and a-wonderin' next Sunday mornin' when the second bell was a-tollin', and the minister walked up the broad aisle with Huldy, all in white, arm in arm with him, and he opened the minister's pew, and handed her in as if she was a princess; for, you see, Parson Carryl come of a good family, and was a born gentleman, and had a sort o' grand way o' bein' polite to womenfolks. Wal, I guess there was a-rus'lin' among the bunnets. Mis' Pipperidge gin a great bounce, like corn poppin' on a shovel, and her eyes glared through her glasses at Huldy as if they'd a' sot her afire; and everybody in the meetin'-house was a-starin', I tell yew. But they could n't none of 'em say nothin' agin Huldy's looks; for there wa'n't a crimp nor a frill about her that wa'n't jis' *so*; and her frock was white as the driven snow, and she had her bunnet all trimmed up with white ribbins; and all the fellows said the old doctor had stole a march, and got the handsomest gal in the parish.

"Wal, arter meetin' they all come round the parson and Huldy at the door, shakin' hands and laughin'; for by that time they was about agreed that they'd got to let putty well alone.

" 'Why, Parson Carryl,' says Mis' Deakin Blodgett, 'how you've come it over us.'[2]

" 'Yes,' says the parson, with a kind o' twinkle in his eye. 'I thought,' says he, 'as folks wanted to talk about Huldy and me, I'd give'em somethin' wuth talkin' about.' "

1872

2. I.e., fooled or surprised us.

ELIZABETH CADY STANTON
1815–1902

"In thought and sympathy we were one," Elizabeth Cady Stanton wrote about herself and Susan B. Anthony, "and in the division of labor we exactly complemented each other. I am the better writer, she the better critic. She supplied the facts and statistics, I the philosophy and rhetoric, and, together, we have made arguments that stood unshaken through the storms of long years; arguments that no one has answered. Our speeches may be considered the united product of our two brains." Through Anthony's efficiency and Stanton's eloquence, these two reformers managed to dislodge feminist demands from the margins of other liberal movements. As different as they were temperamentally, together they formed the National Woman Suffrage Association (NWSA), which shaped the women's movement in America.

The woman who took literary responsibility for this effective collaboration was the fourth child of Daniel and Margaret (Livingson) Cady. After studying at home in Johnstown, New York, at the Johnstown Academy, and later at Emma Willard's Troy Female Seminary, Elizabeth Cady married Henry Brewster Stanton, a journalist and reformer, in 1840, and they attended the World Anti-Slavery Convention in London on their honeymoon. There, with Lucretia Mott, Stanton became involved in a protest against the exclusion of women delegates, and planned a women's rights convention which was to take place on July 19, 1848, at Seneca Falls, New York. Stanton's draft of the *Declaration of Sentiments* for the Seneca Falls Convention initiated a writing career that included the articles she published under the pseudonym "Sun Flower" in Amelia Bloomer's paper, *The Lily*, and the numerous speeches she delivered first in New York and later during several trips to the Western states, tours which were undertaken, in part, to finance the education of her seven children. Stanton had met Anthony in 1851, when they began working together in the temperance and abolitionist movements. Before, during, and after the Civil War, they devoted themselves to the cause of women, organizing women's rights conventions and editing the weekly paper *Revolution*. As the president of NWSA for twenty-one years, Stanton became the major spokesperson for the women's movement. After the death of her husband in 1887, she extended her interest beyond suffrage, especially in her controversial feminist critique of the masculine bias in Judeo-Christian tradition, *The Woman's Bible* (1895, 1898). At this time, too, she published her lively autobiography, *Eighty Years and More* (1898). She continued lecturing on divorce, religion, and women's rights until she died in her sleep at the age of eighty-six, just after writing a letter to President Theodore Roosevelt in which she urged him to support women's suffrage.

From Address to the New York State Legislature, 1860[1]

You who have read the history of nations, from Moses[2] down to our last election, where have you ever seen one class looking after the interests of another? Any of you can readily see the defects in other governments, and pronounce sentence against those who have sacrificed the masses to themselves; but when we come to our own case, we are blinded by custom and self-interest. Some of you who have no capital can see the injustice which the laborer suffers; some of you who have no slaves, can see the cruelty of his oppression; but who of you appreciate the galling humiliation, the refinements of degradation, to which women (the mothers, wives, sisters, and daughters of freemen) are subject, in this the last half of the nineteenth century? How many of you have ever read even the laws concerning them that now disgrace your statute-books? In cruelty and tyranny, they are not surpassed by

---

1. This speech, delivered by Stanton, was, like all the work of Stanton and Anthony (1881–1886), the product of intensive collaboration. Anthony declared that it was up to Stanton to "move the hearts of our law-makers at this time"; moreover, she came to live with Stanton to write the speech with her and to help in the household.

2. In the Old Testament, leader of the Jews out of Egypt to the Promised Land.

any slaveholding code in the Southern states; in fact they are worse, by just so far as woman, from her social position, refinement, and education, is on a more equal ground with the oppressor.

Allow me just here to call the attention of that party now so much interested in the slave of the Carolinas, to the similarity in his condition and that of the mothers, wives, and daughters of the Empire State.[3] The Negro has no name. He is Cuffy Douglas or Cuffy Brooks, just whose Cuffy he may chance to be. The woman has no name. She is Mrs. Richard Roe or Mrs. John Doe, just whose Mrs. she may chance to be. Cuffy has no right to his earnings; he can not buy or sell, or lay up anything that he can call his own. Mrs. Roe has no right to her earnings; she can neither buy nor sell, make contracts, nor lay up anything that she can call her own. Cuffy has no right to his children; they can be sold from him at any time. Mrs. Roe has no right to her children; they may be bound out to cancel a father's debts of honor. The unborn child, even, by the last will of the father, may be placed under the guardianship of a stranger and a foreigner. Cuffy has no legal existence; he is subject to restraint and moderate chastisement. Mrs. Roe has no legal existence; she has not the best right to her own person. The husband has the power to restrain, and administer moderate chastisement.

Blackstone[4] declares that the husband and wife are one, and learned commentators have decided that that one is the husband. In all civil codes, you will find them classified as one. Certain rights and immunities, such and such privileges are to be secured to white male citizens. What have women and Negroes to do with rights? What know they of government, war, or glory?

The prejudice against color, of which we hear so much, is no stronger than that against sex. It is produced by the same cause, and manifested very much in the same way. The Negro's skin and the woman's sex are both *prima facie*[5] evidence that they were intended to be in subjection to the white Saxon man. The few social privileges which the man gives the woman, he makes up to the Negro in civil rights. The woman may sit at the same table and eat with the white man; the free Negro may hold property and vote. The woman may sit in the same pew with the white man in church; the free Negro may enter the pulpit and preach. Now, with the black man's right to suffrage, the right unquestioned, even by Paul, to minister at the altar,[6] it is evident that the prejudice against sex is more deeply rooted and more unreasonably maintained than that against color. * * *

---

3. New York State.
4. Sir William Blackstone, author of the influential *Commentaries on the Laws of England* (1765–1769), had articulated the principle that "by marriage the very being or legal existence of a woman is suspended."
5. On the first view.
6. In 1 Timothy 2:12, St. Paul refuses to allow "a woman to teach"; she must "be in silence."

Just imagine an inhabitant of another planet entertaining himself some pleasant evening in searching over our great national compact, our Declaration of Independence, our Constitutions, or some of our statute-books; what would he think of those "women and Negroes" that must be so fenced in, so guarded against? Why, he would certainly suppose we were monsters, like those fabulous giants or Brobdingnagians[7] of olden times, so dangerous to civilized man, from our size, ferocity, and power. Then let him take up our poets, from Pope down to Dana;[8] let him listen to our Fourth of July toasts, and some of the sentimental adultations of social life, and no logic could convince him that this creature of the law, and this angel of the family altar, could be one and the same being. Man is in such a labyrinth of contradictions with his marital and property rights; he is so befogged on the whole question of maidens, wives, and mothers, that from pure benevolence we should relieve him from this troublesome branch of legislation. We should vote, and make laws for ourselves. Do not be alarmed, dear ladies! You need spend no time reading Grotius, Coke, Puffendorf, Blackstone, Bentham, Kent, and Story[9] to find out what you need. We may safely trust the shrewd selfishness of the white man, and consent to live under the same broad code where he has so comfortably ensconced himself. Any legislation that will do for man, we may abide by most cheerfully. * * *

Now do not think, gentlemen, we wish you to do a great many troublesome things for us. We do not ask our legislators to spend a whole session in fixing up a code of laws to satisfy a class of most unreasonable women. We ask no more than the poor devils in the Scripture asked, "Let us alone." In mercy, let us take care of ourselves, our property, our children, and our homes. True, we are not so strong, so wise, so crafty as you are, but if any kind friend leaves us a little money, or we can by great industry earn fifty cents a day, we would rather buy bread and clothes for our children than cigars and champagne for our legal protectors. There has been a great deal written and said about protection. We, as a class, are tired of one kind of protection, that which leaves us everything to do, to dare, and to suffer, and strips us of all means for its accomplishment. We would not tax man to take care of us. No, the Great Father has endowed all his creatures with the necessary powers for self-support, self-defense, and protection. We do not ask man to represent us; it is hard enough in times like these for man to carry backbone enough to represent himself. So long as the mass of men spend most of their time on the fence, not knowing which way to jump,

7. The race of giants in Jonathan Swift's *Gulliver's Travels* (1735).
8. Alexander Pope (1688–1744) and Richard Henry Dana, Sr. (1787–1879), male authors who wrote about women either satirically or romantically.
9. All, like Blackstone, writers on the law.

they are surely in no condition to tell us where we had better stand. In pity for man, we would no longer hang like a mill-stone round his neck. Undo what man did for us in the Dark Ages, and strike out all special legislation for us; strike the words "white male" from all your constitutions, and then, with fair sailing, let us sink or swim, live or die, survive or perish together.

1860　　　　　　　　　　　　　　　　　　　　　　1881–1886

CHARLOTTE BRONTË
1816–1855

"Ten years ago we professed an orthodox system of novel-making. Our lovers were humble and devoted," remembered the Victorian journalist Margaret Oliphant in 1855, "when suddenly, without warning, *Jane Eyre* stole upon the scene, and the most alarming revolution of modern times has followed the invasion of *Jane Eyre*." When she spoke of "orthodox . . . novel-making," Oliphant no doubt meant to refer to the sentimental novels of manners that had been so popular in the earlier decades of the century. Certainly nothing could have been more different from such books than *Jane Eyre*. Indeed, although in our own century this revolutionary work has usually been thought of as a romance, the model for hundreds of best-selling love stories about darkly mysterious heroes and frail but feisty heroines, it is considerably more than that, as its first readers quickly understood. "Jane Eyre is throughout the personification of an unregenerate and undisciplined spirit," declared the reviewer Elizabeth Rigney in 1848, a year after the novel was published, and in 1853, another reviewer, Anne Mozley, recalled that the book seemed to many to have been written by "an alien . . . from society [who was] amenable to none of its laws."

The author of this electrifying best seller was born on April 21, 1816, the third child of Patrick Brontë, a clergyman of Irish descent, and his wife, Maria Branwell. In 1820, the family settled in the small Yorkshire town of Haworth, where the Reverend Brontë was curate of the local church. Both parents were evidently literary—Reverend Brontë produced several books of poetry, a novel, and a collection of sermons, and his wife wrote essays—but what might, despite modest means, have been a pleasant home became sorrowful when Mrs. Brontë died of cancer after giving birth to six children in rapid succession. Her husband tried in vain to remarry and finally invited his wife's sister, Elizabeth Branwell, to help care for his orphaned family. A strict and forbidding woman, "Aunt Branwell" lived with the Brontës until her death in 1842, but she seems never to have provided the warmth that they lost with their mother's death. Another catastrophe added further gloom to the household: in 1824, seeking to enrich his children's lives, Reverend Brontë sent his four oldest girls to Cowan Bridge School, a charitable institution for the daughters of impoverished clergymen that Charlotte Brontë was later to memorialize as *Jane Eyre*'s grim Lowood. By all accounts, her description in the novel was unfailingly accurate.

Not only were the students subject to a tyrannical disciplinary system, they were so badly fed and housed that many became ill. Among the sickest were the Brontës. Maria and Elizabeth, the two oldest girls, succumbed to a combination of typhoid fever and consumption before their anxious relatives realized how dangerous conditions were; Charlotte and Emily were withdrawn from the school just in time to save their lives.

Isolated in their north of England village on the edge of the Yorkshire moors, the four surviving children—Charlotte, Branwell, Emily, and Anne—drew together for comfort and eventually transformed Reverend Brontë's lonely parsonage into their own literary community. When their father brought Branwell a set of wooden soldiers, each child chose one, named it, and invented a history for it. Soon the tales they wove around these visionary beings evolved into a series of continuing fantasies about two imaginary kingdoms, "Angria" and "Gondal." Eventually, Branwell and Charlotte began to collaborate in recording the chronicles of "Angria," while Emily and Anne transcribed the history of "Gondal." Voracious readers, they reproduced the styles and themes of writers like the popular Scottish novelist Sir Walter Scott and the Romantic poet Lord Byron, as well as the formats of journals like *Blackwood's*, in tiny volumes "printed" in a microscopic hand so as to look like miniaturized versions of real books.

What is more striking still, the Brontës continued creating and transcribing these romantic tales even after Charlotte had once again been sent away to school—this time, in 1831–1832, to Roe Head, a far more comfortable and convenient establishment than Cowan Bridge had been—and even after she had returned to Roe Head in 1835 as a member of the teaching staff. In fact, in some ways Brontë's fantasizings about Angria intensified as she entered the workaday world of the schoolroom, where, as she noted, she had to toil in "irritation and weariness" to teach recalcitrant pupils "the distinction between an article and a substantive." Feeling herself trapped in "wretched bondage" to a career for which she had no natural vocation, she confided to her journal, "I should be agonised if I had not the dream [of Angria] to repose on," and in moments of "divine leisure" she transcribed the "fascinating spell" that the "infernal world" of her daydreams cast upon her, writing in a kind of trance, with her eyes closed and her mind full of visions.

Despite Charlotte Brontë's sense that as a teacher or governess she was in "bondage," she knew that such jobs offered the only source of income to genteel but impoverished young women. As the unmarried daughter of a country clergyman with small means, Brontë had to find a way of supporting herself. Marriage was always, of course, a solution to a spinster's financial problems, but this independent young woman was determined to marry only a man she could respect, and though she had several proposals, none came from such a person. Inevitably, then, she was consigned to the schoolroom or the nursery. After teaching at Roe Head, she went on to several "situations" as private governess, and it is no doubt from these that she learned a truth which stands behind so many of the pained exclamations of her governess-heroine, Jane Eyre: "a private governess has no existence, is not considered as a living and rational being except as connected with the wearisome duties she has to fulfill."

In the summer of 1842, however, Charlotte Brontë and her younger sister

Emily were suddenly given a chance for escape from such "wearisome duties." Troubled by her nieces' dilemma, the Brontës' severe "Aunt Branwell" quite unexpectedly offered them a small sum of money so that they could open a school of their own. But if they were to attempt such an enterprise, they would have to be better educated than they were, and so a second plan was set in motion: Charlotte and Emily were to be sent to Brussels, to a finishing school for young ladies called the Pensionnat Héger, where they would acquire the facility in foreign languages and the continental polish that would fit them to be self-employed headmistresses.

Run by Constantin Héger, an impetuous but brilliant teacher, and his wife, Zoe, the daughter of a cultivated French emigré family, the Pensionnat was a small but exceptionally enlightened educational institution. It was here, however, that Charlotte Brontë found herself involved in real life in the kind of romantic struggle that she had up till now only encountered in her Angrian daydreams. For, perhaps within a few months of her arrival in Brussels, she began to fall in love with M. Héger, although, as a married man and a devout Catholic, he gave no sign of returning her feelings. At the end of a year, "Aunt Branwell" died and the sisters returned to Haworth, where Emily decided to stay and keep house for her father. But Charlotte could not repress her feelings; in the words of her fine recent biographer Winifred Gerin, she was drawn as by a "somnambulist's compulsion" to return to Brussels, where she spent a year as a teacher at the Pensionnat and where both the charisma and the increasing coolness of the "master" she loved gave her what was to become essential material for all four of her novels.

Those novels were not begun until two years after Charlotte had retreated to England in an effort to cure her unrequited passion. Still hoping to begin their school, the Brontë sisters drew up circulars and mailed them to prospective pupils, while in the meantime Charlotte wrote a series of pathetic letters to Héger, declaring that her correspondence with him was now her "only joy on earth." But there was little or no response to either the school circulars or the love letters. Not a single pupil expressed interest in "The Misses Brontë's Establishment," and Héger replied to Charlotte's pleas for understanding at first with perfunctory friendliness and then with prolonged silence. By 1845, it was clear that this rebellious governess would not find redemption either in romance or in private enterprise. Her salvation lay in the writing that had always been her vocation, and in the community of imagination which she shared with her sisters, Anne and Emily.

It was Emily who provided the first impulse toward the creative resurrection that marked the years 1845 to 1848 for Charlotte Brontë. Accidentally discovering some of the verses the author-to-be of *Wuthering Heights* had been composing for years about the inhabitants of *her* fantasy kingdom, "Gondal," Charlotte was struck by their distinctive intensity. Always decisive when she thought she saw a way out of the poverty in which the sisters were ensnared, she resolved at once to send the poems to a publisher, adding some works of her own and Anne's for good measure. Before doing so, she rechristened the three newly professional writers with *noms de plume* that were deliberately ambiguous in gender: Charlotte, Emily, and Anne Brontë became Currer, Ellis, and Acton Bell, ostensibly because, as Charlotte was somewhat disingenuously to explain later, "What author would be without the advantage of being able to walk invisible?" but more likely because women's works were not usually received with sufficient seriousness by reviewers.

The volume called *Poems by Currer, Ellis, and Acton Bell* was hardly received at all, in any case, for it sold only two copies in the year after its publication. Undaunted by this failure, however, the three Brontës turned to fiction, and here Charlotte's painful love for M. Héger, together with her years of transforming her daydreams about Angria into vivid romances, stood her in good stead. Her first novel, *The Professor* (published posthumously), drew directly upon her experiences in Brussels, although it was told by a male narrator, as if its author were trying to disguise her own pain from herself. Her third novel, *Shirley* (1849), featured a hero who was a French tutor. Her fourth, *Villette* (1853), was set again in Brussels, and it was in good part devoted to an extraordinarily accurate portrait of the "master" she loved. Despite a surface realism, moreover, all three works were infused by Romantic and Gothic elements—dreams, visions, dramatic encounters—as well as by an energy of imagination that transformed biographical materials into compelling art.

But it was in Charlotte Brontë's second novel, *Jane Eyre*, that all the elements of her life were most effectively transmuted into a powerful work of fiction. Her early trauma at Cowan Bridge, her hardships as a governess, and her love for Héger—all these experiences helped shape the fictional autobiography of a heroine who, like Brontë herself, seemed small, plain, and decorous even while her apparently "unregenerate spirit" brought about "the most alarming revolution of modern times." At the same time, this book in which a determined female narrator spoke with what was in 1847 surprising authority about a woman's desire for liberty—"for liberty I gasped; for liberty I uttered a prayer" —was also shaped and strengthened by a fantastic subplot for which there was no real-life precedent: the story of Bertha Mason Rochester. As if commenting on Jane's apparent decorum, Bertha's fierce mutterings and secret midnight wanderings suggest more sinister and subversive strategies to which women might be driven in their search for "liberty."

It should not be surprising, then, that when *Jane Eyre* appeared, this unprecedented romance—combining an account of an independent woman's dreams and desires with a fantasy about explosive madness—took the reading public by storm. Shy by nature and profoundly unused to the sophistication of London circles, "Currer Bell" found herself almost overnight a literary "lion." Years later Anne Ritchie, the daughter of the novelist William Makepeace Thackeray, still remembered her father's first meeting with the acclaimed author, and Elizabeth Gaskell reverently recorded her first impressions of Charlotte Brontë in a letter she later reprinted in her 1857 *Life of Charlotte Brontë*. Despite the fact that she continued to live quietly in Haworth, the governess who had seemed to have "no existence" had now a dramatic public life.

For Brontë herself, however, such success was bittersweet. Soon after the publication of *Jane Eyre*, her brother Branwell died in painful circumstances. Ostensibly an art student and painter, he had for years been both an alcoholic and a drug addict, and, like his sister Charlotte but without her resilience, he had endured the pains of unrequited love. Within months, his death was followed by the deaths from tuberculosis of Emily and Anne. Bereft of the sisters who had constituted the only literary society she really wanted to join, Charlotte could not be consoled by her newly won fame. A determined survivor, she went on writing and keeping house for her father, but the Brontë parsonage was now lonelier and more sorrowful than ever, so that when Mrs. Gaskell visited in 1853 she was as struck by the silence as by the "exquisite" cleanliness of the household.

Perhaps in an attempt to cheer her solitude and her father's, Charlotte Brontë married Arthur Bell Nicholls, the Reverend Brontë's curate, in 1854. The marriage seems to have been reasonably content, although the new Mrs. Nicholls did complain to a friend that "the married woman can call but a very small portion of each day her own." Toward the end of the year, however, she became pregnant and suffered so severe a case of what it is almost an understatement to call "morning sickness" that by March of 1855 she was bedridden and emaciated. Some biographers have speculated that her illness was complicated by the same tuberculosis that killed her sisters; others have suggested that she could no longer continue the life that had consumed so many of those she loved. Whatever the medical causes, she died on March 31, 1855, and was buried near her sisters and brother in Haworth Churchyard.

If Brontë's body had not been equal to the task of survival, however, her imagination had been more than equal to that job. "Imagination is a strong, restless faculty which claims to be heard and exercised: are we to be quite deaf to her cry and insensate to her struggles?" she once wrote to the man of letters George Henry Lewes. For her, such a question had only one answer. Through all the hardships of an exceptionally difficult life, Brontë herself had attended with special intensity to the claims of imagination, so that, as Virginia Woolf declared seventy years after this writer's death, even now when we read *Jane Eyre* "we are steeped through and through with the genius, the vehemence, the indignation of Charlotte Brontë."

Jane Eyre

Chapter I

There was no possibility of taking a walk that day. We had been wandering, indeed, in the leafless shrubbery an hour in the morning; but since dinner (Mrs. Reed, when there was no company, dined early) the cold winter wind had brought with it clouds so sombre, and a rain so penetrating, that further outdoor exercise was now out of the question.

I was glad of it: I never liked long walks, especially on chilly afternoons: dreadful to me was the coming home in the raw twilight, with nipped fingers and toes, and a heart saddened by the chidings of Bessie, the nurse, and humbled by the consciousness of my physical inferiority to Eliza, John, and Georgiana Reed.

The said Eliza, John, and Georgiana were now clustered round their mamma in the drawing-room: she lay reclined on the sofa by the fireside, and with her darlings about her (for the time neither quarrelling nor crying) looked perfectly happy. Me, she had dispensed from joining the group; saying, 'She regretted to be under the necessity of keeping me at a distance; but that until she heard from Bessie and could discover by her own observation that I was endeavouring in good earnest to acquire a more sociable and childlike disposition, a more attractive and sprightly manner—something lighter, franker, more natural, as it were —she really must exclude me from privileges intended only for contented, happy, little children.'

'What does Bessie say I have done?' I asked.

'Jane, I don't like cavillers or questioners: besides, there is something truly forbidding in a child taking up her elders in that manner. Be seated somewhere; and until you can speak pleasantly, remain silent.'

A small breakfast-room adjoined the drawing-room. I slipped in there. It contained a bookcase: I soon possessed myself of a volume, taking care that it should be one stored with pictures. I mounted into the window-seat: gathering up my feet, I sat cross-legged like a Turk; and, having drawn the red moreen curtain nearly close, I was shrined in double retirement.

Folds of scarlet drapery shut in my view to the right hand; to the left were the clear panes of glass, protecting, but not separating me from the drear November day. At intervals, while turning over the leaves of my book, I studied the aspect of that winter afternoon. Afar, it offered a pale blank of mist and cloud; near, a scene of wet lawn and storm-beat shrub, with ceaseless rain sweeping away wildly before a long and lamentable blast.

I returned to my book—Bewick's History of British Birds:[1] the letter-press thereof I cared little for, generally speaking; and yet there were certain introductory pages that, child as I was, I could not pass quite as a blank. They were those which treat of the haunts of sea-fowl; of 'the solitary rocks and promontories' by them only inhabited; of the coast of Norway, studded with isles from its southern extremity, the Lindeness, or Naze, to the North Cape——

> Where the Northern Ocean, in vast whirls,
> Boils round the naked, melancholy isles
> Of farthest Thule; and the Atlantic surge
> Pours in among the stormy Hebrides.

Nor could I pass unnoticed the suggestion of the bleak shores of Lapland, Siberia, Spitzbergen, Nova Zembla, Iceland, Greenland, with the

1. Thomas Bewick, *History of British Birds* (1804). "Letterpress": i.e., the text. The verse passage is quoted by Bewick from James Thomson's *Seasons, Autumn*, lines 862–865. We are indebted to Richard J. Dunn for information contained in his notes to the Norton Critical Edition of *Jane Eyre*.

'vast sweep of the Arctic Zone, and those forlorn regions of dreary space—that reservoir of frost and snow, where firm fields of ice, the accumulation of centuries of winters, glazed in Alpine heights above heights, surround the pole, and concentre the multiplied rigors of extreme cold.' Of these death-white realms I formed an idea of my own: shadowy, like all the half-comprehended notions that float dim through children's brains, but strangely impressive. The words in these introductory pages connected themselves with the succeeding vignettes, and gave significance to the rock standing up alone in a sea of billow and spray; to the broken boat stranded on a desolate coast; to the cold and ghastly moon glancing through bars of cloud at a wreck just sinking.

I cannot tell what sentiment haunted the quite solitary churchyard, with its inscribed headstone; its gate, its two trees, its low horizon, girdled by a broken wall, and its newly-risen crescent, attesting the hour of eventide.

The two ships becalmed on a torpid sea I believed to be marine phantoms.

The fiend pinning down the thief's pack behind him I passed over quickly: it was an object of terror.

So was the black, horned thing seated aloof on a rock, surveying a distant crowd surrounding a gallows.

Each picture told a story; mysterious often to my undeveloped understanding and imperfect feelings, yet ever profoundly interesting: as interesting as the tales Bessie sometimes narrated on winter evenings, when she chanced to be in good humour; and when, having brought her ironing-table to the nursery-hearth, she allowed us to sit about it, and while she got up Mrs. Reed's lace frills, and crimped her night-cap borders, fed our eager attention with passages of love and adventure taken from old fairy tales and older ballads; or (as at a later period I discovered) from the pages of 'Pamela,' and 'Henry, Earl of Moreland.' [2]

With Bewick on my knee, I was then happy: happy at least in my way. I feared nothing but interruption and that came too soon. The breakfast-room door opened.

'Bah! Madame Mope!' cried the voice of John Reed; then he paused: he found the room apparently empty.

'Where the dickens is she?' he continued. 'Lizzy! Georgy! (calling to his sisters) Joan[3] is not here: tell mamma she is run out into the rain —bad animal!'

'It is well I drew the curtain,' thought I; and I wished fervently he might not discover my hiding-place: nor would John Reed have found it out himself; he was not quick either of vision or conception; but Eliza

2. Popular eighteenth-century novels by Samuel Richardson and Henry Brooke.   3. "Jane" is a variant of "Joan."

just put her head in at the door, and said at once:—'She is in the window-seat, to be sure, Jack.'

And I came out immediately, for I trembled at the idea of being dragged forth by the said Jack.

'What do you want?' I asked, with awkward diffidence.

'Say, "what do you want, Master Reed?"' was the answer. 'I want you to come here;' and sitting himself in an arm-chair, he intimated by a gesture that I was to approach and stand before him.

John Reed was a schoolboy of fourteen years old; four years older than I, for I was but ten; large and stout for his age, with a dingy and unwholesome skin; thick lineaments in a spacious visage, heavy limbs and large extremities. He gorged himself habitually at table, which made him bilious, and gave him a dim and bleared eye and flabby cheeks. He ought now to have been at school; but his mamma had taken him home for a month or two, 'on account of his delicate health.' Mr. Miles, the master, affirmed that he would do very well if he had fewer cakes and sweetmeats sent him from home; but the mother's heart turned from an opinion so harsh, and inclined rather to the more refined idea that John's sallowness was owing to over-application and, perhaps, to pining after home.

John had not much affection for his mother and sisters, and an antipathy to me. He bullied and punished me; not two or three times in the week, nor once or twice in the day, but continually: every nerve I had feared him, and every morsel of flesh on my bones shrank when he came near. There were moments when I was bewildered by the terror he inspired, because I had no appeal whatever against either his menaces or his inflictions; the servants did not like to offend their young master by taking my part against him, and Mrs. Reed was blind and deaf on the subject: she never saw him strike or heard him abuse me, though he did both now and then in her very presence; more frequently, however, behind her back.

Habitually obedient to John, I came up to his chair: he spent some three minutes in thrusting out his tongue at me as far as he could without damaging the roots: I knew he would soon strike, and while dreading the blow, I mused on the disgusting and ugly appearance of him who would presently deal it. I wonder if he read that notion in my face; for, all at once, without speaking, he struck suddenly and strongly. I tottered, and regaining my equilibrium retired back a step or two from his chair.

'That is for your impudence in answering mamma a while since,' said he, 'and for your sneaking way of getting behind curtains, and for the look you had in your eyes two minutes since, you rat!'

Accustomed to John Reed's abuse, I never had an idea of replying to it; my care was how to endure the blow which would certainly follow the insult.

'What were you doing behind the curtain?' he asked.

'I was reading.'

'Show the book.'

I returned to the window and fetched it thence.

'You have no business to take our books; you are a dependent, mamma says; you have no money; your father left you none; you ought to beg, and not live here with gentlemen's children like us, and eat the same meals we do, and wear clothes at our mamma's expense. Now, I'll teach you to rummage my book-shelves: for they *are* mine; all the house belongs to me, or will do in a few years. Go and stand by the door, out of the way of the mirror and the windows.'

I did so, not at first aware what was his intention; but when I saw him lift and poise the book and stand in act to hurl it, I instinctively started aside with a cry of alarm: not soon enough, however; the volume was flung, it hit me, and I fell, striking my head against the door and cutting it. The cut bled, the pain was sharp: my terror had passed its climax; other feelings succeeded.

'Wicked and cruel boy!' I said. 'You are like a murderer—you are like a slave-driver—you are like the Roman emperors!'

I had read Goldsmith's 'History of Rome,'[4] and had formed my opinion of Nero, Caligula, &c. Also I had drawn parallels in silence, which I never thought thus to have declared aloud.

'What! what!' he cried. 'Did she say that to me? Did you hear her, Eliza and Georgiana? Won't I tell mamma? but first——'

He ran headlong at me: I felt him grasp my hair and my shoulder: he had closed with a desperate thing. I really saw in him a tyrant: a murderer. I felt a drop or two of blood from my head trickle down my neck, and was sensible of somewhat pungent suffering: these sensations for the time predominated over fear, and I received him in frantic sort. I don't very well know what I did with my hands, but he called me 'Rat! rat!' and bellowed out aloud. Aid was near him: Eliza and Georgiana had run for Mrs. Reed, who was gone upstairs; she now came upon the scene, followed by Bessie and her maid Abbot. We were parted: I heard the words:—'Dear! dear! What a fury to fly at Master John!'

'Did ever anybody see such a picture of passion!'

Then Mrs. Reed subjoined:—'Take her away to the red-room, and lock her in there.' Four hands were immediately laid upon me, and I was borne upstairs.

Chapter II

I resisted all the way: a new thing for me, and a circumstance which greatly strengthened the bad opinion Bessie and Miss Abbot were disposed to entertain of me. The fact is, I was a trifle beside myself; or

4. Oliver Goldsmith, *The Roman History* (1769).

rather *out* of myself, as the French would say: I was conscious that a moment's mutiny had already rendered me liable to strange penalties, and, like any other rebel slave, I felt resolved, in my desperation, to go all lengths.

'Hold her arms, Miss Abbot: she's like a mad cat.'

'For shame! for shame!' cried the lady's-maid. 'What shocking conduct, Miss Eyre, to strike a young gentleman, your benefactress's son! Your young master.'

'Master! How is he my master? Am I a servant?'

'No; you are less than a servant, for you do nothing for your keep. There, sit down, and think over your wickedness.'

They had got me by this time into the apartment indicated by Mrs. Reed, and had thrust me upon a stool: my impulse was to rise from it like a spring; their two pairs of hands arrested me instantly.

'If you don't sit still, you must be tied down,' said Bessie. 'Miss Abbot, lend me your garters; she would break mine directly.'

Miss Abbot turned to divest a stout leg of the necessary ligature. This preparation for bonds, and the additional ignominy it inferred, took a little of the excitement out of me.

'Don't take them off,' I cried; 'I will not stir.'

In guarantee whereof I attached myself to my seat by my hands.

'Mind you don't,' said Bessie; and when she had ascertained that I was really subsiding, she loosened her hold of me; then she and Miss Abbot stood with folded arms, looking darkly and doubtfully on my face, as incredulous of my sanity.

'She never did so before,' at last said Bessie, turning to the Abigail.

'But it was always in her,' was the reply. 'I've told Missis often my opinion about the child, and Missis agreed with me. She's an underhand little thing: I never saw a girl of her age with so much cover.'[5]

Bessie answered not; but ere long, addressing me, she said:

'You ought to be aware, Miss, that you are under obligations to Mrs. Reed: she keeps you: if she were to turn you off,[6] you would have to go to the poor-house.'

I had nothing to say to these words: they were not new to me: my very first recollections of existence included hints of the same kind. This reproach of my dependence had become a vague singsong in my ear; very painful and crushing, but only half intelligible. Miss Abbot joined in:—'And you ought not to think yourself on an equality with the Misses Reed and Master Reed, because Missis kindly allows you to be brought up with them. They will have a great deal of money, and you will have none: it is your place to be humble, and to try to make yourself agreeable to them.'

5. Deception. "The Abigail": the maidservant (after a character in a play by Beaumont and Fletcher).

6. Turn you out.

'What we tell you is for your good,' added Bessie, in no harsh voice: 'you should try to be useful and pleasant, then, perhaps, you would have a home here; but if you become passionate and rude, Missis will send you away, I am sure.'

'Besides,' said Miss Abbot, 'God will punish her: He might strike her dead in the midst of her tantrums, and then where would she go? Come, Bessie, we will leave her: I wouldn't have her heart for anything. Say your prayers, Miss Eyre, when you are by yourself; for if you don't repent, something bad might be permitted to come down the chimney, and fetch you away.'

They went, shutting the door, and locking it behind them.

The red-room was a spare chamber, very seldom slept in; I might say never, indeed, unless when a chance influx of visitors at Gateshead Hall rendered it necessary to turn to account all the accommodation it contained: yet it was one of the largest and stateliest chambers in the mansion. A bed supported on massive pillars of mahogany, hung with curtains of deep red damask, stood out like a tabernacle in the centre; the two large windows, with their blinds always drawn down, were half shrouded in festoons and falls of similar drapery; the carpet was red; the table at the foot of the bed was covered with a crimson cloth; the walls were a soft fawn colour, with a blush of pink in it; the wardrobe, the toilet-table, the chairs were of darkly-polished old mahogany. Out of these deep surrounding shades rose high, and glared white, the piled-up mattresses and pillows of the bed, spread with a snowy Marseilles counterpane. Scarcely less prominent was an ample, cushioned easy-chair near the head of the bed, also white, with a footstool before it; and looking, as I thought, like a pale throne.

This room was chill, because it seldom had a fire; it was silent, because remote from the nursery and kitchens; solemn, because it was known to be so seldom entered. The housemaid alone came here on Saturdays, to wipe from the mirrors and the furniture a week's quiet dust: and Mrs. Reed herself, at far intervals, visited it to review the contents of a certain secret drawer in the wardrobe, where were stored divers parchments, her jewel-casket, and a miniature of her deceased husband; and in those last words lies the secret of the red-room—the spell which kept it so lonely in spite of its grandeur.

Mr. Reed had been dead nine years: it was in this chamber he breathed his last; here he lay in state; hence his coffin was borne by the undertaker's men; and, since that day, a sense of dreary consecration had guarded it from frequent intrusion.

My seat, to which Bessie and the bitter Miss Abbot had left me riveted, was a low ottoman near the marble chimney-piece; the bed rose before me; to my right hand there was the high, dark wardrobe, with subdued, broken reflections varying the gloss of its panels; to my left

were the muffled windows; a great looking-glass between them repeated the vacant majesty of the bed and room. I was not quite sure
whether they had locked the door; and, when I dared move, I got up,
and went to see. Alas! yes: no jail was ever more secure. Returning, I
had to cross before the looking-glass; my fascinated glance involuntarily
explored the depth it revealed. All looked colder and darker in that visionary hollow than in reality: and the strange little figure there gazing
at me, with a white face and arms specking the gloom, and glittering
eyes of fear moving where all else was still, had the effect of a real spirit:
I thought it like one of the tiny phantoms, half fairy, half imp, Bessie's
evening stories represented as coming out of lone, ferny dells in moors,
and appearing before the eyes of belated travellers. I returned to my
stool.

Superstition was with me at that moment; but it was not yet her hour
for complete victory: my blood was still warm; the mood of the revolted
slave was still bracing me with its bitter vigour; I had to stem a rapid rush
of retrospective thought before I quailed to the dismal present.

All John Reed's violent tyrannies, all his sisters' proud indifference,
all his mother's aversion, all the servant's partiality, turned up in my
disturbed mind like a dark deposit in a turbid well. Why was I always
suffering, always browbeaten, always accused, for ever condemned?
Why could I never please? Why was it useless to try to win any one's
favour? Eliza, who was headstrong and selfish, was respected. Georgiana, who had a spoiled temper, a very acrid spite, a captious and insolent carriage, was universally indulged. Her beauty, her pink cheeks
and golden curls, seemed to give delight to all who looked at her, and to
purchase indemnity for every fault. John, no one thwarted, much less
punished; though he twisted the necks of the pigeons, killed the little
pea-chicks,[7] set the dogs at the sheep, stripped the hothouse vines of
their fruit, and broke the buds off the choicest plants in the conservatory: he called his mother 'old girl,' too; sometimes reviled her for her
dark skin, similar to his own; bluntly disregarded her wishes; not unfrequently tore and spoiled her silk attire; and he was still 'her own darling.' I dared commit no fault; I strove to fulfil every duty; and I was
termed naughty and tiresome, sullen and sneaking, from morning to
noon, and from noon to night.

My head still ached and bled with the blow and fall I had received: no
one had reproved John for wantonly striking me; and because I had
turned against him to avert farther irrational violence, I was loaded with
general opprobrium.

'Unjust!—unjust!' said my reason, forced by the agonising stimulus
into precocious though transitory power; and Resolve, equally wrought

7. Peacock chicks.

up, instigated some strange expedient to achieve escape from insupportable oppression—as running away, or, if that could not be effected, never eating or drinking more, and letting myself die.

What a consternation of soul was mine that dreary afternoon! How all my brain was in tumult, and all my heart in insurrection! Yet in what darkness, what dense ignorance, was the mental battle fought! I could not answer the ceaseless inward question—*why* I thus suffered; now, at the distance of—I will not say how many years, I see it clearly.

I was a discord in Gateshead Hall; I was like nobody there; I had nothing in harmony with Mrs. Reed or her children, or her chosen vassalage. If they did not love me, in fact, as little did I love them. They were not bound to regard with affection a thing that could not sympathise with one amongst them; a heterogeneous thing, opposed to them in temperament, in capacity, in propensities; a useless thing, incapable of serving their interest, or adding to their pleasure; a noxious thing, cherishing the germs of indignation at their treatment, of contempt of their judgment. I know that had I been a sanguine, brilliant, careless, exacting, handsome, romping child—though equally dependent and friendless—Mrs. Reed would have endured my presence more complacently; her children would have entertained for me more of the cordiality of fellow-feeling; the servants would have been less prone to make me the scapegoat of the nursery.

Daylight began to forsake the red-room; it was past four o'clock, and the beclouded afternoon was tending to drear twilight. I heard the rain still beating continuously on the staircase window, and the wind howling in the grove behind the hall; I grew by degrees cold as a stone, and then my courage sank. My habitual mood of humiliation, self-doubt, forlorn depression, fell damp on the embers of my decaying ire. All said I was wicked, and perhaps I might be so: what thought had I been but just conceiving of starving myself to death? That certainly was a crime: and was I fit to die? Or was the vault under the chancel of Gateshead Church an inviting bourne? In such vault I had been told did Mr. Reed lie buried; and led by this thought to recall his idea, I dwelt on it with gathering dread. I could not remember him; but I knew that he was my own uncle—my mother's brother—that he had taken me when a parentless infant to his house; and that in his last moments he had required a promise of Mrs. Reed that she would rear and maintain me as one of her own children. Mrs. Reed probably considered she had kept this promise; and so she had, I dare say, as well as her nature would permit her; but how could she really like an interloper not of her race,[8] and unconnected with her, after her husband's death, by any tie? It must have been most irksome to find herself bound by a hard-wrung pledge

8. I.e., family.

to stand in the stead of a parent to a strange child she could not love, and to see an uncongenial alien permanently intruded on her own family group.

A singular notion dawned upon me. I doubted not—never doubted —that if Mr. Reed had been alive he would have treated me kindly; and now, as I sat looking at the white bed and overshadowed walls—occasionally also turning a fascinated eye towards the dimly gleaming mirror—I began to recall what I had heard of dead men, troubled in their graves by the violation of their last wishes, revisiting the earth to punish the perjured and avenge the oppressed; and I thought Mr. Reed's spirit, harassed by the wrongs of his sister's child, might quit its abode— whether in the church vault, or in the unknown world of the departed —and rise before me in this chamber. I wiped my tears and hushed my sobs, fearful lest any sign of violent grief might waken a preternatural voice to comfort me, or elicit from the gloom some haloed face, bending over me with strange pity. This idea, consolatory in theory, I felt would be terrible if realised: with all my might I endeavoured to stifle it—I endeavoured to be firm. Shaking my hair from my eyes, I lifted my head and tried to look boldly round the dark room. At this moment a light gleamed on the wall. Was it, I asked myself, a ray from the moon penetrating some aperture in the blind? No; moonlight was still, and this stirred; while I gazed, it glided up to the ceiling and quivered over my head. I can now conjecture readily that this streak of light was, in all likelihood, a gleam from a lantern, carried by some one across the lawn: but then, prepared as my mind was for horror, shaken as my nerves were by agitation, I thought the swift-darting beam was a herald of some coming vision from another world. My heart beat thick, my head grew hot; a sound filled my ears, which I deemed the rushing of wings: something seemed near me; I was oppressed, suffocated: endurance broke down; I rushed to the door and shook the lock in desperate effort. Steps came running along the outer passage; the key turned, Bessie and Abbot entered.

'Miss Eyre, are you ill?' said Bessie.

'What a dreadful noise! it went quite through me!' exclaimed Abbot.

'Take me out! let me go into the nursery!' was my cry.

'What for? Are you hurt? Have you seen something?' again demanded Bessie.

'Oh! I saw a light, and I thought a ghost would come.' I had now got hold of Bessie's hand, and she did not snatch it from me.

'She has screamed out on purpose,' declared Abbot, in some disgust. 'And what a scream! If she had been in great pain one would have excused it, but she only wanted to bring us all here: I know her naughty tricks.'

'What is all this?' demanded another voice, peremptorily; and Mrs.
Reed came along the corridor, her cap flying wide, her gown rustling
stormily. 'Abbot and Bessie, I believe I gave orders that Jane Eyre
should be left in the red-room till I came to her myself.'

'Miss Jane screamed so loud, ma'am,' pleaded Bessie.

'Let her go,' was the only answer. 'Loose Bessie's hand, child: you
cannot succeed in getting out by these means, be assured. I abhor artifice, particularly in children; it is my duty to show you that tricks will
not answer: you will now stay here an hour longer, and it is only on
condition of perfect submission and stillness that I shall liberate you
then.'

'Oh aunt, have pity! Forgive me! I cannot endure it—let me be
punished some other way! I shall be killed if———'

'Silence! This violence is all most repulsive:' and so, no doubt, she
felt it. I was a precocious actress in her eyes: she sincerely looked on me
as a compound of virulent passions, mean spirit, and dangerous duplicity.

Bessie and Abbot having retreated, Mrs. Reed, impatient of my now
frantic anguish and wild sobs, abruptly thrust me back and locked me in,
without farther parley. I heard her sweeping away; and soon after she
was gone I suppose I had a species of fit: unconsciousness closed the
scene.

Chapter III

The next thing I remember is, waking up with a feeling as if I had
had a frightful nightmare, and seeing before me a terrible red glare,
crossed with thick black bars. I heard voices, too, speaking with a hollow
sound, as if muffled by a rush of wind or water: agitation, uncertainty,
and an all-predominating sense of terror confused my faculties. Ere
long I became aware that some one was handling me; lifting me up and
supporting me in a sitting posture, and that more tenderly than I had
ever been raised or upheld before. I rested my head against a pillow or
an arm, and felt easy.

In five minutes more the cloud of bewilderment dissolved: I knew
quite well that I was in my own bed, and that the red glare was the nursery fire. It was night: a candle burnt on the table; Bessie stood at the
bed-foot with a basin in her hand, and a gentleman sat in a chair near
my pillow, leaning over me.

I felt an inexpressible relief, a soothing conviction of protection and
security, when I knew that there was a stranger in the room, an individual not belonging to Gateshead, and not related to Mrs. Reed. Turning

from Bessie (though her presence was far less obnoxious to me than that of Abbot, for instance, would have been), I scrutinised the face of the gentleman: I knew him; it was Mr. Lloyd, an apothecary, sometimes called in by Mrs. Reed when the servants were ailing: for herself and the children she employed a physician.

'Well, who am I?' he asked.

I pronounced his name, offering him at the same time my hand: he took it, smiling and saying, 'We shall do very well by-and-by.' Then he laid me down, and addressing Bessie, charged her to be very careful that I was not disturbed during the night. Having given some further directions, and intimated that he should call again the next day, he departed —to my grief: I felt so sheltered and befriended while he sat in the chair near my pillow; and as he closed the door after him all the room darkened and my heart again sank: inexpressible sadness weighed it down.

'Do you feel as if you should sleep, Miss?' asked Bessie, rather softly.

Scarcely dared I answer her; for I feared the next sentence might be rough. 'I will try.'

'Would you like to drink, or could you eat anything?'

'No, thank you, Bessie.'

'Then I think I shall go to bed, for it is past twelve o'clock; but you may call me if you want anything in the night.'

Wonderful civility this! It emboldened me to ask a question.

'Bessie, what is the matter with me? Am I ill?'

'You fell sick, I suppose, in the red-room with crying; you'll be better soon, no doubt.'

Bessie went into the housemaid's apartment, which was near. I heard her say—'Sarah, come and sleep with me in the nursery; I daren't for my life be alone with that poor child to-night; she might die; it's such a strange thing she should have that fit: I wonder if she saw anything. Missis was rather too hard.'

Sarah came back with her; they both went to bed; they were whispering together for half an hour before they fell asleep. I caught scraps of their conversation, from which I was able only too distinctly to infer the main subject discussed.

'Something passed her, all dressed in white, and vanished'—'A great black dog behind him'—'Three loud raps on the chamber door'—'A light in the churchyard just over his grave'—&c. &c.

At last both slept: the fire and the candle went out. For me, the watches of that long night passed in ghastly wakefulness; ear, eye, and mind were alike strained by dread: such dread as children only can feel.

No severe or prolonged bodily illness followed this incident of the red-room: it only gave my nerves a shock, of which I feel the reverberation to this day. Yes, Mrs. Reed, to you I owe some fearful pangs of mental suffering. But I ought to forgive you, for you knew not what you did:[9] while rending my heart-strings, you thought you were only uprooting my bad propensities.

Next day, by noon, I was up and dressed, and sat wrapped in a shawl by the nursery hearth. I felt physically weak and broken down; but my worst ailment was an unutterable wretchedness of mind: a wretchedness which kept drawing from me silent tears; no sooner had I wiped one salt drop from my cheek than another followed. Yet I thought I ought to have been happy, for none of the Reeds were there, they were all gone out in the carriage with their mamma: Abbot, too, was sewing in another room, and Bessie, as she moved hither and thither, putting away toys and arranging drawers, addressed to me every now and then a word of unwonted kindness. This state of things should have been to me a paradise of peace, accustomed as I was to a life of ceaseless reprimand and thankless fagging;[1] but, in fact, my racked nerves were now in such a state that no calm could soothe, and no pleasure excite them agreeably.

Bessie had been down into the kitchen, and she brought up with her a tart on a certain brightly painted china plate, whose bird of paradise, nestling in a wreath of convolvuli and rosebuds, had been wont to stir in me a most enthusiastic sense of admiration; and which plate I had often petitioned to be allowed to take in my hand in order to examine it more closely, but had always hitherto been deemed unworthy of such a privilege. This precious vessel was now placed on my knee, and I was cordially invited to eat the circlet of delicate pastry upon it. Vain favour! coming, like most other favours long deferred and often wished for, too late! I could not eat the tart: and the plumage of the bird, the tints of the flowers, seemed strangely faded: I put both plate and tart away. Bessie asked if I would have a book: the word *book* acted as a transient stimulus, and I begged her to fetch Gulliver's Travels from the library.[2] This book I had again and again perused with delight. I considered it a narrative of facts and discovered in it a vein of interest deeper than what I found in fairy tales: for as to the elves, having sought them in vain among foxglove leaves and bells, under mushrooms and beneath the ground-ivy mantling old wall-nooks, I had at length made up my mind to the sad truth, that they were all gone out of England to some savage country where the woods were wilder and thicker, and the population more scant; whereas, Lilliput and Brobdingnag being, in my creed, solid parts of the earth's surface, I doubted not that I might one day, by taking a long voyage, see with my own eyes the little fields, houses, and trees, the diminutive people, the tiny cows, sheep, and birds of the one realm; and the corn-fields forest-high, the mighty mastiffs, the monster

9. An echo of Christ's words on the Cross: "Father, forgive them; for they know not what they do" (Luke 23:34).

1. Hard work.
2. Jonathan Swift, *Gulliver's Travels* (1726).

cats, the tower-like men and women, of the other. Yet when this cherished volume was now placed in my hand—when I turned over its leaves, and sought in its marvellous pictures the charm I had, till now, never failed to find—all was eerie and dreary; the giants were gaunt goblins, the pigmies malevolent and fearful imps, Gulliver a most desolate wanderer in most dread and dangerous regions. I closed the book, which I dared no longer peruse, and put it on the table, beside the untasted tart.

Bessie had now finished dusting and tidying the room, and having washed her hands, she opened a certain little drawer, full of splendid shreds of silk and satin, and began making a new bonnet for Georgiana's doll. Meantime she sang: her song was—

> In the days when we went gipsying,
>   A long time ago.[3]

I had often heard the song before, and always with lively delight; for Bessie had a sweet voice—at least I thought so. But now, though her voice was still sweet, I found in its melody an indescribable sadness. Sometimes, preoccupied with her work, she sang the refrain very low, very lingeringly; 'A long time ago' came out like the saddest cadence of a funeral hymn. She passed into another ballad, this time a really doleful one.

> My feet they are sore, and my limbs they are weary;
>   Long is the way, and the mountains are wild;
> Soon will the twilight close moonless and dreary
>   Over the path of the poor orphan child.
>
> Why did they send me so far and so lonely,
>   Up where the moors spread and grey rocks are piled?
> Men are hard-hearted, and kind angels only
>   Watch o'er the steps of a poor orphan child.
>
> Yet distant and soft the night-breeze is blowing,
>   Clouds there are none, and clear stars beam mild;
> God, in His mercy, protection is showing,
>   Comfort and hope to the poor orphan child.
>
> Ev'n should I fall o'er the broken bridge passing,
>   Or stray in the marshes, by false lights beguiled,
> Still will my Father, with promise and blessing,
>   Take to His bosom the poor orphan child.

3. A popular song of the period.

There is a thought that for strength should avail me,
  Though both of shelter and kindred despoiled;
Heaven is a home, and a rest will not fail me;
  God is a friend to the poor orphan child.

'Come, Miss Jane, don't cry,' said Bessie, as she finished. She might as well have said to the fire, 'don't burn!' but how could she divine the morbid suffering to which I was a prey? In the course of the morning Mr. Lloyd came again.

'What, already up!' said he, as he entered the nursery. 'Well, nurse, how is she?'

Bessie answered that I was doing very well.

'Then she ought to look more cheerful. Come here, Miss Jane; your name is Jane, is it not?'

'Yes, sir, Jane Eyre.'

'Well, you have been crying, Miss Jane Eyre; can you tell me what about? Have you any pain?'

'No, sir.'

'Oh! I daresay she is crying because she could not go out with Missis in the carriage,' interposed Bessie.

'Surely not! why, she is too old for such pettishness.'

I thought so too; and my self-esteem being wounded by the false charge, I answered promptly, 'I never cried for such a thing in my life: I hate going out in the carriage. I cry because I am miserable.'

'Oh fie, Miss!' said Bessie.

The good apothecary appeared a little puzzled. I was standing before him; he fixed his eyes on me very steadily: his eyes were small and grey: not very bright, but I daresay I should think them shrewd now: he had a hard-featured yet good-natured looking face. Having considered me at leisure, he said: 'What made you ill yesterday?'

'She had a fall,' said Bessie, again putting in her word.

'Fall! why that is like a baby again! Can't she manage to walk at her age? She must be eight or nine years old.'

'I was knocked down,' was the blunt explanation jerked out of me by another pang of mortified pride: 'but that did not make me ill,' I added; while Mr. Lloyd helped himself to a pinch of snuff.

As he was returning the box to his waistcoat pocket, a loud bell rang for the servants' dinner; he knew what it was. 'That's for you, nurse,' said he; 'you can go down; I'll give Miss Jane a lecture till you come back.'

Bessie would rather have stayed, but she was obliged to go, because punctuality at meals was rigidly enforced at Gateshead Hall.

'The fall did not make you ill; what did, then?' pursued Mr. Lloyd, when Bessie was gone.

'I was shut up in a room where there is a ghost till after dark.'

I saw Mr. Lloyd smile and frown at the same time: 'Ghost! What, you are a baby after all! You are afraid of ghosts?'

'Of Mr. Reed's ghost I am: he died in that room, and was laid out there. Neither Bessie nor any one else will go into it at night, if they can help it; and it was cruel to shut me up alone without a candle,—so cruel that I think I shall never forget it.'

'Nonsense! And is it that makes you so miserable? Are you afraid now in daylight?'

'No: but night will come again before long: and besides,—I am unhappy,—very unhappy, for other things.'

'What other things? Can you tell me some of them?'

How much I wished to reply fully to this question! How difficult it was to frame any answer. Children can feel, but they cannot analyse their feelings; and if the analysis is partially effected in thought, they know not how to express the result of the process in words. Fearful, however, of losing this first and only opportunity of relieving my grief by imparting it, I, after a disturbed pause, contrived to frame a meagre, though, as far as it went, true response.

'For one thing, I have no father or mother, brothers or sisters.'

'You have a kind aunt and cousins.'

Again I paused; then bunglingly enounced: 'But John Reed knocked me down, and my aunt shut me up in the red-room.'

Mr. Lloyd a second time produced his snuff-box.

'Don't you think Gateshead Hall a very beautiful house?' asked he. 'Are you not very thankful to have such a fine place to live at?'

'It is not my house, sir; and Abbot says I have less right to be here than a servant.'

'Pooh! you can't be silly enough to wish to leave such a splendid place?'

'If I had anywhere else to go, I should be glad to leave it; but I can never get away from Gateshead till I am a woman.'

'Perhaps you may—who knows? Have you any relations besides Mrs. Reed?'

'I think not, sir.'

'None belonging to your father?'

'I don't know: I asked aunt Reed once, and she said possibly I might have some poor, low relations called Eyre, but she knew nothing about them.'

'If you had such, would you like to go to them?'

I reflected. Poverty looks grim to grown people; still more so to children: they have not much idea of industrious, working, respectable poverty; they think of the word only as connected with ragged clothes, scanty food, fireless grates, rude manners, and debasing vices: poverty for me was synonymous with degradation.

'No; I should not like to belong to poor people,' was my reply.

'Not even if they were kind to you?'

I shook my head: I could not see how poor people had the means of being kind; and then to learn to speak like them, to adopt their manners, to be uneducated, to grow up like one of the poor women I saw sometimes nursing their children or washing their clothes at the cottage doors of the village of Gateshead: no, I was not heroic enough to purchase liberty at the price of caste.

'But are your relatives so very poor? Are they working people?'

'I cannot tell; aunt Reed says, if I have any, they must be a beggarly set: I should not like to go a begging.'

'Would you like to go to school?'

Again I reflected: I scarcely knew what school was; Bessie sometimes spoke of it as a place where young ladies sat in the stocks, wore back-boards,[4] and were expected to be exceedingly genteel and precise: John Reed hated his school, and abused his master; but John Reed's tastes were no rule for mine, and if Bessie's accounts of school discipline (gathered from the young ladies of a family where she had lived before coming to Gateshead) were somewhat appalling, her details of certain accomplishments attained by these same young ladies were, I thought, equally attractive. She boasted of beautiful paintings of landscapes and flowers by them executed; of songs they could sing and pieces they could play, of purses they could net, of French books they could translate; till my spirit was moved to emulation as I listened. Besides, school would be a complete change: it implied a long journey, an entire separation from Gateshead, an entrance into a new life.

'I should indeed like to go to school,' was the audible conclusion of my musings.

'Well, well; who knows what may happen?' said Mr. Lloyd, as he got up: 'The child ought to have change of air and scene,' he added, speaking to himself; 'nerves not in a good state.'

Bessie now returned; at the same moment the carriage was heard rolling up the gravel-walk.

'Is that your mistress, nurse?' asked Mr. Lloyd. 'I should like to speak to her before I go.'

Bessie invited him to walk into the breakfast-room, and led the way out. In the interview which followed between him and Mrs. Reed, I presume, from after-occurrences, that the apothecary ventured to rec-

---

4. Boards to which nineteenth-century young women were strapped to improve their posture; "stocks": a wooden frame which restrained a culprit's feet and hands.

ommend my being sent to school; and the recommendation was no doubt readily enough adopted; for as Abbot said, in discussing the subject with Bessie when both sat sewing in the nursery one night, after I was in bed, and, as they thought, asleep, 'Missis was, she dared say, glad enough to get rid of such a tiresome, ill-conditioned child, who always looked as if she were watching everybody, and scheming plots underhand.' Abbot, I think, gave me credit for being a sort of infantine Guy Fawkes.[5]

On that same occasion I learned, for the first time, from Miss Abbot's communications to Bessie, that my father had been a poor clergyman; that my mother had married him against the wishes of her friends, who considered the match beneath her; that my grandfather Reed was so irritated at her disobedience, he cut her off without a shilling; that after my mother and father had been married a year, the latter caught the typhus fever while visiting among the poor of a large manufacturing town where his curacy was situated, and where that disease was then prevalent; that my mother took the infection from him, and both died within a month of each other.

Bessie, when she heard this narrative, sighed and said, 'Poor Miss Jane is to be pitied, too, Abbot.'

'Yes,' responded Abbot, 'if she were a nice, pretty child, one might compassionate her forlornness; but one really cannot care for such a little toad as that.'

'Not a great deal, to be sure,' agreed Bessie: 'at any rate, a beauty like Miss Georgiana would be more moving in the same condition.'

'Yes, I doat on Miss Georgiana!' cried the fervent Abbot. 'Little darling!—with her long curls and her blue eyes, and such a sweet colour as she has; just as if she were painted!—Bessie, I could fancy a Welsh rabbit for supper.'

'So could I—with a roast onion. Come, we'll go down.' They went.

Chapter IV

From my discourse with Mr. Lloyd, and from the above-reported conference between Bessie and Abbot, I gathered enough of hope to suffice as a motive for wishing to get well: a change seemed near,—I desired and waited it in silence. It tarried, however: days and weeks passed: I had regained my normal state of health, but no new allusion was made to the subject over which I brooded. Mrs. Reed surveyed me at times with a severe eye, but seldom addressed me: since my illness she had drawn a more marked line of separation than ever between me

---

5. Famous sixteenth-century English traitor who conspired to blow up the houses of Parliament.

and her own children; appointing me a small closet to sleep in by myself, condemning me to take my meals alone, and pass all my time in the nursery, while my cousins were constantly in the drawing-room. Not a hint, however, did she drop about sending me to school: still I felt an instinctive certainty that she would not long endure me under the same roof with her; for her glance, now more than ever, when turned on me, expressed an insuperable and rooted aversion.

Eliza and Georgiana, evidently acting according to orders, spoke to me as little as possible: John thrust his tongue in his cheek whenever he saw me, and once attempted chastisement; but as I instantly turned against him, roused by the same sentiment of deep ire and desperate revolt which had stirred my corruption before, he thought it better to desist, and ran from me, uttering execrations, and vowing I had burst his nose. I had indeed levelled at that prominent feature as hard a blow as my knuckles could inflict; and when I saw that either that or my look daunted him, I had the greatest inclination to follow up my advantage to purpose; but he was already with his mamma. I heard him in a blubbering tone commence the tale of how 'that nasty Jane Eyre' had flown at him like a mad cat: he was stopped rather harshly—'Don't talk to me about her, John: I told you not to go near her; she is not worthy of notice; I do not choose that either you or your sisters should associate with her.'

Here, leaning over the banister, I cried out suddenly, and without at all deliberating on my words,—'They are not fit to associate with me.'

Mrs. Reed was rather a stout woman; but on hearing this strange and audacious declaration, she ran nimbly up the stair, swept me like a whirlwind into the nursery, and crushing me down on the edge of my crib, dared me in an emphatic voice to rise from that place, or utter one syllable, during the remainder of the day.

'What would uncle Reed say to you, if he were alive?' was my scarcely voluntary demand. I say scarcely voluntary, for it seemed as if my tongue pronounced words without my will consenting to their utterance: something spoke out of me over which I had no control.

'What?' said Mrs. Reed under her breath: her usually cold composed grey eye became troubled with a look like fear; she took her hand from my arm, and gazed at me as if she really did not know whether I were child or fiend. I was now in for it.

'My uncle Reed is in heaven, and can see all you do and think; and so can papa and mamma: they know how you shut me up all day long, and how you wish me dead.'

Mrs. Reed soon rallied her spirits: she shook me most soundly, she boxed both my ears, and then left me without a word. Bessie supplied the hiatus by a homily of an hour's length, in which she proved beyond a doubt that I was the most wicked and abandoned child ever reared under a roof. I half believed her; for I felt indeed only bad feelings surging in my breast.

November, December, and half of January passed away. Christmas and the New Year had been celebrated at Gateshead with the usual festive cheer; presents had been interchanged, dinners and evening parties given. From every enjoyment I was, of course, excluded: my share of the gaiety consisted in witnessing the daily apparelling of Eliza and Georgiana, and seeing them descend to the drawing-room, dressed out in thin muslin frocks and scarlet sashes, with hair elaborately ring-letted; and afterwards, in listening to the sound of the piano or the harp played below, to the passing to and fro of the butler and footman, to the jingling of glass and china as refreshments were handed, to the broken hum of conversation as the drawing-room doors opened and closed. When tired of this occupation, I would retire from the stairhead to the solitary and silent nursery: there, though somewhat sad, I was not miserable. To speak truth, I had not the least wish to go into company, for in company I was very rarely noticed; and if Bessie had but been kind and companionable, I should have deemed it a treat to spend the evenings quietly with her, instead of passing them under the formidable eye of Mrs. Reed, in a room full of ladies and gentlemen. But Bessie, as soon as she had dressed her young ladies, used to take herself off to the lively regions of the kitchen and the house-keeper's room, generally bearing the candle along with her. I then sat with my doll on my knee, till the fire got low, glancing round occasionally to make sure that nothing worse than myself haunted the shadowy room; and when the embers sank to a dull red, I undressed hastily, tugging at knots and strings as I best might, and sought shelter from cold and darkness in my crib. To this crib I always took my doll; human beings must love something, and in the dearth of worthier objects of affection, I contrived to find a pleasure in loving and cherishing a faded graven image, shabby as a miniature scarecrow. It puzzles me now to remember with what absurd sincerity I doated on this little toy, half fancying it alive and capable of sensation. I could not sleep unless it was folded in my night-gown; and when it lay there safe and warm, I was comparatively happy, believing it to be happy likewise.

Long did the hours seem while I waited the departure of the company, and listened for the sound of Bessie's step on the stairs: sometimes she would come up in the interval to seek her thimble or her scissors, or perhaps to bring me something by way of supper—a bun or a cheese-cake—then she would sit on the bed while I ate it, and when I had finished, she would tuck the clothes round me, and twice she kissed me, and said, 'Good night, Miss Jane.' When thus gentle, Bessie seemed to me the best, prettiest, kindest being in the world; and I wished most intensely that she would always be so pleasant and amiable, and never push me about, or scold, or task me unreasonably, as she was too often wont to do. Bessie Lee must, I think, have been a girl of good natural capacity, for she was smart in all she did, and had a remarkable knack of narrative; so, at least, I judge from the impression made on me by her nursery tales. She was pretty, too, if my recollections of her face and person are correct. I remember her as a slim young woman, with black hair, dark eyes, very nice features, and good, clear complexion; but she had a capricious and hasty temper, and indifferent ideas of principle or justice: still, such as she was, I preferred her to any one else at Gateshead Hall.

It was the fifteenth of January, about nine o'clock in the morning: Bessie was gone down to breakfast; my cousins had not yet been summoned to their mamma; Eliza was putting on her bonnet and warm garden-coat to go and feed her poultry, an occupation of which she was fond: and not less so of selling the eggs to the housekeeper and hoarding up the money she thus obtained. She had a turn for traffic,[6] and a marked propensity for saving; shown not only in the vending of eggs and chickens, but also in driving hard bargains with the gardener about flower-roots, seeds, and slips of plants; that functionary having orders from Mrs. Reed to buy of his young lady all the products of her parterre she wished to sell: and Eliza would have sold the hair off her head if she could have made a handsome profit thereby. As to her money, she first secreted it in odd corners, wrapped in a rag or an old curl-paper; but some of these hoards having been discovered by the housemaid, Eliza, fearful of one day losing her valued treasure, consented to intrust it to her mother, at a usurious rate of interest—fifty or sixty per cent.; which interest she exacted every quarter, keeping her accounts in a little book with anxious accuracy.

Georgiana sat on a high stool, dressing her hair at the glass, and interweaving her curls with artificial flowers and faded feathers, of which she had found a store in a drawer in the attic. I was making my bed, having received strict orders from Bessie to get it arranged before she returned (for Bessie now frequently employed me as a sort of undernurserymaid, to tidy the room, dust the chairs, &c.). Having spread the quilt, and folded my night-dress, I went to the window-seat to put in order some picture-books and doll's house furniture scattered there; an abrupt command from Georgiana to let her playthings alone (for the tiny chairs and mirrors, the fairy plates and cups were her property) stopped my proceedings; and then, for lack of other occupation, I fell to breathing on the frost-flowers with which the window was fretted, and

6. Bartering.

thus clearing a space in the glass through which I might look out on the grounds, where all was still and petrified under the influence of a hard frost.

From this window were visible the porter's lodge and the carriage-road, and just as I had dissolved so much of the silver-white foliage veiling the panes as left room to look out, I saw the gates thrown open and a carriage roll through. I watched it ascending the drive with indifference: carriages often came to Gateshead, but none ever brought visitors in whom I was interested; it stopped in front of the house, the door-bell rang loudly, the new-comer was admitted. All this being nothing to me, my vacant attention soon found livelier attraction in the spectacle of a little hungry robin, which came and chirruped on the twigs of the leafless cherry-tree nailed against the wall near the casement. The remains of my breakfast of bread and milk stood on the table, and having crumbled a morsel of roll, I was tugging at the sash to put out the crumbs on the window-sill, when Bessie came running upstairs into the nursery.

'Miss Jane, take off your pinafore: what are you doing there? Have you washed your hands and face this morning?' I gave another tug before I answered, for I wanted the bird to be secure of its bread: the sash yielded; I scattered the crumbs, some on the stone sill, some on the cherry-tree bough, then, closing the window, I replied:—'No, Bessie; I have only just finished dusting.'

'Troublesome, careless child! and what are you doing now? You look quite red, as if you had been about some mischief: what were you opening the window for?'

I was spared the trouble of answering, for Bessie seemed in too great a hurry to listen to explanations: she hauled me to the wash-stand, inflicted a merciless, but happily brief scrub on my face and hands with soap, water, and a coarse towel; disciplined my head with a bristly brush, denuded me of my pinafore, and then, hurrying me to the top of the stairs, bid me go down directly, as I was wanted in the breakfast-room.

I would have asked who wanted me: I would have demanded if Mrs. Reed was there; but Bessie was already gone, and had closed the nursery-door upon me: I slowly descended. For nearly three months I had never been called to Mrs. Reed's presence: restricted so long to the nursery, the breakfast, dining, and drawing-rooms were become for me awful regions, on which it dismayed me to intrude.

I now stood in the empty hall; before me was the breakfast-room door, and I stopped, intimidated and trembling. What a miserable little poltroon had fear, engendered of unjust punishment, made of me in those days! I feared to return to the nursery, and feared to go forward to

the parlour; ten minutes I stood in agitated hesitation: the vehement
ringing of the breakfast-room bell decided me; I *must* enter.

'Who could want me?' I asked inwardly, as with both hands I turned
the stiff door-handle, which, for a second or two, resisted my efforts.
'What should I see besides aunt Reed in the apartment?—a man or a
woman?' The handle turned, the door unclosed, and passing through
and curtseying low I looked up at—a black pillar! such, at least, appeared to me, at first sight, the straight, narrow, sable-clad shape standing erect on the rug: the grim face at the top was like a carved mask,
placed above the shaft by way of capital.

Mrs. Reed occupied her usual seat by the fireside: she made a signal
to me to approach: I did so, and she introduced me to the stony stranger
with the words: 'This is the little girl respecting whom I applied to you.'

He, for it was a man, turned his head slowly towards where I stood,
and having examined me with the two inquisitive-looking grey eyes
which twinkled under a pair of bushy brows, said solemnly, and in a bass
voice: 'Her size is small: what is her age?'

'Ten years.'

'So much?' was the doubtful answer; and he prolonged his scrutiny
for some minutes. Presently he addressed me:

'Your name, little girl?'

'Jane Eyre, sir.'

In uttering these words I looked up: he seemed to me a tall gentleman; but then I was very little: his features were large, and they and all
the lines of his frame were equally harsh and prim.

'Well, Jane Eyre, and are you a good child?'

Impossible to reply to this in the affirmative: my little world held a
contrary opinion: I was silent. Mrs. Reed answered for me by an expressive shake of the head, adding soon, 'Perhaps the less said on that
subject the better, Mr. Brocklehurst.'

'Sorry indeed to hear it! she and I must have some talk;' and bending
from the perpendicular, he installed his person in the arm-chair, opposite Mrs. Reed's. 'Come here,' he said.

I stepped across the rug; he placed me square and straight before
him. What a face he had, now that it was almost on a level with mine!
what a great nose! and what a mouth! and what large prominent teeth!

'No sight so sad as that of a naughty child,' he began, 'especially a
naughty little girl. Do you know where the wicked go after death?'

'They go to hell,' was my ready and orthodox answer.

'And what is hell? Can you tell me that?'

'A pit full of fire.'

'And should you like to fall into that pit, and to be burning there for
ever?'

'No, sir.'

'What must you do to avoid it?'

I deliberated a moment; my answer, when it did come, was objectionable: 'I must keep in good health and not die.'

'How can you keep in good health? Children younger than you die daily. I buried a little child of five years old only a day or two since,—a good little child, whose soul is now in heaven. It is to be feared the same could not be said of you, were you to be called hence.'

Not being in a condition to remove his doubt, I only cast my eyes down on the two large feet planted on the rug, and sighed, wishing myself far enough away.

'I hope that sigh is from the heart, and that you repent of ever having been the occasion of discomfort to your excellent benefactress.'

'Benefactress! benefactress!' said I, inwardly: 'they all call Mrs. Reed my benefactress; if so, a benefactress is a disagreeable thing.'

'Do you say your prayers night and morning?' continued my interrogator.

'Yes, sir.'

'Do you read your Bible?'

'Sometimes.'

'With pleasure? Are you fond of it?'

'I like Revelations, and the book of Daniel, and Genesis and Samuel, and a little bit of Exodus, and some parts of Kings and Chronicles, and Job and Jonah.'

'And the Psalms? I hope you like them?'

'No, sir.'

'No? Oh, shocking! I have a little boy, younger than you, who knows six Psalms by heart: and when you ask him which he would rather have, a gingerbread-nut to eat, or a verse of a Psalm to learn he says: "Oh! the verse of a Psalm! angels sing Psalms," says he; "I wish to be a little angel here below;" he then gets two nuts in recompense for his infant piety.'

'Psalms are not interesting,' I remarked.

'That proves you have a wicked heart; and you must pray to God to change it: to give you a new and clean one: to take away your heart of stone and give you a heart of flesh.'

I was about to propound a question, touching the manner in which that operation of changing my heart was to be performed, when Mrs. Reed interposed, telling me to sit down; she then proceeded to carry on the conversation herself.

'Mr. Brocklehurst, I believe I intimated in the letter which I wrote to you three weeks ago, that this little girl has not quite the character and disposition I could wish: should you admit her into Lowood school, I should be glad if the superintendent and teachers were requested to keep a strict eye on her, and above all, to guard against her worst fault, a tendency to deceit. I mention this in your hearing, Jane, that you may not attempt to impose on Mr. Brocklehurst.'

Well might I dread, well might I dislike Mrs. Reed; for it was her nature to wound me cruelly: never was I happy in her presence: however carefully I obeyed, however strenuously I strove to please her, my efforts were still repulsed and repaid by such sentences as the above. Now, uttered before a stranger, the accusation cut me to the heart: I dimly perceived that she was already obliterating hope from the new phase of existence which she destined me to enter; I felt, though I could not have expressed the feeling, that she was sowing aversion and unkindness along my future path; I saw myself transformed under Mr. Brocklehurst's eye into an artful noxious child, and what could I do to remedy the injury?

'Nothing, indeed,' thought I, as I struggled to repress a sob, and hastily wiped away some tears, the impotent evidences of my anguish.

'Deceit is, indeed, a sad fault in a child,' said Mr. Brocklehurst; 'it is akin to falsehood, and all liars will have their portion in the lake burning with fire and brimstone: she shall, however, be watched, Mrs. Reed; I will speak to Miss Temple and the teachers.'

'I should wish her to be brought up in a manner suiting her prospects,' continued my benefactress; 'to be made useful, to be kept humble: as for the vacations, she will, with your permission, spend them always at Lowood.'

'Your decisions are perfectly judicious, madam,' returned Mr. Brocklehurst. 'Humility is a Christian grace, and one peculiarly appropriate to the pupils of Lowood: I, therefore, direct that especial care shall be bestowed on its cultivation amongst them. I have studied how best to mortify in them the worldly sentiment of pride; and, only the other day, I had a pleasing proof of my success. My second daughter, Augusta, went with her mamma to visit the school, and on her return she exclaimed: "Oh, dear papa, how quiet and plain all the girls at Lowood look; with their hair combed behind their ears, and their long pinafores, and those little holland[7] pockets outside their frocks—they are almost like poor people's children! and," said she, "they looked at my dress and mamma's, as if they had never seen a silk gown before."'

'This is the state of things I quite approve.' returned Mrs. Reed; 'had I sought all England over, I could scarcely have found a system more exactly fitting a child like Jane Eyre. Consistency, my dear Mr. Brocklehurst; I advocate consistency in all things.'

'Consistency, madam, is the first of Christian duties; and it has been observed in every arrangement connected with the establishment of Lowood: plain fare, simple attire, unsophisticated accommodations,

---

7. Plain-weave heavy fabric.

hardy and active habits; such is the order of the day in the house and its inhabitants.'

'Quite right, sir. I may then depend upon this child being received as a pupil at Lowood, and there being trained in conformity to her position and prospects?'

'Madam, you may: she shall be placed in that nursery of chosen plants—and I trust she will show herself grateful for the inestimable privilege of her election.'

'I will send her, then, as soon as possible, Mr. Brocklehurst; for, I assure you, I feel anxious to be relieved of a responsibility that was becoming too irksome.'

'No doubt, no doubt, madam, and now I wish you good morning. I shall return to Brocklehurst Hall in the course of a week or two: my good friend, the Archdeacon, will not permit me to leave him sooner. I shall send Miss Temple notice that she is to expect a new girl, so that there wll be no difficulty about receiving her. Good-bye.'

'Good-bye, Mr. Brocklehurst; remember me to Mrs. and Miss Brocklehurst, and to Augusta and Theodore, and Master Broughton Brocklehurst.'

'I will, madam. Little girl, here is a book entitled the "Child's Guide";[8] read it with prayer, especially that part containing "an account of the awfully sudden death of Martha G——, a naughty child addicted to falsehood and deceit."

With these words Mr. Brocklehurst put into my hand a thin pamphlet sewn in a cover, and having rung for his carriage he departed.

Mrs. Reed and I were left alone: some minutes passed in silence: she was sewing, I was watching her. Mrs. Reed might be at that time some six or seven and thirty; she was a woman of robust frame, square-shouldered and strong-limbed, not tall, and, though stout, not obese: she had a somewhat large face, the under-jaw being much developed and very solid; her brow was low, her chin large and prominent, mouth and nose sufficiently regular; under her light eyebrows glimmered an eye devoid of ruth; her skin was dark and opaque, her hair nearly flaxen; her constitution was sound as a bell—illness never came near her; she was an exact, clever manager, her household and tenantry were thoroughly under her control; her children, only, at times defied her authority, and laughed it to scorn; she dressed well, and had a presence and port[9] calculated to set off handsome attire.

Sitting on a low stool, a few yards from her arm-chair, I examined her figure; I perused her features. In my hand I held the tract containing the sudden death of the Liar: to which narrative my attention had been pointed as to an appropriate warning. What had just passed; what Mrs.

8. One of the heavily didactic and religious children's magazines of the period, such as The *Children's Friend.*
9. Manner.

Reed had said concerning me to Mr. Brocklehurst; the whole tenor of their conversation, was recent, raw, and stinging in my mind; I had felt every word as acutely as I had heard it plainly, and a passion of resentment fomented now within me.

Mrs. Reed looked up from her work; her eye settled on mine, her fingers at the same time suspended their nimble movements.

'Go out of the room; return to the nursery,' was her mandate. My look or something else must have struck her as offensive, for she spoke with extreme, though suppressed irritation. I got up, I went to the door; I came back again; I walked to the window, across the room, then close up to her.

Speak I must; I had been trodden on severely, and *must* turn: but how? What strength had I to dart retaliation at my antagonist? I gathered my energies and launched them in this blunt sentence:—'I am not deceitful: if I were, I should say I loved *you*; but I declare I do not love you: I dislike you the worst of anybody in the world except John Reed; and this book about the liar, you may give to your girl, Georgiana, for it is she who tells lies, and not I.'

Mrs. Reed's hands still lay on her work inactive: her eye of ice continued to dwell freezingly on mine.

'What more have you to say?' she asked, rather in the tone in which a person might address an opponent of adult age than such as is ordinarily used to a child.

That eye of hers, that voice stirred every antipathy I had. Shaking from head to foot, thrilled with ungovernable excitement, I continued: —'I am glad you are no relation of mine: I will never call you aunt again as long as I live. I will never come to see you when I am grown up; and if any one asks me how I liked you, and how you treated me, I will say the very thought of you makes me sick, and that you treated me with miserable cruelty.'

'How dare you affirm that, Jane Eyre?'

'How dare I, Mrs. Reed? How dare I? Because it is the *truth*. You think I have no feelings, and that I can do without one bit of love or kindness; but I cannot live so: and you have no pity. I shall remember how you thrust me back—roughly and violently thrust me back—into the red-room, and locked me up there, to my dying day; though I was in agony; though I cried out, while suffocating with distress, "Have mercy! Have mercy, aunt Reed!" And that punishment you made me suffer because your wicked boy struck me—knocked me down for nothing. I will tell anybody who asks me questions this exact tale. People think you a good woman, but you are bad; hard-hearted. *You* are deceitful!'

Ere I had finished this reply my soul began to expand, to exult, with the strangest sense of freedom, of triumph, I ever felt. It seemed as if an invisible bond had burst, and that I had struggled out into unhoped-for liberty. Not without cause was this sentiment: Mrs. Reed looked frightened; her work had slipped from her knee; she was lifting up her hands, rocking herself to and fro, and even twisting her face as if she would cry.

'Jane, you are under a mistake: what is the matter with you? Why do you tremble so violently? Would you like to drink some water?'

'No, Mrs. Reed.'

'Is there anything else you wish for, Jane? I assure you, I desire to be your friend.'

'Not you. You told Mr. Brocklehurst I had a bad character, a deceitful disposition; and I'll let everybody at Lowood know what you are, and what you have done.'

'Jane, you don't understand these things: children must be corrected for their faults.'

'Deceit is not my fault!' I cried out in a savage, high voice.

'But you are passionate, Jane, that you must allow: and now return to the nursery—there's a dear—and lie down a little.'

'I am not your dear; I cannot lie down: send me to school soon, Mrs. Reed, for I hate to live here.'

'I will indeed send her to school soon,' murmured Mrs. Reed, *sotto voce*; and gathering up her work, she abruptly quitted the apartment.

I was left there alone—winner of the field. It was the hardest battle I had fought, and the first victory I had gained: I stood awhile on the rug, where Mr. Brocklehurst had stood, and I enjoyed my conqueror's solitude. First, I smiled to myself and felt elate; but this fierce pleasure subsided in me as fast as did the accelerated throb of my pulses. A child cannot quarrel with its elders, as I had done; cannot give its furious feelings uncontrolled play, as I had given mine, without experiencing afterwards the pang of remorse and the chill of reaction. A ridge of lighted heath, alive, glancing, devouring, would have been a meet[1] emblem of my mind when I accused and menaced Mrs. Reed: the same ridge, black and blasted after the flames are dead, would have represented as meetly my subsequent condition, when half an hour's silence and reflection had shown me the madness of my conduct, and the dreariness of my hated and hating position.

Something of vengeance I had tasted for the first time; as aromatic wine it seemed, on swallowing, warm and racy: its afterflavour, metallic and corroding, gave me a sensation as if I had been poisoned. Willingly would I now have gone and asked Mrs. Reed's pardon; but I knew, partly from experience and partly from instinct, that was the way to make her repulse me with double scorn, thereby re-exciting every turbulent impulse of my nature.

1. Proper.

I would fain exercise some better faculty than that of fierce speaking; fain find nourishment for some less fiendish feeling than that of sombre indignation. I took a book—some Arabian tales; I sat down and endeavoured to read. I could make no sense of the subject; my own thoughts swam always between me and the page I had usually found fascinating. I opened the glass-door in the breakfast-room: the shrubbery was quite still: the black frost reigned, unbroken by sun or breeze, through the grounds. I covered my head and arms with the skirt of my frock, and went out to walk in a part of the plantation which was quite sequestered: but I found no pleasure in the silent trees, the falling fir-cones, the congealed relics of autumn, russet leaves, swept by past winds in heaps, and now stiffened together. I leaned against a gate, and looked into an empty field where no sheep were feeding, where the short grass was nipped and blanched. It was a very grey day; a most opaque sky, 'onding on snaw,'[2] canopied all; thence flakes fell at intervals, which settled on the hard path and on the hoary lea without melting. I stood, a wretched child enough, whispering to myself over and over again, 'What shall I do?—what shall I do?'

All at once I heard a clear voice call, 'Miss Jane! where are you? Come to lunch!'

It was Bessie, I knew well enough; but I did not stir; her light step came tripping down the path.

'You naughty little thing!' she said. 'Why don't you come when you are called?'

Bessie's presence, compared with the thoughts over which I had been brooding, seemed cheerful; even though, as usual, she was somewhat cross. The fact is, after my conflict with and victory over Mrs. Reed, I was not disposed to care much for the nursemaid's transitory anger; and I *was* disposed to bask in her youthful lightness of heart. I just put my two arms round her, and said, 'Come, Bessie! don't scold.'

The action was more frank and fearless than any I was habituated to indulge in: somehow it pleased her.

'You are a strange child, Miss Jane,' she said, as she looked down at me: 'a little, roving, solitary thing: and you are going to school, I suppose?'

I nodded.

'And won't you be sorry to leave poor Bessie?'

'What does Bessie care for me? She is always scolding me.'

'Because you're such a queer, frightened, shy, little thing. You should be bolder.'

'What! to get more knocks?'

'Nonsense! But you are rather put upon, that's certain. My mother

2. Northern dialect: "appearing ready to snow."

said, when she came to see me last week, that she would not like a little one of her own to be in your place. Now, come in, and I've some good news for you.'

'I don't think you have, Bessie.'

'Child! what do you mean? What sorrowful eyes you fix on me! Well! but Missis and the young ladies and Master John are going out to tea this afternoon, and you shall have tea with me. I'll ask cook to bake you a little cake, and then you shall help me to look over your drawers; for I am soon to pack your trunk. Missis intends you to leave Gateshead in a day or two, and you shall choose what toys you like to take with you.'

'Bessie, you must promise not to scold me any more till I go.'

'Well, I will: but mind you are a very good girl, and don't be afraid of me. Don't start when I chance to speak rather sharply: it's so provoking.'

'I don't think I shall ever be afraid of you again, Bessie, because I have got used to you; and I shall soon have another set of people to dread.'

'If you dread them, they'll dislike you.'

'As you do, Bessie?'

'I don't dislike you, Miss; I believe I am fonder of you than of all the others.'

'You don't show it.'

'You little sharp thing! you've got quite a new way of talking. What makes you so venturesome and hardy?'

'Why, I shall soon be away from you, and besides—' I was going to say something about what had passed between me and Mrs. Reed; but on second thoughts I considered it better to remain silent on that head.

'And so you're glad to leave me?'

'Not at all, Bessie; indeed, just now I am rather sorry.'

'Just now! and rather! How coolly my little lady says it! I daresay now if I were to ask you for a kiss you wouldn't give it me: you'd say you'd *rather* not.'

'I'll kiss you and welcome: bend your head down.' Bessie stooped; we mutually embraced, and I followed her into the house quite comforted. That afternoon lapsed in peace and harmony; and in the evening Bessie told me some of her most enchanting stories, and sang me some of her sweetest songs. Even for me life had its gleams of sunshine.

Chapter V

Five o'clock had hardly struck on the morning of the 19th of January, when Bessie brought a candle into my closet, and found me already up and nearly dressed. I had risen half an hour before her entrance, and had washed my face, and put on my clothes by the light of a half-moon just setting, whose rays streamed through the narrow window near my crib. I was to leave Gateshead that day by a coach which passed the lodge gates at six A.M. Bessie was the only person yet risen; she had lit a fire in the nursery, where she now proceeded to make my breakfast. Few children can eat when excited with the thoughts of a journey; nor could I. Bessie, having pressed me in vain to take a few spoonfuls of the boiled milk and bread she had prepared for me, wrapped up some biscuits in a paper and put them into my bag; then she helped me on with my pelisse and bonnet, and wrapping herself in a shawl, she and I left the nursery. As we passed Mrs. Reed's bedroom, she said, 'Will you go in and bid Missis good-bye?'

'No, Bessie: she came to my crib last night when you were gone down to supper, and said I need not disturb her in the morning, or my cousins either; and she told me to remember that she had always been my best friend, and to speak of her and be grateful to her accordingly.'

'What did you say, Miss?'

'Nothing: I covered my face with the bed-clothes, and turned from her to the wall.'

'That was wrong, Miss Jane.'

'It was quite right, Bessie: your Missis has not been my friend: she has been my foe.'

'Oh, Miss Jane! don't say so!'

'Good-bye to Gateshead!' cried I, as we passed through the hall and went out at the front door.

The moon was set, and it was very dark; Bessie carried a lantern, whose light glanced on wet steps and gravel road sodden by a recent thaw. Raw and chill was the winter morning: my teeth chattered as I hastened down the drive. There was a light in the porter's lodge: when we reached it, we found the porter's wife just kindling her fire: my trunk, which had been carried down the evening before, stood corded at the door. It wanted but a few minutes of six, and shortly after that hour had struck the distant roll of wheels announced the coming coach; I went to the door, and watched its lamps approach rapidly through the gloom.

'Is she going by herself?' asked the porter's wife.

'Yes.'

'And how far is it?'

'Fifty miles.'

'What a long way! I wonder Mrs. Reed is not afraid to trust her so far alone.'

The coach drew up; there it was at the gates with its four horses and its top laden with passengers: the guard and coachman loudly urged haste; my trunk was hoisted up; I was taken from Bessie's neck, to which I clung with kisses.

'Be sure and take good care of her,' cried she to the guard, as he lifted me into the inside.

'Ay, ay!' was the answer: the door was slapped to, a voice exclaimed, 'All right,' and on we drove. Thus was I severed from Bessie and Gateshead: thus whirled away to unknown, and, as I then deemed, remote and mysterious regions.

I remember but little of the journey: I only know that the day seemed to me of a preternatural length, and that we appeared to travel over hundreds of miles of road. We passed through several towns, and in one, a very large one, the coach stopped; the horses were taken out, and the passengers alighted to dine. I was carried into an inn, where the guard wanted me to have some dinner; but, as I had no appetite, he left me in an immense room with a fire-place at each end, a chandelier pendent from the ceiling, and a little red gallery high up against the wall filled with musical instruments. Here I walked about for a long time, feeling very strange, and mortally apprehensive of some one coming in and kidnapping me; for I believed in kidnappers, their exploits having frequently figured in Bessie's fireside chronicles. At last the guard returned: once more I was stowed away in the coach, my protector mounted his own seat, sounded his hollow horn, and away we rattled over the 'stony street' of L——

The afternoon came on wet and somewhat misty: as it waned into dusk I began to feel that we were getting very far indeed from Gateshead: we ceased to pass through towns; the country changed; great grey hills heaved up round the horizon: as twilight deepened we descended a valley, dark with wood, and long after night had overclouded the prospect I heard a wild wind rushing amongst trees.

Lulled by the sound, I at last dropped asleep: I had not long slumbered when the sudden cessation of motion awoke me; the coach-door was open, and a person like a servant was standing at it: I saw her face and dress by the light of the lamps.

'Is there a little girl called Jane Eyre here?' she asked. I answered 'Yes,' and was then lifted out; my trunk was handed down, and the coach instantly drove away.

I was stiff with long sitting, and bewildered with the noise and motion of the coach: gathering my faculties, I looked about me. Rain, wind, and darkness filled the air; nevertheless, I dimly discerned a wall before me and a door open in it; through this door I passed with my new guide: she shut and locked it behind her. There was now visible a house or houses—for the building spread far—with many windows, and lights burning in some; we went up a broad pebbly path, splashing wet, and were admitted at a door; then the servant led me through a passage into a room with a fire, where she left me alone.

I stood and warmed my numbed fingers over the blaze, then I looked round; there was no candle, but the uncertain light from the hearth showed, by intervals, papered walls, carpet, curtains, shining mahogany furniture: it was a parlour, not so spacious or splendid as the drawing-room at Gateshead, but comfortable enough. I was puzzling to make out the subject of a picture on the wall, when the door opened, and an individual carrying a light entered; another followed close behind.

The first was a tall lady with dark hair, dark eyes, and a pale and large forehead; her figure was partly enveloped in a shawl, her countenance was grave, her bearing erect.

'The child is very young to be sent alone,' said she, putting her candle down on the table. She considered me attentively for a minute or two, then further added:

'She had better be put to bed soon; she looks tired: are you tired?' she asked, placing her hand on my shoulder.

'A little, ma'am.'

'And hungry too, no doubt: let her have some supper before she goes to bed, Miss Miller. Is this the first time you have left your parents to come to school, my little girl?'

I explained to her that I had no parents. She inquired how long they had been dead; then how old I was, what was my name, whether I could read, write, and sew a little: then she touched my cheek gently with her forefinger, and saying, 'She hoped I should be a good child,' dismissed me along with Miss Miller.

The lady I had left might be about twenty-nine; the one who went with me appeared some years younger: the first impressed me by her voice, look, and air. Miss Miller was more ordinary; ruddy in complexion, though of a careworn countenance; hurried in gait and action, like one who had always a multiplicity of tasks on hand: she looked, indeed, what I afterwards found she really was, an under-teacher. Led by her, I passed from compartment to compartment, from passage to passage, of a large and irregular building; till, emerging from the total and somewhat dreary silence pervading that portion of the house we had traversed, we came upon the hum of many voices, and presently entered a wide, long room, with great deal tables, two at each end, on each of which burnt a pair of candles, and seated all round on benches a congregation of girls of every age, from nine or ten to twenty. Seen by the dim light of the dips, their number to me appeared countless, though not in reality exceeding eighty; they were uniformly dressed in brown stuff frocks of quaint fashion, and long holland pinafores. It was the hour of study; they were engaged in conning over their to-morrow's task, and the hum I had heard was the combined result of their whispered repetitions.

Miss Miller signed to me to sit on a bench near the door, then walking up to the top of the long room, she cried out:

'Monitors, collect the lesson-books and put them away!'

Four tall girls arose from different tables, and going round, gathered the books and removed them. Miss Miller again gave the word of command:

'Monitors, fetch the supper-trays!'

The tall girls went out, and returned presently, each bearing a tray, with portions of something, I knew not what, arranged thereon, and a pitcher of water and mug in the middle of each tray. The portions were handed round; those who liked took a draught of the water, the mug being common to all. When it came to my turn, I drank, for I was thirsty, but did not touch the food, excitement and fatigue rendering me incapable of eating: I now saw, however, that it was a thin oaten cake, shared into fragments.

The meal over, prayers were read by Miss Miller, and the classes filed off, two and two, upstairs. Overpowered by this time with weariness, I scarcely noticed what sort of a place the bedroom was; except that, like the schoolroom, I saw it was very long. To-night I was to be Miss Miller's bedfellow; she helped me to undress: when laid down I glanced at the long rows of beds, each of which was quickly filled with two occupants; in ten minutes the single light was extinguished; amidst silence and complete darkness, I fell asleep.

The night passed rapidly: I was too tired even to dream; I only once awoke to hear the wind rave in furious gusts, and the rain fall in torrents, and to be sensible that Miss Miller had taken her place by my side. When I again unclosed my eyes, a loud bell was ringing: the girls were up and dressing; day had not yet begun to dawn, and a rush-light or two burnt in the room. I too rose reluctantly; it was bitter cold, and I dressed as well as I could for shivering, and washed when there was a basin at liberty, which did not occur soon, as there was but one basin to six girls on the stands down the middle of the room. Again the bell rang: all formed in file, two and two, and in that order descended the stairs and entered the cold and dimly-lit schoolroom: here prayers were read by Miss Miller; afterwards she called out:—'Form classes!'

A great tumult succeeded for some minutes, during which Miss Miller repeatedly exclaimed, 'Silence!' and 'Order!' When it subsided, I saw them all drawn up in four semicircles, before four chairs, placed at the four tables; all held books in their hands, and a great book, like a Bible, lay on each table, before the vacant seat. A pause of some seconds succeeded, filled up by the low, vague hum of numbers; Miss Miller walked from class to class, hushing this indefinite sound.

A distant bell tinkled: immediately three ladies entered the room, each walked to a table and took her seat; Miss Miller assumed the fourth vacant chair, which was that nearest the door, and around which the smallest of the children were assembled: to this inferior class I was called, and placed at the bottom of it.

Business now began: the day's Collect was repeated, then certain texts of Scripture were said, and to these succeeded a protracted reading of chapters in the Bible, which lasted an hour. By the time that exercise was terminated day had fully dawned. The indefatigable bell now sounded for the fourth time: the classes were marshalled and marched into another room to breakfast: how glad I was to behold a prospect of getting something to eat! I was now nearly sick from inanition, having taken so little the day before.

The refectory was a great, low-ceiled, gloomy room; on two long tables smoked basins of something hot, which, however, to my dismay, sent forth an odour far from inviting. I saw a universal manifestation of discontent when the fumes of the repast met the nostrils of those destined to swallow it: from the van of the procession, the tall girls of the first class, rose the whispered words:—'Disgusting! The porridge is burnt again!'

'Silence!' ejaculated a voice; not that of Miss Miller, but one of the upper teachers, a little and dark personage, smartly dressed, but of somewhat morose aspect, who installed herself at the top of one table, while a more buxom lady presided at the other. I looked in vain for her I had first seen the night before; she was not visible: Miss Miller occupied the foot of the table where I sat, and a strange, foreign looking, elderly lady, the French teacher, as I afterwards found, took the corresponding seat at the other board. A long grace was said and a hymn sung; then a servant brought in some tea for the teachers, and the meal began.

Ravenous, and now very faint, I devoured a spoonful or two of my portion without thinking of its taste; but the first edge of hunger blunted, I perceived I had got in hand a nauseous mess: burnt porridge is almost as bad as rotten potatoes; famine itself soon sickens over it. The spoons were moved slowly: I saw each girl taste her food and try to swallow it; but in most cases the effort was soon relinquished. Breakfast was over, and none had breakfasted. Thanks being returned for what we had not got, and a second hymn chanted, the refectory was evacuated for the schoolroom. I was one of the last to go out, and in passing the tables, I saw one teacher take a basin of the porridge and taste it; she looked at the others; all their countenances expressed displeasure, and one of them, the stout one, whispered:—'Abominable stuff! How shameful!'

A quarter of an hour passed before lessons again began, during which the schoolroom was in a glorious tumult; for that space of time, it seemed to be permitted to talk loud and more freely, and they used their privilege. The whole conversation ran on the breakfast, which one and all abused roundly. Poor things! it was the sole consolation they had. Miss Miller was now the only teacher in the room: a group of great girls standing about her, spoke with serious and sullen gestures. I heard the name of Mr. Brocklehurst pronounced by some lips; at which Miss

Miller shook her head disapprovingly; but she made no great effort to check the general wrath: doubtless she shared in it.

A clock in the schoolroom struck nine; Miss Miller left her circle, and standing in the middle of the room, cried:—'Silence! To your seats!'

Discipline prevailed: in five minutes the confused throng was resolved into order, and comparative silence quelled the Babel clamour of tongues. The upper teachers now punctually resumed their posts: but still, all seemed to wait. Ranged on benches down the sides of the room, the eighty girls sat motionless and erect: a quaint assemblage they appeared, all with plain locks combed from their faces, not a curl visible; in brown dresses, made high and surrounded by a narrow tucker about the throat, with little pockets of holland (shaped something like a Highlander's purse) tied in front of their frocks, and destined to serve the purpose of a work-bag: all too wearing woollen stockings and country-made shoes, fastened with brass buckles. Above twenty of those clad in this costume were full-grown girls, or rather young women; it suited them ill, and gave an air of oddity even to the prettiest.

I was still looking at them, and also at intervals examining the teachers—none of whom precisely pleased me; for the stout one was a little coarse, the dark one not a little fierce, the foreigner harsh and grotesque, and Miss Miller, poor thing! looked purple, weatherbeaten, and overworked—when, as my eye wandered from face to face, the whole school rose simultaneously, as if moved by a common spring.

What was the matter? I had heard no order given: I was puzzled. Ere I had gathered my wits, the classes were again seated: but as all eyes were now turned to one point, mine followed the general direction, and encountered the personage who had received me last night. She stood at the bottom of the long room, on the hearth; for there was a fire at each end: she surveyed the two rows of girls silently and gravely. Miss Miller approaching, seemed to ask her a question, and having received her answer, went back to her place, and said aloud,—'Monitor of the first class, fetch the globes!'

While the direction was being executed, the lady consulted moved slowly up the room. I suppose I have a considerable organ of Veneration,[3] for I retain yet the sense of admiring awe with which my eyes traced her steps. Seen now, in broad daylight, she looked tall, fair, and shapely; brown eyes, with a benignant light in their irids, and a fine pencilling of long lashes round, relieved the whiteness of her large front; on each of her temples her hair, of a very dark brown, was clustered in round curls, according to the fashion of those times, when nei-

---

3. A reference to the "science" of phrenology, much in vogue in the nineteenth century, ac- cording to which a person's mental character could be determined by the shape of the skull.

ther smooth bands nor long ringlets were in vogue; her dress, also in the mode of the day, was of purple cloth, relieved by a sort of Spanish trimming of black velvet; a gold watch (watches were not so common then as now) shone at her girdle. Let the reader add, to complete the picture, refined features; a complexion, if pale, clear; and a stately air and carriage, and he will have, at least, as clearly as words can give it, a correct idea of the exterior of Miss Temple—Maria Temple, as I afterwards saw the name written in a prayer-book entrusted to me to carry to church.

The superintendent of Lowood (for such was this lady) having taken her seat before a pair of globes placed on one of the tables, summoned the first class round her, and commenced giving a lesson in geography; the lower classes were called by the teachers: repetitions in history, grammar, &c., went on for an hour; writing and arithmetic succeeded, and music lessons were given by Miss Temple to some of the elder girls. The duration of each lesson was measured by the clock, which at last struck twelve. The superintendent rose:—'I have a word to address to the pupils,' said she.

The tumult of cessation from lessons was already breaking forth, but it sank at her voice. She went on:—'You had this morning a breakfast which you could not eat; you must be hungry. I have ordered that a lunch of bread and cheese shall be served to all.'

The teachers looked at her with a sort of surprise.

'It is to be done on my responsibility,' she added, in an explanatory tone to them, and immediately afterwards left the room.

The bread and cheese was presently brought in and distributed, to the high delight and refreshment of the whole school. The order was now given, 'To the garden!' Each put on a coarse straw bonnet, with strings of coloured calico, and a cloak of grey frieze. I was similarly equipped, and, following the stream, I made my way into the open air.

The garden was a wide inclosure, surrounded with walls so high as to exclude every glimpse of prospect; a covered verandah ran down one side, and broad walks bordered a middle space divided into scores of little beds: these beds were assigned as gardens for the pupils to cultivate, and each bed had an owner. When full of flowers they would doubtless look pretty; but now, at the latter end of January, all was wintry blight and brown decay. I shuddered as I stood and looked around me: it was an inclement day for outdoor exercise; not positively rainy, but darkened by a drizzling yellow fog; all underfoot was still soaking wet with the floods of yesterday. The stronger among the girls ran about and engaged in active games, but sundry pale and thin ones herded together for shelter and warmth in the verandah; and amongst these, as the dense mist penetrated to their shivering frames, I heard frequently the sound of a hollow cough.

As yet I had spoken to no one, nor did anybody seem to take notice of me; I stood lonely enough: but to that feeling of isolation I was accustomed; it did not oppress me much. I leant against a pillar of the verandah, drew my grey mantle close about me, and trying to forget the cold which nipped me without, and the unsatisfied hunger which gnawed me within, delivered myself up to the employment of watching and thinking. My reflections were too undefined and fragmentary to merit record: I hardly yet knew where I was; Gateshead and my past life seemed floated away to an immeasurable distance; the present was vague and strange, and of the future I could form no conjecture. I looked round the convent-like garden, and then up at the house; a large building, half of which seemed grey and old, the other half quite new. The new part, containing the schoolroom and dormitory, was lit by mullioned and latticed windows, which gave it a church-like aspect; a stone tablet over the door, bore this inscription:—

LOWOOD INSTITUTION.
THIS PORTION WAS REBUILT A.D. ———, BY NAOMI BROCKLEHURST, OF BROCKLEHURST HALL, IN THIS COUNTY.

'Let your light so shine before men that they may see your good works, and glorify your Father which is in heaven.'—St. Matt. V. 16.

I read these words over and over again: I felt that an explanation belonged to them, and was unable fully to penetrate their import. I was still pondering the signification of 'Institution,' and endeavouring to make out a connection between the first words and the verse of Scripture, when the sound of a cough close behind me, made me turn my head. I saw a girl sitting on a stone bench near; she was bent over a book, on the perusal of which she seemed intent: from where I stood I could see the title—it was 'Rasselas;'[4] a name that struck me as strange, and consequently attractive. In turning a leaf she happened to look up, and I said to her directly:—'Is your book interesting?' I had already formed the intention of asking her to lend it to me some day.

'I like it,' she answered, after a pause of a second or two, during which she examined me.

'What is it about?' I continued. I hardly know where I found the hardihood thus to open a conversation with a stranger; the step was contrary to my nature and habits: but I think her occupation touched a chord of sympathy somewhere; for I too liked reading, though of a frivolous and childish kind; I could not digest or comprehend the serious or substantial.

---

4. *The History of Rasselas, Prince of Abyssinia* was a popular didactic romance by Samuel   Johnson (1759).

'You may look at it,' replied the girl, offering me the book.

I did so; a brief examination convinced me that the contents were less taking than the title: 'Rasselas' looked dull to my trifling taste; I saw nothing about fairies, nothing about genii; no bright variety seemed spread over the closely printed pages. I returned it to her; she received it quietly, and without saying anything she was about to relapse into her former studious mood: again I ventured to disturb her:—'Can you tell me what the writing on that stone over the door means? What is Lowood Institution?'

'This house where you are come to live.'

'And why do they call it Institution? Is it in any way different from other schools?'

'It is partly a charity-school: you and I, and all the rest of us, are charity children. I suppose you are an orphan: are not either your father or your mother dead?'

'Both died before I can remember.'

'Well, all the girls here have lost either one or both parents, and this is called an institution for educating orphans.'

'Do we pay no money? Do they keep us for nothing?'

'We pay, or our friends pay, fifteen pounds a year for each.'

'Then why do they call us charity children?'

'Because fifteen pounds is not enough for board and teaching, and the deficiency is supplied by subscription.'

'Who subscribes?'

'Different benevolent-minded ladies and gentlemen in this neighborhood and in London.'

'Who was Naomi Brocklehurst?'

'The lady who built the new part of this house as that tablet records, and whose son overlooks and directs everything here.'

'Why?'

'Because he is treasurer and manager of the establishment.'

'Then this house does not belong to that tall lady who wears a watch, and who said we were to have some bread and cheese.'

'To Miss Temple? Oh, no! I wish it did: she has to answer to Mr. Brocklehurst for all she does. Mr. Brocklehurst buys all our food and all our clothes.'

'Does he live here?'

'No—two miles off, at a large hall.'

'Is he a good man?'

'He is a clergyman, and is said to do a great deal of good.'

'Did you say that tall lady was called Miss Temple?'

'Yes.'

'And what are the other teachers called?'

'The one with red cheeks is called Miss Smith; she attends to the

work, and cuts out—for we make our own clothes, our frocks, and pelisses, and everything; the little one with black hair is Miss Scatcherd;
she teaches history and grammar, and hears the second class repetitions;
and the one who wears a shawl, and has a pocket-handkerchief tied to
her side with a yellow riband, is Madame Pierrot: she comes from Lisle,
in France, and teaches French.'

'Do you like the teachers?'

'Well enough.'

'Do you like the little black one, and the Madame ————?—I cannot pronounce her name as you do.'

'Miss Scatcherd is hasty—you must take care not to offend her; Madame Pierrot is not a bad sort of person.'

'But Miss Temple is the best—isn't she?'

'Miss Temple is very good, and very clever: she is above the rest, because she knows far more than they do.'

'Have you been long here?'

'Two years.'

'Are you an orphan?'

'My mother is dead.'

'Are you happy here?'

'You ask rather too many questions. I have given you answers
enough for the present: now I want to read.'

But at the moment the summons sounded for dinner: all re-entered
the house. The odour which now filled the refectory was scarcely more
appetising than that which had regaled our nostrils at breakfast: the
dinner was served in two huge tin-plated vessels, whence rose a strong
steam redolent of rancid fat. I found the mess to consist of indifferent
potatoes and strange shreds of rusty meat, mixed and cooked together.
Of this preparation a tolerably abundant plateful was opportioned to
each pupil. I ate what I could, and wondered within myself whether
every day's fare would be like this.

After dinner, we immediately adjourned to the schoolroom: lessons
recommenced, and were continued till five o'clock.

The only marked event of the afternoon was, that I saw the girl with
whom I had conversed in the verandah, dismissed in disgrace, by Miss
Scatcherd, from a history class, and sent to stand in the middle of the
large schoolroom. The punishment seemed to me in a high degree ig-
nominious, especially for so great a girl—she looked thirteen or upwards. I expected she would show signs of great distress and shame; but
to my surprise she neither wept nor blushed: composed, though grave,
she stood, the central mark of all eyes. 'How can she bear it so quietly
—so firmly?' I asked of myself. 'Were I in her place, it seems to me I
should wish the earth to open and swallow me up. She looks as if she
were thinking of something beyond her punishment—beyond her situ-

ation: of something not round her nor before her. I have heard of day-dreams—is she in a daydream now? Her eyes are fixed on the floor, but I am sure they do not see it—her sight seems turned in, gone down into her heart: she is looking at what she can remember, I believe; not at what is really present. I wonder what sort of a girl she is—whether good or naughty?'

Soon after five P.M. we had another meal, consisting of a small mug of coffee, and half a slice of brown bread. I devoured my bread and drank my coffee with relish; but I should have been glad of as much more—I was still hungry. Half an hour's recreation succeeded, then study: then the glass of water and the piece of oat-cake, prayers and bed. Such was my first day at Lowood.

Chapter VI

The next day commenced as before, getting up and dressing by rush-light; but this morning we were obliged to dispense with the ceremony of washing: the water in the pitchers was frozen. A change had taken place in the weather the preceding evening, and a keen north-east wind, whistling through the crevices of our bed-room windows all night long, had made us shiver in our beds, and turned the contents of the ewers to ice.

Before the long hour and a half of prayers and Bible reading was over, I felt ready to perish with cold. Breakfast-time came at last, and this morning the porridge was not burnt; the quality was eatable, the quantity small; how small my portion seemed! I wished it had been doubled.

In the course of the day I was enrolled a member of the fourth class, and regular tasks and occupations were assigned me: hitherto, I had only been a spectator of the proceedings at Lowood, I was now to become an actor therein. At first, being little accustomed to learn by heart, the lessons appeared to me both long and difficult: the frequent change from task to task, too, bewildered me; and I was glad, when, about three o'clock in the afternoon, Miss Smith put into my hands a border of muslin two yards long, together with needle, thimble, &c., and sent me to sit in a quiet corner of the schoolroom, with directions to hem the same. At that hour most of the others were sewing likewise; but one class still stood round Miss Scatcherd's chair reading, and as all was quiet, the subject of their lessons could be heard, together with the manner in which each girl acquitted herself, and the animadversions or commendations of Miss Scatcherd on the performance. It was English history: among the readers, I observed my acquaintance of the verandah: at the commencement of the lesson, her place had been at the top of the class, but for some error of pronunciation or some inattention to stops, she was suddenly sent to the very bottom. Even in that obscure position, Miss Scatcherd continued to make her an object of constant notice: she was continually addressing to her such phrases as the following:—

'Burns' (such it seems was her name: the girls here were all called by their surnames, as boys are elsewhere), 'Burns, you are standing on the side of your shoe, turn your toes out immediately.' 'Burns, you poke your chin out most unpleasantly, draw it in.' 'Burns, I insist on your holding your head up: I will not have you before me in that attitude,' &c., &c.

A chapter having been read through twice, the books were closed and the girls examined. The lesson had comprised part of the reign of Charles I, and there were sundry questions about tonnage and poundage, and ship-money, which most of them appeared unable to answer; still, every little difficulty was solved instantly when it reached Burns: her memory seemed to have retained the substance of the whole lesson, and she was ready with answers on every point. I kept expecting that Miss Scatcherd would praise her attention; but, instead of that, she suddenly cried out:—

'You dirty, disagreeable girl! you have never cleaned your nails this morning!'

Burns made no answer: I wondered at her silence.

'Why,' thought I, 'does she not explain that she could neither clean her nails nor wash her face, as the water was frozen?'

My attention was now called off by Miss Smith desiring me to hold a skein of thread: while she was winding it, she talked to me from time to time, asking whether I had ever been at school before, whether I could mark, stitch, knit, &c.; till she dismissed me, I could not pursue my observations on Miss Scatcherd's movements. When I returned to my seat, that lady was just delivering an order, of which I did not catch the import; but Burns immediately left the class, and, going into the small inner room where the books were kept, returned in half a minute, carrying in her hand a bundle of twigs tied together at one end. This ominous tool she presented to Miss Scatcherd with a respectful curtsy; then she quietly, and without being told, unloosed her pinafore, and the teacher instantly and sharply inflicted on her neck a dozen strokes with the bunch of twigs. Not a tear rose to Burns' eye; and, while I paused from my sewing, because my fingers quivered at this spectacle with a sentiment of unavailing and impotent anger, not a feature of her pensive face altered its ordinary expression.

'Hardened girl!' exclaimed Miss Scatcherd; 'nothing can correct you of your slatternly habits: carry the rod away.'

Burns obeyed: I looked at her narrowly as she emerged from the book-closet; she was just putting back her handkerchief into her pocket, and the trace of a tear glistened on her thin cheek.

The play-hour in the evening I thought the pleasantest fraction of the day at Lowood: the bit of bread, the draught of coffee swallowed at five o'clock had revived vitality, if it had not satisfied hunger; the long restraint of the day was slackened; the schoolroom felt warmer than in the morning—its fires being allowed to burn a little more brightly to supply, in some measure, the place of candles, not yet introduced; the ruddy gloaming, the licensed uproar, the confusion of many voices, gave one a welcome sense of liberty.

On the evening of the day on which I had seen Miss Scatcherd flog her pupil, Burns, I wandered as usual among the forms and tables and laughing groups without a companion, yet not feeling lonely; when I passed the windows, I now and then lifted a blind and looked out; it snowed fast, a drift was already forming against the lower panes; putting my ear close to the window, I could distinguish from the gleeful tumult within, the disconsolate moan of the wind outside.

Probably, if I had lately left a good home and kind parents, this would have been the hour when I should most keenly have regretted the separation: that wind would then have saddened my heart; this obscure chaos would have disturbed my peace: as it was, I derived from both a strange excitement, and reckless and feverish, I wished the wind to howl more wildly, the gloom to deepen to darkness, and the confusion to rise to clamour.

Jumping over forms, and creeping under tables, I made my way to one of the fire-places: there, kneeling by the high wire fender, I found Burns, absorbed, silent, abstracted from all round her by the companionship of a book, which she read by the dim glare of the embers.

'Is it still "Rasselas"?' I asked, coming behind her.

'Yes,' she said, 'and I have just finished it.'

And in five minutes more she shut it up. I was glad of this.

'Now,' thought I, 'I can perhaps get her to talk.' I sat down by her on the floor.

'What is your name besides Burns?'

'Helen.'

'Do you come a long way from here?'

'I come from a place further north; quite on the borders of Scotland.'

'Will you ever go back?'

'I hope so; but nobody can be sure of the future.'

'You must wish to leave Lowood?'

'No: why should I? I was sent to Lowood to get an education; and it would be of no use going away until I have attained that object.'

'But that teacher, Miss Scatcherd, is so cruel to you?'

'Cruel? Not at all! She is severe: she dislikes my faults.'

'And if I were in your place I should dislike her; I should resist her; if she struck me with that rod, I should get it from her hand; I should break it under her nose.'

'Probably you would do nothing of the sort: but if you did, Mr. Brocklehurst would expel you from the school; that would be a great grief to your relations. It is far better to endure patiently a smart which nobody feels but yourself, than to commit a hasty action whose evil consequences will extend to all connected with you; and, besides, the Bible bids us return good for evil.'

'But then it seems disgraceful to be flogged, and to be sent to stand in the middle of a room full of people; and you are such a great girl: I am far younger than you, and I could not bear it.'

'Yet it would be your duty to bear it, if you could not avoid it: it is weak and silly to say you *cannot bear* what it is your fate to be required to bear.'

I heard her with wonder: I could not comprehend this doctrine of endurance; and still less could I understand or sympathise with the forbearance she expressed for her chastiser. Still I felt that Helen Burns considered things by a light invisible to my eyes. I suspected she might be right and I wrong; but I would not ponder the matter deeply: like Felix, I put it off to a more convenient season.[5]

'You say you have faults, Helen: what are they? To me you seem very good.'

'Then learn from me, not to judge by appearances: I am, as Miss Scatcherd said, slatternly; I seldom put, and never keep, things in order; I am careless; I forget rules; I read when I should learn my lessons; I have no method; and sometimes I say, like you, I cannot *bear* to be subjected to systematic arrangements. This is all very provoking to Miss Scatcherd, who is naturally neat, punctual, and particular.'

'And cross and cruel,' I added; but Helen Burns would not admit my addition: she kept silence.

'Is Miss Temple as severe to you as Miss Scatcherd?'

At the utterance of Miss Temple's name, a soft smile flitted over her grave face.

'Miss Temple is full of goodness: it pains her to be severe to any one, even the worst in the school; she sees my errors, and tells me of them gently; and, if I do anything worthy of praise, she gives me my meed liberally. One strong proof of my wretchedly defective nature is, that even her expostulations, so mild, so rational, have not influence to cure me of my faults; and even her praise, though I value it most highly, cannot stimulate me to continued care and foresight.'

'That is curious,' said I: 'it is so easy to be careful.'

'For *you* I have no doubt it is. I observed you in your class this morning, and saw you were closely attentive: your thoughts never seemed to wander while Miss Miller explained the lesson and questioned you.

5. Felix, the Roman governor of Judea, was impressed by the eloquence of the apostle Paul, and so put off his trial for two years (Acts 24:24–27).

Now, mine continually rove away: when I should be listening to Miss Scatcherd, and collecting all she says with assiduity, often I lose the very sound of her voice; I fall into a sort of dream. Sometimes I think I am in Northumberland, and that the noises I hear round me are the bubbling of a little brook which runs through Deepden near our house;—then, when it comes to my turn to reply, I have to be wakened; and, having heard nothing of what was read for listening to the visionary brook, I have no answer ready.'

'Yet how well you replied this afternoon.'

'It was mere chance: the subject on which we had been reading had interested me. This afternoon, instead of dreaming of Deepden, I was wondering how a man who wished to do right could act so unjustly and unwisely as Charles the First sometimes did; and I thought what a pity it was that, with his integrity and conscientiousness, he could see no farther than the prerogatives of the crown. If he had but been able to look to a distance, and see to what they call the spirit of the age was tending! Still, I like Charles—I respect him—I pity him, poor murdered king! Yes, his enemies were the worst: they shed blood they had no right to shed. How dared they kill him!'

Helen was talking to herself now: she had forgotten I could not very well understand her—that I was ignorant, or nearly so, of the subject she discussed. I recalled her to my level.

'And when Miss Temple teaches you, do your thoughts wander then?'

'No, certainly, not often; because Miss Temple has generally something to say which is newer than my own reflections: her language is singularly agreeable to me, and the information she communicates is often just what I wished to gain.'

'Well, then, with Miss Temple you are good?'

'Yes, in a passive way: I make no effort; I follow as inclination guides me. There is no merit in such goodness.'

'A great deal: you are good to those who are good to you. It is all I ever desire to be. If people were always kind and obedient to those who are cruel and unjust, the wicked people would have it all their own way; they would never feel afraid, and so they would never alter, but would grow worse and worse. When we are struck at without a reason, we should strike back again very hard; I am sure we should—so hard as to teach the person who struck us never to do it again.'

'You will change your mind, I hope, when you grow older: as yet you are but a little untaught girl.'

'But I feel this, Helen: I must dislike those who, whatever I do to please them, persist in disliking me; I must resist those who punish me unjustly. It is as natural as that I should love those who show me affection, or submit to punishment when I feel it is deserved.'

'Heathens and savage tribes hold that doctrine; but Christians and civilised nations disown it.'

'How? I don't understand.'

'It is not violence that best overcomes hate—nor vengeance that most certainly heals injury.'

'What then?'

'Read the New Testament, and observe what Christ says, and how he acts; make his word your rule, and his conduct your example.'

'What does he say?'

'Love your enemies; bless them that curse you; do good to them that hate you and despitefully use you.'[6]

'Then I should love Mrs. Reed, which I cannot do; I should bless her son John, which is impossible.'

In her turn, Helen Burns asked me to explain, and I proceeded forthwith to pour out, in my own way, the tale of my sufferings and resentments. Bitter and truculent when excited, I spoke as I felt, without reserve or softening.

Helen heard me patiently to the end: I expected she would then make a remark, but she said nothing.

'Well,' I asked impatiently, 'is not Mrs. Reed a hard-hearted, bad woman?'

'She has been unkind to you, no doubt; because, you see, she dislikes your cast of character, as Miss Scatcherd does mine: but how minutely you remember all she has done and said to you! What a singularly deep impression her injustice seems to have made on your heart! No ill-usage so brands its record on my feelings. Would you not be happier if you tried to forget her severity, together with the passionate emotions it excited? Life appears to me too short to be spent in nursing animosity, or registering wrongs. We are, and must be, one and all, burdened with faults in this world: but the time will soon come when, I trust, we shall put them off in putting off our corruptible bodies; when debasement and sin will fall from us with this cumbrous frame of flesh, and only the spark of the spirit will remain,—the impalpable principle of life and thought, pure as when it left the Creator to inspire the creature: whence it came it will return; perhaps again to be communicated to some being higher than man—perhaps to pass through gradations of glory, from the pale human soul to brighten to the seraph! Surely it will never, on the contrary, be suffered to degenerate from man to fiend? No; I cannot believe that: I hold another creed; which no one ever taught me, and which I seldom mention; but in which I delight, and to which I cling: for it extends hope to all: it makes Eternity a rest—a mighty home, not a terror and an abyss. Besides, with this creed, I can

6. Matthew 5:44.

so clearly distinguish between the criminal and his crime; I can so sincerely forgive the first while I abhor the last: with this creed revenge never worries my heart, degradation never too deeply disgusts me, injustice never crushes me too low: I live in calm, looking to the end.'

Helen's head, always drooping, sank a little lower as she finished this sentence. I saw by her look she wished no longer to talk to me, but rather to converse with her own thoughts. She was not allowed much time for meditation: a monitor, a great rough girl, presently came up, exclaiming in a strong Cumberland accent,—

'Helen Burns, if you don't go and put your drawer in order, and fold up your work this minute, I'll tell Miss Scatcherd to come and look at it!'

Helen sighed as her reverie fled, and getting up, obeyed the monitor without reply as without delay.

Chapter VII

My first quarter at Lowood seemed an age; and not the golden age either: it comprised an irksome struggle with difficulties in habituating myself to new rules and unwonted tasks. The fear of failure in these points harassed me worse than the physical hardships of my lot; though these were no trifles.

During January, February, and part of March, the deep snows, and, after their melting, the almost impassable roads, prevented our stirring beyond the garden walls, except to go to church; but within these limits we had to pass an hour every day in the open air. Our clothing was insufficient to protect us from the severe cold: we had no boots, the snow got into our shoes and melted there; our ungloved hands became numbed and covered with chilblains, as were our feet: I remember well the distracting irritation I endured from this cause every evening, when my feet inflamed; and the torture of thrusting the swelled, raw, and stiff toes into my shoes in the morning. Then the scanty supply of food was distressing: with the keen appetites of growing children, we had scarcely sufficient to keep alive a delicate invalid. From this deficiency of nourishment resulted an abuse, which pressed hardly on the younger pupils: whenever the famished great girls had an opportunity, they would coax or menace the little ones out of their portion. Many a time I have shared between two claimants the precious morsel of brown bread distributed at tea-time; and after relinquishing to a third, half the contents of my mug of coffee, I have swallowed the remainder with an accompaniment of secret tears, forced from me by the exigency of hunger.

Sundays were dreary days in that wintry season. We had to walk two miles to Brocklebridge Church, where our patron officiated. We set out cold, we arrived at church colder: during the morning service we became almost paralysed. It was too far to return to dinner, and an allowance of cold meat and bread, in the same penurious proportion observed in our ordinary meals, was served round between the services.

At the close of the afternoon service we returned by an exposed and hilly road, where the bitter winter wind, blowing over a range of snowy summits to the north, almost flayed the skin from our faces.

I can remember Miss Temple walking lightly and rapidly along our drooping line, her plaid cloak, which the frosty wind fluttered, gathered close about her, and encouraging us, by precept and example, to keep up our spirits, and march forward, as she said, 'like stalwart soldiers.' The other teachers, poor things, were generally themselves too much dejected to attempt the task of cheering others.

How we longed for the light and heat of a blazing fire when we got back! But, to the little ones at least, this was denied: each hearth in the schoolroom was immediately surrounded by a double row of great girls, and behind them the younger children crouched in groups, wrapping their starved[7] arms in their pinafores.

A little solace came at tea-time, in the shape of a double ration of bread—a whole, instead of a half, slice—with the delicious addition of a thin scrape of butter: it was the hebdomadal treat to which we all looked forward from Sabbath to Sabbath. I generally contrived to reserve a moiety of this bounteous repast for myself; but the remainder I was invariably obliged to part with.

The Sunday evening was spent in repeating, by heart, the Church Catechism, and the fifth, sixth, and seventh chapters of St. Matthew; and in listening to a long sermon, read by Miss Miller, whose irrepressible yawns attested her weariness. A frequent interlude of these performances was the enactment of the part of Eutychus by some half dozen of little girls; who, overpowered with sleep, would fall down, if not out of the third loft, yet off the fourth form, and be taken up half dead.[8] The remedy was, to thrust them forward into the centre of the schoolroom, and oblige them to stand there till the sermon was finished. Sometimes their feet failed them, and they sank together in a heap; they were then propped up with the monitors' high stools.

I have not yet alluded to the visits of Mr. Brocklehurst; and indeed that gentleman was from home during the greater part of the first month after my arrival; perhaps prolonging his stay with his friend the archdeacon: his absence was a relief to me. I need not say that I had my own reasons for dreading his coming: but come he did at last.

One afternoon (I had then been three weeks at Lowood), as I was sitting with a slate in my hand, puzzling over a sum in long division, my eyes, raised in abstraction to the window, caught sight of a figure just

---

7. Frozen: literally, starved for warmth. "Hebdomadal": weekly.

8. Eutychus fell asleep while listening to the apostle Paul, and consequently fell from a third-story window ("third loft") (Acts 20:7–12).

passing: I recognized almost instinctively that gaunt outline; and when two minutes after, all the school, teachers included, rose *en masse*, it was not necessary for me to look up in order to ascertain whose entrance they thus greeted. A long stride measured the schoolroom, and presently beside Miss Temple, who herself had risen, stood the same black column which had frowned on me so ominously from the hearth-rug of Gateshead. I now glanced sideways at this piece of architecture. Yes, I was right: it was Mr. Brocklehurst, buttoned up in a surtout,[9] and looking longer, narrower, and more rigid than ever.

I had my own reasons for being dismayed at this apparition: too well I remembered the perfidious hints given by Mrs. Reed about my disposition, &c.; the promise pledged by Mr. Brocklehurst to apprise Miss Temple and the teachers of my vicious nature. All along I had been dreading the fulfilment of this promise,—I had been looking out daily for the 'Coming Man,' whose information respecting my past life and conversation was to brand me as a bad child for ever: now there he was. He stood at Miss Temple's side; he was speaking low in her ear: I did not doubt he was making disclosures of my villainy; and I watched her eye with painful anxiety, expecting every moment to see its dark orb turn on me a glance of repugnance and contempt. I listened too; and as I happened to be seated quite at the top of the room, I caught most of what he said: its import relieved me from immediate apprehension.

'I suppose, Miss Temple, the thread I bought at Lowton will do; it struck me that it would be just of the quality for the calico chemises, and I sorted the needles to match. You may tell Miss Smith that I forgot to make a memorandum of the darning needles, but she shall have some papers sent in next week; and she is not, on any account, to give out more than one at a time to each pupil: if they have more, they are apt to be careless and lose them. And, oh ma'am! I wish the woollen stockings were better looked to!—when I was here last, I went into the kitchen-garden and examined the clothes drying on the line; there was a quantity of black hose in a very bad state of repair: from the size of the holes in them I was sure they had not been well mended from time to time.'

He paused.

'Your directions shall be attended to, sir,' said Miss Temple.

'And, ma'am,' he continued, 'the laundress tells me some of the girls have two clean tuckers in the week: it is too much; the rules limit them to one.'

'I think I can explain that circumstance, sir. Agnes and Catherine Johnstone were invited to take tea with some friends at Lowton last Thursday, and I gave them leave to put on clean tuckers for the occasion.'

9. Long, close-fitting overcoat.

Mr. Brocklehurst nodded.

'Well, for once it may pass; but please not to let the circumstance occur too often. And there is another thing which surprised me: I find, in settling accounts with the housekeeper, that a lunch, consisting of bread and cheese, has twice been served out to the girls during the past fortnight. How is this? I look over the regulations, and I find no such meal as lunch mentioned. Who introduced this innovation? and by what authority?'

'I must be responsible for the circumstance, sir,' replied Miss Temple: 'the breakfast was so ill-prepared that the pupils could not possibly eat it; and I dared not allow them to remain fasting till dinnertime.'

'Madam, allow me an instant. You are aware that my plan in bringing up these girls is, not to accustom them to habits of luxury and indulgence, but to render them hardy, patient, self-denying. Should any little accidental disappointment of the appetite occur, such as the spoiling of a meal, the under or the over dressing of a dish, the incident ought not to be neutralised by replacing with something more delicate the comfort lost, thus pampering the body and obviating the aim of this institution; it ought to be improved to the spiritual edification of the pupils, by encouraging them to evince fortitude under the temporary privation. A brief address on those occasions would not be mistimed, wherein a judicious instructor would take the opportunity of referring to the sufferings of the primitive Christians; to the torments of martyrs; to the exhortations of our blessed Lord himself, calling upon his disciples to take up their cross and follow him; to his warnings that man shall not live by bread alone, but by every word that proceedeth out of the mouth of God; to his divine consolations, "if ye suffer hunger or thirst for my sake, happy are ye." Oh, madam, when you put bread and cheese, instead of burnt porridge, into these children's mouths, you may indeed feed their vile bodies, but you little think how you starve their immortal souls!'

Mr. Brocklehurst again paused—perhaps overcome by his feelings. Miss Temple had looked down when he first began to speak to her; but she now gazed straight before her, and her face, naturally pale as marble, appeared to be assuming also the coldness and fixity of that material; especially her mouth, closed as if it would have required a sculptor's chisel to open it, and her brow settled gradually into petrified severity.

Meantime, Mr. Brocklehurst, standing on the hearth with his hands behind his back, majestically surveyed the whole school. Suddenly his eye gave a blink, as if it had met something that either dazzled or shocked its pupil; turning, he said in more rapid accents than he had hitherto used:—'Miss Temple, Miss Temple, what—*what* is that girl with curled hair? Red hair, ma'am, curled—curled all over?' And extending his cane he pointed to the awful object, his hand shaking as he did so.

'It is Julia Severn,' replied Miss Temple, very quietly.

'Julia Severn, ma'am! And why has she, or any other, curled hair? Why, in defiance of every precept and principle of this house, does she conform to the world so openly—here in an evangelical, charitable establishment—as to wear her hair one mass of curls?'

'Julia's hair curls naturally,' returned Miss Temple, still more quietly.

'Naturally! Yes, but we are not to conform to nature: I wish these girls to be the children of Grace: and why that abundance? I have again and again intimated that I desire the hair to be arranged closely, modestly, plainly. Miss Temple, that girl's hair must be cut off entirely; I will send a barber to-morrow: and I see others who have far too much of the excrescence—that tall girl, tell her to turn round. Tell all the first form to rise up and direct their faces to the wall.'

Miss Temple passed her handkerchief over her lips, as if to smooth away the involuntary smile that curled them; she gave the order, however, and when the first class could take in what was required of them, they obeyed. Leaning a little back on my bench, I could see the looks and grimaces with which they commented on this manoeuvre: it was a pity Mr. Brocklehurst could not see them too; he would perhaps have felt that, whatever he might do with the outside of the cup and platter, the inside was further beyond his interference than he imagined.[1]

He scrutinised the reverse of these living medals some five minutes, then pronounced sentence. These words fell like the knell of doom:—
'All those top-knots must be cut off.'

Miss Temple seemed to remonstrate.

'Madam,' he pursued, 'I have a master to serve whose kingdom is not of this world: my mission is to mortify in these girls the lusts of the flesh; to teach them to clothe themselves with shamefacedness and sobriety, not with braided hair and costly apparel; and each of the young persons before us has a string of hair twisted in plaits which vanity itself might have woven: these, I repeat, must be cut off; think of the time wasted, of——'

Mr. Brocklehurst was here interrupted: three other visitors, ladies, now entered the room. They ought to have come a little sooner to have heard his lecture on dress, for they were splendidly attired in velvet, silk, and furs. The two younger of the trio (fine girls of sixteen and seventeen) had grey beaver hats, then in fashion, shaded with ostrich plumes, and from under the brim of this graceful head-dress fell a profusion of

---

1. "Woe to you, scribes and Pharisees, hypocrites! for you cleanse the outside of the cup and of the plate, but inside they are full of extortion and rapacity" (Matthew 23:25).

light tresses, elaborately curled; the elder lady was enveloped in a costly velvet shawl, trimmed with ermine, and she wore a false front of French curls.

These ladies were deferentially received by Miss Temple, as Mrs. and the Misses Brocklehurst, and conducted to seats of honour at the top of the room. It seems they had come in the carriage with their reverend relative, and had been conducting a rummaging scrutiny of the rooms upstairs, while he transacted business with the housekeeper, questioned the laundress, and lectured the superintendent. They now proceeded to address divers remarks and reproofs to Miss Smith, who was charged with the care of the linen and the inspection of the dormitories: but I had no time to listen to what they said; other matters called off and enchained my attention.

Hitherto, while gathering up the discourse of Mr. Brocklehurst and Miss Temple, I had not, at the same time, neglected precautions to secure my personal safety; which I thought would be effected, if I could only elude observation. To this end, I had sat well back on the form, and while seeming to be busy with my sum, had held my slate in such a manner as to conceal my face: I might have escaped notice, had not my treacherous slate somehow happened to slip from my hand and falling with an obtrusive crash, directly drawn every eye upon me; I knew it was all over now, and, as I stooped to pick up the two fragments of slate, I rallied my forces for the worst. It came.

'A careless girl!' said Mr. Brocklehurst, and immediately after—'It is the new pupil, I perceive.' And before I could draw breath, 'I must not forget I have a word to say respecting her.' Then aloud: how loud it seemed to me! 'Let the child who broke her slate, come forward!'

Of my own accord, I could not have stirred: I was paralysed: but the two great girls who sat on each side of me, set me on my legs and pushed me towards the dread judge, and then Miss Temple gently assisted me to his very feet, and I caught her whispered counsel,—'Don't be afraid, Jane, I saw it was an accident; you shall not be punished.'

The kind whisper went to my heart like a dagger.

'Another minute, and she will despise me for a hypocrite,' thought I; and an impulse of fury against Reed, Brocklehurst, and Co. bounded in my pulses at the conviction. I was no Helen Burns. 'Fetch that stool,' said Mr. Brocklehurst, pointing to a very high one from which a monitor had just risen: it was brought.

'Place the child upon it.'

And I was placed there, by whom I don't know: I was in no condition to note particulars: I was only aware that they had hoisted me up to the height of Mr. Brocklehurst's nose, that he was within a yard of me, and that a spread of shot orange and purple silk pelisses, and a cloud of silvery plumage extended and waved below me.

Mr. Brocklehurst hemmed.

'Ladies,' said he, turning to his family; 'Miss Temple, teachers, and children, you all see this girl?'

Of course they did; for I felt their eyes directed like burning-glasses against my scorched skin.

'You see she is yet young; you observe she possesses the ordinary form of childhood; God has graciously given her the shape that he has given to all of us; no signal deformity points her out as a marked character. Who would think that the Evil One had already found a servant and agent in her? Yet such, I grieve to say, is the case.'

A pause—in which I began to steady the palsy of my nerves, and to feel that the Rubicon was passed;[2] and that the trial, no longer to be shirked, must be firmly sustained.

'My dear children,' pursued the black marble clergyman, with pathos, 'this is a sad, a melancholy occasion; for it becomes my duty to warn you, that this girl, who might be one of God's own lambs, is a little castaway: not a member of the true flock, but evidently an interloper and an alien. You must be on your guard against her; you must shun her example: if necessary, avoid her company, exclude her from your sports, and shut her out from your converse. Teachers, you must watch her: keep your eyes on her movements, weigh well her words, scrutinise her actions, punish her body to save her soul: if, indeed, such salvation be possible, for (my tongue falters while I tell it) this girl, this child, the native of a Christian land, worse than many a little heathen who says its prayers to Brahma and kneels before Juggernaut[3]—this girl is—a liar!'

Now came a pause of ten minutes; during which I, by this time in perfect possession of my wits, observed all the female Brocklehursts produce their pocket-handkerchiefs and apply them to their optics, while the elderly lady swayed herself to and fro, and the two younger ones whispered, 'How shocking!'

Mr. Brocklehurst resumed.

'This I learned from her benefactress; from the pious and charitable lady who adopted her in her orphan state, reared her as her own daughter, and whose kindness, whose generosity the unhappy girl repaid by an ingratitude so bad, so dreadful, that at last her excellent patroness was obliged to separate her from her own young ones, fearful lest her vicious example should contaminate their purity: she has sent her here to be healed, even as the Jews of old sent their diseased to the troubled pool of Bethesda;[4] and, teachers, superintendent, I beg of you not to allow the waters to stagnate round her.'

2. I.e., the boundary was crossed.
3. Hindu gods.
4. Bethesda, literally "house of grace," was the place where Jesus healed an invalid (John 5:2–9).

With this sublime conclusion, Mr. Brocklehurst adjusted the top button of his surtout, muttered something to his family, who rose, bowed to Miss Temple, and then all the great people sailed in state from the room. Turning at the door, my judge said:—'Let her stand half an hour longer on that stool, and let no one speak to her during the remainder of the day.'

There was I, then, mounted aloft: I, who had said I could not bear the shame of standing on my natural feet in the middle of the room, was now exposed to general view on a pedestal of infamy. What my sensations were, no language can describe: but just as they all rose, stifling my breath and constricting my throat, a girl came up and passed me: in passing, she lifted her eyes. What a strange light inspired them! What an extraordinary sensation that ray sent through me! How the new feeling bore me up! It was as if a martyr, a hero, had passed a slave or victim, and imparted strength in the transit. I mastered the rising hysteria, lifted up my head, and took a firm stand on the stool. Helen Burns asked some slight question about her work of Miss Smith, was chidden for the triviality of the inquiry, returned to her place, and smiled at me as she again went by. What a smile! I remember it now, and I know that it was the effluence of fine intellect, of true courage; it lit up her marked lineaments, her thin face, her sunken grey eye, like a reflection from the aspect of an angel. Yet at that moment Helen Burns wore on her arm 'the untidy badge'; scarcely an hour ago I had heard her condemned by Miss Scatcherd to a dinner of bread and water on the morrow, because she had blotted an exercise in copying it out. Such is the imperfect nature of man! such spots are there on the disc of the clearest planet; and eyes like Miss Scatcherd's can only see those minute defects, and are blind to the full brightness of the orb.

Chapter VIII

Ere the half-hour ended, five o'clock struck; school was dismissed and all were gone into the refectory to tea. I now ventured to descend: it was deep dusk; I retired into a corner and sat down on the floor. The spell by which I had been so far supported began to dissolve; reaction took place, and soon, so overwhelming was the grief that seized me, I sank prostrate with my face to the ground. Now I wept: Helen Burns was not here; nothing sustained me; left to myself I abandoned myself, and my tears watered the boards. I had meant to be so good, and to do so much at Lowood: to make so many friends, to earn respect, and win affection. Already I had made visible progress: that very morning I had reached the head of my class; Miss Miller had praised me warmly; Miss Temple had smiled approbation; she had promised to teach me drawing, and to let me learn French, if I continued to make similar improve-

ment two months longer: and then I was well-received by my
fellow-pupils; treated as an equal by those of my own age, and not mo-
lested by any; now, here I lay again crushed and trodden on; and could I
ever rise more?

'Never,' I thought; and ardently I wished to die. While sobbing out
this wish in broken accents, some one approached: I started up—again
Helen Burns was near me; the fading fires just showed her coming up
the long, vacant room; she brought my coffee and bread.

'Come, eat something,' she said; but I put both away from me, feeling as if a drop or a crumb would have choked me in my present condition. Helen regarded me, probably with surprise: I could not now abate
my agitation, though I tried hard; I continued to weep aloud. She sat
down on the ground near me, embraced her knees with her arms, and
rested her head upon them; in that attitude she remained silent as an
Indian. I was the first who spoke:—'Helen, why do you stay with a girl
whom everybody believes to be a liar?'

'Everybody, Jane? Why, there are only eighty people who have
heard you called so, and the world contains hundreds of millions.'

'But what have I to do with millions? The eighty I know despise me.'

'Jane, you are mistaken: probably not one in the school either despises or dislikes you: many, I am sure, pity you much.'

'How can they pity me after what Mr. Brocklehurst said?'

'Mr. Brocklehurst is not a god: nor is he even a great and admired
man: he is little liked here; he never took steps to make himself liked.
Had he treated you as an especial favourite, you would have found enemies, declared or covert, all around you: as it is, the greater number
would offer you sympathy if they dared. Teachers and pupils may look
coldly on you for a day or two, but friendly feelings are concealed in
their hearts; and if you persevere in doing well, these feelings will ere
long appear so much the more evident for their temporary suppression.
Besides, Jane,'——she paused.

'Well, Helen?' said I, putting my hand into hers: she chafed my
fingers gently to warm them, and went on:—

'If all the world hated you, and believed you wicked, while your own
conscience approved you, and absolved you from guilt, you would not
be without friends.'

'No; I know I should think well of myself; but that is not enough: if
others don't love me, I would rather die than live—I cannot bear to be
solitary and hated, Helen. Look here; to gain some real affection from
you, or Miss Temple, or any other whom I truly love, I would willingly
submit to have the bone of my arm broken, or to let a bull toss me, or
to stand behind a kicking horse, and let it dash its hoof at my
chest,'—

'Hush, Jane! you think too much of the love of human beings, you are too impulsive, too vehement: the sovereign hand that created your frame, and put life into it, has provided you with other resources than your feeble self, or than creatures feeble as you. Besides this earth, and besides the race of men, there is an invisible world and a kingdom of spirits: that world is round us, for it is everywhere; and those spirits watch us, for they are commissioned to guard us; and if we were dying in pain and shame, if scorn smote us on all sides, and hatred crushed us, angels see our tortures, recognise our innocence (if innocent we be: as I know you are of this charge which Mr. Brocklehurst has weakly and pompously repeated at second-hand from Mrs. Reed; for I read a sincere nature in your ardent eyes and on your clear front), and God waits only the separation of spirit from flesh to crown us with a full reward. Why, then, should we ever sink overwhelmed with distress, when life is so soon over, and death is so certain an entrance to happiness—to glory?'

I was silent: Helen had calmed me; but in the tranquility she imparted there was an alloy of inexpressible sadness. I felt the impression of woe as she spoke, but I could not tell whence it came; and when, having done speaking, she breathed a little fast and coughed a short cough, I momentarily forgot my own sorrows to yield to a vague concern for her.

Resting my head on Helen's shoulder, I put my arms round her waist; she drew me to her, and we reposed in silence. We had not sat long thus, when another person came in. Some heavy clouds, swept from the sky by a rising wind, had left the moon bare; and her light, streaming in through a window near, shone full both on us and on the approaching figure, which we at once recognised as Miss Temple.

'I came on purpose to find you, Jane Eyre,' said she; 'I want you in my room; and as Helen Burns is with you, she may come too.'

We went; following the superintendent's guidance, we had to thread some intricate passages, and mount a staircase before we reached her apartment; it contained a good fire, and looked cheerful. Miss Temple told Helen Burns to be seated in a low arm-chair on one side of the hearth, and herself taking another, she called me to her side.

'Is it all over?' she asked, looking down at my face. 'Have you cried your grief away?'

'I am afraid I never shall do that.'

'Why?'

'Because I have been wrongly accused; and you, ma'am, and everybody else will now think me wicked.'

'We shall think you what you prove yourself to be, my child. Continue to act as a good girl, and you will satisfy me.'

'Shall I, Miss Temple?'

'You will,' said she, passing her arm round me. 'And now tell me who is the lady whom Mr. Brocklehurst called your benefactress?'

'Mrs. Reed, my uncle's wife. My uncle is dead, and left me to her care.'

'Did she not, then, adopt you of her own accord?'

'No, ma'am; she was sorry to have to do it: but my uncle, as I have often heard the servants say, got her to promise before he died, that she would always keep me.'

'Well, now, Jane, you know, or at least I will tell you, that when a criminal is accused, he is always allowed to speak in his own defence. You have been charged with falsehood; defend yourself to me as well as you can. Say whatever your memory suggests as true; but add nothing and exaggerate nothing.'

I resolved, in the depth of my heart, that I would be most moderate —most correct; and, having reflected a few minutes in order to arrange coherently what I had to say, I told her all the story of my sad childhood. Exhausted by emotion, my language was more subdued than it generally was when it developed that sad theme; and mindful of Helen's warnings against the indulgence of resentment, I infused into the narrative far less of gall and wormwood than ordinary. Thus restrained and simplified, it sounded more credible: I felt as I went on that Miss Temple fully believed me.

In the course of the tale I had mentioned Mr. Lloyd as having come to see me after the fit: for I never forgot the, to me, frightful episode of the red-room; in detailing which, my excitement was sure, in some degree, to break bounds; for nothing could soften in my recollection the spasm of agony which clutched my heart when Mrs. Reed spurned my wild supplication for pardon, and locked me a second time in the dark and haunted chamber.

I had finished: Miss Temple regarded me a few minutes in silence; she then said:—'I know something of Mr. Lloyd; I shall write to him; if his reply agrees with your statement, you shall be publicly cleared from every imputation: to me, Jane, you are clear now.'

She kissed me, and still keeping me at her side (where I was well contented to stand, for I derived a child's pleasure from the contemplation of her face, her dress, her one or two ornaments, her white forehead, her clustered and shining curls, and beaming dark eyes), she proceeded to address Helen Burns.

'How are you to-night, Helen? Have you coughed much to-day?'

'Not quite so much, I think, ma'am.'

'And the pain in your chest?'

'It is a little better.'

Miss Temple got up, took her hand and examined her pulse; then she returned to her own seat: as she resumed it, I heard her sigh low. She was pensive a few minutes, then rousing herself, she said cheerfully:—'But you two are my visitors to-night; I must treat you as such.' She rang her bell.

'Barbara,' she said to the servant who answered it, 'I have not yet had tea; bring the tray, and place cups for these two young ladies.'

And a tray was soon brought. How pretty, to my eyes, did the china cups and bright teapot look, placed on the little round table near the fire! How fragrant was the steam of the beverage, and the scent of the toast! of which, however, I, to my dismay (for I was beginning to be hungry), discerned only a very small portion: Miss Temple discerned it too:—'Barbara,' said she, 'can you not bring a little more bread and butter? There is not enough for three.'

Barbara went out: she returned soon:—'Madam, Mrs. Harden says she has sent up the usual quantity.'

Mrs. Harden, be it observed, was the housekeeper: a woman after Mr. Brocklehurst's own heart, made up of equal parts of whalebone and iron.

'Oh, very well!' returned Miss Temple; 'we must make it do, Barbara, I suppose.' And as the girl withdrew, she added, smiling, 'Fortunately, I have it in my power to supply deficiencies for this once.'

Having invited Helen and me to approach the table, and placed before each of us a cup of tea with one delicious but thin morsel of toast, she got up, unlocked a drawer, and taking from it a parcel wrapped in paper, disclosed presently to our eyes a good-sized seed-cake.

'I meant to give each of you some of this to take with you,' said she; 'but as there is so little toast, you must have it now,' and she proceeded to cut slices with a generous hand.

We feasted that evening as on nectar and ambrosia; and not the least delight of the entertainment was the smile of gratification with which our hostess regarded us, as we satisfied our famished appetites on the delicate fare she liberally supplied. Tea over and the tray removed, she again summoned us to the fire; we sat one on each side of her, and now a conversation followed between her and Helen, which it was indeed a privilege to be admitted to hear.

Miss Temple had always something of serenity in her air, of state in her mien, of refined propriety in her language, which precluded deviation into the ardent, the excited, the eager: something which chastened the pleasure of those who looked on her and listened to her, by a controlling sense of awe; and such was my feeling now; but as to Helen Burns, I was struck with wonder.

The refreshing meal, the brilliant fire, the presence and kindness of her beloved instructress, or, perhaps, more than all these, something in her own unique mind, had roused her powers within her. They woke, they kindled: first, they glowed in the bright tint of her cheek, which till this hour I had never seen but pale and bloodless; then they shone in the liquid lustre of her eyes, which had suddenly acquired a beauty more singular than that of Miss Temple's—a beauty neither of fine col-

our nor long eyelash, nor pencilled brow, but of meaning, of movement, of radiance. Then her soul sat on her lips, and language flowed,
from what source I cannot tell: has a girl of fourteen a heart large
enough, vigorous enough, to hold the swelling spring of pure full, fervid eloquence? Such was the characteristic of Helen's discourse on
that, to me, memorable evening; her spirit seemed hastening to live
within a very brief span as much as many live during a protracted existence.

They conversed of things I had never heard of: of nations and times
past; of countries far away: of secrets of nature discovered or guessed at:
they spoke of books: how many they had read! What stores of knowledge they possessed! Then they seemed so familiar with French names
and French authors: but my amazement reached its climax when Miss
Temple asked Helen if she sometimes snatched a moment to recall the
Latin her father had taught her, and taking a book from a shelf, bade her
read and construe a page of 'Virgil'; and Helen obeyed, my organ of
Veneration expanding at every sounding line. She had scarcely finished
ere the bell announced bedtime: no delay could be admitted; Miss
Temple embraced us both, saying, as she drew us to her heart:—'God
bless you, my children!'

Helen she held a little longer than me: she let her go more reluctantly; it was Helen her eye followed to the door; it was for her she a second time breathed a sad sigh; for her she wiped a tear from her cheek.

On reaching the bedroom, we heard the voice of Miss Scatcherd: she
was examining drawers; she had just pulled out Helen Burns' and when
we entered Helen was greeted with a sharp reprimand, and told that
to-morrow she should have half a dozen of untidily-folded articles
pinned to her shoulder.

'My things were indeed in shameful disorder,' murmured Helen to
me, in a low voice: 'I intended to have arranged them, but I forgot.'

Next morning, Miss Scatcherd wrote in conspicuous characters on a
piece of pasteboard the word 'Slattern,' and bound it like a phylactery[5]
round Helen's large, mild, intelligent, and benign-looking forehead.
She wore it till evening, patient, unresentful, regarding it as a deserved
punishment. The moment Miss Scatcherd withdrew after afternoon-
school, I ran to Helen, tore it off, and thrust it into the fire: the fury of
which she was incapable had been burning in my soul all day, and tears,
hot and large, had continually been scalding my cheek; for the spectacle
of her sad resignation gave me an intolerable pain at the heart.

About a week subsequently to the incidents above narrated, Miss
Temple, who had written to Mr. Lloyd, received his answer: it appeared that what he said went to corroborate my account. Miss Tem-

5. Box containing scriptural passages, worn by Jewish men during prayers.

ple, having assembled the whole school, announced that inquiry had been made into the charges alleged against Jane Eyre, and that she was most happy to be able to pronounce her completely cleared from every imputation. The teachers then shook hands with me and kissed me, and a murmur of pleasure ran through the ranks of my companions.

Thus relieved of a grievous load, I from that hour set to work afresh, resolved to pioneer my way through every difficulty: I toiled hard, and my success was proportionate to my efforts; my memory, not naturally tenacious, improved with practice: exercise sharpened my wits; in a few weeks I was promoted to a higher class; in less than two months I was allowed to commence French and drawing. I learned the first two tenses of the verb *Être*,[6] and sketched my first cottage (whose walls, by-the-by, outrivalled in slope those of the leaning tower of Pisa), on the same day. That night, on going to bed, I forgot to prepare in imagination the Barmecide supper[7] of hot roast potatoes, or white bread and new milk, with which I was wont to amuse my inward cravings: I feasted instead on the spectacle of ideal drawings, which I saw in the dark; all the work of my own hands: freely pencilled houses and trees, picturesque rocks and ruins, Cuyplike groups of cattle,[8] sweet paintings of butterflies hovering over unblown roses, of birds picking at ripe cherries, of wrens' nests enclosing pearl-like eggs, wreathed about with young ivy sprays. I examined, too, in thought, the possibility of my ever being able to translate currently[9] a certain little French story-book which Madame Pierrot had that day shown me; nor was the problem solved to my satisfaction ere I fell sweetly asleep.

Well has Solomon said—'Better is a dinner of herbs where love is, than a stalled ox and hatred therewith.'

I would not now have exchanged Lowood with all its privations, for Gateshead and its daily luxuries.

Chapter IX

But the privations, or rather the hardships, of Lowood lessened. Spring drew on: she was indeed already come; the frosts of winter had ceased; its snows were melted, its cutting winds ameliorated. My wretched feet, flayed and swollen to lameness by the sharp air of January, began to heal and subside under the gentler breathings of April; the nights and mornings no longer by their Canadian temperature froze the very blood in our veins; we could now endure the play-hour passed in the garden: sometimes on a sunny day it began even to be pleasant and genial, and a greenness grew over those brown beds,

6. French: to be.
7. Barmecide is a wealthy man in *The Arabian Nights* who invites a beggar to an imaginary banquet.

8. Albert Cuyp (1620–1691), Dutch landscape painter; "unblown": unblossomed.
9. Jane transliterates the French word *courament,* "fluently."

which, freshening daily, suggested the thought that Hope traversed them at night, and left each morning brighter traces of her steps. Flowers peeped out amongst the leaves; snowdrops, crocuses, purple auriculas, and golden-eyed pansies. On Thursday afternoons (half-holidays) we now took walks, and found still sweeter flowers opening by the wayside, under the hedges.

I discovered, too, that a great pleasure, an enjoyment which the horizon only bounded, lay all outside the high and spike-guarded walls of our garden: this pleasure consisted in prospect of noble summits girdling a great hill-hollow, rich in verdure and shadow; in a bright beck, full of dark stones and sparkling eddies. How different had this scene looked when I viewed it laid out beneath the iron sky of winter, stiffened in frost, shrouded with snow!—when mists as chill as death wandered to the impulse of east winds along those purple peaks, and rolled down 'ing' and holm till they blended with the frozen fog of the beck.[1] That beck itself was then a torrent, turbid and curbless: it tore asunder the wood, and sent a raving sound through the air, often thickened with wild rain or whirling sleet; and for the forest on its banks, *that* showed only ranks of skeletons.

April advanced to May: a bright, serene May it was; days of blue sky, placid sunshine, and soft western or southern gales filled up its duration. And now vegetation matured with vigour; Lowood shook loose its tresses; it became all green, all flowery; its great elm, ash, and oak skeletons were restored to majestic life; woodland plants sprang up profusely in its recesses; unnumbered varieties of moss filled its hollows, and it made a strange ground-sunshine out of the wealth of its wild primrose plants: I have seen their pale gold gleam in overshadowed spots like scatterings of the sweetest lustre. All this I enjoyed often and fully, free, unwatched, and almost alone: for this unwonted liberty and pleasure there was a cause, to which it now becomes my task to advert.

Have I not described a pleasant site for a dwelling, when I speak of it as bosomed in hill and wood, and rising from the verge of a stream? Assuredly, pleasant enough: but whether healthy or not is another question.

That forest-dell, where Lowood lay, was the cradle of fog and fog-bred pestilence; which, quickening with the quickening spring, crept into the Orphan Asylum, breathed typhus through its crowded schoolroom and dormitory, and, ere May arrived, transformed the seminary into a hospital.

Semi-starvation and neglected colds had predisposed most of the pupils to receive infection: forty-five out of the eighty girls lay ill at one time. Classes were broken up, rules relaxed. The few who continued

1. Brook. "Ing": meadow. "Holm": low ground beside a brook.

well were allowed almost unlimited licence; because the medical attendant insisted on the necessity of frequent exercise to keep them in
health: and had it been otherwise, no one had leisure to watch or restrain them. Miss Temple's whole attention was absorbed by the patients: she lived in the sick-room, never quitting it except to snatch a
few hours' rest at night. The teachers were fully occupied with packing
up and making other necessary preparations for the departure of those
girls who were fortunate enough to have friends and relations able and
willing to remove them from the seat of contagion. Many, already
smitten, went home only to die: some died at the school, and were buried quietly and quickly, the nature of the malady forbidding delay.

While disease had thus become an inhabitant of Lowood, and death
its frequent visitor; while there was gloom and fear within its walls;
while its rooms and passages steamed with hospital smells, the drug and
the pastille striving vainly to overcome the effluvia of mortality, that
bright May shone unclouded over the bold hills and beautiful woodland
out of doors. Its garden, too, glowed with flowers; hollyhocks had
sprung up tall as trees, lilies had opened, tulips and roses were in bloom;
the borders of the little beds were gay with pink thrift and crimson dou-
ble-daisies; the sweetbriers gave out, morning and evening, their scent
of spice and apples; and these fragrant treasures were all useless for most
of the inmates of Lowood, except to furnish now and then a handful of
herbs and blossoms to put in a coffin.

But I, and the rest who continued well, enjoyed fully the beauties of
the scene and season: they let us ramble in the wood, like gipsies, from
morning till night; we did what we liked, went where we liked: we lived
better too. Mr. Brocklehurst and his family never came near Lowood
now: household matters were not scrutinised into; the cross housekeeper was gone, driven away by the fear of infection; her successor,
who had been matron at the Lowton Dispensary, unused to the ways of
her new abode, provided with comparative liberality. Besides, there
were fewer to feed: the sick could eat little; our breakfast-basins were
better filled: when there was no time to prepare a regular dinner, which
often happened, she would give us a large piece of cold pie, or a thick
slice of bread and cheese, and this we carried away with us to the wood,
where we each chose the spot we liked best, and dined sumptuously.

My favourite seat was a smooth and broad stone, rising white and dry
from the very middle of the beck, and only to be got at by wading
through the water; a feat I accomplished barefoot. The stone was just
broad enough to accommodate, comfortably, another girl and me, at
that time my chosen comrade—one Mary Ann Wilson; a shrewd, observant personage, whose society I took pleasure in, partly because she
was witty and original, and partly because she had a manner which set
me at my ease. Some years older than I, she knew more of the world,

and could tell me many things I liked to hear: with her my curiosity found gratification: to my faults also she gave ample indulgence, never imposing curb or rein on anything I said. She had a turn for narrative, I for analysis; she liked to inform, I to question; so we got on swimmingly together, deriving much entertainment, if not much improvement, from our mutual intercourse.

And where, meantime, was Helen Burns? Why did I not spend these sweet days of liberty with her? Had I forgotten her? or was I so worthless as to have grown tired of her pure society? Surely the Mary Ann Wilson I have mentioned was inferior to my first acquaintance: she could only tell me amusing stories, and reciprocate any racy and pungent gossip I chose to indulge in; while, if I have spoken truth of Helen, she was qualified to give those who enjoyed the privilege of her converse, a taste of far higher things.

True, reader; and I knew and felt this: and though I am a defective being, with many faults and few redeeming points, yet I never tired of Helen Burns; nor ever ceased to cherish for her a sentiment of attachment, as strong, tender, and respectful as any that ever animated my heart. How could it be otherwise, when Helen, at all times and under all circumstances, evinced for me a quiet and faithful friendship, which ill-humour never soured, nor irritation ever troubled? But Helen was ill at present: for some weeks she had been removed from my sight to I knew not what room upstairs. She was not, I was told, in the hospital portion of the house with the fever patients; for her complaint was consumption, not typhus: and by consumption I, in my ignorance, understood something mild, which time and care would be sure to alleviate.

I was confirmed in this idea by the fact of her once or twice coming downstairs on very warm sunny afternoons, and being taken by Miss Temple into the garden: but, on these occasions, I was not allowed to go and speak to her; I only saw her from the schoolroom window, and then not distinctly; for she was much wrapped up, and sat at a distance under the verandah.

One evening, in the beginning of June, I had stayed out very late with Mary Ann in the wood; we had, as usual, separated ourselves from the others and had wandered far: so far that we lost our way, and had to ask it at a lonely cottage, where a man and woman lived, who looked after a herd of half-wild swine that fed on the mast in the wood. When we got back it was after moon-rise: a pony, which we knew to be the surgeon's, was standing at the garden door. Mary Ann remarked that she supposed some one must be very ill, as Mr. Bates had been sent for at that time of the evening. She went into the house; I stayed behind a few minutes to plant in my garden a handful of roots I had dug up in the forest, and which I feared would wither if I left them till the morning.

This done, I lingered yet a little longer: the flowers smelt so sweet as the dew fell; it was such a pleasant evening, so serene, so warm; the still glowing west promised so fairly another fine day on the morrow; the moon rose with such majesty in the grave east. I was noting these things and enjoying them as a child might, when it entered my mind as it had never done before:—

'How sad to be lying now on a sick bed, and to be in danger of dying! This world is pleasant—it would be dreary to be called from it, and to have to go who knows where?'

And then my mind made its first earnest effort to comprehend what had been infused into it concerning heaven and hell: and for the first time it recoiled, baffled; and for the first time glancing behind, on each side, and before it, it saw all round an unfathomed gulf: it felt the one point where it stood—the present; all the rest was formless cloud and vacant depth: and it shuddered at the thought of tottering, and plunging amid that chaos. While pondering this new idea, I heard the front door open; Mr. Bates came out, and with him was a nurse. After she had seen him mount his horse and depart, she was about to close the door, but I ran up to her.

'How is Helen Burns?'

'Very poorly,' was the answer.

'Is it her Mr. Bates has been to see?'

'Yes.'

'And what does he say about her?'

'He says she'll not be here long.'

This phrase, uttered in my hearing yesterday, would have only conveyed the notion that she was about to be removed to Northumberland, to her own home. I should not have suspected that it meant she was dying; but I knew instantly now: it opened clear on my comprehension that Helen Burns was numbering her last days in this world, and that she was going to be taken to the region of spirits, if such region there were. I experienced a shock of horror, then a strong thrill of grief, then a desire—a necessity to see her, and I asked in what room she lay.

'She is in Miss Temple's room,' said the nurse.

'May I go up and speak to her?'

'Oh, no, child! It is not likely; and now it is time for you to come in; you'll catch the fever if you stop out when the dew is falling.'

The nurse closed the front door; I went in by the side entrance which led to the schoolroom: I was just in time; it was nine o'clock, and Miss Miller was calling the pupils to go to bed.

It might be two hours later, probably near eleven, when I—not having been able to fall asleep, and deeming, from the perfect silence of the dormitory, that my companions were all wrapt in profound repose—rose softly, put on my frock over my night-dress, and, without shoes, crept from the apartment, and set off in quest of Miss Temple's room. It was quite at the other end of the house; but I knew my way; and the light of the unclouded summer moon, entering here and there at passage windows, enabled me to find it without difficulty. An odour of camphor and burnt vinegar warned me when I came near the fever room: and I passed its door quickly, fearful lest the nurse who sat up all night should hear me. I dreaded being discovered and sent back; for I *must* see Helen,—I must embrace her before she died,—I must give her one last kiss, exchange with her one last word.

Having descended a staircase, traversed a portion of the house below, and succeeded in opening and shutting, without noise, two doors, I reached another flight of steps; these I mounted, and then just opposite to me was Miss Temple's room. A light shone through the key-hole, and from under the door; a profound stillness pervaded the vicinity. Coming near, I found the door slightly ajar; probably to admit some fresh air into the close abode of sickness. Indisposed to hesitate, and full of impatient impulses—soul and senses quivering with keen throes—I put it back and looked in. My eye sought Helen, and feared to find death.

Close by Miss Temple's bed, and half covered with its white curtains, there stood a little crib. I saw the outline of a form under the clothes, but the face was hid by the hangings: the nurse I had spoken to in the garden sat in an easy-chair, asleep; an unsnuffed candle burnt dimly on the table. Miss Temple was not to be seen; I knew afterwards that she had been called to a delirious patient in the fever-room. I advanced; then paused by the crib side: my hand was on the curtain, but I preferred speaking before I withdrew it. I still recoiled at the dread of seeing a corpse.

'Helen!' I whispered softly, 'are you awake?'

She stirred herself, put back the curtain, and I saw her face, pale, wasted, but quite composed: she looked so little changed that my fear was instantly dissipated.

'Can it be you, Jane?' she asked in her own gentle voice.

'Oh!' I thought, 'she is not going to die: they are mistaken: she could not speak and look so calmly if she were.'

I got on to her crib and kissed her: her forehead was cold, and her cheek both cold and thin, and so were her hand and wrist; but she smiled as of old.

'Why are you come here, Jane? It is past eleven o'clock: I heard it strike some minutes since.'

'I came to see you, Helen: I heard you were very ill, and I could not sleep till I had spoken to you.'

'You came to bid me good-bye, then: you are just in time probably.'

'Are you going somewhere, Helen? Are you going home?'

'Yes; to my long home—my last home.'

'No, no, Helen!' I stopped distressed. While I tried to devour my tears, a fit of coughing seized Helen; it did not, however, wake the nurse; when it was over, she lay some minutes exhausted; then she whispered:—'Jane, your little feet are bare; lie down and cover yourself with my quilt.'

I did so: she put her arm over me, and I nestled close to her. After a long silence, she resumed; still whispering,—

'I am very happy, Jane; and when you hear that I am dead, you must be sure and not grieve: there is nothing to grieve about. We all must die one day, and the illness which is removing me is not painful; it is gentle and gradual: my mind is at rest. I leave no one to regret me much: I have only a father; and he is lately married, and will not miss me. By dying young, I shall escape great sufferings. I had not qualities or talents to make my way very well in the world; I should have been continually at fault.'

'But where are you going to, Helen? Can you see? Do you know?'

'I believe: I have faith: I am going to God.'

'Where is God? What is God?'

'My Maker and yours, who will never destroy what he created. I rely implicitly on his power, and confide wholly in his goodness: I count the hours till that eventful one arrives which shall restore me to him, reveal him to me.'

'You are sure, then, Helen, that there is such a place as heaven; and that our souls can get to it when we die?'

'I am sure there is a future state; I believe God is good; I can resign my immortal part to him without any misgiving. God is my father; God is my friend: I love him; I believe he loves me.'

'And shall I see you again, Helen, when I die?'

'You will come to the same region of happiness: be received by the same mighty, universal Parent, no doubt, dear Jane.'

Again I questioned; but this time only in thought. 'Where is that region? Does it exist?' And I clasped my arms closer round Helen; she seemed dearer to me than ever; I felt as if I could not let her go; I lay with my face hidden on her neck. Presently she said in the sweetest tone,—'How comfortable I am! That last fit of coughing has tired me a little; I feel as if I could sleep: but don't leave me, Jane; I like to have you near me.'

'I'll stay with you, *dear* Helen: no one shall take me away.'

'Are you warm, darling?'

'Yes.'

'Goodnight, Jane.'

'Good-night, Helen.'

She kissed me, and I her; and we both soon slumbered.

When I awoke it was day: an unusual movement roused me, I looked up; I was in somebody's arms; the nurse held me; she was carrying me through the passage back to the dormitory. I was not reprimanded for leaving my bed; people had something else to think about: no explanation was afforded then to my many questions; but a day or two afterwards I learned that Miss Temple, on returning to her own room at dawn, had found me laid in a little crib; my face against Helen Burns' shoulder, my arms around her neck. I was asleep, and Helen was— dead.

Her grave is in Brocklebridge churchyard: for fifteen years after her death it was only covered by a grassy mound; but now a grey marble tablet marks the spot, inscribed with her name, and the word 'Resurgam.'[2]

Chapter X

Hitherto I have recorded in detail the events of my insignificant existence: to the first ten years of my life, I have given almost as many chapters. But this is not to be a regular autobiography: I am only bound to invoke memory where I know her responses will possess some degree of interest; therefore I now pass a space of eight years almost in silence: a few lines only are necessary to keep up the links of connection.

When the typhus fever had fulfilled its mission of devastation at Lowood, it gradually disappeared from thence; but not till its virulence and the number of its victims had drawn public attention on the school. Inquiry was made into the origin of the scourge, and by degrees various facts came out which excited public indignation in a high degree. The unhealthy nature of the site; the quantity and quality of the children's food; the brackish, fetid water used in its preparation; the pupils' wretched clothing and accommodation: all these things were discovered; and the discovery produced a result mortifying to Mr. Brocklehurst, but beneficial to the institution.

Several wealthy and benevolent individuals in the county subscribed largely for the erection of a more convenient building in a better situation; new regulations were made; improvements in diet and clothing introduced; the funds of the school were entrusted to the management of a committee. Mr. Brocklehurst, who, from his wealth and family connections, could not be overlooked, still retained the post of treasurer; but he was aided in the discharge of his duties by gentlemen of rather more enlarged and sympathising minds: his office of inspector, too, was shared by those who knew how to combine reason with strictness, comfort with economy, compassion with uprightness. The school, thus improved, became in time a truly useful and noble institution. I re-

2. Latin: I shall rise again.

mained an inmate of its walls, after its regeneration, for eight years: six as pupil, and two as teacher; and in both capacities I bear my testimony to its value and importance.

During these eight years my life was uniform: but not unhappy, because it was not inactive. I had the means of an excellent education placed within my reach. A fondness for some of my studies, and a desire to excel in all, together with a great delight in pleasing my teachers, especially such as I loved, urged me on: I availed myself fully of the advantages offered me. In time I rose to be the first girl of the first class; then I was invested with the office of teacher; which I discharged with zeal for two years; but at the end of that time I altered.

Miss Temple, through all changes, had thus far continued superintendent of the seminary: to her instruction I owed the best part of my acquirements; her friendship and society had been my continual solace: she had stood me in the stead of mother, governess, and, latterly, companion. At this period she married, removed with her husband (a clergyman, an excellent man, almost worthy of such a wife) to a distant county, and consequently was lost to me.

From the day she left I was no longer the same: with her was gone every settled feeling, every association that had made Lowood in some degree a home to me. I had imbibed from her something of her nature and much of her habits: more harmonious thoughts: what seemed better-regulated feelings had become the inmates of my mind. I had given in allegiance to duty and order; I was quiet; I believed I was content: to the eyes of others, usually even to my own, I appeared a disciplined and subdued character.

But destiny, in the shape of the Rev. Mr. Nasmyth, came between me and Miss Temple: I saw her in her travelling dress step into a post-chaise, shortly after the marriage ceremony; I watched the chaise mount the hill and disappear beyond its brow; and then retired to my own room, and there spent in solitude the greatest part of the half-holiday granted in honour of the occasion.

I walked about the chamber most of the time. I imagined myself only to be regretting my loss, and thinking how to repair it; but when my reflections were concluded, and I looked up and found that the afternoon was gone, and evening far advanced, another discovery dawned on me, namely, that in the interval I had undergone a transforming process; that my mind had put off all it had borrowed of Miss Temple—or rather that she had taken with her the serene atmosphere I had been breathing in her vicinity—and that now I was left in my natural element, and beginning to feel the stirring of old emotions. It did not seem as if a prop were withdrawn, but rather as if a motive were gone; it was not the power to be tranquil which had failed me, but the reason for tranquility was no more. My world had for some years been in Lowood:

my experience had been of its rules and systems; now I remembered that the real world was wide, and that a varied field of hopes and fears, of sensations and excitements, awaited those who had courage to go forth into its expanse, to seek real knowledge of life amidst its perils.

I went to my window, opened it, and looked out. There were the two wings of the building; there was the garden; there were the skirts of Lowood; there was the hilly horizon. My eye passed all other objects to rest on those most remote, the blue peaks: it was those I longed to sur-mount; all within their boundary of rock and heath seemed prison-ground, exile limits. I traced the white road winding round the base of one mountain, and vanishing in a gorge between two: how I longed to follow it further! I recalled the time when I had travelled that very road in a coach; I remembered descending that hill at twilight: an age seemed to have elapsed since the day which brought me first to Lo-wood, and I had never quitted it since. My vacations had all been spent at school: Mrs. Reed had never sent for me to Gateshead; neither she nor any of her family had ever been to visit me. I had had no communi-cation by letter or message with the outer world: school-rules, school-duties, school-habits and notions, and voices, and faces, and phrases, and costumes, and preferences, and antipathies: such was what I knew of existence. And now I felt that it was not enough: I tired of the routine of eight years in one afternoon. I desired liberty; for liberty I gasped; for liberty I uttered a prayer; it seemed scattered on the wind then faintly blowing. I abandoned it and framed a humbler supplication; for change, stimulus: that petition, too, seemed swept off into vague space: 'Then,' I cried, half desperate, 'grant me at least a new servitude!'

Here a bell, ringing the hour of supper, called me downstairs.

I was not free to resume the interrupted chain of my reflections till bedtime: even then a teacher who occupied the same room with me kept me from the subject to which I longed to recur, by a prolonged ef-fusion of small talk. How I wished sleep would silence her! It seemed as if, could I but go back to the idea which had last entered my mind as I stood at the window, some inventive suggestion would rise for my re-lief.

Miss Gryce snored at last; she was a heavy Welshwoman, and till now her habitual nasal strains had never been regarded by me in any other light than as a nuisance; to-night I hailed the first deep notes with satisfaction; I was debarrassed[3] of interruption; my half-effaced thought instantly revived.

'A new servitude! There is something in that,' I soliloquised (men-tally, be it understood; I did not talk aloud). 'I know there is, because it does not sound too sweet; it is not like such words as Liberty, Excite-

---

3. Jane transliterates the French *debarassée*, literally, "freed of."

ment, Enjoyment: delightful sounds truly; but no more than sounds for me; and so hollow and fleeting that it is mere waste of time to listen to them. But Servitude! That must be matter of fact. Any one may serve: I have served here eight years; now all I want is to serve elsewhere. Can I not get so much of my own will? Is not the thing feasible? Yes—yes—the end is not so difficult; if I had only a brain active enough to ferret out the means of attaining it.'

I sat up in bed by way of arousing this said brain: it was a chilly night; I covered my shoulders with a shawl, and then I proceeded to *think* again with all my might.

'What do I want? A new place, in a new house, amongst new faces, under new circumstances: I want this because it is of no use wanting anything better. How do people do to get a new place? They apply to friends, I suppose: I have no friends. There are many others who have no friends, who must look about for themselves and be their own helpers; and what is their resource?'

I could not tell: nothing answered me; I then ordered my brain to find a response, and quickly. It worked and worked faster: I felt the pulses throb in my head and temples; but for nearly an hour it worked in chaos, and no result came of its efforts. Feverish with vain labour, I got up and took a turn in the room; undrew the curtain, noted a star or two, shivered with cold, and again crept to bed.

A kind fairy, in my absence, had surely dropped the required suggestion on my pillow; for as I lay down it came quietly and naturally to my mind:—'Those who want situations advertise; you must advertise in the ——shire Herald.'

'How? I know nothing about advertising.'

Replies rose smooth and prompt now:—'You must inclose the advertisement and the money to pay for it under a cover directed to the Editor of the *Herald*; you must put it, the first opportunity you have, into the post at Lowton; answers must be addressed to J. E. at the post-office there: you can go and inquire in about a week after you send your letter, if any are come, and act accordingly.'

This scheme I went over twice, thrice; it was then digested in my mind: I had it in a clear practical form; I felt satisfied, and fell asleep.

With earliest day I was up: I had my advertisement written, inclosed, and directed before the bell rang to rouse the school: it ran thus:—

'A young lady accustomed to tuition' (had I not been a teacher two years?) 'is desirous of meeting with a situation in a private family where the children are under fourteen' (I thought that as I was barely eighteen, it would not do to undertake the guidance of pupils nearer my own age). 'She is qualified to teach the usual branches of a good English education, together with French, Drawing, and Music' (in those days, reader, this now narrow catalogue of accomplishments would have been held tolerably comprehensive). 'Address, J. E., Post-office, Lowton, ——shire.'

This document remained locked in my drawer all day: after tea, I asked leave of the new superintendent to go to Lowton, in order to perform some small commissions for myself and one or two of my fellow-teachers; permission was readily granted: I went. It was a walk of two miles, and the evening was wet, but the days were still long; I visited a shop or two, slipped the letter into the post-office, and came back through heavy rain, with streaming garments, but with a relieved heart.

The succeeding week seemed long: it came to an end at last, however, like all sublunary things, and once more, towards the close of a pleasant autumn day, I found myself afoot on the road to Lowton. A picturesque track it was, by the way, lying along the side of the beck and through the sweetest curves of the dale: but that day I thought more of the letters, that might or might not be awaiting me at the little burgh whither I was bound, than of the charms of lea and water.

My ostensible errand on this occasion was to get measured for a pair of shoes; so I discharged that business first, and when it was done, I stepped across the clean and quiet little street from the shoemaker's to the post-office; it was kept by an old dame, who wore horn spectacles on her nose and black mittens on her hands.

'Are there any letters for J. E.?' I asked.

She peered at me over her spectacles, and then she opened a drawer, and fumbled among its contents for a long time—so long that my hopes began to falter. At last, having held a document before her glasses for nearly five minutes, she presented it across the counter, accompanying the act by another inquisitive and mistrustful glance—it was for J. E.

'Is there only one?' I demanded.

'There are no more,' said she; and I put it in my pocket and turned my face homeward: I could not open it then; rules obliged me to be back by eight, and it was already half-past seven.

Various duties awaited me on my arrival: I had to sit with the girls during their hour of study; then it was my turn to read prayers; to see them to bed: afterwards I supped with the other teachers. Even when we finally retired for the night, the inevitable Miss Gryce was still my companion: we had only a short end of candle in our candlestick, and I dreaded lest she should talk till it was all burnt out: fortunately, however, the heavy supper she had eaten produced a soporific effect: she was already snoring before I had finished undressing. There still remained an inch of candle: I now took out my letter; the seal was an initial F.; I broke it: the contents were brief.

'If J. E., who advertised in the ——shire Herald of last Thursday, possesses the acquirements mentioned, and if she is in a position to give satisfactory references as to character and competency; a situation can be offered her where there is but one pupil—a little girl, under ten years of age—and where the salary is thirty pounds per annum. J. E. is requested to send references, name, address, and all particulars to the direction, "Mrs. Fairfax, Thornfield, near Millcote, ——shire."

I examined the document long: the writing was old-fashioned and rather uncertain, like that of an elderly lady. This circumstance was satisfactory: a private fear had haunted me that, in thus acting for myself, and by my own guidance, I ran the risk of getting into some scrape! and, above all things, I wished the result of my endeavours to be respectable, proper, *en règle*.[4] I now felt that an elderly lady was no bad ingredient in the business I had on hand. Mrs. Fairfax! I saw her in a black gown and widow's cap,—frigid, perhaps, but not uncivil: a model of elderly English respectability. Thornfield! that, doubtless, was the name of her house—a neat, orderly spot, I was sure, though I failed in my efforts to conceive a correct plan of the premises. Millcote, ——shire. I brushed up my recollections of the map of England; yes, I saw it, both the shire and the town. ——shire was seventy miles nearer London than the remote county where I now resided; that was a recommendation to me. I longed to go where there was life and movement. Millcote was a large manufacturing town on the banks of the A——: a busy place, enough, doubtless: so much the better; it would be a complete change at least. Not that my fancy was much captivated by the idea of long chimneys and clouds of smoke—'but,' I argued, 'Thornfield will, probably, be a good way from the town.'

Here the socket of the candle dropped, and the wick went out.

Next day new steps were to be taken; my plans could no longer be confined to my own breast; I must impart them in order to achieve their success. Having sought and obtained an audience of the superintendent during the noontide recreation, I told her I had a prospect of getting a new situation where the salary would be double what I now receive (for at Lowood I only got fifteen pounds per annum), and requested she would break the matter for me to Mr. Brocklehurst, or some of the committee, and ascertain whether they would permit me to mention them as references. She obligingly consented to act as mediatrix in the matter. The next day she laid the affair before Mr. Brocklehurst, who said that Mrs. Reed must be written to, as she was my natural guardian. A note was accordingly addressed to that lady, who returned for answer, that 'I might do as I pleased: she had long relinquished all interference in my affairs.' This note went the round of the committee, and, at last, after what appeared to me most tedious delay, formal leave was given me to better my condition if I could; and an assurance added that, as I had always conducted myself well, both as

4. By the rule.

teacher and pupil, at Lowood, a testimonial of character and capacity, signed by the inspectors of that institution, should forthwith be furnished me.

This testimonial I accordingly received in about a month, forwarded a copy of it to Mrs. Fairfax, and got that lady's reply, stating that she was satisfied, and fixing that day fortnight as the period for my assuming the post of governess in her house.

I now busied myself in preparations: the fortnight passed rapidly. I had not a very large wardrobe, though it was adequate to my wants; and the last day sufficed to pack my truck,—the same I had brought with me eight years ago from Gateshead.

The box was corded, the card nailed on. In half an hour the carrier was to call for it to take it to Lowton, whither I myself was to repair at an early hour the next morning to meet the coach. I had brushed my black stuff travelling dress, prepared my bonnet, gloves, and muff; sought in all my drawers to see that no article was left behind; and now, having nothing more to do, I sat down and tried to rest. I could not, though I had been on foot all day—I could not now repose an instant—I was too much excited. A phase of my life was closing to-night, a new one opening tomorrow: impossible to slumber in the interval; I must watch feverishly while the change was being accomplished.

'Miss,' said a servant who met me in the lobby, where I was wandering like a troubled spirit, 'a person below wishes to see you.'

'The carrier, no doubt,' I thought, and ran downstairs without inquiry. I was passing the back parlour, or teachers' sitting-room, the door of which was half-open, to go to the kitchen, when someone ran out.

'It's her, I am sure!—I could have told her anywhere!' cried the individual who stopped my progress and took my hand.

I looked. I saw a woman attired like a well-dressed servant, matronly, yet still young; very good-looking, with black hair and eyes, and lively complexion.

'Well, who is it?' she asked, in a voice and with a smile I half recognised! 'You've not quite forgotten me, I think, Miss Jane?'

In another second I was embracing and kissing her rapturously. 'Bessie! Bessie! Bessie!' that was all I said; whereat she half laughed, half cried, and we both went into the parlour. By the fire stood a little fellow of three years old, in plaid frock and trousers.

'That is my little boy,' said Bessie, directly.

'Then you are married, Bessie?'

'Yes: nearly five years since, to Robert Leaven, the coachman, and I've a little girl besides Bobby there that I've christened Jane.'

'And you don't live at Gateshead?'

'I live at the lodge: the old porter has left.'

'Well, and how do they all get on? Tell me everything about them,

Bessie: but sit down first; and, Bobby, come and sit on my knee, will you?' But Bobby preferred sidling over to his mother.

'You're not grown so very tall, Miss Jane, nor so very stout,' continued Mrs. Leaven. 'I dare say they've not kept you too well at school: Miss Reed is the head and shoulders taller than you are; and Miss Georgiana would make two of you in breadth.'

'Georgiana is handsome, I suppose, Bessie?'

'Very. She went up to London last winter with her mamma, and there everybody admired her, and a young lord fell in love with her: but his relations were against the match; and—what do you think?—he and Miss Georgiana made it up to run away: but they were found out and stopped. It was Miss Reed that found them out: I believe she was envious; and now she and her sister lead a cat and dog life together; they are always quarrelling.'

'Well, and what of John Reed?'

'Oh, he is not doing so well as his mamma could wish. He went to college, and he got—plucked,[5] I think they call it: and then his uncles wanted him to be a barrister, and study the law: but he is such a dissipated young man, they will never make much of him, I think.'

'What does he look like?'

'He is very tall: some people call him a fine-looking young man; but he has such thick lips.'

'And Mrs. Reed?'

'Missis looks stout and well enough in the face, but I think she's not quite easy in her mind: Mr. John's conduct does not please her—he spends a deal of money.'

'Did she send you here, Bessie?'

'No, indeed: but I have long wanted to see you, and when I heard that there had been a letter from you, and that you were going to another part of the country, I thought I'd just set off, and get a look at you before you were quite out of my reach.'

'I am afraid you are disappointed in me, Bessie.' I said this laughing: I perceived that Bessie's glance, though it expressed regard, did in no shape denote admiration.

'No, Miss Jane, not exactly: you are genteel enough; you look like a lady, and it is as much as ever I expected of you: you were no beauty as a child.'

I smiled at Bessie's frank answer: I felt that it was correct, but I confess I was not quite indifferent to its import: at eighteen most people wish to please, and the conviction that they have not an exterior likely to second that desire brings anything but gratification.

---

5. Expelled for failing examinations.

'I dare say you are clever, though,' continued Bessie, by way of solace. 'What can you do? Can you play on the piano?'

'A little.'

There was one in the room; Bessie went and opened it, and then asked me to sit down and give her a tune: I played a waltz or two, and she was charmed.

'The Miss Reeds could not play as well!' said she exultingly. 'I always said you would surpass them in learning: and can you draw?'

'That is one of my paintings over the chimney-piece.' It was a landscape in water colours, of which I had made a present to the superintendent, in acknowledgment of her obliging mediation with the committee on my behalf, and which she had framed and glazed.

'Well, that is beautiful, Miss Jane! It is as fine a picture as any Miss Reed's drawing-master could paint, let alone the young ladies themselves, who could not come near it: and have you learnt French?'

'Yes, Bessie, I can both read it and speak it.'

'And you can work on muslin and canvas?'

'I can.'

'Oh, you are quite a lady, Miss Jane! I knew you would be: you will get on whether your relations notice you or not. There was something I wanted to ask you. Have you ever heard anything from your father's kinsfolk, the Eyres?'

'Never in my life.'

'Well, you know Missis always said they were poor and quite despicable: and they may be poor; but I believe they are as much gentry as the Reeds are; for one day, nearly seven years ago, a Mr. Eyre came to Gateshead and wanted to see you. Missis said you were at school fifty miles off. He seemed so much disappointed, for he could not stay: he was going on a voyage to a foreign country, and the ship was to sail from London in a day or two. He looked quite a gentleman, and I believe he was your father's brother.'

'What foreign country was he going to, Bessie?'

'An island thousands of miles off, where they make wine—the butler did tell me'—

'Madeira?' I suggested.

'Yes, that is it—that is the very word.'

'So he went?'

'Yes; he did not stay many minutes in the house: Missis was very high with him; she called him afterwards a "sneaking tradesman." My Robert believes he was a wine-merchant.'

'Very likely,' I returned; 'or perhaps clerk or agent to a wine-merchant.'

Bessie and I conversed about old times an hour longer, and then she was obliged to leave me. I saw her again for a few minutes the next morning at Lowton, while I was waiting for the coach. We parted finally at the door of the 'Brocklehurst Arms' there. Each went our separate way: she set off for the brow of Lowood Fell to meet the conveyance which was to take her back to Gateshead; I mounted the vehicle which was to bear me to new duties and a new life in the unknown environs of Millcote.

Chapter XI

A new chapter in a novel is something like a new scene in a play: and when I draw up the curtain this time, reader, you must fancy you see a room in the 'George Inn' at Millcote, with such large figured papering on the walls as inn rooms have; such a carpet, such furniture, such ornaments on the mantelpiece, such prints; including a portrait of George the Third, and another of the Prince of Wales, and a representation of the death of Wolfe. All this is visible to you by the light of an oil lamp hanging from the ceiling, and by that of an excellent fire, near which I sit in my cloak and bonnet; my muff and umbrella lie on the table, and I am warming away the numbness and chill contracted by sixteen hours' exposure to the rawness of an October day: I left Lowton at four o'clock A.M., and the Millcote town clock is now just striking eight.

Reader, though I look comfortably accommodated, I am not very tranquil in my mind. I thought when the coach stopped here there would be someone to meet me; I looked anxiously round as I descended the wooden steps the 'boots' placed for my convenience, expecting to hear my name pronounced, and to see some description of carriage waiting to convey me to Thornfield. Nothing of the sort was visible; and when I asked a waiter if any one had been to inquire after a Miss Eyre, I was answered in the negative: so I had no resource but to request to be shown into a private room: and here I am waiting, while all sorts of doubts and fears are troubling my thoughts.

It is a very strange sensation to inexperienced youth to feel itself quite alone in the world, cut adrift from every connection, uncertain whether the port to which it is bound can be reached, and prevented by many impediments from returning to that it has quitted. The charm of adventure sweetens that sensation, the glow of pride warms it; but then the throb of fear disturbs it; and fear with me became predominant, when half an hour elapsed and still I was alone. I bethought myself to ring the bell.

'Is there a place in this neighbourhood called Thornfield?' I asked of the waiter who answered the summons.

'Thornfield? I don't know, ma'am; I'll inquire at the bar.' He vanished, but reappeared instantly:—'Is your name Eyre, Miss?'

'Yes.'

'Person here waiting for you.'

I jumped up, took my muff and umbrella, and hastened into the inn-passage: a man was standing by the open door, and in the lamp-lit street I dimly saw a one-horse conveyance.

'This will be your luggage, I suppose?' said the man rather abruptly when he saw me, pointing to my trunk in the passage.

'Yes.' He hoisted it on to the vehicle, which was a sort of car, and then I got in: before he shut me up I asked him how far it was to Thornfield.

'A matter of six miles.'

'How long shall we be before we get there?'

'Happen an hour and a half.'

He fastened the car door, climbed to his own seat outside, and we set off. Our progress was leisurely, and gave me ample time to reflect; I was content to be at length so near the end of my journey; and as I leaned back in the comfortable though not elegant conveyance, I meditated much at my ease.

'I suppose,' thought I, 'judging from the plainness of the servant and carriage, Mrs. Fairfax is not a very dashing person: so much the better; I never lived amongst fine people but once, and I was very miserable with them. I wonder if she lives alone except this little girl; if so, and if she is in any degree amiable, I shall surely be able to get on with her! I will do my best: it is a pity that doing one's best does not always answer. At Lowood, indeed, I took that resolution, kept it, and succeeded in pleasing; but with Mrs. Reed, I remember, my best was always spurned with scorn. I pray God Mrs. Fairfax may not turn out a second Mrs. Reed; but if she does, I am not bound to stay with her! let the worst come to the worst, I can advertise again. How far are we on our road now, I wonder?'

I let down the window and looked out: Millcote was behind us; judging by the number of its lights, it seemed a place of considerable magnitude, much larger than Lowton. We were now, as far as I could see, on a sort of common; but there were houses scattered all over the district; I felt we were in a different region to Lowood, more populous, less picturesque; more stirring, less romantic.

The roads were heavy, the night misty; my conductor let his horse walk all the way, and the hour and a half extended, I verily believe, to two hours; at last he turned in his seat and said: 'You're noan so far fro' Thornfield now.'

Again I looked out: we were passing a church: I saw its low broad tower against the sky, and its bell was tolling a quarter; I saw a narrow galaxy of lights too, on a hillside, marking a village or hamlet. About ten minutes after the driver got down and opened a pair of gates; we passed through, and they clashed to behind us. We now slowly ascended a drive, and came upon the long front of a house: candle-light gleamed from one curtained bow-window; all the rest were dark. The car stopped at the front door; it was opened by a maidservant; I alighted and went in.

'Will you walk this way, ma'am,' said the girl; and I followed her across a square hall with high doors all round: she ushered me into a room whose double illumination of fire and candle at first dazzled me, contrasting as it did with the darkness to which my eyes had been for two hours inured; when I could see, however, a cozy and agreeable picture presented itself to my view.

A snug, small room; a round table by a cheerful fire; an arm-chair high-backed and old-fashioned, wherein sat the neatest imaginable little elderly lady, in widow's cap, black silk gown, and snowy muslin apron: exactly like what I had fancied Mrs. Fairfax, only less stately and milder-looking. She was occupied in knitting; a large cat sat demurely at her feet; nothing in short was wanting to complete the beau ideal of domestic comfort. A more reassuring introduction for a new governess could scarcely be conceived: there was no grandeur to overwhelm, no stateliness to embarrass; and then, as I entered, the old lady got up, and promptly and kindly came forward to meet me.

'How do you do, my dear? I am afraid you have had a tedious ride; John drives so slowly: you must be cold; come to the fire.'

'Mrs. Fairfax, I suppose?' said I.

'Yes, you are right: do sit down.'

She conducted me to her own chair, and then began to remove my shawl and untie my bonnet-strings. I begged she would not give herself so much trouble.

'Oh, it is no trouble; I dare say your own hands are almost numbed with cold. Leah, make a little hot negus[6] and cut a sandwich or two: here are the keys of the storeroom.'

And she produced from her pocket a most housewifely bunch of keys, and delivered them to the servant.

'Now, then, draw nearer to the fire,' she continued. 'You've brought your luggage with you, haven't you, my dear?'

'Yes, ma'am.'

'I'll see it carried into your room,' she said, and bustled out.

'She treats me like a visitor,' thought I. 'I little expected such a reception; I anticipated only coldness and stiffness: this is not like what I

---

6. A wine punch.

have heard of the treatment of governesses; but I must not exult too soon.'

She returned, with her own hands cleared her knitting apparatus and a book or two from the table, to make room for the tray which Leah now brought, and then herself handed me the refreshments. I felt rather confused at being the object of more attention than I had ever before received, and that, too, shown by my employer and superior; but as she did not herself seem to consider she was doing anything out of her place, I thought it better to take her civilities quietly.

'Shall I have the pleasure of seeing Miss Fairfax to-night?' I asked, when I had partaken of what she offered me.

'What did you say, my dear? I am a little deaf,' returned the good lady, approaching her ear to my mouth.

I repeated the question more distinctly.

'Miss Fairfax? Oh, you mean Miss Varens! Varens is the name of your future pupil.'

'Indeed! Then she is not your daughter?'

'No,—I have no family.'

I should have followed up my first inquiry by asking in what way Miss Varens was connected with her; but I recollected it was not polite to ask too many questions: besides, I was sure to hear in time.

'I am so glad,' she continued, as she sat down opposite to me, and took the cat on her knee; 'I am so glad you are come; it will be quite pleasant living here now with a companion. To be sure it is pleasant at any time; for Thornfield is a fine old hall, rather neglected of late years perhaps, but still it is a respectable place; yet you know in winter time one feels dreary quite alone, in the best quarters. I say alone—Leah is a nice girl to be sure, and John and his wife are very decent people; but then you see they are only servants, and one can't converse with them on terms of equality: one must keep them at due distance, for fear of losing one's authority. I'm sure last winter (it was a very severe one, if you recollect, and when it did not snow, it rained and blew) not a creature but the butcher and postman came to the house from November till February; and I really got quite melancholy with sitting night after night alone. I had Leah in to read to me sometimes; but I don't think the poor girl liked the task much: she felt it confining. In spring and summer one got on better: sunshine and long days make such a difference; and then, just at the commencement of this autumn, little Adela Varens came and her nurse: a child makes a house alive all at once; and now you are here I shall be quite gay.'

My heart really warmed to the worthy lady as I heard her talk: and I drew my chair a little nearer to her, and expressed my sincere wish that she might find my company as agreeable as she anticipated.

'But I'll not keep you sitting up late to-night,' said she; 'it is on the stroke of twelve now, and you have been travelling all day: you must feel tired. If you have got your feet well warmed I'll show you your bedroom. I've had the room next to mine prepared for you; it is only a small apartment, but I thought you would like it better than one of the large front chambers: to be sure they have finer furniture, but they are so dreary and solitary, I never sleep in them myself.'

I thanked her for her considerate choice, and as I really felt fatigued with my long journey, expressed my readiness to retire. She took her candle, and I followed her from the room. First she went to see if the hall-door was fastened; having taken the key from the lock, she led the way upstairs. The steps and banisters were of oak; the staircase window was high and latticed; both it and the long gallery into which the bedroom doors opened looked as if they belonged to a church rather than a house. A very chill and vaultlike air pervaded the stairs and gallery, suggesting cheerless ideas of space and solitude; and I was glad when finally ushered into my chamber to find it of small dimensions, and furnished in ordinary modern style.

When Mrs. Fairfax had bidden me a kind good-night, and I had fastened my door, gazed leisurely round, and in some measure effaced the eerie impression made by that wide hall, that dark and spacious staircase, and that long, cold gallery, by the livelier aspect of my little room, I remembered that after a day of bodily fatigue and mental anxiety I was now at last in safe haven. The impulse of gratitude swelled my heart, and I knelt down at the bedside, and offered up thanks where thanks were due; not forgetting, ere I rose, to implore aid on my further path, and the power of meriting the kindness which seemed so frankly offered me before it was earned. My couch had no thorns in it that night; my solitary room no fears. At once weary and content, I slept soon and soundly: when I awoke it was broad day.

The chamber looked such a bright little place to me as the sun shone in between the gay blue chintz window curtains, showing papered walls and a carpeted floor, so unlike the bare planks and stained plaster of Lowood that my spirits rose at the view. Externals have a great effect on the young: I thought that a fairer era of life was beginning for me, one that was to have its flowers and pleasures, as well as its thorns and toils. My faculties, roused by the change of scene, the new field offered to hope, seemed all astir. I cannot precisely define what they expected, but it was something pleasant: not perhaps that day or that month, but at an indefinite future period.

I rose; I dressed myself with care: obliged to be plain—for I had no article of attire that was not made with extreme simplicity—I was still by nature solicitous to be neat. It was not my habit to be disregardful of appearance, or careless of the impression I made: on the contrary, I ever wished to look as well as I could, and to please as much as my want of beauty would permit. I sometimes regretted that I was not handsomer: I sometimes wished to have rosy cheeks, a straight nose, and small cherry mouth; I desired to be tall, stately, and finely developed in figure; I felt it a misfortune that I was so little, so pale, and had features so irregular and so marked. And why had I these aspirations and these regrets? It would be difficult to say: I could not then distinctly say it to myself; yet I had a reason, and a logical, natural reason too. However, when I had brushed my hair very smooth, and put on my black frock—which, Quaker-like as it was, at least had the merit of fitting to a nicety—and adjusted my clean white tucker, I thought I should do respectably enough to appear before Mrs. Fairfax; and that my new pupil would not at least recoil from me with antipathy. Having opened my chamber window, and seen that I left all things straight and neat on the toilet table, I ventured forth.

Traversing the long and matted gallery, I descended the slippery steps of oak; then I gained the hall: I halted there a minute: I looked at some pictures on the walls (one I remember represented a grim man in a cuirass, and one a lady with powdered hair and a pearl necklace), at a bronze lamp pendent from the ceiling, at a great clock whose case was of oak curiously carved, and ebon black with time and rubbing. Everything appeared very stately and imposing to me: but then I was so little accustomed to grandeur. The hall-door, which was half of glass, stood open; I stepped over the threshold. It was a fine autumn morning; the early sun shone serenely on embrowned groves and still green fields: advancing on to the lawn, I looked up and surveyed the front of the mansion. It was three stories high, of proportions not vast, though considerable: a gentleman's manor-house, not a nobleman's seat: battlements round the top gave it a picturesque look. Its grey front stood out well from the background of a rookery, whose cawing tenants were now on the wing: they flew over the lawn and grounds to alight in a great meadow, from which these were separated by a sunk fence, and where an array of mighty old thorn trees, strong, knotty, and broad as oaks, at once explained the etymology of the mansion's designation. Farther off were hills: not so lofty as those round Lowood, nor so craggy, nor so like barriers of separation from the living world; but yet quiet and lonely hills enough, and seeming to embrace Thornfield with a seclusion I had not expected to find existent so near the stirring locality of Millcote. A little hamlet whose roofs were blent with trees straggled up the side of one of these hills; the church of the district stood nearer Thornfield: its old tower-top looked over a knoll between the house and gates.

I was yet enjoying the calm prospect and pleasant fresh air, yet listening with delight to the cawing of the rooks, yet surveying the wide, hoary front of the hall, and thinking what a great place it was for one lonely little dame like Mrs. Fairfax to inhabit, when that lady appeared at the door.

'What! out already?' said she. 'I see you are an early riser.' I went up to her, and was received with an affable kiss and shake of the hand.

'How do you like Thornfield?' she asked. I told her I liked it very much.

'Yes,' she said, 'it is a pretty place: but I fear it will be getting out of order, unless Mr. Rochester should take it into his head to come and reside here permanently; or, at least, visit it rather oftener: great houses and fine grounds require the presence of the proprietor.'

'Mr. Rochester!' I exclaimed. 'Who is he?'

'The owner of Thornfield,' she responded quietly. 'Did you not know he was called Rochester?'

Of course I did not—I had never heard of him before; but the old lady seemed to regard his existence as a universally understood fact, with which everybody must be acquainted by instinct.

'I thought,' I continued, 'Thornfield belonged to you.'

'To me? Bless you, child; what an idea! To me? I am only the house-keeper—the manager. To be sure I am distantly related to the Roches-ters by the mother's side; or, at least, my husband was: he was a clergyman, incumbent of Hay—that little village yonder on the hill—and that church near the gates was his. The present Mr. Rochester's mother was a Fairfax, and second cousin to my husband; but I never presume on the connection—in fact it is nothing to me; I consider my-self quite in the light of an ordinary house-keeper: my employer is always civil, and I expect nothing more.'

'And the little girl—my pupil?'

'She is Mr. Rochester's ward; he commissioned me to find a govern-ess for her. He intends to have her brought up in ——shire, I believe. Here she comes with her "bonne," as she calls her nurse.' The enigma then was explained: this affable and kind little widow was no great dame, but a dependent like myself. I did not like her the worse for that; on the contrary, I felt better pleased than ever. The equality between her and me was real; not the mere result of condescension on her part: so much the better—my position was all the freer.

As I was meditating on this discovery, a little girl, followed by her at-tendant, came running up the lawn. I looked at my pupil, who did not at first appear to notice me: she was quite a child, perhaps seven or eight years old, slightly built, with a pale, small-featured face, and a redun-dancy of hair falling in curls to her waist.

'Good-morning, Miss Adela,' said Mrs. Fairfax. 'Come and speak to the lady who is to teach you, and to make you a clever woman some day.' She approached.

'C'est là ma gouvernante?' said she, pointing to me, and addressing her nurse; who answered: 'Mais oui, certainement.'[7]

'Are they foreigners?' I inquired, amazed at hearing the French language.

"The nurse is a foreigner, and Adela was born on the Continent, and, I believe, never left it till within six months ago. When she first came here she could speak no English; now she can make shift to talk it a little: I don't understand her, she mixes it so with French; but you will make out her meaning very well, I daresay.'

Fortunately I had had the advantage of being taught French by a French lady; and as I had always made a point of conversing with Madame Pierrot as often as I could, and had, besides, during the last seven years, learnt a portion of French by heart daily—applying myself to take pains with my accent, and imitating as closely as possible the pronunciation of my teacher—I had acquired a certain degree of readiness and correctness in the language, and was not likely to be much at a loss with Mademoiselle Adela. She came and shook hands with me when she heard that I was her governess; and as I led her into breakfast I addressed some phrases to her in her own tongue: she replied briefly at first, but after we were seated at the table, and she had examined me some ten minutes with her large hazel eyes, she suddenly commenced chattering fluently.

'Ah!' cried she, in French, 'you speak my language as well as Mr. Rochester does: I can talk to you as I can to him, and so can Sophie. She will be glad: nobody here understands her: Madame Fairfax is all English. Sophie is my nurse; she came with me over the sea in a great ship with a chimney that smoked—how it did smoke!—and I was sick, and so was Sophie, and so was Mr. Rochester. Mr. Rochester lay down on a sofa in a pretty room called the salon, and Sophie and I had little beds in another place. I nearly fell out of mine; it was like a shelf. And Mademoiselle—what is your name?'

'Eyre—Jane Eyre.'

'Aire?[8] Bah! I cannot say it. Well: our ship stopped in the morning, before it was quite daylight, at a great city—a huge city, with very dark houses and all smoky; not at all like the pretty clean town I came from; and Mr. Rochester carried me in his arms over a plank to the land, and Sophie came after, and we all got into a coach, which took us to a beautiful large house, larger than this and finer, called an hotel. We stayed there nearly a week. I and Sophie used to walk every day in a great green place full of trees, called the Park; and there were many children

---

7. French: "That is my governess?" . . . "But of course."
8. In French *aire* means, among other things, "threshing ground," "nest for a bird of prey," and "area."

there besides me, and a pond with beautiful birds in it, that I fed with crumbs.'

'Can you understand her when she runs on so fast?' asked Mrs. Fairfax.

I understood her very well, for I had been accustomed to the fluent tongue of Madame Pierrot.

'I wish,' continued the good lady, 'you would ask her a question or two about her parents: I wonder if she remembers them?'

'Adèle,' I inquired, 'with whom did you live when you were in that pretty clean town you spoke of?'

'I lived long ago with mamma; but she is gone to the Holy Virgin. Mamma used to teach me to dance and sing, and to say verses. A great many gentlemen and ladies came to see mamma, and I used to dance before them, or to sit on their knees and sing to them: I liked it. Shall I let you hear me sing now?'

She had finished her breakfast, so I permitted her to give a specimen of her accomplishments. Descending from her chair, she came and placed herself on my knee; then, folding her little hands demurely before her, shaking back her curls and lifting her eyes to the ceiling, she commenced singing a song from some opera. It was the strain of a forsaken lady, who, after bewailing the perfidy of her lover, calls pride to her aid; desires her attendant to deck her in her brightest jewels and richest robes, and resolves to meet the false one that night at a ball, and prove to him, by the gaiety of her demeanour, how little his desertion has affected her.

The subject seemed strangely chosen for an infant singer; but I suppose the point of the exhibition lay in hearing the notes of love and jealousy warbled with the lisp of childhood; and in very bad taste that point was: at least I thought so.

Adèle sang the canzonette tunefully enough, and with the naïveté of her age. This achieved, she jumped from my knee and said, 'Now, Mademoiselle, I will repeat you some poetry.'

Assuming an attitude, she began 'La Ligue des Rats: fable de la Fontaine.'[9] She then declaimed the little piece with an attention to punctuation and emphasis, a flexibility of voice and an appropriateness of gesture, very unusual indeed at her age, and which proved she had been carefully trained.

'Was it your mamma who taught you that piece?' I asked.

'Yes; and she just used to say it in this way: "Qu'avez vous donc? lui dit un de ces rats; parlez!"[1] She made me lift my hand—so—to remind me to raise my voice at the question. Now shall I dance for you?'

---

9. "The League of Rats: A Fable by La Fontaine." In this fable a mouse is eaten by a cat when the rescue attempts of other rodents fail.

1. French: "What's the matter?" says one of the rats to her; "speak!"

'No, that will do: but after your mamma went to the Holy Virgin, as you say, with whom did you live then?'

'With Madame Frédéric and her husband: she took care of me, but she is nothing related to me. I think she is poor, for she had not so fine a house as mamma. I was not long there. Mr. Rochester asked me if I would like to go and live with him in England, and I said yes; for I knew Mr. Rochester before I knew Madame Frédéric, and he was always kind to me and gave me pretty dresses and toys. But you see he has not kept his word, for he has brought me to England, and now he is gone back again himself, and I never see him.'

After breakfast Adèle and I withdrew to the library; which room, it appears, Mr. Rochester had directed should be used as the schoolroom. Most of the books were locked up behind glass doors; but there was one bookcase left open, containing everything that could be needed in the way of elementary works, and several volumes of light literature, poetry, biography, travels, a few romances, &c. I suppose he had considered that these were all the governess would require for her private perusal; and, indeed, they contented me amply for the present; compared with the scanty pickings I had now and then been able to glean at Lowood, they seemed to offer an abundant harvest of entertainment and information. In this room, too, there was a cabinet piano,[2] quite new and of superior tone; also an easel for painting, and a pair of globes.

I found my pupil sufficiently docile, though disinclined to apply: she had not been used to regular occupation of any kind. I felt it would be injudicious to confine her too much at first; so, when I had talked to her a great deal, and got her to learn a little, and when the morning had advanced to noon, I allowed her to return to her nurse. I then proposed to occupy myself till dinner-time in drawing some little sketches for her use.

As I was going upstairs to fetch my portfolio and pencils, Mrs. Fairfax called to me: 'Your morning school-hours are over now, I suppose,' said she. She was in a room the folding-doors of which stood open: I went in when she addressed me. It was a large, stately apartment, with purple chairs and curtains, a Turkey carpet, walnut-panelled walls, one vast window rich in stained glass, and a lofty ceiling, nobly moulded. Mrs. Fairfax was dusting some vases of fine purple spar, which stood on a sideboard.

'What a beautiful room!' I exclaimed, as I looked round; for I had never before seen any half so imposing.

'Yes; this is the dining-room. I have just opened the window, to let in a little air and sunshine; for everything gets so damp in apartments that are seldom inhabited: the drawing-room yonder feels like a vault.'

2. Small upright piano.

She pointed to a wide arch corresponding to the window, and hung like it with a Tyrian-dyed curtain, now looped up. Mounting to it by two broad steps and looking through, I thought I caught a glimpse of a fairy place, so bright to my novice eyes appeared the view beyond. Yet it was merely a very pretty drawing-room, and within it a boudoir, both spread with white carpets, on which seemed laid brilliant garlands of flowers; both ceiled with snowy mouldings of white grapes and vine-leaves, beneath which glowed in rich contrast crimson couches and ottomans; while the ornaments on the pale Parian mantelpiece were of sparkling Bohemian glass, ruby red; and between the windows large mirrors repeated the general blending of snow and fire.

'In what order you keep these rooms, Mrs. Fairfax!' said I. 'No dust, no canvas coverings: except that the air feels chilly, one would think they were inhabited daily.'

'Why, Miss Eyre, though Mr. Rochester's visits here are rare, they are always sudden and unexpected; and as I observed that it put him out to find everything swathed up, and to have a bustle of arrangement on his arrival, I thought it best to keep the rooms in readiness.'

'Is Mr. Rochester an exacting, fastidious sort of man?'

'Not particularly so; but he has a gentleman's tastes and habits, and he expects to have things managed in conformity to them.'

'Do you like him? Is he generally liked?'

'Oh, yes; the family have always been respected here. Almost all the land in this neighbourhood, as far as you can see, has belonged to the Rochesters time out of mind.'

'Well, but, leaving his land out of the question, do you like him? Is he liked for himself?'

'I have no cause to do otherwise than like him; and I believe he is considered a just and liberal landlord by his tenants: but he has never lived much amongst them.'

'But has he no peculiarities? What, in short, is his character?'

'Oh! his character is unimpeachable, I suppose. He is rather peculiar, perhaps: he has travelled a great deal, and seen a great deal of the world, I should think. I daresay he is clever: but I never had much conversation with him.'

'In what way is he peculiar?'

'I don't know—it is not easy to describe—nothing striking, but you feel it when he speaks to you: you cannot be always sure whether he is in jest or earnest, whether he is pleased or the contrary; you don't thoroughly understand him, in short—at least, I don't: but it is of no consequence, he is a very good master.'

This was all the account I got from Mrs. Fairfax of her employer and mine. There are people who seem to have no notion of sketching a character, or observing and describing salient points, either in persons or things: the good lady evidently belonged to this class; my queries puzzled, but did not draw her out. Mr. Rochester was Mr. Rochester in her eyes; a gentleman, a landed proprietor—nothing more: she inquired and searched no further, and evidently wondered at my wish to gain a more definite notion of his identity.

When we left the dining-room, she proposed to show me over the rest of the house; and I followed her upstairs and downstairs, admiring as I went; for all was well arranged and handsome. The large front chambers I thought especially grand; and some of the third-story rooms, though dark and low, were interesting from their air of antiquity. The furniture once appropriated to the lower apartments had from time to time been removed here, as fashions changed; and the imperfect light entering by their narrow casements showed bedsteads of a hundred years old; chests in oak or walnut, looking with their strange carvings of palm branches and cherubs' heads, like types of the Hebrew ark;[3] rows of venerable chairs, high-backed and narrow; stools still more antiquated, on whose cushioned tops were yet apparent traces of half-effaced embroideries, wrought by fingers that for two generations had been coffin-dust. All these relics gave to the third story of Thornfield Hall the aspect of a home of the past: a shrine of memory. I liked the hush, the gloom, the quaintness of these retreats in the day; but I by no means coveted a night's repose on one of those wide and heavy beds: shut in, some of them, with doors of oak; shaded, others, with wrought old-English hangings crusted with thick work, portraying effigies of strange flowers, and stranger birds, and strangest human beings,—all which would have looked strange, indeed, by the pallid gleam of moonlight.

'Do the servants sleep in these rooms?' I asked.

'No; they occupy a range of smaller apartments to the back; no one ever sleeps here: one would almost say that, if there were a ghost at Thornfield Hall, this would be its haunt.'

'So I think: you have no ghost, then?'

'None that I ever heard of,' returned Mrs. Fairfax, smiling.

'Nor any traditions of one? no legends or ghost stories?'

'I believe not. And yet it is said the Rochesters have been rather a violent than a quiet race in their time: perhaps, though, that is the reason they rest tranquilly in their graves now.'

'Yes—"after life's fitful fever they sleep well," '[4] I muttered. 'Where are you going now, Mrs. Fairfax?' for she was moving away.

'On to the leads; will you come and see the view from thence?' I followed still, up a very narrow staircase to the attics, and thence by a lad-

3. The sacred chest containing the Ten Commandments, described in Exodus 25:18–22.

4. Shakespeare's *Macbeth* 3.2.23. "Leads": roof.

der and through a trap-door to the roof of the hall. I was now on a level with the crow colony, and could see into their nests. Leaning over the battlements and looking far down, I surveyed the grounds laid out like a map: the bright and velvet lawn closely girdling the grey base of the mansion; the field, wide as a park, dotted with its ancient timber; the wood, dun and sere, divided by a path visibly overgrown, greener with moss than the trees were with foliage; the church at the gates, the road, the tranquil hills, all reposing in the autumn day's sun: the horizon bounded by a propitious sky, azure, marbled with pearly white. No feature in the scene was extraordinary, but all was pleasing. When I turned from it and repassed the trap-door, I could scarcely see my way down the ladder: the attic seemed black as a vault compared with that arch of blue air to which I had been looking up, and to that sunlit scene of grove, pasture, and green hill of which the hall was the centre, and over which I had been gazing with delight.

Mrs. Fairfax stayed behind a moment to fasten the trap-door; I, by dint of groping, found the outlet from the attic, and proceeded to descend the narrow garret staircase. I lingered in the long passage to which this led, separating the front and back rooms of the third story: narrow, low, and dim, with only one little window at the far end, and looking, with its two rows of small black doors all shut, like a corridor in some Bluebeard's castle.[5]

While I paced softly on the last sound I expected to hear in so still a region, a laugh, struck my ear. It was a curious laugh; distinct, formal, mirthless. I stopped: the sound ceased, only for an instant; it began again louder: for at first, though distinct, it was very low. It passed off in a clamorous peal that seemed to wake an echo in every lonely chamber; though it originated but in one, and I could have pointed out the door whence the accents issued.

'Mrs. Fairfax!' I called out: for I now heard her descending the great stairs. 'Did you hear that loud laugh? Who is it?'

'Some of the servants, very likely,' she answered: 'perhaps Grace Poole.'

'Did you hear it?' I again inquired.

'Yes, plainly: I often hear her; she sews in one of these rooms. Sometimes Leah is with her: they are frequently noisy together.'

The laugh was repeated in its low, syllabic tone, and terminated in an odd murmur.

'Grace!' exclaimed Mrs. Fairfax.

I really did not expect any Grace to answer; for the laugh was as tragic, as preternatural a laugh as any I ever heard; and, but that it was

5. In the fairy tale *Bluebeard*, by Charles Perrault, the young wife is allowed to enter all the rooms in her husband's castle but one, where the bodies of his former wives are kept.

high noon, and that no circumstance of ghostliness accompanied the curious cachinnation, but that neither scene nor season favoured fear, I should have been superstitiously afraid. However, the event showed me I was a fool for entertaining a sense even of surprise.

The door nearest me opened, and a servant came out,—a woman of between thirty and forty; a set, square-made figure, red-haired, and with a hard, plain face: any apparition less romantic or less ghostly could scarcely be conceived.

'Too much noise, Grace,' said Mrs. Fairfax. 'Remember directions!' Grace curtseyed silently and went in.

'She is a person we have to sew and assist Leah in her house-maid's work,' continued the widow; 'not altogether unobjectionable in some points, but she does well enough. By-the-by, how have you got on with your new pupil this morning?'

The conversation, thus turned on Adèle, continued till we reached the light and cheerful region below. Adèle came running to meet us in the hall, exclaiming,—'Mesdames, vous êtes servies!' adding, 'J'ai bien faim, moi!'[6]

We found dinner ready and waiting for us in Mrs. Fairfax's room.

Chapter XII

The promise of a smooth career, which my first calm introduction to Thornfield Hall seemed to pledge, was not belied on a longer acquaintance with the place and its inmates. Mrs. Fairfax turned out to be what she appeared, a placid-tempered, kind-natured woman, of competent education and average intelligence. My pupil was a lively child, who had been spoilt and indulged, and therefore was sometimes wayward; but as she was committed entirely to my care, and no injudicious interference from any quarter ever thwarted my plans for her improvement, she soon forgot her little freaks, and became obedient and teachable. She had no great talents, no marked traits of character, no peculiar development of feeling or taste which raised her one inch above the ordinary level of childhood; but neither had she any deficiency or vice which sunk her below it. She made reasonable progress, entertained for me a vivacious, though perhaps not very profound, affection; and by her simplicity, gay prattle, and efforts to please, inspired me, in return, with a degree of attachment sufficient to make us both content in each other's society.

This, *par parenthèse*,[7] will be thought cool language by persons who entertain solemn doctrines about the angelic nature of children, and the duty of those charged with their education to conceive for them an idol-

6. "My ladies, dinner is served! . . . I am very hungry!"   7. Parenthetically.

atrous devotion: but I am not writing to flatter parental egotism, to echo cant, or prop up humbug; I am merely telling the truth. I felt a conscientious solicitude for Adèle's welfare and progress, and a quiet liking to her little self; just as I cherished towards Mrs. Fairfax a thankfulness for her kindness, and a pleasure in her society proportionate to the tranquil regard she had for me, and the moderation of her mind and character.

Anybody may blame me who likes when I add further that now and then, when I took a walk by myself in the grounds, when I went down to the gates and looked through them along the road, or when, while Adèle played with her nurse, and Mrs. Fairfax made jellies in the storeroom, I climbed the three staircases, raised the trap-door of the attic, and having reached the leads, looked out afar over sequestered field and hill, and along dim sky-line—that then I longed for a power of vision which might overpass that limit; which might reach the busy world, towns, regions full of life I had heard of but never seen: that then I desired more of practical experience than I possessed; more of intercourse with my kind, of acquaintance with variety of character, than was here within my reach. I valued what was good in Mrs. Fairfax, and what was good in Adèle; but I believed in the existence of other and more vivid kinds of goodness, and what I believed in I wished to behold.

Who blames me? Many, no doubt; and I shall be called discontented. I could not help it: the restlessness was in my nature; it agitated me to pain sometimes. Then my sole relief was to walk along the corridor of the third story, backwards and forwards, safe in the silence and solitude of the spot and allow my mind's eye to dwell on whatever bright visions rose before it—and, certainly, they were many and glowing; to let my heart be heaved by the exultant movement, which, while it swelled it in trouble, expanded it with life; and, best of all, to open my inward ear to a tale that was never ended—a tale my imagination created, and narrated continuously; quickened with all of incident, life, fire, feeling, that I desired and had not in my actual existence.

It is in vain to say human beings ought to be satisfied with tranquillity: they must have action; and they will make it if they cannot find it. Millions are condemned to a stiller doom than mine, and millions are in silent revolt against their lot. Nobody knows how many rebellions besides political rebellions ferment in the masses of life which people earth. Women are supposed to be very calm generally: but women feel just as men feel; they need exercise for their faculties and a field for their efforts as much as their brothers do; they suffer from too rigid a restraint, too absolute a stagnation, precisely as men would suffer; and it is narrow-minded in their more privileged fellow-creatures to say that they ought to confine themselves to making puddings and knitting stockings, to playing on the piano and embroidering bags. It is thoughtless to condemn them, or laugh at them, if they seek to do more or learn more than custom has pronounced necessary for their sex.

When thus alone I not unfrequently heard Grace Poole's laugh: the same peal, the same low, slow ha! ha! which, when first heard, had thrilled me: I heard, too, her eccentric murmurs; stranger than her laugh. There were days when she was quite silent; but there were others when I could not account for the sounds she made. Sometimes I saw her; she would come out of her room with a basin, or a plate, or a tray in her hand, go down to the kitchen, and shortly return, generally (oh, romantic reader, forgive me for telling the plain truth:) bearing a pot of porter.[8] Her appearance always acted as a damper to the curiosity raised by her oral oddities: hard-featured and staid, she had no point to which interest could attach. I made some attempts to draw her into conversation, but she seemed a person of few words: a monosyllabic reply usually cut short every effort of that sort.

The other members of the household, viz. John and his wife, Leah the housemaid, and Sophie the French nurse, were decent people: but in no respect remarkable. With Sophie I used to talk French, and sometimes I asked her questions about her native country; but she was not of a descriptive or narrative turn, and generally gave such vapid and confused answers as were calculated rather to check than encourage inquiry.

October, November, December passed away. One afternoon in January Mrs. Fairfax had begged a holiday for Adèle because she had a cold; and, as Adèle seconded the request with an ardour that reminded me how precious occasional holidays had been to me in my own childhood, I accorded it, deeming that I did well in showing pliability on the point. It was a fine, calm day, though very cold; I was tired of sitting still in the library through a whole long morning: Mrs. Fairfax had just written a letter which was waiting to be posted, so I put on my bonnet and cloak and volunteered to carry it to Hay; the distance, two miles, would be a pleasant winter afternoon walk. Having seen Adèle comfortably seated in her little chair by Mrs. Fairfax's parlour fireside, and given her her best wax doll (which I usually kept enveloped in silver paper in a drawer) to play with, and a story-book for change of amusement; and having replied to her 'Revenez bientôt, ma bonne amie, ma chère Mdlle. Jeannette,'[9] with a kiss, I set out.

The ground was hard, the air was still, my road was lonely; I walked fast till I got warm, and then I walked slowly to enjoy and analyse the species of pleasure brooding for me in the hour and situation. It was three o'clock; the church bell tolled as I passed under the belfry: the charm of the hour lay in its approaching dimness, in the low-gliding and pale-beaming sun. I was a mile from Thornfield, in a lane noted for wild roses in summer, for nuts and blackberries in autumn, and even

8. Weak stout.
9. "Come back soon, my good friend, my dear Miss Janie."

now possessing a few coral treasures in hips and haws, but whose best winter delight lay in its utter solitude and leafless repose. If a breath of air stirred, it made no sound here; for there was not a holly, not an evergreen to rustle, and the stripped hawthorn and hazel bushes were as still as the white, worn stones which causewayed the middle of the path. Far and wide, on each side, there were only fields, where no cattle now browsed; and the little brown birds, which stirred occasionally in the hedge, looked like single russet leaves that had forgotten to drop.

This lane inclined uphill all the way to Hay: having reached the middle I sat down on a stile which led thence into a field. Gathering my mantle about me, and sheltering my hands in my muff, I did not feel the cold, though it froze keenly; as was attested by a sheet of ice cover- ing the causeway, where a little brooklet, now congealed, had over- flowed after a rapid thaw some days since. From my seat I could look down on Thornfield: the grey and battlemented hall was the principal object in the vale below me; its woods and dark rookery rose against the west. I lingered till the sun went down amongst the trees, and sank crimson and clear behind them. I then turned eastward.

On the hilltop above me sat the rising moon; pale yet as a cloud, but brightening momently: she looked over Hay, which, half lost in trees, sent up a blue smoke from its few chimneys; it was yet a mile distant, but in the absolute hush I could hear plainly its thin murmurs of life. My ear too felt the flow of currents; in what dales and depths I could not tell: but there were many hills beyond Hay, and doubtless many becks threading their passes. That evening calm betrayed alike the tinkle of the nearest streams, the sough of the most remote.

A rude noise broke on these fine ripplings and whisperings, at once so far away and so clear: a positive tramp, tramp; a metallic clatter, which effaced the soft wave-wanderings; as, in a picture, the solid mass of a crag, or the rough boles of a great oak, drawn in dark and strong on the foreground, efface the aërial distance of azure hill, sunny horizon, and blended clouds, where tint melts into tint.

The din was on the causeway; a horse was coming; the windings of the lane yet hid it, but it approached. I was just leaving the stile; yet, as the path was narrow, I sat still to let it go by. In those days I was young, and all sorts of fancies bright and dark tenanted my mind: the memories of nursery stories were there amongst other rubbish; and when they re- curred, maturing youth added to them a vigour and vividness beyond what childhood could give. As this horse approached, and as I watched for it to appear through the dusk, I remembered certain of Bessie's tales, wherein figured a North-of-England spirit, called a 'Gytrash,' which, in the form of horse, mule, or large dog, haunted solitary ways, and some- times came upon belated travellers, as this horse was now coming upon me.

It was very near, but not yet in sight, when, in addition to the tramp, tramp, I heard a rush under the hedge, and close down by the hazel stems glided a great dog, whose black and white colour made him a distinct object against the trees. It was exactly one mask of Bessie's Gytrash,—a lion-like creature with long hair and a huge head: it passed me, however, quietly enough; not staying to look up, with strange pretercanine eyes, in my face, as I half expected it would. The horse followed,—a tall steed, and on its back a rider. The man, the human being, broke the spell at once. Nothing ever rode the Gytrash: it was always alone; and goblins, to my notions, though they might tenant the dumb carcasses of beasts, could scarce covet shelter in the commonplace human form. No Gytrash was this,—only a traveller taking the short cut to Millcote. He passed, and I went on: a few steps, and I turned: a sliding sound and an exclamation of 'What the deuce is to do now?' and a clattering tumble, arrested my attention. Man and horse were down; they had slipped on the sheet of ice which glazed the causeway. The dog came bounding back, and seeing his master in a predicament, and hearing the horse groan, barked till the evening hills echoed the sound, which was deep in proportion to his magnitude. He snuffed round the prostrate group, and then he ran up to me; it was all he could do,—there was no other help at hand to summon. I obeyed him, and walked down to the traveller, by this time struggling himself free of his steed. His efforts were so vigorous I thought he could not be much hurt; but I asked him the question:—'Are you injured, sir?'

I think he was swearing, but am not certain; however, he was pronouncing some formula which prevented him from replying to me directly.

'Can I do anything?' I asked again.

'You must just stand on one side,' he answered as he rose, first to his knees, and then to his feet. I did; whereupon began a heaving, stamping, clattering process, accompanied by a barking and baying which removed me effectually some yards' distance; but I would not be driven quite away till I saw the event. This was finally fortunate; the horse was re-established, and the dog was silenced with a 'Down, Pilot!' The traveller now, stooping, felt his foot and leg, as if trying whether they were sound; apparently something ailed them, for he halted to the stile whence I had just risen, and sat down.

I was in the mood for being useful, or at least officious, I think, for I now drew near him again.

'If you are hurt, and want help, sir, I can fetch some one either from Thornfield Hall or from Hay.'

'Thank you; I shall do: I have no broken bones—only a sprain;' and again he stood up and tried his foot, but the result extorted an involuntary 'Ugh!'

Something of daylight still lingered, and the moon was waxing bright: I could see him plainly. His figure was enveloped in a riding cloak, fur collared, and steel clasped; its details were not apparent, but I traced the general points of middle height, and considerable breadth of chest. He had a dark face, with stern features and a heavy brow; his eyes and gathered eyebrows looked ireful and thwarted just now; he was past youth, but had not reached middle age; perhaps he might be thirty-five. I felt no fear of him, and but little shyness. Had he been a handsome, heroic-looking young gentleman, I should not have dared to stand thus questioning him against his will, and offering my services unasked. I had hardly ever seen a handsome youth; never in my life spoken to one. I had a theoretical reverence and homage for beauty, elegance, gallantry, fascination; but had I met those qualities incarnate in masculine shape, I should have known instinctively that they neither had nor could have sympathy with anything in me, and should have shunned them as one would fire, lightning, or anything else that is bright but antipathetic.

If even this stranger had smiled and been good-humoured to me when I addressed him; if he had put off my offer of assistance gaily and with thanks, I should have gone on my way and not felt any vocation to renew inquiries: but the frown, the roughness of the traveller, set me at my ease: I retained my station when he waved to me to go, and announced:—'I cannot think of leaving you, sir, at so late an hour, in this solitary lane, till I see you are fit to mount your horse.'

He looked at me when I said this: he had hardly turned his eyes in my direction before.

'I should think you ought to be at home yourself,' said he, 'if you have a home in this neighbourhood: where do you come from?'

'From just below; and I am not at all afraid of being out late when it is moonlight: I will run over to Hay for you with pleasure, if you wish it; indeed, I am going there to post a letter.'

'You live just below—do you mean at that house with the battlements?' pointing to Thornfield Hall, on which the moon cast a hoary gleam, bringing it out distinct and pale from the woods, that, by contrast with the western sky, now seemed one mass of shadow.

'Yes, sir.'

'Whose house is it?'

'Mr. Rochester's.'

'Do you know Mr. Rochester?'

'No, I have never seen him.'

'He is not resident, then?'

'No.'

'Can you tell me where he is?'

'I cannot.'

'You are not a servant at the hall, of course. You are—' He

stopped, ran his eye over my dress, which, as usual, was quite simple: a
black merino cloak, a black beaver bonnet: neither of them half fine
enough for a lady's maid. He seemed puzzled to decide what I was: I
helped him.

'I am the governess.'

'Ah, the governess!' he repeated; 'deuce take me, if I had not forgotten! The governess!' and again my raiment underwent scrutiny. In two
minutes he rose from the stile: his face expressed pain when he tried to
move.

'I cannot commission you to fetch help,' he said; 'but you may help
me a little yourself, if you will be so kind.'

'Yes, sir.'

'You have not an umbrella that I can use as a stick?'

'No.'

'Try to get hold of my horse's bridle and lead him to me: you are not
afraid!'

I should have been afraid to touch a horse when alone, but when told
to do it I was disposed to obey. I put down my muff on the stile, and
went up to the tall steed; I endeavoured to catch the bridle, but it was a
spirited thing, and would not let me come near its head; I made effort
on effort, though in vain: meantime, I was mortally afraid of its trampling fore-feet. The traveller waited and watched for some time, and at
last he laughed.

'I see,' he said, 'the mountain will never be brought to Mahomet, so
all you can do is to aid Mahomet to go to the mountain; I must beg of
you to come here.'[1]

I came. 'Excuse me,' he continued: 'necessity compels me to make
you useful.' He laid a heavy hand on my shoulder, and leaning on me
with some stress, limped to his horse. Having once caught the bridle, he
mastered it directly, and sprang to his saddle; grimacing grimly as he
made the effort, for it wrenched his sprain.

'Now,' said he, releasing his under lip from a hard bite, 'just hand me
my whip; it lies there under the hedge.'

I sought it and found it.

'Thank you: now make haste with the letter to Hay, and return as fast
as you can.'

A touch of a spurred heel made his horse first start and rear, and then
bound away; the dog rushed in his traces: all three vanished,

> Like heath that, in the wilderness,
>   The wild wind whirls away.[2]

1. According to legend, the Moslem prophet
Mohammed summoned Mount Safa to come to
him, in order to display his powers. When the
mountain did not come, he told the spectators he
would go to it.
2. From Thomas Moore's *Fallen Is Thy
Throne, Sacred Songs.*

I took up my muff and walked on. The incident had occurred and was gone for me: it *was* an incident of no moment, no romance, no interest in a sense; yet it marked with change one single hour of a monotonous life. My help had been needed and claimed; I had given it: I was pleased to have done something; trivial, transitory though the deed was, it was yet an active thing, and I was weary of an existence all passive. The new face, too, was like a new picture introduced to the gallery of memory; and it was dissimilar to all the others hanging there: firstly, because it was masculine; and, secondly, because it was dark, strong, and stern. I had it still before me when I entered Hay, and slipped the letter into the post-office; I saw it as I walked fast down hill all the way home. When I came to the stile, I stopped a minute, looked round and listened, with an idea that a horse's hoof might ring on the causeway again, and that a rider in a cloak, and a Gytrash-like Newfoundland dog, might be again apparent: I saw only the hedge and a pollard willow before me, rising up still and straight to meet the moonbeams; I heard only the faintest waft of wind roaming fitful among the trees round Thornfield, a mile distant; and when I glanced down in the direction of the murmur, my eye, traversing the hall-front, caught a light kindling in a window: it reminded me that I was late, and I hurried on.

I did not like re-entering Thornfield. To pass its threshold was to return to stagnation; to cross the silent hall, to ascend the darksome staircase, to seek my own lonely little room, and then to meet tranquil Mrs. Fairfax, and spend the long winter evening with her, and her only, was to quell wholly the faint excitement wakened by my walk,—to slip again over my faculties the viewless fetters of an uniform and too still existence; of an existence whose very privileges of security and ease I was becoming incapable of appreciating. What good it would have done me at that time to have been tossed in the storms of an uncertain struggling life, and to have been taught by rough and bitter experience to long for the calm amidst which I now repined! Yes, just as much good as it would do a man tired of sitting still in a 'too easy chair'[3] to take a long walk; and just as natural was the wish to stir, under my circumstances, as it would be under his.

I lingered at the gates; I lingered on the lawn; I paced backwards and forwards on the pavement: the shutters of the glass door were closed; I could not see into the interior; and both my eyes and spirit seemed drawn from the gloomy house—from the grey hollow filled with rayless cells, as it appeared to me—to that sky expanded before me,—a blue sea absolved from taint of cloud; the moon ascending it in solemn march; her orb seeming to look up as she left the hilltops, from behind which she had come, far and farther below her, and aspired to the zenith, midnight-dark in its fathomless depth and measureless distance:

3. Alexander Pope, *The Dunciad* 4.342.

and for those trembling stars that followed her course; they made my heart tremble, my veins glow when I viewed them. Little things recall us to earth: the clock struck in the hall; that sufficed; I turned from moon and stars, opened a side door, and went in.

The hall was not dark, nor yet was it lit, only by the high-hung bronze lamp: a warm glow suffused both it and the lower steps of the oak staircase. This ruddy shine issued from the great dining-room, whose two-leaved door stood open, and showed a genial fire in the grate, glancing on marble hearth and brass fire-irons, and revealing purple draperies and polished furniture, in the most pleasant radiance. It revealed, too, a group near the mantelpiece: I had scarcely caught it, and scarcely become aware of a cheerful mingling of voices, amongst which I seemed to distinguish the tones of Adèle, when the door closed.

I hastened to Mrs. Fairfax's room: there was a fire there too, but no candle, and no Mrs. Fairfax. Instead, all alone, sitting upright on the rug, and gazing with gravity at the blaze, I beheld a great black and white long-haired dog, just like the Gytrash of the lane. It was so like it that I went forward and said—'Pilot,' and the thing got up and came to me and snuffed me. I caressed him, and he wagged his great tail: but he looked an eerie creature to be alone with, and I could not tell whence he had come. I rang the bell, for I wanted a candle; and I wanted, too, to get an account of this visitant. Leah entered.

'What dog is this?'

'He came with master.'

'With whom?'

'With master—Mr. Rochester—he is just arrived.'

'Indeed! and is Mrs. Fairfax with him?'

'Yes, and Miss Adèla; they are in the dining-room, and John is gone for a surgeon: for master has had an accident; his horse fell and his ankle is sprained.'

'Did the horse fall in Hay Lane?'

'Yes, coming down hill; it slipped on some ice.'

'Ah! Bring me a candle, will you, Leah?'

Leah brought it; she entered, followed by Mrs. Fairfax, who repeated the news; adding that Mr. Carter the surgeon was come, and was now with Mr. Rochester: then she hurried out to give orders about tea, and I went upstairs to take off my things.

Chapter XIII

Mr. Rochester, it seems, by the surgeon's orders, went to bed early that night; nor did he rise soon next morning. When he did come down, it was to attend to business: his agent and some of his tenants were arrived, and waiting to speak with him.

Adèle and I had now to vacate the library: it would be in daily requisition as a reception-room for callers. A fire was lit in an apartment upstairs, and there I carried our books, and arranged it for the future schoolroom. I discerned in the course of the morning that Thornfield Hall was a changed place: no longer silent as a church, it echoed every hour or two to a knock at the door, or a clang of the bell; steps, too, often traversed the hall, and new voices spoke in different keys below; a rill from the outer world was flowing through it; it had a master: for my part I liked it better.

Adèle was not easy to teach that day; she could not apply: she kept running to the door and looking over the banisters to see if she could get a glimpse of Mr. Rochester; then she coined pretexts to go downstairs, in order, as I shrewdly suspected, to visit the library, where I knew she was not wanted; then, when I got a little angry, and made her sit still, she continued to talk incessantly of her 'ami, Monsieur Edouard Fairfax *de* Rochester,' as she dubbed him[4] (I had not before heard his prenomens), and to conjecture what presents he had brought her: for it appears he had intimated the night before, that when his luggage came from Millcote there would be found amongst it a little box in whose contents she had an interest.

'Et cela doit signifier,' said she, 'qu'il y aura là dedans un cadeau pour moi, et peut-être pour vous aussi, mademoiselle. Monsieur a parlé de vous: il m'a demandé le nom de ma gouvernante, et si elle n'était pas une petite personne, assez mince et un peu pâle. J'ai dit qu'oui: car c'est vrai, n'est-ce pas, mademoiselle?'[5]

I and my pupil dined as usual in Mrs. Fairfax's parlour; the afternoon was wild and snowy, and we passed it in the schoolroom. At dark I allowed Adèle to put away books and work, and to run downstairs; for, from the comparative silence below, and from the cessation of appeals to the doorbell, I conjectured that Mr. Rochester was now at liberty. Left alone, I walked to the window; but nothing was to be seen thence: twilight and snowflakes together thickened the air, and hid the very shrubs on the lawn. I let down the curtain and went back to the fireside.

In the clear embers I was tracing a view, not unlike a picture I remembered to have seen of the castle of Heidelberg, on the Rhine, when Mrs. Fairfax came in, breaking up by her entrance the fiery mosaic I had been piecing together, and scattering too some heavy unwelcome thoughts that were beginning to throng on my solitude.

'Mr. Rochester would be glad if you and your pupil would take tea with him in the drawing-room this evening,' said she: 'he has been so much engaged all day that he could not ask to see you before.'

---

4. She adds the "de" as a sign of nobility. "Ami": friend.
5. "And that must mean," said she, "that there will be a present inside for me, and perhaps for you, too, Miss Eyre. Mr. Rochester talked about you; he asked me my governess's name, and if she wasn't a small person, rather thin and a little pale. I said yes: because it's true, isn't it, Miss Eyre?"

'When is his tea-time?' I inquired.

'Oh, at six o'clock: he keeps early hours in the country. You had better change your frock now; I will go with you and fasten it. Here is a candle.'

'Is it necessary to change my frock?'

'Yes, you had better: I always dress for the evening when Mr. Rochester is here.'

This additional ceremony seemed somewhat stately: however, I repaired to my room, and, with Mrs. Fairfax's aid, replaced my black stuff dress by one of black silk: the best and the only additional one I had, except one of light grey, which, in my Lowood notions of the toilette, I thought too fine to be worn, except on first-rate occasions.

'You want a brooch,' said Mrs. Fairfax. I had a single little pearl ornament which Miss Temple gave me as a parting keepsake: I put it on, and then we went downstairs. Unused as I was to strangers, it was rather a trial to appear thus formally summoned in Mr. Rochester's presence. I let Mrs. Fairfax precede me into the dining-room, and kept in her shade as we crossed that apartment; and, passing the arch, whose curtain was now dropped, entered the elegant recess beyond.

Two wax candles stood lighted on the table, and two on the mantelpiece; basking in the light and heat of a superb fire lay Pilot—Adèle knelt near him. Half reclined on a couch appeared Mr. Rochester, his foot supported by the cushion; he was looking at Adèle and the dog: the fire shone full on his face. I knew my traveller with his broad and jetty eyebrows; his square forehead, made squarer by the horizontal sweep of his black hair. I recognised his decisive nose, more remarkable for character than beauty; his full nostrils, denoting, I thought, choler;[6] his grim mouth, chin, and jaw—yes, all three were very grim, and no mistake. His shape, now divested of cloak, I perceived harmonised in squareness with his physiognomy: I suppose it was a good figure in the athletic sense of the term—broad-chested and thin-flanked, though neither tall nor graceful.

Mr. Rochester must have been aware of the entrance of Mrs. Fairfax and myself; but it appeared he was not in the mood to notice us, for he never lifted his head as we approached.

'Here is Miss Eyre, sir,' said Mrs. Fairfax, in her quiet way. He bowed, still not taking his eyes from the group of the dog and child.

'Let Miss Eyre be seated,' said he: and there was something in the forced stiff bow, in the impatient yet formal tone, which seemed further to express, 'What the deuce is it to me whether Miss Eyre be there or not? At this moment I am not disposed to accost her.'

I sat down quite disembarrassed. A reception of finished politeness would probably have confused me: I could not have returned or repaid

6. Anger (originally, one of the four humors thought to dominate a person's make-up).

it by answering grace and elegance on my part; but harsh caprice laid me under no obligation; on the contrary, a decent quiescence, under the freak of manner, gave me advantage. Besides, the eccentricity of the proceeding was piquant: I felt interested to see how he would go on.

He went on as a statue would, that is, he neither spoke nor moved. Mrs. Fairfax seemed to think it necessary that some one should be amiable, and she began to talk. Kindly, as usual—and, as usual, rather trite—she condoled with him on the pressure of business he had had all day; on the annoyance it must have been to him with that painful sprain: then she commended his patience and perseverance in going through with it.

'Madam, I should like some tea,' was the sole rejoinder she got. She hastened to ring the bell; and, when the tray came, she proceeded to arrange the cups, spoons, &c., with assiduous celerity. I and Adèle went to the table; but the master did not leave his couch.

'Will you hand Mr. Rochester's cup?' said Mrs. Fairfax to me; 'Adèle might perhaps spill it.'

I did as requested. As he took the cup from my hand, Adèle, thinking the moment propitious for making a request in my favour, cried out:— N'est-ce pas, monsieur, qu'il y a un cadeau pour Mademoiselle Eyre, dans votre petit coffre?[7]

'Who talks of cadeaux?' said he gruffly: 'did you expect a present, Miss Eyre? Are you fond of presents?' and he searched my face with eyes that I saw were dark, irate, and piercing.

'I hardly know, sir; I have little experience of them: they are generally thought pleasant things.'

'Generally thought? But what do *you* think?'

'I should be obliged to take time, sir, before I could give you an answer worthy of your acceptance: a present has many faces to it, has it not? and one should consider all before pronouncing an opinion as to its nature.'

'Miss Eyre, you are not so unsophisticated as Adèle: she demands a "cadeau," clamorously, the moment she sees me: you beat about the bush.'

'Because I have less confidence in my deserts than Adèle has: she can prefer the claim of old acquaintance, and the right too of custom; for she says you have always been in the habit of giving her playthings; but if I had to make a case I should be puzzled, since I am a stranger, and have done nothing to entitle me to an acknowledgment.'

'Oh, don't fall back on over-modesty! I have examined Adèle, and find you have taken great pains with her; she is not bright, she has no talents; yet in a short time she has made much improvement.'

7. "Isn't it so, sir, that there is a present for Miss Eyre, in your little chest?"

'Sir, you have now given me my "cadeau"; I am obliged to you: it is the meed teachers most covet; praise of their pupil's progress.'

'Humph!' said Mr. Rochester, and he took his tea in silence.

'Come to the fire,' said the master, when the tray was taken away, and Mrs. Fairfax had settled into a corner with her knitting; while Adèle was leading me by the hand round the room, showing me the beautiful books and ornaments on the consoles and chiffonnières. We obeyed, as in duty bound; Adèle wanted to take a seat on my knee, but she was ordered to amuse herself with Pilot.

'You have been resident in my house three months?'

'Yes, sir.'

'And you come from——?'

'From Lowood school, in ——shire.'

'Ah! a charitable concern.—How long were you there?'

'Eight years.'

'Eight years! you must be tenacious of life. I thought half the time in such a place would have done up any constitution! No wonder you have rather the look of another world. I marvelled where you had got that sort of face. When you came on me in Hay Lane last night, I thought unaccountably of fairy tales, and had half a mind to demand whether you had bewitched my horse: I am not sure yet. Who are your parents?'

'I have none.'

'Nor ever had, I suppose: do you remember them?'

'No.'

'I thought not. And so you were waiting for your people when you sat on the stile?'

'For whom, sir?'

'For the men in green: it was a proper moonlight evening for them. Did I break through one of your rings,[8] that you spread that damned ice on the causeway?'

I shook my head. 'The men in green all forsook England a hundred years ago,' said I, speaking as seriously as he had done. 'And not even in Hay Lane, or the fields about it, could you find a trace of them. I don't think either summer or harvest, or winter moon, will ever shine on their revels more.'

Mrs. Fairfax had dropped her knitting, and, with raised eyebrows, seemed wondering what sort of talk this was.

'Well,' resumed Mr. Rochester, 'if you disown parents you must have some sort of kinsfolk: uncles and aunts?'

'No; none that I ever saw.'

'And your home?'

8. Enchanted circles where fairies dance.

'I have none.'

'Where do your brothers and sisters live?'

'I have no brothers and sisters.'

'Who recommended you to come here?'

'I advertised, and Mrs. Fairfax answered my advertisement.'

'Yes,' said the good lady, who now knew what ground we were upon, 'and I am daily thankful for the choice Providence led me to make. Miss Eyre has been an invaluable companion to me, and a kind and careful teacher to Adèle.'

'Don't trouble yourself to give her a character,' returned Mr. Rochester: 'eulogiums will not bias me; I shall judge for myself. She began by felling my horse.'

'Sir?' said Mrs. Fairfax.

'I have to thank her for this sprain.'

The widow looked bewildered.

'Miss Eyre, have you ever lived in a town?'

'No, sir.'

'Have you seen much society?'

'None but the pupils and teachers of Lowood; and now the inmates of Thornfield.'

'Have you read much?'

'Only such books as came in my way; and they have not been numerous or very learned.'

'You have lived the life of a nun: no doubt you are well drilled in religious forms;—Brocklehurst, who I understand directs Lowood, is a parson, is he not?'

'Yes, sir.'

'And you girls probably worshipped him, as a convent full of religieuses[9] would worship their director?'

'Oh, no.'

'You are very cool! No! What! A novice not worship her priest! That sounds blasphemous.'

'I disliked Mr. Brocklehurst; and I was not alone in the feeling. He is a harsh man; at once pompous and meddling: he cut off our hair; and for economy's sake bought us bad needles and thread, with which we could hardly sew.'

'That was very false economy,' remarked Mrs. Fairfax, who now again caught the drift of the dialogue.

'And was that the head and front of his offending?'[1] demanded Mr. Rochester.

'He starved us when he had the sole superintendence of the provision department, before the committee was appointed; and he bored us

9. Nuns.   1. A quotation from *Othello* 1.3.80.

with long lectures once a week, and with evening readings from books of his own inditing,[2] about sudden deaths and judgments, which made us afraid to go to bed.'

'What age were you when you went to Lowood?'

'About ten.'

'And you stayed there eight years: you are now, then, eighteen?'

I assented.

'Arithmetic, you see, is useful; without its aid I should hardly have been able to guess your age. It is a point difficult to fix where the features and countenance are so much at variance as in your case. And now, what did you learn at Lowood? Can you play?'

'A little.'

'Of course: that is the established answer. Go into the library—I mean, if you please. (Excuse my tone of command; I am used to say "Do this," and it is done: I cannot alter my customary habits for one new inmate.) Go then, into the library; take a candle with you; leave the door open; sit down to the piano, and play a tune.'

I departed, obeying his directions.

'Enough!' he called out in a few minutes. 'You play *a little*, I see, like any other English schoolgirl: perhaps rather better than some, but not well.'

I closed the piano and returned. Mr. Rochester continued:

'Adèle showed me some sketches this morning which she said were yours. I don't know whether they were entirely of your doing: probably a master aided you?'

'No, indeed!' I interjected.

'Ah! that pricks pride. Well, fetch me your portfolio, if you can vouch for its contents being original; but don't pass your word unless you are certain: I can recognize patchwork.'

'Then I will say nothing, and you shall judge for yourself, sir.'

I brought the portfolio from the library.

'Approach the table,' said he; and I wheeled it to his couch. Adèle and Mrs. Fairfax drew near to see the pictures.

'No crowding,' said Mr. Rochester: 'take the drawings from my hand as I finish with them; but don't push your faces up to mine.'

He deliberately scrutinised each sketch and painting. Three he laid aside; the others, when he had examined them, he swept from him.

'Take them off to the other table, Mrs. Fairfax,' said he, 'and look at them with Adèle;—you' (glancing at me) 'resume your seat, and answer my questions. I perceive these pictures were done by one hand: was that hand yours?'

'Yes.'

2. Written by him.

'And when did you find time to do them? They have taken much time, and some thought.'

'I did them in the last two vacations I spent at Lowood, when I had no other occupation.'

'Where did you get your copies?'

'Out of my head.'

'That head I see now on your shoulders?'

'Yes, sir.'

'Has it other furniture of the same kind within?'

'I should think it may have: I should hope—better.'

He spread the pictures before him, and again surveyed them alternately.

While he is so occupied I will tell you, reader, what they are: and first, I must premise that they are nothing wonderful. The subjects had, indeed, risen vividly on my mind. As I saw them with the spiritual eye, before I attempted to embody them, they were striking; but my hand would not second my fancy, and in each case it had wrought out but a pale portrait of the thing I had conceived.

These pictures were in water-colours. The first represented clouds low and livid, rolling over a swollen sea: all the distance was in eclipse; so, too, was the foreground; or, rather, the nearest billows, for there was no land. One gleam of light lifted into relief a half-submerged mast, on which sat a cormorant, dark and large, with wings flecked with foam: its beak held a gold bracelet, set with gems, that I had touched with as brilliant tints as my palette could yield, and as glittering distinctness as my pencil could impart. Sinking below the bird and mast, a drowned corpse glanced through the green water; a fair arm was the only limb clearly visible, whence the bracelet had been washed or torn.

The second picture contained for foreground only the dim peak of a hill, with grass and some leaves slanting as if by a breeze. Beyond and above spread an expanse of sky, dark blue as at twilight: rising into the sky was a woman's shape to the bust, portrayed in tints as dusk and soft as I could combine. The dim forehead was crowned with a star; the lineaments below were seen as through the suffusion of vapour; the eyes shone dark and wild; the hair streamed shadowy, like a beamless cloud torn by storm or by electric travail. On the neck lay a pale reflection like moonlight; the same faint lustre touched the train of thin clouds from which rose and bowed this vision of the Evening Star.

The third showed the pinnacle of an iceberg piercing a polar winter sky: a muster of northern lights reared their dim lances, close serried, along the horizon. Throwing these into distance, rose, in the foreground, a head,—a colossal head, inclined towards the iceberg, and resting against it. Two thin hands, joined under the forehead, and supporting it, drew up before the lower features a sable veil; a brow quite bloodless, white as bone, and an eye hollow and fixed, blank of meaning but for the glassiness of despair, alone were visible. Above the temples, amidst wreathed turban folds of black drapery, vague in its character and consistency as cloud, gleamed a ring of white flame, gemmed with sparkles of a more lurid tinge. This pale crescent was 'The likeness of a Kingly Crown'; what it diademed was 'the shape which shape had none.'[3]

'Were you happy when you painted these pictures?' asked Mr. Rochester, presently.

'I was absorbed, sir: yes, and I was happy. To paint them, in short, was to enjoy one of the keenest pleasures I have ever known.'

'That is not saying much. Your pleasures, by your own account, have been few; but I daresay you did exist in a kind of artist's dreamland while you blent and arranged these strange tints. Did you sit at them long each day?'

'I had nothing else to do, because it was the vacation, and I sat at them from morning till noon, and from noon till night: the length of the midsummer days favoured my inclination to apply.'

'And you felt self-satisfied with the result of your ardent labours?'

'Far from it. I was tormented by the contrast between my idea and my handiwork: in each case I had imagined something which I was quite powerless to realise.'

'Not quite: you have secured the shadow of your thought: but no more, probably. You had not enough of the artist's skill and science to give it full being: yet the drawings are, for a schoolgirl, peculiar. As to the thoughts, they are elfish. These eyes in the Evening Star you must have seen in a dream. How could you make them look so clear, and yet not at all brilliant? for the planet above quells their rays. And what meaning is that in their solemn depth? And who taught you to paint wind? There is a high gale in that sky, and on this hilltop. Where did you see Latmos?[4] For that is Latmos. There,—put the drawings away!'

I had scarce tied the strings of the portfolio, when, looking at his watch, he said abruptly,—'It is nine o'clock: what are you about, Miss Eyre, to let Adèle sit up so long? Take her to bed.'

Adèle went to kiss him before quitting the room: he endured the caress, but scarcely seemed to relish it more than Pilot would have done, nor so much.

'I wish you all good-night, now,' said he, making a movement of the hand towards the door, in token that he was tired of our company, and wished to dismiss us. Mrs. Fairfax folded up her knitting: I took my portfolio: we curtseyed to him, received a frigid bow in return, and so withdrew.

3. From Milton's *Paradise Lost* 2.666–673. These lines are a description of Death, the son of Satan.

4. A mythic mountain.

'You said Mr. Rochester was not strikingly peculiar, Mrs. Fairfax,' I observed, when I rejoined her in her room, after putting Adèle to bed.

'Well, is he?'

'I think so: he is very changeful and abrupt.'

'True: no doubt he may appear so to a stranger, but I am so accustomed to his manner I never think of it; and then, if he has peculiarities of temper, allowance should be made.'

'Why?'

'Partly because it is his nature—and we can none of us help our nature; and, partly, he has painful thoughts, no doubt, to harass him, and make his spirits unequal.'

'What about?'

'Family troubles, for one thing.'

'But he has no family.'

'Not now, but he has had—or, at least, relatives. He lost his elder brother a few years since.'

'His *elder* brother?'

'Yes. The present Mr. Rochester has not been very long in possession of the property; only about nine years.'

'Nine years is a tolerable time. Was he so very fond of his brother as to be still inconsolable for his loss?'

'Why, no—perhaps not. I believe there were some misunderstandings between them. Mr. Rowland Rochester was not quite just to Mr. Edward; and, perhaps, he prejudiced his father against him. The old gentleman was fond of money, and anxious to keep the family estate together. He did not like to diminish the property by division, and yet he was anxious that Mr. Edward should have wealth too, to keep up the consequence of the name; and, soon after he was of age, some steps were taken that were not quite fair, and made a great deal of mischief. Old Mr. Rochester and Mr. Rowland combined to bring Mr. Edward into what he considered a painful position, for the sake of making his fortune: what the precise nature of that position was I never clearly knew, but his spirit could not brook what he had to suffer in it. He is not very forgiving: he broke with his family, and now for many years he has led an unsettled kind of life. I don't think he has ever been resident at Thornfield for a fortnight together since the death of his brother without a will left him master of the estate; and, indeed, no wonder he shuns the old place.'

'Why should he shun it?'

'Perhaps he thinks it gloomy.'

The answer was evasive—I should have liked something clearer; but Mrs. Fairfax either could not, or would not, give me more explicit information of the origin and nature of Mr. Rochester's trials. She averred they were a mystery to herself, and that what she knew was chiefly from conjecture. It was evident, indeed, that she wished me to drop the subject, which I did accordingly.

Chapter XIV

For several subsequent days I saw little of Mr. Rochester. In the mornings he seemed much engaged with business, and in the afternoon gentlemen from Millcote or the neighbourhood called, and sometimes stayed to dine with him. When his sprain was well enough to admit of horse exercise, he rode out a good deal; probably to return these visits, as he generally did not come back till late at night.

During this interval even Adèle was seldom sent for to his presence, and all my acquaintance with him was confined to an occasional rencontre in the hall, on the stairs, or in the gallery, when he would sometimes pass me haughtily and coldly, just acknowledging my presence by a distant nod or a cool glance, and sometimes bow and smile with gentlemanlike affability. His changes of mood did not offend me, because I saw that I had nothing to do with their alternation; the ebb and flow depended on causes quite disconnected with me.

One day he had had company to dinner, and had sent for my portfolio; in order, doubtless, to exhibit its contents. The gentlemen went away early, to attend a public meeting at Millcote, as Mrs. Fairfax informed me; but the night being wet and inclement, Mr. Rochester did not accompany them. Soon after they were gone, he rang the bell: a message came that I and Adèle were to go downstairs. I brushed Adèle's hair and made her neat, and having ascertained that I was myself in my usual Quaker trim, where there was nothing to retouch—all being too close and plain, braided locks included, to admit of disarrangement— we descended, Adèle wondering whether the *petit coffre*[5] was at length come; for, owing to some mistake, its arrival had hitherto been delayed. She was gratified: there it stood, a little carton, on the table when we entered the dining-room. She appeared to know it by instinct.

'Ma boîte! ma boîte!' exclaimed she, running towards it.

'Yes—there is your "boîte" at last: take it into a corner, you genuine daughter of Paris, and amuse yourself with disembowelling it,' said the deep and rather sarcastic voice of Mr. Rochester, proceeding from the depths of an immense easy-chair at the fireside. 'And mind,' he continued, 'don't bother me with any details of the anatomical process, or any notice of the condition of the entrails: let your operation be conducted in silence: tiens-toi tranquille, enfant; comprends-tu?'[6]

Adèle seemed scarcely to need the warning; she had already retired to a sofa with her treasure, and was busy untying the cord which se-

5. Little chest.
6. "My box! my box!" . . . "Keep still, child; do you understand?"

cured the lid. Having removed this impediment, and lifted certain silvery envelopes of tissue-paper, she merely exclaimed:—'Oh ciel! Que
c'est beau!'[7] and then remained absorbed in ecstatic contemplation.

'Is Miss Eyre there?' now demanded the master, half rising from his
seat to look round to the door, near which I still stood.

'Ah! well; come forward: be seated here.' He drew a chair near his
own. 'I am not fond of the prattle of children,' he continued; 'for, old
bachelor as I am, I have no pleasant associations connected with their
lisp. It would be intolerable to me to pass a whole evening *tête-à-tête*
with a brat. Don't draw that chair further off, Miss Eyre; sit down exactly where I placed it—if you please, that is. Confound these civilities!
I continually forget them. Nor do I particularly affect simple-minded
old ladies. By-the-bye, I must have mine in mind; it won't do to neglect
her; she is a Fairfax, or wed to one; and blood is said to be thicker than
water.'

He rang and dispatched an invitation to Mrs. Fairfax, who soon arrived, knitting-basket in hand.

'Good-evening, madam; I sent to you for a charitable purpose: I have
forbidden Adèle to talk to me about her presents, and she is bursting
with repletion; have the goodness to serve her as auditress and interloc-
utrice:[8] it will be one of the most benevolent acts you ever performed.'

Adèle, indeed, no sooner saw Mrs. Fairfax than she summoned her
to the sofa, and there quickly filled her lap with the porcelain, the ivory,
the waxen contents of her 'boîte'; pouring out, meantime, explanations
and raptures in such broken English as she was mistress of.

'Now I have performed the part of a good host,' pursued Mr. Rochester, 'put my guests into the way of amusing each other, I ought to be
at liberty to attend to my own pleasure. Miss Eyre, draw your chair still
a little further forward: you are yet too far back; I cannot see you without disturbing my position in this comfortable chair, which I have no
mind to do.'

I did as I was bid, though I would much rather have remained somewhat in the shade: but Mr. Rochester had such a direct way of giving
orders, it seemed a matter of course to obey him promptly.

We were, as I have said, in the dining-room: the lustre, which had
been lit for dinner, filled the room with a festal breadth of light; the
large fire was all red and clear; the purple curtains hung rich and ample
before the lofty windows and loftier arch; everything was still, save the
subdued chat of Adèle (she dared not speak loud), and, filling up each
pause, the beating of winter rain against the panes.

Mr. Rochester, as he sat in his damask-covered chair, looked different to what I had seen him look before; not quite so stern—much less

---

7. "Oh heavens! How beautiful!"   8. Female interlocutor or fellow speaker.

gloomy. There was a smile on his lips, and his eyes sparkled, whether with wine or not I am not sure; but I think it very probable. He was, in short, in his after-dinner mood; more expanded and genial, and also more self-indulgent than the frigid and rigid temper of the morning: still he looked preciously grim, cushioning his massive head against the swelling back of his chair, and receiving the light of the fire on his granite-hewn features, and in his great, dark eyes; for he had great, dark eyes, and very fine eyes too—not without a certain change in their depths sometimes, which, if it was not softness, reminded you, at least, of that feeling.

He had been looking two minutes at the fire, and I had been looking the same length of time at him, when turning suddenly, he caught my gaze fastened on his physiognomy.

'You examine me, Miss Eyre,' said he: 'do you think me handsome?'

I should, if I had deliberated, have replied to this question by something conventionally vague and polite; but the answer somehow slipped from my tongue before I was aware:—'No, sir.'

'Ah! By my word! there is something singular about you,' said he: 'you have the air of a little nonnette,[9] quaint, quiet, grave, and simple, as you sit with your hands before you, and your eyes generally bent on the carpet (except, by-the-bye, when they are directed piercingly to my face; as just now, for instance); and when one asks you a question, or makes a remark to which you are obliged to reply, you rap out a round rejoinder, which, if not blunt, is at least brusque. What do you mean by it?'

'Sir, I was too plain: I beg your pardon. I ought to have replied that it was not easy to give an impromptu answer to a question about appearances; that tastes differ; that beauty is of little consequence, or something of that sort.'

'You ought to have replied no such thing. Beauty of little consequence, indeed! And so, under pretence of softening the previous outrage, of stroking and soothing me into placidity, you stick a sly penknife under my ear! Go on: what fault do you find with me, pray? I suppose I have all my limbs and all my features like any other man?'

'Mr. Rochester, allow me to disown my first answer. I intended no pointed repartee: it was only a blunder.' 'Just so: I think so: and you shall be answerable for it. Criticise me: does my forehead not please you?'

He lifted up the sable waves of hair which lay horizontally over his brow, and showed a solid enough mass of intellectual organs, but an abrupt deficiency where the suave sign of benevolence should have risen.

9. A young nun.

'Now, ma'am, am I a fool?'

'Far from it, sir. You would, perhaps, think me rude if I inquired in return whether you are a philanthropist?'

'There again! Another stick of the penknife, when she pretended to pat my head: and that is because I said I did not like the society of children and old women (low be it spoken!). No, young lady, I am not a general philanthropist; but I bear a conscience;' and he pointed to the prominences which are said to indicate that faculty, and which, fortunately for him, were sufficiently conspicuous; giving, indeed, a marked breadth to the upper part of his head: 'and, besides, I once had a kind of rude tenderness of heart. When I was as old as you I was a feeling fellow enough; partial to the unfledged, unfostered, and unlucky; but fortune has knocked me about since: she has even kneaded me with her knuckles, and now I flatter myself I am hard and tough as an India-rubber ball; pervious, though, through a chink or two still, and with one sentient point in the middle of the lump. Yes: does that leave hope for me?'

'Hope of what, sir?'

'Of my final re-transformation from India-rubber back to flesh?'

'Decidedly he has had too much wine,' I thought; and I did not know what answer to make to his queer question: how could I tell whether he was capable of being re-transformed?

'You look very much puzzled, Miss Eyre; and though you are not pretty any more than I am handsome, yet a puzzled air becomes you; besides, it is convenient, for it keeps those searching eyes of yours away from my physiognomy, and busies them with the worsted flowers of the rug; so puzzle on. Young lady, I am disposed to be gregarious and communicative to-night.'

With this announcement he rose from his chair, and stood, leaning his arm on the marble mantelpiece: in that attitude his shape was seen plainly as well as his face; his unusual breadth of chest, disproportionate almost to his length of limb. I am sure most people would have thought him an ugly man; yet there was so much unconscious pride in his port; so much ease in his demeanour; such a look of complete indifference to his own external appearance; so haughty a reliance on the power of other qualities, intrinsic or adventitious, to atone for the lack of mere personal attractiveness, that, in looking at him, one inevitably shared the indifference, and, even in a blind, imperfect sense, put faith in the confidence.

'I am disposed to be gregarious and communicative to-night,' he repeated; 'and that is why I sent for you: the fire and the chandelier were not sufficient company for me; nor would Pilot have been, for none of these can talk. Adèle is a degree better, but still far below the mark; Mrs. Fairfax ditto; you, I am persuaded, can suit me if you will: you puzzled me the first evening I invited you down here. I have almost forgotten you since: other ideas have driven yours from my head; but to-night I am resolved to be at ease; to dismiss what importunes, and recall what pleases. It would please me now to draw you out—to learn more of you—therefore speak.'

Instead of speaking, I smiled; and not a very complacent or submissive smile either.

'Speak,' he urged.

'What about, sir?'

'Whatever you like. I leave both the choice of subject and the manner of treating it entirely to yourself.'

Accordingly I sat and said nothing: 'If he expects me to talk for the mere sake of talking and showing off, he will find he has addressed himself to the wrong person,' I thought.

'You are dumb, Miss Eyre.'

I was dumb still. He bent his head a little towards me, and with a single hasty glance seemed to dive into my eyes.

'Stubborn?' he said, 'and annoyed. Ah, it is consistent. I put my request in an absurd, almost insolent form. Miss Eyre, I beg your pardon. The fact is, once for all, I don't wish to treat you like an inferior: that is (correcting himself), I claim only such superiority as must result from twenty years' difference in age and a century's advance in experience. This is legitimate, et j'y tiens,[1] as Adèle would say; and it is by virtue of this superiority and this alone that I desire you to have the goodness to talk to me a little now, and divert my thoughts, which are galled with dwelling on one point—cankering as a rusty nail.'

He had deigned an explanation; almost an apology: I did not feel insensible to his condescension, and would not seem so.

'I am willing to amuse you if I can, sir: quite willing; but I cannot introduce a topic, because how do I know what will interest you? Ask me questions, and I will do my best to answer them.'

'Then, in the first place, do you agree with me that I have a right to be a little masterful, abrupt; perhaps exacting, sometimes, on the grounds I stated; namely, that I am old enough to be your father, and that I have battled through a varied experience with many men of many nations, and roamed over half the globe, while you have lived quietly with one set of people in one house?'

'Do as you please, sir.'

'That is no answer; or rather it is a very irritating, because a very evasive one; reply clearly.'

'I don't think, sir, you have a right to command me merely because

---

1. And I accept it.

you are older than I, or because you have seen more of the world than I
have; your claim to superiority depends on the use you have made of
your time and experience.'

'Humph! Promptly spoken. But I won't allow that, seeing that it
would never suit my case; as I have made an indifferent, not to say a
bad, use of both advantages. Leaving superiority out of the question,
then, you must still agree to receive my orders now and then, without
being piqued or hurt by the tone of command—will you?'

I smiled: I thought to myself Mr. Rochester *is* peculiar—he seems to
forget that he pays me £30 per annum for receiving his orders.

'The smile is very well,' said he, catching instantly the passing expression; 'but speak too.'

'I was thinking, sir, that very few masters would trouble themselves to
inquire whether or not their paid subordinates were piqued and hurt by
their orders.'

'Paid subordinates! What, you are my paid subordinate, are you?
Oh, yes, I had forgotten the salary! Well, then, on that mercenary
ground, will you agree to let me hector a little?'

'No, sir, not on that ground: but, on the ground that you did forget it,
and that you care whether or not a dependent is comfortable in his dependency, I agree heartily.'

'And will you consent to dispense with a great many conventional
forms and phrases, without thinking that the omission arises from insolence?'

'I am sure, sir, I should never mistake informality for insolence: one I
rather like, the other nothing free-born would submit to, even for a salary.'

'Humbug! Most things free-born will submit to anything for a salary;
therefore, keep to yourself, and don't venture on generalities of which
you are intensely ignorant. However, I mentally shake hands with you
for your answer, despite its inaccuracy; and as much for the manner in
which it was said as for the substance of the speech: the manner was
frank and sincere; one does not often see such a manner: no, on the
contrary, affectation, or coldness, or stupid, coarse-minded misappre-
hension of one's meaning are the usual rewards of candour. Not three
in three thousand raw school-girl governesses would have answered me
as you have just done. But I don't mean to flatter you: if you are cast in a
different mould to the majority, it is no merit of yours: Nature did it.
And then, after all, I go too fast in my conclusions: for what I yet know,
you may be no better than the rest; you may have intolerable defects to
counterbalance your few good points.'

'And so may you,' I thought. My eye met his as the idea crossed my
mind: he seemed to read the glance, answering as if its import had been
spoken as well as imagined:—

'Yes, yes, you are right,' said he; 'I have plenty of faults of my own: I know it, and I don't wish to palliate them, I assure you. God wot I need not be too severe about others; I have a past existence, a series of deeds, a colour of life to contemplate within my own breast, which might well call my sneers and censures from my neighbours to myself. I started, or rather (for, like other defaulters, I like to lay half the blame on ill fortune and adverse circumstances) was thrust on to a wrong tack at the age of one-and-twenty, and have never recovered the right course since: but I might have been very different; I might have been as good as you—wiser, almost as stainless. I envy you your peace of mind, your clean conscience, your unpolluted memory. Little girl, a memory without blot or contamination must be an exquisite treasure—an inexhaustible source of pure refreshment: is it not?'

'How was your memory when you were eighteen, sir?'

'All right then; limpid, salubrious: no gush of bilge water had turned it to fetid puddle. I was your equal at eighteen—quite your equal. Nature meant me to be, on the whole, a good man, Miss Eyre: one of the better kind; and you see I am not so. You would say you don't see it: at least I flatter myself I read as much in your eye (beware, by-the-bye, what you express with that organ, I am quick at interpreting its language). Then take my word for it,—I am not a villain: you are not to suppose that—not to attribute to me any such bad eminence; but, owing, I verily believe, rather to circumstances than to my natural bent, I am a trite commonplace sinner, hackneyed in all the poor petty dissipations with which the rich and worthless try to put on life. Do you wonder that I avow this to you? Know, that in the course of your future life you will often find yourself elected the involuntary confidant of your acquaintances' secrets: people will instinctively find out, as I have done, that it is not your forte to tell of yourself, but to listen while others talk of themselves; they will feel, too, that you listen with no malevolent scorn of their indiscretion, but with a kind of innate sympathy; not the less comforting and encouraging because it is very unobstrusive in its manifestations.'

'How do you know?—how can you guess all this, sir?'

'I know it well; therefore I proceed almost as freely as if I were writing my thoughts in a diary. You would say, I should have been superior to circumstances; so I should—so I should; but you see I was not. When fate wronged me, I had not the wisdom to remain cool: I turned desperate; then I degenerated. Now, when any vicious simpleton excites my disgust by his paltry ribaldry, I cannot flatter myself that I am better than he: I am forced to confess that he and I are on a level. I wish I had stood firm—God knows I do! Dread remorse when you are tempted to err, Miss Eyre: remorse is the poison of life.'

'Repentance is said to be its cure, sir.'

'It is not its cure. Reformation may be its cure; and I could reform—I have strength yet for that—if—but where is the use of thinking of it, hampered, burdened, cursed as I am? Besides, since happiness is irrevocably denied me, I have a right to get pleasure out of life: and I *will* get it, cost what it may.'

'Then you will degenerate still more, sir.'

'Possibly: yet why should I, if I can get sweet, fresh pleasure? And I may get it as sweet and fresh as the wild honey the bee gatherers on the moor.'

'It will sting—it will taste bitter, sir.'

'How do you know?—you never tried it. How very serious—how very solemn you look: and you are as ignorant of the matter as this cameo head' (taking one from the mantelpiece). 'You have no right to preach to me, you neophyte, that have not passed the porch of life, and are absolutely unacquainted with its mysteries.'

'I only remind you of your own words, sir: you said error brought remorse, and you pronounced remorse the poison of existence.'

'And who talks of error now? I scarcely think the notion that flitted across my brain was an error. I believe it was an inspiration rather than a temptation: it was very genial, very soothing,—I know that. Here it comes again! It is no devil, I assure you; or if it be, it has put on the robes of an angel of light. I think I must admit so fair a guest when it asks entrance to my heart.'

'Distrust it, sir, it is not a true angel.'

'Once more, how do you know? By what instinct do you pretend to distinguish between a fallen seraph of the abyss and a messenger from the eternal throne—between a guide and a seducer?'

'I judged by your countenance, sir; which was troubled: when you said the suggestion had returned upon you. I feel sure it will work you more misery if you listen to it.'

'Not at all—it bears the most gracious message in the world: for the rest, you are not my conscience-keeper, so don't make yourself uneasy. Here, come in, bonny wanderer!'

He said this as if he spoke to a vision, viewless to any eye but his own; then, folding his arms, which he had half extended, on his chest, he seemed to enclose in their embrace the invisible being.

'Now,' he continued, again addressing me, 'I have received the pilgrim—a disguised deity, as I verily believe. Already it has done me good: my heart was a sort of charnel; it will now be a shrine.'

'To speak truth, sir, I don't understand you at all: I cannot keep up the conversation, because it has got out of my depth. Only one thing I know: you said you were not as good as you should like to be, and that you regretted your own imperfection;—one thing I can comprehend: you intimated that to have a sullied memory was a perpetual bane. It seems to me, that if you tried hard, you would in time find it possible to become what you yourself would approve; and that if from this day you began with resolution to correct your thoughts and actions, you would in a few years have laid up a new and stainless store of recollections, to which you might revert with pleasure.'

'Justly thought; rightly said, Miss Eyre; and, at this moment, I am paving hell with energy.'

'Sir?'

'I am laying down good intentions, which I believe durable as flint. Certainly, my associates and pursuits shall be other than they have been.'

'And better?'

'And better—so much better as pure ore is than foul dross. You seem to doubt me; I don't doubt myself: I know what my aim is, what my motives are; and at this moment I pass a law, unalterable as that of the Medes and Persians,[2] that both are right.'

'They cannot be, sir, if they require a new statute to legalise them.'

'They are, Miss Eyre, though they absolutely require a new statute; unheard-of combinations of circumstances demand unheard-of-rules.'

'That sounds a dangerous maxim, sir; because one can see at once that it is liable to abuse.'

'Sententious sage! so it is: but I swear by my household gods not to abuse it.'

'You are human and fallible.'

'I am: so are you—what then?'

'The human and fallible should not arrogate a power with which the divine and perfect alone can be safely entrusted.'

'What power?'

'That of saying of any strange, unsanctioned line of action,—"Let it be right."'

' "Let it be right"—the very words: you have pronounced them.'

'*May* it be right then,' I said, as I rose, deeming it useless to continue a discourse which was all darkness to me; and, besides, sensible that the character of my interlocutor was beyond my penetration; at least, beyond its present reach; and feeling the uncertainty, the vague sense of insecurity, which accompanies a conviction of ignorance.

'Where are you going?'

'To put Adèle to bed: it is past her bedtime.'

'You are afraid of me, because I talk like a Sphinx.'

'Your language is enigmatical, sir: but though I am bewildered, I am certainly not afraid.'

'You *are* afraid—your self-love dreads a blunder.'

2. Two nations noted for the strictness of their legislative procedures.

'In that sense I do feel apprehensive—I have no wish to talk nonsense.'

'If you did, it would be in such a grave, quiet manner, I should mistake it for sense. Do you never laugh, Miss Eyre? Don't trouble yourself to answer—I see, you laugh rarely; but you can laugh very merrily: believe me, you are not naturally austere, any more than I am naturally vicious. The Lowood constraint still clings to you somewhat; controlling your features, muffling your voice, and restricting your limbs; and you fear in the presence of a man and a brother—or father, or master, or what you will—to smile too gaily, speak too freely, or move too quickly: but, in time, I think you will learn to be natural with me, as I find it impossible to be conventional with you; and then your looks and movements will have more vivacity and variety than they dare offer now. I see at intervals the glance of a curious sort of bird through the close-set bars of a cage; a vivid, restless, resolute captive is there; were it but free, it would soar cloud-high. You are still bent on going?'

'It has struck nine, sir.'

'Never mind,—wait a minute: Adèle is not ready to go to bed yet. My position, Miss Eyre, with my back to the fire, and my face to the room, favours observation. While talking to you, I have also occasionally watched Adèle; (I have my own reasons for thinking her a curious study,—reasons that I may, nay that I shall, impart to you some day;) she pulled out of her box, about ten minutes ago, a little pink silk frock; rapture lit her face as she unfolded it; coquetry runs in her blood, blends with her brains, and seasons the marrow of her bones. "Il faut que je l'essaie," cried she; "et à l'instant même!"[3] and she rushed out of the room. She is now with Sophie, undergoing a robing process: in a few minutes she will re-enter; and I know what I shall see,—a miniature of Céline Varens, as she used to appear on the boards at the rising of——: but never mind that. However, my tenderest feelings are about to receive a shock: such is my presentiment; stay now, to see whether it will be realised.'

Ere long Adèle's little foot was heard tripping across the hall. She entered, transformed as her guardian had predicted. A dress of rose-coloured satin, very short, and as full in the skirt as it could be gathered, replaced the brown frock she had previously worn; a wreath of rosebuds circled her forehead; her feet were dressed in silk stockings and small white satin sandals.

'Est-ce que ma robe va bien?' cried she, bounding forwards; 'et mes souliers? et mes bas? Tenez, je croix que je vais danser.'[4]

And spreading out her dress, she chasséed across the room; till, hav-

3. "I must try it, . . . and this very instant!"   my stockings? Wait, I think I'm going to dance."
4. "Is my dress all right? . . . and my shoes? and

ing reached Mr. Rochester, she wheeled lightly round before him on tiptoe, then dropped on one knee at his feet, exclaiming:—

'Monsieur, je vous remercie mille fois de votre bonté'; then rising, she added, 'C'est comme cela que maman faisait, n'est-ce pas, monsieur?'[5]

'Pre-cise-ly!' was the answer; 'and, "comme cela,"[6] she charmed my English gold out of my British breeches pocket. I have been green, too, Miss Eyre,—ay, grass green: not a more vernal tint freshens you now than once freshened me. My Spring is gone, however: but it has left me that French floweret on my hands; which, in some moods, I would fain be rid of. Not valuing now the root whence it sprang; having found that it was of a sort which nothing but gold dust could manure, I have but half a liking to the blossom: especially when it looks so artificial as just now. I keep it and rear it rather on the Roman Catholic principle of expiating numerous sins, great or small, by one good work. I'll explain all this some day. Good-night.'

Chapter XV

Mr. Rochester did, on a future occasion, explain it.

It was one afternoon, when he chanced to meet me and Adèle in the grounds; and while she played with Pilot and her shuttlecock, he asked me to walk up and down a long beech avenue within sight of her.

He then said that she was the daughter of a French opera-dancer, Céline Varens, towards whom he had once cherished what he called a 'grande passion.'[7] This passion Céline had professed to return with even superior ardour. He thought himself her idol; ugly as he was: he believed, as he said, that she preferred his 'taille d'athlète'[8] to the elegance of the Apollo Belvidere.

'And, Miss Eyre, so much was I flattered by this preference of the Gallic sylph for her British gnome, that I installed her in an hotel; gave her a complete establishment of servants, a carriage, cashmeres, diamonds, dentelles,[9] &c. In short, I began the process of ruining myself in the received style, like any other spoony. I had not, it seems, the originality to chalk out a new road to shame and destruction, but trod the old track with stupid exactness not to deviate an inch from the beaten centre. I had—as I deserved to have—the fate of all other spoonies. Happening to call one evening when Céline did not expect me, I found her out; but it was a warm night, and I was tired with strolling through Paris, so I sat down in her boudoir; happy to breathe the air consecrated

---

5. "Sir, I thank you a thousand times for your goodness; . . . It's just as Mamma used to do it, isn't it, sir?"
6. Like that.

7. Great passion.
8. Athletic figure. A famous statue of Apollo is housed in the Belvedere wing of the Vatican.
9. Laces. "Spoony": fool.

so lately by her presence. No,—I exaggerate; I never thought there was any consecrating virtue about her: it was rather a sort of pastille perfume she had left, a scent of musk and amber, than an odour of sanctity. I was just beginning to stifle with the fumes of conservatory flowers and sprinkled essences, when I bethought myself to open the window and step out on to the balcony. It was moonlight and gas-light besides, and very still and serene. The balcony was furnished with a chair or two; I sat down, took out a cigar,—I will take one now, if you will excuse me.'

Here ensued a pause, filled up by the producing and lighting of a cigar; having placed it to his lips and breathed a trail of Havannah incense on the freezing and sunless air, he went on:—

'I liked bonbons too, in those days, Miss Eyre, and I was *croquant*— overlook the barbarism—*croquant*[1] chocolate comfits, and smoking alternately, watching meantime the equipages that rolled along the fashionable streets towards the neighbouring opera-house, when in an elegant close carriage drawn by a beautiful pair of English horses, and distinctly seen in the brilliant city-night, I recognised the "voiture"[2] I had given Céline. She was returning: of course my heart thumped with impatience against the iron rails I leant upon. The carriage stopped, as I had expected, at the hotel door; my flame (that is the very word for an opera inamorata)[3] alighted: though muffled in a cloak—an unnecessary encumbrance, by-the-bye, on so warm a June evening—I knew her instantly by her little foot, seen peeping from the skirt of her dress, as she skipped from the carriage-step. Bending over the balcony, I was about to murmur, "Mon ange"[4]—in a tone, of course, which should be audible to the ear of love alone—when a figure jumped from the carriage after her; cloaked also; but that was a spurred heel which had rung on the pavement, and that was a hatted head which now passed under the arched *porte-cochère* of the hotel.

'You never felt jealousy, did you, Miss Eyre? Of course not: I need not ask you: because you never felt love. You have both sentiments yet to experience: your soul sleeps; the shock is yet to be given which shall waken it. You think all existence lapses in as quiet a flow as that in which your youth has hitherto slid away. Floating on with closed eyes and muffled ears, you neither see the rocks bristling not far off in the bed of the flood, nor hear the breakers boil at their base. But I tell you —and you may mark my words—you will come some day to a craggy pass of the channel, where the whole of life's stream will be broken up into whirl and tumult, foam and noise: either you will be dashed to atoms on crag points, or lifted up and borne on by some master wave into a calmer current—as I am now.

1. Crunching; Rochester's "barbarism" may be his use of an English grammatical construction with a French verb.
2. Carriage.
3. Beloved woman.
4. My angel.

'I like this day: I like that sky of steel; I like the sternness and stillness of the world under this frost. I like Thornfield: its antiquity; its retirement; its old crow-trees and thorn-trees; its grey façade, and lines of dark windows reflecting that metal welkin: and yet how long have I abhorred the very thought of it; shunned it like a great plague-house! How I do still abhor——'

He ground his teeth and was silent: he arrested his step and struck his boot against the hard ground. Some hated thought seemed to have him in its grip, and to hold him so tightly that he could not advance.

We were ascending the avenue when he thus paused; the hall was before us. Lifting his eye to its battlements, he cast over them a glare such as I never saw before or since. Pain, shame, ire—impatience, disgust, detestation—seemed momentarily to hold a quivering conflict in the large pupil dilating under his ebon eyebrow. Wild was the wrestle which should be paramount; but another feeling rose and triumphed: something hard and cynical; self-willed and resolute: it settled his passion and petrified his countenance: he went on:—'During the moment I was silent, Miss Eyre, I was arranging a point with my destiny. She stood there, by that beech-trunk—a hag like one of those who appeared to "Macbeth" on the heath of Forres. "You like Thornfield?" she said, lifting her finger; and then she wrote in the air a memento, which ran in lurid hieroglyphics all along the house-front, between the upper and lower row of windows. "Like it if you can! Like it if you dare!"

' "I will like it," said I. "I dare like it;" and (he subjoined moodily) I will keep my word: I will break obstacles to happiness, to goodness—yes, goodness; I wish to be a better man than I have been; than I am—as Job's leviathan broke the spear, the dart and the habergeon, hindrances which others count as iron and brass I will esteem but straw and rotten wood.'[5]

Adèle here ran before him with her shuttlecock. 'Away!' he cried harshly; 'keep at a distance, child; or go in to Sophie!' Continuing then to pursue his walk in silence, I ventured to recall him to the point whence he had abruptly diverged:—'Did you leave the balcony, sir,' I asked, 'when Mdlle. Varens entered?'

I almost expected a rebuff for this hardly well-timed question: but, on the contrary, waking out of his scowling abstraction, he turned his eyes towards me, and the shade seemed to clear off his brow. 'Oh, I had forgotten Céline! Well, to resume. When I saw my charmer thus come in accompanied by a cavalier, I seemed to hear a hiss, and the green snake of jealousy, rising on undulating coils from the moonlit balcony, glided within my waistcoat, and ate its way in two minutes to my heart's core. Strange!' he exclaimed, suddenly starting again from the point.

5. Job 41:26–27.

'Strange that I should choose you for the confidant of all this, young lady: passing strange that you should listen to me quietly, as if it were the most usual thing in the world for a man like me to tell stories of his opera-mistresses to a quaint, inexperienced girl like you! But the last singularity explains the first, as I intimated once before: you, with your gravity, considerateness, and caution, were made to be the recipient of secrets. Besides, I know what sort of a mind I have placed in communication with my own: I know it is one not liable to take infection: it is a peculiar mind; it is an unique one. Happily I do not mean to harm it: but, if I did, it would not take harm from me. The more you and I converse, the better; for while I cannot blight you, you may refresh me.' After this digression, he proceeded:—'I remained in the balcony. "They will come to her boudoir, no doubt," thought I: "let me prepare an ambush." So putting my hand in through the open window, I drew the curtain over it, leaving only an opening through which I could take observations; then I closed the casement, all but a chink just wide enough to furnish an outlet to lovers' whispered vows: then I stole back to my chair; and as I resumed it the pair came in. My eye was quickly at the aperture. Céline's chambermaid entered, lit a lamp, left it on the table, and withdrew. The couple were thus revealed to me clearly: both removed their cloaks, and there was "the Varens"[6] shining in satin and jewels,—my gifts of course,—and there was her companion in an officer's uniform; and I knew him for a young roué of a vicomte[7]—a brainless and vicious youth whom I had sometimes met in society, and had never thought of hating because I despised him so absolutely. On recognising him, the fang of the snake, jealousy, was instantly broken; because at the same moment my love for Céline sank under an extinguisher. A woman who could betray me for such a rival was not worth contending for: she deserved only scorn; less, however, than I, who had been her dupe.

'They began to talk; their conversation eased me completely: frivolous, mercenary, heartless, and senseless, it was rather calculated to weary than enrage a listener. A card of mine lay on the table; this being perceived, brought my name under discussion. Neither of them possessed energy or wit to belabour me soundly; but they insulted me as coarsely as they could in their little way: especially Céline; who even waxed rather brilliant on my personal defects—deformities she termed them. Now it had been her custom to launch out into fervent admiration of what she called my "beauté mâle":[8] wherein she differed diametrically from you, who told me point-blank, at the second interview,

6. Literal translation of the French "la Varens"; a common Gallic idiom for identifying a well-known female stage performer was to use her last name, preceded by "la."
7. Viscount: a nobleman.
8. Masculine beauty.

that you did not think me handsome. The contrast struck me at the time, and—'

Adèle here came running up again.

'Monsieur, John has just been to say that your agent has called and wishes to see you.'

'Ah! in that case I must abridge. Opening the window, I walked in upon them; liberated Céline from my protection; gave her notice to vacate her hotel; offered her a purse for immediate exigencies; disregarded screams, hysterics, prayers, protestations, convulsions; made an appointment with the vicomte for a meeting at the Bois de Boulogne. Next morning I had the pleasure of encountering him; left a bullet in one of his poor etiolated arms, feeble as the wing of a chicken in the pip, and then thought I had done with the whole crew. But unluckily the Varens, six months before, had given me this filette[9] Adèle; who she affirmed was my daughter; and perhaps she may be, though I see no proofs of such grim paternity written in her countenance. Pilot is more like me than she. Some years after I had broken with the mother she abandoned her child and ran away to Italy with a musician or singer. I acknowledged no natural claim on Adèle's part to be supported by me; nor do I now acknowledge any, for I am not her father; but hearing that she was quite destitute, I e'en took the poor thing out of the slime and mud of Paris, and transplanted it here, to grow up clean in the wholesome soil of an English country garden. Mrs. Fairfax found you to train it; but now you know that it is the illegitimate offspring of a French opera-girl, you will perhaps think differently of your post and protégée. You will be coming to me some day with notice that you have found another place—that you beg me to look out for a new governess, &c. —eh?'

'No. Adèle is not answerable for either her mother's faults or yours. I have a regard for her, and now that I know she is, in a sense, parentless —forsaken by her mother and disowned by you, sir—I shall cling closer to her than before. How could I possibly prefer the spoilt pet of a wealthy family, who would hate her governess as a nuisance, to a lonely little orphan, who leans towards her as a friend?'

'Oh, that is the light in which you view it! Well, I must go in now; and you too: it darkens.'

But I stayed out a few minutes longer with Adèle and Pilot—ran a race with her, and played a game of battledore and shuttlecock. When we went in, and I had removed her bonnet and coat, I took her on my knee; kept her there an hour, allowing her to prattle as she liked, not rebuking even some little freedoms and trivialities into which she was apt to stray when much noticed; and which betrayed in her a superfi-

9. Little girl.

ciality of character, inherited probably from her mother, hardly congenial to an English mind. Still she had her merits; and I was disposed to appreciate all that was good in her to the utmost. I sought in her countenance and features a likeness to Mr. Rochester, but found none —no trait, no turn of expression announced relationship. It was a pity: if she could but have been proved to resemble him, he would have thought more of her.

It was not till after I had withdrawn to my own chamber for the night that I steadily reviewed the tale Mr. Rochester had told me. As he had said, there was probably nothing at all extraordinary in the substance of the narrative itself—a wealthy Englishman's passion for a French dancer, and her treachery to him, were everyday matters enough, no doubt, in society—but there was something decidedly strange in the paroxysm of emotion which had suddenly seized him, when he was in the act of expressing the present contentment of his mood, and his newly-revived pleasure in the old hall and its environs. I meditated wonderingly on this incident: but gradually quitting it, as I found it for the present inexplicable, I turned to the consideration of my master's manner to myself. The confidence he had thought fit to repose in me seemed a tribute to my discretion. I regarded and accepted it as such. His deportment had now for some weeks been more uniform towards me than at the first. I never seemed in his way; he did not take fits of chilling hauteur; when he met me unexpectedly, the encounter seemed welcome—he had always a word and sometimes a smile for me; when summoned by formal invitation to his presence, I was honoured by a cordiality of reception that made me feel I really possessed the power to amuse him, and that these evening conferences were sought as much for his pleasure as for my benefit.

I, indeed, talked comparatively little; but I heard him talk with relish. It was his nature to be communicative—he liked to open to a mind unacquainted with the world glimpses of its scenes and ways (I do not mean its corrupt scenes and wicked ways, but such as derived their interest from the great scale on which they were acted, the strange novelty by which they were characterised); and I had a keen delight in receiving the new ideas he offered, in imagining the new pictures he portrayed, and following him in thought through the new regions he disclosed, never startled or troubled by one noxious allusion.

The ease of his manner freed me from painful restraint; the friendly frankness, as correct as cordial, with which he treated me, drew me to him. I felt at times as if he were my relation, rather than my master: yet he was imperious sometimes still; but I did not mind that; I saw it was his way. So happy, so gratified did I become with this new interest added to life, that I ceased to pine after kindred. My thin crescent-destiny seemed to enlarge; the blanks of existence were filled up; my bodily health improved; I gathered flesh and strength.

And was Mr. Rochester now ugly in my eyes? No, reader. Gratitude, and many associations, all pleasurable and genial, made his face the object I best liked to see; his presence in a room was more cheering than the brightest fire. Yet I had not forgotten his faults—indeed, I could not, for he brought them frequently before me. He was proud, sardonic, harsh to inferiority of every description. In my secret soul I knew that his great kindness to me was balanced by unjust severity to many others. He was moody, too—unaccountably so. I more than once, when sent for to read to him, found him sitting in his library alone, with his head bent on his folded arms; and, when he looked up, a morose, almost a malignant scowl, blackened his features. But I believed that his moodiness, his harshness, and his former faults of morality (I say *former*, for now he seemed corrected of them) had their source in some cruel cross of fate. I believed he was naturally a man of better tendencies, higher principles, and purer tastes than such as circumstances had developed, education instilled, or destiny encouraged. I thought there were excellent materials in him; though for the present they hung together somewhat spoiled and tangled. I cannot deny that I grieved for his grief, whatever that was, and would have given much to assuage it.

Though I had now extinguished my candle and was laid down in bed, I could not sleep for thinking of his look when he paused in the avenue, and told how his destiny had risen up before him, and dared him to be happy at Thornfield.

'Why not?' I asked myself. 'What alienates him from the house? Will he leave it again soon? Mrs. Fairfax said he seldom stayed here longer than a fortnight at a time, and he has now been resident eight weeks. If he does go, the change will be doleful. Suppose he should be absent spring, summer, and autumn: how joyless sunshine and fine days will seem.'

I hardly know whether I had slept or not after this musing; at any rate, I started wide awake on hearing a vague murmur, peculiar and lugubrious, which sounded, I thought, just above me. I wished I had kept my candle burning: the night was drearily dark; my spirits were depressed. I rose and sat up in bed, listening. The sound was hushed.

I tried again to sleep; but my heart beat anxiously: my inward tranquillity was broken. The clock, far down in the hall, struck two. Just then it seemed my chamber-door was touched; as if fingers had swept the panels in groping a way along the dark gallery outside. I said, 'Who is there?' Nothing answered. I was chilled with fear.

All at once I remembered that it might be Pilot: who, when the kitchen-door chanced to be left open, not unfrequently found his way up to the threshold of Mr. Rochester's chamber: I had seen him lying there myself, in the mornings. The idea calmed me somewhat: I lay down. Silence composes the nerves; and as an unbroken hush now reigned again through the whole house, I began to feel the return of slumber. But it was not fated that I should sleep that night. A dream had scarcely approached my ear, when it fled affrighted, scared by a marrow-freezing incident enough.

This was a demoniac laugh—low, suppressed, and deep—uttered, as it seemed, at the very key-hole of my chamber-door. The head of my bed was near the door, and I thought at first the goblin-laughter stood at my bedside—or rather, crouched by my pillow: but I rose, looked round, and could see nothing; while, as I still gazed, the unnatural sound was reiterated: and I knew it came from behind the panels. My first impulse was to rise and fasten the bolt; my next again, to cry out, 'Who is there?'

Something gurgled and moaned. Ere long, steps retreated up the gallery towards the third story staircase: a door had lately been made to shut in that staircase; I heard it open and close, and all was still.

'Was that Grace Poole? and is she possessed with a devil?' thought I. Impossible now to remain longer by myself: I must go to Mrs. Fairfax. I hurried on my frock and a shawl; I withdrew the bolt, and opened the door with a trembling hand. There was a candle burning just outside, left on the matting in the gallery. I was surprised at this circumstance: but still more was I amazed to perceive the air quite dim, as if filled with smoke; and, while looking to the right hand and left, to find whence these blue wreaths issued, I became further aware of a strong smell of burning.

Something creaked: it was a door ajar; and that door was Mr. Rochester's, and the smoke rushed in a cloud from thence. I thought no more of Mrs. Fairfax; I thought no more of Grace Poole or the laugh: in an instant, I was within the chamber. Tongues of flame darted round the bed: the curtains were on fire. In the midst of blaze and vapour, Mr. Rochester lay stretched motionless, in deep sleep.

'Wake! wake!' I cried—I shook him, but he only murmured and turned: the smoke had stupefied him. Not a moment could be lost: the very sheets were kindling. I rushed to his basin and ewer; fortunately, one was wide and the other deep, and both were filled with water. I heaved them up, deluged the bed and its occupant, flew back to my own room, brought my own water-jug, baptized the couch afresh, and, by God's aid, succeeded in extinguishing the flames which were devouring it.

The hiss of the quenched element, the breakage of a pitcher which I flung from my hand when I had emptied it, and, above all, the splash of the shower-bath I had liberally bestowed, roused Mr. Rochester at last. Though it was now dark, I knew he was awake; because I heard him fulminating strange anathemas at finding himself lying in a pool of water.

'Is there a flood?' he cried.

'No, sir,' I answered; 'but there has been a fire: get up, do, you are quenched now; I will fetch you a candle.'

'In the name of all the elves in Christendom, is that Jane Eyre?' he demanded. 'What have you done with me, witch, sorceress? Who is in the room beside you? Have you plotted to drown me?'

'I will fetch you a candle, sir; and, in Heaven's name, get up. Somebody has plotted something: you cannot too soon find out who and what it is.'

'There—I am up now; but at your peril you fetch a candle yet: wait two minutes till I get into some dry garments, if any dry there be—yes, here is my dressing-gown. Now run!'

I did run; I brought the candle which still remained in the gallery. He took it from my hand, held it up, and surveyed the bed, all blackened and scorched, the sheets drenched, the carpet round swimming in water.

'What is it? and who did it?' he asked.

I briefly related to him what had transpired: the strange laugh I had heard in the gallery: the step ascending to the third story; the smoke,— the smell of fire which had conducted me to his room; in what state I had found matters there, and how I had deluged him with all the water I could lay hands on.

He listened very gravely; his face, as I went on, expressed more concern than astonishment; he did not immediately speak when I had concluded.

'Shall I call Mrs. Fairfax?' I asked.

'Mrs. Fairfax? No: what the deuce would you call her for? What can she do? Let her sleep unmolested.'

'Then I will fetch Leah, and wake John and his wife.'

'Not at all: just be still. You have a shawl on? If you are not warm enough, you may take my cloak yonder; wrap it about you, and sit down in the arm-chair: there,—I will put it on. Now place your feet on the stool, to keep them out of the wet. I am going to leave you a few minutes. I shall take the candle. Remain where you are till I return: be as still as a mouse. I must pay a visit to the third story. Don't move, remember, or call any one.'

He went: I watched the light withdraw. He passed up the gallery very softly, unclosed the staircase door with as little noise as possible, shut it after him, and the last ray vanished. I was left in total darkness. I listened for some noise, but heard nothing. A very long time elapsed. I grew weary: it was cold, in spite of the cloak; and then I did not see the use of staying, as I was not to rouse the house. I was on the point of risking Mr. Rochester's displeasure, by disobeying his orders, when the light once more gleamed dimly on the gallery-wall, and I heard his unshod feet tread the matting. 'I hope it is he,' thought I, 'and not something worse.'

He re-entered, pale and very gloomy. 'I have found it all out,' said he, setting his candle down on the wash-stand; 'it is as I thought.'

'How, sir?'

He made no reply, but stood with his arms folded, looking on the ground. At the end of a few minutes, he inquired in rather a peculiar tone:—'I forget whether you said you saw anything when you opened your chamber door.'

'No, sir, only the candlestick on the ground.'

'But you heard an odd laugh? You have heard that laugh before, I should think, or something like it?'

'Yes, sir: there is a woman who sews here, called Grace Poole—she laughs in that way. She is a singular person.'

'Just so. Grace Poole—you have guessed it. She is, as you say, singular,—very. Well, I shall reflect on the subject. Meantime, I am glad that you are the only person, besides myself, acquainted with the precise details of to-night's incident. You are no talking fool: say nothing about it. I will account for this state of affairs (pointing to the bed): and now return to your own room. I shall do very well on the sofa in the library for the rest of the night. It is near four:—in two hours the servants will be up.'

'Good-night, then, sir,' said I, departing.

He seemed surprised—very inconsistently so, as he had just told me to go.

'What!' he exclaimed, 'are you quitting me already: and in that way?'

'You said I might go, sir.'

'But not without taking leave; not without a word or two of acknowledgment and good will: not, in short, in that brief, dry fashion. Why, you have saved my life!—snatched me from a horrible and excruciating death!—and you walk past me as if we were mutual strangers! At least shake hands.'

He held out his hand; I gave him mine: he took it first in one, then in both his own.

'You have saved my life: I have a pleasure in owing you so immense a debt. I cannot say more. Nothing else that has being would have been tolerable to me in the character of creditor for such an obligation: but you: it is different;—I feel your benefits no burden, Jane.'

He paused; gazed at me: words almost visible trembled on his lips, —but his voice was checked.

'Good night again, sir. There is no debt, benefit, burden, obligation, in the case.'

'I knew,' he continued, 'you would do me good in some way, at some time;—I saw it in your eyes when I first beheld you: their expression and smile did not—(again he stopped)—did not (he proceeded hastily) strike delight to my very inmost heart so for nothing. People talk of natural sympathies; I have heard of good genii—there are grains of truth in the wildest fable. My cherished preserver, good night!'

Strange energy was in his voice, strange fire in his look.

'I am glad I happened to be awake,' I said; and then I was going.

'What! you *will* go?'

'I am cold, sir.'

'Cold? Yes,—and standing in a pool! Go, then, Jane; go!' But he still retained my hand, and I could not free it. I bethought myself of an expedient.

'I think I hear Mrs. Fairfax move, sir,' said I.

'Well, leave me.' He relaxed his fingers, and I was gone.

I regained my couch, but never thought of sleep. Till morning dawned I was tossed on a buoyant but unquiet sea, where billows of trouble rolled under surges of joy. I thought sometimes I saw beyond its wild waters a shore, sweet as the hills of Beulah[1]; and now and then a freshening gale wakened by hope, bore my spirit triumphantly towards the bourne; but I could not reach it, even in fancy,—a counteracting breeze blew off land, and continually drove me back. Sense would resist delirium, judgment would warn passion. Too feverish to rest, I rose as soon as day dawned.

Chapter XVI

I both wished and feared to see Mr. Rochester on the day which followed this sleepless night. I wanted to hear his voice again, yet feared to meet his eye. During the early part of the morning, I momentarily expected his coming. He was not in the frequent habit of entering the schoolroom; but he did step in for a few minutes sometimes, and I had the impression that he was sure to visit it that day.

But the morning passed just as usual. Nothing happened to interrupt the quiet course of Adèle's studies; only, soon after breakfast, I heard some bustle in the neighbourhood of Mr. Rochester's chamber, Mrs. Fairfax's voice, and Leah's, and the cook's—that is, John's wife—and even John's own gruff tones. There were exclamations of, 'What a mercy master was not burnt in his bed!' 'It is always dangerous to keep a candle lit at night.' 'How providential that he had presence of mind to think of the water-jug!' 'I wonder he waked nobody!' 'It is to be hoped he will not take cold with sleeping on the library sofa,' &c.

To much confabulation succeeded a sound of scrubbing and setting to rights; and when I passed the room, in going downstairs to dinner, I saw through the open door that all was again restored to complete order—only the bed was stripped of its hangings. Leah stood up in the window-seat, rubbing the panes of glass dimmed with smoke. I was about to address her, for I wished to know what account had been given

---

1. Name given by the Jews to the promised land (Isaiah 62:4).

of the affair; but, on advancing, I saw a second person in the chamber —a woman sitting on a chair by the bedside, and sewing rings to new curtains. That woman was no other than Grace Pole.

There she sat, staid and taciturn-looking, as usual, in her brown stuff gown, her check apron, white handkerchief, and cap. She was intent on her work, in which her whole thoughts seemed absorbed. On her hard forehead, and in her commonplace features, was nothing either of the paleness or desperation one would have expected to see marking the countenance of a woman who had attempted murder, and whose intended victim had followed her last night to her lair, and (as I believed) charged her with the crime she wished to perpetrate. I was amazed—confounded. She looked up, while I still gazed at her: no start, no increase or failure of colour betrayed emotion, consciousness of guilt, or fear of detection. She said, 'Good morning, Miss,' in her usual phlegmatic and brief manner; and taking up another ring and more tape, went on with her sewing.

'I will put her to some test,' thought I. 'Such absolute impenetrability is past comprehension.'

'Good morning, Grace,' I said. 'Has anything happened here? I thought I heard the servants all talking together a while ago.'

'Only master had been reading in his bed last night. He fell asleep with his candle lit, and the curtains got on fire; but, fortunately, he awoke before the bed-clothes or the wood-work caught, and contrived to quench the flame with the water in the ewer.'

'A strange affair!' I said, in a low voice; then, looking at her fixedly, 'Did Mr. Rochester wake nobody? Did no one hear him move?'

She again raised her eyes to me; and this time there was something of consciousness in their expression. She seemed to examine me warily; then she answered, 'The servants sleep so far off, you know, Miss, they would not be likely to hear. Mrs. Fairfax's room and yours are the nearest to master's; but Mrs. Fairfax said she heard nothing: when people get elderly, they often sleep heavy.' She paused, and then added, with a sort of assumed indifference, but still in a marked and significant tone, 'But you are young, Miss, and I should say a light sleeper. Perhaps you may have heard a noise?'

'I did,' said I, dropping my voice, so that Leah, who was still polishing the panes, could not hear me, 'and at first I thought it was Pilot; but Pilot cannot laugh, and I am certain I heard a laugh, and a strange one.'

She took a new needleful of thread, waxed it carefully, threaded her needle with a steady hand, and then observed, with perfect composure, —'It is hardly likely master would laugh, I should think, Miss, when he was in such danger: you must have been dreaming.'

'I was not dreaming,' I said, with some warmth, for her brazen coolness provoked me. Again she looked at me, and with the same scrutinising and conscious eye.

'Have you told master that you heard a laugh?' she inquired.

'I have not had the opportunity of speaking to him this morning.'

'You did not think of opening your door and looking out into the gallery?' she further asked.

She appeared to be cross-questioning me—attempting to draw from me information unawares. The idea struck me that if she discovered I knew or suspected her guilt, she would be playing off some of her malignant pranks on me. I thought it advisable to be on my guard.

'On the contrary,' said I, 'I bolted my door.'

'Then you are not in the habit of bolting your door every night before you get into bed?'

'Fiend! she wants to know my habits, that she may lay her plans accordingly!' Indignation again prevailed over prudence; I replied sharply, 'Hitherto I have often omitted to fasten the bolt: I did not think it necessary. I was not aware any danger or annoyance was to be dreaded at Thornfield Hall; but in future' (and I laid marked stress on the words) 'I shall take good care to make all secure before I venture to lie down.'

'It will be wise so to do,' was her answer. 'This neighbourhood is as quiet as any I know, and I never heard of the hall being attempted by robbers since it was a house though there are hundreds of pounds' worth of plate in the plate-closet, as is well known. And you see, for such a large house, there are very few servants, because master has never lived here much, and when he does come, being a bachelor, he needs little waiting on; but I always think it best to err on the safe side: a door is soon fastened, and it is as well to have a drawn bolt between one and any mischief that may be about. A deal of people, Miss, are for trusting all to Providence; but I say Providence will not dispense with the means, though He often blesses them when they are used discreetly.' And here she closed her harangue: a long one for her, and uttered with the demureness of a Quakeress.

I still stood absolutely dumfounded at what appeared to me her miraculous self-possession and most inscrutable hypocrisy, when the cook entered.

'Mrs. Poole,' said she, addressing Grace, 'the servants' dinner will soon be ready. Will you come down?'

'No. Just put my pint of porter and bit of pudding on a tray, and I'll carry it upstairs.'

'You'll have some meat?'

'Just a morsel, and a taste of cheese, that's all.'

'And the sago?'[2]

'Never mind it at present. I shall be coming down before tea-time. I'll make it myself.'

2. A cereal eaten in the West Indies, made from palm tree trunks.

The cook here turned to me, saying that Mrs. Fairfax was waiting for me: so I departed.

I hardly heard Mrs. Fairfax's account of the curtain conflagration during dinner, so much was I occupied in puzzling my brains over the enigmatical character of Grace Poole, and still more in pondering the problem of her position at Thornfield; in questioning why she had not been given into custody that morning, or, at the very least, dismissed from her master's service. He had almost as much as declared his conviction of her criminality last night: what mysterious cause withheld him from accusing her? Why had he enjoined me, too, to secrecy? It was strange—a bold, vindictive, and haughty gentleman seemed somehow in the power of one of the meanest of his dependants; so much in her power, that even when she lifted her hand against his life, he dared not openly charge her with the attempt, much less punish her for it.

Had Grace been young and handsome, I should have been tempted to think that tenderer feelings than prudence or fear influenced Mr. Rochester in her behalf; but, hard-favoured and matronly as she was, the idea could not be admitted. 'Yet,' I reflected, 'she has been young once; her youth would be contemporary with her master's. Mrs. Fairfax told me once she had lived here many years. I don't think she can ever have been pretty; but, for aught I know, she may possess originality and strength of character to compensate for the want of personal advantages. Mr. Rochester is an amateur of the decided and eccentric— Grace is eccentric at least. What if a former caprice (a freak very possible to a nature so sudden and headstrong as his) has delivered him into her power, and she now exercises over his actions a secret influence, the result of his own indiscretion, which he cannot shake off, and dare not disregard?' But, having reached this point of conjecture, Mrs. Poole's square, flat figure, and uncomely, dry, even coarse face, recurred so distinctly to my mind's eye, that I thought, 'No; impossible! my supposition cannot be correct. Yet,' suggested the secret voice which talks to us in our own hearts, '*you* are not beautiful either, and perhaps Mr. Rochester approves you—at any rate, you have often felt as if he did; and last night—remember his words; remember his look; remember his voice!'

I well remembered all—language, glance, and tone seemed at the moment vividly renewed. I was now in the schoolroom. Adèle was drawing. I bent over her and directed her pencil. She looked up with a sort of start.

'Qu'avez-vous, mademoiselle?' said she; 'Vos doigts tremblent comme la feuille, et vos joues sont rouges: mais, rouges comme des cerises!'[3]

---

3. "What's wrong, miss? . . . Your fingers are trembling like a leaf, and your cheeks are red: red as cherries!"

'I am hot, Adèle, with stooping!' She went on sketching, I went on thinking.

I hastened to drive from my mind the hateful notion I had been conceiving respecting Grace Poole: it disgusted me. I compared myself with her, and found we were different. Bessie Leaven had said I was quite a lady; and she spoke truth: I was a lady. And now I looked much better than I did when Bessie saw me: I had more colour and more flesh; more life, more vivacity; because I had brighter hopes and keener enjoyments.

'Evening approaches,' said I, as I looked towards the window. 'I have never heard Mr. Rochester's voice or step in the house to-day; but surely I shall see him before night: I feared the meeting in the morning: now I desire it, because expectation has been so long baffled that it is grown impatient.'

When dusk actually closed, and when Adèle left me to go and play in the nursery with Sophie, I did most keenly desire it. I listened for the bell to ring below; I listened for Leah coming up with a message; I fancied sometimes I heard Mr. Rochester's own tread, and I turned to the door, expecting it to open and admit him. The door remained shut: darkness only came in through the window. Still it was not late: he often sent for me at seven and eight o'clock, and it was yet but six. Surely I should not be wholly disappointed to-night, when I had so many things to say to him! I wanted again to introduce the subject of Grace Poole, and to hear what he would answer; I wanted to ask him plainly if he really believed it was she who had made last night's hideous attempt; and if so, why he kept her wickedness a secret. It little mattered whether my curiosity irritated him; I knew the pleasure of vexing and soothing him by turns; it was one I chiefly delighted in, and a sure instinct always prevented me from going too far: beyond the verge of provocation I never ventured; on the extreme brink I liked well to try my skill. Retaining every minute form of respect, every propriety of my station, I could still meet him in argument without fear or uneasy restraint: this suited both him and me.

A tread creaked on the stairs at last; Leah made her appearance, but it was only to intimate that tea was ready in Mrs. Fairfax's room. Thither I repaired, glad at least to go downstairs, for that brought me, I imagined, nearer to Mr. Rochester's presence.

'You must want your tea,' said the good lady, as I joined her, 'you ate so little at dinner. I am afraid,' she continued, 'you are not well to-day, you looked flushed and feverish.'

'Oh, quite well! I never felt better.'

'Then you must prove it by evincing a good appetite; will you fill the tea-pot while I knit off this needle?' Having completed her task, she rose to draw down the blind which she had hitherto kept up, by way, I suppose, of making the most of daylight: though dusk was now fast deepening into total obscurity.

'It is fair to-night,' said she, as she looked through the panes, 'though not starlight; Mr. Rochester has, on the whole, had a favourable day for his journey.'

'Journey!—Is Mr. Rochester gone anywhere? I did not know he was out.'

'Oh, he set off the moment he had breakfasted! He is gone to the Leas, Mr. Eshton's place, ten miles on the other side Millcote; I believe there is quite a party assembled there—Lord Ingram, Sir George Lynn, Colonel Dent, and others.'

'Do you expect him back to-night?'

'No—nor tomorrow either; I should think he is very likely to stay a week or more. When these fine, fashionable people get together, they are so surrounded by elegance and gaiety, so well provided with all that can please and entertain, they are in no hurry to separate. Gentlemen, especially, are often in request on such occasions; and Mr. Rochester is so talented and so lively in society, that I believe he is a general favourite—the ladies are very fond of him—though you would not think his appearance calculated to recommend him particularly in their eyes; but I suppose his acquirements and abilities, perhaps his wealth and good blood, make amends for any little fault of looks.'

'Are there ladies at the Leas?'

'There are Mrs. Eshton and her three daughters—very elegant young ladies, indeed; and there are the Honourable Blanche and Mary Ingram—most beautiful women, I suppose: indeed, I have seen Blanche, six or seven years since, when she was a girl of eighteen. She came here to a Christmas ball and party Mr. Rochester gave. You should have seen the dining-room that day—how richly it was decorated, how brilliantly lit up! I should think there were fifty ladies and gentlemen present—all of the first county families; and Miss Ingram was considered the belle of the evening.'

'You saw her, you say, Mrs. Fairfax: what was she like?'

'Yes, I saw her. The dining-room doors were thrown open, and, as it was Christmas-time, the servants were allowed to assemble in the hall, to hear some of the ladies sing and play. Mr. Rochester would have me to come in, and I sat down in a quiet corner and watched them. I never saw a more splendid scene: the ladies were magnificently dressed; most of them—at least most of the younger ones—looked handsome, but Miss Ingram was certainly the queen.'

'And what was she like?'

'Tall, fine bust, sloping shoulders, long, graceful neck; olive complexion, dark and clear; noble features; eyes rather like Mr. Rochester's, large and black, and as brilliant as her jewels. And then she had such a fine head of hair, raven-black, and so becomingly arranged; a crown of thick plaits behind, and in front the longest, the glossiest curls I ever saw. She was dressed in pure white, an amber-coloured scarf was passed over her shoulder and across her breast, tied at the side, and descending in long, fringed ends below her knee. She wore an amber-coloured flower, too, in her hair: it contrasted well with the jetty mass of her curls.'

'She was greatly admired, of course?'

'Yes, indeed, and not only for her beauty, but for her accomplishments. She was one of the ladies who sang; a gentleman accompanied her on the piano. She and Mr. Rochester sang a duet.'

'Mr. Rochester? I was not aware he could sing.'

'Oh! he has a fine bass voice, and an excellent taste for music.'

'And Miss Ingram, what sort of a voice had she?'

'A very rich and powerful one—she sang delightfully—it was a treat to listen to her; and she played afterwards. I am no judge of music, but Mr. Rochester is, and I heard him say her execution was remarkably good.'

'And this beautiful and accomplished lady is not yet married?'

'It appears not: I fancy neither she nor her sister have very large fortunes. Old Lord Ingram's estates were chiefly entailed, and the eldest son came in for everything almost.'

'But I wonder no wealthy nobleman or gentleman has taken a fancy to her: Mr. Rochester, for instance. He is rich, is he not?'

'Oh! yes. But you see there is a considerable difference in age: Mr. Rochester is near forty; she is but twenty-five.'

'What of that? More unequal matches are made every day.'

'True: yet I should scarcely fancy Mr. Rochester would entertain an idea of the sort. But you eat nothing: you have scarcely tasted since you began tea.'

'No: I am too thirsty to eat. Will you let me have another cup?'

I was about again to revert to the probability of a union between Mr. Rochester and the beautiful Blanche; but Adèle came in, and the conversation was turned into another channel.

When once more alone, I reviewed the information I had got; looked into my heart, examined its thoughts and feelings, and endeavoured to bring back with a strict hand such as had been straying through imagination's boundless and trackless waste, into the safe fold of common sense.

Arraigned at my own bar, Memory having given her evidence of the hopes, wishes, sentiments I had been cherishing since last night—of the general state of mind in which I had indulged for nearly a fortnight past; Reason having come forward and told in her own quiet way, a plain, unvarnished tale, showing how I had rejected the real, and rabidly devoured the ideal;—I pronounced judgment to this effect:—That a greater fool than Jane Eyre had never breathed the breath of life: that a more fantastic idiot had never surfeited herself on sweet lies, and swallowed poison as if it were nectar.

'*You*,' I said, 'a favourite with Mr. Rochester? *You* gifted with the power of pleasing him? *You* of importance to him in any way? Go! your folly sickens me. And you have derived pleasure from occasional tokens of preference—equivocal tokens, shown by a gentleman of family, and a man of the world, to a dependant and a novice. How dared you? Poor stupid dupe!—Could not even self-interest make you wiser? You repeated to yourself this morning the brief scene of last night?—Cover your face and be ashamed! He said something in praise of your eyes, did he? Blind puppy! Open their bleared lids and look on your own accursed senselessness! It does good to no woman to be flattered by her superior, who cannot possibly intend to marry her; and it is madness in all women to let a secret love kindle within them, which, if unreturned and unknown, must devour the life that feeds it; and, if discovered and responded to, must lead, *ignis-fatuus*-like,[4] into miry wilds, whence there is no extrication.

'Listen, then, Jane Eyre, to your sentence: to-morrow, place the glass before you, and draw in chalk your own picture, faithfully; without softening one defect: omit no harsh line, smooth away no displeasing irregularity; write under it, "Portrait of a Governess, disconnected, poor, and plain."

'Afterwards, take a piece of smooth ivory—you have one prepared in your drawing-box: take your palette, mix your freshest, finest, clearest tints; choose your most delicate camel-hair pencils; delineate carefully the loveliest face you can imagine; paint it in your softest shades and sweetest hues, according to the description given by Mrs. Fairfax of Blanche Ingram: remember the raven ringlets, the Oriental eye;— what! you revert to Mr. Rochester as a model! Order! No snivel!—no sentiment!—no regret! I will endure only sense and resolution. Recall the august yet harmonious lineaments, the Grecian neck and bust: let the round and dazzling arm be visible, and the delicate hand; omit neither diamond ring nor gold bracelet; portray faithfully the attire, aërial lace and glistening satin, graceful scarf and golden rose: call it "Blanche, an accomplished lady of rank."

'Whenever, in future, you should chance to fancy Mr. Rochester thinks well of you, take out these two pictures and compare them: say, "Mr. Rochester might probably win that noble lady's love, if he chose to strive for it; is it likely he would waste a serious thought on this indigent and insignificant plebian?"'

4. Like a will-of-the-wisp.

'I'll do it,' I resolved: and having framed this determination, I grew calm, and fell asleep.

I kept my word. An hour or two sufficed to sketch my own portrait in crayons; and in less than a fortnight I had completed an ivory miniature of an imaginary Blanche Ingram. It looked a lovely face enough, and when compared with the real head in chalk, the contrast was as great as self-control could desire. I derived benefit from the task: it had kept my head and hands employed, and had given force and fixedness to the new impressions I wished to stamp indelibly on my heart.

Ere long, I had reason to congratulate myself on the course of wholesome discipline to which I had thus forced my feelings to submit: thanks to it, I was able to meet subsequent occurrences with a decent calm; which, had they found me unprepared, I should probably have been unequal to maintain, even externally.

Chapter XVII

A week passed, and no news arrived of Mr. Rochester: ten days, and still he did not come. Mrs. Fairfax said she should not be surprised if he were to go straight from the Leas to London, and thence to the Continent and not show his face again at Thornfield for a year to come: he had not unfrequently quitted it in a manner quite as abrupt and unexpected. When I heard this I was beginning to feel a strange chill and failing at the heart. I was actually permitting myself to experience a sickening sense of disappointment: but rallying my wits, and recollecting my principles, I at once called my sensations to order; and it was wonderful how I got over the temporary blunder—how I cleared up the mistake of supposing Mr. Rochester's movements a matter in which I had any cause to take a vital interest. Not that I humbled myself by a slavish notion of inferiority: on the contrary, I just said—'You have nothing to do with the master of Thornfield, further than to receive the salary he gives you for teaching his protégée, and to be grateful for such respectful and kind treatment as, if you do your duty, you have a right to expect at his hands. Be sure that is the only tie he seriously acknowledges between you and him: so don't make him the object of your fine feelings, your raptures, agonies, and so forth. He is not of your order: keep to your caste, and be too self-respecting to lavish the love of the whole heart, soul, and strength, where such a gift is not wanted and would be despised.'

I went on with my day's business tranquilly, but ever and anon vague suggestions kept wandering across my brain of reasons why I should quit Thornfield; and I kept involuntarily framing advertisements and pondering conjectures about new situations; these thoughts I did not think it necessary to check; they might germinate and bear fruit if they could.

Mr. Rochester had been absent upwards of a fortnight, when the post brought Mrs. Fairfax a letter.

'It is from the master,' said she as she looked at the direction. 'Now I suppose we shall know whether we are to expect his return or not.'

And while she broke the seal and perused the document, I went on taking my coffee (we were at breakfast); it was hot, and I attributed to that circumstance a fiery glow which suddenly rose to my face. Why my hand shook, and why I involuntarily spilt half the contents of my cup into my saucer, I did not choose to consider.

'Well—I sometimes think we are too quiet; but we run a chance of being busy enough now: for a little while at least,' said Mrs. Fairfax, still holding the note before her spectacles.

Ere I permitted myself to request an explanation, I tied the string of Adèle's pinafore, which happened to be loose: having helped her also to another bun, and refilled her mug with milk, I said, nonchalantly:—
'Mr. Rochester is not likely to return soon, I suppose?'

'Indeed, he is—in three days, he says; that will be next Thursday; and not alone either. I don't know how many of the fine people at the Leas are coming with him. He sends directions for all the best bed-rooms to be prepared; and the library and drawing-rooms are to be cleaned out; and I am to get more kitchen hands from the George Inn, at Millcote, and from wherever else I can; and the ladies will bring their maids and the gentlemen their valets: so we shall have a full house of it.' And Mrs. Fairfax swallowed her breakfast and hastened away to commence operations.

The three days were, as she had foretold, busy enough. I had thought all the rooms at Thornfield beautifully clean and well-arranged, but it appears I was mistaken. Three women were got to help; and such scrubbing, such brushing, such washing of paint and beating of carpets, such taking down and putting up of pictures, such polishing of mirrors and lustres, such lighting of fires in bedrooms, such airing of sheets and feather-beds on hearths, I never beheld either before or since. Adèle ran quite wild in the midst of it: the preparations for company, and the prospect of their arrival, seemed to throw her into ecstasies. She would have Sophie to look over all her 'toilettes,' as she called frocks; to furbish up any that were 'passées,'[5] and to air and arrange the new. For herself, she did nothing but caper about in the front chambers, jump on and off the bedsteads, and lie on the mattresses and piled-up bolsters and pillows before the enormous fires roaring in the chimneys. From school duties she was exonerated: Mrs. Fairfax had pressed me into her ser-

5. Out of style.

vice, and I was all day in the storeroom, helping (or hindering) her and the cook; learning to make custards and cheesecakes and French pastry, to truss game and garnish dessert dishes.

The party were expected to arrive on Thursday afternoon, in time for dinner at six. During the intervening period I had no time to nurse chimeras; and I believe I was as active and gay as anybody—Adèle excepted. Still, now and then, I received a damping check to my cheerfulness; and was, in spite of myself, thrown back on the region of doubts and portents, and dark conjectures. This was when I chanced to see the third story staircase door (which of late had always been kept locked) open slowly, and give passage to the form of Grace Poole, in prim cap, white apron, and handerchief; when I watched her glide along the gallery, her quiet tread muffled in a list slipper; when I saw her look into the bustling, topsy-turvy bedrooms,—just say a word, perhaps, to the charwoman about the proper way to polish a grate, or clean a marble mantlepiece, or take stains from papered walls, and then pass on. She would thus descend to the kitchen once a day, eat her dinner, smoke a moderate pipe on the hearth, and go back, carrying her pot of porter with her, for her private solace, in her own gloomy, upper haunt. Only one hour in the twenty-four did she pass with her fellow-servants below; all the rest of her time was spent in some low-ceiled, oaken chamber of the third story: there she sat and sewed—and probably laughed drearily to herself—as companionless as a prisoner in his dungeon.

The strangest thing of all was, that not a soul in the house, except me, noticed her habits, or seemed to marvel at them; no one discussed her position or employment; no one pitied her solitude or isolation. I once, indeed, overheard part of a dialogue between Leah and one of the charwomen, of which Grace formed the subject. Leah had been saying something I had not caught, and the charwoman remarked— 'She gets good wages, I guess?'

'Yes,' said Leah; 'I wish I had as good; not that mine are to complain of,—there's no stinginess at Thornfield; but they're not one-fifth of the sum Mrs. Poole receives. And she is laying by: she goes every quarter to the bank at Millcote. I should not wonder but she has saved enough to keep her independent if she liked to leave; but I suppose she's got used to the place; and then she's not forty yet, and strong and able for anything. It is too soon for her to give up business.'

'She is a good hand, I daresay,' said the charwoman.

'Ah! she understands what she has to do,—nobody better,'—rejoined Leah, significantly; 'and it is not every one could fill her shoes; not for all the money she gets.'

'That it is not!' was the reply. 'I wonder whether master——'

The charwoman was going on; but here Leah turned and perceived me, and she instantly gave her companion a nudge.

'Doesn't she know?' I heard the woman whisper.

Leah shook her head, and the conversation was of course dropped. All I had gathered from it amounted to this,—that there was a mystery at Thornfield; and that from participation in that mystery I was purposely excluded.

Thursday came: all work had been completed the previous evening; carpets were laid down, bed-hangings festooned, radiant white counterpanes spread, toilet-tables arranged, furniture rubbed, flowers piled in vases: both chambers and saloons looked as fresh and bright as hands could make them. The hall, too, was scoured; and the great carved clock, as well as the steps and banisters of the staircase, were polished to the brightness of glass: in the dining-room, the sideboard flashed resplendent with plate; in the drawing-room and boudoir, vases of exotics bloomed on all sides.

Afternoon arrived: Mrs. Fairfax assumed her best black satin gown, her gloves, and her gold watch; for it was her part to receive the company—to conduct the ladies to their rooms, &c. Adèle, too, would be dressed: though I thought that she had little chance of being introduced to the party that day, at least. However, to please her, I allowed Sophie to apparel her in one of her short, full muslin frocks. For myself, I had no need to make any change; I should not be called upon to quit my sanctum of the schoolroom; for a sanctum it was now become to me—'a very pleasant refuge in time of trouble.'[6]

It had been a mild, serene spring day; one of those days which, towards the end of March or the beginning of April, rise shining over the earth as heralds of summer. It was drawing to an end now; but the evening was even warm, and I sat at work in the schoolroom with the window open.

'It gets late,' said Mrs. Fairfax, entering in rustling state. 'I am glad I ordered dinner an hour after the time Mr. Rochester mentioned; for it is past six now. I have sent John down to the gates to see if there is anything on the road: one can see a long way from thence in the direction of Millcote.' She went to the window. 'Here he is!' said she. 'Well, John' (leaning out), 'any news?'

'They're coming, ma'am,' was the answer. 'They'll be here in ten minutes.'

Adèle flew to the window. I followed; taking care to stand on one side, so that, screened by the curtain, I could see without being seen.

The ten minutes John had given seemed very long, but at last wheels were heard; four equestrians galloped up the drive, and after them came two open carriages. Fluttering veils and waving plumes filled the vehicles; two of the cavaliers were young, dashing-looking gentlemen;

6. Psalms 46:1.

the third was Mr. Rochester, on his black horse, Mesrour;[7] Pilot bounding before him: at his side rode a lady, and he and she were the first of the party. Her purple riding-habit almost swept the ground, her veil streamed long on the breeze; mingling with its transparent folds, and gleaming through them, shone rich raven ringlets.

'Miss Ingram!' exclaimed Mrs. Fairfax, and away she hurried to her post below.

The cavalcade, following the sweep of the drive, quickly turned the angle of the house, and I lost sight of it. Adèle now petitioned to go down; but I took her on my knee and gave her to understand that she must not on any account think of venturing in sight of the ladies, either now or at any other time, unless expressly sent for; that Mr. Rochester would be very angry, &c. 'Some natural tears she shed'[8] on being told this; but as I began to look very grave, she consented at last to wipe them.

A joyous stir was now audible in the hall; gentlemen's deep tones and ladies' silvery accents blent harmoniously together, and distinguishable above all, though not loud, was the sonorous voice of the master of Thornfield Hall, welcoming his fair and gallant guests under its roof. Then light steps ascended the stairs; and there was a tripping through the gallery, and soft cheerful laughs, and opening and closing doors, and for a time, a hush.

'Elles changent de toilettes,'[9] said Adèle; who, listening attentively, had followed every movement; and she sighed.

'Chez maman,' said she, 'quand il y avait du monde, je le suivais partout, au salon et à leurs chambres; souvent je regardais les femmes de chambre coiffer et habiller les dames, et c'était si amusant: comme cela on apprend.'[1]

'Don't you feel hungry, Adèle?'

'Mais oui, mademoiselle: voilà cinq ou six heures que nous n'avons pas mangé.'[2]

'Well now, while the ladies are in their rooms, I will venture down and get you something to eat.'

And issuing from my asylum with precaution, I sought a backstairs which conducted directly to the kitchen. All in that region was fire and commotion; the soup and fish were in the last stage of projection, and the cook hung over her crucibles in a frame of mind and body threatening spontaneous combustion.[3] In the servants' hall two coachmen and

7. The name of a royal executioner in *The Arabian Nights*.
8. *Paradise Lost* 12.645.
9. "They are changing clothes."
1. "At mama's, . . . when there were a lot of people, I would follow them everywhere, in the drawing room and to their rooms; I often

watched the maids dress and groom the ladies, and it was so amusing: that is how one learns."
2. "Yes, of course, miss: it's been five or six hours since we've eaten."
3. A playful reference to alchemy, in which metals and powders are placed in crucibles in an attempt to make gold.

three gentlemen's gentlemen stood or sat round the fire; the Abigails, I suppose, were upstairs with their mistresses: the new servants that had been hired from Millcote were bustling about everywhere. Threading this chaos, I at last reached the larder; there I took possession of a cold chicken, a roll of bread, some tarts, a plate or two, and a knife and fork: with this booty I made a hasty retreat. I had regained the gallery, and was just shutting the back-door behind me, when an accelerated hum warned me that the ladies were about to issue from their chambers. I could not proceed to the schoolroom without passing some of their doors, and running the risk of being surprised with my cargo of victual-age; so I stood still at this end, which, being windowless, was dark: quite dark now, for the sun was set and twilight gathering.

Presently the chambers gave up their fair tenants one after another; each came out gaily and airily, with dress that gleamed lustrous through the dusk. For a moment they stood grouped together at the other extremity of the gallery, conversing in a key of sweet subdued vivacity; they then descended the staircase almost as noiselessly as a bright mist rolls down a hill. Their collective appearance had left on me an impression of high-born elegance, such as I had never before received.

I found Adèle peeping through the schoolroom door, which she held ajar. 'What beautiful ladies!' cried she in English. 'Oh, I wish I might go to them! Do you think Mr. Rochester will send for us by-and-by, after dinner?'

'No, indeed, I don't; Mr. Rochester has something else to think about. Never mind the ladies to-night; perhaps you will see them to-morrow; here is your dinner.'

She was really hungry, so the chicken and tarts served to divert her attention for a time. It was well I secured this forage; or both she, I and Sophie, to whom I conveyed a share of our repast, would have run a chance of getting no dinner at all: every one downstairs was too much engaged to think of us. The dessert was not carried out till after nine; and at ten footmen were still running to and fro with trays and coffee-cups. I allowed Adèle to sit up much later than usual; for she declared she could not possibly go to sleep while the doors kept opening and shutting below, and people bustling about. Besides, she added, a message might possibly come from Mr. Rochester when she was undressed; 'et alors quel dommage!'[4]

I told her stories as long as she would listen to them; and then for a change I took her out into the gallery. The hall lamp was now lit, and it amused her to look over the balustrade and watch the servants passing backwards and forwards. When the evening was far advanced, a sound of music issued from the drawing-room, whither the piano had been

4. "And then what a shame!"

removed. Adèle and I sat down on the top step of the stairs to listen. Presently a voice blent with the rich tones of the instrument; it was a lady who sang, and very sweet her notes were. The solo over, a duet followed, and then a glee: a joyous conversational murmur filled up the intervals. I listened long: suddenly I discovered that my ear was wholly intent on analysing the mingled sounds, and trying to discriminate amidst the confusion of accents those of Mr. Rochester; and when it caught them, which it soon did, it found a further task in framing the tones, rendered by distance inarticulate, into words.

The clock struck eleven. I looked at Adèle, whose head leant against my shoulder; her eyes were waxing heavy, so I took her up in my arms and carried her off to bed. It was near one before the gentlemen and ladies sought their chambers.

The next day was as fine as its predecessor; it was devoted by the party to an excursion to some sight in the neighbourhood. They set out early in the forenoon, some on horseback, the rest in carriages; I witnessed both the departure and the return. Miss Ingram, as before, was the only lady equestrian; and, as before, Mr. Rochester galloped at her side; the two rode a little apart from the rest. I pointed out this circumstance to Mrs. Fairfax, who was standing at the window with me:—

'You said it was not likely they should think of being married,' said I, 'but you see Mr. Rochester evidently prefers her to any of the other ladies.'

'Yes; I daresay: no doubt he admires her.'

'And she him,' I added; 'look how she leans her head towards him as if she were conversing confidentially; I wish I could see her face; I have never had a glimpse of it yet.'

'You will see her this evening,' answered Mrs. Fairfax. 'I happened to remark to Mr. Rochester how much Adèle wished to be introduced to the ladies, and he said: "Oh! let her come into the drawing-room after dinner; and request Miss Eyre to accompany her."'

'Yes—he said that from mere politeness: I need not go, I am sure,' I answered.

'Well, I observed to him that as you were unused to company, I did not think you would like appearing before so gay a party—all strangers —and he replied, in his quick way: "Nonsense! If she objects, tell her it is my particular wish; and if she resists, say I shall come and fetch her in case of contumacy."'

'I will not give him that trouble,' I answered. 'I will go, if no better may be: but I don't like it. Shall you be there, Mrs. Fairfax?'

'No; I pleaded off, and he admitted my plea. I'll tell you how to manage so as to avoid the embarrassment of making a formal entrance, which is the most disagreeable part of the business. You must go into the drawing-room while it is empty, before the ladies leave the dinner-table; choose your seat in any quiet nook you like; you need not stay long after the gentlemen come in, unless you please: just let Mr. Rochester see you are there and then slip away—nobody will notice you.'

'Will these people remain long, do you think?'

'Perhaps two or three weeks; certainly not more. After the Easter recess, Sir George Lynn, who was lately elected member for Millcote, will have to go up to town and take his seat; I daresay Mr. Rochester will accompany him: it surprises me that he has already made so protracted a stay at Thornfield.'

It was with some trepidation that I perceived the hour approach when I was to repair with my charge to the drawing-room. Adèle had been in a state of ecstasy all day, after hearing she was to be presented to the ladies in the evening; and it was not till Sophie commenced the operation of dressing her that she sobered down. Then the importance of the process quickly steadied her; and by the time she had her curls arranged in well-smoothed, drooping clusters, her pink satin frock put on, her long sash tied, and her lace mittens adjusted, she looked as grave as any judge. No need to warn her not to disarrange her attire: when she was dressed, she sat demurely down in her little chair, taking care previously to lift up the satin skirt for fear she should crease it, and assured me she would not stir thence till I was ready. This I quickly was; my best dress (the silver-grey one, purchased for Miss Temple's wedding, and never worn since) was soon put on; my hair was soon smoothed; my sole ornament, the pearl brooch, soon assumed. We descended.

Fortunately there was another entrance to the drawing-room than that through the saloon where they were all seated at dinner. We found the apartment vacant, a large fire burning silently on the marble hearth, and wax candles shining in bright solitude, amid the exquisite flowers with which the tables were adorned. The crimson curtain hung before the arch: slight as was the separation this drapery formed from the party in the adjoining saloon, they spoke in so low a key that nothing of their conversation could be distinguished beyond a soothing murmur.

Adèle, who appeared to be still under the influence of a most solemnising impression, sat down, without a word, on the footstool I pointed out to her. I retired to a window-seat, and, taking a book from a table near, endeavoured to read. Adèle brought her stool to my feet; ere long she touched my knee.

'What is it, Adèle?'

'Est-ce que je ne puis pas prendre une seule de ces fleurs magnifiques, mademoiselle? Seulement pour completer ma toilette.'[5]

'You think too much of your "toilette," Adèle, but you may have a

---

5. "Couldn't I take just one of these magnificent flowers, miss? Just to complete my costume."

flower.' And I took a rose from a vase and fastened it in her sash. She sighed a sigh of ineffable satisfaction, as if her cup of happiness were now full. I turned my face away to conceal a smile I could not suppress: there was something ludicrous as well as painful in the little Parisienne's earnest and innate devotion to matters of dress.

A soft sound of rising now became audible; the curtain was swept back from the arch; through it appeared the dining-room, with its lit lustre pouring down light on the silver and glass of a magnificent dessert-service covering a long table; a band of ladies stood in the opening; they entered, and the curtain fell behind them.

There were but eight, yet somehow as they flocked in, they gave the impression of a much larger number. Some of them were very tall, many were dressed in white, and all had a sweeping amplitude of array that seemed to magnify their persons as a mist magnifies the moon. I rose and curtseyed to them; one or two bent their heads in return, the others only stared at me.

They dispersed about the room, reminding me, by the lightness and buoyancy of their movements, of a flock of white plumy birds. Some of them threw themselves in half-reclining positions on the sofas and ottomans, some bent over the tables and examined the flowers and books, the rest gathered in a group round the fire—all talked in a low but clear tone which seemed habitual to them. I knew their names afterwards, and may as well mention them now.

First there was Mrs. Eshton and two of her daughters. She had evidently been a handsome woman, and was well preserved still. Of her daughters, the eldest, Amy, was rather little; naïve, and childlike in face and manner, and piquant in form: her white muslin dress and blue sash became her well. The second, Louisa, was taller and more elegant in figure, with a very pretty face, of that order the French term 'minois chiffonné':[6] both sisters were fair as lilies.

Lady Lynn was a large and stout personage of about forty, very erect, very haughty-looking, richly dressed in a satin robe of changeful sheen: her dark hair shone glossily under the shade of an azure plume, and within the circlet of a band of gems.

Mrs. Colonel Dent was less showy, but, I thought, more ladylike. She had a slight figure, a pale, gentle face, and fair hair. Her black satin dress, her scarf of rich foreign lace, and her pearl ornaments, pleased me better than the rainbow radiance of the titled dame.

But the three most distinguished—partly, perhaps, because the tallest figures of the band—were the Dowager Lady Ingram and her daughters, Blanche and Mary. They were all three of the loftiest stature of woman. The dowager might be between forty and fifty; her shape

6. A sweet, slightly petulant face.

was still fine; her hair (by candlelight at least) still black; her teeth, too, were still apparently perfect. Most people would have termed her a splendid woman of her age: and so she was, no doubt, physically speaking; but then there was an expression of almost insupportable haughtiness in her bearing and countenance. She had Roman features and a double chin, disappearing into a throat like a pillar: these features appeared to me not only inflated and darkened, but even furrowed with pride; and the chin was sustained by the same principle, in a position of almost preternatural erectness. She had, likewise, a fierce and a hard eye: it reminded me of Mrs. Reed's; she mouthed her words in speaking; her voice was deep, its inflections very pompous, very dogmatical —very intolerable, in short. A crimson velvet robe, and a shawl turban of some gold-wrought Indian fabric, invested her (I suppose she thought) with a truly imperial dignity.

Blanche and Mary were of equal stature—straight and tall as poplars. Mary was too slim for her height; but Blanche was moulded like a Dian.[7] I regarded her, of course, with special interest. First, I wished to see whether her appearance accorded with Mrs. Fairfax's description; secondly, whether it at all resembled the fancy miniature I had painted of her; and thirdly—it will out!—whether it were such as I should fancy likely to suit Mr. Rochester's taste.

As far as person went, she answered point for point, both to my picture and Mrs. Fairfax's description. The noble bust, the sloping shoulders, the graceful neck, the dark eyes and black ringlets were all there—but her face? Her face was like her mother's; a youthful unfurrowed likeness: the same low brow, the same high features, the same pride. It was not, however, so saturnine a pride: she laughed continually; her laugh was satirical, and so was the habitual expression of her arched and haughty lip.

Genius is said to be self-conscious: I cannot tell whether Miss Ingram was a genius, but she was self-conscious—remarkably self-conscious indeed. She entered into a discourse on botany with the gentle Mrs. Dent. It seems Mrs. Dent had not studied that science: though, as she said, she liked flowers, 'especially wild ones'; Miss Ingram had, and she ran over its vocabulary with an air. I presently perceived she was (what is vernacularly termed) *trailing* Mrs. Dent; that is playing on her ignorance; her *trail* might be clever, but it was decidedly not good-natured. She played; her execution was brilliant; she sang; her voice was fine; she talked French apart to her mamma; and she talked it well, with fluency and with a good accent.

Mary had a milder and more open countenance than Blanche; softer features too, and a skin some shades fairer (Miss Ingram was dark as a

7. Beautiful Greek goddess of hunting.

Spaniard)—but Mary was deficient in life; her face lacked expression, her eye lustre; she had nothing to say, and having once taken her seat, remained fixed like a statue in its niche. The sisters were both attired in spotless white.

And did I now think Miss Ingram such a choice as Mr. Rochester would be likely to make? I could not tell—I did not know his taste in female beauty. If he liked the majestic, she was the very type of majesty: then she was accomplished, sprightly. Most gentlemen would admire her, I thought; and that he *did* admire her, I already seemed to have obtained proof: to remove the last shade of doubt, it remained but to see them together.

You are not to suppose, reader, that Adèle has all this time been sitting, motionless, on the stool at my feet: no; when the ladies entered, she rose, advanced to meet them, made a stately reverence, and said, with gravity,—'Bon jour, mesdames.'[8]

And Miss Ingram had looked down at her with a mocking air, and exclaimed, 'Oh, what a little puppet!'

Lady Lynn had remarked, 'It is Mr. Rochester's ward, I suppose—the little French girl he was speaking of.'

Mrs. Dent had kindly taken her hand, and given her a kiss. Amy and Louisa Eshton had cried out simultaneously—

'What a love of a child!'

And then they had called her to a sofa, where she now sat, ensconced between them, chattering alternately in French and broken English: absorbing not only the young ladies' attention, but that of Mrs. Eshton and Lady Lynn, and getting spoilt to her heart's content.

At last coffee is brought in, and the gentlemen are summoned. I sit in the shade—if any shade there be in this brilliantly-lit apartment; the window curtain half hides me. Again the arch yawns: they come. The collective appearance of the gentlemen, like that of the ladies, is very imposing: they are all costumed in black; most of them are tall, some young. Henry and Frederick Lynn are very dashing sparks, indeed; and Colonel Dent is a fine soldierly man. Mr. Eshton, the magistrate of the district, is gentleman-like: his hair is quite white, his eyebrows and whiskers still dark, which gives him something of the appearance of a 'père noble de théâtre.'[9] Lord Ingram, like his sisters, is very tall; like them, also, he is handsome; but he shares Mary's apathetic and listless look: he seems to have more length of limb than vivacity of blood or vigour of brain.

And where is Mr. Rochester?

He comes in last: I am not looking at the arch, yet I see him enter. I

8. "Hello, ladies."
9. Distinguished old gentleman, as portrayed in the theater.

try to concentrate my attention on those netting-needles, on the meshes of the purse I am forming—I wish to think only of the work I have in my hands, to see only the silver beads and silk threads that lie in my lap; whereas, I distinctly behold his figure, and I inevitably recall the moment when I last saw it: just after I had rendered him, what he deemed an essential service—and he, holding my hand, and looking down on my face, surveyed me with eyes that revealed a heart full and eager to overflow; in whose emotions I had a part. How near had I approached him at that moment! What had occurred since, calculated to change his and my relative positions? Yet now, how distant, how far estranged we were! So far estranged, that I did not expect him to come and speak to me. I did not wonder, when, without looking at me, he took a seat at the other side of the room, and began conversing with some of the ladies.

No sooner did I see that his attention was riveted on them, and that I might gaze without being observed, than my eyes were drawn involuntarily to his face: I could not keep their lids under control: they would rise, and the irids[1] would fix on him. I looked, and had an acute pleasure in looking,—a precious, yet poignant pleasure; pure gold, with a steely point of agony: a pleasure like what the thirst-perishing man might feel who knows the well to which he has crept is poisoned, yet stoops and drinks divine draughts nevertheless.

Most true is it that 'beauty is in the eye of the gazer.' My master's colorless, olive face, square, massive brow, broad and jetty eyebrows, deep eyes, strong features, firm, grim mouth,—all energy, decision, will,—were not beautiful, according to rule; but they were more than beautiful to me: they were full of an interest, an influence that quite mastered me,—that took my feelings from my own power and fettered them in his. I had not intended to love him: the reader knows I had wrought hard to extirpate from my soul the germs of love there detected; and now, at the first renewed view of him, they spontaneously revived, green and strong! He made me love him without looking at me.

I compared him with his guests. What was the gallant grace of the Lynns, the languid elegance of Lord Ingram,—even the military distinction of Colonel Dent, contrasted with his look of native pith and genuine power? I had no sympathy with their appearance, their expression; yet I could imagine that most observers would call them attractive, handsome, imposing; while they would pronounce Mr. Rochester at once harsh-featured and melancholy-looking. I saw them smile, laugh—it was nothing; the light of the candles had as much soul in it as their smile; the tinkle of the bell as much significance as their

---

1. Plural of "iris."

laugh. I saw Mr. Rochester smile—his stern features softened; his eye grew both brilliant and gentle, its ray both searching and sweet. He was talking, at the moment, to Louisa and Amy Eshton. I wondered to see them receive with calm that look which seemed to me so penetrating; I expected their eyes to fall, their colour to rise under it; yet I was glad when I found they were in no sense moved. 'He is not to them what he is to me,' I thought: 'he is not of their kind. I believe he is of mine;—I am sure he is,—I feel akin to him,—I understand the language of his countenance and movements; though rank and wealth sever us widely, I have something in my brain and heart, in my blood and nerves, that assimilates me mentally to him. Did I say, a few days since, that I had nothing to do with him but to receive my salary at his hands? Did I forbid myself to think of him in any other light than as a paymaster? Blasphemy against nature! Every good, true, vigorous feeling I have, gathers impulsively round him. I know I must conceal my sentiments; I must smother hope; I must remember that he cannot care much for me. For when I say that I am of his kind, I do not mean that I have his force to influence, and his spell to attract; I mean only that I have certain tastes and feelings in common with him. I must then repeat continually that we are for ever sundered;—and yet, while I breathe and think I must love him.'

Coffee is handed. The ladies, since the gentlemen entered, have become lively as larks; conversation waxes brisk and merry. Colonel Dent and Mr. Eshton argue on politics; their wives listen. The two proud dowagers, Lady Lynn and Lady Ingram, confabulate together. Sir George—whom, by-the-by, I have forgotten to describe—a very big and very fresh-looking country gentleman, stands before their sofa, coffee-cup in hand, and occasionally puts in a word. Mr. Frederick Lynn has taken a seat beside Mary Ingram, and is showing her the engravings of a splendid volume; she looks, smiles now and then, but apparently says little. The tall and phlegmatic Lord Ingram leans with folded arms on the chair-back of the little and lively Amy Eshton; she glances up at him, and chatters like a wren: she likes him better than she does Mr. Rochester. Henry Lynn has taken possession of an ottoman at the feet of Louisa; Adèle shares it with him: he is trying to talk French with her, and Louisa laughs at his blunders. With whom will Blanche Ingram pair? She is standing alone at the table, bending gracefully over an album. She seems waiting to be sought; but she will not wait too long: she herself selects a mate.

Mr. Rochester, having quitted the Eshtons, stands on the hearth as solitary as she stands by the table; she confronts him, taking her station on the opposite side of the mantelpiece.

'Mr. Rochester, I thought you were not fond of children?'

'Nor am I.'

'Then, what induced you to take charge of such a little doll as that?' (pointing to Adèle). 'Where did you pick her up?'

'I did not pick her up, she was left on my hands.'

'You should have sent her to school.'

'I could not afford it; schools are so dear.'

'Why, I suppose you have a governess for her; I saw a person with her just now—is she gone? Oh, no, there she is still behind the window-curtain. You pay her, of course. I should think it quite as expensive—more so, for you have them both to keep in addition.'

I feared—or should I say, hoped—the allusion to me would make Mr. Rochester glance my way; and I involuntarily shrank further into the shade; but he never turned his eyes.

'I have not considered the subject,' said he indifferently, looking straight before him.

'No—you men never do consider economy and common sense. You should hear mamma on the chapter of governess. Mary and I have had, I should think, a dozen at least in our day; half of them detestable and the rest ridiculous, and all incubi—were they not, mamma?'

'Did you speak, my own?'

The young lady thus claimed as the dowager's special property reiterated her question with an explanation.

'My dearest, don't mention governesses; the word makes me nervous. I have suffered a martyrdom from their incompetency and caprice; I thank Heaven I have now done with them!'

Mrs. Dent here bent over to the pious lady, and whispered something in her ear; I suppose, from the answer elicited, it was a reminder that one of the anathematised race was present.

'Tant pis!'[2] said her ladyship, 'I hope it may do her good.' Then, in a lower tone, but still loud enough for me to hear, 'I noticed her; I am a judge of physiognomy, and in hers I see all the faults of her class.'

'What are they, madam?' inquired Mr. Rochester aloud.

'I will tell you in your private ear,' replied she, wagging her turban three times with portentous significancy.

'But my curiosity will be past its appetite; it craves food now.'

'Ask Blanche; she is nearer you than I.'

'Oh, don't refer him to me, mamma! I have just one word to say of the whole tribe; they are a nuisance. Not that I ever suffered much from them; I took care to turn the tables. What tricks Theodore and I used to play on our Miss Wilsons, and Mrs. Greys, and Madame Jouberts! Mary was always too sleepy to join in a plot with spirit. The best fun was with Madame Joubert. Miss Wilson was a poor sickly thing, lachrymose and low-spirited: not worth the trouble of vanquishing, in short; and

2. "Too bad!"

Mrs. Grey was coarse and insensible: no blow took effect on her. But poor Madame Joubert! I see her yet in her raging passions, when we had driven her to extremities—spilt our tea, crumbled our bread and butter, tossed our books up to the ceiling, and played a charivari[3] with the ruler and desk, the fender and fire-irons. Theodore, do you remember those merry days?'

'Yaas, to be sure I do,' drawled Lord Ingram; 'and the poor old stick used to cry out, "Oh, you villains[4] childs!" and then we sermonised her on the presumption of attempting to teach such clever blades as we were, when she was herself so ignorant.'

'We did; and Tedo, you know I helped you in prosecuting (or persecuting) your tutor, whey-faced Mr. Vining—the parson in the pip,[5] as we used to call him. He and Miss Wilson took the liberty of falling in love with each other—at least Tedo and I thought so; we surprised sundry tender glances and sighs which we interpreted as tokens of "la belle passion,"[6] and I promise you the public soon had the benefit of our discovery; we employed it as a sort of lever to hoist our dead-weights from the house. Dear mamma, there, as soon as she got an inkling of the business, found out that it was of an immoral tendency. Did you not, my lady-mother?'

'Certainly, my best. And I was quite right, depend on that: there are a thousand reasons why liaisons between governesses and tutors should never be tolerated a moment in any well-regulated house; firstly,——.'

'Oh, gracious, mamma! Spare us the enumeration! Au reste,[7] we all know them: danger of bad example to innocence of childhood—distractions and consequent neglect of duty on the part of the attached—mutual alliance and reliance; confidence thence resulting—insolence accompanying—mutiny and general blow-up. Am I right, Baroness Ingram, of Ingram Park?'

'My lily-flower, you are right now, as always.'

'Then no more need be said; change the subject.'

Amy Eshton, not hearing or not heeding this dictum, joined in with her soft infantine tone: 'Louisa and I used to quiz our governess too; but she was such a good creature, she would bear anything; nothing put her out. She was never cross with us; was she, Louisa?'

'No, never; we might do what we pleased—ransack her desk and her workbox, and turn her drawers inside out; and she was so good-natured, she would give us anything we asked for.'

'I suppose now,' said Miss Ingram, curling her lips sarcastically, 'we shall have an abstract of the memoirs of all the governesses extant; in

3. A noisy serenade to newlyweds.
4. Naughty.
5. Like a chick in its shell.

6. The beautiful passion.
7. At any rate.

order to avert such a visitation, I again move the introduction of a new topic. Mr. Rochester, do you second my motion?'

'Madam, I support you on this point as on every other.'

'Then on me be the onus of bringing it forward. Signor Eduardo, are you in voice to-night?'

'Donna Bianca,[8] if you command it, I will be.'

'Then, signor, I lay on you my sovereign behest to furbish up your lungs and other vocal organs, as they will be wanted on my royal service.'

'Who would not be the Rizzio of so divine a Mary?'

'A fig for Rizzio!' cried she, tossing her head with all its curls, as she moved to the piano. 'It is my opinion the fiddler David must have been an insipid sort of fellow; I like black Bothwell better. To my mind a man is nothing without a spice of the devil in him; and history may say what it will of James Hepburn, but I have a notion he was just the sort of wild, fierce, bandit hero whom I could have consented to gift with my hand.'[9]

'Gentlemen, you hear! Now which of you most resembles Bothwell?' cried Mr. Rochester.

'I should say the preference lies with you,' responded Colonel Dent.

'On my honour, I am much obliged to you,' was the reply.

Miss Ingram, who had now seated herself with proud grace at the piano, spreading out her snowy robes in queenly amplitude, commenced a brilliant prelude; talking meantime. She appeared to be on her high-horse to-night; both her words and her air seemed intended to excite not only the admiration, but the amazement of her auditors; she was evidently bent on striking them as something very dashing and daring indeed.

'Oh, I am so sick of the young men of the present day!' exclaimed she, rattling away at the instrument. 'Poor puny things not fit to stir a step beyond papa's park-gates: nor to go even so far without mamma's permission and guardianship! Creatures so absorbed in care about their pretty faces and their white hands, and their small feet; as if a man had anything to do with beauty! As if loveliness were not the special prerogative of woman—her legitimate appanage[1] and heritage! I grant an ugly *woman* is a blot on the fair face of creation; but as to the *gentlemen*, let them be solicitous to possess only strength and valour: let their motto be—Hunt, shoot, and fight; the rest is not worth a fillip. Such should be my device, were I a man.'

'Whenever I marry,' she continued after a pause which none interrupted, 'I am resolved my husband shall not be a rival, but a foil to me. I

8. "Mr. Edward . . . Miss Blanche" (Italian).

9. David Rizzio was an Italian who joined the household of Mary, Queen of Scots as a singer, then became the queen's confidant and lover. Her second husband, Lord Darnley, had Rizzio killed. James Hepburn, fourth earl of Bothwell, in turn had Darnley murdered and married the queen, becoming her third husband.

1. I.e., endowment.

will suffer no competitor near the throne; I shall exact an undivided homage; his devotions shall not be shared between me and the shape he sees in his mirror. Mr. Rochester, now sing, and I will play for you.'

'I am all obedience,' was the response.

'Here then is a Corsair-song. Know that I doat on Corsairs; and for that reason, sing it "con spirito." '[2]

'Commands from Miss Ingram's lips would put spirit into a mug of milk and water.'

'Take care, then: if you don't please me, I will shame you by showing how such things *should* be done.'

'That is offering a premium on incapacity; I shall now endeavour to fail.'

'Gardez-vous en bien![3] If you err wilfully, I shall devise a proportionate punishment.'

'Miss Ingram ought to be clement, for she has it in her power to inflict a chastisement beyond mortal endurance.'

'Ha! explain!' commanded the lady.

'Pardon me, madam; no need of explanation; your own fine sense must inform you that one of your frowns would be a sufficient substitute for capital punishment.'

'Sing!' said she, and again touching the piano, she commenced an accompaniment in spirited style.

'Now is my time to slip away,' thought I; but the tones that then severed the air arrested me. Mrs. Fairfax had said Mr. Rochester possessed a fine voice; he did—a mellow powerful bass, into which he threw his own feeling, his own force; finding a way through the ear to the heart, and there waking sensation strangely. I waited till the last deep and full vibration had expired—till the tide of talk, checked an instant, had resumed its flow; I then quitted my sheltered corner and made my exit by the side-door, which was fortunately near. Thence a narrow passage led into the hall; in crossing it, I perceived my sandal was loose; I stopped to tie it, kneeling down for that purpose on the mat at the foot of the staircase. I heard the dining-room door unclose; a gentleman came out; rising hastily, I stood face to face with him; it was Mr. Rochester.

'How do you do?' he asked.

'I am very well, sir.'

'Why did you not come and speak to me in the room?'

I thought I might have retorted the question on him who put it; but I would not take that freedom. I answered:—'I did not wish to disturb you, as you seemed engaged, sir.'

'What have you been doing during my absence?'

'Nothing particular; teaching Adèle as usual.'

2. With spirit.   3. I.e., be very careful.

'And getting a good deal paler than you were—as I saw at first sight. What is the matter?'

'Nothing at all, sir.'

'Did you take any cold that night you half drowned me?'

'Not the least.'

'Return to the drawing-room; you are deserting too early.'

'I am tired, sir.'

He looked at me for a minute.

'And a little depressed,' he said. 'What about? Tell me.'

'Nothing—nothing, sir. I am not depressed.'

'But I affirm that you are: so much depressed that a few more words would bring tears to your eyes—indeed, they are there now, shining and swimming; and a bead has slipped from the lash and fallen on to the flag. If I had time, and was not in mortal dread of some prating prig of a servant passing, I would know what all this means. Well, to-night I excuse you; but understand that so long as my visitors stay, I expect you to appear in the drawing-room every evening; it is my wish; don't neglect it. Now go, and send Sophie for Adèle. Good-night, my ——' He stopped, bit his lip, and abruptly left me.

Chapter XVIII

Merry days were these at Thornfield Hall; and busy days too: how different from the first three months of stillness, monotony, and solitude I had passed beneath its roof! All sad feelings seemed now driven from the house, all gloomy associations forgotten: there was life everywhere, movement all day long. You could not now traverse the gallery, once so hushed, nor enter the front chambers, once so tenantless, without encountering a smart lady's maid, or a dandy valet.

The kitchen, the butler's pantry, the servants' hall, the entrance hall, were equally alive; and the saloons were only left void and still when the blue sky and halcyon sunshine of the genial spring weather called their occupants out into the grounds. Even when that weather was broken, and continuous rain set in for some days, no damp seemed cast over enjoyment; indoor amusements only became more lively and varied, in consequence of the stop put to outdoor gaiety.

I wondered what they were going to do the first evening a change of entertainment was proposed; they spoke of 'playing charades,' but in my ignorance I did not understand the term. The servants were called in, the dining-room tables wheeled away, the lights otherwise disposed, the chairs placed in a semicircle opposite the arch. While Mr. Rochester and the other gentlemen directed these alterations, the ladies were running up and down stairs ringing for their maids. Mrs. Fairfax was summoned to give information respecting the resources of the house in

shawls, dresses, draperies of any kind; and certain wardrobes of the third
story were ransacked, and their contents, in the shape of brocaded and
hooped petticoats, satin sacques, black modes, lace lappets, &c., were
brought down in armfuls by the Abigails; then a selection was made,
and such things as were chosen were carried to the boudoir within the
drawing-room.

Meantime, Mr. Rochester had again summoned the ladies round
him, and was selecting certain of their number to be of his party. 'Miss
Ingram is mine, of course,' said he; afterwards he named the two Misses
Eshton, and Mrs. Dent. He looked at me; I happened to be near him, as
I had been fastening the clasp of Mrs. Dent's bracelet, which had got
loose.

'Will you play?' he asked. I shook my head. He did not insist, which I
rather feared he would have done; he allowed me to return quietly to
my usual seat.

He and his aids now withdrew behind the curtain; the other party,
which was headed by Colonel Dent, sat down on the crescent of chairs.
One of the gentlemen, Mr. Eshton, observing me, seemed to propose
that I should be asked to join them; but Lady Ingram instantly nega-
tived the notion.

'No,' I heard her say: 'she looks too stupid for any game of the sort.'

Ere long, a bell tinkled, and the curtain drew up. Within the arch the
bulky figure of Sir George Lynn, whom Mr. Rochester had likewise
chosen, was seen enveloped in a white sheet; before him, on a table, lay
open a large book; and at his side stood Amy Eshton, draped in Mr.
Rochester's cloak, and holding a book in her hand. Somebody, unseen,
rang the bell merrily; then Adèle (who had insisted on being one of her
guardian's party), bounded forward, scattering round her the contents
of a basket of flowers she carried on her arm. Then appeared the magnificent figure of Miss Ingram, clad in white, a long veil on her head,
and a wreath of roses round her brow; by her side walked Mr. Rochester, and together they drew near the table. They knelt, while Mrs. Dent
and Louisa Eshton, dressed also in white, took up their stations behind
them. A ceremony followed, in dumb show, in which it was easy to recognise the pantomime of a marriage. At its termination Colonel Dent
and his party consulted in whispers for two minutes, then the Colonel
called out,—'Bride!' Mr. Rochester bowed, and the curtain fell.

A considerable interval elapsed before it again rose. Its second rising
displayed a more elaborately prepared scene than the last. The drawing-room, as I have before observed, was raised two steps above the
dining-room, and on the top of the upper step, placed a yard or two
back within the room, appeared a large marble basin, which I recognised as an ornament of the conservatory—where it usually stood, surrounded by exotics, and tenanted by gold fish—and whence it must

have been transported with some trouble, on account of its size and weight.

Seated on the carpet, by the side of this basin, was seen Mr. Rochester, costumed in shawls, with a turban on his head. His dark eyes and swarth skin and Paynim features suited the costume exactly: he looked the very model of an Eastern emir; an agent or a victim of the bowstring. Presently advanced into view Miss Ingram. She, too, was attired in Oriental fashion: a crimsom scarf tied sashlike round the waist; an embroidered handkerchief knotted about her temples; her beautifully-moulded arms bare, one of them up-raised in the act of supporting a pitcher, poised gracefully on her head. Both her cast of form and feature, her complexion and her general air, suggested the idea of some Israelitish princess of the patriarchal days; and such was doubtless the character she intended to represent.

She approached the basin, and bent over it as if to fill her pitcher; she again lifted it to her head. The personage on the well-brink now seemed to accost her; to make some request,—'She hasted, let down her pitcher on her hand and gave him to drink.' From the bosom of his robe he then produced a casket, opened it and showed magnificent bracelets and earrings; she acted astonishment and admiration; kneeling, he laid the treasure at her feet; incredulity and delight were expressed by her looks and gestures; the stranger fastened the bracelets on her arms, and the rings in her ears. It was Eliezer and Rebecca; the camels only were wanting.[4]

The divining party again laid their heads together; apparently they could not agree about the word or syllable this scene illustrated. Colonel Dent, their spokesman, demanded 'the tableau of the Whole';[5] whereupon the curtain again descended.

On its third rising only a portion of the drawing-room was disclosed; the rest being concealed by a screen, hung with some sort of dark and coarse drapery. The marble basin was removed; in its place stood a deal table and a kitchen chair: these objects were visible by a very dim light proceeding from a horn lantern, the wax candles being all extinguished.

Amidst this sordid scene sat a man with his clenched hands resting on his knees, and his eyes bent on the ground. I knew Mr. Rochester; though the begrimed face, the disordered dress (his coat hanging loose from one arm, as if it had been almost torn from his back in a scuffle), the desperate and scowling countenance, the rough, bristling hair might well have disguised him. As he moved a chain clanked; to his wrists were attached fetters.

---

4. A servant of Abraham was instructed to find a wife for Abraham's son Isaac; the servant resolved to approach the first woman who was willing to serve water to him and his camels. In this way he met and wooed Rebecca, who became Isaac's wife (Genesis 24:14–67).

5. Tableau which represents the entire word, rather than a single syllable.

'Bridewell!'[6] exclaimed Colonel Dent, and the charade was solved.

A sufficient interval having elapsed for the performers to resume their ordinary costume, they re-entered the dining-room. Mr. Rochester led in Miss Ingram; she was complimenting him on his acting.

'Do you know,' said she, 'that, of the three characters, I liked you in the last best? Oh, had you but lived a few years earlier, what a gallant gentleman-highwayman you would have made!'

'Is all the soot washed from my face?' he asked, turning it towards her.

'Alas, yes; the more's the pity! Nothing could be more becoming to your complexion than that ruffian's rouge.'

'You would like a hero of the road then?'

'An English hero of the road would be the next best thing to an Italian bandit; and that could only be surpassed by a Levantine pirate.'

'Well, whatever I am, remember you are my wife; we were married an hour since, in the presence of all these witnesses.' She giggled, and her colour rose.

'Now, Dent,' continued Mr. Rochester, 'it is your turn.' And as the other party withdrew, he and his band took the vacated seats. Miss Ingram placed herself at her leader's right hand; the other diviners filled the chairs on each side of him and her. I did not now watch the actors; I no longer waited with interest for the curtain to rise; my attention was absorbed by the spectators; my eyes, erewhile fixed on the arch, were now irresistibly attracted to the semicircle of chairs. What charade Colonel Dent and his party played, what word they chose, how they acquitted themselves, I no longer remember; but I still see the consultation which followed each scene: I see Mr. Rochester turn to Miss Ingram, and Miss Ingram to him; I see her incline her head towards him till the jetty curls almost touch his shoulder and wave against his cheek; I hear their mutual whisperings; I recall their interchanged glances; and something even of the feeling roused by the spectacle returns in memory at this moment.

I have told you, reader, that I had learnt to love Mr. Rochester; I could not unlove him now, merely because I found that he had ceased to notice me—because I might pass hours in his presence and he would never once, turn his eyes in my direction—because I saw all his attentions appropriated by a great lady, who scorned to touch me with the hem of her robes as she passed; who, if ever her dark and imperious eye fell on me by chance, would withdraw it instantly as from an object too mean to merit observation. I could not unlove him, because I felt sure he would soon marry this very lady—because I read daily in her a proud security in his intentions respecting her—because I witnessed hourly in

6. A prison.

him a style of courtship which, if careless and choosing rather to be
sought than to seek, was yet, in its very carelessness, captivating, and in
its very pride, irresistible.

There was nothing to cool or banish love in these circumstances;
though much to create despair. Much too, you will think, reader, to engender jealousy; if a woman, in my position, could presume to be jealous of a woman in Miss Ingram's. But I was not jealous; or very
rarely;—the nature of the pain I suffered could not be explained by that
word. Miss Ingram was a mark beneath jeaousy: she was too inferior to
excite the feeling. Pardon the seeming paradox; I mean what I say. She
was very showy, but she was not genuine: she had a fine person, many
brilliant attainments; but her mind was poor, her heart barren by nature; nothing bloomed spontaneously on that soil; no unforced natural
fruit delighted by its freshness. She was not good; she was not original:
she used to repeat sounding phrases from books: she never offered, nor
had, an opinion of her own. She advocated a high tone of sentiment;
but she did not know the sensations of sympathy and pity; tenderness
and truth were not in her. Too often she betrayed this, by the undue
vent she gave to a spiteful antipathy she had conceived against little
Adèle: pushing her away with some contumelious epithet if she happened to approach her; sometimes ordering her from the room, and
always treating her with coldness and acrimony. Other eyes besides
mine watched these manifestations of character—watched them
closely, keenly, shrewdly. Yes: the future bridegroom, Mr. Rochester
himself, exercised over his intended a ceaseless surveillance: and it was
from this sagacity—this guardedness of his—this perfect, clear consciousness of his fair one's defects—this obvious absence of passion in
his sentiments towards her, that my ever-torturing pain arose.

I saw he was going to marry her, for family, perhaps political reasons;
because her rank and connexions suited him; I felt he had not given her
his love, and that her qualifications were ill adapted to win from him
that treasure. This was the point—this was where the nerve was
touched and teased—this was where the fever was sustained and fed:
she could not charm him.

If she had managed the victory at once, and he had yielded and sincerely laid his heart at her feet, I should have covered my face, turned to
the wall, and (figuratively) have died to them. If Miss Ingram had been
a good and noble woman, endowed with force, fervour, kindness,
sense, I should have had one vital struggle with two tigers—jealousy
and despair: then, my heart torn out and devoured, I should have admired her—acknowledged her excellence, and been quiet for the rest
of my days: and the more absolute her superiority, the deeper would
have been my admiration—the more truly tranquil my quiescence. But
as matters really stood, to watch Miss Ingram's efforts at fascinating Mr.

Rochester; to witness their repeated failure—herself unconscious that they did fail; vainly fancying that each shaft launched hit the mark, and infatuatedly pluming herself on success, when her pride and self-complacency repelled further and further what she wished to allure—to witness *this*, was to be at once under ceaseless excitation and ruthless restraint.

Because, when she failed, I saw how she might have succeeded. Arrows that continually glanced off from Mr. Rochester's breast and fell harmless at his feet, might, I knew, if shot by a surer hand, have quivered keen in his proud heart—have called love into his stern eye and softness into his sardonic face; or, better still, without weapons a silent conquest might have been won.

'Why can she not influence him more, when she is privileged to draw so near to him?' I asked myself. 'Surely she cannot truly like him, or not like him with true affection. If she did, she need not coin her smiles so lavishly, flash her glances so unremittingly, manufacture airs so elaborate, graces so multitudinous. It seems to me that she might, by merely sitting quietly at his side, saying little and looking less, get nigher his heart. I have seen in his face a far different expression from that which hardens it now while she is so vivaciously accosting him; but then it came of itself, it was not elicited by meretricious arts and calculated manoeuvres; and one had but to accept it—to answer what he asked without pretension, to address him when needful without grimace—and it increased and grew kinder and more genial, and warmed one like a fostering sunbeam. How will she manage to please him when they are married? I do not think she will manage it; and yet it might be managed and his wife might, I verily believe, be the very happiest woman the sun shines on.'

I have not yet said anything condemnatory of Mr. Rochester's project of marrying for interest and connexions. It surprised me when I first discovered that such was his intention; I had thought him a man unlikely to be influenced by motives so commonplace in his choice of a wife; but the longer I considered the position, education, &c., of the parties, the less I felt justified in judging and blaming either him or Miss Ingram, for acting in conformity to ideas and principles instilled into them, doubtless, from their childhood. All their class held these principles; I supposed, then, they had reasons for holding them such as I could not fathom. It seemed to me that, were I a gentleman like him, I would take to my bosom only such a wife as I could love; but the very obviousness of the advantages to the husband's own happiness, offered by this plan, convinced me that there must be arguments against its general adoption of which I was quite ignorant; otherwise I felt sure all the world would act as I wished to act.

But in other points, as well as this, I was growing very lenient to my master: I was forgetting all his faults, for which I had once kept a sharp look-out. It had formerly been my endeavour to study all sides of his character; to take the bad with the good; and from the just weighing of both to form an equitable judgment. Now I saw no bad. The sarcasm that had repelled, the harshness that had startled me once, were only like keen condiments in a choice dish: their presence was pungent, but their absence would be felt as comparatively insipid. And as for the vague something—was it a sinister or a sorrowful, a designing or a desponding expression?—that opened upon a careful observer, now and then, in his eye and closed again before one could fathom the strange depth partially disclosed; that something which used to make me fear and shrink, as if I had been wandering amongst volcanic-looking hills, and had suddenly felt the ground quiver, and seen it gape; that something I at intervals beheld still, and with throbbing heart, but not with palsied nerves. Instead of wishing to shun, I longed only to dare—to divine it; and I thought Miss Ingram happy, because one day she might look into the abyss at her leisure, explore its secrets, and analyse their nature.

Meantime, while I thought only of my master and his future bride —saw only them, heard only their discourse, and considered only their movements of importance—the rest of the party were occupied with their own separate interests and pleasures. The ladies Lynn and Ingram continued to consort in solemn conferences, when they nodded their two turbans at each other, and held up their four hands in confronting gestures of surprise, or mystery, or horror, according to the theme on which their gossip ran, like a pair of magnified puppets. Mild Mrs. Dent talked with good-natured Mrs. Eshton; and the two sometimes bestowed a courteous word or smile on me. Sir George Lynn, Colonel Dent, and Mr. Eshton discussed politics, or county affairs, or justice business. Lord Ingram flirted with Amy Eshton; Louisa played and sang to and with one of the Messrs. Lynn; and Mary Ingram listened languidly to the gallant speeches of the other. Sometimes all, as with one consent, suspended their by-play to observe and listen to the principal actors; for, after all, Mr. Rochester, and—because closely connected with him—Miss Ingram, were the life and soul of the party. If he was absent from the room an hour, a perceptible dulness seemed to steal over the spirits of his guests, and his re-entrance was sure to give a fresh impulse to the vivacity of conversation.

The want of his animating influence appeared to be peculiarly felt one day that he had been summoned to Millcote on business, and was not likely to return till late. The afternoon was wet: a walk the party had proposed to take to see a gipsy camp, lately pitched on a common beyond Hay, was consequently deferred. Some of the gentlemen were gone to the stables; the younger ones, together with the younger ladies, were playing billiards in the billiard-room. The dowagers Ingram and Lynn sought solace in a quiet game at cards. Blanche Ingram, after having repelled, by supercilious taciturnity, some efforts of Mrs. Dent and Mrs. Eshton to draw her into conversation, had first murmured over some sentimental tunes and airs on the piano, and then, having fetched a novel from the library, had flung herself in haughty listlessness on a sofa, and prepared to beguile, by the spell of fiction, the tedious hours of absence. The room and the house were silent; only now and then the merriment of the billiard players was heard from above.

It was verging on dusk, and the clock had already given warning of the hour to dress for dinner, when little Adèle, who knelt by me in the drawing-room window-seat, exclaimed,—'Voilà Monsieur Rochester, qui revient!'[7]

I turned, and Miss Ingram darted forwards from her sofa; the others, too, looked up from their several occupations; for at the same time a crunching of wheels, and a splashing tramp of horse-hoofs became audible on the wet gravel. A post-chaise was aproaching.

'What can possess him to come home in that style?' said Miss Ingram. 'He rode Mesrour (the black horse), did he not, when he went out? and Pilot was with him,—what has he done with the animals?'

As she said this, she approached her tall person and ample garments so near the window, that I was obliged to bend back almost to the breaking of my spine; in her eagerness she did not observe me at first, but when she did, she curled her lip and moved to another casement. The post-chaise stopped, the driver rang the door bell, and a gentleman alighted, attired in travelling garb; but it was not Mr. Rochester; it was a tall, fashionable-looking man, a stranger.

'Provoking!' exclaimed Miss Ingram: 'you tiresome monkey!' (apostrophising Adèle) 'who perched you up in the window to give false intelligence?' and she cast on me an angry glance, as if I were in fault.

Some parleying was audible in the hall, and soon the new-comer entered. He bowed to Lady Ingram, as deeming her the eldest lady present.

'It appears I come at an inopportune time, madam,' said he; 'when my friend, Mr. Rochester, is from home; but I arrive from a very long journey, and I think I may presume so far on old and intimate acquaintance as to instal myself here till he returns.'

His manner was polite; his accent, in speaking, struck me as being somewhat unusual,—not precisely foreign, but still not altogether English; his age might be about Mr. Rochester's,—between thirty and forty; his complexion was singularly sallow; otherwise he was a fine-looking man, at first sight especially. On closer examination you de-

7. "Here is Mr. Rochester, he's returned!"

tected something in his face that displeased; or rather, that failed to please. His features were regular, but too relaxed; his eye was large and well cut, but the life looking out of it was a tame, vacant life—at least so I thought.

The sound of the dressing-bell dispersed the party. It was not till after dinner that I saw him again; he then seemed quite at his ease. But I liked his physiognomy even less than before; it struck me as being, at the same time, unsettled and inanimate. His eye wandered, and had no meaning in its wandering; this gave him an odd look, such as I never remembered to have seen. For a handsome and not an unamiable-looking man, he repelled me exceedingly; there was no power in that smooth-skinned face of a full oval shape; no firmness in that aquiline nose, and small cherry mouth; there was no thought on the low, even forehead; no command in that blank, brown eye.

As I sat in my usual nook, and looked at him with the light of the girandoles on the mantelpiece beaming full over him—for he occupied an arm-chair, drawn close to the fire, and kept shrinking still nearer, as if he were cold—I compared him with Mr. Rochester. I think (with deference be it spoken) the contrast could not be much greater between a sleek gander and a fierce falcon: between a meek sheep and the rough-coated keen-eyed dog, its guardian.

He had spoken of Mr. Rochester as an old friend. A curious friendship theirs must have been: a pointed illustration, indeed, of the old adage that 'extremes meet.'

Two or three of the gentlemen sat near him, and I caught at times scraps of their conversation across the room. At first I could not make much sense of what I heard; for the discourse of Louisa Eshton and Mary Ingram, who sat nearer to me, confused the fragmentary sentences that reached me at intervals. These last were discussing the stranger: they both called him a 'beautiful man.' Louisa said he was 'a love of a creature,' and she 'adored him': and Mary instanced his 'pretty little mouth, and nice nose,' as her ideal of the charming.

'And what a sweet-tempered forehead he has!' cried Louisa,—'so smooth—none of those frowning irregularities I dislike so much: and such a placid eye and smile!'

And then, to my great relief, Mr. Henry Lynn summoned them to the other side of the room, to settle some point about the deferred excursion to Hay Common.

I was now able to concentrate my attention on the group by the fire, and I presently gathered that the new-comer was called Mr. Mason: then I learnt that he was but just arrived in England, and that he came from some hot country: which was the reason, doubtless, his face was so sallow, and that he sat so near the hearth, and wore a surtout in the house. Presently the words, Jamaica, Kingston, Spanish Town, indicated the West Indies as his residence; and it was with no little surprise I gathered, ere long, that he had there first seen and become acquainted with Mr. Rochester. He spoke of his friend's dislike of the burning heats, the hurricanes, and rainy seasons of that region. I knew Mr. Rochester had been a traveller: Mrs. Fairfax had said so; but I thought the continent of Europe had bounded his wanderings: till now I had never heard a hint given of visits to more distant shores.

I was pondering these things, when an incident, and a somewhat unexpected one, broke the thread of my musing. Mr. Mason, shivering as some one chanced to open the door, asked for more coal to be put on the fire, which had burnt out its flame, though its mass of cinder still shone hot and red. The footman who brought in the coal, in going out, stopped near Mr. Eshton's chair, and said something to him in a low voice, of which I heard only the words, 'old woman,'—'quite trouble-some.'

'Tell her she shall be put in the stocks if she does not take herself off,' replied the magistrate.

'No—stop!' interrupted Colonel Dent. 'Don't send her away, Esh-ton; we might turn the thing to account; better consult the ladies.' And speaking aloud, he continued, 'Ladies, you talked of going to Hay Common to visit the gipsy camp; Sam, here, says that one of the old Mother Bunches[8] is in the servants' hall at this moment, and insists upon being brought in before "the quality," to tell them their fortunes. Would you like to see her?'

'Surely, colonel,' cried Lady Ingram, 'you would not encourage such a low impostor. Dismiss her, by all means, at once!'

'But I cannot persuade her to go away, my lady,' said the footman; 'nor can any of the servants: Mrs. Fairfax is with her just now, entreat-ing her to be gone; but she has taken a chair in the chimney-corner, and says nothing shall stir her from it till she gets leave to come in here.'

'What does she want?' asked Mrs. Eshton.

' "To tell the gentry their fortunes," she says, ma'am; and she swears she must and will do it.'

'What is she like?' inquired the Misses Eshton in a breath.

'A shockingly ugly old creature, miss; almost as black as a crock.'

'Why, she's a real sorceress!' cried Frederick Lynn. 'Let us have her in, of course.'

'To be sure,' rejoined his brother; 'it would be a thousand pities to throw away such a chance of fun.'

'My dear boys, what are you thinking about?' exclaimed Mrs. Lynn.

'I cannot possibly countenance any such inconsistent proceeding,' chimed in the Dowager Ingram.

---

8. A sixteenth-century London alewife whose name was used in many seventeenth-century jestbooks.

'Indeed, mamma, but you can—and will,' pronounced the haughty voice of Blanche, as she turned round on the piano-stool; where till now she had sat silent, apparently examining sundry sheets of music. 'I have a curiosity to hear my fortune told: therefore, Sam, order the beldame[9] forwards.'

'My darling Blanche! recollect——'

'I do—I recollect all you can suggest; and I must have my will—quick, Sam!'

'Yes—yes—yes!' cried all the juveniles, both ladies and gentlemen. 'Let her come—it will be excellent sport!'

The footman still lingered. 'She looks such a rough one,' said he.

'Go!' ejaculated Miss Ingram, and the man went.

Excitement instantly seized the whole party: a running fire of raillery and jests was proceeding when Sam returned.

'She won't come now,' said he. 'She says it's not her mission to appear before the "vulgar herd" (them's her words). I must show her into a room by herself, and then those who wish to consult her must go to her one by one.'

'You see now, my queenly Blanche,' began Lady Ingram, 'she encroaches. Be advised, my angel girl—and——'

'Show her into the library, of course,' cut in the 'angel girl.' 'It is not my mission to listen to her before the vulgar herd either: I mean to have her all to myself. Is there a fire in the library?'

'Yes, ma'am—but she looks such a tinker.'[1]

'Cease that chatter, blockhead! and do my bidding.'

Again Sam vanished; and mystery, animation, expectation rose to full flow once more.

'She's ready now,' said the footman, as he reappeared. 'She wishes to know who will be her first visitor.'

'I think I had better just look in upon her before any of the ladies go,' said Colonel Dent.

'Tell her, Sam, a gentleman is coming.'

Sam went and returned.

'She says, sir, that she'll have no gentlemen; they need not trouble themselves to come near her: nor,' he added, with difficulty suppressing a titter, 'any ladies either, except the young and single.'

'By Jove, she has taste!' exclaimed Henry Lynn.

Miss Ingram rose solemnly: 'I go first,' she said, in a tone which might have befitted the leader of a forlorn hope, mounting a breach in the van of his men.

'Oh, my best! oh, my dearest! pause—reflect!' was her mamma's cry;

9. Old woman.   1. Itinerant metal-worker, often a gypsy.

but she swept past her in stately silence, passed through the door which
Colonel Dent held open, and we heard her enter the library.

A comparative silence ensued. Lady Ingram thought it 'le cas'[2] to
wring her hands: which she did accordingly. Miss Mary declared she
felt, for her part, she never dared venture. Amy and Louisa Eshton tittered under their breath, and looked a little frightened.

The minutes passed very slowly: fifteen were counted before the li-
brary-door again opened. Miss Ingram returned to us through the arch.

Would she laugh? Would she take it as a joke? All eyes met her with
a glance of curiosity, and she met all eyes with one of rebuff and coldness: she looked neither flurried nor merry; she walked stiffly to her
seat, and took it in silence.

'Well, Blanche?' said Lord Ingram.

'What did she say, sister?' asked Mary.

'What did you think? How do you feel? Is she a real fortune-teller?'
demanded the Misses Eshton.

'Now, now, good people,' returned Miss Ingram, 'don't press upon
me. Really your organs of wonder and credulity are easily excited: you
seem by the importance you all—my good mamma included—ascribe
to this matter—absolutely to believe we have a genuine witch in the
house, who is in close alliance with the old gentleman.[3] I have seen a
gipsy-vagabond; she has practised in hackneyed fashion the science of
palmistry, and told me what such people usually tell. My whim is gratified; and now I think Mr. Eshton will do well to put the hag in the
stocks to-morrow morning, as he threatened.'

Miss Ingram took a book, leant back in her chair, and so declined further conversation. I watched her for nearly half an hour: during all that
time she never turned a page, and her face grew momently darker,
more dissatisfied, and more sourly expressive of disappointment. She
had obviously not heard anything to her advantage: and it seemed to
me, from her prolonged fit of gloom and taciturnity, that she herself,
notwithstanding her professed indifference, attached undue importance to whatever revelations had been made her.

Meantime, Mary Ingram, Amy and Louisa Eshton, declared they
dared not go alone; and yet they all wished to go. A negotiation was
opened through the medium of the ambassador, Sam; and after much
pacing to and fro, till, I think, the said Sam's calves must have ached
with the exercise, permission was at last, with great difficulty extorted
from the rigorous Sibyl, for the three to wait upon her in a body.

Their visit was not so still as Miss Ingram's had been: we heard hysterical giggling and little shrieks proceeding from the library; and at the

2. The right moment.   3. I.e., the devil.

end of about twenty minutes they burst the door open, and came running across the hall, as if they were half-scared out of their wits.

'I'm sure she is something not right!' they cried one and all. 'She told us such things! She knows all about us!' and they sank breathless into the various seats the gentlemen hastened to bring them.

Pressed for further explanation they declared she had told them of things they had said and done when they were mere children; described books and ornaments they had in their boudoirs at home; keepsakes that different relations had presented to them. They affirmed that she had even divined their thoughts, and had whispered in the ear of each the name of the person she liked best in the world, and informed them of what they most wished for.

Here the gentlemen interposed with earnest petitions to be further enlightened on these two last-named points; but they got only blushes, ejaculations, tremors, and titters, in return for their importunity. The matrons, meantime, offered vinaigrettes and wielded fans; and again and again reiterated the expression of their concern that their warning had not been taken in time; and the elder gentlemen laughed, and the younger urged their services on the agitated fair ones.

In the midst of the tumult, and while my eyes and ears were fully engaged in the scene before me, I heard a hem close at my elbow: I turned and saw Sam.

'If you please, miss, the gipsy declares that there is another young single lady in the room who has not been to her yet, and she swears she will not go till she has seen all. I thought it must be you: there is no one else for it. What shall I tell her?'

'Oh, I will go by all means,' I answered; and I was glad of the unexpected opportunity to gratify my much-excited curiosity. I slipped out of the room, unobserved by any eye—for the company were gathered in one mass about the trembling trio just returned—and I closed the door quietly behind me.

'If you like, miss,' said Sam, 'I'll wait in the hall for you; and if she frightens you, just call and I'll come in.'

'No, Sam, return to the kitchen: I am not in the least afraid.' Nor was I; but I was a good deal interested and excited.

Chapter XIX

The library looked tranquil enough as I entered it, and the Sibyl—if Sibyl she were—was seated snugly enough in an easy chair at the chimney-corner. She had on a red cloak and a black bonnet: or rather, a broad-brimmed gipsy hat, tied down with a striped handkerchief under her chin. An extinguished candle stood on the table: she was bending over the fire, and seemed reading in a little black book, like a prayer-book, by the light of the blaze: she muttered the words to herself, as most old women do, while she read; she did not desist immediately on my entrance: it appeared she wished to finish a paragraph.

I stood on the rug and warmed my hands, which were rather cold with sitting at a distance from the drawing-room fire. I felt now as composed as ever I did in my life: there was nothing indeed in the gipsy's appearance to trouble one's calm. She shut her book and slowly looked up; her hat-brim partially shaded her face, yet I could see as she raised it, that it was a strange one. It looked all brown and black: elf-locks bristled out from beneath a white band which passed under her chin, and came half over her cheeks or rather jaws; her eye confronted me at once, with a bold and direct gaze.

'Well, and you want your fortune told?' she said in a voice as decided as her glance, as harsh as her features.

'I don't care about it, mother; you may please yourself; but I ought to warn you, I have no faith.'

'It's like your impudence to say so: I expected it of you; I heard it in your step as you crossed the threshold.'

'Did you? You've a quick ear.'

'I have; and a quick eye, and a quick brain.'

'You need them all in your trade.'

'I do; especially when I've customers like you to deal with. Why don't you tremble?'

'I'm not cold.'

'Why don't you turn pale?'

'I am not sick.'

'Why don't you consult my art?'

'I'm not silly.'

The old crone 'nichered' a laugh under her bonnet and bandage: she then drew out a short, black pipe, and lighting it began to smoke. Having indulged a while in this sedative, she raised her bent body, took the pipe from her lips, and while gazing steadily at the fire, said very deliberately:—'You are cold; you are sick; and you are silly.'

'Prove it,' I rejoined.

'I will; in few words. You are cold, because you are alone: no contact strikes the fire from you that is in you. You are sick: because the best of feelings, the highest and the sweetest given to man, keeps far away from you. You are silly, because, suffer as you may, you will not beckon it to approach; nor will you stir one step to meet it where it waits you.'

She again put her short, black pipe to her lips, and renewed her smoking with vigour.

'You might say all that to almost any one who, you knew, lived as a solitary dependant in a great house.'

'I might say it to almost any one; but would it be true of almost any one?'

'In my circumstances.'

'Yes; just so, in *your* circumstances: but find me another precisely placed as you are.'

'It would be easy to find you thousands.'

'You could scarcely find me one. If you knew it, you are peculiarly situated: very near happiness; yes; within reach of it. The materials are all prepared; there only wants a movement to combine them. Chance laid them somewhat apart; let them be once approached and bliss results.'

'I don't understand enigmas. I never could guess a riddle in my life.'

'If you wish me to speak more plainly, show me your palm.'

'And I must cross it with silver, I suppose?'

'To be sure.'

I gave her a shilling: she put it into an old stocking-foot which she took out of her pocket, and having tied it round and returned it, she told me to hold out my hand. I did. She approached her face to the palm, and pored over it without touching it.

'It is too fine,' said she. 'I can make nothing of such a hand as that; almost without lines: besides, what is in a palm? Destiny is not written there.'

'I believe you,' said I.

'No,' she continued, 'it is in the face: on the forehead, about the eyes, in the eyes themselves, in the lines of the mouth. Kneel, and lift up your head.'

'Ah! now you are coming to reality,' I said as I obeyed her. 'I shall begin to put some faith in you presently.'

I knelt within half a yard of her. She stirred the fire, so that a ripple of light broke from the disturbed coal: the glare, however, as she sat, only threw her face into deeper shadow: mine, it illumined.

'I wonder with what feelings you came to me to-night,' she said, when she had examined me a while. 'I wonder what thoughts are busy in your heart during all the hours you sit in yonder room with the fine people flitting before you like shapes in a magic lantern: just as little sympathetic communion passing between you and them, as if they were really mere shadows of human forms and not the actual substance.'

'I feel tired often, sleepy sometimes; but seldom sad.'

'Then you have some secret hope to buoy you up and please you with whispers of the future?'

'Not I. The utmost I hope is, to save money enough out of my earnings to set up a school some day in a little house rented by myself.'

'A mean nutriment for the spirit to exist on: and sitting in that window-seat (you see I know your habits)——'

'You have learned them from the servants.'

'Ah! you think yourself sharp. Well—perhaps I have: to speak truth, I have an acquaintance with one of them—Mrs. Poole——'

I started to my feet when I heard the name.

'You have—have you?' thought I; 'there is diablerie[4] in the business after all, then!'

'Don't be alarmed,' continued the strange being; 'she's a safe hand, is Mrs. Poole: close and quiet: any one may repose confidence in her. But, as I was saying: sitting in that window-seat, do you think of nothing but your future school? Have you no present interest in any of the company who occupy the sofas and chairs before you? Is there not one face you study? One figure whose movements you follow with, at least, curiosity?

'I like to observe all the faces, and all the figures.'

'But do you never single one from the rest—or it may be, two?'

'I do frequently; when the gestures or looks of a pair seem telling a tale: it amuses me to watch them.'

'What tale do you like best to hear?'

'Oh, I have not much choice! They generally run on the same theme—courtship; and promise to end in the same catastrophe—marriage.'

'And do you like that monotonous theme?'

'Positively, I don't care about it: it is nothing to me.'

'Nothing to you? When a lady, young and full of life and health, charming with beauty and endowed with the gifts of rank and fortune, sits and smiles in the eyes of a gentleman you——'

'I what?'

'You know—and, perhaps, think well of?'

'I don't know the gentlemen here. I have scarcely interchanged a syllable with one of them; and as to thinking well of them, I consider some respectable and stately, and middle-aged, and others young, dashing, handsome and lively: but certainly they are all at liberty to be the recipients of whose smiles they please, without my feeling disposed to consider the transaction of any moment to me.'

'You don't know the gentlemen here? You have not exchanged a syllable with one of them? Will you say that of the master of the house?'

'He is not at home.'

'A profound remark! A most ingenious quibble! He went to Millcote this morning, and will be back here to-night, or to-morrow: does that circumstance exclude him from the list of your acquaintance—blot him, as it were, out of existence?'

'No: but I can scarcely see what Mr. Rochester has to do with the theme you had introduced.'

4. Devilry.

'I was talking of ladies smiling in the eyes of gentlemen; and of late so many smiles have been shed into Mr. Rochester's eyes that they overflow like two cups filled above the brim: have you never remarked that?'

'Mr. Rochester has a right to enjoy the society of his guests.'

'No question about his right: but have you never observed that, of all the tales told here about matrimony, Mr. Rochester has been favoured with the most lively and the most continuous?'

'The eagerness of a listener quickens the tongue of a narrator.' I said this rather to myself than to the gipsy; whose strange talk, voice, manner, had by this time wrapped me in a kind of dream. One unexpected sentence came from her lips after another, till I got involved in a web of mystification; and wondered what unseen spirit had been sitting for weeks by my heart watching its workings and taking record of every pulse.

'Eagerness of a listener!' repeated she: 'yes; Mr. Rochester has sat by the hour, his ear inclined to the fascinating lips that took such delight in their task of communicating; and Mr. Rochester was so willing to receive and looked so grateful for the pastime given him: you have noticed this?'

'Grateful! I cannot remember detecting gratitude in his face.'

'Detecting! You have analysed, then. And what did you detect, if not gratitude?'

I said nothing.

'You have seen love: have you not?—and, looking forward, you have seen him married and beheld his bride happy?'

'Humph! Not exactly. Your witch's skill is rather at fault sometimes.'

'What the devil have you seen, then?'

'Never mind: I came here to inquire, not to confess. Is it known that Mr. Rochester is to be married?'

'Yes; and to the beautiful Miss Ingram.'

'Shortly?'

'Appearances would warrant that conclusion; and, no doubt (though, with an audacity that wants chastising out of you, you seem to question it), they will be a superlatively happy pair. He must love such a handsome, noble, witty, accomplished lady; and probably she loves him: or, if not his person, at least his purse. I know she considers the Rochester estate eligible to the last degree; though (God pardon me!) I told her something on that point about an hour ago, which made her look wondrous grave: the corners of her mouth fell half an inch. I would advise her blackaviced[5] suitor to look out: if another comes with a longer, or clearer rent-roll,—he's dished——'

'But, mother, I did not come to hear Mr. Rochester's fortune: I came to hear my own; and you have told me nothing of it.'

---

5. "Blackavised"; i.e., of a dark complexion.

'Your fortune is yet doubtful: when I examined your face, one trait contradicted another. Chance has meted you a measure of happiness: that I know. I knew it before I came here this evening. She has laid it carefully on one side for you. I saw her do it. It depends on yourself to stretch out your hand, and take it up; but whether you will do so, is the problem I study. Kneel again on the rug.'

'Don't keep me long; the fire scorches me.'

I knelt. She did not stoop towards me, but only gazed leaning back in her chair. She began muttering,—'The flame flickers in the eye, the eye shines like dew: it looks soft and full of feeling; it smiles at my jargon: it is susceptible; impression follows impression through its clear sphere; where it ceases to smile, it is sad; an unconscious lassitude weighs on the lid: that signifies melancholy resulting from loneliness. It turns from me; it will not suffer farther scrutiny; it seems to deny, by a mocking glance, the truth of the discoveries I have already made,—to disown the charge both of sensibility and chagrin: its pride and reserve only confirm me in my opinion. The eye is favourable.

'As to the mouth, it delights at times in laughter; it is disposed to impart all that the brain conceives; though I daresay it would be silent on much the heart experiences. Mobile and flexible, it was never intended to be compressed in the eternal silence of solitude: it is a mouth which should speak much and smile often and have human affection for its interlocutor. That feature too is propitious.

'I see no enemy to a fortunate issue but in the brow; and that brow professes to say,—"I can live alone, if self-respect and circumstances require me so to do. I need not sell my soul to buy bliss. I have an inward treasure, born with me, which can keep me alive if all extraneous delights should be withheld; or offered only at a price I cannot afford to give." The forehead declares, "Reason sits firm and holds the reins, and she will not let the feelings burst away and hurry her to wild chasms. The passions may rage furiously, like true heathens, as they are; and the desires may imagine all sorts of vain things: but judgment shall still have the last word in every argument, and the casting vote in every decision. Strong wind, earthquake-shock, and fire may pass by: but I shall follow the guiding of that still small voice which interprets the dictates of conscience."

'Well said, forehead; your declaration shall be respected. I have formed my plans—right plans I deem them—and in them I have attended to the claims of conscience, the counsels of reason. I know how soon youth would fade and bloom perish, if, in the cup of bliss offered, but one dreg of shame, or one flavour of remorse were detected; and I do not want sacrifice, sorrow, dissolution—such is not my taste. I wish to foster, not to blight—to earn gratitude, not to wring tears of blood— no, nor of brine: my harvest must be in smiles, in endearments, in sweet—That will do. I think I rave in a kind of exquisite delirium. I should wish now to protract this moment *ad infinitum*; but I dare not. So far I have governed myself thoroughly. I have acted as I inwardly swore I would act; but farther might try me beyond my strength. Rise, Miss Eyre: leave me; "the play is played out."[6]

Where was I? Did I wake or sleep? Had I been dreaming? Did I dream still? The old woman's voice had changed: her accent, her gesture, and all were familiar to me as my own face in a glass—as the speech of my own tongue. I got up, but did not go. I looked; I stirred the fire, and I looked again: but she drew her bonnet and her bandage closer about her face, and again beckoned me to depart. The flame illuminated her hand stretched out: roused now, and on the alert for discoveries, I at once noticed that hand. It was no more the withered limb of eld than my own; it was a rounded supple member, with smooth fingers, symmetrically turned; a broad ring flashed on the little finger, and stooping forward, I looked at it, and saw a gem I had seen a hundred times before. Again I looked at the face; which was no longer turned from me—on the contrary, the bonnet was doffed, the bandage displaced, the head advanced.

'Well, Jane, do you know me?' asked the familiar voice.

'Only take off the red cloak, sir, and then——'

'But the string is in a knot—help me.'

'Break it, sir.'

'There, then—"Off, ye lendings!"'[7]

And Mr. Rochester stepped out of his disguise.

'Now, sir, what a strange idea!'

'But well carried out, eh? Don't you think so?'

'With the ladies you must have managed well.'

'But not with you?'

'You did not act the character of a gipsy with me.'

'What character did I act? My own?'

'No; some unaccountable one. In short, I believe you have been trying to draw me out—or in; you have been talking nonsense to make me talk nonsense. It is scarcely fair, sir.'

'Do you forgive me, Jane?'

'I cannot tell till I have thought it all over. If, on reflection, I find I have fallen into no great absurdity, I shall try to forgive you; but it was not right.'

'Oh! you have been very correct—very careful, very sensible.'

I reflected, and thought, on the whole, I had. It was a comfort; but, indeed, I had been on my guard almost from the beginning of the interview. Something of masquerade I suspected. I knew gipsies and for-

---

6. The penultimate line of Shakespeare's *Twelfth Night* is "But that's all one, our play is done"; see also *I Henry IV* 2.4.531, "Play out the play." 7. *King Lear* 3.4.114.

tune-tellers did not express themselves as this seeming old woman had expressed herself; besides, I had noted her feigned voice, her anxiety to conceal her features. But my mind had been running on Grace Poole —that living enigma, that mystery of mysteries, as I considered her. I had never thought of Mr. Rochester.

'Well,' said he, 'what are you musing about? What does that grave smile signify?'

'Wonder and self-congratulation, sir. I have your permission to retire now, I suppose?'

'No; stay a moment; and tell me what the people in the drawing-room yonder are doing.'

'Discussing the gipsy, I daresay.'

'Sit down!—Let me hear what they said about me.'

'I had better not stay long, sir; it must be near eleven o'clock. Oh! are you aware, Mr. Rochester, that a stranger has arrived here since you left this morning?'

'A stranger!—no; who can it be? I expected no one; is he gone?'

'No; he said he had known you long, and that he could take the liberty of installing himself here till you returned.'

'The devil he did! Did he give his name?'

'His name is Mason, sir; and he comes from the West Indies; from Spanish Town, in Jamaica, I think.'

Mr. Rochester was standing near me; he had taken my hand, as if to lead me to a chair. As I spoke, he gave my wrist a convulsive grip; the smile on his lips froze: apparently a spasm caught his breath.

'Mason!—the West Indies!' he said, in the tone one might fancy a speaking automaton to enounce its single words; 'Mason!—the West Indies!' he reiterated; and he went over the syllables three times, growing, in the intervals of speaking, whiter than ashes: he hardly seemed to know what he was doing.

'Do you feel ill, sir?' I inquired.

'Jane, I've got a blow;—I've got a blow, Jane!' he staggered.

'Oh!—lean on me, sir.'

'Jane, you offered me your shoulder once before; let me have it now.'

'Yes, sir, yes; and my arm.'

He sat down, and made me sit beside him. Holding my hand in both his own, he chafed it; gazing on me, at the same time, with the most troubled and dreary look.

'My little friend!' said he, 'I wish I were in a quiet island with only you; and trouble, and danger, and hideous recollections removed from me.'

'Can I help you, sir?—I'd give my life to serve you.'

'Jane, if aid is wanted, I'll seek it at your hands; I promise you that.'

'Thank you, sir; tell me what to do,—I'll try, at least, to do it.'

'Fetch me now, Jane, a glass of wine from the dining-room; they will be at supper there; and tell me if Mason is with them, and what he is doing.'

I went. I found all the party in the dining-room at supper, as Mr. Rochester had said; they were not seated at table,—the supper was arranged on the side-board; each had taken what he chose, and they stood about here and there in groups, their plates and glasses in their hands. Every one seemed in high glee; laughter and conversation were general and animated. Mr. Mason stood near the fire, talking to Colonel and Mrs. Dent, and appeared as merry as any of them. I filled a wine-glass (I saw Miss Ingram watch me frowningly as I did so: she thought I was taking a liberty, I daresay), and I returned to the library.

Mr. Rochester's extreme pallor had disappeared, and he looked once more firm and stern. He took the glass from my hand.

'Here is to your health, ministrant spirit!' he said: he swallowed the contents and returned it to me. 'What are they doing, Jane?'

'Laughing and talking, sir.'

'They don't look grave and mysterious, as if they had heard something strange?'

'Not at all—they are full of jests and gaiety.'

'And Mason?'

'He was laughing too.'

'If all these people came in a body and spat at me, what would you do, Jane?'

'Turn them out of the room, sir, if I could.'

He half smiled. 'But if I were to go to them, and they only looked at me coldly, and whispered sneeringly amongst each other, and then dropt off and left me one by one, what then? Would you go with them?'

'I rather think not, sir: I should have more pleasure in staying with you.'

'To comfort me?'

'Yes, sir, to comfort you, as well as I could.'

'And if they laid you under a ban for adhering to me?'

'I, probably, should know nothing about their ban; and if I did, I should care nothing about it.'

'Then, you could dare censure for my sake?'

'I could dare it for the sake of any friend who deserved my adherence; as you, I am sure, do.'

'Go back now into the room; step quietly up to Mason, and whisper in his ear that Mr. Rochester is come and wishes to see him: show him in here and then leave me.'

'Yes, sir.'

I did his behest. The company all stared at me as I passed straight among them. I sought Mr. Mason, delivered the message, and preceded him from the room: I ushered him into the library, and then I went upstairs.

At a late hour, after I had been in bed some time, I heard the vistors repair to their chambers: I distinguished Mr. Rochester's voice, and heard him say, 'This way, Mason; this is your room.'

He spoke cheerfully: the gay tones set my heart at ease. I was soon asleep.

Chapter XX

I had forgotten to draw my curtain, which I usually did; and also to let down my window-blind. The consequence was, that when the moon, which was full and bright (for the night was fine), came in her course to that space in the sky opposite my casement, and looked in at me through the unveiled panes, her glorious gaze roused me. Awaking in the dead of night, I opened my eyes on her disk—silver-white and crystal-clear. It was beautiful, but too solemn: I half rose, and stretched my arm to draw the curtain.

Good God! What a cry!

The night—its silence—its rest, was rent in twain, by a savage, a sharp, a shrilly sound that ran from end to end of Thornfield Hall.

My pulse stopped: my heart stood still; my stretched arm was paralysed. The cry died, and was not renewed. Indeed, whatever being uttered that fearful shriek could not soon repeat it: not the widest-winged condor on the Andes could, twice in succession, send out such a yell from the cloud shrouding his eyrie. The thing delivering such utterance must rest ere it could repeat the effort.

It came out of the third story; for it passed overhead. And overhead —yes, in the room just above my chamber ceiling—I now heard a struggle: a deadly one it seemed from the noise; and a half-smothered voice shouted—'Help! help! help!' three times rapidly.

'Will no one come?' it cried; and then, while the staggering and stamping went on wildly, I distinguished through plank and plaster:—'Rochester! Rochester! for God's sake, come!'

A chamber door opened: some one ran, or rushed, along the gallery. Another step stamped on the flooring above, and something fell; and there was silence.

I had put on some clothes, though horror shook all my limbs: I issued from my apartment. The sleepers were all aroused: ejaculations, terrified murmurs, sounded in every room; door after door unclosed: one looked out and another looked out; the gallery filled. Gentlemen and ladies alike had quitted their beds; and 'Oh! what is it?'—'Who is hurt?'—'What has happened?'—'Fetch a light!'—'Is it fire?'—'Are there robbers?'—'Where shall we run?' was demanded confusedly on all hands. But for the moonlight they would have been in complete darkness. They ran to and fro; they crowded together; some sobbed, some stumbled: the confusion was inextricable.

'Where the devil is Rochester?' cried Colonel Dent. 'I cannot find him in his bed.'

'Here! here!' was shouted in return. 'Be composed, all of you: I'm coming.'

And the door at the end of the gallery opened, and Mr. Rochester advanced with a candle: he had just descended from the upper story. One of the ladies ran to him directly; she seized his arm: it was Miss Ingram.

'What awful event has taken place?' said she. 'Speak! let us know the worst at once!'

'But don't pull me down or strangle me,' he replied: for the Misses Eshton were clinging about him now; and the two dowagers, in vast white wrappers, were bearing down on him like ships in full sail.

'All's right!—all's right!' he cried. 'It's a mere rehearsal of Much Ado About Nothing. Ladies, keep off; or I shall wax dangerous.'

And dangerous he looked: his black eyes darted sparks. Calming himself by an effort, he added:—'A servant has had the nightmare; that is all. She's an excitable, nervous person: she construed her dream into an apparition, or something of that sort, no doubt; and has taken a fit with fright. Now, then, I must see you all back into your rooms; for, till the house is settled she cannot be looked after. Gentlemen, have the goodness to set the ladies the example. Miss Ingram, I am sure you will not fail in evincing superiority to idle terrors. Amy and Louisa, return to your nests like a pair of doves, as you are. Mesdames' (to the dowagers), 'you will take cold to a dead certainty, if you stay in this chill gallery any longer.'

And so, by dint of alternate coaxing and commanding, he contrived to get them all once more enclosed in their separate dormitories. I did not wait to be ordered back to mine; but retreated unnoticed: as unnoticed I had left it.

Not, however, to go to bed: on the contrary, I began and dressed myself carefully. The sounds I had heard after the scream, and the words that had been uttered, had probably been heard only by me; for they had proceeded from the room above mine: but they assured me that it was not a servant's dream which had thus struck horror through the house; and that the explanation Mr. Rochester had given was merely an invention framed to pacify his guests. I dressed, then, to be ready for emergencies. When dressed, I sat a long time by the window, looking out over the silent grounds and silvered fields, and waiting for I knew not what. It seemed to me that some event must follow the strange cry, struggle, and call.

No: stillness returned: each murmur and movement ceased gradually, and in about an hour Thornfield Hall was again as hushed as a desert. It seemed that sleep and night had resumed their empire. Meantime the moon declined: she was about to set. Not liking to sit in the cold and darkness, I thought I would lie down on my bed, dressed as I was. I left the window, and moved with little noise across the carpet; as I stooped to take off my shoes, a cautious hand tapped low at the door.

'Am I wanted?' I asked.

'Are you up?' asked the voice I expected to hear, viz. my master's.

'Yes, sir.'

'And dressed?'

'Yes.'

'Come out, then, quietly.'

I obeyed. Mr. Rochester stood in the gallery, holding a light.

'I want you,' he said: 'come this way: take your time and make no noise.'

My slippers were thin: I could walk the matted floor as softly as a cat. He glided up the gallery and up the stairs, and stopped in the dark, low corridor of the fateful third story: I had followed and stood at his side.

'Have you a sponge in your room?' he asked in a whisper.

'Yes, sir.'

'Have you any salts—volatile salts?'

'Yes.'

'Go back and fetch both.'

I returned, sought the sponge on the wash-stand, the salts in my drawer, and once more retraced my steps. He still waited; he held a key in his hand: approaching one of the small, black doors, he put it in the lock; he paused and addressed me again.

'You don't turn sick at the sight of blood?'

'I think I shall not: I have never been tried yet.'

I felt a thrill while I answered him; but no coldness, and no faintness.

'Just give me your hand,' he said; 'it will not do to risk a fainting fit.'

I put my fingers into his. 'Warm and steady,' was his remark: he turned the key and opened the door.

I saw a room I remembered to have seen before; the day Mrs. Fairfax showed me over the house: it was hung with tapestry; but the tapestry was now looped up in one part, and there was a door apparent, which had then been concealed. This door was open; a light shone out of the room within: I heard thence a snarling, snatching sound, almost like a dog quarrelling. Mr. Rochester, putting down his candle, said to me, 'Wait a minute,' and he went forward to the inner apartment. A shout of laughter greeted his entrance; noisy at first, and terminating in Grace Poole's own goblin ha! ha! *She* then was there. He made some sort of arrangement, without speaking; though I heard a low voice address him: he came out and closed the door behind him.

'Here, Jane!' he said; and I walked round to the other side of a large
bed, which with its drawn curtains concealed a considerable portion of
the chamber. An easy-chair was near the bed-head: a man sat in it,
dressed with the exception of his coat; he was still; his head leant back;
his eyes were closed. Mr. Rochester held the candle over him; I recognised in his pale and seemingly lifeless face—the stranger, Mason: I saw
too that his linen on one side, and one arm, was almost soaked in blood.

'Hold the candle,' said Mr. Rochester, and I took it; he fetched a
basin of water from the wash-stand: 'Hold that,' said he. I obeyed. He
took the sponge, dipped it in and moistened the corpse-like face: he
asked for my smelling-bottle, and applied it to the nostrils. Mr. Mason
shortly unclosed his eyes; he groaned. Mr. Rochester opened the shirt
of the wounded man, whose arm and shoulder were bandaged: he
sponged away blood, trickling fast down.

'Is there immediate danger?' murmured Mr. Mason.

'Pooh! No—a mere scratch. Don't be so overcome, man: bear up!
I'll fetch a surgeon for you now, myself: you'll be able to be removed by
morning, I hope. Jane,' he continued.

'Sir?'

'I shall have to leave you in this room with this gentleman, for an
hour, or perhaps two hours; you will sponge the blood as I do when it
returns: if he feels faint, you will put the glass of water on that stand to
his lips, and your salts to his nose. You will not speak to him on any
pretext—and—Richard—it will be at the peril of your life if you speak
to her: open your lips—agitate yourself—and I'll not answer for the
consequences.'

Again the poor man groaned: he looked as if he dared not move: fear,
either of death or of something else, appeared almost to paralyse him.
Mr. Rochester put the now bloody sponge into my hand, and I proceeded to use it as he had done. He watched me a second, then saying,
'Remember!—No conversation,' he left the room. I experienced a
strange feeling as the key grated in the lock, and the sound of his retreating step ceased to be heard.

Here then I was in the third story, fastened into one of its mystic
cells; night around me; a pale and bloody spectacle under my eyes and
hands; a murderess hardly separated from me by a single door: yes—
that was appalling—the rest I could bear; but I shuddered at the
thought of Grace Poole bursting out upon me.

I must keep to my post, however. I must watch this ghastly countenance—these blue, still lips forbidden to unclose—these eyes now
shut, now opening, now wandering through the room, now fixing on
me, and ever glazed with the dulness of horror. I must dip my hand
again and again in the basin of blood and water, and wipe away the
trickling gore. I must see the light of the unsnuffed candle wane on my

employment; the shadows darken on the wrought-antique tapestry round me, and grow black under the hangings of the vast old bed, and quiver strangely over the doors of a great cabinet opposite—whose front, divided into twelve panels, bore in grim design the heads of the twelve apostles, each inclosed in its separate panel as in a frame; while above them at the top rose an ebon crucifix and a dying Christ.

According as the shifting obscurity and flickering gleam hovered here or glanced there, it was now the bearded physician, Luke, that bent his brow; now St. John's long hair that waved; and anon the devilish face of Judas, that grew out of the panel, and seemed gathering life and threatening a revelation of the arch-traitor—of Satan himself—in his subordinate's form.

Amidst all this, I had to listen as well as watch: to listen for the movements of the wild beast or the fiend in yonder side den. But since Mr. Rochester's visit it seemed spell-bound: all the night I heard but three sounds at three long intervals,—a step creak, a momentary renewal of the snarling, canine noise, and a deep human groan.

Then my own thoughts worried me. What crime was this, that lived incarnate in this sequestered mansion, and could neither be expelled nor subdued by the owner?—What mystery, that broke out, now in fire and now in blood, at the deadest hours of night? What creature was it, that, masked in an ordinary woman's face and shape, uttered the voice, now of a mocking demon, and anon of a carrion-seeking bird of prey?

And this man I bent over—this commonplace, quiet stranger—how had he become involved in the web of horror? and why had the Fury flown at him? What made him seek this quarter of the house at an untimely season, when he should have been asleep in bed? I had heard Mr. Rochester assign him an apartment below—what brought him here? And why, now, was he so tame under the violence or treachery done him? Why did he so quietly submit to the concealment Mr. Rochester enforced? Why *did* Mr. Rochester enforce this concealment? His guest had been outraged, his own life on a former occasion had been hideously plotted against; and both attempts he smothered in secrecy and sank in oblivion! Lastly, I saw Mr. Mason was submissive to Mr. Rochester; that the impetuous will of the latter held complete sway over the inertness of the former: the few words which had passed between them assured me of this. It was evident that in their former intercourse, the passive disposition of the one had been habitually influenced by the active energy of the other: whence then had arisen Mr. Rochester's dismay when he heard of Mr. Mason's arrival? Why had the mere name of this unresisting individual—whom his word now sufficed to control like a child—fallen on him, a few hours since, as a thunderbolt might fall on an oak?

Oh! I could not forget his look and his paleness when he whispered:

'Jane, I have got a blow—I have got a blow, Jane.' I could not forget how the arm had trembled which he had rested on my shoulder: and it was no light matter which could thus bow the resolute spirit and thrill the vigorous frame of Fairfax Rochester.

'When will he come? When will he come?' I cried inwardly, as the night lingered and lingered—as my bleeding patient drooped, moaned, sickened: and neither day nor aid arrived. I had, again and again, held the water to Mason's white lips; again and again offered him the stimulating salts: my efforts seemed ineffectual: either bodily or mental suffering, or loss of blood, or all three combined, were fast prostrating his strength. He moaned so, and looked so weak, wild, and lost, I feared he was dying; and I might not even speak to him.

The candle, wasted at last, went out; as it expired, I perceived streaks of grey light edging the window curtains: dawn was then approaching. Presently I heard Pilot bark far below, out of his distant kennel in the courtyard: hope revived. Nor was it unwarranted: in five minutes more the grating key, the yielding lock, warned me my watch was relieved. It could not have lasted more than two hours: many a week has seemed shorter.

Mr. Rochester entered, and with him the surgeon he had been to fetch.

'Now, Carter, be on the alert,' he said to this last: 'I give you but half an hour for dressing the wound, fastening the bandages, getting the patient downstairs and all.'

'But is he fit to move, sir?'

'No doubt of it; it is nothing serious: he is nervous, his spirits must be kept up. Come, set to work.'

Mr. Rochester drew back the thick curtain, drew up the holland blind, let in all the daylight he could; and I was surprised and cheered to see how far dawn was advanced: what rosy streaks were beginning to brighten the east. Then he approached Mason, whom the surgeon was already handling.

'Now, my good fellow, how are you?' he asked.

'She's done for me, I fear,' was the faint reply.

'Not a whit!—courage! This day fortnight you'll hardly be a pin the worse of it: you've lost a little blood; that's all. Carter, assure him there's no danger.'

'I can do that conscientiously,' said Carter, who had now undone the bandages; 'only I wish I could have got here sooner: he would not have bled so much—but how is this? The flesh on the shoulder is torn as well as cut. This wound was not done with a knife: there have been teeth here!'

'She bit me,' he murmured. 'She worried me like a tigress, when Rochester got the knife from her.'

'You should not have yielded: you should have grappled with her at once,' said Mr. Rochester.

'But under such circumstances, what could one do?' returned Mason. 'Oh, it was frightful!' he added, shuddering. 'And I did not expect it: she looked so quiet at first.'

'I warned you,' was his friend's answer; 'I said—be on your guard when you go near her. Besides, you might have waited till to-morrow, and had me with you: it was mere folly to attempt the interview to-night and alone.'

'I thought I could have done some good.'

'You thought! you thought! Yes; it makes me impatient to hear you: but, however, you have suffered, and are likely to suffer enough for not taking my advice; so I'll say no more. Carter—hurry!—hurry! The sun will soon rise, and I must have him off.'

'Directly, sir; the shoulder is just bandaged. I must look to this other wound in the arm: she has had her teeth here too, I think.'

'She sucked the blood: she said she'd drain my heart,' said Mason.

I saw Mr. Rochester shudder: a singularly marked expression of disgust, horror, hatred, warped his countenance almost to distortion; but he only said:—'Come, be silent, Richard, and never mind her gibberish: don't repeat it.'

'I wish I could forget it,' was the answer.

'You will when you are out of the country: when you get back to Spanish Town, you may think of her as dead and buried—or rather, you need not think of her at all.'

'Impossible to forget this night!'

'It is not impossible: have some energy, man. You thought you were as dead as a herring two hours since, and you are all alive and talking now. There!—Carter has done with you or nearly so; I'll make you decent in a trice. Jane' (he turned to me for the first time since his re-entrance), 'take this key: go down into my bedroom, and walk straight forward into my dressing-room; open the top drawer of the wardrobe and take out a clean shirt and neck-handkerchief: bring them here; and be nimble.'

I went; sought the repository he had mentioned, found the articles named and returned with them.

'Now,' said he, 'go to the other side of the bed while I order his toilet; but don't leave the room: you may be wanted again.'

I retired as directed.

'Was anybody stirring below when you went down, Jane?' inquired Mr. Rochester, presently.

'No, sir; all was very still.'

'We shall get you off cannily, Dick: and it will be better, both for your sake, and for that of the poor creature in yonder. I have striven long to avoid exposure, and I should not like it to come at last. Here, Carter, help him on with his waistcoat. Where did you leave your furred cloak? You can't travel a mile without that, I know, in this damned cold climate. In your room?—Jane, run down to Mr. Mason's room,—the one next mine,—and fetch a cloak you will see there.'

Again I ran, and again returned, bearing an immense mantle lined and edged with fur.

'Now I've another errand for you,' said my untiring master; 'you must away to my room again. What a mercy you are shod with velvet, Jane!—a clod-hopping messenger would never do at this juncture. You must open the middle drawer of my toilet-table and take out a little phial and a little glass you will find there,—quick!'

I flew thither and back, bringing the desired vessels.

'That's well! Now, doctor, I shall take the liberty of administering a dose myself; on my own responsibility. I got this cordial at Rome of an Italian charlatan—a fellow you would have kicked, Carter. It is not a thing to be used indiscriminately, but it is good upon occasion: as now, for instance. Jane, a little water.'

He held out the tiny glass, and I half filled it from the water bottle on the wash-stand.

'That will do—now wet the lip of the phial.'

I did so: he measured twelve drops of a crimson liquid, and presented it to Mason.

'Drink, Richard: it will give you the heart you lack, for an hour or so.'

'But will it hurt me?—is it inflammatory?'

'Drink! drink! drink!'

Mr. Mason obeyed, because it was evidently useless to resist. He was dressed now: he still looked pale, but he was no longer gory and sullied. Mr. Rochester let him sit three minutes after he had swallowed the liquid; he then took his arm.

'Now I am sure you can get on your feet,' he said—'try.'

The patient rose.

'Carter, take him under the other shoulder. Be of good cheer, Richard; step out—that's it!'

'I do feel better,' remarked Mr. Mason.

'I am sure you do. Now, Jane, trip on before us away to the back-stairs; unbolt the side-passage door, and tell the driver of the post-chaise you will see in the yard—or just outside, for I told him not to drive his rattling wheels over the pavement—to be ready; we are coming: and, Jane, if any one is about, come to the foot of the stairs and hem.'[8]

It was by this time half-past five, and the sun was on the point of rising; but I found the kitchen still dark and silent. The side-passage door

8. Cough.

was fastened; I opened it with as little noise as possible: all the yard was quiet; but the gates stood wide open, and there was a post-chaise, with horses ready harnessed, and driver seated on the box, stationed outside. I approached him, and said the gentlemen were coming; he nodded: then I looked carefully round and listened. The stillness of early morning slumbered everywhere; the curtains were yet drawn over the servants' chamber windows; little birds were just twittering in the blossom-blanched orchard trees, whose boughs drooped like white garlands over the wall enclosing one side of the yard; the carriage horses stamped from time to time in their closed stables: all else was still.

The gentlemen now appeared. Mason, supported by Mr. Rochester and the surgeon, seemed to walk with tolerable ease: they assisted him into the chaise; Carter followed.

'Take care of him,' said Mr. Rochester to the latter, 'and keep him at your house till he is quite well: I shall ride over in a day or two to see how he gets on. Richard, how is it with you?'

'The fresh air revives me, Fairfax.'

'Leave the window open on his side, Carter; there is no wind—good-bye, Dick.'

'Fairfax——'

'Well, what is it?'

'Let her be taken care of; let her be treated as tenderly as may be: let her——' he stopped and burst into tears.

'I do my best; and have done it, and will do it,' was the answer: he shut up the chaise door, and the vehicle drove away.

'Yet would to God there was an end of all this!' added Mr. Rochester, as he closed and barred the heavy yard-gates. This done, he moved with slow step and abstracted air towards a door in the wall bordering the orchard. I, supposing he had done with me, prepared to return to the house; again, however, I heard him call 'Jane!' He had opened the portal and stood at it, waiting for me.

'Come where there is some freshness, for a few moments,' he said; 'that house is a mere dungeon: don't you feel it so?'

'It seems to me a splendid mansion, sir.'

'The glamour of inexperience is over your eyes,' he answered; 'and you see it through a charmed medium: you cannot discern that the gilding is slime and the silk draperies cobwebs; that the marble is sordid slate, and the polished woods mere refuse chips and scaly bark. Now *here*' (he pointed to the leafy enclosure we had entered) 'all is real, sweet, and pure.'

He strayed down a walk edged with box; with apple trees, pear trees, and cherry trees on one side, and a border on the other, full of all sorts of old-fashioned flowers, stocks, sweet-williams, primroses, pansies, mingled with southern-wood, sweet-briar, and various fragrant herbs.

They were fresh now as a succession of April showers and gleams, followed by a lovely spring morning, could make them: the sun was just entering the dappled east, and his light illumined the wreathed and dewy orchard trees and shone down the quiet walks under them.

'Jane, will you have a flower?'

He gathered a half-blown rose, the first on the bush, and offered it to me.

'Thank you, sir.'

'Do you like this sunrise, Jane? That sky with its high and light clouds which are sure to melt away as the day waxes warm—this placid and balmy atmosphere?'

'I do, very much.'

'You have passed a strange night, Jane.'

'Yes, sir.'

'And it has made you look pale—were you afraid when I left you alone with Mason?'

'I was afraid of some one coming out of the inner room.'

'But I had fastened the door—I had the key in my pocket: I should have been a careless shepherd if I had left a lamb—my pet lamb—so near a wolf's den, unguarded: you were safe.'

'Will Grace Poole live here still, sir?'

'Oh, yes! don't trouble your head about her—put the thing out of your thoughts.'

'Yet it seems to me your life is hardly secure while she stays.'

'Never fear—I will take care of myself.'

'Is the danger you apprehended last night gone by now sir?'

'I cannot vouch for that till Mason is out of England: nor even then. To live, for me, Jane, is to stand on a crater-crust which may crack and spue fire any day.'

'But Mr. Mason seems a man easily led. Your influence, sir, is evidently potent with him: he will never set you at defiance, or wilfully injure you.'

'Oh, no! Mason will not defy me; nor, knowing it, will he hurt me—but, unintentionally, he might in a moment, by one careless word, deprive me, if not of life, yet for ever of happiness.'

'Tell him to be cautious, sir: let him know what you fear, and show him how to avert the danger.'

He laughed sardonically, hastily took my hand, and as hastily threw it from him.

'If I could do that, simpleton, where would the danger be? Annihilated in a moment. Ever since I have known Mason I have only had to say to him "Do that," and the thing has been done. But I cannot give him orders in this case: I cannot say "Beware of harming me, Richard"; for it is imperative that I should keep him ignorant that harm to me is possible. Now you look puzzled; and I will puzzle you farther. You are my little friend, are you not?'

'I like to serve you, sir, and to obey you in all that is right.'

'Precisely: I see you do. I see genuine contentment in your gait and mien, your eye and face, when you are helping me and pleasing me— working for me, and with me, in, as you characteristically say, ' *all that is right*': for if I bid you do what you thought wrong, there would be no light-footed running, no neat-handed alacrity, no lively glance and ani-mated complexion. My friend would then turn to me, quiet and pale, and would say, "No, sir; that is impossible: I cannot do it, because it is wrong;" and would become immutable as a fixed star. Well, you too have power over me, and may injure me: yet I dare not show you where I am vulnerable, lest, faithful and friendly as you are, you should trans-fix me at once.'

'If you have no more to fear from Mr. Mason than you have from me, sir, you are very safe.'

'God grant it may be so! Here, Jane, is an arbour; sit down.'

The arbour was an arch in the wall, lined with ivy; it contained a rustic seat. Mr. Rochester took it, leaving room, however, for me: but I stood before him.

'Sit,' he said; 'the bench is long enough for two. You don't hesitate to take a place at my side, do you? Is that wrong, Jane?'

I answered him by assuming it: to refuse would, I felt, have been un-wise.

'Now, my little friend, while the sun drinks the dew—while all the flowers in this old garden awake and expand, and the birds fetch their young ones' breakfast out of the cornfield, and the early bees do their first spell of work—I'll put a case to you; which you must endeavour to suppose your own: but first, look at me, and tell me you are at ease, and not fearing that I err in detaining you, or that you err in staying.'

'No, sir; I am content.'

'Well then, Jane, call to aid your fancy—suppose you were no longer a girl well reared and disciplined, but a wild boy indulged from child-hood upwards; imagine yourself in a remote foreign land; conceive that you there commit a capital error, no matter of what nature or from what motives, but one whose consequences must follow you through life and taint all your existence. Mind, I don't say a *crime*; I am not speaking of shedding of blood or any other guilty act, which might make the per-petrator amenable to the law: my word is *error*. The results of what you have done become in time to you utterly insupportable; you take meas-ures to obtain relief: unusual measures, but neither unlawful nor cul-pable. Still you are miserable; for hope has quitted you on the very confines of life: your sun at noon darkens in an eclipse, which you feel will not leave it till the time of setting. Bitter and base associations have become the sole food of your memory: you wander here and there, seeking rest in exile: happiness in pleasure—I mean in heartless, sensual pleasure—such as dulls intellect and blights feeling. Heart-weary and soul-withered, you come home after years of voluntary banishment; you make a new acquaintance—how or where no matter: you find in this stranger much of the good and bright qualities which you have sought for twenty years, and never before encountered; and they are all fresh, healthy, without soil and without taint. Such society revives, regenerates: you feel better days come back—higher wishes, purer feelings; you desire to recommence your life, and to spend what remains to you of days in a way more worthy of an immortal being. To attain this end, are you justified in overleaping an obstacle of custom—a mere conventional impediment, which neither your conscience sanctifies nor your judgment approves?'

He paused for an answer: and what was I to say? Oh, for some good spirit to suggest a judicious and satisfactory response! Vain aspiration! The west wind whispered in the ivy round me; but no gentle Ariel borrowed its breath as a medium of speech: the birds sang in the tree-tops; but their song, however sweet, was inarticulate.

Again Mr. Rochester propounded his query.

'Is the wandering and sinful, but now rest-seeking and repentant, man justified in daring the world's opinion, in order to attach to him for ever this gentle, gracious, genial stranger; thereby securing his own peace of mind and regeneration of life?'

'Sir,' I answered, 'a wanderer's repose or a sinner's reformation should never depend on a fellow-creature. Men and women die; philosophers falter in wisdom, and Christians in goodness: if any one you know has suffered and erred, let him look higher than his equals for strength to amend, and solace to heal.'

'But the instrument—the instrument! God, who does the work, ordains the instrument. I have myself—I tell it you without parable—been a worldly, dissipated, restless man; and I believe I have found the instrument for my cure, in——'

He paused: the birds went on carolling, the leaves lightly rustling. I almost wondered they did not check their songs and whispers to catch the suspended revelation: but they would have had to wait many minutes—so long was the silence protracted. At last I looked up at the tardy speaker: he was looking eagerly at me.

'Little friend,' said he, in quite a changed tone—while his face changed too; losing all its softness and gravity, and becoming harsh and sarcastic—'you have noticed my tender penchant for Miss Ingram: don't you think if I married her she would regenerate me with a vengeance?'

He got up instantly, went quite to the other end of the walk, and when he came back he was humming a tune.

'Jane, Jane,' said he, stopping before me, 'you are quite pale with your vigils: don't you curse me for disturbing your rest?'

'Curse you? No sir.'

'Shake hands in confirmation of the word. What cold fingers! They were warmer last night when I touched them at the door of the mysterious chamber. Jane, when will you watch with me again?'

'Whenever I can be useful, sir.'

'For instance, the night before I am married! I am sure I shall not be able to sleep. Will you promise to sit up with me to bear me company? To you I can talk of my lovely one: for now you have seen her and know her.'

'Yes, sir.'

'She's a rare one, is she not, Jane?'

'Yes, sir.'

'A strapper—a real strapper, Jane: big, brown, and buxom; with hair just such as the ladies of Carthage must have had. Bless me! there's Dent and Lynn in the stables! Go in by the shrubbery, through that wicket.'

As I went one way, he went another, and I heard him in the yard, saying cheeringly:—'Mason got the start of you all this morning; he was gone before sunrise: I rose at four to see him off.'

Chapter XXI

Presentiments are strange things! and so are sympathies; and so are signs: and the three combined make one mystery to which humanity has not yet found the key. I never laughed at presentiments in my life; because I have had strange ones of my own. Sympathies, I believe, exist: (for instance, between far-distant, long-absent, wholly estranged relatives; asserting, notwithstanding their alienation, the unity of the source to which each traces his origin) whose workings baffle mortal comprehension. And signs, for aught we know, may be but the sympathies of Nature with man.

When I was a little girl, only six years old, I, one night, heard Bessie Leaven say to Martha Abbot that she had been dreaming about a little child; and that to dream of children was a sure sign of trouble, either to one's self or one's kin. The saying might have worn out of my memory, had not a circumstance immediately followed which served indelibly to fix it there. The next day Bessie was sent for home to the deathbed of her little sister.

Of late I had often recalled this saying and this incident; for during the past week scarcely a night had gone over my couch that had not brought with it a dream of an infant: which I sometimes hushed in my arms, sometimes dandled on my knee, sometimes watched playing with daisies on a lawn; or again, dabbling its hands in running water. It was a wailing child this night, and a laughing one the next: now it nestled close to me, and now it ran from me; but whatever mood the apparition evinced, whatever aspect it wore, it failed not for seven successive nights to meet me the moment I entered the land of slumber.

I did not like this iteration of one idea—this strange recurrence of one image; and I grew nervous as bedtime approached, and the hour of the vision drew near. It was from companionship with this baby-phantom I had been roused on that moonlight night when I heard the cry; and it was on the afternoon of the day following I was summoned downstairs by a message that some one wanted me in Mrs. Fairfax's room. On repairing thither, I found a man waiting for me, having the appearance of a gentleman's servant: he was dressed in deep mourning, and the hat he held in his hand was surrounded with a crape band.

'I daresay you hardly remember me, miss,' he said, rising as I entered; 'but my name is Leaven: I lived coachman with Mrs. Reed when you were at Gateshead eight or nine years since, and I live there still.'

'Oh, Robert! how do you do? I remember you very well: you used to give me a ride sometimes on Miss Georgiana's bay pony. And how is Bessie? You are married to Bessie?'

'Yes, miss: my wife is very hearty, thank you; she brought me another little one about two months since—we have three now—and both mother and child are thriving.'

'And are the family well at the house, Robert?'

'I am sorry I can't give better news of them, miss: they are very badly at present—in great trouble.'

'I hope no one is dead,' I said glancing at his black dress. He too looked down at the crape round his hat and replied,—'Mr. John died yesterday was a week, at his chambers in London.'

'Mr. John?'

'Yes.'

'And how does his mother bear it?'

'Why you see, Miss Eyre, it is not a common mishap: his life has been very wild: these last three years he gave himself up to strange ways; and his death was shocking.'

'I heard from Bessie he was not doing well.'

'Doing well! He could not do worse: he ruined his health and his estate amongst the worst men and the worst women. He got into debt and into jail: his mother helped him out twice, but as soon as he was free he returned to his old companions and habits. His head was not strong: the knaves he lived amongst fooled him beyond anything I ever heard. He came down to Gateshead about three weeks ago and wanted Missis to give up all to him. Missis refused: her means have long been much reduced by his extravagance; so he went back again, and the next news was that he was dead. How he died, God knows!—they say he killed himself.'

I was silent: the tidings were frightful. Robert Leaven resumed:—'Missis had been out of health herself for some time: she had got very stout, but was not strong with it; and the loss of money and fear of poverty were quite breaking her down. The information about Mr. John's death and the manner of it came too suddenly: it brought on a stroke. She was three days without speaking; but last Tuesday she seemed rather better: she appeared as if she wanted to say something, and kept making signs to my wife and mumbling. It was only yesterday morning, however, that Bessie understood she was pronouncing your name; and at last she made out the words, "Bring Jane—fetch Jane Eyre: I want to speak to her." Bessie is not sure whether she is in her right mind, or means anything by the words; but she told Miss Reed and Miss Georgiana, and advised them to send for you. The young ladies put it off at first: but their mother grew so restless, and said, "Jane, Jane," so many times, that at last they consented. I left Gateshead yesterday; and if you can get ready, miss, I should like to take you back with me early to-morrow morning.'

'Yes, Robert, I shall be ready: it seems to me that I ought to go.'

'I think so too, miss. Bessie said she was sure you would not refuse: but I suppose you will have to ask leave before you can get off?'

'Yes; and I will do it now'; and having directed him to the servants' hall, and recommended him to the care of John's wife, and the attentions of John himself, I went in search of Mr. Rochester.

He was not in any of the lower rooms; he was not in the yard, the stables, or the grounds. I asked Mrs. Fairfax if she had seen him;—yes: she believed he was playing billiards with Miss Ingram. To the billiard-room I hastened: the click of balls and the hum of voices resounded thence: Mr. Rochester, Miss Ingram, the two Misses Eshton, and their admirers, were all busied in the game. It required some courage to disturb so interesting a party; my errand, however, was one I could not defer, so I approached the master where he stood at Miss Ingram's side. She turned as I drew near and looked at me haughtily: her eyes seemed to demand, 'What can the creeping creature want now?' and when I said, in a low voice, 'Mr. Rochester,' she made a movement as if tempted to order me away. I remember her appearance at the moment,—it was very graceful and very striking: she wore a morning robe of sky-blue crape; a gauzy azure scarf was twisted in her hair. She had been all animation with the game, and irritated pride did not lower the expression of her haughty lineaments.

'Does that person want you?' she inquired of Mr. Rochester; and Mr. Rochester turned to see who the 'person' was. He made a curious grimace,—one of his strange and equivocal demonstrations—threw down his cue and followed me from the room.

'Well, Jane?' he said, as he rested his back against the schoolroom door, which he had shut.

'If you please, sir, I want leave of absence for a week or two.'

'What to do?—Where to go?'

'To see a sick lady who has sent for me.'

'What sick lady?—Where does she live?'

'At Gateshead, in ——shire.'

'——shire? That is a hundred miles off! Who may she be that sends for people to see her that distance?'

'Her name is Reed, sir,—Mrs. Reed.'

'Reed of Gateshead? There was a Reed of Gateshead, a magistrate.'

'It is his widow, sir.'

'And what have you to do with her? How do you know her?'

'Mr. Reed was my uncle,—my mother's brother.'

'The deuce he was! You never told me that before: you always said you had no relations.'

'None that would own me, sir. Mr. Reed is dead, and his wife cast me off.'

'Why?'

'Because I was poor, and burdensome, and she disliked me.'

'But Reed left children?—you must have cousins? Sir George Lynn was talking of a Reed of Gateshead, yesterday—who, he said, was one of the veriest rascals in town; and Ingram was mentioning a Georgiana Reed of the same place, who was much admired for her beauty, a season or two ago, in London.'

'John Reed is dead, too, sir: he ruined himself and half-ruined his family, and is supposed to have committed suicide. The news so shocked his mother that it brought on an apoplectic attack.'

'And what good can you do her? Nonsense, Jane! I would never think of running a hundred miles to see an old lady who will, perhaps, be dead before you reach her: besides, you say she cast you off.'

'Yes, sir, but that is long ago; and when her circumstances were very different: I could not be easy to neglect her wishes now.'

'How long will you stay?'

'As short a time as possible, sir.'

'Promise me only to stay a week——'

'I had better not pass my word: I might be obliged to break it.'

'At all events you *will* come back: you will not be induced under any pretext to take up a permanent residence with her.'

'Oh, no! I shall certainly return if all be well.'

'And who goes with you? You don't travel a hundred miles alone.'

'No, sir, she has sent her coachman.'

'A person to be trusted?'

'Yes, sir, he has lived ten years in the family.'

Mr. Rochester meditated. 'When do you wish to go?'

'Early to-morrow morning, sir.'

'Well, you must have some money; you can't travel without money, and I daresay you have not much: I have given you no salary yet. How much have you in the world, Jane?' he asked, smiling.

I drew out my purse; a meagre thing it was. 'Five shillings, sir.' He took the purse, poured the hoard into his palm and chuckled over it as if its scantiness pleased him. Soon he produced his pocket-book: 'Here,' said he, offering me a note: it was fifty pounds, and he owed me but fifteen. I told him I had no change.

'I don't want change: you know that. Take your wages.'

I declined accepting more than was my due. He scowled at first; then, as if recollecting something, he said:—'Right, right! Better not give you all now: you would, perhaps, stay away three months if you had fifty pounds. There are ten: is it not plenty?'

'Yes, sir, but now you owe me five.'

'Come back for it then: I am your banker for forty pounds.'

'Mr. Rochester, I may as well mention another matter of business to you while I have the opportunity.'

'Matter of business? I'm curious to hear it.'

'You have as good as informed me, sir, that you are going shortly to be married?'

'Yes: what then?'

'In that case, sir, Adèle ought to go to school: I am sure you will perceive the necessity of it.'

'To get her out of my bride's way; who might otherwise walk over her rather too emphatically. There's sense in the suggestion; not a doubt of it: Adèle, as you say, must go to school; and you, of course, must march straight to—the devil?'

'I hope not, sir: but I must seek another situation somewhere.'

'In course!' he exclaimed, with a twang of voice and a distortion of features equally fantastic and ludicrous. He looked at me some minutes.

'And old Madam Reed, or the Misses, her daughters, will be solicited by you to seek a place, I suppose?'

'No, sir; I am not on such terms with my relatives as would justify me in asking favours of them—but I shall advertise.'

'You shall walk up the pyramids of Egypt!' he growled. 'At your peril you advertise! I wish I had only offered you a sovereign instead of ten pounds. Give me back nine pounds, Jane; I've a use for it.'

'And so have I, sir,' I returned, putting my hands and my purse behind me. 'I could not spare the money on any account.'

'Little niggard!' said he, 'refusing me a pecuniary request! Give me five pounds, Jane.'

'Not five shillings, sir; nor five pence.'

'Just let me look at the cash.'

'No, sir; you are not to be trusted.'

'Jane!'

'Sir?'

'Promise me one thing.'

'I'll promise you anything, sir, that I think I am likely to perform.'

'Not to advertise: and to trust this quest of a situation to me. I'll find you one in time.'

'I shall be glad so to do, sir, if you, in your turn, will promise that I and Adèle shall be both safe out of the house before your bride enters it.'

'Very well! very well! I'll pledge my word on it. You go to-morrow, then?'

'Yes, sir; early.'

'Shall you come down to the drawing-room after dinner?'

'No, sir, I must prepare for the journey.'

'Then you and I must bid good-bye for a little while?'

'I suppose so, sir.'

'And how do people perform that ceremony of parting, Jane? Teach me; I'm not quite up to it.'

'They say, Farewell; or any other form they prefer.'

'Then say it.'

'Farewell, Mr. Rochester, for the present.'

'What must I say?'

'The same, if you like, sir.'

'Farewell, Miss Eyre, for the present: is that all?'

'Yes.'

'It seems stingy, to my notions, and dry and unfriendly. I should like something else: a little addition to the rite. If one shook hands, for instance; but no—that would not content me either. So you'll do no more than say Farewell, Jane?'

'It is enough, sir: as much good will may be conveyed in one hearty word as in many.'

'Very likely; but it is blank and cool—"farewell."'

'How long is he going to stand with his back against the door?' I asked myself; 'I want to commence my packing.' The dinner-bell rang, and suddenly away he bolted, without another syllable: I saw him no more during the day, and was off before he had risen in the morning.

I reached the lodge at Gateshead about five o'clock in the afternoon of the first of May: I stepped in there before going up to the hall. It was very clean and neat: the ornamental windows were hung with little white curtains; the floor was spotless; the grate and fire-irons were burnished bright, and the fire burnt clear. Bessie sat on the hearth nursing her last-born, and Robert and his sister played quietly in a corner.

'Bless you!—I knew you would come!' exclaimed Mrs. Leaven, as I entered.

'Yes, Bessie,' said I, after I had kissed her; 'and I trust I am not too late. How is Mrs. Reed?—Alive still, I hope.'

'Yes, she is alive; and more sensible and collected than she was. The doctor says she may linger a week or two yet; but he hardly thinks she will finally recover.'

'Has she mentioned me lately?'

'She was talking of you only this morning, and wishing you would come: but she is sleeping now; or was ten minutes ago, when I was up at the house. She generally lies in a kind of lethargy all the afternoon, and wakes up about six or seven. Will you rest yourself here an hour, miss, and then I will go up with you?'

Robert here entered, and Bessie laid her sleeping child in the cradle and went to welcome him: afterwards she insisted on my taking off my bonnet and having some tea; for she said I looked pale and tired. I was glad to accept her hospitality; and I submitted to be relieved of my travelling garb just as passively as I used to let her undress me when a child.

Old times crowded fast back on me as I watched her bustling about —setting out the tea-tray with her best china, cutting bread-and-butter, toasting a tea-cake, and, between whiles, giving little Robert or Jane an occasional tap or push, just as she used to give me in former days. Bessie had retained her quick temper as well as her light foot and good looks.

Tea ready, I was going to approach the table; but she desired me to sit still, quite in her old, peremptory tones. I must be served at the fireside, she said; and she placed before me a little round stand with my cup and a plate of toast, absolutely as she used to accommodate me with some privately purloined dainty on a nursery chair: and I smiled and obeyed her as in bygone days.

She wanted to know if I was happy at Thornfield Hall, and what sort of a person the mistress was; and when I told her there was only a master, whether he was a nice gentleman, and if I liked him. I told her he was rather an ugly man, but quite a gentleman; and that he treated me kindly, and I was content. Then I went on to describe to her the gay company that had lately been staying at the house: and to these details Bessie listened with interest: they were precisely of the kind she relished.

In such conversation an hour was soon gone: Bessie restored to me my bonnet, &c., and, accompanied by her, I quitted the lodge for the hall. It was also accompanied by her that I had, nearly nine years ago, walked down the path I was now ascending. On a dark, misty, raw morning in January, I had left a hostile roof with a desperate and embittered heart—a sense of outlawry and almost of reprobation—to seek the chilly harbourage of Lowood: that bourne so far away and unexplored. The same hostile roof now again rose before me: my prospects were doubtful yet; and I had yet an aching heart. I still felt as a wanderer on the face of the earth; but I experienced firmer trust in myself and my own powers, and less withering dread of oppression. The gaping wound of my wrongs, too, was now quite healed; and the flame of resentment extinguished.

'You shall go into the breakfast-room first,' said Bessie, as she preceded me through the hall; 'the young ladies will be there.'

In another moment I was within that apartment. There was every article of furniture looking just as it did on the morning I was first introduced to Mr. Brocklehurst: the very rug he had stood upon still covered the hearth. Glancing at the book-cases, I thought I could distinguish the two volumes of 'Bewick's British Birds' occupying their old place on the third shelf, and 'Gulliver's Travels' and the 'Arabian Nights' ranged just above. The inanimate objects were not changed: but the living things had altered past recognition.

Two young ladies appeared before me; one very tall, almost as tall as Miss Ingram,—very thin too, with a sallow face and severe mien. There was something ascetic in her look, which was augmented by the extreme plainness of a straight-skirted, black, stuff dress, a starched linen collar, hair combed away from the temples, and the nun-like ornament of a string of ebony beads and a crucifix. This I felt sure was Eliza, though I could trace little resemblance to her former self in that elongated and colourless visage.

The other was as certainly Georgiana: but not the Georgiana I remembered—the slim and fairy-like girl of eleven. This was a full-blown, very plump damsel, fair as wax-work; with handsome and regular features, languishing blue eyes, and ringleted yellow hair. The hue of her dress was black too; but its fashion was so different from her sister's—so much more flowing and becoming—it looked as stylish as the other's looked puritanical.

In each of the sisters there was one trait of the mother—and only one: the thin and pallid elder daughter had her parent's Cairngorm eye: the blooming and luxuriant younger girl had her contour of jaw and chin,—perhaps a little softened, but still imparting an indescribable hardness to the countenance, otherwise so voluptuous and buxom.

Both ladies, as I advanced, rose to welcome me, and both addressed me by the name of 'Miss Eyre.' Eliza's greeting was delivered in a short, abrupt voice, without a smile; and then she sat down again, fixed her eyes on the fire, and seemed to forget me. Georgiana added to her 'How d'ye do?' several common-places about my journey, the weather and so on, uttered in rather a drawling tone: and accompanied by sundry side-glances that measured me from head to foot—now traversing the folds of my drab merino pelisse, and now lingering on the plain trimming of my cottage bonnet. Young ladies have a remarkable way of letting you know that they think you a 'quiz' without actually saying the words. A certain superciliousness of look, coolness of manner, nonchalance of tone, express fully their sentiments on the point, without committing them by any positive rudeness in word or deed.

A sneer, however, whether covert or open, had now no longer that power over me it once possessed: as I sat between my cousins, I was surprised to find how easy I felt under the total neglect of the one and the semi-sarcastic attentions of the other—Eliza did not mortify, nor Georgiana ruffle me. The fact was, I had other things to think about; within the last few months feelings had been stirred in me so much more potent than any they could raise—pains and pleasures so much more acute and exquisite had been excited, than any it was in their power to inflict or bestow—that their airs gave me no concern either for good or bad.

'How is Mrs. Reed?' I asked soon, looking calmly at Georgiana; who thought fit to bridle at the direct address, as if it were an unexpected liberty.

'Mrs. Reed? Ah! mama you mean; she is extremely poorly: I doubt if you can see her to-night.'

'If,' said I, 'you would just step upstairs and tell her I am come, I should be much obliged to you.'

Georgiana almost started, and she opened her blue eyes wild and wide. 'I know she had a particular wish to see me,' I added, 'and I would not defer attending to her desire longer than is absolutely necessary.'

'Mama dislikes being disturbed in an evening,' remarked Eliza. I soon rose, quietly took off my bonnet and gloves, uninvited, and said I would just step out to Bessie—who was, I dared say, in the kitchen—and ask her to ascertain whether Mrs. Reed was disposed to receive me or not to-night. I went, and having found Bessie and despatched her on my errand, I proceeded to take further measures. It had heretofore been my habit always to shrink from arrogance: received as I had been to-day, I should, a year ago, have resolved to quit Gateshead the very next morning; now, it was disclosed to me all at once, that that would be a foolish plan. I had taken a journey of a hundred miles to see my aunt, and I must stay with her till she was better—or dead: as to her daughters' pride or folly, I must put it on one side; make myself independent of it. So I addressed the house-keeper; asked her to show me a room, told her I should probably be a visitor here for a week or two, had my trunk conveyed to my chamber, and followed it thither myself: I met Bessie on the landing.

'Missis is awake,' said she; 'I have told her you are here: come and let us see if she will know you.'

I did not need to be guided to the well-known room: to which I had so often been summoned for chastisement or reprimand in former days. I hastened before Bessie, I softly opened the door: a shaded light stood on the table, for it was now getting dark. There was the great four-post bed with amber hangings as of old: there the toilet-table, the arm-chair, and the foot-stool: at which I had a hundred times been sentenced to kneel, to ask pardon for offences, by me uncommitted. I looked into a certain corner near, half-expecting to see the slim outline of a once-dreaded switch; which used to lurk there, waiting to leap out imp-like and lace my quivering palm or shrinking neck. I approached the bed; I opened the curtains and leant over the high-piled pillows.

Well did I remember Mrs. Reed's face, and I eagerly sought the fa-miliar image. It is a happy thing that time quells the longings of ven-geance, and hushes the promptings of rage and aversion: I had left this woman in bitterness and hate, and I came back to her now with no other emotion than a sort of ruth for her great sufferings, and a strong yearning to forget and forgive all injuries—to be reconciled and clasp hands in amity.

The well-known face was there: stern, relentless as ever—there was that peculiar eye which nothing could melt; and the somewhat raised, imperious, despotic eyebrow. How often had it lowered on me menace and hate! and how the recollection of childhood's terrors and sorrows revived as I traced its harsh line now! And yet I stooped down and kissed her: she looked at me.

'Is this Jane Eyre?' she said.

'Yes, aunt Reed. How are you, dear aunt?'

I had once vowed that I would never call her aunt again: I thought it no sin to forget and break that vow now. My fingers had fastened on her hand which lay outside the sheet: had she pressed mine kindly, I should at that moment have experienced true pleasure. But unimpressionable natures are not so soon softened, nor are natural antipathies so readily eradicated: Mrs. Reed took her hand away, and, turning her face rather from me, she remarked that the night was warm. Again she regarded me, so icily, I felt at once that her opinion of me—her feeling towards me—was unchanged, and unchangeable. I knew by her stony eye—opaque to tenderness, indissoluble to tears—that she was resolved to consider me bad to the last; because to believe me good, would give her no generous pleasure: only a sense of mortification.

I felt pain, and then I felt ire; and then I felt a determination to sub-due her—to be her mistress in spite both of her nature and her will. My tears had risen, just as in childhood: I ordered them back to their source. I brought a chair to the bed-head: I sat down and leaned over the pillow.

'You sent for me,' I said, 'and I am here; and it is my intention to stay till I see how you get on.'

'Oh, of course! You have seen my daughters?'

'Yes.'

'Well, you may tell them I wish you to stay till I can talk some things over with you I have on my mind: to-night it is too late, and I have a difficulty in recalling them. But there was something I wished to say— let me see——'

The wandering look and changed utterance told what wreck had taken place in her once-vigorous frame. Turning restlessly, she drew the bed-clothes round her; my elbow, resting on a corner of the quilt, fixed it down: she was at once irritated.

'Sit up!' said she; 'don't annoy me with holding the clothes fast—are you Jane Eyre?'

'I am Jane Eyre.'

'I have had more trouble with that child than any one would believe. Such a burden to be left on my hands—and so much annoyance as she caused me, daily and hourly, with her incomprehensible disposition, and her sudden starts of temper, and her continual, unnatural watchings of one's movements! I declare she talked to me once like something mad, or like a fiend—no child ever spoke or looked as she did; I was glad to get her away from the house. What did they do with her at Lowood? The fever broke out there, and many of the pupils died. She, however, did not die: but I said she did—I wish she had died!'

'A strange wish, Mrs. Reed: why do you hate her so?'

'I had a dislike to her mother always; for she was my husband's only sister, and a great favourite with him: he opposed the family's disowning her when she made her low marriage; and when news came of her death, he wept like a simpleton. He would send for the baby; though I entreated him rather to put it out to nurse and pay for its maintenance. I hated it the first time I set my eyes on it—a sickly, whining, pining thing! It would wail in its cradle all night long—not screaming heartily like any other child, but whimpering and moaning. Reed pitied it; and he used to nurse it and notice it as if it had been his own: more, indeed, than he ever noticed his own at that age. He would try to make my children friendly to the little beggar: the darlings could not bear it, and he was angry with them when they showed their dislike. In his last ill-ness, he had it brought continually to his bedside; and but an hour be-fore he died, he bound me by vow to keep the creature. I would as soon have been charged with a pauper brat out of a workhouse: but he was weak, naturally weak. John does not at all resemble his father, and I am glad of it: John is like me and like my brothers—he is quite a Gibson. Oh, I wish he would cease tormenting me with letters for money! I have no more money to give him: we are getting poor. I must send away half the servants and shut up part of the house; or let it off. I can never submit to do that—yet how are we to get on? Two-thirds of my income goes in paying the interest of mortgages. John gambles dread-

fully, and always loses—poor boy! He is beset by sharpers: John is sunk
and degraded—his look is frightful—I feel ashamed for him when I see
him.'

She was getting much excited. 'I think I had better leave her now,'
said I to Bessie, who stood on the other side of the bed.

'Perhaps you had, miss: but she often talks in this way towards night
—in the morning she is calmer.'

I rose. 'Stop!' exclaimed Mrs. Reed. 'There is another thing I wished
to say. He threatens me—he continually threatens me with his own
death, or mine: and I dream sometimes that I see him laid out with a
great wound in his throat, or with a swollen and blackened face. I am
come to a strange pass: I have heavy troubles. What is to be done? How
is the money to be had?'

Bessie now endeavoured to persuade her to take a sedative draught:
she succeeded with difficulty. Soon after, Mrs. Reed grew more composed, and sank into a dozing state. I then left her.

More than ten days elapsed before I had again any conversation with
her. She continued either delirious or lethargic; and the doctor forbade
every thing which could painfully excite her. Meantime, I got on as
well as I could with Georgiana and Eliza. They were very cold, indeed,
at first. Eliza would sit half the day sewing, reading, or writing, and
scarcely utter a word either to me or her sister. Georgiana would chatter
nonsense to her canary bird by the hour, and take no notice of me. But I
was determined not to seem at a loss for occupation or amusement: I
had brought my drawing materials with me, and they served me for
both.

Provided with a case of pencils, and some sheets of paper, I used to
take a seat apart from them, near the window, and busy myself in
sketching fancy vignettes, representing any scene that happened momentarily to shape itself in the ever-shifting kaleidoscope of imagination: a glimpse of sea between two rocks; the rising moon, and a ship
crossing its disk; a group of reeds and water-flags, and a naiad's head
crowned with lotus-flowers, rising out of them; an elf sitting in a
hedge-sparrow's nest, under a wreath of hawthorn-bloom.

One morning I fell to sketching a face: what sort of a face it was to be,
I did not care or know. I took a soft black pencil, gave it a broad point,
and worked away. Soon I had traced on the paper a broad and prominent forehead, and a square lower outline of visage: that contour gave
me pleasure; my fingers proceeded actively to fill it with features.
Strongly-marked horizontal eyebrows must be traced under that brow;
then followed, naturally, a well-defined nose, with a straight ridge and
full nostrils; then a flexible-looking mouth, by no means narrow; then a
firm chin with a decided cleft down the middle of it: of course, some

black whiskers were wanted, and some jetty hair, tufted on the temples, and waved above the forehead. Now for the eyes: I had left them to the last, because they required the most careful working. I drew them large; I shaped them well: the eyelashes I traced long and sombre; the irids lustrous and large. 'Good! but not quite the thing,' I thought, as I surveyed the effect: 'They want more force and spirit;' and I wrought the shades blacker, that the lights might flash more brilliantly—a happy touch or two secured success. There, I had a friend's face under my gaze; and what did it signify that those young ladies turned their backs on me? I looked at it; I smiled at the speaking likeness: I was absorbed and content.

'Is that a portrait of some one you know?' asked Eliza, who had approached me unnoticed. I responded that it was merely a fancy head, and hurried it beneath the other sheets. Of course, I lied: it was, in fact, a very faithful representation of Mr. Rochester. But what was that to her, or to any one but myself? Georgiana also advanced to look. The other drawings pleased her much, but she called that 'an ugly man.' They both seemed surprised at my skill. I offered to sketch their portraits; and each, in turn, sat for a pencil outline. Then Georgiana produced her album. I promised to contribute a water-colour drawing: this put her at once into good humour. She proposed a walk in the grounds. Before we had been out two hours, we were deep in a confidential conversation: she had favoured me with a description of the brilliant winter she had spent in London two seasons ago—of the admiration she had there excited—the attention she had received: and I even got hints of the titled conquest she had made. In the course of the afternoon and evening these hints were enlarged on: various soft conversations were reported, and sentimental scenes represented; and, in short, a volume of a novel of fashionable life was that day improvised by her for my benefit. The communications were renewed from day to day: they always ran on the same theme—herself, her loves, and woes. It was strange she never once adverted either to her mother's illness, or her brother's death, or the present gloomy state of the family prospects. Her mind seemed wholly taken up with reminiscences of past gaiety, and aspirations after dissipations to come. She passed about five minutes each day in her mother's sick-room and no more.

Eliza still spoke little: she had evidently no time to talk. I never saw a busier person than she seemed to be: yet it was difficult to say what she did: or rather, to discover any result of her diligence. She had an alarum to call her up early. I know not how she occupied herself before breakfast, but after that meal she divided her time into regular portions; and each hour had its allotted task. Three times a day she studied a little book, which I found, on inspection, was a Common Prayer-book. I asked her once what was the great attraction of that volume, and she said 'the Rubric.'[9] Three hours she gave to stitching, with gold thread, the border of a square crimson cloth, almost large enough for a carpet. In answer to my inquiries after the use of this article, she informed me it was a covering for the altar of a new church lately erected near Gateshead. Two hours she devoted to her diary; two to working by herself in the kitchen-garden; and one to the regulation of her accounts. She seemed to want no company; no conversation. I believe she was happy in her way: this routine sufficed to her; and nothing annoyed her so much as the occurrence of any incident which forced her to vary its clock-work regularity.

She told me one evening, when more disposed to be communicative than usual, that John's conduct, and the threatened ruin of the family, had been a source of profound affliction to her: but she had now, she said, settled her mind, and formed her resolution. Her own fortune she had taken care to secure; and when her mother died,—and it was wholly improbable, she tranquilly remarked, that she should either re- cover or linger long,—she would execute a long-cherished project: seek a retirement where punctual habits would be permanently secured from disturbance, and place safe barriers between herself and a frivo- lous world. I asked if Georgiana would accompany her.

'Of course not. Georgiana and she had nothing in common: they never had had. She would not be burdened with her society for any consideration. Georgiana should take her own course; and she, Eliza, would take hers.'

Georgiana, when not unburdening her heart to me, spent most of her time in lying on the sofa, fretting about the dulness of the house, and wishing over and over again that her aunt Gibson would send her an invitation up to town. 'It would be so much better,' she said, 'if she could only get out of the way for a month or two, till all was over.' I did not ask what she meant by 'all being over,' but I suppose she referred to the expected decease of her mother and the gloomy sequel of funeral rites. Eliza generally took no more notice of her sister's indolence and complaints than if no such murmuring, lounging object had been be- fore her. One day, however, as she put away her account book, and unfolded her embroidery, she suddenly took her up thus:—'Georgiana, a more vain and absurd animal than you, was certainly never allowed to cumber the earth. You had no right to be born: for you make no use of life. Instead of living for, in, and with yourself, as a reasonable being ought, you seek only to fasten your feebleness on some other person's strength: if no one can be found willing to burden her or himself with such a fat, weak, puffy, useless thing, you cry out that you are ill-treated,

9. The section stating the rules for services.

neglected, miserable. Then, too, existence for you must be a scene of
continual change and excitement, or else the world is a dungeon: you
must be admired, you must be courted, you must be flattered—you
must have music, dancing, and society—or you languish, you die away.
Have you no sense to devise a system which will make you independent
of all efforts, and all wills, but your own? Take one day; share it into
sections; to each section apportion its task: leave no stray unemployed
quarters of an hour, ten minutes, five minutes, include all; do each
piece of business in its turn with method, with rigid regularity. The day
will close almost before you are aware it has begun; and you are indebted to no one for helping you to get rid of one vacant moment; you
have had to seek no one's company, conversation, sympathy, forbearance: you have lived, in short, as an independent being ought to do.
Take this advice: the first and last I shall offer you; then you will not
want me or anyone else, happen what may. Neglect it—go on as heretofore, craving, whining, and idling—and suffer the results of your idiocy, however bad and insufferable they may be. I tell you this plainly;
and listen: for though I shall no more repeat what I am now about to
say, I shall steadily act on it. After my mother's death, I wash my hands
of you: from the day her coffin is carried to the vault in Gateshead
Church, you and I will be as separate as if we had never known each
other. You need not think that because we chanced to be born of the
same parents, I shall suffer you to fasten me down by even the feeblest
claim; I can tell you this—if the whole human race, ourselves excepted,
were swept away, and we two stood alone on the earth, I would leave
you in the old world, and betake myself to the new.'

She closed her lips.

'You might have spared yourself the trouble of delivering that tirade,'
answered Georgiana. 'Everybody knows you are the most selfish, heartless creature in existence: and I know your spiteful hatred towards me; I
have had a specimen of it before in the trick you played me about Lord
Edwin Vere: you could not bear me to be raised above you, to have a
title, to be received into circles where you dare not show your face, and
so you acted the spy and informer, and ruined my prospects for ever.'
Georgiana took out her handkerchief and blew her nose for an hour afterwards; Eliza sat cold, impassible, and assiduously industrious.

True, generous feeling is made small account of by some: but here
were two natures rendered, the one intolerably acrid, the other despi-
cably savourless for the want of it. Feeling without judgment is a washy
draught indeed; but judgment untempered by feeling is too bitter and
husky a morsel for human deglutition.

It was a wet and windy afternoon: Georgiana had fallen asleep on the
sofa over the perusal of a novel; Eliza was gone to attend a saint's-day
service at the new church—for in matters of religion she was a rigid

formalist: no weather ever prevented the punctual discharge of what she considered her devotional duties: fair or foul, she went to church thrice every Sunday, and as often on week-days as there were prayers.

I bethought myself to go upstairs and see how the dying woman sped, who lay there almost unheeded: the very servants paid her but a remittent attention: the hired nurse, being little looked after, would slip out of the room whenever she could. Bessie was faithful; but she had her own family to mind, and could only come occasionally to the hall. I found the sick-room unwatched, as I had expected: no nurse was there; the patient lay still, and seemingly lethargic; her livid face sunk in the pillows: the fire was dying in the grate. I renewed the fuel, re-arranged the bedclothes, gazed awhile on her who could not now gaze on me, and then I moved away to the window.

The rain beat strongly against the panes, the wind blew tempestuously: 'One lies there,' I thought, 'who will soon be beyond the war of earthly elements. Whither will that spirit—now struggling to quit its material tenement—flit when at length released?'

In pondering the great mystery, I thought of Helen Burns, recalled her dying words—her faith—her doctrine of equality of disembodied souls. I was still listening in thought to her well-remembered tones—still picturing her pale and spiritual aspect, her wasted face and sublime gaze, as she lay on her placid deathbed, and whispered her longing to be restored to her divine Father's bosom—when a feeble voice murmured from the couch behind: 'Who is that?'

I knew Mrs. Reed had not spoken for days: was she reviving? I went up to her.

'It is I, aunt Reed.'

'Who—I?' was her answer. 'Who are you?' looking at me with surprise and a sort of alarm, but still not wildly. 'You are quite a stranger to me—where is Bessie?'

'She is at the lodge, aunt.'

'Aunt!' she repeated. 'Who calls me aunt? You are not one of the Gibsons; and yet I know you—that face, and the eyes and forehead are quite familiar to me: you are like—why you are like Jane Eyre!'

I said nothing: I was afraid of occasioning some shock by declaring my identity.

'Yet,' said she, 'I am afraid it is a mistake: my thoughts deceive me. I wished to see Jane Eyre, and I fancy a likeness where none exists: besides, in eight years she must be so changed.'

I now gently assured her that I was the person she supposed and desired me to be: and seeing that I was understood, and that her senses were quite collected, I explained how Bessie had sent her husband to fetch me from Thornfield.

'I am very ill, I know,' she said ere long. 'I was trying to turn myself a few minutes since, and find I cannot move a limb. It is as well I should ease my mind before I die: what we think little of in health, burdens us at such an hour as the present is to me. Is the nurse here? or is there no one in the room but you?'

I assured her we were alone.

'Well, I have twice done you a wrong which I regret now. One was in breaking the promise which I gave my husband to bring you up as my own child; the other—' she stopped. 'After all it is of no great importance, perhaps,' she murmured to herself: 'and then I may get better; and to humble myself so to her is painful.'

She made an effort to alter her position, but failed: her face changed; she seemed to experience some inward sensation—the precursor, perhaps, of the last pang.

'Well: I must get it over. Eternity is before me: I had better tell her. —Go to my dressing-case, open it, and take out a letter you will see there.'

I obeyed her directions.

'Read the letter,' she said.

It was short and thus conceived:

'Madam,—

'Will you have the goodness to send me the address of my niece, Jane Eyre, and to tell me how she is: it is my intention to write shortly and desire her to come to me at Madeira. Providence has blessed my endeavours to secure a competency; and as I am unmarried and child-less, I wish to adopt her during my life, and bequeath her at my death whatever I may have to leave.

'I am, Madam, &c. &c.
'John Eyre, Madeira.'

It was dated three years back.

'Why did I never hear of this?' I asked.

'Because I disliked you too fixedly and thoroughly ever to lend a hand in lifting you to prosperity. I could not forget your conduct to me, Jane—the fury with which you once turned on me; the tone in which you declared you abhorred me the worst of anybody in the world; the unchildlike look and voice with which you affirmed that the very thought of me made you sick, and asserted that I had treated you with miserable cruelty. I could not forget my own sensations when you thus started up and poured out the venom of your mind: I felt fear, as if an animal that I had struck or pushed had looked up at me with human eyes and cursed me in a man's voice.—Bring me some water! Oh, make haste!'

'Dear Mrs. Reed,' said I, as I offered her the draught she required, 'think no more of all this, let it pass away from your mind. Forgive me for my passionate language: I was a child then; eight, nine years have passed since that day.'

She heeded nothing of what I said; but when she had tasted the water and drawn breath, she went on thus:—'I tell you I could not forget it; and I took my revenge: for you to be adopted by your uncle, and placed in a state of ease and comfort, was what I could not endure. I wrote to him; I said I was sorry for his disappointment, but Jane Eyre was dead: she had died of typhus fever at Lowood. Now act as you please: write and contradict my assertion—expose my falsehood as soon as you like. You were born, I think, to be my torment: my last hour is racked by the recollection of a deed which, but for you, I should never have been tempted to commit.'

'If you could but be persuaded to think no more of it, aunt, and to regard me with kindness and forgiveness'——

'You have a very bad disposition,' said she, 'and one to this day I feel it impossible to understand: how for nine years you could be patient and quiescent under any treatment, and in the tenth break out all fire and violence, I can never comprehend.'

'My disposition is not so bad as you think: I am passionate, but not vindictive. Many a time, as a little child, I should have been glad to love you if you would have let me; and I long earnestly to be reconciled to you now: kiss me, aunt.'

I approached my cheek to her lips: she would not touch it. She said I oppressed her by leaning over the bed; and again demanded water. As I laid her down—for I raised her and supported her on my arm while she drank—I covered her ice-cold and clammy hand with mine: the feeble fingers shrank from my touch—the glazing eyes shunned my gaze.

'Love me, then, or hate me, as you will,' I said at last; 'you have my full and free forgiveness: ask now for God's; and be at peace.'

Poor, suffering woman! it was too late for her to make now the effort to change her habitual frame of mind: living, she had ever hated me—dying, she must hate me still.

The nurse now entered, and Bessie followed. I yet lingered half an hour longer, hoping to see some sign of amity: but she gave none. She was fast relapsing into stupor; nor did her mind again rally: at twelve o'clock that night she died. I was not present to close her eyes; nor were either of her daughters. They came to tell us the next morning that all was over. She was by that time laid out. Eliza and I went to look at her: Georgiana, who had burst out into loud weeping, said she dared not go. There was stretched Sarah Reed's once robust and active frame, rigid and still: her eye of flint was covered with its cold lid; her brow and strong traits wore yet the impress of her inexorable soul. A strange and solemn object was that corpse to me. I gazed on it with gloom and pain: nothing soft, nothing sweet, nothing pitying, or hopeful, or subduing, did it inspire; only a grating anguish for *her* woes—not *my* loss—and a sombre tearless dismay at the fearfulness of death in such a form.

Eliza surveyed her parent calmly. After a silence of some minutes she observed, 'With her constitution she should have lived to a good old age: her life was shortened by trouble.' And then a spasm constricted her mouth for an instant: as it passed away she turned and left the room, and so did I. Neither of us had dropped a tear.

Chapter XXII

Mr. Rochester had given me but one week's leave of absence: yet a month elapsed before I quitted Gateshead. I wished to leave immediately after the funeral; but Georgiana entreated me to stay till she could get off to London: whither she was now at last invited by her uncle, Mr. Gibson; who had come down to direct his sister's interment and settle the family affairs. Georgiana said she dreaded being left alone with Eliza; from her she got neither sympathy in her dejection, support in her fears, nor aid in her preparations; so I bore with her feeble-minded quailings, and selfish lamentations, as well as I could, and did my best in sewing for her, and packing her dresses. It is true that while I worked she would idle; and I thought to myself, 'If you and I were destined to live always together, cousin, we would commence matters on a different footing. I should not settle tamely down into being the forbearing party; I should assign you your share of labour, and compel you to accomplish it, or else it should be left undone: I should insist, also, on your keeping some of those drawling, half-insincere complaints hushed in your own breast. It is only because our connection happens to be very transitory, and comes at a peculiarly mournful season, that I consent thus to render it so patient and compliant on my part.'

At last I saw Georgiana off; but now it was Eliza's turn to request me to stay another week. Her plans required all her time and attention, she said: she was about to depart for some unknown bourne; and all day long she stayed in her own room, her door bolted within, filling trunks, emptying drawers, burning papers, and holding no communication with anyone. She wished me to look after the house, to see callers, and answers notes of condolence.

One morning she told me I was at liberty. 'And,' she added, 'I am obliged to you for your valuable services and discreet conduct! There is some difference between living with such a one as you, and with Georgiana: you perform you own part in life, and burden no one. To-morrow,' she continued, 'I set out for the Continent. I shall take up my abode in a religious house near Lisle—a nunnery you would call it: there I shall be quiet and unmolested. I shall devote myself for a time to the examination of the Roman Catholic dogmas, and to a careful study of the workings of their system; if I find it to be, as I half suspect it is, the one best calculated to ensure the doing of all things decently and in order, I shall embrace the tenets of Rome and probably take the veil.'

I neither expressed surprise at this resolution nor attempted to dissuade her from it. 'The vocation will fit you to a hair,' I thought: 'much good may it do you!'

When we parted, she said: 'Good-bye, cousin Jane Eyre; I wish you well: you have some sense.'

I then returned: 'You are not without sense, cousin Eliza; but what you have I suppose in another year will be walled up alive in a French convent. However, it is not my business, and so it suits you—I don't much care.'

'You are in the right,' said she: and with these words we each went our separate way. As I shall not have occasion to refer either to her or her sister again, I may as well mention here that Georgiana made an advantageous match with a wealthy worn-out man of fashion; and that Eliza actually took the veil, and is at this day superior of the convent where she passed the period of her novitiate: and which she endowed with her fortune.

How people feel when they are returning home from an absence, long or short, I did not know: I had never experienced the sensation. I had known what it was to come back to Gateshead when a child, after a long walk—to be scolded for looking cold or gloomy; and later, what it was to come back from church to Lowood—to long for a plenteous meal and a good fire, and to be unable to get either. Neither of these returnings were very pleasant or desirable: no magnet drew me to a given point, increasing in its strength of attraction the nearer I came. The return to Thornfield was yet to be tried.

My journey seemed tedious—very tedious: fifty miles one day, a night spent at an inn; fifty miles the next day. During the first twelve hours I thought of Mrs. Reed in her last moments: I saw her disfigured and discoloured face, and heard her strangely altered voice. I mused on the funeral day, the coffin, the hearse, the black train of tenants and servants—few was the number of relatives—the gaping vault, the silent church, the solemn service. Then I thought of Eliza and Georgiana: I beheld one the cynosure of a ball-room, the other the inmate of a convent cell; and I dwelt on and analysed their separate peculiarities of person and character. The evening arrival at the great town of ——— scattered these thoughts; night gave them quite another turn: laid down on my traveller's bed, I left reminiscence for anticipation.

I was going back to Thornfield: but how long was I to stay there? Not long; of that I was sure. I had heard from Mrs. Fairfax in the interim of my absence: the party at the hall was dispersed; Mr. Rochester had left for London three weeks ago, but he was then expected to return in a fortnight. Mrs. Fairfax surmised that he was gone to make arrangements for his wedding, as he had talked of purchasing a new carriage: she said the idea of his marrying Miss Ingram still seemed strange to her; but from what everybody said, and from what she had herself seen, she could no longer doubt that the event would shortly take place. 'You would be strangely incredulous if you did doubt it,' was my mental comment. 'I don't doubt it.'

The question followed, 'Where was I to go?' I dreamt of Miss Ingram all the night: in a vivid morning dream I saw her closing the gates of Thornfield against me and pointing me out another road; and Mr. Rochester looked on with his arms folded—smiling sardonically, as it seemed, at both her and me.

I had not notified to Mrs. Fairfax the exact day of my return; for I did not wish either car or carriage to meet me at Millcote. I proposed to walk the distance quietly by myself; and very quietly, after leaving my box in the ostler's care, did I slip away from the George Inn, about six o'clock of a June evening, and take the old road to Thornfield: a road which lay chiefly through fields, and was now little frequented.

It was not a bright or splendid summer evening, though fair and soft: the haymakers were at work all along the road; and the sky, though far from cloudless, was such as promised well for the future: its blue—where blue was visible—was mild and settled, and its cloud strata high and thin. The west, too, was warm: no watery gleam chilled it—it seemed as if there was a fire lit, an altar burning behind its screen of marbled vapour, and out of apertures shone a golden redness.

I felt glad as the road shortened before me: so glad that I stopped once to ask myself what that joy meant: and to remind reason that it was not to my home I was going, or to a permanent resting-place, or to a place where fond friends looked out for me and waited my arrival. 'Mrs. Fairfax will smile you a calm welcome, to be sure,' said I; 'and little Adèle will clap her hands and jump to see you; but you know very well you are thinking of another than they; and that he is not thinking of you.'

But what is so headstrong as youth? What so blind as inexperience? These affirmed that it was pleasure enough to have the privilege of again looking on Mr. Rochester, whether he looked on me or not; and they added—'Hasten! hasten! be with him while you may: but a few more days or weeks, at most, and you are parted with him for ever!' And then I strangled a new-born agony—a deformed thing which I could not persuade myself to own and rear—and ran on.

They are making hay, too, in Thornfield meadows: or, rather, the labourers are just quitting their work, and returning home with their rakes on their shoulders: now, at the hour I arrive. I have but a field or two to traverse, and then I shall cross the road and reach the gates. How full the hedges are of roses! But I have no time to gather any; I want to be at the house. I passed a tall briar, shooting leafy and flowery branches across the path; I see the narrow stile with stone steps; and I see—Mr. Rochester sitting there, a book and a pencil in his hand: he is writing.

Well, he is not a ghost; yet every nerve I have is unstrung: for a mo-

ment I am beyond my own mastery. What does it mean? I did not think
I should tremble in this way when I saw him—or lose my voice or the
power of motion in his presence. I will go back as soon as I can stir: I
need not make an absolute fool of myself. I know another way to the
house. It does not signify if I knew twenty ways; for he has seen me.

'Hallo!' he cries; and he puts up his book and his pencil. 'There you
are! Come on, if you please.'

I suppose I do come on; though in what fashion I know not: being
scarcely cognisant of my movements, and solicitous only to appear
calm; and, above all, to control the working muscles of my face—which
I feel rebel insolently against my will, and struggle to express what I had
resolved to conceal. But I have a veil—it is down: I may make shift yet
to behave with decent composure.

'And this is Jane Eyre? Are you coming from Millcote, and on foot?
Yes—just one of your tricks: not to send for a carriage, and come clattering over the street and road like a common mortal, but to steal into
the vicinage of your home along with twilight, just as if you were a
dream or a shade. What the deuce have you done with yourself this last
month?'

'I have been with my aunt, sir, who is dead.'

'A true Janian reply! Good angels be my guard! She comes from the
other world—from the abode of people who are dead; and tells me so
when she meets me alone here in the gloaming! If I dared, I'd touch
you, to see if you are substance or shadow, you elf!—but I'd as soon
offer to take hold of a blue *ignis fatuus* light in a marsh. Truant! truant!'
he added, when he had paused an instant. 'Absent from me a whole
month: and forgetting me quite, I'll be sworn!'

I knew there would be pleasure in meeting my master again; even
though broken by the fear that he was so soon to cease to be my master,
and by the knowledge that I was nothing to him: but there was ever in
Mr. Rochester (so at least I thought) such a wealth of the power of communicating happiness, that to taste but of the crumbs he scattered to
stray and stranger birds like me was to feast genially. His last words were
balm: they seemed to imply that it imported something to him whether
I forgot him or not. And he had spoken of Thornfield as my home—
would that it were my home!

He did not leave the stile, and I hardly liked to ask to go by. I inquired
soon if he had not been to London.

'Yes: I suppose you found that out by second-sight.'

'Mrs. Fairfax told me in a letter.'

'And did she inform you what I went to do?'

'Oh, yes, sir! Everybody knew your errand.'

'You must see the carriage, Jane, and tell me if you don't think it will
suit Mrs. Rochester exactly; and whether she won't look like Queen

Boadicea,[1] leaning back against those purple cushions. I wish, Jane, I were a trifle better adapted to match with her externally. Tell me now, fairy as you are,—can't you give me a charm, or a philter, or something of that sort, to make me a handsome man?'

'It would be past the power of magic, sir;' and, in thought, I added, 'A loving eye is all the charm needed: to such you are handsome enough; or rather, your sternness has a power beyond beauty.'

Mr. Rochester had sometimes read my unspoken thoughts with an acumen to me incomprehensible: in the present instance he took no notice of my abrupt vocal response; but he smiled at me with a certain smile he had of his own, and which he used but on rare occasions. He seemed to think it too good for common purposes: it was the real sunshine of feeling—he shed it over me now.

'Pass, Janet,' said he, making room for me to cross the stile: 'go up home, and stay your weary little wandering feet at a friend's threshold.'

All I had now to do was to obey him in silence: no need for me to colloquise further. I got over the stile without a word, and meant to leave him calmly. An impulse held me fast,—a force turned me round. I said—or something in me said for me, and in spite of me:—

'Thank you, Mr. Rochester, for your great kindness. I am strangely glad to get back again to you; and wherever you are is my home—my only home.'

I walked on so fast that even he could hardly have overtaken me had he tried. Little Adèle was half wild with delight when she saw me. Mrs. Fairfax received me with her usual plain friendliness. Leah smiled; and even Sophie bid me 'bon soir'[2] with glee. This was very pleasant: there is no happiness like that of being loved by your fellow creatures, and feeling that your presence is an addition to their comfort.

I, that evening, shut my eyes resolutely against the future: I stopped my ears against the voice that kept warning me of near separation and coming grief. When tea was over and Mrs. Fairfax had taken her knitting, and I had assumed a low seat near her, and Adèle, kneeling on the carpet, had nestled close up to me, and a sense of mutual affection seemed to surround us with a ring of golden peace, I uttered a silent prayer that we might not be parted far or soon; but when, as we thus sat, Mr. Rochester entered, unannounced, and looking at us, seemed to take pleasure in the spectacle of a group so amicable—when he said he supposed the old lady was all right now that she had got her adopted daughter back again, and added that he saw Adèle was 'prête à croquer sa petite maman Anglaise'[3]—I half ventured to hope that he would, even after his marriage, keep us together somewhere under the shelter

1. Early British queen, who led a revolt against   2. Good evening.
the Romans.   3. "Ready to devour her little English mother."

of his protection, and not quite exiled from the sunshine of his presence.

A fortnight of dubious calm succeeded my return to Thornfield Hall. Nothing was said of the master's marriage, and I saw no preparation going on for such an event. Almost every day I asked Mrs. Fairfax if she had yet heard anything decided: her answer was always in the negative. Once, she said, she had actually put the question to Mr. Rochester as to when he was going to bring his bride home; but he had answered her only by a joke, and one of his queer looks, and she could not tell what to make of him.

One thing specially surprised me, and that was, there were no journeyings backward and forward, no visits to Ingram Park: to be sure it was twenty miles off, on the borders of another county; but what was that distance to an ardent lover? To so practised and indefatigable a horseman as Mr. Rochester it would be but a morning's ride. I began to cherish hopes I had no right to conceive: that the match was broken off; that rumour had been mistaken; that one or both parties had changed their minds. I used to look at my master's face to see if it were sad or fierce; but I could not remember the time when it had been so uniformly clear of clouds or evil feelings. If, in the moments I and my pupil spent with him, I lacked spirits and sank into inevitable dejection, he became even gay. Never had he called me more frequently to his presence; never been kinder to me when there—and, alas! never had I loved him so well.

Chapter XXIII

A splendid Midsummer shone over England: skies so pure, suns so radiant as were then seen in long succession, seldom favour, even singly, our wave-girt land. It was as if a band of Italian days had come from the South, like a flock of glorious passenger birds, and lighted to rest them on the cliffs of Albion. The hay was all got in; the fields round Thornfield were green and shorn; the roads white and baked; the trees were in their dark prime; hedge and wood, full-leaved and deeply tinted, contrasted well with the sunny hue of the cleared meadows between.

On Midsummer-eve, Adèle, weary with gathering wild strawberries in Hay Lane half the day, had gone to bed with the sun. I watched her drop asleep, and when I left her I sought the garden.

It was now the sweetest hour of the twenty-four:—'Day its fervid fires had wasted,'[4] and dew fell cool on panting plain and scorched summit. Where the sun had gone down in simple state—pure of the

---

4. From Thomas Campbell's *The Turkish Lady*.

pomp of clouds—spread a solemn purple, burning with the light of red jewel and furnace flame at one point, on one hill-peak, and extending high and wide, soft and still softer, over half heaven. The east had its own charm of fine, deep blue, and its own modest gem, a rising and solitary star: soon it would boast the moon; but she was yet beneath the horizon.

I walked a while on the pavement; but a subtle, well-known scent—that of a cigar—stole from some window; I saw the library casement open a handbreath; I knew I might be watched thence; so I went apart into the orchard. No nook in the grounds more sheltered and more Eden-like; it was full of trees, it bloomed with flowers: a very high wall shut it out from the court, on one side; on the other, a beech avenue screened it from the lawn. At the bottom was a sunk fence; its sole separation from lonely fields; a winding walk, bordered with laurels and terminating in a giant horse-chestnut, circled at the base by a seat, led down to the fence. Here one could wander unseen. While such honey-dew fell, such silence reigned, such gloaming gathered, I felt as if I could haunt such shade for ever: but in threading the flower and fruit parterres at the upper part of the inclosure, enticed there by the light the now-rising moon casts on this more open quarter, my step is stayed—not by sound, not by sight, but once more by a warning fragrance.

Sweet briar and southernwood, jasmine, pink, and rose, have long been yielding their evening sacrifice of incense: this new scent is neither of shrub nor flower; it is—I know it well—it is Mr. Rochester's cigar. I look round, and I listen. I see trees laden with ripening fruit. I hear a nightingale warbling in a wood half a mile off; no moving form is visible, no coming step audible; but that perfume increases: I must flee. I make for the wicket leading to the shrubbery, and I see Mr. Rochester entering. I step aside into the ivy recess; he will not stay long: he will soon return whence he came, and if I sit still he will never see me.

But no—eventide is as pleasant to him as to me, and this antique garden as attractive; and he strolls on, now lifting the gooseberry tree branches to look at the fruit, large as plums, with which they are laden; now taking a ripe cherry from the wall; now stooping towards a knot of flowers, either to inhale their fragrance or to admire the dew-beads on their petals. A great moth goes humming by me; it alights on a plant at Mr. Rochester's foot: he sees it, and bends to examine it.

'Now he has his back towards me,' thought I, 'and he is occupied too; perhaps, if I walk softly, I can slip away unnoticed.'

I trod on an edging of turf that the crackle of the pebbly gravel might not betray me: he was standing among the beds at a yard or two distant from where I had to pass; the moth apparently engaged him. 'I shall get by very well,' I meditated. As I crossed his shadow, thrown long over the garden by the moon, not yet risen high, he said quietly without turning:—'Jane, come and look at this fellow.'

I had made no noise: he had not eyes behind—could his shadow feel? I started at first, and then I approached him.

'Look at his wings,' said he; 'he reminds me rather of a West Indian insect; one does not often see so large and gay a night-rover in England: there! he is flown.'

The moth roamed away. I was sheepishly retreating also; but Mr. Rochester followed me, and when we reached the wicket, he said:— 'Turn back: on so lovely a night it is a shame to sit in the house; and surely no one can wish to go to bed while sunset is thus at meeting with moonrise.'

It is one of my faults that, though my tongue is sometimes prompt enough at an answer, there are times when it sadly fails me in framing an excuse; and always the lapse occurs at some crisis, when a facile word or plausible pretext is specially wanted to get me out of painful embarrassment. I did not like to walk at this hour alone with Mr. Rochester in the shadowy orchard; but I could not find a reason to allege for leaving him. I followed with lagging step, and thoughts busily bent on discovering a means of extrication; but he himself looked so composed, and so grave also, I became ashamed of feeling any confusion: the evil—if evil existent or prospective there was—seemed to lie with me only; his mind was unconscious and quiet.

'Jane,' he recommenced, as we entered the laurel walk, and slowly strayed down in the direction of the sunk fence and the horse-chestnut, 'Thornfield is a pleasant place in summer, is it not?'

'Yes, sir.'

'You must have become in some degree attached to the house,— you, who have an eye for natural beauties, and a good deal of the organ of Adhesiveness?'

'I am attached to it, indeed.'

'And though I don't comprehend how it is, I perceive you have acquired a degree of regard for that foolish little child, Adèle, too; and even for simple dame Fairfax?'

'Yes, sir; in different ways, I have an affection for both.'

'And would be sorry to part with them?'

'Yes.'

'Pity!' he said, and sighed and paused. 'It is always the way of events in this life,' he continued presently: 'no sooner have you got settled in a pleasant resting-place, than a voice calls out to you to rise and move on, for the hour of repose is expired.'

'Must I move on, sir?' I asked. 'Must I leave Thornfield?'

'I believe you must, Jane. I am sorry, Janet, but I believe indeed you must.'

This was a blow: but I did not let it prostrate me.

'Well, sir, I shall be ready when the order to march comes.'

'It is come now—I must give it to-night.'

'Then you are going to be married, sir?'

'Ex-act-ly—pre-cise-ly: with your usual acuteness, you have hit the nail straight on the head.'

'Soon, sir?'

'Very soon, my——that is, Miss Eyre: and you'll remember, Jane, the first time I, or Rumour, plainly intimated to you that it was my intention to put my old bachelor's neck into the sacred noose, to enter into the holy estate of matrimony—to take Miss Ingram to my bosom, in short (she's an extensive armful: but that's not to the point—one can't have too much of such a very excellent thing as my beautiful Blanche): well, as I was saying—listen to me, Jane! You're not turning your head to look after more moths, are you? That was only a lady-clock,[5] child, 'flying away home.' I wish to remind you that it was you who first said to me, with that discretion I respect in you—with that foresight, prudence, and humility which befit your responsible and dependent position—that in case I married Miss Ingram—both you and little Adèle had better trot forthwith. I pass over the sort of slur conveyed in this suggestion on the character of my beloved; indeed, when you are far away, Janet, I'll try to forget it: I shall notice only its wisdom; which is such that I have made it my law of action. Adèle must go to school; and you, Miss Eyre, must get a new situation.'

'Yes, sir, I will advertise immediately: and meantime, I suppose'——I was going to say, 'I suppose I may stay here till I find another shelter to betake myself to:' but I stopped, feeling it would not do to risk a long sentence, for my voice was not quite under command.

'In about a month I hope to be a bridegroom,' continued Mr. Rochester; 'and in the interim I shall myself look out for employment and an asylum for you.'

'Thank you, sir; I am sorry to give——'

'Oh, no need to apologise! I consider that when a dependent does her duty as well as you have done yours, she has a sort of claim upon her employer for any little assistance he can conveniently render her; indeed I have already, through my future mother-in-law, heard of a place that I think will suit: it is to undertake the education of the five daughters of Mrs. Dionysius O'Gall, of Bitternutt Lodge, Connaught, Ireland. You'll like Ireland, I think: they're such warm-hearted people there, they say.'

'It is a long way off, sir.'

5. Ladybug.

'No matter—a girl of your sense will not object to the voyage or the distance.'

'Not the voyage, but the distance: and then the sea is a bar-rier——'

'From what, Jane?'

'From England and from Thornfield: and——'

'Well?'

'From *you*, sir.'

I said this almost involuntarily; and, with as little sanction of free will, my tears gushed out. I did not cry so as to be heard, however; I avoided sobbing. The thought of Mrs. O'Gall and Bitternutt Lodge struck cold to my heart; and colder the thought of all the brine and foam, destined, as it seemed, to rush between me and the master at whose side I now walked! and coldest the remembrance of the wider ocean—wealth, caste, custom intervened between me and what I naturally and inevitably loved.

'It is a long way,' I again said.

'It is to be sure; and when you get to Bitternutt Lodge, Connaught, Ireland, I shall never see you again, Jane: that's morally certain. I never go over to Ireland, not having myself much of a fancy for the country. We have been good friends, Jane; have we not?'

'Yes, sir.'

'And when friends are on the eve of separation, they like to spend the little time that remains to them close to each other. Come—we'll talk over the voyage and the parting quietly, half an hour or so, while the stars enter into their shining life up in heaven yonder: here is the chest-nut tree: here is the bench at its old roots. Come, we will sit there in peace to-night, though we should never more be destined to sit there together.' He seated me and himself.

'It is a long way to Ireland, Janet, and I am sorry to send my little friend on such weary travels; but if I can't do better, how is it to be helped? Are you anything akin to me, do you think, Jane?'

I could risk no sort of answer by this time: my heart was full.

'Because,' he said, 'I sometimes have a queer feeling with regard to you—especially when you are near me, as now: it is as if I had a string somewhere under my left ribs, tightly and inextricably knotted to a sim-ilar string situated in the corresponding quarter of your little frame. And if that boisterous channel, and two hundred miles or so of land come broad between us, I am afraid that cord of communion will be snapt; and then I've a nervous notion I should take to bleeding inwardly. As for you—you'd forget me.'

'That I *never* should, sir: you know'——impossible to proceed.

'Jane, do you hear that nightingale singing in the wood? Listen!'

In listening, I sobbed convulsively; for I could repress what I endured no longer; I was obliged to yield, and I was shaken from head to foot with acute distress. When I did speak, it was only to express an impetuous wish that I had never been born, or never come to Thornfield.

'Because you are sorry to leave it?'

The vehemence of emotion, stirred by grief and love within me, was claiming mastery, and struggling for full sway; and asserting a right to predominate: to overcome, to live, rise, and reign at last; yes,—and to speak.

'I grieve to leave Thornfield: I love Thornfield—I love it, because I have lived in it a full and delightful life,—momentarily at least. I have not been trampled on. I have not been petrified. I have not been buried with inferior minds, and excluded from every glimpse of communion with what is bright and energetic, and high. I have talked, face to face, with what I reverence; with what I delight in,—with an original, a vigorous, an expanded mind. I have known you, Mr. Rochester; and it strikes me with terror and anguish to feel I absolutely must be torn from you for ever. I see the necessity of departure; and it is like looking on the necessity of death.'

'Where do you see the necessity?' he asked, suddenly.

'Where? You, sir, have placed it before me.'

'In what shape?'

'In the shape of Miss Ingram; a noble and beautiful woman,—your bride.'

'My bride! What bride? I have no bride!'

'But you will have.'

'Yes;—I will!—I will!' He set his teeth.

'Then I must go—you have said it yourself.'

'No: you must stay! I swear it—and the oath shall be kept.'

'I tell you I must go!' I retorted, roused to something like passion. 'Do you think I can stay to become nothing to you? Do you think I am an automaton?—a machine without feelings? and can bear to have my morsel of bread snatched from my lips, and my drop of living water dashed from my cup? Do you think, because I am poor, obscure, plain, and little, I am soulless and heartless? You think wrong!—I have as much soul as you,—and full as much heart! And if God had gifted me with some beauty and much wealth, I should have made it as hard for you to leave me, as it is now for me to leave you. I am not talking to you now through the medium of custom, conventionalities, nor even of mortal flesh—it is my spirit that addresses your spirit; just as if both had passed through the grave, and we stood at God's feet, equal,—as we are!'

'As we are!' repeated Mr. Rochester—'so,' he added, enclosing me in his arms, gathering me to his breast, pressing his lips on my lips: 'so, Jane!'

'Yes, so, sir,' I rejoined: 'and yet not so; for you are a married man— or as good as a married man, and wed to one inferior to you—to one with whom you have no sympathy—whom I do not believe you truly love; for I have seen and heard you sneer at her. I would scorn such a union: therefore I am better than you—let me go!'

'Where, Jane? To Ireland?'

'Yes—to Ireland. I have spoken my mind, and can go anywhere now.'

'Jane, be still; don't struggle so, like a wild, frantic bird that is rending its own plumage in its desperation.'

'I am no bird; and no net ensnares me: I am a free human being with an independent will; which I now exert to leave you.'

Another effort set me at liberty, and I stood erect before him.

'And your will shall decide your destiny,' he said: 'I offer you my hand, my heart, and a share of all my possessions.'

'You play a farce, which I merely laugh at.'

'I ask you to pass through life at my side—to be my second self, and best earthly companion.'

'For that fate you have already made your choice, and must abide by it.'

'Jane, be still a few moments; you are over-excited: I will be still too.'

A waft of wind came sweeping down the laurel walk, and trembled through the boughs of the chestnut: it wandered away—away—to an indefinite distance—it died. The nightingale's song was then the only voice of the hour: in listening to it, I again wept. Mr. Rochester sat quiet, looking at me gently and seriously. Some time passed before he spoke; he at last said:—'Come to my side, Jane, and let us explain and understand one another.'

'I will never again come to your side: I am torn away now, and cannot return.'

'But, Jane, I summon you as my wife: it is you only I intend to marry.'

I was silent: I thought he mocked me.

'Come, Jane—come hither.'

'Your bride stands between us.'

He rose, and with a stride reached me.

'My bride is here,' he said, again drawing me to him, 'because my equal is here, and my likeness. Jane, will you marry me?'

Still I did not answer, and still I writhed myself from his grasp: for I was still incredulous.

'Do you doubt me, Jane?'

'Entirely.'

'You have no faith in me?'

'Not a whit.'

'Am I a liar in your eyes?' he asked passionately. 'Little sceptic, you *shall* be convinced. What love have I for Miss Ingram? None: and that you know. What love has she for me? None: as I have taken pains to prove; I caused a rumour to reach her that my fortune was not a third of what was supposed, and after that I presented myself to see the result; it was coldness both from her and her mother. I would not—I could not —marry Miss Ingram. You—you strange—you almost unearthly thing!—I love as my own flesh. You—poor and obscure, and small and plain as you are—I entreat to accept me as a husband.'

'What, me!' I ejaculated: beginning in his earnestness—and especially in his incivility—to credit his sincerity: 'me who have not a friend in the world but you—if you are my friend: not a shilling but what you have given me?'

'You, Jane. I must have you for my own—entirely my own. Will you be mine? Say yes, quickly.'

'Mr. Rochester, let me look at your face: turn to the moonlight.'

'Why?'

'Because I want to read your countenance; turn!'

'There: you will find it scarcely more legible than a crumpled, scratched page. Read on: only make haste, for I suffer.'

His face was very much agitated and very much flushed, and there were strong workings in the features, and strange gleams in the eyes.

'Oh, Jane, you torture me!' he exclaimed. 'With that searching and yet faithful and generous look, you torture me!'

'How can I do that? If you are true, and your offer real, my only feelings to you must be gratitude and devotion—they cannot torture.'

'Gratitude!' he ejaculated; and added wildly—'Jane, accept me quickly. Say, Edward—give me my name—Edward—I will marry you.'

'Are you in earnest?—Do you truly love me? Do you sincerely wish me to be your wife?'

'I do; and if an oath is necessary to satisfy you, I swear it.'

'Then, sir, I will marry you.'

'Edward—my little wife!'

'Dear Edward!'

'Come to me—come to me entirely now,' said he: and added, in his deepest tone, speaking in my ear as his cheek was laid on mine, 'Make my happiness—I will make yours.'

'God pardon me!' he subjoined ere long; 'and man meddle not with me: I have her, and will hold her.'

'There is no one to meddle, sir. I have no kindred to interfere.'

'No—that is the best of it,' he said.

And if I loved him less I should have thought his accent and look of exultation savage; but, sitting by him, roused from the nightmare of parting—called to the paradise of union—I thought only of the bliss given me to drink in so abundant a flow. Again and again he said, 'Are you happy, Jane?' and again and again I answered, 'Yes.' After which he murmured, 'It will atone—it will atone. Have I not found her friendless, and cold, and comfortless? Will I not guard, and cherish, and solace her? Is there not love in my heart, and constancy in my resolves? It will expiate at God's tribunal. I know my Maker sanctions what I do. For the world's judgment—I wash my hands thereof. For man's opinion—I defy it.'

But what had befallen the night? The moon was not yet set, and we were all in shadow: I could scarcely see my master's face, near as I was. And what ailed the chestnut tree? it writhed and groaned; while wind roared in the laurel walk, and came sweeping over us.

'We must go in,' said Mr. Rochester: 'the weather changes. I could have sat with thee till morning, Jane.'

'And so,' thought I, 'could I with you.' I should have said so, perhaps, but a livid, vivid spark leapt out of a cloud at which I was looking, and there was a crack, a crash, and a close rattling peal; and I thought only of hiding my dazzled eyes against Mr. Rochester's shoulder.

The rain rushed down. He hurried me up the walk, through the grounds, and into the house; but we were quite wet before we could pass the threshold. He was taking off my shawl in the hall, and shaking the water out of my loosened hair, when Mrs. Fairfax emerged from her room. I did not observe her at first, nor did Mr. Rochester. The lamp was lit. The clock was on the stroke of twelve.

'Hasten to take off your wet things,' said he; 'and before you go, good-night—good-night, my darling!'

He kissed me repeatedly. When I looked up, on leaving his arms, there stood the widow, pale, grave, and amazed. I only smiled at her, and ran upstairs. 'Explanation will do for another time,' thought I. Still, when I reached my chamber, I felt a pang at the idea that she should even temporarily misconstrue what she had seen. But joy soon effaced every other feeling; and loud as the wind blew, near and deep as the thunder crashed, fierce and frequent as the lightning gleamed, cataract-like as the rain fell during a storm of two hour's duration, I experienced no fear, and little awe. Mr. Rochester came thrice to my door in the course of it, to ask if I was safe and tranquil: and that was comfort, that was strength for anything.

Before I left my bed in the morning, little Adèle came running in to tell me that the great horse-chestnut at the bottom of the orchard had been struck by lightning in the night, and half of it split away.

Chapter XXIV

As I rose and dressed, I thought over what had happened, and wondered if it were a dream. I could not be certain of the reality till I had seen Mr. Rochester again, and heard him renew his words of love and promise.

While arranging my hair, I looked at my face in the glass, and felt it was no longer plain: there was hope in its aspect, and life in its colour; and my eyes seemed as if they had beheld the fount of fruition, and borrowed beams from the lustrous ripple. I had often been unwilling to look at my master, because I feared he could not be pleased at my look; but I was sure I might lift my face to his now, and not cool his affection by its expression. I took a plain but clean and light summer dress from my drawer and put it on: it seemed no attire had ever so well become me; because none had I ever worn in so blissful a mood.

I was not suprised, when I ran down into the hall, to see that a brilliant June morning had succeeded to the tempest of the night; and to feel, through the open glass door, the breathing of a fresh and fragrant breeze. Nature must be gladsome when I was so happy. A beggar-woman and her little boy—pale, ragged objects both—were coming up the walk, and I ran down and gave them all the money I happened to have in my purse—some three or four shillings: good or bad, they must partake of my jubilee. The rooks cawed, and blither birds sang; but nothing was so merry or so musical as my own rejoicing heart.

Mrs. Fairfax surprised me by looking out of the window with a sad countenance, and saying gravely:—'Miss Eyre, will you come to breakfast?' During the meal she was quiet and cool: but I could not undeceive her then. I must wait for my master to give explanations; and so must she. I ate what I could, and then I hastened upstairs. I met Adèle leaving the school-room.

'Where are you going? It is time for lessons.'

'Mr. Rochester has sent me away to the nursery.'

'Where is he?'

'In there,' pointing to the apartment she had left; and I went in, and there he stood.

'Come and bid me good-morning,' said he. I gladly advanced; and it was not merely a cold word now, or even a shake of the hand that I received, but an embrace and a kiss. It seemed natural; it seemed genial to be so well-loved, so caressed by him.

'Jane, you look blooming, and smiling, and pretty,' said he: 'truly pretty this morning. Is this my pale, little elf? Is this my mustard-seed?[6] This little sunny-faced girl with the dimpled cheek and rosy lips; the satin-smooth hazel hair, and the radiant hazel eyes?' (I had green eyes, reader; but you must excuse the mistake: for him they were new-dyed, I suppose.)

6. Name of one of the fairies in Shakespeare's A *Midsummer Night's Dream*.

'It is Jane Eyre, sir.'

'Soon to be Jane Rochester,' he added: 'in four weeks, Janet, not a day more. Do you hear that?'

I did, and I could not quite comprehend it: it made me giddy. The feeling, the announcement sent through me, was something stronger than was consistent with joy—something that smote and stunned: it was, I think, almost fear.

'You blushed, and now you are white, Jane: what is that for?'

'Because you gave me a new name—Jane Rochester; and it seems so strange.'

'Yes, Mrs. Rochester,' said he; 'young Mrs. Rochester—Fairfax Rochester's girl-bride.'

'It can never be, sir; it does not sound likely. Human beings never enjoy complete happiness in this world. I was not born for a different destiny to the rest of my species: to imagine such a lot befalling me is a fairy tale—a day-dream.'

'Which I can and will realise. I shall begin to-day. This morning I wrote to my banker in London to send me certain jewels he has in his keeping,—heirlooms for the ladies of Thornfield. In a day or two I hope to pour them into your lap: for every privilege, every attention shall be yours, that I would accord a peer's daughter, if about to marry her.'

'Oh, sir!—never mind jewels! I don't like to hear them spoken of. Jewels for Jane Eyre sounds unnatural and strange: I would rather not have them.'

'I will myself put the diamond chain round your neck, and the circlet on your forehead,—which it will become: for nature, at least, has stamped her patent of nobility on this brow, Jane; and I will clasp the bracelets on these fine wrists, and load these fairy-like fingers with rings.'

'No, no, sir! think of other subjects, and speak of other things, and in another strain. Don't address me as if I were a beauty; I am your plain, Quakerish governess.'

'You are a beauty, in my eyes; and a beauty just after the desire of my heart,—delicate and aërial.'

'Puny and insignificant, you mean. You are dreaming, sir,—or you are sneering. For God's sake, don't be ironical!'

'I will make the world acknowledge you a beauty too,' he went on, while I really became uneasy at the strain he had adopted; because I felt he was either deluding himself, or trying to delude me. 'I will attire my Jane in satin and lace, and she shall have roses in her hair; and I will cover the head I love best with a priceless veil.'

'And then you won't know me, sir; and I shall not be your Jane Eyre any longer, but an ape in a harlequin's[7] jacket,—a jay in borrowed plumes. I would as soon see you, Mr. Rochester, tricked out in stage-trappings, as myself clad in a court-lady's robe; and I don't call you handsome, sir, though I love you most dearly: far too dearly to flatter you. Don't flatter me.'

He pursued his theme, however, without noticing my deprecation. 'This very day I shall take you in the carriage to Millcote, and you must choose some dresses for yourself. I told you we shall be married in four weeks. The wedding is to take place quietly, in the church down below yonder; and then I shall waft you away at once to town. After a brief stay there, I shall bear my treasure to regions nearer the sun: to French vine-yards and Italian plains; and she shall see whatever is famous in old story and in modern record: she shall taste, too, of the life of cities; and she shall learn to value herself by just comparison with others.'

'Shall I travel?—and with you, sir?'

'You shall sojourn at Paris, Rome, and Naples: at Florence, Venice, and Vienna: all the ground I have wandered over shall be re-trodden by you: wherever I stamped my hoof, your sylph's foot shall step also. Ten years since, I flew through Europe half mad; with disgust, hate, and rage, as my companions; now I shall revisit it healed and cleansed, with a very angel as my comforter.'

I laughed at him as he said this. 'I am not an angel,' I asserted; 'and I will not be one till I die: I will be myself. Mr. Rochester, you must nei-ther expect nor exact anything celestial of me—for you will not get it, any more than I shall get it of you: which I do not at all anticipate.'

'What do you anticipate of me?'

'For a little while you will perhaps be as you are now,—a very little while; and then you will turn cool; and then you will be capricious; and then you will be stern, and I shall have much ado to please you: but when you get well used to me, you will perhaps like me again—*like* me, I say, not *love* me. I suppose your love will effervesce in six months, or less. I have observed in books written by men, that period assigned as the farthest to which a husband's ardour extends. Yet, after all, as a friend and companion, I hope never to become quite distasteful to my dear master.'

'Distasteful! and like you again! I think I shall like you again and yet again: and I will make you confess I do not only *like*, but *love* you—with truth, fervour, constancy.'

'Yet are you not capricious, sir?'

'To women who please me only by their faces, I am the very devil when I find out they have neither souls nor hearts—when they open to

7. I.e., clown's.

me a perspective of flatness, triviality, and perhaps imbecility, coarseness, and ill-temper: but to the clear eye and eloquent tongue, to the soul made of fire, and the character that bends but does not break—at once supple and stable, tractable and consistent—I am ever tender and true.'

'Had you ever experience of such a character, sir? Did you ever love such an one?'

'I love it now.'

'But before me: if I, indeed, in any respect come up to that difficult standard?'

'I never met your likeness. Jane: you please me, and you master me—you seem to submit, and I like the sense of pliancy you impart: and while I am twining the soft, silken skein round my finger, it sends a thrill up my arm to my heart. I am influenced—conquered; and the influence is sweeter than I can express; and the conquest I undergo has a witchery beyond any triumph I can win. Why do you smile, Jane? What does that inexplicable, that uncanny turn of countenance mean?'

'I was thinking, sir (you will excuse the idea; it was involuntary), I was thinking of Hercules and Samson with their charmers——'[8]

'You were, you little elfish——'

'Hush, sir! You don't talk very wisely just now; any more than those gentlemen acted very wisely. However, had they been married, they would no doubt by their severity as husbands have made up for their softness as suitors; and so will you, I fear. I wonder how you will answer me a year hence, should I ask a favour it does not suit your convenience or pleasure to grant.'

'Ask me something now, Janet—the least thing: I desire to be entreated——'

'Indeed, I will, sir; I have my petition all ready.'

'Speak! But if you look up and smile with that countenance, I shall swear concession before I know to what, and that will make a fool of me.'

'Not at all, sir; I ask only this: don't send for the jewels, and don't crown me with roses: you might as well put a border of gold lace round that plain pocket handkerchief you have there.'

'I might as well "gild refined gold."[9] I know it: your request is granted then—for the time. I will remand the order I despatched to my banker. But you have not yet asked for anything; you have prayed a gift to be withdrawn: try again.'

'Well, then, sir; have the goodness to gratify my curiosity, which is much piqued on one point.'

---

8. Hercules was "charmed" by various women, especially by his wife, Deianira, who had him killed; Samson was charmed by Delilah.
9. Shakespeare's *King John* 4.2.11.

He looked disturbed. 'What? what?' he said hastily. 'Curiosity is a dangerous petition: it is well I have not taken a vow to accord every request——'

'But there can be no danger in complying with this, sir.'

'Utter it, Jane: but I wish that instead of a mere inquiry into perhaps, a secret, it was a wish for half my estate.'

'Now, king Ahasuerus![1] What do I want with half your estate? Do you think I am a Jew-usurer, seeking good investment in land? I would much rather have all your confidence. You will not exclude me from your confidence, if you admit me to your heart?'

'You are welcome to all my confidence that is worth having, Jane: but for God's sake don't desire a useless burden! Don't long for poison —don't turn out a downright Eve on my hands!'

'Why not, sir? You have just been telling me how much you like to be conquered, and how pleasant over-persuasion is to you. Don't you think I had better take advantage of the confession, and begin and coax, and entreat—even cry and be sulky if necessary for the sake of a mere essay of my power?'

'I dare you to any such experiment. Encroach, presume, and the game is up.'

'Is it, sir? You soon give in. How stern you look now! Your eyebrows have become as thick as my finger, and your forehead resembles, what, in some very astonishing poetry, I once saw styled "a blue-piled thunderloft." That will be your married look, sir, I suppose?'

'If that will be *your* married look, I, as a Christian, will soon give up the notion of consorting with a mere sprite or salamander. But what had you to ask, thing?—out with it!'

'There, you are less than civil now; and I like rudeness a great deal better than flattery. I had rather be a *thing* than an angel. This is what I have to ask:—Why did you take such pains to make me believe you wished to marry Miss Ingram?'

'Is that all? Thank God, it is no worse!'

And now he unknit his black brows; looked down, smiling at me, and stroked my hair, as if well pleased at seeing a danger averted.

'I think I may confess,' he continued, 'even although I should make you a little indignant, Jane—and I have seen what a fire-spirit you can be when you are indignant. You glowed in the cool moonlight last night, when you mutinied against fate, and claimed your rank as my equal. Janet, by-the-by, it was you who made me the offer.'

'Of course, I did. But to the point if you please, sir—Miss Ingram?'

'Well, I feigned courtship of Miss Ingram, because I wished to render you as madly in love with me as I was with you; and I knew jeal-

---

1. Fabulously rich Persian king in the Book of Esther.

ousy would be the best ally I could call in for the furtherance of that end.'

'Excellent!—now you are small—not one whit bigger than the end of my little finger. It was a burning shame, and a scandalous disgrace to act in that way. Did you think nothing of Miss Ingram's feelings, sir?'

'Her feelings are concentrated in one—pride; and that needs humbling. Were you jealous, Jane?'

'Never mind, Mr. Rochester: it is in no way interesting to you to know that. Answer me truly once more. Do you think Miss Ingram will not suffer from your dishonest coquetry? Won't she feel forsaken and deserted?'

'Impossible!—when I told you how she, on the contrary, deserted me: the idea of my insolvency cooled, or rather extinguished, her flame in a moment.'

'You have a curious designing mind, Mr. Rochester. I am afraid your principles on some points are eccentric.'

'My principles were never trained, Jane: they may have grown a little awry for want of attention.'

'Once again, seriously; may I enjoy the great good that has been vouchsafed to me, without fearing that any one else is suffering the bitter pain I myself felt a while ago?'

'That you may, my good little girl: there is not another being in the world has the same pure love for me as yourself—for I lay that pleasant unction to my soul, Jane, a belief in your affection.'

I turned my lips to the hand that lay on my shoulder. I loved him very much—more than I could trust myself to say—more than words had power to express.

'Ask something more,' he said presently; 'it is my delight to be entreated, and to yield.'

I was again ready with my request.

'Communicate your intentions to Mrs. Fairfax, sir: she saw me with you last night in the hall, and she was shocked. Give her some explanation before I see her again. It pains me to be misjudged by so good a woman.'

'Go to your room, and put on your bonnet,' he replied. 'I mean you to accompany me to Millcote this morning; and while you prepare for the drive, I will enlighten the old lady's understanding. Did she think, Janet, you had given the world for love, and considered it well lost?'[2]

'I believe she thought I had forgotten my station, and yours, sir.'

'Station! station!—your station is in my heart, and on the necks of those who would insult you, now or hereafter—Go.'

I was soon dressed; and when I heard Mr. Rochester quit Mrs. Fair-

---

2. *All for Love; or, The World Well Lost*, is the title of a heroic tragedy by John Dryden.

fax's parlour, I hurried down to it. The old lady had been reading her morning portion of Scripture—the lesson for the day; her Bible lay open before her, and her spectacles were upon it. Her occupation, suspended by Mr. Rochester's announcement, seemed now forgotten: her eyes, fixed on the blank wall opposite, expressed the surprise of a quiet mind, stirred by unwonted tidings. Seeing me, she roused herself: she made a sort of effort to smile, and framed a few words of congratulation; but the smile expired, and the sentence was abandoned unfinished. She put up her spectacles, shut the Bible, and pushed her chair back from the table.

'I feel so astonished,' she began, 'I hardly know what to say to you, Miss Eyre. I have surely not been dreaming, have I? Sometimes I half fall asleep when I am sitting alone, and fancy things that have never happened. It has seemed to me more than once when I have been in a doze, that my dear husband, who died fifteen years since, has come in and sat down beside me; and that I have even heard him call me by my name, Alice, as he used to do. Now, can you tell me whether it is actually true that Mr. Rochester has asked you to marry him? Don't laugh at me. But I really thought he came in here five minutes ago, and said, that in a month you would be his wife.'

'He has said the same thing to me,' I replied.

'He has! Do you believe him? Have you accepted him?'

'Yes.'

She looked at me bewildered.

'I could never have thought it. He is a proud man: all the Rochesters were proud: and his father, at least, liked money. He, too, has always been called careful. He means to marry you?'

'He tells me so.'

She surveyed my whole person: in her eyes I read that they had there found no charm powerful enough to solve the enigma.

'It passes me!' she continued: 'but no doubt it is true since you say so. How it will answer, I cannot tell: I really don't know. Equality of position and fortune is often advisable in such cases; and there are twenty years of difference in your ages. He might almost be your father.'

'No, indeed, Mrs. Fairfax!' exclaimed I, nettled: 'he is nothing like my father! No one, who saw us together, would suppose it for an instant. Mr. Rochester looks as young, and is as young, as some men at five-and-twenty.'

'Is it really for love he is going to marry you?' she asked.

I was so hurt by her coldness and scepticism that the tears rose to my eyes.

'I am sorry to grieve you,' pursued the widow; 'but you are so young, and so little acquainted with men, I wished to put you on your guard. It is an old saying that "all is not gold that glitters;" and in this case I do fear there will be something found to be different to what either you or I expect.'

'Why?—am I a monster?' I said: 'is it impossible that Mr. Rochester should have a sincere affection for me?'

'No: you are very well; and much improved of late: and Mr. Rochester, I daresay, is fond of you. I have always noticed that you were a sort of pet of his. There are times when, for your sake, I have been a little uneasy at his marked preference, and have wished to put you on your guard: but I did not like to suggest even the possibility of wrong. I knew such an idea would shock, perhaps offend you; and you were so discreet, and so thoroughly modest and sensible, I hoped you might be trusted to protect yourself. Last night I cannot tell you what I suffered when I sought all over the house, and could find you nowhere, nor the master either; and then, at twelve o'clock, saw you come in with him.'

'Well, never mind that now,' I interrupted impatiently: 'it is enough that all was right.'

'I hope all will be right in the end,' she said: 'but believe me, you cannot be too careful. Try and keep Mr. Rochester at a distance: distrust yourself as well as him. Gentlemen in his station are not accustomed to marry their governesses.'

I was growing truly irritated: happily, Adèle ran in.

'Let me go,—let me go to Millcote too!' she cried. 'Mr. Rochester won't: though there is so much room in the new carriage. Beg him to let me go, mademoiselle.'

'That I will, Adèle,' and I hastened away with her, glad to quit my gloomy monitress. The carriage was ready: they were bringing it round to the front, and my master was pacing the pavement, Pilot following him backwards and forwards.

'Adèle may accompany us, may she not, sir?'

'I told her no. I'll have no brats!—I'll have only you.'

'Do let her go, Mr. Rochester, if you please: it would be better.'

'Not it: she will be a restraint.'

He was quite peremptory, both in look and voice. The chill of Mrs. Fairfax's warnings, and the damp of her doubts were upon me: something of unsubstantiality and uncertainty had beset my hopes. I half lost the sense of power over him. I was about mechanically to obey him, without further remonstrance; but as he helped me into the carriage, he looked at my face.

'What is the matter?' he asked; 'all the sunshine is gone. Do you really wish the bairn to go? Will it annoy you if she is left behind?'

'I would far rather she went, sir.'

'Then off for your bonnet, and back, like a flash of lightning!' cried he to Adèle.

She obeyed him with what speed she might.

'After all, a single morning's interruption will not matter much,' said he, 'when I mean shortly to claim you—your thoughts, conversation, and company—for life.'

Adèle, when lifted in, commenced kissing me, by way of expressing her gratitude for my intercession: she was instantly stowed away into a corner on the other side of him. She then peeped round to where I sat; so stern a neighbour was too restrictive: to him, in his present fractious mood she dared whisper no observations, nor ask of him any information.

'Let her come to me,' I entreated: 'she will, perhaps, trouble you, sir: there is plenty of room on this side.'

He handed her over as if she had been a lap-dog; 'I'll send her to school yet,' he said, but now he was smiling.

Adèle heard him, and asked if she was to go school 'sans[3] mademoiselle.'

'Yes,' he replied, 'absolutely sans mademoiselle; for I am to take mademoiselle to the moon, and there I shall seek a cave in one of the white valleys among the volcano-tops, and mademoiselle shall live with me there, and only me.'

'She will have nothing to eat: you will starve her,' observed Adèle.

'I shall gather manna for her morning and night: the plains and hillsides in the moon are bleached with manna, Adèle.'

'She will want to warm herself: what will she do for a fire?'

'Fire rises out of the lunar mountains: when she is cold, I'll carry her up to a peak and lay her down on the edge of a crater.'

'Oh, qu'elle y sera mal—peu confortable![4] And her clothes, they will wear out: how can she get new ones?'

Mr. Rochester professed to be puzzled. 'Hem?' said he. 'What would you do, Adèle? Cudgel your brains for an expedient. How would a white or a pink cloud answer for a gown, do you think? And one could cut a pretty enough scarf out of a rainbow.'

'She is far better as she is,' concluded Adèle, after musing some time: 'besides, she would get tired of living with only you in the moon. If I were mademoiselle, I would never consent to go with you.'

'She has consented: she has pledged her word.'

'But you can't get her there: there is no road to the moon: it is all air; and neither you nor she can fly.'

'Adèle, look at that field.' We were now outside Thornfield gates, and bowling lightly along the smooth road to Millcote, where the dust was well-laid by the thunder-storm, and where the low hedges and lofty timber trees on each side glistened green, and rain-refreshed.

'In that field, Adèle, I was walking late one evening about a fortnight

---

3. "Without."   4. "Oh, she'll be uncomfortable there!"

since—the evening of the day you helped me to make hay in the orchard meadows; and as I was tired with raking swaths, I sat down to rest
me on a stile; and there I took out a little book and a pencil, and began
to write about a misfortune that befell me long ago and a wish I had for
happy days to come: I was writing away very fast, though daylight was
fading from the leaf, when something came up the path and stopped
two yards off me. I looked at it. It was a little thing with a veil of gossamer on its head. I beckoned it to come near me; it stood soon at my
knee. I never spoke to it, and it never spoke to me, in words: but I read
its eyes, and it read mine; and our speechless colloquy was to this effect:—It was a fairy, and come from Elf-land, it said; and its errand was
to make me happy: I must go with it out of the common world to a
lonely place—such as the moon, for instance—and it nodded its head
towards her horn, rising over Hay-hill: it told me of the alabaster cave
and silver vale where we might live. I said I should like to go; but reminded it, as you did me, that I had no wings to fly.

' "Oh," returned the fairy, "that does not signify! Here is a talisman
will remove all difficulties;" and she held out a pretty gold ring. "Put
it," she said, "on the fourth finger of my left hand, and I am yours, and
you are mine; and we shall leave earth, and make our own heaven
yonder." She nodded again at the moon. The ring, Adèle, is in my
breeches-pocket, under the disguise of a sovereign: but I mean soon to
change it to a ring again.'

'But what has mademoiselle to do with it? I don't care for the fairy:
you said it was mademoiselle you would take to the moon?'——

'Mademoiselle is a fairy,' he said, whispering mysteriously. Whereupon I told her not to mind his badinage; and she, on her part, evinced a
fund of genuine French scepticism: denominating Mr. Rochester 'un
vrai menteur,'[5] and assuring him that she had made no account whatever of his 'Contes de fée,' and that 'du reste, il n'y avait pas de fées, et
quand même il y en avait,'[6] she was sure they would never appear to
him, nor ever give him rings, or offer to live with him in the moon. The
hour spent at Millcote was a somewhat harassing one to me. Mr. Rochester obliged me to go to a certain silk warehouse: there I was ordered to
choose half a dozen dresses. I hated the business, I begged leave to
defer it: no—it should be gone through with now. By dint of entreaties
expressed in energetic whispers I reduced the half-dozen to two: these,
however, he vowed he would select himself. With anxiety I watched his
eye rove over the gay stores: he fixed on a rich silk of the most brilliant
amethyst dye, and a superb pink satin. I told him in a new series of whispers, that he might as well buy me a gold gown and a silver bonnet at

5. "A real liar."
6. "Fairy tales," and that "furthermore, there
were no fairies, and even so there were some"

(quand même may be Brontë's error for même se,
"even if").

once: I should certainly never venture to wear his choice. With infinite difficulty, for he was stubborn as a stone, I persuaded him to make an exchange in favour of a sober black satin and pearl-grey silk. 'It might pass for the present,' he said; 'but he would yet see me glittering like a parterre.'

Glad was I to get him out of the silk warehouse, and then out of a jeweller's shop: the more he bought me, the more my cheek burned with a sense of annoyance and degradation. As we re-entered the carriage, and I sat back feverish and fagged, I remembered what in the hurry of events, dark and bright, I had wholly forgotten—the letter of my uncle, John Eyre, to Mrs. Reed: his intention to adopt me and make me his legatee. 'It would, indeed, be a relief,' I thought, 'if I had ever so small an independency; I never can bear being dressed like a doll by Mr. Rochester, or sitting like a second Danae with the golden shower falling daily round me.[7] I will write to Madeira the moment I get home, and tell my uncle John I am going to be married, and to whom: if I had but a prospect of one day bringing Mr. Rochester an accession of fortune, I could better endure to be kept by him now.' And somewhat relieved by this idea (which I failed not to execute that day), I ventured once more to meet my master's and lover's eye; which most pertinaciously sought mine, though I averted both face and gaze. He smiled; and I thought his smile was such as a sultan might, in a blissful and fond moment, bestow on a slave his gold and gems had enriched: I crushed his hand, which was ever hunting mine, vigorously, and thrust it back to him red with the passionate pressure—

'You need not look in that way,' I said: 'if you do I'll wear nothing but my old Lowood frocks to the end of the chapter. I'll be married in this lilac gingham—you may make a dressing-gown for yourself out of the pearl-grey silk, and an infinite series of waist-coats out of the black satin.'

He chuckled; he rubbed his hands: 'Oh, it is rich to see and hear her!' he exclaimed. 'Is she original? Is she piquant? I would not exchange this one little English girl for the grand Turk's whole seraglio;[8] gazelle-eyes, houri forms, and all!'

The Eastern allusion bit me again: 'I'll not stand you an inch in the stead of a seraglio,' I said; 'so don't consider me an equivalent for one; if you have a fancy for anything in that line, away with you, sir, to the bazaars of Stamboul without delay; and lay out in extensive slave-purchases some of that spare cash you seem at a loss to spend satisfactorily here.'

'And what will you do, Janet, while I am bargaining for so many tons of flesh and such an assortment of black eyes?'

7. Zeus, as a shower of gold, made love to   8. I.e., harem.
Danae.

'I'll be preparing myself to go out as a missionary to preach liberty to them that are enslaved—your harem inmates amongst the rest. I'll get admitted there, and I'll stir up mutiny; and you, three-tailed bashaw[9] as you are, sir, shall in a trice find yourself fettered amongst our hands: nor will I, for one, consent to cut your bonds till you have signed a charter, the most liberal that despot ever yet conferred.'

'I would consent to be at your mercy, Jane.'

'I would have no mercy, Mr. Rochester, if you supplicated for it with an eye like that. While you looked so, I should be certain that whatever charter you might grant under coercion, your first act, when released, would be to violate its conditions.'

'Why, Jane, what would you have? I fear you will compel me to go through a private marriage ceremony, besides that performed at the altar. You will stipulate, I see, for peculiar terms—what will they be?'

'I only want an easy mind, sir; not crushed by crowded obligations. Do you remember what you said of Céline Varens?—of the diamonds, the cashmeres you gave her? I will not be your English Céline Varens. I shall continue to act as Adèle's governess; by that I shall earn my board and lodging, and thirty pounds a year besides, I'll furnish my own wardrobe out of that money, and you shall give me nothing but'——

'Well, but what?'

'Your regard: and if I give you mine in return, that debt will be quit.'

'Well, for cool native impudence, and pure innate pride, you haven't your equal,' said he. We were now approaching Thornfield. 'Will it please you to dine with me to-day?' he asked, as we re-entered the gates.

'No, thank you, sir.'

'And what for, "no, thank you," if one may inquire?'

'I never have dined with you, sir: and I see no reason why I should now: till'——

'Till what? You delight in half-phrases.'

'Till I can't help it.'

'Do you suppose I eat like an ogre, or a ghoul, that you dread being the companion of my repast?'

'I have formed no supposition on the subject, sir; but I want to go on as usual for another month.'

'You will give up your governessing slavery at once.'

'Indeed! begging your pardon, sir, I shall not. I shall just go on with it as usual. I shall keep out of your way all day, as I have been accustomed to do: you may send for me in the evening, when you feel disposed to see me, and I'll come then; but at no other time.'

'I want a smoke, Jane, or a pinch of snuff, to comfort me under all

9. Pasha (grand Turk).

this, "pour me donner une contenance,"[1] as Adèle would say: and unfortunately I have neither my cigar-case, nor my snuff-box. But listen —whisper—it is your time now, little tyrant, but it will be mine presently: and when once I have fairly seized you, to have and to hold, I'll just—figuratively speaking—attach you to a chain like this' (touching his watch-guard). 'Yes, bonny wee thing, I'll wear you in my bosom, lest my jewel I should tyne.'[2]

He said this as he helped me to alight from the carriage; and while he afterwards lifted out Adèle, I entered the house, and made good my retreat upstairs.

He duly summoned me to his presence in the evening. I had prepared an occupation for him; for I was determined not to spend the whole time in a *tête-à-tête* conversation. I remembered his fine voice; I knew he liked to sing—good singers generally do. I was no vocalist myself, and, in his fastidious judgment, no musician either; but I delighted in listening when the performance was good. No sooner had twilight, that hour of romance, begun to lower her blue and starry banner over the lattice, than I rose, opened the piano, and entreated him, for the love of heaven, to give me a song. He said I was a capricious witch, and that he would rather sing another time; but I averred that no time was like the present.

'Did I like his voice?' he asked.

'Very much.' I was not fond of pampering that susceptible vanity of his; but for once, and from motives of expediency, I would e'en soothe and stimulate it.

'Then, Jane, you must play the accompaniment.'

'Very well, sir; I will try.'

I did try, but was presently swept off the stool and denominated 'a little bungler.' Being pushed unceremoniously to one side—which was precisely what I wished—he unsurped my place, and proceeded to accompany himself: for he could play as well as sing. I hied me to the window-recess; and while I sat there and looked out on the still trees and dim lawn, to a sweet air was sung in mellow tones the following strain:—

> The truest love that ever heart
>   Felt at its kindled core
> Did through each vein, in quickened start,
>   The tide of being pour.
>
> Her coming was my hope each day,
>   Her parting was my pain;
> The chance that did her steps delay
>   Was ice in every vein.

---

1. "To steady me."   2. Lose.

I dreamed it would be nameless bliss,
    As I loved, loved to be;
And to this object did I press
    As blind as eagerly.

But wide as pathless was the space
    That lay, our lives, between,
And dangerous as the foamy race
    Of ocean-surges green.

And haunted as a robber-path
    Through wilderness or wood;
For Might and Right, and Woe and Wrath,
    Between our spirits stood.

I dangers dared; I hind'rance scorned;
    I omens did defy:
Whatever menaced, harassed, warned,
    I passed impetuous by.

On sped my rainbow, fast as light;
    I flew as in a dream;
For glorious rose upon my sight
    That child of Shower and Gleam.

Still bright on clouds of suffering dim
    Shines that soft, solemn joy;
Nor care I now, how dense and grim
    Disasters gather nigh.

I care not in this moment sweet,
    Though all I have rushed o'er
Should come on pinion, strong and fleet,
    Proclaiming vengeance sore:

Though haughty Hate should strike me down,
    Right, bar approach to me,
And grinding Might, with furious frown,
    Swear endless enmity.

My love has placed her little hand
    With noble faith in mine,
And vowed that wedlock's sacred band
    Our nature shall entwine.

My love has sworn, with sealing kiss,
    With me to live—to die;
I have at last my nameless bliss:
    As I love—loved am I!

He rose and came towards me, and I saw his face all kindled, and his full falcon-eye flashing, and tenderness and passion in every lineament. I quailed momentarily—then I rallied. Soft scene, daring demonstration, I would not have; and I stood in peril of both: a weapon of defence must be prepared—I whetted my tongue: as he reached me, I asked with asperity, 'whom he was going to marry now?'

'That was a strange question to be put by his darling Jane.'

'Indeed! I considered it a very natural and necessary one: he had talked of his future wife dying with him. What did he mean by such a pagan idea? I had no intention of dying with him—he might depend on that.'

'Oh, all he longed, all he prayed for, was that I might live with him! Death was not for such as I.'

'Indeed it was: I had as good a right to die when my time came as he had: but I should bide that time, and not be hurried away in a suttee.'[3]

'Would I forgive him for the selfish idea, and prove my pardon by a reconciling kiss?'

'No: I would rather be excused.'

Here I heard myself apostrophised as a 'hard little thing;' and it was added, 'any other woman would have been melted to marrow at hearing such stanzas crooned in her praise.'

I assured him I was naturally hard—very flinty, and that he would often find me so; and that, moreover, I was determined to show him divers rugged points in my character before the ensuing four weeks elapsed: he should know fully what sort of a bargain he had made, while there was yet time to rescind it.

'Would I be quiet, and talk rationally?'

'I would be quiet if he liked; and as to talking rationally, I flattered myself I was doing that now.'

He fretted, pished and pshawed. 'Very good,' I thought; 'you may fume and fidget as you please: but this is the best plan to pursue with you, I am certain. I like you more than I can say; but I'll not sink into a bathos of sentiment: and with this needle of repartee I'll keep you from the edge of the gulf too; and, moreover, maintain by its pungent aid that distance between you and myself most conducive to our real mutual advantage.'

From less to more, I worked him up to considerable irritation; then, after he had retired, in dudgeon, quite to the other end of the room, I got up, and saying, 'I wish you good-night, sir,' in my natural and wonted respectful manner, I slipped out by the side-door and got away.

The system thus entered on I pursued during the whole season of probation; and with the best success. He was kept, to be sure, rather cross and crusty: but on the whole I could see he was excellently enter-

---

3. Custom according to which a Hindu widow was cremated on her husband's funeral pyre.

tained; and that a lamb-like submission and turtle-dove sensibility, while fostering his despotism more, would have pleased his judgment, satisfied his common-sense, and even suited his taste, less.

In other people's presence I was, as formerly, deferential and quiet; any other line of conduct being uncalled for: it was only in the evening conferences I thus thwarted and afflicted him. He continued to send for me punctually the moment the clock struck seven; though when I appeared before him now, he had no such honeyed terms as 'love' and 'darling' on his lips: the best words at my service were 'provoking puppet,' 'malicious elf,' 'sprite,' 'changeling,' &c. For caresses, too, I now got grimaces; for a pressure of the hand, a pinch on the arm; for a kiss on the cheek, a severe tweak of the ear. It was all right: at present I decidely preferred these fierce favours to anything more tender. Mrs. Fairfax, I saw, approved me: her anxiety on my account vanished; therefore I was certain I did well. Meantime, Mr. Rochester affirmed I was wearing him to skin and bone, and threatened awful vengeance for my present conduct at some period fast coming. I laughed in my sleeve at his menaces: 'I can keep you in reasonable check now,' I reflected; 'and I don't doubt to be able to do it hereafter: if one expedient loses its virtue, another must be devised.'

Yet after all my task was not an easy one; often I would rather have pleased than teased him. My future husband was becoming to me my whole world; and more than the world: almost my hope of heaven. He stood between me and every thought of religion, as an eclipse intervenes between man and the broad sun. I could not, in those days, see God for his creature: of whom I had made an idol.

Chapter XXV

The month of courtship had wasted: its very last hours were being numbered. There was no putting off the day that advanced—the bridal day; and all preparations for its arrival were complete. I, at least, had nothing more to do: there were my trunks, packed, locked, corded, ranged in a row along the wall of my little chamber: to-morrow, at this time, they would be far on their road to London: and so should I (D.V.),[4]—or rather, not I, but one Jane Rochester, a person whom as yet I knew not. The cards of address alone remained to nail on: they lay, four little squares, on the drawer. Mr. Rochester had himself written the direction, 'Mrs. Rochester, ———Hotel, London,' on each: I could not persuade myself to affix them, or to have them affixed. Mrs. Rochester! She did not exist: she would not be born till to-morrow, some time after eight o'clock A.M.; and I would wait to be assured she had come into the world alive before I assigned to her all that property.

4. *Deo volente* ("God willing").

It was enough that in yonder closet, opposite my dressing-table, garments said to be hers had already displaced my black stuff Lowood frock and straw bonnet: for not to me appertained that suit of wedding raiment, the pearl-coloured robe, the vapoury veil, pendent from the usurped portmanteau. I shut the closet, to conceal the strange, wraith-like apparel it contained; which, at this evening hour—nine o'clock— gave out certainly a most ghostly shimmer through the shadow of my apartment. 'I will leave you by yourself, white dream,' I said. 'I am feverish: I hear the wind blowing: I will go out of doors and feel it.'

It was not only the hurry of preparation that made me feverish; not only the anticipation of the great change—the new life which was to commence to-morrow: both these circumstances had their share, doubtless, in producing that restless, excited mood which hurried me forth at this late hour into the darkening grounds; but a third cause influenced my mind more than they.

I had at heart a strange and anxious thought. Something had happened which I could not comprehend; no one knew of or had seen the event but myself: it had taken place the preceding night. Mr. Rochester that night was absent from home; nor was he yet returned: business had called him to a small estate of two or three farms he possessed thirty miles off—business it was requisite he should settle in person, previously to his meditated departure from England. I waited now his return; eager to disburthen my mind, and to seek of him the solution of the enigma that perplexed me. Stay till he comes, reader; and, when I disclose my secret to him, you shall share the confidence.

I sought the orchard: driven to its shelter by the wind, which all day had blown strong and full from the south; without, however, bringing a speck of rain. Instead of subsiding as night drew on, it seemed to augment its rush and deepen its roar: the trees blew steadfastly one way, never writhing round, and scarcely tossing back their boughs once in an hour; so continuous was the strain bending their branchy heads northward—the clouds drifted from pole to pole, fast following, mass on mass: no glimpse of blue sky had been visible that July day.

It was not without a certain wild pleasure I ran before the wind delivering my trouble of mind to the measureless air-torrent thundering through space. Descending the laurel-walk, I faced the wreck of the chestnut-tree; it stood up, black and riven: the trunk, split down the centre, gasped ghastly. The cloven halves were not broken from each other, for the firm base and strong roots kept them unsundered below; though community of vitality was destroyed—the sap could flow no more: their great boughs on each side were dead, and next winter's tempests would be sure to fell one or both to earth: as yet, however, they might be said to form one tree—a ruin, but an entire ruin.

'You did right to hold fast to each other,' I said: as if the monster splinters were living things, and could hear me. 'I think, scathed as you look, and charred and scorched, there must be a little sense of life in you yet; rising out of that adhesion at the faithful, honest roots: you will never have green leaves more—never more see birds making nests and singing idyls in your boughs; the time of pleasure and love is over with you; but you are not desolate: each of you has a comrade to sympathise with him in his decay.' As I looked up at them, the moon appeared momentarily in that part of the sky which filled their fissure; her disk was blood-red and half overcast; she seemed to throw on me one bewildered, dreary glance, and buried herself again instantly in the deep drift of cloud. The wind fell, for a second, round Thornfield; but far away over wood and water, poured a wild, melancholy wail: it was sad to listen to, and I ran off again.

Here and there I strayed through the orchard, gathered up the apples with which the grass round the tree roots was thickly strewn: then I employed myself in dividing the ripe from the unripe; I carried them into the house and put them away in the store-room. Then I repaired to the library to ascertain whether the fire was lit; for, though summer, I knew on such a gloomy evening Mr. Rochester would like to see a cheerful hearth when he came in: yes, the fire had been kindled some time, and burnt well. I placed his arm-chair by the chimney-corner: I wheeled the table near it: I let down the curtain, and had the candles brought in ready for lighting. More restless than ever, when I had completed these arrangements I could not sit still, nor even remain in the house: a little timepiece in the room and the old clock in the hall simultaneously struck ten.

'How late it grows!' I said: 'I will run down to the gates: it is moonlight at intervals; I can see a good way on the road. He may be coming now, and to meet him will save some minutes of suspense.

The wind roared high in the great trees which enbowered the gates; but the road as far as I could see, to the right hand and the left, was all still and solitary: save for the shadows of clouds crossing it at intervals, as the moon looked out, it was but a long pale line, unvaried by one moving speck.

A puerile tear dimmed my eye while I looked—a tear of disappointment and impatience: ashamed of it, I wiped it away. I lingered; the moon shut herself wholly within her chamber, and drew close her curtain of dense cloud; the night grew dark; rain came driving fast on the gale.

'I wish he would come! I wish he would come!' I exclaimed, seized with hypochondriac foreboding. I had expected his arrival before tea; now it was dark: what could keep him? Had an accident happened? The event of last night again recurred to me. I interpreted it as a warning of disaster. I feared my hopes were too bright to be realised; and I had enjoyed so much bliss lately that I imagined my fortune had passed its meridian, and must now decline.

'Well, I cannot return to the house,' I thought; 'I cannot sit by the fireside while he is abroad in inclement weather: better tire my limbs than strain my heart; I will go forward and meet him.'

I set out; I walked fast, but not far: ere I had measured a quarter of a mile I heard the tramp of hoofs; a horseman came on, full gallop; a dog ran by his side. Away with evil presentiment! It was he: here he was, mounted on Mesrour, followed by Pilot. He saw me; for the moon had opened a blue field in the sky, and rode in it watery bright: he took his hat off, and waved it round his head. I now ran to meet him.

'There!' he exclaimed, as he stretched out his hand and bent from the saddle: 'You can't do without me, that is evident. Step on my boot-toe; give me both hands: mount!'

I obeyed; joy made me agile: I sprang up before him. A hearty kissing I got for a welcome; and some boastful triumph; which I swallowed as well as I could. He checked himself in his exultation to demand, 'But is there anything the matter, Janet, that you come to meet me at such an hour? Is there anything wrong?'

'No; but I thought you would never come. I could not bear to wait in the house for you, especially with this rain and wind.'

'Rain and wind, indeed! Yes, you are dripping like a mermaid; pull my cloak round you: but I think you are feverish, Jane: both your cheek and hand are burning hot. I ask again, is there anything the matter?'

'Nothing, now: I am neither afraid nor unhappy.'

'Then you have been both?'

'Rather: but I'll tell you all about it by-and-by, sir; and I daresay you will only laugh at me for my pains.'

'I'll laugh at you heartily when to-morrow is past; till then I dare not: my prize is not certain. This is you; who have been as slippery as an eel this last month, and as thorny as a briar-rose. I could not lay a finger anywhere but I was pricked; and now I seem to have gathered up a stray lamb in my arms: you wandered out of the fold to seek your shepherd, did you, Jane?'

'I wanted you: but don't boast. Here we are at Thornfield: now let me get down.'

He landed me on the pavement. As John took his horse, and he followed me into the hall, he told me to make haste and put something dry on, and then return to him in the library; and he stopped me, as I made for the staircase, to extort a promise that I would not be long: nor was I long: in five minutes I rejoined him. I found him at supper.

'Take a seat and bear me company, Jane: please God, it is the last meal but one you will eat at Thornfield Hall for a long time.'

I sat down near him; but told him I could not eat.

'Is it because you have the prospect of a journey before you, Jane? Is it the thoughts of going to London that takes away your appetite?'

'I cannot see my prospects clearly to-night, sir; and I hardly know what thoughts I have in my head. Everything in life seems unreal.'

'Except me: I am substantial enough:—touch me.'

'You, sir, are the most phantom-like of all: you are a mere dream.'

He held out his hand, laughing: 'Is that a dream?' said he, placing it close to my eyes. He had a rounded, muscular, and vigorous hand, as well as a long, strong arm.

'Yes; though I touch it, it is a dream,' said I, as I put it down from before my face. 'Sir, have you finished supper?'

'Yes, Jane.'

I rang the bell, and ordered away the tray. When we were again alone, I stirred the fire, and then took a low seat at my master's knee.

'It is near midnight,' I said.

'Yes: but remember, Jane, you promised to wake with me the night before my wedding.'

'I did; and I will keep my promise, for an hour or two at least: I have no wish to go to bed.'

'Are all your arrangements complete?'

'All, sir.'

'And on my part, likewise,' he returned. 'I have settled everything; and we shall leave Thornfield to-morrow, within half an hour after our return from church.'

'Very well, sir.'

'With what an extraordinary smile you uttered that word—"very well," Jane! What a bright spot of colour you have on each cheek! and how strangely your eyes glitter! Are you well?'

'I believe I am.'

'Believe! What is the matter?—Tell me what you feel.'

'I could not, sir: no words could tell you what I feel. I wish this present hour would never end: who knows with what fate the next may come charged?'

'This is hypochondria, Jane. You have been over-excited, or over-fatigued.'

'Do you, sir, feel calm and happy?'

'Calm?—no: but happy—to the heart's core.'

I looked up at him to read the signs of bliss in his face: it was ardent and flushed.

'Give me your confidence, Jane,' he said: 'relieve your mind of any weight that oppresses it by imparting it to me. What do you fear?—that I shall not prove a good husband?'

'It is the idea farthest from my thoughts.'

'Are you apprehensive of the new sphere you are about to enter?—
of the new life into which you are passing?'

'No.'

'You puzzle me, Jane: your look and tone of sorrowful audacity perplex and pain me. I want an explanation.'

'Then, sir—listen. You were from home last night?'

'I was: I know that; and you hinted a while ago at something which
had happened in my absence:—nothing, probably, of consequence;
but, in short, it has disturbed you. Let me hear it. Mrs. Fairfax has said
something, perhaps? or you have overheard the servants talk?—your
sensitive self-respect has been wounded?'

'No, sir.' It struck twelve—I waited till the timepiece had concluded
its silver chime, and the clock its hoarse, vibrating stroke, and then I
proceeded.

'All day yesterday I was very busy, and very happy in my ceaseless
bustle; for I am not, as you seem to think, troubled by any haunting
fears about the new sphere, et cetera: I think it a glorious thing to have
the hope of living with you, because I love you. No, sir, don't caress me
now—let me talk undisturbed. Yesterday I trusted well in Providence,
and believed that events were working together for your good and
mine: it was a fine day, if you recollect—the calmness of the air and sky
forbade apprehensions respecting your safety or comfort on your journey. I walked a little while on the pavement after tea, thinking of you;
and I beheld you in imagination so near me I scarcely missed your actual presence. I thought of the life that lay before me—*your* life, sir—
an existence more expansive and stirring than my own: as much more
so as the depths of the sea to which the brook runs are than the shallows
of its own strait channel. I wondered why moralists call this world a
dreary wilderness; for me it blossomed like a rose. Just at sunset the air
turned cold and the sky cloudy: I went in. Sophie called me upstairs to
look at my wedding-dress, which they had just brought; and under it in
the box I found your present—the veil which, in your princely extravagance, you sent for from London: resolved, I suppose, since I would
not have jewels, to cheat me into accepting something as costly. I
smiled as I unfolded it, and devised how I would tease you about your
aristocratic tastes, and your efforts to masque your plebeian bride in the
attributes of a peeress. I thought how I would carry down to you the
square of unembroidered blond[5] I had myself prepared as a covering for
my low-born head, and ask if that was not good enough for a woman
who could bring her husband neither fortune, beauty, nor connections.
I saw plainly how you would look; and heard your impetuous republi-

5. A kind of silk lace.

can answers, and your haughty disavowal of any necessity on your part to augment your wealth, or elevate your standing, by marrying either a purse or a coronet.'

'How well you read me, you witch!' interposed Mr. Rochester; 'but what did you find in the veil besides its embroidery? Did you find poison, or a dagger, that you look so mournful now?'

'No, no, sir; besides the delicacy and richness of the fabric, I found nothing save Fairfax Rochester's pride; and that did not scare me, because I am used to the sight of the demon. But, sir, as it grew dark the wind rose: it blew yesterday evening, not as it blows now—wild and high—but "with a sullen, moaning sound"[6] far more eerie. I wished you were at home. I came into this room, and the sight of the empty chair and fireless hearth chilled me. For some time after I went to bed I could not sleep—a sense of anxious excitement distressed me. The gale still rising seemed to my ear to muffle a mournful under-sound; whether in the house or abroad I could not at first tell, but it recurred, doubtful, yet doleful at every lull: at last I made out it must be some dog howling at a distance. I was glad when it ceased. On sleeping, I continued in dreams the idea of a dark and gusty night. I continued also the wish to be with you, and experienced a strange, regretful consciousness of some barrier dividing us. During all my first sleep I was following the windings of an unknown road; total obscurity environed me; rain pelted me; I was burdened with the charge of a little child: a very small creature, too young and feeble to walk, and which shivered in my cold arms and wailed piteously in my ear. I thought, sir, that you were on the road a long way before me; and I strained every nerve to overtake you, and made effort on effort to utter your name and entreat you to stop—but my movements were fettered; and my voice still died away inarticulate; while you, I felt, withdrew farther and farther every moment.'

'And these dreams weigh on your spirits now, Jane, when I am close to you? Little nervous subject! Forget visionary woe, and think only of real happiness! You say you love me, Janet: yes—I will not forget that; and you cannot deny it. *Those* words did not die inarticulate on your lips. I heard them clear and soft: a thought too solemn perhaps, but sweet as music—"I think it is a glorious thing to have the hope of living with you, Edward, because I love you."—Do you love me, Jane? Repeat it.'

'I do, sir.—I do with my whole heart.'

'Well,' he said, after some minutes' silence, 'it is strange; but that sentence has penetrated my breast painfully. Why? I think because you said it with such an earnest, religious energy: and because your upward

6. Sir Walter Scott's *The Lay of the Last Minstrel* 1.13.1.

gaze at me now is the very sublime of faith, truth, and devotion: it is too much as if some spirit were near me. Look wicked, Jane; as you know well how to look; coin one of your wild, shy, provoking smiles; tell me you hate me—tease me, vex me; do anything but move me: I would rather be incensed than saddened.'

'I will tease you and vex you to your heart's content when I have finished my tale: but hear me to the end.'

'I thought, Jane, you had told me all. I thought I had found the source of your melancholy in a dream!'

I shook my head. 'What! is there more? But I will not believe it to be anything important. I warn you of incredulity beforehand. Go on.'

The disquietude of his air, the somewhat apprehensive impatience of his manner, surprised me: but I proceeded.

'I dreamt another dream, sir: that Thornfield Hall was a dreary ruin, the retreat of bats and owls. I thought that of all the stately front nothing remained but a shell-like wall, very high, and very fragile-looking. I wandered, on a moonlight night, through the grass-grown enclosure within: here I stumbled over a marble hearth, and there over a fallen fragment of cornice. Wrapped up in a shawl, I still carried the unknown little child: I might not lay it down anywhere, however tired were my arms—however much its weight impeded my progress, I must retain it. I heard the gallop of a horse at a distance on the road: I was sure it was you; and you were departing for many years, and for a distant country. I climbed the thin wall with frantic, perilous haste, eager to catch one glimpse of you from the top: the stones rolled from under my feet, the ivy branches I grasped gave way, the child clung round my neck in ter-ror, and almost strangled me: at last I gained the summit. I saw you like a speck on a white track, lessening every moment. The blast blew so strong I could not stand. I sat down on the narrow ledge; I hushed the scared infant in my lap: you turned an angle of the road; I bent forward to take a last look; the wall crumbled; I was shaken; the child rolled from my knee, I lost my balance, fell, and woke.'

'Now, Jane, that is all.'

'All the preface, sir; the tale is yet to come. On waking, a gleam daz-zled my eyes: I thought—oh, it is daylight! But I was mistaken: it was only candlelight. Sophie, I supposed, had come in. There was a light on the dressing-table, and the door of the closet, where, before going to bed, I had hung my wedding-dress and veil, stood open: I heard a rus-tling there. I asked, "Sophie, what are you doing?" No one answered; but a form emerged from the closet: it took the light, held it aloft, and surveyed the garments pendent from the portmanteau. "Sophie! So-phie!" I again cried: and still it was silent. I had risen up in bed; I bent forward: first, surprise, then bewilderment, came over me; and then my blood crept cold through my veins. Mr. Rochester, this was not Sophie, it was not Leah, it was not Mrs. Fairfax: It was not—no, I was sure of it, and am still—it was not even that strange woman, Grace Poole.'

'It must have been one of them,' interrupted my master.

'No, sir, I solemnly assure you to the contrary. The shape standing before me had never crossed my eyes within the precincts of Thornfield Hall before; the height, the contour, were new to me.'

'Describe it, Jane.'

'It seemed, sir, a woman, tall and large, with thick and dark hair hanging long down her back. I know not what dress she had on: it was white and straight; but whether gown, sheet, or shroud, I cannot tell.'

'Did you see her face?'

'Not at first. But presently she took my veil from its place; she held it up, gazed at it long, and then she threw it over her own head, and turned to the mirror. At that moment I saw the reflection of the visage and features quite distinctly in the dark oblong glass.'

'And how were they?'

'Fearful and ghastly to me—oh, sir, I never saw a face like it! It was a discoloured face—it was a savage face. I wish I could forget the roll of the red eyes and the fearful blackened inflation of the lineaments.'

'Ghosts are usually pale, Jane.'

'This, sir, was purple: the lips were swelled and dark; the brow furrowed; the black eyebrows widely raised over the bloodshot eyes. Shall I tell you of what it reminded me?'

'You may.'

'Of the foul German spectre—the Vampyre.'

'Ah?—What did it do?'

'Sir, it removed my veil from its gaunt head, rent it in two parts, and flinging both on the floor, trampled on them.'

'Afterwards?'

'It drew aside the window-curtain and looked out: perhaps it saw dawn approaching, for, taking the candle, it retreated to the door. Just at my bedside the figure stopped: the fiery eye glared upon me—she thrust up her candle close to my face, and extinguished it under my eyes. I was aware her lurid visage flamed over mine, and I lost consciousness: for the second time in my life—only the second time—I became insensible from terror.'

'Who was with you when you revived?'

'No one, sir; but the broad day. I rose, bathed my head and face in water, drank a long draught; felt that though enfeebled I was not ill, and determined that to none but you would I impart this vision. Now, sir, tell me who and what that woman was?'

'The creature of an over-stimulated brain; that is certain. I must be careful of you, my treasure: nerves like yours were not made for rough handling.'

'Sir, depend on it, my nerves were not in fault; the thing was real: the transaction actually took place.'

'And your previous dreams: were they real too? Is Thornfield Hall a ruin? Am I severed from you by insuperable obstacles? Am I leaving you without a tear—without a kiss—without a word?'

'Not yet.'

'Am I about to do it?—Why, the day is already commenced which is to bind us indissolubly; and when we are once united, there shall be no recurrence of these mental terrors: I guarantee that.'

'Mental terrors, sir! I wish I could believe them to be only such: I wish it more now than ever; since even you cannot explain to me the mystery of that awful visitant.'

'And since I cannot do it, Jane, it must have been unreal.'

'But, sir, when I said so to myself on rising this morning, and when I looked round the room to gather courage and comfort from the cheerful aspect of each familiar object in full daylight, there—on the carpet —I saw what gave the distinct lie to my hypothesis,—the veil, torn from top to bottom, in two halves!'

I felt Mr. Rochester start and shudder; he hastily flung his arms round me.

'Thank God!' he exclaimed, 'that if anything malignant did come near you last night, it was only the veil that was harmed.—Oh, to think what might have happened!'

He drew his breath short, and strained me so close to him I could scarcely pant. After some minutes' silence, he continued, cheerily:— 'Now, Janet, I'll explain to you all about it. It was half dream, half reality: a woman did, I doubt not, enter your room: and that woman was—must have been—Grace Poole. You call her a strange being yourself: from all you know you have reason so to call her—what did she do to me? what to Mason? In a state between sleeping and waking you noticed her entrance and her actions; but feverish, almost delirious as you were, you ascribed to her goblin appearance different from her own: the long dishevelled hair, the swelled black face, the exaggerated stature, were figments of imagination; results of nightmare: the spiteful tearing of the veil was real: and it is like her. I see you would ask why I keep such a woman in my house: when we have been married a year and a day, I will tell you; but not now. Are you satisfied, Jane? Do you accept my solution of the mystery?'

I reflected, and in truth it appeared to me the only possible one: satisfied I was not, but to please him I endeavoured to appear so—relieved, I certainly did feel; so I answered him with a contented smile. And now, as it was long past one, I prepared to leave him.

'Does not Sophie sleep with Adèle in the nursery?' he asked, as I lit my candle.

'Yes, sir.'

'And there is room enough in Adèle's little bed for you. You must share it with her to-night, Jane: it is no wonder that the incident you have related should make you nervous, and I would rather you did not sleep alone: promise me to go to the nursery.'

'I shall be very glad to do so, sir.'

'And fasten the door securely on the inside. Wake Sophie when you go upstairs, under pretence of requesting her to rouse you in good time to-morrow; for you must be dressed and have finished breakfast before eight. And now, no more sombre thoughts: chase dull care away, Janet. Don't you hear to what soft whispers the wind has fallen? and there is no more beating of rain against the window-panes: look here' (he lifted up the curtain)—'it is a lovely night!'

It was. Half heaven was pure and stainless: the clouds, now trooping before the wind, which had shifted to the west, were filing off eastward in long, silvered columns. The moon shone peacefully.

'Well,' said Mr. Rochester, gazing inquiringly into my eyes, 'how is my Janet now?'

'The night is serene, sir; and so am I.'

'And you will not dream of separation and sorrow to-night; but of happy love and blissful union.'

This prediction was but half fulfilled: I did not indeed dream of sorrow, but as little did I dream of joy; for I never slept at all. With little Adèle in my arms, I watched the slumber of childhood—so tranquil, so passionless, so innocent—and waited for the coming day: all my life was awake and astir in my frame; and as soon as the sun rose I rose too. I remember Adèle clung to me as I left her; I remember I kissed her as I loosened her little hands from my neck; and I cried over her with strange emotion, and quitted her because I feared my sobs would break her still sound repose. She seemed the emblem of my past life; and he, I was now to array myself to meet, the dread, but adored, type of my unknown future day.

Chapter XXVI

Sophie came at seven to dress me; she was very long indeed in accomplishing her task—so long that Mr. Rochester, grown, I suppose, impatient of my delay, sent up to ask why I did not come. She was just fastening my veil (the plain square of blond after all) to my hair with a brooch; I hurried from under her hands as soon as I could.

'Stop!' she cried in French. 'Look at yourself in the mirror: you have not taken one peep.'

So I turned at the door: I saw a robed and veiled figure, so unlike my usual self that it seemed almost the image of a stranger. 'Jane!' called a voice, and I hastened down. I was received at the foot of the stairs by Mr. Rochester.

'Lingerer,' he said, 'my brain is on fire with impatience; and you tarry so long!'

He took me into the dining-room, surveyed me keenly all over, pronounced me 'fair as a lily, and not only the pride of his life, but the desire of his eyes,' and then, telling me he would give me but ten minutes to eat some breakfast, he rang the bell. One of his lately hired servants, a footman, answered it.

'Is John getting the carriage ready?'

'Yes, sir.'

'Is the luggage brought down?'

'They are bringing it down, sir.'

'Go you to the church: see if Mr. Wood (the clergyman) and the clerk are there: return and tell me.'

The church, as the reader knows, was but just beyond the gates; the footman soon returned.

'Mr. Wood is in the vestry, sir, putting on his surplice.'

'And the carriage?'

'The horses are harnessing.'

'We shall not want it to go to church; but it must be ready the moment we return, all the boxes and luggage arranged and strapped on, and the coachman in his seat.'

'Yes, sir.'

'Jane, are you ready?'

I rose. There were no groomsmen, no bridesmaids, no relatives to wait for or marshal: none but Mr. Rochester and I. Mrs. Fairfax stood in the hall as we passed. I would fain have spoken to her, but my hand was held by a grasp of iron: I was hurried along by a stride I could hardly follow; and to look at Mr. Rochester's face was to feel that not a second of delay would be tolerated for any purpose. I wonder what other bridegroom ever looked as he did—so bent up to a purpose, so grimly resolute: or who, under such steadfast brows, ever revealed such flaming and flashing eyes.

I know not whether the day was fair or foul; in descending the drive, I gazed neither on sky nor earth; my heart was with my eyes; and both seemed migrated into Mr. Rochester's frame. I wanted to see the invisible thing on which, as we went along, he appeared to fasten a glance fierce and fell.[7] I wanted to feel the thoughts whose force he seemed breasting and resisting.

At the churchyard wicket he stopped: he discovered I was quite out of breath.

7. Piercing.

'Am I cruel in my love?' he said. 'Delay an instant: lean on me, Jane.'

And now I can recall the picture of the grey old house of God rising calm before me, of a rook wheeling round the steeple, of a ruddy morning sky beyond. I remember something, too, of the green grave-mounds; and I have not forgotten, either, two figures of strangers, straying amongst the low hillocks, and reading the mementoes graven on the few mossy head-stones. I noticed them, because, as they saw us, they passed round to the back of the church; and I doubted not they were going to enter by the side-aisle door, and witness the ceremony. By Mr. Rochester they were not observed; he was earnestly looking at my face, from which the blood had, I daresay, momentarily fled: for I felt my forehead dewy, and my cheeks and lips cold. When I rallied, which I soon did, he walked gently with me up the path to the porch.

We entered the quiet and humble temple; the priest waited in his white surplice at the lowly altar, the clerk beside him. All was still: two shadows only moved in a remote corner. My conjecture had been correct: the strangers had slipped in before us, and they now stood by the vault of the Rochesters, their backs towards us, viewing through the rails the old time-stained marble tomb, where a kneeling angel guarded the remains of Damer de Rochester, slain at Marston Moor[8] in the time of the civil wars; and of Elizabeth, his wife.

Our place was taken at the communion rails. Hearing a cautious step behind me, I glanced over my shoulder: one of the strangers—a gentleman, evidently—was advancing up the chancel. The service began. The explanation of the intent of matrimony was gone through; and then the clergyman came a step further forward, and, bending slightly towards Mr. Rochester, went on.

'I require and charge you both (as ye will answer at the dreadful day of judgment, when the secrets of all hearts shall be disclosed), that if either of you know any impediment why ye may not lawfully be joined in matrimony, ye do now confess it; for be ye well assured that so many as are coupled together otherwise than God's word doth allow, are not joined together by God, neither is their matrimony lawful.'

He paused, as the custom is. When is the pause after that sentence ever broken by reply? Not, perhaps, once in a hundred years. And the clergyman, who had not lifted his eyes from his book, and had held his breath but for a moment, was proceeding: his hand was already stretched towards Mr. Rochester, as his lips unclosed to ask, 'Wilt thou have this woman for thy wedded wife?'—when a distinct and near voice said:—'The marriage cannot go on: I declare the existence of an impediment.'

The clergyman looked up at the speaker, and stood mute; the clerk

---

8. Parliamentarian victory over the Royalists (July 2, 1644) during the English Civil War.

did the same; Mr. Rochester moved slightly, as if an earthquake had rolled under his feet: taking a firmer footing, and not turning his head or eyes; he said, 'Proceed.'

Profound silence fell when he had uttered that word, with deep but low intonation. Presently Mr. Wood said:—'I cannot proceed without some investigation into what has been asserted, and evidence of its truth or falsehood.'

'The ceremony is quite broken off,' subjoined the voice behind us. 'I am in a condition to prove my allegation: an insuperable impediment to this marriage exists.'

Mr. Rochester heard, but heeded not: he stood stubborn and rigid: making no movement, but to possess himself of my hand. What a hot and strong grasp he had!—and how like quarried marble was his pale, firm, massive front at this moment! How his eye shone, still, watchful, and yet wild beneath!

Mr. Wood seemed at a loss. 'What is the nature of the impediment?' he asked. 'Perhaps it may be got over—explained away?'

'Hardly,' was the answer: 'I have called it insuperable, and I speak advisedly.'

The speaker came forwards, and leaned on the rails. He continued, uttering each word distinctly, calmly, steadily, but not loudly.

'It simply consists in the existence of a previous marriage. Mr. Rochester has a wife now living.'

My nerves vibrated to those low-spoken words as they had never vibrated to thunder—my blood felt their subtle violence as it had never felt frost or fire: but I was collected, and in no danger of swooning. I looked at Mr. Rochester: I made him look at me. His whole face was colourless rock: his eye was both spark and flint. He disavowed nothing: he seemed as if he would defy all things. Without speaking, without smiling, without seeming to recognise in me a human being, he only twined my waist with his arm, and riveted me to his side.

'Who are you?' he asked of the intruder.

'My name is Briggs—a solicitor of —— Street, London.

'And you would thrust on me a wife?'

'I would remind you of your lady's existence, sir; which the law recognises, if you do not.'

'Favour me with an account of her—with her name, her parentage, her place of abode.'

'Certainly.' Mr. Briggs calmly took a paper from his pocket, and read out in a sort of official, nasal voice:—

' "I affirm and can prove that on the 20th of October, A.D. ——— (a date of fifteen years back), Edward Fairfax Rochester, of Thornfield Hall, in the county of ———, and of Ferndean Manor, in —— shire, England, was married to my sister, Bertha Antoinetta Mason, daughter

of Jonas Mason, merchant, and of Antoinetta his wife, a Creole—at
—— church, Spanish Town, Jamaica. The record of the marriage will
be found in the register of that church—a copy of it is now in my possession. Signed, Richard Mason." '

'That—if a genuine document—may prove I have been married,
but it does not prove that the woman mentioned therein as my wife is
still living.'

'She was living three months ago,' returned the lawyer.

'How do you know?'

'I have a witness to the fact, whose testimony even you, sir, will
scarcely controvert.'

'Produce him—or go to hell.'

'I will produce him first—he is on the spot: Mr. Mason, have the
goodness to step forward.'

Mr. Rochester, on hearing the name, set his teeth; he experienced,
too, a sort of strong convulsive quiver; near to him as I was, I felt the
spasmodic movement of fury or despair run through his frame. The
second stranger, who had hitherto lingered in the background, now
drew near; a pale face looked over the solicitor's shoulder—yes, it was
Mason himself. Mr. Rochester turned and glared at him. His eye, as I
have often said, was a black eye: it had now a tawny, nay a bloody light
in its gloom; and his face flushed—olive cheek and hueless forehead
received a glow, as from spreading, ascending heart-fire: and he stirred,
lifted his strong arm—he could have struck Mason—dashed him on the
church-floor—shocked by ruthless blow the breath from his body—but
Mason shrank away, and cried faintly, 'Good God!' Contempt fell cool
on Mr. Rochester—his passion died as if a blight had shrivelled it up: he
only asked, 'What have *you* to say?'

An inaudible reply escaped Mason's white lips.

'The devil is in it if you cannot answer distinctly. I again demand,
what have *you* to say?'

'Sir—sir'—interrupted the clergyman, 'do not forget you are in a
sacred place.' Then, addressing Mason, he inquired gently, 'Are you
aware, sir, whether or not this gentleman's wife is still living?'

'Courage,' urged the lawyer,—'speak out.'

'She is now living at Thornfield Hall,' said Mason, in more articulate
tones: 'I saw her there last April. I am her brother.'

'At Thornfield Hall!' ejaculated the clergyman. 'Impossible! I am an
old resident in this neighbourhood, sir, and I never heard of a Mrs.
Rochester at Thornfield Hall.'

I saw a grim smile contort Mr. Rochester's lip, and he muttered:—
'No—by God! I took care that none should hear of it—or of her under
that name.' He mused—for ten minutes he held counsel with himself:

he formed his resolve, and announced it:—'Enough—all shall bolt out at once, like a bullet from the barrel.—Wood, close your book, and take off your surplice; John Green (to the clerk) leave the church: there will be no wedding to-day:' the man obeyed.

Mr. Rochester continued, hardily and recklessly: 'Bigamy is an ugly word!—I meant, however, to be a bigamist; but fate has outmanœuvered me; or Providence has checked me,—perhaps the last. I am little better than a devil at this moment; and, as my pastor there would tell me, deserve no doubt the sternest judgments of God,—even to the quenchless fire and deathless worm. Gentlemen, my plan is broken up!—what this lawyer and his client say is true: I have been married; and the woman to whom I was married lives! You say you never heard of a Mrs. Rochester at the house up yonder, Wood: but I dare say you have many a time inclined your ear to gossip about the mysterious lunatic kept there under watch and ward. Some have whispered to you that she is my bastard half-sister: some, my cast-off mistress; I now inform you that she is my wife, whom I married fifteen years ago,—Bertha Mason by name; sister of this resolute personage, who is now, with his quivering limbs and white cheeks, showing you what a stout heart men may bear. Cheer up, Dick!—never fear me!—I'd almost as soon strike a woman as you. Bertha Mason is mad; and she came of a mad family;—idiots and maniacs through three generations! Her mother, the Creole, was both a mad-woman and a drunkard!—as I found out after I had wed the daughter: for they were silent on family secrets before. Bertha, like a dutiful child, copied her parent in both points. I had a charming partner—pure, wise, modest: you can fancy I was a happy man.—I went through rich scenes! Oh! my experience has been heavenly, if you only knew it! But I owe you no further explanation. Briggs, Wood, Mason,—I invite you all to come up to the house and visit Mrs. Poole's patient, and *my wife*! You shall see what sort of a being I was cheated into espousing, and judge whether or not I had a right to break the compact, and seek sympathy with something at least human. This girl,' he continued, looking at me, 'knew no more than you, Wood, of the disgusting secret: she thought all was fair and legal; and never dreamt she was going to be entrapped into a feigned union with a defrauded wretch, already bound to a bad, mad, and embruted partner! Come, all of you, follow.'

Still holding me fast, he left the church: the three gentlemen came after. At the front door of the hall we found the carriage.

'Take it back to the coach-house, John,' said Mr. Rochester, coolly; 'it will not be wanted to-day.'

At our entrance Mrs. Fairfax, Adèle, Sophie, Leah, advanced to meet and greet us.

'To the right about—every soul!' cried the master: 'away with your
congratulations! Who wants them?—Not I!—they are fifteen years too
late!'

He passed on and ascended the stairs, still holding my hand, and still
beckoning the gentlemen to follow him; which they did. We mounted
the first staircase, passed up the gallery, proceeded to the third storey:
the low, black door, opened by Mr. Rochester's master key, admitted us
to the tapestried room, with its great bed and its pictorial cabinet.

'You know this place, Mason,' said our guide; 'she bit and stabbed
you here.'

He lifted the hangings from the wall, uncovering the second door:
this, too, he opened. In a room without a window there burnt a fire,
guarded by a high and strong fender, and a lamp suspended from the
ceiling by a chain. Grace Poole bent over the fire, apparently cooking
something in a saucepan. In the deep shade, at the further end of the
room, a figure ran backwards and forwards. What it was, whether beast
or human being, one could not, at first sight, tell: it grovelled, seemingly, on all fours; it snatched and growled like some strange wild animal: but it was covered with clothing; and a quantity of dark, grizzled
hair, wild as a mane, hid its head and face.

'Good-morrow, Mrs. Poole!' said Mr. Rochester. 'How are you? and
how is your charge to-day?'

'We're tolerable, sir, I thank you,' replied Grace, lifting the boiling
mess carefully on to the hob: 'rather snappish, but not 'rageous.'

A fierce cry seemed to give the lie to her favourable report: the
clothed hyena rose up, and stood tall on its hind feet.

'Ah, sir, she sees you!' exclaimed Grace: 'you'd better not stay.'

'Only a few moments, Grace: you must allow me a few moments.'

'Take care then, sir!—for God's sake, take care!'

The maniac bellowed: she parted her shaggy locks from her visage,
and gazed wildly at her visitors. I recognised well that purple face—
those bloated features. Mrs. Poole advanced.

'Keep out of the way,' said Mr. Rochester, thrusting her aside: 'she
has no knife now, I suppose? and I'm on my guard.'

'One never knows what she has, sir: she is so cunning: it is not in
mortal discretion to fathom her craft.'

'We had better leave her,' whispered Mason.

'Go to the devil!' was his brother-in-law's recommendation.

''Ware!' cried Grace. The three gentlemen retreated simultaneously.
Mr. Rochester flung me behind him: the lunatic sprang and grappled
his throat viciously, and laid her teeth to his cheek: they struggled. She
was a big woman, in stature almost equalling her husband, and corpulent besides: she showed virile force in the contest—more than once
she almost throttled him, athletic as he was. He could have settled her

with a well-planted blow; but he would not strike: he would only wrestle. At last he mastered her arms; Grace Poole gave him a cord, and he pinioned them behind her: with more rope, which was at hand, he bound her to a chair. The operation was performed amidst the fiercest yells and the most convulsive plunges. Mr. Rochester then turned to the spectators: he looked at them with a smile both acrid and desolate.

'That is *my wife*,' said he. 'Such is the sole conjugal embrace I am ever to know—such are the endearments which are to solace my leisure hours! And *this* is what I wished to have' (laying his hand on my shoulder): 'this young girl, who stands so grave and quiet at the mouth of hell, looking collectedly at the gambols of a demon. I wanted her just as a change after that fierce ragout. Wood and Briggs, look at the difference! Compare these clear eyes with the red balls yonder—this face with that mask—this form with that bulk; then judge me, priest of the gospel and man of the law, and remember, with what judgment ye judge ye shall be judged![9] Off with you now. I must shut up my prize.'

We all withdrew. Mr. Rochester stayed a moment behind us to give some further order to Grace Poole. The solicitor addressed me as he descended the stair.

'You, madam,' said he, 'are cleared from all blame: your uncle will be glad to hear it—if, indeed, he should be still living—when Mr. Mason returns to Madeira.'

'My uncle! What of him? Do you know him?'

'Mr. Mason does: Mr. Eyre has been the Funchal correspondent of his house for some years. When your uncle received your letter intimating the contemplated union between yourself and Mr. Rochester, Mr. Mason, who was staying at Madeira to recruit his health, on his way back to Jamaica, happened to be with him. Mr. Eyre mentioned the intelligence; for he knew that my client here was acquainted with a gentleman of the name of Rochester. Mr. Mason, astonished and distressed as you may suppose, revealed the real state of matters. Your uncle, I am sorry to say, is now on a sick bed; from which, considering the nature of his disease—decline—and the stage it has reached, it is unlikely he will ever rise. He could not then hasten to England himself, to extricate you from the snare into which you had fallen, but he implored Mr. Mason to lose no time in taking steps to prevent the false marriage. He referred him to me for assistance. I used all despatch, and am thankful I was not too late: as you, doubtless, must be also. Were I not morally certain that your uncle will be dead ere you reach Madeira, I would advise you to accompany Mr. Mason back: but as it is, I think you had better remain in England till you can hear further, either from or of Mr. Eyre. Have we anything else to stay for?' he inquired of Mr. Mason.

9. Matthew 7:1–2.

'No, no—let us be gone,' was the anxious reply; and without waiting to take leave of Mr. Rochester, they made their exit at the hall door. The clergyman stayed to exchange a few sentences, either of admonition or reproof, with his haughty parishioner: this duty done, he too departed.

I heard him go as I stood at the half-open door of my own room, to which I had now withdrawn. The house cleared, I shut myself in, fastened the bolt that none might intrude, and proceeded—not to weep, not to mourn, I was yet too calm for that, but—mechanically to take off the wedding-dress, and replace it by the stuff gown I had worn yesterday, as I thought, for the last time. I then sat down: I felt weak and tired. I leaned my arms on a table, and my head dropped on them. And now I thought: till now I had only heard, seen, moved—followed up and down where I was led or dragged—watched event rush on event, disclosure open beyond disclosure: but *now, I thought.*

The morning had been a quiet morning enough—all except the brief scene with the lunatic: the transaction in the church had not been noisy; there was no explosion of passion, no loud altercation, no dispute, no defiance or challenge, no tears, no sobs: a few words had been spoken, a calmly pronounced objection to the marriage made; some stern, short questions put by Mr. Rochester; answers, explanations given, evidence adduced; an open admission of the truth had been uttered by my master; then the living proof had been seen: the intruders were gone, and all was over.

I was in my own room as usual—just myself, without obvious change: nothing had smitten me, or scathed me, or maimed me. And yet, where was the Jane Eyre of yesterday?—where was her life?— where were her prospects?

Jane Eyre, who had been an ardent, expectant woman—almost a bride—was a cold, solitary girl again: her life was pale; her prospects were desolate. A Christmas frost had come at midsummer; a white December storm had whirled over June; ice glazed the ripe apples, drifts crushed the blowing roses; on hay-field and corn-field lay a frozen shroud: lanes which last night blushed full of flowers, to-day were pathless with untrodden snow; and the woods, which twelve hours since waved leafy and fragrant as groves between the tropics, now spread, waste, wild, and white as pine-forests in wintry Norway. My hopes were all dead—struck with a subtle doom, such as in one night, fell on all the first-born in the land of Egypt.[1] I looked on my cherished wishes, yesterday so blooming and glowing: they lay stark, chill, livid corpses that could never revive. I looked at my love: that feeling which was my master's—which he had created; it shivered in my heart, like a suffering

1. Exodus 12.

child in a cold cradle; sickness and anguish had seized it; it could not seek Mr. Rochester's arms—it could not derive warmth from his breast. Oh, never more could it turn to him; for faith was blighted—confidence destroyed! Mr. Rochester was not to me what he had been; for he was not what I had thought him. I would not ascribe vice to him; I would not say he had betrayed me: but the attribute of stainless truth was gone from his idea; and from his presence I must go; *that* I perceived well. When—how—whither, I could not yet discern; but he himself, I doubted not, would hurry me from Thornfield. Real affection, it seemed, he could not have for me; it had been only fitful passion: that was balked; he would want me no more. I should fear even to cross his path now: my view must be hateful to him. Oh, how blind had been my eyes! How weak my conduct!

My eyes were covered and closed: eddying darkness seemed to swim round me, and reflection came in as black and confused a flow. Self-abandoned, relaxed, and effortless, I seemed to have laid me down in the dried-up bed of a great river; I heard a flood loosened in remote mountains, and felt the torrent come: to rise I had no will, to flee I had no strength. I lay faint; longing to be dead. One idea only still throbbed life-like within me—a remembrance of God: it begot an unuttered prayer: these words went wandering up and down in my rayless mind, as something that should be whispered; but no energy was found to express them:—'Be not far from me, for trouble is near: there is none to help.[2]

It was near: and as I had lifted no petition to Heaven to avert it—as I had neither joined my hands, nor bent my knees, nor moved my lips—it came: in full, heavy swing the torrent poured over me. The whole consciousness of my life lorn, my love lost, my hope quenched, my faith death-struck, swayed full and mighty above me in one sullen mass. That bitter hour cannot be described: in truth, 'the waters came into my soul; I sank in deep mire: I felt no standing; I came into deep waters; the floods overflowed me.'[3]

Chapter XXVII

Some time in the afternoon I raised my head, and looking round and seeing the western sun gilding the sign of its decline on the wall, I asked, 'What am I to do?'

But the answer my mind gave—'Leave Thornfield at once'—was so prompt, so dread, that I stopped my ears: I said, I could not bear such words now. 'That I am not Edward Rochester's bride is the least part of my woe,' I alleged: 'that I have wakened out of most glorious dreams, and found them all void and vain, is a horror I could bear and master;

2. Psalms 22:11.   3. Psalms 69:1.

but that I must leave him decidedly, instantly, entirely, is intolerable. I cannot do it.'

But, then, a voice within me averred that I could do it; and foretold that I should do it. I wrestled with my own resolution: I wanted to be weak that I might avoid the awful passage of further suffering I saw laid out for me; and conscience, turned tyrant, held passion by the throat, told her tauntingly she had yet but dipped her dainty foot in the slough, and swore that with that arm of iron he would thrust her down to unsounded depths of agony.

'Let me be torn away, then!' I cried. 'Let another help me!'

'No; you shall tear yourself away, none shall help you: you shall, yourself, pluck out your right eye: yourself cut off your right hand: your heart shall be the victim; and you, the priest, to transfix it.'[4]

I rose up suddenly, terror-struck at the solitude which so ruthless a judge haunted,—at the silence which so awful a voice filled. My head swam as I stood erect: I perceived that I was sickening from excitement and inanition; neither meat nor drink had passed my lips that day, for I had taken no breakfast. And, with a strange pang, I now reflected that, long as I had been shut up here, no message had been sent to ask how I was, or to invite me to come down: not even little Adèle had tapped at the door; not even Mrs. Fairfax had sought me. 'Friends always forget those whom fortune forsakes,' I murmured, as I undrew the bolt and passed out. I stumbled over an obstacle: my head was still dizzy, my sight was dim, and my limbs were feeble. I could not soon recover myself. I fell, but not on to the ground; an out-stretched arm caught me; I looked up—I was supported by Mr. Rochester, who sat in a chair across my chamber threshold.

'You come out at last,' he said. 'Well, I have been waiting for you long, and listening: yet not one movement have I heard, nor one sob: five minutes more of that death-like hush, and I should have forced the lock like a burglar. So, you shun me?—you shut yourself up and grieve alone! I would rather you had come and upbraided me with vehemence. You are passionate: I expected a scene of some kind. I was prepared for the hot rain of tears; only I wanted them to be shed on my breast: now a senseless floor has received them, or your drenched handkerchief. But I err: you have not wept at all! I see a white cheek and a faded eye, but no trace of tears. I suppose, then, your heart has been weeping blood?

'Well, Jane; not a word of reproach? Nothing bitter—nothing poignant? Nothing to cut a feeling or sting a passion? You sit quietly where I have placed you, and regard me with a weary, passive look.

'Jane, I never meant to wound you thus. If the man who had but one

---

4. In Matthew 5:27–30 Jesus redefines the Old Testament concept of adultery.

little ewe lamb that was dear to him as a daughter, that ate of his bread and drank of his cup, and lay in his bosom, had by some mistake slaughtered it at the shambles, he would not have rued his bloody blunder more than I now rue mine.[5] Will you ever forgive me?'

Reader!—I forgave him at the moment, and on the spot. There was such deep remorse in his eye, such true pity in his tone, such manly energy in his manner; and, besides, there was such unchanged love in his whole look and mien—I forgave him all: yet not in words, not outwardly; only at my heart's core.

'You know I am a scoundrel, Jane?' ere long he inquired wistfully—wondering, I suppose, at my continued silence and tameness: the result rather of weakness than of will.

'Yes, sir.'

'Then tell me so roundly and sharply—don't spare me.'

'I cannot: I am tired and sick. I want some water.' He heaved a sort of shuddering sigh, and taking me in his arms, carried me downstairs. At first I did not know to what room he had borne me; all was cloudy to my glazed sight: presently I felt the reviving warmth of a fire; for, summer as it was, I had become icy cold in my chamber. He put wine to my lips; I tasted it and revived; then I ate something he offered me, and was soon myself. I was in the library—sitting in his chair—he was quite near. 'If I could go out of life now, without too sharp a pang, it would be well for me,' I thought; 'then I should not have to make the effort of cracking my heart-strings in rending them from among Mr. Rochester's. I must leave him, it appears. I do not want to leave him—I cannot leave him.'

'How are you now, Jane?'

'Much better, sir: I shall be well soon.'

'Taste the wine again, Jane.'

I obeyed him; then he put the glass on the table, stood before me, and looked at me attentively. Suddenly he turned away, with an inarticulate exclamation, full of passionate emotion of some kind; he walked fast through the room and came back: he stooped towards me as if to kiss me; but I remembered caresses were now forbidden. I turned my face away, and put his aside.

'What!—How is this?' he exclaimed hastily. 'Oh, I know! you won't kiss the husband of Bertha Mason? You consider my arms filled and my embraces appropriated?'

'At any rate, there is neither room nor claim for me, sir.'

'Why, Jane? I will spare you the trouble of much talking: I will answer for you—because I have a wife already, you would reply.—I guess rightly?'

5. 2 Samuel 12:1–4 tells of the rich man's deliberate slaughter of the poor man's lamb.

'Yes.'

'If you think so, you must have a strange opinion of me: you must regard me as a plotting profligate—a base and low rake who has been simulating disinterested love in order to draw you into a snare deliberately laid, and strip you of honour, and rob you of self-respect. What do you say to that? I see you can say nothing: in the first place, you are faint still, and have enough to do to draw your breath; in the second place, you cannot yet accustom yourself to accuse and revile me; and, besides, the flood-gates of tears are opened, and they would rush out if you spoke much; and you have no desire to expostulate, to upbraid, to make a scene: you are thinking how to *act*,—*talking*, you consider, is of no use. I know you—I am on my guard.'

'Sir, I do not wish to act against you,' I said; and my unsteady voice warned me to curtail my sentence.

'Not in *your* sense of the word, but in *mine*, you are scheming to destroy me. You have as good as said that I am a married man—as a married man you will shun me, keep out of my way: just now you have refused to kiss me. You intend to make yourself a complete stranger to me; to live under this roof only as Adèle's governess: if ever I say a friendly word to you, if ever a friendly feeling inclines you again to me, you will say,—"That man had nearly made me his mistress: I must be ice and rock to him;" and ice and rock you will accordingly become.'

I cleared and steadied my voice to reply: 'All is changed about me, sir; I must change too—there is no doubt of that; and to avoid fluctuations of feeling, and continual combats with recollections and associations, there is only one way—Adèle must have a new governess, sir.'

'Oh, Adèle will go to school—I have settled that already; nor do I mean to torment you with the hideous associations and recollections of Thornfield Hall—this accursed place—this tent of Achan[6]—this insolent vault, offering the ghastliness of living death to the light of the open sky—this narrow stone hell, with its one real fiend, worse than a legion of such as we imagine.—Jane, you shall not stay here, nor will I. I was wrong ever to bring you to Thornfield Hall, knowing as I did how it was haunted. I charged them to conceal from you, before I ever saw you, all knowledge of the curse of the place; merely because I feared Adèle never would have a governess to stay if she knew with what inmate she was housed, and my plans would not permit me to remove the maniac elsewhere—though I possess an old house, Ferndean Manor, even more retired and hidden than this, where I could have lodged her safely enough, had not a scruple about the unhealthiness of the situation, in the heart of a wood, made my conscience recoil from the arrangement. Probably those damp walls would soon have eased me of her charge:

6. Achan concealed stolen treasure in his tent (Joshua 7).

but to each villain his own vice; and mine is not a tendency to indirect assassination, even of what I most hate.

'Concealing the mad-woman's neighbourhood from you, however, was something like covering a child with a cloak, and laying it down near a upas-tree:[7] that demon's vicinage is poisoned, and always was. But I'll shut up Thornfield Hall: I'll nail up the front door, and board the lower windows; I'll give Mrs. Poole two hundred a year to live here with *my wife*, as you term that fearful hag: Grace will do much for money, and she shall have her son, the keeper at Grimsby Retreat, to bear her company and be at hand to give her aid in the paroxysms when *my wife* is prompted by her familiar to burn people in their beds at night, to stab them, to bite their flesh from their bones, and so on'—

'Sir,' I interrupted him, 'you are inexorable for that unfortunate lady: you speak of her with hate—with vindictive antipathy. It is cruel—she cannot help being mad.'

'Jane, my little darling (so I will call you, for so you are), you don't know what you are talking about; you misjudge me again: it is not because she is mad I hate her. If you were mad, do you think I should hate you?'

'I do indeed, sir.'

'Then you are mistaken, and you know nothing about me, and nothing about the sort of love of which I am capable. Every atom of your flesh is as dear to me as my own: in pain and sickness it would still be dear. Your mind is my treasure, and if it were broken, it would be my treasure still: if you raved, my arms should confine you, and not a strait waistcoat—your grasp, even in fury, would have a charm for me: if you flew at me as wildly as that woman did this morning, I should receive you in an embrace at least as fond as it would be restrictive. I should not shrink from you with disgust as I did from her: in your quiet moments you should have no watcher and no nurse but me; and I could hang over you with untiring tenderness, though you gave me no smile in return; and never weary of gazing into your eyes, though they had no longer a ray of recognition for me.—But why do I follow that train of ideas? I was talking of removing you from Thornfield. All, you know, is prepared for prompt departure: to-morrow you shall go. I only ask you to endure one more night under this roof, Jane: and then, farewell to its miseries and terrors for ever! I have a place to repair to which will be a secure sanctuary from hateful reminiscences, from unwelcome intrusion—even from falsehood and slander.'

'And take Adèle with you, sir,' I interrupted; 'she will be a companion for you.'

'What do you mean, Jane? I told you I would send Adèle to school:

7. A legendary poisonous tree that killed all the life around it.

and what do I want with a child for a companion? and not my own child,—a French dancer's bastard. Why do you importune me about her? I say, why do you assign Adèle to me for a companion?'

'You spoke of a retirement, sir; and retirement and solitude are dull: too dull for you.'

'Solitude! solitude!' he reiterated, with irritation. 'I see I must come to an explanation. I don't know what sphinx-like expression is forming in your countenance. *You* are to share my solitude. Do you understand?'

I shook my head: it required a degree of courage, excited as he was becoming, even to risk that mute sign of dissent. He had been walking fast about the room, and he stopped, as if suddenly rooted to one spot. He looked at me long and hard: I turned my eyes from him, fixed them on the fire, and tried to assume and maintain a quiet, collected aspect.

'Now for the hitch in Jane's character,' he said at last, speaking more calmly than from his look I had expected him to speak. 'The reel of silk has run smoothly enough so far; but I always knew there would come a knot and a puzzle: here it is. Now for vexation, and exasperation, and endless trouble! By God! I long to exert a fraction of Samson's strength, and break the entanglement like tow!'

He recommenced his walk: but soon again stopped, and this time just before me.

'Jane! will you hear reason?' (he stooped and approached his lips to my ear) 'because, if you won't, I'll try violence.' His voice was hoarse; his look that of a man who is just about to burst an insufferable bond and plunge headlong into wild license. I saw that in another moment, and with one impetus of frenzy more, I should be able to do nothing with him. The present—the passing second of time—was all I had in which to control and restrain him: a movement of repulsion, flight, fear, would have sealed my doom,—and his. But I was not afraid: not in the least. I felt an inward power; a sense of influence, which supported me. The crisis was perilous; but not without its charm: such as the Indian, perhaps, feels when he slips over the rapid in his canoe. I took hold of his clenched hand; loosened the contorted fingers, and said to him, soothingly,—'Sit down; I'll talk to you as long as you like, and hear all you have to say, whether reasonable or unreasonable.'

He sat down: but he did not get leave to speak directly. I had been struggling with tears for some time; I had taken great pains to repress them, because I knew he would not like to see me weep. Now, however, I considered it well to let them flow as freely and as long as they liked. If the flood annoyed him, so much the better. So I gave way and cried heartily.

Soon I heard him earnestly entreating me to be composed. I said I could not while he was in such a passion.

'But I am not angry, Jane: I only love you too well; and you had steeled your little pale face with such a resolute, frozen look, I could not endure it. Hush, now, and wipe your eyes.'

His softened voice announced that he was subdued; so I, in my turn, became calm. Now he made an effort to rest his head on my shoulder; but I would not permit it. Then he would draw me to him: no.

'Jane! Jane!' he said, in such an accent of bitter sadness it thrilled along every nerve I had, 'you don't love me, then? It was only my station, and the rank of my wife, that you valued? Now that you think me disqualified to become your husband you recoil from my touch as if I were some toad or ape.'

These words cut me: yet what could I do or say? I ought probably to have done or said nothing: but I was so tortured by a sense of remorse at thus hurting his feelings I could not control the wish to drop balm where I had wounded.

'I *do* love you,' I said, 'more than ever: but I must not show or indulge the feeling: and this is the last time I must express it.'

'The last time, Jane! What! do you think you can live with me, and see me daily, and yet, if you still love me, be always cold and distant?'

'No, sir; that I am certain I could not; and therefore I see there is but one way: but you will be furious if I mention it.'

'Oh, mention it! If I storm, you have the art of weeping.'

'Mr. Rochester, I must leave you.'

'For how long, Jane? For a few minutes, while you smooth your hair—which is somewhat dishevelled; and bathe your face—which looks feverish?'

'I must leave Adèle and Thornfield. I must part with you for my whole life: I must begin a new existence amongst strange faces and strange scenes.'

'Of course: I told you you should. I pass over the madness about parting from me. You mean you must become a part of me. As to the new existence, it is all right: you shall yet be my wife: I am not married. You shall be Mrs. Rochester—both virtually and nominally. I shall keep only to you so long as you and I live. You shall go to a place I have in the south of France: a white-washed villa on the shores of the Mediterranean. There you shall live a happy, and guarded, and most innocent life. Never fear that I wish to lure you into error—to make you my mistress. Why do you shake your head? Jane, you must be reasonable; or in truth I shall again become frantic.'

His voice and hand quivered; his large nostrils dilated; his eye blazed; still I dared to speak:—'Sir, your wife is living: that is a fact acknowledged this morning by yourself. If I lived with you as you desire, I should then be your mistress: to say otherwise is sophistical—is false.'

'Jane, I am not a gentle-tempered man—you forget that: I am not

long-enduring; I am not cool and dispassionate. Out of pity to me and
yourself, put your finger on my pulse, feel how it throbs, and—beware!'

He bared his wrist and offered it to me: the blood was forsaking his
cheek and lips; they were growing livid; I was distressed on all hands.
To agitate him thus deeply, by a resistance he so abhorred, was cruel: to
yield was out of the question. I did what human beings do instinctively
when they are driven to utter extremity—looked for aid to one higher
than man: the words 'God help me!' burst involuntarily from my lips.

'I am a fool!' cried Mr. Rochester suddenly. 'I keep telling her I am
not married, and do not explain to her why. I forget she knows nothing
of the character of that woman, or of the circumstances attending my
infernal union with her. Oh, I am certain Jane will agree with me in
opinion when she knows all that I know! Just put your hand in mine,
Janet, that I may have the evidence of touch as well as sight to prove
you are near me—and I will in a few words show you the real state of
the case. Can you listen to me?'

'Yes, sir; for hours if you will.'

'I ask only minutes. Jane, did you ever hear or know that I was not
the eldest son of my house; that I had once a brother older than I?'

'I remember Mrs. Fairfax told me so once.'

'And did you ever hear that my father was an avaricious grasping
man?'

'I have understood something to that effect.'

'Well, Jane, being so, it was his resolution to keep the property together; he could not bear the idea of dividing his estate and leaving me a
fair portion: all, he resolved, should go to my brother Rowland. Yet as
little could he endure that a son of his should be a poor man. I must be
provided for by a wealthy marriage. He sought me a partner betimes.
Mr. Mason, a West India planter and merchant, was his old acquaintance. He was certain his possessions were real and vast: he made inquiries. Mr. Mason, he found, had a son and daughter; and he learned
from him that he could and would give the latter a fortune of thirty
thousand pounds: that sufficed. When I left college I was sent out to
Jamaica, to espouse a bride already courted for me. My father said
nothing about her money: but he told me Miss Mason was the boast of
Spanish Town for her beauty: and this was no lie. I found her a fine
woman, in the style of Blanche Ingram; tall, dark, and majestic. Her
family wished to secure me, because I was of a good race; and so did
she. They showed her to me in parties, splendidly dressed. I seldom saw
her alone, and had very little private conversation with her. She flattered me, and lavishly displayed for my pleasure her charms and accomplishments. All the men in her circle seemed to admire her and
envy me. I was dazzled, stimulated: my senses were excited; and being
ignorant, raw, and inexperienced, I thought I loved her. There is no

folly so besotted that the idiotic rivalries of society, the prurience, the rashness, the blindness of youth, will not hurry a man to its commission. Her relatives encouraged me; competitors piqued me; she allured me: a marriage was achieved almost before I knew where I was. Oh, I have no respect for myself when I think of that act!—an agony of inward contempt masters me. I never loved, I never esteemed, I did not even know her. I was not sure of the existence of one virtue in her nature: I had marked neither modesty, nor benevolence, nor candour, nor refinement in her mind or manners—and, I married her:—gross, grovelling, mole-eyed blockhead that I was! With less sin I might have—but let me remember to whom I am speaking.

'My bride's mother I had never seen: I understood she was dead. The honeymoon over, I learned my mistake; she was only mad, and shut up in a lunatic asylum. There was a younger brother, too, a complete dumb idiot. The elder one, whom you have seen (and whom I cannot hate, whilst I abhor all his kindred, because he has some grains of affection in his feeble mind; shown in the continued interest he takes in his wretched sister, and also in a dog-like attachment he once bore me), will probably be in the same state one day. My father, and my brother Rowland, knew all this; but they thought only of the thirty thousand pounds, and joined in the plot against me.

'These were vile discoveries; but, except for the treachery of concealment, I should have made them no subject of reproach to my wife: even when I found her nature wholly alien to mine; her tastes obnoxious to me; her cast of mind common, low, narrow, and singularly incapable of being led to anything higher, expanded to anything larger—when I found that I could not pass a single evening, nor even a single hour of the day, with her in comfort: that kindly conversation could not be sustained between us, because whatever topic I started immediately received from her a turn at once coarse and trite, perverse and imbecile—when I perceived that I should never have a quiet or settled household, because no servant would bear the continued outbreaks of her violent and unreasonable temper, or the vexations of her absurd, contradictory, exacting orders—even then I restrained myself: I eschewed upbraiding, I curtailed remonstrance; I tried to devour my repentance and disgust in secret; I repressed the deep antipathy I felt.

'Jane, I will not trouble you with abominable details: some strong words shall express what I have to say. I lived with that woman upstairs four years, and before that time she had tried me indeed: her character ripened and developed with frightful rapidity; her vices sprang up fast and rank: they were so strong, only cruelty could check them; and I would not use cruelty. What a pigmy intellect she had—and what giant propensities! How fearful were the curses those propensities entailed on me! Bertha Mason,—the true daughter of an infamous mother,—

dragged me through all the hideous and degrading agonies which must attend a man bound to a wife at once intemperate and unchaste.

'My brother in the interval was dead; and at the end of the four years my father died too. I was rich enough now—yet poor to hideous indigence: a nature the most gross, impure, depraved, I ever saw, was associated with mine, and called by the law and by society a part of me. And I could not rid myself of it by any legal proceedings: for the doctors now discovered that *my wife* was mad—her excesses had prematurely developed the germs of insanity:—Jane, you don't like my narrative; you look almost sick—shall I defer the rest to another day?'

'No, sir, finish it now: I pity you—I do earnestly pity you.'

'Pity, Jane, from some people is a noxious and insulting sort of tribute, which one is justified in hurling back in the teeth of those who offer it; but that is the sort of pity native to callous, selfish hearts: it is a hybrid, egotistical pain at hearing of woes, crossed with ignorant contempt for those who have endured them. But that is not your pity, Jane: it is not the feeling of which your whole face is full at this moment—with which your eyes are now almost overflowing—with which your heart is heaving—with which your hand is trembling in mine. Your pity, my darling, is the suffering mother of love: its anguish is the very natal pang of the divine passion. I accept it, Jane; let the daughter have free advent —my arms wait to receive her.'

'Now, sir, proceed: what did you do when you found she was mad?'

'Jane—I approached the verge of despair: a remnant of self-respect was all that intervened between me and the gulf. In the eyes of the world I was doubtless covered with grimy dishonour: but I resolved to be clean in my own sight—and to the last I repudiated the contamination of her crimes, and wrenched myself from connection with her mental defects. Still, society associated my name and person with hers! I yet saw her and heard her daily: something of her breath (faugh!) mixed with the air I breathed; and, besides, I remembered I had once been her husband—that recollection was then, and is now, inexpressibly odious to me: moreover, I knew that while she lived I could never be the husband of another and better wife; and though five years my senior (her family and her father had lied to me even in the particular of her age), she was likely to live as long as I, being as robust in frame as she was infirm in mind. Thus, at the age of twenty-six, I was hopeless.

'One night I had been awakened by her yells—(since the medical men had pronounced her mad she had of course been shut up)—it was a fiery West Indian night; one of the description that frequently precede the hurricanes of those climates; being unable to sleep in bed, I got up and opened the window. The air was like sulphur-steams—I could find no refreshment anywhere. Mosquitoes came buzzing in and hummed sullenly round the room; the sea, which I could hear from thence, rumbled dull like an earthquake—black clouds were casting up over it; the moon was setting in the waves, broad and red, like a hot cannon-ball—she threw her last bloody glance over a world quivering with the ferment of tempest. I was physically influenced by the atmosphere and scene, and my ears were filled with the curses the maniac still shrieked out; wherein she momentarily mingled my name with such a tone of demon-hate, with such language!—no professed harlot ever had a fouler vocabulary than she: though two rooms off, I heard every word—the thin partitions of the West India house opposing but slight obstruction to her wolfish cries.

'"This life," said I at last, "is hell! this is the air—those are the sounds of the bottomless pit! I have a right to deliver myself from it if I can. The sufferings of this mortal state will leave me with the heavy flesh that now cumbers my soul. Of the fanatic's burning eternity I have no fear; there is not a future state worse than this present one—let me break away, and go home to God!"

'I said this whilst I knelt down at and unlocked a trunk which contained a brace of loaded pistols: I meant to shoot myself. I only entertained the intention for a moment; for not being insane, the crisis of exquisite and unalloyed despair which had originated the wish and design of self-destruction was past in a second.

'A wind fresh from Europe blew over the ocean and rushed through the open casement: the storm broke, streamed, thundered, blazed, and the air grew pure. I then framed and fixed a resolution. While I walked under the dripping orange-trees of my wet garden, and amongst its drenched pomegranates and pine-apples, and while the refulgent dawn of the tropics kindled round me—I reasoned thus, Jane:—and now listen; for it was true Wisdom that consoled me in that hour, and showed me the right path to follow.

'The sweet wind from Europe was still whispering in the refreshed leaves, and the Atlantic was thundering in glorious liberty; my heart, dried up and scorched for a long time, swelled to the tone, and filled with living blood—my being longed for renewal—my soul thirsted for a pure draught. I saw Hope revive—and felt Regeneration possible. From a flowery arch at the bottom of my garden I gazed over the sea —bluer than the sky: the old world was beyond; clear prospects opened thus:—

'"Go," said Hope, "and live again in Europe: there it is not known what a sullied name you bear, nor what a filthy burden is bound to you. You may take the maniac with you to England; confine her with due attendance and precautions at Thornfield: then travel yourself to what clime you will, and form what new tie you like. That woman, who has so abused your long-suffering—so sullied your name; so outraged your honour; so blighted your youth—is not your wife; nor are you her husband. See that she is cared for as her condition demands, and you have done all that God and Humanity require of you. Let her identity, her connection with yourself, be buried in oblivion: you are bound to impart them to no living being. Place her in safety and comfort: shelter her degradation with secrecy, and leave her."

'I acted precisely on this suggestion. My father and brother had not made my marriage known to their acquaintance; because, in the very first letter I wrote to apprise them of the union—having already begun to experience extreme disgust of its consequences; and from the family character and constitution seeing a hideous future opening to me—I added an urgent charge to keep it secret; and very soon the infamous conduct of the wife my father had selected for me was such as to make him blush to own her as his daughter-in-law. Far from desiring to publish the connection, he became as anxious to conceal it as myself.

'To England, then, I conveyed her; a fearful voyage I had with such a monster in the vessel. Glad was I when I at last got her to Thornfield, and saw her safely lodged in that third-storey room, of whose secret inner cabinet she has now for ten years made a wild beast's den—a goblin's cell. I had some trouble in finding an attendant for her: as it was necessary to select one on whose fidelity dependence could be placed; for her ravings would inevitably betray my secret: besides, she had lucid intervals of days—sometimes weeks—which she filled up with abuse of me. At last I hired Grace Poole, from the Grimsby Retreat. She and the surgeon, Carter (who dressed Mason's wounds that night he was stabbed and worried), are the only two I have ever admitted to my confidence. Mrs. Fairfax may indeed have suspected something; but she could have gained no precise knowledge as to facts. Grace has, on the whole, proved a good keeper; though, owing partly to a fault of her own, of which it appears nothing can cure her, and which is incident to her harassing profession, her vigilance has been more than once lulled and baffled. The lunatic is both cunning and malignant; she has never failed to take advantage of her guardian's temporary lapses; once to secrete the knife with which she stabbed her brother, and twice to possess herself of the key of her cell, and issue therefrom in the night-time. On the first of these occasions she perpetrated the attempt to burn me in my bed; on the second she paid that ghastly visit to you. I thank Providence, who watched over you, that she then spent her fury on your wedding apparel; which perhaps brought back vague reminiscences of her own bridal days; but on what might have happened I cannot endure to reflect. When I think of the thing which flew at my throat this morning hanging its black and scarlet visage over the nest of my dove my blood curdles'——

'And what, sir,' I asked, while he paused, 'did you do when you had settled her here? Where did you go?'

'What did I do, Jane? I transformed myself into a Will-o'-the-wisp. Where did I go? I pursued wanderings as wild as those of the March-spirit. I sought the Continent, and went devious through all its lands. My fixed desire was to seek and find a good and intelligent woman whom I could love: a contrast to the fury I left at Thornfield'——

'But you could not marry, sir.'

'I had determined, and was convinced that I could and ought. It was not my original intention to deceive, as I have deceived you. I meant to tell my tale plainly, and make my proposals openly: and it appeared to me so absolutely rational that I should be considered free to love and be loved, I never doubted some woman might be found willing and able to understand my case and accept me, in spite of the curse with which I was burdened.'

'Well, sir?'

'When you are inquisitive, Jane, you always make me smile. You open your eyes like an eager bird, and make every now and then a restless movement; as if answers in speech did not flow fast enough for you, and you wanted to read the tablet of one's heart. But before I go on tell me what you mean by your "Well, sir?" It is a small phrase very frequent with you; and which many a time has drawn me on and on through interminable talk: I don't very well know why.'

'I mean—What next? How did you proceed? What came of such an event?'

'Precisely: and what do you wish to know now?'

'Whether you found any one you liked: whether you asked her to marry you; and what she said.'

'I can tell you whether I found any one I liked, and whether I asked her to marry me: but what she said is yet to be recorded in the book of Fate. For ten long years I roved about, living first in one capital, then another: sometimes in St. Petersburg; oftener in Paris; occasionally in Rome, Naples, and Florence. Provided with plenty of money and the passport of an old name, I could choose my own society: no circles were closed against me. I sought my ideal of a woman amongst English ladies, French countesses, Italian signoras, and German gräfinnen.[8] I could not find her. Sometimes, for a fleeting moment, I thought I caught a glance, heard a tone, beheld a form, which announced the realisation of my dream: but I was presently undeceived. You are not to suppose that I desired perfection either of mind or person. I longed only for what suited me—for the antipodes of the Creole: and I longed vainly. Amongst them all I found not one whom, had I been ever so free, I—warned as I was of the risks, the horrors, the loathings of incongruous unions—would have asked to marry me. Disappointment made

8. Countesses.

me reckless. I tried dissipation—never debauchery: that I hated, and hate. That was my Indian Messalina's[9] attribute: rooted disgust at it and her restrained me much, even in pleasure. Any enjoyment that bordered on riot seemed to approach me to her and her vices, and I eschewed it.

'Yet I could not live alone; so I tried the companionship of mistresses. The first I chose was Céline Varens—another of those steps which make a man spurn himself when he recalls them. You already know what she was, and how my liaison with her terminated. She had two successors: an Italian, Giacinta, and a German, Clara; both considered singularly handsome. What was their beauty to me in a few weeks? Giacinta was unprincipled and violent: I tired of her in three months. Clara was honest and quiet; but heavy, mindless, unimpressible: not one whit to my taste. I was glad to give her a sufficient sum to set her up in a good line of business, and so get decently rid of her. But, Jane, I see by your face you are not forming a very favourable opinion of me just now. You think me an unfeeling, loose-principled rake: don't you?'

'I don't like you so well as I have done sometimes, indeed, sir. Did it not seem to you in the least wrong to live in that way: first with one mistress and then another? You talk of it as a mere matter of course.'

'It was with me: and I did not like it. It was a grovelling fashion of existence: I should never like to return to it. Hiring a mistress is the next worst thing to buying a slave: both are often by nature, and always by position, inferior: and to live familiarly with inferiors is degrading. I now hate the recollection of the time I passed with Céline, Giacinta, and Clara.'

I felt the truth of these words; and I drew from them the certain inference, that if I were so far to forget myself and all the teaching that had ever been instilled into me as—under any pretext—with any justification—through any temptation—to become the successor of these poor girls, he would one day regard me with the same feeling which now in his mind desecrated their memory. I did not give utterance to this conviction: it was enough to feel it. I impressed it on my heart, that it might remain there to serve me as aid in the time of trial.

'Now, Jane, why don't you say "Well, sir?" I have not done. You are looking grave. You disapprove of me still, I see. But let me come to the point. Last January, rid of all mistresses—in a harsh, bitter frame of mind, the result of a useless, roving, lonely life—corroded with disappointment, sourly disposed against all men, and especially against all *woman*kind (for I began to regard the notion of an intellectual, faithful, loving woman as a mere dream), recalled by business, I came back to England.

9. Dissipated wife of the Roman emperor Claudius.

'On a frosty winter afternoon I rode in sight of Thornfield Hall. Abhorred spot! I expected no peace—no pleasure there. On a stile in Hay
Lane I saw a quiet little figure sitting by itself. I passed it as negligently
as I did the pollard willow opposite to it; I had no presentiment of what
it would be to me; no inward warning that the arbitress of my life—my
genius for good or evil—waited there in humble guise. I did not know it
even when, on the occasion of Mesrour's accident, it came up and
gravely offered me help. Childish and slender creature! It seemed as if a
linnet had hopped on my foot and proposed to bear me on its tiny wing.
I was surly; but the thing would not go: it stood by me with strange perseverance, and looked and spoke with a sort of authority. I must be
aided, and by that hand: and aided I was.

'When once I had pressed the frail shoulder, something new—a
fresh sap and sense—stole into my frame. It was well I had learnt that
this elf must return to me—that it belonged to my house down below
—or I could not have felt it pass away from under my hand, and seen it
vanish behind the dim hedge, without singular regret. I heard you come
home that night, Jane: though probably you were not aware that I
thought of you, or watched for you. The next day I observed you—
myself unseen—for half an hour, while you played with Adèle in the
gallery. It was a snowy day, I recollect, and you could not go out of
doors. I was in my room; the door was ajar: I could both listen and
watch. Adèle claimed your outward attention for a while; yet I fancied
your thoughts were elsewhere: but you were very patient with her, my
little Jane; you talked to her and amused her a long time. When at last
she left you, you lapsed at once into deep reverie: you betook yourself
slowly to pace the gallery. Now and then, in passing a casement you
glanced out at the thick-falling snow; you listened to the sobbing wind,
and again you paced gently on and dreamed. I think those day visions
were not dark; there was a pleasurable illumination in your eye occasionally, a soft excitement in your aspect, which told of no bitter, bilious, hypochondriac brooding: your look revealed rather the sweet
musings, of youth, when its spirit follows on willing wings the flight of
Hope, up and on to an ideal heaven. The voice of Mrs. Fairfax, speaking to a servant in the hall, wakened you: and how curiously you smiled
to and at yourself, Janet! There was much sense in your smile: it was
very shrewd, and seemed to make light of your own abstraction. It
seemed to say—"My fine visions are all very well, but I must not forget
they are absolutely unreal. I have a rosy sky, and a green flowery Eden
in my brain; but without, I am perfectly aware, lies at my feet a rough
tract to travel, and around me gather black tempests to encounter." You
ran downstairs and demanded of Mrs. Fairfax some occupation: the
weekly house accounts to make up, or something of that sort, I think it
was. I was vexed with you for getting out of my sight.

'Impatiently I waited for evening, when I might summon you to my presence. An unusual—to me—a perfectly new character I suspected was yours: I desired to search it deeper, and know it better. You entered the room with a look and air at once shy and independent: you were quaintly dressed—much as you are now. I made you talk—ere long I found you full of strange contrasts. Your garb and manner were restricted by rule; your air was often diffident, and altogether that of one refined by nature, but absolutely unused to society, and a good deal afraid of making herself disadvantageously conspicuous by some solecism or blunder; yet when addressed you lifted a keen, a daring, and a glowing eye to your interlocutor's face: there was penetration and power in each glance you gave; when plied by close questions, you found ready and round answers. Very soon you seemed to get used to me; I believe you felt the existence of sympathy between you and your grim and cross master, Jane; for it was astonishing to see how quickly a certain pleasant ease tranquillised your manner: snarl as I would, you showed no surprise, fear, annoyance, or displeasure at my moroseness; you watched me, and now and then smiled at me with a simple yet sagacious grace I cannot describe. I was at once content and stimulated with what I saw: I liked what I had seen, and wished to see more. Yet, for a long time, I treated you distantly, and sought your company rarely. I was an intellectual epicure, and wished to prolong the gratification of making this novel and piquant acquaintance: besides, I was for a while troubled with a haunting fear that if I handled the flower freely its bloom would fade—the sweet charm of freshness would leave it. I did not then know that it was no transitory blossom; but rather the radiant resemblance of one, cut in an indestructible gem. Moreover, I wished to see whether you would seek me if I shunned you—but you did not: you kept in the school-room as still as your own desk and easel; if by chance I met you, you passed me as soon, and with as little token of recognition, as was consistent with respect. Your habitual expression in those days, Jane, was a thoughtful look; not despondent, for you were not sickly; but not buoyant, for you had little hope, and no actual pleasure. I wondered what you thought of me—or if you ever thought of me; to find this out I resumed my notice of you. There was something glad in your glance and genial in your manner when you conversed: I saw you had a social heart; it was the silent schoolroom—it was the tedium of your life—that made you mournful. I permitted myself the delight of being kind to you; kindness stirred emotion soon: your face became soft in expression, your tones gentle; I liked my name pronounced by your lips in a grateful, happy accent. I used to enjoy a chance meeting with you, Jane, at this time: there was a curious hesitation in your manner: you glanced at me with a slight trouble—a hovering doubt: you did not know what my caprice might be—whether I was going to play the master and be stern, or the friend and be benignant. I was now too fond of you often to stimulate the first whim; and, when I stretched my hand out cordially, such bloom and light and bliss rose to your young, wistful features, I had much ado often to avoid straining you then and there to my heart.'

'Don't talk any more of those days, sir,' I interrupted, furtively dashing away some tears from my eyes; his language was torture to me; for I knew what I must do—and do soon—and all these reminiscences and these revelations of his feelings only made my work more difficult.

'No, Jane,' he returned: 'what necessity is there to dwell on the Past, when the Present is so much surer—the Future so much brighter?'

I shuddered to hear the infatuated assertion.

'You see now how the case stands—do you not?' he continued. 'After a youth and manhood passed half in unutterable misery and half in dreary solitude, I have for the first time found what I can truly love —I have found *you*. You are my sympathy—my better self—my good angel—I am bound to you with a strong attachment. I think you good, gifted, lovely: a fervent, a solemn passion is conceived in my heart; it leans to you, draws you to my centre and spring of life, wraps my existence about you—and, kindling in pure, powerful flame, fuses you and me in one.

'It was because I felt and knew this that I resolved to marry you. To tell me that I had already a wife is empty mockery: you know now that I had but a hideous demon. I was wrong to attempt to deceive you; but I feared a stubbornness that exists in your character. I feared early instilled prejudice: I wanted to have you safe before hazarding confidences. This was cowardly: I should have appealed to your nobleness and magnanimity at first, as I do now—opened to you plainly my life of agony —described to you my hunger and thirst after a higher and worthier existence—shown to you, not my *resolution* (that word is weak), but my resistless *bent* to love faithfully and well where I am faithfully and well loved in return. Then I should have asked you to accept my pledge of fidelity, and to give me yours: Jane—give it me now.'

A pause.

'Why are you silent, Jane?'

I was experiencing an ordeal: a hand of fiery iron grasped my vitals. Terrible moment: full of struggle, blackness, burning! Not a human being that ever lived could wish to be loved better than I was loved; and him who thus loved me I absolutely worshipped: and I must renounce love and idol. One drear word comprised my intolerable duty—'Depart!'

'Jane, you understand what I want of you? Just this promise—"I will be yours, Mr. Rochester."'

'Mr. Rochester, I will *not* be yours.'

Another long silence.

'Jane!' recommenced he, with a gentleness that broke me down with grief, and turned me stone-cold with ominous terror—for this still voice was the pant of a lion rising—'Jane, do you mean to go one way in the world, and to let me go another?'

'I do.'

'Jane' (bending towards and embracing me), 'do you mean it now?'

'I do.'

'And now?' softly kissing my forehead and cheek.

'I do'—extricating myself from restraint rapidly and completely.

'Oh, Jane, this is bitter! This—this is wicked. It would not be wicked to love me.'

'It would to obey you.'

A wild look raised his brows—crossed his features: he rose; but he forbore yet. I laid my hand on the back of the chair for support: I shook, I feared—but I resolved.

'One instant, Jane. Give one glance to my horrible life when you are gone. All happiness will be torn away with you. What then is left? For a wife I have but the maniac upstairs: as well might you refer me to some corpse in yonder churchyard. What shall I do, Jane? Where turn for a companion, and for some hope?'

'Do as I do: trust in God and yourself. Believe in heaven. Hope to meet again there.'

'Then you will not yield?'

'No.'

'Then you condemn me to live wretched, and to die accursed?' His voice rose.

'I advise you to live sinless; and I wish you to die tranquil.'

'Then you snatch love and innocence from me? You fling me back on lust for a passion—vice for an occupation?'

'Mr. Rochester, I no more assign this fate to you than I grasp at it for myself. We were born to strive and endure—you as well as I: do so. You will forget me before I forget you.'

'You make me a liar by such language: you sully my honour. I declared I could not change: you tell me to my face I shall change soon. And what a distortion in your judgment, what a perversity in your ideas, is proved by your conduct! Is it better to drive a fellow-creature to despair than to transgress a mere human law—no man being injured by the breach? For you have neither relatives nor acquaintances whom you need fear to offend by living with me.'

This was true: and while he spoke my very conscience and reason turned traitors against me, and charged me with crime in resisting him. They spoke almost as loud as Feeling: and that clamoured wildly. 'Oh, comply!' it said. 'Think of his misery; think of his danger—look at his state when left alone; remember his headlong nature; consider the recklessness following on despair—soothe him; save him; love him; tell him you love him and will be his. Who in the world cares for *you?* or who will be injured by what you do?'

Still indomitable was the reply—'I care for myself. The more solitary, the more friendless, the more unsustained I am, the more I will respect myself. I will keep the law given by God; sanctioned by man. I will hold to the principles received by me when I was sane, and not mad—as I am now. Laws and principles are not for the times when there is no temptation: they are for such moments as this, when body and soul rise in mutiny against their rigour; stringent are they; inviolate they shall be. If at my individual convenience I might break them, what would be their worth? They have a worth—so I have always believed; and if I cannot believe it now, it is because I am insane—quite insane: with my veins running fire, and my heart beating faster than I can count its throbs. Preconceived opinions, foregone determinations, are all I have at this hour to stand by: there I plant my foot.'

I did. Mr. Rochester, reading my countenance, saw I had done so. His fury was wrought to the highest: he must yield to it for a moment, whatever followed; he crossed the floor and seized my arm, and grasped my waist. He seemed to devour me with his flaming glance: physically, I felt, at the moment, powerless as stubble exposed to the draught and glow of a furnace—mentally, I still possessed my soul, and with it the certainty of ultimate safety. The soul, fortunately, has an interpreter—often an unconscious, but still a truthful interpreter—in the eye. My eye rose to his; and while I looked in his fierce face, I gave an involuntary sigh: his grip was painful, and my overtasked strength almost exhausted.

'Never,' said he, as he ground his teeth, 'never was anything at once so frail and so indomitable. A mere reed she feels in my hand! (And he shook me with the force of his hold.) 'I could bend her with my finger and thumb: and what good would it do if I bent, if I uptore, if I crushed her? Consider that eye: consider the resolute, wild, free thing looking out of it, defying me, with more than courage—with a stern triumph. Whatever I do with its cage, I cannot get at it—the savage, beautiful creature! If I tear, if I rend the slight prison, my outrage will only let the captive loose. Conqueror I might be of the house; but the inmate would escape to heaven before I could call myself possessor of its clay dwelling-place. And it is you, spirit—with will and energy, and virtue and purity—that I want: not alone your brittle frame. Of yourself, you could come with soft flight and nestle against my heart, if you would: seized against your will you will elude the grasp like an essence—you will vanish ere I inhale your fragrance. Oh! come, Jane, come!'

As he said this he released me from his clutch, and only looked at me.

The look was far worse to resist than the frantic strain: only an idiot, however, would have succumbed now. I had dared and baffled his fury; I must elude his sorrow: I retired to the door.

'You are going, Jane?'

'I am going, sir.'

'You are leaving me?'

'Yes.'

'You will not come?—You will not be my comforter, my rescuer? —My deep love, my wild woe, my frantic prayer, are all nothing to you?'

What unutterable pathos was in his voice! How hard it was to reiterate firmly, 'I am going.'

'Jane!'

'Mr. Rochester!'

'Withdraw, then,—I consent—but remember, you leave me here in anguish. Go up to your own room; think over all I have said, and, Jane, cast a glance on my sufferings—think of me.'

He turned away; he threw himself on his face on the sofa. 'Oh, Jane! my hope—my love—my life!' broke in anguish from his lips. Then came a deep, strong sob.

I had already gained the door: but, reader, I walked back—walked back as determinedly as I had retreated. I knelt down by him; I turned his face from the cushion to me; I kissed his cheek; I smoothed his hair with my hand.

'God bless you, my dear master!' I said. 'God keep you from harm and wrong—direct you, solace you—reward you well for your past kindness to me.'

'Little Jane's love would have been my best reward,' he answered: 'without it, my heart is broken. But Jane will give me her love: yes— nobly, generously.'

Up the blood rushed to his face; forth flashed the fire from his eyes; erect he sprang; he held his arms out; but I evaded the embrace, and at once quitted the room.

'Farewell!' was the cry of my heart as I left him. Despair added, 'Farewell, for ever!'

That night I never thought to sleep; but a slumber fell on me as soon as I lay down in bed. I was transported in thought to the scenes of childhood; I dreamt I lay in the red-room at Gateshead; that the night was dark, and my mind impressed with strange fears. The light that long ago had struck me into syncope, recalled in this vision, seemed glidingly to mount the wall, and tremblingly to pause in the centre of the obscured ceiling. I lifted up my head to look: the roof resolved to clouds, high and dim; the gleam was such as the moon imparts to vapours she is

about to sever. I watched her come—watched with the strangest anticipation; as though some word of doom were to be written on her disk.
She broke forth as never moon yet burst from cloud: a hand first penetrated the sable folds and waved them away; then, not a moon, but a
white human form shone in the azure, inclining a glorious brow earthward. It gazed and gazed and gazed on me. It spoke to my spirit: immeasurably distant was the tone, yet so near, it whispered in my
heart—'My daughter, flee temptation!'

'Mother, I will.'

So I answered after I had waked from the trance-like dream. It was
yet night, but July nights are short: soon after midnight dawn comes. 'It
cannot be too early to commence the task I have to fulfil,' thought I. I
rose: I was dressed; for I had taken off nothing but my shoes. I knew
where to find in my drawers some linen, a locket, a ring. In seeking
these articles I encountered the beads of a pearl necklace Mr. Rochester
had forced me to accept a few days ago. I left that; it was not mine: it
was the visionary bride's, who had melted in air. The other articles I
made up in a parcel; my purse, containing twenty shillings (it was all I
had), I put in my pocket: I tied on my straw bonnet, pinned my shawl,
took the parcel and my slippers, which I would not put on yet, and stole
from my room.

'Farewell, kind Mrs. Fairfax!' I whispered, as I glided past her door.
'Farewell, my darling Adèle!' I said, as I glanced towards the nursery.
No thought could be admitted of entering to embrace her. I had to de-
ceive a fine ear: for aught I knew, it might now be listening.

I would have got past Mr. Rochester's chamber without a pause; but
my heart momentarily stopping its beat at that threshold, my foot was
forced to stop also. No sleep was there: the inmate was walking restlessly from wall to wall; and again and again he sighed while I listened.
There was a heaven—a temporary heaven—in this room for me, if I
chose: I had but to go in and to say—'Mr. Rochester, I will love you and
live with you through life till death,' and a fount of rapture would spring
to my lips. I thought of this.

That kind master, who could not sleep now, was waiting with impatience for day. He would send for me in the morning; I should be gone.
He would have me sought for: vainly. He would feel himself forsaken;
his love rejected: he would suffer; perhaps grow desperate. I thought of
this too. My hand moved towards the lock; I caught it back, and glided
on.

Drearily I wound my way downstairs: I knew what I had to do, and I
did it mechanically. I sought the key of the side-door in the kitchen; I
sought, too, a phial of oil and a feather; I oiled the key and the lock. I got
some water, I got some bread: for perhaps I would have to walk far; and
my strength, sorely shaken of late, must not break down. All this I did

without one sound. I opened the door, passed out, shut it softly. Dim dawn glimmered in the yard. The great gates were closed and locked; but a wicket in one of them was only latched. Through that I departed: it, too, I shut; and now I was out of Thornfield.

A mile off, beyond the fields, lay a road which stretched in the contrary direction to Millcote; a road I had never travelled, but often noticed, and wondered where it led: thither I bent my steps. No reflection was to be allowed now: not one glance was to be cast back; not even one forward. Not one thought was to be given either to the past or the future. The first was a page so heavenly sweet—so deadly sad—that to read one line of it would dissolve my courage and break down my energy. That last was an awful blank: something like the world when the deluge was gone by.

I skirted fields, and hedges, and lanes, till after sunrise. I believe it was a lovely summer morning: I know my shoes, which I had put on when I left the house, were soon wet with dew. But I looked neither to rising sun, nor smiling sky, nor wakening nature. He who is taken out to pass through a fair scene to the scaffold thinks not of the flowers that smile on his road, but of the block and axe-edge; of the disseverment of bone and vein; of the grave gaping at the end: and I thought of drear flight and homeless wandering—and, oh! with agony I thought of what I left. I could not help it. I thought of him now—in his room—watching the sunrise; hoping I should soon come to say I would stay with him, and be his. I longed to be his; I panted to return: it was not too late; I could yet spare him the bitter pang of bereavement. As yet my flight, I was sure, was undiscovered. I could go back and be his comforter—his pride; his redeemer from misery; perhaps from ruin. Oh, that fear of his self-abandonment—far worse than my abandonment—how it goaded me! It was a barbed arrow-head in my breast; it tore me when I tried to extract it; it sickened me when remembrance thrust it further in. Birds began singing in brake and copse: birds were faithful to their mates; birds were emblems of love. What was I? In the midst of my pain of heart, and frantic effort of principle, I abhorred myself. I had no solace from self approbation: none even from self-respect. I had injured—wounded—left my master. I was hateful in my own eyes. Still I could not turn, nor retrace one step. God must have led me on. As to my own will or conscience, impassioned grief had trampled one and stifled the other. I was weeping wildly as I walked along my solitary way: fast, fast I went, like one delirious. A weakness, beginning inwardly, extending to the limbs, seized me, and I fell: I lay on the ground some minutes, pressing my face to the wet turf. I had some fear—or hope—that here I should die: but I was soon up; crawling forwards on my hands and knees, and then again raised to my feet—as eager and as determined as ever to reach the road.

When I got there I was forced to sit to rest me under the hedge; and while I sat, I heard wheels, and saw a coach come on. I stood up and lifted my hand; it stopped. I asked where it was going: the driver named a place a long way off, and where I was sure Mr. Rochester had no connections. I asked for what sum he would take me there; he said thirty shillings; I answered I had but twenty; well, he would try to make it do. He further gave me leave to get into the inside, as the vehicle was empty: I entered, was shut in, and it rolled on its way.

Gentle reader, may you never feel what I then felt! May your eyes never shed such stormy, scalding, heart-wrung tears as poured from mine. May you never appeal to Heaven in prayers so hopeless and so agonised as in that hour left my lips: for never may you, like me, dread to be the instrument of evil to what you wholly love.

Chapter XXVIII

Two days are passed. It is a summer evening; the coachman has set me down at a place called Whitcross; he could take me no farther for the sum I had given, and I was not possessed of another shilling in the world. The coach is a mile off by this time; I am alone. At this moment I discover that I forgot to take my parcel out of the pocket of the coach, where I had placed it for safety; there it remains, there it must remain; and now, I am absolutely destitute.

Whitcross is no town, nor even a hamlet; it is but a stone pillar set up where four roads meet: white-washed, I suppose, to be more obvious at a distance and in darkness. Four arms spring from its summit: the nearest town to which these point is, according to the inscription, distant ten miles; the farthest, above twenty. From the well-known names of these towns I learn in what county I have lighted; a north-midland shire, dusk with moorland, ridged with mountain: this I see. There are great moors behind and on each hand of me; there are waves of mountains far beyond that deep valley at my feet. The population here must be thin, and I see no passengers on these roads: they stretch out east, west, north, and south—white, broad, lonely; they are all cut in the moor, and the heather grows deep and wild to their very verge. Yet a chance traveller might pass by; and I wish no eye to see me now: strangers would wonder what I am doing, lingering here at the sign-post, evidently objectless and lost. I might be questioned: I could give no answer but what would sound incredible and excite suspicion. Not a tie holds me to human society at this moment—not a charm or hope calls me where my fellow-creatures are—none that saw me would have a kind thought or a good wish for me. I have no relative but the universal mother, Nature: I will seek her breast and ask repose.

I struck straight into the heath; I held on to a hollow I saw deeply furrowing the brown moorside; I waded knee-deep in its dark growth; I turned with its turnings, and finding a moss-blackened granite crag in a hidden angle, I sat down under it. High banks of moor were about me; the crag protected my head: the sky was over that.

Some time passed before I felt tranquil even here: I had a vague dread that wild cattle might be near, or that some sportsman or poacher might discover me. If a gust of wind swept the waste. I looked up, fearing it was the rush of a bull; if a plover whistled, I imagined it a man. Finding my apprehensions unfounded, however, and calmed by the deep silence that reigned as evening declined at nightfall, I took confidence. As yet I had not thought; I had only listened, watched, dreaded; now I regained the faculty of reflection.

What was I to do? Where to go? Oh, intolerable questions, when I could do nothing and go nowhere!—when a long way must yet be measured by my weary, trembling limbs, before I could reach human habitation—when cold charity must be entreated before I could get a lodging: reluctant sympathy importuned: almost certain repulse incurred: before my tale could be listened to, or one of my wants relieved!

I touched the heath: it was dry, and yet warm with the heat of the summer-day. I looked at the sky; it was pure: a kindly star twinkled just above the chasm ridge. The dew fell, but with propitious softness; no breeze whispered. Nature seemed to me benign and good; I thought she loved me, outcast as I was; and I, who from man could anticipate only mistrust, rejection, insult, clung to her with filial fondness. To-night, at least, I would be her guest—as I was her child: my mother would lodge me without money and without price. I had one morsel of bread yet: the remnant of a roll I had bought in a town we passed through at noon with a stray penny—my last coin. I saw ripe bilberries gleaming here and there, like jet beads in the heath: I gathered a handful and ate them with the bread. My hunger, sharp before, was, if not satisfied, appeased by this hermit's meal. I said my evening prayers at its conclusion, and then chose my couch.

Beside the crag the heath was very deep: when I lay down my feet were buried in it; rising high on each side, it left only a narrow space for the night-air to invade. I folded my shawl double, and spread it over me for a coverlet; a low, mossy swell was my pillow. Thus lodged, I was not, at least at the commencement of the night, cold.

My rest might have been blissful enough, only a sad heart broke it. It plained of its gaping wounds, its inward bleeding, its riven chords, It trembled for Mr. Rochester and his doom: it bemoaned him with bitter pity; it demanded him with ceaseless longing: and, impotent as a bird with both wings broken, it still quivered its shattered pinions in vain attempts to seek him.

Worn out with this torture of thought, I rose to my knees. Night was come, and her planets were risen: a safe, still night; too serene for the companionship of fear. We know that God is everywhere; but certainly we feel His presence most when His works are on the grandest scale spread before us: and it is in the unclouded night-sky, where His worlds wheel their silent course, that we read clearest His infinitude, His omnipotence, His omnipresence. I had risen to my knees to pray for Mr. Rochester. Looking up, I, with tear-dimmed eyes, saw the mighty Milky Way. Remembering what it was—what countless systems there swept space like a soft trace of light—I felt the might and strength of God. Sure was I of His efficiency to save what He had made: convinced I grew that neither earth should perish nor one of the souls it treasured. I turned my prayer to thanksgiving: the Source of Life was also the Saviour of spirits. Mr. Rochester was safe: he was God's, and by God would he be guarded. I again nestled to the breast of the hill; and ere long, in sleep, forgot sorrow.

But next day Want came to me, pale and bare. Long after the little birds had left their nests; long after bees had come in the sweet prime of day to gather the heath honey before the dew was dried—when the long morning shadows were curtailed, and the sun filled earth and sky —I got up, and I looked round me.

What a still, hot, perfect day! What a golden desert this spreading moor! Everywhere sunshine. I wished I could live in it and on it. I saw a lizard run over the crag; I saw a bee busy among the sweet bilberries. I would fain at the moment have become bee or lizard, that I might have found fitting nutriment, permanent shelter here. But I was a human being, and had a human being's wants: I must not linger where there was nothing to supply them. I rose; I looked back at the bed I had left. Hopeless of the future, I wished but this—that my Maker had that night thought good to require my soul of me while I slept; and that this weary frame, absolved by death from further conflict with fate, had now but to decay quietly, and mingle in peace with the soil of this wilderness. Life, however, was yet in my possession; with all its requirements, and pains, and responsibilities. The burden must be carried; the want provided for; the suffering endured; the responsibility fulfilled. I set out.

Whitcross regained, I followed a road which led from the sun, now fervent and high. By no other circumstance had I will to decide my choice. I walked a long time, and when I thought I had nearly done enough, and might conscientiously yield to the fatigue that almost overpowered me—might relax this forced action, and, sitting down on a stone I saw near, submit resistlessly to the apathy that clogged heart and limb—I heard a bell chime—a church bell.

I turned in the direction of the sound, and there, amongst the romantic hills, whose changes and aspect I had ceased to note an hour ago, I saw a hamlet and a spire. All the valley at my right hand was full of pasture-fields, and corn-fields, and wood; and a glittering stream ran zig-zag through the varied shades of green, the mellowing grain, the sombre wood-land, the clear and sunny lea. Recalled by the rumbling of wheels to the road before me, I saw a heavily-laden waggon labouring up the hill; and not far beyond were two cows and their drover. Human life and human labour were near. I must struggle on: strive to live and bend to toil like the rest.

About two o'clock P.M. I entered the village. At the bottom of its one street there was a little shop with some cakes of bread in the window. I coveted a cake of bread. With that refreshment I could perhaps regain a degree of energy; without it, it would be difficult to proceed. The wish to have some strength and some vigour returned to me as soon as I was amongst my fellow-beings. I felt it would be degrading to faint with hunger on the causeway of a hamlet. Had I nothing about me I could offer in exchange for one of these rolls? I considered. I had a small silk handkerchief tied round my throat; I had my gloves. I could hardly tell how men and women in extremities of destitution proceeded. I did not know whether either of these articles would be accepted: probably they would not; but I must try.

I entered the shop: a woman was there. Seeing a respectably-dressed person, a lady as she supposed, she came forward with civility. How could she serve me? I was seized with shame: my tongue would not utter the request I had prepared. I dared not offer her the half-worn gloves, the creased handkerchief: besides, I felt it would be absurd. I only begged permission to sit down a moment, as I was tired. Disappointed in the expectation of a customer, she coolly acceded to my request. She pointed to a seat; I sank into it. I felt sorely urged to weep; but conscious how unseasonable such a manifestation would be, I restrained it. Soon I asked her, 'if there were any dressmaker or plain-work-woman in the village?'

'Yes; two or three. Quite as many as there was employment for.'

I reflected. I was driven to the point now. I was brought face to face with Necessity. I stood in the position of one without a resource: without a friend; without a coin. I must do something. What? I must apply somewhere. Where?

'Did she know of any place in the neighbourhood where a servant was wanted?'

'Nay; she couldn't say.'

'What was the chief trade in this place? What did most of the people do?'

'Some were farm labourers; a good deal worked at Mr. Oliver's needle-factory, and at the foundry.'

'Did Mr. Oliver employ women?'

'Nay; it was men's work.'

'And what do the women do?'

'I knawn't,' was the answer. 'Some does one thing, and some another. Poor folk mun get on as they can.'

She seemed to be tired of my questions: and, indeed, what claim had I to importune her? A neighbour or two came in; my chair was evidently wanted. I took leave.

I passed up the street, looking as I went at all the houses to the right hand and to the left: but I could discover no pretext, nor see an inducement, to enter any. I rambled round the hamlet, going sometimes to a little distance and returning again, for an hour or more. Much exhausted, and suffering greatly now for want of food, I turned aside into a lane and sat down under the hedge. Ere many minutes had elapsed I was again on my feet, however, and again searching for something—a resource, or at least an informant. A pretty little house stood at the top of the lane, with a garden before it; exquisitely neat, and brilliantly blooming. I stopped at it. What business had I to approach the white door or touch the glittering knocker? In what way could it possibly be the interest of the inhabitants of that dwelling to serve me? Yet I drew near and knocked. A mild-looking, cleanly-attired young woman opened the door. In such a voice as might be expected from a hopeless heart and fainting frame—a voice wretchedly low and faltering—I asked if a servant was wanted here?

'No,' said she; 'we do not keep a servant.'

'Can you tell me where I could get employment of any kind?' I continued. 'I am a stranger, without acquaintance, in this place. I want some work: no matter what.'

But it was not her business to think for me, or to seek a place for me: besides, in her eyes, how doubtful must have appeared my character, position, tale. She shook her head; she 'was sorry she could give me no information,' and the white door closed, quite gently and civilly: but it shut me out. If she had held it open a little longer, I believe I should have begged a piece of bread; for I was now brought low.

I could not bear to return to the sordid village; where, besides, no prospect of aid was visible. I should have longed rather to deviate to a wood I saw not far off, which appeared in its thick shade to offer inviting shelter; but I was so sick, so weak, so gnawed with nature's cravings, instinct kept me roaming round abodes where there was a chance of food. Solitude would be no solitude—rest no rest—while the vulture, hunger, thus sank beak and talons in my side.

I drew near houses; I left them, and came back again, and again I wandered away: always repelled by the consciousness of having no claim to ask—no right to expect interest in my isolated lot. Meantime the afternoon advanced, while I thus wandered about like a lost and starving dog. In crossing a field I saw the church spire before me: I hastened towards it. Near the churchyard, and in the middle of a garden, stood a well-built though small house, which I had no doubt was the parsonage. I remembered that strangers who arrive at a place where they have no friends, and who want employment, sometimes apply to the clergyman for introduction and aid. It is the clergyman's function to help—at least with advice—those who wished to help themselves. I seemed to have something like a right to seek counsel here. Renewing, then, my courage, and gathering my feeble remains of strength, I pushed on. I reached the house, and knocked at the kitchen-door. An old woman opened: I asked was this the parsonage?

'Yes.'

'Was the clergyman in?'

'No.'

'Would he be in soon?'

'No, he was gone from home.'

'To a distance?'

Not so far—happen three mile. He had been called away by the sudden death of his father: he was at Marsh End now, and would very likely stay there a fortnight longer.

'Was there any lady of the house?'

'Nay, there was naught but her, and she was housekeeper;' and of her, reader, I could not bear to ask the relief for want of which I was sinking; I could not yet beg; and again I crawled away.

Once more I took off my handkerchief—once more I thought of the cakes of bread in the little shop. Oh, for but a crust! for but one mouthful to allay the pang of famine! Instinctively I turned my face again to the village; I found the shop again, and I went in; and though others were there besides the woman, I ventured the request: 'Would she give me a roll for this handkerchief?'

She looked at me with evident suspicion: 'Nay, she never sold stuff i' that way.'

Almost desperate, I asked for half a cake; she again refused. 'How could she tell where I had got the handkerchief?' she said.

'Would she take my gloves?'

'No! what could she do with them?'

Reader, it is not pleasant to dwell on these details. Some say there is enjoyment in looking back to painful experience past; but at this day I can scarcely bear to review the times to which I allude: the moral degradation, blent with the physical suffering, form too distressing a recollection ever to be willingly dwelt on. I blamed none of those who repulsed me. I felt it was what was to be expected, and what could not be helped: an ordinary beggar is frequently an object of suspicion; a well-dressed beggar inevitably so. To be sure what I begged was employment: but whose business was it to provide me with employment? Not, certainly, that of persons who saw me then for the first time, and who knew nothing about my character. And as to the woman who would not take my handkerchief in exchange for her bread, why, she was right; if the offer appeared to her sinister, or the exchange unprofitable. Let me condense now. I am sick of the subject.

A little before dark I passed a farm-house, at the open door of which the farmer was sitting, eating his supper of bread and cheese; I stopped, and said:—'Will you give me a piece of bread? for I am very hungry.' He cast on me a glance of surprise; but without answering he cut a thick slice from his loaf, and gave it to me. I imagine he did not think I was a beggar, but only an eccentric sort of lady, who had taken a fancy to his brown loaf. As soon as I was out of sight of his house, I sat down and ate it.

I could not hope to get a lodging under a roof, and sought it in the wood I have before alluded to. But my night was wretched, my rest broken: the ground was damp, the air cold: besides intruders passed near me more than once, and I had again and again to change my quarters: no sense of safety or tranquillity befriended me. Towards morning it rained; the whole of the following day was wet. Do not ask me, reader, to give a minute account of that day; as before, I sought work; as before, I was repulsed; as before, I starved; but once did food pass my lips. At the door of a cottage I saw a little girl about to throw a mess of cold porridge into a pig trough. 'Will you give me that?' I asked.

She stared at me. 'Mother!' she exclaimed; 'there is a woman wants me to give her this porridge.'

'Well, lass,' replied a voice within, 'give it her if she's a beggar. T' pig doesn't want it.'

The girl emptied the stiffened mould into my hand, and I devoured it ravenously.

As the wet twilight deepened, I stopped in a solitary bridle-path, which I had been pursuing an hour or more.

'My strength is quite failing me,' I said, in soliloquy. 'I feel I cannot go much further. Shall I be an outcast again this night? While the rain descends so, must I lay my head on the cold, drenched ground? I fear I cannot do otherwise: for who will receive me? But it will be very dreadful: with this feeling of hunger, faintness, chill, and this sense of desolation—this total prostration of hope. In all likelihood, though, I should die before morning. And why cannot I reconcile myself to the prospect of death? Why do I struggle to retain a valueless life? Because I know, or believe, Mr. Rochester is still living: and then, to die of want and cold, is a fate to which nature cannot submit passively. Oh, Providence! sustain me a little longer! Aid—direct me!'

My glazed eye wandered over the dim and misty landscape. I saw I had strayed far from the village: it was quite out of sight. The very cultivation surrounding it had disappeared. I had, by cross-ways and by-paths, once more drawn near the tract of moorland; and now, only a few fields, almost as wild and unproductive as the heath from which they were scarcely reclaimed, lay between me and the dusky hill.

'Well, I would rather die yonder than in a street, or on a frequented road,' I reflected. 'And far better that crows and ravens—if any ravens there be in these regions—should pick my flesh from my bones, than that they should be prisoned in a workhouse coffin and moulder in a pauper's grave.'

To the hill, then, I turned. I reached it. It remained now only to find a hollow where I could lie down, and feel at least hidden, if not secure: but all the surface of the waste looked level. It showed no variation but of tint; green, where rush and moss overgrew the marshes; black, where the dry soil bore only heath. Dark as it was getting, I could still see these changes; though but as mere alternations of light and shade: for colour had faded with the day-light.

My eye still roved over the sullen swell, and along the moor-edge, vanishing amidst the wildest scenery; when at one dim point, far, in among the marshes and the ridges, a light sprang up. 'That is an *ignis fatuus*,'[1] was my first thought; and I expected it would soon vanish. It burnt on, however, quite steadily; neither receding nor advancing. 'Is it, then, a bonfire just kindled?' I questioned. I watched to see whether it would spread: but no; as it did not diminish, so it did not enlarge. 'It may be a candle in a house,' I then conjectured: 'but if so, I can never reach it. It is much too far away: and were it within a yard of me, what would it avail? I should but knock at the door to have it shut in my face.'

And I sank down where I stood, and hid my face against the ground. I lay still a while: the night-wind swept over the hill and over me, and died moaning in the distance; the rain fell fast, wetting me afresh to the skin. Could I but have stiffened to the still frost—the friendly numbness of death—it might have pelted on: I should not have felt it; but my yet living flesh shuddered to its chilling influence. I rose ere long.

The light was yet there: shining dim, but constant, through the rain. I tried to walk again: I dragged my exhausted limbs slowly towards it. It led me aslant over the hill, through a wide bog; which would have been impassable in winter, and was splashy and shaking even now, in the height of summer. Here I fell twice; but as often I rose and rallied my faculties. This light was my forlorn hope: I must gain it.

Having crossed the marsh, I saw a trace of white over the moor. I approached it; it was a road or a track: it led straight up to the light, which now beamed from a sort of knoll, amidst a clump of trees—firs, apparently, from what I could distinguish of the character of their forms

1. Light from marsh gas.

and foliage through the gloom. My star vanished as I drew near: some obstacle had intervened between me and it. I put out my hand to feel the dark mass before me; I discriminated the rough stones of a low wall —above it, something like palisades, and within, a high and prickly hedge. I groped on. Again a whitish object gleamed before me: it was a gate—a wicket; it moved on its hinges as I touched it. On each side stood a sable bush—holly or yew.

Entering the gate and passing the shrubs, the silhouette of a house rose to view; black, low, and rather long; but the guiding light shone nowhere. All was obscurity. Were the inmates retired to rest? I feared it must be so. In seeking the door, I turned an angle: there shot out the friendly gleam again, from the lozenged panes of a very small latticed window, within a foot of the ground; made still smaller by the growth of ivy or some other creeping plant, whose leaves clustered thick over the portion of the house wall in which it was set. The aperture was so screened and narrow that curtain or shutter had been deemed unnecessary; and when I stooped down and put aside the spray of foliage shooting over it, I could see all within. I could see clearly a room with a sanded floor, clean scoured; a dresser of walnut, with pewter plates ranged in rows, reflecting the redness and radiance of a glowing peat-fire. I could see a clock, a white deal table, some chairs. The candle, whose ray had been my beacon, burnt on the table; and by its light an elderly woman, somewhat rough-looking, but scrupulously clean, like all about her, was knitting a stocking.

I noticed these objects cursorily only—in them there was nothing extraordinary. A group of more interest appeared near the hearth, sitting still amidst the rosy peace and warmth suffusing it. Two young, graceful women—ladies in every point—sat, one in a low rocking-chair, the other on a lower stool; both wore deep mourning of crape and bombazeen, which sombre garb singularly set off very fair necks and faces: a large old pointer dog rested its massive head on the knee of one girl—in the lap of the other was cushioned a black cat.

A strange place was this humble kitchen for such occupants! Who were they? They could not be the daughters of the elderly person at the table; for she looked like a rustic, and they were all delicacy and cultivation. I had nowhere seen such faces as theirs: and yet, as I gazed on them, I seemed intimate with every lineament. I cannot call them handsome—they were too pale and grave for the word: as they each bent over a book, they looked thoughtful almost to severity. A stand between them supported a second candle and two great volumes, to which they frequently referred; comparing them seemingly with the smaller books they held in their hands, like people consulting a dictionary to aid them in the task of translation. This scene was as silent as if all the figures had been shadows, and the fire-lit apartment a picture: so hushed was it, I could hear the cinders fall from the grate, the clock tick in its obscure corner; and I even fancied I could distinguish the click-click of the woman's knitting-needles. When, therefore, a voice broke the strange stillness at last, it was audible enough to me.

'Listen, Diana,' said one of the absorbed students; 'Franz and old Daniel are together in the night-time, and Franz is telling a dream from which he has awakened in terror—listen!' And in a low voice she read something, of which not one word was intelligible to me; for it was in an unknown tongue—neither French nor Latin. Whether it were Greek or German I could not tell.

'That is strong,' she said, when she had finished: 'I relish it.' The other girl, who had lifted her head to listen to her sister, repeated, while she gazed at the fire, a line of what had been read. At a later day, I knew the language and the book; therefore I will here quote the line: though when I first heard it it was only like a stroke on sounding brass to me—conveying no meaning:—' "Da trat hervor Einer, anzusehen wie die Sternen Nacht." Good! good!' she exclaimed, while her dark and deep eye sparkled. 'There you have a dim and mighty archangel fitly set before you! The line is worth a hundred pages of fustian. "Ich wäge die Gedanken in der Schale meines Zornes und die Werke mit dem Gewichte meines Grimms."[2] I like it!'

Both were again silent.

'Is there ony country where they talk i' that way?' asked the old woman, looking up from her knitting.

'Yes, Hannah—a far larger country than England; where they talk in no other way.'

'Well, for sure case, I knawn't how they can understand t' one t' other: and if either o' ye went there, ye could tell what they said, I guess?'

'We could probably tell something of what they said, but not all—for we are not as clever as you think us, Hannah. We don't speak German, and we cannot read it without a dictionary to help us.'

'And what good does it do you?'

'We mean to teach it some time—or at least the elements, as they say; and then we shall get more money than we do now.'

'Varry like: but give ower studying: ye've done enough for to-night.'

'I think we have: at least I'm tired. Mary, are you?'

'Mortally: after all, it's tough work fagging away at a language with no master but a lexicon.'

'It is: especially such a language as this crabbed but glorious Deutsch. I wonder when St. John will come home.'

2. "Then there stepped forth one, in appearance like the starry sky. . . . I weigh thoughts in the scale of my anger, and deeds with the weight of my wrath!" From Johann von Schiller's *The Robbers* 5.1. "Fustian": pretentious writing.

'Surely he will not be long now: it is just ten' (looking at a little gold watch she drew from her girdle). 'It rains fast. Hannah, will you have the goodness to look at the fire in the parlour?'

The woman rose: she opened a door, through which I dimly saw a passage: soon I heard her stir a fire in an inner room; she presently came back.

'Ah, childer!' said she, 'it fair troubles me to go into yond' room now: it looks so lonesome wi' the chair empty and set back in a corner.'

She wiped her eyes with her apron: the two girls, grave before, looked sad now.

'But he is in a better place,' continued Hannah: 'we shouldn't wish him here again. And then, nobody need to have a quieter death nor he had.'

'You say he never mentioned us?' inquired one of the ladies.

'He hadn't time, bairn: he was gone in a minute—was your father. He had been a bit ailing like the day before, but naught to signify; and when Mr. St. John asked if he would like either o' ye to be sent for, he fair laughed at him. He began again with a bit of a heaviness in his head the next day—that is, a fortnight sin'—and he went to sleep and niver wakened: he wor' a'most stark when your brother went into t' chamber and fand him. Ah, childer! that's t' last o' t' old stock—for ye and Mr. St. John is like of a different soart to them 'at's gone; for all your mother wor mich i' your way; and a'most as book-learned. She wor the pictur' o' ye, Mary: Diana is more like your father.'

I thought them so similar I could not tell where the old servant (for such I now concluded her to be) saw the difference. Both were fair complexioned and slenderly made; both possessed faces full of distinction and intelligence. One, to be sure, had hair a shade darker than the other, and there was a difference in their style of wearing it: Mary's pale brown locks were parted and braided smooth; Diana's duskier tresses covered her neck with thick curls. The clock struck ten.

'Ye'll want your supper, I am sure,' observed Hannah; 'and so will Mr. St. John when he comes in.'

And she proceeded to prepare the meal. The ladies rose; they seemed about to withdraw to the parlour. Till this moment I had been so intent on watching them, their appearance and conversation had excited in me so keen an interest, I had half-forgotten my own wretched position: now it recurred to me. More desolate, more desperate than ever, it seemed from contrast. And how impossible did it appear to touch the inmates of this house with concern on my behalf; to make them believe in the truth of my wants and woes—to induce them to vouchsafe a rest for my wanderings! As I groped out the door, and knocked at it hesitatingly, I felt that last idea to be a mere chimera. Hannah opened.

'What do you want?' she inquired, in a voice of surprise, as she surveyed me by the light of the candle she held.

'May I speak to your mistresses?' I said.

'You had better tell me what you have to say to them. Where do you come from?'

'I am a stranger.'

'What is your business here at this hour?'

'I want a night's shelter in an outhouse or anywhere, and a morsel of bread to eat.'

Distrust, the very feeling I dreaded, appeared in Hannah's face. 'I'll give you a piece of bread,' she said, after a pause; 'but we can't take in a vagrant to lodge. It isn't likely.'

'Do let me speak to your mistresses.'

'No; not I. What can they do for you? You should not be roving about now; it looks very ill.'

'But where shall I go if you drive me away? What shall I do?'

'Oh, I'll warrant you know where to go, and what to do. Mind you don't do wrong, that's all. Here is a penny; now go'——

'A penny cannot feed me, and I have no strength to go farther. Don't shut the door:—oh, don't, for God's sake!'

'I must; the rain is driving in'——

'Tell the young ladies.—Let me see them'——

'Indeed, I will not. You are not what you ought to be or you wouldn't make such a noise. Move off.'

'But I must die if I am turned away.'

'Not you. I'm fear'd you have some ill plans agate,[3] that bring you about folk's houses at this time o' night. If you've any followers—housebreakers or such like—anywhere near, you may tell them we are not by ourselves in the house; we have a gentleman, and dogs, and guns.' Here the honest but inflexible servant clapped the door to and bolted it within.

This was the climax. A pang of exquisite suffering—a throe of true despair—rent and heaved my heart. Worn out, indeed, I was; not another step could I stir. I sank on the wet door-step: I groaned—I wrung my hands—I wept in utter anguish. Oh, this spectre of death! Oh, this last hour, approaching in such horror! Alas, this isolation—this banishment from my kind! Not only the anchor of home, but the footing of fortitude was gone—at least for a moment: but the last I soon endeavoured to regain.

'I can but die,' I said, 'and I believe in God. Let me try to wait His will in silence.'

These words I not only thought, but uttered; and thrusting back all

---

3. Under way (literally, "on gate").

my misery into my heart, I made an effort to compel it to remain there
—dumb and still.

'All men must die,' said a voice quite close at hand; 'but all are not
condemned to meet a lingering and premature doom, such as yours
would be if you perished here of want.'

'Who or what speaks?' I asked, terrified at the unexpected sound,
and incapable now of deriving from any occurrence a hope of aid. A
form was near—what form the pitch-dark night and my enfeebled vision prevented me from distinguishing. With a loud long knock the
new comer appealed to the door.

'Is it you, Mr. St. John?' cried Hannah.

'Yes—yes; open quickly.'

'Well, how wet and cold you must be, such a wild night as it is! Come
in—your sisters are quite uneasy about you, and I believe there are bad
folks about. There has been a beggar-woman—I declare she is not gone
yet!—laid down there. Get up! for shame! Move off, I say!'

'Hush, Hannah! I have a word to say to the woman. You have done
your duty in excluding, now let me do mine in admitting her. I was
near, and listened to both you and her. I think this is a peculiar case—I
must at least examine into it. Young woman, rise, and pass before me
into the house.'

With difficulty I obeyed him. Presently I stood within that clean,
bright kitchen—on the very hearth—trembling, sickening; conscious
of an aspect in the last degree ghastly, wild and weatherbeaten. The two
ladies, their brother, Mr. St. John, the old servant, were all gazing at
me.

'St. John, who is it?' I heard one ask.

'I cannot tell: I found her at the door,' was the reply.

'She does look white,' said Hannah.

'As white as clay or death,' was responded. 'She will fall: let her sit.'

And indeed my head swam: I dropped; but a chair received me. I still
possessed my senses; though just now I could not speak.

'Perhaps a little water would restore her. Hannah, fetch some. But
she is worn to nothing. How very thin, and how very bloodless!'

'A mere spectre!'

'Is she ill, or only famished?'

'Famished, I think. Hannah, is that milk? Give it me, and a piece of
bread.'

Diana (I knew her by the long curls which I saw drooping between
me and the fire as she bent over me) broke some bread, dipped it in
milk, and put it to my lips. Her face was near mine: I saw there was pity
in it, and I felt sympathy in her hurried breathing. In her simple words,
too, the same balm-like emotion spoke: 'Try to eat.'

'Yes—try,' repeated Mary gently; and Mary's hand removed my

sodden bonnet and lifted my head. I tasted what they offered me: feebly at first, eagerly soon.

'Not too much at first—restrain her,' said the brother; 'she has had enough.' And he withdrew the cup of milk and the plate of bread.

'A little more, St. John—look at the avidity in her eyes.'

'No more at present, sister. Try if she can speak now—ask her her name.'

I felt I could speak, and I answered—'My name is Jane Elliott.' Anxious as ever to avoid discovery, I had before resolved to assume an *alias*.

'And where do you live? Where are your friends?'

I was silent.

'Can we send for any one you know?'

I shook my head.

'What account can you give of yourself?'

Somehow, now that I had once crossed the threshold of this house, and once was brought face to face with its owners, I felt no longer outcast, vagrant, and disowned by the wide world. I dared to put off the mendicant—to resume my natural manner and character. I began once more to know myself; and when Mr. St. John demanded an account—which at present I was far too weak to render—I said after a brief pause,—'Sir, I can give you no details to-night.'

'But what, then,' said he, 'do you expect me to do for you?'

'Nothing,' I replied. My strength sufficed for but short answers. Diana took the word:—

'Do you mean,' she asked, 'that we have now given you what aid you require? and that we may dismiss you to the moor and the rainy night?'

I looked at her. She had, I thought, a remarkable countenance; instinct both with power and goodness. I took sudden courage. Answering her compassionate gaze with a smile, I said: 'I will trust you. If I were a masterless and stray dog, I know that you would not turn me from your hearth to-night: as it is, I really have no fear. Do with me and for me as you like; but excuse me from much discourse—my breath is short—I feel a spasm when I speak.' All three surveyed me, and all three were silent.

'Hannah,' said Mr. St. John at last, 'let her sit there at present, and ask her no questions; in ten minutes more, give her the remainder of that milk and bread. Mary and Diana, let us go into the parlour and talk the matter over.'

They withdrew. Very soon one of the ladies returned—I could not tell which. A kind of pleasant stupor was stealing over me as I sat by the genial fire. In an undertone she gave some directions to Hannah. Ere long, with the servant's aid, I contrived to mount a staircase; my dripping clothes were removed; soon a warm, dry bed received me. I thanked God—experienced amidst unutterable exhaustion a glow of grateful joy—and slept.

Chapter XXIX

The recollection of about three days and nights succeeding this is very dim in my mind. I can recall some sensations felt in that interval; but few thoughts framed, and no actions performed. I knew I was in a small room, and in a narrow bed. To that bed I seemed to have grown; I lay on it motionless as a stone; and to have torn me from it would have been almost to kill me. I took no note of the lapse of time—of the change from morning to noon, from noon to evening. I observed when any one entered or left the apartment; I could even tell who they were; I could understand what was said when the speaker stood near to me; but I could not answer; to open my lips or move my limbs was equally impossible. Hannah, the servant, was my most frequent visitor. Her coming disturbed me. I had a feeling that she wished me away: that she did not understand me or my circumstances: that she was prejudiced against me. Diana and Mary appeared in the chamber once or twice a day. They would whisper sentences of this sort at my bedside:—

'It is very well we took her in.'

'Yes; she would certainly have been found dead at the door in the morning, had she been left out all night. I wonder what she has gone through?'

'Strange hardships, I imagine—poor, emaciated, pallid wanderer!'

'She is not an uneducated person, I should think, by her manner of speaking; her accent was quite pure; and the clothes she took off, though splashed and wet, were little worn and fine.'

'She has a peculiar face; fleshless and haggard as it is, I rather like it; and when in good health and animated, I can fancy her physiognomy would be agreeable.'

Never once in their dialogues did I hear a syllable of regret at the hospitality they had extended to me; or of suspicion of, or aversion to, myself. I was comforted.

Mr. St. John came but once: he looked at me, and said my state of lethargy was the result of reaction from excessive and protracted fatigue. He pronounced it needless to send for a doctor: nature, he was sure, would manage best left to herself. He said every nerve had been overstrained in some way, and the whole system must sleep torpid awhile. There was no disease. He imagined my recovery would be rapid enough when once commenced. These opinions he delivered in a few words, in a quiet, low voice; and added, after a pause, in the tone of a man little accustomed to expansive comment, 'rather an unusual physiognomy; certainly not indicative of vulgarity or degradation.'

'Far otherwise,' responded Diana. 'To speak truth, St. John, my heart rather warms to the poor little soul. I wish we may be able to benefit her permanently.'

'That is hardly likely,' was the reply. 'You will find she is some young lady who has had a misunderstanding with her friends and has probably injudiciously left them. We may, perhaps, succeed in restoring her to them, if she is not obstinate: but I trace lines of force in her face which make me sceptical of her tractability.' He stood considering me some minutes; then added, 'She looks sensible, but not at all handsome.'

'She is so ill, St. John.'

'Ill or well, she would always be plain. The grace and harmony of beauty are quite wanting in those features.'

On the third day I was better; on the fourth, I could speak, move, rise in bed, and turn. Hannah had brought me some gruel and dry toast, about, as I supposed, the dinner hour. I had eaten with relish: the food was good—void of the feverish flavour which had hitherto poisoned what I had swallowed. When she left me, I felt comparatively strong and revived; ere long satiety of repose and desire for action stirred me. I wished to rise; but what could I put on? Only my damp and bemired apparel, in which I had slept on the ground and fallen in the marsh. I felt ashamed to appear before my benefactors so clad. I was spared the humiliation.

On a chair by the bedside were all my own things, clean and dry. My black silk frock hung against the wall. The traces of the bog were removed from it; the creases left by the wet smoothed out: it was quite decent. My very shoes and stockings were purified and rendered presentable. There were the means of washing in the room, and a comb and brush to smooth my hair. After a weary process, and resting every five minutes, I succeeded in dressing myself. My clothes hung loose on me, for I was much wasted; but I covered deficiencies with a shawl, and once more, clean and respectable-looking—no speck of the dirt, no trace of the disorder I so hated, and which seemed so to degrade me, left—I crept down a stone staircase with the aid of the banisters to a narrow low passage, and found my way presently to the kitchen.

It was full of the fragrance of new bread and the warmth of a generous fire. Hannah was baking. Prejudices, it is well known, are most difficult to eradicate from the heart whose soil has never been loosened or fertilised by education: they grow there, firm as weeds among stones. Hannah had been cold and stiff, indeed, at the first: latterly she had begun to relent a little; and when she saw me come in tidy and well-dressed, she even smiled.

'What, you have got up?' she said. 'You are better, then. You may sit you down in my chair on the hearthstone, if you will.'

She pointed to the rocking-chair: I took it. She bustled about, examining me every now and then with the corner of her eye. Turning to me, as she took some loaves from the oven, she asked, bluntly—'Did you ever go a-begging afore you came here?'

I was indignant for a moment; but remembering that anger was out of the question, and that I had indeed appeared as a begger to her, I answered quietly, but still not without a certain marked firmness—'You are mistaken in supposing me a beggar. I am no beggar: any more than yourself or your young ladies.'

After a pause, she said, 'I dunnut understand that: you've like no house, nor no brass, I guess?'

'The want of house or brass (by which I suppose you mean money) does not make a beggar in your sense of the word.'

'Are you book-learned?' she inquired, presently.

'Yes, very.'

'But you've never been to a boarding-school!'

'I was at a boarding-school eight years.'

She opened her eyes wide.

'Whatever cannot ye keep yourself for, then?'

'I have kept myself; and, I trust, shall keep myself again. What are you going to do with these gooseberries?' I inquired, as she brought out a basket of the fruit.

'Mak'em into pies.'

'Give them to me and I'll pick them.'

'Nay; I dunnut want ye to do nought.'

'But I must do something. Let me have them.'

She consented; and she even brought me a clean towel to spread over my dress, 'lest,' as she said, 'I should mucky it.'

'Ye've not been used to a sarvant's wark, I see by your hands,' she remarked. 'Happen ye've been a dressmaker.'

'No, you are wrong. And, now, never mind what I have been: don't trouble your head further about me; but tell me the name of the house where we are.'

'Some calls it Marsh End, and some calls it Moor House.'

'And the gentleman who lives here is called Mr. St. John?'

'Nay; he doesn't live here: he is only staying a while. When he is at home, he in his own parish at Morton.'

'That village a few miles off?'

'Aye.'

'And what is he?'

'He is a parson.'

I remembered the answer of the old housekeeper at the parsonage, when I had asked to see the clergyman. 'This, then, was his father's residence?'

'Aye; old Mr. Rivers lived here, and his father, and grandfather, and gurt (great) grandfather afore him.'

'The name, then, of that gentleman is Mr. St. John Rivers?'

'Aye; St. John is like his kirstened name.'

'And his sisters are called Diana and Mary Rivers?'

'Yes.'

'Their father is dead?'

'Dead three weeks sin' of a stroke.'

'They have no mother?'

'The mistress has been dead this mony a year.'

'Have you lived with the family long?'

'I've lived here thirty year. I nursed them all three.'

'That proves you must have been an honest and faithful servant. I will say so much for you, though you have had the incivility to call me a beggar.'

She again regarded me with a surprised stare. 'I believe,' she said, 'I was quite mista'en in my thoughts of you: but there is so mony cheats goes about, you mun forgie me.'

'And though,' I continued, rather severely, 'you wished to turn me from the door, on a night when you should not have shut out a dog.'

'Well, it was hard: but what can a body do? I thought more o' th' childer nor of mysel': poor things! They've like nobody to tak' care on 'em but me. I'm like to look sharpish.'

I maintained a grave silence for some minutes.

'You munnut think too hardly of me,' she again remarked.

'But I do think hardly of you,' I said; 'and I'll tell you why—not so much because you refused to give me shelter, or regarded me as an impostor, as because you just now made it a species of reproach that I had no "brass," and no house. Some of the best people that ever lived have been as destitute as I am; and if you are a Christian, you ought not to consider poverty a crime.'

'No more I ought,' said she: 'Mr. St. John tells me so too; and I see I wor wrang—but I've clear a different notion on you now to what I had. You look a raight down dacent little crater.'

'That will do—I forgive you now. Shake hands.'

She put her floury and horny hand into mine: another and heartier smile illumined her rough face: and from that moment we were friends.

Hannah was evidently fond of talking. While I picked the fruit and she made the paste for the pies, she proceeded to give me sundry details about her deceased master and mistress, and 'the childer,' as she called the young people.

Old Mr. Rivers, she said, was a plain man enough; but a gentleman, and of as ancient a family as could be found. Marsh End had belonged to the Rivers' ever since it was a house: and it was, she affirmed, 'aboon two hundred year old—for all it looked but a small, humble place, naught to compare wi' Mr. Oliver's grand hall down i' Morton Vale. But she could remember Bill Oliver's father a journeyman needle-maker; and th' Rivers' wor gentry i' thi' owd days o' th' Henrys, as onybody might see by looking into th' registers i' Morton Church vestry.' Still, she allowed, 'the owd maister was like other folk—naught mich out o' t' common way: stark mad o' shooting, and farming, and sich like.' The mistress was different. She was a great reader, and studied a deal; and the 'bairns' had taken after her. There was nothing like them in these parts, nor ever had been; they had liked learning, all three, almost from the time they could speak; and they had always been 'of a mak' of their own.' Mr. St. John, when he grew up, would go to college and be a parson; and the girls, as soon as they left school, would seek places as governesses: for they had told her their father had some years ago lost a great deal of money by a man he had trusted turning bankrupt; and as he was now not rich enough to give them fortunes, they must provide for themselves. They had lived very little at home for a long while, and were only come now to stay a few weeks on account of their father's death: but they did so like Marsh End and Morton, and all these moors and hills about. They had been in London, and many other grand towns; but they always said there was no place like home; and then they were so agreeable with each other—never fell out nor 'threaped.'[4] She did not know where there was such a family for being united.

Having finished my task of gooseberry picking, I asked where the two ladies and their brother were now.

'Gone over to Morton for a walk; but they would be back in half an hour to tea.'

They returned within the time Hannah had allotted them: they entered by the kitchen door. Mr. St. John, when he saw me, merely bowed and passed through; the two ladies stopped: Mary, in a few words, kindly and calmly expressed the pleasure she felt in seeing me well enough to be able to come down; Diana took my hand: she shook her head at me.

'You should have waited for my leave to descend,' she said. 'You still look very pale—and so thin! Poor child!—poor girl!'

Diana had a voice toned, to my ear, like the cooing of a dove. She possessed eyes whose gaze I delighted to encounter. Her whole face seemed to me full of charm. Mary's countenance was equally intelligent—her features equally pretty: but her expression was more reserved; and her manners, though gentle, more distant. Diana looked and spoke with a certain authority: she had a will, evidently. It was my nature to feel pleasure in yielding to an authority supported like hers: and to bend, where my conscience and self-respect permitted, to an active will.

'And what business have you here?' she continued. 'It is not your

4. Quarreled.

place. Mary and I sit in the kitchen sometimes, because at home we like to be free, even to licence—but you are a visitor, and must go into the parlour.'

'I am very well here.'

'Not at all—with Hannah bustling about and covering you with flour.'

'Besides, the fire is too hot for you,' interposed Mary.

'To be sure,' added her sister. 'Come, you must be obedient.' And still holding my hand, she made me rise, and led me into the inner room.

'Sit there,' she said, placing me on the sofa, 'while we take our things off and get the tea ready; it is another privilege we exercise in our little moorland home—to prepare our own meals when we are so inclined; or when Hannah is baking, brewing, washing, or ironing.'

She closed the door, leaving me solus with Mr. St. John, who sat opposite, a book or newspaper in his hand. I examined, first, the parlour, and then its occupant.

The parlour was rather a small room, very plainly furnished; yet comfortable, because clean and neat. The old-fashioned chairs were very bright, and the walnut-wood table was like a looking-glass. A few strange antique portraits of the men and women of other days decorated the stained walls; a cupboard with glass doors contained some books and an ancient set of china. There was no superfluous ornament in the room—not one modern piece of furniture, save a brace of work-boxes and a lady's desk in rosewood, which stood on a side-table: everything —including the carpet and curtains—looked at once well worn and well saved.

Mr. St. John—sitting as still as one of the dusky pictures on the walls, keeping his eyes fixed on the page he perused and his lips mutely sealed, was easy enough to examine. Had he been a statue instead of a man, he could not have been easier. He was young—perhaps from twenty-eight to thirty—tall, slender; his face riveted the eye; it was like a Greek face, very pure in outline: quite a straight, classic nose; quite an Athenian mouth and chin. It is seldom, indeed, an English face comes so near the antique models as did his. He might well be a little shocked at the irregularity of my lineaments, his own being so harmonious. His eyes were large and blue, with brown lashes; his high forehead, colourless as ivory, was partially streaked over by careless locks of fair hair.

This is a gentle delineation, is it not, reader? Yet he whom it describes scarcely impressed one with the idea of a gentle, a yielding, an impressible, or even of a placid nature. Quiescent as he now sat, there was something about his nostril, his mouth, his brow, which, to my perceptions, indicated elements within either restless, or hard, or eager. He did not speak to me one word, nor even direct to me one glance, till his sisters returned. Diana, as she passed in and out in the course of preparing tea, brought me a little cake, baked on the top of the oven.

'Eat that now,' she said: 'you must be hungry. Hannah says you have had nothing but some gruel since breakfast.'

I did not refuse it, for my appetite was awakened and keen. Mr. Rivers now closed his book, approached the table, and, as he took a seat, fixed his blue pictorial-looking eyes full on me. There was an unceremonious directness, a searching, decided steadfastness in his gaze now, which told that intention, and not diffidence, had hitherto kept it averted from the stranger.

'You are very hungry,' he said.

'I am, sir.' It is my way—it always was my way, by instinct—ever to meet the brief with brevity, the direct with plainness.

'It is well for you that a low fever has forced you to abstain for the last three days: there would have been danger in yielding to the cravings of your appetite at first. Now you may eat; though still not immoderately.'

'I trust I shall not eat long at your expense, sir,' was my very clumsily-contrived, unpolished answer.

'No,' he said coolly: 'when you have indicated to us the residence of your friends, we can write to them, and you may be restored to home.'

'That, I must plainly tell you, is out of my power to do; being absolutely without home and friends.'

The three looked at me, but not distrustfully; I felt there was no suspicion in their glances: there was more of curiosity. I speak particularly of the young ladies. St. John's eyes, though clear enough in a literal sense, in a figurative one were difficult to fathom. He seemed to use them rather as instruments to search other people's thoughts, than as agents to reveal his own: the which combination of keenness and reserve was considerably more calculated to embarrass than to encourage.

'Do you mean to say,' he asked, 'that you are completely isolated from every connection?'

'I do. Not a tie links me to any living thing: not a claim do I possess to admittance under any roof in England.'

'A most singular position at your age!'

Here I saw his glance directed to my hands, which were folded on the table before me. I wondered what he sought there: his words soon explained the quest.

'You have never been married? You are a spinster?'

Diana laughed.

'Why, she can't be above seventeen or eighteen years old, St. John,' said she.

'I am near nineteen: but I am not married. No.'

I felt a burning glow mount to my face; for bitter and agitating recollections were awakened by the allusion to marriage. They all saw the embarrassment and the emotion. Diana and Mary relieved me by turning their eyes elsewhere than to my crimsoned visage; but the colder and sterner brother continued to gaze, till the trouble he had excited forced out tears as well as colour.

'Where did you last reside?' he now asked.

'You are too inquisitive, St. John,' murmured Mary, in a low voice; but he leaned over the table and required an answer by a second firm and piercing look.

'The name of the place where, and of the person with whom I lived, is my secret,' I replied, concisely.

'Which, if you like, you have, in my opinion, a right to keep both from St. John and every other questioner,' remarked Diana.

'Yet if I know nothing about you or your history, I cannot help you,' he said. 'And you need help: do you not?'

'I need it, and I seek it; so far, sir, that some true philanthropist will put me in the way of getting work which I can do, and the remuneration for which will keep me: if but in the barest necessaries of life.'

'I know not whether I am a true philanthropist; yet I am willing to aid you to the utmost of my power, in a purpose so honest. First, then, tell me what you have been accustomed to do, and what you *can* do.'

I had now swallowed my tea. I was mightily refreshed by the beverage; as much so as a giant with wine: it gave new tone to my unstrung nerves, and enabled me to address this penetrating young judge steadily.

'Mr. Rivers,' I said, turning to him, and looking at him, as he looked at me, openly and without diffidence, 'you and your sisters have done me a great service—the greatest man can do his fellow-being; you have rescued me, by your noble hospitality, from death. This benefit conferred gives you an unlimited claim on my gratitude; and a claim, to a certain extent, on my confidence. I will tell you as much of the history of the wanderer you have harboured as I can tell without compromising my own peace of mind—my own security, moral and physical, and that of others.

'I am an orphan; the daughter of a clergyman. My parents died before I could know them. I was brought up a dependent; educated in a charitable institution. I will even tell you the name of the establishment where I passed six years as a pupil and two as a teacher—Lowood Orphan Asylum, ——shire: you will have heard of it, Mr. Rivers?—the Rev. Robert Brocklehurst is the treasurer.'

'I have heard of Mr. Brocklehurst, and I have seen the school.'

'I left Lowood nearly a year since to become a private governess. I obtained a good situation, and was happy. This place I was obliged to leave four days before I came here. The reason of my departure I cannot and ought not to explain: it would be useless—dangerous; and would sound incredible. No blame attached to me; I am as free from culpability as any one of you three. Miserable I am, and must be for a time; for the catastrophe which drove me from a house I had found a paradise was of a strange and direful nature. I observed but two points in planning my departure—speed, secrecy: to secure these I had to leave behind me everything I possessed except a small parcel; which, in my hurry and trouble of mind, I forgot to take out of the coach that brought me to Whitcross. To this neighbourhood, then, I came, quite destitute. I slept two nights in the open air, and wandered about two days without crossing a threshold: but twice in that space of time did I taste food; and it was when brought by hunger, exhaustion and despair almost to the last gasp that you, Mr. Rivers, forbade me to perish of want at your door, and took me under the shelter of your roof. I know all your sisters have done for me since—for I have not been insensible during my seeming torpor—and I owe to their spontaneous, genuine, genial compassion, as large a debt as to your evangelical charity.'

'Don't make her talk any more now, St. John,' said Diana, as I paused; 'she is evidently not yet fit for excitement. Come to the sofa, and sit down now, Miss Elliott.'

I gave an involuntary half-start at hearing the alias; I had forgotten my new name. Mr. Rivers, whom nothing seemed to escape, noticed it at once.

'You said your name was Jane Elliott?' he observed.

'I did say so; and it is the name by which I think it expedient to be called at present: but it is not my real name, and when I hear it, it sounds strange to me.'

'Your real name you will not give?'

'No: I fear discovery above all things; and whatever disclosure would lead to it, I avoid.'

'You are quite right, I am sure,' said Diana. 'Now do, brother, let her be at peace a while.'

But when St. John had mused a few moments, he recommenced, as imperturbably, and with as much acumen as ever.

'You would not like to be long dependent on our hospitality—you would wish, I see, to dispense as soon as may be with my sisters' compassion; and, above all, with my *charity* (I am quite sensible of the distinction drawn, nor do I resent it—it is just): you desire to be independent of us?'

'I do: I have already said so. Show me how to work, or how to seek work: that is all I now ask; then let me go, if it be but to the meanest cottage—but *till then* allow me to stay here: I dread another essay of the horrors of homeless destitution.'

'Indeed, you *shall* stay here,' said Diana, putting her white hand on my head.

'You *shall*,' repeated Mary, in the tone of undemonstrative sincerity which seemed natural to her.

'My sisters, you see, have a pleasure in keeping you,' said Mr. St. John, 'as they would have a pleasure in keeping and cherishing a half-frozen bird some wintry wind might have driven through their casement. I feel more inclination to put you in the way of keeping yourself: and shall endeavour to do so: but observe, my sphere is narrow. I am but the incumbent of a poor country parish: my aid must be of the humblest sort. And if you are inclined to despise the day of small things, seek some more efficient succour than such as I can offer.'

'She has already said that she is willing to do anything honest she *can* do,' answered Diana for me; 'and you know, St. John, she has no choice of helpers: she is forced to put up with such crusty people as you.'

'I will be a dressmaker: I will be a plain-work-woman; I will be a servant, a nurse-girl, if I can be no better,' I answered.

'Right,' said Mr. St. John, quite coolly. 'If such is your spirit, I promise to aid you; in my own time and way.'

He now resumed the book with which he had been occupied before tea. I soon withdrew; for I had talked as much, and sat up as long, as my present strength would permit.

Chapter XXX

The more I knew of the inmates of Moor House, the better I liked them. In a few days I had so far recovered my health that I could sit up all day, and walk out sometimes. I could join with Diana and Mary in all their occupations; converse with them as much as they wished, and aid them when and where they would allow me. There was a reviving pleasure in this intercourse, of a kind now tasted by me for the first time—the pleasure arising from perfect congeniality of tastes, sentiments, and principles.

I liked to read what they liked to read: what they enjoyed, delighted me; what they approved, I reverenced. They loved their sequestered home. I, too, in the grey, small, antique structure, with its low roof, its latticed casements, its mouldering walls, its avenue of aged firs—all grown aslant under the stress of mountain winds; its garden, dark with yew and holly—and where no flowers but of the hardiest species would bloom—found a charm both potent and permanent. They clung to the purple moors behind and around their dwelling—to the hollow vale into which the pebbly bridle-path leading from their gate descended; and which wound between fern-banks first, and then amongst a few of the wildest little pasture-fields that ever bordered a wilderness of heath, or gave sustenance to a flock of grey moorland sheep, with their little mossy-faced lambs:—they clung to this scene, I say, with a perfect enthusiasm of attachment. I could comprehend the feeling, and share both its strength and truth. I saw the fascination of the locality. I felt the consecration of its loneliness: my eye feasted on the outline of swell and sweep—on the wild colouring communicated to ridge and dell by moss, by heath-bell, by flower-sprinkled turf, by brilliant bracken and mellow granite crag. These details were just to me what they were to them—so many pure and sweet sources of pleasure. The strong blast and the soft breeze; the rough and the halcyon day; the hours of sunrise and sunset; the moonlight and the clouded night, developed for me, in these regions, the same attraction as for them—wound round my faculties the same spell that entranced theirs.

Indoors we agreed equally well. They were both more accomplished and better read than I was: but with eagerness I followed in the path of knowledge they had trodden before me. I devoured the books they lent me: then it was full satisfaction to discuss with them in the evening what I had perused during the day. Thought fitted thought; opinion met opinion: we coincided, in short, perfectly.

If in our trio there was a superior and a leader, it was Diana. Physically, she far excelled me: she was handsome; she was vigorous. In her animal spirits there was an affluence of life and certainty of flow, such as excited my wonder, while it baffled my comprehension. I could talk a while when the evening commenced: but the first gush of vivacity and fluency gone, I was fain to sit on a stool at Diana's feet, to rest my head on her knee, and listen alternately to her and Mary; while they sounded thoroughly the topic on which I had but touched. Diana offered to teach me German. I liked to learn of her: I saw the part of instructress pleased and suited her; that of scholar pleased and suited me no less. Our natures dovetailed: mutual affection—of the strongest kind—was the result. They discovered I could draw: their pencils and colour-boxes were immediately at my service. My skill, greater in this one point than theirs, surprised and charmed them. Mary would sit and watch me by the hour together: then she would take lessons; and a docile, intelligent, assiduous pupil she made. Thus occupied, and mutually entertained, days passed like hours and weeks like days.

As to Mr. St. John, the intimacy which had arisen so naturally and rapidly between me and his sisters did not extend to him. One reason of the distance yet observed between us was that he was comparatively seldom at home: a large proportion of his time appeared devoted to visiting the sick and poor among the scattered population of his parish.

No weather seemed to hinder him in these pastoral excursions: rain or fair, he would, when his hours of morning study were over, take his hat, and, followed by his father's old pointer Carlo, go out on his mission of love or duty—I scarcely know in which light he regarded it. Sometimes, when the day was very unfavourable, his sisters would expostulate. He would then say, with a peculiar smile, more solemn than cheerful,—'And if I let a gust of wind or a sprinkling of rain turn me aside from these easy tasks, what preparation would such sloth be for the future I propose to myself?'

Diana and Mary's general answer to this question was a sigh, and some minutes of apparently mournful meditation.

But besides his frequent absences, there was another barrier to friendship with him: he seemed of a reserved, an abstracted, and even of a brooding nature. Zealous in his ministerial labours, blameless in his life and habits, he yet did not appear to enjoy that mental serenity, that inward content, which should be the reward of every sincere Christian and practical philanthropist. Often, of an evening, when he sat at the window, his desk and papers before him, he would cease reading or writing, rest his chin on his hand, and deliver himself up to I know not what course of thought; but that it was perturbed and exciting might be seen in the frequent flash and changeful dilation of his eye.

I think, moreover, that Nature was not to him that treasury of delight it was to his sisters. He expressed once, and but once in my hearing, a strong sense of the rugged charm of the hills, and an inborn affection for the dark roof and hoary walls he called his home; but there was more of gloom than pleasure in the tone and words in which the sentiment was manifested; and never did he seem to roam the moors for the sake of their soothing silence—never seek out or dwell upon the thousand peaceful delights they could yield.

Incommunicative as he was, some time elapsed before I had an opportunity of gauging his mind. I first got an idea of its calibre when I heard him preach in his own church at Morton. I wish I could describe that sermon; but it is past my power. I cannot even render faithfully the effect it produced on me.

It began calm—and indeed, as far as delivery and pitch of voice went, it was calm to the end: an earnestly felt, yet strictly restrained zeal breathed soon in the distinct accents, and prompted the nervous language. This grew to force—compressed, condensed, controlled. The heart was thrilled, the mind astonished, by the power of the preacher: neither was softened. Throughout there was a strange bitterness; an absence of consolatory gentleness; stern allusions to Calvinistic doctrines—election, predestination, reprobation—were frequent; and each reference to these points sounded like a sentence pronounced for doom. When he had done, instead of feeling better, calmer, more enlightened by his discourse, I experienced an inexpressible sadness; for it seemed to me—I know not whether equally so to others—that the eloquence to which I had been listening had sprung from a depth where lay turbid dregs of disappointment—where moved troubling impulses of insatiate yearnings and disquieting aspirations. I was sure St. John

Rivers—pure-lived, conscientious, zealous as he was—had not yet found that peace of God which passeth all understanding;[5] he had no more found it, I thought, then had I; with my concealed and racking regrets for my broken idol and lost elysium[6]—regrets to which I have latterly avoided referring; but which possessed me and tyrannised over me ruthlessly.

Meantime a month was gone. Diana and Mary were soon to leave Moor House, and return to the far different life and scene which awaited them, as governesses in a large, fashionable, south-of-England city; where each held a situation in families, by whose wealthy and haughty members they were regarded only as humble dependents, and who neither knew nor sought one of their innate excellences, and appreciated only their acquired accomplishments as they appreciated the skill of their cook or the taste of their waiting-woman. Mr. St. John had said nothing to me yet about the employment he had promised to obtain for me; yet it became urgent that I should have a vocation of some kind. One morning, being left alone with him a few minutes in the parlour, I ventured to approach the window-recess—which his table, chair, and desk consecrated as a kind of study—and I was going to speak; though not very well knowing in what words to frame my inquiry—for it is at all times difficult to break the ice of reserve glassing over such natures as his—when he saved me the trouble by being the first to commence a dialogue.

Looking up as I drew near—'You have a question to ask of me?' he said.

'Yes; I wish to know whether you have heard of any service I can offer myself to undertake.'

'I found or devised something for you three weeks ago; but as you seemed both useful and happy here—as my sisters had evidently become attached to you, and your society gave them unusual pleasure—I deemed it inexpedient to break in on your mutual comfort till their approaching departure from Marsh End should render yours necessary.'

'And they will go in three days now?' I said.

'Yes; and when they go I shall return to the parsonage at Morton: Hannah will accompany me; and this old house will be shut up.'

I waited for a few moments, expecting he would go on with the subject first broached; but he seemed to have entered another train of reflection; his look denoted abstraction from me and my business. I was obliged to recall him to a theme which was of necessity one of close and anxious interest to me.

'What is the employment you had in view, Mr. Rivers? I hope this delay will not have increased the difficulty of securing it.'

5. Philippians 4:7.   6. I.e., paradise.

'Oh, no; since it is an employment which depends only on me to give, and you to accept.'

He again paused: there seemed a reluctance to continue. I grew impatient: a restless movement or two, and an eager and exacting glance fastened on his face, conveyed the feeling to him as effectually as words could have done, and with less trouble.

'You need be in no hurry to hear,' he said; 'let me frankly tell you, I have nothing eligible or profitable to suggest. Before I explain, recall, if you please, my notice, clearly given, that if I helped you, it must be as the blind man would help the lame. I am poor; for I find that, when I have paid my father's debts, all the patrimony remaining to me will be this crumbling grange, the row of scathed firs behind, and the patch of moorish soil, with the yew-trees and holly-bushes in front. I am obscure: Rivers is an old name; but of the three sole descendants of the race, two earn the dependent's crust among strangers, and the third considers himself an alien from his native country—not only for life, but in death. Yes, and deems, and is bound to deem, himself honoured by the lot, and aspires but after the day when the cross of separation from fleshly ties shall be laid on his shoulders, and when the Head of that church-militant, of whose humblest members he is one, shall give the word, "Rise, follow Me!"'

St. John said these words as he pronounced his sermons, with a quiet, deep voice; with an unflushed cheek, and a coruscating radiance of glance. He resumed:—'And since I am myself poor and obscure, I can offer you but a service of poverty and obscurity. You may even think it degrading—for I see now your habits have been what the world calls refined: your tastes lean to the ideal; and your society has at least been amongst the educated—but I consider that no service degrades which can better our race. I hold that the more arid and unreclaimed the soil where the Christian labourer's task of tillage is appointed him—the scantier the meed his toil brings—the higher the honour. His, under such circumstances, is the destiny of the pioneer; and the first pioneers of the Gospel were the Apostles—their captain was Jesus, the Redeemer, Himself.'

'Well?' I said, as he again paused—'proceed.'

He looked at me before he proceeded: indeed, he seemed leisurely to read my face, as if its features and lines were characters on a page. The conclusions drawn from this scrutiny he partially expressed in his succeeding observations.

'I believe you will accept the post I offer you,' said he; 'and hold it for a while: not permanently, though: any more than I could permanently keep the narrow and narrowing—the tranquil, hidden office of English country incumbent: for in your nature is an alloy as detrimental to repose as that in mine; though of a different kind.'

'Do explain,' I urged, when he halted once more.

'I will; and you shall hear how poor the proposal is,—how trivial—how cramping. I shall not stay long at Morton, now that my father is dead, and that I am my own master. I shall leave the place probably in the course of a twelve-month: but while I do stay I will exert myself to the utmost for its improvement. Morton, when I came to it two years ago, had no school: the children of the poor were excluded from every hope of progress. I established one for boys: I mean now to open a second school for girls. I have hired a building for the purpose, with a cottage of two rooms attached to it for the mistress's house. Her salary will be thirty pounds a year; her house is already furnished, very simply, but sufficiently, by the kindness of a lady, Miss Oliver; the only daughter of the sole rich man in my parish—Mr. Oliver, the proprietor of a needle-factory and iron-foundry in the valley. The same lady pays for the education and clothing of an orphan from the workhouse; on condition that she shall aid the mistress in such menial offices connected with her own house and the school as her occupation of teaching will prevent her having time to discharge in person. Will you be this mistress?'

He put the question rather hurriedly; he seemed half to expect an indignant, or at least a disdainful, rejection of the offer: not knowing all my thoughts and feelings, though guessing some, he could not tell in what light the lot would appear to me. In truth it was humble—but then it was sheltered, and I wanted a safe asylum: it was plodding—but then, compared with that of a governess in a rich house, it was independent; and the fear of servitude with strangers entered my soul like iron: it was not ignoble—not unworthy—not mentally degrading. I made my decision.

'I thank you for the proposal, Mr. Rivers; and I accept it with all my heart.'

'But you comprehend me?' he said. 'It is a village school; your scholars will be only poor girls—cottagers' children—at the best, farmers' daughters. Knitting, sewing, reading, writing, cyphering, will be all you will have to teach. What will you do with your accomplishments? What with the largest portion of your mind—sentiments—tastes?'

'Save them till they are wanted. They will keep.'

'You know what you undertake; then?'

'I do.'

He now smiled: and not a bitter or a sad smile, but one well pleased and deeply gratified.

'And when will you commence the exercise of your function?'

'I will go to my house to-morrow; and open the school, if you like, next week.'

'Very well: so be it.'

He rose and walked through the room. Standing still, he again looked at me. He shook his head.

'What do you disapprove of, Mr. Rivers?' I asked.

'You will not stay at Morton long: no, no!'

'Why! What is your reason for saying so?'

'I read it in your eye; it is not of that description which promises the maintenance of an even tenor in life.'

'I am not ambitious.'

He started at the word 'ambitious.' He repeated, 'No. What made you think of ambition? Who is ambitious? I know I am: but how did you find it out?'

'I was speaking of myself.'

'Well, if you are not ambitious, you are'——He paused.

'What?'

'I was going to say, impassioned: but perhaps you would have misunderstood the word, and been displeased. I mean, that human affections and sympathies have a most powerful hold on you. I am sure you cannot long be content to pass your leisure in solitude, and to devote your working hours to a monotonous labour wholly void of stimulus; any more than I can be content,' he added, with emphasis, 'to live here buried in morass, pent in with mountain—my nature, that God gave me, contravened; my faculties, heaven-bestowed, paralysed—made useless. You hear now how I contradict myself. I, who preached contentment with a humble lot, and justified the vocation even of hewers of wood, and drawers of water, in God's service—I, His ordained minister, almost rave in my restlessness. Well, propensities and principles must be reconciled by some means.'

He left the room. In this brief hour I had learnt more of him than in the whole previous month: yet still he puzzled me.

Diana and Mary Rivers became more sad and silent as the day approached for leaving their brother and their home. They both tried to appear as usual; but the sorrow they had to struggle against was one that could not be entirely conquered or concealed. Diana intimated that this would be a different parting from any they had ever yet known. It would probably, as far as St. John was concerned, be a parting for years: it might be a parting for life.

'He will sacrifice all to his long-framed resolves,' she said: 'natural affection and feelings more potent still. St. John looks quiet, Jane; but he hides a fever in his vitals. You would think him gentle, yet in some things he is inexorable as death; and the worst of it is, my conscience will hardly permit me to dissuade him from his severe decision: certainly, I cannot for a moment blame him for it. It is right, noble, Christian: yet it breaks my heart.' And the tears gushed to her fine eyes. Mary bent her head low over her work.

'We are now without father: we shall soon be without home and brother,' she murmured.

At that moment a little accident supervened which seemed decreed by fate purposely to prove the truth of the adage that 'misfortunes never come singly:' and to add to their distresses the vexing one of the slip between the cup and the lip. St. John passed the window reading a letter. He entered.

'Our uncle John is dead,' said he.

Both the sisters seemed struck: not shocked or appalled; the tidings appeared in their eyes rather momentous than afflicting.

'Dead?' repeated Diana.

'Yes.'

She riveted a searching gaze on her brother's face. 'And what then?' she demanded, in a low voice.

'What then, Di?' he replied, maintaining a marble immobility of feature. 'When then? Why—nothing. Read.'

He threw the letter into her lap. She glanced over it, and handed it to Mary. Mary perused it in silence, and returned it to her brother. All three looked at each other, and all three smiled—a dreary, pensive smile enough.

'Amen! We can yet live,' said Diana at last.

'At any rate, it makes us no worse off than we were before,' remarked Mary.

'Only it forces rather strongly on the mind the picture of what *might have been*,' said Mr. Rivers; 'and contrasts it somewhat too vividly with what *is*.'

He folded the letter, locked it in his desk, and again went out.

For some minutes no one spoke. Diana then turned to me.

'Jane, you will wonder at us and our mysteries,' she said, 'and think us hard-hearted beings not to be more moved at the death of so near a relation as an uncle; but we have never seen him or known him. He was my mother's brother. My father and he quarrelled long ago. It was by his advice that my father risked most of his property in the speculation that ruined him. Mutual recrimination passed between them: they parted in anger, and were never reconciled. My uncle engaged afterwards in more prosperous undertakings: it appears he realised a fortune of twenty thousand pounds. He was never married, and had no near kindred but ourselves, and one other person, not more closely related than we. My father always cherished the idea that he would atone for his error by leaving his possessions to us: that letter informs us that he has bequeathed every penny to the other relation; with the exception of thirty guineas, to be divided between St. John, Diana, and Mary Rivers, for the purchase of three mourning rings. He had a right, of course, to do as he pleased: and yet a momentary damp is cast on the spirits by the receipt of such news. Mary and I would have esteemed ourselves rich with a thousand pounds each; and to St. John such a sum would have been valuable, for the good it would have enabled him to do.'

This explanation given, the subject was dropped, and no further reference made to it, by either Mr. Rivers or his sisters. The next day I left Marsh End for Morton. The day after, Diana and Mary quitted it for distant B———. In a week, Mr. Rivers and Hannah repaired to the parsonage: and so the old grange was abandoned.

Chapter XXXI

My home, then,—when I at last find a home,—is a cottage: a little room with white-washed walls and a sanded floor; containing four painted chairs and a table, a clock, a cupboard, with two or three plates and dishes, and a set of tea-things in delf.[7] Above, a chamber of the same dimensions as the kitchen, with a deal bedstead, and chest of drawers; small, yet too large to be filled with my scanty wardrobe: though the kindness of my gentle and generous friends has increased that by a modest stock of such things as are necessary.

It is evening. I have dismissed, with the fee of an orange, the little orphan who serves me as a handmaid. I am sitting alone on the hearth. This morning the village school opened. I had twenty scholars. But three of the number can read: none write or cypher. Several knit, and a few sew a little. They speak with the broadest accent of the district. At present they and I have a difficulty in understanding each other's language. Some of them are unmannered, rough, intractable, as well as ignorant; but others are docile, have a wish to learn, and evince a disposition that pleases me. I must not forget that these coarsely-clad little peasants are of flesh and blood as good as the scions of gentlest genealogy; and that the germs of native excellence, refinement, intelligence, kind feeling, are as likely to exist in their hearts as in those of the best-born. My duty will be to develop these germs: surely I shall find some happiness in discharging that office. Much enjoyment I do not expect in the life opening before me: yet it will, doubtless, if I regulate my mind, and exert my powers as I ought, yield me enough to live on from day to day.

Was I very gleeful, settled, content, during the hours I passed in yonder bare, humble schoolroom this morning and afternoon? Not to deceive myself, I must reply—No: I felt desolate to a degree. I felt— yes, idiot that I am—I felt degraded. I doubted I had taken a step which sank instead of raising me in the scale of social existence. I was weakly dismayed at the ignorance, the poverty, the coarseness of all I heard and saw round me. But let me not hate and despise myself too much for

7. I.e., delft, Dutch pottery.

these feelings: I know them to be wrong—that is a great step gained; I shall strive to overcome them. To-morrow, I trust, I shall get the better of them partially; and in a few weeks, perhaps, they will be quite subdued. In a few months, it is possible, the happiness of seeing progress, and a change for the better in my scholars, may substitute gratification for disgust.

Meantime, let me ask myself one question—Which is better?—To have surrendered to temptation; listened to passion; made no painful effort—no struggle;—but to have sunk down in the silken snare; fallen asleep on the flowers covering it; wakened in a southern clime, amongst the luxuries of a pleasure villa: to have been now living in France, Mr. Rochester's mistress; delirious with his love half my time—for he would—oh, yes, he would have loved me well for a while. He *did* love me—no one will ever love me so again. I shall never more know the sweet homage given to beauty, youth, and grace—for never to any one else shall I seem to possess these charms. He was fond and proud of me —it is what no man besides will ever be.—But where am I wondering, and what am I saying; and, above all, feeling? Whether is it better, I ask, to be a slave in a fool's paradise at Marseilles—fevered with delusive bliss one hour—suffocating with the bitterest tears of remorse and shame the next—or to be a village schoolmistress, free and honest, in a breezy mountain nook in the healthy heart of England?

Yes; I feel now that I was right when I adhered to principle and law, and scorned and crushed the insane promptings of a frenzied moment. God directed me to a correct choice: I thank His providence for the guidance.

Having brought my eventide musings to this point, I rose, went to my door, and looked at the sunset of the harvest-day, and at the quiet fields before my cottage; which, with the school, was distant half a mile from the village. The birds were singing their last strains—

'The air was mild; the dew was balm.'[8]

While I looked, I thought myself happy, and was surprised to find myself ere long weeping—and why? For the doom which had reft me from adhesion to my master: for him I was no more to see; for the desperate grief and fatal fury—consequences of my departure—which might now, perhaps, be dragging him from the path of right, too far to leave hope of ultimate restoration thither. As this thought, I turned my face aside from the lovely sky of eve and lonely vale of Morton—I say *lonely*, for in that bend of it visible to me there was no building apparent save the church and the parsonage, half-hid in trees; and, quite at the

8. From Sir Walter Scott's *The Lay of the Last Minstrel* 3.24.3–4.

extremity, the roof of Vale Hall, where the rich Mr. Oliver and his daughter lived. I hid my eyes, and leant my head against the stone frame of my door; but soon a slight noise near the wicket which shut in my tiny garden from the meadow beyond it made me look up. A dog —old Carlo, Mr. Rivers' pointer, as I saw in a moment—was pushing the gate with his nose, and St. John himself leant upon it with folded arms; his brow knit, his gaze, grave almost to displeasure, fixed on me. I asked him to come in.

'No, I cannot stay; I have only brought you a little parcel my sisters left for you. I think it contains a colour-box, pencils, and paper.'

I approached to take it: a welcome gift it was. He examined my face, I thought, with austerity, as I came near: the traces of tears were doubtless very visible upon it.

'Have you found your first day's work harder than you expected?' he asked.

'Oh, no! On the contrary, I think in time I shall get on with my scholars very well.'

'But perhaps your accommodations—your cottage—your furniture —have disappointed your expectations? They are, in truth, scanty enough; but——'

I interrupted:—'My cottage is clean and weather-proof; my furniture sufficient and commodious. All I see has made me thankful, not despondent. I am not absolutely such a fool and sensualist as to regret the absence of a carpet, a sofa, and silver plate: besides, five weeks ago I had nothing—I was an outcast, a beggar, a vagrant; now I have acquaintance, a home, a business. I wonder at the goodness of God; the generosity of my friends; the bounty of my lot. I do not repine.'

'But you feel solitude an oppression? The little house there behind you is dark and empty.'

'I have hardly had time yet to enjoy a sense of tranquillity, much less to grow impatient under one of loneliness.'

'Very well; I hope you feel the content you express: at any rate, your good sense will tell you that it is too soon yet to yield to the vacillating fears of Lot's wife.[9] What you had left before I saw you, of course I do not know; but I counsel you to resist, firmly, every temptation which would incline you to look back: pursue your present career steadily, for some months at least.'

'It is what I mean to do,' I answered.

St. John continued:—'It is hard work to control the workings of inclination, and turn the bent of nature: but that it may be done I know from experience. God has given us, in a measure, the power to make our

___

9. Fleeing the destruction of Sodom, Lot's wife looked backward and was turned into a pillar of salt (Genesis 19:24–26).

own fate; and when our energies seem to demand a sustenance they cannot get—when our will strains after a path we may not follow—we need neither starve from inanition, nor stand still in despair: we have but to seek another nourishment for the mind, as strong as the forbidden fruit it longed to taste—and perhaps purer; and to hew out for the adventurous foot a road as direct and broad as the one Fortune has blocked up against us, if rougher than it.

'A year ago I was myself intensely miserable, because I thought I had made a mistake in entering the ministry: its uniform duties wearied me to death. I burnt for the more active life of the world—for the more exciting toils of a literary career—for the destiny of an artist, author, orator; anything rather than that of a priest: yes, the heart of a politician, of a soldier, of a votary of glory, a lover of renown, a luster after power, beat under my curate's surplice. I considered; my life was so wretched, it must be changed, or I must die. After a season of darkness and struggling, light broke and relief fell: my cramped existence all at once spread out to a plain without bounds—my powers heard a call from heaven to rise, gather their full strength, spread their wings, and mount beyond ken. God had an errand for me; to bear which afar, to deliver it well, skill and strength, courage and eloquence, the best qualifications of soldier, statesman, and orator, were all needed: for these all centre in the good missionary.

'A missionary I resolved to be. From that moment my state of mind changed; the fetters dissolved and dropped from every faculty, leaving nothing of bondage but its galling soreness—which time only can heal. My father, indeed, opposed the determination, but since his death I have not a legitimate obstacle to contend with; some affairs settled, a successor for Morton provided, an entanglement or two of the feelings broken through or cut asunder—a last conflict with human weakness, in which I know I shall overcome, because I have vowed that I *will* overcome—and I leave Europe for the East.'

He said this in his peculiar, subdued, yet emphatic voice; looking, when he had ceased speaking, not at me, but at the setting sun, at which I looked too. Both he and I had our backs towards the path leading up the field to the wicket. We had heard no step on that grass-grown track; the water running in the vale was the one lulling sound of the hour and scene; we might well then start when a gay voice, sweet as a silver bell, exclaimed:—'Good evening, Mr. Rivers. And good evening, old Carlo. Your dog is quicker to recognise his friends than you are, sir; he pricked his ears and wagged his tail when I was at the bottom of the field, and you have your back towards me now.'

It was true. Though Mr. Rivers had started at the first of those musical accents, as if a thunderbolt had split a cloud over his head, he stood yet, at the close of the sentence, in the same attitude in which the speaker had surprised him—his arm resting on the gate, his face directed towards the west. He turned at last, with measured deliberation. A vision, as it seemed to me, had risen at his side. There appeared, within three feet of him, a form clad in pure white—a youthful, graceful form: full, yet fine in contour; and when, after bending to caress Carlo, it lifted up its head, and threw back a long veil, there bloomed under his glance a face of perfect beauty. Perfect beauty is a strong expression; but I do not retrace or qualify it: as sweet features as ever the temperate clime of Albion moulded; as pure hues of rose and lily as ever her humid gales and vapoury skies generated and screened justified, in this instance, the term. No charm was wanting, no defect was perceptible; the young girl had regular and delicate lineaments; eyes shaped and coloured as we see them in lovely pictures, large, and dark, and full; the long and shadowy eyelash which encircles a fine eye with so soft a fascination; the pencilled brow which gives such clearness; the white, smooth forehead which adds such repose to the livelier beauties of tint and ray; the cheek, oval, fresh, and smooth; the lips, fresh too, ruddy, healthy, sweetly formed; the even and gleaming teeth without flaw; the small dimpled chin; the ornament of rich, plenteous tresses—all advantages, in short, which, combined, realise the ideal of beauty were fully hers. I wondered, as I looked at this fair creature: I admired her with my whole heart. Nature had surely formed her in a partial mood; and, forgetting her usual stinted stepmother dole of gifts, had endowed this, her darling, with a granddame's bounty.

What did St. John Rivers think of this earthly angel? I naturally asked myself that question as I saw him turn to her and look at her; and, as naturally, I sought the answer to the inquiry in his countenance. He had already withdrawn his eye from the Peri, and was looking at a humble tuft of daisies which grew by the wicket.

'A lovely evening, but late for you to be out alone,' he said, as he crushed the snowy heads of the closed flowers with his foot.

'Oh, I only came home from S——' (she mentioned the name of a large town some twenty miles distant) 'this afternoon. Papa told me you had opened your school, and that the new mistress was come; and so I put on my bonnet after tea, and ran up the valley to see her: this is she?' pointing to me.

'It is,' said St. John.

'Do you think you shall like Morton?' she asked of me, with a direct and naïve simplicity of tone and manner, pleasing, if childlike.

'I hope I shall. I have many inducements to do so.'

'Did you find your scholars as attentive as you expected?'

'Quite.'

'Do you like your house?'

'Very much.'

'Have I furnished it nicely?'

'Very nicely indeed.'

'And made a good choice of an attendant for you in Alice Wood?'

'You have, indeed. She is teachable and handy.' (This, then, I thought, is Miss Oliver, the heiress; favoured, it seems, in the gifts of fortune, as well as in those of nature! What happy combination of the planets presided over her birth, I wonder?)

'I shall come up and help you to teach sometimes,' she added. 'It will be a change for me to visit you now and then; and I like a change. Mr. Rivers, I have been so gay during my stay at S——. Last night, or rather this morning, I was dancing till two o'clock. The ——th regiment are stationed there since the riots; and the officers are the most agreeable men in the world: they put all our young knife-grinders and scissor merchants to shame.'

It seemed to me that Mr. St. John's under lip protruded, and his upper lip curled a moment. His mouth certainly looked a good deal compressed, and the lower part of his face unusually stern and square, as the laughing girl gave him this information. He lifted his gaze, too, from the daisies, and turned it on her. An unsmiling, a searching, a meaning gaze it was. She answered it with a second laugh, and laughter well became her youth, her roses, her dimples, her bright eyes.

As he stood, mute and grave, she again fell to caressing Carlo. 'Poor Carlo loves me,' said she. '*He* is not stern and distant to his friends; and if he could speak, he would not be silent.'

As she patted the dog's head, bending with native grace before his young and austere master, I saw a glow rise to that master's face. I saw his solemn eye melt with sudden fire, and flicker with resistless emotion. Flushed and kindled thus, he looked nearly as beautiful for a man as she for a woman. His chest heaved once, as if his large heart, weary of despotic constriction, had expanded, despite the will, and made a vigorous bound for the attainment of liberty. But he curbed it, I think, as a resolute rider would curb a rearing steed. He responded neither by word nor movement to the gentle advances made him.

'Papa says you never come to see us now,' continued Miss Oliver, looking up. 'You are quite a stranger at Vale Hall. He is alone this evening, and not very well: will you return with me and visit him?'

'It is not a seasonable hour to intrude on Mr. Oliver,' answered St. John.

'Not a seasonable hour! But I declare it is. It is just the hour when papa most wants company: when the works are closed, and he has no business to occupy him. Now, Mr. Rivers, *do* come. Why are you so very shy, and so very sombre?'

She filled up the hiatus his silence left by a reply of her own.

'I forgot!' she exclaimed, shaking her beautiful curled head, as if shocked at herself. 'I am so giddy and thoughtless! *Do* excuse me. It had slipped my memory that you have good reasons to be indisposed for joining in my chatter. Diana and Mary have left you, and Moor House is shut up, and you are so lonely. I am sure I pity you. Do come and see papa.'

'Not to-night, Miss Rosamond, not to-night.'

Mr. St. John spoke almost like an automaton: himself only knew the effort it cost him thus to refuse.

'Well, if you are so obstinate, I will leave you; for I dare not stay any longer: the dew begins to fall. Good-evening!'

She held out her hand. He just touched it. 'Good-evening!' he repeated, in a voice low and hollow as an echo. She turned; but in a moment returned.

'Are you well?' she asked. Well might she put the question: his face was blanched as her gown.

'Quite well,' he enunciated; and, with a bow, he left the gate. She went one way; he another. She turned twice to gaze after him, as she tripped fairy-like down the field; he, as he strode firmly across, never turned at all.

This spectacle of another's suffering and sacrifice rapt my thoughts from exclusive meditation on my own. Diana Rivers had designated her brother 'inexorable as death.' She had not exaggerated.

Chapter XXXII

I continued the labours of the village-school as actively and faithfully as I could. It was truly hard work at first. Some time elapsed before, with all my efforts, I could comprehend my scholars and their nature. Wholly untaught, with faculties quite torpid, they seemed to me hopelessly dull; and, at first sight, all dull alike: but I soon found I was mistaken. There was a difference amongst them as amongst the educated; and when I got to know them, and they me, this difference rapidly developed itself. Their amazement at me, my language, my rules, and ways, once subsided, I found some of these heavy-looking, gaping rustics wake up into sharp-witted girls enough. Many showed themselves obliging, and amiable too; and I discovered amongst them not a few examples of natural politeness and innate self-respect, as well as of excellent capacity, that won both my goodwill and my admiration. These soon took a pleasure in doing their work well; in keeping their persons neat; in learning their tasks regularly; in acquiring quiet and orderly manners. The rapidity of their progress, in some instances, was even surprising; and an honest and happy pride I took in it: besides, I began personally to like some of the best girls; and they liked me. I had amongst my scholars several farmers' daughters: young women grown, almost. These could already read, write, and sew; and to them I taught the elements of grammar, geography, history, and the finer kinds of needlework. I found estimable characters amongst them—characters desirous of information, and disposed for improvement—with whom I passed many a pleasant evening hour in their own homes. Their parents then (the farmer and his wife) loaded me with attentions. There was an enjoyment in accepting their simple kindness, and in repaying it by a consideration—a scrupulous regard to their feelings—to which they were not, perhaps, at all times accustomed, and which both charmed and benefited them; because, while it elevated them in their own eyes, it made them emulous to merit the deferential treatment they received.

I felt I became a favourite in the neighbourhood. Whenever I went out, I heard on all sides cordial salutations, and was welcomed with friendly smiles. To live amidst general regard, though it be but the regard of working-people, is like 'sitting in sunshine, calm and sweet:'[1] serene inward feelings bud and bloom under the ray. At this period of my life my heart far oftener swelled with thankfulness than sank with dejection: and yet, reader, to tell you all, in the midst of this calm, this useful existence—after a day passed in honourable exertion amongst my scholars, an evening spent in drawing or reading contentedly alone —I used to rush into strange dreams at night: dreams many-coloured, agitated, full of the ideal, the stirring, the stormy—dreams where, amidst unusual scenes, charged with adventure, with agitating risk and romantic chance, I still again and again met Mr. Rochester, always at some exciting crisis; and then the sense of being in his arms, hearing his voice, meeting his eye, touching his hand and cheek, loving him, being loved by him—the hope of passing a lifetime at his side, would be renewed, with all its first force and fire. Then I awoke. Then I recalled where I was, and how situated. Then I rose up on my curtainless bed, trembling and quivering; and then the still, dark night witnessed the convulsion of despair and heard the burst of passion. By nine o'clock the next morning I was punctually opening the school; tranquil, settled, prepared for the steady duties of the day.

Rosamond Oliver kept her word in coming to visit me. Her call at the school was generally made in the course of her morning ride. She would canter up to the door on her pony, followed by a mounted livery servant. Anything more exquisite than her appearance, in her purple habit, with her Amazon's cap of black velvet placed gracefully above the long curls that kissed her cheek and floated to her shoulders, can scarcely be imagined: and it was thus she would enter the rustic building, and glide through the dazzled ranks of the village children. She

1. From Thomas Moore's *Lalla Rookh, Third Day*, 346.

generally came at the hour when Mr. Rivers was engaged in giving his daily catechising lesson. Keenly, I fear, did the eye of the visitress pierce the young pastor's heart. A sort of instinct seemed to warn him of her entrance, even when he did not see it; and when he was looking quite away from the door, if she appeared at it his cheek would glow and his marble-seeming features, though they refused to relax, changed indescribably: and in their very quiescence became expressive of a repressed fervour, stronger than working muscle or darting glance could indicate.

Of course she knew her power: indeed, he did not, because he could not, conceal it from her. In spite of his Christian stoicism, when she went up and addressed him, and smiled gaily, encouragingly, even fondly in his face, his hand would tremble and his eye burn. He seemed to say, with his sad and resolute look, if he did not say it with his lips, 'I love you, and I know you prefer me. It is not despair of success that keeps me dumb. If I offered my heart, I believe you would accept it. But that heart is already laid on a sacred altar: the fire is arranged round it. It will soon be no more than a sacrifice consumed.'

And then she would pout like a disappointed child; a pensive cloud would soften her radiant vivacity; she would withdraw her hand hastily from his, and turn in transient petulance from his aspect, at once so heroic and so martyr-like. St. John, no doubt, would have given the world to follow, recall, retain her, when she thus left him: but he would not give one chance of Heaven; nor relinquish, for the elysium of her love, one hope of the true, eternal Paradise. Besides, he could not bound all that he had in his nature—the rover, the aspirant, the poet, the priest—in the limits of a single passion. He could not—he would not—renounce his wide field of mission warfare for the parlours and the peace of Vale Hall. I learnt so much from himself, in an inroad I once, despite his reserve, had the daring to make on his confidence.

Miss Oliver already honoured me with frequent visits to my cottage. I had learnt her whole character; which was without mystery or disguise: she was coquettish, but not heartless; exacting, but not worthlessly selfish. She had been indulged from her birth, but was not absolutely spoilt. She was hasty, but good-humoured; vain (she could not help it, when every glance in the glass showed her such a flush of loveliness), but not affected; liberal-handed; innocent of the pride of wealth; ingenuous; sufficiently intelligent; gay, lively, and unthinking: she was very charming, in short, even to a cool observer of her own sex like me; but she was not profoundly interesting or thoroughly impressive. A very different sort of mind was hers from that, for instance, of the sisters of St. John. Still, I liked her almost as I liked my pupil Adèle: except that for a child whom we have watched over and taught a closer affection is engendered than we can give an equally attractive adult acquaintance.

She had taken an amiable caprice to me. She said I was like Mr. Rivers (only, certainly, she allowed, 'not one-tenth so handsome: though I was a nice neat little soul enough, but he was an angel'). I was, however, good, clever, composed, and firm, like him. I was a *lusus naturae*,[2] she affirmed, as a village schoolmistress: she was sure my previous history, if known, would make a delightful romance.

One evening, while, with her usual childlike activity, and thoughtless yet not offensive inquisitiveness, she was rummaging the cupboard and the table-drawer of my little kitchen, she discovered first two French books, a volume of Schiller, a German grammar and dictionary; and then my drawing-materials and some sketches, including a pencil-head of a pretty little cherub-like girl, one of my scholars, and sundry views from nature, taken in the Vale of Morton and on the surrounding moors. She was first transfixed with surprise, and then electrified with delight.

'Had I done these pictures? Did I know French and German? What a love—what a miracle I was! I drew better than her master in the first school in S——. Would I sketch a portrait of her, to show to papa?'

'With pleasure,' I replied; and I felt a thrill of artist-delight at the idea of copying from so perfect and radiant a model. She had then on a dark-blue silk dress; her arms and her neck were bare; her only ornament was her chestnut tresses, which waved over her shoulders with all the wild grace of natural curls. I took a sheet of fine cardboard, and drew a careful outline. I promised myself the pleasure of colouring it; and, as it was getting late then, I told her she must come and sit another day.

She made such a report of me to her father that Mr. Oliver himself accompanied her next evening—a tall, massive-featured, middle-aged, and grey-headed man, at whose side his lovely daughter looked like a bright flower near a hoary turret. He appeared a taciturn, and perhaps a proud personage; but he was very kind to me. The sketch of Rosamond's portrait pleased him highly: he said I must make a finished picture of it. He insisted, too, on my coming the next day to spend the evening at Vale Hall.

I went. I found it a large, handsome residence, showing abundant evidences of wealth in the proprietor. Rosamond was full of glee and pleasure all the time I stayed. Her father was affable; and when he entered into conversation with me after tea, he expressed in strong terms his approbation of what I had done in Morton school; and said he only feared, from what he saw and heard, I was too good for the place, and would soon quit it for one more suitable.

2. Sport of nature.

'Indeed!' cried Rosamond, 'she is clever enough to be a governess in a high family, papa.'

I thought—I would far rather be where I am than in any high family in the land. Mr. Oliver spoke of Mr. Rivers—of the Rivers family—with great respect. He said it was a very old name in that neighbour-hood; that the ancestors of the house were wealthy; that all Morton had once belonged to them, that even now he considered the representative of that house might, if he liked, make an alliance with the best. He ac-counted it a pity that so fine and talented a young man should have formed the design of going out as a missionary; it was quite throwing a valuable life away. It appeared, then, that her father would throw no obstacle in the way of Rosamond's union with St. John. Mr. Oliver evidently regarded the young clergyman's good birth, old name, and sacred profession as sufficient compensation for the want of fortune.

It was the 5th of November, and a holiday.[3] My little servant, after helping me to clean my house, was gone, well satisfied with the fee of a penny for her aid. All about me was spotless and bright—scoured floor, polished grate, and well-rubbed chairs. I had also made myself neat, and had now the afternoon before me to spend as I would.

The translation of a few pages of German occupied an hour; then I got my palette and pencils, and fell to the more soothing, because easier occupation, of completing Rosamond Oliver's miniature. The head was finished already: there was but the background to tint and the drap-ery to shade off; a touch of carmine, too, to add to the ripe lips—a soft curl here and there to the tresses—a deeper tinge to the shadow of the lash under the azured eyelid. I was absorbed in the execution of these nice details when, after one rapid tap, my door unclosed, admitting St. John Rivers.

'I am come to see how you are spending your holiday,' he said. 'Not, I hope, in thought? No, that is well: while you draw you will not feel lonely. You see, I mistrust you still: though you have borne up won-derfully so far. I have brought you a book for evening solace,' and he laid on the table a new publication—a poem: one of those genuine pro-ductions so often vouchsafed to the fortunate public of those days—the golden age of modern literature. Alas! the readers of our era are less fa-voured. But, courage! I will not pause either to accuse or repine. I know poetry is not dead, nor genius lost; nor has Mammon[4] gained power over either, to bind or slay: they will both assert their existence, their presence, their liberty and strength again one day. Powerful angels, safe in heaven! they smile when sordid souls triumph, and feeble ones weep over their destruction. Poetry destroyed? Genius banished? No! Medi-ocrity, no: do not let envy prompt you to the thought. No; they not only

---

3. I.e., Guy Fawkes Day, anniversary of the ill-fated Gunpowder Plot of 1605.   4. I.e., money.

live, but reign, and redeem: and without their divine influence spread everywhere you would be in hell—the hell of your own meanness.

While I was eagerly glancing at the bright pages of Marmion[5] (for Marmion it was) St. John stooped to examine my drawing. His tall figure sprang erect again with a start: he said nothing. I looked up at him: he shunned my eye. I knew his thoughts well, and could read his heart plainly; at the moment I felt calmer and cooler than he: I had then temporarily the advantage of him; and I conceived an inclination to do him some good, if I could.

'With all his firmness and self-control,' thought I, 'he tasks himself too far: locks every feeling and pang within—expresses, confesses, imparts nothing. I am sure it would benefit him to talk a little about this sweet Rosamond, whom he thinks he ought not to marry: I will make him talk.'

I said first: 'Take a chair, Mr. Rivers.' But he answered, as he always did, that he could not stay. 'Very well,' I responded, mentally, 'stand if you like; but you shall not go just yet, I am determined: solitude is at least as bad for you as it is for me. I'll try if I cannot discover the secret spring of your confidence, and find an aperture in that marble breast through which I can shed one drop of the balm of sympathy.'

'Is this portrait like?' I asked bluntly.

'Like! Like whom? I did not observe it closely.'

'You did, Mr. Rivers.'

He almost started at my sudden and strange abruptness: he looked at me astonished. 'Oh, that is nothing yet,' I muttered within. 'I don't mean to be baffled by a little stiffness on your part; I'm prepared to go to considerable lengths.' I continued, 'You observed it closely and distinctly: but I have no objection to your looking at it again,' and I rose and placed it in his hand.

'A well-executed picture,' he said; 'very soft, clear colouring; very graceful and correct drawing.'

'Yes, yes; I know all that. But what of the resemblance? Who is it like?'

Mastering some hesitation, he answered, 'Miss Oliver, I presume.'

'Of course. And now, sir, to reward you for the accurate guess I will promise to paint you a careful and faithful duplicate of this very picture, provided you admit that the gift would be acceptable to you. I don't wish to throw away my time and trouble on an offering you would deem worthless.'

He continued to gaze at the picture: the longer he looked, the firmer he held it, the more he seemed to covet it. 'It is like!' he murmured; 'the eye is well managed: the colour, light, expression, are perfect. It smiles!'

5. Sir Walter Scott's *Marmion* (1808).

'Would it comfort or would it wound you to have a similar painting? Tell me that. When you are at Madagascar, or at the Cape, or in India, would it be a consolation to have that memento in your possession? or would the sight of it bring recollections calculated to enervate and distress?'

He now furtively raised his eyes: he glanced at me, irresolute, disturbed; he again surveyed the picture.

'That I should like to have it is certain: whether it would be judicious or wise is another question.'

Since I had ascertained that Rosamond really preferred him, and that her father was not likely to oppose the match, I—less exalted in my views than St. John—had been strongly disposed in my own heart to advocate their union. It seemed to me that, should he become the possessor of Mr. Oliver's large fortune, he might do as much good with it as if he went and laid his genius out to wither and his strength to waste under a tropical sun. With this persuasion I now answered:—'As far as I can see, it would be wiser and more judicious if you were to take to yourself the original at once.'

By this time he had sat down: he had laid the picture on the table before him, and with his brow supported on both hands hung fondly over it. I discerned he was now neither angry nor shocked at my audacity. I saw even that to be thus frankly addressed on a subject he had deemed unapproachable—to hear it thus freely handled—was beginning to be felt by him as a new pleasure—an unhoped-for relief. Reserved people often really need the frank discussion of their sentiments and griefs more than the expansive. The sternest-seeming stoic is human after all; and to 'burst' with boldness and goodwill into 'the silent sea'[6] of their souls is often to confer on them the first of obligations.

'She likes you, I am sure,' said I, as I stood behind his chair, 'and her father respects you. Moreover, she is a sweet girl—rather thoughtless; but you would have sufficient thought for both yourself and her. You ought to marry her.'

'*Does* she like me?' he asked.

'Certainly; better than she likes any one else. She talks of you continually: there is no subject she enjoys so much or touches upon so often.'

'It is very pleasant to hear this,' he said—'very: go on for another quarter of an hour.' And he actually took out his watch and laid it upon the table to measure the time.

'But where is the use of going on,' I asked, 'when you are probably preparing some iron blow of contradiction, or forging a fresh chain to fetter your heart?'

6. Samuel Taylor Coleridge's *The Rime of the Ancient Mariner*, lines 105–106.

'Don't imagine such hard things. Fancy me yielding and melting, as I am doing: human love rising like a freshly opened fountain in my mind and overflowing with sweet inundation all the field I have so carefully, and with such labour prepared—so assiduously sown with the seeds of good intentions, of self-denying plans. And now it is deluged with a nectarous flood—the young germs swamped—delicious poison cankering them: now I see myself stretched on an ottoman in the drawing-room at Vale Hall, at my bride Rosamond Oliver's feet: she is talking to me with her sweet voice—gazing down on me with those eyes your skilful hand has copied so well—smiling at me with these coral lips. She is mine—I am hers—this present life and passing world suffice to me. Hush! say nothing—my heart is full of delight—my senses are entranced—let the time I marked pass in peace.'

I humoured him: the watch ticked on: he breathed fast and low: I stood silent. Amidst this hush the quarter sped; he replaced the watch, laid the picture down, rose, and stood on the hearth.

'Now,' said he, 'that little space was given to delirium and delusion. I rested my temples on the breast of temptation, and put my neck voluntarily under her yoke of flowers; I tasted her cup. The pillow was burning; there is an asp in the garland; the wine has a bitter taste; her promises are hollow—her offers false; I see and know all this.'

I gazed at him in wonder.

'It is strange,' pursued he, 'that while I love Rosamond Oliver so wildly—with all the intensity, indeed, of a first passion, the object of which is exquisitely beautiful, graceful, and fascinating—I experience at the same time a calm, unwarped consciousness that she would not make me a good wife; that she is not the partner suited to me; that I should discover this within a year after marriage; and that to twelve months' rapture would succeed a lifetime of regret. This I know.'

'Strange, indeed!' I could not help ejaculating.

'While something in me,' he went on, 'is acutely sensible to her charms, something else is as deeply impressed with her defects; they are such that she could sympathise in nothing I aspired to—co-operate in nothing I undertook. Rosamond a sufferer, a labourer, a female apostle? Rosamond a missionary's wife? No!'

'But you need not be a missionary. You might relinquish that scheme.'

'Relinquish! What! my vocation? My great work? My foundation laid on earth for a mansion in heaven? My hopes of being numbered in the band who have merged all ambition in the glorious one of bettering their race—of carrying knowledge into the realms of ignorance—of substituting peace for war—freedom for bondage—religion for superstition—the hope of heaven for the fear of hell? Must I relinquish that? It is dearer than the blood in my veins. It is what I have to look forward to and to live for.'

After a considerable pause, I said,—'And Miss Oliver? Are her disappointment and sorrow of no interest to you?'

'Miss Oliver is ever surrounded by suitors and flatterers; in less than a month my image will be effaced from her heart. She will forget me; and will marry, probably some one who will make her far happier than I should do.'

'You speak coolly enough; but you suffer in the conflict. You are wasting away.'

'No. If I get a little thin, it is with anxiety about my prospects, yet unsettled—my departure, continually procrastinated. Only this morning I received intelligence that the successor, whose arrival I have been so long expecting, cannot be ready to replace me for three months to come yet; and perhaps the three months may extend to six.'

'You tremble and become flushed whenever Miss Oliver enters the schoolroom.'

Again the surprised expression crossed his face. He had not imagined that a woman would dare to speak so to a man. For me, I felt at home in this sort of discourse. I could never rest in communication with strong, discreet, and refined minds, whether male or female, till I had passed the outworks of conventional reserve, and crossed the threshold of confidence, and won a place by their heart's very hearthstone.

'You *are* original,' said he, 'and not timid. There is something brave in your spirit, as well as penetrating in your eye; but allow me to assure you that you partially misinterpret my emotions. You think them more profound and potent than they are. You give me a larger allowance of sympathy than I have a just claim to. When I colour, and when I shake before Miss Oliver, I do not pity myself. I scorn the weakness. I know it is ignoble; a mere fever of the flesh: not, I declare, a convulsion of the soul. *That* is just as fixed as a rock firm set in the depths of a restless sea. Know me to be what I am—a cold, hard man.'

I smiled incredulously.

'You have taken my confidence by storm,' he continued: 'and now it is much at your service. I am simply, in my original state—stripped of that blood-bleached robe with which Christianity covers human deformity—a cold, hard, ambitious man. Natural affection only, of all the sentiments, has permanent power over me. Reason, and not Feeling, is my guide: my ambition is unlimited; my desire to rise higher, to do more than others, insatiable. I honour endurance, perseverance, industry, talent; because these are the means by which men achieve great ends and mount to lofty eminence. I watch your career with interest, because I consider you a speciment of a diligent, orderly, energetic woman; not because I deeply compassionate what you have gone through, or what you still suffer.'

'You would describe yourself as a mere pagan philosopher,' I said.

'No. There is this difference between me and deistic philosophers: I believe; and I believe the Gospel. You missed your epithet. I am not a pagan, but a Christian philosopher—a follower of the sect of Jesus. As His disciple I adopt His pure, His merciful, His benignant doctrines. I advocate them: I am sworn to spread them. Won in youth to religion, she has cultivated my original qualities thus:—From the minute germ, natural affection, she has developed the overshadowing tree, philanthropy. From the wild, stringy root of human uprightness, she has reared a due sense of the Divine justice. Of the ambition to win power and renown for my wretched self, she has formed the ambition to spread my Master's kingdom; to achieve victories for the standard of the cross. So much has religion done for me; turning the original materials to the best account; pruning and training nature. But she could not eradicate nature: nor will it be eradicated "till this mortal shall put on immortality." '[7]

Having said this, he took his hat, which lay on the table beside my palette. Once more he looked at the portrait.

'She *is* lovely,' he murmured. 'She is well named the Rose of the World, indeed!'

'And may I not paint one like it for you?'

'*Cui bono?*[8] No.'

He drew over the picture the sheet of thin paper on which I was accustomed to rest my hand in painting to prevent the cardboard from being sullied. What he suddenly saw on this blank paper it was impossible for me to tell: but something had caught his eye. He took it up with a snatch; he looked at the edge; then shot a glance at me, inexpressibly peculiar and quite incomprehensible: a glance that seemed to take and make note of every point in my shape, face, and dress; for it traversed all, quick, keen as lightning. His lips parted, as if to speak: but he checked the coming sentence, whatever it was.

'What is the matter?' I asked.

'Nothing in the world,' was the reply; and, replacing the paper, I saw him dexterously tear a narrow slip from the margin. It disappeared in his glove; and, with one hasty nod and 'good-afternoon,' he vanished.

'Well!' I exclaimed, using an expression of the district, 'that caps the globe,[9] however!'

I, in my turn, scrutinised the paper, but saw nothing on it save a few dingy stains of paint where I had tried the tint in my pencil. I pondered the mystery a minute or two; but finding it insolvable, and being certain it could not be of much moment, I dismissed and soon forgot it.

Chapter XXXIII

When Mr. St. John went it was beginning to snow; the whirling storm continued all night. The next day a keen wind brought fresh and

---

7. 1 Corinthians 15:53–54.
8. Who stands to benefit?

9. Tops everything.

blinding falls; by twilight the valley was drifted up and almost impassable. I had closed my shutter, laid a mat to the door to prevent the snow from blowing in under it, trimmed my fire, and after sitting nearly an hour on the hearth listening to the muffled fury of the tempest, I lit a candle, took down Marmion, and beginning—

> Day set on Norham's castled steep,
> And Tweed's fair river broad and deep,
>   And Cheviot's mountains lone;
> The massive towers, the donjon keep,
> The flanking walls that round them sweep,
>   In yellow lustre shone,

I soon forgot storm in music.

I heard a noise: the wind, I thought, shook the door. No; it was St. John Rivers, who, lifting the latch, came in out of the frozen hurricane —the howling darkness—and stood before me: the cloak that covered his tall figure all white as a glacier. I was almost in consternation; so little had I expected any guest from the blocked-up vale that night.

'Any ill news?' I demanded. 'Has anything happened?'

'No. How very easily alarmed you are!' he answered, removing his cloak and hanging it up against the door, towards which he again coolly pushed the mat which his entrance had deranged. He stamped the snow from his boots.

'I shall sully the purity of your floor,' said he, 'but you must excuse me for once.' Then he approached the fire: 'I have had hard work to get here, I assure you,' he observed, as he warmed his hands over the flame. 'One drift took me up to the waist; happily the snow is quite soft yet.'

'But why are you come?' I could not forbear saying.

'Rather an inhospitable question to put to a visitor; but since you ask it, I answer simply to have a little talk with you; I got tired of my mute books and empty rooms. Besides, since yesterday I have experienced the excitement of a person to whom a tale has been half-told, and who is impatient to hear the sequel.'

He sat down. I recalled his singular conduct of yesterday, and really I began to fear his wits were touched. If he were insane, however, his was a very cool and collected insanity: I had never seen that handsome-featured face of his look more like chiselled marble than it did just now, as he put aside his snow-wet hair from his forehead and let the firelight shine free on his pale brow and cheek as pale, where it grieved me to discover the hollow trace of care or sorrow now so plainly graved. I waited, expecting he would say something I could at least comprehend; but his hand was now at his chin, his finger on his lip: he was thinking. It struck me that his hand looked wasted like his face. A perhaps uncalled-for gush of pity came over my heart: I was moved to say:—'I wish Diana or Mary would come and live with you: it is too bad that you should be quite alone; and you are recklessly rash about your own health.'

'Not at all,' said he: 'I care for myself when necessary; I am well now. What do you see amiss in me?'

This was said with a careless, abstracted indifference, which showed that my solicitude was, at least in his opinion, wholly superfluous. I was silenced.

He still slowly moved his finger over his upper lip, and still his eye dwelt dreamily on the glowing grate. Thinking it urgent to say something, I asked him presently if he felt any cold draught from the door, which was behind him.

'No, no,' he responded, shortly and somewhat testily.

'Well,' I reflected, 'if you won't talk, you may be still; I'll let you alone now, and return to my book.'

So I snuffed the candle, and resumed the perusal of Marmion. He soon stirred; my eye was instantly drawn to his movements; he only took out a morocco pocket-book, thence produced a letter, which he read in silence, folded it, put it back, relapsed into meditation. It was vain to try to read with such an inscrutable fixture before me; nor could I, in my impatience, consent to be dumb; he might rebuff me if he liked, but talk I would.

'Have you heard from Diana and Mary lately?'

'Not since the letter I showed you a week ago.'

'There has not been any change made about your own arrangements? You will not be summoned to leave England sooner than you expected?'

'I fear not, indeed: such chance is too good to befall me.' Baffled so far I changed my ground—I bethought myself to talk about the school and my scholars.

'Mary Garrett's mother is better, and Mary came back to the school this morning, and I shall have four new girls next week from the Foundry Close—they would have come to-day but for the snow.'

'Indeed!'

'Mr. Oliver pays for two.'

'Does he?'

'He means to give the whole school a treat at Christmas.'

'I know.'

'Was it your suggestion?'

'No.'

'Whose, then?'

'His daughter's, I think.'

'It is like her: she is so good-natured.'

'Yes.'

Again came the blank of a pause: the clock struck eight strokes. It aroused him; he uncrossed his legs, sat erect, turned to me.

'Leave your book a moment, and come a little nearer the fire,' he said.

Wondering, and of my wonder finding no end, I complied.

'Half an hour ago,' he pursued, 'I spoke of my impatience to hear the sequel of a tale: on reflection, I find the matter will be better managed by my assuming the narrator's part, and converting you into a listener. Before commencing it is but fair to warn you that the story will sound somewhat hackneyed in your ears: but stale details often regain a degree of freshness when they pass through new lips. For the rest, whether trite or novel, it is short.

'Twenty years ago a poor curate—never mind his name at this moment—fell in love with a rich man's daughter; she fell in love with him, and married him, against the advice of all her friends; who consequently disowned her immediately after the wedding. Before two years passed the rash pair were both dead, and laid quietly side by side under one slab. (I have seen their grave; it formed part of the pavement of a huge churchyard surrounding the grim, soot-black old cathedral of an overgrown manufacturing town in ——shire.) They left a daughter, which, at its very birth, Charity received in her lap—cold as that of the snow-drift I almost stuck fast in to-night. Charity carried the friendless thing to the house of its rich maternal relations; it was reared by an aunt-in-law called (I come to names now) Mrs. Reed, of Gateshead—you start—did you hear a noise? I daresay it is only a rat scrambling along the rafters of the adjoining schoolroom: it was a barn before I had it repaired and altered, and barns are generally haunted by rats.—To proceed. Mrs. Reed kept the orphan ten years: whether it was happy or not with her I cannot say, never having been told; but at the end of that time she transferred it to a place you know—being no other than Lowood School, where you so long resided yourself. It seems her career there was very honourable: from a pupil she became a teacher, like yourself—really it strikes me there are parallel points in her history and yours—she left it to be a governess: there, again, your fates were analogous; she undertook the education of the ward of a certain Mr. Rochester.'

'Mr. Rivers!' I interrupted.

'I can guess your feelings,' he said, 'but restrain them for a while: I have nearly finished; hear me to the end. Of Mr. Rochester's character I know nothing, but the one fact that he professed to offer honourable marriage to this young girl, and that at the very altar she discovered he had a wife yet alive, though a lunatic. What his subsequent conduct and proposals were is a matter of pure conjecture; but when an event transpired which rendered inquiry after the governess necessary, it was discovered she was gone—no one could tell when, where, or how. She had left Thornfield Hall in the night; every research after her course had been vain: the country had been scoured far and wide; no vestige of information could be gathered respecting her. Yet that she should be found is become a matter of serious urgency: advertisements have been put in all the papers; I myself have received a letter from one Mr. Briggs, a solicitor, communicating the details I have just imparted. Is it not an odd tale?'

'Just tell me this,' said I, 'and since you know so much you surely *can* tell it me—what of Mr. Rochester? How and where is he? What is he doing? Is he well?'

'I am ignorant of all concerning Mr. Rochester: the letter never mentions him but to narrate the fraudulent and illegal attempt I have adverted to. You should rather ask the name of the governess—the nature of the event which requires her appearance.'

'Did no one go to Thornfield Hall then? Did no one see Mr. Rochester?'

'I suppose not.'

'But they wrote to him?'

'Of course.'

'And what did he say? Who has his letters?'

'Mr. Briggs intimates that the answer to his application was not from Mr. Rochester, but from a lady: it is signed "Alice Fairfax." '

I felt cold and dismayed: my worst fears then were probably true: he had in all probability left England, and rushed in reckless desperation to some former haunt on the Continent. And what opiate for his severe sufferings—what object for his strong passions—had he sought there? I dared not answer the question. Oh, my poor master—once almost my husband—whom I had often called 'my dear Edward!'

'He must have been a bad man,' observed Mr. Rivers.

'You don't know him—don't pronounce an opinion upon him,' I said, with warmth.

'Very well,' he answered, quietly: 'and indeed my head is otherwise occupied than with him: I have my tale to finish. Since you won't ask the governess's name, I must tell it of my own accord—stay—I have it here—it is always more satisfactory to see important points written down, fairly committed to black and white.'

And the pocket-book was again deliberately produced, opened, sought through; from one of its compartments was extracted a shabby slip of paper, hastily torn off: I recognised in its texture and its stains of ultramarine and lake and vermilion the ravished margin of the portrait-cover. He got up, held it close to my eyes: and I read, traced in Indian ink, in my own handwriting, the words 'Jane Eyre'—the work doubtless of some moment of abstraction.

'Briggs wrote to me of a Jane Eyre,' he said; 'the advertisements demanded a Jane Eyre: I knew a Jane Elliott.—I confess I had my suspicions, but it was only yesterday afternoon they were at once resolved into certainty. You own the name and renounce the *alias*?'

'Yes—yes—but where is Mr. Briggs? He perhaps knows more of Mr. Rochester than you do.'

'Briggs is in London; I should doubt his knowing anything at all about Mr. Rochester; it is not in Mr. Rochester he is interested. Meantime you forget essential points in pursuing trifles: you do not inquire why Mr. Briggs sought after you—what he wanted with you.'

'Well, what did he want?'

'Merely to tell you that your uncle, Mr. Eyre of Madeira, is dead; that he has left you all his property, and that you are now rich—merely that—nothing more.'

'I! rich?'

'Yes, you, rich—quite an heiress.'

Silence succeeded.

'You must prove your identity, of course,' resumed St. John, presently: 'a step which will offer no difficulties: you can then enter on immediate possession. Your fortune is vested in the English funds; Briggs has the will and the necessary documents.'

Here was a new card turned up! It is a fine thing, reader, to be lifted in a moment from indigence to wealth—a very fine thing: but not a matter one can comprehend, or consequently enjoy, all at once. And then there are other chances in life far more thrilling and rapture-giving; *this* is solid, an affair of the actual world, nothing ideal about it: all its associations are solid and sober, and its manifestations are the same. One does not jump, and spring, and shout hurrah! at hearing one has got a fortune; one begins to consider responsibilities and to ponder business; on a base of steady satisfaction rise certain grave cares—and we contain ourselves, and brood over our bliss with a solemn brow.

Besides, the words Legacy, Bequest, go side by side with the words Death, Funeral. My uncle I had heard was dead—my only relative; ever since being made aware of his existence I had cherished the hope of one day seeing him: now, I never should. And then this money came only to me: not to me and a rejoicing family, but to my isolated self. It was a grand boon doubtless; and independence would be glorious—yes, I felt that—*that* thought swelled my heart.

'You unbend your forehead at last,' said Mr. Rivers: 'I thought Medusa[1] had looked at you, and that you were turning to stone—perhaps now you will ask how much you are worth?'

---

1. Mythological Gorgon who turned to stone any upon whom she fixed her eyes.

'How much am I worth?'

'Oh, a trifle! Nothing of course to speak of—twenty thousand pounds, I think they say—but what is that?'

'Twenty thousand pounds?'

Here was a new stunner—I had been calculating on four or five thousand. This news actually took my breath for a moment: Mr. St. John, whom I had never heard laugh before, laughed now.

'Well,' said he, 'if you had committed a murder, and I had told you your crime was discovered, you could scarcely look more aghast.'

'It is a large sum—don't you think there is a mistake?'

'No mistake at all.'

'Perhaps you have read the figures wrong—it may be 2,000!'

'It is written in letters, not figures,—twenty thousand.'

I again felt rather like an individual of but average gastronomical powers sitting down to feast alone at a table spread with provisions for a hundred. Mr. Rivers rose now and put his cloak on.

'If it were not such a very wild night,' he said, 'I would send Hannah down to keep you company: you look too desperately miserable to be left alone. But Hannah, poor woman! could not stride the drifts so well as I: her legs are not quite so long: so I must e'en leave you to your sorrows. Good-night.'

He was lifting the latch: a sudden thought occurred to me.

'Stop one minute!' I cried.

'Well?'

'It puzzles me to know why Mr. Briggs wrote to you about me; or how he knew you, or could fancy that you, living in such an out-of-the-way place, had the power to aid in my discovery.'

'Oh! I am a clergyman,' he said; 'and the clergy are often appealed to about odd matters.'

Again the latch rattled.

'No: that does not satisfy me!' I exclaimed: and, indeed, there was something in the hasty and unexplanatory reply which, instead of allaying, piqued my curiosity more than ever.

'It is a very strange piece of business,' I added. 'I must know more about it.'

'Another time.'

'No: to-night!—to-night!' and as he turned from the door I placed myself between it and him. He looked rather embarrassed.

'You certainly shall not go till you have told me all!' I said.

'I would rather not, just now.'

'You shall!—you must!'

'I would rather Diana or Mary informed you.'

Of course these objections wrought my eagerness to a climax: gratified it must be, and that without delay; and I told him so.

'But I apprised you that I was a hard man,' said he; 'difficult to persuade.'

'And I am a hard woman,—impossible to put off.'

'And then,' he pursued, 'I am cold: no fervour infects me.'

'Whereas I am hot, and fire dissolves ice. The blaze there has thawed all the snow from your cloak; by the same token it has streamed on to my floor, and made it like a trampled street. As you hope ever to be forgiven, Mr. Rivers, the high crime and misdemeanour of spoiling a sanded kitchen, tell me what I wish to know.'

'Well, then,' he said, 'I yield; if not to your earnestness, to your perseverance: as stone is worn by continual dropping. Besides, you must know some day,—as well now as later. Your name is Jane Eyre?'

'Of course: that was all settled before.'

'You are not, perhaps, aware that I am your namesake?—that I was christened St. John Eyre Rivers?'

'No, indeed! I remember now seeing the letter E comprised in your initials written in books you have at different times lent me; but I never asked for what name it stood. But what then? Surely'——

I stopped: I could not trust myself to entertain, much less to express, the thought that rushed upon me—that embodied itself,—that, in a second, stood out a strong, solid probability. Circumstances knit themselves, fitted themselves, shot into order: the chain that had been lying hitherto a formless lump of links was drawn out straight,—every ring was perfect, the connection complete. I knew, by instinct, how the matter stood before St. John had said another word: but I cannot expect the reader to have the same intuitive perception, so I must repeat his explanation.

'My mother's name was Eyre; she had two brothers; one a clergyman, who married Miss Jane Reed, of Gateshead; the other, John Eyre, Esq., merchant, late of Funchal, Madeira. Mr. Briggs, being Mr. Eyre's solicitor, wrote to us last August to inform us of our uncle's death; and to say that he had left his property to his brother the clergyman's orphan daughter; overlooking us, in consequence of a quarrel, never forgiven, between him and my father. He wrote again a few weeks since, to intimate that the heiress was lost; and asking if we knew anything of her. A name casually written on a slip of paper has enabled me to find her out. You know the rest.' Again he was going, but I set my back against the door.

'Do let me speak,' I said; 'let me have one moment to draw breath and reflect.' I paused—he stood before me, hat in hand, looking composed enough. I resumed: 'Your mother was my father's sister?'

'Yes.'

'My aunt, consequently?'

He bowed.

'My uncle John was your uncle John? You, Diana and Mary, are his sister's children; as I am his brother's child?'

'Undeniably.'

'You three, then, are my cousins; half our blood on each side flows from the same source?'

'We are cousins; yes.'

I surveyed him. It seemed I had found a brother: one I could be proud of,—one I could love; and two sisters whose qualities were such that, when I knew them but as mere strangers, they had inspired me with genuine affection and admiration. The two girls on whom, kneeling down on the wet ground, and looking through the low, latticed window of Moor House kitchen, I had gazed with so bitter a mixture of interest and despair were my near kinswomen; and the young and stately gentleman who had found me almost dying at his threshold was my blood relation. Glorious discovery to a lonely wretch! This was wealth indeed!—wealth to the heart!—a mine of pure, genial affections. This was a blessing, bright, vivid, and exhilarating;—not like the ponderous gift of gold: rich and welcome enough in its way, but sobering from its weight. I now clapped my hands in sudden joy—my pulse bounded, my veins thrilled.

'Oh, I am glad!—I am glad!' I exclaimed.

St. John smiled. 'Did I not say you neglected essential points to pursue trifles?' he asked. 'You were serious when I told you you had got a fortune; and now, for a matter of no moment, you are excited.'

'What *can* you mean? It may be of no moment to you; you have sisters, and don't care for a cousin; but I had nobody; and now three relations,—or two, if you don't choose to be counted,—are born into my world full grown. I say again, I am glad!'

I walked fast through the room: I stopped, half suffocated with the thoughts that rose faster than I could receive, comprehend, settle them:—thoughts of what might, could, would, and should be, and that ere long. I looked at the blank wall: it seemed a sky, thick with ascending stars,—every one lit me to a purpose or delight. Those who had saved my life, whom till this hour I had loved barrenly, I could now benefit. They were under a yoke: I could free them: they were scattered,—I could reunite them—the independence, the affluence which was mine might be theirs too. Were we not four? Twenty thousand pounds shared equally would be five thousand each, enough and to spare: justice would be done,—mutual happiness secured. Now the wealth did not weigh on me: now it was not a mere bequest of coin,—it was a legacy of life, hope, enjoyment.

How I looked while these ideas were taking my spirit by storm I cannot tell; but I perceived soon that Mr. Rivers had placed a chair behind me, and was gently attempting to make me sit down on it. He also ad-

vised me to be composed: I scorned the insinuation of helplessness and
distraction, shook off his hand, and began to walk about again.

'Write to Diana and Mary to-morrow,' I said, 'and tell them to come
home directly; Diana said they would both consider themselves rich
with a thousand pounds, so with five thousand they will do very well.'

'Tell me where I can get you a glass of water,' said St. John; 'you
must really make an effort to tranquillise your feelings.'

'Nonsense! and what sort of an effect will the bequest have on you?
Will it keep you in England, induce you to marry Miss Oliver, and settle down like an ordinary mortal?'

'You wander: your head becomes confused. I have been too abrupt
in communicating the news; it has excited you beyond your strength.'

'Mr. Rivers! you quite put me out of patience; I am rational enough;
it is you who misunderstand; or rather who affect to misunderstand.'

'Perhaps if you explained yourself a little more fully I should comprehend better.'

'Explain! What is there to explain? You cannot fail to see that twenty
thousand pounds, the sum in question, divided equally between the
nephew and three nieces of our uncle will give five thousand to each?
What I want is, that you should write to your sisters and tell them of the
fortune that has accrued to them.'

'To you, you mean.'

'I have intimated my view of the case: I am incapable of taking any
other. I am not brutally selfish, blindly unjust, or fiendishly ungrateful.
Besides, I am resolved I will have a home and connections. I like Moor
House, and I will live at Moor House; I like Diana and Mary, and I will
attach myself for life to Diana and Mary. It would please and benefit me
to have five thousand pounds; it would torment and oppress me to have
twenty thousand; which, moreover, could never be mine in justice,
though it might in law. I abandon to you, then, what is absolutely superfluous to me. Let there be no opposition, and no discussion about it; let
us agree amongst each other, and decide the point at once.'

'This is acting on first impulses; you must take days to consider such
a matter, ere your word can be regarded as valid.'

'Oh! if all you doubt is my sincerity, I am easy: you see the justice of
the case?'

'I do see a certain justice; but it is contrary to all custom. Besides, the
entire fortune is your right: my uncle gained it by his own efforts; he
was free to leave it to whom he would: he left it to you. After all, justice
permits you to keep it: you may, with a clear conscience, consider it absolutely your own.'

'With me,' said I, 'it is fully as much a matter of feeling as of conscience: I must indulge my feelings; I so seldom have had an opportunity of doing so. Were you to argue, object, and annoy me for a year, I

could not forego the delicious pleasure of which I have caught a glimpse—that of repaying, in part, a mighty obligation, and winning to myself life-long friends.'

'You think so now,' rejoined St. John; 'because you do not know what it is to possess, nor consequently to enjoy wealth: you cannot form a notion of the importance twenty thousand pounds would give you; of the place it would enable you to take in society; of the prospects it would open to you: you cannot——'

'And you,' I interrupted, 'cannot at all imagine the craving I have for fraternal and sisterly love. I never had a home, I never had brothers and sisters; I must and will have them now: you are not reluctant to admit me and own me, are you?'

'Jane: I will be your brother—my sisters will be your sisters—without stipulating for this sacrifice of your just rights.'

'Brother? Yes; at the distance of a thousand leagues! Sisters? Yes; slaving amongst strangers! I, wealthy—gorged with gold I never earned and do not merit! You, penniless! Famous equality and fraternisation! Close union! Intimate attachment!'

'But, Jane, your aspirations after family ties and domestic happiness may be realised otherwise than by the means you contemplate: you may marry.'

'Nonsense again! Marry! I don't want to marry, and never shall marry.'

'That is saying too much: such hazardous affirmations are a proof of the excitement under which you labour.'

'It is not saying too much: I know what I feel, and how averse are my inclinations to the bare thought of marriage. No one would take me for love; and I will not be regarded in the light of a mere money-specula-tion. And I do not want a stranger—unsympathising alien, different from me; I want my kindred: those with whom I have full fellow-feel-ing. Say again you will be my brother: when you uttered the words I was satisfied, happy; repeat them, if you can repeat them sincerely.'

'I think I can. I know I have always loved my own sisters; and I know on what my affection for them is grounded,—respect for their worth and admiration of their talents. You too have principle and mind: your tastes and habits resemble Diana's and Mary's; your presence is always agreeable to me; in your conversation I have already for some time found a salutary solace. I feel I can easily and naturally make room in my heart for you, as my third and youngest sister.'

'Thank you: that contents me for to-night. Now you had better go; for if you stay longer you will perhaps irritate me afresh by some mis-trustful scruple.'

'And the school, Miss Eyre? It must now be shut up, I suppose?'

'No. I will retain my post of mistress till you get a substitute.'

He smiled approbation: we shook hands, and he took leave.

I need not narrate in detail the further struggles I had and arguments I used to get matters regarding the legacy settled as I wished. My task was a very hard one: but, as I was absolutely resolved—as my cousins saw at length that my mind was really and immutably fixed on making a just division of the property—as they would have done precisely what I wished to do—they yielded at length so far as to consent to put the affair to arbitration. The judges chosen were Mr. Oliver and an able lawyer: both coincided in my opinion: I carried my point. The instruments of transfer were drawn out: St. John, Diana, Mary, and I, each became possessed of a competency.[2]

Chapter XXXIV

It was near Christmas by the time all was settled: the season of general holiday approached. I now closed Morton school, taking care that the parting should not be barren on my side. Good fortune opens the hand as well as the heart wonderfully; and to give somewhat when we have largely received, is but to afford a vent to the unusual ebullition of the sensations. I had long felt with pleasure that many of my rustic scholars liked me, and when we parted that consciousness was confirmed: they manifested their affection plainly and strongly. Deep was my gratification to find I had really a place in their unsophisticated hearts: I promised them that never a week should pass in future that I did not visit them, and give them an hour's teaching in their school.

Mr. Rivers came up, as—having seen the classes, now numbering sixty girls, file out before me, and locked the door—I stood with the key in my hand, exchanging a few words of special farewell with some half-dozen of my best scholars: as decent, respectable, modest, and well-informed young women as could be found in the ranks of the British peasantry. And that is saying a great deal; for after all the British peasantry are the best taught, best mannered, most self-respecting of any in Europe: since those days I have seen paysannes and Bäuerinnen:[3] and the best of them seemed to me ignorant, coarse, and besotted, compared with my Morton girls.

'Do you consider you have got your reward for a season of exertion?' asked Mr. Rivers when they were gone. 'Does not the consciousness of having done some real good in your day and generation give pleasure?'

'Doubtless.'

'And you have only toiled a few months! Would not a life devoted to the task of regenerating your race be well spent?'

'Yes,' I said; 'but I could not go on for ever so: I want to enjoy my

---

2. I.e., sufficient money.   3. Peasant women.

own faculties as well as to cultivate those of other people. I must enjoy them now; don't recall either my mind or body to the school: I am out of it, and disposed for full holiday.'

He looked grave. 'What now? What sudden eagerness is this you evince? What are you going to do?'

'To be active: as active as I can. And first I must beg you to set Hannah at liberty, and get somebody else to wait on you.'

'Do you want her?'

'Yes, to go with me to Moor House: Diana and Mary will be at home in a week, and I want to have everything in order against their arrival.'

'I understand: I thought you were for flying off on some excursion. It is better so: Hannah shall go with you.'

'Tell her to be ready by to-morrow then; and here is the schoolroom key: I will give you the key of my cottage in the morning.'

He took it. 'You give it up very gleefully,' said he: 'I don't quite understand your light-heartedness; because I cannot tell what employment you propose to yourself as a substitute for the one you are relinquishing. What aim, what purpose, what ambition in life have you now?'

'My first aim will be to *clean down* (do you comprehend the full force of the expression?) to *clean down* Moor House from chamber to cellar; my next to rub it up with beeswax, oil, and an indefinite number of cloths, till it glitters again; my third, to arrange every chair, table, bed, carpet, with mathematical precision; afterwards I shall go near to ruin you in coals and peat to keep up good fires in every room; and lastly, the two days preceding that on which your sisters are expected will be devoted by Hannah and me to such a beating of eggs, sorting of currants, grating of spices, compounding of Christmas cakes, chopping up of materials for mince-pies, and solemnising of other culinary rites, as words can convey but an inadequate notion of to the uninitiated like you. My purpose, in short, is to have all things in an absolutely perfect state of readiness for Diana and Mary before next Thursday; and my ambition is to give them a beau-ideal of a welcome when they come.'

St. John smiled slightly: still he was dissatisfied.

'It is all very well for the present,' said he: 'but seriously, I trust that when the first flush of vivacity is over you will look a little higher than domestic endearments and household joys.'

'The best things the world has!' I interrupted.

'No, Jane, no: this world is not the scene of fruition; do not attempt to make it so: nor of rest; do not turn slothful.'

'I mean, on the contrary, to be busy.'

'Jane, I excuse you for the present: two months' grace I allow you for the full enjoyment of your new position, and for pleasing yourself with this late-found charm of relationship; but *then* I hope you will begin to

look beyond Moor House and Morton, and sisterly society, and the selfish calm and sensual comfort of civilised affluence. I hope your energies will then once more trouble you with their strength.'

I looked at him with surprise.

'St. John,' I said, 'I think you are almost wicked to talk so. I am disposed to be as content as a queen, and you try to stir me up to restlessness! To what end?'

'To the end of turning to profit the talents which God has committed
to your keeping; and of which He will surely one day demand a strict
account. Jane, I shall watch you closely and anxiously—I warn you of
that. And try to restrain the disproportionate fervour with which you
throw yourself into common-place home pleasures. Don't cling so te-
naciously to ties of the flesh; save your constancy and ardour for an adequate cause; forbear to waste them on trite transient objects. Do you
hear, Jane?'

'Yes; just as if you were speaking Greek. I feel I have adequate cause
to be happy, and I *will* be happy. Good-bye!'

Happy at Moor House I was, and hard I worked; and so did Hannah:
she was charmed to see how jovial I could be amidst the bustle of a
house turned topsy-turvy—how I could brush, and dust, and clean, and
cook. And really after a day or two of confusion worse confounded it
was delightful, by degrees, to invoke order from the chaos ourselves had
made. I had previously taken a journey to S—— to purchase some new
furniture: my cousins having given me carte blanche to effect what alterations I pleased, and a sum having been set aside for that purpose.
The ordinary sitting-room and bedrooms I left much as they were: for I
knew Diana and Mary would derive more pleasure from seeing again
the old homely tables and chairs and beds than from the spectacle of the
smartest innovations. Still some novelty was necessary, to give to their
return the piquancy with which I wished it to be invested. Dark handsome new carpets and curtains, an arrangement of some carefully selected antique ornaments in porcelain and bronze, new coverings, and
mirrors, and dressing-cases for the toilet-tables, answered the end: they
looked fresh without being glaring. A spare parlour and bedroom I re-
furnished entirely with old mahogany and crimson upholstery: I laid
canvas on the passage and carpets on the stairs. When all was finished, I
thought Moor House as complete a model of bright modest snugness
within as it was, at this season, a specimen of wintry waste and desert
dreariness without.

The eventful Thursday at length came. They were expected about
dark, and ere dusk fires were lit upstairs and below; the kitchen was in
perfect trim; Hannah and I were dressed, and all was in readiness.

St. John arrived first. I had entreated him to keep quite clear of the
house till everything was arranged: and, indeed, the bare idea of the

commotion, at once sordid and trivial, going on within its walls sufficed to scare him to estrangement. He found me in the kitchen, watching the progress of certain cakes for tea, then baking. Approaching the hearth, he asked, 'If I was at last satisfied with housemaid's work?' I answered by inviting him to accompany me on a general inspection of the result of my labours. With some difficulty I got him to make the tour of the house. He just looked in at the doors I opened; and when he had wandered upstairs and downstairs, he said I must have gone through a great deal of fatigue and trouble to have effected such considerable changes in so short a time: but not a syllable did he utter indicating pleasure in the improved aspect of his abode.

This silence damped me. I thought perhaps the alterations had disturbed some old associations he valued. I inquired whether this was the case: no doubt in a somewhat crestfallen tone.

'Not at all; he had, on the contrary, remarked that I had scrupulously respected every association: he feared, indeed, I must have bestowed more thought on the matter than it was worth. How many minutes, for instance, had I devoted to studying the arrangement of this very room? —By-the-bye, could I tell him where such a book was?'

I showed him the volume on the shelf: he took it down, and withdrawing to his accustomed window recess, he began to read it.

Now, I did not like this, reader. St. John was a good man; but I began to feel he had spoken truth of himself when he said he was hard and cold. The humanities and amenities of life had no attraction for him— its peaceful enjoyments no charm. Literally, he lived only to aspire— after what was good and great, certainly; but still he would never rest; nor approve of others resting round him. As I looked at his lofty forehead, still and pale as a white stone—at his fine lineaments fixed in study—I comprehended all at once that he would hardly make a good husband: that it would be a trying thing to be his wife. I understood, as by inspiration, the nature of his love for Miss Oliver; I agreed with him that it was but a love of the senses. I comprehended how he should despise himself for the feverish influence it exercised over him; how he should wish to stifle and destroy it; how he should mistrust its ever conducing permanently to his happiness, or hers. I saw he was of the material from which nature hews her heroes—Christian and Pagan—her lawgivers, her statesmen, her conquerors; a steadfast bulwark for great interests to rest upon; but, at the fireside, too often a cold cumbrous column, gloomy and out of place.

'This parlour is not his sphere,' I reflected; 'the Himalayan ridge, or Caffre[4] bush, even the plague-cursed Guinea Coast swamp, would suit him better. Well may he eschew the calm of domestic life; it is not his

4. Kaffir, African.

element: there his faculties stagnate—they cannot develop or appear to advantage. It is in scenes of strife and danger—where courage is proved, and energy exercised, and fortitude tasked—that he will speak and move, the leader and superior. A merry child would have the advantage of him on this hearth. He is right to choose a missionary's career—I see it now.'

'They are coming! they are coming!' cried Hannah, throwing open the parlour door. At the same moment old Carlo barked joyfully. Out I ran. It was now dark: but a rumbling of wheels was audible. Hannah soon had a lantern lit. The vehicle had stopped at the wicket; the driver opened the door: first one well-known form, then another, stepped out. In a minute I had my face under their bonnets, in contact first with Mary's soft cheek, then with Diana's flowing curls. They laughed—kissed me—then Hannah: patted Carlo, who was half wild with delight, asked eagerly if all was well; and being assured in the affirmative, hastened into the house.

They were stiff with their long and jolting drive from Whitcross, and chilled with the frosty night-air; but their pleasant countenances expanded to the cheerful fire-light. While the driver and Hannah brought in the boxes, they demanded St. John. At this moment he advanced from the parlour. They both threw their arms round his neck at once. He gave each one quiet kiss, said in a low tone a few words of welcome, stood a while to be talked to, and then, intimating that he supposed they would soon rejoin him in the parlour, withdrew there as to a place of refuge.

I had lit their candles to go upstairs, but Diana had first to give hospitable orders respecting the driver; this done, both followed me. They were delighted with the renovation and decoration of their rooms; with the new drapery, and fresh carpets, and rich tinted china vases: they expressed their gratification ungrudgingly. I had the pleasure of feeling that my arrangements met their wishes exactly; and that what I had done added a vivid charm to their joyous return home.

Sweet was that evening. My cousins, full of exhilaration, were so eloquent in narrative and comment, that their fluency covered St. John's taciturnity: he was sincerely glad to see his sisters; but in their glow of fervour and flow of joy he could not sympathise. The event of the day —that is, the return of Diana and Mary—pleased him; but the accompaniments of that event, the glad tumult, the garrulous glee of reception, irked him: I saw he wished the calmer morrow was come. In the very meridian of the night's enjoyment, about an hour after tea, a rap was heard at the door. Hannah entered with the intimation that 'a poor lad was come, at that unlikely time, to fetch Mr. Rivers to see his mother, who was drawing away.'

'Where does she live, Hannah?'

'Clear up at Whitcross Brow, almost four miles off; and moor and moss all the way.'

'Tell him I will go.'

'I'm sure, sir, you had better not. It's the worst road to travel after dark that can be: there's no track at all over the bog. And then it is such a bitter night—the keenest wind you ever felt. You had better send word, sir, that you will be there in the morning.'

But he was already in the passage, putting on his cloak; and without one objection, one murmur, he departed. It was then nine o'clock: he did not return till midnight. Starved and tired enough he was: but he looked happier than when he set out. He had performed an act of duty; made an exertion; felt his own strength to do and deny, and was on better terms with himself.

I am afraid the whole of the ensuing week tried his patience. It was Christmas week: we took to no settled employment, but spent it in a sort of merry domestic dissipation. The air of the moors, the freedom of home, the dawn of prosperity, acted on Diana and Mary's spirits like some life-giving elixir: they were gay from morning till noon, and from noon till night. They could always talk; and their discourse, witty, pithy, original, had such charms for me, that I preferred listening to, and sharing in it, to doing anything else. St. John did not rebuke our vivacity; but he escaped from it: he was seldom in the house; his parish was large, the population scattered, and he found daily business in visiting the sick and poor in its different districts.

One morning, at breakfast, Diana, after looking a little pensive for some minutes, asked him, 'If his plans were yet unchanged?'

'Unchanged and unchangeable,' was the reply. And he proceeded to inform us that his departure from England was now definitively fixed for the ensuing year.

'And Rosamond Oliver?' suggested Mary: the words seeming to escape her lips involuntarily: for no sooner had she uttered them, than she made a gesture as if wishing to recall them. St. John had a book in his hand—it was his unsocial custom to read at meals—he closed it, and looked up.

'Rosamond Oliver,' said he, 'is about to be married to Mr. Granby; one of the best connected and most estimable residents in S——, grandson and heir to Sir Frederic Granby: I had the intelligence from her father yesterday.'

His sisters looked at each other, and at me; we all three looked at him: he was serene as glass.

'The match must have been got up hastily,' said Diana: 'they cannot have known each other long.'

'But two months: they met in October at the county ball at S——. But where there are no obstacles to a union, as in the present case, where the connection is in every point desirable, delays are unnecessary: they will be married as soon as S—— Place, which Sir Frederic gives up to them, can be refitted for their reception.'

The first time I found St. John alone after this communication, I felt tempted to inquire if the event distressed him: but he seemed so little to need sympathy, that, so far from venturing to offer him more, I experienced some shame at the recollection of what I had already hazarded. Besides, I was out of practice in talking to him: his reserve was again frozen over, and my frankness was congealed beneath it. He had not kept his promise of treating me like his sisters; he continually made little chilling differences between us, which did not at all tend to the development of cordiality: in short, now that I was acknowledged his kinswoman, and lived under the same roof with him, I felt the distance between us to be far greater than when he had known me only as the village schoolmistress. When I remembered how far I had once been admitted to his confidence, I could hardly comprehend his present frigidity.

Such being the case, I felt not a little surprised when he raised his head suddenly from the desk over which he was stooping, and said:— 'You see, Jane, the battle is fought and the victory won.'

Startled at being thus addressed, I did not immediately reply: after a moment's hesitation I answered:—'But are you sure you are not in the position of those conquerors whose triumphs have cost them too dear? Would not such another ruin you?'

'I think not; and if I were, it does not much signify; I shall never be called upon to contend for such another. The event of the conflict is decisive: my way is now clear; I thank God for it!' So saying, he returned to his papers and his silence.

As our mutual happiness (*i.e.* Diana's, Mary's, and mine) settled into a quieter character, and we resumed our usual habits and regular studies, St. John stayed more at home: he sat with us in the same room, sometimes for hours together. While Mary drew, Diana pursued a course of encyclopaedic reading she had (to my awe and amazement) undertaken, and I fagged away at German, he pondered a mystic lore of his own: that of some Eastern tongue, the acquisition of which he thought necessary to his plans.

Thus engaged, he appeared, sitting in his own recess, quiet and absorbed enough; but that blue eye of his had a habit of leaving the outlandish-looking grammar, and wandering over, and sometimes fixing upon us, his fellow students, with a curious intensity of observation: if caught, it would be instantly withdrawn; yet ever and anon it returned searchingly to our table. I wondered what it meant: I wondered, too, at the punctual satisfaction he never failed to exhibit on an occasion that seemed to me of small moment, namely,—my weekly visit to Morton school; and still more was I puzzled when, if the day was unfavourable, if there was snow, or rain, or high wind, and his sisters urged me not to go, he would invariably make light of their solicitude, and encourage me to accomplish the task without regard to the elements.

'Jane is not such a weakling as you would make her,' he would say: 'she can bear a mountain blast, or a shower, or a few flakes of snow, as well as any of us. Her constitution is both sound and elastic;—better calculated to endure variations of climate than many more robust.'

And when I returned, sometimes a good deal tired and not a little weather-beaten, I never dared complain, because I saw that to murmur would be to vex him: on all occasions fortitude pleased him; the reverse was a special annoyance.

One afternoon, however, I got leave to stay at home, because I really had a cold. His sisters were gone to Morton in my stead: I sat reading Schiller; he, deciphering his crabbed Oriental scrolls. As I exchanged a translation for an exercise, I happened to look his way: there I found myself under the influence of the ever-watchful blue eye. How long it had been searching me through and through, and over and over, I cannot tell: so keen was it, and yet so cold, I felt for the moment superstitious—as if I were sitting in the room with something uncanny.

'Jane, what are you doing?'

'Learning German.'

'I want you to give up German, and learn Hindostanee.'

'You are not in earnest?'

'In such earnest that I must have it so: and I will tell you why.'

He then went on to explain that Hindostanee was the language he was himself at present studying: that, as he advanced, he was apt to forget the commencement; that it would assist him greatly to have a pupil with whom he might again and again go over the elements, and so fix them thoroughly in his mind; that his choice had hovered for some time between me and his sisters; but that he had fixed on me, because he saw I could sit at a task the longest of the three. Would I do him this favour? I should not, perhaps, have to make the sacrifice long; as it wanted now barely three months to his departure.

St. John was not a man to be lightly refused: you felt that every impression made on him, either for pain or pleasure, was deep-graved and permanent. I consented. When Diana and Mary returned, the former found her scholar transferred from her to her brother: she laughed; and both she and Mary agreed that St. John should never have persuaded them to such a step. He answered, quietly: 'I know it.'

I found him a very patient, very forbearing, and yet an exacting master: he expected me to do a great deal; and when I fulfilled his expectations, he, in his own way, fully testified his approbation. By degrees, he acquired a certain influence over me that took away my liberty of mind: his praise and notice were more restraining than his indifference. I could no longer talk or laugh freely when he was by, because a tiresomely importunate instinct reminded me that vivacity (at least in me) was distasteful to him. I was so fully aware that only serious moods and occupations were acceptable, that in his presence every effort to sustain or follow any other became vain: I fell under a freezing spell. When he said 'go,' I went; 'come,' I came; 'do this,' I did it. But I did not love my servitude: I wished, many a time, he had continued to neglect me.

One evening when, at bedtime, his sisters and I stood round him, bidding him good-night, he kissed each of them, as was his custom; and, as was equally his custom, he gave me his hand. Diana, who chanced to be in a frolicsome humour (*she* was not painfully controlled by his will; for hers, in another way, was as strong), exclaimed:—'St. John! you used to call Jane your third sister, but you don't treat her as such: you should kiss her too.'

She pushed me towards him. I thought Diana very provoking, and felt uncomfortably confused; and while I was thus thinking and feeling, St. John bent his head; his Greek face was brought to a level with mine, his eyes questioned my eyes piercingly—he kissed me. There are no such things as marble kisses, or ice kisses, or I should say my ecclesiastical cousin's salute belonged to one of these classes; but there may be experiment kisses, and his was an experiment kiss. When given, he viewed me to learn the result; it was not striking: I am sure I did not blush; perhaps I might have turned a little pale, for I felt as if this kiss were a seal affixed to my fetters. He never omitted the ceremony afterwards, and the gravity and quiescence with which I underwent it seemed to invest it for him with a certain charm.

As for me, I daily wished more to please him: but to do so, I felt daily more and more that I must disown half my nature, stifle half my faculties, wrest my tastes from their original bent, force myself to the adoption of pursuits for which I had no natural vocation. He wanted to train me to an elevation I could never reach; it racked me hourly to aspire to the standard he uplifted. The thing was as impossible as to mould my irregular features to his correct and classic pattern, to give to my changeable green eyes the sea-blue tint and solemn lustre of his own.

Not his ascendancy alone, however, held me in thrall at present. Of late it had been easy enough for me to look sad: a cankering evil sat at my heart and drained my happiness at its source—the evil of suspense.

Perhaps you think I had forgotten Mr. Rochester, reader, amidst these changes of place and fortune. Not for a moment. His idea was still with me; because it was not a vapour sunshine could disperse; nor a sand-traced effigy storms could wash away: it was a name graven on a tablet, fated to last as long as the marble it inscribed. The craving to know what had become of him followed me everywhere; when I was at Morton, I re-entered my cottage every evening to think of that: and now at Moor House, I sought my bedroom each night to brood over it.

In the course of my necessary correspondence with Mr. Briggs about the will, I had inquired if he knew anything of Mr. Rochester's present residence and state of health; but, as St. John had conjectured, he was quite ignorant of all concerning him. I then wrote to Mrs. Fairfax, entreating information on the subject. I had calculated with certainty on this step answering my end: I felt sure it would elicit an early answer. I was astonished when a fortnight passed without reply; but when two months wore away, and day after day the post arrived and brought nothing for me, I fell a prey to the keenest anxiety.

I wrote again: there was a chance of my first letter having missed. Renewed hope followed renewed effort: it shone like the former for some weeks, then, like it, it faded, flickered: not a line, not a word reached me. When half a year wasted in vain expectancy my hope died out: and then I felt dark indeed.

A fine spring shone round me, which I could not enjoy. Summer approached; Diana tried to cheer me: she said I looked ill, and wished to accompany me to the sea-side. This St. John opposed; he said I did not want dissipation, I wanted employment; my present life was too purposeless, I required an aim; and, I suppose, by way of supplying deficiencies, he prolonged still further my lessons in Hindostanee, and grew more urgent in requiring their accomplishment: and I, like a fool, never thought of resisting him—I could not resist him.

One day I had come to my studies in lower spirits than usual; the ebb was occasioned by a poignantly felt disappointment: Hannah had told me in the morning there was a letter for me, and when I went down to take it, almost certain that the long looked-for tidings were vouchsafed me at last, I found only an unimportant note from Mr. Briggs on business. The bitter check had wrung from me some tears; and now as I sat poring over the crabbed characters and flourishing tropes of an Indian scribe, my eyes filled again.

St. John called me to his side to read; in attempting to do this my voice failed me: words were lost in sobs. He and I were the only occupants of the parlour: Diana was practising her music in the drawing-room, Mary was gardening—it was a very fine May-day, clear, sunny, and breezy. My companion expressed no surprise at this emotion, nor did he question me as to its cause; he only said:—'We will wait a few minutes, Jane, till you are more composed.' And while I smothered the paroxysm with all haste, he sat calm and patient, leaning on his desk and looking like a physician watching with the eye of science an expected and fully understood crisis in a patient's malady. Having stifled my sobs, wiped my eyes, and muttered something about not being very well that morning, I resumed my task, and succeeded in completing it. St. John put away my books and his, locked his desk, and said:—'Now, Jane, you shall take a walk; and with me.'

'I will call Diana and Mary.'

'No. I want only one companion this morning, and that must be you: put on your things; go out by the kitchen door; take the road towards the head of Marsh Glen: I will join you in a moment.'

I know no medium: I never in my life have known any medium in my dealings with positive, hard characters, antagonistic to my own, between absolute submission and determined revolt. I have always faithfully observed the one, up to the very moment of bursting, sometimes with volcanic vehemence, into the other; and as neither present circumstances warranted, nor my present mood inclined me to mutiny, I observed careful obedience to St. John's directions; and in ten minutes I was treading the wild track of the glen, side by side with him.

The breeze was from the west: it came over the hill, sweet with scents of heath and rush; the sky was of stainless blue; the stream descending the ravine, swelled with past spring rains, poured along plentiful and clear, catching golden gleams from the sun, and sapphire tints from the firmament. As we advanced and left the track, we trod a soft turf, mossy fine and emerald green, minutely enamelled with a tiny white flower and spangled with a star-like yellow blossom: the hills, meantime, shut us quite in; for the glen, towards its head, wound to the very core.

'Let us rest here,' said St. John, as we reached the first stragglers of a battalion of rocks, guarding a sort of pass, beyond which the beck rushed down a waterfall; and where, still a little further, the mountain shook off turf and flower, had only heath for raiment, and crag for gem —where it exaggerated the wild to the savage, and exchanged the fresh for the frowning—where it guarded the forlorn hope of solitude, and a last refuge for silence.

I took a seat: St. John stood near me. He looked up the pass and down the hollow; his glance wandered away with the stream, and returned to traverse the unclouded heaven which coloured it; he removed his hat, let the breeze stir his hair and kiss his brow. He seemed in communion with the genius of the haunt: with his eye he bade farewell to something.

'And I shall see it again,' he said aloud, 'in dreams, when I sleep by the Ganges: and again, in a more remote hour—when another slumber overcomes me—on the shore of a darker stream.'

Strange words of a strange love! An austere patriot's passion for his fatherland! He sat down; for half an hour we never spoke; neither he to me nor I to him: that interval past, he recommenced:—'Jane, I go in six weeks; I have taken my berth in an East Indiaman which sails on the twentieth of June.'

'God will protect you; for you have undertaken His work,' I answered.

'Yes,' said he, 'there is my glory and joy. I am the servant of an infallible master. I am not going out under human guidance, subject to the defective laws and erring control of my feeble fellow-worms: my king, my lawgiver, my captain, is the All-perfect. It seems strange to me that all round me do not burn to enlist under the same banner,—to join in the same enterprise.'

'All have not your powers: and it would be folly for the feeble to wish to march with the strong.'

'I do not speak to the feeble, or think of them: I address only such as are worthy of the work, and competent to accomplish it.'

'Those are few in number, and difficult to discover.'

'You say truly: but when found, it is right to stir them up—to urge and exhort them to the effort—to show them what their gifts are, and why they were given—to speak Heaven's message in their ear,—to offer them, direct from God, a place in the ranks of His chosen.'

'If they are really qualified for the task, will not their own hearts be the first to inform them of it?'

I felt as if an awful charm was framing round and gathering over me: I trembled to hear some fatal word spoken which would at once declare and rivet the spell.

'And what does *your* heart say?' demanded St. John.

'My heart is mute,—my heart is mute,' I answered, struck and thrilled.

'Then I must speak for it,' continued the deep, relentless voice. 'Jane, come with me to India: come as my help-meet and fellow-labourer.'

The glen and sky spun round: the hills heaved! It was as if I had heard a summons from Heaven—as if a visionary messenger, like him of Macedonia, had enounced, 'Come over and help us!'[5] But I was no apostle,—I could not behold the herald,—I could not receive his call.

'Oh, St. John!' I cried, 'have some mercy!'

I appealed to one who, in the discharge of what he believed his duty, knew neither mercy nor remorse. He continued:—'God and nature intended you for a missionary's wife. It is not personal, but mental endowments they have given you: you are formed for labour, not for love. A missionary's wife you must—shall be. You shall be mine: I claim you—not for my pleasure, but for my Sovereign's service.'

5. A Macedonian appeared in a vision to Paul, asking him to come and help the Macedonians (Acts 16:9).

'I am not fit for it: I have no vocation,' I said.

He had calculated on these first objections: he was not irritated by them. Indeed, as he leaned back against the crag behind him, folded his arms on his chest, and fixed his countenance, I saw he was prepared for a long and trying opposition, and had taken in a stock of patience to last him to its close—resolved, however, that that close should be conquest for him.

'Humility, Jane,' said he, 'is the groundwork of Christian virtues: you say right that you are not fit for the work. Who is fit for it? Or who, that ever was truly called, believed himself worthy of the summons? I, for instance, am but dust and ashes. With St. Paul, I acknowledge myself the chiefest of sinners: but I do not suffer this sense of my personal vileness to daunt me. I know my Leader: that He is just as well as mighty; and while He has chosen a feeble instrument to perform a great task, He will, from the boundless stores of His providence, supply the inadequacy of the means to the end. Think like me, Jane—trust like me. It is the Rock of Ages I ask you to lean on: do not doubt but it will bear the weight of your human weakness.'

'I do not understand a missionary life: I have never studied mission-ary labours.'

'There, I, humble as I am, can give you the aid you want: I can set you your task from hour to hour; stand by you always; help you from moment to moment. This I could do in the beginning: soon (for I know your powers) you would be as strong and apt as myself, and would not require my help.'

'But my powers—where are they for this undertaking? I do not feel them. Nothing speaks or stirs in me while you talk. I am sensible of no light kindling—no life quickening—no voice counselling or cheering. Oh, I wish I could make you see how much my mind is at this moment like a rayless dungeon, with one shrinking fear fettered in its depths— the fear of being persuaded by you to attempt what I cannot accom-plish!'

'I have an answer for you—hear it. I have watched you ever since we first met: I have made you my study for ten months. I have proved you in that time by sundry tests: and what have I seen and elicited? In the village school I found you could perform well, punctually, uprightly, labour uncongenial to your habits and inclinations; I saw you could perform it with capacity and tact: you could win while you controlled. In the calm with which you learnt you had become suddenly rich, I read a mind clear of the vice of Demas:—lucre had no undue power over you.[6] In the resolute readiness with which you cut your wealth into four shares, keeping but one to yourself, and relinquishing the

6. Demas's love of the world made him desert Paul (2 Timothy 4:10).

three others to the claim of abstract justice, I recognised a soul that revelled in the flame and excitement of sacrifice. In the tractability with
which, at my wish, you forsook a study in which you were interested,
and adopted another because it interested me; in the untiring assiduity
with which you have since persevered in it—in the unflagging energy
and unshaken temper with which you have met its difficulties—I acknowledge the complement of the qualities I seek. Jane, you are docile,
diligent, disinterested, faithful, constant, and courageous; very gentle,
and very heroic: cease to mistrust yourself—I can trust you unreservedly. As a conductress of Indian schools, and a helper amongst Indian
women, your assistance will be to me invaluable.'

My iron shroud contracted round me; persuasion advanced with
slow sure step. Shut my eyes as I would, these last words of his succeeded in making the way, which had seemed blocked up, comparatively clear. My work, which had appeared so vague, so hopelessly
diffuse, condensed itself as he proceeded, and assumed a definite form
under his shaping hand. He waited for an answer. I demanded a quarter
of an hour to think, before I again hazarded a reply.

'Very willingly,' he rejoined: and rising, he strode a little distance up
the pass, threw himself down on a swell of heath, and there lay still.

'I *can* do what he wants me to do: I am forced to see and acknowledge that,' I meditated—'That is, if life be spared me. But I feel mine is
not the existence to be long protracted under an Indian sun.—What
then? He does not care for that: when my time came to die he would
resign me, in all serenity and sanctity, to the God who gave me. The
case is very plain before me. In leaving England, I should leave a loved
but empty land—Mr. Rochester is not there: and if he were, what is,
what can that ever be to me? My business is to live without him now:
nothing so absurd, so weak as to drag on from day to day, as if I were
waiting some impossible change in circumstances, which might reunite
me to him. Of course (as St. John once said) I must seek another interest in life to replace the one lost: is not the occupation he now offers me
truly the most glorious man can adopt or God assign? Is it not, by its
noble cares and sublime results, the one best calculated to fill the void
left by uptorn affections and demolished hopes? I believe I must say,
Yes—and yet I shudder. Alas! If I join St. John, I abandon half myself:
if I go to India, I go to premature death. And how will the interval between leaving England for India, and India for the grave, be filled? Oh,
I know well! That, too, is very clear to my vision. By straining to satisfy
St. John till my sinews ache, I *shall* satisfy him—to the finest central
point and farthest outward circle of his expectations. If I *do* go with
him—if I *do* make the sacrifice he urges, I will make it absolutely: I will
throw all on the altar—heart, vitals, the entire victim. He will never
love me; but he shall approve me; I will show him energies he has not

yet seen, resources he was never suspected. Yes: I can work as hard as he can; and with as little grudging.

'Consent, then, to his demand is possible: but for one item—one dreadful item. It is—that he asks me to be his wife, and has no more of a husband's heart for me than that frowning giant of a rock, down which the stream is foaming in yonder gorge. He prizes me as a soldier would a good weapon; and that is all. Unmarried to him, this would never grieve me; but can I let him complete his calculations—coolly put into practice his plans—go through the wedding ceremony? Can I receive from him the bridal ring, endure all the forms of love (which I doubt not he would scrupulously observe) and know that the spirit was quite absent? Can I bear the consciousness that every endearment he bestows is a sacrifice made on principle? No: such a martyrdom would be monstrous. I will never undergo it. As his sister, I might accompany him— not as his wife: I will tell him so.'

I looked toward the knoll: there he lay, still as a prostrate column; his face turned to me: his eye beaming, watchful, and keen. He started to his feet, and approached me.

'I am ready to go to India, if I may go free.'

'Your answer requires a commentary,' he said; 'it is not clear.'

'You have hitherto been my adopted brother: I, your adopted sister; let us continue as such: you and I had better not marry.'

He shook his head. 'Adopted fraternity will not do in this case. If you were my real sister it would be different: I should take you and seek no wife. But as it is, either our union must be consecrated and sealed by marriage, or it cannot exist: practical obstacles oppose themselves to any other plan. Do you not see it, Jane? Consider a moment—your strong sense will guide you.'

I did consider: and still my sense, such as it was, directed me only to the fact that we did not love each other as man and wife should; and therefore it inferred we ought not to marry. I said so. 'St. John,' I returned, 'I regard you as a brother—you, me as a sister: so let us continue.'

'We cannot—we cannot,' he answered, with short, sharp determination: 'it would not do. You have said you will go with me to India: remember—you have said that.'

'Conditionally.'

'Well—well. To the main point—the departure with me from England, the co-operation with me in my future labours—you do not object. You have already as good as put your hand to the plough: you are too consistent to withdraw it. You have but one end to keep in view— how the work you have undertaken can best be done. Simplify your complicated interests, feelings, thoughts, wishes, aims; merge all considerations in one purpose: that of fulfilling with effect—with power—

the mission of your great Master. To do so, you must have a coadjutor—not a brother; that is a loose tie: but a husband. I, too, do not want a sister; a sister might any day be taken from me. I want a wife: the sole helpmeet I can influence efficiently in life and retain absolutely till death.'

I shuddered as he spoke: I felt his influence in my marrow—his hold on my limbs.

'Seek one elsewhere than in me, St. John: seek one fitted to you.'

'One fitted to my purpose, you mean—fitted to my vocation. Again I tell you it is not the insignificant private individual—the mere man, with the man's selfish senses—I wish to mate: it is the missionary.'

'And I will give the missionary my energies—it is all he wants—but not myself: that would be only adding the husk and shell to the kernel. For them he has no use: I retain them.'

'You cannot—you ought not. Do you think God will be satisfied with half an oblation?[7] Will He accept a mutilated sacrifice? It is the cause of God I advocate: it is under His standard I enlist you. I cannot accept on His behalf a divided allegiance: it must be entire.'

'Oh! I will give my heart to God,' I said. '*You* do not want it.'

I will not swear, reader, that there was not something of repressed sarcasm both in the tone in which I uttered this sentence, and in the feeling that accompanied it. I had silently feared St. John till now, because I had not understood him. He had held me in awe, because he had held me in doubt. How much of him was saint, how much mortal, I could not heretofore tell: but revelations were being made in this conference: the analysis of his nature was proceeding before my eyes. I saw his fallibilities: I comprehended them. I understood that, sitting there where I did, on the bank of heath, and with that handsome form before me, I sat at the feet of a man, erring as I. The veil fell from his hardness and despotism. Having felt in him the presence of these qualities, I felt his imperfection, and took courage. I was with an equal—one with whom I might argue—one whom, if I saw good, I might resist.

He was silent after I had uttered the last sentence, and I presently risked an upward glance at his countenance. His eye, bent on me, expressed at once stern surprise and keen inquiry. 'Is she sarcastic, and sarcastic to *me*!' it seemed to say. 'What does this signify?'

'Do not let us forget that this is a solemn matter,' he said ere long: 'one of which we may neither think nor talk lightly without sin. I trust, Jane, you are in earnest when you say you will give your heart to God: it is all I want. Once wrench your heart from man, and fix it on your Maker, the advancement of that Maker's spiritual kingdom on earth will be your chief delight and endeavour; you will be ready to do at once

7. Offering.

whatever furthers that end. You will see what impetus would be given to your efforts and mine by our physical and mental union in marriage: the only union that gives a character of permanent conformity to the destinies and designs of human beings: and, passing over all minor caprices—all trivial difficulties and delicacies of feeling—all scruple about the degree, kind, strength or tenderness of mere personal inclination—you will hasten to enter into that union at once.'

'Shall I?' I said briefly; and I looked at his features, beautiful in their harmony, but strangely formidable in their still severity; at his brow, commanding but not open; at his eyes, bright and deep, and searching, but never soft; at his tall, imposing figure; and fancied myself in idea *his wife*. Oh! it would never do! As his curate, his comrade, all would be right: I would cross oceans with him in that capacity; toil under eastern suns, in Asia deserts with him in that office; admire and emulate his courage and devotion, and vigour; accommodate quietly to his masterhood; smile undisturbed at his ineradicable ambition; discriminate the Christian from the man: profoundly esteem the one, and freely forgive the other. I should suffer often, no doubt, attached to him only in this capacity: my body would be under rather a stringent yoke, but my heart and mind would be free. I should still have my unblighted self to turn to: my natural unenslaved feelings with which to communicate in moments of loneliness. There would be recesses in my mind which would be only mine, to which he never came; and sentiments growing there fresh and sheltered, which his austerity could never blight, nor his measured warrior-march trample down: but as his wife—at his side always, and always restrained, and always checked—forced to keep the fire of my nature continually low, to compel it to burn inwardly and never utter a cry, though the imprisoned flame consumed vital after vital—*this* would be unendurable.

'St. John!' I exclaimed, when I had got so far in my meditation.

'Well?' he answered icily.

'I repeat: I freely consent to go with you as your fellow-missionary; but not as your wife; I cannot marry you and become part of you.'

'A part of me you must become,' he answered steadily; 'otherwise the whole bargain is void. How can I, a man not yet thirty, take out with me to India a girl of nineteen, unless she be married to me? How can we be for ever together—sometimes in solitudes, sometimes amidst savage tribes—and unwed?'

'Very well,' I said shortly; 'under the circumstances, quite as well as if I were either your real sister, or a man and a clergyman like yourself.'

'It is known that you are not my sister; I cannot introduce you as such: to attempt it would be to fasten injurious suspicions on us both. And for the rest, though you have a man's vigorous brain, you have a woman's heart, and—it would not do.'

'It would do,' I affirmed with some disdain, 'perfectly well. I have a woman's heart; but not where you are concerned; for you I have only a comrade's constancy; a fellow-soldier's frankness, fidelity, fraternity, if you like; a neophyte's respect and submission to his hierophant:[8] nothing more—don't fear.'

'It is what I want,' he said, speaking to himself; 'it is just what I want. And there are obstacles in the way: they must be hewn down. Jane, you would not repent marrying me; be certain of that; we *must* be married. I repeat it: there is no other way; and undoubtedly enough of love would follow upon marriage to render the union right even in your eyes.'

'I scorn your idea of love,' I could not help saying, as I rose up and stood before him, leaning my back against the rock. 'I scorn the counterfeit sentiment you offer: yes, St. John, and I scorn you when you offer it.'

He looked at me fixedly: compressing his well-cut lips while he did so. Whether he was incensed or surprised, or what, it was not easy to tell: he could command his countenance thoroughly.

'I scarcely expected to hear that expression from you,' he said: 'I think I have done and uttered nothing to deserve scorn.'

I was touched by his gentle tone, and overawed by his high, calm mien.

'Forgive me the words, St. John: but it is your own fault that I have been roused to speak so unguardedly. You have introduced a topic on which our natures are at variance—a topic we should never discuss: the very name of love is an apple of discord[9] between us—if the reality were required what should we do? How should we feel? My dear cousin, abandon your scheme of marriage—forget it.'

'No,' said he; 'it is a long-cherished scheme, and the only one which can secure my great end: but I shall urge you no further at present. To-morrow I leave home for Cambridge: I have many friends there to whom I should wish to say farewell. I shall be absent a fortnight—take that space of time to consider my offer: and do not forget that if you reject it, it is not me you deny, but God. Through my means, He opens to you a noble career; as my wife only can you enter upon it. Refuse to be my wife, and you limit yourself for ever to a track of selfish ease and barren obscurity. Tremble lest in that case you should be numbered with those who have denied the faith, and are worse than infidels!'

He had done. Turning from me, he once more

Looked to river, looked to hill:[1]

---

8. Priest (in ancient Greece).
9. Mythical apple thrown among the Greek goddesses by Eris, goddess of strife.

1. Sir Walter Scott's *The Lay of the Last Minstrel* 5.26.1.

But this time his feelings were all pent in his heart: I was not worthy to hear them uttered. As I walked by his side homeward, I read well in his iron silence all he felt towards me: the disappointment of an austere and despotic nature, which has met resistance where it expected submission—the disapprobation of a cool, inflexible judgment, which has detected in another feelings and views in which it has no power to sympathise: in short, as a man, he would have wished to coerce me into obedience: it was only as a sincere Christian he bore so patiently with my perversity, and allowed so long a space for reflection and repentance.

That night, after he had kissed his sisters, he thought proper to forget even to shake hands with me; but left the room in silence. I—who, though I had no love, had much friendship for him—was hurt by the marked omission: so much hurt that tears started to my eyes.

'I see you and St. John have been quarrelling, Jane,' said Diana, 'during your walk on the moor. But go after him; he is now lingering in the passage, expecting you—he will make it up.'

I have not much pride under such circumstances: I would always rather be happy than dignified; and I ran after him—he stood at the foot of the stairs.

'Good-night, St. John,' said I.

'Good-night, Jane,' he replied calmly.

'Then shake hands,' I added.

What a cold, loose touch he impressed on my fingers! He was deeply displeased by what had occurred that day: cordiality would not warm, nor tears move him. No happy reconciliation was to be had with him —no cheering smile or generous word: but still the Christian was patient and placid; and when I asked him if he forgave me, he answered that he was not in the habit of cherishing the remembrance of vexation; that he had nothing to forgive: not having been offended.

And with that answer he left me. I would much rather he had knocked me down.

Chapter XXXV

He did not leave for Cambridge the next day, as he had said he would. He deferred his departure a whole week; and during that time he made me feel what severe punishment a good yet stern, a conscientious yet implacable man can inflict on one who has offended him. Without one overt act of hostility, one upbraiding word, he contrived to impress me momently with the conviction that I was put beyond the pale of his favour.

Not that St. John harboured a spirit of unchristian vindictiveness—

not that he would have injured a hair of my head, if it had been fully in his power to do so. Both by nature and principle he was superior to the mean gratification of vengeance: he had forgiven me for saying I scorned him and his love, but he had not forgotten the words; and as long as he and I lived he never would forget them. I saw by his look, when he turned to me, that they were always written on the air between me and him; whenever I spoke, they sounded in my voice to his ear; and their echo toned every answer he gave me.

He did not abstain from conversing with me: he even called me as usual each morning to join him at his desk; and I fear the corrupt man within him had a pleasure unimparted to, and unshared by, the pure Christian, in evincing with what skill he could, while acting and speaking apparently just as usual, extract from every deed and every phrase the spirit of interest and approval which had formerly communicated a certain austere charm to his language and manner. To me, he was in reality become no longer flesh, but marble; his eye was a cold, bright, blue gem; his tongue, a speaking instrument—nothing more.

All this was torture to me—refined, lingering torture. It kept up a slow fire of indignation, and a trembling trouble of grief, which harassed and crushed me altogether. I felt how, if I were his wife, this good man, pure as the deep sunless source, could soon kill me: without drawing from my veins a single drop of blood, or receiving on his own crystal conscience the faintest stain of crime. Especially I felt this when I made any attempt to propitiate him. No ruth met my ruth. *He* experienced no suffering from estrangement—no yearning after reconciliation; and though, more than once, my fast falling tears blistered the page over which we both bent, they produced no more effect on him than if his heart had been really a matter of stone or metal. To his sisters, meantime, he was somewhat kinder than usual: as if afraid that mere coldness would not sufficiently convince me how completely I was banished and banned, he added the force of contrast: and this I am sure he did, not by malice, but on principle.

The night before he left home, happening to see him walking in the garden about sunset, and remembering, as I looked at him, that this man, alienated as he now was, had once saved my life, and that we were near relations, I was moved to make a last attempt to regain his friendship. I went out and approached him, as he stood leaning over the little gate: I spoke to the point at once.

'St. John, I am unhappy, because you are still angry with me. Let us be friends.'

'I hope we are friends,' was the unmoved reply; while he still watched the rising of the moon, which he had been contemplating as I approached.

'No, St. John, we are not friends as we were. You know that.'

'Are we not? That is wrong. For my part, I wish you no ill and all good.'

'I believe you, St. John; for I am sure you are incapable of wishing any one ill: but, as I am your kinswoman, I should desire somewhat more of affection than that sort of general philanthropy you extend to mere strangers.'

'Of course,' he said. 'Your wish is reasonable; and I am far from regarding you as a stranger.'

This, spoken in a cool, tranquil tone, was mortifying and baffling enough. Had I attended to the suggestions of pride and ire, I should immediately have left him: but something worked within me more strongly than those feelings could. I deeply venerated my cousin's talent and principle. His friendship was of value to me: to lose it tried me severely. I would not so soon relinquish the attempt to reconquer it.

'Must we part in this way, St. John? And when you go to India, will you leave me so, without a kinder word than you have yet spoken?'

He now turned quite from the moon, and faced me.

'When I go to India, Jane, will I leave you? What! do you not go to India?'

'You said I could not, unless I married you.'

'And you will not marry me? You adhere to that resolution?'

Reader, do you know, as I do, what terror those cold people can put into the ice of their questions? How much of the fall of the avalanche is in their anger? of the breaking up of the frozen sea in their displeasure?

'No, St. John, I will not marry you. I adhere to my resolution.'

The avalanche had shaken and slid a little forward; but it did not yet crash down.

'Once more, why this refusal?' he asked.

'Formerly,' I answered, 'because you did not love me; now, I reply, because you almost hate me. If I were to marry you, you would kill me. You are killing me now.'

His lips and cheeks turned white—quite white.

'*I should kill you—I am killing you?* Your words are such as ought not to be used: violent, unfeminine, and untrue. They betray an unfortunate state of mind: they merit severe reproof: they would seem inexcusable; but that it is the duty of man to forgive his fellow, even until seventy-and-seven times.'[2]

I had finished the business now. While earnestly wishing to erase from his mind the trace of my former offence, I had stamped on that tenacious surface another and far deeper impression: I had burnt it in.

---

2. Matthew 18:21–22.

'Now, you will indeed hate me,' I said. 'It is useless to attempt to conciliate you: I see I have made an eternal enemy of you.'

A fresh wrong did these words inflict: the worse because they touched on the truth. That bloodless lip quivered to a temporary spasm. I knew the steely ire I had whetted. I was heart-wrung.

'You utterly misinterpret my words,' I said, at once seizing his hand: 'I have no intention to grieve or pain you—indeed, I have not.'

Most bitterly he smiled—most decidedly he withdrew his hand from mine. 'And now you recall your promise, and will not go to India at all, I presume?' said he, after a considerable pause.

'Yes I will, as your assistant,' I answered.

A very long silence succeeded. What struggle there was in him between Nature and Grace in this interval I cannot tell; only singular gleams scintillated in his eyes, and strange shadows passed over his face. He spoke at last.

'I before proved to you the absurdity of a single woman of your age proposing to accompany abroad a single man of mine. I proved it to you in such terms as, I should have thought, would have prevented your ever again alluding to the plan. That you have done so, I regret—for your sake.'

I interrupted him. Anything like a tangible reproach gave me courage at once. 'Keep to common sense, St. John: you are verging on nonsense. You pretend to be shocked by what I have said. You are not really shocked; for, with your superior mind, you cannot be either so dull or so conceited as to misunderstand my meaning. I say again, I will be your curate, if you like, but never your wife.'

Again he turned lividly pale; but, as before, controlled his passion perfectly. He answered emphatically, but calmly: 'A female curate, who is not my wife, would never suit me. With me, then, it seems, you cannot go: but if you are sincere in your offer, I will, while in town, speak to a married missionary, whose wife needs a coadjutor. Your own fortune will make you independent of the Society's aid; and thus you may still be spared the dishonour of breaking your promise, and deserting the band you engaged to join.'

Now I never had, as the reader knows, either given any formal promise, or entered into any engagement; and this language was all much too hard, and much too despotic for the occasion. I replied: 'There is no dishonour; no breach of promise; no desertion in the case. I am not under the slightest obligation to go to India: especially with strangers. With you I would have ventured much; because I admire, confide in, and, as a sister, I love you: but I am convinced that, go when and with whom I would, I should not live long in that climate.'

'Ah! you are afraid of yourself,' he said, curling his lip.

'I am. God did not give me my life to throw away; and to do as you wish me would, I begin to think, be almost equivalent to committing suicide. Moreover, before I definitively resolve in quitting England, I will know for certain whether I cannot be of greater use by remaining in it than by leaving it.'

'What do you mean?'

'It would be fruitless to attempt to explain: but there is a point on which I have long endured painful doubt; and I can go nowhere till by some means that doubt is removed.'

'I know where your heart turns and to what it clings. The interest you cherish is lawless and unconsecrated. Long since you ought to have crushed it: now you should blush to allude to it. You think of Mr. Rochester?'

It was true. I confessed it by silence.

'Are you going to seek Mr. Rochester?'

'I must find out what is become of him.'

'It remains for me, then,' he said, 'to remember you in my prayers; and to entreat God for you, in all earnestness, that you may not indeed become a castaway. I had thought I recognised in you one of the chosen. But God sees not as man sees: *His* will be done.'

He opened the gate, passed through it, and strayed away down the glen. He was soon out of sight.

On re-entering the parlour, I found Diana standing at the window, looking very thoughtful. Diana was a great deal taller than I: she put her hand on my shoulder, and, stooping, examined my face.

'Jane,' she said, 'you are always agitated and pale now. I am sure there is something the matter. Tell me what business St. John and you have on hand. I have watched you this half-hour from the window: you must forgive my being such a spy, but for a long time I have fancied I hardly know what. St. John is a strange being——'

She paused—I did not speak: soon she resumed:—'That brother of mine cherishes peculiar views of some sort respecting you, I am sure: he has long distinguished you by a notice and interest he never showed to any one else—to what end? I wish he loved you—does he Jane?'

I put her cool hand to my hot forehead: 'No, Di, not one whit.'

'Then why does he follow you so with his eyes—and get you so frequently alone with him, and keep you so continually at his side? Mary and I had both concluded he wished you to marry him.'

'He does—he has asked me to be his wife.'

Diana clapped her hands. 'That is just what we hoped and thought! And you will marry him, Jane, won't you? And then he will stay in England.'

'Far from that, Diana; his sole idea in proposing to me is to procure a fitting fellow-labourer in his Indian toils.'

'What! He wishes you to go to India?'

'Yes.'

'Madness!' she exclaimed. 'You would not live three months there, I am certain. You never shall go: you have not consented—have you, Jane?'

'I have refused to marry him——'

'And have consequently displeased him?' she suggested.

'Deeply: he will never forgive me, I fear: yet I offered to accompany him as his sister.'

'It was frantic folly to do so, Jane. Think of the task you undertook —one of incessant fatigue: where fatigue kills even the strong; and you are weak. St. John—you know him—would urge you to impossibilities: with him there would be no permission to rest during the hot hours; and unfortunately, I have noticed, whatever he exacts, you force yourself to perform. I am astonished you found courage to refuse his hand. You do not love him then, Jane?'

'Not as a husband.'

'Yet he is a handsome fellow.'

'And I am so plain, you see, Di. We should never suit.'

'Plain! You? Not at all. You are much too pretty, as well as too good, to be grilled alive in Calcutta.' And again she earnestly conjured me to give up all thoughts of going out with her brother.

'I must, indeed,' I said; 'for when just now I repeated the offer of serving him for a deacon, he expressed himself shocked at my want of decency. He seemed to think I had committed an impropriety in pro- posing to accompany him unmarried: as if I had not from the first hoped to find in him a brother; and habitually regarded him as such.'

'What makes you say he does not love you, Jane?'

'You should hear himself on the subject. He has again and again ex- plained that it is not himself, but his office he wishes to mate. He has told me I am formed for labour—not for love: which is true, no doubt. But, in my opinion, if I am not formed for love, it follows that I am not formed for marriage. Would it not be strange, Di, to be chained for life to a man who regarded one but as a useful tool?'

'Insupportable—unnatural—out of the question!'

'And then,' I continued, 'though I have only sisterly affection for him now, yet, if forced to be his wife, I can imagine the possibility of conceiving an inevitable, strange, torturing kind of love for him: be- cause he is so talented; and there is often a certain heroic grandeur in his look, manner, and conversation. In that case, my lot would become unspeakably wretched. He would not want me to love him; and if I showed the feeling, he would make me sensible that it was a superfluity, urequired by him, unbecoming in me. I know he would.'

'And yet St. John is a good man,' said Diana.

'He is a good and a great man: but he forgets, pitilessly, the feelings and claims of little people, in pursuing his own large views. It is better, therefore, for the insignificant to keep out of his way; lest, in his progress, he should trample them down. Here he comes! I will leave you, Diana.' And I hastened upstairs, as I saw him entering the garden.

But I was forced to meet him again at supper. During that meal he appeared just as composed as usual. I had thought he would hardly speak to me, and I was certain he had given up the pursuit of his matrimonial scheme: the sequel showed I was mistaken on both points. He addressed me precisely in his ordinary manner; or what had, of late, been his ordinary manner; one scrupulously polite. No doubt he had invoked the help of the Holy Spirit to subdue the anger I had roused in him, and now believed he had forgiven me once more.

For the evening reading before prayers, he selected the twenty-first chapter of Revelation. It was at all times pleasant to listen while from his lips fell the words of the Bible: never did his fine voice sound at once so sweet and full—never did his manner become so impressive in its noble simplicity, as when he delivered the oracles of God: and to-night that voice took a more solemn tone—that manner a more thrilling meaning—as he sat in the midst of his household circle (the May moon shining in through the uncurtained window, and rendering almost unnecessary the light of the candle on the table): as he sat there, bending over the great old Bible, and described from its page the vision of the new heaven and the new earth—told how God would come to dwell with men, how He would wipe away all tears from their eyes, and promised that there should be no more death, neither sorrow nor crying, nor any more pain, because the former things were passed away.

The succeeding words thrilled me strangely as he spoke them: especially as I felt, by the slight, indescribable alteration in sound, that in uttering them, his eye had turned on me.

'He that overcometh shall inherit all things; and I will be his God, and he shall be my son. But,' was slowly, distinctly read, 'the fearful, the unbelieving, &c. shall have their part in the lake which burneth with fire and brimstone, which is the second death.'

Henceforth I knew what fate St. John feared for me.

A calm, subdued triumph, blent with a longing earnestness, marked his enunciation of the last glorious verses of that chapter. The reader believed his name was already written in the Lamb's book of life, and he yearned after the hour which should admit him to the city to which the kings of the earth bring their glory and honour; which has no need of sun or moon to shine in it, because the glory of God lightens it, and the Lamb is the light thereof.

In the prayer following the chapter, all his energy gathered—all his stern zeal woke: he was in deep earnest, wrestling with God, and resolved on a conquest. He supplicated strength for the weak-hearted;

guidance for wanderers from the fold: a return, even at the eleventh hour, for those whom the temptations of the world and the flesh were luring from the narrow path. He asked, he urged, he claimed the boon of a brand snatched from the burning. Earnestness is ever deeply solemn: first, as I listened to that prayer, I wondered at his; then, when it continued and rose, I was touched by it, and at last awed. He felt the greatness and goodness of his purpose so sincerely: others who heard him plead for it, could not but feel it too.

The prayer over, we took leave of him: he was to go at a very early hour in the morning. Diana and Mary having kissed him, left the room —in compliance, I think, with a whispered hint from him: I tendered my hand, and wished him a pleasant journey.

'Thank you, Jane. As I said, I shall return from Cambridge in a fortnight: that space, then, is yet left you for reflection. If I listened to human pride, I should say no more to you of marriage with me; but I listen to my duty, and keep steadily in view my first aim—to do all things to the glory of God. My Master was long-suffering: so will I be. I cannot give you up to perdition as a vessel of wrath: repent—resolve; while there is yet time. Remember, we are bid to work while it is day— warned that "the night cometh when no man shall work." Remember the fate of Dives, who had his good things in this life.[3] God give you strength to choose that better part which shall not be taken from you!'

He laid his hand on my head as he uttered the last words. He had spoken earnestly, mildly: his look was not, indeed, that of a lover beholding his mistress; but it was that of a pastor recalling his wandering sheep—or better, of a guardian angel watching the soul for which he is responsible. All men of talent, whether they be men of feeling or not; whether they be zealots, or aspirants, or despots—provided only they be sincere—have their sublime moments: when they subdue and rule. I felt veneration for St. John—veneration so strong that its impetus thrust me at once to the point I had so long shunned. I was tempted to cease struggling with him—to rush down the torrent of his will into the gulf of his existence, and there lose my own. I was almost as hard beset by him now as I had been once before, in a different way, by another. I was a fool both times. To have yielded then would have been an error of principle; to have yielded now would have been an error of judgment. So I think at this hour, when I look back to the crisis through the quiet medium of time: I was unconscious of folly at the instant.

I stood motionless under my hierophant's touch. My refusals were forgotten—my fears overcome—my wrestlings paralysed. The impossible—*i.e.* my marriage with St. John—was fast becoming the Possible. All was changing utterly, with a sudden sweep. Religion called—

3. John 9:4; in Luke 16:19–31, Dives the rich man goes to hell.

Angels beckoned—God commanded—life rolled together like a scroll
—death's gates opening, showed eternity beyond: it seemed, that for
safety and bliss there, all here might be sacrificed in a second. The dim
room was full of visions.

'Could you decide now?' asked the missionary. The inquiry was put
in gentle tones: he drew me to him as gently. Oh, that gentleness! how
far more potent is it than force! I could resist St. John's wrath: I grew
pliant as a reed under his kindness. Yet I knew all the time, if I yielded
now, I should not the less be made to repent, some day, of my former
rebellion. His nature was not changed by one hour of solemn prayer: it
was only elevated.

'I could decide if I were but certain,' I answered: 'were I but convinced that it is God's will I should marry you, I could vow to marry you
here and now—come afterwards what would!'

'My prayers are heard!' ejaculated St. John. He pressed his hand
firmer on my head, as if he claimed me: he surrounded me with his
arm, *almost* as if he loved me (I say *almost*—I knew the difference—for
I had felt what it was to be loved; but, like him, I had now put love out of
the question, and thought only of duty): I contended with my inward
dimness of vision, before which clouds yet rolled. I sincerely, deeply,
fervently longed to do what was right; and only that. 'Show me, show
me the path!' I entreated of Heaven. I was excited more than I had ever
been; and whether what followed was the effect of excitement, the
reader shall judge.

All the house was still; for I believe all, except St. John and myself,
were now retired to rest. The one candle was dying out: the room was
full of moonlight. My heart beat fast and thick: I heard its throb. Suddenly it stood still to an inexpressible feeling that thrilled it through, and
passed at once to my head and extremities. The feeling was not like an
electric shock; but it was quite as sharp, as strange, as startling: it acted
on my senses as if their utmost activity hitherto had been but torpor;
from which they were now summoned, and forced to wake. They rose
expectant: eye and ear waited, while the flesh quivered on my bones.

'What have you heard? What do you see?' asked St. John. I saw
nothing: but I heard a voice somewhere cry—'Jane! Jane! Jane!' nothing more.

'Oh God! what is it?' I gasped.

I might have said, 'Where is it?' for it did not seem in the room—nor
in the house—nor in the garden: it did not come out of the air—nor
from under the earth—nor from overhead. I had heard it—where, or
whence, for ever impossible to know! And it was the voice of a human
being—a known, loved, well-remembered voice—that of Edward
Fairfax Rochester; and it spoke in pain and woe wildly, eerily, urgently.

'I am coming!' I cried. 'Wait for me! Oh, I will come!' I flew to the door, and looked into the passage: it was dark. I ran out into the garden: it was void.

'Where are you?' I exclaimed.

The hills beyond Marsh Glen sent the answer faintly back—'Where are you?' I listened. The wind sighed low in the firs: all was moorland loneliness and midnight hush.

'Down superstition!' I commented, as that spectre rose up black by the black yew at the gate. 'This is not thy deception, nor thy witchcraft: it is the work of nature. She was roused, and did—no miracle—but her best.'

I broke from St. John, who had followed, and would have detained me. It was *my* time to assume ascendancy. *My* powers were in play, and in force. I told him to forbear question or remark; I desired him to leave me: I must, and would be alone. He obeyed at once. Where there is energy to command well enough, obedience never fails. I mounted to my chamber; locked myself in; fell on my knees; and prayed in my way —a different way to St. John's, but effective in its own fashion. I seemed to penetrate very near a Mighty Spirit; and my soul rushed out in gratitude at His feet. I rose from the thanksgiving—took a resolve— and lay down, unscared, enlightened—eager but for the daylight.

Chapter XXXVI

The daylight came. I rose at dawn. I busied myself for an hour or two with arranging my things in my chamber, drawers, and wardrobe, in the order wherein I should wish to leave them during a brief absence. Meantime, I heard St. John quit his room. He stopped at my door: I feared he would knock—no, but a slip of paper was passed under the door. I took it up. It bore these words—

'You left me too suddenly last night. Had you stayed but a little longer, you would have laid your hand on the Christian's cross and the angel's crown. I shall expect your clear decision when I return this day fortnight. Meantime, watch and pray that you enter not into tempta-tion: the spirit, I trust, is willing, but the flesh, I see, is weak.[4] I shall pray for you hourly,—Yours, St. John.'

'My Spirit,' I answered mentally, 'is willing to do what is right; and my flesh, I hope, is strong enough to accomplish the will of Heaven, when once that will is distinctly known to me. At any rate, it shall be strong enough to search—inquire—to grope an outlet from this cloud of doubt, and find the open day of certainty.

It was the first of June; yet the morning was overcast and chilly: rain beat fast on my casement. I heard the front-door open, and St. John

4. Matthew 26:41.

pass out. Looking through the window, I saw him traverse the garden. He took the way over the misty moors in the direction of Whitcross— there he would meet the coach.

'In a few more hours I shall succeed you in that track, cousin,' thought I: 'I too have a coach to meet at Whitcross. I too have some to see and ask after in England, before I depart for ever.'

It wanted yet two hours of breakfast-time. I filled the interval in walking softly about my room, and pondering the visitation which had given my plans their present bent. I recalled that inward sensation I had experienced: for I could recall it, with all its unspeakable strangeness. I recalled the voice I had heard; again I questioned whence it came, as vainly as before: it seemed in *me* —not in the external world. I asked, was it a mere nervous impression—a delusion? I could not conceive or believe: it was more like an inspiration. The wondrous shock of feeling had come like the earthquake which shook the foundations of Paul and Silas's prison:[5] it had opened the doors of the soul's cell, and loosed its bands—it had wakened it out of its sleep, whence it sprang trembling, listening, aghast; then vibrated thrice a cry on my startled ear, and in my quaking heart, and through my spirit; which neither feared nor shook, but exulted as if in joy over the success of one effort it had been privileged to make, independent of the cumbrous body.

'Ere many days,' I said, as I terminated my musings, 'I will know something of him whose voice seemed last night to summon me. Letters have proved of no avail—personal inquiry shall replace them.'

At breakfast I announced to Diana and Mary that I was going a journey, and should be absent at least four days.

'Alone, Jane?' they asked.

'Yes; it was to see, or hear news of, a friend about whom I had for some time been uneasy.'

They might have said, as I have no doubt they thought, that they had believed me to be without any friends save them: for, indeed, I had often said so; but with their true natural delicacy, they abstained from comment; except that Diana asked me if I was sure I was well enough to travel. I looked very pale, she observed. I replied, that nothing ailed me save anxiety of mind, which I hoped soon to alleviate.

It was easy to make my further arrangements; for I was troubled with no inquiries—no surmises. Having once explained to them that I could not now be explicit about my plans, they kindly and wisely acquiesced in the silence with which I pursued them; according to me the privilege of free action I should, under similar circumstances, have accorded them.

I left Moor House at three o'clock P.M., and soon after four I stood

5. Acts 16:25–26.

at the foot of the sign-post of Whitcross, waiting the arrival of the coach which was to take me to distant Thornfield. Amidst the silence of those solitary roads and desert hills, I heard it approach from a great distance. It was the same vehicle whence, a year ago, I had alighted one summer evening on this very spot—how desolate, and hopeless, and objectless! It stopped as I beckoned. I entered—not now obliged to part with my whole fortune as the price of its accommodation. Once more on the road to Thornfield, I felt like the messenger-pigeon flying home.

It was a journey of six-and-thirty hours. I had set out from Whitcross on a Tuesday afternoon, and early on the succeeding Thursday morning the coach stopped to water the horses at a wayside inn, situated in the midst of scenery whose green hedges and large fields and low pastoral hills (how mild of feature and verdant of hue compared with the stern north-midland moors of Morton!) met my eye like the lineaments of a once familiar face. Yes, I knew the character of this landscape: I was sure we were near my bourne.

'How far is Thornfield Hall from here?' I asked of the ostler.

'Just two miles, ma'am, across the fields.'

'My journey is closed,' I thought to myself. I got out of the coach, gave a box I had into the ostler's charge, to be kept till I called for it; paid my fare; satisfied the coachman, and was going: the brightening day gleamed on the sign of the inn, and I read in gilt letters, 'The Rochester Arms.' My heart leapt up: I was already on my master's very lands. It fell again: the thought struck it:—

'Your master himself may be beyond the British Channel, for aught you know: and then, if he is at Thornfield Hall, towards which you hasten, who besides him is there? His lunatic wife: and you have nothing to do with him: you dare not speak to him or seek his presence. You have lost your labour—you had better go no farther,' urged the monitor. 'Ask information of the people at the inn; they can give you all you seek: they can solve your doubts at once. Go up to that man, and inquire if Mr. Rochester be at home.'

The suggestion was sensible; and yet I could not force myself to act on it. I so dreaded a reply that would crush me with despair. To prolong doubt was to prolong hope. I might yet once more see the Hall under the ray of her star. There was the stile before me—the very fields through which I had hurried, blind, deaf, distracted, with a revengeful fury tracking and scourging me, on the morning I fled from Thornfield: ere I well knew what course I had resolved to take, I was in the midst of them. How fast I walked! How I ran sometimes! How I looked forward to catch the first view of the well-known woods! With what feelings I welcomed single trees I knew, and familiar glimpses of meadow and hill between them!

At last the woods rose; the rookery clustered dark; a loud cawing broke the morning stillness. Strange delight inspired me: on I hastened. Another field crossed—a lane threaded—and there were the courtyard walls—the back offices: the house itself, the rookery still hid. 'My first view of it shall be in front,' I determined, 'where its bold battlements will strike the eye nobly at once, and where I can single out my master's very window: perhaps he will be standing at it—he rises early: perhaps he is now walking in the orchard, or on the pavement in front. Could I but see him!—but a moment! Surely, in that case, I should not be so mad as to run to him? I cannot tell—I am not certain. And if I did— what then? God bless him! What then? Who would be hurt by my once more tasting the life his glance can give me?—I rave: perhaps at this moment he is watching the sun rise over the Pyrenees, or on the tide-less sea of the south.'

I had coasted along the lower wall of the orchard—turned its angle: there was a gate just there, opening into the meadow, between two stone pillars, crowned by stone balls. From behind one pillar I could peep round quietly at the full front of the mansion. I advanced my head with precaution, desirous to ascertain if any bedroom window-blinds were yet drawn up: battlements, windows, long front—all from this sheltered station were at my command.

The crows sailing overhead perhaps watched me while I took this survey. I wonder what they thought: they must have considered I was very careful and timid at first, and that gradually I grew very bold and reckless. A peep, and then a long stare; and then a departure from my niche and a straying out into the meadow; and a sudden stop full in front of the great mansion, and a protracted, hardy gaze towards it. 'What affectation of diffidence was this at first?' they might have de-manded. 'What stupid regardlessness now?'

Hear an illustration, reader.

A lover finds his mistress asleep on a mossy bank; he wishes to catch a glimpse of her fair face without waking her. He steal softly over the grass, careful to make no sound; he pauses—fancying she has stirred: he withdraws; not for worlds would be be seen. All is still: he again ad-vances: he bends above her; a light veil rests on her features: he lifts it, bends lower; now his eyes anticipate the vision of beauty—warm, and blooming, and lovely, in rest. How hurried was their first glance! But how they fix! How he starts! How he suddenly and vehemently clasps in both arms the form he dared not, a moment since, touch with his finger! How he calls aloud a name, and drops his burden, and gazes on it wildly! He thus grasps and cries, and gazes, because he no longer fears to waken by any sound he can utter—by any movement he can make. He thought his love slept sweetly: he finds she is stone-dead.

I looked with timorous joy towards a stately house: I saw a blackened ruin.

No need to cower behind a gate-post, indeed!—to peep up at chamber lattices, fearing life was astir behind them! No need to listen for doors opening—to fancy steps on the pavement or the gravel-walk! The lawn, the grounds were trodden and waste: the portal yawned void. The front was, as I had once seen it in a dream, but a shell-like wall, very high and very fragile looking, perforated with paneless windows: no roof, no battlements, no chimneys—all had crashed in.

And there was the silence of death about it: the solitude of a lonesome wild. No wonder that letters addressed to people here had never received an answer: as well despatch epistles to a vault in a church aisle. The grim blackness of the stones told by what fate the Hall had fallen —by conflagration: but how kindled? What story belonged to this disaster? What loss, besides mortar and marble and wood-work, had followed upon it? Had life been wrecked, as well as property? If so, whose? Dreadful question: there was no one here to answer it—not even dumb sign, mute token.

In wandering round the shattered walls and through the devastated interior, I gathered evidence that the calamity was not of late occurrence. Winter snows, I thought, had drifted through that void arch; winter rains beaten in at those hollow casements; for, amidst the drenched piles of rubbish, spring had cherished vegetation: grass and weed grew here and there between the stones and fallen rafters. And oh! where, meantime, was the hapless owner of this wreck? In what land? Under what auspices? My eye involuntarily wandered to the grey church tower near the gates, and I asked, 'Is he with Damer de Rochester, sharing the shelter of his narrow marble house?'

Some answer must be had to these questions. I could find it nowhere but at the inn, and thither, ere long, I returned. The host himself brought my breakfast into the parlour. I requested him to shut the door and sit down: I had some questions to ask him. But when he complied, I scarcely knew how to begin; such horror had I of the possible answers. And yet the spectacle of desolation I had just left prepared me in a measure for a tale of misery. The host was a respectable-looking, middle-aged man.

'You know Thornfield Hall, of course?' I managed to say at last.

'Yes, ma'am; I lived there once.'

'Did you?' Not in my time, I thought: you are a stranger to me.

'I was the late Mr. Rochester's butler,' he added.

The late! I seemed to have received with full force the blow I had been trying to evade.

'The late!' I gasped. 'Is he dead?'

'I mean the present gentleman Mr. Edward's father,' he explained.

I breathed again: my blood resumed its flow. Fully assured by these words that Mr. Edward—*my* Mr. Rochester (God bless him, wherever

he was!)—was at least alive: was, in short, 'the present gentleman.'
Gladdening words! It seemed I could hear all that was to come—whatever the disclosures might be—with comparative tranquillity. Since he
was not in the grave, I could bear, I thought, to learn that he was at the
Antipodes.

'Is Mr. Rochester living at Thornfield Hall now?' I asked, knowing,
of course, what the answer would be, but yet desirous of deferring the
direct question as to where he really was.

'No, ma'am—oh, no! No one is living there. I suppose you are a
stranger in these parts, or you would have heard what happened last
autumn,—Thornfield Hall is quite a ruin: it was burnt down just about
harvest time. A dreadful calamity! such an immense quantity of valuable property destroyed: hardly any of the furniture could be saved.
The fire broke out at dead of night, and before the engines arrived from
Millcote, the building was one mass of flame. It was a terrible spectacle:
I witnessed it myself.'

'At dead of night!' I muttered. Yes, that was ever the hour of fatality
at Thornfield. 'Was it known how it originated?' I demanded.

'They guessed, ma'am: they guessed. Indeed, I should say it was
ascertained beyond a doubt. You are not perhaps aware,' he continued,
edging his chair a little nearer the table, and speaking low, 'that there
was a lady,—a—a lunatic, kept in the house?'

'I have heard something of it.'

'She was kept in very close confinement, ma'am; people even for
some years was not absolutely certain of her existence. No one saw her:
they only knew by rumour that such a person was at the Hall; and who
or what she was it was difficult to conjecture. They said Mr. Edward
had brought her from abroad; and some believed she had been his mistress. But a queer thing happened a year since—a very queer thing.'

I feared now to hear my own story. I endeavoured to recall him to the
main fact.

'And this lady?'

'This lady, ma'am,' he answered, 'turned out to be Mr. Rochester's
wife! The discovery was brought about in the strangest way. There was
a young lady, a governess at the Hall, that Mr. Rochester fell
in——'

'But the fire,' I suggested.

'I'm coming to that, ma'am—that Mr. Edward fell in love with. The
servants say they never saw anybody so much in love as he was: he was
after her continually. They used to watch him—servants will, you
know, ma'am—and he set store on her past everything: for all, nobody
but him thought her so very handsome. She was a little small thing, they
say, almost like a child. I never saw her myself; but I've heard Leah, the
housemaid, tell of her. Leah liked her well enough. Mr. Rochester was

about forty, and this governess not twenty; and you see, when gentlemen of his age fall in love with girls, they are often like as if they were bewitched: well, he would marry her.'

'You shall tell me this part of the story another time,' I said; 'but now I have a particular reason for wishing to hear all about the fire. Was it suspected that this lunatic, Mrs. Rochester, had any hand in it?'

'You've hit it, ma'am: it's quite certain that it was her and nobody but her, that set it going. She had a woman to take care of her called Mrs. Poole—an able woman in her line, and very trustworthy, but for one fault—a fault common to a deal of them nurses and matrons—*she kept a private bottle of gin by her,* and now and then took a drop over much. It is excusable, for she had a hard life of it: but still it was dangerous; for when Mrs. Poole was fast asleep, after the gin-and-water, the mad lady, who was as cunning as a witch, would take the keys out of her pocket, let herself out of her chamber, and go roaming about the house, doing any wild mischief that came into her head. They say she had nearly burnt her husband in his bed once: but I don't know about that. However, on this night, she set fire first to the hangings of the room next her own; and then she got down to a lower story, and made her way to the chamber that had been the governess's—(she was like as if she knew somehow how matters had gone on, and had a spite at her)—and she kindled the bed there; but there was nobody sleeping in it fortunately. The governess had run away two months before; and for all Mr. Rochester sought her as if she had been the most precious thing he had in the world, he never could hear a word of her; and he grew savage—quite savage in his disappointment: he never was a wild man, but he got dangerous after he lost her. He would be alone, too. He sent Mrs. Fairfax, the housekeeper, away to her friends at a distance; but he did it handsomely, for he settled an annuity on her for life: and she deserved it— she was a very good woman. Miss Adèle, a ward he had, was put to school. He broke off acquaintance with all the gentry, and shut himself up, like a hermit, at the Hall.'

'What! did he not leave England?'

'Leave England? Bless you, no! He would not cross the door-stones of the house; except at night, when he walked just like a ghost about the grounds and in the orchard as if he had lost his senses—which it is my opinion he had; for a more spirited, bolder, keener gentleman than he was before that midge of a governess crossed him, you never saw, ma'am. He was not a man given to wine, or cards, or racing, as some are, and he was not so very handsome; but he had a courage and a will of his own, if ever man had. I knew him from a boy, you see: and for my part I have often wished that Miss Eyre had been sunk in the sea before she came to Thornfield Hall.'

'Then Mr. Rochester was at home when the fire broke out?'

'Yes, indeed was he; and he went up to the attics when all was burn-ing above and below, and got the servants out of their beds and helped them down himself—and went back to get his mad wife out of her cell. And then they called out to him that she was on the roof; where she was standing, waving her arms, above the battlements, and shouting out till they could hear her a mile off; I saw her and heard her with my own eyes. She was a big woman, and had long black hair: we could see it streaming against the flames as she stood. I witnessed, and several more witnessed Mr. Rochester ascend through the skylight on to the roof: we heard him call "Bertha!" We saw him approach her; and then, ma'am, she yelled, and gave a spring, and the next minute she lay smashed on the pavement.'

'Dead?'

'Dead? Ay, dead as the stones on which her brains and blood were scattered.'

'Good God!'

'You may well say so, ma'am: it was frightful!'

He shuddered.

'And afterwards?' I urged.

'Well, ma'am, afterwards the house was burnt to the ground: there are only some bits of walls standing now.'

'Were any other lives lost?'

'No—perhaps it would have been better if there had.'

'What do you mean?'

'Poor Mr. Edward!' he ejaculated, 'I little thought ever to have seen it! Some say it was a just judgment on him for keeping his first marriage secret, and wanting to take another wife while he had one living: but I pity him, for my part.'

'You said he was alive?' I exclaimed.

'Yes, yes: he is alive; but many think he had better be dead.'

'Why? How?' My blood was again running cold.

'Where is he?' I demanded. 'Is he in England?'

'Ay—ay—he's in England; he can't get out of England, I fancy—he's a fixture now.'

What agony was this! And the man seemed resolved to protract it.

'He is stone-blind,' he said at last. 'Yes—he is stone-blind—is Mr. Edward.'

I had dreaded worse. I had dreaded he was mad. I summoned strength to ask what had caused this calamity.

'It was all his own courage, and a body may say, his kindness, in a way, ma'am: he wouldn't leave the house till every one else was out before him. As he came down the great staircase at last, after Mrs. Rochester had flung herself from the battlements, there was a great crash—all fell. He was taken out from under the ruins, alive, but sadly hurt: a beam had fallen in such a way as to protect him partly; but one eye was knocked out, and one hand so crushed that Mr. Carter, the surgeon, had to amputate it directly. The other eye inflamed: he lost the sight of that also. He is now helpless, indeed—blind and a cripple.'

'Where is he? Where does he now live?'

'At Ferndean, a manor-house on a farm he has, about thirty miles off: quite a desolate spot.'

'Who is with him?'

'Old John and his wife: he would have none else. He is quite broken down, they say.'

'Have you any sort of conveyance?'

'We have a chaise, ma'am, a very handsome chaise.'

'Let it be got ready instantly; and if your post-boy can drive me to Ferndean before dark this day, I'll pay both you and him twice the hire you usually demand.'

Chapter XXXVII

The manor-house of Ferndean was a building of considerable antiquity, moderate size, and no architectural pretensions, deep buried in a wood. I had heard of it before. Mr. Rochester often spoke of it, and sometimes went there. His father had purchased the estate for the sake of the game covers. He would have let the house; but could find no tenant, in consequence of its ineligible and insalubrious site. Ferndean then remained uninhabited and unfurnished; with the exception of some two or three rooms fitted up for the accommodation of the squire when he went there in the season to shoot.

To this house I came, just ere dark, on an evening marked by the characteristics of sad sky, cold gale, and continued small, penetrating rain. The last mile I performed on foot, having dismissed the chaise and driver with the double remuneration I had promised. Even when within a very short distance of the manor-house you could see nothing of it; so thick and dark grew the timber of the gloomy wood about it. Iron gates between granite pillars showed me where to enter, and passing through them, I found myself at once in the twilight of close-ranked trees. There was a grass-grown track descending the forest aisle, between hoar and knotty shafts and under branched arches. I followed it, expecting soon to reach the dwelling; but it stretched on and on, it wound far and farther: no sign of habitation or grounds was visible.

I thought I had taken a wrong direction and lost my way. The darkness of natural as well as of sylvan dusk gathered over me. I looked round in search of another road. There was none: all was interwoven stem, columnar trunk, dense, summer foliage—no opening anywhere.

I proceeded: at last my way opened, the trees thinned a little: presently I beheld a railing, then the house—scarce, by this dim light, distinguishable from the trees; so dank and green were its decaying walls. Entering a portal, fastened only by a latch, I stood amidst a space of enclosed ground, from which the wood swept away in a semicircle. There were no flowers, no garden-beds; only a broad gravel-walk girdling a grass-plat, and this set in the heavy frame of the forest. The house presented two pointed gables in its front; the windows were latticed and narrow; the front door was narrow too, one step led up to it. The whole looked, as the host of the Rochester Arms had said, 'quite a desolate spot.' It was as still as a church on a week-day: the pattering rain on the forest leaves was the only sound audible in its vicinage.

'Can there be life here?' I asked.

Yes: life of some kind there was: for I heard a movement—that narrow front door was unclosing, and some shape was about to issue from the grange.

It opened slowly: a figure came out into the twilight and stood on the step; a man without a hat: he stretched forth his hand as if to feel whether it rained. Dusk as it was, I had recognised him—it was my master, Edward Fairfax Rochester, and no other.

I stayed my step, almost my breath, and stood to watch him—to examine him, myself unseen, and alas! to him invisible. It was a sudden meeting, and one in which rapture was kept well in check by pain. I had no difficulty in restraining my voice from exclamation, my step from hasty advance.

His form was of the same strong and stalwart contour as ever: his port was still erect, his hair was still raven-black; nor were his features altered or sunk: not in one year's space, by any sorrow, could his athletic strength be quelled, or his vigorous prime blighted. But in his countenance I saw a change: that looked desperate and brooding—that reminded me of some wronged and fettered wild beast or bird, dangerous to approach in his sullen woe. The caged eagle, whose gold-ringed eyes cruelty has extinguished, might look as looked that sightless Samson.

And, reader, do you think I feared him in his blind ferocity?—if you do, you little know me. A soft hope blent with my sorrow that soon I should dare to drop a kiss on that brow of rock, and on those lips so sternly sealed beneath it: but not yet. I would not accost him yet.

He descended the one step, and advanced slowly and gropingly towards the grass-plat. Where was his daring stride now? Then he paused, as if he knew not which way to turn. He lifted his hand and opened his eyelids; gazed blank, and with a straining effort, on the sky, and towards the amphitheatre of trees: one saw that all to him was void darkness. He stretched his right hand (the left arm, the mutilated one, he kept hidden in his bosom); he seemed to wish by touch to gain an idea of what lay around him: he met but vacancy still; for the trees were some yards off where he stood. He relinquished the endeavour, folded his arms, and stood quiet and mute in the rain, now falling fast on his uncovered head. At this moment John approached him from some quarter.

'Will you take my arm, sir?' he said; 'there is a heavy shower coming on: had you not better go in?'

'Let me alone,' was the answer.

John withdrew, without having observed me. Mr. Rochester now tried to walk about: vainly,—all was too uncertain. He groped his way back to the house, and, reentering it, closed the door.

I now drew near and knocked: John's wife opened for me. 'Mary,' I said, 'how are you?'

She started as if she had seen a ghost: I calmed her. To her hurried 'Is it really you, miss, come at this late hour to this 'only place?' I answered by taking her hand; and then I followed her into the kitchen, where John now sat by a good fire. I explained to them, in few words, that I had heard all which had happened since I left Thornfield, and that I was come to see Mr. Rochester. I asked John to go down to the turnpike-house, where I had dismissed the chaise, and bring my trunk, which I had left there: and then, while I removed my bonnet and shawl, I questioned Mary as to whether I could be accommodated at the Manor House for the night; and finding that arrangements to that effect, though difficult, would not be impossible, I informed her I should stay. Just at this moment the parlour-bell rang.

'When you go in,' said I, 'tell your master that a person wishes to speak to him, but do not give my name.'

'I don't think he will see you,' she answered; 'he refuses everybody.'

When she returned I inquired what he had said.

'You are to send in your name and your business,' she replied. She then proceeded to fill a glass with water, and place it on a tray, together with candles.

'Is that what he rang for?' I asked.

'Yes: he always has candles brought in at dark, though he is blind.'

'Give the tray to me, I will carry it in.'

I took it from her hand: she pointed me out the parlour door. The tray shook as I held it; the water spilt from the glass; my heart struck my ribs loud and fast. Mary opened the door for me, and shut it behind me.

This parlour looked gloomy: a neglected handful of fire burnt low in the grate; and, leaning over it, with his head supported against the high, old-fashioned mantelpiece, appeared the blind tenant of the room. His old dog, Pilot, lay on one side, removed out of the way, and coiled up as if afraid of being inadvertently trodden upon. Pilot pricked up his ears when I came in: then he jumped up with a yelp and a whine, and bounded towards me: he almost knocked the tray from my hands. I set it on the table; then patted him, and said softly, 'Lie down!' Mr. Rochester turned mechanically to *see* what the commotion was: but as he *saw* nothing, he re-turned and sighed.

'Give me the water, Mary,' he said.

I approached him with the now only half-filled glass. Pilot followed me, still excited.

What is the matter?' he inquired.

'Down, Pilot!' I again said. He checked the water on its way to his lips, and seemed to listen: he drank, and put the glass down. 'This is you, Mary, is it not?'

'Mary is in the kitchen,' I answered.

He put out his hand with a quick gesture, but not seeing where I stood, he did not touch me. 'Who is this? Who is this?' he demanded, trying, as it seemed, to *see* with those sightless eyes—unavailing and distressing attempt! 'Answer me—speak again!' he ordered, imperiously and aloud.

'Will you have a little more water, sir? I spilt half of what was in the glass,' I said.

'*Who* is it? *What* is it? Who speaks?'

'Pilot knows me, and John and Mary know I am here. I came only this evening,' I answered.

'Great God!—what delusion has come over me? What sweet madness has seized me?'

'No delusion—no madness: your mind, sir, is too strong for delusion, your health too sound for frenzy.'

'And where is the speaker? Is it only a voice? Oh! I *cannot* see, but I must feel, or my heart will stop and my brain burst. Whatever—whoever you are—be perceptible to the touch or I cannot live!'

He groped; I arrested his wandering hand, and prisoned it in both mine.

'Her very fingers!' he cried; 'her small, slight fingers! If so, there must be more of her.'

The muscular hand broke from my custody; my arm was seized, my shoulder—neck—waist—I was entwined and gathered to him.

'Is it Jane? *What* is it? This is her shape—this is her size——'

'And this her voice,' I added. 'She is all here: her heart, too. God bless you, sir! I am glad to be so near you again.'

'Jane Eyre!—Jane Eyre!' was all he said.

'My dear master,' I answered, 'I am Jane Eyre: I have found you out —I am come back to you.'

'In truth?—in the flesh? My living Jane?'

'You touch me, sir,—you hold me, and fast enough; I am not cold like a corpse, nor vacant like air, am I?'

'My living darling! These are certainly her limbs, and these her features; but I cannot be so blest, after all my misery. It is a dream; such dreams as I have had at night when I have clasped her once more to my heart, as I do now; and kissed her, as thus—and felt that she loved me, and trusted that she would not leave me.'

'Which I never will, sir, from this day.'

'Never will, says the vision? But I always woke and found it an empty mockery; and I was desolate and abandoned—my life dark, lonely, hopeless—my soul athirst and forbidden to drink—my heart famished and never to be fed. Gentle, soft dream, nestling in my arms now, you will fly, too, as your sisters have all fled before you: but kiss me before you go—embrace me, Jane.'

'There, sir—and there!'

I pressed my lips to his once brilliant and now rayless eyes—I swept his hair from his brow, and kissed that too. He suddenly seemed to arouse himself: the conviction of the reality of all this seized him.

'It is you—is it Jane? You are come back to me then?'

'I am.'

'And you do not lie dead in some ditch under some stream? And you are not a pining outcast amongst strangers?'

'No, sir; I am an independent woman now.'

'Independent! What do you mean, Jane?'

'My uncle in Madeira is dead, and he left me five thousand pounds.'

'Ah, this is practical—this is real!' he cried: 'I should never dream that. Besides, there is that peculiar voice of hers, so animating and pi-quant, as well as soft: it cheers my withered heart; it puts life into it.—What, Janet! Are you an independent woman? A rich woman?'

'Quite rich, sir. If you won't let me live with you, I can build a house of my own close up to your door, and you may come and sit in my par-lour when you want company of an evening.'

'But as you are rich, Jane, you have now, no doubt, friends who will look after you, and not suffer you to devote yourself to a blind lameter[6] like me?'

'I told you I am independent, sir, as well as rich: I am my own mis-tress.'

'And you will stay with me?'

'Certainly—unless you object. I will be your neighbour, your nurse, your housekeeper. I find you lonely: I will be your companion—to read to you, to walk with you, to sit with you, to wait on you, to be eyes and hands to you. Cease to look so melancholy, my dear master; you shall not be left desolate, so long as I live.'

He replied not: he seemed serious—abstracted; he sighed; he half-opened his lips as if to speak: he closed them again. I felt a little embar-

6. Cripple.

rassed. Perhaps I had too rashly overleaped conventionalities; and he, like St. John, saw impropriety in my inconsiderateness. I had indeed made my proposal from the idea that he wished and would ask me to be his wife: an expectation, not the less certain because unexpressed, had buoyed me up, that he would claim me at once as his own. But no hint to that effect escaping him, and his countenance becoming more overcast, I suddenly remembered that I might have been all wrong and was perhaps playing the fool unwittingly; and I began gently to withdraw myself from his arms—but he eagerly snatched me closer.

'No—no—Jane: you must not go. No—I have touched you, heard you, felt the comfort of your presence—the sweetness of your consolation: I cannot give up these joys. I have little left in myself—I must have you. The world may laugh—may call me absurd, selfish—but it does not signify. My very soul demands you: it will be satisfied: or it will take deadly vengeance on its frame.'

'Well, sir, I will stay with you: I have said so.'

'Yes—but you understand one thing by staying with me; and I understand another. You, perhaps, could make up your mind to be about my hand and chair—to wait on me as a kind little nurse (for you have an affectionate heart and a generous spirit, which prompt you to make sacrifices for those you pity), and that ought to suffice for me no doubt. I suppose I should now entertain none but fatherly feelings for you: do you think so? Come—tell me.'

'I will think what you like, sir: I am content to be only your nurse, if you think it better.'

'But you cannot always be my nurse, Janet: you are young—you must marry one day.'

'I don't care about being married.'

'You should care, Janet: if I were what I once was, I would try to make you care—but—a sightless block!'

He relapsed again into gloom. I, on the contrary, became more cheerful, and took fresh courage: these last words gave me an insight as to where the difficulty lay; and as it was no difficulty with me, I felt quite relieved from my previous embarrassment. I resumed a livelier vein of conversation.

'It is time some one undertook to rehumanise you,' said I, parting his thick and long uncut locks; 'for I see you are being metamorphosed into a lion, or something of that sort. You have "a faux air" of Nebuchadnezzar in the fields[7] about you, that is certain: your hair reminds me of eagle's feathers; whether your nails are grown like bird's claws or not, I have not yet noticed.'

'On this arm I have neither hand nor nails,' he said, drawing the

---

7. "Faux air": semblance. In Daniel 4:32–37 Nebuchadnezzar is driven into the fields to repent.

multilated limb from his breast, and showing it to me. 'It is a mere stump—a ghastly sight! Don't you think so, Jane?'

'It is a pity to see it; and a pity to see your eyes—and the scar of fire on your forehead: and the worst of it is, one is in danger of loving you too well for all this; and making too much of you.'

'I thought you would be revolted, Jane, when you saw my arm and cicatrised visage.'

'Did you? Don't tell me so—lest I should say something disparaging to your judgment. Now, let me leave you an instant, to make a better fire, and have the hearth swept up. Can you tell when there is a good fire?'

'Yes, with the right eye I see a glow—a ruddy haze.'

'And you see the candles?'

'Very dimly—each is a luminous cloud.'

'Can you see me?'

'No, my fairy: but I am only too thankful to hear and feel you.'

'When do you take supper?'

'I never take supper.'

'But you shall have some to-night. I am hungry: so are you, I daresay, only you forget.'

Summoning Mary, I soon had the room in more cheerful order: I prepared him, likewise, a comfortable repast. My spirits were excited, and with pleasure and ease I talked to him during supper, and for a long time after. There was no harassing restraint, no repressing of glee and vivacity with him; for with him I was at perfect ease, because I knew I suited him: all I said or did seemed either to console or revive him. Delightful consciousness! It brought to life and light my whole nature: in his presence I thoroughly lived; and he lived in mine. Blind as he was, smiles played over his face, joy dawned on his forehead; his lineaments softened and warmed.

After supper he began to ask me many questions, of where I had been, what I had been doing, how I had found him out; but I gave him only very partial replies: it was too late to enter into particulars that night. Besides, I wished to touch no deep-thrilling chord—to open no fresh well of emotion in his heart: my sole present aim was to cheer him. Cheered, as I have said, he was: and yet but by fits. If a moment's silence broke the conversation, he would turn restless, touch me, then say, 'Jane.'

'You are altogether a human being, Jane? You are certain of that?'

'I conscientiously believe so, Mr. Rochester.'

'Yet how, on this dark and doleful evening, could you so suddenly rise on my lone hearth? I stretched my hand to take a glass of water from a hireling, and it was given me by you: I asked a question, expecting John's wife to answer me, and your voice spoke at my ear.'

'Because I had come in, in Mary's stead, with the tray.'

'And there is enchantment in the very hour I am now spending with you. Who can tell what a dark, dreary, hopeless life I have dragged on for months past? Doing nothing, expecting nothing; merging night in day; feeling but the sensation of cold when I let the fire go out, of hunger when I forgot to eat: and then a ceaseless sorrow, and, at times, a very delirium of desire to behold my Jane again. Yes: for her restoration I longed, far more than for that of my lost sight. How can it be that Jane is with me, and says she loves me? Will she not depart as suddenly as she came? To-morrow, I fear, I shall find her no more.'

A common-place, practical reply, out of the train of his own disturbed ideas, was, I was sure, the best and most reassuring for him in this frame of mind. I passed my finger over his eyebrows, and remarked that they were scorched, and that I would apply something which should make them grow as broad and black as ever.

'Where is the use of doing me good in any way, beneficent spirit, when, at some fatal moment, you will again desert me—passing like a shadow, whither and how to me unknown; and for me remaining afterwards undiscoverable?'

'Have you a pocket comb about you, sir?'

'What for, Jane?'

'Just to comb out this shaggy black mane. I find you rather alarming when I examine you close at hand: you talk of my being a fairy; but I am sure you are more like a brownie.'

'Am I hideous, Jane?'

'Very, sir: you always were, you know.'

'Humph! The wickedness has not been taken out of you, wherever you have sojourned.'

'Yet I have been with good people; far better than you: a hundred times better people; possessed of ideas and views you never entertained in your life: quite more refined and exalted.'

'Who the deuce have you been with?'

'If you twist in that way you will make me pull the hair out of your head; and then I think you will cease to entertain doubts of my substantiality.'

'Who have you been with, Jane?'

'You shall not get it out of me to-night, sir; you must wait till to-morrow; to leave my tale half told will, you know, be a sort of security that I shall appear at your breakfast table to finish it. By-the-bye, I must mind not to rise on your hearth with only a glass of water, then: I must bring an egg at the least, to say nothing of fried ham.'

'You mocking changeling—fairy-born and human-bred! You make me feel as I have not felt these twelve months. If Saul could have had you for his David, the evil spirit would have been exorcised without the aid of the harp.'[8]

'There, sir, you are redd up and made decent. Now I'll leave you: I have been travelling these last three days, and I believe I am tired. Good-night.'

'Just one word, Jane: were there only ladies in the house where you have been?'

I laughed and made my escape, still laughing as I ran upstairs. 'A good idea!' I thought, with glee. 'I see I have the means of fretting him out of his melancholy for some time to come.'

Very early the next morning I heard him up and astir, wandering from one room to another. As soon as Mary came down I heard the question: 'Is Miss Eyre here?' Then: 'Which room did you put her into? Was it dry? Is she up? Go and ask if she wants anything; and when she will come down.'

I came down as soon as I thought there was a prospect of breakfast. Entering the room very softly, I had a view of him before he discovered my presence. It was mournful indeed to witness the subjugation of that vigorous spirit to a corporeal infirmity. He sat in his chair,—still, but not at rest: expectant evidently; the lines of now habitual sadness marking his strong features. His countenance reminded one of a lamp quenched, waiting to be relit—and alas! it was not himself that could now kindle the lustre of animated expression: he was dependent on another for that office! I had meant to be gay and careless, but the powerlessness of the strong man touched my heart to the quick: still I accosted him with what vivacity I could: 'It is a bright, sunny morning, sir,' I said. 'The rain is over and gone, and there is a tender shining after it: you shall have a walk soon.'

I had wakened the glow: his features beamed.

'Oh, you are indeed there, my sky-lark! Come to me. You are not gone: not vanished? I heard one of your kind an hour ago, singing high over the wood: but its song had no music for me, any more than the rising sun had rays. All the melody on earth is concentrated in my Jane's tongue to my ear (I am glad it is not naturally a silent one): all the sunshine I can feel is in her presence.'

The water stood in my eyes to hear this avowal of his dependence: just as if a royal eagle, chained to a perch, should be forced to entreat a sparrow to become its purveyor. But I would not be lachrymose: I dashed off the salt drops, and busied myself with preparing breakfast.

Most of the morning was spent in the open air. I led him out of the wet and wild wood into some cheerful fields: I described to him how

8. 1 Samuel 16:23.

brilliantly green they were; how the flowers and hedges looked refreshed; how sparklingly blue was the sky. I sought a seat for him in a
hidden and lovely spot: a dry stump of a tree: nor did I refuse to let him,
when seated, place me on his knee: why should I, when both he and I
were happier near than apart? Pilot lay beside us: all was quiet. He
broke out suddenly while clasping me in his arms: 'Cruel, cruel de-
serter! Oh, Jane, what did I feel when I discovered you had fled from
Thornfield, and when I could nowhere find you; and, after examining
your apartment, ascertained that you had taken no money, nor anything which could serve as an equivalent! A pearl necklace I had given
you lay untouched in its little casket; your trunks were left corded and
locked as they had been prepared for the bridal tour. What could my
darling do, I asked, left destitute and penniless? And what did she do?
Let me hear now.'

Thus urged, I began the narrative of my experience for the last year.
I softened considerably what related to the three days of wandering and
starvation, because to have told him all would have been to inflict unnecessary pain: the little I did say lacerated his faithful heart deeper than
I wished.

I should not have left him thus, he said, without any means of making my way: I should have told him my intention. I should have confided in him: he would never have forced me to be his mistress. Violent
as he had seemed in his despair, he, in truth, loved me far too well and
too tenderly to constitute himself my tyrant: he would have given me
half his fortune, without demanding so much as a kiss in return, rather
than I should have flung myself friendless on the wide world. I had endured, he was certain, more than I had confessed to him.

'Well, whatever my sufferings had been, they were very short,' I answered: and then I proceeded to tell him how I had been received at
Moor House; how I had obtained the office of schoolmistress, &c. The
accession of fortune, the discovery of my relations, followed in due
order. Of course St. John Rivers' name came in frequently in the progress of my tale. When I had done that name was immediately taken up.

'This St. John, then, is your cousin?'

'Yes.'

'You have spoken of him often: do you like him?'

'He was a very good man, sir; I could not help liking him.'

'A good man? Does that mean a respectable, well-conducted man of
fifty? Or what does it mean?'

'St. John was only twenty-nine, sir.'

' "*Jeune encore*,"⁹ as the French say. Is he a person of low stature,

9. Still young.

phlegmatic, and plain? A person whose goodness consists rather in his guiltlessness of vice than in his prowess in virtue?'

'He is untiringly active. Great and exalted deeds are what he lives to perform.'

'But his brain? That is probably rather soft? He means well: but you shrug your shoulders to hear him talk?'

'He talks little, sir: what he does say is ever to the point. His brain is first-rate, I should think not impressible, but vigorous.'

'Is he an able man, then?'

'Truly able.'

'A thoroughly educated man?'

'St. John is an accomplished and profound scholar.'

'His manners, I think, you said are not to your taste?—priggish and parsonic?'

'I never mentioned his manners; but, unless I had a very bad taste, they must suit it; they are polished, calm, and gentlemanlike.'

'His appearance,—I forget what description you gave of his appearance;—a sort of raw curate, half-strangled with his white neckcloth, and stilted up on his thick-soled high-lows,[1] eh?'

'St. John dresses well. He is a handsome man: tall, fair, with blue eyes and a Grecian profile.'

(*Aside.*) 'Damn him!'—(*To me.*) 'Did you like him, Jane?'

'Yes, Mr. Rochester, I liked him: but you asked me that before.'

I perceived, of course, the drift of my interlocutor. Jealousy had got hold of him: she stung him; but the sting was salutary: it gave him respite from the gnawing fang of melancholy. I would not, therefore, immediately charm the snake.

'Perhaps you would rather not sit any longer on my knee, Miss Eyre?' was the next somewhat unexpected observation.

'Why not, Mr. Rochester?'

'The picture you have just drawn is suggestive of a rather too overwhelming contrast. Your words have delineated very prettily a graceful Apollo: he is present to your imagination,—tall, fair, blue-eyed, and with a Grecian profile. Your eyes dwell on a Vulcan,—a real blacksmith, brown, broad-shouldered; and blind and lame into the bargain.'[2]

'I never thought of it before; but you certainly are rather like Vulcan, sir.'

'Well,—you can leave me, ma'am: but before you go' (and he retained me by a firmer grasp than ever), 'you will be pleased just to answer me a question or two.' He paused.

---

1. High-fastening shoes.
2. Apollo was the handsome sun god of Greek mythology, Vulcan, the lame blacksmith of the gods.

'What questions, Mr. Rochester?'

Then followed this cross-examination.

'St. John made you schoolmistress of Morton before he knew you were his cousin?'

'Yes.'

'You would often see him? He would visit the school sometimes?'

'Daily.'

'He would approve of your plans, Jane? I know they would be clever, for you are a talented creature.'

'He approved of them—yes.'

'He would discover many things in you he could not have expected to find? Some of your accomplishments are not ordinary.'

'I don't know about that.'

'You had a little cottage near the school, you say: did he ever come there to see you?'

'Now and then.'

'Of an evening?'

'Once or twice.'

A pause.

'How long did you reside with him and his sisters after the cousinship was discovered?'

'Five months.'

'Did Rivers spend much time with the ladies of his family?'

'Yes; the back parlour was both his study and ours: he sat near the window, and we by the table.'

'Did he study much?'

'A good deal.'

'What?'

'Hindostanee.'

'And what did you do meantime?'

'I learnt German, at first.'

'Did he teach you?'

'He did not understand German.'

'Did he teach you nothing?'

'A little Hindostanee.'

'Rivers taught you Hindostanee?'

'Yes, sir.'

'And his sisters also?'

'No.'

'Only you?'

'Only me.'

'Did you ask to learn?'

'No.'

'He wished to teach you?'

'Yes.'

A second pause.

'Why did he wish it? Of what use could Hindostanee be to you?'

'He intended me to go with him to India.'

'Ah! here I reach the root of the matter. He wanted you to marry him?'

'He asked me to marry him.'

'That is a fiction—an impudent invention to vex me.'

'I beg your pardon, it is the literal truth: he asked me more than once, and was as stiff about urging his point as ever you could be.'

'Miss Eyre, I repeat, you can leave me. How often am I to say the same thing? Why do you remain pertinaciously perched on my knee, when I have given you notice to quit?'

'Because I am comfortable there.'

'No, Jane, you are not comfortable there, because your heart is not with me: it is with this cousin—this St. John. Oh, till this moment I thought my little Jane was all mine! I had a belief she loved me even when she left me: that was an atom of sweet in much bitter. Long as we have been parted, hot tears as I have wept over our separation, I never thought that while I was mourning her she was loving another! But it is useless grieving. Jane, leave me: go and marry Rivers.'

'Shake me off, then, sir—push me away, for I'll not leave you of my own accord.'

'Jane, I ever like your tone of voice: it still renews hope, it sounds so truthful. When I hear it, it carries me back a year. I forget that you have formed a new tie. But I am not a fool—go——'

'Where must I go, sir?'

'Your own way—with the husband you have chosen.'

'Who is that?'

'You know—this St. John Rivers.'

'He is not my husband, nor ever will be. He does not love me: I do not love him. He loves (as he *can* love, and that is not as you love) a beautiful young lady called Rosamond. He wanted to marry me only because he thought I should make a suitable missionary's wife, which she would not have done. He is good and great, but severe; and, for me, cold as an iceberg. He is not like you, sir: I am not happy at his side, nor near him, nor with him. He has no indulgence for me—no fondness. He sees nothing attractive in me; not even youth—only a few useful mental points.—Then I must leave you, sir, to go to him?'

I shuddered involuntarily, and clung instinctively closer to my blind but beloved master. He smiled.

'What, Jane! Is this true? Is such really the state of matters between you and Rivers?'

'Absolutely, sir. Oh, you need not be jealous! I wanted to tease you a little to make you less sad: I thought anger would be better than grief. But if you wish me to love you, could you but see how much I *do* love you, you would be proud and content. All my heart is yours, sir: it belongs to you; and with you it would remain were fate to exile the rest of me from your presence for ever.'

Again, as he kissed me, painful thoughts darkened his aspect.

'My seared vision! my crippled strength!' he murmured regretfully.

I caressed, in order to soothe him. I knew of what he was thinking, and wanted to speak for him; but dared not. As he turned aside his face a minute I saw a tear slide from under the sealed eyelid, and trickle down the manly cheek. My heart swelled.

'I am no better than the old lightning-struck chestnut-tree in Thornfield orchard,' he remarked ere long. 'And what right would that ruin have to bid a budding woodbine cover its decay with freshness?'

'You are no ruin, sir—no lightning-struck tree: you are green and vigorous. Plants will grow about your roots, whether you ask them or not, because they take delight in your bountiful shadow; and as they grow they will lean towards you, and wind round you, because your strength offers them so safe a prop.'

Again he smiled: I gave him comfort.

'You speak of friends, Jane?' he asked.

'Yes: of friends,' I answered rather hesitatingly: for I knew I meant more than friends, but could not tell what other word to employ. He helped me.

'Ah! Jane. But I want a wife.'

'Do you, sir?'

'Yes: is it news to you?'

'Of course: you said nothing about it before.'

'Is it unwelcome news?'

'That depends on circumstances, sir—on your choice.'

'Which you shall make for me, Jane. I will abide by your decision.'

'Choose then, sir—*her who loves you best.*'

'I will at least choose—*her I love best.* Jane, will you marry me?'

'Yes, sir.'

'A poor blind man, whom you will have to lead about by the hand?'

'Yes, sir.'

'A crippled man, twenty years older than you, whom you will have to wait on?'

'Yes, sir.'

'Truly, Jane?'

'Most truly, sir.'

'Oh! my darling! God bless you and reward you!'

'Mr. Rochester, if ever I did a good deed in my life—if ever I thought a good thought—if ever I prayed a sincere and blameless prayer—if ever I wished a righteous wish,—I am rewarded now. To be your wife is, for me, to be as happy as I can be on earth.'

'Because you delight in sacrifice.'

'Sacrifice! What do I sacrifice? Famine for food, expectation for content. To be privileged to put my arms round what I value—to press my lips to what I love—to repose on what I trust: is that to make a sacrifice? If so, then certainly I delight in sacrifice.'

'And to bear with my infirmities, Jane: to overlook my deficiencies.'

'Which are none, sir, to me. I love you better now, when I can really be useful to you, than I did in your state of proud independence, when you disdained every part but that of the giver and protector.'

'Hitherto I have hated to be helped—to be led: henceforth, I feel, I shall hate it no more. I did not like to put my hand into a hireling's, but it is pleasant to feel it circled by Jane's little fingers. I preferred utter loneliness to the constant attendance of servants; but Jane's soft ministry will be a perpetual joy. Jane suits me: do I suit her?'

'To the finest fibre of my nature, sir.'

'The case being so, we have nothing in the world to wait for: we must be married instantly.'

He looked and spoke with eagerness: his old impetuosity was rising.

'We must become one flesh without any delay, Jane: there is but the license to get—then we marry.'

'Mr. Rochester, I have just discovered the sun is far declined from its meridian, and Pilot is actually gone home to his dinner. Let me look at your watch.'

'Fasten it into your girdle, Janet, and keep it hence-forward: I have no use for it.'

'It is nearly four o'clock in the afternoon, sir. Don't you feel hungry?'

'The third day from this must be our wedding-day, Jane. Never mind fine clothes and jewels now: all that is not worth a fillip.'

'The sun has dried up all the rain-drops, sir. The breeze is still: it is quite hot.'

'Do you know, Jane, I have your little pearl necklace at this moment fastened round my bronze scrag under my cravat? I have worn it since the day I lost my only treasure: as a memento of her.'

'We will go home through the wood: that will be the shadiest way.'

He pursued his own thoughts without heeding me.

'Jane! you think me, I daresay, an irreligious dog: but my heart swells with gratitude to the beneficent God of this earth just now. He sees not as man sees, but far clearer: judges not as man judges, but far more wisely. I did wrong: I would have sullied my innocent flower— breathed guilt on its purity: the Omnipotent snatched it from me. I, in my stiff-necked rebellion, almost cursed the dispensation: instead of bending to the decree, I defied it. Divine justice pursued its course; disasters came thick on me: I was forced to pass through the valley of the shadow of death. *His* chastisements are mighty; and one smote me which has humbled me for ever. You know I was proud of my strength; but what is it now, when I must give it over to foreign guidance, as a child does its weakness? Of late, Jane—only—only of late—I began to see and acknowledge the hand of God in my doom. I began to experience remorse, repentance; the wish for reconcilement to my Maker. I began sometimes to pray: very brief prayers they were, but very sincere.

'Some days since: nay, I can number them—four; it was last Monday night, a singular mood came over me: one in which grief replaced frenzy—sorrow, sullenness. I had long had the impression that since I could nowhere find you, you must be dead. Late that night—perhaps it might be between eleven and twelve o'clock—ere I retired to my dreary rest, I supplicated God that, if it seemed good to Him, I might soon be taken from this life, and admitted to that world to come, where there was still hope of rejoining Jane.

'I was in my own room, and sitting by the window, which was open: it soothed me to feel the balmy night-air: though I could see no stars and only by a vague, luminous haze, knew the presence of a moon. I longed for thee, Janet! Oh, I longed for thee both with soul and flesh! I asked of God, at once in anguish and humility, if I had not been long enough desolate, afflicted, tormented; and might not soon taste bliss and peace once more. That I merited all I endured I acknowledged—that I could scarcely endure more I pleaded; and the Alpha and Omega of my heart's wishes broke involuntarily from my lips in the words—"Jane! Jane! Jane!"'

'Did you speak these words aloud?'

'I did, Jane. If any listener had heard me, he would have thought me mad: I pronounced them with such frantic energy.'

'And it was last Monday night: somewhere near midnight?'

'Yes; but the time is of no consequence: what followed is the strange point. You will think me superstitious,—some superstition I have in my blood, and always had: nevertheless, this is true—true at least it is that I heard what I now relate.

'As I exclaimed "Jane! Jane! Jane!" a voice—I cannot tell whence the voice came, but I know whose voice it was—replied, "I am coming: wait for me;" and a moment after went whispering on the wind the words—"Where are you?"

'I'll tell you, if I can, the idea, the picture these words opened to my mind: yet it is difficult to express what I want to express. Ferndean is buried, as you see, in a heavy wood, where sound falls dull, and dies unreverberating. "Where are you?" seemed spoken amongst mountains; for I heard a hill-sent echo repeat the words. Cooler and fresher at the moment the gale seemed to visit my brow: I could have deemed that in some wild, lone scene, I and Jane were meeting. In spirit, I believe, we must have met. You no doubt were, at that hour, in unconscious sleep, Jane: perhaps your soul wandered from its cell to comfort mine; for those were your accents—as certain as I live—they were yours!'

Reader, it was on Monday night—near midnight—that I too had received the mysterious summons: those were the very words by which I replied to it. I listened to Mr. Rochester's narrative; but made no disclosure in return. The coincidence struck me as too awful and inexplicable to be communicated or discussed. If I told anything, my tale would be such as must necessarily make a profound impression on the mind of my hearer: and that mind, yet from its sufferings too prone to gloom, needed not the deeper shade of the supernatural. I kept these things then, and pondered them in my heart.[3]

'You cannot now wonder,' continued my master, 'that when you rose upon me so unexpectedly last night I had difficulty in believing you any other than a mere voice and vision: something that would melt to silence and annihilation, as the midnight whisper and mountain echo had melted before. Now, I thank God! I know it to be otherwise. Yes, I thank God!'

He put me off his knee, rose, and reverently lifting his hat from his brow, and bending his sightless eyes to the earth, he stood in mute devotion. Only the last words of the worship were audible.

'I thank my Maker that in the midst of judgment He has remembered mercy. I humbly entreat my Redeemer to give me strength to lead henceforth a purer life than I have done hitherto!'

Then he stretched his hand out to be led. I took that dear hand, held it a moment to my lips, then let it pass round my shoulder: being so much lower of stature than he, I served both for his prop and guide. We entered the wood, and wended homeward.

Chapter XXXVIII

CONCLUSION

Reader, I married him. A quiet wedding we had: he and I, the parson and clerk, were alone present. When we got back from church, I went into the kitchen of the manor-house, where Mary was cooking the dinner, and John cleaning the knives, and I said: 'Mary, I have been married to Mr. Rochester this morning.' The housekeeper and her husband were both of that decent phlegmatic order of people to whom one may at any time safely communicate a remarkable piece of news without incurring the danger of having one's ears pierced by some shrill

3. Luke 2:19.

ejaculation, and subsequently stunned by a torrent of wordy wonderment. Mary did look up, and she did stare at me: the ladle with which she was basting a pair of chickens roasting at the fire did for some three minutes hang suspended in air; and for the same space of time John's knives also had rest from the polishing process: but Mary, bending again over the roast, said only: 'Have you, Miss? Well, for sure!'

A short time after she pursued: 'I seed you go out with the master, but I didn't know you were gone to church to be wed;' and she basted away. John, when I turned to him, was grinning from ear to ear.

'I telled Mary how it would be,' he said: 'I knew what Mr. Edward' (John was an old servant, and had known his master when he was the cadet[4] of the house, therefore he often gave him his Christian name) —'I knew what Mr. Edward would do; and I was certain he would not wait long neither: and he's done right, for aught I know. I wish you joy, Miss!' and he politely pulled his forelock.

'Thank you, John. Mr. Rochester told me to give you and Mary this.' I put into his hand a five-pound note. Without waiting to hear more, I left the kitchen. In passing the door of that sanctum some time after I caught the words: 'She'll happen do better for him nor ony o' t' grand ladies.' And again, 'If she ben't one o' th' handsomest, she's noan faâl[5] and varry good-natured; and i' his een she's fair beautiful, onybody may see that.'

I wrote to Moor House and to Cambridge immediately to say what I had done: fully explaining also why I had thus acted. Diana and Mary approved the step unreservedly. Diana announced that she would just give me time to get over the honeymoon, and then she would come and see me.

'She had better not wait till then, Jane,' said Mr. Rochester, when I read her letter to him; 'if she does, she will be too late, for our honeymoon will shine our life-long: its beams will only fade over your grave or mine.'

How St. John received the news I don't know; he never answered the letter in which I communicated it: yet six months after he wrote to me; without, however, mentioning Mr. Rochester's name, or alluding to my marriage. His letter was then calm: and though very serious, kind. He has maintained a regular, though not frequent correspondence ever since: he hopes I am happy, and trusts I am not of those who live without God in the world, and only mind earthly things.

You have not quite forgotten little Adèle, have you, reader? I had not; I soon asked and obtained leave of Mr. Rochester to go and see her at the school where he had placed her. Her frantic joy at beholding me again moved me much. She looked pale and thin: she said she was not

4. Younger son.   5. No fool; "een": eyes.

happy. I found the rules of the establishment were too strict, its course of study too severe, for a child of her age: I took her home with me. I meant to become her governess once more; but I soon found this impracticable; my time and cares were now required by another—my husband needed them all. So I sought out a school conducted on a more indulgent system; and near enough to permit of my visiting her often, and bringing her home sometimes. I took care she should never want for anything that could contribute to her comfort: she soon settled in her new abode, became very happy there, and made fair progress in her studies. As she grew up a sound English education corrected in a great measure her French defects; and when she left school I found in her a pleasing and obliging companion: docile, good-tempered, and well-principled. By her grateful attention to me and mine she has long since well repaid any little kindness I ever had in my power to offer her.

My tale draws to its close: one word respecting my experience of married life, and one brief glance at the fortunes of those whose names have most frequently recurred in this narrative, and I have done.

I have now been married ten years. I know what it is to live entirely for and with what I love best on earth. I hold myself supremely blest—blest beyond what language can express; because I am my husband's life as fully as he is mine. No woman was ever nearer to her mate than I am; ever more absolutely bone of his bone and flesh of his flesh.[6]

I know no weariness of my Edward's society: he knows none of mine, any more than we each do of the pulsation of the heart that beats in our separate bosoms; consequently, we are ever together. To be together is for us to be at once as free as in solitude, as gay as in company. We talk, I believe, all day long: to talk to each other is but a more animated and an audible thinking. All my confidence is bestowed on him, all his confidence is devoted to me; we are precisely suited in character —perfect concord is the result.

Mr. Rochester continued blind the first two years of our union: perhaps it was that circumstance that drew us so very near—that knit us so very close! for I was then his vision, as I am still his right hand. Literally, I was (what he often called me) the apple of his eye. He saw nature—he saw books through me; and never did I weary of gazing for his behalf, and of putting into words the effect of field, tree, town, river, cloud, sunbeam—of the landscape before us; of the weather round us—and impressing by sound on his ear what light could no longer stamp on his eye. Never did I weary of reading to him: never did I weary of conducting him where he wished to go: of doing for him what he wished to be done. And there was a pleasure in my services, most full, most exquisite, even though sad—because he claimed these services without

6. Genesis 2:23.

painful shame or damping humiliation. He loved me so truly that he knew no reluctance in profiting by my attendance: he felt I loved him so fondly that to yield that attendance was to indulge my sweetest wishes.

One morning at the end of the two years, as I was writing a letter to his dictation, he came and bent over me, and said—'Jane, have you a glittering ornament round your neck?'

I had a gold watch-chain: I answered, 'Yes.'

'And have you a pale blue dress on?'

I had. He informed me then that for some time he had fancied the obscurity clouding one eye was becoming less dense; and that now he was sure of it.

He and I went up to London. He had the advice of an eminent oculist; and he eventually recovered the sight of that one eye. He cannot now see very distinctly: he cannot read or write much; but he can find his way without being led by the hand: the sky is no longer a blank to him—the earth no longer a void. When his firstborn was put into his arms, he could see that the boy had inherited his own eyes, as they once were—large, brilliant, and black. On that occasion he again, with a full heart, acknowledged that God had tempered judgment with mercy.

My Edward and I, then, are happy: and the more so because those we most love are happy likewise. Diana and Mary Rivers are both married: alternately, once every year, they come to see us, and we go to see them. Diana's husband is a captain in the navy; a gallant officer and a good man. Mary's is a clergyman: a college friend of her brother's; and, from his attainments and principles, worthy of the connection. Both Captain Fitzjames and Mr. Wharton love their wives, and are loved by them.

As to St. John Rivers, he left England: he went to India. He entered on the path he had marked for himself; he pursues it still. A more resolute, indefatigable pioneer never wrought amidst rocks and dangers. Firm, faithful, and devoted; full of energy, and zeal, and truth, he labours for his race: he clears their painful way to improvement: he hews down like a giant the prejudices of creed and caste that encumber it. He may be stern; he may be exacting: he may be ambitious yet; but his is the sternness of the warrior Greatheart, who guards his pilgrim convoy from the onslaught of Apollyon.[7] His is the exaction of the apostle, who speaks but for Christ when he says—'Whosoever will come after Me, let him deny himself, and take up his cross and follow Me.[8] His is the ambition of the high master-spirit, which aims to fill a place in the first rank of those who are redeemed from the earth—who stand without fault before the throne of God; who share the last mighty victories of the Lamb; who are called, and chosen, and faithful.

7. In Bunyan's *The Pilgrim's Progress*, Apol-   heart the Christian warrior.
lyon is the angel of the bottomless pit; Great-   8. Mark 8:34.

St. John is unmarried: he never will marry now. Himself has hitherto sufficed to the toil; and the toil draws near its close: his glorious sun hastens to its setting. The last letter I received from him drew from my eyes human tears, and yet filled my heart with Divine joy: he anticipated his sure reward, his incorruptible crown. I know that a stranger's hand will write to me next, to say that the good and faithful servant has been called at length into the joy of his Lord. And why weep for this? No fear of death will darken St. John's last hour: his mind will be unclouded; his heart will be undaunted; his hope will be sure; his faith steadfast. His own words are a pledge of this:—'My Master,' he says, 'has forewarned me. Daily he announces more distinctly,—"Surely I come quickly!"[9] and hourly I more eagerly respond,—"Amen; even so come, Lord Jesus!"'

1847

9. Revelation 22:20, the next-to-last line of the Bible.

EMILY BRONTË
1818–1848

"Stronger than a man, simpler than a child, her nature stood alone," wrote Charlotte Brontë of her sister Emily in a *Biographical Notice of Ellis and Acton Bell* that she published after the deaths of the authors of *Wuthering Heights* and *Agnes Grey*. A few years later, Constantin Héger, Emily's schoolmaster for a year in Brussels, added an equally striking tribute: "She should have been a man—a great navigator . . . her strong, imperious will would never have been daunted by opposition or difficulty." Paradoxically, however, the woman who inspired such dramatic statements appeared to many as a shy yet practical housekeeper who baked bread that was "always light and excellent" while studying German and scribbling poems on odd scraps of paper. Perhaps, indeed, it is because of such contradictions that the life story of Emily Brontë has long haunted biographers as well as more casual readers of her work.

Born in 1818, Emily Brontë was the fifth child of Patrick Brontë, a literarily inclined clergyman, and his wife, Maria Branwell Brontë, a lively but fragile woman who died not long after the birth of her last child, Anne. Like her equally famous sister Charlotte, Emily was raised at Haworth Parsonage in Yorkshire by her mother's pious sister, Elizabeth Branwell, who moved from Cornwall to her brother-in-law's home in order to care for his motherless children when he failed to remarry after his wife's death. Like Charlotte, too, Emily was briefly enrolled in the Clergy Daughters' School at Cowan Bridge, where she was one of the youngest pupils and was summarily brought home after her older sisters, Maria and Elizabeth, fell ill and died of a combination of typhoid fever and tuberculosis. Unlike Charlotte, however, Emily appeared—at least on the surface—to have transcended that traumatic experience unscathed, or so her biographer, Winifred Gérin, has argued.

After the deaths of Maria and Elizabeth, Emily received a haphazard education at home, along with her older brother, Branwell, and her remaining sisters, Charlotte and Anne. Because their father was an intellectual of sorts, the children had access to a literary collection which included not only the works of writers like Milton, Byron, and Scott but also the latest issues of contemporary periodicals like *Blackwood's* magazine. Equally obsessed with politics and poetry, history and fiction, they began early to incorporate such matters into what Charlotte called their "Bed Plays"—elaborate fantasies which were eventually to become more real to Emily than her daily life. Most notably, when their father brought Branwell a set of wooden soldiers, each child chose a figure with which to identify. Emily's was "Parry," named (as if in anticipation of Héger's later description of her) after her childhood hero Edward Parry, the Arctic explorer, and at first this dashing character figured in "plays" primarily of Charlotte and Branwell's invention. Eventually, however, Emily, together with her sister Anne, incorporated his adventures into a series of sagas that were uniquely their own. These were the chronicles of "Gondal," an imaginary country in the North Pacific that was ruled by a tempestuous queen known, variously, as Augusta Geraldine Almeda, A. G. A., Rosina of Alcona, A. S., "Sidonia's deity," and "Gondal's queen." Astonishingly, these two young women sustained their involvement in the "history" of this imaginary country long past their teens: much of Emily Brontë's poetry, the critic Fannie Ratchford has shown, was conceived as part of a "Gondal cycle" whose prose portions have been lost.

What is perhaps even more impressive about Emily Brontë's commitment to "Gondal" is the way she was able both to extend and to elaborate her fantasy in the midst of an apparently prosaic reality. The "Diary Papers" she and her sister Anne wrote on their birthdays indicate the ease with which Emily moved from her existence as a housekeeping daughter to her imaginative experience as "Gondal's queen." In 1834, for instance, when she was just sixteen, she juxtaposed domestic detail and mysterious drama in a statement that began by noting "I fed Rainbow, Diamond Snowflake Jasper" (pet birds), went on to observe that "Taby" (the family servant) "said just now Come Anne pilloputate" (peel a potato) and then declared that "the Gondals are discovering the interior of Gaaldine" (their exotic continent). Rarely have English writers combined such minutely accurate transcriptions of ordinary life—kitchens and potato peels— with such imaginings of high adventure. Yet it is precisely this configuration of the prosaic and the poetic that gives Emily Brontë's one novel, *Wuthering Heights*, its distinctive power.

As her "Diary Papers" suggest, Emily's housekeeping life at Haworth Parsonage was by no means an imprisonment. Rather, she felt constrained and confined on the few occasions when she had to leave home. In 1835, she briefly attended Roe Head, a girls' boarding school where Charlotte was employed as a teacher, and in 1837 she herself spent some six months teaching at Law Hill, a similar institution. Both experiences were unpleasant, indeed almost disastrous, for her. "I felt in my heart she would die, if she did not go home," Charlotte remembered about her sister's time at Roe Head, explaining that "liberty was the breath of Emily's nostrils; without it, she perished." Nevertheless, despite her attachment to such "liberty"—which she evidently found only on the moors near Haworth—Emily accompanied Charlotte to Brussels in 1841, where the two studied at a Belgian school, the Pensionnat Héger, in the hope that they might prepare themselves to found an educational establishment of their own. In November 1842, however, receiving word that their "Aunt Branwell" had died, the sisters returned to Haworth, and although Charlotte went back to Brussels for another term, Emily was never really to leave home again.

Despite its apparent quietness, Emily's life in Yorkshire from 1842 to 1848 was eventful. In the autumn of 1845, Charlotte "accidentally alighted," as she later put it, "on a MS volume of verses in my sister Emily's handwriting," and finding that these works had "a peculiar music—wild, melancholy, and elevating," she conceived a plan to publish them, along with poems by herself and Anne; thus, in 1846, a volume entitled *Poems by Currer, Ellis, and Acton Bell* appeared in London. The pseudonyms had been chosen because they concealed the femininity of the three authors at the same time that they were "not positively masculine." Yet Ellis Bell's gender was an important factor in her sister's appreciation of her work: "I know no woman that ever lived who wrote such poetry before," she exclaimed in a letter to her publisher. No doubt she was referring to the visionary sternness that set Emily's poems apart from the sentimental effusions that "ladies" were supposed to produce. But although a few reviewers received the verse of the Bells with approbation, and at least one singled out "Ellis's" "power of wing" for special praise, the reading public did not share either his admiration or Charlotte's. In the year after the Bells' *Poems* appeared, only two copies were sold.

Undaunted, the sisters set out to try their fortunes as fiction writers. The books they produced were Charlotte's *Jane Eyre*, Anne's *Agnes Grey*, and Emily's *Wuthering Heights*, a novel that was not greeted with anything like the wave of popular enthusiasm that met *Jane Eyre*. Some reviewers, generally the most sympathetic, thought it an early, immature work by "Currer Bell" himself. Others, shocked at the book's frank portrayals of passion and dissolution, commented that it was "a disagreeable story" and speculated that, like the novel, its author must be "dogged, brutal, and morose." In fact, *Wuthering Heights* is none of these: brilliantly organized by an interlocking series of first-person narratives, it is a tale of love, revenge, and redemption that comments on the tensions of nineteenth-century society even while it offers a vision of a spiritual region beyond ordinary "reality." Like Wordsworth and Carlyle, Brontë invested the world with a kind of "Natural Supernaturalism" that gave mystical radiance to the earthly realm of moors and cliffs, and even to the emotional relationships of men and women, parents and children. Like Blake and Byron, she defined her visionary system as one that was beyond good and evil. Indeed, in *Wuthering Heights'* satanic hero, Heathcliff, she created a figure who "stalked apart" from ordinary mortals and conventional morality as so many of Byron's heroes did, a figure whose fierce passions, like those of his beloved Catherine Earnshaw Linton, often seem to represent the author's own desire for the subversive *Marriage of Heaven and Hell* that William Blake had imagined some fifty years earlier.

That Emily Brontë quite consciously shaped *Wuthering Heights* not just as a Gothic romance but also as a radically visionary work becomes quite clear when one studies her poems. Here, in verses spoken in her "own" voice as well as in dramatic monologues written for Gondalian characters like "A. G. A." and her band of troubled lovers, the poet expressed her own alienation from social conventions and her own yearning for the "dazzling sea" of infinity, her own defiance of time and mortality, and her own commitment to the inspiring "Night Wind" of Imagination. *No Coward Soul Is Mine*, perhaps her most famous poem, articulated the severe yet ecstatic creed by which she lived and which informs her other verses, along with her one novel. "No trembler in the world's storm-troubled sphere," she relied in true Romantic fashion on the "God within my breast" to redeem her from pain, and, in true mystical fashion, she saw that inner "God" as one with an outer spirit of "Undying Life." At the same time, however, in a poem that her sister Charlotte published after her death, Emily Brontë insisted that she would not renounce the reality of nature, for "The earth that wakes *one* human heart to feeling / Can centre both the worlds of Heaven and Hell."

If she had experienced a kind of terrestrial "Heaven" on the moors, however, Brontë was destined to live through a domestic "Hell" in her own household. Never a man of strong character, her brother Branwell had dramatically deteriorated over the years, and when he was rejected by a married woman with whom he had been in love, he declined into alcoholism and opium addiction. By all accounts, it was Emily who watched over him in his last days, waiting up night after night to lead him to bed when he came home drunk or drugged. In September of 1848, "his constitution shattered," as Charlotte put it, he died, and October 1, the day of his funeral, was the last day on which Emily went out of her house. Apparently she caught a cold at the funeral service, but what might have been a minor ailment quickly turned into consumption, possibly hastened by the trauma through which she had just lived. Characteristically, she refused to see a doctor and forced herself to go about her usual business during the entire two-month period of her fatal sickness. Even on the day of her death, she stubbornly rose and dressed. Yet the extent of her illness can be judged from the report of the carpenter who made her coffin in December 1848: he claimed he had never made so narrow a coffin for an adult; it was, he said, five feet six inches in length, sixteen inches in width.

Always stoic, Emily Brontë had sworn to the end that "I'll walk where my own nature would be leading: / It vexes me to choose another guide." After her death, such independence was to be recognized as one of the qualities that gave her writing extraordinary power. But even in her lifetime, those closest to her had recognized her special genius: her poems "stirred my heart like the sound of a trumpet when I read them alone and in secret," Charlotte once confided to a friend, "for Ellis Bell is of no . . . ordinary materials."

[Tell me, tell me, smiling child]

Tell me, tell me, smiling child,
What the past is like to thee?
"An Autumn evening soft and mild
With a wind that sighs mournfully."

Tell me, what is the present hour?   5
"A green and flowery spray
Where a young bird sits gathering its power
To mount and fly away."

And what is the future, happy one?
"A sea beneath a cloudless sun;   10
A mighty, glorious, dazzling sea
Stretching into infinity."

1836   1941

[I am the only being whose doom]

I am the only being whose doom[1]
No tongue would ask, no eye would mourn;
I never caused a thought of gloom,
A smile of joy, since I was born.

In secret pleasure, secret tears,   5
This changeful life has slipped away,
As friendless after eighteen years,
As lone as on my natal day.

There have been times I cannot hide,
There have been times when this was drear,   10
When my sad soul forgot its pride
And longed for one to love me here.

But those were in the early glow
Of feelings since subdued by care;
And they have died so long ago,   15
I hardly now believe they were.[2]

First melted off the hope of youth,
Then fancy's[3] rainbow fast withdrew;
And then experience told me truth
In mortal bosoms never grew.   20

'Twas grief enough to think mankind
All hollow, servile, insincere;
But worse to trust to my own mind
And find the same corruption there.

May 17, 1837   1910

1. Death or fate.   3. Imagination's.
2. I.e., existed.

[Alone I sat; the summer day]

Alone I sat; the summer day
Had died in smiling light away;
I saw it die, I watched it fade
From misty hill and breezeless glade:

And thoughts in my soul were gushing, 5
And my heart bowed beneath their power;
And tears within my eyes were rushing
Because I could not speak the feeling,
The solemn joy around me stealing
In that divine, untroubled hour. 10

I asked myself, "O why has heaven
Denied the precious gift to me,
The glorious gift to many given
To speak their thoughts in poetry?

"Dreams have encircled me," I said, 15
"From careless childhood's sunny time;
Visions by ardent fancy fed
Since life was in its morning prime."[4]

But now, when I had hoped to sing,
My fingers strike a tuneless string; 20
And still the burden[5] of the strain
Is "Strive no more; 'tis all in vain."

August, 1837   1941

F. de Samara to A. G. A.[6]

Light up thy halls! 'Tis closing day;
I'm drear and lone and far away—
Cold blows on my breast the northwind's bitter sigh,
And oh, my couch is bleak beneath the rainy sky!

Light up thy halls—and think not of me; 5
That face is absent now, thou hast hated so to see—
Bright be thine eyes, undimmed their dazzling shine,
For never, never more shall they encounter mine!

---

4. First hour, beginning.
5. Bass or accompanying part. "Strain": tune.
6. A.G.A. is Augusta Geraldine Almeda, the heroine of an intricate dynastic story set in the mythological kingdom of Gondal. Both Anne and Emily Brontë participated in creating the story. The speaker of the poem is one of A.G.A.'s betrayed lovers. C.W. Hatfield argues that Emily Brontë made a mistake in copying the poem and that the speaker is really Lord Alfred of Aspin Castle, A.G.A.'s deserted husband, and not the youth Fernando de Samara (see Hatfield's edition of *The Complete Poems of EB*, p. 16).

The desert[7] moor is dark; there is tempest in the air;
I have breathed my only wish in one last, one burning prayer—   10
A prayer that would come forth, although it lingered long;
That set on fire my heart, but froze upon my tongue.

And now, it shall be done before the morning rise:
I will not watch the sun ascend in yonder skies.
One task alone remains—thy pictured face to view;   15
And then I go to prove[8] if God, at least, be true!

Do I not see thee now? Thy black resplendent hair;
Thy glory-beaming brow, and smile, how heavenly fair!
Thine eyes are turned away—those eyes I would not see;
Their dark, their deadly ray, would more than madden me.   20

There, go, Deceiver, go! My hand is streaming wet;
My heart's blood flows to buy the blessing—To forget!
Oh could that lost heart give back, back again to thine,
One tenth part of the pain that clouds my dark decline![9]

Oh could I see thy lids weighed down in cheerless woe;   25
Too full to hide their tears, too stern to overflow;
Oh could I know thy soul with equal grief was torn,
This fate might be endured—this anguish might be borne!

How gloomy grows the night! 'Tis Gondal's wind that blows;
I shall not tread again the deep glens where it rose—   30
I feel it on my face—"Where, wild blast, dost thou roam?
What do we, wanderer,[1] here, so far away from home?

"I do not need thy breath to cool my death-cold brow;
But go to that far land, where she is shining now;
Tell Her my latest wish, tell Her my dreary doom;[2]   35
Say that *my* pangs are past, but *Hers* are yet to come."

Vain words—vain, frenzied thoughts! No ear can hear me call—
Lost in the vacant air my frantic curses fall—
And could she see me now, perchance her lip would smile,
Would smile in careless pride and utter scorn the while!   40

And yet for all her hate, each parting glance would tell
A stronger passion breathed, burned, in this last farewell.
Unconquered in my soul the Tyrant[3] rules me still;
Life bows to my control, but *Love* I cannot kill!

November 1, 1838   1941

---

7. Deserted.   1. The speaker addresses the wind.
8. Test.   2. The speaker's death or fate; also his curse.
9. End, death.   3. I.e, love.

The Night-Wind

In summer's mellow midnight,
A cloudless moon shone through
Our open parlour window
And rosetrees wet with dew.

I sat in silent musing,   5
The soft wind waved my hair:
It told me Heaven was glorious,
And sleeping Earth was fair.

I needed not its breathing
To bring such thoughts to me,   10
But still it whispered lowly,
"How dark the woods will be!

"The thick leaves in my murmur
Are rustling like a dream,
And all their myriad voices   15
Instinct[4] with spirit seem."

I said, "Go, gentle singer,
Thy wooing voice is kind,
But do not think its music
Has power to reach my mind.   20

"Play with the scented flower,
The young tree's supple bough,
And leave my human feelings
In their own course to flow."

The wanderer would not leave[5] me;   25
Its kiss grew warmer still—
"O come," it sighed so sweetly,
"I'll win thee 'gainst thy will.

"Have we not been from childhood friends?
Have I not loved thee long?   30
As long as thou hast loved the night
Whose silence wakes my song.

"And when thy heart is laid at rest
Beneath the church-yard stone

4. Infused.
5. An alternative reading of the manuscript is "heed."

I shall have time enough to mourn   35
And thou to be alone."

September 11, 1840   1850

[Riches I hold in light esteem]

Riches I hold in light esteem
And Love I laugh to scorn
And lust of Fame was but a dream
That vanished with the morn—

And if I pray, the only prayer   5
That moves my lips for me
Is—"Leave the heart that now I bear
And give me liberty."

Yes, as my swift days near their goal
'Tis all that I implore—   10
Through life and death, a chainless soul
With courage to endure!

March 1, 1841   1846

[Aye, there it is! It wakes to-night][6]

Aye, there it[7] is! It wakes to-night
Sweet thoughts that will not die
And feeling's fires flash all as bright
As in the years gone by!

And I can tell by thine altered cheek   5
And by thy kindled gaze
And by the words thou scarce dost speak,
How wildly fancy[8] plays.

Yes, I could swear that glorious wind
Has swept the world aside,   10
Has dashed its memory from thy mind
Like foam-bells[9] from the tide—

6. Possibly addressed to one of Emily Brontë's
siblings. Charlotte Brontë supplied the following
note: "In these stanzas a louder gale has roused
the sleeper on her pillow: the wakened soul
struggles to blend with the storm by which it is
swayed."
7. I.e., the gale wind.
8. Imagination.
9. Bubbles.

And thou art now a spirit pouring
Thy presence into all—
The essence of the Tempest's roaring   15
And of the Tempest's fall—

A universal influence
From Thine own influence free;
A principle of life, intense,
Lost to mortality.   20

Thus truly when that breast is cold
Thy prisoned soul shall rise,
The dungeon mingle with the mould—[1]
The captive with the skies.

July 6, 1841   1850

A Day Dream

On a sunny brae[2] alone I lay
One summer afternoon;
It was the marriage-time of May
With her young lover, June.[3]

From her Mother's[4] heart seemed loath to part   5
That queen of bridal charms,
But her Father[5] smiled on the fairest child
He ever held in his arms.

The trees did wave their plumy crests,
The glad birds carolled clear;   10
And I, of all the wedding guests,
Was only sullen there.

There was not one but wished to shun
My aspect void of cheer;
The very grey rocks, looking on,   15
Asked, "What do you do here?"

And I could utter no reply:
In sooth I did not know
Why I had brought a clouded eye
To greet the general glow.   20

---

1. Earth or decaying flesh in the earth.   4. The earth's.
2. Hillside along a river.   5. The sun.
3. I.e., it was the end of May.

So, resting on a heathy bank,
I took my heart to me;
And we together sadly sank
Into a reverie.

We thought, "When winter comes again,   25
Where will these bright things be?
All vanished, like a vision vain,
An unreal mockery!

"The birds that now so blithely sing,
Through deserts frozen dry,   30
Poor spectres of the perished Spring
In famished troops will fly.

"And why should we be glad at all?
The leaf is hardly green,
Before a token of the fall[6]   35
Is on its surface seen."

Now whether it were really so
I never could be sure;
But as, in fit of peevish woe,
I stretched me on the moor,   40

A thousand thousand glancing fires
Seemed kindling in the air;
A thousand thousand silvery lyres
Resounded far and near:

Methought the very breath I breathed   45
Was full of sparks divine,
And all my heather-couch was wreathed
By that celestial shine.

And while the wide Earth echoing rang
To their strange minstrelsy,   50
The little glittering spirits sang,
Or seemed to sing, to me:

"O mortal, mortal, let them die;
Let Time and Tears destroy,
That we may overflow the sky   55
With universal joy.

6. Both autumn and the fall of man.

"Let Grief distract the sufferer's breast,
And Night obscure his way;
They hasten him to endless rest,
And everlasting day.   60

"To Thee the world is like a tomb,
A desert's naked shore;
To us, in unimagined bloom,
It brightens more and more.

"And could we lift the veil and give   65
One brief glimpse to thine eye
Thou would'st rejoice for those that live,
Because they live to die."

The music ceased—the noonday Dream
Like dream of night withdrew   70
But Fancy still will sometimes deem
Her fond[7] creation true.

March 5, 1844   1846

R. Alcona to J. Brenzaida[8]

Cold in the earth, and the deep snow piled above thee!
Far, far removed, cold in the dreary grave!
Have I forgot, my Only Love, to love thee,
Severed at last by Time's all-wearing wave?

Now, when alone, do my thoughts no longer hover   5
Over the mountains on Angora's shore;
Resting their wings where heath and fern-leaves cover
That noble heart for ever, ever more?

Cold in the earth, and fifteen wild Decembers
From those brown hills have melted into spring—   10
Faithful indeed is the spirit that remembers
After such years of change and suffering!

Sweet Love of youth, forgive if I forget thee
While the World's tide is bearing me along;
Sterner desires and darker hopes beset me,   15
Hopes which obscure but cannot do thee wrong.

7. Foolish. "Fancy": imagination.
8. Rosina Alcona is another name for A.G.A., the heroine of the Gondal stories. C. W. Hat- field suggests that Brenzaida may be A.G.A.'s first love as well as her last husband. Here he is deceased.

No other Sun has lightened up my heaven;
No other Star has ever shone for me:
All my life's bliss from thy dear life was given—
All my life's bliss is in the grave with thee.   20

But when the days of golden dreams had perished
And even Despair was powerless to destroy,
Then did I learn how existence could be cherished,
Strengthened and fed without the aid of joy;

Then did I check the tears of useless passion,   25
Weaned my young soul from yearning after thine;
Sternly denied its burning wish to hasten
Down to that tomb already more than mine!

And even yet, I dare not let it languish,
Dare not indulge in Memory's rapturous pain;   30
Once drinking deep of that divinest anguish,
How could I seek the empty world again?

March 3, 1845   1846

[Ah! why, because the dazzling sun]

Ah! why, because the dazzling sun
Restored my earth to joy
Have you[9] departed, every one,
And left a desert sky?

All through the night, your glorious eyes   5
Were gazing down in mine,
And with a full heart's thankful sighs
I blessed that watch divine!

I was at peace, and drank your beams
As they were life to me   10
And revelled in my changeful dreams
Like petrel[1] on the sea.

Thought followed thought—star followed star
Through boundless regions on,
While one sweet influence, near and far,   15
Thrilled through and proved us one.

Why did the morning rise to break
So great, so pure a spell,

9. The speaker addresses the stars.   1. Sea birds.

And scorch with fire the tranquil cheek
Where your cool radiance fell?   20

Blood-red he rose,[2] and arrow-straight
His fierce beams struck my brow:
The soul of Nature sprang elate,
But mine sank sad and low!

My lids closed down—yet through their veil   25
I saw him blazing still;
And bathe in gold the misty dale,
And flash upon the hill.

I turned me to the pillow then
To call back Night, and see   30
Your worlds of solemn light, again
Throb with my heart and me!

It would not do—the pillow glowed
And glowed both roof and floor,
And birds sang loudly in the wood,   35
And fresh winds shook the door.

The curtains waved, the wakened flies
Were murmuring round my room,
Imprisoned there, till I should rise
And give them leave to roam.   40

O Stars and Dreams and Gentle Night;
O Night and Stars return!
And hide me from the hostile light
That does not warm, but burn—

That drains the blood of suffering men;   45
Drinks tears, instead of dew:
Let me sleep through his blinding reign,
And only wake with you!

April 14, 1845   1846

The Prisoner

A *Fragment*

In the dungeon crypts[3] idly did I stray,
Reckless of the lives wasting there away;

---

2. The sun. Possibly an echo of Coleridge's *The Ancient Mariner*: "All in a hot and copper sky, / The bloody sun, at noon . . ." (11.111–112).

3. Underground vaults. The speaker, a man, is wandering through the dungeon in the castle of his father.

"Draw the ponderous bars! open, Warder stern!"
He dared not say me nay—the hinges harshly turn.

"Our guests are darkly lodged," I whispered, gazing through   5
The vault, whose grated eye showed heaven more gray than blue
(This was when glad Spring laughed in awaking pride);
"Aye, darkly lodged enough!" returned my sullen guide.

Then, God forgive my youth! forgive my careless tongue!
I scoffed, as the chill chains on the damp flagstones rung: 10
"Confined in triple walls, art thou so much to fear,
That we must bind thee down and clench thy fetters here?"

The captive raised her face; it was as soft and mild
As sculptured marble saint; or slumbering unweaned child;
It was so soft and mild, it was so sweet and fair,   15
Pain could not trace a line, or grief a shadow there!

The captive raised her hand and pressed it to her brow;
"I have been struck," she said, "and I am suffering now;
Yet these are little worth, your bolts and irons strong:
And, were they forged in steel, they could not hold me long."   20

Hoarse laughed the jailor grim: "Shall I be won to hear;
Dost think, fond,[4] dreaming wretch, that *I* shall grant thy prayer?
Or, better still, wilt melt my master's heart with groans?
Ah! sooner might the sun thaw down these granite stones.

"My master's voice is low, his aspect bland and kind,   25
But hard as hardest flint the soul that lurks behind;
And I am rough and rude, yet not more rough to see
Than is the hidden ghost that has its home in me."

About her lips there played a smile of almost scorn.
"My friend," she gently said, "you have not heard me mourn;   30
When you my kindred's lives, *my* lost life can restore,
Then may I weep and sue—but never, friend, before!

"Still, let my tyrants know, I am not doomed to wear
Year after year in gloom, and desolate despair;
A messenger of Hope comes every night to me,   35
And offers for short life, eternal liberty.

"He comes with western winds, with evening's wandering airs,
With that clear dusk of heaven that brings the thickest stars,
Winds take a pensive tone, and stars a tender fire,
And visions rise, and change, that kill me with desire.   40

4. Foolish.

"Desire for nothing known in my maturer years,
When Joy grew mad with awe, at counting future tears.
When, if my spirit's sky was full of flashes warm,
I knew not whence they came, from sun or thunderstorm.

"But, first, a hush of peace—a soundless calm descends;   45
The struggle of distress and fierce impatience ends;
Mute music soothes my breast—unuttered harmony,
That I could never dream, till Earth was lost to me.

"Then dawns the Invisible; the Unseen its truth reveals;
My outward sense is gone, my inward essence feels: 50
Its wings are almost free—its home, its harbor found,
Measuring the gulf, it stoops—and dares the final bound.

"Oh! dreadful is the check—intense the agony—
When the ear begins to hear, and the eye begins to see;
When the pulse begins to throb, the brain to think again;   55
The soul to feel the flesh, and the flesh to feel the chain.

"Yet I would lose no sting, would wish no torture less;
The more that anguish racks, the earlier it will bless;
And robed in fires of hell, or bright with heavenly shine,
If it but herald death, the vision is divine!"   60

She ceased to speak, and we, unanswering, turned to go—
We had no further power to work the captive woe:
Her cheek, her gleaming eye, declared that man had given
A sentence, unapproved, and overruled by Heaven.

October 9, 1845   1846

[No coward soul is mine]

No coward soul is mine[5]
No trembler in the world's storm-troubled sphere
I see Heaven's glories shine
And Faith shines equal arming me from Fear

O God within my breast   5
Almighty ever-present Deity
Life, that in me hast rest
As I Undying Life, have power in Thee

Vain are the thousand creeds
That move men's hearts, unutterably vain,   10

5. "The following are the last lines my sister Emily ever wrote" [Charlotte's note].

Worthless as withered weeds
Or idlest froth amid the boundless main

To waken doubt in one
Holding so fast by thy infinity
So surely anchored on   15
The steadfast rock of Immortality

With wide-embracing love
Thy spirit animates eternal years
Pervades and broods above,
Changes, sustains, dissolves, creates and rears   20

Though Earth and moon were gone
And suns and universes ceased to be
And thou wert left alone
Every Existence would exist in thee

There is not room for Death   25
Nor atom that his might could render void
Since thou art Being and Breath
And what thou art may never be destroyed.

January 2, 1846   1850

Stanzas[6]

Often rebuked, yet always back returning
    To those first feelings that were born with me,
And leaving busy chase of wealth and learning
    For idle dreams of things which cannot be:

To-day, I will seek not the shadowy region;[7]   5
    Its unsustaining vastness waxes drear;
And visions rising, legion after legion,
    Bring the unreal world too strangely near.

I'll walk, but not in old heroic traces,[8]
    And not in paths of high morality,   10
And not among the half-distinguished faces,
    The clouded forms of long-past history.

6. As no manuscript exists for this poem, there is
some speculation that Charlotte may have written it instead of Emily; however, the poem
seems to summarize much of Emily's characteristic vision.

7. The shadowy world of the imagination, specifically the private myth of Gondal.
8. Paths or, alternatively, straps that form a harness.

I'll walk where my own nature would be leading:
   It vexes[9] me to choose another guide:
Where the gray flocks in ferny glens are feeding;   15
   Where the wild wind blows on the mountain side.

What have those lonely mountains worth revealing?
   More glory and more grief than I can tell:
The earth that wakes *one* human heart to feeling
   Can centre both the worlds of Heaven and Hell.   20

1850

9. Provokes.

LINDA BRENT
1818–1896

"Slavery is terrible for men; but it is far more terrible for women. Superadded to the burden common to all, *they* have wrongs, and sufferings, and
mortifications peculiarly their own": Linda Brent dramatically documented this
claim in her 1861 autobiography, *Incidents in the Life of a Slave Girl*. From
her description of her sexual harassment by her owner, Dr. Flint, to her account of how she was prevented from marrying, Brent analyzed the wrongs inflicted on slave women. In spite of Victorian taboos against so-called indelicate
subjects, moreover, she also explained why women like her were drawn into
sexual relationships with white men other than their masters ("It seems less degrading to give one's self, than to submit to compulsion"), and the difficulty
these women had in obtaining freedom for their children. Although both the
names and the locations in her narrative are fictitious (to protect the safety of
those who helped her), she deals directly with the racial impact of slave revolts
like the Nat Turner uprising of 1831 and legislation like the Fugitive Slave Act
of 1850, which subjected runaways in the North to deportation back to the
South.

Linda Brent's real name was Harriet Brent Jacobs. She was a mulatto who
lived her first twenty-seven years in slavery. After the death of her parents, she
was nurtured by her maternal grandmother, a freed slave of extraordinary industry and piety. At fifteen years of age, Brent began resisting her owner's efforts at sexual exploitation. Much to Dr. Flint's outrage, she gave birth to a son
and a daughter, both fathered by a white man she calls Mr. Sands, who promised to buy them for her. Much of her narrative is taken up with her efforts to
secure freedom from both Dr. Flint and Mr. Sands for herself and her children.
More than ten years after her escape, she met the white historical novelist and
abolitionist Lydia Maria Child, who introduced and edited Brent's account.
"With trifling exceptions, both the ideas and the language are her own," Child
explained, adding that Brent's first mistress taught her how to read and write.

For both Child and Brent, the publication of *Incidents in the Life of a Slave Girl* was a political effort to help other "sisters in bondage." Our selection has been taken from that point in the narrative when Linda Brent has convinced her owner that she has fled to New York. Actually, after running away to a swamp, where she encountered "large, venomous snakes [that] were less dreadful to my imagination than the white men in that community called civilization," she has hidden out in the same Southern town in which Dr. Flint and Mr. Sands live, at her grandmother's house. Determined to shield herself and her children from harm, she has not revealed to her son or daughter her presence in the house where they, too, are living.

From Incidents in the Life of a Slave Girl

Chapter XXI. The Loophole of Retreat

A small shed had been added to my grandmother's house years ago. Some boards were laid across the joists at the top, and between these boards and the roof was a very small garret, never occupied by any thing but rats and mice. It was a pent roof, covered with nothing but shingles, according to the southern custom for such buildings. The garret was only nine feet long and seven wide. The highest part was three feet high, and sloped down abruptly to the loose board floor. There was no admission for either light or air. My uncle Phillip, who was a carpenter, had very skilfully made a concealed trap-door, which communicated with the storeroom. He had been doing this while I was waiting in the swamp. The storeroom opened upon a piazza. To this hole I was conveyed as soon as I entered the house. The air was stifling; the darkness total. A bed had been spread on the floor. I could sleep quite comfortably on one side; but the slope was so sudden that I could not turn on the other without hitting the roof. The rats and mice ran over my bed; but I was weary, and I slept such sleep as the wretched may, when a tempest has passed over them. Morning came. I knew it only by the noises I heard; for in my small den day and night were all the same. I suffered for air even more than for light. But I was not comfortless. I heard the voices of my children. There was joy and there was sadness in the sound. It made my tears flow. How I longed to speak to them! I was eager to look on their faces; but there was no hole, no crack, through which I could peep. This continued darkness was oppressive. It seemed horrible to sit or lie in a cramped position day after day, without one gleam of light. Yet I would have chosen this, rather than my lot as a slave, though white people considered it an easy one; and it was so compared with the fate of others. I was never cruelly overworked; I was never lacerated with the whip from head to foot; I was never so beaten and bruised that I could not turn from one side to the other; I never had my heel-strings cut to prevent my running away; I was never chained to a log and forced to drag it about, while I toiled in the fields from morning till night; I was never branded with hot iron, or torn by bloodhounds. On the contrary, I had always been kindly treated, and tenderly cared for, until I came into the hands of Dr. Flint.[1] I had never wished for freedom till then. But though my life in slavery was comparatively devoid of hardships, God pity the woman who is compelled to lead such a life!

My food was passed up to me through the trap-door my uncle had contrived; and my grandmother, my uncle Phillip, and aunt Nancy would seize such opportunities as they could, to mount up there and chat with me at the opening. But of course this was not safe in the daytime. It must all be done in darkness. It was impossible for me to move in an erect position, but I crawled about my den for exercise. One day I hit my head against something, and found it was a gimlet. My uncle had left it sticking there when he made the trap-door. I was as rejoiced as Robinson Crusoe[2] could have been at finding such a treasure. It put a lucky thought into my head. I said to myself, "Now I will have some light. Now I will see my children." I did not dare to begin my work during the daytime, for fear of attracting attention. But I groped round; and having found the side next the street, where I could frequently see my children, I stuck the gimlet in and waited for evening. I bored three rows of holes, one above another; then I bored out the interstices between. I thus succeeded in making one hole about an inch long and an inch broad. I sat by it till late into the night, to enjoy the little whiff of air that floated in. In the morning I watched for my children. The first person I saw in the street was Dr. Flint. I had a shuddering, superstitious feeling that it was a bad omen. Several familiar faces passed by. At last I heard the merry laugh of children, and presently two sweet little faces were looking up at me, as though they knew I was there, and were conscious of the joy they imparted. How I longed to *tell* them I was there!

My condition was now a little improved. But for weeks I was tormented by hundreds of little red insects, fine as a needle's point, that pierced through my skin, and produced an intolerable burning. The good grandmother gave me herb teas and cooling medicines, and finally I got rid of them. The heat of my den was intense, for nothing but thin shingles protected me from the scorching summer's sun. But I had my consolations. Through my peeping-hole I could watch the children, and when they were near enough, I could hear their talk. Aunt Nancy brought me all the news she could hear at Dr. Flint's. From her I

1. Brent's owner.
2. Shipwrecked hero of the novel (1719) by Daniel Defoe. "Gimlet": a small tool used for boring.

learned that the doctor had written to New York to a colored woman, who had been born and raised in our neighborhood, and had breathed his contaminating atmosphere. He offered her a reward if she could find out any thing about me. I know not what was the nature of her reply; but he soon after started for New York in haste, saying to his family that he had business of importance to transact. I peeped at him as he passed on his way to the steamboat. It was a satisfaction to have miles of land and water between us, even for a little while; and it was a still greater satisfaction to know that he believed me to be in the Free States. My little den seemed less dreary than it had done. He returned, as he did from his former journey to New York, without obtaining any satisfactory information. When he passed our house next morning, Benny[3] was standing at the gate. He had heard them say that he had gone to find me, and he called out, "Dr. Flint, did you bring my mother home? I want to see her." The doctor stamped his foot at him in a rage, and exclaimed, "Get out of the way, you little damned rascal! If you don't, I'll cut off your head."

Benny ran terrified into the house, saying, "You can't put me in jail again. I don't belong to you now." It was well that the wind carried the words away from the doctor's ear. I told my grandmother of it, when we had our next conference at the trap-door; and begged of her not to allow the children to be impertinent to the irascible old man.

Autumn came, with a pleasant abatement of heat. My eyes had become accustomed to the dim light, and by holding my book or work in a certain position near the aperture I contrived to read and sew. That was a great relief to the tedious monotony of my life. But when winter came, the cold penetrated through the thin shingle roof, and I was dreadfully chilled. The winters there are not so long, or so severe, as in northern latitudes; but the houses are not built to shelter from cold, and my little den was peculiarly comfortless. The kind grandmother brought me bed-clothes and warm drinks. Often I was obliged to lie in bed all day to keep comfortable; but with all my precautions, my shoulders and feet were frostbitten. O, those long, gloomy days, with no object for my eye to rest upon, and no thoughts to occupy my mind, except the dreary past and the uncertain future! I was thankful when there came a day sufficiently mild for me to wrap myself up and sit at the loophole to watch the passers by. Southerners have the habit of stopping and talking in the streets, and I heard many conversations not intended to meet my ears. I heard slave-hunters planning how to catch some poor fugitive. Several times I heard allusions to Dr. Flint, myself, and the history of my children, who, perhaps, were playing near the gate. One would say, "I wouldn't move my little finger to catch her, as old Flint's property,"

3. Her son; her daughter's name is Ellen.

Another would say, "I'll catch *any* nigger for the reward. A man ought
to have what belongs to him, if he *is* a damned brute." The opinion was
often expressed that I was in the Free States. Very rarely did any one
suggest that I might be in the vicinity. Had the least suspicion rested on
my grandmother's house, it would have been burned to the ground.
But it was the last place they thought of. Yet there was no place, where
slavery existed, that could have afforded me so good a place of concealment.

Dr. Flint and his family repeatedly tried to coax and bribe my children to tell something they had heard said about me. One day the doctor took them into a shop, and offered them some bright little silver
pieces and gay handkerchiefs if they would tell where their mother was.
Ellen shrank away from him, and would not speak; but Benny spoke up,
and said, "Dr. Flint, I don't know where my mother is. I guess she's in
New York; and when you go there again, I wish you'd ask her to come
home, for I want to see her; but if you put her in jail, or tell her you'll
cut her head off, I'll tell her to go right back."

From *Chapter XXIX. Preparations for Escape*[4]

I hardly expect that the reader will credit me, when I affirm that I
lived in that little dismal hole, almost deprived of light and air, and with
no space to move my limbs, for nearly seven years. But it is a fact; and to
me a sad one, even now; for my body still suffers from the effects of that
long imprisonment, to say nothing of my soul. Members of my family,
now living in New York and Boston, can testify to the truth of what I
say.

Countless were the nights that I sat late at the little loophole scarcely
large enough to give me a glimpse of one twinkling star. There, I heard
the patrols and slave-hunters conferring together about the capture of
runaways, well knowing how rejoiced they would be to catch me.

Season after season, year after year, I peeped at my children's faces,
and heard their sweet voices, with a heart yearning all the while to say,
"Your mother is here." Sometimes it appeared to me as if ages had
rolled away since I entered upon that gloomy, monotonous existence.
At times, I was stupefied and listless; at other times I became very impatient to know when these dark years would end, and I should again be
allowed to feel the sunshine, and breathe the pure air. * * *

* * * My restlessness increased. I had lived too long in bodily pain
and anguish of spirit. Always I was in dread that by some accident, or
some contrivance, slavery would succeed in snatching my children
from me. This thought drove me nearly frantic, and I determined to

4. In the omitted chapters, Brent reveals herself to her daughter Ellen, who subsequently escapes to
the North.

steer for the North Star[5] at all hazards. At this crisis, Providence opened an unexpected way for me to escape. My friend Peter came one evening, and asked to speak with me. "Your day has come, Linda," said he. "I have found a chance for you to go to the Free States. You have a fortnight to decide." The news seemed too good to be true; but Peter explained his arrangements, and told me all that was necessary was for me to say I would go.[6] * * *

The anticipation of being a free woman proved almost too much for my weak frame. The excitement stimulated me, and at the same time bewildered me. I made busy preparations for my journey, and for my son to follow me. I resolved to have an interview with him before I went, that I might give him cautions and advice, and tell him how anxiously I should be waiting for him at the north. Grandmother stole up to me as often as possible to whisper words of counsel. She insisted upon my writing to Dr. Flint, as soon as I arrived in the Free States, and asking him to sell me to her. She said she would sacrifice her house, and all she had in the world, for the sake of having me safe with my children in any part of the world. If she could only live to know *that* she could die in peace. I promised the dear old faithful friend that I would write to her as soon as I arrived, and put the letter in a safe way to reach her; but in my own mind I resolved that not another cent of her hard earnings should be spent to pay rapacious slave-holders for what they called their property. And even if I had not been unwilling to buy what I had already a right to possess, common humanity would have prevented me from accepting the generous offer, at the expense of turning my aged relative out of house and home, when she was trembling on the brink of the grave.

I was to escape in a vessel; but I forbear to mention any further particulars.[7] * * *

I made all my arrangements to go on board as soon as it was dusk. The intervening time I resolved to spend with my son. I had not spoken to him for seven years, though I had been under the same roof, and seen him every day, when I was well enough to sit at the loophole. I did not dare to venture beyond the storeroom; so they brought him there, and locked us up together, in a place concealed from the piazza door. It was an agitating interview for both of us. After we had talked and wept together for a little while, he said, "Mother, I'm glad you're going away.

5. "This was the only guide of many a fleeing slave, hiding by day and running by night" (note by Walter Teller, editor of our text).
6. In the omitted passage, Brent at first hesitates to escape because of her son, but is persuaded by her uncle Phillip to "seize the chance so unexpectedly offered"; Phillip also tells her grandmother.

7. In the omitted passage, Brent's grandmother is frightened by the murder of another fugitive slave. Brent therefore at first decides to remain with her grandmother and sends her friend Fanny to the ship in her place; Brent is, however, discovered by a neighbor when talking to her grandmother, who now tells her that she must go, too.

I wish I could go with you. I knew you was here; and I have been *so* afraid they would come and catch you!"

I was greatly surprised, and asked him how he had found it out.

He replied, "I was standing under the eaves, one day, before Ellen went away, and I heard somebody cough up over the wood shed. I don't know what made me think it was you, but I did think so. I missed Ellen, the night before she went away; and grandmother brought her back into the room in the night;[8] and I thought maybe she'd been to see *you*, before she went, for I heard grandmother whisper to her, 'Now go to sleep; and remember never to tell.' "

I asked him if he ever mentioned his suspicions to his sister. He said he never did; but after he heard the cough, if he saw her playing with other children on that side of the house, he always tried to coax her round to the other side, for fear they would hear me cough, too. He said he had kept a close lookout for Dr. Flint, and if he saw him speak to a constable, or a patrol, he always told grandmother. I now recollected that I had seen him manifest uneasiness, when people were on that side of the house, and I had at the time been puzzled to conjecture a motive for his actions. Such prudence may seem extraordinary in a boy of twelve years, but slaves, being surrounded by mysteries, deceptions, and dangers, early learn to be suspicious and watchful, and prematurely cautious and cunning. He had never asked a question of grandmother, or uncle Phillip, and I had often heard him chime in with other children, when they spoke of my being at the north.

I told him I was now really going to the Free States, and if he was a good, honest boy, and a loving child to his dear old grandmother, the Lord would bless him, and bring him to me, and we and Ellen would live together. * * *

1861

8. Ellen had spent her last night with her mother.

GEORGE ELIOT
1819–1880

Known as Mary Anne, Mary Ann, and Marian Evans to her family, "Clematis" (meaning mental beauty) to a youthful friend, "Deutera" (which "*means* second and *sounds* a little like daughter") to her first scholarly mentor, Mrs. Lewes to her correspondents, "Our Lady" to the women she considered her spiritual daughters, "Mutter" to her adopted sons, and Mrs. John W. Cross to her eulogists, one of the most celebrated sages of Victorian England was best known to the reading public as "George Eliot." By adopting this name, she paid tribute to the man who nurtured her literary efforts, George Henry Lewes, but she also placed herself in a tradition that goes back to George Sand (Aurore Dupin Dudevant) and the Bells (the Brontës). It was the name "George Eliot" that her readers associated with the blend of compassion, wisdom, and humor that characterizes the omniscient voice of her novels. However, as Ruby Redinger has demonstrated in her recent biography, the very proliferation of feminine names by which Eliot was known dramatizes the problem she had to solve when she began to publish fiction under a male pseudonym at the age of thirty-eight. Although she would eventually attain the appropriate distinction of being represented in the *English Men of Letters* series, Eliot was aware that her identification with masculine achievement threatened to undermine her consciousness of herself as a woman: a talented but embittered female artist in Eliot's last novel exclaims, "You may try, but you cannot imagine what it is to have a man's force of genius in you, yet to suffer the slavery of being a girl." Nevertheless, Eliot's greatest accomplishment may have been her dramatization of just this contradiction.

In Eliot's most autobiographical novel, *The Mill on the Floss* (1860), Maggie Tulliver's acute sense of her own female "slavery" reflects some of the early frustration that resulted in the headaches, depressions, and sensitivity toward cold that Eliot suffered all of her adult life. Maggie's imaginative curiosity earns, from an otherwise affectionate father, the sardonic comment that "an over-'cute [over-acute] woman's no better nor a long-tailed sheep—she'll fetch none the bigger price for that." While Eliot's father was more prosperous as a farmer and agent for a neighboring estate than the miller who is Maggie's father, Robert Evans was just as traditional in his support of the Church of England, the Tory party, and their implicitly conservative assumptions about the appropriate sphere of women. Maggie's mother, Mrs. Tulliver, seems more attached to her son, and even to her monographed linen, than to her daughter, just as Eliot always believed her own mother favored her older brother, Isaac. Similarly, in *The Mill on the Floss*, the sister who is destined never to receive the affection she craves from her brother associates her emotional deprivation with Lucy Dean, the conventionally pretty cousin who is as neat as Maggie is messy, as obedient as Maggie is rebellious; in Eliot's childhood this role was played by her older sister Chrissey. From her depiction of Maggie's angry torturing of her doll to her portrayal of the girl's voracious reading and her running away to become Queen of the Gypsies, Eliot dramatizes the "hunger of the heart" for sympathy it never receives. Maggie's warring impulses—her desire for intellectual stimulation as opposed to her dutiful efforts at renunciation—reflect Eliot's own self-division as well as her awareness of the constraints of provincial life.

Yet looking backward on provincial life remained the motivating impulse and subject of most of Eliot's fiction. Her nostalgia for the everyday scenes of the preindustrial past turned them into "the mother tongue of our imagination," but what she herself humorously portrayed as the shrewd narrow-mindedness of rural characters was precisely what hindered her own development. From the age of five, Eliot attended three different schools, making friends with at least one headmistress, Maria Lewis. From the time she left school at fifteen, when her mother died, until she was thirty, when her father died, however, she was hampered by the household and nursing duties she assiduously performed. At home, she continued to study Italian, German, and music, corresponding frequently with Miss Lewis, who developed an evangelical strain of puritanism in the young girl. Only when Isaac married and she moved with her father from Griff to a house in Coventry did Eliot begin to find acquaintances who would pose challenging philosophic questions to her.

People like Charles Bray, the author of *The Philosophy of Necessity*, and his wife, Caroline (Hennell) Bray, whose brother wrote *An Inquiry concerning the Origins of Christianity*, encouraged Eliot's intellectual development, which issued in a typically Victorian crisis of faith. After a painful struggle, she renounced traditional Christianity, but she could make peace with her father only by promising to accompany him to church on Sundays. During this time, she completed her first major translation, David Friedrich Strauss's *Das Leben Jesu* (*The Life of Jesus*, 1846). Published anonymously, it contributed, as did her other translations, to the belief that animated her subsequent fiction, "that the idea of God, so far as it has been a highly spiritual influence, is the ideal of a goodness entirely human." The struggle with her spiritual Father was an index of her struggle with her own father, whose death evoked contradictory responses: "What shall I be without my father?" Eliot mused during his dying. "It will seem as if part of my moral nature were gone. I had a vision of myself last night becoming earthly sensual and devilish for want of that purifying restraining influence." Retrospectively, however, her comment that his dying days were "the happiest" of her life indicates some intimation that his death meant her release.

After a recuperative trip to Switzerland, Eliot was introduced by the Brays to John Chapman, editor of the *Westminster Review*, and she moved to London, where she worked hard to become a member of the literary establishment. As assistant editor of the *Westminster*, she corresponded and negotiated with authors, read proofs, and wrote reviews of philosophic and religious books. She met such eminent Victorians as Charles Dickens, James Froude, Harriet Martineau, John Stuart Mill, and, most importantly, the philosopher Herbert Spencer. As the biographer Gordon Haight has demonstrated, her earlier propensity to glorify a father figure to whom she could dedicate her labor now meant that she did not receive the credit she deserved for turning the *Westminster* into one of England's leading reviews. Ensconced in Chapman's household, she found herself contending with his jealous wife and mistress. In the presence of Chapman and Spencer, moreover, she became even more acutely self-conscious about what Hallam Tennyson would call her "strong masculine face."

This painful but stimulating period was ended when Spencer introduced Eliot to the writer and editor George Henry Lewes, a married man who had separated from his wife. After they began seeing each other, they made the highly unconventional decision to live together despite the fact that Lewes could not obtain a divorce. Although she faced the censure not only of her brother, Isaac, but also of polite London society, Eliot went off to the Continent in 1854 to begin life with Lewes as an unmarried wife. No wonder, then, that she objected to the plot of *Jane Eyre*, specifically to Jane's refusal to live with the married Rochester: "All self-sacrifice is good," she characteristically

conceded, "but one would like it to be in a somewhat nobler cause than a diabolical law which chains a man body and soul to a putrifying carcass." The
number of those who refused to visit the woman who returned to London calling herself "Marian Lewes" should not be minimized: even so tolerant a writer
as Mrs. Gaskell wrote to her, "I wish you *were* Mrs. Lewes."

By 1856, Eliot was clearly assessing the current state of fiction, specifically
condemning "silly novels" by "lady novelists." In the *Westminster Review*, she
asked, "Why can we not have pictures of religious life among the industrial
classes in England, as interesting as Mrs. Stowe's pictures of religious life
among the Negroes?" Not to be discounted in considering Eliot's late productivity is the intellectual stimulation that Lewes's own work supplied: a versatile
physiologist, biographer, novelist, essayist, and editor, he was the author of a
Biographical History of Philosophy (1854–1856) and an article on *The Lady
Novelists* (1852). It was he who encouraged her to compose and publish her
first stories in *Blackwood's* "Maga," which were collected in *Scenes of Clerical
Life* (1858). Here, as so often, her title was deceptive, for these three stories actually focus on three female characters, a patient but dying wife-mother, a foreign girl goaded into murderous rage by a faithless lover, and a woman who,
having been physically abused by her husband, takes refuge in alcohol.

Lewes had believed that "people would have sniffed" at Eliot's first novel,
Adam Bede (1859), "if they had known the writer to be a woman," and its instant success did place George Eliot in the ranks of major novelists such as
Dickens and Thackeray. Even after her true identity became known, Lewes
continued to protect her career, writing letters for her to publishers, keeping
back unfavorable reviews that would have troubled her, and suggesting certain
scenes for novels in progress. Because Lewes and Eliot had to support themselves and his three sons through their writing, they welcomed the twelve thousand pounds *Adam Bede* brought. *Silas Marner* (1861) was so popular that her
publisher, Blackwood, had to double the original edition of four thousand
copies within a month after publication. By this time Eliot had become a careful
businesswoman who negotiated herself for the seven thousand pounds she received for *Romola* (1863).

How are the private lives of men and women related to the public issues of
culture and society? This question was the recurrent subject of Eliot's mature
novels: *Felix Holt* (1866), *Middlemarch* (1871–1872), and *Daniel Deronda*
(1874–1876). Perhaps *Middlemarch*, with its subtitle, *A Study of Provincial
Life*, best exemplifies Eliot's panoramic range. Set in the 1830s, with its aristocratic landlords and clergymen, its middle-class bankers and doctors, and its
working-class grocers and horse dealers, the novel insists on the complex interrelationships between the sexes and the classes by developing a metaphor of a
web or labyrinth and even by elaborating an image of the multitudinous
scratches on the surface of a pier glass (a mirror): "place now against it a lighted
candle as a centre of illumination, and lo! the scratches will seem to arrange
themselves in a fine series of concentric circles round that little sun." Eliot explained that this "parable" signifies the egoism produced by any single perspective, the "flattering illusion" of a concentric arrangement of events which
both delights and deludes. For her narrator, who studies this "exclusive optical
selection" with patient omniscience, the novel becomes a philosophic study of
domestic incompatibility and religious hypocrisy, political discord and legal in-

trigue. As a composite of the novel's chorus of characters, the narrator maintains a tolerant tone and sympathetic stance which assume that even the most common lives illustrate how "the growing good of the world is partly dependent on unhistoric acts."

Of course the unhistoric acts of Eliot's heroine, Dorothea Brooke, play a central role in *Middlemarch*. As the critic Barbara Hardy has observed, the heroines of all of Eliot's novels share "the *ex-officio* disability of being a woman." For Dorothea, as for the others, this disability is associated with ignorance, the absence of a vocation, and the desire for knowledge "such as great men know." Married to an aging scholar because she wishes to become wise herself in order to do good works, Dorothea discovers not only that she cannot learn from her husband, the author of a projected "Key to All Mythologies," but that he is hardly wise himself. Thus she becomes a "foundress of nothing," for Eliot consistently denied her heroines the worldly success she herself achieved. Yet, through her suffering, Dorothea attains the growth in sympathy which is always an index of ethical maturity in Eliot's world. For a contemporary like Emily Dickinson, Eliot's achievement was monumental: "What do I think of *Middlemarch*? What do I think of glory?" she wrote, adding that "the mysteries of human nature surpass the 'mysteries of redemption.'"

When Lewes died in 1878, Eliot went into mourning. Previously, in times of stress she had relied on a succession of close female friends: Maria Lewis, Sara Hennell, Barbara Smith Bodichon, and Edith Simcox. But if Eliot felt that her pseudonym encoded her special dependency on Lewes ("To L——— I owe it"), then she must have known that no one could take his place and that her writing career was over. Yet, on May 6, 1880, much to her friends' surprise and dismay, Eliot announced her marriage to John Walter Cross. More than twenty years her junior, he had met her in 1867 when he was traveling on the Continent with his mother. The marriage ended seven months after the wedding, when Eliot died. Cross used her letters to write the first and most laudatory of her biographies, but, in spite of his efforts, the next generation of readers considered Eliot's fiction too moralistic, earnest, and diffuse. Women writers from Eliza Linton and Mrs. Oliphant to Katherine Mansfield envied the protection Eliot had received from Lewes, but they distrusted her assumption of masculine superiority. Nevertheless, by integrating philosophy and fiction, Eliot exerted a profound influence on the shape of the novel as it was developed by writers as diverse as Henry James, D. H. Lawrence, and Margaret Drabble.

The following selections represent two different aspects of Eliot's career. *The Lifted Veil* (1859), which appeared anonymously in *Blackwood's*, reflects her reaction to the lifting of her own veil of anonymity when the public was discovering her identity. Eccentric though it is in her *oeuvre*, the tale questions the ideal of sympathetic identification Eliot usually espoused, for, as a surrogate of the author, Latimer experiences nothing but pain from the telepathy that reveals to him the subjectivity of others. *The Lifted Veil* also extends the tradition of female Gothic established in Shelley's *The Mortal Immortal* and Brontë's *Jane Eyre*. *Brother and Sister* represents Eliot as a poet. Written in the period when she composed *The Spanish Gypsy* (1868) and *Armgart* (1871), it explores the same sibling relationship she had placed at the center of her semi-autobiographical *The Mill on the Floss*.

The Lifted Veil

Give me no light, great Heaven, but such as turns
To energy of human fellowship;
No powers beyond the growing heritage
That makes completer manhood.[1]

Chapter I

The time of my end approaches. I have lately been subject to attacks of *angina pectoris*;[2] and in the ordinary course of things, my physician tells me, I may fairly hope that my life will not be protracted many months. Unless, then, I am cursed with an exceptional physical constitution, as I am cursed with an exceptional mental character, I shall not much longer groan under the wearisome burden of this earthly existence. If it were to be otherwise,—if I were to live on to the age most men desire and provide for,—I should for once have known whether the miseries of delusive expectation can outweigh the miseries of true prevision. For I foresee when I shall die, and everything that will happen in my last moments.

Just a month from this day, on the 20th of September, 1850, I shall be sitting in this chair, in this study, at ten o'clock at night, longing to die, weary of incessant insight and foresight, without delusions and without hope. Just as I am watching a tongue of blue flame rising in the fire, and my lamp is burning low, the horrible contraction will begin at my chest. I shall only have time to reach the bell, and pull it violently, before the sense of suffocation will come. No one will answer my bell. I know why. My two servants are lovers, and will have quarrelled. My housekeeper will have rushed out of the house in a fury, two hours before, hoping that Perry will believe she has gone to drown herself. Perry is alarmed at last, and is gone out after her. The little scullery-maid is asleep on a bench: she never answers the bell; it does not wake her. The sense of suffocation increases: my lamp goes out with a horrible stench: I make a great effort, and snatch at the bell again. I long for life, and there is no help. I thirsted for the unknown: the thirst is gone. O God, let me stay with the known, and be weary of it: I am content. Agony of pain and suffocation,—and all the while the earth, the fields, the pebbly brook at the bottom of the rookery,[3] the fresh scent after the rain, the light of the morning through my chamber-window, the warmth of the hearth after the frosty air,—will darkness close over them forever?

Darkness,—darkness,—no pain,—nothing but darkness: but I am passing on and on through the darkness: my thought stays in the darkness, but always with a sense of moving onward. . . .

1. The epigraph is by Eliot.
2. A painful heart disease.

3. A nest of rooks or ravens.

Before that time comes, I wish to use my last hours of ease and strength in telling the strange story of my experience. I have never fully unbosomed myself to any human being; I have never been encouraged to trust much in the sympathy of my fellow-men. But we have all a chance of meeting with some pity, some tenderness, some charity, when we are dead: it is the living only who cannot be forgiven,—the living only from whom men's indulgence and reverence are held off, like the rain by the hard east wind. While the heart beats, bruise it,—it is your only opportunity; while the eye can still turn towards you with moist timid entreaty, freeze it with an icy unanswering gaze; while the ear, that delicate messenger to the inmost sanctuary of the soul, can still take in the tones of kindness, put it off with hard civility, or sneering compliment, or envious affectation of indifference; while the creative brain can still throb with the sense of injustice, with the yearning for brotherly recognition,—make haste,—oppress it with your ill-considered judgments, your trivial comparisons, your careless misrepresentations. The heart will by and by be still,—*ubi sæva indignatio ulterius cor lacerare nequit;*[4] the eye will cease to entreat; the ear will be deaf; the brain will have ceased from all wants as well as from all work. Then your charitable speeches may find vent; then you may remember and pity the toil and the struggle and the failure; then you may give due honour to the work achieved; then you may find extenuation for errors, and may consent to bury them.

That is a trivial schoolboy text; why do I dwell on it? It has little reference to me, for I shall leave no works behind me for men to honour. I have no near relatives who will make up, by weeping over my grave, for the wounds they inflicted on me when I was among them. It is only the story of my life that will perhaps win a little more sympathy from strangers when I am dead, than I ever believed it would obtain from my friends while I was living.

My childhood perhaps seems happier to me than it really was, by contrast with all the after-years. For then the curtain of the future was as impenetrable to me as to other children: I had all their delight in the present hour, their sweet indefinite hopes for the morrow; and I had a tender mother: even now, after the dreary lapse of long years, a slight trace of sensation accompanies the remembrance of her caress as she held me on her knee,—her arms round my little body, her cheek pressed on mine. I had a complaint of the eyes that made me blind for a little while, and she kept me on her knee from morning till night. That unequalled love soon vanished out of my life, and even to my childish consciousness it was as if that life had become more chill. I rode my lit-

---

4. "Inscription on Swift's tombstone" [Eliot's note]: "Where fierce indignation can no longer tear his heart."

tle white pony with the groom by my side as before, but there were no loving eyes looking at me as I mounted, no glad arms opened to me when I came back. Perhaps I missed my mother's love more than most children of seven or eight would have done, to whom the other pleasures of life remained as before; for I was certainly a very sensitive child. I remember still the mingled trepidation and delicious excitement with which I was affected by the tramping of the horses on the pavement in the echoing stables, by the loud resonance of the grooms' voices, by the booming bark of the dogs as my father's carriage thundered under the archway of the courtyard, by the din of the gong as it gave notice of luncheon and dinner. The measured tramp of soldiery which I sometimes heard—for my father's house lay near a country town where there were large barracks—made me sob and tremble; and yet when they were gone past, I longed for them to come back again.

I fancy my father thought me an odd child, and had little fondness for me; though he was very careful in fulfilling what he regarded as a parent's duties. But he was already past the middle of life, and I was not his only son. My mother had been his second wife, and he was five-and-forty when he married her. He was a firm, unbending, intensely orderly man, in root and stem a banker, but with a flourishing graft[5] of the active landholder, aspiring to county influence: one of those people who are always like themselves from day to day, who are uninfluenced by the weather, and neither know melancholy nor high spirits. I held him in great awe, and appeared more timid and sensitive in his presence than at other times; a circumstance which, perhaps, helped to confirm him in the intention to educate me on a different plan from the prescriptive one with which he had complied in the case of my elder brother, already a tall youth at Eton.[6] My brother was to be his representative and successor; he must go to Eton and Oxford, for the sake of making connections, of course: my father was not a man to underrate the bearing of Latin satirists or Greek dramatists on the attainment of an aristocratic position. But, intrinsically, he had slight esteem for "those dead but sceptred spirits;" having qualified himself for forming an independent opinion by reading Potter's "Æschylus," and dipping into Francis's "Horace."[7] To this negative view he added a positive one, derived from a recent connection with mining speculations; namely, that a scientific education was the really useful training for a younger son. Moreover, it was clear that a shy, sensitive boy like me was not fit to encounter the rough experience of a public school. Mr. Letherall had said so very decidedly. Mr. Letherall was a large man in spectacles, who one day took my small head between his large hands, and

5. Part of a plant that has been attached to another plant of a different species.
6. Famous English private school.

7. English translations of the Greek tragedian and Latin poet.

pressed it here and there in an exploratory, suspicious manner,—then placed each of his great thumbs on my temples, and pushed me a little way from him, and stared at me with glittering spectacles. The contemplation appeared to displease him, for he frowned sternly, and said to my father, drawing his thumbs across my eyebrows,—

"The deficiency is there, sir,—there; and here," he added, touching the upper sides of my head,—"here is the excess. That must be brought out, sir, and this must be laid to sleep."[8]

I was in a state of tremor, partly at the vague idea that I was the object of reprobation, partly in the agitation of my first hatred,—hatred of this big, spectacled man, who pulled my head about as if he wanted to buy and cheapen it.

I am not aware how much Mr. Letherall had to do with the system afterwards adopted towards me, but it was presently clear that private tutors, natural history, science, and the modern languages were the appliances by which the defects of my organization were to be remedied. I was very stupid about machines, so I was to be greatly occupied with them; I had no memory for classification, so it was particularly necessary that I should study systematic zoölogy and botany; I was hungry for human deeds and human emotions, so I was to be plentifully crammed with the mechanical powers, the elementary bodies, and the phenomena of electricity and magnetism. A better-constituted boy would certainly have profited under my intelligent tutors, with their scientific apparatus; and would, doubtless, have found the phenomena of electricity and magnetism as fascinating as I was, every Thursday, assured they were. As it was, I could have paired off, for ignorance of whatever was taught me, with the worst Latin scholar that was ever turned out of a classical academy. I read Plutarch, and Shakespeare, and Don Quixote[9] by the sly, and supplied myself in that way with wandering thoughts, while my tutor was assuring me that "an improved man, as distinguished from an ignorant one, was a man who knew the reason why water ran down-hill." I had no desire to be this improved man; I was glad of the running water; I could watch it and listen to it gurgling among the pebbles, and bathing the bright green water-plants, by the hour together. I did not want to know *why* it ran; I had perfect confidence that there were good reasons for what was so very beautiful.

There is no need to dwell on this part of my life. I have said enough to indicate that my nature was of the sensitive, unpractical order, and that it grew up in an uncongenial medium, which could never foster it into happy, healthy development. When I was sixteen I was sent to

8. Letherall is practicing the "science" of phrenology, much in vogue in the later nineteenth century, according to which a person's mental character could be determined by the shape of his skull.
9. Plutarch was a Greek historian and biographer; *Don Quixote* is the comic novel by Cervantes.

Geneva[1] to complete my course of education; and the change was a very happy one to me, for the first sight of the Alps, with the setting sun on them, as we descended the Jura,[2] seemed to me like an entrance into heaven; and the three years of my life there were spent in a perpetual sense of exaltation, as if from a draught of delicious wine, at the presence of Nature in all her awful loveliness. You will think, perhaps, that I must have been a poet, from this early sensibility[3] to Nature. But my lot was not so happy as that. A poet pours forth his song and *believes* in the listening ear and answering soul, to which his song will be floated sooner or later. But the poet's sensibility without his voice,—the poet's sensibility that finds no vent but in silent tears on the sunny bank, when the noonday light sparkles on the water or in an inward shudder at the sound of harsh human tones, the sight of a cold human eye,—this dumb passion brings with it a fatal solitude of soul in the society of one's fellow-men. My least solitary moments were those in which I pushed off in my boat, at evening, towards the centre of the lake; it seemed to me that the sky, and the glowing mountain-tops, and the wide blue water surrounded me with a cherishing love such as no human face had shed on me since my mother's love had vanished out of my life. I used to do as Jean Jacques[4] did,—lie down in my boat and let it glide where it would, while I looked up at the departing glow leaving one mountain-top after the other, as if the prophet's chariot of fire[5] were passing over them on its way to the home of light. Then, when the white summits were all sad and corpse-like, I had to push homeward, for I was under careful surveillance, and was allowed no late wanderings. This disposition of mine was not favourable to the formation of intimate friendships among the numerous youths of my own age who are always to be found studying at Geneva. Yet I made *one* such friendship; and, singularly enough, it was with a youth whose intellectual tendencies were the very reverse of my own. I shall call him Charles Meunier; his real surname —an English one, for he was of English extraction—having since become celebrated. He was an orphan, who lived on a miserable pittance while he pursued the medical studies for which he had a special genius. Strange! that with my vague mind, susceptible and unobservant, hating inquiry and given up to contemplation, I should have been drawn towards a youth whose strongest passion was science. But the bond was not an intellectual one; it came from a source that can happily blend the stupid with the brilliant, the dreamy with the practical: it came from community of feeling. Charles was poor and ugly, derided by Genevese

1. A city in Switzerland known for its fine schools.
2. A mountain rante in Germany.
3. I.e., sensitivity. "Awful": awe-inspiring.
4. Jean Jacques Rousseau (1712–1778),

French philosopher who believed in the goodness of nature.
5. The prophet Elijah was carried into heaven on a flaming chariot (2 Kings 2).

gamins,[6] and not acceptable in drawing-rooms. I saw that he was isolated, as I was, though from a different cause, and, stimulated by a sympathetic resentment, I made timid advances towards him. It is enough
to say that there sprang up as much comradeship between us as our different habits would allow; and in Charles's rare holidays we went up the
Salève together, or took the boat to Vevey, while I listened dreamily to
the monologues in which he unfolded his bold conceptions of future
experiment and discovery. I mingled them confusedly in my thought
with glimpses of blue water and delicate floating cloud, with the notes
of birds and the distant glitter of the glacier. He knew quite well that my
mind was half absent, yet he liked to talk to me in this way; for don't we
talk of our hopes and our projects even to dogs and birds, when they
love us? I have mentioned this one friendship because of its connection
with a strange and terrible scene which I shall have to narrate in my
subsequent life.

This happier life at Geneva was put an end to by a severe illness,
which is partly a blank to me, partly a time of dimly remembered suffering, with the presence of my father by my bed from time to time. Then
came the languid monotony of convalescence, the days gradually
breaking into variety and distinctness as my strength enabled me to take
longer and longer drives. On one of these more vividly remembered
days, my father said to me, as he sat beside my sofa,—

"When you are quite well enough to travel, Latimer, I shall take you
home with me. The journey will amuse you and do you good, for I shall
go through the Tyrol and Austria, and you will see many new places.
Our neighbours, the Filmores, are come; Alfred will join us at Basle,
and we shall all go together to Vienna, and back by Prague—"

My father was called away before he had finished his sentence, and
he left my mind resting on the word *Prague*, with a strange sense that a
new and wondrous scene was breaking upon me: a city under the broad
sunshine, that seemed to me as if it were the summer sunshine of a
long-past century arrested in its course,—unrefreshed for ages by the
dews of night or the rushing rain-cloud; scorching the dusty, weary,
time-eaten grandeur of a people doomed to live on in the stale repetition of memories, like deposed and superannuated kings in their regal
gold-inwoven tatters. The city looked so thirsty that the broad river
seemed to me a sheet of metal; and the blackened statues, as I passed
under their blank gaze, along the unending bridge, with their ancient
garments and their saintly crowns, seemed to me the real inhabitants
and owners of this place, while the busy, trivial men and women, hurrying to and fro, were a swarm of ephemeral visitants infesting it for a
day. It is such grim, stony beings as these, I thought, who are the fathers

6. Street urchins.

of ancient faded children, in those tanned time-fretted dwellings that crowd the steep before me; who pay their court in the worn and crumbling pomp of the palace which stretches its monotonous length on the height; who worship wearily in the stifling air of the churches, urged by no fear or hope, but compelled by their doom to be ever old and undying, to live on in the rigidity of habit, as they live on in perpetual midday, without the repose of night or the new birth of morning.

A stunning clang of metal suddenly thrilled through me, and I became conscious of the objects in my room again: one of the fire-irons had fallen as Pierre opened the door to bring me my draught.[7] My heart was palpitating violently, and I begged Pierre to leave my draught beside me; I would take it presently.

As soon as I was alone again, I began to ask myself whether I had been sleeping. Was this a dream,—this wonderfully distinct vision,—minute in its distinctness down to a patch of rainbow light on the pavement, transmitted through a coloured lamp in the shape of a star,—of a strange city, quite unfamiliar to my imagination? I had seen no picture of Prague: it lay in my mind as a mere name, with vaguely remembered historical associations,—ill-defined memories of imperial grandeur and religious wars.

Nothing of this sort had ever occurred in my dreaming experience before, for I had often been humiliated because my dreams were only saved from being utterly disjointed and commonplace by the frequent terrors of nightmare. But I could not believe that I had been asleep, for I remembered distinctly the gradual breaking-in of the vision upon me, like the new images in a dissolving view, or the growing distinctness of the landscape as the sun lifts up the veil of the morning mist. And while I was conscious of this incipient vision, I was also conscious that Pierre came to tell my father Mr. Filmore was waiting for him, and that my father hurried out of the room. No, it was not a dream; was it,—the thought was full of tremulous exultation,—was it the poet's nature in me, hitherto only a troubled yearning sensibility, now manifesting itself suddenly as spontaneous creation? Surely it was in this way that Homer saw the plain of Troy, that Dante saw the abodes of the departed, that Milton saw the earthward flight of the Tempter.[8] Was it that my illness had wrought some happy change in my organization,—given a firmer tension to my nerves,—carried off some dull obstruction? I had often read of such effects,—in works of fiction at least. Nay; in genuine biographies I had read of the subtilizing or exalting influence of some diseases on the mental powers. Did not Novalis[9] feel his inspiration intensified under the progress of consumption?

---

7. Drink.
8. In the *Iliad*, the *Divine Comedy*, and *Para-* *dise Lost* respectively.
9. German Romantic poet (1772–1801).

When my mind had dwelt for some time on this blissful idea, it seemed to me that I might perhaps test it by an exertion of my will. The vision had begun when my father was speaking of our going to Prague. I did not for a moment believe it was really a representation of that city; I believed—I hoped it was a picture that my newly liberated genius had painted in fiery haste, with the colours snatched from lazy memory. Suppose I were to fix my mind on some other place,—Venice, for example, which was far more familiar to my imagination than Prague: perhaps the same sort of result would follow. I concentrated my thoughts on Venice; I stimulated my imagination with poetic memories, and strove to feel myself present in Venice, as I had felt myself present in Prague. But in vain. I was only colouring the Canaletto[1] engravings that hung in my old bedroom at home; the picture was a shifting one, my mind wandering uncertainly in search of more vivid images; I could see no accident of form or shadow without conscious labour after the necessary conditions. It was all prosaic effort, not rapt passivity, such as I had experienced half an hour before. I was discouraged; but I remembered that inspiration was fitful.

For several days I was in a state of excited expectation, watching for a recurrence of my new gift. I sent my thoughts ranging over my world of knowledge, in the hope that they would find some object which would send a reawakening vibration through my slumbering genius. But no; my world remained as dim as ever, and that flash of strange light refused to come again, though I watched for it with palpitating eagerness.

My father accompanied me every day in a drive, and a gradually lengthening walk as my powers of walking increased; and one evening he had agreed to come and fetch me at twelve the next day, that we might go together to select a musical box, and other purchases rigorously demanded of a rich Englishman visiting Geneva. He was one of the most punctual of men and bankers, and I was always nervously anxious to be quite ready for him at the appointed time. But, to my surprise, at a quarter past twelve he had not appeared. I felt all the impatience of a convalescent who has nothing particular to do, and who has just taken a tonic[2] in the prospect of immediate exercise that would carry off the stimulus.

Unable to sit still and reserve my strength, I walked up and down the room, looking out on the current of the Rhone, just where it leaves the dark-blue lake; but thinking all the while of the possible causes that could detain my father.

Suddenly I was conscious that my father was in the room, but not alone: there were two persons with him. Strange! I had heard no footstep, I had not seen the door open; but I saw my father, and at his right

1. Venetian painter (1697–1768).   2. An invigorating drug.

hand our neighbour Mrs. Filmore, whom I remembered very well, though I had not seen her for five years. She was a commonplace middle-aged woman, in silk and cashmere; but the lady on the left of my father was not more than twenty, a tall, slim, willowy figure, with luxuriant blond hair, arranged in cunning braids and folds that looked almost too massive for the slight figure and the small-featured, thin-lipped face they crowned. But the face had not a girlish expression: the features were sharp, the pale gray eyes at once acute, restless, and sarcastic. They were fixed on me in half-smiling curiosity, and I felt a painful sensation as if a sharp wind were cutting me. The pale-green dress, and the green leaves that seemed to form a border about her pale blond hair, made me think of a Water-Nixie[3]—for my mind was full of German lyrics, and this pale, fatal-eyed woman, with the green weeds, looked like a birth from some cold sedgy stream, the daughter of an aged river.

"Well, Latimer, you thought me long," my father said. . . .

But while the last word was in my ears, the whole group vanished, and there was nothing between me and the Chinese painted folding-screen that stood before the door. I was cold and trembling; I could only totter forward and throw myself on the sofa. This strange new power had manifested itself again. . . . But *was* it a power? Might it not rather be a disease,—a sort of intermittent delirium, concentrating my energy of brain into moments of unhealthy activity, and leaving my saner hours all the more barren? I felt a dizzy sense of unreality in what my eye rested on; I grasped the bell convulsively, like one trying to free himself from nightmare, and rang it twice. Pierre came with a look of alarm in his face.

"Monsieur ne se trouve pas bien?"[4] he said anxiously.

"I'm tired of waiting, Pierre," I said, as distinctly and emphatically as I could, like a man determined to be sober in spite of wine; "I'm afraid something has happened to my father,—he's usually so punctual. Run to the Hôtel des Bergues and see if he is there."

Pierre left the room at once, with a soothing "Bien, Monsieur;" and I felt the better for this scene of simple, waking prose. Seeking to calm myself still further, I went into my bedroom, adjoining the *salon*, and opened a case of eau-de-Cologne; took out a bottle; went through the process of taking out the cork very neatly, and then rubbed the reviving spirit over my hands and forehead, and under my nostrils, drawing a new delight from the scent because I had procured it by slow details of labour, and by no strange sudden madness. Already I had begun to taste something of the horror that belongs to the lot of a human being whose nature is not adjusted to simple human conditions.

3. A nymph who inhabits rivers.   4. "Monsieur is not well?"

Still enjoying the scent, I returned to the *salon*, but it was not unoccupied, as it had been before I left it. In front of the Chinese folding-screen there was my father, with Mrs. Filmore on his right hand, and on his left, the slim blond-haired girl, with the keen face and the keen eyes fixed on me in half-smiling curiosity.

"Well, Latimer, you thought me long," my father said. . . .

I heard no more, felt no more, till I became conscious that I was lying with my head low on the sofa, Pierre and my father by my side. As soon as I was thoroughly revived, my father left the room, and presently returned, saying,—

"I've been to tell the ladies how you are, Latimer. They were waiting in the next room. We shall put off our shopping expedition to-day."

Presently he said, "That young lady is Bertha Grant, Mrs. Filmore's orphan niece. Filmore has adopted her, and she lives with them, so you will have her for a neighbour when we go home,—perhaps for a near relation; for there is a tenderness between her and Alfred, I suspect, and I should be gratified by the match, since Filmore means to provide for her in every way as if she were his daughter. It had not occurred to me that you knew nothing about her living with the Filmores."

He made no further allusion to the fact of my having fainted at the moment of seeing her, and I would not for the world have told him the reason: I shrank from the idea of disclosing to any one what might be regarded as a pitiable peculiarity, most of all from betraying it to my father, who would have suspected my sanity ever after.

I do not mean to dwell with particularity on the details of my experience. I have described these two cases at length, because they had definite, clearly traceable results in my after-lot.

Shortly after this last occurrence—I think the very next day—I began to be aware of a phase in my abnormal sensibility, to which, from the languid and slight nature of my intercourse with others since my illness, I had not been alive before. This was the obtrusion on my mind of the mental process going forward in first one person, and then another, with whom I happened to be in contact: the vagrant, frivolous ideas and emotions of some uninteresting acquaintance—Mrs. Filmore, for example—would force themselves on my consciousness like an importunate, ill-played musical instrument, or the loud activity of an imprisoned insect. But this unpleasant sensibility was fitful, and left me moments of rest, when the souls of my companions were once more shut out from me, and I felt a relief such as silence brings to wearied nerves. I might have believed this importunate insight to be merely a diseased activity of the imagination, but that my prevision of incalculable words and actions proved it to have a fixed relation to the mental process in other minds. But this superadded consciousness, wearying and annoying enough when it urged on me the trivial experience of indifferent people, became an intense pain and grief when it seemed to be opening to me the souls of those who were in a close relation to me,— when the rational talk, the graceful attentions, the wittily turned phrases, and the kindly deeds, which used to make the web of their characters, were seen as if thrust asunder by a microscopic vision, that showed all the intermediate frivolities, all the suppressed egoism, all the struggling chaos of puerilities, meanness, vague capricious memories, and indolent make-shift thoughts, from which human words and deeds emerge like leaflets[5] covering a fermenting heap.

At Basle we were joined by my brother Alfred, now a handsome self-confident man of six-and-twenty,—a thorough contrast to my fragile, nervous, ineffectual self. I believe I was held to have a sort of half-womanish, half-ghostly beauty; for the portrait-painters, who are thick as weeds at Geneva, had often asked me to sit to them, and I had been the model of a dying minstrel in a fancy picture. But I thoroughly disliked my own *physique*, and nothing but the belief that it was a condition of poetic genius would have reconciled me to it. That brief hope was quite fled, and I saw in my face now nothing but the stamp of a morbid organization, framed for passive suffering,—too feeble for the sublime resistance of poetic production. Alfred, from whom I had been almost constantly separated, and who, in his present stage of character and appearance, came before me as a perfect stranger, was bent on being extremely friendly and brother-like to me. He had the superficial kindness of a good-humoured, self-satisfied nature, that fears no rivalry, and has encountered no contrarieties. I am not sure that my disposition was good enough for me to have been quite free from envy towards him, even if our desires had not clashed, and if I had been in the healthy human condition which admits of generous confidence and charitable construction.[6] There must always have been an antipathy between our natures. As it was, he became in a few weeks an object of intense hatred to me; and when he entered the room, still more when he spoke, it was as if a sensation of grating metal had set my teeth on edge. My diseased consciousness was more intensely and continually occupied with his thoughts and emotions than with those of any other person who came in my way. I was perpetually exasperated with the petty promptings of his conceit and his love of patronage, with his self-complacent belief in Bertha Grant's passion for him, with his half-pitying contempt for me —seen not in the ordinary indications of intonation and phrase and slight action, which an acute and suspicious mind is on the watch for, but in all their naked skinless complication.

For we were rivals, and our desires clashed, though he was not aware of it. I have said nothing yet of the effect Bertha Grant produced in me

5. Small leaves.   6. Interpretation.

on a nearer acquaintance. That effect was chiefly determined by the fact that she made the only exception, among all the human beings about me, to my unhappy gift of insight. About Bertha I was always in a state of uncertainty: I could watch the expression of her face, and speculate on its meaning; I could ask for her opinion with the real interest of ignorance; I could listen for her words and watch for her smile with hope and fear: she had for me the fascination of an unravelled destiny. I say it was this fact that chiefly determined the strong effect she produced on me: for, in the abstract, no womanly character could seem to have less affinity for that of a shrinking, romantic, passionate youth than Bertha's. She was keen, sarcastic, unimaginative, prematurely cynical, remaining critical and unmoved in the most impressive scenes, inclined to dissect all my favourite poems, and especially contemptuous towards the German lyrics which were my pet literature at that time. To this moment I am unable to define my feeling towards her: it was not ordinary boyish admiration, for she was the very opposite, even to the colour of her hair, of the ideal woman who still remained to me the type[7] of loveliness; and she was without that enthusiasm for the great and good, which, even at the moment of her strongest dominion over me, I should have declared to be the highest element of character. But there is no tyranny more complete than that which a self-centred negative nature exercises over a morbidly sensitive nature perpetually craving sympathy and support. The most independent people feel the effect of a man's silence in heightening their value for his opinion,—feel an additional triumph in conquering the reverence of a critic habitually captious and satirical: no wonder, then, that an enthusiastic self-distrusting youth should watch and wait before the closed secret of a sarcastic woman's face, as if it were the shrine of the doubtfully benignant deity who ruled his destiny. For a young enthusiast is unable to imagine the total negation in another mind of the emotions which are stirring his own: they may be feeble, latent, inactive, he thinks, but they are there, —they may be called forth; sometimes, in moments of happy hallucination, he believes they may be there in all the greater strength because he sees no outward sign of them. And this effect, as I have intimated, was heightened to its utmost intensity in me, because Bertha was the only being who remained for me in the mysterious seclusion of soul that renders such youthful delusion possible. Doubtless there was another sort of fascination at work,—that subtle physical attraction which delights in cheating our psychological predictions, and in compelling the men who paint sylphs to fall in love with some *bonne et brave femme*,[8] heavy-heeled and freckled.

7. Standard, ideal.
8. Good and hearty woman. "Sylphs": slender, airy creatures.

Bertha's behaviour towards me was such as to encourage all my illusions, to heighten my boyish passion, and make me more and more dependent on her smiles. Looking back with my present wretched knowledge, I conclude that her vanity and love of power were intensely gratified by the belief that I had fainted on first seeing her purely from the strong impression her person had produced on me. The most prosaic woman likes to believe herself the object of a violent, a poetic passion; and without a grain of romance in her, Bertha had that spirit of intrigue which gave piquancy to the idea that the brother of the man she meant to marry was dying with love and jealousy for her sake. That she meant to marry my brother was what at that time I did not believe; for though he was assiduous in his attentions to her, and I knew well enough that both he and my father had made up their minds to this result, there was not yet an understood engagement,—there had been no explicit declaration; and Bertha habitually, while she flirted with my brother, and accepted his homage in a way that implied to him a thorough recognition of its intention, made me believe, by the subtlest looks and phrases,—feminine nothings which could never be quoted against her,—that he was really the object of her secret ridicule; that she thought him, as I did, a coxcomb,[9] whom she would have pleasure in disappointing. Me she openly petted in my brother's presence, as if I were too young and sickly ever to be thought of as a lover; and that was the view he took of me. But I believe she must inwardly have delighted in the tremors into which she threw me by the coaxing way in which she patted my curls, while she laughed at my quotations. Such caresses were always given in the presence of our friends; for when we were alone together, she affected a much greater distance towards me, and now and then took the opportunity, by words or slight actions, to stimulate my foolish timid hope that she really preferred me. And why should she not follow her inclination? I was not in so advantageous a position as my brother, but I had fortune, I was not a year younger than she was, and she was an heiress, who would soon be of age to decide for herself.

The fluctuations of hope and fear, confined to this one channel, made each day in her presence a delicious torment. There was one deliberate act of hers which especially helped to intoxicate me. When we were at Vienna her twentieth birthday occurred, and as she was very fond of ornaments, we all took the opportunity of the splendid jewellers' shops in that Teutonic Paris to purchase her a birthday present of jewelry. Mine, naturally, was the least expensive; it was an opal ring, —the opal was my favourite stone, because it seems to blush and turn pale as if it had a soul. I told Bertha so when I gave it her, and said that it was an emblem of the poetic nature, changing with the changing light

9. A conceited young man.

of heaven and of woman's eyes. In the evening she appeared elegantly dressed, and wearing conspicuously all the birthday presents except mine. I looked eagerly at her fingers, but saw no opal. I had no opportunity of noticing this to her during the evening; but the next day, when I found her seated near the window alone, after breakfast, I said: "You scorn to wear my poor opal. I should have remembered that you despised poetic natures, and should have given you coral, or turquoise, or some other opaque unresponsive stone." "Do I despise it?" she answered, taking hold of a delicate gold chain which she always wore round her neck and drawing out the end from her bosom with my ring hanging to it; "it hurts me a little, I can tell you," she said, with her usual dubious smile, "to wear it in that secret place; and since your poetical nature is so stupid as to prefer a more public position, I shall not endure the pain any longer."

She took off the ring from the chain and put it on her finger, smiling still, while the blood rushed to my cheeks, and I could not trust myself to say a word of entreaty that she would keep the ring where it was before.

I was completely fooled by this, and for two days shut myself up in my own room whenever Bertha was absent, that I might intoxicate myself afresh with the thought of this scene and all it implied.

I should mention that during these two months,—which seemed a long life to me from the novelty and intensity of the pleasures and pains I underwent,—my diseased participation in other people's consciousness continued to torment me; now it was my father, and now my brother, now Mrs. Filmore or her husband, and now our German courier, whose stream of thought rushed upon me like a ringing in the ears not to be got rid of, though it allowed my own impulses and ideas to continue their uninterrupted course. It was like a preternaturally heightened sense of hearing, making audible to one a roar of sound where others find perfect stillness. The weariness and disgust of this involuntary intrusion into other souls was counteracted only by my ignorance of Bertha, and my growing passion for her,—a passion enormously stimulated, if not produced, by that ignorance. She was my oasis of mystery in the dreary desert of knowledge. I had never allowed my diseased condition to betray itself, or to drive me into any unusual speech or action, except once, when, in a moment of peculiar bitterness against my brother, I had forestalled some words which I knew he was going to utter,—a clever observation, which he had prepared beforehand. He had occasionally a slightly affected hesitation in his speech, and when he paused an instant after the second word, my impatience and jealousy impelled me to continue the speech for him, as if it were something we had both learned by rote. He coloured and looked astonished, as well as annoyed; and the words had no sooner escaped my lips than I felt a shock of alarm lest such an anticipation of words—very far from being words of course, easy to divine—should have betrayed me as an exceptional being, a sort of quiet energumen,[1] whom every one, Bertha above all, would shudder at and avoid. But I magnified, as usual, the impression any word or deed of mine could produce on others; for no one gave any sign of having noticed my interruption as more than a rudeness, to be forgiven me on the score of my feeble nervous condition.

While this superadded consciousness of the actual was almost constant with me, I had never had a recurrence of that distinct prevision which I have described in relation to my first interview with Bertha; and I was waiting with eager curiosity to know whether or not my vision of Prague would prove to have been an instance of the same kind. A few days after the incident of the opal ring, we were paying one of our frequent visits to the Lichtenberg Palace. I could never look at many pictures in succession; for pictures, when they are at all powerful, affect me so strongly that one or two exhaust all my capability of contemplation. This morning I had been looking at Giorgione's picture of the cruel-eyed woman, said to be a likeness of Lucrezia Borgia.[2] I had stood long alone before it, fascinated by the terrible reality of that cunning, relentless face, till I felt a strange poisoned sensation, as if I had long been inhaling a fatal odour, and was just beginning to be conscious of its effects. Perhaps even then I should not have moved away, if the rest of the party had not returned to this room, and announced that they were going to the Belvedere Gallery to settle a bet which had arisen between my brother and Mr. Filmore about a portrait. I followed them dreamily, and was hardly alive to what occurred till they had all gone up to the gallery, leaving me below; for I refused to come within sight of another picture that day. I made my way to the Grand Terrace, since it was agreed that we should saunter in the gardens when the dispute had been decided. I had been sitting here a short space, vaguely conscious of trim gardens, with a city and green hills in the distance, when, wishing to avoid the proximity of the sentinel, I rose and walked down the broad stone steps, intending to seat myself farther on in the gardens. Just as I reached the gravel-walk, I felt an arm slipped within mine, and a light hand gently pressing my wrist. In the same instant a strange intoxicating numbness passed over me, like the continuance or climax of the sensation I was still feeling from the gaze of Lucrezia Borgia. The gardens, the summer sky, the consciousness of Bertha's arm being within mine, all vanished, and I seemed to be suddenly in darkness, out of which there gradually broke a dim firelight, and I felt myself sitting in

1. One who is possessed by a devil.
2. Lucretia Borgia (1480–1519), daughter of a family of Italian nobles, was reputed to be vicious and wanton in her treatment of others. Giorgione: Italian painter (1478–1511).

my father's leather chair in the library at home. I knew the fireplace,—
the dogs for the wood-fire,—the black marble chimney-piece with the
white marble medallion of the dying Cleopatra[3] in the centre. Intense
and hopeless misery was pressing on my soul; the light became
stronger, for Bertha was entering with a candle in her hand,—Bertha,
my wife,—with cruel eyes, with green jewels and green leaves on her
white ball-dress; every hateful thought within her present to me. . . .
"Madman, idiot! why don't you kill yourself, then?" It was a moment
of hell. I saw into her pitiless soul,—saw its barren worldliness, its
scorching hate,—and felt it clothe me round like an air I was obliged to
breathe. She came with her candle and stood over me with a bitter smile
of contempt; I saw the great emerald brooch on her bosom, a studded
serpent with diamond eyes. I shuddered,—I despised this woman with
the barren soul and mean thoughts; but I felt helpless before her, as if
she clutched my bleeding heart, and would clutch it till the last drop of
life-blood ebbed away. She was my wife, and we hated each other.
Gradually the hearth, the dim library, the candle-light disappeared,—
seemed to melt away into a background of light, the green serpent with
the diamond eyes remaining a dark image on the retina. Then I had a
sense of my eyelids quivering, and the living daylight broke in upon me;
I saw gardens, and heard voices; I was seated on the steps of the Belvedere Terrace, and my friends were round me.

The tumult of mind into which I was thrown by this hideous vision
made me ill for several days, and prolonged our stay at Vienna. I shuddered with horror as the scene recurred to me; and it recurred constantly, with all its minutiæ, as if they had been burnt into my memory;
and yet, such is the madness of the human heart under the influence of
its immediate desires, I felt a wild hell-braving joy that Bertha was to be
mine; for the fulfilment of my former prevision concerning her first appearance before me, left me little hope that this last hideous glimpse of
the future was the mere diseased play of my own mind, and had no relation to external realities. One thing alone I looked towards as a possible means of casting doubt on my terrible conviction,—the discovery
that my vision of Prague had been false,—and Prague was the next city
on our route.

Meanwhile I was no sooner in Bertha's society again, than I was as
completely under her sway as before. What if I saw into the heart of
Bertha, the matured woman,—Bertha, my wife? Bertha, the *girl*, was a
fascinating secret to me still: I trembled under her touch; I felt the witchery of her presence; I yearned to be assured of her love. The fear of
poison is feeble against the sense of thirst. Nay, I was just as jealous of
my brother as before,—just as much irritated by his small patronizing

3. Egyptian queen (69–30 B.C.) who killed herself by letting a poisonous asp bite her.

ways; for my pride, my diseased sensibility, were there as they had
always been, and winced as inevitably under every offence as my eye
winced from an intruding mote. The future, even when brought within
the compass of feeling by a vision that made me shudder, had still no
more than the force of an idea, compared with the force of present
emotion,—of my love for Bertha, of my dislike and jealousy towards my
brother.

It is an old story, that men sell themselves to the tempter, and sign a
bond with their blood, because it is only to take effect at a distant day;
then rush on to snatch the cup their souls thirst after with an impulse
not the less savage because there is a dark shadow beside them forever-
more. There is no short cut, no patent tram-road[4] to wisdom: after all
the centuries of invention, the soul's path lies through the thorny wilderness which must be still trodden in solitude, with bleeding feet, with
sobs for help, as it was trodden by them of old time.

My mind speculated eagerly on the means by which I should become my brother's successful rival, for I was still too timid, in my ignorance of Bertha's actual feeling, to venture on any step that would urge
from her an avowal of it. I thought I should gain confidence even for
this, if my vision of Prague proved to have been veracious; and yet, the
horror of that certitude! Behind the slim girl Bertha, whose words and
looks I watched for, whose touch was bliss, there stood continually that
Bertha with the fuller form, the harder eyes, the more rigid mouth,—
with the barren selfish soul laid bare; no longer a fascinating secret, but
a measured fact, urging itself perpetually on my unwilling sight. Are
you unable to give me your sympathy,—you who read this? Are you
unable to imagine this double consciousness at work within me, flowing
on like two parallel streams which never mingle their waters and blend
into a common hue? Yet you must have known something of the presentiments that spring from an insight at war with passion; and my visions were only like presentiments intensified to horror. You have
known the powerlessness of ideas before the might of impulse; and my
visions, when once they had passed into memory, were mere ideas,—
pale shadows that beckoned in vain, while my hand was grasped by the
living and the loved.

In after days I thought with bitter regret that if I had foreseen something more or something different,—if instead of that hideous vision
which poisoned the passion it could not destroy, or if even along with it
I could have had a foreshadowing of that moment when I looked on my
brother's face for the last time, some softening influence would have
been shed over my feeling towards him: pride and hatred would surely
have been subdued into pity, and the record of those hidden sins would

4. A road made of metal rails for streetcars.

have been shortened. But this is one of the vain thoughts with which we men flatter ourselves. We try to believe that the egoism within us would have easily been melted, and that it was only the narrowness of our knowledge which hemmed in our generosity, our awe, our human piety, and hindered them from submerging our hard indifference to the sensations and emotions of our fellow. Our tenderness and self-renunciation seem strong when our egoism has had its day,—when, after our mean striving for a triumph that is to be another's loss, the triumph comes suddenly, and we shudder at it, because it is held out by the chill hand of death.

Our arrival in Prague happened at night, and I was glad of this, for it seemed like a deferring of a terribly decisive moment, to be in the city for hours without seeing it. As we were not to remain long in Prague, but to go on speedily to Dresden, it was proposed that we should drive out the next morning and take a general view of the place, as well as visit some of its specially interesting spots, before the heat became oppressive,—for we were in August, and the season was hot and dry. But it happened that the ladies were rather late at their morning toilet,[5] and to my father's politely repressed but perceptible annoyance, we were not in the carriage till the morning was far advanced. I thought with a sense of relief, as we entered the Jews' quarter, where we were to visit the old synagogue, that we should be kept in this flat, shut-up part of the city, until we should all be too tired and too warm to go farther, and so we should return without seeing more than the streets through which we had already passed. That would give me another day's suspense,— suspense, the only form in which a fearful spirit knows the solace of hope. But as I stood under the blackened, groined arches of that old synagogue, made dimly visible by the seven thin candles in the sacred lamp, while our Jewish cicerone[6] reached down the Book of the Law, and read to us in its ancient tongue,—I felt a shuddering impression that this strange building, with its shrunken lights, this surviving withered remnant of mediæval Judaism, was of a piece with my vision. Those darkened dusty Christian saints, with their loftier arches and their larger candles, needed the consolatory scorn with which they might point to a more shrivelled death-in-life than their own.

As I expected, when we left the Jews' quarter the elders of our party wished to return to the hotel. But now, instead of rejoicing in this, as I had done beforehand, I felt a sudden overpowering impulse to go on at once to the bridge, and put an end to the suspense I had been wishing to protract. I declared, with unusual decision, that I would get out of the carriage and walk on alone; they might return without me. My father, thinking this merely a sample of my usual "poetic nonsense," objected

5. Bathing and dressing.   6. Guide.

that I should only do myself harm by walking in the heat; but when I persisted, he said angrily that I might follow my own absurd devices, but that Schmidt (our courier) must go with me. I assented to this, and set off with Schmidt towards the bridge. I had no sooner passed from under the archway of the grand old gate leading on to the bridge, than a trembling seized me, and I turned cold under the mid-day sun; yet I went on: I was in search of something,—a small detail which I remembered with special intensity as part of my vision. There it was,—the patch of rainbow light on the pavement transmitted through a lamp in the shape of a star.

Chapter II

Before the autumn was at an end, and while the brown leaves still stood thick on the beeches in our park, my brother and Bertha were engaged to each other, and it was understood that their marriage was to take place early in the next spring. In spite of the certainty I had felt from that moment on the bridge at Prague, that Bertha would one day be my wife, my constitutional timidity and distrust had continued to benumb me, and the words in which I had sometimes premeditated a confession of my love had died away unuttered. The same conflict had gone on within me as before,—the longing for an assurance of love from Bertha's lips, the dread lest a word of contempt and denial should fall upon me like a corrosive acid. What was the conviction of a distant necessity to me? I trembled under a present glance, I hungered after a present joy, I was clogged and chilled by a present fear. And so the days passed on: I witnessed Bertha's engagement and heard her marriage discussed as if I were under a conscious nightmare,—knowing it was a dream that would vanish, but feeling stifled under the grasp of hard-clutching fingers.

When I was not in Bertha's presence,—and I was with her very often, for she continued to treat me with a playful patronage that wakened no jealousy in my brother,—I spent my time chiefly in wandering, in strolling, or taking long rides while the daylight lasted, and then shutting myself up with my unread books; for books had lost the power of chaining my attention. My self-consciousness was heightened to that pitch of intensity in which our own emotions take the form of a drama which urges itself imperatively on our contemplation, and we begin to weep, less under the sense of our suffering than at the thought of it. I felt a sort of pitying anguish over the pathos of my own lot: the lot of a being finely organized for pain, but with hardly any fibres that responded to pleasure,—to whom the idea of future evil robbed the present of its joy, and for whom the idea of future good did not still the uneasiness of a present yearning or a present dread. I went dumbly through that stage of the poet's suffering, in which he feels the delicious pang of utterance, and makes an image of his sorrows.

I was left entirely without remonstrance concerning this dreamy wayward life: I knew my father's thought about me: "That lad will never be good for anything in life: he may waste his years in an insignificant way on the income that falls to him: I shall not trouble myself about a career for him."

One mild morning in the beginning of November, it happened that I was standing outside the portico patting lazy old Cæsar, a Newfoundland almost blind with age, the only dog that ever took any notice of me,—for the very dogs shunned me, and fawned on the happier people about me,—when the groom brought up my brother's horse which was to carry him to the hunt, and my brother himself appeared at the door, florid, broad-chested, and self-complacent, feeling what a good-natured fellow he was not to behave insolently to us all on the strength of his great advantages.

"Latimer, old boy," he said to me in a tone of compassionate cordiality, "what a pity it is you don't have a run with the hounds now and then! The finest thing in the world for low spirits!"

"Low spirits!" I thought bitterly, as he rode away; "that is the sort of phrase with which coarse, narrow natures like yours think to describe experience of which you can know no more than your horse knows. It is to such as you that the good of this world falls: ready dulness, healthy selfishness, good-tempered conceit,—these are the keys to happiness."

The quick thought came, that my selfishness was even stronger than his,—it was only a suffering selfishness instead of an enjoying one. But then, again, my exasperating insight into Alfred's self-complacent soul, his freedom from all the doubts and fears, the unsatisfied yearnings, the exquisite tortures of sensitiveness, that had made the web of my life, seemed to absolve me from all bonds towards him. This man needed no pity, no love; those fine influences would have been as little felt by him as the delicate white mist is felt by the rock it caresses. There was no evil in store for *him*: if he was not to marry Bertha, it would be because he had found a lot pleasanter to himself.

Mr. Filmore's house lay not more than half a mile beyond our own gates, and whenever I knew my brother was gone in another direction, I went there for the chance of finding Bertha at home. Later on in the day I walked thither. By a rare accident she was alone, and we walked out in the grounds together, for she seldom went on foot beyond the trimly swept gravel-walks. I remember what a beautiful sylph she looked to me as the low November sun shone on her blond hair, and she tripped along teasing me with her usual light banter, to which I listened half fondly, half moodily; it was all the sign Bertha's mysterious inner self ever made to me. To-day perhaps the moodiness predominated, for I had not yet shaken off the access[7] of jealous hate which my brother had raised in me by his parting patronage. Suddenly I interrupted and startled her by saying, almost fiercely, "Bertha, how can you love Alfred?"

She looked at me with surprise for a moment, but soon her light smile came again, and she answered sarcastically, "Why do you suppose I love him?"

"How can you ask that, Bertha?"

"What! your wisdom thinks I must love the man I'm going to marry? The most unpleasant thing in the world. I should quarrel with him; I should be jealous of him; our *ménage*[8] would be conducted in a very ill-bred manner. A little quiet contempt contributes greatly to the elegance of life."

"Bertha, that is not your real feeling. Why do you delight in trying to deceive me by inventing such cynical speeches?"

"I need never take the trouble of invention in order to deceive you, my small Tasso"[9] (that was the mocking name she usually gave me). "The easiest way to deceive a poet is to tell him the truth."

She was testing the validity of her epigram in a daring way, and for a moment the shadow of my vision—the Bertha whose soul was no secret to me—passed between me and the radiant girl, the playful sylph whose feelings were a fascinating mystery. I suppose I must have shuddered, or betrayed in some other way my momentary chill of horror.

"Tasso!" she said, seizing my wrist and peeping round into my face, "are you really beginning to discern what a heartless girl I am? Why, you are not half the poet I thought you were; you are actually capable of believing the truth about me."

The shadow passed from between us, and was no longer the object nearest to me. The girl whose light fingers grasped me, whose elfish charming face looked into mine,—who, I thought, was betraying an interest in my feelings that she would not have directly avowed,—this warm-breathing presence again possessed my senses and imagination like a returning siren[1] melody which had been overpowered for an instant by the roar of threatening waves. It was a moment as delicious to me as the waking up to a consciousness of youth after a dream of middle age. I forgot everything but my passion, and said with swimming eyes,—

"Bertha, shall you love me when we are first married? I wouldn't mind if you really loved me only for a little while."

Her look of astonishment, as she loosed my hand and started away

---

7. Sudden fit.
8. Household.
9. Torquato Tasso (1544–1595), Italian poet, author of the religious epic *Gerusalemme*

Liberata.
1. The sirens are mythological maidens who lure sailors toward rocks by the power of their song.

from me, recalled me to a sense of my strange, my criminal indiscretion.

"Forgive me," I said hurriedly, as soon as I could speak again; "I did not know what I was saying."

"Ah, Tasso's mad fit has come on, I see," she answered quietly, for she had recovered herself sooner than I had. "Let him go home and keep his head cool. I must go in, for the sun is setting."

I left her,—full of indignation against myself. I had let slip words which, if she reflected on them, might rouse in her a suspicion of my abnormal mental condition,—a suspicion which of all things I dreaded. And besides that, I was ashamed of fhe apparent baseness I had committed in uttering them to my brother's betrothed wife. I wandered home slowly, entering our park through a private gate instead of by the lodges.[2] As I approached the house, I saw a man dashing off at full speed from the stable-yard across the park. Had any accident happened at home? No; perhaps it was only one of my father's peremptory business errands that required this headlong haste. Nevertheless I quickened my pace without any distinct motive, and was soon at the house. I will not dwell on the scene I found there. My brother was dead,—had been pitched from his horse, and killed on the spot by a concussion of the brain.

I went up to the room where he lay, and where my father was seated beside him with a look of rigid despair. I had shunned my father more than any one since our return home, for the radical antipathy between our natures made my insight into his inner self a constant affliction to me. But now, as I went up to him, and stood beside him in sad silence, I felt the presence of a new element that blended us as we had never been blent before. My father had been one of the most successful men in the money-getting world: he had had no sentimental sufferings, no illness. The heaviest trouble that had befallen him was the death of his first wife. But he married my mother soon after; and I remember he seemed exactly the same, to my keen childish observation, the week after her death as before. But now, at last, a sorrow had come,—the sorrow of old age, which suffers the more from the crushing of its pride and its hopes, in proportion as the pride and hope are narrow and prosaic. His son was to have been married soon,—would probably have stood for the borough[3] at the next election. That son's existence was the best motive that could be alleged for making new purchases of land every year to round off the estate. It is a dreary thing to live on doing the same things year after year, without knowing why we do them. Perhaps the tragedy of

---

2. Small houses on large private estates used by caretakers, gamekeepers, and other servants.

3. I.e., have run as a parliamentary representative for his district.

disappointed youth and passion is less piteous than the tragedy of disappointed age and worldliness.

As I saw into the desolation of my father's heart, I felt a movement of deep pity towards him, which was the beginning of a new affection,—an affection that grew and strengthened in spite of the strange bitterness with which he regarded me in the first month or two after my brother's death. If it had not been for the softening influence of my compassion for him,—the first deep compassion I had ever felt,—I should have been stung by the perception that my father transferred the inheritance of an eldest son to me with a mortified sense that fate had compelled him to the unwelcome course of caring for me as an important being. It was only in spite of himself that he began to think of me with anxious regard. There is hardly any neglected child for whom death has made vacant a more favoured place, who will not understand what I mean.

Gradually, however, my new deference to his wishes, the effect of that patience which was born of my pity for him, won upon his affection, and he began to please himself with the endeavour to make me fill my brother's place as fully as my feebler personality would admit. I saw that the prospect which by and by presented itself of my becoming Bertha's husband was welcome to him, and he even contemplated in my case what he had not intended in my brother's,—that his son and daughter-in-law should make one household with him. My softened feeling towards my father made this the happiest time I had known since childhood;—these last months in which I retained the delicious illusion of loving Bertha, of longing and doubting and hoping that she might love me. She behaved with a certain new consciousness and distance towards me after my brother's death; and I too was under a double constraint,—that of delicacy towards my brother's memory, and of anxiety as to the impression my abrupt words had left on her mind. But the additional screen this mutual reserve erected between us only brought me more completely under her power: no matter how empty the adytum,[4] so that the veil be thick enough. So absolute is our soul's need of something hidden and uncertain for the maintenance of that doubt and hope and effort which are the breath of its life, that if the whole future were laid bare to us beyond to-day, the interest of all mankind would be bent on the hours that lie between; we should pant after the uncertainties of our one morning and our one afternoon; we should rush fiercely to the Exchange for our last possibility of speculation, of success, of disappointment; we should have a glut of political prophets foretelling a crisis or a no-crisis within the only twenty-four hours left open to prophecy. Conceive the condition of the human

4. Innermost sanctuary of a temple, not to be entered except by priests.

mind if all propositions whatsoever were self-evident except one, which was to become self-evident at the close of a summer's day, but in the mean time might be the subject of question, of hypothesis, of debate. Art and philosophy, literature and science, would fasten like bees on that one proposition which had the honey of probability in it, and be the more eager because their enjoyment would end with sunset. Our impulses, our spiritual activities, no more adjust themselves to the idea of their future nullity, than the beating of our heart, or the irritability of our muscles.

Bertha, the slim, fair-haired girl, whose present thoughts and emotions were an enigma to me amidst the fatiguing obviousness of the other minds around me, was as absorbing to me as a single unknown to-day,—as a single hypothetic proposition to remain problematic till sunset; and all the cramped, hemmed-in belief and disbelief, trust and distrust, of my nature welled out in this one narrow channel.

And she made me believe that she loved me. Without ever quitting her tone of *badinage*[5] and playful superiority, she intoxicated me with the sense that I was necessary to her, that she was never at ease unless I was near her, submitting to her playful tyranny. It costs a woman so little effort to besot us in this way! A half-repressed word, a moment's unexpected silence, even an easy fit of petulance on our account, will serve us as *hashish* for a long while. Out of the subtlest web of scarcely perceptible signs, she set me weaving the fancy that she had always unconsciously loved me better than Alfred, but that, with the ignorant fluttered sensibility of a young girl, she had been imposed on by the charm that lay for her in the distinction of being admired and chosen by a man who made so brilliant a figure in the world as my brother. She satirized herself in a very graceful way for her vanity and ambition. What was it to me that I had the light of my wretched prevision on the fact that now it was I who possessed at least all but the personal part of my brother's advantages? Our sweet illusions are half of them conscious illusions, like effects of colour that we know to be made up of tinsel, broken glass, and rags.

We were married eighteen months after Alfred's death, one cold, clear morning in April, when there came hail and sunshine both together; and Bertha, in her white silk and pale-green leaves, and the pale hues of her hair and face, looked like the spirit of the morning. My father was happier than he had thought of being again: my marriage, he felt sure, would complete the desirable modification of my character, and make me practical and worldly enough to take my place in society among sane men. For he delighted in Bertha's tact and acuteness, and felt sure she would be mistress of me, and make me what she chose: I

5. Joking, trifling.

was only twenty-one, and madly in love with her. Poor father! He kept that hope a little while after our first year of marriage, and it was not quite extinct when paralysis came and saved him from utter disappointment.

I shall hurry through the rest of my story, not dwelling so much as I have hitherto done on my inward experience. When people are well known to each other, they talk rather of what befalls them externally, leaving their feelings and sentiments to be inferred.

We lived in a round of visits for some time after our return home, giving splendid dinner-parties, and making a sensation in our neighbourhood by the new lustre of our equipage, for my father had reserved this display of his increased wealth for the period of his son's marriage; and we gave our acquaintances liberal opportunity for remarking that it was a pity I made so poor a figure as an heir and a bridegroom. The nervous fatigue of this existence, the insincerities and platitudes which I had to live through twice over,—through my inner and outward sense, —would have been maddening to me, if I had not had that sort of intoxicated callousness which came from the delights of a first passion. A bride and bride-groom, surrounded by all the appliances of wealth, hurried through the day by the whirl of society, filling their solitary moments with hastily snatched caresses, are prepared for their future life together as the *novice* is prepared for the cloister,—by experiencing its utmost contrast.

Through all these crowded excited months, Bertha's inward self remained shrouded from me, and I still read her thoughts only through the language of her lips and demeanour: I had still the human interest of wondering whether what I did and said pleased her, of longing to hear a word of affection, of giving a delicious exaggeration of meaning to her smile. But I was conscious of a growing difference in her manner towards me; sometimes strong enough to be called haughty coldness, cutting and chilling me as the hail had done that came across the sunshine on our marriage morning; sometimes only perceptible in the dexterous avoidance of a *tête-à-tête* walk or dinner to which I had been looking forward. I had been deeply pained by this,—had even felt a sort of crushing of the heart, from the sense that my brief day of happiness was near its setting; but still I remained dependent on Bertha, eager for the last rays of a bliss that would soon be gone forever, hoping and watching for some after-glow more beautiful from the impending night.

I remember—how should I not remember?—the time when that dependence and hope utterly left me, when the sadness I had felt in Bertha's growing estrangement became a joy that I looked back upon with longing, as a man might look back on the last pains in a paralyzed limb. It was just after the close of my father's last illness, which had necessarily withdrawn us from society and thrown us more upon each other. It was the evening of my father's death. On that evening the veil which had shrouded Bertha's soul from me—had made me find in her alone among my fellow-beings the blessed possibility of mystery and doubt and expectation—was first withdrawn. Perhaps it was the first day since the beginning of my passion for her, in which that passion was completely neutralized by the presence of an absorbing feeling of another kind. I had been watching by my father's death-bed: I had been witnessing the last fitful yearning glance his soul had cast back on the spent inheritance of life,—the last faint consciousness of love he had gathered from the pressure of my hand. What are all our personal loves when we have been sharing in that supreme agony? In the first moments when we come away from the presence of death, every other relation to the living is merged, to our feeling, in the great relation of a common nature and a common destiny.

In that state of mind I joined Bertha in her private sitting-room. She was seated in a leaning posture on a settee, with her back towards the door; the great rich coils of her pale blond hair surmounting her small neck, visible above the back of the settee. I remember, as I closed the door behind me, a cold tremulousness seizing me, and a vague sense of being hated and lonely,—vague and strong, like a presentiment. I know how I looked at that moment, for I saw myself in Bertha's thought as she lifted her cutting gray eyes, and looked at me: a miserable ghost-seer, surrounded by phantoms in the noonday, trembling under a breeze when the leaves were still, without appetite for the common objects of human desire, but pining after the moonbeams. We were front to front with each other, and judged each other. The terrible moment of complete illumination had come to me, and I saw that the darkness had hidden no landscape from me, but only a blank prosaic wall: from that evening forth, through the sickening years which followed, I saw all round the narrow room of this woman's soul,—saw petty artifice and mere negation where I had delighted to believe in coy sensibilities and in wit at war with latent feeling,—saw the light floating vanities of the girl defining themselves into the systematic coquetry, the scheming selfishness, of the woman,—saw repulsion and antipathy harden into cruel hatred, giving pain only for the sake of wreaking itself.

For Bertha too; after her kind, felt the bitterness of disillusion. She had believed that my wild poet's passion for her would make me her slave; and that, being her slave, I should execute her will in all things. With the essential shallowness of a negative, unimaginative nature, she was unable to conceive the fact that sensibilities were anything else than weaknesses. She had thought my weaknesses would put me in her power, and she found them unmanageable forces. Our positions were reversed. Before marriage she had completely mastered my imagination, for she was a secret to me; and I created the unknown thought before which I trembled as if it were hers. But now that her soul was laid open to me, now that I was compelled to share the privacy of her motives, to follow all the petty devices that preceded her words and acts, she found herself powerless with me, except to produce in me the chill shudder of repulsion,—powerless, because I could be acted on by no lever within her reach. I was dead to worldly ambitions, to social vanities, to all the incentives within the compass of her narrow imagination, and I lived under influences utterly invisible to her.

She was really pitiable to have such a husband, and so all the world thought. A graceful, brilliant woman, like Bertha, who smiled on morning callers, made a figure in ball-rooms, and was capable of that light repartee which, from such a woman, is accepted as wit, was secure of carrying off all sympathy from a husband who was sickly, abstracted, and, as some suspected, crack-brained. Even the servants in our house gave her the balance of their regard and pity. For there were no audible quarrels between us; our alienation, our repulsion from each other, lay within the silence of our own hearts; and if the mistress went out a great deal, and seemed to dislike the master's society, was it not natural, poor thing? The master was odd. I was kind and just to my dependants, but I excited in them a shrinking, half-contemptuous pity; for this class of men and women are but slightly determined in their estimate of others by general considerations, or even experience, of character. They judge of persons as they judge of coins, and value those who pass current at a high rate.

After a time I interfered so little with Bertha's habits, that it might seem wonderful how her hatred towards me could grow so intense and active as it did. But she had begun to suspect, by some involuntary betrayals of mine, that there was an abnormal power of penetration in me,—that fitfully, at least, I was strangely cognizant of her thoughts and intentions, and she began to be haunted by a terror of me, which alternated every now and then with defiance. She meditated continually how the incubus[6] could be shaken off her life,—how she could be freed from this hateful bond to a being whom she at once despised as an imbecile, and dreaded as an inquisitor. For a long while she lived in the hope that my evident wretchedness would drive me to the commission of suicide; but suicide was not in my nature. I was too completely swayed by the sense that I was in the grasp of unknown forces, to believe in my power of self-release. Towards my own destiny I had become entirely passive; for my one ardent desire had spent itself, and impulse no longer predominated over knowledge. For this reason I never thought of taking any steps towards a complete separation, which

6. Evil spirit thought in medieval times to have sexual intercourse with women while they are asleep.

would have made our alienation evident to the world. Why should I rush for help to a new course, when I was only suffering from the consequences of a deed which had been the act of my intensest will? That would have been the logic of one who had desires to gratify, and I had no desires. But Bertha and I lived more and more aloof from each other. The rich find it easy to live married and apart.

That course of our life which I have indicated in a few sentences filled the space of years. So much misery, so slow and hideous a growth of hatred and sin, may be compressed into a sentence! And men judge of each other's lives through this summary medium. They epitomize the experience of their fellow-mortal, and pronounce judgment on him in neat syntax, and feel themselves wise and virtuous,—conquerors over the temptations they define in well-selected predicates. Seven years of wretchedness glide glibly over the lips of the man who has never counted them out in moments of chill disappointment, of head and heart throbbings, of dread and vain wrestling, of remorse and despair. We learn *words* by rote, but not their meaning; *that* must be paid for with our life-blood, and printed in the subtle fibres of our nerves.

But I will hasten to finish my story. Brevity is justified at once to those who readily understand, and to those who will never understand.

Some years after my father's death, I was sitting by the dim firelight in my library one January evening,—sitting in the leather chair that used to be my father's,—when Bertha appeared at the door, with a candle in her hand, and advanced towards me. I knew the ball-dress she had on,—the white ball-dress with the green jewels, shone upon by the light of the wax candle which lit up the medallion of the dying Cleopatra on the mantelpiece. Why did she come to me before going out? I had not seen her in the library, which was my habitual place, for months. Why did she stand before me with the candle in her hand, with her cruel contemptuous eyes fixed on me, and the glittering serpent, like a familiar demon, on her breast? For a moment I thought this fulfilment of my vision at Vienna marked some dreadful crisis in my fate, but I saw nothing in Bertha's mind, as she stood before me, except scorn for the look of overwhelming misery with which I sat before her.... "Fool, idiot, why don't you kill yourself, then?"—that was her thought. But at length her thoughts reverted to her errand, and she spoke aloud. The apparently indifferent nature of the errand seemed to make a ridiculous anticlimax to my prevision and my agitation.

"I have had to hire a new maid. Fletcher is going to be married, and she wants me to ask you to let her husband have the public-house and farm at Molton. I wish him to have it. You must give the promise now, because Fletcher is going to-morrow morning,—and quickly, because I'm in a hurry."

"Very well; you may promise her," I said indifferently; and Bertha swept out of the library again.

I always shrank from the sight of a new person, and all the more when it was a person whose mental life was likely to weary my reluctant insight with worldly ignorant trivialities. But I shrank especially from the sight of this new maid, because her advent had been announced to me at a moment to which I could not cease to attach some fatality: I had a vague dread that I should find her mixed up with the dreary drama of my life,—that some new sickening vision would reveal her to me as an evil genius.[7] When at last I did unavoidably meet her, the vague dread was changed into definite disgust. She was a tall, wiry, dark-eyed woman, this Mrs. Archer, with a face handsome enough to give her coarse hard nature the odious finish of bold, self-confident coquetry. That was enough to make me avoid her, quite apart from the contemptuous feeling with which she contemplated me. I seldom saw her; but I perceived that she rapidly became a favourite with her mistress, and, after the lapse of eight or nine months, I began to be aware that there had arisen in Bertha's mind towards this woman a mingled feeling of fear and dependence, and that this feeling was associated with ill-defined images of candle-light scenes in her dressing-room, and the locking up of something in Bertha's cabinet. My interviews with my wife had become so brief and so rarely solitary that I had no opportunity of perceiving these images in her mind with more definiteness. The recollections of the past become contracted in the rapidity of thought till they sometimes bear hardly a more distinct resemblance to the external reality than the forms of an oriental alphabet to the objects that suggested them.

Besides, for the last year or more a modification had been going forward in my mental condition, and was growing more and more marked. My insight into the minds of those around me was becoming dimmer and more fitful, and the ideas that crowded my double consciousness became less and less dependent on any personal contact. All that was personal in me seemed to be suffering a gradual death, so that I was losing the organ through which the personal agitations and projects of others could affect me. But along with this relief from wearisome insight, there was a new development of what I concluded—as I have since found rightly,—to be a prevision of external scenes. It was as if the relation between me and my fellow-men was more and more deadened, and my relation to what we call the inanimate was quickened into new life. The more I lived apart from society, and in proportion as my wretchedness subsided from the violent throb of agonized passion into the dulness of habitual pain, the more frequent and vivid became such visions as that I had had of Prague,—of strange cities, of sandy plains, of gigantic ruins, of midnight skies with strange bright constellations, of mountain-passes, of grassy nooks flecked with the afternoon sunshine

---

7. Spirit or influence.

through the boughs: I was in the midst of such scenes, and in all of them one presence seemed to weigh on me in all these mighty shapes,—the presence of something unknown and pitiless. For continual suffering had annihilated religious faith within me: to the utterly miserable—the unloving and the unloved—there is no religion possible, no worship but a worship of devils. And beyond all these, and continually recurring, was the vision of my death,—the pangs, the suffocation, the last struggle, when life would be grasped at in vain.

Things were in this state near the end of the seventh year. I had become entirely free from insight, from my abnormal cognizance of any other consciousness than my own, and, instead of intruding involuntarily into the world of other minds, was living continually in my own solitary future. Bertha was aware that I was greatly changed. To my surprise she had of late seemed to seek opportunities of remaining in my society, and had cultivated that kind of distant yet familiar talk which is customary between a husband and wife who live in polite and irrevocable alienation. I bore this with languid submission, and without feeling enough interest in her motives to be roused into keen observation; yet I could not help perceiving something triumphant and excited in her carriage and the expression of her face,—something too subtle to express itself in words or tones, but giving one the idea that she lived in a state of expectation or hopeful suspense. My chief feeling was satisfaction that her inner self was once more shut out from me; and I almost revelled for the moment in the absent melancholy that made me answer her at cross purposes, and betray utter ignorance of what she had been saying. I remember well the look and the smile with which she one day said, after a mistake of this kind on my part: "I used to think you were a clairvoyant, and that was the reason why you were so bitter against other clairvoyants, wanting to keep your monopoly; but I see now you have become rather duller than the rest of the world."

I said nothing in reply. It occurred to me that her recent obtrusion of herself upon me might have been prompted by the wish to test my power of detecting some of her secrets; but I let the thought drop again at once: her motives and her deeds had no interest for me, and whatever pleasures she might be seeking, I had no wish to balk her. There was still pity in my soul for every living thing, and Bertha was living,—was surrounded with possibilities of misery.

Just at this time there occurred an event which roused me somewhat from my inertia, and gave me an interest in the passing moment that I had thought impossible for me. It was a visit from Charles Meunier, who had written me word that he was coming to England for relaxation from too strenuous labour, and would like to see me. Meunier had now a European reputation; but his letter to me expressed that keen remembrance of an early regard, an early debt of sympathy, which is inseparable from nobility of character: and I too felt as if his presence would be to me like a transient resurrection into a happier preexistence.

He came, and as far as possible, I renewed our old pleasure of making *tête-à-tête* excursions, though, instead of mountains and glaciers and the wide blue lake, we had to content ourselves with mere slopes and ponds and artificial plantations. The years had changed us both, but with what different result! Meunier was now a brilliant figure in society, to whom elegant women pretended to listen, and whose acquaintance was boasted of by noblemen ambitious of brains. He repressed with the utmost delicacy all betrayal of the shock which I am sure he must have received from our meeting, or of a desire to penetrate into my condition and circumstances, and sought by the utmost exertion of his charming social powers to make our reunion agreeable. Bertha was much struck by the unexpected fascinations of a visitor whom she had expected to find presentable only on the score of his celebrity, and put forth all her coquetries and accomplishments. Apparently she succeeded in attracting his admiration, for his manner towards her was attentive and flattering. The effect of his presence on me was so benignant, especially in those renewals of our old *tête-à-tête* wanderings, when he poured forth to me wonderful narratives of his professional experience, that more than once, when his talk turned on the psychological relations of disease, the thought crossed my mind that, if his stay with me were long enough, I might possibly bring myself to tell this man the secrets of my lot. Might there not lie some remedy for *me*, too, in his science? Might there not at least lie some comprehension and sympathy ready for me in his large and susceptible mind? But the thought only flickered feebly now and then, and died out before it could become a wish. The horror I had of again breaking in on the privacy of another soul made me, by an irrational instinct, draw the shroud of concealment more closely around my own, as we automatically perform the gesture we feel to be wanting in another.

When Meunier's visit was approaching its conclusion, there happened an event which caused some excitement in our household, owing to the surprisingly strong effect it appeared to produce on Bertha,—on Bertha, the self-possessed, who usually seemed inaccessible to feminine agitations, and did even her hate in a self-restrained hygienic manner. This event was the sudden severe illness of her maid, Mrs. Archer. I have reserved to this moment the mention of a circumstance which had forced itself on my notice shortly before Meunier's arrival, namely, that there had been some quarrel between Bertha and this maid, apparently during a visit to a distant family, in which she had accompanied her mistress. I had overheard Archer speaking in a tone of bitter insolence, which I should have thought an adequate reason for immediate dismissal. No dismissal followed; on the contrary, Bertha seemed to be silently putting up with personal inconveniences from the exhibitions of this woman's temper. I was the more astonished to observe that her illness seemed a cause of strong solicitude to Bertha; that she was at the bedside night and day, and would allow no one else to officiate as head-nurse. It happened that our family doctor was out on a holiday, an accident which made Meunier's presence in the house doubly welcome, and he apparently entered into the case with an interest which seemed so much stronger than the ordinary professional feeling, that one day when he had fallen into a long fit of silence after visiting her, I said to him,—

"Is this a very peculiar case of disease, Meunier?"

"No," he answered, "it is an attack of peritonitis, which will be fatal, but which does not differ physically from many other cases that have come under my observation. But I'll tell you what I have on my mind. I want to make an experiment on this woman, if you will give me permission. It can do her no harm,—will give her no pain,—for I shall not make it until life is extinct to all purposes of sensation. I want to try the effect of transfusing blood into her arteries after the heart has ceased to beat for some minutes. I have tried the experiment again and again with animals that have died of this disease, with astounding results, and I want to try it on a human subject. I have the small tubes necessary, in a case I have with me, and the rest of the apparatus could be prepared readily. I should use my own blood,—take it from my own arm. This woman won't live through the night, I'm convinced, and I want you to promise me your assistance in making the experiment. I can't do without another hand, but it would perhaps not be well to call in a medical assistant from among your provincial doctors. A disagreeable foolish version of the thing might get abroad."

"Have you spoken to my wife on the subject?" I said, "because she appears to be peculiarly sensitive about this woman: she has been a favourite maid."

"To tell you the truth," said Meunier, "I don't want her to know about it. There are always insuperable difficulties with women in these matters, and the effect on the supposed dead body may be startling. You and I will sit up together, and be in readiness. When certain symptoms appear I shall take you in, and at the right moment we must manage to get every one else out of the room."

I need not give our farther conversation on the subject. He entered very fully into the details, and overcame my repulsion from them, by exciting in me a mingled awe and curiosity concerning the possible results of his experiment.

We prepared everything, and he instructed me in my part as assistant. He had not told Bertha of his absolute conviction that Archer would not survive through the night, and endeavoured to persuade her to leave the patient and take a night's rest. But she was obstinate, suspecting the fact that death was at hand, and supposing that he wished merely to save her nerves. She refused to leave the sick-room. Meunier and I sat up together in the library, he making frequent visits to the sick-room, and returning with the information that the case was taking precisely the course he expected. Once he said to me, "Can you imagine any cause of ill feeling this woman has against her mistress, who is so devoted to her?"

"I think there was some misunderstanding between them before her illness. Why do you ask?"

"Because I have observed for the last five or six hours,—since, I fancy, she has lost all hope of recovery,—there seems a strange prompting in her to say something which pain and failing strength forbid her to utter; and there is a look of hideous meaning in her eyes, which she turns continually towards her mistress. In this disease the mind often remains singularly clear to the last."

"I am not surprised at an indication of malevolent feeling in her," I said. "She is a woman who has always inspired me with distrust and dislike, but she managed to insinuate herself into her mistress's favour." He was silent after this, looking at the fire with an air of absorption, till he went upstairs again. He stayed away longer than usual, and on returning, said to me quietly, "Come now."

I followed him to the chamber where death was hovering. The dark hangings of the large bed made a background that gave a strong relief to Bertha's pale face as I entered. She started forward as she saw me enter, and then looked at Meunier with an expression of angry inquiry; but he lifted up his hand as if to impose silence, while he fixed his glance on the dying woman and felt her pulse. The face was pinched and ghastly, a cold perspiration was on the forehead, and the eyelids were lowered so as almost to conceal the large dark eyes. After a minute or two, Meunier walked round to the other side of the bed where Bertha stood, and with his usual air of gentle politeness towards her begged her to leave the patient under our care,—everything should be done for her,—she was no longer in a state to be conscious of an affectionate presence. Bertha was hesitating, apparently almost willing to believe his assurance and to comply. She looked round at the ghastly dying face, as if to read the confirmation of that assurance, when for a moment the lowered eyelids were raised again, and it seemed as if the eyes were looking towards Bertha, but blankly. A shudder passed through Bertha's frame, and she returned to her station near the pillow, tacitly implying that she would not leave the room.

The eyelids were lifted no more. Once I looked at Bertha as she watched the face of the dying one. She wore a rich *peignoir*, and her blond hair was half covered by a lace cap: in her attire she was, as always, an elegant woman, fit to figure in a picture of modern aristocratic life: but I asked myself how that face of hers could ever have seemed to me the face of a woman born of woman, with memories of childhood, capable of pain, needing to be fondled? The features at that moment seemed so preternaturally sharp, the eyes were so hard and eager,—she looked like a cruel immortal, finding her spiritual feast in the agonies of a dying race. For across those hard features there came something like a flash when the last hour had been breathed out, and we all felt that the dark veil had completely fallen. What secret was there between Bertha and this woman? I turned my eyes from her with a horrible dread lest my insight should return, and I should be obliged to see what had been breeding about two unloving women's hearts. I felt that Bertha had been watching for the moment of death as the sealing of her secret: I thanked Heaven it could remain sealed for me.

Meunier said quietly, "She is gone." He then gave his arm to Bertha, and she submitted to be led out of the room.

I suppose it was at her order that two female attendants came into the room, and dismissed the younger one who had been present before. When they entered, Meunier had already opened the artery in the long thin neck that lay rigid on the pillow, and I dismissed them, ordering them to remain at a distance till we rang: the doctor, I said, had an operation to perform,—he was not sure about the death. For the next twenty minutes I forgot everything but Meunier and the experiment in which he was so absorbed that I think his senses would have been closed against all sounds or sights which had no relation to it. It was my task at first to keep up the artificial respiration in the body after the transfusion had been effected, but presently Meunier relieved me, and I could see the wondrous slow return of life; the breast began to heave, the inspirations became stronger, the eyelids quivered, and the soul seemed to have returned beneath them. The artificial respiration was withdrawn: still the breathing continued, and there was a movement of the lips.

Just then I heard the handle of the door moving: I suppose Bertha had heard from the women that they had been dismissed: probably a vague fear had arisen in her mind, for she entered with a look of alarm. She came to the foot of the bed and gave a stifled cry.

The dead woman's eyes were wide open, and met hers in full recognition,—the recognition of hate. With a sudden strong effort, the hand that Bertha had thought forever still was pointed towards her, and the haggard face moved. The gasping eager voice said,—

"You mean to poison your husband . . . the poison is in the black cabinet . . . I got it for you . . . you laughed at me, and told lies about me behind my back, to make me disgusting . . . because you were jealous . . . are you sorry . . . now?"

The lips continued to murmur, but the sounds were no longer distinct. Soon there was no sound,—only a slight movement: the flame had leaped out, and was being extinguished the faster. The wretched woman's heart-strings had been set to hatred and vengeance; the spirit of life had swept the chords for an instant, and was gone again forever. Great God! Is this what it is to live again . . . to wake up with our unstilled thirst upon us, with our unuttered curses rising to our lips, with our muscles ready to act out their half-committed sins?

Bertha stood pale at the foot of the bed, quivering and helpless, despairing of devices,[8] like a cunning animal whose hiding-places are surrounded by swift-advancing flame. Even Meunier looked paralyzed; life for that moment ceased to be a scientific problem to him. As for me, this scene seemed of one texture with the rest of my existence: horror was my familiar,[9] and this new revelation was only like an old pain recurring with new circumstances.

Since then Bertha and I have lived apart,—she in her own neighbourhood, the mistress of half our wealth; I as a wanderer in foreign countries, until I came to this Devonshire nest to die. Bertha lives pitied and admired; for what had I against that charming woman, whom every one but myself could have been happy with? There had been no witness of the scene in the dying room except Meunier, and while Meunier lived his lips were sealed by a promise to me.

Once or twice, weary of wandering, I rested in a favourite spot, and my heart went out towards the men and women and children whose faces were becoming familiar to me; but I was driven away again in terror at the approach of my old insight,—driven away to live continually with the one Unknown Presence revealed and yet hidden by the moving curtain of the earth and sky. Till at last disease took hold of me and forced me to rest here,—forced me to live in dependence on my servants. And then the curse of insight, of my double consciousness, came again, and has never left me. I know all their narrow thoughts, their feeble regard, their half-wearied pity.

It is the 20th of September, 1850. I know these figures I have just written, as if they were a long familiar inscription. I have seen them on this page in my desk unnumbered times, when the scene of my dying struggle has opened upon me. . . .

1859

8. I.e., without means to protect herself.   9. Familiar spirit or demon.

Brother and Sister[1]

I

I cannot choose but think upon the time
When our two lives grew like two buds that kiss
At lightest thrill from the bee's swinging chime,
Because the one so near the other is.

He was the elder and a little man 5
Of forty inches, bound to show no dread,
And I the girl that puppy-like now ran,
Now lagged behind my brother's larger tread.

I held him wise, and when he talked to me
Of snakes and birds, and which God loved the best, 10
I thought his knowledge marked the boundary
Where men grew blind, though angels knew the rest.

If he said "Hush!" I tried to hold my breath;
Wherever he said "Come!" I stepped in faith.

II

Long years have left their writing on my brow, 15
But yet the freshness and the dew-fed beam
Of those young mornings are about me now,
When we two wandered toward the far-off stream

With rod and line. Our basket held a store
Baked for us only, and I thought with joy 20
That I should have my share, though he had more,
Because he was the elder and a boy.

The firmaments of daisies since to me
Have had those mornings in their opening eyes,
The bunchèd cowslip's pale transparency 25
Carries that sunshine of sweet memories,

And wild-rose branches take their finest scent
From those blest hours of infantine content.

III

Our mother bade us keep the trodden ways,
Stroked down my tippet,[2] set my brother's frill, 30
Then with the benediction of her gaze
Clung to us lessening, and pursued us still

Across the homestead to the rookery[3] elms,
Whose tall old trunks had each a grassy mound,

---

1. George Eliot is remembering her childhood
affection for her brother, Isaac Evans.
2. A shoulder cape of fur or cloth.
3. Nesting place of rooks or ravens.

So rich for us, we counted them as realms   35
With varied products: here were earth-nuts found,

And here the Lady-fingers in deep shade;
Here sloping toward the Moat the rushes grew,
The large to split for pith,[4] the small to braid:
While over all the dark rooks cawing flew,   40

    And made a happy strange solemnity,
    A deep-toned chant from life unknown to me.
                IV
Our meadow-path had memorable spots:
One where it bridged a tiny rivulet,
Deep hid by tangled blue Forget-me-nots;   45
And all along the waving grasses met

My little palm, or nodded to my cheek,
When flowers with upturned faces gazing drew
My wonder downward, seeming all to speak
With eyes of souls that dumbly heard and knew.   50

Then came the copse,[5] where wild things rushed unseen,
And black-scathed grass betrayed the past abode
Of mystic gypsies, who still lurked between
Me and each hidden distance of the road.

    A gypsy once had startled me at play,   55
    Blotting with her dark smile my sunny day
                V
Thus rambling we were schooled in deepest lore,
And learned the meanings that give words a soul,
The fear, the love, the primal passionate store,
Whose shaping impulses make manhood whole.   60

Those hours were seed to all my after good;
My infant gladness, through eye, ear, and touch,
Took easily as warmth a various food
To nourish the sweet skill of loving much.

For who in age shall roam the earth and find   65
Reasons for loving that will strike out love
With sudden rod from the hard year-pressed mind?
Were reasons sown as thick as stars above,

    'Tis love must see them, as the eye sees light:
    Day is but Number[6] to the darkened sight.   70

4. Spongy interior of plant stalks.   6. I.e., an abstraction unrelated to experience.
5. Small thicket or grove.

VI

Our brown canal was endless to my thought;
And on its banks I sat in dreamy peace,
Unknowing how the good I loved was wrought,
Untroubled by the fear that it would cease.

Slowly the barges floated into view   75
Rounding a grassy hill to me sublime
With some Unknown beyond it, whither flew
The parting cuckoo toward a fresh spring time.

The wide-arched bridge, the scented elder-flowers,
The wondrous watery rings that died too soon,   80
The echoes of the quarry, the still hours
With white robe sweeping on the shadeless noon,

    Were but my growing self, are part of me,
    My present Past, my root of piety.

VII

Those long days measured by my little feet   85
Had chronicles which yield me many a text;
Where irony still finds an image meet[7]
Of full-grown judgments in this world perplext.

One day my brother left me in high charge,
To mind the rod, while he went seeking bait,   90
And bade me, when I saw a nearing barge,
Snatch out the line, lest he should come too late.

Proud of the task, I watched with all my might
For one whole minute, till my eyes grew wide,
Till sky and earth took on a strange new light   95
And seemed a dream-world floating on some tide—

    A fair pavilioned boat for me alone
    Bearing me onward through the vast unknown.

VIII

But sudden came the barge's pitch-black prow,
Nearer and angrier came my brother's cry,   100
And all my soul was quivering fear, when lo!
Upon the imperilled line, suspended high,

A silver perch! My guilt that won the prey,
Now turned to merit, had a guerdon[8] rich
Of hugs and praises, and made merry play,   105
Until my triumph reached its highest pitch

7. Suitable.   8. Reward.

When all at home were told the wondrous feat,
And how the little sister had fished well.
In secret, though my fortune tasted sweet,
I wondered why this happiness befell.   110

    "The little lass had luck," the gardener said:
    And so I learned, luck was with glory wed.
                IX
We had the self-same world enlarged for each
By loving difference of girl and boy:
The fruit that hung on high beyond my reach   115
He plucked for me, and oft he must employ

A measuring glance to guide my tiny shoe
Where lay firm stepping-stones, or call to mind
"This thing I like my sister may not do
For she is little, and I must be kind."   120

Thus boyish Will the nobler mastery learned
Where inward vision over impulse reigns,
Widening its life with separate life discerned,
A Like unlike, a Self that self restrains.

    His years with others must the sweeter be   125
    For those brief days he spent in loving me.
                X
His sorrow was my sorrow, and his joy
Sent little leaps and laughs through all my frame;
My doll seemed lifeless and no girlish toy
Had any reason when my brother came.   130

I knelt with him at marbles, marked his fling
Cut the ringed stem and make the apple drop,
Or watched him winding close the spiral string
That looped the orbits of the humming top.

Grasped by such fellowship my vagrant thought   135
Ceased with dream-fruit dream-wishes to fulfil;
My aëry-picturing fantasy was taught
Subjection to the harder, truer skill

    That seeks with deeds to grave[9] a thought-tracked line,
    And by "What is," "What will be" to define.   140
                XI
School parted us; we never found again
That childish world where our two spirits mingled

---

9. I.e., engrave, trace.

Like scents from varying roses that remain
One sweetness, nor can evermore be singled.

Yet the twin habit of that early time	145
Lingered for long about the heart and tongue:
We had been natives of one happy clime,
And its dear accents to our utterance clung.

Till the dire years whose awful name is Change
Had grasped our souls still yearning in divorce,[1]	150
And pitiless shaped them in two forms that range
Two elements which sever their life's course.[2]

But were another childhood-world my share,
I would be born a little sister there.

1869	1874

---

1. Separation.
2. I.e., their souls have now become separate elements.

FLORENCE NIGHTINGALE
1820–1910

Florence Nightingale was famous in her lifetime as a nurse, hospital administrator, sanitation reformer, and founder of the Nightingale School for Nursing as well as the Training School for Midwives. She was also the author of a polemical tract entitled *Cassandra*. The title of this protest against the feminization of women dramatizes Nightingale's anxious awareness that her own complaint might be just as ineffectual as that of Cassandra, the virgin-priestess of Apollo whose divinely inspired prophecy is destined to go unheeded.

Nightingale's protest was part of a personal rebellion against her family's traditionally Victorian expectations for her. The family was extremely well-to-do, with residences in Derbyshire, the New Forest, and London's fashionable Mayfair district. It was her mother, Fanny, and her older sister, Parthenope, who represented a feminine ideal that Nightingale found stultifying. Although William Edward Nightingale educated his two children in Greek and Latin, history and philosophy, both girls were clearly intended to grace a fairly typical upper-class household and to marry well. Florence Nightingale reacted to such values by falling into trances, depressions, and daydreams: "The whole occupation of Parthe and Mama," Nightingale later wrote, "was to lie on two sofas and tell one another not to get tired by putting flowers into water." In 1837 the first of what she described as four calls from God enjoined her to a life of active service. Strengthened in her resolve to defy the family's prescriptions, she rejected a marriage proposal from Richard Monckton Milnes, a prosperous social reformer. Between her seventeenth and thirty-second years she struggled to free herself from her mother's acceptance of Parthenope's extreme emotional dependency. In her guilt over this conflict, Nightingale resembled the speaker whose suicidal speeches frame *Cassandra*: "My present life is suicide," she wrote in her diary. "In my 31st year I see nothing desirable but death; What am I that their life is not good enough for me? Oh God what am I?"

Cassandra, which was originally part of a work entitled *Suggestions for Thought to Searchers after Religious Truth*, dates from this period in 1851 and 1852 when Nightingale was struggling with the issue of her own self-definition. This three-volume book has never been publicly printed, and *Cassandra* was not available until 1928, when Ray Strachey included it in *The Cause*, her history of the women's movement. The writing of *Suggestions for Thought*, however, cleared a way for Nightingale herself: at thirty-two years of age, she left home to train as a nurse at the Institute for Deaconesses at Kaiserwerth on the Rhine. In spite of her family's disapprobation, in 1853 she returned to England to become the Superintendent of the Institute for the Care of Sick Gentlewomen in Distressed Circumstances, when her father agreed to settle an annual five hundred pounds on her to ensure her independence. The next year she began her famous work at Scutari in the Crimea.

With ten Roman Catholic nuns, fourteen Anglican sisters, and fourteen hospital nurses, Nightingale confronted the cholera, typhus, gangrene, dysentery, and scurvy that were destroying the British army. In spite of the initial hostility of army officials, Nightingale was determined to help the thousands of men who were dying because of lack of sanitation, lack of equipment, and lack of space in the barracks hospital. She dispensed food and clothing, organized a laundry, built a new wing, and equipped it with everything from towels to arrowroot in huge milk pails. On her return, a national heroine at the age of thirty-six, the "Lady of the Lamp" suffered an illness that at least one scholar, George Pickering, concludes was "a weapon to protect herself from her family."

An invalid's life guaranteed Nightingale's privacy so she could devote herself to the two hundred–odd books and reports she wrote on world hunger, education, taxation, hospital construction, reform of the Poor Law, and the administration of the army in India. Significantly, too, after her mother's death in 1880 and Parthenope's in 1890, her health began to improve; however, she never relinquished her horror of what her mother and sister had represented. During her years of invalidism, she had worked through the agency of a succession of prominent men, including Sidney Herbert, Arthur Clough, and Sir John Sutherland. Friendly with each "exactly like two men," she had declared earlier to Harriet Martineau that "I am brutally indifferent to the wrongs or rights of my sex." Paradoxically, however, in *Cassandra*, the work that liberated her to reject the idleness of her mother and sister, Nightingale produced what the critic Elaine Showalter has aptly termed "a major text of English feminism, a link between Wollstonecraft and Woolf."

From Cassandra

[*Women's Time*][1]

"Yet I would spare no pang,
Would wish no torture less,
The more that anguish racks,
The earlier it will bless."

Give us back our suffering, we cry to Heaven in our hearts—suffering rather than indifferentism; for out of nothing comes nothing.[2] But out of suffering may come the cure. Better have pain than paralysis! A hundred struggle and drown in the breakers. One discovers the new world. But rather, ten times rather, die in the surf, heralding the way to that new world, than stand idly on the shore!

Passion, intellect, moral activity—these three have never been satisfied in a woman. In this cold and oppressive conventional atmosphere, they cannot be satisfied. To say more on this subject would be to enter into the whole history of society, of the present state of civilisation.

Look at that lizard—"It is not hot," he says, "I like it. The atmosphere which enervates you is life to me." The state of society which some complain of makes others happy. Why should these complain to those? *They* do not suffer. *They* would not understand it, any more than that lizard would comprehend the sufferings of a Shetland sheep.

The progressive[3] world is necessarily divided into two classes—those who take the best of what there is and enjoy it—those who wish for something better and try to create it. Without these two classes the world would be badly off. They are the very conditions of progress, both the one and the other. Were there none who were discontented with what they have, the world would never reach anything better. And, through the other class, which is constantly taking the best of what the first is creating for them, a balance is secured, and that which is conquered is held fast. But with neither class must we quarrel for not possessing the privileges of the other. The laws of the nature of each make it impossible.

Is discontent a privilege?

Yes, it is a privilege for you to suffer for your race—a privilege not reserved to the Redeemer,[4] and the martyrs alone, but one enjoyed by numbers in every age.

The common-place life of thousands; and in that is its only interest—its only merit as a history; viz. that it is the type of common suffer-

---

1. Part II of *Cassandra*.
2. An echo of *King Lear* I.i.90: "Nothing will come of nothing."

3. I.e., progressing or developing.
4. Christ.

ings—the story of one who has not the courage to resist nor to submit to the civilisation of her time—is this.

Poetry and imagination begin life. A child will fall on its knees on the gravel walk at the sight of a pink hawthorn in full flower, when it is by itself, to praise God for it.

Then comes intellect. It wishes to satisfy the wants which intellect creates for it. But there is a physical, not moral, impossibility of supplying the wants of the intellect in the state of civilisation at which we have arrived. The stimulus, the training, the time, are all three wanting to us; or, in other words, the means and inducements are not there.

Look at the poor lives we lead. It is a wonder that we are so good as we are, not that we are so bad. In looking round we are struck with the power of the organisations we see, not with their want[5] of power. Now and then, it is true, we are conscious that *there* is an inferior organisation, but, in general, just the contrary. Mrs A. has the imagination, the poetry of a Murillo,[6] and has sufficient power of execution to show that she might have had a great deal more. Why is she not a Murillo? From a material difficulty, not a mental one. If she has a knife and fork in her hands for three hours of the day, she cannot have a pencil or brush. Dinner is the great sacred ceremony of this day, the great sacrament. To be absent from dinner is equivalent to being ill. Nothing else will excuse us from it. Bodily incapacity is the only apology valid. If she has a pen and ink in her hands during other three hours, writing answers for the penny post, again, she cannot have her pencil,[7] and *so ad infinitum* through life. People have no type[8] before them in their lives, neither fathers nor mothers, nor the children themselves. They look at things in detail. They say, "It is very desirable that A., my daughter, should go to such a party, should know such a lady, should sit by such a person." It is true. But what standard have they before them of the nature and destination of man? The very words are rejected as pedantic. But might they not, at least, have a type in their minds that such an one might be a discoverer through her intellect, such another through her art, a third through her moral power?

Women often try one branch of intellect after another in their youth, *e.g.* mathematics. But that, least of all is compatible with the life of "society." It is impossible to follow up anything systematically. Women often long to enter some man's profession where they would find direction, competition (or rather opportunity of measuring the intellect with others) and, above all, time.

In those wise institutions, mixed as they are with many follies, which

---

5. Lack.
6. Bartolomé Murillo (1618–1682), Spanish painter of religious and peasant subjects.

7. Artist's pencil or brush.
8. Model.

will last as long as the human race lasts, because they are adapted to the wants of the human race; those institutions which we call monasteries, and which, embracing much that is contrary to the laws of nature, are yet better adapted to the union of the life of action and that of thought than any other mode of life with which we are acquainted; in many such, four and a half hours, at least, are daily set aside for thought, rules are given for thought, training and opportunity afforded. Among us there is *no* time appointed for this purpose, and the difficulty is that, in our social life, we must be always doubtful whether we ought not to be with somebody else or be doing something else.

Are men better off than women in this?

If one calls upon a friend in London and sees her son in the drawing-room, it strikes one as odd to find a young man sitting idle in his mother's drawing-room in the morning. For men, who are seen much in those haunts, there is no end of the epithets we have: "knights of the carpet," "drawing-room heroes," "ladies' men." But suppose we were to see a number of men in the morning sitting round a table in the drawing-room, looking at prints, doing worsted work,[9] and reading little books, how we should laugh! A member of the House of Commons was once known to do worsted work. Of another man was said, "His only fault is that he is too good; he drives out with his mother every day in the carriage, and if he is asked anywhere he answers that he must dine with his mother, but, if she can spare him, he will come in to tea, and he does not come."

Now, why is it more ridiculous for a man than for a woman to do worsted work and drive out every day in the carriage? Why should we laugh if we were to see a parcel of men sitting round a drawing-room table in the morning, and think it all right if they were women?

Is man's time more valuable than woman's? or is the difference between man and woman this, that woman has confessedly nothing to do?

Women are never supposed to have any occupation of sufficient importance *not* to be interrupted, except "suckling their fools";[1] and women themselves have accepted this, have written books to support it, and have trained themselves so as to consider whatever they do as *not* of such value to the world or to others, but that they can throw it up at the first "claim of social life." They have accustomed themselves to consider intellectual occupation as a merely selfish amusement, which it is their "duty" to give up for every trifler more selfish than themselves.

A young man (who was afterwards useful and known in his day and generation) when busy reading and sent for by his proud mother to shine in some morning visit, came; but, after it was over, he said, "Now,

9. Knitting.
1. Iago on women's role: "To suckle fools and chronicle small beer" (*Othello* II.i.159).

remember, this is not to happen again. I came that you might not think me sulky, but I shall not come again." But for a young woman to send such a message to her mother and sisters, how impertinent it would be! A woman of great administrative powers said that she never undertook anything which she "could not throw by at once, if necessary."

How do we explain then the many cases of women who have distinguished themselves in classics, mathematics, even in politics?

Widowhood, ill-health, or want of bread, these three explanations or excuses are supposed to justify a woman taking up an occupation. In some cases, no doubt, an indomitable force of character will suffice without any of these three, but such are rare.

But see how society fritters away the intellects of those comitted to her charge! It is said that society is necessary to sharpen the intellect. But what do we seek society for? It does sharpen the intellect, because it is a kind of *tour-de-force* to say something at a pinch,—unprepared and uninterested with any subject, to improvise something under difficulties. But what "go we out for to seek"? To take the chance of some one having something to say which we want to hear? or of finding something to say which *they* want to hear? You have a little to say, but not much. You often make a stipulation with someone else, "Come in ten minutes, for I shall not be able to find enough to spin out longer than that." You are not to talk of anything very interesting, for the essence of society is to prevent any long conversations and all tête-à-têtes. *Glissez, n'appuyez pas*[2] is its very motto. The praise of a good *maîtresse de maison* consists in this, that she allows no one person to be too much absorbed in, or too long about, a conversation. She always recalls them to their "duty." People do not go into the company of their fellow-creatures for what would seem a very sufficient reason, namely, that they have something to say to them, or something that they want to hear from them; but in the vague hope that they may find something to say.

Then as to solitary opportunities. Women never have an half-hour in all their lives (excepting before or after anybody is up in the house) that they can call their own, without fear of offending or of hurting someone. Why do people sit up so late, or, more rarely, get up so early? Not because the day is not long enough, but because they have "no time in the day to themselves."

If we do attempt to do anything in company, what is the system of literary exercise which we pursue? Everybody reads aloud out of their own book or newspaper—or, every five minutes, something is said. And what is it to be "read aloud to"? The most miserable exercise of the human intellect. Or rather, is it any exercise at all? It is like lying on

---

2. French: Slide, don't lean. "Maitresse de maison": mistress of the house.

one's back, with one's hands tied and having liquid poured down one's throat. Worse than that, because suffocation would immediately ensue and put a stop to this operation. But no suffocation would stop the other.

So much for the satisfaction of the intellect. Yet for a married woman in society, it is even worse. A married woman was heard to wish that she could break a limb that she might have a little time to herself. Many take advantage of the fear of "infection" to do the same.

It is a thing so accepted among women that they have nothing to do, that one woman has not the least scruple in saying to another, "I will come and spend the morning with you." And you would be thought quite surly and absurd, if you were to refuse it on the plea of occupation. Nay, it is thought a mark of amiability and affection, if you are "on such terms" that you can "come in" "any morning you please."

In a country house, if there is a large party of young people, "You will spend the morning with us," they say to the neighbours, "we will drive together in the afternoon," "to-morrow we will make an expedition, and we will spend the evening together." And this is thought friendly and spending time in a pleasant manner. So women play through life. Yet time is the most valuable of all things. If they had come every morning and afternoon and robbed us of half-a-crown we should have had redress from the police. But it is laid down, that our time is of no value. If you offer a morning visit to a professional man, and say, "I will just stay an hour with you, if you will allow me, till so and so comes back to fetch me"; it costs him the earnings of an hour, and therefore he has a right to complain. But women have no right, because it is "only their time."

Women have no means given them, whereby they can resist the "claims of social life." They are taught from their infancy upwards that it is a wrong, ill-tempered, and a misunderstanding of "woman's mission" (with a great M) if they do not allow themselves willingly to be interrupted at all hours. If a woman has once put in a claim to be treated as a man by some work of science or art or literature, which she can show as the "fruit of her leisure," then she will be considered justified in having leisure (hardly, perhaps, even then). But if not, not. If she has nothing to show, she must resign herself to her fate.

[The Saviour of Her Race][3]
V

"L'enthousiasme est la faiblesse d'un temps où l'intelligence monte très haut, entraînée par l'imagination, et tombe très bas, écrasée par une réalité, sans poésie et sans grandeur."[4]

3. Parts V, VI, and VII.
4. "Enthusiasm is the weakness of a time when intelligence mounts very high, dragged by the imagination, and falls very low, crushed by a reality without poetry and without grandeur."

Women dream till they have no longer the strength to dream; those dreams against which they so struggle, so honestly, vigorously, and conscientiously, and so in vain, yet which are their life, without which they could not have lived; those dreams go at last. All their plans and visions seem vanished, and they know not where; gone, and they cannot recall them. They do not even remember them. And they are left without the food of reality or of hope.

Later in life, they neither desire nor dream, neither of activity, nor of love, nor of intellect. The last often survives the longest. They wish, if their experiences would benefit anybody, to give them to someone. But they never find an hour free in which to collect their thoughts, and so discouragement becomes ever deeper and deeper, and they less and less capable of undertaking anything.

It seems as if the female spirit of the world were mourning everlastingly over blessings, not *lost,* but which she has never had, and which, in her discouragement she feels that she never will have, they are so far off.

The more complete a woman's organisation, the more she will feel it, till at last there shall arise a woman, who will resume,[5] in her own soul, all the sufferings of her race, and that woman will be the Saviour of her race.

Jesus Christ raised women above the condition of mere slaves, mere ministers to the passions of the man, raised them by His sympathy, to be Ministers of God. He gave them moral activity. But the Age, the World, Humanity, must give them the means to exercise this moral activity, must give them intellectual cultivation, spheres of action.

There is perhaps no century where the woman shows so meanly as in this.[6] Because her education seems entirely to have parted company with her vocation; there is no longer unity between the woman as inwardly developed, and as outwardly manifested.

In the last century it was not so. In the succeeding one let us hope that it will no longer be so.

But now she is like the Archangel Michael as he stands upon Saint Angelo at Rome. She has an immense provision of wings, which seem as if they would bear her over earth and heaven; but when she tries to use them, she is petrified into stone, her feet are grown into the earth, chained to the bronze pedestal.

Nothing can well be imagined more painful than the present position of woman, unless, on the one hand, she renounces all outward activity

---

5. Encompass, go through in summary form.

6. "At almost every period of social life, we find, as it were, two undercurrents running different ways. There is the noble woman who dreams the following out her useful vocation; but there is also the selfish dreamer now, who is ever turning to something new, regardless of the expectations she has voluntarily excited, who is ever talking about 'making a life for herself,' heedless that she is spoiling another life, undertaken, perhaps, at her own bidding. This is the ugly reverse of the medal" [Nightingale's note].

and keeps herself within the magic sphere, the bubble of her dreams; or, on the other, surrendering all aspiration, she gives herself to her real life, soul and body. For those to whom it is possible, the latter is best; for out of activity may come thought, out of mere aspiration can come nothing.

But now—when the young imagination is so high and so developed, and reality is so narrow and conventional—there is no more parallelism between life in the thought and life in the actual than between the corpse, which lies motionless in its narrow bed, and the spirit, which, in our imagination, is at large among the stars.

The ideal life is passed in noble schemes of good consecutively followed up, of devotion to a great object, of sympathy given and received for high ideas and generous feelings. The actual life is passed in sympathy given and received for a dinner, a party, a piece of furniture, a house built or a garden laid out well, in devotion to your guests—(a too real devotion, for it implies that of all your time)—in schemes of schooling for the poor, which you follow up perhaps in an odd quarter of an hour, between luncheon and driving out in the carriage—broth and dripping are included in the plan[7]—and the rest of your time goes in ordering the dinner, hunting for a governess for your children, and sending pheasants and apples to your poorer relations. Is there anything in *this* life which can be called an Incarnation of the ideal life within? Is it a wonder that the unhappy woman should prefer to keep them entirely separate? not to take the bloom off her Ideal by mixing it up with her Actual; not to make her Actual still more unpalatable by trying to *inform* it with her Ideal? And then she is blamed, and her own sex unites against her, for not being content with the "day of small things." She is told that "trifles make the sum of human things"; they do indeed. She is contemptuously asked, "Would she abolish domestic life?" Men are afraid that their houses will not be so comfortable, that their wives will make themselves "remarkable" women that they will make themselves distasteful to men; they write books (and very wisely) to teach themselves to dramatise "little things," to persuade themselves that "domestic life is their sphere" and to idealise the "sacred hearth." Sacred it is indeed. Sacred from the touch of their sons almost as soon as they are out of childhood—from its dulness and its tyrannous trifling *these* recoil. Sacred from the grasp of their daughters' affections upon which it has so light a hold that they seize the first opportunity of marriage, *their* only chance of emancipation. The "sacred hearth"; sacred to their husband's sleep, their sons' absence in the body and their daughters' in mind.

---

7. I.e., little bits of time are intermingled like broth and dripping.

Oh! mothers, who talk about this hearth, how much do you know of your son's real life, how much of your daughter's imaginary one? Awake, ye women, all ye that sleep, awake! If this domestic life were so very good, would your young men wander away from it, your maidens think of something else?

The time is come when women must do something more than the "domestic hearth," which means nursing the infants, keeping a pretty house, having a good dinner and an entertaining party.

You say, "It is true, our young men see visions, and our maidens dream dreams," but what of? Does not the woman intend to marry, and have over again what she has at home? and the man ultimately too? Yes, but not the same; she *will* have the same, that is, if circumstances are not altered to prevent it; but her *ideal* is very different, though that ideal and the reality will never come together to mould each other. And it is not only the unmarried woman who dreams. The married woman also holds long imaginary conversations but too often.

VI

We live in the world, it is said, and must walk in its ways.

Was Christ called a complainer against the world? Yet all these great teachers and preachers must have had a most deep and ingrained sense, a continual feeling of the miseries and wrongs of the world. Otherwise they would not have been impelled to devote life and death to redress them. Christ, Socrates, Howard,[8] they must have had no ear for the joys, compared to that which they had for the sorrows of the world.

They acted, however, and we complain. The great reformers of the world turn into the great misanthropists, if circumstances or organisation do not permit them to act. Christ, if He had been a woman, might have been nothing but a great complainer. Peace be with the misanthropists! They have made a step in progress; the next will make them great philanthropists; they are divided but by a line.

The next Christ will perhaps be a female Christ. But do we see one woman who looks like a female Christ? or even like "the messenger before" her "face," to go before her and prepare the hearts and minds for her?

To this will be answered that half the inmates of Bedlam begin in this way, by fancying that they are "the Christ."[9]

---

8. Probably a reference to John Howard (1726–1790), an English prison reformer.
9. "It is quite true that insanity, sensuality, and monstrous fraud have constantly assumed to be 'the Christ,' *vide* the *Agapemone* and the Mormons. 'Believing' a man of the name of Prince 'to be the tabernacle of God on earth,' poor deluded women transfer to him all their stock in the Three per Cents. We hear of the Mormons, etc., being the 'recipients and mouthpieces of God's Spirit.' They profess to be 'incarnations of the Deity,' 'witnesses of the Almighty,' 'solely knowing God's will, and being the medium of communicating it to man,' and so forth. It does not appear to us that this blasphemy is very dangerous to the cause of true religion in general, any more than forgery is very dangerous to commerce in general. It is the universal dishonesty in religion, as in trade, which is really dangerous" [Nightingale's note].

People talk about imitating Christ, and imitate Him in the little tri-fling formal things, such as washing the feet, saying His prayer, and so on; but if anyone attempts the real imitation of Him, there are no bounds to the outcry with which the presumption of that person is condemned.

For instance, Christ was saying something to the people one day, which interested Him very much, and interested them very much; and Mary and His brothers came in the middle of it, and wanted to interrupt Him, and take Him home to dinner, very likely—(how natural that story is! does it not speak more home than any historic evidences of the Gospel's reality?), and He, instead of being angry with their interrup-tion of Him in such an important work for some trifling thing, answers, "Who is my mother? and who are my brethren? Whosoever shall do the will of my Father which is in heaven, the same is my brother and sister and mother." But if *we* were to say that, we should be accused of "destroying the family tie, of diminishing the obligation of the home duties."

He might well say, "Heaven and earth shall pass away, but my words shall not pass away."[1] His words will never pass away. If He had said, "Tell them that I am engaged at this moment in something very im-portant; that the instruction of the multitude ought to go before any personal ties; that I will remember to come when I have done," no one would have been impressed by His words; but how striking is that, "Behold my mother and my brethren!"

VII

The dying woman to her mourners:—"Oh! if you knew how gladly I leave this life, how much more courage I feel to take the chance of an-other, than of anything I see before me in this, you would put on your wedding-clothes instead of mourning for me!"

"But," they say, "so much talent! so many gifts! such good which you might have done!"

"The world will be put back some little time by my death," she says; "you see I estimate my powers at least as highly as you can; but it is by the death which has taken place some years ago in me, not by the death which is about to take place now." And so is the world put back by the death of every one who has to sacrifice the development of his or her peculiar gifts (which were meant, not for selfish gratification, but for the improvement of that world) to conventionality.

"My people were like children playing on the shore of the eight-eenth century. I was their hobby-horse, their plaything; and they drove me to and fro, dear souls! never weary of the play themselves, till I, who had grown to woman's estate and to the ideas of the nineteenth cen-

1. Matthew 24:35

tury, lay down exhausted, my mind closed to hope, my heart to strength.

"Free—free—oh! divine freedom, art thou come at last? Welcome, beautiful death!"

Let neither name nor date be placed on her grave, still less the expression of regret or of admiration; but simply the words, "I believe in God."

1852–1859   1928

ELIZABETH DREW STODDARD
1823–1901

She "was not cursed with mediocrity, but [had] the misfortune to be original," commented the writer R. H. Stoddard about his novelist-wife, Elizabeth Drew Stoddard. She produced "tales of New England life . . . but what a New England!" observed the critic Mary Moss three months after Stoddard's death, explaining that this artist's locale was "a country of uncurbed desire, of hereditary taints, of families divided against themselves, of violence, of excess." Perhaps it was the originality and daring that led Stoddard to explore such a setting which also caused her to be largely forgotten for almost a century after her death and frequently ignored or underestimated even during her lifetime. Much influenced by Charlotte and Emily Brontë but with a uniquely ironic vision of her own, this insistently individual writer refused to abide by the conventions of domesticity and purity which inspired so many of her female contemporaries to produce sentimental fiction; instead, she wrote novels and tales that were both sardonic and Gothic, often witty and almost always unorthodox in their transcriptions of "uncurbed desire."

The daughter of a wealthy shipbuilder-father, Elizabeth Drew Barstow was born in Mattapoisett, Massachusetts, and educated at the Wheaton Female Seminary at Norton, Massachusetts, where she was evidently a difficult, even rebellious student. In 1852, she married Richard Henry Stoddard, a journalist and poet; with him, she settled in New York City and had three children, two of whom died young and the third of whom—an actor and playwright—predeceased her in 1901. During the fifties, Stoddard began writing articles and reviews for the *Daily Alta California*, then stories for the *Atlantic*, *Harper's*, and other important American magazines. Her first novel, *The Morgesons*, appeared in 1862, followed by several other novels and a children's book, but, no doubt because of her boldly unconventional perspective on society, much of this work was widely criticized as immoral.

Not until the novelist and editor William Dean Howells expressed enthusiasm for her fiction did Stoddard receive some measure of praise: after Howells wrote about her, three of her novels were reprinted in 1888 and 1889, and in 1895 she published a collection of her verse, *Poems*. Nevertheless, after her death her reputation again declined, and her work lapsed once more into ob-

scurity. Just recently, however, the scholars Lawrence Buell and Sandra Zagarell have produced an edition of her work, *The Morgesons and Other Stories*,
which should do much to reacquaint readers with what Mary Moss called this
writer's "strange visions" of a daringly different New England, visions that
clearly inform the disturbingly sardonic Gothic plot of *Lemorne* versus *Huell*.

Lemorne *versus* Huell

The two months I spent at Newport[1] with Aunt Eliza Huell, who
had been ordered to the sea-side for the benefit of her health, were the
months that created all that is dramatic in my destiny. My aunt was
troublesome, for she was not only out of health, but in a lawsuit. She
wrote to me, for we lived apart, asking me to accompany her—not because she was fond of me, or wished to give me pleasure, but because I
was useful in various ways. Mother insisted upon my accepting her invitation, not because she loved her late husband's sister, but because she
thought it wise to cotton to her in every particular, for Aunt Eliza was
rich, and we—two lone women—were poor.

I gave my music-pupils a longer and earlier vacation than usual, took
a week to arrange my wardrobe—for I made my own dresses—and
then started for New York, with the five dollars which Aunt Eliza had
sent for my fare thither. I arrived at her house in Bond Street[2] at 7 A.M.,
and found her man James in conversation with the milkman. He informed me that Miss Huell was very bad, and that the housekeeper was
still in bed. I supposed that Aunt Eliza was in bed also, but I had hardly
entered the house when I heard her bell ring as she only could ring it
—with an impatient jerk.

"She wants hot milk," said James, "and the man has just come."

I laid my bonnet down, and went to the kitchen. Saluting the cook,
who was an old acquaintance, and who told me that the "divil" had
been in the range that morning, I took a pan, into which I poured some
milk, and held it over the gaslight till it was hot; then I carried it up to
Aunt Eliza.

"Here is your milk, Aunt Eliza. You have sent for me to help you,
and I begin with the earliest opportunity."

"I looked for you an hour ago. Ring the bell."

I rang it.

"Your mother is well, I suppose. She would have sent you, though,
had she been sick in bed."

"She has done so. She thinks better of my coming than I do."

---

1. Newport, Rhode Island. For information
contained in these notes, we are indebted to
Hershel Parker's text of the story in *The Norton*

Anthology of American Literature.
2. A fashionable street.

The housekeeper, Mrs. Roll, came in, and Aunt Eliza politely requested her to have breakfast for her niece as soon as possible.

"I do not go down of mornings yet," said Aunt Eliza, "but Mrs. Roll presides. See that the coffee is good, Roll."

"It is good generally, Miss Huell."

"You see that Margaret brought me my milk."

"Ahem!" said Mrs. Roll, marching out.

At the beginning of each visit to Aunt Eliza I was in the habit of dwelling on the contrast between her way of living and ours. We lived from "hand to mouth." Every thing about her wore a hereditary air; for she lived in my grandfather's house, and it was the same as in his day. If I was at home when these contrasts occurred to me I should have felt angry; as it was, I felt them as in a dream—the china, the silver, the old furniture, and the excellent fare soothed me.

In the middle of the day Aunt Eliza came down stairs, and after she had received a visit from her doctor, decided to go to Newport on Saturday. It was Wednesday; and I could, if I chose, make any addition to my wardrobe. I had none to make, I informed her. What were my dresses?—had I a black silk? she asked. I had no black silk, and thought one would be unnecessary for hot weather.

"Who ever heard of a girl of twenty-four having no black silk! You have slimsy[3] muslins, I dare say?"

"Yes."

"And you like them?"

"For present wear."

That afternoon she sent Mrs. Roll out, who returned with a splendid heavy silk for me, which Aunt Eliza said should be made before Saturday, and it was. I went to a fashionable dress-maker of her recommending, and on Friday it came home, beautifully made and trimmed with real lace.

"Even the Pushers could find no fault with this," said Aunt Eliza, turning over the sleeves and smoothing the lace. Somehow she smuggled into the house a white straw-bonnet, with white roses; also a handsome mantilla. She held the bonnet before me with a nod, and deposited it again in the box, which made a part of the luggage for Newport.

On Sunday morning we arrived in Newport, and went to a quiet hotel in the town. James was with us, but Mrs. Roll was left in Bond Street, in charge of the household. Monday was spent in an endeavor to make an arrangement regarding the hire of a coach and coachman. Several livery-stable keepers were in attendance, but nothing was settled, till I suggested that Aunt Eliza should send for her own carriage.

3. Flimsy, slightly made.

James was sent back the next day, and returned on Thursday with coach, horses, and William her coachman. That matter being finished, and the trunks being unpacked, she decided to take her first bath in the sea, expecting me to support her through the trying ordeal of the surf. As we were returning from the beach we met a carriage containing a number of persons with a family resemblance.

When Aunt Eliza saw them she angrily exclaimed, "Am I to see those Uxbridges every day?"

Of the Uxbridges this much I knew—that the two brothers Uxbridge were the lawyers of her opponents in the lawsuit which had existed three or four years. I had never felt any interest in it, though I knew that it was concerning a tract of ground in the city which had belonged to my grandfather, and which had, since his day, become very valuable. Litigation was a habit of the Huell family. So the sight of the Uxbridge family did not agitate me as it did Aunt Eliza.

"The sly, methodical dogs! but I shall beat Lemorne yet!"

"How will you amuse yourself then, aunt?"

"I'll adopt some boys to inherit what I shall save from his clutches."

The bath fatigued her so she remained in her room for the rest of the day; but she kept me busy with a hundred trifles. I wrote for her, computed interest, studied out bills of fare, till four o'clock came, and with it a fog. Nevertheless I must ride on the Avenue, and the carriage was ordered.

"Wear your silk, Margaret; it will just about last your visit through —the fog will use it up."

"I am glad of it," I answered.

"You will ride every day. Wear the bonnet I bought for you also."

"Certainly; but won't that go quicker in the fog than the dress?"

"Maybe; but wear it."

I rode every day afterward, from four to six, in the black silk, the mantilla, and the white straw. When Aunt Eliza went she was so on the alert for the Uxbridge family carriage that she could have had little enjoyment of the ride. Rocks never were a passion with her, she said, nor promontories, chasms, or sand. She came to Newport to be washed with salt-water; when she had washed up to the doctor's prescription she should leave, as ignorant of the peculiar pleasures of Newport as when she arrived. She had no fancy for its conglomerate societies, its literary cottages, its parvenue suits of rooms, its saloon habits, and its bathing herds.

I considered the rides a part of the contract of what was expected in my two months' performance. I did not dream that I was enjoying them, any more than I supposed myself to be enjoying a sea-bath while pulling Aunt Eliza to and fro in the surf. Nothing in the life around me stirred me, nothing in nature attracted me. I liked the fog; somehow it seemed to emanate from me instead of rolling up from the ocean, and to represent me. Whether I went alone or not, the coachman was ordered to drive a certain round; after that I could extend the ride in whatever direction I pleased, but I always said, "Any where, William." One afternoon, which happened to be a bright one, I was riding on the road which led to the glen, when I heard the screaming of a flock of geese which were waddling across the path in front of the horses. I started, for I was asleep probably, and, looking forward, saw the Uxbridge carriage, filled with ladies and children, coming toward me; and by it rode a gentleman on horseback. His horse was rearing among the hissing geese, but neither horse nor geese appeared to engage him; his eyes were fixed upon me. The horse swerved so near that its long mane almost brushed against me. By an irresistible impulse I laid my ungloved hand upon it, but did not look at the rider. Carriage and horseman passed on, and William resumed his pace. A vague idea took possession of me that I had seen the horseman before on my various drives. I had a vision of a man galloping on a black horse out of the fog, and into it again. I was very sure, however, that I had never seen him on so pleasant a day as this! William did not bring his horses to time; it was after six when I went into Aunt Eliza's parlor, and found her impatient for her tea and toast. She was crosser than the occasion warranted; but I understood it when she gave me the outlines of a letter she desired me to write to her lawyer in New York. Something had turned up, he had written her; the Uxbridges believed that they had ferreted out what would go against her. I told her that I had met the Uxbridge carriage.

"One of them is in New York; how else could they be giving me trouble just now?"

"There was a gentleman on horseback beside the carriage."

"Did he look mean and cunning?"

"He did not wear his legal beaver[4] up, I think; but he rode a fine horse and sat it well."

"A lawyer on horseback should, like the beggar of the adage, ride to the devil."[5]

"Your business now is the 'Lemorne?' "

"You know it is."

"I did not know but that you had found something besides to litigate."

"It must have been Edward Uxbridge that you saw. He is the brain of the firm."

---

4. *Hamlet* (I.ii.229): "O yes, my lord; he wore his beaver [face-guard for a helmet] up."
5. "The Taylor-Whiting *Dictionary of American Proverbs and Proverbial Phrases, 1820–80* cites Nathaniel Hawthorne's *Old News* in *The Snow-Image* (1851): "Now is the day, when every beggar gets on horse-back. And is not the whole land like a beggar on horse-back, riding post to the devil?" [Parker's note].

"You expect Mr. Van Horn?"

"Oh, he must come; I can not be writing letters."

We had been in Newport two weeks when Mr. Van Horn, Aunt Eliza's lawyer, came. He said that he would see Mr. Edward Uxbridge. Between them they might delay a term, which he thought would be best. "Would Miss Huell ever be ready for a compromise?" he jestingly asked.

"Are you suspicious?" she inquired.

"No; but the Uxbridge chaps are clever."

He dined with us; and at four o'clock Aunt Eliza graciously asked him to take a seat in the carriage with me, making some excuse for not going herself.

"Hullo! said Mr. Van Horn when we had reached the country road, "there's Uxbridge now." And he waved his hand to him.

It was indeed the black horse and the same rider that I had met. He reined up beside us, and shook hands with Mr. Van Horn.

"We are required to answer this new complaint?" said Mr. Van Horn.

Mr. Uxbridge nodded.

"And after that the judgment?"

Mr. Uxbridge laughed.

"I wish that certain gore[6] of land had been sunk instead of being mapped in 1835."

"The surveyor did his business well enough, I am sure."

They talked together in a low voice for a few minutes, and then Mr. Van Horn leaned back in his seat again. "Allow me," he said, "to introduce you, Uxbridge, to Miss Margaret Huell, Miss Huell's niece. Huell *vs.* Brown; you know," he added, in an explanatory tone; for I was Huell *vs.* Brown's daughter.

"Oh!" said Mr. Uxbridge, bowing, and looking at me gravely. I looked at him also; he was a pale, stern-looking man, and forty years old certainly. I derived the impression at once that he had a domineering disposition, perhaps from the way in which he controlled his horse.

"Nice beast that," said Mr. Van Horn.

"Yes," he answered, laying his hand on its mane, so that the action brought immediately to my mind the recollection that I had done so too. I would not meet his eye again, however.

"How long shall you remain, Uxbridge?"

"I don't know. You are not interested in the lawsuit, Miss Huell?" he said, putting on his hat.

"Not in the least; nothing of mine is involved."

"We'll gain it for your portion yet, Miss Margaret," said Mr. Van

---

6. Small triangular piece of land.

Horn, nodding to Mr. Uxbridge, and bidding William drive on. He returned the next day, and we settled into the routine of hotel life. A few mornings after, she sent me to a matinée, which was given by some of the Opera people, who were in Newport strengthening the larynx with applications of brine. When the concert was half over, and the audience were making the usual hum and stir, I saw Mr. Uxbridge against a pillar, with his hands incased in pearl-colored gloves, and holding a shiny hat. He turned half away when he caught my eye, and then darted toward me.

"You have not been much more interested in the music than you are in the lawsuit," he said, seating himself beside me.

"The *tutoyer*[7] of the Italian voice is agreeable, however."

"It makes one dreamy."

"A child."

"Yes, a child; not a man nor a woman."

"I teach music. I can not dream over 'one, two, three.' "

"*You*—a music teacher!"

"For six years."

I was aware that he looked at me from head to foot, and I picked at the lace on my invariable black silk; but what did it matter whether I owned that I was a genteel pauper, representing my aunt's position for two months, or not?

"Where?"

"In Waterbury."[8]

"Waterbury differs from Newport."

"I suppose so."

"You suppose!"

A young gentleman sauntered by us, and Mr. Uxbridge called to him to look up the Misses Uxbridge, his nieces, on the other side of the hall.

"Paterfamilias Uxbridge has left his brood in my charge," he said. "I try to do my duty," and he held out a twisted pearl-colored glove, which he had pulled off while talking. What white nervous fingers he had! I thought they might pinch like steel.

"You suppose," he repeated.

"I do not look at Newport."

"Have you observed Waterbury?"

"I observe what is in my sphere."

"Oh!"

He was silent then. The second part of the concert began; but I could not compose myself to appreciation. Either the music or I grew chaotic. So many tumultuous sounds I heard—of hope, doubt, inquiry, melancholy, and desire; or did I feel the emotions which these words express?

7. I.e., intimate quality.   8. Village noted for the manufacture of clocks.

Or was there magnetism[9] stealing into me from the quiet man beside me? He left me with a bow before the concert was over, and I saw him making his way out of the hall when it was finished.

I had been sent in the carriage, of course; but several carriages were in advance of it before the walk, and I waited there for William to drive up. When he did so, I saw by the oscillatory motion of his head, though his arms and whiphand were perfectly correct, that he was inebriated. It was his first occasion of meeting fellow-coachmen in full dress, and the occasion had proved too much for him. My hand, however, was on the coach door, when I heard Mr. Uxbridge say, at my elbow,

"It is not safe for you."

"Oh, Sir, it is in the programme that I ride home from the concert." And I prepared to step in.

"I shall sit on the box, then."

"But your nieces?"

"They are walking home, squired by a younger knight."

Aunt Eliza would say, I thought, "Needs must when a lawyer drives;" and I concluded to allow him to have his way, telling him that he was taking a great deal of trouble. He thought it would be less if he were allowed to sit inside; both ways were unsafe.

Nothing happened. William drove well from habit; but James was obliged to assist him to dismount. Mr. Uxbridge waited a moment at the door, and so there was quite a little sensation, which spread its ripples till Aunt Eliza was reached. She sent for William, whose only excuse was "dampness."

"Uxbridge knew my carriage, of course," she said, with a complacent voice.

"He knew me," I replied.

"You do not look like the Huells."

"I look precisely like the young woman to whom he was introduced by Mr. Van Horn."

"Oh ho!"

"He thought it unsafe for me to come alone under William's charge."

"Ah ha!"

No more was said on the subject of his coming home with me. Aunt Eliza had several fits of musing in the course of the evening while I read aloud to her, which had no connection with the subject of the book. As I put it down she said that it would be well for me to go to church the next day. I acquiesced, but remarked that my piety would not require the carriage, and that I preferred to walk. Besides, it would be well for

9. I.e., hypnotic sexual attraction.

William and James to attend divine service. She could not spare James, and thought William had better clean the harness, by way of penance.

The morning proved to be warm and sunny. I donned a muslin dress of home manufacture and my own bonnet, and started for church. I had walked but a few paces when the consciousness of being *free* and *alone* struck me. I halted, looked about me, and concluded that I would not go to church, but walk into the fields. I had no knowledge of the whereabouts of the fields; but I walked straight forward, and after a while came upon some barren fields, cropping with coarse rocks, along which ran a narrow road. I turned into it, and soon saw beyond the rough coast the blue ring of the ocean—vast, silent, and splendid in the sunshine. I found a seat on the ruins of an old stone-wall, among some tangled bushes and briers. There being no Aunt Eliza to pull through the surf, and no animated bathers near, I discovered the beauty of the sea, and that I loved it.

Presently I heard the steps of a horse, and, to my astonishment, Mr. Uxbridge rode past. I was glad he did not know me. I watched him as he rode slowly down the road, deep in thought. He let drop the bridle, and the horse stopped, as if accustomed to the circumstance, and pawed the ground gently, or yawed his neck for pastime. Mr. Uxbridge folded his arms and raised his head to look seaward. It seemed to me as if he were about to address the jury. I had dropped so entirely from my observance of the landscape that I jumped when he resumed the bridle and turned his horse to come back. I slipped from my seat to look among the bushes, determined that he should not recognize me; but my attempt was a failure—he did not ride by the second time.

"Miss Huell!" And he jumped from his saddle, slipping his arm through the bridle.

"I am a runaway. What do you think of the Fugitive Slave Bill?"[1]

"I approve of returning property to its owners."

"The sea must have been God's temple first,[2] instead of the groves."

"I believe the Saurians[3] were an Orthodox tribe."

"Did you stop yonder to ponder the sea?"

"I was pondering 'Lemorne *vs.* Huell.'"

He looked at me earnestly, and then gave a tug at the bridle, for his steed was inclined to make a crude repast from the bushes.

"How was it that I did not detect you at once?" he continued.

"My apparel is Waterbury apparel."

"Ah!"

---

1. The Fugitive Slave Bill, part of the Compromise of 1850, was passed on September 18, 1850.

2. "Stoddard's readers would have recognized this alusion to the first line of Bryant's *A Forest Hymn* (1825): "The groves were God's first temples" [Parker's note].

3. Lizards.

We walked up the road slowly till we came to the end of it; then I stopped for him to understand that I thought it time for him to leave me. He sprang into the saddle.

"Give us good-by!" he said, bringing his horse close to me.

"We are not on equal terms; I feel too humble afoot to salute you."

"Put your foot on the stirrup then."

A leaf stuck in the horse's forelock, and I pulled it off and waved it in token of farewell. A powerful light shot into his eyes when he saw my hand close on the leaf.

"May I come and see you?" he asked, abruptly. "I will."

"I shall say neither 'No' nor 'Yes.'"

He rode on at a quick pace, and I walked homeward, forgetting the sense of liberty I had started with, and proceeded straightway to Aunt Eliza.

"I have not been to church, aunt, but to walk beyond the town; it was not so nominated in the bond, but I went. The taste of freedom was so pleasant that I warn you there is danger of my 'striking.'[4] When will you have done with Newport?"

"I am pleased with Newport now," she answered, with a curious intonation. "I like it."

"I do also."

Her keen eyes sparkled.

"Did you ever like any thing when you were with me before?"

"Never. I will tell you why I like it: because I have met, and shall probably meet, Mr. Uxbridge. I saw him to-day. He asked permission to visit me."

"Let him come."

"He will come."

But we did not see him either at the hotel or when we went abroad. Aunt Eliza rode with me each afternoon, and each morning we went to the beach. She engaged me every moment when at home, and I faithfully performed all my tasks. I clapped to the door on self-investigation —locked it against any analysis or reasoning upon any circumstance connected with Mr. Uxbridge. The only piece of treachery to my code that I was guilty of was the putting of the leaf which I brought home on Sunday between the leaves of that poem whose motto is,

"Mariana in the moated grange."[5]

---

4. I.e., striking out on her own.

5. "Tennyson's *Mariana* takes the quoted motto from Shakespeare's *Measure for Measure* (III.i.277): 'there, at the moated grange, resides this dejected Mariana.' (Grange: secluded country house.) The act of putting the leaf in the poem is an avowal of passionate love which the narrator thinks will never be fulfilled; *Mariana* ends: 'Then, said she, "I am very dreary, He will not come," she said; / She wept. "I am aweary, aweary, / Oh God, that I were dead!"' " [Parker's note].

On Saturday morning, nearly a week after I saw him on my walk, Aunt Eliza proposed that we should go to Turo Street on a shopping excursion; she wanted a cap, and various articles besides. As we went into a large shop I saw Mr. Uxbridge at a counter buying gloves; her quick eye caught sight of him, and she edged away, saying she would look at some goods on the other side; I might wait where I was. As he turned to go out he saw me and stopped.

"I have been in New York since I saw you," he said. "Mr. Lemorne sent for me."

"There is my aunt," I said.

He shrugged his shoulders.

"I shall not go away soon again," he remarked. "I missed Newport greatly."

I made some foolish reply, and kept my eyes on Aunt Eliza, who dawdled unaccountably. He appeared amused, and after a little talk went away.

Aunt Eliza's purchase was a rose-colored moire antique, which she said was to be made for me; for Mrs. Bliss, one of our hotel acquaintances, had offered to chaperon me to the great ball which would come off in a few days, and she had accepted the offer for me.

"There will be no chance for you to take a walk instead," she finished with.

"I can not dance, you know."

"But you will be *there*."

I was sent to a dress-maker of Mrs. Bliss's recommending; but I ordered the dress to be made after my own design, long plain sleeves, and high plain corsage, and requested that it should not be sent home till the evening of the ball. Before it came off Mr. Uxbridge called, and was graciously received by Aunt Eliza, who could be gracious to all except her relatives. I could not but perceive, however, that they watched each other in spite of their lively conversation. To me he was deferential, but went over the ground of our acquaintance as if it had been the most natural thing in the world. But for my life-long habit of never calling in question the behavior of those I came in contact with, and of never expecting any thing different from that I received, I might have wondered over his visit. Every person's individuality was sacred to me, from the fact, perhaps, that my own individuality had never been respected by any person with whom I had any relation—not even by my own mother.

After Mr. Uxbridge went, I asked Aunt Eliza if she thought he looked mean and cunning? She laughed, and replied that she was bound to think that Mr. Lemorne's lawyer could not look otherwise.

When, on the night of the ball, I presented myself in the rose-colored moire antique for her inspection, she raised her eyebrows, but said nothing about it.

"I need not be careful of it, I suppose, aunt?"

"Spill as much wine and ice-cream on it as you like."

In the dressing-room Mrs. Bliss surveyed me.

"I think I like this mass of rose-color," she said. "Your hair comes out in contrast so brilliantly. Why, you have not a single ornament on!"

"It is so easy to dress without."

This was all the conversation we had together during the evening, except when she introduced some acquaintance to fulfill her matronizing duties. As I was no dancer I was left alone most of the time, and amused myself by gliding from window to window along the wall, that it might not be observed that I was a fixed flower. Still I suffered the annoyance of being stared at by wandering squads of young gentlemen, the "curled darlings"[6] of the ball-room. I borrowed Mrs. Bliss's fan in one of her visits for a protection. With that, and the embrasure of a remote window where I finally stationed myself, I hoped to escape further notice. The music of the celebrated band which played between the dances recalled the chorus of spirits which charmed Faust:[7]

> "And the fluttering
> Ribbons of drapery
> Cover the plains,
> Cover the bowers,
> Where lovers,
> Deep in thought,
> Give themselves for life."

The voice of Mrs. Bliss broke its spell.

"I bring an old friend, Miss Huell, and he tells me an acquaintance of yours."

It was Mr. Uxbridge.

"I had no thought of meeting you, Miss Huell."

And he coolly took the seat beside me in the window, leaving to Mrs. Bliss the alternative of standing or of going away; she chose the latter.

"I saw you as soon as I came in," he said, "gliding from window to window, like a vessel hugging the shore in a storm."

"With colors at half-mast; I have no dancing partner."

"How many have observed you?"

"Several young gentlemen."

"Moths."

"Oh no, butterflies."

"They must keep away now."

6. Shakespeare's *Othello*, I.iii.68.
7. Goethe's *Faust*, Act III (the "Exorcism" section).

"Are you Rhadamanthus?"[8]

"And Charon, too. I would have you row in the same boat with me."

"Now you are fishing."

"Won't you compliment me. Did I ever look better?"

His evening costume *was* becoming, but he looked pale, and weary, and disturbed. But if we were engaged for a tournament, as his behavior indicated, I must do my best at telling. So I told him that he never looked better, and asked him how I looked. He would look at me presently, he said, and decide. Mrs. Bliss skimmed by us with nods and smiles; as she vanished our eyes followed her, and we talked vaguely on various matters, sounding ourselves and each other. When a furious redowa[9] set in which cut our conversation into rhythm he pushed up the window and said, "Look out."

I turned my face to him to do so, and saw the moon at the full, riding through the strip of sky which our vision commanded. From the moon our eyes fell on each other. After a moment's silence, during which I returned his steadfast gaze, for I could not help it, he said:

"If we understand the impression we make upon each other, what must be said?"

I made no reply, but fanned myself, neither looking at the moon, nor upon the redowa, nor upon any thing.

He took the fan from me.

"Speak of yourself," he said.

"Speak you."

"I am what I seem, a man within your sphere. By all the accidents of position and circumstance suited to it. Have you not learned it?"

"I am not what I seem. I never wore so splendid a dress as this till to-night, and shall not again."

He gave the fan such a twirl that its slender sticks snapped, and it drooped like the broken wing of a bird.

"Mr. Uxbridge, that fan belongs to Mrs. Bliss."

He threw it out of the window.

"You have courage, fidelity, and patience—this character with a passionate soul. I am sure that you have such a soul?"

"I do not know."

"I have fallen in love with you. It happened on the very day when I passed you on the way to the Glen. I never got away from the remembrance of seeing your hand on the mane of my horse."

He waited for me to speak, but I could not; the balance of my mind was gone. Why should this have happened to me—a slave? As it had happened, why did I not feel exultant in the sense of power which the chance for freedom with him should give?

---

8. In Greek mythology, a judge of the dead in Hades, who were rowed there, over the river Styx, by Charon.

9. A Bohemian waltz.

"What is it, Margaret? Your face is as sad as death."

"How do you call me 'Margaret?' "

"As I would call my wife—Margaret."

He rose and stood before me to screen my face from observation. I supposed so, and endeavored to stifle my agitation.

"You are better," he said, presently. "Come go with me and get some refreshment." And he beckoned to Mrs. Bliss, who was down the hall with an unwieldy gentleman.

"Will you go to supper now?" she asked.

"We are only waiting for you," Mr. Uxbridge answered, offering me his arm.

When we emerged into the blaze and glitter of the supper-room I sought refuge in the shadow of Mrs. Bliss's companion, for it seemed to me that I had lost my own.

"Drink this Champagne," said Mr. Uxbridge. "Pay no attention to the Colonel on your left; he won't expect it."

"Neither must you."

"Drink."

The Champagne did not prevent me from reflecting on the fact that he had not yet asked whether I loved him.

The spirit chorus again floated through my mind:

> "Where lovers,
> Deep in thought,
> *Give* themselves for life."

I was not allowed to *give* myself—I was *taken*.

"No heel-taps,"[1] he whispered, "to the bottom quaff."

"Take me home, will you?"

"Mrs. Bliss is not ready."

"Tell her that I must go."

He went behind her chair and whispered something, and she nodded to me to go without her.

When her carriage came up, I think he gave the coachman an order to drive home in a roundabout way, for we were a long time reaching it. I kept my face to the window, and he made no effort to divert my attention. When we came to a street whose thick rows of trees shut out the moonlight my eager soul longed to leap out into the dark and demand of him his heart, soul, life, for *me*.

I struck him lightly on the shoulder; he seized my hand.

"Oh, I know you, Margaret; you are mine!"

"We are at the hotel."

He sent the carriage back, and said that he would leave me at my

---

1. Small amount of liquor left in a glass.

aunt's door. He wished that he could see her then. Was it magic that made her open the door before I reached it?

"Have you come on legal business?" she asked him.

"You have divined what I come for."

"Step in, step in; it's very late. I should have been in bed but for neuralgia. Did Mr. Uxbridge come home with you, Margaret?"

"Yes, in Mrs. Bliss's carriage; I wished to come before she was ready to leave."

"Well, Mr. Uxbridge is old enough for your protector, certainly."

"I *am* forty, ma'am."

"Do you want Margaret?"

"I do."

"You know exactly how much is involved in your client's suit?"

"Exactly."

"You know also that his claim is an unjust one."

"Do I?"

"I shall not be poor if I lose; if I gain, Margaret will be rich."

" 'Margaret will be rich!' " he repeated, absently.

"What! have you changed your mind respecting the orphans, aunt?"

"She has, and is—nothing," she went on, not heeding my remark. "Her father married below his station; when he died his wife fell back to her place—for he spent his fortune—and there she and Margaret must remain, unless Lemorne is defeated."

"Aunt, for your succinct biography of my position many thanks."

"Sixty thousand dollars," she continued. "Van Horn tells me that, as yet, the firm of Uxbridge Brothers have only an income—no capital."

"It is true," he answered, musingly.

The clock on the mantle struck two.

"A thousand dollars for every year of my life," she said. "You and I, Uxbridge, know the value and beauty of money."

"Yet, there is beauty in money, and"—looking at me—"beauty without it."

"The striking of the clock," I soliloquized, "proves that this scene is not a phantasm."

"Margaret is fatigued," he said, rising. "May I come to-morrow?"

"It is my part only," replied Aunt Eliza, "to see that she is, or is not, Cinderella."

"If you have ever thought of me, aunt, as an individual, you must have seen that I am not averse to ashes."

He held my hand a moment, and then kissed me with a kiss of appropriation.

"He is in love with you," she said, after he had gone. "I think I know him. He has found beauty ignorant of itself; he will teach you to develop it."

The next morning Mr. Uxbridge had an interview with Aunt Eliza before he saw me.

When we were alone I asked him how her eccentricities affected him; he could not but consider her violent, prejudiced, warped, and whimsical. I told him that I had been taught to accept all that she did on this basis. Would this explain to him my silence in regard to her?

"Can you endure to live with her in Bond Street for the present, or would you rather return to Waterbury?"

"She desires my company while she is in Newport only. I have never been with her so long before."

"I understand her. Law is a game, in her estimation, in which cheating can as easily be carried on as at cards."

"Her soul is in this case."

"Her soul is not too large for it. Will you ride this afternoon?"

I promised, of course. From that time till he left Newport we saw each other every day, and though I found little opportunity to express my own peculiar feelings, he comprehended many of my wishes, and all my tastes. I grew fond of him hourly. Had I not reason? Never was friend so considerate, never was lover more devoted.

When he had been gone a few days, Aunt Eliza declared that she was ready to depart from Newport. The rose-colored days were ended! In two days we were on the Sound,[2] coach, horses, servants, and ourselves.

It was the 1st of September when we arrived in Bond Street. A week from that date Samuel Uxbridge, the senior partner of Uxbridge Brothers, went to Europe with his family, and I went to Waterbury, accompanied by Mr. Uxbridge. He consulted mother in regard to our marriage, and appointed it in November. In October Aunt Eliza sent for me to come back to Bond Street and spend a week. She had some fine marking[3] to do, she wrote. While there I noticed a restlessness in her which I had never before observed, and conferred with Mrs. Roll on the matter. "She do be awake nights a deal, and that's the reason," Mrs. Roll said. Her manner was the same in other respects. She said she would not give me any thing for my wedding outfit, but she paid my fare from Waterbury and back.

She could not spare me to go out, she told Mr. Uxbridge, and in consequence I saw little of him while there.

In November we were married. Aunt Eliza was not at the wedding, which was a quiet one. Mr. Uxbridge desired me to remain in Waterbury till spring. He would not decide about taking a house in New York till then; by that time his brother might return, and if possible we would go to Europe for a few months. I acquiesced in all his plans. Indeed I

---

2. Long Island Sound.
3. I.e., marking of patterns for Eliza's new clothes.

was not consulted; but I was happy—happy in him, and happy in every thing.

The winter passed in waiting for him to come to Waterbury every Saturday; and in the enjoyment of the two days he passed with me. In March Aunt Eliza wrote me that Lemorne was beaten! Van Horn had taken up the whole contents of his snuff-box in her house the evening before in amazement at the turn things had taken.

That night I dreamed of the scene in the hotel at Newport. I heard Aunt Eliza saying, "If I gain, Margaret will be rich." And I heard also the clock strike two. As it struck I said, "*My husband is a scoundrel*," and woke with a start.[4]

1863

4. "The ending depends upon knowledge of property laws. Among the injustices of men toward women in the Seneca Falls Declaration of Sentiments and Resolutions (July 19, 1848) were these: 'He has made her, if married, in the eye of the law, civilly dead. He has taken from her all right in property, even to the wages she earns.' ('Civilly': legally.)" [Parker's note].

FRANCES E. W. HARPER
1825–1911

Of the black women writers who contributed to the abolition movement, the one with the most successful publishing career was Frances Ellen Watkins Harper. Although her first collection of poetry and prose, *Forest Leaves* (c. 1845), is no longer available, her volume of antislavery verse, *Poems on Miscellaneous Subjects* (1845), sold twelve thousand copies by 1858 and went through some twenty editions by 1874. Her narrative poems, which dramatized her protest against white injustice to blacks, were exceptionally popular with lecture audiences. Just as the *The Two Offers* (*Anglo-African Magazine*, 1859) was described as "the first short story published by an American Negro," *Iola Leroy; or, Shadows Uplifted* (1892) was recognized as the first novel by a black author to describe the Reconstruction. Throughout her life, Harper integrated her literary career with public service dedicated to the moral education of whites and blacks.

Born in Baltimore, Maryland, to free Negro parents, Frances Watkins was orphaned at the age of three and raised by her uncle, the Reverend William Watkins. At thirteen, after attending his school for free Negroes, she supported herself as a nursemaid and later as a seamstress and teacher. Through contacts with abolitionists involved in the Underground Railroad in the early 1850s, she lectured widely for antislavery societies in Massachusetts, Pennsylvania, Maine, New Jersey, New York, and Ohio, sometimes using the lecture podium for readings of her poetry. On November 22, 1860, she married Fenton Harper, a widower who died four years later. When she resumed her lecturing, she toured the South, addressing both black and mixed audiences. From

1871, when she settled in Philadelphia with her daughter, until her death at eighty-five, Harper worked actively in social and civic organizations, as a participant in two conventions of the American Woman Suffrage Association, as the director of the American Association of Education of Colored Youth, and as the vice-president of the National Association of Colored Women.

Her verse, written to dramatize her political commitments, was sometimes as sentimental as the poetry of her contemporary, Felicia Hemans. Yet, at her best, Harper used biblical characters and black dialect to define the terrible experience of slavery from the point of view of black women, and to record the subversive survival skills such women contributed to slave culture.

Vashti[1]

She leaned her head upon her hand
    And heard the king's decree—
"My lords are feasting in my halls,
    Bid Vashti come to me.

"I've shown the treasures of my house,   5
    My costly jewels rare,
But with the glory of her eyes
    No rubies can compare.

"Adorn'd and crown'd I'd have her come,
    With all her queenly grace,   10
And, 'mid my lords and mighty men,
    Unveil her lovely face.

"Each gem that sparkles in my crown,
    Or glitters on my throne,
Grows poor and pale when she appears,   15
    My beautiful, my own!"

All waiting stood the chamberlains
    To hear the Queen's reply,
They saw her cheek grow deathly pale,
    But light flash'd to her eye: 20

"Go, tell the King," she proudly said,
    "That I am Persia's Queen,
And by his crowds of merry men
    I never will be seen.

"I'll take the crown from off my head   25
    And tread it 'neath my feet

1. The queen of Ahasuerus refused to dance before him and was banished from his sight (Esther 1: 9–19).

Before their rude and careless gaze
    My shrinking eyes shall meet.

"A queen unveil'd before the crowd!—
    Upon each lip my name!—   30
Why, Persia's women all would blush
    And weep for Vashti's shame!

"Go back!" she cried, and waived her hand,
    And grief was in her eye:
"Go, tell the King," she sadly said,   35
    "That I would rather die."

They brought her message to the King,
    Dark flash'd his angry eye;
'Twas as the lightning ere the storm
    Hath swept in fury by.   40

Then bitterly outspoke the King,
    Through purple lips of wrath—
"What shall be done to her who dares
    To cross your monarch's path?"

Then spake his wily counsellors—   45
    "O King of this fair land!
From distant Ind to Ethiop,
    All bow to thy command.

"But if, before thy servants' eyes,
    This thing they plainly see,   50
That Vashti doth not heed thy will
    Nor yield herself to thee,

"The women, restive 'neath our rule,
    Would learn to scorn our name,
And from her deed to us would come   55
    Reproach and burning shame.

"Then, gracious King, sign with thy hand
    This stern but just decree,
That Vashti lay aside her crown,
    Thy Queen no more to be."   60

She heard again the King's command,
    And left her high estate,[2]

2. Position in society.

Strong in her earnest womanhood,
   She calmly met her fate,

And left the palace of the King,   65
   Proud of her spotless name—
A woman who could bend to grief,
   But would not bow to shame.

1871

Aunt Chloe's Politics

Of course, I don't know very much
   About these politics,
But I think that some who run 'em,
   Do mighty ugly tricks.

I've seen 'em honey-fugle[3] round,   5
   And talk so awful sweet,
That you'd think them full of kindness,
   As an egg is full of meat.[4]

Now I don't believe in looking
   Honest people in the face,   10
And saying when you're doing wrong,
   That "I haven't sold my race."[5]

When we want to school our children,
   If the money isn't there,
Whether black or white have took it,   15
   The love we all must share.

And this buying up each other
   Is something worse than mean,
Though I thinks a heap of voting,
   I go for voting clean.[6]   20

1872

Learning to Read

Very soon the Yankee teachers
   Came down and set up school;

---

3. Sweet-talk, deceive through empty rhetoric.
4. I.e., yolk and albumen.
5. I.e., wronged my people.

6. During the post–Civil War period white politicians (known as carpetbaggers) tried to buy Negro votes.

But, oh! how the Rebs[7] did hate it,—
    It was agin' their rule.

Our masters always tried to hide   5
    Book learning from our eyes;
Knowledge didn't agree with slavery—
    'Twould make us all too wise.

But some of us would try to steal
    A little from the book,   10
And put the words together,
    And learn by hook or crook.

I remember Uncle Caldwell,
    Who took pot liquor fat[8]
And greased the pages of his book,   15
    And hid it in his hat

And had his master ever seen
    The leaves upon his head,
He'd have thought them greasy papers,
    But nothing to be read.   20

And there was Mr. Turner's Ben,
    Who heard the children spell,
And picked the words right up by heart,
    And learned to read 'em well.

Well, the Northern folks kept sending   25
    The Yankee teachers down;
And they stood right up and helped us,
    Though Rebs did sneer and frown.

And, I longed to read my Bible,
    For precious words it said;   30
But when I begun to learn it,
    Folks just shook their heads,

And said there is no use trying,
    Oh! Chloe, you're too late;
But as I was rising sixty,[9]   35
    I had no time to wait.

So I got a pair of glasses,
    And straight to work I went,

---

7. The southern "rebels." The poem takes place after the Civil War, during the period of Reconstruction when northern teachers came to the South to educate the newly freed slaves.
8. The fat that floats to the top of the pot.
9. Nearing sixty.

> And never stopped till I could read
>   The hymns and Testament.   40
>
> Then I got a little cabin
>   A place to call my own—
> And I felt as independent
>   As the queen upon her throne.

                                                            1872

HARRIET E. ADAMS WILSON
1828?–1860?

Harriet E. Wilson was the first black woman to publish a novel in English and the first Afro-American to publish a novel in the United States. Her sardonically entitled *Our Nig* was printed (apparently at her own expense) by the Massachusetts firm of George C. Rand and Avery in September 1859. Even more than the phrase "our nig"—a phrase that would have been as shocking in the nineteenth century as it is today—the book's full title emphasized the author's political motivation, as well as her irony, for it read:

OUR NIG.

or,
*Sketches from the
Life of a Free Black,*
In a Two-Story White House, North.
SHOWING THAT SLAVERY'S SHADOWS
FALL EVEN THERE.

by "OUR NIG."

Our Nig received no reviews, evidently had hardly any sales, and was almost completely forgotten until the scholar Henry Louis Gates, Jr., reissued it in a facsimile edition in 1983.

As Gates observes, Wilson's use of the controversial, emotionally charged word "nig" in her title may in fact have been partly responsible for the obscurity into which the novel fell; in addition, he argues that the opening of the tale, which portrays a comparatively happy marriage between a black man and a white woman, may have made the work unacceptable to black and white readers alike. In any case, the book's failure undoubtedly accounts for the paucity of information about Wilson herself. She was probably born in New Hampshire, she may have been trained as a hat maker, she married and was evidently deserted by a sailor named Wilson, and she subsequently gave birth in a "county house" (a poor house) to a child named George Mason Wilson, who died in 1860 at the age of seven: these are among the few facts known about her. Nevertheless, *Our Nig* itself offers a vivid picture of the kind of life she must have lived as a free black in New England, for the novel appears to be based on personal experiences.

The selection included here, for instance, recounts the circumstances of the childhood of "our nig," a mulatto girl named Alfrado, or "Frado" for short. When this passage begins, the child is seven, her father has died, and her mother has deserted her, leaving her with a wealthy white family, the Bellmonts, who have decided to keep her in the household as a servant.

From Our Nig

[*Frado's Childhood*]

Frado was called early in the morning by her new mistress. Her first work was to feed the hens. She was shown how it was *always* to be done, and in no other way; any departure from this rule to be punished by a whipping. She was then accompanied by Jack[1] to drive the cows to pasture, so she might learn the way. Upon her return she was allowed to eat her breakfast, consisting of a bowl of skimmed milk, with brown bread crusts, which she was told to eat, standing, by the kitchen table, and must not be over ten minutes about it. Meanwhile the family were taking their morning meal in the dining-room. This over, she was placed on a cricket[2] to wash the common dishes; she was to be in waiting always to bring wood and chips, to run hither and thither from room to room.

A large amount of dish-washing for small hands followed dinner. Then the same after tea and going after the cows finished her first day's work. It was a new discipline to the child. She found some attractions about the place, and she retired to rest at night more willing to remain. The same routine followed day after day, with slight variation; adding a little more work, and spicing the toil with "words that burn," and frequent blows on her head. These were great annoyances to Frado, and had she known where her mother was, she would have gone at once to her. She was often greatly wearied, and silently wept over her sad fate. At first she wept aloud, which Mrs. Bellmont noticed by applying a rawhide,[3] always at hand in the kitchen. It was a symptom of discontent and complaining which must be "nipped in the bud," she said.

Thus passed a year. No intelligence of Mag.[4] It was now certain Frado was to become a permanent member of the family. Her labors were multiplied; she was quite indispensable, although but seven years old. She had never learned to read, never heard of a school until her residence in the family.

---

1. The son of the Bellmont family.   3. I.e., a whip.
2. A footstool.   4. Frado's mother.

Mrs. Bellmont was in doubt about the utility of attempting to educate people of color, who were incapable of elevation. This subject occasioned a lengthy discussion in the family. Mr. Bellmont, Jane and Jack arguing for Frado's education; Mary and her mother objecting. At last Mr. Bellmont declared decisively that she *should* go to school. He was a man who seldom decided controversies at home. The word once spoken admitted of no appeal; so, notwithstanding Mary's objection that she would have to attend the same school she did, the word became law.

It was to be a new scene to Frado, and Jack had many queries and conjectures to answer. He was himself too far advanced to attend the summer school, which Frado regretted, having had too many opportunities of witnessing Miss Mary's temper to feel safe in her company alone.

The opening day of school came. Frado sauntered on far in the rear of Mary, who was ashamed to be seen "walking with a nigger." As soon as she appeared, with scanty clothing and bared feet, the children assembled, noisily published her approach: "See that nigger," shouted one. "Look! look!" cried another. "I won't play with her," said one little girl. "Nor I neither," replied another.

Mary evidently relished these sharp attacks, and saw a fair prospect of lowering Nig where, according to her views, she belonged. Poor Frado, chagrined and grieved, felt that her anticipations of pleasure at such a place were far from being realized. She was just deciding to return home, and never come there again, when the teacher appeared, and observing the downcast looks of the child, took her by the hand, and led her into the school-room. All followed, and, after the bustle of securing seats was over, Miss Marsh inquired if the children knew "any cause for the sorrow of that little girl?" pointing to Frado. It was soon all told. She then reminded them of their duties to the poor and friendless; their cowardice in attacking a young innocent child; referred them to one who looks not on outward appearances, but on the heart. "She looks like a good girl; I think I shall love her, so lay aside all prejudice, and vie with each other in shewing kindness and good-will to one who seems different from you," were the closing remarks of the kind lady. Those kind words! The most agreeable sound which ever meets the ear of sorrowing, grieving childhood.

Example rendered her words efficacious. Day by day there was a manifest change of deportment towards "Nig." Her speeches often drew merriment from the children; no one could do more to enliven their favorite pastimes than Frado. Mary could not endure to see her thus noticed, yet knew not how to prevent it. She could not influence her schoolmates as she wished. She had not gained their effections by winning ways and yielding points of controversy. On the contrary, she was self-willed, domineering; every day reported "mad" by some of her companions. She availed herself of the only alternative, abuse and taunts, as they returned from school. This was not satisfactory; she wanted to use physical force "to subdue her," to "keep her down."

There was, on their way home, a field intersected by a stream over which a single plank was placed for a crossing. It occurred to Mary that it would be a punishment to Nig to compel her to cross over; so she dragged her to the edge, and told her authoritatively to go over. Nig hesitated, resisted. Mary placed herself behind the child, and, in the struggle to force her over, lost her footing and plunged into the stream. Some of the larger scholars being in sight, ran, and thus prevented Mary from drowning and Frado from falling. Nig scampered home fast as possible, and Mary went to the nearest house, dripping, to procure a change of garments. She came loitering home, half crying, exclaiming, "Nig pushed me into the stream!" She then related the particulars. Nig was called from the kitchen. Mary stood with anger flashing in her eyes. Mr. Bellmont sat quietly reading his paper. He had witnessed too many of Miss Mary's outbreaks to be startled. Mrs. Bellmont interrogated Nig.

"I did n't do it! I did n't do it!" answered Nig, passionately, and then related the occurrence truthfully.

The discrepancy greatly enraged Mrs. Bellmont. With loud accusations and angry gestures she approached the child. Turning to her husband, she asked.

"Will you sit still, there, and hear that black nigger call Mary a liar?"

"How do we know but she has told the truth? I shall not punish her," he replied, and left the house, as he usually did when a tempest threatened to envelop him. No sooner was he out of sight than Mrs. B. and Mary commenced beating her inhumanly; then propping her mouth open with a piece of wood, shut her up in a dark room, without any supper. For employment, while the tempest raged within, Mr. Bellmont went for the cows, a task belonging to Frado, and thus unintentionally prolonged her pain. At dark Jack came in, and seeing Mary, accosted her with, "So you thought you'd vent your spite on Nig, did you? Why can't you let her alone? It was good enough for you to get a ducking, only you did not stay in half long enough."

"Stop!" said his mother. "You shall never talk so before me. You would have that little nigger trample on Mary, would you? She came home with a lie; it made Mary's story false."

"What was Mary's story?" asked Jack.

It was related.

"Now," said Jack, sallying into a chair, "the school-children happened to see it all, and they tell the same story Nig does. Which is most likely to be true, what a dozen agree they saw, or the contrary?"

"It is very strange you will believe what others say against your sister," retorted his mother, with flashing eye. "I think it is time your father subdued you."

"Father is a sensible man," argued Jack. "He would not wrong a dog. Where *is* Frado?" he continued.

"Mother gave her a good whipping and shut her up," replied Mary.

Just then Mr. Bellmont entered, and asked if Frado was "shut up yet."

The knowledge of her innocence, the perfidy of his sister, worked fearfully on Jack. He bounded from his chair, searched every room till he found the child; her mouth wedged apart, her face swollen, and full of pain.

How Jack pitied her! He relieved her jaws, brought her some supper, took her to her room, comforted her as well as he knew how, sat by her till she fell asleep, and then left for the sitting room. As he passed his mother, he remarked, "If that was the way Frado was to be treated, he hoped she would never wake again!" He then imparted her situation to his father, who seemed untouched, till a glance at Jack exposed a tearful eye. Jack went early to her next morning. She awoke sad, but refreshed. After breakfast Jack took her with him to the field, and kept her through the day. But it could not be so generally. She must return to school, to her household duties. He resolved to do what he could to protect her from Mary and his mother. He bought her a dog, which became a great favorite with both. The invalid, Jane, would gladly befriend her; but she had not the strength to brave the iron will of her mother. Kind words and affectionate glances were the only expressions of sympathy she could safely indulge in. The men employed on the farm were always glad to hear her prattle; she was a great favorite with them. Mrs. Bellmont allowed them the privilege of talking with her in the kitchen. She did not fear but she should have ample opportunity of subduing her when they were away. Three months of schooling, summer and winter, she enjoyed for three years. Her winter over-dress was a cast-off overcoat, once worn by Jack, and a sun-bonnet. It was a source of great merriment to the scholars, but Nig's retorts were so mirthful, and their satisfaction so evident in attributing the selection to "Old Granny Bellmont," that it was not painful to Nig or pleasurable to Mary. Her jollity was not to be quenched by whipping or scolding. In Mrs. Bellmont's presence she was under restraint; but in the kitchen, and among her schoolmates, the pent up fires burst forth. She was ever at some sly prank when unseen by her teacher, in school hours; not unfrequently some outburst of merriment, of which she was the original, was charged upon some innocent mate, and punishment inflicted which she merited. They enjoyed her antics so fully that any of them would suffer wrongfully to keep open the avenues of mirth. She would venture far beyond propriety, thus shielded and countenanced.

The teacher's desk was supplied with drawers, in which were stored his books and other *et ceteras* of the profession. The children observed Nig very busy there one morning before school, as they flitted in occasionally from their play outside. The master came; called the children to order; opened a drawer to take the book the occasion required; when out poured a volume of smoke. "Fire! fire!" screamed he, at the top of his voice. By this time he had become sufficiently acquainted with the peculiar odor, to know he was imposed upon. The scholars shouted with laughter to see the terror of the dupe, who, feeling abashed at the needless fright, made no very strict investigation, and Nig once more escaped punishment. She had provided herself with cigars, and puffing, puffing away at the crack of the drawer, had filled it with smoke, and then closed it tightly to deceive the teacher, and amuse the scholars. The interim of terms was filled up with a variety of duties new and peculiar. At home, no matter how powerful the heat when sent to rake hay or guard the grazing herd, she was never permitted to shield her skin from the sun. She was not many shades darker than Mary now; what a calamity it would be ever to hear the contrast spoken of. Mrs. Bellmont was determined the sun should have full power to darken the shade which nature had first bestowed upon her as best befitting.

1859

EMILY DICKINSON
1830–1886

In 1881 a young woman named Mabel Loomis Todd wrote her parents about "the *character* of Amherst . . . a lady whom the people call the '*Myth*': She has not been outside of her own house in fifteen years. . . . She dresses wholly in white, and her mind is said to be perfectly wonderful." So began the legend of Emily Dickinson, one of the greatest poets of the nineteenth century, who was for years portrayed by biographers and critics as an eccentric recluse, a "little home-keeping person," a mad spinster who had been disappointed in love. For, four years after this New England woman in white died in 1886, the same Mabel Loomis Todd brought out a volume containing selections from 1,776 strange and passionate poems which had been found, neatly sewed into booklets, in her bureau drawers, and the imagination of the public was immediately seized by the mysterious discrepancy between what seemed to be the isolation of Dickinson's life and the intensity of her art. To many, indeed, the "case" of Emily Dickinson—only eight of whose poems had been published in her lifetime—seemed to offer a crucial model for the situation of the woman poet. Eccentricity, reclusiveness, and, most of all, thwarted romance—these appeared to be the conditions that might drive a woman to what was, for women, the perversity of writing verse.

Despite the equivocal glamour of the legend Mabel Loomis Todd helped create, however, the "Myth of Amherst" had a conventional enough childhood, and, even in its apparent isolation, her adult life was marked not so much by longing for lost love as by aesthetic and intellectual commitment to her art, in whose cause she continually demanded "severer service" of herself. The second child of Edward Dickinson, an austere but ambitious lawyer, and his retiring wife, Emily, she was born on December 10, 1830 into one of Amherst's leading families. With her older brother, Austin, and her younger sister, Lavinia, she seems to have had a cheerful home and, by the standards of her time and place, a good education at Amherst Academy. When she was seventeen, moreover, she even went for a year to what was to become one of the first women's colleges—Mount Holyoke Female Seminary, a few miles outside Amherst.

It was at Mount Holyoke that Dickinson's independence and imagination began to manifest themselves. Two episodes, in particular, tell us something about the kind of resourceful and rebellious girl she was. The first, about which Mabel Loomis Todd heard from the poet's sister, has to do with geometry: "When the [geometry] examination came and [Emily] had never studied it, she went to the blackboard and gave such a glib exposition of imaginary figures that the dazed teacher passed her with the highest mark." The second, which was reported by a classmate, has to do with religion: when Mary Lyon, the school principal, was proselytizing for an evangelical revival, she "asked all those who wanted to be Christians to rise," but, because Emily could not "honestly accede to" the request, she, and only she, "remained seated."

Geometry may have been a subject that the young Emily Dickinson was able to "imagine," but orthodox religious conversion evidently was not, and, as many biographers have speculated, it was quite possibly Miss Lyon's evangelical revival that decided the poet upon leaving Mount Holyoke, though her father's desire to have his older daughter back at home also played a part in the move. In any case, after only a year she left school, never to return, and from then on her life became increasingly withdrawn, as she slowly developed the fear of public places (known as agoraphobia) that marked her later years. Her trips out of town were few. As a girl, she traveled to Boston, Cambridge, and Worcester several times to vacation with relatives. In 1855, she and her sister "Vinnie" accompanied their congressman father to Washington and Philadelphia for a visit of almost two months. Finally, in 1864, she spent some weeks in Cambridge because she was being treated by a Boston specialist for what recent scholars have theorized was a bad case of an eye disorder called exotropia. Except for these excursions, she remained in Amherst—a kind of Yankee princess deliberately training herself to see, as she put it, "New Englandly"—until her death in 1886 of Bright's disease.

But even in Amherst, what Dickinson called the "circumference" of her daily life gradually narrowed. At first a high-spirited girl, helping to hostess her father's parties, paying visits to neighbors, and composing whimsical valentines for undergraduates at Amherst College, she eventually took to dressing "wholly in white," assured the editor Thomas Wentworth Higginson—one of her major correspondents—that "I do not cross my Father's ground to any house in town," refused for the most part to appear before callers, and even in her last illness allowed a doctor to "examine" her only as she walked past a partially opened door in the next room. Becoming a "Myth," she "manifested" her presence, like a priestess of some mysterious religion, only through tokens of flowers, cakes, and wine, transmitted by her sister or the family servant, or, as one famous story has it, through playful gifts of sweets to children, arranged in a basket let down from her bedroom window.

What could have accounted for such behavior in a woman who had been a witty and energetic girl? For years, biographers of Dickinson assumed that sometime in the early 1860s she had fallen hopelessly in love with a man whose identity has never been established, though the leading candidate for the position was long supposed to be the Reverend Charles Wadsworth, a glamorous but married clergyman, whom she was thought to have met during her 1855 stay in Philadelphia. A series of tormented, often frankly erotic letters to a man enigmatically addressed as "Master," in which Dickinson variously defines herself as a wounded bird, a childlike "Daisy," a "culprit," a "smaller life," reinforced the sense of such biographers that both this writer's withdrawal from the world and her impassioned art were inspired by a tragic romance. More recently, however, critics have begun to question the sentimental assumptions upon which such interpretations of her life and work were based.

To be sure, as these scholars concede, there may well have been an emotional event which inspired both Dickinson's poetry and her self-protectiveness. Yet her "Master" letters, with their deliberate effacement of the addressee's identity, are just as clearly explorations of the general relationship between male power and female powerlessness, male authority and female dependency, as they are pleas for romantic reassurance from a particular man. Moreover, in these letters as in so many of her most impassioned verses, the poet is obviously both disguising and dramatizing herself, as if to document a crucial confession that she made to Thomas Wentworth Higginson, the *Atlantic Monthly* editor who became her literary mentor: "When I state myself, as the Representative of the Verse—it does not mean—me—but a supposed person."

Anticipating modern theories of the poet's "persona," Dickinson's definition of herself as a "supposed person" reveals just how self-consciously literary she was, even while its suggestion of a commitment to fantasy recalls the imaginary geometry she sketched on a Mount Holyoke blackboard. In many other ways, moreover, her correspondence with Higginson reinforces these points, as contemporary critics have begun to notice. Struck by an essay entitled *A Letter to a Young Contributor*, which the *Atlantic* editor published in 1862, Dickinson began to write to Higginson in that year, inquiring if her verses were "alive" and asking if she might be his "scholar." Though his responses were sometimes equivocal—he often objected to her eccentric language or to the meters that she called "the Bells whose jingling cooled my tramp"—his basic reaction was encouraging, and in 1870 he even journeyed to Amherst to meet her, becoming one of the few visitors to whom she appeared in person in her later life. For all his faults of perception, he seems to have understood, as many Dickinson biographers after him did not, the extent and intensity of her aesthetic vocation.

A further indication of Dickinson's literary intensity—her professionalism, even—can be found in records of her reading, yet another matter which is only now beginning to be investigated by scholars. According to family members, the walls of this poet's bedroom were hung with pictures of favorite writers— George Eliot, Thomas Carlyle, Elizabeth Barrett Browning, a selection which reveals how she ranged from the male to the female literary traditions and from prose to poetry in her search for intellectual models. Most persistently, however, she defined herself as a *woman* writer, reading the works of female precursors with special care, attending to the implications of novels like Charlotte Brontë's *Jane Eyre*, Emily Brontë's *Wuthering Heights*, and George Eliot's *Middlemarch* with the same absorbed delight that characterized her devotion to Elizabeth Barrett Browning's *Aurora Leigh*. Finally, then, the key to her enigmatic identity as a "supposed person" who was called the "Myth of Amherst" may rest, not in investigations of her questionable romance, but in studies of her unquestionably serious reading as well as in analyses of her disquietingly powerful writing. Elliptically phrased, intensely compressed, her poems are more linguistically innovative than any other nineteenth-century verses, with the possible exception of some works by Walt Whitman and Gerard Manley Hopkins, her two most radical male contemporaries. Throughout her largely secret but always brilliant career, moreover, she confronted precisely the questions about the individual and society, time and death, flesh and spirit, that major precursors from Milton to Keats had faced. Dreaming of "Amplitude and Awe," she recorded sometimes vengeful, sometimes mystical visions of social and personal transformation in poems as inventively phrased and imaginatively constructed as any in the English language.

Clearly such accomplishments required not only extraordinary talent but also some measure of freedom. Yet because she was the unmarried daughter of conservative New Englanders, Dickinson was obliged to take on many household tasks; as a nineteenth-century New England wife, she would have had the same number of obligations, if not more. Some of these she performed with pleasure; in 1856, for instance, she was judge of a bread-baking contest, and in 1857 she won a prize in that contest. But as Higginson's "scholar," as a voracious reader and an ambitious writer, Dickinson had to win herself time for "Amplitude and Awe," and it is increasingly clear that she did so through a strategic withdrawal from her ordinary world. A story related by her niece Martha Dickinson Bianchi reveals that the poet herself knew from the first what both the price and the prize might be: on one occasion, said Mrs. Bianchi, Dickinson took her up to the room in which she regularly sequestered herself, and, mimicking locking herself in, "thumb and forefinger closed on an imaginary key," said "with a quick turn of her wrist, 'It's just a turn—and freedom, Matty!' "

In the freedom of her solitary, but not lonely, room, Dickinson may have become what her Amherst neighbors saw as a bewildering "myth." Yet there, too, she created myths of her own. Reading the Brontës and Barrett Browning,

studying Transcendentalism and the Bible, she contrived a theology which is
powerfully expressed in many of her poems. That it was at its most hopeful a
female-centered theology is revealed in verses like those she wrote about the
women artists she admired, as well as in more general works like her gravely
pantheistic address to the "Sweet Mountains" who "tell me no lie," with its
definition of the hills around Amherst as "strong Madonnas" and its description
of the writer herself as "The Wayward Nun—beneath the Hill— / Whose
service is to You—." As Dickinson's admirer and descendant Adrienne Rich
has accurately observed, this passionate poet consistently chose to confront her
society—to "have it out"—"on her own premises."

24

There is a morn by men unseen—
Whose maids upon remoter green
Keep their Seraphic[1] May—
And all day long, with dance and game,
And gambol I may never name—   5
Employ their holiday.

Here to light measure, move the feet
Which walk no more the village street—
Nor by the wood are found—
Here are the birds that sought the sun   10
When last year's distaff[2] idle hung
And summer's brows were bound.

Ne'er saw I such a wondrous scene—
Ne'er such a ring on such a green—
Nor so serene array—   15
As if the stars some summer night
Should swing their cups of Chrysolite[3]—
And revel till the day—

Like thee to dance—like thee to sing—
People upon the mystic green—   20
I ask, each new May Morn.
I wait thy far, fantastic[4] bells—
Announcing me in other dells—
Unto the different dawn!

c. 1858   1945

---

1. Angelic.   3. A goldlike mineral.
2. Staff that holds unspun wool.   4. Imaginary.

211

Come slowly—Eden!
Lips unused to Thee—
Bashful—sip thy Jessamines[5]—
As the fainting Bee—

Reaching late his flower,   5
Round her chamber hums—
Counts his nectars—
Enters—and is lost in Balms.[6]

c. 1860   1890

249

Wild Nights—Wild Nights!
Were I with thee
Wild Nights should be
Our luxury!

Futile—the Winds—   5
To a Heart in port—
Done with the Compass—
Done with the Chart!

Rowing in Eden—
Ah, the Sea!
Might I but moor—Tonight—   10
In Thee!

c. 1861   1891

258

There's a certain Slant of light,
Winter Afternoons—
That oppresses, like the Heft[7]
Of Cathedral Tunes—

Heavenly Hurt, it gives us—   5
We can find no scar,
But internal difference,
Where the Meanings, are—

5. Jasmines.   7. Weight.
6. Perfumes.

None may teach it—Any—
'Tis the Seal Despair—   10
An imperial affliction
Sent us of the Air—

When it comes, the Landscape listens—
Shadows—hold their breath—
When it goes, 'tis like the Distance   15
On the look of Death—

c. 1861   1890

271

A solemn thing—it was—I said—
A woman—white—to be—
And wear—if God should count me fit—
Her blameless mystery—

A hallowed thing—to drop a life   5
Into the purple well—
Too plummetless[8]— that it return—
Eternity—until—

I pondered how the bliss would look—
And would it feel as big—   10
When I could take it in my hand—
As hovering—seen—through fog—

And then—the size of this "small" life—
The Sages—call it small—
Swelled—like Horizons—in my vest[9]—   15
And I sneered—softly—"small"!

c. 1861   1896

280

I felt a Funeral, in my Brain,
And Mourners to and fro
Kept treading—treading—till it seemed
That Sense was breaking through[1]—

And when they all were seated,   5
A Service, like a Drum—

8. Bottomless.   1. I.e., sense or reason was collapsing.
9. Clothing.

Kept beating—beating—till I thought
My Mind was going numb—

And then I heard them lift a Box
And creak across my Soul   10
With those same Boots of Lead, again,
Then Space—began to toll,

As all the Heavens were a Bell,
And Being, but an Ear,
And I, and Silence, some strange Race   15
Wrecked, solitary, here—

And then a Plank in Reason, broke,
And I dropped down, and down—
And hit a World, at every plunge,
And Finished knowing—then—   20

c. 1861   1896

288

I'm Nobody! Who are you?
Are you—Nobody—Too?
Then there's a pair of us?
Don't tell! they'd advertise[2]—you know!

How dreary—to be—Somebody!   5
How public—like a Frog—
To tell one's name—the livelong June—
To an admiring Bog!

c. 1861   1891

303

The Soul selects her own Society—
Then—shuts the Door—
To her divine Majority—
Present no more—

Unmoved—she notes the Chariots—pausing—   5
At her low Gate—
Unmoved—an Emperor be kneeling
Upon her Mat—

2. Announce, publicize.

I've known her—from an ample nation—
Choose One—   10
Then—close the Valves of her attention—
Like Stone—

c. 1862   1890

312

Her—"last Poems"[3]—
Poets—ended—
Silver—perished—with her Tongue—
Not on Record—bubbled other,
Flute—or Woman—   5
So divine—
Not unto its Summer—Morning
Robin—uttered Half the Tune—
Gushed too free for the Adoring—
From the Anglo-Florentine[4]—   10
Late—the Praise—
'Tis dull—conferring
On the Head too High to Crown—
Diadem—or Ducal Showing[5]—
Be its Grave—sufficient sign—   15
Nought—that We—No Poet's Kinsman—
Suffocate—with easy woe—
What, and if, Ourself a Bridegroom—
Put Her down—in Italy?[6]

c. 1862   1914

341

After great pain, a formal feeling comes—
The Nerves sit ceremonious, like Tombs—
The stiff Heart questions was it He, that bore,
And Yesterday, or Centuries before?

The Feet, mechanical, go round—   5
Of Ground, or Air, or Ought—
A Wooden way

---

3. This poem is an homage to Elizabeth Barrett
Browning (1806–1861), whose *Last Poems*
were posthumously published in 1862.
4. Barrett Browning lived with her husband,
Robert Browning, in Florence during the last

years of her life.
5. I.e., ducal crown.
6. I.e., how much would I grieve for her were I
her husband and had buried her in Italy?

Regardless grown,
A Quartz contentment, like a stone—

This is the Hour of Lead—   10
Remembered, if outlived,
As Freezing persons, recollect the Snow—
First—Chill—then Stupor—then the letting go—

c. 1862   1929

365

Dare you see a Soul *at the White Heat*?
Then crouch within the door—
Red—is the Fire's common tint—
But when the vivid Ore
Has vanquished Flame's conditions,   5
It quivers from the Forge
Without a color, but the light
Of unanointed Blaze.
Least[7] Village has its Blacksmith
Whose Anvil's even ring   10
Stands symbol for the finer Forge
That soundless tugs—within—
Refining these impatient Ores
With Hammer, and with Blaze
Until the Designated Light   15
Repudiate the Forge[8]—

c. 1862   1891

384

No Rack[9] can torture me—
My Soul—at Liberty—
Behind this mortal Bone
There knits a bolder One[1]—

You cannot prick with saw—   5
Nor pierce with Scimitar—
Two Bodies—therefore be—
Bind One—The Other fly—

---

7. I.e., the smallest.
8. Metaphorically, the world in which her soul has been refined.

9. A device used to torture prisoners.
1. I.e., bone.

The Eagle of his Nest
No easier divest[2]—   10
And gain the Sky
Than mayest Thou—

Except[3] Thyself may be
Thine Enemy—
Captivity is Consciousness—   15
So's Liberty.

c. 1862   1890

392

Through the Dark Sod—as Education—
The Lily passes sure[4]—
Feels her white foot—no trepidation—
Her faith—no fear—

Afterward—in the Meadow—   5
Swinging her Beryl[5] Bell—
The Mold-life[6]—all forgotten—now—
In Ecstasy—and Dell—

c. 1862   1929

401

What Soft—Cherubic Creatures—
These Gentlewomen are—
One would as soon assault a Plush[7]—
Or violate a Star—

Such Dimity[8] Convictions—   5
A Horror so refined
Of freckled Human Nature—
Of Deity—ashamed—

It's such a common—Glory—
A Fisherman's—Degree—   10
Redemption—Brittle Lady—
Be so—ashamed of Thee—

c. 1862   1896

2. I.e., it is no easier for the eagle to leave his
nest. . . .
3. Unless.
4. Both the sod and the lily's passage through it
are comparable to education.

5. Blue.
6. Its life in the soil.
7. A thick, rich fabric.
8. A sheer cotton fabric.

425

Good Morning—Midnight—
I'm coming Home—
Day—got tired of Me—
How could I—of Him?

Sunshine was a sweet place—   5
I liked to stay—
But Morn—didn't want me—now—
So—Goodnight—Day!

I can look—can't I—
When the East is Red?   10
The Hills—have a way—then—
That puts the Heart—abroad—

You—are not so fair—Midnight—
I chose—Day—
But—please take a little Girl—   15
He turned away!

c. 1862   1929

435

Much Madness is divinest Sense—
To a discerning Eye—
Much Sense—the starkest Madness—
'Tis the Majority
In this, as All, prevail—   5
Assent—and you are sane—
Demur—you're straightway dangerous—
And handled with a Chain—

c. 1862   1890

441

This is my letter to the World
That never wrote to Me—
The simple News that Nature told—
With tender Majesty

Her[9] Message is committed   5
To Hands I cannot see—

9. I.e., Nature's.

For love of Her—Sweet—countrymen[1]—
Judge tenderly—of Me

c. 1862   1890

462

Why make it[2] doubt—it hurts it so—
So sick—to guess—
So strong—to know—
So brave—upon its little Bed
To tell the very last They said   5
Unto Itself—and smile—And shake—
For that dear—distant—dangerous—Sake—
But—the Instead—the Pinching fear
That Something—it did do—or dare—
Offend the Vision—and it flee—   10
And They no more remember me—
Nor ever turn to tell me why—
Oh, Master, This is Misery—

c. 1862   1929

465

I heard a Fly buzz—when I died—
The Stillness in the Room
Was like the Stillness in the Air—
Between the Heaves of Storm—

The Eyes around—had wrung them dry—   5
And Breaths were gathering firm
For that last Onset—when the King
Be witnessed—in the Room—

I willed my Keepsakes—Signed away
What portion of me be   10
Assignable—and then it was
There interposed a Fly—

With Blue—uncertain stumbling Buzz—
Between the light—and me—
And then the Windows failed—and then   15
I could not see to see—

c. 1862   1896

1. I.e., her readers.
2. For Dickinson's use of "it" to describe herself and for her reference to her "Master," see
letters 233 and 248.

508

I'm ceded—I've stopped being Theirs—
The name They dropped upon my face
With water, in the country church
Is finished using, now,
And They can put it with my Dolls,   5
My childhood, and the string of spools,
I've finished threading—too—

Baptized, before, without the choice,
But this time, consciously, of Grace—
Unto supremest name—   10
Called to my Full—The Crescent dropped[3]—
Existence's whole Arc, filled up,
With one small Diadem.

My second Rank—too small the first—
Crowned—Crowing—on my Father's breast—   15
A half unconscious Queen—
But this time—Adequate—Erect,
With Will to choose, or to reject,
And I choose, just a Crown—

c. 1862   1890

512

The Soul has Bandaged moments—
When too appalled to stir—
She feels some ghastly Fright come up
And stop to look at her—

Salute her—with long fingers—   5
Caress her freezing hair—
Sip, Goblin, from the very lips
The Lover—hovered—o'er—
Unworthy, that a thought so mean
Accost a Theme—so—fair—   10

The soul has moments of Escape—
When bursting all the doors—
She dances like a Bomb, abroad,
And swings upon the Hours,

3. I.e., the crescent moon, symbolizing the immature self, as compared with the full moon, representing maturity.

As do the Bee—delirious borne— 15
Long Dungeoned from his Rose—
Touch Liberty—then know no more,
But Noon, and Paradise—

The Soul's retaken moments—
When, Felon led along, 20
With shackles on the plumed feet,[4]
And staples, in the Song,

The Horror welcomes her, again,
These, are not brayed of Tongue—

c. 1862   1945

528

Mine—by the Right of the White Election!
Mine—by the Royal Seal!
Mine—by the Sign in the Scarlet prison—
Bars—cannot conceal!

Mine—here—in Vision—and in Veto! 5
Mine—by the Grave's Repeal—
Titled—Confirmed—
Delirious Charter!
Mine—long as Ages steal!

c. 1862   1890

569

I reckon[5]—when I count at all—
First—Poets—Then the Sun—
Then Summer—Then the Heaven of God—
And then—the List is done—

But, looking back—the First so seems 5
To Comprehend the Whole—
The Others look a needless Show—
So I write—Poets—All—

Their Summer—lasts a Solid Year—
They can afford a Sun 10

---

4. I.e., winged feet.   5. Take into account, add up.

The East—would deem extravagant—
And if the Further Heaven—

Be Beautiful as they prepare[6]
For Those who worship Them—
It is too difficult a Grace—   15
To justify the Dream—

c. 1862   1929

579

I had been hungry, all the Years—
My Noon had Come—to dine—
I trembling drew the Table near—
And touched the Curious Wine—

'Twas this on Tables I had seen—   5
When turning, hungry, Home
I looked in Windows, for the Wealth
I could not hope—for Mine—

I did not know the ample Bread—
'Twas so unlike the Crumb   10
The Birds and I, had often shared
In Nature's—Dining Room—

The Plenty hurt me—'twas so new—
Myself felt ill—and odd—
As Berry—of a Mountain Bush—   15
Transplanted—to the Road—

Nor was I hungry—so I found
That Hunger—was a way
Of Persons outside Windows—
The Entering—takes away—   20

c. 1862   1891

593

I think I was enchanted
When first a sombre Girl—

6. I.e., as the one which they prepare.

I read that Foreign Lady[7]—
The Dark—felt beautiful—

And whether it was noon at night—   5
Or only Heaven—at Noon—
For very Lunacy of Light
I had not power to tell—

The Bees—became as Butterflies—
The Butterflies—as Swans—   10
Approached—and spurned the narrow Grass—
And just the meanest Tunes

That Nature murmured to herself
To keep herself in Cheer—
I took for Giants—practising   15
Titanic Opera—

The Days—to Mighty Metres stept—
The Homeliest—adorned
As if unto a Jubilee
'Twere suddenly confirmed—   20

I could not have defined the change—
Conversion of the Mind
Like Sanctifying in the Soul—
Is witnessed—not explained—

'Twas a Divine Insanity—   25
The Danger to be Sane
Should I again experience—
'Tis Antidote to turn—

To Tomes of solid Witchcraft—
Magicians be asleep—   30
But Magic—hath an Element
Like Deity—to keep—

c. 1862   1935

613

They shut me up in Prose—
As when a little Girl

---

7. A reference to Elizabeth Barrett Browning.

They put me in the Closet—
Because they liked me "still"—

Still! Could themself have peeped—   5
And seen my Brain—go round—
They might as wise have lodged a Bird
For Treason—in the Pound[8]—

Himself has but to will
And easy as a Star   10
Abolish his Captivity—
And laugh—No more have I[9]—

c. 1862   1935

642

Me from Myself—to banish—
Had I Art[1]—
Impregnable my Fortress
Unto All Heart—

But since Myself—assault Me—   5
How have I peace
Except by subjugating
Consciousness?

And since We're mutual Monarch
How this be   10
Except by Abdication—
Me—of Me?

c. 1862   1929

657

I dwell in Possibility—
A fairer House than Prose—
More numerous of Windows—
Superior—for Doors—

Of Chambers as the Cedars—   5
Impregnable of Eye—

---

8. A roofless enclosure for animals.   to be free.
9. I.e., I have to do no more than the bird   1. Skill.

And for an Everlasting Roof
The Gambrels[2] of the Sky—

Of Visitors—the fairest—
For Occupation[3]—This—   10
The spreading wide my narrow Hands
To gather Paradise—

c. 1862   1929

669

No Romance sold unto[4]
Could so enthrall a Man
As the perusal of
His individual One—
'Tis Fiction's—to dilute to Plausibility
Our Novel—When 'tis small enough
To Credit[5]—'Tisn't true!

c. 1862   1914

670

One need not be a Chamber—to be Haunted—
One need not be a House—
The Brain has Corridors—surpassing
Material Place—

Far safer, of a Midnight Meeting   5
External Ghost
Than its interior Confronting—
That Cooler Host.

Far safer, through an Abbey gallop,
The Stones a'chase—   10
Than Unarmed, one's a' self encounter—
In lonesome Place—

Ourself behind ourself, concealed—
Should startle most—
Assassin hid in our Apartment   15
Be Horror's least.

2. Slanted roofs.   4. I.e., no fantastic tale sold to [a man]. . . .
3. Pastime.   5. Believe.

The Body—borrows a Revolver—
He bolts the Door—
O'erlooking a superior spectre—
Or More—   20

c. 1863   1891

709

Publication—is the Auction
Of the Mind of Man—
Poverty—be justifying
For so foul a thing

Possibly—but We—would rather   5
From Our Garret go
White—Unto the White Creator—
Than invest—Our Snow—

Thought belong to Him who gave it—
Then—to Him Who bear   10
Its Corporeal illustration—Sell
The Royal Air—

In the Parcel—Be the Merchant
Of the Heavenly Grace—
But reduce no Human Spirit   15
To Disgrace of Price—

c. 1863   1929

712

Because I could not stop for Death—
He kindly stopped for me—
The Carriage held but just Ourselves—
And Immortality.

We slowly drove—He knew no haste   5
And I had put away
My labor and my leisure too,
For His Civility—

We passed the School, where Children strove
At Recess—in the Ring—   10

We passed the Fields of Gazing Grain—
We passed the Setting Sun—

Or rather—He passed Us—
The Dews drew quivering and chill—
For only Gossamer, my Gown—   15
My Tippet—only Tulle[6]—

We paused before a House that seemed
A Swelling of the Ground[7]—
The Roof was scarcely visible—
The Cornice—in the Ground—   20

Since then—'tis Centuries—and yet
Feels shorter than the Day
I first surmised the Horses' Heads
Were toward Eternity—

c. 1863   1890

722

Sweet Mountains—Ye tell Me no lie—
Never deny Me—Never fly—
Those same unvarying Eyes
Turn on Me—when I fail—or feign,
Or take the Royal names in vain—   5
Their far—slow—Violet Gaze—

My Strong Madonnas[8]—Cherish still—
The Wayward Nun—beneath the Hill—
Whose service—is to You—
Her latest[9] Worship—When the Day   10
Fades from the Firmament away—
To lift Her Brows on You[1]—

c. 1863   1945

732

She rose to His Requirement—dropt
The Playthings of Her life

---

6. A fine silk net. "Tippet": a feminine garment
that covers the shoulders.
7. I.e., a grave.
8. Italian name for the Virgin Mary; not normally plural.
9. Last.
1. I.e., to look at you.

To take the honorable Work
Of Woman, and of Wife—

If ought She missed in Her new Day,   5
Of Amplitude, or Awe—
Or first Prospective—Or the Gold
In using, wear away,

It lay unmentioned—as the Sea
Develop Pearl, and Weed,   10
But only to Himself—be known
The Fathoms they abide—

c. 1863   1890

754

My Life had stood—a Loaded Gun—
In Corners—till a Day
The Owner passed—identified—
And carried Me away—

And now We roam in Sovereign Woods—   5
And now We hunt the Doe—
And every time I speak for Him—
The Mountains straight reply—

And do I smile, such cordial light
Upon the Valley glow—   10
It is as a Vesuvian face[2]
Had let its pleasure through—

And when at Night—Our good Day done—
I guard My Master's Head—
'Tis better than the Eider Duck's[3]   15
Deep Pillow—to have shared—

To foe of His—I'm deadly foe—
None stir the second time—
On whom I lay a Yellow Eye—
Or an emphatic Thumb—   20

Though I than He—may longer live
He longer must—than I—

2. Volcanic, after Mount Vesuvius.   3. From which eiderdown is taken.

For I have but the power to kill,
Without—the power to die—

c. 1863 1929

959

A loss of something ever felt I—
The first that I could recollect
Bereft I was—of what I knew not
Too young that any should suspect

A Mourner walked among the children   5
I notwithstanding went about
As one bemoaning a Dominion
Itself[4] the only Prince cast out—

Elder, Today, a session wiser
And fainter, too, as Wiseness is—   10
I find myself still softly searching
For my Delinquent[5] Palaces—

And a Suspicion, like a Finger
Touches my Forehead now and then
That I am looking oppositely   15
For the site of the Kingdom of Heaven—

c. 1864 1945

986

A narrow Fellow in the Grass
Occasionally rides—
You may have met Him—did you not
His notice sudden is—

The Grass divides as with a Comb—   5
A spotted shaft is seen—
And then it closes at your feet
And opens further on—

He likes a Boggy Acre
A Floor too cool for Corn—   10
Yet when a Boy, and Barefoot—

---

4. I.e., the one bemoaning.   5. Lost.

I more than once at Noon
Have passed, I thought, a Whip lash
Unbraiding in the Sun
When stooping to secure it[6]   15
It wrinkled, and was gone—

Several of Nature's People
I know, and they know me—
I feel for them a transport
Of cordiality—   20

But never met this Fellow
Attended,[7] or alone
Without a tighter breathing
And Zero at the Bone—

c. 1865   1866

1072

Title divine—is mine!
The Wife—without the Sign!
Acute Degree—conferred on me—
Empress of Calvary![8]
Royal—all but the Crown!   5
Betrothed—without the swoon
God sends us Women—
When you—hold—Garnet to Garnet[9]—
Gold—to Gold—
Born—Bridalled—Shrouded—   10
In a Day—
Tri Victory
"My Husband"—women say—
Stroking the Melody—
Is *this*—the way?   15

c. 1862   1924

1129

Tell all the Truth but tell it slant—
Success in Circuit[1] lies

6. I.e., take it.   9. A dark gemstone.
7. I.e., with others.   1. I.e., circuitousness.
8. The hill on which Christ was crucified.

Too bright for our infirm Delight
The Truth's superb surprise

As Lightning to the Children eased 5
With explanation kind
The Truth must dazzle gradually
Or every man be blind—

c. 1868 1945

1138

A Spider sewed at Night
Without a Light
Upon an Arc of White.

If Ruff[2] it was of Dame
Or Shroud of Gnome 5
Himself himself inform.[3]

Of Immortality
His Strategy
Was Physiognomy.

c. 1869 1891

1445

Death is the supple Suitor
That wins at last—
It is a stealthy Wooing
Conducted first
By pallid innuendoes 5
And dim approach
But brave at last with Bugles
And a bisected Coach
It bears away in triumph
To Troth unknown 10
And Kindred as responsive
As Porcelain.

c. 1878 1945

2. A frilly collar.   3. I.e., only he could tell himself.

1562

Her Losses[4] make our Gains ashamed—
She bore Life's empty Pack
As gallantly as if the East
Were swinging at her Back.
Life's empty Pack is heaviest,   5
As every Porter knows—
In vain to punish Honey—
It only sweeter grows.

c. 1883   1894

1651

A Word made Flesh[5] is seldom
And tremblingly partook
Nor then perhaps reported
But have I not mistook
Each one of us has tasted   5
With ecstasies of stealth
The very food debated
To our specific strength—

A Word that breathes distinctly
Has not the power to die   10
Cohesive as the Spirit
It may expire if He—
"Made Flesh and dwelt among us"
Could condescension be
Like this consent of Language   15
This loved Philology.[6]

?   1955

1657

Eden is that old-fashioned House
We dwell in every day
Without suspecting our abode
Until we drive away.

4. George Eliot's. Dickinson wrote this poem immediately after reading John Cross's biography of the late novelist, and enclosed it in a letter to the publisher Thomas Niles, in which she wrote, "The Life of Marian Evans had much I never knew. A Doom of Fruit without the Bloom, like the Niger Fig."
5. A biblical description of Christ: "And the Word was made flesh" (John 1:14).
6. The study of language.

How fair on looking back, the Day   5
We sauntered from the Door—
Unconscious our returning,
But discover it no more.

?   1914

1670

In Winter in my Room
I came upon a Worm—
Pink, lank and warm—
But as he was a worm
And worms presume   5
Not quite with him at home—
Secured him by a string
To something neighboring
And went along.

A Trifle afterward[7]   10
A thing occurred
I'd not believe it if I heard
But state with creeping blood—
A snake with mottles rare
Surveyed my chamber floor   15
In feature as the worm before
But ringed with power—
The very string with which
I tied him—too
When he was mean[8] and new   20
That string was there—

I shrank—"How fair you are"!
Propitiation's claw—
"Afraid," he hissed
"Of me"?   25
"No cordiality"—
He fathomed me—
Then to a Rhythm *Slim*
Secreted in his Form
As Patterns swim   30
Projected him.[9]

7. I.e., shortly afterward.   9. I.e., he advanced.
8. Low, small.

That time I flew
Both eyes his way
Lest he pursue
Nor ever ceased to run   35
Till in a distant Town
Towns on from mine
I set me down
This was a dream.

?   1914

1705

Volcanoes be in Sicily
And South America
I judge from my Geography—
Volcanos nearer here
A Lava step at any time   5
Am I inclined to climb—
A Crater I may contemplate
Vesuvius[1] at Home.

?   1914

1737

Rearrange a "Wife's" affection!
When they dislocate my Brain!
Amputate my freckled Bosom!
Make me bearded like a man!

Blush, my spirit, in thy Fastness[2]—   5
Blush, my unacknowledged clay[3]—
Seven years of troth[4] have taught thee
More than Wifehood ever may!

Love that never leaped its socket—
Trust entrenched in narrow pain—   10
Constancy thro' fire—awarded—
Anguish—bare of anodyne![5]

Burden—borne so far triumphant—
None suspect me of the crown,

---

1. A volcano near Naples, Italy.   4. Fidelity, betrothal.
2. Firm, secure, or constrained position. 5. Medicine that relieves pain.
3. Flesh.

For I wear the "Thorns"[6] till *Sunset*—   15
Then—my Diadem put on.

Big my Secret but it's *bandaged*—
It will never get away
Till the Day its Weary Keeper
Leads it through the Grave to thee.   20

?   1945

Letters

233 [*Daisy and Her Master*]

To *recipient unknown*   *about* 1861
Master.

If you saw a bullet hit a Bird—and he told you he was'nt shot—you might weep at his courtesy, but you would certainly doubt his word.

One drop more from the gash that stains your Daisy's bosom[1]—then would you *believe*? Thomas' faith in Anatomy, was stronger than his faith in faith.[2] God made me—[Sir][3] Master—I did'nt be—myself. I dont know how it was done. He built the heart in me—Bye and bye it outgrew me—and like the little mother—with the big child—I got tired holding him. I heard of a thing called "Redemption"—which rested men and women. You remember I asked you for it—you gave me something else. I forgot the Redemption [in the Redeemed—I did'nt tell you for a long time, but I knew you had altered me—I] and was tired—no more—[so dear did this stranger become that were it, or my breath—the Alternative—I had tossed the fellow away with a smile.] I am older—tonight, Master—but the love is the same—so are the moon and the crescent. If it had been God's will that I might breathe where you breathed—and find the place—myself—at night—if I (can) never forget that I am not with you—and that sorrow and frost are nearer than I—if I wish with a might I cannot repress—that mine were the Queen's place—the love of the Plantagenet[4] is my only apology—To come nearer than presbyteries[5]—and nearer than the new Coat—that the

6. Christ was made to wear a crown of thorns at his crucifixion.
1. "Daisy" is Dickinson's name for herself when writing to her "Master," whose identity is unknown.
2. In John 20:25, "doubting Thomas" refuses to believe in Christ's resurrection until "I shall see in his hands the print of the nails, and put my finger into the print of the nails, and thrust my hand into his side."

3. "Words which ED crossed out are here enclosed in brackets; alternative readings are in parentheses" [note by Thomas H. Johnson, Dickinson's editor].
4. I.e., the love of royalty for royalty (the Plantagenets were an English royal family).
5. Pertaining to the rule of a church. There has been some speculation that the "Master" was one Reverend Charles Wadsworth.

Tailor made—the prank of the Heart at play on the Heart—in holy Holiday—is forbidden me—You make me say it over—I fear you laugh—when I do not see—[but] "Chillon"[6] is not funny. Have you the Heart in your breast—Sir—is it set like mine—a little to the left— has it the misgiving—if it wake in the night—perchance—itself to it—a timbrel[7] is it—itself to it a tune?

These things are [reverent] holy, Sir, I touch them [reverently] hallowed, but persons who pray—dare remark [our] "Father"! You say I do not tell you all—Daisy confessed—and denied not.

Vesuvius dont talk—Etna[8]—dont—[Thy] one of them—said a syllable—a thousand years ago, and Pompeii heard it, and hid forever— She could'nt look the world in the face, afterward—I suppose—Bashfull Pompeii! "Tell you of the want"—you know what a leech is, dont you—and [remember that] Daisy's arm is small—and you have felt the horizon hav'nt you—and did the sea—never come so close as to make you dance?

I dont know what you can do for it—thank you—Master—but if I had the Beard on my cheek—like you—and you—had Daisy's petals —and you cared so for me—what would become of you? Could you forget me in fight, or flight—or the foreign land? Could'nt Carlo,[9] and you and I walk in the meadows an hour—and nobody care but the Bobolink—and *his*—a *silver* scruple? I used to think when I died—I could see you—so I died as fast as I could—but the "Corporation"[1] are going Heaven too so [Eternity] wont be sequestered—now [at all]—Say I may wait for you—say I need go with no stranger to the to me—untried [country] fold—I waited a long time—Master—but I can wait more— wait till my hazel hair is dappled—and you carry the cane—then I can look at my watch—and if the Day is too far declined—we can take the chances [of] for Heaven—What would you do with me if I came "in white?" Have you the little chest to put the Alive—in?

I want to see you more—Sir—than all I wish for in this world—and the wish—altered a little—will be my only one—for the skies.

Could you come to New England—[this summer—could] would you come to Amherst—Would you like to come—Master?

[Would it do harm—yet we both fear God—] Would Daisy disappoint you—no—she would'nt—Sir—it were comfort forever—just to look in your face, while you looked in mine—then I could play in the woods till Dark—till you take me where Sundown cannot find us—and the true keep coming—till the town is full. [Will you tell me if you will?]

---

6. A reference, probably, to Byron's poem *The Prisoner of Chillon* (1816).
7. Small drum or tambourine.
8. Volcanoes in Italy; Pompeii, a Roman town, was buried by an eruption of Mt. Vesuvius in 79 A.D.
9. Dickinson's dog.
1. The ruling elders of a church.

I did'nt think to tell you, you did'nt come to me "in white," nor ever told me why,

> No Rose, yet felt myself a'bloom,
> No Bird—yet rode in Ether.

248 ["*Daisy Kneels a Culprit*"]

To recipient unknown   *early 1862?*

Oh, did I offend it—[Did'nt it want me to tell it the truth] Daisy—Daisy—offend it—who bends her smaller life to his (it's) meeker (lower) every day—who only asks—a task—[who] something to do for love of it—some little way she cannot guess to make that master glad—

A love so big it scares her, rushing among her small heart—pushing aside the blood and leaving her faint (all) and white in the gust's arm—

Daisy—who never flinched thro' that awful parting, but held her life so tight he should not see the wound—who would have sheltered him in her childish bosom (Heart)—only it was'nt big eno' for a Guest so large—*this* Daisy—grieve her Lord—and yet it (she) often blundered—Perhaps she grieved (grazed) his taste—perhaps her odd—Backwoodsman [life] ways [troubled] teased his finer nature (sense). Daisy [fea] knows all that—but must she go unpardoned—teach her, preceptor grace—teach her majesty—Slow (Dull) at patrician things—Even the wren upon her nest learns (knows) more than Daisy dares—

Low at the knee that bore her once unto [royal] wordless rest [now] Daisy [stoops a] kneels a culprit—tell her her [offence] fault—Master—if it is [not so] small eno' to cancel with her life, [Daisy] she is satisfied—but punish [do not] dont banish her—shut her in prison, Sir—only pledge that you will forgive—sometime—before the grave, and Daisy will not mind—She will awake in [his] your likeness.

Wonder stings me more than the Bee—who did never sting me—but made gay music with his might wherever I [may] [should] did go—Wonder wastes my pound, you said I had so size to spare—

You send the water over the Dam in my brown eyes—

I've got a cough as big as a thimble—but I dont care for that—I've got a Tomahawk in my side but that dont hurt me much. [If you] Her master stabs her more—

Wont he come to her—or will he let her seek him, never minding [whatever] so long wandering [out] if to him at last.

Oh how the sailor strains, when his boat is filling—Oh how the dying tug, till the angel comes. Master—open your life wide, and take me in forever, I will never be tired—I will never be noisy when you want to be still. I will be [glad] [as the] your best little girl—nobody else will see me, but you—but that is enough—I shall not want any more—and all that Heaven only will disappoint me—will be because it's not so dear

260 ["Is My Verse Alive?"]

To T. W. Higginson[2]   15 April 1862

Mr Higginson,

Are you too deeply occupied to say if my Verse is alive?

The Mind is so near itself—it cannot see, distinctly—and I have none to ask—

Should you think it breathed—and had you the leisure to tell me, I should feel quick gratitude—

If I make the mistake—that you dared to tell me—would give me sincerer honor—toward you—

I enclose my name—asking you, if you please—Sir—to tell me what is true?

That you will not betray me—it is needless to ask—since Honor is its own pawn—

261 [My "Companions"]

To T. W. Higginson   25 April 1862

Mr Higginson,

Your kindness claimed earlier gratitude—but I was ill—and write today, from my pillow.

Thank you for the surgery—it was not so painful as I supposed. I bring you others—as you ask—though they might not differ—

While my thought is undressed—I can make the distinction, but when I put them in the Gown—they look alike, and numb.

You asked how old I was? I made no verse—but one or two—until this winter—Sir—

I had a terror—since September—I could tell to none—and so I sing, as the Boy does by the Burying Ground—because I am afraid—

You inquire my Books—For Poets—I have Keats—and Mr and Mrs Browning. For Prose—Mr Ruskin—Sir Thomas Browne—and the Revelations.[3] I went to school—but in your manner of the phrase—had no education. When a little Girl, I had a friend, who taught me Immortality—but venturing too near, himself—he never returned—Soon after, my Tutor, died—and for several years, my Lexicon—was my only companion—Then I found one more—but he was not contented I be his scholar—so he left the Land.

You ask of my Companions Hills—Sir—and the Sundown—and a

---

2. Thomas Wentworth Higginson (1823–1911), a clergyman and then an essayist and lecturer, had published a *Letter to a Young Contributor* in the *Atlantic Monthly*. Dickinson wrote this letter in response, beginning a correspondence that lasted the rest of Dickinson's life.
3. The English Romantic poet John Keats (1795–1821); the poets Robert Browning (1812–1889) and Elizabeth Barrett Browning (1806–1861); the art critic and essayist John Ruskin (1819–1900); the seventeenth-century writer Sir Thomas Browne, noted for his ornate prose style; and the visionary last book of the Bible.

Dog—large as myself, that my Father bought me—They are better than Beings—because they know—but do not tell—and the noise in the Pool, at Noon—excels my Piano. I have a Brother and Sister—My Mother does not care for thought—and Father, too busy with his Briefs—to notice what we do—He buys me many Books—but begs me not to read them—because he fears they joggle the Mind. They are religious—except me—and address an Eclipse, every morning—whom they call their "Father." But I fear my story fatigues you—I would like to learn—Could you tell me how to grow—or is it unconveyed—like Melody—or Witchcraft?

You speak of Mr Whitman[4]—I never read his Book—but was told that he was disgraceful—

I read Miss Prescott's[5] "Circumstance," but it followed me, in the Dark—so I avoided her—

Two Editors of Journals came to my Father's House, this winter—and asked me for my Mind—and when I asked them "Why," they said I was penurious—and they, would use it for the World—

I could not weigh myself—Myself—

My size felt small—to me—I read your Chapters in the Atlantic—and experienced honor for you—I was sure you would not reject a confiding question—

Is this—Sir—what you asked me to tell you?

Your friend,
E—Dickinson.

265 ["Fame"]

To T. W. Higginson   *7 June 1862*
Dear friend.

Your letter gave no Drunkenness, because I tasted Rum before—Domingo[6] comes but once—yet I have had few pleasures so deep as your opinion, and if I tried to thank you, my tears would block my tongue—

My dying Tutor told me that he would like to live till I had been a poet, but Death was much of Mob as I could master[7]—then—And when far afterward—a sudden light on Orchards, or a new fashion in the wind troubled my attention—I felt a palsy, here—the Verses just relieve—

---

4. A number of contemporary reviewers had attacked the sexually frank *Leaves of Grass*, by the American poet Walt Whitman (1819–1892), which included poems described as "coarse," "vulgar," and "indecent."
5. Harriet Prescott (1835–1921), popular short-story writer.
6. Santo Domingo, capital of the Dominican Republic in the West Indies. Dickinson used the name in several poems; here it is invoked as a source of rum.
7. I.e., I was unable to write for a "mob"—a popular audience.

Your second letter surprised me, and for a moment, swung—I had not supposed it. Your first—gave no dishonor, because the True—are not ashamed—I thanked you for your justice—but could not drop the Bells whose jingling cooled my Tramp—Perhaps the Balm, seemed better, because you bled me, first.

I smile when you suggest that I delay "to publish"—that being foreign to my thought, as Firmament to Fin—

If fame belonged to me, I could not escape her—if she did not, the longest day would pass me on the chase—and the approbation of my Dog, would forsake me—then—My Barefoot-Rank is better—

You think my gait "spasmodic"[8]—I am in danger—Sir—

You think me "uncontrolled"—I have no Tribunal.

Would you have time to be the "friend" you should think I need? I have a little shape—it would not crowd your Desk—nor make much Racket as the Mouse, that dents your Galleries—

If I might bring you what I do—not so frequent to trouble you—and ask you if I told it clear—'twould be control, to me—

The Sailor cannot see the North—but knows the Needle[9] can—

The "hand you stretch me in the Dark," I put mine in, and turn away—I have no Saxon,[1] now—

> As if I asked a common Alms,
> And in my wondering hand
> A Stranger pressed a Kingdom,
> And I, bewildered, stand—
> As if I asked the Orient
> Had it for me a Morn—
> And it should lift it's purple Dikes,
> And shatter me with Dawn!

But, will you be my Preceptor, Mr Higginson?

Your friend
E Dickinson—

268 ["My Business is Circumference"]

To T. W. Higginson   *July 1862*

Could you believe me—without? I had no portrait, now, but am small, like the Wren, and my Hair is bold, like the Chestnut Bur—and my eyes, like the Sherry in the Glass, that the Guest leaves—Would this do just as well?

It often alarms Father—He says Death might occur, and he has Molds[2] of all the rest—but has no Mold of me, but I noticed the Quick

---

8. I.e., does not scan in proper measures.   1. "Language fails me" [Johnson's note].
9. Compass needle.   2. I.e., photographs or pictures.

wore off those things, in a few days, and forestall the dishonor—You will think no caprice of me—

You said "Dark." I know the Butterfly—and the Lizard—and the Orchis[3]—

Are not those *your* Countrymen?

I am happy to be your scholar, and will deserve the kindness, I cannot repay.

If you truly consent, I recite, now—

Will you tell me my fault, frankly as to yourself, for I had rather wince, than die. Men do not call the surgeon, to commend—the Bone, but to set it, Sir, and fracture within, is more critical. And for this, Preceptor, I shall bring you—Obedience—the Blossom from my Garden, and every gratitude I know. Perhaps you smile at me. I could not stop for that—My Business is Circumference[4]—An ignorance, not of Customs, but if caught with the Dawn—or the Sunset see me—Myself the only Kangaroo among the Beauty, Sir, if you please, it afflicts me, and I thought that instruction would take it away.

Because you have much business, beside the growth of me—you will appoint, yourself, how often I shall come—without your inconvenience. And if at any time—you regret you received me, or I prove a different fabric to that you supposed—you must banish me—

When I state myself, as the Representative of the Verse—it does not mean—me—but a supposed person. You are true, about the "perfection."

Today, makes Yesterday mean.

You spoke of Pippa Passes[5]—I never heard anybody speak of Pippa Passes—before.

You see my posture is benighted.

To thank you, baffles me. Are you perfectly powerful? Had I a pleasure you had not, I could delight to bring it.

Your Scholar

3. Small orchid; Higginson had written a number of nature essays.
4. This important Dickinsonian word has been defined by Johnson as "a projection of her imagination into all relationships of man, nature, and spirit."
5. Dramatic poem (1841) by Robert Browning.

CHRISTINA ROSSETTI
1830–1894

Admired by such varied contemporaries and descendants as Algernon Charles Swinburne and Gerard Manley Hopkins, Virginia Woolf and Edith Sitwell, Christina Rossetti has often been considered a sort of nun of art, a reclusive poet who lived an uneventful life of austere piety. Yet this apparently retiring woman of letters began her days as a rebelliously willful child, and what her brother referred to as her "hushed life-drama" informed a long literary career marked by struggle and success. Born in 1830, Rossetti was the youngest of four children in an exuberant Anglo-Italian family. Her father, Gabriele Rossetti, had been a famous poet and politician in Naples. Forced to emigrate because he was a member of the Carbonari, a revolutionary group seeking to establish a Neapolitan republic, he settled in London. There he taught Italian, wrote long scholarly treatises on Dante, and married Frances Polidori, a lively sometime governess who was the daughter of Gaetano Polidori, another distinguished Italian emigré, and an Englishwoman named Anna Louisa Pierce. Not surprisingly, all the children of the Rossetti marriage were energetic and ambitious. Maria, the oldest, wrote her own study of Dante and eventually joined an Anglican sisterhood devoted to social work; Dante Gabriel, the second child (known in the family as Gabriel), became a poet and painter, one of the members of the so-called Pre-Raphaelite Brotherhood, a group of young men whose radical ideas about aesthetic style were to influence English art for several generations; and William Michael, the third, became a well-known man of letters.

Like the four Brontë children, the four young Rossettis read voraciously and produced several family journals for which both Gabriel and Christina supplied poems from an early age. Unlike the Brontës, however, the Rossetti children grew up in a cosmopolitan setting. William later recalled that, bilingual from their youth, they listened, fascinated, as numerous Italian expatriates "engaged in animated talk on the affairs of Europe . . . with frequent and fervent recitations of poetry." In addition, they spent many summers at the country cottage of their grandfather Polidori, who introduced them to the pleasures of rural life and who, in 1847, when Christina was seventeen, published her first volume of verses on his private printing press. Then, in the summer of 1848, when Gabriel and six friends formed the Pre-Raphaelite Brotherhood, Christina became romantically involved with James Collinson, a poet-painter who was one of the "brothers," and the pair were engaged that autumn. Though their relationship did not finally end in marriage, it is likely that through Collinson, as well as through Gabriel, the young poet was exposed to some of the most advanced cultural and aesthetic ideas then current in London, including a neo-Romantic revival of medievalism that marked some of her early poems and ballads. Certainly her work appeared in several issues of *The Germ*, a short-lived journal that was published by the Brotherhood, and she sometimes posed as a model for various artists in the group.

Educated at home, Christina Rossetti was raised a strict Anglican, so strict that one of her reasons for breaking her engagement to Collinson was said to be his conversion in 1850 to Roman Catholicism. But she began early to read secular as well as religious poetry from both the Italian and English traditions. Like her sister, Maria, she was meant to follow in her mother's footsteps and become a governess, but such employment seemed hopelessly dreary to her. Perhaps it was no coincidence, then, that in her adolescence she developed a number of mysterious ailments which made it difficult for her to work outside her home.

As early as 1855, when she was temporarily employed as a governess, she confessed in a note to William that "I am rejoiced to feel that my health does really unfit me for miscellaneous governessing *en permanence.*"

From the fifties on, therefore, Christina Rossetti lived mostly at home with her parents, helping to nurse her father, who had become seriously ill in 1843, and after his death in 1854 helping her mother to run the household. Still, she was by no means a recluse. From 1860 to 1870, she did social work at the St. Mary Magdalen Home for Fallen Women on Highgate Hill, and in 1854 she volunteered for service with Florence Nightingale's expedition of nurses to Scutari; evidently, it was only because of her youth that she was not accepted. Besides her involvement in welfare organizations, she led an active social life. In 1862, her brother Gabriel, who had been rootless and depressed after the 1861 suicide of his wife (and onetime mistress), the former Elizabeth Siddal, leased a luxurious residence called Tudor House. There he became the center of a glittering circle that included Meredith, Swinburne, Browning, and Lewis Carroll. Much admired by members of this set, Christina spent a good deal of time at Tudor House.

It was in the fifties and sixties, too, that Christina Rossetti had what seem to have been several love affairs whose vicissitudes she may have recorded in the stream of intensely erotic and sometimes painfully renunciatory poems that she produced in this period, including a sequence of love poems in Italian—*Il Rossegiao dell'oriente* (The Reddening Dawn)—that was discovered after her death. Her brother William consistently claimed that some of her most sorrowful poems were written about her failed relationship with James Collinson, and that others were responses to an amorous entanglement with Charles Bagot Cayley, who proposed to her (and was refused) in 1866. More recently, Lona Mosk Packer, the author of a 1963 biography, has argued that for much of her life Christina was hopelessly in love with William Bell Scott, a friend of the family and a married man, who only briefly returned her affection. Whatever the facts—and it is always possible that Christina's tragic "affair" was more imaginary than real—her poems suggest that at this time she was both scrupulous and sensual, both rigorously moral and richly romantic.

Most important, however, Rossetti's poems of this period reveal that she was already an accomplished artist. Her first collection, *Goblin Market, and Other Poems*, appeared in 1862, with a second edition in 1865. Her second book, *The Prince's Progress, and Other Poems*, was published in 1866. Both volumes included illustrations by her brother Gabriel, and both met with critical acclaim. Thus, by the seventies Christina had become a seasoned writer with a considerable reputation. In 1870 she published a collection of short stories, in 1872 a book of inventive and charming nursery rhymes, and in 1874 a Lewis Carroll–like tale for children entitled *Speaking Likenesses*. In addition, she produced four more books of poems in the course of her career as well as several essays on Dante and six volumes of religious essays. The subject of many critical tributes and the object of a few literary pilgrimages, she developed a briskly professional attitude toward her own work. At a time when there were not yet any international copyright laws to protect the interests of authors, she entered vigorously into royalty negotiations, pressed publishers to see that her books were issued promptly and printed properly, and energetically insisted on retaining what she called "my dear Copyright."

Such professional keenness may at first seem rather at odds with the character of the voice that emerges from Rossetti's poems. For the most part, her verses are marked by a delicate austerity of style that appears incompatible with some of her businesslike correspondence. Yet it is important to remember that Rossetti was always a highly conscious craftswoman and that she came from a family of aesthetically sophisticated intellectuals, with her brothers, in particular, frequently helping her to revise her work and always helping to guard her professional interests. At the same time, it is important to consider the possibility that Rossetti was quite aware of the distinction between her own position in the world and that occupied by the very brothers for whose assistance she had often to be grateful. Though she had been glad to be liberated from the prison of "governessing *en permanence*," she was then obliged to live decorously at home, a chaste Victorian "spinster," while Gabriel, along with his Pre-Raphaelite Brothers, sowed wild oats and took London by storm, and William pursued a more sedate but equally unconstrained career as a critic and editor.

Even though her letters to publishers hint that she knew her own literary worth, therefore, Rossetti's poems suggest that she often had to struggle to renounce or at least moderate worldly ambition as well as to reconcile herself to losses in love. In their various ways, for instance, works like *Goblin Market* and *The World* meditate on the dangers of desire, especially the dangers of female desire, while such pieces as *Shut Out, Symbols*, and *The Convent Threshold* explore the arduous difficulties of renunciation. More specifically, poems like *A Triad, A Soul, In an Artist's Studio, Eve*, and *Enrica, 1865* contemplate the limited and sometimes limiting (but sometimes enlivening) range of alternatives available to women, and so-called "mortuary verses" like *After Death* and *Dead before Death*—verses written about or from the vantage point of the dead—mourn those limitations. Finally, however, an exuberant fantasy like *Venus's Looking Glass* hints at the possibility of a transfigured world in which female power would be liberated and celebrated.

That Rossetti did allow herself to record hopeful visions is significant in view of the increasingly intense religiosity as well as the undeniable somberness that characterized her later life. In 1871 she suffered a severe attack of Graves' disease, a thyroid disorder that seriously disfigured and debilitated her, and around this time she began to write the devotional essays collected in six volumes published by the Society for the Propagation of Christian Knowledge. When she recovered, her brother William, with whom she, her mother, and two elderly aunts had been living, married Lucy Brown, the daughter of Ford Madox Brown, another one of the Pre-Raphaelite Brotherhood. Tensions arose between Christina and Lucy; though the poet tried hard to assuage these strains, within two years she, her mother, and her aunts established a separate household of their own.

After the three older women died, Christina was left alone, and in 1894 she succumbed to cancer. During the last weeks of her life, a neighbor complained that she could be heard screaming for several hours every evening, and one wonders if such outbursts—which her physician attributed to "hysteria" rather than pain—might represent some portion of the cost exacted by her long renunciation of desire. Despite that cost, however, and though she herself often dreamed of dying into another, more spiritually loving world, the works of this woman whom an admirer once described as a "playful saint" won through to many significant artistic triumphs.

Song

When I am dead, my dearest,
    Sing no sad songs for me;
Plant thou no roses at my head,
    Nor shady cypress tree:
Be the green grass above me   5
    With showers and dewdrops wet;
And if thou wilt, remember,
    And if thou wilt, forget.

I shall not see the shadows,
    I shall not feel the rain;   10
I shall not hear the nightingale
    Sing on, as if in pain:
And dreaming through the twilight
    That doth not rise nor set,
Haply[1] I may remember,   15
    And haply may forget.

1848   1862

Symbols

I watched a rosebud very long
    Brought on by dew and sun and shower,
    Waiting to see the perfect[2] flower:
Then, when I thought it should be strong,
    It opened at the matin[3] hour   5
        And fell at evensong.

I watched a nest from day to day,
    A green nest full of pleasant shade,
    Wherein three speckled eggs were laid:
But when they should have hatched in May,   10
    The two old birds had grown afraid
        Or tired, and flew away.

1. Perhaps; by chance.   3. Morning.
2. Finished, full-grown.

Then in my wrath I broke the bough
    That I had tended so with care,
    Hoping its scent should fill the air;
I crushed the eggs, not heeding how
    Their ancient promise had been fair: 15
        I would have vengeance now.

But the dead branch spoke from the sod,[4]
    And the eggs answered me again: 20
    Because we failed dost thou complain?
Is thy wrath just? And what if God,
    Who waiteth for thy fruits in vain,
        Should also take the rod?[5]

1849   1862

After Death

The curtains were half drawn, the floor was swept
    And strewn with rushes, rosemary and may[6]
    Lay thick upon the bed on which I lay,
Where thro' the lattice ivy-shadows crept.
He leaned above me, thinking that I slept   5
    And could not hear him; but I heard him say:
    "Poor child, poor child:" and as he turned away
Came a deep silence, and I knew he wept.
He did not touch the shroud, or raise the fold
    That hid my face, or take my hand in his,   10
    Or ruffle the smooth pillows for my head:
    He did not love me living; but once dead
He pitied me; and very sweet it is
To know he still is warm tho' I am cold.

1849   1862

A Soul

She stands as pale as Parian statues[7] stand;
    Like Cleopatra when she turned at bay,
    And felt her strength above the Roman sway,[8]

4. In Genesis 4, God says to Cain, who has murdered his brother Abel, "the voice of thy brother's blood crieth unto me from the ground."
5. I.e., punishment.
6. Green, flowering branches associated with spring.
7. Ancient statues made with marble from the Greek island of Paros.

8. Leadership. Cleopatra (69–30 B.C.), queen of Egypt, was captured by the Romans, who planned to parade her before the populace. Rather than become a public spectacle, she killed herself by letting a poisonous snake bite her; she feels her strength to be greater because she has taken control of her destiny. "Aspic": variation of "asp," a venomous Egyptian snake.

And felt the aspic writhing in her hand.
Her face is steadfast toward the shadowy land,   5
   For dim beyond it looms the land of day:
   Her feet are steadfast, all the arduous way
That foot-track doth not waver on the sand.
She stands there like a beacon through the night,
   A pale clear beacon where the storm-drift is—   10
She stands alone, a wonder deathly-white:
She stands there patient nerved with inner might,
   Indomitable in her feebleness,
Her face and will athirst against the light.

1854   1896

The World

By day she[9] wooes me, soft, exceeding fair:
   But all night as the moon so changeth she;
   Loathsome and foul with hideous leprosy
And subtle serpents gliding in her hair.
By day she wooes me to the outer air,   5
   Ripe fruits, sweet flowers, and full satiety:
   But thro' the night, a beast she grins at me,
A very monster void of love and prayer.
By day she stands a lie: by night she stands
   In all the naked horror of the truth   10
With pushing horns and clawed and clutching hands.
Is this a friend indeed; that I should sell
   My soul to her, give her my life and youth,
Till my feet, cloven[1] too, take hold on hell?

1854   1862

Dead before Death

Ah! changed and cold, how changed and very cold!
   With stiffened smiling lips and cold calm eyes:
   Changed, yet the same; much knowing, little wise;
This was the promise of the days of old!
Grown hard and stubborn in the ancient mould,[2]   5
   Grown rigid in the sham of lifelong lies:
   We hoped for better things as years would rise,
But it is over as a tale once told.

---

9. I.e., the world.
1. The devil is traditionally thought to have cloven hooves.

2. Both a hollow form in which something is given shape, and soil rich in decaying organic matter.

All fallen the blossom that no fruitage bore,
   All lost the present and the future time,   10
All lost, all lost, the lapse[3] that went before:
So lost till death shut-to the opened door,
   So lost from chime to everlasting chime,
So cold and lost for ever evermore.

1854   1862

Cobwebs

It is a land with neither night nor day,
   Nor heat nor cold, nor any wind nor rain,
   Nor hills nor valleys: but one even plain
Stretches through long unbroken miles away,
While through the sluggish air a twilight grey   5
   Broodeth: no moons or seasons wax and wane,
   No ebb and flow are there along the main,[4]
No bud-time, no leaf-falling, there for aye:[5]—
   No ripple on the sea, no shifting sand,
   No beat of wings to stir the stagnant space: 10
   No pulse of life through all the loveless land
And loveless sea; no trace of days before,
   No guarded home, no toil-won resting-place,
No future hope, no fear for evermore.

1855   1896

Shut Out

The door was shut. I looked between
   Its iron bars; and saw it lie,
   My garden, mine, beneath the sky,
Pied[6] with all flowers bedewed and green:

From bough to bough the song-birds crossed,   5
   From flower to flower the moths and bees;
   With all its nests and stately trees
It had been mine, and it was lost.

A shadowless spirit kept the gate,
   Blank and unchanging like the grave.   10

---

3. Fall (perhaps a reference to the Fall of Man   5. Ever.
in Genesis).   6. Covered with multicolored patches.
4. Sea.

        I peering thro' said: "Let me have
    Some buds to cheer my outcast state."

    He answered not. "Or give me, then,
        But one small twig from shrub or tree;
        And bid my home remember me   15
    Until I come to it again."

    The spirit was silent; but he took
        Mortar and stone to build a wall;
        He left no loophole great or small
    Thro' which my straining eyes might look: 20

    So now I sit here quite alone
        Blinded with tears; nor grieve for that,
        For nought is left worth looking at
    Since my delightful land is gone.

    A violet bed is budding near,   25
        Wherein a lark has made her nest:
        And good they are, but not the best;
    And dear they are, but not so dear.

1856   1862

A Triad[7]

Three sang of love together: one with lips
    Crimson, with cheeks and bosom in a glow,
Flushed to the yellow hair and finger tips;
    And one there sang who soft and smooth as snow
    Bloomed like a tinted hyacinth at a show;   5
And one was blue with famine after love,
    Who like a harpstring snapped rang harsh and low
The burden[8] of what those were singing of.
One shamed herself in love; one temperately
    Grew gross[9] in soulless love, a sluggish wife;   10
One famished died for love. Thus two of three
    Took death for love and won him after strife;
One droned in sweetness like a fattened bee:
    All on the threshold, yet all short of life.

1856   1862

---

7. A musical chord formed of three notes; also,   8. In music, a bass part.
simply, a group of three.   9. Fat.

A Birthday

My heart is like a singing bird
    Whose nest is in a watered shoot;
My heart is like an apple tree
    Whose boughs are bent with thickset fruit;
My heart is like a rainbow shell   5
    That paddles in a halcyon sea;
My heart is gladder than all these
    Because my love is come to me.

Raise me a dais[1] of silk and down;
    Hang it with vair[2] and purple dyes;   10
Carve it in doves and pomegranates,
    And peacocks with a hundred eyes;
Work it in gold and silver grapes,
    In leaves and silver fleurs-de-lys,[3]
Because the birthday of my life   15
    Is come, my love is come to me.

1857   1861

Up-hill

Does the road wind up-hill all the way?
    Yes, to the very end.
Will the day's journey take the whole long day?
    From morn to night, my friend.

But is there for the night a resting-place?   5
    A roof for when the slow dark hours begin.
May not the darkness hide it from my face?
    You cannot miss that inn.[4]

Shall I meet other wayfarers at night?
    Those who have gone before.   10
Then must I knock, or call when just in sight?
    They will not keep you standing at that door.

Shall I find comfort, travel-sore and weak?
    Of labour you shall find the sum.
Will there be beds for me and all who seek?   15
    Yea, beds for all who come.

1858   1861

1. A platform, often hung with cloth and ornately decorated.
2. Gray and white squirrel fur.

3. Conventionalized emblem of an iris, used in heraldry.
4. I.e., death.

The Convent Threshold

There's blood between us, love, my love,
There's father's blood, there's brother's blood;
And blood's a bar I cannot pass:
I choose the stairs that mount above,
Stair after golden skyward stair,   5
To city and to sea of glass.
My lily feet are soiled with mud,
With scarlet mud which tells a tale
Of hope that was, of guilt that was,
Of love that shall not yet avail;   10
Alas, my heart, if I could bare
My heart, this selfsame stain is there:
I seek the sea of glass and fire[5]
To wash the spot, to burn the snare;[6]
Lo, stairs are meant to lift us higher: 15
Mount with me, mount the kindled stair.

Your eyes look earthward, mine look up.
I see the far-off city grand,
Beyond the hills a watered land,
Beyond the gulf a gleaming strand   20
Of mansions where the righteous sup;
Who sleep at ease among their trees,
Or wake to sing a cadenced hymn
With Cherubim and Seraphim;[7]
They bore the Cross, they drained the cup,[8]   25
Racked, roasted, crushed, wrenched limb from limb,
They the offscouring[9] of the world:
The heaven of starry heavens unfurled,
The sun before their face is dim.

You looking earthward, what see you?   30
Milk-white, wine-flushed among the vines,
Up and down leaping, to and fro,
Most glad, most full, made strong with wines,
Blooming as peaches pearled with dew,
Their golden windy hair afloat,   35
Love-music warbling in their throat,
Young men and women come and go.

You linger, yet the time is short:
Flee for your life, gird up your strength

5. An image taken from St. John's vision of the
Day of Judgment in Revelation 15:2.
6. The spot and the snare are emblems of
worldly sin and temptation.

7. Two orders of angels in heaven.
8. Jesus's crucifixion is spoken of in the New
Testament as a bitter cup.
9. Garbage, filth.

To flee; the shadows stretched at length   40
Show that day wanes, that night draws nigh;
Flee to the mountain, tarry not.
Is this a time for smile and sigh,
For songs among the secret trees
Where sudden blue birds nest and sport?   45
The time is short and yet you stay:
Today while it is called today
Kneel, wrestle, knock, do violence, pray:
Today is short, tomorrow nigh:
Why will[1] you die? why will you die?   50

You sinned with me a pleasant sin:
Repent with me, for I repent.
Woe's me the lore I must unlearn!
Woe's me that easy way we went,
So rugged when I would return!   55
How long until my sleep begin,
How long shall stretch these nights and days?
Surely, clean Angels cry, she prays;
She laves[2] her soul with tedious tears:
How long must stretch these years and years?   60

I turn from you my cheeks and eyes,
My hair which you shall see no more—
Alas for joy that went before,
For joy that dies, for love that dies.
Only my lips still turn to you,   65
My livid lips that cry, Repent.
Oh weary life, Oh weary Lent,[3]
Oh weary time whose stars are few.

How should I rest in Paradise,
Or sit on steps of heaven alone?   70
If Saints and Angels spoke of love
Should I not answer from my throne:
Have pity upon me, ye my friends,
For I have heard the sound thereof:
Should I not turn with yearning eyes,   75
Turn earthwards with a pitiful pang?
Oh save me from a pang in heaven.
By all the gifts we took and gave,
Repent, repent, and be forgiven:
This life is long, but yet it ends;   80

1. I.e., do you wish?
2. Washes.
3. In the Christian church, a period of forty days
commemorating Christ's fasting in the wilderness. More generally, a time of pious self-deprivation.

Repent and purge your soul and save:
No gladder song the morning stars
Upon their birthday morning sang
Than Angels sing when one repents.

I tell you what I dreamed last night: 85
A spirit with transfigured face
Fire-footed clomb[4] an infinite space.
I heard his hundred pinions clang,
Heaven-bells rejoicing rang and rang,
Heaven-air was thrilled with subtle scents,   90
Worlds spun upon their rushing cars:[5]
He mounted shrieking: "Give me light."
Still light was poured on him, more light;
Angels, Archangels[6] he outstripped
Exultant in exceeding might,   95
And trod the skirts of Cherubim.
Still "Give me light," he shrieked; and dipped
His thirsty face, and drank a sea,
Athirst with thirst it could not slake.
I saw him, drunk with knowledge, take   100
From aching brows the aureole[7] crown—
His locks writhed like a cloven snake—
He left his throne to grovel down
And lick the dust of Seraphs' feet:
For what is knowledge duly weighed?   105
Knowledge is strong, but love is sweet;
Yea all the progress he had made
Was but to learn that all is small
Save love, for love is all in all.

I tell you what I dreamed last night: 110
It was not dark, it was not light,
Cold dews had drenched my plenteous hair
Thro' clay;[8] you came to seek me there.
And "Do you dream of me?" you said.
My heart was dust that used to leap   115
To you; I answered half asleep:
"My pillow is damp, my sheets are red,
There's a leaden tester[9] to my bed:
Find you a warmer playfellow,
A warmer pillow for your head,   120
A kinder love to love than mine."
You wrung your hands; while I like lead

4. Climbed. "Pinions": wings.   7. Halo.
5. Chariots.   8. The clay of the grave.
6. The highest order of angels.   9. Canopy; here, the coffin's lid.

Crushed downwards thro' the sodden earth:
You smote your hands but not in mirth,
And reeled but were not drunk with wine.   125

For all night long I dreamed of you:
I woke and prayed against my will,
Then slept to dream of you again.
At length I rose and knelt and prayed:
I cannot write the words I said,   130
My words were slow, my tears were few;
But thro' the dark my silence spoke
Like thunder. When this morning broke,
My face was pinched, my hair was grey,
And frozen blood was on the sill   135
Where stifling in my struggle I lay.

If now you saw me you would say:
Where is the face I used to love?
And I would answer: Gone before;
It tarries veiled in paradise.   140
When once the morning star shall rise,
When earth with shadow flees away
And we stand safe within the door,
Then you shall lift the veil thereof.
Look up, rise up: for far above   145
Our palms[1] are grown, our place is set;
There we shall meet as once we met
And love with old familiar love.

1858   1862

Goblin Market

Morning and evening
Maids heard the goblins cry:
"Come buy our orchard fruits,
Come buy, come buy:
Apples and quinces,   5
Lemons and oranges,
Plump unpecked cherries,
Melons and raspberries,
Bloom-down-cheeked peaches,
Swart-headed[2] mulberries,   10
Wild free-born cranberries,
Crabapples, dewberries,

---

1. Trees associated with victory, triumph.   2. Black-headed.

Pineapples, blackberries,
Apricots, strawberries;—
All ripe together   15
In summer weather,—
Morns that pass by,
Fair eyes that fly;
Come buy, come buy:
Our grapes fresh from the vine,   20
Pomegranates full and fine,
Dates and sharp bullaces,
Rare pears and greengages,
Damsons[3] and bilberries,
Taste them and try: 25
Currants and gooseberries,
Bright-fire-like barberries,
Figs to fill your mouth,
Citrons from the South,
Sweet to tongue and sound to eye;   30
Come buy, come buy."
Evening by evening
Among the brookside rushes,
Laura bowed her head to hear,
Lizzie veiled her blushes: 35
Crouching close together
In the cooling weather,
With clasping arms and cautioning lips,
With tingling cheeks and finger tips.
"Lie close," Laura said,   40
Pricking up her golden head:
"We must not look at goblin men,
We must not buy their fruits:
Who knows upon what soil they fed
Their hungry thirsty roots?"   45
"Come buy," call the goblins
Hobbling down the glen.
"Oh," cried Lizzie, "Laura, Laura,
You should not peep at goblin men."
Lizzie covered up her eyes,   50
Covered close lest they should look;
Laura reared her glossy head,
And whispered like the restless brook:
"Look, Lizzie, look, Lizzie,
Down the glen tramp little men.   55
One hauls a basket,
One bears a plate,
One lugs a golden dish

---

3. Bullaces, greengages, and damsons are plums.

Of many pounds' weight.
How fair the vine must grow 60
Whose grapes are so luscious;
How warm the wind must blow
Through those fruit bushes."
"No," said Lizzie: "No, no, no;
Their offers should not charm us, 65
Their evil gifts would harm us."
She thrust a dimpled finger
In each ear, shut eyes and ran:
Curious Laura chose to linger
Wondering at each merchant man. 70
One had a cat's face,
One whisked a tail,
One tramped at a rat's pace,
One crawled like a snail,
One like a wombat prowled obtuse and furry, 75
One like a ratel[4] tumbled hurry skurry.
She heard a voice like voice of doves
Cooing all together:
They sounded kind and full of loves
In the pleasant weather. 80

Laura stretched her gleaming neck
Like a rush-imbedded swan,
Like a lily from the beck,[5]
Like a moonlit poplar branch,
Like a vessel at the launch 85
When its last restraint is gone.

Backwards up the mossy glen
Turned and trooped the goblin men,
With their shrill repeated cry,
"Come buy, come buy." 90
When they reached where Laura was
They stood stock still upon the moss,
Leering at each other,
Brother with queer brother;
Signaling each other, 95
Brother with sly brother.
One set his basket down,
One reared his plate;
One began to weave a crown
Of tendrils, leaves, and rough nuts brown 100
(Men sell not such in any town);
One heaved the golden weight

---

4. A South African badgerlike creature.   5. Small brook.

Of dish and fruit to offer her:
"Come buy, come buy," was still their cry.
Laura stared but did not stir,   105
Longed but had no money.
The whisk-tailed merchant bade her taste
In tones as smooth as honey,
The cat-faced purr'd,
The rat-paced spoke a word   110
Of welcome, and the snail-paced even was heard;
One parrot-voiced and jolly
Cried "Pretty Goblin" still for "Pretty Polly";
One whistled like a bird.

But sweet-tooth Laura spoke in haste: 115
"Good Folk, I have no coin;
To take were to purloin:
I have no copper in my purse,
I have no silver either,
And all my gold is on the furze   120
That shakes in windy weather
Above the rusty heather."
"You have much gold upon your head."
They answered all together:
"Buy from us with a golden curl."   125
She clipped a precious golden lock,
She dropped a tear more rare than pearl,
Then sucked their fruit globes fair or red.
Sweeter than honey from the rock,
Stronger than man-rejoicing wine,   130
Clearer than water flowed that juice;
She never tasted such before,
How should it cloy with length of use?
She sucked and sucked and sucked the more
Fruits which that unknown orchard bore,   135
She sucked until her lips were sore;
Then flung the emptied rinds away
But gathered up one kernel stone,
And knew not was it night or day
As she turned home alone.   140

Lizzie met her at the gate
Full of wise upbraidings:
"Dear, you should not stay so late,
Twilight is not good for maidens;
Should not loiter in the glen   145
In the haunts of goblin men.
Do you not remember Jeanie,
How she met them in the moonlight,

Took their gifts both choice and many,
Ate their fruits and wore their flowers   150
Plucked from bowers
Where summer ripens at all hours?
But ever in the noonlight
She pined and pined away;
Sought them by night and day,   155
Found them no more, but dwindled and grew gray;
Then fell with the first snow,
While to this day no grass will grow
Where she lies low:
I planted daisies there a year ago   160
That never blow.
You should not loiter so."
"Nay, hush," said Laura:
"Nay, hush, my sister:
I ate and ate my fill,   165
Yet my mouth waters still:
Tomorrow night I will
Buy more"; and kissed her.
"Have done with sorrow;
I'll bring you plums tomorrow   170
Fresh on their mother twigs,
Cherries worth getting;
You cannot think what figs
My teeth have met in,
What melons icy-cold   175
Piled on a dish of gold
Too huge for me to hold,
What peaches with a velvet nap,
Pellucid grapes without one seed:
Odorous indeed must be the mead   180
Whereon they grow, and pure the wave they drink
With lilies at the brink,
And sugar-sweet their sap."

Golden head by golden head,
Like two pigeons in one nest   185
Folded in each other's wings,
They lay down in their curtained bed:
Like two blossoms on one stem,
Like two flakes of new-fallen snow,
Like two wands of ivory   190
Tipped with gold for awful[6] kings.
Moon and stars gazed in at them,
Wind sang to them lullaby,

6. Awe-inspiring.

Lumbering owls forebore to fly,
Not a bat flapped to and fro   195
Round their nest:
Cheek to cheek and breast to breast
Locked together in one nest.

Early in the morning
When the first cock crowed his warning.   200
Neat like bees, as sweet and busy,
Laura rose with Lizzie:
Fetched in honey, milked the cows,
Aired and set to rights the house,
Kneaded cakes of whitest wheat,   205
Cakes for dainty mouths to eat,
Next churned butter, whipped up cream,
Fed their poultry, sat and sewed;
Talked as modest maidens should:
Lizzie with an open heart,   210
Laura in an absent dream,
One content, one sick in part;
One warbling for the mere bright day's delight,
One longing for the night.

At length slow evening came: 215
They went with pitchers to the reedy brook;
Lizzie most placid in her look,
Laura most like a leaping flame,
They drew the gurgling water from its deep.
Lizzie plucked purple and rich golden flags,   220
Then turning homeward said: "The sunset flushes
Those furthest loftiest crags;
Come, Laura, not another maiden lags.
No willful squirrel wags,
The beasts and birds are fast asleep."   225
But Laura loitered still among the rushes.
And said the bank was steep.

And said the hour was early still,
The dew not fallen, the wind not chill;
Listening ever, but not catching   230
The customary cry,
"Come buy, come buy,"
With its iterated jingle
Of sugar-baited words:
Not for all her watching   235
Once discerning even one goblin
Racing, whisking, tumbling, hobbling—
Let alone the herds

That used to tramp along the glen,
In groups or single,   240
Of brisk fruit-merchant men.
Till Lizzie urged, "O Laura, come;
I hear the fruit-call, but I dare not look:
You should not loiter longer at this brook:
Come with me home.   245
The stars rise, the moon bends her arc,
Each glow-worm winks her spark,
Let us get home before the night grows dark:
For clouds may gather
Though this is summer weather,   250
Put out the lights and drench us through;
Then if we lost our way what should we do?"

Laura turned cold as stone
To find her sister heard that cry alone,
That goblin cry,   255
"Come buy our fruits, come buy."
Must she then buy no more such dainty fruit?
Must she no more such succous pasture find,
Gone deaf and blind?
Her tree of life dropped from the root: 260
She said not one word in her heart's sore ache:
But peering through the dimness, nought discerning,
Trudged home, her pitcher dripping all the way;
So crept to bed, and lay
Silent till Lizzie slept;   265
Then sat up in a passionate yearning.
And gnashed her teeth for balked desire, and wept
As if her heart would break.

Day after day, night after night,
Laura kept watch in vain   270
In sullen silence of exceeding pain.
She never caught again the goblin cry,
"Come buy, come buy";—
She never spied the goblin men
Hawking their fruits along the glen: 275
But when the noon waxed bright
Her hair grew thin and gray;
She dwindled, as the fair full moon doth turn
To swift decay and burn
Her fire away.   280

One day remembering her kernelstone
She set it by a wall that faced the south:
Dewed it with tears, hoped for a root,

Watched for a waxing shoot,
But there came none. 285
It never saw the sun,
It never felt the trickling moisture run:
While with sunk eyes and faded mouth
She dreamed of melons, as a traveler sees
False waves in desert drouth 290
With shade of leaf-crowned trees,
And burns the thirstier in the sandful breeze.

She no more swept the house,
Tended the fowls or cows,
Fetched honey, kneaded cakes of wheat, 295
Brought water from the brook:
But sat down listless in the chimneynook
And would not eat.

Tender Lizzie could not bear
To watch her sister's cankerous care, 300
Yet not to share. ,
She night and morning
Caught the goblins' cry:
"Come buy our orchard fruits,
Come buy, come buy":— 305
Beside the brook, along the glen,
She heard the tramp of goblin men,
The voice and stir
Poor Laura could not hear;
Longed to buy fruit to comfort her, 310
But feared to pay too dear.
She thought of Jeanie in her grave,
Who should have been a bride;
But who for joys brides hope to have
Fell sick and died 315
In her gay prime,
In earliest winter time,
With the first glazing rime,
With the first snow-fall of crisp winter time.

Till Laura dwindling 320
Seemed knocking at Death's door.
Then Lizzie weighed no more
Better and worse;
But put a silver penny in her purse,
Kissed Laura, crossed the heath with clumps of furze 325
At twilight, halted by the brook:
And for the first time in her life
Began to listen and look.

Laughed every goblin
When they spied her peeping: 330
Came towards her hobbling,
Flying, running, leaping,
Puffing and blowing,
Chuckling, clapping, crowing,
Cluckling and gobbling,   335
Mopping and mowing,
Full of airs and graces,
Pulling wry faces,
Demure grimaces,
Cat-like and rat-like,   340
Ratel- and wombat-like,
Snail-paced in a hurry,
Parrot-voiced and whistler,
Helter skelter, hurry skurry,
Chattering like magpies,   345
Fluttering like pigeons,
Gliding like fishes,—
Hugged her and kissed her:
Squeezed and caressed her:
Stretched up their dishes,   350
Panniers, and plates:
"Look at our apples
Russet and dun,
Bob at our cherries,
Bite at our peaches,   355
Citrons and dates,
Grapes for the asking,
Pears red with basking
Out in the sun,
Plums on their twigs;   360
Pluck them and suck them,—
Pomegranates, figs."

"Good folk," said Lizzie,
Mindful of Jeanie:
"Give me much and many":   365
Held out her apron,
Tossed them her penny
"Nay, take a seat with us,
Honor and eat with us,"
They answered grinning: 370
"Our feast is but beginning.
Night yet is early,
Warm and dew-pearly,
Wakeful and starry:
Such fruits as these   375

No man can carry;
Half their bloom would fly,
Half their dew would dry,
Half their flavor would pass by.
Sit down and feast with us,   380
Be welcome guest with us,
Cheer you and rest with us."—
"Thank you, said Lizzie: "But one waits
At home alone for me:
So without further parleying,   385
If you will not sell me any
Of your fruits though much and many,
Give me back my silver penny
I tossed you for a fee."—
They began to scratch their pates,   390
No longer wagging, purring,
But visibly demurring,
Grunting and snarling.
One called her proud,
Cross-grained, uncivil;   395
Their tones waxed loud,
Their looks were evil.
Lashing their tails
They trod and hustled her,
Elbowed and jostled her,   400
Clawed with their nails,
Barking, mewing, hissing, mocking,
Tore her gown and soiled her stocking,
Twitched her hair out by the roots,
Stamped upon her tender feet,   405
Held her hands and squeezed their fruits
Against her mouth to make her eat.

White and golden Lizzie stood,
Like a lily in a flood,—
Like a rock of blue-veined stone   410
Lashed by tides obstreperously,—
Like a beacon left alone
In a hoary roaring sea,
Sending up a golden fire,—
Like a fruit-crowned orange-tree   415
White with blossoms honey-sweet
Sore beset by wasp and bee,—
Like a royal virgin town
Topped with gilded dome and spire
Close beleaguered by a fleet   420
Mad to tug her standard down.

One may lead a horse to water,
Twenty cannot make him drink.
Though the goblins cuffed and caught her,
Coaxed and fought her,   425
Bullied and besought her,
Scratched her, pinched her black as ink,
Kicked and knocked her,
Mauled and mocked her,
Lizzie uttered not a word;   430
Would not open lip from lip
Lest they should cram a mouthful in:
But laughed in heart to feel the drip
Of juice that syruped all her face,
And lodged in dimples of her chin,   435
And streaked her neck which quaked like curd.
At last the evil people,
Worn out by her resistance,
Flung back her penny, kicked their fruit
Along whichever road they took,   440
Not leaving root or stone or shoot;
Some writhed into the ground,
Some dived into the brook
With ring and ripple,
Some scudded on the gale without a sound.   445
Some vanished in the distance.

In a smart, ache, tingle,
Lizzie went her way;
Knew not was it night or day;
Sprang up the bank, tore through the furze,   450
Threaded copse and dingle,
And heard her penny jingle
Bouncing in her purse,—
Its bounce was music to her ear.
She ran and ran   455
As if she feared some goblin man
Dogged her with gibe or curse
Or something worse:
But not one goblin skurried after,
Nor was she pricked by fear;   460
The kind heart made her windy-paced
That urged her home quite out of breath with haste
And inward laughter.

She cried, "Laura," up the garden,
"Did you miss me?   465
Come and kiss me.
Never mind my bruises,

Hug me, kiss me, suck my juices
Squeezed from goblin fruits for you,
Goblin pulp and goblin dew.   470
Eat me, drink me, love me;
Laura, make much of me;
For your sake I have braved the glen
And had to do with goblin merchant men."

Laura started from her chair,   475
Flung her arms up in the air,
Clutched her hair:
"Lizzie, Lizzie, have you tasted
For my sake the fruit forbidden?
Must your light like mine be hidden,   480
Your young life like mine be wasted,
Undone in mine undoing,
And ruined in my ruin,
Thirsty, cankered, goblin-ridden?"—
She clung about her sister,   485
Kissed and kissed and kissed her:
Tears once again
Refreshed her shrunken eyes,
Dropping like rain
After long sultry drouth;   490
Shaking with anguish, fear, and pain,
She kissed and kissed her with a hungry mouth.

Her lips began to scorch,
That juice was wormwood to her tongue,
She loathed the feast: 495
Writhing as one possessed she leaped and sung,
Rent all her robe, and wrung
Her hands in lamentable haste,
And beat her breast,
Her locks streamed like the torch   500
Borne by a racer at full speed,
Or like the mane of horses in their flight,
Or like an eagle when she stems[7] the light
Straight toward the sun,
Or like a caged thing freed,   505
Or like a flying flag when armies run.

Swift fire spread through her veins, knocked at her heart,
Met the fire smoldering there
And overbore its lesser flame;
She gorged on bitterness without a name: 510

7. Makes headway against.

Ah fool, to choose such part
Of soul-consuming care!
Sense failed in the mortal strife:
Like the watch-tower of a town
Which an earthquake shatters down,   515
Like a lightning-stricken mast,
Like a wind-uprooted tree
Spun about,
Like a foam-topped waterspout
Cast down headlong in the sea,   520
She fell at last;
Pleasure past and anguish past,
Is it death or is it life?

Life out of death.
That night long Lizzie watched by her,   525
Counted her pulse's flagging stir,
Felt for her breath,
Held water to her lips, and cooled her face
With tears and fanning leaves.
But when the first birds chirped about their eaves,   530
And early reapers plodded to the place
Of golden sheaves,
And dew-wet grass
Bowed in the morning winds so brisk to pass,
And new buds with new day   535
Opened of cup-like lilies on the stream,
Laura awoke as from a dream,
Laughed in the innocent old way,
Hugged Lizzie but not twice or thrice;
Her gleaming locks showed not one thread of gray,   540
Her breath was sweet as May,
And light danced in her eyes.

Days, weeks, months, years
Afterwards, when both were wives
With children of their own;   545
Their mother-hearts beset with fears,
Their lives bound up in tender lives:
Laura would call the little ones
And tell them of her early prime,
Those pleasant days long gone   550
Of not-returning time:
Would talk about the haunted glen,
The wicked quaint fruit-merchant men,
Their fruits like honey to the throat
But poison in the blood   555
(Men sell not such in any town):

Would tell them how her sister stood
In deadly peril to do her good,
And win the fiery antidote:
Then joining hands to little hands   560
Would bid them cling together,—
"For there is no friend like a sister
In calm or stormy weather;
To cheer one on the tedious way,
To fetch one if one goes astray,   565
To lift one if one totters down,
To strengthen whilst one stands."

1859   1862

In an Artist's Studio

One face looks out from all his[8] canvases,
   One selfsame figure sits or walks or leans:
   We found her hidden just behind those screens,[9]
That mirror gave back all her loveliness.
A queen in opal or in ruby dress,   5
   A nameless girl in freshest summer-greens,
   A saint, an angel—every canvas means
The same one meaning, neither more nor less.
He feeds upon her face by day and night,
   And she with true kind eyes looks back on him,   10
Fair as the moon and joyful as the light:
   Not wan with waiting, not with sorrow dim;
Not as she is, but was when hope shone bright;
   Not as she is, but as she fills his dream.

1861   1896

Eve[1]

"While I sit at the door
Sick to gaze within
Mine eye weepeth sore
For sorrow and sin:
As a tree my sin stands   5

---

8. "His": Dante Gabriel Rossetti, Christina Rossetti's brother. The "face" is that of Elizabeth Siddall, whom Dante Gabriel later married. Christina herself also posed for many of his paintings.
9. The paintings; however, nude models were protected from the eyes of visitors to the artist's studio by screens, so the word creates an ambiguity throughout the poem. "Mirror": the artist's eye and/or his painting.
1. The first woman and wife of Adam, who, in Genesis 3, is cajoled by the serpent into eating an apple from the forbidden Tree of Knowledge and in turn tempts Adam to eat, thus bringing about the expulsion from Eden and the emergence of death into the world.

To darken all lands;
Death is the fruit it bore.

"How have Eden bowers grown
Without Adam to bend them!
How have Eden flowers blown[2]   10
Squandering their sweet breath
Without me to tend them!
The Tree of Life was ours,
Tree twelvefold-fruited,
Most lofty tree that flowers,   15
Most deeply rooted:
I chose the tree of death.

"Hadst thou but said me nay,
Adam, my brother,
I might have pined away;   20
I, but none other:
God might have let thee stay
Safe in our garden,
By putting me away
Beyond all pardon.   25

"I, Eve, sad mother
Of all who must live,
I, not another,
Plucked bitterest fruit to give
My friend, husband, lover;—   30
O wanton eyes, run over;
Who but I should grieve?—
Cain hath slain his brother:[3]
Of all who must die mother,
Miserable Eve!"   35

Thus she sat weeping,
Thus Eve our mother,
Where one lay sleeping
Slain by his brother.
Greatest and least   40
Each piteous beast
To hear her voice
Forgot his joys
And set aside his feast.

The mouse paused in his walk   45
And dropped his wheaten stalk;

2. Blossomed.
3. In Genesis 4, Adam and Eve's son Cain kills his brother Abel.

Grave cattle wagged their heads
In rumination;[4]
The eagle gave a cry
From his cloud station;   50
Larks on thyme beds
Forbore to mount or sing;
Bees drooped upon the wing;
The raven perched on high
Forgot his ration;   55
The conies[5] in their rock,
A feeble nation,
Quaked sympathetical;
The mocking-bird left off to mock;
Huge camels knelt as if   60
In deprecation;
The kind hart's tears were falling;
Chattered the wistful stork;
Dove-voices with a dying fall[6]
Cooed desolation   65
Answering grief by grief.

Only the serpent in the dust
Wriggling and crawling,
Grinned an evil grin and thrust
His tongue out with its fork.   70

1865   1866

Enrica, 1865[7]

She came among us from the South
　And made the North her home awhile;
　Our dimness brightened in her smile,
Our tongue[8] grew sweeter in her mouth.

We chilled beside her liberal[9] glow,   5
　She dwarfed us by her ampler scale,
　Her full-blown blossom made us pale,
She summer-like and we like snow.

---

4. Both chewing cud and, usually in human application, deep thought.
5. Rabbits.
6. Dying away, trailing off, but also with a suggestion of the Fall of Man.
7. The poem is about a woman of Rossetti's acquaintance named Enrica Barile, who had been abandoned by her husband (a rather eccentric man who changed his name to Filopanti, "all-loving"), and subsequently moved to London.
8. Language.
9. Generous, abundant.

We Englishwomen, trim, correct,
    All minted[1] in the selfsame mould,   10
    Warm-hearted but of semblance cold,
All-courteous out of self-respect.

She woman in her natural grace,
    Less trammelled[2] she by lore of school,
    Courteous by nature not by rule,   15
Warm-hearted and of cordial face.

So for awhile she made her home
    Among us in the rigid North,
    She who from Italy came forth
And scaled the Alps and crossed the foam.   20

But if she found us like our sea,
    Of aspect colourless and chill,
    Rock-girt; like it she found us still
Deep at our deepest, strong and free.

1865   1875

Venus's Looking-Glass

I marked where lovely Venus[3] and her court
    With song and dance and merry laugh went by;
    Weightless, their wingless feet seemed made to fly,
Bound from the ground and in mid air to sport.
Left far behind I heard the dolphins snort,   5
    Tracking their goddess with a wistful eye,
    Around whose head white doves rose, wheeling high
Or low, and cooed after their tender sort.
All this I saw in Spring. Thro' Summer heat
    I saw the lovely Queen of Love no more.   10
      But when flushed Autumn thro' the woodlands went
I spied sweet Venus walk amid the wheat:
    Whom seeing, every harvester gave o'er
      His toil, and laughed and hoped and was content.

1872   1875

1. Stamped, like coins.   3. The Roman name for Aphrodite, the Greek
2. Confined, restrained.   goddess of love. "Marked": saw.

REBECCA HARDING DAVIS
1831–1910

For Tillie Olsen, the twentieth-century working-class writer who recovered *Life in the Iron-Mills* from a century of critical neglect, Rebecca Harding Davis's novella represents the triumph of a "house-bound, class-bound, sex-bound" author who was somehow able to envision the grim realities of mid-nineteenth-century industrialization in America: labor's alienated relations with managers and owners, the degradation of ignored and unjust poverty, the pollution caused by industrial waste. *Life in the Iron-Mills*, which appeared anonymously in an 1861 issue of the *Atlantic Monthly*, was immediately acknowledged as a literary landmark by Nathaniel Hawthorne and Louisa May Alcott, Henry Ward Beecher and Ralph Waldo Emerson. Some six years before the French novelist Émile Zola began publishing what were called "naturalistic" novels, a thirty-year-old Virginian had brilliantly dramatized the socioeconomic implications of environmental determinism. Yet, by the end of her life, this innovative writer was mainly remembered as the mother of the distinguished reporter Richard Harding Davis.

Little is known about the circumstances that turned Harding Davis into a sometimes inspired, always prolific author. The eldest of five children, she was born in Washington County, Pennsylvania, but moved with her family in 1836 to the city of Wheeling (then in Virginia and now in West Virginia). Wheeling was not only a center of the booming steel industry in the late fifties; inside a border state, it was also increasingly involved in the turbulent antagonisms preceding the Civil War. The Harding family was middle class. Richard W. Harding, an Englishman from Ireland, was successful in business, conservative in his political views, and autocratic in his demands on the family. Rachel Leet (Wilson) Harding first educated her daughter at home and then sent her to the Washington Female Seminary in Pennsylvania. After graduating in 1848 with the highest honors in her class, Rebecca Harding lived her life inside the family, educating the younger children, studying the books brought home by her brother, William, when he attended Washington College, and, perhaps most important, walking through the mills and factories of the town.

During this period, Harding sent *Life in the Iron-Mills* to the prestigious magazine that was run by James T. Fields. His acceptance letter, accompanied by fifty dollars, must have seemed like the beginning of an exciting new life, and, in fact, it did lead to a longer work serialized in the *Atlantic* and later published in book form as *Margaret Howth* (1862), as well as to several dramatic stories about the devastating costs of the Civil War. It also resulted in a visit to Fields, which initiated a long-lasting friendship with his wife, Annie Fields, and shorter exchanges with Hawthorne and Emerson, among others. And it precipitated a correspondence with a reader-admirer whom Harding met in 1862 and married in 1863: three years her junior, Lemuel Clarke Davis was studying for the bar and writing journalism when he decided to settle with his wife in Philadelphia.

Although Harding Davis continued to pursue an ever more professional career in journalism and fiction, the rest of her life hardly met the expectations of these exciting years. First, nursing her father through a long illness, she found little refuge back at her new home, which was shared initially with her husband's sister and her children. Next, Harding Davis fell ill with what might have been nervous exhaustion. Then, to supplement the family's income, she began writing for magazines that could pay her more than the *Atlantic*. Subsequent novels suffered from the time pressures imposed by serialization. A late book like *Pro Ares et Focis—A Plea for Our Altars and Hearths* (1870) proclaimed the joys of domesticity; however, her own domestic life seems to have been arduous. With her husband increasingly occupied by abolitionist activities and as editor of the *Philadelphia Public Ledger*, she must have found it difficult to combine her position as contributing editor of the *New York Tribune* with the raising of their two sons and daughter. Yet, in her forties, she retained her earlier determination to extend the subject of fiction to wider social and economic issues: *Put Out of the Way* (1871), for example, focuses on the laws relating to lunacy; *Earthen Pitchers* (1873–1877) on two young professional women; *John Andross* (1874) on monetary corruption in government. A number of short stories collected in *Silhouettes of American Life* (1892) further developed her self-defined literary project, "to dig into this commonplace, this vulgar American life, and see what is in it."

By the time she died at seventy-nine years of age, Harding Davis had witnessed the decline of interest in her work. Yet she must have known that, by writing *Life in the Iron-Mills*, she had herself confronted just the inhibitions to creativity that she had analyzed with such clarity in her portrait of a working-class sculptor's efforts to construct the form of his desire out of the refuse (the korl) of the iron-mill. It is no wonder, then, that, when Fields initially objected to the title, Harding Davis's alternative was "The Korl Woman" or "Beyond," for this huge figure of a woman imbued with longing signifies not only the thwarted work of the korl cutter but also Harding Davis's own protest against a world in which she saw that class, race, and gender could condemn human beings to frustration and pain.

Life in the Iron-Mills

> "Is this the end?
> O Life, as futile, then, as frail!
> What hope of answer or redress?"[1]

A cloudy day: do you know what that is in a town of iron-works? The sky sank down before dawn, muddy, flat, immovable. The air is thick, clammy with the breath of crowded human beings. It stifles me. I open the window, and, looking out, can scarcely see through the rain the

---

1. The first line is Davis's; the next two are from Alfred, Lord Tennyson's *In Memoriam* 56.25–27.

grocer's shop opposite, where a crowd of drunken Irishmen are puffing Lynchburg tobacco[2] in their pipes. I can detect the scent through all the foul smells ranging loose in the air.

The idiosyncrasy of this town is smoke. It rolls sullenly in slow folds from the great chimneys of the iron-foundries, and settles down in black, slimy pools on the muddy streets. Smoke on the wharves, smoke on the dingy boats, on the yellow river,—clinging in a coating of greasy soot to the house-front, the two faded poplars, the faces of the passers-by. The long train of mules, dragging masses of pig-iron[3] through the narrow street, have a foul vapor hanging to their reeking sides. Here, inside, is a little broken figure of an angel pointing upward from the mantel-shelf; but even its wings are covered with smoke, clotted and black. Smoke everywhere! A dirty canary chirps desolately in a cage beside me. Its dream of green fields and sunshine is a very old dream, —almost worn out, I think.

From the back-window I can see a narrow brick-yard sloping down to the river-side, strewed with rain-butts[4] and tubs. The river, dull and tawny-colored, (*la belle rivière!*)[5] drags itself sluggishly along, tired of the heavy weight of boats and coal-barges. What wonder? When I was a child, I used to fancy a look of weary, dumb appeal upon the face of the negro-like river slavishly bearing its burden day after day. Something of the same idle notion comes to me to-day, when from the street-window I look on the slow stream of human life creeping past, night and morning, to the great mills. Masses of men, with dull, besotted faces bent to the ground, sharpened here and there by pain or cunning; skin and muscle and flesh begrimed with smoke and ashes; stooping all night over boiling caldrons of metal, laired by day in dens of drunkenness and infamy; breathing from infancy to death an air saturated with fog and grease and soot, vileness for soul and body. What do you make of a case like that, amateur psychologist? You call it an altogether serious thing to be alive: to these men it is a drunken jest, a joke, —horrible to angels perhaps, to them commonplace enough. My fancy about the river was an idle one: it is no type of such a life. What if it be stagnant and slimy here? It knows that beyond there waits for it odorous sunlight,—quaint old gardens, dusky with soft, green foliage of apple-trees, and flushing crimson with roses,—air, and fields, and mountains. The future of the Welsh puddler[6] passing just now is not so pleasant. To be stowed away, after his grimy work is done, in a hole in the muddy graveyard, and after that,—*not* air, nor green fields, nor curious roses.

Can you see how foggy the day is? As I stand here, idly tapping the

---

2. An inferior tobacco grown in Virginia.
3. Crude iron formed in blocks.
4. Large casks for catching rainwater.
5. "The beautiful river!"—an ironic recollec-

tion of the Ohio's former purity.
6. One who "puddles" or refines metal by stirring molten vats.

window-pane, and looking out through the rain at the dirty back-yard and the coal-boats below, fragments of an old story float up before me, —a story of this old house into which I happened to come to-day. You may think it a tiresome story enough, as foggy as the day, sharpened by no sudden flashes of pain or pleasure.—I know: only the outline of a dull life, that long since, with thousands of dull lives like its own, was vainly lived and lost: thousands of them,—massed, vile, slimy lives, like those of the torpid lizards in yonder stagnant water-butt.—Lost? There is a curious point for you to settle, my friend, who study psychology in a lazy, *dilettante* way. Stop a moment. I am going to be honest. This is what I want you to do. I want you to hide your disgust, take no heed to your clean clothes, and come right down with me,—here, into the thickest of the fog and mud and foul effluvia. I want you to hear this story. There is a secret down here, in this nightmare fog, that has lain dumb for centuries: I want to make it a real thing to you. You, Egoist, or Pantheist, or Arminian,[7] busy in making straight paths for your feet on the hills, do not see it clearly,—this terrible question which men here have gone mad and died trying to answer. I dare not put this secret into words. I told you it was dumb. These men, going by with drunken faces and brains full of unawakened power, do not ask it of Society or of God. Their lives ask it; their deaths ask it. There is no reply. I will tell you plainly that I have a great hope; and I bring it to you to be tested. It is this: that this terrible dumb question is its own reply; that it is not the sentence of death we think it, but, from the very extremity of its dark-ness, the most solemn prophecy which the world has known of the Hope to come. I dare make my meaning no clearer, but will only tell my story. It will, perhaps, seem to you as foul and dark as this thick vapor about us, and as pregnant with death; but if your eyes are free as mine are to look deeper, no perfume-tinted dawn will be so fair with promise of the day that shall surely come.

My story is very simple,—only what I remember of the life of one of these men,—a furnace-tender in one of Kirby & John's rolling-mills,[8] —Hugh Wolfe. You know the mills? They took the great order for the Lower Virginia railroads there last winter; run usually with about a thousand men. I cannot tell why I choose the half-forgotten story of this Wolfe more than that of myriads of these furnace-hands. Perhaps be-cause there is a secret underlying sympathy between that story and this day with its impure fog and thwarted sunshine,—or perhaps simply for the reason that this house is the one where the Wolfes lived. There were the father and son,—both hands, as I said, in one of Kirby & John's mills for making railroad-iron,—and Deborah, their cousin, a

---

7. Respectively, one who believes in self-inter-est, one who believes that God is present in all things, and one who believes in free will.

8. Mills where metal is rolled into sheets, bars, and other forms.

picker[9] in some of the cotton-mills. The house was rented then to half a dozen families. The Wolfes had two of the cellar-rooms. The old man, like many of the puddlers and feeders[1] of the mills, was Welsh,—had spent half of his life in the Cornish tin-mines.[2] You may pick the Welsh emigrants, Cornish miners, out of the throng passing the windows, any day. They are a trifle more filthy; their muscles are not so brawny; they stoop more. When they are drunk, they neither yell, nor shout, nor stagger, but skulk along like beaten hounds. A pure, unmixed blood, I fancy: shows itself in the slight angular bodies and sharply-cut facial lines. It is nearly thirty years since the Wolfes lived here. Their lives were like those of their class: incessant labor, sleeping in kennel-like rooms, eating rank pork and molasses, drinking—God and the distillers only know what; with an occasional night in jail, to atone for some drunken excess. Is that all of their lives?—of the portion given to them and these their duplicates swarming the streets to-day?—nothing beneath?—all? So many a political reformer will tell you,—and many a private reformer, too, who has gone among them with a heart tender with Christ's charity, and come out outraged, hardened.

One rainy night, about eleven o'clock, a crowd of half-clothed women stopped outside of the cellar-door. They were going home from the cotton-mill.

"Good-night, Deb," said one, a mulatto,[3] steadying herself against the gas-post. She needed the post to steady her. So did more than one of them.

"Dah's a ball to Miss Potts' to-night. Ye'd best come."

"Inteet, Deb, if hur'll come, hur'll hef fun,"[4] said a shrill Welsh voice in the crowd.

Two or three dirty hands were thrust out to catch the gown of the woman, who was groping for the latch of the door.

"No."

"No? Where's Kit Small, then?"

"Begorra! on the spools.[5] Alleys behint, though we helped her, we dud. An wid ye! Let Deb alone! It's ondacent frettin' a quite body. Be the powers, an' we'll have a night of it! there'll be lashin's[6] o' drink,— the Vargent be blessed and praised for 't!"

They went on, the mulatto inclining for a moment to show fight, and drag the woman Wolfe off with them; but, being pacified, she staggered away.

9. Operator of a machine that separates cotton fibers.
1. Workers who feed more molten metal into the casting forms.
2. Cornwall is in the west of England, where much mining is done.
3. A person who is half black in ancestry.
4. Welsh dialect: "Indeed, Deb, if she'll come, she'll have fun."
5. I.e., working on the spools where cotton is wound. "Begorra": Irish euphemism for "By God."
6. Plenty; "Vargent": the Virgin Mary.

Deborah groped her way into the cellar, and, after considerable stumbling, kindled a match, and lighted a tallow dip, that sent a yellow glimmer over the room. It was low, damp,—the earthen floor covered with a green, slimy moss,—a fetid air smothering the breath. Old Wolfe lay asleep on a heap of straw, wrapped in a torn horse-blanket. He was a pale, meek little man, with a white face and red rabbit-eyes. The woman Deborah was like him; only her face was even more ghastly, her lips bluer, her eyes more watery. She wore a faded cotton gown and a slouching bonnet. When she walked, one could see that she was deformed, almost a hunchback. She trod softly, so as not to waken him, and went through into the room beyond. There she found by the half-extinguished fire an iron saucepan filled with cold boiled potatoes, which she put upon a broken chair with a pint-cup of ale. Placing the old candlestick beside this dainty repast, she untied her bonnet, which hung limp and wet over her face, and prepared to eat her supper. It was the first food that had touched her lips since morning. There was enough of it, however: there is not always. She was hungry,—one could see that easily enough,—and not drunk, as most of her companions would have been found at this hour. She did not drink, this woman,—her face told that, too,—nothing stronger than ale. Perhaps the weak, flaccid wretch had some stimulant in her pale life to keep her up,—some love or hope, it might be, or urgent need. When that stimulant was gone, she would take to whiskey. Man cannot live by work alone. While she was skinning the potatoes, and munching them, a noise behind her made her stop.

"Janey!" she called, lifting the candle and peering into the darkness. "Janey, are you there?"

A heap of ragged coats was heaved up, and the face of a young girl emerged, staring sleepily at the woman.

"Deborah," she said, at last, "I'm here the night."

"Yes, child. Hur's welcome," she said, quietly eating on.

The girl's face was haggard and sickly; her eyes were heavy with sleep and hunger: real Milesian[7] eyes they were, dark, delicate blue, glooming out from black shadows with a pitiful fright.

"I was alone," she said, timidly.

"Where's the father?" asked Deborah, holding out a potato, which the girl greedily seized.

"He's beyant,—wid Haley,—in the stone house." (Did you ever hear the word *jail* from an Irish mouth?) "I came here. Hugh told me never to stay me-lone."

"Hugh?"

"Yes."

7. Irish.

A vexed frown crossed her face. The girl saw it, and added quickly,—
"I have not seen Hugh the day, Deb. The old man says his watch[8]
lasts till the mornin'."

The woman sprang up, and hastily began to arrange some bread and
flitch[9] in a tin pail, and to pour her own measure of ale into a bottle.
Tying on her bonnet, she blew out the candle.

"Lay ye down, Janey dear," she said, gently, covering her with the
old rags. "Hur can eat the potatoes, if hur's hungry."

"Where are ye goin', Deb? The rain's sharp."

"To the mill, with Hugh's supper."

"Let him bide till th' morn. Sit ye down."

"No, no,"—sharply pushing her off. "The boy'll starve."

She hurried from the cellar, while the child wearily coiled herself up
for sleep. The rain was falling heavily, as the woman, pail in hand,
emerged from the mouth of the alley, and turned down the narrow
street, that stretched out, long and black, miles before her. Here and
there a flicker of gas lighted an uncertain space of muddy footwalk and
gutter; the long rows of houses, except an occasional lager-bier shop,
were closed; now and then she met a band of mill-hands skulking to or
from their work.

Not many even of the inhabitants of a manufacturing town know the
vast machinery of system by which the bodies of workmen are governed, that goes on unceasingly from year to year. The hands of each
mill are divided into watches that relieve each other as regularly as the
sentinels of an army. By night and day the work goes on, the unsleeping
engines groan and shriek, the fiery pools of metal boil and surge. Only
for a day in the week, in half-courtesy to public censure, the fires are
partially veiled; but as soon as the clock strikes midnight, the great furnaces break forth with renewed fury, the clamor begins with fresh,
breathless vigor, the engines sob and shriek like "gods in pain."

As Deborah hurried down through the heavy rain, the noise of these
thousand engines sounded through the sleep and shadow of the city like
far-off thunder. The mill to which she was going lay on the river, a mile
below the city-limits. It was far, and she was weak, aching from standing
twelve hours at the spools. Yet it was her almost nightly walk to take this
man his supper, though at every square she sat down to rest, and she
knew she should receive small word of thanks.

Perhaps, if she had possessed an artist's eye, the picturesque oddity of
the scene might have made her step stagger less, and the path seem
shorter; but to her the mills were only "summat deilish[1] to look at by
night."

8. Workshift.   1. "Somewhat devilish."
9. Rank salt pork.

The road leading to the mills had been quarried from the solid rock, which rose abrupt and bare on one side of the cinder-covered road, while the river, sluggish and black, crept past on the other. The mills for rolling iron are simply immense tent-like roofs, covering acres of ground, open on every side. Beneath these roofs Deborah looked in on a city of fires, that burned hot and fiercely in the night. Fire in every horrible form: pits of flame waving in the wind; liquid metal-flames writhing in tortuous streams through the sand; wide caldrons filled with boiling fire, over which bent ghastly wretches stirring the strange brewing; and through all, crowds of half-clad men, looking like revengeful ghosts in the red light, hurried, throwing masses of glittering fire. It was like a street in Hell. Even Deborah muttered, as she crept through, " 'T looks like t' Devil's place!" It did,—in more ways than one.

She found the man she was looking for, at last, heaping coal on a furnace. He had not time to eat his supper; so she went behind the furnace, and waited. Only a few men were with him, and they noticed her only by a "Hyur comes t' hunchback, Wolfe."

Deborah was stupid with sleep; her back pained her sharply; and her teeth chattered with cold, with the rain that soaked her clothes and dripped from her at every step. She stood, however, patiently holding the pail, and waiting.

"Hout, woman! ye look like a drowned cat. Come near to the fire," —said one of the men, approaching to scrape away the ashes.

She shook her head. Wolfe had forgotten her. He turned, hearing the man, and came closer.

"I did no' think; gi' me my supper, woman."

She watched him eat with a painful eagerness. With a woman's quick instinct, she saw that he was not hungry,—was eating to please her. Her pale, watery eyes began to gather a strange light.

"Is't good, Hugh? T'ale was a bit sour, I feared."

"No, good enough." He hesitated a moment. "Ye're tired, poor lass! Bide here till I go. Lay down there on that heap of ash, and go to sleep."

He threw her an old coat for a pillow, and turned to his work. The heap was the refuse of the burnt iron, and was not a hard bed; the half-smothered warmth, too, penetrated her limbs, dulling their pain and cold shiver.

Miserable enough she looked, lying there on the ashes like a limp, dirty rag,—yet not an unfitting figure to crown the scene of hopeless discomfort and veiled crime: more fitting, if one looked deeper into the heart of things,—at her thwarted woman's form, her colorless life, her waking stupor that smothered pain and hunger,—even more fit to be a type of her class. Deeper yet if one could look, was there nothing worth reading in this wet, faded thing, half-covered with ashes? no story of a soul filled with groping passionate love, heroic unselfishness, fierce jealousy? of years of weary trying to please the one human being whom she loved, to gain one look of real heart-kindness from him? If anything like this were hidden beneath the pale, bleared eyes, and dull, washed-out-looking face, no one had ever taken the trouble to read its faint signs: not the half-clothed furnace-tender, Wolfe, certainly. Yet he was kind to her: it was his nature to be kind, even to the very rats that swarmed in the cellar; kind to her in just the same way. She knew that. And it might be that very knowledge had given to her face its apathy and vacancy more than her low, torpid life. One sees that dead, vacant look steal sometimes over the rarest, finest of women's faces,—in the very midst, it may be, of their warmest summer's day; and then one can guess at the secret of intolerable solitude that lies hid beneath the delicate laces and brilliant smile. There was no warmth, no brilliancy, no summer for this woman; so the stupor and vacancy had time to gnaw into her face perpetually. She was young, too, though no one guessed it; so the gnawing was the fiercer.

She lay quiet in the dark corner, listening, through the monotonous din and uncertain glare of the works, to the dull plash of the rain in the far distance,—shrinking back whenever the man Wolfe happened to look towards her. She knew, in spite of all his kindness, that there was that in her face and form which made him loathe the sight of her. She felt by instinct, although she could not comprehend it, the finer nature of the man, which made him among his fellow-workmen something unique, set apart. She knew, that, down under all the vileness and coarseness of his life, there was a groping passion for whatever was beautiful and pure,—that his soul sickened with disgust at her deformity, even when his words were kindest. Through this dull consciousness, which never left her, came, like a sting, the recollection of the dark blue eyes and lithe figure of the little Irish girl she had left in the cellar. The recollection struck through even her stupid intellect with a vivid glow of beauty and of grace. Little Janey, timid, helpless, clinging to Hugh as her only friend: that was the sharp thought, the bitter thought, that drove into the glazed eyes a fierce light of pain. You laugh at it? Are pain and jealousy less savage realities down here in this place I am taking you to than in your own house or your own heart,—your heart, which they clutch at sometimes? The note is the same, I fancy, be the octave high or low.

If you could go into this mill where Deborah lay, and drag out from the hearts of these men the terrible tragedy of their lives, taking it as a symptom of the disease of their class, no ghost Horror would terrify you more. A reality of soul-starvation, of living death, that meets you every day under the besotted faces on the street,—I can paint nothing of this, only give you the outside outlines of a night, a crisis in the life of one man: whatever muddy depth of soul-history lies beneath you can read according to the eyes God has given you.

Wolfe, while Deborah watched him as a spaniel its master, bent over the furnace with his iron pole, unconscious of her scrutiny, only stopping to receive orders. Physically, Nature had promised the man but little. He had already lost the strength and instinct vigor of a man, his muscles were thin, his nerves weak, his face (a meek, woman's face) haggard, yellow with consumption. In the mill he was known as one of the girl-men: "Molly Wolfe" was his *sobriquet*.[2] He was never seen in the cockpit,[3] did not own a terrier, drank but seldom; when he did, desperately. He fought sometimes, but was always thrashed, pommelled to a jelly. The man was game enough, when his blood was up: but he was no favorite in the mill; he had the taint of school-learning on him,—not to a dangerous extent, only a quarter or so in the free-school in fact,[4] but enough to ruin him as a good hand in a fight.

For other reasons, too, he was not popular. Not one of themselves, they felt that, though outwardly as filthy and ash-covered; silent, with foreign thoughts and longings breaking out through his quietness in innumerable curious ways: this one, for instance. In the neighboring furnace-buildings lay great heaps of the refuse from the ore after the pig-metal is run. *Korl* we call it here: a light, porous substance, of a delicate, waxen, flesh-colored tinge. Out of the blocks of this korl, Wolfe, in his off-hours from the furnace, had a habit of chipping and moulding figures,—hideous, fantastic enough, but sometimes strangely beautiful: even the mill-men saw that, while they jeered at him. It was a curious fancy in the man, almost a passion. The few hours for rest he spent hewing and hacking with his blunt knife, never speaking, until his watch came again,—working at one figure for months, and, when it was finished, breaking it to pieces perhaps, in a fit of disappointment. A morbid, gloomy man, untaught, unled, left to feed his soul in grossness and crime, and hard, grinding labor.

I want you to come down and look at this Wolfe, standing there among the lowest of his kind, and see him just as he is, that you may judge him justly when you hear the story of this night. I want you to look back, as he does every day, at his birth in vice, his starved infancy; to remember the heavy years he has groped through as boy and man, —the slow, heavy years of constant, hot work. So long ago he began, that he thinks sometimes he has worked there for ages. There is no hope that it will ever end. Think that God put into this man's soul a

---

2. Nickname.
3. Place where cockfights are held, a violent game in which roosters are made to kill each other; terriers were bred as hunters.

4. "Most workers in the mills were illiterate, public schools almost nonexistent" [Olsen's note].

fierce thirst for beauty,—to know it, to create it; to *be*—something, he knows not what,—other than he is. There are moments when a passing cloud, the sun glinting on the purple thistles, a kindly smile, a child's face, will rouse him to a passion of pain,—when his nature starts up with a mad cry of rage against God, man, whoever it is that has forced this vile, slimy life upon him. With all this groping, this mad desire, a great blind intellect stumbling through wrong, a loving poet's heart, the man was by habit only a coarse, vulgar laborer, familiar with sights and words you would blush to name. Be just: when I tell you about this night, see him as he is. Be just,—not like man's law, which seizes on one isolated fact, but like God's judging angel, whose clear, sad eye saw all the countless cankering days of this man's life, all the countless nights, when, sick with starving, his soul fainted in him, before it judged him for this night, the saddest of all.

I called this night the crisis of his life. If it was, it stole on him un-awares. These great turning-days of life cast no shadow before, slip by unconsciously. Only a trifle, a little turn of the rudder, and the ship goes to heaven or hell.

Wolfe, while Deborah watched him, dug into the furnace of melting iron with his pole, dully thinking only how many rails the lump would yield. It was late,—nearly Sunday morning; another hour, and the heavy work would be done,—only the furnaces to replenish and cover for the next day. The workmen were growing more noisy, shouting, as they had to do, to be heard over the deep clamor of the mills. Suddenly they grew less boisterous,—at the far end, entirely silent. Something unusual had happened. After a moment, the silence came nearer; the men stopped their jeers and drunken choruses. Deborah, stupidly lifting up her head, saw the cause of the quiet. A group of five or six men were slowly approaching, stopping to examine each furnace as they came. Visitors often came to see the mills after night: except by growing less noisy, the men took no notice of them. The furnace where Wolfe worked was near the bounds of the works; they halted there hot and tired: a walk over one of these great foundries is no trifling task. The woman, drawing out of sight, turned over to sleep. Wolfe, seeing them stop, suddenly roused from his indifferent stupor, and watched them keenly. He knew some of them: the overseer, Clarke,—a son of Kirby, one of the mill-owners,—and a Doctor May, one of the town-physicians. The other two were strangers. Wolfe came closer. He seized eagerly every chance that brought him into contact with this mysterious class that shone down on him perpetually with the glamour of another order of being. What made the difference between them? That was the mystery of his life. He had a vague notion that perhaps to-night he could find it out. One of the strangers sat down on a pile of bricks, and beckoned young Kirby to his side.

"This *is* hot, with a vengeance. A match, please?"—lighting his cigar. "But the walk is worth the trouble. If it were not that you must have heard it so often, Kirby, I would tell you that your works look like Dante's Inferno."[5]

Kirby laughed.

"Yes. Yonder is Farinata himself in the burning tomb,"[6]—pointing to some figure in the shimmering shadows.

"Judging from some of the faces of your men," said the other, "they bid fair to try the reality of Dante's vision, some day."

Young Kirby looked curiously around, as if seeing the faces of his hands for the first time.

"They're bad enough, that's true. A desperate set, I fancy. Eh, Clarke?"

The overseer did not hear him. He was talking of net profits just then,—giving, in fact, a schedule of the annual business of the firm to a sharp peering little Yankee, who jotted down notes on a paper laid on the crown of his hat: a reporter for one of the city-papers, getting up a series of reviews of the leading manufactories. The other gentlemen had accompanied them merely for amusement. They were silent until the notes were finished, drying their feet at the furnaces, and sheltering their faces from the intolerable heat. At last the overseer concluded with—

"I believe that is a pretty fair estimate, Captain."

"Here, some of you men!" said Kirby, "bring up those boards. We may as well sit down, gentlemen, until the rain is over. It cannot last much longer at this rate."

"Pig-metal,"—mumbled the reporter,—"um!—coal facilities,—um!—hands employed, twelve hundred,—bitumen,—um!—all right, I believe, Mr. Clarke;—sinking-fund,—what did you say was your sinking-fund?"[7]

"Twelve hundred hands?" said the stranger, the young man who had first spoken. "Do you control their votes, Kirby?"

"Control? No." The young man smiled complacently. "But my father brought seven hundred votes to the polls for his candidate last November. No force-work, you understand,—only a speech or two, a hint to form themselves into a society, and a bit of red and blue bunting to make them a flag. The Invincible Roughs,—I believe that is their name. I forget the motto: 'Our country's hope,' I think."

There was a laugh. The young man talking to Kirby sat with an amused light in his cool gray eye, surveying critically the half-clothed figures of the puddlers, and the slow swing of their brawny muscles. He

---

5. I.e., of Dante's vision of hell in the *Inferno*.
6. Farinata degli Uberti, one of the heretics in Canto 10 of the *Inferno*.

7. Fund accumulated to pay off a corporate debt.

was a stranger in the city,—spending a couple of months in the borders of a Slave State, to study the institutions of the South,[8]—a brother-in-law of Kirby's,—Mitchell. He was an amateur gymnast,—hence his anatomical eye; a patron, in a *blasé* way, of the prize-ring; a man who sucked the essence out of a science or philosophy in an indifferent, gentlemanly way; who took Kant, Novalis, Humboldt,[9] for what they were worth in his own scales; accepting all, despising nothing, in heaven, earth, or hell, but one-idead men; with a temper yielding and brilliant as summer water, until his Self was touched, when it was ice, though brilliant still. Such men are not rare in the States.

As he knocked the ashes from his cigar, Wolfe caught with a quick pleasure the contour of the white hand, the blood-glow of a red ring he wore. His voice, too, and that of Kirby's, touched him like music,—low, even, with chording cadences. About this man Mitchell hung the impalpable atmosphere belonging to the thoroughbred gentleman. Wolfe, scraping away the ashes beside him, was conscious of it, did obeisance to it with his artist sense, unconscious that he did so.

The rain did not cease. Clark and the reporter left the mills; the others, comfortably seated near the furnace, lingered, smoking and talking in a desultory way. Greek would not have been more unintelligible to the furnace-tenders, whose presence they soon forgot entirely. Kirby drew out a newspaper from his pocket and read aloud some article, which they discussed eagerly. At every sentence, Wolfe listened more and more like a dumb, hopeless animal, with a duller, more stolid look creeping over his face, glancing now and then at Mitchell, marking acutely every smallest sign of refinement, then back to himself, seeing as in a mirror his filthy body, his more stained soul.

Never! He had no words for such a thought, but he knew now, in all the sharpness of the bitter certainty, that between them there was a great gulf never to be passed.[1] Never!

The bells of the mills rang for midnight. Sunday morning had dawned. Whatever hidden message lay in the tolling bells floated past these men unknown. Yet it was there. Veiled in the solemn music ushering the risen saviour was a key-note to solve the darkest secrets of a world gone wrong,—even this social riddle which the brain of the grimy puddler grappled with madly to-night.

The men began to withdraw the metal from the caldrons. The mills were deserted on Sundays, except by the hands who fed the fires, and those who had no lodgings and slept usually on the ash-heaps. The three stangers sat still during the next hour, watching the men cover the furnaces, laughing now and then at some jest of Kirby's.

8. I.e., the institutions of slavery.
9. Three very different eighteenth- and nineteenth-century German thinkers.

1. In Luke 16:26, Christ speaks of the "great gulf fixed" between Dives, the rich man, in hell, and Lazarus, the beggar, in heaven.

"Do you know," said Mitchell, "I like this view of the works better than when the glare was fiercest? These heavy shadows and the amphitheatre of smothered fires are ghostly, unreal. One could fancy these red smouldering lights to be the half-shut eyes of wild beasts, and the spectral figures their victims in the den."

Kirby laughed. "You are fanciful. Come, let us get out of the den. The spectral figures, as you call them, are a little too real for me to fancy a close proximity in the darkness,—unarmed, too."

The others rose, buttoning their over-coats, and lighting cigars.

"Raining, still," said Doctor May, "and hard. Where did we leave the coach, Mitchell?"

"At the other side of the works.—Kirby, what's that?"

Mitchell started back, half-frightened, as, suddenly turning a corner, the white figure of a woman faced him in the darkness,—a woman, white, of giant proportions, crouching on the ground, her arms flung out in some wild gesture of warning.

"Stop! Make that fire burn there!" cried Kirby, stopping short.

The flame burst out, flashing the gaunt figure into bold relief.

Mitchell drew a long breath.

"I thought it was alive," he said, going up curiously.

The others followed.

"Not marble, eh?" asked Kirby, touching it.

One of the lower overseers stopped.

"Korl, Sir."

"Who did it?"

"Can't say. Some of the hands; chipped it out in off-hours."

"Chipped to some purpose, I should say. What a flesh-tint the stuff has! Do you see, Mitchell?"

"I see."

He had stepped aside where the light fell boldest on the figure, looking at it in silence. There was not one line of beauty or grace in it: a nude woman's form, muscular, grown coarse with labor, the powerful limbs instinct with some one poignant longing. One idea: there it was in the tense, rigid muscles, the clutching hands, the wild, eager face, like that of a starving wolf's. Kirby and Doctor May walked around it, critical, curious. Mitchell stood aloof, silent. The figure touched him strangely.

"Not badly done," said Doctor May. "Where did the fellow learn that sweep of the muscles in the arm and hand? Look at them! They are groping,—do you see?—clutching: the peculiar action of a man dying of thirst."

"They have ample facilities for studying anatomy," sneered Kirby, glancing at the half-naked figures.

"Look," continued the Doctor, "at this bony wrist, and the strained sinews of the instep! A working-woman,—the very type of her class."

"God forbid!" muttered Mitchell.

"Why?" demanded May. "What does the fellow intend by the figure? I cannot catch the meaning."

"Ask him," said the other, dryly. "There he stands,"—pointing to Wolfe, who stood with a group of men, leaning on his ash-rake.

The Doctor beckoned him with the affable smile which kind-hearted men put on, when talking with these people.

"Mr. Mitchell has picked you out as the man who did this,—I'm sure I don't know why. But what did you mean by it?"

"She be hungry."

Wolfe's eyes answered Mitchell, not the Doctor.

"Oh-h! But what a mistake you have made, my fine fellow! You have given no sign of starvation to the body. It is strong,—terribly strong. It has the mad, half-despairing gesture of drowning."

Wolfe stammered, glanced appealingly at Mitchell, who saw the soul of the thing, he knew. But the cool, probing eyes were turned on himself now,—mocking, cruel, relentless.

"Not hungry for meat," the furnace-tender said at last.

"What then? Whiskey?" jeered Kirby, with a coarse laugh.

Wolfe was silent a moment, thinking.

"I dunno," he said, with a bewildered look. "It mebbe. Summat to make her live, I think,—like you. Whiskey ull do it, in a way."

The young man laughed again. Mitchell flashed a look of disgust somewhere,—not at Wolfe.

"May," he broke out impatiently, "are you blind? Look at that woman's face! It asks questions of God, and says, 'I have a right to know.' Good God, how hungry it is!"

They looked a moment; then May turned to the mill-owner:—

"Have you many such hands as this? What are you going to do with them? Keep them at puddling iron?"

Kirby shrugged his shoulders. Mitchell's look had irritated him.

"*Ce n'est pas mon affaire.*[2] I have no fancy for nursing infant geniuses. I suppose there are some stray gleams of mind and soul among these wretches. The Lord will take care of his own; or else they can work out their own salvation. I have heard you call our American system a ladder which any man can scale. Do you doubt it? Or perhaps you want to banish all social ladders, and put us all on a flat table-land, —eh, May?"

The Doctor looked vexed, puzzled. Some terrible problem lay hid in

2. "That's not my business."

this woman's face, and troubled these men. Kirby waited for an answer, and, receiving none, went on, warming with his subject.

"I tell you, there's something wrong that no talk of '*Liberté*' or '*Égalité*' will do away.[3] If I had the making of men, these men who do the lowest part of the world's work should be machines,—nothing more, —hands. It would be kindness. God help them! What are taste, reason, to creatures who must live such lives as that?" He pointed to Deborah, sleeping on the ash-heap. "So many nerves to sting them to pain. What if God had put your brain, with all its agony of touch, into your fingers, and bid you work and strike with that?"

"You think you could govern the world better?" laughed the Doctor.

"I do not think at all."

"That is true philosophy. Drift with the stream, because you cannot dive deep enough to find bottom, eh?"

"Exactly," rejoined Kirby. "I do not think. I wash my hands of all social problems,—slavery, caste, white or black. My duty to my operatives[4] has a narrow limit,—the pay-hour on Saturday night. Outside of that, if they cut korl, or cut each other's throats, (the more popular amusement of the two,) I am not responsible."

The Doctor sighed,—a good honest sigh, from the depths of his stomach.

"God help us! Who is responsible?"

"Not I, I tell you," said Kirby, testily. "What has the man who pays them money to do with their souls' concerns, more than the grocer or butcher who takes it?"

"And yet," said Mitchell's cynical voice, "look at her! How hungry she is!"

Kirby tapped his boot with his cane. No one spoke. Only the dumb face of the rough image looking into their faces with the awful question, "What shall we do to be saved?"[5] Only Wolfe's face, with its heavy weight of brain, its weak, uncertain mouth, its desperate eyes, out of which looked the soul of his class,—only Wolfe's face turned towards Kirby's. Mitchell laughed,—a cool, musical laugh.

"Money has spoken!" he said, seating himself lightly on a stone with the air of an amused spectator at a play. "Are you answered?"—turning to Wolfe his clear, magnetic face.

Bright and deep and cold as Arctic air, the soul of the man lay tranquil beneath. He looked at the furnace-tender as he had looked at a rare mosaic in the morning; only the man was the more amusing study of the two.

---

3. The slogan of the French Revolution was "Liberté, Égalité, Fraternité" (Liberty, Equality, Brotherhood).
4. Workers.

5. The words of the keeper of the prison in Philippi after an earthquake opens the doors of his prison (Acts 16:30).

"Are you answered? Why, May, look at him! 'De profundis cla-mavi.'[6] Or, to quote in English, 'Hungry and thirsty, his soul faints in him.' And so Money sends back its answer into the depths through you, Kirby! Very clear the answer, too!—I think I remember reading the same words somewhere:—washing your hands in Eau de Cologne, and saying, 'I am innocent of the blood of this man. See ye to it!' "[7]

Kirby flushed angrily.

"You quote Scripture freely."

"Do I not quote correctly? I think I remember another line, which may amend my meaning: 'Inasmuch as ye did it unto one of the least of these, ye did it unto me.'[8] Deist? Bless you, man, I was raised on the milk of the Word. Now, Doctor, the pocket of the world having uttered its voice, what has the heart to say? You are a philanthropist, in a small way,—n'est ce pas?[9] Here, boy, this gentleman can show you how to cut korl better,—or your destiny. Go on, May!"

"I think a mocking devil possesses you to-night," rejoined the Doctor, seriously.

He went to Wolfe and put his hand kindly on his arm. Something of a vague idea possessed the Doctor's brain that much good was to be done here by a friendly word or two: a latent genius to be warmed into life by a waited-for sun-beam. Here it was: he had brought it. So he went on complacently:—

"Do you know, boy, you have it in you to be a great sculptor, a great man?—do you understand?" (talking down to the capacity of his hearer: it is a way people have with children, and men like Wolfe,)—"to live a better, stronger life than I, or Mr. Kirby here? A man may make himself anything he chooses. God has given you stronger powers than many men,—me, for instance."

May stopped, heated, glowing with his own magnanimity. And it was magnanimous. The puddler had drunk in every word, looking through the Doctor's flurry, and generous heat, and self-approval, into his will, with those slow, absorbing eyes of his.

"Make yourself what you will. It is your right."

"I know," quietly. "Will you help me?"

Mitchell laughed again. The Doctor turned now, in a passion,—

"You know, Mitchell, I have not the means. You know, if I had, it is in my heart to take this boy and educate him for"—

"The glory of God, and the glory of John May."

May did not speak for a moment; then, controlled, he said,—

6. "I have cried out of the deep unto thee, O Lord" (Latin version of Psalm 130).
7. The words of Pontius Pilate, the Roman judge who permitted Christ to be crucified but refused to take responsibility (Matthew 27:24).

8. Christ's words in Matthew 25:40. "Deist": believer in a God who created the universe and its laws but who thereafter refrains from interfering with those laws.
9. "Isn't that right?"

"Why should one be raised, when myriads are left?—I have not the money, boy," to Wolfe, shortly.

"Money?" He said it over slowly, as one repeats the guessed answer to a riddle, doubtfully. "That is it? Money?"

"Yes, money,—that is it," said Mitchell, rising, and drawing his furred coat about him. "You've found the cure for all the world's diseases.—Come, May, find your good-humor, and come home. This damp wind chills my very bones. Come and preach your Saint-Simonian[1] doctrines to-morrow to Kirby's hands. Let them have a clear idea of the rights of the soul, and I'll venture next week they'll strike for higher wages. That will be the end of it."

"Will you send the coach-driver to this side of the mills?" asked Kirby, turning to Wolfe.

He spoke kindly: it was his habit to do so. Deborah, seeing the puddler go, crept after him. The three men waited outside. Doctor May walked up and down, chafed. Suddenly he stopped.

"Go back, Mitchell! You say the pocket and the heart of the world speak without meaning to these people. What has its head to say? Taste, culture, refinement? Go!"

Mitchell was leaning against a brick wall. He turned his head indolently, and looked into the mills. There hung about the place a thick, unclean odor. The slightest motion of his hand marked that he perceived it, and his insufferable disgust. That was all. May said nothing, only quickened his angry tramp.

"Besides," added Mitchell, giving a corollary to his answer, "it would be of no use. I am not one of them."

"You do not mean"—said May, facing him.

"Yes, I mean just that. Reform is born of need, not pity. No vital movement of the people's has worked down, for good or evil; fermented, instead, carried up the heaving, cloggy mass. Think back through history, and you will know it. What will this lowest deep— thieves, Magdalens,[2] negroes—do with the light filtered through ponderous Church creeds, Baconian theories, Goethe schemes? Some day, out of their bitter need will be thrown up their own light-bringer,— their Jean Paul, their Cromwell, their Messiah."[3]

"Bah!" was the Doctor's inward criticism. However, in practice, he adopted the theory; for, when, night and morning, afterwards, he prayed that power might be given these degraded souls to rise, he glowed at heart, recognizing an accomplished duty.

1. Socialist; after Claude Henri de Rouvroy, Comte de Saint-Simon (1760–1825), French social theorist.
2. Prostitutes (from Mary Magdalen in Matthew 16:9).
3. Oliver Cromwell (1599–1658) led the revolt against the British monarchy. Jean Paul Richter (1763–1825) was a German novelist. Francis Bacon (1561–1626) and Johann Wolfgang von Goethe (1749–1832) were a philosopher and a poet who developed complicated abstract theories.

Wolfe and the woman had stood in the shadow of the works as the coach drove off. The Doctor had held out his hand in a frank, generous way, telling him to "take care of himself, and to remember it was his right to rise." Mitchell had simply touched his hat, as to an equal, with a quiet look of thorough recognition. Kirby had thrown Deborah some money, which she found, and clutched eagerly enough. They were gone now, all of them. The man sat down on the cinder-road, looking up into the murky sky.

"'T be late, Hugh. Wunnot hur come?"

He shook his head doggedly, and the woman crouched out of his sight against the wall. Do you remember rare moments when a sudden light flashed over yourself, your world, God? when you stood on a mountain-peak, seeing your life as it might have been, as it is? one quick instant, when custom lost its force and every-day usage? when your friend, wife, brother, stood in a new light? your soul was bared, and the grave,—a foretaste of the nakedness of the Judgment-Day? So it came before him, his life, that night. The slow tides of pain he had borne gathered themselves up and surged against his soul. His squalid daily life, the brutal coarseness eating into his brain, as the ashes into his skin: before, these things had been a dull aching into his consciousness; to-night, they were reality. He gripped the filthy red shirt that clung, stiff with soot, about him, and tore it savagely from his arm. The flesh beneath was muddy with grease and ashes,—and the heart beneath that! And the soul? God knows.

Then flashed before his vivid poetic sense the man who had left him,—the pure face, the delicate, sinewy limbs, in harmony with all he knew of beauty or truth. In his cloudy fancy he had pictured a Some-thing like this. He had found it in this Mitchell, even when he idly scoffed at his pain: a Man all-knowing, all-seeing, crowned by Nature, reigning,—the keen glance of his eye falling like a sceptre on other men. And yet his instinct taught him that he too—He! He looked at himself with sudden loathing, sick, wrung his hands with a cry, and then was silent. With all the phantoms of his heated, ignorant fancy, Wolfe had not been vague in his ambitions. They were practical, slowly built up before him out of his knowledge of what he could do. Through years he had day by day made this hope a real thing to himself,—a clear, projected figure of himself, as he might become.

Able to speak, to know what was best, to raise these men and women working at his side up with him: sometimes he forgot this defined hope in the frantic anguish to escape,—only to escape,—out of the wet, the pain, the ashes, somewhere, anywhere,—only for one moment of free air on a hill-side, to lie down and let his sick soul throb itself out in the sunshine. But to-night he panted for life. The savage strength of his nature was roused; his cry was fierce to God for justice.

"Look at me!" he said to Deborah, with a low, bitter laugh, striking his puny chest savagely. "What am I worth, Deb? Is it my fault that I am no better? My fault? My fault?"

He stopped, stung with a sudden remorse, seeing her hunchback shape writhing with sobs. For Deborah was crying thankless tears, according to the fashion of women.

"God forgi' me, woman! Things go harder wi' you nor me. It's a worse share."

He got up and helped her to rise; and they went doggedly down the muddy street, side by side.

"It's all wrong," he muttered, slowly,—"all wrong! I dunnot understan'. But it'll end some day."

"Come home, Hugh!" she said, coaxingly; for he had stopped, looking around bewildered.

"Home,—and back to the mill!" He went on saying this over to himself, as if he would mutter down every pain in this dull despair.

She followed him through the fog, her blue lips chattering with cold. They reached the cellar at last. Old Wolfe had been drinking since she went out, and had crept nearer the door. The girl Janey slept heavily in the corner. He went up to her, touching softly the worn white arm with his fingers. Some bitterer thought stung him, as he stood there. He wiped the drops from his forehead, and went into the room beyond, livid, trembling. A hope, trifling, perhaps, but very dear, had died just then out of the poor puddler's life, as he looked at the sleeping, innocent girl,—some plan for the future, in which she had borne a part. He gave it up that moment, then and forever. Only a trifle, perhaps, to us: his face grew a shade paler,—that was all. But, somehow, the man's soul, as God and the angels looked down on it, never was the same afterwards.

Deborah followed him into the inner room. She carried a candle, which she placed on the floor, closing the door after her. She had seen the look on his face, as he turned away: her own grew deadly. Yet, as she came up to him her eyes glowed. He was seated on an old chest, quiet, holding his face in his hands.

"Hugh!" she said, softly.

He did not speak.

"Hugh, did hur hear what the man said,—him with the clear voice? Did hur hear? Money, money,—that it wud do all?"

He pushed her away,—gently, but he was worn out; her rasping tone fretted him.

"Hugh!"

The candle flared a pale yellow light over the cobwebbed brick walls, and the woman standing there. He looked at her. She was young, in deadly earnest; her faded eyes, and wet, ragged figure caught from their frantic eagerness a power akin to beauty.

"Hugh, it is true! Money ull do it! Oh, Hugh, boy, listen till me! He said it true! It is money!"

"I know. Go back! I do not want you here."

"Hugh, it is t' last time. I'll never worrit hur again."[4]

There were tears in her voice now, but she choked them back.

"Hear till me only to-night! If one of t' witch people wud come, them we heard of t' home, and gif hur all hur wants, what then? Say, Hugh!"

"What do you mean?"

"I mean money."

Her whisper shrilled through his brain.

"If one of t' witch dwarfs wud come from t' lane moors to-night, and gif hur money, to go out,—*out*, I say,—out, lad, where t' sun shines, and t' heath grows, and t' ladies walk in silken gownds, and God stays all t' time,—where t' man lives that talked to us to-night,—Hugh knows,—Hugh could walk there like a king!"

He thought the woman mad, tried to check her, but she went on, fierce in her eager haste.

"If *I* were t' witch dwarf, if I had t' money, wud hur thank me? Wud hur take me out o' this place wid hur and Janey? I wud not come into the gran' house hur wud build, to vex hur wid t' hunch,—only at night, when t' shadows were dark, stand far off to see hur."

Mad? Yes! Are many of us mad in this way?

"Poor Deb! poor Deb!" he said, soothingly.

"It is here," she said, suddenly jerking into his hand a small roll. "I took it! I did it! Me, me!—not hur! I shall be hanged, I shall be burnt in hell, if anybody knows I took it! Out of his pocket, as he leaned against t' bricks. Hur knows?"

She thrust it into his hand, and then, her errand done, began to gather chips together to make a fire, choking down hysteric sobs.

"Has it come to this?"

That was all he said. The Welsh Wolfe blood was honest. The roll was a small green pocket-book containing one or two gold pieces, and a check for an incredible amount, as it seemed to the poor puddler. He laid it down, hiding his face again in his hands.

"Hugh, don't be angry wud me! It's only poor Deb,—hur knows?"

He took the long skinny fingers kindly in his.

"Angry? God help me, no! Let me sleep. I am tired."

He threw himself heavily down on the wooden bench, stunned with pain and weariness. She brought some old rags to cover him.

4. Welsh dialect: "I'll never bother her again."

It was late on Sunday evening before he awoke. I tell God's truth, when I say he had then no thought of keeping this money. Deborah had hid it in his pocket. He found it there. She watched him eagerly, as he took it out.

"I must gif it to him," he said, reading her face.

"Hur knows," she said with a bitter sigh of disappointment. "But it is hur right to keep it."

His right! The word struck him. Doctor May had used the same. He washed himself, and went out to find this man Mitchell. His right! Why did this chance word cling to him so obstinately? Do you hear the fierce devils whisper in his ear, as he went slowly down the darkening street?

The evening came on, slow and calm. He seated himself at the end of an alley leading into one of the larger streets. His brain was clear to-night, keen, intent, mastering. It would not start back, cowardly, from any hellish temptation, but meet it face to face. Therefore the great temptation of his life came to him veiled by no sophistry, but bold, defiant, owning its own vile name, trusting to one bold blow for victory.

He did not deceive himself. Theft! That was it. At first the word sickened him; then he grappled with it. Sitting there on a broken cart-wheel, the fading day, the noisy groups, the church-bells' tolling passed before him like a panorama,[5] while the sharp struggle went on within. This money! He took it out, and looked at it. If he gave it back, what then? He was going to be cool about it.

People going by to church saw only a sickly mill-boy watching them quietly at the alley's mouth. They did not know that he was mad, or they would not have gone by so quietly: mad with hunger; stretching out his hands to the world, that had given so much to them, for leave to live the life God meant him to live. His soul within him was smothering to death; he wanted so much, thought so much, and *knew*—nothing. There was nothing of which he was certain, except the mill and things there. Of God and heaven he had heard so little, that they were to him what fairy-land is to a child: something real, but not here; very far off. His brain, greedy, dwarfed, full of thwarted energy and unused powers, questioned these men and women going by, coldly, bitterly, that night. Was it not his right to live as they,—a pure life, a good, true-hearted life, full of beauty and kind words? He only wanted to know how to use the strength within him. His heart warmed, as he thought of it. He suffered[6] himself to think of it longer. If he took the money?

Then he saw himself as he might be, strong, helpful, kindly. The night crept on, as this one image slowly evolved itself from the crowd of other thoughts and stood triumphant. He looked at it. As he might be!

5. I.e., like the continuous scenes painted on rolls of canvas that were unrolled before an audience; a popular nineteenth-century theatrical pastime.
6. Allowed.

What wonder, if it blinded him to delirium,—the madness that under-lies all revolution, all progress, and all fall?

You laugh at the shallow temptation? You see the error underlying its argument so clearly,—that to him a true life was one of full develop-ment rather than self-restraint? that he was deaf to the higher tone in a cry of voluntary suffering for truth's sake than in the fullest flow of spontaneous harmony? I do not plead his cause. I only want to show you the mote in my brother's eye: then you can see clearly to take it out.[7]

The money,—there it lay on his knee, a little blotted slip of paper, nothing in itself; used to raise him out of the pit; something straight from God's hand. A thief! Well, what was it to be a thief? He met the question at last, face to face, wiping the clammy drops of sweat from his forehead. God made this money—the fresh air, too—for his children's use. He never made the difference between poor and rich. The Some-thing who looked down on him that moment through the cool gray sky had a kindly face, he knew,—loved his children alike. Oh, he knew that!

There were times when the soft floods of color in the crimson and purple flames, or the clear depth of amber in the water below the bridge, had somehow given him a glimpse of another world than this, —of an infinite depth of beauty and of quiet somewhere,—some-where,—a depth of quiet and rest and love. Looking up now, it became strangely real. The sun had sunk quite below the hills, but his last rays struck upward, touching the zenith. The fog had risen, and the town and river were steeped in its thick, gray damp; but overhead, the sun-touched smoke-clouds opened like a cleft ocean,—shifting, rolling seas of crimson mist, waves of billowy silver veined with blood-scarlet, inner depths unfathomable of glancing light. Wolfe's artist-eye grew drunk with color. The gates of that other world! Fading, flashing before him now! What, in that world of Beauty, Content, and Right, were the pretty laws, the mine and thine, of mill-owners and mill-hands?

A consciousness of power stirred within him. He stood up. A man, —he thought, stretching out his hands,—free to work, to live, to love! Free! His right! He folded the scrap of paper in his hand. As his nervous fingers took it in, limp and blotted, so his soul took in the mean temp-tation, lapped it in fancied rights, in dreams of improved existences, drifting and endless as the cloud-seas of color. Clutching it, as if the tightness of his hold would strengthen his sense of possession, he went aimlessly down the street. It was his watch at the mill. He need not go,

7. In the Sermon on the Mount Christ asks, "And why beholdest thou the mote that is in thy brother's eye, but considerest not the beam that is in thine own eye? Or how wilt thou say to thy brother, Let me pull out the mote out of thine eye, and, behold, a beam is in thine own eye?" (Matthew 7:3–4); a mote is a speck of dust; a beam, a large timber.

need never go again, thank God!—shaking off the thought with unspeakable loathing.

Shall I go over the history of the hours of that night? how the man wandered from one to another of his old haunts, with a half-consciousness of bidding them farewell,—lanes and alleys and back-yards where the mill-hands lodged,—noting, with a new eagerness, the filth and drunkenness, the pig-pens, the ash-heaps covered with potato-skins, the bloated, pimpled women at the doors,—with a new disgust, a new sense of sudden triumph, and, under all, a new, vague dread, unknown before, smothered down, kept under, but still there? It left him but once during the night, when, for the second time in his life, he entered a church. It was a sombre Gothic pile,[8] where the stained light lost itself in far-retreating arches; built to meet the requirements and sympathies of a far other class than Wolfe's. Yet it touched, moved him uncontrollably. The distances, the shadows, the still, marble figures, the mass of silent kneeling worshippers, the mysterious music, thrilled, lifted his soul with a wonderful pain. Wolfe forgot himself, forgot the new life he was going to live, the mean terror gnawing underneath. The voice of the speaker strengthened the charm; it was clear, feeling, full, strong. An old man, who had lived much, suffered much; whose brain was keenly alive, dominant; whose heart was summer-warm with charity. He taught it to-night. He held up Humanity in its grand total; showed the great world-cancer to his people. Who could show it better? He was a Christian reformer; he had studied the age thoroughly; his outlook at man had been free, world-wide, over all time. His faith stood sublime upon the Rock of Ages;[9] his fiery zeal guided vast schemes by which the gospel was to be preached to all nations. How did he preach it to-night? In burning, light-laden words he painted the incarnate Life, Love, the universal Man: words that became reality in the lives of these people, —that lived again in beautiful words and actions, trifling, but heroic. Sin, as he defined it, was a real foe to them; their trials, temptations, were his. His words passed far over the furnace-tender's grasp, toned to suit another class of culture; they sounded in his ears a very pleasant song in an unknown tongue. He meant to cure this world-cancer with a steady eye that had never glared with hunger, and a hand that neither poverty nor strychnine-whiskey[1] had taught to shake. In this morbid, distorted heart of the Welsh puddler he had failed.

Wolfe rose at last, and turned from the church down the street. He looked up; the night had come on foggy, damp; the golden mists had vanished, and the sky lay dull and ash-colored. He wandered again aimlessly down the street, idly wondering what had become of the

---

8. Large building.
9. I.e., strong Christian faith.

1. Especially dangerous kind of whisky.

cloud-sea of crimson and scarlet. The trial-day of this man's life was over, and he had lost the victory. What followed was mere drifting circumstance,—a quicker walking over the path,—that was all. Do you want to hear the end of it? You wish me to make a tragic story out of it? Why, in the police-reports of the morning paper you can find a dozen such tragedies: hints of shipwrecks unlike any that ever befell on the high seas; hints that here a power was lost to heaven,—that there a soul went down where no tide can ebb or flow. Commonplace enough the hints are,—jocose sometimes, done up in rhyme.

Doctor May, a month after the night I have told you of, was reading to his wife at breakfast from this fourth column of the morning-paper: an unusual thing,—these police-reports not being, in general, choice reading for ladies; but it was only one item he read.

"Oh, my dear! You remember that man I told you of, that we saw at Kirby's mill?—that was arrested for robbing Mitchell? Here he is; just listen:—'Circuit Court. Judge Day. Hugh Wolfe, operative in Kirby & John's Loudon Mills. Charge, grand larceny. Sentence, nineteen years hard labor in penitentiary.'—Scoundrel! Serves him right! After all our kindness that night! Picking Mitchell's pocket at the very time!"

His wife said something about the ingratitude of that kind of people, and then they began to talk of something else.

Nineteen years! How easy that was to read! What a simple word for Judge Day to utter! Nineteen years! Half a lifetime![2]

Hugh Wolfe sat on the window-ledge of his cell, looking out. His ankles were ironed. Not usual in such cases; but he had made two desperate efforts to escape. "Well," as Haley, the jailer, said, "small blame to him! Nineteen years' imprisonment was not a pleasant thing to look forward to." Haley was very good-natured about it, though Wolfe had fought him savagely.

"When he was first caught," the jailer said afterwards, in telling the story, "before the trial, the fellow was cut down at once,—laid there on that pallet like a dead man, with his hands over his eyes. Never saw a man so cut down in my life. Time of the trial, too, came the queerest dodge of any customer I ever had. Would choose no lawyer. Judge gave him one, of course. Gibson it was. He tried to prove the fellow crazy; but it wouldn't go. Thing was plain as day-light: money found on him. 'Twas a hard sentence,—all the law allows; but it was for 'xample's sake. These mill-hands are gettin' onbearable. When the sentence was read, he just looked up, and said the money was his by rights, and that all the world had gone wrong. That night, after the trial, a gentleman

---

2. "Nineteen years was literally half a lifetime. Life expectancy for a male in the 1850's was thirty-seven years. Hugh Wolfe is nineteen years old, for all his 'lifetime' in the mills, the 'slow heavy years of constant hot work.' As was common at the time, he had probably been in the mills since he was nine or ten" [Olsen's note].

came to see him here, name of Mitchell,—him as he stole from. Talked to him for an hour. Thought he came for curiosity, like. After he was gone, thought Wolfe was remarkable quiet, and went into his cell. Found him very low; bed all bloody. Doctor said he had been bleeding at the lungs. He was as weak as a cat; yet, if ye'll b'lieve me, he tried to get a-past me and get out. I just carried him like a baby, and threw him on the pallet. Three days after, he tried it again: that time reached the wall. Lord help you! he fought like a tiger,—giv' some terrible blows. Fightin' for life, you see; for he can't live long, shut up in the stone crib down yonder. Got a death-cough now. 'T took two of us to bring him down that day; so I just put the irons on his feet. There he sits, in there. Goin' to-morrow, with a batch more of 'em. That woman, hunchback, tried with him,—you remember?—she's only got three years. 'Complice. But *she's* a woman, you know. He's been quiet ever since I put on irons: giv' up, I suppose. Looks white, sick-lookin'. It acts different on 'em, bein' sentenced. Most of 'em gets reckless, devilish-like. Some prays awful, and sings them vile songs of the mills, all in a breath. That woman, now, she's desper't'. Been beggin' to see Hugh, as she calls him, for three days. I'm a-goin' to let her in. She don't go with him. Here she is in this next cell. I'm a-goin' now to let her in."

He let her in. Wolfe did not see her. She crept into a corner of the cell, and stood watching him. He was scratching the iron bars of the window with a piece of tin which he had picked up, with an idle, uncertain, vacant stare, just as a child or idiot would do.

"Tryin' to get out, old boy?" laughed Haley. "Them irons will need a crow-bar beside your tin, before you can open 'em."

Wolfe laughed, too, in a senseless way.

"I think I'll get out," he said.

"I believe his brain's touched," said Haley, when he came out.

The puddler scraped away with the tin for half an hour. Still Deborah did not speak. At last she ventured nearer, and touched his arm.

"Blood?" she said, looking at some spots on his coat with a shudder.

He looked up at her. "Why, Deb!" he said, smiling,—such a bright, boyish smile, that it went to poor Deborah's heart directly, and she sobbed and cried out loud.

"Oh, Hugh, lad! Hugh! dunnot look at me, when it wur my fault! To think I brought hur to it! And I loved hur so! Oh, lad, I dud!"

The confession, even in this wretch, came with the woman's blush through the sharp cry.

He did not seem to hear her,—scraping away diligently at the bars with the bit of tin.

Was he going mad? She peered closely into his face. Something she saw there made her draw suddenly back,—something which Haley had not seen, that lay beneath the pinched, vacant look it had caught since the trial, or the curious gray shadow that rested on it. That gray shadow,—yes, she knew what that meant. She had often seen it creeping over women's faces for months, who died at last of slow hunger or consumption. That meant death, distant, lingering: but this—Whatever it was the woman saw, or thought she saw, used as she was to crime and misery, seemed to make her sick with a new horror. Forgetting her fear of him, she caught his shoulders, and looked keenly, steadily, into his eyes.

"Hugh!" she cried, in a desperate whisper,—"oh, boy, not that! for God's sake, not *that!*"

The vacant laugh went off his face, and he answered her in a muttered word or two that drove her away. Yet the words were kindly enough. Sitting there on his pallet, she cried silently a hopeless sort of tears, but did not speak again. The man looked up furtively at her now and then. Whatever his own trouble was, her distress vexed him with a momentary sting.

It was market-day. The narrow window of the jail looked down directly on the carts and wagons drawn up in a long line, where they had unloaded. He could see, too, and hear distinctly the clink of money as it changed hands, the busy crowd of whites and blacks shoving, pushing one another, and the chaffering[3] and swearing at the stalls. Somehow, the sound, more than anything else had done, wakened him up,—made the whole real to him. He was done with the world and the business of it. He let the tin fall, and looked out, pressing his face close to the rusty bars. How they crowded and pushed! And he,—he should never walk that pavement again! There came Neff Sanders, one of the feeders at the mill, with a basket on his arm. Sure enough, Neff was married the other week. He whistled, hoping he would look up; but he did not. He wondered if Neff remembered he was there,—if any of the boys thought of him up there, and thought that he never was to go down that old cinder-road again. Never again! He had not quite understood it before; but now he did. Not for days or years, but never!—that was it.

How clear the light fell on that stall in front of the market! and how like a picture it was, the dark-green heaps of corn, and the crimson beets, and golden melons! There was another with game: how the light flickered on that pheasant's breast, with the purplish blood dripping over the brown feathers! He could see the red shining of the drops, it was so near. In one minute he could be down there. It was just a step. So easy, as it seemed, so natural to go! Yet it could never be—not in all the thousands of years to come—that he should put his foot on that street again! He thought of himself with a sorrowful pity, as of some one else. There was a dog down in the market, walking after his master with

3. Bargaining.

such a stately, grave look!—only a dog, yet he could go backwards and forwards just as he pleased: he had good luck! Why, the very vilest cur, yelping there in the gutter, had not lived his life, had been free to act out whatever thought God had put into his brain; while he—No, he would not think of that! He tried to put the thought away, and to listen to a dispute between a countryman and a woman about some meat; but it would come back. He, what had he done to bear this?

Then came the sudden picture of what might have been, and now. He knew what it was to be in the penitentiary,—how it went with men there. He knew how in these long years he should slowly die, but not until soul and body had become corrupt and rotten,—how, when he came out, if he lived to come, even the lowest of the mill-hands would jeer him,—how his hands would be weak, and his brain senseless and stupid. He believed he was almost that now. He put his hand to his head, with a puzzled, weary look. It ached, his head, with thinking. He tried to quiet himself. It was only right, perhaps; he had done wrong. But was there right or wrong for such as he? What was right? And who had ever taught him? He thrust the whole matter away. A dark, cold quiet crept through his brain. It was all wrong; but let it be! It was nothing to him more than the others. Let it be!

The door grated, as Haley opened it.

"Come, my woman! Must lock up for t' night. Come, stir yerself!"

She went up and took Hugh's hand.

"Good-night, Deb," he said, carelessly.

She had not hoped he would say more; but the tired pain on her mouth just then was bitterer than death. She took his passive hand and kissed it.

"Hur'll never see Deb again!" she ventured, her lips growing colder and more bloodless.

What did she say that for? Did he not know it? Yet he would not be impatient with poor old Deb. She had trouble of her own, as well as he.

"No, never again," he said, trying to be cheerful.

She stood just a moment, looking at him. Do you laugh at her, standing there, with her hunchback, her rags, her bleared, withered face, and the great despised love tugging at her heart?

"Come, you!" called Haley, impatiently.

She did not move.

"Hugh!" she whispered.

It was to be her last word. What was it?

"Hugh, boy, not *THAT*!"

He did not answer. She wrung her hands, trying to be silent, looking in his face in an agony of entreaty. He smiled again, kindly.

"It is best, Deb. I cannot bear to be hurted any more."

"Hur knows," she said, humbly.

"Tell my father good-bye; and—and kiss little Janey."

She nodded, saying nothing, looked in his face again, and went out of the door. As she went, she staggered.

"Drinkin' to-day?" broke out Haley, pushing her before him. "Where the Devil did you get it? Here, in with ye!" and he shoved her into her cell, next to Wolfe's, and shut the door.

Along the wall of her cell there was a crack low down by the floor, through which she could see the light from Wolfe's. She had discovered it days before. She hurried in now, and, kneeling down by it, listened, hoping to hear some sound. Nothing buy the rasping of the tin on the bars. He was at his old amusement again. Something in the noise jarred on her ear, for she shivered as she heard it. Hugh rasped away at the bars. A dull old bit of tin, not fit to cut korl with.

He looked out of the window again. People were leaving the market now. A tall mulatto girl, following her mistress, her basket on her head, crossed the street just below, and looked up. She was laughing; but, when she caught sight of the haggard face peering out through the bars, suddenly grew grave, and hurried by. A free, firm, step, a clear-cut olive face, with a scarlet turban tied on one side, dark, shining eyes, and on the head the basket poised, filled with fruit and flowers, under which the scarlet turban and bright eyes looked out half-shadowed. The picture caught his eye. It was good to see a face like that. He would try to-morrow, and cut one like it. *To-morrow!* He threw down the tin, trembling, and covered his face with his hands. When he looked up again, the daylight was gone.

Deborah, crouching near by on the other side of the wall, heard no noise. He sat on the side of the low pallet, thinking. Whatever was the mystery which the woman had seen on his face, it came out now slowly, in the dark there, and became fixed,—a something never seen on his face before. The evening was darkening fast. The market had been over for an hour; the rumbling of the carts over the pavement grew more infrequent: he listened to each, as it passed, because he thought it was to be for the last time. For the same reason, it was, I suppose, that he strained his eyes to catch a glimpse of each passer-by, wondering who they were, what kind of homes they were going to, if they had children,—listening eagerly to every chance word in the street, as if—(God be merciful to the man! what strange fancy was this?)—as if he never should hear human voices again.

It was quite dark at last. The street was a lonely one. The last passenger, he thought, was gone. No,—there was a quick step: Joe Hill, lighting the lamps. Joe was a good old chap; never passed a fellow without some joke or other. He remembered once seeing the place where he lived with his wife. "Granny Hill" the boys called her. Bedridden she was; but so kind as Joe was to her! kept the room so clean!—and the old

woman, when he was there, was laughing at "some of t' lad's foolishness." The step was far down the street; but he could see him place the
ladder, run up, and light the gas. A longing seized him to be spoken to
once more.

"Joe!" he called, out of the grating. "Good-bye, Joe!"

The old man stopped a moment, listening uncertainly; then hurried
on. The prisoner thrust his hand out of the window, and called again,
louder; but Joe was too far down the street. It was a little thing; but it
hurt him,—this disappointment.

"Good-bye, Joe!" he called, sorrowfully enough.

"Be quiet!" said one of the jailers, passing the door, striking on it with
his club.

Oh, that was the last, was it?

There was an inexpressible bitterness on his face, as he lay down on
the bed, taking the bit of tin, which he had rasped to a tolerable degree
of sharpness, in his hand,—to play with, it may be. He bared his arms,
looking intently at their corded veins and sinews. Deborah, listening in
the next cell, heard a slight clicking sound, often repeated. She shut her
lips tightly, that she might not scream, the cold drops of sweat broke
over her, in her dumb agony.

"Hur knows best," she muttered at last, fiercely clutching the boards
where she lay.

If she could have seen Wolfe, there was nothing about him to
frighten her. He lay quite still, his arms outstretched, looking at the
pearly stream of moonlight coming into the window. I think in that one
hour that came then he lived back over all the years that had gone before. I think that all the low, vile life, all his wrongs, all his starved hopes,
came then, and stung him with a farewell poison that made him sick
unto death. He made neither moan nor cry, only turned his worn face
now and then to the pure light, that seemed so far off, as one that said,
"How long, O Lord? how long?"[4]

The hour was over at last. The moon, passing over her nightly path,
slowly came nearer, and threw the light across his bed on his feet. He
watched it steadily, as it crept up, inch by inch, slowly. It seemed to him
to carry with it a great silence. He had been so hot and tired there
always in the mills! The years had been so fierce and cruel! There was
coming now quiet and coolness and sleep. His tense limbs relaxed, and
settled in a calm languor. The blood ran fainter and slow from his heart.
He did not think now with a savage anger of what might be and was not;
he was conscious only of deep stillness creeping over him. At first he
saw a sea of faces: the mill-men,—women he had known, drunken and
bloated,—Janeys timid and pitiful,—poor old Debs: then they floated

---

4. From Thomas Babington Macaulay (1800–1859), *Marriage of Tirzah and Ahirad.*

together like a mist, and faded away, leaving only the clear, pearly moonlight.

Whether, as the pure light crept up the stretched-out figure, it brought with it calm and peace, who shall say? His dumb soul was alone with God in judgment. A Voice may have spoken for it from far-off Calvary, "Father, forgive them, for they know not what they do!"[5] Who dare say? Fainter and fainter the heart rose and fell, slower and slower the moon floated from behind a cloud, until, when at last its full tide of white splendor swept over the cell, it seemed to wrap and fold into a deeper stillness the dead figure that never should move again. Silence deeper than the Night! Nothing that moved, save the black nauseous stream of blood dripping slowly from the pallet to the floor!

There was outcry and crowd enough in the cell the next day. The coroner and his jury, the local editors, Kirby himself, and boys with their hands thrust knowingly into their pockets and heads on one side, jammed into the corners. Coming and going all day. Only one woman. She came late, and outstayed them all. A Quaker, or Friend, as they call themselves.[6] I think this woman was known by that name in heaven. A homely body, coarsely dressed in gray and white. Deborah (for Haley had let her in) took notice of her. She watched them all—sitting on the end of the pallet, holding his head in her arms—with the ferocity of a watch-dog, if any of them touched the body. There was no meekness, or sorrow, in her face; the stuff out of which murderers are made, instead. All the time Haley and the woman were laying straight the limbs and cleaning the cell, Deborah sat still, keenly watching the Quaker's face. Of all the crowd there that day, this woman alone had not spoken to her,—only once or twice had put some cordial to her lips. After they all were gone, the woman, in the same still, gentle way, brought a vase of wood-leaves and berries, and placed it by the pallet, then opened the narrow window. The fresh air blew in, and swept the woody fragrance over the dead face. Deborah looked up with a quick wonder.

"Did hur know my boy wud like it? Did hur know Hugh?"

"I know Hugh now."

The white fingers passed in a slow, pitiful way over the dead, worn face. There was a heavy shadow in the quiet eyes.

"Did hur know where they'll bury Hugh?" said Deborah in a shrill tone, catching her arm.

This had been the question hanging on her lips all day.

"In t' town-yard? Under t' mud and ash? T' lad'll smother, woman! He wur born on t' lane moor, where t' air is frick[7] and strong. Take hur out, for God's sake, take hur out where t' air blows!"

5. Christ's words on the cross (Luke 23:34).   gious sect.
6. The Society of Friends, an American reli-   7. Fresh.

The Quaker hesitated, but only for a moment. She put her strong arm around Deborah and led her to the window.

"Thee sees the hills, friend, over the river? Thee sees how the light lies warm there, and the winds of God blow all the day? I live there,— where the blue smoke is, by the trees. Look at me." She turned Deborah's face to her own, clear and earnest. "Thee will believe me? I will take Hugh and bury him there to-morrow."

Deborah did not doubt her. As the evening wore on, she leaned against the iron bars, looking at the hills that rose far off, through the thick sodden clouds, like a bright, unattainable calm. As she looked, a shadow of their solemn repose fell on her face: its fierce discontent faded into a pitiful, humble quiet. Slow, solemn tears gathered in her eyes: the poor weak eyes turned so hopelessly to the place where Hugh was to rest, the grave heights looking higher and brighter and more solemn than ever before. The Quaker watched her keenly. She came to her at last, and touched her arm.

"When thee comes back," she said, in a low, sorrowful tone, like one who speaks from a strong heart deeply moved with remorse or pity, "thee shall begin thy life again,—there on the hills. I came too late; but not for thee,—by God's help, it may be."

Not too late. Three years after, the Quaker began her work. I end my story here. At evening-time it was light. There is no need to tire you with the long years of sunshine, and fresh air, and slow, patient Christ-love, needed to make healthy and hopeful this impure body and soul. There is a homely pine house, on one of these hills, whose windows overlook broad, wooded slopes and clover-crimsoned meadows,— niched into the very place where the light is warmest, the air freest. It is the Friends' meeting-house. Once a week they sit there, in their grave, earnest way, waiting for the Spirit of Love to speak, opening their simple hearts to receive His words. There is a woman, old, deformed, who takes a humble place among them: waiting like them: in her gray dress, her worn face, pure and meek, turned now and then to the sky. A woman much loved by these silent, restful people; more silent than they, more humble, more loving. Waiting: with her eyes turned to hills higher and purer than these on which she lives,—dim and far off now, but to be reached some day. There may be in her heart some latent hope to meet there the love denied her here,—that she shall find him whom she lost, and that then she will not be all-unworthy. Who blames her? Something is lost in the passage of every soul from one eternity to the other,—something pure and beautiful, which might have been and was not: a hope, a talent, a love, over which the soul mourns, like Esau[8]

---

8. The son of Isaac and Rebecca, who sold his birthright to his brother Jacob (Genesis 25:25).

deprived of his birthright. What blame to the meek Quaker, if she took her lost hope to make the hills of heaven more fair?

Nothing remains to tell that the poor Welsh puddler once lived, but this figure of the mill-woman cut in korl. I have it here in a corner of my library. I keep it hid behind a curtain,—it is such a rough, ungainly thing. Yet there are about it touches, grand sweeps of outline, that show a master's hand. Sometimes,—to-night, for instance,—the curtain is accidentally drawn back, and I see a bare arm stretched out imploringly in the darkness, and an eager, wolfish face watching mine: a wan, woful face, through which the spirit of the dead korl-cutter looks out, with its thwarted life, its mighty hunger, its unfinished work. Its pale, vague lips seem to tremble with a terrible question. "Is this the End?" they say,— "nothing beyond?—no more?" Why, you tell me you have seen that look in the eyes of dumb brutes,—horses dying under the lash. I know.

The deep of the night is passing while I write. The gas-light wakens from the shadows here and there the objects which lie scattered through the room: only faintly, though; for they belong to the open sunlight. As I glance at them, they each recall some task or pleasure of the coming day. A half-moulded child's head; Aphrodite;[9] a bough of forest-leaves; music; work; homely fragments, in which lie the secrets of all eternal truth and beauty. Prophetic all! Only this dumb, woful face seems to belong to and end with the night. I turn to look at it. Has the power of its desperate need commanded the darkness away? While the room is yet steeped in heavy shadow, a cool, gray light suddenly touches its head like a blessing hand, and its groping arm points through the broken cloud to the far East, where, in the flickering, nebulous crimson, God has set the promise of the Dawn.

1861

9. The Greek goddess of love.

LOUISA MAY ALCOTT
1832–1888

If American girls between 1870 and the present were to vote for their favorite fictional heroine, Louisa May Alcott's Jo March would be among the election's finalists. The central character of Alcott's *Little Women* (1869), high-spirited Jo is a literarily inclined tomboy, the second oldest of four sisters whose domestic adventures have had an enduring appeal for generations of young readers. Though the novel in which they appear is frequently didactic, drawing for both its narrative structure and its moral strictures on John Bunyan's allegorical *Pilgrim's Progress* (1678), it is continually enlivened by realistic details of New

England home life during the Civil War period as well as by incisive depictions of the pressures associated with growing up female in nineteenth-century America. More specifically, the tale is made dramatic by its sympathetic examination of rambunctious Jo's initial rebellion against, and ultimate reconciliation to, what the historian Nancy Cott has called "the bonds of womanhood."

No doubt one factor that gave this portrait of the artist as a "little woman" special force was that in many ways the tale of Jo's pilgrim's progress toward maturity was Alcott's own story. Born in 1832, Louisa May Alcott was, like Jo, the second of four sisters; her older sister, Anna, inspired the character of Jo's sister Meg; her younger sisters, Elizabeth and Abbie, were depicted in barely disguised forms as Jo's sisters Beth and Amy. Like gentle philosophical Mr. March, who is away fighting in the Civil War for much of the book, "Lu" Alcott's father was an unworldly philosopher who was often absent from home on lecture and walking tours. The friend of such notable New England intellectuals as Emerson and Thoreau, Bronson Alcott was an experimental educator, a Transcendentalist, and a social reformer whose commitment to idealistic causes—for instance, the short-lived utopian community called "Fruitlands" —frequently left his family on the edge of poverty. Like *Little Women*'s patient and diligent "Marmee," his wife, Abba, was a strong, supportive woman who kept the household going, both emotionally and financially, through all kinds of vicissitudes. Most likely it was from her example that the young Louisa gained the determination to shoulder what *Little Women*, following *Pilgrim's Progress*, calls the "burdens" of life. Certainly it was to assist her overworked mother that she resolved, at the age of eighteen, to become self-supporting, and, more, to make enough money so that Abba Alcott could "have a lovely, quiet home . . . with no debts or troubles."

Although, as she herself observed, the range of careers available to nineteenth-century girls was severely limited, Alcott held positions as a seamstress, a domestic servant, a governess, a teacher, a lady's "companion," and an army nurse—all jobs whose oppressions and rewards she was later to describe in her novel *Work* (1873) and in several other volumes. Even while she labored at these often menial occupations, however, she was steadily writing fiction, poetry, and journalistic sketches. Like Jo March, she had always been an imaginative girl, and, like Jo, she composed Gothic thrillers (which she published under the pseudonym A. M. Barnard) when she was still a teenager. Again like Jo— who learns to renounce her desire for romantic "blood and thunder" in a chapter of *Little Women* called "Literary Lessons"—Alcott moved during her career from romance to realism, from melodramatizing to moralizing. In 1863, she published a well-received collection of *Hospital Sketches*, describing her experiences as a Civil War army nurse with poignant accuracy, and in 1864, she published a promising first novel, *Moods*. Then, early in 1868, she became the editor of *Merry's Museum*, a magazine for girls, and, when a Boston publisher suggested that she herself might write a novel for young people, she composed *Little Women* in two six-week periods. The book was an instant success, establishing her as one of America's best-selling writers. For the next twenty years, until her death in 1888, she was to maintain and enhance her reputation, producing, on the average, a book a year, including seven more novels for girls and two for adults, as well as sixteen collections of stories and sketches for children and adolescents.

Though Alcott is best known for *Little Women* and its sequels—*Little Men* and *Jo's Boys*—a fiction like *Work* reveals her continuing concern with social reform, especially her sense of the ways in which young women were exploited by a society that obliged them to support themselves but offered them few opportunities for self-improvement. Similarly, her early thrillers, recently collected in two volumes—*Behind a Mask* and *Plots and Counterplots*—frequently suggest a secret rage at female powerlessness, a rage that is briefly expressed by even the ever-patient Marmee in *Little Women*, when she confesses that "I have been angry every day of my life." Not surprisingly, then, Louisa May Alcott was active in the nineteenth-century feminist movement. She was the first woman to register in Concord when Massachusetts gave women limited suffrage in 1879, for instance, and she helped facilitate the 1881 publication of Harriet Hanson Robinson's *Massachusetts in the Woman Suffrage Movement*, claiming that she took "more pride" in such gestures toward political reform "than in all the books I ever wrote."

Perhaps it was because her responsibilities had been so heavy and of such long standing that Alcott's success as a writer brought her comparatively little satisfaction. Despite the fact that she was lionized on literary tours and treated as a celebrity in her home town of Concord, she disliked the attentions of her many admirers, complaining that "I asked for bread, and got a stone,—in the shape of a pedestal." Sadly, her last years were shadowed by a range of ailments, many very likely psychosomatic in nature, while her family, particularly her aging father and her widowed sister Anna, continued to be burdens to her. It may be no coincidence that she died, of what was diagnosed as either meningitis or apoplexy, on the very day of her father's funeral: the moral responsibilities of her pilgrim's progress ended only with the end of her life.

From Work

[*In Service*][1]

* * * After several disappointments, Christie decided that her education was too old-fashioned for the city, and gave up the idea of teaching. Sewing she resolved not to try till every thing else failed; and, after a few more attempts to get writing to do, she said to herself, in a fit of humility and good sense: "I'll begin at the beginning, and work my way up. I'll put my pride in my pocket, and go out to service. Housework I like, and can do well, thanks to Aunt Betsey. I never thought it degradation to do it for her, so why should I mind doing it for others if they pay for it? It isn't what I want, but it's better than idleness, so I'll try it!"

---

1. This selection appears early in the novel, in Chapter 2, "Servant"; the heroine has resolved to make her own living, independent of the support of her family.

Full of this wise resolution, she took to haunting that purgatory of the poor, an intelligence office.[2] Mrs. Flint gave her a recommendation, and she hopefully took her place among the ranks of buxom German, incapable Irish, and "smart" American women; for in those days foreign help had not driven farmers' daughters out of the field, and made domestic comfort a lost art.

At first Christie enjoyed the novelty of the thing, and watched with interest the anxious housewives who flocked in demanding that *rara avis*,[3] an angel at nine shillings a week; and not finding it, bewailed the degeneracy of the times. Being too honest to profess herself absolutely perfect in every known branch of house-work, it was some time before she suited herself. Meanwhile, she was questioned and lectured, half engaged and kept waiting, dismissed for a whim, and so worried that she began to regard herself as the incarnation of all human vanities and shortcomings.

"A desirable place in a small, genteel family," was at last offered her, and she posted away to secure it, having reached a state of desperation and resolved to go as a first-class cook rather than sit with her hands before her any longer.

A well-appointed house, good wages, and light duties seemed things to be grateful for, and Christie decided that going out to service was not the hardest fate in life, as she stood at the door of a handsome house in a sunny square waiting to be inspected.

Mrs. Stuart, having just returned from Italy, affected the artistic, and the new applicant found her with a Roman scarf about her head, a rosary like a string of small cannon balls at her side, and azure draperies which became her as well as they did the sea-green furniture of her marine boudoir, where unwary walkers tripped over coral and shells, grew sea-sick looking at pictures of tempestuous billows engulfing every sort of craft, from a man-of-war to a hencoop[4] with a ghostly young lady clinging to it with one hand, and had their appetites effectually taken away by a choice collection of water-bugs and snakes in a glass globe, that looked like a jar of mixed pickles in a state of agitation.

Madame was intent on a water-color copy of Turner's[5] "Rain, Wind, and Hail," that pleasing work which was sold upsidedown and no one found it out. Motioning Christie to a seat she finished some delicate sloppy process before speaking. In that little pause Christie examined her, and the impression then received was afterward confirmed.

Mrs. Stuart possessed some beauty and chose to think herself a queen of society. She assumed majestic manners in public and could not entirely divest herself of them in private, which often produced

2. Employment agency.
3. Rare bird; Latin.
4. A small boat. "Man-of-war": a warship.

5. J. M. W. Turner (1775–1851), British painter of seascapes and sunsets.

comic effects. Zenobia troubled about fish-sauce, or Aspasia[6] indignant at the price of eggs will give some idea of this lady when she condescended to the cares of housekeeping.

Presently she looked up and inspected the girl as if a new servant were no more than a new bonnet, a necessary article to be ordered home for examination. Christie presented her recommendation, made her modest little speech, and awaited her doom.

Mrs. Stuart read, listened, and then demanded with queenly brevity: "Your name?"

"Christie Devon."

"Too long; I should prefer to call you Jane as I am accustomed to the name."

"As you please, ma'am."

"Your age?"

"Twenty-one."

"You are an American?"

"Yes, ma'am."

Mrs. Stuart gazed into space a moment, then delivered the following address with impressive solemnity.

"I wish a capable, intelligent, honest, neat, well-conducted person who knows her place and keeps it. The work is light, as there are but two in the family. I am very particular and so is Mr. Stuart. I pay two dollars and a half, allow one afternoon out, one service on Sunday, and no followers.[7] My table-girl must understand her duties thoroughly, be extremely neat, and always wear white aprons."

"I think I can suit you, ma'am, when I have learned the ways of the house," meekly replied Christie.

Mrs. Stuart looked graciously satisfied and returned the paper with a gesture that Victoria[8] might have used in restoring a granted petition, though her next words rather marred the effect of the regal act, "My cook is black."

"I have no objection to color, ma'am."

An expression of relief dawned upon Mrs. Stuart's countenance, for the black cook had been an insurmountable obstacle to all the Irish ladies who had applied. Thoughtfully tapping her Roman nose with the handle of her brush Madame took another survey of the new applicant, and seeing that she looked neat, intelligent, and respectful, gave a sigh of thankfulness and engaged her on the spot.

Much elated Christie rushed home, selected a bag of necessary articles, bundled the rest of her possessions into an empty closet (lent her rent-free owing to a profusion of cockroaches), paid up her board, and

---

6. A Greek courtesan. "Zenobia": an ancient queen of the Near East.

7. Male visitors, especially suitors.
8. The then-reigning queen of England.

at two o'clock introduced herself to Hepsey Johnson, her fellow servant.

Hepsey was a tall, gaunt woman, bearing the tragedy of her race written in her face, with its melancholy eyes, subdued expression, and the pathetic patience of a wronged dumb animal. She received Christie with an air of resignation, and speedily bewildered her with an account of the duties she would be expected to perform.

A long and careful drill enabled Christie to set the table with but few mistakes, and to retain a tolerably clear recollection of the order of performances. She had just assumed her badge of servitude, as she called the white apron, when the bell rang violently and Hepsey, who was hurrying away to "dish up," said:

"It's de marster. You has to answer de bell, honey, and he likes it done bery spry."

Christie ran and admitted an impetuous, stout gentleman, who appeared to be incensed against the elements, for he burst in as if blown, shook himself like a Newfoundland dog, and said all in one breath:

"You're the new girl, are you? Well, take my umbrella and pull off my rubbers."

"Sir?"

Mr. Stuart was struggling with his gloves, and, quite unconscious of the astonishment of his new maid, impatiently repeated his request.

"Take this wet thing away, and pull off my over-shoes. Don't you see it's raining like the very deuce!"

Christie folded her lips together in a peculiar manner as she knelt down and removed a pair of muddy over-shoes, took the dripping umbrella, and was walking away with her agreeable burden when Mr. Stuart gave her another shock by calling over the banister:

"I'm going out again; so clean those rubbers, and see that the boots I sent down this morning are in order."

"Yes, sir," answered Christie meekly, and immediately afterward startled Hepsey by casting overshoes and umbrella upon the kitchen floor, and indignantly demanding:

"Am I expected to be a boot-jack to that man?"

"I'spects you is, honey."

"Am I also expected to clean his boots?"

"Yes, chile. Katy did, and de work ain't hard when you gits used to it."

"It isn't the work; it's the degradation; and I won't submit to it."

Christie looked fiercely determined; but Hepsey shook her head, saying quietly as she went on garnishing a dish:

"Dere's more 'gradin' works dan dat, chile, and dem dat's bin 'bliged to do um finds dis sort bery easy. You's paid for it, honey; and if you does it willin, it won't hurt you more dan washin' de marster's dishes, or sweepin' his rooms."

"There ought to be a boy to do this sort of thing. *Do* you think it's right to ask it of me?" cried Christie, feeling that being servant was not as pleasant a task as she had thought it.

"Dunno, chile. I'se shore I'd never ask it of any woman if I was a man, 'less I was sick or ole. But folks don't seem to 'member dat we've got feelin's, and de best way is not to mind dese ere little trubbles. You jes leave de boots to me; blackin' can't do dese ole hands no hurt, and dis ain't no deggydation to me now; I's a free woman."

"Why, Hepsey, were you ever a slave?" asked the girl, forgetting her own small injury at this suggestion of the greatest of all wrongs.

"All my life, till I run away five year ago. My ole folks and eight brudders and sisters, is down dere in de pit[9] now, waitin' for the Lord to set 'em free. And He's gwine to do it soon, *soon!*" As she uttered the last words, a sudden light chased the tragic shadow from Hepsey's face, and the solemn fervor of her voice thrilled Christie's heart. All her anger died out in a great pity, and she put her hand on the woman's shoulder, saying earnestly:

"I hope so; and I wish I could help to bring that happy day at once!"

For the first time Hepsey smiled, as she said gratefully, "De Lord bress you for dat wish, chile." Then, dropping suddenly into her old, quiet way, she added, turning to her work:

"Now you tote up de dinner, and I'll be handy by to 'fresh your mind 'bout how de dishes goes, for missis is bery 'ticular, and don't like no 'stakes in tendin.' "

Thanks to her own neat-handed ways and Hepsey's prompting through the slide,[1] Christie got on very well; managed her salver dexterously, only upset one glass, clashed one dish-cover, and forgot to sugar the pie before putting it on the table; an omission which was majestically pointed out, and graciously pardoned as a first offence.

By seven o'clock the ceremonial was fairly over, and Christie dropped into a chair quite tired out with frequent pacings to and fro. In the kitchen she found the table spread for one, and Hepsey busy with the boots.

"Aren't you coming to your dinner, Mrs. Johnson?" she asked, not pleased at the arrangement.

"When you's done, honey; dere's no hurry 'bout me. Katy liked dat way best, and I'se used ter waitin'."

"But *I* don't like that way, and I won't have it. I suppose Katy

---

9. Metaphoric; a place where slaves are kept.
1. A small window between kitchen and dining
room through which dishes are passed. "Salver":
tray.

thought her white skin gave her a right to be disrespectful to a woman old enough to be her mother just because she was black. I don't; and while I'm here, there must be no difference made. If we can work together, we can eat together; and because you have been a slave is all the more reason I should be good to you now."

If Hepsey had been surprised by the new girl's protest against being made a boot-jack of, she was still more surprised at this sudden kindness, for she had set Christie down in her own mind as "one ob dem toppin' smart[2] ones dat don't stay long nowheres." She changed her opinion now, and sat watching the girl with a new expression on her face, as Christie took boot and brush from her, and fell to work energetically, saying as she scrubbed:

"I'm ashamed of complaining about such a little thing as this, and don't mean to feel degraded by it, though I should by letting you do it for me. I never lived out[3] before: that's the reason I made a fuss. There's a polish, for you, and I'm in a good humor again; so Mr. Stuart may call for his boots whenever he likes, and we'll go to dinner like fashionable people, as we are."

There was something so irresistible in the girl's hearty manner, that Hepsey submitted at once with a visible satisfaction, which gave a relish to Christie's dinner, though it was eaten at a kitchen table, with a bare-armed cook sitting opposite, and three rows of burnished dish-covers reflecting the dreadful spectacle.

After this, Christie got on excellently, for she did her best, and found both pleasure and profit in her new employment. It gave her real satisfaction to keep the handsome rooms in order, to polish plate, and spread bountiful meals. There was an atmosphere of ease and comfort about her which contrasted agreeably with the shabbiness of Mrs. Flint's boarding-house, and the bare simplicity of the old home. Like most young people, Christie loved luxury, and was sensible enough to see and value the comforts of her situation, and to wonder why more girls placed as she was did not choose a life like this rather than the confinements of a sewing-room, or the fatigue and publicity of a shop.

She did not learn to love her mistress, because Mrs. Stuart evidently considered herself as one belonging to a superior race of beings, and had no desire to establish any of the friendly relations that may become so helpful and pleasant to both mistress and maid. She made a royal progress through her dominions every morning, issued orders, found fault liberally, bestowed praise sparingly, and took no more personal interest in her servants than if they were clocks, to be wound up once a day, and sent away the moment they got out of repair.

Mr. Stuart was absent from morning till night, and all Christie ever

2. Conceited.   3. I.e., as a servant.

knew about him was that he was a kind-hearted, hot-tempered, and very conceited man; fond of his wife, proud of the society they managed to draw about them, and bent on making his way in the world at any cost.

If masters and mistresses knew how skilfully they are studied, criticised, and imitated by their servants, they would take more heed to their ways, and set better examples, perhaps. Mrs. Stuart never dreamed that her quiet, respectful Jane kept a sharp eye on all her movements, smiled covertly at her affectations, envied her accomplishments, and practised certain little elegancies that struck her fancy.

Mr. Stuart would have become apoplectic with indignation if he had known that this too intelligent table-girl often contrasted her master with his guests, and dared to think him wanting[4] in good breeding when he boasted of his money, flattered a great man, or laid plans to lure some lion[5] into his house. When he lost his temper, she always wanted to laugh, he bounced and bumbled about so like an angry blue-bottle fly; and when he got himself up elaborately for a party, this disrespectful hussy confided to Hepsey her opinion that "master was a fat dandy, with nothing to be vain of but his clothes,"—a sacrilegious remark which would have caused her to be summarily ejected from the house if it had reached the august ears of master or mistress.

"My father was a gentleman; and I shall never forget it, though I do go out to service. I've got no rich friends to help me up, but, sooner or later, I mean to find a place among cultivated people; and while I'm working and waiting, I can be fitting myself to fill that place like a gentlewoman, as I am."

With this ambition in her mind, Christie took notes of all that went on in the polite world, of which she got frequent glimpses while "living out." Mrs. Stuart received[6] one evening of each week, and on these occasions Christie, with an extra frill on her white apron, served the company, and enjoyed herself more than they did, if the truth had been known.

While helping the ladies with their wraps, she observed what they wore, how they carried themselves, and what a vast amount of prinking[7] they did, not to mention the flood of gossip they talked while shaking out their flounces and settling their topknots.

Later in the evening, when she passed cups and glasses, this demure-looking damsel heard much fine discourse, saw many famous beings, and improved her mind with surreptitious studies of the rich and great when on parade. But her best time was after supper, when, through the crack of the door of the little room where she was supposed to be clearing away the relics of the feast, she looked and listened at her

---

4. Lacking.
5. I.e., person of high social standing.

6. Entertained guests.
7. Primping, adorning; "flounces": ruffles.

ease; laughed at the wits, stared at the lions, heard the music, was impressed by the wisdom, and much edified by the gentility of the whole affair.

After a time, however, Christie got rather tired of it, for there was an elegant sameness about these evenings that became intensely wearisome to the uninitiated, but she fancied that as each had his part to play he managed to do it with spirit. Night after night the wag told his stories, the poet read his poems, the singers warbled, the pretty women simpered and dressed, the heavy scientific was duly discussed by the elect precious, and Mrs. Stuart, in amazing costumes, sailed to and fro in her most swan-like manner; while my lord stirred up the lions he had captured, till they roared their best, great and small.

"Good heavens! why don't they do or say something new and interesting, and not keep twaddling on about art, and music, and poetry, and cosmos? The papers are full of appeals for help for the poor, reforms of all sorts, and splendid work that others are doing; but these people seem to think it isn't genteel enough to be spoken of here. I suppose it is all very elegant to go on like a set of trained canaries, but it's very dull fun to watch them, and Hepsey's stories are a deal more interesting to me."

Having come to this conclusion, after studying dilettanteism through the crack of the door for some months, Christie left the "trained canaries" to twitter and hop about their gilded cage, and devoted herself to Hepsey, who gave her glimpses into another sort of life so bitterly real that she never could forget it.

Friendship had prospered in the lower regions, for Hepsey had a motherly heart, and Christie soon won her confidence by bestowing her own. Her story was like many another; yet, being the first Christie had ever heard, and told with the unconscious eloquence of one who had suffered and escaped, it made a deep impression on her, bringing home to her a sense of obligation so forcibly that she began at once to pay a little part of the great debt which the white race owes the black.

Christie loved books; and the attic next her own was full of them. To this store she found her way by a sort of instinct as sure as that which leads a fly to a honey-pot, and, finding many novels, she read her fill. This amusement lightened many heavy hours, peopled the silent house with troops of friends, and, for a time, was the joy of her life.

Hepsey used to watch her as she sat buried in her book when the day's work was done, and once a heavy sigh roused Christie from the most exciting crisis of "The Abbot."[8]

"What's the matter? Are you very tired, Aunty?" she asked, using the name that came most readily to her lips.

"No, honey; I was only wishin' I could read fast like you does. I's

8. A novel about Mary Queen of Scots, by Sir Walter Scott.

berry slow 'bout readin' and I want to learn a heap," answered Hepsey, with such a wistful look in her soft eyes that Christie shut her book, saying briskly:

"Then I'll teach you. Bring out your primer[9] and let's begin at once."

"Dear chile, it's orful hard work to put learnin' in my ole head, and I wouldn't 'cept such a ting from you only I needs dis sort of help so bad, and I can trust you to gib it to me as I wants it."

Then in a whisper that went straight to Christie's heart, Hepsey told her plan and showed what help she craved.

For five years she had worked hard, and saved her earnings for the purpose of her life. When a considerable sum had been hoarded up, she confided it to one whom she believed to be a friend, and sent him to buy her old mother. But he proved false, and she never saw either mother or money. It was a hard blow, but she took heart and went to work again, resolving this time to trust no one with the dangerous part of the affair, but when she had scraped together enough to pay her way she meant to go South and steal her mother at the risk of her life.

"I don't want much money, but I must know little 'bout readin' and countin' up, else I'll get lost and cheated. You'll help me do dis, honey, and I'll bless you all my days, and so will my old mammy, if I ever gets her safe away."

With tears of sympathy shining on her cheeks, and both hands stretched out to the poor soul who implored this small boon of her, Christie promised all the help that in her lay, and kept her word religiously.

From that time, Hepsey's cause was hers; she laid by a part of her wages for "ole mammy," she comforted Hepsey with happy prophecies of success, and taught with an energy and skill she had never known before. Novels lost their charms now, for Hepsey could give her a comedy and tragedy surpassing any thing she found in them, because truth stamped her tales with a power and pathos the most gifted fancy could but poorly imitate.

The select receptions upstairs seemed duller than ever to her now, and her happiest evenings were spent in the tidy kitchen, watching Hepsey laboriously shaping A's and B's, or counting up on her worn fingers the wages they had earned by months of weary work, that she might purchase one treasure,—a feeble, old woman, worn out with seventy years of slavery far away there in Virginia.

For a year Christie was a faithful servant to her mistress, who appreciated her virtues, but did not encourage them; a true friend to poor Hepsey, who loved her dearly, and found in her sympathy and affection

9. Elementary spelling and grammar book.

a solace for many griefs and wrongs. But Providence had other lessons for Christie, and when this one was well learned she was sent away to learn another phase of woman's life and labor.

While their domestics amused themselves with privy conspiracy and rebellion at home, Mr. and Mrs. Stuart spent their evenings in chasing that bright bubble called social success, and usually came home rather cross because they could not catch it.

On one of these occasions they received a warm welcome, for, as they approached the house, smoke was seen issuing from an attic window, and flames flickering behind the half-drawn curtain. Bursting out of the carriage with his usual impetuosity, Mr. Stuart let himself in and tore upstairs shouting "Fire!" like an engine company.

In the attic Christie was discovered lying dressed upon her bed, asleep or suffocated by the smoke that filled the room. A book had slipped from her hand, and in falling had upset the candle on a chair beside her; the long wick leaned against a cotton gown hanging on the wall, and a greater part of Christie's wardrobe was burning brilliantly.

"I forbade her to keep the gas lighted so late, and see what the deceitful creature has done with her private candle!" cried Mrs. Stuart with a shrillness that roused the girl from her heavy sleep more effectually than the anathemas Mr. Stuart was fulminating against the fire.

Sitting up she looked dizzily about her. The smoke was clearing fast, a window having been opened; and the tableau was a striking one. Mr. Stuart with an excited countenance was dancing frantically on a heap of half-consumed clothes pulled from the wall. He had not only drenched them with water from bowl and pitcher, but had also cast those articles upon the pile like extinguishers, and was skipping among the fragments with an agility which contrasted with his stout figure in full evening costume, and his besmirched face, made the sight irresistibly ludicrous.

Mrs. Stuart, though in her most regal array, seemed to have left her dignity downstairs with her opera cloak, for with skirts gathered closely about her, tiara all askew, and face full of fear and anger, she stood upon a chair and scolded like any shrew.

The comic overpowered the tragic, and being a little hysterical with the sudden alarm, Christie broke into a peal of laughter that sealed her fate.

"Look at her! look at her!" cried Mrs. Stuart gesticulating on her perch as if about to fly. "She has been at the wine, or lost her wits. She must go, Horatio, she must go! I cannot have my nerves shattered by such dreadful scenes. She is too fond of books, and it has turned her brain. Hepsey can watch her to-night, and at dawn she shall leave the house for ever."

"Not till after breakfast, my dear. Let us have that in comfort I beg, for upon my soul we shall need it," panted Mr. Stuart, sinking into a chair exhausted with the vigorous measures which had quenched the conflagration.

Christie checked her untimely mirth, explained the probable cause of the mischief, and penitently promised to be more careful for the future.

Mr. Stuart would have pardoned her on the spot, but Madame was inexorable, for she had so completely forgotten her dignity that she felt it would be impossible ever to recover it in the eyes of this disrespectful menial. Therefore she dismissed her with a lecture that made both mistress and maid glad to part.

She did not appear at breakfast, and after that meal Mr. Stuart paid Christie her wages with a solemnity which proved that he had taken a curtain lecture[1] to heart. There was a twinkle in his eye, however, as he kindly added a recommendation, and after the door closed behind him Christie was sure that he exploded into a laugh at the recollection of his last night's performance.

This lightened her sense of disgrace very much, so, leaving a part of her money to repair damages, she packed up her dilapidated wardrobe, and, making Hepsey promise to report progress from time to time, Christie went back to Mrs. Flint's to compose her mind and be ready *à la* Micawber "for something to turn up."[2]

1873

1. I.e., a speech made in private.
2. Mr. Micawber, in Charles Dickens's novel *David Copperfield*, is, in spite of his poverty, always confident that improvement is around the corner.

Turn-of-the-Century
Literature

A MAJOR SHIFT IN GENDER RELATIONS

Speaking about women's labor, the rebellious heroine of Olive Schreiner's *The Story of an African Farm* (1883) exclaims, "*we* bear the world, and *we* make it." Her brash affirmation of female creative primacy would be symbolized ten years later in America by the Woman's Building at the World's Columbian Exposition in Chicago. This building—the first that was funded, managed, and designed entirely by women—included Mary Cassatt's mural depicting "woman apart from her relations to man," and exhibits dedicated to British nurses, Afro-American and American inventors, Continental artisans, and Eastern explorers, as well as the first international collection of women's books gathered by women. Opening in the same year that New Zealand granted women the vote and the English Parliament passed the last of the Married Woman's Property Acts, the Woman's Building expressed the confidence that women felt in looking back on more than a century of unusual accomplishments.

By 1900, women had become, in the words of the feminist historian Ray Strachey, "free both in their persons and their properties, their money and their consciences, their bodies and their souls." For this reason, as another cultural historian, Theodore Roszak, has recently demonstrated, "the 'woman problem' had become one of the most earthshattering debates in the Western world" and "by the final decades of the century, it permeated everything." Between the 1880s and the outbreak of World War I in 1914, female lives and letters on both sides of the Atlantic were transformed by the entrance of large numbers of women into the labor force and by the emergence of militant suffragism. It is hardly surprising, then, that many literary figures in this period felt that they were living between two worlds, one dead and the other struggling to be born. Nor is it surprising that both sexes frequently associated accelerating historical changes with the rapidly shifting situation of women. For, as the Victorian age turned into the modern period, women's revolt was a dramatic component in a series of violent challenges to the social order that were posed by artists, workers, colonized peoples, social reformers, and free thinkers.

A TRANSITIONAL AGE

While it may be convenient to mark the end of the Victorian period as the year 1901, when Queen Victoria died after a sixty-four-year-long reign and Theodore Roosevelt began to make the White House his "bully pulpit," there was a growing realization throughout the last three decades of the nineteenth century and the first decade of the twentieth century that a major historical revolution was in the making. Already in 1873, Mark Twain and Charles Dudley Warner had called the age "gilded," rather than golden, for they were appalled by the crass materialism that was turning America into a world power, a rival to England in industrial leadership. Many intellectuals agreed that Victorianism was dead, though they disagreed about the exact date of its demise: the English libertarian Edward Carpenter and the American historian Henry Adams associated this transition with the eighties and nineties respectively, while the poet William Butler Yeats triumphantly announced that "Victorianism had been defeated in the year 1900," and the novelist Virginia Woolf dated that defeat in 1910, the year when Victoria's successor, King Edward VII, died. At the same time, some of Woolf's friends took the publication of Lytton Strachey's *Eminent Victorians* (1918) as the symbolic end of the nineteenth century, for Strachey's book attacked head-on the respectability, earnestness, industriousness, piety, and propriety of his parents' generation.

Strachey's scathing rejection of the bourgeois values he associated with Victorian complacency had, however, been anticipated in the 1870s, when the novelist Samuel Butler criticized the patriarchal family, the Church, the law, scientific theories based on evolution, and faith in progress through technology. But throughout the late nineteenth century there were other symptoms of a breakdown of certainty and a growing alienation of intellectuals from society. Late Victorians and early modernists alike confronted nineteenth-century economic prosperity from a disillusioned perspective, born in part of their dissatisfaction with the literary marketplace, for the rapid commercialization of literature, accelerated when compulsory elementary school education in the nineties resulted in a higher literacy rate, had led to the formation of a mass reading audience. Not a few writers echoed the protests of the novelist George Gissing, who deplored the mediocrity encouraged by the economics of the literary marketplace. At the same time, however, a number of artists felt constrained by the moralistic standards still maintained by publishers. Outrage over the sexual explicitness of *Jude the Obscure* (1896) so angered Thomas Hardy that it served him as an excuse to devote himself exclusively to writing poetry. Thus both England and America began to witness a schism between a financially successful popular culture and what was considered genuine, "high" art.

The writers who most flamboyantly thumbed their noses at respectable Victorian virtues, even as they sought to elevate the status of art by eliminating its utilitarian function, were the so-called aesthetes. In England, the aesthetic movement espoused the slogan "art for art's sake," the doctrine that the true artistic spirit eschews conventional morality to maintain the integrity of individual vision. As the phrase *fin de siècle* (end of the century) itself suggests, the aesthetes' stylization of the self and of art was profoundly affected by French ideas, especially the ideas of poets like Charles Baudelaire and Arthur Rimbaud, both of whom were represented in Arthur Symons's *The Symbolist Movement in Literature* (1899). According to these thinkers, the artist was not to preach societal reformation, but, in the words of Walter Pater in *Studies in the History of the Renaissance* (1873), "to burn always with [a] hard gem-like flame," for "art comes to you proposing frankly to give nothing but the highest quality to your moments as they pass, and simply for those moments' sake."

The erotic poetry of Algernon Charles Swinburne, the baroque and some-times pornographic drawings of Aubrey Beardsley, and the figure of the dandy began to epitomize the so-called decadence of this movement, while Oscar Wilde's homosexuality became a notorious emblem of bohemian defiance that was castigated in America from countless pulpits. Wilde's hero in *The Portrait of Dorian Gray* (1891) perfectly captured the era's mood of exhausted satiety when he responded to the *fin de siècle* by sighing, "I wish it were *fin du globe*." Throughout "the mauve decade" or "the gay nineties," such periodicals as *The Yellow Book* and *The Chap-Book* flaunted the quest for a deliberately abnor-mal, exotic, and titillating style. Frank Harris's eleven-volume history of his sex-ual escapades, *My Secret Life* (c. 1890), and the dances of the American Isadora Duncan, performed in free-flowing robes and bare feet, flouted puri-tanical codes as assiduously as did the art of the aesthetes.

Of course, many writers rejected the sensationalism and world-weariness of the aesthetes; however, even the eminent late Victorians George Meredith and Rudyard Kipling developed highly innovative styles: Meredith used an elabo-rately elliptical prose in novels that ridicule the presumption of masculine su-periority, while Kipling wrote stories and poems in dialects that capture the unique perspectives of everyday soldiers and citizens. A major transformation in literary history was reflected, too, in the lyrical and novelistic experimenta-tion of many other artists in this period. Throughout the seventies and eighties, Walt Whitman issued revised editions of *Leaves of Grass*, to the acclaim of such English men of letters as William Michael Rossetti and Swinburne. Sev-eral years later, Emily Dickinson's unconventional lyrics began to appear in America, while in England the Jesuit poet Gerard Manley Hopkins revived ar-chaic words, coined compound phrases, and invented a new theory of rhythm in startlingly alliterative poetry that would not be published until 1918. In addi-tion, novelists like Henry James and Joseph Conrad exploited in their work, and explained in their critical prefaces, complex uses of multiple narrators and points of view, and so helped to transform the novel into a more self-con-sciously literary form than it had ever been before.

Like the modernists Ezra Pound, Gertrude Stein, and James Joyce, Henry James was an expatriate in an art world that defined itself as an interna-tional elite. International experimentation also characterized the age's music and painting. The art critic Roger Fry selected for exhibition in London can-vases by impressionists such as Manet, Cézanne, and Van Gogh, together with paintings by postimpressionists like Matisse and Picasso. Through such differ-ent events in music history as the dramatist George Bernard Shaw's defense of Richard Wagner's mythically structured operas in *The Perfect Wagnerite* (1898) and Anton von Webern's creation of atonal scores (*Passacaglia*, 1908), conventional ideas of representation and reality were being broken down, as they were also in the literature that began to appear in newly created "little" magazines. With the emergence of modernism in the years directly before the outbreak of World War I, many artists had begun to engage in an open rebel-lion against society at large, for they were demonstrating how all established forms of intellectual and moral certainty had lost their legitimacy.

Industrialization

What intensified such artists' feelings that they were living in a transitional time were the rise of the industrial city and the rapid advances in national wealth and population that were associated with the development of capitalism in this period. Both American and English society were transformed by mass-production techniques employed in large factories powered by ever more complicated machines. Exciting new technological prospects also opened up with the production of radio shortwaves (1887), the invention of wireless telegraphy (1895), the discovery of radiation by the Curies (1897–1901), and the first flight by the Wright Brothers (1903). In 1895, newly invented automobiles were entered in their first race (only six were able to start and their speed averaged 5.25 miles per hour) and the Underwood Typewriter Company began to market machines that enabled the typist to see what was being typed: both the car and the typewriter would quickly become enormously popular. Louis Sullivan's soaring office buildings, the construction of the Brooklyn Bridge (1883), and the first motion picture, *The Great Train Robbery* (1903), were only the most dramatic signs of how the new technology would shape modern architecture and art. Exhilarated by unfolding possibilities for personal success, popular novelists like Horatio Alger continued to publish best-selling books promulgating an ethic of individual enterprise.

But many social critics felt that, when the mid-nineteenth-century Civil "War for freedom" had been replaced by the "war for the dollar," all the inequities of industrialization were dramatized. In America, a number of so-called robber barons or captains of industry had amassed huge fortunes which they displayed in the ornate mansions of New York and Chicago. Such ostentation led the American economist Thorstein Veblen to develop his *Theory of the Leisure Class* (1899). For the American novelist Edith Wharton, the conspicuous consumption of New York high society—its lavish garden parties, silver-backed hair brushes, visiting cards, and Italian opera—illustrated the immorality of a class that considered only bankruptcy a sin. While industrial development proceeded more slowly in England than in the United States, both countries witnessed the growth of joint stock companies, syndicates, trusts, mergers, holding companies, and interlocking boards of directors. With the introduction of electrical energy for domestic lighting and industrial power, diesel engines, subways, plastics, refrigeration, and canning, the Industrial Revolution began to bring comparative comfort to many people for the first time. But the extension of manhood suffrage, the institution of minimum wage laws, and the passage of child labor laws could not alleviate the economic suffering that resulted from recurrent unemployment, overproduction, and wage cutbacks.

Thus, although a number of religious leaders claimed that "God has intended the great to be great and the little to be little," and so-called social Darwinists argued that the poor had proven themselves to be "evolutionary misfits" who deserved to be destroyed by the economic system, the working class began in this period to organize for collective bargaining to attain job security, shorter hours, better conditions, and higher wages. Labor unions in England developed comparatively peacefully until 1906, when their effort to get working-class spokesmen into Parliament resulted in the creation of the Labour Party; but in America the rise of unions was dramatic and bloody. After more than

110,000 miles of railroad track were built across the American continent in the sixties and seventies, for example, the railroad strikes of 1877, 1886, and 1894 provoked judicial and governmental opposition. The Homestead steel strike (1892) was matched in England by the 1888 strike of Bryant and May's match girls, many of whom suffered from a cancer called "phossy-jaw," caused by the phosphorus into which they dipped matches. Both skilled and unskilled workers in England and America used meetings, leaflets, lockouts, boycotts, picketing, strikes, syndicalism (general strikes), and legislative lobbying to cope with the exploitation and oppression that Karl Marx had outlined in *Das Kapital* (1867–1895) and that the socialists Beatrice and Sidney Webb had described in their massive work *Poverty* (1911).

Besides leading to such public activity and political theory, utopian socialism was at least in part responsible for the growth of fantastic fiction at the turn of the century. On the one hand, H. G. Wells believed that the split between rich and poor had produced two distinct races, and in *The Time Machine* (1895), a pioneering science-fiction novel, he implied that the working-class tenders of machines would cannibalize the effete and idle rich. Edward Bellamy, on the other hand, wrote a popular "fairy tale of social felicity" entitled *Looking Backward* (1888), in which future collectivity eradicates all the evils of private enterprise. In addition, the poet William Morris developed utopian ideas about the aesthetic manufacturing of furniture and home decorations, ideas that contributed to the formation of the arts and crafts movement.

Growing social militancy also resulted in an interest in literary "realism" and "naturalism." In France, the realistic presentation of average people in middle-class society by the novelist Honoré de Balzac (1799–1850) had been succeeded by naturalism, the movement in fiction that approached working-class characters in terms of biological inheritance and economic determinism. The Goncourt brothers and Émile Zola attempted to present their readers "with a living model, or rather life itself with its entrails warm and active, its guts palpitating." As early as 1900, the Philadelphia painter Thomas Eakins discouraged his students from studying classical busts and took them instead to a bone-boiling establishment to dissect horses. George Moore, Arnold Bennett, and John Galsworthy carried on the realistic tradition in English novels about the manners of the genteel and the morals of the poor, while Frank Norris, Upton Sinclair, and Theodore Dreiser developed naturalism in America.

Given their quasi-scientific interest in cultural subsections of the population, a number of these writers appeared to agree with the novelist William Dean Howells that "our life is too large for our art to be broad." Both in ethnic and in regional literature, turn-of-the-century artists charted the rapid changes in society, which had affected different portions of the population in various ways. Ethnic voices began to articulate the special perspective of the some thirteen million immigrants who arrived in New York City between 1890 and 1919 from Eastern Europe and southern Italy. Among Jewish writers, for example, Emma Lazarus wrote *The New Colossus*, for the "huddled masses yearning to breathe free." The Danish-American reformer Jacob Riis portrayed slum life in *How the Other Half Lives* (1890). Similarly, whether addressing the problems of rural villages in England or New England, such turn-of-the-century regionalists as Thomas Hardy and Mary E. Wilkins Freeman attempted to capture the uniqueness of the local customs and landscapes that frame their characters' lives. In poetry, too, A. E. Housman and Edwin Arlington Robinson described the obscure destinies of Shropshire lads and Maine butchers. Whether, like Housman and Robinson, they were resigned or, like Wells and Bellamy, they were rebellious, writers had turned their attention to much distinctively new subject matter.

The Rise and Fall of Empire

Just as nineteenth-century monopoly capitalism had developed huge corporations, nineteenth-century imperialism had portioned the entire globe into so-called spheres of influence. Strong national pride and economic expediency caused both the English and the American governments to consolidate their colonial holdings throughout this period. The rise of imperialist fervor was perhaps most striking in America, for the expanding United States strengthened its hold on the American West, even as it began to exert its influence over foreign states. On the domestic front, large firms controlled the many trans-Atlantic railroad lines that, for the first time, connected the Eastern states to what had been the Western wilderness. A vast section of northern Oklahoma Territory was leased to settler-farmers in 1893, the year that Frederick Jackson Turner attended the World's Columbian Exposition to present his famous thesis about the closing of the frontier. In 1912, the last states of the original forty-eight— New Mexico and Arizona—were admitted to the union.

The subjugation of the native American Indians—a process that concluded in this period—was accompanied by opportunities for foreign conquest offered by a new policy of international imperialism. The Spanish-American War (1898) led to America's first acquisition of noncontiguous colonies with substantial populations: Hawaii, Puerto Rico, the Philippines, and Cuba were colonized in a course of action that President McKinley described as America's "manifest destiny." His successor, Theodore Roosevelt, believed that "the nation that has trained itself to a cancer of unwarlike and isolated ease is bound, in the end, to go down before other nations which have not lost the manly and adventurous virtues." Countless legislators lauded what the English writer Rudyard Kipling called the "white man's burden." Although the Monroe Doctrine (1823) was supposed to prevent European intervention in the Western hemisphere, the construction of the Panama Canal (1907–1914) demonstrated how this doctrine could be used to justify the intervention of the United States in Latin America.

The glamorization of militaristic nationalism in America reflected widespread European jingoism. An ideology of aggression, which some historians associate with the international events that led to World War I, was implicit in the imperialist expansion of England. Disraeli's "Big England" policy had resulted in the purchase of Suez Canal shares in 1875 and his proclamation of Queen Victoria as "Empress of India" in 1876. By 1894, England was signing the Congo Treaty with King Leopold II of Belgium, gaining both countries leases in Africa. In 1900, the British Empire covered nearly twenty million square miles and contained three hundred million people, and the newly created Girl Guides were themselves guided by a *Handbook* that was subtitled "How Girls Can Help Build the Empire."

Even in the heyday of empire-building, however, there were strong voices of dissent. The Boer War in South Africa (1899–1902) not only showed that a small number of Dutch settlers could challenge English right and might, but it was also the first war protested by many British intellectuals. In 1905, a pamphlet on *The Decline and Fall of the British Empire* sold thousands of copies in several months, reflecting widespread belief that the empire might have passed its peak. Moreover, just when it seemed literally the fact that the sun could not set on the British Empire, Joseph Conrad provided one of the more scathing critiques of the European invasion of Africa in *Heart of Darkness* (1902): the "white man's burden," Conrad implied, was less an ennobling mission to civilize the natives than a mercenary effort to wrest wealth from them.

While Cecil Rhodes, prime minister of the Cape Colony (South Africa), and the South African writer Olive Schreiner were disagreeing about the moral influence of the English presence in Africa, a number of black intellectuals in America were redefining their situation through an effort to reimagine their relationship to their race's native continent. To some extent, the dialogues between men like Booker T. Washington, W. E. B. DuBois, and Marcus Garvey presented what in our time remain the parameters of Afro-American identity, for each proposed a different course of liberation to blacks, disillusioned by the racism rampant in America after the abolition of slavery. The legalization of public segregation in 1896 and the growth of the Ku Klux Klan meant that blacks were in some sense colonized people who had to decide between two goals: integration with the dominant culture or an ideology of separatism. While in *Up from Slavery* (1901) Washington counseled self-improvement, which he gauged by white standards, DuBois espoused "Pan-Africanism" during his editorship of the magazine *The Crisis*, and Garvey headed the Universal Negro Improvement Association in an effort to raise racial pride and liberate Africa from colonial rule.

Both DuBois and Garvey understood the need for cultural identity that was informing the growth of jazz in black urban communities. By 1904, "Ma" Rainey was touring America in a song and dance team with her husband, and, by 1907, Bessie Smith was singing the blues at the Ivory Theatre in Chattanooga, Tennessee. Similarly, on numerous reservations throughout the southwest, Indian communities attempted to preserve their traditional rituals and languages after the genocide perpetrated by the government's "pacification" programs. In 1879, Susette La Flesche (or Inshta Theumba, which means Bright Eyes) began the lecture tours on behalf of Indian rights that would inspire Helen Hunt Jackson to write her pro-Indian works *A Century of Dishonor* (1881) and *Ramona* (1884).

While white supremacy came under attack in America, England experienced the growing dissent expressed by colonial rebellions that gained momentum throughout this period. Perhaps in response to such agitation, independence movements (which often excluded aboriginal inhabitants) helped convert Canada into a federation in 1867, Australia into a commonwealth in 1900, and New Zealand into a separate dominion in 1907, as well as establishing the Union of South Africa in 1909. But, most dramatically, in Ireland Charles Stewart Parnell led the Home Rule party in its demands for a separate Irish legislature. Parnell suffered political disaster in 1890, after he was named as a corespondent in a divorce suit; however, rising Irish protests against British rule continued up to the beginning of the century, when the radical Sinn Fein movement became more violent, and through World War I, when Irish patriots sought help from England's enemy, Germany. The Irish Literary Revival, or the Irish Renaissance, as it is sometimes called, was the literary expression of Irish nationalism.

Standish James O'Grady's histories of Ireland (1878, 1880) and Douglas Hyde's translations of Gaelic poetry shaped William Butler Yeats's poems on Irish heroic legends. Indeed, whether Yeats expressed disillusionment with public response to the nationalist movement ("romantic Ireland's dead and gone"), or sympathy with the suffering of the militants ("a terrible beauty is born"), his poetry was as grounded in Celtic mythology and Irish politics, as were the plays of Lady Augusta Gregory, the aristocrat who directed Dublin's Abbey Theatre with him. From the middle of the nineteenth century, when Oscar Wilde's mother wrote for *The Nation*, to 1914, when James Joyce's short stories, *Dubliners*, appeared in print, Ireland witnessed an extraordinary literary revival.

The Death of God

In the face of widespread discontent with the distribution of wealth and intense debates about the imperialist mission, it is hardly surprising that organized religion also came under attack. If God was thought to have disappeared earlier in the century, he was now declared dead by the German philosopher Friedrich Nietzsche (1844–1900). After several decades of Darwinian speculation on the origins of the universe and a quarter century of scholarship investigating the historical backgrounds of the Bible, even so conservative a writer as the British novelist Mrs. Humphrey Ward questioned the literal truth of revelation. Like Thomas Hardy, moreover, a number of artists felt "God-Forsaken" by a deity indifferent to human suffering or, again like Hardy, they believed the world to be determined by mere chance or "Crass Casualty." In England, but more especially in America, many intellectuals and artists were disaffected by the crusading fervor of the evangelicalism that fueled the temperance and worldwide mission movements, for the rhetoric of some Protestant crusaders seemed dangerously antiforeigner, antiblack, anti-Catholic, and anti-Semitic. In the place of orthodox faith, what the American philosopher William James called "varieties of religious experience" began to proliferate.

An explosion of interest in alternative religions was fostered by and in turn fostered the development of anthropology. Sir James Frazer's study of primitive rituals in *The Golden Bough* (1890–1915) and Andrew Lang's *Myth, Ritual, and Religion* (1887, 1899) contributed to the dethronement of religious orthodoxy through their analyses of pagan mythology and folklore. In addition, Madame Blavatsky, the founder of the Theosophic Society (1875), conflated Christianity and other religions when she argued in *The Secret Doctrine* (1888) that Jesus was an incarnation of Buddha. The Tarot, astrology, and the Kabbalah were studied in occult groups like the Golden Dawn, which supplied the poet Yeats—an inveterate attender of séances—with much of his esoteric imagery. At the same time, psychologists, and in particular the psychologists of religion, emphasized the human origins of all faiths: not only did William James analyze how all religions seek to heal humanity's sense of unease, but the philosopher George Santayana claimed that "religion and poetry are identical in essence," for he was elevating the human imagination to a redemptive force.

But the so-called death of God also resulted in an ideology of sexual liberation. The birth-control advocate Annie Besant, for example, was drawn to Eastern forms of mysticism that she viewed as less puritanical than Christianity. With the publication of Edward Carpenter's *Love's Coming of Age* (1896, 1906) and Havelock Ellis's *Studies in the Psychology of Sex* (1897–1910), the subject of human sexuality began to emerge as a field of scientific inquiry, one that was soon to be more closely studied by the Viennese psychoanalyst Sigmund Freud, whose dream interpretations and studies of hysteria began to be translated into English in the first two decades of the twentieth century. Arguing for toleration of homosexuality and for an acceptance of sexuality as part of human behavior, both Carpenter and Ellis saw themselves as liberating modern humanity from Victorian prudery. Although Carpenter, Ellis, and Freud were criticized or censured for their explicit treatment of desire, subjectivity and sexuality would quickly become major subjects for poets and novelists.

IMAGES OF WOMEN

Not only did women participate in all the movements that challenged the balance of power among classes and nations, they were also in the process of fomenting a social revolution that would radically change the relationship between the sexes. As the cultural historian Samuel Hynes has explained, this "revolution had many implications besides the sexual," for it "involved legal, political, and economic issues, and touched on property ownership, the franchise, higher education, the birth rate, laws of marriage and divorce, the protocol of the court, and the future of the empire—in short, on nearly every aspect of . . . society." In this context, it is hardly surprising that by 1920, when Arnold Bennett published *Our Women*, he was arguing that "sex-discord" had "noticeably developed since Coventry Patmore wrote *The Angel in the House*" (1885), a poem that celebrated the virtues of the ideal bride. Patmore's ideology of feminine renunciation and domesticity continued to be influential at the turn of the century, but artists and intellectuals tended to confront what the scholar Martha Vicinus has called women's "widening sphere" more directly and overtly, whether as opponents or advocates, as the period progressed. While moralists, educators, and physicians continued to explain to women why they should lead decorous, selfless private lives as wives and mothers, a number of artists responded angrily or triumphantly to the fact that many women no longer did so.

Patmore's exemplary woman, for example, continued to haunt Henry Adams, who argued in *The Education of Henry Adams* (1907) that modern scientific energy, typified by the dynamo, had to be countered by the eternal beauty and potency he identified with the medieval figure of the Virgin. While Adams viewed the demise of the Virgin and the rise of the dynamo with trepidation, countless writers argued that women could counter the evils of industrial life if they remained within the home. But domesticity was also assumed to constitute women's primary source of satisfaction. John Cordy Jeaffreson's popular novel *A Woman in Spite of Herself* (1872) dramatized the pleasure with which its heroine relinquishes the male costume circumstances had required of her; she is relieved to admit her femininity and accept a marriage proposal which will allow her to demonstrate "the never-ceasing, ever-active delight that a true woman feels" in being the "watchful ministrant, enthusiastic slave of the man to whom she has given her heart."

Even while works like Jeaffreson's and Patmore's celebrated this angelic ministrant and slave, much late-Victorian and early-twentieth-century literature anxiously meditated on her disappearance. Henry A. Jones's play *The Case of Rebellious Susan* (1894), for example, included a scene in which an older man lectures a henpecking, selfish wife who refuses to serve dinner "while the present inequalities between the sexes remain unredressed": "Nature's darling woman," he explains to her, "is a stay-at-home woman, a woman who wants to be a good wife and a good mother, and cares very little for anything else." "Go home!" he concludes, as if anticipating the defensive stridency of the hero in Harley Granville-Barker's play *The Madras House* (1910), who argues that "women haven't morals or intellect in our sense of the words. . . . Shut them away from public life and public exhibition."

At the same time, imperiled as the Victorian cult of feminine purity was felt to be, the ideology of separate sexual spheres was used to argue that women had feminized a previously virile culture. In countless adventure tales where boys like Mark Twain's Huck (in *Huckleberry Finn*, 1884) and Robert Louis Stevenson's Jim Hawkins (in *Treasure Island*, 1883) hear and respond to the call of the wild, they are fleeing from a society associated not only with moralistic women but with women whose refinement symbolizes the confinement of civilization. Turn-of-the-century literature abounded with images of Mrs. Grundy, a priggish puritan whose excessive zeal for gentility makes life unendurable for real men. At the same time, however, women's supposed purity was used by advocates and critics of women's increasingly active role in public life: legislators on both sides of the Atlantic argued, on the one hand, that women would purify politics if they were allowed to participate and, on the other hand, that women would be defiled by such participation. Moreover, even as women's angelic status was being characterized as repressive or endangered, the Victorian cult of feminine selflessness and fragility was also used to prove that, in the words of the antisuffragist James McGrigor Allan, "every woman is . . . always more or less an invalid."

Among the rapidly growing ranks of male gynecologists, obstetricians, and psychologists, hysteria, which was associated with women etymologically through the Greek root *hyster*, or womb, was considered a female disease in which "the patient loses more and more of her energy and self-control, becoming capriciously fanciful about her health, imagining or feigning strange diseases." Indeed, late-nineteenth- and early-twentieth-century physicians like Henry Maudsley and S. Weir Mitchell sought to demonstrate not only that menstruation, pregnancy, and lactation turned women into helpless invalids, but also that higher education and physical or even mental labor would damage women's health. Dr. Mitchell prescribed what became popular as "the rest cure": only complete immobilization—bed rest, constant feeding, and enforced idleness—would center the woman on her primary function, reproduction, and heal her neurasthenic symptoms. When the Victorian angel threatened to turn into an invalid, however, she came perilously close to functioning like her Victorian counterpart, the madwoman, for through illness she had exempted herself from her socially prescribed duties of childbearing, childrearing, and home management. By the turn of the century, however, the angel, the madwoman, and the invalid had all been upstaged by two distinct but related images of rebelliously assertive women: the *femme fatale* and the so-called New Woman.

From the Pre-Raphaelite paintings of Edward Burne-Jones to the *art nouveau* illustrations of Aubrey Beardsley, from Swinburne's sadistic Faustine to Yeats's destructive "daughters of Herodias," the sinister but sensuous figure of the *femme fatale* evoked the same fascination that Walter Pater expressed about Leonardo da Vinci's *La Gioconda* (the *Mona Lisa*). In a famous passage of *Studies in the History of the Renaissance*, Pater portrayed an alluring woman who is "older than the rocks among which she sits; like the vampire, she has been dead many times, and learned the secrets of the grave." Imbued with the sins of the Borgias, the secrets of Leda (mother of Helen of Troy), and the sanctity of Saint Anne (mother of the Virgin Mary), Pater's world-weary beauty is both a lustful vampire and a potent mother, and she therefore epitomizes the contradictory qualities of the fatal female. By the turn of the century, such a figure appeared in so much poetry and fiction that the cultural historian Mario Praz has argued that "in no other literary period . . . has sex been so obviously the mainspring of works of imagination."

As a seductive rebel, for instance, the *femme fatale* emerged in such exceptionally popular late-Victorian fantasies as H. Rider Haggard's best-selling *She* (1887) and George MacDonald's *Lilith* (1895). Endowed with amazing grace, Haggard's She-Who-Must-Be-Obeyed and MacDonald's Lilith are tormented, divided creatures, burning with insatiable, destructive desire, and with a power which implies mounting male anxiety about female energy, specifically those energies associated with the mother transformed into a monster. As if to illustrate this point, the hero of George Bernard Shaw's *Man and Superman* (1903) explains that "of all human struggles there is none so treacherous and remorseless as the struggle between the artist man and the mother woman. Which shall use up the other? That is the issue between them." More generally, however, the realistic novel in this period also dramatized growing male anxiety that men were losing the battle between the sexes. In *Sister Carrie* (1900), Theodore Dreiser described the rise of an actress who triumphs on the stage while her abandoned lover commits suicide. Even in comic or farcical literature, the female seemed indomitable. Max Beerbohm's *Zuleika Dobson* (1911) portrayed the havoc that ensues in Oxford after the entrance of one *femme fatale*: all the undergraduates kill themselves because of their adoration of a flirtatious coquette.

To be sure, a number of American and English writers responded quite differently to women's rising power, for they identified with what they perceived as the growing rebelliousness of women. Following the feminist concerns of the Victorian philosopher John Stuart Mill, George Gissing, George Moore, and John Galsworthy composed novels that implicitly criticized divorce laws, custody provisions, punitive attitudes toward illegitimacy, and the impoverishment of single women. A host of books resembled Stephen Crane's *Maggie: A Girl of the Streets* (1893) in offering sympathetic treatments of the fallen woman. At the same time, moreover, the middle-class American girl emerged in much fiction as a lively representative of the independence of her culture. Praised by Rudyard Kipling, fictionalized by William Dean Howells, and caricatured as "the Gibson girl," she was to acquire spunky innocence, spontaneity, and intelligence in some of the novels of Henry James; in *The Portrait of a Lady* (1881), for example, where he located "the centre of the subject in the young woman's own consciousness," James traced the fastidiousness with which his heroine moved from naive idealism to moral maturity.

Although Howells's and James's audacious innocents often ended up either dead or married, they contributed to the construction of a new character, the New Woman. In portraying this figure, many English and American writers used the novel and the theater to try to make the feminist cause their own. Much of their writing was influenced by the plays of Henrik Ibsen. With its concluding scene in which Nora slams the door as she leaves her husband and children, *A Doll's House* (1879) was only the most famous of the Norwegian dramatist's treatments of women's demands for release from the childish dependency and boredom of domesticity. Following Ibsen in England, Shaw brought imperious heroines on stage, represented by popular actresses like Elizabeth Robins and Ellen Terry. Similarly, the novels of George Meredith (*Diana of the Crossways*, 1885) and Grant Allen (*The Woman Who Did*, 1895) focused on female characters who actively and articulately expressed their dissatisfaction with conventional feminine roles. Frequently as seductive and divided as the *femme fatale*, the New Woman was a rebel who regarded marriage as incompatible with her emancipation, but who just as frequently suffered a tragic penalty for her views, for even while she was often a locus for the male novelist's own discontent with sex roles, she was also often used to dramatize what many men of letters saw as the self-destructiveness of feminism.

For all the irony and ambiguity of Henry James's narrative tone, the suffrage movement is presented in *The Bostonians* (1886) in terms of a manipulative bonding between two women living in what James's hero calls "a feminine, a nervous, hysterical, chattering, canting age." Such a diagnosis of feminism reflected the views of men like Sir Almroth Wright, an eminent bacteriologist and author of *The Unexpurgated Case against Woman's Suffrage* (1913). In a 1912 letter to the *Times* Wright argued that "there is mixed up with the woman's movement much mental disorder"; with a half million "excess women" in Britain, Wright believed that "physiological emergencies" motivated the behavior of the militant suffragist. The idea that the independent woman was sick informed even Havelock Ellis's defense of female homosexuality, for Ellis claimed that the "invert," as he called her, suffered the biological tragedy of being born into the wrong body. Similarly, for all of Thomas Hardy's indisputable sympathies for the sufferings of his New Woman, Sue Bridehead in *Jude the Obscure* (1895), the plot of the novel implies that men will be destroyed by women, whether by a "mere female animal" like Arabella Donn or by the conflicted spirituality of a neurasthenic Sue.

If the New Woman was a source of much imaginative energy at the turn of the century, it may have been because writers like James believed that, in the words of the critic Larzer Ziff, "women, with their free use of leisure, were the chief consumers of novels and therefore were increasingly becoming producers of them. The feminine attitude, now disengaging itself from that of men, was in point of fact coming to be all that the novel was." At least some men responded to the prominence of women writers with attacks whose defensiveness ranged from the sardonic wit that marked Oscar Wilde's discussion of "English Poetesses" in London's *Queen* magazine (1888) to the satiric ferocity that characterized Mark Twain's portrait of the adolescent poet Emmeline Grangerford in *Huckleberry Finn*. Finally, then, the turn-of-the-century obsession with figures like the *femme fatale* and the New Woman reflected not only the importance of women's issues in the public and private lives of Americans and Britons, but also the growth of the female reading public, and the visibility and success of women writers.

WOMEN'S LIVES

In an age when men stopped sporting beards and women started riding bicycles, one sign of the dramatic transformation of women's lives was the change in fashion which began to liberate women from the weight and confinement of crinolines and hoops, replacing them first with bustles and then with simpler, lighter skirts. By the beginning of World War I, many of the necessary conditions for female emancipation were present. As identified by the historian Gerda Lerner, these included a technology that permitted society to remove food preparation and care of the sick from the home; the mechanization of heating and laundry; the spread of health care and birth control; and the availability of education to all children. Yet, while women were, as the suffragist Ray Strachey claimed in *The Cause* (1928), "in the main, free" by 1900, Strachey herself went on to point out that they were still "politically outcast and economically oppressed; under-educated and over-flattered; too much despised and too much admired."

Unlike her mother and her grandmother, the married woman in this period did have some control over her property and her children. By 1883, married women in England were as free as American women to own acquired or inherited property, and after 1886, the Guardianship of Infants' Act provided that, on a father's death, the mother would become either the sole or joint guardian of her offspring. Divorce laws, however, continued to treat the two sexes differently. In England, the husband could sue solely by reason of his wife's adultery, but the wife had to prove cruelty or desertion as well as adultery, and in the United States, too, the laws were inequitable: in the state of Minnesota, for instance, a woman who was divorced by reason of her adultery had to forfeit the real estate which had been her own property, while a man so divorced did not. Still, changes in property, divorce, and custody laws did imply that wives were no longer assumed to be the possessions of their husbands.

Just as legal constraints confining women were being debated and sometimes even loosened, educational restrictions were being questioned, circumvented, and overturned. To be sure, from educators like Dr. Edward H. Clarke, a Harvard professor, women continued to hear that higher education would atrophy women's uteruses. But such claims were countered by M. Carey Thomas, president of Bryn Mawr College, who argued in 1913 that "we know that college women are not only not invalids, but that they are better physically than other women in their own class of life." At the same time, as the historians Barbara Ehrenreich and Deirdre English have demonstrated, the new subject of domestic science, or home economics, became a way of justifying higher education for women, who were now held to need scientific training in order to make housekeeping an efficient profession. As in America, where the daughters of the wealthy could attend Bryn Mawr, Oberlin, Vassar, or the new Harvard annex, Radcliffe, in England women could pursue their higher education not only at Girton, Newnham, and Somerville Colleges, but also within London University; Oxford and Cambridge, however, still did not grant women degrees. A few Afro-American women were given the opportunity of higher education at schools like Bethune-Cookman College: established by Mary McLeod Bethune from sums she raised selling ice cream and sweet-potato pies to workmen on construction jobs, this college was dedicated to Bethune's commitment that all black youngsters should be given a chance to prove their worth.

After 1870, when both boys and girls were for the first time guaranteed an elementary school education by the passage of the Education Act, educational opportunities for the working class were enhanced in England. But such opportunities were limited by the custom of training working-class daughters for domestic service. Public schools and churches in America, moreover, often channeled immigrant women into home economics programs in which they could acquire the laundering, cooking, housecleaning, and sewing skills that would prepare them for low-status, low-paying jobs. But a number of social workers tried to improve the quality of life for urban immigrant women. Most famously, in 1889 Jane Addams established her pioneering settlement house in Chicago's slums. With a kindergarten, courses in arts and crafts, and lectures from the educator John Dewey and the architect Frank Lloyd Wright, the women who ran Hull House provided social and intellectual opportunities for their community even as they helped establish social work as a profession.

Addams's co-workers also agitated along with labor unions for the first meaningful factory laws in Illinois. The number of women workers in America had increased dramatically from approximately four million in 1890 to five and one-third million in 1900 and seven and one-half million in 1910. Many were in domestic occupations, but thousands of others were farm laborers, teachers, sales clerks, factory workers, and textile or garment workers, as well as holders of "white collar" jobs—cashiers, bookkeepers, accountants, typists, and stenographers. Between 1870 and 1914 in England, the number of women clerks in the Civil Service multiplied twenty times, and thousands of women entered textile factories. In spite of this drastic rise in the number of women workers, trade-union leaders were often dubious about organizing women, not infrequently because they believed with the English trade-unionist Henry Broadhurst that "wives should be in their proper place at home." Male fears of job competition also perpetuated the exclusion of women and thereby fostered low pay and limited job options for women.

Although women were not unionized at the rate that men were, many women on both sides of the Atlantic did participate in the trade-union movement. One of the most important early strikes in the history of American unions took place in 1909–1910 among shirtwaist makers in New York and Philadelphia. Early locals of what is now called the International Ladies' Garment

Workers' Union organized in the Triangle Shirt-Waist Company, which two years later was the site of a fire that killed 146 operatives. The terrible conditions created by the so-called "sweating system"—overcrowded tenement buildings, low pay, job insecurity, dangerous and uninspected machinery, employment of very young children—were denounced by the labor organizer Ida M. Van Etten at the national convention of the American Federation of Labor in 1890 and by the English socialist Beatrice Potter (Webb), who wrote *Pages from a Work Girl's Diary* (1888) about London East End tailoring. While the populist orator Mary Elizabeth Lease urged farmers "to raise less corn and more hell" and the organizer Mary ("Mother") Jones agitated among urban laborers, the activist Emma Goldman was repeatedly arrested and eventually deported for anarchist agitation.

That Goldman was eventually to include birth control and free love in her program for human liberation indicates how women were beginning to attempt to gain power over their own bodies. However, Goldman's emphasis in the teens of the twentieth century on women's right to sexual pleasure was far removed from the grounds of earlier pleas for control over reproduction. As the historian Linda Gordon has shown, throughout the last quarter of the nineteenth century women based their arguments for what they called "voluntary motherhood" on their hostility toward men and toward sex. The "fearful strain" of repeated pregnancies and childbirths led nineteenth-century suffragists to attack "the lustful domination of man," just as the threat of "social diseases" like syphilis later led to the suffrage slogan *Votes for Women and Purity for Men*. Social purity campaigns, which emphasized the superior chastity of women, were also efforts to elevate the values of maternal tenderness, patience, and supportiveness. Of course, as in the Victorian era, most middle-class girls at the turn of the century were denied all information about reproduction on the grounds that it would be an affront to their purity. Long after 1901, Vera Brittain, a schoolgirl who would grow up to become a feminist writer, was given newspapers from which all paragraphs about sex had been carefully excised.

When the increasing demand for contraceptive information became evident in this period, it immediately met legal opposition. In the seventies in England, Annie Besant was arrested for publishing George Knowlton's *Fruits of Philosophy*, a book which contained descriptions of contraceptive methods, and in America the Comstock Law (1873) prohibited the sale and the mailing "of obscene literature and articles of immoral use," including birth control information. Many moralists opposed the use of existing methods of contraception such as coitus interruptus, the vaginal sponge, the sheath, and the pessary (intravaginal devices). Just as adamantly, many medical men argued that "continence" (abstinence) was the only suitable form of birth control. Not only did ignorant physicians advise women as late as the eighties and nineties that the "safe" time was midway between the periods of menstruation, the medical attack on birth control also often warned that contraception led to such disasters as hardening of the uterus or moral degeneracy. Yet the use of lamb ceca (intestines) and rubber revolutionized the manufacturing of condoms and resulted in the invention of the Mensinga diaphragm, and the developing birth control movement probably affected the rapidly falling birth rate, which in the United

Kingdom dropped by nearly thirty percent between the mid-seventies and 1910.

The shift from social purity and continence to birth control in the struggle over reproductive rights paralleled a similar ideological shift in the struggle for political rights. Both in England and in America, the activist organizations of women in the seventies and eighties argued for reforms on the grounds of women's ethical superiority. In England, the protest led by Josephine Butler against the Contagious Diseases Acts, which forced accused prostitutes to submit to physical examinations, attacked laws that condoned (male) sexual immorality. Butler's reports of women who had been forced to submit to examinations dwelt on the indignities of "monstrous instruments" used coercively: "They seem to tear the passage open first with their hands," one victim testified, "and then they thrust in instruments, and they pull them out and push them in, and they turn and twist them about; and if you cry out they stifle you." The repeal of the Contagious Diseases Acts in 1886 was based on an ideology of feminine purity that paradoxically involved many middle-class women in public discussions of prostitution and social diseases. Because of its emphasis on deviant or simply excessive male sexual demands, this campaign, like the social purity movement, may have also contributed to what the scholar Lillian Faderman has described as the marked development in quasi-homosexual bonds (so-called Boston marriages) between women living at the beginning of the twentieth century.

Just as committed to a standard of female-defined virtue, the Woman's Christian Temperance Union, which grew to eight hundred thousand members between 1880 and 1920 in America, promoted the slogan "For God and Home and Native Land" to symbolize its effort to bring the purity associated with the home into the national arena. Focusing on temperance (abstinence and legal prohibition of liquor), WCTU organizers argued that women suffered physically, psychologically, and economically from men's consumption of alcohol. Although Frances Willard, the Union's president, eventually placed the temperance cause within a socialist and suffragist context, she never managed to convince all her followers to look forward to "that day when the mothers, and daughters of America shall have a voice [i.e., vote] in the decision by which . . . the rum-shop is opened or shut beside their homes." Throughout the final decades of the nineteenth century, however, women attempted through reform groups to extend their role as nurturers and moral teachers from the domestic to the public sphere. In this context, the sanctification of motherhood even became part of the argument for the vote, for women justified their entrance into public life not only in terms of their domestic responsibilities and their superior morality, but also in terms of their importance as bearers of the race: in spite of its implicitly racist overtones, eugenics, the science of improving humanity through genetic control of heredity, supplied a rhetoric that lent the mother a crucial role in the development of the species.

When women on both sides of the Atlantic began organizing with increased militancy to gain female enfranchisement, their opponents included the novelist Mrs. Humphrey Ward, the poet Christina Rossetti, and even the socialist Beatrice Webb, all of whom signed in 1889 a protest against "an emancipating process [that] has now reached the limits fixed by the physical constitution of women." Turn-of-the-century suffragists were, however, building on the work of early feminists like Elizabeth Cady Stanton and Mary Wollstonecraft, and on their own experiences not only in social purity and temperance organizations, but also in the socialist and labor movements.

While none of the existing political parties in England chose to advocate women's enfranchisement, the ideological underpinnings of the struggle for the vote were established by the South African writer Olive Schreiner, whose novels and tracts identified women's secondary status with "the subjugation of large bodies of other human creatures, either as slaves, subject races, or classes." The granting of women's suffrage in New Zealand in 1893 and in South Australia in 1894 provided new impetus to the cause. After repeated efforts by the moderate National Union, led by Dame Millicent Garrett Fawcett, had failed to get a suffrage bill through Parliament, Emmeline Pankhurst in 1903 formed a new suffrage society, the Women's Social and Political Union. Annie Kenney, a mill hand from Oldham, and Christabel Pankhurst, one of Mrs. Pankhurst's daughters, were among the first to use the tactics—heckling, illegal speaking, seeking arrest, and enduring imprisonment—that would continue to characterize the growing militancy of the WSPU. Meetings and marches multiplied as the militants began pouring acid into letter boxes, throwing bricks and stones through shop windows, cutting telegraph wires, and slashing paintings.

Convinced that they would receive newspaper attention only through dramatic action, those militants sentenced to prison terms refused to eat, and jailors resorted to what was called the "forcible feeding" of hunger strikers. Wardresses pinned the protester to a bed and physicians pushed twenty inches of tubing down her nostrils or throat; milk and eggs were poured through a funnel into the tube. Painful and dangerous, such treatments were publicly condemned when an aristocrat, Lady Constance Lytton, disguised as a working-class woman named "Jane Wharton," was paralyzed by the practice. Nevertheless, the government responded only with what became known as the Cat and Mouse Act (1913), an act that released sick hunger strikers and allowed them to be rearrested without a fresh warrant, to continue serving their sentences when they were well. In spite of growing public support for women's suffrage during the renewed campaigns of 1913 and 1914, many moderates and socialists had been alienated by the Pankhursts' methods or by their exclusive focus on the vote. With the outbreak of war in August 1914, the movement was further split between those women who followed Mrs. Pankhurst in dedicating their energies to the war effort and others, like Olive Schreiner, who worked for world peace.

The splitting of the woman's movement into moderates and militants also occurred in America. In spite of the new leadership of Carrie Chapman Catt and Anna Howard Shaw, between 1896 and 1910 the National American Woman Suffrage Association suffered what the historian Eleanor Flexner has called "the doldrums," for many suffragists were beginning to question their state-by-state strategy, which was both arduous and frequently unsuccessful. When the national movement lost several state campaigns, two splinter groups arose, led by women deeply influenced by their experience with the militant Pankhursts. Harriet Stanton Blatch, Elizabeth Cady Stanton's daughter, traveled back to the United States from England in 1902, dismayed by the comparative inertia of American suffrage organizations. While Blatch's Equality League of Self-Supporting Women began to hold open-air meetings and parades, Alice Paul, who had been jailed in England, undertaken a hunger strike, and undergone forcible feeding, in 1910 returned to America, where she began describing the British movement to American suffrage groups. With the pacifist Crystal Eastman and the historian Mary Beard, Alice Paul began to campaign for a federal suffrage amendment. As different as Alice Paul's and Harriot Stanton Blatch's tactics were from those of Carrie Chapman Catt and Anna Howard Shaw, both militants and moderates depended for their intellectual framework on the analyses of female subordination provided by Charlotte Perkins Gilman, whose *Women and Economics* (1898) hailed "the woman's movement . . . as the best birth of our century." Even as the suffrage movement shaped the writing of women in this period, then, literary women also helped clarify the aims of turn-of-the-century feminism.

THE WOMAN QUESTION AND WOMEN'S ARTISTIC QUEST

In Gilbert and Sullivan's comic opera *The Mikado* (1885), one singer places "that singular anomaly, the lady novelist" on a list of characters who "never would be missed"; in fact, however, women novelists and, for that matter, female poets were hardly anomalies by the turn of the century. Yet many of their contributions have, until recently, been missing from the standard literary histories of this period, for they have been relegated to the footnotes of literary history or placed in a predominantly male context. Not only the prominent role women of letters played but also the uniqueness of their achievement become clearer, however, when we take into account the centrality of the woman question in their lives and works.

Inevitably, the impact of the suffrage movement was greatest on the production of polemical prose. In such books as *Woman and Labour* (1911) and *Women and Economics*, Olive Schreiner and Charlotte Perkins Gilman were contributing to the mass of expository writing that was being published by feminist and antifeminist women alike. In addition, a generation of what we would now call Women's Studies scholars began exploring women's cultural situation. Matilda Joslyn Gage's *Woman, Church and State* (1893) provided a female view of religious history, and Cicely Hamilton's *Marriage as a Trade* (1909) supplied a sociological analysis of the institutions that shaped women's lives. In 1910, Emma Goldman produced *The Traffic in Women*, an essay that connects the exploitation of prostitutes with the subjugation of all women, and Emily James Putnam published *The Lady*, a book about that outmoded and "somewhat dangerous" social type. By 1912, when Harriet Shaw Weaver and Dora Marsden were editing the magazine *The Freewoman*, Anna Garlin Spencer had documented the contributions of women from primitive to modern times in *Woman's Share in Social Culture*. By this time, too, Alice Meynell, Mary Elizabeth Coleridge, Mathilda Blind, and Mrs. Oliphant had produced essays and biographies about literary women.

The effort to document women's cultural situation also led the anthropologist Ruth Underhill to take down the stories of the American Indian Maria Chona, just as it impelled the folkorist Mary Austin to transcribe Indian legends in *The Basket Woman* (1914). The author of two autobiographies, Austin was one of many women in this period who published confessional accounts of their development. A number of Victorian women's diaries and journals were issued at the turn of the century: Elizabeth Cady Stanton's *Eighty Years and More*, which analyzed her role in the feminist movement, appeared in 1898, and Mary Boykin Chestnut's *Diary from Dixie*, which described life on a Southern plantation during the Civil War, was published in an abbreviated form in 1905, while the diaries of Marie Bashkirtseff (translated in 1890) and Mary MacLane (1902) were widely read. In many of these publications, women openly discussed their feelings about the female body, birth control, housework, female friendships, and aging. Alice James's *Diary*, which was privately printed several years after her death in 1892, describes not only her complex attitudes toward her famous brothers, Henry and William James, but also her resentment at a medical establishment that could not save her from an invalid's life. Just as personal and just as focused on the relationship between women and the medical establishment, Charlotte Perkins Gilman's story *The Yellow Wallpaper* (1892) analyzed female madness in terms of women's ambivalent attitudes toward men and maternity.

Besides bringing to the surface the psychological problems that women writers confronted, the feminist movement also provided a utopian vision of a world in which women might experience complete freedom. In verse, drama, fiction, and expository prose, women began to translate the visionary rhetoric of suffragism into utopian works of art. As the literary critic Elaine Showalter has reminded readers, in *Gloriana; or, The Revolution of 1900* (1890), Lady Florence Dixie envisioned a girl who disguises herself as a boy in order to enter Oxford and Parliament, while "Ellis Ethelmer," in *Woman Free* (1893), imagined what would happen if the menstrual cycle were to end. Similarly, Cicely Hamilton's and Christopher St. John's play *How the Vote Was Won* (1910) dramatized the conversion of patriarchal relatives to a triumphant suffrage cause. In addition, Elizabeth Robins's novel *The Convert* (1907) presented suffragists who seem to be "speaking in an unknown tongue," for they desire "a world where beauty exists for beauty's sake—which is love's sake—and not for tricking money or power out of men," a future world that may be "beyond the imagining of many." Gilman herself was to focus on precisely such a world in her utopia, *Herland* (1915), which describes an all-female community of women capable of reproducing themselves without the help of men.

Even when artistic works by women participated in the literary movements dominated or defined by their male contemporaries—for instance, symbolism, naturalism, and regionalism—the contributions of women were characterized by their focus on the issues associated with the turn-of-the-century woman question. Among poets, the women artists who were involved in a revolt against bourgeois conventionality wrote almost exclusively about their defiance of taboos placed on women. The Anglo-American poet Renée Vivien, for example, lived most of her adult life in Paris, where she wrote French verse influenced by Baudelaire and Swinburne: Vivien, who flaunted her alienation from society through her identification with "decadence," undertook to mythologize the lesbian relationships she sustained with, among others, the expatriate writer Natalie Barney. In addition, the British poet Charlotte Mew used sensuous imagery in dramatic monologues frequently narrated by female characters who aspire to a spiritual grace they are destined never to receive, while her contemporary Mary Elizabeth Coleridge portrayed the tormenting self-division of a woman who sees the "hideous wound" of "a woman, wild" in *The Other Side of the Mirror*. Similar symbolist techniques were used by Olive Schreiner in allegorical meditations which explored the spiritual and aesthetic quests that shape women's dreams and dreads.

While prose writers like Vernon Lee and Marie Corelli viewed the seductive *femme fatale* as an image of powerful female beauty, Schreiner analyzed in close detail the effects of narcissism and idleness on women robbed of all functions except the aesthetic. Indeed, her discussion in *Women and Labour* of what she called "sex-parasitism" was partially an analysis of how the role of the *femme fatale* is fatal for women. Just as concerned with the pain experienced by the woman who is perceived as fatally attractive, George Egerton (the pseudonym of Mary Chavelita Dunne) stunned London with what then seemed an erotically explicit volume of stories, *Keynotes* (1894), some of which deal with the frustration of female characters who are hampered by their distrust or ignorance of male sexuality.

In one of her more successful stories, Egerton described the fantasy of a woman who imagines herself performing in front of a male audience that succumbs to her exotic charms. Significantly, the women who were most influenced by the idea of the *femme fatale* were female performers. The Italian actress Eleanora Duse (about whom Amy Lowell was to write a number of poems) and the English-speaking actresses Ellen Terry and Elizabeth Robins, both of whom starred in the plays of Ibsen and Shaw, led visibly eccentric lives, but they were less flamboyant than the very popular entertainer Sarah Bernhardt, who played the role of the *femme fatale* both on and off stage. Attended by a menagerie of wild beasts, engaged in a series of notorious love affairs, sleeping in a satin-lined coffin, Bernhardt reputedly wore a necklace of petrified human eyes. Among dancers, Loie Fuller became famous in *art nouveau* circles for her swirling veil dances, and Isadora Duncan became internationally infamous not only for what she herself called the "fantastic sensuality and ecstasy" of her dances, but also for her bohemian lifestyle.

Just as aestheticism had a distinctive impact on women's art at the turn of the century, the realistic and naturalistic traditions influenced women in a special way. The early pioneer of naturalistic fiction Rebecca Harding Davis continued publishing throughout this period. Similarly, Mrs. Humphrey Ward wrote novels about the degrading conditions of the London poor. But many women writers analyzed social determinism less in terms of governmental or industrial corruption than in terms of the private lives of women. Perhaps the most important novelists in this respect were May Sinclair and Edith Wharton. Unlike those male contemporaries who portrayed the new freedom of the New Woman, moreover, female realists focused for the most part on the continuing confinement women confronted in an increasingly acquisitive society. Wharton, in particular, analyzed the bondage of heroines who are trapped by materialistic societal conventions that turn them into valuable objects.

Like H. H. Richardson, who located a number of her stories and novels in her native Australia, and Wharton, who became famous for her delineations of wealthy New York society, many turn-of-the-century women writers analyzed the unique mores of the local communities that had shaped their own family histories, much as Lady Gregory did in her volumes of Irish legends and in the plays she wrote for the Abbey Theatre. Studying the origins of their own identities and their cultural roots, such authors help explain the importance of regionalism in turn-of-the-century literature by women. Unlike Bret Harte, whose stories about California are dominated by romantic gamblers and sentimental miners, the short-story writers Sarah Orne Jewett and Mary E. Wilkins Freeman described the visiting, gossiping, cooking, and gardening that supplied a network of support for their communities of women. Like such Southern regionalists as Kate Chopin and Grace King, Jewett and Freeman implicitly provided a social history which might otherwise have gone unrecorded by traditional historians. Jewett's *The Country of the Pointed Firs* (1896), no less than Chopin's *Bayou Folk* (1894), set the private problems of daughters, single women, mothers, and widows into the context of economic and social issues at the turn of the century. At the same time, however, such regionalists sometimes also eulogized a pastoral, timeless realm in which women had established a harmonious, almost mythic, relationship with the physical landscape.

Given the ways in which polemical, autobiographical, utopian, realistic, and regional writing by women concentrated on the situation of woman in nature and society, it is hardly surprising that one of the major texts of this age, Kate Chopin's *The Awakening* (1899), focused on a twenty-eight-year-old, married mother of two children who is awakened socially and sexually to "her position in the universe as a human being." Indeed, Chopin's text functions not only polemically, as a plea for women's autonomy, and autobiographically, as a study of the competition between motherhood and artistry, but also as a fantasy of female sensuality, solitude, and self-discovery. Chopin had profited from her reading of Sarah Orne Jewett's stories, just as Jewett and Freeman had developed a tradition pioneered by Harriet Beecher Stowe. Although such American prose writers as Elizabeth Stuart Phelps Ward and Constance Fenimore Woolson published novels and short stories about the impossibility of being both a woman and an artist, many other turn-of-the-century women writers could begin to look back on a tradition of successful women authors.

During the span of years that witnessed the deaths of Victorian sibyls like George Eliot and Harriet Beecher Stowe, women writers felt themselves to be living through a period of transition similar to, yet somewhat different from, the transition period experienced by their male counterparts, for they were writing in an age when thousands of women were crossing the threshold from the private to the public sphere. Unlike many of their Victorian precursors, literary women no longer felt constrained to write covertly about their rebellion against socially prescribed roles. Rather, many of these artists were empowered to record both their protests and their pleas by the idea, articulated in *Woman and Labour*, that "it is the woman who is the final standard of the race." Although two classics of this period—*The Awakening* and *The Yellow Wallpaper*—are overtly pessimistic about women's fates, their pessimism is born of raised expectations for a fully integrated life. Whether the female contemporaries of Chopin and Gilman wrote about the possibility of industrialization ending the necessity of women's domestic service, about the similarity between ethnic discrimination and female subjugation, or about the significance for women of the death of a patriarchal God, they would have agreed with Henry Adams that "the proper study of mankind is woman."

ALICE MEYNELL
1847–1922

"Of all the crying evils in the depraved earth . . . the greatest, judged by all the laws of God and humanity, is the miserable selfishness of men that keeps women from work," wrote the poet Alice Thompson at the age of eighteen. The daughter of cultivated, independently wealthy parents—her mother was a pianist and artist, her father an amateur man of letters—this surprisingly feminist young woman was already beginning to write the elegant verse that would later in her life bring her considerable fame. Raised partly in Italy, where her family lived in what the critic Cora Kaplan has called a "relaxed bohemian style," she had been educated at home and had been taught, as her remark about work suggests, to take herself seriously. In addition, like her mother and sister, she was a convert to Catholicism, organizing her life as well as her art around a strong commitment to her faith.

Alice Thompson's first book of poetry, *Preludes*, appeared in 1875, and a year later she married a young Catholic journalist, Wilfred Meynell. With her husband, she founded and edited several magazines, one of which, *Merry England*, brought her the friendship of well-known contemporary poets like Coventry Patmore, Hilaire Belloc, and Francis Thompson. Besides working on *Merry England*, she also wrote an impressive number of fine essays—many on literary subjects—for such periodicals as *The Spectator* and *The Saturday Review*, and she combined this activity with a busy domestic life: her egalitarian marriage to Wilfred Meynell produced eight children, seven of whom survived.

Alice Meynell's most notable achievement, however, was a body of verse that seemed, in the words of one admirer, Vita Sackville–West, to have been written "with an etching pen." Austerely lyric, poems like *A Father of Women*, *The Sunderland Children*, and *Parentage* reveal the aesthetic craft that elicited for Meynell the praise of such a major figure as John Ruskin. At the same time, the political, and often distinctively feminist, passion that infuses these works reminds us that they were written by the same woman who had longed for significant work at the age of eighteen. Not surprisingly, Meynell became a suffragist in her later years, and, not surprisingly either, she drew upon her deep-seated feminism in singularly powerful poems about the horrors of World War I, a conflict that she saw as having been brought about by cynical "fathers"—for, as she had already observed in *Parentage* (1896), "Theirs are armies. Death is theirs." Perhaps impressed by such intensity, the American poet Amy Lowell remembered, after Meynell's death in 1922, that this English writer's words "rang . . . like bronze cathedral bells / Down ancient lawns."

The Sunderland Children[1]

On the 183 Sunderland children who lost their lives in a panic at the
Victoria Hall, 16th June, 1883

This was the surplus childhood, held as cheap!
   Not worth the care which shields
The lambs that are to stay, the corn to reap—
   The promise of the fields.

The nation guards her future. Fruits and grass   5
   And vegetable life
Are fostered league by league. But oh, the mass
   Of childhood over-rife!

O mass, O units! Oh, the separate story
   Planned for each breather of breath!   10
This futile young mankind, and transitory,
   Is left to stray to Death.

O promise, presage, menace! Upon these
   A certain seal is laid.
Unkept, unbroken, are the auguries   15
   These little children made.

For threat is bound with promise; and the nation
   Holds festival of regret
Over these dead—dead in their isolation—
   Wisely. She feared their threat.   20

1883

Parentage

"When Augustus Caesar legislated against the unmarried citizens of
Rome, he declared them to be, in some sort, slayers of the people."

    Ah no! not these!
These, who were childless, are not they who gave
So many dead unto the journeying wave,
The helpless nurslings of the cradling seas;
Not they who doomed by infallible decrees   5
Unnumbered man to the innumerable grave.

---

1. I.e., from the English mining town of Sunderland.

But those who slay
Are fathers. Theirs are armies. Death is theirs—
The death of innocences and despairs;
The dying of the golden and the grey.   10
The sentence, when these speak it, has no Nay.
And she who slays is she who bears, who bears.

1896

A Father of Women: Ad Sororem E. B.[2]

"Thy father was transfused into thy blood."
        Dryden: *Ode to Mrs. Anne Killigrew*[3]

Our father works in us,
The daughters of his manhood. Not undone
Is he, not wasted, though transmuted thus,
        And though he left no son.

        Therefore on him I cry   5
To arm me: "For my delicate mind a casque,[4]
A breastplate for my heart, courage to die,
        Of thee, captain, I ask.

        "Nor strengthen only; press
A finger on this violent blood and pale,   10
Over this rash will let thy tenderness
        A while pause, and prevail.

        "And shepherd-father, thou
Whose staff folded[5] my thoughts before my birth,
Control them now I am of earth, and now   15
        Thou art no more of earth.

        "O liberal, constant, dear,
Crush in my nature the ungenerous art[6]
Of the inferior; set me high, and here,
        Here garner up thy heart!"   20

        Like to him now are they,
The million living fathers of the War—[7]

2. Latin: "To Sister E. B." E. B. is almost certainly Meynall's sister Elizabeth Thompson
Butler (1844–1933), a painter of military and
battle scenes.
3. Anne Killigrew was a seventeenth-century
poet whose father was a well-known literary

man.
4. Helmet.
5. I.e., guided to the fold, an enclosure for
sheep.
6. Artifice.
7. World War I.

Mourning the crippled world, the bitter day—
Whose striplings are no more.

The crippled world! Come then,   25
Fathers of women with your honour in trust,
Approve, accept, know them daughters of men,
Now that your sons are dust.

1917

ALICE JAMES
1848–1892

The journal Alice James kept for the last three years of her life is acerbic about English customs and medical practices, witty about the gossip and books she received in her sickroom, and sensitively introspective. For the most part, it was dictated to her intimate companion, Katharine Peabody Loring. These two friends, who may have furnished the impetus for Alice's brother Henry's portrait of two emotionally involved suffragists in *The Bostonians* (1886), had traveled to England to cure Katharine's sister and to visit Alice's novelist-brother after the death of her parents in 1882, but Alice's poor health prolonged their stay.

As the only daughter in the illustrious James family and the youngest of five siblings, Alice James was not well equipped to handle either her volatile father, who preached Christian mysticism and intellectual ambition to his children, or her mother, who was worshipped as a self-effacing Madonna within the family. After a childhood punctuated by foreign travel, she grew up in Cambridge, Massachusetts. Her first mental breakdown occurred at sixteen. While her brothers William and Henry were preparing for their eminent careers in psychology and literature, she was treated for stomach pains, "heart attacks," fainting spells, and paralyzed limbs with the remedies of her time: "motor-therapy," "electricity," "blistering" baths, and "sulphuric ether." At thirty years of age, she was tempted to commit suicide during a profound depression, but her father's "permission"—his acknowledgment, on learning of her feelings, of her freedom to choose to die—made even that alternative seem impossible. Before and after her parents' death, she must have compared her own private suffering to her brothers' public accomplishments. A late *Diary* entry lists Henry's *The Tragic Muse* and *The American* along with her philosopher-brother William's *Psychology*: "Not a bad show for one family!" she exulted, ominously adding, "especially if I get myself dead, the hardest job of all."

Because, as her brother Henry explained, "in our family group girls seem scarcely to have had a chance," he believed that Alice's "tragic health was, in a manner, the only solution for her of the practical problem of life." He had not known of the journal during her lifetime; however, Alice James had valued it sufficiently to ask that it be typed, and, after Alice's death from breast cancer at forty-four, Katharine Loring privately printed a copy for each of the surviving brothers and one for herself. A 1934 edition was followed by Leon Edel's 1964 edition, from which we have taken our selections.

From The Diary

May 31st, 1889 [My First Journal!]

I think that if I get into the habit of writing a bit about what happens, or rather doesn't happen, I may lose a little of the sense of loneliness and desolation which abides with me. My circumstances allowing of nothing but the ejaculation of one-syllabled reflections, a written monologue by that most interesting being, *myself*, may have its yet to be discovered consolations. I shall at least have it all my own way and it may bring relief as an outlet to that geyser of emotions, sensations, speculations and reflections which ferments perpetually within my poor old carcass for its sins; so here goes, my first Journal!

July 12th [1889] [My Microscopic Field]

* * * It's amusing to see how, even on my microscopic field, minute events are perpetually taking place illustrative of the broadest facts of human nature. Yesterday Nurse and I had a good laugh but I must allow that decidedly she "had" me. I was thinking of something that interested me very much and my mind was suddenly flooded by one of those luminous waves that sweep out of consciousness all but the living sense and overpower one with joy in the rich, throbbing complexity of life, when suddenly I looked up at Nurse, who was dressing me, and saw her primitive, rudimentary expression (so common here) as of no inherited quarrel with her destiny of putting petticoats over my head; the poverty and deadness of it contrasted to the tide of speculation that was coursing thro' my brain made me exclaim, "Oh! Nurse, don't you wish you were inside of *me!*"—her look of dismay and vehement disclaimer—"Inside of you, Miss, when you have just had a sick headache for five days!"—gave a greater blow to my vanity, than that much battered article has ever received. The headache had gone off in the night and I had clean forgotten it—when the little wretch confronted me with it, at this sublime moment when I was feeling within me the potency of a Bismarck,[1] and left me powerless before the immutable law that however great we may seem to our own consciousness no human being would exchange his for ours, and before the fact that *my* glorious rôle was to stand for *Sick headache* to mankind! What a gro-

---

1. Otto von Bismarck (1815–1898), chancellor of the German Empire, noted for his strength and ruthlessness.

tesque I am to be sure! Lying in this room, with the resistance of a this-
tle-down, having illusory moments of throbbing with the pulse of the
Race, the Mystery to be solved at the next breath and the fountain of all
Happiness within me—the sense of vitality, in short, simply proportionate to the excess of weakness!—To sit by and watch these absurdities is amusing in its way and reminds me of how I used to *listen* to my
"company manners" in the days when I had 'em, and how ridiculous
they sounded.

Ah! Those strange people who have the courage to be unhappy! *Are*
they unhappy, by-the-way?

February 17th [1890] [Pharasaism; Death]

I find myself as the months pass more and more stifled by the all
pervasive sense of pharasaism[2] in the British constitution of things. You
don't feel it at first and you can't put your finger upon it in your friends,
but as the days go by you unfold it with your *Standard*,[3] in the morn. It
rises dense from the *P. M. G.* in the evening, it creeps thro' the cracks
in the window frames like the fog and envelopes you thro' the day. I
asked H.[4] once how it struck him from his wider and varied field not
wanting my view to become cramped upon conclusions drawn from my
centimetre of observation, he said that he didn't think it could be exaggerated. It's woven of a multiplicity of minute details and incidents
which elude you in the telling but which seem to exist in the texture of
things and leave a dent in the mind as they file past. A monarchy to
which they bow down in its tinsel capacity only, denying to it a manly
movement of any sort; a boneless Church broadening itself out, up to
date; the hysterical legislation over a dog with a broken leg whilst Society is engaged making bags of 4,000 pheasants, etc. etc., or gloating
over foxes torn to pieces by a pack of hounds;[5] the docility with which
the classes enslave themselves to respectability or non-respectability as
the "good-form"[6] of the moment may be; the "sense of their betters" in
the masses; the passivity with which the working man allows himself to
be patted and legislated out of all independence; thus the profound in-
eradicables in the bone and sinew conviction that outlying regions are
their preserves, that they alone of human races massacre savages out of
pure virtue. It would ill-become an American to reflect upon the treatment of aboriginal races; but I never heard it suggested that our hideous
dealings with the Indians was brotherly love masquerading under the
disguise of pure cussedness.

2. Strict adherence to the outward forms of
moral and social strictures without regard to their
spirit.
3. The *Morning Standard* and the *Pall Mall
Gazette* were two London newspapers of the

period.
4. Alice's brother Henry James, the famous
novelist.
5. I.e., hunting; "bag": gamebag.
6. I.e., code of behavior.

It would have been highly immoral, when Kath.[7] was here, not to get as much work out of her as possible, so the second week she began upon Woking. I had got discouraged about cremation, having been told that it was very fussy and expensive, so she wrote for the circular[8] to be sent by the Cremation people, when, lo! it's as simple and inexpensive as possible, only six guineas and one extra for a parson. Me ashes are to be put in an urn, and sent home, not as a parlour ornament for William's new house, but to be buried beside Father and Mother in the cemetery at Cam[bridge],—so that we shall not be myths as Harry suggests we might otherwise become. 'Tis a great waste that I didn't die whilst K. was here; she could have carried home the urn in her top berth and as she lay convulsed with seasickness it would have greatly assuaged her grief to have such a palpable assurance that that portion of me hitherto so susceptible to the dread thing was reduced to ashes. It seems delightfully clean to elude in this way that early riser, the unpleasant wurrum, and I am greatly in hopes that

> "The worms crawled in
> And the worms crawled out,"[9]

will not be true of my return to dust.

Then we began upon my Will, which I wanted to make over again, leaving out, of course, those who had offended me since my last, as a cousin of Lilla Walsh's used to do, who re-made hers every few weeks. K. told me that as long as I indulged in no amateur legal terminology but confined myself strictly to my vernacular it would be all right, so she wouldn't allow me even one decorative bequeath. She wrote to the Consul at Birmingham to ask him if it had to be signed in his presence and he said yes, so hearing that Lizzie Putnam was at Banbury and was coming to spend a certain afternoon, K. telegraphed to the Consul, as it was so good to get a Boston witness. The arrival of this august personage the Consul naturally caused me to "go off" and I had to be put to bed—when the most amusing scene followed. I lay in a semi-faint, draped in as many frills as could be found for the occasion, with Nurse at my head with the thickest layer of her anxious-devoted-nurse expression on, as K. told me after, when thro' a mist I vaguely saw five black figures file into my little bower, headed by the most extraordinary little man, all gesticulation and grimace, who planted himself at the foot of the bed and stroking my knees began a long harangue to the effect that he and his wife had both "laid upon a bed of sickness" which seemed to constitute uncontrovertible reason for my immediate recovery. K. with difficulty restrained him from reading the Will aloud there and then—he has doubtless not forgiven this dam thrown across to ar-

7. Katherine P. Loring, James's intimate companion.

8. Advertising pamphlet.

9. From a macabre children's song.

rest the flood of his eloquence—It was so curious for me, just like a
nightmare effect and I felt as if I were assisting at the reading of my own
Will, surrounded by the greedy relatives, as in novels. After they had
filed in and out several times and become tangled in as much resounding red-tape as the creature could reel off for the occasion they went off
downstairs to an "elegant" tea where the Consul entertained them with
his whole history and the digestive processes of his domestic circle,
which seem to be in a sadly disorganized condition. He asked K.
whether she was related to "Our great Minister to Portugal Geo. B.
Loring"—imagine the condition of a Peabody-Loring having such an
insult hurled at her! And he also wanted to know whether Postmaster
James and I were consanguineous.[1] I, not having been *born* (ahem!)
was able to take things more easily, besides Mr. James, I believe, was a
man to be related to whom would have been an honour. Miss Blanche
Leppington, who had been asked to be a witness, told K. after that she
hadn't looked at my face but that she felt as if she "ought to keep her
eye fixed upon Miss James's *hand!*"—she also said the scene—"Will
remain in my thoughts as the most pathetic I ever saw and in my imagination as the most picturesque and American!"—I can't complain of
not being taken seriously and I think it is the first time that *picturesque*
and *American*, which are usually supposed to neutralize one another so
completely, were ever conjoined. In recounting the story to H. he said,
"You can't say you've done nothing for your Race since you've
brought that about in your own person."

October 26th [1890] [My "Hidden Self"]

William uses an excellent expression when he says in his paper on
the "Hidden Self" that the nervous victim "abandons" certain portions
of his consciousness.[2] It may be the word commonly used by his kind. It
is just the right one at any rate, altho' I have never unfortunately been
able to abandon my consciousness and get five minutes' rest. I have
passed thro' an infinite succession of conscious abandonments and in
looking back now I see how it began in my childhood, altho' I wasn't
conscious of the necessity until '67 or '68 when I broke down first,
acutely, and had violent turns of hysteria. As I lay prostrate after the
storm with my mind luminous and active and susceptible of the clearest, strongest impressions, I saw so distinctly that it was a fight simply
between my body and my will, a battle in which the former was to be
triumphant to the end. Owing to some physical weakness, excess of
nervous susceptibility, the moral power *pauses*, as it were for a mo-

---

1. Related.
2. Alice's brother, the philosopher William
James, had published a paper that year called

The Hidden Self, in which he described "con-
tractions in the field of consciousness" in hysterical patients.

ment, and refuses to maintain muscular sanity, worn out with the strain of its constabulary functions. As I used to sit immovable reading in the library with waves of violent inclination suddenly invading my muscles taking some one of their myriad forms such as throwing myself out of the window, or knocking off the head of the benignant pater[3] as he sat with his silver locks, writing at his table, it used to seem to me that the only difference between me and the insane was that I had not only all the horrors and suffering of insanity but the duties of doctor, nurse, and strait-jacket imposed upon me, too. Conceive of never being without the sense that if you let yourself go for a moment your mechanism will fall into pie[4] and that at some given moment you must abandon it all, let the dykes break and the flood sweep in, acknowledging yourself abjectly impotent before the immutable laws. When all one's moral and natural stock in trade is a temperament forbidding the abandonment of an inch or the relaxation of a muscle, 'tis a never-ending fight. When the fancy took me of a morning at school to *study* my lessons by way of variety instead of shirking or wiggling thro' the most impossible sensations of upheaval, violent revolt in my head overtook me so that I had to "abandon" my brain, as it were. So it has always been, anything that sticks of itself is free to do so, but conscious and continuous cerebration is an impossible exercise and from just behind the eyes my head feels like a dense jungle into which no ray of light has ever penetrated. So, with the rest, you abandon the pit of your stomach, the palms of your hands, the soles of your feet, and refuse to keep them sane when you find in turn one moral impression after another producing despair in the one, terror in the other, anxiety in the third and so on until life becomes one long flight from remote suggestion and complicated eluding of the multifold traps set for your undoing.

May 31st [1891] [Going Downhill]

To him who waits, all things come! My aspirations may have been eccentric, but I cannot complain now, that they have not been brilliantly fulfilled. Ever since I have been ill, I have longed and longed for some palpable disease, no matter how conventionally dreadful a label it might have, but I was always driven back to stagger alone under the monstrous mass of subjective sensations, which that sympathetic being "the medical man" had no higher inspiration than to assure me I was personally responsible for, washing his hands of me with a graceful complacency under my very nose. Dr. Torry was the only man who ever treated me like a rational being, who did not assume, because I was

3. Alice's father, the eminent theologian William James, Sr. 4. Into a heap.

victim to many pains, that I was, of necessity, an arrested mental development too.

Nothwithstanding all the happiness and comfort here, I have been going downhill at a steady trot; so they sent for Sir Andrew Clark four days ago, and the blessed being has endowed me not only with cardiac complications, but says that a lump that I have had in one of my breasts for three months, which has given me a great deal of pain, is a tumour, that nothing can be done for me but to alleviate pain, that it is only a question of time, etc. This with a delicate embroidery of "the most distressing case of nervous hyperaesthesia"[5] added to a spinal neurosis that has taken me off my legs for seven years; with attacks of rheumatic gout in my stomach for the last twenty, ought to satisfy the most inflated pathologic vanity. It is decidedly indecent to catalogue oneself in this way, but I put it down in a scientific spirit, to show that though I have no productive worth, I have a certain value as an indestructible quantity.

February 2nd [1892] [*This Long Slow Dying*]

This long slow dying is no doubt instructive, but it is disappointingly free from excitements: "naturalness" being carried to its supreme expression. One sloughs off the activities one by one, and never knows that they're gone, until one suddenly finds that the months have slipped away and the sofa will never more be laid upon, the morning paper read, or the loss of the new book regretted; one revolves with equal content within the narrowing circle until the vanishing point is reached, I suppose.

Vanity, however, maintains its undisputed sway, and I take satisfaction in feeling as much myself as ever, perhaps simply a more concentrated essence in this curtailment. If I could concern myself about the fate of my soul, it would give doubtless a savor of uncertainty to the fleeting moments, but I never felt so absolutely uninterested in the poor, shabby, old thing. The fact is, I have been dead so long and it has been simply such a grim shoving of the hours behind me as I faced a ceaseless possible horror, since that hideous summer of '78, when I went down to the deep sea, its dark waters closed over me and I knew neither hope nor peace; that now it's only the shrivelling of an empty pea pod that has to be completed.

A little while ago we had rather an amusing episode with the kind and usually understanding Tuckey,[6] who was led away into assuring me that I should live a good bit still—I was terribly shocked and when he saw the havoc that he wrought, he reassuringly said: "but you'll be comfortable, too," at which I exclaimed: "Oh I don't care about that, but boo-hoo, it's so *inconvenient!*" and the poor man burst into a roar of

---

5. Abnormal sensitivity to pain.   6. James's doctor.

laughter. I was glad afterwards that it happened, as I was taken quite by surprise, and was able to test the sincerity of my mortuary inclinations. I have always *thought* that I wanted to die, but I felt quite uncertain as to what my muscular demonstrations might be at the moment of transition, for I occasionally have a quiver as of an expected dentistical wrench when I fancy the actual moment. But my substance seemed equally outraged with my mind at Tuckey's dictum, so mayhap I shall be able to maintain a calm befitting so sublimated a spirit!—at any rate there is no humbuggy "strength of mind" about it, 'tis simply physical debility, 'twould be such a bore to be perturbed.

March 4th [1892] [Physical Pain]

I am being ground slowly on the grim grindstone of physical pain, and on two nights I had almost asked for K.'s lethal dose, but one steps hesitantly along such unaccustomed ways and endures from second to second; and I feel sure that it can't be possible but what the bewildered little hammer[7] that keeps me going will very shortly see the decency of ending his distracted career; however this may be, physical pain however great ends in itself and falls away like dry husks from the mind, whilst moral discords and nervous horrors sear the soul. These last, Katharine has completely under the control of her rhythmic hand, so I go no longer in dread. Oh the wonderful moment when I felt myself floated for the first time into the deep sea of divine *cessation*, and saw all the dear old mysteries and miracles vanish into vapour! That first experience doesn't repeat itself, fortunately, for it might become a seduction.

Katharine can't help it, she's made that way, a simple embodiment of Health, as Baldwin called her, "the New England Professor of doing things."

Final Entry by Katharine P. Loring

All through Saturday the 5th and even in the night, Alice was making sentences. One of the last things she said to me was to make a correction in the sentence of March 4th "moral discords and nervous horrors."

This dictation of March 4th was rushing about in her brain all day, and although she was very weak and it tired her much to dictate, she could not get her head quiet until she had had it written: then she was relieved and I finished Miss Woolson's story of "Dorothy"[8] to her.

1894, 1934, 1964

7. I.e., her heart.
8. A story by Constance Fenimore Woolson
(1840–1894), a novelist and friend of Henry James.

SARAH ORNE JEWETT
1849–1909

In one of several tributes to Sarah Orne Jewett, Willa Cather recounted how the more experienced writer "once laughingly told me that her head was full of dear old houses and dear old women, and that when an old house and an old woman came together in her brain with a click, she knew that a story was under way." Jewett, who later advised Cather to relinquish "the masquerade" of her male narrator and write from a female point of view, crafted an art subtle enough to catch the idiomatic language and conservative values of the old women who inhabited the old houses of her native Maine, houses which often situated them in the elegiac splendor of a fading but beautiful world. No wonder, then, that Cather rated *The Country of the Pointed Firs* (1896), along with *The Scarlet Letter* and *Huckleberry Finn*, as one of the three enduring masterpieces of American literature. For, as Cather remarked, these chapters in what amounts to a lyrical novel "are living things caught in the open, with light and freedom and air-spaces about them." Like Jewett's other publications, "they melt into the land and the life of the land until they are not stories at all, but life itself."

That Jewett herself referred to her fiction as "sketches" illustrates her conscious substitution of a meditative lyricism for the neatly sustained conflicts of traditionally plotted stories. Such a focus also reflects the serenity of a life lived for the most part with a profound sense of rootedness, specifically in the southern portion of Maine. The second of the three daughters of Theodore Herman Jewett and Caroline Frances (Perry) Jewett, Theodora Sarah Orne Jewett quickly dropped her first name, which had been bestowed upon her as a tribute to her paternal grandfather. But she was born, was reared, and died in the pre-Revolutionary house in South Berwick this prosperous shipbuilder had bought. Both of her parents came from distinguished, well-educated families: her father, a physician, was descended from the first Bay Colony settlers, and her mother's father was a renowned surgeon. Because she was subject to ill health as a child, Jewett's father thought she would benefit from fresh air and so he took her on his rounds. Through her observation of his country patients, she acquired a deep respect for the everyday lives of common people, and an equally sensitive appreciation of the region's landscape.

In her novel *The Country Doctor* (1884), she would present the struggles of a female character seeking to adopt the role of a father, who is clearly her most important mentor. Jewett's informal education with her own father was supplemented by Miss Olive Rayne's school in South Berwick and the Berwick Academy, from which she graduated in 1865. Three years later, under the pseudonym Alice or A. C. Eliot, she began publishing her first stories in magazines like the *Riverside Magazine for Young People* and the *Atlantic Monthly*. Her father's encouraging admonition—"Don't try to write *about* things: write the things themselves just as they are"—clearly shaped her aesthetic goals. By 1877, Jewett had accepted William Dean Howells's advice to collect her sketches about "things themselves," which had appeared in his *Atlantic*, in the volume she entitled *Deephaven* (1877).

The letters and diaries of Sarah Orne Jewett from this period in her life document her close relationships with a number of female friends. After her father's death in 1878, moreover, her acquaintance with Annie Adams Fields ripened into a thirty-year liaison which the critic Josephine Donovan has recently placed in the context of other so-called Boston marriages: that is, female couples living together in a union comparable to marriage. Annie Fields was the wife of James T. Fields, a prominent Boston publisher who would also become the editor of the *Atlantic*. Mrs. Fields was a hostess, an author, and a social welfare worker. The earliest letters between Fields and Jewett, which were omitted from Fields's 1911 edition of Jewett's letters, are dated 1877, when Fields was forty-three and Jewett was twenty-eight. The correspondence quickly became affectionately intimate, and, after the death of James Fields in 1881, the two women lived together, spending part of each year on Charles Street in Boston, part in Maine, and part traveling in Western Europe.

Sustained by Fields's support and the models provided by her own wide reading in nineteenth-century fiction, Jewett began to produce collections like *A White Heron, and Other Stories* (1886) and *The King of Folly Island* (1888). During her lifetime, she received public acknowledgment of her contribution to American letters from such established writers as John Greenleaf Whittier and James Russell Lowell and from Bowdoin College, her father's alma mater, which made her a Doctor of Letters in 1901. For the last seven years of her life, she suffered the consequences of a spinal concussion caused by an accident in her carriage. By the time she died, in her sixtieth year, however, she had succeeded in portraying the visionary resiliency with which women responded to the economic impoverishment and the physical splendor of rural New England.

The Town Poor

Mrs. William Trimble and Miss Rebecca Wright were driving along Hampden east road, one afternoon in early spring. Their progress was slow. Mrs. Trimble's sorrel horse was old and stiff, and the wheels were clogged by clay mud. The frost was not yet out of the ground, although the snow was nearly gone, except in a few places on the north side of the woods, or where it had drifted all winter against a length of fence.

"There must be a good deal o' snow to the nor'ard of us yet," said weather-wise Mrs. Trimble. "I feel it in the air; 't is more than the ground-damp. We ain't goin' to have real nice weather till the up-country snow's all gone."

"I heard say yesterday that there was good sleddin' yet, all up through Parsley," responded Miss Wright. "I shouldn't like to live in them northern places. My cousin Ellen's husband was a Parsley man, an' he was obliged, as you may have heard, to go up north to his father's second wife's funeral; got back day before yesterday. 'T was about twenty-one miles, an' they started on wheels; but when they'd gone nine or ten miles, they found 't was no sort o' use, an' left their wagon an' took a sleigh. The man that owned it charged 'em four an' six, too.[1] I shouldn't have thought he would; they told him they was goin' to a funeral; an' they had their own buffaloes[2] an' everything."

"Well, I expect it's a good deal harder scratchin', up that way; they have to git money where they can; the farms is very poor as you go north," suggested Mrs. Trimble kindly. " 'T ain't none too rich a country where we be, but I've always been grateful I wa'n't born up to Parsley."

The old horse plodded along, and the sun, coming out from the heavy spring clouds, sent a sudden shine of light along the muddy road. Sister Wright drew her large veil forward over the high brim of her bonnet. She was not used to driving, or to being much in the open air; but Mrs. Trimble was an active business woman, and looked after her own affairs herself, in all weathers. The late Mr. Trimble had left her a good farm, but not much ready money, and it was often said that she was better off in the end than if he had lived. She regretted his loss deeply, however; it was impossible for her to speak of him, even to intimate friends, without emotion, and nobody had ever hinted that this emotion was insincere. She was most warm-hearted and generous, and in her limited way played the part of Lady Bountiful in the town of Hampden.

"Why, there's where the Bray girls lives, ain't it?" she exclaimed, as, beyond a thicket of witch-hazel and scruboak, they came in sight of a weather-beaten, solitary farm-house. The barn was too far away for thrift or comfort, and they could see long lines of light between the shrunken boards as they came nearer. The fields looked both stony and sodden. Somehow, even Parsley itself could be hardly more forlorn.

"Yes'm," said Miss Wright, "that's where they live now, poor things. I know the place, though I ain't been up here for years. You don't suppose, Mis' Trimble—I ain't seen the girls out to meetin' all winter. I've re'lly been covetin' " —

"Why, yes, Rebecca, of course we could stop," answered Mrs. Trimble heartily. "The exercises[3] was over earlier 'n I expected, an' you're goin' to remain over night long o' me, you know. There won't be no tea till we git there, so we can't be late. I'm in the habit o' sendin' a basket to the Bray girls when any o' our folks is comin' this way, but I ain't been to see 'em since they moved up here. Why, it must be a good deal over a year ago. I know 't was in the late winter they had to make the move. 'T was cruel hard, I must say, an' if I hadn't been down with

---

1. Four shillings and sixpence. Inhabitants of the Maine coast were mainly English settlers.
2. Buffalo skin robes or blankets.
3. Church services.

my pleurisy fever I'd have stirred round an' done somethin' about it. There was a good deal o' sickness at the time, an'—well, 't was kind o' rushed through, breakin' of 'em up, an' lots o' folks blamed the selec' men;[4] but when 't was done, 't was done, an' nobody took holt to undo it. Ann an' Mandy looked same 's ever when they come to meetin',[5] 'long in the summer,—kind o' wishful, perhaps. They've always sent me word they was gittin' on pretty comfortable."

"That would be their way," said Rebecca Wright. "They never was any hand to complain, though Mandy's less cheerful than Ann. If Mandy'd been spared such poor eyesight, an' Ann hadn't got her lame wrist that wa'n't set right, they'd kep' off the town fast enough. They both shed tears when they talked to me about havin' to break up, when I went to see 'em before I went over to brother Asa's. You see we was brought up neighbors, an' we went to school together, the Brays an' me. 'T was a special Providence brought us home this road, I've been so covetin' a chance to git to see 'em. My lameness hampers me."

"I'm glad we come this way, myself," said Mrs. Trimble.

"I'd like to see just how they fare," Miss Rebecca Wright continued. "They give their consent to goin' on the town because they knew they'd got to be dependent, an' so they felt 't would come easier for all than for a few to help 'em. They acted real dignified an' right-minded, contrary to what most do in such cases, but they was dreadful anxious to see who would bid 'em off,[6] town-meeting day; they did so hope 't would be somebody right in the village. I just sat down an' cried good when I found Abel Janes's folks had got hold of 'em. They always had the name of bein' slack an' poor-spirited, an' they did it just for what they got out o' the town. The selectmen this last year ain't what we have had. I hope they've been considerate about the Bray girls."

"I should have be'n more considerate about fetchin' of you over," apologized Mrs. Trimble. "I've got my horse, an' you're lame-footed; 't is too far for you to come. But time does slip away with busy folks, an' I forgit a good deal I ought to remember."

"There's nobody more considerate than you be," protested Miss Rebecca Wright.

Mrs. Trimble made no answer, but took out her whip and gently touched the sorrel horse, who walked considerably faster, but did not think it worth while to trot. It was a long, round-about way to the house, farther down the road and up a lane.

"I never had any opinion of the Bray girls' father, leavin' 'em as he did," said Mrs. Trimble.

---

4. Board of officials who govern New England towns.
5. Town meetings are an annual tradition in New England.

6. At the meeting different residents offer to take in the poor for a sum of money paid by the town; the lowest bid is accepted.

"He was much praised in his time, though there was always some said his early life hadn't been up to the mark," explained her companion. "He was a great favorite of our then preacher, the Reverend Daniel Longbrother. They did a good deal for the parish, but they did it their own way. Deacon Bray was one that did his part in the repairs without urging. You know 't was in his time the first repairs was made, when they got out the old soundin'-board an' them handsome square pews. It cost an awful sight o' money, too. They hadn't done payin' up that debt when they set to alter it again an' git the walls frescoed. My grandmother was one that always spoke her mind right out, an' she was dreadful opposed to breakin' up the square pews where she'd always set. They was countin' up what 't would cost in parish meetin', an' she riz right up an' said 't wouldn't cost nothin' to let 'em stay, an' there wa'n't a house carpenter left in the parish that could do such nice work, an' time would come when the great-grandchildren would give their eye-teeth to have the old meetin'-house look just as it did then. But haul the inside to pieces they would and did."

"There come to be a real fight over it, didn't there?" agreed Mrs. Trimble soothingly. "Well, 't wa'n't good taste. I remember the old house well. I come here as a child to visit a cousin o' mother's, an' Mr. Trimble's folks was neighbors, an' we was drawed to each other then, young 's we was. Mr. Trimble spoke of it many's the time,—that first time he ever see me, in a leghorn hat with a feather; 't was one that mother had, an' pressed over."

"When I think of them old sermons that used to be preached in that old meetin'-house of all, I'm glad it's altered over, so's not to remind folks," said Miss Rebecca Wright, after a suitable pause. "Them old brimstone discourses, you know, Mis' Trimble. Preachers is far more reasonable, nowadays. Why, I set an' thought, last Sabbath, as I listened, that if old Mr. Longbrother an' Deacon Bray could hear the difference they'd crack the ground over 'em like pole beans, an' come right up 'long side their headstones."

Mrs. Trimble laughed heartily, and shook the reins three or four times by way of emphasis. "There's no gitting round you," she said, much pleased. "I should think Deacon Bray would want to rise, any way, if 't was so he could, an' knew how his poor girls was farin'. A man ought to provide for his folks he's got to leave behind him, specially if they're women. To be sure, they had their little home; but we've seen how, with all their industrious ways, they hadn't means to keep it. I s'pose he thought he'd got time enough to lay by, when he give so generous in collections; but he didn't lay by, an' there they be. He might have took lessons from the squirrels: even them little wild creatur's makes them their winter hoards, an' menfolks ought to know enough if squirrels does. 'Be just before you are generous:' that's what was always set for the B's in the copy-books, when I was to school, and it often runs through my mind."

" 'As for man, his days are as grass,'[7] that was for A; the two go well together," added Miss Rebecca Wright soberly. "My good gracious, ain't this a starved-lookin' place? It makes me ache to think them nice Bray girls has to brook it here."

The sorrel horse, though somewhat puzzled by an unexpected deviation from his homeward way, willingly came to a stand by the gnawed corner of the door-yard fence, which evidently served as hitching-place. Two or three ragged old hens were picking about the yard, and at last a face appeared at the kitchen window, tied up in a handkerchief, as if it were a case of toothache. By the time our friends reached the side door next this window, Mrs. Janes came disconsolately to open it for them, shutting it again as soon as possible, though the air felt more chilly inside the house.

"Take seats," said Mrs. Janes briefly. "You'll have to see me just as I be. I have been suffering these four days with the ague, and everything to do. Mr. Janes is to court, on the jury. 'T was inconvenient to spare him. I should be pleased to have you lay off your things."

Comfortable Mrs. Trimble looked about the cheerless kitchen, and could not think of anything to say; so she smiled blandly and shook her head in answer to the invitation. "We'll just set a few minutes with you, to pass the time o' day, an' then we must go in an' have a word with the Miss Brays, bein' old acquaintance. It ain't been so we could git to call on 'em before. I don't know 's you're acquainted with Miss R'becca Wright. She's been out of town a good deal."

"I heard she was stopping over to Plainfields with her brother's folks," replied Mrs. Janes, rocking herself with irregular motion, as she sat close to the stove. "Got back some time in the fall, I believe?"

"Yes'm," said Miss Rebecca, with an undue sense of guilt and conviction. "We've been to the installation[8] over to the East Parish, an' thought we'd stop in; we took this road home to see if 't was any better. How is the Miss Brays gettin' on?"

"They're well's common," answered Mrs. Janes grudgingly. "I was put out with Mr. Janes for fetchin' of 'em here, with all I've got to do, an' I own I was kind o' surly to 'em 'long to the first of it. He gits the money from the town, an' it helps him out; but he bid 'em off for five dollars a month, an' we can't do much for 'em at no such price as that. I went an' dealt with the selec'men, an' made 'em promise to find their firewood an' some other things extra. They was glad to get rid o' the matter the fourth time I went, an' would ha' promised 'most anything.

7. Psalm 103:15.
8. Ceremony in which a new pastor takes over a congregation.

But Mr. Janes don't keep me half the time in oven-wood, he's off so much, an' we was cramped o' room, any way. I have to store things up garrit[9] a good deal, an' that keeps me trampin' right through their room. I do the best for 'em I can, Mis' Trimble, but 't ain't so easy for me as 't is for you, with all your means to do with."

The poor woman looked pinched and miserable herself, though it was evident that she had no gift at house or home keeping. Mrs. Trimble's heart was wrung with pain, as she thought of the unwelcome inmates of such a place; but she held her peace bravely, while Miss Rebecca again gave some brief information in regard to the installation.

"You go right up them back stairs," the hostess directed at last. "I'm glad some o' you church folks has seen fit to come an' visit 'em. There ain't been nobody here this long spell, an' they've aged a sight since they come. They always send down a taste out of your baskets, Mis' Trimble, an' I relish it, I tell you. I'll shut the door after you, if you don't object. I feel every draught o' cold air."

"I've always heard she was a great hand to make a poor mouth. Wa'n't she from somewheres up Parsley way?" whispered Miss Rebecca, as they stumbled in the half-light.

"Poor meechin' body,[1] wherever she come from," replied Mrs. Trimble, as she knocked at the door.

There was silence for a moment after this unusual sound; then one of the Bray sisters opened the door. The eager guests stared into a small, low room, brown with age, and gray, too, as if former dust and cobwebs could not be made wholly to disappear. The two elderly women who stood there looked like captives. Their withered faces wore a look of apprehension, and the room itself was more bare and plain than was fitting to their evident refinement of character and self-respect. There was an uncovered small table in the middle of the floor, with some crackers on a plate; and, for some reason or other, this added a great deal to the general desolation.

But Miss Ann Bray, the elder sister, who carried her right arm in a sling, with piteously drooping fingers, gazed at the visitors with radiant joy. She had not seen them arrive.

The one window gave only the view at the back of the house, across the fields, and their coming was indeed a surprise. The next minute she was laughing and crying together. "Oh, sister!" she said, "if here ain't our dear Mis' Trimble!—an' my heart o' goodness, 't is 'Becca Wright, too! What dear good creatur's you be! I've felt all day as if something good was goin' to happen, an' was just sayin' to myself 't was most sundown now, but I wouldn't let on to Mandany I'd give up hope quite yet.

9. I.e, in the attic.   1. Skulking person.

You see, the scissors stuck in the floor this very mornin' an' it's always a reliable sign. There, I've got to kiss ye both again!"

"I don't know where we can all set," lamented sister Mandana. "There ain't but the one chair an' the bed; t' other chair's too rickety; an' we've been promised another these ten days; but first they've forgot it, an' next Mis' Janes can't spare it,—one excuse an' another. I am goin' to git a stump o' wood an' nail a board on to it, when I can git outdoor again," said Mandana, in a plaintive voice. "There, I ain't goin' to complain o' nothin', now you've come," she added; and the guests sat down, Mrs. Trimble, as was proper, in the one chair.

"We've sat on the bed many's the time with you, 'Becca, an' talked over our girl nonsense, ain't we? You know where 't was—in the little back bedroom we had when we was girls, an' used to peek out at our beaux through the strings o' mornin'-glories," laughed Ann Bray delightedly, her thin face shining more and more with joy. "I brought some o' them mornin'-glory seeds along when we come away, we'd raised 'em so many years; an' we got 'em started all right, but the hens found 'em out. I declare I chased them poor hens, foolish as 't was; but the mornin'-glories I'd counted on a sight to remind me o' home. You see, our debts was so large, after my long sickness an' all, that we didn't feel 't was right to keep back anything we could help from the auction."

It was impossible for any one to speak for a moment or two; the sisters felt their own uprooted condition afresh, and their guests for the first time really comprehended the piteous contrast between that neat little village house, which now seemed a palace of comfort, and this cold, unpainted upper room in the remote Janes farmhouse. It was an unwelcome thought to Mrs. Trimble that the well-to-do town of Hampden could provide no better for its poor than this, and her round face flushed with resentment and the shame of personal responsibility. "The girls shall be well settled in the village before another winter, if I pay their board myself," she made an inward resolution, and took another almost tearful look at the broken stove, the miserable bed, and the sisters' one hair-covered trunk, on which Mandana was sitting. But the poor place was filled with a golden spirit of hospitality.

Rebecca was again discoursing eloquently of the installation; it was so much easier to speak of general subjects, and the sisters had evidently been longing to hear some news. Since the late summer they had not been to church, and presently Mrs. Trimble asked the reason.

"Now, don't you go to pouring out our woes, Mandy!" begged little old Ann, looking shy and almost girlish, and as if she insisted upon playing that life was still all before them and all pleasure. "Don't you go to spoilin' their visit with our complaints! They know well's we do that changes must come, an' we'd been so wonted to our home things that this come hard at first; but then they felt for us, I know just as well's can

be. 'T will soon be summer again, an' 't is real pleasant right out in the
fields here, when there ain't too hot a spell. I've got to know a sight o'
singin' birds since we come."

"Give me the folks I've always known," sighed the younger sister,
who looked older than Miss Ann, and less even-tempered. "You may
have your birds, if you want 'em. I do re'lly long to go to meetin' an' see
folks go by up the aisle. Now, I will speak of it, Ann, whatever you say.
We need, each of us, a pair o' good stout shoes an' rubbers,—ours are
all wore out; an' we've asked an' asked, an' they never think to bring
'em, an' "—

Poor old Mandana, on the trunk, covered her face with her arms and
sobbed aloud. The elder sister stood over her, and patted her on the thin
shoulder like a child, and tried to comfort her. It crossed Mrs. Trimble's
mind that it was not the first time one had wept and the other had
comforted. The sad scene must have been repeated many times in that
long, drear winter. She would see them forever after in her mind as
fixed as a picture, and her own tears fell fast.

"You didn't see Mis' Janes's cunning little boy, the next one to the
baby, did you?" asked Ann Bray, turning round quickly at last, and
going cheerfully on with the conversation. "Now, hush, Mandy, dear;
they'll think you're childish! He's a dear, friendly little creatur', an' likes
to stay with us a good deal, though we feel 's if it was too cold for him,
now we are waitin' to get us more wood."

"When I think of the acres o' woodland in this town!" groaned Rebecca Wright. "I believe I'm goin' to preach next Sunday, 'stead o' the
minister, an' I'll make the sparks fly. I've always heard the saying,
'What's everybody's business is nobody's business,' an' I've come to
believe it."

"Now, don't you, 'Becca. You've happened on a kind of a poor time
with us, but we've got more belongings than you see here, an' a good
large cluset, where we can store those things there ain't room to have
about. You an' Mis' Trimble have happened on a kind of poor day, you
know. Soon's I git me some stout shoes an' rubbers, as Mandy says, I
can fetch home plenty o' little dry boughs o' pine; you remember I was
always a great hand to roam in the woods? If we could only have a front
room, so 't we could look out on the road an' see passin', an' was shod
for meetin', I don' know's we should complain. Now we're just goin' to
give you what we've got, an' make out with a good welcome. We make
more tea 'n we want in the mornin', an' then let the fire go down, since
't has been so mild. We've got a *good* cluset" (disappearing as she
spoke), "an' I know this to be good tea, 'cause it's some o' yourn, Mis'
Trimble. An' here's our sprigged chiny cups that R'becca knows by
sight, if Mis' Trimble don't. We kep' out four of 'em, an' put the even
half dozen with the rest of the auction stuff. I've often wondered who'd

got 'em, but I never asked, for fear 't would be somebody that would distress us. They was mother's, you know.''

The four cups were poured, and the little table pushed to the bed, where Rebecca Wright still sat, and Mandana, wiping her eyes, came and joined her. Mrs. Trimble sat in her chair at the end, and Ann trotted about the room in pleased content for a while, and in and out of the closet, as if she still had much to do; then she came and stood opposite Mrs. Trimble. She was very short and small, and there was no painful sense of her being obliged to stand. The four cups were not quite full of cold tea, but there was a clean old tablecloth folded double, and a plate with three pairs of crackers neatly piled, and a small—it must be owned, a very small—piece of hard white cheese. Then, for a treat, in a glass dish, there was a little preserved peach, the last—Miss Rebecca knew it instinctively—of the household stores brought from their old home. It was very sugary, this bit of peach; and as she helped her guests and sister Mandy, Miss Ann Bray said, half unconsciously, as she often had said with less reason in the old days, "Our preserves ain't so good as usual this year; this is beginning to candy." Both the guests protested, while Rebecca added that the taste of it carried her back, and made her feel young again. The Brays had always managed to keep one or two peach-trees alive in their corner of a garden. "I've been keeping this preserve for a treat," said her friend. "I'm glad to have you eat some, 'Becca. Last summer I often wished you was home an' could come an' see us, 'stead o' being away off to Plainfields.''

The crackers did not taste too dry. Miss Ann took the last of the peach on her own cracker; there could not have been quite a small spoonful, after the others were helped, but she asked them first if they would not have some more. Then there was a silence, and in the silence a wave of tender feeling rose high in the hearts of the four elderly women. At this moment the setting sun flooded the poor plain room with light; the unpainted wood was all of a golden-brown, and Ann Bray, with her gray hair and aged face, stood at the head of the table in a kind of aureole. Mrs. Trimble's face was all aquiver as she looked at her; she thought of the text about two or three being gathered together,[2] and was half afraid.

"I believe we ought to 've asked Mis' Janes if she wouldn't come up," said Ann. "She's real good feelin', but[3] she's had it very hard, an' gits discouraged. I can't find that she's ever had anything real pleasant to look back to, as we have. There, next time we'll make a good heartenin' time for her too.''

The sorrel horse had taken a long nap by the gnawed fence-rail, and the cool air after sundown made him impatient to be gone. The two friends

2. Jesus's words in Matthew 18:20: "For where two or three have gathered together in my name, I am there among them."
3. I.e., kindly, well-meaning.

jolted homeward in the gathering darkness, through the stiffening mud, and neither Mrs. Trimble nor Rebecca Wright said a word until they were out of sight as well as out of sound of the Janes house. Time must elapse before they could reach a more familiar part of the road and resume conversation on its natural level.

"I consider myself to blame," insisted Mrs. Trimble at last. "I haven't no words of accusation for nobody else, an' I ain't one to take comfort in calling names to the board o' selec'men. I make no reproaches, an' I take it all on my own shoulders; but I'm goin' to stir about me, I tell you! I shall begin early to-morrow. They're goin' back to their own house,—it's been standin' empty all winter,—an' the town's goin' to give 'em the rent an' what firewood they need; it won't come to more than the board's payin' out now. An' you an' me'll take this same horse an' wagon, an' ride an' go afoot by turns, an' git means enough together to buy back their furniture an' whatever was sold at that plaguey auction; an' then we'll put it all back, an' tell 'em they've got to move to a new place, an' just carry 'em right back again where they come from. An' don't you never tell, R'becca, but here I be a widow woman, layin' up what I make from my farm for nobody knows who, an' I'm goin' to do for them Bray girls all I'm a mind to. I should be sca't⁴ to wake up in heaven, an' hear anybody there ask how the Bray girls was. Don't talk to me about the town o' Hampden, an' don't ever let me hear the name o' town poor! I'm ashamed to go home an' see what's set out for supper. I wish I'd brought 'em right along."

"I was goin' to ask if we couldn't git the new doctor to go up an' do somethin' for poor Ann's arm," said Miss Rebecca. "They say he's very smart. If she could get so's to braid straw or hook rugs again, she'd soon be earnin' a little somethin'. An' may be he could do somethin' for Mandy's eyes. They did use to live so neat an' ladylike. Somehow I couldn't speak to tell 'em there that 't was I bought them six best cups an' saucers, time of the auction; they went very low, as everything else did, an' I thought I could save it some other way. They shall have 'em back an' welcome. You're real whole-hearted, Mis' Trimble. I expect Ann'll be sayin' that her father's child'n wa'n't goin' to be left desolate, an' that all the bread he cast on the water's comin' back through you."⁵

"I don't care what she says, dear creatur'!" exclaimed Mrs. Trimble. "I'm full o' regrets I took time for that installation, an' set there seep on in a lot o' talk this whole day long, except for its kind of bringin' us to the Bray girls. I wish to my heart 't was to-morrow mornin' a'ready, an' I a-startin' for the selec'men."

1890

4. Scared.
5. Ecclesiastes 11:1: "Cast thy bread upon the waters, for thou shalt find it after many days."

KATE CHOPIN
1851–1904

When *The Awakening*, Kate Chopin's frank exploration of a late-nineteenth-century woman's growth toward sexual and emotional independence, first appeared, critics assailed it. The novel tells "an essentially vulgar story," declared one writer; "it is not a pleasant picture of soul-dissection, take it anyway you like," complained another; though "handled with a cunning craft," observed a third, "it is sad and mad and bad." Within months, the libraries of Chopin's native city, St. Louis, had refused to carry the book, and the author herself was actually rebuffed by a number of acquaintances, though she had attempted to defend herself by playfully explaining in a newspaper article that "I never dreamed of Mrs. Pontellier [the novel's heroine] making such a mess of things and working out her own damnation as she did." In fact, though *The Awakening* has by now been recognized as an American classic, Chopin was never to reap the rewards of her achievement. In the years between 1899, when the book was published, and 1904, when she died, she earned hardly any royalties from the novel; her third collection of short stories was rejected by the firm that had published *The Awakening*; and—no doubt disheartened by these failures —she was able to compose only a few tales and poems. For more than three decades after Chopin's death, moreover, her allegedly scandalous masterpiece fell into oblivion; indeed, although one critic attempted to revive the book in the 1930s, *The Awakening* was not really to be recovered for readers until the 1960s.

Even as he attacked the novel, however, at least one contemporary reviewer had noted that *The Awakening* "is hardly the kind of a book some people would look for from" Kate Chopin. A decade later, another literary observer was similarly bemused: "To think of Kate Chopin, who once contented herself with mild yarns about genteel Creole life . . . blowing us a hot blast like that!" The alarm of such critics was not surprising, for the writer who started life as Katherine O'Flaherty would not, at least on the surface, have seemed likely to produce so controversial a work. Born in St. Louis, she was the well-bred daughter of a wealthy family. On her mother's side, she was descended from French Creole aristocrats, while her father was an Irish immigrant who had become a singularly successful merchant before his death in 1855. Coming from such a background, the young Kate received, at home, a typically Victorian training in decorum as well as, at school, a rigorous Catholic education. In 1868, when she made her debut in society, she became one of the belles of St. Louis, and after she married Oscar Chopin, a Creole cotton trader, in 1870, she was evidently a happy and dutiful wife as well as the devoted mother of six children. The young couple had first settled in New Orleans, and then, with their family, they moved to a plantation near Cloutierville, in Natchitoches (pronounced Nack-uh-tush) parish, an area Kate Chopin was eventually to memorialize in a series of brilliant stories and sketches. When Oscar Chopin died of swamp fever in 1883, his bereaved wife was said to be "inconsolable."

Painful as it was, however, Oscar Chopin's untimely death thrust his widow into serious literary activity. She had apparently always "scribbled"—a diary as well as some sketches and poems from her youth are still held by the St. Louis Historical Society—but when she returned to her birthplace with her children, she began to write in earnest. Yet though they were at first received as the "mild yarns about genteel Creole life" which critics were to prefer to *The Awakening*, even Chopin's earliest stories were more radical than many readers understood, suggesting that both the charming debutante and the dutiful wife had always harbored a streak of rebelliousness.

Kate Chopin's family doctor, Frederick Kolbenheyer, had become a very close friend after she resettled in St. Louis. An intellectual and an agnostic, he encouraged her to read the works of such pioneering Victorian thinkers as the scientists Charles Darwin and Thomas Henry Huxley, and to renounce most of the main tenets of Catholicism. In addition, she had begun to read extensively in contemporary fiction, studying, on the one hand, the works of the American regionalists Sarah Orne Jewett and Mary E. Wilkins Freeman, and, on the other hand, the works of the French naturalists Emile Zola, Gustave Flaubert, and Guy de Maupassant. De Maupassant, in particular, had become one of her literary idols, an artist whose defiance of tradition and independence of vision she much admired. If one studies her earliest fictions carefully, it becomes clear that, even at the beginning of her literary career, she was herself defiantly striving to achieve just such philosophical and aesthetic independence. A number of her tales, for instance, examine the inequities of conventional marriage; some explore the arbitrary race distinctions that characterize Southern culture; others question the class divisions that mark even so simple a world as that of Natchitoches parish; finally, one or two actually imagine alternative ways in which society might be structured in order to allow individuals, especially women, more opportunities for emotional, sexual, and intellectual freedom.

But of course it is in *The Awakening* that Chopin most openly and vividly dramatized her own—as well as her heroine's—desire for freedom. Setting her novel in the Louisiana resort town of Grand Isle, where she herself had spent many summers as a young married woman, and in the kind of bourgeois New Orleans neighborhood where she had also lived during her marriage, she used a distinctively turn-of-the-century myth of female sexual independence to show how her protagonist, Edna Pontellier, was defined, and ultimately destroyed, by a society that could not conceive of allowing a woman—especially a wife and mother—the kind of autonomy for which she longed. Specifically, Chopin employed not only realistic strategies learned from such cherished precursors as Jewett and de Maupassant but also images of desire and of the body's holiness drawn from significant literary ancestors like the English poet Algernon Charles Swinburne and the American poet Walt Whitman to explore ideas about the relationship between female sexuality and female creativity that were, in her era, almost entirely forbidden—at least to women writers.

For Edna Pontellier, who explains to her lover that "I give myself where I please," a supposedly "proper" lady has as much right to experience desire as her gentlemanly counterpart might; similarly, for Edna a lady has as much right to feel ambition as might any male peer. Nevertheless, the structure of Chopin's novel is profoundly pessimistic about such desires and ambitions: if Aphrodite, the Greek goddess of love (to whom Edna is at one point in the book compared), were reborn as a late Victorian woman, Chopin suggests, Edna's fate might be *her* fate. Thus, though a number of critics, from the earliest reviewers to the most recent scholars, have felt that Chopin's Edna Pontellier was (in the words of the American novelist Willa Cather) no more than "a Creole Bovary"—a New World revision of Gustave Flaubert's foolishly sentimental Madame Bovary—*The Awakening* seems to elaborate a shadowy story about female erotic freedom and even about feminist emotional independence.

Whether or not Chopin's final illness was related to the failure of her book, her death in her early fifties represented a serious loss to American literature, for when she wrote *The Awakening* she was clearly at the height of her extraordinary power. Yet, despite the pain that evidently put an end to her literary career, Chopin's passionate fantasy about her heroine's fantasizings has impressed a number of readers, especially since 1969, when the scholar Per Seyersted produced a definitive two-volume edition of her works which reintroduced the novel to a wide audience of teachers, critics, and historians. For, in a sense, Edna's story, with its recurrent sea imagery and its persistent emphasis on swimming as a metaphor for autonomy, can be seen as an early and partial but deeply desirous version of a vision that the American writer Muriel Rukeyser was to fully and triumphantly elaborate more than half a century later in a poem called *The Birth of Venus*—a vision of the goddess of love as a freely sensual woman "born in a / tidal wave of the father's overthrow, / the old rule killed and its mutilated sex."

The Awakening

I

A green and yellow parrot, which hung in a cage outside the door, kept repeating over and over:

"*Allez vous-en! Allez vous-en! Sapristi!*[1] That's all right!"

He could speak a little Spanish, and also a language which nobody understood, unless it was the mocking-bird that hung on the other side of the door, whistling his fluty notes out upon the breeze with maddening persistence.

Mr. Pontellier, unable to read his newspaper with any degree of comfort, arose with an expression and an exclamation of disgust. He walked down the gallery and across the narrow "bridges" which connected the Lebrun cottages one with the other. He had been seated before the door of the main house. The parrot and the mocking-bird were the property of Madame Lebrun, and they had the right to make all the noise they wished. Mr. Pontellier had the privilege of quitting their society when they ceased to be entertaining.

He stopped before the door of his own cottage, which was the fourth

---

1. "Go away! Go away! For God's sake!" Notes to *The Awakening* owe much to the Norton Critical Edition prepared by Margaret Culley and to the text prepared by Ronald Gottesman in *The Norton Anthology of American Literature*.

one from the main building and next to the last. Seating himself in a wicker rocker which was there, he once more applied himself to the task of reading the newspaper. The day was Sunday; the paper was a day old. The Sunday papers had not yet reached Grand Isle.[2] He was already acquainted with the market reports, and he glanced restlessly over the editorials and bits of news which he had not had time to read before quitting New Orleans the day before.

Mr. Pontellier wore eye-glasses. He was a man of forty, of medium height and slender build; he stooped a little. His hair was brown and straight, parted on one side. His beard was neatly and closely trimmed.

Once in a while he withdrew his glance from the newspaper and looked about him. There was more noise than ever over at the house. The main building was called "the house," to distinguish it from the cottages. The chattering and whistling birds were still at it. Two young girls, the Farival twins, were playing a duet from "Zampa"[3] upon the piano. Madame Lebrun was bustling in and out, giving orders in a high key to a yard-boy whenever she got inside the house, and directions in an equally high voice to a dining-room servant whenever she got outside. She was a fresh, pretty woman, clad always in white with elbow sleeves. Her starched skirts crinkled as she came and went. Farther down, before one of the cottages, a lady in black was walking demurely up and down, telling her beads. A good many persons of the *pension* had gone over to the *Chênière Caminada*[4] in Beaudelet's lugger to hear mass. Some young people were out under the water-oaks playing croquet. Mr. Pontellier's two children were there—sturdy little fellows of four and five. A quadroon[5] nurse followed them about with a far-away, meditative air.

Mr. Pontellier finally lit a cigar and began to smoke, letting the paper drag idly from his hand. He fixed his gaze upon a white sunshade[6] that was advancing at snail's pace from the beach. He could see it plainly between the gaunt trunks of the water-oaks and across the stretch of yellow camomile. The gulf looked far away melting hazily into the blue of the horizon. The sunshade continued to approach slowly. Beneath its pink-lined shelter were his wife, Mrs. Pontellier, and young Robert Lebrun. When they reached the cottage, the two seated themselves with some appearance of fatigue upon the step of the porch, facing each other, each leaning against a supporting post.

"What folly! to bathe[7] at such an hour in such heat!" exclaimed Mr. Pontellier. He himself had taken a plunge at daylight. That was why the morning seemed long to him.

---

2. Resort island, between the Gulf of Mexico and Caminada Bay, south of New Orleans.
3. Romantic opera by Louis Hérold (1791–1833).
4. Island between Grande Isle and the Louisiana coast; "pension": bed-and-board hotel; "lugger": passenger boat.
5. I.e., with one-fourth ("quad") black ancestry.
6. Parasol.
7. Swim.

"You are burnt beyond recognition," he added, looking at his wife as one looks at a valuable piece of personal property which has suffered some damage. She held up her hands, strong, shapely hands, and surveyed them critically, drawing up her lawn[8] sleeves above the wrists. Looking at them reminded her of her rings, which she had given to her husband before leaving for the beach. She silently reached out to him, and he, understanding, took the rings from his vest pocket and dropped them into her open palm. She slipped them upon her fingers; then clasping her knees, she looked across at Robert and began to laugh. The rings sparkled upon her fingers. He sent back an answering smile.

"What is it?" asked Pontellier, looking lazily and amused from one to the other. It was some utter nonsense; some adventure out there in the water, and they both tried to relate it at once. It did not seem half so amusing when told. They realized this, and so did Mr. Pontellier. He yawned and stretched himself. Then he got up, saying he had half a mind to go over to Klein's hotel and play a game of billiards.

"Come go along, Lebrun," he proposed to Robert. But Robert admitted quite frankly that he preferred to stay where he was and talk to Mrs. Pontellier.

"Well, send him about his business when he bores you, Edna," instructed her husband as he prepared to leave.

"Here, take the umbrella," she exclaimed, holding it out to him. He accepted the sunshade, and lifting it over his head descended the steps and walked away.

"Coming back to dinner?" his wife called after him. He halted a moment and shrugged his shoulders. He felt in his vest pocket; there was a ten-dollar bill there. He did not know; perhaps he would return for the early dinner and perhaps he would not. It all depended upon the company which he found over at Klein's and the size of "the game." He did not say this, but she understood it, and laughed, nodding good-by to him.

Both children wanted to follow their father when they saw him starting out. He kissed them and promised to bring them back bonbons and peanuts.

II

Mrs. Pontellier's eyes were quick and bright; they were a yellowish brown, about the color of her hair. She had a way of turning them swiftly upon an object and holding them there as if lost in some inward maze of contemplation or thought.

Her eyebrows were a shade darker than her hair. They were thick

8. Fine, sheer muslin.

and almost horizontal, emphasizing the depth of her eyes. She was rather handsome than beautiful. Her face was captivating by reason of a certain frankness of expression and a contradictory subtle play of features. Her manner was engaging.

Robert rolled a cigarette. He smoked cigarettes because he could not afford cigars, he said. He had a cigar in his pocket which Mr. Pontellier had presented him with, and he was saving it for his after-dinner smoke.

This seemed quite proper and natural on his part. In coloring he was not unlike his companion. A clean-shaven face made the resemblance more pronounced than it would otherwise have been. There rested no shadow of care upon his open countenance. His eyes gathered in and reflected the light and languor of the summer day.

Mrs. Pontellier reached over for a palmleaf fan that lay on the porch and began to fan herself, while Robert sent between his lips light puffs from his cigarette. They chatted incessantly: about the things around them; their amusing adventure out in the water—it had again assumed its entertaining aspect; about the wind, the trees, the people who had gone to the *Chênière*; about the children playing croquet under the oaks, and the Farival twins, who were now performing the overture to "The Poet and Peasant."[9]

Robert talked a good deal about himself. He was very young, and did not know any better. Mrs. Pontellier talked a little about herself for the same reason. Each was interested in what the other said. Robert spoke of his intention to go to Mexico in the autumn, where fortune awaited him. He was always intending to go to Mexico, but some way never got there. Meanwhile he held on to his modest position in a mercantile house in New Orleans, where an equal familiarity with English, French and Spanish gave him no small value as a clerk and correspondent.

He was spending his summer vacation, as he always did, with his mother at Grand Isle. In former times, before Robert could remember, "the house" had been a summer luxury of the Lebruns. Now flanked by its dozen or more cottages, which were always filled with exclusive visitors from the "*Quartier Français*,"[1] it enabled Madame Lebrun to maintain the easy and comfortable existence which appeared to be her birthright.

Mrs. Pontellier talked about her father's Mississippi plantation and her girlhood home in the old Kentucky blue-grass country. She was an American woman, with a small infusion of French which seemed to have been lost in dilution. She read a letter from her sister, who was away in the East, and who had engaged herself to be married. Robert

9. Operetta by Franz von Suppé (1819–1895).
1. The French Quarter of New Orleans, first settled by the French in the early eighteenth century and occupied at this time by wealthy, older families.

was interested, and wanted to know what manner of girls the sisters were, what the father was like, and how long the mother had been dead.

When Mrs. Pontellier folded the letter it was time for her to dress for the early dinner.

"I see Léonce isn't coming back," she said, with a glance in the direction whence her husband had disappeared. Robert supposed he was not, as there were a good many New Orleans club men over at Klein's.

When Mrs. Pontellier left him to enter her room, the young man descended the steps and strolled over toward the croquet players, where, during the half-hour before dinner, he amused himself with the little Pontellier children, who were very fond of him.

III

It was eleven o'clock that night when Mr. Pontellier returned from Klein's hotel. He was in an excellent humor, in high spirits, and very talkative. His entrance awoke his wife, who was in bed and fast asleep when he came in. He talked to her while he undressed, telling her anecdotes and bits of news and gossip that he had gathered during the day. From his trousers pockets he took a fistful of crumpled bank notes and a good deal of silver coin, which he piled on the bureau indiscriminately with keys, knife, handkerchief, and whatever else happened to be in his pockets. She was overcome with sleep, and answered him with little half utterances.

He thought it very discouraging that his wife, who was the sole object of his existence, evinced so little interest in things which concerned him and valued so little his conversation.

Mr. Pontellier had forgotten the bonbons and peanuts for the boys. Notwithstanding he loved them very much, and went into the adjoining room where they slept to take a look at them and make sure that they were resting comfortably. The result of his investigation was far from satisfactory. He turned and shifted the youngsters about in bed. One of them began to kick and talk about a basket full of crabs.

Mr. Pontellier returned to his wife with the information that Raoul had a high fever and needed looking after. Then he lit a cigar and went and sat near the open door to smoke it.

Mrs. Pontellier was quite sure Raoul had no fever. He had gone to bed perfectly well, she said, and nothing had ailed him all day. Mr. Pontellier was too well acquainted with fever symptoms to be mistaken. He assured her the child was consuming[2] at that moment in the next room.

He reproached his wife with her inattention, her habitual neglect of

---

2. I.e., "consumptive," feverish.

the children. If it was not a mother's place to look after children, whose on earth was it? He himself had his hands full with his brokerage business. He could not be in two places at once; making a living for his family on the street, and staying at home to see that no harm befell them. He talked in a monotonous, insistent way.

Mrs. Pontellier sprang out of bed and went into the next room. She soon came back and sat on the edge of the bed, leaning her head down on the pillow. She said nothing, and refused to answer her husband when he questioned her. When his cigar was smoked out he went to bed, and in half a minute he was fast asleep.

Mrs. Pontellier was by that time thoroughly awake. She began to cry a little, and wiped her eyes on the sleeve of her *peignoir*. Blowing out the candle, which her husband had left burning, she slipped her bare feet into a pair of satin *mules* at the foot of the bed and went out on the porch, where she sat down in the wicker chair and began to rock gently to and fro.

It was then past midnight. The cottages were all dark. A single faint light gleamed out from the hallway of the house. There was no sound abroad except the hooting of an old owl in the top of a water-oak, and the everlasting voice of the sea, that was not uplifted at that soft hour. It broke like a mournful lullaby upon the night.

The tears came so fast to Mrs. Pontellier's eyes that the damp sleeve of her *peignoir* no longer served to dry them. She was holding the back of her chair with one hand; her loose sleeve had slipped almost to the shoulder of her uplifted arm. Turning, she thrust her face, steaming and wet, into the bend of her arm, and she went on crying there, not caring any longer to dry her face, her eyes, her arms. She could not have told why she was crying. Such experiences as the foregoing were not uncommon in her married life. They seemed never before to have weighed much against the abundance of her husband's kindness and a uniform devotion which had come to be tacit and self-understood.

An indescribable oppression, which seemed to generate in some unfamiliar part of her consciousness, filled her whole being with a vague anguish. It was like a shadow, like a mist passing across her soul's summer day. It was strange and unfamiliar; it was a mood. She did not sit there inwardly upbraiding her husband, lamenting at Fate, which had directed her footsteps to the path which they had taken. She was just having a good cry all to herself. The mosquitoes made merry over her, biting her firm, round arms and nipping at her bare insteps.

The little stinging, buzzing imps succeeded in dispelling a mood which might have held her there in the darkness half a night longer.

The following morning Mr. Pontellier was up in good time to take the rockaway[3] which was to convey him to the steamer at the wharf. He

3. Four-wheeled carriage.

was returning to the city to his business, and they would not see him again at the Island till the coming Saturday. He had regained his composure, which seemed to have been somewhat impaired the night before. He was eager to be gone, as he looked forward to a lively week in Carondelet Street.[4]

Mr. Pontellier gave his wife half the money which he had brought away from Klein's hotel the evening before. She liked money as well as most women, and accepted it with no little satisfaction.

"It will buy a handsome wedding present for Sister Janet!" she exclaimed, smoothing out the bills as she counted them one by one.

"Oh! we'll treat Sister Janet better than that, my dear," he laughed, as he prepared to kiss her good-by.

The boys were tumbling about, clinging to his legs, imploring that numerous things be brought back to them. Mr. Pontellier was a great favorite, and ladies, men, children, even nurses, were always on hand to say good-by to him. His wife stood smiling and waving, the boys shouting, as he disappeared in the old rockaway down the sandy road.

A few days later a box arrived for Mrs. Pontellier from New Orleans. It was from her husband. It was filled with *friandises*, with luscious and toothsome bits—the finest of fruits, *pâtés*, a rare bottle or two, delicious syrups, and bonbons in abundance.

Mrs. Pontellier was always very generous with the contents of such a box; she was quite used to receiving them when away from home. The *pâtés* and fruit were brought to the dining-room; the bonbons were passed around. And the ladies, selecting with dainty and discriminating fingers and a little greedily, all declared that Mr. Pontellier was the best husband in the world. Mrs. Pontellier was forced to admit that she knew of none better.

IV

It would have been a difficult matter for Mr. Pontellier to define to his own satisfaction or any one else's wherein his wife failed in her duty toward their children. It was something which he felt rather than perceived, and he never voiced the feeling without subsequent regret and ample atonement.

If one of the little Pontellier boys took a tumble whilst at play, he was not apt to rush crying to his mother's arms for comfort; he would more likely pick himself up, wipe the water out of his eyes and the sand out of his mouth, and go on playing. Tots as they were, they pulled together and stood their ground in childish battles with doubled fists and uplifted voices, which usually prevailed against the other mother-tots. The quadroon nurse was looked upon as a huge encumbrance, only good to

4. The financial center of New Orleans.

button up waists and panties and to brush and part hair; since it seemed to be a law of society that hair must be parted and brushed.

In short, Mrs. Pontellier was not a mother-woman. The mother-women seemed to prevail that summer at Grand Isle. It was easy to know them, fluttering about with extended, protecting wings when any harm, real or imaginary, threatened their precious brood. They were women who idolized their children, worshipped their husbands, and esteemed it a holy privilege to efface themselves as individuals and grow wings as ministering angels.

Many of them were delicious in the rôle; one of them was the embodiment of every womanly grace and charm. If her husband did not adore her, he was a brute, deserving of death by slow torture. Her name was Adèle Ratignolle. There are no words to describe her save the old ones that have served so often to picture the bygone heroine of romance and the fair lady of our dreams. There was nothing subtle or hidden about her charms; her beauty was all there, flaming and apparent: the spun-gold hair that comb nor confining pin could restrain; the blue eyes that were like nothing but sapphires; two lips that pouted, that were so red one could only think of cherries or some other delicious crimson fruit in looking at them. She was growing a little stout, but it did not seem to detract an iota from the grace of every step, pose, gesture. One would not have wanted her white neck a mite less full or her beautiful arms more slender. Never were hands more exquisite than hers, and it was a joy to look at them when she threaded her needle or adjusted her gold thimble to her taper[5] middle finger as she sewed away on the little night-drawers or fashioned a bodice or a bib.

Madame Ratignolle was very fond of Mrs. Pontellier, and often she took her sewing and went over to sit with her in the afternoons. She was sitting there the afternoon of the day the boy arrived from New Orleans. She had possession of the rocker, and she was busily engaged in sewing upon a diminutive pair of night drawers.

She had brought the pattern of the drawers for Mrs. Pontellier to cut out—a marvel of construction, fashioned to enclose a baby's body so effectually that only two small eyes might look out from the garment, like an Eskimo's. They were designed for winter wear, when treacherous drafts came down chimneys and insidious currents of deadly cold found their way through key-holes.

Mrs. Pontellier's mind was quite at rest concerning the present material needs of her children, and she could not see the use of anticipating and making winter night garments the subject of her summer meditations. But she did not want to appear unamiable and uninterested, so she had brought forth newspapers which she spread upon the floor of

5. I.e., tapered.

the gallery, and under Madame Ratignolle's directions she had cut a pattern of the impervious garment.

Robert was there, seated as he had been the Sunday before, and Mrs. Pontellier also occupied her former position on the upper step, leaning listlessly against the post. Beside her was a box of bonbons, which she held out at intervals to Madame Ratignolle.

That lady seemed at a loss to make a selection, but finally settled upon a stick of nugat, wondering if it were not too rich; whether it could possibly hurt her. Madame Ratignolle had been married seven years. About every two years she had a baby. At that time she had three babies, and was beginning to think of a fourth one. She was always talking about her "condition." Her "condition" was in no way apparent, and no one would have known a thing about it but for her persistence in making it the subject of conversation.

Robert started to reassure her, asserting that he had known a lady who had subsisted upon nugat during the entire—but seeing the color mount into Mrs. Pontellier's face he checked himself and changed the subject.

Mrs. Pontellier, though she had married a Creole,[6] was not thoroughly at home in the society of Creoles; never before had she been thrown so intimately among them. There were only Creoles that summer at Lebrun's. They all knew each other, and felt like one large family, among whom existed the most amicable relations. A characteristic which distinguished them and which impressed Mrs. Pontellier most forcibly was their entire absence of prudery. Their freedom of expression was at first incomprehensible to her, though she had no difficulty in reconciling it with a lofty chastity which in the Creole woman seems to be inborn and unmistakable.

Never would Edna Pontellier forget the shock with which she heard Madame Ratignolle relating to old Monsieur Farival the harrowing story of one of her *accouchements*,[7] withholding no intimate detail. She was growing accustomed to like shocks, but she could not keep the mounting color back from her cheeks. Oftener than once her coming had interrupted the droll story with which Robert was entertaining some amused group of married women.

A book had gone the rounds of the *pension*. When it came her turn to read it, she did so with profound astonishment. She felt moved to read the book in secret and solitude, though none of the others had done so—to hide it from view at the sound of approaching footsteps. It was openly criticised and freely discussed at table. Mrs. Pontellier gave over being astonished, and concluded that wonders would never cease.

---

6. Descended from the original French and Spanish settlers of New Orleans, and thus, at this time, an aristocrat.
7. Childbirth.

V

They formed a congenial group sitting there that summer afternoon
—Madame Ratignolle sewing away, often stopping to relate a story or
incident with much expressive gesture of her perfect hands: Robert and
Mrs. Pontellier sitting idle, exchanging occasional words, glances or
smiles which indicated a certain advanced stage of intimacy and *cama-
raderie.*[8]

He had lived in her shadow during the past month. No one thought
anything of it. Many had predicted that Robert would devote himself to
Mrs. Pontellier when he arrived. Since the age of fifteen, which was
eleven years before, Robert each summer at Grand Isle had constituted
himself the devoted attendant of some fair dame or damsel. Sometimes
it was a young girl, again a widow; but as often as not it was some interesting married woman.

For two consecutive seasons he lived in the sunlight of Mademoiselle Duvigné's presence. But she died between summers; then Robert
posed as an inconsolable, prostrating himself at the feet of Madame
Ratignolle for whatever crumbs of sympathy and comfort she might be
pleased to vouchsafe.

Mrs. Pontellier liked to sit and gaze at her fair companion as she
might look upon a faultless Madonna.

"Could any one fathom the cruelty beneath that fair exterior?"
murmured Robert. "She knew that I adored her once, and she let me
adore her. It was 'Robert, come; go; stand up; sit down; do this; do that;
see if the baby sleeps; my thimble, please, that I left God knows where.
Come and read Daudet[9] to me while I sew.'"

"*Par exemple!*"[1] I never had to ask. You were always there under my
feet, like a troublesome cat."

"You mean like an adoring dog. And just as soon as Ratignolle appeared on the scene, then it *was* like a dog. '*Passez! Adieu! Allez vous-
en!*'"[2]

"Perhaps I feared to make Alphonse jealous," she interjoined, with
excessive naïveté. That made them all laugh. The right hand jealous of
the left! The heart jealous of the soul! But for that matter, the Creole
husband is never jealous; with him the gangrene passion is one which
has become dwarfed by disuse.

Meanwhile Robert, addressing Mrs. Pontellier, continued to tell of
his one time hopeless passion for Madame Ratignolle; of sleepless
nights, of consuming flames till the very sea sizzled when he took his

---

8. Friendship.
9. Alphonse Daudet (1840–1887), French
novelist.

1. "For goodness sake!"
2. "Go on! Good-by! Go away!"

daily plunge. While the lady at the needle kept up a little running, contemptuous comment:

"*Blagueur—farceur—gros bête, va!*"[3]

He never assumed this serio-comic tone when alone with Mrs. Pontellier. She never knew precisely what to make of it; at that moment it was impossible for her to guess how much of it was jest and what proportion was earnest. It was understood that he had often spoken words of love to Madame Ratignolle, without any thought of being taken seriously. Mrs. Pontellier was glad he had not assumed a similar rôle toward herself. It would have been unacceptable and annoying.

Mrs. Pontellier had brought her sketching materials, which she sometimes dabbled with in an unprofessional way. She liked the dabbling. She felt in it satisfaction of a kind which no other employment afforded her.

She had long wished to try herself on Madame Ratignolle. Never had that lady seemed a more tempting subject than at that moment, seated there like some sensuous Madonna, with the gleam of the fading day enriching her splendid color.

Robert crossed over and seated himself upon the step below Mrs. Pontellier, that he might watch her work. She handled her brushes with a certain ease and freedom which came, not from long and close acquaintance with them, but from a natural aptitude. Robert followed her work with close attention, giving forth little ejaculatory expressions of appreciation in French, which he addressed to Madame Ratignolle.

"*Mais ce n'est pas mal! Elle s'y connait, elle a de la force, oui.*"[4]

During his oblivious attention he once quietly rested his head against Mrs. Pontellier's arm. As gently she repulsed him. Once again he repeated the offense. She could not but believe it to be thoughtlessness on his part; yet that was no reason she should submit to it. She did not remonstrate, except again to repulse him quietly but firmly. He offered no apology.

The picture completed bore no resemblance to Madame Ratignolle. She was greatly disappointed to find that it did not look like her. But it was a fair enough piece of work, and in many respects satisfying.

Mrs. Pontellier evidently did not think so. After surveying the sketch critically she drew a broad smudge of paint across its surface, and crumpled the paper between her hands.

The youngsters came tumbling up the steps, the quadroon following at the respectful distance which they required her to observe. Mrs. Pontellier made them carry her paints and things into the house. She

3. "Liar—comedian—silly, go on with you!"
4. "But that's not bad at all! She knows what she's doing; yes, she has talent."

sought to detain them for a little talk and some pleasantry. But they were greatly in earnest. They had only come to investigate the contents of the bonbon box. They accepted without murmuring what she chose to give them, each holding out two chubby hands scoop-like, in the vain hope that they might be filled; and then away they went.

The sun was low in the west, and the breeze soft and languorous that came up from the south, charged with the seductive odor of the sea. Children, freshly befurbelowed,[5] were gathering for their games under the oaks. Their voices were high and penetrating.

Madame Ratignolle folded her sewing, placing thimble, scissors and thread all neatly together in the roll, which she pinned securely. She complained of faintness. Mrs. Pontellier flew for the cologne water and a fan. She bathed Madame Ratignolle's face with cologne, while Robert plied the fan with unnecessary vigor.

The spell was soon over, and Mrs. Pontellier could not help wondering if there were not a little imagination responsible for its origin, for the rose tint had never faded from her friend's face.

She stood watching the fair woman walk down the long line of galleries with the grace and majesty which queens are sometimes supposed to possess. Her little ones ran to meet her. Two of them clung about her white skirts, the third she took from its nurse and with a thousand endearments bore it along in her own fond, encircling arms. Though, as everybody well knew, the doctor had forbidden her to lift so much as a pin!

"Are you going bathing?" asked Robert of Mrs. Pontellier. It was not so much a question as a reminder.

"Oh, no," she answered, with a tone of indecision. "I'm tired; I think not." Her glance wandered from his face away toward the Gulf, whose sonorous murmur reached her like a loving but imperative entreaty.

"Oh, come!" he insisted. "You mustn't miss your bath. Come on. The water must be delicious; it will not hurt you. Come."

He reached up for her big, rough straw hat that hung on a peg outside the door, and put it on her head. They descended the steps, and walked away together toward the beach. The sun was low in the west and the breeze was soft and warm.

VI

Edna Pontellier could not have told why, wishing to go to the beach with Robert, she should in the first place have declined, and in the second place have followed in obedience to one of the two contradictory impulses which impelled her.

5. Dressed up.

A certain light was beginning to dawn dimly within her,—the light which, showing the way, forbids it.

At that early period it served but to bewilder her. It moved her to dreams, to thoughtfulness, to the shadowy anguish which had overcome her the midnight when she had abandoned herself to tears.

In short, Mrs. Pontellier was beginning to realize her position in the universe as a human being, and to recognize her relations as an individual to the world within and about her. This may seem like a ponderous weight of wisdom to descend upon the soul of a young woman of twenty-eight—perhaps more wisdom than the Holy Ghost is usually pleased to vouchsafe to any woman.

But the beginning of things, of a world especially, is necessarily vague, tangled, chaotic, and exceedingly disturbing. How few of us ever emerge from such beginning! How many souls perish in its tumult!

The voice of the sea is seductive; never ceasing, whispering, clamoring, murmuring, inviting the soul to wander for a spell in abysses of solitude; to lose itself in mazes of inward contemplation.

The voice of the sea speaks to the soul. The touch of the sea is sensuous, enfolding the body in its soft, close embrace.

VII

Mrs. Pontellier was not a woman given to confidences, a characteristic hitherto contrary to her nature. Even as a child she had lived her own small life all within herself. At a very early period she had apprehended instinctively the dual life—that outward existence which conforms, the inward life which questions.

That summer at Grand Isle she began to loose a little the mantle of reserve that had always enveloped her. There may have been—there must have been—influences, both subtle and apparent, working in their several ways to induce her to do this; but the most obvious was the influence of Adèle Ratignolle. The excessive physical charm of the Creole had first attracted her, for Edna had a sensuous susceptibility to beauty. Then the candor of the woman's whole existence, which everyone might read, and which formed so striking a contrast to her own habitual reserve—this might have furnished a link. Who can tell what metals the gods use in forging the subtle bond which we call sympathy, which we might as well call love.

The two women went away one morning to the beach together, arm in arm, under the huge white sunshade. Edna had prevailed upon Madame Ratignolle to leave the children behind, though she could not induce her to relinquish a diminutive roll of needlework, which Adèle begged to be allowed to slip into the depths of her pocket. In some un-accountable way they had escaped from Robert.

The walk to the beach was no inconsiderable one, consisting as it did of a long, sandy path, upon which a sporadic and tangled growth that bordered it on either side made frequent and unexpected inroads. There were acres of yellow camomile reaching out on either hand. Further away still, vegetable gardens abounded, with frequent small plantations of orange or lemon trees intervening. The dark green clusters glistened from afar in the sun.

The women were both of goodly height, Madame Ratignolle possessing the more feminine and matronly figure. The charm of Edna Pontellier's physique stole insensibly upon you. The lines of her body were long, clean and symmetrical; it was a body which occasionally fell into splendid poses; there was no suggestion of the trim, stereotyped fashion-plate about it. A casual and indiscriminating observer, in passing, might not cast a second glance upon the figure. But with more feeling and discernment he would have recognized the noble beauty of its modeling, and the graceful severity of poise and movement, which made Edna Pontellier different from the crowd.

She wore a cool muslin that morning—white, with a waving vertical line of brown running through it; also a white linen collar and the big straw hat which she had taken from the peg outside the door. The hat rested any way on her yellow-brown hair, that waved a little, was heavy, and clung close to her head.

Madame Ratignolle, more careful of her complexion, had twined a gauze veil about her head. She wore dogskin gloves, white gauntlets that protected her wrists. She was dressed in pure white, with a fluffiness of ruffles that became her. The draperies and fluttering things which she wore suited her rich, luxuriant beauty as a greater severity of line could not have done.

There were a number of bath-houses along the beach, of rough but solid construction, built with small, protecting galleries facing the water. Each house consisted of two compartments, and each family at Lebrun's possessed a compartment for itself, fitted out with all the essential paraphernalia of the bath and whatever other conveniences the owners might desire. The two women had no intention of bathing; they had just strolled down to the beach for a walk and to be alone and near the water. The Pontellier and Ratignolle compartments adjoined one another under the same roof.

Mrs. Pontellier had brought down her key through force of habit. Unlocking the door of her bath-room she went inside, and soon emerged, bringing a rug,[6] which she spread upon the floor of the gal-

6. Blanket; "crash": heavy linen fabric.

lery, and two huge hair pillows covered with crash, which she placed against the front of the building.

The two seated themselves there in the shade of the porch, side by side, with their backs against the pillows and their feet extended. Madame Ratignolle removed her veil, wiped her face with a rather delicate handkerchief, and fanned herself with the fan which she always carried suspended somewhere about her person by a long, narrow ribbon. Edna removed her collar and opened her dress at the throat. She took the fan from Madame Ratignolle and began to fan both herself and her companion. It was very warm, and for a while they did nothing but exchange remarks about the heat, the sun, the glare. But there was a breeze blowing, a choppy stiff wind that whipped the water into froth. It fluttered the skirts of the two women and kept them for a while engaged in adjusting, readjusting, tucking in, securing hair-pins and hat-pins. A few persons were sporting some distance away in the water. The beach was very still of human sound at that hour. The lady in black was reading her morning devotions on the porch of a neighboring bath-house. Two young lovers were exchanging their hearts' yearnings beneath the children's tent, which they had found unoccupied.

Edna Pontellier, casting her eyes about, had finally kept them at rest upon the sea. The day was clear and carried the gaze out as far as the blue sky went; there were a few white clouds suspended idly over the horizon. A lateen[7] sail was visible in the direction of Cat Island, and others to the south seemed almost motionless in the far distance.

"Of whom—of what are you thinking?" asked Adèle of her companion, whose countenance she had been watching with a little amused attention, arrested by the absorbed expression which seemed to have seized and fixed every feature into a statuesque repose.

"Nothing," returned Mrs. Pontellier, with a start, adding at once: "How stupid! But it seems to me it is the reply we make instinctively to such a question. Let me see," she went on, throwing back her head and narrowing her fine eyes till they shone like two vivid points of light. "Let me see. I was really not conscious of thinking of anything; but perhaps I can retrace my thoughts."

"Oh! never mind!" laughed Madame Ratignolle. "I am not quite so exacting. I will let you off this time. It is really too hot to think, especially to think about thinking."

"But for the fun of it," persisted Edna. "First of all, the sight of the water stretching so far away, those motionless sails against the blue sky, made a delicious picture that I just wanted to sit and look at. The hot wind beating in my face made me think—without any connection that I can trace—of a summer day in Kentucky, of a meadow that seemed as

7. Triangular.

big as the ocean to the very little girl walking through the grass, which
was higher than her waist. She threw out her arms as if swimming when
she walked, beating the tall grass as one strikes out in the water. Oh, I
see the connection now!"

"Where were you going that day in Kentucky, walking through the
grass?"

"I don't remember now. I was just walking diagonally across a big
field. My sun-bonnet obstructed the view. I could see only the stretch
of green before me, and I felt as if I must walk on forever, without
coming to the end of it. I don't remember whether I was frightened or
pleased. I must have been entertained.

"Likely as not it was Sunday," she laughed; "and I was running away
from prayers, from the Presbyterian service, read in a spirit of gloom by
my father that chills me yet to think of."

"And have you been running away from prayers ever since, *ma
chère*?" asked Madame Ratignolle, amused.

"No! oh, no!" Edna hastened to say. "I was a little unthinking child
in those days, just following a misleading impulse without question. On
the contrary, during one period of my life religion took a firm hold
upon me; after I was twelve and until—until—why, I suppose until
now, though I never thought much about it—just driven along by
habit. But do you know," she broke off, turning her quick eyes upon
Madame Ratignolle and leaning forward a little so as to bring her face
quite close to that of her companion, "sometimes I feel this summer as
if I were walking through the green meadow again; idly, aimlessly,
unthinking and unguided."

Madame Ratignolle laid her hand over that of Mrs. Pontellier, which
was near her. Seeing that the hand was not withdrawn, she clasped it
firmly and warmly. She even stroked it a little, fondly, with the other
hand, murmuring in an undertone, "*Pauvre chérie.*"[8]

The action was at first a little confusing to Edna, but she soon lent
herself readily to the Creole's gentle caress. She was not accustomed to
an outward and spoken expression of affection, either in herself or in
others. She and her younger sister, Janet, had quarreled a good deal
through force of unfortunate habit. Her older sister, Margaret, was matronly and dignified, probably from having assumed matronly and
house-wifely responsibilities too early in life, their mother having died
when they were quite young. Margaret was not effusive; she was practical. Edna had had an occasional girl friend, but whether accidentally
or not, they seemed to have been all of one type—the self-contained.
She never realized that the reserve of her own character had much,

---

8. "Poor dear."

perhaps everything, to do with this. Her most intimate friend at school had been one of rather exceptional intellectual gifts, who wrote fine-sounding essays which Edna admired and strove to imitate; and with her she talked and glowed over the English classics, and sometimes held religious and political controversies.

Edna often wondered at one propensity which sometimes had inwardly disturbed her without causing any outward show or manifestation on her part. At a very early age—perhaps it was when she traversed the ocean of waving grass—she remembered that she had been passionately enamored of a dignified and sad-eyed cavalry officer who visited her father in Kentucky. She could not leave his presence when he was there, nor remove her eyes from his face which was something like Napoleon's, with a lock of black hair falling across the forehead. But the cavalry officer melted imperceptibly out of her existence.

At another time her affections were deeply engaged by a young gentleman who visited a lady on a neighboring plantation. It was after they went to Mississippi to live. The young man was engaged to be married to the young lady, and they sometimes called upon Margaret, driving over of afternoons in a buggy. Edna was a little miss, just merging into her teens; and the realization that she herself was nothing, nothing, nothing to the engaged young man was a bitter affliction to her. But he, too, went the way of dreams.

She was a grown young woman when she was overtaken by what she supposed to be the climax of her fate. It was when the face and figure of a great tragedian began to haunt her imagination and stir her senses. The persistence of the infatuation lent it an aspect of genuineness. The hopelessness of it colored it with the lofty tones of a great passion.

The picture of the tragedian stood enframed upon her desk. Any one may possess the portrait of a tragedian without exciting suspicion or comment. (This was a sinister reflection which she cherished.) In the presence of others she expressed admiration for his exalted gifts, as she handed the photograph around and dwelt upon the fidelity of the likeness. When alone she sometimes picked it up and kissed the cold glass passionately.

Her marriage to Léonce Pontellier was purely an accident, in this respect resembling many other marriages which masquerade as the decrees of Fate. It was in the midst of her secret great passion that she met him. He fell in love, as men are in the habit of doing, and pressed his suit with an earnestness and an ardor which left nothing to be desired. He pleased her; his absolute devotion flattered her. She fancied there was a sympathy of thought and taste between them, in which fancy she was mistaken. Add to this the violent opposition of her father and her sister Margaret to her marriage with a Catholic, and we need seek no further for the motives which led her to accept Monsieur Pontellier for her husband.

The acme of bliss, which would have been a marriage with the tragedian, was not for her in this world. As the devoted wife of a man who worshiped her, she felt she would take her place with a certain dignity in the world of reality, closing the portals forever behind her upon the realm of romance and dreams.

But it was not long before the tragedian had gone to join the cavalry officer and the engaged young man and a few others; and Edna found herself face to face with the realities. She grew fond of her husband, realizing with some unaccountable satisfaction that no trace of passion or excessive and fictitious warmth colored her affection, thereby threatening its dissolution.

She was fond of her children in an uneven, impulsive way. She would sometimes gather them passionately to her heart; she would sometimes forget them. The year before they had spent part of the summer with their grandmother Pontellier in Iberville. Feeling secure regarding their happiness and welfare, she did not miss them except with an occasional intense longing. Their absence was a sort of relief, though she did not admit this, even to herself. It seemed to free her of a responsibility which she had blindly assumed and for which Fate had not fitted her.

Edna did not reveal so much as all this to Madame Ratignolle that summer day when they sat with faces turned to the sea. But a good part of it escaped her. She had put her head down on Madame Ratignolle's shoulder. She was flushed and felt intoxicated with the sound of her own voice and the unaccustomed taste of candor. It muddled her like wine, or like a first breath of freedom.

There was the sound of approaching voices. It was Robert, surrounded by a troop of children, searching for them. The two little Pontelliers were with him, and he carried Madame Ratignolle's little girl in his arms. There were other children beside, and two nursemaids followed, looking disagreeable and resigned.

The women at once rose and began to shake out their draperies and relax their muscles. Mrs. Pontellier threw the cushions and rug into the bath-house. The children all scampered off to the awning, and they stood there in a line, gazing upon the intruding lovers, still exchanging their vows and sighs. The lovers got up, with only a silent protest, and walked slowly away somewhere else.

The children possessed themselves of the tent, and Mrs. Pontellier went over to join them.

Madame Ratignolle begged Robert to accompany her to the house; she complained of cramp in her limbs and stiffness of the joints. She leaned draggingly upon his arm as they walked.

VIII

"Do me a favor, Robert," spoke the pretty woman at his side, almost as soon as she and Robert had started on their slow, homeward way. She looked up in his face, leaning on his arm beneath the encircling shadow of the umbrella which he had lifted.

"Granted; as many as you like," he returned, glancing down into her eyes that were full of thoughtfulness and some speculation.

"I only ask for one; let Mrs. Pontellier alone."

"*Tiens!*" he exclaimed, with a sudden, boyish laugh. "*Voilà que Madame Ratignolle est jealouse!*"[9]

"Nonsense! I'm in earnest; I mean what I say. Let Mrs. Pontellier alone."

"Why?" he asked; himself growing serious at his companion's solicitation.

"She is not one of us; she is not like us. She might make the unfortunate blunder of taking you seriously."

His face flushed with annoyance, and taking off his soft hat he began to beat it impatiently against his leg as he walked. "Why shouldn't she take me seriously?" he demanded sharply. "Am I a comedian, a clown, a jack-in-the-box? Why shouldn't she? You Creoles! I have no patience with you! Am I always to be regarded as a feature of an amusing programme? I hope Mrs. Pontellier does take me seriously. I hope she has discernment enough to find in me something besides the *blagueur*.[1] If I thought there was any doubt—"

"Oh, enough, Robert!" she broke into his heated outburst. "You are not thinking of what you are saying. You speak with about as little reflection as we might expect from one of those children down there playing in the sand. If your attentions to any married women here were ever offered with any intention of being convincing, you would not be the gentleman we all know you to be, and you would be unfit to associate with the wives and daughters of the people who trust you."

Madame Ratignolle had spoken what she believed to be the law and the gospel. The young man shrugged his shoulders impatiently.

"Oh! well! That isn't it," slamming his hat down vehemently upon his head. "You ought to feel that such things are not flattering to say to a fellow."

"Should our whole intercourse consist of an exchange of compliments? *Ma foi!*[2]

"It isn't pleasant to have a woman tell you—" he went on, unheedingly, but breaking off suddenly: "Now if I were like Arobin—you remember Alcée Arobin and that story of the consul's wife at Biloxi?"[3]

9. "So, Madame Ratignolle is jealous!"   2. "For heaven's sake!"
1. Joker, liar.   3. Coastal resort town near New Orleans.

And he related the story of Alcée Arobin and the consul's wife; and another about the tenor of the French Opera,[4] who received letters which should never have been written; and still other stories, grave and gay, till Mrs. Pontellier and her possible propensity for taking young men seriously was apparently forgotten.

Madame Ratignolle, when they had regained her cottage, went in to take the hour's rest which she considered helpful. Before leaving her. Robert begged her pardon for the impatience—he called it rudeness—with which he had received her well-meant caution.

"You made one mistake, Adèle," he said, with a light smile; "there is no earthly possibility of Mrs. Pontellier ever taking me seriously. You should have warned me against taking myself seriously. Your advice might then have carried some weight and given me subject for some reflection. *Au revoir*. But you look tired," he added, solicitously. "Would you like a cup of bouillon? Shall I stir you a toddy? Let me mix you a toddy with a drop of Angostura."[5]

She acceded to the suggestion of bouillon, which was grateful and acceptable. He went himself to the kitchen, which was a building apart from the cottages and lying to the rear of the house. And he himself brought her the golden-brown bouillon, in a dainty Sèvres[6] cup, with a flaky cracker or two on the saucer.

She thrust a bare, white arm from the curtain which shielded her open door, and received the cup from his hands. She told him he was a *bon garcon*,[7] and she meant it. Robert thanked her and turned away toward "the house."

The lovers were just entering the grounds of the *pension*. They were leaning toward each other as the water-oaks bent from the sea. There was not a particle of earth beneath their feet. Their heads might have been turned upside-down, so absolutely did they tread upon blue ether. The lady in black, creeping behind them, looked a trifle paler and more jaded than usual. There was no sign of Mrs. Pontellier and the children. Robert scanned the distance for any such apparition. They would doubtless remain away till the dinner hour. The young man ascended to his mother's room. It was situated at the top of the house, made up of odd angles and a queer, sloping ceiling. Two broad dormer windows looked out toward the Gulf, and as far across it as a man's eye might reach. The furnishings of the room were light, cool, and practical.

Madame Lebrun was busily engaged at the sewing-machine. A little black girl sat on the floor, and with her hands worked the treadle of the machine. The Creole woman does not take any chances which may be avoided of imperiling her health.

---

4. In New Orleans; perhaps the most distinguished American opera company of the time.
5. Aromatic bitters.

6. Made in Sèvres, France.
7. Both "nice fellow" and "good waiter."

Robert went over and seated himself on the broad sill of one of the dormer windows. He took a book from his pocket and began energetically to read it, judging by the precision and frequency with which he turned the leaves. The sewing-machine made a resounding clatter in the room; it was of a ponderous, by-gone make. In the lulls, Robert and his mother exchanged bits of desultory conversation.

"Where is Mrs. Pontellier?"

"Down at the beach with the children."

"I promised to lend her the Goncourt.[8] Don't forget to take it down when you go; it's there on the bookshelf over the small table." Clatter, clatter, clatter, bang! for the next five or eight minutes.

"Where is Victor going with the rockaway?"

"The rockaway? Victor?"

"Yes; down there in front. He seems to be getting ready to drive away somewhere."

"Call him." Clatter, clatter!

Robert uttered a shrill, piercing whistle which might have been heard back at the wharf.

"He won't look up."

Madame Lebrun flew to the window. She called "Victor!" She waved a handkerchief and called again. The young fellow below got into the vehicle and started the horse off at a gallop.

Madame Lebrun went back to the machine, crimson with annoyance. Victor was the younger son and brother—a *tête montée*,[9] with a temper which invited violence and a will which no ax could break.

"Whenever you say the word I'm ready to thrash any amount of reason into him that he's able to hold."

"If your father had only lived!" Clatter, clatter, clatter, clatter, bang! It was a fixed belief with Madame Lebrun that the conduct of the universe and all things pertaining thereto would have been manifestly of a more intelligent and higher order had not Monsieur Lebrun been removed to other spheres during the early years of their married life.

"What do you hear from Montel?" Montel was a middle-aged gentleman whose vain ambition and desire for the past twenty years had been to fill the void which Monsieur Lebrun's taking off had left in the Lebrun household. Clatter, clatter, bang, clatter!

"I have a letter somewhere," looking in the machine drawer and finding the letter in the bottom of the work-basket. "He says to tell you he will be in Vera Cruz[1] the beginning of next month"—clatter, clatter!—"and if you still have the intention of joining him"—bang! clatter, clatter, bang!

---

8. A French novel by Edmond de Goncourt (1822–1896).

9. Impulsive character.

1. Mexican city on the Gulf of Mexico.

"Why didn't you tell me so before, mother? You know I wanted—"
Clatter, clatter, clatter!

"Do you see Mrs. Pontellier starting back with the children? She will be in late to luncheon again. She never starts to get ready for luncheon till the last minute." Clatter, clatter! "Where are you going?"

"Where did you say the Goncourt was?"

IX

Every light in the hall was ablaze; every lamp turned as high as it could be without smoking the chimney or threatening explosion. The lamps were fixed at intervals against the wall, encircling the whole room. Some one had gathered orange and lemon branches and with these fashioned graceful festoons between. The dark green of the branches stood out and glistened against the white muslin curtains which draped the windows, and which puffed, floated, and flapped at the capricious will of a stiff breeze that swept up from the Gulf.

It was Saturday night a few weeks after the intimate conversation held between Robert and Madame Ratignolle on their way from the beach. An unusual number of husbands, fathers, and friends had come down to stay over Sunday; and they were being suitably entertained by their families, with the material help of Madame Lebrun. The dining tables had all been removed to one end of the hall, and the chairs ranged about in rows and in clusters. Each little family group had had its say and exchanged its domestic gossip earlier in the evening. There was now an apparent disposition to relax; to widen the circle of confidences and give a more general tone to the conversation.

Many of the children had been permitted to sit up beyond their usual bedtime. A small band of them were lying on their stomachs on the floor looking at the colored sheets of the comic papers which Mr. Pontellier had brought down. The little Pontellier boys were permitting them to do so, and making their authority felt.

Music, dancing, and a recitation or two were the entertainments furnished, or rather, offered. But there was nothing systematic about the programme, no appearance of prearrangement nor even premeditation.

At an early hour in the evening the Farival twins were prevailed upon to play the piano. They were girls of fourteen, always clad in the Virgin's colors, blue and white, having been dedicated to the Blessed Virgin at their baptism. They played a duet from "Zampa," and at the earnest solicitation of every one present followed it with the overture to "The Poet and the Peasant."

"*Allez vous-en! Sapristi!*" shrieked the parrot outside the door. He was the only being present who possessed sufficient candor to admit that he was not listening to these gracious performances for the first time that summer. Old Monsieur Farival, grandfather of the twins, grew indignant over the interruption, and insisted upon having the bird removed and consigned to regions of darkness. Victor Lebrun objected; and his decrees were as immutable as those of Fate. The parrot fortunately offered no further interruption to the entertainment, the whole venom of his nature apparently having been cherished up and hurled against the twins in that one impetuous outburst.

Later a young brother and sister gave recitations, which every one present had heard many times at winter evening entertainments in the city.

A little girl performed a skirt dance in the center of the floor. The mother played her accompaniments and at the same time watched her daughter with greedy admiration and nervous apprehension. She need have had no apprehension. The child was mistress of the situation. She had been properly dressed for the occasion in black tulle and black silk tights. Her little neck and arms were bare, and her hair, artificially crimped, stood out like fluffy black plumes over her head. Her poses were full of grace, and her little black-shod toes twinkled as they shot out and upward with a rapidity and a suddenness which were bewildering.

But there was no reason why every one should not dance. Madame Ratignolle could not, so it was she who gaily consented to play for the others. She played very well, keeping excellent waltz time and infusing an expression into the strains which was indeed inspiring. She was keeping up her music on account of the children she said; because she and her husband both considered it a means of brightening the home and making it attractive.

Almost every one danced but the twins, who could not be induced to separate during the brief period when one or the other should be whirling around the room in the arms of a man. They might have danced together, but they did not think of it.

The children were sent to bed. Some went submissively; others with shrieks and protests as they were dragged away. They had been permitted to sit up till after the ice-cream, which naturally marked the limit of human indulgence.

The ice-cream was passed around with cake—gold and silver cake arranged on platters in alternate slices; it had been made and frozen during the afternoon back of the kitchen by two black women, under the supervision of Victor. It was pronounced a great success—excellent if it had only contained a little less vanilla or a little more sugar, if it had been frozen a degree harder, and if the salt might have been kept out of portions of it. Victor was proud of his achievement, and went about recommending it and urging every one to partake of it to excess.

After Mrs. Pontellier had danced twice with her husband, once with Robert, and once with Monsieur Ratignolle, who was thin and tall and swayed like a reed in the wind when he danced, she went out on the gallery and seated herself on the low window-sill, where she commanded a view of all that went on in the hall and could look out toward the Gulf. There was a soft effulgence in the east. The moon was coming up, and its mystic shimmer was casting a million lights across the distant, restless water.

"Would you like to hear Mademoiselle Reisz play?" asked Robert, coming out on the porch where she was. Of course Edna would like to hear Mademoiselle Reisz play; but she feared it would be useless to entreat her.

"I'll ask her," he said. "I'll tell her that you want to hear her. She likes you. She will come." He turned and hurried away to one of the far cottages, where Mademoiselle Reisz was shuffling away. She was dragging a chair in and out of her room, and at intervals objecting to the crying of a baby, which a nurse in the adjoining cottage was endeavoring to put to sleep. She was a disagreeable little woman, no longer young, who had quarreled with almost every one, owing to a temper which was self-assertive and a disposition to trample upon the rights of others. Robert prevailed upon her without any too great difficulty.

She entered the hall with him during a lull in the dance. She made an awkward, imperious little bow as she went in. She was a homely woman, with a small weazened face and body and eyes that glowed. She had absolutely no taste in dress, and wore a batch of rusty black lace with a bunch of artificial violets pinned to the side of her hair.

"Ask Mrs. Pontellier what she would like to hear me play," she requested of Robert. She sat perfectly still before the piano, not touching the keys, while Robert carried her message to Edna at the window. A general air of surprise and genuine satisfaction fell upon every one as they saw the pianist enter. There was a settling down, and a prevailing air of expectancy everywhere. Edna was a trifle embarrassed at being thus signaled out for the imperious little woman's favor. She would not dare to choose, and begged that Mademoiselle Reisz would please herself in selections.

Edna was what she herself called very fond of music. Musical strains, well rendered, had a way of evoking pictures in her mind. She sometimes liked to sit in the room of mornings when Madame Ratignolle played or practiced. One piece which that lady played Edna had entitled "Solitude." It was a short, plaintive, minor strain. The name of the piece was something else, but she called it "Solitude." When she heard it there came before her imagination the figure of a man standing beside a desolate rock on the seashore. He was naked. His attitude was one of hopeless resignation as he looked toward a distant bird winging its flight away from him.

Another piece called to her mind a dainty young woman clad in an Empire gown, taking mincing dancing steps as she came down a long avenue between tall hedges. Again, another reminded her of children at play, and still another of nothing on earth but a demure lady stroking a cat.

The very first chords which Mademoiselle Reisz struck upon the piano sent a keen tremor down Mrs. Pontellier's spinal column. It was not the first time she had heard an artist at the piano. Perhaps it was the first time she was ready, perhaps the first time her being was tempered to take an impress of the abiding truth.

She waited for the material pictures which she thought would gather and blaze before her imagination. She waited in vain. She saw no pictures of solitude, of hope, of longing, or of despair. But the very passions themselves were aroused within her soul, swaying it, lashing it, as the waves daily beat upon her splendid body. She trembled, she was choking, and the tears blinded her.

Mademoiselle had finished. She arose, and bowing her stiff, lofty bow, she went away, stopping for neither thanks nor applause. As she passed along the gallery she patted Edna upon the shoulder.

"Well, how did you like my music?" she asked. The young woman was unable to answer; she pressed the hand of the pianist convulsively. Mademoiselle Reisz perceived her agitation and even her tears. She patted her again upon the shoulder as she said:

"You are the only one worth playing for. Those others? Bah!" and she went shuffling and sidling on down the gallery toward her room.

But she was mistaken about "those others." Her playing had aroused a fever of enthusiasm. "What passion!" "What an artist!" "I have always said no one could play Chopin[2] like Mademoiselle Reisz!" "That last prelude! Bon Dieu![3] It shakes a man!"

It was growing late, and there was a general disposition to disband. But someone, perhaps it was Robert, thought of a bath at that mystic hour and under that mystic moon.

X

At all events Robert proposed it, and there was not a dissenting voice. There was not one but was ready to follow when he led the way. He did not lead the way, however, he directed the way; and he himself loitered behind with the lovers, who had betrayed a disposition to linger and hold themselves apart. He walked between them, whether with malicious or mischievous intent was not wholly clear, even to himself.

The Pontelliers and Ratignolles walked ahead; the women leaning upon the arms of their husbands. Edna could hear Robert's voice be-

2. Frédéric Chopin (1810–1849), Polish composer.   3. "Good Lord!"

hind them, and could sometimes hear what he said. She wondered why he did not join them. It was unlike him not to. Of late he had sometimes held away from her for an entire day, redoubling his devotion upon the next and the next, as though to make up for hours that had been lost. She missed him the days when some pretext served to take him away from her, just as one misses the sun on a cloudy day without having thought much about the sun when it was shining.

The people walked in little groups toward the beach. They talked and laughed; some of them sang. There was a band playing down at Klein's hotel, and the strains reached them faintly, tempered by the distance. There were strange, rare odors abroad—a tangle of the sea smell and of weeds and damp, new-plowed earth, mingled with the heavy perfume of a field of white blossoms somewhere near. But the night sat light upon the sea and the land. There was no weight of darkness; there were no shadows. The white light of the moon had fallen upon the world like the mystery and the softness of sleep.

Most of them walked into the water as though into a native element. The sea was quiet now, and swelled lazily in broad billows that melted into one another and did not break except upon the beach in little foamy crests that coiled back like slow, white serpents.

Edna had attempted all summer to learn to swim. She had received instructions from both the men and women; in some instances from the children. Robert had pursued a system of lessons almost daily; and he was nearly at the point of discouragement in realizing the futility of his efforts. A certain ungovernable dread hung about her when in the water, unless there was a hand near by that might reach out and reassure her.

But that night she was like the little tottering, stumbling, clutching child, who of a sudden realizes its powers, and walks for the first time alone, boldly and with over-confidence. She could have shouted for joy. She did shout for joy, as with a sweeping stroke or two she lifted her body to the surface of the water.

A feeling of exultation overtook her, as if some power of significant import had been given her soul. She grew daring and reckless, overestimating her strength. She wanted to swim far out, where no woman had swum before.

Her unlooked-for achievement was the subject of wonder, applause, and admiration. Each one congratulated himself that his special teachings had accomplished this desired end.

"How easy it is!" she thought. "It is nothing," she said aloud: "why did I not discover before that it was nothing. Think of the time I have lost splashing about like a baby!" She would not join the groups in their sports and bouts, but intoxicated with her newly conquered power, she swam out alone.

She turned her face seaward to gather in an impression of space and solitude, which the vast expanse of water, meeting and melting with moonlit sky, conveyed to her excited fancy. As she swam she seemed to be reaching out for the unlimited in which to lose herself.

Once she turned and looked toward the shore, toward the people she had left there. She had not gone any great distance—that is, what would have been great distance for an experienced swimmer. But to her unaccustomed vision the stretch of water behind her assumed the aspect of a barrier which her unaided strength would never be able to overcome.

A quick vision of death smote her soul, and for a second of time appalled and enfeebled her senses. But by an effort she rallied her staggering faculties and managed to regain the land.

She made no mention of her encounter with death and her flash of terror, except to say to her husband, "I thought I should have perished out there alone."

"You were not so very far, my dear; I was watching you," he told her.

Edna went at once to the bath-house, and she had put on her dry clothes and was ready to return home before the others had left the water. She started to walk away alone. They all called to her and shouted to her. She waved a dissenting hand, and went on paying no further heed to their renewed cries which sought to detain her.

"Sometimes I am tempted to think that Mrs. Pontellier is capricious," said Madame Lebrun, who was amusing herself immensely and feared that Edna's abrupt departure might put an end to the pleasure.

"I know she is," assented Mr. Pontellier; "sometimes, not often."

Edna had not traversed a quarter of the distance on her way home before she was overtaken by Robert.

"Did you think I was afraid?" she asked him, without a shade of annoyance.

"No; I knew you weren't afraid."

"Then why did you come? Why didn't you stay out there with the others?"

"I never thought of it."

"Thought of what?"

"Of anything. What difference does it make?"

"I'm very tired," she uttered, complainingly.

"I know you are."

"You don't know anything about it. Why should you know? I never was so exhausted in my life. But it isn't unpleasant. A thousand emotions have swept through me to-night. I don't comprehend half of them. Don't mind what I'm saying; I am just thinking aloud. I wonder if I shall ever be stirred again as Mademoiselle Reisz's playing moved me to-night. I wonder if any night on earth will ever again be like this one. It is like a night in a dream. The people about me are like some uncanny, half-human beings. There must be spirits abroad to-night."

"There are," whispered Robert. "Didn't you know this was the twenty-eighth of August?

"The twenty-eighth of August?"

"Yes. On the twenty-eighth of August, at the hour of midnight, and if the moon is shining—the moon must be shining—a spirit that has haunted these shores for ages rises up from the Gulf. With its own penetrating vision the spirit seeks some one mortal worthy to hold him company, worthy of being exalted for a few hours into realms of the semi-celestials. His search has always hitherto been fruitless, and he has sunk back, disheartened, into the sea. But tonight he found Mrs. Pontellier. Perhaps he will never wholly release her from the spell. Perhaps she will never again suffer a poor, unworthy earthling to walk in the shadow of her divine presence."

"Don't banter me," she said, wounded at what appeared to be his flippancy. He did not mind the entreaty, but the tone with its delicate note of pathos was like a reproach. He could not explain; he could not tell her that he had penetrated her mood and understood. He said nothing except to offer her his arm, for, by her own admission, she was exhausted. She had been walking alone with her arms hanging limp, letting her white skirts trail along the dewy path. She took his arm, but she did not lean upon it. She let her hand lie listlessly, as though her thoughts were elsewhere—somewhere in advance of her body, and she was striving to overtake them.

Robert assisted her into the hammock which swung from the post before her door out to the trunk of a tree.

"Will you stay out here and wait for Mr. Pontellier?" he asked.

"I'll stay out here. Good-night."

"Shall I get you a pillow?"

"There's one here," she said, feeling about, for they were in the shadow.

"It must be soiled; the children have been tumbling it about."

"No matter." And having discovered the pillow, she adjusted it beneath her head. She extended herself in the hammock with a deep breath of relief. She was not a supercilious or an over-dainty woman. She was not much given to reclining in the hammock, and when she did so it was with no cat-like suggestion of voluptuous ease, but with a beneficent repose which seemed to invade her whole body.

"Shall I stay with you till Mr. Pontellier comes?" asked Robert, seating himself on the outer edge of one of the steps and taking hold of the hammock rope which was fastened to the post.

"If you wish. Don't swing the hammock. Will you get my white shawl which I left on the window-sill over at the house?"

"Are you chilly?"

"No; but I shall be presently."

"Presently?" he laughed. "Do you know what time it is? How long are you going to stay out here?"

"I don't know. Will you get the shawl?"

"Of course I will," he said, rising. He went over to the house, walking along the grass. She watched his figure pass in and out of the strips of moonlight. It was past midnight. It was very quiet.

When he returned with the shawl she took it and kept it in her hand. She did not put it around her.

"Did you say I should stay till Mr. Pontellier came back?"

"I said you might if you wished to."

He seated himself again and rolled a cigarette, which he smoked in silence. Neither did Mrs. Pontellier speak. No multitude of words could have been more significant than those moments of silence, or more pregnant with the first-felt throbbings of desire.

When the voices of the bathers were heard approaching, Robert said good-night. She did not answer him. He thought she was asleep. Again she watched his figure pass in and out of the strips of moonlight as he walked away.

XI

"What are you doing out here, Edna? I thought I should find you in bed," said her husband, when he discovered her lying there. He had walked up with Madame Lebrun and left her at the house. His wife did not reply.

"Are you asleep?" he asked, bending down close to look at her.

"No." Her eyes gleamed bright and intense, with no sleepy shadows, as they looked into his.

"Do you know it is past one o'clock? Come on," and he mounted the steps and went into their room.

"Edna!" called Mr. Pontellier from within, after a few moments had gone by.

"Don't wait for me," she answered. He thrust his head through the door.

"You will take cold out there," he said, irritably. "What folly is this? Why don't you come in?"

"It isn't cold; I have my shawl."

"The mosquitoes will devour you."

"There are no mosquitoes."

She heard him moving about the room; every sound indicating impatience and irritation. Another time she would have gone in at his request. She would, through habit, have yielded to his desire; not with any sense of submission or obedience to his compelling wishes, but unthinkingly, as we walk, move, sit, stand, go through the daily treadmill of the life which has been portioned out to us.

"Edna, dear, are you not coming in soon?" he asked again, this time fondly, with a note of entreaty.

"No; I am going to stay out here."

"This is more than folly," he blurted out. "I can't permit you to stay out there all night. You must come in the house instantly."

With a writhing motion she settled herself more securely in the hammock. She perceived that her will had blazed up, stubborn and resistant. She could not at that moment have done other than denied and resisted. She wondered if her husband had ever spoken to her like that before, and if she had submitted to his command. Of course she had; she remembered that she had. But she could not realize why or how she should have yielded, feeling as she then did.

"Léonce, go to bed," she said. "I mean to stay out here. I don't wish to go in, and I don't intend to. Don't speak to me like that again; I shall not answer you."

Mr. Pontellier had prepared for bed, but he slipped on an extra garment. He opened a bottle of wine, of which he kept a small and select supply in a buffet of his own. He drank a glass of the wine and went out on the gallery and offered a glass to his wife. She did not wish any. He drew up the rocker, hoisted his slippered feet on the rail, and proceeded to smoke a cigar. He smoked two cigars; then he went inside and drank another glass of wine. Mrs. Pontellier again declined to accept a glass when it was offered to her. Mr. Pontellier once more seated himself with elevated feet, and after a reasonable interval of time smoked some more cigars.

Edna began to feel like one who awakens gradually out of a dream, a delicious, grotesque, impossible dream, to feel again the realities pressing into her soul. The physical need for sleep began to overtake her; the exuberance which had sustained and exalted her spirit left her helpless and yielding to the conditions which crowded her in.

The stillest hour of the night had come, the hour before dawn, when the world seems to hold its breath. The moon hung low, and had turned from silver to copper in the sleeping sky. The old owl no longer hooted, and the water-oaks had ceased to moan as they bent their heads.

Edna arose, cramped from lying so long and still in the hammock. She tottered up the steps, clutching feebly at the post before passing into the house.

"Are you coming in, Léonce?" she asked, turning her face toward her husband.

"Yes, dear," he answered, with a glance following a misty puff of smoke. "Just as soon as I have finished my cigar."

XII

She slept but a few hours. They were troubled and feverish hours, disturbed with dreams that were intangible, that eluded her, leaving only an impression upon her half-awakened senses of something unattainable. She was up and dressed in the cool of the early morning. The air was invigorating and steadied somewhat her faculties. However, she was not seeking refreshment or help from any source either external or from within. She was blindly following whatever impulse moved her, as if she had placed herself in alien hands for direction, and freed her soul of responsibility.

Most of the people at that early hour were still in bed and asleep. A few, who intended to go over to the Chênière for mass, were moving about. The lovers, who had laid their plans the night before, were already strolling toward the wharf. The lady in black with her Sunday prayer book, velvet and gold-clasped, and her Sunday silver beads, was following them at no great distance. Old Monsieur Farival was up, and was more than half inclined to do anything that suggested itself. He put on his big straw hat, and taking his umbrella from the stand in the hall, followed the lady in black, never overtaking her.

The little negro girl who worked Madame Lebrun's sewing-machine was sweeping the galleries with long, absent-minded strokes of the broom. Edna sent her up into the house to awaken Robert.

"Tell him I am going to the Chênière. The boat is ready, tell him to hurry."

He had soon joined her. She had never sent for him before. She had never asked for him. She had never seemed to want him before. She did not appear conscious that she had done anything unusual in commanding his presence. He was apparently equally unconscious of anything extraordinary in the situation. But his face was suffused with a quiet glow when he met her.

They went together back to the kitchen to drink coffee. There was no time to wait for any nicety of service. They stood outside the window and the cook passed them their coffee and a roll, which they drank and ate from the window-sill. Edna said it tasted good. She had not thought of coffee nor of anything. He told her he had often noticed that she lacked forethought.

"Wasn't it enough to think of going to the *Chênière* and waking you up?" she laughed. "Do I have to think of everything?—as Léonce says when he's in a bad humor. I don't blame him; he'd never be in a bad humor if it weren't for me."

They took a short cut across the sands. At a distance they could see the curious procession moving toward the wharf—the lovers, shoulder to shoulder, creeping; the lady in black, gaining steadily upon them; old Monsieur Farival, losing ground inch by inch, and a young barefooted Spanish girl, with a red kerchief on her head and a basket on her arm, bringing up the rear.

Robert knew the girl, and he talked to her a little in the boat. No one present understood what they said. Her name was Mariequita. She had a round, sly, piquant face and pretty black eyes. Her hands were small, and she kept them folded over the handle of her basket. Her feet were broad and coarse. She did not strive to hide them. Edna looked at her feet, and noticed the sand and slime between her brown toes.

Beaudelet grumbled because Mariequita was there, taking up so much room. In reality he was annoyed at having old Monsieur Farival, who considered himself the better sailor of the two. But he would not quarrel with so old a man as Monsieur Farival, so he quarreled with Mariequita. The girl was deprecatory at one moment, appealing to Robert. She was saucy the next, moving her head up and down, making "eyes" at Robert and making "mouths" at Beaudelet.

The lovers were all alone. They saw nothing, they heard nothing. The lady in black was counting her beads for the third time. Old Monsieur Farival talked incessantly of what he knew about handling a boat, and of what Beaudelet did not know on the same subject.

Edna liked it all. She looked Mariequita up and down, from her ugly brown toes to her pretty black eyes, and back again.

"Why does she look at me like that?" inquired the girl of Robert.

"Maybe she thinks you are pretty. Shall I ask her?"

"No. Is she your sweetheart?"

"She's a married lady, and has two children."

"Oh! well! Francisco ran away with Sylvano's wife, who had four children. They took all his money and one of the children and stole his boat."

"Shut up!"

"Does she understand?"

"Oh, hush!"

"Are those two married over there—leaning on each other?"

"Of course not," laughed Robert.

"Of course not," echoed Mariequita, with a serious, confirmatory bob of the head.

The sun was high up and beginning to bite. The swift breeze seemed to Edna to bury the sting of it into the pores of her face and hands. Robert held his umbrella over her.

As they went cutting sidewise through the water, the sails bellied taut, with the wind filling and overflowing them. Old Monsieur Farival laughed sardonically at something as he looked at the sails, and Beaudelet swore at the old man under his breath.

Sailing across the bay to the *Chênière Caminada*, Edna felt as if she were being borne away from some anchorage which had held her fast, whose chains had been loosening—had snapped the night before when the mystic spirit was abroad, leaving her free to drift whithersoever she chose to set her sails. Robert spoke to her incessantly; he no longer noticed Mariequita. The girl had shrimps in her bamboo basket. They were covered with Spanish moss. She beat the moss impatiently, and muttered to herself sullenly.

"Let us go to Grande Terre[4] to-morrow?" said Robert in a low voice.

"What shall we do there?"

"Climb up the hill to the old fort and look at the little wriggling gold snakes, and watch the lizards sun themselves."

She gazed away toward Grande Terre and thought she would like to be alone there with Robert, in the sun, listening to the ocean's roar and watching the slimy lizards writhe in and out among the ruins of the old fort.

"And the next day or the next we can sail to the Bayou Brulow,"[5] he went on.

"What shall we do there?"

"Anything—cast bait for fish."

"No; we'll go back to Grande Terre. Let the fish alone."

"We'll go wherever you like," he said. "I'll have Tonie come over and help me patch and trim my boat. We shall not need Beaudelet nor any one. Are you afraid of the pirogue?"[6]

"Oh, no."

"Then I'll take you some night in the pirogue when the moon shines. Maybe your Gulf spirit will whisper to you in which of these islands the treasures are hidden—direct you to the very spot, perhaps."

"And in a day we should be rich!" she laughed. "I'd give it all to you, the pirate gold and every bit of treasure we could dig up. I think you would know how to spend it. Pirate gold isn't a thing to be hoarded or utilized. It is something to squander and throw to the four winds, for the fun of seeing the golden specks fly."

"We'd share it, and scatter it together," he said. His face flushed.

They all went together up to the quaint little Gothic church of Our Lady of Lourdes, gleaming all brown and yellow with paint in the sun's glare.

Only Beaudelet remained behind, tinkering at his boat, and Mariequita walked away with her basket of shrimps, casting a look of childish ill-humor and reproach at Robert from the corner of her eye.

---

4. Another island near Grande Isle.
5. A nearby village built on stilts or platforms in one of the marshy areas called "bayous," and in-habited by Acadians (descendants of French-Ca-nadians expelled from Nova Scotia in 1755).
6. Canoe.

XIII

A feeling of oppression and drowsiness overcame Edna during the service. Her head began to ache, and the lights on the altar swayed before her eyes. Another time she might have made an effort to regain her composure; but her one thought was to quit the stifling atmosphere of the church and reach the open air. She arose, climbing over Robert's feet with a muttered apology. Old Monsieur Farival, flurried, curious, stood up, but upon seeing that Robert had followed Mrs. Pontellier, he sank back into his seat. He whispered an anxious inquiry of the lady in black, who did not notice him or reply, but kept her eyes fastened upon the pages of her velvet prayer-book.

"I felt giddy and almost overcome," Edna said, lifting her hands instinctively to her head and pushing her straw hat up from her forehead. "I couldn't have stayed through the service." They were outside in the shadow of the church. Robert was full of solicitude.

"It was folly to have thought of going in the first place, let alone staying. Come over to Madame Antoine's; you can rest there." He took her arm and led her away, looking anxiously and continuously down into her face.

How still it was, with only the voice of the sea whispering through the reeds that grew in the salt-water pools! The long line of little gray, weather-beaten houses nestled peacefully among the orange trees. It must always have been God's day on that low, drowsy island, Edna thought. They stopped, leaning over a jagged fence made of sea-drift, to ask for water. A youth, a mild-faced Acadian, was drawing water from the cistern, which was nothing more than a rusty buoy, with an opening on one side, sunk in the ground. The water which the youth handed to them in a tin pail was not cold to taste, but it was cool to her heated face, and it greatly revived and refreshed her.

Madame Antoine's cot[7] was at the far end of the village. She welcomed them with all the native hospitality, as she would have opened her door to let the sunlight in. She was fat, and walked heavily and clumsily across the floor. She could speak no English, but when Robert made her understand that the lady who accompanied him was ill and desired to rest, she was all eagerness to make Edna feel at home and to dispose of her comfortably.

The whole place was immaculately clean, and the big, four-posted bed, snow-white, invited one to repose. It stood in a small side room which looked out across a narrow grass plot toward the shed, where there was a disabled boat lying keel upward.

Madame Antoine had not gone to mass. Her son Tonie had, but she supposed he would soon be back, and she invited Robert to be seated

7. Cottage.

and wait for him. But he went and sat outside the door and smoked. Madame Antoine busied herself in the large front room preparing dinner. She was boiling mullets[8] over a few red coals in the huge fireplace.

Edna, left alone in the little side room, loosened her clothes, removing the greater part of them. She bathed her face, her neck and arms in the basin that stood between the windows. She took off her shoes and stockings and stretched herself in the very center of the high, white bed. How luxurious it felt to rest thus in a strange, quaint bed, with its sweet country odor of laurel lingering about the sheets and mattress! She stretched her strong limbs that ached a little. She ran her fingers through her loosened hair for a while. She looked at her round arms as she held them straight up and rubbed them one after the other, observing closely, as if it were something she saw for the first time, the fine, firm quality and texture of her flesh. She clasped her hands easily above her head, and it was thus she fell asleep.

She slept lightly at first, half awake and drowsily attentive to the things about her. She could hear Madame Antoine's heavy, scraping tread as she walked back and forth on the sanded floor. Some chickens were clucking outside the windows, scratching for bits of gravel in the grass. Later she half heard the voices of Robert and Tonie talking under the shed. She did not stir. Even her eyelids rested numb and heavily over her sleepy eyes. The voices went on—Tonie's slow, Acadian drawl, Robert's quick, soft, smooth French. She understood French imperfectly unless directly addressed, and the voices were only part of the other drowsy, muffled sounds lulling her.

When Edna awoke it was with the conviction that she had slept long and soundly. The voices were hushed under the shed. Madame Antoine's step was no longer to be heard in the adjoining room. Even the chickens had gone elsewhere to scratch and cluck. The mosquito bar[9] was drawn over her; the old woman had come in while she slept and let down the bar. Edna arose quietly from the bed, and looking between the curtains of the window, she saw by the slanting rays of the sun that the afternoon was far advanced. Robert was out there under the shed, reclining in the shade against the sloping keel of the overturned boat. He was reading from a book. Tonie was no longer with him. She wondered what had become of the rest of the party. She peeped out at him two or three times as she stood washing herself in the little basin between the windows.

Madame Antoine had laid some coarse, clean towels upon a chair, and had placed a box of *poudre de riz*[1] within easy reach. Edna dabbed the powder upon her nose and cheeks as she looked at herself closely in

8. Small fish.
9. Bar attached to the bedframe holding mosquito netting.
1. Rice powder or talcum powder.

the little distorted mirror which hung on the wall above the basin. Her eyes were bright and wide awake and her face glowed.

When she had completed her toilet she walked into the adjoining room. She was very hungry. No one was there. But there was a cloth spread upon the table that stood against the wall, and a cover was laid for one, with a crusty brown loaf and a bottle of wine beside the plate. Edna bit a piece from the brown loaf, tearing it with her strong, white teeth. She poured some of the wine into the glass and drank it down. Then she went softly out of doors, and plucking an orange from the low-hanging bough of a tree, threw it at Robert, who did not know she was awake and up.

And illumination broke over his whole face when he saw her and joined her under the orange tree.

"How many years have I slept?" she inquired. "The whole island seems changed. A new race of beings must have sprung up, leaving only you and me as past relics. How many ages ago did Madame Antoine and Tonie die? and when did our people from Grand Isle disappear from the earth?"

He familiarly adjusted a ruffle upon her shoulder.

"You have slept precisely one hundred years. I was left here to guard your slumbers; and for one hundred years I have been out under the shed reading a book. The only evil I couldn't prevent was to keep a broiled fowl from drying up."

"If it had turned to stone, still will I eat it," said Edna, moving with him into the house. "But really, what has become of Monsieur Farival and the others?"

"Gone hours ago. When they found that you were sleeping they thought it best not to awake you. Anyway, I wouldn't have let them. What was I here for?"

"I wonder if Lèonce will be uneasy!" she speculated, as she seated herself at table.

"Of course not; he knows you are with me," Robert replied, as he busied himself among sundry pans and covered dishes which had been left standing on the hearth.

"Where are Madame Antoine and her son?" asked Edna.

"Gone to Vespers,[2] and to visit some friends, I believe. I am to take you back in Tonie's boat whenever you are ready to go."

He stirred the smoldering ashes till the broiled fowl began to sizzle afresh. He served her with no mean repast, dripping the coffee anew and sharing it with her. Madame Antoine had cooked little else than the mullets, but while Edna slept Robert had foraged the island. He was childishly gratified to discover her appetite, and to see the relish with which she ate the food which he had procured for her.

---

2. Evening church service.

"Shall we go right away?" she asked, after draining her glass and brushing together the crumbs of the crusty loaf.

"The sun isn't as low as it will be in two hours," he answered.

"The sun will be gone in two hours."

"Well, let it go; who cares!"

They waited a good while under the orange trees, till Madame Antoine came back, panting, waddling, with a thousand apologies to explain her absence. Tonie did not dare to return. He was shy, and would not willingly face any woman except his mother.

It was very pleasant to stay there under the orange trees, while the sun dipped lower and lower, turning the western sky to flaming copper and gold. The shadows lengthened and crept out like stealthy, grotesque monsters across the grass.

Edna and Robert both sat upon the ground—that is, he lay upon the ground beside her, occasionally picking at the hem of her muslin gown.

Madame Antoine seated her fat body, broad and squat, upon a bench beside the door. She had been talking all the afternoon, and had wound herself up to the story-telling pitch.

And what stories she told them! But twice in her life she had left the *Chênière Caminada*, and then for the briefest span. All her years she had squatted and waddled there upon the island, gathering legends of the Baratarians[3] and the sea. The night came on, with the moon to lighten it. Edna could hear the whispering voices of dead men and the click of muffled gold.

When she and Robert stepped into Tonie's boat, with the red lateen sail, misty spirit forms were prowling in the shadows and among the reeds, and upon the water were phantom ships, speeding to cover.

XIV

The youngest boy, Étienne, had been very naughty, Madame Ratignolle said, as she delivered him into the hands of his mother. He had been unwilling to go to bed and had made a scene; where upon she had taken charge of him and pacified him as well as she could. Raoul had been in bed and asleep for two hours.

The youngster was in his long white nightgown, that kept tripping him up as Madame Ratignolle led him along by the hand. With the other chubby fist he rubbed his eyes, which were heavy with sleep and ill humor. Edna took him in her arms, and seating herself in the rocker, began to coddle and caress him, calling him all manner of tender names, soothing him to sleep.

It was not more than nine o'clock. No one had yet gone to bed but the children.

---

3. Pirates who plundered in the area of Barataria Bay.

Léonce had been very uneasy at first, Madame Ratignolle said, and
had wanted to start at once for the *Chênière*. But Monsieur Farival had
assured him that his wife was only overcome with sleep and fatigue, that
Tonie would bring her safely back later in the day; and he had thus been
dissuaded from crossing the bay. He had gone over to Klein's, looking
up some cotton broker whom he wished to see in regard to securities,
exchanges, stocks, bonds, or something of the sort, Madame Ratignolle
did not remember what. He said he would not remain away late. She
herself was suffering from heat and oppression, she said. She carried a
bottle of salts and a large fan. She would not consent to remain with
Edna, for Monsieur Ratignolle was alone, and he detested above all
things to be left alone.

When Étienne had fallen asleep Edna bore him into the back room,
and Robert went and lifted the mosquito bar that she might lay the child
comfortably in his bed. The quadroon had vanished. When they
emerged from the cottage Robert bade Edna good-night. "Do you
know we have been together the whole livelong day, Robert—since
early this morning?" she said at parting.

"All but the hundred years when you were sleeping. Good-night."

He pressed her hand and went away in the direction of the beach. He
did not join any of the others, but walked alone toward the Gulf.

Edna stayed outside, awaiting her husband's return. She had no desire to sleep or to retire; nor did she feel like going over to sit with the
Ratignolles, or to join Madame Lebrun and a group whose animated
voices reached her as they sat in conversation before the house. She let
her mind wander back over her stay at Grand Isle; and she tried to discover wherein this summer had been different from any and every
other summer of her life. She could only realize that she herself—her
present self—was in some way different from the other self. That she
was seeing with different eyes and making the acquaintance of new
conditions in herself that colored and changed her environment, she
did not yet suspect.

She wondered why Robert had gone away and left her. It did not
occur to her to think he might have grown tired of being with her the
livelong day. She was not tired, and she felt that he was not. She regretted that he had gone. It was so much more natural to have him stay,
when he was not absolutely required to leave her.

As Edna waited for her husband she sang low a little song that Robert
had sung as they crossed the bay. It began with "Ah! *Si tu savais*," and
every verse ended with "*si tu savais*."[4]

Robert's voice was not pretentious. It was musical and true. The
voice, the notes, the whole refrain haunted her memory.

---

4. *Couldst Thou but Know*, a song by Michael William Balfe (1808–1870).

XV

When Edna entered the dining-room one evening a little late, as was her habit, an unusually animated conversation seemed to be going on. Several persons were talking at once, and Victor's voice was predominating, even over that of his mother. Edna had returned late from her bath, had dressed in some haste, and her face was flushed. Her head, set off by the dainty white gown, suggested a rich, rare blossom. She took her seat at table between old Monsieur Farival and Madame Ratignolle.

As she seated herself and was about to begin to eat her soup, which had been served when she entered the room, several persons informed her simultaneously that Robert was going to Mexico. She laid her spoon down and looked about her bewildered. He had been with her, reading to her all the morning, and had never even mentioned such a place as Mexico. She had not seen him during the afternoon; she had heard some one say he was at the house, upstairs with his mother. This she had thought nothing of, though she was surprised when he did not join her later in the afternoon, when she went down to the beach.

She looked across at him, where he sat beside Madame Lebrun, who presided. Edna's face was a blank picture of bewilderment, which she never thought of disguising. He lifted his eyebrows with the pretext of a smile as he returned her glance. He looked embarrassed and uneasy.

"When is he going?" she asked of everybody in general, as if Robert were not there to answer for himself.

"To-night!" "This very evening!" "Did you ever!" "What possesses him!" some of the replies she gathered, uttered simultaneously in French and English.

"Impossible!" she exclaimed. "How can a person start off from Grand Isle to Mexico at a moment's notice, as if he were going over to Klein's or to the wharf or down to the beach?"

"I said all along I was going to Mexico; I've been saying so for years!" cried Robert, in an excited and irritable tone, with the air of a man defending himself against a swarm of stinging insects.

Madame Lebrun knocked on the table with her knife handle.

"Please let Robert explain why he is going, and why he is going to-night," she called out. "Really, this table is getting to be more and more like Bedlam[5] every day, with everybody talking at once. Sometimes—I hope God will forgive me—but positively, sometimes I wish Victor would lose the power of speech."

Victor laughed sardonically as he thanked his mother for her holy wish, of which he failed to see the benefit to anybody, except that it might afford her a more ample opportunity and license to talk herself.

5. Famous lunatic asylum in London, hence any madhouse.

Monsieur Farival thought that Victor should have been taken out in mid-ocean in his earliest youth and drowned. Victor thought there would be more logic in thus disposing of old people with an established claim for making themselves universally obnoxious. Madame Lebrun grew a trifle hysterical; Robert called his brother some sharp, hard names.

"There's nothing much to explain, mother," he said; though he explained, nevertheless—looking chiefly at Edna—that he could only meet the gentleman whom he intended to join at Vera Cruz by taking such and such a steamer, which left New Orleans on such a day; that Beaudelet was going out with his lugger-load of vegetables that night, which gave him an opportunity of reaching the city and making his vessel in time.

"But when did you make up your mind to all this?" demanded Monsieur Farival.

"This afternoon," returned Robert, with a shade of annoyance.

"At what time this afternoon?" persisted the old gentleman, with nagging determination, as if he were cross-questioning a criminal in a court of justice.

"At four o'clock this afternoon. Monsieur Farival," Robert replied, in a high voice and with a lofty air, which reminded Edna of some gentleman on the stage.

She had forced herself to eat most of her soup, and now she was picking the flaky bits of a *court bouillon*[6] with her fork.

The lovers were profiting by the general conversation on Mexico to speak in whispers of matters which they rightly considered were interesting to no one but themselves. The lady in black had once received a pair of prayer-beads of curious workmanship from Mexico, with very special indulgence[7] attached to them, but she had never been able to ascertain whether the indulgence extended outside the Mexican border. Father Fochel of the Cathedral had attempted to explain it; but he had not done so to her satisfaction. And she begged that Robert would interest himself, and discover, if possible, whether she was entitled to the indulgence accompanying the remarkably curious Mexican prayer-beads.

Madame Ratignolle hoped that Robert would exercise extreme caution in dealing with the Mexicans, who, she considered, were a treacherous people, unscrupulous and revengeful. She trusted she did them no injustice in thus condemning them as a race. She had known personally but one Mexican, who made and sold excellent tamales, and whom she would have trusted implicitly, so soft-spoken was he. One

---

6. Broth in which fish is poached.
7. According to a Roman Catholic belief, some religious articles, if specifically blessed, could remit part of the punishment for sins after death.

day he was arrested for stabbing his wife. She never knew whether he had been hanged or not.

Victor had grown hilarious, and was attempting to tell an anecdote about a Mexican girl who served chocolate one winter in a restaurant in Dauphine Street. No one would listen to him but old Monsieur Farival, who went into convulsions over the droll story.

Edna wondered if they had all gone mad, to be talking and clamoring at that rate. She herself could think of nothing to say about Mexico or the Mexicans.

"At what time do you leave?" she asked Robert.

"At ten," he told her. "Beaudelet wants to wait for the moon."

"Are you all ready to go?"

"Quite ready. I shall only take a handbag, and shall pack my trunk in the city."

He turned to answer some question put to him by his mother and Edna, having finished her black coffee, left the table.

She went directly to her room. The little cottage was close and stuffy after leaving the outer air. But she did not mind; there appeared to be a hundred different things demanding her attention indoors. She began to set the toilet-stand to rights, grumbling at the negligence of the quadroon, who was in the adjoining room putting the children to bed. She gathered together stray garments that were hanging on the backs of chairs, and put each where it belonged in closet or bureau drawer. She changed her gown for a more comfortable and commodious wrapper. She rearranged her hair, combing and brushing it with unusual energy. Then she went in and assisted the quadroon in getting the boys to bed.

They were very playful and inclined to talk—to do anything but lie quiet and go to sleep. Edna sent the quadroon away to her supper and told her she need not return. Then she sat and told the children a story. Instead of soothing it excited them, and added to their wakefulness. She left them in heated argument, speculating about the conclusion of the tale which their mother promised to finish the following night.

The little black girl came in to say that Madame Lebrun would like to have Mrs. Pontellier go and sit with them over at the house till Mr. Robert went away. Edna returned answer that she had already undressed, that she did not feel quite well, but perhaps she would go over to the house later. She started to dress again, and got as far advanced as to remove her *peignoir*. But changing her mind once more she resumed the *peignoir*, and went outside and sat down before her door. She was overheated and irritable, and fanned herself energetically for a while. Madame Ratignolle came down to discover what was the matter.

"All that noise and confusion at the table must have upset me," replied Edna, "and moreover, I hate shocks and surprises. The idea of Robert starting off in such a ridiculously sudden and dramatic way! As if it were a matter of life and death! Never saying a word about it all morning when he was with me."

"Yes," agreed Madame Ratignolle. "I think it was showing us all—you especially—very little consideration. It wouldn't have surprised me in any of the others; those Lebruns are all given to heroics. But I must say I should never have expected such a thing from Robert. Are you not coming down? Come on, dear; it doesn't look friendly."

"No," said Edna, a little sullenly. "I can't go to the trouble of dressing again; I don't feel like it."

"You needn't dress; you look all right; fasten a belt around your waist. Just look at me!"

"No," persisted Edna; "but you go on. Madame Lebrun might be offended if we both stayed away."

Madame Ratignolle kissed Edna good-night, and went away, being in truth rather desirous of joining in the general and animated conversation which was still in progress concerning Mexico and the Mexicans.

Somewhat later Robert came up, carrying his hand-bag.

"Aren't you feeling well?" he asked.

"Oh, well enough. Are you going right away?"

He lit a match and looked at his watch. "In twenty minutes," he said. The sudden and brief flare of the match emphasized the darkness for a while. He sat down upon a stool which the children had left out on the porch.

"Get a chair," said Edna.

"This will do," he replied. He put on his soft hat and nervously took it off again, and wiping his face with his handkerchief, complained of the heat.

"Take the fan," said Edna, offering it to him.

"Oh, no! Thank you. It does no good; you have to stop fanning some time, and feel all the more uncomfortable afterward."

"That's one of the ridiculous things which men always say. I have never known one to speak otherwise of fanning. How long will you be gone?"

"Forever, perhaps. I don't know. It depends upon a good many things."

"Well, in case it shouldn't be forever, how long will it be?"

"I don't know."

"This seems to me perfectly preposterous and uncalled for. I don't like it. I don't understand your motive for silence and mystery, never saying a word to me about it this morning." He remained silent, not offering to defend himself. He only said, after a moment:

"Don't part from me in an ill-humor. I never knew you to be out of patience with me before."

"I don't want to part in any ill-humor," said she. "But can't you understand? I've grown used to seeing you, to having you with me all the time, and your action seems unfriendly, even unkind. You don't even offer an excuse for it. Why, I was planning to be together, thinking of how pleasant it would be to see you in the city next winter."

"So was I," he blurted. "Perhaps that's the—" He stood up suddenly and held out his hand. "Good-by, my dear Mrs. Pontellier; good-by. You won't—I hope you won't completely forget me." She clung to his hand, striving to detain him.

"Write to me when you get there, won't you, Robert?" she entreated.

"I will, thank you. Good-by."

How unlike Robert! The merest acquaintance would have said something more emphatic than "I will, thank you; good-by," to such a request.

He had evidently already taken leave of the people over at the house, for he descended the steps and went to join Beaudelet, who was out there with an oar across his shoulder waiting for Robert. They walked away in the darkness. She could only hear Beaudelet's voice; Robert had apparently not even spoken a word of greeting to his companion.

Edna bit her handkerchief convulsively, striving to hold back and to hide, even from herself as she would have hidden from another the emotion which was troubling—tearing—her. Her eyes were brimming with tears.

For the first time she recognized anew the symptoms of infatuation which she felt incipiently as a child, as a girl in her earliest teens, and later as a young woman. The recognition did not lessen the reality, the poignancy of the revelation by any suggestion or promise of instability. The past was nothing to her; offered no lesson which she was willing to heed. The future was a mystery which she never attempted to penetrate. The present alone was significant; was hers, to torture her as it was doing then with the biting conviction that she had lost that which she had held, that she had been denied that which her impassioned, newly awakened being demanded.

XVI

"Do you miss your friend greatly?" asked Mademoiselle Reisz one morning as she came creeping up behind Edna, who had just left her cottage on her way to the beach. She spent much of her time in the water since she had acquired finally the art of swimming. As their stay at Grand Isle drew near its close, she felt that she could not give too much time to a diversion which afforded her the only real pleasurable moments that she knew. When Mademoiselle Reisz came and touched her upon the shoulder and spoke to her, the woman seemed to echo the thought which was ever in Edna's mind; or, better, the feeling which constantly possessed her.

Robert's going had some way taken the brightness, the color, the meaning out of everything. The conditions of her life were in no way changed, but her whole existence was dulled, like a faded garment which seems to be no longer worth wearing. She sought him everywhere—in others whom she induced to talk about him. She went up in the mornings to Madame Lebrun's room, braving the clatter of the old sewing-machine. She sat there and chatted at intervals as Robert had done. She gazed around the room at the pictures and photographs hanging upon the wall, and discovered in some corner an old family album, which she examined with the keenest interest, appealing to Madame Lebrun for enlightenment concerning the many figures and faces which she discovered between its pages.

There was a picture of Madame Lebrun with Robert as a baby, seated in her lap, a round-faced infant with a fist in his mouth. The eyes alone in the baby suggested the man. And that was he also in kilts, at the age of five, wearing long curls and holding a whip in his hand. It made Edna laugh, and she laughed, too, at the portrait in his first long trousers; while another interested her, taken when he left for college, looking thin, long-faced, with eyes full of fire, ambition and great intentions. But there was no recent picture, none which suggested the Robert who had gone away five days ago, leaving a void and wilderness behind him.

"Oh, Robert stopped having his pictures taken when he had to pay for them himself! He found wiser use for his money, he says," explained Madame Lebrun. She had a letter from him, written before he left New Orleans. Edna wished to see the letter, and Madame Lebrun told her to look for it either on the table or the dresser, or perhaps it was on the mantelpiece.

The letter was on the bookshelf. It possessed the greatest interest and attraction for Edna; the envelope, its size and shape, the postmark, the handwriting. She examined every detail of the outside before opening it. There were only a few lines, setting forth that he would leave the city that afternoon, that he had packed his trunk in good shape, that he was well, and sent her his love and begged to be affectionately remembered to all. There was no special message to Edna except a postscript saying that if Mrs. Pontellier desired to finish the book which he had been reading to her, his mother would find it in his room, among other books there on the table. Edna experienced a pang of jealousy because he had written to his mother rather than to her.

Every one seemed to take for granted that she missed him. Even her husband, when he came down the Saturday following Robert's departure, expressed regret that he had gone.

"How do you get on without him, Edna?" he asked.

"It's very dull without him," she admitted. Mr. Pontellier had seen Robert in the city, and Edna asked him a dozen questions or more. Where had they met? On Carondelet Street, in the morning. They had gone "in" and had a drink and a cigar together. What had they talked about? Chiefly about his prospects in Mexico, which Mr. Pontellier thought were promising. How did he look? How did he seem—grave, or gay, or how? Quite cheerful, and wholly taken up with the idea of his trip, which Mr. Pontellier found altogether natural in a young fellow about to seek fortune and adventure in a strange, queer country.

Edna tapped her foot impatiently, and wondered why the children persisted in playing in the sun when they might be under the trees. She went down and led them out of the sun, scolding the quadroon for not being more attentive.

It did not strike her as in the least grotesque that she should be making of Robert the object of conversation and leading her husband to speak of him. The sentiment which she entertained for Robert in no way resembled that which she felt for her husband, or had ever felt, or ever expected to feel. She had all her life long been accustomed to harbor thoughts and emotions which never voiced themselves. They had never taken the form of struggles. They belonged to her and were her own, and she entertained the conviction that she had a right to them and that they concerned no one but herself. Edna had once told Madame Ratignolle that she would never sacrifice herself for her children, or for any one. Then had followed a rather heated argument; the two women did not appear to understand each other or to be talking the same language. Edna tried to appease her friend, to explain.

"I would give up the unessential; I would give my money. I would give my life for my children; but I wouldn't give myself. I can't make it more clear; it's only something which I am beginning to comprehend, which is revealing itself to me."

"I don't know what you would call the essential, or what you mean by the unessential," said Madame Ratignolle, cheerfully; "but a woman who would give her life for her children could do no more than that— your Bible tells you so. I'm sure I couldn't do more than that."

"Oh, yes you could!" laughed Edna.

She was not surprised at Mademoiselle Reisz's question the morning that lady, following her to the beach, tapped her on the shoulder and asked if she did not greatly miss her young friend.

"Oh, good morning, Mademoiselle; it is you? Why, of course I miss Robert. Are you going down to bathe?"

"Why should I go down to bathe at the very end of the season when I haven't been in the surf all summer?" replied the woman, disagreeably.

"I beg your pardon," offered Edna, in some embarrassment, for she

should have remembered that Mademoiselle Reisz's avoidance of the
water had furnished a theme for much pleasantry. Some among them
thought it was on account of her false hair, or the dread of getting the
violets wet, while others attributed it to the natural aversion for water
sometimes believed to accompany the artistic temperament. Mademoiselle offered Edna some chocolates in a paper bag, which she took from
her pocket, by way of showing that she bore no ill feeling. She habitually ate chocolates for their sustaining quality; they contained much
nutriment in small compass, she said. They saved her from starvation,
as Madame Lebrun's table was utterly impossible; and no one save so
impertinent a woman as Madame Lebrun could think of offering such
food to people and requiring them to pay for it.

"She must feel very lonely without her son," said Edna, desiring to
change the subject. "Her favorite son, too. It must have been quite hard
to let him go."

Mademoiselle laughed maliciously.

"Her favorite son! Oh dear! Who could have been imposing such a
tale upon you? Aline Lebrun lives for Victor, and for Victor alone. She
has spoiled him into the worthless creature he is. She worships him and
the ground he walks on. Robert is very well in a way, to give up all the
money he can earn to the family, and keep the barest pittance for himself. Favorite son, indeed! I miss the poor fellow myself, my dear. I liked
to see him and to hear him about the place—the only Lebrun who is
worth a pinch of salt. He comes to see me often in the city. I like to play
to him. That Victor! hanging would be too good for him. It's a wonder
Robert hasn't beaten him to death long ago."

"I thought he had great patience with his brother," offered Edna,
glad to be talking about Robert, no matter what was said.

"Oh! he thrashed him well enough a year or two ago," said Mademoiselle. "It was about a Spanish girl, whom Victor considered that he
had some sort of claim upon. He met Robert one day talking to the girl,
or walking with her, or bathing with her, or carrying her basket—I don't
remember what;—and he became so insulting and abusive that Robert
gave him a thrashing on the spot that has kept him comparatively in
order for a good while. It's about time he was getting another."

"Was her name Mariequita?" asked Edna.

"Mariequita—yes, that was it. Mariequita. I had forgotten. Oh, she's
a sly one, and a bad one, that Mariequita!"

Edna looked down at Mademoiselle Reisz and wondered how she
could have listened to her venom so long. For some reason she felt depressed, almost unhappy. She had not intended to go into the water; but
she donned her bathing suit, and left Mademoiselle alone, seated under
the shade of the children's tent. The water was growing cooler as the
season advanced. Edna plunged and swam about with an abandon that

thrilled and invigorated her. She remained a long time in the water, half hoping that Mademoiselle Reisz would not wait for her.

But Mademoiselle waited. She was very amiable during the walk back, and raved much over Edna's appearance in her bathing suit. She talked about music. She hoped that Edna would go to see her in the city, and wrote her address with the stub of a pencil on a piece of card which she found in her pocket.

"When do you leave?" asked Edna.

"Next Monday; and you?"

"The following week," answered Edna, adding, "It has been a pleasant summer, hasn't it, Mademoiselle?"

"Well," agreed Mademoiselle Reisz, with a shrug, "rather pleasant, if it hadn't been for the mosquitoes and the Farival twins."

XVII

The Pontelliers possessed a very charming home on Esplanade Street[8] in New Orleans. It was a large, double cottage, with a broad front veranda, whose round, fluted columns supported the sloping roof. The house was painted a dazzling white; the outside shutters or jalousies, were green. In the yard, which was kept scrupulously neat, were flowers and plants of every description which flourishes in South Louisiana. Within doors the appointments were perfect after the conventional type. The softest carpets and rugs covered the floors; rich and tasteful draperies hung at doors and windows. There were paintings, selected with judgment and discrimination, upon the walls. The cut glass, the silver, the heavy damask which daily appeared upon the table were the envy of many women whose husbands were less generous than Mr. Pontellier.

Mr. Pontellier was very fond of walking about his house examining its various appointments and details, to see that nothing was amiss. He greatly valued his possessions, chiefly because they were his, and derived genuine pleasure from contemplating a painting, a statuette, a rare lace curtain—no matter what—after he had bought it and placed it among his household goods.

On Tuesday afternoons—Tuesday being Mrs. Pontellier's reception day[9]—there was a constant stream of callers—women who came in carriages or in the street cars, or walked when the air was soft and distance permitted. A light-colored mulatto boy, in dress coat and bearing a diminutive silver tray for the reception of cards, admitted them. A maid, in white fluted cap, offered the callers liqueur, coffee, or chocolate, as

---

8. The most exclusive address of the Creole aristocracy.

9. The day when a woman was "at home" to receive visitors.

they might desire. Mrs. Pontellier, attired in a handsome reception gown, remained in the drawing-room the entire afternoon receiving her visitors. Men sometimes called in the evening with their wives.

This had been the programme which Mrs. Pontellier had religiously followed since her marriage, six years before. Certain evenings during the week she and her husband attended the opera or sometimes the play.

Mr. Pontellier left his home in the mornings between nine and ten o'clock, and rarely returned before half-past six or seven in the evening —dinner being served at half-past seven.

He and his wife seated themselves at table on Tuesday evening, a few weeks after their return from Grand Isle. They were alone to-gether. The boys were being put to bed; the patter of their bare, escap-ing feet could be heard occasionally, as well as the pursuing voice of the quadroon, lifted in mild protest and entreaty. Mrs. Pontellier did not wear her usual Tuesday reception gown; she was in ordinary house dress. Mr. Pontellier who was observant about such things, noticed it, as he served the soup and handed it to the boy in waiting.

"Tired out, Edna? Whom did you have? Many callers?" he asked. He tasted his soup and began to season it with pepper, salt, vinegar, mustard—everything within reach.

"There were a good many," replied Edna, who was eating her soup with evident satisfaction. "I found their cards when I got home; I was out."

"Out!" exclaimed her husband, with something like genuine con-sternation in his voice as he laid down the vinegar cruet and looked at her through his glasses. "Why, what could have taken you out on Tuesday? What did you have to do?"

"Nothing. I simply felt like going out, and I went out."

"Well, I hope you left some suitable excuse," said her husband, somewhat appeased, as he added a dash of cayenne pepper to the soup.

"No, I left no excuse. I told Joe to say I was out, that was all."

"Why, my dear, I should think you'd understand by this time that people don't do such things; we've got to observe *les convenances*[1] if we ever expect to get on and keep up with procession. If you felt that you had to leave home this afternoon, you should have left some suitable explanation for your absence.

"This soup is really impossible; it's strange that woman hasn't learned yet to make a decent soup. Any free-lunch stand in town serves a better one. Was Mrs. Belthrop here?"

"Bring the tray with the cards, Joe. I don't remember who was here."

The boy retired and returned after a moment, bringing the tiny silver

___

1. The conventions.

tray, which was covered with ladies' visiting cards. He handed it to Mrs. Pontellier.

"Give it to Mr. Pontellier," she said.

Joe offered the tray to Mr. Pontellier, and removed the soup.

Mr. Pontellier scanned the names of his wife's callers, reading some of them aloud, with comments as he read.

" 'The Misses Delasidas.' I worked a big deal in futures[2] for their father this morning; nice girls; it's time they were getting married. 'Mrs. Belthrop.' I tell you what it is, Edna; you can't afford to snub Mrs. Belthrop. Why, Belthrop could buy and sell us ten times over. His business is worth a good, round sum to me. You'd better write her a note. 'Mrs. James Highcamp.' Hugh! the less you have to do with Mrs. Highcamp, the better. 'Madame Laforcé.' Came all the way from Carrolton,[3] too, poor old soul. 'Miss Wiggs,' 'Mrs. Eleanor Boltons.' " He pushed the cards aside.

"Mercy!" exclaimed Edna, who had been fuming. "Why are you taking the thing so seriously and making such a fuss over it?"

"I'm not making any fuss over it. But it's just such seeming trifles that we've got to take seriously; such things count."

The fish was scorched. Mr. Pontellier would not touch it. Edna said she did not mind a little scorched taste. The roast was in some way not to his fancy, and he did not like the manner in which the vegetables were served.

"It seems to me," he said, "we spend money enough in this house to procure at least one meal a day which a man could eat and retain his self-respect."

"You used to think the cook was a treasure," returned Edna, indifferently.

"Perhaps she was when she first came; but cooks are only human. They need looking after, like any other class of persons that you employ. Suppose I didn't look after the clerks in my office, just let them run things their own way; they'd soon make a nice mess of me and my business."

"Where are you going?" asked Edna, seeing that her husband arose from table without having eaten a morsel except a taste of the highly-seasoned soup.

"I'm going to get my dinner at the club. Good night." He went into the hall, took his hat and stick from the stand, and left the house.

She was somewhat familiar with such scenes. They had often made her very unhappy. On a few previous occasions she had been completely deprived of any desire to finish her dinner. Sometimes she had gone into the kitchen to administer a tardy rebuke to the cook. Once

2. A form of financial speculation.   3. Village to the west of New Orleans.

she went to her room and studied the cookbook during an entire evening, finally writing out a menu for the week, which left her harassed with a feeling that, after all, she had accomplished no good that was worth the name.

But that evening Edna finished her dinner alone, with forced deliberation. Her face was flushed and her eyes flamed with some inward fire that lighted them. After finishing her dinner she went to her room, having instructed the boy to tell any other callers that she was indisposed.

It was a large, beautiful room, rich and picturesque in the soft, dim light which the maid had turned low. She went and stood at an open window and looked out upon the deep tangle of the garden below. All the mystery and witchery of the night seemed to have gathered there amid the perfumes and the dusky and tortuous outlines of flowers and foliage. She was seeking herself and finding herself in just such sweet, half-darkness which met her moods. But the voices were not soothing that came to her from the darkness and the sky above and the stars. They jeered and sounded mournful notes without promise, devoid even of hope. She turned back into the room and began to walk to and fro down its whole length, without stopping, without resting. She carried in her hands a thin handkerchief, which she tore into ribbons, rolled into a ball, and flung from her. Once she stopped, and taking off her wedding ring, flung it upon the carpet. When she saw it lying there, she stamped her heel upon it, striving to crush it. But her small boot heel did not make an indenture, not a mark upon the little glittering circlet.

In a sweeping passion she seized a glass vase from the table and flung it upon the tiles of the hearth. She wanted to destroy something. The crash and clatter were what she wanted to hear.

A maid, alarmed at the din of breaking glass, entered the room to discover what was the matter.

"A vase fell upon the hearth," said Edna. "Never mind; leave it till morning."

"Oh! you might get some of the glass in your feet, ma'am," insisted the young woman, picking up bits of the broken vase that were scattered upon the carpet. "And here's your ring, ma'am, under the chair."

Edna held out her hand, and taking the ring, slipped it upon her finger.

XVIII

The following morning Mr. Pontellier, upon leaving for his office, asked Edna if she would not meet him in town in order to look at some new fixtures for the library.

"I hardly think we need new fixtures, Léonce. Don't let us get anything new; you are too extravagant. I don't believe you ever think of saving or putting by."

"The way to become rich is to make money, my dear Edna, not to save it," he said. He regretted that she did not feel inclined to go with him and select new fixtures. He kissed her good-by, and told her she was not looking well and must take care of herself. She was unusually pale and very quiet.

She stood on the front veranda as he quitted the house, and absently picked a few sprays of jessamine that grew upon a trellis near by. She inhaled the odor of the blossoms and thrust them into the bosom of her white morning gown. The boys were dragging along the banquette[4] a small "express wagon," which they had filled with block and sticks. The quadroon was following them with little quick steps, having assumed a fictitious animation and alacrity for the occasion. A fruit vender was crying his wares in the street.

Edna looked straight before her with a self-absorbed expression upon her face. She felt no interest in anything about her. The street, the children, the fruit vender, the flowers growing there under her eyes, were all part and parcel of an alien world which had suddenly become antagonistic.

She went back into the house. She had thought of speaking to the cook concerning her blunders of the previous night; but Mr. Pontellier had saved her that disagreeable mission, for which she was so poorly fitted. Mr. Pontellier's arguments were usually convincing with those whom he employed. He left home feeling quite sure that he and Edna would sit down that evening, and possibly a few subsequent evenings, to a dinner deserving of the name.

Edna spent an hour or two in looking over some of her old sketches. She could see their shortcomings and defects, which were glaring in her eyes. She tried to work a little, but found she was not in the humor. Finally she gathered together a few of the sketches—those which she considered the least discreditable; and she carried them with her when, a little later, she dressed and left the house. She looked handsome and distinguished in her street gown. The tan of the seashore had left her face, and her forehead was smooth, white, and polished beneath her heavy, yellow-brown hair. There were a few freckles on her face, and a small, dark mole near the under lip and one on the temple, half-hidden in her hair.

As Edna walked along the street she was thinking of Robert. She was still under the spell of her infatuation. She had tried to forget him, realizing the inutility of remembering. But the thought of him was like an

4. Sidewalk.

obsession, ever pressing itself upon her. It was not that she dwelt upon details of their acquaintance, or recalled in any special or peculiar way his personality; it was his being, his existence, which dominated her thought, fading sometimes as if it would melt into the mist of the forgotten, reviving again with an intensity which filled her with an incomprehensible longing.

Edna was on her way to Madame Ratignolle's. Their intimacy, begun at Grand Isle, had not declined, and they had seen each other with some frequency since their return to the city. The Ratignolles lived at no great distance from Edna's home, on the corner of a side street, where Monsieur Ratignolle owned and conducted a drug store which enjoyed a steady and prosperous trade. His father had been in the business before him, and Monsieur Ratignolle stood well in the community and bore an enviable reputation for integrity and clear-headedness. His family lived in commodious apartments over the store, having an entrance on the side within the *porte cochère*.[5] There was something which Edna thought very French, very foreign, about their whole manner of living. In the large and pleasant salon which extended across the width of the house, the Ratignolles entertained their friends once a fortnight with a *soirée musicale*,[6] sometimes diversified by card-playing. There was a friend who played upon the 'cello. One brought his flute and another his violin, while there were some who sang and a number who performed upon the piano with various degrees of taste and agility. The Ratignolles' *soirées musicales* were widely known, and it was considered a privilege to be invited to them.

Edna found her friend engaged in assorting the clothes which had returned that morning from the laundry. She at once abandoned her occupation upon seeing Edna, who had been ushered without ceremony into her presence.

"'Cité can do it as well as I; it is really her business," she explained to Edna, who apologized for interrupting her. And she summoned a young black woman, whom she instructed, in French, to be very careful in checking off the list which she handed her. She told her to notice particularly if a fine linen handkerchief of Monsieur Ratignolle's, which was missing last week, had been returned; and to be sure to set to one side such pieces as required mending and darning.

Then placing an arm around Edna's waist, she led her to the front of the house, to the salon, where it was cool and sweet with the odor of great roses that stood upon the hearth in jars.

Madame Ratignolle looked more beautiful than ever there at home, in a negligé which left her arms almost wholly bare and exposed the rich, melting curves of her white throat.

5. Porch which protects travelers alighting or   6. Musical evening.
boarding from a coach.

"Perhaps I shall be able to paint your picture some day," said Edna with a smile when they were seated. She produced the roll of sketches and started to unfold them. "I believe I ought to work again. I feel as if I wanted to be doing something. What do you think of them? Do you think it worth while to take it up again and study some more? I might study for a while with Laidpore."

She knew that Madame Ratignolle's opinion in such a matter would be next to valueless, that she herself had not alone decided, but determined; but she sought the words and praise and encouragement that would help her to put her heart into her venture.

"Your talent is immense, dear!"

"Nonsense!" protested Edna, well pleased.

"Immense, I tell you," persisted Madame Ratignolle, surveying the sketches one by one, at close range, then holding them at arm's length, narrowing her eyes, and dropping her head on one side. "Surely, this Bavarian peasant is worthy of framing; and this basket of apples! never have I seen anything more lifelike. One might almost be tempted to reach out a hand and take one."

Edna could not control a feeling which bordered upon complacency at her friend's praise, even realizing, as she did, its true worth. She retained a few of the sketches, and gave all the rest to Madame Ratignolle, who appreciated the gift far beyond its value and proudly exhibited the pictures to her husband when he came up from the store a little later for his midday dinner.

Mr. Ratignolle was one of those men who are called the salt of the earth. His cheerfulness was unbounded, and it was matched by his goodness of heart, his broad charity, and common sense. He and his wife spoke English with an accent which was only discernible through its un-English emphasis and a certain carefulness and deliberation. Edna's husband spoke English with no accent whatever. The Ratignolles understood each other perfectly. If ever the fusion of two human beings into one has been accomplished on this sphere it was surely in their union.

As Edna seated herself at table with them she thought, "Better a dinner of herbs,"[7] though it did not take her long to discover that was no dinner of herbs, but a delicious repast, simple, choice, and in every way satisfying.

Monsieur Ratignolle was delighted to see her, though he found her looking not so well as at Grand Isle, and he advised a tonic. He talked a good deal on various topics, a little politics, some city news and neighborhood gossip. He spoke with an animation and earnestness that gave an exaggerated importance to every syllable he uttered. His wife was

7. "Better is a dinner of herbs where love is,   15:15–17).
than a stalled ox and hatred therewith" (Proverbs

keenly interested in everything he said, laying down her fork the better to listen, chiming in, taking the words out of his mouth.

Edna felt depressed rather than soothed after leaving them. The little glimpse of domestic harmony which had been offered her, gave her no regret, no longing. It was not a condition of life which fitted her, and she could see in it but an appalling and hopeless ennui.[8] She was moved by a kind of commiseration for Madame Ratignolle,—a pity for that colorless existence which never uplifted its possessor beyond the region of blind contentment, in which no moment of anguish ever visited her soul, in which she would never have the taste of life's delirium. Edna vaguely wondered what she meant by "life's delirium." It had crossed her thought like some unsought, extraneous impression.

XIX

Edna could not help but think that it was very foolish, very childish, to have stamped upon her wedding ring and smashed the crystal vase upon the tiles. She was visited by no more outbursts, moving her to such futile expedients. She began to do as she liked and to feel as she liked. She completely abandoned her Tuesdays at home, and did not return the visits of those who had called upon her. She made no ineffectual efforts to conduct her household *en bonne ménagère*,[9] going and coming as it suited her fancy, and, so far as she was able, lending herself to any passing caprice.

Mr. Pontellier had been a rather courteous husband so long as he met a certain tacit submissiveness in his wife. But her new and unexpected line of conduct completely bewildered him. It shocked him. Then her absolute disregard for her duties as a wife angered him. When Mr. Pontellier became rude, Edna grew insolent. She had resolved never to take another step backward.

"It seems to me the utmost folly for a woman at the head of a household, and the mother of children, to spend in an atelier[1] days which would be better employed contriving for the comfort of her family."

"I feel like painting," answered Edna. "Perhaps I shan't always feel like it."

"Then in God's name paint! but don't let the family go to the devil. There's Madame Ratignolle; because she keeps up her music, she doesn't let everything go to chaos. And she's more of a musician than you are a painter."

"She isn't a musician, and I'm not a painter. It isn't on account of painting that I let things go."

"On account of what, then?"

"Oh! I don't know. Let me alone; you bother me."

It sometimes entered Mr. Pontellier's mind to wonder if his wife were not growing a little unbalanced mentally. He could see plainly that she was not herself. That is, he could not see that she was becoming herself and daily casting aside that fictitious self which we assume like a garment with which to appear before the world.

Her husband let her alone as she requested, and went away to his office. Edna went up to her atelier—a bright room in the top of the house. She was working with great energy and interest, without accomplishing anything, however, which satisfied her even in the smallest degree. For a time she had the whole household enrolled in the service of art. The boys posed for her. They thought it amusing at first, but the occupation soon lost its attractiveness when they discovered that it was not a game arranged especially for their entertainment. The quadroon sat for hours before Edna's palette, patient as a savage, while the house-maid took charge of the children, and the drawing-room went undusted. But the house-maid, too, served her term as model when Edna perceived that the young woman's back and shoulders were molded on classic lines, and that her hair, loosened from its confining cap, became an inspiration. While Edna worked she sometimes sang low the little air, "*Ah! si tu savais!*"

It moved her with recollections. She could hear again the ripple of the water, the flapping sail. She could see the glint of the moon upon the bay, and could feel the soft, gusty beating of the hot south wind. A subtle current of desire passed through her body, weakening her hold upon the brushes and making her eyes burn.

There were days when she was very happy without knowing why. She was happy to be alive and breathing, when her whole being seemed to be one with the sunlight, the color, the odors, the luxuriant warmth of some perfect Southern day. She liked then to wander alone into strange and unfamiliar places. She discovered many a sunny, sleepy corner, fashioned to dream in. And she found it good to dream and to be alone and unmolested.

There were days when she was unhappy, she did not know why,—when it did not seem worth while to be glad or sorry, to be alive or dead; when life appeared to her like a grotesque pandemonium and humanity like worms struggling blindly toward inevitable annihilation. She could not work on such a day, nor weave fancies to stir her pulses and warm her blood.

XX

It was during such a mood that Edna hunted up Mademoiselle Reisz. She had not forgotten the rather disagreeable impression left upon her by their last interview; but she nevertheless felt a desire to see her—above all, to listen while she played upon the piano. Quite early in the afternoon she started upon her quest for the pianist. Unfortunately she had mislaid or lost Mademoiselle Reisz's card, and looking up her address in the city directory, she found that the woman lived on Bienville Street, some distance away. The directory which fell into her hands was a year or more old, however, and upon reaching the number indicated, Edna discovered that the house was occupied by a respectable family of mulattoes who had *chambres garnies*[2] to let. They had been living there for six months, and knew absolutely nothing of a Mademoiselle Reisz. In fact, they knew nothing of any of their neighbors; their lodgers were all people of the highest distinction, they assured Edna. She did not linger to discuss class distinctions with Madame Pouponne, but hastened to a neighboring grocery store, feeling sure that Mademoiselle would have left her address with the proprietor.

He knew Mademoiselle Reisz a good deal better than he wanted to know her, he informed his questioner. In truth, he did not want to know her at all, anything concerning her—the most disagreeable and unpopular woman who ever lived in Bienville Street. He thanked heaven she had left the neighborhood, and was equally thankful that he did not know where she had gone.

Edna's desire to see Mademoiselle Reisz had increased tenfold since these unlooked for obstacles had arisen to thwart it. She was wondering who could give her the information she sought, when it suddenly occurred to her that Madame Lebrun would be the one most likely to do so. She knew it was useless to ask Madame Ratignolle, who was on the most distant terms with the musician, and preferred to know nothing concerning her. She had once been almost as emphatic in expressing herself upon the subject as the corner grocer.

Edna knew that Madame Lebrun had returned to the city, for it was the middle of November. And she also knew where the Lebruns lived, on Chartres Street.

Their home from the outside looked like a prison, with iron bars before the door and lower windows. The iron bars were a relic of the old *régime*,[3] and no one had ever thought of dislodging them. At the side was a high fence enclosing the garden. A gate or door opening upon the street was locked. Edna rang the bell at this side garden gate, and stood upon the banquette, waiting to be admitted.

It was Victor who opened the gate for her. A black woman, wiping her hands upon her apron, was close at his heels. Before she saw them Edna could hear them in altercation, the woman—plainly an anomaly —claiming the right to be allowed to perform her duties, one of which was to answer the bell.

2. Furnished rooms.   3. I.e., the Spanish regime (1766–1803).

Victor was surprised and delighted to see Mrs. Pontellier, and he made no attempt to conceal either his astonishment or his delight. He was a dark-browed, good-looking youngster of nineteen, greatly resembling his mother, but with ten times her impetuosity. He instructed the black woman to go at once and inform Madame Lebrun that Mrs. Pontellier desired to see her. The woman grumbled a refusal to do part of her duty when she had not been permitted to do it all, and started back to her interrupted task of weeding the garden. Whereupon Victor administered a rebuke in the form of a volley of abuse, which owing to its rapidity and incoherence, was all but incomprehensible to Edna. Whatever it was, the rebuke was convincing, for the woman dropped her hoe and went mumbling into the house.

Edna did not wish to enter. It was very pleasant there on the side porch, where there were chairs, a wicker lounge, and a small table. She seated herself, for she was tired from her long tramp; and she began to rock gently and smooth out the folds of her silk parasol. Victor drew up his chair beside her. He at once explained that the black woman's offensive conduct was all due to imperfect training, as he was not there to take her in hand. He had only come up from the island the morning before, expected to return next day. He stayed all winter at the island; he lived there, and kept the place in order and got things ready for the summer visitors.

But a man needed occasional relaxation, he informed Mrs. Pontellier, and every now and again he drummed up a pretext to bring him to the city. My! but he had had a time of it the evening before! He wouldn't want his mother to know, and he began to talk in a whisper. He was scintillant with recollections. Of course, he couldn't think of telling Mrs. Pontellier all about it, she being a woman and not comprehending such things. But it all began with a girl peeping and smiling at him through the shutters as he passed by. Oh! but she was a beauty! Certainly he smiled back, and went up and talked to her. Mrs. Pontellier did not know him if she supposed he was one to let an opportunity like that escape him. Despite herself, the youngster amused her. She must have betrayed in her look some degree of interest or entertainment. The boy grew more daring, and Mrs. Pontellier might have found herself, in a little while, listening to a highly colored story but for the timely appearance of Madame Lebrun.

That lady was still clad in white, according to her custom of the summer. Her eyes beamed an effusive welcome. Would not Mrs. Pontellier go inside? Would she partake of some refreshment? Why had she not been there before? How was that dear Mr. Pontellier and how were those sweet children? Had Mrs. Pontellier ever known such a warm November?

Victor went and reclined on the wicker lounge behind his mother's chair, where he commanded a view of Edna's face. He had taken her parasol from her hands while he spoke to her, and he now lifted it and twirled it above him as he lay on his back. When Madame Lebrun complained that it was so dull coming back to the city; that she saw so few people now; that even Victor, when he came up from the island for a day or two, had so much to occupy him and engage his time, then it was that the youth went into contortions on the lounge and winked mischievously at Edna. She somehow felt like a confederate in crime, and tried to look severe and disapproving.

There had been but two letters from Robert, with little in them they told her. Victor said it was really not worth while to go inside for the letters, when his mother entreated him to go in search of them. He remembered the contents, which in truth he rattled off very glibly when put to the test.

One letter was written from Vera Cruz and the other from the City of Mexico. He had met Montel, who was doing everything toward his advancement. So far, the financial situation was no improvement over the one he had left in New Orleans, but of course the prospects were vastly better. He wrote of the City of Mexico, the buildings, the people and their habits, the conditions of life which he found there. He sent his love to the family. He inclosed a check to his mother, and hoped she would affectionately remember him to all his friends. That was about the substance of the two letters. Edna felt that if there had been a message for her, she would have received it. The despondent frame of mind in which she had left home began again to overtake her, and she remembered that she wished to find Mademoiselle Reisz.

Madame Lebrun knew where Mademoiselle Reisz lived. She gave Edna the address, regretting that she would not consent to stay and spend the remainder of the afternoon, and pay a visit to Mademoiselle Reisz some other day. The afternoon was already well advanced.

Victor escorted her out upon the banquette, lifted her parasol, and held it over her while he walked to the car with her. He entreated her to bear in mind that the disclosures of the afternoon were strictly confidential. She laughed and bantered him a little, remembering too late that she should have been dignified and reserved.

"How handsome Mrs. Pontellier looked!" said Madame Lebrun to her son.

"Ravishing!" he admitted. "The city atmosphere has improved her. Some way she doesn't seem like the same woman."

XXI

Some people contended that the reason Mademoiselle Reisz always chose apartments up under the roof was to discourage the approach of beggars, peddlars and callers. There were plenty of windows in her little front room. They were for the most part dingy, but as they were nearly always open it did not make so much difference. They often admitted into the room a good deal of smoke and soot; but at the same time all the light and air that there was came through them. From her windows could be seen the crescent of the river, the masts of ships and the big chimneys of the Mississippi steamers. A magnificent piano crowded the apartment. In the next room she slept, and in the third and last she harbored a gasoline stove on which she cooked her meals when disinclined to descend to the neighboring restaurant. It was there also that she ate, keeping her belongings in a rare old buffet, dingy and battered from a hundred years of use.

When Edna knocked at Mademoiselle Reisz's front room door and entered, she discovered that person standing beside the window, engaged in mending or patching an old prunella gaiter.[4] The little musician laughed all over when she saw Edna. Her laugh consisted of a contortion of the face and all the muscles of the body. She seemed strikingly homely, standing there in the afternoon light. She still wore the shabby lace and the artificial bunch of violets on the side of her head.

"So you remembered me at last," said Mademoiselle. "I had said to myself, 'Ah, bah! she will never come.' "

"Did you want me to come?" asked Edna with a smile.

"I had not thought much about it," answered Mademoiselle. The two had seated themselves on a little bumpy sofa which stood against the wall. "I am glad, however, that you came. I have the water boiling back there, and was just about to make some coffee. You will drink a cup with me. And how is *la belle dame*?[5] Always handsome! always healthy! always contented!" She took Edna's hand between her strong wiry fingers, holding it loosely without warmth, and executing a sort of double theme upon the back and palm.

"Yes," she went on; "I sometimes thought: 'She will never come. She promised as those women in society always do, without meaning it. She will not come.' For I really don't believe you like me, Mrs. Pontellier."

"I don't know whether I like you or not," replied Edna, gazing down at the little woman with a quizzical look.

The candor of Mrs. Pontellier's admission greatly pleased Mademoiselle Reisz. She expressed her gratification by repairing forthwith to the region of the gasoline stove and rewarding her guest with the promised cup of coffee. The coffee and the biscuit accompanying it proved very acceptable to Edna, who had declined refreshment at Madame Lebrun's and was now beginning to feel hungry. Mademoiselle set the

4. A cloth button shoe.   5. The lovely lady.

tray which she brought in upon a small table near at hand, and seated herself once again on the lumpy sofa.

"I have had a letter from your friend," she remarked, as she poured a little cream into Edna's cup and handed it to her.

"My friend?"

"Yes, your friend Robert. He wrote to me from the City of Mexico."

"Wrote to *you?*" repeated Edna in amazement, stirring her coffee absently.

"Yes, to me. Why not? Don't stir all the warmth out of your coffee; drink it. Though the letter might as well have been sent to you; it was nothing but Mrs. Pontellier from beginning to end."

"Let me see it," requested the young woman, entreatingly.

"No; a letter concerns no one but the person who writes it and the one to whom it is written."

"Haven't you just said it concerned me from beginning to end?"

"It was written about you, not to you. 'Have you seen Mrs. Pontellier? How is she looking?' he asks. 'As Mrs. Pontellier says,' or 'as Mrs. Pontellier once said.' 'If Mrs. Pontellier should call upon you, play for her that Impromptu of Chopin's, my favorite. I heard it here a day or two ago, but not as you play it. I should like to know how it affects her,' and so on, as if he supposed we were constantly in each other's society."

"Let me see the letter."

"Oh, no."

"Have you answered it?"

"No."

"Let me see the letter."

"No, and again, no."

"Then play the Impromptu for me."

"It is growing late; what time do you have to be home?"

"Time doesn't concern me. Your question seems a little rude. Play the Impromptu."

"But you have told me nothing of yourself. What are you doing?"

"Painting!" laughed Edna. "I am becoming an artist. Think of it!"

"Ah! an artist! You have pretensions, Madame."

"Why pretensions? Do you think I could not become an artist?"

"I do not know you well enough to say. I do not know your talent or your temperament. To be an artist includes much; one must possess many gifts—absolute gifts—which have not been acquired by one's own effort. And, moreover, to succeed, the artist must possess the courageous soul."

"What do you mean by the courageous soul?"

"Courageous, *ma foi!*[6] The brave soul. The soul that dares and defies."

6. In fact (literally, "my faith").

"Show me the letter and play for me the Impromptu. You see that I have persistence. Does that quality count for anything in art?"

"It counts with a foolish old woman whom you have captivated," replied Mademoiselle, with her wriggling laugh.

The letter was right there at hand in the drawer of the little table upon which Edna had just placed her coffee cup. Mademoiselle opened the drawer and drew forth the letter, the topmost one. She placed it in Edna's hands, and without further comment arose and went to the piano.

Mademoiselle played a soft interlude. It was an improvisation. She sat low at the instrument, and the lines of her body settled into ungraceful curves and angles that gave it an appearance of deformity. Gradually and imperceptibly the interlude melted into the soft opening minor chords of the Chopin Impromptu.

Edna did not know when the impromptu began or ended. She sat in the sofa corner reading Robert's letter by the fading light. Mademoiselle had glided from the Chopin into the quivering love-notes of Isolde's song,[7] and back again to the Impromptu with its soulful and poignant longing.

The shadows deepened in the little room. The music grew strange and fantastic—turbulent, insistent, plaintive and soft with entreaty. The shadows grew deeper. The music filled the room. It floated out upon the night, over the housetops, the crescent of the river, losing itself in the silence of the upper air.

Edna was sobbing, just as she had wept one midnight at Grand Isle when strange, new voices awoke in her. She arose in some agitation to take her departure. "May I come again, Mademoiselle?" she asked at the threshold.

"Come whenever you feel like it. Be careful; the stairs and landings are dark; don't stumble."

Mademoiselle reëntered and lit a candle. Robert's letter was on the floor. She stooped and picked it up. It was crumpled and damp with tears. Mademoiselle smoothed the letter out, restored it to the envelope, and replaced it in the table drawer.

XXII

One morning on his way into town Mr. Pontellier stopped at the house of his old friend and family physican, Doctor Mandelet. The Doctor was a semi-retired physician, resting, as the saying is, upon his laurels. He bore a reputation for wisdom rather than skill—leaving the active practice of medicine to his assistants and younger contempo-

7. From Richard Wagner's opera *Tristan und Isolde* (1857–1859); Isolde sings her *Liebestod* ("love-death") as she bids her dead lover farewell and then dies in his arms.

raries—and was much sought for in matters of consultation. A few families, united to him by bonds of friendship, he still attended when they
required the services of a physician. The Pontelliers were among these.

Mr. Pontellier found the Doctor reading at the open window of his
study. His house stood rather far back from the street, in the center of a
delightful garden, so that it was quiet and peaceful at the old gentleman's study window. He was a great reader. He stared up disapprovingly over his eyeglasses as Mr. Pontellier entered, wondering who had
the temerity to disturb him at that hour of the morning.

"Ah, Pontellier! Not sick, I hope. Come and have a seat. What news
do you bring this morning?" He was quite portly, with a profusion of
gray hair, and small blue eyes which age had robbed of much of their
brightness but none of their penetration.

"Oh! I'm never sick, Doctor. You know that I come of tough fiber
—of that old Creole race of Pontelliers that dry up and finally blow
away. I come to consult—no, not precisely to consult—to talk to you
about Edna. I don't know what ails her."

"Madame Pontellier not well?" marveled the Doctor. "Why I saw
her—I think it was a week ago—walking along Canal Street,[8] the picture of health, it seemed to me."

"Yes, yes; she seems quite well," said Mr. Pontellier, leaning forward
and whirling his stick between his two hands; "but she doesn't act well.
She's odd, she's not like herself. I can't make her out, and I thought
perhaps you'd help me."

"How does she act?" inquired the doctor.

"Well, it isn't easy to explain," said Mr. Pontellier, throwing himself
back in his chair. "She lets the housekeeping go to the dickens."

"Well, well; women are not all alike, my dear Pontellier. We've got
to consider—"

"I know that; I told you I couldn't explain. Her whole attitude—toward me and everybody and everything—has changed. You know I
have a quick temper, but I don't want to quarrel or be rude to a woman,
especially my wife; yet I'm driven to it, and feel like ten thousand devils
after I've made a fool of myself. She's making it devilishly uncomfortable for me," he went on nervously. "She's got some sort of notion in
her head concerning the eternal rights of women; and—you understand—we meet in the morning at the breakfast table."

The old gentleman lifted his shaggy eyebrows, protruded his thick
nether lip, and tapped the arms of his chair with his cushioned finger-
tips.

"What have you been doing to her, Pontellier?"

"Doing! *Parbleu!*"[9]

8. The main street of downtown New Orleans.   9. "For heaven's sake!"

"Has she," asked the Doctor, with a smile, "has she been associating of late with a circle of pseudo-intellectual women[1]—superspiritual superior beings? My wife has been telling me about them."

"That's the trouble," broke in Mr. Pontellier, "she hasn't been associating with any one. She has abandoned her Tuesdays at home, has thrown over all her acquaintances, and goes tramping about by herself, moping in the street-cars, getting in after dark. I tell you she's peculiar. I don't like it; I feel a little worried over it."

This was a new aspect for the Doctor. "Nothing hereditary?" he asked, seriously. "Nothing peculiar about her family antecedents, is there?"

"Oh, no, indeed! She comes of sound old Presbyterian Kentucky stock. The old gentleman, her father, I have heard, used to atone for his week-day sins with his Sunday devotions. I know for a fact, that his race horses literally ran away with the prettiest bit of Kentucky farming land I ever laid eyes upon. Margaret—you know Margaret—she has all the Presbyterianism undiluted. And the youngest is something of a vixen. By the way, she gets married in a couple of weeks from now."

"Send your wife up to the wedding," exclaimed the Doctor, foreseeing a happy solution. "Let her stay among her own people for a while; it will do her good."

"That's what I want her to do. She won't go to the marriage. She says a wedding is one of the most lamentable spectacles on earth. Nice thing for a woman to say to her husband!" exclaimed Mr. Pontellier, fuming anew at the recollection.

"Pontellier," said the Doctor, after a moment's reflection, "let your wife alone for a while. Don't bother her, and don't let her bother you. Woman, my dear friend, is a very peculiar and delicate organism—a sensitive and highly organized woman, such as I know Mrs. Pontellier to be, is especially peculiar. It would require an inspired psychologist to deal successfully with them. And when ordinary fellows like you and me attempt to cope with their idiosyncrasies the result is bungling. Most women are moody and whimsical. This is some passing whim of your wife, due to some cause or causes which you and I needn't try to fathom. But it will pass happily over, especially if you let her alone. Send her around to see me."

"Oh! I couldn't do that; there'd be no reason for it," objected Mr. Pontellier.

"Then I'll go around and see her," said the Doctor. "I'll drop in to dinner some evening *en bon ami*."[2]

---

1. "Women's clubs flourished during the late nineteenth century in America. They were a source of education for women as well as an arena for political organization. As the Doctor's remark indicates, the club movement was met with scorn in some quarters [Culley's note].
2. Like an old friend.

"Do! by all means," urged Mr. Pontellier. "What evening will you come? Say Thursday. Will you come Thursday?" he asked, rising to take his leave.

"Very well; Thursday. My wife may possibly have some engagement for me Thursday. In case she has, I shall let you know. Otherwise, you may expect me."

Mr. Pontellier turned before leaving to say:

"I am going to New York on business very soon. I have a big scheme on hand, and want to be on the field proper to pull the ropes and handle the ribbons.[3] We'll let you in on the inside if you say so, Doctor," he laughed.

"No, I thank you, my dear sir," returned the Doctor. "I leave such ventures to you younger men with the fever of life still in your blood."

"What I wanted to say," continued Mr. Pontellier, with his hand on the knob; "I may have to be absent a good while. Would you advise me to take Edna along?"

"By all means, if she wishes to go. If not, leave her here. Don't contradict her. The mood will pass, I assure you. It may take a month, two, three months—possibly longer, but it will pass; have patience."

"Well, good-by, *à jeudi*,"[4] said Mr. Pontellier, as he let himself out.

The Doctor would have liked during the course of conversation to ask, "Is there any man in the case?" but he knew his Creole too well to make such a blunder as that.

He did not resume his book immediately, but sat for a while meditatively looking out into the garden.

XXIII

Edna's father was in the city, and had been with them several days. She was not very warmly or deeply attached to him, but they had certain tastes in common, and when together they were companionable. His coming was in the nature of a welcome disturbance; it seemed to furnish a new direction for her emotions.

He had come to purchase a wedding gift for his daughter, Janet, and an outfit for himself in which he might make a creditable appearance at her marriage. Mr. Pontellier had selected the bridal gift, as every one immediately connected with him always deferred to this taste in such matters. And his suggestions on the question of dress—which too often assumes the nature of a problem—were of inestimable value to his father-in-law. But for the past few days the old gentleman had been upon Edna's hands, and in his society she was becoming acquainted with a new set of sensations. He had been a colonel in the Confederate army,

3. I.e., the reins.   4. "Until Thursday."

and still maintained, with the title, the military bearing which had always accompanied it. His hair and mustache were white and silky, emphasizing the rugged bronze of his face. He was tall and thin, and wore his coats padded, which gave a fictitious breadth and depth to his shoulders and chest. Edna and her father looked very distinguished together, and excited a good deal of notice during their perambulations. Upon his arrival she began by introducing him to her atelier and making a sketch of him. He took the whole matter very seriously. If her talent had been ten-fold greater than it was, it would not have surprised him, convinced as he was that he had bequeathed to all of his daughters the germs of a masterful capability, which only depended upon their own efforts to be directed toward successful achievement.

Before her pencil he sat rigid and unflinching, as he had faced the cannon's mouth in days gone by. He resented the intrusion of the children, who gaped with wondering eyes at him, sitting so stiff up there in their mother's bright atelier. When they drew near he motioned them away with an expressive action of the foot, loath to disturb the fixed lines of his countenance, his arms, or his rigid shoulders.

Edna, anxious to entertain him, invited Mademoiselle Reisz to meet him, having promised him a treat in her piano playing; but Mademoiselle declined the invitation. So together they attended a *soirée musicale* at the Ratignolles'. Monsieur and Madame Ratignolle made much of the Colonel, installing him as the guest of honor and engaging him at once to dine with them the following Sunday, or any day which he might select. Madame coquetted with him in the most captivating and naïve manner, with eyes, gestures, and a profusion of compliments, till the Colonel's old head felt thirty years younger on his padded shoulders. Edna marveled, not comprehending. She herself was almost devoid of coquetry.

There were one or two men whom she observed at the *soirée musicale*; but she would never have felt moved to any kittenish display to attract their notice—to any feline or feminine wiles to express herself toward them. Their personality attracted her in an agreeable way. Her fancy selected them, and she was glad when a lull in the music gave them an opportunity to meet her and talk with her. Often on the street the glance of strange eyes had lingered in her memory, and sometimes had disturbed her.

Mr. Pontellier did not attend these *soirées musicales*. He considered them *bourgeois*, and found more diversion at the club. To Madame Ratignolle he said the music dispensed at her *soirées* was "too heavy," too far beyond his untrained comprehension. His excuse flattered her. But she disapproved of Mr. Pontellier's club, and she was frank enough to tell Edna so.

"It's a pity Mr. Pontellier doesn't stay home more in the evenings. I think you would be more—well, if you don't mind my saying it—more united, if he did."

"Oh! dear no!" said Edna, with a blank look in her eyes. "What should I do if he stayed home? We wouldn't have anything to say to each other."

She had not much of anything to say to her father, for that matter; but he did not antagonize her. She discovered that he interested her, though she realized that he might not interest her long; and for the first time in her life she felt as if she were thoroughly acquainted with him. He kept her busy serving him and ministering to his wants. It amused her to do so. She would not permit a servant or one of the children to do anything for him which she might do herself. Her husband noticed, and thought it was the expression of a deep filial attachment which he had never suspected.

The Colonel drank numerous "toddies" during the course of the day, which left him, however, imperturbed. He was an expert at concocting strong drinks. He had even invented some, to which he had given fantastic names, and for whose manufacture he required diverse ingredients that it devolved upon Edna to procure for him.

When Doctor Mandelet dined with the Pontelliers on Thursday he could discern in Mrs. Pontellier no trace of that morbid condition which her husband had reported to him. She was excited and in a manner radiant. She and her father had been to the race course, and their thoughts when they seated themselves at table were still occupied with the events of the afternoon, and their talk was still of the track. The Doctor had not kept pace with turf affairs. He had certain recollections of racing in what he called "the good old times" when the Lecompte stables flourished,[5] and he drew upon this fund of memories so that he might not be left out and seem wholly devoid of the modern spirit. But he failed to impose upon the Colonel, and was even far from impressing him with this trumped-up knowledge of bygone days. Edna had staked her father on his last venture, with the most gratifying results to both of them. Besides, they had met some very charming people, according to the Colonel's impressions. Mrs. Mortimer Merriman and Mrs. James Highcamp, who were there with Alcée Arobin, had joined them and had enlivened the hours in a fashion that warmed him to think of.

Mr. Pontellier himself had no particular leaning toward horse-racing, and was even rather inclined to discourage it as a pastime, especially when he considered the fate of that blue-grass farm in Kentucky. He endeavored, in a general way, to express a particular disapproval, and only succeeded in arousing the ire and opposition of his father-in-

5. New Orleans had been a celebrated racing center before the Civil War.

law. A pretty dispute followed in which Edna warmly espoused her father's cause and the Doctor remained neutral.

He observed his hostess attentively from under his shaggy brows, and noted a subtle change which had transformed her from the listless woman he had known into a being who, for the moment, seemed palpitant with the forces of life. Her speech was warm and energetic. There was no repression in her glance or gesture. She reminded him of some beautiful, sleek animal waking up in the sun.

The dinner was excellent. The claret was warm and the champagne was cold, and under their beneficent influence the threatened unpleasantness melted and vanished with the fumes of the wine.

Mr. Pontellier warmed up and grew reminiscent. He told some amusing plantation experiences, recollections of old Iberville and his youth, when he hunted 'possum in company with some friendly darky; thrashed the pecan trees, shot the grosbec,[6] and roamed the woods and fields in mischievous idleness.

The Colonel, with little sense of humor and of the fitness of things, related a somber episode of those dark and bitter days, in which he had acted a conspicuous part and always formed a central figure. Nor was the Doctor happier in his selection, when he told the old, ever new and curious story of the waning of a woman's love, seeking strange, new channels, only to return to its legitimate source after days of fierce unrest. It was one of the many little human documents which had been unfolded to him during his long career as a physician. The story did not seem especially to impress Edna. She had one of her own to tell, of a woman who paddled away with her lover one night in a pirogue and never came back. They were lost amid the Barataria Islands, and no one ever heard of them or found trace of them from that day to this. It was a pure invention. She said that Madame Antoine had related it to her. That, also, was an invention. Perhaps it was a dream she had had. But every glowing word seemed real to those who listened. They could feel the hot breath of the Southern night; they could hear the long sweep of the pirogue through the glistening moonlit water, the beating of birds' wings, rising startled from among the reeds in the salt-water pools; they could see the faces of the lovers, pale, close together, rapt in oblivious forgetfulness, drifting into the unknown.

The champagne was cold, and its subtle fumes played fantastic tricks with Edna's memory that night.

Outside, away from the glow of the fire and the soft lamplight, the night was chill and murky. The Doctor doubled his old-fashioned cloak across his breast as he strode home through the darkness. He knew his fellow-creatures better than most men; knew that inner life which so

---

6. Grosbeak, game birds with large ("gros") bills.

seldom unfolds itself to unanointed eyes. He was sorry he had accepted Pontellier's invitation. He was growing old, and beginning to need rest and an imperturbed spirit. He did not want the secrets of other lives thrust upon him.

"I hope it isn't Arobin," he muttered to himself as he walked. "I hope to heaven it isn't Alcée Arobin."

XXIV

Edna and her father had a warm, and almost violent dispute upon the subject of her refusal to attend her sister's wedding. Mr. Pontellier declined to interfere, to interpose either his influence or his authority. He was following Doctor Mandelet's advice, and letting her do as she liked. The Colonel reproached his daughter for her lack of filial kindness and respect, her want of sisterly affection and womanly consideration. His arguments were labored and unconvincing. He doubted if Janet would accept any excuse—forgetting that Edna had offered none. He doubted if Janet would ever speak to her again, and he was sure Margaret would not.

Edna was glad to be rid of her father when he finally took himself off with his wedding garments and his bridal gifts, with his padded shoulders, his Bible reading, his "toddies" and ponderous oaths.

Mr. Pontellier followed him closely. He meant to stop at the wedding on his way to New York and endeavor by every means which money and love could devise to atone somewhat for Edna's incomprehensible action.

"You are too lenient, too lenient by far, Léonce," asserted the Colonel. "Authority, coercion are what is needed. Put your foot down good and hard; the only way to manage a wife. Take my word for it."

The Colonel was perhaps unaware that he had coerced his own wife into her grave. Mr. Pontellier had a vague suspicion of it which he thought it needless to mention at that late day.

Edna was not so consciously gratified at her husband's leaving home as she had been over the departure of her father. As the day approached when he was to leave her for a comparatively long stay, she grew melting and affectionate, remembering his many acts of consideration and his repeated expressions of an ardent attachment. She was solicitous about his health and his welfare. She bustled around, looking after his clothing, thinking about heavy underwear, quite as Madame Ratignolle would have done under similar circumstances. She cried when he went away, calling him her dear, good friend, and she was quite certain she would grow lonely before very long and go to join him in New York.

But after all, a radiant peace settled upon her when she at last found herself alone. Even the children were gone. Old Madame Pontellier had come herself and carried them off to Iberville with their quadroon. The old madame did not venture to say she was afraid they would be neglected during Léonce's absence; she hardly ventured to think so. She was hungry for them—even a little fierce in her attachment. She did not want them to be wholly "children of the pavement," she always said when begging to have them for a space. She wished them to know the country, with its streams, its fields, its woods, its freedom, so delicious to the young. She wished them to taste something of the life their father had lived and known and loved when he, too, was a little child.

When Edna was at last alone, she breathed a big, genuine sigh of relief. A feeling that was unfamiliar but very delicious came over her. She walked all through the house, from one room to another, as if inspecting it for the first time. She tried the various chairs and lounges, as if she had never sat and reclined upon them before. And she perambulated around the outside of the house, investigating, looking to see if windows and shutters were secure and in order. The flowers were like new acquaintances; she approached them in a familiar spirit, and made herself at home among them. The garden walks were damp, and Edna called to the maid to bring out her rubber sandals. And there she stayed, and stooped, digging around the plants, trimming, picking dead, dry leaves. The children's little dog came out, interfering, getting in her way. She scolded him, laughing at him, played with him. The garden smelled so good and looked so pretty in the afternoon sunlight. Edna plucked all the bright flowers she could find, and went into the house with them, she and the little dog.

Even the kitchen assumed a sudden interesting character which she had never before perceived. She went in to give directions to the cook, to say that the butcher would have to bring much less meat, that they would require only half their usual quantity of bread, of milk and groceries. She told the cook that she herself would be greatly occupied during Mr. Pontellier's absence, and she begged her to take all thought and responsibility of the larder upon her own shoulders.

That night Edna dined alone. The candelabra, with a few candles in the center of the table, gave all the light she needed. Outside the circle of light in which she sat, the large dining-room looked solemn and shadowy. The cook, placed upon her mettle, served a delicious repast—a luscious tenderloin broiled à point.[7] The wine tasted good; the marron glacé seemed to be just what she wanted. It was so pleasant, too, to dine in a comfortable *peignoir*.

She thought a little sentimentally about Léonce and the children, and wondered what they were doing. As she gave a dainty scrap or two to the doggie, she talked intimately to him about Étienne and Raoul.

7. To a turn; "marron glacé": glazed chestnuts.

He was beside himself with astonishment and delight over these companionable advances, and showed his appreciation by his little quick, snappy barks and a lively agitation.

Then Edna sat in the library after dinner and read Emerson[8] until she grew sleepy. She realized that she had neglected her reading, and determined to start anew upon a course of improving studies, now that her time was completely her own to do with as she liked.

After a refreshing bath, Edna went to bed. And as she snuggled comfortably beneath the eiderdown a sense of restfulness invaded her, such as she had not known before.

XXV

When the weather was dark and cloudy Edna could not work. She needed the sun to mellow and temper her mood to the sticking point. She had reached a stage when she seemed to be no longer feeling her way, working, when in the humor, with sureness and ease. And being devoid of ambition, and striving not toward accomplishment, she drew satisfaction from the work in itself.

On rainy or melancholy days Edna went out and sought the society of the friends she had made at Grand Isle. Or else she stayed indoors and nursed a mood with which she was becoming too familiar for her own comfort and peace of mind. It was not despair; but it seemed to her as if life were passing by, leaving its promise broken and unfulfilled. Yet there were other days when she listened, was led on and deceived by fresh promises which her youth held out to her.

She went again to the races, and again. Alcée Arobin and Mrs. Highcamp called for her one bright afternoon in Arobin's drag.[9]

Mrs. Highcamp was a worldly but unaffected, intelligent, slim, tall blonde woman in the forties, with an indifferent manner and blue eyes that stared. She had a daughter who served her as a pretext for cultivating the society of young men of fashion. Alcée Arobin was one of them. He was a familiar figure at the race course, the opera, the fashionable clubs. There was a perpetual smile in his eyes, which seldom failed to awaken a corresponding cheerfulness in any one who looked into them and listened to his good-humored voice. His manner was quiet, and at times a little insolent. He possessed a good figure, a pleasing face, not overburdened with depth of thought or feeling; and his dress was that of the conventional man of fashion.

He admired Edna extravagantly, after meeting her at the races with her father. He had met her before on other occasions, but she had seemed to him unapproachable until that day. It was at his instigation

8. Ralph Waldo Emerson (1803–1882), American philosopher.   9. Heavy coach.

that Mrs. Highcamp called to ask her to go with them to the Jockey Club[1] to witness the turf event of the season.

There were possibly a few track men out there who knew the race horse as well as Edna, but there was certainly none who knew it better. She sat between her two companions as one having authority to speak. She laughed at Arobin's pretensions, and deplored Mrs. Highcamp's ignorance. The race horse was a friend and intimate associate of her childhood. The atmosphere of the stables and the breath of the blue grass paddock revived in her memory and lingered in her nostrils. She did not perceive that she was talking like her father as the sleek geldings ambled in review before them. She played for very high stakes, and fortune favored her. The fever of the game flamed in her cheeks and eyes, and it got into her blood and into her brain like an intoxicant. People turned their heads to look at her, and more than one lent an attentive ear to her utterances, hoping thereby to secure the elusive but ever-desired "tip." Arobin caught the contagion of excitement which drew him to Edna like a magnet. Mrs. Highcamp remained, as usual, unmoved, with her indifferent stare and uplifted eyebrows.

Edna stayed and dined with Mrs. Highcamp upon being urged to do so. Arobin also remained and sent away his drag.

The dinner was quiet and uninteresting, save for the cheerful efforts of Arobin to enliven things. Mrs. Highcamp deplored the absence of her daughter from the races, and tried to convey to her what she had missed by going to the "Dante reading"[2] instead of joining them. The girl held a geranium leaf up to her nose and said nothing, but looked knowing and noncommittal. Mr. Highcamp was a plain, bald-headed man, who only talked under compulsion. He was unresponsive. Mrs. Highcamp was full of delicate courtesy and consideration toward her husband. She addressed most of her conversation to him at table. They sat in the library after dinner and read the evening papers together under the drop-light;[3] while the younger people went into the drawing-room near by and talked. Miss Highcamp played some selections from Grieg[4] upon the piano. She seemed to have apprehended all of the composer's coldness and none of his poetry. While Edna listened she could not help wondering if she had lost her taste for music.

When the time came for her to go home, Mr. Highcamp grunted a lame offer to escort her, looking down at his slippered feet with tactless concern. It was Arobin who took her home. The car ride was long, and it was late when they reached Esplanade Street. Arobin asked permission to enter for a second to light his cigarette—his match safe[5] was

1. The exclusive New Louisiana Jockey Club.
2. I.e., her daugher preferred intellectual activities. Dante Alighieri (1265–1321), Italian poet, wrote *The Divine Comedy*.
3. Gas lamp which could be lowered for reading.
4. Edvard Grieg (1843–1907), Norwegian composer.
5. I.e., matchbox.

empty. He filled his match safe, but did not light his cigarette until he left her, after she had expressed her willingness to go to the races with him again.

Edna was neither tired nor sleepy. She was hungry again, for the Highcamp dinner, though of excellent quality, had lacked abundance. She rummaged in the larder and brought forth a slice of "Gruyere"[6] and some crackers. She opened a bottle of beer which she found in the ice-box. Edna felt extremely restless and excited. She vacantly hummed a fantastic tune as she poked at the wood embers on the hearth and munched a cracker.

She wanted something to happen—something, anything; she did not know what. She regretted that she had not made Arobin stay a half hour to talk over the horses with her. She counted the money she had won. But there was nothing else to do, so she went to bed, and tossed there for hours in a sort of monotonous agitation.

In the middle of the night she remembered that she had forgotten to write her regular letter to her husband; and she decided to do so next day and tell him about her afternoon at the Jockey Club. She lay wide awake composing a letter which was nothing like the one which she wrote the next day. When the maid awoke her in the morning Edna was dreaming of Mr. Highcamp playing the piano at the entrance of a music store on Canal Street, while his wife was saying to Alcée Arobin, as they boarded an Esplanade Street car:

"What a pity that so much talent has been neglected! but I must go."

When a few days later, Alcée Arobin again called for Edna in his drag, Mrs. Highcamp was not with him. He said they would pick her up. But as the lady had not been apprised of his intention of picking her up, she was not at home. The daughter was just leaving the house to attend the meeting of a branch Folk Lore Society,[7] and regretted that she could not accompany them. Arobin appeared nonplused, and asked Edna if there were any one else she cared to ask.

She did not deem it worthwhile to go in search of any of the fashionable acquaintances from whom she had withdrawn herself. She thought of Madame Ratignolle, but knew that her fair friend did not leave the house, except to take a languid walk around the block with her husband after nightfall. Mademoiselle Reisz would have laughed at such a request from Edna. Madame Lebrun might have enjoyed the outing, but for some reason Edna did not want her. So they went alone, she and Arobin.

The afternoon was intensely interesting to her. The excitement came back upon her like a remittent fever. Her talk grew familiar and confidential. It was no labor to become intimate with Arobin. His

6. Cheese orginally made in Gruyère, Switzerland.

7. The New Orleans Association of the American Folklore Society.

manner invited easy confidence. The preliminary stage of becoming acquainted was one which he always endeavored to ignore when a pretty and engaging woman was concerned.

He stayed and dined with Edna. He stayed and sat beside the wood fire. They laughed and talked; and before it was time to go he was telling her how different life might have been if he had known her years before. With ingenuous frankness he spoke of what a wicked, ill-disciplined boy he had been, and impulsively drew up his cuff to exhibit upon his wrist the scar from a saber cut which he had received in a duel outside of Paris when he was nineteen. She touched his hand as she scanned the red cicatrice[8] on the inside of his white wrist. A quick impulse that was somewhat spasmodic impelled her fingers to close in a sort of clutch upon his hand. He felt the pressure of her pointed nails in the flesh of his palm.

She arose hastily and walked toward the mantel.

"The sight of a wound or scar always agitates and sickens me," she said. "I shouldn't have looked at it."

"I beg your pardon," he entreated, following her; "it never occurred to me that it might be repulsive."

He stood close to her, and the effrontery in his eyes repelled the old, vanishing self in her, yet drew all her awakening sensousness. He saw enough in her face to impel him to take her hand and hold it while he said his lingering good night.

"Will you go to the races again?" he asked.

"No," she said. "I've had enough of the races. I don't want to lose all the money I've won, and I've got to work when the weather is bright, instead of—"

"Yes; work; to be sure. You promised to show me your work. What morning may I come up to your atelier? To-morrow?"

"No!"

"Day after?"

"No, no."

"Oh, please don't refuse me! I know something of such things, I might help you with a stray suggestion or two."

"No. Good night. Why don't you go after you have said good night? I don't like you," she went on in a high, excited pitch, attempting to draw away her hand. She felt that her words lacked dignity and sincerity, and she knew that he felt it.

"I'm sorry you don't like me. I'm sorry I offended you. How have I offended you? What have I done? Can't you forgive me?" And he bent and pressed his lips upon her hand as if he wished never more to withdraw them.

8. Scar.

"Mr. Arobin," she complained, "I'm greatly upset by the excitement of the afternoon; I'm not myself. My manner must have misled you in some way. I wish you to go, please." She spoke in a monotonous, dull tone. He took his hat from the table, and stood with eyes turned from her, looking into the dying fire. For a moment or two he kept an impressive silence.

"Your manner has not misled me, Mrs. Pontellier," he said finally. "My own emotions have done that. I couldn't help it. When I'm near you, how could I help it? Don't think anything of it, don't bother, please. You see, I go when you command me. If you wish me to stay away, I shall do so. If you let me come back, I—oh! you will let me come back?"

He cast one appealing glance at her, to which she made no response. Alcée Arobin's manner was so genuine that it often deceived even himself.

Edna did not care or think whether it were genuine or not. When she was alone she looked mechanically at the back of her hand which he had kissed so warmly. Then she leaned her head down on the mantelpiece. She felt somewhat like a woman who in a moment of passion is betrayed into an act of infidelity, and realizes the significance of the act without being wholly awakened from its glamour. The thought was passing vaguely through her mind, "what would he think?"

She did not mean her husband; she was thinking of Robert Lebrun. Her husband seemed to her now like a person whom she had married without love as an excuse.

She lit a candle and went up to her room. Alcée Arobin was absolutely nothing to her. Yet his presence, his manners, the warmth of his glances, and above all the touch of his lips upon her hand had acted like a narcotic upon her.

She slept a languorous sleep, interwoven with vanishing dreams.

XXVI

Alcée Arobin wrote Edna an elaborate note of apology, palpitant with sincerity. It embarrassed her; for in a cooler, quieter moment it appeared to her absurd that she should have taken his action so seriously, so dramatically. She felt sure that the significance of the whole occurrence had lain in her own self-consciousness. If she ignored his note it would give undue importance to a trivial affair. If she replied to it in a serious spirit it would still leave in his mind the impression that she had in a susceptible moment yielded to his influence. After all, it was no great matter to have one's hand kissed. She was provoked at his having written the apology. She answered in as light and bantering a spirit as she fancied it deserved, and said she would be glad to have him look in upon her at work whenever he felt the inclination and his business gave him the opportunity.

He responded at once by presenting himself at her home with all his disarming naïveté. And then there was scarcely a day which followed that she did not see him or was not reminded of him. He was prolific in pretexts. His attitude became one of good-humored subservience and tacit adoration. He was ready at all times to submit to her moods, which were as often kind as they were cold. She grew accustomed to him. They became intimate and friendly by imperceptible degrees, and then by leaps. He sometimes talked in a way that astonished her at first and brought the crimson into her face; in a way that pleased her at last, appealing to the animalism that stirred impatiently within her.

There was nothing which so quieted the turmoil of Edna's senses as a visit to Mademoiselle Reisz. It was then, in the presence of that personality which was offensive to her, that the woman, by her divine art, seemed to reach Edna's spirit and set it free.

It was misty, with heavy, lowering atmosphere, one afternoon, when Edna climbed the stairs to the pianist's apartments under the roof. Her clothes were dripping with moisture. She felt chilled and pinched as she entered the room. Mademoiselle was poking at a rusty stove that smoked a little and warmed the room indifferently. She was endeavoring to heat a pot of chocolate on the stove. The room looked cheerless and dingy to Edna as she entered. A bust of Beethoven, covered with a hood of dust, scowled at her from the mantelpiece.

"Ah! here comes the sunlight!" exclaimed Mademoiselle, rising from her knees before the stove. "Now it will be warm and bright enough; I can let the fire alone."

She closed the stove door with a bang, and approaching assisted in removing Edna's dripping mackintosh.

"You are cold; you look miserable. The chocolate will soon be hot. But would you rather have a taste of brandy? I have scarcely touched the bottle which you brought me for my cold." A piece of red flannel was wrapped around Mademoiselle's throat; a stiff neck compelled her to hold her head on one side.

"I will take some brandy," said Edna, shivering as she removed her gloves and overshoes. She drank the liquor from the glass as a man would have done. Then flinging herself upon the uncomfortable sofa she said, "Mademoiselle, I am going to move away from my house on Esplanade Street."

"Ah!" ejaculated the musician, neither surprised nor especially interested. Nothing ever seemed to astonish her very much. She was endeavoring to adjust the bunch of violets which had become loose from its fastening in her hair. Edna drew her down upon the sofa and taking a pin from her own hair, secured the shabby artificial flowers in their accustomed place.

"Aren't you astonished?"

"Passably. Where are you going? To New York? to Iberville? to your father in Mississippi? where?"

"Just two steps away," laughed Edna, "in a little four-room house around the corner. It looks so cozy, so inviting and restful, whenever I pass by; and it's for rent. I'm tired looking after that big house. It never seemed like mine, anyway—like home. It's too much trouble. I have to keep too many servants. I am tired bothering with them."

"That is not your true reason, *ma belle*.[9] There is no use in telling me lies. I don't know your reason, but you have not told me the truth." Edna did not protest or endeavor to justify herself.

"The house, the money that provides for it, are not mine. Isn't that enough reason?"

"They are your husband's," returned Mademoiselle, with a shrug and a malicious elevation of the eyebrows.

"Oh! I see there is no deceiving you. Then let me tell you: it is a caprice. I have a little money of my own from my mother's estate, which my father sends me by driblets. I won a large sum this winter on the races, and I am beginning to sell my sketches. Laidpore is more and more pleased with my work; he says it grows in force and individuality. I cannot judge of that myself, but I feel that I have gained in ease and confidence. However, as I said, I have sold a good many through Laidpore. I can live in the tiny house for little or nothing, with one servant. Old Celestine, who works occasionally for me, says she will come stay with me and do my work. I know I shall like it, like the feeling of freedom and independence.

"What does your husband say?"

"I have not told him yet. I only thought of it this morning. He will think I am demented, no doubt. Perhaps you think so."

Mademoiselle shook her head slowly. "Your reason is not yet clear to me," she said.

Neither was it quite clear to Edna herself; but it unfolded itself as she sat for a while in silence. Instinct had prompted her to put away her husband's bounty in casting off her allegiance. She did not know how it would be when he returned. There would have to be an understanding, an explanation. Conditions would some way adjust themselves, she felt, but whatever came, she had resolved never again to belong to another than herself.

"I shall give a grand dinner before I leave the old house!" Edna ex-

9. My pretty.

claimed. "You will have to come to it, Mademoiselle. I will give you everything that you like to eat and to drink. We shall sing and laugh and be merry for once." And she uttered a sigh that came from the very depth of her being.

If Mademoiselle happened to have received a letter from Robert during the interval of Edna's visits, she would give her the letter unsolicited. And she would seat herself at the piano and play as her humor prompted her while the young woman read the letter.

The little stove was roaring; it was red-hot, and the chocolate in the tin sizzled and sputtered. Edna went forward and opened the stove door, and Mademoiselle rising took a letter from under the bust of Beethoven and handed it to Edna.

"Another! so soon!" she exclaimed, her eyes filled with delight. "Tell me, Mademoiselle, does he know that I see his letters?"

"Never in the world! He would be angry and would never write to me again if he thought so. Does he write to you? Never a line. Does he send you a message? Never a word. It is because he loves you, poor fool, and is trying to forget you, since you are not free to listen to him or to belong to him."

"Why do you show me his letters, then?"

"Haven't you begged for them? Can I refuse you anything? Oh! you cannot deceive me," and Mademoiselle approached her beloved instrument and began to play. Edna did not at once read the letter. She sat holding it in her hand, while the music penetrated her whole being like an effulgence, warming and brightening the dark places of her soul. It prepared her for joy and exultation.

"Oh!" she exclaimed, letting the letter fall to the floor. "Why did you not tell me?" She went and grasped Mademoiselle's hands up from the keys. "Oh! unkind! malicious! Why did you not tell me?"

"That he was coming back? No great news, *ma foi*. I wonder he did not come long ago."

"But when, when?" cried Edna, impatiently. "He does not say when."

"He says 'very soon.' You know as much about it as I do, it is all in the letter."

"But why? Why is he coming? Oh, if I thought—" and she snatched the letters from the floor and turned the pages this way and that way, looking for the reason, which was left untold.

"If I were young and in love with a man," said Mademoiselle, turning on the stool and pressing her wiry hands between her knees as she looked down at Edna, who sat on the floor holding the letter, "it seems to me he would have to be some *grand esprit*,[1] a man with lofty aims

---

1. Noble soul (literally, "grand spirit").

and ability to reach them; one who stood high enough to attract the notice of his fellow-men. It seems to me if I were young and in love I should never deem a man of ordinary caliber worthy of my devotion."

"Now it is you who are telling lies and seeking to deceive me, Mademoiselle; or else you have never been in love, and know nothing about it. Why," went on Edna, clasping her knees and looking up into Mademoiselle's twisted face, "do you suppose a woman knows why she loves? Does she select? Does she say to herself: 'Go to! Here is a distinguished statesman with presidential possibilities: I shall proceed to fall in love with him.' Or, 'I shall set my heart upon this musician, whose fame is on every tongue?' Or, "This financier, who controls the world's money markets?' "

"You are purposely misunderstanding me, *ma reine*.[2] Are you in love with Robert?"

"Yes," said Edna. It was the first time she had admitted it, and a glow overspread her face, blotching it with red spots.

"Why?" asked her companion. "Why do you love him when you ought not to?"

Edna, with a motion or two, dragged herself on her knees before Mademoiselle Reisz, who took the glowing face between her two hands.

"Why? Because his hair is brown and grows away from his temples; because he opens and shuts his eyes, and his nose is a little out of drawing; because he has two lips and a square chin, and a little finger which he can't straighten from having played baseball too energetically in his youth. Because—"

"Because you do, in short," laughed Mademoiselle. "What will you do when he comes back?" she asked.

"Do? Nothing, except feel glad and happy to be alive."

She was already glad and happy to be alive at the mere thought of his return. The murky, lowering sky, which had depressed her a few hours before, seemed bracing and invigorating as she splashed through the streets on her way home.

She stopped at a confectioner's and ordered a huge box of bonbons for the children in Iberville. She slipped a card in the box, on which she scribbled a tender message and sent an abundance of kisses.

Before dinner in the evening Edna wrote a charming letter to her husband, telling him of her intention to move for a while into the little house around the block, and to give a farewell dinner before leaving, regretting that he was not there to share it, to help her out with the menu and assist her in entertaining the guests. Her letter was brilliant and brimming with cheerfulness.

2. My queen.

XXVII

"What is the matter with you?" asked Arobin that evening. "I never found you in such a happy mood." Edna was tired by that time, and was reclining on the lounge before the fire.

"Don't you know the weather prophet has told us we shall see the sun pretty soon?"

"Well, that ought to be reason enough," he acquiesced. "You wouldn't give me another if I sat here all night imploring you." He sat close to her on a low tabouret,[3] and as he spoke his fingers lightly touched the hair that fell a little over her forehead. She liked the touch of his fingers through her hair, and closed her eyes sensitively.

"One of these days," she said, "I'm going to pull myself together for a while and think—try to determine what character of a woman I am; for, candidly, I don't know. By all the codes which I am acquainted with, I am a devilishly wicked specimen of the sex. But some way I can't convince myself that I am. I must think about it."

"Don't. What's the use? Why should you bother thinking about it when I can tell you what manner of woman you are?" His fingers strayed occasionally down to her warm, smooth cheeks and firm chin, which was growing a little full and double.

"Oh, yes! You will tell me that I am adorable; everything that is captivating. Spare yourself the effort."

"No; I shan't tell you anything of the sort, though I shouldn't be lying if I did."

"Do you know Mademoiselle Reisz?" she asked irrelevantly.

"The pianist? I know her by sight. I've heard her play."

"She says queer things sometimes in a bantering way that you don't notice at the time and you feel yourself thinking about afterward."

"For instance?"

"Well, for instance, when I left her today, she put her arms around me and felt my shoulder blades, to see if my wings were strong, she said. 'The bird that would soar above the level plain of tradition and prejudice must have strong wings. It is a sad spectacle to see the weaklings bruised, exhausted, fluttering back to earth.'"

"Whither would you soar?"

"I'm not thinking of any extraordinary flights. I only half comprehend her."

"I've heard she's partially demented," said Arobin.

"She seems to me wonderfully sane," Edna replied.

"I'm told she's extremely disagreeable and unpleasant. Why have you introduced her at a moment when I desired to talk of you?"

3. Cylindrical stool.

"Oh! talk of me if you like," cried Edna, clasping her hands beneath her head; "but let me think of something else while you do."

"I'm jealous of your thoughts to-night. They're making you a little kinder than usual; but some way I feel as if they were wandering, as if they were not here with me." She only looked at him and smiled. His eyes were very near. He leaned upon the lounge with an arm extended across her, while the other hand still rested upon her hair. They continued silently to look into each other's eyes. When he leaned forward and kissed her, she clasped his head, holding his lips to hers.

It was the first kiss of her life to which her nature had really responded. It was a flaming torch that kindled desire.

XXVIII

Edna cried a little that night after Arobin left her. It was only one phase of the multitudinous emotions which had assailed her. There was with her an overwhelming feeling of irresponsibility. There was the shock of the unexpected and the unaccustomed. There was her husband's reproach looking at her from external existence. There was Robert's reproach making itself felt by a quicker, fiercer, more overpowering love, which had awakened within her toward him. Above all, there was understanding. She felt as if a mist had been lifted from her eyes, enabling her to look upon and comprehend the significance of life, that monster made up of beauty and brutality. But among the conflicting sensations which assailed her, there was neither shame nor remorse. There was a dull pang of regret because it was not the kiss of love which had inflamed her, because it was not love which had held this cup of life to her lips.

XXIX

Without even waiting for an answer from her husband regarding his opinion or wishes in the matter, Edna hastened her preparations for quitting her home on Esplanade Street and moving into the little house around the block. A feverish anxiety attended her every action in that direction. There was no moment of deliberation, no interval of repose between the thought and its fulfillment. Early upon the morning following those hours passed in Arobin's society, Edna set about securing her new abode and hurrying her arrangements for occupying it. Within the precincts of her home she felt like one who has entered and lingered within the portals of some forbidden temple in which a thousand muffled voices bade her begone.

Whatever was her own in the house, everything which she had acquired aside from her husband's bounty, she caused to be transported to the other house, supplying simple and meager deficiencies from her own resources.

Arobin found her with rolled sleeves, working in company with the house-maid when he looked in during the afternoon. She was splendid and robust, and had never appeared handsomer than in the old blue gown, with a red silk handkerchief knotted at random around her head to protect her hair from the dust. She was mounted upon a high step-ladder, unhooking a picture from the wall when he entered. He had found the front door open, and had followed his ring by walking in unceremoniously.

"Come down!" he said. "Do you want to kill yourself?" She greeted him with affected carelessness, and appeared absorbed in her occupation.

If he had expected to find her languishing, reproachful, or indulging in sentimental tears, he must have been greatly surprised.

He was no doubt prepared for any emergency, ready for any one of the foregoing attitudes, just as he bent himself easily and naturally to the situation which confronted him.

"Please come down," he insisted, holding the ladder and looking up at her.

"No," she answered; "Ellen is afraid to mount the ladder. Joe is working at the 'pigeon house'—that's the name Ellen gives it, because it's so small and looks like a pigeon house—and some one has to do this"

Arobin pulled off his coat, and expressed himself ready and willing to tempt fate in her place. Ellen brought him one of her dustcaps, and went into contortions of mirth, which she found it impossible to control, which she saw him put it on before the mirror as grotesquely as he could. Edna herself could not refrain from smiling when she fastened it at his request. So it was he who in turn mounted the ladder, unhooking pictures and curtains, and dislodging ornaments as Edna directed. When he had finished he took off his dustcap and went out to wash his hands.

Edna was sitting on the tabouret, idly brushing the tips of a feather duster along the carpet when he came in again.

"Is there anything more you will let me do?" he asked.

"That is all," she answered. "Ellen can manage the rest." She kept the young woman occupied in the drawing-room, unwilling to be left alone with Arobin.

"What about the dinner?" he asked; "the grand event, the *coup d'état?*"

"It will be day after to-morrow. Why do you call it the *'coup d'état?'* Oh! it will be very fine; all my best of everything—crystal, silver and gold. Sèvres, flowers, music, and champagne to swim in. I'll let Léonce pay the bills. I wonder what he'll say when he sees the bills."

"And you ask me why I call it a *coup d'état?*" Arobin had put on his coat, and he stood before her and asked if his cravat was plumb. She told him it was, looking no higher than the tip of his collar.

"When do you go to the 'pigeon house?'—with all due acknowledgement to Ellen."

"Day after to-morrow, after the dinner. I shall sleep there."

"Ellen, will you very kindly get me a glass of water?" asked Arobin. "The dust in the curtains, if you will pardon me for hinting such a thing, has parched my throat to a crisp."

"While Ellen gets the water," said Edna, rising, "I will say good-by and let you go. I must get rid of this grime, and I have a million things to do and think of."

"When shall I see you?" asked Arobin, seeking to detain her, the maid having left the room.

"At the dinner, of course. You are invited."

"Not before?—not to-night or to-morrow morning or to-morrow noon or night? or the day after morning or noon? Can't you see yourself, without my telling you, what an eternity it is?"

He had followed her into the hall and to the foot of the stairway looking up at her as she mounted with her face half turned to him.

"Not an instant sooner," she said. But she laughed and looked at him with eyes that at once gave him courage to wait and made it torture to wait.

XXX

Though Edna had spoken of the dinner as a very grand affair, it was in truth a very small affair and very select, in so much as the invited were few and were selected with discrimination. She had counted upon an even dozen seating themselves at her round mahogany board, forgetting for the moment that Madame Ratignolle was to the last degree *souffrante*[4] and unpresentable, and not foreseeing that Madame Lebrun would send a thousand regrets at the last moment. So there were only ten, after all, which made a cozy, comfortable number.

There were Mr. and Mrs. Merriman, a pretty vivacious little woman in the thirties; her husband, a jovial fellow, something of a shallowpate,[5] who laughed a good deal at other people's witticisms, and had thereby made himself extremely popular. Mrs. Highcamp had accompanied them. Of course, there was Alcée Arobin; and Mademoiselle Reisz had consented to come. Edna had sent her a fresh bunch of violets with black lace trimmings for her hair. Monsieur Ratignolle

4. Ill.   5. I.e., shallow-minded.

brought himself and his wife's excuses. Victor Lebrun, who happened to be in the city, bent upon relaxation, had accepted with alacrity. There was a Miss Mayblunt, no longer in her teens, who looked at the world through lorgnettes and with the keenest interest. It was thought and said that she was intellectual; it was suspected of her that she wrote under a *nom de guerre*.[6] She had come with a gentleman by the name of Gouvernail, connected with one of the daily papers, of whom nothing special could be said, except that he was observant and seemed quiet and inoffensive. Edna herself made the tenth, and at half-past eight they seated themselves at table, Arobin and Monsieur Ratignolle on either side of their hostess.

Mrs. Highcamp sat between Arobin and Victor Lebrun. Then came Mrs. Merriman, Mr. Gouvernail, Miss Mayblunt, Mr. Merriman, and Mademoiselle Reisz next to Monsieur Ratignolle.

There was something extremely gorgeous about the appearance of the table, an effect of splendor conveyed by a cover of pale yellow satin under strips of lace-work. There were wax candles in massive brass candelabra, burning softly under yellow silk shades; full, fragrant roses, yellow and red, abounded. There were silver and gold, as she had said there would be, and crystal which glittered like the gems which the women wore.

The ordinary stiff dining chairs had been discarded for the occasion and replaced by the most commodious and luxurious which could be collected throughout the house. Mademoiselle Reisz, being exceedingly diminutive, was elevated upon cushions, as small children are sometimes hoisted at table upon bulky volumes.

"Something new, Edna?" exclaimed Miss Mayblunt, with lorgnette directed toward a magnificent cluster of diamonds that sparkled, that almost sputtered, in Edna's hair, just over the center of her forehead.

"Quite new; 'brand' new, in fact; a present from my husband. It arrived this morning from New York. I may as well admit that this is my birthday, and that I am twenty-nine. In good time I expect you to drink my health. Meanwhile, I shall ask you to begin with this cocktail, composed—would you say 'composed?'" with an appeal to Miss Mayblunt—"composed by my father in honor of Sister Janet's wedding."

Before each guest stood a tiny glass that looked and sparkled like a garnet gem.

"Then, all things considered," spoke Arobin, "it might not be amiss to start out by drinking the Colonel's health in the cocktail which he composed, on the birthday of the most charming of women—the daughter whom he invented."

Mr. Merriman's laugh at this sally was such a genuine outburst and

6. Pseudonym.

so contagious that it started the dinner with an agreeable swing that never slackened.

Miss Mayblunt begged to be allowed to keep her cocktail untouched before her, just to look at. The color was marvelous! She could compare it to nothing she had ever seen, and the garnet lights which it emitted were unspeakably rare. She pronounced the Colonel an artist, and stuck to it.

Monsieur Ratignolle was prepared to take things seriously; the *mets*, and *entre-mets*,[7] the service, the decorations, even the people. He looked up from his pompono[8] and inquired of Arobin if he were related to the gentleman of that name who formed one of the firm of Laitner and Arobin, lawyers. The young man admitted that Laitner was a warm personal friend, who permitted Arobin's name to decorate the firm's letterheads and to appear upon a shingle that graced Perdido Street.

"There are so many inquisitive people and institutions abounding," said Arobin, "that one is really forced as a matter of convenience these days to assume the virtue of an occupation if he has it not."

Monsieur Ratignolle stared a little, and turned to ask Mademoiselle Reisz if she considered the symphony concerts up to the standard which had been set the previous winter. Mademoiselle Reisz answered Monseiur Ratignolle in French, which Edna thought a little rude, under the circumstances, but characteristic. Mademoiselle had only disagreeable things to say of the symphony concerts, and insulting remarks to make of all the musicians of New Orleans, singly and collectively. All her interest seemed to be centered upon the delicacies placed before her.

Mr. Merriman said that Mr. Arobin's remark about inquisitive people reminded him of a man from Waco[9] the other day at the St. Charles Hotel—but as Mr. Merriman's stories were always lame and lacking point, his wife seldom permitted him to complete them. She interrupted him to ask if he remembered the name of the author whose book she had bought the week before to send to a friend in Geneva. She was talking "books" with Mr. Gouvernail and trying to draw from him his opinion upon current literary topics. Her husband told the story of the Waco man privately to Miss Mayblunt, who pretended to be greatly amused and to think it extremely clever.

Mrs. Highcamp hung with languid but unaffected interest upon the warm and impetuous volubility of her left-hand neighbor, Victor Lebrun. Her attention was never for a moment withdrawn from him after seating herself at table; and when he turned to Mrs. Merriman, who was prettier and more vivacious than Mrs. Highcamp, she waited with

---

7. Main course and side dishes.   9. Town in Texas.
8. Pompano fish, a Southern delicacy.

easy indifference for an opportunity to reclaim his attention. There was the occasional sound of music, of mandolins, sufficiently removed to be an agreeable accompaniment rather than an interruption to the conversation. Outside the soft, monotonous splash of a fountain could be heard; the sound penetrated into the room with the heavy odor of jessamine that came through the open windows.

The golden shimmer of Edna's satin gown spread in rich folds on either side of her. There was a soft fall of lace encircling her shoulders. It was the color of her skin, without the glow, the myriad living tints that one may sometimes discover in vibrant flesh. There was something in her attitude, in her whole appearance when she leaned her head against the high-backed chair and spread her arms, which suggested the regal woman, the one who rules, who looks on, who stands alone.

But as she sat there amid her guests, she felt the old ennui overtaking her; the hopelessness which so often assailed her, which came upon her like an obsession, like something extraneous, independent of volition. It was something which announced itself; a chill breath that seemed to issue from some vast cavern wherein discords wailed. There came over her the acute longing which always summoned into her spiritual vision the presence of the beloved one, overpowering her at once with a sense of the unattainable.

The moments glided on, while a feeling of good fellowship passed around the circle like a mystic cord, holding and binding these people together with jest and laughter. Monsieur Ratignolle was the first to break the pleasant charm. At ten o'clock he excused himself. Madame Ratignolle was waiting for him at home. She was *bien souffrante*,[1] and she was filled with vague dread, which only her husband's presence could allay.

Mademoiselle Reisz arose with Monsieur Ratignolle, who offered to escort her to the car. She had eaten well; she had tasted the good rich wines, and they must have turned her head, for she bowed pleasantly to all as she withdrew from table. She kissed Edna upon the shoulder, and whispered: "*Bonne nuit, ma reine; soyez sage.*"[2] She had been a little bewildered upon rising, or rather, descending from her cushions, and Monsieur Ratignolle gallantly took her arm and led her away.

Mrs. Highcamp was weaving a garland of roses, yellow and red. When she had finished the garland, she laid it lightly upon Victor's black curls. He was reclining far back in the luxurious chair, holding a glass of champagne to the light.

As if a magician's wand had touched him, the garland of roses transformed him into a vision of Oriental beauty. His cheeks were the color of crushed grapes, and his dusky eyes glowed with a languishing fire.

1. Very ill.   2. "Good night, my queen; be good."

"*Sapristi!*" exclaimed Arobin.

But Mrs. Highcamp had one more touch to add to the picture. She took from the back of her chair a white silken scarf, with which she had covered her shoulders in the early part of the evening. She draped it across the boy in graceful folds, and in a way to conceal his black, conventional evening dress. He did not seem to mind what she did to him, only smiled, showing a faint gleam of white teeth, while he continued to gaze with narrowing eyes at the light through his glass of champagne.

"Oh! to be able to paint in color rather than in words!" exclaimed Miss Mayblunt, losing herself in a rhapsodic dream as she looked at him.

> " 'There was a graven image of Desire
>   Painted with red blood on a ground of gold' "[3]

murmured Gouvernail, under his breath.

The effect of the wine upon Victor was, to change his accustomed volubility into silence. He seemed to have abandoned himself to a reverie, and to be seeing pleasing visions in the amber bead.

"Sing," entreated Mrs. Highcamp. "Won't you sing to us?"

"Let him alone," said Arobin.

"He's posing," offered Mr. Merriman; "let him have it out."

"I believe he's paralyzed," laughed Mrs. Merriman. And leaning over the youth's chair, she took the glass from his hand and held it to his lips. He sipped the wine slowly, and when he had drained the glass she laid it upon the table and wiped his lips with her little filmy handkerchief.

"Yes, I'll sing for you," he said, turning in his chair toward Mrs. Highcamp. He clasped his hands behind his head, and looking up at the ceiling began to hum a little, trying his voice like a musician tuning an instrument. Then, looking at Edna, he began to sing:

> "Ah! si tu savais!"

"Stop!" she cried, "don't sing that. I don't want you to sing it," and she laid her glass so impetuously and blindly upon the table as to shatter it against a caraffe. The wine spilled over Arobin's legs and some of it trickled down upon Mrs. Highcamp's black gauze gown. Victor had lost all idea of courtesy, or else he thought his hostess was not in earnest, for he laughed and went on:

> "Ah! si tu savais
>   Ce que tes yeux me disent"—

3. From *A Cameo*, by Algernon Charles Swinburne (1837–1909).

"Oh! you mustn't! you mustn't," exclaimed Edna, and pushing back her chair she got up, and going behind him placed her hand over his mouth. He kissed the soft palm that pressed upon his lips.

"No, no, I won't, Mrs. Pontellier. I didn't know you meant it," looking up at her with caressing eyes. The touch of his lips was like a pleasing sting to her hand. She lifted the garland of roses from his head and flung it across the room.

"Come, Victor; you've posed long enough. Give Mrs. Highcamp her scarf."

Mrs. Highcamp undraped the scarf from about him with her own hands. Miss Mayblunt and Mr. Gouvernail suddenly conceived the notion that it was time to say good night. And Mr. and Mrs. Merriman wondered how it could be so late.

Before parting from Victor, Mrs. Highcamp invited him to call upon her daughter, who she knew would be charmed to meet him and talk French and sing French songs with him. Victor expressed his desire and intention to call upon Miss Highcamp at the first opportunity which presented itself. He asked if Arobin were going his way. Arobin was not.

The mandolin players had long since stolen away. A profound stillness had fallen upon the broad, beautiful street. The voices of Edna's disbanding guests jarred like a discordant note upon the quiet harmony of the night.

XXXI

"Well?" questioned Arobin, who had remained with Edna after the others had departed.

"Well," she reiterated, and stood up, stretching her arms, and feeling the need to relax her muscles after having been so long seated.

"What next?" he asked.

"The servants are all gone. They left when the musicians did. I have dismissed them. The house has to be closed and locked, and I shall trot around to the pigeon house, and shall send Celestine over in the morning to straighten things up."

He looked around, and began to turn out some of the lights.

"What about upstairs?" he inquired.

"I think it is all right: but there may be a window or two unlatched. We had better look; you might take a candle and see. And bring me my wrap and hat on the foot of the bed in the middle room."

He went up with the light, and Edna began closing doors and windows. She hated to shut in the smoke and the fumes of the wine. Arobin found her cape and hat, which he brought down and helped her to put on.

When everything was secured and the lights put out, they left through the front door, Arobin locking it and taking the key, which he carried for Edna. He helped her down the steps.

"Will you have a spray of jessamine?" he asked, breaking off a few blossoms as he passed.

"No; I don't want anything."

She seemed disheartened, and had nothing to say. She took his arm, which he offered her, holding up the weight of her satin train with the other hand. She looked down, noticing the black line of his leg moving in and out so close to her against the yellow shimmer of her gown. There was the whistle of a railway train somewhere in the distance, and the midnight bells were ringing. They met no one in their short walk.

The "pigeon-house" stood behind a locked gate, and a shallow *parterre*[4] that had been somewhat neglected. There was a small front porch, upon which a long window and the front door opened. The door opened directly into the parlor; there was no side entry. Back in the yard was a room for servants, in which old Celestine had been ensconced.

Edna had left a lamp burning low upon the table. She had succeeded in making the room look habitable and homelike. There were some books on the table and a lounge near at hand. On the floor was a fresh matting, covered with a rug or two; and on the walls hung a few tasteful pictures. But the room was filled with flowers. These were a surprise to her. Arobin had sent them, and had had Celestine distribute them during Edna's absence. Her bedroom was adjoining, and across a small passage were the dining-room and kitchen.

Edna seated herself with every appearance of discomfort.

"Are you tired?" he asked.

"Yes, and chilled and miserable. I feel as if I had been wound up to a certain pitch—too tight—and something inside of me had snapped." She rested her head against the table upon her bare arm.

"You want to rest," he said, "and to be quiet. I'll go; I'll leave you and let you rest."

"Yes," she replied.

He stood up beside her and smoothed her hair with his soft magnetic hand. His touch conveyed to her a certain physical comfort. She could have fallen quietly asleep there if he had continued to pass his hand over her hair. He brushed the hair upward from the nape of her neck.

"I hope you will feel better and happier in the morning," he said. "You have tried to do too much in the past few days. The dinner was the last straw; you might have dispensed with it."

"Yes," she admitted; "it was stupid."

"No, it was delightful; but it has worn you out." His hand had strayed

4. Garden.

to her beautiful shoulders, and he could feel the response of her flesh to his touch. He seated himself beside her and kissed her lightly upon the shoulder.

"I thought you were going away," she said, in an uneven voice.

"I am, after I have said good night."

"Good night," she murmured.

He did not answer, except to continue to caress her. He did not say good night until she had become supple to his gentle, seductive entreaties.

XXXII

When Mr. Pontellier learned of his wife's intention to abandon her home and take up her residence elsewhere, he immediately wrote her a letter of unqualified disapproval and remonstrance. She had given reasons which he was unwilling to acknowledge as adequate. He hoped she had not acted upon her rash impulse; and he begged her to consider first, foremost, and above all else, what people would say. He was not dreaming of scandal when he uttered this warning; that was a thing which would never have entered into his mind to consider in connection with his wife's name or his own. He was simply thinking of his financial integrity. It might get noised about that the Pontelliers had met with reverses, and were forced to conduct their *ménage*[5] on a humbler scale than heretofore. It might do incalculable mischief to his business prospects.

But remembering Edna's whimsical turn of mind of late, and foreseeing that she had immediately acted upon her impetuous determination, he grasped the situation with his usual promptness and handled it with his well-known business tact and cleverness.

The same mail which brought to Edna his letter of disapproval carried instructions—the most minute instructions—to a well-known architect concerning the remodeling of his home, changes which he had long contemplated, and which he desired carried forward during his temporary absence.

Expert and reliable packers and movers were engaged to convey the furniture, carpets, pictures—everything movable, in short—to places of security. And in an incredibly short time the Pontellier house was turned over to the artisans. There was to be an addition—a small snuggery;[6] there was to be frescoing, and hardwood flooring was to be put into such rooms as had not yet been subjected to this improvement.

Furthermore, in one of the daily papers appeared a brief notice to the effect that Mr. and Mrs. Pontellier were contemplating a summer so-

5. Household.   6. Den.

journ abroad, and that their handsome residence on Esplanade Street was undergoing sumptuous alterations, and would not be ready for occupancy until their return. Mr. Pontellier had saved appearances!

Edna admired the skill of his maneuver, and avoided any occasion to balk his intentions. When the situation as set forth by Mr. Pontellier was accepted and taken for granted, she was apparently satisfied that it should be so.

The pigeon-house pleased her. It at once assumed the intimate character of a home, while she herself invested it with a charm which it reflected like a warm glow. There was with her a feeling of having descended in the social scale, with a corresponding sense of having risen in the spiritual. Every step which she took toward relieving herself from obligations added to her strength and expansion as an individual. She began to look with her own eyes; to see and to apprehend the deeper undercurrents of life. No longer was she content to "feed upon opinion" when her own soul had invited her.

After a little while, a few days, in fact, Edna went up and spent a week with her children in Iberville. They were delicious February days, with all the summer's promises hovering in the air.

How glad she was to see the children! She wept for very pleasure when she felt their little arms clasping her; their hard, ruddy cheeks pressed against her own glowing cheeks. She looked into their faces with hungry eyes that could not be satisfied with looking. And what stories they had to tell their mother! About the pigs, the cows, the mules! About riding to the mill behind Gluglu; fishing back in the lake with their Uncle Jasper; picking pecans with Lidie's little black brood, and hauling chips in their express wagon. It was a thousand times more fun to haul real chips for old lame Susie's real fire than to drag painted blocks along the banquette on Esplanade Street!

She went with them herself to see the pigs and the cows, to look at the darkies laying the cane, to thrash the pecan trees, and catch fish in the back lake. She lived with them a whole week long, giving them all of herself, and gathering and filling herself with their young existence. They listened, breathless, when she told them the house in Esplanade Street was crowded with workmen, hammering, nailing, sawing, and filling the place with clatter. They wanted to know where their bed was; what had been done with their rocking-horse; and where did Joe sleep, and where had Ellen gone, and the cook? But, above all, they were fired with a desire to see the little house around the block. Was there any place to play? Were there any boys next door? Raoul, with pessimistic foreboding, was convinced that there were only girls next door. Where would they sleep, and where would papa sleep? She told them the fairies would fix it all right.

The old Madame was charmed with Edna's visit, and showered all manner of delicate attentions upon her. She was delighted to know that the Esplanade Street house was in a dismantled condition. It gave her the promise and pretext to keep the children indefinitely.

It was with a wrench and a pang that Edna left her children. She carried away with her the sound of their voices and the touch of their cheeks. All along the journey homeward their presence lingered with her like the memory of a delicious song. But by the time she had regained the city the song no longer echoed in her soul. She was again alone.

XXXIII

It happened sometimes when Edna went to see Mademoiselle Reisz that the little musician was absent, giving a lesson or making some small necessary household purchase. The key was always left in a secret hiding-place in the entry, which Edna knew. If Mademoiselle happened to be away, Edna would usually enter and wait for her return.

When she knocked at Mademoiselle Reisz's door one afternoon there was no response; so unlocking the door, as usual, she entered and found the apartment deserted, as she had expected. Her day had been quite filled up, and it was for a rest, for a refuge, and to talk about Robert, that she sought out her friend.

She had worked at her canvas—a young Italian character study—all the morning, completing the work without the model; but there had been many interruptions, some incident to her modest housekeeping, and others of a social nature.

Madame Ratignolle had dragged herself over, avoiding the too public thoroughfares, she said. She complained that Edna had neglected her much of late. Besides, she was consumed with curiosity to see the little house and the manner in which it was conducted. She wanted to hear all about the dinner party; Monsieur Ratignolle had left so early. What had happened after he left? The champagne and grapes which Edna sent over were *too* delicious. She had so little appetite; they had refreshed and toned her stomach. Where on earth was she going to put Mr. Pontellier in that little house, and the boys? And then she made Edna promise to go to her when her hour of trial overtook her.

"At any time—any time of the day or night, dear," Edna assured her.

Before leaving Madame Ratignolle said:

"In some way you seem to me like a child, Edna. You seem to act without a certain amount of reflection which is necessary in this life. That is the reason I want to say you mustn't mind if I advise you to be a little careful while you are living here alone. Why don't you have some one come and stay with you? Wouldn't Mademoiselle Reisz come?"

"No; she wouldn't wish to come, and I shouldn't want her always with me."

"Well, the reason—you know how evil-minded the world is—some one was talking of Alcée Arobin visiting you. Of course, it wouldn't matter if Mr. Arobin had not such a dreadful reputation. Monsieur Ratignolle was telling me that his attentions alone are considered enough to ruin a woman's name."

"Does he boast of his successes?" asked Edna, indifferently, squinting at her picture.

"No, I think not. I believe he is a decent fellow as far as that goes. But his character is so well known among the men. I shan't be able to come back and see you; it was very, very imprudent today."

"Mind the step!" cried Edna.

"Don't neglect me," entreated Madame Ratignolle; "and don't mind what I said about Arobin, or having some one to stay with you."

"Of course not," Edna laughed. "You may say anything you like to me." They kissed each other good-bye. Madame Ratignolle had not far to go, and Edna stood on the porch a while watching her walk down the street.

Then in the afternoon Mrs. Merriman and Mrs. Highcamp had made their "party call." Edna felt that they might have dispensed with the formality. They had also come to invite her to play *vingt-et-un*[7] one evening at Mrs. Merriman's. She was asked to go early, to dinner, and Mr. Merriman or Mr. Arobin would take her home. Edna accepted in a half-hearted way. She sometimes felt very tired of Mrs. Highcamp and Mrs. Merriman.

Late in the afternoon she sought refuge with Mademoiselle Reisz, and stayed there alone, waiting for her, feeling a kind of repose invade her with the very atmosphere of the shabby, unpretentious little room.

Edna sat at the window, which looked out over the house-tops and across the river. The window frame was filled with pots of flowers, and she sat and picked the dry leaves from a rose geranium. The day was warm, and the breeze which blew from the river was very pleasant. She removed her hat and laid it on the piano. She went on picking the leaves and digging around the plants with her hat pin. Once she thought she heard Mademoiselle Reisz approaching. But it was a young black girl, who came in, bringing a small bundle of laundry, which she deposited in the adjoining room, and went away.

Edna seated herself at the piano, and softly picked out with one hand the bars of a piece of music which lay open before her. A half-hour went by. There was the occasional sound of people going and coming in the lower hall. She was growing interested in her occupation of picking out the aria, when there was a second rap at the door. She vaguely wondered what these people did when they found Mademoiselle's door locked.

7. Twenty-one, a card game.

"Come in," she called. turning her face toward the door. And this time it was Robert Lebrun who presented himself. She attempted to rise; she could not have done so without betraying the agitation which mastered her at sight of him, so she fell back upon the stool, only exclaiming, "Why Robert!"

He came and clasped her hand, seemingly without knowing what he was saying or doing.

"Mrs. Pontellier! How do you happen—oh! how well you look! Is Mademoiselle Reisz not here? I never expected to see you."

"When did you come back?" asked Edna in an unsteady voice, wiping her face with her handkerchief. She seemed ill at ease on the piano stool, and he begged her to take the chair by the window. She did so, mechanically, while he seated himself on the stool.

"I returned day before yesterday," he answered, while he leaned his arm on the keys, bringing forth a crash of discordant sound.

"Day before yesterday!" she repeated, aloud, and went on thinking to herself, "day before yesterday," in a sort of an uncomprehending way. She had pictured him seeking her at the very first hour, and he had lived under the same sky since day before yesterday; while only by accident had he stumbled upon her. Mademoiselle must have lied when she said, "Poor fool, he loves you."

"Day before yesterday," she repeated, breaking off a spray of Mademoiselle's geranium; "then if you had not met me here to-day you wouldn't—when—that is, didn't you mean to come and see me?"

"Of course, I should have gone to see you. There have been so many things—" he turned the leaves of Mademoiselle's music nervously. "I started in at once yesterday with the old firm. After all there is as much chance for me here as there was there—that is, I might find it profitable some day. The Mexicans were not very congenial."

So he had come back because the Mexicans were not congenial; because business was as profitable here as there; because of any reason, and not because he cared to be near her. She remembered the day she sat on the floor, turning the pages of his letter, seeking the reason which was left untold.

She had not noticed how he looked—only feeling his presence; but she turned deliberately and observed him. After all, he had been absent but a few months, and was not changed. His hair—the color of hers—waved back from his temples in the same way as before. His skin was not more burned than it had been at Grand Isle. She found in his eyes, when he looked at her for one silent moment, the same tender caress, with an added warmth and entreaty which had not been there before—the same glance which had penetrated to the sleeping places of her soul and awakened them.

A hundred times Edna had pictured Robert's return, and imagined their first meeting. It was usually at her home, whither he had sought her out at once. She always fancied him expressing or betraying in some way his love for her. And here, the reality was that they sat ten feet apart, she at the window, crushing geranium leaves in her hand and smelling them, he twirling around on the piano stool, saying:

"I was very much surprised to hear of Mr. Pontellier's absence; it's a wonder Mademoiselle Reisz did not tell me; and your moving— mother told me yesterday. I should think you would have gone to New York with him, or to Iberville with the children, rather than be bothered here with housekeeping. And you are going abroad, too, I hear. We shan't have you at Grand Isle next summer; it won't seem—do you see much of Mademoiselle Reisz? She often spoke of you in the few letters she wrote."

"Do you remember that you promised to write to me when you went away?" A flush overspread his whole face.

"I couldn't believe that my letters would be of any interest to you."

"That is an excuse; it isn't the truth." Edna reached for her hat on the piano. She adjusted it, sticking the hat pin through the heavy coil of hair with some deliberation.

"Are you not going to wait for Mademoiselle Reisz?" asked Robert.

"No; I have found when she is absent this long, she is liable not to come back till late." She drew on her gloves, and Robert picked up his hat.

"Won't you wait for her?" asked Edna.

"Not if you think she will not be back till late," adding, as if suddenly aware of some discourtesy in his speech, "and I should miss the pleasure of walking home with you." Edna locked the door and put the key back in its hiding place.

They went together, picking their way across muddy streets and sidewalks encumbered with the cheap display of small tradesmen. Part of the distance they rode in the car, and after disembarking, passed the Pontellier mansion, which looked broken and half torn asunder. Robert had never known the house, and looked at it with interest.

"I never knew you in your home," he remarked.

"I am glad you did not."

"Why?" She did not answer. They went on around the corner, and it seemed as if her dreams were coming true after all, when he followed her into the little house.

"You must stay and dine with me, Robert. You see I am all alone, and it is so long since I have seen you. There is so much I want to ask you."

She took off her hat and gloves. He stood irresolute, making some excuse about his mother who expected him; he even muttered something about an engagement. She struck a match and lit the lamp on the table; it was growing dusk. When he saw her face in the lamplight, looking pained, with all the soft lines gone out of it, he threw his hat aside and seated himself.

"Oh! you know I want to stay if you will let me!" he exclaimed. All the softness came back. She laughed, and went and put her hand on his shoulder.

"This is the first moment you have seemed like the old Robert. I'll go tell Celestine." She hurried away to tell Celestine to set an extra place. She even sent her off in search of some added delicacy which she had not thought of for herself. And she recommended great care in dripping the coffee and having the omelet done to a proper turn.

When she reëntered, Robert was turning over magazines, sketches, and things that lay upon the table in great disorder. He picked up a photograph, and exclaimed:

"Alcée Arobin! What on earth is his picture doing here?"

"I tried to make a sketch of his head one day," answered Edna, "and he thought the photograph might help me. It was at the other house. I thought it had been left there. I must have picked it up with my drawing materials."

"I should think you would give it back to him if you have finished with it."

"Oh! I have a great many such photographs. I never think of returning them. They don't amount to anything." Robert kept on looking at the picture.

"It seems to me—do you think his head worth drawing? Is he a friend of Mr. Pontellier's? You never said you knew him."

"He isn't a friend of Mr. Pontellier's; he's a friend of mine. I always knew him—that is, it is only of late that I know him pretty well. But I'd rather talk about you, and know what you have been seeing and doing and feeling out there in Mexico." Robert threw aside the picture.

"I've been seeing the waves and the white beach of Grand Isle; the quiet, grassy street of the *Chênière*; the old fort at Grande Terre. I've been working like a machine, and feeling like a lost soul. There was nothing interesting."

She leaned her head upon her hand to shade her eyes from the light.

"And what have you been seeing and doing and feeling all these days?" he asked.

"I've been seeing the waves and the white beach of Grand Isle; the quiet, grassy street of the *Chênière Caminada*; the old sunny fort at Grande Terre. I've been working with little more comprehension than a machine, and still feeling like a lost soul. There was nothing interesting."

"Mrs. Pontellier, you are cruel," he said, with feeling, closing his eyes and resting his head back in his chair. They remained in silence till old Celestine announced dinner.

XXXIV

The dining-room was very small. Edna's round mahogany would have almost filled it. As it was there was but a step or two from the little table in the kitchen, to the mantel, the small buffet, and the side door that opened out on the narrow brick-paved yard.

A certain degree of ceremony settled upon them with the announcement of dinner. There was no return to personalities. Robert related incidents of his sojourn in Mexico, and Edna talked of events likely to interest him, which had occurred during his absence. The dinner was of ordinary quality, except for the few delicacies which she had sent out to purchase. Old Celestine, with a bandana *tignon*[8] twisted about her head, hobbled in and out, taking a personal interest in everything; and she lingered occasionally to talk *patois*[9] with Robert, whom she had known as a boy.

He went out to a neighboring cigar stand to purchase cigarette papers, and when he came back he found that Celestine had served the black coffee in the parlor.

"Perhaps I shouldn't have come back," he said. "When you are tired of me, tell me to go."

"You never tire me. You must have forgotten the hours and hours at Grand Isle in which we grew accustomed to each other and used to being together."

"I have forgotten nothing at Grand Isle," he said, not looking at her, but rolling a cigarette. His tobacco pouch, which he laid upon the table, was a fantastic embroidered silk affair, evidently the handiwork of a woman.

"You used to carry your tobacco in a rubber pouch," said Edna, picking up the pouch and examining the needlework.

"Yes; it was lost."

"Where did you buy this one? In Mexico?"

"It was given to me by a Vera Cruz girl; they are very generous," he replied, striking a match and lighting his cigarette.

"They are very handsome, I suppose, those Mexican women; very picturesque, with their black eyes and their lace scarfs."

"Some are; others are hideous. Just as you find women everywhere."

"What was she like—the one who gave you the pouch? You must have known her very well."

_____

8. I.e., her hair is tied up with a scarf.   9. Dialect.

"She was very ordinary. She wasn't of the slightest importance. I knew her well enough."

"Did you visit at her house? Was it interesting? I should like to know and hear about the people you met, and the impressions they made on you."

"There are some people who leave impressions not so lasting as the imprint of an oar upon the water."

"Was she such a one?"

"It would be ungenerous for me to admit that she was of that order and kind." He thrust the pouch back in his pocket, as if to put away the subject with the trifle which had brought it up.

Arobin dropped in with a message from Mrs. Merriman, to say that the card party was postponed on account of the illness of one of her children.

"How do you do, Arobin?" said Robert, rising from the obscurity.

"Oh! Lebrun. To be sure! I heard yesterday you were back. How did they treat you down in Mexico?"

"Fairly well."

"But not well enough to keep you there. Stunning girls, though, in Mexico. I thought I should never get away from Vera Cruz when I was down there a couple of years ago."

"Did they embroider slippers and tobacco pouches and hat bands and things for you?" asked Edna.

"Oh! my! no! I didn't get so deep in their regard. I fear they made more impression on me than I made on them."

"You were less fortunate than Robert, then."

"I am always less fortunate than Robert. Has he been imparting tender confidences?"

"I've been imposing myself long enough," said Robert, rising, and shaking hands with Edna. "Please convey my regards to Mr. Pontellier when you write."

He shook hands with Arobin and went away.

"Fine fellow, that Lebrun," said Arobin when Robert had gone. "I never heard you speak of him."

"I knew him last summer at Grand Isle," she replied. "Here is that photograph of yours. Don't you want it?"

"What do I want with it? Throw it away." She threw it back on the table.

"I'm not going to Mrs. Merriman's," she said. "If you see her, tell her so. But perhaps I had better write. I think I shall write now, and say that I am sorry her child is sick, and tell her not to count on me."

"It would be a good scheme," acquiesced Arobin. "I don't blame you; stupid lot!"

Edna opened the blotter, and having procured paper and pen, began to write a note. Arobin lit a cigar and read the evening paper, which he had in his pocket.

"What is the date?" she asked. He told her.

"Will you mail this for me when you go out?"

"Certainly." He read to her little bits out of the newspaper, while she straightened things on the table.

"What do you want to do?" he asked, throwing aside the paper. "Do you want to go for a walk or a drive or anything? It would be a fine night to drive."

"No; I don't want to do anything but just be quiet. You go away and amuse yourself. Don't stay."

"I'll go away if I must; but I shan't amuse myself. You know that I only live when I am near you."

He stood up to bid her good night.

"Is that one of the things you always say to women?"

"I have said it before, but I don't think I ever came so near meaning it," he answered with a smile. There were no warm lights in her eyes; only a dreamy, absent look.

"Good night. I adore you. Sleep well," he said, and he kissed her hand and went away.

She stayed alone in a kind of reverie—a sort of stupor. Step by step she lived over every instant of the time she had been with Robert after he had entered Mademoiselle Reisz's door. She recalled his words, his looks. How few and meager they had been for her hungry heart! A vision—a transcendently seductive vision of a Mexican girl arose before her. She writhed with a jealous pang. She wondered when he would come back. He had not said he would come back. She had been with him, had heard his voice and touched his hand. But some way he had seemed nearer to her off there in Mexico.

XXXV

The morning was full of sunlight and hope. Edna could see before her no denial—only the promise of excessive joy. She lay in bed awake, with bright eyes full of speculation. "He loves you, poor fool." If she could but get that conviction firmly fixed in her mind, what mattered about the rest? She felt she had been childish and unwise the night before in giving herself over to despondency. She recapitulated the motives which no doubt explained Robert's reserve. They were not insurmountable; they would not hold if he really loved her; they could not hold against her own passion, which he must come to realize in time. She pictured him going to his business that morning. She even saw how he was dressed; how he walked down one street, and turned the corner of another; saw him bending over his desk, talking to people

...ne office, going to his lunch, and perhaps watching for
...e street. He would come to her in the afternoon or evening, sit
..a roll his cigarette, talk a little, and go away as he had done the night
before. But how delicious it would be to have him there with her! She
would have no regrets, nor seek to penetrate his reserve if he still chose
to wear it.

Edna ate her breakfast only half dressed. The maid brought her a
delicious printed scrawl from Raoul, expressing his love, asking her to
send him some bonbons, and telling her they had found that morning
ten tiny white pigs all lying in a row beside Lidie's big white pig.

A letter also came from her husband, saying he hoped to be back
early in March, and then they would get ready for that journey abroad
which he had promised her so long, which he felt now fully able to afford; he felt able to travel as people should, without any thought of
small economies—thanks to his recent speculations in Wall Street.

Much to her surprise she received a note from Arobin, written at
midnight from the club. It was to say good morning to her, to hope that
she had slept well, to assure her of his devotion, which he trusted she in
some faintest manner returned.

All these letters were pleasing to her. She answered the children in a
cheerful frame of mind, promising them bonbons, and congratulating
them upon their happy find of the little pigs.

She answered her husband with friendly evasiveness,—not with any
fixed design to mislead him, only because all sense of reality had gone
out of her life, she had abandoned herself to Fate, and awaited the consequences with indifference.

To Arobin's note she made no reply. She put it under Celestine's
stove-lid.

Edna worked several hours with much spirit. She saw no one but a
picture dealer, who asked her if it were true that she was going abroad to
study in Paris.

She said possibly she might, and he negotiated with her for some
Parisian studies to reach him in time for the holiday trade in December.

Robert did not come that day. She was keenly disappointed. He did
not come the following day, nor the next. Each morning she awoke
with hope, and each night she was a prey to despondency. She was
tempted to seek him out. But far from yielding to the impulse, she
avoided any occasion which might throw her in his way. She did not go
to Mademoiselle Reisz's nor pass by Madame Lebrun's, as she might
have done if he had still been in Mexico.

When Arobin, one night, urged her to drive with him, she went—
out to the lake, on the Shell Road.[1] His horses were full of mettle, and

1. Road by Lake Pontchartrain.

even a little unmanageable. She liked the rapid gait at which they spun along, and the quick, sharp sound of the horses' hoofs on the hard road. They did not stop anywhere to eat or to drink. Arobin was not needlessly imprudent. But they ate and they drank when they regained Edna's little dining-room—which was comparatively early in the evening.

It was late when he left her. It was getting to be more than a passing whim with Arobin to see her and be with her. He had detected the latent sensuality, which unfolded under his delicate sense of her nature's requirements like a torpid, torrid, sensitive blossom.

There was no despondency when she fell asleep that night; nor was there hope when she awoke in the morning.

XXXVI

There was a garden out in the suburbs; a small, leafy corner, with a few green tables under the orange trees. An old cat slept all day on the stone step in the sun, and an old *mulatresse*[2] slept her idle hours away in her chair at the open window, till some one happened to knock on one of the green tables. She had milk and cream cheese to sell, and bread and butter. There was no one who could make such excellent coffee or fry a chicken so golden brown as she.

The place was too modest to attract the attention of people of fashion, and so quiet as to have escaped the notice of those in search of pleasure and dissipation. Edna had discovered it accidentally one day when the high-board gate stood ajar. She caught sight of a little green table, blotched with the checkered sunlight that filtered through the quivering leaves overhead. Within she had found the slumbering *mulatresse*, the drowsy cat, and a glass of milk which reminded her of the milk she had tasted in Iberville.

She often stopped there during her perambulations; sometimes taking a book with her, and sitting an hour or two under the trees when she found the place deserted. Once or twice she took a quiet dinner there alone, having instructed Celestine beforehand to prepare no dinner at home. It was the last place in the city where she would have expected to meet any one she knew.

Still she was not astonished when, as she was partaking of a modest dinner late in the afternoon, looking into an open book, stroking the cat, which had made friends with her—she was not greatly astonished to see Robert come in at the tall garden gate.

"I am destined to see you only by accident," she said, shoving the cat

---

2. A mulatto woman, of mixed black and white ancestry.

off the chair beside her. He was surprised, ill at ease, almost embarrassed at meeting her thus so unexpectedly.

"Do you come here often?" he asked.

"I almost live here," she said.

"I used to drop in very often for a cup of Catiche's good coffee. This is the first time since I came back."

"She'll bring you a plate, and you will share my dinner. There's always enough for two—even three." Edna had intended to be indifferent and as reserved as he when she met him; she had reached the determination by a laborious train of reasoning, incident to one of her despondent moods. But her resolve melted when she saw him before her, seated there beside her in the little garden, as if a designing Providence had led him into her path.

"Why have you kept away from me, Robert?" she asked, closing the book that lay open upon the table.

"Why are you so personal, Mrs. Pontellier? Why do you force me to idiotic subterfuges?" he exclaimed with sudden warmth. "I suppose there's no use telling you I've been very busy, or that I've been sick, or that I've been to see you and not found you at home. Please let me off with any one of those excuses."

"You are the embodiment of selfishness," she said. "You save yourself something—I don't know what—but there is some selfish motive, and in sparing yourself you never consider for a moment what I think, or how I feel your neglect and indifference. I suppose this is what you would call unwomanly; but I have got into a habit of expressing myself. It doesn't matter to me, and you may think me unwomanly if you like."

"No; I only think you cruel, as I said the other day. Maybe not intentionally cruel; but you seem to be forcing me into disclosures which can result in nothing; as if you would have me bare a wound for the pleasure of looking at it, without the intention or power of healing it."

"I'm spoiling your dinner, Robert; never mind what I say. You haven't eaten a morsel."

"I only came in for a cup of coffee." His sensitive face was all disfigured with excitement.

"Isn't this a delightful place?" she remarked. "I am so glad it has never actually been discovered. It is so quiet, so sweet here. Do you notice there is scarcely a sound to be heard? It's so out of the way; and a good walk from the car. However, I don't mind walking. I always feel so sorry for women who don't like to walk; they miss so much—so many rare little glimpses of life; and we women learn so little of life on the whole.

"Catiche's coffee is always hot. I don't know how she manages it, here in the open air. Celestine's coffee gets cold bringing it from the kitchen to the dining-room. Three lumps! How can you drink it so sweet? Take some of the cress with your chop; it's so biting and crisp. Then there's the advantage of being able to smoke with your coffee out here. Now, in the city—aren't you going to smoke?"

"After a while," he said, laying a cigar on the table.

"Who gave it to you?" she laughed.

"I bought it. I suppose I'm getting reckless; I bought a whole box." She was determined not to be personal again and make him uncomfortable.

The cat made friends with him, and climbed into his lap when he smoked his cigar. He stroked her silky fur, and talked a little about her. He looked at Edna's book, which he had read; and he told her the end, to save her the trouble of wading through it, he said.

Again he accompanied her back to her home; and it was after dusk when they reached the little "pigeon-house." She did not ask him to remain, which he was grateful for, as it permitted him to stay without the discomfort of blundering through an excuse which he had no intention of considering. He helped her to light the lamp; then she went into her room to take off her hat and to bathe her face and hands.

When she came back Robert was not examining the pictures and magazines as before; he sat off in the shadow, leaning his head back on the chair as if in a reverie. Edna lingered a moment beside the table, arranging the books there. Then she went across the room to where he sat. She bent over the arm of his chair and called his name.

"Robert," she said, "are you asleep?"

"No," he answered, looking up at her.

She leaned over and kissed him—a soft, cool, delicate kiss, whose voluptuous sting penetrated his whole being—then she moved away from him. He followed, and took her in his arms, just holding her close to him. She put her hand up to his face and pressed his cheek against her own. The action was full of love and tenderness. He sought her lips again. Then he drew her down upon the sofa beside him and held her hand in both of his.

"Now you know," he said, "now you know what I have been fighting against since last summer at Grand Isle; what drove me away and drove me back again."

"Why have you been fighting against it?" she asked. Her face glowed with soft lights.

"Why? Because you were not free; you were Léonce Pontellier's wife. I couldn't help loving you if you were ten times his wife, but so long as I went away from you and kept away I could help telling you so." She put her free hand up to his shoulder, and then against his cheek, rubbing it softly. He kissed her again. His face was warm and flushed.

"There in Mexico I was thinking of you all the time, and longing for you."

"But not writing to me," she interrupted.

"Something put into my head that you cared for me; and I lost my senses. I forgot everything but a wild dream of your some way becoming my wife."

"Your wife!"

"Religion, loyalty, everything would give way if only you cared."

"Then you must have forgotten that I was Léonce Pontellier's wife."

"Oh! I was demented, dreaming of wild, impossible things, recalling men who had set their wives free, we have heard of such things."

"Yes, we have heard of such things."

"I came back full of vague, mad intentions. And when I got here—"

"When you got here you never came near me!" She was still caressing his cheek.

"I realized what a cur I was to dream of such a thing, even if you had been willing."

She took his face between her hands and looked into it as if she would never withdraw her eyes more. She kissed him on the forehead, the eyes, the cheeks, and the lips.

"You have been a very, very foolish boy, wasting your time dreaming of impossible things when you speak of Mr. Pontellier setting me free! I am no longer one of Mr. Pontellier's possessions to dispose of or not. I give myself where I choose. If he were to say, 'Here, Robert, take her and be happy; she is yours,' I should laugh at you both."

His face grew a little white. "What do you mean?" he asked.

There was a knock at the door. Old Celestine came in to say that Madame Ratignolle's servant had come around the back way with a message that Madame had been taken sick and begged Mrs. Pontellier to go to her immediately.

"Yes, yes," said Edna, rising: "I promised. Tell her yes—to wait for me. I'll go back with her."

"Let me walk over with you," offered Robert.

"No," she said; "I will go with the servant." She went into her room to put on her hat, and when she came in again she sat once more upon the sofa beside him. He had not stirred. She put her arms about his neck.

"Good-by, my sweet Robert. Tell me good-by." He kissed her with a degree of passion which had not before entered into his caress, and strained her to him.

"I love you," she whispered, "only you; no one but you. It was you who awoke me last summer out of a life-long, stupid dream. Oh! you have made me so unhappy with your indifference. Oh! I have suffered, suffered! Now you are here we shall love each other, my Robert. We shall be everything to each other. Nothing else in the world is of any consequence. I must go to my friend; but you will wait for me? No matter how late; you will wait for me, Robert?"

"Don't go; don't go! Oh! Edna, stay with me," he pleaded. "Why should you go? Stay with me, stay with me."

"I shall come back as soon as I can; I shall find you here." She buried her face in his neck, and said good-by again. Her seductive voice, together with his great love for her, had enthralled his senses, had deprived him of every impulse but the longing to hold her and keep her.

XXXVII

Edna looked in at the drug store. Monsieur Ratignolle was putting up a mixture himself, very carefully, dropping a red liquid into a tiny glass. He was grateful to Edna for having come; her presence would be a comfort to his wife. Madame Ratignolle's sister, who had always been with her at such trying times, had not been able to come up from the plantation, and Adèle had been inconsolable until Mrs. Pontellier so kindly promised to come to her. The nurse had been with them at night for the past week, as she lived a great distance away. And Dr. Mandelet had been coming and going all the afternoon. They were then looking for him any moment.

Edna hastened upstairs by a private stairway that led from the rear of the store to the apartments above. The children were all sleeping in a back room. Madame Ratignolle was in the salon, whither she had strayed in her suffering impatience. She sat on the sofa, clad in an ample white *peignoir*, holding a handkerchief tight in her hand with a nervous clutch. Her face was drawn and pinched, her sweet blue eyes haggard and unnatural. All her beautiful hair had been drawn back and plaited. It lay in a long braid on the sofa pillow, coiled like a golden serpent. The nurse, a comfortable looking *Griffe* woman[3] in white apron and cap, was urging her to return to her bedroom.

"There is no use, there is no use," she said at once to Edna. "We must get rid of Mandelet; he is getting too old and careless. He said he would be here at half-past seven; now it must be eight. See what time it is, Joséphine."

The woman was possessed of a cheerful nature, and refused to take any situation too seriously, especially a situation with which she was so familiar. She urged Madame to have courage and patience. But Madame only set her teeth hard into her under lip, and Edna saw the sweat gather in beads on her white forehead. After a moment or two she ut-

---

3. I.e., the offspring of a mulatto and a black or an American Indian.

tered a profound sigh and wiped her face with the handkerchief rolled in a ball. She appeared exhausted. The nurse gave her a fresh handkerchief, sprinkled with cologne water.

"This is too much!" she cried. "Mandelet ought to be killed! Where is Alphonse? Is it possible I am to be abandoned like this—neglected by every one?"

"Neglected, indeed!" exclaimed the nurse. Wasn't she there? And here was Mrs. Pontellier leaving, no doubt, a pleasant evening at home to devote to her? And wasn't Monsieur Ratignolle coming that very instant through the hall? And Joséphine was quite sure she had heard Doctor Mandelet's coupé.[4] Yes, there it was, down at the door.

Adèle consented to go back to her room. She sat on the edge of a little low couch next to her bed.

Doctor Mandelet paid no attention to Madame Ratignolle's upbraidings. He was accustomed to them at such times, and was too well convinced of her loyalty to doubt it.

He was glad to see Edna, and wanted her to go with him into the salon and entertain him. But Madame Ratignolle would not consent that Edna should leave her for an instant. Between agonizing moments, she chatted a little, and said it took her mind off her sufferings.

Edna began to feel uneasy. She was seized with a vague dread. Her own like experiences seemed far away, unreal, and only half remembered. She recalled faintly an ecstasy of pain, the heavy odor of chloroform, a stupor which had deadened sensation, and an awakening to find a little new life to which she had given being, added to the great unnumbered multitude of souls that come and go.

She began to wish she had not come; her presence was not necessary. She might have invented a pretext for staying away; she might even invent a pretext now for going. But Edna did not go. With an inward agony, with a flaming, outspoken revolt against the ways of Nature, she witnessed the scene [of] torture.

She was still stunned and speechless with emotion when later she leaned over her friend to kiss her and softly say good-by. Adèle, pressing her cheek, whispered in an exhausted voice: "Think of the children, Edna. Oh think of the children! Remember them!"

XXXVIII

Edna still felt dazed when she got outside in the open air. The Doctor's coupé had returned for him and stood before the *porte cochère*. She did not wish to enter the coupé, and told Doctor Mandelet she

4. Closed carriage.

would walk; she was not afraid, and would go alone. He directed his carriage to meet him at Mrs. Pontellier's, and he started to walk home with her.

Up—away up, over the narrow street between the tall houses, the stars were blazing. The air was mild and caressing, but cool with the breath of spring and the night. They walked slowly, the Doctor with a heavy, measured tread and his hands behind him; Edna, in an absent-minded way, as she had walked one night at Grand Isle, as if her thoughts had gone ahead of her and she was striving to overtake them.

"You shouldn't have been there, Mrs. Pontellier," he said. "That was no place for you. Adèle is full of whims at such times. There were a dozen women she might have had with her, unimpressionable women. I felt that it was cruel, cruel. You shouldn't have gone."

"Oh, well!" she answered, indifferently. "I don't know that it matters after all. One has to think of the children some time or other; the sooner the better."

"When is Léonce coming back?"

"Quite soon. Some time in March."

"And you are going abroad?"

"Perhaps—no, I am not going. I'm not going to be forced into doing things. I don't want to go abroad. I want to be let alone. Nobody has any right—except children, perhaps—and even then, it seems to me—or it did seem—" She felt that her speech was voicing the incoherency of her thoughts, and stopped abruptly.

"The trouble is," sighed the Doctor, grasping her meaning intuitively, "that youth is given up to illusions. It seems to be a provision of Nature; a decoy to secure mothers for the race. And Nature takes no account of moral consequences, of arbitrary conditions which we create, and which we feel obliged to maintain at any cost."

"Yes," she said. "The years that are gone seem like dreams—if one might go on sleeping and dreaming—but to wake up and find—oh! well! perhaps it is better to wake up after all, even to suffer, rather than to remain a dupe to illusions all one's life."

"It seems to me, my dear child," said the Doctor at parting, holding her hand, "you seem to me to be in trouble. I am not going to ask for your confidence. I will only say that if ever you feel moved to give it to me, perhaps I might help you. I know I would understand, and I tell you there are not many who would—not many, my dear."

"Some way I don't feel moved to speak of things that trouble me. Don't think I am ungrateful or that I don't appreciate your sympathy. There are periods of despondency and suffering which take possession of me. But I don't want anything but my own way. That is wanting a good deal, of course, when you have to trample upon the lives, the hearts, the prejudices of others—but no matter—still, I shouldn't want to trample upon the little lives. Oh! I don't know what I'm saying, Doctor. Good night. Don't blame me for anything."

"Yes, I will blame you if you don't come and see me soon. We will talk of things you never have dreamt of talking about before. It will do us both good. I don't want you to blame yourself, whatever comes. Good night, my child."

She let herself in at the gate, but instead of entering she sat upon the step of the porch. The night was quiet and soothing. All the tearing emotion of the last few hours seemed to fall away from her like a somber, uncomfortable garment, which she had but to loosen to be rid of. She went back to that hour before Adèle had sent for her; and her senses kindled afresh in thinking of Robert's words, the pressure of his arms, and the feeling of his lips upon her own. She could picture at that moment no greater bliss on earth than possession of the beloved one. His expression of love had already given him to her in part. When she thought that he was there at hand, waiting for her, she grew numb with the intoxication of expectancy. It was so late; he should be asleep perhaps. She would awaken him with a kiss. She hoped he would be asleep that she might arouse him with her caresses.

Still, she remembered Adèle's voice whispering, "Think of the children; think of them." She meant to think of them, that determination had driven into her soul like a death wound—but not to-night. To-morrow would be time to think of everything.

Robert was not waiting for her in the little parlor. He was nowhere at hand. The house was empty. But he had scrawled on a piece of paper that lay in the lamplight:

"I love you. Good-by—because I love you."

Edna grew faint when she read the words. She went and sat on the sofa. Then she stretched herself out there, never uttering a sound. She did not sleep. She did not go to bed. The lamp sputtered and went out. She was still awake in the morning, when Celestine unlocked the kitchen door and came in to light the fire.

XXXIX

Victor, with hammer and nails and scraps of scantling,[5] was patching a corner of one of the galleries. Mariequita sat near by, dangling her legs, watching him work, and handing him nails from the tool-box. The sun was beating down upon them. The girl had covered her head with her apron folded into a square pad. They had been talking for an hour or more. She was never tired of hearing Victor describe the dinner at Mrs. Pontellier's. He exaggerated every detail, making it appear a veri-

5. Small bits of wood.

table Lucullean[6] feast. The flowers were in tubs, he said. The champagne was quaffed from huge golden goblets. Venus rising from the foam[7] could have presented no more entrancing a spectacle than Mrs. Pontellier, blazing with beauty and diamonds at the head of the board, while the other women were all of them youthful houris[8] possessed of incomparable charms.

She got it into her head that Victor was in love with Mrs. Pontellier, and he gave her evasive answers, framed so as to confirm her belief. She grew sullen and cried a little, threatening to go off and leave him to his fine ladies. There were a dozen men crazy about her at the *Chênière*; and since it was the fashion to be in love with married people, why she could run away any time she liked to New Orleans with Célina's husband.

Célina's husband was a fool, a coward, and a pig, and to prove it to her, Victor intended to hammer his head into a jelly the next time he encountered him. This assurance was very consoling to Mariequita. She dried her eyes, and grew cheerful at the prospect.

They were still talking of the dinner and the allurements of city life when Mrs. Pontellier herself slipped around the corner of the house. The two youngsters stayed dumb with amazement before what they considered to be an apparition. But it was really she in flesh and blood, looking tired and a little travel-stained.

"I walked up from the wharf," she said, "and heard the hammering. I supposed it was you, mending the porch. It's a good thing. I was always tripping over those loose planks last summer. How dreary and deserted everything looks!"

It took Victor some little time to comprehend that she had come in Beaudelet's lugger, that she had come alone, and for no purpose but to rest.

"There's nothing fixed up yet, you see. I'll give you my room; it's the only place."

"Any corner will do," she assured him.

"And if you can stand Philomel's cooking," he went on, "though I might try to get her mother while you are here. Do you think she would come?" turning to Mariequita.

Mariequita thought that perhaps Philomel's mother might come for a few days, and money enough.

Beholding Mrs. Pontellier make her appearance, the girl had at once suspected a lovers' rendezvous. But Victor's astonishment was so genuine, and Mrs. Pontellier's indifference so apparent, that the disturbing notion did not lodge long in her brain. She contemplated with the

---

6. The first-century Roman general Lucius Licinius Lucullus was noted for his extravagant banquets.

7. The Roman goddess of love and beauty was born out of the sea foam.

8. Beautiful maidens in the Muslim paradise.

greatest interest this woman who gave the most sumptuous dinners in America, and who had all the men in New Orleans at her feet.

"What time will you have dinner?" asked Edna. "I'm very hungry; but don't get anything extra."

"I'll have it ready in little or no time," he said, bustling and packing away his tools. "You may go to my room to brush up and rest yourself. Mariequita will show you."

"Thank you," said Edna. "But, do you know, I have a notion to go down to the beach and take a good wash and even a little swim, before dinner?"

"The water is too cold!" they both exclaimed. "Don't think of it."

"Well, I might go down and try—dip my toes in. Why, it seems to me the sun is hot enough to have warmed the very depths of the ocean. Could you get me a couple of towels? I'd better go right away, so as to be back in time. It would be a little too chilly if I waited till this afternoon."

Mariequita ran over to Victor's room, and returned with some towels, which she gave to Edna.

"I hope you have fish for dinner," said Edna, as she started to walk away; "but don't do anything extra if you haven't."

"Run and find Philomel's mother," Victor instructed the girl. "I'll go to the kitchen and see what I can do. By Gimminy! Women have no consideration! She might have sent me word."

Edna walked on down to the beach rather mechanically, not noticing anything special except that the sun was hot. She was not dwelling upon any particular train of thought. She had done all the thinking which was necessary after Robert went away, when she lay awake upon the sofa till morning.

She had said over and over to herself: "To-day it is Arobin; tomorrow it will be some one else. It makes no difference to me, it doesn't matter about Léonce Pontellier—but Raoul and Étienne!" She understood now clearly what she had meant long ago when she said to Adèle Ratignolle that she would give up the unessential, but she would never sacrifice herself for her children.

Despondency had come upon her there in the wakeful night, and had never lifted. There was no one thing in the world that she desired. There was no human being whom she wanted near her except Robert; and she even realized that the day would come when he, too, and the thought of him would melt out of her existence, leaving her alone. The children appeared before her like antagonists who had overcome her; who had overpowered her and sought to drag her into the soul's slavery for the rest of her days. But she knew a way to elude them. She was not thinking of these things when she walked down to the beach.

The water of the Gulf stretched out before her gleaming with the million lights of the sun. The voice of the sea is seductive, never ceasing, whispering, clamoring, murmuring, inviting the soul to wander in abysses of solitude. All along the white beach, up and down, there was no living thing in sight. A bird with a broken wing was beating the air above, reeling, fluttering, circling disabled down, down to the water.

Edna had found her old bathing suit still hanging, faded, upon its accustomed peg.

She put it on, leaving her clothing in the bath-house. But when she was there beside the sea, absolutely alone, she cast the unpleasant, pricking garments from her, and for the first time in her life she stood naked in the open air, at the mercy of the sun, the breeze that beat upon her, and the waves that invited her.

How strange and awful it seemed to stand naked under the sky! how delicious! She felt like some new-born creature, opening its eyes in a familiar world that it had never known.

The foamy wavelets curled up to her white feet, and coiled like serpents about her ankles. She walked out. The water was chill, but she walked on. The water was deep, but she lifted her white body and reached out with a long, sweeping stroke. The touch of the sea is sensuous, enfolding the body in its soft, close embrace.

She went on and on. She remembered the night she swam far out, and recalled the terror that seized her at the fear of being unable to regain the shore. She did not look back now, but went on and on, thinking of the blue-grass meadow that she had traversed when a little child, believing that it had no beginning and no end.

Her arms and legs were growing tired.

She thought of Léonce and the children. They were a part of her life. But they need not have thought that they could possess her, body and soul. How Mademoiselle Reisz would have laughed, perhaps sneered, if she knew! "And you call yourself an artist! What pretensions, Madame! The artist must possess the courageous soul that dares and defies."

Exhaustion was pressing upon and over-powering her.

"Good-by—because, I love you." He did not know; he did not understand. He would never understand. Perhaps Doctor Mandelet would have understood if she had seen him—but it was too late; the shore was far behind her, and her strength was gone.

She looked into the distance, and the old terror flamed up for an instant, then sank again. Edna heard her father's voice and her sister Margaret's. She heard the barking of an old dog that was chained to the sycamore tree. The spurs of the cavalry officer clanged as he walked across the porch. There was the hum of bees, and the musky odor of pinks filled the air.

1899

MARY E. WILKINS FREEMAN
1852–1930

Mary E. Wilkins Freeman's finest short stories hauntingly explore the lives of aging New England women who confront their destitution with sturdy, even ferocious, independence. Whether, like Louisa Ellis of *A New England Nun*, they refuse marriage in order to protect the seclusion and sanctity of virginity or, like Sarah Penn of *The Revolt of "Mother,"* they assert their right to control the domestic sphere in which they have been placed, Freeman's heroines recognize their isolation and defiantly struggle to preserve their integrity against the demands of the importunate suitors, husbands, and preachers who represent all that is left of a dwindling Puritan culture. Like Sarah Orne Jewett, Freeman wrote in and about a region that had experienced a striking demographic change, namely the decline of the male population after the Civil War, and the depression in New England's rural village economy.

The town in which Freeman spent most of her life, Randolph, Massachusetts, was populated by farmers, cottage workers in the shoe industry, and house carpenters like her father, Warren Wilkins. Both he and his wife, Eleanor (Lothrop) Wilkins, could trace their ancestry back to seventeenth-century New England settlers. Their first surviving infant, Mary Wilkins was seven years old when her sister was born. At this age, too, in the village school, she met Mary Wales, a friend she would cherish throughout her life. At fifteen, she moved to Brattleboro, Vermont, where her father hoped to improve the family's fortunes by becoming part-owner of a dry goods store. But the next sixteen years would be filled with disappointments. After graduating from Brattleboro High School in 1870 and spending one unhappy year at Mount Holyoke Female Seminary, Mary Wilkins apparently fell in love with one Hanson Tyler. While the biographical details of this failed relationship are obscure, it is clear that it was accompanied by a series of other difficulties: Mary Wilkins's father went out of business, her one friend left town, her younger sister died, and the family moved into the house of Hanson Tyler's father, with Eleanor Wilkins employed as the Reverend Tyler's housekeeper. When she died suddenly in 1880 and Warren Wilkins died three years later, the thirty-one-year-old Mary Wilkins found herself alone and impoverished.

What saved Freeman from destitution and depression was the literary success she had already begun to achieve. Children's poems in a local magazine, *Wide Awake*, had brought small sums, but in 1882 she had won a fifty-dollar prize offered by a leading Boston magazine for adult fiction, and that same year *Harper's Bazaar* sent her twenty-five dollars with an encouraging acceptance letter. Returning to Randolph, this time to live in the Wales household, Mary Wilkins benefited for the next twenty years from the care of her childhood friend, for Mary Wales freed her from housekeeping chores and solaced her during the nightmares that frequently disturbed her sleep and that may have been responsible for her later addiction to sedatives. *A Humble Romance and Other Stories* (1887) and *A New England Nun and Other Stories* (1891) are usually considered Mary Wilkins's best work. After 1895, when she began traveling to Brattleboro, Boston, Chicago, and Paris, she was well established as a "local-color" realist.

In spite of her financial success and fame, one index of Mary Wilkins's troubled state of mind was her decade-long indecision about whether or not to commit herself to marriage. She had met Dr. Charles Freeman, a nonpracticing physician, in 1892. She was forty-nine years old when, after breaking the engagement and postponing the wedding, she married him in 1902. During the first years of their marriage, he was supportive of her writing, and she published a number of stories about the local customs of her new home, Metuchen, New Jersey. But in 1909 Dr. Freeman entered a sanitarium for alcoholism, the first of a series of such confinements. Before his death, his wife had obtained a legal separation, and after it she successfully contested his will, in which he had left most of his property to someone else. Wealthy at the end of her life, she was awarded the Howells Medal for Fiction in 1926, the same year that she and Edith Wharton became the first women to be elected to membership in the National Institute of Arts and Letters. When she died at seventy-eight, Freeman had published twenty volumes of adult fiction—novels and short stories—as well as six volumes of children's stories. While those volumes have not, until recently, received the critical attention they deserve, a story like *Old Woman Magoun* demonstrates the impact of her best work.

Old Woman Magoun

The hamlet of Barry's Ford is situated in a sort of high valley among the mountains. Below it the hills lie in moveless curves like a petrified ocean; above it they rise in green-cresting waves which never break. It is *Barry's* Ford because at one time the Barry family was the most important in the place; and *Ford* because just at the beginning of the hamlet the little turbulent Barry River is fordable. There is, however, now a rude bridge across the river.

Old Woman Magoun was largely instrumental in bringing the bridge to pass. She haunted the miserable little grocery, wherein whiskey and hands of tobacco[1] were the most salient features of the stock in trade, and she talked much. She would elbow herself into the midst of a knot of idlers and talk.

"That bridge ought to be built this very summer," said Old Woman Magoun. She spread her strong arms like wings, and sent the loafers, half laughing, half angry, flying in every direction. "If I were a *man*," said she, "I'd go out this very minute and lay the fust log. If I were a passel[2] of lazy men layin' round, I'd start up for once in my life, I would." The men cowered visibly—all except Nelson Barry; he swore under his breath and strode over to the counter.

---

1. I.e., small bunches of tobacco leaves (for chewing).   2. Group.

Old Woman Magoun looked after him majestically. "You can cuss all you want to, Nelson Barry," said she; "I ain't afraid of you. I don't expect you to lay ary log of the bridge, but I'm goin' to have it built this very summer." She did. The weakness of the masculine element in Barry's Ford was laid low before such strenuous feminine assertion.

Old Woman Magoun and some other women planned a treat—two sucking pigs, and pies, and sweet cake—for a reward after the bridge should be finished. They even viewed leniently the increased consumption of ardent spirits.

"It seems queer to me," Old Woman Magoun said to Sally Jinks, "that men can't do nothin' without havin' to drink and chew to keep their sperits up. Lord! I've worked all my life and never done nuther."

"Men is different," said Sally Jinks.

"Yes, they be," assented Old Woman Magoun, with open contempt.

The two women sat on a bench in front of Old Woman Magoun's house, and little Lily Barry, her granddaughter, sat holding her doll on a small mossy stone near by. From where they sat they could see the men at work on the new bridge. It was the last day of the work.

Lily clasped her doll—a poor old rag thing—close to her childish bosom, like a little mother, and her face, round which curled her long yellow hair, was fixed upon the men at work. Little Lily had never been allowed to run with the other children of Barry's Ford. Her grandmother had taught her everything she knew—which was not much, but tending at least to a certain measure of spiritual growth—for she, as it were, poured the goodness of her own soul into this little receptive vase of another. Lily was firmly grounded in her knowledge that it was wrong to lie or steal or disobey her grandmother. She had also learned that one should be very industrious. It was seldom that Lily sat idly holding her doll-baby, but this was a holiday because of the bridge. She looked only a child, although she was nearly fourteen; her mother had been married at sixteen. That is, Old Woman Magoun said that her daughter, Lily's mother, had married at sixteen; there had been rumors, but no one had dared openly gainsay the old woman. She said that her daughter had married Nelson Barry, and he had deserted her. She had lived in her mother's house, and Lily had been born there, and she had died when the baby was only a week old. Lily's father, Nelson Barry, was the fairly dangerous degenerate of a good old family. Nelson's father before him had been bad. He was now the last of the family, with the exception of a sister of feeble intellect, with whom he lived in the old Barry house. He was a middle-aged man, still handsome. The shiftless population of Barry's Ford looked up to him as to an evil deity. They wondered how Old Woman Magoun dared brave him as she did. But Old Woman Magoun had within her a mighty sense of reliance upon herself as being on the right track in the midst of a maze of evil, which gave her courage. Nelson Barry had manifested no interest whatever in his daughter. Lily seldom saw her father. She did not often go to the store which was his favorite haunt. Her grandmother took care that she should not do so.

However, that afternoon she departed from her usual custom and sent Lily to the store.

She came in from the kitchen, whither she had been to baste the roasting pig. "There's no use talkin'," said she, "I've got to have some more salt. I've jest used the very last I had to dredge over that pig. I've got to go to the store."

Sally Jinks looked at Lily. "Why don't you send her?" she asked.

Old Woman Magoun gazed irresolutely at the girl. She was herself very tired. It did not seem to her that she could drag herself up the dusty hill to the store. She glanced with covert resentment at Sally Jinks. She thought that she might offer to go. But Sally Jinks said again, "Why don't you let her go?" and looked with a languid eye at Lily holding her doll on the stone.

Lily was watching the men at work on the bridge, with her childish delight in a spectacle of any kind, when her grandmother addressed her.

"Guess I'll let you go down to the store an' git some salt, Lily," said she.

The girl turned uncomprehending eyes upon her grandmother at the sound of her voice. She had been filled with one of the innocent reveries of childhood. Lily had in her the making of an artist or a poet. Her prolonged childhood went to prove it, and also her retrospective eyes, as clear and blue as blue light itself, which seemed to see past all that she looked upon. She had not come of the old Barry family for nothing. The best of the strain was in her, along with the splendid stanchness in humble lines which she had acquired from her grandmother.

"Put on your hat," said Old Woman Magoun; "the sun is hot, and you might git a headache." She called the girl to her, and put back the shower of fair curls under the rubber band which confined the hat. She gave Lily some money, and watched her knot it into a corner of her little cotton handkerchief. "Be careful you don't lose it," said she, "and don't stop to talk to anybody, for I am in a hurry for that salt. Of course, if anybody speaks to you answer them polite, and then come right along."

Lily started, her pocket-handkerchief weighted with the small silver dangling from one hand, and her rag doll carried over her shoulder like a baby. The absurd travesty of a face peeped forth from Lily's yellow curls. Sally Jinks looked after her with a sniff.

"She ain't goin' to carry that rag doll to the store?" said she.

"She likes to," replied Old Woman Magoun, in a half-shamed yet defiantly extenuating voice.

"Some girls at her age is thinkin' about beaux instead of rag dolls," said Sally Jinks.

The grandmother bristled, "Lily ain't big nor old for her age," said she. "I ain't in any hurry to have her git married. She ain't none too strong."

"She's got a good color," said Sally Jinks. She was crocheting white cotton lace, making her thick fingers fly. She really knew how to do scarcely anything except to crochet that coarse lace; somehow her heavy brain or her fingers had mastered that.

"I know she's got a beautiful color," replied Old Woman Magoun, with an odd mixture of pride and anxiety, "but it comes an' goes."

"I've heard that was a bad sign," remarked Sally Jinks, loosening some thread from her spool.

"Yes, it is," said the grandmother. "She's nothin' but a baby, though she's quicker than most to learn."

Lily Barry went on her way to the store. She was clad in a scanty short frock of blue cotton; her hat was tipped back, forming an oval frame for her innocent face. She was very small, and walked like a child, with the clap-clap of little feet of babyhood. She might have been considered, from her looks, under ten.

Presently she heard footsteps behind her; she turned around a little timidly to see who was coming. When she saw a handsome, well-dressed man, she felt reassured. The man came alongside and glanced down carelessly at first, then his look deepened. He smiled, and Lily saw he was very handsome indeed, and that his smile was not only reassuring but wonderfully sweet and compelling.

"Well, little one," said the man, "where are you bound, you and your dolly?"

"I am going to the store to buy some salt for grandma," replied Lily, in her sweet treble. She looked up in the man's face, and he fairly started at the revelation of its innocent beauty. He regulated his pace by hers, and the two went on together. The man did not speak again at once. Lily kept glancing timidly up at him, and every time that she did so the man smiled and her confidence increased. Presently when the man's hand grasped her little childish one hanging by her side, she felt a complete trust in him. Then she smiled up at him. She felt glad that this nice man had come along, for just here the road was lonely.

After a while the man spoke. "What is your name, little one?" he asked, caressingly.

"Lily Barry."

The man started. "What is your father's name?"

"Nelson Barry," replied Lily.

The man whistled. "Is your mother dead?"

"Yes, sir."

"How old are you, my dear?"

"Fourteen," replied Lily.

The man looked at her with surprise. "As old as that?"

Lily suddenly shrank from the man. She could not have told why. She pulled her little hand from his, and he let it go with no remonstrance. She clasped both her arms around her rag doll, in order that her hand should not be free for him to grasp again.

She walked a little farther away from the man, and he looked amused.

"You still play with your doll?" he said, in a soft voice.

"Yes, sir," replied Lily. She quickened her pace and reached the store.

When Lily entered the store, Hiram Gates, the owner, was behind the counter. The only man besides in the store was Nelson Barry. He sat tipping his chair back against the wall; he was half asleep, and his handsome face was bristling with a beard of several days' growth and darkly flushed. He opened his eyes when Lily entered, the strange man following. He brought his chair down on all fours, and he looked at the man—not noticing Lily at all—with a look compounded of defiance and uneasiness.

"Hullo, Jim!" he said.

"Hullo, old man!" returned the stranger.

Lily went over to the counter and asked for the salt, in her pretty little voice. When she had paid for it and was crossing the store, Nelson Barry was on his feet.

"Well, how are you, Lily? It is Lily, isn't it?" he said.

"Yes, sir," replied Lily, faintly.

Her father bent down and, for the first time in her life, kissed her, and the whiskey odor of his breath came into her face.

Lily involuntarily started, and shrank away from him. Then she rubbed her mouth violently with her little cotton handkerchief, which she held gathered up with the rag doll.

"Damn it all! I believe she is afraid of me," said Nelson Barry, in a thick voice.

"Looks a little like it," said the other man, laughing.

"It's that damned old woman," said Nelson Barry. Then he smiled again at Lily. "I didn't know what a pretty little daughter I was blessed with," said he, and he softly stroked Lily's pink cheek under her hat.

Now Lily did not shrink from him. Hereditary instincts and nature itself were asserting themselves in the child's innocent, receptive breast.

Nelson Barry looked curiously at Lily. "How old are you, anyway, child?" he asked.

"I'll be fourteen in September," replied Lily.

"But you still play with your doll?" said Barry, laughing kindly down at her.

Lily hugged her doll more tightly, in spite of her father's kind voice. "Yes, sir," she replied.

Nelson glanced across at some glass jars filled with sticks of candy. "See here, little Lily, do you like candy?" said he.

"Yes, sir."

"Wait a minute."

Lily waited while her father went over to the counter. Soon he returned with a package of the candy.

"I don't see how you are going to carry so much," he said, smiling. "Suppose you throw away your doll?"

Lily gazed at her father and hugged the doll tightly, and there was all at once in the child's expression something mature. It became the reproach of a woman. Nelson's face sobered.

"Oh, it's all right, Lily," he said; "keep your doll. Here, I guess you can carry this candy under your arm."

Lily could not resist the candy. She obeyed Nelson's instructions for carrying it, and left the store laden. The two men also left, and walked in the opposite direction, talking busily.

When Lily reached home, her grandmother, who was watching for her, spied at once the package of candy.

"What's that?" she asked, sharply.

"My father gave it to me," answered Lily, in a faltering voice. Sally regarded her with something like alertness.

"Your father?"

"Yes, ma'am."

"Where did you see him?"

"In the store."

"He gave you this candy?"

"Yes, ma'am."

"What did he say?"

"He asked me how old I was, and—"

"And what?"

"I don't know," replied Lily; and it really seemed to her that she did not know, she was so frightened and bewildered by it all, and, more than anything else, by her grandmother's face as she questioned her.

Old Woman Magoun's face was that of one upon whom a long-anticipated blow had fallen. Sally Jinks gazed at her with a sort of stupid alarm.

Old Woman Magoun continued to gaze at her grandchild with that look of terrible solicitude, as if she saw the girl in the clutch of a tiger. "You can't remember what else he said?" she asked, fiercely, and the child began to whimper softly.

"No, ma'am," she sobbed. "I—don't know, and—"

"And what? Answer me."

"There was another man there. A real handsome man."

"Did he speak to you?" asked Old Woman Magoun.

"Yes ma'am; he walked along with me a piece," confessed Lily, with a sob of terror and bewilderment.

"What did *he* say to you?" asked Old Woman Magoun, with a sort of despair.

Lily told, in her little, faltering, frightened voice, all of the conversation which she could recall. It sounded harmless enough, but the look of the realization of a long-expected blow never left her grandmother's face.

The sun was getting low, and the bridge was nearing completion. Soon the workmen would be crowding into the cabin for their promised supper. There became visible in the distance, far up the road, the heavily plodding figure of another woman who had agreed to come and help. Old Woman Magoun turned again to Lily.

"You go right up-stairs to your own chamber now," said she.

"Good land! ain't you goin' to let that poor child stay up and see the fun?" said Sally Jinks.

"You jest mind your own business," said Old Woman Magoun, forcibly, and Sally Jinks shrank. "You go right up there now, Lily," said the grandmother, in a softer tone, "and grandma will bring you up a nice plate of supper."

"When be you goin' to let that girl grow up?" asked Sally Jinks, when Lily had disappeared.

"She'll grow up in the Lord's good time," replied Old Woman Magoun, and there was in her voice something both sad and threatening. Sally Jinks again shrank a little.

Soon the workmen came flocking noisily into the house. Old Woman Magoun and her two helpers served the bountiful supper. Most of the men had drunk as much as, and more than, was good for them, and Old Woman Magoun had stipulated that there was to be no drinking of anything except coffee during supper.

"I'll git you as good a meal as I know how," she said, "but if I see ary one of you drinkin' a drop, I'll run you all out. If you want anything to drink, you can go up to the store afterward. That's the place for you to to go, if you've got to make hogs of yourselves. I ain't goin' to have no hogs in my house."

Old Woman Magoun was implicitly obeyed. She had a curious authority over most people when she chose to exercise it. When the supper was in full swing, she quietly stole up-stairs and carried some food to Lily. She found the girl, with the rag doll in her arms, crouching by the window in her little rocking-chair—a relic of her infancy, which she still used.

"What a noise they are makin', grandma!" she said, in a terrified whisper, as her grandmother placed the plate before her on a chair."

"They've 'most all of 'em been drinkin'. They air a passel of hogs," replied the old woman.

"Is the man that was with—with my father down there?" asked Lily, in a timid fashion. Then she fairly cowered before the look in her grandmother's eyes.

"No, he ain't; and what's more, he never will be down there if I can help it," said Old Woman Magoun, in a fierce whisper. "I know who he is. They can't cheat me. He's one of them Willises—that family the Barrys married into. They're worse than the Barrys, ef they *have* got money. Eat your supper, and put him out of your mind, child."

It was after Lily was asleep, when Old Woman Magoun was alone, clearing away her supper dishes, that Lily's father came. The door was closed, and he knocked, and the old woman knew at once who was there. The sound of that knock meant as much to her as the whir of a bomb to the defender of a fortress. She opened the door, and Nelson Barry stood there.

"Good-evening, Mrs. Magoun," he said.

Old Woman Magoun stood before him, filling up the doorway with her firm bulk.

"Good-evening, Mrs. Magoun," said Nelson Barry again.

"I ain't got no time to waste," replied the old woman, harshly. "I've got my supper dishes to clean up after them men."

She stood there and looked at him as she might have looked at a rebellious animal which she was trying to tame. The man laughed.

"It's no use," said he. "You know me of old. No human being can turn me from my way when I am once started in it. You may as well let me come in."

Old Woman Magoun entered the house, and Barry followed her.

Barry began without any preface. "Where is the child?" asked he.

"Up-stairs. She has gone to bed."

"She goes to bed early."

"Children ought to," returned the old woman, polishing a plate.

Barry laughed. "You are keeping her a child a long while," he remarked, in a soft voice which had a sting in it.

"She *is* a child," returned the old woman, defiantly.

"Her mother was only three years older when Lily was born."

The old woman made a sudden motion toward the man which seemed fairly menacing. Then she turned again to her dish-washing.

"I want her," said Barry.

"You can't have her," replied the old woman, in a still stern voice.

"I don't see how you can help yourself. You have always acknowledged that she was my child."

The old woman continued her task, but her strong back heaved. Barry regarded her with an entirely pitiless expression.

"I am going to have the girl, that is the long and short of it," he said, "and it is for her best good, too. You are a fool, or you would see it."

"Her best good?" muttered the old woman.

"Yes, her best good. What are you going to do with her, anyway? The girl is a beauty, and almost a woman grown, although you try to make out that she is a baby. You can't live forever."

"The Lord will take care of her," replied the old woman, and again she turned and faced him, and her expression was that of a prophetess.

"Very well, let Him," said Barry, easily. "All the same I'm going to have her, and I tell you it is for her best good. Jim Willis saw her this afternoon, and—"

Old Woman Magoun looked at him. "Jim Willis!" she fairly shrieked.

"Well, what of it?"

"One of them Willises!" repeated the old woman, and this time her voice was thick. It seemed almost as if she were stricken with paralysis. She did not enunciate clearly.

The man shrank a little. "Now what is the need of your making such a fuss?" he said. "I will take her, and Isabel will look out for her."

"Your half-witted sister?" said Old Woman Magoun.

"Yes, my half-witted sister. She knows more than you think."

"More wickedness."

"Perhaps. Well, a knowledge of evil is a useful thing. How are you going to avoid evil if you don't know what it is like? My sister and I will take care of my daughter."

The old woman continued to look at the man, but his eyes never fell. Suddenly her gaze grew inconceivably keen. It was as if she saw through all externals.

"I know what it is!" she cried. "You have been playing cards and you lost, and this is the way you will pay him."

Then the man's face reddened, and he swore under his breath.

"Oh, my God!" said the old woman; and she really spoke with her eyes aloft as if addressing something outside of them both. Then she turned again to her dish-washing.

The man cast a dogged look at her back. "Well, there is no use talking. I have made up my mind," said he, "and you know me and what that means. I am going to have the girl."

"When?" said the old woman, without turning around.

"Well, I am willing to give you a week. Put her clothes in good order before she comes."

The old woman made no reply. She continued washing dishes. She even handled them so carefully that they did not rattle.

"You understand," said Barry. "Have her ready a week from to-day."

"Yes," said Old Woman Magoun, "I understand."

Nelson Barry, going up the mountain road, reflected that Old Woman Magoun had a strong character, that she understood much better than her sex in general the futility of withstanding the inevitable.

"Well," he said to Jim Willis when he reached home, "the old woman did not make such a fuss as I expected."

"Are you going to have the girl?"

"Yes; a week from to-day. Look here, Jim; you've got to stick to your promise."

"All right," said Willis. "Go you one better."

The two were playing at cards in the old parlor, once magnificent, now squalid, of the Barry house. Isabel, the half-witted sister, entered, bringing some glasses on a tray. She had learned with her feeble intellect some tricks, like a dog. One of them was the mixing of sundry drinks. She set the tray on a little stand near the two men, and watched them with her silly simper.

"Clear out now and go to bed," her brother said to her, and she obeyed.

Early the next morning Old Woman Magoun went up to Lily's little sleeping-chamber, and watched her a second as she lay asleep, with her yellow locks spread over the pillow. Then she spoke. "Lily," said she —"Lily, wake up. I am going to Greenham across the new bridge, and you can go with me."

Lily immediately sat up in bed and smiled at her grandmother. Her eyes were still misty, but the light of awakening was in them.

"Get right up," said the old woman. "You can wear your new dress if you want to."

Lily gurgled with pleasure like a baby. "And my new hat?" asked she.

"I don't care."

Old Woman Magoun and Lily started for Greenham before Barry Ford, which kept late hours, was fairly awake. It was three miles to Greenham. The old woman said that, since the horse was a little lame, they would walk. It was a beautiful morning, with a diamond radiance of dew over everything. Her grandmother had curled Lily's hair more punctiliously than usual. The little face peeped like a rose out of two rows of golden spirals. Lily wore her new muslin dress with a pink sash, and her best hat of a fine white straw trimmed with a wreath of rosebuds; also the neatest black open-work stockings and pretty shoes. She even had white cotton gloves. When they set out, the old, heavily stepping woman, in her black gown and cape and bonnet, looked down at the little pink fluttering figure. Her face was full of the tenderest love and admiration, and yet there was something terrible about it. They crossed the new bridge—a primitive structure built of logs in a slovenly fashion. Old Woman Magoun pointed to a gap.

"Jest see that," said she. "That's the way men work."

"Men ain't very nice, be they?" said Lily, in her sweet little voice.

"No, they ain't, take them all together," replied her grandmother.

"That man that walked to the store with me was nicer than some, I guess," Lily said, in a wishful fashion. Her grandmother reached down and took the child's hand in its small cotton glove. "You hurt me, holding my hand so tight," Lily said presently, in a deprecatory little voice.

The old woman loosened her grasp. "Grandma didn't know how tight she was holding your hand," said she. "She wouldn't hurt you for nothin', except it was to save your life, or somethin' like that." She spoke with an undertone of tremendous meaning which the girl was too childish to grasp. They walked along the country road. Just before they reached Greenham they passed a stone wall overgrown with blackberry-vines, and, an unusual thing in that vicinity, a lusty spread of deadly nightshade full of berries.

"Those berries look good to eat, grandma," Lily said.

At that instant the old woman's face became something terrible to see. "You can't have any now," she said, and hurried Lily along.

"They look real nice," said Lily.

When they reached Greenham, Old Woman Magoun took her way straight to the most pretentious house there, the residence of the lawyer, whose name was Mason. Old Woman Magoun bade Lily wait in the yard for a few moments, and Lily ventured to seat herself on a bench beneath an oak-tree; then she watched with some wonder her grandmother enter the lawyer's office door at the right of the house. Presently the lawyer's wife came out and spoke to Lily under the tree. She had in her hand a little tray containing a plate of cake, a glass of milk, and an early apple. She spoke very kindly to Lily; she even kissed her, and offered her the tray of refreshments, which Lily accepted gratefully. She sat eating, with Mrs. Mason watching her, when Old Woman Magoun came out of the lawyer's office with a ghastly face.

"What are you eatin'?" she asked Lily, sharply. "Is that a sour apple?"

"I thought she might be hungry," said the lawyer's wife, with loving, melancholy eyes upon the girl.

Lily had almost finished the apple. "It's real sour, but I like it; it's real nice, grandma," she said.

"You ain't been drinkin' milk with a sour apple?"

"It was real nice milk, grandma."

"You ought never to have drunk milk and eat a sour apple," said her grandmother. "Your stomach was all out of order this mornin', an' sour apples and milk is always apt to hurt anybody."

"I don't know but they are," Mrs. Mason said, apologetically, as she stood on the green lawn with her lavender muslin sweeping around her. "I am real sorry, Mrs. Magoun. I ought to have thought. Let me get some soda for her."

"Soda never agrees with her," replied the old woman, in a harsh voice. "Come," she said to Lily, "it's time we were goin' home."

After Lily and her grandmother had disappeared down the road, Lawyer Mason came out of his office and joined his wife, who had seated herself on the bench beneath the tree. She was idle, and her face wore the expression of those who review joys forever past. She had lost a little girl, her only child, years ago, and her husband always knew when she was thinking about her. Lawyer Mason looked older than his wife; he had a dry, shrewd, slightly one-sided face.

"What do you think, Maria?" he said. "That old woman came to me with the most pressing entreaty to adopt that little girl."

"She is a beautiful little girl," said Mrs. Mason, in a slightly husky voice.

"Yes, she is a pretty child," assented the lawyer, looking pityingly at his wife; "but it is out of the question, my dear. Adopting a child is a serious measure, and in this case a child who comes from Barry's Ford."

"But the grandmother seems a very good woman," said Mrs. Mason.

"I rather think she is. I never heard a word against her. But the father! No, Maria, we cannot take a child with Barry blood in her veins. The stock has run out; it is vitiated physically and morally. It won't do, my dear."

"Her grandmother had her dressed up as pretty as a little girl could be," said Mrs. Mason, and this time the tears welled into her faithful, wistful eyes.

"Well, we can't help that," said the lawyer, as he went back to his office.

Old Woman Magoun and Lily returned, going slowly along the road to Barry's Ford. When they came to the stone wall where the blackberry-vines and the deadly nightshade grew, Lily said she was tired, and asked if she could not sit down for a few minutes. The strange look on her grandmother's face had deepened. Now and then Lily glanced at her and had a feeling as if she were looking at a stranger.

"Yes, you can set down if you want to," said Old Woman Magoun, deeply and harshly.

Lily started and looked at her, as if to make sure that it was her grandmother who spoke. Then she sat down on a stone which was comparatively free of the vines.

"Ain't you goin' to set down, grandma?" Lily asked, timidly.

"No; I don't want to get into that mess," replied her grandmother. "I ain't tired. I'll stand here."

Lily sat still; her delicate little face was flushed with heat. She extended her tiny feet in her best shoes and gazed at them. "My shoes are all over dust," said she.

"It will brush off," said her grandmother, still in that strange voice.

Lily looked around. An elm-tree in the field behind her cast a spray of branches over her head; a little cool puff of wind came on her face. She gazed at the low mountains on the horizon, in the midst of which she lived, and she sighed, for no reason that she knew. She began idly picking at the blackberry-vines; there were no berries on them; then she put her little fingers on the berries of the deadly nightshade. "These look like nice berries," she said.

Old Woman Magoun, standing stiff and straight in the road, said nothing.

"They look good to eat," said Lily.

Old Woman Magoun still said nothing, but she looked up into the ineffable blue of the sky, over which spread at intervals great white clouds shaped like wings.

Lily picked some of the deadly nightshade berries and ate them. "Why, they are real sweet," said she. "They are nice." She picked some more and ate them.

Presently her grandmother spoke. "Come," she said, "it is time we were going. I guess you have set long enough."

Lily was still eating the berries when she slipped down from the wall and followed her grandmother obediently up the road.

Before they reached home, Lily complained of being very thirsty. She stopped and made a little cup of a leaf and drank long at a mountain brook. "I am dreadful dry, but it hurts me to swallow," she said to her grandmother when she stopped drinking and joined the old woman waiting for her in the road. Her grandmother's face seemed strangely dim to her. She took hold of Lily's hand as they went on. "My stomach burns," said Lily, presently. "I want some more water."

"There is another brook a little farther on," said Old Woman Magoun, in a dull voice.

When they reached that brook, Lily stopped and drank again, but she whimpered a little over her difficulty in swallowing. "My stomach burns, too," she said, walking on, "and my throat is so dry, grandma." Old Woman Magoun held Lily's hand more tightly. "You hurt me holding my hand so tight, grandma," said Lily, looking up at her grandmother, whose face she seemed to see through a mist, and the old woman loosened her grasp.

When at last they reached home, Lily was very ill. Old Woman Magoun put her on her own bed in the little bedroom out of the kitchen. Lily lay there and moaned, and Sally Jinks came in.

"Why, what ails her?" she asked. "She looks feverish."

Lily unexpectedly answered for herself. "I ate some sour apples and drank some milk," she moaned.

"Sour apples and milk are dreadful apt to hurt anybody," said Sally Jinks. She told several people on her way home that Old Woman Magoun was dreadful careless to let Lily eat such things.

Meanwhile Lily grew worse. She suffered cruelly from the burning in her stomach, the vertigo, and the deadly nausea. "I am so sick, I am so sick, grandma," she kept moaning. She could no longer see her grandmother as she bent over her, but she could hear her talk.

Old Woman Magoun talked as Lily had never heard her talk before, as nobody had ever heard her talk before. She spoke from the depths of her soul; her voice was as tender as the coo of a dove, and it was grand and exalted. "You'll feel better very soon, little Lily," said she.

"I am so sick, grandma."

"You will feel better very soon, and then—"

"I am sick."

"You shall go to a beautiful place."

Lily moaned.

"You shall go to a beautiful place," the old woman went on.

"Where?" asked Lily, groping feebly with her cold little hands. Then she moaned again.

"A beautiful place, where the flowers grow tall."

"What color? Oh, grandma, I am so sick."

"A blue color," replied the old woman. Blue was Lily's favorite color. "A beautiful blue color, and as tall as your knees, and the flowers always stay there, and they never fade."

"Not if you pick them, grandma? Oh!"

"No, not if you pick them; they never fade, and they are so sweet you can smell them a mile off; and there are birds that sing, and all the roads have gold stones in them, and the stone walls are made of gold."

"Like the ring grandpa gave you? I am so sick, grandma."

"Yes, gold like that. And all the houses are built of silver and gold, and the people all have wings, so when they get tired walking they can fly, and—"

"I am so sick, grandma."

"And all the dolls are alive," said Old Woman Magoun. "Dolls like yours can run, and talk, and love you back again."

Lily had her poor old rag doll in bed with her, clasped close to her agonized little heart. She tried very hard with her eyes, whose pupils were so dilated that they looked black, to see her grandmother's face when she said that, but she could not. "It is dark," she moaned, feebly.

"There where you are going it is always light," said the grandmother, "and the commonest things shine like that breastpin Mrs. Lawyer Mason had on to-day."

Lily moaned pitifully, and said something incoherent. Delirium was commencing. Presently she sat straight up in bed and raved; but even then her grandmother's wonderful compelling voice had an influence over her.

"You will come to a gate with all the colors of the rainbow," said her grandmother; "and it will open, and you will go right in and walk up the gold street, and cross the field where the blue flowers come up to your knees, until you find your mother, and she will take you home where you are going to live. She has a little white room all ready for you, white curtains at the windows, and a little white looking-glass, and when you look in it you will see—"

"What will I see? I am so sick, grandma."

"You will see a face like yours, only it's an angel's; and there will be a little white bed, and you can lay down an' rest."

"Won't I be sick, grandma?" asked Lily. Then she moaned and babbled wildly, although she seemed to understand through it all what her grandmother said.

"No, you will never be sick anymore. Talkin' about sickness won't mean anything to you."

It continued. Lily talked on wildly, and her grandmother's great voice of soothing never ceased, until the child fell into a deep sleep, or what resembled sleep; but she lay stiffly in that sleep, and a candle flashed before her eyes made no impression on them.

Then it was that Nelson Barry came. Jim Willis waited outside the door. When Nelson entered he found Old Woman Magoun on her knees beside the bed, weeping with dry eyes and a might of agony which fairly shook Nelson Barry, the degenerate of a fine old race.

"Is she sick?" he asked, in a hushed voice.

Old Woman Magoun gave another terrible sob, which sounded like the gasp of one dying.

"Sally Jinks said that Lily was sick from eating milk and sour apples," said Barry, in a tremulous voice. "I remember that her mother was very sick once from eating them."

Lily lay still, and her grandmother on her knees shook with her terrible sobs.

Suddenly Nelson Barry started. "I guess I had better go to Greenham for a doctor if she's as bad as that," he said. He went close to the bed and looked at the sick child. He gave a great start. Then he felt of her hands and reached down under the bedclothes for her little feet. "Her hands and feet are like ice," he cried out. "Good God! why didn't you send for some one—for me—before? Why, she's dying; she's almost gone!"

Barry rushed out and spoke to Jim Willis, who turned pale and came in and stood by the bedside.

"She's almost gone," he said, in a hushed whisper.

"There's no use going for the doctor, she'd be dead before he got here," said Nelson, and he stood regarding the passing child with a strange, sad face—unutterably sad, because of his incapability of the truest sadness.

"Poor little thing, she's past suffering, anyhow," said the other man, and his own face also was sad with a puzzled, mystified sadness.

Lily died that night. There was quite a commotion in Barry's Ford until after the funeral, it was all so sudden, and then everything went on as usual. Old Woman Magoun continued to live as she had done before. She supported herself by the produce of her tiny farm; she was very industrious, but people said that she was a trifle touched, since every time she went over the log bridge with her eggs or her garden vegetables to sell in Greenham, she carried with her, as one might have carried an infant, Lily's old rag doll.

1909

LADY AUGUSTA GREGORY
1852–1932

"Lady Gregory was friend and hostess," wrote the Irish poet W. B. Yeats of the woman who had been his lifelong patroness, but "neither she nor we thought her a possible creator." Yet when she herself began to write, he added, "she became the founder of modern Irish dialect literature." Specifically, Lady Gregory produced, first, a collection of traditional tales about the ancient Gaelic hero Cuchulain (*Cuchulain of Muirthemne*, 1902); then, another important volume of Irish legends (*Gods and Fighting Men*, 1904); finally—and most importantly—a group of spirited, inventive, and distinctively Irish plays which made a notable mark on the theater of their time. In yet another way, moreover, this onetime "hostess" helped influence the course of twentieth-century art, for in 1898, with Yeats and the poet-playwright Edward Martyn, she founded the famous Abbey Theatre, an institution that was as important to the history of drama as it was central in the rise of the turn-of-the-century Irish nationalist movement.

Born to a wealthy, landowning family in County Galway, in the west of Ireland, Isabella Augusta Persse married Sir William Gregory, a former governor of Ceylon, in 1880; after his death in 1892, she edited his memoirs and his grandfather's letters. By that time, however, she had already begun to meet, befriend, and subsidize such Irish literary men as W. B. Yeats, George Moore, Edward Martyn, John Synge, and James Joyce, all of whom—along with Lady Gregory herself—were variously concerned with reestablishing the indigenous Irish culture that had been shattered when the English conquered the country in the sixteenth century. Her volumes of Irish tales represented a significant step toward reviving lost traditions, while her work for the Abbey Theatre, with its emphasis on plays written in an accurately transcribed Irish dialect and created around plots that elaborated Irish themes and myths, was another such step. Of at least equal importance, however, were her own creations, especially witty plays like *Spreading the News*, a one-act drama that vividly evokes the world of the Irish peasantry even while it reveals a keen concern with a uniquely female realm of humorous gossip and "scandal."

Not surprisingly, Lady Gregory's pieces for the Abbey Theatre had far more drawing power than Yeats's sometimes greater but usually more arcane offerings: as one observer put it, "Yeats spells empty benches . . . Lady Gregory popularity." Yet despite the solidity of her achievement, this significant woman dramatist always had a tenuous reputation. Though George Bernard Shaw defined her as "the greatest living Irishwoman," he also sardonically remarked that she was "the charwoman of the Abbey Theatre," no doubt because, as a born "hostess" and patroness, she was willing to handle so many details of what Yeats once called "theatre business, management of men." Nevertheless, at least upon Yeats himself her artistic as well as her personal talent made an indelible impression: in two great late poems—*Coole Park, 1929* and *Coole Park and Ballylee, 1931*—both devoted to her deep connections with the places where she lived, he memorialized his sense of her genius, noting in *Coole Park, 1929* that this "woman's powerful character / Could keep a swallow to its first intent."

Spreading the News

Persons

BARTLEY FALLON	JAMES RYAN
MRS. FALLON	MRS. TARPEY
JACK SMITH	MRS. TULLY
SHAWN EARLY	A POLICEMAN, JO MULDOON
TIM CASEY	A REMOVABLE MAGISTRATE

SCENE

[*The outskirts of a Fair. An Apple Stall.* MRS. TARPEY *sitting at it.* MAGISTRATE *and* POLICEMAN *enter.*]

MAGISTRATE. So that is the Fair Green. Cattle and sheep and mud. No system. What a repulsive sight!

POLICEMAN. That is so, indeed.

MAGISTRATE. I suppose there is a good deal of disorder in this place?

POLICEMAN. There is.

MAGISTRATE. Common assault?

POLICEMAN. It's common enough.

MAGISTRATE. Agrarian crime, no doubt?

POLICEMAN. That is so.

MAGISTRATE. Boycotting? Maiming of cattle? Firing into houses?

POLICEMAN. There was one time, and there might be again.

MAGISTRATE. That is bad. Does it go any farther than that?

POLICEMAN. Far enough, indeed.

MAGISTRATE. Homicide, then! This district has been shamefully neglected! I will change all that. When I was in the Andaman Islands,[1]
my system never failed. Yes, yes, I will change all that. What has that
woman on her stall?

POLICEMAN. Apples mostly—and sweets.

MAGISTRATE. Just see if there are any unlicensed goods underneath—
spirits or the like. We had evasions of the salt tax in the Andaman Islands.

POLICEMAN. [*Sniffing cautiously and upsetting a heap of apples.*] I see
no spirits here—or salt.

MAGISTRATE. [*To* MRS. TARPEY.] Do you know this town well, my good
woman?

MRS. TARPEY. [*Holding out some apples.*] A penny the half-dozen, your
honour.

POLICEMAN. [*Shouting.*] The gentleman is asking do you know the
town! He's the new magistrate!

MRS. TARPEY. [*Rising and ducking.*] Do I know the town? I do, to be
sure.

MAGISTRATE. [*Shouting.*] What is its chief business?

MRS. TARPEY. Business, is it? What business would the people here have
but to be minding one another's business?

MAGISTRATE. I mean what trade have they?

MRS. TARPEY. Not a trade. No trade at all but to be talking.

MAGISTRATE. I shall learn nothing here.

[JAMES RYAN *comes in, pipe in mouth. Seeing* MAGISTRATE *he retreats
quickly, taking pipe from mouth.*]

MAGISTRATE. The smoke from that man's pipe had a greenish look; he
may be growing unlicensed tobacco at home. I wish I had brought
my telescope to this district. Come to the postoffice, I will telegraph
for it. I found it very useful in the Andaman Islands.

[MAGISTRATE *and* POLICEMAN *go out left.*]

MRS. TARPEY. Bad luck to Jo Muldoon, knocking my apples this way and
that way. [*Begins arranging them.*] Showing off he was to the new
magistrate.

___

1. Islands governed by Great Britain, south of India.

[*Enter* BARTLEY FALLON *and* MRS. FALLON.]

BARTLEY. Indeed it's a poor country and a scarce country to be living in. But I'm thinking if I went to America it's long ago the day I'd be dead!

MRS. FALLON. So you might, indeed.

[*She puts her basket on a barrel and begins putting parcels in it, taking them from under her cloak.*]

BARTLEY. And it's a great expense for a poor man to be buried in America.

MRS. FALLON. Never fear, Bartley Fallon, but I'll give you a good burying the day you'll die.

BARTLEY. Maybe it's yourself will be buried in the graveyard of Cloonmara before me, Mary Fallon, and I myself that will be dying unbeknownst some night, and no one a-near me. And the cat itself may be gone straying through the country, and the mice squealing over the quilt.

MRS. FALLON. Leave off talking of dying. It might be twenty years you'll be living yet.

BARTLEY. [*With a deep sigh.*] I'm thinking if I'll be living at the end of twenty years, it's a very old man I'll be then!

MRS. TARPEY. [*Turns and sees them.*] Good morrow, Bartley Fallon; good morrow, Mrs. Fallon. Well, Bartley, you'll find no cause for complaining today; they are all saying it was a good fair.

BARTLEY. [*Raising his voice.*] It was not a good fair, Mrs. Tarpey. It was a scattered sort of a fair. If we didn't expect more, we got less. That's the way with me always; whatever I have to sell goes down and whatever I have to buy goes up. If there's ever any misfortune coming to this world, it's on myself it pitches, like a flock of crows on seed potatoes.[2]

MRS. FALLON. Leave off talking of misfortunes, and listen to Jack Smith that is coming the way, and he singing.

[*Voice of* JACK SMITH *heard singing.*]

> I thought, my first love,
>   There'd be but one house between you and me,
> And I thought I would find
>   Yourself coaxing my child on your knee.
> Over the tide
>   I would leap with the leap of a swan,
> Till I came to the side
>   Of the wife of the Red-haired man![3]

[JACK SMITH *comes in; he is a red-haired man, and is carrying a hayfork.*]

MRS. TARPEY. That should be a good song if I had my hearing.

---

2. Potatoes newly planted.   3. A traditional Irish ballad.

MRS. FALLON. [*Shouting.*] It's "The Red-haired Man's Wife."

MRS. TARPEY. I know it well. That's the song that has a skin on it!
[*She turns her back to them and goes on arranging her apples.*]

MRS. FALLON. Where's herself, Jack Smith?

JACK SMITH. She was delayed with her washing; bleaching the clothes on
the hedge she is, and she daren't leave them, with all the tinkers[4] that
do be passing to the fair. It isn't to the fair I came myself, but up to
the Five Acre Meadow I'm going, where I have a contract for the
hay. We'll get a share of it into tramps[5] today. [*He lays down hayfork
and lights his pipe.*]

BARTLEY. You will not get it into tramps today. The rain will be down
on it by evening, and on myself too. It's seldom I ever started on a
journey but the rain would come down on me before I'd find any
place of shelter.

JACK SMITH. If it didn't itself, Bartley, it is my belief you would carry a
leaky pail on your head in place of a hat, the way you'd not be without some cause of complaining.
[*A voice heard, "Go on, now, go on out o' that. Go on I say."*]

JACK SMITH. Look at that young mare of Pat Ryan's that is backing into
Shaughnessy's bullocks with the dint[6] of the crowd! Don't be
daunted, Pat, I'll give you a hand with her.
[*He goes out, leaving his hayfork.*]

MRS. FALLON. It's time for ourselves to be going home. I have all I
bought put in the basket. Look at there, Jack Smith's hayfork he left
after him! He'll be wanting it. [*Calls.*] Jack Smith! Jack Smith!—
He's gone through the crowd—hurry after him, Bartley, he'll be
wanting it.

BARTLEY. I'll do that. This is no safe place to be leaving it. [*He takes up
fork awkwardly and upsets the basket.*] Look at that now! If there is
any basket in the fair upset, it must be our own basket! [*He goes out to
right.*]

MRS. FALLON. Get out of that! It is your own fault, it is. Talk of misfortunes and misfortunes will come. Glory be! Look at my new egg-
cups rolling in every part—and my two pound of sugar with the
paper broke—

MRS. TARPEY. [*Turning from stall.*] God help us, Mrs. Fallon, what
happened your basket?

MRS. FALLON. It's himself that knocked it down, bad manners to him.
[*Putting things up.*] My grand sugar that's destroyed, and he'll not
drink his tea without it. I had best go back to the shop for more, much
good may it do him! [*Enter* TIM CASEY.]

TIM CASEY. Where is Bartley Fallon, Mrs. Fallon? I want a word with
him before he'll leave the fair. I was afraid he might have gone home
by this, for he's a temperate man.

MRS. FALLON. I wish he did go home! It'd be best for me if he went

4. Gypsies.   6. Pressure.
5. I.e., bales of hay.

home straight from the fair green, or if he never came with me at all! Where is he, is it? He's gone up the road [*jerks elbow*] following Jack Smith with a hayfork.

[*She goes out to left.*]

TIM CASEY. Following Jack Smith with a hayfork! Did ever anyone hear the like of that. [*Shouts.*] Did you hear that news, Mrs. Tarpey?

MRS. TARPEY. I heard no news at all.

TIM CASEY. Some dispute I suppose it was that rose between Jack Smith and Bartley Fallon, and it seems Jack made off, and Bartley is following him with a hayfork!

MRS. TARPEY. Is he now? Well, that was quick work! It's not ten minutes since the two of them were here, Bartley going home and Jack going to the Five Acre Meadow; and I had my apples to settle up, that Jo Muldoon of the police had scattered, and when I looked round again Jack Smith was gone, and Bartley Fallon was gone, and Mrs. Fallon's basket upset, and all in it strewed upon the ground—the tea here— the two pound of sugar there—the eggs-cups there—Look, now, what a great hardship the deafness puts upon me, that I didn't hear the commencement of the fight! Wait till I tell James Ryan that I see below; he is a neighbour of Bartley's, it would be a pity if he wouldn't hear the news!

[*She goes out. Enter* SHAWN EARLY *and* MRS. TULLY.]

TIM CASEY. Listen, Shawn Early! Listen, Mrs. Tully, to the news! Jack Smith and Bartley Fallon had a falling out, and Jack knocked Mrs. Fallon's basket into the road, and Bartley made an attack on him with a hayfork, and away with Jack, and Bartley after him. Look at the sugar here yet on the road!

SHAWN EARLY. Do you tell me so? Well, that's a queer thing, and Bartley Fallon so quiet a man!

MRS. TULLY. I wouldn't wonder at all. I would never think well of a man that would have that sort of a mouldering[7] look. It's likley he has overtaken Jack by this.

[*Enter* JAMES RYAN *and* MRS. TARPEY.]

JAMES RYAN. That is great news Mrs. Tarpey was telling me! I suppose that's what brought the police and the magistrate up this way. I was wondering to see them in it a while ago.

SHAWN EARLY. The police after them? Bartley Fallon must have injured Jack so. They wouldn't meddle in a fight that was only for show!

MRS. TULLY. Why wouldn't he injure him? There was many a man killed with no more of a weapon than a hayfork.

JAMES RYAN. Wait till I run north as far as Kelly's bar to spread the news! [*He goes out.*]

TIM CASEY. I'll go tell Jack Smith's first cousin that is standing there south of the church after selling his lambs. [*Goes out.*]

MRS. TULLY. I'll go telling a few of the neighbours I see beyond to the west. [*Goes out.*]

---

7. Wasted.

SHAWN EARLY. I'll give word of it beyond at the east of the green.

[*Is going out when* MRS. TARPEY *seizes hold of him.*]

MRS. TARPEY. Stop a minute, Shawn Early, and tell me did you see red Jack Smith's wife, Kitty Keary, in any place?

SHAWN EARLY. I did. At her own house she was, drying clothes on the hedge as I passed.

MRS. TARPEY. What did you say she was doing?

SHAWN EARLY. [*Breaking away.*] Laying out a sheet on the hedge. [*He goes.*]

MRS. TARPEY. Laying out a sheet for the dead! The Lord have mercy on us! Jack Smith dead, and his wife laying out a sheet for his burying! [*Calls out.*] Why didn't you tell me that before, Shawn Early? Isn't the deafness the great hardship? Half the world might be dead without me knowing of it or getting word of it at all! [*She sits down and rocks herself.*] O my poor Jack Smith! To be going to his work so nice and so hearty, and to be left stretched on the ground in the full light of the day!

[*Enter* TIM CASEY.]

TIM CASEY. What is it, Mrs. Tarpey? What happened since?

MRS. TARPEY. O my poor Jack Smith!

TIM CASEY. Did Bartley overtake him?

MRS. TARPEY. O the poor man!

TIM CASEY. Is it killed he is?

MRS. TARPEY. Stretched in the Five Acre Meadow!

TIM CASEY. The Lord have mercy on us! Is that a fact?

MRS. TARPEY. Without the rites of the Church or a ha'porth![8]

TIM CASEY. Who was telling you?

MRS. TARPEY. And the wife laying out a sheet for his corpse. [*Sits up and wipes her eyes.*] I suppose they'll wake him the same as another?

[*Enter* MRS. TULLY, SHAWN EARLY, *and* JAMES RYAN.]

MRS. TULLY. There is great talk about this work in every quarter of the fair.

MRS. TARPEY. Ochone![9] cold and dead. And myself maybe the last he was speaking to!

JAMES RYAN. The Lord save us! Is it dead he is?

TIM CASEY. Dead surely, and the wife getting provision for the wake.

SHAWN EARLY. Well, now, hadn't Bartley Fallon great venom in him?

MRS. TULLY. You may be sure he had some cause. Why would he have made an end of him if he had not? [*To* MRS. TARPEY, *raising her voice.*] What was it rose the dispute at all, Mrs. Tarpey?

MRS. TARPEY. Not a one of me knows. The last I saw of them, Jack Smith was standing there, and Bartley Fallon was standing there, quiet and easy, and he listening to "The Red-haired Man's Wife."

MRS. TULLY. Do you hear that, Tim Casey? Do you hear that, Shawn Early and James Ryan? Bartley Fallon was here this morning listen-

---

8. Halfpenny-worth; possibly also a mistake for *habeas corpus*.   9. "Alas" (Gaelic).

ing to red Jack Smith's wife, Kitty Keary that was! Listening to her and whispering with her! It was she started the fight so!

SHAWN EARLY. She must have followed him from her own house. It is likely some person roused him.

TIM CASEY. I never knew, before, Bartley Fallon was great[1] with Jack Smith's wife.

MRS. TULLY. How would you know it? Sure it's not in the streets they would be calling it. If Mrs. Fallon didn't know of it, and if I that have the next house to them didn't know of it, and if Jack Smith himself didn't know of it, it is not likely you would know of it, Tim Casey.

SHAWN EARLY. Let Bartley Fallon take charge of her from this out so, and let him provide for her. It is little pity she will get from any person in this parish.

TIM CASEY. How can he take charge of her? Sure he has a wife of his own. Sure you don't think he'd turn souper[2] and marry her in a Protestant church?

JAMES RYAN. It would be easy for him to marry her if he brought her to America.

SHAWN EARLY. With or without Kitty Keary, believe me it is for America he's making at this minute. I saw the new magistrate and Jo Muldoon of the police going into the postoffice as I came up—there was hurry on them—you may be sure it was to telegraph they went, the way he'll be stopped in the docks at Queenstown!

MRS. TULLY. It's likely Kitty Keary is gone with him, and not minding a sheet or a wake at all. The poor man, to be deserted by his own wife, and the breath hardly gone out yet from his body that is lying bloody in the field!

[*Enter* MRS. FALLON.]

MRS. FALLON. What is it the whole of the town is talking about? And what is it you yourselves are talking about? Is it about my man Bartley Fallon you are talking? Is it lies about him you are telling, saying that he went killing Jack Smith? My grief that ever he came into this place at all!

JAMES RYAN. Be easy now, Mrs. Fallon. Sure there is no one at all in the whole fair but is sorry for you!

MRS. FALLON. Sorry for me, is it? Why would anyone be sorry for me? Let you be sorry for yourselves, and that there may be shame on you for ever and at the day of judgment, for the words you are saying and the lies you are telling to take away the character of my poor man, and to take the good name off of him, and to drive him to destruction! That is what you are doing!

SHAWN EARLY. Take comfort now, Mrs. Fallon. The police are not so smart as they think. Sure he might give them the slip yet, the same as Lynchehaun.[3]

---

1. Intimate.
2. Roman Catholic converted to Protestantism by the attractions of free soup and other charity.

3. I.e., James Lynchehaun, a criminal who escaped to America with the help of the people of Achill Island.

MRS. TULLY. If they do get him, and if they do put a rope around his neck, there is no one can say he does not deserve it!

MRS. FALLON. Is that what you are saying, Bridget Tully, and is that what you think? I tell you it's too much talk you have, making yourself out to be such a great one, and to be running down every respectable person! A rope, is it? It isn't much of a rope was needed to tie up your own furniture the day you came into Martin Tully's house, and you never bringing as much as a blanket, or a penny, or a suit of clothes with you and I myself bringing seventy pounds and two feather beds. And now you are stiffer than a woman would have a hundred pounds! It is too much talk the whole of you have. A rope is it? I tell you the whole of this town is full of liars and schemers that would hang you up for half a glass of whisky. [*Turning to go.*] People they are you wouldn't believe as much as daylight from without you'd get up to have a look at it yourself. Killing Jack Smith indeed! Where are you at all, Bartley, till I bring you out of this? My nice quiet little man! My decent comrade! He that is as kind and as harmless as an innocent beast of the field! He'll be doing no harm at all if he'll shed the blood of some of you after this day's work! That much would be no harm at all. [*Calls out.*] Bartley! Bartley Fallon! Where are you? [*Going out.*] Did anyone see Bartley Fallon?

[*All turn to look after her.*]

JAMES RYAN. It is hard for her to believe any such a thing, God help her!

[*Enter* BARTLEY FALLON *from right, carrying hayfork.*]

BARTLEY. It is what I often said to myself, if there is ever any misfortune coming to this world it is on myself it is sure to come!

[*All turn round and face him.*]

BARTLEY. To be going about with this fork and to find no one to take it, and no place to leave it down, and I wanting to be gone out of this— Is that you, Shawn Early? [*Holds out fork.*] It's well I met you. You have no call to be leaving the fair for a while the way I have, and how can I go till I'm rid of this fork? Will you take it and keep it until such time as Jack Smith—

SHAWN EARLY. [*Backing.*] I will not take it, Bartley Fallon, I'm very thankful to you!

BARTLEY. [*Turning to apple stall.*] Look at it now, Mrs. Tarpey, it was here I got it; let me thrust it in under the stall. It will lie there safe enough, and no one will take notice of it until such time as Jack Smith—

MRS. TARPEY. Take your fork out of that! Is it to put trouble on me and to destroy me you want? Putting it there for the police to be rooting it out maybe. [*Thrusts him back.*]

BARTLEY. That is a very unneighbourly thing for you to do, Mrs. Tarpey. Hadn't I enough care on me with that fork before this, running up and down with it like the swinging of a clock, and afeard to lay it down in any place! I wish I never touched it or meddled with it at all!

JAMES RYAN. It is a pity, indeed, you ever did.

BARTLEY. Will you yourself take it, James Ryan? You were always a neighbourly man.

JAMES RYAN. [*Backing.*] There is many a thing I would do for you, Bartley Fallon, but I won't do that!

SHAWN EARLY. I tell you there is no man will give you any help or any encouragement for this day's work. If it was something agrarian now—

BARTLEY. If no one at all will take it, maybe it's best to give it up to the police.

TIM CASEY. There'd be a welcome for it with them surely!

[*Laughter.*]

MRS. TULLY. And it is to the police Kitty Keary herself will be brought.

MRS. TARPEY. [*Rocking to and fro.*] I wonder now who will take the expense of the wake for poor Jack Smith?

BARTLEY. The wake for Jack Smith!

TIM CASEY. Why wouldn't he get a wake as well as another? Would you begrudge him that much? Red Jack Smith dead! Who was telling you?

BARTLEY. Red Jack Smith dead! Who was telling you?

SHAWN EARLY. The whole town knows of it by this.

BARTLEY. Do they say what way did he die?

JAMES RYAN. You don't know that yourself, I suppose, Bartley Fallon? You don't know he was followed and that he was laid dead with the stab of a hayfork?

BARTLEY. The stab of a hayfork!

SHAWN EARLY. You don't know, I suppose, that the body was found in the Five Acre Meadow?

BARTLEY. The Five Acre Meadow!

TIM CASEY. It is likely you don't know that the police are after the man that did it?

BARTLEY. The man that did it!

MRS. TULLY. You don't know, maybe, that he was made away with for the sake of Kitty Keary, his wife?

BARTLEY. Kitty Keary, his wife!

[*Sits down bewildered.*]

MRS. TULLY. And what have you to say now, Bartley Fallon?

BARTLEY. [*Crossing himself.*] I to bring that fork here, and to find that news before me! It is much if I can ever stir from this place at all, or reach as far as the road!

TIM CASEY. Look, boys, at the new magistrate, and Jo Muldoon along with him! It's best for us to quit this.

SHAWN EARLY. That is so. It is best not to be mixed in this business at all.

JAMES RYAN. Bad as he is, I wouldn't like to be an informer against any man.

[*All hurry away except* MRS. TARPEY, *who remains behind her stall. Enter* MAGISTRATE *and* POLICEMAN.]

MAGISTRATE. I knew the district was in a bad state, but I did not expect to be confronted with a murder at the first fair I came to.

POLICEMAN. I am sure you did not, indeed.

MAGISTRATE. It was well I had not gone home. I caught a few words here and there that roused my suspicions.

POLICEMAN. So they would, too.

MAGISTRATE. You heard the same story from everyone you asked?

POLICEMAN. The same story—or if it was not altogether the same, anyway it was no less than the first story.

MAGISTRATE. What is that man doing? He is sitting alone with a hayfork. He has a guilty look. The murder was done with a hayfork!

POLICEMAN. [In a whisper.] That's the very man they say did the act; Bartley Fallon himself!

MAGISTRATE. He must have found escape difficult—he is trying to brazen it out. A convict in the Andaman Islands tried the same game, but he could not escape my system! Stand aside—Don't go far—have the handcuffs ready. [He walks up to BARTLEY, folds his arms, and stands before him.] Here, my man, do you know anything of John Smith?

BARTLEY. Of John Smith! Who is he, now?

POLICEMAN. Jack Smith, sir—Red Jack Smith!

MAGISTRATE. [Coming a step nearer and tapping him on the shoulder.] Where is Jack Smith?

BARTLEY. [With a deep sigh, and shaking his head slowly.] Where is he, indeed?

MAGISTRATE. What have you to tell?

BARTLEY. It is where he was this morning, standing in this spot, singing his share of songs—no, but lighting his pipe—scraping a match on the sole of his shoe—

MAGISTRATE. I ask you, for the third time, where is he?

BARTLEY. I wouldn't like to say that. It is a great mystery, and it is hard to say of any man, did he earn hatred or love.

MAGISTRATE. Tell me all you know.

BARTLEY. All that I know—Well, there are the three estates; there is Limbo, and there is Purgatory, and there is[4]—

MAGISTRATE. Nonsense! This is trifling! Get to the point.

BARTLEY. Maybe you don't hold with the clergy so? That is the teaching of the clergy. Maybe you hold with the old people. It is what they do be saying, that the shadow goes wandering, and the soul is tired, and the body is taking a rest—The shadow! [Starts up.] I was nearly sure I saw Jack Smith not ten minutes ago at the corner of the forge, and I lost him again—Was it his ghost I saw, do you think?

MAGISTRATE. [To POLICEMAN.] Conscience-struck! He will confess all now!

BARTLEY. His ghost to come before me! It is likely it was on account of the fork! I to have it and he to have no way to defend himself the time he met with his death!

---

4. Fallon confuses the "three estates" [nobility, clergy, and common people] of medieval France with the parts of Hell.

MAGISTRATE. [*To* POLICEMAN.] I must note down his words. [*Takes out notebook.*] [*To* BARTLEY.] I warn you that your words are being noted.

BARTLEY. If I had ha' run faster in the beginning, this terror would not be on me at the latter end! Maybe he will cast it up against me at the day of judgment—I wouldn't wonder at all at that.

MAGISTRATE. [*Writing.*] At the day of judgment—

BARTLEY. It was soon for his ghost to appear to me—it is coming after me always by day it will be, and stripping the clothes off in the night time?—I wouldn't wonder at all at that, being as I am an unfortunate man!

MAGISTRATE. [*Sternly.*] Tell me this truly. What was the motive of this crime?

BARTLEY. The motive, is it?

MAGISTRATE. Yes, the motive; the cause.

BARTLEY. I'd sooner not say that.

MAGISTRATE. You had better tell me truly. Was it money?

BARTLEY. Not at all! What did poor Jack Smith ever have in his pockets unless it might be his hands that would be in them?

MAGISTRATE. Any dispute about land?

BARTLEY. [*Indignantly.*] Not at all! He never was a grabber or grabbed from any one!

MAGISTRATE. You will find it better for you if you tell me at once.

BARTLEY. I tell you I wouldn't for the whole world wish to say what it was—it is a thing I would not like to be talking about.

MAGISTRATE. There is no use in hiding it. It will be discovered in the end.

BARTLEY. Well, I suppose it will, seeing that mostly everybody knows it before. Whisper here now. I will tell no lie; where would be the use? [*Puts his hand to his mouth, and* MAGISTRATE *stoops.*] Don't be putting the blame on the parish, for such a thing was never done in the parish before—it was done for the sake of Kitty Keary, Jack Smith's wife.

MAGISTRATE. [*To* POLICEMAN.] Put on the handcuffs. We have been saved some trouble. I knew he would confess if taken in the right way.

[POLICEMAN *puts on handcuffs.*]

BARTLEY. Handcuffs now! Glory be! I always said, if there was ever any misfortune coming to this place it was on myself it would fall. I to be in handcuffs! There's no wonder at all in that.

[*Enter* MRS. FALLON, *followed by the rest. She is looking back at them as she speaks.*]

MRS. FALLON. Telling lies the whole of the people of this town are; telling lies, telling lies as fast as a dog will trot! Speaking against my poor respectable man! Saying he made an end of Jack Smith! My decent comrade! There is no better man and no kinder man in the whole of the five parishes! It's little annoyance he ever gave to anyone! [*Turns and sees him.*] What in the earthly world do I see before me? Bartley

Fallon in charge[5] of the police! Handcuffs on him! O Bartley, what
did you do at all at all?

BARTLEY. O Mary, there has a great misfortune come upon me! It is
what I always said, that if there is ever any misfortune—

MRS. FALLON. What did he do at all, or is it bewitched I am?

MAGISTRATE. This man has been arrested on a charge of murder.

MRS. FALLON. Whose charge is that? Don't believe them! They are all
liars in this place! Give me back my man!

MAGISTRATE. It is natural you should take his part, but you have no
cause of complaint against your neighbours. He has been arrested for
the murder of John Smith, on his own confession.

MRS. FALLON. The saints of heaven protect us! And what did he want
killing Jack Smith?

MAGISTRATE. It is best you should know all. He did it on account of a
love affair with the murdered man's wife.

MRS. FALLON. [*Sitting down.*] With Jack Smith's wife! With Kitty
Keary!—Ochone, the traitor!

THE CROWD. A great shame, indeed. He is a traitor, indeed.

MRS. TULLY. To America he was bringing her, Mrs. Fallon.

BARTLEY. What are you saying, Mary? I tell you—

MRS. FALLON. Don't say a word! I won't listen to any word you'll say!
[*Stops her ears.*] O, isn't he the treacherous villain? Ochone go deo![6]

BARTLEY. Be quiet till I speak! Listen to what I say!

MRS. FALLON. Sitting beside me on the ass-car[7] coming to the town, so
quiet and so respectable, and treachery like that in his heart!

BARTLEY. Is it your wits you have lost or is it I myself that have lost my
wits?

MRS. FALLON. And it's hard I earned you, slaving, slaving—and you
grumbling, and sighing, and coughing, and discontented, and the
priest wore out anointing you, with all the times you threatened to
die!

BARTLEY. Let you be quiet till I tell you!

MRS. FALLON. You to bring such a disgrace into the parish. A thing that
was never heard of before!

BARTLEY. Will you shut your mouth and hear me speaking?

MRS. FALLON. And if it was for any sort of a fine handsome woman, but
for a little fistful of a woman like Kitty Keary, that's not four feet high
hardly, and not three teeth in her head unless she got new ones! May
God reward you, Bartley Fallon, for the black treachery in your heart
and the wickedness in your mind, and the red blood of poor Jack
Smith that is wet upon your hand!

[*Voice of* JACK SMITH *heard singing.*]

> The sea shall be dry,
>   The earth under mourning and ban!

---

5. I.e., taken by.   7. Cart drawn by a donkey.
6. "Alas, my God!" (Gaelic).

Then loud shall he cry
For the wife of the red-haired man!

BARTLEY. It's Jack Smith's voice—I never knew a ghost to sing before
—It is after myself and the fork he is coming! [*Goes back. Enter* JACK
SMITH.] Let one of you give him the fork and I will be clear of him
now and for eternity!

MRS. TARPEY. The Lord have mercy on us! Red Jack Smith! The man
that was going to be waked![8]

JAMES RYAN. Is it back from the grave you are come?

SHAWN EARLY. Is it alive you are, or is it dead you are?

TIM CASEY. Is it yourself at all that's in it?

MRS. TULLY. Is it letting on you were to be dead?

MRS. FALLON. Dead or alive, let you stop Kitty Keary, your wife, from
bringing my man away with her to America!

JACK SMITH. It is what I think, the wits are gone astray on the whole of
you. What would my wife want bringing Bartley Fallon to America?

MRS. FALLON. To leave yourself, and to get quit of you she wants, Jack
Smith, and to bring him away from myself. That's what the two of
them has settled together.

JACK SMITH. I'll break the head of any man that says that! Who is it says
it? [*To* TIM CASEY:] Was it you said it? [*To* SHAWN EARLY:] Was it
you?

ALL TOGETHER. [*Backing and shaking their heads.*] It wasn't I said it!

JACK SMITH. Tell me the name of any man that said it!

ALL TOGETHER. [*Pointing to* BARTLEY.] It was *him* that said it!

JACK SMITH. Let me at him till I break his head!

[BARTLEY *backs in terror. Neighbours hold* JACK SMITH *back.*]

JACK SMITH. [*Trying to free himself.*] Let me at him! Isn't he the pleasant sort of a scarecrow for any woman to be crossing the ocean with!
It's back from the docks of New York he'd be turned [*trying to rush
at him again*], with a lie in his mouth and treachery in his heart, and
another man's wife by his side, and he passing her off as his own! Let
me at him can't you.

[*Makes another rush, but is held back.*]

MAGISTRATE. [*Pointing to* JACK SMITH.] Policeman, put the handcuffs on
this man. I see it all now. A case of false impersonation, a conspiracy
to defeat the ends of justice. There was a case in the Andaman Islands, a murderer of the Mopsa tribe, a religious enthusiast—

POLICEMAN. So he might be, too.

MAGISTRATE. We must take both these men to the scene of the murder.
We must confront them with the body of the real Jack Smith.

JACK SMITH. I'll break the head of any man that will find my dead body!

MAGISTRATE. I'll call more help from the barracks. [*Blows* POLICEMAN'S
whistle.]

BARTLEY. It is what I am thinking, if myself and Jack Smith are put to-

---

8. I.e., given a wake (drinking party held in honor of a dead man).

gether in the one cell for the night, the handcuffs will be taken off him, and his hands will be free, and murder will be done that time surely!

MAGISTRATE. Come on! [*They turn to the right.*]

1904

OLIVE SCHREINER
1855–1920

South African novelist, feminist, anti-imperialist, socialist, and pacifist, Olive Schreiner was a celebrity in turn-of-the-century England. Her first published novel, *The Story of an African Farm* (1883), was a best seller; her first volume of allegorical *Dreams* (1890) was reprinted twenty-four times by 1930; her protest against the racist atrocities of white "pioneers" in Africa, *Trooper Peter Halket* (1897), was quickly translated into German, Swedish, Danish, Dutch, and French; *Woman and Labour* (1911), like its American analogue, Charlotte Perkins Gilman's *Women and Economics* (1898), was hailed by suffragists for its analysis of the historical subjection of women. Yet not only did Schreiner continue to suffer the debilitating consequences of asthma, eating disorders, headaches, and a restlessness that denied her a home, but her most ambitious projects were left unfinished at her death. "Sometimes I don't seem to be alive at all," she admitted at the height of her fame, "No one wants me. I'm [in] no relation with the life or thought in England or Africa or anywhere else." If Schreiner's work is sometimes marred by the self-indulgence that characterizes this remark, it is also frankly ambitious in its effort to align the life and thought of England and Africa with the idealism that imbued her own life and thought.

Such ambition seems especially remarkable given the bleak destitution of Schreiner's early childhood. Born in a Wesleyan mission house, Olive Schreiner was the ninth child of Gottlieb and Rebecca (Lyndall) Schreiner. She was six when the family began to travel over the *karroo* (the South African plains). Her father, a deeply religious missionary, was eventually expelled from the rigid London Missionary Society when he was driven by the family's dire economic need to resort to private trading. If he was sternly orthodox and naïvely impractical, her mother was unbending in her belief in British superiority over black natives and Boers (Dutch settlers in Africa) and in her commitment to conventionally Victorian ideas about female decorum. The youthfully impetuous Olive Schreiner was physically punished if, for example, she used the Boer expression "Ach." Later she explained that these beatings instilled "bitter wild fierce agony in my heart of hatred against God and man" which resulted in the resolve "to spend all my life in helping weak things against strong." The central tragedy of her youth, the death of her two-year-old sister Ellie, had similar repercussions.

Both Schreiner's religious doubts and her feminism reflected prevailing intellectual trends in the late Victorian period, and she did read widely in the philosophical works of Herbert Spencer, John Stuart Mill, and Ralph Waldo Emerson. But she received little formal schooling: at eleven, she was sent to live with an older brother and sister; at the age of fifteen, she took the first of a series of positions as governess in Boer farming families. In these inauspicious situations, after a mysteriously broken engagement and the death of her father in 1876, she composed her first two novels, *Undine* and *The Story of an African Farm*. The latter, written under the pseudonym Ralph Iron, she brought with her to England in 1881 when seeking to train herself as a doctor. Although poor health prevented her from gaining a medical education, the successful publication of *The Story of an African Farm* won her entrance into two pioneering intellectual organizations, the Fellowship of the New Life and the Men and Women's Club. Throughout the 1880s, she lived in London rooming houses, where she wrote essays on prostitution and birth control, planned an edition of Mary Wollstonecraft's *A Vindication of the Rights of Woman*, and spoke on and for the woman question.

At the age of thirty-four, Schreiner returned to South Africa, where she became involved in the antagonisms preceding the Anglo-Boer War (1899–1902). Samuel Cron Cronwright, also an anti-imperialist, was a successful cattle breeder when he and Schreiner decided to marry. Following her wishes, he took her last name and supported her efforts to write, but a series of catastrophes made writing nearly impossible. In 1895, Schreiner gave birth to a nine-pound, nine-ounce daughter, who died mysteriously after only sixteen hours of life. Subsequent miscarriages, imprisonment during the Anglo-Boer War (for her radical political stance), the looting of her Johannesburg home, and the burning of her lengthy manuscript on women and labor (presumably by British troops) only exacerbated her asthma and her writing difficulties. Still, she worked for women's suffrage and women's trade unions until 1913. Indeed, she resigned as vice-president of the Women's Enfranchisement League in South Africa when the organization refused to allow "colored" women to vote.

When she returned alone to London, where she resided during World War I, she was again persecuted for taking an unpopular stance, specifically for her defense of conscientious objectors. A placard inscribed with her words decorated the platform of a 1914 meeting of the Women's Political Union at Carnegie Hall, aptly summarizing her desire for "a society in which all women of all races on earth should equally find their place." For Schreiner, such a society "should overstep the miserable little bounds of nationality and race which lie at the root of the world's evil and war today." Yet in spite of the celebrity her radicalism had won her, she was unable to complete her most ambitious novel, *From Man to Man* (1927), and she frequently expressed great loneliness in her letters. A month after her husband joined her in London in 1920, however, Schreiner inexplicably embarked for South Africa, where she died alone in a boardinghouse at the age of sixty-five.

Perhaps it was both the pain and the courage of Schreiner's life that made her work so influential. Torn between her love for the physical beauty of Africa and her desire for the intellectual stimulation of England, she was also caught between Victorian certainties and modernist skepticism. As if to announce the advent of a new age, even before Schreiner embarked on her unconventional life she had created the most flamboyant representative of the so-called New Woman in *The Story of an African Farm*. Ironically or not, this rebellious heroine is endowed with Schreiner's mother's maiden name: Lyndall. Lyndall's rage against female socialization results in a diatribe analyzing how "the world makes men and women" out of the "little plastic beings" born into it: "To you," she explains to her male companion, "it says—*Work!* and to us it says— *Seem!*" Refusing such dissembling, Lyndall never relinquishes her faith in "a new time" that would liberate women and thereby bring about the fellowship between the sexes that Schreiner herself craved.

Dream Life and Real Life; A Little African Story

Little Jannita sat alone beside a milk-bush. Before her and behind her stretched the plain, covered with red sand and thorny "Karroo" bushes; and here and there a milk-bush, looking like a bundle of pale green rods tied together. Not a tree was to be seen anywhere, except on the banks of the river, and that was far away, and the sun beat on her head. Round her fed the Angora goats she was herding; pretty things, especially the little ones, with white silky curls that touched the ground. But Jannita sat crying. If an angel should gather up in his cup all the tears that have been shed, I think the bitterest would be those of children.

By and by she was so tired, and the sun was so hot, she laid her head against the milk-bush, and dropped asleep.

She dreamed a beautiful dream. She thought that when she went back to the farmhouse in the evening, the walls were covered with vines and roses, and the "kraals" (*sheepfolds*) were not made of red stone, but of lilac trees full of blossom. And the fat old Boer[1] smiled at her, and the stick he held across the door for the goats to jump over, was a lily rod with seven blossoms at the end. When she went to the house her mistress gave her a whole roaster-cake for her supper, and the mistress's daughter had stuck a rose in the cake; and her mistress's son-in-law said "Thank you!" when she pulled off his boots, and did not kick her.

It was a beautiful dream.

While she lay thus dreaming, one of the little kids came and licked her on her cheek, because of the salt from her dried-up tears. And in her dream she was not a poor indentured child any more, living with Boers. It was her father who kissed her. He said he had only been asleep—that day when he lay down under the thorn-bush; he had not really died. He felt her hair, and said it was grown long and silky, and he said they would go back to Denmark now. He asked her why her feet were bare, and what the marks on her back were. Then he put her head on his shoulder, and picked her up, and carried her away, away! She laughed

1. Dutch colonists who fought the British in Africa.

—she could feel her face against his brown beard. His arms were so strong.

As she lay there dreaming with the ants running over her naked feet, and with her brown curls lying in the sand, a Hottentot[2] came up to her. He was dressed in ragged yellow trousers, and a dirty shirt, and torn jacket. He had a red handkerchief round his head, and a felt hat above that. His nose was flat, his eyes like slits, and the wool on his head was gathered into little round balls. He came to the milk-bush, and looked at the little girl lying in the hot sun. Then he walked off, and caught one of the fattest little Angora goats, and held its mouth fast, as he stuck it under his arm. He looked back to see that she was still sleeping, and jumped down into one of the "sluits." (*The deep fissures, generally dry, in which the superfluous torrents of water are carried from the "Karroo" plains after thunderstorms.*) He walked down the bed of the "sluit" a little way and came to an overhanging bank, under which, sitting on the red sand, were two men. One was a tiny, ragged, old bushman, four feet high; the other was an English navvy,[3] in a dark blue blouse. They cut the kid's throat with the navvy's long knife, and covered up the blood with sand, and buried the entrails and skin. Then they talked, and quarrelled a little; and then they talked quietly again.

The Hottentot man put a leg of the kid under his coat and left the rest of the meat for the two in the "sluit," and walked away.

When little Jannita awoke it was almost sunset. She sat up very frightened, but her goats were all about her. She began to drive them home. "I do not think there are any lost," she said.

Dirk, the Hottentot, had brought his flock home already, and stood at the "kraal" door with his ragged yellow trousers. The fat old Boer put his stick across the door, and let Jannita's goats jump over, one by one. He counted them. When the last jumped over: "Have you been to sleep to-day?" he said; "there is one missing."

Then little Jannita knew what was coming, and she said, in a low voice, "No." And then she felt in her heart that deadly sickness that you feel when you tell a lie; and again she said, "Yes."

"Do you think you will have any supper this evening?" said the Boer.

"No," said Jannita.

"What do you think you will have?"

"I don't know," said Jannita.

"Give me your whip," said the Boer to Dirk, the Hottentot.

The moon was all but full that night. Oh, but its light was beautiful! The little girl crept to the door of the outhouse where she slept, and

---

2. Member of a South African people.   3. Laborer.

looked at it. When you are hungry, and very, very sore, you do not cry. She leaned her chin on one hand, and looked, with her great dove's eyes—the other hand was cut open, so she wrapped it in her pinafore. She looked across the plain at the sand and the low karroo-bushes, with the moonlight on them.

Presently, there came slowly, from far away, a wild spring-buck. It came close to the house, and stood looking at it in wonder, while the moonlight glinted on its horns, and in its great eyes. It stood wondering at the red brick walls, and the girl watched it. Then, suddenly, as if it scorned it all, it curved its beautiful back and turned; and away it fled over the bushes and sand, like a sheeny streak of white lightning. She stood up to watch it. So free, so free! Away, away! She watched, till she could see it no more on the wide plain.

Her heart swelled, larger, larger, larger: she uttered a low cry; and without waiting, pausing, thinking, she followed on its track. Away, away, away! "I—I also!" she said, "I—I also!"

When at last her legs began to tremble under her, and she stopped to breathe, the house was a speck behind her. She dropped on the earth, and held her panting sides.

She began to think now.

If she stayed on the plain they would trace her footsteps in the morning and catch her; but if she waded in the water in the bed of the river they would not be able to find her footmarks; and she would hide, there where the rocks and the "kopjes" were.

(*"Kopjes," in the karroo, are hillocks of stones, that rise up singly or in clusters, here and there; presenting sometimes the fantastic appearance of old ruined castles or giant graves, the work of human hands.*)

So she stood up and walked towards the river. The water in the river was low; just a line of silver in the broad bed of sand, here and there broadening into a pool. She stepped into it, and bathed her feet in the delicious cold water. Up and up the stream she walked, where it rattled over the pebbles, and past where the farmhouse lay; and where the rocks were large, she leaped from one to the other. The night wind in her face made her strong—she laughed. She had never felt such night wind before. So the night smells to the wild bucks, because they are free! A free thing feels as a chained thing never can.

At last she came to a place where the willows grew on each side of the river, and trailed their long branches on the sandy bed. She could not tell why, she could not tell the reason, but a feeling of fear came over her.

On the left bank rose a chain of "kopjes" and a precipice of rocks. Between the precipice and the river bank there was a narrow path covered by the fragments of fallen rock. And upon the summit of the precipice a kippersol tree grew, whose palm-like leaves were clearly cut out against the night sky. The rocks cast a deep shadow, and the willow trees, on either side of the river. She paused, looked up and about her, and then ran on, fearful.

"What was I afraid of? How foolish I have been!" she said, when she came to a place where the trees were not so close together. And she stood still and looked back and shivered.

At last her steps grew wearier and wearier. She was very sleepy now, she could scarcely lift her feet. She stepped out of the riverbed. She only saw that the rocks about her were wild, as though many little "kopjes" had been broken up and strewn upon the ground, lay down at the foot of an aloe, and fell asleep.

But, in the morning, she saw what a glorious place it was. The rocks were piled on one another, and tossed this way and that. Prickly pears[4] grew among them, and there were no less than six kippersol trees scattered here and there among the broken "kopjes." In the rocks there were hundreds of homes for the coneys,[5] and from the crevices wild asparagus hung down. She ran to the river, bathed in the clear cold water, and tossed it over her head. She sang aloud. All the songs she knew were sad, so she could not sing them now, she was glad, she was so free; but she sang the notes without the words, as the cock-o-veets do. Singing and jumping all the way, she went back, and took a sharp stone, and cut at the root of a kippersol, and got out a large piece, as long as her arm, and sat to chew it. Two coneys came out on the rock above her head and peeped at her. She held them out a piece, but they did not want it, and ran away.

It was very delicious to her. Kippersol is like raw quince, when it is very green; but she liked it. When good food is thrown at you by other people, strange to say, it is very bitter; but whatever you find yourself is sweet!

When she had finished she dug out another piece, and went to look for a pantry to put it in. At the top of a heap of rocks up which she clambered she found that some large stones stood apart but met at the top, making a room.

"Oh, this is my little home!" she said.

At the top and all round it was closed, only in the front it was open. There was a beautiful shelf in the wall for the kippersol, and she scrambled down again. She brought a great branch of prickly pear, and stuck it in a crevice before the door, and hung wild asparagus over it, till it looked as though it grew there. No one could see that there was a room there, for she left only a tiny opening, and hung a branch of feathery asparagus over it. Then she crept in to see how it looked. There was a glorious soft green light. Then she went out and picked some of those purple little ground flowers—you know them—those that keep their faces close to the ground, but when you turn them up and looked at them they are deep blue eyes looking into yours! She took them with a little earth, and put them in the crevices between the rocks; and so the room was quite furnished. Afterwards she went down to the river and brought her arms full of willow, and made a lovely bed; and, because the weather was very hot, she lay down to rest upon it.

She went to sleep soon, and slept long, for she was very weak. Late in the afternoon she was awakened by a few cold drops falling on her face. She sat up. A great and fierce thunderstorm had been raging, and a few of the cool drops had fallen through the crevice in the rocks. She pushed the asparagus branch aside, and looked out, with her little hands folded about her knees. She heard the thunder rolling, and saw the red torrents rush among the stones on their way to the river. She heard the roar of the river as it now rolled, angry and red, bearing away stumps and trees on its muddy water. She listened and smiled, and pressed closer to the rock that took care of her. She pressed the palm of her hand against it. When you have no one to love you, you love the dumb things very much. When the sun set, it cleared up. Then the little girl ate some kippersol, and lay down again to sleep. She thought there was nothing so nice as to sleep. When one has had no food but kippersol juice for two days, one doesn't feel strong.

"It is so nice here," she thought, as she went to sleep, "I will stay here always."

Afterwards the moon rose. The sky was very clear now, there was not a cloud anywhere; and the moon shone in through the bushes in the door, and made a lattice-work of light on her face. She was dreaming a beautiful dream. The loveliest dreams of all are dreamed when you are hungry. She thought she was walking in a beautiful place, holding her father's hand, and they both had crowns on their head, crowns of wild asparagus. The people whom they passed smiled and kissed her; some gave her flowers, and some gave her food, and the sunlight was every-where. She dreamed the same dream over and over, and it grew more and more beautiful; till, suddenly, it seemed as though she were stand-ing quite alone. She looked up: on one side of her was the high preci-pice, on the other was the river, with the willow trees, drooping their branches into the water; and the moonlight was over all. Up, against the night sky the pointed leaves of the kippersol trees were clearly marked, and the rocks and the willow trees cast dark shadows.

In her sleep she shivered, and half awoke.

"Ah, I am not there, I am here," she said; and she crept closer to the rock, and kissed it, and went to sleep again.

It must have been about three o'clock, for the moon had begun to sink towards the western sky, when she woke, with a violent start. She sat up, and pressed her hand against her heart.

"What can it be? A coney must surely have run across my feet and frightened me!" she said, and she turned to lie down again; but soon she sat up. Outside, there was the distinct sound of thorns crackling in a fire.

She crept to the door and made an opening in the branches with her fingers.

A large fire was blazing in the shadow, at the foot of the rocks. A little Bushman sat over some burning coals that had been raked from it, cooking meat. Stretched on the ground was an Englishman, dressed in a blouse, and with a heavy, sullen face. On the stone beside him was Dirk, the Hottentot, sharpening a bowie knife.

She held her breath. Not a coney in all the rocks was so still.

"They can never find me here," she said; and she knelt, and listened to every word they said. She could hear it all.

"You may have all the money," said the Bushman; "but I want the cask of brandy. I will set the roof alight in six places, for a Dutchman burnt my mother once alive in a hut, with three children."

"You are sure there is no one else on the farm?" said the navvy.

"No, I have told you till I am tired," said Dirk; "the two Kaffirs[6] have gone with the son to town; and the maids have gone to a dance; there is only the old man and the two women left."

"But suppose," said the navvy, "he should have the gun at his bed-side, and loaded!"

"He never has," said Dirk; "it hangs in the passage, and the cartridges too. He never thought when he bought it what work it was for! I only wish the little white girl was there still," said Dirk; "but she is drowned. We traced her footmarks to the great pool that has no bottom."

She listened to every word, and they talked on.

Afterwards, the little Bushman, who crouched over the fire, sat up suddenly, listening.

"Ha! what is that?" he said.

A Bushman is like a dog: his ear is so fine he knows a jackal's tread from a wild dog's.

"I heard nothing," said the navvy.

"I heard," said the Hottentot; "but it was only a coney on the rocks."

"No coney, no coney," said the Bushman; "see, what is that there moving in the shade round the point?"

---

6. Derogatory term for South African blacks.

"Nothing! you idiot," said the navvy. "Finish your meat; we must start now."

There were two roads to the homestead. One went along the open plain, and was by far the shortest; but you might be seen half a mile off. The other ran along the river bank, where there were rocks, and holes, and willow-trees to hide among. And all down the river bank ran a little figure.

The river was swollen by the storm full to its banks, and the willow-trees dipped their half-drowned branches into its water. Wherever there was a gap between them, you could see it flow, red and muddy, with the stumps upon it. But the little figure ran on and on; never looking, never thinking; panting, panting! There, where the rocks were the thickest; there, where on the open space the moonlight shone; there, where the prickly pears were tangled, and the rocks cast shadows, on it ran; the little hands clenched, the little heart beating, the eyes fixed always ahead.

It was not far to run now. Only the narrow path between the high rocks and the river.

At last she came to the end of it, and stood for an instant. Before her lay the plain, and the red farm-house, so near, that if persons had been walking there you might have seen them in the moonlight. She clasped her hands. "Yes, I will tell them, I will tell them!" she said; "I am almost there!" She ran forward again, then hesitated. She shaded her eyes from the moonlight, and looked. Between her and the farm-house there were three figures moving over the low bushes.

In the sheeny moonlight you could see how they moved on, slowly and furtively; the short one, and the one in light clothes, and the one in dark.

"I cannot help them now!" she cried, and sank down on the ground, with her little hands clasped before her.

"Awake, awake!" said the farmer's wife; "I hear a strange noise; something calling, calling, calling!"

The man rose, and went to the window.

"I hear it also," he said; "surely some jackal's at the sheep. I will load my gun and go and see."

"It sounds to me like the cry of no jackal," said the woman; and when he was gone she woke her daughter.

"Come, let us go and make a fire, I can sleep no more," she said; "I have heard a strange thing to-night. Your father said it was a jackal's cry, but no jackal cries so. It was a child's voice, and it cried, 'Master, master, wake!'"

The women looked at each other; then they went to the kitchen, and made a great fire; and they sang psalms all the while.

At last the man came back; and they asked him, "What have you seen?" "Nothing," he said, "but the sheep asleep in their kraals, and the moonlight on the walls. And yet, it did seem to me," he added, "that far away near the 'krantz' [precipice] by the river, I saw three figures moving. And afterwards—it might have been fancy—I thought I heard the cry again; but since that, all has been still there."

Next day a navvy had returned to the railway works.

"Where have you been so long?" his comrades asked.

"He keeps looking over his shoulder," said one, "as though he thought he should see something there."

"When he drank his grog to-day," said another, "he let it fall, and looked round."

Next day, a small old Bushman, and a Hottentot, in ragged yellow trousers, were at a wayside canteen. When the Bushman had had brandy, he began to tell how something (he did not say whether it was man, woman, or child) had lifted up its hands and cried for mercy; had kissed a white man's hands, and cried to him to help it. Then the Hottentot took the Bushman by the throat, and dragged him out.

Next night, the moon rose up, and mounted the quiet sky. She was full now, and looked in at the little home; at the purple flowers stuck about the room, and the kippersol on the shelf. Her light fell on the willow trees, and on the high rocks, and on a little new-made heap of earth and round stones. Three men knew what was under it; and no one else ever will.

1893

From Woman and Labour

[*Sex-parasitism*]

* * * There never has been, and as far as can be seen, there never will be, a time when the majority of the males in any society will be supported by the rest of the males in a condition of perfect mental and physical inactivity. *"Find labour or die,"* is the choice ultimately put before the human male today, as in the past; and *this* constitutes his labour problem.[1]

---

1. "The nearest approach to complete parasitism on the part of a vast body of males occurred, perhaps, in ancient Rome at the time of the decay and downfall of the Empire, when the bulk of the population, male as well as female, was fed on imported corn, wine, and oil, and supplied even with entertainment, almost entirely without exertion or labor of any kind; but

The labour of the man may not always be useful in the highest sense to his society, or it may even be distinctly harmful and antisocial, as in the case of the robber-barons of the Middle Ages, who lived by capturing and despoiling all who passed by their castles; or as in the case of the share speculators, stock-jobbers, ring-and-corner capitalists, and monopolists of the present day, who feed upon the productive labours of society without contributing anything to its welfare. But even males so occupied are compelled to expend a vast amount of energy and even a low intelligence in their callings; and, however injurious to their societies, they run no personal risk of handing down effete and enervated constitutions to their race. Whether beneficially or unbeneficially, the human male must, generally speaking, employ his intellect, or his muscle, or die.

The position of the unemployed modern female is one wholly different. The choice before her, as her ancient fields of domestic labour slip from her, is not generally or often at the present day the choice between finding new fields of labour, or death; but one far more serious in its ultimate reaction on humanity as a whole—it is the choice between finding new forms of labour or sinking slowly into a condition of more or less complete and passive *sex-parasitism!*[2]

Again and again in the history of the past, when among human creatures a certain stage of material civilization has been reached, a curious tendency has manifested itself for the human female to become more or less parasitic; social conditions tend to rob her of all forms of

this condition was of short duration, and speedily contributed to the downfall of the diseased Empire itself. Among the wealthy and so-called upper classes, the males of various aristocrats have frequently tended to become completely parasitic after a lapse of time, but such a condition has always been met by a short and sharp remedy; and the class has fallen, or become extinct. The condition of the males of the upper classes in France before the Revolution affords an interesting illustration of this point" [Schreiner's note].

2. "It is not without profound interest to note the varying phenomena of sex-parasitism as they present themselves in the animal world, both in the male and in the female form. Though among the greater number of species in the animal world the female form is larger and more powerful rather than the male (*e.g.*, among birds of prey, such as eagles, falcons, vultures, &c., and among fishes, insects, &c.), yet sex-parasitism appears among both sex forms. In certain sea-creatures, for example, the female carries about in the folds of her covering three or four minute and quite inactive males, who are entirely passive and dependent upon her.

"Among termites, on the other hand, the female has so far degenerated that she has entirely lost the power of locomotion; she can no longer provide herself or her offspring with nourishment, or defend or even clean herself; she has become a mere passive, distended, bag of eggs, without intelligence or activity, she and her offspring existing through the exertions of the slaves and workers of the community. Among other insects, such, for example, as certain ticks, another form of female parasitism prevails, and while the male remains a complex, highly active, and winged creature, the female, fastening herself by the head into the flesh of some living animal and sucking its blood, has lost wings and all activity, and power of locomotion, having become a mere distended bladder, which when filled with eggs bursts and ends a parasitic existence which has hardly been life. It is not impossible, and it appears, indeed, highly probable, that it has been this degeneration and parasitism on the part of the female which has set its limitation to the evolution of ants, creatures which, having reached a point of mental development in some respects almost as high as that of man, have yet become curiously and immovably arrested. The whole question of sex-parasitism among the lower animals is one throwing suggestive and instructive side-lights on human social problems, but is too extensive to be here entered on" [Schreiner's note].

active conscious social labour, and to reduce her, like the field-bug, to the passive exercise of her sex functions alone. And the result of this parasitism has invariably been the decay in vitality and intelligence of the female, followed after a longer or shorter period by that of her male descendants and her entire society.

Nevertheless, in the history of the past the dangers of the sex-parasitism have never threatened more than a small section of the females of the human race, those exclusively of some dominant race or class; the mass of women beneath them being still compelled to assume many forms of strenuous activity. It is at the present day, and under the peculiar conditions of our modern civilization, that for the first time sex-parasitism has become a danger, more or less remote, to the mass of civilized women, perhaps ultimately to all.

In the very early stages of human growth, the sexual parasitism and degeneration of the female formed no possible source of social danger. Where the conditions of life rendered it inevitable that all the labour of a community should be performed by the members of that community for themselves, without the assistance of slaves or machinery, the tendency has always been rather to throw an excessive amount of social labour on the female. Under no conditions, at no time, in no place, in the history of the world have the males of any period, of any nation, or of any class, shown the slightest inclination to allow their own females to become inactive or parasitic, so long as the actual muscular labour of feeding and clothing them would in that case have devolved upon *themselves*!

The parasitism of the human female becomes a possibility only when a point in civilization is reached (such as that which was attained in the ancient civilizations of Greece, Rome, Persia, Assyria, India, and such as today exists in many of the civilizations of the East, such as those of China and Turkey), when, owing to the extensive employment of the labour of slaves, or of subject races or classes, the dominant race or class has become so liberally supplied with the material goods of life that mere physical toil on the part of its own female members has become unnecessary.

It is when this point has been reached, and never before, that the symptoms of female parasitism have in the past almost invariably tended to manifest themselves, and have become a social danger. The males of the dominant class have almost always contrived to absorb to themselves the new intellectual occupations, which the absence of necessity for the old forms of physical toil made possible in their societies; and the females of the dominant class or race, for whose muscular labours there was now also no longer any need, not succeeding in grasping or attaining to these new forms of labour, have sunk into a state in which, performing no species of active social duty, they have existed through the passive performance of sexual functions alone, with how much or how little of discontent will now never be known, since no literary record has been made by the woman of the past, of her desires or sorrows. Then, in place of the active labouring woman, upholding society by her toil, has come the effete wife, concubine or prostitute, clad in fine raiment, the work of others' fingers; fed on luxurious viands, the result of others' toil, waited on and tended by the labour of others. The need for her physical labour having gone, and mental industry not having taken its place, she bedecked and scented her person, or had it bedecked and scented for her, she lay upon her sofa, or drove or was carried out in her vehicle, and, loaded with jewels, she sought by dissipations and amusements to fill up the inordinate blank left by the lack of productive activity. And the hand whitened and frame softened, till, at last, the very duties of motherhood, which were all the constitution of her life left her, became distasteful, and, from the instant when her infant came damp from her womb, it passed into the hands of others, to be tended and reared by them; and from youth to age her offspring often owed nothing to her personal toil. In many cases so complete was her enervation, that at last the very joy of giving life, the glory and beatitude of a virile womanhood, became distasteful; and she sought to evade it, not because of its interference with more imperious duties to those already born of her, or to her society, but because her existence of inactivity had robbed her of all joy in strenuous exertion and endurance in any form. Finely clad, tenderly housed, life became for her merely the gratification of her own physical and sexual appetites, and the appetites of the male, through the stimulation of which she could maintain herself. And, whether as kept wife, kept mistress, or prostitute, she contributed nothing to the active and sustaining labors of her society. She had attained to the full development of that type which, whether in modern Paris or New York or London, or in ancient Greece, Assyria, or Rome, is essentially one in its features, its nature, and its results. She was the "fine lady," the human female parasite—the most deadly microbe which can make its appearance on the surface of any social organism.[3]

Wherever in the history of the past this type has reached its full development and has comprised the bulk of the females belonging to any dominant class or race, it has heralded its decay. In Assyria, Greece,

---

3. "The relation of female parasitism generally to the peculiar phenomenon of prostitution is fundamental. Prostitution can never be adequately dealt with, either from the moral or the scientific standpoint, unless its relation to the general phenomenon of female parasitism be fully recognized. It is the failure to do this which leaves so painful a sense of abortion on the mind, after listening to most modern utterances on the question, whether made from the emotional platform of the moral reformer, or the intellectual platform of the would-be scientist. We are left with a feeling that the matter has been handled but not dealt with: that the knife has not reached the core" [Schreiner's note].

Rome, Persia, as in Turkey today, the same material conditions have produced the same social disease among wealthy and dominant races; and again and again when the nation so affected has come into contact with nations more healthily constituted, this diseased condition has contributed to its destruction.

1911

CHARLOTTE PERKINS GILMAN
1860–1935

In her autobiography, *The Living of Charlotte Perkins Gilman* (1935), Charlotte Perkins Gilman described the "dark fog" that enveloped her after she gave birth to her daughter, Katharine, and was treated by the prominent physician Dr. S. Weir Mitchell. This major proponent of the so-called "rest cure" put her to bed, where she was fed, bathed, rubbed, and advised to have her child with her at all times. Only further troubled by the treatment, the twenty-five-year-old wife and mother "made a rag baby, hung it on a doorknob and played with it. I would crawl into remote closets and under beds—to hide from the grinding pressure of that profound distress." Two years later, in the fall of 1887, she knew that she had to choose "not . . . between going and staying" with her husband and child, "but between going, insane, and staying, sane." She left her husband in 1888, but this early nervous collapse marked the rest of her life, disrupting her concentration and draining her energies. Yet it also led to the writing of her now classic short story, *The Yellow Wallpaper* (1892), and to the lecturing and publishing that would establish her reputation during her lifetime as the leading feminist-theorist in America.

Gilman's early breakdown, which might today be diagnosed as postpartum depression, probably had its origin in the emotional deprivation she suffered as a child. Born in 1860, in Hartford, Connecticut, she and her older brother were raised by their mother, Mary A. (Fitch) Perkins, after their father left the family because Mrs. Perkins had been warned against another pregnancy, or so Gilman suggests in her autobiography. In any case, the young girl found it difficult to sustain through letters a relationship with a father who was so remote, although she identified her own intellectual ambition with his relatives, the famous Beechers: "The word Father," she explained in her autobiography, "means nothing to me, save indeed in advice about books and the care of them—which seems more the librarian than the father." The great-niece of Catharine Beecher and Harriet Beecher Stowe, Gilman also suffered from her mother's poverty, a problem which caused the family to move nineteen times in eighteen years. Just as difficult to accept was Mary Perkins's apparently principled decision to spare her children the expectation of emotional fulfillment by refusing them any physical signs of tenderness: "She would not let me caress her, and would not caress me, unless I was asleep." Understandably, the young girl would keep herself awake, "even using pins to prevent dropping off," so as to feign sleep and gain the "raptur[ous]" enjoyment of "being gathered into her arms, held close and kissed."

For a short period of time, Charlotte Perkins attended the Rhode Island School of Design, where she obtained the training that enabled her to work as an art teacher and governess. Her first husband, Charles Walter Stetson, was a Providence artist whom she married in 1884, although even during their courtship she was aware of the difficulty of combining marriage, motherhood, and work. After her breakdown, she moved with her daughter to Pasadena, California. There she obtained a divorce and decided to send her daughter, Katharine, to live with her ex-husband and his new wife, her friend Grace Ellery Channing. The resulting publicity, generated by Massachusetts and California newspapers, condemned Charlotte Perkins Stetson as unfeeling and unnatural. In spite of her anguish over both the decision and the notoriety, she struggled to support herself first in Oakland and then in San Francisco by lecturing, editing, writing, and teaching. *The Yellow Wallpaper*, which was published in May 1892 in *The New England Magazine* and later reprinted by William Dean Howells in *Great Modern American Stories* (1920), was followed by the feminist polemic *Women and Economics* (1898). Hailed as "the Bible" of the women's movement and translated into seven languages, the latter work established the argument Gilman would extend in many other publications, namely, the claim that women's economic dependency on men had arrested not only their intellectual and emotional growth, but also the healthy development of the human species.

Two years after the publication of *Women and Economics*, Charlotte Perkins Stetson married George Houghton Gilman, a first cousin who had corresponded extensively with her about her doubts and desires concerning marriage. For the next three decades they lived together, first in New York and then in Norwich, Connecticut. His support, as well as the household help provided by Helen Campbell, a close friend she had made in California, allowed Gilman to develop more fully the socialist ideas of Edward Bellamy and the principles of the American sociologist Frank Ward. As in *Women and Economics*, she continued to argue that the subordination of the female sex had been necessary in the past for human evolution, but that in the twentieth century masculine assertiveness had to be complemented by a female culture grounded in cooperation and nurturance. Attacking what she called a "masculinist" society, Gilman explored alternative social organizations to free women from domestic subservience: in *Concerning Children* (1900), *The Home* (1903), and *Human Work* (1904), she suggested day-care centers, the professionalization of housecleaning, laundry, and sewing, and kitchenless houses. Later books like *Man-Made World* (1911) and *His Religion and Hers* (1923) posit the female as the primary type of the human species, arguing that women's commitment to sustaining life directly contrasts with men's engagement with war, an involvement which results in a theology of sacrificial violence. From 1909 until 1916, Gilman's editorials, poems, and fiction appeared in the *Forerunner*, the monthly magazine she edited and published. It was there that she serialized her feminist utopia, *Herland* (1915), a fantasy about a world of parthenogenetic women whose culture explicitly dramatizes the ecological and ethical superiority of matriarchy while implicitly demonstrating the inferiority of patriarchy.

Although Gilman played an important role in the feminist movement, addressing the International Suffrage Convention in Budapest in 1913 and helping to found the Woman's Peace Party in 1915, when that movement declined in the 1920s she began to lose her audience. After her husband's sudden death in 1934, she returned to California to live near her daughter. There she was joined by the widowed Grace Channing Stetson. After discovering that she was suffering from breast cancer, she ended her life with chloroform, not because of the pain she suffered, she explained, but because her career of service was over. After her death, Gilman and her work were relegated to a minor place in history. For almost fifty years, *The Yellow Wallpaper* went unprinted and unread. For more than sixty years, *Herland* was unavailable. The editorial and biographical work of Ann J. Lane, Gail Parker, Elaine R. Hedges, Carl Degler, and Mary A. Hill has only recently made possible a critical reappraisal of this socialist-feminist whose fiction furnishes a poetics for the feminist politics she developed at the turn of the century.

The Yellow Wallpaper

It is very seldom that mere ordinary people like John and myself secure ancestral halls for the summer.

A colonial mansion, a hereditary estate, I would say a haunted house and reach the height of romantic felicity—but that would be asking too much of fate!

Still I will proudly declare that there is something queer about it.

Else, why should it be let so cheaply? And why have stood so long untenanted?

John laughs at me, of course, but one expects that.

John is practical in the extreme. He has no patience with faith, an intense horror of superstition, and he scoffs openly at any talk of things not to be felt and seen and put down in figures.

John is a physician, and *perhaps*—(I would not say it to a living soul, of course, but this is dead paper and a great relief to my mind)—*perhaps* that is one reason I do not get well faster.

You see, he does not believe I am sick! And what can one do?

If a physician of high standing, and one's own husband, assures friends and relatives that there is really nothing the matter with one but temporary nervous depression—a slight hysterical tendency[1]—what is one to do?

My brother is also a physician, and also of high standing, and he says the same thing.

---

1. "Hysteria" was, at the time, a loose term covering various kinds of "female" emotional disorders—depression, anxiety, nervousness, and so on.

So I take phosphates or phosphites—whichever it is—and tonics, and air and exercise, and journeys, and am absolutely forbidden to "work" until I am well again.

Personally, I disagree with their ideas.

Personally, I believe that congenial work, with excitement and change, would do me good.

But what is one to do?

I did write for a while in spite of them; but it *does* exhaust me a good deal—having to be so sly about it, or else meet with heavy opposition.

I sometimes fancy that in my condition, if I had less opposition and more society and stimulus—but John says the very worst thing I can do is to think about my condition, and I confess it always makes me feel bad.

So I will let it alone and talk about the house.

The most beautiful place! It is quite alone, standing well back from the road, quite three miles from the village. It makes me think of English places that you read about, for there are hedges and walls and gates that lock, and lots of separate little houses for the gardeners and people.

There is a *delicious* garden! I never saw such a garden—large and shady, full of box-bordered paths, and lined with long grape-covered arbors with seats under them.

There were greenhouses, but they are all broken now.

There was some legal trouble, I believe, something about the heirs and co-heirs; anyhow, the place has been empty for years.

That spoils my ghostliness, I am afraid, but I don't care—there is something strange about the house—I can feel it.

I even said so to John one moonlight evening, but he said what I felt was a draught, and shut the window.

I get unreasonably angry with John sometimes. I'm sure I never used to be so sensitive. I think it is due to this nervous condition.

But John says if I feel so I shall neglect proper self-control; so I take pains to control myself—before him, at least, and that makes me very tired.

I don't like our room a bit. I wanted one downstairs that opened onto the piazza and had roses all over the window, and such pretty old-fashioned chintz hangings! But John would not hear of it.

He said there was only one window and not room for two beds, and no near room for him if he took another.

He is very careful and loving, and hardly lets me stir without special direction.

I have a schedule prescription for each hour in the day; he takes all care from me, and so I feel basely ungrateful not to value it more.

He said he came here solely on my account, that I was to have perfect rest and all the air I could get. "Your exercise depends on your strength, my dear," said he, "and your food somewhat on your appetite; but air you can absorb all the time." So we took the nursery at the top of the house.

It is a big, airy room, the whole floor nearly, with windows that look all ways, and air and sunshine galore. It was nursery first, and then playroom and gymnasium, I should judge, for the windows are barred for little children, and there are rings and things in the walls.

The paint and paper look as if a boys' school had used it. It is stripped off—the paper—in great patches all around the head of my bed, about as far as I can reach, and in a great place on the other side of the room low down. I never saw a worse paper in my life. One of those sprawling, flamboyant patterns committing every artistic sin.

It is dull enough to confuse the eye in following, pronounced enough constantly to irritate and provoke study, and when you follow the lame uncertain curves for a little distance they suddenly commit suicide—plunge off at outrageous angles, destroy themselves in un-heard-of contradictions.

The color is repellent, almost revolting: a smouldering unclean yel-low, strangely faded by the slow-turning sunlight. It is a dull yet lurid orange in some places, a sickly sulphur tint in others.

No wonder the children hated it! I should hate it myself if I had to live in this room long.

There comes John, and I must put this away—he hates to have me write a word.

We have been here two weeks, and I haven't felt like writing before, since that first day.

I am sitting by the window now, up in this atrocious nursery, and there is nothing to hinder my writing as much as I please, save lack of strength.

John is away all day, and even some nights when his cases are serious.

I am glad my case is not serious!

But these nervous troubles are dreadfully depressing.

John does not know how much I really suffer. He knows there is no reason to suffer, and that satisfies him.

Of course it is only nervousness. It does weigh on me so not to do my duty in any way!

I meant to be such a help to John, such a real rest and comfort, and here I am a comparative burden already!

Nobody would believe what an effort it is to do what little I am able —to dress and entertain, and order things.

It is fortunate Mary is so good with the baby. Such a dear baby!

And yet I *cannot* be with him, it makes me so nervous.

I suppose John never was nervous in his life. He laughs at me so about this wallpaper!

At first he meant to repaper the room, but afterward he said that I was letting it get the better of me, and that nothing was worse for a nervous patient than to give way to such fancies.

He said that after the wallpaper was changed it would be the heavy bedstead, and then the barred windows, and then that gate at the head of the stairs, and so on.

"You know the place is doing you good," he said, "and really, dear, I don't care to renovate the house just for a three months' rental."

"Then do let us go downstairs," I said. "There are such pretty rooms there."

Then he took me in his arms and called me a blessed little goose, and said he would go down cellar, if I wished, and have it whitewashed into the bargain.

But he is right enough about the beds and windows and things.

It is as airy and comfortable a room as anyone need wish, and, of course, I would not be so silly as to make him uncomfortable just for a whim.

I'm really getting quite fond of the big room, all but that horrid paper.

Out of one window I can see the garden—those mysterious deep-shaded arbors, the riotous old-fashioned flowers, and bushes and gnarly trees.

Out of another I get a lovely view of the bay and a little private wharf belonging to the estate. There is a beautiful shaded lane that runs down there from the house. I always fancy I see people walking in these numerous paths and arbors, but John has cautioned me not to give way to fancy in the least. He says that with my imaginative power and habit of story-making, a nervous weakness like mine is sure to lead to all manner of excited fancies, and that I ought to use my will and good sense to check the tendency. So I try.

I think sometimes that if I were only well enough to write a little it would relieve the press of ideas and rest me.

But I find I get pretty tired when I try.

It is so discouraging not to have any advice and companionship about my work. When I get really well, John says we will ask Cousin Henry and Julia down for a long visit; but he says he would as soon put fire-works in my pillow-case as to let me have those stimulating people about now.

I wish I could get well faster.

But I must not think about that. This paper looks to me as if it *knew* what a vicious influence it had!

There is a recurrent spot where the pattern lolls like a broken neck and two bulbous eyes stare at you upside down.

I get positively angry with the impertinence of it and the everlastingness. Up and down and sideways they crawl, and those absurd unblinking eyes are everywhere. There is one place where two breadths didn't match, and the eyes go all up and down the line, one a little higher than the other.

I never saw so much expression in an inanimate thing before, and we all know how much expression they have! I used to lie awake as a child and get more entertainment and terror out of blank walls and plain furniture than most children could find in a toy-store.

I remember what a kindly wink the knobs of our big old bureau used to have, and there was one chair that always seemed like a strong friend.

I used to feel that if any of the other things looked too fierce I could always hop into that chair and be safe.

The furniture in this room is no worse than inharmonious, however, for we had to bring it all from downstairs. I suppose when this was used as a playroom they had to take the nursery things out, and no wonder! I never saw such ravages as the children have made here.

The wallpaper, as I said before, is torn off in spots, and it sticketh closer than a brother—they must have had perseverance as well as hatred.

Then the floor is scratched and gouged and splintered, the plaster itself is dug out here and there, and this great heavy bed, which is all we found in the room, looks as if it had been through the wars.

But I don't mind it a bit—only the paper.

There comes John's sister. Such a dear girl as she is, and so careful of me! I must not let her find me writing.

She is a perfect and enthusiastic housekeeper, and hopes for no better profession. I verily believe she thinks it is the writing which made me sick!

But I can write when she is out, and see her a long way off from these windows.

There is one that commands the road, a lovely shaded winding road, and one that just looks off over the country. A lovely country, too, full of great elms and velvet meadows.

This wallpaper has a kind of sub-pattern in a different shade, a particularly irritating one, for you can only see it in certain lights, and not clearly then.

But in the places where it isn't faded and where the sun is just so—I can see a strange, provoking, formless sort of figure that seems to skulk about behind that silly and conspicuous front design.

There's sister on the stairs!

Well, the Fourth of July is over! The people are all gone, and I am tired out. John thought it might do me good to see a little company, so we just had Mother and Nellie and the children down for a week.

Of course I didn't do a thing. Jennie sees to everything now.

But it tired me all the same.

John says if I don't pick up faster he shall send me to Weir Mitchell[2] in the fall.

But I don't want to go there at all. I had a friend who was in his hands once, and she says he is just like John and my brother, only more so!

Besides, it is such an undertaking to go so far.

I don't feel as if it was worthwhile to turn my hand over for anything, and I'm getting dreadfully fretful and querulous.

I cry at nothing, and cry most of the time.

Of course I don't when John is here, or anybody else, but when I am alone.

And I am alone a good deal just now. John is kept in town very often by serious cases, and Jennie is good and lets me alone when I want her to.

So I walk a little in the garden or down that lovely lane, sit on the porch under the roses, and lie down up here a good deal.

I'm getting really fond of the room in spite of the wallpaper. Perhaps *because* of the wallpaper.

It dwells in my mind so!

I lie here on this great immovable bed—it is nailed down, I believe —and follow that pattern about by the hour. It is as good as gymnastics, I assure you. I start, we'll say, at the bottom, down in the corner over there where it has not been touched, and I determine for the thousandth time that I *will* follow that pointless pattern to some sort of a conclusion.

I know a little of the principle of design, and I know this thing was not arranged on any laws of radiation, or alternation, or repetition, or symmetry, or anything else that I ever heard of.

It is repeated, of course, by the breadths, but not otherwise.

Looked at in one way, each breadth stands alone; the bloated curves and flourishes—a kind of "debased Romanesque" with delirium tremens[3]—go waddling up and down in isolated columns of fatuity.

But, on the other hand, they connect diagonally, and the sprawling outlines run off in great slanting waves of optic horror, like a lot of wallowing sea-weeds in full chase.

The whole thing goes horizontally, too, at least it seems so, and I exhaust myself trying to distinguish the order of its going in that direction.

2. Silas Weir Mitchell (1829–1914), American nerve specialist who popularized the "rest cure," and who treated Gilman herself.
3. A highly decorative style of architecture.

They have used a horizontal breadth for a frieze, and that adds wonderfully to the confusion.

There is one end of the room where it is almost intact, and there, when the crosslights fade and the low sun shines directly upon it, I can almost fancy radiation after all—the interminable grotesque seems to form around a common center and rush off in headlong plunges of equal distraction.

It makes me tired to follow it. I will take a nap, I guess.

I don't know why I should write this.

I don't want to.

I don't feel able.

And I know John would think it absurd. But I *must* say what I feel and think in some way—it is such a relief!

But the effort is getting to be greater than the relief.

Half the time now I am awfully lazy, and lie down ever so much. John says I mustn't lose my strength, and has me take cod liver oil and lots of tonics and things, to say nothing of ale and wine and rare meat.

Dear John! He loves me very dearly, and hates to have me sick. I tried to have a real earnest reasonable talk with him the other day, and tell him how I wish he would let me go and make a visit to Cousin Henry and Julia.

But he said I wasn't able to go, nor able to stand it after I got there; and I did not make out a very good case for myself, for I was crying before I had finished.

It is getting to be a great effort for me to think straight. Just this nervous weakness, I suppose.

And dear John gathered me up in his arms, and just carried me upstairs and laid me on the bed, and sat by me and read to me till it tired my head.

He said I was his darling and his comfort and all he had, and that I must take care of myself for his sake, and keep well.

He says no one but myself can help me out of it, that I must use my will and self-control and not let any silly fancies run away with me.

There's one comfort—the baby is well and happy, and does not have to occupy this nursery with the horrid wallpaper.

If we had not used it, that blessed child would have! What a fortunate escape! Why, I wouldn't have a child of mine, an impressionable little thing, live in such a room for worlds.

I never thought of it before, but it is lucky that John kept me here after all; I can stand it so much easier than a baby, you see.

Of course I never mention it to them any more—I am too wise—but I keep watch for it all the same.

There are things in that wallpaper that nobody knows about but me, or ever will.

Behind that outside pattern the dim shapes get clearer every day.

It is always the same shape, only very numerous.

And it is like a woman stooping down and creeping about behind that pattern. I don't like it a bit. I wonder—I begin to think—I wish John would take me away from here!

It is so hard to talk with John about my case, because he is so wise, and because he loves me so.

But I tried it last night.

It was moonlight. The moon shines in all around just as the sun does.

I hate to see it sometimes, it creeps so slowly, and always comes in by one window or another.

John was asleep and I hated to waken him, so I kept still and watched the moonlight on that undulating wallpaper till I felt creepy.

The faint figure behind seemed to shake the pattern, just as if she wanted to get out.

I got up softly and went to feel and see if the paper *did* move, and when I came back John was awake.

"What is it, little girl?" he said. "Don't go walking about like that— you'll get cold."

I thought it was a good time to talk, so I told him that I really was not gaining here, and that I wished he would take me away.

"Why, darling!" said he. "Our lease will be up in three weeks, and I can't see how to leave before.

"The repairs are not done at home, and I cannot possibly leave town just now. Of course, if you were in any danger, I could and would, but you really are better, dear, whether you can see it or not. I am a doctor, dear, and I know. You are gaining flesh and color, your appetite is better, I feel really much easier about you."

"I don't weigh a bit more," said I, "nor as much; and my appetite may be better in the evening when you are here but it is worse in the morning when you are away!"

"Bless her little heart!" said he with a big hug. "She shall be as sick as she pleases! But now let's improve the shining hours[4] by going to sleep, and talk about it in the morning!"

"And you won't go away?" I asked gloomily.

"Why, how can I, dear? It is only three weeks more and then we will take a nice little trip of a few days while Jennie is getting the house ready. Really, dear, you are better!"

"Better in body perhaps—" I began, and stopped short, for he sat up

4. From the popular moral poem by Isaac Watts (1674–1748), *Against Idleness and Mischief:* "How doth the little busy bee / Improve each shining hour, / And gather honey all the day / From every opening flower!"

straight and looked at me with such a stern, reproachful look that I could not say another word.

"My darling," said he, "I beg of you, for my sake and for our child's sake, as well as for your own, that you will never for one instant let that idea enter your mind! There is nothing so dangerous, so fascinating, to a temperament like yours. It is a false and foolish fancy. Can you not trust me as a physician when I tell you so?"

So of course I said no more on that score, and we went to sleep before long. He thought I was asleep first, but I wasn't and lay there for hours trying to decide whether that front pattern and the back pattern really did move together or separately.

On a pattern like this, by daylight, there is a lack of sequence, a defiance of law, that is a constant irritant to a normal mind.

The color is hideous enough, and unreliable enough, and infuriating enough, but the pattern is torturing.

You think you have mastered it, but just as you get well under way in following, it turns a back-somersault and there you are. It slaps you in the face, knocks you down, and tramples upon you. It is like a bad dream.

The outside pattern is a florid arabesque, reminding one of a fungus. If you can imagine a toadstool in joints, an interminable string of toadstools, budding and sprouting in endless convolutions—why, that is something like it.

That is, sometimes!

There is one marked peculiarity about this paper, a thing nobody seems to notice but myself, and that is that it changes as the light changes.

When the sun shoots in through the east window—I always watch for that first long, straight ray—it changes so quickly that I never can quite believe it.

That is why I watch it always.

By moonlight—the moon shines in all night when there is a moon —I wouldn't know it was the same paper.

At night in any kind of light, in twilight, candlelight, lamplight, and worst of all by moonlight, it becomes bars! The outside pattern, I mean, and the woman behind it is as plain as can be.

I didn't realize for a long time what the thing was that showed behind, that dim sub-pattern, but now I am quite sure it is a woman.

By daylight she is subdued, quiet. I fancy it is the pattern that keeps her so still. It is so puzzling. It keeps me quiet by the hour.

I lie down ever so much now. John says it is good for me, and to sleep all I can.

Indeed he started the habit by making me lie down for an hour after each meal.

It is a very bad habit, I am convinced, for you see, I don't sleep.

And that cultivates deceit, for I don't tell them I'm awake—oh, no!

The fact is I am getting a little afraid of John.

He seems very queer sometimes, and even Jennie has an inexplicable look.

It strikes me occasionally, just as a scientific hypothesis, that perhaps it is the paper!

I have watched John when he did not know I was looking, and come into the room suddenly on the most innocent excuses, and I've caught him several times *looking at the paper!* And Jennie too. I caught Jennie with her hand on it once.

She didn't know I was in the room, and when I asked her in a quiet, a very quiet voice, with the most restrained manner possible, what she was doing with the paper, she turned around as if she had been caught stealing, and looked quite angry—asked me why I should frighten her so!

Then she said that the paper stained everything it touched, that she had found yellow smooches on all my clothes and John's and she wished we would be more careful!

Did not that sound innocent? But I know she was studying that pattern, and I am determined that nobody shall find it out but myself!

Life is very much more exciting now than it used to be. You see, I have something more to expect, to look forward to, to watch. I really do eat better, and am more quiet than I was.

John is so pleased to see me improve! He laughed a little the other day, and said I seemed to be flourishing in spite of my wallpaper.

I turned it off with a laugh. I had no intention of telling him it was *because* of the wallpaper—he would make fun of me. He might even want to take me away.

I don't want to leave now until I have found it out. There is a week more, and I think that will be enough.

I'm feeling so much better!

I don't sleep much at night, for it is so interesting to watch developments; but I sleep a good deal during the daytime.

In the daytime it is tiresome and perplexing.

There are always new shoots on the fungus, and new shades of yellow all over it. I cannot keep count of them, though I have tried conscientiously.

It is the strangest yellow, that wallpaper! It makes me think of all the yellow things I ever saw—not beautiful ones like buttercups, but old, foul, bad yellow things.

But there is something else about that paper—the smell! I noticed it the moment we came into the room, but with so much air and sun it was not bad. Now we have had a week of fog and rain, and whether the windows are open or not, the smell is here.

It creeps all over the house.

I find it hovering in the dining-room, skulking in the parlor, hiding in the hall, lying in wait for me on the stairs.

It gets into my hair.

Even when I go to ride, if I turn my head suddenly and surprise it— there is that smell!

Such a peculiar odor, too! I have spent hours in trying to analyze it, to find what it smelled like.

It is not bad—at first—and very gentle, but quite the subtlest, most enduring odor I ever met.

In this damp weather it is awful. I wake up in the night and find it hanging over me.

It used to disturb me at first. I thought seriously of burning the house—to reach the smell.

But now I am used to it. The only thing I can think of that it is like is the *color* of the paper! A yellow smell.

There is a very funny mark on this wall, low down, near the mop-board. A streak that runs round the room. It goes behind every piece of furniture, except the bed, a long, straight, even *smooch*, as if it had been rubbed over and over.

I wonder how it was done and who did it, and what they did it for. Round and round and round—round and round and round—it makes me dizzy!

I really have discovered something at last.

Through watching so much at night, when it changes so, I have finally found out.

The front pattern *does* move—and no wonder! The woman behind shakes it!

Sometimes I think there are a great many women behind, and sometimes only one, and she crawls around fast, and her crawling shakes it all over.

Then in the very bright spots she keeps still, and in the very shady spots she just takes hold of the bars and shakes them hard.

And she is all the time trying to climb through. But nobody could climb through that pattern—it strangles so; I think that is why it has so many heads.

They get through, and then the pattern strangles them off and turns them upside down, and makes their eyes white!

If those heads were covered or taken off it would not be half so bad.

I think that woman gets out in the daytime!

And I'll tell you why—privately—I've seen her!

I can see her out of every one of my windows!

It is the same woman, I know, for she is always creeping, and most women do not creep by daylight.

I see her in that long shaded lane, creeping up and down. I see her in those dark grape arbors, creeping all around the garden.

I see her on that long road under the trees, creeping along, and when a carriage comes she hides under the blackberry vines.

I don't blame her a bit. It must be very humiliating to be caught creeping by daylight!

I always lock the door when I creep by daylight. I can't do it at night, for I know John would suspect something at once.

And John is so queer now that I don't want to irritate him. I wish he would take another room! Besides, I don't want anybody to get that woman out at night but myself.

I often wonder if I could see her out of all the windows at once.

But, turn as fast as I can, I can only see out of one at one time.

And though I always see her, she *may* be able to creep faster than I can turn! I have watched her sometimes away off in the open country, creeping as fast as a cloud shadow in a wind.

If only that top pattern could be gotten off from the under one! I mean to try it, little by little.

I have found out another funny thing, but I shan't tell it this time! It does not do to trust people too much.

There are only two more days to get this paper off, and I believe John is beginning to notice. I don't like the look in his eyes.

And I heard him ask Jennie a lot of professional questions about me. She had a very good report to give.

She said I slept a good deal in the daytime.

John knows I don't sleep very well at night, for all I'm so quiet!

He asked me all sorts of questions, too, and pretended to be very loving and kind.

As if I couldn't see through him!

Still, I don't wonder he acts so, sleeping under this paper for three months.

It only interests me, but I feel sure John and Jennie are affected by it.

Hurrah! This is the last day, but it is enough. John is to stay in town over night, and won't be out until this evening.

Jennie wanted to sleep with me—the sly thing; but I told her I should undoubtedly rest better for a night all alone.

That was clever, for really I wasn't alone a bit! As soon as it was moonlight and that poor thing began to crawl and shake the pattern, I got up and ran to help her.

I pulled and she shook. I shook and she pulled, and before morning we had peeled off yards of that paper.

A strip about as high as my head and half around the room.

And then when the sun came and that awful pattern began to laugh at me, I declared I would finish it today!

We go away tomorrow, and they are moving all my furniture down again to leave things as they were before.

Jennie looked at the wall in amazement, but I told her merrily that I did it out of pure spite at the vicious thing.

She laughed and said she wouldn't mind doing it herself, but I must not get tired.

How she betrayed herself that time!

But I am here, and no person touches this paper but Me—not *alive!*

She tried to get me out of the room—it was too patent! But I said it was so quiet and empty and clean now that I believed I would lie down again and sleep all I could, and not to wake me even for dinner—I would call when I woke.

So now she is gone, and the servants are gone, and the things are gone, and there is nothing left but that great bedstead nailed down, with the canvas mattress we found on it.

We shall sleep downstairs tonight, and take the boat home tomorrow.

I quite enjoy the room, now it is bare again.

How those children did tear about here!

This bedstead is fairly gnawed!

But I must get to work.

I have locked the door and thrown the key down into the front path.

I don't want to go out, and I don't want to have anybody come in, till John comes.

I want to astonish him.

I've got a rope up here that even Jennie did not find. If that woman does get out, and tries to get away, I can tie her!

But I forgot I could not reach far without anything to stand on!

This bed will *not* move!

I tried to lift and push it until I was lame, and then I got so angry I bit off a little piece at one corner—but it hurt my teeth.

Then I peeled off all the paper I could reach standing on the floor. It sticks horribly and the pattern just enjoys it! All those strangled heads and bulbous eyes and waddling fungus growths just shriek with derision!

I am getting angry enough to do something desperate. To jump out of the window would be admirable exercise, but the bars are too strong even to try.

Besides I wouldn't do it. Of course not. I know well enough that a step like that is improper and might be misconstrued.

I don't like to *look* out of the windows even—there are so many of those creeping women, and they creep so fast.

I wonder if they all come out of that wallpaper as I did?

But I am securely fastened now by my well-hidden rope—you don't get *me* out in the road there!

I suppose I shall have to get back behind the pattern when it comes night, and that is hard!

It is so pleasant to be out in this great room and creep around as I please!

I don't want to go outside. I won't, even if Jennie asks me to.

For outside you have to creep on the ground, and everything is green instead of yellow.

But here I can creep smoothly on the floor, and my shoulder just fits in that long smooch around the wall, so I cannot lose my way.

Why, there's John at the door!

It is no use, young man, you can't open it!

How he does call and pound!

Now he's crying to Jennie for an axe.

It would be a shame to break down that beautiful door!

"John, dear!" said I in the gentlest voice. "The key is down by the front steps, under a plantain leaf!"

That silenced him for a few moments.

Then he said, very quietly indeed, "Open the door, my darling!"

"I can't," said I. "The key is down by the front door under a plantain leaf!" And then I said it again, several times, very gently and slowly, and said it so often that he had to go and see, and he got it of course, and came in. He stopped short by the door.

"What is the matter?" he cried. "For God's sake, what are you doing!"

I kept on creeping just the same, but I looked at him over my shoulder.

"I've got out at last," said I, "in spite of you and Jane. And I've pulled off most of the paper, so you can't put me back!"

Now why should that man have fainted? But he did, and right across my path by the wall, so that I had to creep over him every time!

1892

MARY ELIZABETH COLERIDGE
1861–1907

The great-great-niece of the Romantic poet Samuel Taylor Coleridge, Mary Elizabeth Coleridge was once called "the tail of the comet S. T. C.," and she herself declared that "I have no fairy god-mother, but lay claim to a fairy great-

great uncle, which is perhaps the reason that I am condemned to wander restlessly around the Gates of Fairyland, although I have never yet passed them." In fact, in a number of uncannily imaginative verses, this late Victorian woman does seem to have "passed" such gates to peer into the realm of fantasy that her Romantic ancestor inhabited. At the same time, perhaps at least in part because she was raised to be a dutiful nineteenth-century lady, Coleridge never achieved her great-great-uncle's literary importance. Although she published several successful novels in her lifetime, she refused to release, or even discuss, most of her verse. Because a friend of the family, the poet Robert Bridges, discovered and admired some of her work, she allowed two small volumes—*Fancy's Following* and *Fancy's Guerdon*—to be privately printed in the nineties, but the rest of her poetry remained unpublished until 1908, the year after her death.

The daughter of a charitable, domestic mother, and a literary lawyer who frequently entertained such notables as Tennyson and Browning, Coleridge lived all her life at home with her parents, and on the surface her existence was uneventful. She was exceptionally well educated, however: according to her friend Edith Sichel, "by the time she was nineteen she was well versed in [Hebrew], as well as in German, French, Italian; and a little later she became a keen reader of Greek." In addition, she undertook ambitious studies of philosophy and literature; participated in intellectual circles; traveled on the continent; wrote a number of stories and essays for *The Cornhill Magazine*, *The Times Literary Supplement*, and *The Reflector*; and during the last twelve years of her life taught English literature at a working women's college, a job she did with passionate commitment. When she died at the early age of forty-six, she left a substantial body of work, in particular a series of luminously phrased, visionary poems. A piece like *The Other Side of a Mirror*, for instance, reminds us that despite all its comforts and satisfactions, her life may not have been as serene as it seemed.

The Other Side of a Mirror

I sat before my glass one day,
    And conjured up a vision bare,
Unlike the aspects glad and gay,
    That erst were found reflected there—
The vision of a woman, wild   5
    With more than womanly despair.

Her hair stood back on either side
    A face bereft of loveliness.
It had no envy[1] now to hide
    What once no man on earth could guess.   10
It formed the thorny aureole
    Of hard unsanctified distress.

---

1. Desire.

Her lips were open—not a sound
   Came through the parted lines of red.
Whate'er it was, the hideous wound   15
   In silence and in secret bled.
No sigh relieved her speechless woe,
   She had no voice to speak her dread.

And in her lurid eyes there shone
   The dying flame of life's desire,
Made mad because its hope was gone,   20
   And kindled at the leaping fire
Of jealousy, and fierce revenge,
   And strength that could not change nor tire.

Shade of a shadow in the glass,   25
   O set the crystal surface free!
Pass—as the fairer visions pass—
   Nor ever more return, to be
The ghost of a distracted hour,
   That heard me whisper, "I am she!"   30

1882   1908

Regina[2]

My Queen her sceptre did lay down,
She took from her head the golden crown
Worn by right of her royal birth.
Her purple robe she cast aside,
And the scarlet vestures of her pride,   5
That was the pride of the earth.
In her nakedness was she
Queen of the world, herself and me.

My Queen took up her sceptre bright,
Her crown more radiant than the light,   10
The rubies gleaming out of the gold.
She donned her robe of purple rare,
And did a deed that none may dare,
That makes the blood run cold.
And in her bravery is she   15
Queen of herself, the world and me.

1884   1908

2. Latin for "queen."

The Devil's Funeral

The Devil is dead, good people all!
Who are the bearers that bear the pall?

One of them thinks he has slain God too,
With the self-same sword that Satan slew.

One of them thinks he has saved God's life;   5
The Devil was ever the God of strife.

A purple pall above him spread!
A king it is that is lying dead.

The worst of kings never ruled so well
As this magnificent King of Hell.   10

What is the guerdon[3] of all his pains?
He is dead himself, but Hell remains.

He forged his coffin before he died.
'Twas made of gold that was seven times tried:[4]

The glittering golden words of those,   15
Who counted themselves his chiefest foes.

Where will you bury him? Not on earth!
In poison flowers he would come to birth.

We will not cast him into the sea.
The winds and the waves would set him free.   20

Lay him out straight on the funeral pyre!
All his life he has lived in fire.

And lo! as the crackling flame burns bright,
Satan transformed to an angel of light,

That he may work more utter woe   25
Than ever he worked when he dwelt below.

1890   1908

The Witch

I have walked a great while over the snow,
And I am not tall nor strong.

---

3. Reward.   4. Tempered.

My clothes are wet, and my teeth are set,
And the way was hard and long.
I have wandered over the fruitful earth,   5
But I never came here before.
Oh, lift me over the threshold, and let me in at the door!

The cutting wind is a cruel foe.
I dare not stand in the blast.
My hands are stone, and my voice a groan,   10
And the worst of death is past.
I am but a little maiden still,
My little white feet are sore.
Oh, lift me over the threshold, and let me in at the door!

Her voice was the voice that women have,   15
Who plead for their heart's desire.
She came—she came—and the quivering flame
Sank and died in the fire.
It never was lit again on my hearth
Since I hurried across the floor,   20
To lift her over the threshold, and let her in at the door!

1892   1908

Doubt

Two forms of darkness are there. One is Night,
When I have been an animal, and feared
I knew not what, and lost my soul, nor dared
Feel aught save hungry longing for the light.
And one is Blindness. Absolute and bright,   5
The Sun's rays smote me till they masked the Sun;
The Light itself was by the light undone;
The day was filled with terrors and affright.

Then did I weep, compassionate of those
Who see no friend in God—in Satan's host no foes.   10

1892   1908

The White Women[5]

Where dwell the lovely, wild white women folk,
        Mortal to man?

5. "From a legend of Malay, told by Hugh Clifford" [Coleridge's note].

They never bowed their necks beneath the yoke,
They dwelt alone when the first morning broke
    And Time began.   5

Taller are they than man, and very fair,
    Their cheeks are pale,
At sight of them the tiger in his lair,
The falcon hanging in the azure air,
    The eagles quail.   10

The deadly shafts their nervous hands let fly
    Are stronger than our strongest—in their form
Larger, more beauteous, carved amazingly,
And when they fight, the wild white women cry
    The war-cry of the storm.

Their words are not as ours. If man might go
    Among the waves of Ocean when they break
And hear them—hear the language of the snow
Falling on torrents—he might also know
    The tongue they speak.   20

Pure are they as the light; they never sinned,
    But when the rays of the eternal fire
Kindle the West, their tresses they unbind
And fling their girdles to the Western wind,
    Swept by desire.   25

Lo, maidens to the maidens then are born,
    Strong children of the maidens and the breeze,
Dreams are not—in the glory of the morn,
Seen through the gates of ivory and horn[6]—
    More fair than these.   30

And none may find their dwelling. In the shade
    Primeval of the forest oaks they hide.
One of our race, lost in an awful glade,
Saw with his human eyes a wild white maid,
    And gazing, died.   35

1900   1908

Marriage

No more alone sleeping, no more alone waking,
    Thy dreams divided, thy prayers in twain;

6. The two gates through which dreams pass up from the underworld, according to Greek myth.

Thy merry sisters to-night forsaking,
  Never shall we see thee, maiden, again.

Never shall we see thee, thine eyes glancing,   5
  Flashing with laughter and wild in glee,
Under the mistletoe kissing and dancing,
  Wantonly free.

There shall come a matron walking sedately,
  Low-voiced, gentle, wise in reply.   10
Tell me, O tell me, can I love her greatly?
  All for her sake must the maiden die!

1900   1908

EDITH WHARTON
1862–1937

When Edith Wharton was forty-five, at the height of her considerable personal and literary powers, her longtime mentor and friend, the American novelist Henry James, began to characterize her (as he would for the rest of his life) in a series of striking phrases: as Wharton's biographer Cynthia Griffin Wolff reports, he called her "the whirling princess, the great and glorious pendulum, the gyrator, the devil-dancer, the golden eagle, the Fire Bird, the Shining One, the angel of desolation or of devastation, the historic ravager." Already the author of twelve books—including collections of poems, essays, and short stories as well as successful major novels and novellas like *The House of Mirth* (1905) and *Madame de Trêymes* (1907)—Wharton, as James understood, was well on her way to becoming a major force in American literature. Within a few decades, in fact, she would be the highest-paid novelist in the country. Yet only a few years earlier, in 1898 (when she was thirty-six), this "whirling princess" had suffered a severe mental breakdown; in the words of her biographer R. W. B. Lewis, she had experienced a "terrible and long drawn-out period . . . of paralyzing melancholy, extreme exhaustion, constant fits of nausea, and no capacity whatever to make choices and decisions."

Born in New York City to a wealthy family, Edith Newbold Jones was raised to be a decorous, even aristocratic, young lady. Long established in high society, her parents summered in the elite resort community of Newport, Rhode Island, and, when Edith was three, took her to live abroad—in Italy, France, and Germany—because their income had been reduced by the economic depression that followed the American Civil War. Educated at home, by a governess, the girl made her debut at seventeen.

At the same time, however, even while following the course that had been plotted for debutantes by generations of conservative forebears, this novelist-to-be was transforming herself into an artist. At sixteen, she wrote a volume of poetry which her parents (although they generally disapproved of literary activity) arranged to have privately printed. Even earlier, moreover, she had begun to read voraciously, sensing that her genteel education was inadequate to her intellectual ambitions. If she had not had "the leave to range in my father's library," she later remembered, "my mind would have starved at the age when the mental muscles are most in need of feeding," adding that "I was enthralled by *words*. . . . Wherever I went, they sang to me like the birds in an enchanted forest."

Despite her consciousness of her literary "enthrallment," however, the tension between what appeared to be Edith Jones's social role and what she had gradually begun to understand were her creative aspirations continued well into her twenties and thirties. In 1885, at the age of twenty-three, she married Edward Robbins Wharton (known as Teddy), a wealthy Bostonian who was thirteen years older than she, and the couple settled into a life of conventional gentility, dividing their time between New York, Boston, Newport, and Europe, where they moved in politely idle circles. A kind and decent but not especially intellectual man, "Teddy" Wharton had little sympathy for his wife's literary interests, and it soon became clear that their childless marriage was not a happy one, though they preserved a façade of compatibility for many years. In fact, what Wharton herself called "the slow, stammering beginnings" of her artistic career did not seriously manifest themselves until she and her husband returned in 1888 from a yacht tour of the Aegean. At this point, perhaps energized by new insights and experiences, the young wife began to write with fresh vigor and even to publish verses and stories in such major periodicals as *Scribner's, Harper's,* and the *Century.* A few years later, too, she collaborated with Ogden Codman, Jr., a Boston architect, on *The Decoration of Houses* (1897). Despite her increasing productivity, however, she evidently felt conflicted about yielding herself entirely to her newly awakened ambition, for it was at about this time that she sought and received S. Weir Mitchell's "rest cure" treatment for the "paralyzing melancholy" which suddenly and inexplicably afflicted her.

But by 1899, when she published two collections of short stories, Edith Wharton had recovered from her nervous illness and definitively committed herself to the world of letters. From then on, indeed, she was to publish, on the average, a book a year for the rest of her life. As the critic Louis Auchincloss observes, however, her "major period" began with her composition of *The House of Mirth,* which appeared in 1905. Tracing the decline of Lily Bart, an elegantly polished young lady in straitened circumstances who cannot bring herself to marry for money and consequently falls into hopeless poverty and alienation, this haunting masterpiece exposes the hypocrisies of the old New York society that its author had been educated to honor and obey. In particular, the novel examines both the problems associated with the artificial construction of woman-as-ornament and the pains inflicted by the secret but often savage dynamics of the marriage market on which such a decorative creature is supposed to be an object of exchange, a realm of social trade in which even the links of Lily's bracelet seem "like manacles chaining her to her fate."

In the novels that followed *The House of Mirth,* Wharton continued to dissect the pretensions and conventions of the civilization that destroyed Lily Bart. *The Reef* (1912), *The Custom of the Country* (1913), and *The Age of Inno-*

cence (1920), for instance, all deal in one way or another with the imprisonment of women—often unorthodox or even rebellious women—by the social
"manacles chaining" them to their fates. Often considered a female Henry
James, Wharton did, in these works, explore the social and psychological
nuances that were of such compelling interest to that artful novelist. At the
same time, however, Wharton also began to become a kind of modern mythol-
ogist in these years. Studying the symbolist fictions of the Polish-born British
novelist Joseph Conrad and admiring the innovative music of the Russian composer Igor Stravinsky, she composed starkly structured, almost legendary tales
of people whose fierce but forgotten lives were lived largely outside the urban
and urbane society in which she herself traveled with innate authority. *Ethan
Frome* (1911) and *Summer* (1917) are her two most important novels in this
mode, but she also composed a number of ghost stories which reveal an abiding
interest in the uncanny, the supernatural, the asocial.

Throughout this period of intense productivity, Wharton's marriage was
slowly but inexorably deteriorating. During her middle forties, as the biographers R. W. B. Lewis and Cynthia Griffin Wolff have recently revealed, she
had a passionate affair with Morton Fullerton, a literary man who was also one
of Henry James's protégés, an affair which may well have forced both her and
her husband to confront the inadequacies of their marriage. In any case, in
1910, as the relationship worsened, they sold "The Mount," a lavish mansion
they had built together near Lenox, Massachusetts, and moved to France,
where Teddy had a nervous breakdown and was sent to a Swiss sanitorium.
Then, in 1913, the couple divorced, and Edith Wharton settled permanently in
Europe, eventually purchasing two beautifully maintained French houses,
where she was to spend the rest of her life.

Wharton evidently experienced her single state as a liberation. Traveling indefatigably, entertaining spectacularly, and writing energetically, she formed
friendships with many well-known men of letters, including—along with
Henry James—the critic Percy Lubbock and the art historian Bernard Berenson. In addition, she became far more active in public affairs than she had been
earlier. During World War I, in particular, she organized shelters and
workrooms for refugees and did much other charitable work. In the view of
some critics, however, her writings—with a few exceptions—declined in quality during the 1920s.

Nevertheless, in the last years of her life Wharton was at the peak of her
fame. In 1930 she was elected to the National Institute of Arts and Letters, and
in 1934 to the American Academy of Arts and Letters. When she died of a
stroke at the age of seventy-five, she had produced a body of work that is extraordinarily impressive in its range and richness. Though they date from comparatively early in her literary career, *The Angel at the Grave* (1901) and *The
Other Two* (1904) reveal in miniature the sardonic skill with which she could
analyze the social pressures that had produced even her own complex personality. Each is, in a phrase she herself used to describe a successful short fiction, "a
shaft driven straight into the heart of experience." Specifically, moreover, each
is a dissection of the female condition: *The Angel at the Grave* examines the
nature of a woman inheritor's problematic relationship to the male literary tradition she feels she has been appointed to carry on, and *The Other Two*—a tale

R. W. B. Lewis has called "very likely the best story Mrs. Wharton ever wrote"—explores the artifice of the supposedly romantic process by which a woman is constructed as a "perfect wife." Scholars have customarily assumed that James applied epithets like "the whirling princess" and "the Fire Bird" to Wharton because of the energy with which she traveled and entertained. Yet, despite their sometimes coolly ironic surfaces, stories like these, along with novels like *The House of Mirth* and *Ethan Frome*, have a fiercely subversive force which more than justifies such phrases.

The Angel at the Grave

I

The House stood a few yards back from the elm-shaded village street, in that semi-publicity sometimes cited as a democratic protest against old-world standards of domestic exclusiveness. This candid exposure to the public eye is more probably a result of the gregariousness which, in the New England bosom, oddly coexists with a shrinking from direct social contact; most of the inmates of such houses preferring that furtive intercourse which is the result of observations through shuttered windows and a categorical acquaintance with the neighboring clothes-lines. The House, however, faced its public with a difference. For sixty years it had written itself with a capital letter, had self-consciously squared itself in the eye of an admiring nation. The most searching inroads of village intimacy hardly counted in a household that opened on the universe; and a lady whose door-bell was at any moment liable to be rung by visitors from London or Vienna was not likely to flutter up-stairs when she observed a neighbor "stepping over."

The solitary inmate of the Anson House owed this induration of the social texture to the most conspicuous accident in her annals: the fact that she was the only granddaughter of the great Orestes Anson.[1] She had been born, as it were, into a museum, and cradled in a glass case with a label; the first foundations of her consciousness being built on the rock of her grandfather's celebrity. To a little girl who acquires her earliest knowledge of literature through a *Reader* embellished with fragments of her ancestor's prose, that personage necessarily fills an heroic space in the foreground of life. To communicate with one's past through the impressive medium of print, to have, as it were, a footing in every library in the country, and an acknowledged kinship with that world-diffused clan, the descendants of the great, was to be pledged to a standard of manners that amazingly simplified the lesser relations of life. The village street on which Paulina Anson's youth looked out led to all the capitals of Europe; and over the roads of intercommunication

---

1. Probably a reference to Orestes Brownson (1803–1870), a prominent New England clergyman, editor, and writer who was interested in Transcendentalism.

unseen caravans bore back to the elm-shaded House the tribute of an admiring world.

Fate seemed to have taken a direct share in fitting Paulina for her part as the custodian of this historic dwelling. It had long been secretly regarded as a "visitation" by the great man's family that he had left no son and that his daughters were not "intellectual." The ladies themselves were the first to lament their deficiency, to own that nature had denied them the gift of making the most of their opportunities. A profound veneration for their parent and an unswerving faith in his doctrines had not amended their congenital incapacity to understand what he had written. Laura, who had her moments of mute rebellion against destiny, had sometimes thought how much easier it would have been if their progenitor had been a poet; for she could recite, with feeling, portions of *The Culprit Fay* and of the poems of Mrs. Hemans;[2] and Phœbe, who was more conspicuous for memory than imagination, kept an album filled with "selections." But the great man was a philosopher; and to both daughters respiration was difficult on the cloudy heights of metaphysic. The situation would have been intolerable but for the fact that, while Phœbe and Laura were still at school, their father's fame had passed from the open ground of conjecture to the chill privacy of certitude. Dr. Anson had in fact achieved one of those anticipated immortalities not uncommon at a time when people were apt to base their literary judgments on their emotions, and when to affect plain food and despise England went a long way toward establishing a man's intellectual pre-eminence. Thus, when the daughters were called on to strike a filial attitude about their parent's pedestal, there was little to do but to pose gracefully and point upward; and there are spines to which the immobility of worship is not a strain. A legend had by this time crystallized about the great Orestes, and it was of more immediate interest to the public to hear what brand of tea he drank, and whether he took off his boots in the hall, than to rouse the drowsy echo of his dialectic. A great man never draws so near his public as when it has become unnecessary to read his books and is still interesting to know what he eats for breakfast.

As recorders of their parent's domestic habits, as pious scavengers of his waste-paper basket, the Misses Anson were unexcelled. They always had an interesting anecdote to impart to the literary pilgrim, and the tact with which, in later years, they intervened between the public and the growing inaccessibility of its idol, sent away many an enthusiast satisfied to have touched the veil before the sanctuary. Still it was felt, especially by old Mrs. Anson, who survived her husband for some years, that Phœbe and Laura were not worthy of their privileges. There

---

2. Felicia Hemans (1793–1835), popular English poet.

had been a third daughter so unworthy of hers that she had married a distant cousin, who had taken her to live in a new Western community where the *Works of Orestes Anson* had not yet become a part of the civic consciousness; but of this daughter little was said, and she was tacitly understood to be excluded from the family heritage of fame. In time, however, it appeared that the traditional penny with which she had been cut off had been invested to unexpected advantage; and the interest on it, when she died, returned to the Anson House in the shape of a granddaughter who was at once felt to be what Mrs. Anson called a "compensation." It was Mrs. Anson's firm belief that the remotest operations of nature were governed by the centripetal force of her husband's greatness and that Paulina's exceptional intelligence could be explained only on the ground that she was designed to act as the guardian of the family temple.

The House, by the time Paulina came to live in it, had already acquired the publicity of a place of worship; not the perfumed chapel of a romantic idolatry but the cold clean empty meetinghouse of ethical enthusiasms. The ladies lived on its outskirts, as it were, in cells that left the central fane undisturbed. The very position of the furniture had come to have a ritual significance: the sparse ornaments were the offerings of kindred intellects, the steel engravings by Raphael Morghen marked the Via Sacra[3] of a European tour, and the black-walnut desk with its bronze inkstand modelled on the Pantheon was the altar of this bleak temple of thought.

To a child compact of enthusiasms, and accustomed to pasture them on the scanty herbage of a new social soil, the atmosphere of the old house was full of floating nourishment. In the compressed perspective of Paulina's outlook it stood for a monument of ruined civilizations, and its white portico opened on legendary distances. Its very aspect was impressive to eyes that had first surveyed life from the jig-saw "residence" of a raw-edged Western town. The high-ceilinged rooms, with their panelled walls, their polished mahogany, their portraits of triple-stocked[4] ancestors and of ringleted "females" in crayon, furnished the child with the historic scenery against which a young imagination constructs its vision of the past. To other eyes the cold spotless thinly-furnished interior might have suggested the shuttered mind of a maiden-lady who associates fresh air and sunlight with dust and discoloration; but it is the eye which supplies the coloring-matter, and Paulina's brimmed with the richest hues.

Nevertheless, the House did not immediately dominate her. She had her confused out-reachings toward other centres of sensation, her

---

3. Raphael Morghen (1758–1833), Italian engraver. "Via Sacra": holy route.

vague intuition of a heliocentric system; but the attraction of habit, the
steady pressure of example, gradually fixed her roving allegiance and
she bent her neck to the yoke. Vanity had a share in her subjugation; for
it had early been discovered that she was the only person in the family
who could read her grandfather's works. The fact that she had perused
them with delight at an age when (even presupposing a metaphysical
bias) it was impossible for her to understand them, seemed to her aunts
and grandmother sure evidence of predestination. Paulina was to be the
interpreter of the oracle, and the philosophic fumes so vertiginous to
meaner minds would throw her into the needed condition of clairvoyance. Nothing could have been more genuine than the emotion on
which this theory was based. Paulina, in fact, delighted in her grandfather's writings. His sonorous periods,[5] his mystic vocabulary, his bold
flights into the rarefied air of the abstract, were thrilling to a fancy un-
hampered by the need of definitions. This purely verbal pleasure was
supplemented later by the excitement of gathering up crumbs of
meaning from the rhetorical board. What could have been more stimulating than to construct the theory of a girlish world out of the fragments of this Titanic cosmogony? Before Paulina's opinions had
reached the stage when ossification sets in their form was fatally prede-
termined.

The fact that Dr. Anson had died and that his apotheosis had taken
place before his young priestess's induction to the temple, made her
ministrations easier and more inspiring. There were no little personal
traits—such as the great man's manner of helping himself to salt, or the
guttural cluck that started the wheels of speech—to distract the eye of
young veneration from the central fact of his divinity. A man whom
one knows only through a crayon portrait and a dozen yellowing tomes
on free-will and intuition is at least secure from the belittling effects of
intimacy.

Paulina thus grew up in a world readjusted to the fact of her grandfather's greatness; and as each organism draws from its surroundings the
kind of nourishment most needful to its growth, so from this somewhat
colorless conception she absorbed warmth, brightness and variety.
Paulina was the type of woman who transmutes thought into sensation
and nurses a theory in her bosom like a child.

In due course Mrs. Anson "passed away"—no one died in the
Anson vocabulary—and Paulina became more than ever the foremost
figure of the commemorative group. Laura and Phœbe, content to
leave their father's glory in more competent hands, placidly lapsed into
needlework and fiction, and their niece stepped into immediate prominence as the chief "authority" on the great man. Historians who were

5. Sentences.

"getting up" the period wrote to consult her and to borrow documents; ladies with inexplicable yearnings begged for an interpretation of phrases which had "influenced" them, but which they had not quite understood; critics applied to her to verify some doubtful citation or to decide some disputed point in chronology; and the great tide of thought and investigation kept up a continuous murmur on the quiet shores of her life.

An explorer of another kind disembarked there one day in the shape of a young man to whom Paulina was primarily a kissable girl, with an after-thought in the shape of a grandfather. From the outset it had been impossible to fix Hewlett Winsloe's attention on Dr. Anson. The young man behaved with the innocent profanity of infants sporting on a tomb. His excuse was that he came from New York, a Cimmerian[6] out-skirt which survived in Paulina's geography only because Dr. Anson had gone there once or twice to lecture. The curious thing was that she should have thought it worth while to find excuses for young Winsloe. The fact that she did so had not escaped the attention of the village; but people, after a gasp of awe, said it was the most natural thing in the world that a girl like Paulina Anson should think of marrying. It would certainly seem a little odd to see a man in the House, but young Wins-loe would of course understand that the Doctor's books were not to be disturbed, and that he must go down to the orchard to smoke—. The village had barely framed this *modus vivendi*[7] when it was convulsed by the announcement that young Winsloe declined to live in the House on any terms. Hang going down to the orchard to smoke! He meant to take his wife to New York. The village drew its breath and watched.

Did Persephone,[8] snatched from the warm fields of Enna, peer half-consentingly down the abyss that opened at her feet? Paulina it must be owned, hung a moment over the black gulf of temptation. She would have found it easy to cope with a deliberate disregard of her grandfa-ther's rights; but young Winsloe's unconsciousness of that shadowy claim was as much a natural function as the falling of leaves on a grave. His love was an embodiment of the perpetual renewal which to some tender spirits seems a crueller process than decay.

On women of Paulina's mould this piety toward implicit demands, toward the ghosts of dead duties walking unappeased among usurping passions, has a stronger hold than any tangible bond. People said that she gave up young Winsloe because her aunts disapproved of her leav-ing them; but such disapproval as reached her was an emanation from the walls of the House, from the bare desk, the faded portraits, the dozen yellowing tomes that no hand but hers ever lifted from the shelf.

6. Gloomy; from the Homeric myth of a coun-try of perpetual darkness.
7. Way of life.

8. In Greek myth, the queen of the underworld, stolen from the earth by Hades.

II

After that the House possessed her. As if conscious of its victory, it imposed a conqueror's claims. It had once been suggested that she should write a life of her grandfather, and the task from which she had shrunk as from a too-oppressive privilege now shaped itself into a justification of her course. In a burst of filial pantheism she tried to lose herself in the vast ancestral consciousness. Her one refuge from scepticism was a blind faith in the magnitude and the endurance of the idea to which she had sacrificed her life, and with a passionate instinct of self-preservation she labored to fortify her position.

The preparations for the *Life* led her through byways that the most scrupulous of the previous biographers had left unexplored. She accumulated her material with a blind animal patience unconscious of fortuitous risks. The years stretched before her like some vast blank page spread out to receive the record of her toil; and she had a mystic conviction that she would not die till her work was accomplished.

The aunts, sustained by no such high purpose, withdrew in turn to their respective divisions of the Anson "plot,"[9] and Paulina remained alone with her task. She was forty when the book was completed. She had travelled little in her life, and it had become more and more difficult to her to leave the House even for a day; but the dread of entrusting her document to a strange hand made her decide to carry it herself to the publisher. On the way to Boston she had a sudden vision of the loneliness to which this last parting condemned her. All her youth, all her dreams, all her renunciations lay in that neat bundle on her knee. It was not so much her grandfather's life as her own that she had written; and the knowledge that it would come back to her in all the glorification of print was of no more help than, to a mother's grief, the assurance that the lad she must part with will return with epaulets.[1]

She had naturally addressed herself to the firm which had published her grandfather's works. Its founder, a personal friend of the philosopher's, had survived the Olympian[2] group of which he had been a subordinate member, long enough to bestow his octogenarian approval on Paulina's pious undertaking. But he had died soon afterward; and Miss Anson found herself confronted by his grandson, a person with a brisk commercial view of his trade, who was said to have put "new blood" into the firm.

This gentleman listened attentively, fingering her manuscript as though literature were a tactile substance; then, with a confidential twist of his revolving chair, he emitted the verdict: "We ought to have had this ten years sooner."

9. Burial plot.
1. Shoulder ornaments worn by soldiers.

2. Olympus is the mountain where the Greek gods live.

Miss Anson took the words as an allusion to the repressed avidity of her readers. "It has been a long time for the public to wait," she solemnly assented.

The publisher smiled. "They haven't waited," he said.

She looked at him strangely. "Haven't waited?"

"No—they've gone off; taken another train. Literature's like a big railway-station now, you know: there's a train starting every minute. People are not going to hang round the waiting-room. If they can't get to a place when they want to they go somewhere else."

The application of this parable cost Miss Anson several minutes of throbbing silence. At length she said: "Then I am to understand that the public is no longer interested in—in my grandfather?" She felt as though heaven must blast the lips that risked such a conjecture.

"Well, it's this way. He's a name still, of course. People don't exactly want to be caught not knowing who he is; but they don't want to spend two dollars finding out, when they can look him up for nothing in any biographical dictionary."

Miss Anson's world reeled. She felt herself adrift among mysterious forces, and no more thought of prolonging the discussion than of opposing an earthquake with argument. She went home carrying the manuscript like a wounded thing. On the return journey she found herself travelling straight toward a fact that had lurked for months in the background of her life, and that now seemed to await her on the very threshold: the fact that fewer visitors came to the House. She owned to herself that for the last four or five years the number had steadily diminished. Engrossed in her work, she had noted the change only to feel thankful that she had fewer interruptions. There had been a time when, at the travelling season, the bell rang continuously, and the ladies of the House lived in a chronic state of "best silks" and expectancy. It would have been impossible then to carry on any consecutive work; and she now saw that the silence which had gathered round her task had been the hush of death.

Not of *his* death! The very walls cried out against the implication. It was the world's enthusiasm, the world's faith, the world's loyalty that had died. A corrupt generation that had turned aside to worship the brazen serpent.[3] Her heart yearned with a prophetic passion over the lost sheep straying in the wilderness. But all great glories had their interlunar period; and in due time her grandfather would once more flash full-orbed upon a darkling world.

The few friends to whom she confided her adventure reminded her with tender indignation that there were other publishers less subject to the fluctuations of the market; but much as she had braved for her

3. I.e., false idol.

grandfather she could not again brave that particular probation. She found herself, in fact, incapable of any immediate effort. She had lost her way in a labyrinth of conjecture where her worst dread was that she might put her hand upon the clue.

She locked up the manuscript and sat down to wait. If a pilgrim had come just then the priestess would have fallen on his neck; but she continued to celebrate her rites alone. It was a double solitude; for she had always thought a great deal more of the people who came to see the House than of the people who came to see her. She fancied that the neighbors kept a keen eye on the path to the House; and there were days when the figure of a stranger strolling past the gate seemed to focus upon her the scorching sympathies of the village. For a time she thought of travelling; of going to Europe, or even to Boston; but to leave the House now would have seemed like deserting her post. Gradually her scattered energies centred themselves in the fierce resolve to understand what had happened. She was not the woman to live long in an unmapped country or to accept as final her private interpretation of phenomena. Like a traveller in unfamiliar regions she began to store for future guidance the minutest natural signs. Unflinchingly she noted the accumulating symptoms of indifference that marked her grandfather's descent toward posterity. She passed from the heights on which he had been grouped with the sages of his day to the lower level where he had come to be "the friend of Emerson," "the correspondent of Hawthorne,"[4] or (later still) "the Dr. Anson" mentioned in their letters. The change had taken place as slowly and imperceptibly as a natural process. She could not say that any ruthless hand had stripped the leaves from the tree: it was simply that, among the evergreen glories of his group, her grandfather's had proved deciduous.

She had still to ask herself why. If the decay had been a natural process, was it not the very pledge of renewal? It was easier to find such arguments than to be convinced by them. Again and again she tried to drug her solicitude with analogies; but at last she saw that such expedients were but the expression of a growing incredulity. The best way of proving her faith in her grandfather was not to be afraid of critics. She had no notion where these shadowy antagonists lurked; for she had never heard of the great man's doctrine being directly combated. Oblique assaults there must have been, however, Parthian shots[5] at the giant that none dared face; and she thirsted to close with such assailants. The difficulty was to find them. She began by re-reading the *Works*; thence she passed to the writers of the same school, those whose rhetoric bloomed perennial in *First Readers* from which her grandfather's

---

4. Ralph Waldo Emerson (1803–1882), American poet and essayist, founder of the Transcendentalist movement. Nathaniel Hawthorne (1804–1864), American fiction writer.
5. Shots delivered while retreating (after Parthian archers).

prose had long since faded. Amid that clamor of far-off enthusiasms she detected no controversial note. The little knot of Olympians held their views in common with an early-Christian promiscuity.[6] They were continually proclaiming their admiration for each other, the public joining as chorus in this guileless antiphon of praise; and she discovered no traitor in their midst.

What then had happened? Was it simply that the main current of thought had set another way? Then why did the others survive? Why were they still marked down as tributaries to the philosophic stream? This question carried her still farther afield, and she pressed on with the passion of a champion whose reluctance to know the worst might be construed into a doubt of his cause. At length—slowly but inevitably— an explanation shaped itself. Death had overtaken the doctrines about which her grandfather had draped his cloudy rhetoric. They had disintegrated and been re-absorbed, adding their little pile to the dust drifted about the mute lips of the Sphinx.[7] The great man's contemporaries had survived not by reason of what they taught, but of what they were; and he, who had been the mere mask through which they mouthed their lesson, the instrument on which their tune was played, lay buried deep among the obsolete tools of thought.

The discovery came to Paulina suddenly. She looked up one evening from her reading and it stood before her like a ghost. It had entered her life with stealthy steps, creeping close before she was aware of it. She sat in the library, among the carefully-tended books and portraits; and it seemed to her that she had been walled alive into a tomb hung with the effigies of dead ideas. She felt a desperate longing to escape into the outer air, where people toiled and loved, and living sympathies went hand in hand. It was the sense of wasted labor that oppressed her; of two lives consumed in that ruthless process that uses generations of effort to build a single cell. There was a dreary parallel between her grandfather's fruitless toil and her own unprofitable sacrifice. Each in turn had kept vigil by a corpse.

III

The bell rang—she remembered it afterward—with a loud thrilling note. It was what they used to call the "visitor's ring"; not the tentative tinkle of a neighbor dropping in to borrow a sauce-pan or discuss parochial incidents, but a decisive summons from the outer world.

Miss Anson put down her knitting and listened. She sat upstairs now, making her rheumatism an excuse for avoiding the rooms below. Her

6. I.e., like the early Christians, who banded together to preserve their faith.
7. In Greek myth, the Sphinx was a monster who killed all who could not answer her riddles; here a figure for inscrutable mysteries.

interests had insensibly adjusted themselves to the perspective of her neighbors' lives, and she wondered—as the bell re-echoed—if it could mean that Mrs. Heminway's baby had come. Conjecture had time to ripen into certainty, and she was limping toward the closet where her cloak and bonnet hung, when her little maid fluttered in with the announcement: "A gentleman to see the house."

"The *House?*"

"Yes, m'm. I don't know what he means," faltered the messenger, whose memory did not embrace the period when such announcements were a daily part of the domestic routine.

Miss Anson glanced at the proffered card. The name it bore—*Mr. George Corby*—was unknown to her, but the blood rose to her languid cheek. "Hand me my Mechlin cap, Katy," she said, trembling a little, as she laid aside her walking stick. She put her cap on before the mirror, with rapid unsteady touches. "Did you draw up the library blinds?" she breathlessly asked.

She had gradually built up a wall of commonplace between herself and her illusions, but at the first summons of the past filial passion swept away the frail barriers of expediency.

She walked down-stairs so hurriedly that her stick clicked like a girlish heel; but in the hall she paused, wondering nervously if Katy had put a match to the fire. The autumn air was cold and she had the reproachful vision of a visitor with elderly ailments shivering by her inhospitable hearth. She thought instinctively of the stranger as a survivor of the days when such a visit was a part of the young enthusiast's itinerary.

The fire was unlit and the room forbiddingly cold; but the figure which, as Miss Anson entered, turned from a lingering scrutiny of the book-shelves, was that of a fresh-eyed sanguine youth clearly independent of any artificial caloric.[8] She stood still a moment, feeling herself the victim of some anterior impression that made this robust presence an insubstantial thing; but the young man advanced with an air of genial assurance which rendered him at once more real and more reminiscent.

"Why this, you know," he exclaimed, "is simply immense!"

The words, which did not immediately present themselves as slang to Miss Anson's unaccustomed ear, echoed with an odd familiarity through the academic silence.

"The room, you know, I mean," he explained with a comprehensive gesture. "These jolly portraits, and the books—that's the old gentleman himself over the mantelpiece, I suppose—and the elms outside, and—and the whole business. I do like a congruous background—don't you?"

---

8. An imaginary fluid thought to produce and transfer heat.

His hostess was silent. No one but Hewlett Winsloe had ever spoken of her grandfather as "the old gentleman."

"It's a hundred times better than I could have hoped," her visitor continued, with a cheerful disregard of her silence. "The seclusion, the remoteness, the philosophic atmosphere—there's so little of that kind of flavor left! I should have simply hated to find that he lived over a grocery, you know.—I had the deuce of a time finding out where he *did* live," he began again, after another glance of parenthetical enjoyment. "But finally I got on the trail through some old book on Brook Farm.[9] I was bound I'd get the environment right before I did my article."

Miss Anson, by this time, had recovered sufficient self-possession to seat herself and assign a chair to her visitor.

"Do I understand," she asked slowly, following his rapid eye about the room, "that you intend to write an article about my grandfather?"

"That's what I'm here for," Mr. Corby genially responded; "that is, if you're willing to help me; for I can't get on without your help," he added with a confident smile.

There was another pause, during which Miss Anson noticed a fleck of dust on the faded leather of the writing-table and a fresh spot of discoloration in the right-hand upper corner of Raphael Morghen's "Parnassus."

"Then you believe in him?" she said, looking up. She could not tell what had prompted her; the words rushed out irresistibly.

"Believe in him?" Corby cried, springing to his feet. "Believe in Orestes Anson? Why, I believe he's simply the greatest—the most stupendous—the most phenomenal figure we've got!"

The color rose to Miss Anson's brow. Her heart was beating passionately. She kept her eyes fixed on the young man's face, as though it might vanish if she looked away.

"You—you mean to say this in your article?" she asked.

"Say it? Why, the facts will say it," he exulted. "The baldest kind of a statement would make it clear. When a man is as big as that he doesn't need a pedestal!"

Miss Anson sighed. "People used to say that when I was young," she murmured. "But now—"

Her visitor stared. "When you were young? But how did they know —when the thing hung fire as it did?[1] When the whole edition was thrown back on his hands?"

"The whole edition—what edition?" It was Miss Anson's turn to stare.

9. A cooperative community (1841–1847)   1. **Was delayed.**
founded by the Transcendentalists.

"Why, of his pamphlet—*the* pamphlet—the one thing that counts, that survives, that makes him what he is! For heaven's sake," he tragically adjured her, "don't tell me there isn't a copy of it left!"

Miss Anson was trembling slightly. "I don't think I understand what you mean," she faltered, less bewildered by his vehemence than by the strange sense of coming on an unexplored region in the very heart of her dominion.

"Why, his account of the *amphioxus*,[2] of course! You can't mean that his family didn't know about it—that *you* don't know about it? I came across it by the merest accident myself, in a letter of vindication that he wrote in 1830 to an old scientific paper; but I understood there were journals—early journals; there must be references to it somewhere in the 'twenties. He must have been at least ten or twelve years ahead of Yarrell; and he saw the whole significance of it, too—he saw where it led to. As I understand it, he actually anticipated in his pamphlet Saint Hilaire's theory of the universal type, and supported the hypothesis by describing the notochord of the *amphioxus* as a cartilaginous vertebral column. The specialists of the day jeered at him, of course, as the specialists in Goethe's time jeered at the plant-metamorphosis.[3] As far as I can make out, the anatomists and zoologists were down on Dr. Anson to a man; that was why his cowardly publishers went back on their bargain. But the pamphlet must be here somewhere —he writes as though, in his first disappointment, he had destroyed the whole edition; but surely there must be at least one copy left?"

His scientific jargon was as bewildering as his slang; and there were even moments in his discourse when Miss Anson ceased to distinguish between them; but the suspense with which he continued to gaze on her acted as a challenge to her scattered thoughts.

"The *amphioxus*," she murmured, half-rising. "It's an animal, isn't it—a fish? Yes, I think I remember." She sank back with the inward look of one who retraces some lost line of association.

Gradually the distance cleared, the details started into life. In her researches for the biography she had patiently followed every ramification of her subject, and one of these overgrown paths now led her back to the episode in question. The great Orestes's title of "Doctor" had in fact not been merely the spontaneous tribute of a national admiration; he had actually studied medicine in his youth, and his diaries, as his granddaughter now recalled, showed that he had passed through a brief phase of anatomical ardor before his attention was diverted to supersensual problems. It had indeed seemed to Paulina, as she scanned those early pages, that they revealed a spontaneity, a freshness of feeling

2. A primitive organism.
3. The poet Johann Wolfgang von Goethe   (1749–1832) developed a controversial botanical theory.

somehow absent from his later lucubrations—as though this one emotion had reached him directly, the others through some intervening medium. In the excess of her commemorative zeal she had even struggled through the unintelligible pamphlet to which a few lines in the journal had bitterly directed her. But the subject and the phraseology were alien to her and unconnected with her conception of the great man's genius; and after a hurried perusal she had averted her thoughts from the episode as from a revelation of failure. At length she rose a little unsteadily, supporting herself against the writing-table. She looked hesitatingly about the room; then she drew a key from her old fashioned reticule[4] and unlocked a drawer beneath one of the book-cases. Young Corby watched her breathlessly. With a tremulous hand she turned over the dusty documents that seemed to fill the drawer. "Is this it?" she said, holding out a thin discolored volume.

He seized it with a gasp. "Oh, by George," he said, dropping into the nearest chair.

She stood observing him strangely as his eye devoured the mouldy pages.

"Is this the only copy left?" he asked at length, looking up for a moment as a thirsty man lifts his head from his glass.

"I think it must be. I found it long ago, among some old papers that my aunts were burning up after my grandmother's death. They said it was of no use—that he'd always meant to destroy the whole edition and that I ought to respect his wishes. But it was something *he* had written; to burn it was like shutting the door against his voice—against something he had once wished to say, and that nobody had listened to. I wanted him to feel that I was always here, ready to listen, even when others hadn't thought it worth while; and so I kept the pamphlet, meaning to carry out his wish and destroy it before my death."

Her visitor gave a groan of retrospective anguish. "And but for me —but for to-day—you would have?"

"I should have thought it my duty."

"Oh, by George—by George," he repeated, subdued afresh by the inadequacy of speech.

She continued to watch him in silence. At length he jumped up and impulsively caught her by both hands.

"He's bigger and bigger!" he almost shouted. "He simply leads the field! You'll help me go to the bottom of this, won't you? We must turn out all the papers—letters, journals, memoranda. He must have made notes. He must have left some record of what led up to this. We must leave nothing unexplored. By Jove," he cried, looking up at her with his

4. Woman's handbag.

bright convincing smile, "do you know you're the granddaughter of a Great Man?"

Her color flickered like a girl's. "Are you—sure of him?" she whispered, as though putting him on his guard against a possible betrayal of trust.

"Sure! Sure! My dear lady—" he measured her again with his quick confident glance. "Don't *you* believe in him?"

She drew back with a confused murmur. "I—used to." She had left her hands in his: their pressure seemed to send a warm current to her heart. "It ruined my life!" she cried with sudden passion. He looked at her perplexedly.

"I gave up everything," she went on wildly, "to keep *him* alive. I sacrificed myself—others—I nursed his glory in my bosom and it died—and left me—left me here alone." She paused and gathered her courage with a gasp. "Don't make the same mistake!" she warned him.

He shook his head, still smiling. "No danger of that! You're not alone, my dear lady. He's here with you—he's come back to you today. Don't you see what's happened? Don't you see that it's your love that has kept him alive? If you'd abandoned your post for an instant—let things pass into other hands—if your wonderful tenderness hadn't perpetually kept guard—this might have been—must have been—irretrievably lost." He laid his hand on the pamphlet. "And then—then he *would* have been dead!"

"Oh," she said, "don't tell me too suddenly!" And she turned away and sank into a chair.

The young man stood watching her in an awed silence. For a long time she sat motionless, with her face hidden, and he thought she must be weeping.

At length he said, almost shyly: "You'll let me come back, then? You'll help me work this thing out?"

She rose calmly and held out her hand. "I'll help you," she declared.

"I'll come to-morrow, then. Can we get to work early?"

"As early as you please."

"At eight o'clock, then," he said briskly. "You'll have the papers ready?"

"I'll have everything ready." She added with a half-playful hesitancy: "And the fire shall be lit for you."

He went out with his bright nod. She walked to the window and watched his buoyant figure hastening down the elm-shaded street. When she turned back into the empty room she looked as though youth had touched her on the lips.

1901

The Other Two

Waythorn, on the drawing-room hearth, waited for his wife to come down to dinner.

It was their first night under his own roof, and he was surprised at his thrill of boyish agitation. He was not so old, to be sure—his glass gave him little more than the five-and-thirty years to which his wife confessed—but he had fancied himself already in the temperate zone; yet here he was listening for her step with a tender sense of all it symbolized, with some old trail of verse about the garlanded nuptial doorposts floating through his enjoyment of the pleasant room and the good dinner just beyond it.

They had been hastily recalled from their honeymoon by the illness of Lily Haskett, the child of Mrs. Waythorn's first marriage. The little girl, at Waythorn's desire, had been transferred to his house on the day of her mother's wedding, and the doctor, on their arrival, broke the news that she was ill with typhoid, but declared that all the symptoms were favorable. Lily could show twelve years of unblemished health, and the case promised to be a light one. The nurse spoke as reassuringly, and after a moment of alarm Mrs. Waythorn had adjusted herself to the situation. She was very fond of Lily—her affection for the child had perhaps been her decisive charm in Waythorn's eyes—but she had the perfectly balanced nerves which her little girl had inherited, and no woman ever wasted less tissue in unproductive worry. Waythorn was therefore quite prepared to see her come in presently, a little late because of a last look at Lily, but as serene and well-appointed as if her good-night kiss had been laid on the brow of health. Her composure was restful to him; it acted as ballast to his somewhat unstable sensibilities. As he pictured her bending over the child's bed he thought how soothing her presence must be in illness: her very step would prognosticate recovery.

His own life had been a gray one, from temperament rather than circumstance, and he had been drawn to her by the unperturbed gaiety which kept her fresh and elastic at an age when most women's activities are growing either slack or febrile. He knew what was said about her; for, popular as she was, there had always been a faint undercurrent of detraction. When she had appeared in New York, nine or ten years earlier, as the pretty Mrs. Haskett whom Gus Varick had unearthed somewhere—was it in Pittsburgh or Utica?—society, while promptly accepting her, had reserved the right to cast a doubt on its own indiscrimination. Inquiry, however, established her undoubted connection with a socially reigning family, and explained her recent divorce as the natural result of a runaway match at seventeen; and as nothing was known of Mr. Haskett it was easy to believe the worst of him.

Alice Haskett's remarriage with Gus Varick was a passport to the set whose recognition she coveted, and for a few years the Varicks were the most popular couple in town. Unfortunately the alliance was brief and stormy, and this time the husband had his champions. Still, even Varick's stanchest supporters admitted that he was not meant for matrimony, and Mrs. Varick's grievances were of a nature to bear the inspection of the New York courts.[1] A New York divorce is in itself a diploma of virtue, and in the semiwidowhood of this second separation Mrs. Varick took on an air of sanctity, and was allowed to confide her wrongs to some of the most scrupulous ears in town. But when it was known that she was to marry Waythorn there was a momentary reaction. Her best friends would have preferred to see her remain in the role of the injured wife, which was as becoming to her as crepe to a rosy complexion. True, a decent time had elapsed, and it was not even suggested that Waythorn had supplanted his predecessor. People shook their heads over him, however, and one grudging friend, to whom he affirmed that he took the step with his eyes open, replied oracularly: "Yes—and with your ears shut."

Waythorn could afford to smile at these innuendoes. In the Wall Street phrase, he had "discounted" them. He knew that society has not yet adapted itself to the consequences of divorce, and that till the adaptation takes place every woman who uses the freedom the law accords her must be her own social justification. Waythorn had an amused confidence in his wife's ability to justify herself. His expectations were fulfilled, and before the wedding took place Alice Varick's group had rallied openly to her support. She took it all imperturbably: she had a way of surmounting obstacles without seeming to be aware of them, and Waythorn looked back with wonder at the trivialities over which he had worn his nerves thin. He had the sense of having found refuge in a richer, warmer nature than his own, and his satisfaction, at the moment, was humorously summed up in the thought that his wife, when she had done all she could for Lily, would not be ashamed to come down and enjoy a good dinner.

The anticipation of such enjoyment was not, however, the sentiment expressed by Mrs. Waythorn's charming face when she presently joined him. Though she had put on her most engaging tea gown she had neglected to assume the smile that went with it, and Waythorn thought he had never seen her look so nearly worried.

"What is it?" he asked. "Is anything wrong with Lily?"

"No; I've just been in and she's still sleeping." Mrs. Waythorn hesitated. "But something tiresome has happened."

---

1. At the time, a divorce in New York State could be granted only on grounds of adultery.

He had taken her two hands, and now perceived that he was crushing a paper between them.

"This letter?"

"Yes—Mr. Haskett has written—I mean his lawyer has written."

Waythorn felt himself flush uncomfortably. He dropped his wife's hands.

"What about?"

"About seeing Lily. You know the courts—"

"Yes, yes," he interrupted nervously.

Nothing was known about Haskett in New York. He was vaguely supposed to have remained in the outer darkness from which his wife had been rescued, and Waythorn was one of the few who were aware that he had given up his business in Utica and followed her to New York in order to be near his little girl. In the days of his wooing, Waythorn had often met Lily on the doorstep, rosy and smiling, on her way "to see papa."

"I am so sorry," Mrs. Waythorn murmured.

He roused himself. "What does he want?"

"He wants to see her. You know she goes to him once a week."

"Well—he doesn't expect her to go to him now, does he?"

"No—he has heard of her illness; but he expects to come here."

"*Here?*"

Mrs. Waythorn reddened under his gaze. They looked away from each other.

"I'm afraid he has the right . . . You'll see. . . . ." She made a proffer of the letter.

Waythorn moved away with a gesture of refusal. He stood staring about the softly-lighted room, which a moment before had seemed so full of bridal intimacy.

"I'm so sorry," she repeated. "If Lily could have been moved—"

"That's out of the question," he returned impatiently.

"I suppose so."

Her lip was beginning to tremble, and he felt himself a brute.

"He must come, of course," he said. "When is—his day?"

"I'm afraid—tomorrow."

"Very well. Send a note in the morning."

The butler entered to announce dinner.

Waythorn turned to his wife. "Come—you must be tired. It's beastly, but try to forget about it," he said, drawing her hand through his arm.

"You're so good, dear. I'll try," she whispered back.

Her face cleared at once, and as she looked at him across the flowers, between the rosy candleshades, he saw her lips waver back into a smile.

"How pretty everything is!" she sighed luxuriously.

He turned to the butler. "The champagne at once, please. Mrs. Waythorn is tired."

In a moment or two their eyes met above the sparkling glasses. Her own were quite clear and untroubled: he saw that she had obeyed his injunction and forgotten.

II

Waythorn, the next morning, went downtown earlier than usual. Haskett was not likely to come till the afternoon, but the instinct of flight drove him forth. He meant to stay away all day—he had thoughts of dining at his club. As his door closed behind him he reflected that before he opened it again it would have admitted another man who had as much right to enter it as himself, and the thought filled him with a physical repugnance.

He caught the elevated[2] at the employees' hour, and found himself crushed between two layers of pendulous humanity. At Eighth Street the man facing him wriggled out, and another took his place. Waythorn glanced up and saw that it was Gus Varick. The men were so close together that it was impossible to ignore the smile of recognition on Varick's handsome overblown face. And after all—why not? They had always been on good terms, and Varick had been divorced before Waythorn's attentions to his wife began. The two exchanged a word on the perennial grievance of the congested trains, and when a seat at their side was miraculously left empty the instinct of self-preservation made Waythorn slip into it after Varick.

The latter drew the stout man's breath of relief. "Lord—I was beginning to feel like a pressed flower." He leaned back, looking unconcernedly at Waythorn. "Sorry to hear that Sellers is knocked out again."

"Sellers?" echoed Waythorn, starting at his partner's name.

Varick looked surprised. "You didn't know he was laid up with the gout?"

"No. I've been away—I only got back last night." Waythorn felt himself reddening in anticipation of the other's smile.

"Ah—yes; to be sure. And Sellers' attack came on two days ago. I'm afraid he's pretty bad. Very awkward for me, as it happens, because he was just putting through a rather important thing for me."

"Ah?" Waythorn wondered vaguely since when Varick had been dealing in "important things." Hitherto he had dabbled only in the shallow pools of speculation, with which Waythorn's office did not usually concern itself.

It occurred to him that Varick might be talking at random, to relieve

2. The elevated train, a form of public transportation in New York City.

the strain of their propinquity. That strain was becoming momentarily more apparent to Waythorn, and when, at Cortlandt Street, he caught sight of an acquaintance and had a sudden vision of the picture he and Varick must present to an initiated eye, he jumped up with a muttered excuse.

"I hope you'll find Sellers better," said Varick civilly, and he stammered back: "If I can be of any use to you—" and let the departing crowd sweep him to the platform.

At his office he heard that Sellers was in fact ill with the gout, and would probably not be able to leave the house for some weeks.

"I'm sorry it should have happened so, Mr. Waythorn," the senior clerk said with affable significance. "Mr. Sellers was very much upset at the idea of giving you such a lot of extra work just now."

"Oh, that's no matter," said Waythorn hastily. He secretly welcomed the pressure of additional business, and was glad to think that, when the day's work was over, he would have to call at his partner's on the way home.

He was late for luncheon, and turned in at the nearest restaurant instead of going to his club. The place was full, and the waiter hurried him to the back of the room to capture the only vacant table. In the cloud of cigar smoke Waythorn did not at once distinguish his neighbors: but presently, looking about him, he saw Varick seated a few feet off. This time, luckily, they were too far apart for conversation, and Varick, who faced another way, had probably not even seen him; but there was an irony in their renewed nearness.

Varick was said to be fond of good living, and as Waythorn sat dispatching his hurried luncheon he looked across half enviously at the other's leisurely degustation of his meal. When Waythorn first saw him he had been helping himself with critical deliberation to a bit of Camembert at the ideal point of liquefaction, and now, the cheese removed, he was just pouring his *café double* [3] from its little two-storied earthen pot. He poured slowly, his ruddy profile bent over the task, and one beringed white hand steadying the lid of the coffeepot; then he stretched his other hand to the decanter of cognac at his elbow, filled a liqueur glass, took a tentative sip, and poured the brandy into his coffee cup.

Waythorn watched him in a kind of fascination. What was he thinking of—only of the flavor of the coffee and the liqueur? Had the morning's meeting left no more trace in his thoughts than on his face? Had his wife so completely passed out of his life that even this odd encounter with her present husband, within a week after her remarriage, was no

3. Very strong coffee.

more than an incident in his day? And as Waythorn mused, another idea struck him: had Haskett ever met Varick as Varick and he had just met? The recollection of Haskett perturbed him, and he rose and left the restaurant, taking a circuitous way out to escape the placid irony of Varick's nod.

It was after seven when Waythorn reached home. He thought the footman who opened the door looked at him oddly.

"How is Miss Lily?" he asked in haste.

"Doing very well, sir. A gentleman—"

"Tell Barlow to put off dinner for half an hour," Waythorn cut him off, hurrying upstairs.

He went straight to his room and dressed without seeing his wife. When he reached the drawing room she was there, fresh and radiant. Lily's day had been good; the doctor was not coming back that evening.

At dinner Waythorn told her of Sellers' illness and of the resulting complications. She listened sympathetically, adjuring him not to let himself be overworked, and asking vague feminine questions about the routine of the office. Then she gave him the chronicle of Lily's day; quoted the nurse and doctor, and told him who had called to inquire. He had never seen her more serene and unruffled. It struck him with a curious pang, that she was very happy in being with him, so happy that she found a childish pleasure in rehearsing the trivial incidents of her day.

After dinner they went to the library, and the servant put the coffee and liqueurs on a low table before her and left the room. She looked singularly soft and girlish in her rosy-pale dress, against the dark leather of one of his bachelor armchairs. A day earlier the contrast would have charmed him.

He turned away now, choosing a cigar with affected deliberation.

"Did Haskett come?" he asked, with his back to her.

"Oh, yes—he came."

"You didn't see him, of course?"

She hesitated a moment. "I let the nurse see him."

That was all. There was nothing more to ask. He swung round toward her, applying a match to his cigar. Well, the thing was over for a week, at any rate. He would try not to think of it. She looked up at him, a trifle rosier than usual, with a smile in her eyes.

"Ready for your coffee, dear?"

He leaned against the mantelpiece, watching her as she lifted the coffeepot. The lamplight struck a gleam from her bracelets and tipped her soft hair with brightness. How light and slender she was, and how each gesture flowed into the next! She seemed a creature all compact of harmonies. As the thought of Haskett receded, Waythorn felt himself yielding again to the joy of possessorship. They were his, those white hands with their flitting motions, his the light haze of hair, the lips and eyes. . . .

She set down the coffeepot, and reaching for the decanter of cognac, measured off a liqueur glass and poured it into his cup.

Waythorn uttered a sudden exclamation.

"What is the matter?" she said, startled.

"Nothing; only—I don't take cognac in my coffee."

"Oh, how stupid of me," she cried.

Their eyes met, and she blushed a sudden agonized red.

III

Ten days later, Mr. Sellers, still housebound, asked Waythorn to call on his way downtown.

The senior partner, with his swaddled foot propped up by the fire, greeted his associate with an air of embarrassment.

"I'm sorry, my dear fellow; I've got to ask you to do an awkward thing for me."

Waythorn waited, and the other went on, after a pause apparently given to the arrangement of his phrases: "The fact is, when I was knocked out I had just gone into a rather complicated piece of business for—Gus Varick."

"Well?" said Waythorn, with an attempt to put him at his ease.

"Well—it's this way: Varick came to me the day before my attack. He had evidently had an inside tip from somebody, and had made about a hundred thousand. He came to me for advice, and I suggested his going in with Vanderlyn."

"Oh, the deuce!" Waythorn exclaimed. He saw in a flash what had happened. The investment was an alluring one, but required negotiation. He listened quietly while Sellers put the case before him, and the statement ended, he said: "You think I ought to see Varick?"

"I'm afraid I can't as yet. The doctor is obdurate. And this thing can't wait. I hate to ask you, but no one else in the office knows the ins and outs of it."

Waythorn stood silent. He did not care a farthing[4] for the success of Varick's venture, but the honor of the office was to be considered, and he could hardly refuse to oblige his partner.

"Very well," he said, "I'll do it."

That afternoon, apprised by telephone, Varick called at the office. Waythorn, waiting in his private room, wondered what the others thought of it. The newspapers, at the time of Mrs. Waythorn's marriage, had acquainted their readers with every detail of her previous

4. Smallest British monetary unit.

matrimonial ventures, and Waythorn could fancy the clerks smiling behind Varick's back as he was ushered in.

Varick bore himself admirably. He was easy without being undignified, and Waythorn was conscious of cutting a much less impressive figure. Varick had no experience of business, and the talk prolonged itself for nearly an hour while Waythorn set forth with scrupulous precision the details of the proposed transaction.

"I'm awfully obliged to you," Varick said as he rose. "The fact is I'm not used to having much money to look after, and I don't want to make an ass of myself—" He smiled, and Waythorn could not help noticing that there was something pleasant about his smile. "It feels uncommonly queer to have enough cash to pay one's bills. I'd have sold my soul for it a few years ago!"

Waythorn winced at the allusion. He had heard it rumored that a lack of funds had been one of the determining causes of the Varick separation, but it did not occur to him that Varick's words were intentional. It seemed more likely that the desire to keep clear of embarrassing topics had fatally drawn him into one. Waythorn did not wish to be outdone in civility.

"We'll do the best we can for you," he said. "I think this is a good thing you're in."

"Oh, I'm sure it's immense. It's awfully good of you—" Varick broke off, embarrassed. "I suppose the thing's settled now—but if—"

"If anything happens before Sellers is about, I'll see you again," said Waythorn quietly. He was glad, in the end, to appear the more self-possessed of the two.

The course of Lily's illness ran smooth, and as the days passed Waythorn grew used to the idea of Haskett's weekly visit. The first time the day came round, he stayed out late, and questioned his wife as to the visit on his return. She replied at once that Haskett had merely seen the nurse downstairs, as the doctor did not wish anyone in the child's sickroom till after the crisis.

The following week Waythorn was again conscious of the recurrence of the day, but had forgotten it by the time he came home to dinner. The crisis of the disease came a few days later, with a rapid decline of fever, and the little girl was pronounced out of danger. In the rejoicing which ensued the thought of Haskett passed out of Waythorn's mind, and one afternoon, letting himself into the house with a latchkey, he went straight to his library without noticing a shabby hat and umbrella in the hall.

In the library he found a small effaced-looking man with a thinnish gray beard sitting on the edge of a chair. The stranger might have been a piano tuner, or one of those mysteriously efficient persons who are summoned in emergencies to adjust some detail of the domestic machinery. He blinked at Waythorn through a pair of gold-rimmed spectacles and said mildly: "Mr. Waythorn, I presume? I am Lily's father."

Waythorn flushed. "Oh—" he stammered uncomfortably. He broke off, disliking to appear rude. Inwardly he was trying to adjust the actual Haskett to the image of him projected by his wife's reminiscences. Waythorn had been allowed to infer that Alice's first husband was a brute.

"I am sorry to intrude," said Haskett, with his over-the-counter politeness.

"Don't mention it," returned Waythorn, collecting himself. "I suppose the nurse has been told?"

"I presume so. I can wait," said Haskett. He had a resigned way of speaking, as though life had worn down his natural powers of resistance.

Waythorn stood on the threshold, nervously pulling off his gloves.

"I'm sorry you've been detained. I will send for the nurse," he said; and as he opened the door he added with an effort: "I'm glad we can give you a good report of Lily." He winced as the *we* slipped out, but Haskett seemed not to notice it.

"Thank you, Mr. Waythorn, it's been an anxious time for me."

"Ah, well, that's past. Soon she'll be able to go to you." Waythorn nodded and passed out.

In his own room he flung himself down with a groan. He hated the womanish sensibility which made him suffer so acutely from the grotesque chances of life. He had known when he married that his wife's former husbands were both living, and that amid the multiplied contacts of modern existence there were a thousand chances to one that he would run against one or the other, yet he found himself as much disturbed by his brief encounter with Haskett as though the law had not obligingly removed all difficulties in the way of their meeting.

Waythorn sprang up and began to pace the room nervously. He had not suffered half as much from his two meetings with Varick. It was Haskett's presence in his own house that made the situation so intolerable. He stood still, hearing steps in the passage.

"This way, please," he heard the nurse say. Haskett was being taken upstairs, then: not a corner of the house but was open to him. Waythorn dropped into another chair, staring vaguely ahead of him. On his dressing table stood a photograph of Alice, taken when he had first known her. She was Alice Varick then—how fine and exquisite he had thought her! Those were Varick's pearls about her neck. At Waythorn's instance they had been returned before her marriage. Had Haskett ever given her any trinkets—and what had become of them, Waythorn wondered? He realized suddenly that he knew very little of Haskett's past or present situation; but from the man's appearance and

manner of speech he could reconstruct with curious precision the surroundings of Alice's first marriage. And it startled him to think that she
had, in the background of her life, a phase of existence so different from
anything with which he had connected her. Varick, whatever his faults,
was a gentleman, in the conventional, traditional sense of the term: the
sense which at that moment seemed, oddly enough, to have most
meaning to Waythorn. He and Varick had the same social habits, spoke
the same language, understood the same allusions. But this other man
. . . it was grotesquely uppermost in Waythorn's mind that Haskett had
worn a made-up tie attached with an elastic. Why should that ridiculous
detail symbolize the whole man? Waythorn was exasperated by his own
paltriness, but the fact of the tie expanded, forced itself on him, became
as it were the key to Alice's past. He could see her, as Mrs. Haskett, sitting in a "front parlor" furnished in plush, with a pianola, and copy of
Ben Hur[5] on the center table. He could see her going to the theater
with Haskett—or perhaps even to a "Church Sociable"—she in a
"picture hat" and Haskett in a black frock coat, a little creased, with the
made-up tie on an elastic. On the way home they would stop and look
at the illuminated shop windows, lingering over the photographs of
New York actresses. On Sunday afternoons Haskett would take her for
a walk, pushing Lily ahead of them in a white enameled perambulator,
and Waythorn had a vision of the people they would stop and talk to.
He could fancy how pretty Alice must have looked, in a dress adroitly
constructed from the hints of a New York fashion paper, and how she
must have looked down on the other women, chafing at her life, and
secretly feeling that she belonged in a bigger place.

For the moment his foremost thought was one of wonder at the way
in which she had shed the phase of existence which her marriage with
Haskett implied. It was as if her whole aspect, every gesture, every inflection, every allusion, were a studied negation of that period of her
life. If she had denied being married to Haskett she could hardly have
stood more convicted of duplicity than in this obliteration of the self
which had been his wife.

Waythorn started up, checking himself in the analysis of her motives.
What right had he to create a fantastic effigy of her and then pass judgment on it? She had spoken vaguely of her first marriage as unhappy,
had hinted, with becoming reticence, that Haskett had wrought havoc
among her young illusions. . . . It was a pity for Waythorn's peace of
mind that Haskett's very inoffensiveness shed a new light on the nature
of those illusions. A man would rather think that his wife has been bru-
talized by her first husband than that the process has been reversed.

5. A very popular novel by Lew Wallace.

IV

"Mr. Waythorn, I don't like that French governess of Lily's."

Haskett, subdued and apologetic, stood before Waythorn in the library, revolving his shabby hat in his hand.

Waythorn, surprised in his armchair over the evening paper, stared back perplexedly at his visitor.

"You'll excuse my asking to see you," Haskett continued. "But this is my last visit, and I thought if I could have a word with you it would be a better way than writing to Mrs. Waythorn's lawyer."

Waythorn rose uneasily. He did not like the French governess either; but that was irrelevant.

"I am not so sure of that," he returned stiffly; "but since you wish it I will give your message to—my wife." He always hesitated over the possessive pronoun in addressing Haskett.

The latter sighed. "I don't know as that will help much. She didn't like it when I spoke to her."

Waythorn turned red. "When did you see her?" he asked.

"Not since the first day I came to see Lily—right after she was taken sick. I remarked to her then that I didn't like the governess."

Waythorn made no answer. He remembered distinctly that, after that first visit, he had asked his wife if she had seen Haskett. She had lied to him then, but she had respected his wishes since; and the incident cast a curious light on her character. He was sure she would not have seen Haskett that first day if she had divined that Waythorn would object, and the fact that she did not divine it was almost as disagreeable to the latter as the discovery that she had lied to him.

"I don't like the woman," Haskett was repeating with mild persistency. "She ain't straight, Mr. Waythorn—she'll teach the child to be underhand. I've noticed a change in Lily—she's too anxious to please —and she don't always tell the truth. She used to be the straightest child. Mr. Waythorn—" He broke off, his voice a little thick. "Not but what I want her to have a stylish education," he ended.

Waythorn was touched. "I'm sorry, Mr. Haskett; but frankly, I don't quite see what I can do."

Haskett hesitated. Then he laid his hat on the table, and advanced to the hearthrug, on which Waythorn was standing. There was nothing aggressive in his manner, but he had the solemnity of a timid man resolved on a decisive measure.

"There's just one thing you can do, Mr. Waythorn," he said. "You can remind Mrs. Waythorn that, by the decree of the courts, I am entitled to have a voice in Lily's bringing-up." He paused, and went on more deprecatingly: "I am not the kind to talk about enforcing my rights, Mr. Waythorn. I don't know as I think a man is entitled to rights he hasn't known how to hold on to; but this business of the child is different. I've never let go there—and I never mean to."

The scene left Waythorn deeply shaken. Shamefacedly, in indirect ways, he had been finding out about Haskett; and all that he had learned was favorable. The little man, in order to be near his daughter, had sold out his share in a profitable business in Utica, and accepted a modest clerkship in a New York manufacturing house. He boarded in a shabby street and had few acquaintances. His passion for Lily filled his life. Waythorn felt that this exploration of Haskett was like groping about with a dark lantern in his wife's past; but he saw now that there were recesses his lantern had not explored. He had never inquired into the exact circumstances of his wife's first matrimonial rupture. On the surface all had been fair. It was she who had obtained the divorce, and the court had given her the child. But Waythorn knew how many ambiguities such a verdict might cover. The mere fact that Haskett retained a right over his daughter implied an unsuspected compromise. Waythorn was an idealist. He always refused to recognize unpleasant contingencies till he found himself confronted with them, and then he saw them followed by a spectral train of consequences. His next days were thus haunted, and he determined to try to lay the ghosts by conjuring them up in his wife's presence.

When he repeated Haskett's request a flame of anger passed over her face; but she subdued it instantly and spoke with a slight quiver of outraged motherhood.

"It is very ungentlemanly of him," she said.

The word grated on Waythorn. "That is neither here nor there. It's a bare question of rights."

She murmured: "It's not as if he could ever be a help to Lily—"

Waythorn flushed. This was even less to his taste. "The question is," he repeated, "what authority has he over her?"

She looked downward, twisting herself a little in her seat. "I am willing to see him—I thought you objected," she faltered.

In a flash he understood that she knew the extent of Haskett's claims. Perhaps it was not the first time she had resisted them.

"My objecting has nothing to do with it," he said coldly; "if Haskett has a right to be consulted you must consult him."

She burst into tears, and he saw that she expected him to regard her as a victim.

Haskett did not abuse his rights. Waythorn had felt miserably sure that he would not. But the governess was dismissed, and from time to time the little man demanded an interview with Alice. After the first outburst she accepted the situation with her usual adaptability. Haskett had once reminded Waythorn of the piano tuner, and Mrs. Waythorn, after a month or two, appeared to class him with that domestic familiar. Waythorn could not but respect the father's tenacity. At first he had tried to cultivate the suspicion that Haskett might be "up to" something, that he had an object in securing a foothold in the house. But in his heart Waythorn was sure of Haskett's single-mindedness; he even guessed in the latter a mild contempt for such advantages as his relation with the Waythorns might offer. Haskett's sincerity of purpose made him invulnerable, and his successor had to accept him as a lien on the property.

Mr. Sellers was sent to Europe to recover from his gout, and Varick's affairs hung on Waythorn's hands. The negotiations were prolonged and complicated; they necessitated frequent conferences between the two men, and the interests of the firm forbade Waythorn's suggesting that his client should transfer his business to another office.

Varick appeared well in the transaction. In moments of relaxation his coarse streak appeared, and Waythorn dreaded his geniality; but in the office he was concise and clear-headed, with a flattering deference to Waythorn's judgment. Their business relations being so affably established, it would have been absurd for the two men to ignore each other in society. The first time they met in a drawing room, Varick took up their intercourse in the same easy key, and his hostess' grateful glance obliged Waythorn to respond to it. After that they ran across each other frequently, and one evening at a ball Waythorn, wandering through the remoter rooms, came upon Varick seated beside his wife. She colored a little, and faltered in what she was saying; but Varick nodded to Waythorn without rising, and the latter strolled on.

In the carriage, on the way home, he broke out nervously: "I didn't know you spoke to Varick."

Her voice trembled a little. "It's the first time—he happened to be standing near me; I didn't know what to do. It's so awkward, meeting everywhere—and he said you had been very kind about some business."

"That's different," said Waythorn.

She paused a moment. "I'll do just as you wish," she returned pliantly. "I thought it would be less awkward to speak to him when we meet."

Her pliancy was beginning to sicken him. Had she really no will of her own—no theory about her relation to these men? She had accepted Haskett—did she mean to accept Varick? It was "less awkward," as she had said, and her instinct was to evade difficulties or to circumvent them. With sudden vividness Waythorn saw how the instinct had developed. She was "as easy as an old shoe"—a shoe that too many feet had worn. Her elasticity was the result of tension in too many different directions. Alice Haskett—Alice Varick—Alice Waythorn—she had been each in turn, and had left hanging to each name a little of her privacy, a little of her personality, a little of the inmost self where the unknown god abides.

"Yes—it's better to speak to Varick," said Waythorn wearily.

V

The winter wore on, and society took advantage of the Waythorns' acceptance of Varick. Harassed hostesses were grateful to them for bridging over a social difficulty, and Mrs. Waythorn was held up as a miracle of good taste. Some experimental spirits could not resist the diversion of throwing Varick and his former wife together, and there were those who thought he found a zest in the propinquity. But Mrs. Waythorn's conduct remained irreproachable. She neither avoided Varick nor sought him out. Even Waythorn could not but admit that she had discovered the solution of the newest social problem.

He had married her without giving much thought to that problem. He had fancied that a woman can shed her past like a man. But now he saw that Alice was bound to hers both by the circumstances which forced her into continued relation with it, and by the traces it had left on her nature. With grim irony Waythorn compared himself to a member of a syndicate. He held so many shares in his wife's personality and his predecessors were his partners in the business. If there had been any element of passion in the transaction he would have felt less deteriorated by it. The fact that Alice took her change of husbands like a change of weather reduced the situation to mediocrity. He could have forgiven her for blunders, for excesses: for resisting Haskett, for yielding to Varick; for anything but her acquiescence and her tact. She reminded him of a juggler tossing knives; but the knives were blunt and she knew they would never cut her.

And then, gradually, habit formed a protecting surface for his sensibilities. If he paid for each day's comfort with the small change of his illusions, he grew daily to value the comfort more and set less store upon the coin. He had drifted into a dulling propinquity with Haskett and Varick and he took refuge in the cheap revenge of satirizing the situation. He even began to reckon up the advantages which accrued from it, to ask himself if it were not better to own a third of a wife who knew how to make a man happy than a whole one who had lacked opportunity to acquire the art. For it *was* an art, and made up, like all others, of concessions, eliminations and embellishments; of lights judiciously thrown and shadows skillfully softened. His wife knew exactly how to manage the lights, and he knew exactly to what training she owed her skill. He even tried to trace the source of his obligations, to discriminate between the influences which had combined to produce his domestic happiness: he perceived that Haskett's commonness had made Alice worship good breeding, while Varick's liberal construction of the marriage bond had taught her to value the conjugal virtues; so that he was directly indebted to his predecessors for the devotion which made his life easy if not inspiring.

From this phrase he passed into that of complete acceptance. He ceased to satirize himself because time dulled the irony of the situation and the joke lost its humor with its sting. Even the sight of Haskett's hat on the hall table had ceased to touch the springs of epigram. The hat was often seen there now, for it had been decided that it was better for Lily's father to visit her than for the little girl to go to his boardinghouse. Waythorn, having acquiesced in this arrangement, had been surprised to find how little difference it made. Haskett was never obtrusive, and the few visitors who met him on the stairs were unaware of his identity. Waythorn did not know how often he saw Alice, but with himself Haskett was seldom in contact.

One afternoon, however, he learned on entering that Lily's father was waiting to see him. In the library he found Haskett occupying a chair in his usual provisional way. Waythorn always felt grateful to him for not leaning back.

"I hope you'll excuse me, Mr. Waythorn," he said rising. "I wanted to see Mrs. Waythorn about Lily, and your man asked me to wait here till she came in."

"Of course," said Waythorn, remembering that a sudden leak had that morning given over the drawing room to the plumbers.

He opened his cigar case and held it out to his visitor, and Haskett's acceptance seemed to mark a fresh stage in their intercourse. The spring evening was chilly, and Waythorn invited his guest to draw up his chair to the fire. He meant to find an excuse to leave Haskett in a moment; but he was tired and cold, and after all the little man no longer jarred on him.

The two were enclosed in the intimacy of their blended cigar smoke when the door opened and Varick walked into the room. Waythorn rose abruptly. It was the first time that Varick had come to the house, and the surprise of seeing him, combined with the singular inopportuneness of his arrival, gave a new edge to Waythorn's blunted sensibilities. He stared at his visitor without speaking.

Varick seemed too preoccupied to notice his host's embarrassment.

"My dear fellow," he exclaimed in his most expansive tone, "I must apologize for tumbling in on you in this way, but I was too late to catch you downtown, and so I thought—"

He stopped short, catching sight of Haskett, and his sanguine color deepened to a flush which spread vividly under his scant blond hair. But in a moment he recovered himself and nodded slightly. Haskett returned the bow in silence, and Waythorn was still groping for speech when the footman came in carrying a tea table.

The intrusion offered a welcome vent to Waythorn's nerves. "What the deuce are you bringing this here for?" he said sharply.

"I beg your pardon, sir, but the plumbers are still in the drawing room, and Mrs. Waythorn said she would have tea in the library." The footman's perfectly respectful tone implied a reflection on Waythorn's reasonableness.

"Oh, very well," said the latter resignedly, and the footman proceeded to open the folding tea table and set out its complicated appointments. While this interminable process continued the three men stood motionless, watching it with a fascinated stare, till Waythorn, to break the silence, said to Varick, "Won't you have a cigar?"

He held out the case he had just tendered to Haskett, and Varick helped himself with a smile. Waythorn looked about for a match, and finding none, proffered a light from his own cigar. Haskett, in the background, held his ground mildly, examining his cigar tip now and then, and stepping forward at the right moment to knock its ashes into the fire.

The footman at last withdrew, and Varick immediately began: "If I could just say half a word to you about this business—"

"Certainly," stammered Waythorn; "in the dining room—"

But as he placed his hand on the door it opened from without, and his wife appeared on the threshold.

She came in fresh and smiling, in her street dress and hat, shedding a fragrance from the boa which she loosened in advancing.

"Shall we have tea in here, dear?" she began; and then she caught sight of Varick. Her smile deepened, veiling a slight tremor of surprise.

"Why, how do you do?" she said with a distinct note of pleasure.

As she shook hands with Varick she saw Haskett standing behind him. Her smile faded for a moment, but she recalled it quickly, with a scarcely perceptible side glance at Waythorn.

"How do you do, Mr. Haskett?" she said, and shook hands with him a shade less cordially.

The three men stood awkwardly before her, till Varick, always the most self-possessed, dashed into an explanatory phrase.

"We—I had to see Waythorn a moment on business," he stammered, brick-red from chin to nape.

Haskett stepped forward with his air of mild obstinacy. "I am sorry to intrude; but you appointed five o'clock—" he directed his resigned glance to the timepiece on the mantel.

She swept aside their embarrassment with a charming gesture of hospitality.

"I'm so sorry—I'm always late; but the afternoon was so lovely." She stood drawing off her gloves, propitiatory and graceful, diffusing about her a sense of ease and familiarity in which the situation lost its grotesqueness. "But before talking business," she added brightly, "I'm sure everyone wants a cup of tea."

She dropped into her low chair by the tea table, and the two visitors, as if drawn by her smile, advanced to receive the cups she held out.

She glanced about for Waythorn, and he took the third cup with a laugh.

MAY SINCLAIR
1863–1946

Through her generous literary patronage, May Sinclair helped defend and define early modernist efforts to break free of Victorian literary conventions. Not only did she protest the censorship of D. H. Lawrence's *The Rainbow*, she also was the first to use William James's phrase "stream of consciousness" to praise Dorothy Richardson's fictional technique in *Pilgrimage*. An early promoter of experimental poets like Ezra Pound and H. D. (Hilda Doolittle), Sinclair also helped Charlotte Mew publish her verse and defended T. S. Eliot's first book against detractors. In the twenty-four works she wrote between 1897 and 1927, moreover, Sinclair herself moved from realistic protests against Victorian constraints to psychological narratives that attempt to capture the inner growth of her characters' consciousness. In the best of these novels—*The Three Sisters* (1914), *Mary Olivier* (1919), and *Life and Death of Harriett Frean* (1920)—Sinclair focused on the efforts of women to escape the sexual repression and domestic confinement that clearly shaped her own early environment.

The youngest child and only girl in a family of five boys, Mary Amelia St. Clair Sinclair lived in an affluent suburb of Liverpool until the bankruptcy of her father's shipowning business caused the family to move in the 1870s to Ilford, Essex. Sinclair's semi-autobiographical novel *Mary Olivier* portrayed her father as an ineffectual alcoholic while her mother was presented as a dogmatic Christian determined to make her children conform to her puritanical will. Like her heroine, Sinclair assimilated her mother's passionate commitment to service, but rebelled against her narrow-minded social conformity. Like Mary Olivier, Sinclair educated herself in Greek, German philosophy, and English literature by reading her brothers' books, although she did spend one year at Cheltenham Ladies' College. Like Mary Olivier, too, Sinclair witnessed the deaths of her father and brothers, and devoted her life to her aging mother. Just as Mary Olivier was inspired by her reading of Walt Whitman to translate Euripides' *Bacchae* and to compose her own poetry, Sinclair supported her mother throughout the nineties by publishing translations, poetry, and her first novel, *Audrey Craven* (1897).

After her mother died in 1901, Sinclair went on to become a major intellectual presence in London. She worked with both the Women's Freedom League and the Women Writers' Suffrage League. When she returned to England from service in an ambulance unit in Belgium, she published *The Tree of Heaven* (1917), an exploration of feminism in the context of the Great War. Founder-member of the Medico-Psychological Clinic in London, Sinclair wrote essays on the work of Sigmund Freud and C. G. Jung before psychoanalysis was widely known. Throughout the early twenties, her London apartment and country cottage continued to serve as meeting places for artists like Pound, H. D., Robert Frost, Edith Wharton, and Ford Madox Ford. By this time, however, she was beginning to suffer from the neuromuscular deterioration that incapacitated her for more than a decade. Besides her novels and essays, Sinclair had produced two novellas and five volumes of short stories, as well as a biographical study of *The Three Brontës* (1912), in which she praised Charlotte Brontë's "new voice," which, she declared, uncovered everything "that proud, decorous mid-Victorian reticence most sedulously sought to hide." Not only in her novels but also in short stories like *The Bambino*, Sinclair contributed to the "subtler and more intimate psychology" that she believed Brontë had pioneered.

The Bambino[1]

No. That isn't mine. It's a thing of Frances Archdale's, her sister-in-law, Mrs. Jack Archdale. You know the man I mean. He buys pictures.

You think it's odd he didn't buy this one? Wait till you've heard the story.

I've seen her sitting like that, like a Flemish Madonna:[2] sloping knees, and the naked slip of the child standing between her hands; her hands half holding, half adoring. *He* must have seen her—and her hands. They're in the centre of the picture, large and white and important; as if Frances had known.

You'd have thought it wasn't possible to hate a woman so unfortunate as she was. She ought to have been immune. Yet I believe I'd have hated her even if she hadn't smashed that incomparable old Chinese bowl poor Lawrence left me. But no doubt that began it: the sight of the precious thing slipping through those large, awkward hands that were always in movement, always seizing and dropping things, the long fingers splaying; and her husky drawl: "I'm so sor-ry, Mr. Simp-son." She sent me a blue and white bowl from Liberty's[3] the next day, and seemed to think that, if anything, that left me in her debt.

On the whole she was let off easily, because, with all her multiplied misfortunes, she never faced the full implications of disaster. She was too complacent.

I remember the season when Jack Archdale brought her to town and we all raved about her, his slender Flemish Madonna, with her long, slender shoulders, her long, slender, skim-milk face, her long, slender nose that overhung her upper lip that overhung the lower one that overhung the soft round of her chin sloping away into her neck. And the thin gold rain of hair on her cheeks, loosened from the two sleek bands, untidily. There was something so helplessly yielding and retreating about that profile that you weren't prepared for her obstinacy, that obstinacy which——

1. Affectionate term for a small child, from Italian.
2. Painting of the Virgin Mary from the Flemish school, which flourished from the 14th to 17th centuries, and was noted for its realistic portrayals of everyday life.
3. A London department store.

Well, it was the helplessness that caught Jack Archdale.

The first time I saw her, at their house-warming, she was unfortunate, standing on a priceless Persian rug and pouring claret-cup[4] over it
from the glass she tilted, following Archdale with her pale, moony eyes.
Her name was Adela.

He adored her in a funny, abject way, sitting dumb (you couldn't talk
to Adela) and staring at her. When the baby came he adored the baby;
they both adored it, and they were both jealous of the adoration. You'd
come in and find them quarrelling about which was to hold it. He'd be
saying: "Give him to me. I want him." And she, with her queer drawl:
"You might let me have him, Jack. He's more mine than yours."

And he'd shout back at her: "He *isn't*." Not ragging,[5] you know, but
quite fierce and serious.

He talked about the Bambino half the time; he'd bring the conversation round to him from anywhere. I remember dining with them one
night before they left London. (They were always asking me because of
Frances.) He'd bought a picture of mine that year, and he thought it
funny to say: "Roly doesn't come to see *us*, he comes to see his old picture."

She sat there, stretching her white goose neck to get out her drawl.
"Aren't you aw-w-fly glad when pee-ple buy your pictures?"

He tried to head her off. "He isn't. He feels as I should if somebody
bought the Bambino."

And she went blundering on. "He knows it's safe with us. He knows
it's all in the family."

I said he didn't know anything of the sort. Frances had chucked me[6]
the week before, and I was still bitter about it and afraid of Adela because she had an unpleasant way of throwing Frances at me. (You
summed Adela up when you said she had no tact.) I could see Archdale
making signs to her, but she did it again with her lazy air of not being
able to help it.

"What are you going to do with yourself this winter?" The poor
woman couldn't see she hadn't changed the subject. She was like that.

In the smoke-room he worked round to *his* subject again. I'd asked
him how he liked his country house, and he said, "It'll be a jolly place
for the Bambino to grow up in. And to step into when I'm dead.

"It's all very well," he said. "He's delicious to kiss and all that, and
he'll never be prettier than he is now. But I wish one could skip fifteen
years or so. I want the Bambino grown up, *now*. I can't wait twenty
years to know what he's going to do, the sort of things he'll say, what his
mind'll be like. He's got no end of a mind, Roly, already. At thirteen
months. You wouldn't believe it.

---

4. A punch made of wine and fruit juice.   6. I.e., thrown me out.
5. Joking.

"Women are funny," he said. "Adela doesn't want him to grow up. She'd keep him a Bambino always if she had her way."

I can see him with that queer, ironic face of his, gripping his old briar pipe with his teeth while he smiled, thinking of the things the Bambino would do when he grew up.

It was four years before I got the rest of the story; and what I couldn't make out, what I couldn't even have tried to get from either of them, Frances told me.

I'd lost sight of them somehow all that time; then one day I met Jack Archdale at Frances', and he motored us both down to that place of theirs in Buckinghamshire. I can't say I enjoyed the run. Archdale was a sulky, nervous driver. He stopped dead to change his gear, and he took his corners badly. That wasn't like him; he used to be so cool and careful and efficient, and I remember wondering why on earth he was so jumpy and why he sulked so now. He didn't even rise when I asked after the blessed Bambino.

And we weren't in his house five minutes before he let us see that he'd grown a temper. He hadn't the ghost of one to start with; that I can swear to. I supposed it was the fruit of seven years' marriage with a goose-faced Madonna.

She hadn't changed, except that she seemed much more glad to see us than she used to be; so glad, in fact, that it struck me she was positively afraid to be left alone with Archdale and his temper.

I expected every minute that he'd say: "Where's the Bambino?" I said it myself at last, to create a diversion.

Adela seemed gratified, and went out to get him, and Archdale got up and stood by the window with his back to us, pretending to stare at things in his garden. Frances looked round at him uneasily, and I supposed then that he and Adela had quarrelled about the kiddy. It was what they would do. I began to long for the Bambino to appear and break the tension. I think I expected an excited, dramatic entry; I reminded myself that the Bambino was now five years old.

So I wasn't prepared to see Adela come back with a baby in her arms —a baby too young to display excitement, too young to talk. It could only make queer, immature noises.

I said: "What? A new Bambino? And you never told me!"

Adela was smiling stupidly, and Archdale kept his station by the window. The new baby looked as if it didn't see any of us. There was something odd, something morbid about its detachment, and I touched its soft magnolia cheek to feel if it were real.

"I can see it's new," I said, "but—isn't it awfully like the old Bambino?"

"It *is* the old Bambino. There isn't any other."

She put it to the ground. Then I saw.

She had got her way. The Bambino would be a baby all its life. Its mind had stopped dead at fifteen months.

Archdale turned, as if he had got up courage at last to stand with her and see her through. He had braced himself to look at the Bambino.

It couldn't walk; it sort of toddled, with a series of little headlong, shambling rushes, wagging its head till the heavy bulging forehead swung forward and upset its balance. It hadn't sense to grab at things and save itself.

When it fell Archdale rushed to it with a sudden gasping cry. He held it up in his arms, turning with it to Frances and me sternly, as if he defied us to see anything in it but its beauty.

Oh, yes, it was beautiful. It isn't true that idiots always have vacant faces. The Bambino's face was full, full of a heavy, sleeping mournfulness—mournfulness carved into the exquisite, morbid bow of his little mouth, into the straight pure line of his nose, and fixed in his black, drowsy eyes. But an unutterable, not human, mournfulness, without any reminiscence of foreboding. Animals—the unmoving sadness of a cat's eyes would be near it, only that has something human in it.

Adela began talking. "He *is* a little backward. But I tell Jack it's because his mind's too big for his body. He's going to be something wonderful. You've only got to look at his face to see he's thinking." She really thought that.

I believe even Jack thought then it wasn't quite hopeless. He had theories; tried experiments; took infinite precautions. He had the nurseries moved to the ground floor so that Adela shouldn't carry him up and down stairs, and a gate put at the bottom of the staircase so that he shouldn't crawl up and fall down it. The day nursery was hung with glittering balls, and glass prisms that shook in the sun and sent rainbow patches darting about the walls and ceiling. He thought if you could once catch the Bambino's attention you might draw his mind out of its hiding-place. They gave him yards and yards of paper ribbons, pink and green and blue, to play with. The Bambino had dark days when he sat on his big mackintosh[7] mattress like a porcelain idol, doing nothing but wag his head. And he had bright days when he seized the paper ribbons and tore them to bits. And days of surpassing brilliance when he shambled along the garden walks and tore down Jack's delphiniums and gladioli from their borders. His progress was marked by a trail of decaying blue and scarlet spears.

Frances told me how it happened. Yes, it was Adela; Adela's hands that couldn't hold things; Adela's obstinacy. He had told her not to carry the Bambino up and down stairs. So she did it. The hall stairs were very long and steep, very narrow at the turn. She was coming down

7. Waterproof.

them with the Bambino on one arm and the tail of her gown on the other. He caught sight of Archdale in the hall, and was struggling to get to him. . . .

Adela doesn't see the connection between that fall and his "backwardness." She doesn't see yet what's happening to Archdale. She doesn't see why they have separate rooms. Nor why he was terrified the other night when she came in with the big lamp in her hands flaring. He jumped up and took it from her, and she stood there splaying her hands and smiling, while he growled at her: "You—"

He didn't say it. It was the one word his mind shied at, the word you hoped he'd never have to hear. If you'll believe me, she positively shrieked it. "Really, Jack, anybody'd think I was an idiot!"

He looked at her, and Frances and I looked at each other. We'd both seen the same thing, only I didn't know what it was till Frances told me.

"He can't help it," she said. "He's afraid of everything. . . . She wants to have more babies, and he won't let her. He simply couldn't stand seeing her hold them."

I said it was rather cruel; and Frances said: "Oh yes, cruel. That's the awful thing, how it's changed him."

I suggested that it hadn't changed Adela, and she put it to me. Could I see anything changing Adela?

I couldn't. After all I was sorrier for him, and I said so. I knew Frances didn't like Adela.

But she shook her head, and said: "I'm not sure. He knows the worst, and she doesn't. It'll be awful when she sees it. She can't go on pretending when the Bambino. . . . Besides, she may have to see what you've seen."

"And that is—?"

She stuck it straight in front of me. "Why, that he hates her."

I suppose that's what I saw.

I wish Frances would take the damned thing away. But she's afraid of it. She's got in too much: the sweet, milk-white, fatuous beauty. And the hands, the terrible, imbecile hands; the insecurity.

1930

CHARLOTTE MEW
1870–1928

When Charlotte Mew died in 1928, she was so obscure that one newspaper report of her death described her as "Charlotte New [sic], said to be a writer." Yet in her earlier years Mew had been a well-known literary woman whose works were admired by a number of contemporaries, including such notable artists as John Masefield, Walter de la Mare, and Thomas Hardy. Even during her lifetime, however, Mew was a paradoxical figure. The author of vividly detailed dramatic monologues that were surprising in their era for their frank depictions of both female and male sexuality, she was extraordinarily rigorous in maintaining her own moral standards and would, as one scholar explains, "drop anyone whom scandal had touched." Raised by genteel parents as a typical Victorian lady, she was, according to her friend Alida Monroe, "passionately attached to another woman," and she became virtually a transvestite in middle age, dressing in a tweed topcoat, a pork pie hat, and "size-two custom-made boots."

Mew was born in London, one of four children in a comfortable middle-class family. But the pleasures of her youth were short-lived: the two younger Mew children became mentally ill and were confined to asylums, while her father's death, when she was in her late twenties, left Charlotte, her sister, and her mother nearly impoverished, for, she later recollected, he had "spent all his available capital on living." To support themselves and their mother, Charlotte and her sister attempted various odd jobs; most notably, Charlotte wrote stories and poems for journals like *The Egoist, The English Woman,* and *The Yellow Book.* But despite a modicum of literary success, she always had to economize and never recaptured the gaiety of her childhood home.

Mew's most important verses appeared in a 1916 collection, *The Farmer's Bride,* whose title poem is still much anthologized. In this monologue, as in the equally powerful *The Quiet House,* she demonstrates the vitality and inventiveness that must have especially appealed to a fellow dramatic poet like Thomas Hardy. At the same time, though, both pieces suggest the intensity with which she herself may have secretly rebelled against the veneer of docility she had been taught to cultivate. When the speaker of *The Quiet House* exclaims, "I think that my soul is red / Like the soul of a sword or a scarlet flower," one feels that she may be expressing Mew's own sexual and emotional frustrations. Similarly, when the same speaker wistfully and wishfully looks forward to the day when "I *shall* not think; I shall not *be*," one fears that her nihilistic desire predicts the day when Mew herself, alone and impoverished, put an end to her conflicted life by drinking a bottle of Lysol.

The Farmer's Bride

Three Summers since I chose a maid,
Too young maybe—but more's to do
At harvest-time than bide and woo.
    When us was wed she turned afraid
Of love and me and all things human;   5
Like the shut of a winter's day
Her smile went out, and 'twadn't a woman—
    More like a little frightened fay.
    One night, in the Fall, she runned away.

"Out 'mong the sheep, her be," they said,   10
Should properly have been abed;
But sure enough she wadn't there
Lying awake with her wide brown stare.
So over seven-acre field and up-along across the down[1]
We chased her, flying like a hare   15
Before our lanterns. To Church-Town
    All in a shiver and a scare
We caught her, fetched her home at last
    And turned the key upon her, fast.

She does the work about the house
As well as most, but like a mouse: 20
    Happy enough to chat and play
    With birds and rabbits and such as they,
    So long as men-folk keep away.

"Not near, not near!" her eyes beseech   25
When one of us comes within reach.
    The women say that beasts in stall
    Look round like children at her call.
    I've hardly heard her speak at all.

Shy as a leveret,[2] swift as he,   30
Straight and slight as a young larch tree,
Sweet as the first wild violets, she,
To her wild self. But what to me?

The short days shorten and the oaks are brown,
    The blue smoke rises to the low grey sky,   35
One leaf in the still air falls slowly down,
    A magpie's spotted feathers lie
On the black earth spread white with rime,
The berries redden up to Christmas-time.
    What's Christmas-time without there be   40
    Some other in the house than we!

    She sleeps up in the attic there
    Alone, poor maid. 'Tis but a stair
Betwixt us. Oh! my God! the down,
The soft young down of her, the brown,   45
The brown of her—her eyes, her hair, her hair!

1916

---

1. Meadow used for grazing.   2. A young hare.

The Quiet House

When we were children old Nurse used to say,
   The house was like an auction or a fair
Until the lot of us were safe in bed.
   It has been quiet as the country-side
   Since Ted and Janey and then Mother died   5
And Tom crossed³ Father and was sent away.
After the lawsuit he could not hold up his head,
    Poor Father, and he does not care
    For people here, or to go anywhere.

To get away to Aunt's for that week-end   10
    Was hard enough; (since then, a year ago,
    He scarcely lets me slip out of his sight—)
At first I did not like my cousin's friend,
    I did not think I should remember him:
    His voice has gone, his face is growing dim   15
And if I like him now I do not know.
    He frightened me before he smiled—
    He did not ask me if he might—
    He said that he would come one Sunday night,
    He spoke to me as if I were a child.   20

No year has been like this that has just gone by;
    It may be that what Father says is true,
If things are so it does not matter why:
    But everything has burned, and not quite through.
    The colours of the world have turned   25
    To flame, the blue, the gold has burned
In what used to be such a leaden sky.
When you are burned quite through you die.

    Red is the strangest pain to bear;
In Spring the leaves on the budding trees;   30
In Summer the roses are worse than these,
    More terrible than they are sweet:
    A rose can stab you across the street
      Deeper than any knife:
    And the crimson haunts you everywhere—   35
Thin shafts of sunlight, like the ghosts of reddened swords
      have struck our stair
As if, coming down, you had spilt your life.

    I think that my soul is red
Like the soul of a sword or a scarlet flower:

---

3. Disobeyed.

But when these are dead
    They have had their hour.   40

I shall have had mine, too,
    For from head to feet
I am burned and stabbed half through,
    And the pain is deadly sweet.   45

The things that kill us seem
    Blind to the death they give:
It is only in our dream
    The things that kill us live.

The room is shut where Mother died,   50
    The other rooms are as they were,
The world goes on the same outside,
    The sparrows fly across the Square,
The children play as we four did there,
    The trees grow green and brown and bare,   55
The sun shines on the dead Church spire,
    And nothing lives here but the fire.
While Father watches from his chair
        Day follows day
The same, now and then a different grey,   60
    Till, like his hair,
Which Mother said was wavy once and bright,
    They will all turn white.

    To-night I heard a bell again—
Outside it was the same mist of fine rain,   65
The lamps just lighted down the long, dim street,
        No one for me—
    I think it is myself I go to meet:
I do not care; some day I *shall* not think; I shall not be.

1916

HENRY HANDEL RICHARDSON
1870–1946

H. H. Richardson left Australia at the age of seventeen, returning only once in 1912 for "a flying six-weeks' visit." Yet she has been claimed as one of Australia's most important novelists. Her trilogy, *The Fortunes of Richard Mahony* (1917, 1925, 1929), describes the psychological impact of colonialism on a character based upon her father: a Dublin-born physician, he reestablished his practice in a series of provincial Australian towns, but he eventually lost his sanity. Her mother, who supported the family as postmistress in Koroit, is sympathetically presented as resourcefully practical in *The Getting of Wisdom* (1910). This satiric novel provides a fictional portrait of the author as she moved at the age of twelve from her home to the Presbyterian Ladies' College in Melbourne. Richardson's surrogate, Laura Ramsbotham, is a rebellious, imaginative adolescent who is unable—no matter how she tries—to conform to the mindless proprieties of the school or to stifle her artistic creativity.

Laura's musical accomplishments reflect Richardson's training as a concert pianist in Leipzig in 1887. There she met and married J. G. Robertson, who subsequently became a professor of German languages at the University of London. Two works—*Maurice Guest* (1908) and *The Young Cosima* (1939) —deal directly with the development of musical genius, a subject of central importance to a literary artist who took "Handel" as her middle name.

After the death of her husband, Richardson survived the bombings of Sussex during World War II, but she did not live to complete her autobiography, *Myself When Young* (1948). *Two Hanged Women* portrays with economy the same competition between heterosexuality and female bonding that *The Getting of Wisdom* traces in its divided heroine.

Two Hanged Women

Hand in hand the youthful lovers sauntered along the esplanade. It was a night in midsummer; a wispy moon had set, and the stars glittered. The dark mass of the sea, at flood, lay tranquil, slothfully lapping the shingle.[1]

"Come on, let's make for the usual," said the boy.

But on nearing their favourite seat they found it occupied. In the velvety shade of the overhanging sea-wall, the outlines of two figures were visible.

"Oh, blast!" said the lad. "That's torn it. What now, Baby?"

"Why, let's stop here, Pincher, right close up, till we frighten 'em off."

And very soon loud, smacking kisses, amatory pinches and ticklings, and skittish squeals of pleasure did their work. Silently the intruders rose and moved away.

But the boy stood gaping after them, open-mouthed.

"Well, I'm *damned*! If it wasn't just two hanged[2] women!"

Retreating before a salvo of derisive laughter, the elder of the girls said: "We'll go out on the breakwater."[3] She was tall and thin, and walked with a long stride.

---

1. Beach gravel.
2. A British slang word, used as an intensifier.

3. Barrier protecting the shore from strong waves.

Her companion, shorter than she by a bobbed head of straight flaxen hair, was hard put to it to keep pace. As she pegged along she said doubtfully, as if in self-excuse: "Though I really ought to go home. It's getting late. Mother will be angry."

They walked with finger-tips lightly in contact; and at her words she felt what was like an attempt to get free, on the part of the fingers crooked in hers. But she was prepared for this, and held fast, gradually working her own up till she had a good half of the other hand in her grip.

For a moment neither spoke. Then, in a low, muffled voice, came the question: "Was she angry last night, too?"

The little fair girl's reply had an unlooked-for vehemence. "You know she wasn't!" And, mildly despairing: "But you never *will* understand. Oh, what's the good of . . . of anything!"

And on sitting down she let the prisoned hand go, even putting it from her with a kind of push. There it lay, palm upwards, the fingers still curved from her hold, looking like a thing with a separate life of its own; but a life that was ebbing.

On this remote seat, with their backs turned on lovers, lights, the town, the two girls sat and gazed wordlessly at the dark sea, over which great Jupiter was flinging a thin gold line. There was no sound but the lapping, sucking, sighing, of the ripples at the edge of the breakwater, and the occasional screech of an owl in the tall trees on the hillside.

But after a time, having stolen more than one side glance at her companion, the younger seemed to take heart of grace. With a childish toss of the head that set her loose hair swaying, she said, in a tone of meaning emphasis: "I like Fred."

The only answer was a faint, contemptuous shrug.

"I tell you I *like* him!"

"Fred? Rats!"

"No it isn't . . . that's just where you're wrong, Betty. But you think you're so wise. Always."

"I know what I know."

"Or imagine you do! But it doesn't matter. Nothing you can say makes any difference. I like him and always shall. In heaps of ways. He's so big and strong, for one thing: it gives you such a safe sort of feeling to be with him . . . as if nothing could happen while you were. Yes, it's . . . it's . . . well, I can't help it, Betty, there's something *comfy* in having a boy to go about with—like other girls do. One they'd eat their hats to get, too! I can see it in their eyes when we pass; Fred with his great long legs and broad shoulders—I don't nearly come up to them—and his blue eyes with the black lashes, and his shiny black hair. And I like his tweeds, the Harris[4] smell of them, and his dirty old pipe, and the way he

4. Popular type of tweed clothing made of cloth woven on an island in the Hebrides.

shows his teeth—he's got *topping* teeth—when he laughs and says 'ra-*ther!*' And other people, when they see us, look . . . well I don't quite know how to say it, but they look sort of pleased; and they make room for us and let us into the dark corner-seats at the pictures, just as if we'd a right to them. And they never laugh. (Oh, I can't *stick*[5] being laughed at!—and that's the truth.) Yes, it's so comfy, Betty darling . . . such a warm cosy comfy feeling. Oh, *won't* you understand?"

"Gawd! why not make a song of it?" But a moment later, very fiercely: "And who is it's taught you to think all this? Who's hinted it and suggested it till you've come to believe it? . . . believe it's what you really feel."

"She hasn't! Mother's never said a word . . . about Fred."

"Words?—why waste words? . . . when she can do it with a cock of the eye. For your Fred, that!" and the girl called Betty held her fingers aloft and snapped them viciously. "But your mother's a different propo-sition."

"I think you're simply horrid."

To this there was no reply.

"*Why* have you such a down on her? What's she ever done to you? . . . except not get ratty when I stay out late with Fred. And I don't see how you can expect . . . being what she is . . . and with nobody but me—after all she *is* my mother . . . you can't alter that. I know very well—and you know, too—I'm not *too* putrid-looking. But"—beseechingly—"I'm *nearly* twenty-five now, Betty. And other girls . . . well, she sees them, every one of them, with a boy of their own, even though they're ugly, or fat, or have legs like sausages—they've only got to ogle them a bit—the girls, I mean . . . and there they are. And Fred's a good sort—he is, really!—and he dances well, and doesn't drink, and so . . . so why *shouldn't* I like him? . . . and off my own bat . . . without it having to be all Mother's fault, and me nothing but a parrot, and without any will of my own?"

"Why? Because I know her too well, my child! I can read her as you'd never dare to . . . even if you could. She's sly, your mother is, so sly there's no coming to grips with her . . . one might as well try to fill one's hand with cobwebs. But she's got a hold on you, a stranglehold, that nothing'll loosen. Oh! mothers aren't fair—I mean it's not fair of nature to weigh us down with them and yet expect us to be our own true selves. The handicap's too great. All those months, when the same blood's running through two sets of veins—there's no getting away from that, ever after. Take yours. As I say, does she need to open her mouth? Not she! She's only got to let it hang at the corners, and you reek, you drip with guilt."

5. Bear.

Something in these words seemed to sting the younger girl. She hit back. "I know what it is, you're jealous, that's what you are! . . . and you've no other way of letting it out. But I tell you this. If ever I marry —yes, *marry!*—it'll be to please myself, and nobody else. Can you imagine me doing it to oblige her?"

Again silence.

"If I only think what it would be like to be fixed up and settled, and able to live in peace, without this eternal dragging two ways . . . just as if I was being torn in half. And see Mother smiling and happy again, like she used to be. Between the two of you I'm nothing but a punch-ball. Oh, I'm fed up with it! . . . fed up to the neck. As for you . . . And yet you can sit there as if you were made of stone! Why don't you *say* something? *Betty!* Why won't you speak?"

But no words came.

"I can *feel* you sneering. And when you sneer I hate you more than any one on earth. If only I'd never seen you!"

"Marry your Fred, and you'll never need to again."

"I will, too! I'll marry him, and have a proper wedding like other girls, with a veil and bridesmaids and bushels of flowers. And I'll live in a house of my own, where I can do as I like, and be left in peace, and there'll be no one to badger and bully me—Fred wouldn't . . . ever! Besides, he'll be away all day. And when he came back at night, he'd . . . I'd . . . I mean I'd—" But here the flying words gave out; there came a stormy breath and a cry of: "Oh, Betty, Betty! . . . I couldn't, no, I couldn't! It's when I think of *that* . . . Yes, it's quite true! I like him all right, I do indeed, but only as long as he doesn't come too near. If he even sits too close, I have to screw myself up to bear it"—and flinging herself down over her companion's lap, she hid her face. "And if he tries to touch me, Betty, or even takes my arm or puts his round me . . . And then his face . . . when it looks like it does sometimes . . . all wrong . . . as if it had gone all wrong—oh! then I feel I shall have to scream— out loud. I'm afraid of him . . . when he looks like that. Once . . . when he kissed me . . . I could have died with the horror of it. His breath . . . his breath . . . and his mouth—like fruit pulp—and the black hairs on his wrists . . . and the way he looked—and . . . and everything! No, I can't, I can't . . . nothing will make me . . . I'd rather die twice over. But what am I to do? Mother'll *never* understand. Oh, why has it got to be like this? I want to be happy, like other girls, and to make her happy, too . . . and everything's all wrong. You tell me, Betty darling, you help me, you're older . . . you *know* . . . and you can help me, if you will . . . if you only will!" And locking her arms round her friend she drove her face deeper into the warmth and darkness, as if, from the very fervour of her clasp, she could draw the aid and strength she needed.

Betty had sat silent, unyielding, her sole movement being to loosen her own arms from her sides and point her elbows outwards, to hinder them touching the arms that lay round her. But at this last appeal she melted; and gathering the young girl to her breast, she held her fast.— And so for long she continued to sit, her chin resting lightly on the fair hair, that was silky and downy as an infant's, and gazing with sombre eyes over the stealthily heaving sea.

1934

Modernist Literature

In *Everybody's Autobiography* (1937), the experimental writer Gertrude Stein remembered a conversation with the mystery novelist Dashiell Hammett. "In the nineteenth century men were confident, the women were not," she reports Hammett as having observed, "but in the twentieth century the men have no confidence." Hammett's comment summarizes a major change in social dynamics that characterized the life and literature of almost all English-speaking countries in the era (roughly between 1914 and 1939) which is usually called the "modernist" period. Many literary men experienced this quarter century as what W. H. Auden was to call an "Age of Anxiety," while many of their female counterparts experienced the time—to be sure, with important qualifications—as an era of exuberance. One reason for such strikingly different reactions was the increase in female power which marked the new culture of the twentieth century. In the second two decades of the century, women on both sides of the Atlantic not only achieved the vote after a seventy-five-year struggle, they also entered all the professions in ever greater numbers. "The modern young man," wrote the British novelist D. H. Lawrence in an essay entitled *Matriarchy* (1929), talks "rather feebly about man being master again. He knows perfectly well that he will never be master again."

Between the years 1914 and 1939 there were, of course, many reasons, besides the altered position of women, for both sexes, but especially men, to feel anxious about the rapidly changing world in which they lived. The phenomenon that has been called the "shock of the new" was profoundly disturbing to people who had been born and brought up in what now seemed comparatively serene late-Victorian times, for "the new" in this period included a scientific revolution that virtually transformed the physical and social landscapes of England and America while producing a technology of destruction that shaped World War I, the deadliest war yet fought in Europe. In addition, because "the new" in these years also implied a complete disruption of the few traditional ideas about God and human nature that had emerged intact from the onslaughts of nineteenth-century skepticism, it was responsible for a widespread sense of intellectual doubt and social alienation. Finally, because the scientific revolution that shocked early-twentieth-century culture also meant the development of mass-communications systems on a startling scale, it greatly intensified the rift between so-called high culture and so-called low culture, leading to what seemed an unbridgeable gulf between serious artists and popular, commercial artists. Not surprisingly, a number of literary figures responded with some trepidation to all these changes. But because women had never perceived themselves as the chosen heirs of a stable and orderly culture, it was especially male thinkers who felt themselves to be living in unprecedentedly threatening times. Assaulted in the public sphere by the machinery of a new age, and haunted in the private sphere by women who would no longer agree to stay in their traditional places, a number of men saw themselves as increasingly marginal and powerless.

BEGINNINGS OF THE "MODERN" WORLD

The Georgian Afternoon

Despite the drastic cultural transformations that would soon become obvious to many observers, the modernist period began, at least in England, with what is often described (referring to the accession to the throne in 1910 of King George V) as a long "Georgian" afternoon, a kind of extension of the Victorian era in which large social changes were by and large disguised by smug and apparently secure continuations of traditional modes and manners. Thus, while experimental painters, poets, and musicians wrote manifestos, mounted art shows, and performed concerts that clamored for attention in Paris, London, and New York, much business—in the provinces and even, to some extent, in the cities—went on as usual.

Between 1910 and 1918, for instance, the American novelists Edith Wharton and Henry James as well as the more radical English writer Virginia Woolf recorded the doings of an upper-class pre–World War I society that continued to be concerned with conventional tea-parties and elegant libraries, while the American novelist Willa Cather, the British novelists Arnold Bennett and D. H. Lawrence, and the Irish novelists George Moore and James Joyce portrayed middle- and lower-class figures whose motivations were no less monetary than were those of characters in middle- and late-nineteenth-century works by Dickens, Hardy, and Dreiser. Finally, in England the editor Edward Marsh's *Georgian Anthologies* (1912, 1915, 1917, 1919, 1922) offered the public verses by such poets as John Masefield and Walter de la Mare, verses which generally celebrated bucolic landscapes or recounted romantic stories.

The New Technology

Nevertheless, even while the long Georgian "afternoon" seemed to suggest that old customs could still be preserved, the swift growth of a new technology, a long-term consequence of the Industrial Revolution, was eroding traditional ways of life. The first decade of the century had seen the invention of radio, the introduction of theaters called nickelodeons for the showing of moving pictures, the development of a viable airplane, and the production (by Henry Ford) of an inexpensive automobile which could be manufactured on what was for the first time called an "assembly line." Along with such late-nineteenth-century innovations as the phonograph, the typewriter, the telephone, and the telegraph, these new devices were to have far-reaching effects on travel, business, and communication.

To begin with, a number of artists on both sides of the Atlantic hailed the industrial inventiveness of the age in much the way that their nineteenth-century predecessors had welcomed the powers promised by, in William Wordsworth's phrase, "Steamboats, Viaducts, and Railways." It is perhaps not surprising that the best-selling British writer Rudyard Kipling, often considered an apologist for the ambitions of the Empire, should have exulted in the glamour of modern railroads ("Romance brings up the 9:15") nor is it surprising that a wealthy novelist like Edith Wharton should have been the devoted owner of an expensive motorcar, but the early reactions to technology of a range of passionately revolutionary artists are rather more unexpected. In the June 1914 issue of the short-lived little magazine *Blast*, for instance, such rebels against the old order as the British painter-writer Wyndham Lewis and the American poet Ezra Pound signed a series of manifestos declaring that "machinery is the greatest Earth-medium." Within a decade or two, their enthusiasm would be seconded by the American poets William Carlos Williams, whose *Overture to a Dance of Locomotives* (1921) portrayed the exuberance of train travel from a perspective remarkably similar to Kipling's, and Hart Crane, whose *The Bridge* (1930) characterized the engineering marvel of the Brooklyn Bridge as a "harp and altar" of the future. As late as 1945, moreover, the iconoclastic Gertrude Stein exuberantly proclaimed that "America began to live in the twentieth century in the [eighteen] eighties with the Ford car."

Even while many writers were eulogizing modern technology as the harbinger of a transfigured world, though, others were beginning to examine its darker implications; indeed, some of those who had originally been most optimistic were eventually to express skepticism. If mass communications like radio and film turned people into mere disembodied voices or images, these thinkers argued, mass manufacturing methods like the assembly line made individuals into interchangeable parts or robots. In addition, they claimed that the capitalist system which had fostered such developments severely widened the gap between what the Victorian writer Thomas Carlyle had called the "captains of industry" and the working classes whose labor served their needs. Thus, from the teens of the century on, critiques of the effects of technology and the intentions of industrial capitalism quickened in pace, focusing both on the psychology of the economic "masters" whose business triumphs were remaking society and the sociology of the alienated masses whose lives were being remade. In *The Financier* (1912), *The Titan* (1914), and *The Stoic* (not published until 1947), for instance, three novels which he called his *Trilogy of Desire*, Theodore Dreiser examined the power of what one critic has called "the businessman as buccaneer." At around the same time, the English novelist-poet D. H. Lawrence was composing a series of books which studied not only the lives of coal miners and factory workers in the industrial Midlands but also the minds of the magnates who shaped their fates. In particular, *Sons and Lovers* (1912), *Women in Love* (1921), and *Lady Chatterley's Lover* (1918) analyzed the deadened and deadening consciousness of the modern "captain of industry" while vividly dramatizing the "soulless ugliness of the coal-and-iron Midlands . . . the cruelty of iron and the smoke of coal, and the endless, endless greed that drove it all."

Even more extravagant than the hostile critiques of novelists were the attacks of poets on the alienated world produced by modern technology. Though T. S. Eliot's despairing depiction of contemporary culture is not simply confined to a portrayal of the effects of mercantile industrialism, his *The Waste Land* (1922) includes perhaps the most famous scenes of alienation that were created in this period, notably its almost hallucinatory vision of a zombie-like mass of urban pedestrians ("A crowd flowed over London Bridge, so many / I had not thought death had undone so many"). Similarly, Eliot's friend and mentor Ezra Pound, who had originally joined Wyndham Lewis in welcoming the new age of the machine, soon saw the negative implications of an era of mechanization. "The 'age demanded' chiefly a mould in plaster," he noted in his sardonic *Hugh Selwyn Mauberly* (1920), "Made with no loss of time, / A prose kinema [cinema], not, not assuredly, alabaster / Or the 'sculpture' of rhyme." Later, in his radically experimental long poem called the *Cantos* (published serially between 1925 and 1959), Pound would go on to attack the foundations of the economic system, which he identified as "Usura" (usury), that had fostered such vulgarity.

Verse attacks like those by Eliot and Pound were both anticipated and echoed by a number of other poets. As if predicting Eliot's *Waste Land* vision of a deadened London crowd, the American poet Carl Sandburg wrote in a 1916 poem called *Halsted Street Car* of the blank faces—"Tired of wishes, / Empty of dreams"—of working-class passengers on a Chicago trolley, and in a 1920 verse entitled *Manual System* he described the workday of a telephone operator: "Mary has a thingamajig clamped on her ears / And sits all day taking plugs out and sticking plugs in," while in his brief *Modern Prayer*, D. H. Lawrence summarized the culture of greedy materialism that had fostered such alienation:

> Almighty Mammon, make me rich!
> Make me rich quickly, with never a hitch
> in my fine prosperity! Kick those in the ditch
> who hinder me, Mammon, great son of a bitch!

Finally, beginning in 1930, such English poets as W. H. Auden, Stephen Spender, and Louis MacNeice produced a rich range of work based on the apocalyptic assumption that modern technology might virtually self-destruct. Though Auden, for instance, had begged in one early poem for "new styles of architecture, a change of heart," he and his contemporaries soon saw the "new" technology as wholly pernicious.

What particularly fostered the disillusionment of the Auden group was the economic depression that had struck both England and America at around the time these writers were beginning their literary careers, a trans-Atlantic calamity that had been precipitated, especially in America, by the perilous practice of buying stocks "on margin" (for a fraction of their real price) and that resulted in the great New York stock market crash of 1929. Though both the British and American governments struggled to counteract the effects of the "crash"— which included breadlines, soup kitchens, and "tent cities" of the unemployed —by instituting new social welfare programs (in America known as Franklin Delano Roosevelt's 1933 "New Deal"), the Great Depression persisted in both countries throughout the thirties, and it is clearly reflected in the works of Auden, Spender, and others, who vividly depicted a ruined and ruinous industrial landscape—in Auden's words, "Smokeless chimneys, damaged bridges, rotting wharves and choked canals." At the same time, adopting a Marxist belief in the inevitability of a revolution that would replace industrial capitalism with a new order, these writers predicted the end of the "businessman as buccaneer." Auden's warning to captains of industry in *Consider This and in Our Time* (1930) was marked by a grimly prophetic exhilaration that permeated the verse of many of his contemporaries both in England and America: "Financier, leaving your little room / Where the money is made but not spent, / You'll need your typist and your boy no more; / The game is up for you and for the others."

World War I

In a sense, a technological "apocalypse"—a seeming end to the known world —*had* already occurred in Europe, for World War I, defined by leaders as "the war to end all wars" but experienced by participants as an unprecedented triumph of death-dealing military technology, functioned in these years as an extraordinary historical turning point. The critic Paul Fussell has shown that many of the young men who went to the front during World War I were imbued with almost chivalric ideals of heroism, ideals that were rapidly destroyed by the horror of the conflict, only to be replaced by the kind of pervasive irony that Ezra Pound expressed in his *Hugh Selwyn Mauberley*: "There died a myriad, / And of the best, among them, / For an old bitch gone in the teeth, / For a botched civilization." But even in the minds of those who might have thought culture still deserved defense, the new technological realities of trenches and poison gas, land mines and machine guns—devices of destruction that had been expressly invented for this "Great War" and that led to a higher fatality rate than has ever been seen in any war before or since—subverted idealism.

As the historian Eric Leed has observed, the practice of digging trenches in order to hold established positions left foot-soldiers with the feeling that they were living in a realm of pollution. Buried beneath the soil, assaulted by the continuous rumble of big guns, threatened by mines from below and poison gas from above, these young men experienced themselves as helpless rather than heroic, and they saw the apparently empty landscape of the battlefield—a landscape that was really "saturated" with enemies who were enclosed in trenches of their own—as nightmarishly threatening, even uncanny. Moreover, because, as the war veteran and poet Robert Graves reported, "the average life expectancy of an infantry subaltern [lieutenant] on the western front was, at some stages of the war, only about three months," the despairing anxiety of such combatants was more than justified.

Many responded with a form of nervous breakdown called "shell shock." Others became permanently embittered and alienated. Some blamed civilians, often—like the English poet Siegfried Sassoon in his *Glory of Women* (1918)—reproaching women because "you love us when we're heroes, home on leave. . . . You worship decorations. . . . You make us shells." Some—like the English poet Wilfred Owen (who was killed at the front in 1918)—held not only women civilians but "fathers" responsible for the conflict, arguing, as Owen did in his *Dulce et Decorum Est* (1920), that "if . . . you [could see] the white eyes writhing in [the] face" of a victim of poison gas, "you would not tell with such high zest / To children ardent for some desperate glory, / The old Lie: Dulce et decorum est / Pro patria mori" (It is sweet and proper to die for one's country).

As the comments of noncombatants like Pound reveal, moreover, even civilians were profoundly affected by the enormity of the catastrophe. In England, figures as diverse as the poet-suffragist Alice Meynell and the colonial apologist Rudyard Kipling shared Owen's belief that "fathers"—meaning an avaricious male ruling class—were responsible for the disaster. In A *Father of Women* (1917), Meynell reproached the "million living fathers of the war," while in *Common Form*, one of his *Epitaphs of the War* (1914–1918), Kipling—whose son was killed early in the war—imagined a dead soldier saying, "If any question why we died, / Tell them, because our fathers lied." Though the United States did not enter the war until 1917—and only, then, after considerable national debate about the issue—a number of American writers expressed equal revulsion toward the conflict, with pacifists like the activist-feminist writers Charlotte Perkins Gilman and Crystal Eastman holding a patriarchal system accountable for its horrors in much the way that Meynell had.

Not surprisingly, much of the most intensely disillusioned World War I literature was written not during but after the war. Works like Ernest Hemingway's *The Sun Also Rises* (1926), a portrait of an artist made impotent by a war wound, as well as Lawrence's *Lady Chatterley's Lover* and Virginia Woolf's *Mrs. Dalloway* (1925), a portrait of a society lady shadowed by a portrait of a young man made mad by the war, suggest the many ways in which this apocalyptic European conflict had deadened or sickened both participants and onlookers. For many thinkers, moreover, such alienation widened into a deeper sense of cultural fragmentation. Before the war, the Viennese psychoanalyst Sigmund Freud (1856–1939) wrote in 1915, "he who was not by stress of circumstances confined to one spot, could also confer upon himself . . . a new, a wider fatherland, wherein he moved unhindered and unsuspected," but after the war, he noted, "that civilized cosmopolitan . . . stand[s] helpless in a world grown strange to him—his all-embracing patrimony disintegrated, the common estates in it laid waste, the fellow-citizens embroiled and debased!"

Intellectual Anxiety

Interestingly, Freud's own theories about the human psyche, as well as the ideas of such fellow analysts as Alfred Adler (1870–1937) and the speculations of such contemporary scientists as Albert Einstein (1879–1955), had dramatically contributed to just the alienation that Freud thought had been fostered by the war. Though Freud's and Einstein's radically disruptive scientific theories were formulated early in the twentieth century, they were to have their most powerful impact in the decades between 1910 and 1940, and we are still feeling their effects today. Specifically, Freud's concept of psychoanalysis, first definitively set out in his *The Interpretation of Dreams* (1900) and then elaborated in a series of studies that were published through the 1930s, implied that what the human mind experiences as "knowable" is not necessarily all that there is of the mind: the self, argued Freud, is constituted not only by the conscious personality ("the ego") but also by such warring forces as the desirous unconscious ("the id") and the moralistic, socially learned "upper"-conscious ("the superego").

More problematic still, this complex and layered self is, in Freud's view, constructed out of an interaction between the urgently voracious, primitive in-

fant and the adult world, represented by the parents, whose repressive or seductive actions inexorably shape the child's development. Somewhat in the way
that Charles Darwin's account of human evolution from animal forms (in *The
Origin of Species*, 1859) had seemed to destroy the concept of human singularity, Freud's vision of an essentially amoral secret self, together with his insistence that that self was helplessly conditioned by external forces, seemed to
subvert traditional beliefs in free will and morality, and this subversion was intensified by the claims of such other thinkers as Freud's former colleague Alfred
Adler, who argued that the individual was driven by a "will to power" and—
failing to achieve sufficient parental support—subject to disorders like the "inferiority complex."

The new physics outlined by Albert Einstein and other scientists mirrored
these disturbing concepts of the "inner" world with equally troublesome visions
of the "outer" world, while new philosophical ideas further fractured traditional
ideas of time, reality, experience, and language. Einstein's special theory of relativity (1905), for instance, followed by his general theory of relativity (1916),
invited doubts about even such apparently absolute categories as space and
time, implying that the physical universe was far more complex than earlier,
Newtonian physics had asserted it was. Diverse as they were, moreover, the
questionings of received reality produced by the speculations of Henri Bergson
(1859–1941), Edmund Husserl (1859–1938), and Martin Heidegger (1889–
1976), the revisions of logic and mathematics undertaken by Alfred North
Whitehead (1861–1947), and the linguistic analyses of Ludwig Wittgenstein
(1889–1951) also tended to undercut the confidence of intellectuals in both
the "knowability" of a material world and the plausibility of a moral order.

To complicate matters further, the new researches of anthropologists and
archaeologists led to a kind of cultural relativism that fostered skepticism about
the nature of human society itself. Increasingly, such investigators of primitive
societies and artifacts had come to the conclusion that neither the origins nor
the structure of society were necessarily patriarchal, and that indeed there was
no one fixed social system that governed the behavior of human groups around
the world. By the turn of the century, moreover, the work of figures like the
British anthropologist Sir James Frazer (1854–1941) and his classicist colleague Jane Ellen Harrison (1850–1928) suggested—to the distress of many
religious readers—that Western Christianity was as deeply shaped by the codes
of archaic fertility cults as any supposedly primitive theology. In particular,
Frazer's *The Golden Bough* (1890) implied a connection between the figure of
the Christian Messiah and the "dying and rising god" of such cults. Extensively
revised between 1911 and 1915 and issued in an abridged edition in 1922, the
book had an enormous impact on a number of modernist writers, as did the
speculations of Freud's former associate the psychoanalyst Carl Jung (1875–
1961), who postulated that human thought was shaped by primitive "archetypal" images drawn from a "collective unconscious," and the work of Frazer's
disciple Jessie Weston, whose *From Ritual to Romance* (1920)—a study of the
relationship between fertility religions and the medieval cult of the Holy Grail
—was adopted by T. S. Eliot to help provide a narrative framework for *The
Waste Land*. Indeed, from Eliot's *The Waste Land* and Joyce's *Ulysses* to
Hemingway's *The Sun Also Rises* and H. D.'s *Trilogy* (1944, 1945, 1946),

many twentieth-century works were inspired by the researches of anthropologists and mythographers.

At the same time, a number of literary figures welcomed the annihilation of traditional faith that was brought about by all these scientific and philosophical movements. In his *Sunday Morning* (1923), for instance, the American poet Wallace Stevens celebrated "the heavenly fellowship / Of men that perish and of summer morn," rejecting the old pieties of paradise, while in England, D. H. Lawrence vigorously redefined God as no more than "the great urge that has not yet found a body," and in Ireland, the poet William Butler Yeats concluded that "we are blest by everything, / Everything we look upon is blest." The case of Yeats is a telling one, however, for before affirming the blessedness of material reality, this poet had struggled for years to define a redemptive spiritual reality; repudiating traditional Christian dogma, he studied the occult, engaged in psychic research, and sought to strengthen his art with images of transcendence.

In this last respect, Yeats's early career was surprisingly similar to the later careers of such disparate poets as T. S. Eliot and W. H. Auden, both of whom—after periods of skepticism—took refuge in orthodox Christianity from what seemed to them a culture of disbelief. Following the publication of *The Waste Land*, that classic of modernist despair, Eliot in particular became increasingly religious, as if proposing that the best way to allay the intellectual anxieties of the twentieth century was to revive the verities of former ages. At the same time, in keeping with his conscious orthodoxy, his politics and his social views became notably conservative, even reactionary, charting a course that would be followed in their various ways by such American writers as the poet-critics John Crowe Ransom and Allen Tate. Manifesting itself during the 1930s, the conservatism of these figures represented one major response to skepticism about reality and signaled a deep political split between two sets of twentieth-century writers, a split that would become more significant as the twenties darkened into the thirties, and the intellectual anxiety fueled by contemporary science and philosophy was coupled with a more specifically political anxiety fostered by a new series of critical international developments.

International Anxiety

World War I was not the only disturbing international event that marked the years between 1914 and 1939, though it was the most striking. Specifically, this period saw the continuing decline of the British Empire; the intensification of so-called "isolationism" in the United States; the growth of such threateningly revolutionary movements as anarchism, socialism, and communism; the worldwide trauma caused by the Russian Revolution of 1917; and the rise of international fascism, first manifested by Benito Mussolini's takeover of Italy (1928) and Adolf Hitler's accession to dictatorship in Germany (1933), and then most vividly dramatized by the Spanish civil war (1936–1939).

In a sense, the slow but inexorable disintegration of the British Empire may have served as a portent of things to come, foreshadowing what the German historian Oswald Spengler was to call, in a gloomy theoretical volume, *The Decline of the West* (1922). In the once-crucial British colony of Ireland, for instance, the Easter Rising of 1916 was followed first by the so-called Irish troubles—guerrilla warfare, between British troops called "Black and Tans" and Irish rebels, that lasted from 1918 to 1920—and then by the establishment of the Irish Free State in 1921. At about the same time, agitation for freedom began in India, where Mohandas K. Gandhi returned from years spent in England and South Africa to lead an independence movement in 1915. The nation was not to achieve Gandhi's goal until 1949, but his radicalism—though manifested by "passive resistance" rather than overt violence—was so threatening that he was imprisoned by the British in 1930–1931 and again from 1942 to 1944, and English anxiety about the troublesome "otherness" now asserting itself in a major colony was brilliantly represented in E. M. Forster's *A Passage to India* (1920). Other subject domains also gradually freed themselves from England in this period: Egypt achieved independence in 1923, while the establishment of the British Commonwealth in 1931 granted equal and independent status to such nations as Canada, Australia, and New Zealand.

Perhaps in part because of the monitory example of Britain's decline, the mood in the United States became increasingly conservative and isolationist in these years. Northern anxiety about blacks, for instance, was intensified when, between 1910 and 1920, the mass migration of Southern blacks to New York City made the upper-Manhattan neighborhood of Harlem one of the largest black communities in the United States and—because of poor living conditions and the underemployment of many of its citizens—the site of racial unrest throughout the twenties and thirties. At the same time, the white supremacist Ku Klux Klan gained strength in the South and the Midwest as well as in such Northern states as Maine and Oregon. Founded in 1915, the Klan grew in membership to a peak in the mid-twenties; its power was symbolic of a widespread American racism that also led to the controversial 1931 trial of the so-called Scottsboro boys, nine young Alabama black men who were accused (unjustly, in the view of many liberals) of having raped two young white women.

Besides feeling assaulted from within, however, many conservative Americans felt threatened from without. In response to the country's isolationist mood, the government sought to stem the tide of immigration that brought thirty-eight million new citizens to the land between 1820 and 1930. In 1917, a literacy requirement was imposed on all immigrants, and in 1921 and 1924 quota systems were established, severely restricting the number of southern and eastern Europeans and Asians who could enter the country. Still, despite such measures, American anxiety about international involvement was clearly responsible for the reluctance of President Woodrow Wilson (who was elected on a platform of neutrality) to enter the First World War, and it was responsible, too, for a terror of Communist infiltration—a "Red scare"—that dominated the 1920s.

It was not the American 1920s alone that were haunted by the threat of such revolutionary movements as anarchism, socialism, and communism. Significantly, however, a number of British socialists were such comparatively respected figures as the playwright George Bernard Shaw, the novelist H. G. Wells, the journalist Rebecca West, and the writer-editor Leonard Woolf (husband of Virginia Woolf), unlike the situation in the United States, where anarchism and rebellion were usually associated with immigrants who were perceived as both unsavory and lawless. Such a perception in America fostered the passage of the Volstead Act (1918), which instituted the prohibition of liquor sales in the United States until its repeal in 1933, for the consumption of alcohol was often connected with just the immigrant groups that, during the Prohibition years, bootlegged sales of "bathtub" wine and gin. More specifically, this attitude led to the persecution in America of radical immigrants like Emma Goldman, Nicola Sacco, and Bartolomeo Vanzetti.

The political agitator and free-love advocate Emma Goldman was a Russian Jew popularly called "Red Emma" and "the Queen of the Anarchists"; her *Living My Life* (1931) recorded a brilliant but controversial career as a rebel against oppression, a career for which she was deported to Russia in 1919. The Italian-born left-wing labor agitators Nicola Sacco and Bartolomeo Vanzetti, who were tried in 1920 and executed in 1927 for an alleged payroll robbery, were the focus of fierce American debate throughout the 1920s because it was believed by radicals and liberals alike that they were innocent, and that their "alien" ethnic origins and their political convictions had led to their deaths.

Even before the deportation of Emma Goldman and the Sacco-Vanzetti case had aroused American political passions, the Russian Revolution of 1917 had brought anxieties about left-wing agitation to a kind of climax. To many thinkers, it appeared that the assassination of the tsar and his family represented an apotheosis of the anarchy that had been troubling Europe for more than a century, ever since the French Revolution of 1789, and especially after Karl Marx and Friedrich Engels had produced their *Communist Manifesto* (1848). Certainly for William Butler Yeats the 1917 turmoil in Russia constituted an historical crux, a moment when he felt obliged to concede that what Spengler had called "the decline of the West" was a reality. In his famous poem *The Second Coming* (1920), Yeats suggested that the historical cycle represented by Western Christianity had at last come to an end: "Things fall apart; the center cannot hold," he wrote. "Mere anarchy is loosed upon the world, / The blood-dimmed tide is loosed," and later, according to one scholar, he "accepted the poem" not only as a comment on the Russian Revolution but as "an unconscious prophecy of the rise of fascism."

Again, however, Yeats is emblematic here, for despite his later repudiation of fascism, he had actually, in 1934, written a sequence of poems that were intended to be inspiriting to the Irish "brownshirt" (Fascist) movement. His gesture revealed a political ambivalence that was characteristic of a number of the major modernists. In 1926, for instance, D. H. Lawrence published a novel fantasizing the redemption of Mexico by what he called a "blood-brotherhood" of revolutionaries whose common creed was almost shockingly fascistic because based on the assumption that natural leaders must always command unquestioning loyalty from their subordinates, and in 1933, just before Hitler was to rise to power in Germany with the plan of finding a "final solution" to the "Jewish problem," T. S. Eliot gave a series of lectures (entitled *After Strange Gods*) in which he declared that populations "should be homogeneous" both in race and in religion, adding that "reasons of race and religion combine to make any large number of free-thinking Jews undesirable" and that "a spirit of excessive tolerance is to be deprecated."

Even while these writers were flirting with fascism, however, another group of modernists were passionately attacking their reactionary orthodoxy. With its radical double assault on patriarchal culture and Fascist ideology, *Three Guineas* (1938), by Eliot's friend and publisher Virginia Woolf, was perhaps this period's fiercest critique of the intertwined Nazi notions of leadership and the Fatherland. But during the thirties the Englishmen W. H. Auden and George Orwell, and the Americans John Dos Passos, John Steinbeck, Langston Hughes, Edna St. Vincent Millay, and Muriel Rukeyser, also wrote novels and poems that mourned the oppression of what the poet Carl Sandburg had once called "the people, yes" while advocating strong rebellion against both Fascist and capitalist domination. On both sides of the Atlantic, moreover, many of these younger artists—including Ernest Hemingway, George Orwell, and Virginia Woolf's nephew Julian Bell—journeyed to Spain to fight on the side of the Loyalists (Republicans) against Franco's Falangists (Fascists). Speaking for all these activists, Auden's *Spain 1937* said: "We are left alone with our day, and the time is short and / History to the defeated / May say alas but cannot help or pardon."

Artistic Innovation

Given the age of rapid cultural, economic, and intellectual change in which modern artists found themselves, it is not surprising that many responded with an urgent sense that new aesthetic modes were needed to mirror the newness of the century, and not surprising, either, that many gathered into informal communities for which the creation of such modes became a kind of group project. Three intertwined phenomena were associated with the development of these radical intellectual communities. First, because the new availability and speed of steamships, railroads, and motorcars had made long-range travel easy, a number of artists chose to journey abroad: Americans became expatriates in London and Paris; English writers settled in Paris, Mexico, Berlin, and the United States; German, Russian, and Spanish artists traveled to Paris or New York; and wherever they went, these figures tended to establish cosmopolitan groups that shared innovative aesthetic ideas. Second, because so many of these groups were bonded by common artistic goals, a number of "little magazines" and anthologies sprang up in these years, journals disseminating a range of new literary views. Third, the availability of such periodicals fostered the development of the genre of the "manifesto," a statement in which groups of artists outlined their aesthetic principles, usually in revolutionary language.

Charting the movements of twentieth-century writers, painters, and musicians can be dizzying. Ezra Pound, T. S. Eliot, Robert Frost, and H. D. (Hilda Doolittle) established themselves in London during the first two decades of the century, but though Eliot was by and large to remain in England for the rest of his life, Pound was later to travel to Italy (where he would broadcast pro-fascist propaganda for the Mussolini government), Frost was eventually to return to his New England home, and, after the twenties, H. D. was to live intermittently in Switzerland. The same complexities mark the itineraries of many other writers. Though Gertrude Stein—perhaps this century's most famous expatriate—moved to Paris in 1903, where she settled permanently, as did Edith Wharton (who hardly left France after 1914), Ernest Hemingway, Sherwood Anderson, Henry Miller, Djuna Barnes, and Anaïs Nin lived in Paris during the twenties and thirties (where Hemingway and Anderson, in particular, were members of the "Stein circle"), but then departed for points elsewhere. Similarly, though James Joyce was ultimately to settle in Paris, he did not do so until he had spent some years living in Trieste and Zurich, while W. B. Yeats, though he was deeply identified with the so-called Irish Renaissance, actually spent most of his life journeying between London, Paris, Dublin, and the west of Ireland. Considering the complexity of these international movements, it was probably inevitable that such travelers should have produced a literature that is always singularly cosmopolitan even while it expresses a deep sense of uprootedness.

To be sure, little magazines did provide writers with aesthetic "homes" of a sort. *Poetry* and *The Little Review* in Chicago, *Broom* and the *Dial* in New York, *Blast*, the *Egoist*, and the *Criterion* in London, and *transition* in Paris, along with annual anthologies like *The Imagist Anthology* (edited first by Ezra Pound, then by Amy Lowell) and *Wheels* (edited by Edith Sitwell) offered experimental writers a rich range of outlets for their talents, as well as an array of pages that could be filled with manifestoes explaining the new aesthetic assumptions on which these artists operated. The *Blast* manifestoes of 1914, quoted earlier, were typical of these productions, but the *Imagist Manifesto* of 1915, written to justify the sharply chiseled free verse that had been composed from 1908 on by Pound and H. D., was more crucially influential, with its admonitions to "employ always the *exact* word," "to create new rhythms—as the expression of new moods," "to present an image," and "to produce poetry that is hard and clear" because "concentration is of the very essence of poetry."

Having slightly less impact on poetry in English, but almost equally representative in their radical repudiation of old forms and their enthusiasm for shockingly new methods, were the *Surrealist Manifesto* (1924) and *Manifesto: The Revolution of the Word*, which was published in *transition* in the early thirties. In the first, the French poet André Breton confided that the "Secrets of the Magical/Surrealist Art"—an art based on dreams and visions, wild associations and images of the world that were "sur" (or super-) real—included automatic writing, for the poet must "trust . . . the inexhaustible nature of the murmur." In the second, a series of axioms attacking linguistic and narrative "realism," such diverse figures as Kay Boyle and Hart Crane agreed that "THE LITERARY CREATOR HAS THE RIGHT TO DISINTEGRATE THE PRIMAL MATTER OF WORDS."

A number of individual writers produced critical statements of their own that also functioned as manifestos of a sort. Quite early in his career, for instance, Ezra Pound had advised all his contemporaries to "make it new" and paid tribute to Walt Whitman, the nineteenth-century American artist who virtually pioneered free verse, with the words "it was you that broke the new wood." Similarly, in a lecture called *Composition as Explanation* (1926), Gertrude Stein sought both to justify her use of what she called "the continuous present" and to account for what seemed the obscurity of her *avant-garde* writing with the observation that "the creator of the new composition in the arts is an outlaw until he is a classic." In an article on *Modern Fiction* (1919), Virginia Woolf insisted that it is "the task of the novelist to convey" a "varying . . . unknown and uncircumscribed spirit" rather than fixed and discrete external realities, while in an analysis of *The Novel Démeublé* ("The Unfurnished Novel,"

1936) Willa Cather argued for a fiction stripped of the stuffy furniture of circumstantial detail that had cluttered the works of "naturalists" and Victorians alike. Though other modernists did not make quite such hortatory statements, their critical analyses of literature past and present often acted as equally passionate personal manifestos. Certainly Eliot's *Tradition and the Individual Talent* or his *The Metaphysical Poets* can be read in such a way, as can William Carlos Williams's praise of the brilliance with which the American poet Marianne Moore cut "soiled words" out of "greasy" traditional contexts.

The experimental impulses articulated both in group and personal literary manifestoes were strengthened by the intense experimentation that was being conducted by artists in other media. Since the late nineteenth century, painters from Auguste Renoir, Mary Cassatt, Marie Laurencin, and Edvard Munch to Georges Bracque and Pablo Picasso had used the techniques of impressionism, expressionism, and cubism to break down traditional modes of representing the material world, substituting for strictly pictorial images more abstract forms, forms either determined by unique individual perceptions or governed by larger principles of design. It was during the modernist period, however, that the innovations of these artists began to seem most compelling to their literary contemporaries. Picasso, in particular, became a kind of hero of the *avant-garde*: Gertrude Stein, one of the first great collectors of modern art and the subject of what was perhaps the Spanish painter's most famous portrait, wrote in an ironic understatement that he was "one whom some were certainly following." Similarly exhilarating to many literary figures were the daring works of such composers as Igor Stravinsky (whose ballet *Le Sacre du Printemps*, 1913 —*The Rite of Spring*—shocked even cosmopolitan Paris with its ferocious primitivism) and Arnold Schoenberg (whose theory of the "twelve-tone row" seemed to many conservatives to threaten to substitute mathematical formulas for traditional melodies).

Both the poetry and the fiction produced by writers who participated in this experimental culture were also often unnervingly controversial. To some, the Imagists' liberation of verse from traditional rhyme and rhythm, along with their turn toward such alien forms as the Japanese *haiku*, seemed to signal the end of poetry; to others, such liberation—particularly as it appeared in the beautifully crafted poems of H. D. and the early Pound—promised the beginning of a style that might, as William Carlos Williams thought, capture the inflections of the voice (and especially the American voice) more accurately than any conventional meter ever had. Similarly, to some the fragmented narratives of such ambitious works as Eliot's *The Waste Land*, Pound's *Cantos*, H. D.'s *Trilogy*, and Williams's *Paterson*, as well as the more modest poems of Marianne Moore, together with these artists' use of literary allusions—quotations from writings in a range of languages—appeared willfully obscurantist, while to others the freeing of poetry from a straightforward narrative or argumentative line promised a new richness in the art.

Equally crucial but controversial innovations marked the development of modernist fiction. Most notable perhaps was the development in this period of the so-called stream-of-consciousness novel, a genre that seemed to many readers quite as obscure as the fragmented and allusive poetry of Eliot and Pound but which was destined to become no less influential. First defined by the English writer May Sinclair, who borrowed the phrase "stream of consciousness" from the American philosopher William James, this kind of novel generally focused on the mental processes—the thoughts, responses, and interior emotional experiences—of a single central character (although sometimes the writer switched "points of view" among several key figures). Not surprisingly in an era obsessed by the hypotheses of Sigmund Freud and other psychoanalysts, the novelists who worked in this mode strove to represent not only the fluid movements of what might be considered the surface of the mind, but also the irrational disruptions of thought that signaled the explosions of unconscious material into the consciousness.

James Joyce's *Ulysses* (1922) was unquestionably the most famous work in this mode; indeed, with its searching examinations of the phases of the mind of its protagonist Leopold Bloom and its equally innovative dramatizations of the thoughts of Bloom's counterhero Stephen Daedalus, the book represented a turning point in modern novelistic technique. But this important work's strategies were prepared for not only by Joyce's earlier *A Portrait of the Artist as a Young Man* (1916), a *Bildungsroman* (development novel) which traced Stephen Daedalus's growth to maturity, but also by such equally radical experimentations as Dorothy Richardson's *Pointed Roofs* (1915), the first novel in a series called *Pilgrimage* that explored the mental evolution of its heroine, Miriam Henderson. Moreover, stream-of-consciousness techniques were further implemented in the work of such artists as May Sinclair, whose *Mary Olivier* (1919) was only one of several fictions by this writer that explored the lights and shadows of a protagonist's mind; Virginia Woolf, whose *Mrs. Dalloway* (1925), *To the Lighthouse* (1927), and *The Waves* (1933) were particularly notable examples of what Woolf called a "tunneling" technique through which she "excavated" the dreams and desires of her characters; and William Faulkner, whose *The Sound and the Fury* (1929) and *As I Lay Dying* (1930) consisted of brilliantly sewn-together "interior monologues."

Modernist fiction writers also undertook other revisionary strategies. What the critic Michael Hoffman has called Gertrude Stein's "abstractionism"—a method of emphasizing language itself rather than its narrative components—led not only to the experiment in "the continuous present" of Stein's own *Three Lives* (1909) but also, because of the force of Stein's personality and example, to the highly stylized and stripped repetitions of Ernest Hemingway's *The Sun Also Rises* (1926) and *A Farewell to Arms* (1929). In the writings of Joyce (*Dubliners*, 1916), Lawrence, and Katherine Mansfield (*The Garden Party*, 1922), moreover, this period saw what was in effect the invention of the modern short story. Influenced by the work of the continental artists Maupassant, Turgenev, and Chekhov, these writers struggled to create a genre whose plot would reflect, not the complexity of an extended chain of causes and effects, but the purity of what Woolf called a "timeless moment" or, in Joyce's words, an "epiphany" (a revelation) that functions as the turning point of a life. Similarly, particularly in the United States, a group of experimental dramatists —notably those associated with the Provincetown Players, headquartered both on Cape Cod and in Greenwich Village, in New York City—sought to import new life into the theater: writers like Eugene O'Neill and Susan Glaspell produced plays that were striking for such "expressionistic" techniques as the use of archaic masks and symbols (in O'Neill's *The Emperor Jones*, 1922) or for their oblique, even mysterious narrative forms (in Glaspell's *Trifles*, 1916).

Even while these largely elite artists were striving to articulate manifestos, to experiment with styles, and to pioneer new genres, however, a number of more popular literary modes and movements were developing. Perhaps the most impressive of these was the so-called Harlem Renaissance, a movement led by the American black writers Jean Toomer, Nella Larson, Langston Hughes, Countee Cullen, and Zora Neale Hurston, all of whom agreed, despite major philosophical differences among them, that it was now essential for Afro-Americans to become conscious of, and write about, their uniquely rich culture. In the 1920s, Harlem had in any case become, along with the bohemian quarter of Greenwich Village, a center of New York's aesthetic life: the increasingly fascinating new musical form of jazz, with its improvisational intensity, had at last obliged many white intellectuals to pay attention to their black contemporaries. Finally, therefore, it seemed possible for these writers to dramatize not only what Cullen called in *Heritage* (1925) the history of Africa's lost "copper sun or scarlet sea"—the history of a forgotten past—but also the distinctive pain of the black mother who represents the oppression of all her people when she tells her child in Hughes's *Mother to Son* (1926) that "life for me ain't been no crystal stair." While the work of these writers clearly had an impact on that of their white contemporaries, it was to be most dramatically carried on in the writing of their black descendants LeRoi Jones (Imamu Amiri Baraka), Ishmael Reed, Toni Morrison, Toni Cade Bambara, Audre Lorde, and Alice Walker.

Other movements that major modernists sometimes defined as "popular" also had important effects. Joyce, Stein, Woolf, and Lawrence, for instance, may have in various ways scorned such vulgar genres as science fiction and the detective novel as well as such media as radio, musical comedy, and film. However, the rapid development of all these modes inevitably impinged upon the careers of these artists as well as upon the styles of their descendants. For one thing, the commercial appeal of best-selling thrillers and hit musicals contrasted sharply with the small sales achieved by the works of elite modernists, whose difficult experimental novels and poems often earned little money even when they were greeted with critical praise. Thus the gap between the aesthetically ambitious artist and the hack writer, a gap first perceived in the nineteenth century, widened dramatically in these years, intensifying the sense of alienation experienced by many serious novelists and poets.

Modernist writers could not, however, simply ignore the rise of popular media. Some actually led double lives, supporting themselves by writing for money while doing their "real" work on the side. William Faulkner, F. Scott Fitzgerald, and Dorothy Parker, for instance, went to Hollywood to write for the movies. In addition, a number of supposedly hack writers who produced only commercial works were ultimately to be perceived as more serious than they had at first seemed. H. L. Mencken's and George Jean Nathan's *Black Mask* magazine developed the talents of the powerful and influential artist Dashiell Hammett, whose style and subject matter have been frequently compared to those of Ernest Hemingway. In addition, this period—often referred to as the "Golden Age" of detective fiction—fostered the work of mystery writers like Agatha Christie and Dorothy L. Sayers, novelists whose supposedly popular plots left indelible marks on the consciousness of the era. Ultimately, as much as the innovations of the so-called "high modernists," the pioneering contributions of such artists may represent the extraordinarily transfigurative quality of the age, an era whose literary no less than its intellectual and social changes were perhaps the most radical ones experienced in Western history.

MODERNIST IMAGES OF WOMEN

Perhaps because of the sense of cultural cataclysm inspired by the new technology, together with the widespread male anxiety about a female "takeover" that characterized the years from 1914 to 1939, the images of women produced by modernist men (and even some produced by their female contemporaries) were largely negative. To be sure, a number of writers created attractive female characters (and a number depicted unpleasant male characters), but by and large much literature of the period is notable for its obsession with what women should—and should not—be. In particular, threatened by suffragists, immobilized and unmanned by the war, alienated from both the industrial modes and the commercial media of what seemed an increasingly hectic society, many male novelists and poets tended to blame women for the sense of lost mastery that Lawrence outlined in his essay *Matriarchy*. If man would never, in Lawrence's words, "be master again," these writers implied, that was because women had in effect conspired with the new technology to render their male contemporaries socially and even sexually impotent. Thus, where late-nineteenth-century literary men had become obsessed by the threatening and predatory figure of the *femme fatale*, a merciless siren whose wiles were associated with the deadly potential of nature, modernist men were haunted by a new kind of destructive female: the flapper, a figure whose daunting ease with technology and unnerving sexual freedom were manifested by her short skirts and bobbed hair, her feverish dancing and wild drinking, her skillful driving and willful wandering.

Perhaps the most famously destructive flappers in modernist fiction were Brett Ashley, the anti-heroine of Ernest Hemingway's *The Sun Also Rises* (1926), and Daisy Buchanan, the equally problematic heroine of F. Scott Fitzgerald's *The Great Gatsby* (1925). A "damned good-looking" woman whose almost mechanically sleek sexuality is emphasized by the narrator's notation that she "was built with curves like the hull of a racing yacht," Hemingway's Brett rules over a novel whose hero, Jake Barnes, has been rendered literally impotent by a World War I wound and whose other male characters are shown to be in one way or another figuratively impotent. Similarly seductive, Fitzgerald's narcissistic Daisy is a rich and faithless young married woman who incarnates the corrupted morals of the society over which she presides: her voice "was full of money—that was the inexhaustible charm that rose and fell in it, the jingle of it, the cymbals' song of it," and her mechanistic deathliness reaches a climax when she casually slams her lover's expensive automobile into her husband's mistress in a hit-and-run accident that leads not only to the woman's death but later to the deaths of two men.

If few other flappers were quite as metaphorically murderous as Brett Ashley and Daisy Buchanan, many were characterized as either decadent or danger-

MODERNIST LITERATURE [*Introduction*] 1231

ous. In Richard Aldington's World War I novel *The Death of a Hero* (1929), for instance, the soldier-protagonist's wife and mistress—indifferent to his suffering in the trenches—are described as "terribly at ease upon the Zion of sex, abounding in masochism, Lesbianism, sodomy, etcetera," while in T. S. Eliot's *The Waste Land* the loveless and even anaesthetized sexuality of a "typist home at teatime" is echoed by the robotlike eroticism of a number of other female figures, all of whom the poet sees as having been liberated from traditional moral standards to no good end. Moreover, in countless bitterly misogynistic poems and stories written toward the close of his life, D. H. Lawrence held newly energetic women responsible for most social ills, implying that the apocalypse of modernism had been set in motion by what he variously defined as "energetic women," "dominant women," and "volcanic Venuses," for, as he explained in one verse, "Vengeance is mine, saith the Lord, / but the women are my favorite vessels of wrath."

In picturing women as such "vessels of wrath," however, Lawrence was moving to a more general concept of the destructiveness implicit in all female ambition. Particularly the newly liberated intellectual or literary woman—the figure whom turn-of-the-century observers had labeled "the New Woman"— was seen by this writer and others as a flawed and potentially evil personage. Gudrun Brangwen, one of the two female protagonists of his *Women in Love*, for example, is no flapper but a serious artist, yet her commitment to her works is frequently shown to be narcissistic, her consciousness is often characterized as coldly "glittering," and her turbulent love affair with Gerald Crich, one of the book's major male figures, leads directly to his death. In creating such a deadly female intellectual Lawrence was expressing an attitude that would also permeate the writings of the modernists W. B. Yeats, Ernest Hemingway, William Faulkner, and Nathanael West.

Imagining ideal womanhood in his *A Prayer for My Daughter* (1919), for instance, Yeats transcribed his own ambivalence toward the activism of Maude Gonne, the Irish actress and revolutionary whom he had loved almost all his life, with the imperative "let her [his infant daughter] think opinions are accursed" and the comment "Have I not seen the loveliest woman born / Out of the mouth of Plenty's horn / Because of her opinionated mind / Barter that horn and every good / By quiet natures understood / For an old bellows full of angry wind?" A similar ambivalence toward the female intellect appears in West's *Miss Lonelyhearts*, in which a group of male reporters curse lady writers with three names: "Mary Roberts Wilcox, Ella Wheeler Catheter . . . what they all needed was a good rape." As for suffragists, many were characterized as insane man-haters, and, if they were not seen as mad, many—along with female intellectuals and New Women—were often labeled as lesbians. If they actually *were* lesbians, moreover, they were almost always described with horror or nervous scorn: in his *Autobiography* (1952), William Carlos Williams recalls a visit to the salon of the lesbian expatriate Natalie Barney, where women were "sneaking off together into a side room while casting surreptitious glances about them," and was reminded of the behavior of a French deputy who, confronted with the same scene, "undid his pants buttons, took out his tool and, shaking it right and left, yelled out in a rage, 'Have you never seen one of these?'"

Single women who did not define themselves as New Women or intellectuals fared little better at the hands of twentieth-century male artists, for the
Victorian myth of the frustrated spinster lingered on, at least through the thirties. Faulkner's short story *A Rose for Emily* (written 1931) told the morbid tale
of an unmarried Southern heiress who keeps the skeleton of her lover in her bed
for decades after his death while she herself grows increasingly bloated, as if fat-
tening on his decay. In an equally savage vein, Auden's ballad *Miss Gee* (1937)
recounted the case history of a churchgoing spinster who wears "her clothes
buttoned up to her neck" and gets cancer from sexual frustration; the medical
men who operate on her find the sight of her sick body hilarious: "They laid her
on the table, / The students began to laugh; / And Mr. Rose the surgeon / He
cut Miss Gee in half." Even the images of women who *had* dutifully married
did not necessarily escape such opprobrium, for widows were often depicted as
prissy, fussy creatures. Wallace Stevens's *A High-Toned Old Christian
Woman* (1923), for instance, complained that the joy generated by the "supreme fiction" of poetry "will make widows wince," but defiantly contended
that "fictive things / Wink as they will. Wink most when widows wince."

Nor can the male modernists' portrayals of "properly" heterosexual women
—married women, mothers, mistresses, whores—have been very much more
inspiriting for female readers. Perhaps the most famous female character in
early twentieth-century fiction was Molly Bloom, the heroine of *Ulysses*, an
insatiably lusty earth-goddess who never gets out of bed in the course of the
novel, and whose last words in the book—"yes I said yes I will Yes"—express
her passionate acquiescence in her purely sexual destiny. From Lawrence's desirous Lady Chatterley to the obscene female figures in Samuel Beckett's poem
Whoroscope (1929) to the prostitutes who haunt Henry Miller's *Tropic of
Cancer* (1934) and his *Tropic of Capricorn* (1938), Molly Bloom's descendants proliferated in twentieth-century fiction, frequently described in terms of
body parts, with Miller's whores usually appraised as "cunts." Even the former
Victorian ideals of mothers and motherhood were now castigated, moreover,
for psychoanalysts increasingly tended to blame the sins of the mothers for the
neuroses of the sons. By 1942, the American writer Philip Wylie was to inveigh
in *Generation of Vipers* against "the destroying mother," arguing that "we
must face the dynasty of the dames at once."

Finally, with perhaps a few exceptions—Mrs. Wilcox and Margaret Schle-
gel in Forster's *Howard's End* (1912) come to mind, for instance—it began to
seem that the only "good" women in male-authored modern literature were,
on the one hand, little girls who had not yet *become* women, and, on the other
hand, adults who were willing to sacrifice themselves completely to the imperatives of male desire and need. An example of the first group is "Littless," the
prepubescent tomboy heroine of Hemingway's *The Last Good Country*
(1st. pub. 1972), Nick Adams's younger sister who is beloved by the hero partly
for her impassioned loyalty and partly for her intense innocence. Examples of
the second group would include the nameless heroine of Lawrence's *The
Woman Who Rode Away* (1923), a white woman who allows herself to be
stripped and sacrificed by the priests of an Indian tribe so that they can "regain
the mastery that man must hold," and Rose of Sharon, the daughter of the
Joads in John Steinbeck's *The Grapes of Wrath* (1939), who also allows herself

to be stripped and then willingly offers her milk-filled breast to a starving tramp she has never seen before. What distinguished both these groups of women was their absence of self-will, their vulnerable passivity, their dutiful instrumentality, qualities that seemed to their creators to be increasingly lacking in the real behavior of real women.

WOMEN'S NEW LIVES

When Virginia Woolf meditated in her essay *Mr. Bennett and Mrs. Brown* on the change in "human character" that took place "on or about December, 1910," her examples were telling. First, she noted that while the "Victorian cook lived like a leviathan in the lower depths . . . the Georgian cook is a creature of sunshine and fresh air." Then, she observed that contemporary readers of Aeschylus's drama *Agamemnon* will find that their "sympathies are . . . almost entirely with Clytemnestra," the rebellious wife whose betrayal of her husband was traditionally vilified. Finally, she argued that readers who study the biographies of the Victorian sage Thomas Carlyle and his wife will dislike "the horrible domestic tradition" that confined "a woman of genius" like Jane Carlyle to the kitchen. For, declared Woolf, "all human relations have shifted" —and especially, as her images of change indicate, the relations between the sexes.

Woolf's analysis was characteristically acute, for the technological and intellectual innovations of the early twentieth century had a striking impact on women of all classes. Though workers on both sides of the Atlantic continued to suffer from economic exploitation—and in particular from the effects of widespread postwar unemployment in the 1920s and of the Great Depression in the 1930s—trade unionism and social welfare programs had begun to insulate them to some extent from the horrors experienced by, for instance, Victorian women in the mines or sweatshops, while universal public education, together with new systems of mass communication, gave them access to cultural institutions from which they had earlier been excluded. Similarly, both middle- and upper-class women, no longer bound by the preceding century's ideology of femininity, entered universities and professions in ever-increasing numbers while exulting in a new intellectual and sexual freedom. Finally, after nearly a century of struggle, women of all classes in both England and America at last gained the right to vote, a right that—at least legally—for the first time acknowledged their full citizenship in the human community.

Just before England entered the Great War in the summer of 1914, suffragist militancy had reached a new intensity. In 1913, British feminists, led by the Pankhursts, engaged in hunger strikes, window smashings, and other radical actions, and five thousand American feminists, led by Alice Paul, marched on Washington in January of that year. When war broke out, however, British suffrage societies immediately suspended their protests, and the government issued an amnesty to all its hunger-striking female prisoners. Although a splinter group of pacifist women, led by the socialist Sylvia Pankhurst, refused to support "this capitalist war," most suffrage workers abandoned their struggle for the vote in favor of war work on the home front, and major figures in the W.S.P.U.—most notably Sylvia Pankhurst's mother, Mrs. Emmeline Pankhurst, and her sister, Christabel Pankhurst—became passionately patriotic, supporting (in the words of the historian Sheila Rowbotham) "military conscription for men, industrial conscription for women." In fact, the suffrage battle did not resume in England until 1916, when the National Union of Women's Suffrage Societies, led by Millicent Garrett Fawcett, pressured Parliament to introduce a new Franchise Bill and managed at last to win the support of prominent politicians. By June 1917, the House of Commons had actually passed a women's suffrage bill, and, by January 1918, the more conservative House of Lords had also accepted the bill.

Although the United States did not actually enter the war until 1917, events paralleled those in Great Britain to some extent. To be sure, between 1914 and 1916 the struggle for suffrage did not lapse in America as it had in England; on the contrary, two parties with rather different philosophies pressed the issue vigorously. Led by Carrie Chapman Catt, the National American Woman Suffrage Association organized state referenda while also proselytizing for an amendment to the Constitution. At the same time, led by Alice Paul, the Congressional Union (later the Woman's Party) directed its energies entirely toward the passage of a constitutional amendment, and—in doing so—adopted increasingly militant tactics. As it had in England, the tide of political opinion began to turn in America in 1916 and 1917, although, again as in England, the already divided women's movement split further over the issue of America's entrance into the war: the N.A.W.S.A.—like the W.S.P.U.—patriotically supported war work, and the Woman's Party—like Sylvia Pankhurst's faction—took a pacifist line. Despite these rifts, however, the Nineteenth Amendment, granting women the vote, finally came before the House of Representatives in January 1918, and, with the support of President Woodrow Wilson, passed by a two-thirds majority while cheering throngs in the galleries and corridors of the Capital sang the hymn "Old Hundred." Although another year and a half of struggle—including elaborate maneuvers in the Senate and arduous state-by-state campaigning—was necessary before the amendment became law, thirty-six states had finally ratified it by August 1920.

Most historians agree that, in addition to decades of struggle and hard work, a major factor in achieving the right to vote was women's contributions to the war effort. For, in fact, one of the most striking discontinuities between male and female experience in the modernist period was generated by the Great War. Specifically, as young men were sent off to a front where their chances for survival were often slim, and as they became increasingly immured in the muck and blood of "No Man's Land," their mothers, wives, sisters, and daughters on the home front seemed to become ever more powerful. Filling the places soldiers had left behind in mines and munitions factories, farms and railroads, women found themselves confronted for the first time with opportunities to do remunerative and meaningful work in the public sphere. By 1918, a visitor to London observed that "England was a world of women—women in uniforms," and the English poet Nina Macdonald proudly proclaimed that "Girls are doing things / They've never done before. . . . All the world is topsy-turvy / Since the War began."

That the world *was* in some sense "topsy-turvy" contributed, of course, to the soldiers' sickened sense of anxiety and exclusion from the homes they had left behind. Nevertheless, despite the massive tragedy that the conflict represented for thousands of grieving wives and mothers, such a reversal of the old order contributed enormously to the liberation—and the new exuberance—of women, who felt for the first time not only needed but appreciated. The American writer Harriot Stanton Blatch declared that war "make[s] the blood course through the veins" because, by compelling "women to work," it sends them "over the top . . . up the scaling-ladder, and out into 'All Man's Land.' " Similarly, women who were for the first time invited to work as nurses and ambulance drivers at the front itself, found their experiences exhilarating as well as painful: the English novelist May Sinclair—an ambulance driver in Belgium —confided that "[you think] 'What a fool I would have been if I hadn't come. I wouldn't have missed this run for the world.' "

By the end of the war, the number of working women had increased by almost fifty percent in England, and seven hundred thousand of the women employed had directly replaced men in the work force; similar statistics obtained in the United States. In both countries, moreover, it was not only working-class women who delighted in new usefulness and prosperity; many a middle- or upper-class woman could rejoice with the English doctor Caroline Matthews, who asserted that because her medical services were needed at last, "life was worth living in those days." Not surprisingly, then, Prime Minister Asquith, repudiating his former opposition to women's suffrage, admitted that women "have aided in the most effective way in the prosecution of the war" while President Wilson declared that "the services of the women—services rendered in every sphere . . . wherever men have worked, and upon the very skirts and edges of the battle itself" should be rewarded with the full rights of citizenship.

There were a number of other ways in which the social disruption fostered by the war seemed also to help facilitate the liberation of women. Although nineteenth-century factory and farm workers had always had more freedom of movement than their upper-class counterparts, "war girls" were among the first "respectable" female groups in Western history who could stroll the public streets unescorted, go to theaters and dances without chaperones, and even travel on their own without incurring the suspicion that they were "fallen" women. In addition, such female workers were the first group to shed traditional women's costumes in significant numbers: though the American suffragist Amelia Bloomer had devised the divided skirt (known as "the bloomer") as early as 1850, that garment had only been a passing fad among radical free-thinkers; now, however, impelled by the necessities of hard labor on the land, at the front, or in factories, most women shortened their skirts, and many took to wearing breeches or overalls. Even after the war, the trend they pioneered proved irreversible. As one historian has observed, flappers' clothing—short skirts, brassieres instead of corsets, silk stockings—"weighed one-tenth as much as [women's clothing] in the Victorian period."

To be sure, some of the most crucial social changes that marked women's lives in this era had already been set in motion by turn-of-the-century feminists; the birth-control movement as well as the free-love and child-care movements, for example, had prewar origins. Nevertheless, all three came to considerable prominence in the years between 1914 and 1921. The American nurse and birth-control advocate Margaret Sanger, for instance, founded a journal, *The Woman Rebel*, in 1914, designed to give working women advice on birth control, and in 1916 she established the first birth-control clinic in America. Also in 1916, the anarchist and free-love theorist Emma Goldman was arrested in New York for lecturing on birth control, while in England the suffragist and scientist Marie Stopes published her *Married Love*—a book offering contraceptive advice—in 1918, and in 1921 she opened a London birth-control clinic. Margaret Sanger summarized the long-standing feminist assumptions of all these women when she declared in *Woman and the New Race* (1920) that "the most far-reaching social development of modern times is the revolt of women against sex servitude."

Besides the advocacy of birth control, other elements of this revolt were agitation for communal child-care centers (and in some cases communal domestic centers) and proselytizing for free love or at least for the sort of egalitarian conjugal relationship that came to be called "companionate marriage." In 1914, the British feminist Sylvia Pankhurst opened a small nursery for the children of factory workers which became so successful that it was moved to a pub formerly called "The Gunmaker's Arms" and now renamed "The Mother's Arms." At around the same time, free-love advocates in England and the United States, ranging from the activist Emma Goldman and the writer Neith Boyce to self-proclaimed male feminists like Bertrand Russell and Floyd Dell, championed the cause of sexual liberation. In her *Hypatia* (1925), the British suffragist Dora Russell, wife of the philosopher Bertrand Russell, declared that "sex, even without children and without marriage is . . . a thing of dignity, beauty, and delight."

Russell's view was distinctively new both in its departure from the Victorian ideal of what the scholar Nancy Cott has called female "passionlessness" and in its repudiation of the vision of male sexual brutality implicit in the writings of turn-of-the-century feminists like Charlotte Perkins Gilman. Yet this new view was quickly to become characteristic of an age marked by the publication of some of the earliest marriage manuals to emphasize female pleasure: not only Marie Stopes's *Married Love* but also Theodore Hendrik van de Velde's *Ideal Marriage: Its Physiology and Technique* (1928, trans. 1930) for the first time encouraged women, the way Dora Russell did, to experience sex as a "thing of . . . delight" rather than an act of submission, and, as researchers subsequently discovered, countless women did just that. The psychologist Lewis Terman found in 1938 that among 777 middle-class wives, 74 percent of those born between 1890 and 1900 remained virgins until marriage, but only 31.7 percent of those born after 1910 did so.

What contributed to the unprecedented feelings of female autonomy that fostered such a new emphasis on women's sexual desires may, paradoxically enough, have been the fact that—in Virginia Woolf's phrase—"Professions for Women" seemed finally to have become seriously possible. The historian William Chafe has noted that in America during the first two decades of the twentieth century "female enrollment increased 1,000 per cent in public colleges and 485 per cent in private schools," and "the number of women employed in the professions increased by over 450,000 and in business by over 100,000." While the figures for England were not quite so dramatic, they were almost equally impressive to contemporary observers. Certainly, among activists, an increasing number seem to have been professional women. Of seventeen female contributors to a symposium on *These Modern Women* sponsored by *The Nation* in 1927–1928, four had Ph.D.s, two were lawyers, one was an artist, one was a cartoonist, one was a politician, and three were journalists, while the editor of *The Nation*, Freda Kirchwey, was herself a successful professional woman. In addition, during these years a number of other professional women rose to national prominence on both sides of the Atlantic, including the anthropologists Margaret Mead, Ruth Benedict, and Zora Neale Hurston, the psychologists Lorine Pruette and Lillian Gilbreth, and the psychoanalysts Karen Horney, Helene Deutsch, and Melanie Klein.

Despite all these advances, however, the twenties and thirties saw the inauguration of, in the phrase of the literary critic Elaine Showalter, "feminism's awkward age." As Chafe has observed, the statistics representing American women's professional advances were misleading, for, despite some gains, most career women tended to gravitate toward such traditionally "feminine" occupations as teaching and nursing, while the number of female medical students "actually diminished" between 1902–1903 and 1926; in addition, women academicians rarely achieved the status of full professor, and "prospects for career women" actually "grew worse rather than better" during the economic difficulties of the thirties. Similarly, many vocational opportunities for English women closed down in the postwar years, a fact for which some female workers wrongly tended to blame themselves. By 1925, moreover, the feminist movement had significantly disintegrated, for the suffragists' utopian expectation that the achievement of the vote would mark a turning point into a better world was proven wrong when most female voters either failed to register or, if they did vote, cast ballots for the candidates recommended by husbands and fathers. Many sometime suffragists discovered, too, that "anti-feminism" was, in the words of Rebecca West, "strikingly the correct fashion . . . among . . . the intellectuals" in this period.

Even the ideal of companionate marriage now appeared to collapse; a number of women realized, with Crystal Eastman, that a woman "wants work of her own" but she also "wants husband, home, and children"—for whose care she was still obliged to bear primary responsibility—so that "how to reconcile these two desires in real life" was a perplexing question. As for the freedom of costume in which "war girls" had delighted, flappers learned that, as Sheila Rowbotham puts it, "going out to work in short skirts and fragile shoes was a problem," and the exhortations of a booming cosmetics industry along with the rise of "beauty parlors" threatened to turn even the most liberated New Woman back into a revised version of the living doll who had been the goal of her Victorian grandmother. Indeed, the masklike faces of movie stars like Mary Pickford, Jean Harlow, and Clara Bow symbolized a return to the artificial ideal of "femininity" that was rapidly replacing the assertive ideas of feminism.

Nevertheless, the dreams and demands of feminists from Mary Wollstonecraft to Elizabeth Cady Stanton still lived in some quarters. Virginia Woolf's *A Room of One's Own* (1929) was no doubt the most brilliant contemporary analysis of woman's situation, while her *Orlando* (1928)—with its portrait of a four-hundred-year-old heroine who changes her sex from male to female in the late seventeenth century—was probably the wittiest contemporary dramatization of the feminist desire to revise and reconstruct history as what some recent writers have called "herstory," but neither work was anomalous. From Elizabeth Robins's *Ancilla's Share* (1924) to Dora Russell's *Hypatia* (1925) to the feminist essays included in V. F. Calverton's and Samuel Schmalhausen's *Woman's Coming of Age* (1931), women continued to express the wish for a transformed society. From Ray Strachey's *The Cause* (1928) to Mary Beard's *On Understanding Women* (1931), I. B. O'Malley's *Women in Subjection* (1933), and Winifred Holtby's *Women and a Changing Civilization* (1935), women historians—both amateurs and professionals—continued to excavate and reconstruct a feminist past. Furthermore, in spite of the setbacks that fragmented the women's movement in the twenties and thirties, all these thinkers would have agreed with Woolf that they *were* living astonishingly new lives. "Am I the Christian gentlewoman my mother slaved to make me?" asked the poet Genevieve Taggard, and answered her own question with vehemence: "No indeed. I am a poet, a wine-bibber, a radical; a non-churchgoer who will no longer sing in the choir or lead prayer-meeting with a testimonial." In the same vein, the politician Cornelia Bryce Pinchot declared that "my feminism tells me that woman can bear children, charm her lovers, boss a business, swim the Channel, stand at Armageddon and battle for the Lord—all in the day's work!"

FEMINISM AND MODERNISM: THE NEW WOMAN'S LITERARY HISTORY

The exuberance of feminists like Woolf and Russell, Taggard and Pinchot suggests that, although the women's movement *per se* had suffered a series of defeats in the twenties, a significant number of individuals felt themselves to be in possession of a new source of strength, a source that did not entirely depend on the vagaries of contemporary politics. Given the concern with "herstory" that permeated the writings of so many theorists who continued to espouse the feminist cause in the face of increasingly widespread indifference or hostility, what seems to have functioned as a wellspring of energy was a new realization that women did have a history, and particularly a history of cultural achievement. "We think back through our mothers if we are women," wrote Virginia Woolf in *A Room of One's Own*, explaining that a crucial problem of early-nineteenth-century women novelists was "that they had no tradition behind them, or one so short and partial that it was of little help." Elsewhere, she contrasted her own situation with that of her literary ancestresses: "The road [to female literary accomplishment] was cut many years ago . . . many famous women, and many more unknown and forgotten have been before me, making the path smooth, and regulating my steps." In other words, the very existence of the nineteenth century's golden age of women's writing seems to have made a difference in Woolf's self-definition as a woman writer. For if women *had* written, and written successfully, women *could* write, and it was no longer necessary to ask, with the eighteenth-century poet Anne Finch, "How are we fal'n? Fal'n by mistaken rules?" The poet or novelist "in" a woman was no longer what Aphra Behn had called "my masculine part"; rather, "it" was a powerful female self for whom Emily and Charlotte Brontë, Elizabeth Barrett Browning and Emily Dickinson (as well as Finch and Behn themselves) provided patterns.

Of course, as the critic Harold Bloom has argued, the high achievements of literary precursors can in themselves constitute a source of anxiety for writers: Virginia Woolf and other literary women of her generation may well have wondered if their art could ever be as successful as the art of their great predecessors. In addition, women in Woolf's era had to contend with an intense male reaction not only against the present triumphs of suffragists but also against the past cultural achievements of women, whose history was now for the first time being adequately recounted. On balance, however, the records of women who had made the way "smooth" for Woolf and her peers seem to have been empowering rather than intimidating, and they seem to have persuaded writers of the teens, twenties, and thirties that any talented woman could be, in Taggard's words, "a poet, a wine-bibber, a radical."

Perhaps, too, the distinction between women writers' exuberant recognition that they at last had a strong female past and men writers' anxiety about the turmoil of the present accounts for the subtle but significant ways in which the texts produced by the two sexes often differ in this period. To be sure, as in earlier periods, women worked in most of the same modes and genres as their male contemporaries. The popular novelists Edith Wharton, Willa Cather, Katharine Susannah Prichard, Dorothy Sayers, and Agatha Christie had their counterparts in Sinclair Lewis, F. Scott Fitzgerald, John Galsworthy, Ellery Queen, and Rex Stout. The fictional experiments of Gertrude Stein, Dorothy Richardson, Virginia Woolf, and Djuna Barnes paralleled the fictional experiments of James Joyce, D. H. Lawrence, Ernest Hemingway, and William Faulkner. Women poets who employed traditional forms and meters—Anna Wickham, Edna St. Vincent Millay, Eleanor Wylie, Ruth Pitter, and Anne Spencer— were matched by male poets who employed comparable strategies—John Masefield, Stephen Vincent Benét, Robert Frost, and Countee Cullen. Finally, women innovators in verse—H. D., Marianne Moore, and Edith Sitwell —were influenced by (and influenced) the experiments of male innovators—Ezra Pound, T. S. Eliot, and William Carlos Williams. Nevertheless, both in theme and in technique the works of modernist women in all four categories frequently swerved from the works of modernist men.

Popular women novelists and memoirists, for instance, ranging from the best-selling writers Wharton and Cather to the autobiographers Vera Brittain and the mystery writer Christie, were distinctly concerned to explore the dynamics, and often the triumphs, of female lives. In the modernist period, Wharton, who had criticized the social system that sacrificed her heroine Lily Bart in her early *The House of Mirth* (1905), moved increasingly toward an affirmation of female strength. Ellen Olenska, the heroine of Wharton's Pulitzer Prize-winning *The Age of Innocence* (1920), expatriates herself to Paris (as her author, too, did during these years) and becomes an emblem of independence for the book's self-imprisoned hero, Newland Archer. In *My Ántonia* (1918) Willa Cather—though she spoke through a male narrator and often wrote novels and stories with male protagonists (for instance, *Coming, Aphrodite!*)— explored the virtually matriarchal energies of Ántonia Shimerda Cusack, a pioneer woman whose genius for survival transforms her into a symbol of natural endurance and fertility. Working in a different mode and with entirely different materials, Vera Brittain developed a surprisingly similar theme: her *Testament of Youth* (1933), a memoir of the World War I years, recounted her discovery of her own capacities, her commitment to service in the world, and her ability to surmount the tragedies of the war. Even the detective story writers Sayers and Christie—women who might seem to have been merely producing entertainment for a popular market—created and celebrated strong women characters: Sayers's Harriet Vane, the heroine of *Gaudy Night* (1935), a mystery set in one of Oxford's women's colleges, is at least as smart and tough as Lord Peter Wimsey, the novel's detective hero, while Christie's Miss Jane Marple, the brilliant detective heroine of a series of novels, is arguably smarter and tougher than Christie's detective hero Hercule Poirot, who is often portrayed as foppish and effete.

Women who composed more consciously experimental books elaborated similar ideas about female power. From Virginia Woolf and Katherine Mansfield to Gertrude Stein and Zora Neale Hurston, such artists excavated the lives and strengths of heroines and their ancestresses. Woolf's Clarissa Dalloway, the protagonist of her *Mrs. Dalloway*, and her Mrs. Ramsay, the mystical and mysterious mother in *To the Lighthouse* (1927), become emblems of independence and endurance as resonant as Ellen Olenska or Ántonia Cusack, while Mansfield's Mrs. Fairfield, the grandmother who presides over a group of fine stories about the author's New Zealand childhood, is equally energetic and inspiring. Similarly, the figure of Saint Therese in Stein's libretto for the opera *Four Saints in Three Acts* (1927) is characterized as magically charismatic, and Janie, the heroine of Hurston's *Their Eyes Were Watching God* (1937), is depicted as a triumphant survivor. The artists who created these figures did not, however, limit themselves to portraying what we would today call "positive role models" for women. Rather, in literary essays and experiments they meditated on fundamental questions having to do with the nature of writing itself, questions that ranged from the kind of language a woman author inherited to the kinds of aesthetic traditions and conventions that were passed down to her.

In *A Room of One's Own*, for example, Woolf called for "a woman's sentence," a sentence that would be different from the "common sentence . . . [the] man's sentence" that female writers had learned from "Thackeray . . . Dickens, De Quincey," for, she observed, "the weight, the pace, the stride of a man's mind are too unlike" those of female minds for women "to lift anything substantial" from male precursors. Whether or not they had read Woolf's proposal, her contemporaries Dorothy Richardson, Gertrude Stein, and Djuna Barnes—writing in very different ways—attempted stylistic innovations that would meet the kind of need she expressed. *Pilgrimage*, Richardson's ambitious sequence of novels (published between 1915 and 1935), was composed in a freely flowing language that transcribed her heroine's stream of consciousness so effectively that Woolf thought this writer *had* "invented the psychological sentence of the feminine gender." In the meantime, Gertrude Stein, experimenting in Paris, sought to subvert the grammatical and narrative conventions of what she called "patriarchal poetry" by putting words together in an entirely unprecedented (and often enigmatic) fashion because, as she argued in *Composition as Explanation*, "composition is the difference which makes each and all of them then different from other generations." Less drastically but perhaps just as dramatically, Djuna Barnes, in *Nightwood* (1937) and other works, wrote in an ornate and archaic style, as if by doing so she could create a new ancestral past for herself and other women. In remaking language so that it might more accurately reflect female experience, while revising conventions so that female artists might, as Stein put it, "Reject" what was oppressive in tradition, "Rejoice" in what was possible for the future, and "Rejuvenate" what was stale in the present, all these writers were employing the experimental strategies of male modernists to achieve distinctively feminist goals.

Many of the women poets who were their contemporaries used a variety of techniques toward the same ends. The poets Wylie, Millay, Spencer, and Pitter, for instance—none of whom were consciously experimental—nevertheless emphasized women's experiences and female perspectives. The sonnet sequences of Millay and Wylie appropriated and revised a genre traditionally used by male writers to praise a female beloved in order to express the dreams and desires of a female writer about a male beloved. Similarly, Spencer and Pitter used apparently conventional forms to record the unconventional feelings of passionate women or to recount the case histories of obscure but unique heroines. As for the more experimental poets H. D., Marianne Moore, and Edith Sitwell, all quested with the same urgency that marked the work of writers like Woolf and Stein for styles and forms that would free them from the burdensome conventions which infected "patriarchal poetry." Each in her own way —Moore slyly and sardonically, Sitwell with jazzy exuberance, and H. D. through overt re-creations of matriarchal images as well as through inventive wordplay—sought to annihilate the inherited forms and formulas of tradition so as to release her individual talent.

Finally, then, while many feminist modernists worked to excavate a specifically female past, all modernist women, even those who were not consciously feminists, in some sense strove to bring into being what H. D. called in *Trilogy* (1944, 1945, 1946) "the unwritten book of the new." Besides manifesting itself in linguistic experimentation and in the development of uniquely female perspectives, moreover, that "book of the new" now included a number of unprecedentedly frank and forceful writings from artists working in the suddenly burgeoning lesbian tradition (including Radclyffe Hall and Amy Lowell), in a newly rich ethnic and working-class tradition (including Meridel Le Sueur and Anzia Yezierska), in a growing colonial tradition (including Jean Rhys and Katharine Susannah Prichard), and in a lively tradition of revisionary feminist myth-making (including Isak Dinesen and Laura Riding).

As she so often did, Virginia Woolf summarized at least one aspect of the project upon which so many of these artists were engaged. Toward the end of *A Room of One's Own*, she described a novel by an imaginary female author named Mary Carmichael, who had "broken the sequence" of traditional fiction because, instead of focusing upon a conventional romance between hero and heroine, she had written about a friendship between two women: " 'Chloe liked Olivia,' I read," noted Woolf. "And then it struck me how immense a change was there. Chloe liked Olivia perhaps for the first time in literature." Almost as significant, from Woolf's point of view, was the occupation that had fostered the new friendship of these two characters: "They shared a laboratory together." Entering the new world of the professions, as Woolf and many of her contemporaries saw, women were no longer to be primarily defined through their erotic relationships with men. Thus the task of the woman writer was, for the first time, the task of tracing the prospects and problems of an expanding female intellectual community. No wonder, then, that in 1932, in the first serious study of Virginia Woolf's work, the novelist and essayist Winifred Holtby made a statement about the author of A *Room of One's Own* and *Mrs. Dalloway* that has resonant implications for our understanding of most female modernists: "When Virginia Woolf wrote of women," declared Holtby, "she wrote of a generation as adventurous in its exploration of experience as the Elizabethan men had been in their exploration of the globe. The women whom Mrs. Woolf knew were exploring the professional world, the political world, the world of business, discovering that they themselves had legs as well as wombs, brains as well as nerves, reason as well as sensibility; their Americas lay within themselves, and altered the map as profoundly as any added by Cabot or Columbus."

ELLEN GLASGOW
1873–1945

The eighth of ten children of an old Virginia family, Ellen Glasgow, whose novels were to record and explore the vagaries of Southern society, was born in Richmond to a frail, hospitable mother and a Calvinist-businessman father. As a girl, she had been supposed to make a debut and pursue a genteel career that would, in the words of one biographer, "follow the expected pattern of a Southern lady in her position." Instead, although she was not formally educated, she read voraciously—paying special attention to the works of such radical nineteenth-century intellectuals as Charles Darwin—and began to compose stories and poems at an early age, in the hope of becoming a successful writer. When she was only seventeen, she drafted her first novel, entitled *Sharp Realities*, and though it was rejected by a New York literary agent, she persistently rewrote the book until it was finally published anonymously as *The Descendant* (1897) and greeted with praise by reviewers, including the novelist Hamlin Garland.

When Glasgow was twenty, her much loved mother died, and the young writer became exceptionally close to her older sister Cary McCormack, a widow and an active feminist; to a brother, Frank, who reminded her of her mother; and to a married man (identified as "Gerald B——" in her memoirs), with whom she fell in love. In the early part of the century, all of these crucial figures also died, and Glasgow moved to New York for a period, during which she traveled extensively abroad and met Thomas Hardy, Arnold Bennett, John Galsworthy, Joseph Conrad, and other notable writers. Increasingly successful, she had begun to publish novels in rapid sucession, and her reputation soared. Yet, besides suffering from deafness, she evidently felt isolated and lonely, remarking that no "living creature ever came quite so close to me" as Jeremy, her Sealyham terrier.

In 1916, after her father's death, Glasgow returned to Richmond, Virginia, where she was to reside for the rest of her life. Here she entered into what one writer calls "an intermittent romance" with a well-known lawyer-politician, and here she wrote her finest novels—*Barren Ground* (1925), *The Sheltered Life* (1932), and *Vein of Iron* (1935)—as well as her posthumously published autobiography *The Woman Within* (1954), which her friend the Virginia novelist James Branch Cabell thought a "beautiful and wise volume which contains a large deal of her very best fiction." By the time she died at the age of seventy-two, Glasgow had been awarded many honors, including the Pulitzer Prize in 1942, and she had been widely recognized as a major American novelist, with the critics Carl Van Doren, J. Donald Adams, and Van Wyck Brooks vehemently arguing for her importance. Though her reputation has declined in the years since her death, a story like *Jordan's End* vividly justifies the success she achieved, dramatizing her ambivalent commitment to that "barren ground" of the South in which she found for herself a "vein of iron."

Jordan's End

At the fork of the road there was the dead tree where buzzards were roosting, and through its bough I saw the last flare of the sunset. On either side the November woods were flung in broken masses against the sky. When I stopped they appeared to move closer and surround me with vague, glimmering shapes. It seemed to me that I had been driving for hours; yet the ancient negro who brought the message had told me to follow the Old Stage Road till I came to Buzzard's Tree at the fork. "F'om dar on hit's moughty nigh ter Marse Jur'dn's place," the old man had assured me, adding tremulously, "en young Miss she sez you mus' come jes' ez quick ez you kin." I was young then (that was more than thirty years ago), and I was just beginning the practice of medicine in one of the more remote counties of Virginia.

My mare stopped, and leaning out, I gazed down each winding road, where it branched off, under half bared boughs, into the autumnal haze of the distance. In a little while the red would fade from the sky, and the chill night would find me still hesitating between those dubious ways which seemed to stretch into an immense solitude. While I waited uncertainly there was a stir in the boughs overhead, and a buzzard's feather floated down and settled slowly on the robe over my knees. In the effort to drive off depression, I laughed aloud and addressed my mare in a jocular tone:

"We'll choose the most God-forsaken of the two, and see where it leads us."

To my surprise the words brought an answer from the trees at my back. "If you're goin' to Isham's store, keep on the Old Stage Road," piped a voice from the underbrush.

Turning quickly, I saw the dwarfed figure of a very old man, with a hunched back, who was dragging a load of pine knots out of the woods. Though he was so stooped that his head reached scarcely higher than my wheel, he appeared to possess unusual vigour for one of his age and infirmities. He was dressed in a rough overcoat of some wood brown shade, beneath which I could see his overalls of blue jeans. Under a thatch of grizzled hair his shrewd little eyes twinkled cunningly, and his bristly chin jutted so far forward that it barely escaped the descending curve of his nose. I remember thinking that he could not be far from a hundred; his skin was so wrinkled and weather-beaten that, at a distance, I had mistaken him for a negro.

I bowed politely. "Thank you, but I am going to Jordan's End," I replied.

He cackled softly. "Then you take the bad road. Thar's Jur'dn's turn-out." He pointed to the sunken trail, deep in mud, on the right. "An' if you ain't objectin' to a little comp'ny, I'd be obleeged if you'd give me a lift. I'm bound thar on my own o' count, an' it's a long ways to tote these here lightwood knots."

While I drew back my robe and made room for him, I watched him heave the load of resinous pine into the buggy, and then scramble with agility to his place at my side.

"My name is Peterkin," he remarked by way of introduction. "They call me Father Peterkin along o'[1] the gran'child'en." He was a garrulous soul, I suspected, and would not be averse to imparting the information I wanted.

"There's not much travel this way," I began, as we turned out of the cleared space into the deep tunnel of the trees. Immediately the twilight enveloped us, though now and then the dusky glow in the sky was still visible. The air was sharp with the tang of autumn; with the effluvium of rotting leaves, the drift of wood smoke, the ripe flavour of crushed apples.

"Thar's nary a stranger, thoughten he was a doctor, been to Jur'dn's End as fur back as I kin recollect. Ain't you the new doctor?"

"Yes, I am the doctor." I glanced down at the gnomelike shape in the wood brown overcoat. "Is it much farther?"

"Naw, suh, we're all but thar jest as soon as we come out of Whitten woods."

"If the road is so little travelled, how do you happen to be going there?"

Without turning his head, the old man wagged his crescent shaped profile. "Oh, I live on the place. My son Tony works a slice of the farm

---

1. I.e., in the presence of, or because of.

on shares,[2] and I manage to lend a hand at the harvest or corn shuckin', and, now-and-agen, with the cider. The old gentleman used to run the place that away afore he went deranged, an' now that the young one is laid up, thar ain't nobody to look after the farm but Miss Judith. Them old ladies don't count. Thar's three of 'em, but they're all addle-brained an' look as if the buzzards had picked 'em. I reckon that comes from bein' shut up with crazy folks in that thar old tumbledown house. The roof ain't been patched fur so long that the shingles have most rotted away, an' thar's times, Tony says, when you kin skearcely hear yo' years fur the rumpus the wrens an' rats are makin' overhead."

"What is the trouble with them—the Jordans, I mean?"

"Jest run to seed, suh, I reckon."

"Is there no man of the family left?"

For a minute Father Peterkin made no reply. Then he shifted the bundle of pine knots, and responded warily. "Young Alan, he's still livin' on the old place, but I hear he's been took now, an' is goin' the way of all the rest of 'em. 'Tis a hard trial for Miss Judith, po' young thing, an' with a boy nine year old that's the very spit an' image of his pa. Wall, wall, I kin recollect away back yonder when old Mr. Timothy Jur'dn was the proudest man anywhar aroun' in these parts; but arter the War things sorter begun to go down hill with him, and he was ob-leeged to draw in his horns."

"Is he still living?"

The old man shook his head. "Mebbe he is, mebbe he ain't. Nobody knows but the Jur'dn's, an' they ain't tellin' fur the axin'."

"I suppose it was this Miss Judith who sent for me?"

" 'Twould most likely be she, suh. She was one of the Yardlys that lived over yonder at Yardly's Field; an' when young Mr. Alan begun to take notice of her, 'twas the first time sence way back that one of the Jur'dn's had gone courtin' outside the family. That's the reason the blood went bad like it did, I reckon. Thar's a sayin' down aroun' here that Jur'dn an' Jur'dn won't mix." The name was invariably called Jur-din by all classes; but I had already discovered that names are rarely pro-nounced as they are spelled in Virginia.

"Have they been married long?"

"Ten year or so, suh. I remember as well as if 'twas yestiddy the day young Alan brought her home as a bride, an' thar warn't a soul besides the three daft old ladies to welcome her. They drove over in my son Tony's old buggy, though 'twas spick an' span then. I was goin' to the house on an arrant, an' I was standin' right down thar at the ice pond

---

2. Sharecroppers are farmers who work a piece of land in exchange for a share of the profits from the owner.

when they come by. She hadn't been much in these parts, an' none of us had ever seed her afore. When she looked up at young Alan her face was pink all over and her eyes war shinin' bright as the moon. Then the front do' opened an' them old ladies, as black as crows, flocked out on the po'ch. Thar never was anybody as peart-lookin' as Miss Judith was when she come here; but soon arterwards she begun to peak an' pine, though she never lost her sperits an' went mopin' roun' like all the other women folks at Jur'dn's End. They married sudden, an' folks do say she didn't know nothin' about the family, an' young Alan didn't know much mo' than she did. The old ladies had kep' the secret away from him, sorter believin' that what you don't know cyarn' hurt you. Anyways they never let it leak out tell arter his chile was born. Thar ain't never been but that one, an' old Aunt Jerusly declars he was born with a caul[3] over his face, so mebbe things will be all right fur him in the long run."

"But who are the old ladies? Are their husbands living?"

When Father Peterkin answered the question he had dropped his voice to a hoarse murmur. "Deranged. All gone deranged," he replied.

I shivered, for a chill depression seemed to emanate from the November woods. As we drove on, I remembered grim tales of enchanted forests filled with evil faces and whispering voices. The scents of wood earth and rotting leaves invaded my brain like a magic spell. On either side the forest was as still as death. Not a leaf quivered, not a bird moved, not a small wild creature stirred in the underbush. Only the glossy leaves and the scarlet berries of the holly appeared alive amid the bare interlacing branches of the trees. I began to long for an autumn clearing and the red light of the afterglow.

"Are they living or dead?" I asked presently.

"I've hearn strange tattle," answered the old man nervously, "but nobody kin tell. Folks do say as young Alan's pa is shut up in a padded place, and that his gran'pa died thar arter thirty years. His uncles went crazy too, an' the daftness is beginnin' to crop out in the women. Up tell now it has been mostly the men. One time I remember old Mr. Peter Jur'dn tryin' to burn down the place in the dead of the night. Thar's the end of the wood, suh. If you'll jest let me down here, I'll be gittin' along home across the old-field, an' thanky too."

At last the woods ended abruptly on the edge of an abandoned field which was thickly sown with scrub pine and broomsedge. The glow in the sky had faded now to a thin yellow-green, and a melancholy twilight pervaded the landscape. In this twilight I looked over the few sheep huddled together on the ragged lawn, and saw the old brick house

---

3. A membrane covering the head at birth; supposed to imply semimagical powers in a child born with it.

crumbling beneath its rank growth of ivy. As I drew nearer I had the feeling that the surrounding desolation brooded there like some sinister influence.

Forlorn as it appeared at this first approach, I surmised that Jordan's End must have possessed once charm as well as distinction. The proportions of the Georgian front were impressive, and there was beauty of design in the quaint doorway, and in the steps of rounded stone which were brocaded now with a pattern of emerald moss. But the whole place was badly in need of repair. Looking up, as I stopped, I saw that the eaves were falling away, that crumbled shutters were sagging from loosened hinges, that odd scraps of hemp sacking or oil cloth were stuffed into windows where panes were missing. When I stepped on the floor of the porch, I felt the rotting boards give way under my feet.

After thundering vainly on the door, I descended the steps, and followed the beaten path that led round the west wing of the house. When I had passed an old boxwood tree at the corner, I saw a woman and a boy of nine years or so come out of a shed, which I took to be the smokehouse,[4] and begin to gather chips from the woodpile. The woman carried a basket made of splits on her arm, and while she stooped to fill this, she talked to the child in a soft musical voice. Then, at a sound that I made, she put the basket aside, and rising to her feet, faced me in the pallid light from the sky. Her head was thrown back, and over the dress of some dark calico, a tattered gray shawl clung to her figure. That was thirty years ago; I am not young any longer; I have been in many countries since then, and looked on many women; but her face, with that wan light on it, is the last one I shall forget in my life. Beauty! Why, that woman will be beautiful when she is a skeleton, was the thought that flashed into my mind.

She was very tall, and so thin that her flesh seemed faintly luminous, as if an inward light pierced the transparent substance. It was the beauty, not of earth, but of triumphant spirit. Perfection, I suppose, is the rarest thing we achieve in this world of incessant compromise with inferior forms; yet the woman who stood there in that ruined place appeared to me to have stepped straight out of legend or allegory. The contour of her face was Italian in its pure oval; her hair swept in wings of dusk above her clear forehead; and, from the faintly shadowed hollows beneath her brows, the eyes that looked at me were purple-black, like dark pansies.

"I had given you up," she began in a low voice, as if she were afraid of being overheard. "You are the doctor?"

"Yes, I am the doctor. I took the wrong road and lost my way. Are you Mrs. Jordan?"

---

4. A small building where meat is cured by means of dense smoke.

She bowed her head. "Mrs. Alan Jordan. There are three Mrs. Jordans besides myself. My husband's grandmother and the wives of his two uncles."

"And it is your husband who is ill?"

"My husband, yes. I wrote a few days ago to Doctor Carstairs." (Thirty years ago Carstairs, of Baltimore, was the leading alienist[5] in the country.) "He is coming to-morrow morning; but last night my husband was so restless that I sent for you to-day." Her rich voice, vibrating with suppressed feeling, made me think of stained glass windows and low organ music.

"Before we go in," I asked, "will you tell me as much as you can?"

Instead of replying to my request, she turned and laid her hand on the boy's shoulder. "Take the chips to Aunt Agatha, Benjamin," she said, "and tell her that the doctor has come."

While the child picked up the basket and ran up the sunken steps to the door, she watched him with breathless anxiety. Not until he had disappeared into the hall did she lift her eyes to my face again. Then, without answering my question, she murmured, with a sigh which was like the voice of that autumn evening, "We were once happy here." She was trying, I realized, to steel her heart against the despair that threatened it.

My gaze swept the obscure horizon, and returned to the mouldering woodpile where we were standing. The yellow-green had faded from the sky, and the only light came from the house where a few scattered lamps were burning. Through the open door I could see the hall, as bare as if the house were empty, and the spiral staircase which crawled to the upper story. A fine old place once, but repulsive now in its abject decay, like some young blood of former days who has grown senile.

"Have you managed to wring a living out of the land?" I asked, because I could think of no words that were less compassionate.

"At first a poor one," she answered slowly. "We worked hard, harder than any negro in the fields, to keep things together, but we were happy. Then three years ago this illness came, and after that everything went against us. In the beginning it was simply brooding, a kind of melancholy, and we tried to ward it off by pretending that it was not real, that we imagined it. Only of late, when it became so much worse, have we admitted the truth, have we faced the reality—"

This passionate murmur, which had almost the effect of a chant rising out of the loneliness, was addressed, not to me, but to some abstract and implacable power. While she uttered it her composure was like the tranquillity of the dead. She did not lift her hand to hold her shawl,

---

5. Obsolete word for psychiatrist.

which was slipping unnoticed from her shoulders, and her eyes, so like dark flowers in their softness, did not leave my face.

"If you will tell me all, perhaps I may be able to help you," I said.

"But you know our story," she responded. "You must have heard it."

"Then it is true? Heredity, intermarriage, insanity?"

She did not wince at the bluntness of my speech. "My husband's grandfather is in an asylum, still living after almost thirty years. His father—my husband's, I mean—died there a few years ago. Two of his uncles are there. When it began I don't know, or how far back it reaches. We have never talked of it. We have tried always to forget it —Even now I cannot put the thing into words—My husband's mother died of a broken heart, but the grandmother and the two others are still living. You will see them when you go into the house. They are old women now, and they feel nothing."

"And there have been other cases?"

"I do not know. Are not four enough?"

"Do you know if it has assumed always the same form?" I was trying to be as brief as I could.

She flinched, and I saw that her unnatural calm was shaken at last. "The same, I believe. In the beginning there is melancholy, moping, Grandmother calls it, and then—" She flung out her arms with a despairing gesture, and I was reminded again of some tragic figure of legend.

"I know, I know," I was young, and in spite of my pride, my voice trembled. "Has there been in any case partial recovery, recurring at intervals?"

"In his grandfather's case, yes. In the others none. With them it has been hopeless from the beginning."

"And Carstairs is coming?"

"In the morning. I should have waited, but last night—" Her voice broke, and she drew the tattered shawl about her with a shiver. "Last night something happened. Something happened," she repeated, and could not go on. Then, collecting her strength with an effort which made her tremble like a blade of grass in the wind, she continued more quietly, "To-day he has been better. For the first time he has slept, and I have been able to leave him. Two of the hands from the fields are in the room." Her tone changed suddenly, and a note of energy passed into it. Some obscure resolution brought a tinge of colour to her pale cheek. "I must know," she added, "if this is as hopeless as all the others."

I took a step toward the house. "Carstairs's opinion is worth as much as that of any man living," I answered.

"But will he tell me the truth?"

I shook my head. "He will tell you what he thinks. No man's judgment is infallible."

Turning away from me, she moved with an energetic step to the house. As I followed her into the hall the threshold creaked under my tread, and I was visited by an apprehension, or, if you prefer, by a superstitious dread of the floor above. Oh, I got over that kind of thing before I was many years older; though in the end I gave up medicine, you know, and turned to literature as a safer outlet for a suppressed imagination.

But the dread was there at that moment, and it was not lessened by the glimpse I caught, at the foot of the spiral staircase, of a scantily furnished room, where three lean black-robed figures, as impassive as the Fates,[6] were grouped in front of a wood fire. They were doing something with their hands. Knitting, crocheting, or plaiting straw?

At the head of the stairs the woman stopped and looked back at me. The light from the kerosene lamp on the wall fell over her, and I was struck afresh not only by the alien splendour of her beauty, but even more by the look of consecration, of impassioned fidelity that illumined her face.

"He is very strong," she said in a whisper. "Until this trouble came on him he had never had a day's illness in his life. We hoped that hard work, not having time to brood, might save us; but it has only brought the thing we feared sooner."

There was a question in her eyes, and I responded in the same subdued tone. "His health, you say, is good?" What else was there for me to ask when I understood everything?

A shudder ran through her frame. "We used to think that a blessing, but now—" She broke off and then added in a lifeless voice, "We keep two field hands in the room day and night, lest one should forget to watch the fire, or fall asleep."

A sound came from a room at the end of the hall, and, without finishing her sentence, she moved swiftly toward the closed door. The apprehension, the dread, or whatever you choose to call it, was so strong upon me, that I was seized by an impulse to turn and retreat down the spiral staircase. Yes, I know why some men turn cowards in battle.

"I have come back, Alan," she said in a voice that wrung my heartstrings.

The room was dimly lighted; and for a minute after I entered, I could see nothing clearly except the ruddy glow of the wood fire in front of which two negroes were seated on low wooden stools. They had kindly faces, these men; there was a primitive humanity in their features, which might have been modelled out of the dark earth of the fields.

6. Three sisters, Greek goddesses of human destiny.

Looking round the next minute, I saw that a young man was sitting away from the fire, huddled over in a cretonne-covered chair with a high back and deep wings. At our entrance the negroes glanced up with surprise; but the man in the winged chair neither lifted his head nor turned his eyes in our direction. He sat there, lost within the impenetrable wilderness of the insane, as remote from us and from the sound of our voices as if he were the inhabitant of an invisible world. His head was sunk forward; his eyes were staring fixedly at some image we could not see; his fingers, moving restlessly, were plaiting and unplaiting the fringe of a plaid shawl. Distraught as he was, he still possessed the dignity of mere physical perfection. At his full height he must have measured not under six feet three; his hair was the colour of ripe wheat, and his eyes, in spite of their fixed gaze, were as blue as the sky after rain. And this was only the beginning, I realized. With that constitution, that physical frame, he might live to be ninety.

"Alan!" breathed his wife again in her pleading murmur.

If he heard her voice, he gave no sign of it. Only when she crossed the room and bent over his chair, he put out his hand, with a gesture of irritation, and pushed her away, as if she were a veil of smoke which came between him and the object at which he was looking. Then his hand fell back to its old place, and he resumed his mechanical plaiting of the fringe.

The woman lifted her eyes to mine. "His father did that for twenty years," she said in a whisper that was scarcely more than a sigh of anguish.

When I had made my brief examination, we left the room as we had come, and descended the stairs together. The three old women were still sitting in front of the wood fire. I do not think they had moved since we went upstairs; but, as we reached the hall below, one of them, the youngest, I imagine, rose from her chair, and came out to join us. She was crocheting something soft and small, an infant's sacque,[7] I perceived as she approached, of pink wool. The ball had rolled from her lap as she stood up, and it trailed after her now, like a woolen rose, on the bare floor. When the skein pulled at her, she turned back and stooped to pick up the ball, which she rewound with caressing fingers. Good God, an infant's sacque in that house!

"Is it the same thing?" she asked.

"Hush!" responded the younger woman kindly. Turning to me she added, "We cannot talk here," and opening the door, passed out on the porch. Not until we had reached the lawn, and walked in silence to where my buggy stood beneath an old locust tree, did she speak again.

Then she said only, "You know now?"

---

7. A jacket for a baby.

"Yes, I know," I replied, averting my eyes from her face while I gave my directions as briefly as I could. "I will leave an opiate," I said. "To-morrow, if Carstairs should not come, send for me again. If he does come," I added, "I will talk to him and see you afterward."

"Thank you," she answered gently; and taking the bottle from my hand, she turned away and walked quickly back to the house.

I watched her as long as I could; and then getting into my buggy. I turned my mare's head toward the woods, and drove by moonlight, past Buzzard's Tree and over the Old Stage Road, to my home. "I will see Carstairs to-morrow," was my last thought that night before I slept.

But, after all, I saw Carstairs only for a minute as he was taking the train. Life at its beginning and its end had filled my morning; and when at last I reached the little station, Carstairs had paid his visit, and was waiting on the platform for the approaching express. At first he showed a disposition to question me about the shooting,[8] but as soon as I was able to make my errand clear, his jovial face clouded.

"So you've been there?" he said. "They didn't tell me. An interesting case, if it were not for that poor woman. Incurable, I'm afraid, when you consider the predisposing causes. The race is pretty well deteriorated, I suppose. God! what isolation! I've advised her to send him away. There are three others, they tell me, at Staunton."

The train came; he jumped on it, and was whisked away while I gazed after him. After all, I was none the wiser because of the great reputation of Carstairs.

All that day I heard nothing more from Jordan's End; and then, early next morning, the same decrepit negro brought me a message.

"Young Miss, she tole me ter ax you ter come along wid me jes' ez soon ez you kin git ready."

"I'll start at once. Uncle, and I'll take you with me."

My mare and buggy stood at the door. All I needed to do was to put on my overcoat, pick up my hat, and leave word, for a possible patient, that I should return before noon. I knew the road now, and I told myself, as I set out, that I would make as quick a trip as I could. For two nights I had been haunted by the memory of that man in the armchair, plaiting and unplaiting the fringe of the plaid shawl. And his father had done that, the woman told me, for twenty years!

It was a brown autumn morning, raw, windless, with an overcast sky and a peculiar illusion of nearness about the distance. A high wind had blown all night, but at dawn it had dropped suddenly, and now there was not so much as a ripple in the broomsedge. Over the fields, when we came out of the woods, the thin trails of blue smoke were as motion-less as cobwebs. The lawn surrounding the house looked smaller than it

8. Hunting.

had appeared to me in the twilight, as if the barren fields had drawn closer since my last visit. Under the trees, where the few sheep were browsing, the piles of leaves lay in windrifts along the sunken walk and against the wings of the house.

When I knocked the door was opened immediately by one of the old women, who held a streamer of black cloth or rusty crape in her hands.

"You may go straight upstairs," she croaked; and, without waiting for an explanation, I entered the hall quickly, and ran up the stairs.

The door of the room was closed, and I opened it noiselessly, and stepped over the threshold. My first sensation, as I entered, was one of cold. Then I saw that the windows were wide open, and that the room seemed to be full of people, though, as I made out presently, there was no one there except Alan Jordan's wife, her little son, the two old aunts, and an aged crone of a negress. On the bed there was something under a yellowed sheet of fine linen (what the negroes call "a burial sheet." I suppose), which had been handed down from some more affluent generation.

When I went over, after a minute, and turned down one corner of the covering, I saw that my patient of the other evening was dead. Not a line of pain marred his features, not a thread of gray dimmed the wheaten gold of his hair. So he must have looked, I thought, when she first loved him. He had gone from life, not old, enfeebled and repulsive, but enveloped still in the romantic illusion of their passion.

As I entered, the two old women, who had been fussing about the bed, drew back to make way for me, but the witch of a negress did not pause in the weird chant, an incantation of some sort, which she was mumbling. From the rag carpet in front of the empty fireplace, the boy, with his father's hair and his mother's eyes, gazed at me silently, broodingly, as if I were trespassing; and by the open window, with her eyes on the ashen November day, the young wife stood as motionless as a statue. While I looked at her a redbird flew out of the boughs of a cedar, and she followed it with her eyes.

"You sent for me?" I said to her.

She did not turn. She was beyond the reach of my voice, of any voice, I imagine; but one of the palsied old women answered my question.

"He was like this when we found him this morning," she said. "He had a bad night, and Judith and the two hands were up with him until daybreak. Then he seemed to fall asleep, and Judith sent the hands, turn about,[9] to get their breakfast."

While she spoke my eyes were on the bottle I had left there. Two nights ago it had been full, and now it stood empty, without a cork, on

9. One at a time, in shifts.

the mantelpiece. They had not even thrown it away. It was typical of the pervading inertia of the place that the bottle should still be standing there awaiting my visit.

For an instant the shock held me speechless; when at last I found my voice it was to ask mechanically.

"When did it happen?"

The old woman who had spoken took up the story. "Nobody knows. We have not touched him. No one but Judith has gone near him." Her words trailed off into unintelligible muttering. If she had ever had her wits about her, I dare-say fifty years at Jordan's End had unsettled them completely.

I turned to the woman at the window. Against the gray sky and the black intersecting branches of the cedar, her head, with its austere perfection, was surrounded by that visionary air of legend. So Antigone[1] might have looked on the day of her sacrifice, I reflected. I had never seen a creature who appeared so withdrawn, so detached, from all human associations. It was as if some spiritual isolation divided her from her kind.

"I can do nothing," I said.

For the first time she looked at me, and her eyes were unfathomable. "No, you can do nothing," she answered. "He is safely dead."

The negress was still crooning on; the other old women were fussing helplessly. It was impossible in their presence, I felt, to put in words the thing I had to say.

"Will you come downstairs with me?" I asked, "Outside of this house?"

Turning quietly, she spoke to the boy. "Run out and play, dear. He would have wished it."

Then, without a glance toward the bed, or the old women gathered about it, she followed me over the threshold, down the stairs, and out on the deserted lawn. The ashen day could not touch her, I saw then. She was either so remote from it, or so completely a part of it, that she was impervious to its sadness. Her white face did not become more pallid as the light struck it; her tragic eyes did not grow deeper; her frail figure under the thin shawl did not shiver in the raw air. She felt nothing, I realized suddenly.

Wrapped in that silence as in a cloak, she walked across the windrifts of leaves to where my mare was waiting. Her step was so slow, so unhurried, that I remember thinking she moved like one who had all eternity before her. Oh, one has strange impressions, you know, at such moments!

---

1. Heroine of Sophocles' *Antigone*, she sacrificed herself in order to bury her brother, against the king's decree.

In the middle of the lawn, where the trees had been stripped bare in the night, and the leaves were piled in long mounds like double graves, she stopped and looked in my face. The air was so still that the whole place might have been in a trance or asleep. Not a branch moved, not a leaf rustled on the ground, not a sparrow twittered in the ivy; and even the few sheep stood motionless, as if they were under a spell. Farther away, beyond the sea of broomsedge, where no wind stirred, I saw the flat desolation of the landscape. Nothing moved on the earth, but high above, under the leaden clouds, a buzzard was sailing.

I moistened my lips before I spoke. "God knows I want to help you!" At the back of my brain a hideous question was drumming. How had it happened? Could she have killed him? Had that delicate creature nerved her will to the unspeakable act? It was incredible. It was inconceivable. And yet. . . .

"The worst is over," she answered quietly, with that tearless agony which is so much more terrible than any outburst of grief. "Whatever happens, I can never go through the worst again. Once in the beginning he wanted to die. His great fear was that he might live too long, until it was too late to save himself. I made him wait then. I held him back by a promise."

So she had killed him, I thought. Then she went on steadily, after a minute, and I doubted again.

"Thank God, it was easier for him than he feared it would be," she murmured.

No, it was not conceivable. He must have bribed one of the negroes. But who had stood by and watched without intercepting? Who had been in the room? Well, either way! "I will do all I can to help you," I said.

Her gaze did not waver. "There is so little that any one can do now," she responded, as if she had not understood what I meant. Suddenly, without the warning of a sob, a cry of despair went out of her, as if it were torn from her breast. "He was my life," she cried, "and I must go on!"

So full of agony was the sound that it seemed to pass like a gust of wind over the broomsedge. I waited until the emptiness had opened and closed over it. Then I asked as quietly as I could:

"What will you do now?"

She collected herself with a shudder of pain. "As long as the old people live, I am tied here. I must bear it out to the end. When they die, I shall go away and find work. I am sending my boy to school. Doctor Carstairs will look after him, and he will help me when the time comes. While my boy needs me, there is no release."

While I listened to her, I knew that the question on my lips would never be uttered. I should always remain ignorant of the truth. The thing I feared most, standing there alone with her, was that some accident might solve the mystery before I could escape. My eyes left her face and wandered over the dead leaves at our feet. No, I had nothing to ask her.

"Shall I come again?" That was all.

She shook her head. "Not unless I send for you. If I need you, I will send for you," she answered; but in my heart I knew that she would never send for me.

I held out my hand, but she did not take it; and I felt that she meant me to understand, by her refusal, that she was beyond all consolation and all companionship. She was nearer to the bleak sky and the deserted fields than she was to her kind.

As she turned away, the shawl slipped from her shoulders to the dead leaves over which she was walking; but she did not stoop to recover it, nor did I make a movement to follow her. Long after she had entered the house I stood there, gazing down on the garment that she had dropped. Then climbing into my buggy, I drove slowly across the field and into the woods.

1923

WILLA CATHER
1873–1947

Willa Cather's novels commemorate an obdurate, primordial landscape that had almost been erased by the time she began writing. Her fictional frontiers—the shaggy midwestern plains of *O Pioneers!* (1913) or the cliffs, canyons, and caves of the Southwest in *The Professor's House* (1925)—evoke the grandeur of eternal, mysterious forces that call forth the exertions characteristic of her early settlers. But the pioneer is only one type of the determined, willful character who absorbed Cather throughout her highly successful career. Another is the artist, whom she portrayed first in the opera singer of *The Song of the Lark* (1915) and later in the actresses and vocalists of *Coming, Aphrodite!* (1920), *My Mortal Enemy* (1926), and *Lucy Gayheart* (1940). Whether she focused on pioneering settlers or pioneering artists, however, Cather was frequently drawn to powerful female figures.

Possibly the most momentous event in Cather's early life was the move from Virginia to Nebraska that her family undertook in 1883. For her first nine years, she lived in a spacious, three-story, brick farmhouse near Winchester, Virginia. Wilella Cather was the first of seven children born to Charles Cather, an easygoing farmer who turned to real estate in later life, and Mary Virginia (Boak) Cather, an imperious woman remembered with some ambivalence by her daughter. But Willie, as she liked to call herself, was primarily educated by her maternal grandmother, whose portrait she lovingly drew in the short story *Old Mrs. Harris* (1932). When the family moved to Webster County, Nebraska, Cather must have experienced the same shock at the primitive sod houses and the ice-encrusted wilderness that her narrator Jim Burden expresses in *My Ántonia* (1918). Less a country than the vast "material out of which countries are made," the county in which her family settled was, in her own words, "naked as the back of your hand."

Like Jim, too, when Cather moved with her family to neighboring Red Cloud, a town of twenty-five hundred situated on the Burlington railroad line, she identified with other uprooted immigrants: Swedish, Bohemian, and Russian settlers struggling to make a new life in the New World while preserving the cultural traditions of the old world. In school at Red Cloud, Cather frequently dressed in boyish clothes and dreamed of becoming William Cather, M.D. At home, she read widely in British and American literature in her parents' library and in French and German translations at her neighbors'. At the University of Nebraska, in Lincoln, moreover, she began studying the classics while publishing her writing in the undergraduate literary magazine. Before and after graduation in 1895, she reviewed cultural events for the Lincoln newspaper, and then moved to Pittsburgh to edit the *Home Monthly* magazine for another year.

Cather's personal life during her ten-year residence in Pittsburgh is no less shrouded in obscurity than her later life in New York because she burned as many of her letters as she could and because in her will she forbade publication of the surviving letters. Her biographers James Woodress and Leon Edel have argued, however, that what saved Cather from loneliness in those years was her relationship with Isabelle McClung. This daughter of a conservative Pittsburgh judge invited Cather to live in her house, where the two shared a bedroom. Cather began writing her fiction in an attic room in the McClung house, but she continued to work at the *Pittsburgh Daily Leader*. As music, drama, and book reviewer, Cather wrote about the Pittsburgh Symphony's performance of Dvořák's *New World Symphony*, Helen Modjeska's acting in *Mary Stuart*, and Kate Chopin's predilection for romanticism in *The Awakening*. As a free-lance artist, she composed the verse that would appear in *April Twilights* (1903) and the stories collected in *The Troll Garden* (1905).

In 1906 Cather moved to New York to join the staff of *McClure's Magazine*. An assignment in Boston led to a meaningful friendship with Sarah Orne Jewett: in subsequent essays, Cather praised Jewett's sparse but evocative prose style, a style she would strive toward in her own later fiction. In New York, Cather lived in a studio apartment at 60 South Washington Square, a building that also housed the woman who would become her lifelong companion, Edith Lewis. Cather decided to resign as managing editor of *McClure's* after her first novel, *Alexander's Bridge*, was serialized in the 1912 issues. From the architect Alexander, she moved on to the pioneer Alexandra in her next novel, *O Pioneers!*, which she dedicated to Jewett. Although Cather wrote both *O Pioneers!* and *The Song of the Lark* during stays in Isabelle McClung's house, by 1913 she had moved to 5 Bank Street with Edith Lewis. Cather was apparently extremely upset at Isabelle McClung's decision to marry in 1915. Yet she and Edith Lewis had already become close friends. Indeed, they had embarked on a series of trips to the Southwest which would shape the writer's novels.

My Ántonia, the next novel Cather composed, was strongly autobiographical. Although it presents her memories of her Nebraskan childhood through a male narrator, its main subject is Ántonia, a female character who heroically survives the suicide of her father, arduous farm work, town employment as a hired girl, and an illegitimate pregnancy, to become "a rich mine of life, like the founders of early races." The tension between Ántonia's sturdy earthiness and Jim Burden's commitment to the sophistication and learning he associates with the East would inform a number of Cather's finest stories, as well as later works like her Pulitzer Prize-winning war novel, *One of Ours* (1922). Yet, although she was gaining a literary reputation, Cather was becoming disillusioned with modern life. "The world was broken in two in 1922 or thereabouts," she wrote in her collected essays, *Not under Forty* (1936), expressing her distress over poor health, her disappointment about her books' receptions, and her growing contempt for contemporary values. From this point on, she would turn with nostalgia to historically remote periods.

Later novels like *The Professor's House* (1925), *Death Comes for the Archbishop* (1927), and *Shadows on the Rock* (1931) continue to explore the individual's withdrawal from society, frequently depicting a quest for integrity through male characters who are often placed in a Catholic context. Typical in this respect are the European missionaries in New Mexico of *Death Comes for the Archbishop* and the seventeenth-century French Canadian settlers of *Shadows on the Rock*. With her last novel, however, Cather returned to the questions about female identity that had absorbed her earlier in her career. *Sapphira and the Slave Girl* (1940) focuses on the Shenandoah Valley of the writer's early childhood and on the reconciliation of a domineering mother with her equally willful daughter. As in Cather's earlier fiction, romantic plot elements are far less important than suggestive tableaux in which the self is tested and shaped by experience.

Cather had already received a number of honorary degrees and literary prizes when, in 1937, she prepared a complete edition of her works for Scribner's. *Coming, Aphrodite!*, which appeared in her collection *Youth and the Bright Medusa*, integrates mythic material and social analysis to explore both the triumphs and the irrevocable personal costs of the artistic ambition that clearly propelled her own career.

Coming, Aphrodite![1]

I

Don Hedger had lived for four years on the top floor of an old house on the south side of Washington Square,[2] and nobody had ever disturbed him. He occupied one big room with no outside exposure except on the north, where he had built in a many-paned studio window

---

that looked upon a court and upon the roofs and walls of other buildings. His room was very cheerless, since he never got a ray of direct
sunlight; the south corners were always in shadow. In one of the
corners was a clothes closet, built against the partition, in another a
wide divan, serving as a seat by day and a bed by night. In the front
corner, the one farther from the window, was a sink, and a table with
two gas burners where he sometimes cooked his food. There, too, in
the perpetual dusk, was the dog's bed, and often a bone or two for his
comfort.

The dog was a Boston bull terrier, and Hedger explained his surly
disposition by the fact that he had been bred to the point where it told
on his nerves. His name was Caesar III, and he had taken prizes at very
exclusive dog shows. When he and his master went out to prowl about
University Place or to promenade along West Street, Caesar III was
invariably fresh and shining. His pink skin showed through his mottled
coat, which glistened as if it had just been rubbed with olive oil, and he
wore a brass-studded collar, bought at the smartest saddler's. Hedger, as
often as not, was hunched up in an old striped blanket coat, with a
shapeless felt hat pulled over his bushy hair, wearing black shoes that
had become grey, or brown ones that had become black, and he never
put on gloves unless the day was biting cold.

Early in May, Hedger learned that he was to have a new neighbour
in the rear apartment—two rooms, one large and one small, that faced
the west. His studio was shut off from the larger of these rooms by double doors, which, though they were fairly tight, left him a good deal at
the mercy of the occupant. The rooms had been leased, long before he
came there, by a trained nurse who considered herself knowing in old
furniture. She went to auction sales and bought up mahogany and dirty
brass and stored it away here, where she meant to live when she retired
from nursing. Meanwhile, she sub-let her rooms, with their precious
furniture, to young people who came to New York to "write" or to
"paint"—who proposed to live by the sweat of the brow rather than of
the hand, and who desired artistic surroundings. When Hedger first
moved in, these rooms were occupied by a young man who tried to
write plays,—and who kept on trying until a week ago, when the nurse
had put him out for unpaid rent.

A few days after the playwright left, Hedger heard an ominous murmur of voices through the bolted double doors: the lady-like intonation
of the nurse—doubtless exhibiting her treasures—and another voice,
also a woman's, but very different; young, fresh, unguarded, confident.
All the same, it would be very annoying to have a woman in there. The
only bath-room on the floor was at the top of the stairs in the front hall,
and he would always be running into her as he came or went from his
bath. He would have to be more careful to see that Caesar didn't leave

bones about the hall, too; and she might object when he cooked steak and onions on his gas burner.

As soon as the talking ceased and the women left, he forgot them. He was absorbed in a study of paradise fish at the Aquarium, staring out at people through the glass and green water of their tank. It was a highly gratifying idea; the incommunicability of one stratum of animal life with another,—though Hedger pretended it was only an experiment in unusual lighting. When he heard trunks knocking against the sides of the narrow hall, then he realized that she was moving in at once. Toward noon, groans and deep gasps and the creaking of ropes, made him aware that a piano was arriving. After the tramp of the movers died away down the stairs, somebody touched off a few scales and chords on the instrument, and then there was peace. Presently he heard her lock her door and go down the hall humming something; going out to lunch, probably. He stuck his brushes in a can of turpentine and put on his hat, not stopping to wash his hands. Caesar was smelling along the crack under the bolted doors; his bony tail stuck out hard as a hickory withe, and the hair was standing up about his elegant collar.

Hedger encouraged him. "Come along, Caesar. You'll soon get used to a new smell."

In the hall stood an enormous trunk, behind the ladder that led to the roof, just opposite Hedger's door. The dog flew at it with a growl of hurt amazement. They went down three flights of stairs and out into the brilliant May afternoon.

Behind the Square, Hedger and his dog descended into a basement oyster house where there were no tablecloths on the tables and no handles on the coffee cups, and the floor was covered with sawdust, and Caesar was always welcome,—not that he needed any such precautionary flooring. All the carpets of Persia would have been safe for him. Hedger ordered steak and onions absentmindedly, not realizing why he had an apprehension that this dish might be less readily at hand hereafter. While he ate, Caesar sat beside his chair, gravely disturbing the sawdust with his tail.

After lunch Hedger strolled about the Square for the dog's health and watched the stages[3] pull out;—that was almost the very last summer of the old horse stages on Fifth Avenue. The fountain had but lately begun operations for the season and was throwing up a mist of rainbow water which now and then blew south and sprayed a bunch of Italian babies that were being supported on the outer rim by older, very little older, brothers and sisters. Plump robins were hopping about on the soil; the grass was newly cut and blindingly green. Looking up the Avenue through the Arch, one could see the young poplars with their

3. Public horse-drawn vehicles.

bright, sticky leaves, and the Brevoort[4] glistening in its spring coat of paint, and shining horses and carriages,—occasionally an automobile, mis-shapen and sullen, like an ugly threat in a stream of things that were bright and beautiful and alive.

While Caesar and his master were standing by the fountain, a girl approached them, crossing the Square. Hedger noticed her because she wore a lavender cloth suit and carried in her arms a big bunch of fresh lilacs. He saw that she was young and handsome,—beautiful, in fact, with a splendid figure and good action. She, too, paused by the fountain and looked back through the Arch up the Avenue. She smiled rather patronizingly as she looked, and at the same time seemed delighted. Her slowly curving upper lip and half-closed eyes seemed to say: "You're gay, you're exciting, you are quite the right sort of thing; but you're none too fine for me!"

In the moment she tarried, Caesar stealthily approached her and sniffed at the hem of her lavender skirt, then, when she went south like an arrow, he ran back to his master and lifted a face full of emotion and alarm, his lower lip twitching under his sharp white teeth and his hazel eyes pointed with a very definite discovery. He stood thus, motionless, while Hedger watched the lavender girl go up the steps and through the door of the house in which he lived.

"You're right, my boy, it's she! She might be worse looking, you know."

When they mounted to the studio, the new lodger's door, at the back of the hall, was a little ajar, and Hedger caught the warm perfume of lilacs just brought in out of the sun. He was used to the musty smell of the old hall carpet. (The nurse-lessee had once knocked at his studio door and complained that Caesar must be somewhat responsible for the particular flavour of that mustiness, and Hedger had never spoken to her since.) He was used to the old smell, and he preferred it to that of the lilacs, and so did his companion, whose nose was so much more discriminating. Hedger shut his door vehemently, and fell to work.

Most young men who dwell in obscure studios in New York have had a beginning, come out of something, have somewhere a home town, a family, a paternal roof. But Don Hedger had no such background. He was a foundling, and had grown up in a school for homeless boys, where book-learning was a negligible part of the curriculum. When he was sixteen, a Catholic priest took him to Greensburg, Pennsylvania, to keep house for him. The priest did something to fill in the large gaps in the boy's education,—taught him to like "Don Quixote" and "The Golden Legend,"[5] and encouraged him to mess with paints

---

4. A fashionable hotel.
5. A poem of medieval chivalry by Henry Wadsworth Longfellow (1807–1882); *Don*

Quixote is the famous novel of an aging knight longing for adventure, by Miguel de Cervantes (1547–1616).

and crayons in his room up under the slope of the mansard. When Don wanted to go to New York to study at the Art League, the priest got him a night job as packer in one of the big department stores. Since then, Hedger had taken care of himself; that was his only responsibility. He was singularly unencumbered; had no family duties, no social ties, no obligations toward any one but his landlord. Since he travelled light, he had travelled rather far. He had got over a good deal of the earth's surface, in spite of the fact that he never in his life had more than three hundred dollars ahead at any one time, and he had already outlived a succession of convictions and revelations about his art.

Though he was now but twenty-six years old, he had twice been on the verge of becoming a marketable product; once through some studies of New York streets he did for a magazine, and once through a collection of pastels he brought home from New Mexico, which Remington,[6] then at the height of his popularity, happened to see, and generously tried to push. But on both occasions Hedger decided that this was something he didn't wish to carry further,—simply the old thing over again and got nowhere,—so he took enquiring dealers experiments in a "later manner," that made them put him out of the shop. When he ran short of money, he could always get any amount of commercial work; he was an expert draughtsman and worked with lightning speed. The rest of his time he spent in groping his way from one kind of painting into another, or travelling about without luggage, like a tramp, and he was chiefly occupied with getting rid of ideas he had once thought very fine.

Hedger's circumstances, since he had moved to Washington Square, were affluent compared to anything he had ever known before. He was now able to pay advance rent and turn the key on his studio when he went away for four months at a stretch. It didn't occur to him to wish to be richer than this. To be sure, he did without a great many things other people think necessary, but he didn't miss them, because he had never had them. He belonged to no clubs, visited no houses, had no studio friends, and he ate his dinner alone in some decent little restaurant, even on Christmas and New Year's. For days together he talked to nobody but his dog and the janitress and the lame oysterman.

After he shut the door and settled down to his paradise fish on that first Tuesday in May, Hedger forgot all about his new neighbour. When the light failed, he took Caesar out for a walk. On the way home he did his marketing on West Houston Street, with a one-eyed Italian woman who always cheated him. After he had cooked his beans and scallopini, and drunk half a bottle of Chianti, he put his dishes in the sink and went up on the roof to smoke. He was the only person in the

6. Frederic Remington (1861–1909), popular American painter.

house who ever went to the roof, and he had a secret understanding with the janitress about it. He was to have "the privilege of the roof," as she said, if he opened the heavy trapdoor on sunny days to air out the upper hall, and was watchful to close it when rain threatened. Mrs. Foley was fat and forty and hated to climb stairs,—besides, the roof was reached by a perpendicular iron ladder, definitely inaccessible to a woman of her bulk, and the iron door at the top of it was too heavy for any but Hedger's stong arm to lift. Hedger was not above medium height, but he practised with weights and dumb-bells, and in the shoulders he was as strong as a gorilla.

So Hedger had the roof to himself. He and Caesar often slept up there on hot nights, rolled in blankets he had brought home from Arizona. He mounted with Caesar under his left arm. The dog had never learned to climb a perpendicular ladder, and never did he feel so much his master's greatness and his own dependence upon him, as when he crept under his arm for this perilous ascent. Up there was even gravel to scratch in and a dog could do whatever he liked, so long as he did not bark. It was a kind of Heaven, which no one was strong enough to reach but his great paint-smelling master.

On this blue May night there was a slender girlish looking young moon in the west, playing with a whole company of silver stars. Now and then one of them darted away from the ground and shot off into the gauzy blue with a soft little trail of light, like laughter. Hedger and his dog were delighted when a star did this. They were quite lost in watching the glittering game, when they were suddenly diverted by a sound, —not from the stars, though it was music. It was not the Prologue to Pagliacci,[7] which rose ever and anon on hot evenings from an Italian tenement on Thompson Street, with the gasps of the corpulent baritone who got behind it; nor was it the hurdy-gurdy[8] man, who often played at the corner in the balmy twilight. No, this was a woman's voice, singing the tempestuous, over-lapping phrases of Signor Puccini,[9] then comparatively new in the world, but already so popular that even Hedger recognized his unmistakable gusts of breath. He looked about over the roofs; all was blue and still, with the well-built chimneys that were never used now standing up dark and mournful. He moved softly toward the yellow quadrangle where the gas from the hall shone up through the half-lifted trapdoor. Oh yes! It came up through the hole like a strong draught, a big, beautiful voice, and it sounded rather like a professional's. A piano had arrived in the morning, Hedger remembered. This might be a very great nuisance. It would be pleasant enough to listen to, if you could turn it on and off as you wished; but

7. Popular Italian opera by Ruggiero Leoncavallo (1858–1919).
8. Portable instrument which plays popular
tunes when a crank is turned.
9. Giacomo Puccini (1858–1924), popular Italian opera composer.

you couldn't. Caesar, with the gas light shining on his collar and his ugly but sensitive face, panted and looked up for information. Hedger put down a reassuring hand.

"I don't know. We can't tell yet. It may not be so bad."

He stayed on the roof until all was still below, and finally descended, with quite a new feeling about his neighbour. Her voice, like her figure, inspired respect,—if one did not choose to call it admiration. Her door was shut, the transom was dark; nothing remained of her but the obtrusive trunk, unrightfully taking up room in the narrow hall.

II

For two days Hedger didn't see her. He was painting eight hours a day just then, and only went out to hunt for food. He noticed that she practised scales and exercises for about an hour in the morning; then she locked her door, went humming down the hall, and left him in peace. He heard her getting her coffee ready at about the same time he got his. Earlier still, she passed his room on her way to her bath. In the evening she sometimes sang, but on the whole she didn't bother him. When he was working well he did not notice anything much. The morning paper lay before his door until he reached out for his milk bottle, then he kicked the sheet inside and it lay on the floor until evening. Sometimes he read it and sometimes he did not. He forgot there was anything of importance going on in the world outside of his third floor studio. Nobody had ever taught him that he ought to be interested in other people; in the Pittsburgh steel strike, in the Fresh Air Fund, in the scandal about the Babies' Hospital. A grey wolf, living in a Wyoming canyon, would hardly have been less concerned about these things than was Don Hedger.

One morning he was coming out of the bath-room at the front end of the hall, having just given Caesar his bath and rubbed him into a glow with a heavy towel. Before the door, lying in wait for him, as it were, stood a tall figure in a flowing blue silk dressing gown that fell away from her marble arms. In her hands she carried various accessories of the bath.

"I wish," she said distinctly, standing in his way, "I wish you wouldn't wash your dog in the tub. I never heard of such a thing! I've found his hair in the tub, and I've smelled a doggy smell, and now I've caught you at it. It's an outrage!"

Hedger was badly frightened. She was so tall and positive, and was fairly blazing with beauty and anger. He stood blinking, holding on to his sponge and dog-soap, feeling that he ought to bow very low to her. But what he actually said was:

"Nobody has ever objected before. I always wash the tub,—and, anyhow, he's cleaner than most people."

"Cleaner than me?" her eyebrows went up, her white arms and neck and her fragrant person seemed to scream at him like a band of out-raged nymphs. Something flashed through his mind about a man who was turned into a dog, or was pursued by dogs, because he unwittingly intruded upon the bath of beauty.[1]

"No, I didn't mean that," he muttered, turning scarlet under the bluish stubble of his muscular jaws. "But I know he's cleaner than I am."

"That I don't doubt!" Her voice sounded like a soft shivering of crystal, and with a smile of pity she drew the folds of her voluminous blue robe close about her and allowed the wretched man to pass. Even Caesar was frightened; he darted like a streak down the hall, through the door and to his own bed in the corner among the bones.

Hedger stood still in the doorway, listening to indignant sniffs and coughs and great swishing of water about the sides of the tub. He had washed it; but as he had washed it with Caesar's sponge, it was quite possible that a few bristles remained; the dog was shedding now. The playwright had never objected, nor had the jovial illustrator who occu-pied the front apartment,—but he, as he admitted, "was usually pye-eyed,[2] when he wasn't in Buffalo." He went home to Buffalo sometimes to rest his nerves.

It had never occurred to Hedger that any one would mind using the tub after Caesar;—but then, he had never seen a beautiful girl capari-soned for the bath before. As soon as he beheld her standing there, he realized the unfitness of it. For that matter, she ought not to step into a tub that any other mortal had bathed in; the illustrator was sloppy and left cigarette ends on the moulding.

All morning as he worked he was gnawed by a spiteful desire to get back at her. It rankled that he had been so vanquished by her disdain. When he heard her locking her door to go out for lunch, he stepped quickly into the hall in his messy painting coat, and addressed her.

"I don't wish to be exigent, Miss,"—he had certain grand words that he used upon occasion—"but if this is your trunk, it's rather in the way here."

"Oh, very well!" she exclaimed carelessly, dropping her keys into her handbag. "I'll have it moved when I can get a man to do it," and she went down the hall with her free, roving stride.

Her name, Hedger discovered from her letters, which the postman left on the table in the lower hall, was Eden Bower.

III

In the closet that was built against the partition separating his room from Miss Bower's, Hedger kept all his wearing apparel, some of it on

---

1. In Greek myth, the hunter Actaeon was pun-ished by the goddess Diana when he spied on her while she was bathing; he was turned into a stag and torn apart by his own hounds.
2. Drunk.

hooks and hangers, some of it on the floor. When he opened his closet door now-a-days, little dust-coloured insects flew out on downy wing, and he suspected that a brood of moths were hatching in his winter overcoat. Mrs. Foley, the janitress, told him to bring down all his heavy clothes and she would give them a beating and hang them in the court. The closet was in such disorder that he shunned the encounter, but one hot afternoon he set himself to the task. First he threw out a pile of for-gotten laundry and tied it up in a sheet. The bundle stood as high as his middle when he had knotted the corners. Then he got his shoes and overshoes together. When he took his over-coat from its place against the partition, a long ray of yellow light shot across the dark enclosure, —a knot hole, evidently, in the high wainscoting of the west room. He had never noticed it before, and without realizing what he was doing, he stooped and squinted through it.

Yonder, in a pool of sunlight, stood his new neighbour, wholly un-clad, doing exercises of some sort before a long gilt mirror. Hedger did not happen to think how unpardonable it was of him to watch her. Nudity was not improper to any one who had worked so much from the figure, and he continued to look, simply because he had never seen a woman's body so beautiful as this one,—positively glorious in action. As she swung her arms and changed from one pivot of motion to an-other, muscular energy seemed to flow through her from her toes to her finger-tips. The soft flush of exercise and the gold of afternoon sun played over her flesh together, enveloped her in a luminous mist which, as she turned and twisted, made now an arm, now a shoulder, now a thigh, dissolve in pure light and instantly recover its outline with the next gesture. Hedger's fingers curved as if he were holding a crayon; mentally he was doing the whole figure in a single running line, and the charcoal seemed to explode in his hand at the point where the energy of each gesture was discharged into the whirling disc of light, from a foot or shoulder, from the up-thrust chin or the lifted breasts.

He could not have told whether he watched her for six minutes or sixteen. When her gymnastics were over, she paused to catch up a lock of hair that had come down, and examined with solicitude a little red-dish mole that grew under her left arm-pit. Then, with her hand on her hip, she walked unconcernedly across the room and disappeared through the door into her bedchamber.

Disappeared—Don Hedger was crouching on his knees, staring at the golden shower which poured in through the west windows, at the lake of gold sleeping on the faded Turkish carpet. The spot was en-chanted; a vision out of Alexandria, out of the remote pagan past, had bathed itself there in Helianthine fire.[3]

---

3. Fire of the sun.

When he crawled out of his closet, he stood blinking at the grey sheet stuffed with laundry, not knowing what had happened to him. He felt a little sick as he contemplated the bundle. Everything here was different; he hated the disorder of the place, the grey prison light, his old shoes and himself and all his slovenly habits. The black calico curtains that ran on wires over his big window were white with dust. There were three greasy frying pans in the sink, and the sink itself— He felt desperate. He couldn't stand this another minute. He took up an armful of winter clothes and ran down four flights into the basement.

"Mrs. Foley," he began, "I want my room cleaned this afternoon, thoroughly cleaned. Can you get a woman for me right away?"

"Is it company you're having?" the fat, dirty janitress enquired. Mrs. Foley was the widow of a useful Tammany man,[4] and she owned real estate in Flatbush. She was huge and soft as a feather bed. Her face and arms were permanently coated with dust, grained like wood where the sweat had trickled.

"Yes, company. That's it."

"Well, this is a queer time of the day to be asking for a cleaning woman. It's likely I can get you old Lizzie, if she's not drunk. I'll send Willy round to see."

Willy, the son of fourteen, roused from the stupor and stain of his fifth box of cigarettes by the gleam of a quarter, went out. In five minutes he returned with old Lizzie,—she smelling strong of spirits and wearing several jackets which she had put on one over the other, and a number of skirts, long and short, which made her resemble an animated dish-clout. She had, of course, to borrow her equipment from Mrs. Foley, and toiled up the long flights, dragging mop and pail and broom. She told Hedger to be of good cheer, for he had got the right woman for the job, and showed him a great leather strap she wore about her wrist to prevent dislocation of tendons. She swished about the place, scattering dust and splashing soapsuds, while he watched her in nervous despair. He stood over Lizzie and made her scour the sink, directing her roughly, then paid her and got rid of her. Shutting the door on his failure, he hurried off with his dog to lose himself among the stevedores and dock labourers on West Street.

A strange chapter began for Don Hedger. Day after day, at that hour in the afternoon, the hour before his neighbour dressed for dinner, he crouched down in his closet to watch her go through her mysterious exercises. It did not occur to him that his conduct was detestable; there was nothing shy or retreating about this unclad girl,—a bold body, studying itself quite coolly and evidently well pleased with itself, doing all this for a purpose. Hedger scarcely regarded his action as conduct at

4. I.e., member of the corrupt New York political organization.

all; it was something that had happened to him. More than once he went out and tried to stay away for the whole afternoon, but at about five o'clock he was sure to find himself among his old shoes in the dark. The pull of that aperture was stronger than his will,—and he had always considered his will the strongest thing about him. When she threw herself upon the divan and lay resting, he still stared, holding his breath. His nerves were so on edge that a sudden noise made him start and brought out the sweat on his forehead. The dog would come and tug at his sleeve, knowing that something was wrong with his master. If he attempted a mournful whine, those strong hands closed about his throat.

When Hedger came slinking out of his closet, he sat down on the edge of the couch, sat for hours without moving. He was not painting at all now. This thing, whatever it was, drank him up as ideas had sometimes done, and he sank into a stupor of idleness as deep and dark as the stupor of work. He could not understand it; he was no boy, he had worked from models for years, and a woman's body was no mystery to him. Yet now he did nothing but sit and think about one. He slept very little, and with the first light of morning he awoke as completely possessed by this woman as if he had been with her all the night before. The unconscious operations of life went on in him only to perpetuate this excitement. His brain held but one image now—vibrated, burned with it. It was a heathenish feeling; without friendliness, almost without tenderness.

Women had come and gone in Hedger's life. Not having had a mother to begin with, his relations with them, whether amorous or friendly, had been casual. He got on well with janitresses and wash-women, with Indians and with the peasant women of foreign countries. He had friends among the silk-skirt factory girls who came to eat their lunch in Washington Square, and he sometimes took a model for a day in the country. He felt an unreasoning antipathy toward the well-dressed women he saw coming out of big shops, or driving in the Park. If, on his way to the Art Museum, he noticed a pretty girl standing on the steps of one of the houses on upper Fifth Avenue, he frowned at her and went by with his shoulders hunched up as if he were cold. He had never known such girls, or heard them talk, or seen the inside of the houses in which they lived; but he believed them all to be artificial and, in an aesthetic sense, perverted. He saw them enslaved by desire of merchandise and manufactured articles, effective only in making life complicated and insincere and in embroidering it with ugly and meaningless trivialities. They were enough, he thought, to make one almost forget woman as she existed in art, in thought, and in the universe.

He had no desire to know the woman who had, for the time at least, so broken up his life,—no curiosity about her every-day personality. He shunned any revelation of it, and he listened for Miss Bower's coming and going, not to encounter, but to avoid her. He wished that the girl who wore shirt-waists and got letters from Chicago would keep out of his way, that she did not exist. With her he had naught to make. But in a room full of sun, before an old mirror, on a little enchanted rug of sleeping colours, he had seen a woman who emerged naked through a door, and disappeared naked. He thought of that body as never having been clad, or as having worn the stuffs and dyes of all the centuries but his own. And for him she had no geographical associations; unless with Crete, or Alexandria, or Veronese's[5] Venice. She was the immortal conception, the perennial theme.

The first break in Hedger's lethargy occurred one afternoon when two young men came to take Eden Bower out to dine. They went into her music room, laughed and talked for a few minutes, and then took her away with them. They were gone a long while, but he did not go out for food himself; he waited for them to come back. At last he heard them coming down the hall, gayer and more talkative than when they left. One of them sat down at the piano, and they all began to sing. This Hedger found absolutely unendurable. He snatched up his hat and went running down the stairs. Caesar leaped beside him, hoping that old times were coming back. They had supper in the oysterman's basement and then sat down in front of their own doorway. The moon stood full over the Square, a thing of regal glory; but Hedger did not see the moon; he was looking, murderously, for men. Presently two, wearing straw hats and white trousers and carrying canes, came down the steps from his house. He rose and dogged them across the Square. They were laughing and seemed very much elated about something. As one stopped to light a cigarette, Hedger caught from the other:

"Don't you think she has a beautiful talent?"

His companion threw away his match. "She has a beautiful figure." They both ran to catch the stage.

Hedger went back to his studio. The light was shining from her transom. For the first time he violated her privacy at night, and peered through that fatal aperture. She was sitting fully dressed, in the window, smoking a cigarette and looking out over the housetops. He watched her until she rose, looked about her with a disdainful, crafty smile, and turned out the light.

The next morning, when Miss Bower went out Hedger followed her. Her white skirt gleamed ahead of him as she sauntered about the Square. She sat down behind the Garibaldi statue[6] and opened a music book she carried. She turned the leaves carelessly, and several times glanced in his direction. He was on the point of going over to her, when

---

5. Paolo Veronese (1528–1588), Venetian painter.

6. Statue of Giuseppe Garibaldi (1807–1882), Italian patriot and champion of independence.

she rose quickly and looked up at the sky. A flock of pigeons had risen from somewhere in the crowded Italian quarter to the south, and were wheeling rapidly up through the morning air, soaring and dropping, scattering and coming together, now grey, now white as silver, as they caught or intercepted the sunlight. She put up her hand to shade her eyes and followed them with a kind of defiant delight in her face.

Hedger came and stood beside her. "You've surely seen them before?"

"Oh, yes," she replied, still looking up. "I see them every day from my windows. They always come home about five o'clock. Where do they live?"

"I don't know. Probably some Italian raises them for the market. They were here long before I came, and I've been here four years."

"In that same gloomy room? Why didn't you take mine when it was vacant?"

"It isn't gloomy. That's the best light for painting."

"Oh, is it? I don't know anything about painting. I'd like to see your pictures sometime. You have such a lot in there. Don't they get dusty, piled up against the wall like that?"

"Not very. I'd be glad to show them to you. Is your name really Eden Bower? I've seen your letters on the table."

"Well, it's the name I'm going to sing under. My father's name is Bowers, but my friend Mr. Jones, a Chicago newspaper man who writes about music, told me to drop the 's.' He's crazy about my voice."

Miss Bower didn't usually tell the whole story,—about anything. Her first name, when she lived in Huntington, Illinois, was Edna, but Mr. Jones had persuaded her to change it to one which he felt would be worthy of her future. She was quick to take suggestions, though she told him she "didn't see what was the matter with 'Edna.' "

She explained to Hedger that she was going to Paris to study. She was waiting in New York for Chicago friends who were to take her over but who had been detained. "Did you study in Paris?" she asked.

"No, I've never been in Paris. But I was in the south of France all last summer, studying with C——. He's the biggest man among the moderns,—at least I think so."

Miss Bower sat down and made room for him on the bench. "Do tell me about it. I expected to be there by this time, and I can't wait to find out what it's like."

Hedger began to relate how he had seen some of this Frenchman's work in an exhibition, and deciding at once that this was the man for him, he had taken a boat for Marseilles the next week going over steerage. He proceeded at once to the little town on the coast where his painter lived, and presented himself. The man never took pupils, but because Hedger had come so far he let him stay. Hedger lived at the

master's house and every day they went out together to paint, sometimes on the blazing rocks down by the sea. They wrapped themselves
in light woollen blankets and didn't feel the heat. Being there and working with C—— was being in Paradise, Hedger concluded; he learned
more in three months than in all his life before.

Eden Bower laughed. "You're a funny fellow. Didn't you do anything but work? Are the women very beautiful? Did you have awfully
good things to eat and drink?"

Hedger said some of the women were fine looking, especially one
girl who went about selling fish and lobsters. About the food there was
nothing remarkable,—except the ripe figs, he liked those. They drank
sour wine, and used goat-butter, which was strong and full of hair, as it
was churned in a goat skin.

"But don't they have parties or banquets? Aren't there any fine
hotels down there?"

"Yes, but they are all closed in summer, and the country people are
poor. It's a beautiful country, though."

"How, beautiful?" she persisted.

"If you want to go in, I'll show you some sketches, and you'll see."

Miss Bower rose. "All right. I won't go to my fencing lesson this
morning. Do you fence? Here comes your dog. You can't move but
he's after you. He always makes a face at me when I meet him in the
hall, and shows his nasty little teeth as if he wanted to bite me."

In the studio Hedger got out his sketches, but to Miss Bower, whose
favourite pictures were Christ Before Pilate and a redhaired Magdalen
of Henner,[7] these landscapes were not at all beautiful, and they gave
her no idea of any country whatsoever. She was careful not to commit
herself, however. Her vocal teacher had already convinced her that she
had a great deal to learn about many things.

"Why don't we go out to lunch somewhere?" Hedger asked, and
began to dust his fingers with a handkerchief—which he got out of sight
as swiftly as possible.

"All right, the Brevoort," she said carelessly. "I think that's a good
place, and they have good wine. I don't care for cocktails."

Hedger felt his chin uneasily. "I'm afraid I haven't shaved this morning. If you could wait for me in the Square? It won't take me ten minutes."

Left alone, he found a clean collar and handkerchief, brushed his
coat and blacked his shoes, and last of all dug up ten dollars from the
bottom of an old copper kettle he had brought from Spain. His winter

---

7. A painting of Mary Magdalen, a reformed
prostitute in the New Testament, by Jean
Jacques Henner (1829–1905), French painter
of religious subjects. Pilate is the judge who permitted Christ's crucifixion.

hat was of such complexion that the Brevoort hall boy winked at the porter as he took it and placed it on the rack in a row of fresh straw ones.

IV

That afternoon Eden Bower was lying on the couch in her music room, her face turned to the window, watching the pigeons. Reclining thus she could see none of the neighbouring roofs, only the sky itself and the birds that crossed and recrossed her field of vision, white as scraps of paper blowing in the wind. She was thinking that she was young and handsome and had had a good lunch, that a very easy-going, light-hearted city lay in the streets below her; and she was wondering why she found this queer painter chap, with his lean, bluish cheeks and heavy black eyebrows, more interesting than the smart young men she met at her teacher's studio.

Eden Bower was, at twenty, very much the same person that we all know her to be at forty, except that she knew a great deal less. But one thing she knew: that she was to be Eden Bower. She was like some one standing before a great show window full of beautiful and costly things, deciding which she will order. She understands that they will not all be delivered immediately, but one by one they will arrive at her door. She already knew some of the many things that were to happen to her; for instance, that the Chicago millionaire who was going to take her abroad with his sister as chaperone, would eventually press his claim in quite another manner. He was the most circumspect of bachelors, afraid of everything obvious, even of women who were too flagrantly handsome. He was a nervous collector of pictures and furniture, a nervous patron of music, and a nervous host; very cautious about his health, and about any course of conduct that might make him ridiculous. But she knew that he would at last throw all his precautions to the winds.

People like Eden Bower are inexplicable. Her father sold farming machinery in Huntington, Illinois, and she had grown up with no acquaintances or experiences outside of that prairie town. Yet from her earliest childhood she had not one conviction or opinion in common with the people about her,—the only people she knew. Before she was out of short dresses she had made up her mind that she was going to be an actress, that she would live far away in great cities, that she would be much admired by men and would have everything she wanted. When she was thirteen, and was already singing and reciting for church entertainments, she read in some illustrated magazine a long article about the late Czar of Russia, then just come to the throne or about to come to it. After that, lying in the hammock on the front porch on summer evenings, or sitting through a long sermon in the family pew, she amused herself by trying to make up her mind whether she would or would not be the Czar's mistress when she played in his Capital. Now

Edna had met this fascinating word only in the novels of Ouida,[8]—her hard-worked little mother kept a long row of them in the upstairs storeroom, behind the linen chest. In Huntington, women who bore that relation to men were called by a very different name, and their lot was not an enviable one; of all the shabby and poor, they were the shabbiest. But then, Edna had never lived in Huntington, not even before she began to find books like "Sapho" and "Mademoiselle de Maupin,"[9] secretly sold in paper covers throughout Illinois. It was as if she had come into Huntington, into the Bowers family, on one of the trains that puffed over the marshes behind their back fence all day long, and was waiting for another train to take her out.

As she grew older and handsomer, she had many beaux, but these small-town boys didn't interest her. If a lad kissed her when he brought her home from a dance, she was indulgent and she rather liked it. But if he pressed her further, she slipped away from him, laughing. After she began to sing in Chicago, she was consistently discreet. She stayed as a guest in rich people's houses, and she knew that she was being watched like a rabbit in a laboratory. Covered up in bed, with the lights out, she thought her own thoughts, and laughed.

This summer in New York was her first taste of freedom. The Chicago capitalist, after all his arrangements were made for sailing, had been compelled to go to Mexico to look after oil interests. His sister knew an excellent singing master in New York. Why should not a discreet, well-balanced girl like Miss Bower spend the summer there, studying quietly? The capitalist suggested that his sister might enjoy a summer on Long Island; he would rent the Griffiths' place for her, with all the servants, and Eden could stay there. But his sister met this proposal with a cold stare. So it fell out, that between selfishness and greed, Eden got a summer all her own,—which really did a great deal toward making her an artist and whatever else she was afterward to become. She had time to look about, to watch without being watched; to select diamonds in one window and furs in another, to select shoulders and moustaches in the big hotels where she went to lunch. She had the easy freedom of obscurity and the consciousness of power. She enjoyed both. She was in no hurry.

While Eden Bower watched the pigeons, Don Hedger sat on the other side of the bolted doors, looking into a pool of dark turpentine, at his idle brushes, wondering why a woman could do this to him. He, too, was sure of his future and knew that he was a chosen man. He could not know, of course, that he was merely the first to fall under a fascination which was to be disastrous to a few men and pleasantly stimulating to

---

8. Pseudonym of Louise de la Ramée (1839–1908), English author of popular romantic novels.

9. *Mademoiselle de Maupin* (1835), by Théophile Gautier, and *Sapho* (1884), by Alphonse Daudet, novels about illicit love.

many thousands. Each of these two young people sensed the future, but not completely. Don Hedger knew that nothing much would ever happen to him. Eden Bower understood that to her a great deal would happen. But she did not guess that her neighbour would have more tempestuous adventures sitting in his dark studio than she would find in all the capitals of Europe, or in all the latitude of conduct she was prepared to permit herself.

V

One Sunday morning Eden was crossing the Square with a spruce young man in a white flannel suit and a panama hat. They had been breakfasting at the Brevoort and he was coaxing her to let him come up to her rooms and sing for an hour.

"No, I've got to write letters. You must run along now. I see a friend of mine over there, and I want to ask him about something before I go up."

"That fellow with the dog? Where did you pick him up?" The young man glanced toward the seat under a sycamore where Hedger was reading the morning paper.

"Oh, he's an old friend from the West," said Eden easily. "I won't introduce you, because he doesn't like people. He's a recluse. Goodbye. I can't be sure about Tuesday. I'll go with you if I have time after my lesson." She nodded, left him, and went over to the seat littered with newspapers. The young man went up the Avenue without looking back.

"Well, what are you going to do today? Shampoo this animal all morning?" Eden enquired teasingly.

Hedger made room for her on the seat. "No, at twelve o'clock I'm going out to Coney Island.[1] One of my models is going up in a balloon this afternoon. I've often promised to go and see her, and now I'm going."

Eden asked if models usually did such stunts. No, Hedger told her, but Molly Welch added to her earnings in that way. "I believe," he added, "she likes the excitement of it. She's got a good deal of spirit. That's why I like to paint her. So many models have flaccid bodies."

"And she hasn't, eh? Is she the one who comes to see you? I can't help hearing her, she talks so loud."

"Yes, she has a rough voice, but she's a fine girl. I don't suppose you'd be interested in going?"

"I don't know," Eden sat tracing patterns on the asphalt with the end of her parasol. "Is it any fun? I got up feeling I'd like to do something

---

1. Amusement park on the beach in Brooklyn.

different today. It's the first Sunday I've not had to sing in church. I had that engagement for breakfast at the Brevoort, but it wasn't very exciting. That chap can't talk about anything but himself."

Hedger warmed a little. "If you've never been to Coney Island, you ought to go. It's nice to see all the people; tailors and bar-tenders and prize-fighters with their best girls, and all sorts of folks taking a holiday."

Eden looked sidewise at him. So one ought to be interested in people of that kind, ought one? He was certainly a funny fellow. Yet he was never, somehow, tiresome. She had seen a good deal of him lately, but she kept wanting to know him better, to find out what made him different from men like the one she had just left—whether he really was as different as he seemed. "I'll go with you," she said at last, "if you'll leave that at home." She pointed to Caesar's flickering ears with her sunshade.

"But he's half the fun. You'd like to hear him bark at the waves when they come in."

"No, I wouldn't. He's jealous and disagreeable if he sees you talking to any one else. Look at him now."

"Of course, if you make a face at him. He knows what that means, and he makes a worse face. He likes Molly Welch, and she'll be disappointed if I don't bring him."

Eden said decidedly that he couldn't take both of them. So at twelve o'clock when she and Hedger got on the boat at Desbrosses street, Caesar was lying on his pallet, with a bone.

Eden enjoyed the boat-ride. It was the first time she had been on the water, and she felt as if she were embarking for France. The light warm breeze and the plunge of the waves made her very wide awake, and she liked crowds of any kind. They went to the balcony of a big, noisy restaurant and had a shore dinner, with tall steins of beer. Hedger had got a big advance from his advertising firm since he first lunched with Miss Bower ten days ago, and he was ready for anything.

After dinner they went to the tent behind the bathing beach, where the tops of two balloons bulged out over the canvas. A red-faced man in a linen suit stood in front of the tent, shouting in a hoarse voice and telling the people that if the crowd was good for five dollars more, a beautiful young woman would risk her life for their entertainment. Four little boys in dirty red uniforms ran about taking contributions in their pill-box hats. One of the balloons was bobbing up and down in its tether and people were shoving forward to get nearer the tent.

"Is it dangerous, as he pretends?" Eden asked.

"Molly says it's simple enough if nothing goes wrong with the balloon. Then it would be all over, I suppose."

"Wouldn't you like to go up with her?"

"I? Of course not. I'm not fond of taking foolish risks."

Eden sniffed. "I shouldn't think sensible risks would be very much fun."

Hedger did not answer, for just then every one began to shove the other way and shout, "Look out. There she goes!" and a band of six pieces commenced playing furiously.

As the balloon rose from its tent enclosure, they saw a girl in green tights standing in the basket, holding carelessly to one of the ropes with one hand and with the other waving to the spectators. A long rope trailed behind to keep the balloon from blowing out to sea.

As it soared, the figure in green tights in the basket diminished to a mere spot, and the balloon itself, in the brilliant light, looked like a big silver-grey bat, with its wings folded. When it began to sink, the girl stepped through the hole in the basket to a trapeze that hung below, and gracefully descended through the air, holding to the rod with both hands, keeping her body taut and her feet close together. The crowd, which had grown very large by this time, cheered vociferously. The men took off their hats and waved, little boys shouted, and fat old women, shining with the heat and a beer lunch, murmured admiring comments upon the balloonist's figure. "Beautiful legs, she has!"

"That's so," Hedger whispered. "Not many girls would look well in that position." Then, for some reason, he blushed a slow, dark, painful crimson.

The balloon descended slowly, a little way from the tent, and the red-faced man in the linen suit caught Molly Welch before her feet touched the ground, and pulled her to one side. The band struck up "Blue Bell" by way of welcome, and one of the sweaty pages ran forward and presented the balloonist with a large bouquet of artificial flowers. She smiled and thanked him, and ran back across the sand to the tent.

"Can't we go inside and see her?" Eden asked. "You can explain to the door man. I want to meet her." Edging forward, she herself addressed the man in the linen suit and slipped something from her purse into his hand.

They found Molly seated before a trunk that had a mirror in the lid and a "make-up" outfit spread upon the tray. She was wiping the cold cream and powder from her neck with a discarded chemise.

"Hello, Don," she said cordially. "Brought a friend?"

Eden liked her. She had an easy, friendly manner, and there was something boyish and devil-may-care about her.

"Yes, it's fun. I'm mad about it," she said in reply to Eden's questions. "I always want to let go, when I come down on the bar. You don't feel your weight at all, as you would on a stationary trapeze."

The big drum boomed outside, and the publicity man began shouting to newly arrived boat-loads. Miss Welch took a last pull at her cigarette. "Now you'll have to get out, Don. I change for the next act. This time I go up in a black evening dress, and lose the skirt in the basket before I start down."

"Yes, go along," said Eden. "Wait for me outside the door. I'll stay and help her dress."

Hedger waited and waited, while women of every build bumped into him and begged his pardon, and the red pages ran about holding out their caps for coins, and the people ate and perspired and shifted parasols against the sun. When the band began to play a two-step, all the bathers ran up out of the surf to watch the ascent. The second balloon bumped and rose, and the crowd began shouting to the girl in a black evening dress who stood leaning against the ropes and smiling. "It's a new girl," they called. "It ain't the Countess this time. You're a peach, girlie!"

The balloonist acknowledged these compliments, bowing and looking down over the sea of upturned faces,—but Hedger was determined she should not see him, and he darted behind the tent-fly. He was suddenly dripping with cold sweat, his mouth was full of the bitter taste of anger and his tongue felt stiff behind his teeth. Molly Welch, in a shirtwaist and a white tam-o'-shanter cap, slipped out from the tent under his arm and laughed up in his face. "She's a crazy one you brought along. She'll get what she wants!"

"Oh, I'll settle with you, all right!" Hedger brought out with difficulty.

"It's not my fault, Donnie. I couldn't do anything with her. She bought me off. What's the matter with you? Are you soft on her? She's safe enough. It's as easy as rolling off a log, if you keep cool." Molly Welch was rather excited herself, and she was chewing gum at a high speed as she stood beside him, looking up at the floating silver cone. "Now watch," she exclaimed suddenly. "She's coming down on the bar. I advised her to cut that out, but you see she does it first-rate. And she got rid of the skirt, too. Those black tights show off her legs very well. She keeps her feet together like I told her, and makes a good line along the back. See the light on those silver slippers,—that was a good idea I had. Come along to meet her. Don't be a grouch; she's done it fine!"

Molly tweaked his elbow, and then left him standing like a stump, while she ran down the beach with the crowd.

Though Hedger was sulking, his eye could not help seeing the low blue welter of the sea, the arrested bathers, standing in the surf, their arms and legs stained red by the dropping sun, all shading their eyes and gazing upward at the slowly falling silver star.

Molly Welch and the manager caught Eden under the arms and lifted her aside, a red page dashed up with a bouquet, and the band struck up "Blue Bell." Eden laughed and bowed, took Molly's arm, and ran up the sand in her black tights and silver slippers, dodging the friendly old women, and the gallant sports[2] who wanted to offer their homage on the spot.

When she emerged from the tent, dressed in her own clothes, that part of the beach was almost deserted. She stepped to her companion's side and said carelessly: "Hadn't we better try to catch this boat? I hope you're not sore at me. Really, it was lots of fun."

Hedger looked at his watch. "Yes, we have fifteen minutes to get to the boat," he said politely.

As they walked toward the pier, one of the pages ran up panting. "Lady, you're carrying off the bouquet," he said, aggrievedly.

Eden stopped and looked at the bunch of spotty cotton roses in her hand. "Of course. I want them for a souvenir. You gave them to me yourself."

"I give 'em to you for looks, but you can't take 'em away. They belong to the show."

"Oh, you always use the same bunch?"

"Sure we do. There ain't too much money in this business."

She laughed and tossed them back to him.

"Why are you angry?" she asked Hedger. "I wouldn't have done it if I'd been with some fellows, but I thought you were the sort who wouldn't mind. Molly didn't for a minute think you would."

"What possessed you to do such a fool thing?" he asked roughly.

"I don't know. When I saw her coming down, I wanted to try it. It looked exciting. Didn't I hold myself as well as she did?"

Hedger shrugged his shoulders, but in his heart he forgave her.

The return boat was not crowded, though the boats that passed them, going out, were packed to the rails. The sun was setting. Boys and girls sat on the long benches with their arms about each other, singing. Eden felt a strong wish to propitiate her companion, to be alone with him. She had been curiously wrought up by her balloon trip; it was a lark, but not very satisfying unless one came back to something after the flight. She wanted to be admired and adored. Though Eden said nothing, and sat with her arms limp on the rail in front of her, looking languidly at the rising silhouette of the city and the bright path of the sun, Hedger felt a strange drawing near to her. If he but brushed her white skirt with his knee, there was an instant communication between them, such as there had never been before. They did not talk at all, but when they went over the gangplank she took his arm and kept her shoulder close to his. He felt as if they were enveloped in a highly charged atmosphere, an in-

2. Jaunty young men.

visible network of subtle, almost painful sensibility. They had somehow taken hold of each other.

An hour later, they were dining in the back garden of a little French hotel on Ninth Street, long since passed away. It was cool and leafy there, and the mosquitoes were not very numerous. A party of South Americans at another table were drinking champagne, and Eden murmured that she thought she would like some, if it were not too expensive. "Perhaps it will make me think I am in the balloon again. That was a very nice feeling. You've forgiven me, haven't you?"

Hedger gave her a quick straight look from under his black eyebrows, and something went over her that was like a chill, except that it was warm and feathery. She drank most of the wine: her companion was indifferent to it. He was talking more to her tonight than he had ever done before. She asked him about a new picture she had seen in his room; a queer thing full of stiff, supplicating female figures. "It's Indian, isn't it?"

"Yes. I call it Rain Spirits, or maybe, Indian Rain. In the Southwest, where I've been a good deal, the Indian traditions make women have to do with the rain-fall. They were supposed to control it, somehow, and to be able to find springs and make moisture come out of the earth. You see I'm trying to learn to paint what people think and feel; to get away from all that photographic stuff. When I look at you, I don't see what a camera would see, do I?"

"How can I tell?"

"Well, if I should paint you, I could make you understand what I see." For the second time that day Hedger crimsoned unexpectedly, and his eyes fell and steadily contemplated a dish of little radishes. "That particular picture I got from a story a Mexican priest told me; he said he found it in an old manuscript book in a monastery down there, written by some Spanish Missionary, who got his stories from the Aztecs. This one he called 'The Forty Lovers of the Queen,' and it was more or less about rain-making."

"Aren't you going to tell it to me?" Eden asked.

Hedger fumbled among the radishes. "I don't know if it's the proper kind of story to tell a girl."

She smiled; "Oh, forget about that! I've been balloon riding today. I like to hear you talk."

Her low voice was flattering. She had seemed like clay in his hands ever since they got on the boat to come home. He leaned back in his chair, forgot his food, and, looking at her intently, began to tell his story, the theme of which he somehow felt was dangerous tonight.

The tale began, he said, somewhere in Ancient Mexico, and concerned the daughter of a king. The birth of this Princess was preceded by unusual portents. Three times her mother dreamed that she was delivered of serpents, which betokened that the child she carried would have power with the rain gods. The serpent was the symbol of water. The Princess grew up dedicated to the gods, and wise men taught her the rain-making mysteries. She was with difficulty restrained from men and was guarded at all times, for it was the law of the Thunder that she be maiden until her marriage. In the years of her adolescence, rain was abundant with her people. The oldest man could not remember such fertility. When the Princess had counted eighteen summers, her father went to drive out a war party that harried his borders on the north and troubled his prosperity. The King destroyed the invaders and brought home many prisoners. Among the prisoners was a young chief, taller than any of his captors, of such strength and ferocity that the King's people came a day's journey to look at him. When the Princess beheld his great stature, and saw that his arms and breast were covered with the figures of wild animals, bitten into the skin and coloured, she begged his life from her father. She desired that he should practise his art upon her, and prick upon her skin the signs of Rain and Lightning and Thunder, and stain the wounds with herb-juices, as they were upon his own body. For many days, upon the roof of the King's house, the Princess submitted herself to the bone needle, and the women with her marvelled at her fortitude. But the Princess was without shame before the Captive, and it came about that he threw from him his needles and his stains, and fell upon the Princess to violate her honour; and her women ran down from the roof screaming, to call the guard which stood at the gateway of the King's house, and none stayed to protect their mistress. When the guard came, the Captive was thrown into bonds, and he was gelded, and his tongue was torn out, and he was given for a slave to the Rain Princess.

The country of the Aztecs to the east was tormented by thirst, and their king, hearing much of the rain-making arts of the Princess, sent an embassy to her father, with presents and an offer of marriage. So the Princess went from her father to be the Queen of the Aztecs, and she took with her the Captive, who served her in everything with entire fidelity and slept upon a mat before her door.

The King gave his bride a fortress on the outskirts of the city, whither she retired to entreat the rain gods. This fortress was called the Queen's House, and on the night of the new moon the Queen came to it from the palace. But when the moon waxed and grew toward the round, because the god of Thunder had had his will of her, then the Queen returned to the King. Drouth abated in the country and rain fell abundantly by reason of the Queen's power with the stars.

When the Queen went to her own house she took with her no servant but the Captive, and he slept outside her door and brought her food after she had fasted. The Queen had a jewel of great value, a turquoise that had fallen from the sun, and had the image of the sun upon it. And when she desired a young man whom she had seen in the army or among the slaves, she sent the Captive to him with the jewel, for a sign that he should come to her secretly at the Queen's House upon business concerning the welfare of all. And some, after she had talked with them, she sent away with rewards; and some she took into her chamber and kept them by her for one night or two. Afterward she called the Captive and bade him conduct the youth by the secret way he had come, underneath the chambers of the fortress. But for the going away of the Queen's lovers the Captive took out the bar that was beneath a stone in the floor of the passage, and put in its stead a rush-reed, and the youth stepped upon it and fell through into a cavern that was the bed of an underground river, and whatever was thrown into it was not seen again. In this service nor in any other did the Captive fail the Queen.

But when the Queen sent for the Captain of the Archers, she detained him four days in her chamber, calling often for food and wine, and was greatly content with him. On the fourth day she went to the Captive outside her door and said:

"Tomorrow take this man up by the sure way, by which the King comes, and let him live."

In the Queen's door were arrows, purple and white. When she desired the King to come to her publicly, with his guard, she sent him a white arrow; but when she sent the purple, he came secretly, and covered himself with his mantle to be hidden from the stone gods at the gate. On the fifth night that the Queen was with her lover, the Captive took a purple arrow to the King, and the King came secretly and found them together. He killed the Captain with his own hand, but the Queen he brought to public trial. The Captive, when he was put to the question, told on his fingers forty men that he had let through the underground passage into the river. The Captive and the Queen were put to death by fire, both on the same day, and afterward there was scarcity of rain.

Eden Bower sat shivering a little as she listened. Hedger was not trying to please her, she thought, but to antagonize and frighten her by his brutal story. She had often told herself that his lean, big-boned lower jaw was like his bull-dog's, but tonight his face made Caesar's most savage and determined expression seem an affectation. Now she was looking at the man he really was. Nobody's eyes had ever defied her like this. They were searching her and seeing everything; all she had concealed from Livingston, and from the millionaire and his friends, and from the newspaper men. He was testing her, trying her out, and she was more ill at ease than she wished to show.

"That's quite a thrilling story," she said at last, rising and winding her scarf about her throat. "It must be getting late. Almost every one has gone."

They walked down the Avenue like people who have quarrelled, or who wish to get rid of each other. Hedger did not take her arm at the street crossings, and they did not linger in the Square. At her door he tried none of the old devices of the Livingston boys. He stood like a post, having forgotten to take off his hat, gave her a harsh, threatening glance, muttered "goodnight," and shut his own door noisily.

There was no question of sleep for Eden Bower. Her brain was working like a machine that would never stop. After she undressed, she tried to calm her nerves by smoking a cigarette, lying on the divan by the open window. But she grew wider and wider awake, combating the challenge that had flamed all evening in Hedger's eyes. The balloon had been one kind of excitement, the wine another; but the thing that had roused her, as a blow rouses a proud man, was the doubt, the contempt, the sneering hostility with which the painter had looked at her when he told his savage story. Crowds and balloons were all very well, she reflected, but woman's chief adventure is man. With a mind over active and a sense of life over strong, she wanted to walk across the roofs in the starlight, to sail over the sea and face at once a world of which she had never been afraid.

Hedger must be asleep; his dog had stopped sniffing under the double doors. Eden put on her wrapper and slippers and stole softly down the hall over the old carpet; one loose board creaked just as she reached the ladder. The trap-door was open, as always on hot nights. When she stepped out on the roof she drew a long breath and walked across it, looking up at the sky. Her foot touched something soft; she heard a low growl, and on the instant Caesar's sharp little teeth caught her ankle and waited. His breath was like steam on her leg. Nobody had ever intruded upon his roof before, and he panted for the movement or the word that would let him spring his jaw. Instead, Hedger's hand seized his throat.

"Wait a minute. I'll settle with him," he said grimly. He dragged the dog toward the manhole and disappeared. When he came back, he found Eden standing over by the dark chimney, looking away in an offended attitude.

"I caned him unmercifully," he panted. "Of course you didn't hear anything; he never whines when I beat him. He didn't nip you, did he?"

"I don't know whether he broke the skin or not," she answered aggrievedly, still looking off into the west.

"If I were one of your friends in white pants, I'd strike a match to find whether you were hurt, though I know you are not, and then I'd see your ankle, wouldn't I?"

"I suppose so."

He shook his head and stood with his hands in the pockets of his old painting jacket. "I'm not up to such boy-tricks. If you want the place to yourself, I'll clear out. There are plenty of places where I can spend the night, what's left of it. But if you stay here and I stay here—" He shrugged his shoulders.

Eden did not stir, and she made no reply. Her head drooped slightly, as if she were considering. But the moment he put his arms about her they began to talk, both at once, as people do in an opera. The instant avowal brought out a flood of trivial admissions. Hedger confessed his crime, was reproached and forgiven, and now Eden knew what it was in his look that she had found so disturbing of late.

Standing against the black chimney, with the sky behind and blue shadows before, they looked like one of Hedger's own paintings of that period; two figures, one white and one dark, and nothing whatever distinguishable about them but that they were male and female. The faces were lost, the contours blurred in shadow, but the figures were a man and a woman, and that was their whole concern and their mysterious beauty,—it was the rhythm in which they moved, at last, along the roof and down into the dark hole; he first, drawing her gently after him. She came down very slowly. The excitement and bravado and uncertainty of that long day and night seemed all at once to tell upon her. When his feet were on the carpet and he reached up to lift her down, she twined her arms about his neck as after a long separation, and turned her face to him, and her lips, with their perfume of youth and passion.

One Saturday afternoon Hedger was sitting in the window of Eden's music room. They had been watching the pigeons come wheeling over the roofs from their unknown feeding grounds.

"Why," said Eden suddenly, "don't we fix those big doors into your studio so they will open? Then, if I want you, I won't have to go through the hall. That illustrator is loafing about a good deal of late."

"I'll open them, if you wish. The bolt is on your side."

"Isn't there one on yours, too?"

"No. I believe a man lived there for years before I came in, and the nurse used to have these rooms herself. Naturally, the lock was on the lady's side."

Eden laughed and began to examine the bolt. "It's all stuck up with paint." Looking about, her eye lighted upon a bronze Buddah which was one of the nurse's treasures. Taking him by his head, she struck the bolt a blow with his squatting posteriors. The two doors creaked, sagged, and swung weakly inward a little way, as if they were too old for such escapades. Eden tossed the heavy idol into a stuffed chair. "That's better," she exclaimed exultantly. "So the bolts are always on the lady's side? What a lot society takes for granted!"

Hedger laughed, sprang up and caught her arms roughly. "Whoever takes you for granted— Did anybody, ever?"

"Everybody does. That's why I'm here. You are the only one who knows anything about me. Now I'll have to dress if we're going out for dinner."

He lingered, keeping his hold on her. "But I won't always be the only one, Eden Bower. I won't be the last."

"No, I suppose not," she said carelessly. "But what does that matter? You are the first."

As a long, despairing whine broke in the warm stillness, they drew apart. Caesar, lying on his bed in the dark corner, had lifted his head at this invasion of sunlight, and realized that the side of his room was broken open, and his whole world shattered by change. There stood his master and this woman, laughing at him! The woman was pulling the long black hair of this mightiest of men, who bowed his head and permitted it.

VI

In time they quarrelled, of course, and about an abstraction,—as young people often do, as mature people almost never do. Eden came in late one afternoon. She had been with some of her musical friends to lunch at Burton Ives' studio, and she began telling Hedger about its splendours. He listened a moment and then threw down his brushes. "I know exactly what it's like," he said impatiently. "A very good department-store conception of a studio. It's one of the show places."

"Well, it's gorgeous, and he said I could bring you to see him. The boys tell me he's awfully kind about giving people a lift,[3] and you might get something out of it."

Hedger started up and pushed his canvas out of the way. "What could I possibly get from Burton Ives? He's almost the worst painter in the world; the stupidest, I mean."

Eden was annoyed. Burton Ives had been very nice to her and had begged her to sit for him. "You must admit that he's a very successful one," she said coldly.

3. I.e., help.

"Of course he is! Anybody can be successful who will do that sort of thing. I wouldn't paint his pictures for all the money in New York."

"Well, I saw a lot of them, and I think they are beautiful."

Hedger bowed stiffly.

"What's the use of being a great painter if nobody knows about you?" Eden went on persuasively. "Why don't you paint the kind of pictures people can understand, and then, after you're successful, do whatever you like?"

"As I look at it," said Hedger brusquely, "I am successful."

Eden glanced about. "Well, I don't see any evidences of it," she said, biting her lip. "He has a Japanese servant and a wine cellar, and keeps a riding horse."

Hedger melted a little. "My dear, I have the most expensive luxury in the world, and I am much more extravagant than Burton Ives, for I work to please nobody but myself."

"You mean you could make money and don't? That you don't try to get a public?"

"Exactly. A public only wants what has been done over and over. I'm painting for painters—who haven't been born."

"What would you do if I brought Mr. Ives down here to see your things?"

"Well, for God's sake, don't! Before he left I'd probably tell him what I thought of him."

Eden rose. "I give you up. You know very well there's only one kind of success that's real."

"Yes, but it's not the kind you mean. So you've been thinking me a scrub painter, who needs a helping hand from some fashionable studio man? What the devil have you had anything to do with me for, then?"

"There's no use talking to you," said Eden walking slowly toward the door. "I've been trying to pull wires for you all afternoon, and this is what it comes to." She had expected that the tidings of a prospective call from the great man would be received very differently, and had been thinking as she came home in the stage how, as with a magic wand, she might gild Hedger's future, float him out of his dark hole on a tide of prosperity, see his name in the papers and his pictures in the windows on Fifth Avenue.

Hedger mechanically snapped the midsummer leash on Caesar's collar and they ran downstairs and hurried through Sullivan Street off toward the river. He wanted to be among rough, honest people, to get down where the big drays bumped over stone paving blocks and the men wore corduroy trowsers and kept their shirts open at the neck. He stopped for a drink in one of the sagging bar-rooms on the water front. He had never in his life been so deeply wounded; he did not know he could be so hurt. He had told this girl all his secrets. On the roof, in these warm, heavy summer nights, with her hands locked in his, he had been able to explain all his misty ideas about an unborn art the world was waiting for; had been able to explain them better than he had ever done to himself. And she had looked away to the chattels of this uptown studio and coveted them for him! To her he was only an unsuccessful Burton Ives.

Then why, as he had put it to her, did she take up with him? Young, beautiful, talented as she was, why had she wasted herself on a scrub? Pity? Hardly; she wasn't sentimental. There was no explaining her. But in this passion that had seemed so fearless and so fated to be, his own position now looked to him ridiculous; a poor dauber without money or fame,—it was her caprice to load him with favours. Hedger ground his teeth so loud that his dog, trotting beside him, heard him and looked up.

While they were having supper at the oysterman's, he planned his escape. Whenever he saw her again, everything he had told her, that he should never have told any one, would come back to him; ideas he had never whispered even to the painter whom he worshipped and had gone all the way to France to see. To her they must seem his apology for not having horses and a valet, or merely the puerile boastfulness of a weak man. Yet if she slipped the bolt tonight and came through the doors and said, "Oh, weak man, I belong to you!" what could he do? That was the danger. He would catch the train out to Long Beach tonight, and tomorrow he would go on to the north end of Long Island, where an old friend of his had a summer studio among the sand dunes. He would stay until things came right in his mind. And she could find a smart painter, or take her punishment.

When he went home, Eden's room was dark; she was dining out somewhere. He threw his things into a hold-all he had carried about the world with him, strapped up some colours and canvases, and ran downstairs.

VII

Five days later Hedger was a restless passenger on a dirty, crowded Sunday train, coming back to town. Of course he saw now how unreasonable he had been in expecting a Huntington girl to know anything about pictures; here was a whole continent full of people who knew nothing about pictures and he didn't hold it against them. What had such things to do with him and Eden Bower? When he lay out on the dunes, watching the moon come up out of the sea, it had seemed to him that there was no wonder in the world like the wonder of Eden Bower. He was going back to her because she was older than art, because she was the most overwhelming thing that had ever come into his life.

He had written her yesterday, begging her to be at home this evening, telling her that he was contrite, and wretched enough.

Now that he was on his way to her, his stronger feeling unaccountably changed to a mood that was playful and tender. He wanted to share everything with her, even the most trivial things. He wanted to tell her about the people on the train, coming back tired from their holiday with bunches of wilted flowers and dirty daisies; to tell her that the fish-man, to whom she had often sent him for lobsters, was among the passengers, disguised in a silk shirt and a spotted tie, and how his wife looked exactly like a fish, even to her eyes on which cataracts were forming. He could tell her, too, that he hadn't as much as unstrapped his canvases,—that ought to convince her.

In those days passengers from Long Island came into New York by ferry. Hedger had to be quick about getting his dog out of the express car in order to catch the first boat. The East River, and the bridges, and the city to the west, were burning in the conflagration of the sunset; there was that great home-coming reach of evening in the air.

The car changes from Thirty-fourth Street were too many and too perplexing; for the first time in his life Hedger took a hansom cab for Washington Square. Caesar sat bolt upright on the worn leather cushion beside him, and they jogged off, looking down on the rest of the world.

It was twilight when they drove down lower Fifth Avenue into the Square, and through the Arch behind them were the two long rows of pale violet lights that used to bloom so beautifully against the grey stone and asphalt. Here and yonder about the Square hung globes that shed a radiance not unlike the blue mists of evening, emerging softly when daylight died, as the stars emerged in the thin blue sky. Under them the sharp shadows of the trees fell on the cracked pavement and the sleeping grass. The first stars and the first lights were growing silver against the gradual darkening, when Hedger paid his driver and went into the house,—which, thank God, was still there! On the hall table lay his letter of yesterday, unopened.

He went upstairs with every sort of fear and every sort of hope clutching at his heart; it was as if tigers were tearing him. Why was there no gas burning in the top hall? He found matches and the gas bracket. He knocked, but got no answer; nobody was there. Before his own door were exactly five bottles of milk, standing in a row. The milk-boy had taken spiteful pleasure in thus reminding him that he forgot to stop his order.

Hedger went down to the basement; it, too, was dark. The janitress was taking her evening airing on the basement steps. She sat waving a palm-leaf fan majestically, her dirty calico dress open at the neck. She told him at once that there had been "changes." Miss Bower's room was to let again, and the piano would go tomorrow. Yes, she left yesterday, she sailed for Europe with friends from Chicago. They arrived on Friday, heralded by many telegrams. Very rich people they were said to be, though the man had refused to pay the nurse a month's rent in lieu of notice,—which would have been only right, as the young lady had agreed to take the rooms until October. Mrs. Foley had observed, too, that he didn't overpay her or Willy for their trouble, and a great deal of trouble they had been put to, certainly. Yes, the young lady was very pleasant, but the nurse said there were rings on the mahogany table where she had put tumblers and wine glasses. It was just as well she was gone. The Chicago man was uppish in his ways, but not much to look at. She supposed he had poor health, for there was nothing to him inside his clothes.

Hedger went slowly up the stairs—never had they seemed so long, or his legs so heavy. The upper floor was emptiness and silence. He unlocked his room, lit the gas, and opened the windows. When he went to put his coat in the closet, he found, hanging among his clothes, a pale, flesh-tinted dressing gown he had liked to see her wear, with a perfume —oh, a perfume that was still Eden Bower! He shut the door behind him and there, in the dark, for a moment he lost his manliness. It was when he held this garment to him that he found a letter in the pocket.

The note was written with a lead pencil, in haste: She was sorry that he was angry, but she still didn't know just what she had done. She had thought Mr. Ives would be useful to him; she guessed he was too proud. She wanted awfully to see him again, but Fate came knocking at her door after he had left her. She believed in Fate. She would never forget him, and she knew he would become the greatest painter in the world. Now she must pack. She hoped he wouldn't mind her leaving the dressing gown; somehow, she could never wear it again.

After Hedger read this, standing under the gas, he went back into the closet and knelt down before the wall; the knot hole had been plugged up with a ball of wet paper,—the same blue note-paper on which her letter was written.

He was hard hit. Tonight he had to bear the loneliness of a whole lifetime. Knowing himself so well, he could hardly believe that such a thing had ever happened to him, that such a woman had lain happy and contented in his arms. And now it was over. He turned out the light and sat down on his painter's stool before the big window. Caesar, on the floor beside him, rested his head on his master's knee. We must leave Hedger thus, sitting in his tank with his dog, looking up at the stars.

COMING, APHRODITE! This legend, in electric lights over the Lexington Opera House, had long announced the return of Eden Bower to New York after years of spectacular success in Paris. She came at last, under the management of an American Opera Company, but bringing her own *chef d'orchestre*.[4]

4. Orchestra leader. *Aphrodite* (1906) is an opera by Camille Erlanger (1863–1919), based on Pierre Loüy's novel, *Aphrodite* (1896).

One bright December afternoon Eden Bower was going down Fifth Avenue in her car, on the way to her broker, in Williams Street. Her thoughts were entirely upon stocks,—Cerro de Pasco, and how much she should buy of it,—when she suddenly looked up and realized that she was skirting Washington Square. She had not seen the place since she rolled out of it in an old-fashioned four-wheeler to seek her fortune, eighteen years ago.

"*Arrêtez, Alphonse. Attendez moi,*"[5] she called, and opened the door before he could reach it. The children who were streaking over the asphalt on roller skates saw a lady in a long fur coat, and short, high-heeled shoes, alight from a French car and pace slowly about the Square, holding her muff to her chin. This spot, at least, had changed very little, she reflected; the same trees, the same fountain, the white arch, and over yonder, Garibaldi, drawing the sword for freedom. There, just opposite her, was the old red brick house.

"Yes, that is the place," she was thinking. "I can smell the carpets now, and the dog,—what was his name? That grubby bathroom at the end of the hall, and that dreadful Hedger—still, there was something about him, you know—" She glanced up and blinked against the sun. From somewhere in the crowded quarter south of the Square a flock of pigeons rose, wheeling quickly upward into the brilliant blue sky. She threw back her head, pressed her muff closer to her chin, and watched them with a smile of amazement and delight. So they still rose, out of all that dirt and noise and squalor, fleet and silvery, just as they used to rise that summer when she was twenty and went up in a balloon on Coney Island!

Alphonse opened the door and tucked her robes about her. All the way down town her mind wandered from Cerro de Pasco, and she kept smiling and looking up at the sky.

When she had finished her business with the broker, she asked him to look in the telephone book for the address of M. Gaston Jules, the picture dealer, and slipped the paper on which he wrote it into her glove. It was five o'clock when she reached the French Galleries, as they were called. On entering she gave the attendant her card, asking him to take it to M. Jules. The dealer appeared very promptly and begged her to come into his private office, where he pushed a great chair toward his desk for her and signalled his secretary to leave the room.

"How good your lighting is in here," she observed, glancing about. "I met you at Simon's studio, didn't I? Oh, no! I never forget anybody who interests me." She threw her muff on his writing table and sank into the deep chair. "I have come to you for some information that's

5. French: "Stop, Alphonse. Wait for me."

not in my line. Do you know anything about an American painter named Hedger?"

He took the seat opposite her. "Don Hedger? But, certainly! There are some very interesting things of his in an exhibition at V——'s. If you would care to—"

She held up her hand. "No, no. I've no time to go to exhibitions. Is he a man of any importance?"

"Certainly. He is one of the first men among the moderns. That is to say, among the very moderns. He is always coming up with something different. He often exhibits in Paris, you must have seen—"

"No, I tell you I don't go to exhibitions. Has he had great success? That is what I want to know."

M. Jules pulled at his short grey moustache. "But, Madame, there are many kinds of success," he began cautiously.

Madame gave a dry laugh. "Yes, so he used to say. We once quarrelled on that issue. And how would you define his particular kind?"

M. Jules grew thoughtful. "He is a great name with all the young men, and he is decidedly an influence in art. But one can't definitely place a man who is original, erratic, and who is changing all the time."

She cut him short. "Is he much talked about at home? In Paris, I mean? Thanks. That's all I want to know." She rose and began buttoning her coat. "One doesn't like to have been an utter fool, even at twenty."

"*Mais, non!*"[6] M. Jules handed her her muff with a quick, sympathetic glance. He followed her out through the carpeted show-room, now closed to the public and draped in cheesecloth, and put her into her car with words appreciative of the honour she had done him in calling.

Leaning back in the cushions, Eden Bower closed her eyes, and her face, as the street lamps flashed their ugly orange light upon it, became hard and settled, like a plaster cast; so a sail, that has been filled by a strong breeze, behaves when the wind suddenly dies. Tomorrow night the wind would blow again, and this mask would be the golden face of Aphrodite. But a "big" career takes its toll, even with the best of luck.

1920

6. "But no!"

DOROTHY RICHARDSON
1873–1957

"She has invented a sentence that we might call the psychological sentence of the feminine gender," wrote Virginia Woolf about Dorothy Richardson's fluid and flexible transcriptions of female consciousness. She is "the greatest woman genius of our time," asserted the writer John Cowper Powys. Yet though Richardson's authorship of a ground-breaking, eleven-volume novel sequence entitled *Pilgrimage* won her such acclaim from intellectuals, as well as the financial patronage of the novelist Bryher (Winifred Ellerman, a shipping heiress who was the close friend of the poet H. D.), she lived and worked in comparative obscurity, and she earned minimal royalties from her books, which, after her death, were largely overlooked except by literary historians, who regarded them as experimental curiosities. Her ambition, however, was extraordinary: in the eleven volumes of *Pilgrimage*, each a self-contained text yet all intricately interrelated, Richardson set out to recount the subtlest details of the living-and-learning process by which her heroine, Miriam Henderson, forges an identity.

As many contemporary critics observed, Miriam Henderson *was* in some sense Dorothy Richardson, or at least a crucial "aspect" of that artist, for Richardson endowed her protagonist with a family background and an early life almost exactly the equivalent of her own. Born in Abingdon, in the English county of Berkshire, Richardson, like Miriam Henderson, was the third of four daughters. Her father was a proud, independently wealthy man who lost most of his money during the nineties; her mother was charming but mentally fragile. In 1895, while Dorothy was staying with her in the seaside resort of Hastings, where the two had gone for the sake of Mrs. Richardson's health, the older woman committed suicide in an episode that Richardson records with hallucinatory vividness at the end of *Honeycomb* (1917), the third book of *Pilgrimage*. Even before this drastic event, however, the young writer-to-be had had to confront a number of difficulties. Because of her father's bankruptcy, she had accepted two arduous teaching jobs—one at a girls' school in Germany, another at a school in the north of London; again, both situations are described with subtlety and sensitivity in the two first books of *Pilgrimage, Pointed Roofs* (1915) and *Backwater* (1916).

After her mother's death, Richardson moved to London, where she found an inexpensive "room of her own" in Bloomsbury and worked for eight years as a dental assistant. Here she began to write sketches, articles, and reviews; she encountered a number of London intellectuals who were to be lifelong friends; she became involved in the feminist and socialist movements; and—perhaps most important—she met the rising novelist H. G. Wells. The husband of one of Richardson's schoolfriends, Wells grew intensely interested in this lively and thoughtful young woman, and soon the two had entered upon a prolonged affair, which Richardson used as the basis for a later volume of *Pilgrimage*.

In 1912, Richardson embarked upon the composition of what was to become *Pilgrimage*. A few years earlier, she had left her job as dental assistant and begun to eke out a thin living as a writer, publishing sketches and reviews as well as articles about dentistry in a number of journals, and producing several books about Quakerism, a subject that fascinated her throughout her career. Now, staying sometimes in London and sometimes in country cottages lent her by friends, she devoted herself almost exclusively to the massive work that would take her three decades to complete. Shortly after the first volume (*Pointed Roofs*) appeared, she met and, in 1917, married the artist Allan Odle. A skillful illustrator who was widely regarded as the heir of the sardonic turn-of-the-century aesthete Aubrey Beardsley, Odle was considerably younger than Richardson and evidently almost ethereally frail, so that her feelings for him appear to have been mostly maternal. Yet—despite some ambivalence on Richardson's part—the marriage was a strong one, lasting until Odle died of a heart attack in 1948.

In an early review of *Pointed Roofs*, the novelist May Sinclair borrowed a phrase from the American philosopher William James to describe Richardson's literary technique. "Every definite image of the mind is steeped and dyed in the free water that flows around it," James had written, adding, "Let us call [that water] the stream of thought, of consciousness, or of subjective life." Though Richardson herself objected to what she called the "label" of "stream of consciousness," the phrase became standard for historians of modernism seeking to characterize not only her work but also the work of such major contemporaries as James Joyce, Virginia Woolf, and Sinclair herself. As the critic Walter Allen remarks of Richardson's ambitious novel sequence, "Reading *Pilgrimage*, we are within Miriam as in life we are within ourselves; we share in her extraordinary capacity for continuous and never-blunted response to current existence, the ultimate astonisher." Similarly, in a story like *Death*—a brief tale which nevertheless demonstrates Richardson's technique in miniature—we share in the fluidity, the ceaseless streaming, of her protagonist's gradually lapsing consciousness.

In 1957, Dorothy Richardson died in a nursing home in southeast London where she had been residing for some five years. Despite the influence she had had on novelists like Sinclair and Woolf, no one at the home had ever heard of her; when she claimed to be a writer, the nurses, according to her biographer Gloria Fromm, "believed at first that she had delusions." Yet in recent years critics and scholars have begun to reread *Pilgrimage*, to recognize the significance both of its contribution to a modernist aesthetic and of its feminist emphasis on a single *woman's* mind, and thus to acknowledge the importance of Dorothy Richardson. For interestingly, in recounting the process by which Miriam Henderson forged her identity, Richardson had also forged an indelible identity for herself: though her given name was really Dorothy Miller Richardson, her tombstone—through an error that seems more crucial than coincidental—was inscribed "To the Memory of Dorothy *Miriam* Odle, Authoress D. M. Richardson."

Death

This was death this time, no mistake. Her cheeks flushed at the indecency of being seen, dying and then dead. If only she could get it over and lay herself out decent before anyone came in to see and meddle. Mrs. Gworsh winning, left out there in the easy world, coming in to see her dead and lay her out and talk about her. . . . While there's life there's hope. Perhaps she wasn't dying. Only afraid. People can be so mighty bad and get better. But no. Not after that feeling rolling up within, telling her in words, her whom it knew, that this time she was going to be overwhelmed. That was the beginning, the warning and the certainty. To be more and more next time, any minute, increasing till her life flowed out for all to see. Her heart thumped. The rush of life beating against the walls of her body, making her head spin, numbed the pain and brought a mist before her eyes. Death. What she'd always feared so shocking, and put away. But no one knows what it is, how awful beyond everything, till they're in for it. Nobody knows death is this rush of life in all your parts.

The mist cleared. Her face was damp. The spinning in her head had ceased. She drew a careful breath. Without pain. Some of the pain had driven through her without feeling. But she was heavier. It wasn't gone either. Only waiting. She saw the doctor on his way. Scorn twisted her lips against her empty gums. Scores of times she'd waited for him. Felt him drive fear away. Joked. This time he'd say nothing. Watch, for her secret life to come up and out. When his turn came he'd know what it was like letting your life out; and all of them out there. No good telling. You can't know till you're in for it. They're all in for it, rich and poor alike. No help. The great enormous creature driving your innards up, what nobody knows. What *you* don't know. . . . Life ain't worth death.

It's got to be stuck, shame or no . . . but how do you do it?

She lay still and listened for footsteps. They knew next door by now. That piece[1] would never milk Snowdrop dry. Less cream, less butter. Everything going back. Slip-slop, go as you please, and never done. Where'd us be to now if I hadn't? That's it. What they don't think of. Slip-slop. Grinning and singing enough to turn the milk. I've got a tongue. I know it. You've got to keep on and keep on at them. Or nothing done. I been young, but never them silly ways. Snowdrop'll go back; for certain. . . .

But I shan't ever *see* it no more . . . the thought flew lifting through her mind. See no more. Work no more. Worry no more. Then what had been the good of it? Why had she gone on year in year out since Tom died and she began ailing, tramping all weathers up to the field, toiling and aching, and black as thunder most times. What was the good? Nobody knew her. Tom never had. And now there was only that piece downstairs, and what she did didn't matter any more. Except to herself, and she'd go on being slip-slop; not knowing she was in for

1. Girl (pejorative).

death that makes it all one whatever you do. Good and bad they're all dying and don't know it's the most they've got to do.

Her mind looked back up and down her life. Tom. What a fool she'd been to think him any different. Then when he died she'd thought him the same as at first, and cried because she'd let it all all slip in the worries. Little Joe. Tearing her open, then snuggled in her arms, sucking. And all outside bright and peaceful; better than the beginning with Tom. But they'd all stop if they knew where it led. Joe, and his wife, and his little ones, in for all of it, getting the hard of it now, and death waiting for them. She could tell them all now what it was like, all of them, the squire, all the same. All going the same way, rich and poor.

The Bible was right, "Remember now thy Creator in the days of thy youth."[2] What she had always wanted. She had always wanted to be good. Now it was too late. Nothing mattering, having it all lifted away, made the inside of you come back as it was at the first, ready to begin. Too late. Shocking she had thought it when parson said prepare for death, live as if you were going to die tonight. But it's true. If every moment was your last on earth you could be yourself. You'd dare. Everybody would dare. People is themselves when they are children, and not again till they know they'm dying. But conscience knows all the time. I've a heavy bill for all my tempers. God forgive me. But why should He? He was having his turn now, anyhow, with all this dying to do. Death must be got through as life had been, just somehow. But how?

When the doctor had gone she knew she was left to do it alone. While there's life there's hope. But the life in her was too much smaller than the great weight and pain. He made her easier, numb. Trying to think and not thinking. Everything unreal. The piece coming up and downstairs like something in another world. Perhaps God would let her go easy. Then it was all over? Just fading to nothing with everything still to do. . . .

The struggle came unexpectedly. She heard her cries, and then the world leapt upon her and grappled, and even in the midst of the agony of pain was the surprise of her immense strength. The strength that struggled against the huge stifling, the body that leapt and twisted against the heavy darkness, a shape within her shape, that she had not known. Her unknown self rushing forward through all her limbs to fight. Leaping out and curving in a great sweep away from where she lay to the open sill, yet pinned back, unwrenchable from the bed. Back and back she slid, down a long tunnel at terrific speed, cool, her brow cool and wet, with wind blowing upon it. Darkness in front. Back and back into her own young body, alone. In front on the darkness came the

2. Ecclesiastes 12:1

garden, the old garden in April, the crab-apple blossom, all as it was before she began, but brighter. . . .

1924

AMY LOWELL
1874–1925

"I am ugly, fat, conspicuous & dull," Amy Lowell confided to her diary when she was fifteen, adding, soon after, that "I should like best of anything to be literary." Although she *was* overweight, Lowell's adolescent self-definition was otherwise quite inaccurate. As the daughter of a prominent Boston family, she had inherited a confident manner bred by generations of privilege: her grandfathers on both sides had founded important textile businesses; one of her cousins was the poet James Russell Lowell; her father was a member of the governing board of the Massachusetts Institute of Technology; her brother Percival was the founder of the Lowell Observatory at Harvard; and her brother Abbott Lawrence was a president of Harvard. She herself, moreover, was evidently a gifted child who discovered that she liked best "to be literary" mainly by ranging through her father's excellent library. By the time she was in her early teens she had begun to read the Romantic poets, and she had produced a first book entitled *Dream Drops, or Stories from Fairy Land, by a Dreamer* (1887), which her mother arranged for her to sell at a charity bazaar.

To be sure, as the daughter of a distinguished family Amy Lowell was expected to lead a genteel life. After making her debut in society, she took several long trips abroad, and at one point she almost became engaged to a "proper" Bostonian. In addition, both before and after the deaths of her parents in the last years of the century, she served on numerous civic boards and committees. At the same time, however, she continued to be tormented by personal problems; she suffered from bouts of "nervous prostration" and was intransigently overweight despite countless attempts at severe dieting, even while, persistently "literary," she converted several rooms of Sevenels—the Lowell family mansion—into what one biographer has called "a baronial library."

It was during the Boston theater season of 1902 that this ambivalent former debutante first seriously defined herself as a poet. She experienced her literary awakening because of an encounter with Eleanora Duse, the Italian actress, who was appearing in a play written by her lover, the poet Gabriel D'Annunzio. Lowell attended the work's opening-night performance, where she was so overcome by Duse's dramatic presence that she returned home and wrote, as she later remembered, "seventy-one lines of bad blank verse," including a tribute to the actress's "woman's soul" and "woman's heart." After this, and after attending all the other performances of the D'Annunzio play, Lowell claimed to know that verse writing was her true vocation. Struggling to perfect her art, she read, studied, founded a little theater group, and in 1912 published her first collection, a somewhat derivative volume entitled A *Dome of Many-Coloured*

Glass in deference to *Adonais*, the Romantic poet Shelley's elegy for her beloved John Keats.

Shortly before *A Dome* appeared and ten years after her crucial encounter with Duse, Lowell met another woman who was to inspire her even more than the Italian celebrity had. Ada Dwyer Russell, a divorced actress eleven years Lowell's senior, was introduced to the poet at a women's "lunch club," and the attraction between the two was evidently both mutual and instantaneous. By 1914, Ada Russell had moved into Sevenels, where she was to live with Amy Lowell for the rest of the writer's life, acting—the way Alice B. Toklas did for Gertrude Stein—as beloved companion, general amanuensis, resident critic, and nurturing muse. For her, Lowell composed many of her most poignant love poems, including *Madonna of the Evening Flowers*, *The Letter*, *Venus Transiens*, and *Opal*. At the same time, the relationship between the two women was evidently so deeply collaborative that Lowell sometimes joked that they should put up a sign above the doorway at Sevenels reading "Lowell & Russell, Makers of Fine Poems."

Also significantly influential on Lowell's evolving art was the founding in 1912 of *Poetry* magazine. Edited in Chicago by the innovative woman of letters Harriet Monroe, this journal immediately began to publish the works of Ezra Pound, T. S. Eliot, D. H. Lawrence, John Gould Fletcher, Richard Aldington, and H. D. (Hilda Doolittle), among others. Upon Lowell, H. D.'s free verse, with its irregular lines and crisp, Greek-inspired images, had the greatest impact; as one critic observes, "When in the January 1913 number [of *Poetry*] she saw the signature 'H. D., Imagiste,' she recognized in a flash her own as yet unrealized poetic identity," for she felt that she too ought to be writing verse in the deliberately stripped, cool, vividly pictorial style employed by the group of aesthetic radicals who, under the leadership of the revolutionary Ezra Pound, called themselves "Imagists." Journeying to London in 1913, Lowell and Russell met Pound; the following year, just before the outbreak of World War I, the pair returned to England to make the acquaintance of John Gould Fletcher, H. D., Henry James, D. H. Lawrence, and Robert Frost; with Lawrence and Frost, in particular, Lowell formed important, long-lasting friendships.

No doubt encouraged by her participation in these innovative aesthetic circles as well as by her relationship with Russell, Lowell now began to produce and edit volumes of poetry and criticism at an increasingly energetic pace. Works like *Can Grande's Castle* (1918) and *Pictures of the Floating World* (1919) firmly established her reputation as a leader of the Imagist movement, which its founder, Ezra Pound, sardonically renamed "Amygism." Books like *Tendencies in Modern American Poetry* (1917) gave her an equally solid reputation as a critic. Eccentric in her personal behavior—she was, for instance, famous for smoking what most people thought were "big black cigars" (really slim cigarillos)—she became a celebrity.

During her last years, Lowell's lifetime of ambitious activity combined with serious overweight led to ill health. In 1918, she had the first of a series of operations (for an umbilical hernia) that drastically weakened her. Still, she continued indefatigably writing, lecturing, reviewing, and maintaining many friendships. Her most important project in the early twenties was a massive biography of John Keats, the Romantic poet she had admired since her youth.

Published early in 1925, the book aroused much controversy, especially in England, and the author was planning to travel to London to defend it when she died of a cerebral hemorrhage in May 1925, at fifty-one. The following year her posthumously published volume of poems, *What's O'Clock*, was awarded the Pulitzer Prize. The honor, as her biographer Jean Gould observes, was fitting, for this collection featured a number of Lowell's finest verses, including her long meditation on the lot of female poets entitled *The Sisters*, a work that might well stand as a vindication of the rights of women like Amy Lowell to abandon genteel New England society and, instead, create poems, compose criticism, edit anthologies, write biographies, love women like Ada Russell, and smoke slim, elegant cigarillos.

The Letter

Little cramped words scrawling all over the paper
Like draggled fly's legs,
What can you tell of the flaring moon
Through the oak leaves?
Or of my uncurtained window and the bare floor   5
Spattered with moonlight?
Your silly quirks and twists have nothing in them
Of blossoming hawthorns,
And this paper is dull, crisp, smooth, virgin of loveliness
Beneath my hand.   10

I am tired, Beloved, of chafing my heart against
The want of you;
Of squeezing it into little inkdrops,
And posting[1] it.
And I scald alone, here, under the fire   15
Of the great moon.

1919

Venus Transiens[2]

Tell me,
Was Venus more beautiful
Than you are,
When she topped
The crinkled waves,   5
Drifting shoreward
On her plaited shell?

1. Mailing.
2. Latin: Venus passing over. Venus is the Greek goddess of love.

Was Botticelli's vision[3]
Fairer than mine;
And were the painted rosebuds   10
He tossed his lady,
Of better worth
Than the words I blow about you
To cover your too great loveliness
As with a gauze   15
Of misted silver?
For me,
You stand poised
In the blue and buoyant air,
Cinctured by bright winds,   20
Treading the sunlight.
And the waves which precede you
Ripple and stir
The sands at my feet.

                                           1919

Madonna of the Evening Flowers[4]

All day long I have been working,
Now I am tired.
I call: "Where are you?"
But there is only the oak-tree rustling in the wind.
The house is very quiet,   5
The sun shines in on your books,
On your scissors and thimble just put down,
But you are not there.
Suddenly I am lonely:
Where are you?   10
I go about searching.

Then I see you,
Standing under a spire of pale blue larkspur,
With a basket of roses on your arm.
You are cool, like silver,   15
And you smile.
I think the Canterbury bells[5] are playing little tunes.

You tell me that the peonies need spraying,
That the columbines have overrun all bounds,

3. Sandro Botticelli (1444–1510) executed a
famous painting called *The Birth of Venus*, in
which the goddess stands on a large scalloped
seashell riding on the ocean waves.

4. Madonna: my lady; in Italian painting, the
phrase is applied to the Virgin Mary.
5. The bells of the famous cathedral at Canterbury, England.

That the pyrus japonica should be cut back and rounded. 20
You tell me these things.
But I look at you, heart of silver,
White heart-flame of polished silver,
Burning beneath the blue steeples of the larkspur,
And I long to kneel instantly at your feet, 25
While all about us peal the loud, sweet *Te Deums*[6] of the
    Canterbury bells.

1919

The Weather-Cock Points South

I put your leaves aside,
One by one:
The stiff, broad outer leaves;
The smaller ones,
Pleasant to touch, veined with purple; 5
The glazed inner leaves.
One by one
I parted you from your leaves,
Until you stood up like a white flower
Swaying slightly in the evening wind. 10

White flower,
Flower of wax, of jade, of unstreaked agate;
Flower with surfaces of ice,
With shadows faintly crimson.
Where in all the garden is there such a flower? 15
The stars crowd through the lilac leaves
To look at you.
The low moon brightens you with silver.

The bud is more than the calyx.
There is nothing to equal a white bud, 20
Of no colour, and of all,
Burnished by moonlight,
Thrust upon by a softly-swinging wind.

1919

Opal

You are ice and fire,
The touch of you burns my hands like snow.

6. An ancient Latin hymn: *Te deum laudamus,* we praise thee, God.

You are cold and flame.
You are the crimson of amaryllis,
The silver of moon-touched magnolias.
When I am with you,
My heart is a frozen pond
Gleaming with agitated torches.

                                                    5

                                                  1919

Decade

When you came, you were like red wine and honey,
And the taste of you burnt my mouth with its sweetness.
Now you are like morning bread,
Smooth and pleasant.
I hardly taste you at all for I know your savour,   5
But I am completely nourished.

                                                  1919

The Sisters

Taking us by and large, we're a queer lot
We women who write poetry. And when you think
How few of us there've been, it's queerer still.
I wonder what it is that makes us do it,
Singles us out to scribble down, man-wise,   5
The fragments of ourselves. Why are we
Already mother-creatures, double-bearing,
With matrices in body and in brain?
I rather think that there is just the reason
We are so sparse a kind of human being;   10
The strength of forty thousand Atlases[7]
Is needed for our every-day concerns.
There's Sapho,[8] now I wonder what was Sapho.
I know a single slender thing about her:
That, loving, she was like a burning birch-tree   15
All tall and glittering fire, and that she wrote
Like the same fire caught up to Heaven and held there,
A frozen blaze before it broke and fell.
Ah, me! I wish I could have talked to Sapho,
Surprised her reticences by flinging mine   20
Into the wind. This tossing off of garments

7. In Greek mythology, one of a giant race   holding up the earth.
called the Titans, who was assigned the task of   8. Greek lyric poet of the seventh century B.C.

Which cloud the soul is none too easy doing
With us to-day. But still I think with Sapho
One might accomplish it, were she in the mood
To bare her loveliness of words and tell 25
The reasons, as she possibly conceived them,
Of why they are so lovely. Just to know
How she came at them, just to watch
The crisp sea sunshine playing on her hair,
And listen, thinking all the while 'twas she 30
Who spoke and that we two were sisters
Of a strange, isolated little family.
And she is Sapho—Sapho—not Miss or Mrs.,
A leaping fire we call so for convenience;
But Mrs. Browning[9]—who would ever think 35
Of such presumption as to call her "Ba."
Which draws the perfect line between sea-cliffs
And a close-shuttered room in Wimpole Street.
Sapho could fly her impulses like bright
Balloons tip-tilting to a morning air 40
And write about it. Mrs. Browning's heart
Was squeezed in stiff conventions. So she lay
Stretched out upon a sofa, reading Greek
And speculating, as I must suppose,
In just this way on Sapho; all the need, 45
The huge, imperious need of loving, crushed
Within the body she believed so sick.
And it was sick, poor lady, because words
Are merely simulacra after deeds
Have wrought a pattern; when they take the place 50
Of actions they breed a poisonous miasma
Which, though it leave the brain, eats up the body.
So Mrs. Browning, aloof and delicate,
Lay still upon her sofa, all her strength
Going to uphold her over-topping brain. 55
It seems miraculous, but she escaped
To freedom and another motherhood
Than that of poems. She was a very[1] woman
And needed both.
          If I had gone to call, 60
Would Wimpole Street have been the kindlier place,
Or Casa Guidi,[2] in which to have met her?
I am a little doubtful of that meeting,
For Queen Victoria was very young and strong
And all-pervading in her apogee 65

---

9. Elizabeth Barrett Browning (1806–1861), English poet; she lived as an invalid in her father's house in Wimpole Street, until the poet Robert Browning courted and married her.

1. True.
2. The house in Florence where the Brownings resided after their marriage.

At just that time. If we had stuck to poetry,
Sternly refusing to be drawn off by mesmerism
Or Roman revolutions,[3] it might have done.
For, after all, she is another sister,
But always, I rather think, an older sister   70
And not herself so curious a technician
As to admit newfangled modes of writing—
"Except, of course, in Robert, and that is neither
Here nor there for Robert is a genius."
I do not like the turn this dream is taking,   75
Since I am very fond of Mrs. Browning
And very much indeed should like to hear her
Graciously asking me to call her "Ba."
But then the Devil of Verisimilitude
Creeps in and forces me to know she wouldn't.   80
Convention again, and how it chafes my nerves,
For we are such a little family
Of singing sisters, and as if I didn't know
What those years felt like tied down to the sofa.
Confound Victoria, and the slimy inhibitions   85
She loosed on all us Anglo-Saxon creatures!
Suppose there hadn't been a Robert Browning,
No *Sonnets from the Portuguese*[4] would have been written.
They are the first of all her poems to be,
One might say, fertilized. For, after all,   90
A poet is flesh and blood as well as brain
And Mrs. Browning, as I said before,
Was very, very woman. Well, there are two
Of us, and vastly unlike that's for certain.
Unlike at least until we tear the veils   95
Away which commonly gird souls. I scarcely think
Mrs. Browning would have approved the process
In spite of what had surely been relief;
For speaking souls must always want to speak
Even when bat-eyed, narrow-minded Queens   100
Set prudishness to keep the keys of impulse.
Then do the frowning Gods invent new banes
And make the need of sofas. But Sapho was dead
And I, and others, not yet peeped above
The edge of possibility. So that's an end   105
To speculating over tea-time talks
Beyond the movement of pentameters
With Mrs. Browning.
                              But I go dreaming on,

---

3. At the time of the Brownings' residence, Italy
was struggling for independence from foreign
rule.

4. A sequence of love sonnets by Barrett
Browning addressed to her husband, Robert.

In love with these my spiritual relations.   110
I rather think I see myself walk up
A flight of wooden steps and ring a bell
And send a card in to Miss Dickinson.[5]
Yet that's a very silly way to do.
I should have taken the dream twist-ends about   115
And climbed over the fence and found her deep
Engrossed in the doings of a humming-bird
Among nasturtiums. Not having expected strangers,
She might forget to think me one, and holding up
A finger say quite casually: "Take care.   120
Don't frighten him, he's only just begun."
"Now this," I well believe I should have thought,
"Is even better than Sapho. With Emily
You're really here, or never anywhere at all
In range of mind." Wherefore, having begun   125
In the strict centre, we could slowly progress
To various circumferences, as we pleased.
We could, but should we? That would quite depend
On Emily. I think she'd be exacting,
Without intention possibly, and ask   130
A thousand tight-rope tricks of understanding.
But, bless you, I would somersault all day
If by so doing I might stay with her.
I hardly think that we should mention souls
Although they might just round the corner from us   135
In some half-quizzical, half-wistful metaphor.
I'm very sure that I should never seek
To turn her parables to stated fact.
Sapho would speak, I think, quite openly,
And Mrs. Browning guard a careful silence,   140
But Emily would set doors ajar and slam them
And love you for your speed of observation.

Strange trio of my sisters, most diverse,
And how extraordinarily unlike
Each is to me, and which way shall I go?   145
Sapho spent and gained; and Mrs. Browning,
After a miser girlhood, cut the strings
Which tied her money-bags and let them run;
But Emily hoarded—hoarded—only giving
Herself to cold, white paper. Starved and tortured,   150
She cheated her despair with games of patience[6]
And fooled herself by winning. Frail little elf,
The lonely brain-child of a gaunt maturity,

---

5. Emily Dickinson (1830–1886), American   6. Solitaire card games.
poet.

She hung her womanhood upon a bough
And played ball with the stars—too long—too long—   155
The garment of herself hung on a tree
Until at last she lost even the desire
To take it down. Whose fault? Why let us say,
To be consistent, Queen Victoria's.
But really, not to over-rate the queen,   160
I feel obliged to mention Martin Luther,[7]
And behind him the long line of Church Fathers
Who draped their prurience like a dirty cloth
About the naked majesty of God.
Good-bye, my sisters, all of you are great,   165
And all of you are marvellously strange,
And none of you has any word for me.
I cannot write like you, I cannot think
In terms of Pagan or of Christian now.
I only hope that possibly some day   170
Some other woman with an itch for writing
May turn to me as I have turned to you
And chat with me a brief few minutes. How
We lie, we poets! It is three good hours
I have been dreaming. Has it seemed so long   175
To you? And yet I thank you for the time
Although you leave me sad and self-distrustful,
For older sisters are very sobering things.
Put on your cloaks, my dears, the motor's waiting.
No, you have not seemed strange to me, but near,   180
Frightfully near, and rather terrifying.
I understand you all, for in myself—
Is that presumption? Yet indeed it's true—
We are one family. And still my answer
Will not be any one of yours, I see.   185
Well, never mind that now. Good night! Good night!

1925

7. German monk and the founder of the Protestant church (1483–1546).

⌐GERTRUDE STEIN
1874–1946

In paintings by Pablo Picasso (1906) and Pavel Tchelitchew (1930), sculptures by Jacques Lipchitz (1920) and Jo Davidson (1920), and the many photographs by Carl Van Vechten and Cecil Beaton, Gertrude Stein sometimes looks like the Roman emperor Ernest Hemingway took her to be and sometimes like the great Jewish Buddha many of her other friends thought she resembled. Whether, in a reference to the derisively experimental movement called "dadaism," she was hailed as the "the Mama of dada" or ridiculed as "the Mother Goose of Montparnasse," Stein herself was hardly embarrassed about her growing celebrity, for she believed that "Einstein was the creative philosophic mind of the century and I have been the creative literary mind of the century." But as late in her career as 1937 she admitted, "It always did bother me that the American public were more interested in me than in my work." If her *oeuvre* has been neglected because it sometimes seems opaque or even incomprehensible, that is because it includes short stories, portraits, novels, autobiographies, dramas, and poems that develop the radical linguistic experimentation associated with modernism.

Stein was a first-generation American, the youngest of seven children. In 1841, her German-Jewish father, Daniel Stein, emigrated from Bavaria to Baltimore, where he established a profitable clothing business and married Amelia (Keyser) Stein before moving to Allegheny, Pennsylvania, in 1862 to start his family. Stein's earliest memories dated from the age of four, when the family lived in Austria and Paris before settling down in Oakland, California, in 1879. Although she had prattled in German and French, she soon began reading English poetry and fiction, and, more idiosyncratically, Congressional records and constitutional histories of England. After the death of her mother in 1888 and the death of her father three years later, she and her closest sibling, Leo, traveled to Baltimore, where they were cared for by their mother's sister, Fannie Bachrach, and provided for by an independent income secured for them by their eldest brother, Michael.

Stein's identification with Leo continued to inform her early development. After Leo transferred from the University of California to Harvard, Gertrude enrolled as a special student at the Annex that would become Radcliffe College. There she studied with the philosopher George Santayana and the psychologist William James. With the encouragement of James, she joined Leo in Baltimore in 1897 to pursue a medical education at Johns Hopkins, where her formal class training was supplemented by obstetrical work and by her friendship with Claribel and Etta Cone, two well-to-do and well-educated young women. But after two years, Stein abandoned her plans to complete the medical degree. She was probably depressed by her involvement in an erotic triangle with Mabel Haynes and May Bookstaver: Stein fictionalized her sense of misery at the futility of this relationship in *Q.E.D. or Things as They Are*, a work published posthumously in 1950. In 1902, she joined Leo, who had been studying in Italy with the art critic Bernard Berenson. After a summer in Bloomsbury and a winter in New York, she again returned to Leo, who occupied rooms at 27 rue de Fleurus that would soon become famous as a center of *avant-garde* activity in Paris.

It was from this early period in Paris that Stein's fascination with modern art dated. Attached by a courtyard to the rooms the Steins shared was an atelier (a studio) which was quickly filled with the many paintings they purchased from art dealers like Amboise Vollard. Stein herself recounted how they found Matisse's *La Femme au Chapeau* at the Petit Palais show where some viewers were so infuriated by this picture that they laughed and tried to scratch off the paint. What attracted Stein to the impressionist and postimpressionist work of

Cézanne, Renoir, Rousseau, Braque, Matisse, and Picasso was their effort to use deformation to intensify and clarify visual effect. Soon she began her own efforts to intensify and clarify English so as to liberate language from representation. The three stories that comprise *Three Lives* (1909)—*The Good Anna, Melanctha,* and *The Gentle Lena*—were composed while the writer studied Cézanne's portrait of his wife and while she sat for Picasso's portrait of her. They are what she called "the first definite step away from the nineteenth century and into the twentieth century in literature." Early in her career, moreover, Stein began working in "the continuous present": derived from William James, her notion of time as a series of discrete moments, rather than a linear progression, allowed her to move toward a language drained of conventional meaning and charged, through repetition, with the insistent, recurrent obsessions of her characters' consciousnesses.

When Stein finally found a publisher for *Three Lives,* she willingly allowed her new friend, Alice B. Toklas, to proofread the manuscript for her. Just arrived from California, Alice quickly supplanted Leo both in Gertrude's affections and in the atelier. Much later, Stein would cheerfully explain that she stopped being interested in Leo when it became clear that "it was I who was the genius, there was no reason for it but I was, and he was not." For a contemporary poet like Diane Wakoski, Stein and Toklas epitomize the genius and the devoted wife: Stein's "craggy, grand / stony ideas" were in some sense made possible by Toklas's embroidery, baking, and secretarial skills. Yet the Stein-Toklas relationship was not just based on Toklas's renunciatory adulation or Stein's energetic egotism. Stein's earlier depression in Baltimore was ended by the lifelong companionship of Toklas, who created the Plain Edition Press to publish Stein when she was feeling "a little bitter" about all her unpublished manuscripts. Even more importantly, Toklas helped free Stein's style. In the early experimental portrait *Ada* and in the erotic poem *Lifting Belly,* Stein developed an encoded language to articulate her erotic and linguistic play with Toklas. In her first commercial success, moreover, Stein wrote using Toklas's voice: in *The Autobiography of Alice B. Toklas* (1933), Gertrude's Alice describes the formative influence Stein had on younger writers like Ernest Hemingway and Sherwood Anderson, even as she provides titillating gossip about the postimpressionists and modernists who populated the Stein-Toklas salon.

The books Stein completed before and after World War I are markedly different from each other and from works produced in the realistic tradition in fiction. Her thousand-page history, *The Making of Americans* (1911), attempted to delineate every sort of American "who ever can or is or was or will be living," while the prose poems of *Tender Buttons* (1914) supplied impressionistic definitions that are sometimes witty ("A White Hunter: A white hunter is nearly crazy") and sometimes enigmatic ("Cream: Cream cut. Any where crumb. Left hop chambers"). Within a small circle of artists, Stein was gaining a reputation as a prolific and daring inventor of new forms. Judging from *The Autobiography,* the Great War was a great adventure for Toklas and Stein, who enlisted in an American ambulance unit in France. After the war, they reestablished their salon, which was frequented by many American expatriates and visitors. Stein continued to produce experimental poems, but she also began writing plays (*Four Saints in Three Acts,* 1927) and giving lectures at Oxford and Cambridge, speeches that issued in books like *Composition as Explanation* (1926), which was published by the Woolfs' Hogarth Press. In the 1930s, Stein profited from the commercial success of both the *Autobiography of Alice B. Toklas* and Virgil Thompson's opera version of her play *Four Saints in Three Acts*, which led to a long American lecture tour and a contract that assured her continued publication in America.

During the German occupation of France in the early forties, Stein and Toklas were forced to take refuge in the area around Bilignin, where they had a summer house. Always productive, Stein continued to write novels (*Ida, a Novel*, 1941), plays (*The Mother of Us All*, 1946), and memoirs (*Wars I Have Seen*, 1945). Generous and friendly to the many G.I.s still in Paris after 1944, she was by this time a celebrity in the American press. Two years after her return to Paris, she entered the American Hospital at Neuilly-sur-Seine because of an abdominal tumor. On her deathbed, she was said to have asked, "What is the answer?" When no one spoke, she replied to herself with characteristic aplomb: "What is the question?" Alice B. Toklas, who died twenty-one years later, was buried beside Stein in the cemetery of Père-Lachaise in Paris.

The Gentle Lena

Lena was patient, gentle, sweet and german. She had been a servant for four years and had liked it very well.

Lena had been brought from Germany to Bridgepoint by a cousin and had been in the same place there for four years.

This place Lena had found very good. There was a pleasant, unexacting mistress and her children, and they all liked Lena very well.

There was a cook there who scolded Lena a great deal but Lena's german patience held no suffering and the good incessant woman really only scolded so for Lena's good.

Lena's german voice when she knocked and called the family in the morning was as awakening, as soothing, and as appealing, as a delicate soft breeze in midday, summer. She stood in the hallway every morning a long time in her unexpectant and unsuffering german patience calling to the young ones to get up. She would call and wait a long time and then call again, always even, gentle, patient, while the young ones fell back often into that precious, tense, last bit of sleeping that gives a strength of joyous vigor in the young, over them that have come to the readiness of middle age, in their awakening.

Lena had good hard work all morning, and on the pleasant, sunny afternoons she was sent out into the park to sit and watch the little two year old girl baby of the family.

The other girls, all them that make the pleasant, lazy crowd, that watch the children in the sunny afternoons out in the park, all liked the simple, gentle, german Lena very well. They all, too, liked very well to tease her, for it was so easy to make her mixed and troubled, and all helpless, for she could never learn to know just what the other quicker girls meant by the queer things they said.

The two or three of these girls, the ones that Lena always sat with, always worked together to confuse her. Still it was pleasant, all this life for Lena.

The little girl fell down sometimes and cried, and then Lena had to soothe her. When the little girl would drop her hat, Lena had to pick it up and hold it. When the little girl was bad and threw away her playthings, Lena told her she could not have them and took them from her to hold until the little girl should need them.

It was all a peaceful life for Lena, almost as peaceful as a pleasant leisure. The other girls, of course, did tease her, but then that only made a gentle stir within her.

Lena was a brown and pleasant creature, brown as blonde races often have them brown, brown, not with the yellow or the red or the chocolate brown of sun burned countries, but brown with the clear color laid flat on the light toned skin beneath, the plain, spare brown that makes it right to have been made with hazel eyes, and not too abundant straight, brown hair, hair that only later deepens itself into brown from the straw yellow of a german childhood.

Lena had the flat chest, straight back and forward falling shoulders of the patient and enduring working woman, though her body was now still in its milder girlhood and work had not yet made these lines too clear.

The rarer feeling that there was with Lena, showed in all the even quiet of her body movements, but in all it was the strongest in the patient, old-world ignorance, and earth made pureness of her brown, flat, soft featured face. Lena had eyebrows that were a wondrous thickness. They were black, and spread, and very cool, with their dark color and their beauty, and beneath them were her hazel eyes, simple and human, with the earth patience of the working, gentle, german woman.

Yes it was all a peaceful life for Lena. The other girls, of course, did tease her, but then that only made a gentle stir within her.

"What you got on your finger Lena," Mary, one of the girls she always sat with, one day asked her. Mary was good natured, quick, intelligent and Irish.

Lena had just picked up the fancy paper made accordion that the little girl had dropped beside her, and was making it squeak sadly as she pulled it with her brown strong, awkward finger.

"Why, what is it, Mary, paint?" said Lena, putting her finger to her mouth to taste the dirt spot.

"That's awful poison Lena, don't you know?" said Mary, "that green paint that you just tasted."

Lena had sucked a good deal of the green paint from her finger. She stopped and looked hard at the finger. She did not know just how much Mary meant by what she said.

"Ain't it poison, Nellie, that green paint, that Lena sucked just now," said Mary. "Sure it is Lena, its real poison, I ain't foolin' this time anyhow."

Lena was a little troubled. She looked hard at her finger where the paint was, and she wondered if she had really sucked it.

It was still a little wet on the edges and she rubbed it off a long time on the inside of her dress, and in between she wondered and looked at the finger and thought, was it really poison that she had just tasted.

"Ain't it too bad, Nellie, Lena should have sucked that," Mary said.

Nellie smiled and did not answer. Nellie was dark and thin, and looked Italian. She had a big mass of black hair that she wore high up on her head, and that made her face look very fine.

Nellie always smiled and did not say much, and then she would look at Lena to perplex her.

And so they all three sat with their little charges in the pleasant sunshine a long time. And Lena would often look at her finger and wonder if it was really poison that she had just tasted and then she would rub her finger on her dress a little harder.

Mary laughed at her and teased her and Nellie smiled a little and looked queerly at her.

Then it came time, for it was growing cooler, for them to drag together the little ones, who had begun to wander, and to take each one back to its own mother. And Lena never knew for certain whether it was really poison, that green stuff that she had tasted.

During these four years of service, Lena always spent her Sundays out at the house of her aunt, who had brought her four years before to Bridgepoint.

This aunt, who had brought Lena, four years before, to Bridgepoint, was a hard, ambitious, well meaning, german woman. Her husband was a grocer in the town, and they were very well to do. Mrs. Haydon, Lena's aunt, had two daughters who were just beginning as young ladies, and she had a little boy who was not honest and who was very hard to manage.

Mrs. Haydon was a short, stout, hard built, german woman. She always hit the ground very firmly and compactly as she walked. Mrs. Haydon was all a compact and well hardened mass, even to her face, reddish and darkened from its early blonde, with its hearty, shiny, cheeks, and doubled chin well covered over with the up-roll from her short, square neck.

The two daughters, who were fourteen and fifteen, looked like unkneaded, unformed mounds of flesh beside her.

The elder girl, Mathilda, was blonde, and slow, and simple, and quite fat. The younger, Bertha, who was almost as tall as her sister, was dark, and quicker, and she was heavy, too, but not really fat.

These two girls the mother had brought up very firmly. They were well taught for their position. They were always both well dressed, in the same kinds of hats and dresses, as is becoming in two german sisters. The mother liked to have them dressed in red. Their best clothes were red dresses, made of good heavy cloth, and strongly trimmed with braid of a glistening black. They had stiff, red felt hats, trimmed with black velvet ribbon, and a bird. The mother dressed matronly, in a bonnet and in black, always sat between her two big daughters, firm, directing, and repressed.

The only weak spot in this good german woman's conduct was the way she spoiled her boy, who was not honest and who was very hard to manage.

The father of this family was a decent, quiet, heavy, and uninterfering german man. He tried to cure the boy of his bad ways, and make him honest, but the mother could not make herself let the father manage, and so the boy was brought up very badly.

Mrs. Haydon's girls were now only just beginning as young ladies, and so to get her niece, Lena, married, was just then the most important thing that Mrs. Haydon had to do.

Mrs. Haydon had four years before gone to Germany to see her parents, and had taken the girls with her. This visit had been for Mrs. Haydon most successful, though her children had not liked it very well.

Mrs. Haydon was a good and generous woman, and she patronized her parents grandly, and all the cousins who came from all about to see her. Mrs. Haydon's people were of the middling class of farmers. They were not peasants, and they lived in a town of some pretension, but it all seemed very poor and smelly to Mrs. Haydon's american born daughters.

Mrs. Haydon liked it all. It was familiar, and then here she was so wealthy and important. She listened and decided, and advised all of her relations how to do things better. She arranged their present and their future for them, and showed them how in the past they had been wrong in all their methods.

Mrs. Haydon's only trouble was with her two daughters, whom she could not make behave well to her parents. The two girls were very nasty to all their numerous relations. Their mother could hardly make them kiss their grandparents, and every day the girls would get a scolding. But then Mrs. Haydon was so very busy that she did not have time to really manage her stubborn daughters.

These hard working, earth-rough german cousins were to these american born children, ugly and dirty and as far below them as were italian or negro workmen, and they could not see how their mother could ever bear to touch them, and then all the women dressed so funny, and were worked all rough and different.

The two girls stuck up their noses at them all, and always talked in English to each other about how they hated all these people and how they wished their mother would not do so. The girls could talk some German, but they never chose to use it.

It was her eldest brother's family that most interested Mrs. Haydon. Here there were eight children, and out of the eight, five of them were girls.

Mrs. Haydon thought it would be a fine thing to take one of these girls back with her to Bridgepoint and get her well started. Everybody liked that she should do so and they were all willing that it should be Lena.

Lena was the second girl in her large family. She was at this time just seventeen years old. Lena was not an important daughter in the family. She was always sort of dreamy and not there. She worked hard and went very regularly at it, but even good work never seemed to bring her near.

Lena's age just suited Mrs. Haydon's purpose. Lena could first go out to service, and learn how to do things, and then, when she was a little older, Mrs. Haydon could get her a good husband. And then Lena was so still and docile, she would never want to do things her own way. And then, too, Mrs. Haydon, with all her hardness had wisdom, and she could feel the rarer strain there was in Lena.

Lena was willing to go with Mrs. Haydon. Lena did not like her ger-man life very well. It was not the hard work but the roughness that disturbed her. The people were not gentle, and the men when they were glad were very boisterous, and would lay hold of her and roughly tease her. They were good people enough around her, but it was all harsh and dreary for her.

Lena did not really know that she did not like it. She did not know that she was always dreamy and not there. She did not think whether it would be different for her away off there in Bridgepoint. Mrs. Haydon took her and got her different kinds of dresses, and then took her with them to the steamer. Lena did not really know what it was that had happened to her.

Mrs. Haydon, and her daughters, and Lena traveled second class on the steamer. Mrs. Haydon's daughters hated that their mother should take Lena. They hated to have a cousin, who was to them, little better than a nigger, and then everybody on the steamer there would see her. Mrs. Haydon's daughters said things like this to their mother, but she never stopped to hear them, and the girls did not dare to make their meaning very clear. And so they could only go on hating Lena hard, together. They could not stop her from going back with them to Bridgepoint.

Lena was very sick on the voyage. She thought, surely before it was over that she would die. She was so sick she could not even wish that she had not started. She could not eat, she could not moan, she was just blank and scared, and sure that every minute she would die. She could not hold herself in, nor help herself in her trouble. She just staid where she had been put, pale, and scared, and weak, and sick, and sure that she was going to die.

Mathilda and Bertha Haydon had no trouble from having Lena for a cousin on the voyage, until the last day that they were on the ship, and by that time they had made their friends and could explain.

Mrs. Haydon went down every day to Lena, gave her things to make her better, held her head when it was needful, and generally was good and did her duty by her.

Poor Lena had no power to be strong in such trouble. She did not know how to yield to her sickness nor endure. She lost all her little sense of being in her suffering. She was so scared, and then at her best, Lena, who was patient, sweet and quiet, had not self-control, nor any active courage.

Poor Lena was so scared and weak, and every minute she was sure that she would die.

After Lena was on land again a little while, she forgot all her bad suffering. Mrs. Haydon got her the good place, with the pleasant unexacting mistress, and her children, and Lena began to learn some English and soon was very happy and content.

All her Sundays out Lena spent at Mrs. Haydon's house. Lena would have liked much better to spend her Sundays with the girls she always sat with, and who often asked her, and who teased her and made a gentle stir within her, but it never came to Lena's unexpectant and unsuffering german nature to do something different from what was expected of her, just because she would like it that way better. Mrs. Haydon had said that Lena was to come to her house every other Sunday, and so Lena always went there.

Mrs. Haydon was the only one of her family who took any interest in Lena. Mr. Haydon did not think much of her. She was his wife's cousin and he was good to her, but she was for him stupid, and a little simple, and very dull, and sure some day to need help and to be in trouble. All young poor relations, who were brought from Germany to Bridgepoint were sure, before long, to need help and to be in trouble.

The little Haydon boy was always very nasty to her. He was a hard child for any one to manage, and his mother spoiled him very badly.

Mrs. Haydon's daughters as they grew older did not learn to like Lena any better. Lena never knew that she did not like them either. She did not know that she was only happy with the other quicker girls, she always sat with in the park, and who laughed at her and always teased her.

Mathilda Haydon, the simple, fat, blonde, older daughter felt very badly that she had to say that this was her cousin Lena, this Lena who was little better for her than a nigger. Mathilda was an overgrown, slow, flabby, blonde, stupid, fat girl, just beginning as a woman; thick in her speech and dull and simple in her mind, and very jealous of all her family and of other girls, and proud that she could have good dresses and new hats and learn music, and hating very badly to have a cousin who was a common servant. And then Mathilda remembered very strongly that dirty nasty place that Lena came from and that Mathilda had so turned up her nose at, and where she had been made so angry because her mother scolded her and liked all those rough cow-smelly people.

Then, too, Mathilda would get very mad when her mother had Lena at their parties, and when she talked about how good Lena was, to certain german mothers in whose sons, perhaps, Mrs. Haydon might find Lena a good husband. All this would make the dull, blonde, fat Mathilda very angry. Sometimes she would get so angry that she would, in her thick, slow way, and with jealous anger blazing in her light blue eyes, tell her mother that she did not see how she could like that nasty Lena; and then her mother would scold Mathilda, and tell her that she knew her cousin Lena was poor and Mathilda must be good to poor people.

Mathilda Haydon did not like relations to be poor. She told all her girl friends what she thought of Lena, and so the girls would never talk to Lena at Mrs. Haydon's parties. But Lena in her unsuffering and unexpectant patience never really knew that she was slighted. When Mathilda was with her girls in the street or in the park and would see Lena, she always turned up her nose and barely nodded to her, and then she would tell her friends how funny her mother was to take care of people like that Lena, and how, back in Germany, all Lena's people lived just like pigs.

The younger daughter, the dark, large, but not fat, Bertha Haydon, who was very quick in her mind, and in her ways, and who was the favorite with her father, did not like Lena, either. She did not like her because for her Lena was a fool and so stupid, and she would let those Irish and Italian girls laugh at her and tease her, and everybody always made fun of Lena, and Lena never got mad, or even had sense enough to know that they were all making an awful fool of her.

Bertha Haydon hated people to be fools. Her father, too, thought

Lena was a fool, and so neither the father nor the daughter ever paid any attention to Lena, although she came to their house every other Sunday.

Lena did not know how all the Haydons felt. She came to her aunt's house all her Sunday afternoons that she had out, because Mrs. Haydon had told her she must do so. In the same way Lena always saved all of her wages. She never thought of any way to spend it. The german cook, the good woman who always scolded Lena, helped her to put it in the bank each month, as soon as she got it. Sometimes before it got into the bank to be taken care of, somebody would ask Lena for it. The little Haydon boy sometimes asked and would get it, and sometimes some of the girls, the ones Lena always sat with, needed some more money; but the german cook, who always scolded Lena, saw to it that this did not happen very often. When it did happen she would scold Lena very sharply, and for the next few months she would not let Lena touch her wages, but put it in the bank for her on the same day that Lena got it.

So Lena always saved her wages, for she never thought to spend them, and she always went to her aunt's house for her Sundays because she did not know that she could do anything different.

Mrs. Haydon felt more and more every year that she had done right to bring Lena back with her, for it was all coming out just as she had expected. Lena was good and never wanted her own way, she was learning English, and saving all her wages, and soon Mrs. Haydon would get her a good husband.

All these four years Mrs. Haydon was busy looking around among all the german people that she knew for the right man to be Lena's husband, and now at last she was quite decided.

The man Mrs. Haydon wanted for Lena was a young german-american tailor, who worked with his father. He was good and all the family were very saving, and Mrs. Haydon was sure that this would be just right for Lena, and then too, this young tailor always did whatever his father and his mother wanted.

This old german tailor and his wife, the father and the mother of Herman Kreder, who was to marry Lena Mainz, were very thrifty, careful people. Herman was the only child they had left with them, and he always did everything they wanted. Herman was now twenty-eight years old, but he had never stopped being scolded and directed by his father and his mother. And now they wanted to see him married.

Herman Kreder did not care much to get married. He was a gentle soul and a little fearful. He had a sullen temper, too. He was obedient to his father and his mother. He always did his work well. He often went out on Saturday nights and on Sundays, with other men. He liked it with them but he never became really joyous. He liked to be with men and he hated to have women with them. He was obedient to his mother, but he did not care much to get married.

Mrs. Haydon and the elder Kreders had often talked the marriage over. They all three liked it very well. Lena would do anything that Mrs. Haydon wanted, and Herman was always obedient in everything to his father and his mother. Both Lena and Herman were saving and good workers and neither of them ever wanted their own way.

The elder Kreders, everybody knew, had saved up all their money, and they were hard, good german people, and Mrs. Haydon was sure that with these people Lena would never be in any trouble. Mr. Haydon would not say anything about it. He knew old Kreder had a lot of money and owned some good houses, and he did not care what his wife did with that simple, stupid Lena, so long as she would be sure never to need help or to be in trouble.

Lena did not care much to get married. She liked her life very well where she was working. She did not think much about Herman Kreder. She thought he was a good man and she always found him very quiet. Neither of them ever spoke much to the other. Lena did not care much just then about getting married.

Mrs. Haydon spoke to Lena about it very often. Lena never answered anything at all. Mrs. Haydon thought, perhaps Lena did not like Herman Kreder. Mrs. Haydon could not believe that any girl not even Lena, really had no feeling about getting married.

Mrs. Haydon spoke to Lena very often about Herman. Mrs. Haydon sometimes got very angry with Lena. She was afraid that Lena, for once, was going to be stubborn, now when it was all fixed right for her to be married.

"Why you stand there so stupid, why don't you answer, Lena," said Mrs. Haydon one Sunday, at the end of a long talking that she was giving Lena about Herman Kreder, and about Lena's getting married to him.

"Yes ma'am," said Lena, and then Mrs. Haydon was furious with this stupid Lena. "Why don't you answer with some sense, Lena, when I ask you if you don't like Herman Kreder. You stand there so stupid and don't answer just like you ain't heard a word what I been saying to you. I never see anybody like you, Lena. If you going to burst out at all, why don't you burst out sudden instead of standing there so silly and don't answer. And here I am so good to you, and find you a good husband so you can have a place to live in all your own. Answer me, Lena, don't you like Herman Kreder? He is a fine young fellow, almost too good for you, Lena, when you stand there so stupid and don't make no answer. There ain't many poor girls that get the chance you got now to get married."

"Why, I do anything you say, Aunt Mathilda. Yes, I like him. He don't say much to me, but I guess he is a good man, and I do anything you say for me to do."

"Well then Lena, why you stand there so silly all the time and not answer when I asked you."

"I didn't hear you say you wanted I should say anything to you. I didn't know you wanted me to say nothing. I do whatever you tell me it's right for me to do. I marry Herman Kreder, if you want me."

And so for Lena Mainz the match was made.

Old Mrs. Kreder did not discuss the matter with her Herman. She never thought that she needed to talk such things over with him. She just told him about getting married to Lena Mainz who was a good worker and very saving and never wanted her own way, and Herman made his usual little grunt in answer to her.

Mrs. Kreder and Mrs. Haydon fixed the day and made all the arrangements for the wedding and invited everybody who ought to be there to see them married.

In three months Lena Mainz and Herman Kreder were to be married.

Mrs. Haydon attended to Lena's getting all the things that she needed. Lena had to help a good deal with the sewing. Lena did not sew very well. Mrs. Haydon scolded because Lena did not do it better, but then she was very good to Lena, and she hired a girl to come and help her. Lena still stayed on with her pleasant mistress, but she spent all her evenings and her Sundays with her aunt and all the sewing.

Mrs. Haydon got Lena some nice dresses. Lena liked that very well. Lena liked having new hats even better, and Mrs. Haydon had some made for her by a real milliner who made them very pretty.

Lena was nervous these days, but she did not think much about getting married. She did not know really what it was, that, which was always coming nearer.

Lena liked the place where she was with the pleasant mistress and the good cook, who always scolded, and she liked the girls she always sat with. She did not ask if she would like being married any better. She always did whatever her aunt said and expected, but she was always nervous when she saw the Kreders with their Herman. She was excited and she liked her new hats, and everybody teased her and every day her marrying was coming nearer, and yet she did not really know what it was, this that was about to happen to her.

Herman Kreder knew more what it meant to be married and he did not like it very well. He did not like to see girls and he did not want to have to have one always near him. Herman always did everything that his father and his mother wanted and now they wanted that he should be married.

Herman had a sullen temper; he was gentle and he never said much. He liked to go out with other men, but he never wanted that there should be any women with them. The men all teased him about getting married. Herman did not mind the teasing but he did not like very well the getting married and having a girl always with him.

Three days before the wedding day, Herman went away to the country to be gone over Sunday. He and Lena were to be married Tuesday afternoon. When the day came Herman had not been seen or heard from.

The old Kreder couple had not worried much about it. Herman always did everything they wanted and he would surely come back in time to get married. But when Monday night came, and there was no Herman, they went to Mrs. Haydon to tell her what had happened.

Mrs. Haydon got very much excited. It was hard enough to work so as to get everything all ready, and then to have that silly Herman go off that way, so no one could tell what was going to happen. Here was Lena and everything all ready, and now they would have to make the wedding later so that they would know that Herman would be sure to be there.

Mrs. Haydon was very much excited, and then she could not say much to the old Kreder couple. She did not want to make them angry, for she wanted very badly now that Lena should be married to their Herman.

At last it was decided that the wedding should be put off a week longer. Old Mr. Kreder would go to New York to find Herman, for it was very likely that Herman had gone there to his married sister.

Mrs. Haydon sent word around, about waiting until a week from that Tuesday, to everybody that had been invited, and then Tuesday morning she sent for Lena to come down to see her.

Mrs. Haydon was very angry with poor Lena when she saw her. She scolded her hard because she was so foolish, and now Herman had gone off and nobody could tell where he had gone to, and all because Lena always was so dumb and silly. And Mrs. Haydon was just like a mother to her, and Lena always stood there so stupid and did not answer what anybody asked her, and Herman was so silly too, and now his father had to go and find him. Mrs. Haydon did not think that any old people should be good to their children. Their children always were so thankless, and never paid any attention, and older people were always doing things for their good. Did Lena think it gave Mrs. Haydon any pleasure, to work so hard to make Lena happy, and get her a good husband, and then Lena was so thankless and never did anything that anybody wanted. It was a lesson to poor Mrs. Haydon not to do things any more for anybody. Let everybody take care of themselves and never come to her with any troubles; she knew better now than to meddle to make

other people happy. It just made trouble for her and her husband did
not like it. He always said she was too good, and nobody ever thanked
her for it, and there Lena was always standing stupid and not answering
anything anybody wanted. Lena could always talk enough to those silly
girls she liked so much, and always sat with, but who never did anything
for her except to take away her money, and here was her aunt who tried
so hard and was so good to her and treated her just like one of her own
children and Lena stood there, and never made any answer and never
tried to please her aunt, or to do anything that her aunt wanted. "No, it
ain't no use your standin' there and cryin', now, Lena. Its too late now
to care about that Herman. You should have cared some before, and
then you wouldn't have to stand and cry now, and be a disappointment
to me, and then I get scolded by my husband for taking care of everybody, and nobody ever thankful. I am glad you got the sense to feel
sorry now, Lena, anyway, and I try to do what I can to help you out in
your trouble, only you don't deserve to have anybody take any trouble
for you. But perhaps you know better next time. You go home now and
take care you don't spoil your clothes and that new hat, you had no
business to be wearin' that this morning, but you ain't got no sense at
all, Lena. I never in my life see anybody be so stupid."

Mrs. Haydon stopped and poor Lena stood there in her hat, all
trimmed with pretty flowers, and the tears coming out of her eyes, and
Lena did not know what it was that she had done, only she was not
going to be married and it was a disgrace for a girl to be left by a man on
the very day she was to be married.

Lena went home all alone, and cried in the street car.

Poor Lena cried very hard all alone in the street car. She almost
spoiled her new hat with her hitting it against the window in her crying.
Then she remembered that she must not do so.

The conductor was a kind man and he was very sorry when he saw
her crying. "Don't feel so bad, you get another feller, you are such a
nice girl," he said to make her cheerful. "But Aunt Mathilda said now, I
never get married," poor Lena sobbed out for her answer. "Why you
really got trouble like that," said the conductor, "I just said that now to
josh you. I didn't ever think you really was left by a feller. He must be a
stupid feller. But don't you worry, he wasn't much good if he could go
away and leave you, lookin' to be such a nice girl. You just tell all your
trouble to me, and I help you." The car was empty and the conductor
sat down beside her to put his arm around her, and to be a comfort to
her. Lena suddenly remembered where she was, and if she did things
like that her aunt would scold her. She moved away from the man into
the corner. He laughed, "Don't be scared," he said, "I wasn't going to
hurt you. But you just keep up your spirit. You are a real nice girl, and

you'll be sure to get a real good husband. Don't you let nobody fool you. You're all right and I don't want to scare you."

The conductor went back to his platform to help a passenger get on the car. All the time Lena stayed in the street car, he would come in every little while and reassure her, about her not to feel so bad about a man who hadn't no more sense than to go away and leave her. She'd be sure yet to get a good man, she needn't be so worried, he frequently assured her.

He chatted with the other passenger who had just come in, a very well dressed old man, and then with another who came in later, a good sort of a working man, and then another who came in, a nice lady, and he told them all about Lena's having trouble, and it was too bad there were men who treated a poor girl so badly. And everybody in the car was sorry for poor Lena and the workman tried to cheer her, and the old man looked sharply at her, and said she looked like a good girl, but she ought to be more careful and not be so careless, and things like that would not happen to her, and the nice lady went and sat beside her and Lena liked it, though she shrank away from being near her.

So Lena was feeling a little better when she got off the car, and the conductor helped her, and he called out to her, "You be sure you keep up a good heart now. He wasn't no good that feller and you were lucky for to lose him. You'll get a real man yet, one that will be better for you. Don't you be worried, you're a real nice girl as I ever see in such trouble," and the conductor shook his head and went back into his car to talk it over with the other passengers he had there.

The german cook, who always scolded Lena, was very angry when she heard the story. She never did think Mrs. Haydon would do so much for Lena, though she was always talking so grand about what she could do for everybody. The good german cook always had been a little distrustful to her. People who always thought they were so much never did really do things right for anybody. Not that Mrs. Haydon wasn't a good woman. Mrs. Haydon was a real, good, german woman, and she did really mean to do well by her niece Lena. The cook knew that very well, and she had always said so, and she always had liked and respected Mrs. Haydon, who always acted very proper to her, and Lena was so backward, when there was a man to talk to, Mrs. Haydon did have hard work when she tried to marry Lena. Mrs. Haydon was a good woman, only she did talk sometimes too grand. Perhaps this trouble would make her see it wasn't always so easy to do, to make everybody do everything just like she wanted. The cook was very sorry now for Mrs. Haydon. All this must be such a disappointment, and such a worry to her, and she really had always been very good to Lena. But Lena had better go and put on her other clothes and stop with all that crying. That wouldn't do nothing now to help her, and if Lena would be a good girl, and just be real patient, her aunt would make it all come out right yet for her. "I just tell Mrs. Aldrich, Lena, you stay here yet a little longer. You know she is always so good to you, Lena, and I know she let you, and I tell her all about that stupid Herman Kreder. I got no patience, Lena, with anybody who can be so stupid. You just stop now with your crying, Lena, and take off them good clothes and put them away so you don't spoil them when you need them, and you can help me with the dishes and everything will come off better for you. You see if I ain't right by what I tell you. You just stop crying now Lena quick, or else I scold you."

Lena still choked a little and was very miserable inside her but she did everything just as the cook told her.

The girls Lena always sat with were very sorry to see her look so sad with her trouble. Mary the Irish girl sometimes got very angry with her. Mary was always very hot when she talked of Lena's aunt Mathilda, who thought she was so grand, and had such stupid, stuck up daughters. Mary wouldn't be a fat fool like that ugly tempered Mathilda Haydon, not for anything anybody could ever give her. How Lena could keep on going there so much when they all always acted as if she was just dirt to them, Mary never could see. But Lena never had any sense of how she should make people stand round for her, and that was always all the trouble with her. And poor Lena, she was so stupid to be sorry for losing that gawky fool who didn't ever know what he wanted and just said "ja"[1] to his mamma and his papa, like a baby, and was scared to look at a girl straight, and then sneaked away the last day like as if somebody was going to do something to him. Disgrace, Lena talking about disgrace! It was a disgrace for a girl to be seen with the likes of him, let alone to be married to him. But that poor Lena, she never did know how to show herself off for what she was really. Disgrace to have him go away and leave her. Mary would just like to get a chance to show him. If Lena wasn't worth fifteen like Herman Kreder, Mary would just eat her own head all up. It was a good riddance Lena had of that Herman Kreder and his stingy, dirty parents, and if Lena didn't stop crying about it,— Mary would just naturally despise her.

Poor Lena, she knew very well how Mary meant it all, this she was always saying to her. But Lena was very miserable inside her. She felt the disgrace it was for a decent german girl that a man should go away and leave her. Lena knew very well that her aunt was right when she said the way Herman had acted to her was a disgrace to everyone that knew her. Mary and Nellie and the other girls she always sat with were always very good to Lena but that did not make her trouble any better.

---

1. German: "yes."

It was a disgrace the way Lena had been left, to any decent family, and that could never be made any different to her.

And so the slow days wore on, and Lena never saw her Aunt Mathilda. At last on Sunday she got word by a boy to go and see her aunt Mathilda. Lena's heart beat quick for she was very nervous now with all this that had happened to her. She went just as quickly as she could to see her Aunt Mathilda.

Mrs. Haydon quick, as soon as she saw Lena, began to scold her for keeping her aunt waiting so long for her, and for not coming in all the week to see her, to see if her aunt should need her, and so her aunt had to send a boy to tell her. But it was easy, even for Lena, to see that her aunt was not really angry with her. It wasn't Lena's fault, went on Mrs. Haydon, that everything was going to happen all right for her. Mrs. Haydon was very tired taking all this trouble for her, and when Lena couldn't even take trouble to come and see her aunt, to see if she needed anything to tell her. But Mrs. Haydon really never minded things like that when she could do things for anybody. She was tired now, all the trouble she had been taking to make things right for Lena, but perhaps now Lena heard it she would learn a little to be thankful to her. "You get all ready to be married Tuesday. Lena, you hear me," said Mrs. Haydon to her. "You come here Tuesday morning and I have everything all ready for you. You wear your new dress I got you, and your hat with all them flowers on it, and you be very careful coming you don't get your things all dirty, you so careless all the time, Lena, and not thinking, and you act sometimes you never got no head at all on you. You go home now, and you tell your Mrs. Aldrich that you leave her Tuesday. Don't you go forgetting now, Lena, anything I ever told you what you should do to be careful. You be a good girl, now Lena. You get married Tuesday to Herman Kreder." And that was all Lena ever knew of what had happened all this week to Herman Kreder. Lena forgot there was anything to know about it. She was really to be married Tuesday, and her Aunt Mathilda said she was a good girl, and now there was no disgrace left upon her.

Lena now fell back into the way she always had of being always dreamy and not there, the way she always had been, except for the few days she was so excited, because she had been left by a man the very day she was to have been married. Lena was a little nervous all these last days, but she did not think much about what it meant for her to be married.

Herman Kreder was not so content about it. He was quiet and was sullen and he knew he could not help it. He knew now he just had to let himself get married. It was not that Herman did not like Lena Mainz. She was as good as any other girl could be for him. She was a little better perhaps than other girls he saw, she was so very quiet, but Herman did not like to always have to have a girl around him. Herman had always done everything that his mother and his father wanted. His father had found him in New York, where Herman had gone to be with his married sister.

Herman's father when he had found him coaxed Herman a long time and went on whole days with his complaining to him, always troubled but gentle and quite patient with him, and always he was worrying to Herman about what was the right way his boy Herman should always do, always whatever it was his mother ever wanted from him, and always Herman never made him any answer.

Old Mr. Kreder kept on saying to him, he did not see how Herman could think now, it could be any different. When you make a bargain you just got to stick right to it, that was the only way old Mr. Kreder could ever see it, and saying you would get married to a girl and she got everything all ready, that was a bargain just like one you make in business and Herman he had made it, and now Herman he would just have to do it, old Mr. Kreder didn't see there was any other way a good boy like his Herman had, to do it. And then too that Lena Mainz was such a nice girl and Herman hadn't ought to really give his father so much trouble and make him pay out all that money, to come all the way to New York just to find him, and they both lose all that time from their working, when all Herman had to do was just to stand up, for an hour, and then he would be all right married, and it would be all over for him, and then everything at home would never be any different to him.

And his father went on; there was his poor mother saying always how her Herman always did everything before she ever wanted, and now just because he got notions in him, and wanted to show people how he could be stubborn, he was making all this trouble for her, and making them pay all that money just to run around and find him. "You got no idea Herman, how bad mama is feeling about the way you been acting Herman," said old Mr. Kreder to him. "She says she never can understand how you can be so thankless Herman. It hurts her very much you been so stubborn, and she find you such a nice girl for you, like Lena Mainz who is always just so quiet and always saves up all her wages, and she never wanting her own way at all like some girls are always all the time to have it, and your mama trying so hard, just so you could be comfortable Herman to be married, and then you act so stubborn Herman. You like all young people Herman, you think only about yourself, and what you are just wanting, and your mama she is thinking only what is good for you to have, for you in the future. Do you think your mama wants to have a girl around to be a bother, for herself, Herman. Its just for you Herman she is always thinking, and she talks always about how happy she will be, when she sees her Herman married to a nice girl, and then when she fixed it all up so good for you, so it never would be any bother to you, just the way she wanted you should like it, and you say yes all right, I do it, and then you go away like this act stubborn, and make all this trouble everybody to take for you, and we spend money, and I got to travel all round to find you. You come home now with me Herman and get married, and I tell your mama she better not say anything to you about how much it cost me to come all the way to look for you—Hey Herman," said his father coaxing, "Hey, you come home now and get married. All you got to do Herman is just to stand up for an hour Herman, and then you don't never to have any more bother to it —Hey Herman!—you come home with me to-morrow and get married. Hey Herman."

Herman's married sister liked her brother Herman, and she had always tried to help him, when there was anything she knew he wanted. She liked it that he was so good and always did everything that their father and their mother wanted, but still she wished it could be that he could have more his own way, if there was anything he ever wanted.

But now she thought Herman with his girl was very funny. She wanted that Herman should be married. She thought it would do him lots of good to get married. She laughed at Herman when she heard the story. Until his father came to find him, she did not know why it was Herman had come just then to New York to see her. When she heard the story she laughed a good deal at her brother Herman and teased him a good deal about his running away, because he didn't want to have a girl to be all the time around him.

Herman's married sister liked her brother Herman, and she did not want him not to like to be with women. He was good, her brother Herman, and it would surely do him good to get married. It would make him stand up for himself stronger. Herman's sister always laughed at him and always she would try to reassure him. "Such a nice man as my brother Herman acting like as if he was afraid of women. Why the girls all like a man like you Herman, if you didn't always run away when you saw them. It do you good really Herman to get married, and then you got somebody you can boss around when you want to. It do you good Herman to get married, you see if you don't like it, when you really done it. You go along home now with papa, Herman and get married to that Lena. You don't know how nice you like it Herman when you try once how you can do it. You just don't be afraid of nothing, Herman. You good enough for any girl to marry, Herman. Any girl be glad to have a man like you to be always with them Herman. You just go along home with papa and try it what I say, Herman. Oh you so funny Herman, when you sit there, and then run away and leave your girl behind you. I know she is crying like anything Herman for to lose you. Don't be bad to her Herman. You go along home with papa now and get married Herman. I'd be awful ashamed Herman, to really have a brother didn't have spirit enough to get married, when a girl is just dying for to have him. You always like me to be with you Herman. I don't see why you say you don't want a girl to be all the time around you. You always been good to me Herman, and I know you always be good to that Lena, and you soon feel just like as if she had always been there with you. Don't act like as if you wasn't a nice strong man, Herman. Really I laugh at you Herman, but you know I like awful well to see you real happy. You go home and get married to that Lena, Herman. She is a real pretty girl and real nice and good and quiet and she make my brother Herman very happy. You just stop your fussing now with Herman, papa. He go with you to-morrow papa, and you see he like it so much to be married, he make everybody laugh just to see him be so happy. Really truly, that's the way it will be with you Herman. You just listen to me what I tell you Herman." And so his sister laughed at him and reassured him, and his father kept on telling what the mother always said about her Herman, and he coaxed him and Herman never said anything in answer, and his sister packed his things up and was very cheerful with him, and she kissed him, and then she laughed and then she kissed him, and his father went and brought the tickets for the train, and at last late on Sunday he brought Herman back to Bridgepoint with him.

It was always very hard to keep Mrs. Kreder from saying what she thought, to her Herman, but her daughter had written her a letter, so as to warn her not to say anything about what he had been doing, to him, and her husband came in with Herman and said, "Here we are come home mama, Herman and me, and we are very tired it was so crowded coming," and then he whispered to her. "You be good to Herman, mama, he didn't mean to make us so much trouble," and so old Mrs. Kreder, held in what she felt was so strong in her to say to her Herman. She just said very stiffly to him, "I'm glad to see you come home to-day, Herman." Then she went to arrange it all with Mrs. Haydon.

Herman was now again just like he always had been, sullen and very good, and very quiet, and always ready to do whatever his mother and his father wanted. Tuesday morning came, Herman got his new clothes on and went with his father and his mother to stand up for an hour and get married. Lena was there in her new dress, and her hat with all the pretty flowers, and she was very nervous for now she knew she was really very soon to be married. Mrs. Haydon had everything all ready. Everybody was there just as they should be and very soon Herman Kreder and Lena Mainz were married.

When everything was really over, they went back to the Kreder house together. They were all now to live together, Lena and Herman and the old father and the old mother, in the house where Mr. Kreder had worked so many years as a tailor, with his son Herman always there to help him.

Irish Mary had often said to Lena she never did see how Lena could ever want to have anything to do with Herman Kreder and his dirty stingy parents. The old Kreders were to an Irish nature, a stingy, dirty couple. They had not the free-hearted, thoughtless, fighting, mud be-spattered, ragged, peat-smoked cabin dirt that irish Mary knew and could forgive and love. Theirs was the german dirt of saving, of being dowdy and loose and foul in your clothes so as to save them and yourself in washing, having your hair greasy to save it in the soap and drying, having your clothes dirty, not in freedom, but because so it was cheaper, keeping the house close and smelly because so it cost less to get it heated, living so poorly not only so as to save money but so they should never even know themselves that they had it, working all the time not only because from their nature they just had to and because it made them money but also that they never could be put in any way to make them spend their money.

This was the place Lena now had for her home and to her it was very different than it could be for an irish Mary. She too was german and was thrifty, though she was always so dreamy and not there. Lena was always careful with things and she always saved her money, for that was the only way she knew how to do it. She never had taken care of her own money and she never had thought how to use it.

Lena Mainz had been, before she was Mrs. Herman Kreder, always clean and decent in her clothes and in her person, but it was not be-cause she ever thought about it or really needed so to have it, it was the way her people did in the german country where she came from, and her Aunt Mathilda and the good german cook who always scolded, had kept her on and made her, with their scoldings, always more careful to keep clean and to wash real often. But there was no deep need in all this for Lena and so, though Lena did not like the old Kreders, though she really did not know that, she did not think about their being stingy dirty people.

Herman Kreder was cleaner than the old people, just because it was his nature to keep cleaner, but he was used to his mother and his father, and he never thought that they should keep things cleaner. And Her-man too always saved all his money, except for that little beer he drank when he went out with other men of an evening the way he always liked to do it, and he never thought of any other way to spend it. His father had always kept all the money for them and he always was doing business with it. And then too Herman really had no money, for he always had worked for his father, and his father had never thought to pay him.

And so they began all four to live in the Kreder house together, and Lena began soon with it to look careless and a little dirty, and to be more lifeless with it, and nobody ever noticed much what Lena wanted, and she never really knew herself what she needed.

The only real trouble that came to Lena with their living all four there together, was the way old Mrs. Kreder scolded. Lena had always been used to being scolded, but this scolding of old Mrs. Kreder was very different from the way she ever before had had to endure it.

Herman, now he was married to her, really liked Lena very well. He did not care very much about her but she never was a bother to him being there around him, only when his mother worried and was nasty to them because Lena was so careless, and did not know how to save things right for them with their eating, and all the other ways with money, that the old woman had to save it.

Herman Kreder had always done everything his mother and his father wanted but he did not really love his parents very deeply. With Herman it was always only that he hated to have any struggle. It was all always all right with him when he could just go along and do the same thing over every day with his working, and not to hear things, and not to have people make him listen to their anger. And now his marriage, and he just knew it would, was making trouble for him. It made him hear more what his mother was always saying, with her scolding. He had to really hear it now because Lena was there, and she was so scared and dull always when she heard it. Herman knew very well with his mother, it was all right if one ate very little and worked hard all day and did not learn her when she scolded, the way Herman always had done before they were so foolish about his getting married and having a girl there to be all the time around him, and now he had to help her so the girl could learn too, not to hear it when his mother scolded, and not to look so scared, and not to eat much, and always to be sure to save it.

Herman really did not know very well what he could do to help Lena to understand it. He could never answer his mother back to help Lena, that never would make things any better for her, and he never could feel in himself any way to comfort Lena, to make her strong not to hear his mother, in all the awful ways she always scolded. It just worried Herman to have it like that all the time around him. Herman did not know much about how a man could make a struggle with a mother, to do much to keep her quiet, and indeed Herman never knew much how to make a struggle against anyone who really wanted to have anything very badly. Herman all his life never wanted anything so badly, that he would really make a struggle against any one to get it. Herman all his life only wanted to live regular and quiet, and not talk much and to do the same way every day like every other with his working. And now his mother had made him get married to this Lena and now with his mother making all that scolding, he had all this trouble and this worry always on him.

Mrs. Haydon did not see Lena now very often. She had not lost her interest in her niece Lena, but Lena could not come much to her house to see her, it would not be right, now Lena was a married woman. And then too Mrs. Haydon had her hands full just then with her two daughters, for she was getting them ready to find them good husbands, and then too her own husband now worried her very often about her always spoiling that boy of hers, so he would be sure to turn out no good and be a disgrace to a german family, and all because his mother always spoiled him. All these things were very worrying now to Mrs. Haydon, but still she wanted to be good to Lena, though she could not see her very often. She only saw her when Mrs. Haydon went to call on Mrs. Kreder or when Mrs. Kreder came to see Mrs. Haydon, and that never could be very often. Then too these days Mrs. Haydon could not scold Lena, Mrs. Kreder was always there with her, and it would not be right to scold Lena when Mrs. Kreder was there, who had now the real right to do it. And so her aunt always said nice things now to Lena, and though Mrs. Haydon sometimes was a little worried when she saw Lena looking sad and not careful, she did not have time just then to really worry much about it.

Lena now never any more saw the girls she always used to sit with. She had no way now to see them and it was not in Lena's nature to search out ways to see them, nor did she now ever think much of the days when she had been used to see them. They never any of them had come to the Kreder house to see her. Not even Irish Mary had ever thought to come to see her. Lena had been soon forgotten by them. They had soon passed away from Lena and now Lena never thought any more that she had ever known them.

The only one to her old friends who tried to know what Lena liked and what she needed, and who always made Lena come to see her, was the good german cook who had always scolded. She now scolded Lena hard for letting herself go so, and going out when she was looking so untidy. "I know you going to have a baby Lena, but that's no way for you to be looking. I am ashamed most to see you come and sit here in my kitchen, looking so sloppy and like you never used to Lena. I never see anybody like you Lena. Herman is very good to you, you always say so, and he don't treat you bad ever though you don't deserve to have anybody good to you, you so careless all the time, Lena, letting yourself go like you never had anybody tell you what was the right way you should know how to be looking. No, Lena, I don't see no reason you should let yourself go so and look so untidy Lena, so I am ashamed to see you sit there looking so ugly, Lena. No Lena that ain't no way ever I see a woman make things come out better, letting herself go so every way and crying all the time like as if you had real trouble. I never wanted to see you marry Herman Kreder, Lena, I knew what you got to stand with that old woman always, and that old man, he is so stingy too and he don't say things out but he ain't any better in his heart than his wife with her bad ways, I know that Lena, I know they don't hardly give you enough to eat, Lena, I am real sorry for you Lena, you know that Lena, but that ain't any way to be going round so untidy Lena, even if you have got all that trouble. You never see me do like that Lena, though sometimes I got a headache so I can't see to stand to be working hardly, and nothing comes right with all my cooking, but I always see Lena, I look decent. That's the only way a german girl can make things come out right Lena. You hear me what I am saying to you Lena. Now you eat something nice Lena, I got it all ready for you, and you wash up and be careful Lena and the baby will come all right to you, and then I make your Aunt Mathilda see that you live in a house soon all alone with Herman and your baby, and then everything go better for you. You hear me what I say to you Lena. Now don't let me ever see you come looking like this any more Lena, and you just stop with that always crying. You ain't got no reason to be sitting there now with all that crying, I never see anybody have trouble it did them any good to be the way you are doing, Lena. You hear me Lena. You go home now and you be good the way I tell you Lena, and I see what I can do. I make your Aunt Mathilda make old Mrs. Kreder let you be till you get your baby all right. Now don't you be scared and so silly Lena. I don't like to see you act so Lena when really you got a nice man and so many things really any girl should be grateful to be having. Now you go home Lena to-day and you do the way I say, to you, and I see what I can do to help you."

"Yes Mrs. Aldrich" said the good german woman to her mistress later, "Yes Mrs. Aldrich that's the way it is with them girls when they want so to get married. They don't know when they got it good Mrs. Aldrich. They never know what it is they're really wanting when they got it, Mrs. Aldrich. There's that poor Lena, she just been here crying and looking so careless so I scold her, but that was no good that marrying for that poor Lena, Mrs. Aldrich. She do look so pale and sad now Mrs. Aldrich, it just break my heart to see her. She was a good girl was Lena, Mrs. Aldrich, and I never had no trouble with her like I got with so many young girls nowadays, Mrs. Aldrich, and I never see any girl any better to work right than our Lena, and now she got to stand it all the time with that old woman Mrs. Kreder. My! Mrs. Aldrich, she is a bad old woman to her. I never see Mrs. Aldrich how old people can be so bad to young girls and not have no kind of patience with them. If Lena could only live with her Herman, he ain't so bad the way men are, Mrs. Aldrich, but he is just the way always his mother wants him, he ain't got no spirit in him, and so I don't really see no help for that poor Lena. I know her aunt, Mrs. Haydon, meant it all right for her Mrs. Aldrich, but poor Lena, it would be better for her if her Herman had stayed there in New York that time he went away to leave her. I don't like it the way Lena is looking now, Mrs. Aldrich. She looks like as if she don't have no life left in her hardly, Mrs. Aldrich, she just drags around and looks so dirty and after all the pains I always took to teach her and to keep her nice in her ways and looking. It don't do no good to them, for them girls to get married Mrs. Aldrich, they are much better when they only know it, to stay in a good place when they got it, and keep on regular with their working. I don't like it the way Lena looks now Mrs. Aldrich. I wish I knew some way to help that poor Lena, Mrs. Aldrich, but she is a bad old woman, that old Mrs. Kreder, Herman's mother. I speak to Mrs. Haydon real soon, Mrs. Aldrich, I see what we can do now to help that poor Lena."

These were really bad days for poor Lena. Herman always was real good to her and now he even sometimes tried to stop his mother from scolding Lena. "She ain't well now mama, you let her be now you hear me. You tell me what it is you want she should be doing, I tell her. I see she does it right just the way you want it mama. You let be, I say now mama, with that always scolding Lena. You let be, I say now, you wait till she is feeling better." Herman was getting really strong to struggle, for he could see that Lena with that baby working hard inside her, really could not stand it any longer with his mother and the awful ways she always scolded.

It was a new feeling Herman now had inside him that made him feel he was strong to make a struggle. It was new for Herman Kreder really to be wanting something, but Herman wanted strongly now to be a father, and he wanted badly that his baby should be a boy and healthy. Herman never had cared really very much about his father and his mother, though always, all his life, he had done everything just as they wanted, and he had never really cared much about his wife, Lena, though he always had been very good to her, and had always tried to keep his mother off her, with the awful way she always scolded, but to be really a father of a little baby, that feeling took hold of Herman very deeply. He was almost ready, so as to save his baby from all trouble, to really make a strong struggle with his mother and with his father, too, if he would not help him to control his mother.

Sometimes Herman even went to Mrs. Haydon to talk all this trouble over. They decided then together, it was better to wait there all four together for the baby, and Herman could make Mrs. Kreder stop a little with her scolding, and then when Lena was a little stronger, Herman should have his own house for her, next door to his father, so he could always be there to help him in his working, but so they could eat and sleep in a house where the old woman could not control them and they could not hear her awful scolding.

And so things went on, the same way, a little longer. Poor Lena was not feeling any joy to have a baby. She was scared the way she had been when she was so sick on the water. She was scared now every time when anything would hurt her. She was scared and still and lifeless, and sure that every minute she would die. Lena had no power to be strong in this kind of trouble, she could only sit still and be scared, and dull, and lifeless, and sure that every minute she would die.

Before very long, Lena had her baby. He was a good, healthy little boy, the baby. Herman cared very much to have the baby. When Lena was a little stronger he took a house next door to the old couple, so he and his own family could eat and sleep and do the way they wanted. This did not seem to make much change now for Lena. She was just the same as when she was waiting with her baby. She just dragged around and was careless with her clothes and all lifeless, and she acted always and lived on just as if she had no feeling. She always did every-thing regular with the work, the way she always had had to do it, but she never got back any spirit in her. Herman was always good and kind, and always helped her with her working. He did everything he knew to help her. He always did all the active new things in the house and for the baby. Lena did what she had to do the way she always had been taught it. She always just kept going now with her working, and she was always careless, and dirty, and a little dazed, and lifeless. Lena never got any better in herself of this way of being that she had had ever since she had been married.

Mrs. Haydon never saw any more of her niece, Lena. Mrs. Haydon had now so much trouble with her own house, and her daughters get-ting married, and her boy, who was growing up, and who always was getting so much worse to manage. She knew she had done right by Lena. Herman Kreder was a good man, she would be glad to get one so good, sometimes, for her own daughters, and now they had a home to live in together, separate from the old people, who had made their trou-ble for them. Mrs. Haydon felt she had done very well by her niece, Lena, and she never thought now she needed any more to go and see her. Lena would do very well now without her aunt to trouble herself any more about her.

The good german cook who had always scolded, still tried to do her duty like a mother to poor Lena. It was very hard now to do right by Lena. Lena never seemed to hear now what anyone was saying to her. Herman was always doing everything he could to help her. Herman always, when he was home, took good care of the baby. Herman loved to take care of his baby. Lena never thought to take him out or to do anything she didn't have to.

The good cook sometimes made Lena come to see her. Lena would come with her baby and sit there in the kitchen, and watch the good woman cooking, and listen to her sometimes a little, the way she used to, while the good german woman scolded her for going around looking so careless when now she had no trouble, and sitting there so dull, and always being just so thankless. Sometimes Lena would wake up a little and get back into her face her old, gentle, patient, and unsuffering sweetness, but mostly Lena did not seem to hear much when the good german woman scolded. Lena always liked it when Mrs. Aldrich her good mistress spoke to her kindly, and then Lena would seem to go back and feel herself to be like she was when she had been in service. But mostly Lena just lived along and was careless in her clothes, and dull, and lifeless.

By and by Lena had two more little babies. Lena was not so much scared now when she had the babies. She did not seem to notice very much when they hurt her, and she never seemed to feel very much now about anything that happened to her.

They were very nice babies, all these three that Lena had, and Herman took good care of them always. Herman never really cared much about his wife, Lena. The only things Herman ever really cared for were his babies. Herman always was very good to his children. He always had a gentle, tender way when he held them. He learned to be very handy with them. He spent all the time he was not working, with them. By the by he began to work all day in his own home so that he could have his children always in the same room with him.

Lena always was more and more lifeless and Herman now mostly never thought about her. He more and more took all the care of their three children. He saw to their eating right and their washing, and he dressed them every morning, and he taught them the right way to do things, and he put them to their sleeping, and he was now always every minute with them. Then there was to come to them, a fourth baby. Lena went to the hospital near by to have the baby. Lena seemed to be going to have much trouble with it. When the baby was come out at last, it was like its mother lifeless. While it was coming, Lena had grown very pale and sicker. When it was all over Lena had died, too, and nobody knew just how it had happened to her.

The good german cook who had always scolded Lena, and had always to the last day tried to help her, was the only one who ever missed her. She remembered how nice Lena had looked all the time she was in service with her, and how her voice had been so gentle and sweet-sounding, and how she always was a good girl, and how she never had to have any trouble with her, the way she always had with all the other girls who had been taken into the house to help her. The good cook sometimes spoke so of Lena when she had time to have a talk with

Mrs. Aldrich, and this was all the remembering there now ever was of Lena.

Herman Kreder now always lived very happy, very gentle, very quiet, very well content alone with his three children. He never had a woman any more to be all the time around him. He always did all his own work in his house, when he was through every day with the work he was always doing for his father. Herman always was alone, and he always worked alone, until his little ones were big enough to help him. Herman Kreder was very well content now and he always lived very regular and peaceful, and with every day just like the next one, always alone now with his three good, gentle children.

Finis[2]

1909

Picasso[3]

One whom some were certainly following was one who was completely charming. One whom some were certainly following was one who was charming. One whom some were following was one who was completely charming. One whom some were following was one who was certainly completely charming.

Some were certainly following and were certain that the one they were then following was one working and was one bringing out of himself then something. Some were certainly following and were certain that the one they were then following was one bringing out of himself then something that was coming to be a heavy thing, a solid thing and a complete thing.

One whom some were certainly following was one working and certainly was one bringing something out of himself then and was one who had been all his living had been one having something coming out of him.

Something had been coming out of him, certainly it had been coming out of him, certainly it was something, certainly it had been coming out of him and it had meaning, a charming meaning, a solid meaning, a struggling meaning, a clear meaning.

One whom some were certainly following and some were certainly following him, one whom some were certainly following was one certainly working.

One whom some were certainly following was one having something

2. The end.   Pablo Picasso (1881–1973) when she lived in
3. Stein became a friend of the Spanish artist   Paris.

coming out of him something having meaning and this one was certainly working then.

This one was working and something was coming then, something was coming out of this one then. This one was one and always there was something coming out of this one and always there had been something coming out of this one. This one had never been one not having something coming out of this one. This one was one having something coming out of this one. This one had been one whom some were following. This one was one whom some were following. This one was being one whom some were following. This one was one who was working.

This one was one who was working. This one was one being one having something being coming out of him. This one was one going on having something come out of him. This one was one going on working. This one was one whom some were following. This one was one who was working.

This one always had something being coming out of this one. This one was working. This one always had been working. This one was always having something that was coming out of this one that was a solid thing, a charming thing, a lovely thing, a perplexing thing, a disconcerting thing, a simple thing, a clear thing, a complicated thing, an interesting thing, a disturbing thing, a repellant thing, a very pretty thing. This one was one certainly being one having something coming out of him. This one was one whom some were following. This one was one who was working.

This one was one who was working and certainly this one was needing to be working so as to be one being working. This one was one having something coming out of him. This one would be one all his living having something coming out of him. This one was working and then this one was working and this one was needing to be working, not to be one having something coming out of him something having meaning, but was needing to be working so as to be one working.

This one was certainly working and working was something this one was certain this one would be doing and this one was doing that thing, this one was working. This one was not one completely working. This one was not ever completely working. This one certainly was not completely working.

This one was one having always something being coming out of him, something having completely a real meaning. This one was one whom some were following. This one was one who was working. This one was one who was working and he was one needing this thing needing to be working so as to be one having some way of being one having some way of working. This one was one who was working. This one was one having something come out of him something having meaning. This one was one always having something come out of him and this thing the thing coming out of him always had real meaning. This one was one who was working. This one was one who was almost always working. This one was not one completely working. This one was one not ever completely working. This one was not one working to have anything come out of him. This one did have something having meaning that did come out of him. He always did have something come out of him. He was working, he was not ever completely working. He did have some following. They were always following him. Some were certainly following him. He was one who was working. He was one having something coming out of him something having meaning. He was not ever completely working.

1912, 1934

Ada[4]

Barnes Colhard did not say he would not do it but he did not do it. He did it and then he did not do it, he did not ever think about it. He just thought some time he might do something.

His father Mr. Abram Colhard spoke about it to every one and very many of them spoke to Barnes Colhard about it and he always listened to them.

Then Barnes fell in love with a very nice girl and she would not marry him. He cried then, his father Mr. Abram Colhard comforted him and they took a trip and Barnes promised he would do what his father wanted him to be doing. He did not do the thing, he thought he would do another thing, he did not do the other thing, his father Mr. Colhard did not want him to do the other thing. He really did not do anything then. When he was a good deal older he married a very rich girl. He had thought perhaps he would not propose to her but his sister wrote to him that it would be a good thing. He married the rich girl and she thought he was the most wonderful man and one who knew everything. Barnes never spent more than the income of the fortune he and his wife had then, that is to say they did not spend more than the income and this was a surprise to very many who knew about him and about his marrying the girl who had such a large fortune. He had a happy life while he was living and after he was dead his wife and children remembered him.

He had a sister who also was successful enough in being one being living. His sister was one who came to be happier than most people come to be in living. She came to be a completely happy one. She was

ADA

twice as old as her brother. She had been a very good daughter to her mother. She and her mother had always told very pretty stories to each other. Many old men loved to hear her tell these stories to her mother. Every one who ever knew her mother liked her mother. Many were sorry later that not every one liked the daughter. Many did like the daughter but not every one as every one had liked the mother. The daughter was charming inside in her, it did not show outside in her to every one, it certainly did to some. She did sometimes think her mother would be pleased with a story that did not please her mother, when her mother later was sicker the daughter knew that there were some stories she could tell her that would not please her mother. Her mother died and really mostly altogether the mother and the daughter had told each other stories very happily together.

The daughter then kept house for her father and took care of her brother. There were many relations who lived with them. The daughter did not like them to live with them and she did not like them to die with them. The daughter, Ada they had called her after her grandmother who had delightful ways of smelling flowers and eating dates and sugar, did not like it at all then as she did not like so much dying and she did not like any of the living she was doing then. Every now and then some old gentlemen told delightful stories to her. Mostly then there were not nice stories told by any one then in her living. She told her father Mr. Abram Colhard that she did not like it at all being one being living then. He never said anything. She was afraid then, she was one needing charming stories and happy telling of them and not having that thing she was always trembling. Then every one who could live with them were dead and there were then the father and the son a young man then and the daughter coming to be that one then. Her grandfather had left some money to them each one of them. Ada said she was going to use it to go away from them. The father said nothing then, then he said something and she said nothing then, then they both said nothing and then it was that she went away from them. The father was quite tender then, she was his daughter then. He wrote her tender letters then, she wrote him tender letters then, she never went back to live with him. He wanted her to come and she wrote him tender letters then. He liked the tender letters she wrote to him. He wanted her to live with him. She answered him by writing tender letters to him and telling very nice stories indeed in them. He wrote nothing and then he wrote again and there was some waiting and then he wrote tender letters again and again.

She came to be happier than anybody else who was living then. It is easy to believe this thing. She was telling some one, who was loving every story that was charming. Some one who was living was almost always listening. Some one who was loving was almost always listening. That one who was loving was almost always listening. That one who was loving was telling about being one then listening. That one being loving was then telling stories having a beginning and a middle and an ending. That one was then one always completely listening. Ada was then one and all her living then one completely telling stories that were charming, completely listening to stories having a beginning and a middle and an ending. Trembling was all living, living was all loving, some one was then the other one. Certainly this one was loving this Ada then. And certainly Ada all her living then was happier in living than any one else who ever could, who was, who is, who ever will be living.

1909–1910   1922

ALICE DUNBAR-NELSON
1875–1935

Short-story writer, poet, teacher, and black political activist, Alice Dunbar-Nelson was born Alice Ruth Moore in New Orleans, Louisiana, the second daughter of a seaman father and a seamstress mother. After attending a two-year teachers' training program, she had her first book, *Violets and Other Tales*—a collection of twelve poems and seventeen sketches—privately printed in 1895. When one of the poems in this volume was first published in the Boston *Monthly Review*, it caught the fancy of the young black poet Paul Laurence Dunbar, who began to correspond with her. A few years later, the pair met and married, and Nelson began teaching in the New York City school system while also serving as recording secretary of the National Association of Colored Women. In 1899, her second book, *The Goodness of St. Rocque and Other Stories*, appeared, and in 1902, after she and Dunbar separated (later to divorce), she began teaching at the Howard High School in Wilmington, Delaware, where she was to be a popular instructor and the head of the English department for eighteen years.

In 1916, Alice Moore Dunbar remarried; her second husband, Robert John Nelson, was the publisher of the *Wilmington Advocate*, a weekly newspaper dedicated to the cause of black rights. Continually energetic, she edited several anthologies in these years—*Masterpieces of Negro Eloquence* (1914) and *The Dunbar Speaker and Entertainer* (1920)—and, besides working on many councils and committees, wrote a regular column for the *Washington Eagle*. In 1920, she risked—and lost—her teaching position because she insisted (despite her school district's rules forbidding employees to engage in political activity) on attending a meeting at which the presidential candidate Warren Harding's racial policies were to be formulated. From 1928 to 1931, she served as executive secretary of the American Interracial Peace Committee, a group sponsored by the American Friends Service Committee which worked to encourage black support for world peace. Not coincidentally, a poem like *I Sit and Sew*, one of the comparatively few verses she wrote, expresses Nelson's distinctively female frustration at the "wasted fields" of a world at war, a world she consistently tried to improve.

I Sit and Sew

I sit and sew—a useless task it seems,
My hands grown tired, my head weighed down with dreams—
The panoply of war, the martial tread of men,
Grim-faced, stern-eyed, gazing beyond the ken
Of lesser souls, whose eyes have not seen Death   5
Nor learned to hold their lives but as a breath—
But—I must sit and sew.

I sit and sew—my heart aches with desire—
That pageant terrible, that fiercely pouring fire
On wasted fields, and writhing grotesque things   10
Once men. My soul in pity flings
Appealing cries, yearning only to go
There in that holocaust of hell, those fields of woe—
But—I must sit and sew.

The little useless seam, the idle patch;   15
Why dream I here beneath my homely thatch,
When there they lie in sodden mud and rain,
Pitifully calling me, the quick[1] ones and the slain?
You need me, Christ! It is no roseate dream
That beckons me—this pretty futile seam,   20
It stifles me—God, must I sit and sew?

1920

1. Living.

ANNA HEMPSTEAD BRANCH
1875–1937

The daughter of a comfortable professional family—her father was a lawyer, her mother a poet and writer of children's books—Anna Hempstead Branch was born in New London, Connecticut, and, after graduating from Smith College in 1897, she achieved a considerable reputation in the early years of the century with two collections of verse, *The Shoes That Danced* (1905) and *Rose of the Wind* (1910), both of which were significantly influenced by the art of the English Pre-Raphaelites, especially by the poetry of Christina Rossetti. Later her reputation was enhanced by *Sonnets from a Lock Box* (1929), a volume that is generally considered her finest book. Throughout her career, she was both devout and philosophical, pursuing studies of mysticism and numerology as well as more orthodox Christian theology, so that at least one critic felt some of her work was reminiscent not only of Rossetti's devotional poetry but also of the meditative verse produced by the seventeenth-century Anglican lyricist George Herbert.

Putting her religious principles into practice, Branch devoted a good deal of time and energy to social service at Christadora House, a settlement house on New York's Lower East Side. In the belief that poetry was a sacred and redemptive activity which would foster human fellowship, she organized a series of readings at the House, as well as a successful youth club; then, along with Edwin Arlington Robinson, William Rose Benét, and other notable writers, she become a founding member of the Poets' Guild, an organization whose classes, readings, and dramatic performances lent what one scholar describes as a special "intellectual aura" to the House. Yet although a number of Branch's poems brood on the "stolid, homely, visible things" which manifest divinity, pieces like the *Sonnets from a Lock Box*, excerpted here, reveal a deeply rebellious and unorthodox strain in her thinking.

From Sonnets from a Lock Box

XIV

What witchlike spell weaves here its deep design,
And sells its pattern to the ignorant buyer.
Oh lacelike cruelty with stitches fine—
Which stings the flesh with its sharp mesh of fire.
God of the Thief and Patron of the Liar,   5
I think that it is best not to inquire
Upon whose wheel was spun this mortal thread;
What dyed this curious robe so rich a red;
With shivering hues it is embroidered.
With changing colors like unsteady eyes.   10
I think the filigree is Medea's wreath.[1]
Oh, treacherous splendor! In this lustrous prize
Of gold and silver weaving, madness lies.
Who purchases this garment—Sire—buys death.

XXV

Into the void behold my shuddering flight,
Plunging straight forward through unhuman space,
My wild hair backward blown and my white face
Set like a wedge of ice. My chattering teeth
Cut like sharp knives my swiftly freezing breath.   5
Perched upon straightness I seek a wilder zone.
My Flying Self—on this black steed alone—
Drives out to God or else to utter death.
Beware straight lines which do subdue man's pride!
'Tis on a broomstick that great witches ride.   10
Wild, dangerous and holy are the runes

---

1. Medea was a sorceress who helped Jason, a Greek hero, win the Golden Fleece. She became his wife and bore him two sons, but when they returned to Greece, Jason took a new wife, Creusa. In revenge, Medea sent Creusa a splendid "wreath" or tiara and wedding robes; when Creusa put them on, they clung to her flesh and killed her.

Which shift the whirling atoms with their tunes.
Oh like a witch accursed shall she be burned
Who having flown on straightness has returned.

XXXI

I say that words are men and when we spell
In alphabets we deal with living things;
With feet and thighs and breasts, fierce heads, strong wings;
Material Powers, great Bridals, Heaven and Hell.
There is a menace in the tales we tell.   5
From out the throne from which all language springs
Voices proceed and fires and thunderings.
Oh when we speak, Great God, let us speak well.
Beware of shapes, beware of letterings,
For in them lies such magic as alters dream,   10
Shakes cities down and moves the inward scheme.
Beware the magic of the coin that sings.
These coins are graved with supernatural powers
And magic wills that are more strong than ours.

1929

VIRGINIA WOOLF
1882–1941

In a memoir entitled A *Sketch of the Past* (1939), the mature Virginia Woolf asked "Who was I . . . ? Adeline Virginia Stephen, the second daughter of Leslie and Julia Prinsep Stephen, born on 25th January 1882, descended from a great many people, some famous, others obscure; born into a large connection, born not of rich parents, but of well-to-do parents, born into a very communicative, literate, letter writing, visiting, articulate, late-nineteenth-century world." At the height of her fame as a novelist, essayist, editor, feminist, and influential force in English life and letters, Woolf had moved far from the Victorian origins she outlined in her reminiscence, yet—as she herself understood with greater clarity than many of her contemporaries—what her first biographer, Winifred Holtby, had called "the advantages of being Virginia Stephen" had consistently shaped both her consciousness and her career.

Woolf's father, Leslie Stephen, was a distinguished literary man, the editor, first, of *The Cornhill Magazine*, and, then, of *The Dictionary of National Biography*, as well as the author of numerous critical, biographical, and philosophical studies. His friends, frequent visitors to the Stephen household, included the American poet and ambassador James Russell Lowell, the English novelist-poet George Meredith, and the American novelist Henry James. Woolf's lively and beautiful mother, Julia Stephen, also had important artistic connections. As a girl, Julia had spent much time at Little Holland House, the

Kensington estate where the painters William Holman Hunt, Edward Burne-Jones, and G. F. Watts, the actress Ellen Terry, and the poet Alfred, Lord Tennyson frequently gathered, and as a young widow she had seriously devoted herself to the profession of nursing, about which she wrote a useful and witty little book entitled *Notes from Sick Rooms* (1883).

The union of these two was the second for both. As a young man, Leslie Stephen had been married to a daughter of the Victorian novelist William Makepeace Thackeray, by whom he had one child, a retarded girl who lived at home with the Stephen family during the years when Virginia was growing up. Similarly, his wife Julia had been married at the age of nineteen to a promising attorney, Herbert Duckworth, by whom she had three children—Stella, George, and Gerald—who were to figure importantly in Virginia's life. Widower and widow, the pair met and eventually wed when they were London neighbors, living in an upper-middle-class quarter near London's Hyde Park Gate. Together, they had four more children: Vanessa (who became a painter), Thoby (who died at the age of twenty-six, after a promising university career), Virginia, and Adrian (who became a physician).

Woolf's childhood at 22 Hyde Park Gate was for the most part rich and exhilarating but, at times, bewildering. As she recalled in another memoir, the house itself consisted "of innumerable small oddly shaped rooms built to accommodate not one family but three" (the two Stephen families along with the Duckworths), and here "eleven people aged between eight and sixty lived . . . and were waited upon by seven servants," so that "the place seemed tangled and matted with emotion." Nevertheless, many of the children's activities were perfectly normal for their class and era. Summers the family spent at Talland House in Cornwall, a late-nineteenth-century country home of which Woolf has left an idyllic record in her 1927 novel *To the Lighthouse*. Winters, in London, were occupied with standard Victorian pedagogical routines: the boys were sent away to school, the girls were taught at home by their mother and by a series of tutors and governesses, an inequitable education that was later to inspire considerable bitterness in Woolf. Still, despite such familial adherence to convention, the novelist's childhood was distinctively intellectual: not only was she continually brought in touch with what she once called the "old men of recognized genius" who were her father's friends, she was also early given the freedom of her father's extraordinarily well stocked library, and she began, too, when she was quite young, to demonstrate her own imaginative talents, writing stories that her mother proudly circulated to friends, and editing (at first with her brother Thoby and later alone) a family bulletin called *The Hyde Park Gate News*.

Although she had a few painful childhood experiences—evidently including bizarre sexual advances from her stepbrothers Gerald and George Duckworth—Woolf herself identified the death in 1895 of her adored mother as the first and perhaps the most significant trauma of her life, an event from which she would not recover until she had in effect exorcized her mother's ghost through her characterization of Julia Stephen as Mrs. Ramsay in *To the Lighthouse*. "With mother's death the merry, various family life which she had held in being shut for ever," Woolf later remembered. "In its place a dark cloud settled over us. . . . A finger seemed laid on one's lips." To make matters worse, the girl's older half-sister, Stella Duckworth, who had become hostess and surrogate mother in the Stephen house, married within two years of Julia Stephen's death and died, apparently from complications of pregnancy worsened by appendicitis, three months after her marriage. For the next seven years, Virginia and her sister Vanessa were to be left largely at the mercy of their lugubrious father, now a mournful and deaf old man, and their social-climbing half brother George Duckworth, the central subject of her scathing autobiographical sketch *22 Hyde Park Gate*. Perhaps because of these difficulties, or perhaps, as she herself speculated, because of inherited sensitivities, it was in this period that the novelist-to-be suffered the first of a series of mental breakdowns that were certainly to mark, and significantly to mar, the rest of her life.

In her own way, Woolf clearly loved Leslie Stephen, yet she experienced his death in 1904 as a kind of liberation. Years later, she remarked in her diary that, had her father lived, "his life would have entirely ended mine. What would have happened? No writing, no books:—inconceivable." Certainly, after Stephen's demise, the ambition manifested by "writing" and "books" became possible for her as it had never been before. Packing up the relics of 22 Hyde Park Gate that they still wished to keep, the four youngest Stephens—Thoby, Vanessa, Virginia, and Adrian—left Kensington and settled at 46 Gordon Square in Bloomsbury, where the two young women, at last freed from the constraints of the Victorian society George Duckworth had so cherished, quickly became acquainted with a group of their brother Thoby's most brilliant Cambridge friends—Lytton Strachey, Saxon Sydney-Turner, John Maynard Keynes, Clive Bell, Leonard Woolf, Duncan Grant, and, eventually, E. M. Forster.

Many of these young men had been members of a college group known as the "Apostles," and a number were to become prominent in English intellectual circles, Strachey as an iconoclastic biographer, Keynes as a groundbreaking economist, Forster as a novelist, and Woolf as a man of letters, a socialist politician, and the husband of Virginia Stephen. In these early Bloomsbury years, however, they functioned primarily as messengers of a freedom that Virginia, in particular, seems hardly to have allowed herself to imagine before she met them. From late-night discussions of beauty and truth, the group moved to frank analyses of their own sexuality, especially of the homosexuality that had characterized many of the men's public (secondary) school and college careers. For the young woman who was to become the novelist Virginia Woolf, the Victorian period, with its covert suppression of the female intellect and its overt disapproval of everybody's sexuality, seems definitively to have ended.

To be sure, just before and right after the move to Gordon Square, Virginia Woolf had been actively engaged in a number of radical projects, studying Greek (still at that time an unusual undertaking for a young woman), teaching in a working women's college in South London, doing office chores for the suffrage movement, and writing reviews for the prestigious *Times Literary Supplement*. Plainly she was already quite aware that her vocation was to be a literary one, and, more, she was already quite conscious of her own deeply feminist inclinations. Yet one more trauma was to darken her life in this period: her brother Thoby's sudden death from typhoid fever on a trip that the four Stephens took to Greece in 1906. Like the loss of her mother, this family calamity may well have slowed Woolf's aesthetic growth; certainly it weakened her own mental and physical health for a time (in fact, she herself had a bad case of the illness that killed Thoby). Perhaps for this reason, it was not until after her marriage to Leonard Woolf in 1912 that she was able sufficiently to focus her energies so that she could finish her first novel, *The Voyage Out* (1915), a book on which she had been working for seven years when it was finally published.

Only a year before her wedding, Virginia Stephen had brooded on the contrast between her sister, Vanessa—now married, a mother, and a productive painter—and herself: "To be 29 and unmarried—to be a failure—childless—insane too, no writer." But when she married Woolf, after the fiasco of a twenty-four-hour engagement to the homosexual Lytton Strachey, she appears to have felt that she had found a husband with whom she could be perfectly happy. Although their relationship may have been in some ways unusual—it seems hardly to have existed sexually, for example—the "Woolves," as Leonard and Virginia were called in their circle, were evidently an exceptionally compatible couple. A former colonial administrator and, in his wife's words, a "penniless Jew," Leonard Woolf was passionately devoted to the sensitive yet powerfully ambitious literary woman he had married, nursing her through periods of mental illness, guarding her time and supporting her work when she was well. As a combination of Jewish "outsider" and Cambridge "insider," moreover, he may well have provided the former Virginia Stephen with just the oblique perspective on her culture that she needed. Thus, though the fact that she and Leonard remained childless did sometimes continue to trouble her, Woolf was in most ways satisfied, indeed sustained, by her relationship with him.

In the years after her marriage, Woolf worked with increasing intensity at the craft of fiction, publishing a series of novels that made her, by the middle twenties, one of the best-known innovative literary artists in England. *The Voyage Out* was followed in 1919 by *Night and Day*, an exploration of the trials of a young woman who was, like the writer herself, a kind of anxious literary heiress. Comparatively conventional in form and substance, this book gave little indication of the more profoundly experimental works that were to come: *Jacob's Room* (1922), a deliberately fragmented meditation on the life and death of a young man who seemed, like Woolf's brother Thoby, to have been a confident inheritor of the patriarchal culture represented by institutions like Cambridge and Oxford; *Mrs. Dalloway* (1925), a daringly structured analysis of post–World War I London society that shifts from one character's mind to another's even while it focuses on a single day in the life of Clarissa Dalloway, a well-born Westminister hostess, and her mad double, Septimus Warren Smith, a shell-shocked veteran, who paradoxically functions as a kind of "other self" for her; and *To the Lighthouse* (1927), partly a nostalgic memoir of Woolf's own childhood summers at Talland House and partly a sardonic critique of the Victorian mores that made Talland House both a stimulating and a suffocating environment, especially for girls like the rebellious Virginia Stephen.

In the period when she was writing these books, Woolf and her husband also undertook to found a press. The Hogarth Press, as they called it, began at first as a hobby, an attempt on Leonard Woolf's part to offer his wife a species of what would today be called "occupational therapy." But the enterprise quickly grew into a serious publishing venture; the "Woolves" produced editions of, among other notable works, the poems of T. S. Eliot, the short stories of Katherine Mansfield, and the writings of Sigmund Freud in translation. Dominating what had come to be called "the Bloomsbury Group" both with her art and with her press, Leslie Stephen's youngest daughter had become, in her own right, an intellectual force to be reckoned with.

Central as she was to London literary life, however, Woolf continued to perceive herself as, in many ways, an outsider, and specifically as an outsider because she was a woman. From the first—as the critical essays included here suggest—she had been obsessed with reconstructing a uniquely female aesthetic heritage, a heritage which she implicitly opposed to the predominantly male tradition represented by her father's *Dictionary of National Biography*, and which she herself was eventually to define as, at least in its inceptions, one of marginality. But when, in the early twenties, Woolf met and fell in love with a younger writer named Victoria Sackville-West, her commitment to women's lives and works was dramatically intensified. The daughter of an ancient and aristocratic family, Sackville-West was a lesbian poet-novelist who had been married for some years to Harold Nicolson, a literarily inclined diplomat who was evidently an unusually congenial and sympathetic husband. The mother of two sons, she nevertheless quite frankly led what she and Woolf called a "Sapphic" life, though over the years the ambiguity of her sexual identity had given her considerable pain.

Despite the comfort of her marriage to Leonard, Woolf's relationship with Vita, as she was called, became, in one biographer's words, the "great passion" of the older novelist's career. More, it inspired at least one book: *Orlando* (1928), a parodic biography of a four-hundred-year-old character who changes from male to female in the late seventeenth century and whose fantastic, centuries-long development represents not only the history of the Sackville-West family but also the evolution of English literature from the Renaissance to the twentieth century. In addition, Woolf's feelings for Sackville-West may have energized her composition of a text that is in a sense *Orlando*'s "sister" book: *A Room of One's Own* (1929), a luminous extended essay on "women and fiction" which is, as most literary historians would agree, the first major achievement of feminist criticism in the English language.

After the exuberant blossoming represented by *Orlando* and *A Room of One's Own*, Woolf's life and work slowly darkened. Though her friendship with Vita was never completely disrupted, it gradually dissolved, never to be replaced by another truly erotic passion. In some ways, *The Waves* (1931) represents Woolf at the height of her avant-garde experimental powers. A "poemplay," as she called it, this innovative novel consists of a series of meditatively lyric monologues spoken by six central characters, yet the book is already notably elegiac: each figure is, in one way or another, an aspect of the central human self, and all are haunted by the untimely death of an ambiguously heroic youth named Percival, who seems significantly related to Woolf's lost brother, Thoby. Following *The Waves*, Woolf achieved great popular success with what would now be called a "family chronicle" novel, *The Years* (1937), a book which traced the lives of the upper-class Pargiter clan from the Victorian 1880s to "the present moment" in the 1930s. But as Europe began to sink beneath the shadow of fascism, her own existence became increasingly painful. During the thirties, her nephew Julian Bell, the oldest son of her sister, Vanessa, was killed in the Spanish civil war, and she herself had never, in any case, struggled free of the recurrent mental illness that had tormented her since adolescence. Her last novel, *Between the Acts* (posthumously published in 1941), was written at a time when she felt herself to be precariously balanced between health and disease. A few years earlier, she had produced her most radically feminist work, *Three Guineas* (1938), whose title refered to monetary contributions she had been asked to give to various political causes. The book had taken a number of years—and three scrapbooks full of notes and clippings—to compose, and, in its examination of the modes of social oppression, it made overt what Woolf saw as the covert connections between the West's patriarchal social structures and Hitler's jackbooted Nazis marching for the Fatherland.

As German planes began to appear over the once bucolic Sussex countryside, where the "Woolves" had a weekend home in the small village of Rodmell, Virginia Woolf evidently became increasingly anxious, not only about her own sanity but about her society's health. Her physician brother, Adrian, had provided her and Leonard with a painless poison, in case of a German invasion (which would, of course, have been a particularly disastrous event for the couple, considering Leonard's Jewish origins). But no doctor, apparently, could offer her a cure for the "voices" she had begun to hear; no one could provide a panacea to prevent, in her words, "another of those terrible times" when she would sink into madness. On March 28, 1941, she weighted her pockets with stones and walked into the river Ouse, a stream near her cottage at Rodmell, leaving a note for Leonard that explained, "I feel certain I am going mad again," but concluded with the reassurance that "I don't think two people could have been happier than we have been."

Dramatic and disturbing as it was, Woolf's suicide should not be taken as her life's ultimate gesture. Certainly, when one sets that gray, precarious moment in 1941—a moment when the sky above Sussex was heavy with bombers and the novelist's own head buzzing with "voices"—against this artist's lifetime of energetic achievement, the sad instant dissipates. Had Woolf lived, she would surely have written more and just as well, revising *Between the Acts* and perhaps reworking even such other posthumously published works included here as *22 Hyde Park Gate*. Yet stories like *The New Dress* and *Slater's Pins Have No Points*, along with essays like *Professions for Women* or *"Jane Eyre" and "Wuthering Heights*," demonstrate that her vitality was continually intense. "The advantages of being Virginia Stephen," after all, had been manifold: they had taught her not only how to write but how not to think: not to think like a Victorian, not to think like an "insider," not to think like what she called "a patriarch." Instead, defining herself, the way she had in *Three Guineas*, as the founder of a "Society of Outsiders," Woolf had spent most of her life setting herself against both literal and figurative death: the death of the mind symbolized by mental illness as well as the death of the soul manifested by deadening social structures. The last line of *The Waves*, spoken by a character who is perhaps her most significant alter ego—the novelist, Bernard—summarizes an attitude that informed all her finest achievements: "Against you I will fling myself, unvanquished and unyielding, O Death!"

Jane Eyre and *Wuthering Heights* [1]

Of the hundred years that have passed since Charlotte Brontë was born, she, the centre now of so much legend, devotion, and literature, lived but thirty-nine. It is strange to reflect how different those legends might have been had her life reached the ordinary human span. She might have become, like some of her famous contemporaries, a figure familiarly met with in London and elsewhere, the subject of pictures and anecdotes innumerable, the writer of many novels, of memoirs possibly, removed from us well within the memory of the middle-aged in all the splendour of established fame. She might have been wealthy, she might have been prosperous. But it is not so. When we think of her we have to imagine some one who had no lot in our modern world; we have to cast our minds back to the 'fifties of the last century, to a remote parsonage upon the wild Yorkshire moors. In that parsonage, and on those moors, unhappy and lonely, in her poverty and her exaltation, she remains for ever.

These circumstances, as they affected her character, may have left their traces on her work. A novelist, we reflect, is bound to build up his structure with much very perishable material which begins by lending it reality and ends by cumbering it with rubbish. As we open *Jane Eyre* once more we cannot stifle the suspicion that we shall find her world of imagination as antiquated, mid-Victorian, and out of date as the parsonage on the moor, a place only to be visited by the curious, only preserved by the pious. So we open *Jane Eyre*; and in two pages every doubt is swept clean from our minds.

> Folds of scarlet drapery shut in my view to the right hand; to the left were the clear panes of glass, protecting, but not separating me from the drear November day. At intervals, while turning over the leaves of my book, I studied the aspect of that winter afternoon. Afar, it offered a pale blank of mist and cloud; near, a scene of wet lawn and storm-beat shrub, with ceaseless rain sweeping away wildly before a long and lamentable blast.

There is nothing there more perishable than the moor itself, or more subject to the sway of fashion than the "long and lamentable blast." Nor is this exhilaration short-lived. It rushes us through the entire volume, without giving us time to think, without letting us lift our eyes from the page. So intense is our absorption that if some one moves in the room the movement seems to take place not there but up in Yorkshire. The writer has us by the hand, forces us along her road, makes us see what

---

1. Two famous novels, the first by Charlotte   Emily Brontë (1818–1848).
Brontë (1816–1855), the second by her sister

she sees, never leaves us for a moment or allows us to forget her.[2] At the end we are steeped through and through with the genius, the vehemence, the indignation of Charlotte Brontë. Remarkable faces, figures of strong outline and gnarled feature have flashed upon us in passing; but it is through her eyes that we have seen them. Once she is gone, we seek for them in vain. Think of Rochester and we have to think of Jane Eyre. Think of the moor, and again, there is Jane Eyre. Think of the drawing-room, even, those "white carpets on which seemed laid brilliant garlands of flowers," that "pale Parian mantelpiece" with its Bohemia glass of "ruby red" and the "general blending of snow and fire"—what is all that except Jane Eyre?

The drawbacks of being Jane Eyre are not far to seek. Always to be a governess and always to be in love is a serious limitation in a world which is full, after all, of people who are neither one nor the other. The characters of a Jane Austen or of a Tolstoi[3] have a million facets compared with these. They live and are complex by means of their effect upon many different people who serve to mirror them in the round. They move hither and thither whether their creators watch them or not, and the world in which they live seems to us an independent world which we can visit, now that they have created it, by ourselves. Thomas Hardy[4] is more akin to Charlotte Brontë in the power of his personality and the narrowness of his vision. But the differences are vast. As we read *Jude the Obscure* we are not rushed to a finish; we brood and ponder and drift away from the text in plethoric trains of thought which build up round the characters an atmosphere of question and suggestion of which they are themselves, as often as not, unconscious. Simple peasants as they are, we are forced to confront them with destinies and questionings of the hugest import, so that often it seems as if the most important characters in a Hardy novel are those which have no names. Of this power, of this speculative curiosity, Charlotte Brontë has no trace. She does not attempt to solve the problems of human life; she is even unaware that such problems exist; all her force, and it is the more tremendous for being constricted, goes into the assertion, "I love," "I hate," "I suffer."

2. "Charlotte and Emily Brontë had much the same sense of colour. '... we saw—ah! it was beautiful—a splendid place carpeted with crimson, and crimson-covered chairs and tables, and a pure white ceiling bordered by gold, a shower of glass drops hanging in silver chains from the centre, and shimmering with little soft tapers' (*Wuthering Heights*). Yet it was merely a very pretty drawing-room, and within it a boudoir, both spread with white carpets, on which seemed laid brilliant garlands of flowers; both ceiled with snowy mouldings of white grapes and vine leaves, beneath which glowed in rich contrast crimson couches and ottomans; while the ornaments on the pale Parian mantelpiece were of sparkling Bohemia glass, ruby red; and between the windows large mirrors repeated the general blending of snow and fire" [Woolf's note].

3. Jane Austen (1775–1817), English novelist; Count Leo Tolstoi (1828–1910), Russian novelist.

4. Thomas Hardy (1840–1928), English novelist, author of *Jude the Obscure*.

For the self-centred and self-limited writers have a power denied the more catholic and broad-minded. Their impressions are close packed and strongly stamped between their narrow walls. Nothing issues from their minds which has not been marked with their own impress. They learn little from other writers, and what they adopt they cannot assimilate. Both Hardy and Charlotte Brontë appear to have founded their styles upon a stiff and decorous journalism. The staple of their prose is awkward and unyielding. But both with labour and the most obstinate integrity by thinking every thought until it has subdued words to itself, have forged for themselves a prose which takes the mould of their minds entire; which has, into the bargain, a beauty, a power, a swiftness of its own. Charlotte Brontë, at least, owed nothing to the reading of many books. She never learnt the smoothness of the professional writer, or acquired his ability to stuff and sway his language as he chooses. "I could never rest in communication with strong, discreet, and refined minds, whether male or female," she writes, as any leader-writer[5] in a provincial journal might have written; but gathering fire and speed goes on in her own authentic voice "till I had passed the outworks of conventional reserve and crossed the threshold of confidence, and won a place by their hearts' very hearthstone." It is there that she takes her seat; it is the red and fitful glow of the heart's fire which illumines her page. In other words, we read Charlotte Brontë not for exquisite observation of character—her characters are vigorous and elementary; not for comedy—hers is grim and crude; not for a philosophic view of life —hers is that of a country parson's daughter; but for her poetry. Probably that is so with all writers who have, as she has, an overpowering personality, who, as we should say in real life, have only to open the door to make themselves felt. There is in them some untamed ferocity perpetually at war with the accepted order of things which makes them desire to create instantly rather than to observe patiently. This very ardour, rejecting half shades and other minor impediments, wings its way past the daily conduct of ordinary people and allies itself with their more inarticulate passions. It makes them poets, or, if they choose to write in prose, intolerant of its restrictions. Hence it is that both Emily and Charlotte are always invoking the help of nature. They both feel the need of some more powerful symbol of the vast and slumbering passions in human nature than words or actions can convey. It is with a description of a storm that Charlotte ends her finest novel *Villette*. "The skies hang full and dark—a wrack sails from the west; the clouds cast themselves into strange forms." So she calls in nature to describe a state of mind which could not otherwise be expressed. But neither of the sisters observed nature accurately as Dorothy Wordsworth ob-

5. Editorial writer.

served it, or painted it minutely as Tennyson painted it.[6] They seized those aspects of the earth which were most akin to what they themselves felt or imputed to their characters, and so their storms, their moors, their lovely spaces of summer weather are not ornaments applied to decorate a dull page of display the writer's powers of observation—they carry on the emotion and light up the meaning of the book.

The meaning of a book, which lies so often apart from what happens and what is said and consists rather in some connection which things in themselves different have had for the writer, is necessarily hard to grasp. Especially this is so when, like the Brontës, the writer is poetic, and his meaning inseparable from his language, and itself rather a mood than a particular observation. *Wuthering Heights* is a more difficult book to understand than *Jane Eyre*, because Emily was a greater poet than Charlotte. When Charlotte wrote she said with eloquence and splendour and passion "I love," "I hate," "I suffer." Her experience, though more intense, is on a level with our own. But there is no "I" in *Wuthering Heights*. There are no governesses. There are no employers. There is love, but it is not the love of men and women. Emily was inspired by some more general conception. The impulse which urged her to create was not her own suffering or her own injuries. She looked out upon a world cleft into gigantic disorder and felt within her the power to unite it in a book. That gigantic ambition is to be felt throughout the novel—a struggle, half thwarted but of superb conviction, to say something through the mouths of her characters which is not merely "I love" or "I hate," but "we, the whole human race" and "you, the eternal powers . . . " the sentence remains unfinished. It is not strange that it should be so; rather it is astonishing that she can make us feel what she had it in her to say at all. It surges up in the half-articulate words of Catherine Earnshaw,[7] "If all else perished and *he* remained, I should still continue to be; and if all else remained and he were annihilated, the universe would turn to a mighty stranger; I should not seem part of it." It breaks out again in the presence of the dead. "I see a repose that neither earth nor hell can break, and I feel an assurance of the endless and shadowless hereafter—the eternity they have entered—where life is boundless in its duration, and love in its sympathy and joy in its fulness." It is this suggestion of power underlying the apparitions of human nature, and lifting them up into the presence of greatness that gives the book its huge stature among other novels. But it was not enough for Emily Brontë to write a few lyrics, to utter a cry, to express a creed. In her poems she did this once and for all, and her poems will perhaps outlast her novel. But she was novelist as well as poet. She must

6. Dorothy Wordsworth (1771–1855), English poet and diarist; Alfred, Lord Tennyson (1809–1892), English poet.

7. The central female character of *Wuthering Heights*; the "he" in her speech is Heathcliff, her adoptive brother and lover.

take upon herself a more laborious and a more ungrateful task. She must face the fact of other existences, grapple with the mechanism of external things, build up, in recognisable shape, farms and houses and report the speeches of men and women who existed independently of herself. And so we reach these summits of emotion not by rant or rhapsody but by hearing a girl sing old songs to herself as she rocks in the branches of a tree; by watching the moor sheep crop the turf; by listening to the soft wind breathing through the grass. The life at the farm with all its absurdities and its improbability is laid open to us. We are given every opportunity of comparing *Wuthering Heights* with a real farm and Heathcliff with a real man. How, we are allowed to ask, can there be truth or insight or the finer shades of emotion in men and women who so little resemble what we have seen ourselves? But even as we ask it we see in Heathcliff the brother that a sister of genius might have seen; he is impossible, we say, but nevertheless no boy in literature has so vivid an existence as his. So it is with the two Catherines; never could women feel as they do or act in their manner, we say. All the same, they are the most lovable women in English fiction. It is as if she could tear up all that we know human beings by, and fill these unrecognisable transparences with such a gust of life that they transcend reality. Hers, then, is the rarest of all powers. She could free life from its dependence on facts; with a few touches indicate the spirit of a face so that it needs no body; by speaking of the moor make the wind blow and the thunder roar.

1925

22 Hyde Park Gate[1]

As I have said, the drawing room at Hyde Park Gate was divided by black folding doors picked out with thin lines of raspberry red. We were still much under the influence of Titian.[2] Mounds of plush, Watts' portraits,[3] busts shrined in crimson velvet, enriched the gloom of a room naturally dark and thickly shaded in summer by showers of Virginia Creeper.

But it is of the folding doors that I wish to speak. How could family life have been carried on without them? As soon dispense with waterclosets or bathrooms as with folding doors in a family of nine men and women, one of whom into the bargain was an idiot. Suddenly there

---

1. Written by Woolf to be read aloud to the Memoir Club, a group consisting of the members of the famous Bloomsbury circle. All members of the club were expected to read memoirs characterized by "absolute frankness."

2. Tiziano Vecellio (c. 1490–1576), Venetian painter of rich, dark interiors.
3. George Frederick Watts (1817–1904), English painter strongly influenced by Titian.

would be a crisis—a servant dismissed, a lover rejected, pass books[4] opened, or poor Mrs. Tyndall who had lately poisoned her husband by mistake come for consolation. On one side of the door Cousin Adeline, Duchess of Bedford, perhaps would be on her knees—the Duke had died tragically at Woburn; Mrs. Dolmetsch would be telling how she had found her husband in bed with the parlour-maid or Lisa Stillman would be sobbing that Walter Headlam had chalked her nose with a billiard cue—"which," she cried, "is what comes of smoking a pipe before gentlemen"—and my mother had much ado to persuade her that life had still to be faced, and the flower of virginity was still unplucked in spite of a chalk mark on the nose.

Though dark and agitated on one side, the other side of the door, especially on Sunday afternoons, was cheerful enough. There round the oval tea table with its pink china shell full of spice buns would be found old General Beadle, talking of the Indian Mutiny; or Mr. Haldane, or Sir Frederick Pollock—talking of all things under the sun; or old C. B. Clarke, whose name is given to three excessively rare Himalayan ferns; and Professor Wolstenholme, capable, if you interrupted him, of spouting two columns of tea not unmixed with sultanas[5] through his nostrils; after which he would relapse into a drowsy ursine torpor, the result of eating opium to which he had been driven by the unkindness of his wife and the untimely death of his son Oliver who was eaten, somewhere off the coast of Coromandel, by a shark. These gentlemen came and came again; and they were often reinforced by Mr. Frederick Gibbs, sometime tutor to the Prince of Wales, whose imperturbable common sense and fund of information about the colonies in general and Canada in particular were a perpetual irritation to my father who used to wonder whether a brain fever at college in the year 1863 had not something to do with it. These old gentlemen were generally to be found, eating very slowly, staying very late and making themselves agreeable at Christmas-time with curious presents of Indian silver work, and hand bags made from the skin of the ornithorhynchus —as I seem to remember.

The tea table however was also fertilized by a ravishing stream of female beauty--the three Miss Lushingtons, the three Miss Stillmans, and the three Miss Montgomeries—all triplets, all ravishing, but of the nine the paragon for wit, grace, charm and distinction was undoubtedly the lovely Kitty Lushington—now Mrs. Leo Maxse. (Their engagement under the jackmanii in the Love Corner at St. Ives was my first introduction to the passion of love.) At the time I speak of she was in process of disengaging herself from Lord Morpeth, and had, I suspect, to ex-

---

4. Bankbooks.   5. Raisins.

plain her motives to my mother, a martinet[6] in such matters, for first promising to marry a man and then breaking it off. My mother believed that all men required an infinity of care. She laid all the blame, I feel sure, upon Kitty. At any rate I have a picture of her as she issued from the secret side of the folding doors bearing on her delicate pink cheeks two perfectly formed pear-shaped crystal tears. They neither fell nor in the least dimmed the lustre of her eyes. She at once became the life and soul of the tea table—perhaps Leo Maxse was there—perhaps Ronny Norman—perhaps Esmé Howard—perhaps Arthur Studd, for the gentlemen were not all old, or all professors by any means—and when my father groaned beneath his breath but very audibly, "Oh Gibbs, what a bore you are!" it was Kitty whom my mother instantly threw into the breach. "Kitty wants to tell you how much she loved your lecture," my mother would cry, and Kitty still with the tears on her cheeks would improvise with the utmost gallantry some compliment or opinion which pacified my father who was extremely sensitive to female charm and largely depended upon female praise. Repenting of his irritation he would press poor Gibbs warmly by the hand and beg him to come soon again—which needless to say, poor Gibbs did.

And then there would come dancing into the room rubbing his hands, wrinkling his forehead, the most remarkable figure, as I sometimes think, that our household contained. I have alluded to a grisly relic of another age which we used to disinter from the nursery wardrobe—Herbert Duckworth's wig. (Herbert Duckworth had been a barrister.) Herbert Duckworth's son—George Herbert—was by no means grisly. His hair curled naturally in dark crisp ringlets; he was six foot high; he had been in the Eton Eleven;[7] he was now cramming at Scoones[8] in the hope of passing the Foreign Office examination. When Miss Willett of Brighton saw him 'throwing off his ulster' in the middle of her drawing room she was moved to write an Ode Comparing George Duckworth to the Hermes of Praxiteles[9]—which Ode my mother kept in her writing table drawer, along with a little Italian medal that George had won for saving a peasant from drowning. Miss Willett was reminded of the Hermes; but if you looked at him closely you noticed that one of his ears was pointed; and the other round; you also noticed that though he had the curls of a God and the ears of a faun he had unmistakably the eyes of a pig. So strange a compound can seldom have existed. And in the days I speak of, God, faun and pig were all in all alive, all in opposition, and in their conflicts producing the most astonishing eruptions.

---

6. Strict disciplinarian.
7. I.e., on the cricket team at Eton, a prestigious English boy's school.
8. I.e., intensively preparing for examinations at
a "cram school."
9. A statue of Hermes, the Greek messenger god, by a Greek sculptor of the fourth century B.C., Praxiteles.

To begin with the God—well, he was only a plaster cast perhaps of Miss Willett's Hermes, but I cannot deny that the benign figure of George Duckworth teaching his small half-brothers and sisters by the hour on a strip of coco-nut matting to play forward with a perfectly straight bat[1] had something Christlike about it. He was certainly Christian rather than Pagan in his divinity, for it soon became clear that this particular forward stroke to be applied to every ball indifferently, was a symbol of moral rectitude, and that one could neither slog nor bowl a sneak[2] without paltering rather dangerously (as poor Gerald Duckworth used to do) with the ideals of a sportsman and an English gentleman. Then, he would run miles to fetch cushions; he was always shutting doors and opening windows; it was always George who said the tactful thing, and broke bad news, and braved my father's irritation, and read aloud to us when we had the whooping cough, and remembered the birthdays of aunts, and sent turtle soup to the invalids, and attended funerals, and took children to the pantomime—oh yes, whatever else George might be he was certainly a saint.

But then there was the faun. Now this animal was at once sportive and demonstrative and thus often at variance with the self-sacrificing nature of the God. It was quite a common thing to come into the drawing room and find George on his knees with his arms extended, addressing my mother, who might be adding up the weekly books, in tones of fervent adoration. Perhaps he had been staying with the Chamberlains for the week-end. But he lavished caresses, endearments, enquiries and embraces as if, after forty years in the Australian bush, he had at last returned to the home of his youth and found an aged mother still alive to welcome him. Meanwhile we gathered round—the dinner bell had already rung—awkward, but appreciative. Few families, we felt, could exhibit such a scene as this. Tears rushed to his eyes with equal abandonment. For example when he had a tooth out he flung himself into the cook's arms in a paroxysm of weeping. When Judith Blunt refused him he sat at the head of the table sobbing loudly, but continuing to eat. He cried when he was vaccinated. He was fond of sending telegrams which began "My darling mother" and went on to say that he would be dining out. (I copied this style of his, I regret to say, with disastrous results on one celebrated occasion. "She is an angel" I wired, on hearing that Flora Russell had accepted him, and signed my nickname 'Goat.' "She is an aged Goat" was the version that arrived, at Islay, and had something to do, George said, with Flora's reluctance to ally herself with the Stephen family.) But all this exuberance of emotion was felt to be wholly to George's credit. It proved not only how

---

1. I.e., properly using a cricket bat.　　　2. Unsportsmanlike strategies in cricket.

deep and warm his feelings were, but how marvellously he had kept the open heart and simple manners of a child.

But when nature refused him two pointed ears and gave him only one she knew, I think, what she was about. In his wildest paroxysms of emotion, when he bellowed with grief, or danced round the room, leaping like a kid, and flung himself on his knees before the Dowager Lady Carnarvon there was always something self conscious, a little uneasy about him, as though he were not quite sure of the effect—as though the sprightly faun had somehow been hobbled together with a timid and conventional old sheep.

It is true that he was abnormally stupid. He passed the simplest examinations with incredible difficulty. For years he was crammed by Mr. Scoones; and again and again he failed to pass the Foreign Office examination. He had existed all his life upon jobs found for him by his friends. His small brown eyes seemed perpetually to be boring into something too hard for them to penetrate. But when one compares them to the eyes of a pig, one is alluding not merely to their stupidity, or to their greed—George, I have been told, had the reputation of being the greediest young man in London ball-rooms—but to something obstinate and pertinacious in their expression as if the pig were grouting for truffles with his snout and would by sheer persistency succeed in unearthing them. Never shall I forget the pertinacity with which he learnt "Love in the Valley" by heart in order to impress Flora Russell; or the determination with which he mastered the first volume of *Middlemarch*[3] for the same purpose; and how immensely he was relieved when he left the second volume in a train and got my father, whose set was ruined, to declare that in his opinion one volume of *Middlemarch* was enough. Had his obstinacy been directed solely to self-improvement there would have been no call for us to complain. I myself might even have been of use to him. But it gradually became clear that he was muddling out a scheme, a plan of campaign, a system of life—I scarcely know what to call it—and then we had every reason to feel the earth tremble beneath our feet and the heavens darken. For George Duckworth had become after my mother's death, for all practical purposes, the head of the family. My father was deaf, eccentric, absorbed in his work, and entirely shut off from the world. The management of affairs fell upon George. It was usually said that he was father and mother, sister and brother in one—and all the old ladies of Kensington and Belgravia added with one accord that Heaven had blessed those poor Stephen girls beyond belief, and it remained for them to prove that they were worthy of such devotion.

3. Long novel by George Eliot (1819–1880).

But what was George Duckworth thinking and what was there alarming in the sight of him as he sat in the red leather arm-chair after dinner, mechanically stroking the dachshund Schuster, and lugu-briously glancing at the pages of George Eliot? Well, he might be thinking about the crest on the post office notepaper, and how nice it would look picked out in red (he was now Austen Chamberlain's pri-vate secretary) or he might be thinking how the Duchess of St. Albans had given up using fish knives at dinner; or how Mrs. Grenfell had asked him to stay and he had created as he thought a good impression by refusing; at the same time he was revolving in the slow whirlpool of his brain schemes of the utmost thoughtfulness—plans for sending us for treats; for providing us with riding lessons; for finding jobs for some of poor Augusta Croft's innumerable penniless children. But the alarming thing was that he looked not merely muddled and emotional but obstinate. He looked as if he had made up his mind about some-thing and would refuse to budge an inch. At the time it was extremely difficult to say what he had made up his mind to, but after the lapse of many years I think it may be said brutally and baldly, that George had made up his mind to rise in the social scale. He had a curious inborn reverence for the British aristocracy; the beauty of our great aunts had allied us in the middle of the nineteenth century with, I think I am right in saying, two dukes and quite a number of earls and countesses. They naturally showed no particular wish to remember the connection but George did his best to live up to it. His reverence for the symbols of greatness now that he was attached to a Cabinet Minister had fuller scope. His talk was all of ivory buttons that the coachmen of Cabinet Ministers wear in their coats; of having the entrée at Court; of baronies descending in the female line; of countesses secreting the diamonds of Marie Antoinette in black boxes under their beds. His secret dreams as he sat in the red leather chair stroking Schuster were all of marrying a wife with diamonds, and having a coachman with a button, and having the entrée at Court. But the danger was that his dreams were secret even to himself. Had you told him—and I think Vanessa did once—that he was a snob, he would have burst into tears. What he liked, he explained, was to know 'nice people'; Lady Jeune was nice; so were Lady Sligo, Lady Carnarvon and Lady Leitrim. Poor Mrs. Clifford, on the other hand, was not; nor was old Mr. Wolstenholme; of all our old friends, Kitty Maxse, who might have been Lady Morpeth, came near-est to his ideal. It was not a question of birth or wealth; it was—and then if you pressed him further he would seize you in his arms and cry out that he refused to argue with those he loved. "Kiss me, kiss me, you beloved", he would vociferate; and the argument was drowned in kisses. Everything was drowned in kisses. He lived in the thickest emo-tional haze, and as his passions increased and his desires became more vehement—he lived, Jack Hills assured me, in complete chastity until his marriage—one felt like an unfortunate minnow shut up in the same tank with an unwieldy and turbulent whale.

Nothing stood in the way of his advancement. He was a bachelor of prepossessing appearance though inclined to fat, aged about thirty years, with an independent income of something over a thousand a year. As private secretary to Austen Chamberlain he was as a matter of course invited to all the great parties of all the great peers. Hostesses had no time to remember, if they had ever known, that the Duckworths had made their money in cotton, or coal, not a hundred years ago, and did not really rank, as George made out, among the ancient families of Somersetshire. For I have it on the best authority that when the original Duckworth acquired Orchardleigh about the year 1810 he filled it with casts from the Greek to which he had attached not merely fig leaves for the Gods but aprons for the Goddesses—much to the amusement of the Lords of Longleat who never forgot that old Duckworth had sold cotton by the yard and probably bought his aprons cheap. George, as I say, could have mounted alone to the highest pinnacles of London society. His mantelpiece was a gallery of invitation cards from every house in London. Why then did he insist upon cumbering himself with a couple of half-sisters who were more than likely to drag him down? It is probably useless to enquire. George's mind swam and steamed like a cauldron of rich Irish stew. He believed that aristocratic society was possessed of all the virtues and all the graces. He believed that his family had been entrusted to his care. He believed that it was his sacred duty —but when he reached that point his emotions overcame him; he began to sob; he flung himself on his knees; he seized Vanessa in his arms; he implored her in the name of her mother, of her grandmother, by all that was sacred in the female sex and holy in the traditions of our family to accept Lady Arthur Russell's invitation to dinner, to spend the week-end with the Chamberlains at Highbury.

I cannot conceal my own opinion that Vanessa was to blame; not indeed that she could help herself, but if, I sometimes think, she had been born with one shoulder higher than another, with a limp, with a squint, with a large mole on her left cheek, both our lives would have been changed for the better. As it was, George had a good deal of reason on his side. It was plain that Vanessa in her white satin dress made by Mrs. Young, wearing a single flawless amethyst round her neck, and a blue enamel butterfly in her hair—the gifts, of course, of George himself— beautiful, motherless, aged only eighteen, was a touching spectacle, an ornament for any dinner table, a potential peeress, anything might be made of such precious material as she was—outwardly at least; and to be seen hovering round her, providing her with jewels, and Arab horses, and expensive clothes, whispering encouragement, lavishing embraces which were not entirely concealed from the eyes of strangers, redounded to the credit of George himself and invested his figure with a pathos which it would not otherwise have had in the eyes of the dowagers of Mayfair. Unfortunately, what was inside Vanessa did not altogether correspond with what was outside. Underneath the necklaces and the enamel butterflies was one passionate desire—for paint and turpentine, for turpentine and paint. But poor George was no psychologist. His perceptions were obtuse. He never saw within. He was completely at a loss when Vanessa said she did not wish to stay with the Chamberlains at Highbury; and would not dine with Lady Arthur Russell—a rude, tyrannical old woman, with a bloodstained complexion and the manners of a turkey cock. He argued, he wept, he complained to Aunt Mary Fisher, who said that she could not believe her ears. Every battery was turned upon Vanessa. She was told that she was selfish, unwomanly, callous and incredibly ungrateful considering the treasures of affection that had been lavished upon her—the Arab horse she rode and the slabs of bright blue enamel which she wore. Still she persisted. She did not wish to dine with Lady Arthur Russell. As the season wore on, every morning brought its card of invitation for Mr Duckworth and Miss Stephen; and every evening witnessed a battle between them. For the first year or so George, I suppose, was usually the victor. Off they went, in the hansom cab of those days and late at night Vanessa would come into my room complaining that she had been dragged from party to party, where she knew no one, and had been bored to death by the civilities of young men from the Foreign Office and the condescensions of old ladies of title. The more Vanessa resisted, the more George's natural obstinacy persisted. At last there was a crisis. Lady Arthur Russell was giving a series of select parties on Thursday evenings in South Audley Street. Vanessa had sat through one entire evening without opening her lips. George insisted that she must go next week and make amends, or he said, "Lady Arthur will never ask you to her house again." They argued until it was getting too late to dress. At last Vanessa, more in desperation than in concession, rushed upstairs, flung on her clothes and announced that she was ready to go. Off they went. What happened in the cab will never be known. But whenever they reached 2 South Audley Street—and they reached it several times in the course of the evening—one or the other was incapable of getting out. George refused to enter with Vanessa in such a passion; and Vanessa refused to enter with George in tears. So the cabman had to be told to drive once more round the Park. Whether they ever managed to alight I do not know.

But next morning as I was sitting spelling out my Greek George came into my room carrying in his hand a small velvet box. He presented me with the jewel it contained—a Jews' harp made of enamel with a pinkish blob of matter swinging in the centre which I regret to say only fetched a few shillings when I sold it the other day. But his face showed that he had come upon a different errand. His face was sallow and scored with innumerable wrinkles, for his skin was as loose and flexible as a pug dog's, and he would express his anguish in the most poignant manner by puckering lines, folds, and creases from forehead to chin. His manner was stern. His bearing rigid. If Miss Willett of Brighton could have seen him then she would certainly have compared him to Christ on the cross. After giving me the Jews' harp he stood before the fire in complete silence. Then, as I expected, he began to tell me his version of the preceding night—wrinkling his forehead more than ever, but speaking with a restraint that was at once bitter and manly. Never, never again, he said, would he ask Vanessa to go out with him. He had seen a look in her eyes which positively frightened him. It should never be said of him that he made her do what she did not wish to do. Here he quivered, but checked himself. Then he went on to say that he had only done what he knew my mother would have wished him to do. His two sisters were the most precious things that remained to him. His home had always meant more to him—more than he could say, and here he became agitated, struggled for composure, and then burst into a statement which was at once dark and extremely lurid. We were driving Gerald from the house, he cried—when a young man was not happy at home—he himself had always been content—but if his sisters—if Vanessa refused to go out with him—if he could not bring his friends to the house—in short, it was clear that the chaste, the immaculate George Duckworth would be forced into the arms of whores. Needless to say he did not put it like that; and I could only conjure up in my virgin consciousness, dimly irradiated by having read the "Symposium"[4] with Miss Case, horrible visions of the vices to which young men were driven whose sisters did not make them happy at home. So we went on talking for an hour or two. The end of it was that he begged me, and I agreed, to go a few nights later to the Dowager Marchioness of Sligo's ball. I had already been to May Week[5] at Cambridge, and my recollections of gallopading round the room with Hawtrey, or sitting on the stairs and quizzing the dancers with Clive,[6] were such as to make me wonder why Vanessa found dances in London so utterly detestable. A few nights later I discovered for myself. After two hours of standing about in Lady Sligo's ball-room, of waiting to be introduced to strange young men, of dancing a round with Conrad Russell or with Esmé Howard, of dancing very badly, of being left without a

---

4. Dialogue on the subject of love, by the Greek philosopher Plato (427–347 B.C.).
5. A traditional week of festivities at the English

university.
6. Clive Bell, later to be Vanessa's husband.

partner, of being told by George that I looked lovely but must hold myself upright, I retired to an ante-room and hoped that a curtain concealed me. For some time it did. At length old Lady Sligo discovered me, judged the situation for herself and being a kind old peeress with a face like a rubicund sow's carried me off to the dining room, cut me a large slice of iced cake, and left me to devour it by myself in a corner.

On that occasion George was lenient. We left about two o'clock, and on the way home he praised me warmly, and assured me that I only needed practice to be a great social success. A few days later he told me that the Dowager Countess of Carnarvon particularly wished to make my acquaintance, and had invited me to dinner. As we drove across the Park he stroked my hand, and told me how he hoped that I should make friends with Elsie—for so both he and Vanessa had called her for some time at her own request—how I must not be frightened—how though she had been vice-reine of Canada and vice-reine of Ireland she was simplicity itself—always since the death of her husband dressed in black—refused to wear any of her jewels though she had inherited the diamonds of Marie Antoinette—and was the one woman, he said, with a man's sense of honour. The portrait he drew was of great distinction and bereavement. There would also be present her sister, Mrs. Popham of Littlecote, a lady also of distinction and also bereaved, for her husband, Dick Popham of Littlecote, came of an ancient unhappy race, cursed in the reign of Henry the Eighth, since which time the property had never descended from father to son. Sure enough Mary Popham was childless, and Dick Popham was in a lunatic asylum. I felt that I was approaching a house of grandeur and desolation, and was not a little impressed. But I could see nothing alarming either in Elsie Carnarvon or in Mrs. Popham of Littlecote. They were a couple of spare prim little women, soberly dressed in high black dresses, with grey hair strained off their foreheads, rather prominent blue eyes, and slightly protruding front teeth. We sat down to dinner.

The conversation was mild and kindly. Indeed I soon felt that I could not only reply to their questions—was I fond of painting?—was I fond of reading?—did I help my father in his work?—but could initiate remarks of my own. George had always complained of Vanessa's silence. I would prove that I could talk. So off I started. Heaven knows what devil prompted me—or why to Lady Carnarvon and Mrs. Popham of Littlecote of all people in the world I, a chit of eighteen, should have chosen to discourse upon the need of expressing the emotions! That, I said, was the great lack of modern life. The ancients, I said, discussed everything in common. Had Lady Carnavon ever read the dialogues of Plato? "We—both men and women—" once launched it was difficult to stop, nor was I sure that my audacity was not holding them spell-bound with admiration. I felt that I was earning George's gratitude for ever.

Suddenly a twitch, a shiver, a convulsion of amazing expressiveness, shook the Countess by my side; her diamonds, of which she wore a chaste selection, flashed in my eyes; and stopping, I saw George Duckworth blushing crimson on the other side of the table. I realized that I had committed some unspeakable impropriety. Lady Carnarvon and Mrs. Popham began at once to talk of something entirely different; and directly dinner was over George, pretending to help me on with my cloak, whispered in my ear in a voice of agony, "They're not used to young women saying anything—." And then as if to apologize to Lady Carnarvon for my ill breeding, I saw him withdraw with her behind a pillar in the hall, and though Mrs. Popham of Littlecote tried to attract my attention to a fine specimen of Moorish metal work which hung on the wall, we both distinctly heard them kiss. But the evening was not over. Lady Carnarvon had taken tickets for the French actors, who were then appearing in some play whose name I have forgotten. We had stalls[7] of course, and filed soberly to our places in the very centre of the crowded theatre. The curtain went up. Snubbed, shy, indignant, and uncomfortable, I paid little attention to the play. But after a time I noticed that Lady Carnarvon on one side of me, and Mrs. Popham on the other, were both agitated by the same sort of convulsive twitching which had taken them at dinner. What could be the matter? They were positively squirming in their seats. I looked at the stage. The hero and heroine were pouring forth a flood of voluble French which I could not disentangle. Then they stopped. To my great astonishment the lady leapt over the back of a sofa; the gentleman followed her. Round and round the stage they dashed, the lady shrieking, the man groaning and grunting in pursuit. It was a fine piece of realistic acting. As the pursuit continued, the ladies beside me held to the arms of their stalls with claws of iron. Suddenly, the actress dropped exhausted upon the sofa, and the man with a howl of gratification, loosening his clothes quite visibly, leapt on top of her. The curtain fell. Lady Carnarvon, Mrs. Popham of Littlecote and George Duckworth rose simultaneously. Not a word was said. Out we filed. And as our procession made its way down the stalls I saw Arthur Cane leap up in his seat like a jack-in-the-box, amazed and considerably amused that George Duckworth and Lady Carnarvon of all people should have taken a girl of eighteen to see the French actors copulate upon the stage.

The brougham[8] was waiting, and Mrs. Popham of Littlecote, without speaking a word or even looking at me, immediately secreted herself inside it. Nor could Lady Carnarvon bring herself to face me. She took my hand, and said in a tremulous voice—her elderly cheeks were flushed with emotion—"I do hope, Miss Stephen, that the evening has

---

7. Expensive seats.   8. Closed carriage.

not tired you very much." Then she stepped into the carriage, and the two bereaved ladies returned to Bruton Street. George meanwhile had secured a cab. He was much confused, and yet very angry. I could see that my remarks at dinner upon the dialogues of Plato rankled bitterly in his mind. And he told the cabman to go, not back to Hyde Park Gate as I hoped, but on to Melbury Road.

"It's quite early still," he said in his most huffy manner as he sat down. "And I think you want a little practice in how to behave to strangers. It's not your fault of course, but you have been out much less than most girls of your age." So it appeared that my education was to be continued, and that I was about to have another lesson in the art of behaviour at the house of Mrs. Holman Hunt.[9] She was giving a large evening party. Melbury Road was lined with hansoms, four-wheelers, hired flies, and an occasional carriage drawn by a couple of respectable family horses. "A very *dritte*[1] crowd", said George disdainfully as we took our place in the queue. Indeed all our old family friends were gathered together in the Moorish Hall, and directly I came in I recognised the Stillmans, the Lushingtons, the Montgomeries, the Morrises, the Burne-Joneses—Mr. Gibbs, Professor Wolstenholme and General Beadle would certainly have been there too had they not all been sleeping for many years beneath the sod. The effect of the Moorish Hall, after Bruton Street, was garish, a little eccentric, and certainly very dowdy. The ladies were intense and untidy; the gentlemen had fine foreheads and short evening trousers, in some cases revealing a pair of bright red Pre-Raphaelite socks. George stepped among them like a Prince in disguise. I soon attached myself to a little covey of Kensington ladies who were being conveyed by Gladys Holman Hunt across the Moorish Hall to the studio. There we found old Holman Hunt himself dressed in a long Jaeger dressing gown, holding forth to a large gathering about the ideas which had inspired him in painting "The Light of the World," a copy of which stood upon an easel. He sipped cocoa and stroked his flowing beard as he talked, and we sipped cocoa and shifted our shawls—for the room was chilly—as we listened. Occasionally some of us strayed off to examine with reverent murmurs other bright pictures upon other easels, but the tone of the assembly was devout, high-minded, and to me after the tremendous experiences of the evening, soothingly and almost childishly simple. George was never lacking in respect for old men of recognised genius, and he now advanced with his opera hat pressed beneath his arm; drew his feet together, and made a profound bow over Holman Hunt's hand. Holman Hunt had no notion who he was, or indeed who any of us were; but went on sip-

---

9. Wife of William Holman Hunt (1827–1910), well-known Victorian painter; one of his most famous paintings is *The Light of the World*.
1. I.e., third-rate (German: third).

ping his cocoa, stroking his beard, and explaining what ideas had inspired him in painting "The Light of the World," until we left.

At last—at last—the evening was over.

I went up to my room, took off my beautiful white satin dress, and unfastened the three pink carnations which had been pinned to my breast by the Jews' harp. Was it really possible that tomorrow I should open my Greek dictionary and go on spelling out the dialogues of Plato with Miss Case? I felt I knew much more about the dialogues of Plato than Miss Case could ever do. I felt old and experienced and disillusioned and angry, amused and excited, full of mystery, alarm and bewilderment. In a confused whirlpool of sensation I stood slipping off my petticoats, withdrew my long white gloves, and hung my white silk stockings over the back of a chair. Many different things were whirling round in my mind—diamonds and countesses, copulations, the dialogues of Plato, Mad Dick Popham and "The Light of the World." Ah, how pleasant it would be to stretch out in bed, fall asleep and forget them all!

Sleep had almost come to me. The room was dark. The house silent. Then, creaking stealthily, the door opened; treading gingerly, someone entered. "Who?" I cried. "Don't be frightened," George whispered. "And don't turn on the light, oh beloved. Beloved—" and he flung himself on my bed, and took me in his arms.

Yes, the old ladies of Kensington and Belgravia never knew that George Duckworth was not only father and mother, brother and sister to those poor Stephen girls; he was their lover also.

1921?   1976

A Woman's College from Outside

The feathery-white moon never let the sky grow dark; all night the chestnut blossoms were white in the green, and dim was the cow-parsley in the meadows. Neither to Tartary nor to Arabia went the wind of the Cambridge courts, but lapsed dreamily in the midst of grey-blue clouds over the roofs of Newnham.[1] There, in the garden, if she needed space to wander, she might find it among the trees; and as none but women's faces could meet her face, she might unveil it, blank, featureless, and gaze into rooms where at that hour, blank, featureless, eyelids white over eyes, ringless hands extended upon sheets, slept innumerable women. But here and there a light still burned.

A double light one might figure in Angela's room, seeing how bright

1. A woman's college at Cambridge, England, connected with Cambridge University.

Angela herself was, and how bright came back the reflection of herself from the square glass. The whole of her was perfectly delineated—perhaps the soul. For the glass held up an untrembling image—white and gold, red slippers, pale hair with blue stones in it, and never a ripple or shadow to break the smooth kiss of Angela and her reflection in the glass, as if she were glad to be Angela. Anyhow the moment was glad—the bright picture hung in the heart of night, the shrine hollowed in the nocturnal blackness. Strange indeed to have this visible proof of the rightness of things; this lily floating flawless upon Time's pool, fearless, as if this were sufficient—this reflection. Which meditation she betrayed by turning, and the mirror held nothing at all, or only the brass bedstead, and she, running here and there, patting, and darting, became like a woman in a house, and changed again, pursing her lips over a black book and marking with her finger what surely could not be a firm grasp of the science of economics. Only Angela Williams was at Newnham for the purpose of earning her living, and could not forget even in moments of impassioned adoration the cheques of her father at Swansea: her mother washing in the scullery: pink frocks out to dry on the line; tokens that even the lily no longer floats flawless upon the pool, but has a name on a card like another.

A. Williams—one may read it in the moonlight; and next to it some Mary or Eleanor, Mildred, Sarah, Phoebe upon square cards on their doors. All names, nothing but names. The cool white light withered them and starched them until it seemed as if the only purpose of all these names was to rise martially in order should there be a call on them to extinguish a fire, suppress an insurrection, or pass an examination. Such is the power of names written upon cards pinned upon doors. Such too the resemblance, what with tiles, corridors, and bedroom doors, to dairy or nunnery, a place of seclusion or discipline, where the bowl of milk stands cool and pure and there's a great washing of linen.

At that very moment soft laughter came from behind a door. A prim-voiced clock struck the hour—one, two. Now if the clock were issuing his commands, they were disregarded. Fire, insurrection, examination, were all snowed under by laughter, or softly uprooted, the sound seeming to bubble up from the depths and gently waft away the hour, rules, discipline. The bed was strewn with cards. Sally was on the floor. Helena in the chair. Good Bertha clasping her hands by the fireplace. A. Williams came in yawning.

"Because it's utterly and intolerably damnable," said Helena.

"Damnable," echoed Bertha. Then yawned.

"We're not eunuchs."

"I saw her slipping in by the back gate with that old hat on. They don't want us to know."

"They?" said Angela. "She."

Then the laughter.

The cards were spread, falling with their red and yellow faces on the table, and hands were dabbled in the cards. Good Bertha, leaning with her head against the chair, sighed profoundly. For she would willingly have slept, but since night is free pasturage, a limitless field, since night is unmoulded richness, one must tunnel into its darkness. One must hang it with jewels. Night was shared in secret, day browsed on by the whole flock. The blinds were up. A mist was on the garden. Sitting on the floor by the window (while the others played), body, mind, both together, seemed blown through the air, to trail across the bushes. Ah, but she desired to stretch out in bed and to sleep! She believed that no one felt her desire for sleep; she believed humbly—sleepily—with sudden nods and lurchings, that other people were wide awake. When they laughed all together a bird chirped in its sleep out in the garden, as if the laughter—

Yes, as if the laughter (for she dozed now) floated out much like mist and attached itself by soft elastic shreds to plants and bushes, so that the garden was vaporous and clouded. And then, swept by the wind, the bushes would bow themselves and the white vapours blow off across the world.

From all the rooms where women slept this vapour issued, attaching itself to shrubs, like mist, and then blew freely out into the open. Elderly women slept, who would on waking immediately clasp the ivory rod of office. Now smooth and colourless, reposing deeply, they lay surrounded, lay supported, by the bodies of youth recumbent or grouped at the window; pouring forth into the garden this bubbling laughter, this irresponsible laughter: this laughter of mind and body floating away rules, hours, discipline: immensely fertilising, yet formless, chaotic, trailing and straying and tufting the rose-bushes with shreds of vapour.

"Ah," breathed Angela, standing at the window in her nightgown. Pain was in her voice. She leant her head out. The mist was cleft as if her voice parted it. She had been talking, while the others played, to Alice Avery, about Bamborough Castle;[2] the colour of the sands at evening; upon which Alice said she would write and settle the day, in August, and stooping, kissed her, at least touched her head with her hand, and Angela, positively unable to sit still, like one possessed of a wind-lashed sea in her heart, roamed up and down the room (the witness of such a scene) throwing her arms out to relieve this excitement, this astonishment at the incredible stooping of the miraculous tree with the golden fruit at its summit—hadn't it dropped into her arms? She held it glowing to her breast, a thing not to be touched, thought of, or spoken about, but left to glow there. And then, slowly putting there her stock-

2. A medieval castle on the northeastern coast of England.

ings, there her slippers, folding her petticoat neatly on top, Angela, her other name being Williams, realised—how could she express it?—that after the dark churning of myriad ages here was light at the end of the tunnel; life; the world. Beneath her it lay—all good; all lovable. Such was her discovery.

Indeed, how could one then feel surprise if, lying in bed, she could not close her eyes?—something irresistibly unclosed them—if in the shallow darkness chair and chest of drawers looked stately, and the looking-glass precious with its ashen hint of day? Sucking her thumb like a child (her age nineteen last November), she lay in this good world, this new world, this world at the end of the tunnel, until a desire to see it or forestall it drove her, tossing her blankets, to guide herself to the window, and there, looking out upon the garden, where the mist lay, all the windows open, one fiery-bluish, something murmuring in the distance, the world of course, and the morning coming, "Oh," she cried, as if in pain.

1926, 1977

The New Dress

Mabel had her first serious suspicion that something was wrong as she took her cloak off and Mrs. Barnet, while handing her the mirror and touching the brushes and thus drawing her attention, perhaps rather markedly, to all the appliances for tidying and improving hair, complexion, clothes, which existed on the dressing table, confirmed the suspicion—that it was not right, not quite right, which growing stronger as she went upstairs and springing at her, with conviction as she greeted Clarissa Dalloway, she went straight to the far end of the room, to a shaded corner where a looking-glass hung and looked. No! It was not right. And at once the misery which she always tried to hide, the profound dissatisfaction—the sense she had had, ever since she was a child, of being inferior to other people—set upon her, relentlessly, remorselessly, with an intensity which she could not beat off, as she would when she woke at night at home, by reading Borrow or Scott;[1] for oh these men, oh these women, all were thinking—"What's Mabel wearing? What a fright she looks! What a hideous new dress!"—their eyelids flickering as they came up and then their lids shutting rather tight. It was her own appalling inadequacy; her cowardice; her mean, water-sprinkled blood that depressed her. And at once the whole of the

---

1. George Borrow (1803–1881), English author of adventure novels; Sir Walter Scott (1771–1832), popular author of historical adventures and romances.

room where, for ever so many hours, she had planned with the little dressmaker how it was to go, seemed sordid, repulsive; and her own drawing-room so shabby, and herself, going out, puffed up with vanity as she touched the letters on the hall table and said: "How dull!" to show off—all this now seemed unutterably silly, paltry, and provincial. All this had been absolutely destroyed, shown up, exploded, the moment she came into Mrs. Dalloway's drawing-room.

What she had thought that evening when, sitting over the teacups, Mrs. Dalloway's invitation came, was that, of course, she could not be fashionable. It was absurd to pretend it even—fashion meant cut, meant style, meant thirty guineas at least—but why not be original? Why not be herself, anyhow? And, getting up, she had taken that old fashion book of her mother's, a Paris fashion book of the time of the Empire, and had thought how much prettier, more dignified, and more womanly they were then, and so set herself—oh, it was foolish—trying to be like them, pluming herself in fact, upon being modest and old-fashioned and very charming, giving herself up, no doubt about it, to an orgy of self-love, which deserved to be chastised, and so rigged herself out like this.

But she dared not look in the glass. She could not face the whole horror—the pale yellow, idiotically old-fashioned silk dress with its long skirt and its high sleeves and its waist and all the things that looked so charming in the fashion book, but not on her, not among all these ordinary people. She felt like a dressmaker's dummy standing there, for young people to stick pins into.

"But, my dear, it's perfectly charming!" Rose Shaw said, looking her up and down with that little satirical pucker of the lips which she expected—Rose herself being dressed in the height of the fashion, precisely like everybody else, always.

We are all like flies trying to crawl over the edge of the saucer, Mabel thought, and repeated the phrase as if she were crossing herself, as if she were trying to find some spell to annul this pain, to make this agony endurable. Tags of Shakespeare, lines from books she had read ages ago, suddenly came to her when she was in agony, and she repeated them over and over again. "Flies trying to crawl," she repeated. If she could say that over often enough and make herself see the flies, she would become numb, chill, frozen, dumb. Now she could see flies crawling slowly out of a saucer of milk with their wings stuck together; and she strained and strained (standing in front of the looking-glass, listening to Rose Shaw) to make herself see Rose Shaw and all the other people there as flies, trying to hoist themselves out of something, or into something, meagre, insignificant, toiling flies. But she could not see them like that, not other people. She saw herself like that—she was a fly, but the others were dragonflies, butterflies, beautiful insects, dancing, fluttering, skimming, while she alone dragged herself up out of the saucer. (Envy and spite, the most detestable of the vices, were her chief faults.)

"I feel like some dowdy, decrepit, horribly dingy old fly," she said, making Robert Haydon stop just to hear her say that, just to reassure herself by furbishing up a poor weak-kneed phrase and so showing how detached she was, how witty, that she did not feel in the least out of anything. And, of course, Robert Haydon answered something quite polite, quite insincere, which she saw through instantly, and said to herself, directly he went (again from some book), "Lies, lies, lies!" For a party makes things either much more real, or much less real, she thought; she saw in a flash to the bottom of Robert Haydon's heart; she saw through everything. She saw the truth. *This* was true, this drawing-room, this self, and the other false. Miss Milan's little workroom was really terribly hot, stuffy, sordid. It smelt of clothes and cabbage cooking; and yet, when Miss Milan put the glass in her hand, and she looked at herself with the dress on, finished, an extraordinary bliss shot through her heart. Suffused with light, she sprang into existence. Rid of cares and wrinkles, what she had dreamed of herself was there—a beautiful woman. Just for a second (she had not dared look longer, Miss Milan wanted to know about the length of the skirt), there looked at her, framed in the scrolloping[2] mahogany, a grey-white, mysteriously smiling, charming girl, the core of herself, the soul of herself; and it was not vanity only, not only self-love that made her think it good, tender, and true. Miss Milan said that the skirt could not well be longer; if anything the skirt, said Miss Milan, puckering her forehead, considering with all her wits about her, must be shorter; and she felt, suddenly, honestly, full of love for Miss Milan, much, much fonder of Miss Milan than of any one in the whole world, and could have cried for pity that she should be crawling on the floor with her mouth full of pins, and her face red and her eyes bulging—that one human being should be doing this for another, and she saw them all as human beings merely, and herself going off to her party, and Miss Milan pulling the cover over the canary's cage, or letting him pick a hemp-seed from between her lips, and the thought of it, of this side of human nature and its patience and its endurance and its being content with such miserable, scanty, sordid, little pleasures filled her eyes with tears.

And now the whole thing had vanished. The dress, the room, the love, the pity, the scrolloping looking-glass, and the canary's cage—all had vanished, and here she was in a corner of Mrs. Dalloway's drawing-room, suffering tortures, woken wide awake to reality.

But it was all so paltry, weak-blooded, and petty-minded to care so much at her age with two children, to be still so utterly dependent on

---

2. Carved with scrollwork.

people's opinions and not have principles or convictions, not to be able to say as other people did, "There's Shakespeare! There's death! We're all weevils in a captain's biscuit"—or whatever it was that people did say.

She faced herself straight in the glass; she pecked at her left shoulder; she issued out into the room, as if spears were thrown at her yellow dress from all sides. But instead of looking fierce or tragic, as Rose Shaw would have done—Rose would have looked like Boadicea[3]—she looked foolish and self-conscious, and simpered like a schoolgirl and slouched across the room, positively slinking, as if she were a beaten mongrel, and looked at a picture, an engraving. As if one went to a party to look at a picture! Everybody knew why she did it—it was from shame, from humiliation.

"Now the fly's in the saucer," she said to herself, "right in the middle, and can't get out, and the milk," she thought, rigidly staring at the picture, "is sticking its wings together."

"It's so old-fashioned," she said to Charles Burt, making him stop (which by itself he hated) on his way to talk to some one else.

She meant, or she tried to make herself think that she meant, that it was the picture and not her dress, that was old-fashioned. And one word of praise, one word of affection from Charles would have made all the difference to her at the moment. If he had only said, "Mabel, you're looking charming to-night!" it would have changed her life. But then she ought to have been truthful and direct. Charles said nothing of the kind, of course. He was malice itself. He always saw through one, especially if one were feeling particularly mean, paltry, or feeble-minded.

"Mabel's got a new dress!" he said, and the poor fly was absolutely shoved into the middle of the saucer. Really, he would like her to drown, she believed. He had no heart, no fundamental kindness, only a veneer of friendliness. Miss Milan was much more real, much kinder. If only one could feel that and stick to it, always. "Why," she asked herself—replying to Charles much too pertly, letting him see that she was out of temper, or "ruffled" as he called it ("Rather ruffled?" he said and went on to laugh at her with some woman over there)—"Why," she asked herself "can't I feel one thing always, feel quite sure that Miss Milan is right, and Charles wrong and stick to it, feel sure about the canary and pity and love and not be whipped all round in a second by coming into a room full of people? It was her odious, weak, vacillating character again, always giving at the critical moment and not being seriously interested in conchology,[4] etymology, botany, archeology, cut-

---

3. Ancient queen of Britain, who gathered tribes against the invading Romans.   4. Study of shells.

ting up potatoes and watching them fructify like Mary Dennis, like Violet Searle.

Then Mrs. Holman, seeing her standing there, bore down upon her. Of course a thing like a dress was beneath Mrs. Holman's notice, with her family always tumbling downstairs or having the scarlet fever. Could Mable tell her if Elmthorpe was ever let for August and September? Oh, it was a conversation that bored her unutterably!—it made her furious to be treated like a house agent or a messenger boy, to be made use of. Not to have value, that was it, she thought, trying to grasp something hard, something real, while she tried to answer sensibly about the bathroom and the south aspect and the hot water to the top of the house; and all the time she could see little bits of her yellow dress in the round looking-glass which made them all the size of boot-buttons or tadpoles; and it was amazing to think how much humiliation and agony and self-loathing and effort and passionate ups and downs of feeling were contained in a thing the size of a threepenny bit. And what was still odder, this thing, this Mabel Waring, was separate, quite disconnected; and though Mrs. Holman (the black button) was leaning forward and telling her how her eldest boy had strained his heart running, she could see her, too, quite detached in the looking-glass, and it was impossible that the black dot, leaning forward, gesticulating, should make the yellow dot, sitting solitary, self-centred, feel what the black dot was feeling, yet they pretended.

"So impossible to keep boys quiet"—that was the kind of thing one said.

And Mrs. Holman, who could never get enough sympathy and snatched what little there was greedily, as if it were her right (but she deserved much more for there was her little girl who had come down this morning with a swollen knee-joint), took this miserable offering and looked at it suspiciously, grudgingly, as if it were a halfpenny when it ought to have been a pound and put it away in her purse, must put up with it, mean and miserly though it was, times being hard, so very hard; and on she went, creaking, injured Mrs. Holman, about the girl with the swollen joints. Ah, it was tragic, this greed, this clamour of human beings, like a row of cormorants, barking and flapping their wings for sympathy—it was tragic, could one have felt it and not merely pretended to feel it!

But in her yellow dress to-night she could not wring out one drop more; she wanted it all, all for herself. She knew (she kept on looking into the glass, dipping into that dreadfully showing-up blue pool) that she was condemned, despised, left like this in a backwater, because of her being like this a feeble, vacillating creature; and it seemed to her that the yellow dress was a penance which she had deserved, and if she had been dressed like Rose Shaw, in lovely, clinging green with a ruffle of swansdown, she would have deserved that; and she thought that there was no escape for her—none whatever. But it was not her fault altogether, after all. It was being one of a family of ten; never having money enough, always skimping and paring; and her mother carrying great cans, and the linoleum worn on the stair edges, and one sordid little domestic tragedy after another—nothing catastrophic, the sheep farm failing, but not utterly; her eldest brother marrying beneath him but not very much—there was no romance, nothing extreme about them all. They petered out respectably in seaside resorts; every watering-place had one of her aunts even now asleep in some lodging with the front windows not quite facing the sea. That was so like them—they had to squint at things always. And she had done the same—she was just like her aunts. For all her dreams of living in India, married to some hero like Sir Henry Lawrence,[5] some empire builder (still the sight of a native in a turban filled her with romance), she had failed utterly. She had married Hubert, with his safe, permanent underling's job in the Law Courts, and they managed tolerably in a smallish house, without proper maids, and hash when she was alone or just bread and butter, but now and then—Mrs. Holman was off, thinking her the most dried-up, unsympathetic twig she had ever met, absurdly dressed, too, and would tell every one about Mabel's fantastic appearance—now and then, thought Mabel Waring, left alone on the blue sofa, punching the cushion in order to look occupied, for she would not join Charles Burt and Rose Shaw, chattering like magpies and perhaps laughing at her by the fireplace—now and then, there did come to her delicious moments, reading the other night in bed, for instance, or down by the sea on the sand in the sun, at Easter—let her recall it—a great tuft of pale sandgrass standing all twisted like a shock of spears against the sky, which was blue like a smooth china egg, so firm, so hard, and then the melody of the waves—"Hush, hush," they said, and the children's shouts paddling—yes, it was a divine moment, and there she lay, she felt, in the hand of the Goddess who was the world; rather a hard-hearted, but very beautiful Goddess, a little lamb laid on the altar (one did think these silly things, and it didn't matter so long as one never said them). And also with Hubert sometimes she had quite unexpectedly—carving the mutton for Sunday lunch, for no reason, opening a letter, coming into a room—divine moments, when she said to herself (for she would never say this to anybody else), "This is it. This has happened. This is it!" And the other way about it was equally surprising—that is, when everything was arranged—music, weather, holidays, every reason for happiness was there—then nothing happened at all. One wasn't happy. It was flat, just flat, that was all.

Her wretched self again, no doubt! She had always been a fretful, weak, unsatisfactory mother, a wobbly wife, lolling about in a kind of twilight existence with nothing very clear or very bold, or more one thing than another, like all her brothers and sisters, except perhaps

5. English general in India (1806–1857), who died in battle.

Fanny stooped, with her ears full of the music, to look for the pin on the floor.

The words gave her an extraordinary shock, as Miss Craye struck the last chord of the Bach fugue. Did Miss Craye actually go to Slater's and buy pins then, Fanny Wilmot asked herself, transfixed for a moment. Did she stand at the counter waiting like anybody else, and was she given a bill with coppers wrapped in it, and did she slip them into her purse and then, an hour later, stand by her dressing table and take out the pins? What need had she of pins? For she was not so much dressed as cased, like a beetle compactly in its sheath, blue in winter, green in summer. What need had she of pins—Julia Craye—who lived, it seemed, in the cool glassy world of Bach fugues, playing to herself what she liked, and only consenting to take one or two pupils at the Archer Street College of Music (so the Principal, Miss Kingston, said) as a special favour to herself, who had "the greatest admiration for her in every way." Miss Craye was left badly off, Miss Kingston was afraid, at her brother's death. Oh, they used to have such lovely things, when they lived at Salisbury, and her brother Julius was, of course, a very well-known man: a famous archæologist. It was a great privilege to stay with them, Miss Kingston said ("My family had always known them—they were regular Canterbury[1] people," Miss Kingston said), but a little frightening for a child; one had to be careful not to slam the door or bounce into the room unexpectedly. Miss Kingston, who gave little character sketches like this on the first day of term while she received cheques and wrote out receipts for them, smiled here. Yes, she had been rather a tomboy; she had bounced in and set all those green Roman glasses and things jumping in their case. The Crayes were not used to children. The Crayes were none of them married. They kept cats; the cats, one used to feel, knew as much about the Roman urns and things as anybody.

"Far more than I did!" said Miss Kingston brightly, writing her name across the stamp in her dashing, cheerful, full-bodied hand, for she had always been practical. That was how she made her living, after all.

Perhaps then, Fanny Wilmot thought, looking for the pin, Miss Craye said that about "Slater's pins having no points," at a venture. None of the Crayes had ever married. She knew nothing about pins—nothing whatever. But she wanted to break the spell that had fallen on the house; to break the pane of glass which separated them from other people. When Polly Kingston, that merry little girl, had slammed the door and made the Roman vases jump, Julius, seeing that no harm was done (that would be his first instinct) looked, for the case was stood in the window, at Polly skipping home across the fields; looked with the look his sister often had, that lingering, driving look.

1. A city in the south of England.

"Stars, sun, moon," it seemed to say, "the daisy in the grass, fires, frost on the window pane, my heart goes out to you. But," it always seemed to add, "you break, you pass, you go." And simultaneously it covered the intensity of both these states of mind with "I can't reach you—I can't get at you," spoken wistfully, frustratedly. And the stars faded, and the child went. That was the kind of spell that was the glassy surface, that Miss Craye wanted to break by showing, when she had played Bach beautifully as a reward to a favourite pupil (Fanny Wilmot knew that she was Miss Craye's favourite pupil), that she, too, knew, like other people, about pins. Slater's pins had no points.

Yes, the "famous archæologist" had looked like that too. "The famous archæologist"—as she said that, endorsing cheques, ascertaining the day of the month, speaking so brightly and frankly, there was in Miss Kingston's voice an indescribable tone which hinted at something odd; something queer in Julius Craye; it was the very same thing that was odd perhaps in Julia too. One could have sworn, thought Fanny Wilmot, as she looked for the pin, that at parties, meetings (Miss Kingston's father was a clergyman), she had picked up some piece of gossip, or it might only have been a smile, or a tone when his name was mentioned, which had given her "a feeling" about Julius Craye. Needless to say, she had never spoken about it to anybody. Probably she scarcely knew what she meant by it. But whenever she spoke of Julius, or heard him mentioned, that was the first thing that came to mind; and it was a seductive thought; there was something odd about Julius Craye.

It was so that Julia looked too, as she sat half turned on the music stool, smiling. It's on the field, it's on the pane, it's in the sky—beauty; and I can't get at it; I can't have it—I, she seemed to add, with that little clutch of the hand which was so characteristic, who adore it so passionately, would give the whole world to possess it! And she picked up the carnation which had fallen on the floor, while Fanny searched for the pin. She crushed it, Fanny felt, voluptuously in her smooth veined hands stuck about with water-coloured rings set in pearls. The pressure of her fingers seemed to increase all that was most brilliant in the flower; to set it off; to make it more frilled, fresh, immaculate. What was odd in her, and perhaps in her brother, too, was that this crush and grasp of the finger was combined with a perpetual frustration. So it was even now with the carnation. She had her hands on it; she pressed it; but she did not possess it, enjoy it, not entirely and altogether.

None of the Crayes had married, Fanny Wilmot remembered. She had in mind how one evening when the lesson had lasted longer than usual and it was dark, Julia Craye had said "it's the use of men, surely, to protect us," smiling at her that same odd smile, as she stood fastening her cloak, which made her, like the flower, conscious to her finger tips of youth and brilliance, but, like the flower, too, Fanny suspected, made her feel awkward.

"Oh, but I don't want protection," Fanny had laughed, and when Julia Craye, fixing on her that extraordinary look, had said she was not so sure of that, Fanny positively blushed under the admiration in her eyes.

It was the only use of men, she had said. Was it for that reason then, Fanny wondered, with her eyes on the floor, that she had never married? After all, she had not lived all her life in Salisbury. "Much the nicest part of London," she had said once, "(but I'm speaking of fifteen or twenty years ago) is Kensington.[2] One was in the Gardens in ten minutes—it was like the heart of the country. One could dine out in one's slippers without catching cold. Kensington—it was like a village then, you know," she had said.

Here she broke off, to denounce acridly the draughts in the Tubes.[3]

"It was the use of men," she had said, with a queer wry acerbity. Did that throw any light on the problem why she had not married? One could imagine every sort of scene in her youth, when with her good blue eyes, her straight firm nose, her air of cool distinction, her piano playing, her rose flowering with chaste passion in the bosom of her muslin dress, she had attracted first the young men to whom such things, the china tea cups and the silver candlesticks and the inlaid table, for the Crayes had such nice things, were wonderful; young men not sufficiently distinguished; young men of the cathedral town with ambitions. She had attracted them first, and then her brother's friends from Oxford or Cambridge. They would come down in the summer; row her on the river; continue the argument about Browning[4] by letter; and arrange perhaps, on the rare occasions when she stayed in London, to show her—Kensington Gardens?

"Much the nicest part of London—Kensington (I'm speaking of fifteen or twenty years ago)," she had said once. One was in the gardens in ten minutes—in the heart of the country. One could make that yield what one liked, Fanny Wilmot thought, single out, for instance, Mr. Sherman, the painter, an old friend of hers; make him call for her, by appointment, one sunny day in June; take her to have tea under the trees. (They had met, too, at those parties to which one tripped in slippers without fear of catching cold.) The aunt or other elderly relative was to wait there while they looked at the Serpentine.[5] They looked at the Serpentine. He may have rowed her across. They compared it with the Avon.[6] She would have considered the comparison very furiously. Views of rivers were important to her. She sat hunched a little, a little angular, though she was graceful then, steering. At the critical moment, for he had determined that he must speak now—it was his only chance

---

2. A fashionable district of London with an elegant park.
3. The London subway.
4. Robert Browning (1812–1889), English poet.
5. An artificial body of water in Hyde Park, London.
6. An English river.

of getting her alone—he was speaking with his head turned at an absurd angle, in his great nervousness, over his shoulder—at that very moment she interrupted fiercely. He would have them into the Bridge,[7] she cried. It was a moment of horror, of disillusionment, of revelation, for both of them. I can't have it, I can't possess it, she thought. He could not see why she had come then. With a great splash of his oar he pulled the boat round. Merely to snub him? He rowed her back and said good-bye to her.

The setting of that scene could be varied as one chose, Fanny Wilmot reflected. (Where had that pin fallen?) It might be Ravenna; or Edinburgh, where she had kept house for her brother. The scene could be changed; and the young man and the exact manner of it all, but one thing was constant—her refusal, and her frown, and her anger with herself afterwards, and her argument, and her relief—yes, certainly her immense relief. The very next day, perhaps, she would get up at six, put on her cloak, and walk all the way from Kensington to the river. She was so thankful that she had not sacrificed her right to go and look at things when they are at their best—before people are up, that is to say she could have her breakfast in bed if she liked. She had not sacrificed her independence.

Yes, Fanny Wilmot smiled, Julia had not endangered her habits. They remained safe; and her habits would have suffered if she had married. "They're ogres," she had said one evening, half laughing, when another pupil, a girl lately married, suddenly bethinking her that she would miss her husband, had rushed off in haste.

"They're ogres," she had said, laughing grimly. An ogre would have interfered perhaps with breakfast in bed; with walks at dawn down to the river. What would have happened (but one could hardly conceive this) had she had children. She took astonishing precautions against chills, fatigue, rich food, the wrong food, draughts, heated rooms, journeys in the Tube, for she could never determine which of these it was exactly that brought on those terrible headaches that gave her life the semblance of a battlefield. She was always engaged in outwitting the enemy, until it seemed as if the pursuit had its interest; could she have beaten the enemy finally she would have found life a little dull. As it was, the tug-of-war was perpetual—on the one side the nightingale or the view which she loved with passion—yes, for views and birds she felt nothing less than passion; on the other the damp path or the horrid long drag up a steep hill which would certainly make her good for nothing next day and bring on one of her headaches. When, therefore, from time to time, she managed her forces adroitly and brought off a visit to Hampton Court the week the crocuses—those glossy bright flowers

---

7. I.e., they were about to run into the bridge.

were her favourite—were at their best, it was a victory. It was something that lasted; something that mattered for ever. She strung the afternoon on the necklace of memorable days, which was not too long for
her to be able to recall this one or that one; this view, that city; to finger
it, to feel it, to savour, sighing, the quality that made it unique.

"It was so beautiful last Friday," she said, "that I determined I must
go there." So she had gone off to Waterloo on her great undertaking
—to visit Hampton Court—alone. Naturally, but perhaps foolishly,
one pitied her for the thing she never asked pity for (indeed she was reticent habitually, speaking of her health only as a warrior might speak of
his foe)—one pitied her for always doing everything alone. Her brother
was dead. Her sister was asthmatic. She found the climate of Edinburgh
good for her. It was too bleak for Julia. Perhaps, too, she found the associations painful, for her brother, the famous archæologist, had died
there; and she had loved her brother. She lived in a little house off the
Brompton Road entirely alone.

Fanny Wilmot saw the pin; she picked it up. She looked at Miss
Craye. Was Miss Craye so lonely? No, Miss Craye was steadily, bliss-
fully, if only for that moment, a happy woman. Fanny had surprised her
in a moment of ecstasy. She sat there, half turned away from the piano,
with her hands clasped in her lap holding the carnation upright, while
behind her was the sharp square of the window, uncurtained, purple in
the evening, intensely purple after the brilliant electric lights which
burnt unshaded in the bare music room. Julia Craye, sitting hunched
and compact holding her flower, seemed to emerge out of the London
night, seemed to fling it like a cloak behind her, it seemed, in its bare-
ness and intensity, the effluence of her spirit, something she had made
which surrounded her. Fanny stared.

All seemed transparent, for a moment, to the gaze of Fanny Wilmot,
as if looking through Miss Craye, she saw the very fountain of her being
spurting its pure silver drops. She saw back and back into the past behind her. She saw the green Roman vases stood in their case; heard the
choristers playing cricket; saw Julia quietly descend the curving steps on
to the lawn; then saw her pour out tea beneath the cedar tree; softly
enclosed the old man's hand in hers; saw her going round and about the
corridors of that ancient Cathedral dwelling place with towels in her
hand to mark them;[8] lamenting, as she went, the pettiness of daily life;
and slowly ageing, and putting away clothes when summer came, because at her age they were too bright to wear; and tending her father's
sickness; and cleaving her way ever more definitely as her will stiffened
towards her solitary goal; travelling frugally; counting the cost and
measuring out of her tight shut purse the sum needed for this journey

8. I.e., mark them for the laundry.

or for that old mirror; obstinately adhering, whatever people might say, in choosing her pleasures for herself. She saw Julia——

Julia blazed. Julia kindled. Out of the night she burnt like a dead white star. Julia opened her arms. Julia kissed her on the lips. Julia possessed it.

"Slater's pins have no points," Miss Craye said, laughing queerly and relaxing her arms as Fanny Wilmot pinned the flower to her breast with trembling fingers.

1928, 1944

From A Room of One's Own

[Shakespeare's Sister][1]

It was disappointing not to have brought back in the evening some important statement, some authentic fact. Women are poorer than men because—this or that. Perhaps now it would be better to give up seeking for the truth, and receiving on one's head an avalanche of opinion hot as lava, discolored as dishwater. It would be better to draw the curtains; to shut out distractions; to light the lamp; to narrow the inquiry and to ask the historian, who records not opinions but facts, to describe under what conditions women lived, not throughout the ages, but in England, say in the time of Elizabeth.

For it is a perennial puzzle why no woman wrote a word of that extraordinary literature when every other man, it seemed, was capable of song or sonnet. What were the conditions in which women lived, I asked myself; for fiction, imaginative work that is, is not dropped like a pebble upon the ground, as science may be; fiction is like a spider's web, attached ever so lightly perhaps, but still attached to life at all four corners. Often the attachment is scarcely perceptible; Shakespeare's plays, for instance, seem to hang there complete by themselves. But when the web is pulled askew, hooked up at the edge, torn in the middle, one remembers that these webs are not spun in midair by incorporeal creatures, but are the work of suffering human beings, and are attached to grossly material things, like health and money and the houses we live in.

I went, therefore, to the shelf where the histories stand and took down one of the latest, Professor Trevelyan's *History of England*.[2]

---

1. This selection is taken from Chapter Three and the conclusion of the final chapter. In the previous chapter Woolf visits the British Museum library in an attempt to trace the different fates of men and women in history.

2. G. M. Trevelyan's *History of England* (1926), then the standard one-volume history.

Once more I looked up Women, found "position of," and turned to the pages indicated. "Wife-beating," I read, "was a recognized right of man, and was practiced without shame by high as well as low. . . . Similarly," the historian goes on, "the daughter who refused to marry the gentleman of her parents' choice was liable to be locked up, beaten, and flung about the room, without any shock being inflicted on public opinion. Marriage was not an affair of personal affection, but of family avarice, particularly in the 'chivalrous' upper classes. . . . Betrothal often took place while one or both of the parties was in the cradle, and marriage when they were scarely out of the nurses' charge." That was about 1470, soon after Chaucer's time. The next reference to the position of women is some two hundred years later, in the time of the Stuarts. "It was still the exception for women of the upper and middle class to choose their own husbands, and when the husband had been assigned, he was lord and master, so far at least as law and custom could make him. Yet even so," Professor Trevelyan concludes, "neither Shakespeare's women nor those of authentic seventeenth-century memoirs, like the Verneys and the Hutchinsons,[3] seem wanting in personality and character." Certainly, if we consider it, Cleopatra must have had a way with her; Lady Macbeth, one would suppose, had a will of her own; Rosalind, one might conclude, was an attractive girl.[4] Professor Trevelyan is speaking no more than the truth when he remarks that Shakespeare's women do not seem wanting in personality and character. Not being a historian, one might go even further and say that women have burnt like beacons in all the works of all the poets from the beginning of time—Clytemnestra, Antigone, Cleopatra, Lady Macbeth, Phèdre, Cressida, Rosalind, Desdemona, the Duchess of Malfi, among the dramatists; then among the prose writers: Millamant, Clarissa, Becky Sharp, Anna Karenina, Emma Bovary, Madame de Guermantes[5]—the names flock to mind, nor do they recall women "lacking in personality and character." Indeed, if woman had no existence save in the fiction written by men, one would imagine her a person of the utmost importance; very various; heroic and mean; splendid and sordid; infinitely beautiful and hideous in the extreme; as great as a man, some

---

3. "The ideal family life of the period [1640–1650] that ended in such tragic political division has been recorded once and for all in the *Memoirs of the Verney Family*" (Trevelyan, *History of England*). Lucy Hutchinson wrote a biography of her husband, Colonel John Hutchinson (1616–1684).
4. Heroines of three plays by Shakespeare, *Antony and Cleopatra*, *Macbeth*, and *As You Like It*.

5. Characters in, respectively, Aeschylus's *Agamemnon*, Sophocles' *Antigone*, Shakespeare's *Antony and Cleopatra* and *Macbeth*, Racine's *Phèdre*, Shakespeare's *Troilus and Cressida*, *As You Like It*, and *Othello*, Webster's *The Duchess of Malfi*, Congreve's *The Way of the World*, Richardson's *Clarissa*, Thackeray's *Vanity Fair*, Tolstoy's *Anna Karenina*, Flaubert's *Madame Bovary*, and Proust's *À la recherche du temps perdu*.

think even greater.[6] But this is woman in fiction. In fact, as Professor Trevelyan points out, she was locked up, beaten, and flung about the room.

A very queer, composite being thus emerges. Imaginatively she is of the highest importance; practically she is completely insignificant. She pervades poetry from cover to cover; she is all but absent from history. She dominates the lives of kings and conquerors in fiction; in fact she was the slave of any boy whose parents forced a ring upon her finger. Some of the most inspired words, some of the most profound thoughts in literature fall from her lips; in real life she could hardly read, could scarcely spell, and was the property of her husband.

It was certainly an odd monster that one made up by reading the historians first and the poets afterwards—a worm winged like an eagle; the spirit of life and beauty in a kitchen chopping up suet. But these monsters, however amusing to the imagination, have no existence in fact. What one must do to bring her to life was to think poetically and prosaically at one and the same moment, thus keeping in touch with fact —that she is Mrs. Martin, aged thirty-six, dressed in blue, wearing a black hat and brown shoes; but not losing sight of fiction either—that she is a vessel in which all sorts of spirits and forces are coursing and flashing perpetually. The moment, however, that one tries this method with the Elizabethan woman, one branch of illumination fails; one is held up by the scarcity of facts. One knows nothing detailed, nothing perfectly true and substantial about her. History scarcely mentions her. And I turned to Professor Trevelyan again to see what history meant to him. I found by looking at his chapter headings that it meant—

"The Manor Court and the Methods of Open-Field Agriculture . . . The Cistercians and Sheep-Farming . . . The Crusades . . . The University . . . The House of Commons . . . The Hundred Years' War . . . The Wars of the Roses . . . The Renaissance Scholars . . . The Dissolution of the Monasteries . . . Agrarian and Religious Strife . . . The Origin of English Sea-Power . . . The Armada . . . " and so on. Occasionally an individual woman is mentioned, an Elizabeth, or a Mary; a queen or a great lady. But by no possible means could

6. " 'It remains a strange and almost inexplicable fact that in Athena's city, where women were kept in almost Oriental suppression as odalisques or drudges, the stage should yet have produced figures like Clytemnestra and Cassandra, Atossa and Antigone, Phèdre and Medea, and all the other heroines who dominate play after play of the "misogynist" Euripides. But the paradox of this world where in real life a respectable woman could hardly show her face alone in the street, and yet on the stage woman equals or surpasses man, has never been satisfactorily explained. In modern tragedy the same predominance exists. At all events, a very cursory survey of Shakespeare's work (similarly with Webster, though not with Marlowe or Jonson) suffices to reveal how this dominance, this initiative of women, persists from Rosalind to Lady Macbeth. So too in Racine; six of his tragedies bear their heroines' names; and what male characters of his shall we set against Hermione and Andromaque, Bérénice and Roxane, Phèdre and Athalie? So again with Ibsen; what men shall we match with Solveig and Nora, Hedda and Hilda Wangel and Rebecca West?'—F. L. Lucas, *Tragedy*, pp. 114–15" [Woolf's note].

middle-class women with nothing but brains and character at their command have taken part in any one of the great movements which, brought together, constitute the historian's view of the past. Nor shall we find her in any collection of anecdotes. Aubrey[7] hardly mentions her. She never writes her own life and scarcely keeps a diary; there are only a handful of her letters in existence. She left no plays or poems by which we can judge her. What one wants, I thought—and why does not some brilliant student at Newnham or Girton[8] supply it?—is a mass of information; at what age did she marry; how many children had she as a rule; what was her house like; had she a room to herself; did she do the cooking; would she be likely to have a servant? All these facts lie somewhere, presumably, in parish registers and account books; the life of the average Elizabethan woman must be scattered about somewhere, could one collect it and make a book of it. It would be ambitious beyond my daring. I thought, looking about the shelves for books that were not there, to suggest to the students of those famous colleges that they should rewrite history, though I own that it often seems a little queer as it is, unreal, lopsided; but why should they not add a supplement to history? calling it, of course, by some inconspicuous name so that women might figure there without impropriety? For one often catches a glimpse of them in the lives of the great, whisking away into the background, concealing, I sometimes think, a wink, a laugh, perhaps a tear. And, after all, we have lives enough of Jane Austen; it scarcely seems necessary to consider again the influence of the tragedies of Joanna Baillie[9] upon the poetry of Edgar Allan Poe; as for myself, I should not mind if the homes and haunts of Mary Russell Mitford[1] were closed to the public for a century at least. But what I find deplorable, I continued, looking about the bookshelves again, is that nothing is known about women before the eighteenth century. I have no model in my mind to turn about this way and that. Here am I asking why women did not write poetry in the Elizabethan age, and I am not sure how they were educated; whether they were taught to write; whether they had sitting rooms to themselves; how many women had children before they were twenty-one; what, in short, they did from eight in the morning till eight at night. They had no money evidently; according to Professor Trevelyan they were married whether they liked it or not before they were out of the nursery, at fifteen or sixteen very likely. It would have been extremely odd, even upon this showing, had one of them suddenly written the plays of Shakespeare, I concluded, and I thought of that old gentleman, who is dead now, but was a bishop, I think, who declared

7. John Aubrey (1626–1697), English diarist.
8. The two women's colleges at Cambridge, England.
9. English poet and dramatist (1762–1851);
Poe (1809–1849), American poet and short story writer.
1. English poet and novelist, (1787–1855) best known for her sketches of rural life.

that it was impossible for any woman, past, present, or to come, to have the genius of Shakespeare. He wrote to the papers about it. He also told a lady who applied to him for information that cats do not as a matter of fact go to heaven, though they have, he added, souls of a sort. How much thinking those old gentlemen used to save one! How the borders of ignorance shrank back at their approach! Cats do not go to heaven. Women cannot write the plays of Shakespeare.

Be that as it may, I could not help thinking, as I looked at the works of Shakespeare on the shelf, that the bishop was right at least in this; it would have been impossible, completely and entirely, for any woman to have written the plays of Shakespeare in the age of Shakespeare. Let me imagine, since facts are so hard to come by, what would have happened had Shakespeare had a wonderfully gifted sister, called Judith, let us say. Shakespeare himself went, very probably—his mother was an heiress —to grammar school, where he may have learnt Latin—Ovid, Virgil, and Horace[2]—and the elements of grammar and logic. He was, it is well known, a wild boy who poached rabbits, perhaps shot a deer, and had, rather sooner than he should have done, to marry a woman in the neighborhood, who bore him a child rather quicker than was right. That escapade sent him to seek his fortune in London. He had, it seemed, a taste for the theater; he began by holding horses at the stage door. Very soon he got work in the theater, became a successful actor, and lived at the hub of the universe, meeting everybody, knowing everybody, practicing his art on the boards, exercising his wits in the streets, and even getting access to the palace of the queen. Meanwhile his extraordinarily gifted sister, let us suppose, remained at home. She was as adventurous, as imaginative, as agog to see the world as he was. But she was not sent to school. She had no chance of learning grammar and logic, let alone of reading Horace and Virgil. She picked up a book now and then, one of her brother's perhaps, and read a few pages. But then her parents came in and told her to mend the stockings or mind the stew and not moon about with books and papers. They would have spoken sharply but kindly, for they were substantial people who knew the conditions of life for a woman and loved their daughter—indeed, more likely than not she was the apple of her father's eye. Perhaps she scribbled some pages up in an apple loft on the sly, but was careful to hide them or set fire to them. Soon, however, before she was out of her teens, she was to be betrothed to the son of a neighboring wool-stapler.[3] She cried out that marriage was hateful to her, and for that she was severely beaten by her father. Then he ceased to scold her. He begged her instead not to hurt him, not to shame him in this matter of her

2. Three Latin poets of the Augustan age (27 B.C.–A.D. 14).

3. A dealer in wool, a "staple" product of sixteenth-century England.

marriage. He would give her a chain of beads or a fine petticoat, he said; and there were tears in his eyes. How could she disobey him? How could she break his heart? The force of her own gift alone drove her to it. She made up a small parcel of her belongings, let herself down by a rope one summer's night, and took the road to London. She was not seventeen. The birds that sang in the hedge were not more musical than she was. She had the quickest fancy, a gift like her brother's, for the tune of words. Like him, she had a taste for the theater. She stood at the stage door; she wanted to act, she said. Men laughed in her face. The manager—a fat, loose-lipped man—guffawed. He bellowed something about poodles dancing and women acting—no woman, he said, could possibly be an actress. He hinted—you can imagine what. She could get no training in her craft. Could she even seek her dinner in a tavern or roam the streets at midnight? Yet her genius was for fiction and lusted to feed abundantly upon the lives of men and women and the study of their ways. At last—for she was very young, oddly like Shakespeare the poet in her face, with the same gray eyes and rounded brows —at last Nick Greene the actor-manager took pity on her; she found herself with child by that gentleman and so—who shall measure the heat and violence of the poet's heart when caught and tangled in a woman's body?—killed herself one winter's night and lies buried at some crossroads where the omnibuses now stop outside the Elephant and Castle![4]

That, more or less, is how the story would run, I think, if a woman in Shakespeare's day had had Shakespeare's genius. But for my part, I agree with the deceased bishop, if such he was—it is unthinkable that any woman in Shakespeare's day should have had Shakespeare's genius. For genius like Shakespeare's is not born among laboring, uneducated, servile people. It was not born in England among the Saxons and the Britons. It is not born today among the working classes. How, then, could it have been born among women whose work began, according to Professor Trevelyan, almost before they were out of the nursery, who were forced to it by their parents and held to it by all the power of law and custom? Yet genius of a sort must have existed among women as it must have existed among the working classes. Now and again an Emily Brontë or a Robert Burns[5] blazes out and proves its presence. But certainly it never got itself on to paper. When, however, one reads of a witch being ducked, of a woman possessed by devils, of a wise woman selling herbs, or even of a very remarkable man who had a mother, then I think we are on the track of a lost novelist, a suppressed

4. Suicides were commonly buried at crossroads; the Elephant and Castle was a tavern located at a busy crossroads in the south of England.

5. Burns (1759–1796) was a working-class Scottish poet who wrote in his native dialect; Emily Brontë (1818–48) was an English poet and novelist.

poet, of some mute and inglorious[6] Jane Austen, some Emily Brontë who dashed her brains out on the moor or mopped and mowed about the highways crazed with the torture that her gift had put her to. Indeed, I would venture to guess that Anon, who wrote so many poems without signing them, was often a woman. It was a woman Edward Fitzgerald,[7] I think, suggested who made the ballads and the folk songs, crooning them to her children, beguiling her spinning with them, or the length of the winter's night.

This may be true or it may be false—who can say?—but what is true in it, so it seemed to me, reviewing the story of Shakespeare's sister as I had made it, is that any woman born with a great gift in the sixteenth century would certainly have gone crazed, shot herself, or ended her days in some lonely cottage outside the village, half witch, half wizard, feared and mocked at. For it needs little skill in psychology to be sure that a highly gifted girl who had tried to use her gift for poetry would have been so thwarted and hindered by other people, so tortured and pulled asunder by her own contrary instincts, that she must have lost her health and sanity to a certainty. No girl could have walked to London and stood at a stage door and forced her way into the presence of actor-managers without doing herself a violence and suffering an anguish which may have been irrational—for chastity may be a fetish invented by certain societies for unknown reasons—but were none the less inevitable. Chastity had then, it has even now, a religious importance in a woman's life, and has so wrapped itself round with nerves and instincts that to cut it free and bring it to the light of day demands courage of the rarest. To have lived a free life in London in the sixteenth century would have meant for a woman who was poet and playwright a nervous stress and dilemma which might well have killed her. Had she survived, whatever she had written would have been twisted and deformed, issuing from a strained and morbid imagination. And undoubtedly, I thought, looking at the shelf where there are no plays by women, her work would have gone unsigned. That refuge she would have sought certainly. It was the relic of the sense of chastity that dictated anonymity to women even so late as the nineteenth century. Currer Bell, George Eliot, George Sand,[8] all the victims of inner strife as their writings prove, sought ineffectively to veil themselves by using the name of a man. Thus they did homage to the convention, which if not implanted by the other sex was liberally encouraged by them (the chief glory of a woman is not to be talked of, said Pericles,[9] himself a much-talked-of man), that publicity in women is detestable. Anonymity runs in their blood. The desire to be veiled still possesses them.

---

6. An echo of Thomas Gray's *Elegy Written in a Country Churchyard* (1751): "Some mute inglorious Milton here may rest."

7. English poet and translator (1809–1883).

8. Male pen names of the novelists Charlotte Brontë, Marian Evans, and Aurore Dupin.

9. Athenian statesman and orator (495–429 B.C.).

I told you in the course of this paper that Shakespeare had a sister; but do not look for her in Sir Sidney Lee's[1] life of the poet. She died young—alas, she never wrote a word. She lies buried where the omnibuses now stop, opposite the Elephant and Castle. Now my belief is that this poet who never wrote a word and was buried at the crossroads still lives. She lives in you and in me, and in many other women who are not here tonight, for they are washing up the dishes and putting the children to bed. But she lives; for great poets do not die; they are continuing presences; they need only the opportunity to walk among us in the flesh. This opportunity, as I think, it is now coming within your power to give her. For my belief is that if we live another century or so —I am talking of the common life which is the real life and not of the little separate lives which we live as individuals—and have five hundred a year each of us and rooms of our own; if we have the habit of freedom and the courage to write exactly what we think; if we escape a little from the common sitting room and see human beings not always in their relation to each other but in relation to reality; and the sky, too, and the trees or whatever it may be in themselves; if we look past Milton's bogey,[2] for no human being should shut out the view; if we face the fact, for it is a fact, that there is no arm to cling to, but that we go alone and that our relation is to the world of reality and not only to the world of men and women, then the opportunity will come and the dead poet who was Shakespeare's sister will put on the body which she has so often laid down. Drawing her life from the lives of the unknown who were her forerunners, as her brother did before her, she will be born. As for her coming without that preparation, without that effort on our part, without that determination that when she is born again she shall find it possible to live and write her poetry, that we cannot expect, for that would be impossible. But I maintain that she would come if we worked for her, and that so to work, even in poverty and obscurity, is worth while.

1929

Professions for Women[1]

When your secretary invited me to come here, she told me that your Society is concerned with the employment of women and she suggested that I might tell you something about my own profesional experiences. It is true that I am a woman; it is true I am employed; but what

---

1. Biographer of Shakespeare (1859–1926).
2. John Milton (1608–1674), English poet; his epic poem *Paradise Lost* retells the story of Genesis 2, and portrays Eve as morally and intellectually inferior to Adam.
1. "A paper read to the Women's Service League" [Woolf's note].

professional experiences have I had? It is difficult to say. My profession is literature; and in that profession there are fewer experiences for women than in any other, with the exception of the stage—fewer, I mean, that are peculiar to women. For the road was cut many years ago—by Fanny Burney, by Aphra Behn, by Harriet Martineau, by Jane Austen, by George Eliot—[2] many famous women, and many more unknown and forgotten, have been before me, making the path smooth, and regulating my steps. Thus, when I came to write, there were very few material obstacles in my way. Writing was a reputable and harmless occupation. The family peace was not broken by the scratching of a pen. No demand was made upon the family purse. For ten and sixpence one can buy paper enough to write all the plays of Shakespeare —if one has a mind that way. Pianos and models, Paris, Vienna, and Berlin, masters and mistresses, are not needed by a writer. The cheapness of writing paper is, of course, the reason why women have succeeded as writers before they have succeeded in the other professions.

But to tell you my story—it is a simple one. You have only got to figure to yourselves a girl in a bedroom with a pen in her hand. She had only to move that pen from left to right—from ten o'clock to one. Then it occurred to her to do what is simple and cheap enough after all—to slip a few of those pages into a envelope, fix a penny stamp in the corner, and drop the envelope into the red box at the corner. It was thus that I became a journalist; and my effort was rewarded on the first day of the following month—a very glorious day it was for me—by a letter from an editor containing a check for one pound ten shillings and sixpence. But to show you how little I deserve to be called a professional woman, how little I know of the struggles and difficulties of such lives, I have to admit that instead of spending that sum upon bread and butter, rent, shoes and stockings, or butcher's bills, I went out and bought a cat—a beautiful cat, a Persian cat, which very soon involved me in bitter disputes with my neighbors.

What could be easier than to write articles and to buy Persian cats with the profits? But wait a moment. Articles have to be about something. Mine, I seem to remember, was about a novel by a famous man. And while I was writing this review, I discovered that if I were going to review books I should need to do battle with a certain phantom. And the phantom was a woman, and when I came to know her better I called her after the heroine of a famous poem, The Angel in the House.[3] It was she who used to come between me and my paper when I was writing reviews. It was she who bothered me and wasted my time and so

---

2. Fanny Burney (1752–1840), English novelist; Aphra Behn (1640–1689), English poet and playwright; Harriet Martineau (1802–1876), English economist, journalist, and novelist; Jane Austen (1775–1817), English novelist; George Eliot (1819–1880), English novelist.

3. A popular Victorian poem of idealized domestic life by Coventry Patmore (1823–1896).

tormented me that at last I killed her. You who come of a younger and happier generation may not have heard of her—you may not know what I mean by The Angel in the House. I will describe her as shortly as I can. She was intensely sympathetic. She was immensely charming. She was utterly unselfish. She excelled in the difficult arts of family life. She sacrificed herself daily. If there was chicken, she took the leg; if there was a draft she sat in it—in short she was so constituted that she never had a mind or a wish of her own, but preferred to sympathize always with the minds and wishes of others. Above all—I need not say it—she was pure. Her purity was supposed to be her chief beauty—her blushes, her great grace. In those days—the last of Queen Victoria— every house had its Angel. And when I came to write I encountered her with the very first words. The shadow of her wings fell on my page; I heard the rustling of her skirts in the room. Directly, that is to say, I took my pen in my hand to review that novel by a famous man, she slipped behind me and whispered: "My dear, you are a young woman. You are writing about a book that has been written by a man. Be sympathetic; be tender; flatter; deceive; use all the arts and wiles of our sex. Never let anybody guess that you have a mind of your own. Above all, be pure." And she made as if to guide my pen. I now record the one act for which I take some credit to myself, though the credit rightly belongs to some excellent ancestors of mine who left me a certain sum of money—shall we say five hundred pounds a year?—so that it was not necessary for me to depend solely on charm for my living. I turned upon her and caught her by the throat. I did my best to kill her. My excuse, if I were to be had up in a court of law, would be that I acted in self-defense. Had I not killed her she would have killed me. She would have plucked the heart out of my writing. For, as I found, directly I put pen to paper, you cannot review even a novel without having a mind of your own, without expressing what you think to be the truth about human relations, morality, sex. And all these questions, according to the Angel of the House, cannot be dealt with freely and openly by women; they must charm, they must conciliate, they must—to put it bluntly—tell lies if they are to succeed. Thus, whenever I felt the shadow of her wing or the radiance of her halo upon my page, I took up the inkpot and flung it at her. She died hard. Her fictitious nature was of great assistance to her. It is far harder to kill a phantom than a reality. She was always creeping back when I thought I had despatched her. Though I flatter myself that I killed her in the end, the struggle was severe; it took much time that had better have been spent upon learning Greek grammar; or in roaming the world in search of adventures. But it was a real experience; it was an experience that was bound to befall all women writers at that time. Killing the Angel in the House was part of the occupation of a woman writer.

But to continue my story. The Angel was dead; what then remained? You may say that what remained was a simple and common object—a young woman in a bedroom with an inkpot. In other words, now that she had rid herself of falsehood, that young woman had only to be herself. Ah, but what is "herself"? I mean, what is a woman? I assure you, I do not know. I do not believe that you know. I do not believe that anybody can know until she has expressed herself in all the arts and professions open to human skill. That indeed is one of the reasons why I have come here—out of respect for you, who are in process of showing us by your experiments what a woman is, who are in process of providing us, by your failures and successes, with that extremely important piece of information.

But to continue the story of my professional experiences. I made one pound ten and six by my first review; and I bought a Persian cat with the proceeds. Then I grew ambitious. A Persian cat is all very well, I said; but a Persian cat is not enough. I must have a motorcar. And it was thus that I became a novelist—for it is a very strange thing that people will give you a motorcar if you will tell them a story. It is a still stranger thing that there is nothing so delightful in the world as telling stories. It is far pleasanter than writing reviews of famous novels. And yet, if I am to obey your secretary and tell you my professional experiences as a novelist, I must tell you about a very strange experience that befell me as a novelist. And to understand it you must try first to imagine a novelist's state of mind. I hope I am not giving away professional secrets if I say that a novelist's chief desire is to be as unconscious as possible. He has to induce in himself a state of perpetual lethargy. He wants life to proceed with the utmost quiet and regularity. He wants to see the same faces, to read the same books, to do the same things day after day, month after month, while he is writing, so that nothing may break the illusion in which he is living—so that nothing may disturb or disquiet the mysterious nosings about, feelings around, darts, dashes, and sudden discoveries of that very shy and illusive spirit, the imagination. I suspect that this state is the same both for men and women. Be that as it may, I want you to imagine me writing a novel in a state of trance. I want you to figure to yourselves a girl sitting with a pen in her hand, which for minutes, and indeed for hours, she never dips into the inkpot. The image that comes to my mind when I think of this girl is the image of a fisherman lying sunk in dreams on the verge of a deep lake with a rod held out over the water. She was letting her imagination sweep unchecked round every rock and cranny of the world that lies submerged in the depths of our unconscious being. Now came the experience that I believe to be far commoner with women writers than with men. The line raced through the girl's fingers. Her imagination had rushed away. It had sought the pools, the depths, the dark places where the largest fish slumber. And then there was a smash. There was an explosion. There was foam and confusion. The imagination had dashed itself against something hard. The girl was roused from her dream. She was indeed in a state of the most acute and difficult distress. To speak without figure, she had thought of something, something about the body, about the passions which it was unfitting for her as a woman to say. Men, her reason told her, would be shocked. The consciousness of what men will say of a woman who speaks the truth about her passions had roused her from her artist's state of unconsciousness. She could write no more. The trance was over. Her imagination could work no longer. This I believe to be a very common experience with women writers—they are impeded by the extreme conventionality of the other sex. For though men sensibly allow themselves great freedom in these respects, I doubt that they realize or can control the extreme severity with which they condemn such freedom in women.

These then were two very genuine experiences of my own. These were two of the adventures of my professional life. The first—killing the Angel in the House—I think I solved. She died. But the second, telling the truth about my own experiences as a body, I do not think I solved. I doubt that any woman has solved it yet. The obstacles against her are still immensely powerful—and yet they are very difficult to define. Outwardly, what is simpler than to write books? Outwardly, what obstacles are there for a woman rather than for a man? Inwardly, I think, the case is very different; she has still many ghosts to fight, many prejudices to overcome. Indeed it will be a long time still, I think, before a woman can sit down to write a book without finding a phantom to be slain, a rock to be dashed against. And if this is so in literature, the freest of all professions for women, how is it in the new professions which you are now for the first time entering?

Those are the questions that I should like, had I time, to ask you. And indeed, if I have laid stress upon these professional experiences of mine, it is because I believe that they are, though in different forms, yours also. Even when the path is nominally open—when there is nothing to prevent a woman from being a doctor, a lawyer, a civil servant—there are many phantoms and obstacles, as I believe, looming in her way. To discuss and define them is I think of great value and importance; for thus only can the labor be shared, the difficulties be solved. But besides this, it is necessary also to discuss the ends and the aims for which we are fighting, for which we are doing battle with these formidable obstacles. Those aims cannot be taken for granted; they must be perpetually questioned and examined. The whole position, as I see it—here in this hall surrounded by women practicing for the first time in history I know not how many different professions—is one of extraordinary interest and importance. You have won rooms of your own in the house hitherto exclusively owned by men. You are able, though not without great labor and effort, to pay the rent. You are earning your five hundred pounds a year. But this freedom is only a beginning; the room is your own, but it is still bare. It has to be furnished; it has to be decorated; it has to be shared. How are you going to furnish it, how are you going to decorate it? With whom are you going to share it, and upon what terms? These, I think are questions of the utmost importance and interest. For the first time in history you are able to ask them; for the first time you are able to decide for yourselves what the answers should be. Willingly would I stay and discuss those questions and answers—but not tonight. My time is up; and I must cease.

1942

SUSAN GLASPELL
1882–1948

Cofounder in 1915 of the Provincetown Playhouse, Susan Glaspell was also a noted dramatist and prolific fiction writer. Her full-length play *The Verge* (1921), which experimented with the psychological portrayal of character, focused on the feminism of the New Woman, while her Pulitzer Prize-winning drama *Alison's House* (1930) presented a fictionalized portrait of a woman artist modeled on Emily Dickinson. She published ten novels and more than forty short stories. A *Jury of Her Peers*—a short-story version of her one-act play *Trifles* (1916)—was included in E. J. O'Brien's edition of *The Best Short Stories of 1917*.

The daughter of Elmer S. Glaspell, a feed dealer, and Alice (Keating) Glaspell, an emigrant from Dublin, Susan Glaspell was born and raised in Davenport, Iowa. After graduating from Drake University in 1899, she worked on the staff of the *Des Moines Daily News* until she could support herself by writing fiction. Her stories appeared in magazines like *Harper's* and the *Ladies' Home Journal*, and her early novels were popular examples of regionalism. In 1911, Glaspell moved to Greenwich Village with a friend, and two years later she married George Cram Cook, a Harvard graduate from her hometown who was soon to become known as a charismatic director. They spent their winters in the Village and their summers in Provincetown, a small town on Cape Cod. Together they organized a group of Provincetown actors who performed one-act plays in a wharf theater. Eugene O'Neill, Edna St. Vincent Millay, John Reed, Michael Gold, and Susan Glaspell were to become the leading playwrights there and in the Playwrights' Theater Glaspell helped found in the Village. Determinedly anticommercial and avant-garde, Glaspell's and Cook's productions fostered the first experimental drama in America. Indeed, when their theaters grew commercially successful, Cook became disillusioned, and he and his wife lived in Greece from 1922 until his death in 1924. Glaspell was remarried between 1925 and 1931. The rest of her life was spent in Provincetown, where she wrote novels that continued to explore the major subject of *Trifles*, the confining environments that frustrate the full development of human potential.

Trifles

Characters

GEORGE HENDERSON, *County Attorney*   MRS. PETERS
HENRY PETERS, *Sheriff*   MRS. HALE
LEWIS HALE, A *Neighboring Farmer*

SCENE

The kitchen in the now abandoned farmhouse of JOHN WRIGHT, *a gloomy kitchen, and left without having been put in order—unwashed pans under the sink, a loaf of bread outside the breadbox, a dish towel on the table—other signs of incompleted work. At the rear the outer door opens and the* SHERIFF *comes in followed by the* COUNTY ATTORNEY *and* HALE. *The* SHERIFF *and* HALE *are men in middle life, the* COUNTY ATTORNEY *is a young man; all are much bundled up and go at once to the stove. They are followed by two women—the* SHERIFF'S *wife first; she is a slight wiry woman, a thin nervous face.* MRS. HALE *is larger and would ordinarily be called more comfortable looking, but she is disturbed now and looks fearfully about as she enters. The women have come in slowly, and stand close together near the door.*

COUNTY ATTORNEY. [*Rubbing his hands.*] This feels good. Come up to the fire, ladies.

MRS. PETERS. [*After taking a step forward.*] I'm not—cold.

SHERIFF. [*Unbuttoning his overcoat and stepping away from the stove as if to mark the beginning of official business.*] Now, Mr. Hale, before we move things about, you explain to Mr. Henderson just what you saw when you came here yesterday morning.

COUNTY ATTORNEY. By the way, has anything been moved? Are things just as you left them yesterday?

SHERIFF. [*Looking about.*] It's just the same. When it dropped below zero last night I thought I'd better send Frank out this morning to make a fire for us—no use getting pneumonia with a big case on, but I told him not to touch anything except the stove—and you know Frank.

COUNTY ATTORNEY. Somebody should have been left here yesterday.

SHERIFF. Oh—yesterday. When I had to send Frank to Morris Center for that man who went crazy—I want you to know I had my hands full yesterday, I knew you could get back from Omaha by today and as long as I went over everything here myself—

COUNTY ATTORNEY. Well, Mr. Hale, tell just what happened when you came here yesterday morning.

HALE. Harry and I had started to town with a load of potatoes. We came along the road from my place and as I got here I said, "I'm going to see if I can't get John Wright to go in with me on a party telephone." I spoke to Wright about it once before and he put me off, saying folks talked too much anyway, and all he asked was peace and quiet—I guess you know about how much he talked himself; but I thought maybe if I went to the house and talked about it before his wife, though I said to Harry that I didn't know as what his wife wanted made much difference to John—

COUNTY ATTORNEY. Let's talk about that later, Mr. Hale. I do want to talk about that, but tell now just what happened when you got to the house.

HALE. I didn't hear or see anything; I knocked at the door, and still it was all quiet inside. I knew they must be up, it was past eight o'clock. So I knocked again, and I thought I heard somebody say, "Come in." I wasn't sure, I'm not sure yet, but I opened the door—this door [*Indicating the door by which the two women are still standing*] and there in that rocker—[*Pointing to it.*] sat Mrs. Wright.

[*They all look at the rocker.*]

COUNTY ATTORNEY. What—was she doing?

HALE. She was rockin' back and forth. She had her apron in her hand and was kind of—pleating it.

COUNTY ATTORNEY. And how did she—look?

HALE. Well, she looked queer.

COUNTY ATTORNEY. How do you mean—queer?

HALE. Well, as if she didn't know what she was going to do next. And kind of done up.

COUNTY ATTORNEY. How did she seem to feel about your coming?

HALE. Why, I don't think she minded—one way or other. She didn't pay much attention. I said, "How do, Mrs. Wright, it's cold, ain't it?" And she said, "Is it?"—and went on kind of pleating at her apron. Well, I was surprised; she didn't ask me to come up to the stove, or to set down, but just sat there, not even looking at me, so I said, "I want to see John." And then she—laughed. I guess you would call it a laugh. I thought of Harry and the team outside, so I said a little sharp: "Can't I see John?" "No," she says, kind o' dull like. "Ain't he home?" says I. "Yes," says she, "he's home." "Then why can't I see him?" I asked her, out of patience. " 'Cause he's dead," says she. "*Dead?*" says I. She just nodded her head, not getting a bit excited, but rockin' back and forth. "Why—where is he?" says I, not knowing what to say. She just pointed upstairs—like that [*Himself pointing to the room above*]. I got up, with the idea of going up there. I walked from there to here—then I says, "Why, what did he die of?" "He died of a rope round his neck," says she, and just went on pleatin' at her apron. Well, I went out and called Harry. I thought I might—need help. We went upstairs and there he was lyin'—

COUNTY ATTORNEY. I think I'd rather have you go into that upstairs, where you can point it all out. Just go on now with the rest of the story.

HALE. Well, my first thought was to get that rope off. It looked . . . [*Stops, his face twitches.*] . . . but Harry, he went up to him, and he said, "No, he's dead all right, and we'd better not touch anything." So we went back down stairs. She was still sitting that same way. "Has anybody been notified?" I asked. "No," says she, unconcerned. "Who did this, Mrs. Wright?" said Harry. He said it businesslike—and she stopped pleatin' of her apron. "I don't know," she says. "You don't *know?*" says Harry. "No," says she. "Weren't you sleepin' in the bed with him?" says Harry. "Yes," says she, "but I was on the inside." "Somebody slipped a rope round his neck and strangled him and you didn't wake up?" says Harry. "I didn't wake up," she said after him. We must 'a looked as if we didn't see how that could be, for after a minute she said, "I sleep sound." Harry was going to ask her more questions but I said maybe we ought to let her tell her story first to the coroner, or the sheriff, so Harry went fast as he could to Rivers' place, where there's a telephone.

COUNTY ATTORNEY. And what did Mrs. Wright do when she knew that you had gone for the coroner?

HALE. She moved from that chair to this one over here [*Pointing to a small chair in the corner.*] and just sat there with her hands held together and looking down. I got a feeling that I ought to make some conversation, so I said I had come in to see if John wanted to put in a telephone, and at that she started to laugh, and then she stopped and looked at me—scared. [*The* COUNTY ATTORNEY, *who has had his notebook out, makes a note.*] I dunno, maybe it wasn't scared. I wouldn't like to say it was. Soon Harry got back, and then Dr. Lloyd came, and you, Mr. Peters, and so I guess that's all I know that you don't.

COUNTY ATTORNEY. [*Looking around.*] I guess we'll go upstairs first—and then out to the barn and around there. [*To the* SHERIFF] You're convinced that there was nothing important here—nothing that would point to any motive.

SHERIFF. Nothing here but kitchen things.

[*The* COUNTY ATTORNEY, *after again looking around the kitchen, opens the door of a cupboard closet. He gets up on a chair and looks on a shelf. Pulls his hand away, sticky.*]

COUNTY ATTORNEY. Here's a nice mess.

[*The women draw nearer.*]

MRS. PETERS. [*To the other woman.*] Oh, her fruit; it did freeze. [*To the* COUNTY ATTORNEY] She worried about that when it turned so cold. She said the fire'd go out and her jars would break.

SHERIFF. Well, can you beat the women! Held for murder and worryin' about her preserves.

COUNTY ATTORNEY. I guess before we're through she may have something more serious than preserves to worry about.

HALE. Well, women are used to worrying over trifles.

[*The two women move a little closer together.*]

COUNTY ATTORNEY. [*With the gallantry of a young politician.*] And yet, for all their worries, what would we do without the ladies? [*The women do not unbend. He goes to the sink, takes a dipperful of water from the pail and pouring it into a basin, washes his hands. Starts to wipe them on the roller towel, turns it for a cleaner place.*] Dirty towels! [*Kicks his foot against the pans under the sink.*] Not much of a housekeeper, would you say, ladies?

MRS. HALE. [*Stiffly.*] There's a great deal of work to be done on a farm.

COUNTY ATTORNEY. To be sure. And yet [*With a little bow to her*] I know there are some Dickson county farmhouses which do not have such roller towels.

[*He gives it a pull to expose its full length again.*]

MRS. HALE. Those towels get dirty awful quick. Men's hands aren't always as clean as they might be.

COUNTY ATTORNEY. Ah, loyal to your sex, I see. But you and Mrs. Wright were neighbors. I suppose you were friends, too.

MRS. HALE. [*Shaking her head.*] I've not seen much of her of late years. I've not been in this house—it's more than a year.

COUNTY ATTORNEY. And why was that? You didn't like her?

MRS. HALE. I liked her all well enough. Farmers' wives have their hands full, Mr. Henderson. And then—

COUNTY ATTORNEY. Yes—?

MRS. HALE. [*Looking about.*] It never seemed a very cheerful place.

COUNTY ATTORNEY. No—it's not cheerful. I shouldn't say she had the homemaking instinct.

MRS. HALE. Well, I don't know as Wright had, either.

COUNTY ATTORNEY. You mean that they didn't get on very well?

MRS. HALE. No, I don't mean anything. But I don't think a place'd be any cheerfuller for John Wright's being in it.

COUNTY ATTORNEY. I'd like to talk more of that a little later. I want to get the lay of things upstairs now.

[*He goes to the left, where three steps lead to a stair door.*]

SHERIFF. I suppose anything Mrs. Peter does'll be all right. She was to take in some clothes for her, you know, and a few little things. We left in such a hurry yesterday.

COUNTY ATTORNEY. Yes, but I would like to see what you take, Mrs. Peters, and keep an eye out for anything that might be of use to us.

MRS. PETERS. Yes, Mr. Henderson.

[*The women listen to the men's steps on the stairs, then look about the kitchen.*]

MRS. HALE. I'd hate to have men coming into my kitchen, snooping around and criticising.

[*She arranges the pans under sink which the* COUNTY ATTORNEY *had shoved out of place.*]

MRS. PETERS. Of course it's no more than their duty.

MRS. HALE. Duty's all right, but I guess that deputy sheriff that came out to make the fire might have got a little of this on. [*Gives the roller towel a pull.*] Wish I'd thought of that sooner. Seems mean to talk about her for not having things slicked up when she had to come away in such a hurry.

MRS. PETERS. [*Who has gone to a small table in the left rear corner of the room, and lifted one end of a towel that covers a pan.*] She had bread set.

[*Stands still.*]

MRS. HALE. [*Eyes fixed on a loaf of bread beside the breadbox, which is on a low shelf at the other side of the room. Moves slowly toward it.*] She was going to put this in there. [*Picks up loaf, then abruptly drops it. In a manner of returning to familiar things.*] It's a shame about her fruit. I wonder if it's all gone. [*Gets up on the chair and looks.*] I think there's some here that's all right, Mrs. Peters. Yes—here; [*Holding it toward the window.*] this is cherries, too. [*Looking again.*] I declare I believe that's the only one. [*Gets down, bottle in her hand. Goes to the sink and wipes it off on the outside.*] She'll feel awful bad after all her hard work in the hot weather. I remember the afternoon I put up my cherries last summer.

[*She puts the bottle on the big kitchen table, center of the room. With a sigh, is about to sit down in the rocking-chair. Before she is seated realizes what chair it is; with a slow look at it, steps back. The chair which she has touched rocks back and forth.*]

MRS. PETERS. Well, I must get those things from the front room closet. [*She goes to the door at the right, but after looking into the other room, steps back.*] You coming with me, Mrs. Hale? You could help me carry them.

[*They go in the other room; reappear,* MRS. PETERS *carrying a dress and skirt,* MRS. HALE *following with a pair of shoes.*]

MRS. PETERS. My, it's cold in there.

[*She puts the clothes on the big table, and hurries to the stove.*]

MRS. HALE. [*Examining her skirt.*] Wright was close. I think maybe that's why she kept so much to herself. She didn't even belong to the Ladies Aid. I suppose she felt she couldn't do her part, and then you don't enjoy things when you feel shabby. She used to wear pretty clothes and be lively, when she was Minnie Foster, one of the town girls singing in the choir. But that—oh, that was thirty years ago. This all you was to take in?

MRS. PETERS. She said she wanted an apron. Funny thing to want, for there isn't much to get you dirty in jail, goodness knows. But I suppose just to make her feel more natural. She said they was in the top drawer in this cupboard. Yes, here. And then her little shawl that always hung behind the door. [*Opens stair door and looks.*] Yes, here it is.

[*Quickly shuts door leading upstairs.*]

MRS. HALE. [*Abruptly moving toward her.*] Mrs. Peters?

MRS. PETERS. Yes, Mrs. Hale?

MRS. HALE. Do you think she did it?

MRS. PETERS. [*In a frightened voice.*] Oh, I don't know.

MRS. HALE. Well, I don't think she did. Asking for an apron and her little shawl. Worrying about her fruit.

MRS. PETERS. [*Starts to speak, glances up, where footsteps are heard in the room above. In a low voice.*] Mr. Peters says it looks bad for her. Mr. Henderson is awful sarcastic in a speech and he'll make fun of her sayin' she didn't wake up.

MRS. HALE. Well, I guess John Wright didn't wake when they was slipping that rope under his neck.

MRS. PETERS. No, it's strange. It must have been done awful crafty and still. They say it was such a—funny way to kill a man, rigging it all up like that.

MRS. HALE. That's just what Mr. Hale said. There was a gun in the house. He says that's what he can't understand.

MRS. PETERS. Mr. Henderson said coming out that what was needed for the case was a motive; something to show anger, or—sudden feeling.

MRS. HALE. [*Who is standing by the table.*] Well, I don't see any signs of anger around here. [*She puts her hand on the dish towel which lies on the table, stands looking down at table, one half of which is clean, the other half messy.*] It's wiped to here. [*Makes a move as if to finish work, then turns and looks at loaf of bread outside the breadbox. Drops towel. In that voice of coming back to familiar things.*] Wonder how they are finding things upstairs. I hope she had it a little more red-up up there. You know, it seems kind of *sneaking.* Locking her up in town and then coming out here and trying to get her own house to turn against her!

MRS. PETERS. But Mrs. Hale, the law is the law.

MRS. HALE. I s'pose 'tis. [*Unbuttoning her coat.*] Better loosen up your things, Mrs. Peters. You won't feel them when you go out.

[MRS. PETERS *takes off her fur tippet, goes to hang it on hook at back of room, stands looking at the under part of the small corner table.*]

MRS. PETERS. She was piecing a quilt.

[*She brings the large sewing basket and they look at the bright pieces.*]

MRS. HALE. It's log cabin pattern. Pretty, isn't it? I wonder if she was goin' to quilt it or just knot it?

[*Footsteps have been heard coming down the stairs. The* SHERIFF *enters followed by* HALE *and the* COUNTY ATTORNEY.]

SHERIFF. They wonder if she was going to quilt it or just knot it!

[*The men laugh; the women look abashed.*]

COUNTY ATTORNEY. [*Rubbing his hands over the stove.*] Frank's fire didn't do much up there, did it? Well, let's go out to the barn and get that cleared up.

[*The men go outside.*]

MRS. HALE. [*Resentfully.*] I don't know as there's anything so strange, our takin' up our time with little things while we're waiting for them to get the evidence. [*She sits down at the big table smoothing out a block with decision.*] I don't see as it's anything to laugh about.

MRS. PETERS. [*Apologetically*.] Of course they've got awful important things on their minds.

[*Pulls up a chair and joins* MRS. HALE *at the table*.]

MRS. HALE. [*Examining another block*.] Mrs. Peters, look at this one. Here, this is the one she was working on, and look at the sewing! All the rest of it has been so nice and even. And look at this! It's all over the place! Why, it looks as if she didn't know what she was about!

[*After she has said this they look at each other, then start to glance back at the door. After an instant* MRS. HALE *has pulled at a knot and ripped the sewing*.]

MRS. PETERS. Oh, what are you doing, Mrs. Hale?

MRS. HALE. [*Mildly*.] Just pulling out a stitch or two that's not sewed very good. [*Threading a needle*.] Bad sewing always made me fidgety.

MRS. PETERS. [*Nervously*.] I don't think we ought to touch things.

MRS. HALE. I'll just finish up this end. [*Suddenly stopping and leaning forward*.] Mrs. Peters?

MRS. PETERS. Yes, Mrs. Hale?

MRS. HALE. What do you suppose she was so nervous about?

MRS. PETERS. Oh—I don't know. I don't know as she was nervous. I sometimes sew awful queer when I'm just tired. [MRS. HALE *starts to say something, looks at* MRS. PETERS, *then goes on sewing*.] Well, I must get these things wrapped up. They may be through sooner than we think. [*Putting apron and other things together*.] I wonder where I can find a piece of paper, and string.

MRS. HALE. In that cupboard, maybe.

MRS. PETERS. [*Looking in cupboard*.] Why, here's a birdcage. [*Holds it up*.] Did she have a bird, Mrs. Hale?

MRS. HALE. Why, I don't know whether she did or not—I've not been here for so long. There was a man around last year selling canaries cheap, but I don't know as she took one; maybe she did. She used to sing real pretty herself.

MRS. PETERS. [*Glancing around*.] Seems funny to think of a bird here. But she must have had one, or why would she have a cage? I wonder what happened to it.

MRS. HALE. I s'pose maybe the cat got it.

MRS. PETERS. No, she didn't have a cat. She's got that feeling some people have about cats—being afraid of them. My cat got in her room and she was real upset and asked me to take it out.

MRS. HALE. My sister Bessie was like that. Queer, ain't it?

MRS. PETERS. [*Examining the cage*.] Why, look at this door. It's broke. One hinge is pulled apart.

MRS. HALE. [*Looking too*.] Looks as if someone must have been rough with it.

MRS. PETERS. Why, yes.

[*She brings the cage forward and puts it on the table*.]

MRS. HALE. I wish if they're going to find any evidence they'd be about it. I don't like this place.

MRS. PETERS. But I'm awful glad you came with me, Mrs. Hale. It would be lonesome for me sitting here alone.

MRS. HALE. It would, wouldn't it? [*Dropping her sewing.*] But I tell you what I do wish, Mrs. Peters. I wish I had come over sometimes when *she* was here. I—[*Looking around the room.*]—wish I had.

MRS. PETERS. But of course you were awful busy, Mrs. Hale—your house and your children.

MRS. HALE. I could've come. I stayed away because it weren't cheerful —and that's why I ought to have come. I—I've never liked this place. Maybe because it's down in a hollow and you don't see the road. I dunno what it is but it's a lonesome place and always was. I wish I had come over to see Minnie Foster sometimes. I can see now—
[*Shakes her head.*]

MRS. PETERS. Well, you mustn't reproach yourself, Mrs. Hale. Some-how we just don't see how it is with other folks until—something comes up.

MRS. HALE. Not having children makes less work—but it makes a quiet house, and Wright out to work all day, and no company when he did come in. Did you know John Wright, Mrs. Peters?

MRS. PETERS. Not to know him; I've seen him in town. They say he was a good man.

MRS. HALEY. Yes—good; he didn't drink, and kept his word as well as most, I guess, and paid his debts. But he was a hard man, Mrs. Peters. Just to pass the time of day with him—[*Shivers.*] Like a raw wind that gets to the bone. [*Pauses, her eye falling on the cage.*] I should think she would 'a wanted a bird. But what do you suppose went with it?

MRS. PETERS. I don't know, unless it got sick and died.
[*She reaches over and swings the broken door, swings it again. Both women watch it.*]

MRS. HALE. You weren't raised round here, were you? [MRS. PETERS *shakes her head.*] You didn't know—her?

MRS. PETERS. Not till they brought her yesterday.

MRS. HALE. She—come to think of it, she was kind of like a bird herself —real sweet and pretty, but kind of timid and—fluttery. How—she —did—change. [*Silence; then as if struck by a happy thought and relieved to get back to every day things.*] Tell you what, Mrs. Peters, why don't you take the quilt in with you? It might take up her mind.

MRS. PETERS. Why, I think that's a real nice idea, Mrs. Hale. There couldn't possibly be any objection to it, could there? Now, just what would I take? I wonder if her patches are in here—and her things.
[*They look in the sewing basket.*]

MRS. HALE. Here's some red. I expect this has got sewing things in it. [*Brings out a fancy box.*] What a pretty box. Looks like something somebody would give you. Maybe her scissors are in here. [*Opens box. Suddenly puts her hand to her nose.*] Why—[MRS. PETERS *bends nearer, then turns her face away.*] There's something wrapped up in this piece of silk.

MRS. PETERS. Why, this isn't her scissors.

MRS. HALE. [*Lifting the silk.*] Oh, Mrs. Peters—its—

[MRS. PETERS *bends closer.*]

MRS. PETERS. It's the bird.

MRS. HALE. [*Jumping up.*] But, Mrs. Peters—look at it! Its neck! Look at its neck! It's all—other side *to.*

MRS. PETERS. Somebody—wrung—its—neck.

[*Their eyes meet. A look of growing comprehension, of horror. Steps are heard outside.* MRS. HALE *slips box under quilt pieces, and sinks into her chair. Enter* SHERIFF *and* COUNTY ATTORNEY. MRS. PETERS *rises.*]

COUNTY ATTORNEY. [*As one turning from serious things to little pleasantries.*] Well, ladies, have you decided whether she was going to quilt it or knot it?

MRS. PETERS. We think she was going to—knot it.

COUNTY ATTORNEY. Well, that's interesting, I'm sure. [*Seeing the birdcage.*] Has the bird flown?

MRS. HALE. [*Putting more quilt pieces over the box.*] We think the—cat got it.

COUNTY ATTORNEY. [*Preoccupied.*] Is there a cat?

[MRS. HALE *glances in a quick covert way at* MRS. PETERS.]

MRS. PETERS. Well, not *now.* They're superstitious, you know. They leave.

COUNTY ATTORNEY. [*To* SHERIFF PETERS, *continuing an interrupted conversation.*] No sign at all of anyone having come from the outside. Their own rope. Now let's go up again and go over it piece by piece. [*They start upstairs.*] It would have to have been someone who knew just the—

[MRS. PETERS *sits down. The two women sit there not looking at one another, but as if peering into something and at the same time holding back. When they talk now it is in the manner of feeling their way over strange ground, as if afraid of what they are saying, but as if they can not help saying it.*]

MRS. HALE. She liked the bird. She was going to bury it in that pretty box.

MRS. PETERS. [*In a whisper.*] When I was a girl—my kitten—there was a boy took a hatchet, and before my eyes—and before I could get there—[*Covers her face an instant.*] If they hadn't held me back I would have—[*Catches herself, looks upstairs where steps are heard, falters weakly.*]—hurt him.

MRS. HALE. [*With a slow look around her.*] I wonder how it would seem never to have had any children around. [*Pause.*] No, Wright wouldn't like the bird—a thing that sang. She used to sing. He killed that, too.

MRS. PETERS. [*Moving uneasily.*] We don't know who killed the bird.

MRS. HALE. I knew John Wright.

MRS. PETERS. It was an awful thing was done in this house that night, Mrs. Hale. Killing a man while he slept, slipping a rope around his neck that choked the life out of him.

MRS. HALE. His neck. Choked the life out of him.

[*Her hand goes out and rests on the birdcage.*]

MRS. PETERS. [*With rising voice.*] We don't know who killed him. We don't *know*.

MRS. HALE. [*Her own feeling not interrupted.*] If there'd been years and years of nothing, then a bird to sing to you, it would be awful—still, after the bird was still.

MRS. PETERS. [*Something within her speaking.*] I know what stillness is. When we homesteaded in Dakota, and my first baby died—after he was two years old, and me with no other then—

MRS. HALE. [*Moving.*] How soon do you suppose they'll be through, looking for the evidence?

MRS. PETERS. I know what stillness is. [*Pulling herself back.*] The law has got to punish crime, Mrs. Hale.

MRS. HALE. [*Not as if answering that.*] I wish you'd seen Minnie Foster when she wore a white dress with blue ribbons and stood up there in the choir and sang. [*A look around the room.*] Oh, I *wish* I'd come over here once in a while! That was a crime! That was a crime! Who's going to punish that?

MRS. PETERS. [*Looking upstairs.*] We mustn't—take on.

MRS. HALE. I might have known she needed help! I know how things can be—for women. I tell you, it's queer, Mrs. Peters. We live close together and we live far apart. We all go through the same things— it's all just a different kind of the same thing. [*Brushes her eyes; noticing the bottle of fruit, reaches out for it.*] If I was you I wouldn't tell her her fruit was gone. Tell her it *ain't*. Tell her it's all right. Take this in to prove it to her. She—she may never know whether it was broke or not.

MRS. PETERS. [*Takes the bottle, looks about for something to wrap it in; takes petticoat from the clothes brought from the other room, very nervously begins winding this around the bottle. In a false voice.*] My, it's a good thing the men couldn't hear us. Wouldn't they just laugh! Getting all stirred up over a little thing like a—dead canary. As if that could have anything to do with—with—wouldn't they *laugh*!

[*The men are heard coming down stairs.*]

MRS. HALE. [*Under her breath.*] Maybe they would—maybe they wouldn't.

COUNTY ATTORNEY. No, Peters, it's all perfectly clear except a reason for doing it. But you know juries when it comes to women. If there was some definite thing. Something to show—something to make a story about—a thing that would connect up with this strange way of doing it—

[*The women's eyes meet for an instant. Enter HALE from outer door.*]

HALE. Well, I've got the team around. Pretty cold out there.

COUNTY ATTORNEY. I'm going to stay here a while by myself. [*To the*

SHERIFF.] You can send Frank out for me, can't you? I want to go over everything. I'm not satisfied that we can't do better.

SHERIFF. Do you want to see what Mrs. Peters is going to take in?

[*The* COUNTY ATTORNEY *goes to the table, picks up the apron, laughs.*]

COUNTY ATTORNEY. Oh, I guess they're not very dangerous things the ladies have picked out. [*Moves a few things about, disturbing the quilt pieces which cover the box. Steps back.*] No, Mrs. Peters doesn't need supervising. For that matter, a sheriff's wife is married to the law. Ever think of it that way, Mrs. Peters?

MRS. PETERS. Not—just that way.

SHERIFF. [*Chuckling.*] Married to the law. [*Moves toward the other room.*] I just want you to come in here a minute, George. We ought to take a look at these windows.

COUNTY ATTORNEY. [*Scoffingly.*] Oh, windows!

SHERIFF. We'll be right out, Mr. Hale.

[HALE *goes outside. The* SHERIFF *follows the* COUNTY ATTORNEY *into the other room. Then* MRS. HALE *rises, hands tight together, looking intensely at* MRS. PETERS, *whose eyes make a slow turn, finally meeting* MRS. HALE'S. *A moment* MRS. HALE *holds her, then her own eyes point the way to where the box is concealed. Suddenly* MRS. PETERS *throws back quilt pieces and tries to put the box in the bag she is wearing. It is too big. She opens box, starts to take bird out, cannot touch it, goes to pieces, stands there helpless. Sound of a knob turning in the other room.* MRS. HALE *snatches the box and puts it in the pocket of her big coat. Enter* COUNTY ATTORNEY *and* SHERIFF.]

COUNTY ATTORNEY. [*Facetiously.*] Well, Henry, at least we found out that she was not going to quilt it. She was going to—what is it you call it, ladies?

MRS. HALE. [*Her hand against her pocket.*] We call it—knot it, Mr. Henderson.

CURTAIN

1916

KATHARINE SUSANNAH PRICHARD
1883–1967

"With Henry Handel Richardson she pioneered the Australian novel as [an] art form," wrote one critic of Katharine Susannah Prichard. The author of twelve novels, a number of short-story collections, two volumes of verse, and a series of Marxist political pamphlets, Prichard is still little known outside Australia, yet her groundbreaking contribution to that nation's literary development was crucial; in addition, as a story like *The Cooboo* reveals, her art transcended regional issues to focus on universal questions of exploitation and justice, freedom and survival.

Born in Levuka, Fiji, Prichard was the daughter of conservative middle-class parents. Her father was a Melbourne journalist who had published a novel in 1891, and the family lived in moderate comfort until his newspaper went out of business and their household goods were sold to pay debts, an event that may have fostered Prichard's later consciousness of economic inequities. Nevertheless, despite straitened circumstances, she was a precocious child who wrote and published her first story at the age of ten, and continued to write, even to publish, short stories thereafter. In 1908, she journeyed to England, where she spent a year studying and writing journalism, a career she continued to pursue when she returned to Australia. In 1915, her novel *The Pioneers* won a major Australian literary prize and, as one biographer reports, she "was accorded public honors unprecedented for a native born writer."

Shortly after the 1917 Russian Revolution, Prichard became a committed Marxist, and in 1919, the year after she married Captain Hugo Throssell, an Australian World War I hero, she joined the Communist party, whose ideology was to influence her world view for the next few decades. In particular, *Working Bullocks* (1926) and *Coonardoo* (1929) were marked by her newly passionate interest in the lives of the working classes and of the Australian aborigines. Among her later novels, the so-called "goldfields trilogy"—*The Roaring Nineties* (1946), *Golden Miles* (1948), and *Winged Seeds* (1950)—is widely regarded as her most significant achievement, partly for its historically realistic exploration of West Australia's prospecting era and partly for its vivid portrayal of an implicitly feminist heroine, Sally Gough. But *The Cooboo*, too, suggests the skill with which this productively political artist could render the social dynamics that shadowed the lives of Australian aborigines and half-castes while shaping the society of settlers who might seem to have traveled far from the oppressions of civilization.

The Cooboo[1]

They had been mustering[2] all day on the wide plains of Murndoo station. Over the red earth, black with ironstone pebbles, through mulga and curari bush, across the ridges which make a blue wall along the horizon. And the rosy, garish light of sunset was on plains, hills, moving cattle, men and horses.

Through red dust the bullocks mooched, restless and scary still, a wild mob from the hills. John Gray, in the rear with Arra, the boy who was his shadow; Wongana, on the right with his gin,[3] Rose; Frank, the half-caste, on the left with Minni.

A steer breaking from the mob before Rose, she wheeled and went

---

1. Australian aborigine dialect: baby.   3. Native wife or woman.
2. Rounding up cattle.

after him. Faint and wailing, a cry followed her, as though her horse had stepped on and crushed some small creature. But the steer was getting away. Arra went after him, stretched along his horse's neck, rounded the beast and rode him back to the mob, sulky and blethering.[4] The mob swayed; it had broken three times that day, but was settling to the road.

John Gray called: "Yienda (you) damn fool, Rosey. Finish!"

The gin, on her slight, rough-haired horse, pulled up scowling.

"Tell Meetchie, Thirty Mile, to-morrow," John Gray said. "Miah, new moon."

Rose slewed[5] her horse away from the mob of men and cattle. That wailing, thin and hard as hair-string, moved with her.

"Minni!"

John Gray jerked his head towards Rose. Minni's bare heels struck her horse's belly; with a turn of the wrist she swung her horse off from the mob, turned, leaned forward, rising in her stirrups, and came up with Rose.

Thin, dark figures on their wiry station-bred horses, the gins rode into the haze of sunset towards the hills. The dull, dirty blue of the trousers wrapped round their legs was torn; their short, fairish hair tousled by the wind. But the glitter and tumult of Rose's eyes, Minni looked away from them.

At a little distance, when men and cattle were a moving cloud of red dust, Rose's anger gushed after them.

"Koo!"[6]

Fierce as the cry of a hawk flew her last note of derision and defiance.

A far-away rattle of laughter drifted back across country. Alone they would have been afraid, as darkness coming up behind, was hovering near them, secreting itself among the low, writhen trees, and bushes; afraid of the evil spirits who wander over the plains and stony ridges when the light of day is withdrawn. But together they were not so afraid. Twenty miles away, over there, below that dent in the hills where Nyedee Creek made a sandy bed for itself among white-bodied gums, was Murndoo homestead and the uloo[7] of their people.

There was no track; and in the first darkness, which would be thick as wool after the glow of sunset faded, only their instinct would keep them moving in the direction of the homestead and their own low, round huts of bagging, rusty tin and dead boughs.

Both were Wongana's women: Rose, tall, gaunt and masterful; Minni, younger, fat and jolly. Rose had been a good stockman[8] in her day: one of the best. Minni did not ride or track nearly as well as Rose.

---

4. Muttering, grumbling.
5. Swung.
6. An aborigine cry.

7. Camp.
8. Herdsman.

And yet, as they rode along, Minni pattered complacently of how well she had worked that day; of how she was flashed, this way and that, heading-off breakaways, dashing after them, turning them back to the mob so smartly that John had said, "Good man, Minni!" There was the white bullock—he had rushed near the yards. Had Rose seen the chestnut mare stumble in a crab-hole and send Arra flying? But Minni had chased the white bullock, chased him for a couple of miles, and brought him back to the yards. No doubt there would be nammery[9] for her and a new gina-gina when the men came in from the muster.

She pulled a pipe from her belt, shook the ashes out, and with reins looped over one arm stuffed the bowl with tobacco from a tin tied to her belt. Stooping down, she struck a match on her stirrup-iron, guarded the flame to the pipe between her short, white teeth, and smoked contentedly.

The scowl on Rose's face deepened, darkened. That thin, fretted wailing came from her breast.

She unslung from her neck the rag rope by which the baby had been against her body, and gave him a sagging breast to suck. Holding him with one arm, she rode slowly, her horse picking his way over the rough, stony earth.

It had been a hard day. The gins were mustering with the men at sunrise. Camped at Nyedee well the night before, in order to get a good start, they had been riding through the timbered ridges all the morning, rounding up the wild cows, calves and young bullocks, and driving them to the yards at Nyedee, where John Gray cut out the fats, left old Jimmy and a couple of boys to brand calves, turn the cows and calves back to the ridge again while he took on the mob for trucking at Meekatharra. The bullocks were as wild as birds: needed watching all day. And all the time that small, whimpering bundle against her breast had hampered Rose's movements.

There was nothing the gins liked better than a muster, riding after cattle. And they could ride, were quicker in their movements, more alert than the men; sharper at picking up tracks. They did not go mustering very often nowadays when there was work to do at the homestead. Since John Gray had married, and there was a woman on Murndoo, she found plenty of washing, scrubbing and sweeping for the gins to do; would not spare them often to go after cattle. But John was short-handed. He had said he must have Rose and Minni to muster Nyedee. And all day her baby's crying had irritated Rose. The cooboo had wailed and wailed as she rode with him tied to her body.

The cooboo was responsible for the wrong things she had done all day. Stupid things. Rose was furious. The men had yelled at her.

9. Reward; "gina-gina": dress.

Wongana, her man, blackguarding her before everybody, had called her "a hen who did not know where she laid her eggs." And John Gray, with his "Yienda, damn fool, Rosey. Finish!" had sent her home like a naughty child.

Now, here was Minni jabbering of the tobacco she would get and the new gina-gina. How pleased Wongana would be with her! And the cooboo, wailing, wailing. He wailed as he chewed Rose's empty breast, squirming against her; wailed and gnawed.

She cried out with hurt and impatience. Rage, irritated to madness, rushed through her; rushed like waters coming down the dry creek-beds after heavy rain. Rose wrenched the cooboo from her breast and flung him from her to the ground. There was a crack as of twigs breaking.

Minni glanced aside. "Wiah!"[1] she gasped with widening eyes. But Rose rode on, gazing ahead over the rosy, garish plains and wall of the hills, darkening from the blue to purple and indigo.

When the women came into the station kitchen, earth, hills and trees were dark; the sky heavy with stars. Minni gave John's wife his message: that he would be home with the new moon, in about a fortnight.

Meetchie, as the blacks called Mrs John Gray, could not make out why the gins were so stiff and quiet: why Rose stalked scowling and sulky-fellow, sombre eyes just glancing, and away again. Meetchie wanted to ask about the muster, what sort of condition the bullocks had on; how many were on the road; if many calves had been branded at Nyedee. But she knew them too well to ask questions when they looked like that.

Only when she had given them bread and a tin of jam, cut off hunks of corned beef for them, filled their billies[2] with strong black tea, put sugar in their empty tins, and they were going off to the uloo, she was surprised to see Rose without her baby.

"Why, Rose," she exclaimed, "where's the cooboo?"

Rose stalked off into the night. Minni glanced back with scared eyes, and followed Rose.

In the dawn, when a cry, remote and anguished flew through the clear air, Meetchie wondered who was dead in the camp by the creek. She remembered Rose: how she had looked the night before. And the cooboo—where was he?

Then she knew that it was Rose wailing for her cooboo in the dawn: Rose cutting herself with stones until her body bled: Rose screaming in a fury of unavailing grief.

1932

---

1. Ho!
2. Cylindrical tin container with close-fitting lid.

ANNA WICKHAM
1884–1947

"I have to thank God I'm a woman," wrote Anna Wickham in a poem entitled *The Affinity*, explaining with some irony that "in these ordered days a woman only / Is free to be very hungry, very lonely." That terse, sardonic couplet defines the difficult liberty which was achieved in verse by this distinctively feminist poet who has now been largely forgotten. Born in Wimbledon, just outside London, Wickham emigrated with her family to Australia at the age of six, where she was evidently raised in a freer environment than that of her English contemporaries. When she was twenty-one, she returned to Europe and studied opera singing in Paris, then entered into a marriage which seems to have been somewhat unsatisfactory, for, as one critic observes, she "was considered a 'rebellious' wife, a woman who lived by her own rules." Yet her problematic marriage appears to have energized her art: after a few years of domesticity, she began to write poetry at an extraordinary pace. Her first collection was privately printed in 1911, and it was followed by three more volumes—*The Contemplative Quarry* (1915), *The Man with a Hammer* (1916), and *The Little Old House* (1922). All in all, in one four-year period of intense creative activity, she produced nine hundred poems.

Among London intellectuals of her era, Wickham was well known, especially in a circle that included the writers T. E. Hulme and D. H. Lawrence as well as the artists Gaudier-Brzeska and Jacob Epstein. Her poems are often as bitterly explicit about the impediments to female achievement as the critical writings of her contemporary Virginia Woolf. In *Dedication of the Cook*, for instance, she declares, "If any ask why there's no great She-Poet, / Let him come live with me, and he will know it." At the same time, a number of her works, like *The Affinity* (quoted earlier), celebrate the aesthetic freedom made possible by woman's status as what Woolf called an "outsider."

Meditation at Kew[1]

Alas! for all the pretty women who marry dull men,
Go into the suburbs and never come out again,
Who lose their pretty faces, and dim their pretty eyes,
Because no one has skill or courage to organize.

What do these pretty women suffer when they marry?   5
They bear a boy who is like Uncle Harry,
A girl, who is like Aunt Eliza, and not new,
These old, dull races must breed true.

---

1. A South London suburb.

I would enclose a common[2] in the sun,
And let the young wives out to laugh and run;   10
I would steal their dull clothes and go away,
And leave the pretty naked things to play.

Then I would make a contract with hard Fate
That they see all the men in the world and choose a mate,
And I would summon all the pipers in the town   15
That they dance with Love at a feast, and dance him down.

From the gay unions of choice
We'd have a race of splendid beauty, and of thrilling voice.
The World whips frank, gay love with rods,
But frankly, gayly shall we get the gods.   20

1915

The Affinity

I have to thank God I'm a woman,
For in these ordered days a woman only
Is free to be very hungry, very lonely.

It is sad for Feminism, but still clear
That man, more often than woman, is pioneer.   5
If I would confide a new thought,
First to a man must it be brought.

Now, for our sins, it is my bitter fate
That such a man wills soon to be my mate,
And so of friendship is quick end: 10
When I have gained a love I lose a friend.

It is well within the order of things
That man should listen when his mate sings;
But the true male never yet walked
Who liked to listen when his mate talked.   15

I would be married to a full man,
As would all women since the world began;
But from a wealth of living I have proved
I must be silent, if I would be loved.

Now of my silence I have much wealth,   20
I have to do my thinking all by stealth.
My thoughts may never see the day;
My mind is like a catacomb where early Christians pray.

2. A piece of land for public use; a park.

And of my silence I have much pain,
But of these pangs I have great gain;   25
For I must take to drugs or drink,
Or I must write the things I think.

If my sex would let me speak,
I would be very lazy and most weak;
I should speak only, and the things I spoke   30
Would fill the air awhile, and clear like smoke.

The things I think now I write down,
And some day I will show them to the Town.
When I am sad I make thought clear;
I can re-read it all next year.   35

I have to thank God I'm a woman,
For in these ordered days a woman only
Is free to be very hungry, very lonely.

                                                 1915

Divorce

A voice from the dark is calling me.
In the close house I nurse a fire.
Out in the dark, cold winds rush free,
To the rock heights of my desire.
I smother in the house in the valley below,   5
Let me out to the night, let me go, let me go!

Spirits that ride the sweeping blast,
Frozen in rigid tenderness,
Wait! For I leave the fire at last,
My little-love's warm loneliness.   10
I smother in the house in the valley below,
Let me out in the night, let me go, let me go!

High on the hills are beating drums,
Clear from a line of marching men
To the rock's edge the hero comes.   15
He calls me, and he calls again.
On the hill there is fighting, victory, or quick death,
In the house is the fire, which I fan with sick breath
I smother in the house in the valley below,
Let me out in the dark, let me go, let me go!   20

                                                 1916

Dedication of the Cook

If any ask why there's no great She-Poet,
Let him come live with me, and he will know it:
If I'd indite an ode or mend a sonnet,
I must go choose a dish or tie a bonnet;
For she who serves in forced virginity   5
Since I am wedded will not have me free;
And those new flowers my garden is so rich in
Must die for clammy odors of my kitchen.

Yet had I chosen Dian's[3] barrenness
I'm not full woman, and I can't be less,   10
So could I state no certain truth for life,
Can I survive and be my good man's wife?

Yes! I will make the servant's cause my own
That she in pity leave me hours alone
So I will tend her mind and feed her wit   15
That she in time have her own joy of it;
And count it pride that not a sonnet's spoiled
Lacking her choice betwixt the baked and boiled.
So those young flowers my garden is so rich in
Will blossom from the ashes of my kitchen!   20

1922

3. Diana, the Roman goddess of chastity.

ELINOR WYLIE
1885–1928

During her lifetime, Elinor Wylie seemed to the writer Carl Van Doren like a "white queen"—pale, elegantly dressed, brilliantly successful, dominating the literary world with glittering poems and eloquent talk—while the critic Edmund Wilson regarded her as "one of the most steadily industrious and most productive writers of my acquaintance." Yet, more recently, at least one essayist has declared that her work "holds little interest; the poems include far too many references to goldfish, moonbeams, and snowflakes for modern taste." The woman who inspired such mixed opinions was born Elinor Hoyt in Somerville, New Jersey, the eldest of five children in a distinguished family, and her early life was marked by what one biographer calls "unruffled gentility." In 1905, at the age of twenty, she married Philip Hichborn, the son of a prominent admiral, but five years later she left him and her young son, Philip, to elope with Horace Wylie, a married lawyer seventeen years older than she. The ensuing scandal clearly altered the well-born young woman's sense of herself and of the world, imbuing her poetry with an enduring irony about society. Wylie's wife refused to grant him a divorce, and, though the lovers sought anonymity in England, they were considered notorious for a number of years.

When the couple returned to the United States just after the outbreak of World War I, they were legally married in 1916, then settled in 1919 in Washington, D.C., where Horace Wylie had a government job and where Elinor Wylie began seriously to write and publish poetry with the sponsorship of a group of new friends, including the novelist Sinclair Lewis and the poet William Rose Benét. In 1912, she had had a small collection of verse, *Incidental Numbers*, privately printed in England, but she herself regarded the book as marred by "incredible immaturity." Her first really ambitious volume, therefore, was *Nets to Catch the Wind* (1921), a book that achieved instantaneous success with what the anthologist Louis Untermeyer called its "brilliance of moonlight coruscating on a plain of ice." It was followed in 1923 by an equally notable collection, *Black Armour*, and by a well-received first novel, *Jennifer Lorn*.

At around the time that *Nets to Catch the Wind* appeared, Wylie had moved to New York, where she became increasingly close to William Rose Benét, now the editor of the prestigious *Saturday Review of Literature*. In 1923, she divorced Wylie and married Benét. Though later she was to travel to England, where she resided for long periods in the late twenties and where, as she confided to the critic Carl Van Doren, she found someone she really loved "for the first time" (the mysterious lover to whom her *Sonnets to One Person* are addressed), her marriage to Benét seems on the whole to have been a good one. She had returned to live with him just before she died of a stroke on the very day that she had finished correcting the proofs for her last collection of verse, *Angels and Earthly Creatures* (posthumously published in 1929). In addition, her years in New York had been both triumphant and productive: publishing three novels after *Jennifer Lorn*, one of which—*The Orphan Angel* (1926)— was a Book-of-the-Month-Club selection, and several other collections of verse, she had become a literary personage; wealthy, beautiful, and fashionably dressed, she had also become a public personality, a friend of many key intellectuals and almost a patron saint to such younger writers as the poet Edna St. Vincent Millay, who wrote a series of moving elegies on her death.

Despite such success, however, Wylie's best poetry is marked by an austere lyricism that suggests a deeply pessimistic cast of mind. "I was, being human, born alone," she confesses in one verse, adding "I am, being woman, hard beset." Elsewhere, moreover, she reveals a sardonic consciousness that her admirers may be mythologizing her, musing that "the woman [might be] moulded by your wish." Perhaps some of the recent rejection of her work as disfigured by "too many references to goldfish [and] moonbeams" is the consequence of such mythologizing, an inability to separate the worldly glamour of the woman from the aesthetic severity of the poet.

The Eagle and the Mole

Avoid the reeking herd,
Shun the polluted flock,

Live like that stoic bird,
The eagle of the rock.

The huddled warmth of crowds   5
Begets and fosters hate;
He keeps, above the clouds,
His cliff inviolate.

When flocks are folded warm,
And herds to shelter run,   10
He sails above the storm,
He stares into the sun.

If in the eagle's track
Your sinews cannot leap,
Avoid the lathered pack,   15
Turn from the steaming sheep.

If you would keep your soul
From spotted sight or sound,
Live like the velvet mole;
Go burrow underground.   20

And there hold intercourse
With roots of trees and stones,
With rivers at their source,
And disembodied bones.

                                                 1921

Atavism[1]

I always was afraid of Somes's Pond:
Not the little pond, by which the willow stands,
Where laughing boys catch alewives[2] in their hands
In brown, bright shallows; but the one beyond.
There, when the frost makes all the birches burn   5
Yellow as cow-lilies, and the pale sky shines
Like a polished shell between black spruce and pines,
Some strange thing tracks us, turning where we turn.

You'll say I dream it, being the true daughter
Of those who in old times endured this dread.   10
Look! Where the lily-stems are showing red
A silent paddle moves below the water,

---

1. Recurrence in a person of genetic traits oc-   2. An Atlantic fish of the herring family.
curring several generations in the past.

A sliding shape has stirred them like a breath;
Tall plumes surmount a painted mask of death.

1921

Wild Peaches

1

When the world turns completely upside down
You say we'll emigrate to the Eastern Shore
Aboard a river-boat from Baltimore;
We'll live among wild peach trees, miles from town,
You'll wear a coonskin cap, and I a gown   5
Homespun, dyed butternut's dark gold colour.
Lost, like your lotus-eating ancestor,[3]
We'll swim in milk and honey till we drown.

The winter will be short, the summer long,
The autumn amber-hued, sunny and hot,   10
Tasting of cider and of scuppernong;[4]
All seasons sweet, but autumn best of all.
The squirrels in their silver fur will fall
Like falling leaves, like fruit, before your shot.

2

The autumn frosts will lie upon the grass   15
Like bloom on grapes of purple-brown and gold.
The misted early mornings will be cold;
The little puddles will be roofed with glass.
The sun, which burns from copper into brass,
Melts these at noon, and makes the boys unfold   20
Their knitted mufflers; full as they can hold,
Fat pockets dribble chestnuts as they pass.

Peaches grow wild, and pigs can live in clover;
A barrel of salted herrings lasts a year;
The spring begins before the winter's over.   25
By February you may find the skins
Of garter snakes and water moccasins
Dwindled and harsh, dead-white and cloudy-clear.

3

When April pours the colours of a shell
Upon the hills, when every little creek   35
Is shot with silver from the Chesapeake
In shoals new-minted by the ocean swell,
When strawberries go begging, and the sleek

3. In Homer's *Odyssey* the lotus-eaters remain
in a constant drugged state due to the flowers
they consume.
4. A sweet golden wine native to America.

Blue plums lie open to the blackbird's beak,
We shall live well—we shall live very well.   30

The months between the cherries and the peaches
Are brimming cornucopias which spill
Fruits red and purple, sombre-bloomed and black;
Then, down rich fields and frosty river beaches
We'll trample bright persimmons, while you kill   40
Bronze partridge, speckled quail, and canvasback.

                                4

Down to the Puritan marrow of my bones
There's something in this richness that I hate.
I love the look, austere, immaculate,
Of landscapes drawn in pearly monotones.   45
There's something in my very blood that owns
Bare hills, cold silver on a sky of slate,
A thread of water, churned to milky spate[5]
Streaming through slanted pastures fenced with stones.
I love those skies, thin blue or snowy gray,   50
Those fields sparse-planted, rendering meagre sheaves:
That spring, briefer than apple-blossom's breath,
Summer, so much too beautiful to stay,
Swift autumn, like a bonfire of leaves,
And sleepy winter, like the sleep of death.   55

                                                              1921

Full Moon

My bands of silk and miniver[6]
Momently grew heavier;
The black gauze was beggarly thin;
The ermine muffled mouth and chin;
I could not suck the moonlight in.   5

Harlequin in lozenges
Of love and hate, I walked in these
Striped and ragged rigmaroles;
Along the pavement my footsoles
Trod warily on living coals.   10

Shouldering the thoughts I loathed,
In their corrupt disguises clothed,
Mortality I could not tear
From my ribs, to leave them bare
Ivory in silver air.   15

---

5. Flood or freshet.   6. A white fur.

There I walked, and there I raged;
The spiritual savage caged
Within my skeleton, raged afresh
To feel, behind a carnal mesh,
The clean bones crying in the flesh.   20

1923

Let No Charitable Hope

Now let no charitable hope
Confuse my mind with images
Of eagle and of antelope:
I am in nature none of these.

I was, being human, born alone;   5
I am, being woman, hard beset;
I live by squeezing from a stone
The little nourishment I get.

In masks outrageous and austere
The years go by in single file;[7]   10
But none has merited my fear,
And none has quite escaped my smile.

1923

From One Person[8]

XII

In our content, before the autumn came
To shower sallow droppings on the mould,
Sometimes you have permitted me to fold
Your grief in swaddling-bands, and smile to name
Yourself my infant, with an infant's claim   5
To utmost adoration as of old,
Suckled with kindness, fondled from the cold,
And loved beyond philosophy or shame.

I dreamt I was the mother of a son
Who had deserved a manger for a crib;   10

---

7. Possibly an echo of Ralph Waldo Emerson's
poem *Days*: "Daughters of Time, the hypocritic
Days, / Muffled and dumb like barefoot der-

vishes, / And marching single in an endless file."
8. From the sonnet sequence *One Person*.

Torn from your body, furbished from your rib,[9]
I am the daughter of your skeleton,
Born of your bitter and excessive pain:
I shall not dream you are my child again.

1929

To a Lady's Countenance

This unphilosophic sight;
This silly mask of silken white;
This thing which has, to hide its grief,
Less than a rose's lesser leaf;
This web a spider might have spun   5
With patience and precision;
This veil concealing sorrow's face,
Arranged with coquetry and grace,
Which shall remain, when all is said,
After sorrow itself is dead;   10
In colour, a camellia flower;
In shape, a whim of the glass-blower;
The mind's eye hollowed and made blind,
But not the brow above the mind;
And, whatsoever may be starved,   15
The little lips uncut, uncarved;
God's power has disdained to mould
This clay so delicate and cold;
Perchance he took it for the flesh
Of mushrooms, or the silkworm's mesh;   20
Stuff too slight to bear the fine
Finger-tip of the divine
In lines of noble heritage;
And so, you do not show your age.

1929

Portrait in Black Paint, with a
Very Sparing Use of Whitewash

"She gives herself;" there's a poetic thought;
She gives you comfort sturdy as a reed;
She gives you fifty things you might have bought,
And half a hundred that you'll never need;
She gives you friendship, but it's such a bother   5
You'd fancy influenza from another.

9. In the Bible God fashions Eve from one of Adam's ribs (Genesis 2:18).

She'd give the shirt from off her back, except that
She doesn't wear a shirt, and most men do;
And often and most bitterly she's wept that
A starving tramp can't eat a silver shoe,   10
Or some poor beggar, slightly alcoholic,
Enjoy with Donne a metaphysical frolic.[1]

She gives away her darling secret hope
At dinner tables between eight and nine,
And she would give Saint Peter's to the Pope,   15
And coals to men of Newcastle-on-Tyne,[2]
She would arrange a match for Solomon
Or give Casanova an adoptive son.[3]

She does not give advice; that I admit;
Here's her sole virtue, and I'll count it double,   20
Forgiving her some crime because of it,
But she gives tiresome and endless trouble.
If you need rest, she'll straight contrive a racket;
If gaiety, she'll fetch a padded jacket.

And she gives love of the least useful kind   25
At which advanced civilization mocks;
Half, a Platonic passion of the mind,
And half, a mad desire to mend the socks;
She's always wishing to turn back the page
And live with children in a golden age.   30

She gives a false impression that she's pretty
Because she has a soft, deceptive skin
Saved from her childhood; yet it seems a pity
That she should be as vain of this as sin;
Her mind might bloom, she might reform the world   35
In those lost hours while her hair is curled.

She gives a vague impression that she's lazy,
But when she writes she grows intense and thorough;
Gone quietly and ecstatically crazy
Among the sea-blue hills of Peterboro;   40
She'll work within her cool, conventual flat
As self-sufficient as a Persian cat.

---

1. John Donne (1571–1631), English poet of
the "Metaphysical" school, known for his witty
and farfetched comparisons.
2. A mining town; "carrying coals to Newcastle" is an idiomatic expression, meaning to bring
something where it is not needed; St. Peter's is
the cathedral in Rome where the Pope officiates.
3. Casanova (1725–1798) was a famous libertine who fathered many illegitimate children.
Solomon was a biblical king with many wives.

And she can live on aspirin and Scotch
Or British ginger beer and bread and butter,
And like them both, and neither very much;   45
And in her infancy she possessed a stutter
Which gives a strong impression that she's shy
When heard today, and this is verity.

But when she clothes herself in gold and silver
In the evening, she gives herself away;   50
Having remained a high, laborious delver
For all the hours of a sunny day,
At night she gives you rather the idea
Of mad Ophelia tutored by Medea.[4]

She gives you nothing worth consideration;   55
The effervescence of enthusiasm
Is trivial stuff; she'll give you adoration
If you belong to her peculiar schism;
As, that a certain English man of letters
Need never call the Trinity his betters.   60

Sometimes she gives her heart; sometimes instead
Her tongue's sharp side. Her will is quick to soften.
She has no strength of purpose in her head
And she gives up entirely too often;
Her manners mingle in disastrous ways   65
"The Lower Depths" and the Court of Louis Seize.[5]

Doubtless, she gives her enemies the creeps
And all her friends a vast amount of worry;
She's given oblivion only when she sleeps;
She says she loves the grave; but she'd be sorry   70
To die, while it is vanity to live;
"She gives herself;" what has she left to give?

She'd give her eyes—but both her eyes are blind—
And her right hand—but both her hands are weak—
To be "Careless to win, unskilled to find,   75
And quick—and quick—to lose what all men seek."
But whether this has truly been her story
She'll never know, this side of purgatory.

1932

4. Sorceress in Greek myth who murdered her children to avenge herself upon her husband Jason, who had abandoned her; Ophelia is a courtly lady who goes mad in Shakespeare's *Hamlet*.

5. The court of the French king Louis XVI was famous for its gentility; *The Lower Depths* is a play by the Russian author Maxim Gorky (1868–1936) which depicts the lives of the extremely poor.

Pastiche

Is not the woman moulded by your wish
A cockatrice[6] of a most intricate kind?
You have, my friend, the high fantastic mind
To clasp the cold enamel of a fish
As breastplate for a bosom tigerish;   5
To make a dove a dragon; or to bind
A panther skin upon the escaping hind:
You mix ambiguous spices in your dish.

Will there remain, when thus embellished I
Sprout wings, or am by cloven heels improved,   10
An atom of the lady that you loved?
Does Christ or Lucifer seal this alchemy?
Is there not lacking from your synthesis
Someone you may occasionally miss?

1932

6. Legendary monster with the head, wings, and legs of a cock and the tail of a serpent.

ISAK DINESEN
1885–1962

Isak Dinesen's writing career did not begin until she reached her late forties, when she believed that she had left her real life behind, although she would survive another thirty years to produce several brilliant volumes of short stories, as well as a fascinating autobiography, a novel, and a collection of essays. She had lost her coffee plantation in Africa, her husband, her health, and her lover when she returned to what she considered the stultifying confinement of her mother's house at Rungstedlund in Denmark. "All sorrows," she believed, "can be borne if you put them into a story or tell a story about them." And she was, by her own admission, "*une conteuse, et rien qu'une conteuse*" (a story-teller and nothing but a storyteller). As a storyteller who transformed the sorrows of her life through the sorcery of her art, she could see herself in her past youth and her future old age as a magical witch or wise sibyl.

Christened Karen Christentze Dinesen in 1885, Dinesen viewed her matri-lineage with dislike, associating her mother, Ingeborg (Westenholz) Dinesen, with bourgeois practicality and puritanical morality. Tanne, as she was called, condescended to her mother and romanticized her father, Wilhelm Dinesen, as the representative of adventurous, aristocratic ancestors, erotically daring in their restless search for intense experiences in love and war. The author of *Letters from the Hunt*, Wilhelm Dinesen had fought in the Dano-Prussian War of 1864, suffered the death of his first "great passion," an eighteen-year-old cousin, and wandered as far as America. Tanne was the second of five children in the family, all of whom must have been shocked by Wilhelm Dinesen's suicide in 1895. Her father left a note admitting that, while he knew his other two daughters would fend for themselves, "my heart aches for Tanne." Certainly, the nine-year-old Tanne felt herself to be especially bereaved, and, as her biographer Judith Thurman has shown, by fifteen Dinesen was obsessed with a fantasy of union with her father that would inform not only her subsequent relationships with men but also her sense of herself as an artist.

Educated in the schoolroom at Rungstedlund with her two sisters while her brothers were sent to boarding school, Dinesen wrote witty essays on Danish proverbs and the French Revolution, plays in which she took the part of Pierrot, and fantasies in which she was a romantic Lord Byron. In 1899, she went with her sisters and mother to Switzerland, where the girls entered the École Bénét and where Dinesen began painting. Although after this her formal education was supposed to be complete, back at home she read the plays of Shakespeare, the poetry of Heine and Shelley, and the novels of Laurence Sterne, as well as Danish writers like the novelist Meïr Aaron Goldschmidt, the lyricist Johannes Ewald, and the storyteller Hans Christian Andersen. Over the objections of her family, moreover, she left for Copenhagen to enroll in the private art classes girls had to take for admission into the Royal Academy of Fine Arts. In 1904, she began work on a group of tales called *Likely Stories*, two of which were published in the Danish journal *Tilskueren* under the pseudonym Osceola, chosen to commemorate a rebellious leader of the Seminole Indians.

After five semesters at the Royal Academy, Dinesen returned home and fell in love with Hans Blixen, a distant and dashing cousin on her father's side. When he did not respond, she married his twin brother, Bror, and convinced her family to support Bror's purchase of several hundred acres of land for a coffee plantation near Nairobi. Embarking in 1913 on the thirteen-day passage to British East Africa, neither Bror nor Tanne knew that the acreage was too acidic and too high in altitude for successful coffee growing. In *Out of Africa* (1937), Dinesen described the beauty of the Ngong hills around Nairobi, the dignified customs of the Masai and the Somali, her passionate love of safari life, and her enjoyment at playing the role of the aristocratic baroness to intelligent servants like Farah Aden, her steward. "Here I am where I ought to be," she explained. But, as a pastoral, *Out of Africa* is reticent about the personal problems she confronted on the farm.

The worst of these presented itself as a recurrent malady which she diagnosed as malaria, although it turned out to be syphilis contracted from her husband. Though she managed to treat her symptoms during a trip to Copenhagen in 1910, the disease would recur throughout her life, causing her repeated "lumbago," shooting pains "like a toothache" in her ears, and spinal degeneration. While she had no desire to separate from Bror, she soon fell in love with another adventurous aristocrat, the handsome, thirty-two-year-old Denys Finch-Hatton. Son of the earl of Winchilsea and Nottingham, Finch-Hatton had become a farmer, trader, flyer, and safari leader in East Africa in 1912, after an Eton and Oxford education. For a while, her lover and her husband shared a bedroom at Ngong, each using it while the other was on safari. But Bror began an affair with a woman he would eventually marry, and by 1922 Tanne had to agree to the divorce he wanted. For ten years, the woman who relished being called "The Lioness" managed the farm alone, although her visiting brother Thomas helped her face the droughts, fires, and disappointing harvests that eventually made it impossible for her to stay. Just before Dinesen's departure, in 1931, Finch-Hatton died in a plane crash and was buried in the Ngong hills.

Dinesen had begun reading Rudyard Kipling, Oscar Wilde, and Robert Louis Stevenson on the African farm, where she also wrote romances for her lover. On her return to Denmark, when she had to rescue herself from bankruptcy, she chose to write in Finch-Hatton's language in order to distance herself from her Danish surroundings, just as she used the pseudonym Isak, "the one who laughs," to cope with her sorrow. In *Seven Gothic Tales* (1934) and *Winter Tales* (1942), she focused with ironic wit on the charades and masquerades that liberate the self from the constraints of a fixed identity. Similarly, she created a myth of herself through her extravagant costumes, a gown that she named Sappho, for example, or a suit she called Sober Truth. Identifying her disease with her fallen father, whose suicide, she had reason to believe, was related to a case of syphilis, she considered "it was worth while having syphilis in order to become a Baroness." As one of the last representatives of the aristocratic spirit, then, she saw herself as a quixotic rebel opposed to a dreary bourgeois realism. In her later years, she was active in Danish intellectual life as a patroness of avant-garde artists, as a hostess of a lively salon, and as a speaker on the radio. Like many of the characters in her parables and fables, Dinesen delighted in her personal and artistic power even in the bleakest of historical moments.

Between the appearance of her thriller *The Angelic Avengers* (1944), published under the pseudonym Pierre Andrezel, and her next volume of stories, *Last Tales* (1957), Dinesen suffered from the syphilis, which was now beyond treatment. Nevertheless, with the help of her companion and secretary, Clara Svendsen, she continued to travel—to America in 1959, for instance, where her books were greeted enthusiastically by admirers like Carson McCullers. After an operation on her spinal cord, and another on her stomach, however, Dinesen would never again weigh more than eighty-five pounds. "The doctor tells me that I have all the symptoms of a concentration camp prisoner," she explained during the time she lived on asparagus, fruit juice, oysters, and dry biscuits. She died of malnutrition.

The Blank Page

By the ancient city gate sat an old coffee-brown, black-veiled woman who made her living by telling stories.

She said:

"You want a tale, sweet lady and gentleman? Indeed I have told many tales, one more than a thousand,[1] since that time when I first let young men tell me, myself, tales of a red rose, two smooth lily buds, and

---

1. A reference to *The Thousand and One Nights*, a collection of Arabian tales told by Scheherezade, a bride trying to delay her execution at the hands of her husband, the Sultan.

four silky, supple, deadly entwining snakes. It was my mother's mother, the black-eyed dancer, the often-embraced, who in the end—wrinkled like a winter apple and crouching beneath the mercy of the veil—took upon herself to teach me the art of story-telling. Her own mother's mother had taught it to her, and both were better story-tellers than I am. But that, by now, is of no consequence, since to the people they and I have become one, and I am most highly honored because I have told stories for two hundred years."

Now if she is well paid and in good spirits, she will go on.

"With my grandmother," she said, "I went through a hard school. 'Be loyal to the story,' the old hag would say to me. 'Be eternally and unswervingly loyal to the story.' 'Why must I be that, Grandmother?' I asked her. 'Am I to furnish you with reasons, baggage?' she cried. 'And you mean to be a story-teller! Why, you are to become a story-teller, and I shall give you my reasons! Hear then: Where the story-teller is loyal, eternally and unswervingly loyal to the story, there, in the end, silence will speak. Where the story has been betrayed, silence is but emptiness. But we, the faithful, when we have spoken our last word, will hear the voice of silence. Whether a small snotty lass understands it or not.'

"Who then," she continues, "tells a finer tale than any of us? Silence does. And where does one read a deeper tale than upon the most perfectly printed page of the most precious book? Upon the blank page. When a royal and gallant pen, in the moment of its highest inspiration, has written down its tale with the rarest ink of all—where, then, may one read a still deeper, sweeter, merrier and more cruel tale than that? Upon the blank page."

The old beldame for a while says nothing, only giggles a little and munches with her toothless mouth.

"We," she says at last, "the old women who tell stories, we know the story of the blank page. But we are somewhat averse to telling it, for it might well, among the uninitiated, weaken our own credit. All the same, I am going to make an exception with you, my sweet and pretty lady and gentleman of the generous hearts. I shall tell it to you."

High up in the blue mountains of Portugal there stands an old convent for sisters of the Carmelite order, which is an illustrious and austere order. In ancient times the convent was rich, the sisters were all noble ladies, and miracles took place there. But during the centuries highborn ladies grew less keen on fasting and prayer, the great dowries flowed scantily into the treasury of the convent, and today the few portionless[2] and humble sisters live in but one wing of the vast crumbling

2. Without dowries.

structure, which looks as if it longed to become one with the gray rock itself. Yet they are still a blithe and active sisterhood. They take much pleasure in their holy meditations, and will busy themselves joyfully with that one particular task which did once, long, long ago, obtain for the convent a unique and strange privilege: they grow the finest flax and manufacture the most exquisite linen of Portugal.

The long field below the convent is plowed with gentle-eyed, milk-white bullocks, and the seed is skillfully sown out by labor-hardened virginal hands with mold under the nails. At the time when the flax field flowers, the whole valley becomes air-blue, the very color of the apron which the blessed virgin put on to go out and collect eggs within St. Anne's poultry yard, the moment before the Archangel Gabriel in mighty wing-strokes lowered himself onto the threshold of the house, and while high, high up a dove, neck-feathers raised and wings vibrating, stood like a small clear silver star in the sky. During this month the villagers many miles round raise their eyes to the flax field and ask one another: "Has the convent been lifted into heaven? Or have our good little sisters succeeded in pulling down heaven to them?"

Later in due course the flax is pulled, scutched and hackled;[3] thereafter the delicate thread is spun, and the linen woven, and at the very end the fabric is laid out on the grass to bleach, and is watered time after time, until one may believe that snow has fallen round the convent walls. All this work is gone through with precision and piety and with such sprinklings and litanies as are the secret of the convent. For these reasons the linen, baled high on the backs of small gray donkeys and sent out through the convent gate, downwards and ever downwards to the towns, is as flower-white, smooth and dainty as was my own little foot when, fourteen years old, I had washed it in the brook to go to a dance in the village.

Diligence, dear Master and Mistress, is a good thing, and religion is a good thing, but the very first germ of a story will come from some mystical place outside the story itself. Thus does the linen of the Convento Velho draw its true virtue from the fact that the very first linseed was brought home from the Holy Land itself by a crusader.

In the Bible, people who can read may learn about the lands of Lecha and Maresha, where flax is grown. I myself cannot read, and have never seen this book of which so much is spoken. But my grandmother's grandmother as a little girl was the pet of an old Jewish rabbi, and the learning she received from him has been kept and passed on in our family. So you will read, in the book of Joshua, of how Achsah the daughter of Caleb lighted from her ass and cried unto her father: "Give

3. Beaten and combed.

me a blessing! For thou hast now given me land; give me also the blessing of springs of water!" And he gave her the upper springs and the nether springs. And in the fields of Lecha and Maresha lived, later on, the families of them that wrought the finest linen of all. Our Portuguese crusader, whose own ancestors had once been great linen weavers of Tomar, as he rode through these same fields was struck by the quality of the flax, and so tied a bag of seeds to the pommel of his saddle.

From this circumstance originated the first privilege of the convent, which was to procure bridal sheets for all the young princesses of the royal house.

I will inform you, dear lady and gentleman, that in the country of Portugal in very old and noble families a venerable custom has been observed. On the morning after the wedding of a daughter of the house, and before the morning gift had yet been handed over, the Chamberlain or High Steward from a balcony of the palace would hang out the sheet of the night and would solemnly proclaim: *Virginem eam tenemus*—"we declare her to have been a virgin." Such a sheet was never afterwards washed or again lain on.

This time-honored custom was nowhere more strictly upheld than within the royal house itself, and it has there subsisted till within living memory.

Now for many hundred years the convent in the mountains, in appreciation of the excellent quality of the linen delivered, has held its second high privilege: that of receiving back that central piece of the snow-white sheet which bore witness to the honor of a royal bride.

In the tall main wing of the convent, which overlooks an immense landscape of hills and valleys, there is a long gallery with a black-and-white marble floor. On the walls of the gallery, side by side, hangs a long row of heavy, gilt frames, each of them adorned with a coroneted plate of pure gold, on which is engraved the name of a princess: Donna Christina, Donna Ines, Donna Jacintha Lenora, Donna Maria. And each of these frames encloses a square cut from a royal wedding sheet.

Within the faded markings of the canvases people of some imagination and sensibility may read all the signs of the zodiac: the Scales, the Scorpion, the Lion, the Twins. Or they may there find pictures from their own world of ideas: a rose, a heart, a sword—or even a heart pierced through with a sword.

In days of old it would occur that a long, stately, richly colored procession wound its way through the stone-gray mountain scenery, upwards to the convent. Princesses of Portugal, who were now queens or queen dowagers of foreign countries, Archduchesses, or Electresses, with their splendid retinue, proceeded here on a pilgrimage which was by nature both sacred and secretly gay. From the flax field upwards the road rises steeply; the royal-lady would have to descend from her coach to be carried this last bit of the way in a palanquin[4] presented to the convent for the very same purpose..

Later on, up to our own day, it has come to pass—as it comes to pass when a sheet of paper is being burnt, that after all other sparks have run along the edge and died away, one last clear little spark will appear and hurry along after them—that a very old highborn spinster undertakes the journey to Convento Velho. She has once, a long long time ago, been playmate, friend and maid-of-honor to a young princess of Portugal. As she makes her way to the convent she looks round to see the view widen to all sides. Within the building a sister conducts her to the gallery and to the plate bearing the name of the princess she has once served, and there takes leave of her, aware of her wish to be alone.

Slowly, slowly a row of recollections passes through the small, venerable, skull-like head under its mantilla[5] of black lace, and it nods to them in amicable recognition. The loyal friend and confidante looks back upon the young bride's elevated married life with the elected royal consort. She takes stock of happy events and disappointments—coronations and jubilees, court intrigues and wars, the birth of heirs to the throne, the alliances of younger generations of princes and princesses, the rise or decline of dynasties. The old lady will remember how once, from the markings on the canvas, omens were drawn; now she will be able to compare the fulfillment to the omen, sighing a little and smiling a little. Each separate canvas with its coroneted name-plate has a story to tell, and each has been set up in loyalty to the story.

But in the midst of the long row there hangs a canvas which differs from the others. The frame of it is as fine and as heavy as any, and as proudly as any carries the golden plate with the royal crown. But on this one plate no name is inscribed, and the linen within the frame is snow-white from corner to corner, a blank page.

I beg of you, you good people who want to hear stories told: look at this page, and recognize the wisdom of my grandmother and of all old story-telling women!

For with what eternal and unswerving loyalty has not this canvas been inserted in the row! The story-tellers themselves before it draw their veils over their faces and are dumb. Because the royal papa and mama who once ordered this canvas to be framed and hung up, had they not had the tradition of loyalty in their blood, might have left it out.

It is in front of this piece of pure white linen that the old princesses of Portugal—worldly wise, dutiful, long-suffering queens, wives and

---

4. Enclosed litter carried on poles.   5. A light shawl (mantle).

mothers—and their noble old playmates, bridesmaids and maids-of-honor have most often stood still.

It is in front of the blank page that old and young nuns, with the Mother Abbess herself, sink into deepest thought.

1957

ANZIA YEZIERSKA
c. 1885–1970

Anzia Yezierska's novel *Bread Givers* (1925) dramatizes the ambivalence of a girl who confronts the misogyny of Jewish laws and learning in the Torah (the Jewish Bible): "Women were always the curse of men," the girl's pious father proclaims, "but when they get older they're devils and witches." Angered though she is, later in the novel, after she rejects a lucrative marriage proposal which would have turned her into "another piece of property," this same daughter believes that her integrity comes from her father's "wiser-than-the-world kind of wisdom," for "he had given up worldly success to drink the wisdom of the Torah." Many of Yezierska's characters are similarly caught between the old world of their fathers, the "shtetl" (village) of Europe transplanted to the Lower East Side of New York, and the New World of America with its promise of advancement through education and economic mobility, a world that, ironically enough, inexorably isolates them from those origins which are the source of their energies.

Born in Poland of poor parents who had nine children, Yezierska emigrated with her family to America in the 1890s. Athough her father continued to maintain the honorable poverty associated with the study of the Talmud (the ancient writings of rabbis), she sought advancement in night school. Married once, for a few months in 1910, and soon again for three years, she eventually decided to leave her only child, a daughter, with her second husband. Her fiction, which began appearing in 1915, won quick acclaim; *The Fat of the Land* was awarded the Edward J. O'Brien prize and her collection *Hungry Hearts* (1920) was purchased by the Hollywood producer Samuel Goldwyn for ten thousand dollars. Although she published story collections (like *Children of Loneliness*, 1923) and novels (like *Salome of the Tenements*, 1922) throughout the twenties, her success had cut her off from the people who had inspired her writing in the first place. For all of the filth, poverty, ignorance, degrading toil, and misogyny of the ghetto, Jewish immigrant culture provided the familiar cadences of the Yiddish language and the warmth of familial customs that animated her fiction.

By the nineteen-thirties and -forties, Yezierska had difficulties finding a publisher for her writing. She was quite poor and more than eighty years old when readers began to rediscover her work. By the time she died, she was being recognized as a sensitive interpreter of the assimilation process.

The Fat of the Land

In an air-shaft so narrow that you could touch the next wall with your bare hands, Hanneh Breineh leaned out and knocked on her neighbor's window.

"Can you loan me your wash-boiler[1] for the clothes?" she called.

Mrs. Pelz threw up the sash.

"The boiler? What's the matter with yours again? Didn't you tell me you had it fixed already last week?"

"A black year on him, the robber, the way he fixed it! If you have no luck in this world, then it's better not to live. There I spent out fifteen cents to stop up one hole, and it runs out another. How I ate out my gall bargaining with him he should let it down to fifteen cents! He wanted yet a quarter, the swindler. Gottuniu![2] My bitter heart on him for every penny he took from me for nothing!"

"You got to watch all those swindlers, or they'll steal the whites out of your eyes," admonished Mrs. Pelz. "You should have tried out your boiler before you paid him. Wait a minute till I empty out my dirty clothes in a pillowcase; then I'll hand it to you."

Mrs. Pelz returned with the boiler and tried to hand it across to Hanneh Breineh, but the soapbox refrigerator on the window sill was in the way.

"You got to come in for the boiler yourself," said Mrs. Pelz.

"Wait only till I tie my Sammy on to the highchair he shouldn't fall on me again. He's so wild that ropes won't hold him."

Hanneh Breineh tied the child in the chair, stuck a pacifier in his mouth, and went in to her neighbor. As she took the boiler Mrs. Pelz said:

"Do you know Mrs. Melker ordered fifty pounds of chicken for her daughter's wedding? And such grand chickens! Shining like gold! My heart melted in me just looking at the flowing fatness of those chickens."

Hanneh Breineh smacked her thin, dry lips, a hungry gleam in her sunken eyes.

"Fifty pounds!" she gasped. "It ain't possible. How do you know?"

"I heard her with my own ears. I saw them with my own eyes. And she said she will chop up the chicken livers with onions and eggs for an appetizer, and then she will buy twenty-five pounds of fish, and cook it sweet and sour with raisins, and she said she will bake all her shtrudels[3] on pure chicken fat."

"Some people work themselves up in the world," sighed Hanneh

---

1. Metal vessel for boiling clothes.
2. Oh, dear God!

3. Pastries of thin dough wrapped around a filling.

Breineh. "For them is America flowing with milk and honey. In Savel,[4] Mrs. Melker used to get shriveled up from hunger. She and her children used to live on potato-peelings and crusts of dry bread picked out from the barrels; and in America she lives to eat chicken, and apple shtrudels soaking in fat."

"The world is a wheel always turning," philosophized Mrs. Pelz. "Those who were high go down low, and those who've been low go up higher. Who will believe me here in America that in Poland I was a cook in a banker's house? I handled ducks and geese every day. I used to bake coffeecake with cream so thick you could cut it with a knife."

"And do you think I was a nobody in Poland?" broke in Hanneh Breineh, tears welling in her eyes as the memories of her past rushed over her. "But what's the use of talking? In America money is everything. Who cares who my father or grandfather was in Poland? Without money I'm a living dead one. My head dries out worrying how to get for the children the eating a penny cheaper."

Mrs. Pelz wagged her head, a gnawing envy contracting her features.

"Mrs. Melker had it good from the day she came," she said, begrudgingly. "Right away she sent all her children to the factory, and she began to cook meat for dinner every day. She and her children have eggs and buttered rolls for breakfast each morning like millionaires."

A sudden fall and a baby's scream, and the boiler dropped from Hanneh Breineh's hands as she rushed into her kitchen, Mrs. Pelz after her. They found the highchair turned on top of the baby.

"Gewalt![5] Save me! Run for a doctor!" cried Hanneh Breineh, as she dragged the child from under the highchair. "He's killed! He's killed! My only child! My precious lamb!" she shrieked as she ran back and forth with the screaming infant.

Mrs. Pelz snatched little Sammy from the mother's hands.

"Meshugeneh![6] What are you running around like a crazy, frightening the child? Let me see. Let me tend to him. He ain't killed yet." She hastened to the sink to wash the child's face, and discovered a swelling lump on his forehead. "Have you a quarter in your house?" she asked.

"Yes, I got one," replied Hanneh Breineh, climbing on a chair. "I got to keep it on a high shelf where the children can't get it."

Mrs. Pelz seized the quarter Hanneh Breineh handed down to her.

"Now pull your left eyelid three times while I'm pressing the quarter, and you'll see the swelling go down."

Hanneh Breineh took the child again in her arms, shaking and cooing over it and caressing it.

---

4. Village in Poland.
5. A cry of fear or astonishment.
6. Crazy woman!

"Ah-ah-ah, Sammy! Ah-ah-ah-ah, little lamb! Ah-ah-ah, little bird! Ah-ah-ah-ah, precious heart! Oh, you saved my life; I thought he was killed," gasped Hanneh Breineh, turning to Mrs. Pelz. "Oi-i!" she sighed, "a mother's heart! Always in fear over her children. The minute anything happens to them all life goes out of me. I lose my head and I don't know where I am anymore."

"No wonder the child fell," admonished Mrs. Pelz. "You should have a red ribbon or red beads on his neck to keep away the evil eye. Wait. I got something in my machine-drawer."

Mrs. Pelz returned, bringing the boiler and a red string, which she tied about the child's neck while the mother proceeded to fill the boiler.

A little later Hanneh Breineh again came into Mrs. Pelz's kitchen, holding Sammy in one arm and in the other an apronful of potatoes. Putting the child down on the floor, she seated herself on the unmade kitchen-bed and began to peel the potatoes in her apron.

"Woe to me!" sobbed Hanneh Breineh. "To my bitter luck there ain't no end. With all my other troubles, the stove got broke. I lighted the fire to boil the clothes, and it's to get choked with smoke. I paid rent only a week ago, and the agent don't want to fix it. A thunder should strike him! He only comes for the rent, and if anything has to be fixed, then he don't want to hear nothing.

"Why comes it to me so hard?" went on Hanneh Breineh, the tears streaming down her cheeks. "I can't stand it no more. I came in to you for a minute to run away from my troubles. It's only when I sit myself down to peel potatoes or nurse the baby that I take time to draw a breath, and beg only for death."

Mrs. Pelz, accustomed to Hanneh Breineh's bitter outbursts, continued her scrubbing.

"Ut!" exclaimed Hanneh Breineh, irritated at her neighbor's silence, "what are you tearing up the world with your cleaning? What's the use to clean up when everything only gets dirty again?"

"I got to shine up my house for the holidays."

"You've got it so good nothing lays on your mind but to clean your house. Look on this little bloodsucker," said Hanneh Breineh, pointing to the wizened child, made prematurely solemn from starvation and neglect. "Could anybody keep that brat clean? I wash him one minute, and he is dirty the minute after." Little Sammy grew frightened and began to cry. "Shut up!" ordered the mother, picking up the child to nurse it again. "Can't you see me take a rest for a minute?"

The hungry child began to cry at the top of its weakened lungs.

"Na, na, you glutton." Hanneh Breineh took out a dirty pacifier from her pocket and stuffed it into the baby's mouth. The grave, pasty-faced infant shrank into a panic of fear, and chewed the nipple nervously, clinging to it with both his thin little hands.

"For what did I need yet the sixth one?" groaned Hanneh Breineh, turning to Mrs. Pelz. "Wasn't it enough five mouths to feed? If I didn't have this child on my neck, I could turn myself around and earn a few cents." She wrung her hands in a passion of despair. "Gottuniu! The earth should only take it before it grows up!"

"Shah![7] Shah!" reproved Mrs. Pelz. "Pity yourself on the child. Let it grow up already so long as it is here. See how frightened it looks on you." Mrs. Pelz took the child in her arms and petted it. "The poor little lamb! What did it done you should hate it so?"

Hanneh Breineh pushed Mrs. Pelz away from her.

"To whom can I open the wounds of my heart?" she moaned. "Nobody has pity on me. You don't believe me, nobody believes me until I'll fall down like a horse in the middle of the street. Oi weh![8] Mine life is so black for my eyes! Some mothers got luck. A child gets run over by a car, some fall from a window, some burn themselves up with a match, some get choked with diphtheria; but no death takes mine away."

"God from the world, stop cursing!" admonished Mrs. Pelz. "What do you want from the poor children? Is it their fault that their father makes small wages? Why do you let it all out on them?" Mrs. Pelz sat down beside Hanneh Breineh. "Wait only till your children get old enough to go to the shop and earn money," she consoled. "Push only through those few years while they are yet small; your sun will begin to shine; you will live on the fat of the land, when they begin to bring you in the wages each week."

Hanneh Breineh refused to be comforted.

"Till they are old enough to go to the shop and earn money they'll eat the head off my bones," she wailed. "If you only knew the fights I got by each meal. Maybe I gave Abe a bigger piece of bread than Fanny. Maybe Fanny got a little more soup in her plate than Jake. Eating is dearer than diamonds. Potatoes went up a cent on a pound, and milk is only for millionaires. And once a week, when I buy a little meat for the Sabbath, the butcher weighs it for me like gold, with all the bones in it. When I come to lay the meat out on a plate and divide it up, there ain't nothing to it but bones. Before, he used to throw me in a piece of fat extra or a piece of lung, but now you got to pay for everything, even for a bone to the soup."

"Never mind; you'll yet come out from all your troubles. Just as soon as your children get old enough to get their working papers the more children you got, the more money you'll have."

"Why should I fool myself with the false shine of hope? Don't I know it's already my black luck not to have it good in this world? Do you think American children will right away give everything they earn to their mother?"

"I know what is with you the matter," said Mrs. Pelz. "You didn't eat yet to-day. When it is empty in the stomach, the whole world looks black. Come, only let me give you something good to taste in the mouth; that will freshen you up." Mrs. Pelz went to the cupboard and brought out the saucepan of gefüllte fisch[9] that she had cooked for dinner and placed it on the table in front of Hanneh Breineh. "Give a taste my fish," she said, taking one slice on a spoon, and handing it to Hanneh Breineh with a piece of bread. "I wouldn't give it to you on a plate because I just cleaned up my house, and I don't want to dirty up more dishes."

"What, am I a stranger you should have to serve me on a plate yet!" cried Hanneh Breineh, snatching the fish in her trembling fingers.

"Oi weh! How it melts through all the bones!" she exclaimed, brightening as she ate. "May it be for good luck to us all!" she exulted, waving aloft the last precious bite.

Mrs. Pelz was so flattered that she even ladled up a spoonful of gravy.

"There is a bit of onion and carrot in it," she said, as she handed it to her neighbor.

Hanneh Breineh sipped the gravy drop by drop, like a connoisseur sipping wine.

"Ah-h-h! A taste of that gravy lifts me up to heaven!" As she disposed leisurely of the slice of onion and carrot she relaxed and expanded and even grew jovial. "Let us wish all our troubles on the Russian Czar![1] Let him burst with our worries for rent! Let him get shriveled with our hunger for bread! Let his eyes dry out of his head looking for work!

"Shah! I'm forgetting from everything," she exclaimed, jumping up. "It must be eleven or soon twelve, and my children will be right away out of school and fall on me like a pack of wild wolves. I better quick run to the market and see what cheaper I can get for a quarter."

Because of the lateness of her coming, the stale bread at the nearest bakeshop was sold out, and Hanneh Breineh had to trudge from shop to shop in search of the usual bargain, and spent nearly an hour to save two cents.

In the meantime the children returned from school, and, finding the door locked, climbed through the fire-escape, and entered the house through the window. Seeing nothing on the table, they rushed to the stove. Abe pulled a steaming potato out of the boiling pot, and so scalded his fingers that the potato fell to the floor, whereupon the three others pounced on it.

9. Savory fish cakes.
1. The Russian czars had been responsible for the segregation and suffering of Jews for generations.

"It was my potato," cried Abe, blowing his burned fingers, while with the other hand and his foot he cuffed and kicked the three who were struggling on the floor. A wild fight ensued, and the potato was smashed under Abe's foot amid shouts and screams. Hanneh Breineh, on the stairs, heard the noise of her famished brood, and topped their cries with curses and invective.

"They are here already, the savages! They are here already to shorten my life! They heard you all over the hall, in all the houses around!"

The children, disregarding her words, pounced on her market-basket, shouting ravenously: "Mamma, I'm hungry! What more do you got to eat?"

They tore the bread and herring out of Hanneh Breineh's basket and devoured it in starved savagery, clamoring for more.

"Murderers!" screamed Hanneh Breineh, goaded beyond endurance. "What are you tearing from me my flesh? From where should I steal to give you more? Here I had already a pot of potatoes and a whole loaf of bread and two herrings, and you swallowed it down in the wink of an eye. I have to have Rockefeller's millions[2] to fill your stomachs."

All at once Hanneh Breineh became aware that Benny was missing. "Oi weh!" she burst out, wringing her hands in a new wave of woe, "where is Benny? Didn't he come home yet from school?"

She ran out into the hall, opened the grime-coated window, and looked up and down the street, but Benny was nowhere in sight.

"Abe, Jake, Fanny, quick, find Benny!" entreated Hanneh Breineh, as she rushed back into the kitchen. But the children, anxious to snatch a few minutes' play before the school-call, dodged past her and hurried out.

With the baby on her arm, Hanneh Breineh hastened to the kindergarten.

"Why are you keeping Benny here so long?" she shouted at the teacher as she flung open the door. "If you had my bitter heart, you would send him home long ago and not wait till I got to come for him."

The teacher turned calmly and consulted her record-cards.

"Benny Safron? He wasn't present this morning."

"Not here?" shrieked Hanneh Breineh. "I pushed him out myself he should go. The children didn't want to take him, and I had no time. Woe is me! Where is my child?" She began pulling her hair and beating her breast as she ran into the street.

Mrs. Pelz was busy at a pushcart, picking over some spotted apples, when she heard the clamor of an approaching crowd. A block off she recognized Hanneh Breineh, her hair disheveled, her clothes awry,

2. I.e., the wealth of the millionaire John D. Rockefeller (1839–1937).

running toward her with her yelling baby in her arms, the crowd following.

"Friend mine," cried Hanneh Breineh, falling on Mrs. Pelz's neck, "I lost my Benny, the best child of all my children." Tears streamed down her red, swollen eyes as she sobbed. "Benny! mine heart, mine life! Oi-i-i!"

Mrs. Pelz took the frightened baby out of the mother's arms.

"Still yourself a little! See how you're frightening your child."

"Woe to me! Where is my Benny? Maybe he's killed already by a car. Maybe he fainted away from hunger. He didn't eat nothing all day long. Gottuniu! Pity yourself on me!"

She lifted her hands full of tragic entreaty.

"People, my child! Get me my child! I'll go crazy out of my head! Get me my child, or I'll take poison before your eyes!"

"Still yourself a little!" pleaded Mrs. Pelz.

"Talk not to me!" cried Hanneh Breineh, wringing her hands. "You're having all your children. I lost mine. Every good luck comes to other people. But I didn't live yet to see a good day in my life. Mine only joy, mine Benny, is lost away from me."

The crowd followed Hanneh Breineh as she wailed through the street, leaning on Mrs. Pelz. By the time she returned to her house the children were back from school; but seeing that Benny was not there, she chased them out in the street, crying:

"Out of here, you robbers, gluttons! Go find Benny!" Hanneh Breineh crumpled into a chair in utter prostration. "Oi weh! he's lost! Mine life; my little bird; mine only joy! How many nights I spent nursing him when he had the measles! And all that I suffered for weeks and months when he had the whooping-cough! How the eyes went out of my head till I learned him how to walk, till I learned him how to talk! And such a smart child! If I lost all the others, it wouldn't tear me so by the heart."

She worked herself up into such a hysteria, crying, and tearing her hair, and hitting her head with her knuckles, that at last she fell into a faint. It took some time before Mrs. Pelz, with the aid of neighbors, revived her.

"Benny, mine angel!" she moaned as she opened her eyes.

Just then a policeman came in with the lost Benny.

"Na, na, here you got him already!" said Mrs. Pelz. "Why did you carry on so for nothing? Why did you tear up the world like a crazy?"

The child's face was streaked with tears as he cowered, frightened and forlorn. Hanneh Breineh sprang toward him, slapping his cheeks, boxing his ears, before the neighbors could rescue him from her.

"Woe on your head!" cried the mother. "Where did you lost yourself? Ain't I got enough worries on my head than to go around looking for you? I didn't have yet a minute's peace from that child since he was born!"

"See a crazy mother!" remonstrated Mrs. Pelz, rescuing Benny from another beating. "Such a mouth! With one breath she blesses him when he is lost, and with the other breath she curses him when he is found."

Hanneh Breineh took from the windowsill a piece of herring covered with swarming flies, and putting it on a slice of dry bread, she filled a cup of tea that had been stewing all day, and dragged Benny over to the table to eat.

But the child, choking with tears, was unable to touch the food.

"Go eat!" commanded Hanneh Breineh. "Eat and choke yourself eating!"

"Maybe she won't remember me no more. Maybe the servant won't let me in," thought Mrs. Pelz, as she walked by the brownstone house on Eighty-Fourth Street where she had been told Hanneh Breineh now lived. At last she summoned up enough courage to climb the steps. She was all out of breath as she rang the bell with trembling fingers. "Oi weh! even the outside smells riches and plenty! Such curtains! And shades on all windows like by millionaires! Twenty years ago she used to eat from the pot to the hand, and now she lives in such a palace."

A whiff of steam-heated warmth swept over Mrs. Pelz as the door opened, and she saw her old friend of the tenements dressed in silk and diamonds like a being from another world.

"Mrs. Pelz, is it you!" cried Hanneh Breineh, overjoyed at the sight of her former neighbor. "Come right in. Since when are you back in New York?"

"We came last week," mumbled Mrs. Pelz, as she was led into a richly carpeted reception-room.

"Make yourself comfortable. Take off your shawl," urged Hanneh Breineh.

But Mrs. Pelz only drew her shawl more tightly around her, a keen sense of her poverty gripping her as she gazed, abashed by the luxurious wealth that shone from every corner.

"This shawl covers up my rags," she said, trying to hide her shabby sweater.

"I'll tell you what; come right into the kitchen," suggested Hanneh Breineh. "The servant is away for this afternoon, and we can feel more comfortable there. I can breathe like a free person in my kitchen when the girl has her day out."

Mrs. Pelz glanced about her in an excited daze. Never in her life had she seen anything so wonderful as a white-tiled kitchen, with its glistening porcelain sink and the aluminum pots and pans that shone like silver.

"Where are you staying now?" asked Hanneh Breineh, as she pinned an apron over her silk dress.

"I moved back to Delancey Street,[3] where we used to live," replied Mrs. Pelz, as she seated herself cautiously in a white enameled chair.

"Oi weh! What grand times we had in that old house when we were neighbors!" sighed Hanneh Breineh, looking at her old friend with misty eyes.

"You still think on Delancey Street? Haven't you more high-class neighbors uptown here?"

"A good neighbor is not to be found every day," deplored Hanneh Breineh. "Uptown here, where each lives in his own house, nobody cares if the person next door is dying or going crazy from loneliness. It ain't anything like we used to have it in Delancey Street, when we could walk into one another's rooms without knocking, and borrow a pinch of salt or a pot to cook in."

Hanneh Breineh went over to the pantry-shelf.

"We are going to have a bite right here on the kitchen-table like on Delancey Street. So long there's no servant to watch us we can eat what we please."

"Oi! How it waters my mouth with appetite, the smell of the herring and onion!" chuckled Mrs. Pelz, sniffing the welcome odors with greedy pleasure.

Hanneh Breineh pulled a dishtowel from the rack and threw one end of it to Mrs. Pelz.

"So long there's no servant around, we can use it together for a napkin. It's dirty, anyhow. How it freshens up my heart to see you!" she rejoiced as she poured out her tea into a saucer. "If you would only know how I used to beg my daughter to write for me a letter to you; but these American children, what is to them a mother's feelings?"

"What are you talking!" cried Mrs. Pelz. "The whole world rings with you and your children. Everybody is envying you. Tell me how began your luck?"

"You heard how my husband died with consumption," replied Hanneh Breineh. "The five hundred dollars lodge money gave me the first lift in life, and I opened a little grocery store. Then my son Abe married himself to a girl with a thousand dollars. That started him in business, and now he has the biggest shirtwaist factory on West Twenty-Ninth Street."

"Yes, I heard your son had a factory." Mrs. Pelz hesitated and stammered; "I'll tell you the truth. What I came to ask you—I thought

3. Street on New York's Lower East Side.

maybe you would beg your son Abe if he would give my husband a job."

"Why not?" said Hanneh Breineh. "He keeps more than five hundred hands. I'll ask him if he should take in Mr. Pelz."

"Long years on you, Hanneh Breineh! You'll save my life if you could only help my husband get work."

"Of course my son will help him. All my children like to do good. My daughter Fanny is a milliner on Fifth Avenue, and she takes in the poorest girls in her shop and even pays them sometimes while they learn the trade." Hanneh Breineh's face lit up, and her chest filled with pride as she enumerated the successes of her children. "And my son Benny he wrote a play on Broadway, and he gave away more than a hundred free tickets for the first night."

"Benny? The one who used to get lost from home all the time? You always did love that child more than all the rest. And what is Sammy your baby doing?"

"He ain't a baby no longer. He goes to college and quarterbacks the football team. They can't get along without him."

"And my son Jake, I nearly forgot him. He began collecting rent in Delancey Street, and now he is boss of renting the swellest apartmenthouses on Riverside Drive."[4]

"What did I tell you? In America children are like money in the bank," purred Mrs. Pelz, as she pinched and patted Hanneh Breineh's silk sleeve. "Oi weh! How it shines from you! You ought to kiss the air and dance for joy and happiness. It is such a bitter frost outside; a pail of coal is so dear, and you got it so warm with steam heat. I had to pawn my feather bed to have enough for the rent, and you are rolling in money."

"Yes, I got it good in some ways, but money ain't everything," sighed Hanneh Breineh.

"You ain't yet satisfied?"

"But here I got no friends," complained Hanneh Breineh.

"Friends?" queried Mrs. Pelz. "What greater friend is there on earth than the dollar?"

"Oi! Mrs. Pelz; if you could only look into my heart! I'm so choked up! You know they say a cow has a long tongue, but can't talk." Hanneh Breineh shook her head wistfully, and her eyes filmed with inward brooding. "My children give me everything from the best. When I was sick, they got me a nurse by day and one by night. They bought me the best wine. If I asked for dove's milk, they would buy it for me; but—but—I can't talk myself out in their language. They want to make me

4. Upper-class neighborhood on New York's Upper West Side; especially high-class at the time of this story.

over for an American lady, and I'm different." Tears cut their way under her eyelids with a pricking pain as she went on: "When I was poor, I was free, and could holler and do what I like in my own house. Here I got to lie still like a mouse under a broom. Between living up to my Fifth-Avenue daughter and keeping up with the servants, I am like a sinner in the next world that is thrown from one hell to another." The doorbell rang, and Hanneh Breineh jumped up with a start.

"Oi weh! It must be the servant back already!" she exclaimed, as she tore off her apron. "Oi weh! Let's quickly put the dishes together in a dishpan. If she sees I eat on the kitchen table, she will look on me like the dirt under her feet."

Mrs. Pelz seized her shawl in haste.

"I better run home quick in my rags before your servant sees me."

"I'll speak to Abe about the job," said Hanneh Breineh, as she pushed a bill into the hand of Mrs. Pelz, who edged out as the servant entered.

"I'm having fried potato lotkes[5] special for you, Benny," said Hanneh Breineh, as the children gathered about the table for the family dinner given in honor of Benny's success with his new play. "Do you remember how you used to lick the fingers from them?"

"Oh, mother!" reproved Fanny. "Any one hearing you would think we were still in the pushcart district."

"Stop your nagging, sis, and let ma alone," commanded Benny, patting his mother's arm affectionately. "I'm home only once a month. Let her feed me what she pleases. My stomach is bomb-proof."

"Do I hear that the President is coming to your play?" said Abe, as he stuffed a napkin over his diamond-studded shirt-front.

"Why shouldn't he come?" returned Benny. "The critics say it's the greatest antidote for the race hatred created by the war. If you want to know, he is coming tonight; and what's more, our box is next to the President's."

"Nu, mammeh,"[6] sallied Jake, "did you ever dream in Delancey Street that we should rub sleeves with the President?"

"I always said that Benny had more head than the rest of you," replied the mother.

As the laughter died away, Jake went on:

"Honor you are getting plenty; but how much mezummen does this play bring you? Can I invest any of it in real estate for you?"

"I'm getting ten per cent royalties of the gross receipts," replied the youthful playwright.

"How much is that?" queried Hanneh Breineh.

---

5. Potato pancakes.   6. Well, mama.

"Enough to buy up all your fish-markets in Delancey Street," laughed Abe in good-natured raillery at his mother.

Her son's jest cut like a knife-thrust in her heart. She felt her heart ache with the pain that she was shut out from their successes. Each added triumph only widened the gulf. And when she tried to bridge this gulf by asking questions, they only thrust her back upon herself.

"Your fame has even helped me get my hat trade solid with the Four Hundred,"[7] put in Fanny. "You bet I let Mrs. Van Suyden know that our box is next to the President's. She said she would drop in to meet you. Of course she let on to me that she hadn't seen the play yet, though my designer said she saw her there on the opening night."

"Oh, Gosh, the toadies!" sneered Benny. "Nothing so sickens you with success as the way people who once shoved you off the sidewalk come crawling to you on their stomachs begging you to dine with them."

"Say, that leading man of yours he's some class!" cried Fanny. "That's the man I'm looking for. Will you invite him to supper after the theater?"

The playwright turned to his mother.

"Say, ma," he said laughingly, "how would you like a real actor for a son-in-law?"

"She should worry," mocked Sam. "She'll be discussing with him the future of the Greek drama. Too bad it doesn't happen to be Warfield,[8] or mother could give him tips on the 'Auctioneer.' "

Jake turned to his mother with a covert grin.

"I guess you'd have no objection if Fanny got next to Benny's leading man. He makes at least fifteen hundred a week. That wouldn't be such a bad addition to the family, would it?"

Again the bantering tone stabbed Hanneh Breineh. Everything in her began to tremble and break loose.

"Why do you ask me?" she cried, throwing her napkin into her plate. "Do I count for a person in this house? If I'll say something, will you even listen to me? What is to me the grandest man that my daughter could pick out? Another enemy in my house! Another person to shame himself from me!" She swept in her children in one glance of despairing anguish as she rose from the table. "What worth is an old mother to American children? The President is coming tonight to the theater, and none of you asked me to go." Unable to check the rising tears, she fled toward the kitchen and banged the door.

They all looked at one another guiltily.

"Say, sis," Benny called out sharply, "what sort of frame-up is this? Haven't you told mother that she was to go with us tonight?"

7. I.e., exclusive social elite.
8. David Warfield (1866–1951), prominent

American actor who starred as a New York East Side Jew in *The Auctioneer* (1900–1903).

"Yes—I—" Fanny bit her lips as she fumbled evasively for words. "I asked her if she wouldn't mind my taking her some other time."

"Now you have made a mess of it!" fumed Benny. "Mother'll be too hurt to go now."

"Well, I don't care," snapped Fanny. "I can't appear with mother in a box at the theater. Can I introduce her to Mrs. Van Suyden? And suppose your leading man should ask to meet me?"

"Take your time, sis. He hasn't asked yet," scoffed Benny.

"The more reason I shouldn't spoil my chances. You know mother. She'll spill the beans that we come from Delancey Street the minute we introduce her anywhere. Must I always have the black shadow of my past trailing after me?"

"But have you no feelings for mother?" admonished Abe.

"I've tried harder than all of you to do my duty. I've *lived* with her." She turned angrily upon them. "I've borne the shame of mother while you bought her off with a present and a treat here and there. God knows how hard I tried to civilize her so as not to have to blush with shame when I take her anywhere. I dressed her in the most stylish Paris models, but Delancey Street sticks out from every inch of her. Whenever she opens her mouth, I'm done for. You fellows had your chance to rise in the world because a man is free to go up as high as he can reach up to; but I, with all my style and pep, can't get a man my equal because a girl is always judged by her mother."

They were silenced by her vehemence, and unconsciously turned to Benny.

"I guess we all tried to do our best for mother," said Benny, thoughtfully. "But wherever there is growth, there is pain and heartbreak. The trouble with us is that the ghetto of the Middle Ages and the children of the twentieth century have to live under one roof, and—"

A sound of crashing dishes came from the kitchen, and the voice of Hanneh Breineh resounded through the diningroom as she wreaked her pent-up fury on the helpless servant.

"Oh, my nerves! I can't stand it any more! There will be no girl again for another week!" cried Fanny.

"Oh, let up on the old lady," protested Abe. "Since she can't take it out on us any more, what harm is it if she cusses the servants?"

"If you fellows had to chase around employment agencies, you wouldn't see anything funny about it. Why can't we move into a hotel that will do away with the need of servants altogether?"

"I got it better," said Jake, consulting a notebook from his pocket. "I have on my list an apartment on Riverside Drive where there's only a small kitchenette; but we can do away with the cooking, for there is a dining service in the building."

The new Riverside apartment to which Hanneh Breineh was re-moved by her socially ambitious children was for the habitually active mother an empty desert of enforced idleness. Deprived of her kitchen, Hanneh Breineh felt robbed of the last reason for her existence. Cook-ing and marketing and puttering busily with pots and pans gave her an excuse for living and struggling and bearing up with her children. The lonely idleness of Riverside Drive stunned all her senses and arrested all her thoughts. It gave her that choked sense of being cut off from air, from life, from everything warm and human. The cold indifference, the each-for-himself look in the eyes of the people about her were like stinging slaps in the face. Even the children had nothing real or human in them. They were starched and stiff miniatures of their elders.

But the most unendurable part of the stifling life on Riverside Drive was being forced to eat in the public diningroom. No matter how hard she tried to learn polite table manners, she always found people staring at her, and her daughter rebuking her for eating with the wrong fork or guzzling the soup or staining the cloth.

In a fit of rebellion Hanneh Breineh resolved never to go down to the public diningroom again, but to make use of the gas-stove in the kitch-enette to cook her own meals. That very day she rode down to Delan-cey Street and purchased a new market-basket. For some time she walked among the haggling pushcart venders, relaxing and swimming in the warm waves of her old familiar past.

A fish-peddler held up a large carp in his black, hairy hand and waved it dramatically:

"Women! Women! Fourteen cents a pound!"

He ceased his raucous shouting as he saw Hanneh Breineh in her rich attire approach his cart.

"How much?" she asked, pointing to the fattest carp.

"Fifteen cents, lady," said the peddler, smirking as he raised his price.

"Swindler! Didn't I hear you call fourteen cents?" shrieked Hanneh Breineh, exultingly, the spirit of the penny chase surging in her blood. Diplomatically, Hanneh Breineh turned as if to go, and the fisherman seized her basket in frantic fear.

"I should live; I'm losing money on the fish, lady," whined the ped-dler. "I'll let it down to thirteen cents for you only."

"Two pounds for a quarter, and not a penny more," said Hanneh Breineh, thrilling again with the rare sport of bargaining, which had been her chief joy in the good old days of poverty.

"Nu, I want to make the first sale for good luck." The peddler threw the fish on the scale.

As he wrapped up the fish, Hanneh Breineh saw the driven look of worry in his haggard eyes, and when he counted out the change from her dollar, she waved it aside. "Keep it for your luck," she said, and hurried off to strike a new bargain at a pushcart of onions.

Hanneh Breineh returned triumphantly with her purchases. The basket under her arm gave forth the old, homelike odors of herring and garlic, while the scaly tail of a four-pound carp protruded from its newspaper wrapping. A gilded placard on the door of the apartment-house proclaimed that all merchandise must be delivered through the trade entrance in the rear; but Hanneh Breineh with her basket strode proudly through the marble-paneled hall and rang nonchalantly for the elevator.

The uniformed hall-man, erect, expressionless, frigid with dignity, stepped forward:

"Just a minute, madam. I'll call a boy to take up your basket for you."

Hanneh Breineh, glaring at him, jerked the basket savagely from his hands. "Mind your own business!" she retorted. "I'll take it up myself. Do you think you're a Russian policeman to boss me in my own house?"

Angry lines appeared on the countenance of the representative of social decorum.

"It is against the rules, madam," he said, stiffly.

"You should sink into the earth with all your rules and brass buttons. Ain't this America? Ain't this a free country? Can't I take up in my own house what I buy with my own money?" cried Hanneh Breineh, reveling in the opportunity to shower forth the volley of invectives that had been suppressed in her for the weeks of deadly dignity of Riverside Drive.

In the midst of this uproar Fanny came in with Mrs. Van Suyden. Hanneh Breineh rushed over to her, crying:

"This bossy policeman won't let me take up my basket in the elevator."

The daughter, unnerved with shame and confusion, took the basket in her white-gloved hand and ordered the hall-boy to take it around to the regular delivery entrance.

Hanneh Breineh was so hurt by her daughter's apparent defense of the hall-man's rules that she utterly ignored Mrs. Van Suyden's greeting and walked up the seven flights of stairs out of sheer spite.

"You see the tragedy of my life?" broke out Fanny, turning to Mrs. Van Suyden.

"You poor child! You go right up to your dear, old lady mother, and I'll come some other time."

Instantly Fanny regretted her words. Mrs. Van Suyden's pity only roused her wrath the more against her mother.

Breathless from climbing the stairs, Hanneh Breineh entered the apartment just as Fanny tore the faultless millinery creation from her head and threw it on the floor in a rage.

"Mother, you are the ruination of my life! You have driven away Mrs. Van Suyden, as you have driven away all my best friends. What do you think we got this apartment for but to get rid of your fish smells and your brawls with the servants? And here you come with a basket on your arm as if you just landed from steerage![9] And this afternoon, of all times, when Benny is bringing his leading man to tea. When will you ever stop disgracing us?"

"When I'm dead," said Hanneh Breineh, grimly. "When the earth will cover me up, then you'll be free to go your American way. I'm not going to make myself over for a lady on Riverside Drive. I hate you and all your swell friends. I'll not let myself be choked up here by you or by that hall-boss policeman that is higher in your eyes than your own mother."

"So that's your thanks for all we've done for you?" cried the daughter.

"All you've done for me!" shouted Hanneh Breineh. "What have you done for me? You hold me like a dog on a chain! It stands in the Talmud;[1] some children give their mothers dry bread and water and go to heaven for it, and some give their mother roast duck and go to Gehenna because it's not given with love."

"You want me to love you yet?" raged the daughter. "You knocked every bit of love out of me when I was yet a kid. All the memories of childhood I have is your everlasting cursing and yelling that we were gluttons."

The bell rang sharply, and Hanneh Breineh flung open the door.

"Your groceries, ma'am," said the boy.

Hanneh Breineh seized the basket from him, and with a vicious fling sent it rolling across the room, strewing its contents over the Persian rugs and inlaid floor. Then seizing her hat and coat, she stormed out of the apartment and down the stairs.

Mr. and Mrs. Pelz sat crouched and shivering over their meager supper when the door opened, and Hanneh Breineh in fur coat and plumed hat charged into the room.

"I come to cry out to you my bitter heart," she sobbed. "Woe is me! It is so black for my eyes!"

"What is the matter with you, Hanneh Breineh?" cried Mrs. Pelz in bewildered alarm.

"I am turned out of my own house by the brass-buttoned policeman

9. Lowest-class passage on a ship.
1. The body of Jewish law and tradition; "Gehenna": hell.

that bosses the elevator. Oi-i-i-i! Weh-h-h-h! What have I from my life? The whole world rings with my son's play. Even the President came to see it, and I, his mother, have not seen it yet. My heart is dying in me like in a prison," she went on wailing. "I am starved out for a piece of real eating. In that swell restaurant is nothing but napkins and forks and lettuce-leaves. There are a dozen plates to every bite of food. And it looks so fancy on the plate, but it's nothing but straw in the mouth. I'm starving, but I can't swallow down their American eating."

"Hanneh Breineh," said Mrs. Pelz, "you are sinning before God. Look on your fur coat; it alone would feed a whole family for a year. I never had yet a piece of fur trimming on a coat, and you are in fur from the neck to the feet. I never had yet a piece of feather on a hat, and your hat is all feathers."

"What are you envying me?" protested Hanneh Breineh. "What have I from all my fine furs and feathers when my children are strangers to me? All the fur coats in the world can't warm up the loneliness inside my heart. All the grandest feathers can't hide the bitter shame in my face that my children shame themselves from me."

Hanneh Breineh suddenly loomed over them like some ancient, heroic figure of the Bible condemning unrighteousness.

"Why should my children shame themselves from me? From where did they get the stuff to work themselves up in the world? Did they get it from the air? How did they get all their smartness to rise over the people around them? Why don't the children of born American mothers write my Benny's plays? It is I, who never had a chance to be a person, who gave him the fire in his head. If I would have had a chance to go to school and learn the language, what couldn't I have been? It is I and my mother and my mother's mother and my father and father's father who had such a black life in Poland; it is our choked thoughts and feelings that are flaming up in my children and making them great in America. And yet they shame themselves from me!"

For a moment Mr. and Mrs. Pelz were hypnotized by the sweep of her words. Then Hanneh Breineh sank into a chair in utter exhaustion. She began to weep bitterly, her body shaking with sobs.

"Woe is me! For what did I suffer and hope on my children? A bitter old age—my end. I'm so lonely!"

All the dramatic fire seemed to have left her. The spell was broken. They saw the Hanneh Breineh of old, ever discontented, ever complaining even in the midst of riches and plenty.

"Hanneh Breineh," said Mrs. Pelz, "the only trouble with you is that you got it too good. People will tear the eyes out of your head because you're complaining yet. If I only had your fur coat! If I only had your diamonds! I have nothing. You have everything. You are living on the fat of the land. You go right back home and thank God that you don't have my bitter lot."

"You got to let me stay here with you," insisted Hanneh Breineh. "I'll not go back to my children except when they bury me. When they will see my dead face, they will understand how they killed me."

Mrs. Pelz glanced nervously at her husband. They barely had enough covering for their one bed; how could they possibly lodge a visitor?

"I don't want to take up your bed," said Hanneh Breineh. "I don't care if I have to sleep on the floor or on the chairs, but I'll stay here for the night."

Seeing that she was bent on staying, Mr. Pelz prepared to sleep by putting a few chairs next to the trunk, and Hanneh Breineh was invited to share the rickety bed with Mrs. Pelz.

The mattress was full of lumps and hollows. Hanneh Breineh lay cramped and miserable, unable to stretch out her limbs. For years she had been accustomed to hair mattresses and ample woolen blankets, so that though she covered herself with her fur coat, she was too cold to sleep. But worse than the cold were the creeping things on the wall. And as the lights were turned low, the mice came through the broken plaster and raced across the floor. The foul odors of the kitchen-sink added to the night of horrors.

"Are you going back home?" asked Mrs. Pelz, as Hanneh Breineh put on her hat and coat the next morning.

"I don't know where I'm going," she replied, as she put a bill into Mrs. Pelz's hand.

For hours Hanneh Breineh walked through the crowded ghetto streets. She realized that she no longer could endure the sordid ugliness of her past, and yet she could not go home to her children. She only felt that she must go on and on.

In the afternoon a cold, drizzling rain set in. She was worn out from the sleepless night and hours of tramping. With a piercing pain in her heart she at last turned back and boarded the subway for Riverside Drive. She had fled from the marble sepulcher of the Riverside apartment to her old home in the ghetto; but now she knew that she could not live there again. She had outgrown her past by the habits of years of physical comforts, and these material comforts that she could no longer do without choked and crushed the life within her.

A cold shudder went through Hanneh Breineh as she approached the apartment-house. Peering through the plate glass of the door she saw the face of the uniformed hallman. For a hesitating moment she remained standing in the drizzling rain, unable to enter, and yet knowing full well that she would have to enter.

Then suddenly Hanneh Breineh began to laugh. She realized that it was the first time she had laughed since her children had become rich. But it was the hard laugh of bitter sorrow. Tears streamed down her furrowed cheeks as she walked slowly up the granite steps.

"The fat of the land!" muttered Hanneh Breineh, with a choking sob as the hall-man with immobile face deferentially swung open the door —"the fat of the land!"

1920

RADCLYFFE HALL
1886–1943

Una, Lady Troubridge, who was Radclyffe Hall's lover for twenty-seven years, supplied in her biography (1945) most of the scanty facts we have about the early life of this pioneering lesbian novelist. Marguerite Radclyffe Hall was born in Bournemouth, Hampshire. She was neglected by her father, who left the family when she was three, and alienated from her mother, who remarried an Italian singing teacher as insensitive to her daughter as she was. By the time she attended day schools and, for one year, King's College, Radclyffe Hall was calling herself "Peter" or "John," as if to express her desire to forge a new sexual identity for herself. At twenty-one, she inherited a fortune from the Radclyffe-Hall Trust, and moved to Kensington with the only affectionate relative she had ever known, her maternal grandmother. Six years later, she began the affair that would really provide her education. Mabel Veronica Batten ("Ladye") was a cultivated patroness of music. Twenty-three years older than Hall, she encouraged her young lover to relinquish sports for more intellectual pursuits, horses and dogs for books. After the death of "Ladye" in 1916, Hall turned to Una Troubridge for consolation, and they lived together for the rest of Hall's life.

Handsome in her tweed suits and cropped hair, Radclyffe Hall had published several volumes of verse and two novels before *Adam's Breed* (1927) won the Femina–Vie Heureuse Prize and the James Tait Black Memorial Book Prize. But she became famous because of the trial and scandal that greeted her next book, *The Well of Loneliness* (1928). Introduced by the psychologist Havelock Ellis, Radclyffe Hall's novel focused on a heroine named Stephen Gordon, a girl brought up by a father who wanted a boy. Stephen lives and loves heroically, engaging in passionate affairs with other women and working in the London Ambulance Column during World War I. Feeling herself to be a man trapped in a female body, however, she suffers the frustrations of the "congenital invert." Through its reliance on this concept of the "invert," *The Well of Loneliness* presents lesbianism as a biological tragedy and has therefore been criticized by a number of contemporary historians of lesbian culture. Yet it nevertheless protests against the persecution of lesbians with unusual explicitness, even as it presents a broodingly attractive portrait of a young woman who aspires to the courage and verve she associates with masculinity. Although Radclyffe Hall responded to the banning of *The Well of Loneliness* in England by going on to write several religious novels, her contribution to literary history is still measured by her portrait of the conflicted but androgynous Stephen, who seems "to combine the strength of a man with the gentler and more subtle strength of a woman." *Miss Ogilvy Finds Herself* meditates on the same themes that inform Hall's lesbian classic.

Miss Ogilvy Finds Herself

Miss Ogilvy stood on the quay at Calais and surveyed the disbanding of her Unit, the Unit that together with the coming of war[1] had completely altered the complexion of her life, at all events for three years.

Miss Ogilvy's thin, pale lips were set sternly and her forehead was puckered in an effort of attention, in an effort to memorise every small detail of every old war-weary battered motor on whose side still appeared the merciful emblem[2] that had set Miss Ogilvy free.

Miss Ogilvy's mind was jerking a little, trying to regain its accustomed balance, trying to readjust itself quickly to this sudden and paralysing change. Her tall, awkward body with its queer look of strength, its broad, flat bosom and thick legs and ankles, as though in response to her jerking mind, moved uneasily, rocking backwards and forwards. She had this trick of rocking on her feet in moments of controlled agitation. As usual, her hands were thrust deep into her pockets, they seldom seemed to come out of her pockets unless it were to light a cigarette, and as though she were still standing firm under fire while the wounded were placed in her ambulances, she suddenly straddled her legs very slightly and lifted her head and listened. She was standing firm under fire at that moment, the fire of a desperate regret.

Some girls came towards her, young, tired-looking creatures whose eyes were too bright from long strain and excitement. They had all been members of that glorious Unit, and they still wore the queer little forage-caps[3] and the short, clumsy tunics of the French Militaire. They still slouched in walking and smoked Caporals in emulation of the Poilus.[4] Like their founder and leader these girls were all English, but like her they had chosen to serve England's ally, fearlessly thrusting right up to the trenches in search of the wounded and dying. They had seen some fine things in the course of three years, not the least fine of which was the cold, hard-faced woman who, commanding, domineer-

---

1. World War I, in 1914.
2. A Red Cross symbol of the ambulance corps.

3. Caps worn by infantry soldiers.
4. French soldiers.

ing, even hectoring at times, had yet been possessed of so dauntless a courage and of so insistent a vitality that it vitalised the whole Unit.

"It's rotten!" Miss Ogilvy heard someone saying. "It's rotten, this breaking up of our Unit!" And the high, rather childish voice of the speaker sounded perilously near to tears.

Miss Ogilvy looked at the girl almost gently, and it seemed, for a moment, as though some deep feeling were about to find expression in words. But Miss Ogilvy's feelings had been held in abeyance so long that they seldom dared become vocal, so she merely said "Oh?" on a rising inflection—her method of checking emotion.

They were swinging the ambulance cars in midair, those of them that were destined to go back to England, swinging them up like sacks of potatoes, then lowering them with much clanging of chains to the deck of the waiting steamer. The porters were shoving and shouting and quarrelling, pausing now and again to make meaningless gestures; while a pompous official was becoming quite angry as he pointed at Miss Ogilvy's own special car—it annoyed him, it was bulky and difficult to move.

"Bon Dieu! Mais dépêchez-vous donc!"[5] he bawled, as though he were bullying the motor.

Then Miss Ogilvy's heart gave a sudden, thick thud to see this undignified, pitiful ending; and she turned and patted the gallant old car as though she were patting a well-beloved horse, as though she would say: "Yes, I know how it feels—never mind, we'll go down together."

2

Miss Ogilvy sat in the railway carriage on her way from Dover to London. The soft English landscape sped smoothly past: small homesteads, small churches, small pastures, small lanes with small hedges; all small like England itself, all small like Miss Ogilvy's future. And sitting there still arrayed in her tunic, with her forage-cap resting on her knees, she was conscious of a sense of complete frustration; thinking less of those glorious years at the Front and of all that had gone to the making of her, than of all that had gone to the marring of her from the days of her earliest childhood.

She saw herself as a queer little girl, aggressive and awkward because of her shyness; a queer little girl who loathed sisters and dolls, preferring the stable-boys as companions, preferring to play with footballs and tops, and occasional catapults. She saw herself climbing the tallest beech trees, arrayed in old breeches illicitly come by. She remembered insisting with tears and some temper that her real name was William and not Wilhelmina. All these childish pretences and illusions she remembered, and the bitterness that came after. For Miss Ogilvy had

5. French: "Good God! Move along, then!"

found as her life went on that in this world it is better to be one with the herd, that the world has no wish to understand those who cannot conform to its stereotyped pattern. True enough, in her youth she had gloried in her strength, lifting weights, swinging clubs and developing muscles, but presently this had grown irksome to her; it had seemed to lead nowhere, she being a woman, and then as her mother had often protested: muscles looked so appalling in evening dress—a young girl ought not to have muscles.

Miss Ogilvy's relation to the opposite sex was unusual and at that time added much to her worries, for no less than three men had wished to propose, to the genuine amazement of the world and her mother. Miss Ogilvy's instinct made her like and trust men, for whom she had a pronounced fellow-feeling; she would always have chosen them as her friends and companions in preference to girls or women; she would dearly have loved to share in their sports, their business, their ideas and their wide-flung interests. But men had not wanted her, except the three who had found in her strangeness a definite attraction, and those would-be suitors she had actually feared, regarding them with aversion. Towards young girls and women she was shy and respectful, apologetic and sometimes admiring. But their fads and their foibles, none of which she could share, while amusing her very often in secret, set her outside the sphere of their intimate lives, so that in the end she must blaze a lone trail through the difficulties of her nature.

"I can't understand you," her mother had said, "you're a very odd creature—now when I was your age . . ."

And her daughter had nodded, feeling sympathetic. There were two younger girls who also gave trouble, though in their case the trouble was fighting for husbands who were scarce enough even in those days. It was finally decided, at Miss Ogilvy's request, to allow her to leave the field clear for her sisters. She would remain in the country with her father when the others went up for the Season.[6]

Followed long, uneventful years spent in sport, while Sarah and Fanny toiled, sweated and gambled in the matrimonial market. Neither ever succeeded in netting a husband, and when the Squire died leaving very little money, Miss Ogilvy found to her great surprise that they looked upon her as a brother. They had so often jibed at her in the past, that at first she could scarcely believe her senses, but before very long it became all too real: she it was who must straighten out endless muddles, who must make the dreary arrangements for the move, who must find a cheap but genteel house in London and, once there, who must cope with the family accounts which she only, it seemed, could balance.

It would be: "You might see to that, Wilhelmina; you write, you've

6. The social season.

got such a good head for business." Or: "I wish you'd go down and explain to that man that we really can't pay his account till next quarter." Or: "This money for the grocer is five shillings short. Do run over my sum, Wilhelmina."

Her mother, grown feeble, discovered in this daughter a staff upon which she could lean with safety. Miss Ogilvy genuinely loved her mother, and was therefore quite prepared to be leaned on; but when Sarah and Fanny began to lean too with the full weight of endless neurotic symptoms incubated in resentful virginity, Miss Ogilvy found herself staggering a little. For Sarah and Fanny were grown hard to bear, with their mania for telling their symptoms to doctors, with their unstable nerves and their acrid tongues and the secret dislike they now felt for their mother. Indeed, when old Mrs. Ogilvy died, she was unmourned except by her eldest daughter who actually felt a void in her life—the unforeseen void that the ailing and weak will not infrequently leave behind them.

At about this time an aunt also died, bequeathing her fortune to her niece Wilhelmina who, however, was too weary to gird up her loins and set forth in search of exciting adventure—all she did was to move her protesting sisters to a little estate she had purchased in Surrey. This experiment was only a partial success, for Miss Ogilvy failed to make friends of her neighbours; thus at fifty-five she had grown rather dour, as is often the way with shy, lonely people.

When the war came she had just begun settling down—people do settle down in their fifty-sixth year—she was feeling quite glad that her hair was grey, that the garden took up so much of her time, that, in fact, the beat of her blood was slowing. But all this was changed when war was declared; on that day Miss Ogilvy's pulses throbbed wildly.

"My God! If only I were a man!" she burst out, as she glared at Sarah and Fanny, "if only I had been born a man!" Something in her was feeling deeply defrauded.

Sarah and Fanny were soon knitting socks and mittens and mufflers and Jaeger trench-helmets.[7] Other ladies were busily working at depots, making swabs at the Squire's, or splints at the Parson's; but Miss Ogilvy scowled and did none of these things—she was not at all like other ladies.

For nearly twelve months she worried officials with a view to getting a job out in France—not in their way but in hers, and that was the trouble. She wished to go up to the front-line trenches, she wished to be actually under fire, she informed the harassed officials.

To all her enquiries she received the same answer: "We regret that

---

7. Woolen caps worn in the trenches, where much of World War I was fought.

we cannot accept your offer." But once thoroughly roused she was hard to subdue, for her shyness had left her as though by magic.

Sarah and Fanny shrugged angular shoulders: "There's plenty of work here at home," they remarked, "though of course it's not quite so melodramatic!"

"Oh . . . ?" queried their sister on a rising note of impatience—and she promptly cut off her hair: "That'll jar them!" she thought with satisfaction.

Then she went up to London, formed her admirable unit and finally got it accepted by the French, despite renewed opposition.

In London she had found herself quite at her ease, for many another of her kind was in London doing excellent work for the nation. It was really surprising how many cropped heads had suddenly appeared as it were out of space; how many Miss Ogilvies, losing their shyness, had come forward asserting their right to serve, asserting their claim to attention.

There followed those turbulent years at the front, full of courage and hardship and high endeavour; and during those years Miss Ogilvy forgot the bad joke that Nature seemed to have played her. She was given the rank of a French lieutenant and she lived in a kind of blissful illusion; appalling reality lay on all sides and yet she managed to live in illusion. She was competent, fearless, devoted and untiring. What then? Could any man hope to do better? She was nearly fifty-eight, yet she walked with a stride, and at times she even swaggered a little.

Poor Miss Ogilvy sitting so glumly in the train with her manly trench-boots and her forage-cap! Poor all the Miss Ogilvies back from the war with their tunics, their trench-boots, and their childish illusions! Wars come and wars go but the world does not change: it will always forget an indebtedness which it thinks it expedient not to remember.

3

When Miss Ogilvy returned to her home in Surrey it was only to find that her sisters were ailing from the usual imaginary causes, and this to a woman who had seen the real thing was intolerable, so that she looked with distaste at Sarah and then at Fanny. Fanny was certainly not prepossessing, she was suffering from a spurious attack of hay fever.

"Stop sneezing!" commanded Miss Ogilvy, in the voice that had so much impressed the Unit. But as Fanny was not in the least impressed, she naturally went on sneezing.

Miss Ogilvy's desk was piled mountain-high with endless tiresome letters and papers: circulars, bills, months-old correspondence, the gardener's accounts, an agent's report on some fields that required land-draining. She seated herself before this collection; then she sighed, it all seemed so absurdly trivial.

"Will you let your hair grow again?" Fanny enquired . . . she and Sarah had followed her into the study. "I'm certain the Vicar would be glad if you did."

"Oh?" murmured Miss Ogilvy, rather too blandly.

"Wilhelmina!"

"Yes?"

"You will do it, won't you?"

"Do what?"

"Let your hair grow; we all wish you would."

"Why should I?"

"Oh, well, it will look less odd, especially now that the war is over—in a small place like this people notice such things."

"I entirely agree with Fanny," announced Sarah.

Sarah had become very self-assertive, no doubt through having mismanaged the estate during the years of her sister's absence. They had quite a heated dispute one morning over the south herbaceous border.

"Whose garden is this?" Miss Ogilvy asked sharply. "I insist on auricula-eyed sweet Williams! I even took the trouble to write from France, but it seems that my letter has been ignored."

"Don't shout," rebuked Sarah, "you're not in France now!"

Miss Ogilvy could gladly have boxed her ears: "I only wish to God I were," she muttered.

Another dispute followed close on its heels, and this time it happened to be over the dinner. Sarah and Fanny were living on weeds—at least that was the way Miss Ogilvy put it.

"We've become vegetarians," Sarah said grandly.

"You've become two damn tiresome cranks!" snapped their sister.

Now it never had been Miss Ogilvy's way to indulge in acid recriminations, but somehow, these days, she forgot to say: "Oh?" quite so often as expediency demanded. It may have been Fanny's perpetual sneezing that had got on her nerves; or it may have been Sarah, or the gardener, or the Vicar, or even the canary; though it really did not matter very much what it was just so long as she found a convenient peg upon which to hang her growing irritation.

"This won't do at all," Miss Ogilvy thought sternly, "life's not worth so much fuss, I must pull myself together." But it seemed this was easier said than done; not a day passed without her losing her temper and that over some trifle: "No, this won't do at all—it just mustn't be," she thought sternly.

Everyone pitied Sarah and Fanny: "Such a dreadful, violent old thing," said the neighbours.

But Sarah and Fanny had their revenge: "Poor darling, it's shell shock,[8] you know," they murmured.

8. A common mental illness during World War I, brought on by the noise and anxiety of battle.

Thus Miss Ogilvy's prowess was whittled away until she herself was beginning to doubt it. Had she ever been that courageous person who had faced death in France with such perfect composure? Had she ever stood tranquilly under fire, without turning a hair, while she issued her orders? Had she ever been treated with marked respect? She herself was beginning to doubt it.

Sometimes she would see an old member of the Unit, a girl who, more faithful to her than the others, would take the trouble to run down to Surrey. These visits, however, were seldom enlivening.

"Oh, well . . . here we are . . ." Miss Ogilvy would mutter.

But one day the girl smiled and shook her blond head: "I'm not— I'm going to be married."

Strange thoughts had come to Miss Ogilvy, unbidden, thoughts that had stayed for many an hour after the girl's departure. Alone in her study she had suddenly shivered, feeling a sense of complete desolation. With cold hands she had lighted a cigarette.

"I must be ill or something," she had mused, as she stared at her trembling fingers.

After this she would sometimes cry out in her sleep, living over in dreams God knows what emotions; returning, maybe to the battlefield of France. Her hair turned snow-white; it was not unbecoming yet she fretted about it.

"I'm growing very old," she would sigh as she brushed her thick mop before the glass; and then she would peer at her wrinkles.

For now that it had happened she hated being old; it no longer appeared such an easy solution of those difficulties that had always beset her. And this she resented most bitterly, so that she became the prey of self-pity, and of other undesirable states in which the body will torment the mind, and the mind, in its turn, the body. Then Miss Ogilvy straightened her ageing back, in spite of the fact that of late it had ached with muscular rheumatism, and she faced herself squarely and came to a resolve.

"I'm off!" she announced abruptly one day; and that evening she packed her kit-bag.

4

Near the south coast of Devon there exists a small island that is still very little known to the world, but which nevertheless can boast an hotel, the only building upon it. Miss Ogilvy had chosen this place quite at random, it was marked on her map by scarcely more than a dot, but somehow she had liked the look of that dot and had set forth alone to explore it.

She found herself standing on the mainland one morning looking at a vague blur of green through the mist, a vague blur of green that rose out of the Channel like a tidal wave suddenly suspended. Miss Ogilvy was filled with a sense of adventure; she had not felt like this since the ending of war.

"I was right to come here, very right indeed. I'm going to shake off all my troubles," she decided.

A fisherman's boat was parting the mist, and before it was properly beached, in she bundled.

"I hope they're expecting me?" she said gaily.

"They du be expecting you," the man answered.

The sea, which is generally rough off that coast, was indulging itself in an oily ground-swell; the broad, glossy swells struck the side of the boat, then broke and sprayed over Miss Ogilvy's ankles.

The fisherman grinned: "Feeling all right?" he queried. "It du be tiresome most times about these parts." But the mist had suddenly drifted away and Miss Ogilvy was staring wide-eyed at the island.

She saw a long shoal of jagged black rocks, and between them the curve of a small sloping beach, and above that the lift of the island itself, and above that again, blue heaven. Near the beach stood the little two-storied hotel which was thatched, and built entirely of timber; for the rest she could make out no signs of life apart from a host of white sea-gulls.

Then Miss Ogilvy said a curious thing. She said: "On the south-west side of that place there was once a cave—a very large cave. I remember that it was some way from the sea."

"There du be a cave still," the fisherman told her, "but it's just above highwater level."

"A-ah," murmured Miss Ogilvy thoughtfully, as though to herself; then she looked embarrassed.

The little hotel proved both comfortable and clean, the hostess both pleasant and comely. Miss Ogilvy started unpacking her bag, changed her mind and went for a stroll round the island. The island was covered with turf and thistles and traversed by narrow green paths thick with daisies. It had four rock-bound coves of which the south-western was by far the most difficult of access. For just here the island descended abruptly as though it were hurtling down to the water; and just here the shale was most treacherous and the tide-swept rocks most aggressively pointed. Here it was that the seagulls, grown fearless of man by reason of his absurd limitations, built their nests on the ledges and reared countless young who multiplied, in their turn, every season. Yes, and here it was that Miss Ogilvy, greatly marvelling, stood and stared across at a cave; much too near the crumbling edge for her safety, but by now completely indifferent to caution.

"I remember . . . I remember . . ." she kept repeating. Then: "That's all very well, but what do I remember?"

She was conscious of somehow remembering all wrong, of her memory being distorted and coloured—perhaps by the endless things she had seen since her eyes had last rested upon that cave. This worried her sorely, far more than the fact that she should be remembering the cave at all, she who had never set foot on the island before that actual morning. Indeed, except for the sense of wrongness when she struggled to piece her memories together, she was steeped in a very profound contentment which surged over her spirit, wave upon wave.

"It's extremely odd," pondered Miss Ogilvy. Then she laughed, so pleased did she feel with its oddness.

5

That night after supper she talked to her hostess who was only too glad, it seemed, to be questioned. She owned the whole island and was proud of the fact, as she very well might be, decided her boarder. Some curious things had been found on the island, according to comely Mrs. Nanceskivel: bronze arrow-heads, pieces of ancient stone celts;[9] and once they had dug up a man's skull and thigh-bone—this had happened while they were sinking a well. Would Miss Ogilvy care to have a look at the bones? They were kept in a cupboard in the scullery.

Miss Ogilvy nodded.

"Then I'll fetch him this moment," said Mrs. Nanceskivel, briskly.

In less than two minutes she was back with the box that contained those poor remnants of a man, and Miss Ogilvy, who had risen from her chair, was gazing down at those remnants. As she did so her mouth was sternly compressed, but her face and her neck flushed darkly.

Mrs. Nanceskivel was pointing to the skull: "Look, miss, he was killed," she remarked rather proudly, "and they tell me that the axe that killed him was bronze. He's thousands and thousands of years old, they tell me. Our local doctor knows a lot about such things and he wants me to send these bones to an expert; they ought to belong to the Nation, he says. But I know what would happen, they'd come digging up my island, and I won't have people digging up my island, I've got enough worry with the rabbits as it is." But Miss Ogilvy could no longer hear the words for the pounding of the blood in her temples.

She was filled with a sudden, inexplicable fury against the innocent Mrs. Nanceskivel: "You . . . you . . ." she began, then checked herself, fearful of what she might say to the woman.

For her sense of outrage was overwhelming as she stared at those bones that were kept in the scullery; moreover, she knew how such men had been buried, which made the outrage seem all the more shameful. They had buried such men in deep, well-dug pits surmounted by four stout stones at their corners—four stout stones there had been and a

_____

9. Prehistoric stone axes.

covering stone. And all this Miss Ogilvy knew as by instinct, having no concrete knowledge on which to draw. But she knew it right down in the depths of her soul, and she hated Mrs. Nanceskivel.

And now she was swept by another emotion that was even more strange and more devastating: such a grief as she had not conceived could exist; a terrible unassuageable grief, without hope, without respite, without palliation, so that with something akin to despair she touched the long gash in the skull. Then her eyes, that had never wept since her childhood, filled slowly with large, hot, difficult tears. She must blink very hard, then close her eyelids, turn away from the lamp and say rather loudly:

"Thanks, Mrs. Nanceskivel. It's past eleven—I think I'll be going upstairs."

6

Miss Ogilvy closed the door of her bedroom, after which she stood quite still to consider: "Is it shell shock?" she muttered incredulously. "I wonder, can it be shell shock?"

She began to pace slowly about the room, smoking a Caporal. As usual her hands were deep in her pockets; she could feel small, familiar things in those pockets and she gripped them, glad of their presence. Then all of a sudden she was terribly tired, so tired that she flung herself down on the bed, unable to stand any longer.

She thought that she lay there struggling to reason, that her eyes were closed in the painful effort, and that as she closed them she continued to puff the inevitable cigarette. At least that was what she thought at one moment—the next, she was out in a sunset evening, and a large red sun was sinking slowly to the rim of a distant sea.

Miss Ogilvy knew that she was herself, that is to say she was conscious of her being, and yet she was not Miss Ogilvy at all, nor had she a memory of her. All that she now saw was very familiar, all that she now did was what she should do, and all that she now was seemed perfectly natural. Indeed, she did not think of these things; there seemed no reason for thinking about them.

She was walking with bare feet on turf that felt springy and was greatly enjoying the sensation; she had always enjoyed it, ever since as an infant she had learned to crawl on this turf. On either hand stretched rolling green uplands, while at her back she knew that there were forests; but in front, far away, lay the gleam of the sea towards which the big sun was sinking. The air was cool and intensely still, with never so much as a ripple or bird song. It was wonderfully pure—one might almost say young—but Miss Ogilvy thought of it merely as air. Having always breathed it she took it for granted, as she took the soft turf and the uplands.

She pictured herself as immensely tall; she was feeling immensely tall at the moment. As a matter of fact she was five feet eight which, however, was quite a considerable height when compared to that of her fellow tribesmen. She was wearing a single garment of pelts which came to her knees and left her arms sleeveless. Her arms and her legs, which were closely tattooed with blue zig-zag lines, were extremely hairy. From a leathern thong twisted about her waist there hung a clumsily made stone weapon, a celt, which in spite of its clumsiness was strongly hafted and useful for killing.

Miss Ogilvy wanted to shout aloud from a glorious sense of physical well-being, but instead she picked up a heavy, round stone which she hurled with great force at some distant rocks.

"Good! Strong!" she exclaimed. "See how far it goes!"

"Yes, strong. There is no one so strong as you. You are surely the strongest man in our tribe," replied her little companion.

Miss Ogilvy glanced at this little companion and rejoiced that they two were all alone together. The girl at her side had a smooth brownish skin, oblique black eyes and short, sturdy limbs. Miss Ogilvy marvelled because of her beauty. She also was wearing a single garment of pelts, new pelts, she had made it that morning. She had stitched at it diligently for hours with short lengths of gut and her best bone needle. A strand of black hair hung over her bosom, and this she was constantly stroking and fondling; then she lifted the strand and examined her hair.

"Pretty," she remarked with childish complacence.

"Pretty," echoed the young man at her side.

"For you," she told him, "all of me is for you and none other. For you this body has ripened."

He shook back his own coarse hair from his eyes; he had sad brown eyes like those of a monkey. For the rest he was lean and steel-strong of loin, broad of chest, and with features not too uncomely. His prominent cheekbones were set rather high, his nose was blunt, his jaw somewhat bestial; but his mouth, though full-lipped, contradicted his jaw, being very gentle and sweet in expression. And now he smiled, showing big, square, white teeth.

"You . . . woman," he murmured contentedly, and the sound seemed to come from the depths of his being.

His speech was slow and lacking in words when it came to expressing a vital emotion, so one word must suffice and this he now spoke, and the word that he spoke had a number of meanings. It meant: "Little spring of exceedingly pure water." It meant: "Hut of peace for a man after battle." It meant: "Ripe red berry sweet to the taste." It meant: "Happy small home of future generations." All these things he must try to express by a word, and because of their loving she understood him.

They paused, and lifting her up he kissed her. Then he rubbed his large shaggy head on her shoulder; and when he released her she knelt at his feet.

"My master; blood of my body," she whispered. For with her it was different, love had taught her love's speech, so that she might turn her heart into sounds that her primitive tongue could utter.

After she had pressed her lips to his hands, and her cheek to his hairy and powerful forearm, she stood up and they gazed at the setting sun, but with bowed heads, gazing under their lids, because this was very sacred.

A couple of mating bears padded toward them from a thicket, and the female rose to her haunches. But the man drew his celt and menaced the beast, so that she dropped down noiselessly and fled, and her mate also fled, for here was the power that few dared to withstand by day or by night, on the uplands or in the forests. And now from across to the left where a river would presently lose itself in the marshes, came a rhythmical thudding, as a herd of red deer with wide nostrils and starting eyes thundered past, disturbed in their drinking by the bears.

After this the evening returned to its silence, and the spell of its silence descended on the lovers, so that each felt very much alone, yet withal more closely united to the other. But the man became restless under that spell, and he suddenly laughed; then grasping the woman he tossed her above his head and caught her. This he did many times for his own amusement and because he knew that his strength gave her joy. In this manner they played together for a while, he with his strength and she with her weakness. And they cried out, and made many guttural sounds which were meaningless save only to themselves. And the tunic of pelts slipped down from her breasts, and her two little breasts were pear-shaped.

Presently, he grew tired of their playing, and he pointed toward a cluster of huts and earthworks that lay to the eastward. The smoke from these huts rose in thick straight lines, bending neither to right nor left in its rising, and the thought of sweet burning rushes and brushwood touched his consciousness, making him feel sentimental.

"Smoke," he said.

And she answered: "Blue smoke."

He nodded: "Yes, blue smoke—home."

Then she said: "I have ground much corn since the full moon. My stones are too smooth. You make me new stones."

"All you have need of, I make," he told her.

She stole closer to him, taking his hand: "My father is still a black cloud full of thunder. He thinks that you wish to be head of our tribe in his place, because he is now very old. He must not hear of these meetings of ours, if he did I think he would beat me!"

So he asked her: "Are you unhappy, small berry?"

But at this she smiled: "What is being unhappy? I do not know what that means any more."

"I do not either," he answered.

Then as though some invisible force had drawn him, his body swung around and he stared at the forests where they lay and darkened, fold upon fold; and his eyes dilated with wonder and terror, and he moved his head quickly from side to side as a wild thing will do that is held between bars and whose mind is pitifully bewildered.

"Water!" he cried hoarsely, "great water—look, look! Over there. This land is surrounded by water!"

"What water?" she questioned.

He answered: "The sea." And he covered his face with his hands.

"Not so," she consoled, "big forests, good hunting. Big forests in which you hunt boar and aurochs.[1] No sea over there but only the trees."

He took his trembling hands from his face: "You are right . . . only trees," he said dully.

But now his face had grown heavy and brooding and he started to speak of a thing that oppressed him: "The Roundheaded-ones, they are devils," he growled, while his bushy black brows met over his eyes, and when this happened it changed his expression which became a little sub-human.

"No matter," she protested, for she saw that he forgot her and she wished him to think an talk only of love. "No matter. My father laughs at your fears. Are we not friends with the Roundheaded-ones? We are friends, so why should we fear them?"

"Our forts, very old, very weak," he went on, "and the Roundheaded-ones have terrible weapons. Their weapons are not made of good stone like ours, but of some dark, devilish substance."

"What of that?" she said lightly. "They would fight on our side, so why need we trouble about their weapons?"

But he looked away, not appearing to hear her. "We must barter all, all for their celts and arrows and spears, and then we must learn their secret. They lust after our women, they lust after our lands. We must barter all, all for their sly brown celts."

"Me . . . bartered?" she queried, very sure of his answer, otherwise she had not dared to say this.

"The Roundheaded-ones may destroy my tribe and yet I will not part with you," he told her. Then he spoke very gravely: "But I think they desire to slay us, and me they will try to slay first because they well know how much I mistrust them—they have seen my eyes fixed many times on their camps."

---

1. Extinct long-horned wild oxen.

She cried: "I will bite out the throats of these people if they so much as scratch your skin!"

And at this his mood changed and he roared with amusement: "You . . . woman!" he roared. "Little foolish white teeth. Your teeth were made for nibbling wild cherries, not for tearing the throats of the Roundheaded-ones!"

"Thoughts of war always make me afraid," she whimpered, still wishing him to talk about love.

He turned his sorrowful eyes upon her, the eyes that were sad even when he was merry, and although his mind was often obtuse, yet he clearly perceived how it was with her then. And his blood caught fire from the flame in her blood, so that he strained her against his body.

"You . . . mine . . ." he stammered.

"Love," she said, trembling, "this is love."

And he answered: "Love."

Then their faces grew melancholy for a moment, because dimly, very dimly in their dawning souls, they were conscious of a longing for something more vast than their earthly passion could compass.

Presently, he lifted her like a child and carried her quickly southward and westward till they came to a place where a gentle descent led down to a marshy valley. Far away, at the line where the marshes ended, they discerned the misty line of the sea; but the sea and the marshes were become as one substance, merging, blending, folding together; and since they were lovers they also would be one, even as the sea and the marshes.

And now they reached the mouth of a cave that was set in the quiet hillside. There was bright green verdure beside the cave, and a number of small, pink, thick-stemmed flowers that when they were crushed smelt of spices. And within the cave there was bracken newly gathered and heaped together for a bed; while beyond, from some rocks, came a low liquid sound as a spring dripped out through a crevice. Abruptly, he set the girl on her feet, and she knew that the days of her innocence were over. And she thought of the anxious virgin soil that was rent and sown to bring forth fruit in season, and she gave a quick little gasp of fear:

"No . . . no . . ." she gasped. For, divining his need, she was weak with the longing to be possessed, yet the terror of love lay heavy upon her. "No . . . no . . ." she gasped.

But he caught her wrist and she felt the great strength of his rough, gnarled fingers, the great strength of the urge that leapt in his loins, and again she must give the quick gasp of fear, the while she clung close to him lest he should spare her.

The twilight was engulfed and possessed by darkness, which in turn was transfigured by the moonrise, which in turn was fulfilled and consumed by dawn. A mighty eagle soared up from his eyrie,[2] cleaving the air with his masterful wings, and beneath him from the rushes that harboured their nests, rose other great birds, crying loudly. Then the heavy-horned elks appeared on the uplands, bending their burdened heads to the sod; while beyond in the forests the fierce wild aurochs stamped as they bellowed their love songs.

But within the dim cave the lord of these creatures had put by his weapon and his instinct for slaying. And he lay there defenceless with tenderness, thinking no longer of death but of life as he murmured the word that had so many meanings. That meant: "Little spring of exceedingly pure water." That meant: "Hut of peace for a man after battle." That meant: "Ripe red berry sweet to the taste." That meant: "Happy small home of future generations."

7

They found Miss Ogilvy the next morning; the fisherman saw her and climbed to the ledge. She was sitting at the mouth of the cave. She was dead, with her hands thrust deep into her pockets.

1926, 1934

2. Nest on a cliff or mountaintop.

H. D. (HILDA DOOLITTLE)
1886–1961

"Take care, do not know me," H. D. warned her readers in her book-length poem *Trilogy*; "shun me; for this reality / is infectious—ecstasy." The infectious ecstasy that H. D. dared to express was an alternative to what she considered the senseless violence of the modern world. Writing, in her periods of greatest productivity, during the two world wars, H. D. rejected the nightmare of history, substituting for it a personal, spiritual quest for resurrection. In search of "what men say is-not," she recovered eternal, mythic patterns in everyday events through what she called "spiritual realism." At their most problematic, H. D.'s equivalencies can be dizzyingly associative, for she traced the multiple meanings of related words, decoding such words as if they were hieroglyphs. At their most powerful, the images of her poetry transformed her own life and the life of her times into a palimpsest, a record that retains traces of a still visible and viable ancient script.

Until quite recently, H. D. has been remembered for a handful of short, intense poems that helped define the literary movement the modernist poet Ezra Pound dubbed Imagism. But the pioneering works of the critic Norman Holmes Pearson, Susan Friedman, and Louis Martz have illuminated the later development of this major modernist. The early Imagist lyrics written at the beginning of this century were followed by long poetic narratives composed at midcentury. In part, H. D.'s development as a poet was the result of the Greek translations, prose fiction, and film criticism she produced throughout the twenties and thirties. In part, too, it was indebted to a series of illustrious men who functioned as "initiators" for the poet. If, as the literary critic Rachel Blau DuPlessis has shown, H. D. sometimes seemed inextricably drawn to a relationship of "romantic thralldom" with such men, what she took away from them was transformed into a revisionary mythology that reflected her lifelong effort to understand her identity as a woman and a poet.

The only surviving daughter in a prominent family that included five sons, Hilda Doolittle lived the first eight years of her life in Bethlehem, Pennsylvania. Her father, Charles Doolittle, was professor of mathematics and astronomy at Lehigh University. In her autobiographical prose, H. D. recurrently associated him with authority and knowledge, for he charted the course of the stars in his study, where the maps and instruments impressed her as sacred symbols. Artistically talented, H. D.'s mother, Helen (Wolle) Doolittle, was a member of the Moravian brotherhood, a Protestant sect noted for its mysticism, and she maintained a close relationship with her own mother and with her father, who was the head of the Moravian seminary. The community had brought with them from Germany a doctrine that taught faith in a direct, sensuous illumination of God. Indeed, for H. D., the "gift" of vision and spiritual wisdom that the Moravians traced from generation to generation was an aspect of her own poetic gift.

In 1895, when H. D.'s father became Flower Professor of Astronomy and director of the Flower Observatory at the University of Pennsylvania, the family moved to a suburb of Philadelphia. Hilda lived at home while attending first the Gordon School, then the Friends Central School, and, finally, Bryn Mawr. She soon left college, however, after failing English and suffering from a breakdown. In her autobiographical novel *HERmione* (1923, published 1981), she analyzed the conflict she experienced at this time between her relationship with the young Ezra Pound, to whom she became engaged, and her growing attachment to a girlfriend, Frances Gregg. An early admirer, the poet William Carlos Williams has described the beauty of the youthful H. D. (which Pound celebrated in his *Is-Hilda Book*) as well as her nervous isolation within her family (which H. D. attributed to her relationship with Frances). By 1911, she had decided to sail to Europe with Frances and Mrs. Gregg, a trip that resulted in her reunion with Pound in London and the beginning of a lifelong expatriation.

Through Pound, H. D. met D. H. Lawrence, William Butler Yeats, May Sinclair, and the poet-translator Richard Aldington. It was at Pound's suggestion, too, that she submitted her first poems to Harriet Monroe's magazine *Poetry*. Indeed, in the tea room of the British Museum in August 1912, Pound signed Hilda Doolittle's poems with the pseudonym "H. D. Imagiste." As the promoter of early Imagism, he defined the poetic principles he saw embodied in H. D.'s verse: direct treatment of the subject, no inessential words, and musical (rather than strictly regular) rhythms. H. D.'s strikingly minimalist poems from this period were collected in her first volume of verse, *Sea Garden* (1916). Before this happened, however, her relationship with Pound had become troubled by his magisterial willfulness and his infidelities. Influenced by Aldington, who had succeeded Pound as the editor of *The New Freewoman* (soon to be-

come *The Egoist*), H. D. had begun to concentrate on her own poetic education, studying Greek lyrics, the French symbolists, and the troubadours of
medieval Provence. In 1913, she married Aldington.

While Pound went on from Imagism to another experimental movement,
Vorticism, and from H. D. to Dorothy Shakespear, whom he married in 1914,
H. D. and Aldington were befriended by the wealthy American poet Amy Low-
ell, who published three anthologies and a critical book publicizing both Ima-
gism and H. D. in America. At this time, too, the couple became intimate with
D. H. and Frieda Lawrence. Much has been written about this relationship:
Lawrence fictionalized H. D. as the bohemian Julia in *Aaron's Rod* (1922);
H. D. portrayed Lawrence in the unpublished "Pilate's Wife" (1924–1929)
and in *Bid Me to Live* (1939, published 1960); and Aldington wrote a biography of D. H. Lawrence entitled *Portrait of a Genius, But . . .* (1950).
Lawrence and H. D., who met on the eve of World War I, shared a common
revulsion against the war. Both were convinced of the necessity for spiritual rebirth, which they sought to attain through writing that drew on esoteric mythology and imagery grounded in the physical details of a natural world. From
H. D.'s point of view, however, Lawrence sometimes seemed to represent an
oppressively masculine smugness. Whether or not Lawrence withdrew from
the sexual relationship H. D. was led to expect, as she implied in *Bid Me to
Live*, she continued to wrestle in writing with her admiration and fear of his creative potency.

By 1915, when H. D. suffered a miscarriage, the catastrophes she identified
with World War I had begun. In 1917, when the Lawrences lived in H. D.'s
London flat, Aldington, who was training to become an army officer, began an
affair with one of H. D.'s acquaintances. In 1918, he was sent to the French
front, and, at about the same time, H. D.'s brother Gilbert was killed in the war.
The next year her father died, and she found herself pregnant after a trip to
Cornwall with Cecil Gray, a wealthy young man who would go on to become a
well-known music critic. After she contracted double pneumonia, H. D. was
terrified that either she or her child would die. As she explains in the novel *Palimpsest* (1926), which fictionalizes much of this autobiographical material, she
was "saved" from this crisis by the intercession of the twenty-four-year-old
woman who would befriend her for the rest of her life, the writer Winifred Ellerman—or "Bryher," as she called herself (after one of the Scilly Islands).

Bryher was the illegitimate daughter of the richest of England's shipping
magnates, a rebellious girl who wanted to be a boy and grew up to write historical adventure novels about boys. She had memorized all of *Sea Garden* before
she met H. D., subsidized the publication of *Hymen* (1921), H. D.'s next volume of verse, continued to pay many of H. D.'s bills, and eventually adopted
H. D.'s daughter, Perdita. In 1919 and 1920, Bryher fulfilled a promise to take
H. D. to Greece, where H. D. had one of her first psychic or visionary experiences. She saw what she later called "writing on the wall" projected in her hotel
room, pictographic images of the helmeted face of a dead airman, a tripod, and
then the winged figure of Niké, goddess of victory. When H. D. was too exhausted to sustain her concentration, Bryher described the last vision, the union
of Niké with the god of the sun, Helios. The two women felt they had glimpsed
a narrative line that, moving beyond the destruction of modern culture to a vi-

sion of female regeneration, would inform H. D.'s later poetry. The visit to
Corfu was the most dramatic of a series of trips that took them to Egypt (1923),
Paris (1924), and America (1921, 1926).

Although H. D. published *Heliodora and Other Poems* in 1924, her *Collected Poems* in 1925, *Red Roses for Bronze* in 1931, and several novels, short
stories, and Greek translations during the late thirties, she was troubled by what
she considered a decline in her creativity, a decline which she related both to
her personal problems and to the confusion of the times. While H. D. resided,
for the most part, in London and Switzerland, Bryher twice embarked on marriages of convenience. H. D., who had an affair with Bryher's second husband,
Kenneth MacPherson, became interested in film through his journal *Close-
Up*; however, her tremulous performance in MacPherson's movie *Borderline*
(1930) seems to dramatize her sense of anxiety during this period. Already acquainted with the psychologists Hans Sachs and Havelock Ellis, H. D. decided
to confront her writing difficulties and her dread of an impending world war by
journeying to 19 Bergasse in Vienna, where she would undergo the still relatively new process of psychoanalysis with the famous psychotherapist Sigmund
Freud.

H. D.'s 1933 and 1934 sessions with Freud are brilliantly portrayed in her
impressionistic *Tribute to Freud* (1944, 1956). The poet accepted Freud's insights into the associative, imagistic workings of the unconscious, as well as his
conviction about the importance of the childhood of the individual and the infancy of the race. But she viewed herself as more intuitive, more attuned to spiritual realities, than Freud was. Analyzing visions like those she had seen in
Greece, he diagnosed H. D.'s "symptoms" in terms of her unresolved attachment to her mother, implying that she was a victim of penis envy; however, she
went on to explore the "inspiration" she associated with her mother in order to
forge a poetry dedicated to the daughter's excavation of the maternal principle.

After surviving the bombings of London in World War II, H. D. composed
two major epics about war, *Trilogy* (1944–1946) and *Helen in Egypt* (1961).
The former begins with the wasteland of war-torn London in *The Walls Do
Not Fall* and moves backward first in *Tribute to the Angels* and then in *The
Flowering of the Rod* to the birth of Christ, which is understood as a miracle of
female creativity, for in the last of these books H. D. meditates on the crucial
roles of the prostitute Mary Magdalene and the virgin mother Mary. Similarly,
Helen in Egypt focuses on Helen of Troy as the scapegoat of a war that reveals
the nihilism of a culture based on masculine values. Helen, who has been reviled as the cause of the war, must recover a less punitive sense of her self.
H. D.'s two Marys and her Helen are each helped in their quests by mentors
who resemble Freud: Kaspar, one of the three Wise Men to visit the Christ
child in *Trilogy*, and Theseus, in *Helen in Egypt*, provide the ancient wisdom
that empowers female rebirth.

After the war, H. D. suffered a mental breakdown and moved from London
to Küsnacht, Switzerland, but she continued to work on *Helen in Egypt* and on
a coda to it entitled *Hermetic Definition* (1972). She also wrote a number of
prose and verse narratives that remain unpublished. Neither her interest in spir-
itualism nor her propensity for "romantic thralldom" was diminished in her
later years. She continued working on occult material, specifically with Tarot

cards, Moravian rituals, and astrology. During World War II, she had become emotionally attached to Sir Hugh Carswell Dowding, Chief Air Marshal of the Royal Air Force Fighter Command, and in her seventies she fell in love with Lionel Durand, a Haitian journalist. Yet, as her memoir of her earlier relationship with Pound, *End to Torment* (1979), indicates, she had matured into the recognition that, while "there was always a challenge" in the creativity of the men whom she admired or even adored, "the mother is the Muse, the Creator." The pseudonym H. D., which had begun as Pound's invention, had transformed itself into the mirror image of D. H. (Lawrence) and the replication of H(ugh) D(owding); however, by the end of the artist's life it seems to have stood for the hermetic definition of Hermes, for her mother, Helen, and for the spirit of Hellas.

In 1960, H. D. visited the United States for the last time, to accept the Award of Merit Medal for Poetry from the American Academy of Arts and Letters. Poets like Robert Duncan and Denise Levertov were among her earliest admirers because, as Levertov succinctly explained, H. D.'s poetry offers "doors, ways in, tunnels through" the "hiddenness before which man must shed his arrogance."

Oread[1]

Whirl up, sea—
whirl your pointed pines,
splash your great pines
on our rocks,
hurl your green over us,   5
cover us with your pools of fir.

                                                1914, 1925

Sea Poppies

Amber husk
fluted with gold,
fruit on the sand
marked with a rich grain,

treasure   5
spilled near the shrub-pines
to bleach on the boulders:

your stalk has caught root
among wet pebbles
and drift flung by the sea   10

---

1. A mountain nymph.

and grated shells
and split conch-shells.

Beautiful, wide-spread,
fire upon leaf,
what meadow yields   15
so fragrant a leaf
as your bright leaf?

                                                      1916

Eurydice[2]

I

So you have swept me back,
I who could have walked with the live souls
above the earth,
I who could have slept among the live flowers
at last;   5

so for your arrogance
and your ruthlessness
I am swept back
where dead lichens drip
dead cinders upon moss of ash;   10

so for your arrogance
I am broken at last,
I who had lived unconscious,
who was almost forgot;

if you had let me wait   15
I had grown from listlessness into peace,
if you had let me rest with the dead,
I had forgot you
and the past.

II

Here only flame upon flame   20
and black among the red sparks,
streaks of black and light
grown colourless;

why did you turn back,
that hell should be reinhabited   25

2. According to Greek myth, the wife of the poet Orpheus, who died and was carried to Hades; Orpheus managed to win her back through the power of his song, but then lost her again when he glanced back as she followed him up from the underworld.

of myself thus
swept into nothingness?

why did you turn?
why did you glance back?
why did you hesitate for that moment?   30
why did you bend your face
caught with the flame of the upper earth,
above my face?

what was it that crossed my face
with the light from yours   35
and your glance?
what was it you saw in my face?
the light of your own face,
the fire of your own presence?

What had my face to offer   40
but reflex of the earth,
hyacinth colour
caught from the raw fissure in the rock
where the light struck,
and the colour of azure crocuses   45
and the bright surface of gold crocuses
and of the wind-flower,
swift in its veins as lightning
and as white.

III

Saffron from the fringe of the earth,   50
wild saffron that has bent
over the sharp edge of earth,
all the flowers that cut through the earth,
all, all the flowers are lost;

everything is lost,   55
everything is crossed with black,
black upon black
and worse than black,
this colourless light.

IV

Fringe upon fringe   60
of blue crocuses,
crocuses, walled against blue of themselves,
blue of that upper earth,
blue of the depth upon depth of flowers,
lost;   65

flowers,
if I could have taken once my breath of them,
enough of them,
more than earth,
even than of the upper earth,   70
had passed with me
beneath the earth;

if I could have caught up from the earth,
the whole of the flowers of the earth,
if once I could have breathed into myself   75
the very golden crocuses
and the red,
and the very golden hearts of the first saffron,
the whole of the golden mass,
the whole of the great fragrance,   80
I could have dared the loss.

                              V
So for your arrogance
and your ruthlessness
I have lost the earth
and the flowers of the earth,   85
and the live souls above the earth,
and you who passed across the light
and reached
ruthless;

you who have your own light,   90
who are to yourself a presence,
who need no presence;

yet for all your arrogance
and your glance,
I tell you this: 95

such loss is no loss,
such terror, such coils and strands and pitfalls
of blackness,
such terror
is no loss;   100

hell is no worse than your earth
above the earth,
hell is no worse,
no, nor your flowers
nor your veins of light   105
nor your presence,
a loss;

my hell is no worse than yours
though you pass among the flowers and speak
with the spirits above earth.   110
VI
Against the black
I have more fervour
than you in all the splendour of that place,
against the blackness
and the stark grey   115
I have more light;

and the flowers,
if I should tell you,
you would turn from your own fit paths
toward hell,   120
turn again and glance back
and I would sink into a place
even more terrible than this.
VIII
At least I have the flowers of myself,
and my thoughts, no god   125
can take that;
I have the fervour of myself for a presence
and my own spirit for light;

and my spirit with its loss
knows this;   130
though small against the black,
small against the formless rocks,
hell must break before I am lost;

before I am lost,
hell must open like a red rose   135
for the dead to pass.

1917, 1925

Fragment Thirty-six

I know not what to do: my mind is divided.
—Sappho.[3]

I know not what to do,
my mind is reft:
is song's gift best?

---

3. This fragment by Sappho, Greek woman poet who lived in about 600 B.C., has, according to H. D.'s note, been "reworked freely" in the poem.

is love's gift loveliest?
I know not what to do,   5
now sleep has pressed
weight on your eyelids.

Shall I break your rest,
devouring, eager?
is love's gift best?   10
nay, song's the loveliest:
yet were you lost,
what rapture
could I take from song?
what song were left?   15

I know not what to do:
to turn and slake
the rage that burns,
with my breath burn
and trouble your cool breath?   20
so shall I turn and take
snow in my arms?
(is love's gift best?)
yet flake on flake
of snow were comfortless,   25
did you lie wondering,
wakened yet unawake.

Shall I turn and take
comfortless snow within my arms?
press lips to lips   30
that answer not,
press lips to flesh
that shudders not nor breaks?

Is love's gift best?
shall I turn and slake   35
all the wild longing?
O I am eager for you!
as the Pleiads[4] shake
white light in whiter water
so shall I take you?   40

My mind is quite divided,
my minds hesitate,
so perfect matched,
I know not what to do:

4. Seven nymphs who, according to legend, were turned into stars (in the constellation Taurus).

each strives with each　　　　　　　　45
as two white wrestlers
standing for a match,
ready to turn and clutch
yet never shake muscle nor nerve nor tendon;
so my mind waits　　　　　　　　50
to grapple with my mind,
yet I lie quiet,
I would seem at rest.

I know not what to do:
strain upon strain,　　　　　　　　55
sound surging upon sound
makes my brain blind;
as a wave-line may wait to fall
yet (waiting for its falling)
still the wind may take　　　　　　　60
from off its crest,
white flake on flake of foam,
that rises,
seeming to dart and pulse
and rend the light,　　　　　　　　65
so my mind hesitates
above the passion
quivering yet to break,
so my mind hesitates
above my mind,　　　　　　　　70
listening to song's delight.

I know not what to do:
will the sound break,
rending the night
with rift on rift of rose　　　　　　75
and scattered light?
will the sound break at last
as the wave hesitant,
or will the whole night pass
and I lie listening awake?　　　　　　80

1924

Helen[5]

All Greece hates
　　the still eyes in the white face,

---

5. The beautiful wife of the Greek leader Menelaus, who was stolen by the Trojan prince Paris, and blamed for the Trojan War.

        the lustre as of olives
        where she stands,
        and the white hands.   5

        All Greece reviles
        the wan face when she smiles,
        hating it deeper still
        when it grows wan and white,
        remembering past enchantments   10
        and past ills.

        Greece sees unmoved,
        God's daughter, born of love,
        the beauty of cool feet
        and slenderest knees,   15
        could love indeed the maid,
        only if she were laid,
        white ash amid funereal cypresses.

                                                        1924

From Tribute to the Angels

        To Osbert Sitwell
        . . . possibly we will reach haven,
                heaven.[6]

                        [1]
Hermes Trismegistus[7]
is patron of alchemists;

his province is thought,
inventive, artful and curious;

his metal is quicksilver,   5
his clients, orators, thieves and poets;

steal then, O orator,
plunder, O poet,

---

6. An echo of the last lines of *The Walls Do Not Fall*, the first part of *Trilogy*. In *Tribute to the Angels*, the second book of *Trilogy*, H. D. revises the biblical Book of Revelation while invoking a series of symbolic angels; in the midst of this invocation, the poet has a vision of "a Lady."

7. Supposed author of the Hermetic Books, dealing with magic, astrology and alchemy; his name combines that of Hermes, the Greek messenger god, with that of Thoth, the Egyptian god of the dead.

take what the old-church
found in Mithra's[8] tomb,   10

candle and script and bell,
take what the new-church spat upon

and broke and shattered;
collect the fragments of the splintered glass

and of your fire and breath,   15
melt down and integrate,

re-invoke, re-create
opal, onyx, obsidian,

now scattered in the shards
men tread upon.   20

[2]

Your walls do not fall, he said,
because your walls are made of jasper;[9]

but not four-square, I thought,
another shape (octahedron?)

slipped into the place   25
reserved by rule and rite

for the *twelve foundations*,
for the *transparent glass*,

for *no need of the sun*
nor *moon to shine*;[1]   30

for the vision as we see
or have seen or imagined it

or in the past invoked
or conjured up or had conjured

by another, was usurped;   35
I saw the shape

8. A chief god of the ancient Persians, associated with the sun.
9. The first line echoes the title of the first part
of *Trilogy*; in Revelation 21:18, the City of God
is described as having a wall of jasper.
1. Other allusions to the City of God in Revelation 21:14–23: the City has "twelve foundations"; its streets are of gold like "transparent
glass"; and there is "no need of the sun" or the
"moon to shine" because it is lighted by the
"glory of God."

which might have been of jasper,
but it was not four-square.

[3]

I John saw.[2] *I testify;*
if any man shall add   40

God shall add unto him the plagues,
but he that sat upon the throne said,

I make all things new.
I John saw. I testify,

but *I make all things new,*   45
said He of the seven stars,

he of the seventy-times-seven
passionate, bitter wrongs,

He of the seventy-times-seven
bitter, unending wars.   50

* * *

[8]

Now polish the crucible
and in the bowl distill

a word most bitter, *marah,*[3]
a word bitterer still, *mar,*

sea, brine, breaker, seducer,   55
giver of life, giver of tears;

now polish the crucible
and set the jet of flame

under, till *marah-mar*
are melted, fuse and join   60

and change and alter,
mer, mere, mère, mater, Maia, Mary,[4]

Star of the Sea,
Mother.

[9]

Bitter, bitter jewel   65
in the heart of the bowl,

---

2. An echo of Revelation 22:8.
3. Hebrew: bitter. "Mar": ocean.
4. H. D. here plays on the common etymologies

of words for "ocean" and "mother" in French
and Latin. Maia: mother of Mercury. Mary:
mother of Jesus.

what is your colour?
what do you offer

to us who rebel?
what were we had you loved other?　　　70

what is this mother-father
to tear at our entrails?

what is this unsatisfied duality
which you can not satisfy?

[10]

In the field-furrow　　　75
the rain-water

showed splintered edge
as of a broken mirror,

and in the glass
as in a polished spear,　　　80

glowed the star Hesperus,[5]
white, far and luminous,

incandescent and near,
Venus, Aphrodite, Astarte,[6]

star of the east,　　　85
star of the west,

Phosphorus[7] at sun-rise,
Hesperus at sun-set.

[11]

O swiftly, re-light the flame
before the substance cool,　　　90

for suddenly we saw your name
desecrated; knaves and fools

have done you impious wrong,
Venus, for venery stands for impurity

and Venus as desire　　　95
is venereous, lascivious,

---

5. The evening star.
6. Semitic goddess of fecundity and love, identified with the crescent moon. "Aphrodite": Greek goddess of love. "Venus": the Roman name for Aphrodite; also the morning star.
7. I.e., light-bearing.

while the very root of the word shrieks
like a mandrake when foul witches pull

its stem at midnight,
and rare mandragora[8] itself   100

is full, they say, of poison,
food for the witches' den.

[12]

Swiftly re-light the flame,
Aphrodite, holy name,

Astarte, hull and spar   105
of wrecked ships lost your star,

forgot the light at dusk,
forgot the prayer at dawn;

return, O holiest one,
Venus whose name is kin   110

to venerate,
venerator.

[13]

"What is the jewel colour?"
green-white, opalescent,

with under-layer of changing blue,   115
with rose-vein; a white agate

with a pulse uncooled that beats yet,
faint blue-violet;

it lives, it breathes,
it gives off—fragrance?   120

I do not know what it gives,
a vibration that we can not name

for there is no name for it;
my patron said, "name it";

I said, I can not name it,   125
there is no name;

he said,
"invent it."

8. Mandrake, so called for the resemblance of its forked root to a human body; used in witchcraft.

[14]

I can not invent it,
I said it was agate,   130

I said it lived, it gave—
fragrance—was near enough

to explain that quality
for which there is no name;

I do not want to name it,   135
I want to watch its faint

heart-beat, pulse-beat
as it quivers, I do not want

to talk about it,
I want to minimize thought,   140

concentrate on it
till I shrink,

dematerialize
and am drawn into it.

* * *

[24]

Every hour, every moment   145
has its specific attendant Spirit;

the clock-hand, minute by minute,
ticks round its prescribed orbit;

but this curious mechanical perfection
should not separate but relate rather,   150

our life, this temporary eclipse
to that other. . . .

[25]

. . . of the *no need*
of the moon to shine in it,

for it was ticking minute by minute   155
(the clock at my bed-head,

with its dim, luminous disc)
when the Lady knocked;

I was talking casually
with friends in the other room,   160

when we saw the outer hall
grow lighter—then we saw where the door was,

there was no door
(this was a dream, of course),

and she was standing there,   165
actually, at the turn of the stair.

[26]
One of us said, how odd,
she is actually standing there,

I wonder what brought her?
another of us said,   170

have we some power between us,
we three together,

that acts as a sort of magnet,
that attracts the super-natural?

(yet it was all natural enough,   175
we agreed);

I do not know what I said
or if I said anything,

for before I had time to speak,
I realized I had been dreaming,

that I lay awake now on my bed,   180
that the luminous light

was the phosphorescent face
of my little clock

and the faint knocking
was the clock ticking.   185

[27]
And yet in some very subtle way,
she was there more than ever,

as if she had miraculously
related herself to time here,

which is no easy trick, difficult   190
even for the experienced stranger,

of whom we must *be not forgetful*
for *some have entertained angels unawares.*[9]

[28]
I had been thinking of Gabriel,[1]
of the moon-cycle, of the moon-shell,   195

of the moon-crescent
and the moon at full:

I had been thinking of Gabriel,
the moon-regent, the Angel,

and I had intended to recall him   200
in the sequence of candle and fire

and the law of the seven;
I had not forgotten

his special attribute
of annunciator; I had thought   205

to address him as I had the others,
Uriel, Annael;[2]

how could I imagine
the Lady herself would come instead?

[29]
We have seen her   210
the world over,

Our Lady of the Goldfinch,
Our Lady of the Candelabra,

Our Lady of the Pomegranate,
Our Lady of the Chair;[3]   215

we have seen her, an empress,
magnificent in pomp and grace,

and we have seen her
with a single flower

or a cluster of garden-pinks   220
in a glass beside her;

9. "Be not forgetful to entertain strangers: for thereby some have entertained angels unawares" (Hebrews 13:2).
1. One of the seven archangels in Christian tradition; thought to be the angel of mercy. He announced the coming of Christ to Mary.
2. Two of the seven archangels.
3. Titles of different iconographic representations of Mary.

we have seen her snood[4]
drawn over her hair,

or her face set in profile
with the blue hood and stars;   225

we have seen her head bowed down
with the weight of a domed crown,

or we have seen her, a wisp of a girl
trapped in a golden halo;

we have seen her with arrow, with doves   230
and a heart like a valentine;

we have seen her in fine silks imported
from all over the Levant,[5]

and hung with pearls brought
from the city of Constantine;   235

we have seen her sleeve
of every imaginable shade

of damask and figured brocade;
it is true,

the painters did very well by her;   240
it is true, they missed never a line

of the suave turn of the head
or subtle shade of lowered eye-lid

or eye-lids half-raised; you find
her everywhere (or did find),   245

in cathedral, museum, cloister,
at the turn of the palace stair.

                          * * *

                            [35]
So she must have been pleased with us,
who did not forgo our heritage

at the grave-edge;   250
she must have been pleased

---

4. Hair net.
5. Countries of the eastern Mediterranean noted for their rich goods; "city of Constantine": Constantinople, the new name given to the ancient city of Byzantium by the great Roman emperor Constantine.

with the straggling company of the brush and quill
who did not deny their birthright;

she must have been pleased with us,
for she looked so kindly at us   255

under her drift of veils,
and she carried a book.

[36]
Ah (you say), this is Holy Wisdom,
Santa Sophia, the SS of the *Sanctus Spiritus*,[6]

so by facile reasoning, logically   260
the incarnate symbol of the Holy Ghost;

your Holy Ghost was an apple-tree
smouldering—or rather now bourgeoning

with flowers; the fruit of the Tree?[7]
this is the new Eve who comes

clearly to return, to retrieve   265
what she lost the race,

given over to sin, to death;
she brings the Book of Life, obviously.

[37]
This is a symbol of beauty (you continue),
she is Our Lady universally,   270

I see her as you project her,
not out of place

flanked by Corinthian capitals,
or in a Coptic nave,[8]

or frozen above the centre door   275
of a Gothic cathedral;

you have done very well by her
(to repeat your own phrase),

you have carved her tall and unmistakable,
a hieratic figure, the veiled Goddess,   280

6. Holy Ghost. "Santa Sophia": holy wisdom, as well as the name of an important church in Constantinople.
7. A reference to the Tree of Knowledge in Genesis 2.
8. Nave in an Egyptian Christian church; "Corinthian capitals": the upper ends of Greek pillars, carved in the lightest and most ornate "Corinthian" style.

whether of the seven delights,
whether of the seven spear-points.

[38]
O yes—you understand, I say,
this is all most satisfactory,

but she wasn't hieratic, she wasn't frozen,   285
she wasn't very tall;

she is the Vestal
from the days of Numa,[9]

she carries over the cult
of the *Bona Dea*,[1]   290

she carries a book but it is not
the tome of the ancient wisdom,

the pages, I imagine, are the blank pages
of the unwritten volume of the new;

all you say, is implicit,   295
all that and much more;

but she is not shut up in a cave
like a Sibyl;[2] she is not

imprisoned in leaden bars
in a coloured window;   300

she is Psyche,[3] the butterfly,
out of the cocoon.

[39]
But nearer than Guardian Angel
or good Daemon,[4]

she is the counter-coin-side   305
of primitive terror;

she is not-fear, she is not-war,
but she is no symbolic figure

---

9. King of Rome associated with the founding of their honored institutions, including the building of the temple of Vesta.
1. Good goddess, another name for Maia/Venus.
2. Female prophet.
3. Human lover of the Greek god of love,

Cupid or Eros, who was eventually deified after performing a number of apparently impossible tasks, including a descent to Hades. Her name means "soul" in Greek; the butterfly is her symbol because its career parallels her own.
4. Indwelling spirit or genius.

of peace, charity, chastity, goodness,
faith, hope, reward;   310

she is not Justice with eyes
blindfolded like Love's;[5]

I grant you the dove's symbolic purity,[6]
I grant you her face was innocent

and immaculate and her veils   315
like the Lamb's Bride,[7]

but the Lamb was not with her,
either as Bridegroom or Child;

her attention is undivided,
we are her bridegroom and lamb;   320

her book is our book; written
or unwritten, its pages will reveal

a tale of a Fisherman,
a tale of a jar or jars,[8]

the same—different—the same attributes,   325
different yet the same as before.

[40]

This is no rune[9] nor symbol,
what I mean is—it is so simple

yet no trick of the pen or brush
could capture that impression;   330

what I wanted to indicate was
a new phase, a new distinction of colour;

I wanted to say, I did say
there was no sheen, no reflection,

no shadow; when I said white,   335
I did not mean sculptor's or painter's white,

---

5. Both Justice and Cupid, the god of love, are traditionally depicted as blindfolded.
6. The spiritual purity of the dove is an important Christian theme.
7. The Lamb is Christ; his bride is traditionally the church.

8. Anticipates the last book of *Trilogy*, *The Flowering of the Rod*, which retells the Gospel story of the wise men's gift of a jar of myrrh to the Christ child; the "fisherman" refers to Christ.
9. A character in the runic alphabet, associated with mysticism.

nor porcelain; dim-white could
not suggest it, for when

is fresh-fallen snow (or snow
in the act of falling) dim?   340

yet even now, we stumble, we are lost—
what can we say?

she was not impalpable like a ghost,
she was not awe-inspiring like a Spirit,

she was not even over-whelming   345
like an Angel.
                          [41]
She carried a book, either to imply
she was one of us, with us,

or to suggest she was satisfied
with our purpose, a tribute to the Angels;   350

yet though the campanili[1] spoke,
Gabriel, Azrael,

though the campanili answered,
Raphael, Uriel,

though a distant note over-water   355
chimed *Annael,* and *Michael*[2]

was implicit from the beginning,
another, deep, un-named, resurging bell

answered, sounding through them all:
remember, where there was   360

no need of the moon to shine. . . .
I saw no temple

                          [42]
Some call that deep-deep bell
Zadkiel,[3] the righteousness of God,

he is regent of Jupiter[4]   365
or Zeus-pater or Theus-pater,

---

1. Bell tower.
2. All archangels previously invoked in the
poem (some in passages not printed here).
3. An archangel.

4. The most powerful of the Roman gods, patriarch of the pantheon; Zeus in Greek. "Pater":
father.

Theus, God; God-the-father, father-god
or the Angel god-father,

himself, heaven yet at home in a star
whose colour is amethyst,   370

whose candle burns deep-violet
with the others.

[43]
And the point in the spectrum
where all lights become one,

is white and white is not no-colour,   375
as we were told as children,

but all-colour;
where the flames mingle

and the wings meet, when we gain
the arc of perfection,   380

we are satisfied, we are happy,
we begin again;

I John saw. I testify
to rainbow feathers, to the span of heaven

and walls of colour,   385
the colonnades of jasper;

but when the jewel
melts in the crucible

we find not ashes, not ash-of-rose,
not a tall vase and a staff of lilies,   390

not *vas spirituale*,[5]
not *rosa mystica* even,

but a cluster of garden-pinks
or a face like a Christmas-rose.

This is the flowering of the rod,[6]   395
this is the flowering of the burnt-out wood,

5. Spiritual vessel; "*rosa mystica*": mystic rose.   6. The title of the next and last book of *Trilogy*.

> *where, Zadkiel, we pause to give*
> *thanks that we rise again from death and live.*

London   1945
May 17–31, 1944

EDITH SITWELL
1887–1964

The daughter of an aristocratic English family, brought up in a sumptuous home, Edith Sitwell nevertheless began her life by feeling that "I was unpopular with my parents from the moment of my birth." Tall and slim, with a markedly aquiline nose for which a London orthopedist provided a special "contraption [turning] the organ in question . . . very firmly to the opposite way which Nature had intended," she must as a girl have seemed an unlikely candidate for the glamorous reputation she later achieved. Yet, with the help of a supportive grandmother, a kind nurse, and an encouraging governess, Sitwell began early to read and write poetry, dismissing her eccentric, scholarly father as a foolish man and her elegant but unloving mother as a woman who cared only about a "silly daily life of bridge and watching the golfers on the golf course." Despite financial difficulties—including a series of debts which at one point sent the extravagant Lady Ida Sitwell to prison—Edith Sitwell settled in London in 1914, sharing a flat with her former governess, and in 1916 began editing *Wheels*, an avant-garde literary anthology featuring experimental writings that shocked conservative critics who might have expected greater decorum from an upper-class heiress.

Sitwell had from the first enjoyed the admiration and respect of her younger brothers, Osbert and Sacheverell, each of whom became a distinguished literary man in his own right, and such powerful ties with her siblings also clearly energized her. Yet that she was innately strong-willed, vigorous, and imaginative is plain from the innovative verse she began to publish during her *Wheels* period. *Clown's Houses* (1918), *The Wooden Pegasus* (1920), and *Façade* (1922) followed each other in rapid succession, proposing surprising alternatives to the more traditional work included in the comparatively sedate *Georgian Anthology* (1911–1920)—an annual collection of poems by such writers as Rupert Brooke, Walter de la Mare, and John Masefield—against which Sitwell was reacting with some violence. Deliberately stylized, even rebelliously artificial, these early works seemed, according to a contemporary critic, to be composed for "the xylophone," written by "a virtuoso in the communication of a half-wooden, half-glassy tone which is seldom without brilliance." The musical analogy is apt, for *Façade* is a jazzy poem-sequence whose syncopated linguistic rhythms are echoed by the background music that the British composer Sir William Walton wrote for it: when the pair first performed this joint production in public—Walton conducting the orchestra, Sitwell reading the poems from behind a screen—the controversial work was, according to one observer, a "sensation."

In her later years, Edith Sitwell became an increasingly dramatic figure on the London literary and artistic scene. As an aristocratic infant she had been painted in a Sitwell family portrait by the renowned American artist John Singer Sargent, but as a more compellingly aquiline adult she was the subject of photographs by Cecil Beaton and paintings by Roger Fry, Alvaro Guevara, Wyndham Lewis, Felix Topolski, and her close friend Pavel Tchelitchew; the Guevara hangs today in London's Tate Gallery. More important, she continued to move—determinedly unmarried and fiercely independent—in major British aesthetic circles, discovering and befriending the young Dylan Thomas and associating with such writers as Virginia Woolf. During the grim years of World War II, when London was being blitzed by German planes, she began to write poems that were less sardonically stylized, more bitterly macabre than any of her earlier works. Yet pieces like *Lullaby* and *Serenade: Any Man to Any Woman* retain the metallic edge—the "xylophone" quality—that had marked even the verses of the lighthearted *Façade*, as if Sitwell had decided, when she was quite young, that her supposedly privileged world was no more and no less than, in the words of *Façade's* Sir Beelzebub, a "hotel in Hell."

En Famille[1]

In the early springtime, after their tea,
Through the young fields of the springing Bohea,[2]
Jemima, Jocasta, Dinah, and Deb
Walked with their father Sir Joshua Jebb—
An admiral red, whose only notion   5
(A butterfly poised on a pigtailed ocean),
Is of the peruked[3] sea whose swell
Breaks on the flowerless rocks of Hell.
Under the thin trees, Deb and Dinah,
Jemima, Jocasta walked, and finer   10
Their black hair seemed (flat-sleek to see)
Than the young leaves of the springing Bohea;
Their cheeks were like nutmeg-flowers when swells
The rain into foolish silver bells.
They said, "If the door you would only slam,   15
Or if, Papa, you would once say 'Damn'—
Instead of merely roaring 'Avast'
Or boldly invoking the nautical Blast—
We should now stand in the street of Hell
Watching siesta shutters that fell   20
With a noise like amber softly sliding;
Our moon-like glances through these gliding

1. French: as a family.   3. Wearing eighteenth-century periwigs.
2. A black Chinese tea.

Would see at her table preened and set
Myrrhina[4] sitting at her toilette
With eyelids closed as soft as the breeze   25
That flows from gold flowers on the incense-trees."

The Admiral said, "You could never call—
I assure you it would not do at all!
She gets down from table without saying 'Please,'
Forgets her prayers and to cross her T's,   30
In short, her scandalous reputation
Has shocked the whole of the Hellish nation;
And every turbaned Chinoiserie,[5]
With whom we should sip our black Bohea,
Would stretch out her simian fingers thin   35
To scratch you, my dears, like a mandoline;
For Hell is just as properly proper
As Greenwich, or as Bath, or Joppa!"[6]

                                                          1922

Sir Beelzebub[7]

When
Sir
Beelzebub called for his syllabub[8] in the hotel in Hell
          Where Proserpine[9] first fell,
Blue as the gendarmerie[1] were the waves of the sea   5

          (Rocking and shocking the bar-maid).

Nobody comes to give him his rum but the
Rim of the sky hippopotamus-glum
Enhances the chances to bless with a benison
Alfred Lord Tennyson crossing the bar[2] laid   10
With cold vegetation from pale deputations
Of temperance workers (all signed In Memoriam)[3]
Hoping with glory to trip up the Laureate's feet[4]

4. Possibly a variation on "Myrrha," in Greek
myth the mother of Adonis, who was transformed into a myrrh tree by the gods to protect
her from her father.
5. A term denoting European adaptations of
Chinese forms and customs; though here it may
simply refer to Chinese people.
6. The first two are English cities; "Joppa" is
the ancient name of the Israeli city of Jaffa, the
center of many religious battles.
7. Beelzebub is one of the fallen angels who was
cast into hell with Satan.
8. A dessert made of sweetened cream and wine

or liquor.
9. Wife of Hades and goddess of the underworld in Greek myth.
1. The French police force.
2. Tennyson (1809–1892) wrote a late poem
called *Crossing the Bar*, in which he said that he
hoped "to see [his] Pilot face to face." A bar is a
narrow ridge of sand near a harbor or beach.
3. The title of Tennyson's long elegy for his
friend Arthur Hallam.
4. Tennyson succeeded Wordsworth as Poet
Laureate, an honorific title bestowed upon English poets by the crown.

(Moving in classical metres) . . .

Like Balaclava,[5] the lava came down from the   15
Roof, and the sea's blue wooden gendarmerie
Took them in charge while Beelzebub roared for his rum.

. . . None of them come!

1922

Aubade[6]

Jane, Jane,
Tall as a crane,
The morning light creaks down again;

Comb your cockscomb-ragged hair,
Jane, Jane, come down the stair.   5

Each dull blunt wooden stalactite
Of rain creaks, hardened by the light,

Sounding like an overtone
From some lonely world unknown.

But the creaking empty light   10
Will never harden into sight,

Will never penetrate your brain
With overtones like the blunt rain.

The light would show (if it could harden)
Eternities of kitchen garden,[7]   15

Cockscomb flowers that none will pluck,
And wooden flowers that 'gin to cluck.

In the kitchen you must light
Flames as staring, red and white,

As carrots or as turnips, shining   20
Where the cold dawn light lies whining.

Cockscomb hair on the cold wind
Hangs limp, turns the milk's weak mind. . . .

5. Site of a battle during the Crimean War in
1854, described by Tennyson in *The Charge of
the Light Brigade*.

6. Dawn poem.
7. Small back gardens used by cooks to grow
herbs and vegetables.

Jane, Jane,
Tall as a crane,
The morning light creaks down again!

1923

Lullaby[8]

Though the world has slipped and gone,
Sounds my loud discordant cry
Like the steel birds' song on high:
"Still one thing is left—the Bone!"
Then out danced the Babioun.[9]   5

She sat in the hollow of the sea—
A socket whence the eye's put out—
She sang to the child a lullaby
(The steel birds' nest was thereabout).

"Do, do, do, do—   10
Thy mother's hied to the vaster race:
The Pterodactyl made its nest
And laid a steel egg in her breast—
Under the Judas-colored[1] sun.
She'll work no more, nor dance, nor moan,   15
And I am come to take her place
Do, do.

There's nothing left but earth's low bed—
(The Pterodactyl fouls its nest):
But steel wings fan thee to thy rest,   20
And wingless truth and larvae lie
And eyeless hope and handless fear—
All these for thee as toys are spread,
Do—do—

Red is the bed of Poland, Spain,[2]   25
And thy mother's breast, who has grown wise
In that fouled nest. If she could rise,
Give birth again,
In wolfish pelt she'd hide thy bones
To shield thee from the world's long cold,   30
And down on all fours shouldst thou crawl
For thus from no height canst thou fall—
Do, do.

8. Written in reaction to World War II.
9. "The phrase 'out-dance the Babioun' occurs
in an Epigram by Ben Jonson" [Sitwell's note].

1. Judas was the apostle who betrayed Jesus.
2. Countries that had recently, after many battles, come under Fascist rule.

She'd give no hands: there's nought to hold
And nought to make: there's dust to sift,   35
But no food for the hands to lift.
Do, do.

Heed my ragged lullaby,
Fear not living, fear not chance;
All is equal—blindness, sight,   40
There is no depth, there is no height:
Do, do.

The Judas-colored sun is gone,
And with the Ape thou art alone—
Do,   45
          Do."

                    1942

Serenade: Any Man to Any Woman

Dark angel who art clear and straight
As cannon shining in the air,
Your blackness doth invade my mind,
And thunderous as the armored wind
That rained on Europe is your hair;   5

And so I love you till I die—
(Unfaithful I, the cannon's mate):
Forgive my love of such brief span,
But fickle is the flesh of man,
And death's cold puts the passion out.   10

I'll woo you with a serenade—
The wolfish howls the starving made;
And lies shall be your canopy
To shield you from the freezing sky.

Yet when I clasp you in my arms—   15
Who are my sleep, the zero hour
That clothes, instead of flesh, my heart—
You in my heaven have no part,
For you, my mirage broken in flower,

Can never see what dead men know!   20
Then die with me and be my love:[3]

3. An ironic variation of a line from Christopher Marlowe's (1564–1593) poem *The Passionate* *Shepherd to His Love*: "Come live with me, and be my love."

The grave shall be your shady grove,
And in your pleasaunce rivers flow

(To ripen this new Paradise)
From a more universal Flood   25
Than Noah knew: but yours is blood.

Yet still you will imperfect be
That in my heart like death's chill grows,
—A rainbow shining in the night,[4]
Born of my tears . . . your lips, the bright   30
Summer-old folly of the rose.

1942

A Bird's Song

The fire high up in air,
The bird, cries, "I am the seed of fire
From the Sun—although I wear
A bird-mask. Now I swoop
Down to the archipelago of suns on the orange-tree in a dark
　　　sea of leaves.   5

O young Medea,[5] fear
The sea in each fire that hangs upon your tree,
The cold in the heart of Man.
O guard that fleece of gold[6] in your breast, your heart of fire;
Too soon it stolen will be!   10

Between smooth leaves where still the drops of night
Lie, the gold cold water-drops, I take my flight,
Shaking down the water-drops like the dark drowsy bees.
Beneath the orange-tree, the sleeper lies—
A bone of fire in a body of thin amber; the umbrageous tree 15
Has changed her to a bird of fire, feathered with shade, like me.

And I, the seed of the Sun in a bird-mask,
Fly where from the perfumed stem and wind-smooth fruits
　　　down-pour
Such amber tears as the rich Sun doth weep   20
In his deep noonday sleep."

---

4. The rainbow was the sign God gave to Noah of the Covenant after the flood (Genesis 9:12).
5. In Greek legend Medea killed her children to avenge herself on her husband, Jason, who had abandoned her.
6. Jason and his men, the Argonauts, won the Golden Fleece after many adventures; the prize was guarded by a dragon in an orange grove.

In this deep night of leaves
And seas in a fire of gold,
If Man, the marauding faithless Jason, came, how should he know
Which is the gilded fleece and which the long and
    legendary Sea—

Which is the Sleeper's long and tangled hair and which the   25
    water-cold gold orange-tree?

                                          1948

Song

to Alberto de Lacerda

Where is all the bright company gone—
The Trojan Elaine and the Knight Sir Gawaine?[7]
Why have they glided out of the rain?
The Queens were bright as the waters' sheen,
Beautiful, bountiful as the grain;   5
The Knights were brighter than stars in the sky
(The moons thick as roses in hot July)—
As bright as the raindrops and roses in June,
And many and merry as notes in a tune.
Alas, they are gone and I am alone,   10
For all they glided out of the rain.
And now I sit under the bright apple tree
And weep that ever the speech was spoken
That the false angel said unto me.
For had I never the apple-branch broken,[8]   15
Death had not fallen on mankind and me.

                                          1954

7. Sir Gawaine was one of the Knights of the Round Table in Arthurian legend; Elaine is Helen of Troy, whose beauty was the cause of the Trojan War.

8. "Lines 13–14 are from Eva's Lament in the Coventry Plays" [Sitwell's note]. Eve brought death into the world by eating an apple from the Tree of Knowledge (Genesis 3:6).

MARIANNE MOORE
1887–1972

"I, too, dislike it," Marianne Moore once remarked about poetry, explaining, "There are things that are important beyond all this fiddle." Yet even as she wrote these words, this reserved and obscure sometime librarian was beginning to earn a distinctive reputation as a poet, and by the end of her career she had become one of the most famous—and famously eccentric—American writers of her generation. Wearing her legendary three-cornered hat, she appeared at baseball games, of which she was notoriously fond, like some character out of a fairytale. Brooding in her Brooklyn apartment, she thought up names for a new Ford car—"The Resilient Bullet," "Mongoose Civique," "Turcotingo" "Utopian Turtletop"—that was eventually, despite her fanciful suggestions, to be called the "Edsel," in honor of one of the company's presidents. Even as a somewhat austere young writer, moreover, she had been praised by such major literary men as William Carlos Williams and T. S. Eliot, and praised not for public idiosyncrasies but for private inspiration. In a way, the contradictions in Moore's history—between early reticence and later reputation, between impassioned aesthetic rigor and ironically eccentric self-presentation—are emblematic of both her life and art.

Born in Kirkwood, Missouri, near St. Louis, Moore moved with her mother and brother to Carlisle, Pennsylvania, in 1894, when her father abandoned the family because of financial and personal problems. After studying at the Metzger Institute, where her mother taught, and graduating in 1909 from Bryn Mawr College, where she found biology classes particularly "exhilarating" and where the poet H. D. (Hilda Doolittle) was a fellow student, she took courses in business at the Carlisle Commercial College, traveled to Europe with her mother, and from 1911 to 1915 taught shorthand, typing, and commercial law at the U.S. Indian School in Carlisle. In 1915, her verse began to appear in *The Egoist* in London and *Poetry* in Chicago, and by the end of the decade she had won a small but distinguished reputation.

Unassuming and shy, Moore continued to live with her mother, as she would throughout most of her life, and the pair moved first to New Jersey, then to Greenwich Village, and finally to Brooklyn, so that they could be near the poet's brother, a Presbyterian minister to whom she was also exceptionally close. Yet, even this early, friends could perceive the paradoxes in her personality. Presenting herself as a kind of anachronism—a dutiful, neo-Victorian daughter, an old-fashioned "lady"—she nevertheless struck William Carlos Williams as "a rafter holding up the superstructure of our uncompleted building, a caryatid, her red hair plaited and wound twice about the fine skull . . . she was surely one of the main supports of the new order." And indeed, though Moore earned her living at conventional jobs—secretary in a girls' school, part-time assistant in a New York City branch library—she was mingling socially with a group of avant-garde painters and writers who were connected with the experimental little magazine *Others*; more important, she was herself composing the disruptive verse, with lines consistently organized into unusual stanza forms and language frequently freed from traditional associations, that would demonstrate her commitment to "the new order." Nevertheless, her first book appeared only because her former schoolmate H. D. and H. D.'s close friend the writer Bryher (Winifred Ellerman) conspired without her knowledge to have the volume, simply entitled *Poems*, issued in London in 1921. After that, Moore herself arranged the publication of *Observations* (1924), which won the prestigious *Dial* award for that year, and the following year she herself became editor of *The Dial*, a position she held from 1925 to 1929.

A major New York literary magazine, *The Dial* brought Moore even further into touch with a number of important figures, including Ezra Pound (whose work she printed in the same issue with work by the neo-Victorian essayist George Saintsbury), Hart Crane (whose poems she attempted rigorously to edit), and James Joyce (portions of whose *Finnegans Wake* she rejected because they seemed to her to be morally and linguistically "offensive"). Although she largely abandoned her own verse writing during her period on this journal, her editorial experience strengthened her aesthetic self-confidence and enriched her imagination. When she began to write and publish again, she produced one of her most significant books, *Selected Poems* (1935), a volume which appeared with a laudatory introduction from T. S. Eliot, and which included among other major works *The Jerboa* and *Poetry*.

Shortly before the publication of *Selected Poems*, Marianne Moore was sought out by a young poet, Elizabeth Bishop, then a student at Vassar, who was to become a lifelong friend and who later remembered the older writer as "not very tall and not in the least intimidating." It was at this time, however, that Moore was composing some of her most formidable verse, carefully constructed stanzas bristling with erudite allusions which were soon to strike the editor Louis Untermeyer as "frankly puzzling" because they "seem to erect a barrier of jagged clauses [and] barbed quotations . . . between herself and her audience." About her characteristic, even notorious, use of quotations, however, Moore herself explained that "I was just trying to be honorable and not to steal things," and about her apparently "jagged" stanza forms, she insisted that "words cluster like chromosomes, determining the procedure [though] I may influence an arrangement or thin it, then try to have successive stanzas identical with the first."

Moore had perhaps more forthrightly formulated her personal aesthetic in her poem *To a Snail* (1924), where, defining " 'compression [as] the first grace of style,' " she added that "contractility is a virtue / as modesty is a virtue," a motto that seems eminently suitable to the quasi-Victorian spinster she so often pretended to be. Still, self-consciously "modest" and compressed as many of Moore's most ambitious early- and middle-period poems are, their serious implications become clear on close reading. Many, for instance, take animals, often quite exotic ones, as their overt subjects. But this poet appears deeply to identify with the ironically "humble" creatures who constitute her distinctive bestiary, especially with those who are in their way as carefully camouflaged or fancifully armored as her own verse.

Moore's later years were increasingly characterized by honors—including the Pulitzer Prize in 1951 and the Bollingen Prize in 1953—and by the kind of public adulation that led to her being asked, at one point, to throw out the ball that would open the Brooklyn Dodgers' baseball season. During World War II, her poetry had become more frankly passionate; pieces like *The Paper Nautilus* openly addressed themselves to issues of love and survival that she might earlier have treated more obliquely. After her mother died in 1947, she continued living in the Brooklyn apartment that the pair had shared since the late twenties, indomitably active to the end and enjoying, as Elizabeth Bishop put it, "an unusually fortunate old age." Even for a close friend like Bishop, however, the contradictions represented by the career and personality of this radically inno-

vative old-fashioned "lady" who made such a mark on modern poetry continued to be haunting. "When I try to [summarize her life]," confessed the
younger woman, "I become foolishly bemused: I have a sort of subliminal
glimpse of the capital letter *M* multiplying . . . Marianne's monogram; mother;
manners; morals; and I catch myself murmuring, 'Manners and morals; manners *as* morals? or is it morals *as* manners?' "

To a Snail

If "compression is the first grace of style,"[1]
you have it. Contractility is a virtue
as modesty is a virtue.
It is not the acquisition of any one thing
that is able to adorn,   5
or the incidental quality that occurs
as a concomitant of something well said,
that we value in style,
but the principle that is hid:
in the absence of feet, "a method of conclusions";   10
"a knowledge of principles,"
in the curious phenomenon of your occipital horn.

1921, 1976

Poetry[2]

I, too, dislike it: there are things that are important beyond all
        this fiddle.
    Reading it, however, with a perfect contempt for it, one
        discovers in
    it after all, a place for the genuine.   5
        Hands that can grasp, eyes
        that can dilate, hair that can rise
            if it must, these things are important not because a

high-sounding interpretation can be put upon them but because
        they are   10
    useful. When they become so derivative as to become
        unintelligible,
        the same thing may be said for all of us, that we
        do not admire what
            we cannot understand: the bat   15

---

1. " 'The very first grace of style is that which
comes from compression.' *Demetrius on Style*,
translated by W. Hamilton Fyfe. Heinemann,
1932" [Moore's note].
2. Moore revised this poem a number of times

after its first publication in 1921. In her *Complete Poems* it is reduced to the first two sentences. The version printed here is that of
Selected Poems (1935).

holding on upside down or in quest of something to

eat, elephants pushing, a wild horse taking a roll, a tireless
       wolf under a tree, the immovable critic twitching his skin
       like a horse that feels a flea, the base-   20
ball fan, the statistician—
   nor is it valid
      to discriminate against 'business documents and

school-books';[3] all these phenomena are important. One must
      make a distinction   25
   however: when dragged into prominence by half poets, the
      result is not poetry,
   nor till the poets among us can be
     'literalists of
     the imagination'[4]—above   30
      insolence and triviality and can present

for inspection, imaginary gardens with real toads in them, shall
      we have
   it. In the meantime, if you demand on the one hand,
   the raw material of poetry in   35
     all its rawness and
     that which is on the other hand
      genuine, then you are interested in poetry.

                                   1921, 1935

Sojourn in the Whale[5]

Trying to open locked doors with a sword, threading
   the points of needles, planting shade trees
   upside down; swallowed by the opaqueness of one whom
                          the seas

love better than they love you, Ireland[6]—

3. *"Diary of Tolstoy* (Dutton), p. 84. "Where the boundary between prose and poetry lies, I shall never be able to understand. The question is raised in manuals of style, yet the answer to it lies beyond me. Poetry is verse; prose is not verse. Or else poetry is everything with the exception of business documents and school books" [Moore's note]. Count Leo Tolstoi (1828–1910), Russian novelist and mystic.
4. "Yeats: *Ideas of Good and Evil* (A. H. Bullen), p. 182. 'The limitation of his view was from the very intensity of his vision; he was a too literal realist of the imagination, as others are of nature; and because he believed that the figures seen by the mind's eye, when exalted by inspiration, were "eternal essences," symbols of divine essences, he hated every grace of style that might obscure their lineaments' " [Moore's note]. William Butler Yeats (1865–1939), Irish poet.
5. Moore alludes to the biblical story of Jonah, who was swallowed by a whale because he disobeyed God, but was then released after praying for help (Jonah 1–2). Text and format follow *Selected Poems* (1935).
6. Ireland had long been politically and economically exploited by England; it had also been the victim of numerous famines.

you have lived and lived on every kind of shortage.   5
    You have been compelled by hags to spin
    gold thread from straw[7] and have heard men say:
"There is a feminine temperament in direct contrast to ours

which makes her do these things. Circumscribed by a
    heritage of blindness and native   10
    incompetence, she will become wise and will be forced to
give in.
Compelled by experience, she will turn back;

water seeks its own level":
    and you have smiled. "Water in motion is far
    from level."[8] You have seen it, when obstacles happened
to bar   15
the path, rise automatically.

1921, 1967

Sea Unicorns and Land Unicorns

with their respective lions—
"mighty monoceroses with immeasured tayles"—[9]
these are those very animals
described by the cartographers of 1539,
defiantly revolving   5
in such a way that
the long keel of white exhibited in tumbling,
disperses giant weeds
and those sea snakes whose forms, looped in the foam,
    "disquiet shippers."[1]
Knowing how a voyager obtained the horn of a sea unicorn   10
to give to Queen Elizabeth,
who thought it worth a hundred thousand pounds,
they persevere in swimming where they like,
finding the place where sea-lions live in herds,
strewn on the beach like stones with lesser stones—   15
and bears are white;

---

7. In the folk tale *Rumplestiltskin*, collected by the brothers Grimm, a maiden is commanded by a king to spin straw into gold.
8. *"Literary Digest"* [Moore's note].
9. An echo of Edmund Spenser (1552–1599), English poet.
1. "Violet A. Wilson, in *Queen Elizabeth's Maids of Honour* (Dutton, 1922), quotes Olaus Magnus, *History of the Goths and Swedes*, with regard to the sea serpent; says of Cavendish as a voyager, 'He sailed up the Thames in splendour, the sails of his ship being cloth of gold and his seamen clad in rich silks. Many were the curiosities which the explorers brought home as presents for the ladies. The Queen naturally had first choice and to her fell the unicorn's horn valued at a hundred thousand pounds, which became one of the treasures of Windsor'" [Moore's note].

discovering Antarctica, its penguin kings and icy spires,
and Sir John Hawkins' Florida
"abounding in land unicorns and lions;
since where the one is,   20
its arch-enemy cannot be missing."[2]
Thus personalities by nature much opposed,
can be combined in such a way
that when they do agree, their unanimity is great,
"in politics, in trade, law, sport, religion,   25
china-collecting, tennis, and church-going."[3]
You have remarked this fourfold combination of strange animals,
upon embroideries
enwrought with "polished garlands" of agreeing difference—
thorns, "myrtle rods, and shafts of bay,"[4]   30
"cobwebs, and knotts, and mulberries"[5]
of lapis lazuli and pomegranate and malachite—
Britannia's sea unicorn with its rebellious child
now ostentatiously indigenous to the new English coast;
and its land lion oddly tolerant of those pacific counterparts to it,   35
the water lions of the west.
This is a strange fraternity—these sea lions and land lions,
land unicorns and sea unicorns:
the lion civilly rampant,
tame and concessive like the long-tailed bear of Ecuador—[6]   40
the lion standing up against this screen of woven air
which is the forest:
the unicorn also, on its hind legs in reciprocity.
A puzzle to the hunters, is this haughtiest of beasts,
to be distinguished from those born without a horn,   45
in use like Saint Jerome's tame lion,[7] as domestics;
rebelling proudly at the dogs
which are dismayed by the chain lightning
playing at them from its horn—
the dogs persistent in pursuit of it as if it could be caught,   50

2. "Sir John Hawkins 'affirmed the existence of land unicorns in the forests of Florida, and from their presence deduced abundance of lions because of the antipathy between the two animals, so that "where the one is the other cannot be missing" ' " [Moore's note].

3. An echo of the American novelist Henry James's (1843–1916) book *English Hours* (1905).

4. Moore takes these phrases from the English poet J. A. Symonds (1840–1893).

5. "Apropos Queen Elizabeth's dresses, 'cobwebs, and knotts and mulberries.' 'A petticoat embroidered all over slightly with snakes of Venice gold and silver and some O's, with a faire border embroidered like seas, cloudes, and rain-

bowes' " [Moore's note].

6. "*The long-tailed bear*. C. H. Prodgers in *Adventures in Bolivia* (Dodd, Mead, 1922), p. 193, tells of a strange animal that he bought: 'It was stuffed with long grass and cost me ten shillings, turning out eventually to be a bear with a tail. In his book on wild life, Rowland Ward says, "Amongst the rarest animals is a bear with a tail; this animal is known to exist, is very rare, and only to be found in the forests of Ecuador," and this was where the man who sold it to me said he got it' " [Moore's note].

7. Saint Jerome, a church father of the fourth century, is traditionally thought to have spent a night unharmed in a lion's den.

"deriving agreeable terror" from its "moonbeam throat"[8]
on fire like its white coat and unconsumed as if of
    salamander's skin.[9]

So wary as to disappear for centuries and reappear,
    yet never to be caught,
the unicorn has been preserved   55
by an unmatched device[1]
wrought like the work of expert blacksmiths,
this animal of that one horn
throwing itself upon which head foremost from a cliff,
it walks away unharmed;   60
proficient in this feat which, like Herodotus,[2]
I have not seen except in pictures.
Thus this strange animal with its miraculous elusiveness,
has come to be unique,
"impossible to take alive,"[3]   65
tamed only by a lady inoffensive like itself—
as curiously wild and gentle;
"as straight and slender as the crest,
or antlet of the one-beam'd beast."[4]
Upon the printed page,   70
also by word of mouth,
we have a record of it all
and how, unfearful of deceit,
etched like an equine monster of an old celestial map,
beside a cloud or dress of Virgin-Mary blue,   75
improved "all over slightly with snakes of Venice gold,
and silver, and some O's,"
the unicorn "with pavon high," approaches eagerly;
until engrossed by what appears of this strange enemy,
upon the map, "upon her lap,"   80
its "mild wild head doth lie."

                                                1921, 1967

An Egyptian Pulled Glass Bottle in the Shape of a Fish

      Here we have thirst
      and patience, from the first,

8. " 'The lover of reading will derive agreeable terror from Sir Bertram and the Haunted Chamber.' Leigh Hunt's *Autobiography*. Lines 52, 80, 82: 'Moonbeam throat,' 'with pavon high,' 'upon her lap.' 'Mediaeval,' an anonymous poem in *Punch*, April 25, 1923" [Moore's notes].
9. Salamanders are traditionally reputed to be immune to flames.
1. "Bulfinch's *Mythology*, under 'Unicorn'" [Moore's note].
2. "Herodotus says of the phoenix, 'I have not seen it myself except in a picture' " [Moore's note]. Herodotus was a Greek historian of the fifth century B.C.
3. Moore quotes Pliny the Elder, a Roman naturalist of the first century A.D.
4. "Charles Cotton, *An Epitaph on M. H.*: 'As soft, and snowy, as that down / Adorns the Blow-ball's frizzled crown; / As straight and slender as the crest / Or antlet of the one-beam'd beast' " [Moore's note]. Charles Cotton (1630–1687), English poet and translator.

and art, as in a wave held up for us to see
in its essential perpendicularity;

not brittle but   5
intense—the spectrum, that
    spectacular and nimble animal the fish,
    whose scales turn aside the sun's sword by their polish.

                                                    1921, 1967

Silence

My father used to say,
"Superior people never make long visits,
have to be shown Longfellow's grave
or the glass flowers at Harvard.[5]
Self-reliant like the cat—   5
that takes it prey to privacy,
the mouse's limp tail hanging like a shoelace from its mouth—
they sometimes enjoy solitude,
and can be robbed of speech
by speech which has delighted them.   10
The deepest feeling always shows itself in silence;
not in silence, but restraint."
Nor was he insincere in saying, "Make my house your inn."[6]
Inns are not residences.

                                                    1921, 1967

No Swan So Fine

"No water so still as the
    dead fountains of Versailles."[7] No swan,
with swart blind look askance
and gondoliering legs, so fine
    as the chintz china one with fawn-   5
brown eyes and toothed gold
collar on to show whose bird it was.

Lodged in the Louis Fifteenth
    candelabrum-tree of cockscomb-

---

5. "My father used to say, 'Superior people
never make long visits. When I am visiting, I like
to go about by myself. I never had to be shown
Longfellow's grave or the glass flowers at Harvard.' Miss A. M. Homans" [Moore's note].
6. Edmund Burke, in *Burke's Life*, by Sir James
Prior (1872). " 'Throw yourself into a coach,'
said he. 'Come down and make my house your
inn' " [Moore's note].

7. "A pair of Louis XV candelabra with Dresden figures of swans belonging to Lord Balfour.
'There is no water so still as in the dead fountains
of Versailles.' Percy Phillip, *New York Times
Magazine*, May 10, 1931" [Moore's note].
Louis XV, the king of France, held court at the
opulent palace of Versailles in the eighteenth
century.

tinted buttons, dahlias,   10
sea urchins, and everlastings,
    it perches on the branching foam
of polished sculptured
flowers—at ease and tall. The king is dead.

1932, 1967

The Jerboa[8]

Too Much

A Roman had an
artist, a freedman,
    contrive a cone—pine cone
    or fir cone-with holes for a fountain. Placed on
        the Prison of St. Angelo,[9] this cone   5
        of the Pompeys which is known

now as the Popes', passed
for art. A huge cast
    bronze, dwarfing the peacock
    statue in the garden of the Vatican,   10
        it looks like a work of art made to give
        to a Pompey, or native

of Thebes.[1] Others could
build, and understood
    making colossi[2] and   15
    how to use slaves, and kept crocodiles and put
        baboons on the necks of giraffes to pick
        fruit, and used serpent magic.

They had their men tie
hippopotami   20
    and bring out dappled dog-
    cats to course antelopes, dikdik,[3] and ibex;
        or used small eagles. They looked on as theirs,
        impalas and onigers,[4]

the wild ostrich herd   25
with hard feet and bird
    necks rearing back in the
dust like a serpent preparing to strike, cranes,

8. A nocturnal jumping rodent.   2. Huge statues of human forms.
9. A prison in Rome.   3. A variety of antelope. "Ibex": wild goats.
1. Greek city. Pompey was a Roman general.   4. African antelopes.

mongooses, storks, anoas,[5] Nile geese;
and there were gardens for these—

combining planes, dates,
limes, and pomegranates,   30
   in avenues—with square
    pools of pink flowers, tame fish, and small frogs. Besides
      yarns dyed with indigo, and red cotton,
       they had a flax which they spun

into fine linen   35
cordage for yachtsmen.
   These people liked small things;
   they gave to boys little paired playthings such as
   nests of eggs, ichneumon[6] and snake, paddle
   and raft, badger and camel;   40

and made toys for them-
selves: the royal totem;
   and toilet boxes marked
   with the contents. Lords and ladies put goose-grease
      paint in round bone boxes—the pivoting   45
       lid incised with a duck-wing

or reverted duck-
head; kept in a buck
   or rhinoceros horn,
   the ground horn; and locust oil in stone locusts.[7]   50
      It was a picture with a fine distance;
      of drought, and of assistance

in time, from the Nile
rising slowly, while
   the pig-tailed monkeys on   55
   slab hands, with arched-up slack-slung gait, and the brown
      dandy looked at the jasmine two-leafed twig
      and bud, cactus pads, and fig.

Dwarfs here and there, lent
to an evident   60
   poetry of frog grays,
   duck-egg greens, and eggplant blues, a fantasy
      and a verisimilitude that were
      right to those with, everywhere,

---

5. Small wild oxen.
6. Mongoose: small ferretlike animal that eats
snakes.

7. "Toilet box dating from about the twenty-
second Egyptian Dynasty. *Illustrated London
News*, July 26, 1930" [Moore's note].

power over the poor.   65
The bees' food is your
    food. Those who tended flower-
      beds and stables were like the king's cane[8] in the
        form of a hand, or the folding bedroom[9]
          made for his mother of whom   70

he was fond. Princes
clad in queens' dresses,
    calla or petunia
      white, that trembled at the edge, and queens in a
        king's underskirt of fine-twilled thread like silk-   75
          worm gut, as bee-man and milk-

maid, kept divine cows
and bees; limestone brows,
    and gold-foil wings. They made
      basalt serpents and portraits of beetles; the   80
        king gave his name to them and he was named
          for them. He feared snakes, and tamed

Pharaoh's rat, the rust-
backed mongoose. No bust
    of it was made, but there   85
      was pleasure for the rat. Its restlessness was
        its excellence; it was praised for its wit;
          and the jerboa,[1] like it,

a small desert rat,
and not famous, that   90
    lives without water, has
      happiness. Abroad seeking food, or at home
        in its burrow, the Sahara fieldmouse
          has a shining silver house

of sand. O rest and   95
joy, the boundless sand,
    the stupendous sandspout,
      no water, no palm trees, no ivory bed,
        tiny cactus; but one would not be he
          who has nothing but plenty.   100

---

8. "Description by J. D. S. Pendlebury, *Illustrated London News*, March 19, 1932" [Moore's note].
9. "The portable bedchamber of Queen Hetepheres presented to her by her son, Cheops. Described by Dr. G. A. Reisner, *Illustrated London News*, May 7, 1932" [Moore's note].

1. " 'There are little rats called jerboas which run on long hindlegs as thin as a match. The forelimbs are mere tiny hands.' Dr. R. L. Ditmars, *Strange Animals I Have Known* (New York: Harcourt Brace, 1931), p. 274" [Moore's note].

Abundance

Africanus[2] meant
the conqueror sent
    from Rome. It should mean the
    untouched: the sand-brown jumping-rat—free-born; and
        the blacks, that choice race with an elegance   105
        ignored by one's ignorance.

Part terrestrial,
and part celestial,
    Jacob saw,[3] cudgel staff
    in claw hand—steps of air and air angels; his   110
        friends were the stones. The translucent mistake
        of the desert, does not make

hardship for one who
can rest and then do
    the opposite—launching   115
    as if on wings, from its match-thin hind legs, in
        daytime or at night; with the tail as a weight,
        undulated out by speed, straight.

Looked at by daylight,
the underside's white,   120
    though the fur on the back
    is buff-brown like the breast of the fawn-breasted
        bower-bird. It hops like the fawn-breast, but has
        chipmunk contours—perceived as

it turns its bird head—   125
the nap directed
    neatly back and blending
    with the ear which reiterates the slimness
        of the body. The fine hairs on the tail,
        repeating the other pale   130

markings, lengthen until
at the tip they fill
    out in a tuft—black and
    white; strange detail of the simplified creature,
        fish-shaped and silvered to steel by the force   135
        of the large desert moon. Course

the jerboa, or
plunder its food store,

---

2. An honorary name bestowed on Roman generals who made conquests in Africa, such as Scipio.

3. During a journey through the desert, Jacob dreams he sees a ladder rising to heaven, carrying God's angels (Genesis 28:12).

and you will be cursed. It
honors the sand by assuming its color;   140
    closed upper paws seeming one with the fur
    in its flight from a danger.

By fifths and sevenths,[4]
in leaps of two lengths,
    like the uneven notes   140
of the Bedouin flute, it stops its gleaning
    on little wheel castors, and makes fern-seed
    footprints with kangaroo speed.

Its leaps should be set
to the flageolet;[5]
    pillar body erect   145
on a three-cornered smooth-working Chippendale[6]
    claw—propped on hind legs, and tail as third toe,
    between leaps to its burrow.

                                                    1935, 1967

Marriage

            This institution,
            perhaps one should say enterprise
            out of respect for which
            one says one need not change one's mind
            about a thing one has believed in,   5
            requiring public promises
            of one's intention
            to fulfil a private obligation:
            I wonder what Adam and Eve[7]
            think of it by this time,   10
            this fire-gilt steel
            alive with goldenness;
            how bright it shows—
            "of circular traditions and impostures,
            committing many spoils,"[8]   15
            requiring all one's criminal ingenuity
            to avoid!
            Psychology which explains everything
            explains nothing,

4. Wide melodic intervals in music.
5. A small flute.
6. An English manufacturer of furniture, often
featuring clawlike feet.
7. The first man and the first woman

(Genesis 3).
8. "Francis Bacon" [Moore's note]. This is the
first of many quotations in the poem; in her
notes, Moore calls them "statements that took
my fancy which I tried to arrange plausibly."

and we are still in doubt.   20
Eve: beautiful woman—
I have seen her
when she was so handsome
she gave me a start,
able to write simultaneously   25
in three languages—
English, German, and French—
and talk in the meantime;[9]
equally positive in demanding a commotion
and in stipulating quiet: 30
"*I should like to be alone*";
to which the visitor replies,
"I should like to be alone;
why not be alone together?"
Below the incandescent stars   35
below the incandescent fruit,
the strange experience of beauty;
its existence is too much;
it tears one to pieces
and each fresh wave of consciousness   40
is poison.
"See her, see her in this common world,"[1]
the central flaw
in that first crystal-fine experiment,
this amalgamation which can never be more   45
than an interesting impossibility,
describing it
as "that strange paradise
unlike flesh, stones,
gold or stately buildings,   50
the choicest piece of my life:
the heart rising
in its estate of peace
as a boat rises
with the rising of the water";[2]   55
constrained in speaking of the serpent—
shed snakeskin in the history of politeness
not to be returned to again—
that invaluable accident
exonerating Adam.   60

9. "Miss A—— will write simultaneously in three languages, English, German, and French, talking in the meantime. [She] takes advantage of her abilities in everyday life, writing her letters simultaneously with both hands; namely, the first, third, and fifth words with her left and the second, fourth, and sixth with her right hand. While generally writing outward she is able as well to write inward with both hands. 'Multiple Consciousness or Reflex Action of Unaccustomed Range,' *Scientific American*, January 1922" [Moore's note].
1. "George Shock" [Moore's note].
2. "Richard Baxter, *The Saints' Everlasting Rest*" [Moore's note].

And he has beauty also;
it's distressing—the O thou
to whom from whom,
without whom nothing—Adam;
"something feline,   65
something colubrine"[3]—how true!
a crouching mythological monster
in that Persian miniature[4] of emerald mines,
raw silk—ivory white, snow white,
oyster white, and six others—   70
that paddock full of leopards and giraffes—
long lemon-yellow bodies
sown with trapezoids of blue.
Alive with words,
vibrating like a cymbal   75
touched before it has been struck,
he has prophesied correctly—
the industrious waterfall,
"the speedy stream
which violently bears all before it,   80
at one time silent as the air
and now as powerful as the wind."
"Treading chasms
on the uncertain footing of a spear,"[5]
forgetting that there is in woman   85
a quality of mind
which as an instinctive manifestation
is unsafe,
he goes on speaking
in a formal customary strain,   90
of "past states, the present state,
seals, promises,
the evil one suffered,
the good one enjoys,
hell, heaven,   95
everything convenient
to promote one's joy."[6]
In him a state of mind
perceives what it was not
intended that he should;   100
"he experiences a solemn joy
in seeing that he has become an idol."[7]

3. " 'We were puzzled and we were fascinated, as if by something feline, by something colubrine.' Philip Littell, reviewing Santayana's *Poems* in *The New Republic*, March 21, 1923" [Moore's note]. "Colubrine": snakelike.
4. Tiny, meticulously detailed paintings, often using other media besides paint, such as silk or ivory.
5. "Hazlitt: 'Essay on Burke's Style' " [Moore's note].
6. "Richard Baxter" [Moore's note].
7. " 'À Travers Champs,' by Anatole France, in *Filles et Garçons* (Hachette)" [Moore's note].

Plagued by the nightingale
in the new leaves,
with its silence—   105
not its silence but its silences,
he says of it:
"It clothes me with a shirt of fire."[8]
"He dares not clap his hands
to make it go on   110
lest it should fly off;
if he does nothing, it will sleep;
if he cries out, it will not understand."[9]
Unnerved by the nightingale
and dazzled by the apple,   115
impelled by "the illusion of a fire
effectual to extinguish fire,"
compared with which
the shining of the earth
is but deformity—a fire   120
"as high as deep
as bright as broad
as long as life itself,"[1]
he stumbles over marriage,
"a very trivial object indeed"[2]   125
to have destroyed the attitude
in which he stood—
the ease of the philosopher
unfathered by a woman.
Unhelpful Hymen![3]   130
a kind of overgrown cupid
reduced to insignificance
by the mechanical advertising
parading as involuntary comment,
by that experiment of Adam's   135
with ways out but no way in—
the ritual of marriage,
augmenting all its lavishness;
its fiddlehead ferns,
lotus flowers, opuntias,[4] white dromedaries,   140
its hippopotamus—
nose and mouth combined
in one magnificent hopper—

8. "Hagop Boghossian in a poem, 'The Nightingale' " [Moore's note].
9. "Edward Thomas, *Feminine Influence on
the Poets* (Martin Secker, 1910)" [Moore's
note].
1. "Richard Baxter" [Moore's note].

2. " 'Marriage is a law, and the worst of all laws
. . . a very trivial object indeed.' Godwin"
[Moore's note].
3. The Greek god of marriage; Cupid was the
child-god of love.
4. Greek: prickly pears.

its snake and the potent apple.[5]
He tells us   145
that "for love that will
gaze an eagle blind,[6]
that is with Hercules
climbing the trees
in the garden of the Hesperides,[7]   150
from forty-five to seventy
is the best age,"
commending it
as a fine art, as an experiment,
a duty or as merely recreation.   155
One must not call him ruffian
nor friction a calamity—
the fight to be affectionate:
"no truth can be fully known
until it has been tried   160
by the tooth of disputation."[8]
The blue panther with black eyes,
the basalt panther with blue eyes,
entirely graceful—
one must give them the path—   165
the black obsidian Diana[9]
who "darkeneth her countenance
as a bear doth,"[1]
the spiked hand
that has an affection for one   170
and proves it to the bone,
impatient to assure you
that impatience is the mark of independence,
not of bondage.
"Married people often look that way"[2]—   175
"seldom and cold, up and down,
mixed and malarial
with a good day and a bad."[3]
We Occidentals are so unemotional,
self lost, the irony preserved   180
in "the Ahasuerus tête-à-tête banquet"[4]
with its small orchids like snakes' tongues,

---

5. The serpent persuaded Eve to eat the apple
of the tree of the knowledge of good and evil—
thus banishing Adam and Eve from the Garden
of Eden.
6. "Anthony Trollope, *Barchester Towers*"
[Moore's note].
7. One of the labors of the mythological hero
Hercules was to fetch the golden apples from the
Garden of the Hesperides.
8. "Robert of Sorbonne" [Moore's note].

9. I.e., a statue of the Roman goddess of chastity, made out of black semiprecious glass.
1. "Ecclesiasticus" [Moore's note].
2. "C. Bertram Hartmann" [Moore's note].
3. "Richard Baxter" [Moore's note].
4. "George Adam Smith, *Expositor's Bible*"
[Moore's note]. The reference is to the banquet
at which Esther, queen of the Israelites, persuades King Ahasuerus of Haman's perfidy
(Esther 7); "tête-à-tête": i.e., intimate.

with its "good monster, lead the way,"[5]
with little laughter
and munificence of humor   185
in that quixotic atmosphere of frankness
in which "four o'clock does not exist,
but at five o'clock
the ladies in their imperious humility
are ready to receive you";[6]   190
in which experience attests
that men have power
and sometimes one is made to feel it.
He says, "What monarch would not blush
to have a wife   195
with hair like a shaving brush?"[7]
The fact of woman
is "not the sound of the flute
but very poison."[8]
She says, "Men are monopolists   200
of 'stars, garters, buttons
and other shining baubles'—
unfit to be the guardians
of another person's happiness.'"[9]
He says, "These mummies   205
must be handled carefully—
'the crumbs from a lion's meal,
a couple of shins and the bit of an ear';[1]
turn to the letter M
and you will find   210
that 'a wife is a coffin,'[2]
that severe object
with the pleasing geometry
stipulating space not people,
refusing to be buried   215
and uniquely disappointing,
revengefully wrought in the attitude
of an adoring child
to a distinguished parent,"
She says, "This butterfly,   220

5. "*The Tempest*" [Moore's note].
6. "Comtesse de Noailles, 'Le Thé,' *Femina*, December 1921" [Moore's note].
7. "From 'The Rape of the Lock,' a parody of Mary Frances Nearing, with suggestions by M. Moore" [Moore's note].
8. "A. Mitram Rihbany, *The Syrian Christ* (Houghton, Mifflin, 1916). Silence of women —'to an Oriental, this is as poetry set to music'" [Moore's note]
9. "Miss M. Carey Thomas, Founder's address, Mount Holyoke, 1921: 'Men practically reserve for themselves stately funerals, splendid monuments, memorial statues, membership in academies, medals, titles, honorary degrees, stars, garters, ribbons, buttons and other shining baubles, so valueless in themselves and yet so infinitely desirable because they are symbols of recognition by their fellow-craftsmen of difficult work well done'" [Moore's note].
1. "Amos iii, 12. Translation by George Adam Smith, *Expositor's Bible*" [Moore's note].
2. "Ezra Pound" [Moore's note].

this waterfly, this nomad
that has 'proposed
to settle on my hand for life'[3]—
What can one do with it?
There must have been more time   225
in Shakespeare's day
to sit and watch a play.
You know so many artists who are fools."
He says, "You know so many fools
who are not artists."   230
The fact forgot
that "some have merely rights
while some have obligations,"[4]
he loves himself so much,
he can permit himself   235
no rival in that love.
She loves herself so much,
she cannot see herself enough—
a statuette of ivory on ivory,
the logical last touch   240
to an expansive splendor
earned as wages for work done:
one is not rich but poor
when one can always seem so right.
What can one do for them—   245
these savages
condemned to disaffect
all those who are not visionaries
alert to undertake the silly task
of making people noble?   250
This model of petrine fidelity
who "leaves her peaceful husband
only because she has seen enough of him"[5]—
that orator reminding you,
"I am yours to command."   255
"Everything to do with love is mystery;[6]
it is more than a day's work
to investigate this science."
One sees that it is rare—
that striking grasp of opposites   260
opposed each to the other, not to unity,
which in cycloid inclusiveness

3. "Charles Reade, *Christie Johnstone*" [Moore's note].
4. "Edmund Burke" [Moore's note].
5. "Simon Puget, advertisement entitled 'Change of Fashion,' *English Review*, June 1914: 'Thus proceed pretty dolls when they leave their old home to renovate their frame, and dear others who may abandon their peaceful husband only because they have seen enough of him'" [Moore's note]. "Petrine": like Saint Peter the Apostle, who, before Christ's crucifixion, denied Him three times (Matthew 26:69–75).
6. "F. C. Tilney, *Fables of La Fontaine*, 'Love and Folly', Book XII, No. 14" [Moore's note].

has dwarfed the demonstration
of Columbus with the egg[7]—
a triumph of simplicity—   265
that charitive Euroclydon[8]
of frightening disinterestedness
which the world hates,
admitting:

"I am such a cow,   270
if I had a sorrow
I should feel it a long time;
I am not one of those
who have a great sorrow
in the morning   275
and a great joy at noon";

which says: "I have encountered it
among those unpretentious
protégés of wisdom,
where seeming to parade   280
as the debater and the Roman,
the statesmanship
of an archaic Daniel Webster[9]
persists to their simplicity of temper
as the essence of the matter: 285

    'Liberty and union
    now and forever';[1]

the Book on the writing table;
the hand in the breast pocket."

1935

The Paper Nautilus[2]

For authorities whose hopes
are shaped by mercenaries?
Writers entrapped by
teatime fame and by

---

7. A reference to the story in which Columbus boasted that he could make an egg stand up; when challenged, he broke an end, thus flattening it.
8. A tempestuous wind (Acts 27:14); "charitive" (or "charitative"): charitable.
9. The ancient Romans prized the skills of rhetoric and debate; Daniel Webster (1782–1852), American statesman, was famous for his oratory.

1. "Daniel Webster (statue with inscription, Central Park, New York City)" [Moore's note].
2. A fish related to the octopus, also known as the Argonaut; the female builds a fragile shell to contain her eggs, carrying it on the surface of the water with two of her eight tentacles, once thought to serve as sails; hence the name, which means "sailor."

commuters' comforts? Not for these   5
        the paper nautilus
        constructs her thin glass shell.

    Giving her perishable
souvenir of hope, a dull
        white outside and smooth-   10
        edged inner surface
glossy as the sea, the watchful
        maker of it guards it
        day and night; she scarcely

        eats until the eggs are hatched.   15
Buried eightfold in her eight
        arms, for she is in
        a sense a devil-
fish, her glass ram's-horn-cradled freight
        is hid but is not crushed;   20
        as Hercules, bitten

    by a crab loyal to the hydra,[3]
was hindered to succeed,
        the intensively
        watched eggs coming from   25
the shell free it when they are freed—
        leaving its wasp-nest flaws
        of white on white, and close-

    laid Ionic chiton[4]-folds
like the lines in the mane of   30
        a Parthenon horse,[5]
        round which the arms had
wound themselves as if they knew love
        is the only fortress
        strong enough to trust to.   35

                                            1941

His Shield

The pin-swin or spine-swine
        (the edgehog miscalled hedgehog) with all his edges out,
    echidna and echinoderm in distressed-
pin-cushion thorn-fur coats, the spiny pig or porcupine,

---

3. In Greek myth, a many-headed monster subdued by the hero Hercules. As he fought the
monster, a crab bit him, and he crushed it underfoot.

4. Ancient Greek linen undergarment, with
long sleeves.
5. Represented in the frieze at the Parthenon, a
temple in Athens.

the rhino with horned snout—   5
everything is battle-dressed.

Pig-fur won't do, I'll wrap
    myself in salamander-skin like Presbyter John.[6]
    A lizard in the midst of flames, a firebrand
that is life, asbestos-eyed asbestos-eared, with tattooed nap   10
    and permanent pig on
    the instep; he can withstand

fire and won't drown. In his
    unconquerable country of unpompous gusto,
    gold was so common none considered it; greed   15
and flattery were unknown. Though rubies large as tennis
    balls conjoined in streams so
    that the mountain seemed to bleed,

the inextinguishable
    salamander[7] styled himself but presbyter. His shield   20
    was his humility. In Carpasian
linen coat, flanked by his household lion cubs and sable
    retinue, he revealed
    a formula safer than

an armorer's: the power of relinquishing   25
    what one would keep; that is freedom. Become dinosaur-
    skulled, quilled or salamander-wooled, more ironshod
and javelin-dressed than a hedgehog battalion of steel, but be
    dull. Don't be envied or
    armed with a measuring-rod.   30

                                                              1951

O to Be a Dragon[8]

If I, like Solomon,[9] . . .
    could have my wish—

    my wish . . . O to be a dragon,
    a symbol of the power of Heaven—of silkworm
    size or immense; at times invisible.   5
        Felicitous phenomenon!

                                                              1957

6. A legendary Christian monarch of the twelfth
century, who was said to perform marvels of all
kinds. "Presbyter": priest.
7. A lizard traditionally thought to be immune
to fire.
8. "See secondary symbols, Volume II of *The*

Tao of Painting, translated and edited by Mai-
mai Sze, Bollingen Series 49 (New York: Pantheon, 1956; Modern Library edition, p. 57)"
[Moore's note].
9. "Solomon's wish: 'an understanding heart.' I
Kings 3:9" [Moore's note].

KATHERINE MANSFIELD
1888–1923

When she was thirty years old, Katherine Mansfield described the two motives of what she called her "writing game" with striking clarity and conviction: "*One* is joy," she explained in a letter to her husband, the critic J. Middleton Murry, adding that in this state of being "in some perfectly blissful way *at peace*," something like a flower "seems to open before my eyes." The other "kick off" consisted of "*a cry against corruption*" that she associated with the hopeless sense that "everything [is] doomed to disaster." It is hardly surprising that the New Zealand–born Kathleen Beauchamp should have felt divided about her identity as a London literary figure called Katherine Mansfield. She came from a conventional Victorian family, but she lived the bohemian life of a New Woman. She referred to herself as a "child" and liked to play with dolls, kittens, and imaginary babies, but she suffered from gonorrhea, had one miscarriage, and seems to have had an abortion. She repeatedly protested that she wanted nothing more than a home of her own, but she spent her life restlessly traveling from England to France and Italy, and back again. She said she adored her husband, but she never relinquished her close ties to her "wife," Ida Baker. Finally, and most tragically, while she searched for spiritual health, she suffered the debilitating consequences of the tuberculosis that killed her at the age of thirty-five.

Kathleen Beauchamp's father, Harold Beauchamp, was an enterprising Wellington businessman who would go on to become a prominent director of the Bank of New Zealand. Her mother, Annie (Dyer) Beauchamp, was a delicate woman who brought her own mother to live in the household. This grandmother provided the affectionate protection Kathleen's self-absorbed, frail mother and upwardly-mobile father could not supply. After the birth of her only brother, Kathleen was sent with her sisters to a series of New Zealand schools; then, at fifteen, she traveled with her family to London, where she studied for three years at Queen's College. By the time she unwillingly returned to New Zealand, she was reading the fiction of Oscar Wilde, Elizabeth Robins, the Brontës, and Leo Tolstoi, and she was beginning to receive payment for vignettes appearing in *The Native Companion*, a New Zealand journal. This sign of success was sufficient to convince her father to allow her to go back to London.

Kathleen had already begun to establish the divided emotional loyalties that would inform the rest of her life. On the one hand, she was writing love letters to the son of her Wellington music teacher, Tom Trowell, whose twin, Garnet, would become her fiancé when she finally managed to return to England. On the other hand, an early journal entry indicates that she felt guilty about her passion for a Wellington schoolfriend, Maata Mahupuka, a Maori (native New Zealand) heiress. At Queen's College, moreover, she met Ida Constance Baker, a motherless girl whose father was to become the model for the tyrannical paterfamilias in *The Daughters of the Late Colonel*. Ida eventually became known as L. M. (Leslie Moore) and Kathleen called herself Katherine Mansfield. When Katherine was rejected by Garnet Trowell's parents and decided on the spur of the moment to marry a new acquaintance, George Bowden, it was L. M. who accompanied the twenty-one-year-old bride, dressed all in black, to the Registry Office; it was also to L. M. that the bride fled on her wedding night. At this point, however, Mrs. Beauchamp arrived in London and packed Katherine off to a German hotel. There, according to her biographer Antony Alpers, she was "treated" for her lesbianism with cold baths, and she suffered a miscarriage.

Mansfield's early stories were first published individually in A. R. Orage's *New Age* and then collected in the caustic volume entitled *In a German Pension* (1911). After she sent one tale, *The Woman at the Store*, to a new review, *Rhythm*, she was visited by its literary editor, J. Middleton Murry, an Oxford undergraduate who came from what Alpers calls "the very bottom of the lower middle class." One year younger than Mansfield, he became in 1912 first a lodger in her flat and then her lover. Although *Rhythm* would soon go bankrupt, Mansfield continued to publish stories to supplement the modest allowance provided by her father, and Murry began earning money from critical essays and reviews.

Their lives, like everyone else's, were shattered by World War I. While L. M. worked as a machinist in an airplane factory, Murry took a job in military intelligence. For Mansfield, however, the reality of the war was brought home by the death of her brother, who was "blown to bits" in France. In *Prelude* (1917) and *At the Bay* (1921), Mansfield went on to reconstruct the "undiscovered country" she had shared with Leslie Beauchamp in stories that depart from conventional narration to convey the mysterious radiance of childhood as it is perceived by a community of women and children. Near the end of her life, moreover, she wrote the startling antiwar story *The Fly* (1922) to express her outrage at the sacrifice of a generation of sons by their fathers, the architects of the war.

When she was not traveling or living on the Continent, Mansfield was befriended by a number of literary celebrities in London, including, most importantly, the novelists D. H. Lawrence and Virginia Woolf. These last two relationships illuminate the tensions in the writer's literary career. Throughout her *Journal* and her numerous letters, Mansfield expressed her admiration for Lawrence, her sense that they were "unthinkably alike" not only in temperament but in their artistic efforts to capture the sensuous feeling of life. Yet she was horrified by the violent, public bickering in which Lawrence and his wife, Frieda, engaged, and she may have also understood that Lawrence was really searching for what he called a "blood brotherhood" with Murry, to whom he was greatly attracted. Even if she did not recognize herself and Murry in Lawrence's portraits of the self-conscious miniaturist Gudrun and her masterfully attractive but flawed lover Gerald in *Women in Love* (1920), Mansfield had been alienated by a shocking letter Lawrence wrote her in 1920: "You revolt me, stewing in your consumption."

Significant as Mansfield's relationship with Lawrence was, her friendship with Virginia Woolf was perhaps equally crucial. In 1917, the "Woolves" published *Prelude* at their Hogarth Press, and Mansfield and Woolf began visiting and writing each other. Sometimes the older, wealthier Woolf criticized Mansfield's bohemian promiscuity, but she nevertheless admitted that beyond Mansfield's "commonness" was an "inscrutable" intelligence. Analyzing their similar literary aims, Mansfield wrote Woolf, "We have the same job, Virginia." After Mansfield died, moreover, Woolf recorded in her diary that Mansfield had produced "the only writing I have ever been jealous of." Although Woolf did not understand why their relationship deteriorated, it is clear from Mansfield's letters that the younger writer envied a woman who had her own home, her own possessions, and her own man within call, for Mansfield's rootlessness was related to her uneasy alliance with Murry.

Mansfield sustained a relationship with Murry from the time she was twenty-four until her death. While she admired the critical intelligence shown in his book on Dostoevsky, she knew the "sham" side of Murry's personality, when he seemed "to uncover" himself "and quiver" in an ecstasy of self-pity. Mansfield was also aware of Murry's physical revulsion against and impatience with her tuberculosis, a reaction she presents brilliantly in her short story *The Man Without a Temperament* (1920). Mansfield's continual search for a healthy place to recuperate meant long separations, and her letters complain of her husband's monetary and emotional stinginess, as well as of her loneliness. The sicker she became, the more she relied on L. M.'s services as a traveling companion, a home nurse, and a cook, but her dependence bred resentment, and L. M. came to seem like "The Albatross" or "a revolting hysterical ghoul." Mansfield's letters from this period remain difficult to interpret, for they were, like her *Journal*, heavily edited by Murry.

After 1918, Mansfield increasingly suffered from night terrors, insomnia, difficulty walking, pains in the chest, and a nausea that made it difficult for her to eat. Yet at this time she wrote the stories that would be published in *Bliss and Other Stories* (1920), as well as many reviews for Murry's journal, the *Atheneum*. Always short of money, she nevertheless began a series of cures that included stays in nursing homes, radium treatments, and X-rays. By 1922, when *The Garden Party and Other Stories* was published to critical acclaim, she was reading P. D. Ouspensky's *Cosmic Anatomy* and contemplating spiritual cures for the physical problems her physicians could not alleviate. Then she became acquainted through Orage with the Caucasian Greek spiritualist George Ivanovich Gurdjieff. He was just establishing his Institute for the Harmonious Development of Man at Fontainebleau, where he recommended drastic shifts in habit, unsettling alterations in living conditions, and rhythmic exercises and dances to accomplish a "centering" that would result in a new self and a new way of seeing. In 1922, Mansfield secretly joined Gurdjieff's community, but soon she invited Murry to visit her. By that time, she had been installed in a hayloft where she could breathe the exhalation of cows, drink fresh milk, and gaze at the ceiling and walls, which were decorated with paintings of flowers, birds, and animals. On the night of Murry's visit, Mansfield suffered a hemorrhage and died almost instantly.

During her short lifetime, the former Kathleen Beauchamp had been recognized for the sardonic, often cynical stories that she wrote as a cry against the corruption of modern English society. But, midway in her career, she had also begun composing joyous narratives, peaceful memories of a blissful New Zealand childhood. For the last few years of her life, moreover, she brilliantly integrated her satiric and sympathetic impulses in portraits of impoverished, single women and imaginative children that transformed the art of the short story. Frequently compared to Anton Chekhov, whom she greatly admired, Mansfield practiced her art with strenuous discipline, for it was a reprieve from the pain of her life.

The Daughters of the Late Colonel

1

The week after was one of the busiest weeks of their lives. Even when they went to bed it was only their bodies that lay down and rested; their minds went on, thinking things out, talking things over, wondering, deciding, trying to remember where . . .

Constantia lay like a statue, her hands by her sides, her feet just overlapping each other, the sheet up to her chin. She stared at the ceiling.

"Do you think father would mind if we gave his top-hat to the porter?"[1]

"The porter?" snapped Josephine. "Why ever the porter? What a very extraordinary idea!"

"Because," said Constantia slowly, "he must often have to go to funerals. And I noticed at—at the cemetery that he only had a bowler." She paused. "I thought then how very much he'd appreciate a top-hat. We ought to give him a present, too. He was always very nice to father."

"But," cried Josephine, flouncing on her pillow and staring across the dark at Constantia, "father's head!" And suddenly, for one awful moment, she nearly giggled. Not, of course, that she felt in the least like giggling. It must have been habit. Years ago, when they had stayed awake at night talking, their beds had simply heaved. And now the porter's head, disappearing, popped out, like a candle, under father's hat. . . . The giggle mounted, mounted; she clenched her hands; she fought it down; she frowned fiercely at the dark and said "Remember" terribly sternly.

"We can decide to-morrow," she sighed.

Constantia had noticed nothing; she sighed.

"Do you think we ought to have our dressing-gowns dyed as well?"

"Black?" almost shrieked Josephine.

"Well, what else?" said Constantia. "I was thinking—it doesn't

---

1. In England, a male servant; originally a gatekeeper.

seem quite sincere, in a way, to wear black out of doors and when we're fully dressed, and then when we're at home—"

"But nobody sees us," said Josephine. She gave the bedclothes such a twitch that both her feet became uncovered, and she had to creep up the pillows to get them well under again.

"Kate does," said Constantia. "And the postman very well might."

Josephine thought of her dark-red slippers, which matched her dressing-gown, and of Constantia's favourite indefinite green ones which went with hers. Black! Two black dressing-gowns and two pairs of black woolly slippers, creeping off to the bathroom like black cats.

"I don't think it's absolutely necessary," said she.

Silence. Then Constantia said, "We shall have to post the papers with the notice in them to-morrow to catch the Ceylon mail. . . . How many letters have we had up till now?"

"Twenty-three."

Josephine had replied to them all, and twenty-three times when she came to "We miss our dear father so much" she had broken down and had to use her handkerchief, and on some of them even to soak up a very light-blue tear with an edge of blotting-paper. Strange! She couldn't have put it on—but twenty-three times. Even now, though when she said over to herself sadly. "We miss our dear father *so* much" she could have cried if she'd wanted to.

"Have you got enough stamps?" came from Constantia.

"Oh, how can I tell?" said Josephine crossly. "What's the good of asking me that now?"

"I was just wondering," said Constantia mildly.

Silence again. There came a little rustle, a scurry, a hop.

"A mouse," said Constantia.

"It can't be a mouse because there aren't any crumbs," said Josephine.

"But it doesn't know there aren't," said Constantia.

A spasm of pity squeezed her heart. Poor little thing! She wished she'd left a tiny piece of biscuit on the dressing-table. It was awful to think of it not finding anything. What would it do?

"I can't think how they manage to live at all," she said slowly.

"Who?" demanded Josephine.

And Constantia said more loudly than she meant to, "Mice."

Josephine was furious. "Oh, what nonsense, Con!" she said. "What have mice got to do with it? You're asleep."

"I don't think I am," said Constantia. She shut her eyes to make sure. She was.

Josephine arched her spine, pulled up her knees, folded her arms so that her fists came under her ears, and pressed her cheek hard against the pillow.

2

Another thing which complicated matters was they had Nurse Andrews staying on with them that week. It was their own fault; they had asked her. It was Josephine's idea. On the morning—well, on the last morning, when the doctor had gone, Josephine had said to Constantia, "Don't you think it would be rather nice if we asked Nurse Andrews to stay on for a week as our guest?"

"Very nice," said Constantia.

"I thought," went on Josephine quickly, "I should just say this afternoon, after I've paid her, 'My sister and I would be very pleased, after all you've done for us, Nurse Andrews, if you would stay on for a week as our guest.' I'd have to put that in about being our guest in case—"

"Oh, but she could hardly expect to be paid!" cried Constantia.

"One never knows," said Josephine sagely.

Nurse Andrews had, of course, jumped at the idea. But it was a bother. It meant they had to have regular sit-down meals at the proper times, whereas if they'd been alone they could just have asked Kate if she wouldn't have minded bringing them a tray wherever they were. And meal-times now that the strain was over were rather a trial.

Nurse Andrews was simply fearful about butter. Really they couldn't help feeling that about butter, at least, she took advantage of their kindness. And she had that maddening habit of asking for just an inch more bread to finish what she had on her plate, and then, at the last mouthful, absent-mindedly—of course it wasn't absent-mindedly—taking another helping. Josephine got very red when this happened, and she fastened her small, bead-like eyes on the tablecloth as if she saw a minute strange insect creeping through the web of it. But Constantia's long, pale face lengthened and set, and she gazed away—away—far over the desert, to where that line of camels unwound like a thread of wool. . . .

"When I was with Lady Tukes," said Nurse Andrews, "she had such a dainty little contrayvance for the buttah. It was a silvah Cupid balanced on the—on the bordah of a glass dish, holding a tayny fork. And when you wanted some buttah you simply pressed his foot and he bent down and speared you a piece. It was quite a gayme."

Josephine could hardly bear that. But "I think those things are very extravagant" was all she said.

"But whey?" asked Nurse Andrews, beaming through her eyeglasses. "No one, surely, would take more buttah than one wanted—would one?"

"Ring, Con," cried Josephine. She couldn't trust herself to reply.

And proud young Kate, the enchanted princess, came in to see what the old tabbies wanted now. She snatched away their plates of mock something or other and slapped down a white, terrified blancmange.[2]

2. A sweet pudding.

"Jam, please, Kate," said Josephine kindly.

Kate knelt and burst open the sideboard, lifted the lid of the jam-pot, saw it was empty, put it on the table, and stalked off.

"I'm afraid," said Nurse Andrews a moment later, "there isn't any."

"Oh, what a bother!" said Josephine. She bit her lip. "What had we better do?"

Constantia looked dubious. "We can't disturb Kate again," she said softly.

Nurse Andrews waited, smiling at them both. Her eyes wandered, spying at everything behind her eye-glasses. Constantia in despair went back to her camels. Josephine frowned heavily—concentrated. If it hadn't been for this idiotic woman she and Con would, of course, have eaten their blancmange without. Suddenly the idea came.

"I know," she said. "Marmalade. There's some marmalade in the sideboard. Get it, Con."

"I hope," laughed Nurse Andrews, and her laugh was like a spoon tinkling against a medicine-glass—"I hope it's not very bittah marmalayde."

3

But, after all, it was not long now, and then she'd be gone for good. And there was no getting over the fact that she had been very kind to father. She had nursed him day and night at the end. Indeed, both Constantia and Josephine felt privately she had rather overdone the not leaving him at the very last. For when they had gone in to say good-bye Nurse Andrews had sat beside his bed the whole time, holding his wrist and pretending to look at her watch. It couldn't have been necessary. It was so tactless, too. Supposing father had wanted to say something—something private to them. Not that he had. Oh, far from it! He lay there, purple, a dark angry purple in the face, and never even looked at them when they came in. Then, as they were standing there, wondering what to do, he had suddenly opened one eye. Oh, what a difference it would have made, what a difference to their memory of him, how much easier to tell people about it, if he had only opened both! But no —one eye only. It glared at them a moment and then . . . went out.

4

It had made it very awkward for them when Mr. Farolles, of St. John's, called the same afternoon.

"The end was quite peaceful, I trust?" were the first words he said as he glided towards them through the dark drawing-room.

"Quite," said Josephine faintly. They both hung their heads. Both of them felt certain that eye wasn't at all a peaceful eye.

"Won't you sit down?" said Josephine.

"Thank you, Miss Pinner," said Mr. Farolles gracefully. He folded his coat-tails and began to lower himself into father's armchair, but just as he touched it he almost sprang up and slid into the next chair instead.

He coughed. Josephine clasped her hands; Constantia looked vague.

"I want you to feel, Miss Pinner," said Mr. Farolles, "and you Miss Constantia, that I'm trying to be helpful. I want to be helpful to you both, if you will let me. These are the times," said Mr. Farolles, very simple and earnestly, "when God means us to be helpful to one another."

"Thank you very much, Mr. Farolles," said Josephine and Constantia.

"Not at all," said Mr. Farolles gently. He drew his kid gloves through his fingers and leaned forward. "And if either of you would like a little Communion,[3] either or both of you, here *and* now, you have only to tell me. A little Communion is often very help—a great comfort," he added tenderly.

But the idea of a little Communion terrified them. What! In the drawing-room by themselves—with no—no altar or anything! The piano would be much too high, thought Constantia, and Mr. Farolles could not possibly lean over it with the chalice. And Kate would be sure to come bursting in and interrupt them, thought Josepine. And supposing the bell rang in the middle? It might be somebody important— about their mourning. Would they get up reverently and go out, or would they have to wait . . . in torture?

"Perhaps you will send round a note by your good Kate if you would care for it later," said Mr. Farolles.

"Oh yes, thank you very much!" they both said.

Mr. Farolles got up and took his black straw hat from the round table.

"And about the funeral," he said softly. "I may arrange that—as your dear father's old friend and yours, Miss Pinner—and Miss Constantia?"

Josephine and Constantia got up too.

"I should like it to be quite simple," said Josephine firmly, "and not too expensive. At the same time, I should like—"

"A good one that will last," thought dreamy Constantia, as if Josephine were buying a nightgown. But of course Josephine didn't say that. "One suitable to our father's position." She was very nervous.

"I'll run round to our good friend Mr. Knight," said Mr. Farolles soothingly. "I will ask him to come and see you. I am sure you will find him very helpful indeed."

5

Well, at any rate, all that part of it was over, though neither of them could possibly believe that father was never coming back. Josephine had had a moment of absolute terror at the cemetery, while the coffin

---

3. The Anglican ceremony in which sacramental wine and bread are consumed, symbolizing the Blood and Body of Christ.

was lowered, to think that she and Constantia had done this thing without asking his permission. What would father say when he found out? For he was bound to find out sooner or later. He always did. "Buried. You two girls had me *buried!*" She heard his stick thumping. Oh, what would they say? What possible excuse could they make? It sounded such an appallingly heartless thing to do. Such a wicked advantage to take of a person because he happened to be helpless at the moment. The other people seemed to treat it all as a matter of course. They were strangers; they couldn't be expected to understand that father was the very last person for such a thing to happen to. No, the entire blame for it all would fall on her and Constantia. And the expense, she thought, stepping into the tight-buttoned cab. When she had to show him the bills. What would he say then?

She heard him absolutely roaring. "And do you expect me to pay for this gimcrack excursion of yours?"

"Oh," groaned poor Josephine aloud, "we shouldn't have done it, Con!"

And Constantia, pale as a lemon in all that blackness, said in a frightened whisper, "Done what, Jug?"

"Let them bu-bury father like that," said Josephine, breaking down and crying into her new, queer-smelling mourning handkerchief.

"But what else could we have done?" asked Constantia wonderingly. "We couldn't have kept him, Jug—we couldn't have kept him unburied. At any rate, not in a flat that size."

Josephine blew her nose; the cab was dreadfully stuffy.

"I don't know," she said forlornly. "It is all so dreadful. I feel we ought to have tried to, just for a time at least. To make perfectly sure. One thing's certain"—and her tears sprang out again—"father will never forgive us for this—never!"

6

Father would never forgive them. That was what they felt more than ever when, two mornings later, they went into his room to go through his things. They had discussed it quite calmly. It was even down on Josephine's list of things to be done. *Go through father's things and settle about them.* But that was a very different matter from saying after breakfast:

"Well, are you ready, Con?"

"Yes, Jug—when you are."

"Then I think we'd better get it over."

It was dark in the hall. It had been a rule for years never to disturb father in the morning, whatever happened. And now they were going to open the door without knocking even. . . . Constantia's eyes were enormous at the idea; Josephine felt weak in the knees.

"You—you go first," she gasped, pushing Constantia.

But Constantia said, as she always had said on those occasions, "No, Jug, that's not fair. You're eldest."

Josephine was just going to say—what at other times she wouldn't have owned to for the world—what she kept for her very last weapon, "But you're tallest," when they noticed that the kitchen door was open, and there stood Kate. . . .

"Very stiff," said Josephine, grasping the door-handle and doing her best to turn it. As if anything ever deceived Kate!

It couldn't be helped. That girl was . . . Then the door was shut behind them, but—but they weren't in father's room at all. They might have suddenly walked through the wall by mistake into a different flat altogether. Was the door just behind them? They were too frightened to look. Josephine knew that if it was it was holding itself tight shut; Constantia felt that, like the doors in dreams, it hadn't any handle at all. It was the coldness which made it so awful. Or the whiteness—which? Everything was covered. The blinds were down, a cloth hung over the mirror, a sheet hid the bed; a huge fan of white paper filled the fireplace. Constantia timidly put out her hand; she almost expected a snowflake to fall. Josephine felt a queer tingling in her nose, as if her nose was freezing. Then a cab klop-klopped over the cobbles below, and the quiet seemed to shake into little pieces.

"I had better pull up a blind," said Josephine bravely.

"Yes, it might be a good idea," whispered Constantia.

They only gave the blind a touch, but it flew up and the cord flew after, rolling round the blindstick, and the little tassel tapped as if trying to get free. That was too much for Constantia.

"Don't you think—don't you think we might put it off for another day?" she whispered.

"Why?" snapped Josephine, feeling, as usual, much better now that she knew for certain that Constantia was terrified. "It's got to be done. But I do wish you wouldn't whisper, Con."

"I didn't know I was whispering," whispered Constantia.

"And why do you keep on staring at the bed?" said Josephine, raising her voice almost defiantly. "There's nothing *on* the bed."

"Oh, Jug, don't say so!" said poor Connie. "At any rate, not so loudly."

Josephine felt herself that she had gone too far. She took a wide swerve over to the chest of drawers, put out her hand, but quickly drew it back again.

"Connie!" she gasped, and she wheeled round and leaned with her back against the chest of drawers.

"Oh, Jug—what?"

Josephine could only glare. She had the most extraordinary feeling that she had just escaped something simply awful. But how could she explain to Constantia that father was in the chest of drawers? He was in the top drawer with his handkerchiefs and neckties, or in the next with his shirts and pyjamas, or in the lowest of all with his suits. He was watching there, hidden away—just behind the door-handle—ready to spring.

She pulled a funny old-fashioned face at Constantia, just as she used to in the old days when she was going to cry.

"I can't open," she nearly wailed.

"No, don't, Jug," whispered Constantia earnestly. "It's much better not to. Don't let's open anything. At any rate, not for a long time."

"But—but it seems so weak," said Josephine, breaking down.

"But why not be weak for once, Jug?" argued Constantia, whispering quite fiercely. "If it is weak." And her pale stare flew from the locked writing-table—so safe—to the huge glittering wardrobe, and she began to breathe in a queer, panting way. "Why shouldn't we be weak for once in our lives, Jug? It's quite excusable. Let's be weak—be weak, Jug. It's much nicer to be weak than to be strong."

And then she did one of those amazingly bold things that she'd done about twice before in their lives; she marched over to the wardrobe, turned the key, and took it out of the lock. Took it out of the lock and held it up to Josephine, showing Josephine by her extraordinary smile that she knew what she'd done, she'd risked deliberately father being in there among his overcoats.

If the huge wardrobe had lurched forward, had crashed down on Constantia, Josephine wouldn't have been surprised. On the contrary, she would have thought it the only suitable thing to happen. But nothing happened. Only the room seemed quieter than ever, and bigger flakes of cold air fell on Josephine's shoulders and knees. She began to shiver.

"Come, Jug," said Constantia, still with that awful callous smile, and Josephine followed just as she had that last time, when Constantia had pushed Benny into the round pond.

7

But the strain told on them when they were back in the dining-room. They sat down, very shaky, and looked at each other.

"I don't feel I can settle to anything," said Josephine, "until I've had something. Do you think we could ask Kate for two cups of hot water?"

"I really don't see why we shouldn't," said Constantia carefully. She was quite normal again. "I won't ring. I'll go to the kitchen door and ask her."

"Yes, do," said Josephine, sinking down into a chair. "Tell her, just two cups, Con, nothing else—on a tray."

"She needn't even put the jug on, need she?" said Constantia, as though Kate might very well complain if the jug had been there.

"Oh no, certainly not! The jug's not at all necessary. She can pour it direct out of the kettle," cried Josephine, feeling that would be a labour-saving indeed.

Their cold lips quivered at the greenish brims. Josephine curved her small red hands round the cup; Constantia sat up and blew on the wavy stream, making it flutter from one side to the other.

"Speaking of Benny," said Josephine.

And though Benny hadn't been mentioned Constantia immediately loked as though he had.

"He'll expect us to sent him something of father's, of course. But it's so difficult to know what to send to Ceylon."

"You mean things get unstuck so on the voyage," murmured Constantia.

"No, lost," said Josephine sharply. "You know there's no post. Only runners."

Both paused to watch a black man in white linen drawers running through the pale fields for dear life, with a large brown-paper parcel in his hands. Josephine's black man was tiny; he scurried along glistening like an ant. But there was something blind and tireless about Constantia's tall, thin fellow, which made him, she decided, a very unpleasant person indeed. . . . On the veranda, dressed all in white and wearing a cork helmet, stood Benny. His right hand shook up and down, as father's did when he was impatient. And behind him, not in the least interested, sat Hilda, the unknown sister-in-law. She swung in a cane rocker and flicked over the leaves of the *Tatler*.

"I think his watch would be the most suitable present," said Josephine.

Constantia looked up; she seemed surprised.

"Oh, would you trust a gold watch to a native?"

"But of course I'd disguise it," said Josephine. "No one would know it was a watch." She liked the idea of having to make a parcel such a curious shape that no one could possibly guess what it was. She even thought for a moment of hiding the watch in a narrow cardboard corset-box that she'd kept by her for a long time, waiting for it to come in for something. It was such beautiful firm cardboard. But, no, it wouldn't be appropriate for this occasion. It had lettering on it: *Medium Women's 28. Extra Firm Busks*. It would be almost too much of a surprise for Benny to open that and find father's watch inside.

"And of course it isn't as though it would be going—ticking, I mean," said Constantia, who was still thinking of the native love of jewellery. "At least," she added, "it would be very strange if after all that time it was."

8

Josephine made no reply. She had flown off on one of her tangents. She had suddenly thought of Cyril. Wasn't it more usual for the only grandson to have the watch? And then dear Cyril was so appreciative, and a gold watch meant so much to a young man. Benny, in all probability, had quite got out of the habit of watches; men so seldom wore waistcoats in those hot climates. Whereas Cyril in London wore them from year's end to year's end. And it would be so nice for her and Constantia, when he came to tea, to know it was there. "I see you've got on grandfather's watch, Cyril." It would be somehow so satisfactory.

Dear boy! What a blow his sweet, sympathetic little note had been! Of course they quite understood; but it was most unfortunate.

"It would have been such a point, having him," said Josephine.

"And he would have enjoyed it so," said Constantia, not thinking what she was saying.

However, as soon as he got back he was coming to tea with his aunties. Cyril to tea was one of their rare treats.

"Now, Cyril, you must't be frightened of our cakes. Your Auntie Con and I bought them at Buszard's this morning. We know what a man's appetite is. So don't be ashamed of making a good tea."

Josephine cut recklessly into the rich dark cake that stood for her winter gloves or the soling and heeling of Constantia's only respectable shoes. But Cyril was most unmanlike in appetite.

"I say, Aunt Josephine, I simply can't. I've only just had lunch, you know."

"Oh, Cyril, that can't be true! It's after four," cried Josephine. Constantia sat with her knife poised over the chocolate-roll.

"It is all the same," said Cyril. "I had to meet a man at Victoria[4] and he kept me hanging about till . . . there was only time to get lunch and to come on here. And he gave me—phew"—Cyril put his hand to his forehead—"a terrific blow-out," he said.

It was disappointing—to-day of all days. But still he couldn't be expected to know.

"But you'll have a meringue, won't you, Cyril?" said Aunt Josephine. "These meringues were bought specially for you. Your dear father was so fond of them. We were sure you are, too."

"I *am*, Aunt Josephine," cried Cyril ardently. "Do you mind if I take half to begin with?"

"Not at all, dear boy; but we mustn't let you off with that."

"Is your dear father still so fond of meringues?" asked Auntie Con gently. She winced faintly as she broke through the shell of hers.

"Well, I don't quite know, Auntie Con," said Cyril breezily.

At that they both looked up.

---

4. A railroad station in London.

"Don't know?" almost snapped Josephine. "Don't know a thing like that about your own father, Cyril?"

"Surely," said Auntie Con softly.

Cyril tried to laugh if off. "Oh well," he said, "it's such a long time since—" He faltered. He stopped. Their faces were too much for him.

"Even *so*," said Josephine.

And Auntie Con looked.

Cyril put down his teacup. "Wait a bit," he cried. "Wait a bit, Aunt Josephine. What am I thinking of?"

He looked up. They were beginning to brighten. Cyril slapped his knee.

"Of course," he said, "it was meringues. How could I have forgotten? Yes, Aunt Josephine, you're perfectly right. Father's most frightfully keen on meringues."

They didn't only beam. Aunt Josephine went scarlet with pleasure; Auntie Con gave a deep, deep sigh.

"And now, Cyril, you must come and see father," said Josephine. "He knows you were coming to-day."

"Right," said Cyril, very firmly and heartily. He got up from his chair; suddenly he glanced at the clock.

"I say, Auntie Con, isn't your clock a bit slow? I've got to meet a man at—at Paddington[5] just after five. I'm afraid I shan't be able to stay very long with grandfather."

"Oh, he won't expect you to stay *very* long!" said Aunt Josephine.

Constantia was still gazing at the clock. She couldn't make up her mind if it was fast or slow. It was one or the other, she felt almost certain of that. At any rate, it had been.

Cyril still lingered. "Aren't you coming along, Auntie Con?"

"Of course," said Josephine, "we shall all go. Come on, Con."

9

They knocked at the door, and Cyril followed his aunts into grandfather's hot, sweetish room.

"Come on," said Grandfather Pinner. "Don't hang about. What is it? What've you been up to?"

He was sitting in front of the roaring fire, clasping his stick. He had a thick rug over his knees. On his lap there lay a beautiful pale yellow silk handkerchief.

"It's Cyril, father," said Josephine shyly. And she took Cyril's hand and led him forward.

"Good afternoon, grandfather," said Cyril, trying to take his hand out of Aunt Josephine's. Grandfather Pinner shot his eyes at Cyril in the way he was famous for. Where was Auntie Con? She stood on the other side of Aunt Josephine; her long arms hung down in front of her;

5. Another London railroad station.

her hands were clasped. She never took her eyes off grandfather.

"Well," said Grandfather Pinner, beginning to thump, "what have you got to tell me?"

What had he, what had he got to tell him? Cyril felt himself smiling like a perfect imbecile. The room was stifling, too.

But Aunt Josephine came to the rescue. She cried brightly, "Cyril says his father is still very fond of meringues, father dear."

"Eh?" said Grandfather Pinner, curving his hand like a purple meringue-shell over one ear.

Josephine repeated, "Cyril says his father is still very fond of meringues."

"Can't hear," said old Colonel Pinner. And he waved Josephine away with his stick, then pointed with his stick to Cyril. "Tell me what she's trying to say," he said.

(My God) "Must I?" said Cyril, blushing and staring at Aunt Josephine.

Do, dear," she smiled. "It will please him so much."

"Come on, out with it!" cried Colonel Pinner testily, beginning to thump again.

And Cyril leaned forward and yelled, "Father's still very fond of meringues."

At that Grandfather Pinner jumped as though he had been shot.

"Don't shout!" he cried. "What's the matter with the boy? *Meringues!* What about 'em?"

Oh, Aunt Josephine, must we go on?" groaned Cyril desperately.

"It's quite all right, dear boy," said Aunt Josephine, as though he and she were at the dentist's together. "He'll understand in a minute." And she whispered to Cyril, "He's getting a bit deaf, you know." Then she leaned forward and really bawled at Grandfather Pinner, "Cyril only wanted to tell you, father dear, that *his* father is still very fond of meringues."

Colonel Pinner heard that time, heard and brooded, looking Cyril up and down.

"What an esstrordinary thing!" said old Grandfather Pinner. "What an esstrordinary thing to come all this way here to tell me!"

And Cyril felt it *was*.

"Yes, I shall send Cyril the watch," said Josephine.

"That would be very nice," said Constantia. "I seem to remember last time he came there was some little trouble about the time."

10

They were interrupted by Kate bursting through the door in her usual fashion, as though she had discovered some secret panel in the wall.

"Fried or boiled?" asked the bold voice.

Fried or boiled? Josephine and Constantia were quiet bewildered for the moment. They could hardly take it in.

"Fried or boiled what, Kate?" asked Josephine, trying to begin to concentrate.

Kate gave a loud sniff. "Fish."

"Well, why didn't you say so immediately?" Josephine reproached her gently. "How could you expect us to understand, Kate? There are a great many things in this world, you know, which are fried or boiled." And after such a display of courage she said quite brightly to Constantia, "Which do you prefer, Con?"

"I think it might be nice to have it fried," said Constantia. "On the other hand, of course boiled fish is very nice. I think I prefer both equally well . . . Unless you . . . In that case—"

"I shall fry it," said Kate, and she bounced back, leaving their door open and slamming the door of her kitchen.

Josephine gazed at Constantia; she raised her pale eyebrows until they rippled away into her pale hair. She got up. She said in a very lofty, imposing way, "Do you mind following me into the drawing-room, Constantia? I've something of great importance to discuss with you."

For it was always to the drawing-room they retired when they wanted to talk over Kate.

Josephine closed the door meaningly. "Sit down, Constantia," she said, still very grand. She might have been receiving Constantia for the first time. And Con looked round vaguely for a chair, as though she felt indeed quite a stranger.

"Now the question is," said Josephine, bending forward, "whether we shall keep her or not."

"That is the question," agreed Constantia.

"And this time," said Josephine firmly. "we must come to a definite decision."

Constantia looked for a moment as though she might begin going over all the other times, but she pulled herself together and said, "Yes, Jug."

"You see, Con," explained Josephine, "everything is so changed now." Constantia looked up quickly. "I mean," went on Josephine, "we're not dependent on Kate as we were." And she blushed faintly. "There's not father to cook for."

"That is perfectly true," agreed Constantia. "Father certainly doesn't want any cooking now, whatever else—"

Josephine broke in sharply. "You're not sleepy, are you, Con?"

"Sleepy, Jug?" Constantia was wide-eyed.

"Well, concentrate more," said Josephine sharply, and she returned to the subject. "What it comes to is, if we did"—and this she barely breathed, glancing at the door—"give Kate notice"—she raised her voice again—"we could manage our own food."

"Why not?" cried Constantia. She couldn't help smiling. The idea was so exciting. She clasped her hands. "What should we live on, Jug?"

"Oh, eggs in various forms!" said Jug, lofty again. "And, besides, there are all the cooked foods."

"But I've always heard," said Constantia, "they are considered so very expensive."

"Not if one buys them in moderation," said Josephine. But she tore herself away from this fascinating bypath and dragged Constantia after her.

"What we've got to decide now, however, is whether we really do trust Kate or not."

Constantia leaned back. Her flat little laugh flew from her lips.

"Isn't it curious, Jug," said she, "that just on this one subject I've never been able to quite make up my mind?"

11

She never had. The whole difficulty was to prove anything. How did one prove things, how could one? Suppose Kate had stood in front of her and deliberately made a face. Mightn't she very well have been in pain? Wasn't it impossible, at any rate, to ask Kate if she was making a face at her? If Kate answered "No"—and of course she would say "No"—what a position! How undignified! Then again Constantia suspected, she was almost certain that Kate went to her chest of drawers when she and Josephine were out, not to take things but to spy. Many times she had come back to find her amethyst cross in the most unlikely places, under her lace ties or on top of her evening Bertha.[6] More than once she had laid a trap for Kate. She had arranged things in a special order and then called Josephine to witness.

"You see, Jug?"

"Quite, Con."

"Now we shall be able to tell."

But, oh dear, when she did go to look, she was as far off from a proof as ever! If anything was displaced, it might so very well have happened as she closed the drawer; a jolt might have done it so easily.

"You come, Jug, and decide. I really can't. It's too difficult."

But after a pause and a long glare Josephine would sigh, "Now you've put the doubt into my mind, Con, I'm sure I can't tell myself."

"Well, we can't postpone it again," said Josephine. "If we postpone it this time—"

6. A detachable lace collar for low-necked dresses.

12

But at that moment in the street below a barrel-organ struck up. Josephine and Constantia sprang to their feet together.

"Run, Con," said Josephine. "Run quickly. There's sixpence on the—"

Then they remembered. It didn't matter. They would never have to stop the organ-grinder again. Never again would she and Constantia be told to make that monkey take his noise somewhere else. Never would sound that loud, strange bellow when father thought they were not hurrying enough. The organ-grinder might play there all day and the stick would not thump.

> It never will thump again.
> It never will thump again,

played the barrel-organ.

What was Constantia thinking? She had such a strange smile; she looked different. She couldn't be going to cry.

"Jug, Jug," said Constantia softly, pressing her hands together. "Do you know what day it is? It's Saturday. It's a week to-day, a whole week."

> A week since father died,
> A week since father died,

cried the barrel-organ. And Josephine, too, forgot to be practical and sensible; she smiled faintly, strangely. On the Indian carpet there fell a square of sunlight, pale red; it came and went and came—and stayed, deepened—until it shone almost golden.

"The sun's out," said Josephine, as though it really mattered.

A perfect fountain of bubbling notes shook from the barrel-organ, round, bright notes, carelessly scattered.

Constantia lifted her big, cold hands as if to catch them, and then her hands fell again. She walked over to the mantelpiece to her favourite Buddha. And the stone and gilt image, whose smile always gave her such a queer feeling, almost a pain and yet a pleasant pain, seemed to-day to be more than smiling. He knew something; he had a secret. "I know something that you don't know," said her Buddha. Oh, what was it, what could it be? And yet she had always felt there was . . . something.

The sunlight pressed through the windows, thieved its way in, flashed its light over the furniture and the photographs. Josephine watched it. When it came to mother's photograph, the enlargement over the piano, it lingered as though puzzled to find so little remained of mother, except the earrings shaped like tiny pagodas and a black feather boa. Why did the photographs of dead people always fade so?

wondered Josephine. As soon as a person was dead their photograph died too. But, of course, this one of mother was very old. It was thirty-five years old. Josephine remembered standing on a chair and pointing out that feather boa to Constantia and telling her that it was a snake that had killed their mother in Ceylon. . . . Would everything have been different if mother hadn't died? She didn't see why. Aunt Florence had lived with them until they had left school, and they had moved three times and had their yearly holiday and . . . and there'd been changes of servants, of course.

Some little sparrows, young sparrows they sounded, chirped on the window-ledge. *Yeep—eyeep—yeep.* But Josephine felt they were not sparrows, not on the window-ledge. It was inside her, that queer little crying noise. *Yeep—eyeep—yeep.* Ah, what was it crying, so weak and forlorn?

If mother had lived, might they have married? But there had been nobody for them to marry. There had been father's Anglo-Indian friends before he quarrelled with them. But after that she and Constantia never met a single man except clergymen. How did one meet men? Or even if they'd met them, how could they have got to know men well enough to be more than strangers? One read of people having adventures, being followed, and so on. But nobody had ever followed Constantia and her. Oh yes, there had been one year at Eastbourne[7] a mysterious man at their boarding-house who had put a note on the jug of hot water outside their bedroom door! But by the time Connie had found it the steam had made the writing too faint to read; they couldn't even make out to which of them it was addressed. And he had left next day. And that was all. The rest had been looking after father, and at the same time keeping out of father's way. But now? But now? The thieving sun touched Josephine gently. She lifted her face. She was drawn over to the window by gentle beams. . . .

Until the barrel-organ stopped playing Constantia stayed before the Buddha, wondering, but not as usual, not vaguely. This time her wonder was like longing. She remembered the times she had come in here, crept out of bed in her nightgown when the moon was full, and lain on the floor with her arms outstretched, as though she was crucified. Why? The big, pale moon had made her do it. The horrible dancing figures on the carved screen had leered at her and she hadn't minded. She remembered too how, whenever they were at the seaside, she had gone off by herself and got as close to the sea as she could, and sung something, something she had made up, while she gazed all over that restless water. There had been this other life, running out, bringing things home in bags, getting things on approval, discussing them with Jug, and taking them back to get more things on approval, and arranging father's trays and trying not to annoy father. But it all seemed to

7. A seaside resort in Sussex.

have happened in a kind of tunnel. It wasn't real. It was only when she came out of the tunnel into the moonlight or by the sea or into a thunderstorm that she really felt herself. What did it mean? What was it she was always wanting? What did it all lead to? Now? Now?

She turned away from the Buddha with one of her vague gestures. She went over to where Josephine was standing. She wanted to say something to Josephine, something frightfully important, about—about the future and what . . .

"Don't you think perhaps—" she began.

But Josephine interrupted her. "I was wondering if now—" she murmured. They stopped; they waited for each other.

"Go on, Con," said Josephine.

"No, no, Jug; after you," said Constantia.

"No, say what you were going to say. You began," said Josephine.

"I . . . I'd rather hear what you were going to say first," said Constantia.

"Don't be absurd, Con."

"Really, Jug."

"Connie!"

"Oh, *Jug!*"

A pause. Then Constantia said faintly, "I can't say what I was going to say, Jug, because I've forgotten what it was . . . that I was going to say."

Josephine was silent for a moment. She stared at a big cloud where the sun had been. Then she replied shortly, "I've forgotten too."

1922

The Doll's House

When dear old Mrs. Hay went back to town after staying with the Burnells she sent the children a doll's house. It was so big that the carter and Pat carried it into the courtyard, and there it stayed, propped up on two wooden boxes beside the feed-room door. No harm could come of it; it was summer. And perhaps the smell of paint would have gone off by the time it had to be taken in. For, really, the smell of paint coming from that doll's house ("Sweet of old Mrs. Hay, of course; most sweet and generous!")—but the smell of paint was quite enough to make any one seriously ill, in Aunt Beryl's opinion. Even before the sacking was taken off. And when it was . . .

There stood the doll's house, a dark, oily, spinach green, picked out with bright yellow. Its two solid little chimneys, glued on to the roof, were painted red and white, and the door, gleaming with yellow varnish, was like a little slab of toffee. Four windows, real windows, were divided into panes by a broad streak of green. There was actually a tiny porch, too, painted yellow, with big lumps of congealed paint hanging along the edge.

But perfect, perfect little house! Who could possibly mind the smell? It was part of the joy, part of the newness.

"Open it quickly, some one!"

The hook at the side was stuck fast. Pat pried it open with his pen-knife, and the whole house-front swung back, and—there you were, gazing at one and the same moment into the drawing-room and dining-room, the kitchen and two bedrooms. That is the way for a house to open! Why don't all houses open like that? How much more exciting than peering through the slit of a door into a mean little hall with a hat-stand and two umbrellas! That is—isn't it?—what you long to know about a house when you put your hand on the knocker. Perhaps it is the way God opens houses at dead of night when He is taking a quiet turn with an angel. . . .

"O-oh!" The Burnell children sounded as though they were in de-spair. It was too marvellous; it was too much for them. They had never seen anything like it in their lives. All the rooms were papered. There were pictures on the walls, painted on the paper, with gold frames complete. Red carpet covered all the floors except the kitchen; red plush chairs in the drawing-room, green in the dining-room; tables, beds with real bedclothes, a cradle, a stove, a dresser with tiny plates and one big jug. But what Kezia liked more than anything, what she liked frightfully, was the lamp. It stood in the middle of the dining-room table, an exquisite little amber lamp with a white globe. It was even filled all ready for lighting, though, of course, you couldn't light it. But there was something inside that looked like oil, and that moved when you shook it.

The father and mother dolls, who sprawled very stiff as though they had fainted in the drawing-room, and their two little children asleep upstairs, were really too big for the doll's house. They didn't look as though they belonged. But the lamp was perfect. It seemed to smile to Kezia, to say, "I live here." The lamp was real.

The Burnell children could hardly walk to school fast enough the next morning. They burned to tell everybody, to describe, to—well—to boast about their doll's house before the school-bell rang.

"I'm to tell," said Isabel, "because I'm the eldest. And you two can join in after. But I'm to tell first."

There was nothing to answer. Isabel was bossy, but she was always right, and Lottie and Kezia knew too well the powers that went with being eldest. They brushed through the thick buttercups at the road edge and said nothing.

"And I'm to choose who's to come and see it first. Mother said I might."

For it had been arranged that while the doll's house stood in the courtyard they might ask the girls at school, two at a time, to come and look. Not to stay to tea, of course, or to come traipsing through the house. But just to stand quietly in the courtyard while Isabel pointed out the beauties, and Lottie and Kezia looked pleased. . . .

But hurry as they might, by the time they had reached the tarred palings of the boys' playground the bell had begun to jangle. They only just had time to whip off their hats and fall into line before the roll was called. Never mind. Isabel tried to make up for it by looking very important and mysterious and by whispering behind her hand to the girls near her, "Got something to tell you at playtime."

Playtime came and Isabel was surrounded. The girls of her class nearly fought to put their arms round her, to walk away with her, to beam flatteringly, to be her special friend. She held quite a court under the huge pine trees at the side of the playground. Nudging, giggling together, the little girls pressed up close. And the only two who stayed outside the ring were the two who were always outside, the little Kelveys. They knew better than to come anywhere near the Burnells.

For the fact was, the school the Burnell children went to was not at all the kind of place their parents would have chosen if there had been any choice. But there was none. It was the only school for miles. And the consequence was all the children in the neighborhood, the Judge's little girls, the doctor's daughters, the store-keeper's children, the milkman's, were forced to mix together. Not to speak of there being an equal number of rude, rough little boys as well. But the line had to be drawn somewhere. It was drawn at the Kelveys. Many of the children, including the Burnells, were not allowed even to speak to them. They walked past the Kelveys with their heads in the air, and as they set the fashion in all matters of behaviour, the Kelveys were shunned by everybody. Even the teacher had a special voice for them, and a special smile for the other children when Lil Kelvey came up to her desk with a bunch of dreadfully common-looking flowers.

They were the daughters of a spry, hardworking little washerwoman, who went about from house to house by the day. This was awful enough. But where was Mr. Kelvey? Nobody knew for certain. But everybody said he was in prison. So they were the daughters of a washerwoman and a gaolbird. Very nice company for other people's children! And they looked it. Why Mrs. Kelvey made them so conspicuous was hard to understand. The truth was they were dressed in "bits" given to her by the people for whom she worked. Lil, for instance, who was a stout, plain child, with big freckles, came to school in a dress made from a green art-serge table-cloth of the Burnells', with red plush sleeves from the Logans' curtains. Her hat, perched on top of her high forehead, was a grown-up woman's hat, once the property of Miss

1. In England a "guy" is a dummy dressed in rags.

Lecky, the postmistress. It was turned up at the back and trimmed with a large scarlet quill. What a little guy[1] she looked! It was impossible not to laugh. And her little sister, our Else, wore a long white dress, rather like a nightgown, and a pair of little boy's boots. But whatever our Else wore she would have looked strange. She was a tiny wishbone of a child, with cropped hair and enormous solemn eyes—a little white owl. Nobody had ever seen her smile; she scarcely ever spoke. She went through life holding on to Lil, with a piece of Lil's skirt screwed up in her hand. Where Lil went our Else followed. In the playground, on the road going to and from school, there was Lil marching in front and our Else holding on behind. Only when she wanted anything, or when she was out of breath, our Else gave Lil a tug, a twitch, and Lil stopped and turned round. The Kelveys never failed to understand each other.

Now they hovered at the edge; you couldn't stop them listening. When the little girls turned round and sneered, Lil, as usual, gave her silly, shamefaced smile, but our Else only looked.

And Isabel's voice, so very proud, went on telling. The carpet made a great sensation, but so did the beds with real bedclothes, and the stove with an oven door.

When she finished Kezia broke in. "You've forgotten the lamp, Isabel."

"Oh, yes," said Isabel, "and there's a teeny little lamp, all made of yellow glass, with a white globe that stands on the dining-room table. You couldn't tell it from a real one."

"The lamp's best of all," cried Kezia. She thought Isabel wasn't making half enough of the little lamp. But nobody paid any attention. Isabel was choosing the two who were to come back with them that afternoon and see it. She chose Emmie Cole and Lena Logan. But when the others knew they were all to have a chance, they couldn't be nice enough to Isabel. One by one they put their arms round Isabel's waist and walked her off. They had something to whisper to her, a secret. "Isabel's *my* friend."

Only the little Kelveys moved away forgotten; there was nothing more for them to hear.

Days passed, and as more children saw the doll's house, the fame of it spread. It became the one subject, the rage. The one question was, "Have you seen Burnells' doll's house?" Oh, ain't it lovely!" "Haven't you seen it? Oh, I say!"

Even the dinner hour was given up to talking about it. The little girls sat under the pines eating their thick mutton sandwiches and big slabs of johnny cake spread with butter. While always, as near as they could get, sat the Kelveys, our Else holding on to Lil, listening too, while they chewed their jam sandwiches out of a newspaper soaked with large red blobs. . . .

"Mother," said Kezia, "can't I ask the Kelveys just once?"

"Certainly not, Kezia."

"But why not?"

"Run away, Kezia; you know quite well why not."

At last everybody had seen it except them. On that day the subject rather flagged. It was the dinner hour. The children stood together under the pine trees, and suddenly, as they looked at the Kelveys eating out of their paper, always by themselves, always listening, they wanted to be horrid to them. Emmie Cole started the whisper.

"Lil Kelvey's going to be a servant when she grows up."

"O-oh, how awful!" said Isabel Burnell, and she made eyes at Emmie.

Emmie swallowed in a very meaning way and nodded to Isabel as she'd seen her mother do on those occasions.

"It's true—it's true—it's true," she said.

Then Lena Logan's little eyes snapped. "Shall I ask her?" she whispered.

"Bet you don't," said Jessie May.

"Pooh, I'm not frightened," said Lena. Suddenly she gave a little squeal and danced in front of the other girls. "Watch! Watch me! Watch me now!" said Lena. And sliding, gliding, dragging one foot, giggling behind her hand, Lena went over to the Kelveys.

Lil looked up from her dinner. She wrapped the rest quickly away. Our Else stopped chewing. What was coming now?

"Is it true you're going to be a servant when you grow up, Lil Kelvey?" shrilled Lena.

Dead silence. But instead of answering, Lil only gave her silly, shame-faced smile. She didn't seem to mind the question at all. What a sell[2] for Lena! The girls began to titter.

Lena couldn't stand that. She put her hands on her hips; she shot forward. "Yah, yer father's in prison!" she hissed, spitefully.

This was such a marvellous thing to have said that the little girls rushed away in a body, deeply, deeply excited, wild with joy. Some one found a long rope, and they began skipping. And never did they skip so high, run in and out so fast, or do such daring things as on that morning.

In the afternoon Pat called for the Burnell children with the buggy and they drove home. There were visitors. Isabel and Lottie, who liked visitors, went upstairs to change their pinafores. But Kezia thieved out at the back. Nobody was about; she began to swing on the big white gates of the courtyard. Presently, looking along the road, she saw two little dots. They grew bigger, they were coming towards her. Now she could see that one was in front and one close behind. Now she could see that they were the Kelveys. Kezia stopped swinging. She slipped off

2. Deception, hoax.

the gate as if she was going to run away. Then she hesitated. The Kelveys came nearer, and beside them walked their shadows, very long, stretching right across the road with their heads in the buttercups. Kezia clambered back on the gate; she had made up her mind; she swung out.

"Hullo," she said to the passing Kelveys.

They were so astounded that they stopped. Lil gave her silly smile. Our Else stared.

"You can come and see our doll's house if you want to," said Kezia, and she dragged one toe on the ground. But at that Lil turned red and shook her head quickly.

"Why not?" asked Kezia.

Lil gasped, then she said, "Your ma told our ma you wasn't to speak to us."

"Oh, well," said Kezia. She didn't know what to reply. "It doesn't matter. You can come and see our doll's house all the same. Come on. Nobody's looking."

But Lil shook her head still harder.

"Don't you want to?" asked Kezia.

Suddenly there was a twitch, a tug at Lil's skirt. She turned round. Our Else was looking at her with big, imploring eyes; she was frowning; she wanted to go. For a moment Lil looked at our Else very doubtfully. But then our Else twitched her skirt again. She started forward. Kezia led the way. Like two little stray cats they followed across the courtyard to where the doll's house stood.

"There it is," said Kezia.

There was a pause. Lil breathed loudly, almost snorted; our Else was still as a stone.

"I'll open it for you," said Kezia kindly. She undid the hook and they looked inside.

"There's the drawing-room and the dining-room, and that's the—"

"Kezia!"

Oh, what a start they gave!

"Kezia!"

It was Aunt Beryl's voice. They turned round. At the back door stood Aunt Beryl, staring as if she couldn't believe what she saw.

"How dare you ask the little Kelveys into the courtyard?" said her cold, furious voice. "You know as well as I do, you're not allowed to talk to them. Run away, children, run away at once. And don't come back again," said Aunt Beryl. And she stepped into the yard and shooed them out as if they were chickens.

"Off you go immediately!" she called, cold and proud.

They did not need telling twice. Burning with shame, shrinking together, Lil huddling along like her mother, our Else dazed, somehow they crossed the big courtyard and squeezed through the white gate.

"Wicked, disobedient little girl!" said Aunt Beryl bitterly to Kezia, and she slammed the doll's house to.

The afternoon had been awful. A letter had come from Willie Brent, a terrifying, threatening letter, saying if she did not meet him that evening in Pulman's Bush, he'd come to the front door and ask the reason why! But now that she had frightened those little rats of Kelveys and given Kezia a good scolding, her heart felt lighter. That ghastly pressure was gone. She went back to the house humming.

When the Kelveys were well out of sight of Burnells', they sat down to rest on a big red drain-pipe by the side of the road. Lil's cheeks were still burning; she took off the hat with the quill and held it on her knee. Dreamily they looked over the hay paddocks, past the creek, to the group of wattles[3] where Logan's cows stood waiting to be milked. What were their thoughts?

Presently our Else nudged up close to her sister. But now she had forgotten the cross lady. She put out a finger and stroked her sister's quill; she smiled her rare smile.

"I seen the little lamp," she said, softly.

Then both were silent once more.

1923

---

3. Wooden poles interwoven with branches or reeds.

MOURNING DOVE (HUM-ISHU-MA)
1888–1936

The first native-American woman to write and publish a novel, Mourning Dove (a translation of Hum-ishu-ma) was a member of the Okanogan tribe, whose communities were located in British Columbia and north-central Washington state. Born near Bonner's Ferry, Idaho, she was given the English name Christal Quintasket but raised in part by a grandmother who taught her to respect the rapidly vanishing traditions of her people. Although she had little formal education—three years at the Sacred Heart Convent in Ward, Washington, and brief periods at government Indian schools—Mourning Dove began early to collect and transcribe Okanogan tribal legends. In 1912, she enrolled in a business school to study English and typing so that she could improve her work on Indian tales and on the novel-in-progress which was to become her *Cogewea the Half Blood: A Depiction of the Great Montana Cattle Range* (1927). Then, in 1914, at a Frontier Days Celebration in Walla Walla, Washington, she met a pioneering ethnographer and advocate of Indian rights, Lucullus V. McWhorter, who offered to help her with her novel while also urging her to turn more of her attention in the future to gathering the folklore that would "perpetuate the story of her people in their primitive simplicity."

Following McWhorter's advice, Mourning Dove spent years traveling through the Northwest and collecting the tales that were eventually published in *Coyote Stories* (1933), although she complained in 1918 that the Okanogans "are such hard people to get anything out from . . . if the Indians find out that their stories will reach print I am sure it will be hard for me to get any more legends without paying the hard cash for them" because "a whiteman" who paid "five dollars a piece for good Indian legends" had "spoiled my field of work." After a brief marriage to Hector McLeod, a Flathead Indian, Mourning Dove married Fred Galler, a Wenatchee, in 1919. Childless, the couple supported themselves as migrant laborers, yet, even while doing such arduous seasonal work as picking hops and thinning apples for one dollar and fifty cents a day, Mourning Dove traveled with a battered typewriter and wrote to McWhorter apologizing that "after working for ten hours in the blazing sun, and cooking my meals, I know I shall not have the time to look over very much mss. . . . between sand, grease, campfire, and real apple dirt I hope I can do the work."

When *Cogewea* was completed in 1916, Mourning Dove and McWhorter had considerable difficulty in finding a publisher, though she had already been hailed in the press as the first American Indian novelist. Finally the Boston publishing house of Four Seas agreed to print the book if the collaborators would help finance the enterprise. According to the scholar Dexter Fisher, "To raise her part of the money, Mourning Dove worked longer hours thinning apples and even opened a lunch stand for a brief time." Yet despite the triumph implied by *Cogewea's* publication, the novel did not represent a pure victory for this aspiring writer: McWhorter had rewritten many passages in what Fisher rightly calls a "stiff, formal, and highly rhetorical" style that was "totally unlike Mourning Dove's own direct and simple" language, and a number of critics claimed that he had actually written the whole book.

Mourning Dove's *Coyote Stories*, from which *The Origin of Diseases*, *Coyote Takes His Daughter as a Wife*, and *Coyote Kills Owl Woman* were taken, have also been edited, but far more lightly, by the scholar Donald M. Hines, who has deleted some of McWhorter's additions and whose perceptive foreword analyzes the achievement of this "remarkable woman: poorly educated, working under impossible conditions," who "sought to bridge two cultures."

The Origin of Diseases

There once lived a man and his wife, and they had two children, a boy and a girl. It was not many snows when the boy showed signs that he was going to be a great warrior, and the little girl grew beautiful. The boy killed much game when he grew up, and his father and mother lived in plenty. They were glad when the little girl bloomed into womanhood. She was sent to her private lodge for one snow, and no one was allowed in her tepee. She was not allowed in her father's tepee for fear that she would cause bad fortunes to come to her people, as was the custom. She lived alone; only food was brought to her lodge by her mother.

One day as the girl took her bath, her brother saw her by accident and he loved her because she was beautiful of figure. After that he went each night to see her at her tepee without the knowledge of his parents. After that the boy killed no more game. He hunted and hunted, but all the game feared him because he had done wrong with his sister. It was not many suns when his mother took notice of things and told his father, but the father refused to believe and listen. At last one day the boy overslept, and his parents knew then. It was decided that the girl would have to be thrown away. So the mother took her across the Big River and left her to her fate.

Her brother did not know where she had gone, so he left his parents and hunted his lover and sister. For many moons he traveled, until at last he saw someone across the Big River. Making himself a canoe, he went across. He was surprised when, on entering the tepee, he found only a small child in the cradle by the fireside. He knew it was his child, and he played with it until he heard footsteps coming. He hid himself to see what his sister's daily habit was. As she came in, she picked up her baby and began to make it dance on her knee saying, "What a naughty little girl you are. Your uncle is your father, and your father is your uncle." This made the warrior very ashamed. He kept hidden until his sister went back to picking berries, leaving her baby in the tepee. He took the baby and crushed her in his shame. Then he left the tepee to go back to his parents, leaving only his moccasin tracks, which were discovered by the girl. She knew that it was her brother.

She picked up the little dead body, and, tying it on her back, she followed him. For many suns she followed, but he was too fast for her. At last she came to a river, and she could not cross. She stopped there and cried. Then taking the decayed corpse off her back, she dipped it in the river and, breaking it into many pieces, she threw it all over the country saying, "You are to follow your father until he dies with sickness. In the future, people will have sickness and not always live in happiness. Punishment will always come to a brother and sister who do wrong." So thus have diseases come from the rotten baby corpse to the people.

1933

Coyote Takes His Daughter as a Wife

Coyote *(Sin-ka'-lip)* had a beautiful daughter, and the warriors came far and near from the surrounding tribes to ask for her hand. She refused them all. One day, as she stretched out her foot, Coyote saw that she had a shapely leg, which made him fall in love with his daughter.

He thought, "What a fool I am to save my virgin daughter for someone else." So Coyote schemed how to get his daughter.

One day Coyote fell ill, and soon he was ready to die. He called his daughter to his bedside and told her that he had a good friend who was coming from the Kootenay tribes. When the friend came, it was his last wish that his daughter would take him as a husband, because he was a great warrior and had much wealth. To this, his daughter consented. And he also made another wish, that his daughter would bring food to where he was to be buried, so that it would be as if he were alive and not dead.

Then Coyote pretended he was dead. His daughter took him on a high hill and buried him. She sadly went back to her people in mourning for her wicked father.

It was not many sundowns when the people said that a stranger had come to their village with a canoe full of valuable robes of fur and skins, and that he spoke the unknown language of the Kootenays. The tribe then looked for Mouse (*Gou'-kouh-ana*) who knew all the languages of the tribes, because she was a great traveler and thief. Mouse was taken as an interpreter, and she said, "The warrior wished to see his friend Coyote." Then the people knew that it was the looked-for friend of Coyote. Coyote's daughter took the Kootenay stranger as her husband because it was the dying wish of her father, Coyote.

It was not many sundowns when she went bathing with other women. She noticed that Coyote hair was among her clothing, and she grew suspicious. Going back to her tepee, she threw dog dung at her husband, who turned into Coyote, her father. She was so ashamed that she ran and threw herself down the *Swah-netk'-qha* falls, becoming a large rock in midstream, where it is to be seen to this day. The people chased Coyote, trying to kill him. But he left for another country to make more mischief, with Mouse following because the people knew that she was aware of Coyote's actions.

1933

Coyote Kills Owl-Woman

Chipmunk (*Co-ge-we-a*) was a little girl who lived with her grandmother. She had a special *ol-la-la* bush that she visited every day to see how many ripe berries she could find. She would climb on the tree and count the berries one by one as she ate them. She would say, "One berry ripe. Two berries ripe. Three berries ripe."

One day while in the tree counting and eating the berries, she put none in the basket that hung at her side. This basket was made out of the hoof of a deer. Chipmunk heard noisy footsteps beneath her. Looking down, she saw Owl-woman (*Sne'-nah*) with her big basket on her back. In this basket were many little children whom Owl-woman had stolen from their parents. These children she would eat as she grew hungry. Owl-woman traveled from camp to camp, from village to village, in search of children. She was the fear of both parents and children. She was the child-eating Owl-woman.

Chipmunk was very much frightened, but she knew that Owl-woman could not reach her up in the tree. The big woman coaxed her to come down. She said to Chipmunk, "Your father wants you."

Chipmunk replied, "I have no father. He died long ago."

Then Owl-woman lied, "Your mother wants you."

Chipmunk spoke back, "My mother died many snows ago."

Owl-woman still lied, "Your aunt wants you home."

Chipmunk laughed, "Ha! ha! My aunt never lived."

Owl-woman lied the more, "Then your uncle wants you."

Chipmunk again laughed, "Ha! ha! I never had an uncle."

Owl-woman coaxed her further, "Your grandfather wants you."

Chipmunk sauced back, "Ha! ha! My grandfather died before I was born."

Then Owl-woman said, "Your grandmother wants you home."

Chipmunk was silent, then spoke, "I will not come down from the tree unless you hide your eyes."

Owl-woman made the pretense of hiding her eyes, putting her hands over them but slightly. But Chipmunk was not easily fooled. She said to Owl-woman, "I can see your big eyes blinking! I will not come down the tree unless you hide all your eyes."

Owl-woman then hid her eyes almost entirely, only leaving a small space through which to watch Chipmunk come down the tree. Chipmunk jumped from the top of the tree, over the Owl-woman. Owl-woman tried to catch her, but only raked her back. The long fingers with their sharp claws left scratches the full length of Chipmunk's back, which she carries to this day.

Running to her grandmother, Chipmunk tried to talk but was so frightened that all she could say was, "*Sing-naw! Sing-naw!* (Owl! Owl!)"

The old grandmother with deafened ears misunderstood. She asked Chipmunk if she had stepped on a thorn. All the answer she received was, "*Sing-naw! Sing-naw!*"

At last the old grandmother understood. She tried to hide Chipmunk in her bed, but Chipmunk ran around under the robes so much with fear that her movements could be seen. The grandmother then put her in the berry basket, but Chipmunk was too noisy. The grandmother tried to hide her in the soup, where poor Chipmunk nearly drowned.

Meadowlark *(Wh-wet'-kula)* flew to a nearby tree and sang,

> "Two little oyster shells
> Hide her in!"

The old grandmother then put Chipmunk between two oyster shells where she was well hid. The grandmother took the necklace from her neck and gave it to Meadowlark that she would not tell where Chipmunk was hid. She knew that Meadowlark was a tattler. Meadowlark flew away.

Owl-woman followed Chipmunk's tracks to the grandmother's tepee. Going inside she asked, "Where is the hunted child that I am tracking?"

The grandmother denied that she knew. Then the mean Owl-woman began hunting for Chipmunk. She looked in the bedding, in the basket, and in the soup. As last she gave up hope of finding Chipmunk when Meadowlark flew back to the tree and sang,

> "I will tell you if you pay me!
> I will tell you if you pay me!
> Where she is! Where she is!"

Owl-woman went outside the tepee and threw Meadowlark a yellow vest. Meadowlark, the tattler, sang,

> "Two little oyster shells,
> Take her out!
> Two little oyster shells,
> Take her out!"

Meadowlark flew away with the necklace and the yellow vest which she had earned for befriending and then tattling on Chipmunk. She wears them to this day.

Owl-woman went back into the tepee. With all the begging of the grandmother, poor little Chipmunk was taken from the oyster shells. She was cut open by the sharp claws of Owl-woman and her heart taken out. Owl-woman swallowed it and said, "*Yum, yum-yum!* It is good. Little girls' hearts are the best." Owl-woman then went on with her big basket filled with children.

The grandmother cried for some time when she again heard the song of the Meadowlark from the tree,

> "Put a berry for a heart!
> Put a berry for a heart!"

At this, the grandmother put a half ripe *ol-la-la* berry in the breast of Chipmunk and sewed it up. She then stepped over her work when Chipmunk jumped up, alive.

Owl-woman had not gone far from the grandmother's tepee when

she met the cunning Coyote (*Sin-ka'-lip*). Coyote knew Owl-woman.
He said to her, "I love to eat all bad little children. If we travel together,
we will have better success finding children." Owl-woman agreed. She
was glad, for she knew the trickery of Coyote. Because of Coyote's evil
powers, she thought that they would be greater than all the monsters of
the earth. The two went traveling together.

They had not gone far until Owl-woman grew hungry. Coyote said,
"We will stop and make a big fire. We will roast the children. They will
taste better roasted than eating them alive and uncooked." Owl-woman
consented. She praised Coyote for his wisdom, while Coyote flattered
Owl-woman with good words. Coyote told her to let all the children out
of the basket so they could do the work. Coyote and Owl-woman would
oversee the work, that it was done right.

By Coyote's orders, the children gathered much pitchwood, piling it
high. When Owl-woman was out of hearing, Coyote said to the children, "Gather the wood with most pitch. Gather the solid pitch in
plenty if you wish to return to your parents." The children took spirit.
They worked hard. Soon they set the big pile on fire.

Coyote said to Owl-woman, "This is to be a big feast. To make it
what it should be, you had better blacken your face with charcoal. To
make the charcoal stick good, you must rub your face over with pitch."
This Owl-woman did, Coyote and the children helping. Coyote covered her arms with their many bracelets with pitch, then painted them
with charcoal. They danced around the fire, singing and shouting for
the roast-feast. They danced while waiting for the coals to grow hot.

When Owl-woman grew anxious to roast the children, Coyote told
her that the pitch smoke would spoil the meat. Coyote said to her, "Let
the children all get sticks, and we will pretend to dance the sun dance.
We will roast the children afterwards." Owl-woman readily consented.
She was flattered. Coyote instructed the children to get forked sticks.

Owl-woman asked Coyote, "Why forked sticks?"

Coyote replied, "We will use the forked sticks in turning the roasting
children."

It was not long before Owl-woman grew tired of dancing. But
Coyote insisted that the coals were not ready. They danced on, Coyote
flattering her on her knowledge of dancing. She danced till she staggered, when Coyote purposely went against her. She fell; Coyote
laughed and danced the harder. Owl-woman got up and began dancing
again. Coyote danced around the fire a few times and then, pretending
to stagger, fell against her again. Owl-woman was knocked into the
blazing fire of pitchwood. Her pitch-covered face and arms blazed.
Coyote told the children to help him with all their forked sticks to keep
Owl-woman in the fire. They did so, and at last she was burned to
death. She was roasted instead of the children.

Coyote then sent all the children back home. After Owl-woman's eyes burst, from them flew a small owl, alighting on a tree where it hooted its night call. Coyote told the bird, "In the future, Owl-woman's remains will only be a thing to scare a bad child into sleep. You will only travel by night because you will be blind in the daylight, only able to see in darkness, because your eyes were burnt out with the pitch." So it is to this day. Indian children are still afraid of Owl-woman.

1933

KATHERINE ANNE PORTER
c. 1890–1980

Writing in her *Journal*, Katherine Anne Porter observed in 1936 that the "constant exercise of memory seems to be the chief occupation of my mind, and all my experience seems to be simply memory, with continuity, marginal notes, constant revision and comparison of one thing with another." When "thousands of memories converge, harmonize, arrange themselves around a central ideal in a coherent form," she continued, "I write a story." Through the memories that are transformed in her twenty-seven works of short fiction and her one novel, *Ship of Fools* (1962), Porter established herself as a fine stylist who could convey what she called "the thumbprint"—the distinctive individuality—of characters "who populate all these enormous migrations, calamities; who fight wars and furnish life for the future; these beings without which, one by one, all the 'broad movements of history' could never take place." Curiously, however, despite her "constant exercise of memory," the episodes from the past that Porter recalled in interviews and autobiographical sketches contain contradictory evidence about her birthdate, her family's religion, her medical history, and even her literary career.

Porter's father and mother lived in Indian Creek, Texas, some 140 miles from Kyle, where her paternal grandmother resided. The third of five children, the young "Callie" was, according to the older Katherine Anne Porter, "precocious, nervous, rebellious, unteachable, and made life very uncomfortable for myself and I suppose for those around me." Porter was not quite two years old when her mother died and the family moved to Kyle, where Katherine was reared by her grandmother in a house that Porter's biographer Joan Givner has described as disorderly and cramped. Yet Aunt Cat, as she was called, was a storyteller who, in Givner's words, "laid the foundation for Porter's literary gifts." In 1901, when her grandmother died, the family moved several times before settling in San Antonio. Although Porter disliked the convent schools she attended, she later boasted that already at this point in her life she was reading Shakespeare, Dante, and Homer and French poetry in translation. At sixteen, she ran away and married. Divorced three years later, she left Texas for Chicago: "I didn't want to be regarded as a freak. That was how they regarded a woman who tried to write."

For several years, Porter worked on newspapers in Chicago, Fort Worth, Texas, and Denver, Colorado, and she also traveled around the South singing ballads and acting in little theater groups. In the period preceding and during

World War I, which she has described in her autobiographical story *Pale Horse, Pale Rider*, she may have suffered from tuberculosis. After a short ghostwriting stint in New York City, Porter traveled to Mexico, where she became involved in politics from 1918 to 1921. The next year she sold her first short story, *Maria Concepcion*, to *Century Magazine*, and began studying and helping to exhibit Mexican folk art. She would return to Mexico in 1931, and, in such stories as *The Mexican Trinity* (1921), *Virgin Violeta* (1924), *Flowering Judas* (1930), and *Hacienda* (1934), she studied the *"chance* of salvation" in Mexican culture as well as the dissolution of that chance for expatriated Americans.

After traveling throughout the late twenties and writing book reviews for *The New Republic* and *The Nation*, Porter collected some of her stories in the volume *Flowering Judas* (1930). Two years later, she left for Europe, where she was briefly married to Eugene Pressly, a member of the American Foreign Service. One year after *Noon Wine* (1937) was published to critical acclaim, she was again briefly married, at this time to Albert Erskine, Jr., of Louisiana State University, and she lived in Baton Rouge for several years. By the time *Pale Horse, Pale Rider* (1939) and *The Leaning Tower, and Other Stories* (1944) appeared, she had established her reputation as a short-story writer. Throughout the fifties, Porter lectured at a number of major American universities. When her novel *Ship of Fools* was published in 1962, it was an instant best seller. Four years later, Porter received the National Book Award and the Pulitzer Prize for her *Collected Stories* (1965). In 1970, she published an expanded edition of her essays.

While *Ship of Fools* deals with an international group of characters set adrift in the violence that preceded the outbreak of World War II, many of Porter's other works focus on conventional family life in her native South. Influenced by Willa Cather, Katherine Mansfield, James Joyce, and Virginia Woolf, Porter produced fictionalized accounts of herself and her childhood memories of her grandmother in such stories as *The Source*, *The Grave*, and *Old Mortality*. *The Jilting of Granny Weatherall* is less overtly autobiographical than those stories in which Porter figures as the character Miranda; however, it presents a strong-willed, older woman who has reared a large family. And, as in so much of her fiction, Porter manages here to convey how past and present events mingle in the consciousness of a character who experiences an epiphany that is linked to her confrontation with death.

The Jilting of Granny Weatherall

She flicked her wrist neatly out of Doctor Harry's pudgy careful fingers and pulled the sheet up to her chin. The brat ought to be in knee breeches. Doctoring around the country with spectacles on his nose! "Get along now, take your schoolbooks and go. There's nothing wrong with me."

Doctor Harry spread a warm paw like a cushion on her forehead where the forked green vein danced and made her eyelids twitch. "Now, now, be a good girl, and we'll have you up in no time."

"That's no way to speak to a woman nearly eighty years old just because she's down. I'd have you respect your elders, young man."

"Well, Missy, excuse me." Doctor Harry patted her cheek. "But I've got to warn you, haven't I? You're a marvel, but you must be careful or you're going to be good and sorry."

"Don't tell me what I'm going to be. I'm on my feet now, morally speaking. It's Cornelia. I had to go to bed to get rid of her."

Her bones felt loose, and floated around in her skin, and Doctor Harry floated like a balloon around the foot of the bed. He floated and pulled down his waistcoat and swung his glasses on a cord. "Well, stay where you are, it certainly can't hurt you."

"Get along and doctor your sick," said Granny Weatherall. "Leave a well woman alone. I'll call for you when I want you. . . . Where were you forty years ago when I pulled through milk-leg[1] and double pneumonia? You weren't even born. Don't let Cornelia lead you on," she shouted, because Doctor Harry appeared to float up to the ceiling and out. "I pay my own bills, and I don't throw my money away on nonsense!"

She meant to wave good-by, but it was too much trouble. Her eyes closed of themselves, it was like a dark curtain drawn around the bed. The pillow rose and floated under her, pleasant as a hammock in a light wind. She listened to the leaves rustling outside the window. No, somebody was swishing newspapers: no, Cornelia and Doctor Harry were whispering together. She leaped broad awake, thinking they whispered in her ear.

"She was never like this, *never* like this!" "Well, what can we expect?" "Yes, eighty years old. . . . "

Well, and what if she was? She still had ears. It was like Cornelia to whisper around doors. She always kept things secret in such a public way. She was always being tactful and kind. Cornelia was dutiful; that was the trouble with her. Dutiful and good: "So good and dutiful," said Granny, "that I'd like to spank her." She saw herself spanking Cornelia and making a fine job of it.

"What'd you say, Mother?"

Granny felt her face tying up in hard knots.

"Can't a body think, I'd like to know?"

"I thought you might want something."

"I do. I want a lot of things. First off, go away and don't whisper."

She lay and drowsed, hoping in her sleep that the children would keep out and let her rest a minute. It had been a long day. Not that she was tired. It was always pleasant to snatch a minute now and then. There was always so much to be done, let me see: tomorrow.

---

1. Swelling of the legs after childbirth.

Tomorrow was far away and there was nothing to trouble about. Things were finished somehow when the time came; thank God there was always a little margin over for peace: then a person could spread out the plan of life and tuck in the edges orderly. It was good to have everything clean and folded away, with the hair brushes and tonic bottles sitting straight on the white embroidered linen: the day started without fuss and the pantry shelves laid out with rows of jelly glasses and brown jugs and white stone-china jars with blue whirligigs and words painted on them: coffee, tea, sugar, ginger, cinnamon, allspice: and the bronze clock with the lion on top nicely dusted off. The dust that lion could collect in twenty-four hours! The box in the attic with all those letters tied up, well, she'd have to go through that tomorrow. All those letters —George's letters and John's letters and her letters to them both— lying around for the children to find afterwards made her uneasy. Yes, that would be tomorrow's business. No use to let them know how silly she had been once.

While she was rummaging around she found death in her mind and it felt clammy and unfamiliar. She had spent so much time preparing for death there was no need for bringing it up again. Let it take care of itself now. When she was sixty she had felt very old, finished, and went around making farewell trips to see her children and grandchildren, with a secret in her mind: This is the very last of your mother, children! Then she made her will and came down with a long fever. That was all just a notion like a lot of other things, but it was lucky too, for she had once for all got over the idea of dying for a long time. Now she couldn't be worried. She hoped she had better sense now. Her father had lived to be one hundred and two years old and had drunk a noggin of strong hot toddy on his last birthday. He told the reporters it was his daily habit, and he owed his long life to that. He had made quite a scandal and was very pleased about it. She believed she'd just plague Cornelia a little.

"Cornelia! Cornelia!" No footsteps, but a sudden hand on her cheek. "Bless you, where have you been?"

"Here, Mother."

"Well, Cornelia, I want a noggin of hot toddy."

"Are you cold, darling?"

"I'm chilly, Cornelia. Lying in bed stops the circulation. I must have told you that a thousand times."

Well, she could just hear Cornelia telling her husband that Mother was getting a little childish and they'd have to humor her. The thing that most annoyed her was that Cornelia thought she was deaf, dumb, and blind. Little hasty glances and tiny gestures tossed around her and over her head saying, "Don't cross her, let her have her way, she's eighty years old," and she sitting there as if she lived in a thin glass cage. Sometimes Granny almost made up her mind to pack up and move back to her own house where nobody could remind her every minute that she was old. Wait, wait, Cornelia, till your own children whisper behind your back!

In her day she had kept a better house and had got more work done. She wasn't too old yet for Lydia to be driving eighty miles for advice when one of the children jumped the track, and Jimmy still dropped in and talked things over: "Now, Mammy, you've a good business head, I want to know what you think of this? . . ." Old. Cornelia couldn't change the furniture around without asking. Little things, little things! They had been so sweet when they were little. Granny wished the old days were back again with the children young and everything to be done over. It had been a hard pull, but not too much for her. When she thought of all the food she had cooked, and all the clothes she had cut and sewed, and all the gardens she had made—well, the children showed it. There they were, made out of her, and they couldn't get away from that. Sometimes she wanted to see John again and point to them and say, Well, I didn't do so badly, did I? But that would have to wait. That was for tomorrow. She used to think of him as a man, but now all the children were older than their father, and he would be a child beside her if she saw him now. It seemed strange and there was something wrong in the idea. Why, he couldn't possibly recognize her. She had fenced in a hundred acres once, digging the post holes herself and clamping the wires with just a negro boy to help. That changed a woman. John would be looking for a young woman with the peaked Spanish comb in her hair and the painted fan. Digging post holes changed a woman. Riding country roads in the winter when women had their babies was another thing: sitting up nights with sick horses and sick negroes and sick children and hardly ever losing one. John, I hardly ever lost one of them! John would see that in a minute, that would be something he could understand, she wouldn't have to explain anything!

It made her feel like rolling up her sleeves and putting the whole place to rights again. No matter if Cornelia was determined to be everywhere at once, there were a great many things left undone on this place. She would start tomorrow and do them. It was good to be strong enough for everything, even if all you made melted and changed and slipped under your hands, so that by the time you finished you almost forgot what you were working for. What was it I set out to do? she asked herself intently, but she could not remember. A fog rose over the valley, she saw it marching across the creek swallowing the trees and moving up the hill like an army of ghosts. Soon it would be at the near edge of the orchard, and then it was time to go in and light the lamps. Come in, children, don't stay out in the night air.

Lighting the lamps had been beautiful. The children huddled up to her and breathed like little calves waiting at the bars[2] in the twilight. Their eyes followed the match and watched the flame rise and settle in a blue curve, then they moved away from her. The lamp was lit, they didn't have to be scared and hang on to Mother any more. Never, never never more. God, for all my life I thank Thee. Without Thee, my God, I could never have done it. Hail, Mary, full of grace.

I want you to pick all the fruit this year and see that nothing is wasted. There's always someone who can use it. Don't let good things rot for want of using. You waste life when you waste good food. Don't let things get lost. It's bitter to lose things. Now, don't let me get to thinking, not when I am tired and taking a little nap before supper. . . .

The pillow rose about her shoulders and pressed against her heart and the memory was being squeezed out of it: oh, push down the pillow, somebody; it would smother her if she tried to hold it. Such a fresh breeze blowing and such a green day with no threats in it. But he had not come, just the same. What does a woman do when she has put on the white veil and set out the white cake for a man and he doesn't come? She tried to remember. No, I swear he never harmed me but in that. He never harmed me but in that . . . and what if he did? There was the day, the day, but a whirl of dark smoke rose and covered it, crept up and over into the bright field where everything was planted so carefully in orderly rows. That was hell, she knew hell when she saw it. For sixty years she had prayed against remembering him and against losing her soul in the deep pit of hell, and now the two things were mingled in one and the thought of him was a smoky cloud from hell that moved and crept in her head when she had just got rid of Doctor Harry and was trying to rest a minute. Wounded vanity, Ellen, said a sharp voice in the top of her mind. Don't let your wounded vanity get the upper hand of you. Plenty of girls get jilted. You were jilted, weren't you? Then stand up to it. Her eyelids wavered and let in streamers of blue-gray light like tissue paper over her eyes. She must get up and pull the shades down or she'd never sleep. She was in bed again and the shades were not down. How could that happen? Better turn over, hide from the light, sleeping in the light gave you nightmares. "Mother, how do you feel now?" and a stinging wetness on her forehead. But I don't like having my face washed in cold water!

Hapsy? George? Lydia? Jimmy? No, Cornelia, and her features were swollen and full of little puddles. "They're coming, darling, they'll all be here soon." Go wash your face, child, you look funny.

Instead of obeying, Cornelia knelt down and put her head on the

2. Pasture gates.

pillow. She seemed to be talking but there was no sound. "Well, are you tongue-tied? Whose birthday is it? Are you going to give a party?"

Cornelia's mouth moved urgently in strange shapes. "Don't do that, you bother me, daughter."

"Oh, no, Mother. Oh, no. . . ."

Nonsense. It was strange about children. They disputed your every word. "No what, Cornelia?"

"Here's Doctor Harry."

"I won't see that boy again. He just left five minutes ago."

"That was this morning, Mother. It's night now. Here's the nurse."

"This is Doctor Harry, Mrs. Weatherall. I never saw you look so young and happy!"

"Ah, I'll never be young again—but I'd be happy if they'd let me lie in peace and get rested."

She thought she spoke up loudly, but no one answered. A warm weight on her forehead, a warm bracelet on her wrist, and a breeze went on whispering, trying to tell her something. A shuffle of leaves in the everlasting hand of God, He blew on them and they danced and rattled. "Mother, don't mind, we're going to give you a little hypodermic." "Look here, daughter, how do ants get in this bed? I saw sugar ants yesterday." Did you send for Hapsy too?

It was Hapsy she really wanted. She had to go a long way back through a great many rooms to find Hapsy standing with a baby on her arm. She seemed to herself to be Hapsy also, and the baby on Hapsy's arm was Hapsy and himself and herself, all at once, and there was no surprise in the meeting. Then Hapsy melted from within and turned flimsy as gray gauze and the baby was a gauzy shadow, and Hapsy came up close and said, "I thought you'd never come," and looked at her very searchingly and said, "You haven't changed a bit!" They leaned forward to kiss, when Cornelia began whispering from a long way off, "Oh, is there anything you want to tell me? Is there anything I can do for you?"

Yes, she had changed her mind after sixty years and she would like to see George. I want you to find George. Find him and be sure to tell him I forgot him. I want him to know I had my husband just the same and my children and my house like any other woman. A good house too and a good husband that I loved and fine children out of him. Better than I hoped for even. Tell him I was given back everything he took away and more. Oh, no, oh, God, no, there was something else besides the house and the man and the children. Oh, surely they were not all? What was it? Something not given back. . . . Her breath crowded down under her ribs and grew into a monstrous frightening shape with cutting edges; it bored up into her head, and the agony was unbelievable: Yes, John, get the Doctor now, no more talk, my time has come.

When this one was born it should be the last. The last. It should have been born first, for it was the one she had truly wanted. Everything came in good time. Nothing left out, left over. She was strong, in three days she would be as well as ever. Better. A woman needed milk in her to have her full health.

"Mother, do you hear me?"

"I've been telling you—"

"Mother, Father Connolly's here."

"I went to Holy Communion only last week. Tell him I'm not so sinful as all that."

"Father just wants to speak to you."

He could speak as much as he pleased. It was like him to drop in and inquire about her soul as if it were a teething baby, and then stay on for a cup of tea and a round of cards and gossip. He always had a funny story of some sort, usually about an Irishman who made his little mistakes and confessed them, and the point lay in some absurd thing he would blurt out in the confessional showing his struggles between native piety and original sin. Granny felt easy about her soul. Cornelia, where are your manners? Give Father Connolly a chair. She had her secret comfortable understanding with a few favorite saints who cleared a straight road to God for her. All as surely signed and sealed as the papers for the new Forty Acres. Forever . . . heirs and assigns forever. Since the day the wedding cake was not cut, but thrown out and wasted. The whole bottom dropped out of the world, and there she was blind and sweating with nothing under her feet and the walls falling away. His hand had caught her under the breast, she had not fallen, there was the freshly polished floor with the green rug on it, just as before. He had cursed like a sailor's parrot and said, "I'll kill him for you." Don't lay a hand on him, for my sake leave something to God. "Now, Ellen, you must believe what I tell you. . . ."

So there was nothing, nothing to worry about any more, except sometimes in the night one of the children screamed in a nightmare, and they both hustled out shaking and hunting for the matches and calling, "There, wait a minute, here we are!" John, get the doctor now, Hapsy's time has come. But there was Hapsy standing by the bed in a white cap. "Cornelia, tell Hapsy to take off her cap. I can't see her plain."

Her eyes opened very wide and the room stood out like a picture she had seen somewhere. Dark colors with the shadows rising towards the ceiling in long angles. The tall black dresser gleamed with nothing on it but John's picture, enlarged from a little one, with John's eyes very black when they should have been blue. You never saw him, so how do you know how he looked? But the man insisted the copy was perfect, it was very rich and handsome. For a picture, yes, but it's not my husband. The table by the bed had a linen cover and a candle and a crucifix. The light was blue from Cornelia's silk lampshades. No sort of light at all, just frippery. You had to live forty years with kerosene lamps to appreciate honest electricity. She felt very strong and she saw Doctor Harry with a rosy nimbus around him.

"You look like a saint, Doctor Harry, and I vow that's as near as you'll ever come to it."

"She's saying something."

"I heard you, Cornelia. What's all this carrying-on?"

"Father Connolly's saying—"

Cornelia's voice staggered and bumped like a cart in a bad road. It rounded corners and turned back again and arrived nowhere. Granny stepped up in the cart very lightly and reached for the reins, but a man sat beside her and she knew him by his hands, driving the cart. She did not look in his face, for she knew without seeing, but looked instead down the road where the trees leaned over and bowed to each other and a thousand birds were singing a Mass. She felt like singing too, but she put her hand in the bosom of her dress and pulled out a rosary, and Father Connolly murmured Latin in a very solemn voice and tickled her feet. My God, will you stop that nonsense? I'm a married woman. What if he did run away and leave me to face the priest by myself? I found another a whole world better. I wouldn't have exchanged my husband for anybody except St. Michael himself, and you may tell him that for me with a thank you in the bargain.

Light flashed on her closed eyelids, and a deep roaring shook her. Cornelia, is that lightning? I hear thunder. There's going to be a storm. Close all the windows. Call the children in. . . . "Mother, here we are, all of us." "Is that you, Hapsy?" "Oh, no, I'm Lydia. We drove as fast as we could." Their faces drifted above her, drifted away. The rosary fell out of her hands and Lydia put it back. Jimmy tried to help, their hands fumbled together, and Granny closed two fingers around Jimmy's thumb. Beads wouldn't do, it must be something alive. She was so amazed her thoughts ran round and round. So, my dear Lord, this is my death and I wasn't even thinking about it. My children have come to see me die. But I can't, it's not time. Oh, I always hated surprises. I wanted to give Cornelia the amethyst set—Cornelia, you're to have the amethyst set, but Hapsy's to wear it when she wants, and, Doctor Harry, do shut up. Nobody sent for you. Oh, my dear Lord, do wait a minute. I meant to do something about the Forty Acres, Jimmy doesn't need it and Lydia will later on, with that worthless husband of hers. I meant to finish the altar cloth and send six bottles of wine to Sister Borgia for her dyspepsia. I want to send six bottles of wine to Sister Borgia, Father Connolly, now don't let me forget.

Cornelia's voice made short turns and tilted over and crashed. "Oh, Mother, oh, Mother, oh, Mother. . . ."

"I'm not going, Cornelia. I'm taken by surprise. I can't go."

You'll see Hapsy again. What about her? "I thought you'd never come." Granny made a long journey outward, looking for Hapsy. What if I don't find her? What then? Her heart sank down and down, there was no bottom to death, she couldn't come to the end of it. The blue light from Cornelia's lampshade drew into a tiny point in the center of her brain, it flickered and winked like an eye, quietly it fluttered and dwindled. Granny lay curled down within herself, amazed and watchful, staring at the point of light that was herself; her body was now only a deeper mass of shadow in an endless darkness and this darkness would curl around the light and swallow it up. God, give a sign!

For the second time there was no sign. Again no bridegroom and the priest in the house.[3] She could not remember any other sorrow because this grief wiped them all away. Oh, no, there's nothing more cruel than this—I'll never forgive it. She stretched herself with a deep breath and blew out the light.

1930

3. In Christ's parable of the wise and foolish virgins, salvation is compared to the arrival of a bridegroom (Matthew 25:1–13).

EDNA ST. VINCENT MILLAY
1892–1950

In the late fifties, the poet Anne Sexton worried that she might be a "reincarnation" of Edna St. Vincent Millay, and at around the same time Sexton's friend Sylvia Plath was expressing similar fears, insisting to her mother that she would not write "simple lyrics like Millay." At least in part, such anxieties were the result of the enormous success that Edna St. Vincent Millay—poet, playwright, feminist, and political activist—achieved, especially in her early youth, by producing fluent and inventive sonnet cycles, verse dramas, and dramatic poems. For indeed, even while Sexton was troubled by the thought that she might be seriously compared to Millay, she was candidly admitting that "2 years ago I had never heard of any poet but Edna St. Vincent."

Born in Rockland, Maine, Edna St. Vincent Millay was the oldest of three daughters whose father deserted them and their mother, a practical nurse, when the child—called "Vincent" in the family—was twelve. According to one biographer, her mother "taught" her to write verse at the age of four; in any case, she soon exhibited a precocious talent, and, when she was only twenty, one of her most famous poems, *Renascence*, was a prize winner in an important contest sponsored by *The Lyric Year*, an anthology of contemporary poetry. Almost immediately, her ability brought her to the attention of a number of older intellectuals, one of whom, Caroline Dow, the executive secretary of the Y.W.C.A.'s national training school in New York, urged her to attend Vassar College, where she had a lively career as a notable undergraduate poet, actress, and playwright.

After graduation from Vassar in 1917, Edna St. Vincent Millay lived a bohemian life in Greenwich Village. Writing articles for popular magazines and innovative plays as well as acting in the Provincetown Players, a radical little theater group, she seemed to be an incarnation of what was in the twenties called "the Jazz Age." Passionately independent, red-haired, green-eyed, she was a celebrity of sorts among artists and intellectuals, with, according to the critic Edmund Wilson (who proposed marriage to her), "an intoxicating effect on people." For her part, she mythologized such intoxication from the heroine's point of view, writing poems that extolled sexual and emotional liberation, poems that would be memorized by generations of young women from her own day to Anne Sexton's. "My candle burns at both ends," she rebelliously proclaimed; "It will not last the night; / But ah, my foes, and oh, my friends—/It gives a lovely light!"

Millay was also undertaking more ambitious tasks. Though financial difficulties drove her to hackwork for magazines, which she wrote under the name "Nancy Boyd," she produced a number of quite serious volumes of verse: *The Harp-Weaver* won the Pulitzer Prize in 1923. In addition, she presented herself as, in the words of her friend the writer Floyd Dell, "very much a revolutionary in all her sympathies, and a whole-hearted Feminist." In 1923—in keeping with this self-definition—she married the widower of the prominent American feminist Inez Milholland, a Dutch businessman named Eugen Jan Boissevain.

After her marriage to Boissevain, Millay's career continued to flourish for a while. In 1925, she was awarded an honorary degree by Tufts College, the first of many such degrees, and in 1927, she became intensely involved in the crusade to stay the execution of the alleged anarchists Sacco and Vanzetti, about whom she wrote a number of passionate verses. In the thirties, however, her reputation began to wane, perhaps because her art did not seem as innovative as the work of modernist contemporaries like T. S. Eliot, Wallace Stevens, and Marianne Moore, writers whose rugged and sometimes seemingly ragged forms appeared to be far in advance of the more traditional modes and meters Millay employed. Although during World War II she continued to work actively for public causes and to write intensely political poetry, she became increasingly isolated. In 1944, she suffered a nervous breakdown, and in 1950, a year after her husband died, she too died of a heart attack while living alone on their country place at Austerlitz, New York. Yet despite the obscurity into which her work fell in the fifties and sixties—decades when former acolytes like Plath and Sexton felt it necessary to repudiate her as an old-fashioned "poetess"—Millay's art has endured and seems, sometimes, surprisingly fresh: indeed, not too long ago one prominent editor remarked that her *Childhood Is the Kingdom* reads like "a twenty-first-century poem."

First Fig

My candle burns at both ends;
    It will not last the night;
But ah, my foes, and oh, my friends—
    It gives a lovely light!

1920

Second Fig

Safe upon the solid rock the ugly houses stand:
Come and see my shining palace built upon the sand!

1920

[Oh, oh, you will be sorry for that word!]

Oh, oh, you will be sorry for that word!
Give back my book and take my kiss instead.
Was it my enemy or my friend I heard,
"What a big book for such a little head!"
Come, I will show you now my newest hat,   5
And you may watch me purse my mouth and prink![1]
Oh, I shall love you still, and all of that.
I never again shall tell you what I think.
I shall be sweet and crafty, soft and sly;
You will not catch me reading any more: 10
I shall be called a wife to pattern by;
And some day when you knock and push the door,
Some sane day, not too bright and not too stormy,
I shall be gone, and you may whistle for me.

1923

[I, being born a woman and distressed]

I, being born a woman and distressed
By all the needs and notions of my kind,
Am urged by your propinquity to find
Your person fair, and feel a certain zest

1. Primp.

To bear your body's weight upon my breast: 5
So subtly is the fume of life designed,
To clarify the pulse and cloud the mind,
And leave me once again undone, possessed.
Think not for this, however, the poor treason
Of my stout blood against my staggering brain,   10
I shall remember you with love, or season
My scorn with pity,—let me make it plain:
I find this frenzy insufficient reason
For conversation when we meet again.

1923

Sonnets from an Ungrafted Tree[2]

I

So she came back into his house again
And watched beside his bed until he died,
Loving him not at all. The winter rain
Splashed in the painted butter-tub outside,
Where once her red geraniums had stood,   5
Where still their rotted stalks were to be seen;
The thin log snapped; and she went out for wood,
Bareheaded, running the few steps between
The house and shed; there, from the sodden eaves
Blown back and forth on ragged ends of twine,   10
Saw the dejected creeping-jinny vine,
(And one, big-aproned, blithe, with stiff blue sleeves
Rolled to the shoulder that warm day in spring,
Who planted seeds, musing ahead to their far blossoming).

II

The last white sawdust on the floor was grown   15
Gray as the first, so long had he been ill;
The axe was nodding in the block; fresh-blown
And foreign came the rain across the sill,
But on the roof so steadily it drummed
She could not think a time it might not be—   20
In hazy summer, when the hot air hummed
With mowing, and locusts rising raspingly,
When that small bird with iridescent wings
And long incredible sudden silver tongue

---

2. A tree to which new branches or cuttings have not been attached.

Had just flashed (and yet maybe not!) among   25
The dwarf nasturtiums—when no sagging springs
Of shower were in the whole bright sky, somehow
Upon this roof the rain would drum as it was drumming now.

III

She filled her arms with wood, and set her chin
Forward, to hold the highest stick in place,   30
No less afraid than she had always been
Of spiders up her arms and on her face,
But too impatient for a careful search
Or a less heavy loading, from the heap
Selecting hastily small sticks of birch,   35
For their curled bark, that instantly will leap
Into a blaze, nor thinking to return
Some day, distracted, as of old, to find
Smooth, heavy, round, green logs with a wet, gray rind
Only, and knotty chunks that will not burn,   40
(That day when dust is on the wood-box floor,
And some old catalogue, and a brown, shriveled apple core).

IV

The white bark writhed and sputtered like a fish
Upon the coals, exuding odorous smoke.
She knelt and blew, in a surging desolate wish   45
For comfort; and the sleeping ashes woke
And scattered to the hearth, but no thin fire
Broke suddenly, the wood was wet with rain.
Then, softly stepping forth from her desire,
(Being mindful of like passion hurled in vain   50
Upon a similar task, in other days)
She thrust her breath against the stubborn coal,
Bringing to bear upon its hilt the whole
Of her still body . . . there sprang a little blaze . . .
A pack of hounds, the flame swept up the flue!—   55
And the blue night stood flattened against the window,
          staring through.

V

A wagon stopped before the house; she heard
The heavy oilskins of the grocer's man
Slapping against his legs. Of a sudden whirred
Her heart like a frightened partridge, and she ran   60
And slid the bolt, leaving his entrance free;

Then in the cellar way till he was gone
Hid, breathless, praying that he might not see
The chair sway she had laid her hand upon
In passing. Sour and damp from that dark vault   65
Arose to her the well-remembered chill;
She saw the narrow wooden stairway still
Plunging into the earth, and the thin salt
Crusting the crocks; until she knew him far,
So stood, with listening eyes upon the empty doughnut jar.   70

VI

Then cautiously she pushed the cellar door
And stepped into the kitchen—saw the track
Of muddy rubber boots across the floor,
The many paper parcels in a stack
Upon the dresser; with accustomed care   75
Removed the twine and put the wrappings by,
Folded, and the bags flat, that with an air
Of ease had been whipped open skillfully,
To the gape of children. Treacherously dear
And simple was the dull, familiar task.   80
And so it was she came at length to ask:
How came the soda there? The sugar here?
Then the dream broke. Silent, she brought the mop,
And forced the trade-slip[3] on the nail that held his razor strop.

VII

One way there was of muting in the mind   85
A little while the ever-clamorous care;
And there was rapture, of a decent kind,
In making mean and ugly objects fair:
Soft-sooted kettle-bottoms, that had been
Time after time set in above the fire,   90
Faucets, and candlesticks, corroded green,
To mine again from quarry; to attire
The shelves in paper petticoats, and tack
New oilcloth in the ringed-and-rotten's place,
Polish the stove till you could see your face,   95
And after nightfall rear an aching back
In a changed kitchen, bright as a new pin,
An advertisement, far too fine to cook a supper in.

---

3. Receipt.

VIII

She let them leave their jellies at the door
And go away, reluctant, down the walk.   100
She heard them talking as they passed before
The blind, but could not quite make out their talk
For noise in the room—the sudden heavy fall
And roll of a charred log, and the roused shower
Of snapping sparks; then sharply from the wall   105
The unforgivable crowing of the hour.
One instant set ajar, her quiet ear
Was stormed and forced by the full rout of day:
The rasp of a saw, the fussy cluck and bray
Of hens, the wheeze of a pump, she needs must hear;   110
She inescapably must endure to feel
Across her teeth the grinding of a backing wagon wheel.

IX

Not over-kind nor over-quick in study
Nor skilled in sports nor beautiful was he,
Who had come into her life when anybody   115
Would have been welcome, so in need was she.
They had become acquainted in this way:
He flashed a mirror in her eyes at school;
By which he was distinguished; from that day
They went about together, as a rule.   120
She told, in secret and with whispering,
How he had flashed a mirror in her eyes;
And as she told, it struck her with surprise
That this was not so wonderful a thing.
But what's the odds?—It's pretty nice to know   125
You've got a friend to keep you company everywhere you go.

X

She had forgotten how the August night
Was level as a lake beneath the moon,
In which she swam a little, losing sight
Of shore; and how the boy, who was at noon   130
Simple enough, not different from the rest,
Wore now a pleasant mystery as he went,
Which seemed to her an honest enough test
Whether she loved him, and she was content.
So loud, so loud the million crickets' choir . . .   135
So sweet the night, so long-drawn-out and late . . .
And if the man were not her spirit's mate,

Why was her body sluggish with desire?
Stark on the open field the moonlight fell,
But the oak tree's shadow was deep and black and secret as a well. 140

XI

It came into her mind, seeing how the snow
Was gone, and the brown grass exposed again,
And clothes-pins, and an apron—long ago,
In some white storm that sifted through the pane
And sent her forth reluctantly at last   145
To gather in, before the line gave way,
Garments, board-stiff, that galloped on the blast
Clashing like angel armies in a fray,
An apron long ago in such a night
Blown down and buried in the deepening drift,   150
To lie till April thawed it back to sight,
Forgotten, quaint and novel as a gift—
It struck her, as she pulled and pried and tore,
That here was spring, and the whole year to be lived through
      once more.

XII

Tenderly, in those times, as though she fed   155
An ailing child—with sturdy propping up
Of its small, feverish body in the bed,
And steadying of its hands about the cup—
She gave her husband of her body's strength,
Thinking of men, what helpless things they were,   160
Until he turned and fell asleep at length,
And stealthily stirred the night and spoke to her.
Familiar, at such moments, like a friend,
Whistled far off the long, mysterious train,
And she could see in her mind's vision plain   165
The magic World, where cities stood on end . . .
Remote from where she lay—and yet—between,
Save for something asleep beside her, only the window screen.

XIII

From the wan dream that was her waking day,
Wherein she journeyed, borne along the ground   170
Without her own volition in some way,
Or fleeing, motionless, with feet fast bound,
Or running silent through a silent house
Sharply remembered from an earlier dream,

Upstairs, down other stairs, fearful to rouse,   175
Regarding him, the wide and empty scream
Of a strange sleeper on a malignant bed,
And all the time not certain if it were
Herself so doing or some one like to her,
From this wan dream that was her daily bread,   180
Sometimes, at night, incredulous, she would wake—
A child, blowing bubbles that the chairs and carpet did not break!

XIV

She had a horror he would die at night.
And sometimes when the light began to fade
She could not keep from noticing how white   185
The birches looked—and then she would be afraid,
Even with a lamp, to go about the house
And lock the windows; and as night wore on
Toward morning, if a dog howled, or a mouse
Squeaked in the floor, long after it was gone   190
Her flesh would sit awry on her. By day
She would forget somewhat, and it would seem
A silly thing to go with just this dream
And get a neighbor to come at night and stay.
But it would strike her sometimes, making the tea: 195
She had kept that kettle boiling all night long, for company.

XV

There was upon the sill a pencil mark,
Vital with shadow when the sun stood still
At noon, but now, because the day was dark,
It was a pencil mark upon the sill.   200
And the mute clock, maintaining ever the same
Dead moment, blank and vacant of itself,
Was a pink shepherdess, a picture frame,
A shell marked Souvenir, there on the shelf.
Whence it occurred to her that he might be,   205
The mainspring being broken in his mind,
A clock himself, if one were so inclined,
That stood at twenty minutes after three—
The reason being for this, it might be said,
That things in death were neither clocks nor people,   210
     but only dead.

XVI

The doctor asked her what she wanted done
With him, that could not lie there many days.

And she was shocked to see how life goes on
Even after death, in irritating ways;
And mused how if he had not died at all   215
'Twould have been easier—then there need not be
The stiff disorder of a funeral
Everywhere, and the hideous industry,
And crowds of people calling her by name
And questioning her, she'd never seen before,   220
But only watching by his bed once more
And sitting silent if a knocking came . . .
She said at length, feeling the doctor's eyes,
"I don't know what you do exactly when a person dies."

XVII

Gazing upon him now, severe and dead,   225
It seemed a curious thing that she had lain
Beside him many a night in that cold bed,
And that had been which would not be again.
From his desirous body the great heat
Was gone at last, it seemed, and the taut nerves   230
Loosened forever. Formally the sheet
Set forth for her today those heavy curves
And lengths familiar as the bedroom door.
She was as one who enters, sly, and proud,
To where her husband speaks before a crowd,   235
And sees a man she never saw before—
The man who eats his victuals at her side,
Small, and absurd, and hers: for once, not hers, unclassified.

FINIS

1923

The Buck in the Snow

White sky, over the hemlocks bowed with snow,
Saw you not at the beginning of evening the antlered buck
      and his doe
Standing in the apple-orchard? I saw them. I saw them
      suddenly go,
Tails up, with long leaps lovely and slow,
Over the stone-wall into the wood of hemlocks bowed with snow. 5

Now lies he here, his wild blood scalding the snow.

How strange a thing is death, bringing to his knees, bringing
      to his antlers
The buck in the snow.

How strange a thing,—a mile away by now, it may be,
Under the heavy hemlocks that as the moments pass   10
Shift their loads a little, letting fall a feather of snow—
Life, looking out attentive from the eyes of the doe.

1928

To Inez Milholland[4]

Read in Washington, November eighteenth, 1923, at the unveiling of a
statue of three leaders in the cause of Equal Rights for Women

Upon this marble bust that is not I
Lay the round, formal wreath that is not fame;
But in the forum of my silenced cry
Root ye the living tree whose sap is flame.
I, that was proud and valiant, am no more;—   5
Save as a dream that wanders wide and late,
Save as a wind that rattles the stout door,
Troubling the ashes in the sheltered grate.
The stone will perish; I shall be twice dust.
Only my standard on a taken hill   10
Can cheat the mildew and the red-brown rust
And make immortal my adventurous will.
Even now the silk is tugging at the staff:
Take up the song; forget the epitaph.

1928

[Women have loved before as I love now][5]

Women have loved before as I love now;
At least, in lively chronicles of the past—
Of Irish waters by a Cornish prow
Or Trojan waters by a Spartan mast[6]
Much to their cost invaded—here and there,   5
Hunting the amorous line, skimming the rest,
I find some woman bearing as I bear
Love like a burning city in the breast.
I think however that of all alive
I only in such utter, ancient way   10
Do suffer love; in me alone survive

---

4. Socialist reformer and activist (1886–1916)
who started the women's suffrage movement at
Vassar, where Millay was a student, and died
from her overexertions on behalf of the women's
vote.

5. From the sonnet sequence "Fatal Interview."
6. An allusion to Isolde, the Irish lover of her
Cornish captor, Tristan, and Helen, the Greek
mistress of the Trojan Paris.

The unregenerate passions of a day
When treacherous queens, with death upon the tread,
Heedless and wilful, took their knights to bed.

1931

[Oh, sleep forever in the Latmian cave]

Oh, sleep forever in the Latmian cave,
Mortal Endymion, darling of the Moon![7]
Her silver garments by the senseless wave
Shouldered and dropped and on the shingle[8] strewn,
Her fluttering hand against her forehead pressed,   5
Her scattered looks that trouble all the sky,
Her rapid footsteps running down the west—
Of all her altered state, oblivious lie!
Whom earthen you, by deathless lips adored,
Wild-eyed and stammering to the grasses thrust,   10
And deep into her crystal body poured
The hot and sorrowful sweetness of the dust:
Whereof she wanders mad, being all unfit
For mortal love, that might not die of it.

1931

Childhood Is the Kingdom Where Nobody Dies

Childhood is not from birth to a certain age and at a certain age
The child is grown, and puts away childish things.
Childhood is the kingdom where nobody dies.

Nobody that matters, that is. Distant relatives of course
Die, whom one never has seen or has seen for an hour,   5
And they gave one candy in a pink-and-green stripéd bag, or a
    jack-knife,
And went away, and cannot really be said to have lived at all.

And cats die. They lie on the floor and lash their tails,
And their reticent fur is suddenly all in motion
With fleas that one never knew were there,   10
Polished and brown, knowing all there is to know,
Trekking off into the living world.
You fetch a shoe-box, but it's much too small, because she won't
    curl up now:
So you find a bigger box, and bury her in the yard, and weep.

---

7. According to Greek myth, Endymion was a beautiful youth who fell asleep in a cave on Mount Latmos; there he was visited by the goddess of the moon, Selene.
8. Pebbly beach.

But you do not wake up a month from then, two months,   15
A year from then, two years, in the middle of the night
And weep, with your knuckles in your mouth, and say Oh, God!
     Oh, God!
Childhood is the kingdom where nobody dies that matters,—
     mothers and fathers don't die.

And if you have said, "For heaven's sake, must you always
     be kissing a person?"
Or, "I do wish to gracious you'd stop tapping on the window
     with your thimble!"   20
Tomorrow, or even the day after tomorrow if you're busy
     having fun,
Is plenty of time to say, "I'm sorry, mother."

To be grown up is to sit at the table with people who have died,
     who neither listen nor speak;
Who do not drink their tea, though they always said
Tea was such a comfort.   25

Run down into the cellar and bring up the last jar of raspberries;
     they are not tempted.
Flatter them, ask them what was it they said exactly
That time, to the bishop, or to the overseer, or to Mrs. Mason;
They are not taken in.
Shout at them, get red in the face, rise,   30
Drag them up out of their chairs by their stiff shoulders and
     shake them and yell at them;
They are not startled, they are not even embarrassed;
     they slide back into their chairs.

Your tea is cold now.
You drink it standing up,
And leave the house.   35

1934

Apostrophe to Man

(on reflecting that the world is ready to go to war again)[9]

Detestable race, continue to expunge yourself, die out.
Breed faster, crowd, encroach, sing hymns, build bombing
     airplanes;

9. Written in the decade before World War II.

Make speeches, unveil statues, issue bonds, parade;
Convert again into explosives the bewildered ammonia
    and the distracted cellulose;
Convert again into putrescent matter drawing flies   5
The hopeful bodies of the young; exhort,
Pray, pull long faces, be earnest, be all but overcome,
    be photographed;
Confer, perfect your formulae, commercialize
Bacteria harmful to human tissue,
Put death on the market;   10
Breed, crowd, encroach, expand, expunge yourself, die out,
Homo called *sapiens*.[1]

                           1934

Rendezvous

Not for these lovely blooms that prank your chambers did I come.
    Indeed,
I could have loved you better in the dark;
That is to say, in rooms less bright with roses, rooms more casual,
    less aware
Of History in the wings about to enter with benevolent air
On ponderous tiptoe, at the cue "Proceed."   5
Not that I like the ash-trays over-crowded and the place
    in a mess,
Or the monastic cubicle too unctuously austere and stark,
But partly that these formal garlands for our Eighth
    Street Aphrodite[2] are a bit too Greek,
And partly that to make the poor walls rich with our unaided
    loveliness
Would have been more *chic*.   10

Yet here I am, having told you of my quarrel with the
    taxi-driver over a line of Milton, and you laugh;
    and you are you, none other.
Your laughter pelts my skin with small delicious blows.
But I am perverse; I wish you had not scrubbed—with pumice,
    I suppose—
The tobacco stains from your beautiful fingers.
    And I wish I did not feel like your mother.

                           1939

---

1. The scientific Latin name for the human   2. Greek goddess of love.
species, meaning "intelligent man."

The Fitting

The fitter said, "*Madame, vous avez maigri*,"[3]
And pinched together a handful of skirt at my hip.
"*Tant mieux*,"[4] I said, and looked away slowly,
          and took my under-lip
Softly between my teeth.

                              Rip—rip!   5

Out came the seam, and was pinned together in another place.
She knelt before me, a hardworking woman with a familiar
          and unknown face,
Dressed in linty black, very tight in the arm's-eye and smelling
          of sweat.
She rose, lifting my arm, and set her cold shears against me,—
          snip-snip;
Her knuckles gouged my breast. My drooped eyes lifted to
          my guarded eyes in the glass, and glanced away as from
          someone they had never met.   10
"*Ah, que madame a maigri!*" cried the *vendeuse*,[5]
          coming in with dresses over her arm.
"*C'est la chaleur*,"[6] I said, looking out into the sunny tops of the
          horse-chestnuts—and indeed it was very warm.

I stood for a long time so, looking out into the afternoon,
          thinking of the evening and you. . . .
While they murmured busily in the distance, turning me, touching
          my secret body, doing what they were paid to do.   15

                                                            1939

[I too beneath your moon, almighty Sex]

I too beneath your moon, almighty Sex,
Go forth at nightfall crying like a cat,
Leaving the lofty tower I laboured at
For birds to foul and boys and girls to vex
With tittering chalk; and you, and the long necks   5
Of neighbours sitting where their mothers sat
Are well aware of shadowy this and that
In me, that's neither noble nor complex.

---

3. French: "Madame, you have grown thin."   thin!"
4. "So much the better."   6."It's the heat."
5. Saleswoman: "Ah, how madame has grown

Such as I am, however, I have brought
To what it is, this tower; it is my own;   10
Though it was reared To Beauty, it was wrought
From what I had to build with: honest bone
Is there, and anguish; pride; and burning thought;
And lust is there, and nights not spent alone.

1939

[The courage that my mother had]

The courage that my mother had
Went with her, and is with her still:
Rock from New England quarried;
Now granite in a granite hill.

The golden brooch my mother wore   5
She left behind for me to wear;
I have no thing I treasure more:
Yet, it is something I could spare.

Oh, if instead she'd left to me
The thing she took into the grave!—   10
That courage like a rock, which she
Has no more need of, and I have.

1954

An Ancient Gesture

I thought, as I wiped my eyes on the corner of my apron:
Penelope[7] did this too.
And more than once: you can't keep weaving all day
And undoing it all through the night;
Your arms get tired, and the back of your neck gets tight;   5
And along towards morning, when you think it will never be light,
And your husband has been gone, and you don't know where,
        for years,
Suddenly you burst into tears;
There is simply nothing else to do.

7. The wife of Odysseus (Ulysses) in Homer's   out the weaving at night in order to keep away
Odyssey, who waited for her husband to return the suitors for her hand.
from the Trojan Wars. She wove all day but tore

And I thought, as I wiped my eyes on the corner of my apron: 10
This is an ancient gesture, authentic, antique,
In the very best tradition, classic, Greek;
Ulysses did this too.
But only as a gesture,—a gesture which implied
To the assembled throng that he was much too moved to speak.   15
He learned it from Penelope . . .
Penelope, who really cried.

                                                                                                    1954

DJUNA BARNES
1892–1982

Few writers have remained as elusive to literary critics, historians, and biographers as Djuna Barnes. Throughout this century, Barnes published journalism, plays, and stories, as well as two novels, one of which, *Nightwood* (1937), has been considered a classic. She also played a major role in two expatriate groups: the modernist movement associated with James Joyce and T. S. Eliot, and the circle of lesbians who frequented the salons of Natalie Barney and Gertrude Stein. Yet, from 1919, when she refused to answer any questions about herself in *The Little Review*, through her return from Europe to America in 1940 and her subsequent life in Greenwich Village, she rejected publicity and lived an ever more reclusive life.

Barnes was raised in upstate New York, near Cornwall-on-Hudson, until her father moved the family to Long Island, where he purchased a 105-acre farm. Wald Barnes, who rejected his father's surname in preference for his mother's, was dedicated to an independent, private, and eccentric life. Little is known about Elizabeth (Chappell) Barnes, Wald Barnes's British-born wife and Djuna Barnes's mother. The major source of Barnes' private education was her father's mother, Zadel Barnes, who was both a feminist and a published journalist. After a brief stint studying art at Pratt Institute and at the Art Students League, Barnes quickly became active in the New York literary world: a slim volume of drawings and poems, *The Book of Repulsive Women* (1915), was published as a chapbook, her poems and stories appeared in a number of periodicals, and she joined the Provincetown Players. Supporting herself as a newspaperwoman, she produced reviews of theatrical events along with stunt stories that required her to be hugged by a gorilla or forcibly fed. After the 1919–1920 season, when three of Barnes's plays were produced by the Provincetown Players, she left for Europe to write interviews for *McCall's* magazine.

In Europe, whether she was interviewing the filmmaker D. W. Griffith, describing "the Jungle folk" at the circus, or depicting her meetings with James Joyce, who later presented her with the original manuscript of *Ulysses*, Barnes continued to make a reputation for herself as a witty, unconventional reporter. Just as she had earlier relished the bohemian sexual freedom of Greenwich Village, in Paris and later in Berlin and London she had a number of affairs: the most important and tempestuous was with the sculptor Thelma Wood. Befriended by such figures as the poet Mina Loy and the wealthy art patron Peggy Guggenheim, Barnes began to compose the stories for which she quickly became famous. Earlier, in *The Book of Repulsive Women*, she had produced macabre portraits of victimized females. In her next volume, *A Book* (1923), and in its 1929 reprint, *A Night among the Horses*, she depicted the baffling instability of relationships among characters who are estranged not only from all societal and religious traditions but also from each other and from themselves.

Barnes's next two books marked the beginning of her fascination with anachronistic literary models. Using Elizabethan diction, the *Ladies Almanack* (1928) records the life story of Dame Evangeline Musset, who had "developed in the Womb of her most gentle Mother to be a Boy," but "came forth an Inch or so less than this." Determined to "do it without the Tools for the Trade," Dame Musset embarks on the affairs that turn her into a lesbian saint or crusader. With its use of elaborate puns and fables, the *Ladies Almanack* presents fictionalized portraits of the expatriate writer Natalie Barney and the members of her salon. *Ryder* (1928), which Barnes described as a "female *Tom Jones*," focuses on the comic arrogance of a man who wants to establish himself as the father of the whole world.

The linguistic exuberance of these two books, along with their emphasis on female sexuality, also characterized Barnes's major work, *Nightwood*, an experimental novel that explores the love affair between two women and records the meditations on that affair furnished by a sage but derelict Doctor O'Connor, a character who made his first appearance in *Ryder*. But, in this work, Barnes presented a more tragic view of what she called the "stop[s] the mind makes between uncertainties," for all of her expatriated characters are lost to themselves and to each other. T. S. Eliot's introduction established the reputation of the novel, which was, he said, closer to Elizabethan poetry than modern prose. "Uncle Tom," as she called him, was Barnes's editor at Faber and Faber during the composition of *Nightwood* and *The Antiphon* (1958), a fact that may explain why the latter has been considered a response to Eliot's *Family Reunion*. A blank verse tragedy, *The Antiphon* is even more Gothic than *Nightwood* in its dramatization of the anguished confusion that is experienced by a mother and daughter during the reunion of a family which is in the process of destroying itself.

Although Eliot, like the critic Edwin Muir, continued to support Barnes after her return to America, she isolated herself in her apartment on Patchin Place, and retreated into decades of silence that were punctuated by quarrels, breakdowns, and hospitalizations or by the inquiries of her neighbor, the poet e.e. cummings, who would occasionally yell out of his window, "—Are ya still alive, Djuna?!" The writer Samuel Beckett, Peggy Guggenheim, Natalie Barney, and, eventually, the National Endowment for the Arts supplemented Barnes's meager income, and the novelists Anaïs Nin and John Hawkes acknowledged her influence on their own work, but, according to her biographer, Andrew Field, she was alienated from her native country, believing Americans to be "—A fierce sadistic race crouching behind radiators."

Cassation[1]

"Do you know Germany, Madame, Germany in the spring? It is charming then, do you not think so? Wide and clean, the Spree[2] winding thin and dark—and the roses! the yellow roses in the windows; and the bright talkative Americans passing through groups of German men staring over their *steins*, at the light and laughing women.

"It was such a spring, three years ago, that I came into Berlin from Russia. I was just sixteen, and my heart was a dancer's heart. It is that way sometimes; one's heart is all one thing for months, then—altogether another thing, *nicht wahr?*[3] I used to sit in the café at the end of the Zelten, eating eggs and drinking coffee, watching the sudden rain of sparrows. Their feet struck the table all together, and all together they cleared the crumbs, and all together they flew into the sky, so that the café was as suddenly without birds as it had been suddenly full of birds.

"Sometimes a woman came here, at about the same hour as myself, around four in the afternoon; once she came with a little man, quite dreamy and uncertain. But I must explain how she looked: *temperamentvoll*[4] and tall, *kraftvoll* and thin. She must have been forty then, dressed richly and carelessly. It seemed as though she could hardly keep her clothes on; her shoulders were always coming out, her skirt would be hanging on a hook, her pocket book would be mislaid, but all the time she was savage with jewels, and something purposeful and dramatic came in with her, as if she were the centre of a whirlpool, and her clothes a temporary debris.

"Sometimes she clucked the sparrows, and sometimes she talked to the *weinschenk*,[5] clasping her fingers together until the rings stood out and you could see through them, she was so vital and so wasted. As for her dainty little man, she would talk to him in English, so that I did not know where they came from.

"Then one week I stayed away from the café because I was trying out for the *Schauspielhaus*,[6] I heard they wanted a ballet dancer, and I was very anxious to get the part, so of course I thought of nothing else. I would wander, all by myself, through the *Tiergarten*,[7] or I would stroll down the *Sieges-Allee* where all the great German emperors' statues are, looking like widows. Then suddenly I thought of the *Zelten*, and of the birds, and of that tall odd woman and so I went back there, and there

---

1. An annullment or cancellation; also the dismissal of a soldier. The story was originally published under the title *A Little Girl Tells a Story to a Lady* in *A Night among the Horses* (1929); it was reprinted under the present title in *Spillway* (1972).
2. A small German river south of Berlin.

3. An idiomatic German expression meaning "Isn't it true?"
4. Temperamental; "kraftvoll": powerful.
5. Wine steward.
6. Theater.
7. Zoo. "Sieges-Allee": Victory Lane.

she was, sitting in the garden sipping beer and chuck-chucking the sparrows.

"When I came in, she got up at once and came over to me and said: 'Why, how do you do, I have missed you. Why did you not tell me that you were going away? I should have seen what I could do about it.' "

"She talked like that; a voice that touched the heart because it was so unbroken and clear. 'I have a house', she said, 'just on the Spree. You could have stayed with me. It is a big, large house, and you could have the room just off my room. It is difficult to live in, but it is lovely—Italian you know, like the interiors you see in Venetian paintings, where young girls lie dreaming of the Virgin. You could find that you could sleep there, because you have dedication.'

"Somehow it did not seem at all out of the way that she should come to me and speak to me. I said I would meet her again some day in the garden, and we could go 'home' together, and she seemed pleased, but did not show surprise.

"Then one evening we came into the garden at the same moment. It was late and the fiddles were already playing. We sat together without speaking, just listening to the music, and admiring the playing of the only woman member of the orchestra. She was very intent on the movement of her fingers, and seemed to be leaning over her chin to watch. Then suddenly the lady got up, leaving a small rain of coin, and I followed her until we came to a big house and she let herself in with a brass key. She turned to the left and went into a dark room and switched on the lights and sat down and said: 'This is where we sleep; this is how it is.'

"Everything was disorderly, and expensive and melancholy. Everything was massive and tall, or broad and wide. A chest of drawers rose above my head. The china stove was enormous and white, enamelled in blue flowers. The bed was so high that you could only think of it as something that might be overcome. The walls were all bookshelves, and all the books were bound in red morocco, on the back of each, in gold, was stamped a coat of arms, intricate and oppressive. She rang for tea and began taking off her hat.

"A great painting hung over the bed; the painting and the bed ran together in encounter, the huge rumps of the stallions reined into the pillows. The generals, with foreign helmets and dripping swords, raging through rolling smoke and the bleeding ranks of the dying, seemed to be charging the bed, so large, so rumpled, so devastated. The sheets were trailing, the counterpane hung torn, and the feathers shivered along the floor, trembling in the slight wind from the open window. The lady was smiling in a sad grave way, but she said nothing, and it was not until some moments later that I saw a child, not more than three years old, a small child, lying in the centre of the pillows, making a thin noise, like the buzzing of a fly, and I thought it was a fly.

"She did not talk to the child, indeed she paid no attention to it, as if it were in her bed and she did not know it. When the tea was brought in she poured it, but she took none, instead she drank small glasses of Rhine wine.

" 'You have seen Ludwig,' she said in her faint and grieving voice, 'we were married a long time ago, he was just a boy then. I? Me? I am an Italian, but I studied English and German because I was with a travelling company. You,' she said abruptly, 'you must give up the ballet—the theatre—acting.' Somehow I did not think it odd that she should know of my ambition, though I had not mentioned it. 'And', she went on, 'you are not for the stage; you are for something quieter, more withdrawn. See here, I like Germany very much, I have lived here a good many years. You will stay and you will see. You have seen Ludwig, you have noticed that he is not strong; he is always declining, you must have noticed it yourself; he must not be distressed, he can't bear anything. He has his room to himself.' She seemed suddenly tired, and she got up and threw herself across the bed, at the foot, and fell asleep, almost instantly, her hair all about her. I went away then, but I came back that night and tapped at the window. She came to the window and signed to me, and presently appeared at another window to the right of the bedroom, and beckoned with her hand, and I came up and climbed in, and did not mind that she had not opened the door for me. The room was dark except for the moon, and two thin candles burning before the Virgin.

"It was a beautiful room, Madame, *'traurig'*[8] as she said. Everything was important and old and gloomy. The curtains about the bed were red velvet, Italian you know, and fringed in gold bullion. The bed cover was a deep red velvet with the same gold fringe: on the floor, beside the bed, a stand on which was a tasselled red cushion, on the cushion a Bible in Italian, lying open.

"She gave me a long nightgown, it came below my feet and came back up again almost to my knees. She loosened my hair, it was long then, and yellow. She plaited it in two plaits; she put me down at her side and said a prayer in German, then in Italian, and ended, 'God bless you', and I got into bed. I loved her very much because there was nothing between us but this strange preparation for sleep. She went away then. In the night I heard the child crying, but I was tired.

"I stayed a year. The thought of the stage had gone out of my heart. I had become a *religieuse*; a gentle religion that began with the prayer I

8. Sad.

had said after her the first night, and the way I had gone to sleep, though we never repeated the ceremony. It grew with the furniture and the air of the whole room, and with the Bible lying open at a page that I could not read; a religion, Madame, that was empty of need, therefore it was not holy perhaps, and not as it should have been in its manner. It was that I was happy, and I lived there for one year. I almost never saw Ludwig, and almost never Valentine, for that was her child's name, a little girl.

"But at the end of that year I knew there was trouble in other parts of the house. I heard her walking in the night, sometimes Ludwig would be with her, I could hear him crying and talking, but I could not hear what was said. It sounded like a sort of lesson, a lesson for a child to repeat, but if so, there would have been no answer, for the child never uttered a sound, except that buzzing cry.

"Sometimes it is wonderful in Germany, Madame, *nicht wahr?* There is nothing like a German winter. She and I used to walk about the Imperial Palace, and she stroked the cannon, and said they were splendid. We talked about philosophy, for she was troubled with too much thinking, but she always came to the same conclusion, that one must be, or try to be, like everyone else. She explained that to be like everyone, all at once, in your own person, was to be holy. She said that people did not understand what was meant by 'Love thy neighbour as thyself.' It meant, she said, that one should be like all people *and* oneself, then, she said, one was both ruined and powerful.

"Sometimes it seemed that she was managing it, that she was all Germany, at least in her Italian heart. She seemed so irreparably collected and yet distressed, that I was afraid of her, and not afraid.

"That is the way it was, Madame, she seemed to wish it to be that way, though at night she was most scattered and distraught, I could hear her pacing in her room.

"Then she came in one night and woke me and said that I must come into her room. It was in a most terrible disorder. There was a small cot bed that had not been there before. She pointed to it and said that it was for me.

"The child was lying in the great bed against a large lace pillow. Now it was four years old and yet it did not walk, and I never heard it say a thing, or make a sound, except that buzzing cry. It was beautiful in the corrupt way of idiot children; a sacred beast without a taker, tainted with innocence and waste time; honey-haired and failing, like those dwarf angels on holy prints and valentines, if you understand me, Madame, something saved for a special day that would not arrive, not for life at all: and my lady was talking quietly, but I did not recognize any of her former state.

" 'You must sleep here now,' she said, 'I brought you here for this if I should need you, and I need you. You must stay, you must stay forever.' Then she said, 'Will you?' And I said no, I could not do that.

"She took up the candle and put it on the floor beside me, and knelt beside it, and put her arms about my knees. 'Are you a traitor?' she said, 'have you come into my house, Ludwig's house, the house of my child, to betray us?' And I said, no, I had not come to betray. 'Then', she said, 'you will do as I tell you. I will teach you slowly, slowly; it will not be too much for you, but you must begin to forget, you must forget *everything*. You must forget all the things people have told you. You must forget arguments and philosophy. I was wrong in talking of such things; I thought it would teach you how to lag with her mind, to undo time for her as it passes, to climb into her bereavement and her dispossession. I brought you up badly; I was vain. You will do better. Forgive me.' She put the palms of her hands on the floor, her face to my face. 'You must never see any other room than this room. It was a great vanity that I took you out walking. Now you will stay here safely, and you will see. You will like it, you will learn to like it the very best of all. I will bring you breakfast, and luncheon, and supper. I will bring it to you both, myself. I will hold you on my lap, I will feed you like the birds. I will rock you to sleep. You must not argue with me—above all we must have no arguments, no talk about man and his destiny—man has no destiny—that is my secret—I have been keeping it from you until today, this very hour. Why not before? Perhaps I was jealous of the knowledge, yes, that must be it, but now I give it to you, I share it with you. I am an old woman,' she said, still holding me by the knees. 'When Valentine was born, Ludwig was only a boy.' She got up and stood behind me. 'He is not strong, he does not understand that the weak are the strongest things in the world, because he is one of them. He cannot help her, they are adamant together. I need you, it must be you.' Suddenly she began talking to me as she talked with the child, and I did not know which of us she was talking to. 'Do not repeat anything after me. Why should children repeat what people say? The whole world is nothing but a noise, as hot as the inside of a tiger's mouth. They call it civilization—that is a lie! But some day you may have to go out, someone will try to take you out, and you will not understand them or what they are saying, unless you understand nothing, absolutely nothing, then you will manage.' She moved around so that she faced us, her back against the wall. 'Look,' she said, 'it is all over, it has gone away, you do not need to be afraid; there is only you. The stars are out, and the snow is falling down and covering the world, the hedges, the houses and the lamps. No, no!' she said to herself, 'wait. I will put you on your feet and tie you up in ribbons, and we will go out together, out into the garden where the swans are, and the flowers and the bees and small beasts. And the students will come because it will be summer, and they will read in their books. . . .' She broke off, then took her wild speech up again, this time as though she were really speaking to the child, 'Katya will go with you. She will instruct you, she will tell you there are no swans, no flowers, no beasts, no boys—*nothing*, nothing at all, just as you like it. No mind no thought, nothing whatsoever else. No bells will ring, no people will talk, no birds will fly, no boys will move, there'll be no birth and no death; no sorrow, no laughing, no kissing, no crying, no terror, no joy; no eating, no drinking, no games, no dancing; no father, no mother, no sisters, no brothers—only you, only you!'

"I stopped her and I said, 'Gaya, why is it that you suffer so, and what am I to do?' I tried to put my arms around her, but she struck them down crying, 'Silence!' Then she said, bringing her face close to my face, 'She has no claws to hang by; she has no hunting foot; she has no mouth for the meat—*vacancy!*'

"Then, Madame, I got up. It was very cold in the room. I went to the window and pulled the curtain, it was a bright and starry night, and I stood leaning my head against the frame, saying nothing. When I turned around, she was regarding me, her hands held apart, and I knew that I had to go away and leave her. So I came up to her and said, 'Good-bye, my Lady.' And I went and put on my street clothes, and when I came back she was leaning against the battle picture, her hands hanging. I said to her, without approaching her, 'Good-bye, my love,' and went away.

"Sometimes it is beautiful in Berlin, Madame, *nicht wahr?* There was something new in my heart, a passion to see Paris, so it was natural that I said *lebe wohl*[9] to Berlin.

"I went for the last time to the café in the Zelten, ate my eggs, drank my coffee and watched the birds coming and going just as they used to come and go—altogether here then altogether gone. I was happy in my spirit, for that is the way it is with my spirit, Madame, when I am going away.

"But I went back to her house just once. I went in quite easily by the door, for all the doors and windows were open—perhaps they were sweeping that day. I came to the bedroom door and knocked, but there was no answer. I pushed, and there she was, sitting up in the bed with the child, and she and the child were making that buzzing cry, and no human sound between them, and as usual, everything was in disorder. I came up to her, but she did not seem to know me. I said, 'I am going away; I am going to Paris. There is a longing in me to be in Paris. So I have come to say farewell.'

"She got down off the bed and came to the door with me. She said, 'Forgive me—I trusted you—I was mistaken. I did not know that I

9. Farewell.

could do it myself, but you see, I can do it myself.' Then she got back on to the bed and said, 'Go away,' and I went.

"Things are like that, when one travels, *nicht wahr*, Madame?"

1929, 1972

REBECCA WEST
1892–1983

"Ladies of Great Britain," Rebecca West exclaimed in 1912, "we are clever, we are trustworthy, we are twice the women that our grandmothers were, but we have not enough evil in us." But West herself published caustic journalism and fiction that led a number of her contemporaries to condemn her as demonically rebellious. Her choice of a pseudonym was part of the rebellion she fomented for women's economic and sexual freedom. Born Cicily Isabel Fairfield, the youngest of three daughters of Isabella McKenzie, a Scots pianist, and Captain Charles Fairfield, an impoverished Irish journalist, West went to school in Edinburgh, but left at sixteen for the London stage. Though her theatrical career was short-lived, it gave her the name that she would quickly make famous: one script she read was Henrik Ibsen's *Rosmersholm* (1886), a play about a radical feminist named Rebecca West. Writing in the feminist journal *The Freewoman* and the socialist weekly *The Clarion*, the nineteen-year-old who now called herself Rebecca West reviewed books by antisuffragists like Mrs. Humphrey Ward and suffragists like Olive Schreiner, even as she argued for free love and women's trade unions and against imperialism and conservative divorce laws.

To an unfortunate extent, West's part in the journalistic radicalism preceding World War I has been obscured in literary history by the attention paid to her ten-year affair with the novelist H. G. Wells and by her son Anthony West's recent attacks on her. As the critic Gordon Ray has shown in his *H. G. Wells and Rebecca West*, West at twenty was understandably drawn to the forty-six-year-old spokesman for societal reform, but she was also convinced that she was right in the review she wrote about the antifeminism of Wells's early novels, an essay that first attracted him to her in 1912. In any case, when West gave birth to Wells's son in 1914, she became responsive to the cause of unwed mothers. Her novel *The Judge* (1922) was the most direct expression of this concern, placing the issues of rape, illegitimacy, and motherhood in the context of the suffrage struggle, but an early war novel like *The Return of the Soldier* (1918) also described the sham conventionalities and desexualization of traditional marriage.

Throughout the twenties, West wrote a series of literary reviews for the *New Statesman*, and, during the thirties, she produced more novels. Moreover, from her study of Henry James (1916) to her biography of St. Augustine (1933), she exploited the insights of psychology, a fact that helps explain her early enthusiasm for the fiction of Virginia Woolf and D. H. Lawrence. In 1930, she married a banker, Henry Maxwell Andrews, and moved with him to a country house in Buckinghamshire. During World War II, she published *Black Lamb and Grey Falcon* (1941), a travel book that was also a powerful attack on Nazism. By the fifties, however, West had been converted from a feminist-socialist to a conservative anti-Communist. In 1959, the year before her husband died, she was created a Dame Commander of the British Empire, a strange fate for the woman who had written forty-seven years earlier that "there are two kinds of imperialists—imperialists and bloody imperialists." Nevertheless, despite her political turnabout, Dame Rebecca never lost sight of the fact that, "like all terrible and wicked things, sex-antagonism has a sound logical basis," and it is the nature of sex-antagonism that she analyzed in *Indissoluble Matrimony*, a story that the scholar Jane Marcus has recently recovered from critical neglect.

Indissoluble Matrimony

When George Silverton opened the front door he found that the house was not empty for all its darkness. The spitting noise of the striking of damp matches and mild, growling exclamations of annoyance told him that his wife was trying to light the dining-room gas. He went in and with some short, hostile sound of greeting lit a match and brought brightness into the little room. Then, irritated by his own folly in bringing private papers into his wife's presence, he stuffed the letters he had brought from the office deep into the pockets of his overcoat. He looked at her suspiciously, but she had not seen them, being busy in unwinding her orange motor-veil.[1] His eyes remained on her face to brood a little sourly on her moving loveliness, which he had not been sure of finding: for she was one of those women who create an illusion alternately of extreme beauty and extreme ugliness. Under her curious dress, designed in some pitifully cheap and worthless stuff by a successful mood of her indiscreet taste—she had black blood in her—her long body seemed pulsing with some exaltation. The blood was coursing violently under her luminous yellow skin, and her lids, dusky with fatigue, drooped contentedly over her great humid black eyes. Perpetually she raised her hand to the mass of black hair that was coiled on her thick golden neck and stroked it with secretive enjoyment, as a cat licks its fur. And her large mouth smiled frankly, but abstractedly, at some digested pleasure.

There was a time when George would have looked on this riot of excited loveliness with suspicion. But now he knew it was almost certainly caused by some trifle—a long walk through stinging weather, the report of a socialist victory at a by-election, or the intoxication of a waltz refrain floating from the municipal bandstand across the flats of the

1. A scarf worn in open automobiles.

local recreation ground. And even if it had been caused by some amorous interlude he would not have greatly cared. In the ten years since their marriage he had lost the quality which would have made him resentful. He now believed that quality to be purely physical. Unless one was in good condition and responsive to the messages sent out by the flesh Evadne could hardly concern one. He turned the bitter thought over in his heart and stung himself by deliberately gazing unmoved upon her beautiful joyful body.

"Let's have supper now!" she said rather greedily.

He looked at the table and saw she had set it before she went out. As usual she had been in an improvident hurry: it was carelessly done. Besides what an absurd supper to set before a hungry solicitor's[2] clerk! In the centre, obviously intended as the principal dish, was a bowl of plums, softly red, soaked with the sun, glowing like jewels in the downward stream of the incandescent light. Beside them was a great yellow melon, its sleek sides fluted with rich growth, and a honeycomb glistening on a willow-pattern dish. The only sensible food to be seen was a plate of tongue laid at his place.

"I can't sit down to supper without washing my hands!"

While he splashed in the bathroom upstairs he heard her pull a chair to the table and sit down to her supper. It annoyed him. There was no ritual about it. While he was eating the tongue she would be crushing honey on new bread, or stripping a plum of its purple skin and holding the golden globe up to the gas to see the light filter through. The meal would pass in silence. She would innocently take his dumbness for a sign of abstraction and forbear to babble. He would find the words choked on his lips by the weight of dullness that always oppressed him in her presence. Then, just about the time when he was beginning to feel able to formulate his obscure grievances against her, she would rise from the table without a word and run upstairs to her work, humming in that uncanny, Negro way of hers.

And so it was. She ate with an appalling catholicity of taste, with a nice child's love of sweet foods, and occasionally she broke into that hoarse, beautiful croon. Every now and then she looked at him with too obvious speculations as to whether his silence was due to weariness or uncertain temper. Timidly she cut him an enormous slice of the melon, which he did not want. Then she rose abruptly and flung herself into the rocking-chair on the hearth. She clasped her hands behind her head and strained backwards so that the muslin stretched over her strong breasts. She sang softly to the ceiling.

There was something about the fantastic figure that made him feel as though they were not properly married.

2. Lawyer's.

"Evadne?"

" 'S?"

"What have you been up to this evening?"

"I was at Milly Stafordale's."

He was silent again. That name brought up the memory of his courting days. It was under the benign eyes of blonde, plebeian Milly that he had wooed the distracting creature in the rocking-chair.

Ten years before, when he was twenty-five, his firm had been reduced to hysteria over the estates of an extraordinarily stupid old woman, named Mrs. Mary Ellerker. Her stupidity, grappling with the complexity of the sources of the vast income which rushed in spate from the properties of four deceased husbands, demanded oceans of explanations even over her weekly rents. Silverton alone in the office, by reason of a certain natural incapacity for excitement, could deal calmly with this marvel of imbecility. He alone could endure to sit with patience in the black-panelled drawing-room amidst the jungle of shiny mahogany furniture and talk to a mass of darkness, who rested heavily in the window-seat and now and then made an idiotic remark in a bright, hearty voice. But it shook even him. Mrs. Mary Ellerker was obscene. Yet she was perfectly sane and although of that remarkable plainness noticeable in most oft-married women, in good enough physical condition. She merely presented the loathsome spectacle of an ignorant mind, contorted by the artificial idiocy of coquetry, lack of responsibility and hatred of discipline, stripped naked by old age. That was the real horror of her. One feared to think how many women were really like Mrs. Ellerker under their armour of physical perfection or social grace. For this reason he turned eyes of hate on Mrs. Ellerker's pretty little companion, Milly Stafordale, who smiled at him over her embroidery with wintry northern brightness. When she was old she too would be obscene.

This horror obsessed him. Never before had he feared anything. He had never lived more than half an hour from a police station and, as he had by some chance missed the melancholy clairvoyance of adolescence, he had never conceived of any horror with which the police could not deal. This disgust of women revealed to him that the world is a place of subtle perils. He began to fear marriage as he feared death. The thought of intimacy with some lovely, desirable and necessary wife turned him sick as he sat at his lunch. The secret obscenity of women! He talked darkly of it to his friends. He wondered why the Church did not provide a service for the absolution of men after marriage. Wife desertion seemed to him a beautiful return of the tainted body to cleanliness.

On his fifth visit to Mrs. Ellerker he could not begin his business at once. One of Milly Stafordale's friends had come in to sing to the old lady. She stood by the piano against the light, so that he saw her washed with darkness. And before he had time to apprehend the sleepy wonder of her beauty, she had begun to sing. Now he knew that her voice was a purely physical attribute, built in her as she lay in her mother's womb, and no index of her spiritual values. But then, as it welled up from the thick golden throat and clung to her lips, it seemed a sublime achievement of the soul. It was a smouldering contralto such as only those of black blood can possess. As she sang her great black eyes lay on him with the innocent shamelessness of a young animal, and he remembered hopefully that he was good-looking. Suddenly she stood in silence, playing with her heavy black plait. Mrs. Ellerker broke into silly thanks. The girl's mother, who had been playing the accompaniment, rose and stood rolling up her music. Silverton, sick with excitement, was introduced to them. He noticed that the mother was a little darker than the conventions permit. Their name was Hannan—Mrs. Arthur Hannan and Evadne. They moved lithely and quietly out of the room, the girl's eyes still lingering on his face.

The thought of her splendour and the rolling echoes of her voice disturbed him all night. Next day, going to his office, he travelled with her on the horse-car that bound his suburb to Petrick. One of the horses fell lame, and she had time to tell him that she was studying at a commercial college. He quivered with distress. All the time he had a dizzy illusion that she was nestling up against him. They parted shyly. During the next few days they met constantly. He began to go and see them in the evening at their home—a mean flat crowded with cheap glories of bead curtains and Oriental hangings that set off the women's alien beauty. Mrs Hannan was a widow and they lived alone, in a wonderful silence. He talked more than he had ever done in his whole life before. He took a dislike to the widow, she was consumed with fiery passions, no fit guardian for the tender girl.

Now he could imagine with what silent rapture Evadne had watched his agitation. Almost from the first she had meant to marry him. He was physically attractive, though not strong. His intellect was gently stimulating like a mild white wine. And it was time she married. She was ripe for adult things. This was the real wound in his soul. He had tasted of a divine thing created in his time for dreams out of her rich beauty, her loneliness, her romantic poverty, her immaculate youth. He had known love. And Evadne had never known anything more than a magnificent physical adventure which she had secured at the right time as she would have engaged a cab to take her to the station in time for the cheapest excursion train. It was a quick way to light-hearted living. With loathing he remembered how in the days of their engagement she used to gaze purely into his blinking eyes and with her unashamed kisses incite him to extravagant embraces. Now he cursed her for having obtained his spiritual revolution on false pretences. Only for a little time had he had his illusion, for their marriage was hastened by Mrs. Hannan's sudden death. After three months of savage mourning Evadne flung herself into marriage, and her excited candour had enlightened him very soon.

That marriage had lasted ten years. And to Evadne their relationship was just the same as ever. Her vitality needed him as it needed the fruit on the table before him. He shook with wrath and a sense of outraged decency.

"Oh George!" She was yawning widely.

"What's the matter?" he said without interest.

"It's so beastly dull."

"I can't help that, can I?"

"No." She smiled placidly at him. "We're a couple of dull dogs, aren't we? I wish we had children."

After a minute she suggested, apparently as an alternative amusement, "Perhaps the post hasn't passed."

As she spoke there was a rat-tat and the slither of a letter under the door. Evadne picked herself up and ran out of the lobby. After a second or two, during which she made irritating inarticulate exclamations, she came in reading the letter and stroking her bust with a gesture of satisfaction.

"They want me to speak at Longton's meeting on the nineteenth," she purred.

"Longton? What's he up to?"

Stephen Longton was the owner of the biggest iron-works in Petrick, a man whose refusal to adopt the livery of busy oafishness thought proper to commercial men aroused the gravest suspicions.

"He's standing as socialist candidate for the town council."

" . . . Socialist!" he muttered.

He set his jaw. That was a side of Evadne he considered as little as possible. He had never been able to assimilate the fact that Evadne had, two years after their marriage, passed through his own orthodox radicalism to a passionate socialism, and that after reading enormously of economics she had begun to write for the socialist Press and to speak successfully at meetings. In the jaundiced recesses of his mind he took it for granted that her work would have the lax fibre of her character: that it would be infected with her Oriental crudities. Although once or twice he had been congratulated on her brilliance, he mistrusted this phase in her activity as a caper of the sensualist. His eyes blazed on her and found the depraved, over-sexed creature, looking milder than a gazelle, holding out a handbill to him.

"They've taken it for granted!"

He saw her name—his name—MRS. EVADNE SILVERTON.

It was at first the blaze of stout scarlet letters on the dazzling white ground that made him blink. Then he was convulsed with rage.

"Georgie dear!"

She stepped forward and caught his weak body to her bosom. He wrenched himself away. Spiritual nausea made him determined to be a better man than her.

"A pair of you! You and Longton!" he snarled scornfully. Then seeing her startled face, he controlled himself.

"I thought it would please you," said Evadne, a little waspishly.

"You mustn't have anything to do with Longton," he stormed.

A change passed over her. She became ugly. Her face was heavy with intellect, her lips coarse with power. He was at arms with a socialist leader. Much would he have preferred the bland sensualist again.

"Why?"

"Because," his lips stuck together like blotting paper "he's not the sort of man my wife should—should—."

With movements which terrified him by their rough energy, she folded up the bills and put them back in the envelope.

"George. I suppose you mean that he's a bad man." He nodded. "I know quite well that the girl who used to be his typist is his mistress." She spoke it sweetly, as if reasoning with an old fool. "But she's got consumption. She'll be dead in six months. In fact, I think it's rather nice of him. To look after her and all that."

"My God!" He leapt to his feet, extending a shaking forefinger. As she turned to him, the smile dying on her lips, his excited weakness wrapped him in a paramnesic illusion: it seemed to him that he had been through all this before—a long, long time ago. "My God, you talk like a woman off the streets!"

Evadne's lips lifted over her strong teeth. With clever cruelty she fixed his eyes with hers, well knowing that he longed to fall forward and bury his head on the table in a transport of hysterical sobs. After a moment of this torture she turned away, herself distressed by a desire to cry.

"How can you say such dreadful, dreadful things!" she protested, chokingly.

He sat down again. His eyes looked little and red, but they blazed on her. "I wonder if you are," he said softly.

"Are what?" she asked petulantly, a tear rolling down her nose.

"You know," he answered, nodding.

"George, George, George!" she cried.

"You've always been keen on kissing and making love, haven't you, my precious. At first you startled me, you did! I didn't know women were like that." From that morass he suddenly stepped on to a high peak of terror. Amazed to find himself sincere, he cried, "I don't believe good women are!"

"Georgie, how can you be so silly!" exclaimed Evadne shrilly. 'You know quite well I've been as true to you as any woman could be." She sought his eyes with a liquid glance of reproach. He averted his gaze, sickened at having put himself in the wrong. For even while he degraded his tongue his pure soul fainted with loathing of her fleshliness.

"I . . . I'm sorry."

Too wily to forgive him at once, she showed him a lowering profile with downcast lids. Of course, he knew it was a fraud. An imputation against her chastity was no more poignant than a reflection on the cleanliness of her nails—rude and spiteful, but that was all. But for a time they kept up the deception, while she cleared the table in steely silence.

"Evadne, I'm sorry. I'm tired." His throat was dry. He could not bear the discord of a row added to the horror of their companionship. "Evadne, do forgive me—I don't know what I meant by. . . ."

"That's all right, silly!" she said suddenly and bent over the table to kiss him. Her brow was smooth. It was evident from her splendid expression that she was preoccupied. Then she finished clearing up the dishes and took them into the kitchen. While she was out of the room he rose from his seat and sat down in the armchair by the fire, setting his bulldog pipe alight. For a very short time he was free of her voluptuous presence. But she ran back soon, having put the kettle on and changed her blouse for a loose dressing-jacket, and sat down on the arm of his chair. Once or twice she bent and kissed his brow, but for the most part she lay back with his head drawn to her bosom, rocking herself rhythmically. Silverton, a little disgusted by their contact, sat quite motionless and passed into a doze. He revolved in his mind the incidents of his day's routine and remembered a snub from a superior. So he opened his eyes and tried to think of something else. It was then that he became conscious that the rhythm of Evadne's movement was not regular. It was broken as though she rocked in time to music. Music? His sense of hearing crept up to hear if there was any sound of music in the breaths she was emitting rather heavily, every now and then. At first he could hear nothing. Then it struck him that each breath was a muttered phrase. He stiffened, and hatred flamed through his veins. The words came clearly through her lips. . . . "The present system of wage-slavery. . . ."

"Evadne!" He sprang to his feet. "You're preparing your speech!"

She did not move. "I am," she said.

"Damn it, you shan't speak!"

"Damn it, I will!"

"Evadne, you shan't speak! If you do I swear to God above I'll turn you out into the streets." She rose and came towards him. She looked black and dangerous. She trod softly like a cat with her head down. In spite of himself, his tongue licked his lips in fear and he cowered a moment before he picked up a knife from the table. For a space she looked down on him and the sharp blade.

"You idiot, can't you hear the kettle's boiling over?"

He shrank back, letting the knife fall on the floor. For three minutes he stood there controlling his breath and trying to still his heart. Then he followed her into the kitchen. She was making a noise with a basinful of dishes.

"Stop that row."

She turned round with a dripping dishcloth in her hand and pondered whether to throw it at him. But she was tired and wanted peace; so that she could finish the rough draft of her speech. So she stood waiting.

"Did you understand what I said then? If you don't promise me here and now. . . . "

She flung her arms upwards with a cry and dashed past him. He made to run after her upstairs, but stumbled on the threshold of the lobby and sat with his ankle twisted under him, shaking with rage. In a second she ran downstairs again, clothed in a big cloak with a black bundle clutched to her breast. For the first time in their married life she was seized with a convulsion of sobs. She dashed out the front door and banged it with such passion that a glass pane shivered to fragments behind her.

"What's this? What's this?" he cried stupidly, standing up. He perceived with an insane certainty that she was going to meet some unknown lover. "I'll come and tell him what a slut you are!" he shouted after her and stumbled to the door. It was jammed now and he had to drag at it.

The night was flooded with the yellow moonshine of midsummer; it seemed to drip from the lacquered leaves of the shrubs in the front garden. In its soft clarity he could see her plainly, although she was now two hundred yards away. She was hastening to the north end of Sumatra Crescent, an end that curled up the hill like a silly kitten's tail and stopped abruptly in green fields. So he knew that she was going to the young man who had just bought the Georgian manor, whose elm trees crowned the hill. Oh, how he hated her! Yet he must follow her, or else she would cover up her adulteries so that he could not take his legal revenge. So he began to run—silently, for he wore his carpet-slippers. He was only a hundred yards behind her when she slipped through a gap in the hedge to tread a field-path. She still walked with pride, for though she was town-bred, night in the open seemed not at all fearful to her. As he shuffled in pursuit his carpet-slippers were engulfed in a shining pool of mud. He raised one with a squelch, the other was left. This seemed the last humiliation. He kicked the other one off his foot and padded on in his socks, snuffling in anticipation of a cold. Then physical pain sent him back to the puddle to pluck out the slippers. It was a dirty job. His heart battered his breast as he saw that Evadne had gained the furthest hedge and was crossing the stile into the lane that ran up to the manor gates.

"Go on, you beast!" he muttered. "Go on, go on!" After a scamper he climbed the stile and thrust his lean neck beyond a mass of wilted hawthorn bloom that crumbled into vagrant petals at his touch.

The lane mounted yellow as cheese to where the moon lay on the iron tracery of the manor gates. Evadne was not there. Hardly believing his eyes he hobbled over into the lane and looked in the other direction. There he saw her disappearing round the bend of the road. Gathering himself up to a run, he tried to think out his bearings. He had seldom passed this way, and like most people without strong primitive instincts he had no sense of orientation. With difficulty he remembered that after a mile's mazy wanderings between high hedges this lane sloped suddenly to the bowl of heather overhung by the moorlands, in which lay the Petrick reservoirs, two untamed lakes.

"Eh! She's going to meet him by the water!" he cursed to himself. He remembered the withered ash tree, seared by lightning to its root, that stood by the road at the bare frontier of the moor. "May God strike her like that," he prayed, "as she fouls the other man's lips with her kisses. Oh God! Let me strangle her. Or bury a knife deep in her breast." Suddenly he broke into a lolloping run. "Oh my Lord, I'll be able to divorce her. I'll be free. Free to live alone. To do my day's work and sleep my night's sleep without her. I'll get a job somewhere else and forget her. I'll bring her to the dogs. No clean man or woman in Petrick will look at her now. They won't have her to speak at that meeting now!" His throat swelled with joy, he leapt high in the air.

"I'll lie about her. If I can prove that she's wrong with this man they'll believe me if I say she's a bad woman and drinks. I'll make her name a joke. And then. . . ."

He flung wide his arms in ecstasy: the left struck against stone. More pain than he had thought his body could hold convulsed him, so that he sank on the ground hugging his aching arm. He looked backwards as he writhed and saw that the hedge had stopped; above him was the great stone wall of the county asylum. The question broke on him—was there any lunatic in its confines so slavered with madness as he himself? Nothing but madness could have accounted for the torrent of ugly words, the sea of uglier thoughts that was now a part of him. "Oh God, for me to turn like this!" he cried, rolling over full-length on the grassy bank by the roadside. That the infidelity of his wife, a thing that should have brought out the stern manliness of his true nature, should have discovered him as lecherous-lipped as any pot-house[3] lounger, was the most infamous accident of his married life. The sense of sin descended on him so that his tears flowed hot and bitterly. "Have I gone to the Unitarian chapel every Sunday morning and to the Ethical Society every evening for nothing?" his spirit asked itself in its travail. "All those Browning lectures[4] for nothing. . . ." He said the Lord's Prayer several times and lay for a minute quietly crying. The relaxation of his muscles brought him a sense of rest which seemed forgiveness falling from God. The tears dried on his cheeks. His calmer consciousness heard the sound of rushing waters mingled with the beating of blood in his ears. He got up and scrambled round the turn of the road that brought him to the withered ash tree.

He walked forward on the parched heatherland to the mound whose scarred sides, heaped with boulders, tufted with mountain grasses, shone before him in the moonlight. He scrambled up to it hurriedly and hoisted himself from ledge to ledge till he fell on his knees with a squeal of pain. His ankle was caught in a crevice of the rock. Gulping down his agony at this final physical humiliation he heaved himself upright and raced on to the summit, and found himself before the Devil's Cauldron, filled to the brim with yellow moonshine and the fiery play of summer lightning. The rugged crags opposite him were a low barricade against the stars to which the mound where he stood shot forward like a bridge. To the left of this the long Lisbech pond lay like a trailing serpent; its silver scales glittered as the wind swept down from the vaster moorlands to the east. To the right under a steep drop of twenty feet was the Whimsey pond, more sinister, shaped in an unnatural oval, sheltered from the wind by the high ridge so that the undisturbed moonlight lay across it like a sharp-edged sword.

He looked about for some sign of Evadne. She could not be on the land by the margin of the lakes, for the light blazed so strongly that each reed could be clearly seen like a black dagger stabbing the silver. He looked down Lisbech and saw far east a knot of red and green and orange lights. Perhaps for some devilish purpose Evadne had sought Lisbech railway station. But his volcanic mind had preserved one grain of sense that assured him that, subtle as Evadne's villainy might be, it would not lead her to walk five miles out of her way to a terminus which she could have reached in fifteen minutes by taking a train from the station down the road. She must be under cover somewhere here. He went down the gentle slope that fell from the top of the ridge to Lisbech pond in a disorder of rough heather, unhappy patches of cultivated

3. Tavern.
4. Lectures given under the auspices of the Browning Society, a popular literary society de-voted chiefly to the works of the English poet Robert Browning (1812–1889).

grass and coppices of silver birch, fringed with flaming broom that seemed faintly tarnished in the moonlight. At the bottom was a roughly hewn path which he followed in hot aimless hurry. In a little he approached a riot of falling waters. There was a slice ten feet broad carved out of the ridge, and to this narrow channel of black shining rock the floods of Lisbech leapt some feet and raced through to Whimsey. The noise beat him back. The gap was spanned by a gaunt thing of paint-blistered iron, on which he stood dizzily and noticed how the wide step that ran on each side of the channel through to the other pond was smeared with sinister green slime. Now his physical distress reminded him of Evadne, whom he had almost forgotten in contemplation of these lonely waters. The idea of her had been present but obscured, as sometimes toothache may cease active torture. His blood-lust set him on and he staggered forward with covered ears. Even as he went something caught his eye in a thicket high up on the slope near the crags. Against the slender pride of some silver birches stood a gnarled hawthorn tree, its branches flattened under the stern moorland winds so that it grew squat like an opened umbrella. In its dark shadows, faintly illumined by a few boughs of withered blossom, there moved a strange bluish light. Even while he did not know what it was it made his flesh stir.

The light emerged. It was the moonlight reflected from Evadne's body. She was clad in a black bathing-dress, and her arms and legs and the broad streak of flesh laid bare by a rent down the back shone brilliantly white, so that she seemed like a grotesquely patterned wild animal as she ran down to the lake. Whirling her arms above her head she trampled down into the water and struck out strongly. Her movements were full of brisk delight and she swam quickly. The moonlight made her the center of a little feathery blur of black and silver, with a comet's tail trailing in her wake.

Nothing in all his married life had ever staggered Silverton so much as this. He had imagined his wife's adultery so strongly that it had come to be. It was now as real as their marriage; more real than their courtship. So this seemed to be the last crime of the adulteress. She had dragged him over those squelching fields and these rough moors and changed him from a man of irritations, but no passions, into a cold designer of murderous treacheries, so that he might witness a swimming exhibition! For a minute he was stunned. Then he sprang down to the rushy edge and ran along in the direction of her course, crying, "Evadne! Evadne!" She did not hear him. At last he achieved a chest-note and shouted, "Evadne! Come here!" The black-and-silver feather shivered in mid-water. She turned immediately and swam back to shore. He suspected sullenness in her slowness, but was glad of it, for after the shock of this extraordinary incident he wanted to go to sleep.

Drowsiness lay on him like lead. He shook himself like a dog and wrenched off his linen collar, winking at the bright moon to keep himself awake. As she came quite near he was exasperated by the happy, snorting breaths she drew, and strolled a pace or two up the bank. To his enragement the face she lifted as she waded to dry land was placid, and she scrambled gaily up the bank to his side.

"Oh George, why did you come!" she exclaimed quite affectionately, laying a damp hand on his shoulder.

"Oh damn it, what does this mean?" he cried, committing a horrid tenor squeak. "What are you doing?"

"Why, George," she said, "I came here for a bathe."

He stared into her face and could make nothing of it. It was only sweet surfaces of flesh, soft radiances of eye and lip, a lovely lie of comeliness. He forgot this present grievance in a cold search for the source of her peculiar hatefulness. Under this sick gaze she pouted and turned away with a peevish gesture. He made no sign and stood silent, watching her saunter to that gaunt iron bridge. The roar of the little waterfall did not disturb her splendid nerves and she drooped sensuously over the hand-rail, sniffing up the sweet night smell; too evidently trying to abase him to another apology.

A mosquito whirred into his face. He killed it viciously and strode off towards his wife, who showed by a common little toss of the head that she was conscious of his coming.

"Look here, Evadne!" he panted. "What did you come here for? Tell me the truth and I promise I'll not . . . I'll not. . . ."

"Not *what*, George?"

"Oh please, please tell me the truth, do Evadne!" he cried pitifully.

"But, dear, what is there to carry on about so? You went on so queerly about my meeting that my head felt fit to split, and I thought the long walk and the dip would do me good." She broke off, amazed at the wave of horror that passed over his face.

His heart sank. From the loose-lipped hurry in the telling of her story, from the bigness of her eyes and the lack of subtlety in her voice, he knew that this was the truth. Here was no adulteress whom he could accuse in the law courts and condemn into the street, no resourceful sinner whose merry crimes he could discover. Here was merely his good wife, the faithful attendant of his hearth, relentless wrecker of his soul.

She came towards him as a cat approaches a displeased master, and hovered about him on the stone coping of the noisy sluice.

"Indeed!" he found himself saying sarcastically. "Indeed!"

"Yes, George Silverton, indeed!" she burst out, a little frightened. "And why shouldn't I? I used to come here often enough on summer nights with poor Mamma.'

"Yes!" he shouted. It was exactly the sort of thing that would appeal to that weird half-black woman from the back of beyond. "Mamma!" he cried tauntingly, "Mamma!"

There was a flash of silence between them before Evadne, clutching her breast and balancing herself dangerously on her heels on the stone coping, broke into gentle shrieks. "You dare talk of my Mamma, my poor Mamma, and she cold in her grave! I haven't been happy since she died and I married you, you silly little misery, you!" Then the rage was suddenly wiped off her brain by the perception of a crisis.

The trickle of silence overflowed into a lake, over which their spirits flew, looking at each other's reflection in the calm waters: in the hurry of their flight they had never before seen each other. They stood facing one another with dropped heads, quietly thinking.

The strong passion which filled them threatened to disintegrate their souls as a magnetic current decomposes the electrolyte,[5] so they fought to organise their sensations. They tried to arrange themselves and their lives for comprehension, but beyond sudden lyric visions of old incidents of hatefulness—such as a smarting quarrel of six years ago as to whether Evadne had or had not cheated the railway company out of one-and-eightpence on an excursion ticket—the past was intangible. It trailed behind this intense event as the pale hair trails behind the burning comet. They were preoccupied with the moment. Quite often George had found a mean pleasure in the thought that by never giving Evadne a child he had cheated her out of one form of experience, and now he paid the price of this unnatural pride of sterility. For now the spiritual offspring of their intercourse came to birth. A sublime loathing was between them. For a little time it was a huge perilous horror, but afterwards, like men aboard a ship whose masts seek the sky through steep waves, they found a drunken pride in the adventure. This was the very absolute of hatred. It cheapened the memory of the fantasias of irritation and ill-will they had performed in the less boring moments of their marriage, and they felt dazed, as amateurs who had found themselves creating a masterpiece. For the first time they were possessed by a supreme emotion and they felt a glad desire to strip away restraint and express it nakedly. It was ecstasy; they felt tall and full of blood.

Like people who, bewitched by Christ, see the whole earth as the breathing body of God, so they saw the universe as the substance and the symbol of their hatred. The stars trembled overhead with wrath. A wind from behind the angry crags set the moonlight on Lisbech quivering with rage, and the squat hawthorn tree creaked slowly like the irritation of a dull little man. The dry moors, parched with harsh anger, waited thirstily and, sending out the murmur of rustling mountain grass

---

5. A substance that conducts electricity.

and the cry of wakening fowl, seemed to huddle closer to the lake. But this sense of the earth's sympathy slipped away from them and they loathed all matter as the dull wrapping of their flame-like passion. At their wishing matter fell away and they saw sarcastic visions. He saw her as a toad squatting on the clean earth, obscuring the stars and pressing down its hot moist body on the cheerful fields. She felt his long boneless body coiled round the roots of the lovely tree of life. They shivered fastidiously. With an uplifting sense of responsibility they realised that they must kill each other.

A bird rose over their heads with a leaping flight that made it seem as though its black body was bouncing against the bright sky. The foolish noise and motion precipitated their thoughts. They were broken into a new conception of life. They perceived that God is war and his creatures are meant to fight. When dogs walk through the world cats must climb trees. The virgin must snare the wanton, the fine lover must put the prude to the sword. The gross man of action walks, spurred on by the bloodless bodies of the men of thought, who lie quiet and cunningly do not tell him where his grossness leads him. The flesh must smother the spirit, the spirit must set the flesh on fire and watch it burn. And those who were gentle by nature and shrank from the ordained brutality were betrayers of their kind, surrendering the earth to the seed of their enemies. In this war there is no discharge. If they succumbed to peace now, the rest of their lives would be dishonourable, like the exile of a rebel who has begged his life as the reward of cowardice. It was their first experience of religious passion, and they abandoned themselves to it so that their immediate personal qualities fell away from them. Neither his weakness nor her prudence stood in the way of the event.

They measured each other with the eye. To her he was a spidery thing against the velvet blackness and hard silver surfaces of the pond. The light soaked her bathing-dress so that she seemed, against the jagged shadows of the rock cutting, as though she were clad in a garment of dark polished mail. Her knees were bent so clearly, her toes gripped the coping so strongly. He understood very clearly that if he did not kill her instantly she would drop him easily into the deep riot of waters. Yet for a space he could not move, but stood expecting a degrading death. Indeed, he gave her time to kill him. But she was without power too, and struggled weakly with a hallucination. The quarrel in Sumatra Crescent with its suggestion of vast and unmentionable antagonisms; her swift race through the moon-drenched countryside, all crepitant with night noises; the swimming in the wine-like lake; their isolation on the moor, which was expressedly hostile to them, as nature always is to lonely man; and this stark contest face to face, with their resentments heaped between them like a pile of naked swords—these things were so strange that her civilised self shrank back appalled. There entered into her the primitive woman who is the curse of all women: a creature of the most utter femaleness, useless, save for childbirth, with no strong brain to make her physical weakness a light accident, abjectly and corruptingly afraid of man. A squaw, she dared not strike her lord.

The illusion passed like a moment of faintness and left her enraged at having forgotten her superiority even for an instant. In the material world she had a thousand times been defeated into making prudent reservations and practising unnatural docilities. But in the world of thought she had maintained unfalteringly her masterfulness in spite of the strong yearning of her temperament towards voluptuous surrenders. That was her virtue. Its violation whipped her to action and she would have killed him at once, had not his moment come a second before hers. Sweating horribly, he had dropped his head forward on his chest; his eyes fell on her feet and marked the plebeian moulding of her ankle, which rose thickly over a crease of flesh from the heel to the calf. The woman was coarse in grain and pattern.

He had no instinct for honourable attack, so he found himself striking her in the stomach. She reeled from pain, not because his strength overcame hers. For the first time her eyes looked into his candidly open, unveiled by languor or lust; their hard brightness told him how she despised him for that unwarlike blow. He cried out as he realised that this was another of her despicable victories and that the whole burden of the crime now lay on him, for he had begun it. But the rage was stopped on his lips as her arms, flung wildly out as she fell backwards, caught him about the waist with abominable justness of eye and evil intention. So they fell body to body into the quarrelling waters.

The feathery confusion had looked so soft, yet it seemed the solid rock they struck. The breath shot out of him and suffocation warmly stuffed his ears and nose. Then the rock cleft and he was swallowed by a brawling blackness in which whirled a vortex that flung him again and again on a sharp thing that burned his shoulder. All about him fought the waters, and they cut his flesh like knives. His pain was past belief. Though God might be war, he desired peace in his time, and he yearned for another God—a child's God, an immense arm coming down from the hills and lifting him to a kindly bosom. Soon his body would burst for breath, his agony would smash in his breast-bone. So great was his pain that his consciousness was strained to apprehend it, as a too tightly stretched canvas splits and rips.

Suddenly the air was sweet on his mouth. The starlight seemed as hearty as a cheer. The world was still there, the world in which he had lived, so he must be safe. His own weakness and lovableness induced enjoyable tears, and there was a delicious moment of abandonment to comfortable whining before he realised that the water would not kindly buoy him up for long, and that even now a hostile current clasped his waist. He braced his flaccid body against the sucking blackness and flung his head back so that the water should not bubble so hungrily against the cords of his throat. Above him the slime of the rock was sticky with moonbeams, and the leprous light brought to his mind a newspaper paragraph, read years ago, which told him that the dawn had discovered floating in some oily Mersey dock, under walls as infected with wet growth as this, a corpse whose blood-encrusted finger-tips were deeply cleft. On the instant his own fingertips seemed hot with blood and deeply cleft from clawing at the impregnable rock. He screamed gaspingly, and beat his hands through the strangling flood. Action, which he had always loathed and dreaded, had broken the hard mould of his self-possession, and the dry dust of his character was blown hither and thither by fear. But one sharp fragment of intelligence which survived this detrition of his personality perceived that a certain gleam on the rock about a foot above the water was not the cold putrescence of the slime, but certainly the hard and merry light of a moon-ray striking on solid metal. His left hand clutched upwards at it, and he swung from a rounded projection. It was, his touch told him, a leaden ring hanging obliquely from the rock, to which his memory could visualise precisely in some past drier time when Lisbech sent no flood to Whimsey, a waterman mooring a boat strewn with pale-bellied perch. And behind the stooping waterman he remembered a flight of narrow steps that led up a buttress to a stone shelf that ran through the cutting. Unquestionably he was safe. He swung in a happy rhythm from the ring, his limp body trailing like a caterpillar through the stream to the foot of the steps, while he gasped in strength. A part of him was in agony, for his arm was nearly dragged out of its socket, and a part of him was embarrassed because his hysteria shook him with a deep rumbling chuckle that sounded as though he meditated on some unseemly joke; the whole was pervaded by a twilight atmosphere of unenthusiastic gratitude for his rescue, like the quietly cheerful tone of a Sunday evening sacred concert. After a minute's deep breathing he hauled himself up by the other hand and prepared to swing himself on to the steps.

But first, to shake off the wet worsted rags, once his socks, that now stuck uncomfortably between his toes, he splashed his feet outwards to midstream. A certain porpoise-like surface met his left foot. Fear dappled his face with goose-flesh. Without turning his head he knew what it was. It was Evadne's fat flesh rising on each side of her deep-furrowed spine through the rent in her bathing-dress.

Once more hatred marched through his soul like a king: a compelling service by his godhead and, like all gods, a little hatred for his harsh lien on his worshipper. He saw his wife as the curtain of flesh between him and celibacy, and solitude and all those delicate abstentions from life which his soul desired. He saw her as the invisible worm destroying the rose of the world with her dark secret love.[6] Now he knelt on the lowest stone step watching her wet seal-smooth head bobbing nearer on the waters. As her strong arms, covered with little dark points where her thick hairs were clotted with moisture, stretched out towards safety he bent forward and laid his hands on her head. He held her face under water. Scornfully he noticed the bubbles that rose to the surface from her protesting mouth and nostrils, and the foam raised by her arms and her thick ankles. To the end the creature persisted in turmoil, in movement, in action. . . .

She dropped like a stone. His hands, with nothing to resist them, slapped the water foolishly and he nearly overbalanced forward into the stream. He rose to his feet very stiffly. 'I must be a very strong man,' he said, as he slowly climbed the steps. 'I must be a very strong man,' he repeated, a little louder, as with hot and painful rigidity of the joints he stretched himself out at full length along the stone shelf. Weakness closed him in like a lead coffin. For a little time the wetness of his clothes persisted in being felt; then the sensation oozed out of him and his body fell out of knowledge. There was neither pain nor joy nor any other reckless ploughing of the brain by nerves. He knew unconsciousness, or rather the fullest consciousness he had ever known. For the world became nothingness, and nothingness which is free from the yeasty nuisance of matter and the ugliness of generation was the law of his being. He was absorbed into vacuity, the untamed substance of the universe, round which he conceived passion and thought to circle as straws caught up by the wind. He saw God and lived.

In Heaven a thousand years are a day. And this little corner of time in which he found happiness shrank to a nutshell as he opened his eyes again. This peace was hardly printed on his heart, yet the brightness of the night was blurred by the dawn. With the grunting carefulness of a man drunk with fatigue, he crawled along the stone shelf to the iron bridge, where he stood with his back to the roaring sluice and rested. All things seemed different now and happier. Like most timid people he disliked the night, and the commonplace hand which the dawn laid on the scene seemed to him a sanctification. The dimmed moon sank to her setting behind the crags. The jewel lights of Lisbech railway station were weak, cheerful twinklings. A steaming bluish milk of morning mist had been spilt on the hard silver surface of the lake, and the reeds no longer stabbed it like little daggers, but seemed a feathery fringe, like the pampas grass in the front garden in Sumatra Crescent. The black crags became brownish, and the mist disguised the sternness of the

---

6. An echo of a poem by William Blake (1757–1827), *The Sick Rose*: "O Rose thou art sick. / The invisible worm / That flies in the night / In the howling storm: / Has found out thy bed / Of crimson joy: / And his dark secret love / Does thy life destroy."

moor. This weakening of effects was exactly what he had always thought the extinction of Evadne would bring the world. He smiled happily at the moon.

Yet he was moved to sudden angry speech. "If I had my time over again," he said, "I wouldn't touch her with the tongs." For the cold he had known all along he would catch had settled in his head, and his handkerchief was wet through.

He leaned over the bridge and looked along Lisbech and thought of Evadne. For the first time for many years he saw her image without spirits, and wondered without indignation why she had so often looked like the cat about to steal the cream. What was the cream? And did she ever steal it? Now he would never know. He thought of her very generously and sighed over the perversity of fate in letting so much comeliness.

"If she had married a butcher or a veterinary surgeon she might have been happy," he said, and shook his head at the glassy black water that slid under the bridge to that boiling sluice.

A gust of ague reminded him that wet clothes clung to his fevered body and that he ought to change as quickly as possible, or expect to be laid up for weeks. He turned along the path that led back across the moor to the withered ash tree, and was learning the torture of bare feet on gravel when he cried out to himself: "I shall be hanged for killing my wife." It did not come as a trumpet-call, for he was one of those people who never quite hear what is said to them, and this deafishness extended in him to emotional things. It stole on him calmly, like a fog closing on a city. When he first felt hemmed in by this certainty he looked over his shoulder to the crags, remembering tales of how Jacobite fugitives[7] had hidden on the moors for many weeks. There lay at least another day of freedom. But he was the kind of man who always goes home. He stumbled on, not very unhappy, except for his feet. Like many people of weak temperament he did not fear death. Indeed, it had a peculiar appeal to him; for while it was important, exciting, it did not, like most important and exciting things, try to create action. He allowed his imagination the vanity of painting pictures. He saw himself standing in their bedroom, plotting this last event, with the white sheet and the high lights of the mahogany wardrobe shining ghostly at him through the darkness. He saw himself raising a thin hand to the gas bracket and turning on the tap. He saw himself staggering to their bed while death crept in at his nostrils. He saw his corpse lying in full daylight, and for the first time knew himself certainly, unquestionably dignified.

He threw back his chest in pride; but at that moment the path

7. The Jacobites supported the monarchy of James II, who was deposed in the "Glorious Revolution" of 1688.

stopped and he found himself staggering down the mound of heather-land and boulders with bleeding feet. Always he had suffered from sore feet, which had not exactly disgusted but, worse still, disappointed Evadne. A certain wistfulness she had always evinced when she found herself the superior animal had enraged and humiliated him many times. He felt that sting him now, and flung himself down the mound cursing. When he stumbled up to the withered ash tree he hated her so much that it seemed as though she were alive again, and a sharp wind blowing down from the moor terrified him like her touch.

He rested there. Leaning against the stripped grey trunk, he smiled up at the sky, which was now so touched to ineffectiveness by the dawn that it looked like a tent of faded silk. There was the peace of weakness in him, which he took to be spiritual, because it had no apparent physical justification, but he lost it as his dripping clothes chilled his tired flesh. His discomfort reminded him that the phantasmic night was passing from him. Daylight threatened him; the daylight in which for so many years he had worked in the solicitor's office and been snubbed and ignored. " 'The garish day,' "[8] he murmured disgustedly, quoting the blasphemy of some hymn-writer. He wanted his death to happen in this phantasmic night.

So he limped his way along the road. The birds had not yet begun to sing, but the rustling noises of the night had ceased. The silent highway was consecrated to his proud progress. He staggered happily like a tired child returning from a lovely birthday walk: his death in the little bed-room, which for the first time he would have to himself, was a culmi-nating treat to be gloated over like the promise of a favourite pudding for supper. As he walked he brooded dozingly on large and swelling thoughts. Like all people of weak passions and enterprise he loved to think of Napoleon, and in the shadow of the great asylum wall he strut-ted a few steps of his advance from murder to suicide, with arms crossed on his breast and thin legs trying to strut massively. He was so happy. He wished that a military band went before him, and pretended that the high hedges were solemn lines of men, stricken in awe to silence as their king rode out to some nobly self-chosen doom. Vast he seemed to himself, and magnificent like music, and solemn like the Sphinx. He had saved the earth from corruption by killing Evadne, for whom he now felt the unremorseful pity a conqueror might bestow on a devas-tated empire. He might have grieved that his victory brought him death, but with immense pride he found that the occasion was exactly described by a text. "He saved others, Himself He could not save."[9] He had missed the stile in the field above Sumatra Crescent and had to go

8. From the hymn *Lead Kindly Light*, by John Henry, Cardinal Newman (1801–1890): "I loved the garish day, and, spite of fears, / Pride ruled my will: remember not past years."
9. I.e., Christ (Matthew 27:42).

back and hunt for it in the hedge. So quickly had his satisfaction borne him home.

The field had the fantastic air that jerry-builders give to land poised on the knife-edge of town and country, so that he walked in romance to his very door. The unmarred grass sloped to a stone-hedge of towers of loose brick, trenches and mounds of shining clay, and the fine intentful spires of the scaffolding round the last unfinished house. And he looked down on Petrick. Though to the actual eye it was but a confusion of dark instances through the twilight, a breaking of velvety perspectives, he saw more intensely than ever before its squalid walls and squalid homes where mean men and mean women enlaced their unwholesome lives. Yet he did not shrink from entering for his great experience, as Christ did not shrink from being born in a stable. He swaggered with humility over the trodden mud of the field and the new white flags of Sumatra Crescent. Down the road before him there passed a dim fig-ure, who paused at each lamp-post and raised a long wand to behead the yellow gas-flowers that were now wilting before the dawn; a ghostly herald preparing the world to be his deathbed. The crescent curved in quiet darkness, save for one house, where blazed a gas-lit room with undrawn blinds. The brightness had the startled quality of a scream. He looked in almost anxiously as he passed, and met the blank eyes of a man in evening clothes who stood by the window shaking a medicine bottle. His face was like a wax mask softened by heat: the features were blurred with the suffering which comes from the spectacle of suffering. His eyes lay unshiftingly on George's face as he went by and he went on shaking the bottle. It seemed as though he would never stop.

In the hour of his grandeur George was not forgetful of the griefs of the little human people, but interceded with God for the sake of this stranger. Everything was beautiful, beautiful, beautiful.

His own little house looked solemn as a temple. He leaned against the lamp-post at the gate and stared at its empty windows and neat bricks. The disorder of the shattered pane of glass could be overlooked by considering a sign that this house was a holy place, like the Passover blood on the lintel.[1] The propriety of the evenly drawn blind pleased him enormously. He had always known that this was how the great tragic things of the world had accomplished themselves: quietly. Evadne's raging activity belonged to trivial or annoying things like spring-cleaning or thunderstorms. Well, the house belonged to him now. He opened the gate and went up the asphalt path, sourly noticing that Evadne had as usual left out the lawnmower, though it might very easily have rained, with the wind coming up as it was. A stray cat that

---

1. The blood on the door was a sign to God on the eve of the Exodus to pass over Hebrew houses while killing the first-born children of the Egyptians (Exodus 12:13). "Jerry-builders": builders whose work is cheap and careless.

had been sleeping in the tuft of pampas grass in the middle of the lawn was roused by his coming, and fled insolently close to his legs. He hated all wild homeless things, and bent for a stone to throw at it. But instead his fingers touched a slug, which reminded him of the feeling of Evadne's flesh through the slit in her bathing-dress. And suddenly the garden was possessed by her presence; she seemed to amble there as she had so often done, sowing seeds unwisely and tormenting the last days of an ailing geranium by insane transplantation, exclaiming absurdly over such mere weeds as morning glory. He caught the very clucking of her voice. . . . The front door opened at his touch.

The little lobby with its closed doors seemed stuffed with expectant silence. He realised that he had come to the theatre of his great adventure. Then panic seized him. Because this was the home where he and she had lived together so horribly he doubted whether he could do this splendid momentous thing, for here he had always been a poor thing with the habit of failure. His heart beat in him more quickly than his raw feet could pad up the oil-clothed stairs. Behind the deal door at the end of the passage was death. Nothingness! It would escape him, even the idea of it would escape him if he did not go to it at once. When he burst at last into its presence he felt so victorious that he sank back against the door waiting for death to come to him without turning on the gas. He was so happy. His death was coming true.

But Evadne lay on his deathbed. She slept there soundly, with her head flung back on the pillows so that her eyes and brow seemed small in shadow, and her mouth and jaw huge above her thick throat in the light. Her wet hair straggled across the pillow on to a broken cane chair covered with her tumbled clothes. Her breast, silvered with sweat, shone in the ray of the street lamp that had always disturbed their nights. The counterpane rose enormously over her hips in rolls of glazed linen. Out of mere innocent sleep her sensuality was distilling a most drunken pleasure.

Not for one moment did he think this a phantasmic appearance. Evadne was not the sort of woman to have a ghost.

Still leaning against the door he tried to think it all out, but his thoughts came brokenly, because the dawnlight flowing in at the window confused him by its pale glare and that lax figure on the bed held his attention. It must have been that when he laid his murderous hands on her head she had simply dropped below the surface and swum a few strokes under water as any expert swimmer can. Probably he had never even put her into danger, for she was a great lusty creature and the weir[2] was a little place. He had imagined the wonder and peril of the

2. A dam or a fenced enclosure in the water for catching fish.

battle as he had imagined his victory. He sneezed exhaustingly, and from his physical distress realised how absurd it was ever to have thought that he had killed her. Bodies like his do not kill bodies like hers.

Now his soul was naked and lonely as though the walls of his body had fallen in at death, and the grossness of Evadne's sleep made him suffer more unlovely a destitution than any old beggarwoman squatting by the roadside in the rain. He had thought he had had what every man most desires: one night of power over a woman for the business of murder or love. But it had been a lie. Nothing beautiful had ever happened to him. He would have wept, but the hatred he had learnt on the moors obstructed all tears in his throat. At least this night had given him passion enough to put an end to it all.

Quietly he went to the window and drew down the sash. There was no fireplace, so that sealed the room. Then he crept over to the gas bracket and raised his thin hand, as he had imagined in his hour of vain glory by the lake. He had forgotten Evadne's thrifty habit of turning off the gas at the main to prevent leakage when she went to bed.

He was beaten. He undressed and got into bed; as he had done every night for ten years, and as he would do every night until he died. Still sleeping, Evadne caressed him with warm arms.

1914, 1982

DOROTHY PARKER
1893–1967

"Brevity is the soul of Lingerie," Dorothy Parker announced in a *Vogue* advertisement that captured the witty brevity which would make her famous in the twenties and thirties. Whether in conversation she dubbed a young man "a rhinestone in the rough" or, as "Constant Reader" in *The New Yorker*, reviewed *The House at Pooh Corner* by protesting that "Tonstant Weader Fwowed Up," the wisecracking Parker epitomized style in New York, but she also managed, through an unfailing sense of humor and an uncanny ear for dialogue, to express her dissatisfaction with herself and with the society she so flamboyantly inhabited.

Dorothy Rothschild was the daughter of a Scottish mother, who died when the writer was a young child, and a Jewish garment manufacturer, who remarried a woman Dorothy disliked as much as she disliked her father. She grew up on the Upper West Side of Manhattan, and attended first a Catholic convent school and then Miss Dana's School in Morristown, New Jersey. After a brief stint writing captions for fashion photographs at *Vogue*, she was hired as a drama critic by Frank Crowninshield, the editor of *Vanity Fair*. Friendly with the playwright Robert Sherwood, the humorist Robert Benchley, and the newspaper writer Harold Ross, she became a prominent member of the Algonquin Hotel's Round Table (a lively lunch group) and, through her sketches and dialogues, she helped shape the character of *The New Yorker*, which Ross founded in 1925.

She had married Edwin Pond Parker II, a Wall Street businessman, in 1917, but they separated soon after his return from World War I and divorced in 1928. Parker's love life was never simple. After an abortion in 1923, she tried unsuccessfully to commit suicide. In the thirties, she married Alan Campbell, a bisexual writer eleven years her junior, and they subsequently divorced (1947), remarried (1950), separated (1953), and reunited (1956) until his death in 1963. Throughout this time, however, Parker continued to produce successful criticism, fiction, and verse. Her reviews and stories appeared in *The New Yorker* at irregular intervals from 1926 until 1955. In 1926, her first collection of verse, *Enough Rope*, was a smash success. Volumes like *Sunset Gun* (1928), *Death and Taxes* (1931), and *Not So Deep as a Well* (1936) were received just as favorably. Parker's protests against the execution of the anarchists Sacco and Vanzetti and her work against fascism during the Spanish civil war made her conspicuous when she and Campbell earned five thousand dollars a week in Hollywood during the late thirties; by the forties the couple were blacklisted for their political views. Her last years were sadly marked by self-doubt about her literary accomplishments and by her reliance on alcohol. Yet in stories like *You Were Perfectly Fine* and in poems like those in *A Pig's-Eye View of Literature*, she had satirized literary, social, and sexual pieties with sardonic exuberance.

Résumé[1]

Razors pain you;
Rivers are damp;
Acids stain you;
And drugs cause cramp.
Guns aren't lawful;   5
Nooses give;
Gas smells awful;
You might as well live.

1926

One Perfect Rose

A single flow'r he sent me, since we met.
All tenderly his messenger he chose;

---

1. Summary.

Deep-hearted, pure, with scented dew still wet—
    One perfect rose.

I knew the language of the floweret;   5
    "My fragile leaves," it said, "his heart enclose."
Love long has taken for his amulet
    One perfect rose.

Why is it no one ever sent me yet
    One perfect limousine, do you suppose?   10
Ah no, it's always just my luck to get
    One perfect rose.

                        1926

News Item

    Men seldom make passes
    At girls who wear glasses.

                        1926

Song of One of the Girls

Here in my heart I am Helen;
    I'm Aspasia and Hero, at least.
I'm Judith, and Jael, and Madame de Staël;
    I'm Salome, moon of the East.[2]

Here in my soul I am Sappho;   5
    Lady Hamilton am I, as well.
In me Recamier vies with Kitty O'Shea,
    With Dido, and Eve, and poor Nell.[3]

I'm of the glamorous ladies
    At whose beckoning history shook.   10

2. Helen of Troy was a Greek woman renowned for her beauty; Aspasia was the consort of the Greek statesman Pericles; Hero was a Greek priestess; Judith was a courageous Jewish woman who killed Israel's enemy Holofernes singlehanded; Jael was a Jewish woman who similarly killed the enemy general Sisera; Madame de Staël (1766–1817) was a French writer; Salome was the beautiful daughter of queen Herodias who demanded that the head of John the Baptist be brought to her.
3. Sappho was a Greek lyric poet of the seventh century B.C.; Lady Hamilton (1765–1815) was the mistress of the English admiral Lord Nelson; Madame Récamier (1777–1849) was a French beauty and friend of Madame de Staël; Kitty O'Shea was the wife of an Irish patriot; her adultery with Charles Parnell (1846–1891), the charismatic Irish leader, brought about his downfall. Dido was the queen of ancient Carthage, abandoned by her lover Aeneas in Virgil's *Aeneid*; Eve was the first woman created by God in the book of Genesis; Nell is a girl who dies in Charles Dickens's novel *The Old Curiosity Shop*.

But you are a man, and see only my pan,[4]
So I stay at home with a book.

1926

From A Pig's-Eye View of Literature

The Lives and Times of John Keats, Percy Bysshe Shelley, and George Gordon Noel, Lord Byron[5]

Byron and Shelley and Keats
Were a trio of lyrical treats.
The forehead of Shelley was cluttered with curls
And Keats never was a descendant of earls,
And Byron walked out with a number of girls,   5
    But it didn't impair the poetical feats
        Of Byron and Shelley,
        Of Byron and Shelley,
Of Byron and Shelley and Keats.

Oscar Wilde[6]

If, with the literate, I am   10
Impelled to try an epigram,
I never seek to take the credit;
We all assume that Oscar said it.

Harriet Beecher Stowe[7]

The pure and worthy Mrs. Stowe
Is one we all are proud to know   15
As mother, wife, and authoress—
Thank God, I am content with less!

D. G. Rossetti[8]

Dante Gabriel Rossetti
Buried all of his *libretti*,[9]
Thought the matter over—then   20
Went and dug them up again.

---

4. Face.
5. Keats (1795–1821), Shelley (1792–1822), and Byron (1788–1824), major Romantic poets; Keats was of working-class descent, and Byron was notorious for his philandering.
6. Irish writer (1854–1900), famous for his wit.
7. American novelist and activist (1811–1896),

the author of the antislavery novel *Uncle Tom's Cabin*.
8. English poet and painter (1828–1882).
9. Italian: books. Rossetti actually buried his manuscripts in his wife's coffin in 1862, then recovered them eight years later.

Thomas Carlyle[1]

Carlyle combined the lit'ry life
With throwing teacups at his wife,
Remarking, rather testily,
"Oh, stop your dodging, Mrs. C.!"   25

Alfred, Lord Tennyson[2]

Should Heaven send me any son,
I hope he's not like Tennyson.
I'd rather have him play a fiddle
Than rise and bow and speak an idyll.[3]

Walter Savage Landor[4]

Upon the work of Walter Landor   30
I am unfit to write with candor.
If you can read it, well and good;
But as for me, I never could.

George Sand[5]

What time the gifted lady took
Away from paper, pen, and book,   35
She spent in amorous dalliance
(They do those things so well in France).

1928

You Were Perfectly Fine

The pale young man eased himself carefully into the low chair, and
rolled his head to the side, so that the cool chintz comforted his cheek
and temple.

"Oh, dear," he said. "Oh, dear, oh, dear, oh, dear. Oh."

The clear-eyed girl, sitting light and erect on the couch, smiled
brightly at him.

"Not feeling so well today?" she said.

"Oh, I'm great," he said. "Corking, I am. Know what time I got up?
Four o'clock this afternoon, sharp. I kept trying to make it, and every
time I took my head off the pillow, it would roll under the bed. This

---

1. Scottish essayist and historian (1795–1881).
2. English poet (1809–1892).
3. A poem describing a scene or episode. Tennyson wrote a long Arthurian poem called *Idylls*

of the King.
4. English lyric poet (1775–1843).
5. The pen name of Aurore Dupin (1804–1876), French novelist.

isn't my head I've got on now. I think this is something that used to belong to Walt Whitman.[6] Oh, dear, oh, dear, oh, dear."

"Do you think maybe a drink would make you feel better?" she said.

"The hair of the mastiff that bit me?"[7] he said. "Oh, no, thank you. Please never speak of anything like that again. I'm through. I'm all, all through. Look at that hand; steady as a humming-bird. Tell me, was I very terrible last night?"

"Oh, goodness," she said, "everybody was feeling pretty high. You were all right."

"Yeah," he said. "I must have been dandy. Is everybody sore at me?"

"Good heavens, no," she said. "Everyone thought you were terribly funny. Of course, Jim Pierson was a little stuffy, there, for a minute at dinner. But people sort of held him back in his chair, and got him calmed down. I don't think anybody at the other tables noticed it at all. Hardly anybody."

"He was going to sock me?" he said. "Oh, Lord. What did I do to him?"

"Why, you didn't do a thing," she said. "You were perfectly fine. But you know how silly Jim gets, when he thinks anybody is making too much fuss over Elinor."

"Was I making a pass at Elinor?" he said. "Did I do that?"

"Of course you didn't," she said. "You were only fooling, that's all. She thought you were awfully amusing. She was having a marvelous time. She only got a little tiny bit annoyed just once, when you poured the clam-juice down her back."

"My God," he said. "Clam-juice down that back. And every vertebra a little Cabot.[8] Dear God. What'll I ever do?"

"Oh, she'll be all right," she said. "Just send her some flowers, or something. Don't worry about it. It isn't anything."

"No, I won't worry," he said. "I haven't got a care in the world. I'm sitting pretty. Oh, dear, oh, dear. Did I do any other fascinating tricks at dinner?"

"You were fine," she said. "Don't be so foolish about it. Everybody was crazy about you. The maître d'hôtel was a little worried because you wouldn't stop singing, but he really didn't mind. All he said was, he was afraid they'd close the place again, if there was so much noise. But he didn't care a bit, himself. I think he loved seeing you have such a good time. Oh, you were just singing away, there, for about an hour. It wasn't so terribly loud, at all."

"So I sang," he said. "That must have been a treat. I sang."

6. American author (1819–1891).
7. I.e., "hair of the dog"—a phrase for taking a

drink after a hangover.
8. Upper-class conservative Boston family.

"Don't you remember?" she said. "You just sang one song after another. Everybody in the place was listening. They loved it. Only you kept insisting that you wanted to sing some song about some kind of fusiliers or other,[9] and everybody kept shushing you, and you'd keep trying to start it again. You were wonderful. We were all trying to make you stop singing for a minute, and eat something, but you wouldn't hear of it. My, you were funny."

"Didn't I eat any dinner?" he said.

"Oh, not a thing," she said. "Every time the waiter would offer you something, you'd give it right back to him, because you said that he was your long-lost brother, changed in the cradle by a gypsy band, and that anything you had was his. You had him simply roaring at you."

"I bet I did," he said. "I bet I was comical. Society's Pet, I must have been. And what happened then, after my overwhelming success with the waiter?"

"Why, nothing much," she said. "You took a sort of dislike to some old man with white hair, sitting across the room, because you didn't like his necktie and you wanted to tell him about it. But we got you out, before he got really mad."

"Oh, we got out," he said. "Did I walk?"

"Walk! Of course you did," she said. "You were absolutely all right. There was that nasty stretch of ice on the sidewalk, and you did sit down awfully hard, you poor dear. But good heavens, that might have happened to anybody."

"Oh, sure," he said. "Louisa Alcott[1] or anybody. So I fell down on the sidewalk. That would explain what's the matter with my—Yes. I see. And then what, if you don't mind?"

"Ah, now, Peter!" she said. "You can't sit there and say you don't remember what happened after that! I did think that maybe you were just a little tight at dinner—oh, you were perfectly all right, and all that, but I did know you were feeling pretty gay. But you were so serious, from the time you fell down—I never knew you to be that way. Don't you know, how you told me I had never seen your real self before? Oh, Peter, I just couldn't bear it, if you didn't remember that lovely long ride we took together in the taxi! Please, you do remember that, don't you? I think it would simply kill me, if you didn't."

"Oh, yes," he said. "Riding in the taxi. Oh, yes, sure. Pretty long ride, hmm?"

"Round and round and round the park," she said. "Oh, and the trees were shining so in the moonlight. And you said you never knew before that you really had a soul."

9. I.e., an old British army song.
1. Louisa May Alcott (1832–1888), thought of, in Parker's time, only as the saccharine author of *Little Women*.

"Yes," he said. "I said that. That was me."

"You said such lovely, lovely things," she said. "And I'd never known, all this time, how you had been feeling about me, and I'd never dared to let you see how I felt about you. And then last night—oh, Peter dear, I think that taxi ride was the most important thing that ever happened to us in our lives."

"Yes," he said. "I guess it must have been."

"And we're going to be so happy," she said. "Oh, I just want to tell everybody! But I don't know—I think maybe it would be sweeter to keep it all to ourselves."

"I think it would be," he said.

"Isn't it lovely?" she said.

"Yes," he said. "Great."

"Lovely!" she said.

"Look here," he said, "do you mind if I have a drink? I mean, just medicinally, you know. I'm off the stuff for life, so help me. But I think I feel a collapse coming on."

"Oh, I think it would do you good," she said. "You poor boy, it's a shame you feel so awful. I'll go make you a whisky and soda."

"Honestly," he said, "I don't see how you could ever want to speak to me again, after I made such a fool of myself, last night. I think I'd better go join a monastery in Tibet."

"You crazy idiot!" she said. "As if I could ever let you go away now! Stop talking like that. You were perfectly fine."

She jumped up from the couch, kissed him quickly on the forehead, and ran out of the room.

The pale young man looked after her and shook his head long and slowly, then dropped it in his damp and trembling hands.

"Oh, dear," he said. "Oh, dear, oh, dear, oh, dear."

1930, 1944

JEAN RHYS
1894–1979

Described by one friend as "a shy, gentle and almost fatally impractical person," the novelist Jean Rhys was nevertheless thought by her mentor and sometime lover, Ford Madox Ford, to have "a terrifying insight, and a terrific . . . passion for stating the case of the underdog." Ford's comment, made early in Rhys's career, was an acute one, for, in five novels and a number of short stories, Rhys established a reputation for subtlety and style; more specifically, exploring the pain of wounded or abandoned women, she created a haunting landscape of anxiety that provides a kind of female equivalent to the wastelands of metaphysical despair constructed by such male contemporaries as the playwright Samuel Beckett and the poet T. S. Eliot.

Like the protagonist of *Wide Sargasso Sea* (1966), one of her most celebrated novels, Rhys was born and raised in Roseau, Dominica, in the West Indies. Educated at a convent school in Roseau, she traveled to London at the age of sixteen, where she studied for a term at the Royal Academy of Dramatic Art, then toured England as a chorus girl in a musical comedy during the years of World War I. Married for a time to the poet Max Hamer, she had one child. Much of her life, however, was spent in Paris and in travels on the Continent, an expatriation whose alienating implications she captured in, for instance, her portrait of the numbed and lonely heroine of *Good Morning, Midnight* (1939).

According to one commentator, Rhys "had always kept 'a sort of diary,' but she didn't think seriously of writing until a time when she was desperate for money, which fortunately coincided with her 'discovery' by . . . Ford." Once she began to write, though, she quickly became a serious professional: throughout her years of wandering, she was producing her poignant yet coolly understated novels and tales, and when she returned to settle in England—chiefly in London and Cornwall—she continued to write, although her reputation fell into an eclipse for some years. After *Good Morning, Midnight* was broadcast in England in the sixties, Rhys was "rediscovered," however, and the subsequent publication of *Wide Sargasso Sea* was defined as "a magnificent comeback."

Whether or not *Wide Sargasso Sea* was a "comeback," it continued and elaborated a mode of psychological analysis that Rhys had already pioneered in earlier works. In particular, it developed a technique of literary allusion hinted at in the title of *Good Morning, Midnight*—a line drawn from one of Emily Dickinson's poems ("Good Morning—Midnight— / I'm coming Home— / Day—got tired of Me—," #425), for *Wide Sargasso Sea* is a disturbing yet brilliantly revisionary retelling of the story of *Jane Eyre* from the point of view of Bertha Mason Rochester, the madwoman sequestered in Thornfield's attic. Describing Bertha's experience as a repressed daughter and an oppressed wife, Rhys continued the delineation of a landscape of female despair that she had begun in her earlier novels, but now she located that countryside of anguish more specifically in the context of the women's literary tradition. Acknowledging the affinity between the anxieties of her protagonists and the pain articulated by such precursors as Dickinson and Brontë, Rhys elaborated what Ford had called her "terrifying insight" into the lives of "underdogs"—forgotten women imprisoned by self or society in attics and rooming houses, rebellious women whose stories she recounted with sympathy and sensitivity.

On Not Shooting Sitting Birds

There is no control over memory. Quite soon you find yourself being vague about an event which seemed so important at the time that you thought you'd never forget it. Or unable to recall the face of someone whom you could have sworn was there for ever. On the other hand, trivial and meaningless memories may stay with you for life. I can still shut my eyes and see Victoria grinding coffee on the pantry steps, the glass bookcase and the books in it, my father's pipe-rack, the leaves of the sandbox tree, the wallpaper of the bedroom in some shabby hotel, the hairdresser in Antibes. It's in this way that I remember buying the pink milanese silk underclothes, the assistant who sold them to me and coming into the street holding the parcel.

I had started out in life trusting everyone and now I trusted no one. So I had few acquaintances and no close friends. It was perhaps in reaction against the inevitable loneliness of my life that I'd find myself doing bold, risky, even outrageous things without hesitation or surprise. I was usually disappointed in these adventures and they didn't have much effect on me, good or bad, but I never quite lost the hope of something better or different.

One day, I've forgotten now where, I met this young man who smiled at me and when we had talked a bit I agreed to have dinner with him in a couple of days' time. I went home excited, for I'd liked him very much, and began to plan what I should wear. I had a dress I quite liked, an evening cloak, shoes, stockings, but my underclothes weren't good enough for the occasion, I decided. Next day I went out and bought the milanese silk chemise and drawers.

So there we were seated at a table having dinner with a bedroom very obvious in the background. He was younger than I'd thought and stiffer and I didn't like him much after all. He kept eyeing me in such a wary, puzzled way. When we had finished our soup and the waiter had taken the plates away, he said: "But you're really a lady, aren't you?" exactly as he might have said, "But you're really a snake or a crocodile, aren't you?"

"Oh no, not that you'd notice," I said, but this didn't work. We looked glumly at each other across the gulf that had yawned between us.

Before I came to England I'd read many English novels and I imagined I knew all about the thoughts and tastes of various sorts of English people. I quickly decided that to distract or interest this man I must talk about shooting.

I asked him if he knew the West Indies at all. He said no, he didn't and I told him a long story of having been lost in the Dominican forest when I was a child. This wasn't true. I'd often been in the woods but never alone. "There are no parrots now," I said, "or very few. There used to be. There's a Dominican parrot in the zoo—have you ever seen it?—a sulky bird, very old I think. However, there are plenty of other birds and we do have shooting parties. Perdrix are very good to eat, but ramiers are rather bitter."

Then I began describing a fictitious West Indian shooting party and all the time I talked I was remembering the real thing. An old shotgun leaning up in one corner of the room, the round table in the middle where we would sit to make cartridges, putting the shot in, ramming it down with a wad of paper. Gunpowder? There was that too, for I remember the smell. I suppose the boys were trusted to be careful.

The genuine shooting party consisted of my two brothers, who shared the shotgun, some hangers-on and me at the end of the procession, for then I couldn't bear to be left out of anything. As soon as the shooting was about to start I would stroll away casually and when I was out of sight run as hard as I could, crouch down behind a bush and put my fingers in my ears. It wasn't that I was sorry for the birds, but I hated and feared the noise of the gun. When it was all over I'd quietly join the others. I must have done this unobtrusively or probably my brothers thought me too insignificant to worry about, for no one ever remarked on my odd behaviour or teased me about it.

On and on I went, almost believing what I was saying, when he interrupted me. "Do you mean to say that your brothers shot sitting birds?" His voice was cold and shocked.

I stared at him. How could I convince this man that I hadn't the faintest idea whether my brothers shot sitting birds or not? How could I explain now what really happened? If I did he'd think me a liar. Also a coward and there he'd be right, for I was afraid of many things, not only the sound of gunfire. But by this time I wasn't sure that I liked him at all so I was silent and felt my face growing as stiff and unsmiling as his.

It was a most uncomfortable dinner. We both avoided looking at the bedroom and when the last mouthful was swallowed he announced that he was going to take me home. The way he said this rather puzzled me. Then I told myself that probably he was curious to see where I lived. Neither of us spoke in the taxi except to say, "Well, goodnight." "Goodnight."

I felt regretful when it came to taking off my lovely pink chemise, but I could still think: Some other night perhaps, another sort of man.

I slept at once.

1976

LOUISE BOGAN
1897–1970

"Women have no wilderness in them, / They are provident instead," wrote Louise Bogan in a famous poem entitled *Women*. Yet this scrupulous artist, who was from 1931 to 1969 the influential and fiercely independent poetry critic for *The New Yorker*, herself wrote poems that constituted rigorous and fearless explorations of an interior "wilderness," poems that—in the words of W. H. Auden, a fellow writer whom she much admired—"wrested beauty and truth out of dark places." Born in Livermore Falls, Maine, Bogan described herself as "the highly charged and neurotically inclined product of an extraordinary childhood and an unfortunate early marriage, into which last state I had rushed to escape the first." Her parents were genteelly impoverished and unhappily married, often separating for long periods, so that she later confessed that "I cannot bring myself to describe the horrors of the pre–1914 lower-middle-class life, in which they found themselves."

The family had moved to Boston in 1909, where the young Bogan entered Girls' Latin School and began to write poetry. In 1915, she enrolled as a freshman at Boston University, where two of her verses were printed in the literary magazine. But though she had been offered a scholarship to Radcliffe for the following year, she decided instead to marry Curt Alexander, a professional soldier, so that she could get away from the turmoil in her home. While living on an army base in the Panama Canal Zone, the couple had a daughter in 1917, but the marriage was indeed, in other ways, "unfortunate," and Bogan left her husband in 1919. The next year he died, and she received a small widow's pension which enabled her to travel to Vienna in 1922, where she studied piano.

In 1923, after she had returned to New York, Bogan met Raymond Holden, a novelist and minor poet, whom she was to marry in 1925. Supporting herself at various odd jobs, she began seriously to write and publish; her work in this period included film criticism and poetry reviews as well as two well-received volumes of verse, *Body of This Death* (1923) and *Dark Summer* (1929). In 1931, just after she had begun her career as a poetry reviewer for *The New Yorker*, Bogan had the first of a series of nervous breakdowns that were to acquaint her with what Auden called "dark places." Recovering, she separated from Holden in 1934 and entered into a relationship with the poet Theodore Roethke, who became her lifelong friend and partisan. Her new collections appeared at regular intervals—*The Sleeping Fury* in 1937 and *Poems and New Poems* in 1941—and a growing number of prizes recognized the nature of her aesthetic achievement. After serving in 1945 as a Consultant in Poetry to the Library of Congress, she was awarded visiting professorships and literary residencies at several major institutions, including the University of Washington and Brandeis University. Her last book of verse, *The Blue Estuaries: Poems 1923–1968*, appeared shortly before she resigned from her job as poetry reviewer for *The New Yorker* and a year before she died of a heart attack.

Throughout her successful and productive career, Bogan had remained an intensely private woman: she made few pronouncements on public events and, as the poem *Women* suggests, did not particularly identify herself as a feminist. Yet in a late essay on women poets she reminded her audience that "the word feminism . . . is a word which has its own honor and radiance," and—though she had once claimed that she disliked "other women poets (jealousy!)"—she catalogued in some detail the achievements of literary women from Sappho to Virginia Woolf. What may seem at first like a puzzling inconsistency in her thought becomes easier to understand when one sets the bitterness this writer

expresses in *Women* against the powerful reimagining of mythology that she
undertakes in works like *Medusa* and *Cassandra*.

Medusa[1]

I had come to the house, in a cave of trees,
Facing a sheer sky.
Everything moved,—a bell hung ready to strike,
Sun and reflection wheeled by.

When the bare eyes were before me   5
And the hissing hair,
Held up at a window, seen through a door.
The stiff bald eyes, the serpents on the forehead
Formed in the air.

This is a dead scene forever now.   10
Nothing will ever stir.
The end will never brighten it more than this,
Nor the rain blur.

The water will always fall, and will not fall,
And the tipped bell make no sound.   15
The grass will always be growing for hay
Deep on the ground.

And I shall stand here like a shadow
Under the great balanced day,
My eyes on the yellow dust, that was lifting in the wind, 20
And does not drift away.

1923

The Crows

The woman who has grown old
And knows desire must die,
Yet turns to love again,
Hears the crows' cry.

She is a stem long hardened,   5
A weed that no scythe mows.
The heart's laughter will be to her
The crying of the crows.

1. In Greek myth, one of three snaky-haired sisters called the Gorgons, the sight of whom turned men
to stone.

Who slide in the air with the same voice
Over what yields not, and what yields,   10
Alike in spring, and when there is only bitter
Winter-burning in the fields.

                                                          1923

Women

Women have no wilderness in them,
They are provident instead,
Content in the tight hot cell of their hearts
To eat dusty bread.

They do not see cattle cropping red winter grass,   5
They do not hear
Snow water going down under culverts
Shallow and clear.

They wait, when they should turn to journeys,
They stiffen, when they should bend.   10
They use against themselves that benevolence
To which no man is friend.

They cannot think of so many crops to a field
Or of clean wood cleft by an axe.
Their love is an eager meaninglessness   15
Too tense, or too lax.

They hear in every whisper that speaks to them
A shout and a cry.
As like as not, when they take life over their door-sills
They should let it go by.   20

                                                          1923

Cassandra[2]

To me, one silly task is like another.
I bare the shambling tricks of lust and pride.
This flesh will never give a child its mother,—
Song, like a wing, tears through my breast, my side,

---

2. Trojan princess with the gift of prophecy, but believed by no one.

And madness chooses out my voice again,   5
Again. I am the chosen no hand saves:
The shrieking heaven lifted over men,
Not the dumb earth, wherein they set their graves.

1929

The Crossed Apple

I've come to give you fruit from out my orchard,
Of wide report.
I have trees there that bear me many apples
Of every sort:

Clear, streakèd; red and russet; green and golden;   5
Sour and sweet.
This apple's from a tree yet unbeholden,
Where two kinds meet,—

So that this side is red without a dapple,
And this side's hue   10
Is clear and snowy. It's a lovely apple.
It is for you.

Within are five black pips as big as peas,
As you will find,
Potent to breed you five great apple trees   15
Of varying kind:

To breed you wood for fire, leaves for shade,
Apples for sauce.
Oh, this is a good apple for a maid,
It is a cross,   20

Fine on the finer, so the flesh is tight,
And grained like silk.
Sweet Burning gave the red side, and the white
Is Meadow Milk.

Eat it; and you will taste more than the fruit;   25
The blossom, too,
The sun, the air, the darkness at the root,
The rain, the dew,

The earth we came to, and the time we flee,
The fire and the breast.   30

I claim the white part, maiden, that's for me.
You take the rest.

1929

The Sleeping Fury[3]

You are here now,
Who were so loud and feared, in a symbol before me,
Alone and asleep, and I at last look long upon you.

Your hair fallen on your cheek, no longer in the
    semblance of serpents,
Lifted in the gale; your mouth, that shrieked so, silent.   5
You, my scourge, my sister, lie asleep, like a child,
Who, after rage, for an hour quiet, sleeps out its tears.

The days close to winter
Rough with strong sound. We hear the sea and the forest,
And the flames of your torches fly, lit by others,   10
Ripped by the wind, in the night. The black sheep for sacrifice
Huddle together. The milk is cold in the jars.

All to no purpose, as before, the knife whetted and plunged,
The shout raised, to match the clamor you have given them.
You alone turn away, not appeased; unaltered, avenger.   15

Hands full of scourges, wreathed with your flames and adders,
You alone turned away, but did not move from my side,
Under the broken light, when the soft nights took the torches.

At thin morning you showed, thick and wrong in that calm,
The ignoble dream and the mask, sly, with slits at the eyes,   20
Pretence and half-sorrow, beneath which a coward's
    hope trembled.

You uncovered at night, in the locked stillness of houses,
False love due the child's heart, the kissed-out lie, the embraces,
Made by the two who for peace tenderly turned to each other.

You who know what we love, but drive us to know it;   25
You with your whips and shrieks, bearer of truth and of solitude;
You who give, unlike men, to expiation your mercy.

Dropping the scourge when at last the scourged advances
    to meet it,

3. In Greek myth, the Furies are three female monsters of revenge and retribution.

You, when the hunted turns, no longer remain the hunter
But stand silent and wait, at last returning his gaze.   30

Beautiful now as a child whose hair, wet with rage and tears
Clings to its face. And now I may look upon you,
Having once met your eyes. You lie in sleep and forget me.
Alone and strong in my peace, I look upon you in yours.

1937

Evening in the Sanitarium[4]

The free evening fades, outside the windows fastened with
    decorative iron grilles.
The lamps are lighted; the shades drawn; the nurses are
    watching a little.
It is the hour of the complicated knitting on the safe
    bone needles; of the games of anagrams and bridge;
The deadly game of chess; the book held up like a mask.   5

The period of the wildest weeping, the fiercest delusion, is over.
The women rest their tired half-healed hearts; they are
    almost well.
Some of them will stay almost well always: the blunt-faced
    woman whose thinking dissolved
Under academic discipline; the manic-depressive girl
Now leveling off; one paranoiac afflicted with jealousy.   10
Another with persecution. Some alleviation has been possible.

O fortunate bride, who never again will become elated after
    childbirth!
O lucky older wife, who has been cured of feeling unwanted!
To the suburban railway station you will return, return,
To meet forever Jim home on the 5:35.   15
You will be again as normal and selfish and heartless as
    anybody else.

There is life left: the piano says it with its octave smile.
The soft carpets pad the thump and splinter of the suicide to be.
Everything will be splendid: the grandmother will not drink
    habitually.
The fruit salad will bloom on the plate like a bouquet   20
And the garden produce the blue-ribbon aquilegia.
The cats will be glad; the fathers feel justified; the
    mothers relieved.

4. Originally published with the subtitle *Imitated from Auden* (W. H. Auden, 1907–1973, English poet).

The sons and husbands will no longer need to pay the bills.
Childhoods will be put away, the obscene nightmare abated.

At the ends of the corridors the baths are running.   25
Mrs. C. again feels the shadow of the obsessive idea.
Miss R. looks at the mantel-piece, which must mean something.

                                                                  1941

Several Voices out of a Cloud

Come, drunks and drug-takers; come, perverts unnerved!
Receive the laurel,[5] given, though late, on merit; to whom and
    wherever deserved.

Parochial punks, trimmers, nice people, joiners true-blue,
Get the hell out of the way of the laurel. It is deathless   5
    And it isn't for you.

                                                                  1941

The Dream

O God, in the dream the terrible horse began
To paw at the air, and make for me with his blows.
Fear kept for thirty-five years poured through his mane,
And retribution equally old, or nearly, breathed through his nose.

Coward complete, I lay and wept on the ground   5
When some strong creature appeared, and leapt for the rein.
Another woman, as I lay half in a swound,
Leapt in the air, and clutched at the leather and chain.

Give him, she said, something of yours as a charm.
Throw him, she said, some poor thing you alone claim.   10
No, no, I cried, he hates me; he's out for harm,
And whether I yield or not, it is all the same.

But, like a lion in a legend, when I flung the glove
Pulled from my sweating, my cold right hand,
The terrible beast, that no one may understand,   15
Came to my side, and put down his head in love.

                                                                  1941

5. In classical Greece, a laurel wreath crowned the victor in an athletic or poetic contest.

RUTH PITTER

1897–

"My purpose has never varied," wrote Ruth Pitter in a foreword to her *Collected Poems* (1968). "It has been simply to capture . . . some of the secret meanings which haunt life and language." Despite years of poverty and obscurity, Pitter has done this in verses that have been acclaimed by a range of literary figures, including the poet Hilaire Belloc and the critic Lord David Cecil, and that have won the Hawthornden Prize, the Heinemann Award, and the Queen's Gold Medal for Poetry. Born in the village of Ilford, in the English county of Essex, Pitter is the daughter of middle-class parents who, she recalls, "loved poetry and were determined to impart it to their children." She herself began to write poems at the age of five, publishing her first book when she was in her early twenties but later acknowledging that "I produced little that I now think worth keeping until about the age of thirty."

After a comparatively sketchy education, Pitter worked in the British War Office during World War I, then studied various handicrafts and opened a shop where she sold (as she still does) hand-painted trays. Her major collections of verse include *A Mad Lady's Garland* (1935), *A Trophy of Arms* (1936), *The Spirit Watches* (1940), and *Collected Poems*. Her best work oscillates between grave meditation and sardonic wit, but throughout her career she has consistently sought to express what she calls "the silent music, the dance in stillness . . . of which everything is full."

The Military Harpist

Strangely assorted, the shape of song and the bloody man.

Under the harp's gilt shoulder and rainlike strings,
Prawn-eyed, with prawnlike bristle, well-waxed moustache,
With long tight cavalry legs, and the spurred boot
Ready upon the swell, the Old Sweat waits.   5

Now dies, and dies hard, the stupid, well-relished fortissimo,
Wood-wind alone inviting the liquid tone,
The voice of the holy and uncontending, the harp.

Ceasing to ruminate interracial fornications,
He raises his hands, and his wicked old mug is David's,[1]   10
Pastoral, rapt, the king and the poet in innocence,

---

1. Ancient king of Israel, both a musician and military leader. As a youth, David sang and played before the previous king, Saul, who later turned against him.

Singing Saul in himself asleep, and the ancient Devil
Clean out of countenance, as with an army of angels.

He is now where his bunion has no existence.
Breathing an atmosphere free of pipeclay[2] and swearing,   15
He wears the starched nightshirt of the hereafter, his halo
Is plain manly brass with a permanent polish,
Requiring no oily rag and no Soldier's Friend.[3]

His place is with the beloved poet of Israel,
With the wandering minnesinger and the loves of Provence,[4]   20
With Blondel[5] footsore and heartsore, the voice in the darkness
Crying like beauty bereaved beneath many a donjon,[6]
O Richard! O king! where is the lion of England?
With Howell, Llewellyn,[7] and far in the feral north
With the savage fame of the hero in glen and in ben,   25
At the morning discourse of saints in the island Eire,[8]
And at nameless doings in the stone-circle, the dreadful grove.

Thus far into the dark do I delve for his likeness:
He harps at the Druid[9] sacrifice, where the golden string
Sings to the golden knife and the victim's shriek.   30
Strangely assorted, the shape of song and the bloody man.

                                                                        1939

The Irish Patriarch

He bathes his soul in women's wrath;
His whiskers twinkle, and it seems
As if he trod some airy path
In that young land of warriors' dreams;
As if he took a needle-bath[1]   5
In mountain falls, in tingling streams.

The man whom nagging drives to drink
Should learn from him, whom female rage
Seems but to make a precious link
With some sweet ancient heritage,   10

---

2. A whitener, for sprucing up military uniforms.
3. A popular brand of metal polish.
4. Traveling poet and musician of the Middle
Ages in Germany and Provence.
5. A French troubadour poet of the twelfth century, companion to the English king Richard the
Lion-Hearted. According to legend, Blondel discovered Richard imprisoned in the castle of

Dürnstein while singing a song they had written
together, to which the king sang back.
6. Massive tower in medieval castles.
7. Prince of northern Wales in the Middle Ages
who revolted against the English king.
8. Ireland.
9. Ancient Celtic priests.
1 I.e., cold shower of water.

With women saying—huh!—what they think!
To the amusement of the sage.

O women, what a boon it is,
With workday worries at their worst,
When hordes of little miseries 15
Force us to speak our mind or burst,
To be Rich-angered Mistresses,[2]
Not Shrews and Vixens, Cross and Curst!

1966

Old Nelly's Birthday

She knows where to get cracked eggs, does Nelly.
Knows where to get them cheap:
Ninepence a dozen from that Mrs. Kelly.
Of course they will not keep,
But Nelly will make them into a jam sandwich[3] 5
Of most portentous size.
Now this jam sandwich is her secret language,
And sacred in her eyes;
And to go with this sandwich, her love, her treasure,
She'll make a pot of tea, 10
Her urn, her cauldron of almost unholy pleasure,
For in that tea will be
Never a drop of shivering starving water,
But milk with all its cream;
A boiling foaming snow, by pleasure's daughter, 15
Obedient to the dream,
Brewed and kept hot and poured out and delected,
This once of all the year,
Most cordial to the hearts of those selected,
Those delicate, those dear, 20
Mystical inmost friends of fervent Nelly,
Who will consume with glee
And blessings on the decent Mrs. Kelly,
That sandwich and that tea.

But this year it was really extra special; 25
For when old Nelly went
Down to the dairy, she beheld a vessel
Of marvellous extent,

2. An echo of John Keats's *Ode to Melancholy*: "Or if thy mistress some rich anger shows, / Imprison her soft hand, and let her rave, / And feed deep, deep upon her peerless eyes."
3. I.e., a layer cake.

Full of fine milk soured by the spring thunder,
With cream on top galore: 30
And Mrs Kelly, who really is the world's wonder,
Skimmed her a quart and more;
And Nelly with light heart and little trouble
Beat it and made it turn
Into lovely butter that made the pleasure double: 35
Her sandwich and her urn,
Flanked by the light new loaf and heavenly butter,
Home-made from magic cream,
Ravished the creature till words could not utter
The glory of the dream.[4]

                                                            1966

Yorkshire Wife's Saga

War was her life, with want and the wild air;
Not for life only; she was out to win.
Houses and ground were cheap, out on the bare
Moor, and the land not bad; they could begin,
Now that the seven sons were mostly men.   5

Two acres and a sow, on hard-saved brass;[5]
Men down the mine, and mother did the rest.
Pity, with all those sons, they had no lass;
No help, no talk, no mutual interest,
Made fourteen slaving hours empty at best.   10

Fierce winter mornings, up at three or four;
Men bawl, pigs shriek against the raving beck.[6]
Off go the eight across the mile of moor,
With well-filled dinner-pail and sweat-ragged neck;
But pigs still shriek, and wind blows door off sneck.[7]   15

Of course they made it; what on earth could stop
People like that? Marrying one by one,
This got a farm, the other got a shop;
Now she was left with but the youngest son,
But she could look about and feel she'd won.   20

Doctor had told her she was clean worn out.
All pulled to bits, and nowt[8] that he could do.

4. An echo of Wordsworth's *Ode: Intimations*   6. Brook.
of Immortality: "Where is it now, the glory and   7. Latch.
the dream?"   8. Nothing.
5. Money.

But plenty get that way, or die, without
Having a ruddy ten-quid[9] note to show.
She'd got seven thriving sons all in a row.   25

And grandchildren. She liked going by bus
Or train, to stay a bit in those snug homes.
They were her colonies, fair glorious.
"Sit by the fire, ma, till the dinner comes.
Sit by the fire and cuddle little lass."   30

1968

9. Ten-pound: English currency.

ELIZABETH BOWEN
1899–1973

Elizabeth Bowen was born in Dublin and identified her early childhood with
her family's estate near Kildorrery, County Cork. Of Welsh extraction, the
Bowens had acquired Bowen's Court in the seventeenth century, and her father wanted a male heir to inherit it. When he realized that Elizabeth was to be
his only child, he suffered a nervous breakdown, and the child was taken away
to England with her mother and governess. Leading a nomadic existence, the
ten-year-old witnessed her mother's suffering from a fatal cancer. From the
ages of fifteen to eighteen, she attended Downe House School in Kent,
the only Bowen to be educated in England and increasingly self-conscious
about belonging neither in England nor in Ireland. In 1918, after nursing
shell-shocked veterans of World War I in Dublin, she went to live in London,
and in 1923 she married Alan C. Cameron, an educator in the Oxford city
school system. Four years later, the death of her father made Elizabeth Bowen
the first female owner of Bowen's Court. But she did not return to live there
until 1952, and in that year her husband died. Seven years later, she was forced
to sell the house. In 1963, it was pulled down.

   Bowen herself attributed her thematic focus on the insecurity of childhood
to her Anglo-Irish personal history. "Motherless since I was thirteen," she
wrote in a preface (1948), "I was in and out of the homes of my different relatives—and, as constantly, shuttling between two countries: Ireland and England." An Irish outsider in England and a guilty English landowner in Ireland,
she nevertheless used her acute sense of "submerged fear" to depict the vulnerability of child-heroines like the orphaned Portia of *The Death of the Heart*
(1938) or to describe the sinister menace of war-torn London in *The Heat of
the Day* (1948). As in *The Demon Lover*, moreover, that sense of fear is often
conveyed through descriptions of physically damaged or psychically damaging
houses. Bowen wrote most of her fiction first in Northampton and then in

London, where she worked for the Ministry of Information during the bombings of the early forties. After a prolific career, in which she published more than twenty novels and collections of short stories, she died at eighty-four, having been made a Commander of the British Empire and having received honorary degrees from Trinity College, Dublin, and from Oxford University.

The Demon Lover

Towards the end of her day in London Mrs. Drover went round to her shut-up house to look for several things she wanted to take away. Some belonged to herself, some to her family, who were by now used to their country life. It was late August; it had been a steamy, showery day: at the moment the trees down the pavement glittered in an escape of humid yellow afternoon sun. Against the next batch of clouds, already piling up ink-dark, broken chimneys and parapets stood out. In her once familiar street, as in any unused channel, an unfamiliar queerness had silted up; a cat wove itself in and out of railings, but no human eye watched Mrs. Drover's return. Shifting some parcels under her arm, she slowly forced round her latchkey in an unwilling lock, then gave the door, which had warped, a push with her knee. Dead air came out to meet her as she went in.

The staircase window having been boarded up, no light came down into the hall. But one door, she could just see, stood ajar, so she went quickly through into the room and unshuttered the big window in there. Now the prosaic woman, looking about her, was more perplexed than she knew by everything that she saw, by traces of her long former habit of life—the yellow smoke-stain up the white marble mantelpiece, the ring left by a vase on the top of the escritoire[1]; the bruise in the wallpaper where, on the door being thrown open widely, the china handle had always hit the wall. The piano, having gone away to be stored, had left what looked like claw-marks on its part of the parquet. Though not much dust had seeped in, each object wore a film of another kind; and, the only ventilation being the chimney, the whole drawing room smelled of the cold hearth. Mrs. Drover put down her parcels on the escritoire and left the room to proceed upstairs; the things she wanted were in the bedroom chest.

She had been anxious to see how the house was—the part-time caretaker she shared with some neighbors was away this week on his holiday, known to be not yet back. At the best of times he did not look in often, and she was never sure that she trusted him. There were some cracks in the structure, left by the last bombing, on which she was anxious to keep an eye. Not that one could do anything—

---

1. Writing desk.

A shaft of refracted daylight now lay across the hall. She stopped dead and stared at the hall table—on this lay a letter addressed to her.

She thought first—then the caretaker *must* be back. All the same, who, seeing the house shuttered, would have dropped a letter in at the box? It was not a circular, it was not a bill. And the post office redirected, to the address in the country, everything for her that came through the post. The caretaker (even if he *were* back) did not know she was due in London today—her call here had been planned to be a surprise—so his negligence in the matter of this letter, leaving it to wait in the dusk and dust, annoyed her. Annoyed, she picked up the letter, which bore no stamp. But it cannot be important, or they would know. . . . She took the letter rapidly upstairs with her, without a stop to look at the writing till she reached what had been her bedroom, where she let in light. The room looked over the garden and other gardens: the sun had gone in; as the clouds sharpened and lowered, the trees and rank lawns seemed already to smoke with dark. Her reluctance to look again at the letter came from the fact that she felt intruded upon—and by someone contemptuous of her ways. However, in the tenseness preceding the fall of rain she read it: it was a few lines.

> Dear Kathleen,
> You will not have forgotten that today is our anniversary, and the day we said. The years have gone by at once slowly and fast. In view of the fact that nothing has changed, I shall rely upon you to keep your promise. I was sorry to see you leave London, but was satisfied that you would be back in time. You may expect me, therefore, at the hour arranged.
> Until then . . .
> K.

Mrs. Drover looked for the date: it was today's. She dropped the letter on to the bedsprings, then picked it up to see the writing again—her lips, beneath the remains of lipstick, beginning to go white. She felt so much the change in her own face that she went to the mirror, polished a clear patch in it and looked at once urgently and stealthily in. She was confronted by a woman of forty-four, with eyes staring out under a hat brim that had been rather carelessly pulled down. She had not put on any more powder since she left the shop where she ate her solitary tea. The pearls her husband had given her on their marriage hung loose round her now rather thinner throat, slipping into the V of the pink wool jumper her sister knitted last autumn as they sat round the fire. Mrs. Drover's most normal expression was one of controlled worry, but of assent. Since the birth of the third of her little boys, attended by a quite serious illness, she had had an intermittent muscular flicker to the left of her mouth, but in spite of this she could always sustain a manner that was at once energetic and calm.

Turning from her own face as precipitately as she had gone to meet it, she went to the chest where the things were, unlocked it, threw up the lid and knelt to search. But as the rain began to come crashing down she could not keep from looking over her shoulder at the stripped bed on which the letter lay. Behind the blanket of rain the clock of the church that still stood struck six—with rapidly heightening apprehension she counted each of the slow strokes. "The hour arranged. . . . My God," she said, "*what* hour? How should I . . . ? After twenty-five years. . ."

The young girl talking to the soldier in the garden had not ever completely seen his face. It was dark; they were saying goodbye under a tree. Now and then—for it felt, from not seeing him at this intense moment, as though she had never seen him at all—she verified his presence for these few moments longer by putting out a hand, which he each time pressed, without very much kindness, and painfully, on to one of the breast buttons of his uniform. That cut of the button on the palm of her hand was, principally, what she was to carry away. This was so near the end of a leave from France that she could only wish him already gone. It was August 1916. Being not kissed, being drawn away from and looked at intimidated Kathleen till she imagined spectral glitters in the place of his eyes. Turning away and looking back up the lawn she saw, through branches of trees, the drawing room window alight: she caught a breath for the moment when she could go running back there into the safe arms of her mother and sister, and cry: "What shall I do, what shall I do? He has gone."

Hearing her catch her breath, her fiancé said, without feeling: "Cold?"

"You're going away such a long way."

"Not so far as you think."

"I don't understand?"

"You don't have to," he said. "You will. You know what we said."

"But that was—suppose you—I mean, suppose."

"I shall be with you," he said, "sooner or later. You won't forget that. You need do nothing but wait."

Only a little more than a minute later she was free to run up the silent lawn. Looking in through the window at her mother and sister, who did not for the moment perceive her, she already felt that unnatural promise drive down between her and the rest of all human kind. No other way of having given herself could have made her feel so apart, lost and forsworn. She could not have plighted a more sinister troth.

Kathleen behaved well when, some months later, her fiancé was reported missing, presumed killed. Her family not only supported her but were able to praise her courage without stint because they could not regret, as a husband for her, the man they knew almost nothing about. They hoped she would, in a year or two, console herself—and had it been only a question of consolation things might have gone much straighter ahead. But her trouble, behind just a little grief, was a complete dislocation from everything. She did not reject other lovers, for these failed to appear: for years she failed to attract men—and with the approach of her thirties she became natural enough to share her family's anxiousness on this score. She began to put herself out, to wonder; and at thirty-two she was very greatly relieved to find herself being courted by William Drover. She married him, and the two of them settled down in this quiet, arboreal part of Kensington:[2] in this house the years piled up, her children were born and they all lived till they were driven out by the bombs of the next war. Her movements as Mrs. Drover were circumscribed, and she dismissed any idea that they were still watched.

As things were—dead or living the letter-writer sent her only a threat. Unable, for some minutes, to go on kneeling with her back exposed to the empty room, Mrs. Drover rose from the chest to sit on an upright chair whose back was firmly against the wall. The desuetude of her former bedroom, her married London home's whole air of being a cracked cup from which memory, with its reassuring power, had either evaporated or leaked away, made a crisis—and at just this crisis the letter-writer had, knowledgeably, struck. The hollowness of the house this evening cancelled years on years of voices, habits and steps. Through the shut windows she only heard rain fall on the roofs around. To rally herself, she said she was in a mood—and, for two or three seconds shutting her eyes, told herself that she had imagined the letter. But she opened them—there it lay on the bed.

On the supernatural side of the letter's entrance she was not permitting her mind to dwell. Who, in London, knew she meant to call at the house today? Evidently, however, this had been known. The caretaker, *had* he come back, had had no cause to expect her: he would have taken the letter in his pocket, to forward it, at his own time, through the post. There was no other sign that the caretaker had been in—but, if not? Letters dropped in at doors of deserted houses do not fly or walk to tables in halls. They do not sit on the dust of empty tables with the air of certainty that they will be found. There is needed some human hand —but nobody but the caretaker had a key. Under circumstances she did not care to consider, a house can be entered without a key. It was possi-

2. Fashionable neighborhood in London.

ble that she was not alone now. She might be being waited for, down-stairs. Waited for—until when? Until "the hour arranged." At least that was not six o'clock: six had struck.

She rose from the chair and went over and locked the door.

The thing was, to get out. To fly? No, not that: she had to catch her train. As a woman whose utter dependability was the keystone of her family life she was not willing to return to the country, to her husband, her little boys and her sister, without the objects she had come up to fetch. Resuming work at the chest she set about making up a number of parcels in a rapid, fumbling-decisive way. These, with her shopping parcels, would be too much to carry; these meant a taxi—at the thought of the taxi her heart went up and her normal breathing resumed. I will ring up the taxi now; the taxi cannot come too soon: I shall hear the taxi out there running its engine, till I walk calmly down to it through the hall. I'll ring up—But no: the telephone is cut off . . . She tugged at a knot she had tied wrong.

The idea of flight . . . He was never kind to me, not really. I don't remember him kind at all. Mother said he never considered me. He was set on me, that was what it was—not love. Not love, not meaning a person well. What did he do, to make me promise like that? I can't re-member.—But she found that she could.

She remembered with such dreadful acuteness that the twenty-five years since then dissolved like smoke and she instinctively looked for the weal left by the button on the palm of her hand. She remembered not only all that he said and did but the complete suspension of *her* ex-istence during that August week. I was not myself—they all told me so at the time. She remembered—but with one white burning blank as where acid has dropped on a photograph: *under no conditions* could she remember his face.

So, wherever he may be waiting, I shall not know him. You have no time to run from a face you do not expect.

The thing was to get to the taxi before any clock struck what could be the hour. She would slip down the street and round the side of the square to where the square gave on the main road. She would return in the taxi, safe, to her own door, and bring the solid driver into the house with her to pick up the parcels from room to room. The idea of the taxi driver made her decisive, bold: she unlocked her door, went to the top of the staircase and listened down.

She heard nothing—but while she was hearing nothing the *passé*[3] air of the staircase was disturbed by a draught that travelled up to her face. It emanated from the basement: down there a door or window was being opened by someone who chose this moment to leave the house.

3. I.e., foul, stuffy.

The rain had stopped; the pavements steamily shone as Mrs. Drover let herself out by inches from her own front door into the empty street. The unoccupied houses opposite continued to meet her look with their damaged stare. Making towards the thoroughfare and the taxi, she tried not to keep looking behind. Indeed, the silence was so intense—one of those creeks of London silence exaggerated this summer by the damage of war—that no tread could have gained on hers unheard. Where her street debouched on the square where people went on living she grew conscious of and checked her unnatural pace. Across the open end of the square two buses impassively passed each other; women, a peram-bulator, cyclists, a man wheeling a barrow signalized, once again, the ordinary flow of life. At the square's most populous corner should be—and was—the short taxi rank. This evening, only one taxi—but this, al-though it presented its blank rump, appeared already to be alertly waiting for her. Indeed, without looking round the driver started his engine as she panted up from behind and put her hand on the door. As she did so, the clock struck seven. The taxi faced the main road: to make the trip back to her house it would have to turn—she had settled back on the seat and the taxi *had* turned before she, surprised by its knowing movement, recollected that she had not "said where." She leaned for-ward to scratch at the glass panel that divided the driver's head from her own.

The driver braked to what was almost a stop, turned round and slid the glass panel back: the jolt of this flung Mrs. Drover forward till her face was almost into the glass. Through the aperture driver and passen-ger, not six inches between them, remained for an eternity eye to eye. Mrs. Drover's mouth hung open for some seconds before she could issue her first scream. After that she continued to scream freely and to beat with her gloved hands on the glass all round as the taxi, accelerat-ing without mercy, made off with her into the hinterland of deserted streets.

1945

MERIDEL LE SUEUR

1900–

During the Great Depression, Meridel Le Sueur recorded the stories of Mid-western women, insisting that "their lives were not defeated, trashed, defense-less but that we as woman contained the real and only seed, and were the granary of the people." She had begun to consider herself a "village scribe" for American Indians and immigrant farm and factory workers when she was a young girl traveling throughout the Midwest and Southwest with her socialist parents. A high school dropout, LeSueur lived in a New York anarchist commune with Emma Goldman, acted in the early movies produced in Hollywood, and directed the Little Theater of Sacramento, California. Married to Harry Rice, a labor organizer, she gave birth to two daughters in the late twenties, the period in which she began to publish the work she had been recording in her journals.

Le Sueur's fifty-year career was shaped by her association with prairie populists (who advocated an equitable redistribution of wealth to help farmers and laborers) and Marxists. During the thirties, both her prize-winning stories and the articles she wrote for left-wing periodicals documented the struggle of working people. According to the critic Elaine Hedges, *Salute to Spring* (1940), a collection of Le Sueur's stories and articles, marked both the high point of Le Sueur's reputation and the beginning of her critical neglect. The first draft of her novel *The Girl* was written in 1939, but the book remained unpublished until 1978. When national sentiment arose against communism during the so-called red scare of the fifties, Le Sueur was informally blacklisted, and she turned to writing children's stories—about Abraham Lincoln's mother, for example, and about Indian-white relationships. An early work, *Annunciation* (1935) looks forward to such a recent publication as *Rites of Ancient Ripening* (1975), for it demonstrates Le Sueur's ongoing fascination with the myths and realities of motherhood; originally written in the form of notes to her first, unborn child, it was, she explained, "the bud of a new flower within the time of the old."

Annunciation[1]

For Rachel

Ever since I have known I was going to have a child I have kept writing things down on these little scraps of paper. There is something I want to say, something I want to make clear for myself and others. One lives all one's life in a sort of way, one is alive and that is about all that there is to say about it. Then something happens.

There is the pear tree I can see in the afternoons as I sit on this porch writing these notes. It stands for something. It has had something to do with what has happened to me. I sit here all afternoon in the autumn sun and then I begin to write something on this yellow paper; something seems to be going on like a buzzing, a flying and circling within me, and then I want to write it down in some way. I have never felt this way before, except when I was a girl and was first in love and wanted then to set things down on paper so that they would not be lost. It is something perhaps like a farmer who hears the swarming of a host of bees and goes out to catch them so that he will have honey. If he does

1. The angel Gabriel's announcement to Mary that she is to give birth to the Son of God (Luke 1:26–38).

not go out right away, they will go, and he will hear the buzzing grow-ing more distant in the afternoon.

My sweater pocket is full of scraps of paper on which I have written. I sit here many afternoons while Karl is out looking for work, writing on pieces of paper, unfolding, reading what I have already written.

We have been here two weeks at Mrs. Mason's boarding house. The leaves are falling and there is a golden haze over everything. This is the fourth month for me and it is fall. A rich powerful haze comes down from the mountains over the city. In the afternoon I go out for a walk. There is a park just two blocks from here. Old men and tramps lie on the grass all day. It is hard to get work. Many people beside Karl are out of work. People are hungry just as I am hungry. People are ready to flower and they cannot. In the evenings we go there with a sack of old fruit we can get at the stand across the way quite cheap, bunches of grapes and old pears. At noon there is a hush in the air and at evening there are stirrings of wind coming from the sky, blowing in the fallen leaves, or perhaps there is a light rain, falling quickly on the walk. Early in the mornings the sun comes up hot in the sky and shines all day through the mist. It is strange, I notice all these things, the sun, the rain falling, the blowing of the wind. It is as if they had a meaning for me as the pear tree has come to have.

In front of Mrs. Mason's house there is a large magnolia tree with its blossoms yellow, hanging over the steps almost within reach. Its giant leaves are motionless and shining in the heat, occasionally as I am going down the steps towards the park one falls heavily on the walk.

This house is an old wooden one, that once was quite a mansion I imagine. There are glass chandeliers in the hall and fancy tile in the bathrooms. It was owned by the rich once and now the dispossessed live in it with the rats. We have a room three flights up. You go into the dark hallway and up the stairs. Broken settees and couches sit in the halls. About one o'clock the girls come down stairs to get their mail and sit on the front porch. The blinds go up in the old wooden house across the street. It is always quite hot at noon.

Next to our room lies a sick woman in what is really a kind of closet with no windows. As you pass you see her face on the pillow and a nauseating odor of sickness comes out the door. I haven't asked her what is the matter with her but everyone knows she is waiting for death. Somehow it is not easy to speak to her. No one comes to see her. She has been a housemaid all her life tending other people's children; now no one comes to see her. She gets up sometimes and drinks a little from the bottle of milk that is always sitting by her bed covered with flies.

Mrs. Mason, the landlady, is letting us stay although we have only paid a week's rent and have been here over a week without paying. But it is a bad season and we may be able to pay later. It is better perhaps for her than having an empty room. But I hate to go out and have to pass her door and I am always fearful of meeting her on the stairs. I go down as quietly as I can but it isn't easy, for the stairs creak frightfully.

The room we have on the top floor is a back room, opening out onto an old porch which seems to be actually tied to the wall of the house with bits of wire and rope. The floor of it slants downward to a rickety railing. There is a box perched on the railing that has geraniums in it. They are large, tough California geraniums. I guess nothing can kill them. I water them since I have been here and a terribly red flower has come. It is on this porch I am sitting. Just over the banisters stand the top branches of a pear tree.

Many afternoons I sit here. It has become a kind of alive place to me. The room is dark behind me, with only the huge walnut tree scraping against the one window over the kitchenette. If I go to the railing and look down I can see far below the back yard which has been made into a garden with two fruit trees and I can see where a path has gone in the summer between a small bed of flowers, now only dead stalks. The ground is bare under the walnut tree where little sun penetrates. There is a dog kennel by the round trunk but there doesn't ever seem to be a dog. An old wicker chair sits outdoors in rain or shine. A woman in an old wrapper comes out and sits there almost every afternoon. I don't know who she is, for I don't know anybody in this house, having to sneak downstairs as I do.

Karl says I am foolish to be afraid of the landlady. He comes home drunk and makes a lot of noise. He says she's lucky in these times to have anybody in her house, but I notice in the mornings he goes down the stairs quietly and often goes out the back way.

I'm alone all day so I sit on this rickety porch. Straight out from the rail so that I can almost touch it is the radiating frail top of the pear tree that has opened a door for me. If the pears were still hanging on it each would be alone and separate with a kind of bloom upon it. Such a bloom is upon me at this moment. Is it possible that everyone, Mrs. Mason who runs this boarding house, the woman next door, the girls downstairs, all in this dead wooden house have hung at one time, each separate in a mist and bloom upon some invisible tree? I wonder if it is so.

I am in luck to have this high porch to sit on and this tree swaying before me through the long afternoons and the long nights. Before we came here, after the show broke up in S.F.[2] we were in an old hotel, a foul smelling place with a dirty chambermaid and an old cat in the halls, and night and day we could hear the radio going in the office. We had a room with a window looking across a narrow way into another room

2. San Francisco.

where a lean man stood in the mornings looking across, shaving his evil face. By leaning out and looking up I could see straight up the sides of the tall building and above the smoky sky.

Most of the time I was sick from the bad food we ate. Karl and I walked the streets looking for work. Sometimes I was too sick to go. Karl would come in and there would be no money at all. He would go out again to perhaps borrow something. I know many times he begged although we never spoke of it, but I could tell by the way he looked when he came back with a begged quarter. He went in with a man selling Mexican beans but he didn't make much. I lay on the bed bad days feeling sick and hungry, sick too with the stale odor of the foul walls. I would lie there a long time listening to the clang of the city outside. I would feel thick with this child. For some reason I remember that I would sing to myself and often became happy as if mesmerised there in the foul room. It must have been because of this child. Karl would come back perhaps with a little money and we would go out to a dairy lunch[3] and there have food I could not relish. The first alleyway I must give it up with the people all looking at me.

Karl would be angry. He would walk on down the street so people wouldn't think he was with me. Once we walked until evening down by the docks. "Why don't you take something?" he kept saying. "Then you wouldn't throw up your food like that. Get rid of it. That's what everybody does nowadays. This isn't the time to have a child. Everything is rotten. We must change it." He kept on saying, "Get rid of it. Take something why don't you?" And he got angry when I didn't say anything but just walked along beside him. He shouted so loud at me that some stevedores loading a boat for L.A.[4] laughed at us and began kidding us, thinking perhaps we were lovers having a quarrel.

Some time later, I don't know how long it was, for I hadn't any time except the nine months I was counting off, but one evening Karl sold enough Mexican jumping beans at a carnival to pay our fare, so we got on a river boat and went up the river to a delta town. There might be a better chance of a job. On this boat you can sit up all night if you have no money to buy a berth. We walked all evening along the deck and then when it got cold we went into the saloon because we had pawned our coats. Already at that time I had got the habit of carrying slips of paper around with me and writing on them, as I am doing now. I had a feeling then that something was happening to me of some kind of loveliness I would want to preserve in some way. Perhaps that was it. At any rate I was writing things down. Perhaps it had something to do with Karl wanting me all the time to take something. "Everybody does it,"

---

3. In Jewish dietary custom, a meal containing   4. Los Angeles.
only fish and dairy products.

he kept telling me. "It's nothing, then it's all over." I stopped talking to him much. Everything I said only made him angry. So writing was a kind of conversation I carried on with myself and with the child.

Well, on the river boat that night after we had gone into the saloon to get out of the cold, Karl went to sleep right away in a chair. But I couldn't sleep. I sat watching him. The only sound was the churning of the paddle wheel and the lap of the water. I had on then this sweater and the notes I wrote are still in the breast pocket. I would look up from writing and see Karl sleeping like a young boy.

"Tonight, the world into which you are coming"—then I was speaking to the invisible child—"is very strange and beautiful. That is, the natural world is beautiful. I don't know what you will think of man, but the dark glisten of vegetation and the blowing of the fertile land wind and the delicate strong step of the sea wind, these things are familiar to me and will be familiar to you. I hope you will be like these things. I hope you will glisten with the glisten of ancient life, the same beauty that is in a leaf or a wild rabbit, wild sweet beauty of limb and eye. I am going on a boat between dark shores, and the river and the sky are so quiet that I can hear the scurryings of tiny animals on the shores and their little breathings seem to be all around. I think of them, wild, carrying their young now, crouched in the dark underbrush with the fruit-scented land wind in their delicate nostrils, and they are looking out at the moon and the fast clouds. Silent, alive, they sit in the dark shadow of the greedy world. There is something wild about us too, something tender and wild about my having you as a child, about your crouching so secretly here. There is something very tender and wild about it. We, too, are at the mercy of many hunters. On this boat I act like the other human beings, for I do not show that I have you, but really I know we are as helpless, as wild, as at bay as some tender wild animals who might be on the ship.

"I put my hand where you lie so silently. I hope you will come glistening with life power, with it shining upon you as upon the feathers of birds. I hope you will be a warrior and fierce for change, so all can live."

Karl woke at dawn and was angry with me for sitting there looking at him. Just to look at me makes him angry now. He took me out and made me walk along the deck although it was hardly light yet. I gave him the "willies" he said, looking at him like that. We walked round and round the decks and he kept talking to me in a low voice, trying to persuade me. It was hard for me to listen. My teeth were chattering with cold, but anyway I found it hard to listen to anyone talking, especially Karl. I remember I kept thinking to myself that a child should be made by machinery now, then there would be no fuss. I kept thinking of all the places I had been with this new child, traveling with the show from Tia Juana to S.F. In trains, over mountains, through deserts, in hotels and rooming houses, and myself in a trance of wonder. There wasn't a person I could have told it to, that I was going to have a child. I didn't want to be pitied. Night after night we played in the tent and the faces were all dust to me, but traveling, through the window the many vistas of the earth meant something—the bony skeleton of the mountains, like the skeleton of the world jutting through its flowery flesh. My child too would be made of bone. There were the fields of summer, the orchards fruiting, the berry fields and the pickers stooping, the oranges and the grapes. Then the city again in September and the many streets I walk looking for work, stopping secretly in doorways to feel beneath my coat.

It is better in this small town with the windy fall days and the sudden rain falling out of a sunny sky. I can't look for work any more. Karl gets a little work washing dishes at a wienie place.[5] I sit here on the porch as if in a deep sleep waiting for this unknown child. I keep hearing this far flight of strange birds going on in the mysterious air about me. This time has come without warning. How can it be explained? Everything is dead and closed, the world a stone, and then suddenly everything comes alive as it has for me, like an anemone on a rock, opening itself, disclosing itself, and the very stones themselves break open like bread. It has all got something to do with the pear tree too. It has come about some way as I have sat here with this child so many afternoons, with the pear tree murmuring in the air.

The pears are all gone from the tree but I imagine them hanging there, ripe curves within the many scimitar leaves, and within them many pears of the coming season. I feel like a pear. I hang secret within the curling leaves, just as the pear would be hanging on its tree. It seems possible to me that perhaps all people at some time feel this, round and full. You can tell by looking at most people that the world remains a stone to them and a closed door. I'm afraid it will become like that to me again. Perhaps after this child is born, then everything will harden and become small and mean again as it was before. Perhaps I would even have a hard time remembering this time at all and it wouldn't seem wonderful. That is why I would like to write it down.

How can it be explained? Suddenly many movements are going on within me, many things are happening, there is an almost unbearable sense of sprouting, of bursting encasements, of moving kernels, expanding flesh. Perhaps it is such an activity that makes a field come alive with millions of sprouting shoots of corn or wheat. Perhaps it is something like that that makes a new world.

I have been sitting here and it seems as if the wooden houses around me had become husks that suddenly as I watched began to swarm with

5. Hotdog stand.

livening seed. The house across becomes a fermenting seed alive with its own movements. Everything seems to be moving along a curve of creation. The alley below and all the houses are to me like an orchard abloom, shaking and trembling, moving outward with shouting. The people coming and going seem to hang on the tree of life, each blossoming from himself. I am standing here looking at the blind windows of the house next door and suddenly the walls fall away, the doors open, and within I see a young girl making a bed from which she had just risen having dreamed of a young man who became her lover . . . she stands before her looking-glass in love with herself.

I see in another room a young man sleeping, his bare arm thrown over his head. I see a woman lying on a bed after her husband has left her. There is a child looking at me. An old woman sits rocking. A boy leans over a table reading a book. A woman who has been nursing a child comes out and hangs clothes on the line, her dress in front wet with milk. A young woman comes to an open door looking up and down the street waiting for her young husband. I get up early to see this young woman come to the door in a pink wrapper and wave to her husband. They have only been married a short time, she stands waving until he is out of sight and even then she stands smiling to herself, her hand upraised.

Why should I be excited? Why should I feel this excitement, seeing a woman waving to her young husband, or a woman who has been nursing a child, or a young man sleeping? Yet I am excited. The many houses have become like an orchard blooming soundlessly. The many people have become like fruits to me, the young girl in the room alone before her mirror, the young man sleeping, the mother, all are shaking with their inward blossoming, shaken by the windy blooming, moving along a future curve.

I do not want it all to go away from me. Now many doors are opening and shutting, light is falling upon darkness, closed places are opening, still things are now moving. But there will come a time when the doors will close again, the shouting will be gone, the sprouting and the movement and the wondrous opening out of everything will be gone. I will be only myself. I will come to look like the women in this house. I try to write it down on little slips of paper, trying to preserve this time for myself so that afterwards when everything is the same again I can remember what all must have.

This is the spring there should be in the world, so I say to myself, "Lie in the sun with the child in your flesh shining like a jewel. Dream and sing, pagan, wise in your vitals. Stand still like a fat budding tree, like a stalk of corn athrob and aglisten in the heat. Lie like a mare panting with the dancing feet of colts against her sides. Sleep at night as the spring earth. Walk heavily as a wheat stalk at its full time bending towards the earth waiting for the reaper. Let your life swell downward so you become like a vase, a vessel. Let the unknown child knock and knock against you and rise like a dolphin within."

I look at myself in the mirror. My legs and head hardly make a difference, just a stem my legs. My hips are full and tight in back as if bracing themselves. I look like a pale and shining pomegranate, hard and tight, and my skin shines like crystal with the veins showing beneath blue and distended. Children are playing outside and girls are walking with young men along the walk. All that seems over for me. I am a pomegranate hanging from an invisible tree with the juice and movement of seed within my hard skin. I dress slowly. I hate the smell of clothes. I want to leave them off and just hang in the sun ripening . . . ripening.

It is hard to write it down so that it will mean anything. I've never heard anything about how a woman feels who is going to have a child, or about how a pear tree feels bearing its fruit. I would like to read these things many years from now, when I am barren and no longer trembling like this, when I get like the women in this house, or like the woman in the closed room, I can hear her breathing through the afternoon.

When Karl has no money he does not come back at night. I go out on the street walking to forget how hungry I am. This is an old town and along the streets are many old strong trees. Night leaves hang from them ready to fall, dark and swollen with their coming death. Trees, dark, separate, heavy with their down hanging leaves, cool surfaces hanging on the dark. I put my hand among the leaf sheaves. They strike with a cool surface, their glossy surfaces surprising me in the dark. I feel like a tree swirling upwards too, muscular sap alive, with rich surfaces hanging from me, flaring outward rocket-like and falling to my roots, a rich strong power in me to break through into a new life. And dark in me as I walk the streets of this decayed town are the buds of my child. I walk alone under the dark flaring trees. There are many houses with the lights shining out but you and I walk on the skirts of the lawns amidst the downpouring darkness. Houses are not for us. For us many kinds of hunger, for us a deep rebellion.

Trees come from a far seed walking the wind, my child too from a far seed blowing from last year's rich and revolutionary dead. My child budding secretly from far walking seed, budding secretly and dangerously in the night.

The woman has come out and sits in the rocker, reading, her fat legs crossed. She scratches herself, cleans her nails, picks her teeth. Across the alley lying flat on the ground is a garage. People are driving in and out. But up here it is very quiet and the movement of the pear tree is the only movement and I seem to hear its delicate sound of living as it moves upon itself silently, and outward and upward.

The leaves twirl and twirl all over the tree, the delicately curving tinkling leaves. They twirl and twirl on the tree and the tree moves far inward upon its stem, moves in an invisible wind, gently swaying. Far below straight down the vertical stem like a stream, black and strong into the ground, runs the trunk; and invisible, spiraling downward and outwards in powerful radiation, lie the roots. I can see it spiraling upwards from below, its stem straight, and from it, spiraling the branches season by season, and from the spiraling branches moving out in quick motion, the forked stems, and from the stems twirling fragilely the tinier stems holding outward until they fall, the half curled pear leaves.

Far below lies the yard, lying flat and black beneath the body of the upshooting tree, for the pear tree from above looks as if it had been shot instantaneously from the ground, shot upward like a rocket to break in showers of leaves and fruits twirling and falling. Its movement looks quick, sudden and rocketing. My child when grown can be looked at in this way as if it suddenly existed . . . but I know the slow time of making. The pear tree knows.

Far inside the vertical stem there must be a movement, a river of sap rising from below and radiating outward in many directions clear to the tips of the leaves. The leaves are the lips of the tree speaking in the wind or they move like many tongues. The fruit of the tree you can see has been a round speech, speaking in full tongue on the tree, hanging in ripe body, the fat curves hung within the small curves of the leaves. I imagine them there. The tree has shot up like a rocket, then stops in midair and its leaves flow out gently and its fruit curves roundly and gently in a long slow curve. All is gentle on the pear tree after its strong upward shooting movement.

I sit here all the afternoon as if in its branches, midst the gentle and curving body of the tree. I have looked at it until it has become more familiar to me than Karl. It seems a strange thing that a tree might come to mean more to one than one's husband. It seems a shameful thing even. I am ashamed to think of it but it is so. I have sat here in the pale sun and the tree has spoken to me with its many tongued leaves, speaking through the afternoon of how to round a fruit. And I listen through the slow hours. I listen to the whisperings of the pear tree, speaking to me, speaking to me. How can I describe what is said by a pear tree? Karl did not speak to me so. No one spoke to me in any good speech.

There is a woman coming up the stairs, slowly. I can hear her breathing. I can hear her behind me at the screen door.

She came out and spoke to me. I know why she was looking at me so closely. "I hear you're going to have a child," she said. "It's too bad."

She is the same color as the dead leaves in the park. Was she once alive too?

I am writing on a piece of wrapping paper now. It is about ten o'clock. Karl didn't come home and I had no supper. I walked through the streets with their heavy, heavy trees bending over the walks and the lights shining from the houses and over the river the mist rising.

Before I came into this room I went out and saw the pear tree standing motionless, its leaves curled in the dark, its radiating body falling darkly, like a stream far below into the earth.

1935

ZORA NEALE HURSTON
c. 1901–1960

Zora Neale Hurston once claimed that she had escaped punishment when arrested for crossing against a red light by explaining to the authorities that "I had seen white folks pass on green and therefore assumed the red light was for me." Both the humor and the audacity of this incident were typical of her. Like a number of her female characters, Hurston was a strong woman, determined to "wrassle me up a future, or die trying," and she was encouraged by another strong woman, her mother, who advised her to "jump at de sun." Not only did Hurston profit from a mother who refused to "squinch" the girl's spirits, she also gained self-confidence from her hometown, the first incorporated, self-governing, all-black town in the United States. Her father, John Hurston, a Baptist preacher, was elected to three terms as the mayor of Eatonville, Florida. Although Eatonville later inspired Hurston to preserve the linguistic exuberance, the protective community, and the spiritual traditions of Southern black culture, when her mother died the nine-year-old girl saw herself as a wanderer. Alienated by her father's remarriage, she worked at fourteen as a wardrobe girl in a traveling Gilbert and Sullivan troupe until—with one dress and one change of underwear—she enrolled at Morgan Academy in Baltimore. There, and later at Howard University in Washington, D.C., she supported herself in jobs ranging from manicurist to maid.

After 1925, when Hurston moved to New York City, she became a frequent guest at the writer Carl Van Vechten's parties, where many distinguished Harlem artists mingled with wealthy whites. She worked first as a secretary and then as a chauffeur and companion to the popular white novelist Fanny Hurst. Early writings at Howard had brought her to the attention of Alain Locke, whose anthology *The New Negro* (1925) hailed the coming of a "new soul" for black America. Hurston contributed a story to Locke's influential volume, and she also helped edit the quarterly *Fire!!*, which the authors Langston Hughes and Wallace Thurman created in 1926. In addition, a number of her plays and stories won literary awards. Although Hughes and Hurston quarreled in 1931 after they tried to collaborate on the play *Mule Bone*, during the two and a half years that Hurston actively participated in the Harlem Renaissance she was appreciated by Hughes and his friends as a flamboyant dresser and a great teller of folk tales.

During her early New York years, Hurston also enrolled at Barnard College, where she studied anthropology on a scholarship. Barnard's only black student, she received her degree in 1928 after working with the noted anthropologist Franz Boas. One year earlier, however, she had already embarked on folklore research in her hometown of Eatonville, research sponsored by Mrs. R. Osgood Mason, a white patron who subsidized a number of other artists besides Hurston. Generous though Mrs. Mason was, both Hurston's biographer Robert Hemenway and the literary critic Mary Helen Washington have shown that Hurston was placed in a situation of childlike dependency on a "godmother" who prohibited the young writer and scholar from publishing both her fiction and her anthropological findings. In addition, Hurston had to write her patroness adulatory letters to get her to agree even to the purchase of a much needed pair of shoes. In 1932, when Mrs. Mason claimed ownership of the material Hurston had collected, the relationship collapsed.

During the thirties, the decade in which she published her most important work, Hurston taught at Bethune-Cookman College (1934), enrolled at Columbia University on a fellowship for graduate study in anthropology (1935), did dramatic coaching for the Federal Theater Project in New York (1935–1936), traveled in the Caribbean on Guggenheim Fellowships (1936 and 1937), and worked as an editor for the Federal Writers' Project in Florida (1938). At the beginning of this period, she was briefly married, to Herbert Sheen, a medical student she had met at Howard University, and, at the end of the decade, she was again briefly married to Albert Price, a younger man. Among the most successful of the works she composed in this time, her collection of folklore *Mules and Men* (1935) and her novel *Their Eyes Were Watching God* (1937) have recently been reissued after years of critical neglect.

These two books established Hurston as an important twentieth-century writer. *Mules and Men* was based on Hurston's anthropological studies in Florida and Louisiana. During her earlier travels, Hurston had participated in hoodoo initiation ceremonies in New Orleans, spending sixty-nine hours, on one occasion, nude on a conjurer's couch, with her navel touching a snakeskin. Hoodoo ceremonies and tall-tale sessions reappear, vividly dramatized, in *Mules and Men*, along with descriptions of such hoodoo rites as *Eulalia—Ritual to Get a Man*. Through her recounting of initiation, cursing, and conjuring ceremonies, Hurston demonstrated that hoodoo was "a suppressed religion" and not "just superstition," even while she rescued black expression from ridicule by illustrating its metaphoric inventiveness. Similarly, *Their Eyes Were Watching God* celebrated the uniqueness of black cultural roots. Hurston's heroine, Janie Woods, is warned by her grandmother that "de nigger woman is de mule uh de world." Yet Janie manages to live the text of a sermon her grandmother had wanted to preach, "a great sermon about colored women sittin' on high." Through her heroine's progress, then, Hurston charted the evolution of Afro-American culture from subjugation through identification with whites, and, finally, into autonomous racial identity and self-celebration.

Hurston received remarkably good reviews not only for these two books but for her novel *Jonah's Gourd Vine* (1934), for her play *Singing Steel* (1934), which attempted to debunk "the current mammy-song-Jolson conception of the Southern Negro," and for her autobiography *Dust Tracks on a Road* (1942); however, she came under attack throughout the forties and fifties. As early as 1937, the celebrated black novelist Richard Wright had criticized *Their Eyes Were Watching God* as a "minstrel" novel intended to make white people laugh at blacks. Her former teacher and friend Alain Locke called *Moses, Man of the Mountain* (1939)—a novel that takes Moses out of the Judeo-Christian tradition by portraying him as an African—"caricature instead of portraiture." Such critics were also opposed to the conservative cast of the political and social essays Hurston published in predominantly white magazines. Yet the basis for Hurston's rejection of Northern liberalism was clarified by a letter she wrote to the editor of a Florida newspaper, in which she attacked the Supreme Court school desegregation decision (1954), for Hurston argued that integration denied the value of already-existing black institutions. By the fifties, like many other journalists Hurston was publishing anticommunist essays. While Hemenway has attributed Hurston's growing conservatism to her inability "to admit that one could both celebrate Afro-American culture and deplore many of the conditions that helped shape it," Washington has associated Hurston's decision to ignore the brutal side of black experience with a refusal to submit to political pressures on black writers, who were expected throughout this period to protest against racism by portraying blacks as degraded or victimized.

In any case, by the time Hurston published her last novel, *Seraph on the Suwanee* (1948), she was beginning to experience the insecurity and pain that would characterize the rest of her life. Although she continued to teach and travel, she began to suffer from gall bladder attacks and an ulcer. In 1948, she was accused in New York of impairing the morals of a minor, a charge that was dismissed but that nevertheless horrified her. In 1950, she was working as a maid in Miami until the woman who employed her discovered an article Hurston had published in the *Saturday Evening Post*. Subsequent free-lance writing earned her some savings, and she managed to spend several years in a house in Eau Gallie, Florida, during the early fifties. But her fiction was being rejected by publishing houses, and in 1956, she was evicted after her landlord decided to sell the property. After a stroke in 1959, she entered the St. Lucie County Welfare Home. Three months later she died penniless, and her body was placed in an unmarked grave.

Both *How It Feels to Be Colored Me* and *Sweat* were published before Hurston attained national visibility as a folklorist and a novelist. Their vitality is typical, however, and helps explain why the contemporary black writer Alice Walker—the editor of a Zora Neale Hurston reader—admires Hurston's vision of "racial health—a sense of black people as complete, complex, *undiminished* human beings."

Sweat

It was eleven o'clock of a Spring night in Florida. It was Sunday. Any other night, Delia Jones would have been in bed for two hours by this time. But she was a washwoman, and Monday morning meant a great deal to her. So she collected the soiled clothes on Saturday when she returned the clean things. Sunday night after church, she sorted them and put the white things to soak. It saved her almost a half day's start. A great hamper in the bedroom held the clothes that she brought home. It was so much neater than a number of bundles lying around.

She squatted in the kitchen floor beside the great pile of clothes, sorting them into small heaps according to color, and humming a song in a mournful key, but wondering through it all where Sykes, her husband, had gone with her horse and buckboard.[1]

Just then something long, round, limp and black fell upon her shoulders and slithered to the floor beside her. A great terror took hold of her. It softened her knees and dried her mouth so that it was a full minute before she could cry out or move. Then she saw that it was the big bull whip her husband liked to carry when he drove.

She lifted her eyes to the door and saw him standing there bent over with laughter at her fright. She screamed at him.

"Sykes, what you throw dat whip on me like dat? You know it would skeer me—looks just like a snake, an' you knows how skeered Ah is of snakes."

"Course Ah knowed it! That's how come Ah done it." He slapped his leg with his hand and almost rolled on the ground in his mirth. "If you such a big fool dat you got to have a fit over a earth worm or a string, Ah don't keer how bad Ah skeer you."

"You aint got no business doing it. Gawd knows it's a sin. Some day Ah'm gointuh drop dead from some of yo' foolishness. 'Nother thing, where you been wid mah rig? Ah feeds dat pony. He aint fuh you to be drivin' wid no bull whip."

"You sho is one aggravatin' nigger woman!" he declared and stepped into the room. She resumed her work and did not answer him at once. "Ah done tole you time and again to keep them white folks' clothes outa dis house."

He picked up the whip and glared down at her. Delia went on with her work. She went out into the yard and returned with a galvanized tub and set it on the washbench. She saw that Sykes had kicked all of the clothes together again, and now stood in her way truculently, his whole manner hoping, *praying*, for an argument. But she walked calmly around him and commenced to re-sort the things.

"Next time, Ah'm gointer kick 'em outdoors," he threatened as he struck a match along the leg of his corduroy breeches.

Delia never looked up from her work, and her thin, stooped shoulders sagged further.

"Ah aint for no fuss t'night, Sykes. Ah just come from taking sacrament at the church house."

1. An open wagon.

He snorted scornfully. "Yeah, you just come from de church house on a Sunday night, but heah you is gone to work on them clothes. You ain't nothing but a hypocrite. One of them amen-corner Christians—sing, whoop, and shout, then come home and wash white folks' clothes on the Sabbath."

He stepped roughly upon the whitest pile of things, kicking them helter-skelter as he crossed the room. His wife gave a little scream of dismay, and quickly gathered them together again.

"Sykes, you quit grindin' dirt into these clothes! How can Ah git through by Sat'day if Ah don't start on Sunday?"

"Ah don't keer if you never git through. Anyhow, Ah done promised Gawd and a couple of other men, Ah aint gointer have it in mah house. Don't gimme no lip neither, else Ah'll throw 'em out and put mah fist up side yo' head to boot."

Delia's habitual meekness seemed to slip from her shoulders like a blown scarf. She was on her feet; her poor little body, her bare knuckly hands bravely defying the strapping hulk before her.

"Looka heah, Sykes, you done gone too fur. Ah been married to you fur fifteen years, and Ah been takin' in washin' fur fifteen years, Sweat, sweat, sweat! Work and sweat, cry and sweat, pray and sweat!"

"What's that got to do with me?" he asked brutally.

"What's it got to do with you, Sykes? Mah tub of suds is filled yo' belly with vittles more times than yo' hands is filled it. Mah sweat is done paid for this house and Ah reckon Ah kin keep on sweatin' in it."

She seized the iron skillet from the stove and struck a defensive pose, which act surprised him greatly, coming from her. It cowed him and he did not strike her as he usually did.

"Naw you won't," she panted, "that ole snaggle-toothed black woman you runnin' with aint comin' heah to pile up on *mah* sweat and blood. You aint paid for nothin' on this place, and Ah'm gointer stay right heah till Ah'm toted out foot foremost."

"Well, you better quit gittin' me riled up, else they'll be totin' you out sooner than you expect. Ah'm so tired of you Ah don't know whut to do. Gawd! how Ah hates skinny wimmen!"

A little awed by this new Delia, he sidled out of the door and slammed the back gate after him. He did not say where he had gone, but she knew too well. She knew very well that he would not return until nearly daybreak also. Her work over, she went on to bed but not to sleep at once. Things had come to a pretty pass!

She lay awake, gazing upon the debris that cluttered their matrimonial trail. Not an image left standing along the way. Anything like flowers had long ago been drowned in the salty stream that had been pressed from her heart. Her tears, her sweat, her blood. She had brought love to the union and he had brought a longing after the flesh.

Two months after the wedding, he had given her the first brutal beating. She had the memory of his numerous trips to Orlando[2] with all of his wages when he had returned to her penniless, even before the first year had passed. She was young and soft then, but now she thought of her knotty, muscled limbs, her harsh knuckly hands, and drew herself up into an unhappy little ball in the middle of the big feather bed. Too late now to hope for love, even if it were not Bertha it would be someone else. This case differed from the others only in that she was bolder than the others. Too late for everything except her little home. She had built it for her old days, and planted one by one the trees and flowers there. It was lovely to her, lovely.

Somehow, before sleep came, she found herself saying aloud: "Oh well, whatever goes over the Devil's back, is got to come under his belly. Sometime or ruther, Sykes, like everybody else, is gointer reap his sowing." After that she was able to build a spiritual earthworks[3] against her husband. His shells could no longer reach her. *Amen*. She went to sleep and slept until he announced his presence in bed by kicking her feet and rudely snatching the covers away.

"Gimme some kivah heah, an' git yo' damn foots over on yo' own side! Ah oughter mash you in yo' mouf fuh drawing dat skillet on me."

Delia went clear to the rail without answering him. A triumphant indifference to all that he was or did.

The week was as full of work for Delia as all other weeks, and Saturday found her behind her little pony, collecting and delivering clothes.

It was a hot, hot day near the end of July. The village men on Joe Clarke's porch even chewed cane listlessly. They did not hurl the caneknots as usual. They let them dribble over the edge of the porch. Even conversation had collapsed under the heat.

"Heah come Delia Jones," Jim Merchant said, as the shaggy pony came 'round the bend of the road toward them. The rusty buckboard was heaped with baskets of crisp, clean laundry.

"Yep," Joe Lindsay agreed. "Hot or col', rain or shine, jes ez reg'lar ez de weeks roll roun' Delia carries 'em an' fetches 'em on Sat'day."

"She better if she wanter eat," said Moss. "Syke Jones aint wuth de shot an' powder hit would tek tuh kill 'em. Not to *huh* he aint."

"He sho' aint," Walter Thomas chimed in. "It's too bad, too, cause she wuz a right pritty lil trick when he got huh. Ah'd uh mah'ied huh mahseff if he hadnter beat me to it."

Delia nodded briefly at the men as she drove past.

"Too much knockin' will ruin *any* 'oman. He done beat huh 'nough

---

2. City in Florida.
3. A ridge of earth of the kind used to protect trench soldiers in World War I.

tuh kill three women, let 'lone change they looks," said Elijah Moseley.
"How Syke kin stommuck dat big black greasy Mogul[4] he's layin' roun'
wid, gits me. Ah swear dat eight-rock couldn't kiss a sardine can Ah
done thowed out de back do' 'way las' yeah."

"Aw, she's fat, thass how come. He's allus been crazy 'bout fat
women," put in Merchant. "He'd a' been tied up wid one long time
ago if he could a' found one tuh have him. Did Ah tell yuh 'bout him
come sidlin' roun' *mah* wife—bringin' her a basket uh peecans outa his
yard fuh a present? Yessir, mah wife! She tol' him tuh take em right
straight back home, cause Delia works so hard ovah dat wash tub she
reckon everything on de place taste lak sweat an' soapsuds. Ah jus' wisht
Ah'd a caught 'im 'roun' dere! Ah'd a' made his hips ketch on fiah
down dat shell road."

"Ah know he done it, too. Ah sees 'im grinnin' at every 'oman dat
passes," Walter Thomas said. "But even so, he useter eat some mighty
big hunks uh humble pie tuh git dat lil' 'oman he got. She wuz ez pritty
ez a speckled pup! Dat wuz fifteen yeahs ago. He useter be so skeered
uh losin' huh, she could make him do some parts of a husband's duty.
Dey never wuz de same in de mind."

"There oughter be a law about him," said Lindsay. "He aint fit tuh
carry guts tuh a bear."

Clarke spoke for the first time. "Taint no law on earth dat kin make a
man be decent if it aint in 'im. There's plenty men dat takes a wife lak
dey do a joint uh sugar-cane. It's round, juicy an' sweet when dey gits it.
But dey squeeze an' grind, squeeze an' grind an' wring tell dey wring
every drop uh pleasure dat's in 'em out. When dey's satisfied dat dey is
wrung dry, dey treats 'em jes lak dey do a cane-chew. Dey thows 'em
away. Dey knows whut dey is doin' while dey is at it, an' hates their-
selves fuh it but they keeps on hangin' after huh tell she's empty. Den
dey hates huh fuh bein' a cane-chew an' in de way."

"We oughter take Syke an' dat stray 'oman uh his'n down in Lake
Howell swamp an' lay on de rawhide till they cain't say Lawd a' mussy.'
He allus wuz uh ovahbearin' niggah, but since dat white 'oman from up
north done teached 'im how to run a automobile, he done got too big-
gety[5] to live—an' we oughter kill 'im." Old Man Anderson advised.

A grunt of approval went around the porch. But the heat was melting
their civic virtue and Elijah Moseley began to bait Joe Clarke.

"Come on, Joe, git a melon outa dere an' slice it up for yo' customers. We'se all sufferin' wid de heat. De bear's done got *me!*"

"Thass right, Joe, a watermelon is jes' whut Ah needs tuh cure de
eppizudicks,"[6] Walter Thomas joined forces with Moseley. "Come on

---

4. I.e., big woman.
5. I.e., full of himself.

6. I.e., "epizootic," used of a disease that attacks
a large number of animals at once.

dere, Joe. We all is steady customers an' you aint set us up in a long time. Ah chooses dat long, bowlegged Floridy favorite."

"A god, an' be dough. You all gimme twenty cents and slice way," Clarke retorted. "Ah needs a col' slice m'self. Heah, everybody chip in. Ah'll lend y'll mah meat knife."

The money was quickly subscribed and the huge melon brought forth. At that moment, Sykes and Bertha arrived. A determined silence fell on the porch and the melon was put away again.

Merchant snapped down the blade of his jackknife and moved toward the store door.

"Come on in, Joe, an' gimme a slab uh sow belly an' uh pound uh coffee—almost fuhgot 'twas Sat'day. Got to git on home." Most of the men left also.

Just then Delia drove past on her way home, as Sykes was ordering magnificently for Bertha. It pleased him for Delia to see.

"Git whutsoever yo' heart desires, Honey. Wait a minute, Joe. Give huh two bottles uh strawberry soda-water, uh quart uh parched ground-peas, an' a block uh chewin' gum."

With all this they left the store, with Sykes reminding Bertha that this was his town and she could have it if she wanted it.

The men returned soon after they left, and held their watermelon feast.

"Where did Syke Jones git da 'oman from nohow?" Lindsay asked.

"Ovah Apopka. Guess dey musta been cleanin' out de town when she lef'. She don't look lak a thing but a hunk uh liver wid hair on it."

"Well, she sho' kin squall," Dave Carter contributed. "When she gits ready tuh laff, she jes' opens huh mouf an' latches it back tuh de las' notch. No ole grandpa alligator down in Lake Bell ain't got nothin' on huh."

Bertha had been in town three months now. Sykes was still paying her room rent at Della Lewis'—the only house in town that would have taken her in. Sykes took her frequently to Winter Park to "stomps."[7] He still assured her that he was the swellest man in the state.

"Sho' you kin have dat lil' ole house soon's Ah kin git dat 'oman outa dere. Everything b'longs tuh me an' you sho' kin have it. Ah sho' 'bominates uh skinny 'oman. Lawdy, you sho' is got one portly shape on you! You kin git *anything* you wants. Dis is *mah* town an' you sho' kin have it."

Delia's work-worn knees crawled over the earth in Gethsemane and up the rocks of Calvary[8] many, many times during these months. She

7. Jazz dances.
8. Gethsemane is the garden where Christ was betrayed (Matthew 26:36–47); Calvary is the hill where he was crucified.

avoided the villagers and meeting places in her efforts to be blind and deaf. But Bertha nullified this to a degree, by coming to Delia's house to call Sykes out to her at the gate.

Delia and Sykes fought all the time now with no peaceful interludes. They slept and ate in silence. Two or three times Delia had attempted a timid friendliness, but she was repulsed each time. It was plain that the breaches must remain agape.

The sun had burned July to August. The heat streamed down like a million hot arrows, smiting all things living upon the earth. Grass withered, leaves browned, snakes went blind in shedding and men and dogs went mad. Dog days!

Delia came home one day and found Sykes there before her. She wondered, but started to go on into the house without speaking, even though he was standing in the kitchen door and she must either stoop under his arm or ask him to move. He made no room for her. She noticed a soap box beside the steps, but paid no particular attention to it, knowing that he must have brought it there. As she was stooping to pass under his outstretched arm, he suddenly pushed her backward, laughingly.

"Look in de box dere Delia, Ah done brung yuh somethin'!"

She nearly fell upon the box in her stumbling, and when she saw what it held, she all but fainted outright.

"Syke! Syke, mah Gawd! You take dat rattlesnake 'way from heah! You *gottuh.* Oh, Jesus, have mussy!"

"Ah aint gut tuh do nuthin' uh de kin'—fact is Ah aint got tuh do nothin' but die. Taint no use uh you puttin' on airs makin' out lak you skeered uh dat snake—he's gointer stay right heah tell he die. He wouldn't bite me cause Ah knows how tuh handle 'im. Nohow he wouldn't risk breakin' out his fangs 'gin yo' skinny laigs."

"Naw, now Syke, don't keep dat thing 'roun' heah tuh skeer me tuh death. You knows Ah'm even feared uh earth worms. Thass de biggest snake Ah evah did see. Kill 'im Syke, please."

"Doan ast me tuh do nothin' fuh yuh. Goin' 'roun' tryin' tuh be so damn asterperious. Naw, Ah aint gonna kill it. Ah think uh damn sight mo' uh him dan you! Dat's a nice snake an' anybody doan lak 'im kin jes' hit de grit."

The village soon heard that Sykes had the snake, and came to see and ask questions.

"How de hen-fire did you ketch dat six-foot rattler, Syke?" Thomas asked.

"He's full uh frogs so he caint hardly move, thass how Ah eased up on 'm. But Ah'm a snake charmer an' knows how tuh handle 'em. Shux, dat aint nothin'. Ah could ketch one eve'y day if Ah so wanted tuh."

"Whut he needs is a heavy hick'ry club leaned real heavy on his head. Dat's de bes 'way tuh charm a rattlesnake."

"Naw, Walt, y'll jes' don't understand dese diamon' backs lak Ah do," said Sykes in a superior tone of voice.

The village agreed with Walter, but the snake stayed on. His box remained by the kitchen door with its screen wire covering. Two or three days later it had digested its meal of frogs and literally came to life. It rattled at every movement in the kitchen or the yard. One day as Delia came down the kitchen steps she saw his chalky-white fangs curved like scimitars hung in the wire meshes. This time she did not run away with averted eyes as usual. She stood for a long time in the doorway in a red fury that grew bloodier for every second that she regarded the creature that was her torment.

That night she broached the subject as soon as Sykes sat down to the table.

"Syke, Ah wants you tuh take dat snake 'way fum heah. You done starved me an' Ah put up widcher, you done beat me an Ah took dat, but you done kilt all mah insides bringin' dat varmint heah."

Sykes poured out a saucer full of coffee and drank it deliberately before he answered her.

"A whole lot Ah keer 'bout how you feels inside uh out. Dat snake aint goin' no damn wheah till Ah gits ready fuh 'im tuh go. So fur as beatin' is concerned, yuh aint took near all dat you gointer take ef yuh stay 'roun' me."

Delia pushed back her plate and got up from the table. "Ah hates you, Sykes," she said calmly. "Ah hates you tuh de same degree dat Ah useter love yuh. Ah done took an' took till mah belly is full up tuh mah neck. Dat's de reason Ah got mah letter fum de church an' moved mah membership tuh Woodbridge—so Ah don't haftuh take no sacrament wid yuh. Ah don't wantuh see yuh 'roun' me atall. Lay 'roun' wid dat 'oman all yuh wants tuh, but gwan 'way fum me an' mah house. Ah hates yuh lak uh suck-egg dog."

Sykes almost let the huge wad of corn bread and collard greens he was chewing fall out of his mouth in amazement. He had a hard time whipping himself up to the proper fury to try to answer Delia.

"Well, Ah'm glad you does hate me. Ah'm sho' tiahed uh you hangin' ontuh me. Ah don't want yuh. Look at yuh stringey ole neck! Yo' rawbony laigs an' arms is enough tuh cut uh man tuh death. You looks jes' lak de devvul's doll-baby tuh *me*. You cain't hate me no worse dan Ah hates you. Ah been hatin' *you* fuh years."

"Yo' ole black hide don't look lak nothin' tuh me, but uh passle uh wrinkled up rubber, wid yo' big ole yeahs flappin' on each side lak uh paih uh buzzard wings. Don't think Ah'm gointuh be run 'way fum mah house neither. Ah'm goin' tuh de white folks bout *you*, mah young man, de very nex' time you lay yo' han's on me. Mah cup is done run ovah."

Delia said this with no signs of fear and Sykes departed from the house, threatening her, but made not the slightest move to carry out any of them.

That night he did not return at all, and the next day being Sunday, Delia was glad she did not have to quarrel before she hitched up her pony and drove the four miles to Woodbridge.

She stayed to the night service—"love feast"—which was very warm and full of spirit. In the emotional winds her domestic trials were borne far and wide so that she sang as she drove homeward,

> "Jurden water,[9] black an' col'
> Chills de body, not de soul
> An' Ah wantah cross Jurden in uh calm time."

She came from the barn to the kitchen door and stopped.

"Whut's de mattah, ol' satan, you aint kickin' up yo' racket?" She addressed the snake's box. Complete silence. She went on into the house with a new hope in its birth struggles. Perhaps her threat to go to the white folks had frightened Sykes! Perhaps he was sorry! Fifteen years of misery and suppression had brought Delia to the place where she would hope *anything* that looked towards a way over or through her wall of inhibitions.

She felt in the match safe behind the stove at once for a match. There was only one there.

"Dat niggah wouldn't fetch nothin' heah tuh save his rotten neck, but he kin run thew whut Ah brings quick enough. Now he done toted off nigh on tuh haff uh box uh matches. He done had dat 'oman heah in mah house too."

Nobody but a woman could tell how she knew this even before she struck the match. But she did and it put her into a new fury.

Presently she brought in the tubs to put the white things to soak. This time she decided she need not bring the hamper out of the bedroom: she would go in there and do the sorting. She picked up the pot-bellied lamp and went in. The room was small and the hamper stood hard by the foot of the white iron bed. She could sit and reach through the bedposts—resting as she worked.

"Ah wantah cross Jurden in uh calm time." She was singing again. The mood of the "love feast" had returned. She threw back the lid of the basket almost gaily. Then, moved by both horror and terror, she sprang back toward the door. *There lay the snake in the basket!* He

9. Jordan water, the river which the Jews had to cross to reach the promised land.

moved sluggishly at first, but even as she turned round and round, jumped up and down in an insanity of fear, he began to stir vigorously. She saw him pouring his awful beauty from the basket upon the bed, then she seized the lamp and ran as fast as she could to the kitchen. The wind from the open door blew out the light and the darkness added to her terror. She sped to the darkness of the yard, slamming the door after her before she thought to set down the lamp. She did not feel safe even on the ground, so she climbed up in the hay barn.

There for an hour or more she lay sprawled upon the hay a gibbering wreck.

Finally she grew quiet, and after that, coherent thought. With this, stalked through her a cold, bloody rage. Hours of this. A period of introspection, a space of retrospection, then a mixture of both. Out of this an awful calm.

"Well, Ah done de bes' Ah could. If things aint right, Gawd knows taint mah fault."

She went to sleep—a twitch sleep—and woke up to a faint gray sky. There was a loud hollow sound below. She peered out. Sykes was at the wood-pile, demolishing a wire-covered box.

He hurried to the kitchen door, but hung outside there some minutes before he entered, and stood some minutes more inside before he closed it after him.

The gray in the sky was spreading. Delia descended without fear now, and crouched beneath the low bedroom window. The drawn shade shut out the dawn, shut in the night. But the thin walls held back no sound.

"Dat ol' scratch is woke up now!" She mused at the tremendous whirr inside, which every woodsman knows, is one of the sound illusions. The rattler is a ventriloquist. His whirr sounds to the right, to the left, straight ahead, behind, close under foot—everywhere but where it is. Woe to him who guesses wrong unless he is prepared to hold up his end of the argument! Sometimes he strikes without rattling at all.

Inside, Sykes heard nothing until he knocked a pot lid off the stove while trying to reach the match safe in the dark. He had emptied his pockets at Bertha's.

The snake seemed to wake up under the stove and Sykes made a quick leap into the bedroom. In spite of the gin he had had, his head was clearing now.

"Mah Gawd!" he chattered, "ef Ah could on'y strack uh light!"

The rattling ceased for a moment as he stood paralyzed. He waited. It seemed that the snake waited also.

"Oh, fuh de light! Ah thought he'd be too sick"—Sykes was muttering to himself when the whirr began again, closer, right underfoot this time. Long before this, Sykes' ability to think had been flattened down to primitive instinct and he leaped—onto the bed.

Outside Delia heard a cry that might have come from a maddened chimpanzee, a stricken gorilla. All the terror, all the horror, all the rage that man possibly could express, without a recognizable human sound.

A tremendous stir inside there, another series of animal screams, the intermittent whirr of the reptile. The shade torn violently down from the window, letting in the red dawn, a huge brown hand seizing the window stick, great dull blows upon the wooden floor punctuating the gibberish of sound long after the rattle of the snake had abruptly subsided. All this Delia could see and hear from her place beneath the window, and it made her ill. She crept over to the four-o'clocks[1] and stretched herself on the cool earth to recover.

She lay there. "Delia, Delia!" She could hear Sykes calling in a most despairing tone as one who expected no answer. The sun crept on up, and he called. Delia could not move—her legs were gone flabby. She never moved, he called, and the sun kept rising.

"Mah Gawd!" She heard him moan, "Mah Gawd fum Heben!" She heard him stumbling about and got up from her flower-bed. The sun was growing warm. As she approached the door she heard him call out hopefully, "Delia, is dat you Ah heah?"

She saw him on his hands and knees as soon as she reached the door. He crept an inch or two toward her—all that he was able, and she saw his horribly swollen neck and his one open eye shining with hope. A surge of pity too strong to support bore her away from that eye that must, could not, fail to see the tubs. He would see the lamp. Orlando with its doctors was too far. She could scarcely reach the Chinaberry tree, where she waited in the growing heat while inside she knew the cold river was creeping up and up to extinguish that eye which must know by now that she knew.

1926

How It Feels to Be Colored Me

I am colored but I offer nothing in the way of extenuating circumstances except the fact that I am the only Negro in the United States whose grandfather on the mother's side was *not* an Indian chief.

I remember the very day that I became colored. Up to my thirteenth year I lived in the little Negro town of Eatonville, Florida. It is exclusively a colored town. The only white people I knew passed through the

---

1. A tropical plant with tubular flowers.

town going to or coming from Orlando. The native whites rode dusty horses, the Northern tourists chugged down the sandy village road in automobiles. The town knew the Southerners and never stopped cane chewing[2] when they passed. But the Northerners were something else again. They were peered at cautiously from behind curtains by the timid. The more venturesome would come out on the porch to watch them go past and got just as much pleasure out of the tourists as the tourists got out of the village.

The front porch might seem a daring place for the rest of the town, but it was a gallery seat for me. My favorite place was atop the gate-post. Proscenium box for a born first-nighter. Not only did I enjoy the show, but I didn't mind the actors knowing that I liked it. I usually spoke to them in passing. I'd wave at them and when they returned my salute, I would say something like this: "Howdy-do-well-I-thank-you-where-you-goin'?" Usually automobile or the horse paused at this, and after a queer exchange of compliments, I would probably "go a piece of the way" with them, as we say in farthest Florida. If one of my family happened to come to the front in time to see me, of course negotiations would be rudely broken off. But even so, it is clear that I was the first "welcome-to-our-state" Floridian, and I hope the Miami Chamber of Commerce will please take notice.

During this period, white people differed from colored to me only in that they rode through town and never lived there. They liked to hear me "speak pieces" and sing and wanted to see me dance the parse-me-la, and gave me generously of their small silver for doing these things, which seemed strange to me for I wanted to do them so much that I needed bribing to stop. Only they didn't know it. The colored people gave no dimes. They deplored any joyful tendencies in me, but I was their Zora nevertheless. I belonged to them, to the nearby hotels, to the county—everybody's Zora.

But changes came in the family when I was thirteen, and I was sent to school in Jacksonville. I left Eatonville, the town of the oleanders, as Zora. When I disembarked from the river-boat at Jacksonville, she was no more. It seemed that I had suffered a sea change. I was not Zora of Orange County any more, I was now a little colored girl. I found it out in certain ways. In my heart as well as in the mirror, I became a fast brown—warranted not to rub nor run.

But I am not tragically colored. There is no great sorrow dammed up in my soul, nor lurking behind my eyes. I do not mind at all. I do not belong to the sobbing school of Negrohood who hold that nature somehow has given them a lowdown dirty deal and whose feelings are all

2. Chewing sugar cane.

hurt about it. Even in the helter-skelter skirmish that is my life, I have seen that the world is to the strong regardless of a little pigmentation more or less. No, I do not weep at the world—I am too busy sharpening my oyster knife.[3]

Someone is always at my elbow reminding me that I am the grand-daughter of slaves. It fails to register depression with me. Slavery is sixty years in the past. The operation was successful and the patient is doing well, thank you. The terrible struggle[4] that made me an American out of a potential slave said "On the line!" The Reconstruction said "Get set!"; and the generation before said "Go!" I am off to a flying start and I must not halt in the stretch to look behind and weep. Slavery is the price I paid for civilization, and the choice was not with me. It is a bully adventure and worth all that I have paid through my ancestors for it. No one on earth ever had a greater chance for glory. The world to be won and nothing to be lost. It is thrilling to think—to know that for any act of mine, I shall get twice as much praise or twice as much blame. It is quite exciting to hold the center of the national stage, with the spectators not knowing whether to laugh or to weep.

The position of my white neighbor is much more difficult. No brown specter pulls up a chair beside me when I sit down to eat. No dark ghost thrusts its leg against mine in bed. The game of keeping what one has is never so exciting as the game of getting.

I do not always feel colored. Even now I often achieve the uncon-scious Zora of Eatonville before the Hegira.[5] I feel most colored when I am thrown against a sharp white background.

For instance at Barnard.[6] "Beside the waters of the Hudson" I feel my race. Among the thousand white persons, I am a dark rock surged upon, and overswept, but through it all, I remain myself. When cov-ered by the waters, I am; and the ebb but reveals me again.

Sometimes it is the other way around. A white person is set down in our midst, but the contrast is just as sharp for me. For instance, when I sit in the drafty basement that is The New World Cabaret with a white person, my color comes. We enter chatting about any little nothing that we have in common and are seated by the jazz waiters. In the abrupt way that jazz orchestras have, this one plunges into a number. It loses no time in circumlocutions, but gets right down to business. It con-stricts the thorax and splits the heart with its tempo and narcotic har-

3. A reference to the popular expression "The world is my oyster."
4. I.e., the Civil War. The Reconstruction was the period immediately following the war, when Northern educators traveled to the South to teach the newly freed slaves.
5. Flight of Muhammed from Mecca in A.D.

622; any journey, especially one undertaken to escape from a dangerous or undesirable situa-tion.
6. American women's college in New York City, near the Hudson River (cf. "by the waters of Zion").

monies. This orchestra grows rambunctious, rears on its hind legs and attacks the tonal veil with primitive fury, rending it, clawing it until it breaks through to the jungle beyond. I follow those heathen—follow them exultingly. I dance wildly inside myself; I yell within, I whoop; I shake my assegai[7] above my head, I hurl it true to the mark *yeeeeooww!* I am in the jungle and living in the jungle way. My face is painted red and yellow and my body is painted blue. My pulse is throbbing like a war drum. I want to slaughter something—give pain, give death to what, I do not know. But the piece ends. The men of the orchestra wipe their lips and rest their fingers. I creep back slowly to the veneer we call civilization with the last tone and find the white friend sitting motionless in his seat, smoking calmly.

"Good music they have here," he remarks, drumming the table with his fingertips.

Music. The great blobs of purple and red emotion have not touched him. He has only heard what I felt. He is far away and I see him but dimly across the ocean and the continent that have fallen between us. He is so pale with his whiteness then and I am *so* colored.

At certain times I have no race, I am *me*. When I set my hat at a certain angle and saunter down Seventh Avenue, Harlem City, feeling as snooty as the lions in front of the Forty-Second Street Library, for instance. So far as my feelings are concerned, Peggy Hopkins Joyce[8] on the Boule Mich with her gorgeous raiment, stately carriage, knees knocking together in a most aristocratic manner, has nothing on me. The cosmic Zora emerges. I belong to no race nor time. I am the eternal feminine with its string of beads.

I have no separate feeling about being an American citizen and colored. I am merely a fragment of the Great Soul that surges within the boundaries. My country, right or wrong.

Sometimes, I feel discriminated against, but it does not make me angry. It merely astonishes me. How *can* any deny themselves the pleasure of my company? It's beyond me.

But in the main, I feel like a brown bag of miscellany propped against a wall. Against a wall in company with other bags, white, red and yellow. Pour out the contents, and there is discovered a jumble of small things priceless and worthless. A first-water diamond, an empty spool, bits of broken glass, lengths of string, a key to a door long since crumbled away, a rusty knife-blade, old shoes saved for a road that never was and never will be, a nail bent under the weight of things too heavy for

7. A light spear used by tribesmen in southern Africa.
8. American beauty and fashion-setter of the twenties. "Boule Mich": the Boulevard Saint-Michel, a fashionable street in Paris.

any nail, a dried flower or two still a little fragrant. In your hand is the brown bag. On the ground before you is the jumble it held—so much like the jumble in the bags, could they be emptied, that all might be dumped in a single heap and the bags refilled without altering the content of any greatly. A bit of colored glass more or less would not matter. Perhaps that is how the Great Stuffer of Bags filled them in the first place—who knows?

1928

Contemporary Literature

Meditating on the woman of the future, the American poet Adrienne Rich mused in *Snapshots of a Daughter-in-Law* (1958–1960) that "she's long about her coming, who must be / more merciless to herself than history." Yet, added Rich in a moment of visionary certitude, "I see her plunge / breasted and glancing through the currents / . . . at least as beautiful as any boy / or helicopter." Rich's vision reflects a major cultural shift that—in a sense reiterating and reemphasizing the moments of change which ushered in turn-of-the-century and modernist crises—occurred in the years between 1940 and 1984, a shift which suggested to many writers and thinkers all over the world that, whether it meant apocalyptic annihilation or ecstatic transformation, the future had at last definitively arrived.

On the one hand, like George Orwell, the author of *1984* (1949), contemporary thinkers brooded on what the novelist James Joyce had earlier called "the nightmare of history," diagnosing social ills in terms of the crises they associated with the rise of totalitarianism and the threat of nuclear catastrophe. On the other hand, like Rich and such social theorists as the Marxist Herbert Marcuse, these thinkers dwelt on the metamorphic possibilities implicit in what the poet Hart Crane (echoing Walt Whitman) had called "Years of the Modern!," prescribing and predicting new and more harmonious relationships between mind and body, culture and nature, as well as among nations, classes, races, and sexes. From the modernist novelist Virginia Woolf to the French feminist theorist Simone de Beauvoir to Adrienne Rich herself, women writers expressed both attitudes toward the contemporary world, but—as the women's movement strengthened during the sixties—the hopes of many feminists became increasingly utopian.

To begin with, pessimistic speculations were fostered in both sexes by a period that saw such major global calamities as the Holocaust (the genocide of millions of Jews and other prisoners during World War II) and the dropping of the first atomic bomb on Hiroshima (in 1945, at the end of that war). Later, however, optimistic speculations were encouraged by an era that witnessed such dramatic impulses toward liberation as those that impelled the rise of many Third World countries and the formation of the international peace movement as well as the development of the civil rights, ecological, feminist, and gay rights movements. Difficult as it is to generalize about a period characterized by radical extremes and rapid change, an era whose deepest implications are still unclear, it is nevertheless true that in the years from 1940 to 1984 almost all the traditional categories through which the Western mind had understood reality were questioned or annihilated. Not only conventional concepts of space, time, authority, and morality but also received ideas about class, race, and gender were dissolved and revised in a world reeling from what the social observer Alvin Toffler has called *Future Shock*.

TOWARD 1984

The Impact of World War II

One of the first systems to be traumatically shaken in this period was the system of capitalism itself, for international crises in the 1930s indicated to many observors on both sides of the Atlantic that a free market economy might no longer be viable. The 1929 New York stock market crash, followed by the Great Depression and serious crop failures (the "Dust Bowl") in America and crippling monetary inflation in Germany, along with business slumps as well as bread lines in England, posed problems which seemed impossible to solve despite the efforts of such a leader as President Franklin Delano Roosevelt, whose "New Deal" constituted an unprecedented social welfare program. The widespread disillusionment that marked the era was vividly recorded in such American novels as John Steinbeck's Pulitzer Prize–winning *The Grapes of Wrath* (1939) and Tillie Olsen's *Yonnondio: From the Thirties* (1974), both of which described the grim lives of agricultural and industrial workers as well as the miseries of the unemployed in the 1930s. In addition, the skepticism about capitalism manifested in books like these fostered a disbelief in the efficacy of government in general. Centered in cities like London, Chicago, and New York, for instance, political unrest in England and America resulted in strikes, riots, marches, and demonstrations.

Similar economic and political discontent on the Continent led to the strengthening of the powers of Benito Mussolini, *Il Duce* ("the leader"), whose blackshirted *Fascisti* had established him as ruler of Italy in 1922, and to the rise of Adolf Hitler, the so-called *Fuehrer* ("leader"), whose goose-stepping Nazis took over Germany and elevated him to absolute dictatorship in 1933. Dreaming of a new Roman Empire, Mussolini annexed Ethiopia in 1936 and Albania in 1939 while advocating the supreme authority of the strong leader and ruthlessly suppressing dissent. Similarly, arguing for the "natural superiority" of Aryans (Nordic-Germanic peoples) and for their right to *Lebensraum* ("living space"), Hitler invaded Austria and the Sudetenland (a province of Czechoslovakia) in 1938 and Poland in 1939. At the same time, he put into practice the brutally totalitarian principles he had outlined in *Mein Kampf* ("My Battle," 1925) and implemented what would be called the "final solution" to "the Jewish problem" as well as to the "problem" of other aliens or dissenters by setting up concentration camps, in whose gas ovens millions would die during his reign.

In Japan and Russia, totalitarian dictatorships had also formed. In 1926, Hirohito became emperor of Japan and began to pursue an aggressively militaristic policy of international expansion, while in 1927 Joseph Stalin rose to power in the Soviet Union and began liquidating opponents in a series of purges. By 1939, the world had been divided into hostile camps by a series of treaties and alliances, including the formation of an Axis (1936) which aligned Fascist Italy, Nazi Germany, and imperialist Japan; the Munich Pact (1938), in which England and France followed a policy of appeasement toward Hitler; and the short-lived Hitler-Stalin pact (1939), in which Germany and Russia entered into a nonaggression treaty. On the brink of World War II, citizens of many countries felt not only disillusioned about government but anxiously at the mercy of the authoritarian men who controlled so many lives.

War broke out in Europe during 1939, and the United States entered the conflict when Japanese planes bombed the American naval base at Pearl Harbor (in Hawaii) in 1941. Although the mortality rate for combatants was not nearly as high as it had been in World War I, enormous numbers of noncombatants were for the first time profoundly vulnerable to attack from the air in homes, schools, and workplaces. What made possible the destruction of whole cities was the swift development of a technology of death even more sinister than that used in the earlier war. While armored tanks and submarines provided some protection to soldiers and sailors, civilians in urban centers like London, Dresden, and Tokyo huddled in shelters or tube (subway) stations that offered little security against blitzes (rains of bombs) and fire bombings. A number of the most significant participants in World War II were aviators who bombed immobilized populations of women, children, and old people. After the Battle of Britain (1941), planes were no longer the kinds of fragile two-seaters in which chivalric pilots had dueled during World War I. Intricate and often large machines, protected by the newly developed device of radar, bombers and transport aircraft insulated their crews and often alienated them from the targets they mapped, surveyed, and destroyed. James Dickey's *The Fire Bombing* (1964) recalled the poet's anesthetized sense of distance from humanity on a bombing run over Japan in terms echoing the infamous remark of Mussolini's pilot son that the flames of a bombed Ethiopian city looked "like a rose unfolding."

To be sure, airmen were also subject to ferocious attacks by anti-aircraft guns or other planes, and the poet Randall Jarrell, who was himself in the Air Force during the war, described the terrible vulnerability of the ball turret gunner, a man who, wrote Jarrell in a note, had to "hunch upside-down . . . like a foetus in the womb" to operate machine guns set into the plexiglass belly of a B-17 or B-24 bomber: "When I died they washed me out of the turret with a hose," explains the dead speaker of *The Death of the Ball Turret Gunner* (1945). In addition, as Jarrell's poem also implied, these men—subject to a universal conscription system that reduced them to mere cyphers—had been assimilated into a gigantic military bureaucracy which sought to deprive them of their individuality by making them standardized and interchangeable parts of what seemed a monstrous whole. "From my mother's sleep I fell into the State," Jarrell's gunner confesses. Similarly, the hero of Joseph Heller's satiric *Catch-22* (1961) discovers that he is helplessly entangled in a logically absurd army hierarchy whose rules contradict and confound each other and him.

Nevertheless, to civilians the assaults by such military men seemed virtually apocalyptic. The American poet H. D., who lived through the blitz of London in the forties, saw England as "an island of wounds," while the expatriate poet T. S. Eliot, a British air raid warden during the same years, characterized an attacking plane as a "dark dove with [a] flickering tongue." Even in the supposedly safe and stable United States, Japanese-American citizens, called *Nisei*, were suspected of collusion with the enemy and imprisoned in camps in California, a development that proved—as if working off the title of Sinclair Lewis's dystopian (anti-utopian) novel *It Can't Happen Here* (1935)—that "it" could happen here.

But despite the difficulties recounted by H. D. and T. S. Eliot, the civilians who suffered the most dramatically during the war and whose experiences were destined to become emblematic of the apocalypse that had engulfed an entire generation were those who endured either the Holocaust in Germany or the American atomic bombing of Hiroshima, the latter a cataclysm which culminated and concluded World War II on the Pacific front. Both these events, too, were facilitated or created by recent technological innovations and by the construction of elaborate bureaucracies which so depersonalized the decision-making process that moral responsibility was obscured for individuals who claimed they were only "following orders." The demonic efficiency with which the Nazis conducted Jews to death factories was documented by victims of the Holocaust like Anne Frank, a thirteen-year-old girl whose *Diary* became famous when it was published after her death in a concentration camp at the age of fifteen, and by survivors like the expatriate Rumanian-Jewish novelist Eli Wiesel and the German-Jewish poet Nelly Sachs, both of whom paradoxically explained how the moral implications of such a mass cultural descent into hell were so drastic that the existence of death camps could never be explained away.

The destruction of most of the inhabitants of Hiroshima and Nagasaki and the debilitation of those who survived were not the result of the same sort of genocidal program, but they nevertheless had similarly resonant implications, not only for citizens of Japan but for a number of Americans, who were horrified by the Truman administration's decision actually to drop the bomb. Later, however, it was not so much this one decision which haunted the whole world as it was the concept of the bomb itself, whose characteristic mushroom cloud began to symbolize a science harnessed to death rather than to life. Only a hundred years after nineteenth-century poets as diverse as Tennyson and Whitman had extolled the virtues of technological progress, the poet Karl Shapiro could write in *The Progress of Faust* (1947) that the sinister scientist-magician of legend had appeared "in an American desert at war's end / Where, at his back, a dome of atoms rose."

It was perhaps inevitable that intellectuals should have responded to such events with writings based on nihilistic assumptions about the world. Existentialism, a philosophical movement led by the French thinkers Jean-Paul Sartre and Albert Camus, posited a meaningless cosmos from which human beings could only derive significance through acts of engagement willed in and for themselves. The movement's theories issued in a number of major works, including Sartre's treatise *Being and Nothingness* (1943) and Camus's novel *The Stranger* (1942), while shaping the spirit of the age in which Samuel Beckett depicted in his play *Waiting for Godot* (1952) the tragicomic fate of two tramps who are pointlessly waiting for a no-one who never arrives. But many other writers of this period also expressed sardonic disillusionment: from Norman

Mailer's *The Naked and the Dead* (1948) to Katherine Anne Porter's *Ship of Fools* (1962) and Thomas Pynchon's *Gravity's Rainbow* (1973), their works explored the irrationality of both culture and nature in a world at war.

The Cold War

It can be argued that the so-called cold war began at the Yalta Conference of 1945, when the British prime minister Winston Churchill and the American president Franklin Delano Roosevelt allowed the Soviet Premier Joseph Stalin to claim portions of conquered Germany as the spoils of war. In a sense, the division of Germany into what were to become two separate states—East and West Germany—represented a splitting of the world into two opposed ideological camps that deeply affected every phase of the life of this period. Internationally, the so-called iron curtain—physically symbolized by the Berlin wall that the Soviets built to keep East Berliners from escaping to the West—shut western Europe off from the eastern sphere of Hungary, Poland, and East Germany, which had been annexed by Russia. The Korean War in the early fifties, followed by the Suez Canal and Cuban crises, dramatized the struggle between Soviet and American powers while manifesting the decline of Great Britain as an imperial force. At the same time, in the United States, citizens anxious about nuclear attack built basement bomb shelters and stockpiled canned goods while anti-Communist sentiment grew in intensity.

During the late forties in Hollywood and New York, "left-wing" writers like Dashiell Hammett and Lillian Hellman, together with prominent film directors and actors, were "blacklisted"—deprived of jobs and reputations—by producers worried about political respectability. By 1953, Senator Joseph McCarthy was acting as, in the words of one historian, an "inquisitor," accusing such diverse figures as the former diplomat Alger Hiss and the American president Dwight Eisenhower of being Communists or Communist sympathizers, while members of the House Un-American Activities Committee promoted patriotism and inveighed against the supposedly subversive doings of liberal intellectuals. From the loyalty oaths that many civic employees were now obliged to sign in order to retain their jobs to the execution in 1953 of Julius and Ethel Rosenberg, a Jewish couple convicted of conspiring to commit espionage in behalf of the Soviet Union, the fifties were permeated by the anxiety of "ordinary" citizens that they were threatened by Communists and by intellectuals' fear that they might be charged with being Communists or Communist sympathizers. "A savage servility / slides by on grease," wrote the poet Robert Lowell about the spirit of the age in *For the Union Dead* (1960).

In a number of other poems that were to become crucially influential on contemporary verse, Lowell further characterized the era with remarks such as, "These are the tranquillized *Fifties*, / and I am forty." It was not only Lowell who felt himself and his age to be middle-aged, for the conservatism of the fifties, as many writers perceived, was social as well as political. In England, to be sure, the years from 1945 to 1951 had seen the ascendancy of a strong Labour government that nationalized major industries and introduced a program of socialized medicine. But by the early fifties England had reinstated the Conservative party, which, led by Winston Churchill, ruled the country throughout the decade. On both sides of the Atlantic, then, but perhaps more in the newly prosperous United States than in still war-devastated England, this was the era of the "man in the gray flannel suit," the title of a 1955 best seller by Sloan Wilson. The phrase perfectly captured the conformity and materialism which characterized the middle-class suburban culture that arose in this period.

Largely created by and for a postwar population exhausted by the calamities of the forties, the suburbs of the fifties were enclaves of nuclear families in a newly nuclear age. Ambitious commuting husbands and dutifully domestic wives produced a record number of children who constituted the so-called baby boom of the period. The workplace was still located in urban centers, but as the bourgeois ideal of home-ownership sent more and more young couples into affordable out-of-town subdivisions, inner cities began to decay and to be associated with the poverty and violence of ghettos—usually slum districts—where many blacks, Chicanos, Puerto Ricans, and other disadvantaged groups were obliged to live. Among the middle classes, an ideology of "togetherness" permeated the age, as did an ethic of "adjustment" and "maturity." Television shows like *I Love Lucy*, *Ozzie and Harriet*, and *Leave It to Beaver* might celebrate the charmingly nutty antics of middle-class wives and children, but in the end everyone professed to agree that, as the title of another series put it, *Father Knows Best*. For those who did not acquiesce in such an idea, a new breed of professionals—psychiatrists, psychologists, advice columnists, and guidance counselors—arose to explain the virtues of "normalcy": to be "well adjusted," they argued, was to "fit in" to a system that was morally right and emotionally healthful.

In a more sophisticated form, this popular ideology of adjustment affected even the increasingly conservative intellectual and literary life of the age. Paralleling the rise of corporations, public universities grew in size and number, aided by monies for education that the government had provided returning veterans through the G.I. Bill, as well as by other federal grants. In the United States, in particular, higher education became a major industry, offering jobs to countless intellectuals. Just at this point, too, an effort to elevate the study of literature to the status already achieved by the sciences resulted in what was called the "New Criticism." Detaching the literary text from its cultural context—its author, its audience, and its historical setting—the New Critics analyzed the ironic and metaphorical complexities within poems that were now considered well-wrought, autonomous objects. Developing sophisticated techniques of reading, these thinkers saw themselves as rebels against the naïveté of traditional scholarship. Yet, significantly, their efforts to divorce art and criticism from culture and society were essentially conservative. Such theorists as Cleanth Brooks and R. P. Blackmur insisted that the literary analyst should adopt a position of political neutrality, while writers like T. S. Eliot, Allan Tate, and John Crowe Ransom actually defined themselves as "reactionaries."

A similar academic professionalization marked the careers of a number of creative writers in this period, some of whom were themselves also practicing critics and many of whom now accepted positions in newly established university creative writing programs. From Tate and Ransom to Theodore Roethke, Robert Lowell, John Berryman, and Randall Jarrell, most of the major American poets of the age were associated with English departments, and many British writers, including Donald Davie and Phillip Larkin, were also connected with universities. Novels such as C. P. Snow's *The Masters* (1951), Mary McCarthy's *The Groves of Academe* (1952), and Randall Jarrell's *Pictures from an Institution* (1954) all dealt with the so-called ivory tower of academia, while the school of poets known as "the Movement," which arose in England in the fifties, produced work that was both stylistically conservative and thematically modest.

Nevertheless, despite the overt decorum of what Lowell called "the tranquillized *Fifties*," a number of dissenting voices were raised throughout the period. In America, for instance, even during the McCarthy investigations, radical folksingers like the Weavers continued to play to large audiences, and left-wing students circulated the so-called Stockholm Peace Petition, a demand for world peace sponsored by a set of radical organizations, while in England the British philosopher Bertrand Russell presided over a series of mass demonstrations demanding nuclear disarmament. Among poets, too, the *dicta* of orthodoxy and depersonalization promulgated by a leader like T. S. Eliot were challenged, first by the flamboyant behavior and neo-Romantic verse of the Welsh poet Dylan Thomas, whose influence was at least as great in America as it was in England, then by the so-called Beat writers, and finally by the group of artists known as the "confessional" poets—most notably, W. D. Snodgrass, Robert Lowell, and John Berryman, but later also Sylvia Plath and Anne Sexton—all of whom insisted, in their different ways, upon defying the values of maturity, adjustment, and normalcy.

In addition, during this period "Southern Gothic" writers like Carson McCullers, Truman Capote, Tennessee Williams, and Flannery O'Connor constructed grotesque fantasies to reveal the immaturity, maladjustment, and perversity endemic to apparently ordinary small-town communities. At the same time, a set of English playwrights known as "Angry Young Men" were producing realistic dramas like John Osborne's *Look Back in Anger* (1956), which attacked the complacency of the welfare state. The rebellious young Allen Ginsberg, a leader of the American Beat movement that would help shape the verse of the sixties, spoke for all these dissenters in his poem *America* (1956), when, referring to left-wing anti-Stalinists, he asked, "America when will you be worthy of your million Trotskyites?," and he cursed the age that produced the cold war as well as his own country's complicity in it, telling "America" to "go fuck yourself with your atom bomb."

The Third World

Even as he excoriated the United States in *America*, Ginsberg mockingly identified with his culture in the line "Asia is rising against me." Parodic though his comment was, it referred to the increasing anxiety with which many American and British citizens responded to the emergence of Third World countries and peoples that began in the late forties and continued throughout the sixties and seventies. As early as 1945, when the United Nations was established, granting responsibility in world councils to a number of small powers, a process of global redefinition had been initiated. When two years later, in 1947, Mohandas Gandhi finally achieved his goal of national independence for India, the final disintegration of the British Empire was under way. In 1948, Burma also achieved independence, and in that year the new state of Israel was established. During the late fifties and sixties, a growing number of African states—Ghana (1967), Nigeria (1960), and Kenya (1963)—won autonomy from Britain, and their victories, paralleled earlier by the liberation of North Vietnam from French rule (1945), were now paralleled by the liberation in 1960 of the French colonies Chad, the Congo Republic, Mali, and Senegal. Counterpointing the emergence of new African, Middle Eastern, and Asian nations was the rise of China to prominence as a world power. In 1949, the Communist party chairman Mao Tse-tung established the Chinese People's Republic, and, though the new state was not officially recognized by the American government until the 1970s, it became ever more important on the international scene, complicating the plot of the cold war with interventions in Korea, Africa, Cuba, and, ultimately, Vietnam.

At least in part inspired by the theorizing of radical critics of imperialism like the black political writer Frantz Fanon, these new nations struggled to recover lost national traditions, and their efforts were reflected in the literature that native artists—Chinua Achebe, Amos Tutuola, Kamala Das, and Ama Ata Aidoo—began to produce. Although frequently writing in English to insure an international audience, poets and novelists of former British colonies or possessions nevertheless often drew heavily upon local myths and legends while recording the conflicts of identity experienced by people inhabiting cultures in transition, cultures that were no longer colonized yet still not free from Western influence. At the same time, the struggle of these countries was also recorded by the African-born white writers Alan Paton, Doris Lessing, and Nadine Gordimer.

Meanwhile, in Latin America, the Chilean poet Pablo Neruda wrote such passionate poems as *The United Fruit Company*, attacking American exploitation, as well as vividly surrealistic works like *The Heights of Macchu Pichu*, recovering legends of the Andes. Mining similar veins were the Peruvian poet César Vallejo, the Mexican writer Octavio Paz, and the Colombian novelist Gabriel García Márquez, all authors whose work was to become extraordinarily influential in the United States during the sixties and seventies. In Australia and Canada, moreover, the poet Judith Wright and the poet-novelist Margaret Atwood were only two among many who sought to memorialize what Wright in *South of My Days* called "my blood's country." Atwood, in particular, epitomized this effort of self-definition in white English-speaking lands resisting engulfment by England and the United States. In *Survival* (1972), for instance, she offered a "thematic guide to Canadian literature," while in her *Oxford Anthology of Canadian Literature* (1982) she established her literary inheritance.

It was not just abroad, however, that oppressed or subordinated peoples sought to claim lost cultural identities and win political power. In the United States, native-Americans became newly conscious of their own traditions and, supported by the reissuing of such classics as *Black Elk Speaks*, a shaman's memoir translated and edited by John Neihardt in 1932, writers like Scott Momaday, Leslie Marmon Silko, and Paula Gunn Allen struggled to reclaim their aesthetic legacy. But perhaps the most important of the libertarian struggles that gained momentum between the fifties and the seventies was the black civil rights movement in America.

Most prominently led by the Nobel Prize–winning clergyman Martin

Luther King, Jr., who advocated nonviolent resistence to white racism, this movement began with so-called freedom riders, who helped register black voters in the South, and progressed to sit-ins, marches, and mass demonstrations in the North, events which helped pass the sweeping Civil Rights Act of 1964, outlawing segregation in public places and guaranteeing legal equality to blacks. More militant than King was the black Muslim leader Malcolm X, who began his career, arguing that whites were inherently evil, by seeking to convert blacks to a revised form of the Islamic religion. Both represented the new passion for self-affirmation that swept black communities in these years. From Rosa Parks, who fought to integrate buses in 1955, to Representative Shirley Chisolm, who ran for the presidency in 1972, to the prisoner-turned-writer Eldridge Cleaver and the group of revolutionaries who called themselves the Black Panthers, black activists struggled against social, economic, legal, and psychological oppression. Yet their battle was marked by tragedy, for Malcolm X and Martin Luther King, Jr., were assassinated in, respectively, 1965 and 1968, while four children killed in a bombed Birmingham, Alabama, Sunday school were just a few among many victims of a violent white backlash.

The civil rights movement produced a rich proliferation of black writing, work marked by a confidence and energy that had not been seen since the Harlem Renaissance of the twenties. From Richard Wright, whose prize-winning novel *Native Son* was published in 1940, to Ralph Ellison, whose novel *Invisible Man* won the National Book Award in 1952, James Baldwin, whose impassioned essay *The Fire Next Time* was widely read when it appeared in 1963, and Toni Morrison, whose *The Bluest Eye* was published in 1970, a new generation of black prose writers arose to express what Baldwin defined as "the sorrow, the rage, and the murderous bitterness which was eating up my life and the lives of those about me." Similarly, from Margaret Walker and Gwendolyn Brooks to Imamu Amiri Baraka (Le Roi Jones), Ishmael Reed, Mari Evans, June Jordan, Audre Lorde, Nikki Giovanni, Lucille Clifton, and Sonia Sanchez, two new generations of black poets appeared to proclaim that—in the words of Lorde's *Coal*—"I / is the total black, being spoken / from the earth's inside" and to demand that the reader "now take my word for jewel in the open light."

The Sixties

Not insignificantly, the styles and strategies of writers like Baraka, Reed, and Lorde were influenced by and influenced a new literary movement that developed on the Lower East Side of New York City and in San Francisco: called the Beats, a term coined by the novelist Jack Kerouac and conflating the words "beaten" and "beatified," writers in this group attained national notoriety early in the sixties, in part because of the impact of Kerouac's *On the Road* (1957) and Allen Ginsberg's long poem *Howl* (1956). With its violent assault on the bourgeois materialism of the fifties, *Howl*, in particular, spoke for a disaffected and rebellious generation. Writing in Whitmanesque lines and in a visionary mode shaped by his studies of the late-eighteenth-century prophetic poet William Blake, Ginsberg exclaimed that "I saw the best minds of my generation destroyed by madness, starving hysterical naked," and excoriated the modern world: "Robot apartments! invisible suburbs! skeleton treasuries! blind capitals! demonic industries! spectral nations! invincible madhouses! granite cocks!

monstrous bombs!" He and his followers earned the label "beatniks," a term which implied that these unorthodox young people were Soviet sympathizers. At the same time however, this poet defined the characteristic stance of a decade that was to be marked by what often seemed like one long howl of protest.

Politically, such protests, which were in part the result of early civil rights activism, took the form of rebellion against censorship, poverty, war, and the destruction of natural resources. As early as 1959, the complaints of publishers and intellectuals had led to the rescinding of bans against the distribution of such supposedly pornographic novels as D. H. Lawrence's *Lady Chatterley's Lover* and Henry Miller's *Tropic of Capricorn*. In the early sixties, however, students at the University of California, Berkeley, led by Mario Savio, organized "sit-ins," conducted rallies, and made speeches to force university authorities to let them use whatever language they pleased in newspapers and journals. Their tactics were adopted by such other groups as Students for a Democratic Society (SDS) and the California Diggers, who tried to draw attention to poverty by demonstrating against what President Eisenhower once called the "military-industrial complex" and by distributing free food to impoverished sections of the population.

Though brief, the tradition of student leafleting, picketing, marching, and meeting that these groups pioneered laid the groundwork for what became a nationwide phenomenon: the antiwar movement. After the United States, under the leadership of John Kennedy and then of Lyndon Johnson, had intervened in South Vietnam to support a series of conservative, even dictatorial, governments against, on the one hand, the revolutionary guerrilla forces of the Viet Cong and, on the other hand, the Communist troops marshaled by Ho Chi Minh, leader of North Vietnam, the outrage of young people, and especially of draft-eligible young men, grew into a mass disaffection which was exacerbated when the Ohio National Guard fired on students demonstrating at Kent State University and killed four of them.

Not only had such protesters as those at Kent State adopted the tactics of the Free Speech movement and the SDS, they had also employed more theatrical strategies: burning draft cards, pouring blood on military files, and organizing "read-ins" to which famous writers drew large audiences. Among the poets who performed on such occasions were Robert Bly and Denise Levertov. "You who go out on schedule / to kill," Levertov exclaimed, "do you know there are eyes that watch you, / eyes whose lids you burned off [?]" "It's because the aluminum window shade business is doing so well in the U.S. that we roll fire over entire villages," noted Bly. "It's because we have new packaging for smoked oysters that bomb holes appear in the rice paddies."

Because, as Bly's line suggests, it involved a critique of Western culture in general, the militancy of the sixties extended from political to social protest. The period, in any case, was marked by a general loosening of authoritarian hierarchies; with the accession in 1958 of Pope John XXIII, and the convening of the Second Vatican Council, even the traditionally conservative Catholic Church had relaxed old rules and substituted services in the vernacular for masses in Latin. But in England and America, as the sixties wore on, popular trends also dramatized change. The Beats gave way to the Beatles, and beatniks became hippies. The rock movement of the fifties, picked up in England and popularized by the Rolling Stones as well as the Beatles, issued in such diverse phenomena as miniskirts, unisex clothes, long hair (for both sexes), and psychedelic drugs. Some British youths defined themselves as "mods" or "rockers," while others became disciples of the radical psychologist R. D. Laing, who preached that the sane were mad and the mad, sane. Some Americans dreamed of running away to the Haight Ashbury district of San Francisco and becoming hippies. What the historian Theodore Roszak called the "counterculture" may have at first seemed juvenile and narcissistic, with its emphasis on flower children and hedonistic self-development, but it was to result in a serious ecology movement, whose spokespersons included the poet Gary Snyder (*Earth Household*, 1957), the feminist writer Susan Griffin (*Woman and Nature*, 1978), and the feminist theologian Mary Daly (*Gyn/Ecology*, 1978).

But Griffin and Daly spoke for another growing constituency, too, for the activism of the sixties functioned, paradoxically, in two ways for women: on the one hand, many women participated with passion in all phases of the political and social movements prevalent in the period; on the other hand, the very intensity of their participation forced them to confront their marginalization both in the reigning culture and in the counterculture. Performing as coffee-makers, secretaries, or sex objects for male rebels, radical women soon became disillusioned and, like the nineteenth-century women who had worked for abolition but discovered that their male contemporaries held them in as low esteem as the oppressive slave system held blacks, they formed a movement of their own. In turn, the women's liberation movement, stressing sexual freedom, fostered the development of the gay (homosexual) rights movement, for gay men and lesbians now began organizing to combat the legal and moral strictures that had ostracized them in the past.

Inevitably so much ferment had its effect on the entertainment and literature of the era. The disillusionment expressed by Allen Ginsberg, for instance, was picked up and popularized by the stand-up comedians Lenny Bruce, Woody Allen, and Joan Rivers, even as it evolved into the genre of "black humor" (grotesque comedy) produced in the United States by Terry Southern, Donald Barthelme, Thomas Pynchon, Vladimir Nabokov, and Stanley Elkin, and matched in England by the witty novels of Kingsley Amis, John Wain, and Iris Murdoch. Similarly comic, but more self-consciously ethnic, were the writings of the Jewish-American writers Philip Roth, Grace Paley, Saul Bellow, Bernard Malamud, and Cynthia Ozick, while the realistic novels of social criticism produced by the British authors Doris Lessing and Margaret Drabble expressed the same disaffection with the status quo.

Irreverent, sometimes vulgar, and often nihilistic, the work of both "black humorists" and Jewish writers was paralleled by the experimental, "guerrilla," and "street" theater that developed in these years, led by such figures as Julian Beck and Judith Malina, whose "Living Theater" attempted through radically disruptive methods to bridge the distance between author, actor, and audience. Finally, a similar comic nihilism also characterized the ironic and sometimes surrealistic verse of the "New York poets" Frank O'Hara, Kenneth Koch, and John Ashbery; and if poets like those who belonged to the so-called Black Mountain school (Charles Olson, Robert Creeley, Denise Levertov, Robert Duncan) were less comic, they were equally rebellious and experimental, as were the Americans Robert Bly, James Wright, and W. S. Merwin, along with the English Ted Hughes. Hughes's *Crow* (1970), for instance, was a poem sequence that drew upon native-American trickster legends and summarized the spirit of the age in a sardonic catechism: "Who owns the whole rainy, stony earth? *Death.*"

Future Shock

The distinction between Hughes's gloom and the hopeful passion that impelled the disparate activists of the sixties symbolizes the thin line that separated dystopian and utopian thinkers in this period. Approaching and passing 1984, the year that George Orwell in 1949 used to date the political, social, and cultural death of "the whole rainy, stony earth," many people all over the globe must have wondered whether, if one is living in the future, one has any future. Certainly, the threats posed by neutron bombs, ICBMs (intercontinental ballistic missiles), nuclear power plants, and industrial pollution seemed to imply a future that might be merely deathly. In particular, a war of the worlds became an increasingly haunting possibility when more nations joined the race to build atomic bombs, many of them countries—like Israel and Syria, India and Pakistan—involved in intense border disputes. But with chemical waste accumulating and with nuclear engineering errors multiplying, apocalypse seemed in any case to be a random accident that could happen now. More, a society based on what Orwell would have called "newspeak" and "doublethink"—in the United States and England, exemplified in advertising language and political euphemisms—surely presented a particular problem to thinkers who no longer felt they had a viable language or a usable past.

At the same time, however, a number of scientific and social breakthroughs in these years seemed to belie Orwell's pessimistic prognoses. Moon landings, space shuttles, and communications satellites promised new horizons for the world, while medical innovations, from polio vaccine to heart transplants, suggested new leases on life for humanity. Home appliances, convenience foods, and computers all offered the possibilities of liberation from drudgery, and the concept of equality implicit not only in large-scale welfare programs but also in humanitarian movements hinted at new societal steps toward moral responsibility.

Finally, though, the future that had arrived was shocking because to many it seemed almost impossible to diagnose the divergent implications of the more than new. DNA research (biochemical investigations of the nature of the cell) might yield either deadly mutations or new life. Similarly, such pioneering surgical procedures as sex-change operations, and such obstetrical procedures as artificial insemination and conception outside the womb, promised either to allow women to control their own reproductive functions or else to replace real women with artificial wombs. No wonder, then, that experimental writers from the French novelist Alain Robbe-Grillet to the Argentinian writer Jorge Luis Borges and science-fiction writers from Isaac Asimov to Ursula K. Le Guin described a world of radical instability—a world also reflected in the philosophy of the French thinker Jacques Derrida, a prototypical postmodernist theorist of indeterminacy. Interestingly, Derrida decided to identify himself in *Spurs* (1978) as "a woman," an extreme self-definition which suggested that, not unlike so different a contemporary as the lesbian feminist Adrienne Rich, this male intellectual associated modernity with the coming of a woman. That Derrida should attempt such an identification revealed how deeply what had been traditionally called the "woman question" was intertwined with the future shock experienced and expressed by so many thinkers in this period. After four decades of social turmoil and intellectual upheaval, not only were the validity of government, the boundaries of the earth, and the integrity of the cell being questioned but even the biological determinacy of gender—the deepest structure through which the self has traditionally been defined and society organized—no longer seemed inevitable.

CONTEMPORARY IMAGES OF WOMEN

Though some thinkers in the eighties were to arrive at radically antibiological positions like that of Derrida, by many other writers and artists from 1940 to 1984 images of women were biologized and sexualized as never before. Indeed, the traditional polarities of angel and monster, virgin and whore, lady and madwoman were consistently eroticized in this period. The nineteenth century had praised women for purity and decorum while blaming them for passion and desire, but the second half of the twentieth century virtually reversed those moral priorities; contemporary writers blamed women for frigidity and praised them for sexiness. The scarlet letter "A" that Hawthorne had used in the nineteenth century to emblematize the crime of the adulteress now dissolved into the pornographic letter "O" that signified both the emptiness and the openness of an obediently serviceable woman in Pauline Réage's *The Story of O* (1954, 1964). To be sure, many thinkers resisted this cultural tendency to eroticize the female, creating women characters who were autonomous and intelligent, yet for many others popular pressures were hard to overcome, and the images constructed in the works of those writers posed particular problems for women readers.

Certainly from the World War II pin-up girl to the *Playboy* playmate of the sixties, from the nymphet of Vladimir Nabokov's *Lolita* (1955) to the nymphomaniac of Terry Southern and Mason Hoffenberg's *Candy* (1964), representations of women often became blatantly titillating to men; indeed, the current male argot objectified the deliciously willing heroine as a cupcake, a muffin, a cookie, a tomato, a honey, a tootsie, a real sugar, a cherry, a sweetie pie, a tart, or a peach while metamorphosing all women into sexy or repellent animals (foxes, birds, chicks, beavers, kittens, pussies, bitches, dogs, pigs). Though there are, of course, distinctions among the attitudes toward women manifested in the texts produced during World War II, during the "tranquilized *Fifties*," and during the rebellious sixties, it is extraordinary how consistently most novelists and poets of the era focused their attention on the female body and its willingness to function as a receptacle for male desire. Even when contemporary male writers seemed to be contemplating such seemingly nonerotic figures as the mother or the literary woman, they tended to sexualize both their dreams and their dreads about femininity.

Even before 1939, a process of frankly eroticizing women had begun with the development of a cultural atmosphere whose ideology was both more permissive and more promiscuous than ever before. The dissemination of birth control information and devices, the publication of sex manuals, new divorce laws, short skirts, silk stockings, brassieres—all these diverse phenomena transformed woman from an untouchable object in a hoop skirt or a bustle to a willing and easily accessible body. By World War II, it was possible, as it had not been during World War I, for armies of sex-starved men to decorate barracks, tanks, and planes with clippings of naked or scantily dressed movie stars or models. Countless war novels and movies recorded the joys of lust and the pleasures of casual sexual encounters, especially with prostitutes and foreigners.

At the same time, the pinning-up of female nudity led to a fetishizing of body parts; breasts, buttocks, and legs were often appraised separately, as if the ideal woman could be put together like a jigsaw puzzle. Such fetishizing was perhaps most dramatically expressed in the quasi-theology of the "cunt" that permeated the writings of the American novelist Henry Miller, who had even before the war published such sexually explicit books as *Tropic of Capricorn* (1939). "The body is hers, but the cunt's yours," Miller was to observe in *Sexus* (1949), but in *Tropic of Capricorn* he had already outlined his credo in a description of "the best fuck" he ever had: the object of his desire was a "simpleton" about whom he noted that "above the belt . . . she was batty . . . Perhaps that was what made her cunt so marvellously impersonal. It was one cunt out of a million."

But of course besides being seductive, those "millions" of "cunts" were threatening: for example, governments constantly urged fighting men to protect themselves against the danger of VD posed by whores and foreigners, a peril which, according to official propagandists, implicitly involved all women. Moreover, just as many World War I soldiers had blamed women for their suffering, combatants in World War II sometimes tended to associate the devastation of war with unleashed female energies. The American poet Stanley Kunitz's *Careless Love* (1944) actually personified the event as an insatiable female, who contaminates and destroys men: "for what / This nymphomaniac enjoys," Kunitz wrote about the machinery of destruction, "Inexhaustibly is boys."

Even while the horror of the war was metaphorized as female, however, fighting men were continually reminded and constantly reminded themselves that they were struggling to preserve both the "girl back home" and the values she represented. In countless movies and popular songs, this good girl was kissed and reluctantly left in railroad stations and on wharves. Karl Shapiro's *V Letter* (1944), perhaps the most famous war poem of the period, was addressed to this girl and summarized both her virtues ("I love you first because your face is fair . . . I love you first because you wait. . . . You are my home and in your spacious love / I dream to march as under flaring flags . . .") and the poet's commitment to die for her, if necessary ("I love you first because your years / Lead to my matter-of-fact and simple death / or to our open marriage").

Yet though Shapiro's poem suggests that his beloved simply waits while he risks death, not every stay-at-home sweetheart was wholly passive. Dutiful and patriotic, many a lady in waiting became Rosie the Riveter and went to work in a munitions factory, for, as the war progressed, government propagandists in both England and America transformed the image of the good girl from that of a wistful dreamer to that of an energetic partner doing her share for the boys abroad. As soon as the conflict was over, however, this image faded; Rosie was turned back into a cheerful housewife or a clean-cut girl-next-door, and admonished in such works as Ferdinand Lundberg and Marynia Farnham's *Modern Woman, the Lost Sex* (1947) that she would lose her sexiness and her sex life if she insisted on continuing to compete with men outside the home.

As "pioneers of the sex frontier," wrote David Riesman, Nathan Glazer, and Reuel Denney in their influential sociological study *The Lonely Crowd* (1950), women "must foster aggressiveness and simulate modesty . . . if they have a profession, both men and women are apt to think that their skill detracts from their sexual life or that their sexual life detracts from their skill." Besides reemphasizing Lundberg and Farnham's point, their comment reminds us that these researchers were writing in the age of the Kinsey report and the sex manual, the sex goddess and the high school date. Whether male writers during these years portrayed women as involuntarily animal or expertly sensual, they frequently saw the women they described as less than fully conscious human beings. In his well-known poem *A Girl in a Library* (1951), for instance, Randall Jarrell depicted his subject as "an object among dreams," and remarked that "one sees in your blurred eyes / The 'uneasy half-soul' Kipling saw in dogs," and in a long story entitled *The Making of Ashenden* (1973) Stanley Elkin's protagonist finds a consummation he devoutly wishes in the luxurious lap of a hairy bear, while both the English writer Kingsley Amis and the American poet Kenneth Koch characterized women as dreamy parts of a dream world: in *A Dream of Fair Women* (1957), Amis imagined a horde of "Lime-lighted dolls guttering in their brain," each one begging him "to sign / Her body's autograph-book," and in *Sleeping with Women* (1969), Koch created a surrealistic landscape in which he could be "Asleep with women, awake with man." Clearly the popular cultural equivalents of all these sexy somnambulists were such stars as Marilyn Monroe and Jayne Mansfield, whose tantalizingly exposed bosoms and thighs revealed them as mindlessly voluptuous embodiments of bodily pleasure even while the artifice of their glamour defined them as no more than fantasy figures.

From the Beat poets of the fifties to the "black humorists" of the sixties and seventies, many writers continued the tendency of earlier artists to reduce females to collections of body parts. As if elaborating upon what we earlier called Henry Miller's theology of the "cunt," Allen Ginsberg in *Sather Gate Illumination* (1956) proclaimed of his friend Neal Cassady that "Neal sees all girls / as visions of their inner cunts," and Gary Snyder in *For a Far-out Friend* (1955) told a woman whom, he confessed, he had once beaten up that "visions of your body / kept me high for weeks," and, in particular, visions of her with "a little golden belt, just above / your naked snatch." Interestingly these celebrations of women's body parts implicitly characterized the male speaker as a voyeur, pruriently peering at female mysteries that the male must master.

For some writers in this period, however, such distancing techniques sometimes collapsed and were replaced by frank and frankly comic acknowledgments of male helplessness about the female body. Not only did Philip Roth in *The Breast* (1971) bemusedly imagine a male narrator's terrified transformation into a female breast, but both the American novelist John Barth in *Night Sea Journey* (1966) and the American filmmaker Woody Allen in *Everything You Wanted to Know about Sex* (1972) recounted the hapless expeditions of nervous sperm up the cavernous labyrinth of the birth canal toward the heart of darkness where female power lurks. Perhaps it was because the distancing strategy of voyeurism did not always work to defuse anxiety about such engulfing femininity that contemporaries of Roth, Barth, and Allen also turned to other defensive strategies, and particularly to a strategy of domesticating female sexuality. In his *Wife Wooing* (1962), for instance, the American writer John Updike praised the dutifully passive wife as "the Wide W, the receptive O. Womb," while in *The Lingam and the Yoni* (1955) the Australian poet A. D. Hope used the Sanskrit words for phallus and vulva to satirize a society that does "the Lingam honor" by keeping "the Yoni in" a cute suburban cottage.

Even this strategy, however, backfired for a number of writers in the era. Novels and stories of suburban sexual intrigue like those of Philip Roth (*Goodbye, Columbus*, 1959) and John Updike (*Couples*, 1969) often depicted the domesticated heroine as spoiled and idle, indeed as so bored that she is driven to plot pointlessly promiscuous or merely pragmatic romantic conquests. Perhaps the paradigm of these banal, bed-hopping predators is Brenda Patimkin in Roth's *Goodbye, Columbus*, a "Jewish-American princess" whose narcissism, heartlessness, and materialism lead her to seduce and abandon her impoverished and ardent lover. In the same vein, for beleaguered mates like the speaker of Robert Creeley's *Ballad of the Despairing Husband* (1955) and protesting prospective mates like the speaker of Gregory Corso's *Marriage* (1959), the woman who is a wife became the traditional "battle axe." Looking for "the darling I did love," Creeley's speaker encounters instead a ferocious female who declares, "I'm free of you, you little prick, / and I'm the one can make it stick," and Corso's speaker, fantasizing "a fat Reichian wife screeching over potatoes Get a job!," argues that "I never wanted to marry a girl who was like my mother, / And Ingrid Bergman was always impossible."

When women characters in contemporary literary texts were perceived as both "real" and "good," they were often defined as "good" because they were willing to be sacrificed by men and for male purposes. In a tradition that goes back to D. H. Lawrence's *The Woman Who Rode Away* (1926), a fisherman/ artist in the Welsh poet Dylan Thomas's *Ballad of the Long-Legged Bait* (1942) "throw[s] to the swift flood / A girl alive with his hooks through her lips" so that he can "catch" the inspiration that he seeks, while in a mode that goes back even further, to the self-immolations of martyrs like St. Cecelia, Celia Coplestone, the heroine of T. S. Eliot's play *The Cocktail Party* (1950), proves her virtue by allowing herself to be "crucified / Very near an ant hill" in the service of a "handful of plague-stricken natives / Who would have died anyway." A number of male writers brought to the surface the hostility implicit in works like those by Thomas and Eliot, constructing revenge fantasies in which autonomous females were punished for their supposed sins. In the British poet Roger McGough's *The Newly Pressed Suit* (1971), for example, the speaker first takes the role of the hero, placing his heroine "gently upon the *bed* / like a *newly pressed suit*," but then "step[s] into the poem" as the villain, to knock out the hero "and with a cruel laugh / Rape the *heroine* / (The raping continues for several stanzas)."

While McGough plainly intended to be sardonic, fictions by Norman Mailer, Hubert Selby, and Thomas Pynchon enacted visions of rape that were also murderous. Mailer's *An American Dream* (1964) not only told the story of a homicidal assault on a wife but associated that assault with a brutal act of anal intercourse; as the critic Kate Millett has observed, "The reader is given to understand that by murdering one woman and buggering another, Rojack [Mailer's hero] became a 'man.'" More grotesquely, male revenge on the "dumb" but desirous female was enacted in Selby's *Last Exit to Brooklyn* (1957), where the whorish Tra La La is gang-raped and finally murdered by being impaled on broomsticks and beerbottles. Even a brilliantly metaphysical comedy like Pynchon's *V* (1963) turned on comparable vengeance dreams. V's lesbian actress-lover Melanie is skewered by a pole in an onstage act in which she has failed to protect herself with a prop chastity belt, while the supposedly charismatic body of V herself is disassembled by children who steal her wooden legs, false teeth, and wig. As the critic Mary Allan has pointed out, "V" is clearly a virgin who thrives on both violence and vulgarity; at the same time, however, she incarnates the vulva, the vagina, and the horrifying void that these female body parts seemed ultimately to epitomize for many contemporary male artists.

Some of this period's fiercest conflicts among men often issued in literal and literary acts of aggression toward women. The revolt of male rock 'n' roll culture against bourgeois conventionality was often dramatized through record albums and posters flaunting images of enchained, seminaked women, while racial battles between black and white males seem to have been fought out, over, and on the body of the female. Although the black prisoner-writer Eldridge Cleaver conceded in his memoir *Soul on Ice* (1968) that he "could not approve the act of rape," he explained that for him sexual assaults on white women had been "insurrectionary act[s]": "I was very resentful over the historical fact of how the white man has used the black woman. I felt I was getting revenge." Precisely such revenge was imagined in *Babylon Revisited* (1969), a curse poem by the black writer Imamu Amiri Baraka (Le Roi Jones), which damns the whorish white woman as "a vast puschamber / of pus(sy) memories / with no organs / nothing to make babies," and prays that "this bitch and her sisters, all of them, / receive my word / in all their orifices / like lye mixed with / cocola and alaga syrup." As if to establish and explain a relationship between *Soul on Ice* and *Babylon Revisited*, moreover, Cleaver quoted from *The Dead Lecturer* (1965), one of Baraka's earlier books: "Rape the white girls. Rape their fathers. Cut the mothers' throats."

Despite, or perhaps because of, its use of a black colloquialism ("mother" for "mother-fucker"), Baraka's last phrase highlighted an anxiety that may underlie a good deal of degrading contemporary rhetoric about women, specifically an anxiety about a generation of viperous and vituperative mothers who were no longer experienced as being the selfless nurturers that their sons wanted them to be. With its definition of the pernicious American disease of "momism," Philip Wylie's *Generation of Vipers* (1942) definitively described the malaise that some men had begun to feel. Arguing that "the male is an attachment of the female in our civilization," Wylie excoriated a "dynasty of the dames," whom he saw as "five-and-ten-cent-store Lilith[s]"—that is, as modern equivalents of the monstrous first woman and first witch in Jewish legend. Ostensibly writing in a more scientific vein, the social historian Ferdinand Lundberg and the psychiatrist Marynia Farnham declared a few years later in *Modern Woman, the Lost Sex* that research had shown "the traditional 'Mom' " to be "the mother of [a] deficient male" and, rhetorically asking "Just what have these women done to their sons?," they replied "They have stripped them of their male powers—that is, they have castrated them."

As late as 1962, a character like "Big Nurse" in Ken Kesey's *One Flew Over the Cuckoo's Nest* was portrayed as embodying exactly the maternal flaws described by Wylie, Lundberg, and Farnham: Kesey's hero seemed to speak for the author when he exclaimed that Big Nurse "may be a mother, but she's big as a damn barn and tough as a knife metal . . . she's a bitch and a buzzard and a ball-cutter." In this period, moreover, even mothers apparently dedicated to the good of their growing boys were pictured as guilty and guilt-inducing. The stereotypical Jewish mother who reigns over Philip Roth's *Portnoy's Complaint* (1970) reveals her love for her son by threatening him with a knife in order to make him eat. Finally, even mothers who were neither castrating nor guilt-inducing often seemed horrifyingly weak and hence grotesquely pathetic. In *Kaddish* (1960), Allen Ginsberg lamented the death of his mad mother, ritually telling her "farewell / with your old dress and a long black beard around the vagina / farewell / with your sagging belly," while in *Sailing Home from Rapallo* (1959) Robert Lowell described bringing his mother's body home from Italy, noting that "Mother travelled first-class in the hold," and adding that "the corpse / was wrapped like *panettone* [a Milanese Christmas bread] in Italian tinfoil."

Perhaps what informed depictions of both maternal power and maternal pathos in this period was a mythology of the mother goddess that can be traced back to the nineteenth century and that was outlined in the mid-twentieth century by the English poet-novelist Robert Graves, the German psychoanalyst Erich Neumann, and the American poet Robert Bly. For Graves, the enduring feminine ideal was a figure he called the "White Goddess," while for both Neumann and Bly she was the four-faceted "Great Mother." In all these cases, however, her differing aspects corresponded significantly with just the aspects of women, and especially mothers, that were praised or blamed by many contemporary male artists. Though such mythological schema and the ideology of sexuality on which they were based might have seemed only indirectly relevant to literary women, these ideals and ideas in fact reverberated through male definitions of female writing that had considerable impact on women of letters.

In *The White Goddess* (1948), Graves claimed that "a woman who concerns herself with poetry" should either be "a Silent Muse" or should "be the Muse in a complete sense . . . and should write . . . with antique authority." If most other writers did not mystify the literary woman as Graves did, many either scornfully trivialized or melodramatically aggrandized her. Theodore Roethke claimed in a glowing review of Louise Bogan's verse that most women poets were guilty of "running between the boudoir and the altar; stamping a tiny foot against God or lapsing into . . . sententiousness," while W. H. Auden praised Adrienne Rich's volume of verse *A Change of World* with the faintly patronizing comment that "the poems are neatly and modestly dressed, speak quietly but do not mumble, respect their elders but are not cowed by them, and do not tell fibs." Similarly, Robert Lowell introduced the first American edition of

Sylvia Plath's *Ariel* (1965) by proclaiming that its author had here become "hardly a person at all, or a woman, certainly not another 'poetess,' but one of those super-real, hypnotic, great classical heroines." More generally, the British novelist-critic Anthony Burgess declared in 1966 that Jane Austen's novels failed because her writing "lacks a strong male thrust," and the American philosopher-novelist William Gass asserted in 1976 that literary women "lack that blood congested genital drive which energizes every great style." Given the impulse simultaneously to sexualize and dehumanize women that seems to have permeated much male thinking in the years between 1940 and 1984, how was it possible for women writers—indeed for women generally—to accomplish anything of importance in this period?

CONTEMPORARY WOMEN'S LIVES

The pervasive eroticizing of women characteristic of so much contemporary male culture may have been in part a reaction against many personal and professional options that had just become open to women of all ages, classes, and races. For with the aid of newly granted legal, economic, social, political, and educational rights, women were in fact able to accomplish a great deal in these years. At the same time, however, it is no doubt true that many of these new rights were not equally available to all women; that all these new rights were controversial and continually threatened by conservative social movements; and, finally, that a number of these new rights often presented problems to those who were supposedly benefiting from them.

During the years between 1940 and 1984, the legal status of women rose in most English-speaking countries. Throughout the twentieth century, divorce had become increasingly common and simple to obtain, with the introduction of a "no-fault" divorce law in California in the 1970s representing perhaps the most dramatic symbol of the way in which the Victorian double standard of morality had been reversed: where in the past a woman could be chastised and divorced for adultery (while, often enough, a man could not), now either partner could dissolve a marriage for any or no reason whatsoever. Nor could a divorced woman's children be taken from her by their father—as they could have been in the nineteenth and early twentieth centuries—without elaborate court battles. In addition, the Abortion Act (1967) in Great Britain, and the landmark Supreme Court decision in the case of *Roe v. Wade* (1973) in the United States, gave women in both countries an unprecedented control over their own reproductive systems, and, though in some English-speaking nations abortion remained illegal, the British and American models were powerful ones, implying that, in the words of the historian Carl Degler, "the law and society [had given] women final authority over the size of the family." Finally, throughout the sixties and seventies, equal-pay acts were passed and equal-opportunity commissions established in a number of English-speaking countries, seeking to rectify traditionally large differentials between male and female wages. The American Equal Pay Act of 1963 formulated for the first time the principle that women should not be paid less money for doing exactly the same work as men, and the Civil Rights Act of 1964 outlawed job discrimination on the basis of gender as well as race.

All these transformations in women's legal status were in one way or another problematic in their consequences. Not only did the ease of divorce lead to un-precedentedly high divorce rates, it was associated with a weakening of alimony and child support arrangements so that, as Degler reports, "in 1970, some 77 per cent of white women and 85 per cent of black women with children but without husbands maintained their own households. Yet as recently as 1940 only 45 per cent of white women and 40 percent of black women did." A di-vorcée, therefore, was frequently impoverished and solely responsible for the welfare of her children. As for abortion legislation, because the so-called right to life of the developing fetus rapidly evolved in many countries from an ethical and religious question to a political issue, such legislation was contin-ually being challenged. Moreover, women's wages remained significantly infe-rior to those of male counterparts; at present in the United States women workers earn fifty-nine cents for every dollar earned by men, while in Great Britain and Canada working women receive sixty per cent of the amount re-ceived by men. Worse still, in Australia until quite recently, the law established minimum wages for women that were lower than those for men performing identical tasks.

The issue of wages for women's work became an increasingly critical one in this period, however, precisely because women now found that they had in-creasing economic opportunities. To begin with—as the recent prize-winning documentary film *Rosie the Riveter* illustrated—World War II brought enor-mous numbers of women into the job market. By 1960, as the historian William Chafe has shown, "twice as many women were at work as in 1940, and 40 per cent of all women over sixteen held a job." In addition, he notes, between 1940 and 1960, "the number of mothers at work leaped 400 per cent—from 1.5 million to 6.6 million—and 39 per cent of women with children ages six to sev-enteen had jobs." Once again, though, the gains achieved by contemporary women were problematic. First, women workers tended to be clustered in low-status, low-paying, or service-oriented jobs: as the sociologists Juanita Kreps and R. John Leaper put it, in 1976 "the working woman [was] a typist, maid, teacher, nurse, cashier, or saleswoman." Second, few married women workers were defined as primary breadwinners even when they were in fact the sole sup-porters of themselves or their families. Third, working women had few support systems to help them cope with what had traditionally been defined as the unique female responsibilities of child-care and housework. Though nursery school and day-care enrollments rose radically in this period, child-care facilities were often either inadequate or expensive, while working wives found them-selves performing two jobs, one paid and one unpaid.

As if to underline the contradictions implicit in the history of women's gains during this period, Degler observes that "the proportion of women graduating from college was higher than ever" while Chafe remarks that "the proportion of women in business and the professions . . . changed hardly at all." Perhaps this paradox reflects a debate over the nature of women's education which goes back at least to the nineteenth century but which intensified in these years when female students flooded into universities, colleges, community colleges, and vocational training programs in every English-speaking country. The nature of this debate was succinctly summarized in 1955 by Lynn White, Jr., then presi-dent of Mills College, in California. In a book called *Educating Our Daugh-*

ters, he proposed a "distinctively feminine curriculum," and speculated that "a beginning course in foods"—perhaps focusing on "the theory and preparation of Basque paella"—might be "as exciting . . . as a course in post-Kantian philosophy." Such ideas had an effect on female students, with a number of studies revealing that many young women who were ambitious to get A's in classes nevertheless felt obliged to "play dumb" on dates. The psychologist Matina Horner's classic essay *Fail: Bright Women* (1969) documented the consequences of such a conflict: precisely the girls who had been the most dutiful students in early life were least likely to succeed later.

Of course, the fact remains that Horner herself, now the president of Radcliffe College, represented a group of women intellectuals who had *not* failed. Between 1940 and 1984, a range of female thinkers rose to prominence in virtually every profession. To name only a few of them: in the United States, the philosopher Hannah Arendt, the critic Susan Sontag, the political theorist Angela Davis, and the biologist Barbara McClintock; in England, the crystallographer Rosalind Franklin, the philosopher-novelist Iris Murdoch, and the critics Helen Gardiner and Muriel Bradbrook. Moreover, although in the forties and fifties women achievers might have appeared to be "singular anomalies," by the seventies female enrollments in graduate and professional schools had risen so sharply that it finally seemed possible that the contradiction posed by Degler and Chafe might be resolved.

The shifts in fashionable styles that can be traced from the forties through the eighties might function as an index of the enormous social changes that marked these years. From the utilitarian suits of the forties, with their padded shoulders and severe lines, to the "New Look" of the fifties, with its long, full, aggressively feminine skirts and decorous Peter Pan blouses, the revealing miniskirts and flowing Indian prints of the sixties, the unisex costumes and pantsuits of the late sixties and early seventies, and the dress-for-success costumes of the early eighties, women's fashions illustrated, successively, the austerity of the forties' war effort, the domestic conservatism of the fifties, the new sexual freedom of the sixties, and the emergence of reactions in the seventies and eighties against the eroticizing of women in the sixties.

What intensified, perhaps even triggered, the debate about female sexual liberation that was enacted through these changes in costume was a series of major advances in birth control techniques. Beginning with the repeal in the forties and fifties of laws forbidding the public dissemination of contraceptive information, birth control devices like the condom and the diaphragm had become more widely available. The development in the sixties of the birth control pill and the IUD (intrauterine device) for women meant that for unmarried women a new morality was now imaginable, a morality no longer grounded in the threat of pregnancy, while for married women a new control over family size was now feasible. In addition, even seemingly minor inventions such as tampons and beltless sanitary pads allowed women far greater flexibility in their activities. Particularly in the sixties, then, women may have seemed to be on the brink of an age of utopian sexuality in which desire could at last be expressed without dread.

Yet, the new emphasis on sex was often in its own way puritanical, even censorious: "coming" together was *de rigueur*; "good girls" always said yes; and proliferating sex manuals as well as how-to-do-it advice columns propounded efficient techniques for amorous encounters that reduced life between the sheets to a series of athletic events. Moreover, with the legalization of pornography in the late fifties, the sexual revolution began to seem like a specifically male revolution which, through such popular magazines as *Playboy* and *Penthouse*, expounded a hedonistic philosophy that turned women into consumable luxury goods. When hardcore pornographic films, journals, and books in the seventies began to emphasize bondage and discipline of women along with "kiddy porn," a number of female thinkers became radically disaffected. Their alienation was increased by their recognition that, despite the apparently enlightened rhetoric of the era, social problems such as child abuse, wife beating, and rape continued unabated. Sexual liberation, they decided, was not identical with women's liberation.

As early as 1963, Betty Friedan's *The Feminine Mystique* had begun to define the difficulties fostered by the cult of suburban domesticity that marked the fifties. Describing "the problem that has no name," Friedan excavated the feelings of almost metaphysical emptiness that were associated with the roles of housewife and consumer. At around the same time, moreover, women involved in the civil rights movement (and not too much later in the peace movement) were discovering that their revolutionary energies were mainly taken up by making coffee and love. These women turned not only to Friedan's book but also to earlier works—notably Simone de Beauvoir's *The Second Sex* (1949)— and began to produce theoretical writings of their own. Together, Mary Ellmann's *Thinking about Women* (1968), Kate Millett's *Sexual Politics* (1969), Shulamith Firestone's *The Dialectic of Sex* (1970), and Germaine Greer's *The Female Eunuch* (1970) sought to rescue liberationist arguments for female freedom from the sexual exploitation their authors believed implicit in male-dominated radical movements.

At the same time, activists who gained public recognition through such dramatic actions as bra burning, integrating all-male bars, and demonstrating at beauty contests began to issue manifestos, even as they helped popularize so-called consciousness-raising groups (small gatherings of women who met to discuss the effects of gender on their lives). In England, militants articulated "the 7 demands of The Women's Liberation Movement": "1. Equal pay, 2. Equal education and job opportunities, 3. Free contraception and abortion on demand, 4. Free twenty-four-hour nurseries under community control, 5. Legal and financial independence, 6. An end to discrimination against lesbians, 7. Freedom from intimidation by . . . assumptions and institutions that perpetuate male dominance." In America, similar demands were formulated by groups like Red Stockings, SCUM (Society for Cutting Up Men), and the Feminists, while more moderate women joined the new movement when Betty Friedan organized the National Organization for Women (NOW) in 1966, and when the magazine *Ms.* was founded under the editorship of the journalist Gloria Steinem in 1972. In addition, in many English-speaking countries, grass-roots projects were founded in these years: child-care centers, women's health collectives, abortion clinics, rape crisis hotlines and centers, as well as shelters for battered women and abused children.

Politically, of course, this sort of activity had a long history. In the United

States, the League of Women Voters had evolved out of the National Woman's Suffrage Association shortly after women gained the vote in 1920. But the first significant political gesture made by feminists and their supporters since the passage of the Nineteenth Amendment was the campaign for congressional approval and state ratification of the Equal Rights Amendment, an amendment to the Constitution declaring that "equality of rights under the law shall not be denied or abridged by the United States or by any State on account of sex." Until 1970, both organized labor and women's leaders had opposed this amendment on the grounds that it threatened protective legislation for working women. But in 1970, Elizabeth B. Koontz, the first black woman to head the Women's Bureau in Washington, arranged for the Bureau to support the amendment; it was easily passed by Congress in 1972 and shortly thereafter ratified by several dozen states. However, at this point the ERA encountered powerful opposition from very different quarters. Led by Phyllis Schlafly, a conservative Republican, women anxious about their rights as wives and their protection as members of the second sex joined with religious fundamentalists and other upholders of traditional familial structures to claim that the amendment would bring about social chaos. Despite prolonged and arduous efforts by feminists, the ERA had not been approved by the necessary minimum of thirty-eight states in 1982, the deadline year by which it would have had to be ratified in order to become law.

That so many women were mobilized to oppose what had been defined as their own liberation dramatizes the anxieties raised by the women's movement. A conservative like Schlafly spoke not only for women who wished to preserve the prerogatives of suburban consumerism but also for women who felt empowered by precisely the fetishizing of female sexuality that characterized this era. The seductive wife described in Marabel Morgan's *The Total Woman* (1973) sought to guarantee her own emotional and material security through strategies of submissiveness and enticement. Moreover, even world leaders like Evita Peron, Indira Gandhi, and Margaret Thatcher—women who had managed what seemed astonishing rises to political power in this era—publicly endorsed Schlafly's ways of thinking, if not Morgan's. As for working-class women, in most English-speaking countries a significant percentage could not see any special advantage in feminist ideals of female autonomy. The American sociologists Louise Kapp Howe and Lillian Rubin have pointed out that many blue-collar women tended to agree with a seventies homemaker who insisted that "a lot of women are much better off married and at home than they would be at some low-paying job and they know this; they've usually worked before, after all. So when they hear some feminist writers or lawyers or something like that say that jobs are so terrific, they know that for the average woman that's a lot of baloney."

Despite these controversies, however, the awareness of women's complex cultural situation manifested in such research as that by Howe and Rubin points to another significant phenomenon in this period: the development of women's studies as an area of intellectual concern in colleges and universities. Humanists (historians, literary critics, and philosophers), social scientists (anthropologists, psychologists, sociologists, linguists, and economists), and scholars of the fine arts (art historians, musicologists, theater historians and film critics) joined during the seventies and eighties to undertake interdisciplinary investigations of women's role in history and society, analyses which sought to transform traditional disciplines and *curricula*. Founding such journals as *Signs*, *Feminist Studies*, and the *International Journal of Women's Studies*, they explored not only the gender pressures all women seemed to share, but also the distinctive perspectives that marked the lives of disparate groups and cultures—blacks, lesbians, Chicanas, working-class women, and others. To be sure, many experienced themselves as marginalized, fearing in particular that their effort to widen the scope of scholarly inquiry from a study of man's culture to a study of human culture would have only a fleeting influence on intellectual institutions. Yet, significantly, their academic endeavors did coincide with an era when women were striving to bring about a number of other large social and ideological changes. In literary criticism, for instance, feminist scholars unearthed and analyzed a tradition of female artistic achievement at just the moment when contemporary women writers were sometimes consciously and sometimes unconsciously extending that tradition into the future.

WOMEN'S WRITING

Whether they defined themselves as feminists or not, women writers between 1940 and 1984 wrote out of a double consciousness: on the one hand, a newly intense awareness of their role as female artists who had inherited an increasingly great tradition, and, on the other hand, a newly protective sense of their vulnerability as women who inhabited a culture hostile to female ambition and haunted by eroticized images of women. Certainly both these strands of thought came together in Adrienne Rich's *Writing as Re-Vision* (1971), an essay which might be said to have functioned as a kind of manifesto for both female writers and feminist critics in these years. Criticizing "the use that the male artist and thinker . . . has made of women, in his life and in his work," Rich resurrected foremothers from Virginia Woolf to Marianne Moore, explaining that "re-vision" of both male imperatives and female ancestresses was "for us more than a chapter in cultural history: it is an act of survival."

In their various ways, many contemporaries of this notable American feminist were engaged in exactly such acts of survival. Essays like Tillie Olsen's *One Out of Twelve* (1972), Joanna Russ's *What Can a Heroine Do?* (1972), and Susan Griffin's *The Show Horse* (1978); poems like Muriel Rukeyser's *Myth*, Denise Levertov's *Hypocrite Women*, P. K. Page's *The Stenographers*, and Sylvia Plath's *Stings*; as well as stories like Doris Lessing's *To Room 19* articulate or enact a deep resistance to male-created social strictures and structures. At the same time, essays like Alice Walker's *In Search of Our Mothers' Gardens* (1974) and Eudora Welty's *The House of Willa Cather* (1974), poems like May Sarton's *My Sisters, O My Sisters*, and Kamala Das's *An Introduction*, as well as stories like Edna O'Brien's *A Rose in the Heart* and Ursula K. Le Guin's *Sur* articulate or enact a deep identification with either literal or literary mothers. In coming to terms with both the male and female forces that shaped them, contemporary writers were consistently struggling to define the cultural forces that had formed their personal and artistic identities.

Such a search for the roots of selfhood was perhaps especially urgent for women writers in Third World and Commonwealth countries, and for writers who inhabited racial, ethnic, and lesbian subcultures in England or America. Though all these authors had in common the medium of the English language, with its comparatively fixed grammatical and lexical conventions, they were influenced by distinctive traits and traditions to use English in very different ways and for notably different ends. Tillie Olsen captured the inflections of an immigrant Russian Jew in *Tell Me a Riddle*; Lucille Clifton used a modified black dialect to retell the story of the Virgin Mary in her "Mary Poems"; and the Anglo-Indian poet Kamala Das confronted head-on her conflicted but nevertheless definitive decision to write in English in *The Introduction*. Writers with such disparate backgrounds as the African Ama Ata Aidoo, the Asian-American Maxine Hong Kingston, the black lesbian Audre Lorde, and the native-American Leslie Marmon Silko filtered their stories of significant ethnicity through an English language which registered diverse cultural and sexual heritages.

By simultaneously defining both themselves and their worlds, such doubly dispossessed women indicated the more general parameters of female writing in this period, for the motivating impulse behind the works of contemporary women of letters can often be located along a continuum that reaches from self-definition to social criticism. Taking the real or figurative self as a subject, the writers whose work depended on processes of self-definition tended to explore not only the dynamics but the dreams of subjectivity itself. Remembering in *In the Waiting Room* how she had learned "I was an Elizabeth," Elizabeth Bishop can stand as a model for the poets Sylvia Plath, Diane Wakoski, Denise Levertov, Audre Lorde, and Ruth Stone, all of whom struggled to articulate— in Levertov's words—"what, woman, and who, myself, I am." Clearly, the diarists and memoirists Anaïs Nin, Maya Angelou, and Mary McCarthy shared this project, but, less obviously, so did fiction writers as diverse as Margaret Laurence and Carson McCullers.

In a quite different mode, those artists who took a real or imagined society as their subject set out, often in a strikingly realistic manner, to describe the world that circumscribes the self. Gwendolyn Brooks's Chicago "bean-eaters," Flannery O'Connor's Georgia country people, Stevie Smith's cartoon Britons, Judy Grahn's bus-stop waitresses, and Nadine Gordimer's South African liberals inhabit markedly different landscapes, yet all their authors explored the everyday worlds in which such characters were situated in order to construct an almost sociological analysis of the relationship between the individual and her community.

To be sure, most contemporary writers oscillated between both these modes, for—or so most would have agreed—to know the society *is* to know the self. Even a tale of black culture like Toni Morrison's *The Bluest Eye* (1970), with its implicit indictment of the ways in which white dominance cripples black men and maddens black women, can be said also to constitute a fable of identity, an act of self-examination as well as of social analysis. For, as Morrison herself remarked in a recent interview, "I do feel a strong connection to 'ancestors.' . . . What is uppermost in my mind . . . is that my life seems to be dominated by information about black women. . . . I feel the authority of those women more than I do my own." Finally, indeed, the fact that Morrison has perceived her exploration of the black female community as a kind of analysis of her own (as well as its) "authority" implies an interdependency between the sociological and the psychological modes of writing.

From this last perspective, Adrienne Rich's celebration of a woman as an icon of the future—her vision of the woman "who must be more merciless to herself than history"—is significant because it draws upon a dream of social transformation to create an image of a transformed self. As Rich herself tells us in a number of her poems, it was her reading of feminist analyses of society that enabled her to convert the eroticized body of the fifties and sixties into a luminous figure, a figure fully "breasted" but also fully self-aware and self-possessed. Perhaps, too, the exuberance of Rich's vision was made possible by her consciousness that she herself belonged to a complex community of women artists.

If we compare the section of this anthology in which Rich's work appears with the first section of the book, we cannot fail to be struck by the vitality and variety of the voices that have been raised in recent years to take up the kinds of questions that only a few medieval and Renaissance women had been able to formulate. Yet we have included here merely a representative selection of authors whose works reveal the new authority with which women are writing today. Nevertheless, the vigorous line of development we have been able to trace from the Middle Ages to the 1980s suggests the ways in which by the late twentieth century women of letters no longer believed themselves to be what May Sarton in *My Sisters, O My Sisters* called "strange monsters." This development reveals, instead, how many female artists had already, in Sarton's words, "come to the deep place where poet becomes woman" while rejoicing in "that great sanity, that sun, the feminine power."

STEVIE SMITH

1902–1971

"Who and what is Stevie Smith? / Is she woman? Is she myth?" asked the American poet-humorist Ogden Nash in 1964, expressing awe at the ways in which this English writer was able "to sing at Man's expense / Songs of deadly innocence." Nash's praise is not surprising, for as a sardonic versifier Smith wrote comic poems significantly akin to his famously witty couplets; at the same time, both more mordant and (occasionally) more morbid than her American counterpart, she frequently achieved what the poet Robert Lowell called a "unique and cheerfully gruesome voice."

Born Florence Margaret Smith in Hull, Yorkshire, Smith (subsequently nicknamed "Stevie" after the famous jockey Steve Donohue, because she was very short) moved to London with her mother and sister when she was only three. There, in the unfashionable suburb of Palmers Green, she and her sister Molly were largely raised by an aunt (whom Smith affectionately called "Auntie Lion") because their father was frequently away, and their mother's health was bad. After graduating from the North London Collegiate School for Girls, Smith became a secretary in the magazine publishing house of Newnes,

Pearson, where she was to work for thirty years, from 1923 to 1953. Continuing to live, as she would all her life, with "Auntie Lion," she began to publish both poetry and fiction when she was in her early thirties. *Novel on Yellow Paper; or, Work It Out for Yourself* appeared in 1936, succeeded by her first volume of verse, *A Good Time Was Had by All* (1937), and later followed by two more novels and more than ten other collections of poetry, including *Not Waving but Drowning* (1957) and *The Frog Prince and Other Poems* (1966).

Ranging from satiric melancholy to ferocious irony, Smith's work both celebrated and criticized the customs of a slowly declining British Empire. Perhaps for this reason, it was some years before her American audience grew as large as her English readership. Yet by the time she was awarded the Queen's Gold Medal for Poetry in 1969, her "cheerfully gruesome voice" had been noted on this side of the Atlantic. "Across the world I hear her still," declared Ogden Nash, "singing underneath the hill."

Papa Love Baby

My mother was a romantic girl
So she had to marry a man with his hair in curl
Who subsequently became my unrespected papa,
But that was a long time ago now.

What folly it is that daughters are always supposed to be   5
In love with papa. It wasn't the case with me
I couldn't take to him at all.
But he took to me
What a sad fate to befall
A child of three.   10
I sat upright in my baby carriage
And wished mama hadn't made such a foolish marriage.
I tried to hide it, but it showed in my eyes unfortunately
And a fortnight later papa ran away to sea.

He used to come home on leave   15
It was always the same
I could not grieve
But I think I was somewhat to blame.

                                                                  1937

This Englishwoman

This Englishwoman is so refined
She has no bosom and no behind.

                                                                  1937

Lord Barrenstock

Lord Barrenstock and Epicene,[1]
What's it to me that you have been
In your pursuit of interdicted[2] joys
Seducer of a hundred little boys?

Your sins are red about your head   5
And many people wish you dead.

You trod the widow in the mire
Wronged the son, deceived the sire.

You put a fence about the land
And made the people's cattle graze on sand.   10

Ratted from many a pool and forced amalgamation[3]
And dealt in shares which never had a stock exchange quotation.

Non flocci facio,[4] I do not care
For wrongs you made the other fellow bear:
'Tis not for these unsocial acts not these   15
I wet my pen. I would not have you tease,
With a repentance smug and overdue
For all the things you still desire to do,
The ears of an outraged divinity:
But oh your tie is crooked and I see   20
Too plain you had an éclair for your tea.

It is this nonchalance about your person—
That is the root of my profound aversion.

You are too fat. In spite of stays[5]
Your shape is painful to the polished gaze;   25
Your uncombed hair grows thin and daily thinner,
In fact you're far too ugly to be such a sinner.

Lord Barrenstock and Epicene, consider all that you have done
Lord Epicene and Barrenstock, yet not two Lords but one,
I think you are an object not of fear but pity   30
Be good, my Lord, since you can not be pretty.

1937

---

1. A sexless or effeminate man. "Barrenstock":
i.e., unable to produce children.
2. Forbidden.

3. I.e., cheated business associates.
4. Latin: I don't give a straw, I don't care.
5. Corsets.

Dear Female Heart

Dear Female Heart, I am sorry for you,
You must suffer, that is all that you can do.
But if you like, in common with the rest of the human race,
You may also look most absurd with a miserable face.

1938

Souvenir de Monsieur Poop[6]

I am the self-appointed guardian of English literature,
I believe tremendously in the significance of age;
I believe that a writer is wise at 50,
Ten years wiser at 60, at 70 a sage.
I believe that juniors are lively, to be encouraged with discretion
    and snubbed,   5
I believe also that they are bouncing, communistic, ill mannered
    and, of course, young.
But I never define what I mean by youth
Because the word undefined is more useful for general purposes
    of abuse.
I believe that literature is a school where only those who
    apply themselves diligently to their tasks acquire merit.
And only they after the passage of a good many years (see above). 10
But then I am an old fogey.
I always write more in sorrow than in anger.
I am, after all, devoted to Shakespeare, Milton,
And, coming to our own times,
Of course   15
Housman.[7]
I have never been known to say a word against the
    established classics,
I am in fact devoted to the established classics.
In the service of literature I believe absolutely in the
    principle of division;
I divide into age groups and also into schools.   20
This is in keeping with my scholastic mind, and enables
    me to trounce
Not only youth
(Which might be thought intellectually frivolous by pedants)
    but also periodical tendencies,
To ventilate, in a word, my own political and moral philosophy.
(When I say that I am an old fogey, I am, of course, joking.)   25

---

6. French: memory of Mister Poop.
7. A. E. Housman (1859–1936), English poet, writer of ballads and other traditional forms.

English literature, as I see it, requires to be defended
By a person of integrity and essential good humour
Against the forces of fanaticism, idiosyncrasy and anarchy.
I perfectly apprehend the perilous nature of my convictions
And I am prepared to go to the stake   30
For Shakespeare, Milton,
And, coming to our own times,
Of course
Housman.
I cannot say more than that, can I?   35
And I do not deem it advisable, in the interests of the editor
    to whom I am spatially contracted,
To say less.

1938

Human Affection

    Mother, I love you so.
    Said the child, I love you more than I know.
    She laid her head on her mother's arm,
    And the love between them kept them warm.

1942

The Wanderer[8]

    Twas the voice of the Wanderer, I heard her exclaim,
    You have weaned me too soon, you must nurse me again,
    She taps as she passes at each window pane,
    Pray, does she not know that she taps in vain?

    Her voice flies away on the midnight wind,   5
    But would she be happier if she were within?
    She is happier far where the night winds fall,
    And there are no doors and no windows at all.

    No man has seen her, this pitiful ghost,
    And no woman either, but heard her at most,   10
    Sighing and tapping and sighing again,
    You have weaned me too soon, you must nurse me again.

1950

8. Compare the moral poem by Isaac Watts (1674–1748), *The Sluggard*: " 'Tis the voice of the sluggard; I heard him complain, / 'You have waked me too soon, I must slumber again.' / As the door on its hinges, so he on his bed, / Turns his sides and his shoulders and his heavy head." See also Lewis Carroll's parody of Watts, *'Twas the Voice of the Lobster*, in *Alice in Wonderland*.

Lightly Bound

You beastly child, I wish you had miscarried,
You beastly husband, I wish I had never married.
You hear the north wind riding fast past the window? He calls me.
Do you suppose I shall stay when I can go so easily?

1950

Not Waving but Drowning

Nobody heard him, the dead man,
But still he lay moaning:
I was much further out than you thought
And not waving but drowning.

Poor chap, he always loved larking   5
And now he's dead
It must have been too cold for him his heart gave way,
They said.

Oh, no no no, it was too cold always
(Still the dead one lay moaning)   10
I was much too far out all my life
And not waving but drowning.

1957

How Cruel Is the Story of Eve[9]

How cruel is the story of Eve
What responsibility
It has in history
For cruelty.

Touch, where the feeling is most vulnerable,   5
Unblameworthy—ah reckless—desiring children,
Touch there with a touch of pain?
Abominable.

Ah what cruelty,
In history   10
What misery.

9. According to the Old Testament, Eve was the first woman, created by God from a rib belonging to Adam, the first man; she disobeyed God by eating an apple from the Tree of Knowledge at the behest of the serpent, thereby bringing death into the world (Genesis 3).

Put up to barter
The tender feelings
Buy her a husband to rule her
Fool her to marry a master   15
She must or rue it
The Lord said it.

And man, poor man,
Is he fit to rule,
Pushed to it?   20
How can he carry it, the governance,
And not suffer for it
Insuffisance?
He must make woman lower then

So he can be higher then.   25
Oh what cruelty,
In history what misery.

Soon woman grows cunning
Masks her wisdom,
How otherwise will he   30
Bring food and shelter, kill enemies?
If he did not feel superior
It would be worse for her
And for the tender children
Worse for them.   35

Oh what cruelty,
In history what misery
Of falsity.

It is only a legend
You say? But what   40
Is the meaning of the legend
If not
To give blame to women most
And most punishment?

This is the meaning of a legend that colours   45
All human thought; it is not found among animals.

How cruel is the story of Eve,
What responsibility it has
In history
For misery.   50

Yet there is this to be said still:
Life would be over long ago
If men and women had not loved each other
Naturally, naturally,
Forgetting their mythology   55
They would have died of it else
Long ago, long ago,
And all would be emptiness now
And silence.

Oh dread Nature, for your purpose,   60
To have made them love so.

                                                                      1966

ANAÏS NIN

1903–1977

In a passage from her critical book *The Novel of the Future* (1968), which typi-
fies the introspective quality of her famous *Diary*, Anaïs Nin analyzed the origins of her creativity: the "traumatic genesis" occurred when she was nine years
old and what later turned out to be an incorrect medical diagnosis that she
would never walk again turned her to writing as a pastime; the "artistic genesis"
of her *Diary* was her separation from her father, for she recorded her impressions in order "to persuade my absent father to return." The self-absorption of
much of Nin's work reflects her lifelong effort to explore her sense of difference
and of separation. Her father, a Spanish pianist and composer, had taken her
with him on his concert tours throughout Europe. But when her parents separated, the eleven-year-old girl and her two brothers left their native Paris for
New York, where they lived with their mother, a French-Danish singer. Nin
did not return to Paris until the thirties, after her marriage to the banker Hugh
Guiler. Under the name Ian Hugo, her husband later became an illustrator of
her books, but she remained surprisingly reticent about him and their relationship. Indeed, for all of the self-scrutiny of her work, Nin fashioned an image of
her life to demonstrate that "it is not only the woman Anaïs who has to speak,
but I who have to speak for many women."

   Nin's first book, a critical evaluation of the novelist D. H. Lawrence, displayed the emotional sensitivity that would continue to characterize her writing. While composing it, the twenty-eight-year-old met Henry Miller, who was
drafting both *Tropic of Cancer* (1934) and his own essay on D. H. Lawrence.
Like Lawrence, Nin and Miller perceived themselves as pioneers in a sexual
revolution and, while Nin explored how—as a woman—she could not accept
Miller's male-dominated perspective, both artists produced fiction about the
nature of eroticism. Nin's other friends were just as fascinated by the relationship between identity and sexuality: they included Henry Miller's wife,

June Miller, the surrealist poet Antonin Artaud, the novelist Lawrence Durrell, and the well-known psychiatrist Dr. Otto Rank, with whom Nin studied.

Although she was forced to leave Europe at the outbreak of World War II, Nin continued her journal in America, where she responded to the difficulty she experienced in getting her work published by buying a printing press. *The Diaries* first received serious critical attention in 1966, when they began to be printed by Alan Swallow. They constitute an extraordinary effort "to capture the living moments" of her emotional reactions to experience, an effort that Miller had earlier compared to the literary self-revelations of St. Augustine, Petronius, Abelard, Rousseau, and Proust. The *Diaries* were significantly complemented and supplemented, moreover, by a series of lyrical prose fictions in which Nin reworked and objectified much of her personal experience. In particular, the sequence of novels called *Cities of the Interior* (1959) —*Ladders to Fire, Children of the Albatross, The Four-Chambered Heart, A Spy in the House of Love,* and *Seduction of the Minotaur*—extended her exploration of the female psyche in lyrical language that attempts to capture the fluid formations and reformations of the self.

From The Diary of Anaïs Nin

[*December 30, 1931*] [*June Miller—The Woman I Want to Be*]

Henry came to Louveciennes with June.[1]

As June walked towards me from the darkness of the garden into the light of the door, I saw for the first time the most beautiful woman on earth. A startlingly white face, burning dark eyes, a face so alive I felt it would consume itself before my eyes. Years ago I tried to imagine a true beauty; I created in my mind an image of just such a woman. I had never seen her until last night. Yet I knew long ago the phosphorescent color of her skin, her huntress profile, the evenness of her teeth. She is bizarre, fantastic, nervous, like someone in a high fever. Her beauty drowned me. As I sat before her, I felt I would do anything she asked of me. Henry suddenly faded. She was color and brilliance and strangeness. By the end of the evening I had extricated myself from her power. She killed my admiration by her talk. Her talk. The enormous ego, false, weak, posturing. She lacks the courage of her personality, which is sensual, heavy with experience. Her role alone preoccupies her. She invents dramas in which she always stars. I am sure she creates genuine dramas, genuine chaos and whirlpools of feelings, but I feel that her share in it is a pose. That night, in spite of my response to her, she sought to be whatever she felt I wanted her to be. She is an actress every moment. I cannot grasp the core of June. Everything Henry had said about her is true.

1. The novelist Henry Miller (1891–1980) and his wife, June.

By the end of the evening I felt as Henry did, fascinated with her face and body which promises so much, but hating her invented self which hides the true one. This false self is composed to stir the admiration of others, inspires others to words and acts about and around her. I feel she does not know what to do when confronted with these legends which are born around her face and body; she feels unequal to them.

That night she never admitted, "I did not read that book." She was obviously repeating what she had heard Henry say. They were not her words. Or she tried to speak the suave language of an English actress.

She tried to subdue her feverishness to harmonize with the serenity of the house, but she could not control her endless smoking and her restlessness. She worried about the loss of her gloves as if it were a serious flaw in her costume, as if wearing gloves were enormously important.

It was strange. I who am not always sincere was astonished and repelled by her insincerity. I recalled Henry's words: "She seems perverse to me." The extent of her falsity was terrifying, like an abyss. Fluidity. Elusiveness. Where was June? Who was June? There is a woman who stirs others' imagination, that is all. She was the essence of the theatre itself, stirring the imagination, promising such an intensity and heightening of experience, such richness, and then failing to appear in person, giving instead a smoke screen of compulsive talk about trivialities. Others are roused, others are moved to write about her, others love her as Henry does, in spite of himself. And June? What does she feel?

June. At night I dreamed of her, not magnificent and overwhelming as she is, but very small and frail, and I loved her. I loved a smallness, a vulnerability which I felt was disguised by her inordinate pride, by her volubility. It is a hurt pride. She lacks confidence, she craves admiration insatiably. She lives on the reflections of herself in the eyes of others. She does not dare to be herself. There is no June to grasp and know. She knows it. The more she is loved, the more she knows it. She knows there is a very beautiful woman who took her cue last night from my inexperience and concealed the depth of her knowledge.

Her face startlingly white as she retreated into the darkness of the garden, she posed for me as she left. I wanted to run out and kiss her fantastic beauty and say: "June, you have killed my sincerity too. I will never know again who I am, what I am, what I love, what I want. Your beauty has drowned me, the core of me. You carry away with you a part of me reflected in you. When your beauty struck me, it dissolved me. Deep down, I am not different from you. I dreamed you, I wished for your existence. You are the woman I want to be. I see in you that part of me which is you. I feel compassion for your childish pride, for your trembling unsureness, your dramatization of events, your enhancing of the loves given to you. I surrender my sincerity because if I love you it means we share the same fantasies, the same madnesses."

Henry hurts her but he keeps her body and soul together. Her love for him is her only wholeness.

June and I have paid with our souls for taking fantasies seriously, for living life as a theatre, for loving costumes and changes of selves, for wearing masks and disguises. But I know always what is real. Does June?

* * *

I look at June's neck which is strong, I listen to her voice which is dark, heavy, husky. I look at her hands which are larger than most women's, and almost those of a peasant woman.

June does not reach the same sexual center of my being as man reaches. She does not touch that. What, then, does she move in me?

I resent Henry injuring her enormous and shallow pride. Henry looks with interest at my homely maid, Emilia. June's superiority arouses his hatred, even a feeling of revenge. He looks lingeringly at stupid, gentle Emilia. His offense makes me love June.

I love June for what she has dared to be, for her hardness and cruelty, her relentlessness, her egoism, her pride, her destructiveness. I am suffocated by my compassions. She is a personality expanded to the limit. I worship that courage to hurt which she has, and I am willing to be sacrificed to it. She will add me to her other admirers, she will boast about my subjection to her. She will be June plus all that I am, all that I give her. I love this magnified woman, bigger than other women.

When she talks, she has the same expression of intensity she must have while making love, that forward thrust of her whole head which gives her the appearance of a woman at the prow of a ship. The coal brown of her eyes turns to cloudy violet.

Is she drugged?

It was not only that June had the body of the women who climbed every night upon the stage of music halls and gradually undressed, but that it was impossible to situate her in any other atmosphere. The luxuriance of the flesh, its vivid tones, the fevered eyes and the weight of the voice, its huskiness, became instantly conjugated with sensual love. Other women lost this erotic phosphorescence as soon as they abandoned their role of dance-hall hostesses. But June's night life was internal, it glowed from within her and it came, in part, from her treating every encounter as either intimate, or to be forgotten. It was as if, before every man, she lighted within herself the lamp lighted by waiting mistresses or wives at the end of the day, only they were her eyes, and it was her face which became like a poem's bedchamber, tapestried with twilight and velvet. As it glowed from within her, it could appear in totally unexpected places, early in the morning, in a neglected café, on a park bench, on a rainy morning in front of a hospital or a morgue, anywhere. It was always the soft light kept through the centuries for the moment of pleasure.

* * *

June came to my house on Monday. I wanted an end to the mysteries, a climax to the suspense. I asked her cruelly and brutally, as Henry might have asked, "Do you love women? Have you faced your impulses towards women?"

She answered me so quietly. "Jean was too masculine. I have faced my feelings. I am fully aware of them. But I have never found anyone I wanted to live them out with, so far. I am not sure what it is I want to live out."

And then she turned away from my questions and said, gazing at me, "What a lovely way you have of dressing. This dress—its rose color, its old-fashioned fullness at the bottom, the little black velvet jacket, the lace collar, the lacing over the breasts. How perfect, how absolutely perfect. I like the way you cover yourself, too. There is very little nudity, only your neck, really. I love your turquoise ring, and the coral earrings." Her hands were shaking, she was trembling. I was ashamed of my directness. I was intensely nervous. She told me that at the restaurant she had wanted to look at my bare feet in sandals but that she could not bring herself to stare. I told her I had been afraid to stare at her body, and how much I had wanted to. We talked brokenly, chaotically. She now looked at my feet in sandals and said, "They are flawless. I have never seen such flawless feet. And I love the way you walk, like an Indian woman."

Our nervousness was unbearable.

I said, "Do you like these sandals?"

"I have always loved sandals and worn them, but lately I could not afford them and I am wearing shoes someone gave me."

I said, "Come up to my room and try another pair I have, just like these."

She tried them on, sitting on my bed. They were too small for her. I saw she was wearing cotton stockings and it hurt me to see June in cotton stockings. I showed her my black cape, which she found beautiful. I made her try it on. Then I saw the beauty of her body I had not dared to look at, I saw its fullness, its heaviness; and the richness of it overwhelmed me.

I could not understand why she was so ill and so timid, so frightened. I told her that I would make her a cape like mine. Once I touched her arm. She moved it away. Had I frightened her? Could there be someone more sensitive and more afraid than I? I could not believe this. I was not afraid at that moment.

When she sat on the couch downstairs, the opening of her black, clinging dress showed the beginning of her full breasts. I was trembling. I was aware of the vagueness of our feelings and desires. She talked ramblingly, but now I knew she was talking to cover a deeper talk, talking against the things we could not express.

I came back from walking with her to the station dazed, exhausted, elated, happy, unhappy. I wanted to ask her forgiveness for my questions. They had been so unsubtle, so unlike me.

We met the next day at the American Express. She came in her tailored suit because I had said that I liked it.

She had said that she wanted nothing from me but the perfume I wore and my wine-colored handkerchief. But I reminded her she had promised she would let me buy her sandals.

First of all, I took her to the ladies' room. I opened my bag and took out a pair of sheer black stockings. "Put them on," I said, pleading and apologizing at the same time. She obeyed. Meanwhile I opened a bottle of perfume. "Put some on."

June had a hole in her sleeve.

I was happy, and June was exultant. We talked simultaneously. "I wanted to call you last night." "I wanted to send you a telegram last night." June said, "I wanted to tell you how unhappy I was on the train, regretting my awkwardness, my nervousness, my pointless talk. There was so much, so much I wanted to say."

We had the same fears of displeasing each other, of disappointing each other. She had gone to the café in the evening to meet Henry. "I felt as if drugged. I was full of thoughts of you. People's voices reached me from afar. I was elated. I could not sleep all night. What have you done to me?"

She added, "I was always poised, I could always talk well. People never overwhelmed me."

When I realized what she was revealing to me, I was overjoyed. I overwhelm *her*? She loved me then? June! She sat beside me in the restaurant, small, timid, unworldly, panic-stricken, and I was moved, I was almost unbearably moved. June different, upset, changed, yielding, when she had made me so different, she had made me impulsive, strong.

She would say something and then beg forgiveness for its stupidity. I could not bear her humility. I told her, "We have both lost ourselves, but that is when one reveals most of one's true self. You've revealed your incredible sensitiveness. I am so moved. You are like me, wishing for such perfect moments, and frightened for fear of spoiling them. Neither one of us was prepared for this, and we had imagined it too long. Let's be overwhelmed, it is so lovely. I love you, June."

And not knowing what else to say, I spread between us on the seat the wine-colored handkerchief she wanted, my coral earrings, my turquoise ring. It was blood I wanted to lay at June's feet, before June's incredible humility.

Then she began to talk beautifully, not hysterically, but deeply.

We walked to the sandal shop. In the shop the ugly woman who waited on us hated us and our obvious happiness. I held June's hand firmly. I commanded: "Bring this. Bring that." I was firm, willful with the woman. When she mentioned the width of June's feet I scolded her. June could not understand the Frenchwoman, but she sensed that she was disagreeable.

We chose sandals like mine. She refused everything else, anything that was not symbolic or representative of me. Everything I wore she would wear, although she said she had never wanted to imitate anyone else ever before.

When we walked the streets, bodies close together, arm in arm, hands locked, I was in such ecstasy I could not talk. The city disappeared, and so did the people. The acute joy of our walking together through the grey streets of Paris I shall never forget, and I shall never be able to describe it. We were walking above the world, above reality, into pure, pure ecstasy.

I discovered June's purity. It was June's purity I was given to possess, what she had given to no one else. To me she gave the secret of her being, the woman whose face and body have aroused instincts around her which left her untouched, which terrified her. As I had sensed, her destructiveness is unconscious. She is imprisoned in it, and detached, and bewildered. When she met me, she revealed her innocent self. She lives in fantasies, not in the world Henry lives in.

[*August, 1937*] [*Gender and Creativity*]

As to all that nonsense Henry and Larry[2] talked about, the necessity of "I am God" in order to create (I suppose they mean "I am God, I am not a woman"). Woman never had direct communication with God anyway, but only through man, the priest. She never created directly except through man, was never able to create as a woman. But what neither Larry nor Henry understands is that woman's creation far from being like man's must be exactly like her creation of children, that is it must come out of her own blood, englobed by her womb, nourished with her own milk. It must be a human creation, of flesh, it must be different from man's abstractions. As to this "I am God," which makes creation an act of solitude and pride, this image of God alone making

2. The novelist Lawrence Durrell (1912–).

sky, earth, sea, it is this image which has confused woman. (Man too, because he thinks God did it all alone, and he thinks he did it all alone. And behind every achievement of man lies a woman, and I am sure God was helped too but never acknowledged it.)

Woman does not forget she needs the fecundator, she does not forget that everything that is born of her is planted in her. If she forgets this she is lost. What will be marvelous to contemplate will not be her solitude but this image of woman being visited at night by man and the marvelous things she will give birth to in the morning. God alone, creating, may be a beautiful spectacle. I don't know. Man's objectivity may be an imitation of this God so detached from us and human emotion. But a woman alone creating is not a beautiful spectacle. The woman was born mother, mistress, wife, sister, she was born to represent union, communion, communication, she was born to give birth to life, and not to insanity. It is man's separateness, his so-called objectivity, which has made him lose contact, and then his reason. Woman was born to *be* the connecting link between man and his human self. Between abstract ideas and the personal pattern which creates them. Man, to create, must become man.

Woman has this life-role, but the woman artist has to fuse creation and life in her own way, or in her own womb if you prefer. She has to create something different from man. Man created a world cut off from nature. Woman has to create within the mystery, storms, terrors, the infernos of sex, the battle against abstractions and art. She has to sever herself from the myth man creates, from being created by him, she has to struggle with her own cycles, storms, terrors which man does not understand. Woman wants to destroy aloneness, recover the original paradise. The art of woman must be born in the womb-cells of the mind. She must be the link between the synthetic products of man's mind and the elements.

I do not delude myself as man does, that I create in proud isolation. I say we are bound, interdependent. Woman is not deluded. She must create without these proud delusions of man, without megalomania, without schizophrenia, without madness. She must create that unity which man first destroyed by his proud consciousness.

Henry and Larry tried to lure me out of the womb. They call it objectivity. No woman died the kind of death Rimbaud[3] died. I have never seen in a woman a skeleton like Fraenkel, killed by the dissections of analysis, the leprosy of egotism, the black pest of the brain cells.

Man today is like a tree that is withering at the roots. And most women painted and wrote nothing but imitations of phalluses. The

---

3. Arthur Rimbaud (1854–1891), French Symbolist poet; he ended his life in a self-imposed exile from France. Ludwig Frankl (1810–1893), Austrian-Jewish poet.

world was filled with phalluses, like totem poles, and no womb anywhere. I must go the opposite way from Proust[4] who found eternal
moments in creation. I must find them in life. My work must be the
closest to the life flow. I must install myself inside of the seed, growth,
mysteries. I must prove the possibility of instantaneous, immediate,
spontaneous art. My art must be like a miracle. Before it goes through
the conduits of the brain and becomes an abstraction, a fiction, a lie. It
must be for woman, more like a personified ancient ritual, where every
spiritual thought was made visible, enacted, represented.

A sense of the infinite in the present, as the child has.

Woman's role in creation should be paralled to her role in life. I
don't mean the good earth. I mean the bad earth too, the demon, the
instincts, the storms of nature. Tragedies, conflicts, mysteries are personal. Man fabricated a detachment which became fatal. Woman must
not fabricate. She must descend into the real womb and expose its secrets and its labyrinths. She must describe it as the city of Fez,[5] with its
Arabian Nights gentleness, tranquility and mystery. She must describe
the voracious moods, the desires, the worlds contained in each cell of it.
For the womb has dreams. It is not as simple as the good earth. I believe
at times that man created art out of fear of exploring woman. I believe
woman stuttered about herself out of fear of what she had to say. She
covered herself with taboos and veils. Man invented a woman to suit his
needs. He disposed of her by identifying her with nature and then paraded his contemptuous domination of nature. But woman is not nature
only.

She is the mermaid with her fish-tail dipped in the unconscious. Her
creation will be to make articulate this obscure world which dominates
man, which he denies being dominated by, but which asserts its domination in destructive proofs of its presence, madness.

1966, 1967

4. Marcel Proust (1871–1922), French novel-   5. A city in north-central Morocco, the coun-
ist.   try's religious center.

KAY BOYLE

1903–

From her first volume, *Wedding Day, and Other Stories* (1930), to her recent
novel *The Underground Woman* (1970), Kay Boyle has explored the human
need for love in the context of desperate historical situations. Inspired by World
War II, such short stories as *Men*, *Defeat*, *Army of Occupation*, and *Winter
Night* dramatized her identification with European suffering before and during

the occupation of France, the bombing of England, the attempted genocide of the Jews, and the annexation of Germany. Illustrating her belief that the writer "must bear the full weight of moral responsibility," Boyle's fiction has often focused on ethical questions associated with combat, expatriation, espionage, and the conflicted or conflicting roles of men and women who inhabit a landscape of stress.

Boyle was born in St. Paul, Minnesota, but at the age of six months she was taken by her parents to Europe. It was the first of many sojourns abroad. After attending school in Washington, D.C., she studied violin at the Cincinnati Conservatory and architecture at the Ohio Mechanics' Institute. She began writing poems and stories when she worked as a telephone operator in her father's garage in Cincinnati. Subsequently married three times, Boyle lived abroad with all three of her husbands. The mother of six children, she established her literary reputation throughout the late twenties and thirties, when she became acquainted with such literary expatriates as Gertrude Stein, James Joyce, Djuna Barnes, and Robert McAlmon. During this period, she resided in England, Austria, and France. After the war, she worked in Germany as a foreign correspondent for *The New Yorker*. Several collections of stories (*The White Horses of Vienna*, 1936; *Thirty Stories*, 1946) and numerous novels (*My Next Pride*, 1934; *Death of a Man*, 1936; *Monday Night*, 1938) gained her O. Henry Awards, Guggenheim Fellowships, and, later, honorary degrees. Since returning to this country, she has taught creative writing at a number of universities, where she actively participated in student demonstrations during the sixties.

Winter Night

There is a time of apprehension which begins with the beginning of darkness, and to which only the speech of love can lend security. It is there, in abeyance, at the end of every day, not urgent enough to be given the name of fear but rather of concern for how the hours are to be reprieved from fear, and those who have forgotten how it was when they were children can remember nothing of this. It may begin around five o'clock on a winter afternoon when the light outside is dying in the windows. At that hour the New York apartment in which Felicia lived was filled with shadows, and the little girl would wait alone in the living room, looking out at the winter-stripped trees that stood black in the park against the isolated ovals of unclean snow. Now it was January, and the day had been a cold one; the water of the artificial lake was frozen fast, but because of the cold and the coming darkness, the skaters had ceased to move across its surface. The street that lay between the park and the apartment house was wide, and the two-way streams of cars and busses, some with their headlamps already shining, advanced and halted, halted and poured swiftly on to the tempo of the traffic signals' altering lights. The time of apprehension had set in, and Felicia, who was seven, stood at the window in the evening and waited before she asked the question. When the signals below would change from red to green again, or when the double-decker bus would turn the corner below, she would ask it. The words of it were already there, tentative in her mouth, when the answer came from the far end of the hall.

"Your mother," said the voice among the sound of kitchen things, "she telephoned up before you came in from nursery school. She won't be back in time for supper. I was to tell you a sitter was coming in from the sitting parents'[1] place."

Felicia turned back from the window into the obscurity of the living room, and she looked toward the open door, and into the hall beyond it where the light from the kitchen fell in a clear yellow angle across the wall and onto the strip of carpet. Her hands were cold, and she put them in her jacket pockets as she walked carefully across the living-room rug and stopped at the edge of light.

"Will she be home late?" she said.

For a moment there was the sound of water running in the kitchen, a long way away, and then the sound of the water ceased, and the high, Southern voice went on:

"She'll come home when she gets ready to come home. That's all I have to say. If she wants to spend two dollars and fifty cents and ten cents' carfare on top of that three or four nights out of the week for a sitting parent to come in here and sit, it's her own business. It certainly ain't nothing to do with you or me. She makes her money, just like the rest of us does. She works all day down there in the office, or whatever it is, just like the rest of us works, and she's entitled to spend her money like she wants to spend it. There's no law in the world against buying your own freedom. Your mother and me, we're just buying our own freedom, that's all we're doing. And we're not doing nobody no harm."

"Do you know who she's having supper with?" said Felicia from the edge of dark. There was one more step to take, and then she would be standing in the light that fell on the strip of carpet, but she did not take the step.

"Do I know who she's having supper with?" the voice cried out in what might have been derision, and there was the sound of dishes striking the metal ribs of the drainboard by the sink. "Maybe it's Mr. Van Johnson, or Mr. Frank Sinatra, or maybe it's just the Duke of Wincers[2] for the evening. All I know is you're having soft-boiled egg and spinach and applesauce for supper, and you're going to have it quick now because the time is getting away."

---

1. Baby sitters'.
2. Popular romantic figures of the time: the duke of Windsor, Edward VIII (1894–1972), abdicated the British throne in 1937 in order to marry Mrs. Simpson, an American divorcée; Van Johnson was a film star; Frank Sinatra was a singer, especially popular with teen-age girls.

The voice from the kitchen had no name. It was as variable as the faces and figures of the women who came and sat in the evenings. Month by month the voice in the kitchen altered to another voice, and the sitting parents were no more than lonely aunts of an evening or two who sometimes returned and sometimes did not to this apartment in which they had sat before. Nobody stayed anywhere very long any more, Felicia's mother told her. It was part of the time in which you lived, and part of the life of the city, but when the fathers came back,[3] all this would be miraculously changed. Perhaps you would live in a house again, a small one, with fir trees on either side of the short brick walk, and Father would drive up every night from the station just after darkness set in. When Felicia thought of this, she stepped quickly into the clear angle of light, and she left the dark of the living room behind her and ran softly down the hall.

The drop-leaf table stood in the kitchen between the refrigerator and the sink, and Felicia sat down at the place that was set. The voice at the sink was speaking still, and while Felicia ate it did not cease to speak until the bell of the front door rang abruptly. The girl walked around the table and went down the hall, wiping her dark palms in her apron, and, from the drop-leaf table, Felicia watched her step from the angle of light into darkness and open the door.

"You put in an early appearance," the girl said, and the woman who had rung the bell came into the hall. The door closed behind her, and the girl showed her into the living room, and lit the lamp on the bookcase, and the shadows were suddenly bleached away. But when the girl turned, the woman turned from the living room too and followed her, humbly and in silence, to the threshold of the kitchen. "Sometimes they keep me standing around waiting after it's time for me to be getting on home, the sitting parents do," the girl said, and she picked up the last two dishes from the table and put them in the sink. The woman who stood in the doorway was a small woman, and when she undid the white silk scarf from around her head, Felicia saw that her hair was black. She wore it parted in the middle, and it had not been cut, but was drawn back loosely into a knot behind her head. She had very clean white gloves on, and her face was pale, and there was a look of sorrow in her soft black eyes. "Sometimes I have to stand out there in the hall with my hat and coat on, waiting for the sitting parents to turn up," the girl said, and, as she turned on the water in the sink, the contempt she had for them hung on the kitchen air. "But you're ahead of time," she said, and she held the dishes, first one and then the other, under the flow of steaming water.

The woman in the doorway wore a neat black coat, not a new-look-

---

3. The fathers are enlisted soldiers fighting World War II in Europe and the Pacific.

ing coat, and it had no fur on it, but it had a smooth velvet collar and
velvet lapels. She did not move, or smile, and she gave no sign that she
had heard the girl speaking above the sound of water at the sink. She
simply stood looking at Felicia, who sat at the table with the milk in her
glass not finished yet.

"Are you the child?" she said at last, and her voice was low, and the
pronunciation of the words a little strange.

"Yes, this here's Felicia," the girl said, and the dark hands dried the
dishes and put them away. "You drink up your milk quick now, Felicia,
so's I can rinse your glass."

"I will wash the glass," said the woman. "I would like to wash the
glass for her," and Felicia sat looking across the table at the face in the
doorway that was filled with such unspoken grief. "I will wash the glass
for her and clean off the table," the woman was saying quietly. "When
the child is finished, she will show me where her night things are."

"The others, they wouldn't do anything like that," the girl said, and
she hung the dishcloth over the rack. "They wouldn't put their hand to
housework, the sitting parents. That's where they got the name for
them," she said.

Whenever the front door closed behind the girl in the evening, it
would usually be that the sitting parent who was there would take up a
book of fairy stories and read aloud for a while to Felicia; or else would
settle herself in the big chair in the living room and begin to tell the
words of a story in drowsiness to her, while Felicia took off her clothes
in the bedroom, and folded them, and put her pajamas on, and brushed
her teeth, and did her hair. But this time, that was not the way it happened. Instead, the woman sat down on the other chair at the kitchen
table, and she began at once to speak, not of good fairies or bad, or of
animals endowed with human speech, but to speak quietly, in spite of
the eagerness behind her words, of a thing that seemed of singular importance to her.

"It is strange that I should have been sent here tonight," she said, her
eyes moving slowly from feature to feature of Felicia's face, "for you
look like a child that I knew once, and this is the anniversary of that
child."

"Did she have hair like mine?" Felicia asked quickly, and she did not
keep her eyes fixed on the unfinished glass of milk in shyness any more.

"Yes, she did. She had hair like yours," said the woman, and her
glance paused for a moment on the locks which fell straight and thick
on the shoulders of Felicia's dress. It may have been that she thought to
stretch out her hand and touch the ends of Felicia's hair, for her fingers
stirred as they lay clasped together on the table, and then they relapsed
into passivity again. "But it is not the hair alone, it is the delicacy of your
face, too, and your eyes the same, filled with the same spring lilac

color," the woman said, pronouncing the words carefully. "She had little coats of golden fur on her arms and legs," she said, "and when we were closed up there, the lot of us in the cold, I used to make her laugh when I told her that the fur that was so pretty, like a little fawn's skin on her arms, would always help to keep her warm."

"And did it keep her warm?" asked Felicia, and she gave a little jerk of laughter as she looked down at her own legs hanging under the table, with the bare calves thin and covered with a down of hair.

"It did not keep her warm enough," the woman said, and now the mask of grief had come back upon her face. "So we used to take everything we could spare from ourselves, and we would sew them into cloaks and other kinds of garments for her and for the other children. . . ."

"Was it a school?" said Felicia when the woman's voice had ceased to speak.

"No," said the woman softly, "it was not a school, but still there were a lot of children there. It was a camp—that was the name the place had; it was a camp. It was a place where they put people until they could decide what was to be done with them."[4] She sat with her hands clasped, silent a moment, looking at Felicia. "That little dress you have on," she said, not saying the words to anybody, scarcely saying them aloud. "Oh, she would have liked that little dress, the little buttons shaped like hearts, and the white collar—"

"I have four school dresses," Felicia said. "I'll show them to you. How many dresses did she have?"

"Well, there, you see, there in the camp," said the woman, "she did not have any dresses except the little skirt and the pullover. That was all she had. She had brought just a handkerchief of her belongings with her, like everybody else—just enough for three days away from home was what they told us, so she did not have enough to last the winter. But she had her ballet slippers," the woman said, and her clasped fingers did not move. "She had brought them because she thought during her three days away from home she would have the time to practice her ballet."

"I've been to the ballet," Felicia said suddenly, and she said it so eagerly that she stuttered a little as the words came out of her mouth. She slipped quickly down from the chair and went around the table to where the woman sat. Then she took one of the woman's hands away from the other that held it fast, and she pulled her toward the door. "Come into the living room and I'll do a pirouette for you," she said, and then she stopped speaking, her eyes halted on the woman's face.

---

4. I.e., one of the concentration camps where, in the late thirties and early forties, the Nazis gathered Jews of occupied Europe and exter-minated them in the service of so-called racial purity.

"Did she—did the little girl—could she do a pirouette very well?" she said.

"Yes, she could. At first she could," said the woman, and Felicia felt uneasy now at the sound of sorrow in her words. "But after that she was hungry. She was hungry all winter," she said in a low voice. "We were all hungry, but the children were the hungriest. Even now," she said, and her voice went suddenly savage, "when I see milk like that, clean, fresh milk standing in a glass, I want to cry out loud, I want to beat my hands on the table, because it did not have to be. . . ." She had drawn her fingers abruptly away from Felicia now, and Felicia stood before her, cast off, forlorn, alone again in the time of apprehension. "That was three years ago," the woman was saying, and one hand was lifted, as in weariness, to shade her face. "It was somewhere else, it was in another country," she said, and behind her hand her eyes were turned upon the substance of a world in which Felicia had played no part.

"Did—did the little girl cry when she was hungry?" Felicia asked, and the woman shook her head.

"Sometimes she cried," she said, "but not very much. She was very quiet. One night when she heard the other children crying, she said to me, 'You know, they are not crying because they want something to eat. They are crying because their mothers have gone away.' "

"Did the mothers have to go out to supper?" Felicia asked, and she watched the woman's face for the answer.

"No," said the woman. She stood up from her chair, and now that she put her hand on the little girl's shoulder, Felicia was taken into the sphere of love and intimacy again. "Shall we go into the other room, and you will do your pirouette for me?" the woman said, and they went from the kitchen and down the strip of carpet on which the clear light fell. In the front room, they paused hand in hand in the glow of the shaded lamp, and the woman looked about her, at the books, the low tables with the magazines and ash trays on them, the vase of roses on the piano, looking with dark, scarcely seeing eyes at these things that had no reality at all. It was only when she saw the little white clock on the mantelpiece that she gave any sign, and then she said quickly: "What time does your mother put you to bed?"

Felicia waited a moment, and in the interval of waiting the woman lifted one hand and, as if in reverence, touched Felicia's hair.

"What time did the little girl you knew in the other place go to bed?" Felicia asked.

"Ah, God, I do not know, I do not remember," the woman said.

"Was she your little girl?" said Felicia softly, stubbornly.

"No," said the woman. "She was not mine. At least, at first she was not mine. She had a mother, a real mother, but the mother had to go away."

"Did she come back late?" asked Felicia.

"No, ah, no, she could not come back, she never came back," the woman said, and now she turned, her arm around Felicia's shoulders, and she sat down in the low soft chair. "Why am I saying all this to you, why am I doing it?" she cried out in grief, and she held Felicia close against her. "I had thought to speak of the anniversary to you, and that was all, and now I am saying these other things to you. Three years ago today, exactly, the little girl became my little girl because her mother went away. That is all there is to it. There is nothing more."

Felicia waited another moment, held close against the woman, and listening to the swift, strong heartbeats in the woman's breast.

"But the mother," she said then in the small, persistent voice, "did she take a taxi when she went?"

"This is the way it used to happen," said the woman, speaking in hopelessness and bitterness in the softly lighted room. "Every week they used to come into the place where we were and they would read a list of names out. Sometimes it would be the names of children they would read out, and then a little later they would have to go away. And sometimes it would be the grown people's names, the names of the mothers or big sisters, or other women's names. The men were not with us. The fathers were somewhere else, in another place."

"Yes," Felicia said. "I know."

"We had been there only a little while, maybe ten days or maybe not so long," the woman went on, holding Felicia against her still, "when they read the name of the little girl's mother out, and that afternoon they took her away."

"What did the little girl do?" Felicia said.

"She wanted to think up the best way of getting out so that she could go find her mother," said the woman, "but she could not think of anything good enough until the third or fourth day. And then she tied her ballet slippers up in the handkerchief again, and she went up to the guard standing at the door." The woman's voice was gentle, controlled now. "She asked the guard please to open the door so that she could go out. 'This is Thursday,' she said, 'and every Tuesday and Thursday I have my ballet lessons. If I miss a ballet lesson, they do not count the money off, so my mother would be just paying for nothing, and she cannot afford to pay for nothing. I missed my ballet lesson on Tuesday,' she said to the guard, 'and I must not miss it again today.'"

Felicia lifted her head from the woman's shoulder, and she shook her hair back and looked in question and wonder at the woman's face.

"And did the man let her go?" she said.

"No, he did not. He could not do that," said the woman. "He was a soldier and he had to do what he was told. So every evening after her mother went, I used to brush the little girl's hair for her," the woman went on saying. "And while I brushed it, I used to tell her the stories of the ballets. Sometimes I would begin with *Narcissus*," the woman said, and she parted Felicia's locks with her fingers, "so if you will go and get your brush now, I will tell it while I brush your hair."

"Oh, yes," said Felicia, and she made two whirls as she went quickly to the bedroom. On the way back, she stopped and held on to the piano with the fingers of one hand while she went up on her toes. "Did you see me? Did you see me standing on my toes?" she called to the woman, and the woman sat smiling in love and contentment at her.

"Yes, wonderful, really wonderful," she said. "I am sure I have never seen anyone do it so well." Felicia came spinning toward her, whirling in pirouette after pirouette, and she flung herself down in the chair close to her, with her thin bones pressed against the woman's soft, wide hip. The woman took the silver-backed, monogrammed brush and the tortoise-shell comb in her hands, and now she began to brush Felicia's hair. "We did not have any soap at all and not very much water to wash in, so I never could fix her as nicely and prettily as I wanted to," she said, and the brush stroked regularly, carefully down, caressing the shape of Felicia's head.

"If there wasn't very much water, then how did she do her teeth?" Felicia said.

"She did not do her teeth," said the woman, and she drew the comb through Felicia's hair. "There were not any toothbrushes or tooth paste, or anything like that."

Felicia waited a moment, constructing the unfamiliar scene of it in silence, and then she asked the tentative question.

"Do I have to do my teeth tonight?" she said.

"No," said the woman, and she was thinking of something else, "you do not have to do your teeth."

"If I am your little girl tonight, can I pretend there isn't enough water to wash?" said Felicia.

"Yes," said the woman, "you can pretend that if you like. You do not have to wash," she said, and the comb passed lightly through Felicia's hair.

"Will you tell me the story of the ballet?" said Felicia, and the rhythm of the brushing was like the soft, slow rocking of sleep.

"Yes," said the woman. "In the first one, the place is a forest glade with little pale birches growing in it, and they have green veils over their faces and green veils drifting from their fingers, because it is the springtime. There is the music of a flute," said the woman's voice softly, softly, "and creatures of the wood are dancing—"

"But the mother," Felicia said as suddenly as if she had been awaked from sleep. "What did the little girl's mother say when she didn't do her teeth and didn't wash at night?"

"The mother was not there, you remember," said the woman, and the brush moved steadily in her hand. "But she did send one little letter back. Sometimes the people who went away were able to do that. The mother wrote it in a train, standing up in a car that had no seats," she said, and she might have been telling the story of the ballet still, for her voice was gentle and the brush did not falter on Felicia's hair. "There were perhaps a great many other people standing up in the train with her, perhaps all trying to write their little letters on the bits of paper they had managed to hide on them, or that they had found in forgotten corners as they traveled. When they had written their letters, then they must try to slip them out through the boards of the car in which they journeyed, standing up," said the woman, "and these letters fell down on the tracks under the train, or they were blown into the fields or onto the country roads, and if it was a kind person who picked them up, he would seal them in envelopes and send them to where they were addressed to go. So a letter came back like this from the little girl's mother," the woman said, and the brush followed the comb, the comb the brush in steady pursuit through Felicia's hair. "It said good-by to the little girl, and it said please to take care of her. It said: 'Whoever reads this letter in the camp, please take good care of my little girl for me, and please have her tonsils looked at by a doctor if this is possible to do.' "

"And then," said Felicia softly, persistently, "what happened to the little girl?"

"I do not know. I cannot say," the woman said. But now the brush and comb had ceased to move, and in the silence Felicia turned her thin, small body on the chair, and she and the woman suddenly put their arms around each other. "They must all be asleep now, all of them," the woman said, and in the silence that fell on them again, they held each other closer. "They must be quietly asleep somewhere, and not crying all night because they are hungry and because they are cold. For three years I have been saying "They must all be asleep, and the cold and the hunger and the seasons or night or day or nothing matters to them—' "

It was after midnight when Felicia's mother put her key in the lock of the front door, and pushed it open, and stepped into the hallway. She walked quickly to the living room, and just across the threshold she slipped the three blue foxskins from her shoulders and dropped them, with her little velvet bag, upon the chair. The room was quiet, so quiet that she could hear the sound of breathing in it, and no one spoke to her in greeting as she crossed toward the bedroom door. And then, as startling as a slap across her delicately tinted face, she saw the woman lying sleeping on the divan, and Felicia, in her school dress still, asleep within the woman's arms.

1946

LILLIAN HELLMAN

1907–1984

Whether her plays analyzed the pain of two women accused of lesbianism (*The Children's Hour*, 1934) or the ruthless pursuit of power (*The Little Foxes*, 1939) or the effects of European fascism on Americans (*Watch on the Rhine*, 1941), Lillian Hellman established herself as one of America's leading dramatists. For a woman, such a career was pioneering, since the theater requires financial backing and extensive collaboration with producers, directors, and actors; both of these support systems have been denied most women artists. Like Lorraine Hansberry, however, Hellman managed to shape the conventions of the Broadway stage to explore the sexual, familial, and social issues that directly affect women's lives. The pragmatism and toughness that enabled her to do this informed the skepticism and irony of her plays, in which characters are often tested against experience and found wanting.

Hellman was born into a Jewish family living in New Orleans, but she moved to New York City when her father decided to make a new start after his shoe store went bankrupt. In New York, she attended Wadleigh High School, New York University, and Columbia University, and in the late twenties, she became a manuscript reader for the publisher Horace Liveright. She described her generation as cynical and worldly even when inexperienced: "The shock of Fitzgerald's flappers was not for us," she explained in her memoir *An Unfinished Woman* (1969); "by the time we were nineteen or twenty we had either slept with a man or pretended that we had." During her seven-year marriage to the writer Arthur Kober, Hellman worked as a theatrical playreader in New York and as a scenario reader in Hollywood. In her late twenties, when she began living with the detective-story writer Dashiell Hammett, her first successful play—*The Children's Hour*—ran for 691 performances on Broadway.

Along with Hellman's close friend, Dorothy Parker, both Hellman and Hammett were active in anti-Fascist work during the Spanish civil war and World War II, and both of them were blacklisted for their left-wing politics during the McCarthy period. While Hellman expressed her willingness to explain her own views to the House of Representatives' Un-American Activities Committee, she refused to inform on others, explaining that "to hurt innocent people whom I knew many years ago in order to save myself is, to me, inhuman and indecent and dishonorable." After Hammett's death in 1961, Hellman began to teach at a number of universities and to publish her memoirs.

An Unfinished Woman, which won the National Book Award in Arts and Letters, describes Hellman's family background and her early literary career in New York. In *Pentimento* (1973), she provides portraits of several family members, of the friend she called "Julia," who worked against fascism in the European resistence, and of her numerous literary acquaintances. Finally, *Scoundrel Time* (1976) focuses on American hysteria about communism during the late forties and fifties. As the critic V. S. Pritchett has noted, Hellman may have become a brilliant autobiographer in her later life because the theater taught her to break up her memories into short, strong scenes.

From Pentimento

[Pentimento *Defined*]

Old paint on canvas, as it ages, sometimes becomes transparent. When that happens it is possible, in some pictures, to see the original lines: a tree will show through a woman's dress, a child makes way for a dog, a large boat is no longer on an open sea. That is called pentimento because the painter "repented," changed his mind. Perhaps it would be as well to say that the old conception, replaced by a later choice, is a way of seeing and then seeing again.

That is all I mean about the people in this book. The paint has aged now and I wanted to see what was there for me once, what is there for me now.

Pentimento

In 1961, a few weeks after Hammett's[1] death, I moved to Cambridge to teach a writing seminar at Harvard. I had thought Hammett would be coming with me and had arranged with the help of Harry and Elena Levin[2] for a room in a nursing home, a pleasant, sprawling nineteenth century house a few blocks away. Now, living with Helen[3] on the top floor of Leverett Towers, a new student building, I could look down on the nursing home from the window and one night, when I couldn't sleep, I went to stand in front of it. That got to be a habit, and two or three times a week I would walk to the house Hammett had never seen, stand until I was too cold to stand any longer, and go back to bed.

The fifth or sixth time I took my late night walk—Helen was a heavy sleeper and I didn't think there was a chance that I could wake her as I dressed quietly in the next room—there had been a snowstorm during the day that made the few blocks hard going and slippery. But I never reached the nursing home that night, turning back for a reason I didn't as yet know, into Athens Street. Long before I reached our corner I saw Helen, looking very black in her useless summer white raincoat, standing with a tall boy who was holding a motorcycle. I felt the combination of gratitude and resentment I had so often felt for her through the years, but I didn't wish to waste time with it that night.

"Bad night," I said as I went past them.

I heard them behind me as I reached the courtyard of the building, and then I heard a misstep and a sound. As I turned, Helen had slipped, but the boy had caught the great weight and was holding to her, sensibly waiting for her to straighten herself. I knew she would not like me to see

---

1. Dashiell Hammett (1894–1961), American novelist and Hellman's longtime companion and closest friend.

2. Harry Levin taught Comparative Literature at Harvard.

3. Hellman's black housekeeper.

this, and so I went on into the building, took one elevator, waited until I heard her take another, heard the boy say something outside our door, and closed my own door against whatever she might say to me.

A few days later I saw her cross the courtyard, the tall boy behind her carrying two large bags of groceries. As she opened our door she took the bags from him and said, "Thank you, son. Come whenever you want your good dinner."

That night I said to her, "You've got a good-looking beau."

She had very little humor, but she liked that kind of simple stuff. Now she didn't answer me and I realized that for the last few days she had said almost nothing to me. She gave me my dinner in silence. After dinner I read for a while, felt restless, and went to get my coat. She came out of her room.

"Death ain't what you think," she said.

"I don't know what it is, do you?"

"A rest. Not for us to understand."

I was used to this palaver, but that night I was ill-humored and made a restless movement.

"I don't want to talk about death."

As I stood waiting for the elevator, she watched me from the doorway.

"You go stand in front of that place because you think you can bring him back. Maybe he don't want to come back, and maybe you don't—" she shrugged, always a sign that she had caught herself at something she considered unwise or useless to continue with.

It was a long time before I knew what she had been about to say, and it was at least a year later, after I had moved back to New York, before I knew that she had discussed me with the tall boy. I thought that was disloyal of her and struggled for months about telling her that, and then knew it wasn't disloyal, and didn't care any more because I had come to like the boy and to understand she had needed him at a lonely time in her own life, in a strange city, living with a woman who did odd things at night.

Soon after the night we had talked about death I came into the apartment to change my clothes for a dinner with friends. The boy was sitting at the table, Helen opposite him. He got up when I came into the room. We shook hands and Helen said to him, "Sit you down and eat your soufflé before it falls." As I went to my room I heard him say to her, "I never ate a soufflé before. It's wonderful."

"You can have one every night," she said, "a different kind."

When I came out of the bath I could see the boy from the hall mopping the kitchen floor. Helen came into my room.

"He eats nice. Two steaks."

I laughed. "*Two* steaks?"

"He asked what you'd think about that. I told him you got some strange sides, getting stranger, but you don't think about things like that."

"Thank you."

"He is taking me for a drive Thursday."

"On that motorcycle?"

"His rich roommate got a car. He says his roommate's on the stuff."

This then new way of saying dope, the only modern phrase I had ever heard Helen use, was no surprise. Years before she had told me her son was on the stuff and she would have to take him back to South Carolina to the farm her family still owned.

That Thursday, her day off, she got ready early in the morning and looked mighty handsome and big in a suit and a great coat.

"This early?" I said. "Doesn't he go to classes?"

"Jimsie is very, very bright," she said.

"What is Jimsie's last name?"

"I don't know," she said, "he's poor."

Jimsie was not as young as his classmates. He was twenty when we met him in his sophomore year. He told me he had had to wait to save a little money and win a scholarship, and when I asked him what his father did he laughed and said that nobody in his family had earned a living for three generations. He came from Oregon and one night he told funny stories about his mother and father, his five sisters and brothers.

I said, "You like them. That's unusual."

"Like them? I don't know."

"You don't know?"

"I don't know what they mean when they use words like that. I like to be around some people, or my motorcycle, and chemistry. I like one thing more than another. But that's all. Is that bad?"

I said I didn't know, I wasn't that kind of teacher. Then he went back to talking about his family and read me a letter from his father. His father wrote that a doctor in Portland had diagnosed stomach cancer but that he himself had cured it with a mixture of hot beer, cloves, and a sweet onion.

Through that first year I spent at Harvard, Jimsie would drop in at least three or four times a week to see Helen, carry her packages from the market, borrow his roommate's car to take her on small trips. Often he would stay to eat dinner with her and sometimes with me.

It was the period of the early student movement and there was a time when he disappeared into Mississippi and came back beaten up around the kidneys, a favorite place, then and now, for a police beating since it doesn't show. Helen moved him in with us for a week, saying that a roommate who was on the stuff would be no good as a nurse. Jimsie was puzzled, uneasy about the fuss she made over him. And her lack of response to the state of the Negro in the South made him stubborn and nagging. It took years for him to know that it had to do with her age and time: her anger was so great, hidden so deep for so long, that it frightened her and she couldn't face it. He didn't understand her at all, in fact, and there was a funny, nice night in which his attempt to explain to her the reasons for the insanity of the Bay of Pigs[4] was hilarious to hear. She didn't like talk like that: she liked best the times when he played his harmonica, and once she told me with pride that while she had not seen his "report card" another boy in the building had told her he was the most brilliant man in the class who played a harmonica.

In May of that year, about a week before we were to leave Cambridge, I woke up, knocked over an ashtray, and lay sweating with the mess I had been dreaming. After a while I got up, put on a coat and walked to the nursing home, certain that I would never go again. I stood in front of it for a long time, and when I turned to go back, Jimsie was directly behind me. I knew, of course, that Helen had telephoned him, but now, as we walked together, I had no concern for either of them. We didn't speak until I heard myself say, "Pentimento."

"What's that mean?" he said.

I said, "Don't follow me again, Jimsie, I don't like it."

But I don't wish to write about Jimsie; that isn't the point here and he wouldn't like it. Everybody else in this book is dead. We have become good friends, although now, twelve years after I met him, I don't understand him, or why he has decided on a life so different from the one he planned the year I met him. He was a chemistry student then and stayed on, after graduation, to work with Robert Woodward, the Nobel laureate, and spoke of the beauties and mysteries of chemistry with an emotion he showed for nothing else. Then he suddenly switched to astrophysics, and the night he tried to tell Helen what that meant she said he gave her a headache for a week, and because she came down with a bad cold after the headache and died from pneumonia a month later, I have always thought of astrophysics as having to do with her last days.

Jimsie was at the funeral in the ugly Harlem funeral place and I saw him standing in the rear, talking to her son. But by the time I reached the back of the place, through the mass of incompetent relatives she had been supporting for years, he had disappeared, and it was only last year that I found out it was he, not her son, who had taken the coffin by train to Camden, South Carolina, and waited with it on the station platform for a night and a day until her sister and brothers came a long distance over country roads to take it from him.

Somewhere in the years before or after that, I can no longer re-

---

4. A futile and abortive invasion of Castro's Cuba by the U.S. (1961).

member, Jimsie won a Marshall Scholarship, harder to earn than a Rhodes or a Fulbright, and went off to study in Cambridge, England. A friend of mine, an old Cambridge graduate, sent me a letter: "He has dazzled them here. I took him out for a drink, less because you wrote than because he is so interesting. But something has gone awry: I don't think he wants astrophysics, I think the world puzzles him."

I guess that was true, because he returned to Harvard, although I am no longer clear about when or why, except that he was there when I went back to teach in 1968, the year of the student riots. I remember that one day, at the height of the protests, we walked together in the Harvard Yard. George Wald,[5] who had been a hero, and may be again, was not doing well that day as he stood before students making a concil-iatory speech, too sure that his audience was with him, he with them. There were angry boos and the boy in front of us took an apple from his pocket and raised his arm for the pitch. Jimsie caught his arm and said, "Put it down, kiddie, a fine way of saying no to an old man." The boy pulled away angrily until he turned and recognized Jimsie, and then he said, "Oh, it's you," and patted him on the shoulder.

I guess he went back to England, because sometime in 1970 I had a short letter: "Do you think I can write? Of course not. But I'm through with astrophysics. I don't intend to work for the bastards and there is no other place to take it." I wrote back to say I didn't think he should try writing and didn't hear again until I had a card with an Albanian post-mark that says, "I like these folks. They're willing to fight everybody and they know the reason why. See you soon."

But it wasn't soon, not until last year during the summer, when I had a letter from Oregon saying he was back there, his father had given him forty acres of ruined land, the way everything his family touched was ruined, things were agreeable, but he was sick of communal life except for Carrie, who was clean and hard-working. A few days before this Christmas he called me, said he was in New York, could he take me to dinner?

It was good to see him again. The too bony face and body had grown now into power and full masculine good looks. We ate in a Greenwich Village fancy joint one of his friends had told him about and he whistled when he saw the prices on the menu.

He said, "I can't buy you dinner. I thought I could, but I can't at these prices."

"I'll buy it for you. It doesn't matter."

"Yes, it does, but never mind. You look tired. Is something wrong?"

"I am tired."

5. Outspoken liberal chemistry professor and Nobel laureate at Harvard (b. 1906).

"Come to Oregon. I'll take care of you. Carrie has learned to cook and she scrubs around. I can't stand dirt. My mother is such a slob. A pretty, nice lady, but a slob."

"You like Carrie?"

"She's O.K."

"That's all?"

"Isn't that enough?"

"No," I said, "I don't think so."

"Not for you," he said. "For me."

"Do you farm the land?"

He laughed. "I have a good vegetable garden and I had a hundred chickens, but my father killed the chickens for a neighborhood celebration. I earn a living as a carpenter and now, *now*, I'm getting rich. Some ass in Portland, a woman decorator, sells what she calls rosettes des bois and I carve them for her. Got that? I make *rosettes des bois*."

"Somewhere I know those words," I said, "but I can't remember—"

"They're rosettes of wood and you stick them on headboards of beds or old armoires, mostly new junk you fix to make old. She started out paying me five bucks apiece but now she pays me twenty-five. I'll get more when I get around to telling her I want it. Good?"

When I didn't answer, he put down his fork. "Good?"

"Stop it," I said. "You know what I think. Do you want another steak?"

He laughed. "If you've got the money, yes. Helen told you about the two steaks she used to cook me?"

"Yes."

"That great, big, fine lady, doing her best in this world. Do you know she gave me this coat?" He pointed to a sheepskin coat, expensive but old, lying on the chair next to him. "And when I brought it to her, said it cost too much, couldn't take presents from a working lady, know what she did? She slapped my face."

"You once told me you didn't understand about like or dislike."

He said, "I loved Helen."

"Too bad you never told her so. Too late now."

"I told it to her," he said, "the night I looked up your word, pentimento."

1973

KATHLEEN RAINE

1908–

Of Kathleen Raine, the British poet-critic G. S. Fraser has written that hers "are the poems of a sibyl, perhaps of a rapt visionary, but not of a saint." Raine herself has said that, though "I began as a poet of spontaneous inspirations, drawing greatly on nature and fortified by my more precise biological studies," and though "I have much sympathy for the young generation now reacting against materialist culture . . . I am too firmly rooted in the civilization of the past to speak their language." Together, such statements accurately summarize this artist's radical commitment to a mystical aesthetic tradition whose best exemplar is the Romantic poet-prophet William Blake, a figure to whom Raine, a scholar and critic as well as a poet, has devoted much of her literary energy. Like Blake, indeed, she has consistently written poetry whose aim is "to see a World in a Grain of Sand . . . Hold Infinity in the palm of your hand."

The author of some fourteen books of criticism—including four studies of Blake and an important book about the modernist Irish poet W. B. Yeats—along with a dozen collections of verse, Raine was born in London and educated at Girton College, Cambridge, where she received an M.A. in natural sciences in 1929. Married several times and the winner of many prizes for both poetry and scholarship, she lives in London but, as a poem like *Heirloom* suggests, often turns her attention to the landscape of her youth, explaining that "though I was born in London, my poetic roots were in wild Northumberland where I lived as a child."

At one time, Raine decided to exclude from her *Collected Poems* all works devoted to "mere human emotion," but fortunately—despite her commitment to "the symbolic language of . . . poets of the 'Romantic' tradition"—she was persuaded not to do so. Exploring the mythology of her own personality as well as the personalities of myth, such poems as *Kore in Hades* and *Heirloom* offer varying but consistently imaginative perspectives on the mystical radiance that this sometime "sibyl" sees at the center of women's lives.

Isis Wanderer[1]

This too is an experience of the soul,
The dismembered world that once was the whole god
Whose broken fragments now lie dead.
This passing of reality itself is real.

Gathering under my black cloak the remnants of life   5
That lie dishonoured among people and places

---

1. Isis was the Egyptian nature goddess; her brother Osiris, the sun god, was slain and dismembered by their brother Set, and Isis wandered through the world gathering up the pieces. When she had finally completed this task, Osiris was restored to life and became the ruler of the dead.

I search the twofold desert of my solitude,
The outward perished world, and the barren mind.

Once he was present, numinous, in the house of the world,
Wearing day like a garment, his beauty manifest   10
In corn and man as he journeyed down the fertile river.
With love he filled my distances of night.

I trace the contour of his hand fading upon a cloud,
And this his blood flows from a dying soldier's wound.
In broken fields his body is scattered and his limbs lie   15
Spreadeagled like wrecked fuselage in the sand.

His skull is a dead cathedral, and his crown's rays
Glitter from worthless tins and broken glass.
His blue eyes are reflected from pools in the gutter,
And his strength is the desolate stone of fallen cities.   20

Oh in the kitchen-midden[2] of my dreams
Turning over the potsherds of past days
Shall I uncover his loved desecrated face?
Are the unfathomed depths of sleep his grave?

Beyond the looming dangerous end of night   25
Beneath the vaults of fear do his bones lie,
And does the maze of nightmare lead to the power within?
Do menacing nether waters cover the fish king?

I piece the divine fragments into the mandala[3]
Whose centre is the lost creative power,   30
The sun, the heart of God, the lotus, the electron
That pulses world upon world, ray upon ray
That he who lived on the first may rise on the last day.

1948

Kore in Hades[4]

I came, yes, dear, dear
Mother for you I came, so I remember,
To lie in your warm

2. Refuse heap, or, more specifically, mound marking the site of a prehistoric dwelling.
3. In Eastern religion, a mystical design thought to symbolize the universe.
4. In Greek myth, Kore or Persephone is the daughter of Demeter, the goddess of fertility and harvest, and the wife of Hades, the ruler of the underworld where the dead dwell (also called Hades). For eight months of the year Kore lives on the surface of the earth, causing plants to blossom; for the remaining four months she must return to Hades.

Bed, to watch the wonder flame:
Burning, golden gentle and bright the light of the living.   5

With you I ran
To see the roadside green
Leaves and small cool bindweed flowers
Living rejoicing to proclaim
We are, we are manifold, in multitude   10
We come, we are near and far,
Past and future innumerable, we are yours,
We are you. I listened
To the sweet bird whose song is for ever,
I was the little girl of the one mother.   15

World you wove me to please a child,
Yet its texture was thinner than light, fleeter
Than flame that burned while it seemed
Leaves and flowers and garden world without end.
Bright those faces closed and were over.   20

Here and now is over, the garden
Lost from time, its sun its moon
Mother, daughter, daughter, mother, never
Is now: there is nothing, nothing for ever.

1965

Heirloom

She gave me childhood's flowers,
Heather and wild thyme,
Eyebright and tormentil,
Lichen's mealy cup
Dry on wind-scored stone,   5
The corbies on the rock,
The rowan by the burn.[5]

Sea-marvels a child beheld
Out in the fisherman's boat,
Fringed pulsing violet   10
Medusa, sea-gooseberries,
Starfish on the sea-floor,
Cowries and rainbow-shells
From pools on a rocky shore,

5. Scottish term for a small brook. "Corbies": ravens.

Gave me her memories,   15
But kept her last treasure:
"When I was a lass," she said,
"Sitting among the heather,
"Suddenly I saw
"That all the moor was alive!   20
"I have told no one before."

That was my mother's tale.
Seventy years had gone
Since she saw the living skein
Of which the world is woven,   25
And having seen, knew all;
Through long indifferent years
Treasuring the priceless pearl.

                                                    1971

[What substance had Euridice][6]

What substance had Euridice,
Or shade?
Unseen he knew that she was near
Whom when with bodily arms he held
Was waterfall, was fleeting flame, was empty air: 5
Yet in that country far
He only cast a shadow, bright was she.

                                                    1973

[On its way I see]

On its way I see
The anew-created
Garden as old as woman; to me
These daisies in the grass are shown, these
Birds in the apple-tree:[7]
Is my sin, then,
Forgiven?

                                                    1978

---

6. In Greek myth, the wife of the singer and
poet Orpheus. When she died, Orpheus tried to
bring her back from the underworld; but as they
were traveling back to the surface of the earth,
Orpheus glanced back at her, breaking the instructions he had received from Hades, the god
of the underworld, and so he lost her permanently.
7. A reference to the story of Eve's eating of the
apple from the Tree of Knowledge in the garden
of Eden, the primal sin, which brought death
into the world (Genesis 3).

DOROTHY LIVESAY

1909–

Dorothy Livesay's mother, Florence (Randal) Livesay, was a writer and her father, John F. B. Livesay, was a general manager of the Canadian Press. After receiving a B.A. from the University of Toronto and a Diplôme d'Études Supérieures from the Sorbonne, she studied social science at Toronto. Before and after she married Duncan Macnair in 1937, she was a social worker in Vancouver, but she has more recently worked as a correspondent for the *Toronto Daily Star*, as a documentary scriptwriter for the Canadian Broadcasting Coportation, as a UNESCO English Specialist in Paris, as an English teacher in Northern Rhodesia, as an editor of Canadian literary journals and anthologies, and as a lecturer and writer-in-residence in many Canadian universities.

A widow with two children, Livesay has described her work as "the evocation of the Canadian scene through the writing of lyrical and documentary poetry." For more than six decades, she has published prize-winning volumes of verse that combine frankly sensual and personal poems with more public, polemical works. Her early Imagistic volumes (*Green Pitcher*, 1928, and *Signpost*, 1932) were followed by the political poems in *Day and Night* (1944), verse that analyzed the threats of poverty and fascism. By the fifties and sixties, however, Livesay had established herself as a lyricist of intimacy. Many of the pieces in her *Collected Poems* (1972) focus, as she has explained, on "love, marriage and its bonds, childbirth, childhood" and on "the need for peace in the world to give children a growing place."

Green Rain

I remember long veils of green rain
Feathered like the shawl of my grandmother—
Green from the half-green of the spring trees
Waving in the valley.

I remember the road   5
Like the one which leads to my grandmother's house,
A warm house, with green carpets,
Geraniums, a trilling canary
And shining horse-hair chairs;
And the silence, full of the rain's falling   10
Was like my grandmother's parlour
Alive with herself and her voice, rising and falling—
Rain and wind intermingled.

I remember on that day
I was thinking only of my love   15

And of my love's house.
But now I remember the day
As I remember my grandmother.
I remember the rain as the feathery fringe of her shawl.

1932   1972

Eve[1]

Beside the highway
at the motel door
            it roots
the last survivor of a pioneer
                    orchard   5
miraculously   still
            bearing.

A thud   another apple falls
            I stoop   and O
that scent, gnarled, ciderish   10
            with sun in it
that woody pulp
            for teeth and tongue
            to bite and curl around
that spurting juice   15
            earth-sweet!

In fifty seconds, fifty summers sweep
            and shake me—
I am alive!   can stand
            up still   20
hoarding this apple
            in my hand.

1967   1972

The Three Emily's[2]

These women crying in my head
Walk alone, uncomforted:
The Emily's, these three

---

1. According to the Bible, Eve was the first
woman, created by God from the rib of Adam,
the first man. She disobeyed God by eating an
apple from the Tree of Knowledge at the behest
of the serpent, thereby bringing death into the
world (Genesis 3).
2. Emily Brontë (1818–1848), English novelist
and poet; Emily Dickinson (1830–1886),
American poet; and Emily Carr (1871–1945),
Canadian painter.

Cry to be set free—
And others whom I will not name   5
Each different, each the same.

Yet they had liberty!
Their kingdom was the sky:
They batted clouds with easy hand,
Found a mountain for their stand;   10
From wandering lonely they could catch
The inner magic of a heath—
A lake their palette, any tree
Their brush could be.

And still they cry to me   15
As in reproach—
I, born to hear their inner storm
Of separate man in woman's form,
I yet possess another kingdom, barred
To them, these three, this Emily.   20
I move as mother in a frame,
My arteries
Flow the immemorial way
Towards the child, the man;
And only for brief span   25
Am I an Emily on mountain snows
And one of these.

And so the whole that I possess
Is still much less—
They move triumphant through my head: 30
I am the one
Uncomforted.

1972

The Children's Letters

They are my secret food
consumed in the most hushed corners
of my room
when no one's looking
I hold them up to sunlight   5
at the window
to see aright
to hear behind the spindly words
a child's tentative
               first footsteps   10

a small voice stuttering
                    at the sky
"bird . . . bird. . . ."

Whether these be
my children or my grandchildren   15
they're ghostly visitors
food of a solitary kind—
they leap on shafts of sunlight
through the mind's
shutters.   20

                                                          1972

EUDORA WELTY

1909–

"Without the love and belief my family gave me, I could not have become a writer to begin with," confessed Eudora Welty in an introduction to her *Collected Short Stories* (1980), adding, as if to argue that love begets further love, "I have been told, both in approval and in accusation, that I seem to love all my characters." In fact, her work has been consistently marked by a celebratory warmth—a sympathy for the deformed, the distorted, and even the demonic in human life, along with a loving insight into the trials and triumphs of daily living. From her earliest to her most recent stories, moreover, Welty has been particularly notable for her creation of powerfully engaging women characters: such tales as *Why I Live at the P.O.* (1941), *A Worn Path* (1941), and *The Wide Net* (1943), along with later stories like *The Bride of the Innisfallen* (1955) and *Circe* (1955), explore the varieties of female experience with grace and wit.

The daughter of an Ohio-born father and a mother who was a native West Virginian, Welty was born and raised in Jackson, Mississippi, where she has continued to live all her life, in a rural Southern setting whose customs and convictions have been as central to her work as they were to the writing of such other Southern regionalists as William Faulkner and Flannery O'Connor. After attending Mississippi State College for Women from 1925 to 1927, Welty earned a B.A. in 1929 from the University of Wisconsin, then studied advertising for a year at Columbia University. Following her father's death in 1931, however, she resettled permanently in Jackson, where, throughout the 1930s, she worked for local newspapers, for the Jackson radio station, and for the WPA (the federally funded Works Progress Administration, which was created to give people jobs during the Great Depression). Her first collection of short fiction, *A Curtain of Green, and Other Stories*, was published in 1941, with an introduction by Katherine Anne Porter, whose "shining bounty," Welty has written, "nourished my life." Subsequent volumes included the short-story collections *The Wide Net, and Other Stories* (1943) and *The Bride of the Innisfallen* (1955) as well as the novels *The Robber Bridegroom* (1942), *Delta Wedding* (1946), *The Ponder Heart* (1954), *The Optimist's Daughter* (for which Welty won the Pulitzer Prize in 1972), and, most recently, the memoir *One Writer's Beginnings* (1983).

Though she has sometimes been accused of—in the words of one critic— not having "often taken the South's social turmoil as subject matter," Welty's longstanding concern for the crises of her culture is clearly revealed in *One Time, One Place* (1971), a collection of photographs of black and white share-croppers and other workers in the Mississippi countryside that she took during her time with the WPA in the thirties, as well as in her delineation of Phoenix Jackson, the heroic black grandmother of *A Worn Path*, who might well have stepped out of one of those pictures, and in her portrayal of the white assassin of Medgar Evers, who narrates the bitter story *Where Is the Voice Coming From?* (1963). Consistently sensitive and sympathetic to "the mind, heart, and skin of" human beings who are "not myself," Welty proves in all her sometimes sorrowful, sometimes amused, but always loving fictions the intensity with which she adheres to her central belief: "It is the act of a writer's imagination that I set most high."

The Wide Net

This story is for John Fraiser Robinson

William Wallace Jamieson's wife Hazel was going to have a baby. But this was October, and it was six months away, and she acted exactly as though it would be tomorrow. When he came in the room she would not speak to him, but would look as straight at nothing as she could, with her eyes glowing. If he only touched her she stuck out her tongue or ran around the table. So one night he went out with two of the boys down the road and stayed out all night. But that was the worst thing yet, because when he came home in the early morning Hazel had vanished. He went through the house not believing his eyes, balancing with both hands out, his yellow cowlick rising on end, and then he turned the kitchen inside out looking for her, but it did no good. Then when he got back to the front room he saw she had left him a little letter, in an envelope. That was doing something behind someone's back. He took out the letter, pushed it open, held it out at a distance from his eyes. . . . After one look he was scared to read the exact words, and he crushed the whole thing in his hand instantly, but what it had said was that she would not put up with him after that and was going to the river to drown herself.

"Drown herself. . . . But she's in mortal fear of the water!"

He ran out front, his face red like the red plums hanging on the bushes there, and down in the road he gave a loud shout for Virgil

Thomas, who was just going in his own house, to come out again. He could just see the edge of Virgil, he had almost got in, he had one foot inside the door.

They met half-way between the farms, under the shade-tree.

"Haven't you had enough of the night?" asked Virgil. There they were, their pants all covered with dust and dew, and they had had to carry the third man home flat between them.

"I've lost Hazel, she's vanished, she went to drown herself."

"Why, that ain't like Hazel," said Virgil.

William Wallace reached out and shook him. "You heard me. Don't you know we have to drag the river?"

"Right this minute?"

"You ain't got nothing to do till spring."

"Let me go set foot inside the house and speak to my mother and tell her a story, and I'll come back."

"This will take the wide net," said William Wallace. His eyebrows gathered, and he was talking to himself.

"How come Hazel to go and do that way?" asked Virgil as they started out.

William Wallace said, "I reckon she got lonesome."

"That don't argue—drown herself for getting lonesome. My mother gets lonesome."

"Well," said William Wallace. "It argues for Hazel."

"How long is it now since you and her was married?"

"Why, it's been a year."

"It don't seem that long to me. A year!"

"It was this time last year. It seems longer," said William Wallace, breaking a stick off a tree in surprise. They walked along, kicking at the flowers on the road's edge. "I remember the day I seen her first, and that seems a long time ago. She was coming along the road holding a little frying-size chicken from her grandma, under her arm, and she had it real quiet. I spoke to her with nice manners. We knowed each other's names, being bound to, just didn't know each other to speak to. I says, 'Where are you taking the fryer?' and she says, 'Mind your manners,' and I kept on till after while she says, 'If you want to walk me home, take littler steps.' So I didn't lose time. It was just four miles across the field and full of blackberries, and from the top of the hill there was Dover below, looking sizeable-like and clean, spread out between the two churches like that. When we got down, I says to her, 'What kind of water's in this well?' and she says, 'The best water in the world.' So I drew a bucket and took out a dipper and she drank and I drank. I didn't think it was that remarkable, but I didn't tell her."

"What happened that night?" asked Virgil.

"We ate the chicken," said William Wallace, "and it was tender. Of course that wasn't all they had. The night I was trying their table out, it sure had good things to eat from one end to the other. Her mama and papa sat at the head and foot and we was face to face with each other across it, with I remember a pat of butter between. They had real sweet butter, with a tree drawed down it, elegant-like. Her mama eats like a man. I had brought her a whole hatful of berries and she didn't even pass them to her husband. Hazel, she would leap up and take a pitcher of new milk and fill up the glasses. I had heard how they couldn't have a singing at the church without a fight over her."

"Oh, she's a pretty girl, all right," said Virgil. "It's a pity for the ones like her to grow old, and get like their mothers."

"Another thing will be that her mother will get wind of this and come after me," said William Wallace.

"Her mother will eat you alive," said Virgil.

"She's just been watching her chance," said William Wallace. "Why did I think I could stay out all night."

"Just something come over you."

"First it was just a carnival at Carthage, and I had to let them guess my weight . . . and after that . . ."

"It was nice to be sitting on your neck in a ditch singing," prompted Virgil, "in the moonlight. And playing on the harmonica like you can play."

"Even if Hazel did sit home knowing I was drunk, that wouldn't kill her," said William Wallace. "What she knows ain't ever killed her yet. . . . She's smart, too, for a girl," he said.

"She's a lot smarter than her cousins in Beulah," said Virgil. "And especially Edna Earle, that never did get to be what you'd call a heavy thinker. Edna Earle could sit and ponder all day on how the little tail of the 'C' got through the 'L' in a Coca-Cola sign."

"Hazel *is* smart," said William Wallace. They walked on. "You ought to see her pantry shelf, it looks like a hundred jars when you open the door. I don't see how she could turn around and jump in the river."

"It's a woman's trick."

"I always behaved before. Till the one night—last night."

"Yes, but the one night," said Virgil. "And she was waiting to take advantage."

"She jumped in the river because she was scared to death of the water and that was to make it worse," he said. "She remembered how I used to have to pick her up and carry her over the oak-log bridge, how she'd shut her eyes and make a dead-weight and hold me round the neck, just for a little creek. I don't see how she brought herself to jump."

"Jumped backwards," said Virgil. "Didn't look."

When they turned off, it was still early in the pink and green fields. The fumes of morning, sweet and bitter, sprang up where they walked. The insects ticked softly, their strength in reserve; butterflies chopped the air, going to the east, and the birds flew carelessly and sang by fits and starts, not the way they did in the evening in sustained and drowsy songs.

"It's a pretty *day* for sure," said William Wallace. "It's a pretty *day* for it."

"I don't see a sign of her ever going along here," said Virgil.

"Well," said William Wallace. "She wouldn't have dropped anything. I never saw a girl to leave less signs of where she's been."

"Not even a plum seed," said Virgil, kicking the grass.

In the grove it was so quiet that once William Wallace gave a jump, as if he could almost hear a sound of himself wondering where she had gone. A descent of energy came down on him in the thick of the woods and he ran at a rabbit and caught it in his hands.

"Rabbit . . . Rabbit. . . ." He acted as if he wanted to take it off to himself and hold it up and talk to it. He laid a palm against its pushing heart. "Now . . . There now . . ."

"Let her go, William Wallace, let her go." Virgil, chewing on an elderberry whistle he had just made, stood at his shoulder: "What do you want with a live rabbit?"

William Wallace squatted down and set the rabbit on the ground but held it under his hand. It was a little, old, brown rabbit. It did not try to move. "See there?"

"Let her go."

"She can go if she wants to, but she don't want to."

Gently he lifted his hand. The round eye was shining at him sideways in the green gloom.

"Anybody can freeze a *rabbit*, that wants to," said Virgil. Suddenly he gave a far-reaching blast on the whistle, and the rabbit went in a streak. "Was you out catching cotton-tails, or was you out catching your wife?" he said, taking the turn to the open fields. "I come along to keep you on the track."

"Who'll we get, now?" They stood on top of a hill and William Wallace looked critically over the countryside. "Any of the Malones?"

"I was always scared of the Malones," said Virgil. "Too many *of* them."

"This is my day with the net, and they would have to watch out," said William Wallace. "I reckon some Malones, and the Doyles, will be enough. The six Doyles and their dogs, and you and me, and two little nigger boys is enough, with just a few Malones."

"That ought to be enough," said Virgil, "no matter what."

"I'll bring the Malones, and you bring the Doyles," said William Wallace, and they separated at the spring.

When William Wallace came back, with a string of Malones just showing behind him on the hilltop, he found Virgil with the two little Rippen boys waiting behind him, solemn little towheads. As soon as he walked up, Grady, the one in front, lifted his hand to signal silence and caution to his brother Brucie, who began panting merrily and untrustworthily behind him.

Brucie bent readily under William Wallace's hand-pat, and gave him a dreamy look out of the tops of his round eyes, which were pure green-and-white like clover tops. William Wallace gave him a nickel. Grady hung his head; his white hair lay in a little tail in the nape of his neck.

"Let's let them come," said Virgil.

"Well, they can come then, but if we keep letting everybody come it is going to be too many," said William Wallace.

"They'll appreciate it, those little-old boys," said Virgil. Brucie held up at arm's length a long red thread with a bent pin tied on the end; and a look of helpless and intense interest gathered Grady's face like a drawstring—his eyes, one bright with a sty, shone pleadingly under his white bangs, and he snapped his jaw and tried to speak. . . . "Their papa was drowned in the Pearl River," said Virgil.

There was a shout from the gully.

"Here come all the Malones," cried William Wallace. "I asked four of them would they come, but the rest of the family invited themselves."

"Did you ever see a time when they didn't," said Virgil. "And yonder from the other direction comes the Doyles, still with biscuit crumbs on their cheeks, I bet, now it's nothing to do but eat as their mother said."

"If two little niggers would come along now, or one big nigger," said William Wallace. And the words were hardly out of his mouth when two little Negro boys came along, going somewhere, one behind the other, stepping high and gay in their overalls, as though they waded in honeydew to the waist.

"Come here, boys. What's your names?"

"Sam and Robbie Bell."

"Come along with us, we're going to drag the river."

"You hear that, Robbie Bell?" said Sam.

They smiled.

The Doyles came noiselessly, their dogs made all the fuss. The Malones, eight giants with great long black eyelashes, were already stamping the ground and pawing each other, ready to go. Everybody went up together to see Doc.

Old Doc owned the wide net. He had a house on top of the hill and he sat and looked out from a rocker on the front porch.

"Climb the hill and come in!" he began to intone across the valley. "Harvest's over . . . slipped up on everybody . . . corn's all in, hogs gettin' ripe . . . hay cut . . . molasses made around here. . . . Big explosion's over, supervisors elected, some pleased, some not. . . . We're hearing talk of war!"

When they got closer, he was saying, "Many's been saved at revival, twenty-two last Sunday including a Doyle, ought to counted two. Hope they'll be a blessing to Dover community besides a shining star in Heaven. Now what?" he asked, for they had arrived and stood gathered in front of the steps.

"If nobody is using your wide net, could we use it?" asked William Wallace.

"You just used it a month ago," said Doc. "It ain't your turn."

Virgil jogged William Wallace's arm and cleared his throat. "This time is kind of special," he said. "We got reason to think William Wallace's wife Hazel is in the river, drowned."

"What reason have you got to think she's in the river drowned?" asked Doc. He took out his old pipe. "I'm asking the husband."

"Because she's not in the house," said William Wallace.

"Vanished?" and he knocked out the pipe.

"Plum vanished."

"Of course a thousand things could have happened to her," said Doc, and he lighted the pipe.

"Hand him up the letter, William Wallace," said Virgil. "We can't wait around till Doomsday for the net while Doc sits back thinkin'."

"I tore it up, right at the first," said William Wallace. "But I know it by heart. It said she was going to jump straight in the Pearl River and that I'd be sorry."

"Where do you come in, Virgil?" asked Doc.

"I was in the same place William Wallace sat on his neck in, all night, and done as much as he done, and come home the same time."

"You-all were out cuttin' up, so Lady Hazel has to jump in the river, is that it? Cause and effect? Anybody want to argue with me? Where do these others come in, Doyles, Malones, and what not?"

"Doc is the smartest man around," said William Wallace, turning to the solidly waiting Doyles, "but it sure takes time."

"These are the ones that's collected to drag the river for her," said Virgil.

"Of course I am not going on record to say so soon that *I* think she's drowned," Doc said, blowing out blue smoke.

"Do you think . . . " William Wallace mounted a step, and his hands both went into fists. "Do you think she was *carried off*?"

"Now that's the way to argue, see it from all sides," said Doc promptly. "But who by?"

Some Malone whistled, but not so you could tell which one.

"There's no booger around the Dover section that goes around carrying off young girls that's married," stated Doc.

"She was always scared of the Gypsies." William Wallace turned scarlet. "She'd sure turn her ring around on her finger if she passed one, and look in the other direction so they couldn't see she was pretty and carry her off. They come in the end of summer."

"Yes, there are the Gypsies, kidnappers since the world began. But was it to be you that would pay the grand ransom?" asked Doc. He pointed his finger. They all laughed then at how clever old Doc was and clapped William Wallace on the back. But that turned into a scuffle and they fell to the ground.

"Stop it, or you can't have the net," said Doc. "You're scaring my wife's chickens."

"It's time we was gone," said William Wallace.

The big barking dogs jumped to lean their front paws on the men's chests.

"My advice remains, Let well enough alone," said Doc. "Whatever this mysterious event will turn out to be, it has kept one woman from talking a while. However, Lady Hazel is the prettiest girl in Mississippi, you've never seen a prettier one and you never will. A golden-haired girl." He got to his feet with the nimbleness that was always his surprise, and said, "I'll come along with you."

The path they always followed was the Old Natchez Trace. It took them through the deep woods and led them out down below on the Pearl River, where they could begin dragging it upstream to a point near Dover. They walked in silence around William Wallace, not letting him carry anything, but the net dragged heavily and the buckets were full of clatter in a place so dim and still.

Once they went through a forest of cucumber trees and came up on a high ridge. Grady and Brucie, who were running ahead all the way, stopped in their tracks; a whistle had blown and far down and far away a long freight train was passing. It seemed like a little festival procession, moving with the slowness of ignorance or a dream, from distance to distance, the tiny pink and gray cars like secret boxes. Grady was counting the cars to himself, as if he could certainly see each one clearly, and Brucie watched his lips, hushed and cautious, the way he would watch a bird drinking. Tears suddenly came to Grady's eyes, but it could only be because a tiny man walked along the top of the train, walking and moving on top of the moving train.

They went down again and soon the smell of the river spread over the woods, cool and secret. Every step they took among the great walls of vines and among the passion-flowers started up a little life, a little flight.

"We're walking along in the changing-time," said Doc. "Any day now the change will come. It's going to turn from hot to cold, and we can kill the hog that's ripe and have fresh meat to eat. Come one of these nights and we can wander down here and tree a nice possum. Old Jack Frost will be pinching things up. Old Mr. Winter will be standing in the door. Hickory tree there will be yellow. Sweet-gum red, hickory yellow, dogwood red, sycamore yellow." He went along rapping the tree trunks with his knuckle. "Magnolia and live-oak never die. Remember that. Persimmons will all get fit to eat, and the nuts will be dropping like rain all through the woods here. And run, little quail, run, for we'll be after you too."

They went on and suddenly the woods opened upon light, and they had reached the river. Everyone stopped, but Doc talked on ahead as though nothing had happened. "Only today," he said, "today, in October sun, it's all gold—sky and tree and water. Everything just before it changes looks to be made of gold."

William Wallace looked down, as though he thought of Hazel with the shining eyes, sitting at home and looking straight before her, like a piece of pure gold, too precious to touch.

Below them the river was glimmering, narrow, soft, and skin-colored, and slowed nearly to stillness. The shining willow trees hung round them. The net that was being drawn out, so old and so long-used, it too looked golden, strung and tied with golden threads.

Standing still on the bank, all of a sudden William Wallace, on whose word they were waiting, spoke up in a voice of surprise. "What is the name of this river?"

They looked at him as if he were crazy not to know the name of the river he had fished in all his life. But a deep frown was on his forehead, as if he were compelled to wonder what people had come to call this river, or to think there was a mystery in the name of a river they all knew so well, the same as if it were some great far torrent of waves that dashed through the mountains somewhere, and almost as if it were a river in some dream, for they could not give him the name of that.

"Everybody knows Pearl River is named the Pearl River," said Doc.

A bird note suddenly bold was like a stone thrown into the water to sound it.

"It's deep here," said Virgil, and jogged William Wallace. "Remember?"

William Wallace stood looking down at the river as if it were still a mystery to him. There under his feet, which hung over the bank, it was transparent and yellow like an old bottle lying in the sun, filling with light.

Doc clattered all his paraphernalia.

Then all of a sudden all the Malones scattered jumping and tumbling down the bank. They gave their loud shout. Little Brucie started after them, and looked back.

"Do you think she jumped?" Virgil asked William Wallace.

II

Since the net was so wide, when it was all stretched it reached from bank to bank of the Pearl River, and the weights would hold it all the way to the bottom. Jug-like sounds filled the air, splashes lifted in the sun, and the party began to move upstream. The Malones with great groans swam and pulled near the shore, the Doyles swam and pushed from behind with Virgil to tell them how to do it best; Grady and Brucie with his thread and pin trotted along the sandbars hauling buckets and lines. Sam and Robbie Bell, naked and bright, guided the old oarless rowboat that always drifted at the shore, and in it, sitting up tall with his hat on, was Doc—he went along without ever touching water and without ever taking his eyes off the net. William Wallace himself did everything but most of the time he was out of sight, swimming about under water or diving, and he had nothing to say any more.

The dogs chased up and down, in and out of the water, and in and out of the woods.

"Don't let her get too heavy, boys," Doc intoned regularly, every few minutes, "and she won't let nothing through."

"She won't let nothing through, she won't let nothing through," chanted Sam and Robbie Bell, one at his front and one at his back.

The sandbars were pink or violet drifts ahead. Where the light fell on the river, in a wandering from shore to shore, it was leaf-shaped spangles that trembled softly, while the dark of the river was calm. The willow trees leaned overhead under muscadine vines, and their trailing leaves hung like waterfalls in the morning air. The thing that seemed like silence must have been the endless cry of all the crickets and locusts in the world, rising and falling.

Every time William Wallace took hold of a big eel that slipped the net, the Malones all yelled, "Rassle with him, son!"

"Don't let her get too heavy, boys," said Doc.

"This is hard on catfish," William Wallace said once.

There were big and little fishes, dark and bright, that they caught, good ones and bad ones, the same old fish.

"This is more shoes than I ever saw got together in any store," said

Virgil when they emptied the net to the bottom. "Get going!" he shouted in the next breath.

The little Rippens who had stayed ahead in the woods stayed ahead on the river. Brucie, leading them all, made small jumps and hops as he went, sometimes on one foot, sometimes on the other.

The winding river looked old sometimes, when it ran wrinkled and deep under high banks where the roots of trees hung down, and sometimes it seemed to be only a young creek, shining with the colors of wildflowers. Sometimes sandbars in the shapes of fishes lay nose to nose across, without the track of even a bird.

"Here comes some alligators," said Virgil. "Let's let them by."

They drew out on the shady side of the water, and three big alligators and four middle-sized ones went by, taking their own time.

"Look at their great big old teeth!" called a shrill voice. It was Grady making his only outcry, and the alligators were not showing their teeth at all.

"The better to eat folks with," said Doc from his boat, looking at him severely.

"Doc, you are bound to declare all you know," said Virgil. "Get going!"

When they started off again the first thing they caught in the net was the baby alligator.

"That's just what we wanted!" cried the Malones.

They set the little alligator down on a sandbar and he squatted perfectly still; they could hardly tell when it was he started to move. They watched with set faces his incredible mechanics, while the dogs after one bark stood off in inquisitive humility, until he winked.

"He's ours!" shouted all the Malones. "We're taking him home with us!"

"He ain't nothing but a little-old baby," said William Wallace.

The Malones only scoffed, as if he might be only a baby but he looked like the oldest and worst lizard.

"What are you going to do with him?" asked Virgil.

"Keep him."

"I'd be more careful what I took out of this net," said Doc.

"Tie him up and throw him in the bucket," the Malones were saying to each other, while Doc was saying, "Don't come running to me and ask me what to do when he gets big."

They kept catching more and more fish, as if there was no end in sight.

"Look, a string of lady's beads," said Virgil. "Here, Sam and Robbie Bell."

Sam wore them around his head, with a knot over his forehead and loops around his ears, and Robbie Bell walked behind and stared at them.

In a shadowy place something white flew up. It was a heron, and it went away over the dark treetops. William Wallace followed it with his eyes and Brucie clapped his hands, but Virgil gave a sigh, as if he knew that when you go looking for what is lost, everything is a sign.

An eel slid out of the net.

"Rassle with him, son!" yelled the Malones. They swam like fiends.

"The Malones are in it for the fish," said Virgil.

It was about noon that there was a little rustle on the bank.

"Who is that yonder?" asked Virgil, and he pointed to a little under-sized man with short legs and a little straw hat with a band around it, who was following along on the other side of the river.

"Never saw him and don't know his brother," said Doc.

Nobody had ever seen him before.

"Who invited you?" cried Virgil hotly. "Hi . . . !" and he made signs for the little undersized man to look at him, but he would not.

"Looks like a crazy man, from here," said the Malones.

"Just don't pay any attention to him and maybe he'll go away," advised Doc.

But Virgil had already swum across and was up on the other bank. He and the stranger could be seen exchanging a word apiece and then Virgil put out his hand the way he would pat a child and patted the stranger to the ground. The little man got up again just as quickly, lifted his shoulders, turned around, and walked away with his hat tilted over his eyes.

When Virgil came back he said, "Little-old man claimed he was harmless as a baby. I told him to just try horning in on this river and anything in it."

"What did he look like up close?" asked Doc.

"I wasn't studying how he looked," said Virgil. "But I don't like anybody to come looking at me that I am not familiar with." And he shouted, "Get going!"

"Things are moving in too great a rush," said Doc.

Brucie darted ahead and ran looking into all the bushes, lifting up their branches and looking underneath.

"Not one of the Doyles has spoke a word," said Virgil.

"That's because they're not talkers," said Doc.

All day William Wallace kept diving to the bottom. Once he dived down and down into the dark water, where it was so still that nothing stirred, not even a fish, and so dark that it was no longer the muddy world of the upper river but the dark clear world of deepness, and he must have believed this was the deepest place in the whole Pearl River, and if she was not here she would not be anywhere. He was gone such a long time that the others stared hard at the surface of the water, through which the bubbles came from below. So far down and all alone, had he found Hazel? Had he suspected down there, like some secret, the real, the true trouble that Hazel had fallen into, about which words in a letter could not speak . . . how (who knew?) she had been filled to the brim with that elation that they all remembered, like their own secret, the elation that comes of great hopes and changes, sometimes simply of the harvest time, that comes with a little course of its own like a tune to run in the head, and there was nothing she could do about it—they knew —and so it had turned into this? It could be nothing but the old trouble that William Wallace was finding out, reaching and turning in the gloom of such depths.

"Look down yonder," said Grady softly to Brucie.

He pointed to the surface, where their reflections lay colorless and still side by side. He touched his brother gently as though to impress him.

"That's you and me," he said.

Brucie swayed precariously over the edge, and Grady caught him by the seat of his overalls. Brucie looked, but showed no recognition. Instead, he backed away, and seemed all at once unconcerned and spiritless, and pressed the nickel William Wallace had given him into his palm, rubbing it into his skin. Grady's inflamed eyes rested on the brown water. Without warning he saw something . . . perhaps the image in the river seemed to be his father, the drowned man—with arms open, eyes open, mouth open. . . . Grady stared and blinked, again something wrinkled up his face.

And when William Wallace came up it was in an agony from submersion, which seemed an agony of the blood and of the very heart, so woeful he looked. He was staring and glaring around in astonishment, as if a long time had gone by, away from the pale world where the brown light of the sun and the river and the little party watching him trembled before his eyes.

"What did you bring up?" somebody called—was it Virgil?

One of his hands was holding fast to a little green ribbon of plant, root and all. He was surprised, and let it go.

It was afternoon. The trees spread softly, the clouds hung wet and tinted. A buzzard turned a few slow wheels in the sky, and drifted upwards. The dogs promenaded the banks.

"It's time we ate fish," said Virgil.

On a wide sandbar on which seashells lay they dragged up the haul and built a fire.

Then for a long time among clouds of odors and smoke, all half-

naked except Doc, they cooked and ate catfish. They ate until the Malones groaned and all the Doyles stretched out on their faces, though
for long after, Sam and Robbie Bell sat up to their own little table on a
cypress stump and ate on and on. Then they all were silent and still, and
one by one fell asleep.

"There ain't a thing better than fish," muttered William Wallace.
He lay stretched on his back in the glimmer and shade of trampled sand.
His sunburned forehead and cheeks seemed to glow with fire. His eye-
lids fell. The shadow of a willow branch dipped and moved over him.
"There is nothing in the world as good as . . . fish. The fish of Pearl
River." Then slowly he smiled. He was asleep.

But it seemed almost at once that he was leaping up, and one by one
up sat the others in their ring and looked at him, for it was impossible to
stop and sleep by the river.

"You're feeling as good as you felt last night," said Virgil, setting his
head on one side.

"The excursion is the same when you go looking for your sorrow as
when you go looking for your joy," said Doc.

But William Wallace answered none of them anything, for he was
leaping all over the place and all, over them and the feast and the bones
of the feast, trampling the sand, up and down, and doing a dance so
crazy that he would die next. He took a big catfish and hooked it to his
belt buckle and went up and down so that they all hollered, and the tears
of laughter streaming down his cheeks made him put his hand up, and
the two days' growth of beard began to jump out, bright red.

But all of a sudden there was an even louder cry, something almost
like a cheer, from everybody at once, and all pointed fingers moved
from William Wallace to the river. In the center of three light-gold
rings across the water was lifted first an old hoary head ("It has
whiskers!" a voice cried) and then in an undulation loop after loop and
hump after hump of a long dark body, until there were a dozen rings of
ripples, one behind the other, stretching all across the river, like a
necklace.

"The King of the Snakes!" cried all the Malones at once, in high
tenor voices and leaning together.

"The King of the Snakes," intoned old Doc in his profound bass.

"He looked you in the eye."

William Wallace stared back at the King of the Snakes with all his
might.

It was Brucie that darted forward, dangling his little thread with the
pin tied to it, going toward the water.

"That's the King of the Snakes!" cried Grady, who always looked
after him.

Then the snake went down.

The little boy stopped with one leg in the air, spun around on the other, and sank to the ground.

"Git up," Grady whispered. "It was just the King of the Snakes. He went off whistling. Git up. It wasn't a thing but the King of the Snakes."

Brucie's green eyes opened, his tongue darted out, and he sprang up; his feet were heavy, his head light, and he rose like a bubble coming to the surface.

Then thunder like a stone loosened and rolled down the bank.

They all stood unwilling on the sandbar, holding to the net. In the eastern sky were the familiar castles and the round towers to which they were used, gray, pink, and blue, growing darker and filling with thunder. Lightning flickered in the sun along their thick walls. But in the west the sun shone with such a violence that in an illumination like a long-prolonged glare of lightning the heavens looked black and white; all color left the world, the goldenness of everything was like a memory, and only heat, a kind of glamor and oppression, lay on their heads. The thick heavy trees on the other side of the river were brushed with mile-long streaks of silver, and a wind touched each man on the forehead. At the same time there was a long roll of thunder that began behind them, came up and down mountains and valleys of air, passed over their heads, and left them listening still. With a small, near noise a mocking-bird followed it, the little white bars of its body flashing over the willow trees.

"We are here for a storm now," Virgil said. "We will have to stay till it's over."

They retreated a little, and hard drops fell in the leathery leaves at their shoulders and about their heads.

"Magnolia's the loudest tree there is in a storm," said Doc.

Then the light changed the water, until all about them the woods in the rising wind seemed to grow taller and blow inward together and suddenly turn dark. The rain struck heavily. A huge tail seemed to lash through the air and the river broke in a wound of silver. In silence the party crouched and stooped beside the trunk of the great tree, which in the push of the storm rose full of a fragrance and unyielding weight. Where they all stared, past their tree, was another tree, and beyond that another and another, all the way down the bank of the river, all towering and darkened in the storm.

"The outside world is full of endurance," said Doc. "Full of endurance."

Robbie Bell and Sam squatted down low and embraced each other from the start.

"Runs in our family to get struck by lightnin'," said Robbie Bell. "Lightnin' drawed a pitchfork right on our grandpappy's cheek, stayed till he died. Pappy got struck by some bolts of lightnin' and was dead three days, dead as that-there axe."

There was a succession of glares and crashes.

"This'n's goin' to be either me or you," said Sam. "Here come a little bug. If he go to the left, be me, and to the right, be you."

But at the next flare a big tree on the hill seemed to turn into fire before their eyes, every branch, twig, and leaf, and a purple cloud hung over it.

"Did you hear that crack?" asked Robbie Bell. "That were its bones."

"Why do you little niggers talk so much!" said Doc. "Nobody's profiting by this information."

"We always talks this much," said Sam, "but now everybody so quiet, they hears us."

The great tree, split and on fire, fell roaring to earth. Just at its moment of falling, a tree like it on the opposite bank split wide open and fell in two parts.

"Hope they ain's goin' to be no balls of fire come rollin' over the water and fry all the fishes with their scales on," said Robbie Bell.

The water in the river had turned purple and was filled with sudden currents and whirlpools. The little willow trees bent almost to its surface, bowing one after another down the bank and almost breaking under the storm. A great curtain of wet leaves was borne along before a blast of wind, and every human being was covered.

"Now us got scales," wailed Sam. "Us is the fishes."

"Hush up, little-old colored children," said Virgil. "This isn't the way to act when somebody takes you out to drag a river."

"Poor lady's-ghost, I bet it is scareder than us," said Sam.

"All I hoping is, us don't find her!" screamed Robbie Bell.

William Wallace bent down and knocked their heads together. After that they clung silently in each other's arms, the two black heads resting, with wind-filled cheeks and tight-closed eyes, one upon the other until the storm was over.

"Right over yonder is Dover," said Virgil. "We've come all the way. William Wallace, you have walked on a sharp rock and cut your foot open."

III

In Dover it had rained, and the town looked somehow like new. The wavy heat of late afternoon came down from the watertank and fell over everything like shiny mosquito-netting. At the wide place where the road was paved and patched with tar, it seemed newly embedded with Coca-Cola tops. The old circus posters on the store were nearly gone, only bits, the snowflakes of white horses, clinging to its side. Morning-glory vines started almost visibly to grow over the roofs and cling round the ties of the railroad track, where bluejays lighted on the rails, and umbrella chinaberry trees hung heavily over the whole town, dripping intermittently upon the tin roofs.

Each with his counted fish on a string, the members of the river-dragging party walked through the town. They went toward the town well, and there was Hazel's mother's house, but no sign of her yet coming out. They all drank a dipper of the water, and still there was not a soul on the street. Even the bench in front of the store was empty, except for a little corn-shuck doll.[1]

But something told them somebody had come, for after one moment people began to look out of the store and out of the post office. All the bird dogs woke up to see the Doyle dogs and such a large number of men and boys materialize suddenly with such a big catch of fish, and they ran out barking. The Doyle dogs joyously barked back. The blue-jays flashed up and screeched above the town, whipping through their tunnels in the chinaberry trees. In the café a nickel clattered inside a music box and a love song began to play. The whole town of Dover began to throb in its wood and tin, like an old tired heart, when the men walked through once more, coming around again and going down the street carrying the fish, so drenched, exhausted, and muddy that no one could help but admire them.

William Wallace walked through the town as though he did not see anybody or hear anything. Yet he carried his great string of fish held high where it could be seen by all. Virgil came next, imitating William Wallace exactly, then the modest Doyles crowded by the Malones, who were holding up their alligator, tossing it in the air, even, like a father tossing his child. Following behind and pointing authoritatively at the ones in front strolled Doc, with Sam and Robbie Bell still chanting in his wake. In and out of the whole little line Grady and Brucie jerked about. Grady, with his head ducked, and stiff as a rod, walked with a springy limp; it made him look forever angry and unapproachable. Under his breath he was whispering, "Sty, sty, git out of my eye, and git on somebody passin' by." He traveled on with narrowed shoulders, and kept his eye unerringly upon his little brother, wary and at the same time proud, as though he held a flying June-bug on a string. Brucie, making a twanging noise with his lips, had shot forth again, and he was darting rapidly everywhere at once, delighted and tantalized, running in circles around William Wallace, pointing to his fish. A frown of pleasure like the print of a bird's foot was stamped between his faint brows, and he trotted in some unknown realm of delight.

1. A doll made from corn husks.

"Did you ever see so many fish?" said the people in Dover.

"How much are your fish, mister?"

"Would you sell your fish?"

"Is that all the fish in Pearl River?"

"How much you sell them all for? Everybody's?"

"Take 'em free," said William Wallace suddenly and loud. The Malones were upon him and shouting, but it was too late. "I don't want no more of 'em. I want my wife!" he yelled, just at the moment when Hazel's mother walked out of her front door.

"You can't head her mother off," said Virgil. "Here she comes in full bloom."

"What have you done with my child?" Hazel's mother shouted.

But William Wallace turned his back on her, that was all, and on everybody, for that matter, and that was the breaking-up of the party.

Just as the sun went down, Doc climbed his back steps, sat in his chair on the back porch where he sat in the evenings, and lighted his pipe. William Wallace hung out the net and came back and Virgil was waiting for him, so they could say good evening to Doc.

"All in all," said Doc, when they came up, "I've never been on a better river-dragging, or seen better behavior. If it took catching catfish to move the Rock of Gibraltar, I believe this outfit could move it."

"Well, we didn't catch Hazel," said Virgil.

"What did you say?" asked Doc.

"He don't really pay attention," said Virgil. "I said, 'We didn't catch Hazel.'"

"Who says Hazel was to be caught?" asked Doc. "She wasn't in there. Girls don't like the water—remember that. Girls don't just haul off and go jumping in the river to get back at their husbands. They got other ways."

"Didn't you ever think she was in there?" asked William Wallace. "The whole time?"

"Nary once," said Doc.

"He's just smart," said Virgil, putting his hand on William Wallace's arm. "It's only because we didn't find her that he wasn't looking for her."

"I'm beholden to you for the net, anyway," said William Wallace.

"You're welcome to borry it again," said Doc.

On the way home Virgil kept saying, "Calm down, calm down, William Wallace."

"If he wasn't such an old skinny man I'd have wrung his neck for him," said William Wallace. "He had no business coming."

"He's too big for his britches," said Virgil. "Don't nobody know everything. And just because it's his net. Why does it have to be his net?"

"If it wasn't for being polite to old men, I'd have skinned him alive," said William Wallace.

"I guess he don't really know nothing about wives at all, his wife's so deaf," said Virgil.

"He don't know Hazel," said William Wallace. "I'm the only man alive knows Hazel: would she jump in the river or not, and I say she would. She jumped in because I was sitting on the back of my neck in a ditch singing, and that's just what she ought to done. Doc ain't got no right to say one word about it."

"Calm down, calm down, William Wallace," said Virgil.

"If it had been you that talked like that, I'd have broke every bone in your body," said William Wallace. "Just let you talk like that. You're my age and size."

"But I ain't going to talk like that," said Virgil. "What have I done the whole time but keep this river-dragging going straight and running even, without no hitches? You couldn't have drug the river a foot without me."

"What are you talking about! Without who!" cried William Wallace. "This wasn't your river-dragging! It wasn't your wife!" He jumped on Virgil and they began to fight.

"Let me up." Virgil was breathing heavily.

"Say it was my wife. Say it was my river-dragging."

"Yours!" Virgil was on the ground with William Wallace's hand putting dirt in his mouth.

"Say it was my net."

"Your net!"

"Get up then."

They walked along getting their breath, and smelling the honey-suckle in the evening. On a hill William Wallace looked down, and at the same time there went drifting by the sweet sounds of music out-doors. They were having the Sacred Harp Sing on the grounds of an old white church glimmering there at the crossroads, far below. He stared away as if he saw it minutely, as if he could see a lady in white take a flowered cover off the organ, which was set on a little slant in the shade, dust the keys, and start to pump and play. . . . He smiled faintly, as he would at his mother, and at Hazel, and at the singing women in his life, now all one young girl standing up to sing under the trees the oldest and longest ballads there were.

Virgil told him good night and went into his own house and the door shut on him.

When he got to his own house, William Wallace saw to his surprise that it had not rained at all. But there, curved over the roof, was something he had never seen before as long as he could remember, a rainbow at night. In the light of the moon, which had risen again, it looked small and of gauzy material, like a lady's summer dress, a faint veil through which the stars showed.

He went up on the porch and in at the door, and all exhausted he had walked through the front room and through the kitchen when he heard his name called. After a moment, he smiled, as if no matter what he might have hoped for in his wildest heart, it was better than that to hear his name called out in the house. The voice came out of the bedroom.

"What do you want?" he yelled, standing stock-still.

Then she opened the bedroom door with the old complaining creak, and there she stood. She was not changed a bit.

"How do you feel?" he said.

"I feel pretty good. Not too good," Hazel said, looking mysterious.

"I cut my foot," said William Wallace, taking his shoe off so she could see the blood.

"How in the world did you do that?" she cried, with a step back.

"Dragging the river. But it don't hurt any longer."

"You ought to have been more careful," she said. "Supper's ready and I wondered if you would ever come home, or if it would be last night all over again. Go and make yourself fit to be seen," she said, and ran away from him.

After supper they sat on the front steps a while.

"Where were you this morning when I came in?" asked William Wallace when they were ready to go in the house.

"I was hiding," she said. "I was still writing on the letter. And then you tore it up."

"Did you watch me when I was reading it?"

"Yes, and you could have put out your hand and touched me. I was so close."

But he bit his lip, and gave her a little tap and slap, and then turned her up and spanked her.

"Do you think you will do it again?" he asked.

"I'll tell my mother on you for this!"

"Will you do it again?"

"No!" she cried.

"Then pick yourself up off my knee."

It was just as if he had chased her and captured her again. She lay smiling in the crook of his arm. It was the same as any other chase in the end.

"I will do it again if I get ready," she said. "Next time will be different, too."

Then she was ready to go in, and rose up and looked out from the top step, out across their yard where the China tree was and beyond, into the dark fields where the lightning-bugs flickered away. He climbed to his feet too and stood beside her, with the frown on his face, trying to look where she looked. And after a few minutes she took him by the hand and led him into the house, smiling as if she were smiling down on him.

1943

ELIZABETH BISHOP
1911–1979

"You sound like Lope de Vega and I sound like Jacob Abbot or Peter Rabbit," wrote the poet Marianne Moore in 1959 to her friend and admirer the poet Elizabeth Bishop. Self-deprecatingly comparing herself to a nineteenth-century American clergyman (Abbot) and a children's book character, Moore glowingly imagined Bishop as Spain's greatest Renaissance playwright: her compliment, if hyperbolical, was a measure of the esteem in which this writer was held by many contemporaries. The friend of—besides Moore—the poets Robert Lowell, Pablo Neruda, and Frank Bidart, Bishop achieved in her lifetime a distinctive reputation as, in the words of the critic Sibyl Estess, a "virtuoso of descriptive poetry." Since her death, however, her work has been increasingly seen as visionary and meditative, acute in its understated but powerful transcription of inner reality as well as accurate in its attention to external objects.

Born in Worcester, Massachusetts, Elizabeth Bishop was raised by two sets of grandparents in Nova Scotia and New England. Her father died when she was eight months old, and, not long after that, her mother had to be hospitalized for mental illness; though at one point Bishop's maternal grandparents had hoped to bring their daughter home to recover, the poet's mother experienced a final breakdown when Elizabeth was five, an event that is recorded in the poignant story *In the Village* (1953), Bishop's semifictionalized account of her last encounter with her mother. A frail child, the poet did not attend school regularly until she was sixteen, when she entered Walnut Hill School. By the time she enrolled at Vassar College at nineteen, however, she was a voracious reader and an aspiring writer. With several other undergraduates, including the novelist-to-be Mary McCarthy, she founded a literary magazine, *The Conspirito*; in addition, she began publishing poems and stories, some of them in nationally known periodicals; and, perhaps most important, the year before her graduation she met and was befriended by Marianne Moore, who encouraged her to devote herself entirely to her writing rather than, as she had planned, attending medical school.

After graduation from Vassar, Bishop traveled extensively, pursuing what one biographer has called a "nomadic" way of life that was to define the rest of her career and provide central metaphors for such volumes of poetry as *North & South* (1946), *Questions of Travel* (1965), and *Geography III* (1976). Her journeys were interrupted, however, for one long and quite significant period: between 1951 and 1966, she settled in Brazil, sharing a house in the mountains and an apartment in Rio de Janeiro with Lota Costellat de Macedo Soares, a Brazilian friend; translating Brazilian poetry; and producing a book about the country—*Brazil* (1962)—for the *Life* World Library series. After leaving Brazil, Bishop returned to the United States, where she taught, first, at the University of Washington, and, then, from 1969 until her retirement in 1977, at Harvard University.

Throughout, Bishop's career was marked by numerous honors, including the Pulitzer Prize in 1955 and the National Book Award in 1969. Despite the acclaim she received, however, she always maintained an ironically understated yet passionately exact perspective on both her self and her society. Her commitments, both to friends and to ideas, were keen: though she had always defined herself as a feminist, for instance, she consistently refused what she considered the ghettoization implied by inclusion in anthologies of women's writing. (With the permission of Alice Methfessel, her literary executrix, we reprint here a quotation from a letter Bishop wrote in 1977, a passage that clarifies the poet's position on this matter.) Yet, as poems like *Roosters* and *Pink Dog* reveal, Bishop was capable of composing fiercely sardonic feminist critiques of her society, and, as *Invitation to Miss Marianne Moore* suggests, she was intensely loyal to her major female literary mentor.

[Gender and Art][1]

Undoubtedly gender does play an important part in the making of any art, but art is art and to separate writings, paintings, musical compositions, etc., into two sexes is to emphasize values in them that are *not* art.

1977

The Man-Moth[2]

Here, above,
cracks in the buildings are filled with battered moonlight.
The whole shadow of Man is only as big as his hat.
It lies at his feet like a circle for a doll to stand on,
and he makes an inverted pin, the point magnetized to the moon.   5
He does not see the moon; he observes only her vast properties,
feeling the queer light on his hands, neither warm nor cold,
of a temperature impossible to record in thermometers.

---

1. From a letter to Joan Keefe, June 8, 1977.
2. "Newspaper misprint for 'mammoth' " [Bishop's note].

But when the Man-Moth
pays his rare, although occasional, visits to the surface,   10
the moon looks rather different to him. He emerges
from an opening under the edge of one of the sidewalks
and nervously begins to scale the faces of the buildings.
He thinks the moon is a small hole at the top of the sky,
proving the sky quite useless for protection.   15
He trembles, but must investigate as high as he can climb.

Up the façades,
his shadow dragging like a photographer's cloth behind him,
he climbs fearfully, thinking that this time he will manage
to push his small head through that round clean opening   20
and be forced through, as from a tube, in black scrolls on the light.
(Man, standing below him, has no such illusions.)
But what the Man-Moth fears most he must do, although
he fails, of course, and falls back scared but quite unhurt.

Then he returns   25
to the pale subways of cement he calls his home. He flits,
he flutters, and cannot get aboard the silent trains
fast enough to suit him. The doors close swiftly.
The Man-Moth always seats himself facing the wrong way
and the train starts at once at its full, terrible speed,   30
without a shift in gears or a gradation of any sort.
He cannot tell the rate at which he travels backwards.

Each night he must
be carried through artificial tunnels and dream recurrent dreams.
Just as the ties recur beneath his train, these underlie   35
his rushing brain. He does not dare look out the window,
for the third rail,[3] the unbroken draught of poison,
runs there beside him. He regards it as a disease
he has inherited the susceptibility to. He has to keep
his hands in his pockets, as others must wear mufflers.   40

If you catch him,
hold up a flashlight to his eye. It's all dark pupil,
an entire night itself, whose haired horizon tightens
as he stares back, and closes up the eye. Then from the lids
one tear, his only possession, like the bee's sting, slips.   45
Slyly he palms it, and if you're not paying attention
he'll swallow it. However, if you watch, he'll hand it over,
cool as from underground springs and pure enough to drink.

1946

---

3. Allusion to the exposed electrified source of power on modern subways.

Roosters

At four o'clock
in the gun-metal blue dark
we hear the first crow of the first cock

just below
the gun-metal blue window   5
and immediately there is an echo

off in the distance,
then one from the backyard fence,
then one, with horrible insistence,

grates like a wet match   10
from the broccoli patch,
flares, and all over town begins to catch.

Cries galore
come from the water-closet door,
from the dropping-plastered henhouse floor,   15

where in the blue blur
their rustling wives admire,
the roosters brace their cruel feet and glare

with stupid eyes
while from their beaks there rise   20
the uncontrolled, traditional cries.

Deep from protruding chests
in green-gold medals dressed,
planned to command and terrorize the rest,

the many wives   25
who lead hens' lives
of being courted and despised;

deep from raw throats
a senseless order floats
all over town. A rooster gloats   30

over our beds
from rusty iron sheds
and fences made from old bedsteads,

over our churches
where the tin rooster perches,   35
over our little wooden northern houses,

making sallies
from all the muddy alleys,
marking out maps like Rand McNally's:[4]

glass-headed pins,   40
oil-golds and copper greens,
anthracite blues, alizarins,[5]

each one an active
displacement in perspective;
each screaming, "This is where I live!"   45

Each screaming
"Get up! Stop dreaming!"
Roosters, what are you projecting?

You, whom the Greeks elected
to shoot at on a post, who struggled   50
when sacrificed, you whom they labeled

"Very combative . . ."[6]
what right have you to give
commands and tell us how to live,

cry "Here!" and "Here!"   55
and wake us here where are
unwanted love, conceit and war?

The crown of red
set on your little head
is charged with all your fighting blood.   60

Yes, the excrescence
makes a most virile presence,
plus all that vulgar beauty of iridescence.

Now in mid-air
by twos they fight each other.   65
Down comes a first flame-feather,

and one is flying,
with raging heroism defying
even the sensation of dying.

---

4. A publisher of road-maps and atlases.
5. An orange or red dye.
6. In classical Greece, roosters were used in tar-

get practice, for sacrifice to the gods, and in
highly popular cockfighting contests.

And one has fallen,   70
but still above the town
his torn-out, bloodied feathers drift down;

and what he sung
no matter. He is flung
on the gray ash-heap, lies in dung   75

with his dead wives
with open, bloody eyes,
while those metallic feathers oxidize.

St. Peter's sin
was worse than that of Magdalen   80
whose sin was of the flesh alone;[7]

of spirit, Peter's,
falling, beneath the flares,
among the "servants and officers."

Old holy sculpture   85
could set it all together
in one small scene, past and future:

Christ stands amazed,
Peter, two fingers raised
to surprised lips, both as if dazed.   90

But in between
a little cock is seen
carved on a dim column in the travertine,

explained by *gallus canit;*
flet Petrus[8] underneath it.   95
There is inescapable hope, the pivot;

yes, and there Peter's tears
run down our chanticleer's[9]
sides and gem his spurs.

---

7. Mary Magdalen was a prostitute who reformed under the influence of Christ's teaching. Peter was one of Christ's Twelve Apostles; shortly before his crucifixion, Christ prophesied that Peter would deny knowing him three times before the cock crowed (Luke 22:34). This prophecy was fulfilled after Christ had been seized by the Romans; three witnesses claimed that Peter was one of Christ's associates, and three times he denied the accusation. After the third denial, a cock was heard crowing. Peter later became the founder of the Christian church, again in fulfillment of Christ's word.
8. Latin: "the cock crows; Peter weeps." The "old holy sculpture" described in these lines was carved c. 400 A.D. and is now in the Vatican.
9. Old name for "rooster."

Tear-encrusted thick   100
as a medieval relic
he waits. Poor Peter, heart-sick,

still cannot guess
those cock-a-doodles yet might bless,
his dreadful rooster come to mean forgiveness,   105

a new weathervane
on basilica and barn,
and that outside the Lateran[1]

there would always be
a bronze cock on a porphyry   110
pillar so the people and the Pope might see

that even the Prince
of the Apostles long since
had been forgiven, and to convince

all the assembly   115
that "Deny deny deny"
is not all the roosters cry.

In the morning
a low light is floating
in the backyard, and gilding   120

from underneath
the broccoli, leaf by leaf;
how could the night have come to grief?

gilding the tiny
floating swallow's belly   125
and lines of pink cloud in the sky,

the day's preamble
like wandering lines in marble.
The cocks are now almost inaudible.

The sun climbs in,
following "to see the end,"[2]   130
faithful as enemy, or friend.

1946

---

1. The cathedral in Rome where the Pope presides; "basilica": church.
2. Probably not a quotation from any particular
source, but an expression akin to the expression
"to stay to the bitter end."

The Fish

I caught a tremendous fish
and held him beside the boat
half out of water, with my hook
fast in a corner of his mouth.
He didn't fight.   5
He hadn't fought at all.
He hung a grunting weight,
battered and venerable
and homely. Here and there
his brown skin hung in strips   10
like ancient wallpaper,
and its pattern of darker brown
was like wallpaper:
shapes like full-blown roses
stained and lost through age.   15
He was speckled with barnacles,
fine rosettes of lime,
and infested
with tiny white sea-lice,
and underneath two or three   20
rags of green weed hung down.
While his gills were breathing in
the terrible oxygen
—the frightening gills,
fresh and crisp with blood,   25
that can cut so badly—
I thought of the coarse white flesh
packed in like feathers,
the big bones and the little bones,
the dramatic reds and blacks   30
of his shiny entrails,
and the pink swim bladder
like a big peony.
I looked into his eyes
which were far larger than mine   35
but shallower, and yellowed,
the irises backed and packed
with tarnished tinfoil
seen through the lenses
of old scratched isinglass.[3]   40
They shifted a little, but not
to return my stare.
—It was more like the tipping

3. Semitransparent substance, originally obtained from the swim-bladders of some freshwater fishes, used for windows.

of an object toward the light.
I admired his sullen face,   45
the mechanism of his jaw,
and then I saw
that from his lower lip
—if you could call it a lip—
grim, wet, and weaponlike,   50
hung five old pieces of fish-line,
or four and a wire leader
with the swivel still attached,
with all their five big hooks
grown firmly in his mouth.   55
A green line, frayed at the end
where he broke it, two heavier lines,
and a fine black thread
still crimped from the strain and snap
when it broke and he got away.   60
Like medals with their ribbons
frayed and wavering,
a five-haired beard of wisdom
trailing from his aching jaw.
I stared and stared   65
and victory filled up
the little rented boat,
from the pool of bilge
where oil had spread a rainbow
around the rusted engine   70
to the bailer rusted orange,
the sun-cracked thwarts,
the oarlocks on their strings,
the gunnels—until everything
was rainbow, rainbow, rainbow!   75
And I let the fish go.

                                                    1946

At the Fishhouses

Although it is a cold evening,
down by one of the fishhouses
an old man sits netting,
his net, in the gloaming almost invisible,
a dark purple-brown,   5
and his shuttle worn and polished.
The air smells so strong of codfish
it makes one's nose run and one's eyes water.
The five fishhouses have steeply peaked roofs

and narrow, cleated gangplanks slant up   10
to storerooms in the gables
for the wheelbarrows to be pushed up and down on.
All is silver: the heavy surface of the sea,
swelling slowly as if considering spilling over,
is opaque, but the silver of the benches,   15
the lobster pots, and masts, scattered
among the wild jagged rocks,
is of an apparent translucence
like the small old buildings with an emerald moss
growing on their shoreward walls.   20
The big fish tubs are completely lined
with layers of beautiful herring scales
and the wheelbarrows are similarly plastered
with creamy iridescent coats of mail,
with small iridescent flies crawling on them.   25
Up on the little slope behind the houses,
set in the sparse bright sprinkle of grass,
is an ancient wooden capstan,[4]
cracked, with two long bleached handles
and some melancholy stains, like dried blood,   30
where the ironwork has rusted.
The old man accepts a Lucky Strike.[5]
He was a friend of my grandfather.
We talk of the decline in the population
and of codfish and herring   35
while he waits for a herring boat to come in.
There are sequins on his vest and on his thumb.
He has scraped the scales, the principal beauty,
from unnumbered fish with that black old knife,
the blade of which is almost worn away.   40

Down at the water's edge, at the place
where they haul up the boats, up the long ramp
descending into the water, thin silver
tree trunks are laid horizontally
across the gray stones, down and down   45
at intervals of four or five feet.

Cold dark deep and absolutely clear,
element bearable to no mortal,
to fish and to seals . . . One seal particularly
I have seen here evening after evening.   50
He was curious about me. He was interested in music;
like me a believer in total immersion,[6]

---

4. A rotating cylinder on which cable is wound
for the purpose of lifting heavy weights.
5. A brand of cigarettes.

6. I.e., a member of the Baptist sect of Christians, who believe that people must be immersed
in water to be baptized.

so I used to sing him Baptist hymns.
I also sang "A Mighty Fortress Is Our God."
He stood up in the water and regarded me   55
steadily, moving his head a little.
Then he would disappear, then suddenly emerge
almost in the same spot, with a sort of shrug
as if it were against his better judgment.
Cold dark deep and absolutely clear,   60
the clear gray icy water . . . Back, behind us,
the dignified tall firs begin.
Bluish, associating with their shadows,
a million Christmas trees stand
waiting for Christmas. The water seems suspended   65
above the rounded gray and blue-gray stones.
I have seen it over and over, the same sea, the same,
slightly, indifferently swinging above the stones,
icily free above the stones,
above the stones and then the world.   70
If you should dip your hand in,
your wrist would ache immediately,
your bones would begin to ache and your hand would burn
as if the water were a transmutation of fire
that feeds on stones and burns with a dark gray flame.   75
If you tasted it, it would first taste bitter,
then briny, then surely burn your tongue.
It is like what we imagine knowledge to be:
dark, salt, clear, moving, utterly free,
drawn from the cold hard mouth   80
of the world, derived from the rocky breasts
forever, flowing and drawn, and since
our knowledge is historical, flowing, and flown.

1955

Invitation to Miss Marianne Moore[7]

From Brooklyn, over the Brooklyn Bridge, on this fine morning,
        please come flying.
In a cloud of fiery pale chemicals,
        please come flying.
to the rapid rolling of thousands of small blue drums   5
descending out of the mackerel sky
over the glittering grandstand of harbor-water,
        please come flying.

7. American poet (1887–1972).

Whistles, pennants and smoke are blowing. The ships
are signaling cordially with multitudes of flags   10
rising and falling like birds all over the harbor.
Enter: two rivers, gracefully bearing
countless little pellucid jellies
in cut-glass epergnes[8] dragging with silver chains.
The flight is safe; the weather is all arranged   15
The waves are running in verses this fine morning.
     Please come flying.

Come with the pointed toe of each black shoe
trailing a sapphire highlight,
with a black capeful of butterfly wings and bon-mots,   20
with heaven knows how many angels all riding
on the broad black brim of your hat,
     please come flying.

Bearing a musical inaudible abacus,
a slight censorious frown, and blue ribbons,   25
     please come flying.
Facts and skyscrapers glint in the tide; Manhattan
is all awash with morals this fine morning,
     so please come flying.

Mounting the sky with natural heroism,   30
above the accidents, above the malignant movies,
the taxicabs and injustices at large,
while horns are resounding in your beautiful ears
that simultaneously listen to
a soft uninvented music, fit for the musk deer,   35
     please come flying.

For whom the grim museums will behave
like courteous male bower birds,
for whom the agreeable lions lie in wait
on the steps of the Public Library,   40
eager to rise and follow through the doors
up into the reading rooms,
     please come flying.
We can sit down and weep; we can go shopping,
or play at a game of constantly being wrong   45
with a priceless set of vocabularies,
or we can bravely deplore, but please
     please come flying.

8. Compartmented serving dishes.

With dynasties of negative constructions
darkening and dying around you,   50
with grammar that suddenly turns and shines
like flocks of sandpipers flying,
    please come flying.

Come like a light in the white mackerel sky,
come like a daytime comet   55
with a long unnebulous train of words,
from Brooklyn, over the Brooklyn Bridge, on this fine morning,
    please come flying.

                                    1955

In the Waiting Room

In Worcester, Massachusetts,
I went with Aunt Consuelo
to keep her dentist's appointment
and sat and waited for her
in the dentist's waiting room.   5
It was winter. It got dark
early. The waiting room
was full of grown-up people,
arctics and overcoats,
lamps and magazines.   10
My aunt was inside
what seemed like a long time
and while I waited I read
the *National Geographic*
(I could read) and carefully   15
studied the photographs:
the inside of a volcano,
black, and full of ashes;
then it was spilling over
in rivulets of fire.   20
Osa and Martin Johnson[9]
dressed in riding breeches,
laced boots, and pith helmets.
A dead man slung on a pole
—"Long Pig,"[1] the caption said.   25
Babies with pointed heads
wound round and round with string;
black, naked women with necks

9. Married team of American explorers and   1. Polynesian cannibals' name for the human
travel writers.   carcass.

wound round and round with wire
like the necks of light bulbs.   30
Their breasts were horrifying.
I read it right straight through.
I was too shy to stop.
And then I looked at the cover:
the yellow margins, the date.   35

Suddenly, from inside,
came an *oh!* of pain
—Aunt Consuelo's voice—
not very loud or long.
I wasn't at all surprised;   40
even then I knew she was
a foolish, timid woman.
I might have been embarrassed,
but wasn't. What took me
completely by surprise   45
was that it was *me:*
my voice, in my mouth.
Without thinking at all
I was my foolish aunt,
I—we—were falling, falling,   50
our eyes glued to the cover
of the *National Geographic*,
February, 1918.

I said to myself: three days
and you'll be seven years old.   55
I was saying it to stop
the sensation of falling off
the round, turning world
into cold, blue-black space.
But I felt: you are an *I,*   60
you are an *Elizabeth,*
you are one of *them.*
Why should you be one, too?
I scarcely dared to look
to see what it was I was.   65
I gave a sidelong glance
—I couldn't look any higher—
at shadowy gray knees,
trousers and skirts and boots
and different pairs of hands   70
lying under the lamps.
I knew that nothing stranger
had ever happened, that nothing
stranger could ever happen.

Why should I be my aunt,   75
or me, or anyone?
What similarities—
boots, hands, the family voice
I felt in my throat, or even
the *National Geographic*   80
and those awful hanging breasts—
held us all together
or made us all just one?
How—I didn't know any
word for it—how "unlikely" . . .   85
How had I come to be here,
like them, and overhear
a cry of pain that could have
got loud and worse but hadn't?

The waiting room was bright   90
and too hot. It was sliding
beneath a big black wave,
another, and another.

Then I was back in it.
The War[2] was on. Outside,   95
in Worcester, Massachusetts,
were night and slush and cold,
and it was still the fifth
of February, 1918.

                                             1976

The Moose

For Grace Bulmer Bowers

From narrow provinces
of fish and bread and tea,
home of the long tides
where the bay leaves the sea
twice a day and takes   5
the herrings long rides,

where if the river
enters or retreats
in a wall of brown foam
depends on if it meets   10

---

2. I.e., World War I.

the bay coming in,
the bay not at home;

where, silted red,
sometimes the sun sets
facing a red sea,   15
and others, veins the flats'
lavender, rich mud
in burning rivulets;

on red, gravelly roads,
down rows of sugar maples,   20
past clapboard farmhouses
and neat, clapboard churches,
bleached, ridged as clamshells,
past twin silver birches,

through late afternoon   25
a bus journeys west,
the windshield flashing pink,
pink glancing off of metal,
brushing the dented flank
of blue, beat-up enamel;   30

down hollows, up rises,
and waits, patient, while
a lone traveller gives
kisses and embraces
to seven relatives   35
and a collie supervises.

Goodbye to the elms,
to the farm, to the dog.
The bus starts. The light
grows richer; the fog,   40
shifting, salty, thin,
comes closing in.

Its cold, round crystals
form and slide and settle
in the white hens' feathers,   45
in gray glazed cabbages,
on the cabbage roses
and lupins like apostles;

the sweet peas cling
to their wet white string   50
on the whitewashed fences;

bumblebees creep
inside the foxgloves,
and evening commences.

One stop at Bass River.   55
Then the Economies—
Lower, Middle, Upper;
Five Islands, Five Houses,[3]
where a woman shakes a tablecloth
out after supper.   60

A pale flickering. Gone.
The Tantramar marshes
and the smell of salt hay.
An iron bridge trembles
and a loose plank rattles   65
but doesn't give way.

On the left, a red light
swims through the dark:
a ship's port lantern.
Two rubber boots show,   70
illuminated, solemn.
A dog gives one bark.

A woman climbs in
with two market bags,
brisk, freckled, elderly.   75
"A grand night. Yes, sir,
all the way to Boston."
She regards us amicably.

Moonlight as we enter
the New Brunswick woods,   80
hairy, scratchy, splintery;
moonlight and mist
caught in them like lamb's wool
on bushes in a pasture.

The passengers lie back.   85
Snores. Some long sighs.
A dreamy divagation
begins in the night,
a gentle, auditory,
slow hallucination. . . .   90

3. Names of New England towns.

In the creakings and noises,
an old conversation
—not concerning us,
but recognizable, somewhere,
back in the bus: 95
Grandparents' voices

uninterruptedly
talking, in Eternity:
names being mentioned,
things cleared up finally;   100
what he said, what she said,
who got pensioned;

deaths, deaths and sicknesses;
the year he remarried;
the year (something) happened.   105
She died in childbirth.
That was the son lost
when the schooner foundered.

He took to drink. Yes.
She went to the bad.   110
When Amos began to pray
even in the store and
finally the family had
to put him away.

"Yes . . ." that peculiar   115
affirmative. "Yes . . ."
A sharp, indrawn breath,
half groan, half acceptance,
that means "Life's like that.
We know *it* (also death)."   120

Talking the way they talked
in the old featherbed,
peacefully, on and on,
dim lamplight in the hall,
down in the kitchen, the dog   125
tucked in her shawl.

Now, it's all right now
even to fall asleep
just as on all those nights.
—Suddenly the bus driver   130
stops with a jolt,
turns off his lights.

A moose has come out of
the impenetrable wood
and stands there, looms, rather,   135
in the middle of the road.
It approaches; it sniffs at
the bus's hot hood.

Towering, antlerless,
high as a church,   140
homely as a house
(or, safe as houses).
A man's voice assures us
"Perfectly harmless. . . . "

Some of the passengers   145
exclaim in whispers,
childishly, softly,
"Sure are big creatures."
"It's awful plain."
"Look! It's a she!"   150

Taking her time,
she looks the bus over,
grand, otherworldly.
Why, why do we feel
(we all feel) this sweet   155
sensation of joy?

"Curious creatures,"
says our quiet driver,
rolling his *r*'s.
"Look at that, would you."   160
Then he shifts gears.
For a moment longer,

by craning backward,
the moose can be seen
on the moonlit macadam;   165
then there's a dim
smell of moose, an acrid
smell of gasoline.

                                              1976

One Art

The art of losing isn't hard to master;
so many things seem filled with the intent
to be lost that their loss is no disaster.

Lose something every day. Accept the fluster
of lost door keys, the hour badly spent.   5
The art of losing isn't hard to master.

Then practice losing farther, losing faster:
places, and names and where it was you meant
to travel. None of these will bring disaster.

I lost my mother's watch. And look! my last, or   10
next-to-last, of three loved houses went.
The art of losing isn't hard to master.

I lost two cities, lovely ones. And, vaster,
some realms I owned, two rivers, a continent.
I miss them, but it wasn't a disaster.   15

—Even losing you (the joking voice, a gesture
I love) I shan't have lied. It's evident
the art of losing's not too hard to master
though it may look like (*Write* it!) like disaster.

                                                          1976

Pink Dog

[Rio de Janeiro]

The sun is blazing and the sky is blue.
Umbrellas clothe the beach in every hue.
Naked, you trot across the avenue.

Oh, never have I seen a dog so bare!
Naked and pink, without a single hair . . .   5
Startled, the passersby draw back and stare.

Of course they're mortally afraid of rabies.
You are not mad; you have a case of scabies[4]
but look intelligent. Where are your babies?

(A nursing mother, by those hanging teats.)   10
In what slum have you hidden them, poor bitch,
while you go begging, living by your wits?

Didn't you know? It's been in all the papers,
to solve this problem, how they deal with beggars?
They take and throw them in the tidal rivers.   15

---

4. A skin disease that causes severe itching.

Yes, idiots, paralytics, parasites
go bobbing in the ebbing sewage, nights
out in the suburbs, where there are no lights.

If they do this to anyone who begs,
drugged, drunk, or sober, with or without legs,   20
what would they do to sick, four-legged dogs?

In the cafés and on the sidewalk corners
the joke is going round that all the beggars
who can afford them now wear life preservers.

In your condition you would not be able   25
even to float, much less to dog-paddle.
Now look, the practical, the sensible

solution is to wear a *fantasia*.[5]
Tonight you simply can't afford to be a-
n eyesore. But no one will ever see a   30

dog in *mascara* this time of year.
Ash Wednesday'll[6] come but Carnival is here.
What sambas[7] can you dance? What will you wear?

They say that Carnival's degenerating
—radios, Americans, or something,   35
have ruined it completely. They're just talking.

Carnival is always wonderful!
A depilated dog would not look well.
Dress up! Dress up and dance at Carnival!

                                    1979

5. "Carnival costume" [Bishop's note].
6. In the Christian calendar, the Wednesday
before Lent (the forty-day period that precedes
the anniversary of Christ's Crucifixion and resurrection), a day when devout Catholics place a
smudge of ash on their foreheads.
7. Popular Brazilian dances.

JOSEPHINE MILES

1911–

The poet and critic Josephine Miles has written that "I like the idea of speech
—not images, not ideas, not music, but people talking—as the material from
which poetry is made." The comment is an important one, for it reveals this artist's strong commitment to the daily reality of people and places while illumi-

nating the success with which she transcribes that reality in evocative yet colloquial language.

Miles was born in Chicago, Illinois, but moved with her family to California —where she has lived since—when she was only five. After earning a B.A. from U.C.L.A. in 1932, she did graduate work at the University of California, Berkeley, and, despite a lifelong struggle with crippling arthritis, she remained at that institution as a faculty member until her retirement in the late seventies. During her long and successful career as a teacher, she published a number of distinguished critical works, including *The Vocabulary of Poetry: Three Studies* (1946) and *Eras and Modes in English Poetry* (1957), as well as ten volumes of poetry, among them *Lines at Intersections* (1939), *Local Measures* (1946), *To All Appearances: Poems New and Selected* (1975), and *Coming to Terms* (1979); most recently, her *Collected Poems* (1984) has appeared.

As the freshness and vitality of her verse suggest, Miles has never seen the university as an ivory tower. Having grown up with, as she puts it, "the feeling that poetry and politics, new writing and the New Deal, went together," she believes instead that "as a teacher of English . . . I have not had the chance to lose sight of new ideas and arguments." "I think my poems are peaceful and peaceable," she has said, "but [I] am glad they got written where the action is."

Reason

Said, Pull her up a bit will you, Mac, I want to unload there.
Said, Pull her up my rear end, first come first serve.
Said, Give her the gun, Bud, he needs a taste of his own bumper
Then the usher came out and got into the act:

Said, Pull her up, pull her up a bit, we need this space, sir.   5
Said, For God's sake, is this still a free country or what?
You go back and take care of Gary Cooper's[1] horse
And leave me handle my own car.

Saw them unloading the lame old lady,
Ducked out under the wheel and gave her an elbow,   10
Said All you needed to do was just explain;
Reason, Reason is my middle name.

                                                    1955

[In the town where every man is king]

In the town where every man is king,
        Every man has one subject,
        Every man bends to his own foot.

---

1. Popular film star of the thirties, forties, and fifties who appeared in many westerns.

Bring on the mirror that he may properly bend.
But who will bring it on?   5

In the castle where is no hunger and no need,
Every man gives gifts and receives
Gifts. But of these only his own
Enhance him, the ring giver.
He must wear his ring.   10

Gradually, as he resolves the oppression of his edicts,
Losing his fellow lords to dim perspectives,
Monoliths of rock and stone, even
Of reinforced concrete, become before him
Mirrors. He licks the glass.   15

1967

[Dear Frank, Here is a poem]

Dear Frank, Here is a poem
    I dreamed of you last night;
    It makes me happy
    Because it makes sense to me.

We went to the Greek Theater[2] to see a play   5
And as we entered were given elaborate menus
    Of the players' names.
    Dinner was three dollars.
    It was served on the little round tables from cocktail lounges.

I kept leaning back against your knees,   10
Because of those backless benches, and you kept moving
Further and further away in the amphitheater,
    I following, until finally you said,
    Jo: I am having the six dollar dinner.

1967

Doll

Though the willows bent down to shelter us where we played
House in the sandy acres, though our dolls,
Especially Lillian, weathered all the action,
I kept getting so much earlier home to rest
That medical consultation led to cast   5

2. A large open-air theater at the University of California, Berkeley.

From head to toe. It was a surprise for my parents
And so for me also, and I railed
Flat out in the back seat on the long trip home
In which three tires blew on our trusty Mitchell.
Home, in a slight roughhouse of my brothers,   10
It turned out Lillian had been knocked to the floor and broken
Across the face. Good, said my mother
In her John Deweyan[3] constructive way,
Now you and Lillian can be mended together.
We made a special trip to the doll hospital   15
To pick her up. But, they can't fix her after all, my father said,
You'll just have to tend her with her broken cheek.
I was very willing. We opened the box, and she lay
In shards mixed among tissue paper. Only her eyes
Set loose on a metal stick so they would open   20
And close, opened and closed, and I grew seasick.
A friend of the family sent me a kewpie doll.[4]
Later Miss Babcox the sitter
After many repetitious card games,
Said, we must talk about bad things.   25
Let me tell you
Some of the bad things I have known in my life.
She did not ask me mine, I could not have told her.
Among the bad things in my life, she said,
Have been many good people, good but without troubles;   30
Her various stories tended
To end with transmigrations of one sort or another,
Dishonest riches to honest poverty; kings and queens
To indians over an adequate space of time.
Take this cat, coming along here, she said,   35
A glossy black cat whom she fed her wages in salmon,
He is a wise one, about to become a person.
Come to think of it, possibly Lillian
Is about to become a cat.
She will have different eyes then, I said.   40
Obviously. Slanted, and what is more,
Able to see in the dark.

1979

Parent

Letting down the isinglass[5] curtains
Between the wet rain and the back seat

---

3. Following the thought of John Dewey
(1859–1952), American pragmatic philosopher
and educator.
4. A doll with a bow-shaped mouth, popular in
the twenties.
5. Semitransparent substance, made from the
swim-bladders of fish, used for the windows in
some makes of early automobiles.

Where new plaster flattened me,
My father said,
Wait here. I will get you the sherbet   5
Of your eight-year-old dreams.
There were no drive-ins then.
The rain roared. Don't go away,
I said to him? He said to me.

                                                    1979

Bureau 2

Skunks fight under the house and keep us
Wakeful, they are down from the hills in the drought.
Lots of colloquial remedies, mothballs, tomato juice
Leave them unmoved. Call the S P C A.
Call the Bureau of Health, call the P G & E[6] where they rest   5
Past the meter box, call the Animal Shelter,
Call commercial exterminators; all reply
With a sigh, and a different number to call
Next month or next year when they're not so busy.
Asking around, getting the number finally   10
Number of the chief health officer of the county,
Mr. Simms. His secretary answers,
What makes you think Mr. Simms will speak to you?
What makes you think Mr. Simms is interested in skunks?
Mr. Simms is animal health officer of this whole county   15
And his chief interest is wolves.

                                                    1979

Concert

I was sitting behind a somewhat neat old person
In creamlined beige matching coat and hat
Neat but that the hat crown
Tilted at a curious angle left to right.
As I deliberated, she turned her head impatiently   5
As at a draft of air,
And pulled the hat from off a mane of hair,
Of wild white hair.

                                                    1979

---

6. Pacific Gas and Electric.

Why We Are Late

A red light is stuck
At the corner of LeConte and Euclid.
Numbers of people are going in and out of the 7 Palms Market,
Some sitting with beer at La Vals.[7]
Lots lugging bags to the Laundromat—Open—   5
A couple thumbing rides up the hill, fog curling in over
    the newsracks,
Low pressures.

You can tell it is about five or six o'clock
And we are coming home from a meeting not bad, not good,
Just coming along, and stop at the red light.   10
Time stands there, we in the midst of it,
The numberless years of our lives.
A late green light later
May let us get home.

                                                                      1979

7. A pizza restaurant popular with students in Berkeley, California.

MARY McCARTHY

1912–

Sardonically associating "the kind of woman writer who's a capital W, capital W" with the production of literature that focuses on decor and drapery, Mary McCarthy claimed in a *Paris Review* interview in 1962 that Jane Austen and George Eliot were not "Women Writers." Should she divide literary women into the categories of "Sense and Sensibility," she explained, "I *am* for the ones who represent sense, and so was Jane Austen." As an accomplished journalist, McCarthy has been hailed for politically astute essays on Vietnam and the Watergate crisis, as well as for intelligent criticism of contemporary drama and fiction. Her reputation as a creative writer rests, however, on the work that illuminates her growth from an emotional sensibility to the tolerant but ironic common sense that so frequently animates her prose style.

The oldest child of parents who were killed in an influenza epidemic in 1918, McCarthy was raised in Minneapolis by a series of relatives, some of whom enjoyed tormenting her and her siblings. In *Memories of a Catholic Girlhood* (1957), she has explored her grief at the loss of her parents as well as her development into "a lapsed Catholic," first in the homes of her Catholic, Protestant, and Jewish relatives, and later at the convent school she attended in Seattle. She began publishing fiction after graduating from Vassar College and divorcing her first husband. While married to the literary critic Edmund Wilson, with whom she had a child, McCarthy wrote *The Company She Keeps* (1942), a successful series of satiric stories. After the marriage broke up in 1945, McCarthy traveled and published extensively. From *The Groves of Academe* (1952) to *Cannibals and Missionaries* (1979), McCarthy delineated the limits and liabilities of modern liberalism. In addition, the novels *A Charmed Life* (1955) and *The Group* (1963) focused with wit and intelligence on the restricted options and sensibilities of well-educated middle-class women. Like her fiction, McCarthy's autobiographical writing is marked by scrupulous detachment; in *Names*, for instance, she meditates on the disjunction between her sense of herself as an adolescent and the sometimes baffling, sometimes degrading identities she was given by teachers and fellow students.

From Memories of a Catholic Girlhood

Names

Anna Lyons, Mary Louise Lyons, Mary von Phul, Emilie von Phul, Eugenia McLellan, Marjorie McPhail, Marie-Louise L'Abbé, Mary Danz, Julia Dodge, Mary Fordyce Blake, Janet Preston—these were the names (I can still tell them over like a rosary)[1] of some of the older girls in the convent: the Virtues and Graces. The virtuous ones wore wide blue or green moire good-conduct ribbons, bandoleer-style,[2] across their blue serge uniforms; the beautiful ones wore rouge and powder or at least were reputed to do so. Our class, the eighth grade, wore pink ribbons (I never got one myself) and had names like Patricia ("Pat") Sullivan, Eileen Donohoe, and Joan Kane. We were inelegant even in this respect; the best name we could show, among us, was Phyllis ("Phil") Chatham, who boasted that her father's name, Ralph, was pronounced "Rafe" as in England.

Names had a great importance for us in the convent, and foreign names, French, German, or plain English (which, to us, were foreign, because of their Protestant sound), bloomed like prize roses among a collection of spuds. Irish names were too common in the school to have any prestige either as surnames (Gallagher, Sheehan, Finn, Sullivan, McCarthy) or as Christian names (Kathleen, Eileen). Anything exotic had value: an "olive" complexion, for example. The pet girl of the convent was a fragile Jewish girl named Susie Lowenstein, who had pale red-gold hair and an exquisite retroussé[3] nose, which, if we had had it, might have been called "pug." We liked her name too and the name of a child in the primary grades: Abbie Stuart Baillargeon. My favorite name, on the whole, though, was Emilie von Phul (pronounced

---

1. A series of prayers in the Catholic church, which are recited while counting a string of special beads.

2. Across the chest.

3. Turned up.

"Pool"); her oldest sister, recently graduated, was called Celeste. Another name that appealed to me was Genevieve Albers, Saint Genevieve being the patron saint of Paris who turned back Attila[4] from the gates of the city.

All these names reflected the still-pioneer character of the Pacific Northwest. I had never heard their like in the parochial school in Minneapolis, where "foreign" extraction, in any case, was something to be ashamed of, the whole drive being toward Americanization of first name and surname alike. The exceptions to this were the Irish, who could vaunt such names as Catherine O'Dea and the name of my second cousin, Mary Catherine Anne Rose Violet McCarthy, while an unfortunate German boy named Manfred was made to suffer for his. But that was Minneapolis. In Seattle, and especially in the convent of the Ladies of the Sacred Heart, foreign names suggested not immigration but emigration—distinguished exile. Minneapolis was a granary; Seattle was a port, which had attracted a veritable Foreign Legion[5] of adventurers—soldiers of fortune, younger sons, gamblers, traders, drawn by the fortunes to be made in virgin timber and shipping and by the Alaska Gold Rush. Wars and revolutions had sent the defeated out to Puget Sound, to start a new life; the latest had been the Russian Revolution, which had shipped us, via Harbin, a Russian colony, complete with restaurant, on Queen Anne Hill. The English names in the convent, when they did not testify to direct English origin, as in the case of "Rafe" Chatham, had come to us from the South and represented a kind of internal exile; such girls as Mary Fordyce Blake and Mary McQueen Street (a class ahead of me; her sister was named Francesca) bore their double-barreled first names like titles of aristocracy from the ante-bellum South. Not all our girls, by any means, were Catholic; some of the very prettiest ones—Julia Dodge and Janet Preston, if I remember rightly—were Protestants. The nuns had taught us to behave with special courtesy to these strangers in our midst, and the whole effect was of some superior hostel for refugees of all the lost causes of the past hundred years. Money could not count for much in such an atmosphere; the fathers and grandfathers of many of our "best" girls were ruined men.

Names, often, were freakish in the Pacific Northwest, particularly girls' names. In the Episcopal boarding school I went to later, in Tacoma, there was a girl called De Vere Utter, and there was a girl called Rocena and another called Hermoine. Was Rocena a mistake for Rowena and Hermoine for Hermione? And was Vere, as we called her, Lady Clara Vere de Vere? Probably. You do not hear names like those

4. Attila the Hun (A.D. 406?–453), notorious invader of Europe.

5. International volunteer army corps that does not inquire into its enlistees' backgrounds.

often, in any case, east of the Cascade Mountains; they belong to the frontier, where books and libraries were few and memory seems to have been oral, as in the time of Homer.

Names have more significance for Catholics than they do for other people; Christian names are chosen for the spiritual qualities of the saints they are taken from; Protestants used to name their children out of the Old Testament and now they name them out of novels and plays, whose heroes and heroines are perhaps the new patron saints of a secular age. But with Catholics it is different. The saint a child is named for is supposed to serve, literally, as a model or pattern to imitate; your name is your fortune and it tells you what you are or must be. Catholic children ponder their names for a mystic meaning, like birthstones; my own, I learned, besides belonging to the Virgin and Saint Mary of Egypt, originally meant "bitter" or "star of the sea." My second name, Therese, could dedicate me either to Saint Theresa or to the saint called the Little Flower, Soeur Thérèse of Lisieux, on whom God was supposed to have descended in the form of a shower of roses. At Confirmation,[6] I had added a third name (for Catholics then rename themselves, as most nuns do, yet another time, when they take orders); on the advice of a nun, I had taken "Clementina," after Saint Clement, an early pope—a step I soon regretted on account of "My Darling Clementine"[7] and her number nine shoes. By the time I was in the convent, I would no longer tell anyone what my Confirmation name was. The name I had nearly picked was "Agnes," after a little Roman virgin martyr, always shown with a lamb, because of her purity. But Agnes would have been just as bad, I recognized in Forest Ridge Convent—not only because of the possibility of "Aggie," but because it was subtly, indefinably *wrong*, in itself. Agnes would have made me look like an ass.

The fear of appearing ridiculous first entered my life, as a governing motive, during my second year in the convent. Up to then, a desire for prominence had decided many of my actions and, in fact, still persisted. But in the eighth grade, I became aware of mockery and perceived that I could not seek prominence without attracting laughter. Other people could, but I couldn't. This laughter was proceeding, not from my classmates, but from the girls of the class just above me, in particular from two boon companions, Elinor Heffernan and Mary Harty, a clownish pair—oddly assorted in size and shape, as teams of clowns generally are, one short, plump, and baby-faced, the other tall, lean, and owlish—who entertained the high-school department by calling attention to the oddities of the younger girls. Nearly every school has such a pair of sati-

6. In the Catholic church, a ceremony admitting adolescents to full membership in the church.

7. A popular American folk song.

rists, whose marks are generally low and who are tolerated just because of their laziness and non-conformity; one of them (in this case, Mary Harty, the plump one) usually appears to be half asleep. Because of their low standing, their indifference to appearances, the sad state of their uniforms, their clowning is taken to be harmless, which, on the whole, it is, their object being not to wound but to divert; such girls are bored in school. We in the eighth grade sat directly in front of the two wits in study hall, so that they had us under close observation; yet at first I was not afraid of them, wanting, if anything, to identify myself with their laughter, to be initiated into the joke. One of their specialties was giving people nicknames, and it was considered an honor to be the first in the eighth grade to be let in by Elinor and Mary on their latest invention. This often happened to me; they would tell me, on the playground, and I would tell the others. As their intermediary, I felt myself almost their friend and it did not occur to me that I might be next on their list.

I had achieved prominence not long before by publicly losing my faith and regaining it at the end of a retreat. I believe Elinor and Mary questioned me about this on the playground, during recess, and listened with serious, respectful faces while I told them about my conversations with the Jesuits. Those serious faces ought to have been an omen, but if the two girls used what I had revealed to make fun of me, it must have been behind my back. I never heard any more of it, and yet just at this time I began to feel something, like a cold breath on the nape of my neck, that made me wonder whether the new position I had won for myself in the convent was as secure as I imagined. I would turn around in study hall and find the two girls looking at me with speculation in their eyes.

It was just at this time, too, that I found myself in a perfectly absurd situation, a very private one, which made me live, from month to month, in horror of discovery. I had waked up one morning, in my convent room, to find a few small spots of blood on my sheet; I had somehow scratched a trifling cut on one of my legs and opened it during the night. I wondered what to do about this, for the nuns were fussy about bedmaking, as they were about our white collars and cuffs, and if we had an inspection those spots might count against me. It was best, I decided, to ask the nun on dormitory duty, tall, stout Mother Slattery, for a clean bottom sheet, even though she might scold me for having scratched my leg in my sleep and order me to cut my toenails. You never know what you might be blamed for. But Mother Slattery, when she bustled in to look at the sheet, did not scold me at all; indeed, she hardly seemed to be listening as I explained to her about the cut. She told me to sit down: she would be back in a minute. "You can be excused from athletics today," she added, closing the door. As I waited, I considered this remark, which seemed to me strangely munificent, in view of the unimportance of the cut. In a moment, she returned, but without the sheet. Instead, she produced out of her big pocket a sort of cloth girdle and a peculiar flannel object which I first took to be a bandage, and I began to protest that I did not need or want a bandage; all I needed was a bottom sheet. "The sheet can wait," said Mother Slattery, succinctly, handing me two large safety pins. It was the pins that abruptly enlightened me; I saw Mother Slattery's mistake, even as she was instructing me as to how this flannel article, which I now understood to be a sanitary napkin, was to be put on.

"Oh, no, Mother," I said, feeling somewhat embarrassed. "You don't understand. It's just a little cut, on my leg." But Mother, again, was not listening; she appeared to have grown deaf, as the nuns had a habit of doing when what you were saying did not fit in with their ideas. And now that I knew what was in her mind, I was conscious of a funny constraint; I did not feel it proper to name a natural process, in so many words, to a nun. It was like trying not to think of their going to the bathroom or trying not to see the straggling iron-grey hair coming out of their coifs (the common notion that they shaved their heads was false). On the whole, it seemed better just to show her my cut. But when I offered to do so and unfastened my black stocking, she only glanced at my leg, cursorily. "That's only a scratch, dear," she said. "Now hurry up and put this on or you'll be late for chapel. Have you any pain?" "No, no, Mother!" I cried. "You don't understand!" "Yes, yes, I understand," she replied soothingly, "and you will too, a little later. Mother Superior will tell you about it some time during the morning. There's nothing to be afraid of. You have become a woman."

"I know all about that," I persisted. "Mother, please listen. I just cut my leg. On the athletic field. Yesterday afternoon." But the more excited I grew, the more soothing, and yet firm, Mother Slattery became. There seemed to be nothing for it but to give up and do as I was bid. I was in the grip of a higher authority, which almost had the power to persuade me that it was right and I was wrong. But of course I was not wrong; that would have been too good to be true. While Mother Slattery waited, just outside my door, I miserably donned the equipment she had given me, for there was no place to hide it, on account of drawer inspection. She led me down the hall to where there was a chute and explained how I was to dispose of the flannel thing, by dropping it down the chute into the laundry. (The convent arrangements were very old-fashioned, dating back, no doubt, to the days of Louis Philippe.)[8]

The Mother Superior, Madame MacIllvra, was a sensible woman,

8. King of France (1773–1850).

and all through my early morning classes, I was on pins and needles, chafing for the promised interview with her which I trusted would clear things up. "*Ma Mère*,"[9] I would begin, "Mother Slattery thinks . . . ." Then I would tell her about the cut and the athletic field. But precisely the same impasse confronted me when I was summoned to her office at recess-time. *I* talked about my cut, and *she* talked about becoming a woman. It was rather like a round, in which she was singing "Scotland's burning, Scotland's burning," and I was singing "Pour on water, pour on water." Neither of us could hear the other, or, rather, I could hear her, but she could not hear me. Owing to our different positions in the convent, she was free to interrupt me, whereas I was expected to remain silent until she had finished speaking. When I kept breaking in, she hushed me, gently, and took me on her lap. Exactly like Mother Slattery, she attributed all my references to the cut to a blind fear of this new, unexpected reality that had supposedly entered my life. Many young girls, she reassured me, were frightened if they had not been prepared. "And you, Mary, have lost your dear mother, who could have made this easier for you." Rocked on Madame MacIllvra's lap, I felt paralysis overtake me and I lay, mutely listening, against her bosom, my face being tickled by her white, starched, fluted wimple, while she explained to me how babies were born, all of which I had heard before.

There was no use fighting the convent. I had to pretend to have become a woman, just as, not long before, I had had to pretend to get my faith back—for the sake of peace. This pretense was decidedly awkward. For fear of being found out by the lay sisters downstairs in the laundry (no doubt an imaginary contingency, but the convent was so very thorough), I reopened the cut on my leg, so as to draw a little blood to stain the napkins, which were issued me regularly, not only on this occasion, but every twenty-eight days thereafter. Eventually, I abandoned this bloodletting, for fear of lockjaw, and trusted to fate. Yet I was in awful dread of detection; my only hope, as I saw it, was either to be released from the convent or to become a woman in reality, which might take a year, at least, since I was only twelve. Getting out of athletics once a month was not sufficient compensation for the farce I was going through. It was not my fault; they had forced me into it; nevertheless, it was I who would look silly—worse than silly; half mad—if the truth ever came to light.

I was burdened with this guilt and shame when the nickname finally found me out. "Found me out," in a general sense, for no one ever did learn the particular secret I bore about with me, pinned to the linen band. "We've got a name for you," Elinor and Mary called out to me, one day on the playground. "What is it?" I asked, half hoping, half

9. French: my mother.

fearing, since not all their sobriquets were unfavorable. "Cye," they answered, looking at each other and laughing. " 'Si'?" I repeated, supposing that it was based on Simple Simon. Did they regard me as a hick? "C.Y.E.," they elucidated, spelling it out in chorus. "The letters stand for something. Can you guess?" I could not and I cannot now. The closest I could come to it in the convent was "Clean Your Ears." Perhaps that was it, though in later life I have wondered whether it did not stand, simply, for "Clever Young Egg" or "Champion Young Eccentric." But in the convent I was certain that it stood for something horrible, something even worse than dirty ears (as far as I knew, my ears were clean), something I could never guess because it represented some aspect of myself that the world could see and I couldn't, like a sign pinned on my back. Everyone in the convent must have known what the letters stood for, but no one would tell me. Elinor and Mary had made them promise. It was like halitosis; not even my best friend, my deskmate, Louise, would tell me, no matter how much I pleaded. Yet everyone assured me that it was "very good," that is, very apt. And it made everyone laugh.

This name reduced all my pretensions and solidified my sense of *wrongness*. Just as I felt I was beginning to belong to the convent, it turned me into an outsider, since I was the only pupil who was not in the know. I liked the convent, but it did not like me, as people say of certain foods that disagree with them. By this, I do not mean that I was actively unpopular, either with the pupils or with the nuns. The Mother Superior cried when I left and predicted that I would be a novelist, which surprised me. And I had finally made friends; even Emilie von Phul smiled upon me softly out of her bright blue eyes from the far end of the study hall. It was just that I did not fit into the convent pattern; the simplest thing I did, like asking for a clean sheet, entrapped me in consequences that I never could have predicted. I was not bad; I did not consciously break the rules; and yet I could never, not even for a week, get a pink ribbon, and this was something I could not understand, because I was trying as hard as I could. It was the same case as with the hated name; the nuns, evidently, saw something about me that was invisible to me.

The oddest part was all that pretending. There I was, a walking mass of lies, pretending to be a Catholic and going to confession while really I had lost my faith, and pretending to have monthly periods by cutting myself with nail scissors; yet all this had come about without my volition and even contrary to it. But the basest pretense I was driven to was the acceptance of the nickname. Yet what else could I do? In the convent, I could not live it down. To all those girls, I had become "Cye McCarthy." That was who I was. That was how I had to identify myself when telephoning my friends during vacations to ask them to the movies: "Hello, this is Cye." I loathed myself when I said it, and yet I succumbed to the name totally, making myself over into a sort of hearty to go with it—the kind of girl I hated. "Cye" was my new patron saint. This false personality stuck to me, like the name, when I entered public high school, the next fall, as a freshman, having finally persuaded my grandparents to take me out of the convent, although they could never get to the bottom of my reasons, since, as I admitted, the nuns were kind, and I had made many nice new friends. What I wanted was a fresh start, a chance to begin life over again, but the first thing I heard in the corridors of the public high school was that name called out to me, like the warmest of welcomes: "Hi, there, Si!" That was the way they thought it was spelled. But this time I was resolute. After the first weeks, I dropped the hearties who called me "Si" and I never heard it again. I got my own name back and sloughed off Clementina and even Therese—the names that did not seem to me any more to be mine but to have been imposed on me by others. And I preferred to think that Mary meant "bitter" rather than "star of the sea."

1957

MAY SARTON

1912–

The woman artist in May Sarton's novel *Mrs. Stevens Hears the Mermaids Singing* (1965) explains about herself that "we are all monsters . . . we women who have chosen to be something more and something less than women!" Yet, as a novelist, a memoirist, and a poet, Sarton has described the everyday and often prosaic details that fill the life of the single and sometimes singular woman writer. For, like Mrs. Stevens, Sarton clearly believes that "we have to dare to be ourselves, however frightening or strange that self may prove to be."

Born in Belgium and raised in Cambridge, Massachusetts, Sarton was the only child of an eminent historian of science, George Sarton, and an English portrait painter, Mabel (Elwes) Sarton. She attended the Shady Hill School in Cambridge and the Institut Belge de Culture Française in Brussels before joining Eva Le Gallienne's Repertory Theatre in New York and experimenting with her own theatrical company. In *I Knew a Phoenix* (1959), Sarton also described her early trips to England, where she met the writers Elizabeth Bowen and Virginia Woolf. In spite of the gregarious personality that emerges from this autobiography, Sarton became famous for the journals that described her solitary life in Nelson, New Hamphire, and for such novels as *The Small Room* (1961), *Joanna and Ulysses* (1963), and *Kinds of Love* (1970) that depict the female friendships and love affairs that save women from loneliness. Until very recently, her many publications have received little critical attention. Yet few writers have dealt as sensitively with such subjects as the roots of identity (*The*

House by the Sea, 1977), aging and death (*As We Are Now*, 1973), and the different forms female creativity takes. In her *Journal of a Solitude* (1973), wondering why "poetry always seems to me so much more a true work of the soul than prose," Sarton explained that it is "because the poem is primarily a dialogue with the self." Significantly, however, both *Letter from Chicago* and *My Sisters, O My Sisters* analyze her own creativity through dialogues with other literary women.

My Sisters, O My Sisters

> *Nous qui voulions poser, image ineffaçable*
> *Comme un delta divin notre main sur le sable*[1]
> Anna de Noailles

I

Dorothy Wordsworth,[2] dying, did not want to read,
"I am too busy with my own feelings," she said.

And all women who have wanted to break out
Of the prison of consciousness to sing or shout

Are strange monsters who renounce the treasure   5
Of their silence for a curious devouring pleasure.

Dickinson, Rossetti, Sappho[3]—they all know it,
Something is lost, strained, unforgiven in the poet.

She abdicates from life or like George Sand[4]
Suffers from the mortality in an immortal hand,   10

Loves too much, spends a whole life to discover
She was born a good grandmother, not a good lover.

Too powerful for men: Madame de Stael. Too sensitive:
Madame de Sévigné[5] who burdened where she meant to give.

Delicate as that burden was and so supremely lovely,   15
It was too heavy for her daughter, much too heavy.

Only when she built inward in a fearful isolation
Did any one succeed or learn to fuse emotion

1. French: "We who wanted to leave an ineffaceable image / Like a divine delta, our hand on the sand." Anna-Elisabeth, comtesse de Noailles (1876–1933), French poet and novelist.
2. English poet and diarist (1771–1855).
3. Emily Dickinson (1830–1886), Christina Rossetti (1830–1894), and Sappho (c.500 B.C.)
were three female lyric poets, American, English, and Greek respectively.
4. Pen name of Aurore Dupin (1804–1876), French novelist known for her many love affairs.
5. Marie de Sévigné (1626–1696), French noblewoman and prolific letter-writer. Germaine de Staël (1766–1817), French woman of letters.

With thought. Only when she renounced did Emily
Begin in the fierce lonely light to learn to be.   20

Only in the extremity of spirit and the flesh
And in renouncing passion did Sappho come to bless.

Only in the farewells or in old age does sanity
Shine through the crimson stains of their mortality.

And now we who are writing women and strange monsters   25
Still search our hearts to find the difficult answers,

Still hope that we may learn to lay our hands
More gently and more subtly on the burning sands.

To be through what we make more simply human,
To come to the deep place where poet becomes woman,   30

Where nothing has to be renounced or given over
In the pure light that shines out from the lover,

In the pure light that brings forth fruit and flower
And that great sanity, that sun, the feminine power.

II

Let us rejoice in   35
The full curve of breast,
The supple thigh
And all riches in
A woman's keeping
For man's comfort and rest   40
(Crimson and ivory)
For children's nourishment
(Magic fruits and flowers).
But when they are sleeping,
The children, the men,   45
Fed by these powers,
We know what is meant
By the wise serpent,
By the gentle dove,
And remember then   50
How we wish to love,

Let us rejoice now
In these great powers
Which are ours alone.
And trust what we know: 55
First the green hand

That can open flowers
In the deathly bone,
And the magic breast
That can feed the child,   60
And is under a hand
A rose of fire in snow
So tender, so wild
All fires come to rest,
All lives can be blest—   65
So sighs the gentle dove,
Wily the serpent so,
Matched in a woman's love.

III

Eve and Mary the mother are our stem;[6]
All our centuries go back to them.   70
And delicate the balance lies
Between the passionate and wise:
Of man's rib, one, and cleaves to him;
And one bears man and then frees him.
This double river has created us,   75
Always the rediscovered, always the cherished.
(But many fail in this. Many have perished.)

Hell is the loss of balance when woman is destroyer.
Each of us has been there.
Each of us knows what the floods can do.   80
How many women mother their husbands
Out of all strength and secret *Virtu*;[7]
How many women love an only son
As a lover loves, binding the free hands.
How many yield up their true power   85
Out of weakness, the moment of passion
Betrayed by years of confused living—
For it is surely a lifetime work,
This learning to be a woman.
Until at the end what is clear   90
Is the marvelous skill to make
Life grow in all its forms.

Is knowing where to ask, where to yield,
Where to sow, where to plough the field,

---

6. In the Book of Genesis, Eve was the first woman, made from the rib of Adam, and was responsible for the Fall; in the New Testament, Mary was the mother of Jesus Christ, whose crucifixion redeemed humanity from sin.
7. The Latin word *virtu* means strength or power.

Where to kill the heart or let it live;   95
To be Eve, the giver of knowledge, the lover;
To be Mary, the shield, the healer and the mother.
The balance is eternal whatever we may wish;
The law can be broken but we cannot change
What is supremely beautiful and strange.   100
Where find the root? Where re-join the source?
The fertile feminine goddess, double river?

                                    IV
We think of all the women hunting for themselves,
Turning and turning to each other with a driving
Need to learn to understand, to live in charity,   105
And above all to be used fully, to be giving
From wholeness, wholeness back to love's deep clarity.
O, all the burning hearts of women unappeased
Shine like great stars, like flowers of fire,
As the sun goes and darkness opens all desire—   110
And we are with a fierce compassion seized.
How lost, how far from home, how parted from
The earth, my sisters, O my sisters, we have come!

For so long asked so little of ourselves and men,
And let the Furies[8] have their way—our treasure,   115
The single antidote to all our world's confusion,
A few gifts to the poor small god of pleasure.
The god of passion has gone back into the mountain,
Is sleeping in the dark, deep in the earth.

We have betrayed a million times the holy fountain,   120
The potent spirit who brings his life to birth,
The masculine and violent joy of pure creation—
And yielded up the sacred fires to sensation.
But we shall never come home to the earth
Until we bring the great god and his mirth   125
Back from the mountain, until we let this stranger
Plough deep into our hearts his joy and anger,
For we shall never find ourselves again
Until we ask men's greatness back from men,
And we shall never find ourselves again   130
Until we match men's greatness with our own.

                                                          1948

---

8. The Eumenides, three monstrous women who avenge all wrongdoing in Greek myth.

Letter from Chicago

For Virginia Woolf[9]

Four years ago I met your death here,
Heard it where I had never been before
In a city of departures, streets of wind,
Soft plumes of smoke dissolving—
City of departures beside an aloof lake.   5
Here where you never were, they said,
"Virginia Woolf is dead."

The city died. I died in the city,
Witness of unreal tears, my own,
For experience involves time   10
And time was gone
The world arrested at the instant of death.
I wept wildly like a child
Who cannot give his present after all:
I met your death and did not recognize you.   15

Now you are dead four years
And there are no more private tears.
The city of departure is the city of arrival,
City of triumphant wind lifting people,
City of spring: yesterday I found you.   20
Wherever I looked was love.
Wherever I went I had presents in my hands.
Wherever I went I recognized you.

You are not, never to be again,
Never, never to be dead,   25
Never to be dead again in this city,
Never to be mourned again,
But to come back yearly,
Hourly, with the spring, with the wind,
Fresh as agony or resurrection;   30
A plume of smoke dissolving,
Remaking itself, never still,
Never static, never lost:
The place where time flows again.

I speak to you and meet my own life.   35
Is it to be poised as the lake beside the city,
Aloof, but given still to air and wind,

9. English novelist and essayist (1882–1941).

Detached from time, but given to the moment—
Is it to be a celebration always?

I send you love forward into the past.   40

                                                          1953

The Muse as Medusa[1]

I saw you once, Medusa; we were alone.
I looked you straight in the cold eye, cold.
I was not punished, was not turned to stone—
How to believe the legends I am told?

I came as naked as any little fish,   5
Prepared to be hooked, gutted, caught;
But I saw you, Medusa, made my wish,
And when I left you I was clothed in thought. . . .

Being allowed, perhaps, to swim my way
Through the great deep and on the rising tide,   10
Flashing wild streams, as free and rich as they,
Though you had power marshaled on your side.

The fish escaped to many a magic reef;
The fish explored many a dangerous sea—
The fish, Medusa, did not come to grief,   15
But swims still in a fluid mystery.

Forget the image: your silence is my ocean,
And even now it teems with life. You chose
To abdicate by total lack of motion,
But did it work, for nothing really froze?   20

It is all fluid still, that world of feeling
Where thoughts, those fishes, silent, feed and rove;
And, fluid, it is also full of healing,
For love is healing, even rootless love.

I turn your face around! It is my face.   25
That frozen rage is what I must explore—
Oh secret, self-enclosed, and ravaged place!
This is the gift I thank Medusa for.

                                                          1971

---

1. The Muse is a poet's personal goddess of inspiration; Medusa is a female monster with
snakes for hair, the sight of whom turns men to
stone, according to Greek myth.

MURIEL RUKEYSER
1913–1980

"Breathe-in experience, breathe-out poetry": Muriel Rukeyser opened the first poem of her first volume of verse, *Theory of Flight* (1935), with a vow to eschew all that might be construed as artificially poetic in favor of a lyrical articulation of personal experience. That those experiences would be shaped by political realities is evidenced later in the poem, when Rukeyser exclaims, "Not Sappho, Sacco." Rejecting the erotic verse of ancient Greece for poetry focusing on the racial, political, and economic issues that led to the execution of the anarchist-immigrants Sacco and Vanzetti, Rukeyser placed herself in the expansive tradition of American verse established by Walt Whitman as well as in the school of modern political poetry led by W. H. Auden, and she thereby dedicated herself throughout her distinguished career to breathing in the ordinary expressions of the victimized and breathing out the songs that linked their lives to her own.

Rukeyser was born and lived most of her life in New York. Her parents were affluent, and she attended the Fieldston School, Vassar College, and Columbia University. But most of her friends were socialists, labor organizers, or artists. At Vassar, she began publishing her work, and in the early thirties, along with Elizabeth Bishop and Mary McCarthy, she founded a literary magazine to protest the policies of the *Vassar Review*. *Theory of Flight*, published in the Yale Series of Younger Poets, was quickly followed by *Mediterranean* (1938), *A Turning Wind* (1939), *The Soul and Body of John Brown* (1940), *Wake Island* (1942), *Beast in View* (1944), and *The Green Wave* (1948). A number of these volumes deal directly with social injustice in America and with the atrocities of World War II, a subject of passionate concern to Rukeyser because of her Jewishness and because of her earlier involvement in the fight against fascism in Spain.

After the war, Rukeyser lived briefly in Berkeley, where she taught at the California Labor School, but she spent much of her time "pushing a baby carriage" after the birth of her child in 1947. Although the biographical details of her relationship with the baby's father are obscure, it is clear that Rukeyser remained a single parent. An anonymous benefactor, who turned out to be the wealthy Californian Henriette Durham, helped finance Rukeyser's return to New York, where she began teaching part-time at Sarah Lawrence College and serving as vice-president of the House of Photography. During the fifties, few of Rukeyser's publications were new compositions, a fact that the critic Louise Kertesz attributes to Rukeyser's childcare responsibilities. In such later volumes as *Body of Waking* (1958), *The Speed of Darkness* (1968), *Breaking Open* (1973), and *The Gates* (1976), giving birth became a major source of her imagery, sometimes providing the only solace against the violence she witnessed and protested both in Korea and in Vietnam.

Although, from her early training in aviation to her later biographies of scientists, Rukeyser never relinquished her fascination with technological and rational quests for transcendence, she increasingly turned to mythic and historical female figures in order to trace an ancestry for herself that could counter the destructiveness she associated with American capitalism. While she was faulted by some literary critics for both her optimism and her philosophizing, toward the end of her life she had clearly found an audience through her teaching and in the younger generation of emerging women writers. The poet Anne Sexton wrote "Muriel, mother of everyone," to thank her for a copy of *The Speed of Darkness*; Sexton added that the volume remained on her desk, "flow[ing] out like an infusion of blood into the body."

Boy with His Hair Cut Short

Sunday shuts down on this twentieth-century evening.
The El[1] passes. Twilight and bulb define
the brown room, the overstuffed plum sofa,
the boy, and the girl's thin hands above his head.
A neighbor radio sings stocks, news, serenade.   5

He sits at the table, head down, the young clear neck exposed,
watching the drugstore sign from the tail of his eye;
tattoo, neon, until the eye blears, while his
solicitous tall sister, simple in blue, bending
behind him, cuts his hair with her cheap shears.   10

The arrow's electric red always reaches its mark,
successful neon! He coughs, impressed by that precision.
His child's forehead, forever protected by his cap,
is bleached against the lamplight as he turns head
and steadies to let the snippets drop.   15

Erasing the failure of weeks with level fingers,
she sleeks the fine hair, combing: "You'll look fine tomorrow!
You'll surely find something, they can't keep turning you down;
the finest gentleman's not so trim as you!" Smiling, he raises
the adolescent forehead wrinkling ironic now.   20

He sees his decent suit laid out, new-pressed,
his carfare on the shelf. He lets his head fall, meeting
her earnest hopeless look, seeing the sharp blades splitting,
the darkened room, the impersonal sign, her motion,
the blue vein, bright on her temple, pitifully beating.   25

1938

1. The elevated train, part of the New York subway system that used to run above the street.

More of a Corpse than a Woman

Give them my regards when you go to the school reunion;
and at the marriage-supper, say that I'm thinking about them.
They'll remember my name; I went to the movies with that one,
feeling the weight of their death where she sat at my elbow;
    she never said a word,   5
    but all of them were heard.

all of them alike, expensive girls, the leaden friends:
one used to play the piano, one of them once wrote a sonnet,
one even seemed awakened enough to photograph wheatfields—
the dull girls with the educated minds and technical passions—   10
    pure love was their employment,
    they tried it for enjoyment.

Meet them at the boat: they've brought the souvenirs of boredom,
a seashell from the faltering monarchy;
the nose of a marble saint; and from the battlefield,   15
an empty shell divulged from a flower-bed.
    The lady's wealthy breath
    perfumes the air with death.

The leaden lady faces the fine, voluptuous woman,
faces a rising world bearing its gifts in its hands.   20
Kisses her casual dreams upon the lips she kisses,
risen, she moves away; takes others; moves away.
    Inadequate to love,
    supposes she's enough.

Give my regards to the well-protected woman,   25
I knew the ice-cream girl, we went to school together.
There's something to bury, people, when you begin to bury.
When your women are ready and rich in their wish for the world,
    destroy the leaden heart,
    we've a new race to start.   30

1938

Who in One Lifetime

Who in one lifetime sees all causes lost,
Herself dismayed and helpless, cities down,
Love made monotonous fear and the sad-faced
Inexorable armies and the falling plane,
Has sickness, sickness. Introspective and whole,   5

She knows how several madnesses are born,
Seeing the integrated never fighting well,
The flesh too vulnerable, the eyes tear-torn.

She finds a pre-surrender on all sides:
Treaty before the war, ritual impatience turn   10
The camps of ambush to chambers of imagery.
She holds belief in the world, she stays and hides
Life in her own defeat, stands, though her whole world burn,
A childless goddess of fertility.

June 1941   1944

From Letter to the Front

VII

To be a Jew in the twentieth century
Is to be offered a gift. If you refuse,
Wishing to be invisible, you choose
Death of the spirit, the stone insanity.
Accepting, take full life. Full agonies: 5
Your evening deep in labyrinthine blood
Of those who resist, fail, and resist; and God
Reduced to a hostage among hostages.

The gift is torment. Not alone the still
Torture, isolation; or torture of the flesh.   10
That may come also. But the accepting wish,
The whole and fertile spirit as guarantee
For every human freedom, suffering to be free,
Daring to live for the impossible.

                                                       1944

The Birth of Venus[2]

Risen in a
welter of waters.

Not as he saw her
standing upon a frayed and lovely surf
clean-riding the graceful leafy breezes   5
clean-poised and easy. Not yet.

2. The Roman name for the Greek goddess of
love and beauty, Aphrodite, who was born from
the ocean. The scene of her birth is depicted in a
famous painting by Sandro Botticelli (1444?–
1510).

But born in a
tidal wave of the father's overthrow,
the old rule killed and its mutilated sex.

The testicles of the father-god, father of fathers,   10
sickled off by his son, the next god Time.
Sickled off. Hurled into the ocean.
In all that blood and foam.
among raving and generation,
of semen and the sea born, the   15
great goddess rises.

           However, possibly,
on the long worldward voyage flowing,
horror gone down in birth, the curse, being changed,
being used, is translated far at the margin into   20
our rose and saving image, curling toward a shore
early and April, with certainly shells, certainly blossoms.

And the girl, the wellborn, goddess, human love—
young-known, new-knowing, mouth flickering, sure eyes—
rides shoreward, from death to us as we are at this moment on   25
the crisp delightful Botticellian wave.

                                         1958

The Poem as Mask

Orpheus[3]

When I wrote of the women in their dances and wildness,
    it was a mask,
on their mountain, gold-hunting, singing, in orgy,
it was a mask; when I wrote of the god,
fragmented, exiled from himself, his life, the love gone down
    with song,
it was myself, split open, unable to speak, in exile from myself.   5

There is no mountain, there is no god, there is memory
of my torn life, myself split open in sleep, the rescued child
beside me among the doctors, and a word
of rescue from the great eyes.

No more masks! No more mythologies!   10

3. The subject of the poem is the mythical Greek singer and poet whose music had magical powers over humans and animals, and who was torn to pieces by the Maenads, a band of wild women. He was the son of Apollo, the god of poetry and the sun.

Now, for the first time, the god lifts his hand,
the fragments join in me with their own music.

                                                          1968

The Power of Suicide[4]

The potflower on the windowsill says to me
In words that are green-edged red leaves:
Flower   flower   flower   flower
Today for the sake of all the dead   Burst into flower.

1963   1968

Käthe Kollwitz[5]

I

Held between wars
my lifetime
                    among wars, the big hands of the world of death
my lifetime
listens to yours.   5

The faces of the sufferers
in the street, in dailiness,
their lives showing
through their bodies
a look as of music   10
the revolutionary look
that says   I am in the world
to change the world
my lifetime
is to love to endure to suffer the music   15
to set its portrait
up as a sheet of the world
the most moving the most alive
Easter and bone
and Faust[6] walking among the flowers of the world   20
and the child alive within the living woman, music of man,
and death holding my lifetime between great hands

---

4. The poem has been read as a response to the
suicide of the American poet Sylvia Plath
(1932–1963).
5. German graphic artist and sculptor (1867–
1945), famous especially for her searing drawings and prints of workers, mothers and children,
and the horrors of war. The poem quotes her
words, and recalls a number of her works.
6. The questing intellectual hero of Johann
Wolfgang von Goethe's epic poem *Faust*. In
one scene, Faust is uplifted when he hears the
church bells and children's choir on Easter
morning.

the hands of enduring life
that suffers the gifts and madness of full life, on earth, in our time,
and through my life, through my eyes, through my arms
     and hands   25
may give the face of this music in portrait waiting for
the unknown person
held in the two hands, you.

II

Woman as gates, saying:
"The process is after all like music,   30
like the development of a piece of music.
The fugues come back and
                   again and again
interweave.
A theme may seem to have been put aside,   35
but it keeps returning—
the same thing modulated,
somewhat changed in form.
Usually richer.
And it is very good that this is so."   40

A woman pouring her opposites.
"After all there are happy things in life too.
Why do you show only the dark side?"
"I could not answer this. But I know—
in the beginning my impulse to know   45
the working life
              had little to do with
pity or sympathy.
           I simply felt
that the life of the workers was beautiful."   50

She said, "I am groping in the dark."

She said, "When the door opens, of sensuality,
then you will understand it too. The struggle begins.
Never again to be free of it,
often you will feel it to be your enemy.   55
Sometimes
you will almost suffocate,
such joy it brings."

Saying of her husband: "My wish
is to die after Karl.   60
I know no person who can love as he can,
with his whole soul.

Often this love has oppressed me;
I wanted to be free.
But often too it has made me   65
so terribly happy."[7]

She said: "We rowed over to Carrara[8] at dawn,
climbed up to the marble quarries
and rowed back at night. The drops of water
fell like glittering stars   70
from our oars."

She said: "As a matter of fact,
I believe
          that bisexuality
is almost   a necessary factor   75
in artistic production; at any rate,
the tinge of masculinity within me
helped me
          in my work."

She said: "The only technique I can still manage.   80
It's hardly a technique at all, lithography.
In it
          only the essentials count."

A tight-lipped man in a restaurant last night saying to me:
"Kollwitz?   She's too black-and-white."[9]   85

III

Held among wars, watching
    all of them
    all these people
    weavers,
    Carmagnole[1]   90

Looking at
    all of them
    death, the children
    patients in waiting-rooms
    famine   95
    the street
    the corpse with the baby
    floating, on the dark river

7. Karl Kollwitz, a pioneering doctor for the
poor, was deeply supportive of his wife's work.
8. City in central Italy, center of the marble industry.
9. Kollwitz worked almost exclusively in black
and white.
1. The title of a famous series of prints (Italian:
revolutionary songs and dances).

A woman seeing
    the violent, inexorable   100
    movement of nakedness
    and the confession of No
    the confession of great weakness, war,
    all streaming to one son killed, Peter;[2]
even the son left living; repeated,   105
    the father, the mother; the grandson
    another Peter killed in another war:[3] firestorm;
    dark, light, as two hands,
    this pole and that pole as the gates.

What would happen if one woman told the truth about her life? 110
    The world would split open

IV / Song : The Calling-Up

Rumor, stir of ripeness
rising within this girl
sensual blossoming
of meaning, its light and form.   115

The birth-cry summoning
out of the male, the father
from the warm woman
a mother in response.

The word of death   120
calls up the fight with stone
wrestle with grief with time
from the material make
an art harder than bronze.

V / Self-Portrait[4]

Mouth looking directly at you   125
eyes in their inwardness looking
directly at you
half light   half darkness
woman, strong, German, young artist
flows into   130
wide sensual mouth meditating
looking right at you
eyes shadowed with brave hand
looking deep at you
flows into   135

---

2. Kollwitz's younger son, Peter, was killed in World War I.

3. Her grandson Peter was killed in Russia dur-ing World War II.

4. Kollwitz drew self-portraits throughout her life.

wounded brave mouth
grieving and hooded eyes
alive, German, in her first War
flows into
strength of the worn face 140
a skein of lines
broods, flows into
mothers among the war graves
bent over death
facing the father 145
stubborn upon the field
flows into
the marks of her knowing—
Nie Wieder Krieg[5]
repeated in the eyes 150
flows into
"Seedcorn must not be ground"[6]
and the grooved cheek
lips drawn fine
the down-drawn grief 155
face of our age
flows into
Pieta,[7] mother and
between her knees
life as her son in death 160
pouring from the sky of
one more war
flows into
face almost obliterated
hand over the mouth forever 165
hand over one eye now
the other great eye
closed

1968

Myth

Long afterward, Oedipus,[8] old and blinded, walked the
roads.   He smelled a familiar smell.   It was

5. "No More War," the title of another famous set of prints.
6. Title of her last work, depicting a mother protecting her young children; the title means that the youth who will provide the next generation must not be destroyed in war.
7. Italian, "pity"; a term traditionally applied to representations of the Virgin Mary sorrowing over the dead body of Christ, and used by Koll-

witz as the title for drawings of mothers mourning their dead children.
8. According to Greek myth, a king of Thebes who saved the city from plague by answering a riddle posed by a monster called the Sphinx, then discovered that he had unknowingly killed his father and married his mother. Horrified by his deeds, he put out his eyes and went into exile.

the Sphinx.   Oedipus said, "I want to ask one question.
Why didn't I recognize my mother?"   "You gave the
wrong answer," said the Sphinx.   "But that was what   5
made everything possible," said Oedipus.   "No," she said.
"When I asked, What walks on four legs in the morning,
two at noon, and three in the evening, you answered,
Man.   You didn't say anything about woman."
"When you say Man," said Oedipus, "you include women   10
too. Everyone knows that."   She said, "That's what
you think."

1973

Along History

Along history, forever
   some woman dancing,
   making shapes on the air;
   forever a man
   riding a good horse,   5
   sitting the dark horse well,
   his penis erect with
      fantasy

1973

TILLIE OLSEN

c. 1913–

"In the twenty years I bore and reared my children, usually had to work on a
paid job as well, the simplest circumstances for creation did not exist," wrote
Tillie Olsen in *Silences* (1962), an essay in which she explored the "relationship of circumstances—including class, color, sex" to "the unnatural thwarting
of what struggles to come into being." Later, in an equally important essay,
One Out of Twelve: Women Who Are Writers in Our Century (1971), Olsen
made the connection between gender and silence even more direct: "We
[women] who write are survivors, '*only's*,'" she declared, defining a "survivor"
as "one who must bear witness for those who foundered," and explaining again
the "cost of 'discontinuity'" in her own life. Yet despite the pressures of such
discontinuity, Olsen herself has managed to produce a significant group of extraordinarily accomplished tales.

  Born in Nebraska, Tillie Olsen dropped out of high school in the eleventh
grade to enter the world of what she calls "everyday" jobs. A member of the
depression generation, she began early to work for social and political causes.
She struggled to organize packinghouse workers in Omaha and Kansas City,
joined the Young Communist League, and was involved in the San Francisco

labor movement, including the general strike of 1934. Even while she was engaged in such activism, however, Olsen had begun to write. A chapter of a novel appeared in the *Partisan Review* in 1934, and for several more years she continued to work on the book. At last, however, "it had," as she herself tells us, "to be set aside, never to come to completion," though a "rewoven" version of it was finally published as *Yonnondio: From the Thirties* (1974).

Married in 1943 to Jack Olsen, a printer and, like herself, an activist passionately committed to the labor movement, Olsen had four children and did not begin to write again until the 1950s, when her youngest daughter was five years old. In eight years, she produced the four stories that were collected in her distinguished volume *Tell Me a Riddle* (1961), a book whose title novella, with its searching examination of the mind and memories of a dying woman, received the O. Henry Award as the best American story in the year when it was published. A prodigious reader ("public libraries were my college") whose interest in women's writing was rekindled by the resurgence of feminism in the sixties, Olsen has been instrumental in bringing important forgotten books back into print. An afterword of hers appears with Rebecca Harding Davis's *Life in the Iron-Mills* (rpt. 1971), while her meticulously documented critical volume *Silences* (1978) further explores the crucial power of circumstance.

Between 1969 and 1974, Olsen taught at Amherst, Stanford, M.I.T., and the University of Massachusetts, Boston. More recently, she has received fellowships from the Guggenheim Foundation and the National Endowment for the Humanities, as well as several honorary degrees. Throughout this period, mindful of her "hatred for all that, societally rooted . . . slows, impairs, silences writers," she has continued her struggle to "re-dedicate and encourage" other women to the powers and possibilities of their own creativity.

Tell Me a Riddle

"These Things Shall Be"

1

For forty-seven years they had been married. How deep back the stubborn, gnarled roots of the quarrel reached, no one could say—but only now, when tending to the needs of others no longer shackled them together, the roots swelled up visible, split the earth between them, and the tearing shook even to the children, long since grown.

Why now, why now? wailed Hannah.

As if when we grew up weren't enough, said Paul.

Poor Ma. Poor Dad. It hurts so for both of them, said Vivi. They never had very much; at least in old age they should be happy.

Knock their heads together, insisted Sammy; tell 'em: you're too old for this kind of thing; no reason not to get along now.

Lennie wrote to Clara: They've lived over so much together; what could possibly tear them apart?

Something tangible enough.

Arthritic hands, and such work as he got, occasional. Poverty all his life, and there was little breath left for running. He could not, could not turn away from this desire: to have the troubling of responsibility, the fretting with money, over and done with; to be free, to be *carefree* where success was not measured by accumulation, and there was use for the vitality still in him.

There was a way. They could sell the house, and with the money join his lodge's Haven, co-operative for the aged. Happy communal life, and was he not already an official; had he not helped organize it, raise funds, served as a trustee?

But she—would not consider it.

"What do we need all this for?" he would ask loudly, for her hearing aid was turned down and the vacuum was shrilling. "Five rooms" (pushing the sofa so she could get into the corner) "furniture" (smoothing down the rug) "floors and surfaces to make work. Tell me, why do we need it?" And he was glad he could ask in a scream.

"Because I'm use't."

"Because you're use't. This is a reason, Mrs. Word Miser? Used to can get unused!"

"Enough unused I have to get used to already. . . . Not enough words?" turning off the vacuum a moment to hear herself answer. "Because soon enough we'll need only a little closet, no windows, no furniture, nothing to make work for but worms. Because now I want room . . . Screech and blow like you're doing, you'll need that closet even sooner . . . Ha, again!" for the vacuum bag wailed, puffed half up, hung stubbornly limp. "This time fix it so it stays; quick before the phone rings and you get too important-busy."

But while he struggled with the motor, it seethed in him. Why fix it? Why have to bother? And if it can't be fixed, have to wring the mind with how to pay the repair? At the Haven they come in with their own machines to clean your room or your cottage; you fish, or play cards, or make jokes in the sun, not with knotty fingers fight to mend vacuums.

Over the dishes, coaxingly: "For once in your life, to be free, to have everything done for you, like a queen."

"I never liked queens."

"No dishes, no garbage, no towel to sop, no worry what to buy, what to eat."

"And what else would I do with my empty hands? Better to eat at my own table when I want, and to cook and eat how I want."

"In the cottages they buy what you ask, and cook it how you like. *You* are the one who always used to say: better mankind born without mouths and stomachs than always to worry for money to buy, to shop, to fix, to cook, to wash, to clean."

"How cleverly you hid that you heard. I said it then because eighteen hours a day I ran. And you never scraped a carrot or knew a dish towel sops. Now—for you and me—who cares? A herring out of a jar is enough. But when *I* want, and nobody to bother." And she turned off her ear button, so she would not have to hear.

But as *he* had no peace, juggling and rejuggling the money to figure: how will I pay for this now?; prying out the storm windows (there they take care of this); jolting in the streetcar on errands (there I would not have to ride to take care of this or that); fending the patronizing relatives just back from Florida (there it matters what one is, not what one can afford), he gave *her* no peace.

"Look! In their bulletin. A reading circle. Twice a week it meets."

"Haumm," her answer of not listening.

"A reading circle. Chekhov they read that you like, and Peretz.[1] Cultured people at the Haven that you would enjoy."

"Enjoy!" She tasted the word. "Now, when it pleases you, you find a reading circle for me. And forty years ago when the children were morsels and there was a Circle, did you stay home with them once so I could go? Even once? You trained me well. I do not need others to enjoy. Others!" Her voice trembled. "Because you want to be there with others. Already it makes me sick to think of you always around others. Clown, grimacer, floormat, yesman, entertainer, whatever they want of you."

And now it was he who turned on the television loud so he need not hear.

Old scar tissue ruptured and the wounds festered anew. Chekhov indeed. She thought without softness of that young wife, who in the deep night hours while she nursed the current baby, and perhaps held another in her lap, would try to stay awake for the only time there was to read. She would feel again the weather of the outside on his cheek when, coming late from a meeting, he would find her so, and stimulated and ardent, sniffing her skin, coax: "I'll put the baby to bed, and you—put the book away, don't read, don't read."

That had been the most beguiling of all the "don't read, put your book away" her life had been. Chekhov indeed!

"Money?" She shrugged him off. "Could we get poorer than once we were? And in America, who starves?"

But as still he pressed:

"Let me alone about money. Was there ever enough? Seven little ones—for every penny I had to ask—and sometimes, remember, there was nothing. But always *I* had to manage. No *you* manage. Rub your nose in it good."

1. I. L. Peretz (1852–1915), Russian author of poems, plays, and stories in Yiddish; "the Jewish Chekhov": Anton Chekov, the Russian writer (1860–1904).

But from those years she had had to manage, old humiliations and terrors rose up, lived again, and forced her to relive them. The children's needings; that grocer's face or this merchant's wife she had had to beg credit from when credit was a disgrace, the scenery of the long blocks walked around when she could not pay; school coming, and the desperate going over the old to see what could yet be remade; the soups of meat bones begged "for-the-dog" one winter. . . .

Enough. Now they had no children. Let *him* wrack his head for how they would live. She would not exchange her solitude for anything. *Never again to be forced to move to the rhythms of others.*

For in this solitude she had won to a reconciled peace.

Tranquillity from having the empty house no longer an enemy, for it stayed clean—not as in the days when it was her family, the life in it, that had seemed the enemy: tracking, smudging, littering, dirtying, engaging her in endless defeating battle—and on whom her endless defeat had been spewed.

The few old books, memorized from rereading; the pictures to ponder (the magnifying glass superimposed on her heavy eye-glasses). Or if she wishes, when he is gone, the phonograph, that if she turns up very loud and strains, she can hear: the ordered sounds and the struggling.

Out in the garden, growing things to nurture. Birds to be kept out of the pear tree, and when the pears are heavy and ripe, the old fury of work, for all must be canned, nothing wasted.

And her one social duty (for she will not go to luncheons or meetings) the boxes of old clothes left with her, as with a life-practised eye for finding what is still wearable within the worn (again the magnifying glass superimposed on the heavy glasses) she scans and sorts—this for rag or rummage, that for mending and cleaning, and this for sending abroad.

Being able at last to live within, and not move to the rhythms of others, as life had helped her to: denying; removing; isolating; taking the children one by one; then deafening, half-blinding—and at last, presenting her solitude.

And in it she had won to a reconciled peace.

Now he was violating it with his constant campaigning: *Sell the house and move to the Haven.* (You sit, you sit—there too you could sit like a stone.) He was making of her a battleground where old grievances tore. (Turn on your ear button—I am talking.) And stubbornly she resisted—so that from wheedling, reasoning, manipulation, it was bitterness he now started with.

And it came to where every happening lashed up a quarrel.

"I will sell the house anyway," he flung at her one night. "I am putting it up for sale. There will be a way to make you sign."

The television blared, as always it did on the evenings he stayed home, and as always it reached her only as noise. She did not know if the tumult was in her or outside. Snap! she turned the sound off. "Shadows," she whispered to him, pointing to the screen, "look, it is only shadows." And in a scream: "Did you say that you will sell the house? Look at me, not at that. I am no shadow. You cannot sell without me."

"Leave on the television. I am watching."

"Like Paulie, like Jenny, a four-year-old. Staring at shadows. *You cannot sell the house.*"

"I will. We are going to the Haven. There you would not hear the television when you do not want it. I could sit in the social room and watch. You could lock yourself up to smell your unpleasantness in a room by yourself—for who would want to come near you?"

"No, no selling." A whisper now.

"The television is shadows. Mrs. Enlightened! Mrs. Cultured! A world comes into your house—and it is shadows. People you would never meet in a thousand lifetimes. Wonders. When you were four years old, yes, like Paulie, like Jenny, did you know of Indian dances, alligators, how they use bamboo in Malaya? No, you scratched in your dirt with the chickens and thought Olshana[2] was the world. Yes, Mrs. Unpleasant, I will sell the house, for there better can we be rid of each other than here."

She did not know if the tumult was outside, or in her. Always a ravening inside, a pull to the bed, to lie down, to succumb.

"Have you thought maybe Ma should let a doctor have a look at her?" asked their son Paul after Sunday dinner, regarding his mother crumpled on the couch, instead of, as was her custom, busying herself in Nancy's kitchen.

"Why not the President too?"

"Seriously, Dad. This is the third Sunday she's lain down like that after dinner. Is she that way at home?"

"A regular love affair with the bed. Every time I start to talk to her."

Good protective reaction, observed Nancy to herself. The workings of hos-til-ity.

"Nancy could take her. I just don't like how she looks. Let's have Nancy arrange an appointment."

"You think she'll go?" regarding his wife gloomily. "All right, we have to have doctor bills, we have to have doctor bills." Loudly: "Something hurts you?"

2. Village in Russia.

She startled, looked to his lips. He repeated: "Mrs. Take It Easy, something hurts?"

"Nothing. . . . Only you."

"A woman of honey. That's why you're lying down?"

"Soon I'll get up to do the dishes, Nancy."

"Leave them, Mother, I like it better this way."

"Mrs. Take It Easy, Paul says you should start ballet. You should go to see a doctor and ask: how soon can you start ballet?"

"A doctor?" she begged. "Ballet?"

"We were talking, Ma," explained Paul, "you don't seem any too well. It would be a good idea for you to see a doctor for a checkup."

"I get up now to do the kitchen. Doctors are bills and foolishness, my son. I need no doctors."

"At the Haven," he could not resist pointing out, "a doctor is *not* bills. He lives beside you. You start to sneeze, he is there before you open up a Kleenex. You can be sick there for free, all you want."

"Diarrhea of the mouth, is there a doctor to make you dumb?"

"Ma. Promise me you'll go. Nancy will arrange it."

"It's all of a piece when you think of it," said Nancy, "the way she attacks my kitchen, scrubbing under every cup hook, doing the inside of the oven so I can't enjoy Sunday dinner, knowing that half-blind or not, she's going to find every speck of dirt. . . ."

"Don't Nancy, I've told you—it's the only way she knows to be useful. What did the *doctor* say?"

"A real fatherly lecture. Sixty-nine is young these days. Go out, enjoy life, find interests. Get a new hearing aid, this one is antiquated. Old age is sickness only if one makes it so. Geriatrics, Inc."

"So there was nothing physical."

"Of course there was. How can you live to yourself like she does without there being? Evidence of a kidney disorder, and her blood count is low. He gave her a diet, and she's to come back for follow-up and lab work. . . . But he was clear enough: Number One prescription —start living like a human being. When I think of your dad, who could really play the invalid with that arthritis of his as active as a teenager, and twice as much fun. . . ."

"You didn't tell me the doctor says your sickness is in you, how you live." He pushed his advantage. "Life and enjoyments you need better than medicine. And this diet, how can you keep it? To weigh each morsel and scrape away the bits of fat to make this soup, that pudding. There, at the Haven, they have a dietician, they would do it for you."

She is silent.

"You would feel better there, I know it," he says gently. "There there is life and enjoyments all around."

"What is the matter, Mr. Importantbusy, you have no card game or meeting you can go to?"—turning her face to the pillow.

For a while he cut his meetings and going out, fussed over her diet, tried to wheedle her into leaving the house, brought in visitors:

"I should come to a fashion tea. I should sit and look at pretty babies in clothes I cannot buy. This is pleasure?"

"Always you are better than everyone else. The doctor said you should go out. Mrs. Brem comes to you with goodness and you turn her away."

"Because *you* asked her to, she asked me."

"They won't come back. People you need, the doctor said. Your own cousins I asked; they were willing to come and make peace as if nothing had happened. . . ."

"No more crushers of people, pushers, hypocrites, around me. No more in *my* house. You go to them if you like."

"Kind he is to visit. And you, like ice."

"A babbler. All my life around babblers. Enough!"

"She's even worse, Dad? Then let her stew a while," advised Nancy. "You can't let it destroy you; it's a psychological thing, maybe too far gone for any of us to help."

So he let her stew. More and more she lay silent in bed, and sometimes did not even get up to make the meals. No longer was the tongue-lashing inevitable if he left the coffee cup where it did not belong, or forgot to take out the garbage or mislaid the broom. The birds grew bold that summer and for once pocked the pears, undisturbed.

A bellyful of bitterness and every day the same quarrel in a new way and a different old grievance the quarrel forced her to enter and relive. And the new torment: I am not really sick, the doctor said it, then why do I feel so sick?

One night she asked him: "You have a meeting tonight? Do not go. Stay . . . with me."

He had planned to watch "This Is Your Life" anyway, but half sick himself from the heavy heat, and sickening therefore the more after the brooks and woods of the Haven, with satisfaction he grated:

"Hah, Mrs. Live Alone And Like It wants company all of a sudden. It doesn't seem so good the time of solitary when she was a girl exile in Siberia. 'Do not go. Stay with me.' A new song for Mrs. Free As A

Bird. Yes, I am going out, and while I am gone chew this aloneness good, and think how you keep us both from where if you want people you do not need to be alone."

"Go, go. All your life you have gone without me."

After him she sobbed curses he had not heard in years, old-country curses from their childhood: Grow, oh shall you grow like an onion, with your head in the ground. Like the hide of a drum shall you be, beaten in life, beaten in death. Oh shall you be like a chandelier, to hang, and to burn. . . .

She was not in their bed when he came back. She lay on the cot on the sun-porch. All week she did not speak or come near him; nor did he try to make peace or care for her.

He slept badly, so used to her next to him. After all the years, old harmonies and dependencies deep in their bodies; she curled to him, or he coiled to her each warmed, warming, turning as the other turned, the nights a long embrace.

It was not the empty bed or the storm that woke him, but a faint singing. *She* was singing. Shaking off the drops of rain, the lightning riving her lifted face, he saw her so; the cot covers on the floor.

"This is a private concert?" he asked. "Come in, you are wet."

"I can breathe now," she answered; "my lungs are rich." Though indeed the sound was hardly a breath.

"Come in, come in." Loosing the bamboo shades.

"Look how wet you are." Half helping, half carrying her, still faint-breathing her song.

A Russian love song of fifty years ago.

He had found a buyer, but before he told her, he called together those children who were close enough to come. Paul, of course, Sammy from New Jersey, Hannah from Connecticut, Vivi from Ohio.

With a kindling of energy for her beloved visitors, she arrayed the house, cooked and baked. She was not prepared for the solemn after-dinner conclave, they too probing in and tearing. Her frightened eyes watched from mouth to mouth as each spoke.

His stories were eloquent and funny of her refusal to go back to the doctor; of the scorned invitations; of her stubborn silences or the bile "Like a Niagara"; of her contrariness: "If I clean it's no good how I cleaned; if I don't clean, I'm still a master who thinks he has a slave."

("Vinegar he poured on me all his life; I am well marinated; how can I be honey now?")

Deftly he marched in the rightness for moving to the Haven; their money from social security free for visiting the children; not sucked into daily needs and into the house; the activities in the Haven for him;

but mostly the Haven for *her*: her health, her need of care, distraction, amusement, friends who shared her interests.

"This does offer an outlet for Dad," said Paul; "he's always been an active person. And economic peace of mind isn't to be sneezed at, either. I could use a little of that myself."

But when they asked: "And you, Ma, how do you feel about it?" could only whisper:

"For him it is good. It is not for me. I can no longer live between people."

"You lived all your life *for* people," Vivi cried.

"Not with." Suffering doubly for the unhappiness on her children's faces.

"You have to find some compromise," Sammy insisted. "Maybe sell the house and buy a trailer. After forty-seven years there's surely some way you can find to live in peace."

"There is no help, my children. Different things we need."

"Then live alone!" He could control himself no longer. "I have a buyer for the house. Half the money for you, half for me. Either alone or with me to the Haven. You think I can live any longer as we are doing now?"

"Ma doesn't have to make a decision this minute, however you feel, Dad," Paul said quickly, "and you wouldn't want her to. Let's let it lay a few months, and then talk some more."

"I think I can work it out to take Mother home with me for a while," Hannah said. "You both look terrible, but especially you, Mother. I'm going to ask Phil to have a look at you."

"Sure," cracked Sammy. "What's the use of a doctor husband if you can't get free service out of him once in a while for the family? And absence might make the heart . . . you know."

"There was something after all," Paul told Nancy in a colorless voice. "That was Hannah's Phil calling. Her gall bladder. . . . Surgery."

"Her *gall* bladder. If that isn't classic. 'Bitter as gall'—talk of psychosom——"

He stepped closer, put his hand over her mouth and said in the same colorless, plodding voice. "We have to get Dad. They operated at once. The cancer was everywhere, surrounding the liver, everywhere. They did what they could . . . at best she has a year. Dad . . . we have to tell him."

II

Honest in his weakness when they told him, and that she was not to know. "I'm not an actor. She'll know right away by how I am. Oh that poor woman. I am old too, it will break me into pieces. Oh that poor

woman. She will spit on me: 'So my sickness was how I live.' Oh Paulie,
how she will be, that poor woman. Only she should not suffer. . . . I
can't stand sickness, Paulie, I can't go with you."

But went. And play-acted.

"A grand opening and you did not even wait for me. . . . A good
thing Hannah took you with her."

"Fashion teas I needed. They cut out what tore in me; just in my
throat something hurts yet. . . . Look! so many flowers, like a funeral.
Vivi called, did Hannah tell you? And Lennie from San Francisco, and
Clara; and Sammy is coming." Her gnome's face pressed happily into
the flowers.

> It is impossible to predict in these cases, but once over the
> immediate effects of the operation, she should have several
> months of comparative well-being.
>
> *The money, where will come the money?*
>
> Travel with her, Dad. Don't take her home to the old associ-
> ations. The other children will want to see her.
>
> *The money, where will I wring the money?*
>
> Whatever happens, she is not to know. No, you can't ask her
> to sign papers to sell the house; nothing to upset her. Borrow in-
> stead. Then, after. . . .
>
> *I had wanted to leave you each a few dollars to make life eas-
> ier, as other fathers do. There will be nothing left now. (Failure!
> you and your "business is exploitation." Why didn't you make it
> when it could be made?—Is that what you're thinking, Sammy?)*
>
> Sure she's unreasonable, Dad—but you have to stay with
> her. If there's to be any happiness in what's left of her life, it de-
> pends on you.
>
> *Prop me up, children, think of me, too. Shuffled, chained
> with her, bitter woman. No Haven, and the little money going. . . .
> How happy she looks, poor creature.*

The look of excitement. The straining to hear everything (the new
hearing aid turned full). Why are you so happy, dying woman?

How the petals are, fold on fold, and the gladioli color. The autumn
air.

Stranger grandsons, tall above the little gnome grandmother, the little spry grandfather. Paul in a frenzy of picture-taking before going.

She, wandering the great house. Feeling the books; laughing at the
maple shoemaker's bench of a hundred years ago used as a table. The
ear turned to music.

"Let us go home. See how good I walk now." "One step from the
hospital," he answers, "and she wants to fly. Wait till Doctor Phil says."

"Look—the birds too are flying home. Very good Phil is and will not show it, but he is sick of sickness by the time he comes home."

"Mrs. Telepathy, to read minds," he answers; "read mine what it says: when the trunks of medicines become a suitcase, then we will go."

The grandboys, they do not know what to say to us. . . . Hannah, she runs around here, there, when is there time for herself?

Let us go home. Let us go home.

Musing; gentleness—*but for the incidents of the rabbi in the hospital, and of the candles of benediction.*

Of the rabbi in the hospital:

Now tell me what happened, Mother.

From the sleep I awoke, Hannah's Phil, and he stands there like a devil in a dream and calls me by name. I cannot hear. I think he prays. Go away, please, I tell him, I am not a believer. Still he stands, while my heart knocks with fright.

You scared *him*, Mother. He thought you were delirious.

Who sent him? Why did he come to me?

It is a custom. The men of God come to visit those of their religion they might help. The hospital makes up the list for them—race, religion—and you are on the Jewish list.

Not for rabbis. At once go and make them change. Tell them to write: Race, human; Religion, none.

And of the candles of benediction:

Look how you have upset yourself, Mrs. Excited Over Nothing. Pleasant memories you should leave.

Go in, go back to Hannah and the lights. Two weeks I saw candles and said nothing. But she asked me.

So what was so terrible? She forgets you never did, she asks you to light the Friday candles and say the benediction like Phil's mother when she visits. If the candles give her pleasure, why shouldn't she have the pleasure?

Not for pleasure she does it. For emptiness. Because his family does. Because all around her do.

That is not a good reason too? But you did not hear her. For heritage, she told you. For the boys, from the past they should have tradition.

Superstition! From our ancestors, savages, afraid of the dark, of themselves: mumbo words and magic lights to scare away ghosts.

She told you: how it started does not take away the goodness. For centuries, peace in the house it means.

Swindler! does she look back on the dark centuries? Candles bought instead of bread and stuck into a potato for a candlestick?

Religion that stifled and said: in Paradise, woman, you will be the
footstool of your husband, and in life—poor chosen Jew—ground
under, despised, trembling in cellars. And cremated. And cremated.

This is religion's fault? You think you are still an orator of the
1905 revolution?[3] Where are the pills for quieting? Which are they?

Heritage. How have we come from our savage past, how no
longer to be savages—this to teach. To look back and learn what hu-
manizes—this to teach. To smash all ghettos that still divide us—not
to go back, not to go back—this to teach. Learned books in the
house, will man live or die, and she gives to her boys—superstition.

Hannah that is so good to you. Take your pill, Mrs. Excited For
Nothing, swallow.

Heritage! But when did I have time to teach? Of Hannah I
asked only hands to help.

Swallow.

Otherwise—musing; gentleness.

Not to travel. To go home.

The children want to see you. We have to show them you are as
thorny a flower as ever.

Not to travel.

Vivi wants you should see her new baby. She sent the tickets—airplane tickets—a Mrs. Roosevelt[4] she wants to make of you. To Vivi's
we have to go.

A new baby. How many warm, seductive babies. She holds him
stiffly, *away* from her, so that he wails. And a long shudder begins,
and the sweat beads on her forehead.

"Hush, shush," croons the grandfather, lifting him back. "You
should forgive your grandmamma, little prince, she has never held
a baby before, only seen them in glass cases. Hush, shush."

"You're tired, Ma," says Vivi. "The travel and the noisy dinner.
I'll take you to lie down."

(*A long travel from, to, what the feel of a baby evokes.*)

In the airplane, cunningly designed to encase from motion (no
wind, no feel of flight), she had sat severely and still, her face turned to
the sky through which they cleaved and left no scar.

So this was how it looked, the determining, the crucial sky, and this
was how man moved through it, remote above the dwindled earth, the
concealed human life. Vulnerable life, that could scar.

3. Attempt to establish a democracy in czarist   President Franklin D. Roosevelt, was famous for
Russia. It was crushed by totalitarian terror.   extensive, frequent travels in the days when air-
4. Eleanor Roosevelt (1884–1962), wife of   plane travel was unusual.

There was a steerage ship[5] of memory that shook across a great, circular sea: clustered, ill human beings; and through the thick-stained air, tiny fretting waters in a window round like the airplane's—sun round, moon round. (The round thatched roofs of Olshana.) Eye round—like the smaller window that framed distance the solitary year of exile when only her eyes could travel, and no voice spoke. And the polar winds hurled themselves across snow trackless and endless and white—like the clouds which had closed together below and hidden the earth.

Now they put a baby in her lap. Do not ask me, she would have liked to beg. Enough the worn face of Vivi, the remembered grandchildren, I cannot, cannot. . . .

Cannot what? Unnatural grandmother, not able to make herself embrace a baby.

She lay there in the bed of the two little girls, her new hearing aid turned full, listening to the sound of the children going to sleep, the baby's fretful crying and hushing, the clatter of dishes being washed and put away. They thought she slept. Still she rode on.

It was not that she had not loved her babies, her children. The love —the passion of tending—had risen with the need like a torrent; and like a torrent drowned and immolated all else. But when the need was done—oh the power that was lost in the painful damming back and drying up of what still surged, but had nowhere to go. Only the thin pulsing left that could not quiet, suffering over lives one felt, but could no longer hold nor help.

On that torrent she had borne them to their own lives, and the riverbed was desert long years now. Not there would she dwell, a memoried wraith. Surely that was not all, surely there was more. Still the springs, the springs were in her seeking. Somewhere an older power that beat for life. Somewhere coherence, transport, meaning. If they would but leave her in the air now stilled of clamor, in the reconciled solitude, to journey on.

And they put a baby in her lap. Immediacy to embrace, and the breath of *that* past: warm flesh like this that had claims and nuzzled away all else and with lovely mouths devoured; hot-living like an animal—intensely and now; the turning maze; the long drunkenness; the drowning into needing and being needed. Severely she looked back— and the shudder seized her again, and the sweat. Not that way. Not there, not now could she, not yet. . . .

And all that visit, she could not touch the baby.

"Daddy, is it the . . . sickness she's like that?" asked Vivi. "I was so glad to be having the baby—for her. I told Tim, it'll give her more hap-

5. I.e., a ship having only the lowest class of accommodations.

piness than anything, being around a baby again. And she hasn't played with him once."

He was not listening, "Aahh little seed of life, little charmer," he crooned, "Hollywood should see you. A heart of ice you would melt. Kick, kick. The future you'll have for a ball. In 2050 still kick. Kick for your grandaddy then."

Attentive with the older children; sat through their performances (command performance; we command you to be the audience); helped Ann sort autumn leaves to find the best for a school program; listened gravely to Richard tell about his rock collection, while her lips mutely formed the words to remember: *igneous, sedimentary, metamorphic*[6]; looked for missing socks, books and bus tickets; watched the children whoop after their grandfather who knew how to tickle, chuck, lift, toss, do tricks, tell secrets, make jokes, match riddle for riddle. (Tell me a riddle, Grammy. I know no riddles, child.) Scrubbed sills and woodwork and furniture in every room; folded the laundry; straightened drawers; emptied the heaped baskets waiting for ironing (while he or Vivi or Tim nagged: You're supposed to rest here, you've been sick) but to none tended or gave food—and could not touch the baby.

After a week she said: "Let us go home. Today call about the tickets."

"You have important business, Mrs. Inahurry? The President waits to consult with you?" He shouted, for the fear of the future raced in him. "The clothes are still warm from the suitcase, your children cannot show enough how glad they are to see you, and you want home. There is plenty of time for home. We cannot be with the children at home."

"Blind to around you as always: the little ones sleep four in a room because we take their bed. We are two more people in a house with a new baby, and no help."

"Vivi is happy so. The children should have their grandparents a while, she told to me. I should have my mommy and daddy. . . . ."

"Babbler and blind. Do you look at her so tired? How she starts to talk and she cries? I am not strong enough yet to help. Let us go home."

(To reconciled solitude.)

For it seemed to her the crowded noisy house was listening to her, listening for her. She could feel it like a great ear pressed under her heart. And everything knocked: quick constant raps: let me in, let me in.

How was it that soft reaching tendrils also became blows that knocked?

---

6. Basic types of rocks.

C'mon, Grandma, I want to show you. . . .

Tell me a riddle, Grandma. (*I know no riddles.*)

Look, Grammy, he's so dumb he can't even find his hands. (Dody and the baby on a blanket over the fermenting autumn mould.)

I made them—for you. (Ann) (Flat paper dolls with aprons that lifted on scalloped skirts that lifted on flowered pants; hair of yarn and great ringed questioning eyes.)

Watch me, Grandma. (Richard snaking up the tree, hanging exultant, free, with one hand at the top. Below Dody hunching over in pretend-cooking.)

(*Climb too, Dody, climb and look*)

Be my nap bed, Grammy. (The "No!" too late.) Morty's abandoned heaviness, while his fingers ladder up and down her hearing-aid cord to his drowsy chant: eentsiebeentsiespider. (*Children trust.*)

It's to start off your own rock collection, Grandma.

That's a trilobite fossil, 200 million years old (millions of years on a boy's mouth) and that one's obsidian, black glass.

Knocked and knocked.

Mother, I *told* you the teacher said we had to bring it back all filled out this morning. Didn't you even ask Daddy? Then tell *me* which plan and I'll check it: evacuate or stay in the city or wait for you to come and take me away. (Seeing the look of straining to hear.) It's for Disaster, Grandma.[7] (*Children trust.*)

Vivi in the maze of the long, the lovely drunkenness. The old old noises: baby sounds; screaming of a mother flayed to exasperation; children quarreling; children playing; singing; laughter.

And Vivi's tears and memories, spilling so fast, half the words not understood.

She had started remembering out loud deliberately, so her mother would know the past was cherished, still lived in her.

Nursing the baby: My friends marvel, and I tell them, oh it's easy to be such a cow. I remember how beautiful my mother seemed nursing my brother, and the milk just flows. . . . Was that Davy? It must have been Davy. . . .

Lowering a hem: How did you ever . . . when I think how you made everything we wore . . . Tim, just think, seven kids and Mommy sewed everything . . . do I remember you sang while you sewed? That white

---

7. During the 1950s, with the encouragement of the federal government, a number of American communities built fallout shelters and drew up evacuation ("Disaster") plans to be used in a nuclear attack.

dress with the red apples on the skirt you fixed over for me, was it Hannah's or Clara's before it was mine?

Washing sweaters: Ma, I'll never forget, one of those days so nice you washed clothes outside; one of the first spring days it must have been. The bubbles just danced up and down while you scrubbed, and we chased after, and you stopped to show us how to blow our own bubbles with green onion stalks . . . you always. . . .

"Strong onion, to still make you cry after so many years," her father said, to turn the tears into laughter.

While Richard bent over his homework: Where is it now, do we still have it, the Book of the Martyrs? It always seemed so, well—exalted, when you'd put it on the round table and we'd all look at it together; there was even a halo from the lamp. The lamp with the beaded fringe you could move up and down; they're in style again, pulley lamps like that, but without the fringe. You know the book I'm talking about, Daddy, the Book of the Martyrs, the first picture was a bust of Spartacus? . . . Socrates? I wish there was something like that for the children, Mommy, to give them what you. . . . (And the tears splashed again.)

(What I intended and did not? Stop it, daughter, stop it, leave that time. And he, the hypocrite, sitting there with tears in his eyes—it was nothing to you then, nothing.)

. . . The time you came to school and I almost died of shame because of your accent and because I knew you knew I was ashamed; how could I? . . . Sammy's harmonica and you danced to it once, yes you did, you and Davy squealing in your arms. . . . That time you bundled us up and walked us down to the railway station to stay the night 'cause it was heated and we didn't have any coal, that winter of the strike, you didn't think I remembered that, did you, Mommy? . . . How you'd call us out to see the sunsets. . . .

Day after day, the spilling memories. Worse now, questions, too. Even the grandchildren: Grandma, in the olden days, when you were little. . . .

It was the afternoons that saved.

While they thought she napped, she would leave the mosaic on the wall (of children's drawings, maps, calendars, pictures, Ann's cardboard dolls with their great ringed questioning eyes) and hunch in the girls' closet, on the low shelf where the shoes stood, and the girls' dresses covered.

For that while she would painfully sheathe against the listening house, the tendrils and noises that knocked, and Vivi's spilling memories. Sometimes it helped to braid and unbraid the sashes that dangled, or to trace the pattern on the hoop slips.

Today she had jacks and children under jet trails to forget. Last night, Ann and Dody silhouetted in the window against a sunset of flaming man-made clouds of jet trail, their jacks ball accenting the peaceful noise of dinner being made. Had she told them, yes she had told them of how they played jacks in her village though there was no ball, no jacks. Six stones, round and flat, toss them out, the seventh on the back of the hand, toss, catch and swoop up as many as possible, toss again. . . .

Of stones (repeating Richard) there are three kinds: earth's fire jetting; rock of layered centuries; crucibled new out of the old (*igneous, sedimentary, metamorphic*). But there was that other—frozen to black glass, never to transform or hold the fossil memory . . . (let not my seed fall on stone). There was an ancient one who fought to heights a great rock that crashed back down eternally—eternal labor, freedom, labor . . . (stone will perish, but the word remain[8]). And you, David, who with a stone slew, screaming: Lord, take my heart of stone and give me flesh.

Who was screaming? Why was she back in the common room of the prison, the sun motes dancing in the shafts of light, and the informer being brought in, a prisoner now, like themselves. And Lisa leaping, yes, Lisa, the gentle and tender, biting at the betrayer's jugular. Screaming and screaming.

No, it is the children screaming. Another of Paul and Sammy's terrible fights?

In Vivi's house. Severely: you are in Vivi's house.

Blows, screams, a call: "Grandma!" For her? Oh please not for her. Hide, hunch behind the dresses deeper. But a trembling little body hurls itself beside her—surprised, smothered laughter, arms surround her neck, tears rub dry on her cheek, and words too soft to understand whisper into her ear (Is this where you hide too, Grammy? It's my secret place, we have a secret now).

And the sweat beads, and the long shudder seizes.

It seemed the great ear pressed inside now, and the knocking. "We have to go home," she told him, "I grow ill here."

"It is your own fault, Mrs. Bodybusy, you do not rest, you do too much." He raged, but the fear was in his eyes. "It was a serious operation, they told you to take care. . . . All right, we will go to where you can rest."

But where? Not home to death, not yet. He had thought to Lennie's, to Clara's; beautiful visits with each of the children. She would have to rest first, be stronger. If they could but go to Florida—it glittered before him, the never-realized promise of Florida. California: of course. (The

8. An allusion to the myth of Sisyphus, who was punished in Tartarus (below Hades) by having to roll a huge stone uphill; each time he approached the top, the stone would roll back.

money, the money, dwindling!) Los Angeles first for sun and rest, then to Lennie's in San Francisco.

He told her the next day, "You saw what Nancy wrote: snow and wind back home, a terrible winter. And look at you—all bones and a swollen belly. I called Phil: he said: 'A prescription, Los Angeles sun and rest.'"

She watched the words on his lips. "You have sold the house," she cried, "that is why we do not go home. That is why you talk no more of the Haven. Why there is money for travel. After the children you will drag me to the Haven."

"The Haven! Who thinks of the Haven any more? Tell her, Vivi, tell Mrs. Suspicious: a prescription, sun and rest, to make you healthy. . . . And how could I sell the house without *you*?"

At the place of farewells and greetings, of winds of coming and winds of going, they say their good-byes.

They look back at her with the eyes of others before them: Richard with her own blue blaze; Ann with the Nordic eyes of Tim; Morty's dreaming brown of a great-grandmother he will never know; Dody with the laughing eyes of him who had been her springtide love (who stands beside her now); Vivi's, all tears.

The baby's eyes are closed in sleep.

Good-bye, my children.

III

It is to the back of the great city he brought her, to the dwelling places of the cast-off old. Bounded by two lines of amusement piers to the north and to the south, and between a long straight paving rimmed with black benches facing the sand—sands so wide the ocean is only a far fluting.

In the brief vacation season, some of the boarded stores fronting the sands open, and families, young people and children, may be seen. A little tasselled tram shuttles between the piers, and the lights of roller coasters prink and tweak over those who come to have sensation made in them.

The rest of the year it is abandoned to the old, all else boarded up and still; seemingly empty, except the occasional days and hours when the sun, like a tide, sucks them out of the low rooming houses, casts them on to the benches and sandy rim of the walk—and sweeps them into decaying enclosures back again.

A few newer apartments glint among the low bleached squares. It is in one of these Lennie's Jeannie has arranged their rooms. "Only a few miles north and south people pay hundreds of dollars a month for just this gorgeous air, Grandaddy, just this ocean closeness."

She had been ill on the plane, lay ill for days in the unfamiliar room. Several times the doctor came by—left medicine she would not take. Several times Jeannie drove in the twenty miles from work, still in her Visiting Nurse uniform, the lightness and brightness of her like a healing.

"Who can believe it is winter?" he asked one morning. "Beautiful it is outside like an ad. Come, Mrs. Invalid, come to taste it. You are well enough to sit in here, you are well enough to sit outside. The doctor said it too."

But the benches were encrusted with people, and the sands at the sidewalk's edge. Besides, she had seen the far ruffle of the sea: "there take me," and though she leaned against him, it was she who led.

Plodding and plodding, sitting often to rest, he grumbling. Patting the sand so warm. Once she scooped up a handful, cradling it close to her better eye; peered, and flung it back. And as they came almost to the brink and she could see the glistening wet, she sat down, pulled off her shoes and stockings, left him and began to run. "You'll catch cold," he screamed, but the sand in his shoes weighed him down—he who had always been the agile one—and already the white spray creamed her feet.

He pulled her back, took a handkerchief to wipe off the wet and the sand. "Oh no," she said, "the sun will dry," seized the square and smoothed it flat, dropped on it a mound of sand, knotted the kerchief corners and tied it to a bag—"to look at with the strong glass" (for the first time in years explaining an action of hers)—and lay down with the little bag against her cheek, looking toward the shore that nurtured life as it first crawled toward consciousness the millions of years ago.

He took her one Sunday in the evil-smelling bus, past flat miles of blister houses, to the home of relatives. Oh what is this? she cried as the light began to smoke and the houses to dim and recede. Smog, he said, everyone knows but you. . . . Outside he kept his arms about her, but she walked with hands pushing the heavy air as if to open it, whispered: who has done this? sat down suddenly to vomit at the curb and for a long while refused to rise.

One's age as seen on the altered face of those known in youth. Is this they he has come to visit? This Max and Rose, smooth and pleasant, introducing them to polite children, disinterested grandchildren, "the whole family, once a month on Sundays. And why not? We have the room, the help, the food."

Talk of cars, of houses, of success: this son that, that daughter this. And *your* children? Hastily skimped over, the intermarriages, the obscure work—"my doctor son-in-law, Phil"—all he has to offer. She silent in a corner. (Car-sick like a baby, he explains.) Years since he has taken her to visit anyone but the children, and old apprehensions prickle: "no incidents," he silently begs, "no incidents." He itched to tell them. "A very sick woman," significantly, indicating her with his eyes, "a very sick woman." Their restricted faces did not react. "Have you thought maybe she'd do better at Palm Springs?" Rose asked. "Or at least a nicer section of the beach, nicer people, a pool." Not to have to say "money" he said instead: "would she have sand to look at through a magnifying glass?" and went on, detail after detail, the old habit betraying of parading the queerness of her for laughter.

After dinner—the others into the living-room in men- or women-clusters, or into the den to watch TV—the four of them alone. She sat close to him, and did not speak. Jokes, stories, people they had known, beginning of reminiscence, Russia fifty-sixty years ago. Strange words across the Duncan Phyfe table: *hunger; secret meetings; human rights; spies; betrayals; prison; escape*—interrupted by one of the grandchildren: "Commercial's on; any Coke left? Gee, you're missing a real hair-raiser." And then a granddaughter (Max proudly: "look at her, an American queen") drove them home on her way back to U.C.L.A. No incident—except that there had been no incidents.

The first few mornings she had taken with her the magnifying glass, but he would sit only on the benches, so she rested at the foot, where slatted bench shadows fell, and unless she turned her hearing aid down, other voices invaded.

Now on the days when the sun shone and she felt well enough, he took her on the tram to where the benches ranged in oblongs, some with tables for draughts or cards. Again the blanket on the sand in the striped shadows, but she no longer brought the magnifying glass. He played cards, and she lay in the sun and looked towards the waters; or they walked—two blocks down to the scaling hotel, two blocks back—past chili-hamburger stands, open-doored bars, Next to New and Perpetual Rummage Sale stores.

Once, out of the aimless walkers, slow and shuffling like themselves, someone ran unevenly towards them, embraced, kissed, wept: "dear friends, old friends." A friend of *hers*, not his: Mrs. Mays who had lived next door to them in Denver when the children were small.

Thirty years are compressed into a dozen sentences; and the present, not even in three. All is told: the children scattered; the husband dead; she lives in a room two blocks up from the sing hall—and points to the domed auditorium jutting before the pier. The leg? phlebitis; the heavy breathing? that, one does not ask. She, too, comes to the benches each day to sit. And tomorrow, tomorrow, are they going to the community sing? Of course he would have heard of it, everybody goes—the big doings they wait for all week. They have never been? She will come for them to dinner tomorrow and they will all go together.

So it is that she sits in the wind of the singing, among the thousand various faces of age.

She had turned off her hearing aid at once they came into the auditorium—as she would have wished to turn off sight.

One by one they streamed by and imprinted on her—and though the savage zest of their singing came voicelessly soft and distant, the faces still roared—the faces densened the air—chorded into

children-chants, mother-croons, singing of the chained
love serenades, Beethoven storms, mad Lucia's scream
drunken joy-songs, keens for the dead, work-singing

> *while from floor to balcony to dome a bare-footed sore-covered lit-tle girl threaded the sound-thronged tumult, danced her ecstasy of grimace to flutes that scratched at a cross-roads village wedding.*

Yes, faces became sound, and the sound became faces; and faces and sound became weight—pushed, pressed

"Air"—her hand claws his.

"Whenever I enjoy myself. . . ." Then he saw the grey sweat on her face. "Here. Up. Help me, Mrs. Mays," and they support her out to where she can gulp the air in sob after sob.

"A doctor, we should get for her a doctor."

"Tch, it's nothing," says Ellen Mays, "I get it all the time. You've missed the tram; come to my place. Fix your hearing aid, honey . . . close . . . tea. My view. See, she *wants* to come. Steady now, that's how." Adding mysteriously: "Remember your advice, easy to keep your head above water, empty things float. Float."

The singing a fading march for them, tall woman with a swollen leg, weaving little man, and the swollen thinness they help between.

The stench in the hall: mildew? decay? "We sit and rest then climb. My gorgeous view. We help each other and here we are."

The stench along into the slab of room. A wash stand for a sink, a box with oilcloth tacked around for a cupboard, a three-burner gas plate. Artificial flowers, colorless with dust. Everywhere pictures foaming: wedding, baby, party, vacation, graduation, family pictures. From the narrow couch under a slit of window, sure enough the view: lurching rooftops and a scallop of ocean heaving, preening, twitching under the moon.

"While the water heats. Excuse me . . . down the hall." Ellen Mays has gone.

"You'll live?" he asks mechanically, sat down to feel his fright; tried to pull her alongside.

She pushed him away. "For air," she said; stood clinging to the dresser. Then, in a terrible voice:

After a lifetime of room. Of many rooms.

Shhh.

You remember how she lived. Eight children. And now   one room   like a coffin.

She pays rent!

Shrinking the life of her   into one room   like a coffin Rooms and rooms like this.   I lie on the quilt and hear them talk.

Please, Mrs. Orator-without-Breath.

Once you went for coffee   I walked   I saw   A Balzac[9] a Chekhov to write it   Rummage   Alone   On scraps

Better old here than in the old country!

On scraps   Yet they sang like . . . like . . . Wondrous.   *Humankind   one has to believe*.   So strong   for what?   To rot   not grow?

Your poor lungs beg you. They sob between each word.

Singing.   Unused   the life in them. She   in this poor room   with her pictures.   Max   You   The children   Everywhere   unused   the life   And who has meaning?   Century after century   still all in us   not   to grow?

Coffins, rummage, plants: sick woman. Oh lay down. We will get for you the doctor.

"And when will it end. Oh, *the end*." *That* nightmare thought, and this time she writhed, crumpled beside him, seized his hand (for a moment again the weight, the soft distant roaring of humanity) and on the strangled-for breath, begged: "Man . . . we'll destroy ourselves?"

And looking for answer—in the helpless pity and fear for her (for *her*) that distorted his face—she understood the last months, and knew that she was dying.

IV

"Let us go home," she said after several days.

"You are in training for a cross-country run? That is why you do not even walk across the room? Here, like a prescription Phil said, till you are stronger from the operation. You want to break doctor's orders?"

She saw the fiction was necessary to him, was silent; then: "At home I will get better. If the doctor here says?"

"And winter? And the visits to Lennie and to Clara? All right," for he saw the tears in her eyes, "I will write Phil, and talk to the doctor."

Days passed. He reported nothing. Jeannie came and took her out for air, past the boarded concessions, the hooded and tented amuse-

9. Honoré de Balzac, French writer (1799–1850).

ment rides, to the end of the pier. They watched the spent waves feeding the new, the gulls in the clouded sky; even up where they sat, the wind-blown sand stung.

She did not ask to go down the crooked steps to the sea.

Back in her bed, while he was gone to the store, she said: "Jeannie, this doctor, he is not one I can ask questions. Ask him for me, can I go home?"

Jeannie looked at her, said quickly: "Of course, poor Granny. You want your own things around you, don't you? I'll call him tonight. . . . Look, I've something to show you," and from her purse unwrapped a large cookie, intricately shaped like a little girl. "Look at the curls—can you hear me well, Granny?—and the darling eyelashes. I just came from a house where they were baking them."

"The dimples," she marvelled, "there in the knees," holding it to the better light, turning, studying, "like art. Each singly they cut, or a mould?"

"Singly," said Jeannie, "and if it is a child only the mother can make them. Oh Granny, it's the likeness of a real little girl who died yesterday—Rosita. She was three years old. *Pan del Muerto*, the Bread of the Dead. It was the custom in the part of Mexico they came from."

Still she turned and inspected. "Look, the hollow in the throat, the little cross necklace. . . . I think for the mother it is a good thing to be busy with such bread. You know the family?"

Jeannie nodded. "On my rounds. I nursed. . . . Oh Granny, it is like a party; they play songs she liked to dance to. The coffin is lined with pink velvet and she wears a white dress. There are candles. . . ."

"In the house?" Surprised, "They keep her in the house?"

"Yes," said Jeannie, "and it is against the health law. I think she is . . . prepared there. The father said it will be sad to bury her in this country; in Oaxaca they have a feast night with candles each year; everyone picnics on the graves of those they loved until dawn."

"Yes, Jeannie, the living must comfort themselves." And closed her eyes.

"You want to sleep, Granny?"

"Yes, tired from the pleasure of you. I may keep the Rosita? There stand it, on the dresser, where I can see; something of my own around me."

In the kitchenette, helping her grandfather unpack the groceries, Jeannie said in her light voice:

"I'm resigning my job, Grandaddy."

"Ah, the lucky young man. Which one is he?"

"Too late. You're spoken for." She made a pyramid of cans, unstacked, and built again.

"Something is wrong with the job?"

"With me. I can't be"—she searched for the word—"What they call professional enough. I let myself feel things. And tomorrow I have to report a family. . . ." The cans clicked again. "It's not that, either. I just don't know what I want to do, maybe go back to school, maybe go to art school. I thought if you went to San Francisco I'd come along and talk it over with Mommy and Daddy. But I don't see how you can go. She wants to go home. She asked me to ask the doctor."

The doctor told her himself. "Next week you may travel, when you are a little stronger." But next week there was the fever of an infection, and by the time that was over, she could not leave the bed—a rented hospital bed that stood beside the double bed he slept in alone now.

Outwardly the days repeated themselves. Every other afternoon and evening he went out to his newfound cronies, to talk and play cards. Twice a week, Mrs. Mays came. And the rest of the time, Jeannie was there.

By the sickbed stood Jeannie's FM radio. Often into the room the shapes of music came. She would lie curled on her side, her knees drawn up, intense in listening (Jeannie sketched her so, coiled, convoluted like an ear), then thresh her hand out and abruptly snap the radio mute—still to lie in her attitude of listening, concealing tears.

Once Jeannie brought in a young Marine to visit, a friend from high-school days she had found wandering near the empty pier. Because Jeannie asked him to, gravely, without self-consciousness, he sat himself cross-legged on the floor and performed for them a dance of his native Samoa.

Long after they left, a tiny thrumming sound could be heard where, in her bed, she strove to repeat the beckon, flight, surrender of his hands, the fluttering footbeats, and his low plaintive calls.

Hannah and Phil sent flowers. To deepen her pleasure, he placed one in her hair. "Like a girl," he said, and brought the hand mirror so she could see. She looked at the pulsing red flower, the yellow skull face; a desolate, excited laugh shuddered from her, and she pushed the mirror away—but let the flower burn.

The week Lennie and Helen came, the fever returned. With it the excited laugh, and incessant words. She, who in her life had spoken but seldom and then only when necessary (never having learned the easy, social uses of words), now in dying, spoke incessantly.

In a half-whisper: "Like Lisa she is, your Jeannie. Have I told you of Lisa, she who taught me to read? Of the highborn she was, but noble in herself. I was sixteen; they beat me; my father beat me so I would not go to her. It was forbidden, she was a Tolstoyan.[1] At night, past dogs that

---

1. I.e., a follower of Leo Tolstoy (1828–1910), Russian novelist, social reformer, and teacher of nonviolence.

howled, terrible dogs, my son, in the snows of winter to the road, I to ride in her carriage like a lady, to books. To her, life was holy, knowledge was holy, and she taught me to read. They hung her. Everything that happens one must try to understand why. She killed one who betrayed many. Because of betrayal, betrayed all she lived and believed. In one minute she killed, before my eyes (there is so much blood in a human being, my son), in prison with me. All that happens, one must try to understand.

"The name?" Her lips would work. "The name that was their pole star; the doors of the death houses fixed to open on it; I read of it my year of penal servitude. Thuban!" very excited, "Thuban, in ancient Egypt the pole star. Can you see, look out to see it, Jeannie, if it swings around *our* pole star that seems to *us* not to move.

"Yes, Jeannie, at your age my mother and grandmother had already buried children . . . yes, Jeannie, it is more than oceans between Olshana and you . . . yes, Jeannie, they danced, and for all the bodies they had they might as well be chickens, and indeed, they scratched and flapped their arms and hopped.

"And Andrei Yefimitch, who was twenty years had never known of it and never wanted to know, said as if he wanted to cry: but why my dear friend this malicious laughter?" Telling to herself half-memorized phrases from her few books. "Pain I answer with tears and cries, baseness with indignation, meanness with repulsion . . . for life may be hated or wearied of, but never despised."

Delirious: "Tell me, my neighbor, Mrs. Mays, the pictures never lived, but what of the flowers? Tell them who ask: no rabbis, no ministers, no priests, no speeches, no ceremonies: ah, false—let the living comfort themselves. Tell Sammy's boy, he who flies, tell him to go to Stuttgart[2] and see where Davy has no grave. And what? And what? where millions have no graves save air."

In delirium or not, wanting the radio on; not seeming to listen, the words still jetting, wanting the music on. Once, silencing it abruptly as of old, she began to cry, unconcealed tears this time. "You have pain, Granny?" Jeannie asked.

"The music," she said, "still it is there and we do not hear; knocks, and our poor human ears too weak. What else, what else we do not hear?"

Once she knocked his hand aside as he gave her a pill, swept the bottles from her bedside table: "no pills, let me feel what I feel," and laughed as on his hands and knees he groped to pick them up.

Nighttimes her hand reached across the bed to hold his.

---

2. City in Germany, figuring in World War II.

A constant retching began. Her breath was too faint for sustained speech now, but still the lips moved:

> *When no longer necessary   to injure others*
> *Pick   pick pick   Blind chicken*
> *As a human being   responsibility for*

"David!" imperious, "Basin!" and she would vomit, rinse her mouth, the wasted throat working to swallow, and begin the chant again.

She will be better off in the hospital now, the doctor said.

He sent the telegrams to the children, was packing her suitcase, when her hoarse voice startled. She had roused, was pulling herself to sitting.

"Where now?" she asked. "Where now do you drag me?"

"You do not even have to have a baby to go this time," he soothed, looking for the brush to pack. "Remember, after Davy you told me—worthy to have a baby for the pleasure of the ten-day rest in the hospital?"

"Where now? Not home yet?" Her voice mourned. "Where *is* my home?"

He rose to ease her back. "The doctor, the hospital," he started to explain, but deftly, like a snake, she had slithered out of bed and stood swaying, propped behind the night table.

"Coward," she hissed, "runner."

"You stand," he said senselessly.

"To take me there and run. Afraid of a little vomit."

He reached her as she fell. She struggled against him, half slipped from his arms, pulled herself up again.

"Weakling," she taunted, "to leave me there and run. Betrayer. All your life you have run."

He sobbed, telling Jeannie. "A Marilyn Monroe to run for her virtue. Fifty-nine pounds she weighs, the doctor said, and she beats at me like a Dempsey.[3] Betrayer, she cries, and I running like a dog when she calls; day and night, running to her, her vomit, the bedpan. . . ."

"She needs you, Grandaddy," said Jeannie. "Isn't that what they call love? I'll see if she sleeps, and if she does, poor worn-out darling, we'll have a party, you and I; I brought us rum babas."

They did not move her. By her bed now stood the tall hooked pillar that held the solutions—blood and dextrose—to feed her veins. Jeannie moved down the hall to take over the sickroom, her face so radiant, her

---

3. Jack Dempsey, world's heavyweight champion boxer in the 1920s.

grandfather asked her once: "you are in love?" (Shameful the joy, the pure overwhelming joy from being with her grandmother; the peace, the serenity that breathed.) "My darling escape," she answered incoherently, "my darling Granny"—as if that explained.

Now one by one the children came, those that were able. Hannah, Paul, Sammy. Too late to ask: and what did you learn with your living, Mother, and what do we need to know?

Clara, the eldest, clenched:

> Pay me back, Mother, pay me back for all you took from me. Those others you crowded into your heart. The hands I needed to be for you, the heaviness, the responsibility.
>
> Is this she? Noises the dying make, the crablike hands crawling over the covers. The ethereal singing.
>
> She hears that music, that singing from childhood; forgotten sound—not heard since, since. . . . And the hardness breaks like a cry: Where did we lose each other, first mother, singing mother?
>
> Annulled: the quarrels, the gibing, the harshness between; the fall into silence and the withdrawal.
>
> I do not know you, Mother. Mother, I never knew you.

Lennie, suffering not alone for her who was dying, but for that in her which never lived (for that which in him might never live). From him too, unspoken words: good-bye Mother who taught me to mother myself.

Not Vivi, who must stay with her children; not Davy, but he is already here, having to die again with her this time, for the living take their dead with them when they die.

Light she grew, like a bird, and, like a bird, sound bubbled in her throat while the body fluttered in agony. Night and day, asleep or awake (though indeed there was no difference now) the songs and the phrases leaping.

And he, who had once dreaded a long dying (from fear of himself, from horror of the dwindling money) now desired her quick death profoundly, for her sake. He no longer went out, except when Jeannie forced him; no longer laughed, except when, in the bright kitchenette, Jeannie coaxed his laughter (and she, who seemed to hear nothing else, would laugh too, conspiratorial wisps of laughter).

Light, like a bird, the fluttering body, the little claw hands, the beaked shadow on her face; and the throat, bubbling, straining.

He tried not to listen, as he tried not to look on the face in which only the forehead remained familiar, but trapped with her the long nights in that little room, the sounds worked themselves into his consciousness, with their punctuation of death swallows, whimpers, gurglings.

Even in reality (swallow) *life's lack of it*
Slaveships   deathtrains   clubs   enough
The bell   Summon   what enables
78,000[4] *in one minute* (whisper of a scream) 78,000 *human beings   we'll destroy ourselves?*

Aah, Mrs. Miserable," he said, as if she could hear, "all your life working, and now in bed you lie, servants to tend, you do not even need to call to be tended, and still you work. Such hard work it is to die? Such hard work?"

The body threshed, her hand clung in his. A melody, ghost-thin, hovered on her lips, and like a guilty ghost, the vision of her vent in listening to it, silencing the record instantly he was near. Now, heedless of his presence, she floated the melody on and on.

"Hid it from me," he complained, "how many times you listened to remember it so?" And tried to think when she had first played it, or first begun to silence her few records when he came near—but could reconstruct nothing. There was only this room with its tall hooked pillar and its swarm of sounds.

No man one   except through others
Strong   with the not yet   in the now
Dogma dead   war dead   one country

"It helps, Mrs. Philosopher, words from books? It helps?" And it seemed to him that for seventy years she had hidden a tape recorder, infinitely microscopic, within her, that it had coiled infinite mile on mile, trapping every song, every melody, every word read, heard and spoken —and that maliciously she was playing back only what said nothing of him, of the children, of their intimate life together.

"Left us indeed, Mrs. Babbler," he reproached, "you who called others babbler and cunningly saved your words. A lifetime you tended and loved, and now not a word of us, for us. Left us indeed? Left me."

And he took out his solitaire deck, shuffled the cards loudly, slapped them down.

Lift high   banner of reason (tatter of an orator's voice) *justice freedom   light*
Humankind   life worthy   capacities
Seeks (blur of shudder) *belong   human being*

"Words, words," he accused, "and what human beings did *you* seek around you, Mrs. Live Alone, and what mankind think worthy?"

Though even as he spoke, he remembered she had not always been isolated, had not always to be alone (as he knew there had been a voice

4. The number killed in Hiroshima by the first atomic bomb.

before this gossamer one; before the hoarse voice that broke from silence to lash, make incidents, shame him—a girl's voice of eloquence that spoke their holiest dreams). But again he could reconstruct, image, nothing of what had been before, or when, or how, it had changed.

Ace, queen, jack. The pillar shadow fell, so, in two tracks; in the mirror depths glistened a moonlike blob, the empty solution bottle. And it worked in him: *reason and justice and freedom. Dogma dead:* he remembered the full quotation, laughed bitterly. "Hah, good you do not know what you say; good Victor Hugo[5] died and did not see it, his twentieth century."

Deuce, ten, five. Dauntlessly she began a song of their youth of belief:

> *These things shall be.[6] A loftier race*
> *than e'er the world hath known shall rise*
> *with flame of freedom in their souls*
> *and light of knowledge in their eyes*

King, four, jack. "In the twentieth century, hah!"

> *They shall be gentle, brave and strong*
> *to spill no drop of blood, but dare*
> *all . . .*

> *on earth and fire and sea and air*

"To spill no drop of blood, hah! So, cadaver, and you too, cadaver Hugo, 'in the twentieth century ignorance will be dead, prejudice will be dead, war will be dead, and for all mankind one country—of fulfillment.' Hah!"

> *And every life* (long strangling cough) *shall be a song*

The cards fell from his fingers. Without warning, the bereavement and betrayal he had sheltered—compounded through the years—hidden even from himself—revealed itself,

    uncoiled,

    released,

    sprung

and with it the monstrous shapes of what had actually happened in the century.

---

5. Victor Hugo (1802–1885), French writer and champion of liberty; he prophesied the triumph of peace and liberty in the twentieth century.

6. Century-old socialist song, now a United Nations hymn. The first line is a translation of the French Revolutionary slogan "Ça ira."

A ravening hunger or thirst seized him. He groped into the kitchenette, switched on all three lights, piled a tray—"you have finished your night snack, Mrs. Cadaver, now I will have mine." And he was shocked at the tears that splashed on the tray.

"Salt tears. For free. I forgot to shake on salt?"

Whispered: "Lost, how much I lost."

Escaped to the grandchildren whose childhoods were childish, who had never hungered, who lived unravaged by disease in warm houses of many rooms, had all the school for which they cared, could walk on any street, stood a head taller than their grandparents, towered above—beautiful skins, straight backs, clear straightforward eyes. "Yes, you in Olshana," he said to the town of sixty years ago, "they would be nobility to you."

And was this not the dream then, come true in ways undreamed? he asked.

And are there no other children in the world? he answered, as if in her harsh voice.

And the flame of freedom, the light of knowledge?

And the drop, to spill no drop of blood?

And he thought that at six Jeannie would get up and it would be his turn to go to her room and sleep, that he could press the buzzer and she would come now; that in the afternoon Ellen Mays was coming, and this time they would play cards and he could marvel at how rouge can stand half an inch on the cheek; that in the evening the doctor would come, and he could beg him to be merciful, to stop the feeding solutions, to let her die.

To let her die, and with her their youth of belief out of which her bright, betrayed words foamed; stained words, that on her working lips came stainless.

Hours yet before Jeannie's turn. He could press the buzzer and wake her to come now; he could take a pill, and with it sleep; he could pour more brandy into his milk glass, though what he had poured was not yet touched.

Instead he went back, checked her pulse, gently tended with his knotty fingers as Jeannie had taught.

She was whimpering; her hand crawled across the covers for his. Compassionately he enfolded it, and with his free hand gathered up the cards again. Still was there thirst or hunger ravening in him.

That world of their youth—dark, ignorant, terrible with hate and disease—how was it that living in it, in the midst of corruption, filth, treachery, degradation, they had not mistrusted man nor themselves; had believed so beautifully, so . . . falsely?

"Aaah, children," he said out loud, "how we believed, how we belonged." And he yearned to package for each of the children, the grandchildren, for everyone, *that joyous certainty, that sense of mattering, of moving and being moved, of being one and indivisible with the great of the past, with all that freed, ennobled.* Package it, stand on corners, in front of stadiums and on crowded beaches, knock on doors, give it as a fabled gift.

"And why not in cereal boxes, in soap packages?" he mocked himself. "Aah. You have taken my senses, cadaver."

Words foamed, died unsounded. Her body writhed; she made kissing motions with her mouth. (Her lips moving as she read, poring over the Book of the Martyrs, the magnifying glass superimposed over the heavy eyeglasses.) *Still she believed?* "Eva!" he whispered. "Still you believed? You lived by it? These Things Shall Be?"

"One pound soup meat," she answered distinctly, "one soup bone."

"My ears heard you. Ellen Mays was witness: 'Man . . . one has to believe.' " Imploringly: "Eva!"

"Bread, day-old." She was mumbling. "Please, in a wooden box . . . for kindling. The thread, hah, the thread breaks. Cheap thread"—and a gurgling, enormously loud, began in her throat.

"I ask for stone; she gives me bread—day-old." He pulled his hand away, shouted: "Who wanted questions? Everything you have to wake?" Then dully, "Ah, let me help you turn, poor creature."

Words jumbled, cleared. In a voice of crowded terror:

"Paul, Sammy, don't fight.

"Hannah, have I ten hands?

"How can I give it, Clara, how can I give it if I don't have?"

"You lie," he said sturdily, "there was joy too." Bitterly: "Ah how cheap you speak of us at the last."

As if to rebuke him, as if her voice had no relationship with her flailing body, she sang clearly, beautifully, a school song the children had taught her when they were little; begged:

"Not look   my hair   where they cut. . . ."

(The crown of braids shorn.) And instantly he left the mute old woman poring over the Book of the Martyrs; went past the mother treadling at the sewing machine, singing with the children; past the girl in her wrinkled prison dress, hiding her hair with scarred hands, lifting to him her awkward, shamed, imploring eyes of love; and took her in his arms, dear, personal, fleshed, in all the heavy passion he had loved to rouse from her.

"Eva!"

Her little claw hand beat the covers. How much, how much can a man stand? He took up the cards, put them down, circled the beds, walked to the dresser, opened, shut drawers, brushed his hair, moved his hand bit by bit over the mirror to see what of the reflection he could blot out with each move, and felt that at any moment he would die of what was unendurable. Went to press the buzzer to wake Jeannie, looked down, saw on Jeannie's sketch pad the hospital bed, with *her*; the double bed alongside, with him; the tall pillar feeding into her veins, and their hands, his and hers, clasped, feeding each other. And as if he had been instructed he went to his bed, lay down, holding the sketch as if it could shield against the monstrous shapes of loss, of betrayal, of death—and with his free hand took hers back into his.

So Jeannie found them in the morning.

That last day the agony was perpetual. Time after time it lifted her almost off the bed, so they had to fight to hold her down. He could not endure and left the room; wept as if there never would be tears enough.

Jeannie came to comfort him. In her light voice she said: Grandaddy, Grandaddy don't cry. She is not there, she promised me. On the last day, she said she would go back to when she first heard music, a little girl on the road of the village where she was born. She promised me. It is a wedding and they dance, while the flutes so joyous and vibrant tremble in the air. Leave her there, Grandaddy, it is all right. She promised me. Come back, come back and help her poor body to die.

> *For two of that generation*
> *Seevya and Genya*
>
> *Infinite, Dauntless, Incorruptible*
>
> *Death deepens the wonder*

1961

RUTH STONE

1915–

"I found that poems came with this mysterious feeling, and it was a kind of peculiar ecstasy," the poet Ruth Stone once explained to an interviewer, noting that "my mother read poetry—Tennyson—to me from the time, apparently, she started suckling me at her breasts." Improvisational as her verse may often seem, however, Stone is an artist who works with notable integrity and intensity to shape the "peculiar ecstasy" of her aesthetic visions. Born in Roanoke, Virginia, she was raised in Indiana and Illinois. After graduating from the University of Illinois, she married twice—her second husband was the critic-novelist Walter Stone, who died in 1958—and she is the mother of three daughters. The winner of several Guggenheim fellowships, she has published three collections of poetry: *In an Iridescent Time* (1958), *Topography* (1970), and

Cheap (1975). Supporting herself as a teacher and poet-in-residence at such institutions as the University of Illinois, the University of Wisconsin, Indiana University, the University of California, Davis, and Brandeis University, she has consistently concentrated her attention on the situations of women as different as the stubborn survivor of *Absinthe Granny* and the acquiescent housewife of *Secondhand Coat*.

In an Iridescent Time

My mother, when young, scrubbed laundry in a tub,
She and her sisters on an old brick walk
Under the apple trees, sweet rub-a-dub.
The bees came round their heads, the wrens made talk.
Four young ladies each with a rainbow board   5
Honed their knuckles, wrung their wrists to red,
Tossed back their braids and wiped their aprons wet.
The Jersey calf beyond the back fence roared;
And all the soft day, swarms about their pet
Buzzed at his big brown eyes and bullish head.   10
Four times they rinsed, they said. Some things they starched,
Then shook them from the baskets two by two,
And pinned the fluttering intimacies of life
Between the lilac bushes and the yew:
Brown gingham, pink, and skirts of Alice blue.[1]   15

                                                                   1958

Periphery

You are not wanted
I said to the older body
Who was listening near the cupboards.
But outside on the porch
They were all eating.   5
The body dared not
Put its fingers in its mouth.
Behave, I whispered,
You have a wart on your cheek
And everyone knows you drink.   10
But that's all right, I relented,
It isn't generally known
How clever you are.
I know you aren't appreciated.
The body hunted for something good to eat,   15

1. A pale shade of blue.

But the food had all been eaten by the others.
They laughed together carelessly outside the kitchen.
The body hid in the pantry near the refrigerator.
After a while it laughed, too.
It listened to all the jokes and it laughed.   20

                                                          1975

The Song of Absinthe[2] Granny

Among some hills there dwelt in parody
A young woman; me.
I was that gone with child
That before I knew it I had three
And they hung whining and twisting.   5
Why I wasn't more than thirty-nine
And sparse as a runt fruit tree.
Three pips[3] that plagued the life out of me.
Ah me. It wore me down,
The grubs, the grubbing.   10
We were two inches thick in dust
For lack of scrubbing.
Diapers and panty-shirts and yolk of eggs.
One day in the mirror I saw my stringy legs
And I looked around   15
And saw string on the floor,
And string on the chair
And heads like wasps' nests
Full of stringy hair.
"Well," I said, "if you have string, knit.   20
Knit something, don't just sit."
We had the orchard drops,[4]
But they didn't keep.
The milk came in bottles.
It came until the bottles were that deep   25
We fell over the bottles.
The milk dried on the floor.
"Drink it up," cried their papa,
And they all began to roar, "More!"
Well, time went on,   30
Not a bone that wasn't frayed.
Every chit[5] was knicked and bit,
And nothing was paid.
We had the dog spayed.

---

2. A strong liqueur made from wormwood.   4. Fruit fallen from trees.
3. Small seeds; anything small.   5. Child, especially a pert girl.

"It looks like a lifetime,"   35
Their papa said.
"It's a good life, it's a good wife,
It's a good bed."
So I got the rifle out
To shoot him through the head.   40
But he went on smiling and sitting
And I looked around for a piece of string
To do some knitting.
Then I picked at the tiling
And the house fell down.   45
"Now you've done it," he said.
"I'm going to town.
Get them up out of there,
Put them to bed."
"I'm afraid to look," I whimpered,   50
"They might be dead."
"We're here, mama, under the shed."
Well, the winters wore on.
We had cats that hung around.
When I fed them they scratched.   55
How the little nippers loved them.
Cats and brats.
I couldn't see for my head was thatched
But they kept coming in when the door unlatched.
"I'll shave my head," I promised,   60
"I'll clip my mop.
This caterwauling has got to stop."
Well, all that's finished,
It's all been done.
Those were high kick summers,   65
It was bald galled fun.
Now the daft time's over
And the string is spun.
I'm all alone
To cull[6] and be furry.   70
Not an extra page in the spanking story.
The wet britches dried
And the teeth came in.
The last one cried
And no new began.   75
Those were long hot summers,
Now the sun won't tarry.
My birds have flocked,
And I'm old and wary.
I'm old and worn and a cunning sipper,   80

6. Gather, collect.

And I'll outlive every little nipper.
And with what's left I'm chary,
And with what's left I'm chary.

                                                        1975

Secondhand Coat

I feel
in her pockets; she wore nice cotton gloves,
kept a handkerchief box, washed her undies,
ate at the Holiday Inn, had a basement freezer,
belonged to a bridge club.   5
I think when I wake in the morning
that I have turned into her.
She hangs in the hall downstairs,
a shadow with pulled threads.
I slip her over my arms, skin of a matron.   10
Where are you? I say to myself, to the orphaned body,
and her coat says,
Get your purse, have you got your keys?

                                                        1981

MARGARET WALKER

1915–

The dedication of Margaret Walker's *For My People*, a volume which was
chosen for the Yale Series of Younger Poets in 1942, acknowledged her indebtedness to and her sense of responsibility for "my people everywhere singing
their slave songs repeatedly: their dirges and their ditties and their blues and jubilees." In many of the poems she included in this book, moreover, Walker
used jazz rhythms and blues meters to present the grace and daring of such folk
characters as Stagolee, Molly Means, Poppa Chicken, Kissie Lee, and Yalluh
Hammuh. Caught in a culture oblivious to the "black and poor and small and
different," Walker's characters reflect her effort "to fashion a world that will
hold all the people, all the faces, all the adams and eves and their countless generations."

One of four children of Sigismund Walker, a Methodist minister, and Marion Walker, a musicologist, Margaret Walker was born in Birmingham, Alabama. Educated at church schools in Mississippi, Alabama, and Louisiana, she
began composing verse at thirteen years of age. During her undergraduate days
at Northwestern University, she "went hungry unless friends fed me." Yet she
received her B.A. in 1935, and her M.A. and Ph.D. from the University of

Iowa in 1940 and 1965. After she married in 1943, she began teaching at Livingstone College in Salisbury, North Carolina. For more than three decades she has been a professor of English at Jackson State College in Mississippi, where she has supported a disabled husband and four children on a salary that remained for many years well under six thousand dollars. In both her academic life and her literary career, Walker has self-consciously attempted to nurture the growth of black culture. *Prophets for a New Day* (1970) and *October Journey* (1973) include a number of sonnets and ballads about the human rights struggle, just as her historical novel *Jubilee* (1966), which won the Houghton Mifflin Literary Fellowship, uses the traditional genre of the slave narrative to celebrate a heroic woman who simultaneously moves into maturity and freedom.

Dark Blood

There were bizarre beginnings in old lands for the making of me.
> There were sugar sands and islands of fern and pearl, palm jungles and stretches of a never-ending sea.

There were the wooing nights of tropical lands and the cool discretion of flowering plains between two stalwart hills. They nurtured my coming with wanderlust. I sucked fevers of adventure through my veins with my mother's milk.

Someday I shall go to the tropical lands of my birth, to the coasts of continents and the tiny wharves of island shores. I shall roam the Balkans[1] and the hot lanes of Africa and Asia. I shall stand on mountain tops and gaze on fertile homes below.

And when I return to Mobile[2] I shall go by the way of Panama and Bocas del Toro to the littered streets and the one-room shacks of my old poverty, and blazing suns of other lands may struggle then to reconcile the pride and pain in me.

1942

Lineage

My grandmothers were strong.
They followed plows and bent to toil.
They moved through fields sowing seed.

---

1. Mountain range in Bulgaria.
2. City in Alabama; Bocas del Toro is a town in Panama.

They touched earth and grain grew.
They were full of sturdiness and singing.   5
My grandmothers were strong.

My grandmothers are full of memories
Smelling of soap and onions and wet clay
With veins rolling roughly over quick hands
They have many clean words to say.   10
My grandmothers were strong.
Why am I not as they?

1942

Molly Means

Old Molly Means was a hag and a witch;
Chile of the devil, the dark, and sitch.
Her heavy hair hung thick in ropes
And her blazing eyes was black as pitch.
Imp at three and wench at 'leben   5
She counted her husbands to the number seben.
    O Molly, Molly, Molly Means
    There goes the ghost of Molly Means.

Some say she was born with a veil on her face
So she could look through unnatchal space   10
Through the future and through the past
And charm a body or an evil place
And every man could well despise
The evil look in her coal black eyes.
    Old Molly, Molly, Molly Means   15
    Dark is the ghost of Molly Means.

And when the tale begun to spread
Of evil and of holy dread:
Her black-hand arts and her evil powers
How she cast her spells and called the dead,   20
The younguns was afraid at night
And the farmers feared their crops would blight.
    Old Molly, Molly, Molly Means
    Cold is the ghost of Molly Means.

Then one dark day she put a spell   25
On a young gal-bride just come to dwell
In the lane just down from Molly's shack
And when her husband come riding back
His wife was barking like a dog

And on all fours like a common hog.   30
   O Molly, Molly, Molly Means
   Where is the ghost of Molly Means?

The neighbors come and they went away
And said she'd die before break of day
But her husband held her in his arms   35
And swore he'd break the wicked charms;
He'd search all up and down the land
And turn the spell on Molly's hand.
   O Molly, Molly, Molly Means
   Sharp is the ghost of Molly Means.   40

So he rode all day and he rode all night
And at the dawn he come in sight
Of a man who said he could move the spell
And cause the awful thing to dwell
On Molly Means, to bark and bleed   45
Till she died at the hands of her evil deed.
   Old Molly, Molly, Molly Means
   This is the ghost of Molly Means.

Sometimes at night through the shadowy trees
She rides along on a winter breeze.   50
You can hear her holler and whine and cry.
Her voice is thin and her moan is high,
And her cackling laugh or her barking cold
Bring terror to the young and old.
   O Molly, Molly, Molly Means   55
   Lean is the ghost of Molly Means.

1942

Kissie Lee

Toughest gal I ever did see
Was a gal by the name of Kissie Lee;
The toughest gal God ever made
And she drew a dirty, wicked blade.

Now this here gal warn't always tough   5
Nobody dreamed she'd turn out rough
But her Grammaw Mamie had the name
Of being the town's sin and shame.

When Kissie Lee was young and good
Didn't nobody treat her like they should   10

Allus gettin' beat by a no-good shine[3]
An' allus quick to cry and whine.

Till her Grammaw said, "Now listen to me,
I'm tiahed of yoah whinin', Kissie Lee.
People don't never treat you right,   15
An' you allus scrappin' or in a fight.

"Whin I was a gal wasn't no soul
Could do me wrong an' still stay whole.
Ah got me a razor to talk for me
An' aftah that they let me be."   20

Well Kissie Lee took her advice
And after that she didn't speak twice
'Cause when she learned to stab and run
She got herself a little gun.

And from that time that gal was mean,   25
Meanest mama you ever seen.
She could hold her likker and hold her man
And she went thoo life jus' raisin' san'.[4]

One night she walked in Jim's saloon
And seen a guy what spoke too soon;   30
He done her dirt long time ago
When she was good and feeling low.

Kissie bought her drink and she paid her dime
Watchin' this guy what beat her time
And he was making for the outside door   35
When Kissie shot him to the floor.

Not a word she spoke but she switched her blade
And flashing that lil ole baby paid:
Evvy livin' guy got out of her way
Because Kissie Lee was drawin' her pay.   40

She could shoot glass doors offa the hinges,
She could take herself on the wildest binges.
And she died with her boots on switching blades
On Talladega Mountain in the likker raids.[5]

1942

---

3. Person with jet-black skin.
4. I.e., raising dust, moving briskly.

5. Police raids made during Prohibition on people manufacturing illegal, "bootleg," liquor.

Whores

When I grew up I went away to work
where painted whores were fascinating sights.
They came on like whole armies through the nights—
their sullen eyes on mine, their mouths a smirk,
and from their hands keys hung suggestively.   5
Old women working by an age-old plan
to make their bread in ways as best they can
would hobble past and beckon tirelessly.

Perhaps one day they'll all die in the streets
or be surprised by bombs in each wide bed;   10
learning too late in unaccustomed dread
that easy ways, like whores on special beats,
no longer have the gift to harbor pride
or bring men peace, or leave them satisfied.

1942

JUDITH WRIGHT

1915–

Lamenting that "the song is gone; the dance / is secret with the dancers in the earth," the Australian poet Judith Wright mourned in *Bora Ring*, an early poem, the dispersal and destruction of the aborigines who inhabited her native land before it was conquered by the British. In part, those lines predicted one major direction her artistic career would take: in producing more than a dozen volumes of verse and a number of collections of essays on criticism and articles on conservation, as well as editing several anthologies of Australian poetry, this prolific writer has memorialized Australia as "my blood's country . . . the high lean country / full of old stories that still go walking in my sleep." At the same time, however, much of her poetry has spoken of such matters from a distinctively female perspective, a point of view explicitly summarized by the title of her second book, *Woman to Man* (1949).

The descendant of what one commentator calls "pioneering rural stock," Wright was born in Armidale, New South Wales, and educated at New England Girls School, Armidale, and the University of Sydney. Married to J. P. McKinney, and the mother of one daughter, she worked for some time as a secretary and civil servant before taking up a position as honors tutor in English at the University of Queensland. In recent years, she has become increasingly involved in political action, including both the antiwar movement of the 1960s and Australia's conservationist movement. Cofounder and former president of the Wild Life Preservation Society of Queensland, she now lives in a wildlife sanctuary near Braidwood.

Such poems as *Ishtar* and *Eve to Her Daughters* suggest the connections that Wright sees between female power and the forces of nature, even while they explore the relationship between Adam's fear that "outside Eden the earth was imperfect" and the twentieth century's assault upon the environment. That this poet identifies deeply with women's literary tradition is also made clear in these works, as well as in her *Rosina Alcona to Julius Brenzaida*, a piece whose title is taken from a poem by another female acolyte of nature—the Victorian poet-novelist Emily Brontë.

Half-Caste[1] Girl

Little Josie buried under the bright moon
is tired of being dead, death lasts too long.
She would like to push death aside, and stand on the hill
and beat with a waddy[2] on the bright moon like a gong.

Across the hills, the hills that belong to no people   5
and so to none are foreign,
once she climbed high to find the native cherry;
the lithe darkhearted lubra[3]
who in her beads like blood
dressed delicately for love   10
moves her long hands among the strings of the wind,
singing the songs of women,
the songs of love and dying.

Against the world's stone walls she thrust her heart—
endless the strength of its beating—   15
atom of flesh that cannot move a stone.
She used her love for lever;
but the wall is cunningly made.
Not even the strong break jail.
So she is restless still under her rootwarm cover,   20
hearing the noise of living,
forgetting the pain of dying.

Little Josie buried under the bright sun
would like to open her eyes and dance in the light.
Who is it has covered the sun and the beautiful moon   25
with a wallaby[4] skin, and left her alone in the night?

1946

---

1. Of mixed racial descent.
2. A club used as a weapon by Australian aborigines.
3. Aboriginal Australian woman.
4. Small kangaroo.

The Sisters

In the vine-shadows on the veranda,
under the yellow leaves, in the cooling sun,
sit the two sisters. Their slow voices run
like little winter creeks dwindled by frost and wind,
and the square of sunlight moves on the veranda.   5

They remember the gay young men on their tall horses
who came courting; the dancing and the smells of leather
and wine, the girls whispering by the fire together:
even their dolls and ponies, all they have left behind
moves in the yellow shadows on the veranda.   10

Thinking of their lives apart and the men they married,
thinking of the marriage-bed and the birth of the first child,
they look down smiling. "My life was wide and wild,
and who can know my heart? There in that golden jungle
I walk alone," say the old sisters on the veranda.   15

1949

Ishtar[5]

When I first saw a woman after childbirth
the room was full of your glance who had just gone away.
And when the mare was bearing her foal
you were with her but I did not see your face.

When in fear I became a woman   5
I first felt your hand.
When the shadow of the future first fell across me
it was your shadow, my grave and hooded attendant.

It is all one whether I deny or affirm you;
it is not my mind you are concerned with.   10
It is no matter whether I submit or rebel;
the event will still happen.

You neither know nor care for the truth of my heart;
but the truth of my body has all to do with you.
You have no need of my thoughts or my hopes,   15
living in the realm of the absolute event.

5. Babylonian goddess of love and fertility.

Then why is it that when I at last see your face
under that hood of slate-blue, so calm and dark,
so worn with the burden of an inexpressible knowledge—
why is it that I begin to worship you with tears?   20

1953

Request to a Year

If the year is meditating a suitable gift,
I should like it to be the attitude
of my great-great-grandmother,
legendary devotee of the arts,

who, having had eight children   5
and little opportunity for painting pictures,
sat one day on a high rock
beside a river in Switzerland

and from a difficult distance viewed
her second son, balanced on a small ice-floe,   10
drift down the current towards a waterfall
that struck rock-bottom eighty feet below,

while her second daughter, impeded,
no doubt, by the petticoats of the day,
stretched out a last-hope alpenstock[6]   15
(which luckily later caught him on his way).

Nothing, it was evident, could be done;
and with the artist's isolating eye
my great-great-grandmother hastily sketched the scene.
The sketch survives to prove the story by.   20

Year, if you have no Mother's Day present planned,
reach back and bring me the firmness of her hand.

1955

To Another Housewife

Do you remember how we went,
on duty bound, to feed the crowd
of hungry dogs your father kept

6. A walking stick used in mountain climbing.

as rabbit-hunters? Lean and loud,
half-starved and furious, how they leapt   5
against their chains, as though they meant
in mindless rage for being fed,
to tear our childish hands instead!

With tomahawk and knife we hacked
the flyblown tatters of old meat,   10
gagged at their carcass-smell, and threw
the scraps and watched the hungry eat.
Then turning faint, we made a pact,
(two greensick girls), crossed hearts and swore
to touch no meat forever more.   15

How many cuts of choice and prime
our housewife hands have dressed since then—
these hands with love and blood imbrued—
for daughters, sons, and hungry men!
How many creatures bred for food   20
we've raised and fattened for the time
they met at last the steaming knife
that serves the feast of death-in-life!

And as the evening meal is served
we hear the turned-down radio   25
begin to tell the evening news
just as the family joint[7] is carved.
O murder, famine, pious wars. . . .
Our children shrink to see us so,
in sudden meditation, stand   30
with knife and fork in either hand.

                                1966

Eve[8] to Her Daughters

It was not I who began it.
Turned out into draughty caves,
hungry so often, having to work for our bread,
hearing the children whining,
I was nevertheless not unhappy.   5
Where Adam went I was fairly contented to go.
I adapted myself to the punishment: it was my life.

7. I.e., joint of roast meat.
8. The first woman, created by God as a companion for Adam in the Garden of Eden;
tempted by the serpent into eating and convincing Adam to eat the forbidden fruit of the Tree
of Knowledge, and so precipitating the Fall, their
expulsion from Eden, and the introduction of
death into the world.

But Adam, you know . . . !
He kept on brooding over the insult,
over the trick They had played on us, over the scolding.   10
He had discovered a flaw in himself
and he had to make up for it.

Outside Eden the earth was imperfect,
the seasons changed, the game was fleet-footed,
he had to work for our living, and he didn't like it.   15
He even complained of my cooking
(it was hard to compete with Heaven).

So he set to work.
The earth must be made a new Eden
with central heating, domesticated animals,   20
mechanical harvesters, combustion engines,
escalators, refrigerators,
and modern means of communication
and multiplied opportunities for safe investment
and higher education for Abel and Cain[9]   25
and the rest of the family.
You can see how his pride had been hurt.

In the process he had to unravel everything,
because he believed that mechanism
was the whole secret—he was always mechanical-minded.   30
He got to the very inside of the whole machine
exclaiming as he went, So this is how it works!
And now that I know how it works, why, I must have invented it.
As for God and the Other, they cannot be demonstrated,
and what cannot be demonstrated   35
doesn't exist.
You see, he had always been jealous.

Yes, he got to the centre
where nothing at all can be demonstrated.
And clearly he doesn't exist; but he refuses   40
to accept the conclusion.
You see, he was always an egotist.

It was warmer than this in the cave;
there was none of this fall-out.
I would suggest, for the sake of the children,   45
that it's time you took over.

---

9. The first two sons of Adam and Eve; Cain   preferred Abel's offerings.
murdered Abel out of jealousy because God

But you are my daughters, you inherit my own faults of character;
you are submissive, following Adam
even beyond existence.
Faults of character have their own logic   50
and it always works out.
I observed this with Abel and Cain.

Perhaps the whole elaborate fable
right from the beginning
is meant to demonstrate this; perhaps it's the whole secret.   55
Perhaps nothing exists but our faults?
At least they can be demonstrated.

But it's useless to make
such a suggestion to Adam.
He has turned himself into God,   60
who is faultless, and doesn't exist.

1966

Naked Girl and Mirror

This is not I. I had no body once—
only what served my need to laugh and run
and stare at stars and tentatively dance
on the fringe of foam and wave and sand and sun.
Eyes loved, hands reached for me, but I was gone   5
on my own currents, quicksilver, thistledown.
Can I be trapped at last in that soft face?

I stare at you in fear, dark brimming eyes.
Why do you watch me with that immoderate plea—
"Look under these curled lashes, recognize   10
that you were always here; know me—be me."
Smooth once-hermaphrodite[1] shoulders, too tenderly
your long slope runs, above those sudden shy
curves furred with light that spring below your space.

No, I have been betrayed. If I had known   15
that this girl waited between a year and a year,
I'd not have chosen her bough to dance upon.
Betrayed, by that little darkness here, and here
this swelling softness and that frightened stare
from eyes I will not answer; shut out here   20
from my own self, by its new body's grace—

---

1. With both female and male characteristics.

for I am betrayed by someone lovely. Yes,
I see you are lovely, hateful naked girl.
Your lips in the mirror tremble as I refuse
to know or claim you. Let me go—let me be gone.   25
You are half of some other who may never come.
Why should I tend you? You are not my own;
you seek that other—he will be your home.

Yet I pity your eyes in the mirror, misted with tears;
I lean to your kiss. I must serve you; I will obey.   30
Some day we may love. I may miss your going, some day,
though I shall always resent your dumb and fruitful years.
Your lovers shall learn better, and bitterly too,
if their arrogance dares to think I am part of you.

                                                          1966

"Rosina Alcona to Julius Brenzaida"[2]

Living long is containing
archaean levels,
buried yet living.
Greek urns, their lovely tranquillity
still and yet moving,   5
directing, surviving.

So driving homewards
full of my present
along the new freeway,
carved straight, rushing forward,   10
I see suddenly there still
that anachronism, the old wooden pub
stranded at the crossways.

Where you and I once
in an absolute present   15
drank laughing
in a day still living,
still laughing, still permanent.

Present crossed past
synchronized, at the junction.   20
The daylight of one day
was deepened, was darkened
by the light of another.

2. The title of a poem by Emily Brontë (1819–1848).

Three faces met,
your vivid face in life,   25
your face of dead marble
touched mine simultaneously.

Holding the steering-wheel
my hands freeze. Out of my eyes
jump these undryable tears   30
from artesian pressures,
from the strata that cover you,
the silt-sift of time.

These gulping dry lines
are not my song for you.   35
That's made already.
Come in, dead Emily.

Have I forgot, my only Love, to love thee,
Severed at last by time's all-wearing wave?

A work of divinest anguish,   40
a Greek urn completed.
I grip the steering-wheel.
No other star has ever shone for me.

The pure poem rises
in lovely tranquillity,   45
as the Greek urn rises
from the soil of the past,
as the lost face rises
and the tears return.

I move through my present   50
gripping the steering-wheel,
repeating, repeating it.

The crossways fade; the freeway rushes forward.
"These days obscure but cannot do thee wrong."

                                                   1971

P. K. PAGE
1916–

Patricia Kathleen Page was born in England and raised in Canada. During the forties, while working as a scriptwriter for the National Film Board, she became associated with the poets contributing to *Preview* (1942–1945), a Montreal magazine founded by Patrick Anderson. The social concerns of her poetry date from this period and help explain her sense of indebtedness to such English poets as Stephen Spender and W. H. Auden. However, in her first two volumes of verse—*As Ten as Twenty* (1946) and *The Metal and the Flower* (1954)—Page also demonstrated her commitment to a visionary poetry of quest that links her to the mystical tradition of Rainer Maria Rilke and W. B. Yeats. In her own words, she has attempted "to copy exactly something which exists in a dimension where worldly senses are inadequate." Page's publishing career was interrupted by the travels through Australia, Brazil, and Mexico she undertook with her husband, the diplomat W. Arthur Irwin, in the fifties. After the couple returned to Canada in 1964, she published *Cry Ararat! Poems New and Selected* (1967), *The Sun and the Moon and Other Fictions* (1973), *Poems Selected and New* (1974), and *Evening Dance of the Grey Flies* (1981). The stenographers, typists, and clerks of Page's poems about office workers illustrate her unique ability to endow realistic portraiture with visionary precision.

The Stenographers

After the brief bivouac[1] of Sunday,
their eyes, in the forced march of Monday to Saturday,
hoist the white flag, flutter in the snow-storm of paper,
haul it down and crack in the mid-sun of temper.

In the pause between the first draft and the carbon   5
they glimpse the smooth hours when they were children—
the ride in the ice-cart, the ice-man's name,
the end of the route and the long walk home;

remember the sea where floats at high tide
were sea marrows growing on the scatter-green vine   10
or spools of grey toffee, or wasps' nests on water;
remember the sand and the leaves of the country.

Bell rings and they go and the voice draws their pencil
like a sled across snow; when its runners are frozen

---

1. Temporary encampment.

rope snaps and the voice then is pulling no burden   15
but runs like a dog on the winter of paper.

Their climates are winter and summer—no wind
for the kites of their hearts—no wind for a flight;
a breeze at the most, to tumble them over
and leave them like rubbish—the boy-friends of blood.   20

In the inch of the noon as they move they are stagnant.
The terrible calm of the noon is their anguish;
the lip of the counter, the shapes of the straws
like icicles breaking their tongues, are invaders.

Their beds are their oceans—salt water of weeping   25
the waves that they know—the tide before sleep;
and fighting to drown they assemble their sheep
in columns and watch them leap desks for their fences
and stare at them with their own mirror-worn faces.

In the felt of the morning the calico-minded,   30
sufficiently starched, insert papers, hit keys,
efficient and sure as their adding machines;
yet they weep in the vault, they are taut as net curtains
stretched upon frames. In their eyes I have seen
the pin men[2] of madness in marathon trim   35
race round the track of the stadium pupil.

1946

Typists

They without message, having read
the running words on their machines,
know every letter as a stamp
cutting the stencils of their ears.
Deep in their hands, like pianists,   5
all longing gropes and moves, is trapped
behind the tensile gloves of skin.

Or blind, sit with their faces locked
away from work. Their varied eyes
are stiff as everlasting flowers.   10
While fingers on a different plane
perform the automatic act

2. "Stick figures, such as children draw" [Page's note].

as questions grope along the dark
and twisting corridors of brain.

Crowded together typists touch   15
softly as ducks and seem to sense
each others' anguish with the swift
sympathy of the deaf and dumb.

1946

CARSON McCULLERS
1917–1967

Mick Kelly, the would-be musician of *The Heart Is a Lonely Hunter* (1940), and Frankie Addams, the would-be poet of *The Member of the Wedding* (1946), are Carson McCullers's most famous characters, adolescents who dream of being wedded to a new world where the children, the blacks, and the homosexuals of their hometowns would no longer be misbegotten mutes or loners. Because of her sometimes grotesque or violent plots, McCullers has been placed in the so-called Southern Gothic tradition of writing associated with her friend the playwright Tennessee Williams. Yet, as Virginia Spencer Carr's recent biography of McCullers demonstrates, the macabre atmosphere of McCullers's art reflected the confusion of her life.

The first child of Lamar Smith, a watch repairman and jewelry store owner, and Vera Marguerite (Waters) Smith, McCullers was born Lula Carson Smith in Columbus, Georgia. Like many of her adolescent heroines, Lula was an imaginative child, devoted to music in general and the piano in particular. When she was fifteen, however, an attack of rheumatic fever forced her to relinquish the strenuous demands of a musical career for a future in writing, and she began to produce for her family plays which were, in her own words, "thick with incest, lunacy, and murder." At seventeen, she arrived in New York, where she worked as a waitress and typist while taking writing courses at Columbia University. *Wunderkind* was one of her first publications, appearing in *Story* magazine when she was nineteen years old. By this time in her life, her rheumatic fever had recurred, sending her back to Georgia to recuperate.

McCullers herself became something of a "Wunderkind" (a prodigy) after the publication of *The Heart Is a Lonely Hunter*. The twenty-three-year-old author was immediately celebrated as a brilliant regionalist and supported by friendships with such established writers as W. H. Auden, Richard Wright, and Jane Bowles. Although *Reflections in a Golden Eye* (1941) was less successful than her first novel, she received fellowships from the Yaddo colony (a retreat for writers), the Guggenheim Foundation, and the American Academy of Arts and Letters. Yet both McCullers's personal friends and her professional acquaintances commented on the insecurity and neediness that made her emotionally demanding and compulsively moody.

Just before the publication of *The Heart Is a Lonely Hunter*, she had married Reeves McCullers, a would-be writer recently released from the army. But the strains of their relationship were only heightened when Carson, as she now called herself, fell in love with Annemarie Clarac-Schwarzenbach, a Swiss writer. Although Schwarzenbach did not reciprocate McCullers's feelings, the McCullerses divorced in 1941, remarried in 1945, broke up again in 1948, and reunited in 1949. Throughout this period, McCullers's literary success was remarkable. *The Ballad of the Sad Café* was chosen for *Best American Stories* in 1944, *The Member of the Wedding* received rave reviews in 1946, and four years later it was hailed as a dramatic triumph when it opened as a play in New York starring Ethel Waters and Julie Harris. Yet in 1948 McCullers tried to commit suicide, and in 1953 Reeves McCullers killed himself.

During her forties, McCullers suffered a heart attack, pneumonia, and breast cancer. With her cropped hair and whimsical smile, however, she looks in photographs from this period like the tormented but gallant adolescents who dominated her fiction. After several strokes, she died at the age of fifty. In her last two publications—the novel *Clock without Hands* (1961) and the play *The Square Root of Wonderful* (1958)—McCullers continued to explore the loneliness of adults chafing from their childhood griefs.

Wunderkind[1]

She came into the living room, her music satchel plopping against her winter-stockinged legs and her other arm weighted down with schoolbooks, and stood for a moment listening to the sounds from the studio. A soft procession of piano chords and the tuning of a violin. Then Mister Bilderbach called out to her in his chunky, guttural tones:

"That you, Bienchen?"

As she jerked off her mittens she saw that her fingers were twitching to the motions of the fugue she had practiced that morning. "Yes," she answered. "It's me."

"I," the voice corrected. "Just a moment."

She could hear Mister Lafkowitz talking—his words spun out in a silky, unintelligible hum. A voice almost like a woman's, she thought, compared to Mister Bilderbach's. Restlessness scattered her attention. She fumbled with her geometry book and *Le Voyage de Monsieur Perrichon*[2] before putting them on the table. She sat down on the sofa and began to take her music from the satchel. Again she saw her hands —the quivering tendons that stretched down from her knuckles, the sore finger tip capped with curled, dingy tape. The sight sharpened the fear that had begun to torment her for the past few months.

Noiselessly she mumbled a few phrases of encouragement to herself.

---

1. German: wonder child, prodigy.   2. A widely used French primer.

A good lesson—a good lesson—like it used to be—Her lips closed as she heard the stolid sound of Mister Bilderbach's footsteps across the floor of the studio and the creaking of the door as it slid open.

For a moment she had the peculiar feeling that during most of the fifteen years of her life she had been looking at the face and shoulders that jutted from behind the door, in a silence disturbed only by the muted, blank plucking of a violin string. Mister Bilderbach. Her teacher, Mister Bilderbach. The quick eyes behind the horn-rimmed glasses; the light, thin hair and the narrow face beneath; the lips full and loose shut and the lower one pink and shining from the bites of his teeth; the forked veins in his temples throbbing plainly enough to be observed across the room.

"Aren't you a little early?" he asked, glancing at the clock on the mantelpiece that had pointed to five minutes of twelve for a month. "Josef's in here. We're running over a little sonatina by someone he knows."

"Good," she said, trying to smile. "I'll listen." She could see her fingers sinking powerless into a blur of piano keys. She felt tired—felt that if he looked at her much longer her hands might tremble.

He stood uncertain, halfway in the room. Sharply his teeth pushed down on his bright, swollen lip. "Hungry, Bienchen?" he asked. "There's some apple cake Anna made, and milk."

"I'll wait till afterward," she said. "Thanks."

"After you finish with a very fine lesson—eh?" His smile seemed to crumble at the corners.

There was a sound from behind him in the studio and Mister Lafkowitz pushed at the other panel of the door and stood beside him.

"Frances?" he said, smiling. "And how is the work coming now?"

Without meaning to, Mister Lafkowitz always made her feel clumsy and overgrown. He was such a small man himself, with a weary look when he was not holding his violin. His eyebrows curved high above his sallow, Jewish face as though asking a question, but the lids of his eyes drowsed languorous and indifferent. Today he seemed distracted. She watched him come into the room for no apparent purpose, holding his pearl-tipped bow in his still fingers, slowly gliding the white horsehair through a chalky piece of rosin. His eyes were sharp bright slits today and the linen handkerchief that flowed down from his collar darkened the shadows beneath them.

"I gather you're doing a lot now," smiled Mister Lafkowitz, although she had not yet answered the question.

She looked at Mister Bilderbach. He turned away. His heavy shoulders pushed the door open wide so that the late afternoon sun came through the window of the studio and shafted yellow over the dusty living room. Behind her teacher she could see the squat long piano, the window, and the bust of Brahms.[3]

"No," she said to Mister Lafkowitz, "I'm doing terribly." Her thin fingers flipped at the pages of her music. "I don't know what's the matter," she said, looking at Mister Bilderbach's stooped muscular back that stood tense and listening.

Mister Lafkowitz smiled. "There are times, I suppose, when one—"

A harsh chord sounded from the piano. "Don't you think we'd better get on with this?" asked Mister Bilderbach.

"Immediately," said Mister Lafkowitz, giving the bow one more scrape before starting toward the door. She could see him pick up his violin from the top of the piano. He caught her eye and lowered the instrument. "You've seen the picture of Heime?"

Her fingers curled tight over the sharp corner of the satchel. "What picture?"

"One of Heime in the *Musical Courier* there on the table. Inside the top cover."

The sonatina began. Discordant yet somehow simple. Empty but with a sharp-cut style of its own. She reached for the magazine and opened it.

There Heime was—in the left-hand corner. Holding his violin with his fingers hooked down over the strings for a pizzicato. With his dark serge knickers strapped neatly beneath his knees, a sweater and rolled collar. It was a bad picture. Although it was snapped in profile his eyes were cut around toward the photographer and his finger looked as though it would pluck the wrong string. He seemed suffering to turn around toward the picture-taking apparatus. He was thinner—his stomach did not poke out now—but he hadn't changed much in six months.

Heime Israelsky, talented young violinist, snapped while at work in his teacher's studio on Riverside Drive.[4] Young Master Israelsky, who will soon celebrate his fifteenth birthday, has been invited to play the Beethoven concerto with—

That morning, after she had practiced from six until eight, her dad had made her sit down at the table with the family for breakfast. She hated breakfast; it gave her a sick feeling afterward. She would rather wait and get four chocolate bars with her twenty cents lunch money and munch them during school—bringing up little morsels from her pocket under cover of her handkerchief, stopping dead when the silver paper rattled. But this morning her dad had put a fried egg on her plate and she had known that if it burst—so that the slimy yellow oozed over the

3. Johannes Brahms (1833–1897), German composer.   4. Upper-class residential area on the Upper West Side of Manhattan.

white—she would cry. And that had happened. The same feeling was upon her now. Gingerly she laid the magazine back on the table and closed her eyes.

The music in the studio seemed to be urging violently and clumsily for something that was not to be had. After a moment her thoughts drew back from Heime and the concerto and the picture—and hovered around the lesson once more. She slid over on the sofa until she could see plainly into the studio—the two of them playing, peering at the notations on the piano, lustfully drawing out all that was there.

She could not forget the memory of Mister Bilderbach's face as he had stared at her a moment ago. Her hands, still twitching unconsciously to the motions of the fugue, closed over her bony knees. Tired, she was. And with a circling, sinking-away feeling like the one that often came to her just before she dropped off to sleep on the nights when she had over-practiced. Like those weary half-dreams that buzzed and carried her out into their own whirling space.

A *Wunderkind—a Wunderkind—a Wunderkind*. The syllables would come out rolling in the deep German way, roar against her ears and then fall to a murmur. Along with the faces circling swelling out in distortion, diminishing to pale blobs—Mister Bilderbach, Mrs. Bilderbach, Heime, Mister Lafkowitz. Around and around in a circle revolving to the guttural *Wunderkind*. Mister Bilderbach looming large in the middle of the circle, his face urging—with the others around him.

Phrases of music seesawing crazily. Notes she had been practicing falling over each other like a handful of marbles dropped downstairs. Bach, Debussy, Prokofieff, Brahms—timed grotesquely to the far-off throb of her tired body and the buzzing circle.

Sometimes—when she had not worked more than three hours or had stayed out from high school—the dreams were not so confused. The music soared clearly in her mind and quick, precise little memories would come back—clear as the sissy "Age of Innocence" picture Heime had given her after their joint concert was over.

A *Wunderkind—a Wunderkind*. That was what Mister Bilderbach had called her when, at twelve, she first came to him. Older pupils had repeated the word.

Not that he had ever said the word to her. "Bienchen—" (She had a plain American name but he never used it except when her mistakes were enormous.) "Bienchen," he would say, "I know it must be terrible. Carrying around all the time a head that thick. Poor Bienchen—"

Mister Bilderbach's father had been a Dutch violinist. His mother was from Prague. He had been born in this country and had spent his youth in Germany. So many times she wished she had not been born and brought up in just Cincinnati. How do you say *cheese* in German? Mister Bilderbach, what is Dutch for *I don't understand you*?

The first day she came to the studio. After she played the whole Second Hungarian Rhapsody[5] from memory. The room graying with twilight. His face as he leaned over the piano.

"Now we begin all over," he said that first day. "It—playing music —is more than cleverness. If a twelve-year-old girl's fingers cover so many keys to a second—that means nothing."

He tapped his broad chest and his forehead with his stubby hand. "Here and here. You are old enough to understand that." He lighted a cigarette and gently blew the first exhalation above her head. "And work—work—work— We will start now with these Bach inventions and these little Schumann pieces." His hands moved again—this time to jerk the cord of the lamp behind her and point to the music. "I will show you how I wish this practiced. Listen carefully now."

She had been at the piano for almost three hours and was very tired. His deep voice sounded as though it had been straying inside her for a long time. She wanted to reach out and touch his muscle-flexed finger that pointed out the phrases, wanted to feel the gleaming gold band ring and the strong hairy back of his hand.

She had lessons Tuesday after school and on Saturday afternoons. Often she stayed, when the Saturday lesson was finished, for dinner, and then spent the night and took the streetcar home the next morning. Mrs. Bilderbach liked her in her calm, almost dumb way. She was much different from her husband. She was quiet and fat and slow. When she wasn't in the kitchen, cooking the rich dishes that both of them loved, she seemed to spend all her time in their bed upstairs, reading magazines or just looking with a half-smile at nothing. When they had married in Germany she had been a *lieder* singer.[6] She didn't sing anymore (she said it was her throat). When he would call her in from the kitchen to listen to a pupil she would always smile and say that it was *gut*, very *gut*.[7]

When Frances was thirteen it came to her one day that the Bilderbachs had no children. It seemed strange. Once she had been back in the kitchen with Mrs. Bilderbach when he had come striding in from the studio, tense with anger at some pupil who had annoyed him. His wife stood stirring the thick soup until his hand groped out and rested on her shoulder. Then she turned—stood placid—while he folded his arms about her and buried his sharp face in the white, nerveless flesh of her neck. They stood that way without moving. And then his face jerked back suddenly, the anger diminished to a quiet inexpressiveness, and he had returned to the studio.

After she had started with Mister Bilderbach and didn't have time to

---

5. A very difficult piece by Franz Liszt (1811–1886).

6. A singer of German art songs.

7. Good.

see anything of the people at high school, Heime had been the only friend of her own age. He was Mister Lafkowitz's pupil and would come with him to Mister Bilderbach's on evenings when she would be there. They would listen to their teachers' playing. And often they themselves went over chamber music together—Mozart sonatas or Bloch.[8]

A *Wunderkind*—a *Wunderkind*.

Heime was a *Wunderkind*. He and she, then.

Heime had been playing the violin since he was four. He didn't have to go to school; Mister Lafkowitz's brother, who was crippled, used to teach him geometry and European history and French verbs in the afternoon. When he was thirteen he had as fine a technique as any violinist in Cincinnati—everyone said so. But playing the violin must be easier than the piano. She knew it must be.

Heime always seemed to smell of corduroy pants and the food he had eaten and rosin.[9] Half the time, too, his hands were dirty around the knuckles and the cuffs of his shirts peeped out dingily from the sleeves of his sweater. She always watched his hands when he played—thin only at the joints with the hard little blobs of flesh bulging over the short-cut nails and the babyish-looking crease that showed so plainly in his bowing wrist.

In the dreams, as when she was awake, she could remember the concert only in a blur. She had not known it was unsuccessful for her until months after. True, the papers had praised Heime more than her. But he was much shorter than she. When they stood together on the stage he came only to her shoulders. And that made a difference with people, she knew. Also, there was the matter of the sonata they played together. The Bloch.

"No, no—I don't think that would be appropriate," Mister Bilderbach had said when the Bloch was suggested to end the programme. "Now that John Powell thing—the Sonate Virginianesque."

She hadn't understood then; she wanted it to be the Bloch as much as Mister Lafkowitz and Heime.

Mister Bilderbach had given in. Later, after the reviews had said she lacked the temperament for that type of music, after they called her playing thin and lacking in feeling, she felt cheated.

"That oie oie stuff," said Mister Bilderbach, crackling the newspapers at her. "Not for you, Bienchen. Leave all that to the Heimes and vitzes and skys."[1]

A *Wunderkind*. No matter what the papers said, that was what he had called her.

---

8. Ernest Bloch (1880–1959), Jewish composer of very expressive, romantic music.
9. A resin used on violin bows.

1. I.e., musicians of Jewish or Slavic background whose names end in suffixes like *-vitz* and *-sky*. "Oie" is a Yiddish word of complaint.

Why was it Heime had done so much better at the concert than she? At school sometimes, when she was supposed to be watching someone do a geometry problem on the blackboard, the question would twist knife-like inside her. She would worry about it in bed, and even sometimes when she was supposed to be concentrating at the piano. It wasn't just the Bloch and her not being Jewish—not entirely. It wasn't that Heime didn't have to go to school and had begun his training so early, either. It was—?

Once she thought she knew.

"Play the Fantasia and Fugue," Mister Bilderbach had demanded one evening a year ago—after he and Mister Lafkowitz had finished reading some music together.

The Bach, as she played, seemed to her well done. From the tail of her eye she could see the calm, pleased expression on Mister Bilderbach's face, see his hands rise climactically from the chair arms and then sink down loose and satisfied when the high points of the phrases had been passed successfully. She stood up from the piano when it was over, swallowing to loosen the bands that the music seemed to have drawn around her throat and chest. But—

"Frances—" Mister Lafkowitz had said then, suddenly, looking at her with his thin mouth curved and his eyes almost covered by their delicate lids. "Do you know how many children Bach had?"

She turned to him, puzzled. "A good many. Twenty some odd."

"Well then—" The corners of his smile etched themselves gently in his pale face. "He could not have been so cold—then."

Mister Bilderbach was not pleased; his guttural effulgence of German words had *Kind*[2] in it somewhere. Mister Lafkowitz raised his eyebrows. She had caught the point easily enough, but she felt no deception in keeping her face blank and immature because that was the way Mister Bilderbach wanted her to look.

Yet such things had nothing to do with it. Nothing very much, at least, for she would grow older. Mister Bilderbach understood that, and even Mister Lafkowitz had not meant just what he said.

In the dreams Mister Bilderbach's face loomed out and contracted in the center of the whirling circle. The lips surging softly, the veins in his temples insisting.

But sometimes, before she slept, there were such clear memories; as when she pulled a hole in the heel of her stocking down, so that her shoe would hide it. "Bienchen, Bienchen!" And bringing Mrs. Bilderbach's work basket in and showing her how it should be darned and not gathered together in a lumpy heap.

And the time she graduated from Junior High.

2. Child.

"What you wear?" asked Mrs. Bilderbach the Sunday morning at breakfast when she told them about how they had practiced to march into the auditorium.

"An evening dress my cousin had last year."

"Ah—Bienchen!" he said, circling his warm coffee cup with his heavy hands, looking up at her with wrinkles around his laughing eyes. "I bet I know what Bienchen wants—"

He insisted. He would not believe her when she explained that she honestly didn't care at all.

"Like this, Anna," he said, pushing his napkin across the table and mincing to the other side of the room, swishing his hips, rolling up his eyes behind his horn-rimmed glasses.

The next Saturday afternoon, after her lessons, he took her to the department stores downtown. His thick fingers smoothed over the filmy nets and crackling taffetas that the saleswomen unwound from their bolts. He held colors to her face, cocking his head to one side, and selected pink. Shoes, he remembered too. He liked best some white kid pumps. They seemed a little like old ladies' shoes to her and the Red Cross label in the instep had a charity look. But it really didn't matter at all. When Mrs. Bilderbach began to cut out the dress and fit it to her with pins, he interrupted his lessons to stand by and suggest ruffles around the hips and neck and a fancy rosette on the shoulder. The music was coming along nicely then. Dresses and commencement and such made no difference.

Nothing mattered much except playing the music as it must be played, bringing out the thing that must be in her, practicing, practicing, playing so that Mister Bilderbach's face lost some of its urging look. Putting the thing into her music that Myra Hess had, and Yehudi Menuhin[3]—even Heime!

What had begun to happen to her four months ago? The notes began springing out with a glib, dead intonation. Adolescence, she thought. Some kids played with promise—and worked and worked until, like her, the least little thing would start them crying, and worn out with trying to get the thing across—the longing thing they felt— something queer began to happen—But not she! She was like Heime. She had to be. She—

Once it was there for sure. And you didn't lose things like that. A *Wunderkind.* . . . A *Wunderkind.* . . . Of her he said it, rolling the words in the sure, deep German way. And in the dreams even deeper, more certain than ever. With his face looming out at her, and the longing phrases of music mixed in with the zooming, circling round, round, round—A *Wunderkind.* A *Wunderkind.* . . .

---

3. Jewish violinist and child prodigy (b. 1916); Dame Myra Hess (1890–1965), English pianist.

This afternoon Mister Bilderbach did not show Mister Lafkowitz to the front door, as he usually did. He stayed at the piano, softly pressing a solitary note. Listening, Frances watched the violinist wind his scarf about his pale throat.

"A good picture of Heime," she said, picking up her music. "I got a letter from him a couple of months ago—telling about hearing Schnabel and Huberman and about Carnegie Hall and things to eat at the Russian Tea Room."[4]

To put off going into the studio a moment longer she waited until Mister Lafkowitz was ready to leave and then stood behind him as he opened the door. The frosty cold outside cut into the room. It was growing late and the air was seeped with the pale yellow of winter twilight. When the door swung to on its hinges, the house seemed darker and more silent than ever before she had known it to be.

As she went into the studio Mister Bilderbach got up from the piano and silently watched her settle herself at the keyboard.

"Well, Bienchen," he said, "this afternoon we are going to begin all over. Start from scratch. Forget the last few months."

He looked as though he were trying to act a part in a movie. His solid body swayed from toe to heel, he rubbed his hands together, and even smiled in a satisfied, movie way. Then suddenly he thrust this manner brusquely aside. His heavy shoulders slouched and he began to run through the stack of music she had brought in. "The Bach—no, not yet," he murmured. "The Beethoven? Yes. The Variation Sonata. Opus 26."

The keys of the piano hemmed her in—stiff and white and deadseeming.

"Wait a minute," he said. He stood in the curve of the piano, elbows propped, and looked at her. "Today I expect something from you. Now this sonata—it's the first Beethoven sonata you ever worked on. Every note is under control—technically—you have nothing to cope with but the music. Only music now. That's all you think about."

He rustled through the pages of her volume until he found the place. Then he pulled his teaching chair halfway across the room, turned it around and seated himself, straddling the back with his legs.

For some reason, she knew, this position of his usually had a good effect on her performance. But today she felt that she would notice him from the corner of her eye and be disturbed. His back was stiffly tilted, his legs looked tense. The heavy volume before him seemed to balance dangerously on the chair back. "Now we begin," he said with a peremptory dart of his eyes in her direction.

4. A famous restaurant near Carnegie Hall, where many classical music recitals are given; Arthur Schnabel (1882–1951), Austrian pianist; Bronislaw Huberman (1882–1947), Polish violinist.

Her hands rounded over the keys and then sank down. The first notes were too loud, the other phrases followed dryly.

Arrestingly his hand rose up from the score. "Wait! Think a minute what you're playing. How is this beginning marked?"

"An-*andante*."

"All right. Don't drag it into an *adagio*[5] then. And play deeply into the keys. Don't snatch it off shallowly that way. A graceful, deep-toned *andante*—"

She tried again. Her hands seemed separate from the music that was in her.

"Listen," he interrupted. "Which of these variations dominates the whole?"

"The dirge," she answered.

"Then prepare for that. This is an *andante*—but it's not salon stuff as you just played it. Start out softly, *piano*, and make it swell out just before the arpeggio. Make it warm and dramatic. And down here—where it's marked *dolce* make the counter melody sing out. You know all that. We've gone over all that side of it before. Now play it. Feel it as Beethoven wrote it down. Feel that tragedy and restraint."

She could not stop looking at his hands. They seemed to rest tentatively on the music, ready to fly up as a stop signal as soon as she would begin, the gleaming flash of his ring calling her to halt. "Mister Bilderbach—maybe if I—if you let me play on through the first variation without stopping I could do better."

"I won't interrupt," he said.

Her pale face leaned over too close to the keys. She played through the first part, and, obeying a nod from him, began the second. There were no flaws that jarred on her, but the phrases shaped from her fingers before she had put into them the meaning that she felt.

When she had finished he looked up from the music and began to speak with dull bluntness: "I hardly heard those harmonic fillings in the right hand. And incidentally, this part was supposed to take on intensity, develop the foreshadowings that were supposed to be inherent in the first part. Go on with the next one, though."

She wanted to start it with subdued viciousness and progress to a feeling of deep, swollen sorrow. Her mind told her that. But her hands seemed to gum in the keys like limp macaroni and she could not imagine the music as it should be.

When the last note had stopped vibrating, he closed the book and deliberately got up from the chair. He was moving his lower jaw from side to side—and between his open lips she could glimpse the pink healthy lane to his throat and his strong, smoke-yellowed teeth. He laid the Bee-

5. A piece whose tempo is very slow; "andante": a moderately slow or "walking" tempo.

thoven gingerly on top of the rest of her music and propped his elbows on the smooth, black piano top once more. "No," he said simply, looking at her.

Her mouth began to quiver. "I can't help it. I—"

Suddenly he strained his lips into a smile. "Listen, Bienchen," he began in a new, forced voice. "You still play the Harmonious Blacksmith,[6] don't you? I told you not to drop it from your repertoire."

"Yes," she said. "I practice it now and then."

His voice was the one he used for children. "It was among the first things we worked on together—remember. So strongly you used to play it—like a real blacksmith's daughter. You see, Bienchen, I know you so well—as if you were my own girl. I know what you have—I've heard you play so many things beautifully. You used to—"

He stopped in confusion and inhaled from his pulpy stub of cigarette. The smoke drowsed out from his pink lips and clung in a gray mist around her lank hair and childish forehead.

"Make it happy and simple," he said, switching on the lamp behind her and stepping back from the piano.

For a moment he stood just inside the bright circle the light made. Then impulsively he squatted down to the floor. "Vigorous," he said.

She could not stop looking at him, sitting on one heel with the other foot resting squarely before him for balance, the muscles of his strong thighs straining under the cloth of his trousers, his back straight, his elbows staunchly propped on his knees. "Simply now," he repeated with a gesture of his fleshy hands. "Think of the blacksmith—working out in the sunshine all day. Working easily and undisturbed."

She could not look down at the piano. The light brightened the hairs on the backs of his outspread hands, made the lenses of his glasses glitter.

"All of it," he urged. "Now!"

She felt that the marrows of her bones were hollow and there was no blood left in her. Her heart that had been springing against her chest all afternoon felt suddenly dead. She saw it gray and limp and shriveled at the edges like an oyster.

His face seemed to throb out in space before her, come closer with the lurching motion in the veins of his temples. In retreat, she looked down at the piano. Her lips shook like jelly and a surge of noiseless tears made the white keys blur in a watery line. "I can't," she whispered. "I don't know why, but I just can't—can't any more."

His tense body slackened and, holding his hand to his side, he pulled himself up. She clutched her music and hurried past him.

6. A technically difficult but unexpressive piano piece by George Frideric Handel (1685–1759), which imitates the hammering of a blacksmith.

Her coat. The mittens and galoshes. The schoolbooks and the satchel he had given her on her birthday. All from the silent room that was hers. Quickly—before he would have to speak.

As she passed through the vestibule she could not help but see his hands—held out from his body that leaned against the studio door, relaxed and purposeless. The door shut to firmly. Dragging her books and satchel she stumbled down the stone steps, turned in the wrong direction, and hurried down the street that had become confused with noise and bicycles and the games of other children.

1936, 1955

GWENDOLYN BROOKS

1917–

In a recent interview, the poet Gwendolyn Brooks declared that "what I'm fighting for now in my work [is] an *expression* relevant to all manner of blacks, poems I could take into a tavern, into the street, into the halls of a housing project." Her impassioned statement reflects a change of literary direction that occurred in the middle of her poetic career, a career she describes as falling into two distinct phases, "pre-1967" and "post-1967." Born in Chicago and graduated from Wilson Junior College in 1936, Brooks began to write poetry from the time she was seven; in the early forties, she entered a poetry workshop at the South Side Community Art Center, where, with the guidance of Inez Cunningham Stark, a Chicago socialite, she studied the major modernists and, in the words of one biographer, was "introduced to the rigors of poetic technique."

The early work that resulted from this education revealed extraordinary verbal skill, particularly an interest in what Brooks herself has called "word play," as well as exceptional accomplishment in the handling of intricate verse forms. Like such writers of the Harlem Renaissance as Langston Hughes and Countee Cullen, Brooks combined black idioms, jazz rhythm, and "street" slang with the traditional "high style" of English poetry. Married in 1939 to Henry Blakely, and the mother of two children, she produced in this period a series of volumes of verse—notably A *Street in Bronzeville* (1945), *Annie Allen* (1949), and *The Bean Eaters* (1960)—which offered vivid depictions of the lives and losses of people in Chicago's black neighborhoods, together with a novel, *Maud Martha* (1953), about a young black girl's growth to adulthood. Yet though she dealt brilliantly—sometimes poignantly and sometimes sardonically—with such distinctively "black" subjects as Bronzeville (the name given by journalists to Chicago's black ghetto), and though she became the first black woman to receive the Pulitzer Prize in poetry (for *Annie Allen*), Brooks has herself explained that "I wasn't writing consciously with the idea that blacks *must address* blacks, *must write* about blacks."

In 1967, when she attended the Second Black Writers' Conference at Fisk

University, Brooks met a number of young black poets who persuaded her that "black poets should write as blacks, about blacks, and address themselves *to* blacks." Revitalized by their commitment, she began to teach a verse-writing workshop for a group of Chicago teenagers called the Blackstone Rangers, and, becoming herself an activist leader, she sought to *"clarify* [her] language" so that she could reach out to wider audiences—specifically "to all manner of blacks." Exploring the tragedies of American racism as well as the triumphs of black endurance, her later works in this mode include several important volumes of verse—notably *In the Mecca* (1968), a book-length poetic sequence examining the diversity of existence in a Chicago housing project; *Riot* (1969); and *Beckonings* (1975)—along with an autobiography, *Report from Part I* (1972), and several books of poetry for children.

Though Brooks does not define herself as a feminist, believing that racial issues must take priority over gender questions, she has always written with extraordinary sympathy about the dilemmas of female characters like those in *Jessie Mitchell's Mother, Bronzeville Woman in a Red Hat,* and *The Mother.* In addition, she has frequently attempted to analyze the roots of what she calls "woman rage," asking, for example, "Why in the world has it been that our men have preferred either white or that pigmentation which is as close to white as possible?" Courageously exploring the real choices that real women confront, she has nevertheless also insisted that, even if "black women have got some problems with black men and vice versa, . . . these are family matters. They must be worked out within the family."

The Mother

Abortions will not let you forget.
You remember the children you got that you did not get,
The damp small pulps with a little or with no hair,
The singers and workers that never handled the air.
You will never neglect or beat   5
Them, or silence or buy with a sweet.
You will never wind up the sucking-thumb
Or scuttle off ghosts that come.
You will never leave them, controlling your luscious sigh,
Return for a snack of them, with gobbling mother-eye.   10

I have heard in the voices of the wind the voices of my dim
        killed children.
I have contracted. I have eased
My dim dears at the breasts they could never suck.
I have said, Sweets, if I sinned, if I seized
Your luck   15
And your lives from your unfinished reach,
If I stole your births and your names,
Your straight baby tears and your games,
Your stilted or lovely loves, your tumults, your marriages,
        aches, and your deaths,

If I poisoned the beginnings of your breaths,   20
Believe that even in my deliberateness I was not deliberate.
Though why should I whine,
Whine that the crime was other than mine?—
Since anyhow you are dead.
Or rather, or instead,   25
You were never made.

But that too, I am afraid,
Is faulty: oh, what shall I say, how is the truth to be said?
You were born, you had body, you died.
It is just that you never giggled or planned or cried.   30

Believe me, I loved you all.
Believe me, I knew you, though faintly, and I loved, I loved you
All.

                                                        1945

From The Womanhood

3

Stand off, daughter of the dusk,
And do not wince when the bronzy lads
Hurry to cream-yellow shining.
It is plausible. The sun is a lode.

True, there is silver under   5
The veils of the darkness.
But few care to dig in the night
For the possible treasure of stars.

                                                        1949

The Bean Eaters

They eat beans mostly, this old yellow pair.
Dinner is a casual affair.
Plain chipware on a plain and creaking wood,
Tin flatware.

Two who are Mostly Good.   5
Two who have lived their day,
But keep on putting on their clothes
And putting things away.

And remembering . . .
Remembering, with twinklings and twinges,   10
As they lean over the beans in their rented back room
        that is full of beads and receipts and dolls and
        cloths, tobacco crumbs, vases and fringes.

                                                    1960

We Real Cool

The Pool Players.
Seven at the Golden Shovel

            We real cool. We
            Left school. We

            Lurk late. We
            Strike straight. We

            Sing sin. We   5
            Thin gin. We

            Jazz June. We
            Die soon.

                                                    1960

Jessie Mitchell's Mother

Into her mother's bedroom to wash the ballooning body.
"My mother is jelly-hearted and she has a brain of jelly:
Sweet, quiver-soft, irrelevant. Not essential.
Only a habit would cry if she should die.
A pleasant sort of fool without the least iron. . . .   5
Are you better, mother, do you think it will come today?"
The stretched yellow rag that was Jessie Mitchell's mother
Reviewed her. Young, and so thin, and so straight.
So straight! as if nothing could ever bend her.
But poor men would bend her, and doing things with poor men,   10
Being much in bed, and babies would bend her over,
And the rest of things in life that were for poor women,
Coming to them grinning and pretty with intent to bend
        and to kill.
Comparisons shattered her heart, ate at her bulwarks:
The shabby and the bright: she, almost hating her daughter,   15
Crept into an old sly refuge: "Jessie's black
And her way will be black, and jerkier even than mine.
Mine, in fact, because I was lovely, had flowers

Tucked in the jerks, flowers were here and there. . . ."
She revived for the moment settled and dried-up triumphs,   20
Forced perfume into old petals, pulled up the droop,
Refueled
Triumphant long-exhaled breaths.
Her exquisite yellow youth . . .

1960

The Crazy Woman

I shall not sing a May song.
A May song should be gay.
I'll wait until November
And sing a song of gray.

I'll wait until November.   5
That is the time for me.
I'll go out in the frosty dark
And sing most terribly.

And all the little people
Will stare at me and say,   10
"That is the Crazy Woman
Who would not sing in May."

1960

Bronzeville[1] Woman in a Red Hat

hires out to Mrs. Miles

I

They had never had one in the house before.
          The strangeness of it all. Like unleashing
A lion, really. Poised
To pounce. A puma. A panther. A black
Bear.   5
There it stood in the door,
Under a red hat that was rash, but refreshing—
In a tasteless way, of course—across the dull dare,
The semi-assault of that extraordinary blackness.
The slackness   10
Of that light pink mouth told little. The eyes told
    of heavy care. . . .
But that was neither here nor there,

1. Name given to the Chicago black ghetto.

And nothing to a wage-paying mistress as should
Be getting her due whether life had been good
For her slave, or bad.   15
There it stood
In the door. They had never had
One in the house before.

But the Irishwoman had left!
A message had come.   20
Something about a murder at home.
A daughter's husband—"berserk," that was the phrase:
The dear man had "gone berserk"
And short work—
With a hammer—had been made   25
Of this daughter and her nights and days.
The Irishwoman (underpaid,
Mrs. Miles remembered with smiles),
Who was a perfect jewel, a red-faced trump,
A good old sort, a baker   30
Of rum cake, a maker
Of Mustard, would never return.
Mrs. Miles had begged the bewitched woman
To finish, at least, the biscuit blending,
To tarry till the curry was done,   35
To show some concern
For the burning soup, to attend to the tending
Of the tossed salad. "Inhuman,"
Patsy Houlihan had called Mrs. Miles.
"Inhuman." And "a fool."   40
And "a cool
One."

The Alert Agency had leafed through its files—
On short notice could offer
Only this dusky duffer[2]   45
That now made its way to her kitchen and sat on her
        kitchen stool.

                              II
Her creamy child kissed by the black maid! square on the mouth!
World yelled, world writhed, world turned to light and rolled
Into her kitchen, nearly knocked her down.

Quotations, of course, from baby books were great   50
Ready armor; (but her animal distress
Wore, too and under, a subtler metal dress,
Inheritance of approximately hate.)

2. Dense or clumsy person.

Say baby shrieked to see his finger bleed,
Wished human humoring—there was a kind   55
Of unintimate love, a love more of the mind
To order the nebulousness of that need.
—This was the way to put it, this the relief.
This sprayed a honey upon marvelous grime.
This told it possible to postpone the reef.   60
Fashioned a huggable darling out of crime.
Made monster personable in personal sight
By cracking mirrors down the personal night.

Disgust crawled through her as she chased the theme.
She, quite supposing purity despoiled,   65
Committed to sourness, disordered, soiled,
Went in to pry the ordure from the cream.
Cooing, "Come." (Come out of the cannibal wilderness,
Dirt, dark, into the sun and bloomful air.
Return to freshness of your right world, wear   70
Sweetness again. Be done with beast, duress.)

Child with continuing cling issued his No in final fire,
          Kissed back the colored maid,
          Not wise enough to freeze or be afraid.
          Conscious of kindness, easy creature bond.   75
          Love had been handy and rapid to respond.

Heat at the hairline, heat between the bowels,
Examining seeming coarse unnatural scene,
She saw all things except herself serene:
Child, big black woman, pretty kitchen towels.   80

                                              1960

Queen of the Blues

          Mame was singing
          At the Midnight Club.
          And the place was red
          With blues.
          She could shake her body   5
          Across the floor.
          For what did she have
          To lose?

          She put her mama
          Under the ground   10

Two years ago.
(Was it three?)
She covered that grave
With roses and tears.
(A handsome thing   15
To see.)

She didn't have any
Legal pa
To glare at her,
To shame   20
Her off the floor
Of the Midnight Club.
Poor Mame.

She didn't have any
Big brother   25
To shout
"No sister of mine! . . ."
She didn't have any
Small brother
To think she was everything   30
Fine.

She didn't have any
Baby girl
With velvet
Pop-open eyes.   35
She didn't have any
Sonny boy
To tell sweet
Sonny boy lies.

"Show me a man   40
What will love me
Till I die.
Now show me a man
What will love me
Till I die.   45
Can't find no such a man
No matter how hard
You try.
Go 'long, baby.
Ain't a true man left   50
In Chi.[3]

3. I.e., Chicago.

"I loved my daddy.
But what did my daddy
Do?
I loved my daddy.   55
But what did my daddy
Do?
Found him a brown-skin chicken
What's gonna be
Black and blue.   60

"I was good to my daddy.
Gave him all my dough.
I say, I was good to my daddy.
I gave him all of my dough.
Scrubbed hard in them white folks'   65
Kitchens
Till my knees was rusty
And so'. "

The M.C. hollered,
"Queen of the blues!   70
Folks, this is strictly
The queen of the blues!"
She snapped her fingers.
She rolled her hips.
What did she have   75
To lose?

But a thought ran through her
Like a fire.
"Men don't tip their
Hats to me.   80
They pinch my arms
And they slap my thighs.
But when has a man
Tipped his hat to me?"

Queen of the blues!   85
Queen of the blues!
Strictly, strictly,
The queen of the blues!

Men are low down
Dirty and mean.   90
Why don't they tip
Their hats to a queen?

1960

Riot

A riot is the language of the unheard.
—Martin Luther King, Jr.[4]

John Cabot, out of Wilma, once a Wycliffe,[5]
all whitebluerose below his golden hair,
wrapped richly in right linen and right wool,
almost forgot his Jaguar and Lake Bluff;
almost forgot Grandtully (which is The   5
Best Thing That Ever Happened To Scotch); almost
forgot the sculpture at the Richard Gray
and Distelheim; the kidney pie at Maxim's,
the Grenadine de Boeuf at Maison Henri.[6]

Because the Negroes were coming down the street.   10

Because the Poor were sweaty and unpretty
(not like Two Dainty Negroes in Winnetka)
and they were coming toward him in rough ranks.
In seas. In windsweep. They were black and loud.
And not detainable. And not discreet.   15

Gross. Gross. *"Que tu es grossier!"*[7] John Cabot
itched instantly beneath the nourished white
that told his story of glory to the World.
"Don't let It touch me! the blackness! Lord!" he whispered
to any handy angel in the sky.   20

But, in a thrilling announcement, on It drove
and breathed on him: and touched him. In that breath
the fume of pig foot, chitterling and cheap chili,
malign, mocked John. And, in terrific touch, old
averted doubt jerked forward decently,   25
cried "Cabot! John! You are a desperate man,
and the desperate die expensively today."

John Cabot went down in the smoke and fire
and broken glass and blood, and he cried "Lord!
Forgive these nigguhs that know not what they do."   30

                                                    1969

---

4. Black civil rights leader (1929–1968).
5. A follower of the fourteenth-century English
religious reformer John Wycliffe. Wilma is a city
in Alabama.

6. A famous French restaurant in New York;
Maxim's is a famous restaurant in Paris. "Grenadine de Boeuf": a gourmet beef dish.
7. French: "How gross you are!"

MURIEL SPARK
1918–

When she was an adolescent, Muriel Camberg composed torrid love letters that she signed with men's names and concealed around the house in the hope of giving her mother a good shock. This fictional gesture forecasts the witty impersonation characteristic of Spark's later writing, novels and short stories that frequently deal with blackmail, literary espionage, and the mysterious interconnections between illusion and reality.

Muriel Camberg was brought up in a prosperous Edinburgh neighborhood by a Presbyterian mother and a Jewish father. After attending James Gillespie's School for Girls, she traveled to South Africa, where she married S. O. Spark and gave birth to a son. When the marriage ended, Spark returned to Great Britain and worked for the Political Intelligence Department until the end of World War II. Then she supported herself as a free-lance writer and editor, publishing several books collaboratively with Derek Stanford, including lives of the Brontës and of Mary Shelley. After converting to Catholicism at the age of thirty-six, Spark completed her first novel, *The Comforters* (1957). Her subsequent stories and novels, set for the most part in England or in Africa, often unmask the hypocrisies of professional Catholics even as they dramatize the dilemmas of authentic spiritual conversions. It was, however, the grotesque comedy of *Memento Mori* (1959) that established Spark's reputation. Later novels—*The Prime of Miss Jean Brodie* (1961), *The Girls of Slender Means* (1963), and *The Abbess of Crewe* (1974), in particular—turn her irony toward the delusions and deceits of communities of women. In *The Fathers' Daughters*, however, she slyly satirizes the ways in which patriarchal structures dominate both life and letters.

The Fathers' Daughters

She left the old man in his deck-chair on the front, having first adjusted the umbrella awning with her own hand, and with her own hand, put his panama hat at a comfortable angle. The beach attendant had been sulky, but she didn't see why one should lay out tips only for adjusting an umbrella and a panama hat. Since the introduction of the new franc[1] it was impossible to tip less than a franc. There seemed to be a conspiracy all along the coast to hide the lesser coins from the visitors, and one could only find franc pieces in one's purse, and one had to be careful not to embarrass Father, and one . . .

She hurried along the Rue Paradis keeping in the hot shade, among

---

1. A new unit of French currency somewhat smaller than the old franc; worth about twenty cents.

all the old, old smells of Nice,[2] not only garlic wafting from the cafés, and of the hot invisible air itself, but the smells from her memory, from thirty-five summers at Nice in apartments of long ago, Father's summer salon, Father's friends' children, Father's friends, writers, young artists dating back five years at Nice, six, nine years; and then, before the war, twenty years ago—when we were at Nice, do you remember, Father? Do you remember the pension on the Boulevard Victor Hugo when we were rather poor? Do you remember the Americans at the Negresco in 1937—how changed, how demure they are now! Do you remember, Father how in the old days we disliked the thick carpets—at least, you disliked them, and what you dislike, I dislike, isn't it so, Father?

Yes, Dora, we don't care for luxury. Comfort, yes, but luxury, no.

I doubt if we can afford to stay at an hotel on the front this year, Father.

What's that? What's that you say?

I said I doubt if we ought to stay on the front this year, Father; the Promenade des Anglais is becoming very trippery. Remember you disliked the thick carpets. . . .

Yes, yes, of course.

Of course, and so we'll go, I suggest, to a little place I've found on the Boulevard Gambetta, and if we don't like that there's a very good place on the Boulevard Victor Hugo. Within our means, Father, modest and . . .

What's that you say?

I said it wasn't a vulgar place, Father.

Ah. No.

And so I'll just drop them a note and book a couple of bedrooms. They may be small, but the food . . .

Facing the sea, Dora.

They are all very vulgar places facing the sea, Father. Very distracting. No peace at all. Times have changed, you know.

Ah. Well, I leave it to you, dear. Tell them I desire a large room, suitable for entertaining. Spare no expense, Dora.

Oh, of course not, Father.

And I hope to God we've won the lottery, she thought, as she hurried up the street to the lottery kiosk. Someone's got to win it out of the whole of France. The dark-skinned blonde at the lottery kiosk took an interest in Dora, who came so regularly each morning rather than buy a newspaper to see the results. She leaned over the ticket, holding her card of numbers, comparing it with Dora's ticket, with an expression of earnest sympathy.

---

2. A popular resort city on the Mediterranean Ocean in the south of France.

"No luck," Dora said.

"Try again tomorrow," said the woman. "One never knows. Life is a lottery . . . " smiled as one who must either smile or weep. On her way back to the sea front she thought, tomorrow I will buy five hundred francs' worth. Then she thought, no, no, I'd better not, I may run short of francs and have to take Father home before time. Dora, the food here is inferior.—I know, Father, but it's the same everywhere in France now, times have changed.—I think we should move to another hotel, Dora.—The others are all very expensive, Father.—What's that? What's that you say?—There are no other rooms available, Father, because of the tourists, these days.

The brown legs of lovely young men and girls passed her as she approached the sea. I ought to appreciate every minute of this, she thought, it may be the last time. This thoroughly blue sea, these brown limbs, these white teeth and innocent inane tongues, these palm trees —all this is what we are paying for.

"Everything all right, Father?"

"Where have you been, dear?"

"Only for a walk round the back streets to smell the savours."

"Dora, you are a chip off the old block. What did you see?"

"Brown limbs, white teeth, men in shirt sleeves behind café windows, playing cards with green bottles in front of them."

"Good—you see everything with my eyes, Dora."

"Heat, smell, brown legs—it's what we are paying for, Father."

"Dora, you are becoming vulgar, if you don't mind my saying so. The eye of the true artist doesn't see life in the way of goods paid for. The world is ours. It is our birthright. We take it without payment."

"I'm not an artist like you, Father. Let me move the umbrella—you mustn't get too much sun."

"Times have changed," he said, glancing along the pebble beach, "the young men today have no interest in life."

She knew what her father meant. All along the beach, the young men playing with the air, girls, the sun; they were coming in from the sea, shaking the water from their heads; they were walking over the pebbles, then splashing into the water; they were taking an interest in their environment with every pore of their skin, as Father would have said in younger days when he was writing his books. What he meant now, when he said, "the young men of today have no interest in life" was that his young disciples, his admirers, had all gone, they were grown old and preoccupied, and had not been replaced. The last young man to seek out Father had been a bloodless-looking youth—not that one judged by appearances—who had called about seven years ago at their house in Essex. Father had made the most of him, giving up many of his mornings to sitting in the library talking about books with the

young man, about life and the old days. But this, the last of Father's disciples, had left after two weeks with a promise to send them the article
he was going to write about Father and his works. Indeed he had sent a
letter: "Dear Henry Castlemaine,—Words cannot express my admiration . . . " After that they heard no more. Dora was not really sorry. He
was a poor specimen compared with the men who, in earlier days, used
to visit Father. Dora in her late teens could have married one of three
or four vigorous members of the Henry Castlemaine set, but she had
not done so because of her widowed father and his needs as a public figure; and now she sometimes felt it would have served Father better if
she had married, because of Father—one could have contributed from
a husband's income, perhaps, to his declining years.

Dora said, "We must be going back to the hotel for lunch."

"Let us lunch somewhere else. The food there is . . . "

She helped her father from the deck-chair and, turning to the sea,
took a grateful breath of the warm blue breeze. A young man, coming
up from the sea, shook his head blindly and splashed her with water;
then noticing what he had done he said—turning and catching her by
the arm—"Oh, I'm so sorry." He spoke in English, was an Englishman, and she knew already how unmistakably she was an Englishwoman. "All right," she said, with a quick little laugh. The father was
fumbling with his stick, the incident had passed, was immediately forgotten by Dora as she took his arm and propelled him across the wide
hot boulevard where the white-suited policemen held up the impetuous traffic. "How would you like to be arrested by one of those, Dora?"
He gave his deep short laugh and looked down at her. "I'd love it, Father." Perhaps he wouldn't insist on lunching elsewhere. If only they
could reach the hotel it would be all right; Father would be too exhausted to insist. But already he was saying, "Let's find somewhere for
lunch."

"Well, we've paid for it at the hotel, Father."

"Don't be vulgar, my love."

In the following March, when Dora met Ben Donadieu for the first
time, she had the feeling she had seen him somewhere before, she
knew not where. Later she told him of this, but he could not recall having seen her. But this sense of having seen him somewhere remained
with Dora all her life. She came to believe she had met him in a former
existence. In fact, it was on the beach at Nice that she had seen him,
when he came up among the pebbles from the sea, and shook his hair,
wetting her, and took her arm, apologising.

"Don't be vulgar, my love. The hotel food is appalling. Not French
at all."

"It's the same all over France, Father, these days."

"There used to be a restaurant—what was its name?—in one of

those little streets behind the Casino. Let's go there. All the writers go there."

"Not any more, Father."

"Well, so much the better. Let's go there in any case. What's the name of the place?—Anyway, come on, I could go there blindfolded. All the writers used to go. . . ."

She laughed, because, after all, he was sweet. As she walked with him towards the Casino she did not say—Not any more, Father, do the writers go there. The writers don't come to Nice, not those of moderate means. But there's one writer here this year, Father, called Kenneth Hope, whom you haven't heard about. He uses our beach, and I've seen him once—a shy, thin, middle-aged man. But he won't speak to anyone. He writes wonderfully, Father. I've read his novels, they open windows in the mind that have been bricked-up for a hundred years. I have read *The Inventors*, which made great fame and fortune for him. It is about the inventors of patent gadgets, what lives they lead, how their minds apply themselves to invention and to love, and you would think, while you were reading *The Inventors*, that the place they live in was dominated by inventors. He has that magic, Father—he can make you believe anything. Dora did not say this, for her father had done great work too, and deserved a revival. His name was revered, his books were not greatly spoken of, they were not read. He would not understand the fame of Kenneth Hope. Father's novels were about the individual consciences of men and women, no one could do the individual conscience like Father. "Here we are, Father—this is the place, isn't it?"

"No, Dora, it's further along."

"Oh, but that's the Tumbril; it's wildly expensive."

"Really, darling!"

She decided to plead the heat, and to order only a slice of melon for lunch with a glass of her father's wine. Both tall and slim, they entered the restaurant. Her hair was drawn back, the bones of her face were good, her eyes were small and fixed ready for humour, for she had decided to be a spinster and do it properly; she looked forty-six and she did not look forty-six; her skin was dry; her mouth was thin, and growing thinner with the worry about money. The father looked eighty years old, as he was. Thirty years ago people used to turn round and say, as he passed, "That's Henry Castlemaine."

Ben lay on his stomach on his mattress on the beach enclosure. Carmelita Hope lay on her mattress, next to him. They were eating rolls and cheese and drinking white wine which the beach attendant had brought to them from the café. Carmelita's tan was like a perfect garment, drawn skintight over her body. Since leaving school she had been in numerous jobs behind the scenes of film and television studios. Now she was out of a job again. She thought of marrying Ben, he was so entirely different from all the other men of her acquaintance, he was joyful and he was serious. He was also good looking: he was half-French, brought up in England. And an interesting age, thirty-one. He was a school teacher, but Father could probably get him a job in advertising or publishing. Father could do a lot of things for them both if only he would exert himself. Perhaps if she got married he would exert himself.

"Did you see your father at all yesterday, Carmelita?"

"No; as a matter of fact he's driven up the coast. I think he's gone to stay at some villa on the Italian border."

"I should like to see more of him," said Ben. "And have a talk with him. I've never really had a chance to have a talk with him."

"He's awfully shy," said Carmelita, "with my friends."

Sometimes she felt a stab of dissatisfaction when Ben talked about her father. Ben had read all his books through and through—that seemed rather obsessive to Carmelita, reading books a second time and a third, as if one's memory was defective. It seemed to her that Ben loved her only because she was Kenneth Hope's daughter, and then, again, it seemed to her that this couldn't be so, for Ben wasn't attracted by money and success. Carmelita knew lots of daughters of famous men, and they were beset by suitors who were keen on their father's money and success. But it was the books that Ben liked about her father.

"He never interferes with me," she said. "He's rather good that way."

"I would like to have a long talk with him," Ben said.

"What about?—He doesn't like talking about his work."

"No, but a man like that. I would like to know his mind."

"What about my mind?"

"You've got a lovely mind. Full of pleasant laziness. No guile." He drew his forefinger from her knee to her ankle. She was wearing a pink bikini. She was very pretty and had hoped to become a starlet before her eighteenth birthday. Now she was very close to twenty-one and was thinking of marrying Ben instead, and was relieved that she no longer wanted to be an actress. He had lasted longer than any other boy-friend. She had often found a boy exciting at first but usually went off him quite soon. Ben was an intellectual, and intellectuals, say what you like, seemed to last longer than anyone else. There was more in them to find out about. One was always discovering new things—she supposed it was Father's blood in her that drew her towards the cultivated type, like Ben.

He was staying at a tiny hotel in a back street near the old quay. The entrance was dark, but the room itself was right at the top of the house, with a little balcony. Carmelita was staying with friends at a villa. She spent a lot of time in Ben's room, and sometimes slept there. It was turning out to be a remarkably happy summer.

"You won't see much of Father," she said, "if we get married. He works and sees nobody. Perhaps he'll get married again and—"

"That's all right," he said, "I don't want to marry your father."

Dora Castlemaine had several diplomas for elocution which she had never put to use. She got a part-time job, after the Christmas holidays that year, in Basil Street Grammar School in London, and her job was to try to reform the more pronounced Cockney accents of the more promising boys into near-standard English. Her father was amazed.

"Money, money, you are always talking about money. Let us run up debts. One is nobody without debts."

"One's credit is limited, Father. Don't be an old goose."

"Have you consulted Waite?" Waite was the publisher's young man who looked after the Castlemaine royalties, diminishing year by year.

"We've drawn more than our due for the present."

"Well, it's a bore, you going out to teach."

"It may be a bore for you," she said at last, "but it isn't for me."

"Dora, do you really mean you want to go to this job in London?"

"Yes, I want to. I'm looking forward to it."

He didn't believe her. But he said, "I suppose I'm a bit of a burden on you, Dora, these days. Perhaps I ought to go off and die."

"Like Oates at the South Pole,"[3] Dora commented.

He looked at her and she looked at him. They were shrewd in their love for each other.

She was the only woman teacher in the school, with hardly the status of a teacher. She had her own corner of the common room and, anxious to reassure the men that she had no intention of intruding upon them, would, during free periods, spread out on the table one of the weekly journals and study it intently, only looking up to say good morning or good afternoon to the masters who came in with piles of exercise books under their arms. Dora had no exercise books to correct, she was something apart, a reformer of vowel sounds. One of the masters, and then another, made conversation with her during morning break, when she passed round the sugar for the coffee. Some were in their early thirties. The ginger-moustached science master was not long graduated from Cambridge. Nobody said to her, as intelligent young men had done as late as fifteen years ago, "Are you any relation, Miss Castlemaine, to Henry Castlemaine the writer?"

3. Lawrence Edward Oates (1880–1912), one of the explorers in the Scott expedition to the South Pole; on the return journey he became crippled by frostbite and walked away from his camp into the blizzard, sacrificing himself for the safety of his companions. Unfortunately the other members perished despite this gesture.

Ben walked with Carmelita under the trees of Lincoln's Inn Fields in the spring of the year, after school, and watched the children at their games. They were a beautiful couple. Carmelita was doing secretarial work in the City. Her father was in Morocco, having first taken them out to dinner to celebrate their engagement.

Ben said, "There's a woman at the school, teaching elocution."

"Oh?" said Carmelita. She was jumpy, because since her father's departure for Morocco Ben had given a new turn to their relationship. He would not let her stay overnight in his flat in Bayswater, not even at the week-ends. He said it would be nice, perhaps, to practise restraint until they were married in the summer, and that would give them something to look forward to. "And I'm interested to see," said Ben, "what we mean to each other without sex."

This made her understand how greatly she had become obsessed with him. She thought perhaps he was practising a form of cruelty to intensify her obsession. In fact, he did want to see what they meant to each other without sex.

She called at his flat unexpectedly and found him reading, with piles of other books set out on the table as if waiting to be read.

She accused him: You only want to get rid of me so that you can read your books.

"The fourth form[4] is reading Trollope," he explained, pointing to a novel of Trollope's among the pile.

"But you aren't studying Trollope just now."

He had been reading a life of James Joyce.[5] He banged it down and said. "I've been reading all my life, and you won't stop me, Carmelita."

She sat down. "I don't want to stop you," she said.

"I know," he said.

"We aren't getting on at all well without sex," she said, and on that occasion stayed the night.

He was writing an essay on her father. She wished that her father had taken more interest in it. Father had taken them out to dinner with his party face, smiling and boyish. Carmelita had seen him otherwise—in his acute dejection, when he seemed hardly able to endure the light of day.

"What's the matter, Father?"

"There's a comedy of errors going on inside me, Carmelita." He sat at his desk most of the day while he was in these moods, doing nothing. Then, during the night, he would perhaps start writing, and sleep all the next morning, and gradually in the following days the weight would pass.

4. British equivalent of ninth grade; Anthony Trollope (1815–1882), English novelist.   5. Irish novelist (1882–1941).

"There's a man on the phone wants you, Father—an interview."

"Tell him I'm in the Middle East."

"What did you think of Ben, Father?"

"A terribly nice man, Carmelita. You've made the right choice, I think."

"An intellectual—I do like them the best, you know."

"I'd say he was the student type. Always will be."

"He wants to write an essay about you, Father. He's absolutely mad about your books."

"Yes."

"I mean, couldn't you help him, Father? Couldn't you talk to him about your work, you know?"

"Oh, God, Carmelita. It would be easier to write the bloody essay myself."

"All right, all right. I was only asking."

"I don't want any disciples, Carmelita. They give me the creeps."

"Yes, yes, all right. I know you're an artist, Father, there's no need to show off your temperament. I only wanted you to help Ben. I only . . ."

I only, she thought as she walked in Lincoln's Inn Fields with Ben, wanted him to help me. I should have said, "I want you to talk more to Ben, to help me." And Father would have said, "How do you mean?" And I would have said, "I don't know, quite." And he would have said, "Well, if you don't know what you mean, how the hell do I?"

Ben was saying, "There's a woman at the school, teaching elocution."

"Oh?" said Carmelita jumpily.

"A Miss Castlemaine. She's been there four months, and I only found out today that she's the daughter of Henry Castlemaine."

"But he's dead!" said Carmelita.

"Well, I thought so too. But apparently he isn't dead, he's very much alive in a house in Essex."

"How old is Miss Castlemaine?" said Carmelita.

"Middle-aged. Middle forties. Perhaps late forties. She's a nice woman, a classic English spinster. She teaches the boys to say 'How now brown cow.' You could imagine her doing wood-engravings in the Cotswolds. I only found out today—"

"You might manage to get invited to meet him, with any luck," Carmelita said.

"Yes, she said I must come and see him, perhaps for a week-end. Miss Castlemaine is going to arrange it. She was awfully friendly when she found I was a Castlemaine admirer. A lot of people think he's dead. Of course, his work belongs to a past world, but it's wonderful. Do you know *The Pebbled Shore*?—that's an early one."

"No, but I've read *Sin of Substance*, I think. It—"

"You mean *The Sinner and the Substance*. Oh, it has fine things in it. Castlemaine's due for a revival."

Carmelita felt a sharp stab of anger with her father, and then a kind of despair which was not yet entirely familiar to her, although already she wondered if this was how Father felt in his great depressions when he sat all day, staring and enduring, and all night miraculously wrote the ache out of his system in prose of harsh merriment.

Helplessly, she said, "Castlemaine's novels aren't as good as Father's, are they?"

"Oh, there's no comparison. Castlemaine is quite different. You can't say one type is *better* than another—goodness me!" He was looking academically towards the chimney stacks of Lincoln's Inn. This was the look in which she loved him most. After all, she thought, the Castlemaines might make everything easier for both of us.

"Father, it's really absurd. A difference of sixteen years. . . . People will say—"

"Don't be vulgar, Dora dear. What does it matter what people say? Mere age makes no difference when there's a true affinity, a marriage of true minds."

"Ben and I have a lot in common."

"I know it," he said, and sat a little higher in his chair.

"I shall be able to give up my job, Father, and spend my time here with you again. I never really wanted that job. And you are so much better in health now. . . . "

"I know."

"And Ben will be here in the evenings and the weekends. You get on well with Ben, don't you?"

"A remarkably fine man, Dora. He'll go far. He's perceptive."

"He's keen to revive your work."

"I know. He should give up that job, as I told him, and devote himself entirely to literary studies. A born essayist."

"Oh, Father, he'll have to keep his job for the meantime, anyhow. We'll need the money. It will help us all; we—"

"What's that? What's that you say?"

"I said he finds work in the grammar school stimulating, Father."

"Do you love the man?"

"It's a little difficult to say, at my age, Father."

"To me, you both seem children. Do you love him?"

"I feel," she said, "that I have known him much longer than I have. Sometimes I think I've known him all my life. I'm sure we have met before, perhaps even in a former existence. That's the decisive factor.

There's something of *destiny* about my marrying Ben; do you know what I mean?"

"Yes, I think I do."

"He was engaged, last year for a short time, to marry quite a young girl," she said. "The daughter of a novelist called Kenneth Hope. Have you heard of him, Father?"

"Vaguely," he said. "Ben," he said, "is a born disciple."

She looked at him and he looked at her, shrewd in their love for each other.

1961

SHIRLEY JACKSON
1919–1965

The author of Gothic "tales"—stories of extraordinary, often apparently supernatural events—and comic essays about childrearing, psychological novels about mental disintegration, and "potboilers" about the trials of suburban life, Shirley Jackson was a productive yet paradoxical artist. Born and raised in California, she moved with her family to Rochester, New York, in 1933, where she briefly attended the University of Rochester, then dropped out because of feelings of "depression." In 1937, she entered Syracuse University, where—with the literary critic Stanley Edgar Hyman, whom she was to marry in 1940—she founded a magazine entitled *The Spectre*. Later, the couple had four children and, while Hyman taught at Bennington, Jackson wrote rueful comedies about housekeeping, along with darker allegories like the famous short story *The Lottery* (1948); the novel *Hangsaman* (1951), about a schizophrenic seventeen-year-old; and the play *We Have Always Lived in the Castle* (1962), about a demonic and disturbed teenage girl. Usually interpreted as an updated, sardonic study of the implications of primitive fertility rituals, her *The Lottery* reveals the extent to which (as in *Hangsaman* and *We Have Always Lived in the Castle*) Jackson was preoccupied with the fates, and with the fatality, of female protagonists.

The Lottery

The morning of June 27th was clear and sunny, with the fresh warmth of a full-summer day; the flowers were blossoming profusely and the grass was richly green. The people of the village began to gather in the square, between the post office and the bank, around ten o'clock; in some towns there were so many people that the lottery took two days and had to be started on June 26th, but in this village, where there were only about three hundred people, the whole lottery took less than two hours, so it could begin at ten o'clock in the morning and still be through in time to allow the villagers to get home for noon dinner.

The children assembled first, of course. School was recently over for the summer, and the feeling of liberty sat uneasily on most of them; they tended to gather together quietly for a while before they broke into boisterous play, and their talk was still of the classroom and the teacher, of books and reprimands. Bobby Martin had already stuffed his pockets full of stones, and the other boys soon followed his example, selecting the smoothest and roundest stones; Bobby and Harry Jones and Dickie Delacroix—the villagers pronounced this name "Dellacroy"—eventually made a great pile of stones in one corner of the square and guarded it against the raids of the other boys. The girls stood aside, talking among themselves, looking over their shoulders at the boys, and the very small children rolled in the dust or clung to the hands of their older brothers or sisters.

Soon the men began to gather, surveying their own children, speaking of planting and rain, tractors and taxes. They stood together, away from the pile of stones in the corner, and their jokes were quiet and they smiled rather than laughed. The women, wearing faded house dresses and sweaters, came shortly after their menfolk. They greeted one another and exchanged bits of gossip as they went to join their husbands. Soon the women, standing by their husbands, began to call to their children, and the children came reluctantly, having to be called four or five times. Bobby Martin ducked under his mother's grasping hand and ran, laughing, back to the pile of stones. His father spoke up sharply, and Bobby came quickly and took his place between his father and his oldest brother.

The lottery was conducted—as were the square dances, the teen-age club, the Halloween program—by Mr. Summers, who had time and energy to devote to civic activities. He was a round-faced, jovial man and he ran the coal business, and people were sorry for him, because he had no children and his wife was a scold. When he arrived in the square, carrying the black wooden box, there was a murmur of conversation among the villagers, and he waved and called, "Little late today." The postmaster, Mr. Graves, followed him, carrying a three-legged stool, and the stool was put in the center of the square and Mr. Summers set the black box down on it. The villagers kept their distance, leaving a space between themselves and the stool, and when Mr. Summers said, "Some of you fellows want to give me a hand?" there was a hesitation before two men, Mr. Martin and his oldest son, Baxter, came forward to hold the box steady on the stool while Mr. Summers stirred up the papers inside it.

The original paraphernalia for the lottery had been lost long ago, and the black box now resting on the stool had been put into use even before Old Man Warner, the oldest man in town, was born. Mr. Summers spoke frequently to the villagers about making a new box, but no one liked to upset even as much tradition as was represented by the black box. There was a story that the present box had been made with some pieces of the box that had preceded it, the one that had been constructed when the first people settled down to make a village here. Every year, after the lottery, Mr. Summers began talking again about a new box, but every year the subject was allowed to fade off without anything's being done. The black box grew shabbier each year; by now it was no longer completely black but splintered badly along one side to show the original wood color, and in some places faded or stained.

Mr. Martin and his oldest son, Baxter, held the black box securely on the stool until Mr. Summers had stirred the papers thoroughly with his hand. Because so much of the ritual had been forgotten or discarded, Mr. Summers had been successful in having slips of paper substituted for the chips of wood that had been used for generations. Chips of wood, Mr. Summers had argued, had been all very well when the village was tiny, but now that the population was more than three hundred and likely to keep on growing, it was necessary to use something that would fit more easily into the black box. The night before the lottery, Mr. Summers and Mr. Graves made up the slips of paper and put them in the box, and it was then taken to the safe of Mr. Summers's coal company and locked up until Mr. Summers was ready to take it to the square next morning. The rest of the year, the box was put away, sometimes one place, sometimes another; it had spent one year in Mr. Graves's barn and another year underfoot in the post office, and sometimes it was set on a shelf in the Martin grocery and left there.

There was a great deal of fussing to be done before Mr. Summers declared the lottery open. There were the lists to make up—of heads of families, heads of households in each family, members of each household in each family. There was the proper swearing-in of Mr. Summers by the postmaster, as the official of the lottery; at one time, some people remembered, there had been a recital of some sort, performed by the official of the lottery, a perfunctory, tuneless chant that had been rattled off duly each year; some people believed that the official of the lottery used to stand just so when he said or sang it, others believed that he was supposed to walk among the people, but years and years ago this part of the ritual had been allowed to lapse. There had been, also, a ritual salute, which the official of the lottery had had to use in addressing each person who came up to draw from the box, but this also had changed with time, until now it was felt necessary only for the official to speak to each person approaching. Mr. Summers was very good at all this; in his clean white shirt and blue jeans, with one hand resting carelessly on the black box, he seemed very proper and important as he talked interminably to Mr. Graves and the Martins.

Just as Mr. Summers finally left off talking and turned to the assembled villagers, Mrs. Hutchinson came hurriedly along the path to the square, her sweater thrown over her shoulders, and slid into place in the back of the crowd. "Clean forgot what day it was," she said to Mrs. Delacroix, who stood next to her, and they both laughed softly. "Thought my old man was out back stacking wood," Mrs. Hutchinson went on, "and then I looked out the window and the kids was gone, and then I remembered it was the twenty-seventh and came a-running." She dried her hands on her apron, and Mrs. Delacroix said, "You're in time, though. They're still talking away up there."

Mrs. Hutchinson craned her neck to see through the crowd and found her husband and children standing near the front. She tapped Mrs. Delacroix on the arm as a farewell and began to make her way through the crowd. The people separated good-humoredly to let her through; two or three people said, in voices just loud enough to be heard across the crowd, "Here comes your Missus, Hutchinson," and "Bill, she made it after all." Mrs. Hutchinson reached her husband, and Mr. Summers, who had been waiting, said cheerfully, "Thought we were going to have to get on without you, Tessie." Mrs. Hutchinson said, grinning, "Wouldn't have me leave m'dishes in the sink, now, would you, Joe?" and soft laughter ran through the crowd as the people stirred back into position after Mrs. Hutchinson's arrival.

"Well, now," Mr. Summers said soberly, "guess we better get started, get this over with, so's we can go back to work. Anybody aint's here?"

"Dunbar," several people said, "Dunbar, Dunbar."

Mr. Summers consulted his list. "Clyde Dunbar," he said. "That's right. He's broke his leg, hasn't he? Who's drawing for him?"

"Me, I guess," a woman said, and Mr. Summers turned to look at her. "Wife draws for her husband," Mr. Summers said. "Don't you have a grown boy to do it for you, Janey?" Although Mr. Summers and everyone else in the village knew the answer perfectly well, it was the business of the official of the lottery to ask such questions formally. Mr. Summers waited with an expression of polite interest while Mrs. Dunbar answered.

"Horace's not but sixteen yet," Mrs. Dunbar said regretfully. "Guess I gotta fill in for the old man this year."

"Right," Mr. Summers said. He made a note on the list he was holding. Then he asked, "Watson boy drawing this year?"

A tall boy in the crowd raised his hand. "Here," he said. "I'm drawing for m'mother and me." He blinked his eyes nervously and ducked his head as several voices in the crowd said things like "Good fellow, Jack," and "Glad to see your mother's got a man to do it."

"Well," Mr. Summers said, "guess that's everyone. Old Man Warner make it?"

"Here," a voice said, and Mr. Summers nodded.

A sudden hush fell on the crowd as Mr. Summers cleared his throat and looked at the list. "All ready?" he called. "Now, I'll read the names—heads of families first—and the men come up and take a paper out of the box. Keep the paper folded in your hand without looking at it until everyone has had a turn. Everything clear?"

The people had done it so many times that they only half listened to the directions; most of them were quiet, wetting their lips, not looking around. Then Mr. Summers raised one hand high and said, "Adams." A man disengaged himself from the crowd and came forward. "Hi, Steve," Mr. Summers said, and Mr. Adams said, "Hi, Joe." They grinned at one another humorlessly and nervously. Then Mr. Adams reached into the black box and took out a folded paper. He held it firmly by one corner as he turned and went hastily back to his place in the crowd, where he stood a little apart from his family, not looking down at his hand.

"Allen," Mr. Summers said, "Anderson . . . Bentham."

"Seems like there's no time at all between lotteries any more," Mrs. Delacroix said to Mrs. Graves in the back row. "Seems like we got through with the last one only last week."

"Time sure goes fast," Mrs. Graves said.

"Clark . . . Delacroix."

"There goes my old man," Mrs. Delacroix said. She held her breath while her husband went forward.

"Dunbar," Mr. Summers said, and Mrs. Dunbar went steadily to the box while one of the women said, "Go on, Janey," and another said, "There she goes."

"We're next," Mrs. Graves said. She watched while Mr. Graves came around from the side of the box, greeted Mr. Summers gravely, and selected a slip of paper from the box. By now, all through the crowd there were men holding the small folded papers in their large hands, turning them over and over nervously. Mrs. Dunbar and her two sons stood together, Mrs. Dunbar holding the slip of paper.

"Harburt . . . Hutchinson."

"Get up there, Bill," Mrs. Hutchinson said, and the people near her laughed.

"Jones."

"They do say," Mr. Adams said to Old Man Warner, who stood next to him, "that over in the north village they're talking of giving up the lottery."

Old Man Warner snorted. "Pack of crazy fools," he said. "Listening to the young folks, nothing's good enough for *them*. Next thing you know, they'll be wanting to go back to living in caves, nobody work any more, live *that* way for a while. Used to be a saying about 'Lottery in June, corn be heavy soon.' First thing you know, we'd all be eating stewed chickweed and acorns. There's *always* been a lottery," he added petulantly. "Bad enough to see young Joe Summers up there joking with everybody."

"Some places have already quit lotteries," Mrs. Adams said.

"Nothing but trouble in *that*," Old Man Warner said stoutly. "Pack of young fools."

"Martin." And Bobby Martin watched his father go forward. "Overdyke . . . Percy."

"I wish they'd hurry," Mrs. Dunbar said to her older son. "I wish they'd hurry."

"They're almost through," her son said.

"You get ready to run tell Dad," Mrs. Dunbar said.

Mr. Summers called his own name and then stepped forward precisely and selected a slip from the box. Then he called, "Warner."

"Seventy-seventh year I been in the lottery," Old Man Warner said as he went through the crowd. "Seventy-seventh time."

"Watson." The tall boy came awkwardly through the crowd. Someone said, "Don't be nervous, Jack," and Mr. Summers said, "Take your time, son."

"Zanini."

After that, there was a long pause, a breathless pause, until Mr. Summers, holding his slip of paper in the air, said, "All right, fellows," For a minute, no one moved, and then all the slips of paper were opened. Suddenly, all the women began to speak at once, saying, "Who is it?" "Who's got it?" "Is it the Dunbars?" "Is it the Watsons?" Then the voices began to say, "It's Hutchinson. It's Bill," "Bill Hutchinson's got it."

"Go tell your father," Mrs. Dunbar said to her older son.

People began to look around to see the Hutchinsons. Bill Hutchinson was standing quiet, staring down at the paper in his hand. Suddenly, Tessie Hutchinson shouted to Mr. Summers, "You didn't give him time enough to take any paper he wanted. I saw you. It wasn't fair!"

"Be a good sport, Tessie," Mrs. Delacroix called, and Mrs. Graves said, "All of us took the same chance."

"Shut up, Tessie," Bill Hutchinson said.

"Well, everyone," Mr. Summers said, "that was done pretty fast, and now we've got to be hurrying a little more to get done in time." He consulted his next list. "Bill," he said, "you draw for the Hutchinson family. You got any other households in the Hutchinsons?"

"There's Don and Eva," Mrs. Hutchinson yelled. "Make *them* take their chance!"

"Daughters draw with their husbands' families, Tessie," Mr. Summers said gently. "You know that as well as anyone else."

"It wasn't *fair*," Tessie said.

"I guess not, Joe," Bill Hutchinson said regretfully. "My daughter draws with her husband's family, that's only fair. And I've got no other family except the kids."

"Then, as far as drawing for families is concerned, it's you," Mr. Summers said in explanation, "and as far as drawing for households is concerned, that's you, too. Right?"

"Right," Bill Hutchinson said.

"How many kids, Bill?" Mr. Summers asked formally.

"Three," Bill Hutchinson said, "There's Bill, Jr., and Nancy, and little Dave. And Tessie and me."

"All right, then," Mr. Summers said. "Harry, you got their tickets back?"

Mr. Graves nodded and held up the slips of paper. "Put them in the box, then," Mr. Summers directed. "Take Bill's and put it in."

"I think we ought to start over," Mrs. Hutchinson said, as quietly as she could. "I tell you it wasn't *fair*. You didn't give him time enough to choose. *Every*body saw that."

Mr. Graves had selected the five slips and put them in the box, and he dropped all the papers but those onto the ground, where the breeze caught them and lifted them off.

"Listen, everybody," Mrs. Hutchinson was saying to the people around her.

"Ready, Bill?" Mr. Summers asked, and Bill Hutchinson, with one quick glance around at his wife and children, nodded.

"Remember," Mr. Summers said, "take the slips and keep them folded until each person has taken one. Harry, you help little Dave." Mr. Graves took the hand of the little boy, who came willingly with him up to the box. "Take a paper out of the box, Davy," Mr. Summers said. Davy put his hand into the box and laughed. "Take just *one* paper," Mr. Summers said. "Harry, you hold it for him." Mr. Graves took the child's hand and removed the folded paper from the tight fist and held it while little Dave stood next to him and looked up at him wonderingly.

"Nancy next," Mr. Summers said. Nancy was twelve, and her school friends breathed heavily as she went forward, switching her skirt, and took a slip daintily from the box. "Bill, Jr.," Mr. Summers said, and

Billy, his face red and his feet overlarge, nearly knocked the box over as he got a paper out. "Tessie," Mr. Summers said. She hesitated for a minute, looking around defiantly, and then set her lips and went up to the box. She snatched a paper out and held it behind her.

"Bill," Mr. Summers said, and Bill Hutchinson reached into the box and felt around, bringing his hand out at last with the slip of paper in it.

The crowd was quiet. A girl whispered, "I hope it's not Nancy," and the sound of the whisper reached the edges of the crowd.

"It's not the way it used to be," Old Man Warner said clearly. "People ain't the way they used to be."

"All right," Mr. Summers said. "Open the papers. Harry, you open little Dave's."

Mr. Graves opened the slip of paper and there was a general sigh through the crowd as he held it up and everyone could see that it was blank. Nancy and Bill, Jr., opened theirs at the same time, and both beamed and laughed, turning around to the crowd and holding their slips of paper above their heads.

"Tessie," Mr. Summers said. There was a pause, and then Mr. Summers looked at Bill Hutchinson, and Bill unfolded his paper and showed it. It was blank.

"It's Tessie," Mr. Summers said, and his voice was hushed. "Show us her paper Bill."

Bill Hutchinson went over to his wife and forced the slip of paper out of her hand. It had a black spot on it, the black spot Mr. Summers had made the night before with the heavy pencil in the coal-company office. Bill Hutchinson held it up, and there was a stir in the crowd.

"All right, folks," Mr. Summers said. "Let's finish quickly."

Although the villagers had forgotten the ritual and lost the original black box, they still remembered to use stones. The pile of stones the boys had made earlier was ready; there were stones on the ground with the blowing scraps of paper that had come out of the box. Mrs. Delacroix selected a stone so large she had to pick it up with both hands and turned to Mrs. Dunbar. "Come on," she said. "Hurry up."

Mrs. Dunbar had small stones in both hands, and she said, gasping for breath, "I can't run at all. You'll have to go ahead and I'll catch up with you."

The children had stones already, and someone gave little Davy Hutchinson a few pebbles.

Tessie Hutchinson was in the center of a cleared space by now, and she held her hands out desperately as the villagers moved in on her. "It isn't fair," she said. A stone hit her on the side of the head.

Old Man Warner was saying, "Come on, come on, everyone." Steve Adams was in the front of the crowd of villagers, with Mrs. Graves beside him.

"It isn't fair, it isn't right," Mrs. Hutchinson screamed, and then they were upon her.

1948

DORIS LESSING

1919–

Doris Lessing has had a remarkably productive and influential career, a career which continues to show signs of developing through yet another of the shifts in fictional technique that have marked its several stages. Her autobiographical tetralogy *Children of Violence* (1950–1969) was praised for its social realism in depicting the growth of a heroine, Martha Quest, who comes to terms with her own identity by confronting the racism of Africa and the class stratifications of England. When Lessing published *The Golden Notebook* (1962), a number of feminists took the novel's analysis of female socialization to be, in Lessing's words, "a useful weapon in the sex war." But, in a preface (1971), the author warned that the book was really about the threat of compartmentalization in the intellectual and moral climate of the mid-twentieth century. While the issues of female identity and aging were at the center of *The Summer before the Dark* (1973), Lessing also published two moral fables: both *Briefing for a Descent into Hell* (1971) and *The Memoirs of a Survivor* (1975) move from realistic portrayals of psychological and cultural entropy to speculative allegories that seek to explain the causes and effects of the illness she associates with the modern world. In her most recent books, those fantasies have transformed themselves into science-fiction novels in which Lessing envisions other life forms on alternative worlds.

Lessing was born Doris Tayler in Kermanshah, which is in what is now Iran. Her father had gone to work in the Imperial Bank of Persia after he had been wounded in World War I and married his nurse. But, when his daughter was six, he moved the family to a three-thousand-acre farm in Southern Rhodesia. Doris Tayler studied at a Catholic convent school and at Girls' High School in the small city of Salisbury, while her parents farmed maize with the help of cheap native laborers. She read and reread the classics of European and American literature but left school at fourteen years of age to work as a nursemaid and a secretary. After she had given birth to two children in her first marriage to Frank Charles Wisdom and one child in her second marriage to Gottfried Anton Lessing, she decided that marriage was not one of her "talents." In 1949, she left Africa for England, where she briefly joined the Communist party and began earning her living as a professional writer.

While Lessing has moved from social realism to science fiction, she has maintained a strong sense of moral responsibility as a writer. A self-described "architect of the soul," she believes that the writer must be especially inventive during this age which is, she claims, "one of the great turning points of history." As a socialist, Lessing has always criticized the inequalities of capitalism. Given the destructive capabilities of technology today, moreover, Lessing believes that only an extraordinary effort of imagination can free humanity so that it will become capable of surviving. Therefore, all of her books study what she analyzed in the *Children of Violence* novels, namely, "the individual conscience in its relation with the collective." Like Martha Quest, then, Lessing is searching for a vision of unity that can empower the individual to survive the fragmentation of modern life, whether that fragmentation is associated with antagonism among races, competition between nations, the battle between men and women, the conflicts of a divided psyche, or the dualistic thinking that sets "them" against "us."

The short story *To Room Nineteen* was published one year after the appearance of *The Golden Notebook* and six years before *The Four-Gated City* (1969), the last novel in the *Children of Violence* series. At this stage of her career, Lessing focused on the problems creativity and solitude pose for women. Anna Wulf, the heroine of *The Golden Notebook*, struggles against her fear of being alone, her dread of her own destructive impulses, and her divided political allegiances, to get beyond a writing block. Like Anna, many of the female characters in *Four-Gated City* experience the so-called normal patterns of women's lives as a maddening form of self-censorship, while their breakdowns into madness lead to visionary breakthroughs that are healing not only for themselves but also for their society. Lessing, who was influenced by the psychologist R. D. Laing's theories of the divided self, sometimes views insanity as a protest against the irrationality of contemporary life, sometimes as a symptom of it, and sometimes as a solution to it.

To Room Nineteen

This is a story, I suppose, about a failure in intelligence: the Rawlingses' marriage was grounded in intelligence.

They were older when they married than most of their married friends: in their well-seasoned late twenties. Both had had a number of affairs, sweet rather than bitter; and when they fell in love—for they did fall in love—had known each other for some time. They joked that they had saved each other "for the real thing." That they had waited so long (but not too long) for this real thing was to them a proof of their sensible discrimination. A good many of their friends had married young, and now (they felt) probably regretted lost opportunities; while others, still unmarried, seemed to them arid, self-doubting, and likely to make desperate or romantic marriages.

Not only they, but others, felt they were well matched: their friends' delight was an additional proof of their happiness. They had played the same roles, male and female, in this group or set, if such a wide, loosely connected, constantly changing constellation of people could be called a set. They had both become, by virtue of their moderation, their humour, and their abstinence from painful experience, people to whom others came for advice. They could be, and were, relied on. It was one of those cases of a man and a woman linking themselves whom no one else had ever thought of linking, probably because of their similarities. But then everyone exclaimed: Of course! How right! How was it we never thought of it before!

And so they married amid general rejoicing, and because of their foresight and their sense for what was probable, nothing was a surprise to them.

Both had well-paid jobs. Matthew was a sub-editor on a large London newspaper, and Susan worked in an advertising firm. He was not the stuff of which editors or publicized journalists are made, but he was much more than "a sub-editor," being one of the essential background people who in fact steady, inspire and make possible the people in the limelight. He was content with this position. Susan had a talent for commercial drawing. She was humorous about the advertisements she was responsible for, but she did not feel strongly about them one way or the other.

Both, before they married, had had pleasant flats, but they felt it unwise to base a marriage on either flat, because it might seem like a submission of personality on the part of the one whose flat it was not. They moved into a new flat in South Kensington on the clear understanding that when their marriage had settled down (a process they knew would not take long, and was in fact more a humorous concession to popular wisdom than what was due to themselves) they would buy a house and start a family.

And this is what happened. They lived in their charming flat for two years, giving parties and going to them, being a popular young married couple, and then Susan became pregnant, she gave up her job, and they bought a house in Richmond. It was typical of this couple that they had a son first, then a daughter, then twins, son and daughter. Everything right, appropriate, and what everyone would wish for, if they could choose. But people did feel these two had chosen; this balanced and sensible family was no more than what was due to them because of their infallible sense for *choosing* right.

And so they lived with their four children in their gardened house in Richmond and were happy. They had everything they had wanted and had planned for.

And yet . . .

Well, even this was expected, that there must be a certain flatness. . . .

Yes, yes, of course, it was natural they sometimes felt like this. Like what?

Their life seemed to be like a snake biting its tail. Matthew's job for the sake of Susan, children, house, and garden—which caravanserai needed a well-paid job to maintain it. And Susan's practical intelligence for the sake of Matthew, the children, the house and the garden—which unit would have collapsed in a week without her.

But there was no point about which either could say: "For the sake of *this* is all the rest." Children? But children can't be a center of life and a reason for being. They can be a thousand things that are delightful, interesting, satisfying, but they can't be a wellspring to live from. Or they shouldn't be. Susan and Matthew knew that well enough.

Matthew's job? Ridiculous. It was an interesting job, but scarcely a reason for living. Matthew took pride in doing it well; but he could hardly be expected to be proud of the newspaper: the newspaper he read, *his* newspaper, was not the one he worked for.

Their love for each other? Well, that was nearest it. If this wasn't a centre, what was? Yes, it was around this point, their love, that the whole extraordinary structure revolved. For extraordinary it certainly was. Both Susan and Matthew had moments of thinking so, of looking in secret disbelief at this thing they had created: marriage, four children, big house, garden, charwomen, friends, cars . . . and this *thing*, this entity, all of it had come into existence, been blown into being out of nowhere, because Susan loved Matthew and Matthew loved Susan. Extraordinary. So that was the central point, the wellspring.

And if one felt that it simply was not strong enough, important enough, to support it all, well whose fault was that? Certainly neither Susan's nor Matthew's. It was in the nature of things. And they sensibly blamed neither themselves nor each other.

On the contrary, they used their intelligence to preserve what they had created from a painful and explosive world: they looked around them, and took lessons. All around them, marriages collapsing, or breaking, or rubbing along (even worse, they felt). They must not make the same mistakes, they must not.

They had avoided the pitfall so many of their friends had fallen into —of buying a house in the country *for the sake of the children*; so that the husband became a weekend husband, a weekend father, and the wife always careful not to ask what went on in the town flat which they called (in joke) a bachelor flat. No. Matthew was a full-time husband, a full-time father, and at nights, in the big married bed in the married bedroom (which had an attractive view of the river) they lay beside each other talking and he told her about his day, and what he had done, and whom he had met; and she told him about her day (not as interesting, but that was not her fault) for both knew of the hidden resentments and deprivations of the woman who has lived her own life—and above all, has earned her own living—and is now dependent on a husband for outside interests and money.

Nor did Susan make the mistake of taking a job for the sake of her in-dependence, which she might very well have done, since her old firm, missing her qualities of humour, balance, and sense, invited her often to go back. Children needed their mother to a certain age, that both par-ents knew and agreed on; and when these four healthy wisely brought-up children were of the right age, Susan would work again, because she knew, and so did he, what happened to women of fifty at the height of their energy and ability, with grown-up children who no longer needed their full devotion.

So here was this couple, testing their marriage, looking after it, treat-ing it like a small boat full of helpless people in a very stormy sea. Well, of course, so it was. . . . The storms of the world were bad, but not too close—which is not to say they were selfishly felt: Susan and Matthew were both well-informed and responsible people. And the inner storms and quicksands were understood and charted. So everything was all right. Everything was in order. Yes, things were under control.

So what did it matter if they felt dry, flat? People like themselves, fed on a hundred books (psychological, anthropological, sociological), could scarcely be unprepared for the dry, controlled wistfulness which is the distinguishing mark of the intelligent marriage. Two people, endowed with education, with discrimination, with judgment, linked together voluntarily from their will to be happy together and to be of use to others—one sees them everywhere, one knows them, one even is that thing oneself: sadness because so much is after all so little. These two, unsurprised, turned towards each other with even more courtesy and gentle love: this was life, that two people, no matter how carefully cho-sen, could not be everything to each other. In fact, even to say so, to think in such a way, was banal, they were ashamed to do it.

It was banal, too, when one night Matthew came home late and confessed he had been to a party, taken a girl home and slept with her. Susan forgave him, of course. Except that forgiveness is hardly the word. Understanding, yes. But if you understand something, you don't forgive it, you are the thing itself: forgiveness is for what you *don't* un-derstand. Nor had he *confessed*—what sort of word is that?

The whole thing was not important. After all, years ago they had joked: Of course I'm not going to be faithful to you, no one can be faithful to one other person for a whole lifetime. (And there was the word *faithful*—stupid, all these words, stupid, belonging to a savage old world.) But the incident left both of them irritable. Strange, but they were both bad-tempered, annoyed. There was something unassimilable about it.

Making love splendidly after he had come home that night, both had felt that the idea that Myra Jenkins, a pretty girl met at a party, could be even relevant was ridiculous. They had loved each other for over a decade, would love each other for years more. Who, then, was Myra Jenkins?

Except, thought Susan, unaccountably bad-tempered, she was (is?) the first. In ten years. So either the ten years' fidelity was not important, or she isn't. (No, no, there is something wrong with this way of thinking, there must be.) But if she isn't important, presumably it wasn't important either when Matthew and I first when to bed with each other that afternoon whose delight even now (like a very long shadow at sundown) lays a long, wandlike finger over us. (Why did I say sundown?) Well, if what we felt that afternoon was not important, nothing is important, because if it hadn't been for what we felt, we wouldn't be Mr. and Mrs. Rawlings with four children, etc., etc. The whole thing is *absurd*—for him to have come home and told me was absurd. For him not to have told me was absurd. For me to care, or for that matter not to care, is absurd . . . and who is Myra Jenkins? Why, no one at all.

There was only one thing to do, and of course these sensible people did it: they put the thing behind them, and consciously, knowing what they were doing, moved forward into a different phase of their marriage, giving thanks for past good fortune as they did so.

For it was inevitable that the handsome, blond, attractive, manly man, Matthew Rawlings, should be at times tempted (oh, what a word!) by the attractive girls at parties she could not attend because of the four children; and that sometimes he would succumb (a word even more repulsive, if possible) and that she, a good-looking woman in the big well-tended garden at Richmond, would sometimes be pierced as by an arrow from the sky with bitterness. Except that bitterness was not in order, it was out of court. Did the casual girls touch the marriage? They did not. Rather it was they who knew defeat because of the handsome Matthew Rawlings's marriage body and soul to Susan Rawlings.

In that case why did Susan feel (though luckily not for longer than a few seconds at a time) as if life had become a desert, and that nothing mattered, and that her children were not her own?

Meanwhile her intelligence continued to assert that all was well. What if her Matthew did have an occasional sweet afternoon, the odd affair? For she knew quite well, except in her moments of aridity, that they were very happy, that the affairs were not important.

Perhaps that was the trouble? It was in the nature of things that the adventures and delights could no longer be hers, because of the four children and the big house that needed so much attention. But perhaps she was secretly wishing, and even knowing that she did, that the wildness and the beauty could be his. But he was married to her. She was married to him. They were married inextricably. And therefore the gods could not strike him with the real magic, not really. Well, was it Susan's fault that after he came home from an adventure he looked harassed rather than fulfilled? (In fact, that was how she knew he had been *unfaithful*, because of his sullen air, and his glances at her, similar to hers at him: What is it that I share with this person that shields all delight from me?) But none of it by anybody's fault. (But what did they feel ought to be somebody's fault?) Nobody's fault, nothing to be at fault, no one to blame, no one to offer or to take it . . . and nothing wrong, either, except that Matthew never was really struck, as he wanted to be, by joy; and that Susan was more and more often threatened by emptiness. (It was usually in the garden that she was invaded by this feeling: she was coming to avoid the garden, unless the children or Matthew were with her.) There was no need to use the dramatic words, unfaithful, forgive, and the rest: intelligence forbade them. Intelligence barred, too, quarrelling, sulking, anger, silences of withdrawal, accusations and tears. Above all, intelligence forbids tears.

A high price has to be paid for the happy marriage with the four healthy children in the large white gardened house.

And they were paying it, willingly, knowing what they were doing. When they lay side by side or breast to breast in the big civilized bedroom overlooking the wild sullied river, they laughed, often, for no particular reason; but they knew it was really because of these two small people, Susan and Matthew, supporting such an edifice on their intelligent love. The laugh comforted them; it saved them both, though from what, they did not know.

They were now both fortyish. The older children, boy and girl, were ten and eight, at school. The twins, six, were still at home. Susan did not have nurses or girls to help her: childhood is short; and she did not regret the hard work. Often enough she was bored, since small children can be boring; she was often very tired; but she regretted nothing. In another decade, she would turn herself back into being a woman with a life of her own.

Soon the twins would go to school, and they would be away from home from nine until four. These hours, so Susan saw it, would be the preparation for her own slow emancipation away from the role of hub-of-the-family into woman-with-her-own-life. She was already planning for the hours of freedom when all the children would be "off her hands." That was the phrase used by Matthew and by Susan and by their friends, for the moment when the youngest child went off to school. "They'll be off your hands, darling Susan, and you'll have time to yourself." So said Matthew, the intelligent husband, who had often enough commended and consoled Susan, standing by her in spirit during the years when her soul was not her own, as she said, but her children's.

What it amounted to was that Susan saw herself as she had been at twenty-eight, unmarried; and then again somewhere about fifty, blossoming from the root of what she had been twenty years before. As if the essential Susan were in abeyance, as if she were in cold storage. Matthew said something like this to Susan one night: and she agreed that it was true—she did feel something like that. What, then, was this essential Susan? She did not know. Put like that it sounded ridiculous, and she did not really feel it. Anyway, they had a long discussion about the whole thing before going off to sleep in each other's arms.

So the twins went off to their school, two bright affectionate children who had no problems about it, since their older brother and sister had trodden this path so successfully before them. And now Susan was going to be alone in the big house, every day of the school term, except for the daily woman who came in to clean.

It was now, for the first time in this marriage, that something happened which neither of them had foreseen.

This is what happened. She returned, at nine-thirty, from taking the twins to the school by car, looking forward to seven blissful hours of freedom. On the first morning she was simply restless, worrying about the twins "naturally enough" since this was their first day away at school. She was hardly able to contain herself until they came back. Which they did happily, excited by the world of school, looking forward to the next day. And the next day Susan took them, dropped them, came back, and found herself reluctant to enter her big and beautiful home because it was as if something was waiting for her there that she did not wish to confront. Sensibly, however, she parked the car in the garage, entered the house, spoke to Mrs. Parkes the daily woman about her duties, and went up to her bedroom. She was possessed by a fever which drove her out again, downstairs, into the kitchen, where Mrs. Parkes was making cake and did not need her, and into the garden. There she sat on a bench, and tried to calm herself, looking at trees, at a brown glimpse of the river. But she was filled with tension, like a panic: as if an enemy was in the garden with her. She spoke to herself severely, thus: All this is quite natural. First, I spent twelve years of my adult life working, *living my own life*. Then I married, and from the moment I became pregnant for the first time I signed myself over, so to speak, to other people. To the children. Not for one moment in twelve years have I been alone, had time to myself. So now I have to learn to be myself again. That's all.

And she went indoors to help Mrs. Parkes cook and clean, and found some sewing to do for the children. She kept herself occupied every day. At the end of the first term she understood she felt two contrary emotions. First: secret astonishment and dismay that during those weeks when the house was empty of children she had in fact been more occupied (had been careful to keep herself occupied) than ever she had been when the children were around her needing her continual attention. Second: that now she knew the house would be full of them, and for five weeks, she resented the fact she would never be alone. She was already looking back at those hours of sewing, cooking (but by herself), as at a lost freedom which would not be hers for five long weeks. And the two months of term which would succeed the five weeks stretched alluringly open to her—freedom. But what freedom—when in fact she had been so careful *not* to be free of small duties during the last weeks? She looked at herself, Susan Rawlings, sitting in a big chair by the window in the bedroom, sewing shirts or dresses, which she might just as well have bought. She saw herself making cakes for hours at a time in the big family kitchen: yet usually she bought cakes. What she saw was a woman alone, that was true, but she had not felt alone. For instance, Mrs. Parkes was always somewhere in the house. And she did not like being in the garden at all, because of the closeness there of the enemy —irritation, restlessness, emptiness, whatever it was, which keeping her hands occupied made less dangerous for some reason.

Susan did not tell Matthew of these thoughts. They were not sensible. She did not recognize herself in them. What should she say to her dear friend and husband Matthew? "When I go into the garden, that is, if the children are not there, I feel as if there is an enemy there waiting to invade me." "What enemy, Susan darling?" "Well I don't know, really. . . ." "Perhaps you should see a doctor?"

No, clearly this conversation should not take place. The holidays began and Susan welcomed them. Four children, lively, energetic, intelligent, demanding: she was never, not for a moment of her day, alone. If she was in a room, they would be in the next room, or waiting for her to do something for them; or it would soon be time for lunch or tea, or to take one of them to the dentist. Something to do: five weeks of it, thank goodness.

On the fourth day of these so welcome holidays, she found she was storming with anger at the twins, two shrinking beautiful children who (and this is what checked her) stood hand in hand looking at her with sheer dismayed disbelief. This was their calm mother, shouting at them. And what for? They had come to her with some game, some bit of nonsense. They looked at each other, moved closer for support, and went off hand in hand, leaving Susan holding on to the windowsill of the living room, breathing deep, feeling sick. She went to lie down, telling the older children she had a headache. She heard the boy Harry telling the little ones: "It's all right, Mother's got a headache." She heard that *It's all right* with pain.

That night she said to her husband: "Today I shouted at the twins, quite unfairly." She sounded miserable, and he said gently: "Well, what of it?"

"It's more of an adjustment than I thought, their going to school."

"But Susie, Susie darling . . . " For she was crouched weeping on the bed. He comforted her: "Susan, what is all this about? You shouted at them? What of it? If you shouted at them fifty times a day it wouldn't be more than the little devils deserve." But she wouldn't laugh. She wept. Soon he comforted her with his body. She became calm. Calm, she wondered what was wrong with her, and why she should mind so much that she might, just once, have behaved unjustly with the children. What did it matter? They had forgotten it all long ago: Mother had a headache and everything was all right.

It was a long time later that Susan understood that that night, when she had wept and Matthew had driven the misery out of her with his big solid body, was the last time, ever in their married life, that they had been—to use their mutual language—with each other. And even that was a lie, because she had not told him of her real fears at all.

The five weeks passed, and Susan was in control of herself, and good and kind, and she looked forward to the holidays with a mixture of fear and longing. She did not know what to expect. She took the twins off to school (the elder children took themselves to school) and she returned to the house determined to face the enemy wherever he was, in the house, or the garden or—where?

She was again restless, she was possessed by restlessness. She cooked and sewed and worked as before, day after day, while Mrs. Parkes remonstrated: "Mrs. Rawlings, what's the need for it? I can do that, it's what you pay me for."

And it was so irrational that she checked herself. She would put the car into the garage, go up to her bedroom, and sit, hands in her lap, forcing herself to be quiet. She listened to Mrs. Parkes moving around the house. She looked out into the garden and saw the branches shake the trees. She sat defeating the enemy, restlessness. Emptiness. She ought to be thinking about her life, about herself. But she did not. Or perhaps she could not. As soon as she forced her mind to think about Susan (for what else did she want to be alone for?) it skipped off to thoughts of butter or school clothes. Or it thought of Mrs. Parkes. She realized that she sat listening for the movements of the cleaning woman, following her every turn, bend, thought. She followed her in her mind from kitchen to bathroom, from table to oven, and it was as if the duster, the cleaning cloth, the saucepan, were in her own hand. She would hear herself saying: No, not like that, don't put that there. . . . Yet she did not give a damn what Mrs. Parkes did, or if she did it at all. Yet she could not prevent herself from being conscious of her, every minute. Yes, this was what was wrong with her: she needed, when she was alone, to be really alone, with no one near. She could not endure the knowledge that in ten minutes or in half an hour Mrs. Parkes would call up the stairs: "Mrs. Rawlings, there's no silver polish. Madam, we're out of flour."

So she left the house and went to sit in the garden where she was screened from the house by trees. She waited for the demon to appear and claim her, but he did not.

She was keeping him off, because she had not, after all, come to an end of arranging herself.

She was planning how to be somewhere where Mrs. Parkes would not come after her with a cup of tea, or a demand to be allowed to telephone (always irritating since Susan did not care who she telephoned or how often), or just a nice talk about something. Yes, she needed a place, or a state of affairs, where it would not be necessary to keep reminding herself: In ten minutes I must telephone Matthew about . . . and at half past three I must leave early for the children because the car needs cleaning. And at ten o'clock tomorrow I must remember . . . She was possessed with resentment that the seven hours of freedom in every day (during weekdays in the school term) were not free, that never, not for one second, ever, was she free from the pressure of time, from having to remember this or that. She could never forget herself; never really let herself go into forgetfulness.

Resentment. It was poisoning her. (She looked at this emotion and thought it was absurd. Yet she felt it.) She was a prisoner. (She looked at this thought too, and it was no good telling herself it was a ridiculous one.) She must tell Matthew—but what? She was filled with emotions that were utterly ridiculous, that she despised, yet that nevertheless she was feeling so strongly she could not shake them off.

The school holidays came round, and this time they were for nearly two months, and she behaved with a conscious controlled decency that nearly drove her crazy. She would lock herself in the bathroom, and sit on the edge of the bath, breathing deep, trying to let go into some kind of calm. Or she went up into the spare room, usually empty, where no one would expect her to be. She heard the children calling "Mother, Mother," and kept silent, feeling guilty. Or she went to the very end of the garden, by herself, and looked at the slow-moving brown river; she looked at the river and closed her eyes and breathed slow and deep, taking it into her being, into her veins.

Then she returned to the family, wife and mother, smiling and responsible, feeling as if the pressure of these people—four lively children and her husband—were a painful pressure on the surface of her skin, a hand pressing on her brain. She did not once break down into irritation during these holidays, but it was like living out a prison sentence, and when the children went back to school, she sat on a white stone seat near the flowing river, and she thought: It is not even a year since the twins went to school, since *they were off my hands* (What on earth did I think I meant when I used that stupid phrase?) and yet I'm a different person. I'm simply not myself. I don't understand it.

Yet she had to understand it. For she knew that this structure—big white house, on which the mortgage still cost four hundred a year, a husband, so good and kind and insightful, four children, all doing so nicely, and the garden where she sat, and Mrs. Parkes the cleaning woman—all this depended on her, and yet she could not understand why, or even what it was she contributed to it.

She said to Matthew in their bedroom: "I think there must be something wrong with me."

And he said: "Surely not, Susan? You look marvellous—you're as lovely as ever."

She looked at the handsome blond man, with his clear, intelligent, blue-eyed face, and thought: Why is it I can't tell him? Why not? And she said: "I need to be alone more than I am."

At which he swung his slow blue gaze at her, and she saw what she had been dreading: Incredulity. Disbelief. And fear. An incredulous blue stare from a stranger who was her husband, as close to her as her own breath.

He said: "But the children are at school and off your hands."

She said to herself: I've got to force myself to say: Yes, but do you realize that I never feel free? There's never a moment I can say to myself: There's nothing I have to remind myself about, nothing I have to do in half an hour, or an hour, or two hours. . . .

But she said: "I don't feel well."

He said: "Perhaps you need a holiday."

She said, appalled: "But not without you, surely?" For she could not imagine herself going off without him. Yet that was what he meant. Seeing her face, he laughed, and opened his arms, and she went into them, thinking: Yes, yes, but why can't I say it? And what is it I have to say?

She tried to tell him, about never being free. And he listened and said: "But Susan, what sort of freedom can you possibly want—short of being dead! Am I ever free? I go to the office, and I have to be there at ten—all right, half past ten, sometimes. And I have to do this or that, don't I? Then I've got to come home at a certain time—I don't mean it, you know I don't—but if I'm not going to be back home at six I telephone you. When can I ever say to myself: I have nothing to be responsible for in the next six hours?"

Susan, hearing this, was remorseful. Because it was true. The good marriage, the house, the children, depended just as much on his volun-

tary bondage as it did on hers. But why did he not feel bound? Why
didn't he chafe and become restless? No, there was something really
wrong with her and this proved it.

And that word *bondage*—why had she used it? She had never felt
marriage, or the children, as bondage. Neither had he, or surely they
wouldn't be together lying in each other's arms content after twelve
years of marriage.

No, her state (whatever it was) was irrelevant, nothing to do with her
real good life with her family. She had to accept the fact that after all,
she was an irrational person and to live with it. Some people had to live
with crippled arms, or stammers, or being deaf. She would have to live
knowing she was subject to a state of mind she could not own.

Nevertheless, as a result of this conversation with her husband, there
was a new regime next holidays.

The spare room at the top of the house now had a cardboard sign
saying: PRIVATE! DO NOT DISTURB! on it. (This sign had been drawn in
coloured chalks by the children, after a discussion between the parents
in which it was decided that was psychologically the right thing.) The
family and Mrs. Parkes knew this was "Mother's Room" and that she
was entitled to her privacy. Many serious conversations took place between Matthew and the children about not taking Mother for granted.
Susan overheard the first, between father and Harry, the older boy, and
was surprised at her irritation over it. Surely she could have a room
somewhere in that big house and retire into it without such a fuss being
made? Without it being so solemnly discussed? Why couldn't she simply have announced: "I'm going to fit out the little top room for myself,
and when I'm in it I'm not to be disturbed for anything short of fire"?
Just that, and finished; instead of long earnest discussions. When she
heard Harry and Matthew explaining it to the twins with Mrs. Parkes
coming in—"Yes, well, a family sometimes gets on top of a woman"
—she had to go right away to the bottom of the garden until the devils
of exasperation had finished their dance in her blood.

But now there was a room, and she could go there when she liked,
she used it seldom: she felt even more caged there than in her bedroom.
One day she had gone up there after a lunch for ten children she had
cooked and served because Mrs. Parkes was not there, and had sat alone
for a while looking into the garden. She saw the children stream out
from the kitchen and stand looking up at the window where she sat behind the curtains. They were all—her children and their friends—discussing Mother's Room. A few minutes later, the chase of children in
some game came pounding up the stairs, but ended as abruptly as if
they had fallen over a ravine, so sudden was the silence. They had remembered she was there, and had gone silent in a great gale of "Hush!

Shhhhhh! Quiet, you'll disturb her. . . ." And they went tiptoeing downstairs like criminal conspirators. When she came down to make tea for them, they all apologized. The twins put their arms around her, from front and back, making a human cage of loving limbs, and promised it would never occur again. "We forgot, Mummy, we forgot all about it!"

What it amounted to was that Mother's Room, and her need for privacy, had become a valuable lesson in respect for other people's rights. Quite soon Susan was going up to the room only because it was a lesson it was a pity to drop. Then she took sewing up there, and the children and Mrs. Parkes came in and out: it had become another family room.

She sighed, and smiled, and resigned herself—she made jokes at her own expense with Matthew over the room. That is, she did from the self she liked, she respected. But at the same time, something inside her howled with impatience, with rage. . . . And she was frightened. One day she found herself kneeling by her bed and praying: "Dear God, keep it away from me, keep him away from me." She meant the devil, for she now thought of it, not caring if she were irrational, as some sort of demon. She imagined him, or it, as a youngish man, or perhaps a middle-aged man pretending to be young. Or a man young-looking from immaturity? At any rate, she saw the young-looking face which, when she drew closer, had dry lines about mouth and eyes. He was thinnish, meager in build. And he had a reddish complexion, and ginger hair. That was he—a gingery, energetic man, and he wore a reddish hairy jacket, unpleasant to the touch.

Well, one day she saw him. She was standing at the bottom of the garden, watching the river ebb past, when she raised her eyes and saw this person, or being, sitting on the white stone bench. He was looking at her, and grinning. In his hand was a long crooked stick, which he had picked off the ground, or broken off the tree above him. He was absent-mindedly, out of an absentminded or freakish impulse of spite, using the stick to stir around in the coils of a blindworm or a grass snake (or some kind of snake-like creature: it was whitish and unhealthy to look at, unpleasant). The snake was twisting about, flinging its coils from side to side in a kind of dance of protest against the teasing prodding stick.

Susan looked at him thinking: Who is the stranger? What is he doing in our garden? Then she recognized the man around whom her terrors had crystallized. As she did so, he vanished. She made herself walk over to the bench. A shadow from a branch lay across thin emerald grass, moving jerkily over its roughness, and she could see why she had taken it for a snake, lashing and twisting. She went back to the house thinking: Right, then, so I've seen him with my own eyes, so I'm not crazy after all—there *is* a danger because I've seen him. He is lurking in the garden and sometimes even in the house, and he wants *to get into me and to take me over*.

She dreamed of having a room or a place, anywhere, where she could go and sit, by herself, no one knowing where she was.

Once, near Victoria, she found herself outside a news agent that had Rooms to Let advertised. She decided to rent a room, telling no one. Sometimes she could take the train in from Richmond and sit alone in it for an hour or two. Yet how could she? A room would cost three or four pounds a week, and she earned no money, and how could she explain to Matthew that she needed such a sum? What for? It did not occur to her that she was taking it for granted she wasn't going to tell him about the room.

Well, it was out of the question, having a room; yet she knew she must.

One day, when a school term was well established, and none of the children had measles or other ailments, and everything seemed in order, she did the shopping early, explained to Mrs. Parkes she was meeting an old school friend, took the train to Victoria, searched until she found a small quiet hotel, and asked for a room for the day. They did not let rooms by the day, the manageress said, looking doubtful, since Susan so obviously was not the kind of woman who needed a room for unrespectable reasons. Susan made a long explanation about not being well, being unable to shop without frequent rests for lying down. At last she was allowed to rent the room provided she paid a full night's price for it. She was taken up by the manageress and a maid, both concerned over the state of her health . . . which must be pretty bad if, living at Richmond (she had signed her name and address in the register), she needed a shelter at Victoria.

The room was ordinary and anonymous, and was just what Susan needed. She put a shilling in the gas fire, and sat, eyes shut, in a dingy armchair with her back to a dingy window. She was alone. She was alone. She was alone. She could feel pressures lifting off her. First the sounds of traffic came very loud; then they seemed to vanish; she might even have slept a little. A knock on the door: it was Miss Townsend the manageress, bringing her a cup of tea with her own hands, so concerned was she over Susan's long silence and possible illness.

Miss Townsend was a lonely woman of fifty, running this hotel with all the rectitude expected of her, and she sensed in Susan the possibility of understanding companionship. She stayed to talk. Susan found herself in the middle of a fantastic story about her illness, which got more and more improbable as she tried to make it tally with the large house at Richmond, well-off husband, and four children. Suppose she said instead: Miss Townsend, I'm here in your hotel because I need to be alone for a few hours, above all *alone and with no one knowing where I am*. She said it mentally, and saw, mentally, the look that would inevitably come on Miss Townsend's elderly maiden's face. "Miss Townsend, my four children and my husband are driving me insane, do you understand that? Yes, I can see from the gleam of hysteria in your eyes that comes from loneliness controlled but only just contained that I've got everything in the world you've ever longed for. Well, Miss Townsend, I don't want any of it. You can have it, Miss Townsend. I wish I was absolutely alone in the world, like you. Miss Townsend, I'm besieged by seven devils, Miss Townsend, Miss Townsend, let me stay here in your hotel where the devils can't get me. . . ." Instead of saying all this, she described her anaemia, agreed to try Miss Townsend's remedy for it, which was raw liver, minced, between whole-meal bread, and said yes, perhaps it would be better if she stayed at home and let a friend do shopping for her. She paid her bill and left the hotel, defeated.

At home Mrs. Parkes said she didn't really like it, no, not really, when Mrs. Rawlings was away from nine in the morning until five. The teacher had telephoned from school to say Joan's teeth were paining her, and she hadn't known what to say; and what was she to make for the children's tea, Mrs. Rawlings hadn't said.

All this was nonsense, of course, Mrs. Parkes's complaint was that Susan had withdrawn herself spiritually, leaving the burden of the big house on her.

Susan looked back at her day of "freedom" which had resulted in her becoming a friend to the lonely Miss Townsend, and in Mrs. Parkes's remonstrances. Yet she remembered the short blissful hour of being alone, really alone. She was determined to arrange her life, no matter what it cost, so that she could have that solitude more often. An absolute solitude, where no one knew her or cared about her.

But how? She thought of saying to her old employer: I want to back you up in a story with Matthew that I am doing part-time work for you. The truth is that . . . but she would have to tell him a lie too, and which lie? She could not say: I want to sit by myself three or four times a week in a rented room. And besides, he knew Matthew, and she could not really ask him to tell lies on her behalf, apart from his being bound to think it meant a lover.

Suppose she really took a part-time job, which she could get through fast and efficiently, leaving time for herself. What job? Addressing envelopes? Canvassing?

And there was Mrs. Parkes, working widow, who knew exactly what she was prepared to give to the house, who knew by instinct when her mistress withdrew in spirit from her responsibilities. Mrs. Parkes was one of the servers of this world, but she needed someone to serve. She had to have Mrs. Rawlings, her madam, at the top of the house or in the garden, so that she could come and get support from her: "Yes, the bread's not what it was when I was a girl. . . . Yes, Harry's got a won- derful appetite, I wonder where he puts it all. . . . Yes, it's lucky the twins are so much of a size, they can wear each other's shoes, that's a saving in these hard times. . . . Yes, the cherry jam from Switzerland is not a patch on the jam from Poland, and three times the price. . . ." And so on. That sort of talk Mrs. Parkes must have, every day, or she would leave, not knowing herself why she left.

Susan Rawlings, thinking these thoughts, found that she was prowl- ing through the great thicketed garden like a wild cat: she was walking up the stairs, down the stairs, through the rooms, into the garden, along the brown running river, back, up through the house, down again. . . . It was a wonder Mrs. Parkes did not think it strange. But on the con- trary, Mrs. Rawlings could do what she liked, she could stand on her head if she wanted, provided she was *there*. Susan Rawlings prowled and muttered through her house, hating Mrs. Parkes, hating poor Miss Townsend, dreaming of her hour of solitude in the dingy respectability of Miss Townsend's hotel bedroom, and she knew quite well she was mad. Yes, she was mad.

She said to Matthew that she must have a holiday. Matthew agreed with her. This was not as things had been once—how they had talked in each other's arms in the marriage bed. He had, she knew, diagnosed her finally as *unreasonable*. She had become someone outside himself that he had to manage. They were living side by side in this house like two tolerably friendly strangers.

Having told Mrs. Parkes, or rather, asked for her permission, she went off on a walking holiday in Wales. She chose the remotest place she knew of. Every morning the children telephoned her before they went off to school, to encourage and support her, just as they had over Mother's Room. Every evening she telephoned them, spoke to each child in turn, and then to Matthew. Mrs. Parkes, given permission to telephone for instructions or advice, did so every day at lunchtime. When, as happened three times, Mrs. Rawlings was out on the moun- tainside, Mrs. Parkes asked that she should ring back at such and such a time, for she would not be happy in what she was doing without Mrs. Rawlings's blessing.

Susan prowled over wild country with the telephone wire holding her to her duty like a leash. The next time she must telephone, or wait to be telephoned, nailed her to her cross. The mountains themselves seemed trammelled by her unfreedom. Everywhere on the mountains, where she met no one at all, from breakfast time to dusk, excepting sheep, or a shepherd, she came face to face with her own craziness which might attack her in the broadest valleys, so that they seemed too small; or on a mountain-top from which she could see a hundred other mountains and valleys, so that they seemed too low, too small, with the sky pressing down too close. She would stand gazing at a hillside brilliant with ferns and bracken, jewelled with running water, and see nothing but her devil, who lifted inhuman eyes at her from where he leaned negligently on a rock, switching at his ugly yellow boots with a leafy twig.

She returned to her home and family, with the Welsh emptiness at the back of her mind like a promise of freedom.

She told her husband she wanted to have an *au pair* girl.

They were in their bedroom, it was late at night, the children slept. He sat, shirted and slippered, in a chair by the window, looking out. She sat brushing her hair and watching him in the mirror. A time hallowed scene in the connubial bedroom. He said nothing, while she heard the arguments coming into his mind, only to be rejected because every one was *reasonable*.

"It seems strange to get one now, after all, the children are in school most of the day. Surely the time for you to have help was when you were stuck with them day and night. Why don't you ask Mrs. Parkes to cook for you? She's even offered to—I can understand if you are tired of cooking for six people. But you know that an *au pair* girl means all kinds of problems, it's not like having an ordinary char in during the day. . . ."

Finally he said carefully: "Are you thinking of going back to work?"

"No," she said, "no, not really." She made herself sound vague, rather stupid. She went on brushing her black hair and peering at herself so as to be oblivious of the short uneasy glances her Matthew kept giving her. "Do you think we can't afford it?" she went on vaguely, not at all the old efficient Susan who knew exactly what they could afford.

"It's not that," he said, looking out of the window at dark trees, so as not to look at her. Meanwhile she examined a round, candid, pleasant face with clear dark brows and clear grey eyes. A sensible face. She brushed thick healthy black hair and thought: Yet that's the reflection of a madwoman. How very strange! Much more to the point if what looked back at me was the gingery green-eyed demon with his dry meagre smile. . . . Why wasn't Matthew agreeing? After all, what else could he do? She was breaking her part of the bargain and there was no way of forcing her to keep it: that her spirit, her soul, should live in this house, so that the people in it could grow like plants in water, and Mrs. Parkes remain content in their service. In return for this, he would be a good loving husband, and responsible towards the children. Well, nothing like this had been true of either of them for a long time. He did his duty, perfunctorily; she did not even pretend to do hers. And he had become like other husbands, with his real life in his work and the people he met there, and very likely a serious affair. All this was her fault.

At last he drew heavy curtains, blotting out the trees, and turned to force her attention: "Susan, are you really sure we need a girl?" But she would not meet his appeal at all: She was running the brush over her hair again and again, lifting fine black clouds in a small hiss of electricity. She was peering in and smiling as if she were amused at the clinging hissing hair that followed the brush.

"Yes, I think it would be a good idea on the whole," she said, with the cunning of a madwoman evading the real point.

In the mirror she could see her Matthew lying on his back, his hands behind his head, staring upwards, his face sad and hard. She felt her heart (the old heart of Susan Rawlings) soften and call out to him. But she set it to be indifferent.

He said: "Susan, the children?" It was an appeal that *almost* reached her. He opened his arms, lifting them from where they had lain by his sides, palms up, empty. She had only to run across and fling herself into them, on to his hard, warm chest, and melt into herself, into Susan. But she could not. She would not see his lifted arms. She said vaguely: "Well, surely it'll be even better for them? We'll get a French or a German girl and they'll learn the language."

In the dark she lay beside him, feeling frozen, a stranger. She felt as if Susan had been spirited away. She disliked very much this woman who lay here, cold and indifferent beside a suffering man, but she could not change her.

Next morning she set about getting a girl, and very soon came Sophie Traub from Hamburg, a girl of twenty, laughing, healthy, blue-eyed, intending to learn English. Indeed, she already spoke a good deal. In return for a room—"Mother's Room"—and her food, she undertook to do some light cooking, and to be with the children when Mrs. Rawlings asked. She was an intelligent girl and understood perfectly what was needed. Susan said: "I go off sometimes, for the morning or for the day—well, sometimes the children run home from school, or they ring up, or a teacher rings up. I should be here, really. And there's the daily woman. . . ." And Sophie laughed her deep fruity *Fräulein*'s laugh, showed her fine white teeth and her dimples, and said: "You want some person to play mistress of the house sometimes, not so?"

"Yes, that is just so," said Susan, a bit dry, despite herself, thinking in secret fear how easy it was, how much nearer to the end she was than she thought. Healthy Fräulein Traub's instant understanding of their position proved this to be true.

The *au pair* girl, because of her own common sense, or (as Susan said to herself with her new inward shudder) because she had been *chosen* so well by Susan, was a success with everyone, the children liking her, Mrs. Parkes forgetting almost at once that she was German, and Matthew finding her "nice to have around the house." For he was now taking things as they came, from the surface of life, withdrawn both as a husband and a father from the household.

One day Susan saw how Sophie and Mrs. Parkes were talking and laughing in the kitchen, and she announced that she would be away until teatime. She knew exactly where to go and what she must look for. She took the District Line to South Kensington, changed to the Circle, got off at Paddington, and walked around looking at the smaller hotels until she was satisfied with one which had FRED'S HOTEL painted on windowpanes that needed cleaning. The façade was a faded shiny yellow, like unhealthy skin. A door at the end of a passage said she must knock; she did, and Fred appeared. He was not at all attractive, not in any way, being fattish, and run-down, and wearing a tasteless striped suit. He had small sharp eyes in a white creased face, and was quite prepared to let Mrs. Jones (she chose the farcical name deliberately, staring him out) have a room three days a week from ten until six. Provided of course that she paid in advance each time she came? Susan produced fifteen shillings (no price had been set by him) and held it out, still fixing him with a bold unblinking challenge she had not known until then she could use at will. Looking at her still, he took up a tenshilling note from her palm between thumb and forefinger, fingered it; then shuffled up two half crowns, held out his own palm with these bits of money displayed thereon, and let his gaze lower broodingly at them. They were standing in the passage, a red-shaded light above, bare boards beneath, and a strong smell of floor polish rising about them. He shot his gaze up at her over the still-extended palm, and smiled as if to say: What do you take me for? "I shan't," said Susan, "be using this room for the purposes of making money." He still waited. She added another five shillings, at which he nodded and said: "You pay, and I ask no questions." "Good," said Susan. He now went past her to the stairs, and there waited a moment: the light from the street door being in her eyes, she lost sight of him momentarily. Then she saw a sober-suited, white-faced, white-balding little man trotting up the stairs like a waiter, and she went after him. They proceeded in utter silence up the stairs of this house where no questions were asked—Fred's Hotel, which could afford the freedom for its visitors that poor Miss Townsend's hotel could not. The room was hideous. It had a single window, with thin green brocade curtains, a three-quarter bed that had a cheap green satin bedspread on it, a fireplace with a gas fire and a shilling meter by it, a chest of drawers, and a green wicker armchair.

"Thank you," said Susan, knowing that Fred (if this was Fred, and not George, or Herbert or Charlie) was looking at her, not so much with curiosity, an emotion he would not own to, for professional reasons, but with a philosophical sense of what was appropriate. Having taken her money and shown her up and agreed to everything, he was clearly disapproving of her for coming here. She did not belong here at all, so his look said. (But she knew, already, how very much she did belong: the room had been waiting for her to join it.) "Would you have me called at five o'clock, please?" and he nodded and went downstairs.

It was twelve in the morning. She was free. She sat in the armchair, she simply sat, she closed her eyes and sat and let herself be alone. She was alone and no one knew where she was. When a knock came on the door she was annoyed, and prepared to show it: but it was Fred himself, it was five o'clock and he was calling her as ordered. He flicked his sharp little eyes over the room—bed, first. It was undisturbed. She might never have been in the room at all. She thanked him, said she would be returning the day after tomorrow, and left. She was back home in time to cook supper, to put the children to bed, to cook a second supper for her husband and herself later. And to welcome Sophie back from the pictures where she had gone with a friend. All these things she did cheerfully, willingly. But she was thinking all the time of the hotel room, she was longing for it with her whole being.

Three times a week. She arrived promptly at ten, looked Fred in the eyes, gave him twenty shillings, followed him up the stairs, went into the room, and shut the door on him with gentle firmness. For Fred, disapproving of her being here at all, was quite ready to let friendship, or at least acquaintanceship, follow his disapproval, if only she would let him. But he was content to go off on her dismissing nod, with the twenty shillings in his hand.

She sat in the armchair and shut her eyes.

What did she *do* in the room? Why, nothing at all. From the chair, when it had rested her, she went to the window, stretching her arms, smiling, treasuring her anonymity, to look out. She was no longer Susan Rawlings, mother of four, wife of Matthew, employer of Mrs. Parkes and of Sophie Traub, with these and those relations with friends, schoolteachers, tradesmen. She no longer was mistress of the big white house and garden, owning clothes suitable for this and that activity or occasion. She was Mrs. Jones, and she was alone, and she had no past and no future. Here I am, she thought, after all these years of being married and having children and playing those roles of responsibility— and I'm just the same. Yet there have been times I thought that nothing existed of me except the roles that went with being Mrs. Matthew Rawlings. Yes, here I am, and if I never saw any of my family again, here I would still be . . . how very strange that is! And she leaned on the sill, and looked into the street, loving the men and women who passed, because she did not know them. She looked at the downtrodden buildings over the street, and the sky, wet and dingy, or sometimes blue, and she felt she had never seen buildings or sky before. And then she went back to the chair, empty, her mind a blank. Sometimes she talked aloud, saying nothing—an exclamation, meaningless, followed by a comment about the floral pattern on the thin rug, or a stain on the green satin coverlet. For the most part, she wool-gathered—what word is there for it?—brooded, wandered, simply went dark, feeling emptiness run deliciously through her veins like the movement of her blood.

This room had become more her own than the house she lived in. One morning she found Fred taking her a flight higher than usual. She stopped, refusing to go up, and demanded her usual room, Number 19. "Well, you'll have to wait half an hour then," he said. Willingly she descended to the dark disinfectant-smelling hall, and sat waiting until the two, man and woman, came down the stairs, giving her swift indifferent glances before they hurried out into the street, separating at the door. She went up to the room, *her* room, which they had just vacated. It was no less hers, though the windows were set wide open, and a maid was straightening the bed as she came in.

After these days of solitude, it was both easy to play her part as mother and wife, and difficult—because it was so easy: she felt an impostor. She felt as if her shell moved here, with her family, answering to Mummy, Mother, Susan, Mrs. Rawlings. She was surprised no one saw through her, that she wasn't turned out of doors, as a fake. On the contrary, it seemed the children loved her more; Matthew and she "got on" pleasantly, and Mrs. Parkes was happy in her work under (for the most part, it must be confessed) Sophie Traub. At night she lay beside her husband, and they made love again, apparently just as they used to, when they were really married. But she, Susan, or the being who answered so readily and improbably to the name of Susan, was not there: she was in Fred's Hotel, in Paddington, waiting for the easing hours of solitude to begin.

Soon she made a new arrangement with Fred and with Sophie. It was for five days a week. As for the money, five pounds, she simply asked Matthew for it. She saw that she was not even frightened he might ask what for: he would give it to her, she knew that, and yet it was terrifying it could be so, for this close couple, these partners, had once known the destination of every shilling they must spend. He agreed to give her five pounds a week. She asked for just so much, not a penny more. He sounded indifferent about it. It was as if he were paying her, she thought: *paying her off*—yes, that was it. Terror came back for a moment, when she understood this, but she stilled it: things had gone too far for that. Now, every week, on Sunday nights, he gave her five pounds, turning away from her before their eyes could meet on the transaction. As for Sophie Traub, she was to be somewhere in or near the house until six at night, after which she was free. She was not to cook, or to clean, she was simply to be there. So she gardened or sewed, and asked friends in, being a person who was bound to have a lot of

friends. If the children were sick, she nursed them. If teachers telephoned, she answered them sensibly. For the five daytimes in the
school week, she was altogether the mistress of the house.

One night in the bedroom, Matthew asked: "Susan, I don't want to
interfere—don't think that, please—but are you sure you are well?"

She was brushing her hair at the mirror. She made two more strokes
on either side of her head, before she replied: "Yes, dear, I am sure I am
well."

He was again lying on his back, his big blond head on his hands, his
elbows angled up and part-concealing his face. He said: "Then Susan, I
have to ask you this question, though you must understand, I'm not
putting any sort of pressure on you." (Susan heard the word pressure
with dismay, because this was inevitable, of course she could not go on
like this.) "Are things going to go on like this?"

"Well," she said, going vague and bright and idiotic again, so as to
escape: "Well, I don't see why not."

He was jerking his elbows up and down, in annoyance or in pain,
and, looking at him, she saw he had got thin, even gaunt; and restless
angry movements were not what she remembered of him. He said:
"Do you want a divorce, is that it?"

At this, Susan only with the greatest difficulty stopped herself from
laughing: she could hear the bright bubbling laughter she *would* have
emitted, had she let herself. He could only mean one thing: she had a
lover, and that was why she spent her days in London, as lost to him as if
she had vanished to another continent.

Then the small panic set in again: she understood that he hoped she
did have a lover, he was begging her to say so, because otherwise it
would be too terrifying.

She thought this out, as she brushed her hair, watching the fine black
stuff fly up to make its little clouds of electricity, hiss, hiss, hiss. Behind
her head, across the room, was a blue wall. She realized she was absorbed in watching the black hair making shapes against the blue. She
should be answering him. "Do *you* want a divorce, Matthew?"

He said: "That surely isn't the point, is it?"

"You brought it up, I didn't," she said, brightly, suppressing meaningless tinkling laughter.

Next day she asked Fred: "Have enquiries been made for me?"

He hesitated, and she said: "I've been coming here a year now. I've
made no trouble, and you've been paid every day. I have a right to be
told."

"As a matter of fact, Mrs. Jones, a man did come asking."

"A man from a detective agency?"

"Well, he could have been, couldn't he?"

"I was asking you . . . well, what did you tell him?"

"I told him a Mrs. Jones came every week day from ten until five or six and stayed in Number 19 by herself."

"Describing me?"

"Well, Mrs. Jones, I had no alternative. Put yourself in my place."

"By rights I should deduct what that man gave you for the information."

He raised shocked eyes: she was not the sort of person to make jokes like this! Then he chose to laugh: a pinkish wet slit appeared across his white crinkled face: his eyes positively begged her to laugh, otherwise he might lose some money. She remained grave, looking at him.

He stopped laughing and said: "You want to go up now?"—returning to the familiarity, the comradeship, of the country where no questions are asked, on which (and he knew it) she depended completely.

She went up to sit in her wicker chair. But it was not the same. Her husband had searched her out. (The world had searched her out.) The pressures were on her. She was here with his connivance. He might walk in at any moment, here, into Room 19. She imagined the report from the detective agency: "A woman calling herself Mrs. Jones, fitting the description of your wife (etc., etc., etc.), stays alone all day in Room No. 19. She insists on this room, waits for it if it is engaged. As far as the proprietor knows, she receives no visitors there, male or female." A report something on these lines, Matthew must have received.

Well of course he was right: things couldn't go on like this. He had put an end to it all simply by sending the detective after her.

She tried to shrink herself back into the shelter of the room, a snail pecked out of its shell and trying to squirm back. But the peace of the room had gone. She was trying consciously to revive it, trying to let go into the dark creative trance (or whatever it was) that she had found there. It was no use, yet she craved for it, she was as ill as a suddenly deprived addict.

Several times she returned to the room, to look for herself there, but instead she found the unnamed spirit of restlessness, a prickling fevered hunger for movement, an irritable self-consciousness that made her brain feel as if it had coloured lights going on and off inside it. Instead of the soft dark that had been the room's air, were now waiting for her demons that made her dash blindly about, muttering words of hate; she was impelling herself from point to point like a moth dashing itself against a windowpane, sliding to the bottom, fluttering off on broken wings, then crashing into the invisible barrier again. And again and again. Soon she was exhausted, and she told Fred that for a while she would not be needing the room, she was going on holiday. Home she went, to the big white house by the river. The middle of a weekday, and she felt guilty at returning to her own home when not expected. She stood unseen, looking in at the kitchen window. Mrs. Parkes, wearing a discarded floral overall of Susan's, was stooping to slide something into the oven. Sophie, arms folded, was leaning her back against a cupboard and laughing at some joke made by a girl not seen before by Susan—a dark foreign girl, Sophie's visitor. In an armchair Molly, one of the twins, lay curled, sucking her thumb and watching the grownups. She must have some sickness, to be kept from school. The child's listless face, the dark circles under her eyes, hurt Susan: Molly was looking at the three grownups working and talking in exactly the same way Susan looked at the four through the kitchen window: she was remote, shut off from them.

But then, just as Susan imagined herself going in, picking up the little girl, and sitting in an armchair with her, stroking her probably heated forehead, Sophie did just that: she had been standing on one leg, the other knee flexed, its foot set against the wall. Now she let her foot in its ribbon-tied red shoe slide down the wall, stood solid on two feet, clapping her hands before and behind her, and sang a couple of lines in German, so that the child lifted her heavy eyes at her and began to smile. Then she walked, or rather skipped, over to the child, swung her up, and let her fall into her lap at the same moment she sat herself. She said: "Hopla! Hopla! Molly . . . " and began stroking the dark untidy young head that Molly laid on her shoulder for comfort.

Well . . . Susan blinked the tears of farewell out of her eyes, and went quietly up the house to her bedroom. There she sat looking at the river through the trees. She felt at peace, but in a way that was new to her. She had no desire to move, to talk, to do anything at all. The devils that had haunted the house, the garden, were not there; but she knew it was because her soul was in Room 19 in Fred's Hotel; she was not really here at all. It was a sensation that should have been frightening: to sit at her own bedroom window, listening to Sophie's rich young voice sing German nursery songs to her child, listening to Mrs. Parkes clatter and move below, and to know that all this had nothing to do with her: she was already out of it.

Later, she made herself go down and say she was home: it was unfair to be here unannounced. She took lunch with Mrs. Parkes, Sophie, Sophie's Italian friend Maria, and her daughter Molly, and felt like a visitor.

A few days later, at bedtime, Matthew said: "Here's your five pounds," and pushed them over to her. Yet he must have known she had not been leaving the house at all.

She shook her head, gave it back to him, and said, in explanation, not in accusation: "As soon as you knew where I was, there was no point."

He nodded, not looking at her. He was turned away from her: thinking, she knew, how best to handle this wife who terrified him.

He said: "I wasn't trying to . . . it's just that I was worried."

"Yes I know."

"I must confess that I was beginning to wonder. . . ."

"You thought I had a lover?"

"Yes, I am afraid I did."

She knew that he wished she had. She sat wondering how to say: "For a year now I've been spending all my days in a very sordid hotel room. It's the place where I'm happy. In fact, without it I don't exist." She heard herself saying this, and understood how terrified he was that she might. So instead she said: "Well, perhaps you're not far wrong."

Probably Matthew would think the hotel proprietor lied: he would want to think so.

"Well," he said, and she could hear his voice spring up, so to speak, with relief: "in that case I must confess I've got a bit of an affair on myself."

She said, detached and interested: "Really? Who is she?" and saw Matthew's startled look because of this reaction.

"It's Phil. Phil Hunt."

She had known Phil Hunt well in the old unmarried days. She was thinking: No, she won't do, she's too neurotic and difficult. She's never been happy yet. Sophie's much better: Well Matthew will see that himself, as sensible as he is.

This line of thought went on in silence, while she said aloud:

"It's no point telling you about mine, because you don't know him."

Quick, quick, invent, she thought. Remember how you invented all that nonsense for Miss Townsend.

She began slowly, careful not to contradict herself: "His name is Michael"—(*Michael What?*)—"Michael Plant." (What a silly name!) "He's rather like you—in looks, I mean." And indeed, she could imagine herself being touched by no one but Matthew himself. "He's a publisher." (Really? Why?) "He's got a wife already and two children."

She brought out this fantasy, proud of herself.

Matthew said: "Are you two thinking of marrying?"

She said, before she could stop herself: "Good God, *no!*"

She realized, if Matthew wanted to marry Phil Hunt, that this was too emphatic, but apparently it was all right, for his voice sounded relieved as he said: "It is a bit impossible to imagine oneself married to anyone else, isn't it?" With which he pulled her to him, so that her head lay on his shoulder. She turned her face into the dark of his flesh, and listened to the blood pounding through her ears saying: I am alone, I am alone, I am alone.

In the morning Susan lay in bed while he dressed.

He had been thinking things out in the night, because now he said: "Susan, why don't we make a foursome?"

Of course, she said to herself, of course he would be bound to say that. If one is sensible, if one is reasonable, if one never allows oneself a base thought or an envious emotion, naturally one says: Let's make a foursome!

"Why not?" she said.

"We could all meet for lunch. I mean, it's ridiculous, you sneaking off to filthy hotels, and me staying late at the office, and all the lies everyone has to tell."

What on earth did I say his name was?—she panicked, then said: "I think it's a good idea, but Michael is away at the moment. When he comes back though—and I'm sure you two would like each other."

"He's away, is he? So that's why you've been . . ." Her husband put his hand to the knot of his tie in a gesture of male coquetry she would not before have associated with him; and he bent to kiss her cheek with the expression that goes with the words: Oh you naughty little puss! And she felt its answering look, naughty and coy, come on to her face.

Inside she was dissolving in horror at them both, at how far they had both sunk from honesty of emotion.

So now she was saddled with a lover, and he had a mistress! How ordinary, how reassuring, how jolly! And now they would make a foursome of it, and go about to theatres and restaurants. After all, the Rawlingses could well afford that sort of thing, and presumably the publisher Michael Plant could afford to do himself and his mistress quite well. No, there was nothing to stop the four of them developing the most intricate relationship of civilized tolerance, all enveloped in a charming afterglow of autumnal passion. Perhaps they would all go off on holidays together? She had known people who did. Or perhaps Matthew would draw the line there? Why should he, though, if he was capable of talking about "foursomes" at all?

She lay in the empty bedroom, listening to the car drive off with Matthew in it, off to work. Then she heard the children clattering off to school to the accompaniment of Sophie's cheerfully ringing voice. She slid down into the hollow of the bed, for shelter against her own irrelevance. And she stretched out her hand to the hollow where her husband's body had lain, but found no comfort there: he was not her husband. She curled herself up in a small tight ball under the clothes: she could stay here all day, all week, indeed, all her life.

But in a few days she must produce Michael Plant, and—but how? She must presumably find some agreeable man prepared to impersonate a publisher called Michael Plant. And in return for which she would—what? Well, for one thing they would make love. The idea made her want to cry with sheer exhaustion. Oh no, she had finished with all that—the proof of it was that the words "make love," or even imagining it, trying hard to revive no more than the pleasures of sensuality, let alone affection, or love, made her want to run away and hide from the sheer effort of the thing. . . . Good Lord, why make love at all? Why make love with anyone? Or if you are going to make love, what does it matter who with? Why shouldn't she simply walk into the street, pick up a man and have a roaring sexual affair with him? Why not? Or even with Fred? What difference did it make?

But she had let herself in for it—an interminable stretch of time with a lover, called Michael, as part of a gallant civilized foursome. Well, she could not, and would not.

She got up, dressed, went down to find Mrs. Parkes, and asked her for the loan of a pound, since Matthew, she said, had forgotten to leave her money. She exchanged with Mrs. Parkes variations on the theme that husbands are all the same, they don't think, and without saying a word to Sophie, whose voice could be heard upstairs from the telephone, walked to the underground, travelled to South Kensington, changed to the Inner Circle, got out at Paddington, and walked to Fred's Hotel. There she told Fred that she wasn't going on holiday after all, she needed the room. She would have to wait an hour, Fred said. She went to a busy tearoom-cum-restaurant around the corner, and sat watching the people flow in and out the door that kept swinging open and shut, watched them mingle and merge and separate, felt her being flow into them, into their movement. When the hour was up she left a half crown for her pot of tea, and left the place without looking back at it, just as she had left her house, the big, beautiful white house, without another look, but silently dedicating it to Sophie. She returned to Fred, received the key of No. 19, now free, and ascended the grimy stairs slowly, letting floor after floor fall away below her, keeping her eyes lifted, so that floor after floor descended jerkily to her level of vision, and fell away out of sight.

No. 19 was the same. She saw everything with an acute, narrow, checking glance: the cheap shine of the satin spread, which had been replaced carelessly after the two bodies had finished their convulsions under it; a trace of powder on the glass that topped the chest of drawers; an intense green shade in a fold of the curtain. She stood at the window, looking down, watching people pass and pass and pass until her mind went dark from the constant movement. Then she sat in the wicker chair, letting herself go slack. But she had to be careful, because she did not want, today, to be surprised by Fred's knock at five o'clock.

The demons were not here. They had gone forever, because she was buying her freedom from them. She was slipping already into the dark fructifying dream that seemed to caress her inwardly, like the movement of her blood . . . but she had to think about Matthew first. Should she write a letter for the coroner? But what should she say? She would like to leave him with the look on his face she had seen this morning—

banal, admittedly, but at least confidently healthy. Well, that was impossible, one did not look like that with a wife dead from suicide. But how to leave him believing she was dying because of a man—because of the fascinating publisher Michael Plant? Oh, how ridiculous! How absurd! How humiliating! But she decided not to trouble about it, simply not to think about the living. If he wanted to believe she had a lover, he would believe it. And he *did* want to believe it. Even when he had found out that there was no publisher in London called Michael Plant, he would think: Oh poor Susan, she was afraid to give me his real name.

And what did it matter whether he married Phil Hunt or Sophie? Though it ought to be Sophie who was already the mother of those children . . . and what hypocrisy to sit here worrying about the children, when she was going to leave them because she had not got the energy to stay.

She had about four hours. She spent them delightfully, darkly, sweetly, letting herself slide gently, gently, to the edge of the river. Then, with hardly a break in her consciousness, she got up, pushed the thin rug against the door, made sure the windows were tight shut, put two shillings in the meter, and turned on the gas. For the first time since she had been in the room she lay on the hard bed that smelled stale, that smelled of sweat and sex.

She lay on her back on the green satin cover, but her legs were chilly. She got up, found a blanket folded into the bottom of the chest of drawers, and carefully covered her legs with it. She was quite content lying there, listening to the faint soft hiss of the gas that poured into the room, into her lungs, into her brain, as she drifted off into the dark river.

1963

MAY SWENSON
1919–

Born and raised in Logan, Utah, where her father was a professor of mechanical engineering at the state university, the poet May Swenson worked as a reporter for the Salt Lake City *Deseret News*, then settled in New York City, where she became an editor for the avant-garde publisher New Directions in 1959. In 1966, after publishing a number of well-received collections of verse—including *Another Animal* (1954) and *To Mix with Time: New and Selected Poems* (1963)—she resigned to devote herself completely to her writing. Since then, with the assistance of Guggenheim and Rockefeller Fellowships among other awards, Swenson has produced a considerable body of poetry, most notably the imaginative and innovative volume of "concrete" poetry *Iconographs* (1970), a book of verses that are all, like *Women* and *Bleeding*, arranged in typographical forms whose shapes reflect the nature of their subject, for her intention, as she has explained, is "to make an existence in space, as well as time, for the poem." About Swenson's early work, the poet Elizabeth Bishop remarked in a letter (1962) that this artist is "one of the few good poets who write good poems about nature . . . not just comparing it to states of mind or society." As the poet-critic Alicia Ostriker has recently observed, in Swenson's later work the scrupulous vision that Bishop was describing has evolved into more radical and metaphysical "shapes of speculation."

Women

```
Women                        Or they
    should be                    should be
      pedestals                    little horses
        moving                       those wooden
          pedestals                    sweet              5
            moving                       oldfashioned
              to the                       painted
                motions                      rocking
                  of men                       horses


        the gladdest things in the toyroom
                                                           10
            The                          feelingly
          pegs                         and then
        of their                     unfeelingly
      ears                          To be
    so familiar                    joyfully             15
  and dear                       ridden
to the trusting                rockingly
fists                        ridden until
To be chafed               the restored


egos dismount and the legs stride away
                                                           20
Immobile                 willing
  sweetlipped              to be set
    sturdy                   into motion
      and smiling             Women
        women                   should be              25
          should always           pedestals
            be waiting               to men
```

1968, 1970

Bleeding

Stop bleeding   said the knife.
I would if I   could said the cut.
Stop bleeding   you make me messy with this blood.
I'm sorry said   the cut.
Stop or I will   sink in farther said the knife.
Don't said the   cut.
The knife did   not say it couldn't help it but it sank in farther.
If only you   didn't bleed said the knife I wouldn't have to do this.
I know said   the cut I bleed too easily I hate that I can't
help it I   wish I were a knife like you and didn't have to bleed.
Meanwhile   stop bleeding will you said the knife.
Yes you   are a mess and sinking in farther said the cut I will
have to   stop.
Have you   stopped by now said the knife.
I've almost   stopped I think
Why must you   bleed in the first place said the knife.
For the reason   maybe that you must do what you must do said the cut.
I can't stand   bleeding said the knife and sank in farther.

I hate it too   said the cut I know it isn't you it's me
you're lucky to   be a knife you ought to be glad about that.
Too many cuts   around said the knife they're messy I don't know
how they stand   themselves
They don't said   the cut.
You're bleeding   again.
No I've stopped   said the cut. See you're coming out now the
blood is drying   it will rub off you'll be shiny again and clean.
If only cuts   wouldn't bleed so much said the knife coming out a little.
But then knives   might become dull said the cut.
Aren't you bleeding   a little said the knife.
I hope not said the   cut.
I feel you are just   a little.
Maybe just a little   but I can stop now.
I feel a little   wetness still said the knife sinking in
a little but then   coming out a little.
Just a little maybe   just enough said the cut.
That's enough now   stop now do you feel better now said the knife.
I feel I have to   bleed to feel I think said the cut.
I don't I don't have   to feel said the knife drying now becoming shiny.

20
25
30
35

1970

ELEANOR ROSS TAYLOR

1920–

Of Eleanor Ross Taylor's first collection of poems, *Wilderness of Ladies* (1960), Adrienne Rich remarked that many pieces in the book "speak of the underground life of women, the Southern white Protestant woman in particular . . . possessed of a will to survive and to see others survive." As *Welcome Eumenides*, the title poem of Taylor's second book, suggests, this artist has continued in the last two decades to chart the "wilderness" of women's lives, expanding her exploration from studies of contemporary American women to analyses of historical figures like Florence Nightingale, the speaker of *Welcome Eumenides*. A native of North Carolina, Eleanor Ross Taylor was educated at the University of North Carolina at Greensboro and at Vanderbilt University. In 1943, she married the writer Peter Taylor, with whom she has had two children. She has worked as a high school teacher of English, as a librarian, and as a creative-writing teacher at the University of Virginia, but in recent years she has increasingly devoted herself to her writing.

Welcome Eumenides[1]

"God called me in the morning and asked me would I do good for Him,
for Him alone without the reputation."

F.N. March 7, 1850

Who calls?
Speak, for thy servant heareth.[2] . . .

Is it the wards at Scutari?[3]
Or the corridors at Waverley,
Where last night eighty slept.   5
Our masks—my pink gown with black lace—
Moving, at five, exhilarated,
Weary from dancing, up the famous stairs. . . .

---

1. In Greek mythology, the "kindly ones"—a euphemism for the (female) Furies, avengers of crimes. The phrase "Welcome Eumenides" comes from an entry (June 7, 1849) in the diary of Florence Nightingale (1820–1910), founder of modern nursing and author of *Cassandra*. According to Taylor, she was then "struggling to reject her worldly dreams and accept her destiny: the Eumenides are these dreams, and she welcomes the struggle to vanquish them." The poem contains other quotations from Nightingale's journals and allusions to her life, and we are indebted to the poet for her invaluable help in annotating them.

2. The words of Samuel to the Lord (1 Samuel 10).

3. Site of the hospital Nightingale founded to care for soldiers during the Crimean War. Nightingale's work was perhaps the only positive result of this war, in which many British soldiers were killed or wounded. Waverley Abbey was the home of Nightingale's aunt and uncle; "actually, Nightingale did not go to this dance, but it was typical of the Nightingale world" [Taylor's note].

Mother!   Nurse!   water! . . .
I come!   10

But now at five they have not slept
Except the men, heads blanketed, who crept
To timeless shadow.
Two thousand deathbeds that one winter.
Last May my window gave   15
On a thousand Turkish flowers,
Two thousand English graves.
Two thousand deathbeds that one winter[4]—
    Who thinks of that now?

    Who calls?   20
Not my child
(*O God no more love*
No more marriage)[5]
    Only my British Army.

(*Dear Aunt Mai,*[6] *kiss all babies for me.*)   25
    Oh my poor men I am a bad mother
    To come home and leave you to your Crimean graves.
    73 percent in 8 regiments in 6 months
    From disease alone. (Who thinks of that now?)

There was a white rose in the New Garden cloister.   30
(The idol of the man I adored)
Richard,[7] the sea breaks against the sea wall.
("You could undertake that,
When you could not undertake me.")
The plough goes over the soul.   35
    My Hilary ateliered,[8]
    Femme espaliered, or, woman staked.[9]
    The apricot bears against the south wall
    Daughters too basked at hearth.
    (No more love, no more marriage!)   40
Which of the chosen ever chose her state?
To hide in love!
Lord, seek Thy servant elsewhere. . . .
    Yet He calls.

---

4. A parapharase of Nightingale's words.
5. Nightingale's words; other phrases in italic type in the poem are also direct quotations.
6. "Mrs. Samuel Smith, Nightingale's aunt and her 'Spiritual' mother from her early years. She sacrificed her own family to Nightingale" [Taylor's note].
7. Richard Monckton Milnes (1809–1892), literary man and friend of Nightingale's. "New Garden cloister" is the garden in New College,

Oxford, where they walked together.
8. "Hilary Bonham-Carter, intimate friend and confidante; a talented painter, allowed to attend only a 'ladies' atelier' [studio] in London" [Taylor's note].
9. I.e., "tied down and sacrificed to domesticity"; "femme espaliered": woman "tortured into conformity" [Taylor's notes]; to "espalier" means, literally, to force a tree to grow flat against a wall.

I was not invited.   45
At home at Embly, Wilton,[1] Waverly,
I, sated with invitations,
I, presented to the poor Queen,
I, worthy of the Deaconesses of Kaiserswerth,[2]
Asked by the birthday child to every fête,   50

I was unwelcome.
The others came.
Two hundred by the shipload,
Jolted from stretchers,
Feverishly crawling up the hill   55
Through the ice-needled puddles.

I guarded the anteroom
Holding my nurses back, immune
To the cries, the sudden retching spasms, the all
But visible odors. (*Abandon hope all ye who enter here.*)[3]   60
The mold grew on the walls.

> *Blessed are the merciful,*[4]
> Says my crowned cross.

Pails of arrowroot,[5] some port. . . .
And then, all Balaclava broke loose.[6]   65
Quick now, old sheets (the dying wait)
Speed, needle! This is no hooped French knot;[7]
A deathbed is required.
        (Where did I yawn
        In the face of the gilt clock   70
        Defying it to reach to?)
Stuff straw for deathbeds, for deathbeds,
For deathbeds.
Not one shall die alone.
I die with each.   75
Now hurry to the next lax hand, loose tongue,
Quick messages for forever.
Mr. Osborne[8] knelt down for dictation.
His pencil skirmished among lice.

---

1. Embley Park was the Nightingales' larger house; Wilton, where Sidney Herbert, secretary of war, lived.
2. Members of a Protestant sisterhood at Kaiserswerth, Germany, where Nightingale studied in 1855.
3. The words over the gates of hell in Dante's *Inferno*.
4. "Blessed are the merciful, for they shall obtain mercy," from Christ's Sermon on the Mount.
5. A starch used in invalid food.
6. "The unloading at Scutari of the wounded from Balaclava" [Taylor's note]; Balaclava was the site of an especially bloody Crimean War battle (October 1854).
7. I.e., no elaborate embroidery stitch.
8. "Rev. Sidney Godolphin Osborne, volunteer-chaplain at Scutari" [Taylor's note].

At last, the chance for a rich and true life.[9]   80

Outside, the wind rises.
    Wood! the fire dies. . . .
        There is no wood.
    The operating table then. Yes, chop it up.
        (For the operation Mr. Osborne   85
        Held up the patient with his arms and knee.)

Pen—paper—*vite!*
They demand supplies . . .
Ah ohhh the engine in my head. . . .
Claret and white flour for the Persian adventurer![1]   90
    Must I repeat:
Do not
    attach to the cutlets
    (1) rags (2) nails (3) buttons
    . . . surgical scissors   95

. . . that you can join me on the twenty-seventh
(Crème Harlequin aux Meringues—or dariolettes?)[2]

And again. Please keep:
    a. Toilets covered.
    b. Windows open.   100
Orderlies: Eat not the rations of those men asleep.
    (*The éclat of this adventure of mine!*)

I dreamed . . .
Compulsive dreaming of the victim.
The rich play in God's garden.[3]   105
Can they be forgiven?
Their errors gambols scintillating
Under the chandeliers like razors honed.
I murder their heaven,
I, starving, desperate, diseased . . .   110
    ("You'll catch something and bring it home.")
Mother, you were willing enough
To part with me to marriage.
No, I must take some things;
They will not be given.   115
I dream.
    Saints are non-conformists,[4]

9. A paraphrase of Nightingale's words.
1. The Persian adventurer "figured in Nightingale's delirium with Crimean fever in May, 1855; she could only be kept quiet by being given pen and paper to write" [Taylor's note].

2. I.e., special culinary delicacies.
3. Another paraphrase of Nightingale's words.
4. Perhaps in the religious sense: dissociated from the Church of England.

Ladies gone into service,
Serving ladies with one talent;[5]
Cast ye the unprofitable servant into outer darkness.   120

Still-room,[6] pantry, linen room.
Green lists, brown lists, red lists.
Come to me, yearbk[7] of statistics
Of the Deaconesses of Kaiserswerth,
My love, my escape;   125
My share.
I dreamed of you; now I dream on you:
A hundred baby prayers;
All days garlanded with birthdays, prayers and flowers,
Rye tea. Elevenses:[8] broth without bread: 130
At last, the chance for a rich and true life.

A girl, desperately fortified in my castle,
The starched pure linen,
Scalded plates, the sanitary air,
The facile word killed soul-ferment.   135
Six courses starved the spirit.
            And I said of laughter, mad,
            And of mirth, what is it doing?
I dreamed of all things at man's mercy.

Another boy reached for my hand.   140

Nurse, keep away. I'm filthy.
My own mother could not touch me.
And I looked sharply down. I was *not*
Wearing my great Paree panjandrum[9] of black velvet.
It was my shawl, my pockets.   145
            (It is not lady's work.)
I got the burned wing ready.
For eight hundred, sheets and warm food.
"I think I am in heaven," one soldier said.

            Bridget looked up. A lady in black   150
            Walked up the Lea Hurst[1] drive.
            Miss Flo! our little beauty—

---

5. These two lines refer to Christ's parable of
the talents, in which the "unprofitable" servant
who has buried his one talent (the word also
means "unit of money") is "cast into outer darkness" (Matthew 25:14–30).
6. Room off the kitchen where tea and other
drinks are prepared.
7. I.e., yearbook.

8. Midmorning snacks.
9. Nonsense word for an imaginary powerful individual; perhaps Nightingale's word for one of
her outfits.
1. The Nightingales' first home. "Bridget" is
"actually Mrs. Watson, the housekeeper. I used
'Bridget' for speed, as a name immediately acceptable as a household worker" [Taylor's note].

Come home to die?
Or come home dead.
I have looked on Hell.   155

I wear black for you O British Army.

At night they flare in this soft room:
The long flickering wards,
The muddy uniforms, and sullied faces,
The black, dried, inky blood.   160

I can never forget.
I stand at the altar of the murdered men
And while I live I fight their cause.

Which of the chosen ever chose her state?
I who looked for some small stanch   165
Found the world's blood,
Armed with my handkerchief.
Armed with statistics:
Halt! wagons of the heavy artillery.
Cease and desist, wheels of the War Office.   170
        ("She wept very much.")
I survive them all.
I am sure I did not mean to . . .
No one ever did give up so much to live
Who longed so much to die.   175
Venez me consoler de n'être pas morte. . . .[2]

. . . Much obliged, Dear George[3]
For your Latin Hey Diddle Diddle
(O God no more love no more marriage.)

Ni lire, ni écrire, ni réfléchir.[4]   180
I wear black for you O British Army.

        Another boy reached for my hand. . . .

Sir George, thank you
For the Greek Humpty Dumpty.
        (Still He calls.)   185
Venez me consoler de n'être pas morte.
Venez chez moi on Harley Street.[5]
Bordure de jambon à la Sauvaroff—

2. Come to console me for not being dead.   [Taylor's note].
3. "Sir George Lewis, classical scholar, secretary of war following Sidney Herbert; Nightingale 'despised [his] powers of administration' "
4. Not to read, not to write, not to reflect.
5. Come to my house on Harley Street (London's fashionable street for doctors' offices).

Or . . . *quenelles de veau à la Villeroi?*[6]
—The pungent meat pots at Scutari   190
Seasoned with iron pins, bolts, rusty nails
Tied to each packet.
A skinned sheep lay in the ward all night
To tempt our appetites.
The backed-up drains,   195
The floor inch-deep in sewage
Seeping under the door.
A thousand diarrheas vs. twenty chamber pots.
Ma'am, I've gone here.

Entry: March 10, 1866.   *O!*[7]   200

    I who could not live
    Without silence and solitude[8]
    Harassed by Parthe's crewel Jesse tree[9] . . .
    (Mother *lied* about the money). . . .
They left my owl locked in the empty house.   205
In my torment come dreams,
Dreams of Athena who left the Parthenon[1]
To keep house in my pocket,
Forsaken in her feathers,
Her head winding and unwinding,   210
Eyes blank of me . . .
Eyes at Scutari following
From cot, from floor, from table, winding-sheet.
For all things at our mercy—
Give us grace.   215

                                1972

---

6. Expensive delicacies.
7. "Complete entry for this date" [Taylor's note].
8. Paraphrase of Nightingale's words.
9. I.e., a genealogical table of the house of David worked out in embroidery ("crewel") by

Parthe, Nightingale's sister. The phrase is "intended to evoke the needle, the thread, the tapestry, the tentacles of the family (Parthe 'devoured' Nightingale)" [Taylor's note].
1. The famous temple to Athena, Greek goddess of wisdom (whose sacred bird was the owl).

GRACE PALEY

1922–

Grace Paley was born in New York into a family of socialist Russian Jews, and she grew up listening to the stories of her father, her mother, and her aunts, stories which were recounted sometimes in English and sometimes in Russian or Yiddish. For this reason, she has explained in a *Shenandoah* interview

(1981), she did not consider herself a writer until she managed to get beyond "me—me—me" through "hear[ing] other people's voices" which she recorded by writing "with an accent." Although Paley composed poetry in the style of W. H. Auden while she attended Hunter College, she did not begin publishing fiction until after she was thirty. Encouraged by her husband, and fascinated by the community of women and children who lived separate lives in the army camps she knew during World War II, she produced the stories that eventually appeared in *The Little Disturbances of Man* (1959); the volume immediately established her reputation as a funny and irreverent urban chronicler, a reputation strengthened by the appearance of her second volume of stories, *Enormous Changes at the Last Minute* (1974).

The mother of two children, Paley captures the everyday cadences and causes of the immigrant Jews, impoverished blacks, and displaced Irish Catholics who inhabit neighborhood playgrounds and P.T.A.s, Brooklyn's Coney Island, and Manhattan's subways. In her short story *A Conversation with My Father*, she explains that her father's insistence on the somber relentlessness of plotted "Tragedy! Plain tragedy!" conflicted with her own sense that "it's a funny world nowadays." This comic yet affirmative vision, along with her determination to tell stories "in order to . . . save a few lives," has animated not only Paley's activism in antiwar and anti-hunger movements and her teaching at Syracuse University and Sarah Lawrence College, but also those stories where—against all odds—her characters seize the opportunity to make "enormous changes at the last minute."

Enormous Changes at the Last Minute

A young man said he wanted to go to bed with Alexandra because she had an interesting mind. He was a cabdriver and she *had* admired the curly back of his head. Still, she was surprised. He said he would pick her up again in about an hour and a half. Because she was fair and a responsible person, she placed between them a barrier of truthful information. She said, I suppose you don't know many middle-aged women.

You don't look so middle-aged to me. I mean, everyone likes what they like. That is, I'm interested in your point of view, your way of life. Anyway, he said, peering into the mirror, your face is nice and your eyebrows are out of sight!

Make it two hours, she said. I'm visiting my father whom I happen to love.

I love mine too, he said. He just doesn't love me. Too too bad.

O.K. That's enough, she said. Because they had already *had* the following factual and introductory conversation.

How old are your kids?

I have none.

Sorry. Then what do you do for a living?

Children. Early teenage. Adoptions, foster homes. Probation. Troubles—well . . .

Where'd you go to school?

City colleges. What about you?

Oh, me. Lots of places. Antioch. Wisconsin. California. I might go back someday. Some place else though. Maybe Harvard. Why not?

He leaned on his horn to move a sixteen-wheel trailer truck delivering Kleenex to the A & P.

I wish you'd stop that, she said. I hate that kind of driving.

Why? Oh! You're an idealist! He looked through his rearview mirror straight into her eyes. But were you married? Ever?

Once. For years.

Who to?

It's hard to describe. A revolutionist.

Really? Could I know him? What's his name? We say revolutionary nowadays.

Oh?

By the way, my name's Dennis. I probably like you, he said.

You do, do you? Well, why should you? And let me ask you something. What do you mean by nowadays?

By the birdseed of St. Francis,[1] he said, taking a tiny brogue to the tip of his tongue. I meant no harm.

Nowadays! she said. What does that mean? I guess you think you're kind of brand-new. You're not so brand-new. The telephone was brand-new. The airplane was brand-new. *You've* been seen on earth before.

Wow! he said. He stopped the cab just short of the hospital entrance. He turned to look at her and make decisions. But you're right, he said sweetly. You know the mind *is* an astonishing, long-living, erotic thing.

Is it? she asked. Then she wondered: What is the life expectancy of the mind?

Eighty years, said her father, glad to be useful. Once he had explained electrical storms before you could find the Book of Knowledge. Now in the cave of old age, he continued to amass wonderful information. But he was sick with oldness. His arteries had a hopeless future, and conversation about all that obsolescent tubing often displaced very interesting subjects.

One day he said, Alexandra! Don't show me the sunset again. I'm not interested any more. You know that. She had just pointed to a simple sunset happening outside his hospital window. It was a red ball—all

---

1. Saint Francis of Assisi (1182?–1226), tradi-   Irish Catholics.
tionally depicted feeding birds, is beloved by

alone, without its evening streaking clouds—a red ball falling hope-lessly west, just missing the Hudson River, Jersey City, Chicago, the Great Plains, the Golden Gate—falling, falling.

Then in Russian he sighed some Pushkin.[2] Not for me, the spring. *Nye dyla menya.* . . . He slept. She read the large-print edition of *The Guns of August.*[3] A half hour later, he opened his eyes and told her how, in that morning's *Times*, the Phoenicians had sailed to Brazil in about 500 B.C. A remarkable people. The Vikings too were remarkable. He spoke well of the Chinese, the Jews, the Greeks, the Indians—all the old commercial people. Actually he had never knocked an entire nation. International generosity had been started in him during the late nineteenth century by his young mother and father, candleholders in-side the dark tyranny of the czars. It was childhood training. Thought-fully, he passed it on.

In the hospital bed next to him, a sufferer named John feared the im-minent rise of the blacks of South Africa, the desperate blacks of Chi-cago, the yellow Chinese, and the Ottoman Turks. He had more reason than Alexandra's father to dread the future because his heart was strong. He would probably live to see it all. He believed the Turks when they came would bring to New York City diseases like cholera, virulent scarlet fever, and particularly leprosy.

Leprosy! for God's sakes! said Alexandra. John! Upset yourself with reality for once! She read aloud from the *Times* about the bombed, burned lepers' colonies in North Vietnam. Her father said, Please, Alexandra, today, no propaganda. Why do you constantly pick on the United States? He remembered the first time he'd seen the American flag on wild Ellis Island.[4] Under its protection and working like a horse, he'd read Dickens, gone to medical school, and shot like a surface-to-air missile right into the middle class.

Then he said, But they shouldn't put a flag in the middle of the choc-olate pudding. It's ridiculous.

It's Memorial Day, said the nurse's aide, removing his tray.

In the early evening Dennis stood at the door of each room of Alex-andra's apartment. He looked this way and that. Underuse in a time of population stress, he muttered. He entered the kitchen and sniffed the kitchen air. It doesn't matter, he said aloud. He took a fingerful of gravy out of the pot on the stove. Beef stew, he whispered. Then he opened the door to the freezer compartment and said, Sweet Jesus! because there were eleven batches of the same, neatly stacked and frozen. They

2. Aleksandr Pushkin (1799–1837), Russian poet.
3. A history of the beginning of World War I by Barbara Tuchman, published in 1962.

4. The island in the harbor of New York City on which immigrants were put through lengthy customs procedures.

were for Alexandra's junkies, whose methadone required lots of protein and carbohydrates.

I wouldn't have them in my house. It's a wonder you got a cup and saucer left. Creeps, said Dennis. However, yes indeed, I will eat this stuff. Why? Does it make me think of home or of something else? he asked. I think, a movie I once saw.

Apple turnovers! You know I have to admit it, our commune isn't working too well. Probably because it's in Brooklyn and the food coop[5] isn't together. But it's cool, they've accepted the criticism.

You have lots of junk in here, he pointed out after dinner. He had decided to give the place some respectful attention. He meant armchairs, lamps, desk sets, her grandmother's wedding portrait, and an umbrella stand with two of her father's canes.

Um, said Alexandra, it's rent-controlled.

You know what I like to do, Alexandra? I like to sit with a girl and look at a late movie, he said. It's an experience common to Americans at this hour. It's important to be like others, to dig the average dude, you have to be him. Be HIM. It's groovier than a lot of phony gab. You'd be surprised how friendly you get.

I'm not against friendliness, she said, I'm not even against Americans.

They watched half of A *Day at the Races*.[6] This is very relaxing, he said. It's kind of long though, isn't it? Then he began to undress. He held out his arms. He said, Alexandra I really can't wait any more. I'm a sunrise person. I like to go to bed early. Can I stay a few days?

He gave reasons: 1. It was a Memorial Day weekend, and the house in Brooklyn was full of tripping visitors. 2. He was disgusted with them anyway because they'd given up the most beautiful batik work for fashionable tie-dying. 3. He and Alexandra could take some good walks in the morning because all the parks to walk in were the lightest green. He had noticed that the tree on the corner though dying of buses was green at the beginning of many twigs. 4. He could talk to her about the kids, help her to understand their hangups, their incredible virtues. He had missed being one of them by about seven useless years.

So many reasons are not essential, Alexandra said. She offered him a brandy. Holy toads! he said furiously. You *know* I'm not into that. Touched by gloom, he began to remove the heavy shoes he wore for mountain walking. He dropped his pants and stamped on them a couple of times to make sure he and they were disengaged.

Alexandra, in the first summer dress of spring, stood still and watched. She breathed deeply because of having been alone for a year

5. Cooperative purchase and preparation of food for the commune.

6. A 1936 film starring the comedy team the Marx Brothers.

or two. She put her two hands over her ribs to hold her heart in place and also out of modesty to quiet its immodest thud. Then they went to bed in the bedroom and made love until that noisy disturbance ended. She couldn't hear one interior sound. Therefore they slept.

In the morning she became interested in reality again, which she had always liked. She wanted to talk about it. She began with a description of John, her father's neighbor in the hospital.

Turks? Far out! Well he's right. And another thing. Leprosy *is* coming. It's coming to the Forest Hills County Fair, the Rikers Island Jamboree, the Fillmore East, and the Ecolocountry Gardens in Westchester.[7] In August.

Reality? A lesson in reality? Am I a cabdriver? No. I drive a cab but I am not a cabdriver. I'm a song hawk. A songmaker. I'm a poet, in other words. Do you know that every black man walking down the street today is a poet? But only one white honky devil in ten. One in ten.

Nowadays I write for the Lepers all the time. Fuck poetry. The Lepers dig me. I dig them.

The Lepers? Alexandra said.

Cool! You know them? No? Well, you may have known them under their old name. They used to be called The Split Atom. But they became too popular and their thing is anonymity. That's what they're known for. They'll probably change their name after the summer festivals. They might move to the country and call themselves Winter Moss.

Do you really make a living now?

Oh yes. I do. I do. Among technicians like myself I do.

Now: I financially carry one third of a twelve-person, three-children commune. I only drive a cab to keep on top of the world of illusion, you know, Alexandra, to rap with the bourgeoisies, the fancy whores, the straight ladies visiting their daddies. Oh, excuse me, he said.

Now, Alexandra, imagine this: two bass guitars, a country violin, one piccolo, and drums. The Lepers' theme song! He sat up in bed. The sun shone on his chest. He had begun to think of breakfast, but he sang so that Alexandra could know him better and dig his substantialness.

> *ooooh*
> *first my finger goes goes goes*
> *then my nose*
>   *then baby my toes*
>
> *if you love me this way anyway any day*
> *I'll go your way*
>   *my Little Neck rose*

7. All locations in the New York area.

Well? he asked. He looked at Alexandra. Was she going to cry? I thought you were such a reality freak. Alexandra. That's the way it is in the real world. Anyway! He then said a small prose essay to explain and buttress the poem:

The kids! the kids! Though terrible troubles hang over them, such as the absolute end of the known world quickly by detonation or slowly through the easygoing destruction of natural resources, they are still, even now, optimistic, humorous, and brave. In fact, they intend enormous changes at the last minute.

Come on, said Alexandra, hardhearted, an enemy of generalization, there are all kinds. My boys aren't like that.

Yes, they are, he said, angry. You bring them around. I'll prove it. Anyway, I love them. He tried for about twenty minutes, forgetting breakfast, to show Alexandra how to look at things in this powerful last-half-of-the-century way. She tried. She had always had a progressive if sometimes reformist disposition, but at that moment, listening to him talk, she could see straight ahead over the thick hot rod of love to solitary age and lonesome death.

But there's nothing to fear my dear girl, her father said. When you get there you will not want to live a hell of a lot. Nothing to fear at all. You will be used up. You are like a coal burning, smoldering. Then there's nothing left to burn. Finished. Believe me, he said, although he hadn't been there yet himself, at that moment you won't mind. Alexandra's face was a bit rumpled, listening.

Don't look at me like that! he said. He was too sensitive to her appearance. He hated her to begin to look older the way she'd had to in the last twenty years. He said, Now *I* have seen people die. A large number. Not one or two. Many. They are good and ready. Pain. Despair. Unconsciousness, nightmares. Perfectly good comas, wrecked by nightmares. They are ready. You will be too, Sashka.[8] Don't worry so much.

Ho ho ho, said John in the next bed listening through the curtains. Doc, I'm not ready. I feel terrible, I got lousy nightmares. I don't sleep a wink. But I'm not ready. I can't piss without this tube. Lonesomeness! Boy! Did you ever see *one* of my kids visiting? No! Still I am *not* ready NOT READY. He spelled it out, looking at the ceiling or through it, to the roof garden for incurables, and from there to God.

---

8. Russian diminutive for Alexandra.

The next morning Dennis said, I would rather die than go to the hospital.

For God's sakes why?

Why? Because I hate to be in the hands of strangers. They don't let you take the pills you got that you know work, then if you need one of their pills, even if you buzz, they don't come. The nurse and three interns are making out in the information booth. I've seen it. It's a high counter, she's answering questions, and they're taking turns banging her from behind.

Dennis! You're too dumb. You sound like some superstitious old lady with rape dreams.

That's cool, he said. I *am* an old lady about my health. I mean I like it. I want my teeth to go right on. Right on sister. He began to sing, then stopped. Listen! Your destiny's in their hands. It's up to them. Do you live? Or are you a hippie crawling creep from their point of view? Then die!

Really. Nobody ever decides to let you die. In fact, that's what's wrong. They decide to keep people alive for years after death has set in.

You mean like your father?

Alexandra leaped out of bed stark naked. My father! Why he's got twenty times your zip.

Cool it! he said. Come back. I was just starting to fuck you and you get so freaked.

And another thing. Don't use that word. I hate it. When you're with a woman you have to use the language that's right for her.

What do you want me to say?

I want you to say, I was just starting to make love to you, etc.

Well, that's true, said Dennis, I was. When she returned to him, he only touched the tips of her fingers, though all of her was present. He kissed each finger and said right after each kiss, I want to make love to you. He did this sweetly, not sarcastically.

Dennis, Alexandra said in an embarrassment of recognition, you look like one of my placements, in fact you look like a kid, Billy Platoon. His real name is Platon but he calls himself Platoon so he can go to Vietnam and get killed like his stepbrother. He's a dreamy boy.

Alexandra, you talk a lot, now hush, no politics.

Alexandra continued for a sentence or two. He carries a stick with a ball full of nails attached, like some medieval weapon, in case an enemy from Suffolk Street CIA's him. That's what they call it.

Never heard that before. Besides I'm jealous. And also I'm the enemy from Suffolk Street.

No, no, said Alexandra. Then she noticed in her mother's bedroom bureau mirror across the room a small piece of her naked self. She said, Ugh!

There, there! said Dennis lovingly, caressing what he thought she'd looked at, a couple of rippled inches between her breast and belly. It's natural, Alexandra. Men don't change as much as women. Among all the animals, human females are the only ones to lose estrogen as they get older.

Is that it? she said.

Then there was nothing to talk about for half an hour.

But how come you knew that? she asked. The things you know, Dennis. What for?

Why—for my art, he said. And despite his youth he rested from love the way artists often do in order to sing. He sang:

> *Camp out*
>   *out in the forest daisy*
>   *under the gallows tree*
> *with the*
>   *ace of pentacles*[9]
>   *and me.*
>   *daisy flower*
> *What of the*
>   *earth's ecology*
> *you're drivin too fast*
> *Daisy you're drivin alone*
>   *Hey Daisy   cut the ignition*
>   *let the oil*
>   *back in the stone.*

Oh, I like that one. I admire it! Alexandra said. But in fact, *is* ecology a good word for a song? It's technical. . . .

Any word is good, it's the big word today anyway, said Dennis. It's what you do with the word. The language and the idea, they work it out together.

Really? Where do you get most of your ideas.

I don't know if I want to eat or sleep, he said. I think I just want to nuzzle your titty. Talk talk talk. Most? Well, I would say the majority are from a magazine, the *Scientific American.*

During breakfast, language remained on his mind. Because of this, he was silent. After the pancakes, he said, Actually Alexandra, I *can* use any words I want. And I have. I proved it last week in a conversation just like this one. I asked these blue-eyed cats to give me a dictionary. I just flipped the pages and jabbed and the word I hit was *ophidious.*[1] But I did it, because the word does the dreaming for you. The WORD.

---

9. Card in the mystical Tarot deck.   1. Involving snakes.

To a tune that was probably "On Top of Old Smoky" he sang:

The ophidious garden
was invented by Freud

   where three ladies murdered
   oh three ladies murdered

the pricks of the birds

the cobra is buried
the rattlesnake writhes

   in the black snaky garden
   in the blue snaky garden

in the hairs of my wives.[2]

More coffee, please, he said with pride and modesty.

It's better than most of your songs, Alexandra said. It's a poem, isn't it? It *is* better.

What? What? It is *not* better, it is not, goddamn. It is not. . . . It just isn't . . . oh, excuse me for losing my cool like that.

Forget it sonny, Alexandra said respectfully. I only meant I liked it, but I know, I'm too frank from living alone so much I think. Anyway, how come you always think about wives? Wives, mothers?

Because that's me, said peaceful Dennis. Haven't you noticed it yet? That's my bag. I'm a motherfucker.

Oh, she said, I see. But I'm not a mother, Dennis.

Yes, you are, Alexandra. I've figured out a lot about you. I know. I act like the weekend stud sometimes. But I wrote you a song. Just last night in the cab. I think about you. The Lepers'll never dig it. They don't know too much about life. They're still baby bees trying to make it to the next flower, but some old-timer'll tape it, some sore dude who's been out of it for a couple of years who wants to grow. He'll smell the shit in it.

   Oh
I know something about you baby

   that's sad
   don't be mad

2. An allusion to the Gorgons, three sisters in Greek mythology with snakes for hair. Sigmund Freud (1856–1939) interprets this myth as containing phallic symbolism.

> baby
>
> That you will never have children at
> rest
> at that beautiful breast
> my love
>
> But see
> everywhere you go, children follow you
> for more
> many more
> are the children of your life
> than the children of the married wife.

That one is out of the Bible, he said.[3] Pa, Alexandra said, don't you think a woman in this life ought to have at least one child?

No doubt about it, he said. You should have when you were married to Granofsky, the Communist. We disagreed. He had no sense of humor. He's probably boring the Cubans to death this minute. But he was an intelligent person otherwise. I would have brilliant grandchildren. They would not necessarily have the same politics.

Then he looked at her, her age and possibilities. He softened. You don't look so bad. You could still marry, dear girl. Then he softened further, thinking of hopeless statistics he had just read about the ratio of women to men. Actually! So what! It's not important, Alexandra. According to the Torah,[4] only the man is commanded to multiply. You are not commanded. You have a child, you don't have, God doesn't care. You don't have one, you call in the maid. You say to your husband, Sweetie, get my maid with child. O.K. Well, your husband has anyway been fooling around with the maid for a couple of years, but now it's a respectable business. Good. You don't have to go through the whole thing, nine months, complications, maybe a Caesarean, no no pronto, a child for the Lord, Hosanna.

Pa, she said, several weeks later, but what if I did have a baby?

Don't be a fool, he said. Then he gave her a terrible long medical look, which included her entire body. He said, Why do you ask this question? He became red in the face, which had never happened. He took hold of his chest with his right hand, the hospital buzzer with the left. First, he said, I want the nurse! Now! Then he ordered Alexandra: marry!

---

3. "Sing, O barren thou that didst not bear; break forth into singing, and cry aloud, thou that didst not travail with child: for more are the children of the desolate than the children of the married wife" (Isaiah 54:1).
4. One of the first five books of the Old Testament; i.e., according to Judaic law.

Dennis said, I don't know how I got into this shit. It's not right, but because your habits and culture are different, I will compromise. What I suggest is this, Alexandra. The three children in our commune belong to us all. No one knows who the father is. It's far out. I swear—by the cock of our hard-up gods, I swear it's beautiful. One of them might be mine. But she doesn't have any distinguishing marks. Why don't you come and live with us and we'll all raise that kid up to be a decent human and humane being in this world. We need a slightly older person, we really do, with a historic sense. We lack that.

Thank you, Alexandra replied. No.

Her father said, Explain it to me, please. For what purpose did you act out this nonsense? For love? At your age. Money? Some conniver flattered you. You probably made him supper. Some starving ne'er-do-well probably wanted a few meals and said, Why not? This middle-aged fool is an easy mark. She'll give me pot roast at night, bacon and eggs in the morning.

No Pa, no, Alexandra said. Please, you'll get sicker.

John in the next bed dying with a strong heart wrote a little note to him. Doc, you're crazy. Don't leave enemies. That girl is loyal! She hasn't missed a Tues., Thurs., or Sat. Did you ever see one of my kids visit? Something else. I feel worse and worse. But I'm still *not ready*.

I want to tell you one more thing, her father said. You are going to embitter my last days and ruin my life.

After that, Alexandra hoped every day for her father's death, so that she could have a child without ruining his interesting life at the very end of it when ruin is absolutely retroactive.

Finally, Dennis said, Then let me at least share the pad with you. It'll be to *your* advantage.

No, Alexandra said. Please, Dennis. I've got to go to work early. I'm sleepy.

I dig. I've been a joke to you. You've used me in a bad way. That's not cool. That smells under heaven.

No, Alexandra said. Please, shut up. Anyway, how do you know you're the father?

Come on, he said, who else would be?

Alexandra smiled, bit her lip to the edge of blood to show pain politely. She was thinking about the continuity of her work, how to be proud and not lose a productive minute. She thought about the members of her case load one by one.

She said, Dennis, I know exactly what I'm going to do.

In that case, this is it, I'm splitting.

This is what Alexandra did in order to make good use of the events of her life. She invited three pregnant clients who were fifteen and sixteen

years old to live with her. She visited each one and explained to them
that she was pregnant too, and that her apartment was very large. Although they had disliked her because she'd always worried more about
the boys, they moved out of the homes of their bad-tempered parents
within a week. At the very first evening meal they began to give Alexandra good advice about men, which she did appreciate years later. She
ensured their health and her own and she took notes as well. She established a precedent in social work which would not be followed or even
mentioned in state journals for about five years.

Alexandra's father's life was not ruined, nor did he have to die.
Shortly before the baby's birth, he fell hard on the bathroom tiles,
cracked his skull, dipped the wires of his brain into his heart's blood.
Short circuit! He lost twenty, thirty years in the flood, the faces of
nephews, in-laws, the names of two Presidents, and a war. His eyes
were rounder, he was often awestruck, but he was smart as ever, and
able to begin again with fewer scruples to notice and appreciate.

The baby was born and named Dennis for his father. Of course his
last name was Granofsky because of Alexandra's husband, Granofsky
the Communist.

The Lepers, who had changed their name to the Edible Amanita,
taped the following song in his tiny honor. It was called "Who? I."

The lyrics are simple. They are:

Who is the father?
Who is the father
Who is the father

                I!   I!   I!   I!

I am the father
I am the father
I am the father

Dennis himself sang the solo which was I! I! I! I! in a hoarse enraged
prophetic voice. He had been brave to acknowledge the lyrics. After a
thirty-eight-hour marathon encounter at his commune, he was asked to
leave. The next afternoon he moved to a better brownstone about four
blocks away where occasional fatherhood was expected.

On the baby's third birthday, Dennis and the Fair Fields of Corn
produced a folk-rock album because that was the new sound and exciting. It was called *For Our Son*. Tuned-in listeners could hear how taps
played by the piccolo about forty times a verse flitted in and out of the
long dark drum rolls, the ordinary banjo chords, and the fiddle tune
which was something but not exactly like "Lullaby and Good Night."

Will you come to see me Jack
     When I'm old and very shaky?
Yes I will for you're my dad
     And you've lost your last old lady
     Though you traveled very far
To the highlands and the badlands
     And ripped off the family car
Still, old dad, I won't forsake you.

Will you come to see me Jack?
     Though I'm really not alone.
Still I'd like to see my boy
     For we're lonesome for our own.
     Yes I will for you're my dad
Though you dumped me and my brothers
     And you sizzled down the road
Loving other fellows' mothers.

Will you come to see me Jack?
     Though I look like time boiled over.
Growing old is not a lark.
     Yes I will for you're my dad
     Though we never saw a nickel
As we struggled up life's ladder
I will call you and together
We will cuddle up and see
     What the weather's like in Key West
On the old-age home TV.

This song was sung coast to coast and became famous from the dark
Maine woods to Texas's shining gulf. It was responsible for a statistical
increase in visitors to old-age homes by the apprehensive middle-aged
and the astonished young.

1974

NADINE GORDIMER

1923–

The government of the Union of South Africa understood that Nadine Gordimer's fiction furnishes a scathing critique of the effects of *apartheid*, the legal
system that bars native blacks from full human and civil rights, and so a number

of her books were banned for several years in her native country. Gordimer, who was born and raised in South Africa, continues to live in Johannesburg. The daughter of Isidore and Nan Gordimer, she attended private schools and, for one year, the University of Witwatersrand, before marrying Reinhold H. Cassirer, the director of the Johannesburg branch of Sotheby Parke Bernet, and giving birth to two children. From her earliest fiction, *The Lying Days* (1953), to her critically acclaimed novels *A Guest of Honour* (1970) and *Burger's Daughter* (1979), Gordimer has written with sensitivity and intelligence about the customs, habits, superstitions, and rituals that distinguish and divide blacks and whites in a society shaped by imperialist history. In several collections of stories, too, she has become what the critic Maxwell Geismar calls "a luminous symbol of at least one white person's understanding of the black man's burden." *Town and Country Lovers* illustrates Gordimer's equally astute understanding of the burdens borne by native African women.

Town and Country Lovers[1]

Dr. Franz-Josef von Leinsdorf is a geologist absorbed in his work; wrapped up in it, as the saying goes—year after year the experience of this work enfolds him, swaddling him away from the landscapes, the cities and the people, wherever he lives: Peru, New Zealand, the United States. He's always been like that, his mother could confirm from their native Austria. There, even as a handsome small boy he presented only his profile to her: turned away to his bits of rock and stone. His few relaxations have not changed much since then. An occasional skiing trip, listening to music, reading poetry—Rainer Maria Rilke[2] once stayed in his grandmother's hunting lodge in the forests of Styria and the boy was introduced to Rilke's poems while very young.

Layer upon layer, country after country, wherever his work takes him—and now he has been almost seven years in Africa. First the Côte d'Ivoire, and the past five years, South Africa. The shortage of skilled manpower brought about his recruitment here. He has no interest in the politics of the countries he works in. His private preoccupation-within-the-preoccupation of his work has been research into underground water-courses, but the mining company that employs him in a senior though not executive capacity is interested only in mineral discovery. So he is much out in the field—which is the veld,[3] here—seeking new gold, copper, platinum and uranium deposits. When he is at home—on this particular job, in this particular country, this city—he lives in a two-roomed flat in a suburban block with a landscaped garden, and does his shopping at a supermarket conveniently across the street. He is not married—yet. That is how his colleagues, and the typists and

---

1. This is the first of two stories which Gordimer published as a sequence, under the title *Town and Country Lovers, One* and *Two*; our selection originally appeared in *The New Yorker* as *City Lovers*.
2. German poet (1875–1926).
3. Open grazing areas in Southern Africa.

secretaries at the mining company's head office, would define his situation. Both men and women would describe him as a good-looking man, in a foreign way, with the lower half of the face dark and middle-aged (his mouth is thin and curving, and no matter how close-shaven his beard shows like fine shot embedded in the skin round mouth and chin) and the upper half contradictorily young, with deep-set eyes (some would say grey, some black), thick eyelashes and brows. A tangled gaze: through which concentration and gleaming thoughtfulness perhaps appear as fire and languor. It is this that the women in the office mean when they remark he's not unattractive. Although the gaze seems to promise, he has never invited any one of them to go out with him. There is the general assumption he probably has a girl who's been picked for him, he's bespoken by one of his own kind, back home in Europe where he comes from. Many of these well-educated Europeans have no intention of becoming permanent immigrants; neither the remnant of white colonial life nor idealistic involvement with Black Africa appeals to them.

One advantage, at least, of living in underdeveloped or half-developed countries is that flats are serviced. All Dr. von Leinsdorf has to do for himself is buy his own supplies and cook an evening meal if he doesn't want to go to a restaurant. It is simply a matter of dropping in to the supermarket on his way from his car to his flat after work in the afternoon. He wheels a trolley up and down the shelves, and his simple needs are presented to him in the form of tins, packages, plastic-wrapped meat, cheeses, fruit and vegetables, tubes, bottles. . . . At the cashiers' counters where customers must converge and queue[4] there are racks of small items uncategorized, for last-minute purchase. Here, as the coloured girl cashier punches the adding machine, he picks up cigarettes and perhaps a packet of salted nuts or a bar of nougat. Or razor-blades, when he remembers he's running short. One evening in winter he saw that the cardboard display was empty of the brand of blades he preferred, and he drew the cashier's attention to this. These young coloured girls are usually pretty unhelpful, taking money and punching their machines in a manner that asserts with the time-serving obstinacy of the half-literate the limit of any responsibility towards customers, but this one ran an alert glance over the selection of razor-blades, apologized that she was not allowed to leave her post, and said she would see that the stock was replenished "next time." A day or two later she recognized him, gravely, as he took his turn before her counter—"I ahssed them, but it's out of stock. You can't get it. I did ahss about it." He said this didn't matter. "When it comes in, I can keep a few packets for you." He thanked her.

---

4. Form lines.

He was away with the prospectors the whole of the next week. He arrived back in town just before nightfall on Friday, and was on his way from car to flat with his arms full of briefcase, suitcase and canvas bags when someone stopped him by standing timidly in his path. He was about to dodge round unseeingly on the crowded pavement but she spoke. "We got the blades in now. I didn't see you in the shop this week, but I kept some for when you come. So . . ."

He recognized her. He had never seen her standing before, and she was wearing a coat. She was rather small and finely-made, for one of them. The coat was skimpy but no big backside jutted. The cold brought an apricot-graining of warm colour to her cheekbones, beneath which a very small face was quite delicately hollowed, and the skin was smooth, the subdued satiny colour of certain yellow wood. That crêpey hair, but worn drawn back flat and in a little knot pushed into one of the cheap wool chignons that (he recognized also) hung in the miscellany of small goods along with the razor-blades, at the supermarket. He said thanks, he was in a hurry, he'd only just got back from a trip—shifting the burdens he carried, to demonstrate. "Oh shame." She acknowledged his load. "But if you want I can run in and get it for you quickly. If you want."

He saw at once it was perfectly clear that all the girl meant was that she would go back to the supermarket, buy the blades and bring the packet to him there where he stood, on the pavement. And it seemed that it was this certainty that made him say, in the kindly tone of assumption used for an obliging underling, "I live just across there—*Atlantis*—that flat building. Could you drop them by, for me—number seven-hundred-and-eighteen, seventh floor—"

She had not before been inside one of these big flat buildings near where she worked. She lived a bus- and train-ride away to the West of the city, but this side of the black townships, in a township for people her tint. There was a pool with ferns, not plastic, and even a little waterfall pumped electrically over rocks, in the entrance of the building *Atlantis*; she didn't wait for the lift marked GOODS but took the one meant for whites and a white woman with one of those sausage-dogs on a lead got in with her but did not pay her any attention. The corridors leading to the flats were nicely glassed-in, not draughty.

He wondered if he should give her a twenty-cent piece for her trouble—ten cents would be right for a black; but she said, "Oh no—please, here—" standing outside his open door and awkwardly pushing back at his hand the change from the money he'd given her for the razor-blades. She was smiling, for the first time, in the dignity of refusing a tip. It was difficult to know how to treat these people, in this country; to know what they expected. In spite of her embarrassing refusal of the coin, she stood there, completely unassuming, fists thrust down the pockets of her cheap coat against the cold she'd come in from, rather pretty thin legs neatly aligned, knee to knee, ankle to ankle.

"Would you like a cup of coffee or something?"

He couldn't very well take her into his study-cum-living-room and offer her a drink. She followed him to his kitchen, but at the sight of her pulling out the single chair to drink her cup of coffee at the kitchen table, he said, "No—bring it in here—" and led the way into the big room where, among his books and his papers, his files of scientific correspondence (and the cigar boxes of stamps from the envelopes) his racks of records, his specimens of minerals and rocks, he lived alone.

It was no trouble to her; she saved him the trips to the supermarket and brought him his groceries two or three times a week. All he had to do was to leave a list and the key under the doormat, and she would come up in her lunch-hour to collect them, returning to put his supplies in the flat after work. Sometimes he was home and sometimes not. He bought a box of chocolates and left it, with a note, for her to find; and that was acceptable, apparently, as a gratuity.

Her eyes went over everything in the flat although her body tried to conceal its sense of being out of place by remaining as still as possible, holding its contours in the chair offered her as a stranger's coat is set aside and remains exactly as left until the owner takes it up to go. "You collect?"

"Well, these are specimens—connected with my work."

"My brother used to collect. Miniatures. With brandy and whisky and that, in them. From all over. Different countries."

The second time she watched him grinding coffee for the cup he had offered her she said, "You always do that? Always when you make coffee?"

"But of course. Is it no good, for you? Do I make it too strong?"

"Oh it's just I'm not used to it. We buy it ready—you know, it's in a bottle, you just add a bit to the milk or water."

He laughed, instructive: "That's not coffee, that's a synthetic flavouring. In my country we drink only real coffee, fresh, from the beans —you smell how good it is as it's being ground?"

She was stopped by the caretaker and asked what she wanted in the building. Heavy with the *bona fides*[5] of groceries clutched to her body, she said she was working at number 718, on the seventh floor. The caretaker did not tell her not to use the whites' lift; after all, she was not black; her family was very light-skinned.

There was the item "grey button for trousers" on one of his shopping lists. She said as she unpacked the supermarket carrier, "Give me

5. Genuine examples, evidence (Latin: good faith).

the pants, so long, then," and sat on his sofa that was always gritty with fragments of pipe tobacco, sewing in and out through the four holes of the button with firm, fluent movements of the right hand, gestures supplying the articulacy missing from her talk. She had a little yokel's, peasant's (he thought of it) gap between her two front teeth when she smiled that he didn't much like, but, face ellipsed to three-quarter angle, eyes cast down in concentration with soft lips almost closed, this didn't matter. He said, watching her sew, "You're a good girl"; and touched her.

She remade the bed every late afternoon when they left it and she dressed again before she went home. After a week there was a day when late afternoon became evening, and they were still in the bed.

"Can't you stay the night?"

"My mother," she said.

"Phone her. Make an excuse." He was a foreigner. He had been in the country five years, but he didn't understand that people don't usually have telephones in their houses, where she lived. She got up to dress. He didn't want that tender body to go out in the night cold and kept hindering her with the interruption of his hands; saying nothing. Before she put on her coat, when the body had already disappeared, he spoke. "But you must make some arrangement."

"Oh my mother!" Her face opened to fear and vacancy he could not read.

He was not entirely convinced the woman would think of her daughter as some pure and unsullied virgin. . . . "Why?"

The girl said, "S'e'll be scared. S'e'll be scared we get caught."

"Don't tell her anything. Say I'm employing you." In this country he was working in now there were generally rooms on the roofs of flat buildings for tenants' servants.

She said: "That's what I told the caretaker."

She ground fresh coffee beans every time he wanted a cup while he was working at night. She never attempted to cook anything until she had watched in silence while he did it the way he liked, and she learned to reproduce exactly the simple dishes he preferred. She handled his pieces of rock and stone, at first admiring the colours—"It'd make a beautiful ring or a necklace, ay." Then he showed her the striations, the formation of each piece, and explained what each was, and how, in the long life of the earth, it had been formed. He named the mineral it yielded, and what that was used for. He worked at his papers, writing, writing, every night, so it did not matter that they could not go out together to public places. On Sundays she got into his car in the basement garage and they drove to the country and picnicked away up in the

Magaliesberg, where there was no one. He read or poked about among the rocks; they climbed together, to the mountain pools. He taught her to swim. She had never seen the sea. She squealed and shrieked in the water, showing the gap between her teeth, as—it crossed his mind—she must do when among her own people. Occasionally he had to go out to dinner at the houses of colleagues from the mining company; she sewed and listened to the radio in the flat and he found her in the bed, warm and already asleep, by the time he came in. He made his way into her body without speaking; she made him welcome without a word. Once he put on evening dress for a dinner at his country's consulate; watching him brush one or two fallen hairs from the shoulders of the dark jacket that sat so well on him, she saw a huge room, all chandeliers and people dancing some dance from a costume film—stately, hand-to-hand. She supposed he was going to fetch, in her place in the car, a partner for the evening. They never kissed when either left the flat; he said, suddenly, kindly, pausing as he picked up cigarettes and keys, "Don't be lonely." And added, "Wouldn't you like to visit your family sometimes, when I have to go out?"

He had told her he was going home to his mother in the forests and mountains of his country near the Italian border (he showed her on the map) after Christmas. She had not told him how her mother, not knowing there was any other variety, assumed he was a medical doctor, so she had talked to her about the doctor's children and the doctor's wife who was a very kind lady, glad to have someone who could help out in the surgery as well as the flat.

She remarked wonderingly on his ability to work until midnight or later, after a day at work. She was so tired when she came home from her cash register at the supermarket that once dinner was eaten she could scarcely keep awake. He explained in a way she could understand that while the work she did was repetitive, undemanding of any real response from her intelligence, requiring little mental or physical effort and therefore unrewarding, his work was his greatest interest, it taxed his mental capacities to their limit, exercised all his concentration, and rewarded him constantly as much with the excitement of a problem presented as with the satisfaction of a problem solved. He said later, putting away his papers, speaking out of a silence: "Have you done other kinds of work?" She said, "I was in a clothing factory before. Sportbeau shirts; you know? But the pay's better in the shop."

Of course. Being a conscientious newspaper-reader in every country he lived in, he was aware that it was only recently that the retail consumer trade in this one had been allowed to employ coloureds as shop assistants; even punching a cash register represented advancement. With the continuing shortage of semi-skilled whites a girl like this might be able to edge a little farther into the white-collar category. He began to teach her to type. He was aware that her English was poor, even though, as a foreigner, in his ears her pronounciation did not offend, nor categorize her as it would in those of someone of his education whose mother tongue was English. He corrected her grammatical mistakes but missed the less obvious ones because of his own sometimes exotic English usage—she continued to use the singular pronoun "it" when what was required was the plural "they." Because he was a foreigner (although so clever, as she saw) she was less inhibited than she might have been by the words she knew she misspelled in her typing. While she sat at the typewriter she thought how one day she would type notes for him, as well as making coffee the way he liked it, and taking him inside her body without saying anything, and sitting (even if only through the empty streets of quiet Sundays) beside him in his car, like a wife.

On a summer night near Christmas—he had already bought and hidden a slightly showy but nevertheless good watch he thought she would like—there was a knocking at the door that brought her out of the bathroom and him to his feet, at his work-table. No one ever came to the flat at night; he had no friends intimate enough to drop in without warning. The summons was an imperious banging that did not pause and clearly would not stop until the door was opened.

She stood in the open bathroom doorway gazing at him across the passage into the living-room; her bare feet and shoulders were free of a big bath-towel. She said nothing, did not even whisper. The flat seemed to shake with the strong unhurried blows.

He made as if to go to the door, at last, but now she ran and clutched him by both arms. She shook her head wildly; her lips drew back but her teeth were clenched, she didn't speak. She pulled him into the bedroom, snatched some clothes from the clean laundry laid out on the bed and got into the wall-cupboard, thrusting the key at his hand. Although his arms and calves felt weakly cold he was horrified, distastefully embarrassed at the sight of her pressed back crouching there under his suits and coat; it was horrible and ridiculous. *Come out!* he whispered. *No! Come out!* She hissed: *Where? Where can I go?*

Never mind! Get out of there!

He put out his hand to grasp her. At bay, she said with all the force of her terrible whisper, baring the gap in her teeth: *I'll throw myself out the window.*

She forced the key into his hand like the handle of a knife. He closed the door on her face and drove the key home in the lock, then dropped it among coins in his trouser pocket.

He unslotted the chain that was looped across the flat door. He turned the serrated knob of the Yale lock. The three policemen, two in plain clothes, stood there without impatience although they had been banging on the door for several minutes. The big dark one with an elaborate moustache held out in a hand wearing a plaited gilt ring some sort of identity card.

Dr. von Leinsdorf said quietly, the blood coming strangely back to legs and arms, "What is it?"

The sergeant told him they knew there was a coloured girl in the flat. They had had information; "I been watching this flat three months, I know."

"I am alone here." Dr. von Leinsdorf did not raise his voice.

"I know, I know who is here. Come—" And the sergeant and his two assistants went into the living-room, the kitchen, the bathroom (the sergeant picked up a bottle of after-shave cologne, seemed to study the French label) and the bedroom. The assistants removed the clean laundry that was laid upon the bed and then turned back the bedding, carrying the sheets over to be examined by the sergeant under the lamp. They talked to one another in Afrikaans, which the Doctor did not understand. The sergeant himself looked under the bed, and lifted the long curtains at the window. The wall cupboard was of the kind that has no knobs; he saw that it was locked and began to ask in Afrikaans, then politely changed to English, "Give us the key."

Dr. von Leinsdorf said, "I'm sorry, I left it at my office—I always lock and take my keys with me in the mornings."

"It's no good, man, you better give me the key."

He smiled a little, reasonably. "It's on my office desk."

The assistants produced a screwdriver and he watched while they inserted it where the cupboard doors met, gave it quick, firm but not forceful leverage. He heard the lock give.

She had been naked, it was true, when they knocked. But now she was wearing a long-sleeved T-shirt with an appliquéd butterfly motif on one breast, and a pair of jeans. Her feet were still bare; she had managed, by feel, in the dark, to get into some of the clothing she had snatched from the bed, but she had no shoes. She had perhaps been weeping behind the cupboard door (her cheeks looked stained) but now her face was sullen and she was breathing heavily, her diaphragm contracting and expanding exaggeratedly and her breasts pushing against the cloth. It made her appear angry; it might simply have been that she was half-suffocated in the cupboard and needed oxygen. She did not look at Dr. von Leinsdorf. She would not reply to the sergeant's questions.

They were taken to the police station where they were at once separated and in turn led for examination by the district surgeon. The man's underwear was taken away and examined, as the sheets had been, for signs of his seed. When the girl was undressed, it was discovered that beneath her jeans she was wearing a pair of men's briefs with his name on the neatly-sewn laundry tag; in her haste, she had taken the wrong garment to her hiding-place.

Now she cried, standing there before the district surgeon in a man's underwear.

He courteously pretended not to notice. He handed briefs, jeans and T-shirt round the door, and motioned her to lie on a white-sheeted high table where he placed her legs apart, resting in stirrups, and put into her where the other had made his way so warmly a cold hard instrument that expanded wider and wider. Her thighs and knees trembled uncontrollably while the doctor looked into her and touched her deep inside with more hard instruments, carrying wafers of gauze.

When she came out of the examining room back to the charge office, Dr. von Leinsdorf was not there; they must have taken him somewhere else. She spent what was left of the night in a cell, as he must be doing; but early in the morning she was released and taken home to her mother's house in the coloured township by a white man who explained he was the clerk of the lawyer who had been engaged for her by Dr. von Leinsdorf. Dr. von Leinsdorf, the clerk said, had also been bailed out that morning. He did not say when, or if, she would see him again.

A statement made by the girl to the police was handed in to Court when she and the man appeared to meet charges of contravening the Immorality Act in a Johannesburg flat on the night of — December, 19—. *I lived with the white man in his flat. He had intercourse with me sometimes. He gave me tablets to take to prevent me becoming pregnant.*

Interviewed by the Sunday papers, the girl said, "I'm sorry for the sadness brought to my mother." She said she was one of nine children of a female laundry worker. She had left school in Standard Three[6] because there was no money at home for gym clothes or a school blazer. She had worked as a machinist in a factory and a cashier in a supermarket. Dr. von Leinsdorf taught her to type his notes.

Dr. Franz-Josef von Leinsdorf, described as the grandson of a baroness, a cultured man engaged in international mineralogical research, said he accepted social distinctions between people but didn't think they should be legally imposed. "Even in my own country it's difficult for a person from a higher class to marry one from a lower class."

The two accused gave no evidence. They did not greet or speak to each other in Court. The Defence argued that the sergeant's evidence that they had been living together as man and wife was hearsay. (The

___

6. South African equivalent of eighth grade.

woman with the dachshund, the caretaker?) The magistrate acquitted
them because the State failed to prove carnal intercourse had taken
place of the night of — December, 19—.

The girl's mother was quoted, with photograph, in the Sunday
papers: "I won't let my daughter work as a servant for a white man
again."

1980

DENISE LEVERTOV

1923–

Born and brought up in Ilford, Essex, England, Denise Levertov has paradoxically become one of the most American of writers, a self-defined disciple of
many of the aesthetic ideas of the American poets William Carlos Williams and
H. D. (Hilda Doolittle). About Williams, for example, Levertov has observed
that "he made available to us the whole range of the language, he showed us the
rhythms of speech *as poetry*," adding that "it is a mistake to suppose that Williams's insistence on 'the American idiom' ever implied a reduction; on the
contrary, it means the recognition of wide resources." Similarly, about H. D.,
she has remarked that the author of *Trilogy* offered "doors, ways in, tunnels
through," noting that H. D. "showed a way to penetrate mystery; which means,
not to flood darkness with light so that darkness is destroyed, but to *enter into*
darkness, mystery, so that it is experienced." In her own work, moreover, Levertov has consistently employed such "natural" speech-rhythms to open the
gates of mystery and enter what she defines in *The Goddess* and *Song to Ishtar*
as the sacred precincts of the Muse.

The younger of two daughters of a Welsh mother and a Russian Jewish father (who later became a clergyman in the Church of England), Levertov was
educated mostly at home; in several memoirs, she has described her English
childhood as bucolic, paying special attention to the influence of her older sister
Olga, about whose death she wrote a poignant elegiac sequence, *The Sorrow
Dance*. During World War II, she became a nurse, and in 1947 she married
the writer Mitchell Goodman (from whom she was divorced in the early seventies). The couple have one son, about whose childhood and adolescence Levertov has also written several moving poems. Emigrating to the United States
in 1948, Levertov became an American citizen in 1955, and began to publish
the suavely cadenced collections of verse on which her reputation is based. In
England, she had already produced one book—*The Double Image* (1946)—
but her American volumes, based on a radical commitment to the idea that "a
poem *is* a sonic, sensuous event and not a statement or a string of ideas," are
more characteristic. Over a dozen in number, they include such influential and
widely read collections as *The Jacob's Ladder* (1961), *O Taste and See* (1964),
The Sorrow Dance (1967), *Relearning the Alphabet* (1970), *The Freeing of the*

Dust (1975), and *Candles in Babylon* (1982), as well as two books of essays, *The Poet in the World* (1973) and *Light up the Cave* (1981).

In recent years, Levertov has taught at a number of universities, including Tufts and Stanford; served as poetry editor of the liberal journal *The Nation*; and—perhaps most important—become a notable activist in the peace movement of the sixties and seventies (protesting the Vietnam War), and in the anti-nuclear and peace movements of the eighties (protesting nuclear proliferation and American intervention in El Salvador). Though she does not define herself as a feminist, her poetry frequently expresses a distinctively female perspective on the world, celebrating the values of nature and nurture while drawing on the details of domesticity to dramatize a mystical reality whose radiance she often sees (for instance, in *Abel's Bride*) as illuminating even the most apparently ordinary objects. In addition, in such poems as *Hypocrite Women*, *In Mind*, and *Stepping Westward*, Levertov turns again and again to questions of female self-definition, exploring the complexity of her own character as an example of the complexity of a woman's being. More generally, however, in their Romantic commitment to both an imagining of moral justice and an intuition of mystical truth, her finest verses consistently reflect her belief that "the written poem" is at its best a "record" of an "inner song."

The Goddess

She in whose lipservice
I passed my time,
whose name I knew, but not her face,
came upon me where I lay in Lie Castle!

Flung me across the room, and   5
room after room (hitting the walls, re-
bounding—to the last
sticky wall—wrenching away from it
pulled hair out!)
till I lay   10
outside the outer walls!

There in cold air
lying still where her hand had thrown me,
I tasted the mud that splattered my lips:
the seeds of a forest were in it,   15
asleep and growing! I tasted
her power!

The silence was answering my silence,
a forest was pushing itself
out of sleep between my submerged fingers.   20

I bit on a seed and it spoke on my tongue
of day that shone already among stars
in the water-mirror of low ground,

and a wind rising ruffled the lights:
she passed near me returning from the encounter,   25
she who plucked me from the close rooms,

without whom nothing
flowers, fruits, sleeps in season,
without whom nothing
speaks in its own tongue, but returns   30
lie for lie!

                                                    1960

Song for Ishtar[1]

The moon is a sow
and grunts in my throat
Her great shining shines through me
so the mud of my hollow gleams
and breaks in silver bubbles   5

She is a sow
and I a pig and a poet

When she opens her white
lips to devour me I bite back
and laughter rocks the moon   10

In the black of desire
we rock and grunt, grunt and
shine

                                                    1964

Hypocrite Women

Hypocrite women, how seldom we speak
of our own doubts, while dubiously
we mother man in his doubt!

---

1. Babylonian goddess of love and fertility.

And if at Mill Valley[2] perched in the trees
the sweet rain drifting through western air   5
a white sweating bull of a poet told us

our cunts are ugly—why didn't we
admit we have thought so too? (And
what shame? They are not for the eye!)

No, they are dark and wrinkled and hairy,   10
caves of the Moon . . .   And when a
dark humming fills us, a

coldness towards life,
we are too much women to
own to such unwomanliness.   15

Whorishly with the psychopomp[3]
we play and plead—and say
nothing of this later.   And our dreams,

with what frivolity we have pared them
like toenails, clipped them like ends of   20
split hair.

                                                    1964

In Mind

There's in my mind a woman
of innocence, unadorned but

fair-featured, and smelling of
apples or grass. She wears

a utopian smock or shift, her hair   5
is light brown and smooth, and she

is kind and very clean without
ostentation—
            but she has
no imagination.   10
            And there's a
turbulent moon-ridden girl

---

2. Town in northern California, location of   3. The soul's guide in a moral or spiritual battle-
Marin College.   field.

or old woman, or both,
dressed in opals and rags, feathers

and torn taffeta,   15
who knows strange songs—

but she is not kind.

1964

The Ache of Marriage

The ache of marriage:

thigh and tongue, beloved,
are heavy with it,
it throbs in the teeth

We look for communion   5
and are turned away, beloved,
each and each

It is leviathan[4] and we
in its belly
looking for joy, some joy   10
not to be known outside it

two by two in the ark[5] of
the ache of it.

1964

The Crack

While snow fell carelessly
floating indifferent in eddies of
rooftop air, circling the black
chimney cowls,

a spring night entered   5
my mind through the tight-closed window,
wearing

---

4. A reference to the story of Jonah in the Old Testament, swallowed by a sea monster, or leviathan.

5. A reference to Noah's ark, in which animals of every species were preserved from the flood that destroyed all other life (Genesis 7).

a loose Russian shirt of
light silk.
      For this, then,   10
that slanting
line was left, that crack, the pane
never replaced.

                 1964

Eros[6] at Temple Stream

The river in its abundance
many-voiced
all about us as we stood
on a warm rock to wash

slowly   5
smoothing in long
             sliding strokes
our soapy hands along each other's
slippery cool bodies

quiet and slow in the midst of   10
the quick of the
sounding river

our hands were
flames
stealing upon quickened flesh until   15

no part of us but was
sleek and
on fire.

                 1964

About Marriage

Don't lock me in wedlock, I want
marriage, an
encounter—

I told you about the
green light of   5
May

6. The Greek god of love.

(a veil of quiet befallen
the downtown park,
late

Saturday after   10
noon, long
shadows and cool

air, scent of
new grass,
fresh leaves,   15

blossom on the threshold of
abundance—

and the birds I met there,
birds of passage breaking their journey,
three birds each of a different species: 20

the azalea-breasted with round poll, dark,
the brindled, merry, mousegliding one,
and the smallest, golden as gorse and wearing
a black Venetian mask[7]

and with them the three douce[8] hen-birds   25
feathered in tender, lively brown—

I stood
a half-hour under the enchantment,
no-one passed near,
the birds saw me and   30

let me be
near them.)

It's not
irrelevant:
I would be   35
met

and meet you
so,
in a green

airy space, not   40
locked in.

1964

---

7. Domino mask, covering the eyes and nose.   8. French: gentle.

The Wings

Something hangs in back of me,
I can't see it, can't move it.

I know it's black,
a hump on my back.

It's heavy. You   5
can't see it.

What's in it? Don't tell me
you don't know. It's

what you told me about—
black   10

inimical power, cold
whirling out of it and

around me and
sweeping you flat.

But what if,   15
like a camel, it's

pure energy I store,
and carry humped and heavy?

Not black, not
that terror, stupidity   20

of cold rage; or black
only for being pent there?

What if released in air
it became a white

source of light, a fountain   25
of light? Could all that weight

be the power of flight?
Look inward: see me

with embryo wings, one
feathered in soot, the other   30

blazing ciliations[9] of ember, pale
flare-pinions. Well—

could I go
on one wing,

the white one?   35

1967

Abel's Bride[1]

Woman fear for man, he goes
out alone to his labors. No mirror
nests in his pocket. His face
opens and shuts with his hopes.
His sex hangs unhidden   5
or rises before him
blind and questing.

She thinks herself
lucky. But sad. When she goes out
she looks in the glass, she remembers   10
herself. Stones, coal,
the hiss of water upon the kindled
branches—her being
is a cave, there are bones at the hearth.

1967

The Son

i   The Disclosure

He-who-came-forth was
it turned out
a man—

Moves among us from room to room of our life
in boots, in jeans, in a cloak of flame   5
pulled out of his pocket along with

---

9. Microscopic hairlike growths.
1. According to the Bible, Abel was the second
son of Adam and Eve, and was murdered by his
brother Cain (Genesis 4). No mention is made
of Abel's wife in the Bible.

old candywrappers, where it had lain
transferred from pants to pants,
folded small as a curl of dust,
from the beginning—   10

unfurled now.

The fine flame
almost unseen in common light.

ii   The Woodblock

He cuts into a slab of wood,
engrossed, violently precise.   15
Thus, yesterday, the day before yesterday,
engines of fantasy were evolved
in poster paints. Tonight
a face forms under the knife,
slashed with stern   20
crisscrosses of longing, downstrokes
of silence endured—
                    his visioned

own face!—
down which from one eye   25

rolls a tear.
            His own face
drawn from the wood,

deep in the manhood his childhood
so swiftly led to, a small brook rock-leaping   30
into the rapt, imperious, seagoing river.

                                1967

Stepping Westward

    What is green in me
    darkens, muscadine.

    If woman is inconstant,
    good, I am faithful to

    ebb and flow, I fall   5
    in season and now

is a time of ripening.
If her part

is to be true,
a north star,   10

good, I hold steady
in the black sky

and vanish by day,
yet burn there

in blue or above   15
quilts of cloud.

There is no savor
more sweet, more salt

than to be glad to be
what, woman,   20

and who, myself,
I am, a shadow

that grows longer as the sun
moves, drawn out

on a thread of wonder.   25
If I bear burdens

they begin to be remembered
as gifts, goods, a basket

of bread that hurts
my shoulders but closes me   30

in fragrance. I can
eat as I go.

1967

The Mutes

Those groans men use
passing a woman on the street
or on the steps of the subway

to tell her she is a female
and their flesh knows it,   5

are they a sort of tune,
an ugly enough song, sung
by a bird with a slit tongue

but meant for music?

Or are they the muffled roaring   10
of deafmutes trapped in a building that is
slowly filling with smoke?

Perhaps both.

Such men most often
look as if groan were all they could do,   15
yet a woman, in spite of herself,

knows it's a tribute:
if she were lacking all grace
they'd pass her in silence:

so it's not only to say she's   20
a warm hole. It's a word

in grief-language, nothing to do with
primitive, not an ur-language;
language stricken, sickened, cast down

in decrepitude. She wants to   25
throw the tribute away, dis-
gusted, and can't,

it goes on buzzing in her ear,
it changes the pace of her walk,
the torn posters in echoing corridors   30

spell it out, it
quakes and gnashes as the train comes in.
Her pulse sullenly

had picked up speed,
but the cars slow down and   35
jar to a stop while her understanding

keeps on translating:
'Life after life after life goes by

without poetry,
without seemliness,   40
without love.'

                                                       1967

A Note to Olga[2] (1966)

i

Of lead and emerald
the reliquary
that knocks my breastbone,

slung round my neck
on a rough invisible rope   5
that rubs the knob of my spine.

Though I forget you
a red coal from your fire
burns in that box.

ii

On the Times Square[3] sidewalk   10
we shuffle along, cardboard signs
—Stop the War[4]—
slung round our necks.

The cops
hurry about,   15
shoulder to shoulder,
comic.

Your high soprano
sings out from just
in back of me—   20

We shall[5]—I turn,
you're, I very well know,
not there,

2. Olga Levertoff (1914–1964) was the poet's sister and a radical activist; Levertov wrote a sequence called *Olga Poems* in her memory (*The Sorrow Dance*, 1966).

3. Busy area in midtown Manhattan.
4. I.e., the Vietnam War.
5. The first words of the protest song "We Shall Overcome."

and your voice, they say,
grew hoarse   25
from shouting at crowds . . .

yet *overcome*
sounds then hoarsely
from somewhere in front,

the paddywagon   30
gapes. —It seems
you that is lifted

limp and ardent
off the dark snow
and shoved in, and driven away.   35

1967

Canción[6]

When I am the sky
a glittering bird
slashes at me with the knives of song.

When I am the sea
fiery clouds plunge into my mirrors,   5
fracture my smooth breath with crimson sobbing.

When I am the earth
I feel my flesh of rock wearing down:
pebbles, grit, finest dust, nothing.

When I am a woman—O, when I am   10
a woman,
my wells of salt brim and brim,
poems force the lock of my throat.

1975

Divorcing

One garland
of flowers, leaves, thorns
was twined round our two necks.

6. Spanish: song or lyric poem.

Drawn tight, it could choke us,
yet we loved its scratchy grace,   5
     our fragrant yoke.

We were Siamese twins.
Our blood's not sure
     if it can circulate,
now we are cut apart.   10
Something in each of us is waiting
     to see if we can survive,
          severed.

1975

FLANNERY O'CONNOR

1925–1964

Because Flannery O'Connor believed that "the novelist with Christian concerns will find in modern life distortions" which are "repugnant" to the writer but "natural" to the reader, in a posthumously published volume of collected essays entitled *Mystery and Manners* (1969) she advocated "violent means" to get her vision across: with a "hostile audience," the writer must make her "vision apparent by shock—to the hard of hearing you shout, and for the almost blind you draw large and startling figures." Christ-haunted prophets, religious hucksters, and visionary farm hands, many of the characters in O'Connor's stories and novels inhabit a South that she associated with the urgency of faith: "The South," she explained in a letter (1957), "still believes that man has fallen and that he is only perfectible by God's grace, not by his own unaided efforts." Her characters are therefore often caught in the grip of a violent spiritual struggle in which they are ultimately saved or lost. Few fiction writers have so successfully resisted religious sentimentality while dramatizing the cost of redemption.

The only child of Regina and Edward Francis O'Connor, Mary Flannery O'Connor grew up in Savannah, Georgia, until her father became ill and the family moved to Milledgeville, Georgia, her mother's hometown. At fifteen, when her father died of lupus erythematosus, an incurable blood disease, she was already committed to Roman Catholicism, the religion of her parents. After graduating in 1942 from Peabody High School, she attended Georgia State College for Women, where she contributed stories and cartoons to the literary magazine. After graduation, she attended the Writers' Workshop at the University of Iowa, where she won the Rinehart-Iowa prize for a work-in-progress, which she completed first at Yaddo (a writers' retreat) and then in the Connecticut home of two friends, Sally and Robert Fitzgerald. A comic masterpiece, this book—*Wise Blood* (1952)—focused on Hazel Motes, the would-be founder of a "church without Christ, where the blind stay blind, the lame stay lame and them that's dead stays that way."

Both the grotesque humor and the rural, Southern dialect of *Wise Blood* characterize the fiction O'Connor later went on to write under difficult circumstances. Three years before the publication of her first novel, she had discovered that she was suffering from the disease that had killed her father. With the aid of cortisone treatments and with her mother's care, she managed to control the disease. Mother and daughter lived on a farm near Milledgeville, where O'Connor raised peacocks and chickens, and wrote her second novel, *The Violent Bear It Away* (1960), as well as the stories that appeared in *A Good Man Is Hard to Find and Others* (1955) and in the posthumous collection *Everything That Rises Must Converge* (1965). She was befriended by the poet Robert Lowell, the editor Robert Giroux, and the short-story writer Caroline Gordon, but the cortisone weakened her bones and made it difficult for her to travel or lecture. When an operation reactivated her lupus, she died at thirty-nine years of age.

Good Country People

Besides the neutral expression that she wore when she was alone, Mrs. Freeman had two others, forward and reverse, that she used for all her human dealings. Her forward expression was steady and driving like the advance of a heavy truck. Her eyes never swerved to left or right but turned as the story turned as if they followed a yellow line down the center of it. She seldom used the other expression because it was not often necessary for her to retract a statement, but when she did, her face came to a complete stop, there was an almost imperceptible movement of her black eyes, during which they seemed to be receding, and then the observer would see that Mrs. Freeman, though she might stand there as real as several grain sacks thrown on top of each other, was no longer there in spirit. As for getting anything across to her when this was the case, Mrs. Hopewell had given it up. She might talk her head off. Mrs. Freeman could never be brought to admit herself wrong on any point. She would stand there and if she could be brought to say anything, it was something like, "Well, I wouldn't of said it was and I wouldn't of said it wasn't," or letting her gaze range over the top kitchen shelf where there was an assortment of dusty bottles, she might remark, "I see you ain't ate many of them figs you put up last summer."

They carried on their most important business in the kitchen at breakfast. Every morning Mrs. Hopewell got up at seven o'clock and lit her gas heater and Joy's. Joy was her daughter, a large blonde girl who had an artificial leg. Mrs. Hopewell thought of her as a child though she was thirty-two years old and highly educated. Joy would get up while her mother was eating and lumber into the bathroom and slam the door, and before long, Mrs. Freeman would arrive at the back door. Joy would hear her mother call, "Come on in," and then they would talk for a while in low voices that were indistinguishable in the bathroom. By the time Joy came in, they had usually finished the weather report and were on one or the other of Mrs. Freeman's daughters, Glynese or Carramae, Joy called them Glycerin and Caramel. Glynese, a redhead, was eighteen and had many admirers; Carramae, a blonde, was only fifteen but already married and pregnant. She could not keep anything on her stomach. Every morning Mrs. Freeman told Mrs. Hopewell how many times she had vomited since the last report.

Mrs. Hopewell liked to tell people that Glynese and Carramae were two of the finest girls she knew and that Mrs. Freeman was a *lady* and that she was never ashamed to take her anywhere or introduce her to anybody they might meet. Then she would tell how she had happened to hire the Freemans in the first place and how they were a godsend to her and how she had had them four years. The reason for her keeping them so long was that they were not trash. They were good country people. She had telephoned the man whose name they had given as a reference and he had told her that Mr. Freeman was a good farmer but that his wife was the nosiest woman ever to walk the earth. "She's got to be into everything," the man said. "If she don't get there before the dust settles, you can bet she's dead, that's all. She'll want to know all your business. I can stand him real good," he had said, "but me nor my wife neither could have stood that woman one more minute on this place." That had put Mrs. Hopewell off for a few days.

She had hired them in the end because there were no other applicants but she had made up her mind beforehand exactly how she would handle the woman. Since she was the type who had to be into everything, then, Mrs. Hopewell had decided, she would not only let her be into everything, she would *see to it* that she was into everything—she would give her the responsibility of everything, she would put her in charge. Mrs. Hopewell had no bad qualities of her own but she was able to use other people's in such a constructive way that she never felt the lack. She had hired the Freemans and she had kept them four years.

Nothing is perfect. This was one of Mrs. Hopewell's favorite sayings. Another was: that is life! And still another, the most important, was: well, other people have their opinions too. She would make these statements, usually at the table, in a tone of gentle insistence as if no one held them but her, and the large hulking Joy, whose constant outrage had obliterated every expression from her face, would stare just a little to the side of her, her eyes icy blue, with the look of someone who has achieved blindness by an act of will and means to keep it.

When Mrs. Hopewell said to Mrs. Freeman that life was like that, Mrs. Freeman would say, "I always said so myself." Nothing had been arrived at by anyone that had not first been arrived at by her. She was quicker than Mr. Freeman. When Mrs. Hopewell said to her after they had been on the place a while, "You know, you're the wheel behind the wheel," and winked, Mrs. Freeman had said, "I know it. I've always been quick. It's some that are quicker than others."

"Everybody is different," Mrs. Hopewell said.

"Yes, most people is," Mrs. Freeman said.

"It takes all kinds to make the world."

"I always said it did myself."

The girl was used to this kind of dialogue for breakfast and more of it for dinner; sometimes they had it for supper too. When they had no guest they ate in the kitchen because that was easier. Mrs. Freeman always managed to arrive at some point during the meal and to watch them finish it. She would stand in the doorway if it were summer but in the winter she would stand with one elbow on top of the refrigerator and look down on them, or she would stand by the gas heater, lifting the back of her skirt slightly. Occasionally she would stand against the wall and roll her head from side to side. At no time was she in any hurry to leave. All this was very trying on Mrs. Hopewell but she was a woman of great patience. She realized that nothing is perfect and that in the Freemans she had good country people and that if, in this day and age, you get good country people, you had better hang onto them.

She had had plenty of experience with trash. Before the Freemans she had averaged one tenant family a year. The wives of these farmers were not the kind you would want to be around you for very long. Mrs. Hopewell, who had divorced her husband long ago, needed someone to walk over the fields with her; and when Joy had to be impressed for these services, her remarks were usually so ugly and her face so glum that Mrs. Hopewell would say, "If you can't come pleasantly, I don't want you at all," to which the girl, standing square and rigid-shouldered with her neck thrust slightly forward, would reply, "If you want me, here I am—LIKE I AM."

Mrs. Hopewell excused this attitude because of the leg (which had been shot off in a hunting accident when Joy was ten). It was hard for Mrs. Hopewell to realize that her child was thirty-two now and that for more than twenty years she had had only one leg. She thought of her still as a child because it tore her heart to think instead of the poor stout girl in her thirties who had never danced a step or had any *normal* good times. Her name was really Joy but as soon as she was twenty-one and away from home, she had had it legally changed. Mrs. Hopewell was certain that she had thought and thought until she had hit upon the ugliest name in any language. Then she had gone and had the beautiful name, Joy, changed without telling her mother until after she had done it. Her legal name was Hulga.

When Mrs. Hopewell thought of the name, Hulga, she thought of the broad blank hull of a battleship. She would not use it. She continued to call her Joy to which the girl responded but in a purely mechanical way.

Hulga had learned to tolerate Mrs. Freeman who saved her from taking walks with her mother. Even Glynese and Carramae were useful when they occupied attention that might otherwise have been directed at her. At first she had thought she could not stand Mrs. Freeman for she had found that it was not possible to be rude to her. Mrs. Freeman would take on strange resentments and for days together she would be sullen but the source of her displeasure was always obscure; a direct attack, a positive leer, blatant ugliness to her face—these never touched her. And without warning one day, she began calling her Hulga.

She did not call her that in front of Mrs. Hopewell who would have been incensed but when she and the girl happened to be out of the house together, she would say something and add the name Hulga to the end of it, and the big spectacled Joy-Hulga would scowl and redden as if her privacy had been intruded upon. She considered the name her personal affair. She had arrived at it first purely on the basis of its ugly sound and then the full genius of its fitness had struck her. She had a vision of the name working like the ugly sweating Vulcan[1] who stayed in the furnace and to whom, presumably, the goddess had to come when called. She saw it as the name of her highest creative act. One of her major triumphs was that her mother had not been able to turn her dust into Joy, but the greater one was that she had been able to turn it herself into Hulga. However, Mrs. Freeman's relish for using the name only irritated her. It was as if Mrs. Freeman's beady steel-pointed eyes had penetrated far enough behind her face to reach some secret fact. Something about her seemed to fascinate Mrs. Freeman and then one day Hulga realized that it was the artificial leg. Mrs. Freeman had a special fondness for the details of secret infections, hidden deformities, assaults upon children. Of diseases, she preferred the lingering or incurable. Hulga had heard Mrs. Hopewell give her the details of the hunting accident, how the leg had been literally blasted off, how she had never lost consciousness. Mrs. Freeman could listen to it any time as if it had happened an hour ago.

When Hulga stumped into the kitchen in the morning (she could walk without making the awful noise but she made it—Mrs. Hopewell was certain—because it was ugly-sounding), she glanced at them and did not speak. Mrs. Hopewell would be in her red kimono with her hair tied around her head in rags. She would be sitting at the table, finishing her breakfast and Mrs. Freeman would be hanging by her elbow outward from the refrigerator, looking down at the table. Hulga always put

---

1. Greek god of fire whom Venus, goddess of love, "presumably" obeyed as her consort.

her eggs on the stove to boil and then stood over them with her arms folded, and Mrs. Hopewell would look at her—a kind of indirect gaze divided between her and Mrs. Freeman—and would think that if she would only keep herself up a little, she wouldn't be so bad looking. There was nothing wrong with her face that a pleasant expression wouldn't help. Mrs. Hopewell said that people who looked on the bright side of things would be beautiful even if they were not.

Whenever she looked at Joy this way, she could not help but feel that it would have been better if the child had not taken the Ph.D. It had certainly not brought her out any and now that she had it, there was no more excuse for her to go to school again. Mrs. Hopewell thought it was nice for girls to go to school to have a good time but Joy had "gone through." Anyhow, she would not have been strong enough to go again. The doctors had told Mrs. Hopewell that with the best of care, Joy might see forty-five. She had a weak heart. Joy had made it plain that if it had not been for this condition, she would be far from these red hills and good country people. She would be in a university lecturing to people who knew what she was talking about. And Mrs. Hopewell could very well picture her there, looking like a scarecrow and lecturing to more of the same. Here she went about all day in a six-year-old skirt and a yellow sweat shirt with a faded cowboy on a horse embossed on it. She thought this was funny; Mrs. Hopewell thought it was idiotic and showed simply that she was still a child. She was brilliant but she didn't have a grain of sense. It seemed to Mrs. Hopewell that every year she grew less like other people and more like herself—bloated, rude, and squint-eyed. And she said such strange things! To her own mother she had said—without warning, without excuse, standing up in the middle of a meal with her face purple and her mouth half full—"Woman! do you ever look inside? Do you ever look inside and see what you are *not*? God!" she had cried sinking down again and staring at her plate, "Malebranche[2] was right: we are not our own light. We are not our own light!" Mrs. Hopewell had no idea to this day what brought that on. She had only made the remark, hoping Joy would take it in, that a smile never hurt anyone.

The girl had taken the Ph.D. in philosophy and this left Mrs. Hopewell at a complete loss. You could say, "My daughter is a nurse," or "My daughter is a schoolteacher," or even, "My daughter is a chemical engineer." You could not say, "My daughter is a philosopher." That was something that had ended with the Greeks and Romans. All day Joy sat on her neck in a deep chair, reading. Sometimes she went for walks but she didn't like dogs or cats or birds or flowers or nature or nice

2. Nicolas Malebranche, French philosopher (1638–1715).

young men. She looked at nice young men as if she could smell their stupidity.

One day Mrs. Hopewell had picked up one of the books the girl had just put down and opening it at random, she read, "Science, on the other hand, has to assert its soberness and seriousness afresh and declare that it is concerned solely with what-is. Nothing—how can it be for science anything but a horror and a phantasm? If science is right, then one thing stands firm: science wishes to know nothing of nothing. Such is after all the strictly scientific approach to Nothing. We know it by wishing to know nothing of Nothing." These words had been underlined with a blue pencil and they worked on Mrs. Hopewell like some evil incantation in gibberish. She shut the book quickly and went out of the room as if she were having a chill.

This morning when the girl came in, Mrs. Freeman was on Carramae. "She thrown up four times after supper," she said, "and was up twict in the night after three o'clock. Yesterday she didn't do nothing but ramble in the bureau drawer. All she did. Stand up there and see what she could run up on."

"She's got to eat," Mrs. Hopewell muttered, sipping her coffee, while she watched Joy's back at the stove. She was wondering what the child had said to the Bible salesman. She could not imagine what kind of a conversation she could possibly have had with him.

He was a tall gaunt hatless youth who had called yesterday to sell them a Bible. He had appeared at the door, carrying a large black suitcase that weighted him so heavily on one side that he had to brace himself against the door facing. He seemed on the point of collapse but he said in a cheerful voice. "Good morning, Mrs. Cedars!" and set the suitcase down on the mat. He was not a bad-looking young man though he had on a bright blue suit and yellow socks that were not pulled up far enough. He had prominent face bones and a streak of sticky-looking brown hair falling across his forehead.

"I'm Mrs. Hopewell," she said.

"Oh!" he said, pretending to look puzzled but with his eyes sparkling, "I saw it said 'The Cedars' on the mailbox so I thought you was Mrs. Cedars!" and he burst out in a pleasant laugh. He picked up the satchel and under cover of a pant, he fell forward into her hall. It was rather as if the suitcase had moved first, jerking him after it. "Mrs. Hopewell!" he said and grabbed her hand. "I hope you are well!" and he laughed again and then all at once his face sobered completely. He paused and gave her a straight earnest look and said, "Lady, I've come to speak of serious things."

"Well, come in," she muttered, none too pleased because her dinner was almost ready. He came into the parlor and sat down on the edge of a straight chair and put the suitcase between his feet and glanced around the room as if he were sizing her up by it. Her silver gleamed on the two sideboards; she decided he had never been in a room as elegant as this.

"Mrs. Hopewell," he began, using her name in a way that sounded almost intimate, "I know you believe in Chrustian service."

"Well yes," she murmured.

"I know," he said and paused, looking very wise with his head cocked on one side, "that you're a good woman. Friends have told me."

Mrs. Hopewell never liked to be taken for a fool. "What are you selling?" she asked.

"Bibles," the young man said and his eye raced around the room before he added, "I see you have no family Bible in your parlor, I see that is the one lack you got!"

Mrs. Hopewell could not say, "My daughter is an atheist and won't let me keep the Bible in the parlor." She said, stiffening slightly, "I keep my Bible by my bedside." This was not the truth. It was in the attic somewhere.

"Lady," he said, "the word of God ought to be in the parlor."

"Well, I think that's a matter of taste," she began. "I think. . . ."

"Lady," he said, "for a Chrustian, the word of God ought to be in every room in the house besides in his heart. I know you're a Chrustian because I can see it in every line of your face."

She stood up and said, "Well, young man, I don't want to buy a Bible and I smell my dinner burning."

He didn't get up. He began to twist his hands and looking down at them, he said softly, "Well lady, I'll tell you the truth—not many people want to buy one nowadays and besides, I know I'm real simple. I don't know how to say a thing but to say it. I'm just a country boy." He glanced up into her unfriendly face. "People like you don't like to fool with country people like me!"

"Why!" she cried, "good country people are the salt of the earth! Besides, we all have different ways of doing, it takes all kinds to make the world go 'round. That's life!"

"You said a mouthful," he said.

"Why, I think there aren't enough good country people in the world!" she said, stirred. "I think that's what's wrong with it!"

His face had brightened. "I didn't inraduce myself," he said. "I'm Manley Pointer from out in the country around Willohobie, not even from a place, just from near a place."

"You wait a minute," she said. "I have to see about my dinner." She went out to the kitchen and found Joy standing near the door where she had been listening.

"Get rid of the salt of the earth," she said, "and let's eat."

Mrs. Hopewell gave her a pained look and turned the heat down under the vegetables. "*I* can't be rude to anybody," she murmured and went back into the parlor.

He had opened the suitcase and was sitting with a Bible on each knee.

"You might as well put those up," she told him. "I don't want one."

"I appreciate your honesty," he said. "You don't see any more real honest people unless you go away out in the country."

"I know," she said, "real genuine folks!" Through the crack in the door she heard a groan.

"I guess a lot of boys come telling you they're working their way through college," he said, "but I'm not going to tell you that. Somehow," he said, "I don't want to go to college. I want to devote my life to Christian service. See," he said, lowering his voice, "I got this heart condition. I may not live long. When you know it's something wrong with you and you may not live long, well then, lady . . . " He paused, with his mouth open, and stared at her.

He and Joy had the same condition! She knew that her eyes were filling with tears but she collected herself quickly and murmured, "Won't you stay for dinner? We'd love to have you!" and was sorry the instant she heard herself say it.

"Yes mam," he said in an abashed voice, "I would sher love to do that!"

Joy had given him one look on being introduced to him and then throughout the meal had not glanced at him again. He had addressed several remarks to her, which she had pretended not to hear. Mrs. Hopewell could not understand deliberate rudeness, although she lived with it, and she felt she had always to overflow with hospitality to make up for Joy's lack of courtesy. She urged him to talk about himself and he did. He said he was the seventh child of twelve and that his father had been crushed under a tree when he himself was eight year old. He had been crushed very badly, in fact, almost cut in two and was practically not recognizable. His mother had got along the best she could by hard working and she had always seen that her children went to Sunday School and that they read the Bible every evening. He was now nineteen year old and he had been selling Bibles for four months. In that time he had sold seventy-seven Bibles and had the promise of two more sales. He wanted to become a missionary because he thought that was the way you could do most for people. "He who losest his life shall find it," he said simply and he was so sincere, so genuine and earnest that Mrs. Hopewell would not for the world have smiled. He prevented his peas from sliding onto the table by blocking them with a piece of bread which he later cleaned his plate with. She could see Joy observing sidewise how he handled his knife and fork and she saw too that every few minutes, the boy would dart a keen appraising glance at the girl as if he were trying to attract her attention.

After dinner Joy cleared the dishes off the table and disappeared and Mrs. Hopewell was left to talk with him. He told her again about his childhood and his father's accident and about various things that had happened to him. Every five minutes or so she would stifle a yawn. He sat for two hours until finally she told him she must go because she had an appointment in town. He packed his Bibles and thanked her and prepared to leave, but in the doorway he stopped and wrung her hand and said that not on any of his trips had he met a lady as nice as her and he asked if he could come again. She had said she would always be happy to see him.

Joy had been standing in the road, apparently looking at something in the distance, when he came down the steps toward her, bent to the side with his heavy valise. He stopped where she was standing and confronted her directly. Mrs. Hopewell could not hear what he said but she trembled to think what Joy would say to him. She could see that after a minute Joy said something and that then the boy began to speak again, making an excited gesture with his free hand. After a minute Joy said something else at which the boy began to speak once more. Then to her amazement, Mrs. Hopewell saw the two of them walk off together, toward the gate. Joy had walked all the way to the gate with him and Mrs. Hopewell could not imagine what they had said to each other, and she had not yet dared to ask.

Mrs. Freeman was insisting upon her attention. She had moved from the refrigerator to the heater so that Mrs. Hopewell had to turn and face her in order to seem to be listening. "Glynese gone out with Harvey Hill again last night," she said. "She had this sty."

"Hill," Mrs. Hopewell said absently, "is that the one who works in the garage?"

"Nome, he's the one that goes to chiropracter school," Mrs. Freeman said. "She had this sty. Been had it two days. So she says when he brought her in the other night he says, 'Lemme get rid of that sty for you,' and she says, 'How?' and he says, 'You just lay yourself down acrost the seat of that car and I'll show you.' So she done it and he popped her neck. Kept on a-popping it several times until she made him quit. This morning," Mrs. Freeman said, "she ain't got no sty. She ain't got no traces of a sty."

"I never heard of that before," Mrs. Hopewell said.

"He ast her to marry him before the Ordinary,"[3] Mrs. Freeman went on, "and she told him she wasn't going to be married in no *office*."

3. Justice of the peace who performs the marriage ceremony in his chambers rather than in public.

"Well, Glynese is a fine girl," Mrs. Hopewell said. "Glynese and Carramae are both fine girls."

"Carramae said when her and Lyman was married Lyman said it sure felt sacred to him. She said he said he wouldn't take five hundred dollars for being married by a preacher."

"How much would he take?" the girl asked from the stove.

"He said he wouldn't take five hundred dollars," Mrs. Freeman repeated.

"Well we all have work to do," Mrs. Hopewell said.

"Lyman said it just felt more sacred to him," Mrs. Freeman said. "The doctor wants Carramae to eat prunes. Says instead of medicine. Says them cramps is coming from pressure. You know where I think it is?"

"She'll be better in a few weeks," Mrs. Hopewell said.

"In the tube," Mrs. Freeman said. "Else she wouldn't be as sick as she is."

Hulga had cracked her two eggs into a saucer and was bringing them to the table along with a cup of coffee that she had filled too full. She sat down carefully and began to eat, meaning to keep Mrs. Freeman there by questions if for any reason she showed an inclination to leave. She could perceive her mother's eye on her. The first round-about question would be about the Bible salesman and she did not wish to bring it on. "How did he pop her neck?" she asked.

Mrs. Freeman went into a description of how he had popped her neck. She said he owned a '55 Mercury but that Glynese said she would rather marry a man with only a '36 Plymouth who would be married by a preacher. The girl asked what if he had a '32 Plymouth and Mrs. Freeman said what Glynese had said was a '36 Plymouth.

Mrs. Hopewell said there were not many girls with Glynese's common sense. She said what she admired in those girls was their common sense. She said that reminded her that they had had a nice visitor yesterday, a young man selling Bibles. "Lord," she said, "he bored me to death but he was so sincere and genuine I couldn't be rude to him. He was just good country people, you know," she said, "—just the salt of the earth."

"I seen him walk up," Mrs. Freeman said, "and then later—I seen him walk off," and Hulga could feel the slight shift in her voice, the slight insinuation, that he had not walked off alone, had he? Her face remained expressionless but the color rose into her neck and she seemed to swallow it down with the next spoonful of egg. Mrs. Freeman was looking at her as if they had a secret together.

"Well, it takes all kinds of people to make the world go 'round," Mrs. Hopewell said. "It's very good we aren't all alike."

"Some people are more alike than others," Mrs. Freeman said.

Hulga got up and stumped, with about twice the noise that was necessary, into her room and locked the door. She was to meet the Bible salesman at ten o'clock at the gate. She had thought about it half the night. She had started thinking of it as a great joke and then she had begun to see profound implications in it. She had lain in bed imagining dialogues for them that were insane on the surface but that reached below to depths that no Bible salesman would be aware of. Their conversation yesterday had been of this kind.

He had stopped in front of her and had simply stood there. His face was bony and sweaty and bright, with a little pointed nose in the center of it, and his look was different from what it had been at the dinner table. He was gazing at her with open curiosity, with fascination, like a child watching a new fantastic animal at the zoo, and he was breathing as if he had run a great distance to reach her. His gaze seemed somehow familiar but she could not think where she had been regarded with it before. For almost a minute he didn't say anything. Then on what seemed an insuck of breath, he whispered, "You ever ate a chicken that was two days old?"

The girl looked at him stonily. He might have just put this question up for consideration at the meeting of a philosophical association. "Yes," she presently replied as if she had considered it from all angles.

"It must have been mighty small!" he said triumphantly and shook all over with little nervous giggles, getting very red in the face, and subsiding finally into his gaze of complete admiration, while the girl's expression remained exactly the same.

"How old are you?" he asked softly.

She waited some time before she answered. Then in a flat voice she said, "Seventeen."

His smiles came in succession like waves breaking on the surface of a little lake. "I see you got a wooden leg," he said. "I think you're brave. I think you're real sweet."

The girl stood blank and solid and silent.

"Walk to the gate with me," he said. "You're a brave sweet little thing and I liked you the minute I seen you walk in the door."

Hulga began to move forward.

"What's your name?" he asked, smiling down on the top of her head.

"Hulga," she said.

"Hulga," he murmured, "Hulga. Hulga. I never heard of anybody name Hulga before. You're shy, aren't you, Hulga?" he asked.

She nodded, watching his large red hand on the handle of the giant valise.

"I like girls that wear glasses," he said. "I think a lot. I'm not like these people that a serious thought don't ever enter their heads. It's because I may die."

"I may die too," she said suddenly and looked up at him. His eyes were very small and brown, glittering feverishly.

"Listen," he said, "don't you think some people was meant to meet on account of what all they got in common and all? Like they both think serious thoughts and all?" He shifted the valise to his other hand so that the hand nearest her was free. He caught hold of her elbow and shook it a little. "I don't work on Saturday," he said. "I like to walk in the woods and see what Mother Nature is wearing. O'er the hills and far away. Pic-nics and things. Couldn't we go on a pic-nic tomorrow? Say yes, Hulga," he said and gave her a dying look as if he felt his insides about to drop out of him. He had even seemed to sway slightly toward her.

During the night she had imagined that she seduced him. She imagined that the two of them walked on the place until they came to the storage barn beyond the two back fields and there, she imagined, that things came to such a pass that she very easily seduced him and that then, of course, she had to reckon with his remorse. True genius can get an idea across even to an inferior mind. She imagined that she took his remorse in hand and changed it into a deeper understanding of life. She took all his shame away and turned it into something useful.

She set off for the gate at exactly ten o'clock, escaping without drawing Mrs. Hopewell's attention. She didn't take anything to eat, forgetting that food is usually taken on a picnic. She wore a pair of slacks and a dirty white shirt, and as an afterthought, she had put some Vapex on the collar of it since she did not own any perfume. When she reached the gate no one was there.

She looked up and down the empty highway and had the furious feeling that she had been tricked, that he had only meant to make her walk to the gate after the idea of him. Then suddenly he stood up, very tall, from behind a bush on the opposite embankment. Smiling, he lifted his hat which was new and wide-brimmed. He had not worn it yesterday and she wondered if he had bought it for the occasion. It was toast-colored with a red and white band around it and was slightly too large for him. He stepped from behind the bush still carrying the black valise. He had on the same suit and the same yellow socks sucked down in his shoes from walking. He crossed the highway and said, "I knew you'd come!"

The girl wondered acidly how he had known this. She pointed to the valise and asked, "Why did you bring your Bibles?"

He took her elbow, smiling down on her as if he could not stop. "You can never tell when you'll need the word of God, Hulga," he said. She had a moment in which she doubted that this was actually happening and then they began to climb the embankment. They went down into the pasture toward the woods. The boy walked lightly by her side, bouncing on his toes. The valise did not seem to be heavy today; he even swung it. They crossed half the pasture without saying anything and then, putting his hand easily on the small of her back, he asked softly, "Where does your wooden leg join on?"

She turned an ugly red and glared at him and for an instant the boy looked abashed. "I didn't mean you no harm," he said. "I only meant you're so brave and all. I guess God takes care of you."

"No," she said, looking forward and walking fast, "I don't even believe in God."

At this he stopped and whistled. "No!" he exclaimed as if he were too astonished to say anything else.

She walked on and in a second he was bouncing at her side, fanning with his hat. "That's very unusual for a girl," he remarked, watching her out of the corner of his eye. When they reached the edge of the wood, he put his hand on her back again and drew her against him without a word and kissed her heavily.

The kiss, which had more pressure than feeling behind it, produced that extra surge of adrenalin in the girl that enables one to carry a packed trunk out of a burning house, but in her, the power went at once to the brain. Even before he released her, her mind, clear and detached and ironic anyway, was regarding him from a great distance, with amusement but with pity. She had never been kissed before and she was pleased to discover that it was an unexceptional experience and all a matter of the mind's control. Some people might enjoy drain water if they were told it was vodka. When the boy, looking expectant but uncertain, pushed her gently away, she turned and walked on, saying nothing as if such business, for her, were common enough.

He came along panting at her side, trying to help her when he saw a root that she might trip over. He caught and held back the long swaying blades of thorn vine until she had passed beyond them. She led the way and he came breathing heavily behind her. Then they came out on a sunlit hillside, sloping softly into another one a little smaller. Beyond, they could see the rusted top of the old barn where the extra hay was stored.

The hill was sprinkled with small pink weeds. "Then you ain't saved?" he asked suddenly, stopping.

The girl smiled. It was the first time she had smiled at him at all. "In my economy," she said, "I'm saved and you are damned but I told you I didn't believe in God."

Nothing seemed to destroy the boy's look of admiration. He gazed at her now as if the fantastic animal at the zoo had put its paw through the bars and given him a loving poke. She thought he looked as if he wanted to kiss her again and she walked on before he had the chance.

"Ain't there somewheres we can sit down sometime?" he murmured, his voice softening toward the end of the sentence.

"In that barn," she said.

They made for it rapidly as if it might slide away like a train. It was a large two-story barn, cool and dark inside. The boy pointed up the ladder that led into the loft and said, "It's too bad we can't go up there."

"Why can't we?" she asked.

"Yer leg," he said reverently.

The girl gave him a contemptuous look and putting both hands on the ladder, she climbed it while he stood below, apparently awe-struck. She pulled herself expertly through the opening and then looked down at him and said, "Well, come on if you're coming," and he began to climb the ladder, awkwardly bringing the suitcase with him.

"We won't need the Bible," she observed.

"You never can tell," he said, panting. After he had got into the loft, he was a few seconds catching his breath. She had sat down in a pile of straw. A wide sheath of sunlight, filled with dust particles, slanted over her. She lay back against a bale, her face turned away, looking out the front opening of the barn where hay was thrown from a wagon into the loft. The two pink-speckled hillsides lay back against a dark ridge of woods. The sky was cloudless and cold blue. The boy dropped down by her side and put one arm under her and the other over her and began methodically kissing her face, making little noises like a fish. He did not remove his hat but it was pushed far enough back not to interfere. When her glasses got in his way, he took them off of her and slipped them into his pocket.

The girl at first did not return any of the kisses but presently she began to and after she had put several on his cheek, she reached his lips and remained there, kissing him again and again as if she were trying to draw all the breath out of him. His breath was clear and sweet like a child's and the kisses were sticky like a child's. He mumbled about loving her and about knowing when he first seen her that he loved her, but the mumbling was like the sleepy fretting of a child being put to sleep by his mother. Her mind, throughout this, never stopped or lost itself for a second to her feelings. "You ain't said you loved me none," he whispered finally, pulling back from her. "You got to say that."

She looked away from him off into the hollow sky and then down at a black ridge and then down farther into what appeared to be two green swelling lakes. She didn't realize he had taken her glasses but this landscape could not seem exceptional to her for she seldom paid any close attention to her surroundings.

"You got to say it," he repeated. "You got to say you love me."

She was always careful how she committed herself. "In a sense," she began, "if you use the word loosely, you might say that. But it's not a word I use. I don't have illusions. I'm one of those people who see *through* to nothing."

The boy was frowning. "You got to say it. I said it and you got to say it," he said.

The girl looked at him almost tenderly. "You poor baby," she murmured. "It's just as well you don't understand," and she pulled him by the neck, face-down, against her. "We are all damned," she said, "but some of us have taken off our blindfolds and see that there's nothing to see. It's a kind of salvation."

The boy's astonished eyes looked blankly through the ends of her hair. "Okay," he almost whined, "but do you love me or don'tcher?"

"Yes," she said and added, "in a sense. But I must tell you something. There mustn't be anything dishonest between us." She lifted his head and looked him in the eye. "I am thirty years old," she said. "I have a number of degrees."

The boy's look was irritated but dogged. "I don't care," he said. "I don't care a thing about what all you done. I just want to know if you love me or don'tcher?" and he caught her to him and wildly planted her face with kisses until she said, "Yes, yes."

"Okay then," he said, letting her go. "Prove it."

She smiled, looking dreamily out on the shifty landscape. She had seduced him without even making up her mind to try. "How?" she asked, feeling that he should be delayed a little.

He leaned over and put his lips to her ear. "Show me where your wooden leg joins on," he whispered.

The girl uttered a sharp little cry and her face instantly drained of color. The obscenity of the suggestion was not what shocked her. As a child she had sometimes been subject to feelings of shame but education had removed the last traces of that as a good surgeon scrapes for cancer; she would no more have felt it over what he was asking than she would have believed in his Bible. But she was as sensitive about the artificial leg as a peacock about his tail. No one ever touched it but her. She took care of it as someone else would his soul, in private and almost with her own eyes turned away. "No," she said.

"I known it," he muttered, sitting up. "You're just playing me for a sucker."

"Oh no no!" she cried. "It joins on at the knee. Only at the knee. Why do you want to see it?"

The boy gave her a long penetrating look. "Because," he said, "it's what makes you different. You ain't like anybody else."

She sat staring at him. There was nothing about her face or her round freezing-blue eyes to indicate that this had moved her; but she felt as if her heart had stopped and left her mind to pump her blood. She decided that for the first time in her life she was face to face with real innocence. This boy, with an instinct that came from beyond wisdom, had touched the truth about her. When after a minute, she said in a hoarse high voice, "All right," it was like surrendering to him completely. It was like losing her own life and finding it again, miraculously, in his.

Very gently he began to roll the slack leg up. The artificial limb, in a white sock and brown flat shoe, was bound in a heavy material like canvas and ended in an ugly jointure where it was attached to the stump. The boy's face and his voice were entirely reverent as he uncovered it and said, "Now show me how to take it off and on."

She took it off for him and put it back on again and then he took it off himself, handling it as tenderly as if it were a real one. "See!" he said with a delighted child's face. "Now I can do it myself!"

"Put it back on," she said. She was thinking that she would run away with him and that every night he would take the leg off and every morning put it back on again. "Put it back on," she said.

"Not yet," he murmured, setting it on its foot out of her reach. "Leave it off for a while. You got me instead."

She gave a little cry of alarm but he pushed her down and began to kiss her again. Without the leg she felt entirely dependent on him. Her brain seemed to have stopped thinking altogether and to be about some other function that it was not very good at. Different expressions raced back and forth over her face. Every now and then the boy, his eyes like two steel spikes, would glance behind him where the leg stood. Finally she pushed him off and said, "Put it back on me now."

"Wait," he said. He leaned the other way and pulled the valise toward him and opened it. It had a pale blue spotted lining and there were only two Bibles in it. He took one of these out and opened the cover of it. It was hollow and contained a pocket flask of whiskey, a pack of cards, and a small blue box with printing on it. He laid these out in front of her one at a time in an evenly-spaced row, like one presenting offerings at the shrine of a goddess. He put the blue box in her hand. THIS PRODUCT TO BE USED ONLY FOR THE PREVENTION OF DISEASE, she read, and dropped it. The boy was unscrewing the top of the flask. He stopped and pointed, with a smile, to the deck of cards. It was not an ordinary deck but one with an obscene picture on the back of each card. "Take a swig," he said, offering her the bottle first. He held it in front of her, but like one mesmerized, she did not move.

Her voice when she spoke had an almost pleading sound. "Aren't you," she murmured, "aren't you just good country people?"

The boy cocked his head. He looked as if he were just beginning to understand that she might be trying to insult him. "Yeah," he said, curling his lip slightly, "but it ain't held me back none. I'm as good as you any day in the week."

"Give me my leg," she said.

He pushed it farther away with his foot. "Come on now, let's begin to have us a good time," he said coaxingly. "We ain't got to know one another good yet."

"Give me my leg!" she screamed and tried to lunge for it but he pushed her down easily.

"What's the matter with you all of a sudden?" he asked, frowning as he screwed the top on the flask and put it quickly back inside the Bible. "You just a while ago said you didn't believe in nothing. I thought you was some girl!"

Her face was almost purple. "You're a Christian!" she hissed. "You're a fine Christian! You're just like them all—say one thing and do another. You're a perfect Christian, you're . . ."

The boy's mouth was set angrily. "I hope you don't think," he said in a lofty indignant tone, "that I believe in that crap! I may sell Bibles but I know which end is up and I wasn't born yesterday and I know where I'm going!"

"Give me my leg!" she screeched. He jumped up so quickly that she barely saw him sweep the cards and the blue box into the Bible and throw the Bible into the valise. She saw him grab the leg and then she saw it for an instant slanted forlornly across the inside of the suitcase with a Bible at either side of its opposite ends. He slammed the lid shut and snatched up the valise and swung it down the hole and then stepped through himself.

When all of him had passed but his head, he turned and regarded her with a look that no longer had any admiration in it. "I've gotten a lot of interesting things," he said. "One time I got a woman's glass eye this way. And you needn't to think you'll catch me because Pointer ain't really my name. I use a different name at every house I call at and don't stay nowhere long. And I'll tell you another thing, Hulga," he said, using the name as if he didn't think much of it, "you ain't so smart. I been believing in nothing ever since I was born!" and then the toast-colored hat disappeared down the hole and the girl was left, sitting on the straw in the dusty sunlight. When she turned her churning face toward the opening, she saw his blue figure struggling successfully over the green speckled lake.

Mrs. Hopewell and Mrs. Freeman, who were in the back pasture, digging up onions, saw him emerge a little later from the woods and head across the meadow toward the highway. "Why, that looks like that nice dull young man that tried to sell me a Bible yesterday," Mrs. Hopewell said, squinting. "He must have been selling them to the Negroes back in there. He was so simple," he said, "but I guess the world would be better off if we were all that simple."

Mrs. Freeman's gaze drove forward and just touched him before he disappeared under the hill. Then she returned her attention to the evil-smelling onion shoot she was lifting from the ground. "Some can't be that simple," she said. "I know I never could."

1955

CAROLYN KIZER

1925–

"From Sappho to myself, consider the fate of women," wrote Carolyn Kizer in 1963, adding, with characteristically acerbic irony, "How unwomanly to discuss it!" Yet "discuss it" Kizer has, in four volumes—*The Ungrateful Garden* (1961), *Knock upon Silence* (1965), *Midnight Was My Cry* (1971), and *Yin* (1984)—that are marked by keen attention to the vicissitudes experienced by women who, like Kizer herself, "must act as handmaidens / To our own goddess." Born in Spokane, Washington, in 1925, Kizer graduated from Sarah Lawrence College in 1945. Subsequently, she traveled widely in China and Japan, translating Tu Fu and other Chinese poets whose terse urbanity was an important influence on her style. Married and the mother of three children, she helped found the prestigious verse journal *Poetry Northwest* in 1959, then was for seven years its editor in chief. In 1966, she was director of literary programs for the National Endowment for the Arts. More recently, she has taught verse writing at many colleges and universities throughout the country. During this crowded career, however, she has continued to "speak about women of letters," explaining that "I'm in the racket." Sometimes jauntily colloquial in its phrasing, sometimes suavely elegant in its formulation, her tough wisdom is consistently based on the knowledge that women writers "are the custodians of the world's best-kept secret: / Merely the private lives of one-half of humanity."

From Pro Femina[1]

Three

I will speak about women of letters, for I'm in the racket.
Our biggest successes to date? Old maids to a woman.
And our saddest conspicuous failures? The married spinsters
On loan to the husbands they treated like surrogate fathers.
Think of that crew of self-pitiers, not-very-distant,   5

1. Latin, "for the woman."

Who carried the torch for themselves and got first-degree
    burns.
Or the sad sonneteers, toast-and-teasdales[2] we loved at
    thirteen;
Middle-aged virgins seducing the puerile anthologists
Through lust-of-the-mind; barbiturate-drenched Camilles[3]
With continuous periods, murmuring softly on sofas   10
When poetry wasn't a craft but a sickly effluvium,
The air thick with incense, musk, and emotional blackmail.

I suppose they reacted from an earlier womanly modesty
When too many girls were scabs[4] to their stricken
    sisterhood,
Impugning our sex to stay in good with the men,   15
Commencing their insecure bluster. How they must have
    swaggered
When women themselves indorsed their own inferiority!
Vestals, vassals[5] and vessels, rolled into several,
They took notes in rolling syllabics, in careful journals,
Aiming to please a posterity that despises them.   20
But we'll always have traitors who swear that a woman
    surrenders
Her Supreme Function, by equating Art with aggression
And failure with Femininity. Still, it's just as unfair
To equate Art with Femininity, like a prettily-packaged
    commodity
When we are the custodians of the world's best-kept
    secret: 25
Merely the private lives of one-half of humanity.

But even with masculine dominance, we mares and
    mistresses
Produced some sleek saboteuses, making their cracks
Which the porridge-brained males of the day were too
    thick to perceive.
Mistaking young hornets for perfectly harmless
    bumblebees.   30
Being thought innocuous rouses some women to frenzy;
They try to be ugly by aping the ways of the men
And succeed. Swearing, sucking cigars and scorching the
    bedspread,
Slopping straight shots, eyes blotted, vanity-blown
In the expectation of glory: *she writes like a man!*   35

---

2. Punning reference to Sara Teasdale (1844–1933), American poet who wrote slight, sensitive verses.
3. Camille is the repentant courtesan in *La Dame aux Camellias* (1852) by Alexandre Dumas *fils*.
4. Laborers who go back to work before a strike has ended.
5. "Vestals": Roman virgin-priestesses; "vassals": person in service to a feudal lord.

This drives other women mad in a mist of chiffon
(one poetess draped her gauze over red flannels, a practical
    feminist).

But we're emerging from all that, more or less,
Except for some lady-like laggards and Quarterly[6]
    priestesses
Who flog men for fun, and kick women to maim
    competition.   40
Now, if we struggle abnormally, we may almost seem
    normal;
If we submerge our self-pity in disciplined industry;
If we stand up and be hated, and swear not to sleep with
    editors;
If we regard ourselves formally, respecting our true
    limitations
Without making an unseemly show of trying to unfreeze
    our assets;   45
Keeping our heads and our pride while remaining
    unmarried;
And if wedded, kill guilt in its tracks when we stack up the
    dishes
And defect to the typewriter. And if mothers, believe in the
    luck of our children,
Whom we forbid to devour us, whom we shall not devour,
And the luck of our husbands and lovers, who keep
    free women.   50

                                 1963, 1965

Semele[7] Recycled

After you left me forever,
I was broken into pieces,
and all the pieces flung into the river.
Then the legs crawled ashore
and aimlessly wandered the dusty cow-track.   5
They became, for a while, a simple roadside shrine:
A tiny table set up between the thighs
held a dusty candle, weed, and fieldflower chains
placed reverently there by children and old women.
My knees were hung with tin triangular medals   10
to cure all forms of hysterical disease.

6. I.e., literary-magazine.
7. In Greek myth, the beloved of Zeus and the mother of Dionysus; she requested Zeus to ap-pear in his radiant divinity; when he did, she burned to death.

After I died forever in the river,
my torso floated, bloated in the stream,
catching on logs or stones among the eddies.
White water foamed around it, then dislodged it;   15
after a whirlwind trip, it bumped ashore.
A grizzled old man who scavenged along the banks
had already rescued my arms and put them by,
knowing everything has its uses, sooner or later.

When he found my torso, he called it his canoe,   20
and, using my arms as paddles,
he rowed me up and down the scummy river.
When catfish nibbled my fingers, he scooped them up
and blessed his re-usable bait.
Clumsy but serviceable, that canoe!   25
The trail of blood that was its wake
attracted the carp and eels, and the river turtle,
easily landed, dazed by my tasty red.

A young lad found my head among the rushes
and placed it on a dry stone.   30
He carefully combed my hair with a bit of shell
and set small offerings before it
which the birds and rats obligingly stole at night,
so it seemed I ate.
And the breeze wound through my mouth and empty sockets 35
so my lungs would sigh and my dead tongue mutter.

Attached to my throat like a sacred necklace
was a circlet of small snails.
Soon the villagers came to consult my oracular head
with its waterweed crown.   40
Seers found occupation, interpreting sighs,
and their papyrus rolls accumulated.

Meanwhile, young boys retrieved my eyes
they used for marbles in a simple game
—till somebody's pretty sister snatched at them   45
and set them, for luck, in her bridal diadem.
Poor girl! When her future groom caught sight of her,
all eyes, he crossed himself in horror,
and stumbled away in haste
through her dowered meadows.   50

What then of my heart and organs,
my sacred slit
which loved you best of all?
They were caught in a fisherman's net

and tossed at night into a pen for swine.   55
But they shone so by moonlight that the sows stampeded,
trampled each other in fear, to get away.
And the fisherman's wife, who had 13 living children
and was contemptuous of holy love,
raked the rest of me onto the compost heap.   60

Then in their various places and helpful functions,
the altar, oracle, offal, canoe, and oars
learned the wild rumor of your return.
The altar leapt up and ran to the canoe,
scattering candle grease and wilted grasses.   65
Arms sprang to their sockets, blind hands with nibbled nails
groped their way, aided by loud lamentation,
to the bed of the bride, snatched up those unlucky eyes
from her discarded veil and diadem,
and rammed them home. O what a bright day it was!   70
This empty body danced on the river bank.
Hollow, it called and searched among the fields
for those parts that steamed and simmered in the sun,
and never would have found them.

But then your great voice rang out under the skies   75
my name!—and all those private names
for the parts and places that had loved you best.
And they stirred in their nest of hay and dung.
The distraught old ladies chasing their lost altar,
and the seers pursuing my skull, their lost employment,   80
and the tumbling boys, who wanted the magic marbles,
and the runaway groom, and the fisherman's 13 children
set up such a clamor, with their cries of "Miracle!"
that our two bodies met like a thunderclap
in mid-day—right at the corner of that wretched field   85
with its broken fenceposts and startled, skinny cattle.
We fell in a heap on the compost heap
and all our loving parts made love at once,
while the bystanders cheered and prayed and hid their eyes
and then went decently about their business.   90

And here it is, moonlight again; we've bathed in the river
and are sweet and wholesome once more.
We kneel side by side in the sand;
we worship each other in whispers.
But the inner parts remember fermenting hay,   95
the comfortable odor of dung, the animal incense,
and passion, its bloody labor,
its birth and rebirth and decay.

MAXINE W. KUMIN

1925–

"Even though she is fascinated by and preoccupied with the irrational unconscious," the critic Sybil Estess has written of Maxine Kumin, "sanity and a
conscious choice within and for life are essential keys to [her] voice." The observation is apt, for though she was the longtime best friend and poetic co-
worker of the troubled, "confessional" artist Anne Sexton—the two frequently
analyzed and revised their poems together and collaborated on several children's books—Kumin is a very different sort of writer from Sexton. While she
sometimes writes poems about pain and suffering, Kumin has a notable drive
for survival along with a deep commitment to memorialize those elements of
everyday life that enrich the existence of the artist and make survival possible.
Children and kitchens, animals and vegetables, friends and family—these are
the stuff of the poems in which she makes a redemptive choice for sanity.

Born in Philadelphia, Pennsylvania, Kumin earned B.A. and M.A. degrees
from Radcliffe College and was married young to Victor M. Kumin, an engineering consultant, with whom she has had three children. At present, she and
her husband live on a farm in New Hampshire, where she grows vegetables and
breeds Arabian and quarter horses while writing both poetry and fiction. Her
first collection, *Halfway*, appeared in 1961 and was followed in rapid succession by a number of other volumes, including five novels, three children's
books coauthored with Sexton, the collection of poems—*Up Country* (1972)
—for which she won the Pulitzer Prize in 1973, and, most recently, *Our
Ground Time Here Will Be Brief* (1982), a volume of selected and new poems.
For two years a fellow at the Radcliffe Institute for Independent Study, she has
also taught verse writing at a number of universities, including Columbia,
Brandeis, and Princeton. Throughout this varied career, she has found ways to
formulate a hopeful if skeptical vision: "Wherever we're going / is Monday
morning. / Wherever we're coming from / is Mother's lap."

Making the Jam without You

for Judy

Old daughter, small traveler
asleep in a German featherbed
under the eaves in a postcard town
of turrets and towers,
I am putting a dream in your head.   5

Listen! Here it is afternoon.
The rain comes down like bullets.
I stand in the kitchen,

that harem of good smells
where we have bumped hips and   10
cracked the cupboards with our talk
while the stove top danced with pots
and it was not clear who did
the mothering. Now I am
crushing blackberries   15
to make the annual jam
in a white cocoon of steam.

Take it, my sleeper. Redo it
in any of your three
languages and nineteen years.   20
Change the geography.
Let there be a mountain,
the fat cows on it belled
like a cathedral. Let
there be someone beside you   25
as you come upon the ruins
of a schloss,[1] all overgrown
with a glorious thicket,
its brambles soft as wool.
Let him bring the buckets   30
crooked on his angel arms
and may the berries, vaster
than any forage in
the mild hills of New Hampshire,
drop in your pail, plum size,   35
heavy as the eyes
of an honest dog
and may you bear them
home together to a square
white unreconstructed kitchen   40
not unlike this one.

Now may your two heads
touch over the kettle,
over the blood of the berries
that drink up sugar and sun,   45
over that tar-thick boil
love cannot stir down.
More plainly than
the bric-a-brac of shelves
filling with jelly glasses,   50
more surely than
the light driving through them

---

1. German: castle.

trite as rubies, I see him
as pale as paraffin beside you.
I see you cutting   55
fresh baked bread to spread it
with the bright royal fur.

At this time
I lift the flap of your dream
and slip out thinner than a sliver   60
as your two mouths open
for the sweet stain of purple.

                                                            1970

The Envelope

It is true, Martin Heidegger,[2] as you have written,
I *fear to cease*, even knowing that at the hour
of my death my daughters will absorb me, even
knowing they will carry me about forever
inside them, an arrested fetus, even as I carry   5
the ghost of my mother under my navel, a nervy
little androgynous person, a miracle
folded in lotus position.

Like those old pear-shaped Russian dolls that open
at the middle to reveal another and another, down   10
to the pea-sized, irreducible minim,
may we carry our mothers forth in our bellies.
May we, borne onward by our daughters, ride
in the Envelope of Almost-Infinity,
that chain letter good for the next twenty-five   15
thousand days of their lives.

                                                            1978

How It Is[3]

Shall I say how it is in your clothes?
A month after your death I wear your blue jacket.
The dog at the center of my life recognizes
you've come to visit, he's ecstatic.

---

2. German existentialist philosopher (1889–
1976) who wrote extensively on the fear of
death.
3. The poem is addressed to Anne Sexton

(1928–1974), poet and close friend of Kumin's
who commited suicide by inhaling carbon mon-
oxide fumes from her car.

In the left pocket, a hole.   5
In the right, a parking ticket
delivered up last August on Bay State Road.
In my heart, a scatter like milkweed,
a flinging from the pods of the soul.
My skin presses your old outline.   10
It is hot and dry inside.

I think of the last day of your life,
old friend, how I would unwind it, paste
it together in a different collage,
back from the death car idling in the garage,   15
back up the stairs, your praying hands unlaced,
reassembling the bits of bread and tuna fish
into a ceremony of sandwich,
running the home movie backward to a space
we could be easy in, a kitchen place   20
with vodka and ice, our words like living meat.

Dear friend, you have excited crowds
with your example. They swell
like wine bags, straining at your seams.
I will be years gathering up our words,   25
fishing out letters, snapshots, stains,
leaning my ribs against this durable cloth
to put on the dumb blue blazer of your death.

                                                               1978

MARGARET LAURENCE
1926–

One of Canada's foremost novelists, Margaret Laurence frequently sets her
fiction in a prairie town similar to the one in which she grew up, Neepawa,
Manitoba. The granddaughter of Irish and Scottish settlers, Jean Margaret
Wemyss lost her mother when she was four years old and her father when she
was nine. Brought up by her mother's sister and her father's widowed mother,
she witnessed the devastating effects of the depression and of World War II on
the lives of her neighbors. In 1944, a scholarship enabled her to leave for the
United College in Winnipeg, where she majored in English and wrote for the
college paper. After a brief stint working as a reporter for *The Winnipeg Citizen*, she married Jack Laurence, a civil engineer, and they moved first to England and then to Africa. *A Tree for Poverty* (1954), *The Prophet's Camel Bell*
(1963), and *The Tomorrow-Tamer* (1963), her earliest publications, reflect
Laurence's seven years in Somali and Ghana: the first is a collection and trans-

lation of African folk tales; the second, a record of her life in British Somaliland; the third, a collection of short stories.

Although the Laurences returned to Canada when Ghana achieved independence, five years later Margaret Laurence separated from her husband and moved with her daughter and son to England. By this time, she had established her reputation as a writer with her first novel, *This Side of Jordan* (1960), and a number of prize-winning stories. Like expatriated writers from H. H. Richardson to Doris Lessing, Laurence began to mythologize her native land while she was living in another country, although in 1972 she did return to settle in Canada. Her series of interrelated novels and stories—*The Stone Angel* (1964), *The Fire-Dwellers* (1969), *A Bird in the House* (1970), and *The Diviners* (1974)— are set in the mythical Manitoba town of Manawaka. Laurence's characters— the ninety-year-old Hagar in *The Stone Angel*, for example, or the middle-aged single schoolteacher Rachel Cameron in *A Jest of God* (1966)—confront the crippling provincialism of small-town life with a courage that lends them a capacity for increased self-knowledge and for joy. *The Loons* is part of *A Bird in the House*, an autobiographical series of stories.

The Loons

Just below Manawaka, where the Wachakwa River ran brown and noisy over the pebbles, the scrub oak and grey-green willow and choke-cherry bushes grew in a dense thicket. In a clearing at the centre of the thicket stood the Tonnerre family's shack. The basis of this dwelling was a small square cabin made of poplar poles and chinked with mud, which had been built by Jules Tonnerre some fifty years before, when he came back from Batoche with a bullet in his thigh, the year that Riel[1] was hung and the voices of the Metis entered their long silence. Jules had only intended to stay the winter in the Wachakwa Valley, but the family was still there in the thirties, when I was a child. As the Tonnerres had increased, their settlement had been added to, until the clearing at the foot of the town hill was a chaos of lean-tos, wooden packing cases, warped lumber, discarded car tyres, ramshackle chicken coops, tangled strands of barbed wire and rusty tin cans.

The Tonnerres were French halfbreeds, and among themselves they spoke a *patois* that was neither Cree[2] nor French. Their English was broken and full of obscenities. They did not belong among the Cree of the Galloping Mountain reservation, further north, and they did not belong among the Scots-Irish and Ukrainians of Manawaka, either. They were, as my Grandmother MacLeod would have put it, neither

---

1. Louis Riel (1844–1885), Canadian insurgent who was tried and hanged for treason in Saskatchewan. Metis: persons of mixed Indian and European, especially French, descent.
2. The language of a tribe of Indians formerly living in Ontario.

flesh, fowl, nor good salt herring. When their men were not working at odd jobs or as section hands on the C.P.R.,[3] they lived on relief. In the summers, one of the Tonnerre youngsters, with a face that seemed totally unfamiliar with laughter, would knock at the doors of the town's brick houses and offer for sale a lard-pail full of bruised wild strawberries, and if he got as much as a quarter he would grab the coin and run before the customer had time to change her mind. Sometimes old Jules, or his son Lazarus, would get mixed up in a Saturday-night brawl, and would hit out at whoever was nearest, or howl drunkenly among the offended shoppers on Main Street, and then the Mountie would put them for the night in the barred cell underneath the Court House, and the next morning they would be quiet again.

Piquette Tonnerre, the daughter of Lazarus, was in my class at school. She was older than I, but she had failed several grades, perhaps because her attendance had always been sporadic and her interest in schoolwork negligible. Part of the reason she had missed a lot of school was that she had had tuberculosis of the bone, and had once spent many months in hospital. I knew this because my father was the doctor who had looked after her. Her sickness was almost the only thing I knew about her, however. Otherwise, she existed for me only as a vaguely embarrassing presence, with her hoarse voice and her clumsy limping walk and her grimy cotton dresses that were always miles too long. I was neither friendly nor unfriendly towards her. She dwelt and moved somewhere within my scope of vision, but I did not actually notice her very much until that peculiar summer when I was eleven.

"I don't know what to do about that kid," my father said at dinner one evening. "Piquette Tonnerre, I mean. The damn bone's flared up again. I've had her in hospital for quite a while now, and it's under control all right, but I hate like the dickens to send her home again."

"Couldn't you explain to her mother that she has to rest a lot?" my mother said.

"The mother's not there," my father replied. "She took off a few years back. Can't say I blame her. Piquette cooks for them, and she says Lazarus would never do anything for himself as long as she's there. Anyway, I don't think she'd take much care of herself, once she got back. She's only thirteen, after all. Beth, I was thinking—what about taking her up to Diamond Lake with us this summer? A couple of months rest would give that bone a much better chance."

My mother looked stunned.

"But Ewen—what about Roddie and Vanessa?"

"She's not contagious," my father said. "And it would be company for Vanessa."

3. Canada Pacific Railroad.

"Oh dear," my mother said in distress, "I'll bet anything she has nits[4] in her hair."

"For Pete's sake," my father said crossly, "do you think Matron would let her stay in the hospital for all this time like that? Don't be silly, Beth."

Grandmother MacLeod, her delicately featured face as rigid as a cameo, now brought her mauve-veined hands together as though she were about to begin a prayer.

"Ewen, if that half-breed youngster comes along to Diamond Lake, I'm not going," she announced. "I'll go to Morag's for the summer."

I had trouble in stifling my urge to laugh, for my mother brightened visibly and quickly tried to hide it. If it came to a choice between Grandmother MacLeod and Piquette, Piquette would win hands down, nits or not.

"It might be quite nice for you, at that," she mused. "You haven't seen Morag for over a year, and you might enjoy being in the city for a while. Well, Ewen dear, you do what you think best. If you think it would do Piquette some good, then we'll be glad to have her, as long as she behaves herself."

So it happened that several weeks later, when we all piled into my father's old Nash, surrounded by suit-cases and boxes of provisions and toys for my ten-month-old brother, Piquette was with us and Grandmother MacLeod, miraculously, was not. My father would only be staying at the cottage for a couple of weeks, for he had to get back to his practice, but the rest of us would stay at Diamond Lake until the end of August.

Our cottage was not named, as many were, "Dew Drop Inn" or "Bide-a-Wee," or "Bonnie Doon." The sign on the roadway bore in austere letters only our name, MacLeod. It was not a large cottage, but it was on the lakefront. You could look out the windows and see, through the filigree of the spruce trees, the water glistening greenly as the sun caught it. All around the cottage were ferns, and sharp-branched raspberry bushes, and moss that had grown over fallen tree trunks. If you looked carefully among the weeds and grass, you could find wild strawberry plants which were in white flower now and in another month would bear fruit, the fragrant globes hanging like miniature scarlet lanterns on the thin hairy stems. The two grey squirrels were still there, gossiping at us from the tall spruce beside the cottage, and by the end of the summer they would again be tame enough to take pieces of crust from my hands. The broad moose antlers that hung above the back door were a little more bleached and fissured after the winter, but otherwise everything was the same. I raced joyfully around

4. The eggs of lice.

my kingdom, greeting all the places I had not seen for a year. My brother, Roderick, who had not been born when we were here last summer, sat on the car rug in the sunshine and examined a brown spruce cone, meticulously turning it round and round in his small and curious hands. My mother and father toted the luggage from car to cottage, exclaiming over how well the place had wintered, no broken windows, thank goodness, no apparent damage from storm-felled branches or snow.

Only after I had finished looking around did I notice Piquette. She was sitting on the swing, her lame leg held stiffly out, and her other foot scuffing the ground as she swung slowly back and forth. Her long hair hung black and straight around her shoulders, and her broad coarse-featured face bore no expression—it was blank, as though she no longer dwelt within her own skull, as though she had gone elsewhere. I approached her very hesitantly.

"Want to come and play?"

Piquette looked at me with a sudden flash of scorn.

"I ain't a kid," she said.

Wounded, I stamped angrily away, swearing I would not speak to her for the rest of the summer. In the days that followed, however, Piquette began to interest me, and I began to want to interest her. My reasons did not appear bizarre to me. Unlikely as it may seem, I had only just realised that the Tonnerre family, whom I had always heard called half-breeds, were actually Indians, or as near as made no difference. My acquaintance with Indians was not extensive. I did not remember ever having seen a real Indian, and my new awareness that Piquette sprang from the people of Big Bear and Poundmaker, of Tecumseh, of the Iroquois who had eaten Father Brebeuf's heart[5]—all this gave her an instant attraction in my eyes. I was a devoted reader of Pauline Johnson at this age, and sometimes would orate aloud and in an exalted voice, *West Wind, blow from your prairie nest; Blow from the mountains, blow from the west*[6]—and so on. It seemed to me that Piquette must be in some way a daughter of the forest, a kind of junior prophetess of the wilds, who might impart to me, if I took the right approach, some of the secrets which she undoubtedly knew—where the whippoorwill made her nest, how the coyote reared her young, or whatever it was that it said in Hiawatha.[7]

I set about gaining Piquette's trust. She was not allowed to go swim-

5. Jean de Brebeuf (1593–1649), French missionary in North America, killed by Indians. Tecumseh (1768?–1813), chief of the Shawnee; Big Bear and Poundmaker (1842–1886), leaders of the Cree.

6. The first two lines from *The Song My Paddle Sings* by Pauline Johnson (1861–1913), Canadian poet who was the daughter of an English woman and a Mohawk chief.

7. *The Song of Hiawatha*, a poem about the lives of American Indians by the American poet Henry Wadsworth Longfellow (1807–1882).

ming, with her bad leg, but I managed to lure her down to the beach—
or rather, she came because there was nothing else to do. The water was
always icy, for the lake was fed by springs, but I swam like a dog,
thrashing my arms and legs around at such speed and with such an out-
put of energy that I never grew cold. Finally, when I had had enough, I
came out and sat beside Piquette on the sand. When she saw me approaching, her hand squashed flat the sand castle she had been building, and she looked at me sullenly, without speaking.

"Do you like this place?" I asked, after a while, intending to lead on
from there into the question of forest lore.

Piquette shrugged. "It's okay. Good as anywhere."

"I love it," I said. "We come here every summer."

"So what?" Her voice was distant, and I glanced at her uncertainly,
wondering what I could have said wrong.

"Do you want to come for a walk?" I asked her. "We wouldn't need
to go far. If you walk just around the point there, you come to a bay
where great big reeds grow in the water, and all kinds of fish hang
around there. Want to? Come on."

She shook her head.

"Your dad said I ain't supposed to do no more walking than I got to."

I tried another line.

"I bet you know a lot about the woods and all that, eh?" I began respectfully.

Piquette looked at me from her large dark unsmiling eyes.

"I don't know what in hell you're talkin' about," she replied. "You
nuts or somethin'? If you mean where my old man, and me, and all
them live, you better shut up, by Jesus, you hear?"

I was startled and my feelings were hurt, but I had a kind of dogged
perserverance. I ignored her rebuff.

"You know something, Piquette? There's loons here, on this lake.
You can see their nests just up the shore there, behind those logs. At
night, you can hear them even from the cottage, but it's better to listen
from the beach. My dad says we should listen and try to remember how
they sound, because in a few years when more cottages are built at
Diamond Lake and more people come in, the loons will go away."

Piquette was picking up stones and snail shells and then dropping
them again.

"Who gives a good goddamn?" she said.

It became increasingly obvious that, as an Indian, Piquette was a
dead loss. That evening I went out by myself, scrambling through the
bushes that overhung the steep path, my feet slipping on the fallen
spruce needles that covered the ground. When I reached the shore, I
walked along the firm damp sand to the small pier that my father had
built, and sat down there. I heard someone else crashing through the

undergrowth and the bracken, and for a moment I thought Piquette had changed her mind, but it turned out to be my father. He sat beside me on the pier and we waited, without speaking.

At night the lake was like black glass with a streak of amber which was the path of the moon. All around, the spruce trees grew tall and close-set, branches blackly sharp against the sky, which was lightened by a cold flickering of stars. Then the loons began their calling. They rose like phantom birds from the nests on the shore, and flew out onto the dark still surface of the water.

No one can ever describe that ululating sound, the crying of the loons, and no one who has heard it can ever forget it. Plaintive, and yet with a quality of chilling mockery, those voices belonged to a world separated by aeons from our neat world of summer cottages and the lighted lamps of home.

"They must have sounded just like that," my father remarked, "before any person ever set foot here."

Then he laughed. "You could say the same, of course, about sparrows, or chipmunks, but somehow it only strikes you that way with the loons."

"I know," I said.

Neither of us suspected that this would be the last time we would ever sit here together on the shore, listening. We stayed for perhaps half an hour, and then we went back to the cottage. My mother was reading beside the fireplace. Piquette was looking at the burning birch log, and not doing anything.

"You should have come along," I said, although in fact I was glad she had not.

"Not me," Piquette said. "You wouldn' catch me walkin' way down there jus' for a bunch of squawkin' birds."

Piquette and I remained ill at ease with one another. I felt I had somehow failed my father, but I did not know what was the matter, nor why she would not or could not respond when I suggested exploring the woods or playing house. I thought it was probably her slow and difficult walking that held her back. She stayed most of the time in the cottage with my mother, helping her with the dishes or with Roddie, but hardly ever talking. Then the Duncans arrived at their cottage, and I spent my days with Mavis, who was my best friend. I could not reach Piquette at all, and I soon lost interest in trying. But all that summer she remained as both a reproach and a mystery to me.

That winter my father died of pneumonia, after less than a week's illness. For some time I saw nothing around me, being completely immersed in my own pain and my mother's. When I looked outward once more, I scarcely noticed that Piquette Tonnerre was no longer at school. I do not remember seeing her at all until four years later, one

Saturday night when Mavis and I were having Cokes in the Regal Café. The jukebox was booming like tuneful thunder, and beside it, leaning lightly on its chrome and its rainbow glass, was a girl.

Piquette must have been seventeen then, although she looked about twenty. I stared at her, astounded that anyone could have changed so much. Her face, so stolid and expressionless before, was animated now with a gaiety that was almost violent. She laughed and talked very loudly with the boys around her. Her lipstick was bright carmine, and her hair was cut short and frizzily permed. She had not been pretty as a child, and she was not pretty now, for her features were still heavy and blunt. But her dark and slightly slanted eyes were beautiful, and her skin-tight skirt and orange sweater displayed to enviable advantage a soft and slender body.

She saw me, and walked over. She teetered a little, but it was not due to her once-tubercular leg, for her limp was almost gone.

"Hi, Vanessa." Her voice still had the same hoarseness. "Long time no see, eh?"

"Hi," I said. "Where've you been keeping yourself, Piquette?"

"Oh, I been around," she said. "I been away almost two years now. Been all over the place—Winnipeg, Regina, Saskatoon. Jesus, what I could tell you! I come back this summer, but I ain't stayin'. You kids goin' to the dance?"

"No," I said abruptly, for this was a sore point with me. I was fifteen, and thought I was old enough to go to the Saturday-night dances at the Flamingo. My mother, however, thought otherwise.

"Y'oughta come," Piquette said. "I never miss one. It's just about the on'y thing in this jerkwater town that's any fun. Boy, you couldn' catch me stayin' here. I don' give a shit about this place. It stinks."

She sat down beside me, and I caught the harsh over-sweetness of her perfume.

"Listen, you wanna know something, Vanessa?" she confided, her voice only slightly blurred. "Your dad was the only person in Mana-waka that ever done anything good to me."

I nodded speechlessly. I was certain she was speaking the truth. I knew a little more than I had that summer at Diamond Lake, but I could not reach her now any more than I had then. I was ashamed, ashamed of my own timidity, the frightened tendency to look the other way. Yet I felt no real warmth towards her—I only felt that I ought to, because of that distant summer and because my father had hoped she would be company for me, or perhaps that I would be for her, but it had not happened that way. At this moment, meeting her again, I had to admit that she repelled and embarrassed me, and I could not help despising the self-pity in her voice. I wished she would go away. I did not want to see her. I did not know what to say to her. It seemed that we had nothing to say to one another.

"I'll tell you something else," Piquette went on. "All the old bitches an' biddies in this town will sure be surprised. I'm gettin' married this fall—my boyfriend, he's an English fella, works in the stockyards in the city there, a very tall guy, got blond wavy hair. Gee, is he ever handsome. Got this real classy name. Alvin Gerald Cummings—some handle, eh? They call him Al."

For the merest instant, then, I saw her. I really did see her, for the first and only time in all the years we had both lived in the same town. Her defiant face, momentarily, became unguarded and unmasked, and in her eyes there was a terrifying hope.

"Gee, Piquette—" I burst out awkwardly, "that's swell. That's really wonderful. Congratulations—good luck—I hope you'll be happy—"

As I mouthed the conventional phrases, I could only guess how great her need must have been, that she had been forced to seek the very things she so bitterly rejected.

When I was eighteen, I left Manawaka and went away to college. At the end of my first year, I came back home for the summer. I spent the first few days in talking non-stop with my mother, as we exchanged all the news that somehow had not found its way into letters—what had happened in my life and what had happened here in Manawaka while I was away. My mother searched her memory for events that concerned people I knew.

"Did I ever write you about Piquette Tonnerre, Vanessa?" she asked one morning.

"No, I don't think so," I replied. "Last I heard of her, she was going to marry some guy in the city. Is she still there?"

My mother looked perturbed, and it was a moment before she spoke, as though she did not know how to express what she had to tell and wished she did not need to try.

"She's dead," she said at last. Then, as I stared at her, "Oh, Vanessa, when it happened, I couldn't help thinking of her as she was that summer—so sullen and gauche and badly dressed. I couldn't help wondering if we could have done something more at that time—but what could we do? She used to be around in the cottage there with me all day, and honestly, it was all I could do to get a word out of her. She didn't even talk to your father very much, although I think she liked him, in her way."

"What happened?" I asked.

"Either her husband left her, or she left him," my mother said. "I don't know which. Anyway, she came back here with two youngsters, both only babies—they must have been born very close together. She kept house, I guess, for Lazarus and her brothers, down in the valley there, in the old Tonnerre place. I used to see her on the street some-times, but she never spoke to me. She'd put on an awful lot of weight, and she looked a mess, to tell you the truth, a real slattern, dressed any old how. She was up in court a couple of times—drunk and disorderly, of course. One Saturday night last winter, during the coldest weather, Piquette was alone in the shack with the children. The Tonnerres made home brew all the time, so I've heard, and Lazarus said later she'd been drinking most of the day when he and the boys went out that evening. They had an old woodstove there—you know the kind, with exposed pipes. The shack caught fire. Piquette didn't get out, and neither did the children."

I did not say anything. As so often with Piquette, there did not seem to be anything to say. There was a kind of silence around the image in my mind of the fire and the snow, and I wished I could put from my memory the look that I had seen once in Piquette's eyes.

I went up to Diamond Lake for a few days that summer, with Mavis and her family. The MacLeod cottage had been sold after my father's death, and I did not even go to look at it, not wanting to witness my long-ago kingdom possessed now by strangers. But one evening I went down to the shore by myself.

The small pier which my father had built was gone, and in its place there was a large and solid pier built by the government, for Galloping Mountain was now a national park, and Diamond Lake had been re-named Lake Wapakata, for it was felt that an Indian name would have a greater appeal to tourists. The one store had become several dozen, and the settlement had all the attributes of a flourishing resort—hotels, a dance-hall, cafés with neon signs, the penetrating odours of potato chips and hot dogs.

I sat on the government pier and looked out across the water. At night the lake at least was the same as it had always been, darkly shining and bearing within its black glass the streak of amber that was the path of the moon. There was no wind that evening, and everything was quiet all around me. It seemed too quiet, and then I realized that the loons were no longer here. I listened for some time, to make sure, but never once did I hear that long-drawn call, half mocking and half plaintive, spearing through the stillness across the lake.

I did not know what had happened to the birds. Perhaps they had gone away to some far place of belonging. Perhaps they had been un-able to find such a place, and had simply died out, having ceased to care any longer whether they lived or not.

I remembered how Piquette had scorned to come along, when my father and I sat there and listened to the lake birds. It seemed to me now that in some unconscious and totally unrecognized way, Piquette might have been the only one, after all, who had heard the crying of the loons.

1970

ANNE SEXTON
1928–1974

According to her best friend, the poet Maxine Kumin, at their first meeting Anne Sexton "looked every inch the fashion model"—a job she had once briefly held: she was "tall, blue-eyed, stunningly slim, her carefully coifed dark hair decorated with flowers, her face skillfully made up." Yet, as Kumin also notes, this artfully lovely and theatrical woman led a "troubled and chaotic life." By the time she met Kumin in the late winter of 1957, she had had several nervous collapses and been intermittently hospitalized, seeking "sanctuary" from "voices that urged her to die." Described by one biographer as "a demanding, rebellious child who felt rejected by her upper-middle-class parents," she had had emotional problems since girlhood. Now the mother of two young daughters, she had married Alfred Sexton in 1948, but the couple's home in a Boston suburb was not a happy one, no doubt in part because of her persistent breakdowns. Nevertheless, though Anne Sexton did not consider herself a good student and had dropped out of Garland Junior College after only a year, she had just enrolled, at the suggestion of her psychiatrist, in a verse-writing workshop taught by the poet John Holmes at the Boston Center for Adult Education.

As Kumin reports, Sexton's literary progress was astonishing once she began to understand that she *could* write poetry. Her first book, *To Bedlam and Part Way Back*, appeared in 1960. Including such searching (if partly disguised) self-explorations as *The Moss of His Skin*, it was influenced not only by the "workshopping" this swiftly developing artist did with Kumin and Holmes but also by the self-examinations of the poet W. D. Snodgrass and by the writings of Robert Lowell (with whom Sexton studied at Boston University) and Sylvia Plath (who was a fellow student of Sexton's in Lowell's class). Later described as "confessional poets," these last three artists had begun to use the details of their personal lives as exemplary images of larger social and metaphysical problems, and their experiments offered Sexton a fruitful mode in which she, too, could work, while her innovative self-analyses also provided models for further "confessional" verse by Lowell and Plath. Fiercely productive, Sexton published a number of volumes in rapid succession, including *All My Pretty Ones* (1962), *Live or Die* (which won the Pulitzer Prize in 1966), *Love Poems* (1969), *Transformations* (1971), *The Book of Folly* (1972), and *The Death Notebooks* (1974). Almost always marked by imaginative and often surrealistic verve and frequently characterized by sardonic wit, her poems struggled against the pain of her past to sing "in celebration of the woman I am."

Despite the honors and awards Sexton received, however, and the dramatic impression she evidently made at the poetry readings she gave, her work inspired much the sort of controversy aroused by the quite different verse of Sylvia Plath, with whom Sexton was often associated. "It would be hard to find a writer who dwells more insistently on the pathetic and disgusting aspects of bodily experience," protested the poet James Dickey in *The New York Times Book Review*, while the poet Muriel Rukeyser, taking precisely the opposite position, declared that Sexton's *In Celebration of My Uterus* was "one of the few poems in which a woman has come to the fact as symbol, the center, after many years of silence and taboo." In part, at least, such conflicting opinions arose because, as Kumin observes, Sexton "wrote openly about menstruation, abortion, masturbation, incest, adultery, and drug addiction at a time when the proprieties embraced none of these as proper topics for poetry."

That Sexton did write with unusual frankness and intensity reflected not only her commitment to her art (she was a tireless reviser and a passionate participant in workshops) but also the extremity of her personal situation. Throughout the years when she was winning prizes and fellowships, she was still under psychiatric care and gradually growing dependent on alcohol and sedatives, besides being dosed with the tranquilizing drug Thorazine, which caused her to gain weight and feel "so overwhelmed with lassitude that she could not write." At the same time, probably because of her persistent problems, she became increasingly obsessed with what the title of a posthumously published volume called *The Awful Rowing toward God* (1975). In the fall of 1974, just a month before her birthday—a time of year when the "voices" urging her to die had always been particularly insistent—Sexton gassed herself in her garage, perhaps influenced by the suicide method her friend Sylvia Plath had chosen some eleven years earlier. Yet though the story of this prolific writer's metamorphosis from model and housewife to famous poet ended tragically, her career, like Plath's, had been marked by extraordinary aesthetic vitality.

Her Kind

I have gone out, a possessed witch,
haunting the black air, braver at night;
dreaming evil, I have done my hitch
over the plain houses, light by light:
lonely thing, twelve-fingered, out of mind.　　　　　5
A woman like that is not a woman, quite.
I have been her kind.

I have found the warm caves in the woods,
filled them with skillets, carvings, shelves,
closets, silks, innumerable goods;　　　　　10
fixed the suppers for the worms and the elves:
whining, rearranging the disaligned.
A woman like that is misunderstood.
I have been her kind.

I have ridden in your cart, driver,   15
waved my nude arms at villages going by,
learning the last bright routes, survivor
where your flames still bite my thigh
and my ribs crack where your wheels wind.
A woman like that is not ashamed to die.   20
I have been her kind.

                                                              1960

The Moss of His Skin

Young girls in old Arabia were often buried alive next to their dead
fathers, apparently as sacrifice to the goddesses of the tribes. . . .
                    Harold Feldman, "Children of the Desert,"
            Psychoanalysis and Psychoanalytic Review, Fall 1958

It was only important
to smile and hold still,
to lie down beside him
and to rest awhile,
to be folded up together   5
as if we were silk,
to sink from the eyes of mother
and not to talk.
The black room took us
like a cave or a mouth   10
or an indoor belly.
I held my breath
and daddy was there,
his thumbs, his fat skull,
his teeth, his hair growing   15
like a field or a shawl.
I lay by the moss
of his skin until
it grew strange. My sisters
will never know that I fall   20
out of myself and pretend
that Allah will not see
how I hold my daddy
like an old stone tree.

                                                              1960

Housewife

Some women marry houses.
It's another kind of skin; it has a heart,

a mouth, a liver and bowel movements.
The walls are permanent and pink.
See how she sits on her knees all day,   5
faithfully washing herself down.
Men enter by force, drawn back like Jonah
into their fleshy mothers.[1]
A woman *is* her mother.
That's the main thing.   10

    1962

Somewhere in Africa

Must you leave, John Holmes,[2] with the prayers and psalms
you never said, said over you? Death with no rage
to weigh you down? Praised by the mild God, his arm
over the pulpit, leaving you timid, with no real age,

whitewashed by belief, as dull as the windy preacher!   5
Dead of a dark thing, John Holmes, you've been lost
in the college chapel, mourned as father and teacher,
mourned with piety and grace under the University Cross.

Your last book unsung, your last hard words unknown,
abandoned by science, cancer blossomed in your throat,   10
rooted like bougainvillea into your gray backbone,
ruptured your pores until you wore it like a coat.

The thick petals, the exotic reds, the purples and whites
covered up your nakedness and bore you up with all
their blind power. I think of your last June nights   15
in Boston, your body swollen but light, your eyes small

as you let the nurses carry you into a strange land.
. . . If this is death and God is necessary let him be hidden
from the missionary, the well-wisher and the glad hand.
Let God be some tribal female who is known but forbidden.   20

Let there be this God who is a woman who will place you
upon her shallow boat, who is a woman naked to the waist,
moist with palm oil and sweat, a woman of some virtue
and wild breasts, her limbs excellent, unbruised and chaste.

1. In the Old Testament, the prophet Jonah is
swallowed by a sea monster.

2. An American poet in whose workshop Sexton had studied.

Let her take you. She will put twelve strong men at the oars   25
for you are stronger than mahogany and your bones fill
the boat high as with fruit and bark from the interior.
She will have you now, you whom the funeral cannot kill.

John Holmes, cut from a single tree, lie heavy in her hold
and go down that river with the ivory, the copra[3] and the gold.   30

July 1, 1962   1966

Consorting with Angels

I was tired of being a woman,
tired of the spoons and the pots,
tired of my mouth and my breasts,
tired of the cosmetics and the silks.
There were still men who sat at my table,   5
circled around the bowl I offered up.
The bowl was filled with purple grapes
and the flies hovered in for the scent
and even my father came with his white bone.
But I was tired of the gender of things.   10

Last night I had a dream
and I said to it . . .
"You are the answer.
You will outlive my husband and my father."
In that dream there was a city made of chains   15
where Joan was put to death in man's clothes[4]
and the nature of the angels went unexplained,
no two made in the same species,
one with a nose, one with an ear in its hand,
one chewing a star and recording its orbit,   20
each one like a poem obeying itself,
performing God's functions,
a people apart.

"You are the answer,"
I said, and entered,   25
lying down on the gates of the city.
Then the chains were fastened around me
and I lost my common gender and my final aspect.

3. Coconut oil.
4. An allusion to Joan of Arc, the medieval peasant girl who, at the behest of her angelic voices, dressed in men's clothes and led the French to victory; later she was captured and put to death.

Adam was on the left of me
and Eve was on the right of me,[5]   30
both thoroughly inconsistent with the world of reason.
We wove our arms together
and rode under the sun.
I was not a woman anymore,
not one thing or the other.   35

O daughters of Jerusalem,
the king has brought me into his chamber.
I am black and I am beautiful.
I've been opened and undressed.
I have no arms or legs.   40
I'm all one skin like a fish.
I'm no more a woman
than Christ was a man.

February, 1963   1966

Sylvia's Death[6]

for Sylvia Plath

O Sylvia, Sylvia,
with a dead box of stones and spoons,

with two children, two meteors
wandering loose in the tiny playroom,

with your mouth into the sheet,   5
into the roofbeam, into the dumb prayer,

(Sylvia, Sylvia,
where did you go
after you wrote me
from Devonshire[7]   10
about raising potatoes
and keeping bees?)

what did you stand by,
just how did you lie down into?

Thief!—   15
how did you crawl into,

---

5. The first man and the first woman (Genesis).
6. Sylvia Plath (1932–1963), American poet

who committed suicide.
7. County in England.

crawl down alone
into the death I wanted so badly and for so long,

the death we said we both outgrew,
the one we wore on our skinny breasts,   20

the one we talked of so often each time
we downed three extra dry martinis in Boston,

the death that talked of analysts and cures,
the death that talked like brides with plots,

the death we drank to,   25
the motives and then the quiet deed?

(In Boston
the dying
ride in cabs,
yes death again,   30
that ride home
with *our* boy.)

O Sylvia, I remember the sleepy drummer
who beat on our eyes with an old story,

how we wanted to let him come   35
like a sadist or a New York fairy

to do his job,
a necessity, a window in a wall or a crib,

and since that time he waited
under our heart, our cupboard,   40

and I see now that we store him up
year after year, old suicides

and I know at the news of your death,
a terrible taste for it, like salt.

(And me,   45
me too.
And now, Sylvia,
you again
with death again,
that ride home   50
with *our* boy.)

And I say only
with my arms stretched out into that stone place,

what is your death
but an old belonging,   55

a mole that fell out
of one of your poems?

(O friend,
while the moon's bad,
and the king's gone,   60
and the queen's at her wit's end
the bar fly ought to sing!)

O tiny mother,
you too!
O funny duchess!   65
O blonde thing!

February 17, 1963   1966

In Celebration of My Uterus

Everyone in me is a bird.
I am beating all my wings.
They wanted to cut you out
but they will not.
They said you were immeasurably empty   5
but you are not.
They said you were sick unto dying
but they were wrong.
You are singing like a school girl.
You are not torn.   10

Sweet weight,
in celebration of the woman I am
and of the soul of the woman I am
and of the central creature and its delight
I sing for you. I dare to live.   15
Hello, spirit. Hello, cup.
Fasten, cover. Cover that does contain.
Hello to the soil of the fields.
Welcome, roots.

Each cell has a life.   20
There is enough here to please a nation.

It is enough that the populace own these goods.
Any person, any commonwealth would say of it,
"It is good this year that we may plant again
and think forward to a harvest.   25
A blight had been forecast and has been cast out."
Many women are singing together of this:
one is in a shoe factory cursing the machine,
one is at the aquarium tending a seal,
one is dull at the wheel of her Ford,   30
one is at the toll gate collecting,
one is tying the cord of a calf in Arizona,
one is straddling a cello in Russia,
one is shifting pots on the stove in Egypt,
one is painting her bedroom walls moon color,   35
one is dying but remembering a breakfast,
one is stretching on her mat in Thailand,
one is wiping the ass of her child,
one is staring out the window of a train
in the middle of Wyoming and one is   40
anywhere and some are everywhere and all
seem to be singing, although some can not
sing a note.

Sweet weight,
in celebration of the woman I am   45
let me carry a ten-foot scarf,
let me drum for the nineteen-year-olds,
let me carry bowls for the offering
(if that is my part).
Let me study the cardiovascular tissue,   50
let me examine the angular distance of meteors,
let me suck on the stems of flowers
(if that is my part).
Let me make certain tribal figures
(if that is my part).   55
For this thing the body needs
let me sing
for the supper,
for the kissing,
for the correct   60
yes.

From O Ye Tongues

Third Psalm

Let Noah build an ark out of the old lady's shoe[8] and
    fill it with the creatures of the Lord.

Let the ark of salvation have many windows so the creatures
    of the Lord will marry mouthfuls of oxygen.

Let the ark of salvation do homage to the Lord and notch his
    belt repeatedly.

Let Anne and Christopher[9] kneel with a buzzard whose
    mouth will bite her toe so that she may offer it up.

Let Anne and Christopher appear with two robins whose
    worms are sweet and pink as lipstick.   5

Let them present a bee, cupped in their palms, zinging the
    electricity of the Lord out into little yellow Z's.

Let them give praise with a bull whose horns are yellow
    with history.

Praise the Lord with an ox who grows sweet in heaven and ties
    the hair ribbons of little girls.

Humble themselves with the fly buzzing like the mother of
    the engine.

Serve with the ape who tore down the Empire State Building
    and won the maid.[1]   10

Dedicate an ant who will crawl toward the Lord like the
    print of this page.

Bless with a sable who bleeds ink across the dresses of
    ladies of the court.

Bless with a rabbit who comes with a whole sackful of
    sperm.

Bless with the locust who dances a curtain over the sky and
    makes the field blind.

---

8. A reference to the old nursery rhyme, "There was an old woman who lived in a shoe, / She had so many children she didn't know what to do."

9. Imaginary twins.

1. In the famous movie *King Kong*, the giant ape does not "win the maid"; shot at from an airplane, he falls from the Empire State Building and is killed.

Bless with the kingfish who melts down dimes into
    slim silver beside Frisco.   15

Rejoice with the day lily for it is born for a day to
    live by the mailbox and glorify the roadside.

Rejoice with the olive for it gives forth a faithful oil and
    eaten alone it will grease the mouth and bury the teeth.

Rejoice with a French angelfish which floats by like a jewel
    glowing like a blue iceberg in the Carribean.

Rejoice with a cottonbush which grows stars and seeds to
    clothe the multitudes of America.

Rejoice with the sea horse who lives in amusement parks
    and poems.

Let Anne and Christopher rejoice with the worm who moves
    into the light like a doll's penis.

                                              1974

MAYA ANGELOU
1928–

At the beginning of her best-selling autobiography *I Know Why the Caged Bird Sings* (1970), Maya Angelou explained that "if growing up is painful for the Southern Black girl, being aware of her displacement is the rust on the razor that threatens the throat. It is an unnecessary insult." Later in the book, Angelou described the insult of displacement associated with her childhood move from her native St. Louis to Stamps, Arkansas, with the sexual abuse she received from her mother's boyfriend, and with the "pride and prejudice" she encountered as a streetcar conductor in San Francisco. But *I Know Why the Caged Bird Sings* also recorded her affectionate respect for the grandmother, Ann Henderson, who raised her in Stamps, as well as Angelou's relish for black religious and social traditions, and her joy in the birth of her son.

As a self-described six-foot, black southwesterner, Angelou currently lives in Sonoma, California, with her husband, the writer Paul Du Feu. She published her first book, *I Know Why the Caged Bird Sings*, after a brief theatrical career. Since then she has lectured at several universities, published a number of sequels—including *Gather Together in My Name* (1974) and *Singin' and Swingin' and Gettin' Merry Like Christmas* (1976)—and written two books of poetry.

From I Know Why the Caged Bird Sings

[*The Peckerwood Dentist and Momma's Incredible Powers*]

The Angel of the candy counter had found me out at last, and was exacting excruciating penance for all the stolen Milky Ways, Mounds, Mr. Goodbars and Hersheys with Almonds. I had two cavities that were rotten to the gums. The pain was beyond the bailiwick of crushed aspirins or oil of cloves. Only one thing could help me, so I prayed earnestly that I'd be allowed to sit under the house and have the building collapse on my left jaw. Since there was no Negro dentist in Stamps,[1] nor doctor either, for that matter, Momma had dealt with previous toothaches by pulling them out (a string tied to the tooth with the other end looped over her fist), pain killers and prayer. In this particular instance the medicine had proved ineffective; there wasn't enough enamel left to hook a string on, and the prayers were being ignored because the Balancing Angel was blocking their passage.

I lived a few days and nights in blinding pain, not so much toying with as seriously considering the idea of jumping in the well, and Momma decided I had to be taken to a dentist. The nearest Negro dentist was in Texarkana, twenty-five miles away, and I was certain that I'd be dead long before we reached half the distance. Momma said we'd go to Dr. Lincoln, right in Stamps, and he'd take care of me. She said he owed her a favor.

I knew there were a number of whitefolks in town that owed her favors. Bailey and I had seen the books which showed how she had lent money to Blacks and whites alike during the Depression, and most still owed her. But I couldn't aptly remember seeing Dr. Lincoln's name, nor had I ever heard of a Negro's going to him as a patient. However, Momma said we were going, and put water on the stove for our baths. I had never been to a doctor, so she told me that after the bath (which would make my mouth feel better) I had to put on freshly starched and ironed underclothes from inside out. The ache failed to respond to the bath, and I knew then that the pain was more serious than that which anyone had ever suffered.

Before we left the Store, she ordered me to brush my teeth and then wash my mouth with Listerine. The idea of even opening my clamped jaws increased the pain, but upon her explanation that when you go to a doctor you have to clean yourself all over, but most especially the part that's to be examined, I screwed up my courage and unlocked my teeth. The cool air in my mouth and the jarring of my molars dislodged what little remained of my reason. I had frozen to the pain, my family nearly

---

1. The town in Arkansas where Angelou grew up.

had to tie me down to take the toothbrush away. It was no small effort to get me started on the road to the dentist. Momma spoke to all the passers-by, but didn't stop to chat. She explained over her shoulder that we were going to the doctor and she'd "pass the time of day" on our way home.

Until we reached the pond the pain was my world, an aura that haloed me for three feet around. Crossing the bridge into whitefolks' country, pieces of sanity pushed themselves forward. I had to stop moaning and start walking straight. The white towel, which was drawn under my chin and tied over my head, had to be arranged. If one was dying, it had to be done in style if the dying took place in whitefolks' part of town.

On the other side of the bridge the ache seemed to lessen as if a whitebreeze blew off the whitefolks and cushioned everything in their neighborhood—including my jaw. The gravel road was smoother, the stones smaller and the tree branches hung down around the path and nearly covered us. If the pain didn't diminish then, the familiar yet strange sights hypnotized me into believing that it had.

But my head continued to throb with the measured insistence of a bass drum, and how could a toothache pass the calaboose,[2] hear the songs of the prisoners, their blues and laughter, and not be changed? How could one or two or even a mouthful of angry tooth roots meet a wagonload of powhitetrash[3] children, endure their idiotic snobbery and not feel less important?

Behind the building which housed the dentist's office ran a small path used by servants and those tradespeople who catered to the butcher and Stamps' one restaurant. Momma and I followed that lane to the backstairs of Dentist Lincoln's office. The sun was bright and gave the day a hard reality as we climbed up the steps to the second floor.

Momma knocked on the back door and a young white girl opened it to show surprise at seeing us there. Momma said she wanted to see Dentist Lincoln and to tell him Annie was there. The girl closed the door firmly. Now the humiliation of hearing Momma describe herself as if she had no last name to the young white girl was equal to the physical pain. It seemed terribly unfair to have a toothache and a headache and have to bear at the same time the heavy burden of Blackness.

It was always possible that the teeth would quiet down and maybe drop out of their own accord. Momma said we would wait. We leaned in the harsh sunlight on the shaky railings of the dentist's back porch for over an hour.

2. Southern slang: the jail.
3. I.e., poor white trash, lower-class white children.

He opened the door and looked at Momma. "Well, Annie, what can I do for you?"

He didn't see the towel around my jaw or notice my swollen face.

Momma said, "Dentist Lincoln. It's my grandbaby here. She got two rotten teeth that's giving her a fit."

She waited for him to acknowledge the truth of her statement. He made no comment, orally or facially.

"She had this toothache purt' near four days now, and today I said, 'Young lady, you going to the Dentist.' "

"Annie?"

"Yes, sir, Dentist Lincoln."

He was choosing words the way people hunt for shells. "Annie, you know I don't treat nigra, colored people."

"I know, Dentist Lincoln. But this here is just my little grandbaby, and she ain't gone be no trouble to you. . . ."

"Annie, everybody has a policy. In this world you have to have a policy. Now, my policy is I don't treat colored people."

The sun had baked the oil out of Momma's skin and melted the Vaseline in her hair. She shone greasily as she leaned out of the dentist's shadow.

"Seem like to me, Dentist Lincoln, you might look after her, she ain't nothing but a little mite. And seems like maybe you owe me a favor or two."

He reddened slightly. "Favor or no favor. The money has all been repaid to you and that's the end of it. Sorry, Annie." He had his hand on the doorknob. "Sorry." His voice was a bit kinder on the second "Sorry," as if he really was.

Momma said, "I wouldn't press on you like this for myself but I can't take No. Not for my grandbaby. When you come to borrow my money you didn't have to beg. You asked me, and I lent it. Now, it wasn't my policy. I ain't no moneylender, but you stood to lose this building and I tried to help you out."

"It's been paid, and raising your voice won't make me change my mind. My policy . . ." He let go of the door and stepped nearer Momma. The three of us were crowded on the small landing. "Annie, my policy is I'd rather stick my hand in a dog's mouth than in a nigger's."

He had never once looked at me. He turned his back and went through the door into the cool beyond. Momma backed up inside herself for a few minutes. I forgot everything except her face which was almost a new one to me. She leaned over and took the doorknob, and in her everyday soft voice she said, "Sister, go on downstairs. Wait for me. I'll be there directly."

Under the most common of circumstances I knew it did no good to argue with Momma. So I walked down the steep stairs, afraid to look back and afraid not to do so. I turned as the door slammed, and she was gone.

Momma walked in that room as if she owned it. She shoved that silly nurse aside with one hand and strode into the dentist's office. He was sitting in his chair, sharpening his mean instruments and putting extra sting into his medicines. Her eyes were blazing like live coals and her arms had doubled themselves in length. He looked up at her just before she caught him by the collar of his white jacket.

"Stand up when you see a lady, you contemptuous scoundrel." Her tongue had thinned and the words rolled off well enunciated. Enunciated and sharp like little claps of thunder.

The dentist had no choice but to stand at R.O.T.C.[4] attention. His head dropped after a minute and his voice was humble. "Yes, ma'am, Mrs. Henderson."

"You knave, do you think you acted like a gentleman, speaking to me like that in front of my granddaughter?" She didn't shake him, although she had the power. She simply held him upright.

"No, ma'am, Mrs. Henderson."

"No, ma'am, Mrs. Henderson, what?" Then she did give him the tiniest of shakes, but because of her strength the action set his head and arms to shaking loose on the ends of his body. He stuttered much worse than Uncle Willie. "No, ma'am, Mrs. Henderson, I'm sorry."

With just an edge of her disgust showing, Momma slung him back in his dentist's chair. "Sorry is as sorry does, and you're about the sorriest dentist I ever laid my eyes on." (She could afford to slip into the vernacular because she had such eloquent command of English.)

"I didn't ask you to apologize in front of Marguerite, because I don't want her to know my power, but I order you, now and herewith. Leave Stamps by sundown."

"Mrs. Henderson, I can't get my equipment. . . ." He was shaking terribly now.

"Now, that brings me to my second order. You will never again practice dentistry. Never! When you get settled in your next place, you will be a vegetarian caring for dogs with the mange, cats with the cholera and cows with the epizootic. Is that clear?"

The saliva ran down his chin and his eyes filled with tears. "Yes, ma'am. Thank you for not killing me. Thank you, Mrs. Henderson."

Momma pulled herself back from being ten feet tall with eight-foot arms and said, "You're welcome for nothing, you varlet, I wouldn't waste a killing on the likes of you."

---

4. Reserve Officers' Training Corps, a program that gives high school and college students mili- tary training.

On her way out she waved her handkerchief at the nurse and turned her into a crocus sack of chicken feed.

Momma looked tired when she came down the stairs, but who wouldn't be tired if they had gone through what she had. She came close to me and adjusted the towel under my jaw (I had forgotten the toothache; I only knew that she made her hands gentle in order not to awaken the pain). She took my hand. Her voice never changed. "Come on, Sister."

I reckoned we were going home where she would concoct a brew to eliminate the pain and maybe give me new teeth too. New teeth that would grow overnight out of my gums. She led me toward the drug-store, which was in the opposite direction from the Store. "I'm taking you to Dentist Baker in Texarkana."

I was glad after all that that I had bathed and put on Mum and Cash-mere Bouquet talcum powder. It was a wonderful surprise. My tooth-ache had quieted to solemn pain, Momma had obliterated the evil white man, and we were going on a trip to Texarkana, just the two of us.

On the Greyhound she took an inside seat in the back, and I sat be-side her. I was so proud of being her granddaughter and sure that some of her magic must have come down to me. She asked if I was scared. I only shook my head and leaned over on her cool brown upper arm. There was no chance that a dentist, especially a Negro dentist, would dare hurt me then. Not with Momma there. The trip was uneventful, except that she put her arm around me, which was very unusual for Momma to do.

The dentist showed me the medicine and the needle before he dead-ened my gums, but if he hadn't I wouldn't have worried. Momma stood right behind him. Her arms were folded and she checked on every-thing he did. The teeth were extracted and she bought me an ice cream cone from the side window of a drug counter. The trip back to Stamps was quiet, except that I had to spit into a very small empty snuff can which she had gotten for me and it was difficult with the bus humping and jerking on our country roads.

At home, I was given a warm salt solution, and when I washed out my mouth I showed Bailey the empty holes, where the clotted blood sat like filling in a pie crust. He said I was quite brave, and that was my cue to reveal our confrontation with the peckerwood[5] dentist and Momma's incredible powers.

I had to admit that I didn't hear the conversation, but what else could she have said than what I said she said? What else done? He agreed with my analysis in a lukewarm way, and I happily (after all, I'd been

5. Originally, very poor Southern white; later, any white person.

sick) flounced into the Store. Momma was preparing our evening meal and Uncle Willie leaned on the door sill. She gave her version.

"Dentist Lincoln got right uppity. Said he'd rather put his hand in a dog's mouth. And when I reminded him of the favor, he brushed it off like a piece of lint. Well, I sent Sister downstairs and went inside. I hadn't never been in his office before, but I found the door to where he takes out teeth, and him and the nurse was in there thick as thieves. I just stood there till he caught sight of me." Crash bang the pots on the stove. "He jumped just like he was sitting on a pin. He said, 'Annie, I done tole you, I ain't gonna mess around in no niggah's mouth.' I said, 'Somebody's got to do it then,' and he said, 'Take her to Texarkana to the colored dentist' and that's when I said, 'If you paid me my money I could afford to take her.' He said, 'It's all been paid.' I tole him everything but the interest been paid. He said. "Twasn't no interest.' I said "Tis now. I'll take ten dollars as payment in full.' You know, Willie, it wasn't no right thing to do, 'cause I lent that money without thinking about it.

"He tole that little snippity nurse of his'n to give me ten dollars and make me sign a 'paid in full' receipt. She gave it to me and I signed the papers. Even though by rights he was paid up before, I figger, he gonna be that kind of nasty, he gonna have to pay for it."

Momma and her son laughed and laughed over the white man's evilness and her retributive sin.

I preferred, much preferred, my version.

1969

URSULA K. LE GUIN
1929–

The daughter of the distinguished anthropologist Alfred L. Kroeber and the writer-folklorist Theodora Kroeber, the science-fiction writer Ursula K. Le Guin has sometimes compared her own work to that of an anthropologist. "Science fiction allows a fiction writer to make up cultures, to *invent*—not only a new world, but a new *culture*," she told an interviewer for the *California Quarterly* in 1978, adding that "my father preferred to go find [other civilizations]; I prefer to invent them." Imaginatively elaborating new possibilities for human society and personality while incisively commenting on the "real" world, Le Guin's invented cultures are described and dramatized in an impressive range of volumes, including the novels *Rocannon's World* (1966), *The Left Hand of Darkness* (1969), and *The Dispossessed* (1974); the short-story collections *The Wind's Twelve Quarters* (1975) and *The Compass Rose* (1982); and the three fantasies for children—*A Wizard of Earthsea* (1968),

The Tombs of Atuan (1971), and *The Farthest Shore* (1972)—which make up the prize-winning Earthsea trilogy.

Born and raised in Berkeley, California, Le Guin attended Radcliffe College and Columbia University. In 1953, while studying in Paris on a Fulbright scholarship, she married the historian Charles A. Le Guin, with whom she eventually settled in Portland, Oregon. From the start, she has explained, her writing always had "what you'd have to call a fantasy element. . . . It took place in an imaginary country or something like that," but it was not until she "got back to reading science fiction in [her] late twenties" that she realized "I could *call* my stuff science fiction." From that time on, even while working and raising three children, she became a productive and distinguished writer of what might be labelled "speculative fiction" as well as "science fiction." Extending the boundaries of her genre so that science fiction could explore the problems and possibilities of human society with a new intensity, she created imaginary creatures who allowed her to raise important questions about the modes and morals of her own world. Particularly in such works as *The Left Hand of Darkness* (which won the Hugo and Nebula awards from the Science Fiction Writers of America in 1969) and *Sur* (1982), she examined the pressures and possibilities of gender with subtlety and wit. What would it "be like to be a man-woman, or a woman-man," she asks in *The Left Hand of Darkness*, a fantasy of life on a planet whose inhabitants are biologically bisexual, and what would it mean if *women* had discovered the South Pole, she wonders in *Sur*. Her answers to such questions are invariably both brilliant and surprising.

Sur[1]

A Summary Report of the Yelcho Expedition to the Antarctic, 1909–1910

Although I have no intention of publishing this report, I think it would be nice if a grandchild of mine, or somebody's grandchild, happened to find it some day; so I shall keep it in the leather trunk in the attic, along with Rosita's christening dress and Juanito's silver rattle and my wedding shoes and finneskos.[2]

The first requisite for mounting an expedition—money—is normally the hardest to come by. I grieve that even in a report destined for a trunk in the attic of a house in a very quiet suburb of Lima[3] I dare not write the name of the generous benefactor, the great soul without whose unstinting liberality the *Yelcho* Expedition would never have been more than the idlest excursion into daydream. That our equipment was the best and most modern—that our provisions were plentiful and fine—that a ship of the Chilean Government, with her brave officers and gallant crew, was twice sent halfway round the world for our

---

1. Spanish: south.
2. Boots made of reindeer skin.
3. Largest city of Peru.

THE MAP IN THE ATTIC

convenience: all this is due to that benefactor whose name, alas! I must not say, but whose happiest debtor I shall be till death.

When I was little more than a child my imagination was caught by a newspaper account of the voyage of the *Belgica*, which, sailing south from Tierra del Fuego, became beset by ice in the Bellingshausen Sea and drifted a whole year with the floe, the men aboard her suffering a great deal from want of food and from the terror of the unending winter darkness. I read and reread that account, and later followed with excitement the reports of the rescue of Dr. Nordenskjold from the South Shetland Isles by the dashing Captain Irizar of the *Uruguay*, and the adventures of the *Scotia* in the Weddell Sea. But all these exploits were to me but forerunners of the British National Antarctic Expedition of 1902–1904, in the *Discovery*, and the wonderful account of that expedition by Captain Scott.[4] This book, which I ordered from London and reread a thousand times, filled me with longing to see with my own eyes that strange continent, last Thule[5] of the South, which lies on our maps and globes like a white cloud, a void, fringed here and there with scraps of coastline, dubious capes, supposititious islands, headlands that may or may not be there: Antarctica. And the desire was as pure as the polar snows: to go, to see—no more, no less. I deeply respect the scientific accomplishments of Captain Scott's expedition, and have read with passionate interest the findings of physicists, meteorologists, biologists, etc.; but having had no training in any science, nor any opportunity for such training, my ignorance obliged me to forego any thought of adding to the body of scientific knowledge concerning Antarctica; and the same is true for all the members of my expedition. It seems a pity; but there was nothing we could do about it. Our goal was limited to observation and exploration. We hoped to go a little farther, perhaps, and see a little more; if not, simply to go and to see. A simple ambition, I think, and essentially a modest one.

Yet it would have remained less than an ambition, no more than a longing, but for the support and encouragement of my dear cousin and friend Juana— —(I use no surnames, lest this report fall into strangers' hands at last, and embarrassment or unpleasant notoriety thus be brought upon unsuspecting husbands, sons, etc.) I had lent Juana my copy of *The Voyage of the Discovery*, and it was she who, as we strolled beneath our parasols across the Plaza de Armas after Mass one Sunday in 1908, said, "Well, if Captain Scott can do it, why can't we?"

It was Juana who proposed that we write Carlota—in Valparaiso.

4. Robert Falcon Scott (1868–1912), British naval officer and antarctic explorer, commanded an expedition to explore the Ross Sea region in 1901–1904.

5. Ultima Thule, an imaginary island north of Britain, thought by ancient geographers to mark the edge of the world.

Through Carlota we met our benefactor, and so obtained our money, our ship, and even the plausible pretext of going on retreat in a Bolivian convent, which some of us were forced to employ (while the rest of us said we were going to Paris for the winter season). And it was my Juana who in the darkest moments remained resolute, unshaken in her determination to achieve our goal.

And there were dark moments, especially in the early months of 1909—times when I did not see how the Expedition would ever become more than a quarter ton of pemmican[6] gone to waste and a lifelong regret. It was so very hard to gather our expeditionary force together! So few of those we asked even knew what we were talking about—so many thought we were mad, or wicked, or both! And of those few who shared our folly, still fewer were able, when it came to the point, to leave their daily duties and commit themselves to a voyage of at least six months, attended with not inconsiderable uncertainty and danger. An ailing parent; an anxious husband beset by business cares; a child at home with only ignorant or incompetent servants to look after it: these are not responsibilities lightly to be set aside. And those who wished to evade such claims were not the companions we wanted in hard work, risk, and privation.

But since success crowned our efforts, why dwell on the setbacks and delays, or the wretched contrivances and downright lies that we all had to employ? I look back with regret only to those friends who wished to come with us but could not, by any contrivance, get free—those we had to leave behind to a life without danger, without uncertainty, without hope.

On the seventeenth of August, 1909, in Punta Arenas, Chile, all the members of the Expedition met for the first time: Juana and I, the two Peruvians; from Argentina, Zoe, Berta, and Teresa; and our Chileans, Carlota and her friends Eva, Pepita, and Dolores. At the last moment I had received word that Maria's husband, in Quito, was ill, and she must stay to nurse him, so we were nine, not ten. Indeed, we had resigned ourselves to being but eight, when, just as night fell, the indomitable Zoe arrived in a tiny pirogue[7] manned by Indians, her yacht having sprung a leak just as it entered the Strait of Magellan.

That night before we sailed we began to get to know one another; and we agreed, as we enjoyed our abominable supper in the abominable seaport inn of Punta Arenas, that if a situation arose of such urgent danger that one voice must be obeyed without present question, the unenviable honor of speaking with that voice should fall first upon my-

---

6. A food originally made by American Indians   7. Canoe made from a hollow tree trunk.
from dried meat and fruit.

self: if I were incapacitated, upon Carlota: if she, then upon Berta. We three were then toasted as "Supreme Inca," "La Araucana,"[8] and "The Third Mate," among a lot of laughter and cheering. As it came out, to my very great pleasure and relief, my qualities as a "leader" were never tested; the nine of us worked things out amongst us from beginning to end without any orders being given by anybody, and only two or three times with recourse to a vote by voice or show of hands. To be sure, we argued a good deal. But then, we had time to argue. And one way or another the arguments always ended up in a decision, upon which action could be taken. Usually at least one person grumbled about the decision, sometimes bitterly. But what is life without grumbling, and the occasional opportunity to say, "I told you so"? How could one bear housework, or looking after babies, let alone the rigors of sledge-hauling in Antarctica, without grumbling? Officers—as we came to understand aboard the *Yelcho*—are forbidden to grumble; but we nine were, and are, by birth and upbringing, unequivocally and irrevocably, all crew.

Though our shortest course to the southern continent, and that originally urged upon us by the captain of our good ship, was to the South Shetlands and the Bellingshausen Sea, or else by the South Orkneys into the Weddell Sea, we planned to sail west to the Ross Sea, which Captain Scott had explored and described, and from which the brave Ernest Shackleton[9] had returned only the previous autumn. More was known about this region than any other portion of the coast of Antarctica, and though that more was not much, yet it served as some insurance of the safety of the ship, which we felt we had no right to imperil. Captain Pardo had fully agreed with us after studying the charts and our planned itinerary; and so it was westward that we took our course out of the Strait next morning.

Our journey half round the globe was attended by fortune. The little *Yelcho* steamed cheerily along through gale and gleam, climbing up and down those seas of the Southern Ocean that run unbroken round the world. Juana, who had fought bulls and the far more dangerous cows on her family's *estancia*, called the ship *"la vaca valiente,"*[1] because she always returned to the charge. Once we got over being seasick we all enjoyed the sea voyage, though oppressed at times by the kindly but officious protectiveness of the captain and his officers, who felt that we were only "safe" when huddled up in the three tiny cabins which they had chivalrously vacated for our use.

8. The Araucanian Indians occupied present-day Chile before the Spanish conquest; like the Incas they were subjugated by the Spanish, but only after much resistance.
9. Sir Ernest Henry Shackleton (1874–1922),

British antarctic explorer, member of the Scott expedition.
1. Spanish: the fine cow. "Estancia": cattle ranch.

We saw our first iceberg much farther south than we had looked for it, and saluted it with Veuve Clicquot[2] at dinner. The next day we entered the ice pack, the belt of floes and bergs, broken loose from the land ice and winter-frozen seas of Antarctica, which drifts northward in the spring. Fortune still smiled on us: our little steamer, incapable, with her unreinforced metal hull, of forcing a way into the ice, picked her way from lane to lane without hesitation, and on the third day we were through the pack, in which ships have sometimes struggled for weeks and been obliged to turn back at last. Ahead of us now lay the dark grey waters of the Ross Sea, and beyond that, on the horizon, the remote glimmer, the cloud-reflected whiteness of the Great Ice Barrier.

Entering the Ross Sea a little east of Longitude West 160°, we came in sight of the Barrier at the place where Captain Scott's party, finding a bight[3] in the vast wall of ice, had gone ashore and sent up their hydrogen-gas balloon for reconnaissance and photography. The towering face of the Barrier, its sheer cliffs and azure and violet water-worn caves, all were as described, but the location had changed: instead of a narrow bight there was a considerable bay, full of the beautiful and terrific orca whales playing and spouting in the sunshine of that brilliant southern spring.

Evidently masses of ice many acres in extent had broken away from the Barrier (which—at least for most of its vast extent—does not rest on land but floats on water) since the *Discovery*'s passage in 1902. This put our plan to set up camp on the Barrier itself in a new light; and while we were discussing alternatives, we asked Captain Pardo to take the ship west along the Barrier face towards Ross Island and McMurdo Sound. As the sea was clear of ice and quite calm, he was happy to do so, and, when we sighted the smoke plume of Mount Erebus, to share in our celebration—another half case of Veuve Clicquot.

The *Yelcho* anchored in Arrival Bay, and we went ashore in the ship's boat. I cannot describe my emotions when I set foot on the earth, on that earth, the barren, cold gravel at the foot of the long volcanic slope. I felt elation, impatience, gratitude, awe, familiarity. I felt that I was home at last. Eight Adélie penguins immediately came to greet us with many exclamations of interest not unmixed with disapproval. "Where on earth have you been? What took you so long? The Hut is around this way. Please come this way. Mind the rocks!" They insisted on our going to visit Hut Point, where the large structure built by Captain Scott's party stood, looking just as in the photographs and drawings that illustrate his book. The area about it, however, was disgusting—a kind of graveyard of seal skins, seal bones, penguin bones, and rubbish, presided over by the mad, screaming skua gulls. Our escorts waddled

---

2. An expensive French champagne.   3. A bend in a shoreline, forming a bay.

past the slaughterhouse in all tranquility, and one showed me personally to the door, though it would not go in.

The interior of the hut was less offensive, but very dreary. Boxes of
supplies had been stacked up into a kind of room within the room; it did
not look as I had imagined it when the *Discovery* party put on their
melodramas and minstrel shows in the long winter night. (Much later,
we learned that Sir Ernest had rearranged it a good deal when he was
there just a year before us.) It was dirty, and had about it a mean disorder. A pound tin of tea was standing open. Empty meat tins lay about;
biscuits were spilled on the floor; a lot of dog turds were underfoot—
frozen, of course, but not a great deal improved by that. No doubt the
last occupants had had to leave in a hurry, perhaps even in a blizzard.
All the same, they could have closed the tea tin. But housekeeping, the
art of the infinite, is no game for amateurs.

Teresa proposed that we use the hut as our camp. Zoe counterpro-
posed that we set fire to it. We finally shut the door and left it as we had
found it. The penguins appeared to approve, and cheered us all the way
to the boat.

McMurdo Sound was free of ice, and Captain Pardo now proposed
to take us off Ross Island and across to Victoria Land, where we might
camp at the foot of the Western Mountains, on dry and solid earth. But
those mountains, with their storm-darkened peaks and hanging cirques
and glaciers, looked as awful as Captain Scott had found them on his
western journey, and none of us felt much inclined to seek shelter
among them.

Aboard the ship that night we decided to go back and set up our base
as we had originally planned, on the Barrier itself. For all available reports indicated that the clear way south was across the level Barrier surface until one could ascend one of the confluent glaciers to the high
plateau which appears to form the whole interior of the continent.
Captain Pardo argued strongly against this plan, asking what would become of us if the Barrier "calved"—if our particular acre of ice broke
away and started to drift northward. "Well," said Zoe, "then you won't
have to come so far to meet us." But he was so persuasive on this theme
that he persuaded himself into leaving one of the *Yelcho's* boats with us
when we camped, as a means of escape. We found it useful for fishing,
later on.

My first steps on Antarctic soil, my only visit to Ross Island, had not
been pleasure unalloyed. I thought of the words of the English poet:

> Though every prospect pleases,
> And only Man is vile.[4]

---

4. From the hymn *From Greenland's Icy Mountains* by Bishop Reginald Heber (1783–1826)

But then, the backside of heroism is often rather sad; women and servants know that. They know also that the heroism may be no less real for that. But achievement is smaller than men think. What is large is the sky, the earth, the sea, the soul. I looked back as the ship sailed east again that evening. We were well into September now, with ten hours or more of daylight. The spring sunset lingered on the twelve-thousand-foot peak of Erebus and shone rosy gold on her long plume of steam. The steam from our own small funnel faded blue on the twilit water as we crept along under the towering pale wall of ice.

On our return to "Orca Bay"—Sir Ernest, we learned years later, had named it the Bay of Whales—we found a sheltered nook where the Barrier edge was low enough to provide fairly easy access from the ship. The *Yelcho* put out her ice anchor, and the next long, hard days were spent in unloading our supplies and setting up our camp on the ice, a half kilometer in from the edge: a task in which the *Yelcho*'s crew lent us invaluable aid and interminable advice. We took all the aid gratefully, and most of the advice with salt.

The weather so far had been extraordinarily mild for spring in this latitude; the temperature had not yet gone below $-20°$ Fahrenheit, and there was only one blizzard while we were setting up camp. But Captain Scott had spoken feelingly of the bitter south winds on the Barrier, and we had planned accordingly. Exposed as our camp was to every wind, we built no rigid structures above ground. We set up tents to shelter in while we dug out a series of cubicles in the ice itself, lined them with hay insulation and pine boarding, and roofed them with canvas over bamboo poles, covered with snow for weight and insulation. The big central room was instantly named Buenos Aires by our Argentineans, to whom the center, wherever one is, is always Buenos Aires. The heating and cooking stove was in Buenos Aires. The storage tunnels and the privy (called Punta Arenas) got some back heat from the stove. The sleeping cubicles opened off Buenos Aires, and were very small, mere tubes into which one crawled feet first; they were lined deeply with hay and soon warmed by one's body warmth. The sailors called them "coffins" and "wormholes," and looked with horror on our burrows in the ice. But our little warren or prairie-dog village served us well, permitting us as much warmth and privacy as one could reasonably expect under the circumstances. If the *Yelcho* was unable to get through the ice in February, and we had to spend the winter in Antarctica, we certainly could do so, though on very limited rations. For this coming summer, our base—Sudamérica del Sur, South South America, but we generally called it the Base—was intended merely as a place to sleep, to store our provisions, and to give shelter from blizzards.

To Berta and Eva, however, it was more than that. They were its chief architect-designers, its most ingenious builder-excavators, and its most diligent and contented occupants, forever inventing an improvement in ventilation, or learning how to make skylights, or revealing to us a new addition to our suite of rooms, dug in the living ice. It was thanks to them that our stores were stowed so handily, that our stove drew and heated so efficiently, and that Buenos Aires, where nine people cooked, ate, worked, conversed, argued, grumbled, painted, played the guitar and banjo, and kept the Expedition's library of books and maps, was a marvel of comfort and convenience. We lived there in real amity; and if you simply had to be alone for a while, you crawled into your sleeping hole head first.

Berta went a little farther. When she had done all she could to make South South America livable, she dug out one more cell just under the ice surface, leaving a nearly transparent sheet of ice like a greenhouse roof; and there, alone, she worked at sculptures. They were beautiful forms, some like a blending of the reclining human figure with the subtle curves and volumes of the Weddell seal, others like the fantastic shapes of ice cornices and ice caves. Perhaps they are there still, under the snow, in the bubble in the Great Barrier. There where she made them they might last as long as stone. But she could not bring them north. That is the penalty for carving in water.

Captain Pardo was reluctant to leave us, but his orders did not permit him to hang about the Ross Sea indefinitely, and so at last, with many earnest injunctions to us to stay put—make no journeys—take no risks —beware of frostbite—don't use edge tools—look out for cracks in the ice—and a heartfelt promise to return to Orca Bay on the twentieth of February, or as near that date as wind and ice would permit, the good man bade us farewell, and his crew shouted us a great goodbye cheer as they weighed anchor. That evening, in the long orange twilight of October, we saw the topmast of the *Yelcho* go down the north horizon, over the edge of the world, leaving us to ice, and silence, and the Pole.

That night we began to plan the Southern Journey.

The ensuing month passed in short practice trips and depotlaying.[5] The life we had led at home, though in its own way strenuous, had not fitted any of us for the kind of strain met with in sledge-hauling at ten or twenty degrees below freezing. We all needed as much working-out as possible before we dared undertake a long haul.

My longest exploratory trip, made with Dolores and Carlota, was southwest towards Mount Markham, and it was a nightmare—blizzards and pressure ice[6] all the way out, crevasses and no view of the mountains when we got there, and white weather and sastrugi[7] all the way back. The trip was useful, however, in that we could begin to esti-

5. Depositing supplies of food along the route to be taken.
6. Ridges formed in the antarctic seas by the pressures of sea ice.
7. Long wavelike ridges of snow.

mate our capacities; and also in that we had started out with a very heavy load of provisions, which we depoted at 100 and 130 miles SSW of Base. Thereafter other parties pushed on farther, till we had a line of snow cairns and depots right down to Latitude 83° 43′, where Juana and Zoe, on an exploring trip, had found a kind of stone gateway opening on a great glacier leading south. We established these depots to avoid, if possible, the hunger that had bedevilled Captain Scott's Southern Party, and the consequent misery and weakness. And we also established to our own satisfaction—intense satisfaction—that we were sledgehaulers at least as good as Captain Scott's husky dogs. Of course we could not have expected to pull as much or as fast as his men. That we did so was because we were favored by much better weather than Captain Scott's party ever met on the Barrier; and also the quantity and quality of our food made a very considerable difference. I am sure that the fifteen percent of dried fruits in our pemmican helped prevent scurvy; and the potatoes, frozen and dried according to an ancient Andean Indian method, were very nourishing yet very light and compact —perfect sledging rations. In any case, it was with considerable confidence in our capacities that we made ready at last for the Southern Journey.

The Southern Party consisted of two sledge teams: Juana, Dolores, and myself; Carlota, Pepita, and Zoe. The support team of supplies, going right up onto the glacier to prospect routes and leave depots of supplies for our return journey. We followed five days behind them, and met them returning between Depot Ercilla and Depot Miranda (see map). That "night"—of course there was no real darkness—we were all nine together in the heart of the level plain of ice. It was the fifteenth of November, Dolores's birthday. We celebrated by putting eight ounces of pisco[8] in the hot chocolate, and became very merry. We sang. It is strange now to remember how thin our voices sounded in that great silence. It was overcast, white weather, without shadows and without visible horizon or any feature to break the level; there was nothing to see at all. We had come to that white place on the map, that void, and there we flew and sang like sparrows.

After sleep and a good breakfast the Base Party continued north, and the Southern Party sledged on. The sky cleared presently. High up, thin clouds passed over very rapidly from southwest to northeast, but down on the Barrier it was calm and just cold enough, five or ten degrees below freezing, to give a firm surface for hauling.

On the level ice we never pulled less than eleven miles, seventeen kilometers, a day, and generally fifteen or sixteen miles, twenty-five kilometers. (Our instruments, being British made, were calibrated in feet,

8. A Peruvian brandy.

miles, degrees Fahrenheit, etc., but we often converted miles to kilometers because the larger numbers sounded more encouraging.) At the
time we left South America, we knew only that Mr. Shackleton had
mounted another expedition to the Antarctic in 1908, had tried to attain the Pole but failed, and had returned to England in June of the
current year, 1909. No coherent report of his explorations had yet
reached South America when we left; we did not know what route he
had gone, or how far he had got. But we were not altogether taken by
surprise when, far across the featureless white plain, tiny beneath the
mountain peaks and the strange silent flight of the rainbow-fringed
cloud wisps, we saw a fluttering dot of black. We turned west from our
course to visit it: a snow heap nearly buried by the winter's storms—a
flag on a bamboo pole, a mere shred of threadbare cloth—an empty
oilcan—and a few footprints standing some inches above the ice. In
some conditions of weather the snow compressed under one's weight
remains when the surrounding soft snow melts or is scoured
away by the wind; and so these reversed footprints had been left standing all these months, like rows of cobbler's lasts[9]—a queer sight.

We met no other such traces on our way. In general I believe our
course was somewhat east of Mr. Shackleton's. Juana, our surveyor,
had trained herself well and was faithful and methodical in her sightings
and readings, but our equipment was minimal—a theodolite on tripod
legs, a sextant with artificial horizon,[1] two compasses, and chrono-
meters. We had only the wheel meter on the sledge to give distance actually travelled.

In any case, it was the day after passing Mr. Shackleton's waymark
that I first saw clearly the great glacier among the mountains to the
southwest, which was to give us a pathway from the sea level of the
Barrier up to the altiplano,[2] ten thousand feet above. The approach was
magnificent: a gateway formed by immense vertical domes and pillars
of rock. Zoe and Juana had called the vast ice river that flowed through
that gateway the Florence Nightingale Glacier,[3] wishing to honor the
British, who had been the inspiration and guide of our expedition; that
very brave and very peculiar lady seemed to represent so much that is
best, and strangest, in the island race. On maps, of course, this glacier
bears the name Mr. Shackleton gave it, the Beardmore.

The ascent of the Nightingale was not easy. The way was open at
first, and well marked by our support party, but after some days we
came among terrible crevasses, a maze of hidden cracks, from a foot to
thirty feet wide and from thirty to a thousand feet deep. Step by step we

9. Foot-shaped blocks used in shoemaking.
1. A sextant measures the altitude of stars; a
theodolite measures angles. Both are used for
surveying and navigation.

2. High plateau.
3. Florence Nightingale (1820–1910), British
nursing pioneer and feminist writer.

went, and step by step, and the way always upward now. We were fifteen days on the glacier. At first the weather was hot, up to 20° F., and the hot nights without darkness were wretchedly uncomfortable in our small tents. And all of us suffered more or less from snowblindness just at the time when we wanted clear eyesight to pick our way among the ridges and crevasses of the tortured ice, and to see the wonders about and before us. For at every day's advance more great, nameless peaks came into view in the west and southwest, summit beyond summit, range beyond range, stark rock and snow in the unending noon.

We gave names to these peaks, not very seriously, since we did not expect our discoveries to come to the attention of geographers. Zoe had a gift for naming, and it is thanks to her that certain sketch maps in various suburban South American attics bear such curious features as "Bolívar's Big Nose," "I Am General Rosas,"[4] "The Cloudmaker," "Whose Toe?" and "Throne of Our Lady of the Southern Cross." And when at last we got up onto the altiplano, the great interior plateau, it was Zoe who called it the pampa,[5] and maintained that we walked there among vast herds of invisible cattle, transparent cattle pastured on the spindrift snow, their gauchos the restless, merciless winds. We were by then all a little crazy with exhaustion and the great altitude—twelve thousand feet—and the cold and the wind blowing and the luminous circles and crosses surrounding the suns, for often there were three or four suns in the sky, up there.

That is not a place where people have any business to be. We should have turned back; but since we had worked so hard to get there, it seemed that we should go on, at least for a while.

A blizzard came with very low temperatures, so we had to stay in the tents, in our sleeping bags, for thirty hours, a rest we all needed; though it was warmth we needed most, and there was no warmth on that terrible plain anywhere at all but in our veins. We huddled close together all that time. The ice we lay on is two miles thick.

It cleared suddenly and became, for the plateau, good weather: twelve below zero and the wind not very strong. We three crawled out of our tent and met the others crawling out of theirs. Carlota told us then that her group wished to turn back. Pepita had been feeling very ill; even after the rest during the blizzard, her temperature would not rise above 90°. Carlota was having trouble breathing. Zoe was perfectly fit, but much preferred staying with her friends and lending them a hand in difficulties to pushing on towards the Pole. So we put the four ounces of pisco which we had been keeping for Christmas into the

---

4. Juan Manuel de Rosas (1793–1877), Argentine dictator. Simon Bolívar (1783–1830), South American soldier and activist who led the revolution against Spain.

5. South American grazing land. "Gauchos": South American cattlemen.

breakfast cocoa, and dug out our tents, and loaded our sledges, and parted there in the white daylight on the bitter plain.

Our sledge was fairly light by now. We pulled on to the south. Juana calculated our position daily. On the twenty-second of December, 1909, we reached the South Pole. The weather was, as always, very cruel. Nothing of any kind marked the dreary whiteness. We discussed leaving some kind of mark or monument, a snow cairn, a tent pole and flag; but there seemed no particular reason to do so. Anything we could do, anything we were, was insignificant, in that awful place. We put up the tent for shelter for an hour and made a cup of tea, and then struck "90° Camp."[6] Dolores, standing patient as ever in her sledging harness, looked at the snow; it was so hard frozen that it showed no trace of our footprints coming, and she said, "Which way?"

"North," said Juana.

It was a joke, because at that particular place there is no other direction. But we did not laugh. Our lips were cracked with frostbite and hurt too much to let us laugh. So we started back, and the wind at our backs pushed us along, and dulled the knife edges of the waves of frozen snow.

All that week the blizzard wind pursued us like a pack of mad dogs. I cannot describe it. I wished we had not gone to the Pole. I think I wish it even now. But I was glad even then that we had left no sign there, for some man longing to be first might come some day, and find it, and know then what a fool he had been, and break his heart.

We talked, when we could talk, of catching up to Carlota's party, since they might be going slower than we. In fact they had used their tent as a sail to catch the following wind and had got far ahead of us. But in many places they had built snow cairns or left some sign for us; once Zoe had written on the lee side of a ten-foot sastruga, just as children write on the sand of the beach at Miraflores, "This Way Out!" The wind blowing over the frozen ridge had left the words perfectly distinct.

In the very hour that we began to descend the glacier, the weather turned warmer, and the mad dogs were left to howl forever tethered to the Pole. The distance that had taken us fifteen days going up we covered in only eight days going down. But the good weather that had aided us descending the Nightingale became a curse down on the Barrier ice, where we had looked forward to a kind of royal progress from depot to depot, eating our fill and taking our time for the last three hundred-odd miles. In a tight place on the glacier I lost my goggles—I was swinging from my harness at the time in a crevasse—and then Juana had broken hers when we had to do some rock climbing coming

---

6. The South Pole is at latitude 90 degrees and longitude 0 degrees.

down to the Gateway. After two days in bright sunlight with only one pair of snow goggles to pass amongst us, we were all suffering badly from snowblindness. It became acutely painful to keep lookout for landmarks or depot flags, to take sightings, even to study the compass, which had to be laid down on the snow to steady the needle. At Concolorcorvo Depot, where there was a particularly good supply of food and fuel, we gave up, crawled into our sleeping bags with bandaged eyes, and slowly boiled alive like lobsters in the tent exposed to the relentless sun. The voices of Berta and Zoe were the sweetest sound I ever heard. A little concerned about us, they had skied south to meet us. They led us home to Base.

We recovered quite swiftly, but the altiplano left its mark. When she was very little, Rosita asked if a dog "had bitted Mama's toes." I told her Yes, a great, white, mad dog named Blizzard! My Rosita and my Juanito heard many stories when they were little, about that fearful dog and how it howled, and the transparent cattle of the invisible gauchos, and a river of ice eight thousand feet high called Nightingale, and how Cousin Juana drank a cup of tea standing on the bottom of the world under seven suns, and other fairy tales.

We were in for one severe shock when we reached Base at last. Teresa was pregnant. I must admit that my first response to the poor girl's big belly and sheepish look was anger—rage—fury. That one of us should have concealed anything, and such a thing, from the others! But Teresa had done nothing of the sort. Only those who had concealed from her what she most needed to know were to blame. Brought up by servants, with four years' schooling in a convent, and married at sixteen, the poor girl was still so ignorant at twenty years of age that she had thought it was "the cold weather" that made her miss her periods. Even this was not entirely stupid, for all of us on the Southern Journey had seen our periods change or stop altogether as we experienced increasing cold, hunger, and fatigue. Teresa's appetite had begun to draw general attention; and then she had begun, as she said pathetically, "to get fat." The others were worried at the thought of all the sledge-hauling she had done, but she flourished, and the only problem was her positively insatiable appetite. As well as could be determined from her shy references to her last night on the hacienda with her husband, the baby was due at just about the same time as the *Yelcho*, the twentieth of February. But we had not been back from the Southern Journey two weeks when, on February 14, she went into labor.

Several of us had borne children and had helped with deliveries, and anyhow most of what needs to be done is fairly self-evident; but a first labor can be long and trying, and we were all anxious, while Teresa was frightened out of her wits. She kept calling for her José till she was as hoarse as a skua.[7] Zoe lost all patience at last and said, "By God, Teresa, if you say 'José!' once more I hope you have a penguin!" But what she had, after twenty long hours, was a pretty little red-faced girl.

Many were the suggestions for that child's name from her eight proud midwife-aunts: Polita, Penguina, McMurdo, Victoria. . . . But Teresa announced, after she had had a good sleep and a large serving of pemmican, "I shall name her Rosa—Rosa del Sur," Rose of the South. That night we drank the last two bottles of Veuve Clicquot (having finished the pisco at 88° 30′ South) in toasts to our little Rose.

On the nineteenth of February, a day early, my Juana came down into Buenos Aires in a hurry. "The ship," she said, "the ship has come," and she burst into tears—she who had never wept in all our weeks of pain and weariness on the long haul.

Of the return voyage there is nothing to tell. We came back safe.

In 1912 all the world learned that the brave Norwegian Amundsen[8] had reached the South Pole; and then, much later, came the accounts of how Captain Scott and his men had come there after him, but did not come home again.

Just this year, Juana and I wrote to the captain of the *Yelcho*, for the newspapers have been full of the story of his gallant dash to rescue Sir Ernest Shackleton's men from Elephant Island, and we wished to congratulate him, and once more to thank him. Never one word has he breathed of our secret. He is a man of honor, Luis Pardo.

I add this last note in 1929. Over the years we have lost touch with one another. It is very difficult for women to meet, when they live so far apart as we do. Since Juana died, I have seen none of my old sledge-mates, though sometimes we write. Our little Rosa del Sur died of the scarlet fever when she was five years old. Teresa had many other children. Carlota took the veil[9] in Santiago ten years ago. We are old women now, with old husbands, and grown children, and grandchildren who might some day like to read about the Expedition. Even if they are rather ashamed of having such a crazy grandmother, they may enjoy sharing in the secret. But they must not let Mr. Amundsen know! He would be terribly embarrassed and disappointed. There is no need for him or anyone else outside the family to know. We left no footprints, even.

1982

7. Predatory sea-bird.
8. Roald Amundsen (1872–1928), Norwegian

explorer, first man to reach the South Pole.
9. I.e., became a nun.

ADRIENNE RICH
1929–

"I am an instrument," wrote Adrienne Rich in her poem *Planetarium* (1968), "in the shape / of a woman trying to translate pulsations / into images for the relief of the body / and the reconstruction of the mind." How she began to change herself into such an "instrument" is the subject of her famous autobiographical essay, *When We Dead Awaken: Writing as Re-Vision* (1972, 1976). Her life—first as "faculty wife" and mother, then as civil-rights and antiwar activist, then as lesbian in the women's liberation movement, teacher and lecturer—and her books—nine of poetry, two of prose—all demonstrate that, as the critic David Kalstone has said, work, for her, "is a jagged present, always pitched toward the future and change." It is this commitment to change, as much as the example of her life, that has made her a crucial figure in contemporary feminist experience.

"*From where does your strength come, you Southern Jew? / split at the root, raised in a castle of air?*" Rich asked in her poem *Sources* (1983). She was born in Baltimore, Maryland, on May 16, 1929, the elder of two sisters; the family was intellectual and well-off ("a castle of air"), but aware of being apart as Jews. She began to write carefully crafted poetry at an early age, above all for her taskmaster father. Her mother, who had studied to be a musician, gave over her life to her husband and children. Rich graduated from Radcliffe in 1951, "where I did not see a woman teacher for four years," and where, as she tells us in *When We Dead Awaken*, she studied exclusively the work of male poets. She also published her first book, *A Change of World*, in the prestigious Yale Younger Poets series. The volume was introduced by the British poet W. H. Auden, who admired her command of diction and meter: the poems, he says, "are neatly and modestly dressed, speak quietly but do not mumble, respect their elders but are not cowed by them, and do not tell fibs." Four years later, when she published *The Diamond Cutters*, the poet Randall Jarrell observed that "the poet whom we see behind" the poems "cannot help seeming to us a sort of princess in a fairy tale."

Meanwhile, "determined to have a 'full' woman's life," Rich had married Alfred Conrad, an economist at Harvard, in 1953, and would have three sons before she was thirty—"a radicalizing experience," as she later called it. Of this period she has said (in *Of Woman Born*, 1976), "I *knew* I had to remake my life; I did not then understand that we—the women of that academic community —as in so many middle-class communities of the period—were expected to fill both the part of the Victorian Lady of Leisure, the Angel in the House, and also of the Victorian cook, scullery maid, laundress, governess, and nurse." In *When We Dead Awaken*, she describes the long struggle to confront, for the first time, her condition as a woman, which resulted in *Snapshots of a Daughter-in-Law*, the title poem of her next book, eight difficult years later. The "modest princess," as Jarrell had defined her, was beginning to change.

In 1966, the Conrads moved to New York, where Alfred had taken a post at City College. There they both became increasingly involved in resistance activities against the Vietnam War. Rich taught in the SEEK Program for disadvantaged young people, and her poems as well as her view of her audience changed. Her vivid political concerns were the subject of many of the verses in *Leaflets* (1969) and *The Will to Change* (1971), while transformations in her poetic style reflected the continuing evolution of her political attitudes. Writing with a new urgency, she broke away from the tight verse forms and neat metrics that had marked much of her early work and began to produce poems that were characterized by a kind of improvisational intensity. As Kalstone usefully reminds us, Rich has also—ever since *Snapshots*—been dating each of her poems, "like entries in a journal where feelings are subject to continual revision." In this respect the title of her 1971 volume is significant: whereas she had called her first book *A Change of World*, as if dependent on changes outside of herself, now she took her title from the poet Charles Olson's line, "What does not change / is the will to change," for "the moment of change," as she wrote, "is the only poem." Rich's life was changing, too: in 1970 she left her marriage, "to do something very common, in my own way" (*A Valediction Forbidding Mourning*). Later that year, Alfred Conrad committed suicide.

In *Diving into the Wreck* (1973), Rich continued her explorations into both the exterior world and the interior self, as the title poem makes clear. The book also contains a poem called *The Phenomenology of Anger*, which articulates the way Rich has worked, in this and previous poems, to use the anger aroused by her political and cultural concerns for positive ends: "anger," as she told her friends the critics Barbara Charlesworth Gelpi and Albert Gelpi, "can be a kind of genius if it's acted on."

Diving into the Wreck received the National Book Award in 1974; Rich rejected the prize as an individual but accepted it, in a statement written with Audre Lorde and Alice Walker, two other nominees, in the name of all women. That same year, she became professor of English at City College and began the research for *Of Woman Born: Motherhood as Experience and Institution*. This prose work, published in 1976, employs personal journals, anthropology, political and medical history, as a background for meditation on a subject which, she said, she had not chosen: "it had, long ago, chosen me." The book examines the experience of motherhood, along with the myths that have been projected on that experience.

In 1976, as well, Rich published *Twenty-one Love Poems*, a verse sequence whose form recalls that of Elizabethan sonnet cycles in which male poets wrote hyperbolically of their lady-loves: these poems, however, record and explore a lesbian relationship. But the term "lesbian," for Rich, was "nothing so simple and dismissible as the fact that two women might go to bed together," as she wrote in *It Is the Lesbian in Us* (1976). Lesbianism, for her,

> was a sense of desiring oneself; choosing oneself; it was also a primary intensity between women, an intensity which in the world at large was trivialized, caricatured, or invested with evil.

> Even before I wholly knew I was a lesbian, it was the lesbian in me who pursued that elusive configuration. And I believe it is the lesbian in every woman

who is compelled by female energy, who gravitates toward strong women, who seeks a literature that will express that energy and strength. It is the lesbian in us who drives us to feel imaginatively, render in language, grasp, the full connection between woman and woman.

Characteristically, for Rich, the points of view expressed in the *Love Poems* and in this essay are significantly interrelated.

For the next three years, Rich was professor of English at Douglass College. She then left the academy and moved to a small town in western Massachusetts, where for several years she edited, with Michelle Cliff, the lesbian-feminist journal *Sinister Wisdom*. Her next volume of poems, *The Dream of a Common Language*, appeared in 1978; her most recent book, *A Wild Patience Has Taken Me This Far*, was published in 1981. In *Dream*, many of the poems are discourses or conversations, "explorations of women-to-woman relationships: mothers and daughters, sister-siblings, lover and lover, friendships, and the spirit-sisters of a collective past and future." But Rich's commitment to exploration and discourse has compelled her, as well, to write *Sources*, a long poem about her complex relationships with her now dead father and husband, and what they represent of her Jewish heritage. Significantly, then, as she prepared in 1984 a new volume selecting her poems from thirty-five years of work, she wrote, "one task for the nineteen- or twenty-year-old who wrote the earliest poems here, was to learn that she was neither unique nor universal, but a person in history, a woman and not a man, a white and also Jewish inheritor of a particular Western consciousness, from the making of which most women have been excluded."

Aunt Jennifer's Tigers

Aunt Jennifer's tigers prance across a screen,
Bright topaz denizens of a world of green.
They do not fear the men beneath the tree;
They pace in sleek chivalric certainty.

Aunt Jennifer's fingers fluttering through her wool   5
Find even the ivory needle hard to pull.
The massive weight of Uncle's wedding band
Sits heavily upon Aunt Jennifer's hand.

When Aunt is dead, her terrified hands will lie
Still ringed with ordeals she was mastered by.   10
The tigers in the panel that she made
Will go on prancing, proud and unafraid.

1951

Snapshots of a Daughter-in-Law

1

You, once a belle in Shreveport,
with henna-colored hair, skin like a peachbud,
still have your dresses copied from that time,
and play a Chopin prelude
called by Cortot: *"Delicious recollections*   5
float like perfume through the memory."[1]

Your mind now, moldering like wedding-cake,
heavy with useless experience, rich
with suspicion, rumor, fantasy,
crumbling to pieces under the knife-edge   10
of mere fact. In the prime of your life.

Nervy, glowering, your daughter
wipes the teaspoons, grows another way.

2

Banging the coffee-pot into the sink
she hears the angels chiding, and looks out   15
past the raked gardens to the sloppy sky.
Only a week since They said: *Have no patience.*

The next time it was: *Be insatiable.*
Then: *Save yourself; others you cannot save,*
Sometimes she's let the tapstream scald her arm,   20
a match burn to her thumbnail,

or held her hand above the kettle's snout
right in the woolly steam. They are probably angels,
since nothing hurts her anymore, except
each morning's grit blowing into her eyes.   25

3

A thinking woman sleeps with monsters.
The beak that grips her, she becomes. And Nature,
that sprung-lidded, still commodious
steamer-trunk of *tempora* and *mores*[2]
gets stuffed with it all: the mildewed orange-flowers,   30

---

1. A remark made by Alfred Cortot (1877–
1962), a well-known French pianist, in his
Chopin: 24 Preludes (1930); he is referring specifically to Chopin's Prelude No. 7, Andantino,
A Major. Frederic François Chopin (1810–
1849), Polish composer and pianist who settled
in Paris in 1831.
2. Literally, "times and customs"—alluding
perhaps to the Roman orator Cicero's famous
phrase, "O Tempora! O Mores!" ("Alas for the
degeneracy of our times and the low standard of
our morals!").

the female pills,[3] the terrible breasts
of Boadicea[4] beneath flat foxes' heads and orchids.

Two handsome women, gripped in argument,
each proud, acute, subtle, I hear scream
across the cut glass and majolica   35
like Furies[5] cornered from their prey:
The argument *ad feminam*,[6] all the old knives
that have rusted in my back, I drive in yours,
ma semblable, ma soeur![7]

4

Knowing themselves too well in one another: 40
their gifts no pure fruition, but a thorn,
the prick filed sharp against a hint of scorn . . .
Reading while waiting
for the iron to heat,
writing, *My Life had stood—a Loaded Gun—*[8]   45
in that Amherst pantry while the jellies boil and scum,
or, more often,
iron-eyed and beaked and purposed as a bird,
dusting everything on the whatnot every day of life.

5

Dulce ridens, dulce loquens,[9]   50
she shaves her legs until they gleam
like petrified mammoth-tusk.

6

When to her lute Corinna sings[1]
neither words nor music are her own;
only the long hair dipping   55
over her cheek, only the song
of silk against her knees
and these
adjusted in reflections of an eye.

Poised, trembling and unsatisfied, before   60
an unlocked door, that cage of cages,

---

3. Remedies for menstrual pain.
4. British queen in the time of the emperor
Nero; she led her people in a large though ultimately unsuccessful revolt against Roman rule.
5. Greek goddesses of vengeance.
6. Feminine version of the phrase *ad hominem*
(literally, "to the man"), referring to an argument directed not to reason but to personal prejudices and emotions.
7. The last line of Charles Baudelaire's poem
Au Lecteur addresses *"Hypocrite lecteur!—mon
semblable—mon frère!"* ("Hypocrite reader,
like me, my brother"); Rich here instead ad-

dresses "ma soeur" ("my sister").
8. "Emily Dickinson, *Complete Poems*, ed. T.
H. Johnson, 1960, p. 369" [Rich's note]; this is
the poem numbered 754 in the Johnson edition.
Amherst, referred to in the next line, is the town
where Dickinson lived her entire life (1830–
1886).
9. Latin, "sweetly laughing, sweetly speaking"
(from Horace, Ode XXII, *"Integer vitae,"* lines
23–24).
1. First line of a poem by Thomas Campion
(1567–1620).

tell us, you bird, you tragical machine—
is this *fertilisante douleur?*[2] Pinned down
by love, for you the only natural action,
are you edged more keen   65
to prise the secrets of the vault? has Nature shown
her household books to you, daughter-in-law,
that her sons never saw?

7

"To have in this uncertain world some stay
which cannot be undermined, is   70
of the utmost consequence."[3]
                                        Thus wrote
a woman, partly brave and partly good,
who fought with what she partly understood.
Few men about her would or could do more,   75
hence she was labeled harpy, shrew and whore.

8

"You all die at fifteen," said Diderot,[4]
and turn part legend, part convention.
Still, eyes inaccurately dream
behind closed windows blankening with steam.   80
Deliciously, all that we might have been,
all that we were—fire, tears,
wit, taste, martyred ambition—
stirs like the memory of refused adultery
the drained and flagging bosom of our middle years.   85

9

Not that it is done well, but
that it is done at all?[5] Yes, think
of the odds! or shrug them off forever.
This luxury of the precocious child,
Time's precious chronic invalid,—   90
would we, darlings, resign it if we could?
Our blight has been our sinecure:
mere talent was enough for us—
glitter in fragments and rough drafts.

Sigh no more, ladies.
                            Time is male   95

---

2. French, "fertilizing (or life-giving) sorrow."
3. "From Mary Wollstonecraft, *Thoughts on
the Education of Daughters*, London, 1787"
[Rich's note]. Wollstonecraft (1759–1797) is
best known for A *Vindication of the Rights of
Woman*.
4. Denis Diderot (1713–1784): French philosopher, encyclopedist, playwright, and critic.
" 'You all die at fifteen': 'Vous mourez toutes a

quinze ans,' from the *Lettres à Sophie Volland*,
quoted by Simone de Beauvoir in *Le Deuxième
Sexe*, Vol. II, pp. 123–24" [Rich's note].
5. An allusion to Samuel Johnson's remark to
Boswell: "Sir, a woman's preaching is like a dog's
walking on his hinder legs. It is not done well;
but you are surprised to find it done at all" (July
31, 1763).

and in his cups drinks to the fair.
Bemused by gallantry, we hear
our mediocrities over-praised,
indolence read as abnegation,   100
slattern thought styled intuition,
every lapse forgiven, our crime
only to cast too bold a shadow
or smash the mold straight off.

For that, solitary confinement,   105
tear gas, attrition shelling.
Few applicants for that honor.

10

       Well,
she's long about her coming, who must be
more merciless to herself than history.   110
Her mind full to the wind, I see her plunge
breasted and glancing through the currents,
taking the light upon her
at least as beautiful as any boy
or helicopter,[6]   115
        poised, still coming,
her fine blades making the air wince

but her cargo
no promise then:
delivered   120
palpable
ours.

1958–1960   1963

"I Am in Danger—Sir—"[7]

"Half-cracked"[8] to Higginson, living,
afterward famous in garbled versions,
your hoard of dazzling scraps a battlefield,
now your old snood

---

6. "She comes down from the remoteness of ages, from Thebes, from Crete, from Chichén-Itzá; and she is also the totem set deep in the African jungle; she is a helicopter and she is a bird; and there is this, the greatest wonder of all: under her tinted hair the forest murmur becomes a thought, and words issue from her breasts" (Simone de Beauvoir, *The Second Sex*, trans. H. M. Parshley, New York, 1953, p. 729). (A translation of the passage from *Le Deuxième Sexe*, Vol.

II, p. 574, cited in French by Rich.)
7. "See the *Letters of Emily Dickinson*, T. H. Johnson, ed., Vol. II, p. 409" [Rich's note]. In one of her letters to her "mentor," the editor Thomas Wentworth Higginson, Dickinson wrote, "You think my gait 'spasmodic'—I am in danger—Sir—You think me 'uncontrolled'—I have no Tribunal."
8. Higginson described Dickinson, in a letter, as "my partially cracked poetess at Amherst."

mothballed at Harvard[9] 5
and you in your variorum monument[1]
equivocal to the end—
who are you?

Gardening the day-lily,
wiping the wine-glass stems, 10
your thought pulsed on behind
a forehead battered paper-thin,

you, woman, masculine
in single-mindedness,
for whom the word was more 15
than a symptom—

a condition of being.
Till the air buzzing with spoiled language
sang in your ears
of Perjury 20

and in your half-cracked way you chose
silence for entertainment,
chose to have it out at last
on your own premises.

1964   1966

Planetarium

Thinking of Caroline Herschel (1750–1848)
astronomer, sister of William;[2] and others.

A woman in the shape of a monster
a monster in the shape of a woman
the skies are full of them

a woman   'in the snow
among the Clocks and instruments 5
or measuring the ground with poles'
in her 98 years to discover
8 comets

9. The Rare Books Library at Harvard has a collection of Dickinson manuscripts and memorabilia, including her "snood" (hairnet).
1. I.e., Thomas H. Johnson's three-volume *Poems of Emily Dickinson* (1955); a "variorum" edition contains all the variant readings of a text.
2. Astronomer (1738–1822) and discoverer of the planet Uranus; Caroline assisted him and became an astronomer in her own right.

she whom the moon ruled
like us   10
levitating into the night sky
riding the polished lenses

Galaxies of women, there
doing penance for impetuousness
ribs chilled   15
in those spaces   of the mind

An eye,

       'virile, precise and absolutely certain'
       from the mad webs of Uranusborg[3]

              encountering the NOVA[4]   20

every impulse of light exploding
from the core
as life flies out of us

       Tycho whispering at last
       'Let me not seem to have lived in vain'[5]   25

What we see, we see
and seeing is changing

the light that shrivels a mountain
and leaves a man alive

Heartbeat of the pulsar[6]   30
heart sweating through my body

The radio impulse
pouring in from Taurus[7]

      I am bombarded yet   I stand

I have been standing all my life in the   35
direct path of a battery of signals
the most accurately transmitted most
untranslatable language in the universe
I am a galactic[8] cloud so deep   so invo-

3. Or Uranienborg, "castle in the sky," the name of the observatory built by Tycho Brahe (1546–1601), Danish astronomer; the preceding phrase was one he used to describe his astronomical observations.
4. The "new Star" discovered in the constella-tion Cassiopeia by Brahe in 1573.
5. Brahe's last words.
6. A short-period variable galactic radio source.
7. Constellation in the Northern Hemisphere.
8. I.e., out of the Milky Way.

luted that a light wave could take 15   40
years to travel through me   And has
taken   I am an instrument in the shape
of a woman trying to translate pulsations
into images   for the relief of the body
and the reconstruction of the mind.   45

1968   1971

I Dream I'm the Death of Orpheus[9]

I am walking rapidly through striations of light and dark
thrown under an arcade.

I am a woman in the prime of life, with certain powers
and those powers severely limited
by authorities whose faces I rarely see.   5
I am a woman in the prime of life
driving her dead poet in a black Rolls-Royce
through a landscape of twilight and thorns.
A woman with a certain mission
which if obeyed to the letter will leave her intact.   10
A woman with the nerves of a panther
a woman with contacts among Hell's Angels[1]
a woman feeling the fullness of her powers
at the precise moment when she must not use them
a woman sworn to lucidity   15
who sees through the mayhem, the smoky fires
of these underground streets
her dead poet learning to walk backward against the wind
on the wrong side of the mirror

1968   1971

Diving into the Wreck

First having read the book of myths,
and loaded the camera,
and checked the edge of the knife-blade,
I put on

---

9. Legendary Greek poet and musician, who
descended into the underworld to recover his
dead wife Eurydice. In Jean Cocteau's film *Or-*
phée (1950) Death is a woman who comes for
Orpheus, riding in a Rolls Royce guarded by
motorcyclists in black leather jackets; she moves
through a mirror from the underworld to this
world. Other images in the poem (the "arcade,"
the "landscape of twilight and thorns") also derive from the film.
1. Tough motorcycle club in California.

the body-armor of black rubber 5
the absurd flippers
the grave and awkward mask.
I am having to do this
not like Cousteau[2] with his
assiduous team 10
aboard the sun-flooded schooner
but here alone.

There is a ladder.
The ladder is always there
hanging innocently 15
close to the side of the schooner.
We know what it is for,
we who have used it.
Otherwise
it's a piece of maritime floss 20
some sundry equipment.

I go down.
Rung after rung and still
the oxygen immerses me
the blue light 25
the clear atoms
of our human air.
I go down.
My flippers cripple me,
I crawl like an insect down the ladder 30
and there is no one
to tell me when the ocean
will begin.

First the air is blue and then
it is bluer and then green and then 35
black I am blacking out and yet
my mask is powerful
it pumps my blood with power
the sea is another story
the sea is not a question of power 40
I have to learn alone
to turn my body without force
in the deep element.
And now: it is easy to forget
what I came for 45
among so many who have always
lived here

2. Jacques Cousteau (1910–), French underwater explorer, author, and filmmaker.

swaying their crenellated[3] fans
between the reefs
and besides   50
you breathe differently down here.

I came to explore the wreck.
The words are purposes.
The words are maps.
I came to see the damage that was done   55
and the treasures that prevail.
I stroke the beam of my lamp
slowly along the flank
of something more permanent
than fish or weed   60

the thing I came for:
the wreck and not the story of the wreck
the thing itself and not the myth

the drowned face always staring
toward the sun   65
the evidence of damage
worn by salt and sway into this threadbare beauty
the ribs of the disaster
curving their assertion
among the tentative haunters.   70

This is the place.
And I am here, the mermaid whose dark hair
streams black, the merman in his armored body
We circle silently
about the wreck   75
we dive into the hold.
I am she: I am he

whose drowned face sleeps with open eyes
whose breasts still bear the stress
whose silver, copper, vermeil[4] cargo lies   80
obscurely inside barrels
half-wedged and left to rot
we are the half-destroyed instruments
that once held to a course
the water-eaten log   85
the fouled compass

---

3. Notched with rounded or scalloped projec-   4. Gilded metal.
tions.

We are, I am, you are
by cowardice or courage
the one who find our way
back to this scene   90
carrying a knife, a camera
a book of myths
in which
our names do not appear.

1972   1973

From a Survivor

The pact that we made was the ordinary pact
of men & women in those days

I don't know who we thought we were
that our personalities
could resist the failures of the race   5

Lucky or unlucky, we didn't know
the race had failures of that order
and that we were going to share them

Like everybody else, we thought of ourselves as special

Your body is as vivid to me   10
as it ever was: even more

since my feeling for it is clearer:
I know what it could and could not do

it is no longer
the body of a god   15
or anything with power over my life

Next year it would have been 20 years
and you are wastefully dead
who might have made the leap
we talked, too late, of making   20

which I live now
not as a leap
but a succession of brief, amazing movements

each one making possible the next

1972   1973

Power

Living   in the earth-deposits   of our history

Today a backhoe divulged   out of a crumbling flank of earth
one bottle   amber   perfect   a hundred-year-old
cure for fever   or melancholy   a tonic
for living on this earth   in the winters of this climate   5

Today I was reading about Marie Curie:[5]
she must have known she suffered   from radiation sickness
her body bombarded for years   by the element
she had purified
It seems she denied to the end   10
the source of the cataracts on her eyes
the cracked and suppurating skin   of her finger-ends
till she could no longer hold   a test-tube or a pencil

She died   a famous woman   denying
her wounds   15
denying
her wounds   came   from the same source as her power

1974   1978

From Twenty-one Love Poems

XI

Every peak is a crater. This is the law of volcanoes,
making them eternally and visibly female.
No height without depth, without a burning core,
though our straw soles shred on the hardened lava.
I want to travel with you to every sacred mountain   5
smoking within like the sibyl stooped over her tripod,
I want to reach for your hand as we scale the path,
to feel your arteries glowing in my clasp,
never failing to note the small, jewel-like flower
unfamiliar to us, nameless till we rename her,   10
that clings to the slowly altering rock—
that detail outside ourselves that brings us to
    ourselves,
was here before us, knew we would come, and sees
    beyond us.   15

5. Physicist and chemist (1867–1934) who, with her husband, Pierre, discovered radium.

(The Floating Poem, Unnumbered)

Whatever happens with us, your body
will haunt mine—tender, delicate
your lovemaking, like the half-curled frond
of the fiddlehead fern in forests
just washed by sun. Your traveled, generous thighs   5
between which my whole face has come and come—
the innocence and wisdom of the place my tongue
   has found there—
the live, insatiate dance of your nipples in my mouth—
your touch on me, firm, protective, searching
me out, your strong tongue and slender fingers   10
reaching where I had been waiting years for you
in my rose-wet cave—whatever happens, this is.

XXI

The dark lintels, the blue and foreign stones
of the great round rippled by stone implements
the midsummer night light rising from beneath
the horizon—when I said "a cleft of light"
I meant this. And this is not Stonehenge[6]   5
simply nor any place but the mind
casting back to where her solitude,
shared, could be chosen without loneliness,
not easily nor without pains to stake out
the circle, the heavy shadows, the great light.   10
I choose to be a figure in that light,
half-blotted by darkness, something moving
across that space, the color of stone
greeting the moon, yet more than stone:
a woman. I choose to walk here. And to draw this circle.   15

1974–1976   1976, 1978

Phantasia for Elvira Shatayev

(leader of a women's climbing team, all of whom died in a storm on
Lenin Peak, August 1974. Later, Shatayev's husband found and buried
the bodies.)

The cold felt cold until our blood
grew colder   then the wind
died down and we slept

6. A great prehistoric structure of stones set in a circle.

If in this sleep I speak
it's with a voice no longer personal   5
(I want to say   *with voices*)
When the wind tore   our breath from us at last
we had no need of words
For months   for years   each one of us
had felt her own *yes*   growing in her   10
slowly forming   as she stood at windows   waited
for trains   mended her rucksack   combed her hair
What we were to learn   was simply   what we had
up here   as out of all words   that *yes*   gathered
its forces   fused itself   and only just in time   15
to meet a No of no degrees
the black hole   sucking the world in

I feel you climbing toward me
your cleated bootsoles leaving   their geometric bite
colossally embossed   on microscopic crystals   20
as when I trailed you in the Caucasus
Now I am further
ahead   than either of us dreamed   anyone would be
I have become
the white snow packed like asphalt by the wind   25
the women I love   lightly flung   against the mountain
that blue sky
our frozen eyes unribboned   through the storm
we could have stitched that blueness   together   like a quilt

You come (I know this)   with your love   your loss   30
strapped to your body   with your tape-recorder   camera
ice-pick   against advisement
to give us burial in the snow   and in your mind
While my body lies out here
flashing like a prism   into your eyes   35
how could you sleep   You climbed here for yourself
we climbed for ourselves

When you have buried us   told your story
ours does not end   we stream
into the unfinished   the unbegun   40
the possible
Every cell's core of heat   pulsed out of us
into the thin air   of the universe
the armature of rock beneath these snows
this mountain   which has taken   the imprint of our minds   45
through changes elemental and minute
as those we underwent
to bring each other here
choosing ourselves   each other   and this life

whose every breath   and grasp   and further foothold   50
is somewhere   still enacted   and continuing

In the diary I wrote: *Now we are ready*
and each of us knows it   I have never loved
like this   I have never seen
my own forces so taken up and shared   55
and given back
After the long training   the early sieges
we are moving almost effortlessly in our love

In the diary as the wind   began to tear
at the tents over us   I wrote: 60
We know now we have always been in danger
down in our separateness
and now up here together   but till now
we had not touched our strength

In the diary torn from my fingers I had written: 65
What does love mean
what does it mean   "to survive"
A cable of blue fire ropes our bodies
burning together in the snow   We will not live
to settle for less   We have dreamed of this   70
all of our lives

1974   1978

Culture and Anarchy[7]

Leafshade stirring on lichened bark
                                        Daylilies
run wild, "escaped" the botanists call it
from dooryard to   meadow to roadside

Life-tingle of angled light
                        late summer
sharpening toward fall, each year more sharply

---

7. "The title is stolen from Matthew Arnold's collection of essays by the same name, first published in London, 1869. The sources for the voices of nineteenth-century women heard in this poem are as follows: Diaries of Susan B. Anthony, 1861; letter from Anthony to her sister, 1883, both from Ida Husted Harper, *The Life and Work of Susan B. Anthony* (Indianapolis and Kansas City: Bowen-Merrill, 1899); Jane Addams, *Twenty Years at Hull House* (New York: Macmillan, 1926); Elizabeth Barrett-Browning, letter to Anna Brownell Jameson, 1852, in Frederick Kenyon, ed., *The Letters of Elizabeth Barrett Browning* (New York: Macmillan, 1898), vol. 2; Ida Husted Harper, introduction to Susan B. Anthony and Ida Husted Harper, *The History of Woman Suffrage* (1902) vol. 4; Elizabeth Cady Stanton, speech 'On Solitude of Self,' in Anthony and Harper, *The History of Woman Suffrage*, vol. 4; Elizabeth Cady Stanton, letter to Susan B. Anthony, in Harper, *The Life and Work of Susan B. Anthony*, vol. 1." [Rich's note].

This headlong, loved, escaping life

Rainy days at the kitchen table typing,
heaped up letters, a dry moth's   10
perfectly mosaiced wings, pamphlets on rape,
forced sterilization, snapshots in color
of an Alabama woman still quilting in her nineties,
The Life and Work of Susan B. Anthony. . . .

> *I stained and varnished*   15
> *the library bookcase today and superintended*
> *the plowing of the orchard. . . .*
> *Fitted out a fugitive slave for Canada*
> *with the help of Harriet Tubman. . . .*
> *The women's committee failed*   20
> *to report. I am mortified to death for them. . . .*
> *Washed every window in the house today.*
> *Put a quilted petticoat in the frame.*
> *Commenced Mrs. Browning's Portuguese*
> *Sonnets. Have just finished*   25
> *Casa Guidi Windows, a grand poem*
> *and so fitting to our struggle. . . .*
> *To forever blot our slavery is the only*
> *possible compensation for this*
> *merciless war. . . .*

> *The all-alone feeling will creep over me. . . .*

Upstairs, long silence, then
again, the sudden torrent of your typing

Rough drafts we share, each reading
her own page over the other's shoulder   35
trying to see afresh

An energy I cannot even yet
take for granted: picking up a book
of the nineteenth century, reading there the name
of the woman whose book you found
in the old town Athenaeum   40
beginning to stitch together
Elizabeth Ellet
Elizabeth Barrett
Elizabeth Blackwell
Frances Kemble   45
Ida B. Wells-Barnett
Susan B. Anthony

On Saturday Mrs. Ford took us to Haworth,
the home of the Brontë sisters. . . .
A most sad day it was to me   50
as I looked into the little parlor where
the sisters walked up and down
with their arms around each other
and planned their novels. . . .
How much the world of literature has lost   55
because of their short and ill-environed lives
we can only guess. . . .

Anarchy of August: as if already
autumnal gases glowed in darkness underground
the meadows roughen, grow guttural   60
with goldenrod, milkweed's late-summer lilac,
cat-tails, the wild lily brazening,
dooryards overflowing in late, rough-headed
bloom: bushes of orange daisies, purple mallow,
the thistle blazing in her clump of knives,   65
and the great SUNFLOWER turns

Haze wiping out the hills. Mornings like milk,
the mind wading, treading water, the line of vision blind
the pages of the book cling to the hand
words hang in a suspension   70
the prism hanging in the windowframe
is blank
A stillness building all day long to thunder
as the weedpod swells and thickens
No one can call this calm   75

                    Jane Addams, marking time
                    in Europe: *During most*
                    of that time I was absolutely at sea
                    so far as any moral purpose was concerned
                    clinging only to the desire to live   80
                    in a really living world
                    refusing to be content
                    with a shadowy intellectual
                    or aesthetic reflection

finally the bursting of the sky   85
power, release
by sheets by ropes of water, wind
driving before or after
the book laid face-down on the table
spirit travelling the lines of storm   90

leaping the torrent   all that water
already smelling of earth

> Elizabeth Barrett to Anna Jameson:
> *. . . and is it possible you think*
> *a woman has no business with questions*   95
> *like the question of slavery?*
> *Then she had better use a pen no more.*
> *She had better subside into slavery*
> *and concubinage herself, I think, . . .*
> *and take no rank among thinkers and speakers.*   100

Early dark; still raining; the electricity
out. On the littered table
a transparent globe half-filled
with liquid light, the soaked wick quietly
drinking, turning to flame   105
that faintly stains the slim glass chimney:
ancient, fragile contrivance

light welling, searching the shadows

Matilda Joslyn Gage; Harriet Tubman;
Ida B. Wells-Barnett; Maria Mitchell;   110
Anna Howard Shaw; Sojourner Truth;
Elizabeth Cady Stanton; Harriet Hosmer,
Clara Barton; Harriet Beecher Stowe;
Ida Husted Harper; Ernestine Rose

and all those without names
because of their short and ill-environed lives

False dawn Gossamer tents in wet grass; leaflets
dissolving within hours,
spun of necessity and
le~~aving no~~ trace   120

The heavy volumes, calf, with titles in smooth
leather, red and black, gilt letters spelling;
THE HISTORY OF HUMAN SUFFERING

I brush my hand across my eyes
—this is a dream, I think—and read: 125
THE HISTORY OF WOMAN SUFFRAGE

> *of a movement*
> *for many years unnoticed*
> *or greatly misrepresented in the public press*
> *its records usually not considered*   130

of sufficient value to be
officially preserved

and conjure up again
THE HISTORY OF HUMAN SUFFERING
like bound back issues of a periodical   135
stretching for miles
OF HUMAN SUFFERING: borne,
tended, soothed, cauterized,
stanched, cleansed, absorbed, endured
by women   140

our records usually not considered
of sufficient value to be
officially preserved

> *The strongest reason*
> *for giving woman all the opportunities*   145
> *for higher education, for the full*
> *development of her forces of mind and body. . . .*
> *the most enlarged freedom of thought and action*
> *a complete emancipation*
> *from all the crippling influences of fear—*   150
> *is the solitude and personal*
> *responsibility*
> *of her own individual life.*

Late afternoon: long silence.
Your notes on yellow foolscap drift on the table   155
you go down to the garden to pick chard
while the strength is in the leaves
crimson stems veining upward into green
How you have given back to me
my dream of a common language   160
my solitude of self.
I slice the beetroots to the core,
each one contains a different landscape
of bloodlight filaments, distinct rose-purple
striations like the oldest   165
strata of a Southwestern canyon
an undiscovered planet laid open in the lens

> *I should miss you more than any other*
> *living being from this earth. . . .*
> *Yes, our work is one,*   170
> *we are one in aim and sympathy*
> *and we should be together. . . .*

When We Dead Awaken: Writing as Re-Vision (1971)[8]

The Modern Language Association is both marketplace and funeral parlor for the professional study of Western literature in North America. Like all gatherings of the professions, it has been and remains a "procession of the sons of educated men" (Virginia Woolf): a congeries of old-boys' networks, academicians rehearsing their numb canons in sessions dedicated to the literature of white males, junior scholars under the lash of "publish or perish" delivering papers in the bizarrely lit drawing-rooms of immense hotels: a ritual competition veering between cynicism and desperation.

However, in the interstices of these gentlemanly rites (or, in Mary Daly's words, on the boundaries of this patriarchal space),[9] some feminist scholars, teachers, and graduate students, joined by feminist writers, editors, and publishers, have for a decade been creating more subversive occasions, challenging the sacredness of the gentlemanly canon, sharing the rediscovery of buried works by women, asking women's questions, bringing literary history and criticism back to life in both senses. The Commission on the Status of Women in the Profession was formed in 1969, and held its first public event in 1970. In 1971 the Commission asked Ellen Peck Killoh, Tillie Olsen, Elaine Reuben, and myself, with Elaine Hedges as moderator, to talk on "The Woman Writer in the Twentieth Century." The essay that follows was written for that forum, and later published, along with the other papers from the forum and workshops, in an issue of College English *edited by Elaine Hedges ("Women Writing and Teaching," vol. 34, no. 1, October 1972). With a few revisions, mainly updating, it was reprinted in* American Poets *in 1976, edited by William Heyen (New York: Bobbs-Merrill, 1976). That later text is the one published here.*

The challenge flung by feminists at the accepted literary canon, at the methods of teaching it, and at the biased and astigmatic view of male "literary scholarship," has not diminished in the decade since the first Women's Forum; it has become broadened and intensified more recently by the challenges of black and lesbian feminists pointing out that feminist literary criticism itself has overlooked or held back from examining the work of black women and lesbians. The dynamic between a political vision and the demand for a fresh vision of literature is clear: without a growing feminist movement, the first inroads of feminist scholarship could not have been made; without the sharpening of a black feminist consciousness, black women's writing would have been

---

8. As Rich explains, this essay—written in 1971 —was first published in 1972 and then included in her volume *On Lies, Secrets, and Silence* (1978). At that time she added the introductory note reprinted here, as well as some notes, identified as "A.R., 1978."

9. "Mary Daly, *Beyond God the Father* (Boston: Beacon, 1971), pp. 40–41" [Rich's note].

left in limbo between misogynist black male critics and white feminists still struggling to unearth a white women's tradition; without an articulate lesbian/feminist movement, lesbian writing would still be lying in that closet where many of us used to sit reading forbidden books "in a bad light."

Much, much more is yet to be done; and university curricula have of course changed very little as a result of all this. What *is* changing is the availability of knowledge, of vital texts, the visible effects on women's lives of seeing, hearing our wordless or negated experience affirmed and pursued further in language.

Ibsen's *When We Dead Awaken* is a play about the use that the male artist and thinker—in the process of creating culture as we know it— has made of women, in his life and in his work; and about a woman's slow struggling awakening to the use to which her life has been put. Bernard Shaw wrote in 1900 of this play:

> [Ibsen] shows us that no degradation ever devized or permitted is as disastrous as this degradation; that through it women can die into luxuries for men and yet can kill them; that men and women are becoming conscious of this; and that what remains to be seen as perhaps the most interesting of all imminent social developments is what will happen "when we dead awaken."[1]

It's exhilarating to be alive in a time of awakening consciousness; it can also be confusing, disorienting, and plainful. This awakening of dead or sleeping consciousness has already affected the lives of millions of women, even those who don't know it yet. It is also affecting the lives of men, even those who deny its claims upon them. The argument will go on whether an oppressive economic class system is responsible for the oppressive nature of male/female relations, or whether, in fact, patriarchy—the domination of males—is the original model of oppression on which all others are based. But in the last few years the women's movement has drawn inescapable and illuminating connections between our sexual lives and our political institutions. The sleepwalkers are coming awake, and for the first time this awakening has a collective reality; it is no longer such a lonely thing to open one's eyes.

Re-vision—the act of looking back, of seeing with fresh eyes, of entering an old text from a new critical direction—is for women more than a chapter in cultural history: it is an act of survival. Until we can understand the assumptions in which we are drenched we cannot know ourselves. And this drive to self-knowledge, for women, is more than a

1. "G. B. Shaw, *The Quintessence of Ibsenism*   [Rich's note].
(New York: Hill & Wang, 1922), p. 139"

search for identity: it is part of our refusal of the self-destructiveness of male-dominated society. A radical critique of literature, feminist in its impulse, would take the work first of all as a clue to how we live, how we have been living, how we have been led to imagine ourselves, how our language has trapped as well as liberated us, how the very act of naming has been till now a male prerogative, and how we can begin to see and name—and therefore live—afresh. A change in the concept of sexual identity is essential if we are not going to see the old political order reassert itself in every new revolution. We need to know the writing of the past, and know it differently than we have ever known it; not to pass on a tradition but to break its hold over us.

For writers, and at this moment for women writers in particular, there is the challenge and promise of a whole new psychic geography to be explored. But there is also a difficult and dangerous walking on the ice, as we try to find language and images for a consciousness we are just coming into, and with little in the past to support us. I want to talk about some aspect of this difficulty and this danger.

Jane Harrison, the great classical anthropologist, wrote in 1914 in a letter to her friend Gilbert Murray:

> By the by, about "Women," it has bothered me often—why do women never want to write poetry about Man as a sex—why is Woman a dream and a terror to man and not the other way around? . . . Is it mere convention and propriety, or something deeper?[2]

I think Jane Harrison's question cuts deep into the myth-making tradition, the romantic tradition; deep into what women and men have been to each other; and deep into the psyche of the woman writer. Thinking about that question, I began thinking of the work of two twentieth-century women poets, Sylvia Plath and Diane Wakoski. It strikes me that in the work of both Man appears as, if not a dream, a fascination and a terror; and that the source of the fascination and the terror is, simply, Man's power—to dominate, tyrannize, choose, or reject the woman. The charisma of Man seems to come purely from his power over her and his control of the world by force, not from anything fertile or life-giving in him. And, in the work of both these poets, it is finally the woman's sense of *herself*—embattled, possessed—that gives the poetry its dynamic charge, its rhythms of struggle, need, will, and female energy. Until recently this female anger and this furious awareness of the Man's power over her were not available materials to the female poet, who tended to write of Love as the source of her suffering, and to view that victimization by Love as an almost inevitable fate. Or, like Mar-

2. "J. G. Stewart, *Jane Ellen Harrison: A Portrait from Letters* (London: Merlin, 1959), p. 140" [Rich's note].

ianne Moore and Elizabeth Bishop, she kept sexuality at a measured
and chiseled distance in her poems.

One answer to Jane Harrison's question has to be that historically
men and women have played very different parts in each others' lives.
Where woman has been a luxury for man, and has served as the
painter's model and the poet's muse, but also as comforter, nurse, cook,
bearer of his seed, secretarial assistant, and copyist of manuscripts, man
has played a quite different role for the female artist. Henry James repeats an incident which the writer Prosper Mérimée described, of how,
while he was living with George Sand,

> he once opened his eyes, in the raw winter dawn, to see his companion, in
> a dressing-gown, on her knees before the domestic hearth, a candle-stick
> beside her and a red *madras* round her head, making bravely, with her
> own hands the fire that was to enable her to sit down betimes to urgent pen
> and paper. The story represents him as having felt that the spectacle
> chilled his ardor and tried his taste; her appearance was unfortunate, her
> occupation an inconsequence, and her industry a reproof—the result of all
> which was a lively irritation and an early rupture.[3]

The specter of this kind of male judgment, along with the misnaming
and thwarting of her needs by a culture controlled by males, has created
problems for the woman writer: problems of contact with herself, problems of language and style, problems of energy and survival.

In rereading Virginia Woolf's *A Room of One's Own* (1929) for the
first time in some years, I was astonished at the sense of effort, of pains
taken, of dogged tentativeness, in the tone of that essay. And I recognized that tone. I had heard it often enough, in myself and in other
women. It is the tone of a woman almost in touch with her anger, who
is determined not to appear angry, who is *willing* herself to be calm,
detached, and even charming in a roomful of men where things have
been said which are attacks on her very integrity. Virginia Woolf is addressing an audience of women, but she is acutely conscious—as she
always was—of being overheard by men: by Morgan and Lytton and
Maynard Keynes[4] and for that matter by her father, Leslie Stephen.[5]
She drew the language out into an exacerbated thread in her determination to have her own sensibility yet protect it from those masculine

3. "Henry James, 'Notes on Novelists,' in *Selected Literary Criticism of Henry James*, Morris
Shapira, ed. (London: Heinemann, 1963), pp.
157–58" [Rich's note].
4. I.e., E. M. Forster, Lytton Strachey, and
John Maynard Keynes, all members of Woolf's
Bloomsbury circle.
5. "A. R., 1978: This intuition of mine was
corroborated when, early in 1978, I read the
correspondence between Woolf and Dame

Ethel Smyth (Henry W. and Albert A. Berg
Collection, The New York Public Library,
Astor, Lenox and Tilden Foundations); in a letter dated June 8, 1933, Woolf speaks of having
kept her own personality out of *A Room of One's
Own* lest she not be taken seriously: ' . . . how
personal, so will they say, rubbing their hands
with glee, women always are; *I even hear them as
I write*.' (Italics mine.)" [Rich's note].

presences. Only at rare moments in that essay do you hear the passion in her voice; she was trying to sound as cool as Jane Austen, as Olympian as Shakespeare, because that is the way the men of the culture thought a writer should sound.

No male writer has written primarily or even largely for women, or with the sense of women's criticism as a consideration when he chooses his materials, his theme, his language. But to a lesser or greater extent, every woman writer has written for men even when, like Virginia Woolf, she was supposed to be addressing women. If we have come to the point when this balance might begin to change, when women can stop being haunted, not only by "convention and propriety" but by internalized fears of being and saying themselves, then it is an extraordinary moment for the woman writer—and reader.

I have hesitated to do what I am going to do now, which is to use myself as an illustration. For one thing, it's a lot easier and less dangerous to talk about other women writers. But there is something else. Like Virginia Woolf, I am aware of the women who are not with us here because they are washing the dishes and looking after the children. Nearly fifty years after she spoke, that fact remains largely unchanged. And I am thinking also of women whom she left out of the picture altogether—women who are washing other people's dishes and caring for other people's children, not to mention women who went on the streets last night in order to feed their children. We seem to be special women here, we have liked to think of ourselves as special, and we have known that men would tolerate, even romanticize us as special, as long as our words and actions didn't threaten their privilege of tolerating or rejecting us and our work according to *their* ideas of what a special woman ought to be. An important insight of the radical women's movement has been how divisive and how ultimately destructive is this myth of the special woman, who is also the token woman. Every one of us here in this room has had great luck—we are teachers, writers, academicians; our own gifts could not have been enough, for we all know women whose gifts are buried or aborted. Our struggles can have meaning and our privileges—however precarious under patriarchy—can be justified only if they can help to change the lives of women whose gifts—and whose very being—continue to be thwarted and silenced.

My own luck was being born white and middle-class into a house full of books, with a father who encouraged me to read and write. So for about twenty years I wrote for a particular man, who criticized and praised me and made me feel I was indeed "special." The obverse side of this, of course, was that I tried for a long time to please him, or rather, not to displease him. And then of course there were other men—writers, teachers—the Man, who was not a terror or a dream but a liter-

WHEN WE DEAD AWAKEN   2049

ary master and a master in other ways less easy to acknowledge. And
there were all those poems about women, written by men: it seemed to
be a given that men wrote poems and women frequently inhabited
them. These women were almost always beautiful, but threatened with
the loss of beauty, the loss of youth—the fate worse than death. Or,
they were beautiful and died young, like Lucy and Lenore. Or, the
woman was like Maud Gonne,[6] cruel and disastrously mistaken, and
the poem reproached her because she had refused to become a luxury
for the poet.

A lot is being said today about the influence that the myths and
images of women have on all of us who are products of culture. I think
it has been a peculiar confusion to the girl or woman who tries to write
because she is peculiarly susceptible to language. She goes to poetry or
fiction looking for *her* way of being in the world, since she too has been
putting words and images together; she is looking eagerly for guides,
maps, possibilities; and over and over in the "words' masculine persuasive force" of literature she comes up against something that negates
everything she is about: she meets the image of Woman in books written by men. She finds a terror and a dream, she finds a beautiful pale
face, she finds La Belle Dame Sans Merci, she finds Juliet or Tess or
Salomé,[7] but precisely what she does not find is that absorbed, drudg-
ing, puzzled, sometimes inspired creature, herself, who sits at a desk
trying to put words together.

So what does she do? What did I do? I read the older women poets
with their peculiar keenness and ambivalence: Sappho, Christina Rossetti, Emily Dickinson, Elinor Wylie, Edna Millay, H. D. I discovered
that the woman poet most admired at the time (by men) was Marianne
Moore, who was maidenly, elegant, intellectual, discreet. But even in
reading these women I was looking in them for the same things I had
found in the poetry of men, because I wanted women poets to be the
equals of men, and to be equal was still confused with sounding the
same.

I know that my style was formed first by male poets: by the men I was
reading as an undergraduate—Frost, Dylan Thomas, Donne, Auden,
MacNeice, Stevens, Yeats. What I chiefly learned from them was
craft.[8] But poems are like dreams: in them you put what you don't know

6. In poems by William Wordsworth and Edgar
Allan Poe; Maud Gonne: Irish revolutionary activist, beautiful beloved of William Butler Yeats,
and subject of many of his poems.
7. *La Belle Dame Sans Merci*, "the beautiful
lady without pity," title of a poem by John Keats;
Juliet, tragic girl heroine of Shakespeare's play;
Tess of the D'Urbervilles, innocent doomed
heroine in Thomas Hardy's novel; Salomé,
dancer responsible for the killing of John the

Baptist in Oscar Wilde's play.
8. "A. R., 1978: Yet I spent months, at sixteen,
memorizing and writing imitations of Millay's
sonnets; and in notebooks of that period I find
what are obviously attempts to imitate Dickinson's metrics and verbal compression. I knew
H. D. only through anthologized lyrics; her epic
poetry was not then available to me." [Rich's
note].

you know. Looking back at poems I wrote before I was twenty-one, I'm startled because beneath the conscious craft are glimpses of the split I even then experienced between the girl who wrote poems, who defined herself in writing poems, and the girl who was to define herself by her relationships with men. "Aunt Jennifer's Tigers" (1951), written while I was a student, looks with deliberate detachment at this split.[9] In writing this poem, composed and apparently cool as it is, I thought I was creating a portrait of an imaginary woman. But this woman suffers from the opposition of her imagination, worked out in tapestry, and her lifestyle, "ringed with ordeals she was mastered by." It was important to me that Aunt Jennifer was a person as distinct from myself as possible —distanced by the formalism of the poem, by its objective, observant tone—even by putting the woman in a different generation.

In those years formalism was part of the strategy—like asbestos gloves, it allowed me to handle materials I couldn't pick up barehanded. A later strategy was to use the persona of a man, as I did in "The Loser" (1958):

> *A man thinks of the woman he once loved: first, after her*
> *wedding, and then nearly a decade later.*

> I
> I kissed you, bride and lost, and went
> home from that bourgeois sacrament,
> your cheek still tasting cold upon
> my lips that gave you benison
> with all the swagger that they knew—
> as losers somehow learn to do.

> Your wedding made my eyes ache; soon
> the world would be worse off for one
> more golden apple dropped to ground
> without the least protesting sound,
> and you would windfall lie, and we
> forget your shimmer on the tree.

> Beauty is always wasted: if
> not Mignon's song sung to the deaf,
> at all events to the unmoved.
> A face like yours cannot be loved
> long or seriously enough.
> Almost, we seem to hold it off.

> II
> Well, you are tougher than I thought.
> Now when the wash with ice hangs taut
> this morning of St. Valentine,

---

9. For the text of the poem, see above.

I see you strip the squeaking line,
your body weighed against the load,
and all my groans can do no good.

Because you are still beautiful,
though squared and stiffened by the pull
of what nine windy years have done.
You have three daughters, lost a son.
I see all your intelligence
flung into that unwearied stance.

My envy is of no avail.
I turn my head and wish him well
who chafed your beauty into use
and lives forever in a house
lit by the friction of your mind.
You stagger in against the wind.

I finished college, published my first book by a fluke, as it seemed to me, and broke off a love affair. I took a job, lived alone, went on writing, fell in love. I was young, full of energy, and the book seemed to mean that others agreed I was a poet. Because I was also determined to prove that as a woman poet I could also have what was then defined as a "full" woman's life, I plunged in my early twenties into marriage and had three children before I was thirty. There was nothing overt in the environment to warn me: these were the fifties, and in reaction to the earlier wave of feminism, middle-class women were making careers of domestic perfection, working to send their husbands through professional schools, then retiring to raise large families. People were moving out to the suburbs, technology was going to be the answer to everything, even sex; the family was in its glory. Life was extremely private; women were isolated from each other by the loyalties of marriage. I have a sense that women didn't talk to each other much in the fifties—not about their secret emptinesses, their frustrations. I went on trying to write; my second book and first child appeared in the same month. But by the time that book came out I was already dissatisfied with those poems, which seemed to me mere exercises for poems I hadn't written. The book was praised, however, for its "gracefulness"; I had a marriage and a child. If there were doubts, if there were periods of null depression or active despairing, these could only mean that I was ungrateful, insatiable, perhaps a monster.

About the time my third child was born, I felt that I had either to consider myself a failed woman and a failed poet, or to try to find some synthesis by which to understand what was happening to me. What frightened me most was the sense of drift, of being pulled along on a current which called itself my destiny, but in which I seemed to be losing touch with whoever I had been, with the girl who had experienced her own will and energy almost ecstatically at times, walking around a city or riding a train at night or typing in a student room. In a poem about my grandmother I wrote (of myself): "A young girl, thought sleeping, is certified dead" ("Halfway"). I was writing very little, partly from fatigue, that female fatigue of suppressed anger and loss of contact with my own being; partly from the discontinuity of female life with its attention to small chores, errands, work that others constantly undo, small children's constant needs. What I did write was unconvincing to me; my anger and frustration were hard to acknowledge in or out of poems because in fact I cared a great deal about my husband and my children. Trying to look back and understand that time I have tried to analyze the real nature of the conflict. Most, if not all, human lives are full of fantasy—passive day-dreaming which need not be acted on. But to write poetry or fiction, or even to think well, is not to fantasize, or to put fantasies on paper. For a poem to coalesce, for a character or an action to take shape, there has to be an imaginative transformation of reality which is no way passive. And a certain freedom of the mind is needed—freedom to press on, to enter the currents of your thought like a glider pilot, knowing that your motion can be sustained, that the buoyancy of your attention will not be suddenly snatched away. Moreover, if the imagination is to transcend and transform experience it has to question, to challenge, to conceive of alternatives, perhaps to the very life you are living at that moment. You have to be free to play around with the notion that day might be night, love might be hate; nothing can be too sacred for the imagination to turn into its opposite or to call experimentally by another name. For writing is re-naming. Now, to be maternally with small children all day in the old way, to be with a man in the old way of marriage, requires a holding-back, a putting-aside of that imaginative activity, and demands instead a kind of conservatism. I want to make it clear that I am *not* saying that in order to write well, or think well, it is necessary to become unavailable to others, or to become a devouring ego. This has been the myth of the masculine artist and thinker; and I do not accept it. But to be a female human being trying to fulfill traditional female functions in a traditional way *is* in direct conflict with the subversive function of the imagination. The word traditional is important here. There must be ways, and we will be finding out more and more about them, in which the energy of creation and the energy of relation can be united. But in those years I always felt the conflict as a failure of love in myself. I had thought I was choosing a full life: the life available to most men, in which sexuality, work, and parenthood could coexist. But I felt, at twenty-nine, guilt toward the people closest to me, and guilty toward my own being.

I wanted, then, more than anything, the one thing of which there was never enough: time to think, time to write. The fifties and early sixties were years of rapid revelations: the sit-ins and marches in the South, the Bay of Pigs,[1] the early antiwar movement, raised large questions—questions for which the masculine world of the academy around me seemed to have expert and fluent answers. But I needed to think for myself—about pacifism and dissent and violence, about poetry and society, and about my own relationship to all these things. For about ten years I was reading in fierce snatches, scribbling in notebooks, writing poetry in fragments; I was looking desperately for clues, because if there were no clues then I thought I might be insane. I wrote in a notebook about this time:

> Paralyzed by the sense that there exists a mesh of relationships—e.g., between my anger at the children, my sensual life, pacifism, sex (I mean sex in its broadest significance, not merely sexual desire)—an interconnectedness which, if I could see it, make it valid, would give me back myself, make it possible to function lucidly and passionately. Yet I grope in and out among these dark webs.

I think I began at this point to feel that politics was not something "out there" but something "in here" and of the essence of my condition.

In the late fifties I was able to write, for the first time, directly about experiencing myself as a woman. The poem was jotted in fragments during children's naps, brief hours in a library, or at 3:00 A.M. after rising with a wakeful child. I despaired of doing any continuous work at this time. Yet I began to feel that my fragments and scraps had a common consciousness and a common theme, one which I would have been very unwilling to put on paper at an earlier time because I had been taught that poetry should be "universal," which meant, of course, nonfemale. Until then I had tried very much *not* to identify myself as a female poet. Over two years I wrote a ten-part poem called "Snapshots of a Daughter-in-Law" (1958–1960), in a longer looser mode than I'd ever trusted myself with before. It was an extraordinary relief to write that poem. It strikes me now as too literary, too dependent on allusion; I hadn't found the courage yet to do without authorities, or even to use the pronoun "I"—the woman in the poem is always "she." One section of it, No. 2, concerns a woman who thinks she is going mad; she is haunted by voices telling her to resist and rebel, voices which she can hear but not obey.

2.
Banging the coffee-pot into the sink
she hears the angels chiding, and looks out

---

1. Site of a failed American invasion of Cuba, intended to overthrow the Castro regime.

past the raked gardens to the sloppy sky.
Only a week since They said: *Have no patience.*

The next time it was: *Be insatiable.*
Then: *Save yourself; others you cannot save.*
Sometimes she's let the tapstream scald her arm,
a match burn to her thumbnail,

or held her hand above the kettle's snout
right in the woolly steam. They are probably angels,
since nothing hurts her anymore, except
each morning's grit blowing into her eyes.

    The poem "Orion," written five years later, is a poem of reconnec-
tion with a part of myself I had felt I was losing—the active principle,
the energetic imagination, the "half-brother" whom I projected, as I
had for many years, into the constellation Orion. It's no accident that
the words "cold and egotistical" appear in this poem, and are applied to
myself.

Far back when I went zig-zagging
through tamarack pastures
you were my genius, you
my cast-iron Viking, my helmed
lion-heart king in prison.
Years later now you're young

my fierce half-brother, staring
down from that simplified west
your breast open, your belt dragged down
by an oldfashioned thing, a sword
the last bravado you won't give over
though it weighs you down as you stride

and the stars in it are dim
and maybe have stopped burning.
But you burn, and I know it;
as I throw back my head to take you in
an old transfusion happens again:
divine astronomy is nothing to it.

Indoors I bruise and blunder,
break faith, leave ill enough
alone, a dead child born in the dark.
Night cracks up over the chimney,
pieces of time, frozen geodes
come showering down in the grate.

A man reaches behind my eyes
and finds them empty
a woman's head turns away

from my head in the mirror
children are dying my death
and eating crumbs of my life.

Pity is not your forte.
Calmly you ache up there
pinned aloft in your crow's nest,
my speechless pirate!
You take it all for granted
and when I look you back

it's with a starlike eye
shooting its cold and egotistical spear
where it can do least damage.
Breathe deep! No hurt, no pardon
out here in the cold with you
you with your back to the wall.

The choice still seemed to be between "love"—womanly, maternal love, altruistic love—a love defined and ruled by the weight of an entire culture; and egotism—a force directed by men into creation, achievement, ambition, often at the expense of others, but justifiably so. For weren't they men, and wasn't that their destiny as womanly, selfless love was ours? We know now that the alternatives are false ones—that the word "love" is itself in need of re-vision.

There is a companion poem to "Orion," written three years later, in which at last the woman in the poem and the woman writing the poem become the same person. It is called "Planetarium," and it was written after a visit to a real planetarium, where I read an account of the work of Caroline Herschel, the astronomer, who worked with her brother William, but whose name remained obscure, as his did not.[2]

In closing I want to tell you about a dream I had last summer. I dreamed I was asked to read my poetry at a mass women's meeting, but when I began to read, what came out were the lyrics of a blues song. I share this dream with you because it seemed to me to say something about the problems and the future of the woman writer, and probably of women in general. The awakening of consciousness is not like the crossing of a frontier—one step and you are in another country. Much of woman's poetry has been of the nature of the blues song: a cry of pain, of victimization, or a lyric of seduction.[3] And today, much poetry by women—and prose for that matter—is charged with anger. I think we need to go through that anger, and we will betray our own reality if we try, as Virginia Woolf was trying, for an objectivity, a detachment,

2. For the text of the poem, see above.
3. "A. R., 1978: When I dreamed that dream, was I wholly ignorant of the tradition of Bessie Smith and other women's blues lyrics which transcended victimization to sing of resistance and independence?" [Rich's note].

that would make us sound more like Jane Austen or Shakespeare. We know more than Jane Austen or Shakespeare knew: more than Jane Austen because our lives are more complex, more than Shakespeare because we know more about the lives of women—Jane Austen and Virginia Woolf included.

Both the victimization and the anger experienced by women are real, and have real sources, everywhere in the environment, built into society, language, the structures of thought. They will go on being tapped and explored by poets, among others. We can neither deny them, nor will we rest there. A new generation of women poets is already working out of the psychic energy released when women begin to move out towards what the feminist philosopher Mary Daly has described as the "new space" on the boundaries of patriarchy.[4] Women are speaking to and of women in these poems, out of a newly released courage to name, to love each other, to share risk and grief and celebration.

To the eye of a feminist, the work of Western male poets now writing reveals a deep, fatalistic pessimism as to the possibilities of change, whether societal or personal, along with a familiar and threadbare use of women (and nature) as redemptive on the one hand, threatening on the other; and a new tide of phallocentric sadism and overt woman-hating which matches the sexual brutality of recent films. "Political" poetry by men remains stranded amid the struggles for power among male groups; in condemning U.S. imperialism or the Chilean junta the poet can claim to speak for the oppressed while remaining, as male, part of a system of sexual oppression. The enemy is always outside the self, the struggle somewhere else. The mood of isolation, self-pity, and self-imitation that pervades "nonpolitical" poetry suggests that a profound change in masculine consciousness will have to precede any new male poetic—or other—inspiration. The creative energy of patriarchy is fast running out; what remains is its self-generating energy for destruction. As women, we have our work cut out for us.

1972, 1976, 1978

4. "Mary Daly, *Beyond God the Father: To-* (Boston: Beacon, 1973)" [Rich's note].
wards a Philosophy of Women's Liberation

LORRAINE HANSBERRY
1930–1965

Born on the South Side of Chicago, Lorraine Hansberry was eight years old when her parents, Nannie and Carl A. Hansberry, decided to move into the affluent, segregated neighborhood of Hyde Park, where the young girl was threatened by cursing, spitting, and brick-wielding whites, and Nannie Hansberry patrolled the house with a gun. After the family was evicted by an Illinois court, Carl Hansberry (a real estate broker) employed NAACP lawyers to bring the issue before the Supreme Court, and in 1941 he won a landmark decision. The fact that Lorraine Hansberry attributed her father's early death to his embitterment over this struggle, however, lends special poignancy to the ending of her most famous work, *A Raisin in the Sun* (1959).

Already considered a classic play, *A Raisin in the Sun* is very much about Hansberry's parents' dream. When ten thousand dollars of insurance money comes to the widowed Lena ("Mama") Younger, she uses it to put a down payment on a spacious house in a white suburb, although her son Walter Lee wants to invest in a liquor store. Mama's conservative convictions and Walter Lee's stymied entrepreneurial desires have been criticized by a number of scholars for recapitulating two stereotypes, those of the domineering "matriarch" and the emasculated black "boy." But, as the critic Margaret B. Wilkerson has demonstrated and as the instant and enduring popularity of the play implies, Hansberry's sympathetic portrayal of both characters undercuts such stereotypes, for Mama willingly renounces her financial power over Walter Lee, just as he, forced by external circumstances to relinquish his enterprising schemes, refuses to sell out to white racists and decides instead to lead the family into the new house. No one knew better than Hansberry, however, what the Younger family had waiting for them there.

The brilliance of *A Raisin in the Sun* was recognized when, at twenty-nine years of age, Hansberry became the only black dramatist ever to win the Best Play of the Year Award of the New York Drama Critics. A stellar Broadway cast—including Claudia McNeil, Sidney Poitier, Ruby Dee, and Diana Sands—helped establish this young woman as the herald of modern black drama. Yet although Hansberry came from an intellectually distinguished family—her uncle, Leo Hansberry, was a pioneer scholar of African history—no one had expected her to turn the story of a black family into a commercial hit. Before coming to New York City in 1950, she had studied at the University of Wisconsin, Roosevelt College, and the School of the Art Institute of Chicago. Three years later, she married Robert Nemiroff, a music publisher and songwriter. Through her work as a journalist for the progressive paper *Freedom*, she met such major black intellectuals as Paul Robeson, W. E. B. DuBois, and Langston Hughes. When she completed *Raisin*, she had to raise money herself to stage the play in New Haven, Philadelphia, and Chicago before Broadway producers were convinced that it would have a successful run. Tragically, by the time her next play, *The Sign in Sidney Brustein's Window* (1965), appeared on Broadway, Hansberry was dying of cancer.

After Hansberry's death at thirty-four, a number of her works were edited and published posthumously by Robert Nemiroff. *To Be Young, Gifted and Black: Lorraine Hansberry in Her Own Words*, a biography drawn from letters, plays, and journals, appeared in 1969. A dramatic adaptation of this portrait of the artist became the longest running off-Broadway drama of 1969 and toured hundreds of college campuses. Three late plays—*Les Blancs*, *The Drinking Gourd*, and *What Use Are Flowers?*—were published in a 1972 volume, again by Nemiroff. Taken together and written before the emergence of the black nationalist and peace movements, they prove that Hansberry was visionary in her awareness of the complexity of Afro-American identity and of the threat of nuclear holocaust. Less well known, however, because still unpublished or uncollected, are Hansberry's equally insightful essays on women's issues.

While working at *Freedom*, Hansberry signed a snapshot of herself with the name "young Ida B.," a reference to the journalist Ida B. Wells, who crusaded against lynching. In 1957, before the appearance of Betty Friedan's *The Feminine Mystique* (1963), Hansberry hailed Simone de Beauvoir's *The Second Sex* as "the most important book in America," while her 1959 speech *The Negro Writer and His Roots: Towards a New Romanticism* ridiculed a culture that conditions people into believing that "women are idiots" and "people are white." As a black woman, Hansberry knew that she had to establish the validity of her protest against social injustice in an age when "any form of radicalism" was viewed as "latent protest against Mom, toilet-training, or heterosexuality." Two years later, she composed the ironically titled *In Defense of the Equality of Men*, an essay which is being printed here for the first time. Writing for a commercial magazine (*The Fair Sex*, which was going to be marketed as an intellectual *Mademoiselle* but which never came into being), she clearly found it necessary to modulate her tone. Yet the prospect of a decidedly middle-class, probably white, and possibly complacent readership did not inhibit Hansberry from protesting what she viewed as absurd assumptions about race and sex. A link between the nineteenth-century visionary Sojourner Truth and contemporary black dramatists like Adrienne Kennedy and Ntozake Shange, she believed that "one cannot live with sighted eyes and feeling heart and not know and react to the miseries which afflict this world."

In Defense of the Equality of Men

There is currently mushrooming in the land, a voluminous body of opinion in which scores of magazine writers, television panelists, and conference speakers with weighted eyebrows and ominous sentences allude to a peril in the Republic such as might herald a second coming of the British. Book, speech, and dissertation titles make the matter explicit: "Modern Woman—The Lost Sex";[1] "Trousered Mothers and Dishwashing Dads"; "American Man in a Woman's World"; etc.

Women, it is said, have ceased being, of all things, *women*. The conclusion has now been drawn in many circles that womanhood's historical insistence on ever-increasing measures of equality has resulted in women becoming "the imitations of men"—and, it is sometimes added, with something of a Calvinist shout: "Very bad imitations!"

The total theme of the alarm is that the "roles of the sexes are disappearing," and according to one analyst: "We are drifting toward a social

---

1. Title of an influential book (1947) by Marynia Farnham and Ferdinand Lundberg.

structure made up of he-women and she-men." Which, all will admit, if it is true, is pretty scary business!

To aid in the terror, some contemporary schools of psychoanalytical thought have been right in there giving leadership, guiding the worried along paths of "explanation" which have to do with their own preoccupations with "phallus envy," "castration complexes," and the rest of it: the inevitable result being that large numbers of people are now inclined to speak of the hardly new quest for universal equality as a neurotic disorder! "A disorder," we are informed, which seems to be sweeping other modern civilizations as well. For what else could be at the root, for example, of the "trouble in Australia," where a study reveals that sixty percent of the husbands in Melbourne reported that they help their wives with the dishes and yet another twenty-two percent get breakfast for the family in the mornings?

It appears that the horrified commentators have taken note of some very real disorders in modern life and deduced, rather automatically, that the causes must lie in the disintegration of our most entrenched traditions. Yet few of these seers, remarkably enough, seem to have seriously considered the alternative: that the problems might in fact lie in the lingering *life* of certain of our traditions.

There are, to be sure, other observers—a counter force holding their own—who suggest that, at best, the alarm is rooted in archaic concepts and, at worst, is in itself presumptuous as the dickens! Striking a note of rationality, they argue that what we are dealing with is the oldest phenomenon of the planet: *change*. The implication being that, contrary to negative legends, the human race possesses an incredible capacity to adapt itself, physically and psychologically, to its own ever-improving technological condition. Thus, modern man—modern urban man in particular—has begun to lose his *reasons* for the retention of formerly rigid notions of occupational, avocational, or even psychic categorizations which were apparently essential to his forebears in their more primitive social systems.

Affairs behind executive or professorial desks have tended to make "brute strength" irrelevant; World War II showed that virtually the same thing was true for the assembly line. And even if there were wild boars and such things still to be hunted for survival, the force required on the trigger of an automatic weapon is hardly the same once needed to pummel something with a stone axe. Increasingly, it is a human being's thinking capacity, not his bulk, which most equips him for modern life; whatever there once was of a realistic reason for physique determining labor is rapidly disappearing. In that light it is not extraordinary to behold the human attitude also changing. If modern trade unionism, white-collar labor, and the eight-hour day have contrived to diminish the laboring hours of the husband, it is to his credit that he has begun of his own volition to apply his new and hard-won leisure to sharing some part of his wife's still often twelve-to-fourteen-hour workday. It suggests that more than being a question for concern, it is one for celebration inasmuch as for the first time in history the family may now be growing toward a circumstantial reality which will allow it to become the truly harmonized, cooperative unit the human dream has always longed for it to be.

The current aspiration for the retention of ancient polarized concepts of strict divisions of labor reflects a social order which has effectively kept womanhood in her well known second-class situation, but which is less often criticised for imposing *upon males* the most unreasonable and unnecessary burdens of "superiority" and "authority," which, in fact, work only to insult their humanness and *deny the reality of their civilized state*.

Most apologists for a male supremacist culture do not dream that they savagely downgrade *men* in their efforts to provide them with a socially guaranteed place of privilege on the human scale. Yet, it was not romanticism alone, but also shimmering human practicality, which led the great humanist thinkers and artists of history to postulate, in poetry and prose, the ideas that, for instance, the rich must be inevitably degraded, in *human* terms, in a world where so many starve; that the educated remain, in large measure, untested for their wisdom when so few can read or write. And, certainly, in our own time, in the United States, it has become increasingly clear that white Americans are among the most compromised people on the face of the earth, because of their steady demonstration of their fear of running a non-handicapped race with their black countrymen.

If modern males are suffering from high percentages of ulcer, heart ailment, and a thousand-and-one nervous disorders, this might well be the burden imposed on their nervous systems from subjecting the reality of present-day life to the totems and taboos[2] of the primeval, medieval, and Victorian past. As in all questions where nonconformity carries heavy penalties, great numbers of males are naturally reticent to articulate their dissent from the "favors" heaped upon them. But, occasionally, usually in the more acceptable guise of "explaining" to women how to give artificially contrived sustenance to the male ego, the plea can be discerned. John Kord Lagemann provides an excellent example in an article in *Redbook*[3] entitled "The Male Sex": "The average male would be happy to drop the he-man pose if he didn't feel it would mean losing face as a man. It isn't because of his male instinct that he shies away from washing dishes, changing diapers, working under a woman boss or enjoying string quartets and modern art. It's

---

2. An allusion to a book by Sigmund Freud.   3. A popular women's magazine.

because he suspects that other people, including his wife—despite their prostestations to the contrary—still look on these chores and pastimes as 'unnatural' for a man."

We have all become so preoccupied with the "usurpation of the male's authority by the female" that we have neglected to analyse the vestigial presumption of that self-awarded authority; in so doing, we have also neglected to be outraged and shocked by the equally widespread assumption that men are in reality inferior human beings who have to be "propped up." The institutional acceptance of woman as a second-class human being carries its own dynamic which inadvertantly must, of necessity, present men as flagrantly unintelligent and somewhat dehumanized creatures. In "Making Marriage Work," featured in a widely read woman's magazine, the professor-analyst author tackled what might seem, to the excessively civilized, a resolved question: "*Should a Husband Strike His Wife?*" Bending to enlightenment, the writer opined, "It is impossible to condone such behavior." He then went on, however, to modify that bit of radical abandon by advising his readers that the "provocation" by wives was undoubtedly far greater than they realized. He offered the following directions to wives as to how best avoid their partially deserved beatings: "Gauge his mood; avoid arguments; indulge his whims; help him relax; share his burdens; keep love alive."

Now it must be clear that any group of human beings who *could* impose such saintly behavior on themselves at will, presumably after their own fairly exhausting and temper-rousing workdays, would be a superior lot indeed. But rather more outrageous is the assumption that men must be placated, outwitted, humored, and patronized like the family pet of whom we do not expect rationality and emotional control. One wonders how the writer supposes the criminal charge of "assault" ever found its way to the law books (evolved as it was by *male* representatives of social authority who could not apparently find within *themselves* justification for such behavior regardless of the sex of the victim).

Many men have cast wary eyes at the false crutches handed their sex: Shakespeare toyed freely with pompous assumptions of masculine superiority in several of his works; Mark Twain in his witticisms; Zola in his novels; Frederick Douglass from the antislavery podium; August Bebel in his great studies; John Stuart Mill in his essays; Whitman in his poetry; William Godwin in the stuff of his life and his writings; Karl Marx in the development of his economic theories; and, of course, in our own time, George Bernard Shaw in almost every wise and irreverent word he wrote. None of these figures found themselves diminished by an impending "threat" of the equality of women; most of them took the position that its accomplishment bode but another aspect of the liberation of *men*, in all senses of that mighty word.

It required, in fact, the industrial revolution and the winds of *égalité* from the American and French revolutions before history could thrust forward a woman to set down the case for the "Rights of Woman" in 1792. That the brilliant Jacobin Englishwoman Mary Wollstonecraft did so raised all the stormy outrage that the conservative thinkers of her time, male and female, could muster.[4] That the outrage has lingered and all but obscured her name and her book is a revealing indicator of the unfinished character of what is sometimes called, improperly, the "sexual revolution."

It is worth the digression to remark that whole generations have come to maturity believing that "feminists," upper- or lowercase, were strident, ludicrous creatures in incongruous costumes of feathered hats and oversized bloomers, who marched about, mainly through the saloons of the land, conking poor, peaceful, beer-guzzling males over the head. The image successfully erases a truer and more cogent picture. In deed and oratory, in their recognition of direct political action as opposed to parlor and bedroom wheedling of husbands and fathers as the true key to social transformation, American Feminist leaders, in particular, set a path that a grateful society will undoubtedly, in time, celebrate. The scope of their understanding of the evils of their times is summed up magnificently in a portion of a speech by Susan B. Anthony[5] as she addressed the court where she was being sentenced to jail for voting in the state of New York in 1879: "Your denial of my right to vote is the denial of my right of consent as one of the governed, the denial of my right of representation as one of the taxed, the denial of my right to a trial by a jury of my peers. . . . But, yesterday, the same man-made forms of law declared it a crime punishable with a $1,000 fine and six months' imprisonment, for you, or me, or any of us, to give a cup of cold water, a crust of bread, or a night's shelter to a panting fugitive as he was tracking his way to Canada. And every man or woman in whose veins coursed a drop of human sympathy violated that wicked law, reckless of consequences, and was justified in doing so. As then, the slaves who got their freedom must yet take it over, or under, or through the unjust forms of law, precisely so now must women, to get their right to a voice in this Government, take it; I have taken mine, and mean to take it at every possible opportunity."

This thrilling American patriot, not less than the Franklin radicals or the Jeffersonian democrats—and like scores of other Feminists—put her comfort, and in some brutal instances her very life, upon the line in order to do no more and certainly no less than enlarge the Constitu-

---

4. A reference to Mary Wollstonecraft's *Vindication of the Rights of Woman*, hardly known when Hansberry was writing this essay.

5. Susan B. Anthony (1820–1906), feminist and temperance worker.

tional promises of the American Republic to include the largest numbers of its people of both sexes. As is apparent from the text of her speech she and the other leaders of the Feminist movement (Lucretia Mott, Elizabeth Cady Stanton, Sojourner Truth, and Harriet Tubman, among many[6]) gave equally of their energies to the greatest issue of their time, the antislavery struggle, as their spiritual descendants were to give theirs, in another period, to prison reform, the eradication of illiteracy, conservation, and the crowning achievement of the abolition of child labor. We might well long for the day when the knowledge of the debt all society owes to organized womanhood in bringing the human race closer together, not pushing it farther apart, will still the laughter in the throats of the now uninformed.

Nonetheless, the lingering infamy in which "feminism" is generally held helps to explain the mystery of the widespread notion that the emancipation of the modern American woman is an accomplished fact, despite all evidence that she does not universally get "equal pay for equal work," that she is discouraged flatly in many occupations and government posts, and that her advance into executive positions is held stringently in check. It also helps to explain the eager mythology of the "tyranny of women" who allegedly rule over the home and even the wealth of the nation. In his book *America as a Civilization*, Max Lerner replies to the myth thusly: "The catch is that women hold their purchasing power largely as wives and have acquired their wealth mainly as widows; economically they are disbursing agents, not principals. . . . The real control of the wealth is in the hands of male trustees, lawyers and bankers. Few women are directors of big corporations, just as there are few who form government policies. . . . The minority of women who are powerful in their ownership of wealth are functionless with respect to their wealth, because they lack strategic control of it."

As for the "tyranny of Mom," Mom has been effectively toppled from her pedestal without society taking a second look to discover, if all those dreadful things are really true about her, *how* she got that way. Our culture has been slow to assume responsibility for ordinary women who have been told, starting with the cradle, that home and husband and children will be the sources of all reward in life, the foundations of all true happiness; it has had almost nothing to say about what she should do with herself when the children are grown and her husband is exhausted and bored with excessive attention, preoccupied as he is with other aspects of the world. Mah-jong and matinees in the city seem to

---

6. Lucretia Mott (1793–1880), feminist and reformer; Elizabeth Cady Stanton (1815–1902), feminist and co-worker with Anthony (see above); Sojourner Truth (c.1797–1883), former slave and feminist (see above); Harriet Tubman (1820?–1913), fugitive slave and rescuer of slaves.

her to lack purpose, and, whether we like it or not, that is the thing that human beings tend to crave: purpose.

The glaring fact is that Mom's life needs liberation as much as everyone else's. To say so is to be thought of as attacking the "bedrock of our way of life" and all of that, but it must be said. Mom must be allowed to think of herself, as Simone de Beauvoir has insisted brilliantly,[7] as a human being first and a mother second. Housewives insist on identifying themselves, to the frustration of the experts, as *"only* housewives" because, apparently, they perceive that housework and care of the family is but humankind's necessity of function: things requisite to existence; essentials which should permit us to . . . something else. We do not live to wash our faces and eat our meals, we wash our faces and eat our meals in order to participate in the world: in the classroom, in the factory, in the office, in the shop, in the national and international halls of government, in the scientific laboratory and in the studios where the arts are created. *The Feminists did not create the housewife's dissatisfaction with her lot—the Feminists came from out of the only place they could have come—the housewives of the world*! Satisfaction for the housewife, then, lies not in a new program of propaganda to exalt what remains, and always will remain, drudgery; but in the continued effort to reduce it to a hardly perceptible (if ever necessary) interruption in the pursuit of productive labors and creative expression. Satisfaction lies in allowing and encouraging men to freely assume more and more equal relationship with their children and their wives. The argument against this is difficult to understand since the more interesting the lives of the parents (both parents), the more interesting we have every right to expect future generations to be.

One area of the national life where the estate of woman is certainly never debated, and may be passed over quickly, is in the newest crop of "for Men Only" magazines where the whole thing has been resolved by reducing the entire relationship between men and women to a long and rather boring (not to add mechanical) tableaux of simple-minded and degrading animal essences. There, Woman the Child, Woman the Animal, Woman Upside-down-and-naked, Woman the Harem Fantasy—is replete with no conflict and no aspiration, the sex-object of men who cannot fathom the nature of their own delusions. The symptomatic fumes of Romanesque decay which exude from the same pages, where some of the world's most established writers are obliged, like musicians in a whorehouse, to appear between "playmates," is stultifying. To say so, however, is not to long for a new wave of "banning": that unfortunate practice always ends up by lynching the brave new thoughts in the world and merely covering up our social filth. It is

7. In her influential book *The Second Sex* (1949).

to long for a deeper appraisal of what we really want for ourselves and our children; to long for a cultural climate where Mrs. Roosevelt's[8] image will be projected to our young men and women with more regularity than the current courtesans.

It is, finally, a longing that another generation of girls will not have to grow up under a certain pragmatism which insists that men do not like "brainy" women. That notion is a terrible cheat to all, and one of the most belittling indictments of men. Girls are better taught to "reach for the stars" even in the matter of seeking or accepting a mate. The grim possibility is that she who "hides her brains" will, more than likely, end up with a mate who is only equal to a woman with "hidden brains" or none at all. That hardly gives the children of such a union a robust start in life. To hide one's mental capacity is a personality disfigurement which is even more grotesque than to flaunt it—which, at least, boasts *pride*.

There *are* men who find love affairs of stature enough. Men who neither desire nor tolerate affected vacuity: who wish mutuality and stimulation. In this writer's experience *those* are the exciting men; they exist. A woman who is willing to be herself and pursue her own potentials—it is time it was said—runs not so much the risk of loneliness as the challenge of exposure to more interesting men—and people in general.

There are, it is true, perhaps larger numbers of men who have mistaken WOMAN herself for the antagonism between the sexes. And, heaven knows, women passionately, often hysterically, feed the delusion. But it *is* a delusion: it is the codified barriers *between* the sexes that cause the trouble. Accordingly, some men are overwhelmed by the pressures upon their "masculinity" as they understand it, and move through life in perpetual states of agitation because, they are certain, of their persecution by women. Some of them, a few, become pathological woman-haters and proceed to hate all women: those in their "place" at home; and those "out of it." They have hatred of the women who will not sleep with them and hatred for those who will. Their hostility should not be met with hostility: they are frightened and pathetic human beings, as much caught in a social trap as their feminine counterparts who, it is true, get more and uglier attention in popular conversation and literature. These people are the most extreme victims of the *inequality* between the sexes; the rest of us are victims in other ways. In their situation, a member of the opposite sex does not have to open his or her mouth, they just have to *be* and they have offended. The weight is put upon our shoulders when we are hardly out of the womb, all of us,

8. Eleanor Roosevelt (1884–1962), widow of President Franklin D. Roosevelt and an influen- tial humanitarian in her own right.

and it is more than a little tragic, this exaggerated sense of alienation from one another that we are taught. Having paid such terrible prices for it, need we despair for its passing?

With the barriers should go many of the arbitrary definitions structured into our very language from out of the past: the classification of occupations, activities, roles by gender; the built-in assumption of maleness in certain words; the adjectives which still confuse and confine us in our thinking and make it possible for serious sociologists and psychologists to draw conclusions from "masculine-feminine" charts which are based on nothing other than conditioned concepts of what is "natural" (for whom?). Within that scale, male journalists, firemen and policemen have scored "less masculine" than other men, such as laborers, because of their occupational interest in "womanish" concerns like the human condition and saving lives! Among women, domestic servants score the highest "femininity" ratings of all—because of their demonstrated "interest" in cleaning house!

At the heart of this incredible mish-mash of nonsense is the time-honored but perfectly silly habit of attributing to a given set of universally human capacities, a qualification which implies that they are unique to one sex, race, or culture. (It is by that outrage that the people of Europe and their descendants in North America innocently go on speaking of objective adjectives such as "modern" or even "progressive" as if they were virtually synonymous with the geographical noun "the West"—to the wonder (and fury) of at least two-thirds of the world. Modern ideas, one notes, function elsewhere and, in some instances, these days especially, with greater acceleration. It was not "the West," after all, that first punctured space[9] and it is the women of Ghana who vote and the women of Switzerland who do not.) Thus, women who seek objective fulfillment as people are not trying to be "men" (or good or bad "imitations" of them)—they are trying to be successful human beings.

Finally, it is not to be doubted that our clinging to the habits of the past gives all of us some comfort in this thus-far-unexplained universe: it is always reassuring to think that our ancestors "did it" the same way. But in medicine the price of dogged superstition has too often been death, and in all human affairs there comes a time—to let go. With regard to the sexual connotations of words, can we all not think of what a dream will be realized for the race when the noun "soldier," for example, ceases to conjure up romantic notions of masculinity, but will instead have been unsexed and (at long last) put in its true place in history by the more accurate associations it recalls: "tragedy . . . the organized waste of human life and potential"?

9. A reference to the Russian launching of Sputnik, the first artificial satellite, in 1957.

None of this, we can rest easy, will dissipate the *true* distinction between the sexes: that will not happen because nobody *desires* for it to happen. The French have remarked on that matter for all time[1]—to which one need only add another *"Vive!"*

1961   1984

1. A reference to the French adage *"Vive la différence"*—"Long live the difference" (between men and women).

TONI MORRISON
1931–

Toni Morrison, who frequently focuses on black, midwestern communities in her fiction, was born Chloe Anthony Wofford and was raised by working-class parents in the small town of Lorain, Ohio. Because Ohio is on the Kentucky border while its main river leads to Canada, Morrison views it as a crucial boundary between North and South. With a history of underground railroad stations and cross burnings, abolitionist activism and Ku Klux Klan persecution, Ohio is, in Morrison's phrase, "neither plantation nor ghetto," and so it provides Morrison with an ideal site for her analysis of the struggle for freedom in which so many of her characters engage.

After graduating from Howard University in 1953, Morrison went north to Cornell University, where she received a master's degree for a thesis on the theme of suicide in the fiction of William Faulkner and Virginia Woolf. While she was teaching at Howard University, she married Harold Morrison, a Jamaican architect, and gave birth to two sons, Harold Ford and Slade. In 1964, she separated from her husband and moved with her children first to Syracuse, New York, and then to New York City, where she worked as a senior editor at Random House. There she helped shape such autobiographies as those by the activist Angela Davis and the boxer Muhammad Ali, as well as an anthology entitled *The Black Book* (1974), a collection that reflects the breadth of the "anonymous Black man's" experience in America. Recently, she has taught at Yale and Rutgers universities.

Morrison's four novels—*The Bluest Eye* (1970), *Sula* (1973), *Song of Solomon* (1977), and *Tar Baby* (1981)—have been widely acclaimed as evocative meditations on black cultural identity in contemporary America. Like Lucille Clifton and Toni Cade Bambara, artists she praises, Morrison has managed to convey racial pain without losing a sense of joy. She does this, in part at least, by exploring the unique cultural inheritence of black Americans in terms of universal ethical issues, namely, the tension between the individual and society and the problem of good and evil. Typical in her work, then, are "outlaw" figures, wild characters like Cholly Breedlove in *The Bluest Eye*, Sula in her second novel, and Guitar in *Song of Solomon*. Rebellious and defiant, such characters are often castigated as evil by the community and cast out as pariahs. For Morrison, however, their energy and verve can never be wholly rejected, for "evil is not an alien force." Just as important, Morrison sees the pariah as a paradigm of the black community, which is, she claims, "a pariah community" in white America.

As a philosophic novelist, Morrison is concerned with the texture of moral issues as they are experienced and understood by black men and women. At the same time, moreover, she is a writer obsessed with words, especially those words that exert a profound psychological impact on the lives of ordinary people. In her depiction of the violent Breedlove family in *The Bluest Eye*, the dead Peace children in *Sula*, and the wise woman Pilate in *Song of Solomon*, Morrison tries to convey the ironic juxtapositions between words and things as well as the equally mysterious connections between personality and the names bestowed upon it. What the word "blue" means to Picola Breedlove is as crucial for an understanding of *The Bluest Eye* as is the disjunction between the language of children's literature, which frames each of Morrison's chapters, and the reality of children's lives.

Although Morrison has portrayed the friendships between women in *Sula*, the search for ancestry in *Song of Solomon*, and the dynamics of eroticism in *Tar Baby*, *The Bluest Eye* focuses most explicitly on what it means to grow up black and female in twentieth-century America. The early maturity black girls must attain in order to cope with the violence that threatens them, the problem of confronting white standards of physical beauty that deem black racial traits "ugly," the ambivalent relationship between black women and the white women who employ or exploit them: all of these issues are analyzed in *The Bluest Eye*. In addition, Morrison explores the unique dynamics of the black family unit. Her language, which has "holes and spaces so the reader can come into [the story]," reflects her effort to encourage what she has called "participatory reading." An early reviewer responded to the metaphorical richness of *The Bluest Eye* by explaining that it is as much "history, sociology, folklore, nightmare, and music" as it is fiction.

The Bluest Eye

To the two who gave me life and the one who made me free

Here is the house. It is green and white. It has a red door. It is very pretty. Here is the family. Mother, Father, Dick, and Jane[1] live in the green-and-white house. They are very happy. See Jane. She has a red dress. She wants to play. Who will play with Jane? See the cat. It goes meow-meow. Come and play. Come play with Jane. The kitten will not play. See Mother. Mother is very nice. Mother, will you play with Jane?

---

1. Cliché names for the innocuous children depicted in pre–Sesame Street elementary school primers. The passage is a parody of such primers and their sanitized version of family life.

Mother laughs. Laugh, Mother, laugh. See Father. He is big and strong. Father, will you play with Jane? Father is smiling. Smile, Father, smile. See the dog. Bowwow goes the dog. Do you want to play with Jane? See the dog run. Run, dog, run. Look, look. Here comes a friend. The friend will play with Jane. They will play a good game. Play, Jane, play.

Here is the house it is green and white it has a red door it is very pretty here is the family mother father dick and jane live in the green-and-white house they are very happy see jane she has a red dress she wants to play who will play with jane see the cat it goes meow-meow come and play come play with jane the kitten will not play see mother mother is very nice mother will you play with jane mother laughs laugh mother laugh see father he is big and strong father will you play with jane father is smiling smile father smile see the dog bowwow goes the dog do you want to play do you want to play with jane see the dog run run dog run look look here comes a friend the friend will play with jane they will play a good game play jane play

Hereisthehouseitisgreenandwhiteitithasareddooritisveryprettyhereisth efamilymotherfatherdickandjaneliveinthegreenandwhitehousetheyar everyhappyseejaneshehasareddressshewantstoplaywhowillplaywithja neseethecatitgoesmeowmeowcomeandplaycomecomeplaywithjaneth ekittenwillnotplaywithjanemotherlaughslaughmotherlaughseefatherh eisbigandstrongfatherwillyouplaywithjanefatherissmilingsmilefathers mileseethedogbowwowgoesthedogdoyouwanttoplaywithjaneseethed ogrunrundogrunlooklookherecomesafriendthefriendwillplaywithjane theywillplayagoodgameplayjaneplay

Quiet as it's kept, there were no marigolds in the fall of 1941. We thought, at the time, that it was because Pecola was having her father's baby that the marigolds did not grow. A little examination and much less melancholy would have proved to us that our seeds were not the only ones that did not sprout; nobody's did. Not even the gardens fronting the lake showed marigolds that year. But so deeply concerned were we with the health and safe delivery of Pecola's baby we could think of nothing but our own magic: if we planted the seeds, and said the right words over them, they would blossom, and everything would be all right.

It was a long time before my sister and I admitted to ourselves that no green was going to spring from our seeds. Once we knew, our guilt was relieved only by fights and mutual accusations about who was to blame.

*For years I thought my sister was right: it was my fault. I had planted
them too far down in the earth. It never occurred to either of us that the
earth itself might have been unyielding. We had dropped our seeds in
our own little plot of black dirt just as Pecola's father had dropped his
seeds in his own plot of black dirt. Our innocence and faith were no
more productive than his lust or despair. What is clear now is that of all
of that hope, fear, lust, love, and grief, nothing remains but Pecola and
the unyielding earth. Cholly Breedlove is dead; our innocence too. The
seeds shriveled and died; her baby too.*

*There is really nothing more to say—except why. But since why is
difficult to handle, one must take refuge in how.*

Autumn

Nuns go by as quiet as lust, and drunken men and sober eyes sing in
the lobby of the Greek hotel. Rosemary Villanucci, our next-door
friend who lives above her father's café, sits in a 1939 Buick eating
bread and butter. She rolls down the window to tell my sister Frieda
and me that we can't come in. We stare at her, wanting her bread, but
more than that wanting to poke the arrogance out of her eyes and
smash the pride of ownership that curls her chewing mouth. When
she comes out of the car we will beat her up, make red marks on her
white skin and she will cry and ask us do we want her to pull her pants
down. We will say no. We don't know what we should feel or do if
she does, but whenever she asks us, we know she is offering us
something precious and that our own pride must be asserted by
refusing to accept.

School has started, and Frieda and I get new brown stockings and
cod-liver oil. Grown-ups talk in tired, edgy voices about Zick's Coal
Company and take us along in the evening to the railroad tracks
where we fill burlap sacks with the tiny pieces of coal lying about.
Later we walk home, glancing back to see the great carloads of slag
being dumped, red hot and smoking, into the ravine that skirts the
steel mill. The dying fire lights the sky with a dull orange glow. Frieda
and I lag behind, staring at the patch of color surrounded by black. It
is impossible not to feel a shiver when our feet leave the gravel path
and sink into the dead grass in the field.

Our house is old, cold, and green. At night a kerosene lamp lights
one large room. The others are braced in darkness, peopled by
roaches and mice. Adults do not talk to us—they give us directions.
They issue orders without providing information. When we trip and
fall down they glance at us; if we cut or bruise ourselves, they ask us

are we crazy. When we catch colds, they shake their heads in disgust at our lack of consideration. How, they ask us, do you expect anybody to get anything done if you all are sick? We cannot answer them. Our illness is treated with contempt, foul Black Draught, and castor oil that blunts our minds.

When, on a day after a trip to collect coal, I cough once, loudly, through bronchial tubes already packed tight with phlegm, my mother frowns. "Great Jesus. Get on in that bed. How many times do I have to tell you to wear something on your head? You must be the biggest fool in this town. Frieda? Get some rags and stuff that window."

Frieda restuffs the window. I trudge off to bed, full of guilt and self-pity. I lie down in my underwear, the metal in my black garters hurts my legs, but I do not take them off, for it is too cold to lie stockingless. It takes a long time for my body to heat its place in the bed. Once I have generated a silhouette of warmth, I dare not move, for there is a cold place one-half inch in any direction. No one speaks to me or asks how I feel. In an hour or two my mother comes. Her hands are large and rough, and when she rubs the Vicks salve on my chest, I am rigid with pain. She takes two fingers' full of it at a time, and massages my chest until I am faint. Just when I think I will tip over into a scream, she scoops out a little of the salve on her forefinger and puts it in my mouth, telling me to swallow. A hot flannel is wrapped about my neck and chest. I am covered up with heavy quilts and ordered to sweat, which I do—promptly.

Later I throw up, and my mother says, "What did you puke on the bed clothes for? Don't you have sense enough to hold your head out the bed? Now, look what you did. You think I got time for nothing but washing up your puke?"

The puke swaddles down the pillow onto the sheet—green-gray, with flecks of orange. It moves like the insides of an uncooked egg. Stubbornly clinging to its own mass, refusing to break up and be removed. How, I wonder, can it be so neat and nasty at the same time?

My mother's voice drones on. She is not talking to me. She is talking to the puke, but she is calling it my name: Claudia. She wipes it up as best she can and puts a scratchy towel over the large wet place. I lie down again. The rags have fallen from the window crack, and the air is cold. I dare not call her back and am reluctant to leave my warmth. My mother's anger humiliates me; her words chafe my cheeks, and I am crying. I do not know that she is not angry at me, but at my sickness. I believe she despises my weakness for letting the sickness "take holt." By and by I will not get sick; I will refuse to. But for now I am crying. I know I am making more snot, but I can't stop.

My sister comes in. Her eyes are full of sorrow. She sings to me:

"When the deep purple falls over sleepy garden walls, someone thinks of me. . . ."[2] I doze, thinking of plums, walls, and "someone."

But was it really like that? As painful as I remember? Only mildly. Or rather, it was a productive and fructifying pain. Love, thick and dark as Alaga syrup,[3] eased up into that cracked window. I could smell it—taste it—sweet, musty, with an edge of wintergreen in its base— everywhere in that house. It stuck, along with my tongue, to the frosted windowpanes. It coated my chest, along with the salve, and when the flannel came undone in my sleep, the clear, sharp curves of air outlined its presence on my throat. And in the night, when my coughing was dry and tough, feet padded into the room, hands repinned the flannel, readjusted the quilt, and rested a moment on my forehead. So when I think of autumn, I think of somebody with hands who does not want me to die.

It was autumn too when Mr. Henry came. Our roomer. Our roomer. The words ballooned from the lips and hovered about our heads—silent, separate, and pleasantly mysterious. My mother was all ease and satisfaction in discussing his coming.

"You know him," she said to her friends. "Henry Washington. He's been living over there with Miss Della Jones on Thirteenth Street. But she's too addled now to keep up. So he's looking for another place."

"Oh, yes." Her friends do not hide their curiosity. "I been wondering how long he was going to stay up there with her. They say she's real bad off. Don't know who he is half the time, and nobody else."

"Well, that old crazy nigger she married up with didn't help her head none."

"Did you hear what he told folks when he left her?"

"Uh-uh. What?"

"Well, he run off with that trifling Peggy—from Elyria. You know."

"One of Old Slack Bessie's girls?"

"That's the one. Well, somebody asked him why he left a nice good church woman like Della for that heifer. You know Della always did keep a good house. And he said the honest-to-God real reason was he couldn't take no more of that violet water Della Jones used. Said he wanted a woman to smell like a woman. Said Della was just too clean for him."

"Old dog. Ain't that nasty!"

"You telling me. What kind of reasoning is that?"

"No kind. Some men just dogs."

---

2. From the popular song "Deep Purple."   3. A molasses-like syrup.

"Is that what give her them strokes?"

"Must have helped. But you know, none of them girls wasn't too bright. Remember that grinning Hattie? She wasn't never right. And their Auntie Julia is still trotting up and down Sixteenth Street talking to herself."

"Didn't she get put away?"

"Naw. County wouldn't take her. Said she wasn't harming anybody."

"Well, she's harming me. You want something to scare the living shit out of you, you get up at five-thirty in the morning like I do and see that old hag floating by in that bonnet. Have mercy!"

They laugh.

Frieda and I are washing Mason jars. We do not hear their words, but with grown-ups we listen to and watch out for their voices.

"Well, I hope don't nobody let me roam around like that when I get senile. It's a shame."

"What they going to do about Della? Don't she have no people?"

"A sister's coming up from North Carolina to look after her. I expect she wants to get aholt of Della's house."

"Oh, come on. That's a evil thought, if ever I heard one."

"What you want to bet? Henry Washington said that sister ain't seen Della in fifteen years."

"I kind of thought Henry would marry her one of these days."

"That old woman?"

"Well, Henry ain't no chicken."

"No, but he ain't no buzzard, either."

"He ever been married to anybody?"

"No."

"How come? Somebody cut it off?"

"He's just picky."

"He ain't picky. You see anything around here you'd marry?"

"Well . . . no."

"He's just sensible. A steady worker with quiet ways. I hope it works out all right."

"It will. How much you charging?"

"Five dollars every two weeks."

"That'll be a big help to you."

"I'll say."

Their conversation is like a gently wicked dance: sound meets sound, curtsies, shimmies, and retires. Another sound enters but is upstaged by still another: the two circle each other and stop. Sometimes their words move in lofty spirals; other times they take strident leaps, and all of it is punctuated with warm-pulsed laughter—

like the throb of a heart made of jelly. The edge, the curl, the thrust of their emotions is always clear to Frieda and me. We do not, cannot, know the meanings of all their words, for we are nine and ten years old. So we watch their faces, their hands, their feet, and listen for truth in timbre.

So when Mr. Henry arrived on a Saturday night, we smelled him. He smelled wonderful. Like trees and lemon vanishing cream, and Nu Nile Hair Oil and flecks of Sen-Sen.[4]

He smiled a lot, showing small even teeth with a friendly gap in the middle. Frieda and I were not introduced to him—merely pointed out. Like, here is the bathroom; the clothes closet is here; and these are my kids, Frieda and Claudia; watch out for this window; it don't open all the way.

We looked sideways at him, saying nothing and expecting him to say nothing. Just to nod, as he had done at the clothes closet, acknowledging our existence. To our surprise, he spoke to us.

"Hello there. You must be Greta Garbo, and you must be Ginger Rogers."[5]

We giggled. Even my father was startled into a smile.

"Want a penny?" He held out a shiny coin to us. Frieda lowered her head, too pleased to answer. I reached for it. He snapped his thumb and forefinger, and the penny disappeared. Our shock was laced with delight. We searched all over him, poking our fingers into his socks, looking up the inside back of his coat. If happiness is anticipation with certainty, we were happy. And while we waited for the coin to reappear, we knew we were amusing Mama and Daddy. Daddy was smiling, and Mama's eyes went soft as they followed our hands wandering over Mr. Henry's body.

We loved him. Even after what came later, there was no bitterness in our memory of him.

She slept in the bed with us. Frieda on the outside because she is brave—it never occurs to her that if in her sleep her hand hangs over the edge of the bed "something" will crawl out from under it and bite her fingers off. I sleep near the wall because that thought *has* occurred to me. Pecola, therefore, had to sleep in the middle.

Mama had told us two days earlier that a "case" was coming—a girl who had no place to go. The county had placed her in our house for a few days until they could decide what to do, or, more precisely, until the family was reunited. We were to be nice to her and not fight. Mama didn't know "what got into people," but that old Dog

4. A breath-freshening candy.
5. Popular female film stars of the thirties, both noted for their beauty.

Breedlove had burned up his house, gone upside[6] his wife's head, and everybody, as a result, was outdoors.

Outdoors, we knew, was the real terror of life. The threat of being outdoors surfaced frequently in those days. Every possibility of excess was curtailed with it. If somebody ate too much, he could end up outdoors. If somebody used too much coal, he could end up outdoors. People could gamble themselves outdoors, drink themselves outdoors. Sometimes mothers put their sons outdoors, and when that happened, regardless of what the son had done, all sympathy was with him. He was outdoors, and his own flesh had done it. To be put outdoors by a landlord was one thing—unfortunate, but an aspect of life over which you had no control, since you could not control your income. But to be slack enough to put oneself outdoors, or heartless enough to put one's own kin outdoors—that was criminal.

There is a difference between being put *out* and being put out*doors*. If you are put out, you go somewhere else; if you are outdoors, there is no place to go. The distinction was subtle but final. Outdoors was the end of something, an irrevocable, physical fact, defining and complementing our metaphysical condition. Being a minority in both caste and class, we moved about anyway on the hem of life, struggling to consolidate our weaknesses and hang on, or to creep singly up into the major folds of the garment. Our peripheral existence, however, was something we had learned to deal with—probably because it was abstract. But the concreteness of being outdoors was another matter—like the difference between the concept of death and being, in fact, dead. Dead doesn't change, and outdoors is here to stay.

Knowing that there was such a thing as outdoors bred in us a hunger for property, for ownership. The firm possession of a yard, a porch, a grape arbor. Propertied black people spent all their energies, all their love, on their nests. Like frenzied, desperate birds, they overdecorated everything; fussed and fidgeted over their hard-won homes; canned, jellied, and preserved all summer to fill the cupboards and shelves; they painted, picked, and poked at every corner of their houses. And these houses loomed like hothouse sunflowers among the rows of weeds that were the rented houses. Renting blacks cast furtive glances at these owned yards and porches, and made firmer commitments to buy themselves "some nice little old place." In the meantime, they saved, and scratched, and piled away what they could in the rented hovels, looking forward to the day of property.

Cholly Breedlove, then, a renting black, having put his family outdoors, had catapulted himself beyond the reaches of human consideration. He had joined the animals; was, indeed, an old dog, a

6. Black slang: struck.

snake, a ratty nigger. Mrs. Breedlove was staying with the woman she worked for; the boy, Sammy, was with some other family; and Pecola was to stay with us. Cholly was in jail.

She came with nothing. No little paper bag with the other dress, or a nightgown, or two pair of whitish cotton bloomers. She just appeared with a white woman and sat down.

We had fun in those few days Pecola was with us. Frieda and I stopped fighting each other and concentrated on our guest, trying hard to keep her from feeling outdoors.

When we discovered that she clearly did not want to dominate us, we liked her. She laughed when I clowned for her, and smiled and accepted gracefully the food gifts my sister gave her.

"Would you like some graham crackers?"

"I don't care."

Frieda brought her four graham crackers on a saucer and some milk in a blue-and-white Shirley Temple cup. She was a long time with the milk, and gazed fondly at the silhouette of Shirley Temple's dimpled face. Frieda and she had a loving conversation about how cu-ute Shirley Temple was. I couldn't join them in their adoration because I hated Shirley. Not because she was cute, but because she danced with Bojangles, who was *my* friend, *my* uncle, *my* daddy, and who ought to have been soft-shoeing it and chuckling with me. Instead he was enjoying, sharing, giving a lovely dance thing with one of those little white girls whose socks never slid down under their heels. So I said, "I like Jane Withers."[7]

They gave me a puzzled look, decided I was incomprehensible, and continued their reminiscing about old squint-eyed Shirley.

Younger than both Frieda and Pecola, I had not yet arrived at the turning point in the development of my psyche which would allow me to love her. What I felt at that time was unsullied hatred. But before that I had felt a stranger, more frightening thing than hatred for all the Shirley Temples of the world.

It had begun with Christmas and the gift of dolls. The big, the special, the loving gift was always a big, blue-eyed Baby Doll. From the clucking sounds of adults I knew that the doll represented what they thought was my fondest wish. I was bemused with the thing itself, and the way it looked. What was I supposed to do with it? Pretend I was its mother? I had no interest in babies or the concept of motherhood. I was interested only in humans my own age and size, and could not generate any enthusiasm at the prospect of being a

7. Shirley Temple was an extremely popular child star of many films during the thirties. She often appeared with the black dancer Bill "Bojangles" Robinson, and with another child actress named Jane Withers. Withers portrayed nasty little girls who tried to get Temple into trouble.

mother. Motherhood was old age, and other remote possibilities. I learned quickly, however, what I was expected to do with the doll: rock it, fabricate storied situations around it, even sleep with it. Picture books were full of little girls sleeping with their dolls. Raggedy Ann dolls usually, but they were out of the question. I was physically revolted by and secretly frightened of those round moronic eyes, the pancake face, and orangeworms hair.

The other dolls, which were supposed to bring me great pleasure, succeeded in doing quite the opposite. When I took it to bed, its hard unyielding limbs resisted my flesh—the tapered fingertips on those dimpled hands scratched. If, in sleep, I turned, the bone-cold head collided with my own. It was a most uncomfortable, patently aggressive sleeping companion. To hold it was no more rewarding. The starched gauze or lace on the cotton dress irritated any embrace. I had only one desire: to dismember it. To see of what it was made, to discover the dearness, to find the beauty, the desirability that had escaped me, but apparently only me. Adults, older girls, shops, magazines, newspapers, window signs—all the world had agreed that a blue-eyed, yellow-haired, pink-skinned doll was what every girl child treasured. "Here," they said, "this is beautiful, and if you are on this day 'worthy' you may have it." I fingered the face, wondering at the single-stroke eyebrows; picked at the pearly teeth stuck like two piano keys between red bowline lips. Traced the turned-up nose, poked the glassy blue eyeballs, twisted the yellow hair. I could not love it. But I could examine it to see what it was that all the world said was lovable. Break off the tiny fingers, bend the flat feet, loosen the hair, twist the head around, and the thing made one sound—a sound they said was the sweet and plaintive cry "Mama," but which sounded to me like the bleat of a dying lamb, or, more precisely, our icebox door opening on rusty hinges in July. Remove the cold and stupid eyeball, it would bleat still. "Ahhhhhh," take off the head, shake out the sawdust, crack the back against the brass bed rail, it would bleat still. The gauze back would split, and I could see the disk with six holes, the secret of the sound. A mere metal roundness.

Grown people frowned and fussed: "You-don't-know-how-to-take-care-of-nothing. I-never-had-a-baby-doll-in-my-whole-life-and-used-to-cry-my-eyes-out-for-them. Now-you-got-one-a-beautiful-one-and-you-tear-it-up-what's-the-matter-with-you?"

How strong was their outrage. Tears threatened to erase the aloofness of their authority. The emotion of years of unfulfilled longing preened in their voices. I did not know why I destroyed those dolls. But I did know that nobody ever asked me what I wanted for Christmas. Had any adult with the power to fulfill my desires taken me seriously and asked me what I wanted, they would have known that I

did not want to have anything to own, or to possess any object. I
wanted rather to feel something on Christmas day. The real question
would have been. "Dear Claudia, what experience would you like on
Christmas?" I could have spoken up, "I want to sit on the low stool in
Big Mama's kitchen with my lap full of lilacs and listen to Big Papa
play his violin for me alone." The lowness of the stool made for my
body, the security and warmth of Big Mama's kitchen, the smell of the
lilacs, the sound of the music, and, since it would be good to have all
of my senses engaged, the taste of a peach, perhaps, afterward.

Instead I tasted and smelled the acridness of tin plates and cups
designed for tea parties that bored me. Instead I looked with loathing
on new dresses that required a hateful bath in a galvanized zinc tub
before wearing. Slipping around on the zinc, no time to play or soak,
for the water chilled too fast, no time to enjoy one's nakedness, only
time to make curtains of soapy water careen down between the legs.
Then the scratchy towels and the dreadful and humiliating absence of
dirt. The irritable, unimaginative cleanliness. Gone the ink marks
from legs and face, all my creations and accumulations of the day
gone, and replaced by goose pimples.

I destroyed white baby dolls.

But the dismembering of dolls was not the true horror. The truly
horrifying thing was the transference of the same impulses to little
white girls. The indifference with which I could have axed them was
shaken only by my desire to do so. To discover what eluded me: the
secret of magic they weaved on others. What made people look at
them and say, "Awwwww," but not for me? The eye slide of black
women as they approached them on the street, and the possessive
gentleness of their touch as they handled them.

If I pinched them, their eyes—unlike the crazed glint of the baby
doll's eyes—would fold in pain, and their cry would not be the sound
of an icebox door, but a fascinating cry of pain. When I learned how
repulsive this disinterested violence was, that it was repulsive because
it was disinterested, my shame floundered about for refuge. The best
hiding place was love. Thus the conversion from pristine sadism to
fabricated hatred, to fraudulent love. It was a small step to Shirley
Temple. I learned much later to worship her, just as I learned to
delight in cleanliness, knowing, even as I learned, that the change was
adjustment without improvement.

"Three quarts of milk. That's what was *in* that icebox yesterday.
Three whole quarts. Now they ain't none. Not a drop. I don't mind
folks coming in and getting what they want, but three quarts of milk!
What the devil does *anybody* need with *three* quarts of milk?"

The "folks" my mother was referring to was Pecola. The three of

us, Pecola, Frieda, and I, listened to her downstairs in the kitchen
fussing about the amount of milk Pecola had drunk. We knew she was
fond of the Shirley Temple cup and took every opportunity to drink
milk out of it just to handle and see sweet Shirley's face. My mother
knew that Frieda and I hated milk and assumed Pecola drank it out of
greediness. It was certainly not for us to "dispute" her. We didn't
initiate talk with grown-ups; we answered their questions.

Ashamed of the insults that were being heaped on our friend, we
just sat there: I picked toe jam, Frieda cleaned her fingernails with her
teeth, and Pecola finger-traced some scars on her knee—her head
cocked to one side. My mother's fussing soliloquies always irritated
and depressed us. They were interminable, insulting, and although
indirect (Mama never named anybody—just talked about folks and
some people), extremely painful in their thrust. She would go on like
that for hours, connecting one offense to another until all of the
things that chagrined her were spewed out. Then, having told
everybody and everything off, she would burst into song and sing the
rest of the day. But it was such a long time before the singing part
came. In the meantime, our stomachs jellying and our necks burning,
we listened, avoided each others's eyes, and picked toe jam or whatever.

" . . . I don't know what I'm suppose to be running here, a charity
ward, I guess. Time for me to get out of the *giving* line and get in the
getting line. I guess I ain't *supposed* to have nothing. I'm *supposed* to
end up in the poorhouse. Look like nothing I do is going to keep me
out of there. Folks just spend all their time trying to figure out ways to
send *me* to the poorhouse. I got about as much business with another
mouth to feed as a cat has with side pockets. As if I don't have trouble
enough trying to feed my own and keep out the poorhouse, now I got
something else in here that's just going to *drink* me on in there. Well,
naw, she ain't. Not long as I got strength in my body and a tongue in
my head. There's a limit to everything. I ain't got nothing to just
throw *away*. Don't *no*body need *three* quarts of milk. Henry *Ford*[8]
don't need three quarts of milk. That's just downright *sin*ful. I'm
willing to do what I can for folks. Can't nobody say I ain't. But this
has got to stop, and I'm just the one to stop it. Bible say watch as *well*
as pray.[9] Folks just dump they children off on you and go on 'bout
they business. Ain't nobody even *peeped* in here to see whether that
child has a loaf of bread. Look like they would just *peep* in to see
whether I had a loaf of bread to give her. But naw. That thought don't
cross they mind. That old trifling Cholly been out of jail *two* whole
days and ain't been here *yet* to see if his own child was 'live or dead.

---

8. American auto manufacturer (1863–1947).
9. The words of Jesus to his disciples the night
before his betrayal by Judas: "Watch and pray,
that ye enter not into temptation: the spirit indeed is willing, but the flesh is weak" (Matthew
26:41, Mark 14:38, Luke 21:36).

She could be *dead* for all he know. And that *mama* neither. What kind of something is that?"

When Mama got around to Henry Ford and all those people who didn't care whether she had a loaf of bread, it was time to go. We wanted to miss the part about Roosevelt and the CCC camps.[1]

Frieda got up and started down the stairs. Pecola and I followed, making a wide arc to avoid the kitchen doorway. We sat on the steps of the porch, where my mother's words could reach us only in spurts.

It was a lonesome Saturday. The house smelled of Fels Naphtha[2] and the sharp odor of mustard greens cooking. Saturdays were lonesome, fussy, soapy days. Second in misery only to those tight, starchy, cough-drop Sundays, so full of "don'ts" and "set'cha self downs."

If my mother was in a singing mood, it wasn't so bad. She would sing about hard times, bad times, and somebody-done-gone-and-left-me times. But her voice was so sweet and her singing-eyes so melty I found myself longing for those hard times, yearning to be grown without "a thin di-i-ime to my name." I looked forward to the delicious time when "my man" would leave me, when I would "hate to see that evening sun go down . . . " 'cause then I would know "my man has left this town." Misery colored by the greens and blues in my mother's voice took all of the grief out of the words and left me with a conviction that pain was not only endurable, it was sweet.

But without song, those Saturdays sat on my head like a coal scuttle, and if Mama was fussing, as she was now, it was like somebody throwing stones at it.

". . . and here I am poor as a bowl of yak-me. What do they think I am? Some kind of Sandy Claus? Well, they can just take they stocking down 'cause it *ain't* Christmas. . . ."

We fidgeted.

"Let's do something," Frieda said.

"What do you want to do?" I asked.

"I don't know. Nothing." Frieda stared at the tops of the trees. Pecola looked at her feet.

"You want to go up to Mr. Henry's room and look at his girlie magazines?"

Frieda made an ugly face. She didn't like to look at dirty pictures. "Well," I continued, "we could look at his Bible. *That's* pretty." Frieda sucked her teeth and made a *phttt* sound with her lips. "O.K., then. We could go thread needles for the half-blind lady. She'll give us a penny."

---

1. The Civilian Conservation Corps was established by President Franklin D. Roosevelt (1882–1945) during the depression to create jobs in forestry for the unemployed.
2. A very strong hand soap.

Frieda snorted. "Her eyes look like snot. I don't feel like looking at them. What *you* want to do, Pecola?"

"I don't care," she said. "Anything you want."

I had another idea. "We could go up the alley and see what's in the trash cans."

"Too cold," said Frieda. She was bored and irritable.

"I know. We could make some fudge."

"You kidding? With Mama in there fussing? When she starts fussing at the walls, you know she's gonna be at it all day. She wouldn't even let us."

"Well, let's go over to the Greek hotel and listen to them cuss."

"Oh, who wants to do *that*? Besides, they say the same old words all the time."

My supply of ideas exhausted, I began to concentrate on the white spots on my fingernails. The total signified the number of boyfriends I would have. Seven.

Mama's soliloquy slid into the silence ". . . Bible say feed the hungry. That's fine. That's all right. But I ain't feeding no elephants. . . . Anybody need three quarts of milk to *live* need to get out of here. They in the wrong place. What is this? Some kind of *dairy* farm?"

Suddenly Pecola bolted straight up, her eyes wide with terror. A whinnying sound came from her mouth.

"What's the matter with *you*?" Frieda stood up too.

Then we both looked where Pecola was staring. Blood was running down her legs. Some drops were on the steps. I leaped up. "Hey. You cut yourself? Look. It's all over your dress."

A brownish-red stain discolored the back of her dress. She kept whinnying, standing with her legs far apart.

Frieda said, "Oh. Lordy! I know. I know what that is!"

"What?" Pecola's fingers went to her mouth.

"That's ministratin'."

"What's that?"

"You know."

"Am I going to die?" she asked.

"Noooo. You won't die. It just means you can have a baby!"

"What?"

"How do you know?" I was sick and tired of Frieda knowing everything.

"Mildred told me, and Mama too."

"I don't believe it."

"You don't have to, dummy. Look. Wait here. Sit down, Pecola. Right here." Frieda was all authority and zest. "And you," she said to me, "you go get some water."

"Water?"

"Yes, stupid. Water. And be quiet, or Mama will hear you."

Pecola sat down again, a little less fear in her eyes. I went into the kitchen.

"What you want, girl?" Mama was rinsing curtains in the sink.

"Some water, ma'am."

"Right where I'm working, naturally. Well, get a glass. Not no clean one neither. Use that jar."

I got a Mason jar and filled it with water from the faucet. It seemed a long time filling.

"Don't nobody never want nothing till they see me at the sink. Then everybody got to drink water. . . ."

When the jar was full, I moved to leave the room.

"Where you going?"

"Outside."

"Drink that water right here!"

"I ain't gonna break nothing."

"You don't know what you gonna do."

"Yes, ma'am. I do. Lemme take it out. I won't spill none."

"You bed' not."

I got to the porch and stood there with the Mason jar of water. Pecola was crying.

"What you crying for? Does it hurt?"

She shook her head.

"Then stop slinging snot."

Frieda opened the back door. She had something tucked in her blouse. She looked at me in amazement and pointed to the jar. "What's that supposed to do?"

"You told me. You *said* get some water."

"Not a little old jar full. Lots of water. To scrub the steps with, dumbbell!"

"How was I supposed to know?"

"Yeah. How was you. Come on." She pulled Pecola up by the arm. "Let's go back here." They headed for the side of the house where the bushes were thick.

"Hey. What about me? I want to go."

"Shut uuuup," Frieda stage-whispered. "Mama will hear you. You wash the steps."

They disappeared around the corner of the house.

I was going to miss something. Again. Here was something important, and I had to stay behind and not see any of it. I poured the water on the steps, sloshed it with my shoe, and ran to join them.

Frieda was on her knees; a white rectangle of cotton was near her on the ground. She was pulling Pecola's pants off. "Come on. Step out of them." She managed to get the soiled pants down and flung them at me. "Here."

"What am I supposed to do with these?"

"Bury them, moron."

Frieda told Pecola to hold the cotton thing between her legs.

"How she gonna walk like that?" I asked.

Frieda didn't answer. Instead she took two safety pins from the hem of her skirt and began to pin the ends of the napkin to Pecola's dress.

I picked up the pants with two fingers and looked about for something to dig a hole with. A rustling noise in the bushes startled me, and turning toward it, I saw a pair of fascinated eyes in a dough-white face. Rosemary was watching us. I grabbed for her face and succeeded in scratching her nose. She screamed and jumped back.

"Mrs. MacTeer! Mrs. MacTeer!" Rosemary hollered. "Frieda and Claudia are out here playing nasty! Mrs. MacTeer!"

Mama opened the window and looked down at us.

"What?"

"They're playing nasty, Mrs. MacTeer. Look. And Claudia hit me 'cause I seen them!"

Mama slammed the window shut and came running out the back door.

"What you all doing? Oh. Uh-huh. Uh-huh. Playing nasty, huh?" She reached into the bushes and pulled off a switch. "I'd rather raise pigs than some nasty girls. Least I can slaughter *them*!"

We began to shriek. "No, Mama. No, ma'am. We wasn't! She's a liar! No, ma'am, Mama! No, ma'am, Mama!"

Mama grabbed Frieda by the shoulder, turned her around, and gave her three or four stinging cuts on her legs. "Gonna be nasty, huh? Naw you ain't!"

Frieda was destroyed. Whippings wounded and insulted her.

Mama looked at Pecola. "You too!" she said. "Child of mine or not!" She grabbed Pecola and spun her around. The safety pin snapped open on one end of the napkin, and Mama saw it fall from under her dress. The switch hovered in the air while Mama blinked. "What the devil is going on here?"

Frieda was sobbing. I, next in line, began to explain. "She was bleeding. We was just trying to stop the blood!"

Mama looked at Frieda for verification. Frieda nodded. "She's ministratin'. We was just helping."

Mama released Pecola and stood looking at her. Then she pulled both of them toward her, their heads against her stomach. Her eyes were sorry. "All right, all right. Now, stop crying. I didn't know.

Come on, now. Get on in the house. Go on home, Rosemary. The show is over."

We trooped in, Frieda sobbing quietly, Pecola carrying a white tail, me carrying the little-girl-gone-to-woman pants.

Mama led us to the bathroom. She prodded Pecola inside, and taking the underwear from me, told us to stay out.

We could hear water running into the bathtub.

"You think she's going to drown her?"

"Oh, Claudia. You so dumb. She's just going to wash her clothes and all."

"Should we beat up Rosemary?"

"No. Leave her alone."

The water gushed, and over its gushing we could hear the music of my mother's laughter.

That night, in bed, the three of us lay still. We were full of awe and respect for Pecola. Lying next to a real person who was really ministratin' was somehow sacred. She was different from us now—grown-up-like. She, herself, felt the distance, but refused to lord it over us.

After a long while she spoke very softly. "Is it true that I can have a baby now?"

"Sure," said Frieda drowsily. "Sure you can."

"But . . . how?" Her voice was hollow with wonder.

"Oh," said Frieda, "somebody has to love you."

"Oh."

There was a long pause in which Pecola and I thought this over. It would involve, I supposed, "my man," who, before leaving me, would love me. But there weren't any babies in the songs my mother sang. Maybe that's why the women were sad: the men left before they could make a baby.

Then Pecola asked a question that had never entered my mind. "How do you do that? I mean, how do you get somebody to love you?" But Frieda was asleep. And I didn't know.

HEREISTHEHOUSEITISGREENANDWH
ITEITHASAREDDOORITISVERYPRETT
YITISVERYPRETTYPRETTYPRETTYP

There is an abandoned store on the southeast corner of Broadway and Thirty-fifth Street in Lorain, Ohio. It does not recede into its background of leaden sky, nor harmonize with the gray frame houses and black telephone poles around it. Rather, it foists itself on the eye of the passerby in a manner that is both irritating and melancholy. Visitors who drive to this tiny town wonder why it has not been torn down, while pedestrians, who are residents of the neighborhood, simply look away when they pass it.

At one time, when the building housed a pizza parlor, people saw only slow-footed teen-aged boys huddled about the corner. These young boys met there to feel their groins, smoke cigarettes, and plan mild outrages. The smoke from their cigarettes they inhaled deeply, forcing it to fill their lungs, their hearts, their thighs, and keep at bay the shiveriness, the energy of their youth. They moved slowly, laughed slowly, but flicked the ashes from their cigarettes too quickly, too often, and exposed themselves, to those who were interested, as novices to the habit. But long before the sound of their lowing and the sight of their preening, the building was leased to a Hungarian baker, modestly famous for his brioche and poppy-seed rolls. Earlier than that, there was a real-estate office there, and even before that, some gypsies used it as a base of operations. The gypsy family gave the large plate-glass window as much distinction and character as it ever had. The girls of the family took turns sitting between yards of velvet draperies and Oriental rugs hanging at the windows. They looked out and occasionally smiled, or winked, or beckoned—only occasionally. Mostly they looked, their elaborate dresses, long-sleeved and long-skirted, hiding the nakedness that stood in their eyes.

So fluid has the population in that area been, that probably no one remembers longer, longer ago, before the time of the gypsies and the time of the teen-agers when the Breedloves lived there, nestled together in the storefront. Festering together in the debris of a realtor's whim. They slipped in and out of the box of peeling gray, making no stir in the neighborhood, no sound in the labor force, and no wave in the mayor's office. Each member of the family in his own cell of consciousness, each making his own patchwork quilt of reality—collecting fragments of experience here, pieces of information there. From the tiny impressions gleaned from one another, they created a sense of belonging and tried to make do with the way they found each other.

The plan of the living quarters was as unimaginative as a first-generation Greek landlord could contrive it to be. The large "store" area was partitioned into two rooms by beaverboard planks that did not reach to the ceiling. There was a living room, which the family called the front room, and the bedroom, where all the living was done. In the front room were two sofas, an upright piano, and a tiny artificial Christmas tree which had been there, decorated and dust-laden, for two years. The bedroom had three beds: a narrow iron bed for Sammy, fourteen years old, another for Pecola, eleven years old, and a double bed for Cholly and Mrs. Breedlove. In the center of the bedroom, for the even distribution of heat, stood a coal stove. Trunks, chairs, a small end table, and a cardboard "wardrobe" closet were placed around the walls. The kitchen was in the back of this apartment, a separate room. There were no bath facilities. Only a toilet bowl, inaccessible to the eye, if not the ear, of the tenants.

There is nothing more to say about the furnishings. They were anything but describable, having been conceived, manufactured, shipped, and sold in various states of thoughtlessness, greed, and indifference. The furniture had aged without ever having become familiar. People had owned it, but never known it. No one had lost a penny or a brooch under the cushions of either sofa and remembered the place and time of the loss or the finding. No one had clucked and said, "But I *had* it just a minute ago. I was sitting right there talking to . . ." or "Here it is. It must have slipped down while I was feeding the baby!" No one had given birth in one of the beds—or remembered with fondness the peeled paint places, because that's what the baby, when he learned to pull himself up, used to pick loose. No thrifty child had tucked a wad of gum under the table. No happy drunk—a friend of the family, with a fat neck, unmarried, you know, but God how he eats!—had sat at the piano and played "You Are My Sunshine." No young girl had stared at the tiny Christmas tree and remembered when she had decorated it, or wondered if that blue ball was going to hold, or if HE would ever come back to see it.

There were no memories among those pieces. Certainly no memories to be cherished. Occasionally an item provoked a physical reaction: an increase of acid irritation in the upper intestinal tract, a light flush of perspiration at the back of the neck as circumstances surrounding the piece of furniture were recalled. The sofa, for example. It had been purchased new, but the fabric had split straight across the back by the time it was delivered. The store would not take the responsibility. . . .

"Looka here, buddy. It was O.K. when I put it on the truck. The store can't do anything about it once it's on the truck. . . ." Listerine and Lucky Strike breath.

"But I don't want no tore couch if'n it's bought new." Pleading eyes and tightened testicles.

"Tough shit, buddy. *Your* tough shit. . . ."

You could hate a sofa, of course—that is, if you could hate a sofa. But it didn't matter. You still had to get together $4.80 a month. If you had to pay $4.80 a month for a sofa that started off split, no good, and humiliating—you couldn't take any joy in owning it. And the joylessness stank, pervading everything. The stink of it kept you from painting the beaverboard walls; from getting a matching piece of material for the chair; even from sewing up the split, which became a gash, which became a gaping chasm that exposed the cheap frame and cheaper upholstery. It withheld the refreshment in a sleep slept on it. It imposed a furtiveness on the loving done on it. Like a sore tooth that is not content to throb in isolation, but must diffuse its own pain to other parts of the body—making breathing difficult, vision limited, nerves unsettled, so a hated piece of furniture produces a fretful malaise that asserts itself throughout the house and limits the delights of things not related to it.

The only living thing in the Breedloves' house was the coal stove, which lived independently of everything and everyone, its fire being "out," "banked," or "up" at its own discretion, in spite of the fact that the family fed it and knew all the details of its regimen: sprinkle, do not dump, not too much. . . . The fire seemed to live, go down, or die according to its own schemata. In the morning, however, it always saw fit to die.

HEREISTHEFAMILYMOTHERFATHER
DICKANDJANETHEYLIVEINTHEGREE
NANDWHITEHOUSETHEYAREVERYH

The Breedloves did not live in a storefront because they were having temporary difficulty adjusting to the cutbacks at the plant. They lived there because they were poor and black, and they stayed there because they believed they were ugly. Although their poverty was traditional and stultifying, it was not unique. But their ugliness was unique. No one could have convinced them that they were not relentlessly and aggressively ugly. Except for the father, Cholly, whose ugliness (the result of despair, dissipation, and violence directed toward petty things and weak people) was behavior, the rest of the family—Mrs. Breedlove, Sammy Breedlove, and Pecola Breedlove—wore their ugliness, put it on, so to speak, although it did not belong to them. The eyes, the small eyes set closely together under narrow foreheads. The low, irregular hairlines, which seemed even more irregular in contrast to the straight, heavy eyebrows which nearly met. Keen but crooked noses, with insolent nostrils. They had high cheekbones, and their ears turned forward. Shapely lips which called attention not to themselves but to the rest of the face. You looked at them and wondered why they were so ugly; you looked closely and could not find the source. Then you realized that it came from conviction, their conviction. It was as though some mysterious all-knowing master had given each one a cloak of ugliness to wear, and they had each accepted it without question. The master had said, "You are ugly people." They had looked about themselves and saw nothing to contradict the statement: saw, in fact, support for it leaning at them from every billboard, every movie, every glance. "Yes," they had said. "You are right." And they took the ugliness in their hands, threw it as a mantle over them, and went about the world with it. Dealing with it each according to his way. Mrs. Breedlove handled hers as an actor does a prop: for the articulation of character, for support of a role she frequently imagined was hers—martyrdom. Sammy used his as a weapon to cause others pain. He adjusted his behavior to it, chose his companions on the basis of it: people who could be fascinated, even intimidated by it. And Pecola. She hid behind hers. Concealed, veiled, eclipsed—peeping out from behind the shroud very seldom, and then only to yearn for the return of her mask.

This family, on a Saturday morning in October, began, one by one, to stir out of their dreams of affluence and vengeance into the anonymous misery of their storefront.

Mrs. Breedlove slipped noiselessly out of bed, put a sweater on over her nightgown (which was an old day dress), and walked toward the kitchen. Her one good foot made hard, bony sounds; the twisted one whispered on the linoleum. In the kitchen she made noises with doors, faucets, and pans. The noises were hollow, but the threats they implied were not. Pecola opened her eyes and lay staring at the dead coal stove. Cholly mumbled, thrashed about in the bed for a minute, and then was quiet.

Even from where Pecola lay, she could smell Cholly's whiskey. The noises in the kitchen became louder and less hollow. There was direction and purpose in Mrs. Breedlove's movements that had nothing to do with the preparation of breakfast. This awareness, supported by ample evidence from the past, made Pecola tighten her stomach muscles and ration her breath.

Cholly had come home drunk. Unfortunately he had been too drunk to quarrel, so the whole business would have to erupt this morning. Because it had not taken place immediately, the oncoming fight would lack spontaneity; it would be calculated, uninspired, and deadly.

Mrs. Breedlove came swiftly into the room and stood at the foot of the bed where Cholly lay.

"I need some coal in this house."

Cholly did not move.

"Hear me?" Mrs. Breedlove jabbed Cholly's foot.

Cholly opened his eyes slowly. They were red and menacing. With no exception, Cholly had the meanest eyes in town.

"Awwwwww, woman!"

"I said I need some coal. It's as cold as a witch's tit in this house. Your whiskey ass wouldn't feel hellfire, but I'm cold. I got to do a lot of things, but I ain't got to freeze."

"Leave me 'lone."

"Not until you get me some coal. If working like a mule don't give me the right to be warm, what am I doing it for? You sure ain't bringing in nothing. If it was left up to you, we'd all be dead. . . . . ." Her voice was like an earache in the brain. " . . . If you think I'm going to wade out in the cold and get it myself, you'd better think again."

"I don't give a shit how you get it." A bubble of violence burst in his throat.

"You going to get your drunk self out of that bed and get me some coal or not?"

Silence.

"Cholly!"

Silence.

"Don't try me this morning, man. You say one more word, and I'll split you open!"

Silence.

"All right. All right. But if I sneeze once, just once, God help your butt!"

Sammy was awake now too, but pretending to be asleep. Pecola still held her stomach muscles taut and conserved her breath. They all knew that Mrs. Breedlove could have, would have, and had, gotten coal from the shed, or that Sammy or Pecola could be directed to get it. But the unquarreled evening hung like the first note of a dirge in sullenly expectant air. An escapade of drunkenness, no matter how routine, had its own ceremonial close. The tiny, undistinguished days that Mrs. Breedlove lived were identified, grouped, and classed by these quarrels. They gave substance to the minutes and hours otherwise dim and unrecalled. They relieved the tiresomeness of poverty, gave grandeur to the dead rooms. In these violent breaks in routine that were themselves routine, she could display the style and imagination of what she believed to be her own true self. To deprive her of these fights was to deprive her of all the zest and reasonableness of life. Cholly, by his habitual drunkenness and orneriness, provided them both with the material they needed to make their lives tolerable. Mrs. Breedlove considered herself an upright and Christian woman, burdened with a no-count man, whom God wanted her to punish. (Cholly was beyond redemption, of course, and redemption was hardly the point—Mrs. Breedlove was not interested in Christ the Redeemer, but rather Christ the Judge.)[3] Often she could be heard discoursing with Jesus about Cholly, pleading with Him to help her "strike the bastard down from his pea-knuckle[4] of pride." And once when a drunken gesture catapulted Cholly into the red-hot stove, she screamed, "Get him, Jesus! Get him!" If Cholly had stopped drinking, she would never have forgiven Jesus. She needed Cholly's sins desperately. The lower he sank, the wilder and more irresponsible he became, the more splendid she and her task became. In the name of Jesus.

No less did Cholly need her. She was one of the few things abhorrent to him that he could touch and therefore hurt. He poured out on her

---

3. I.e., the Christ who presides at the Day of Judgment, deciding which souls will be saved and which damned, rather than the Christ who allowed himself to be crucified to redeem the sins of humanity.

4. Mispronunciation of "pinnacle."

the sum of all his inarticulate fury and aborted desires. Hating her, he could leave himself intact. When he was still very young, Cholly had been surprised in some bushes by two white men while he was newly but earnestly engaged in eliciting sexual pleasure from a little country girl. The men had shone a flashlight right on his behind. He had stopped, terrified. They chuckled. The beam of the flashlight did not move. "Go on," they said. "Go on and finish. And, nigger, make it good." The flashlight did not move. For some reason Cholly had not hated the white men; he hated, despised, the girl. Even a half-remembrance of this episode, along with myriad other humiliations, defeats, and emasculations, could stir him into flights of depravity that surprised himself—but only himself. Somehow he could not astound. He could only be astounded. So he gave that up, too.

Cholly and Mrs. Breedlove fought each other with a darkly brutal formalism that was paralleled only by their lovemaking. Tacitly they had agreed not to kill each other. He fought her the way a coward fights a man—with feet, the palms of his hands, and teeth. She, in turn, fought back in a purely feminine way—with frying pans and pokers, and occasionally a flatiron would sail toward his head. They did not talk, groan, or curse during these beatings. There was only the muted sound of falling things, and flesh on unsurprised flesh.

There was a difference in the reaction of the children to these battles. Sammy cursed for a while, or left the house, or threw himself into the fray. He was known, by the time he was fourteen, to have run away from home no less than twenty-seven times. Once he got to Buffalo and stayed three months. His returns, whether by force or circumstance, were sullen. Pecola, on the other hand, restricted by youth and sex, experimented with methods of endurance. Though the methods varied, the pain was as consistent as it was deep. She struggled between an overwhelming desire that one would kill the other, and a profound wish that she herself could die. Now she was whispering, "Don't, Mrs. Breedlove. Don't." Pecola, like Sammy and Cholly, always called her mother Mrs. Breedlove.

"Don't, Mrs. Breedlove. Don't."

But Mrs. Breedlove did.

By the grace, no doubt, of God, Mrs. Breedlove sneezed. Just once.

She ran into the bedroom with a dishpan full of cold water and threw it in Cholly's face. He sat up, choking and spitting. Naked and ashen, he leaped from the bed, and with a flying tackle, grabbed his wife around the waist, and they hit the floor. Cholly picked her up and knocked her down with the back of his hand. She fell in a sitting position, her back supported by Sammy's bed frame. She had not let go of the dishpan, and began to hit at Cholly's thighs and groin with it. He put his foot in her chest, and she dropped the pan. Dropping to his

knee, he struck her several times in the face, and she might have succumbed early had he not hit his hand against the metal bed frame when
his wife ducked. Mrs. Breedlove took advantage of this momentary suspension of blows and slipped out of his reach. Sammy, who had
watched in silence their struggling at his bedside, suddenly began to hit
his father about the head with both fists, shouting "You naked fuck!"
over and over and over. Mrs. Breedlove, having snatched up the round,
flat stove lid, ran tippy-toe to Cholly as he was pulling himself up from
his knees, and struck him two blows, knocking him right back into the
senselessness out of which she had provoked him. Panting, she threw a
quilt over him and let him lie.

Sammy screamed, "Kill him! Kill him!"

Mrs. Breedlove looked at Sammy with surprise. "Cut out that noise,
boy." She put the stove lid back in place, and walked toward the
kitchen. At the doorway she paused long enough to say to her son, "Get
up from there anyhow. I need some coal."

Letting herself breathe easy now, Pecola covered her head with the
quilt. The sick feeling, which she had tried to prevent by holding in her
stomach, came quickly in spite of her precaution. There surged in her
the desire to heave, but as always, she knew she would not.

"Please, God," she whispered into the palm of her hand. "Please
make me disappear." She squeezed her eyes shut. Little parts of her
body faded away. Now slowly, now with a rush. Slowly again. Her
fingers went, one by one; then her arms disappeared all the way to the
elbow. Her feet now. Yes, that was good. The legs all at once. It was
hardest above the thighs. She had to be real still and pull. Her stomach
would not go. But finally it, too, went away. Then her chest, her neck.
The face was hard, too. Almost done, almost. Only her tight, tight eyes
were left. They were always left.

Try as she might, she could never get her eyes to disappear. So what
was the point? They were everything. Everything was there, in them.
All of those pictures, all of those faces. She had long ago given up the
idea of running away to see new pictures, new faces, as Sammy had so
often done. He never took her, and he never thought about his going
ahead of time, so it was never planned. It wouldn't have worked anyway. As long as she looked the way she did, as long as she was ugly, she
would have to stay with these people. Somehow she belonged to them.
Long hours she sat looking in the mirror, trying to discover the secret of
the ugliness, the ugliness that made her ignored or despised at school,
by teachers and classmates alike. She was the only member of her class
who sat alone at a double desk. The first letter of her last name forced
her to sit in the front of the room always. But what about Marie Appo-
lonaire? Marie was in front of her, but she shared a desk with Luke

Angelino. Her teachers had always treated her this way. They tried never to glance at her, and called on her only when everyone was required to respond. She also knew that when one of the girls at school wanted to be particularly insulting to a boy, or wanted to get an immediate response from him, she could say, "Bobby loves Pecola Breedlove! Bobby loves Pecola Breedlove!" and never fail to get peals of laughter from those in earshot, and mock anger from the accused.

It had occurred to Pecola some time ago that if her eyes, those eyes that held the pictures, and knew the sights—if those eyes of hers were different, that is to say, beautiful, she herself would be different. Her teeth were good, and at least her nose was not big and flat like some of those who were thought so cute. If she looked different, beautiful, maybe Cholly would be different, and Mrs. Breedlove too. Maybe they'd say, "Why, look at pretty-eyed Pecola. We mustn't do bad things in front of those pretty eyes."

Pretty eyes. Pretty blue eyes. Big blue pretty eyes.
Run, Jip, run. Jip runs, Alice runs. Alice has blue eyes.
Jerry has blue eyes. Jerry runs. Alice runs. They run
with their blue eyes. Four blue eyes. Four pretty
blue eyes. Blue-sky eyes. Blue-like Mrs. Forrest's
blue blouse eyes. Morning-glory-blue-eyes.
Alice-and-Jerry-blue-storybook-eyes.

Each night, without fail, she prayed for blue eyes. Fervently, for a year she had prayed. Although somewhat discouraged, she was not without hope. To have something as wonderful as that happen would take a long, long time.

Thrown, in this way, into the binding conviction that only a miracle could relieve her, she would never know her beauty. She would see only what there was to see: the eyes of other people.

She walks down Garden Avenue to a small grocery store which sells penny candy. Three pennies are in her shoe—slipping back and forth between the sock and the inner sole. With each step she feels the painful press of the coins against her foot. A sweet, endurable, even cherished irritation, full of promise and delicate security. There is plenty of time to consider what to buy. Now, however, she moves down an avenue gently buffeted by the familiar and therefore loved images. The dandelions at the base of the telephone pole. Why, she wonders, do people call them weeds? She thought they were pretty. But grownups say, "Miss Dunion keeps her yard so nice. Not a dandelion anywhere." Hunkie women in black babushkas[5] go into the fields with baskets to

---

5. A kind of head-scarf originally worn by Russian peasant women.

pull them up. But they do not want the yellow heads—only the jagged leaves. They make dandelion soup. Dandelion wine. Nobody loves the head of a dandelion. Maybe because they are so many, strong, and soon.

There was the sidewalk crack shaped like a Y, and the other one that lifted the concrete up from the dirt floor. Frequently her sloughing step had made her trip over that one. Skates would go well over this sidewalk—old it was, and smooth; it made the wheels glide evenly, with a mild whirr. The newly paved walks were bumpy and uncomfortable, and the sound of skate wheels on new walks was grating.

These and other inanimate things she saw and experienced. They were real to her. She knew them. They were the codes and touchstones of the world, capable of translation and possession. She owned the crack that made her stumble; she owned the clumps of dandelions whose white heads, last fall, she had blown away; whose yellow heads, this fall, she peered into. And owning them made her part of the world, and the world a part of her.

She climbs four wooden steps to the door of Yacobowski's Fresh Veg. Meat and Sundries Store. A bell tinkles as she opens it. Standing before the counter, she looks at the array of candies. All Mary Janes, she decides. Three for a penny. The resistant sweetness that breaks open at last to deliver peanut butter—the oil and salt which complement the sweet pull of caramel. A peal of anticipation unsettles her stomach.

She pulls off her shoe and takes out the three pennies. The gray head of Mr. Yacobowski looms up over the counter. He urges his eyes out of his thoughts to encounter her. Blue eyes. Blear-dropped. Slowly, like Indian summer moving imperceptibly toward fall, he looks toward her. Somewhere between retina and object, between vision and view, his eyes draw back, hesitate, and hover. At some fixed point in time and space he senses that he need not waste the effort of a glance. He does not see her, because for him there is nothing to see. How can a fifty-two-year-old white immigrant storekeeper with the taste of potatoes and beer in his mouth, his mind honed on the doe-eyed Virgin Mary, his sensibilities blunted by a permanent awareness of loss, *see* a little black girl? Nothing in his life even suggested that the feat was possible, not to say desirable or necessary.

"Yeah?"

She looks up at him and sees the vacuum where curiosity ought to lodge. And something more. The total absence of human recognition —the glazed separateness. She does not know what keeps his glance suspended. Perhaps because he is grown, or a man, and she a little girl. But she has seen interest, disgust, even anger in grown male eyes. Yet this vacuum is not new to her. It has an edge; somewhere in the bottom lid is the distaste. She has seen it lurking in the eyes of all white people.

So. The distaste must be for her, her blackness. All things in her are flux and anticipation. But her blackness is static and dread. And it is the blackness that accounts for, that creates, the vacuum edged with distaste in white eyes.

She points her finger at the Mary Janes—a little black shaft of finger, its tip pressed on the display window. The quietly inoffensive assertion of a black child's attempt to communicate with a white adult.

"Them." The word is more sigh than sense.

"What? These? These?" Phlegm and impatience mingle in his voice.

She shakes her head, her fingertip fixed on the spot which, in her view, at any rate, identifies the Mary Janes. He cannot see her view— the angle of his vision, the slant of her finger, makes it incomprehensible to him. His lumpy red hand plops around in the glass casing like the agitated head of a chicken outraged by the loss of its body.

"Christ. Kantcha talk?"

His fingers brush the Mary Janes.

She nods.

"Well, why'nt you say so? One? How many?"

Pecola unfolds her fist, showing the three pennies. He scoots three Mary Janes toward her—three yellow rectangles in each packet. She holds the money toward him. He hesitates, not wanting to touch her hand. She does not know how to move the finger of her right hand from the display counter or how to get the coins out of her left hand. Finally he reaches over and takes the pennies from her hand. His nails graze her damp palm.

Outside, Pecola feels the inexplicable shame ebb.

Dandelions. A dart of affection leaps out from her to them. But they do not look at her and do not send love back. She thinks, "They *are* ugly. They *are* weeds." Preoccupied with that revelation, she trips on the sidewalk crack. Anger stirs and wakes in her; it opens its mouth, and like a hot-mouthed puppy, laps up the dredges of her shame.

Anger is better. There is a sense of being in anger. A reality and presence. An awareness of worth. It is a lovely surging. Her thoughts fall back to Mr. Yacobowski's eyes, his phlegmy voice. The anger will not hold; the puppy is too easily surfeited. Its thirst too quickly quenched, it sleeps. The shame wells up again, its muddy rivulets seeping into her eyes. What to do before the tears come. She remembers the Mary Janes.

Each pale yellow wrapper has a picture on it. A picture of little Mary Jane, for whom the candy is named. Smiling white face. Blond hair in gentle disarray, blue eyes looking at her out of a world of clean comfort. The eyes are petulant, mischievous. To Pecola they are simply pretty.

She eats the candy, and its sweetness is good. To eat the candy is somehow to eat the eyes, eat Mary Jane. Love Mary Jane. Be Mary Jane.

Three pennies had bought her nine lovely orgasms with Mary Jane. Lovely Mary Jane, for whom a candy is named.

Three whores lived in the apartment above the Breedloves' storefront. China, Poland, and Miss Marie. Pecola loved them, visited them, and ran their errands. They, in turn, did not despise her.

On an October morning, the morning of the stove-lid triumph, Pecola climbed the stairs to their apartment.

Even before the door was opened to her tapping, she could hear Poland singing—her voice sweet and hard, like new strawberries:

> I got blues in my mealbarrel
> Blues up on the shelf
> I got blues in my mealbarrel
> Blues up on the shelf
> Blues in my bedroom
> 'Cause I'm sleepin' by myself

"Hi, dumplin'. Where your socks?" Marie seldom called Pecola the same thing twice, but invariably her epithets were fond ones chosen from menus and dishes that were forever uppermost in her mind.

"Hello, Miss Marie. Hello, Miss China. Hello, Miss Poland."

"You heard me. Where your socks? You as bare-legged as a yard dog."

"I couldn't find any."

"Couldn't find any? Must be somethin' in your house that loves socks."

China chuckled. Whenever something was missing, Marie attributed its disappearance to "something in the house that loved it." "There is somethin' in this house that loves brassieres," she would say with alarm.

Poland and China were getting ready for the evening. Poland, forever ironing, forever singing. China, sitting on a pale-green kitchen chair, forever and forever curling her hair. Marie never got ready.

The women were friendly, but slow to begin talk. Pecola always took the initiative with Marie, who, once inspired, was difficult to stop.

"How come you got so many boyfriends, Miss Marie?"

"*Boy*friends? *Boy*friends? Chittlin', I ain't seen a *boy* since nineteen and twenty-seven."

"You didn't see none then." China stuck the hot curlers into a tin of Nu Nile hair dressing. The oil hissed at the touch of the hot metal.

"How come, Miss Marie?" Pecola insisted.

"How come what? How come I ain't seen a boy since nineteen and twenty-seven? Because they ain't *been* no boys since then. That's when they stopped. Folks started gettin' born old."

"You mean that's when *you* got old," China said.

"I ain't never got old. Just fat."

"Same thing."

"You think 'cause you skinny, folks think you young? You'd make a haint[6] buy a girdle."

"And you look like the north side of a southbound mule."

"All I know is, them bandy little legs of yours is every bit as old as mine."

"Don't worry 'bout my bandy legs. That's the first thing they push aside."

All three of the women laughed. Marie threw back her head. From deep inside, her laughter came like the sound of many rivers, freely, deeply, muddily, heading for the room of an open sea. China giggled spastically. Each gasp seemed to be yanked out of her by an unseen hand jerking an unseen string. Poland, who seldom spoke unless she was drunk, laughed without sound. When she was sober she hummed mostly or chanted blues songs, of which she knew many.

Pecola fingered the fringe of a scarf that lay on the back of a sofa. "I never seen nobody with as many boyfriends as you got, Miss Marie. How come they all love you?"

Marie opened a bottle of root beer. "What else they gone do? They know I'm rich and good-lookin'. They wants to put their toes in my curly hair, and get at my money."

"You rich, Miss Marie?"

"Puddin', I got money's mammy."

"Where you get it from? You don't do no work."

"Yeah," said China, "where you get it from?"

"Hoover[7] give it me. I did him a favor once, for the F.B. and I."

"What'd you do?"

"I did him a favor. They wanted to catch this crook, you see. Name of Johnny. He was as low-down as they come. . . ."

"We *know* that." China arranged a curl.

" . . . the F.B. and I. wanted him bad. He killed more people than TB.[8] And if you *crossed* him? Whoa, Jesus! He'd run you as long as there was ground. Well, I was little and cute then. No more than ninety pounds, soaking wet."

"You ain't never been soaking wet," China said.

"Well, you ain't never been dry. Shut up. Let me tell you, sweetnin'.

6. A ghost.
7. J. Edgar Hoover (1895–1972), then director

of the Federal Bureau of Investigation.
8. Tuberculosis.

To tell it true, I was the only one could handle him. He'd go out and
rob a bank or kill some people, and I'd say to him, soft-like, 'Johnny,
you shouldn't do that.' And he'd say he just had to bring me pretty
things. Lacy drawers and all. And every Saturday we'd get a case of beer
and fry up some fish. We'd fry it in meal and egg batter, you know, and
when it was all brown and crisp—not hard, though—we'd break open
that cold beer. . . ." Marie's eyes went soft as the memory of just such
a meal sometime, somewhere transfixed her. All her stories were subject to breaking down at descriptions of food. Pecola saw Marie's teeth
settling down into the back of crisp sea bass; saw the fat fingers putting
back into her mouth tiny flakes of white, hot meat that had escaped
from her lips; she heard the "pop" of the beer-bottle cap; smelled the
acridness of the first stream of vapor; felt the cold beeriness hit the
tongue. She ended the daydream long before Marie.

"But what about the money?" she asked.

China hooted. "She's makin' like she's the Lady in Red that told on
Dillinger.[9] Dillinger wouldn't have come near you lessen he was going
hunting in Africa and shoot you for a hippo."

"Well, this hippo had a ball back in Chicago. Whoa Jesus, ninety-
nine!"

"How come you always say 'Whoa Jesus' and a number?" Pecola
had long wanted to know.

"Because my mama taught me never to cuss."

"Did she teach you not to drop your drawers?" China asked.

"Didn't have none," said Marie. "Never saw a pair of drawers till I
was fifteen, when I left Jackson and was doing day work in Cincinnati.
My white lady gave me some old ones of hers. I thought they was some
kind of stocking cap. I put it on my head when I dusted. When she saw
me, she liked to fell out."

"You must have been one dumb somebody." China lit a cigarette
and cooled her irons.

"How'd I know?" Marie paused. "And what's the use of putting on
something you got to keep taking off all the time? Dewey never let me
keep them on long enough to get used to them."

"Dewey who?" This was a somebody new to Pecola.

"Dewey who? Chicken! You never heard me tell of *Dewey*?" Marie
was shocked by her negligence.

"No, ma'am."

"Oh, honey, you've missed half your life. Whoa Jesus, one-nine-
five. You talkin' 'bout smooth! I met him when I was fourteen. We ran
away and lived together like married for three years. You know all those

9. John Dillinger (1903–1934), American
gangster and bank robber, who was captured
after a friend named Anna Sage informed on
him; she dressed in red when she was with him
so the FBI would recognize her.

klinker-tops you see runnin' up here? Fifty of 'em in a bowl wouldn't make a Dewey Prince ankle bone. Oh, Lord. How that man loved me!"

China arranged a fingerful of hair into a bang effect. "Then why he left you to sell tail?"

"Girl, when I found out I could sell it—that somebody would pay cold cash for it, you could have knocked me over with a feather."

Poland began to laugh. Soundlessly. "Me too. My auntie whipped me good that first time when I told her I didn't get no money. I said 'Money? For what? He didn't owe me nothin'.' She said, 'The hell he didn't!' "

They all dissolved in laughter.

Three merry gargoyles. Three merry harridans. Amused by a long-ago time of ignorance. They did not belong to those generations of prostitutes created in novels, with great and generous hearts, dedicated, because of the horror of circumstance, to ameliorating the luckless, barren life of men, taking money incidentally and humbly for their "understanding." Nor were they from that sensitive breed of young girl, gone wrong at the hands of fate, forced to cultivate an outward brittleness in order to protect her springtime from further shock, but knowing full well she was cut out for better things, and could make the right man happy. Neither were they the sloppy, inadequate whores who, unable to make a living at it alone, turn to drug consumption and traffic or pimps to help complete their scheme of self-destruction, avoiding suicide only to punish the memory of some absent father or to sustain the misery of some silent mother. Except for Marie's fabled love for Dewey Prince, these women hated men, all men, without shame, apology, or discrimination. They abused their visitors with a scorn grown mechanical from use. Black men, white men, Puerto Ricans, Mexicans, Jews, Poles, whatever—all were inadequate and weak, all came under their jaundiced eyes and were the recipients of their disinterested wrath. They took delight in cheating them. On one occasion the town well knew, they lured a Jew up the stairs, pounced on him, all three, held him up by the heels, shook everything out of his pants pockets, and threw him out of the window.

Neither did they have respect for women, who, although not their colleagues, so to speak, nevertheless deceived their husbands—regularly or irregularly, it made no difference. "Sugar-coated whores," they called them, and did not yearn to be in their shoes. Their only respect was for what they would have described as "good Christian colored women." The woman whose reputation was spotless, and who tended to her family, who didn't drink or smoke or run around. These women had their undying, if covert, affection. They would sleep with their husbands, and take their money, but always with a vengeance.

Nor were they protective and solicitous of youthful innocence. They looked back on their own youth as a period of ignorance, and regretted that they had not made more of it. They were not young girls in whores' clothing, or whores regretting their loss of innocence. They were whores in whores' clothing, whores who had never been young and had no word for innocence. With Pecola they were as free as they were with each other. Marie concocted stories for her because she was a child, but the stories were breezy and rough. If Pecola had announced her intention to live the life they did, they would not have tried to dissuade her or voiced any alarm.

"You and Dewey Prince have any children, Miss Marie?"

"Yeah. Yeah. We had some." Marie fidgeted. She pulled a bobby pin from her hair and began to pick her teeth. That meant she didn't want to talk anymore.

Pecola went to the window and looked down at the empty street. A tuft of grass had forced its way up through a crack in the sidewalk, only to meet a raw October wind. She thought of Dewey Prince and how he loved Miss Marie. What did love feel like? she wondered. How do grown-ups act when they love each other? Eat fish together? Into her eyes came the picture of Cholly and Mrs. Breedlove in bed. He making sounds as though he were in pain, as though something had him by the throat and wouldn't let go. Terrible as his noises were, they were not nearly as bad as the no noise at all from her mother. It was as though she was not even there. Maybe that was love. Choking sounds and silence.

Turning her eyes from the window, Pecola looked at the women.

China had changed her mind about the bangs and was arranging a small but sturdy pompadour. She was adept in creating any number of hair styles, but each one left her with a pinched and harassed look. Then she applied makeup heavily. Now she gave herself surprised eyebrows and a cupid-bow mouth. Later she would make Oriental eyebrows and an evilly slashed mouth.

Poland, in her sweet strawberry voice, began another song:

I know a boy who is sky-soft brown
I know a boy who is sky-soft brown
The dirt leaps for joy when his feet touch the ground.
    His strut is a peacock
    His eye is burning brass
    His smile is sorghum syrup drippin' slow-sweet to the last
I know a boy who is sky-soft brown

Marie sat shelling peanuts and popping them into her mouth. Pecola looked and looked at the women. Were they real? Marie belched, softly, purringly, lovingly.

Winter

My daddy's face is a study. Winter moves into it and presides there.
His eyes become a cliff of snow threatening to avalanche; his
eyebrows bend like black limbs of leafless trees. His skin takes on the
pale, cheerless yellow of winter sun; for a jaw he has the edges of a
snowbound field dotted with stubble; his high forehead is the frozen
sweep of the Erie,[1] hiding currents of gelid thoughts that eddy in
darkness. Wolf killer turned hawk fighter, he worked night and day to
keep one from the door and the other from under the windowsills. A
Vulcan[2] guarding the flames, he gives us instructions about which
doors to keep closed or opened for proper distribution of heat, lays
kindling by, discusses qualities of coal, and teaches us how to rake,
feed, and bank the fire. And he will not unrazor his lips until spring.

Winter tightened our heads with a band of cold and melted our
eyes. We put pepper in the feet of our stockings, Vaseline on our
faces, and stared through dark icebox mornings at four stewed prunes,
slippery lumps of oatmeal, and cocoa with a roof of skin.

But mostly we waited for spring, when there could be gardens.

By the time this winter had stiffened itself into a hateful knot that
nothing could loosen, something did loosen it, or rather someone. A
someone who splintered the knot into silver threads that tangled us,
netted us, made us long for the dull chafe of the previous boredom.

This disrupter of seasons was a new girl in school named Maureen
Peal. A high-yellow dream child with long brown hair braided into
two lynch ropes that hung down her back. She was rich, at least by our
standards, as rich as the richest of the white girls, swaddled in comfort
and care. The quality of her clothes threatened to derange Frieda and
me. Patent-leather shoes with buckles, a cheaper version of which we
got only at Easter and which had disintegrated by the end of May.
Fluffy sweaters the color of lemon drops tucked into skirts with pleats
so orderly they astounded us. Brightly colored knee socks with white
borders, a brown velvet coat trimmed in white rabbit fur, and a
matching muff. There was a hint of spring in her sloe green eyes,
something summery in her complexion, and a rich autumn ripeness
in her walk.

She enchanted the entire school. When teachers called on her,
they smiled encouragingly. Black boys didn't trip her in the halls; white
boys didn't stone her, white girls didn't suck their teeth when she was
assigned to be their work partners; black girls stepped aside when she
wanted to use the sink in the girls' toilet, and their eyes genuflected

---

1. Lake Erie, one of the Great Lakes, located in   tween the U.S. and Canada.
east-central North America on the border be-   2. Greek god of fire.

under sliding lids. She never had to search for anybody to eat with in the cafeteria—they flocked to the table of her choice, where she opened fastidious lunches, shaming our jelly-stained bread with egg-salad sandwiches cut into four dainty squares, pink-frosted cupcakes, stocks of celery and carrots, proud, dark apples. She even bought and liked white milk.

Frieda and I were bemused, irritated, and fascinated by her. We looked hard for flaws to restore our equilibrium, but had to be content at first with uglying up her name, changing Maureen Peal to Meringue Pie. Later a minor epiphany was ours when we discovered that she had a dog tooth—a charming one to be sure—but a dog tooth nonetheless. And when we found out that she had been born with six fingers on each hand and that there was a little bump where each extra one had been removed, we smiled. They were small triumphs, but we took what we could get—snickering behind her back and calling her Six-finger-dog-tooth-meringue-pie. But we had to do it alone, for none of the other girls would cooperate with our hostility. They adored her.

When she was assigned a locker next to mine, I could indulge my jealousy four times a day. My sister and I both suspected that we were secretly prepared to be her friend, if she would let us, but I knew it would be a dangerous friendship, for when my eye traced the white border patterns of those Kelly-green knee socks, and felt the pull and slack of my brown stockings, I wanted to kick her. And when I thought of the unearned haughtiness in her eyes, I plotted accidental slammings of locker doors on her hand.

As locker friends, however, we got to know each other a little, and I was even able to hold a sensible conversation with her without visualizing her fall off a cliff, or giggling my way into what I thought was a clever insult.

One day, while I waited at the locker for Frieda, she joined me.

"Hi."

"Hi."

"Waiting for your sister?"

"Uh-huh."

"Which way do you go home?"

"Down Twenty-first Street to Broadway."

"Why don't you go down Twenty-second Street?"

" 'Cause I live on Twenty-first Street."

"Oh. I can walk that way, I guess. Partly, anyway."

"Free country."

Frieda came toward us, her brown stockings straining at the knees because she had tucked the toe under to hide a hole in the foot.

"Maureen's gonna walk part way with us."

Frieda and I exchanged glances, her eyes begging my restraint, mine promising nothing.

It was a false spring day, which, like Maureen, had pierced the shell of a deadening winter. There were puddles, mud, and an inviting warmth that deluded us. The kind of day on which we draped our coats over our heads, left our galoshes in school, and came down with croup the following day. We always responded to the slightest change in weather, the most minute shifts in time of day. Long before seeds were stirring, Frieda and I were scruffing and poking at the earth, swallowing air, drinking rain. . . .

As we emerged from the school with Maureen, we began to moult immediately. We put our head scarves in our coat pockets, and our coats on our heads. I was wondering how to maneuver Maureen's fur muff into a gutter when a commotion in the playground distracted us. A group of boys was circling and holding at bay a victim, Pecola Breedlove.

Bay Boy, Woodrow Cain, Buddy Wilson, Junie Bug—like a necklace of semiprecious stones they surrounded her. Heady with the smell of their own musk, thrilled by the easy power of a majority, they gaily harassed her.

"Black e mo. Black e mo. Yadaddsleepsnekked. Black e mo black e mo ya dadd sleeps nekked. Black e mo. . . ."

They had extemporized a verse made up of two insults about matters over which the victim had no control: the color of her skin and speculations on the sleeping habits of an adult, wildly fitting in its incoherence. That they themselves were black, or that their own father had similarly relaxed habits was irrelevant. It was their contempt for their own blackness that gave the first insult its teeth. They seemed to have taken all of their smoothly cultivated ignorance, their exquisitely learned self-hatred, their elaborately designed hopelessness and sucked it all up into a fiery cone of scorn that had burned for ages in the hollows of their minds—cooled—and spilled over lips of outrage, consuming whatever was in its path. They danced a macabre ballet around the victim, whom, for their own sake, they were prepared to sacrifice to the flaming pit.

Black e mo Black e mo Ya daddy sleeps nekked.
Stch ta ta stch ta ta
stach ta ta ta ta ta

Pecola edged around the circle crying. She had dropped her notebook, and covered her eyes with her hands.

We watched, afraid they might notice us and turn their energies our way. Then Frieda, with set lips and Mama's eyes, snatched her coat from her head and threw it on the ground. She ran toward them and brought her books down on Woodrow Cain's head. The circle broke. Woodrow Cain grabbed his head.

"Hey, girl!"

"You cut that out, you hear?" I had never heard Frieda's voice so loud and clear.

Maybe because Frieda was taller than he was, maybe because he saw her eyes, maybe because he had lost interest in the game, or maybe because he had a crush on Frieda, in any case Woodrow looked frightened just long enough to give her more courage.

"Leave her 'lone, or I'm gone tell everybody what you did!"

Woodrow did not answer; he just walled his eyes.

Bay Boy piped up, "Go on, gal! Ain't nobody bothering you."

"You shut up, Bullet Head." I had found my tongue.

"Who you calling Bullet Head?"

"I'm calling you Bullet Head, Bullet Head."

Frieda took Pecola's hand. "Come on."

"You want a fat lip?" Bay Boy drew back his fist at me.

"Yeah. Gimme one of yours."

"You gone get one."

Maureen appeared at my elbow, and the boys seemed reluctant to continue under her springtime eyes so wide with interest. They buckled in confusion, not willing to beat up three girls under her watchful gaze. So they listened to a budding male instinct that told them to pretend we were unworthy of their attention.

"Come on, man."

"Yeah. Come on. We ain't got time to fool with them."

Grumbling a few disinterested epithets, they moved away.

I picked up Pecola's notebook and Frieda's coat, and the four of us left the playground.

"Old Bullet Head, he's always picking on girls."

Frieda agreed with me. "Miss Forrester said he was incorrigival."[3]

"Really?" I didn't know what that meant, but it had enough of a doom sound in it to be true of Bay Boy.

While Frieda and I clucked on about the near fight, Maureen, suddenly animated, put her velvet-sleeved arm through Pecola's and began to behave as though they were the closest of friends.

"I just moved here. My name is Maureen Peal. What's yours?"

"Pecola."

"Pecola? Wasn't that the name of the girl in *Imitation of Life*?"[4]

"I don't know. What is that?"

---

3. Mispronunciation of "incorrigible."
4. A 1934 film. (The "mulatto girl" was named Peola, not Pecola.)

"The picture show, you know. Where this mulatto girl hates her mother 'cause she is black and ugly but then cries at the funeral. It was real sad. Everybody cries in it. Claudette Colbert too."

"Oh." Pecola's voice was no more than a sigh.

"Anyway, her name was Pecola too. She was so pretty. When it comes back, I'm going to see it again. My mother has seen it four times."

Frieda and I walked behind them, surprised at Maureen's friendliness to Pecola, but pleased. Maybe she wasn't so bad, after all. Frieda had put her coat back on her head, and the two of us, so draped, trotted along enjoying the warm breeze and Frieda's heroics.

"You're in my gym class, aren't you?" Maureen asked Pecola.

"Yes."

"Miss Erkmeister's legs sure are bow. I bet she thinks they're cute. How come she gets to wear real shorts, and we have to wear those old bloomers? I want to die every time I put them on."

Pecola smiled but did not look at Maureen.

"Hey." Maureen stopped short. "There's an Isaley's. Want some ice cream? I have money."

She unzipped a hidden pocket in her muff and pulled out a multifolded dollar bill. I forgave her those knee socks.

"My uncle sued Isaley's," Maureen said to the three of us. "He sued the Isaley's in Akron. They said he was disorderly and that that was why they wouldn't serve him, but a friend of his, a policeman, came in and beared the witness, so the suit went through."

"What's a suit?"

"It's when you can beat them up if you want to and won't anybody do nothing. Our family does it all the time. We believe in suits."

At the entrance to Isaley's Maureen turned to Frieda and me, asking, "You all going to buy some ice cream?"

We looked at each other. "No," Frieda said.

Maureen disappeared into the store with Pecola.

Frieda looked placidly down the street; I opened my mouth, but quickly closed it. It was extremely important that the world not know that I fully expected Maureen to buy us some ice cream, that for the past 120 seconds I had been selecting the flavor, that I had begun to like Maureen, and that neither of us had a penny.

We supposed Maureen was being nice to Pecola because of the boys, and were embarrassed to be caught—even by each other—thinking that she would treat us, or that we deserved it as much as Pecola did.

The girls came out. Pecola with two dips of orange-pineapple, Maureen with black raspberry.

"You should have got some," she said. "They had all kinds. Don't eat down to the tip of the cone," she advised Pecola.

"Why?"

"Because there's a fly in there."

"How you know?"

"Oh, not really. A girl told me she found one in the bottom of hers once, and ever since then she throws that part away."

"Oh."

We passed the Dreamland Theater, and Betty Grable[5] smiled down at us.

"Don't you just love her?" Maureen asked.

"Uh-huh," said Pecola.

I differed. "Hedy Lamarr is better."

Maureen agreed. "Ooooo yes. My mother told me that a girl named Audrey, she went to the beauty parlor where we lived before, and asked the lady to fix her hair like Hedy Lamarr's, and the lady said, 'Yeah, when you grow some hair like Hedy Lamarr's.' " She laughed long and sweet.

"Sounds crazy," said Frieda.

"She sure is. Do you know she doesn't even menstrate yet, and she's sixteen. Do you, yet?"

"Yes." Pecola glanced at us.

"So do I." Maureen made no attempt to disguise her pride. "Two months ago I started. My girl friend in Toledo, where we lived before, said when she started she was scared to death. Thought she had killed herself."

"Do you know what it's for?" Pecola asked the question as though hoping to provide the answer herself.

"For babies." Maureen raised two pencil-stroke eyebrows at the obviousness of the question. "Babies need blood when they are inside you, and if you are having a baby, then you don't menstrate. But when you're not having a baby, then you don't have to save the blood, so it comes out."

"How do babies get the blood?" asked Pecola.

"Through the like-line. You know. Where your belly button is. That is where the like-line grows from and pumps the blood to the baby."

"Well, if the belly buttons are to grow like-lines to give the baby blood, and only girls have babies, how come boys have belly buttons?"

Maureen hesitated. "I don't know," she admitted. "But boys have

5. Popular American musical comedy film star   ous film star of same period.
of the thirties and forties. Hedy Lamarr: glamor-

all sorts of things they don't need." Her tinkling laughter was somehow stronger than our nervous ones. She curled her tongue around the edge of the cone, scooping up a dollop of purple that made my eyes water. We were waiting for a stop light to change. Maureen kept scooping the ice cream from around the cone's edge with her tongue; she didn't bite the edge as I would have done. Her tongue circled the cone. Pecola had finished hers: Maureen evidently liked her things to last. While I was thinking about her ice cream, she must have been thinking about her last remark, for she said to Pecola, "Did you ever see a naked man?"

Pecola blinked, then looked away. "No. Where would I see a naked man?"

"I don't know. I just asked."

"I wouldn't even look at him, even if I did see him. That's dirty. Who wants to see a naked man?" Pecola was agitated. "Nobody's father would be naked in front of his own daughter. Not unless he was dirty too."

"I didn't say 'father.' I just said 'a naked man.' "

"Well. . . ."

"How come you said 'father'?" Maureen wanted to know.

"Who else would she see, dog tooth?" I was glad to have a chance to show anger. Not only because of the ice cream, but because we had seen our own father naked and didn't care to be reminded of it and feel the shame brought on by the absence of shame. He had been walking down the hall from the bathroom into his bedroom and passed the open door of our room. We had lain there wide-eyed. He stopped and looked in, trying to see in the dark room whether we were really asleep—or was it his imagination that opened eyes were looking at him? Apparently he convinced himself that we were sleeping. He moved away, confident that his little girls would not lie open-eyed like that, staring, staring. When he had moved on, the dark took only him away, not his nakedness. That stayed in the room with us. Friendly-like.

"I'm not talking to you," said Maureen. "Besides, I don't care if she sees her father naked. She can look at him all day if she wants to. Who cares?"

"You do," said Frieda. "That's all you talk about."

"It is not."

"It is so. Boys, babies, and somebody's naked daddy. You must be boy-crazy."

"You better be quiet."

"Who's gonna make me?" Frieda put her hand on her hip and jutted her face toward Maureen.

"You all ready made. Mammy made."

"You stop talking about my mama."

"Well, you stop talking about my daddy."

"Who said anything about your old daddy?"

"You did."

"Well, you started it."

"I wasn't even talking to you. I was talking to Pecola."

"Yeah. About seeing her naked daddy."

"So what if she did see him?"

Pecola shouted, "I never saw my daddy naked. Never."

"You did too," Maureen snapped. "Bay Boy said so."

"I did not."

"You did."

"I did not."

"Did. Your own daddy, too!"

Pecola tucked her head in—a funny, sad, helpless movement. A kind of hunching of the shoulders, pulling in of the neck, as though she wanted to cover her ears.

"You stop talking about her daddy," I said.

"What do I care about her old black daddy?" asked Maureen.

"Black? Who you calling black?"

"You!"

"You think you so cute!" I swung at her and missed, hitting Pecola in the face. Furious at my clumsiness, I threw my notebook at her, but it caught her in the small of her velvet back, for she had turned and was flying across the street against traffic.

Safe on the other side, she screamed at us, "I *am* cute! And you ugly! Black and ugly black e mos. I *am* cute!"

She ran down the street, the green knee socks making her legs look like wild dandelion stems that had somehow lost their heads. The weight of her remark stunned us, and it was a second or two before Frieda and I collected ourselves enough to shout, "Six-finger-dog-tooth-meringue-pie!" We chanted this most powerful of our arsenal of insults as long as we could see the green stems and rabbit fur.

Grown people frowned at the three girls on the curbside, two with their coats draped over their heads, the collars framing the eyebrows like nuns' habits, black garters showing where they bit the tops of brown stockings that barely covered the knees, angry faces knotted like dark cauliflowers.

Pecola stood a little apart from us, her eyes hinged in the direction in which Maureen had fled. She seemed to fold into herself, like a pleated wing. Her pain antagonized me. I wanted to open her up, crisp her edges, ram a stick down that hunched and curving spine, force her to stand erect and spit the misery out on the streets. But she held it in where it could lap up into her eyes.

Frieda snatched her coat from her head. "Come on, Claudia. 'Bye, Pecola."

We walked quickly at first, and then slower, pausing every now and then to fasten garters, tie shoelaces, scratch, or examine old scars. We were sinking under the wisdom, accuracy, and relevance of Maureen's last words. If she was cute—and if anything could be believed, she *was*—then we were not. And what did that mean? We were lesser. Nicer, brighter, but still lesser. Dolls we could destroy, but we could not destroy the honey voices of parents and aunts, the obedience in the eyes of our peers, the slippery light in the eyes of our teachers when they encountered the Maureen Peals of the world. What was the secret? What did we lack? Why was it important? And so what? Guileless and without vanity, we were still in love with ourselves then. We felt comfortable in our skins, enjoyed the news that our senses released to us, admired our dirt, cultivated our scars, and could not comprehend this unworthiness. Jealousy we understood and thought natural—a desire to have what somebody else had; but envy was a strange, new feeling for us. And all the time we knew that Maureen Peal was not the Enemy and not worthy of such intense hatred. The *Thing* to fear was the *Thing* that made *her* beautiful, and not us.

The house was quiet when we opened the door. The acrid smell of simmering turnips filled our cheeks with sour saliva.

"Mama!"

There was no answer, but a sound of feet. Mr. Henry shuffled part of the way down the stairs. One thick, hairless leg leaned out of his bathrobe.

"Hello there, Greta Garbo; hello, Ginger Rogers."

We gave him the giggle he was accustomed to. "Hello, Mr. Henry. Where's Mama?"

"She went to your grandmaw's. Left word for you to cut off the turnips and eat some graham crackers till she got back. They in the kitchen."

We sat in silence at the kitchen table, crumbling the crackers into anthills. In a little while Mr. Henry came back down the stairs. Now he had his trousers on under his robe.

"Say. Wouldn't you all like some cream?"

"Oh, yes, sir."

"Here. Here's a quarter. Gone over to Isaley's and get yourself some cream. You been good girls, ain't you?"

His light-green words restored color to the day. "Yes, sir. Thank you, Mr. Henry. Will you tell Mama for us if she comes?"

"Sure. But she ain't due back for a spell."

Coatless, we left the house and had gotten all the way to the corner when Frieda said, "I don't want to go to Isaley's."

"What?"

"I don't want ice cream. I want potato chips."

"They got potato chips at Isaley's."

"I know, but why go all that long way? Miss Bertha got potato chips."

"But I want ice cream."

"No you don't, Claudia."

"I do too."

"Well, you go on to Isaley's. I'm going to Miss Bertha's."

"But you got the quarter, and I don't want to go all the way up there by myself."

"Then let's go to Miss Bertha's. You like her candy, don't you?"

"It's always stale, and she always runs out of stuff."

"Today is Friday. She orders fresh on Friday."

"And then that crazy old Soaphead Church lives there."

"So what? We're together. We'll run if he does anything at us."

"He scares me."

"Well, I don't want to go up by Isaley's. Suppose Meringue Pie is hanging around. You want to run into her, Claudia?"

"Come on, Frieda. I'll get candy."

Miss Bertha had a small candy, snuff, and tobacco store. One brick room sitting in her front yard. You had to peep in the door, and if she wasn't there, you knocked on the door of her house in back. This day she was sitting behind the counter reading a Bible in a tube of sunlight.

Frieda bought potato chips, and we got three Powerhouse bars for ten cents, and had a dime left. We hurried back home to sit under the lilac bushes on the side of the house. We always did our Candy Dance there so Rosemary could see us and get jealous. The Candy Dance was a humming, skipping, foot-tapping, eating, smacking combination that overtook us when we had sweets. Creeping between the bushes and the side of the house, we heard voices and laughter. We looked into the living-room window, expecting to see Mama. Instead we saw Mr. Henry and two women. In a playful manner, the way grandmothers do with babies, he was sucking the fingers of one of the women, whose laughter filled a tiny place over his head. The other woman was buttoning her coat. We knew immediately who they were, and our flesh crawled. One was China, and the other was called the Maginot Line.[6] The back of my neck itched. These were

---

6. A line of fortifications built by France along its eastern border; the implication may be that she is "built like a fortress."

the fancy women of the maroon nail polish that Mama and Big Mama hated. And in our house.

China was not too terrible, at least not in our imaginations. She was thin, aging, absentminded, and unaggressive. But the Maginot Line. That was the one my mother said she "wouldn't let eat out of one of her plates." That was the one church women never allowed their eyes to rest on. That was the one who had killed people, set them on fire, poisoned them, cooked them in lye. Although I thought the Maginot Line's face, hidden under all that fat, was really sweet, I had heard too many black and red words about her, seen too many mouths go triangle at the mention of her name, to dwell on any redeeming features she might have.

Showing brown teeth, China seemed to be genuinely enjoying Mr. Henry. The sight of him licking her fingers brought to mind the girlie magazines in his room. A cold wind blew somewhere in me, lifting little leaves of terror and obscure longing. I thought I saw a mild lonesomeness cross the face of the Maginot Line. But it may have been my own image that I saw in the slow flaring of her nostrils, in her eyes that reminded me of waterfalls in movies about Hawaii.

The Maginot Line yawned and said, "Come on, China. We can't hang in here all day. Them people be home soon." She moved toward the door.

Frieda and I dropped down to the ground, looking wildly into each other's eyes. When the women were some distance away, we went inside. Mr. Henry was in the kitchen opening a bottle of pop.

"Back already?"

"Yes, sir."

"Cream all gone?" His little teeth looked so kindly and helpless. Was that really our Mr. Henry with China's fingers?

"We got candy instead."

"You did huh? Ole sugar-tooth Greta Garbo."

He wiped the bottle sweat and turned it up to his lips—a gesture that made me uncomfortable.

"Who were those women, Mr. Henry?"

He choked on the pop and looked at Frieda. "What you say?"

"Those women," she repeated, "who just left. Who were they?"

"Oh." He laughed the grown-up getting-ready-to-lie laugh. A heh-heh we knew well.

"Those were some members of my Bible class. We read the scriptures together, and so they came today to read with me."

"Oh," said Frieda. I was looking at his house slippers to keep from seeing those kindly teeth frame a lie. He walked toward the stairs and then turned back to us.

"Bed' not mention it to your mother. She don't take to so much

Bible study and don't like me having visitors, even if they good
Christians."

"No, sir, Mr. Henry. We won't."

He rapidly mounted the stairs.

"Should we?" I asked. "Tell Mama?"

Frieda sighed. She had not even opened her Powerhouse bar or
her potato chips, and now she traced the letters on the candy wrappers
with her fingers. Suddenly she lifted her head and began to look all
around the kitchen.

"No. I guess not. No plates are out."

"Plates? What you talking about now?"

"No plates are out. The Maginot Line didn't eat out of one of
Mama's plates. Besides, Mama would just fuss all day if we told her."

We sat down and looked at the graham-cracker anthills we had
made.

"We better cut off the turnips. They'll burn, and Mama will whip
us," she said.

"I know."

"But if we let them burn, we won't have to eat them."

"Heyyy, what a lovely idea," I thought.

"Which you want? A whipping and no turnips, or turnips and no
whippings?"

"I don't know. Maybe we could burn them just a little so Mama
and Daddy can eat them, but we can say we can't."

"O.K."

I made a volcano out of my anthill.

"Frieda?"

"What?"

"What did Woodrow do that you was gonna tell?"

"Wet the bed. Mrs. Cain told Mama he won't quit."

"Old nasty."

The sky was getting dark; I looked out of the window and saw snow
falling. I poked my finger down into the mouth of my volcano, and it
toppled, dispersing the golden grains into little swirls. The turnip pot
crackled.

SEETHECATITGOESMEOWMEOWCOM
EANDPLAYCOMEPLAYWITHJANETHE
KITTENWILLNOTPLAYPLAYPLAYPLA

They come from Mobile. Aiken. From Newport News. From Mar-
ietta. From Meridian.[7] And the sounds of these places in their mouths
make you think of love. When you ask them where they are from, they

_____

7. Cities in Alabama, Georgia, Virginia, Georgia, and Mississippi respectively.

tilt their heads and say "Mobile" and you think you've been kissed. They say "Aiken" and you see a white butterfly glance off a fence with a torn wing. They say "Nagadoches" and you want to say "Yes, I will." You don't know what these towns are like, but you love what happens to the air when they open their lips and let the names ease out.

Meridian. The sound of it opens the windows of a room like the first four notes of a hymn. Few people can say the names of their home towns with such sly affection. Perhaps because they don't have home towns, just places where they were born. But these girls soak up the juice of their home towns, and it never leaves them. They are thin brown girls who have looked long at hollyhocks in the backyards of Meridian, Mobile, Aiken, and Baton Rouge. And like hollyhocks they are narrow, tall, and still. Their roots are deep, their stalks are firm, and only the top blossom nods in the wind. They have the eyes of people who can tell what time it is by the color of the sky. Such girls live in quiet black neighborhoods where everybody is gainfully employed. Where there are porch swings hanging from chains. Where the grass is cut with a scythe, where rooster combs and sunflowers grow in the yards, and pots of bleeding heart, ivy, and mother-in-law tongue line the steps and windowsills. Such girls have bought watermelon and snapbeans from the fruit man's wagon. They have put in the window the cardboard sign that has a pound measure printed on each of three edges—10 lbs., 25 lbs., 50 lbs.,—and NO ICE on the fourth. These particular brown girls from Mobile and Aiken are not like some of their sisters. They are not fretful, nervous, or shrill; they do not have lovely black necks that stretch as though against an invisible collar; their eyes do not bite. These sugar-brown Mobile girls move through the streets without a stir. They are as sweet and plain as buttercake. Slim ankles; long, narrow feet. They wash themselves with orange-colored Lifebuoy soap, dust themselves with Cashmere Bouquet talc, clean their teeth with salt on a piece of rag, soften their skin with Jergens Lotion. They smell like wood, newspapers, and vanilla. They straighten their hair with Dixie Peach, and part it on the side. At night they curl it on paper from brown bags, tie a print scarf around their heads, and sleep with hands folded across their stomachs. They do not drink, smoke, or swear, and they still call sex "nookey." They sing second soprano in the choir, and although their voices are clear and steady, they are never picked to solo. They are in the second row, white blouses starched, blue skirts almost purple from ironing.

They go to land-grant colleges, normal schools,[8] and learn how to do the white man's work with refinement: home economics to prepare his food; teacher education to instruct black children in obedience; music

8. Schools for teacher preparation; land-grant colleges are state colleges.

to soothe the weary master and entertain his blunted soul. Here they learn the rest of the lesson begun in those soft houses with porch swings and pots of bleeding heart: how to behave. The careful development of thrift, patience, high morals, and good manners. In short, how to get rid of the funkiness. The dreadful funkiness of passion, the funkiness of nature, the funkiness of the wide range of human emotions.

Wherever it erupts, this Funk, they wipe it away; where it crusts, they dissolve it; wherever it drips, flowers, or clings, they find it and fight it until it dies. They fight this battle all the way to the grave. The laugh that is a little too loud; the enunciation a little too round; the gesture a little too generous. They hold their behind in for fear of a sway too free; when they wear lipstick, they never cover the entire mouth for fear of lips too thick, and they worry, worry, worry about the edges of their hair.

They never seem to have boyfriends, but they always marry. Certain men watch them, without seeming to, and know that if such a girl is in his house, he will sleep on sheets boiled white, hung out to dry on juniper bushes, and pressed flat with a heavy iron. There will be pretty paper flowers decorating the picture of his mother, a large Bible in the front room. They feel secure. They know their work clothes will be mended, washed, and ironed on Monday, that their Sunday shirts will billow on hangers from the door jamb, stiffly starched and white. They look at her hands and know what she will do with biscuit dough; they smell the coffee and the fried ham; see the white, smoky grits with a dollop of butter on top. Her hips assure them that she will bear children easily and painlessly. And they are right.

What they do not know is that this plain brown girl will build her nest stick by stick, make it her own inviolable world, and stand guard over its every plant, weed, and doily, even against him. In silence will she return the lamp to where she put it in the first place; remove the dishes from the table as soon as the last bite is taken; wipe the doorknob after a greasy hand has touched it. A sidelong look will be enough to tell him to smoke on the back porch. Children will sense instantly that they cannot come into her yard to retrieve a ball. But the men do not know these things. Nor do they know that she will give him her body sparingly and partially. He must enter her surreptitiously, lifting the hem of her nightgown only to her navel. He must rest his weight on his elbows when they make love, ostensibly to avoid hurting her breasts but actually to keep her from having to touch or feel too much of him.

While he moves inside her, she will wonder why they didn't put the necessary but private parts of the body in some more convenient place —like the armpit, for example, or the palm of the hand. Someplace one could get to easily, and quickly, without undressing. She stiffens when she feels one of her paper curlers coming undone from the activity of love; imprints in her mind which one it is that is coming loose so she can quickly secure it once he is through. She hopes he will not sweat— the damp may get into her hair; and that she will remain dry between her legs—she hates the glucking sound they make when she is moist. When she senses some spasm about to grip him, she will make rapid movements with her hips, press her fingernails into his back, suck in her breath, and pretend she is having an orgasm. She might wonder again, for the six hundredth time, what it would be like to have *that* feeling while her husband's penis is inside her. The closest thing to it was the time she was walking down the street and her napkin slipped free of her sanitary belt. It moved gently between her legs as she walked. Gently, ever so gently. And then a slight and distinctly delicious sensation collected in her crotch. As the delight grew, she had to stop in the street, hold her thighs together to contain it. That must be what it is like, she thinks, but it never happens while he is inside her. When he withdraws, she pulls her nightgown down, slips out of the bed and into the bathroom with relief.

Occasionally some living thing will engage her affections. A cat, perhaps, who will love her order, precision, and constancy; who will be as clean and quiet as she is. The cat will settle quietly on the windowsill and caress her with his eyes. She can hold him in her arms, letting his back paws struggle for footing on her breast and his forepaws cling to her shoulder. She can rub the smooth fur and feel the unresisting flesh underneath. At her gentlest touch he will preen, stretch, and open his mouth. And she will accept the strangely pleasant sensation that comes when he writhes beneath her hand and flattens his eyes with a surfeit of sensual delight. When she stands cooking at the table, he will circle about her shanks, and the trill of his fur spirals up her legs to her thighs, to make her fingers tremble a little in the pie dough.

Or, as she sits reading the "Uplifting Thoughts" in *The Liberty Magazine*, the cat will jump into her lap. She will fondle that soft hill of hair and let the warmth of the animal's body seep over and into the deeply private areas of her lap. Sometimes the magazine drops, and she opens her legs just a little, and the two of them will be still together, perhaps shifting a little together, sleeping a little together, until four o'clock, when the intruder comes home from work vaguely anxious about what's for dinner.

The cat will always know that he is first in her affections. Even after she bears a child. For she does bear a child—easily, and painlessly. But only one. A son. Named Junior.

One such girl from Mobile, or Meridian, or Aiken who did not sweat in her armpits nor between her thighs, who smelled of wood and vanilla, who had made soufflés in the Home Economics Department, moved with her husband, Louis, to Lorain, Ohio. Her name was Geraldine. There she built her nest, ironed shirts, potted bleeding hearts, played with her cat, and birthed Louis Junior.

Geraldine did not allow her baby, Junior, to cry. As long as his needs were physical, she could meet them—comfort and satiety. He was always brushed, bathed, oiled, and shod. Geraldine did not talk to him, coo to him, or indulge him in kissing bouts, but she saw that every other desire was fulfilled. It was not long before the child discovered the difference in his mother's behavior to himself and the cat. As he grew older, he learned how to direct his hatred of his mother to the cat, and spent some happy moments watching it suffer. The cat survived, because Geraldine was seldom away from home, and could effectively soothe the animal when Junior abused him.

Geraldine, Louis, Junior, and the cat lived next to the playground of Washington Irving School. Junior considered the playground his own, and the schoolchildren coveted his freedom to sleep late, go home for lunch, and dominate the playground after school. He hated to see the swings, slides, monkey bars, and seesaws empty and tried to get kids to stick around as long as possible. White kids; his mother did not like him to play with niggers. She had explained to him the difference between colored people and niggers. They were easily identifiable. Colored people were neat and quiet; niggers were dirty and loud. He belonged to the former group: he wore white shirts and blue trousers; his hair was cut as close to his scalp as possible to avoid any suggestion of wool, the part was etched into his hair by the barber. In winter his mother put Jergens Lotion on his face to keep the skin from becoming ashen. Even though he was light-skinned, it was possible to ash. The line between colored and nigger was not always clear; subtle and telltale signs threatened to erode it, and the watch had to be constant.

Junior used to long to play with the black boys. More than anything in the world he wanted to play King of the Mountain and have them push him down the mound of dirt and roll over him. He wanted to feel their hardness pressing on him, smell their wild blackness, and say "Fuck you" with that lovely casualness. He wanted to sit with them on curbstones and compare the sharpness of jackknives, the distance and arcs of spitting. In the toilet he wanted to share with them the laurels of being able to pee far and long. Bay Boy and P. L. had at one time been his idols. Gradually he came to agree with his mother that neither Bay Boy nor P. L. was good enough for him. He played only with Ralph Nisensky, who was two years younger, wore glasses, and didn't want to *do* anything. More and more Junior enjoyed bullying girls. It was easy making them scream and run. How he laughed when they fell down and their bloomers showed. When they got up, their faces red and crinkled, it made him feel good. The nigger girls he did not pick on very much. They usually traveled in packs, and once when he threw a stone at some of them, they chased, caught, and beat him witless. He lied to his mother, saying Bay Boy did it. His mother was very upset. His father just kept on reading the Lorain *Journal*.

When the mood struck him, he would call a child passing by to come play on the swings or the seesaw. If the child wouldn't, or did and left too soon, Junior threw gravel at him. He became a very good shot.

Alternately bored and frightened at home, the playground was his joy. On a day when he had been especially idle, he saw a very black girl taking a shortcut through the playground. She kept her head down as she walked. He had seen her many times before, standing alone, always alone, at recess. Nobody ever played with her. Probably, he thought, because she was ugly.

Now Junior called to her. "Hey! What are you doing walking through my yard?"

The girl stopped.

"Nobody can come through this yard 'less I say so."

"This ain't your yard. It's the school's."

"But I'm in charge of it."

The girl started to walk away.

"Wait." Junior walked toward her. "You can play in it if you want to. What's your name?"

"Pecola. I don't want to play."

"Come on. I'm not going to bother you."

"I got to go home."

"Say, you want to see something? I got something to show you."

"No. What is it?"

"Come on in my house. See, I live right there. Come on. I'll show you."

"Show me what?"

"Some kittens. We got some kittens. You can have one if you want."

"Real kittens?"

"Yeah. Come on."

He pulled gently at her dress. Pecola began to move toward his house. When he knew she had agreed, Junior ran ahead excitedly, stopping only to yell back at her to come on. He held the door open for her, smiling his encouragement. Pecola climbed the porch stairs and hesitated there, afraid to follow him. The house looked dark. Junior said, "There's nobody here. My ma's gone out, and my father's at work. Don't you want to see the kittens?"

Junior turned on the lights. Pecola stepped inside the door.

How beautiful, she thought. What a beautiful house. There was a big red-and-gold Bible on the dining-room table. Little lace doilies were everywhere—on arms and backs of chairs, in the center of a large dining table, on little tables. Potted plants were on all the windowsills. A color picture of Jesus Christ hung on a wall with the prettiest paper flowers fastened on the frame. She wanted to see everything slowly, slowly. But Junior kept saying, "Hey, you. Come on. Come on." He pulled her into another room, even more beautiful than the first. More doilies, a big lamp with green-and-gold base and white shade. There was even a rug on the floor, with enormous dark-red flowers. She was deep in admiration of the flowers when Junior said, "Here!" Pecola turned. "Here is your kitten!" he screeched. And he threw a big black cat right in her face. She sucked in her breath in fear and surprise and felt fur in her mouth. The cat clawed her face and chest in an effort to right itself, then leaped nimbly to the floor.

Junior was laughing and running around the room clutching his stomach delightedly. Pecola touched the scratched place on her face and felt tears coming. When she started toward the doorway, Junior leaped in front of her.

"You can't get out. You're my prisoner," he said. His eyes were merry but hard.

"You let me go."

"No!" He pushed her down, ran out the door that separated the rooms, and held it shut with his hands. Pecola's banging on the door increased his gasping, high-pitched laughter.

The tears came fast, and she held her face in her hands. When something soft and furry moved around her ankles, she jumped, and saw it was the cat. He wound himself in and about her legs. Momentarily distracted from her fear, she squatted down to touch him, her hands wet from the tears. The cat rubbed up against her knee. He was black all over, deep silky black, and his eyes, pointing down toward his nose, were bluish green. The light made them shine like blue ice. Pecola rubbed the cat's head; he whined, his tongue flicking with pleasure. The blue eyes in the black face held her.

Junior, curious at not hearing her sobs, opened the door, and saw her squatting down rubbing the cat's back. He saw the cat stretching its head and flattening its eyes. He had seen that expression many times as the animal responded to his mother's touch.

"Gimme my cat!" His voice broke. With a movement both awkward and sure he snatched the cat by one of its hind legs and began to swing it around his head in a circle.

"Stop that!" Pecola was screaming. The cat's free paws were stiffened, ready to grab anything to restore balance, its mouth wide, its eyes blue streaks of horror.

Still screaming, Pecola reached for Junior's hand. She heard her dress rip under her arm. Junior tried to push her away, but she grabbed the arm which was swinging the cat. They both fell, and in falling, Junior let go the cat, which, having been released in mid-motion, was thrown full force against the window. It slithered down and fell on the radiator behind the sofa. Except for a few shudders, it was still. There was only the slightest smell of singed fur.

Geraldine opened the door.

"What is this?" Her voice was mild, as though asking a perfectly reasonable question. "Who is this girl?"

"She killed our cat," said Junior. "Look." He pointed to the radiator, where the cat lay, its blue eyes closed, leaving only an empty, black, and helpless face.

Geraldine went to the radiator and picked up the cat. He was limp in her arms, but she rubbed her face in his fur. She looked at Pecola. Saw the dirty torn dress, the plaits sticking out on her head, hair matted where the plaits had come undone, the muddy shoes with the wad of gum peeping out from between the cheap soles, the soiled socks, one of which had been walked down into the heel of the shoe. She saw the safety pin holding the hem of the dress up. Up over the hump of the cat's back she looked at her. She had seen this little girl all of her life. Hanging out of windows over saloons in Mobile, crawling over the porches of shotgun houses on the edge of town, sitting in bus stations holding paper bags and crying to mothers who kept saying "Shet up!" Hair uncombed, dresses falling apart, shoes untied and caked with dirt. They had stared at her with great uncomprehending eyes. Eyes that questioned nothing and asked everything. Unblinking and unabashed, they stared up at her. The end of the world lay in their eyes, and the beginning, and all the waste in between.

They were everywhere. They slept six in a bed, all their pee mixing together in the night as they wet their beds each in his own candy-and-potato-chip dream. In the long, hot days, they idled away, picking plaster from the walls and digging into the earth with sticks. They sat in little rows on street curbs, crowded into pews at church, taking space from the nice, neat, colored children; they clowned on the playgrounds, broke things in dime stores, ran in front of you on the street, made ice slides on the sloped sidewalks in winter. The girls grew up knowing nothing of girdles, and the boys announced their manhood by turning the bills of their caps backward. Grass wouldn't grow where they lived. Flowers died. Shades fell down. Tin cans and tires blossomed where they lived. They lived on cold black-eyed peas and orange pop. Like flies they hovered; like flies they settled. And this one had settled in her house. Up over the hump of the cat's back she looked.

"Get out," she said, her voice quiet. "You nasty little black bitch. Get out of my house."

The cat shuddered and flicked his tail.

Pecola backed out of the room, staring at the pretty milk-brown lady in the pretty gold-and-green house who was talking to her through the cat's fur. The pretty lady's words made the cat fur move; the breath of each word parted the fur. Pecola turned to find the front door and saw Jesus looking down at her with sad and unsurprised eyes, his long brown hair parted in the middle, the gay paper flowers twisted around his face.

Outside, the March wind blew into the rip in her dress. She held her head down against the cold. But she could not hold it low enough to avoid seeing the snowflakes falling and dying on the pavement.

Spring

The first twigs are thin, green, and supple. They bend into a complete circle, but will not break. Their delicate, showy hopefulness shooting from forsythia and lilac bushes meant only a change in whipping style. They beat us differently in the spring. Instead of the dull pain of a winter strap, there were these new green switches that lost their sting long after the whipping was over. There was a nervous meanness in these long twigs that made us long for the steady stroke of a strap or the firm but honest slap of a hairbrush. Even now spring for me is shot through with the remembered ache of switchings, and forsythia holds no cheer.

Sunk in the grass of an empty lot on a spring Saturday, I split the stems of milkweed and thought about ants and peach pits and death and where the world went when I closed my eyes. I must have lain long in the grass, for the shadow that was in front of me when I left the house had disappeared when I went back. I entered the house, as the house was bursting with an uneasy quiet. Then I heard my mother singing something about trains and Arkansas. She came in the back door with some folded yellow curtains which she piled on the kitchen table. I sat down on the floor to listen to the song's story, and noticed how strangely she was behaving. She still had her hat on, and her shoes were dusty, as though she had been walking in deep dirt. She put on some water to boil and then swept the porch; then she hauled out the curtain stretcher, but instead of puting the damp curtains on it, she swept the porch again. All the time singing about trains and Arkansas.

When she finished, I went to look for Frieda. I found her upstairs lying on our bed, crying the tired, whimpering cry that follows the first wailings—mostly gasps and shudderings. I lay on the bed and looked at the tiny bunches of wild roses sprinkled over her dress. Many washings had faded their color and dimmed their outlines.

"What happened, Frieda?"

She lifted a swollen face from the crook of her arm. Shuddering still, she sat up, letting her thin legs dangle over the bedside. I knelt on the bed and picked up the hem of my dress to wipe her running nose. She never liked wiping noses on clothes, but this time she let me. It was the way Mama did with her apron.

"Did you get a whipping?"

She shook her head no.

"Then why you crying?"

"Because."

"Because what?"

"Mr. Henry."

"What'd he do?"

"Daddy beat him up."

"What for? The Maginot Line? Did he find out about the Maginot Line?"

"No."

"Well, what, then? Come on, Frieda. How come I can't know?"

"He . . . *picked* at me."

"Picked at you? You mean like Soaphead Church?"

"Sort of."

"He showed his privates at you?"

"Noooo. He touched me."

"Where?"

"Here and here." She pointed to the tiny breasts that, like two fallen acorns, scattered a few faded rose leaves on her dress.

"Really? How did it feel?"

"Oh, Claudia." She sounded put-out. I wasn't asking the right questions.

"It didn't feel like anything."

"But wasn't it supposed to? Feel good, I mean?" Frieda sucked her teeth. "What'd he do? Just walk up and pinch them?"

She sighed. "First he said how pretty I was. Then he grabbed my arm and touched me."

"Where was Mama and Daddy?"

"Over at the garden weeding."

"What'd you say when he did it?"

"Nothing. I just ran out the kitchen and went to the garden."

"Mama said we was never to cross the tracks by ourselves."

"Well, what would you do? Set there and let him pinch you?"

I looked at my chest. "I don't have nothing to pinch. I'm never going to have nothing."

"Oh, Claudia, you're jealous of everything. You *want* him to?"

"No, I just get tired of having everything last."

"You do not. What about scarlet fever? You had that first."

"Yes, but it didn't last. Anyway, what happened at the garden?"

"I told Mama, and she told Daddy, and we all come home, and he was gone, so we waited for him, and when Daddy saw him come up on the porch, he threw our old tricycle at his head and knocked him off the porch."

"Did he die?"

"Naw. He got up and started singing 'Nearer My God to Thee.' Then Mama hit him with a broom and told him to keep the Lord's name out of his mouth, but he wouldn't stop, and Daddy was cussing, and everybody was screaming."

"Oh, shoot, I always miss stuff."

"And Mr. Buford came running out with his gun, and Mama told him to go somewhere and sit down, and Daddy said no, give him the gun, and Mr. Buford did, and Mama screamed, and Mr. Henry shut up and started running, and Daddy shot at him and Mr. Henry jumped out of his shoes and kept on running in his socks. Then Rosemary came out and said that Daddy was going to jail, and I hit her."

"Real hard?"

"Real hard."

"Is that when Mama whipped you?"

"She didn't whip me, I told you."

"Then why you crying?"

"Miss Dunion came in after everybody was quiet, and Mama and Daddy was fussing about who let Mr. Henry in anyway, and she said that Mama should take me to the doctor, because I might be ruined, and Mama started screaming all over again."

"At you?"

"No. At Miss Dunion."

"But why were you crying?"

"I don't want to be *ruined*!"

"What's ruined?"

"You know. Like the Maginot Line. She's ruined. Mama said so." The tears came back.

An image of Frieda, big and fat, came to mind. Her thin legs swollen, her face surrounded by layers of rouged skin. I too begin to feel tears.

"But, Frieda, you could exercise and not eat."

She shrugged.

"Besides, what about China and Poland? They're ruined too, aren't they? And they ain't fat."

"That's because they drink whiskey. Mama says whiskey ate them up."

"You could drink whiskey."

"Where would I get whiskey?"

We thought about this. Nobody would sell it to us; we had no money, anyway. There was never any in our house. Who would have some?

"Pecola," I said. "Her father's always drunk. She can get us some."

"You think so?"

"Sure. Cholly's always drunk. Let's go ask her. We don't have to tell her what for."

"Now?"

"Sure, now."

"What'll we tell Mama?"

"Nothing. Let's just go out the back. One at a time. So she won't notice."

"O.K. You go first, Claudia."

We opened the fence gate at the bottom of the backyard and ran down the alley.

Pecola lived on the other side of Broadway. We had never been in her house, but we knew where it was. A two-story gray building that had been a store downstairs and had an apartment upstairs.

Nobody answered our knock on the front door, so we walked around to the side door. As we approached, we heard radio music and looked to see where it came from. Above us was the second-story porch, lined with slanting, rotting rails, and sitting on the porch was the Maginot Line herself. We stared up and automatically reached for the other's hand. A mountain of flesh, she lay rather than sat in a rocking chair. She had no shoes on, and each foot was poked between a railing: tiny baby toes at the tip of puffy feet; swollen ankles smoothed and tightened the skin; massive legs like tree stumps parted wide at the knees, over which spread two roads of soft flabby inner thigh that kissed each other deep in the shade of her dress and closed. A dark-brown root-beer bottle, like a burned limb, grew out of her dimpled hand. She looked at us down through the porch railings and emitted a low, long belch. Her eyes were as clean as rain, and again I remembered the waterfall. Neither of us could speak. Both of us imagined we were seeing what was to become of Frieda. The Maginot Line smiled at us.

"You all looking for somebody?"

I had to pull my tongue from the roof of my mouth to say, "Pecola —she live here?"

"Uh-huh, but she ain't here now. She gone to her mama's work place to git the wash."

"Yes, ma'am. She coming back?"

"Uh-huh. She got to hang up the clothes before the sun goes down."

"Oh."

"You can wait for her. Wanna come up here and wait?"

We exchanged glances. I looked back up at the broad cinnamon roads that met in the shadow of her dress.

Frieda said, "No, ma'am."

"Well," the Maginot Line seemed interested in our problem. "You can go to her mama's work place, but it's way over by the lake."

"Where by the lake?"

"That big white house with the wheelbarrow full of flowers."

It was a house that we knew, having admired the large white wheelbarrow tilted down on spoked wheels and planted with seasonal flowers.

"Ain't that too far for you all to go walking?"

Frieda scratched her knee.

"Why don't you wait for her? You can come up here. Want some pop?" Those rain-soaked eyes lit up, and her smile was full, not like the pinched and holding-back smile of other grown-ups.

I moved to go up the stairs, but Frieda said, "No, ma'am, we ain't allowed."

I was amazed at her courage, and frightened of her sassiness. The smile of the Maginot Line slipped. "Ain't 'llowed?"

"No'm."

"Ain't 'llowed to what?"

"Go in your house."

"Is that right?" The waterfalls were still. "How come?"

"My mama said so. My mama said you ruined."

The waterfalls began to run again. She put the root-beer bottle to her lips and drank it empty. With a graceful movement of the wrist, a gesture so quick and small we never really saw it, only remembered it afterward, she tossed the bottle over the rail at us. It split at our feet, and shards of brown glass dappled our legs before we could jump back. The Maginot Line put a fat hand on one of the folds of her stomach and laughed. At first just a deep humming with her mouth closed, then a larger, warmer sound. Laughter at once beautiful and frightening. She let her head tilt sideways, closed her eyes, and shook her massive trunk, letting the laughter fall like a wash of red leaves all around us. Scraps and curls of the laughter followed us as we ran. Our breath gave out at the same time our legs did. After we rested against a tree, our heads on crossed forearms, I said, "Let's go home."

Frieda was still angry—fighting, she believed, for her life. "No, we got to get it now."

"We can't go all the way to the lake."

"Yes we can. Come on."

"Mama gone get us."

"No she ain't. Besides, she can't do nothing but whip us."

That was true. She wouldn't kill us, or laugh a terrible laugh at us, or throw a bottle at us.

We walked down tree-lined streets of soft gray houses leaning like tired ladies. . . The streets changed; houses looked more sturdy, their paint was newer, porch posts straighter, yards deeper. Then came brick houses set well back from the street, fronted by yards edged in shrubbery clipped into smooth cones and balls of velvet green.

The lakefront houses were the loveliest. Garden furniture, ornaments, windows like shiny eyeglasses, and no sign of life. The backyards of these houses fell away in green slopes down to a strip of sand, and then the blue Lake Erie, lapping all the way to Canada. The orange-patched sky of the steel-mill section never reached this part of town. This sky was always blue.

We reached Lake Shore Park, a city park laid out with rosebuds, fountains, bowling greens, picnic tables. It was empty now, but sweetly expectant of clean, white, well-behaved children and parents who would play there above the lake in summer before half-running, half-stumbling down the slope to the welcoming water. Black people were not allowed in the park, and so it filled our dreams.

Right before the entrance to the park was the large white house with the wheelbarrow full of flowers. Short crocus blades sheathed the purple-and-white hearts that so wished to be first they endured the chill and rain of early spring. The walkway was flagged in calculated disorder, hiding the cunning symmetry. Only fear of discovery and the knowledge that we did not belong kept us from loitering. We circled the proud house and went to the back.

There on the tiny railed stoop sat Pecola in a light red sweater and blue cotton dress. A little wagon was parked near her. She seemed glad to see us.

"Hi."

"Hi."

"What you all doing here?" She was smiling, and since it was a rare thing to see on her, I was surprised at the pleasure it gave me.

"We're looking for you."

"Who told you I was here?"

"The Maginot Line."

"Who is that?"

"That big fat lady. She lives over you."

"Oh, you mean Miss Marie. Her name is Miss Marie."

"Well, everybody calls her Miss Maginot Line. Ain't you scared?"

"Scared of what?"

"The Maginot Line."

Pecola looked genuinely puzzled. "What for?"

"Your mama let you go in her house? And eat out of her plates?"

"She don't know I go. Miss Marie is nice. They all nice."

"Oh, yeah," I said, "she tried to kill us."

"Who? Miss Marie? She don't bother nobody."

"Then how come your mama don't let you go in her house if she so nice?"

"I don't know. She say she's bad, but they ain't bad. They give me stuff all the time."

"What stuff?"

"Oh, lots of stuff, pretty dresses, and shoes. I got more shoes than I ever wear. And jewelry and candy and money. They take me to the movies, and once we went to the carnival. China gone take me to Cleveland to see the square, and Poland gone take me to Chicago to see the Loop.[9] We going everywhere together."

"You lying. You don't have no pretty dresses."

"I do, too."

"Oh, come on, Pecola, what you telling us all that junk for?" Frieda asked.

"It ain't junk." Pecola stood up ready to defend her words, when the door opened.

Mrs. Breedlove stuck her head out the door and said, "What's going on out here? Pecola, who are these children?"

"That's Frieda and Claudia, Mrs. Breedlove."

"Whose girls are you?" She came all the way out on the stoop. She looked nicer than I had ever seen her, in her white uniform and her hair in a small pompadour.

"Mrs. MacTeer's girls, ma'am."

"Oh, yes. Live over on Twenty-first Street?"

"Yes, ma'am."

"What are you doing 'way over here?"

"Just walking. We came to see Pecola."

"Well, you better get on back. You can walk with Pecola. Come on in while I get the wash."

We stepped into the kitchen, a large spacious room. Mrs. Breedlove's skin glowed like taffeta in the reflection of white porcelain, white woodwork, polished cabinets, and brilliant copperware. Odors of meat, vegetables, and something freshly baked mixed with a scent of Fels Naphtha.

"I'm gone get the wash. You all stand stock still right there and don't mess up nothing." She disappeared behind a white swinging door, and we could hear the uneven flap of her footsteps as she descended into the basement.

9. Downtown area of Chicago.

Another door opened, and in walked a little girl, smaller and younger than all of us. She wore a pink sunback dress and pink fluffy bedroom slippers with two bunny ears pointed up from the tips. Her hair was corn yellow and bound in a thick ribbon. When she saw us, fear danced across her face for a second. She looked anxiously around the kitchen.

"Where's Polly?" she asked.

The familiar violence rose in me. Her calling Mrs. Breedlove Polly, when even Pecola called her mother Mrs. Breedlove, seemed reason enough to scratch her.

"She's downstairs," I said.

"Polly!" she called.

"Look," Frieda whispered, "look at that." On the counter near the stove in a silvery pan was a deep-dish berry cobbler. The purple juice bursting here and there through crust. We moved closer.

"It's still hot," Frieda said.

Pecola stretched her hand to touch the pan, lightly, to see if it was hot.

"Polly, come here," the little girl called again.

It may have been nervousness, awkwardness, but the pan tilted under Pecola's fingers and fell to the floor, splattering blackish blueberries everywhere. Most of the juice splashed on Pecola's legs, and the burn must have been painful, for she cried out and began hopping about just as Mrs. Breedlove entered with a tightly packed laundry bag. In one gallop she was on Pecola, and with the back of her hand knocked her to the floor. Pecola slid in the pie juice, one leg folding under her. Mrs. Breedlove yanked her up by the arm, slapped her again, and in a voice thin with anger, abused Pecola directly and Frieda and me by implication.

"Crazy fool . . . my floor, mess . . . look what you . . . work . . . get on out . . . now that . . . crazy . . . my floor, my floor . . . my floor." Her words were hotter and darker than the smoking berries, and we backed away in dread.

The little girl in pink started to cry. Mrs. Breedlove turned to her. "Hush, baby, hush. Come here. Oh, Lord, look at your dress. Don't cry no more. Polly will change it." She went to the sink and turned tap water on a fresh towel. Over her shoulder she spit out words to us like rotten pieces of apple. "Pick up that wash and get on out of here, so I can get this mess cleaned up."

Pecola picked up the laundry bag, heavy with wet clothes, and we stepped hurriedly out the door. As Pecola put the laundry bag in the wagon, we could hear Mrs. Breedlove hushing and soothing the tears of the little pink-and-yellow girl.

"Who were they, Polly?"

"Don't worry none, baby."

"You gonna make another pie?"

" 'Course I will."

"Who were they, Polly?"

"Hush. Don't worry none," she whispered, and the honey in her words complemented the sundown spilling on the lake.

SEEMOTHERMOTHERISVERYNICEMO
THERWILLYOUPLAYWITHJANEMOTH
ERLAUGHSLAUGHMOTHERLAUGHLA

The easiest thing to do would be to build a case out of her foot. That is what she herself did. But to find out the truth about how dreams die, one should never take the word of the dreamer. The end of her lovely beginning was probably the cavity in one of her front teeth. She preferred, however, to think always of her foot. Although she was the ninth of eleven children and lived on a ridge of red Alabama clay seven miles from the nearest road, the complete indifference with which a rusty nail was met when it punched clear through her foot during her second year of life saved Pauline Williams from total anonymity. The wound left her with a crooked, archless foot that flopped when she walked—not a limp that would have eventually twisted her spine, but a way of lifting the bad foot as though she were extracting it from little whirlpools that threatened to pull it under. Slight as it was, this deformity explained for her many things that would have been otherwise incomprehensible: why she alone of all the children had no nickname; why there were no funny jokes and anecdotes about funny things she had done; why no one ever remarked on her food preferences—no saving of the wing or neck for her—no cooking of the peas in a separate pot without rice because she did not like rice; why nobody teased her; why she never felt at home anywhere, or that she belonged anyplace. Her general feeling of separateness and unworthiness she blamed on her foot. Restricted, as a child, to this cocoon of her family's spinning, she cultivated quiet and private pleasures. She liked, most of all, to arrange things. To line things up in rows—jars on shelves at canning, peach pits on the step, sticks, stones, leaves—and the members of her family let these arrangements be. When by some accident somebody scattered her rows, they always stopped to retrieve them for her, and she was never angry, for it gave her a chance to rearrange them again. Whatever portable plurality she found, she organized into neat lines, according to their size, shape, or gradations of color. Just as she would never align a pine needle with the leaf of a cottonwood tree, she would never put the jars of tomatoes next to the green beans. During all of her four years of going to school, she was enchanted by numbers and depressed by words. She missed—without knowing what she missed—paints and crayons.

Near the beginning of World War I, the Williamses discovered, from returning neighbors and kin, the possibility of living better in another place. In shifts, lots, batches, mixed in with other families, they migrated, in six months and four journeys, to Kentucky, where there were mines and millwork.

> *"When all us left from down home and was waiting down by the depot for the truck, it was nighttime. June bugs was shooting everywhere. They lighted up a tree leaf, and I seen a streak of green every now and again. That was the last time I seen real june bugs. These things up here ain't june bugs. They's something else. Folks here call them fireflies. Down home they was different. But I recollect that streak of green. I recollect it well."*

In Kentucky they lived in a real town, ten to fifteen houses on a single street, with water piped right into the kitchen. Ada and Fowler Williams found a five-room frame house for their family. The yard was bounded by a once-white fence against which Pauline's mother planted flowers and within which they kept a few chickens. Some of her brothers joined the Army, one sister died, and two got married, increasing the living space and giving the entire Kentucky venture a feel of luxury. The relocation was especially comfortable to Pauline, who was old enough to leave school. Mrs. Williams got a job cleaning and cooking for a white minister on the other side of town, and Pauline, now the oldest girl at home, took over the care of the house. She kept the fence in repair, pulling the pointed stakes erect, securing them with bits of wire, collected eggs, swept, cooked, washed, and minded the two younger children—a pair of twins called Chicken and Pie, who were still in school. She was not only good at housekeeping, she enjoyed it. After her parents left for work and the other children were at school or in mines, the house was quiet. The stillness and isolation both calmed and energized her. She could arrange and clean without interruption until two o'clock, when Chicken and Pie came home.

When the war ended and the twins were ten years old, they too left school to work. Pauline was fifteen, still keeping house, but with less enthusiasm. Fantasies about men and love and touching were drawing her mind and hands away from her work. Changes in weather began to affect her, as did certain sights and sounds. These feelings translated themselves to her in extreme melancholy. She thought of the death of newborn things, lonely roads, and strangers who appear out of nowhere simply to hold one's hand, woods in which the sun was always setting.

In church especially did these dreams grow. The songs caressed her, and while she tried to hold her mind on the wages of sin, her body trembled for redemption, salvation, a mysterious rebirth that would simply happen, with no effort on her part. In none of her fantasies was she ever aggressive; she was usually idling by the river bank, or gathering berries in a field when a someone appeared, with gentle and penetrating eyes, who—with no exchange of words—understood; and before whose glance her foot straightened and her eyes dropped. The someone had no face, no form, no voice, no odor. He was a simple Presence, an all-embracing tenderness with strength and a promise of rest. It did not matter that she had no idea of what to do or say to the Presence—after the wordless knowing and the soundless touching, her dreams disintegrated. But the Presence would know what to do. She had only to lay her head on his chest and he would lead her away to the sea, to the city, to the woods . . . forever.

There was a woman named Ivy who seemed to hold in her mouth all of the sounds of Pauline's soul. Standing a little apart from the choir, Ivy sang the dark sweetness that Pauline could not name; she sang the death-defying death that Pauline yearned for; she sang of the Stranger who *knew*. . . .

> Precious Lord take my hand
> Lead me on, let me stand
> I am tired, I am weak, I am worn.
> Through the storms, through the night
> Lead me on to the light
> Take my hand, precious Lord, lead me on.
>
> When my way grows drear
> Precious Lord linger near,
> When my life is almost gone
> Hear my cry hear my call
> Hold my hand lest I fall
> Take my hand, precious Lord, lead me on.

Thus it was that when the Stranger, the someone, did appear out of nowhere, Pauline was grateful but not surprised.

He came, strutting right out of a Kentucky sun on the hottest day of the year. He came big, he came strong, he came with yellow eyes, flaring nostrils, and he came with his own music.

Pauline was leaning idly on the fence, her arms resting on the crossrail between the pickets. She had just put down some biscuit dough and was cleaning the flour from under her nails. Behind her at some distance she heard whistling. One of these rapid, high-note riffs that black boys make up as they go while sweeping, shoveling, or just walking along. A kind of city-street music where laughter belies anxiety, and joy is as short and straight as the blade of a pocketknife. She listened carefully to the music and let it pull her lips into a smile. The whistling got louder, and still she did not turn around, for she wanted it to last. While smiling to herself and holding fast to the break in somber thoughts, she felt something tickling her foot. She laughed aloud and turned to see. The whistler was bending down tickling her broken foot and kissing her leg. She could not stop her laughter—not until he looked up at her and she saw the Kentucky sun drenching the yellow, heavy-lidded eyes of Cholly Breedlove.

"When I first seed Cholly, I want you to know it was like all the bits of color from that time down home when all us chil'ren went berry picking after a funeral and I put some in the pocket of my Sunday dress, and they mashed up and stained my hips. My whole dress was messed with purple, and it never did wash out. Not the dress nor me. I could feel that purple deep inside me. And that lemonade Mama used to make when Pap came in out the fields. It be cool and yellowish, with seeds floating near the bottom. And that streak of green them june bugs made on the trees the night we left from down home. All of them colors was in me. Just sitting there. So when Cholly come up and tickled my foot, it was like them berries, that lemonade, them streaks of green the june bugs made, all come together. Cholly was thin then, with real light eyes. He used to whistle, and when I heerd him, shivers come on my skin."

Pauline and Cholly loved each other. He seemed to relish her company and even to enjoy her country ways and lack of knowledge about city things. He talked with her about her foot and asked, when they walked through the town or in the fields, if she were tired. Instead of ignoring her infirmity, pretending it was not there, he made it seem like something special and endearing. For the first time Pauline felt that her bad foot was an asset.

And he did touch her, firmly but gently, just as she had dreamed. But minus the gloom of setting suns and lonely river banks. She was secure and grateful; he was kind and lively. She had not know there was so much laughter in the world.

They agreed to marry and go 'way up north, where Cholly said steel mills were begging for workers. Young, loving, and full of energy, they came to Lorain, Ohio. Cholly found work in the steel mills right away, and Pauline started keeping house.

And then she lost her front tooth. But there must have been a speck, a brown speck easily mistaken for food but which did not leave, which sat on the enamel for months, and grew, until it cut into the surface and then to the brown putty underneath, finally eating away to the root, but avoiding the nerves, so its presence was not noticeable or uncomfortable. Then the weakened roots, having grown accustomed to the poison, responded one day to severe pressure, and the tooth fell free, leaving a ragged stump behind. But even before the little brown speck, there must have been the conditions, the setting that would allow it to exist in the first place.

In that young and growing Ohio town whose side streets, even, were paved with concrete, which sat on the edge of a calm blue lake, which boasted an affinity with Oberlin, the underground railroad station, just thirteen miles away, this melting pot on the lip of America facing the cold but receptive Canada—What could go wrong?

"Me and Cholly was getting along good then. We come up north; supposed to be more jobs and all. We moved into two rooms up over a furniture store, and I set about housekeeping. Cholly was working at the steel plant, and everything was looking good. I don't know what all happened. Everything changed. It was hard to get to know folks up here, and I missed my people. I weren't used to so much white folks. The ones I seed before was something hateful, but they didn't come around too much. I mean, we didn't have too much truck with them. Just now and then in the fields, or at the commissary. But they want all over us. Up north they was everywhere—next door, downstairs, all over the streets—and colored folks few and far between. Northern colored folk was different too. Dicty-like.[1] No better than whites for meanness. They could make you feel just as no-count, 'cept I didn't expect it from them. That was the lonesomest time of my life. I 'member looking out them front windows just waiting for Cholly to come home at three o'clock. I didn't even have a cat to talk to."

In her loneliness, she turned to her husband for reassurance, entertainment, for things to fill the vacant places. Housework was not enough; there were only two rooms, and no yard to keep or move about in. The women in the town wore high-heeled shoes, and when Pauline tried to wear them, they aggravated her shuffle into a pronounced limp. Cholly was kindness still, but began to resist her total dependence on him. They were beginning to have less and less to say to each other. He had no problem finding other people and other things to occupy him —men were always climbing the stairs asking for him, and he was happy to accompany them, leaving her alone.

---

1. Upper-class, snobbish.

Pauline felt uncomfortable with the few black women she met. They were amused by her because she did not straighten her hair. When she tried to make up her face as they did, it came off rather badly. Their goading glances and private snickers at her way of talking (saying "chil'ren") and dressing developed in her a desire for new clothes. When Cholly began to quarrel about the money she wanted, she decided to go to work. Taking jobs as a day worker helped with the clothes, and even a few things for the apartment, but it did not help with Cholly. He was not pleased with her purchases and began to tell her so. Their marriage was shredded with quarrels. She was still no more than a girl, and still waiting for that plateau of happiness, that hand of a precious Lord who, when her way grew drear, would always linger near. Only now she had a clearer idea of what drear meant. Money became the focus of all their discussions, hers for clothes, his for drink. The sad thing was that Pauline did not really care for clothes and makeup. She merely wanted other women to cast favorable glances her way.

After several months of doing day work, she took a steady job in the home of a family of slender means and nervous, pretentious ways.

"*Cholly commenced to getting meaner and meaner and wanted to fight me all of the time. I give him as good as I got. Had to. Look like working for that woman and fighting Cholly was all I did. Tiresome. But I holt on to my jobs, even though working for that woman was more than a notion. It wasn't so much her meanness as just simpleminded. Her whole family was. Couldn't get along with one another worth nothing. You'd think with a pretty house like that and all the money they could holt on to, they would enjoy one another. She haul off and cry over the leastest thing. If one of her friends cut her short on the telephone, she'd go to crying. She should of been glad she had a telephone. I ain't got one yet. I recollect oncet how her baby brother who she put through dentistry school didn't invite them to some big party he throwed. They was a big to-do about that. Everybody stayed on the telephone for days. Fussing and carrying on. She asked me, 'Pauline, what would you do if your own brother had a party and didn't invite you?' I said ifn I really wanted to go to that party, I reckoned I'd go anyhow. Never mind what he want. She just sucked her teeth a little and made out like what I said was dumb. All the while I was thinking how dumb she was. Whoever told her that her brother was her friend? Folks can't like folks just 'cause they has the same mama. I tried to like that woman myself. She was good about giving me stuff, but I just couldn't like her. Soon as I worked up a good feeling on her account, she'd do something ignorant and start in to telling me how to clean and do. If I left her on her own, she'd drown in dirt. I didn't have to pick up after Chicken and Pie the way I*

had to pick up after them. None of them knew so much as how to wipe
their behinds. I know, 'cause I did the washing. And couldn't pee
proper to save their lives. Her husband ain't hit the bowl yet. Nasty
white folks is about the nastiest things they is. But I would have
stayed on 'cepting for Cholly come over by where I was working and
cut up so. He come there drunk wanting some money. When that
white woman see him, she turned red. She tried to act strong-like, but
she was scared bad. Anyway, she told Cholly to get out or she would
call the police. He cussed her and started pulling on me. I would of
gone upside his head, but I don't want no dealings with the police. So
I taken my things and left. I tried to get back, but she didn't want me
no more if I was going to stay with Cholly. She said she would let me
stay if I left him. I thought about that. But later on it didn't seem
none too bright for a black woman to leave a black man for a white
woman. She didn't never give me the eleven dollars she owned me,
neither. That hurt bad. The gas man had cut the gas off, and I
couldn't cook none. I really begged that woman for my money. I went
to see her. She was mad as a wet hen. Kept on telling me I owed her
for uniforms and some old broken-down bed she give me. I didn't
know if I owed her or not, but I needed my money. She wouldn't let
up none, neither, even when I give her my word that Cholly wouldn't
come back there no more. Then I got so desperate I asked her if she
would loan it to me. She was quiet for a spell, and then she told me I
shouldn't let a man take advantage over me. That I should have more
respect, and it was my husband's duty to pay the bills, and if he
couldn't, I should leave and get alimony. All such simple stuff. What
was he gone give me alimony on? I seen she didn't understand that all
I needed from her was my eleven dollars to pay the gas man so I could
cook. She couldn't get that one thing through her thick head. 'Are you
going to leave him, Pauline?' She kept on saying. I thought she'd give
me my money if I said I would, so I said 'Yes, ma'am.' 'All right,' she
said. 'You leave him, and then come back to work, and we'll let
bygones be bygones.' 'Can I have my money today?' I said. 'No' she
said. 'Only when you leave him. I'm only thinking of you and your
future. What good is he, Pauline, what good is he to you?' How you
going to answer a woman like that, who don't know what good a man
is, and say out of one side of her mouth she's thinking of your future
but won't give you your own money so you can buy you something
besides baloney to eat? So I said, 'No good, ma'am. He ain't no good
to me. But just the same, I think I'd best stay on.' She got up, and I
left. When I got outside, I felt pains in my crotch, I had held my legs
together so tight trying to make that woman understand. But I reckon
now she couldn't understand. She married a man with a slash in his
face instead of a mouth. So how could she understand?"

One winter Pauline discovered she was pregnant. When she told Cholly, he surprised her by being pleased. He began to drink less and come home more often. They eased back into a relationship more like the early days of their marriage, when he asked if she were tired or wanted him to bring her something from the store. In this state of ease, Pauline stopped doing day work and returned to her own housekeeping. But the loneliness in those two rooms had not gone away. When the winter sun hit the peeling green paint of the kitchen chairs, when the smoked hocks were boiling in the pot, when all she could hear was the truck delivering furniture downstairs, she thought about back home, about how she had been all alone most of the time then too, but that this lonesomeness was different. Then she stopped staring at the green chairs, at the delivery truck; she went to the movies instead. There in the dark her memory was refreshed, and she succumbed to her earlier dreams. Along with the idea of romantic love, she was introduced to another—physical beauty. Probably the most destructive ideas in the history of human thought. Both originated in envy, thrived in insecurity, and ended in disillusion. In equating physical beauty with virtue, she stripped her mind, bound it, and collected self-contempt by the heap. She forgot lust and simple caring for. She regarded love as possessive mating, and romance as the goal of the spirit. It would be for her a well-spring from which she would draw the most destructive emotions, deceiving the lover and seeking to imprison the beloved, curtailing freedom in every way.

She was never able, after her education in the movies, to look at a face and not assign it some category in the scale of absolute beauty, and the scale was one she absorbed in full from the silver screen. There at last were the darkened woods, the lonely roads, the river banks, the gently knowing eyes. There the flawed became whole, the blind sighted, and the lame and halt threw away their crutches. There death was dead, and people made every gesture in a cloud of music. There the black-and-white images came together, making a magnificent whole—all projected through the ray of light from above and behind.

It was really a simple pleasure, but she learned all there was to love and all there was to hate.

"The onliest time I be happy seem like was when I was in the picture show. Every time I got, I went. I'd go early, before the show started. They'd cut off the lights, and everything be black. Then the screen would light up, and I'd move right on in them pictures. White men taking such good care of they women, and they all dressed up in big clean houses with the bathtubs right in the same room with the toilet. Them pictures gave me a lot of pleasure, but it made coming home hard, and looking at Cholly hard. I don't know. I 'member one

time I went to see Clark Gable and Jean Harlow.[2] I fixed my hair up
like I'd seen hers on a magazine. A part on the side, with one little
curl on my forehead. It looked just like her. Well, almost just like.
Anyway, I sat in that show with my hair done up that way and had a
good time. I thought I'd see it through to the end again, and I got up
to get me some candy. I was sitting back in my seat, and I taken a big
bite of that candy, and it pulled a tooth right out of my mouth. I could
of cried. I had good teeth, not a rotten one in my head. I don't believe
I ever did get over that. There I was, five months pregnant, trying to
look like Jean Harlow, and a front tooth gone. Everything went then.
Look like I just didn't care no more after that. I let my hair go back,
plaited it up, and settled down to just being ugly. I still went to the
pictures, though, but the meanness got worse. I wanted my tooth back.
Cholly poked fun at me, and we started fighting again. I tried to kill
him. He didn't hit me too hard, 'cause I were pregnant I guess, but
the fights, once they got started up again, kept up. He begin to make
me madder than anything I knowed, and I couldn't keep my hands off
him. Well, I had that baby—a boy—and after that got pregnant
again with another one. But it weren't like I thought it was gone be. I
loved them and all, I guess, but maybe it was having no money, or
maybe it was Cholly, but they sure worried the life out of me.
Sometimes I'd catch myself hollering at them and beating them, and
I'd feel sorry for them, but I couldn't seem to stop. When I had the
second one, a girl, I 'member I said I'd love it no matter what it looked
like. She looked like a black ball of hair. I don't recollect trying to get
pregnant that first time. But that second time, I actually tried to get
pregnant. Maybe 'cause I'd had one already and wasn't scairt to do it.
Anyway, I felt good, and wasn't thinking on the carrying, just the
baby itself. I used to talk to it whilst it be still in the womb. Like good
friends we was. You know. I be hanging wash and I knowed lifting
weren't good for it. I'd say to it holt on now I gone hang up these few
rags, don't get froggy; it be over soon. It wouldn't leap or nothing. Or I
be mixing something in a bowl for the other child and I'd talk to it
then too. You know, just friendly talk. On up til the end I felted good
about that baby. I went to the hospital when my time come. So I could
be easeful. I didn't want to have it at home like I done with the boy.
They put me in a big room with a whole mess of women. The pains
was coming, but not too bad. A little old doctor come to examine me.
He had all sorts of stuff. He gloved his hand and put some kind of
jelly on it and rammed it up between my legs. When he left off, some
more doctors come. One old one and some young ones. The old one
was learning the young ones about babies. Showing them how to do.

2. Popular romantic film stars of the thirties.

When he got to me he said now these here women you don't have any trouble with. They deliver right away and with no pain. Just like horses. The young ones smiled a little. They looked at my stomach and between my legs. They never said nothing to me. Only one looked at me. Looked at my face, I mean. I looked right back at him. He dropped his eyes and turned red. He knowed, I reckon, that maybe I weren't no horse foaling. But them others. They didn't know. They went on. I seed them talking to them white women: 'How you feel? Gonna have twins?' Just shucking[3] them, of course, but nice talk. Nice friendly talk. I got edgy and when them pains got harder, I was glad. Glad to have something else to think about. I moaned something awful. The pains wasn't as bad as I let on, but I had to let them people know having a baby was more than a bowel movement. I hurt just like them white women. Just 'cause I wasn't hooping and hollering before didn't mean I wasn't feeling pain. What'd they think? That just 'cause I knowed how to have a baby with no fuss that my behind wasn't pulling and aching like theirs Besides, that doctor don't know what he talking about. He must never seed no mare foal. Who say they don't have no pain? Just 'cause she don't cry? 'Cause she can't say it, they think it ain't there? If they looks in her eyes and see them eyeballs lolling back, see the sorrowful look, they'd know. Anyways, the baby come. Big old healthy thing. She looked different from what I thought. Reckon I talked to it so much before I conjured up a mind's eye view of it. So when I seed it, it was like looking at a picture of your mama when she was a girl. You knows who she is, but she don't look the same. They give her to me for a nursing, and she liked to pull my nipple off right away. She caught on fast. Not like Sammy, he was the hardest child to feed. But Pecola look like she knowed right off what to do. A right smart baby she was. I used to like to watch her. You know they makes them greedy sounds. Eyes all soft and wet. A cross between a puppy and a dying man. But I knowed she was ugly. Head full of pretty hair, but Lord she was ugly."

When Sammy and Pecola were still young Pauline had to go back to work. She was older now, with no time for dreams and movies. It was time to put all of the pieces together, make coherence where before there had been none. The children gave her this need; she herself was no longer a child. So she became, and her process of becoming was like most of ours: she developed a hatred for things that mystified or obstructed her; acquired virtues that were easy to maintain; assigned herself a role in the scheme of things; and harked back to simpler times for gratification.

---

3. Fooling, flattering.

She took on the full responsibility and recognition of breadwinner and returned to church. First, however, she moved out of the two rooms into a spacious first floor of a building that had been built as a store. She came into her own with the women who had despised her, by being more moral than they; she avenged herself on Cholly by forcing him to indulge in the weaknesses she despised. She joined a church where shouting was frowned upon, served on Stewardess Board No. 3,[4] and became a member of Ladies Circle No. 1. At prayer meeting she moaned and sighed over Cholly's ways, and hoped God would help her keep the children from the sins of the father. She stopped saying "chil'ren" and said "childring" instead. She let another tooth fall, and was outraged by painted ladies who thought only of clothes and men. Holding Cholly as a model of sin and failure, she bore him like a crown of thorns, and her children like a cross.

It was her good fortune to find a permanent job in the home of a well-to-do family whose members were affectionate, appreciative, and generous. She looked at their houses, smelled their linen, touched their silk draperies, and loved all of it. The child's pink nightie, the stacks of white pillow slips edged with embroidery, the sheets with top hems picked out with blue cornflowers. She became what is known as an ideal servant, for such a role filled practically all of her needs. When she bathed the little Fisher girl, it was in a procelain tub with silvery taps running infinite quantities of hot, clear water. She dried her in fluffy white towels and put her in cuddly night clothes. Then she brushed the yellow hair, enjoying the roll and slip of it between her fingers. No zinc tub, no buckets of stove-heated water, no flaky, stiff, grayish towels washed in a kitchen sink, dried in a dusty backyard, no tangled black puffs of rough wool to comb. Soon she stopped trying to keep her own house. The things she could afford to buy did not last, had no beauty or style, and were absorbed by the dingy storefront. More and more she neglected her house, her children, her man—they were like the after-thoughts one has just before sleep, the early-morning and late-evening edges of her day, the dark edges that made the daily life with the Fishers lighter, more delicate, more lovely. Here she could arrange things, clean things, line things up in neat rows. Here her foot flopped around on deep pile carpets, and there was no uneven sound. Here she found beauty, order, cleanliness, and praise. Mr. Fisher said, "I would rather sell her blueberry cobblers than real estate." She reigned over cupboards stacked high with food that would not be eaten for weeks, even months; she was queen of canned vegetables bought by the case, special fondants and ribbon candy curled up in tiny silver dishes. The creditors and service people who humiliated her when she went to them on her

4. Women's groups in the church.

own behalf respected her, were even intimidated by her, when she spoke for the Fishers. She refused beef slightly dark or with edges not properly trimmed. The slightly reeking fish that she accepted for her own family she would all but throw in the fish man's face if he sent it to the Fisher house. Power, praise, and luxury were hers in this household. They even gave her what she had never had—a nickname—Polly. It was her pleasure to stand in her kitchen at the end of a day and survey her handiwork. Knowing there were soap bars by the dozen, bacon by the rasher, and reveling in her shiny pots and pans and polished floors. Hearing, "We'll never let her go. We could never find anybody like Polly. She will *not* leave the kitchen until everything is in order. Really, she is the ideal servant."

Pauline kept this order, this beauty, for herself, a private world, and never introduced it into her storefront, or to her children. Them she bent toward respectability, and in so doing taught them fear: fear of being clumsy, fear of being like their father, fear of not being loved by God, fear of madness like Cholly's mother's. Into her son she beat a loud desire to run away, and into her daughter she beat a fear of growing up, fear of other people, fear of life.

All the meaningfulness of her life was in her work. For her virtues were intact. She was an active church woman, did not drink, smoke, or carouse, defended herself mightily against Cholly, rose above him in every way, and felt she was fulfilling a mother's role conscientiously when she pointed out their father's faults to keep them from having them, or punished them when they showed any slovenliness, no matter how slight, when she worked twelve to sixteen hours a day to support them. And the world itself agreed with her.

It was only sometimes, sometimes, and then rarely, that she thought about the old days, or what her life had turned to. They were musings, idle thoughts, full sometimes of the old dreaminess, but not the kind of thing she cared to dwell on.

"I started to leave him once, but something came up. Once, after he tried to set the house on fire, I was all set in my mind to go. I can't even 'member now what held me. He sure ain't give me much of a life. But it wasn't all bad. Sometimes things wasn't all bad. He used to come easing into bed sometimes, not too drunk. I make out like I'm asleep, 'cause it's late, and he taken three dollars out of my pocketbook that morning or something. I hear him breathing, but I don't look around. I can see in my mind's eye his black arms thrown back behind his head, the muscles like great big peach stones sanded down, with veins running like little swollen rivers down his arms. Without touching him I be feeling those ridges on the tips of my fingers. I see the palms of his hands calloused to granite, and the long fingers

curled up and still. I think about the thick, knotty hair on his chest, and the two big swells his breast muscles make. I want to rub my face hard in his chest and feel the hair cut my skin. I know just where the hair growth slacks out—just above his navel—and how it picks up again and spreads out. Maybe he'll shift a little, and his leg will touch me, or I feel his flank just graze my behind. I don't move even yet. Then he lift his head, turn over, and put his hand on my waist. If I don't move, he'll move his hand over to pull and knead my stomach. Soft and slow-like. I still don't move, because I don't want him to stop. I want to pretend sleep and have him keep on rubbing my stomach. Then he will lean his head down and bite my tit. Then I don't want him to rub my stomach anymore. I want him to put his hand between my legs. I pretend to wake up, and turn to him, but not opening my legs. I want him to open them for me. He does, and I be soft and wet where his fingers are strong and hard. I be softer than I ever been before. All my strength in his hand. My brain curls up like wilted leaves. A funny, empty feeling is in my hands. I want to grab holt of something, so I hold his head. His mouth is under my chin. Then I don't want his hand between my legs no more, because I think I am softening away. I stretch my legs open, and he is on top of me. Too heavy to hold, and too light not to. He puts his thing in me. In me. In me. I wrap my feet around his back so he can't get away. His face is next to mine. The bed springs sounds like them crickets used to back home. He puts his fingers in mine, and we stretches our arms outwise like Jesus on the cross. I hold on tight. My fingers and my feet hold on tight, because everything else is going, going. I know he wants me to come first. But I can't. Not until he does. Not until I feel him loving me. Just me. Sinking into me. Not until I know that my flesh is all that be on his mind. That he couldn't stop if he had to. That he would die rather than take his thing out of me. Of me. Not until he has let go of all he has, and give it to me. To me. To me. When he does, I feel a power. I be strong, I be pretty, I be young. And then I wait. He shivers and tosses his head. Now I be strong enough, pretty enough, and young enough to let him make me come. I take my fingers out of his and put my hands on his behind. My legs drop back onto the bed. I don't make no noise, because the chil'ren might hear. I begin to feel those little bits of color floating up into me—deep in me. That streak of green from the june-bug light, the purple from the berries trickling along my thighs, Mama's lemonade yellow runs sweet in me. Then I feel like I'm laughing between my legs, and the laughing gets all mixed up with the colors, and I'm afraid I'll come, and afraid I won't. But I know I will. And I do. And it be rainbow all inside. And it lasts and lasts and lasts. I want to thank him, but don't know how, so I pat him like you do a baby. He asks me if I'm all right. I say yes. He gets *off me and lies down to sleep. I want to say something, but I don't. I don't want to take my mind offen the rainbow. I should get up and go to the toilet, but I don't. Besides, Cholly is asleep with his leg throwed over me. I can't move and don't want to.*

"But it ain't like that anymore. Most times he's thrashing away inside me before I'm woke, and through when I am. The rest of the time I can't even be next to his stinking drunk self. But I don't care 'bout it no more. My Maker will take care of me. I know He will. I know He will. Besides, it don't make no difference about this old earth. There is sure to be a glory. Only thing I miss sometimes is that rainbow. But like I say, I don't recollect it much anymore."

.SEEFATHERHEISBIGANDSTRONGFATH
ERWILLYOUPLAYWITHJANEFATHER
ISSMILINGSMILEFATHERSMILESMILE

When Cholly was four days old, his mother wrapped him in two blankets and one newspaper and placed him on a junk heap by the railroad. His Great Aunt Jimmy, who had seen her niece carrying a bundle out of the back door, rescued him. She beat his mother with a razor strap and wouldn't let her near the baby after that. Aunt Jimmy raised Cholly herself, but took delight sometimes in telling him of how she had saved him. He gathered from her that his mother wasn't right in the head. But he never had a chance to find out, because she ran away shortly after the razor strap, and no one had heard of her since.

Cholly was grateful for having been saved. Except sometimes. Sometimes when he watched Aunt Jimmy eating collards with her fingers, sucking her four gold teeth, or smelled her when she wore the asafetida bag[5] around her neck, or when she made him sleep with her for warmth in winter and he could see her old, wrinkled breasts sagging in her nightgown—then he wondered whether it would have been just as well to have died there. Down in the rim of a tire under a soft black Georgia sky.

He had four years of school before he got courage enough to ask his aunt who and where his father was.

"That Fuller boy, I believe it was," his aunt said. "He was hanging around then, but he taken off pretty quick before you was born. I think he gone to Macon. Him or his brother Maybe both. I hear old man Fuller say something 'bout it once."

"What name he have?" asked Cholly.

"Fuller Foolish."

5. A bag worn for medicinal purposes, containing an offensive-smelling material obtained from certain roots.

"I mean what his given name?"

"Oh." She closed her eyes to think, and sighed. "Can't recollect nothing no more. Sam, was it? Yeh. Samuel. No. No, it wasn't. It was Samson. Samson Fuller."

"How come you all didn't name me Samson?" Cholly's voice was low.

"What for? He wasn't nowhere around when you was born. Your mama didn't name you nothing. The nine days wasn't up before she throwed you on the junk heap. When I got you I named you myself on the ninth day. You named after my dead brother. Charles Breedlove. A good man. Ain't no Samson never come to no good end."[6]

Cholly didn't ask anything else.

Two years later he quit school to take a job at Tyson's Feed and Grain Store. He swept up, ran errands, weighed bags, and lifted them onto the drays. Sometimes they let him ride with the drayman. A nice old man called Blue Jack. Blue used to tell him old-timey stories about how it was when the Emancipation Proclamation[7] came. How the black people hollered, cried, and sang. And ghost stories about how a white man cut off his wife's head and buried her in the swamp, and the headless body came out at night and went stumbling around the yard, knocking over stuff because it couldn't see, and crying all the time for a comb. They talked about the women Blue had had, and the fights he'd been in when he was younger, about how he talked his way out of getting lynched once, and how others hadn't.

Cholly loved Blue. Long after he was a man, he remembered the good times they had had. How on a July 4 at a church picnic a family was about to break open a watermelon. Several children were standing around watching. Blue was hovering about on the periphery of the circle—a faint smile of anticipation softening his face. The father of the family lifted the melon high over his head—his big arms looked taller then the trees to Cholly, and the melon blotted out the sun. Tall, head forward, eyes fastened on a rock, his arms higher than the pines, his hands holding a melon bigger than the sun, he paused an instant to get his bearing and secure his aim. Watching the figure etched against the bright blue sky, Cholly felt goose pimples popping along his arms and neck. He wondered if God looked like that. No. God was a nice old white man, with long white hair, flowing white beard, and little blue eyes that looked sad when people died and mean when they were bad. It must be the devil who looks like that—holding the world in his hands, ready to dash it to the ground and spill the red guts so niggers could eat

---

6. In the Old Testament the Israelite Samson is captured by the Philistines and blinded; he manages to bring down their temple by pushing out the central pillars, burying himself and them in the wreckage (Judges 16).

7. The proclamation signed by President Lincoln in 1863, decreeing the freedom of slaves in the confederate states.

the sweet, warm insides. If the devil did look like that, Cholly preferred him. He never felt anything thinking about God, but just the idea of the devil excited him. And now the strong, black devil was blotting out the sun and getting ready to split open the world.

Far away somebody was playing a mouth organ; the music slithered over the cane fields and into the pine grove; it spiraled around the trunks and mixed itself with the pine scent, so Cholly couldn't tell the difference between the sound and the odor that hung about the heads of the people.

The man swung the melon down to the edge of a rock. A soft cry of disappointment accompanied the sound of smashed rind. The break was a bad one. The melon was jagged, and hunks of rind and red meat scattered on the grass.

Blue jumped. "Aw—awww," he moaned, "dere go da heart." His voice was both sad and pleased. Everybody looked to see the big red chunk from the very center of the melon, free of rind and sparse of seed which had rolled a little distance from Blue's feet. He stooped to pick it up. Blood red, its planes dull and blunted with sweetness, its edges rigid with juice. Too obvious, almost obscene, in the joy it promised.

"Go 'head, Blue," the father laughed. "You can have it."

Blue smiled and walked away. Little children scrambled for the pieces on the ground. Women picked out the seeds for the smallest ones and broke off little bits of the meat for themselves. Blue's eye caught Cholly's. He motioned to him. "Come on, boy. Le's you and me eat the heart."

Together the old man and the boy sat on the grass and shared the heart of the watermelon. The nasty-sweet guts of the earth.

It was in the spring, a very chilly spring, that Aunt Jimmy died of peach cobbler. She went to a camp meeting that took place after a rainstorm, and the damp wood of the benches was bad for her. For four or five days afterward, she felt poorly. Friends came to see about her. Some made camomile tea; others rubbed her with liniment. Miss Alice, her closest friend, read the Bible to her. Still she was declining. Advice was prolific, if contradictory.

"Don't eat no whites of eggs."

"Drink new milk."

"Chew on this root."

Aunt Jimmy ignored all but Miss Alice's Bible reading. She nodded in drowsy appreciation as the words from First Corinthians[8] droned over her. Sweet amens fell from her lips as she was chastised for all her sins. But her body would not respond.

Finally it was decided to fetch M'Dear. M'Dear was a quiet woman

---

8. A book of the New Testament containing some of the basic doctrines of Christianity.

who lived in a shack near the woods. She was a competent midwife and decisive diagnostician. Few could remember when M'Dear was not around. In any illness that could not be handled by ordinary means—known cures, intuition, or endurance—the word was always, "Fetch M'Dear."

When she arrived at Aunt Jimmy's house, Cholly was amazed at the sight of her. He had always pictured her as shriveled and hunched over, for he knew she was very, very old. But M'Dear loomed taller than the preacher who accompanied her. She must have been over six feet tall. Four big white knots of hair gave power and authority to her soft black face. Standing straight as a poker, she seemed to need her hickory stick not for support but for communication. She tapped it lightly on the floor as she looked down at Aunt Jimmy's wrinkled face. She stroked the knob with the thumb of her right hand while she ran her left one over Aunt Jimmy's body. The backs of her long fingers she placed on the patient's cheek, then placed her palm on the forehead. She ran her fingers through the sick woman's hair, lightly scratching the scalp, and then looking at what the fingernails revealed. She lifted Aunt Jimmy's hand and looked closely at it—fingernails, back skin, the flesh of the palm she pressed with three fingertips. Later she put her ear on Aunt Jimmy's chest and stomach to listen. At M'Dear's request, the women pulled the slop jar from under the bed to show the stools. M'Dear tapped her stick while looking at them.

"Bury the slop jar and everything in it," she said to the women. To Aunt Jimmy she said, "You done caught cold in your womb. Drink pot liquor[9] and nothing else."

"Will it pass?" asked Aunt Jimmy. "Is I'm gone be all right?"

"I reckon."

M'Dear turned and left the room. The preacher put her in his buggy to take her home.

That evening the women brought bowls of pot liquor from black-eyed peas, from mustards, from cabbage, from kale, from collards, from turnips, from beets, from green beans. Even the juice from a boiling hog jowl.

Two evenings later Aunt Jimmy had gained much strength. When Miss Alice and Mrs. Gaines stopped in to check on her, they remarked on her improvement. The three women sat talking about various miseries they had had, their cure or abatement, what had helped. Over and over again they returned to Aunt Jimmy's condition. Repeating its cause, what could have been done to prevent the misery from taking hold, and M'Dear's infallibility. Their voices blended into a threnody of nostalgia about pain. Rising and falling, complex in harmony, un-

9. Broth.

certain in pitch, but constant in the recitative of pain. They hugged the memories of illnesses to their bosoms. They licked their lips and clucked their tongues in fond remembrance of pains they had endured —childbirth, rheumatism, croup, sprains, backaches, piles. All of the bruises they had collected from moving about the earth—harvesting, cleaning, hoisting, pitching, stooping, kneeling, picking—always with young ones underfoot.

But they had been young once. The odor of their armpits and haunches had mingled into a lovely musk; their eyes had been furtive, their lips relaxed, and the delicate turn of their heads on those slim black necks had been like nothing other than a doe's. Their laughter had been more touch than sound.

Then they had grown. Edging into life from the back door. Becoming. Everybody in the world was in a position to give them orders. White women said, "Do this." White children said, "Give me that." White men said, "Come here." Black men said, "Lay down." The only people they need not take orders from were black children and each other. But they took all of that and re-created it in their own image. They ran the houses of white people, and knew it. When white men beat their men, they cleaned up the blood and went home to receive abuse from the victim. They beat their children with one hand and stole for them with the other. The hands that felled trees also cut umbilical cords; the hands that wrung the necks of chickens and butchered hogs also nudged African violets into bloom; the arms that loaded sheaves, bales, and sacks rocked babies into sleep. They patted biscuits into flaky ovals of innocence—and shrouded the dead. They plowed all day and came home to nestle like plums under the limbs of their men. The legs that straddled a mule's back were the same ones that straddled their men's hips. And the difference was all the difference there was.

Then they were old. Their bodies honed, their odor sour. Squatting in a cane field, stooping in a cotton field, kneeling by a river bank, they had carried a world on their heads. They had given over the lives of their own children and tendered their grandchildren. With relief they wrapped their heads in rags, and their breasts in flannel; eased their feet into felt. They were through with lust and lactation, beyond tears and terror. They alone could walk the roads of Mississippi, the lanes of Georgia, the fields of Alabama unmolested. They were old enough to be irritable when and where they chose, tired enough to look forward to death, disinterested enough to accept the idea of pain while ignoring the presence of pain. They were, in fact and at last, free. And the lives of these old black women were synthesized in their eyes—a purée of tragedy and humor, wickedness and serenity, truth and fantasy.

They chattered far into the night. Cholly listened and grew sleepy.

The lullaby of grief enveloped him, rocked him, and at last numbed him. In his sleep the foul odor of an old woman's stools turned into the healthy smell of horse shit, and the voices of the three women were muted into the pleasant notes of a mouth organ. He was aware, in his sleep, of being curled up in a chair, his hands tucked between his thighs. In a dream his penis changed into a long hickory stick, and the hands caressing it were the hands of M'Dear.

On a wet Saturday night, before Aunt Jimmy felt strong enough to get out of the bed, Essie Foster brought her a peach cobbler. The old lady ate a piece, and the next morning when Cholly went to empty the slop jar, she was dead. Her mouth was a slackened O, and her hands, those long fingers with a man's hard nails, having done their laying by, could now be dainty on the sheet. One open eye looked at him as if to say, "Mind how you take holt of that jar, boy." Cholly stared back, unable to move, until a fly settled at the corner of her mouth. He fanned it away angrily, looked back at the eye, and did its bidding.

Aunt Jimmy's funeral was the first Cholly had ever attended. As a member of the family, one of the bereaved, he was the object of a great deal of attention. The ladies had cleaned the house, aired everything out, notified everybody, and stitched together what looked like a white wedding dress for Aunt Jimmy, a maiden lady, to wear when she met Jesus. They even produced a dark suit, white shirt, and tie for Cholly. The husband of one of them cut his hair. He was enclosed in fastidious tenderness. Nobody talked to him; that is, they treated him like the child he was, never engaging him in serious conversation; but they anticipated wishes he never had: meals appeared, hot water for the wooden tub, clothes laid out. At the wake he was allowed to fall asleep, and arms carried him to bed. Only on the third day after the death—the day of the funeral—did he have to share the spotlight. Aunt Jimmy's people came from nearby towns and farms. Her brother O. V., his children and wife, and lots of cousins. But Cholly was still the major figure, because he was "Jimmy's boy, the last thing she loved," and "the one who found her." The solicitude of the women, the head pats of the men, pleased Cholly, and the creamy conversations fascinated him.

"What'd she die from?"

"Essie's pie."

"Don't say?"

"Uh-huh. She was doing fine, I saw her the very day before. Said she wanted me to bring her some black thread to patch some things for the boy. I should of known just from her wanting black thread that was a sign."

"Sure was."

"Just like Emma. 'Member? She kept asking for thread. Dropped dead that very evening."

"Yeah. Well, she was determined to have it. Kept on reminding me. I told her I had some to home, but naw, she wanted it new. So I sent Li'l June to get some that very morning when she was laying dead. I was just fixing to bring it over, 'long with a piece of sweet bread. You know how she craved my sweet bread."

"Sure did. Always bragged on it. She was a good friend to you."

"I believe it. Well, I had no more got my clothes on when Sally bust in the door hollering about how Cholly here had been over to Miss Alice saying she was dead. You could have knocked me over, I tell you."

"Guess Essie feels mighty bad."

"Oh, Lord, yes. But I told her the Lord giveth and the Lord taketh away. Wasn't her fault none. She makes good peach pies. But she bound to believe it was the pie did it, and I 'spect she right."

"Well, she shouldn't worry herself none 'bout that. She was just doing what we all would of done."

"Yeah. 'Cause I was sure wrapping up that sweet bread, and that could of done it too."

"I doubts that. Sweet bread is pure. But a pie is the worse thing to give anybody ailing. I'm surprised Jimmy didn't know better."

"If she did, she wouldn't let on. She would have tried to please. You know how she was. So good."

"I'll say. Did she leave anything?"

"Not even a pocket handkerchief. The house belongs to some white folks in Clarksville."

"Oh, yeah? I thought she owned it."

"May have at one time. But not no more. I hear the insurance folks been down talking to her brother."

"How much do it come to?"

"Eighty-five dollars, I hear."

"That all?"

"Can she get in the ground on that?"

"Don't see how. When my daddy died last year this April it costed one hundred and fifty dollars. 'Course, we had to have everything just so. Now Jimmy's people may all have to chip in. That undertaker that lays out black folks ain't none too cheap."

"Seems a shame. She been paying on that insurance all her life."

"Don't I know?"

"Well, what about the boy? What he gone do?"

"Well, caint nobody find that mama, so Jimmy's brother gone take him back to his place. They say he got a nice place. Inside toilet and everything."

"That's nice. He seems like a good Christian man. And the boy need a man's hand."

"What time's the funeral?"

"Two clock. She ought to be in the ground by four."

"Where's the banquet? I heard Essie wanted it at her house."

"Naw, it's at Jimmy's. Her brother wanted it so."

"Well, it will be a big one. Everybody liked old Jimmy. Sure will miss her in the pew."

The funeral banquet was a peal of joy after the thunderous beauty of the funeral. It was like a street tragedy with spontaneity tucked softly into the corners of a highly formal structure. The deceased was the tragic hero, the survivors the innocent victims; there was the omnipresence of the deity, strophe and antistrophe[1] of the chorus of mourners led by the preacher. There was grief over the waste of life, the stunned wonder at the ways of God, and the restoration of order in nature at the graveyard.

Thus the banquet was the exultation, the harmony, the acceptance of physical frailty, joy in the termination of misery. Laughter, relief, a steep hunger for food.

Cholly had not yet fully realized his aunt was dead. Everything was so interesting. Even at the graveyard he felt nothing but curiosity, and when his turn had come to view the body at the church, he had put his hand out to touch the corpse to see if it were really ice cold like everybody said. But he drew his hand back quickly. Aunt Jimmy looked so private, and it seemed wrong somehow to disturb that privacy. He had trudged back to his pew dry-eyed amid tearful shrieks and shouts of others, wondering if he should try to cry.

Back in his house, he was free to join in the gaiety and enjoy what he really felt—a kind of carnival spirit. He ate greedily and felt good enough to try to get to know his cousins. There was some question, according to the adults, as to whether they were his real cousins or not, since Jimmy's brother O. V. was only a half-brother, and Cholly's mother had been the daughter of Jimmy's sister, but that sister was from the second marriage of Jimmy's father, and O. V. was from the first marriage.

One of these cousins interested Cholly in particular. He was about fifteen or sixteen years old. Cholly went outside and found the boy standing with some others near the tub where Aunt Jimmy used to boil her clothes.

He ventured a tentative "Hey." They responded with another. The fifteen-year-old named Jake offered Cholly a rolled-up cigarette. Cholly took it, but when he held the cigarette at arm's length and stuck the tip of it into the match flame, instead of putting it in his mouth and

1. Alternating verse forms used in Greek tragedies, here compared to the question-response   form used in black churches.

drawing on it, they laughed at him. Shamefaced, he threw the cigarette down. He felt it important to do something to reinstate himself with Jake. So when he asked Cholly if he knew any girls, Cholly said, "Sure."

All the girls Cholly knew were at the banquet, and he pointed to a cluster of them standing, hanging, draping on the back porch. Darlene too. Cholly hoped Jake wouldn't pick her.

"Let's get some and walk around," said Jake.

The two boys sauntered over to the porch. Cholly didn't know how to begin. Jake wrapped his legs around the rickety porch rail and just sat there staring off into space as though he had no interest in them at all. He was letting them look him over, and guardedly evaluating them in return.

The girls pretended they didn't see the boys and kept on chattering. Soon their talk got sharp; the gentle teasing they had been engaged in with each other changed to bitchiness, a serious kind of making fun. That was Jake's clue; the girls were reacting to him. They had gotten a whiff of his manhood and were shivering for a place in his attention.

Jake left the porch rail and walked right up to a girl named Suky, the one who had been most bitter in her making fun.

"Want to show me 'round?" He didn't even smile.

Cholly held his breath, waiting for Suky to shut Jake up. She was good at that, and well known for her sharp tongue. To his enormous surprise, she readily agreed, and even lowered her lashes. Taking courage, Cholly turned to Darlene and said, "Come on 'long. We just going down to the gully." He waited for her to screw up her face and say no, or what for, or some such thing. His feelings about her were mostly fear—fear that she would not like him, and fear that she would.

His second fear materialized. She smiled and jumped down the three leaning steps to join him. Her eyes were full of compassion, and Cholly remembered that he was the bereaved.

"If you want to," she said, "but not too far. Mama said we got to leave early, and it's getting dark."

The four of them moved away. Some of the other boys had come to the porch and were about to begin that partly hostile, partly indifferent, partly desperate mating dance. Suky, Jake, Darlene, and Cholly walked through several backyards until they came to an open field. They ran across it and came to a dry riverbed lined with green. The object of the walk was a wild vineyard where the muscadine grew. Too new, too tight to have much sugar, they were eaten anyway. None of them wanted—not then—the grape's easy relinquishing of all its dark juice. The restraint, the holding off, the promise of sweetness that had yet to unfold, excited them more than full ripeness would have done. At last their teeth were on edge, and the boys diverted themselves by pelting

the girls with the grapes. Their slim black boy wrists made G clefs in the
air as they executed the tosses. The chase took Cholly and Darlene
away from the lip of the gully, and when they paused for breath, Jake
and Suky were nowhere in sight. Darlene's white cotton dress was
stained with juice. Her big blue hair bow had come undone, and the
sundown breeze was picking it up and fluttering it about her head.
They were out of breath and sank down in the green-and-purple grass
on the edge of the pine woods.

Cholly lay on his back panting. His mouth full of the taste of muscadine, listening to the pine needles rustling loudly in their anticipation of
rain. The smell of promised rain, pine, and muscadine made him giddy.
The sun had gone and pulled away its shreds of light. Turning his head
to see where the moon was. Cholly caught sight of Darlene in moonlight behind him. She was huddled into a D—arms encircling drawn-
up knees, on which she rested her head. Cholly could see her bloomers
and the muscles of her young thighs.

"We bed' get on back," he said.

"Yeah." She stretched her legs flat on the ground and began to retie
her hair ribbon. "Mama gone whup me."

"Naw she ain't."

"Uh-huh. She told me she would if I get dirty."

"You ain't dirty."

"I am too. Looka that." She dropped her hands from the ribbon and
smoothed out a place on her dress where the grape stains were heaviest.

Cholly felt sorry for her; it was just as much his fault. Suddenly he realized that Aunt Jimmy was dead, for he missed the fear of being
whipped. There was nobody to do it except Uncle O. V., and he was
the bereaved too.

"Let me," he said. He rose to his knees facing her and tried to tie her
ribbon. Darlene put her hands under his open shirt and rubbed the
damp tight skin. When he looked at her in surprise, she stopped and
laughed. He smiled and continued knotting the bow. She put her hands
back under his shirt.

"Hold still," he said. "How I gone get this?"

She tickled his ribs with her fingertips. He giggled and grabbed his
rib cage. They were on top of each other in a moment. She corkscrew-
ing her hands into his clothes. He returning the play, digging into the
neck of her dress, and then under her dress. When he got his hand in
her bloomers, she suddenly stopped laughing and looked serious.
Cholly, frightened, was about to take his hand away, but she held his
wrist so he couldn't move it. He examined her then with his fingers,
and she kissed his face and mouth. Cholly found her muscadine-lipped
mouth distracting. Darlene released his head, shifted her body, and
pulled down her pants. After some trouble with the buttons, Cholly

dropped his pants down to his knees. Their bodies began to make sense to him, and it was not as difficult as he had thought it would be. She moaned a little, but the excitement collecting inside him made him close his eyes and regard her moans as no more than pine sighs over his head. Just as he felt an explosion threaten, Darlene froze and cried out. He thought he had hurt her, but when he looked at her face, she was staring wildly at something over his shoulder. He jerked around.

There stood two white men. One with a spirit lamp,[2] the other with a flashlight. There was no mistake about their being white; he could smell it. Cholly jumped, trying to kneel, stand, and get his pants up all in one motion. The men had long guns.

"Hee hee hee heeeee." The snicker was a long asthmatic cough.

The other raced the flashlight all over Cholly and Darlene.

"Get on wid it, nigger," said the flashlight one.

"Sir?" said Cholly, trying to find a buttonhole.

"I said, get on wid it. An' make it good, nigger, make it good."

There was no place for Cholly's eyes to go. They slid about furtively searching for shelter, while his body remained paralyzed. The flashlight man lifted his gun down from his shoulder, and Cholly heard the clop of metal. He dropped back to his knees. Darlene had her head averted, her eyes staring out of the lamplight into the surrounding darkness and looking almost unconcerned, as though they had no part in the drama taking place around them. With a violence born of total helplessness, he pulled her dress up, lowered his trousers and underwear.

"Hee hee hee hee heeeeee."

Darlene put her hands over her face as Cholly began to simulate what had gone on before. He could do no more than make-believe. The flashlight made a moon on his behind.

"Hee hee hee hee heeee."

"Come on, coon. Faster. You ain't doing nothing for her."

"Hee hee hee hee heeee."

Cholly, moving faster, looked at Darlene. He hated her. He almost wished he could do it—hard, long, and painfully, he hated her so much. The flashlight wormed its way into his guts and turned the sweet taste of muscadine into rotten fetid bile. He stared at Darlene's hands covering her face in the moon and lamplight. They looked like baby claws.

"Hee hee hee hee heee."

Some dogs howled. "Thas them. Thas them. I know thas Old Honey."

"Yep," said the spirit lamp.

"Come on." The flashlight turned away, and one of them whistled to Honey.

2. A lamp that burns alcohol.

"Wait," said the spirit lamp, "the coon ain't comed yet."

"Well, he have to come on his own time. Good luck, coon baby."

They crushed the pine needles underfoot. Cholly could hear them whistling for a long time, and then the dogs' answer no longer a howl, but warm excited yelps of recognition.

Cholly raised himself and in silence buttoned his trousers. Darlene did not move. Cholly wanted to strangle her, but instead he touched her leg with his foot. "We got to get, girl. Come on!"

She reached for her underwear with her eyes closed, and could not find them. The two of them patted about in the moonlight for the panties. When she found them, she put them on with the movements of an old woman. They walked away from the pine woods toward the road. He in front, she plopping along behind. It started to rain. "That's good," Cholly thought. "It will explain away our clothes."

When they got back to the house, some ten or twelve guests were still there. Jake was gone, Suky too. Some people had gone back for more helpings of food—potato pie, ribs. All were engrossed in early-night reminiscences about dreams, figures, premonitions. Their stuffed comfort was narcotic and had produced recollections and fabrications of hallucinations.

Cholly and Darlene's entrance produced only a mild stir.

"Ya'll soaked, ain't you?"

Darlene's mother was only vaguely fussy. She had eaten and drunk too much. Her shoes were under her chair, and the side snaps of her dress were opened. "Girl. Come on in here. Thought I told you. . . ."

Some of the guests thought they would wait for the rain to slacken. Others, who had come in wagons, thought they'd best leave now. Cholly went into the little storeroom which had been made into a bedroom for him. Three infants were sleeping on his cot. He took off his rain- and pine-soaked clothes and put on his coveralls. He didn't know where to go. Aunt Jimmy's room was out of the question, and Uncle O. V. and his wife would be using it later anyway. He took a quilt from a trunk, spread it on the floor, and lay down. Somebody was brewing coffee, and he had a sharp craving for it, just before falling asleep.

The next day was cleaning-out day, settling accounts, distributing Aunt Jimmy's goods. Mouths were set in downward crescents, eyes veiled, feet tentative.

Cholly floated about aimlessly, doing chores as he was told. All the glamour and warmth the adults had given him on the previous day were replaced by a sharpness that agreed with his mood. He could think only of the flashlight, the muscadines, and Darlene's hands. And when he was not thinking of them, the vacancy in his head was like the space left by a newly pulled tooth still conscious of the rottenness that had once filled it. Afraid of running into Darlene, he would not go far from the house, but neither could he endure the atmosphere of his dead Aunt's house. The picking through her things, the comments on the "condition" of her goods. Sullen, irritable, he cultivated his hatred of Darlene. Never did he once consider directing his hatred toward the hunters. Such an emotion would have destroyed him. They were big, white, armed men. He was small, black, helpless. His subconscious knew what his conscious mind did not guess—that hating them would have consumed him, burned him up like a piece of soft coal, leaving only flakes of ash and a question mark of smoke. He was, in time, to discover that hatred of white men—but not now. Not in impotence but later, when the hatred could find sweet expression. For now, he hated the one who had created the situation, the one who bore witness to his failure, his impotence. The one whom he had not been able to protect, to spare, to cover from the round moon glow of the flashlight. The hee-hee-hee's. He recalled Darlene's dripping hair ribbon, flapping against her face as they walked back in silence in the rain. The loathing that galloped through him made him tremble. There was no one to talk to. Old Blue was too drunk too often these days to make sense. Besides, Cholly doubted if he could reveal his shame to Blue. He would have to lie a little to tell Blue, Blue the woman-killer. It seemed to him that lonely was much better than alone.

The day Cholly's uncle was ready to leave, when everything was packed, when the quarrels about who gets what had seethed down to a sticking gravy on everybody's tongue, Cholly sat on the back porch waiting. It had occurred to him that Darlene might be pregnant. It was a wildly irrational, completely uninformed idea, but the fear it produced was complete enough.

He had to get away. Never mind the fact that he was leaving that very day. A town or two away was not far enough, especially since he did not like or trust his uncle, and Darlene's mother could surely find him, and Uncle O. V. would turn him over to her. Cholly knew it was wrong to run out on a pregnant girl, and recalled, with sympathy, that his father had done just that. Now he understood. He knew then what he must do—find his father. His father would understand. Aunt Jimmy said he had gone to Macon.

With no more thought than a chick leaving its shell, he stepped off the porch. He had gotten a little way when he remembered the treasure; Aunt Jimmy had left something, and he had forgotten all about it. In a stove flue no longer used, she had hidden a little meal bag which she called her treasure. He slipped into the house and found the room empty. Digging into the flue, he encountered webs and soot, and then the soft bag. He sorted the money; fourteen one-dollar bills, two two-dollar bills, and lots of silver change . . . twenty-three dollars in all. Surely that would be enough to get to Macon. What a good, strong-sounding word, *Macon*.

Running away from home for a Georgia black boy was not a great problem. You just sneaked away and started walking. When night came you slept in a barn, if there were no dogs, a cane field, or an empty sawmill. You ate from the ground and bought root beer and licorice in little country stores. There was always an easy tale of woe to tell inquiring black adults, and whites didn't care, unless they were looking for sport.

When he was several days away, he could go to the back door of nice houses and tell the black cook or white mistress that he wanted a job weeding, plowing, picking, cleaning, and that he lived nearby. A week or more there, and he could take off. He lived this way through the turn of summer, and only the following October did he reach a town big enough to have a regular bus station. Dry-mouthed with excitement and apprehension, he went to the colored side of the counter to buy his ticket.

"How much to Macon, sir?"

"Eleven dollars. Five-fifty for children under twelve."

Cholly had twelve dollars and four cents.

"How old you be?"

"Just on twelve, sir, but my mama only give me ten dollars."

"You jest about the biggest twelve I ever seed."

"Please, sir, I got to get to Macon. My mama's sick."

"Thought you said you mama give you ten dollars."

"That's my play mama. My real mama is in Macon, sir."

"I reckon I knows a lying nigger when I sees one, but jest in case you ain't, jest in case one of them mammies is really dyin' and wants to see her little old smoke before she meets her maker, I gone do it."

Cholly heard nothing. The insults were part of the nuisances of life, like lice. He was happier than he had ever remembered being, except that time with Blue and the watermelon. The bus wasn't leaving for four hours, and the minutes of those hours struggled like gnats on fly paper—dying slow, exhausted with the fight to stay alive. Cholly was afraid to stir, even to relieve himself. The bus might leave while he was gone. Finally, rigid with constipation, he boarded the bus to Macon.

He found a window seat in the back all to himself, and all of Georgia slid before his eyes, until the sun shrugged out of sight. Even in the dark, he hungered to see, and only after the fiercest fight to keep his eyes open did he fall asleep. When he awoke it was very well into day, and a fat black lady was nudging him with a biscuit gashed with cold bacon. With the taste of bacon still in his teeth, they sidled into Macon.

At the end of the alley he could see men clustered like grapes. One large whooping voice spiraled over the heads of the bended forms. The kneeling forms, the leaning forms, all intent on one ground spot. As he came closer, he inhaled a rife and stimulating man smell. The men

were gathered, just as the man in the pool hall had said, for and about
dice and money. Each figure was decorated some way with the slight
pieces of green. Some of them had separated their money, folded the
bills around their fingers, clenched the fingers into fists, so the neat
ends of the money stuck out in a blend of daintiness and violence.
Others had stacked their bills, creased them down the middle, and held
the wad as though they were about to deal cards. Still others had left
their money in loosely crumpled balls. One man had money sticking
out from under his cap. Another stroked his bills with a thumb and forefinger. There was more money in those black hands than Cholly had
ever seen before. He shared their excitement, and the dry-mouthed
apprehension on meeting his father gave way to the saliva flow of excitement. He glanced at the faces, looking for the one who might be his
father. How would he know him? Would he look like a larger version of
himself? At that moment Cholly could not remember what his own self
looked like. He only knew he was fourteen years old, black, and already
six feet tall. He searched the faces and saw only eyes, pleading eyes,
cold eyes, eyes gone flat with malice, others laced with fear—all focused on the movement of a pair of dice that one man was throwing,
snatching up, and throwing again. Chanting a kind of litany to which
the others responded, rubbing the dice as though they were two hot
coals, he whispered to them. Then with a whoop the cubes flew from
his hand to a chorus of amazements and disappointments. Then the
thrower scooped up money, and someone shouted, "Take it and crawl,
you water dog, you, the best I know." There was some laughter, and a
noticeable release of tension, during which some men exchanged
money.

   Cholly tapped an old white-haired man on the back.

   "Can you tell me is Samson Fuller 'round here somewhere?"

   "Fuller?" The name was familiar to the man's tongue. "I don't
know, he here somewhere. They he is. In the brown jacket." The man
pointed.

   A man in a light-brown jacket stood at the far end of the group. He
was gesturing in a quarrelsome, agitated manner with another man.
Both of them had folded their faces in anger. Cholly edged around to
where they stood, hardly believing he was at the end of his journey.
There was his father, a man like any other man, but there indeed were
his eyes, his mouth, his whole head. His shoulders lurked beneath that
jacket, his voice, his hands—all real. They existed, really existed, somewhere. Right here. Cholly had always thought of his father as a giant of
a man, so when he was very close it was with a shock that he discovered
that he was taller than his father. In fact, he was staring at a balding spot
on his father's head, which he suddenly wanted to stroke. While thus
fascinated by the pitiable clean space hedged around by neglected tufts
of wool, the man turned a hard, belligerent face to him.

"What you want, boy?"

"Uh. I mean . . . is you Samson Fuller?"

"Who sent you?"

"Huh?"

"You Melba's boy?"

"No, sir, I'm . . . " Cholly blinked. He could not remember his
mother's name. Had he ever known it? What could he say? Whose boy
was he? He couldn't say, "I'm your boy." That sounded disrespectful.

The man was impatient. "Something wrong with your head? Who
told you to come after me?"

"Nobody." Cholly's hands were sweating. The man's eyes frightened him. "I just thought . . . I mean, I was just wandering around,
and, uh, my name is Cholly. . . ."

But Fuller had turned back to the game that was about to begin
anew. He bent down to toss a bill on the ground, and waited for a throw.
When it was gone, he stood up and in a vexed and whiny voice shouted
at Cholly, "Tell that bitch she get her money. Now, get the fuck outta
my face!"

Cholly was a long time picking his foot up from the ground. He was
trying to back up and walk away. Only with extreme effort could he get
the first muscle to cooperate. When it did, he walked back up the alley,
out of its shade, toward the blazing light of the street. As he emerged
into the sun, he felt something in his legs give way. An orange crate
with a picture of clasping hands pasted on its side was upended on the
sidewalk. Cholly sat down on it. The sunshine dropped like honey on
his head. A horse-drawn fruit wagon went by, its driver singing: "Fresh
from the vine, sweet as sugar, red as wine."

Noises seemed to increase in volume. The clic-cloc of the women's
heels, the laughter of idling men in doorways. There was a streetcar
somewhere. Cholly sat. He knew if he was very still he would be all
right. But then the trace of pain edged his eyes, and he had to use everything to send it away. If he was very still, he thought, and kept his eyes
on one thing, the tears would not come. So he sat in the dripping honey
sun, pulling every nerve and muscle into service to stop the fall of water
from his eyes. While straining in this way, focusing every erg[3] of energy
on his eyes, his bowels suddenly opened up, and before he could realize
what he knew, liquid stools were running down his legs. At the mouth
of the alley where his father was, on an orange crate in the sun, on a
street full of grown men and women, he had soiled himself like a baby.

In panic he wondered should he wait there, not moving until night-
time? No. His father would surely emerge and see him and laugh. Oh,
Lord. He would laugh. Everybody would laugh. There was only one
thing to do.

---

3. Unit of energy.

Cholly ran down the street, aware only of silence. People's mouths moved, their feet moved, a car jugged by but with no sound. A door slammed in perfect soundlessness. His own feet made no sound. The air seemed to strangle him, hold him back. He was pushing through a world of invisible pine sap that threatened to smother him. Still he ran, seeing only silent moving things, until he came to the end of buildings, the beginning of open space, and saw the Ocmulgee River winding ahead. He scooted down a gravelly slope to a pier jutting out over the shallow water. Finding the deepest shadow under the pier, he crouched in it, behind one of the posts. He remained knotted there in fetal position, paralyzed, his fists covering his eyes, for a long time. No sound, no sight, only darkness and heat and the press of his knuckles on his eyelids. He even forgot his messed-up trousers.

Evening came. The dark, the warmth, the quiet, enclosed Cholly like the skin and flesh of an elderberry protecting its own seed.

Cholly stirred. The ache in his head was all he felt. Soon, like bright bits of glass, the events of that afternoon cut into him. At first he saw only money in black fingers, then he thought he was sitting on an uncomfortable chair, but when he looked, it turned out to be the head of a man, a head with a bald spot the size of an orange. When finally these bits merged into full memory, Cholly began to smell himself. He stood up and found himself weak, trembling, and dizzy. He leaned for a moment on the pier post, then took off his pants, underwear, socks, and shoes. He rubbed handfuls of dirt on his shoes; then he crawled to the river edge. He had to find the water's beginning with his hands, for he could not see it clearly. Slowly he swirled his clothes in the water and rubbed them until he thought they were clean. Back near his post, he took off his shirt and wrapped it around his waist, then spread his trousers and underwear on the ground. He squatted down and picked at the rotted wood of the pier. Suddenly he thought of his Aunt Jimmy, her asafetida bag, her four gold teeth, and the purple rag she wore around her head. With a longing that almost split him open, he thought of her handing him a bit of smoked hock out of her dish. He remembered just how she held it—clumsy-like, in three fingers, but with so much affection. No words, just picking up a bit of meat and holding it out to him. And then the tears rushed down his cheeks, to make a bouquet under his chin.

Three women are leaning out of two windows. They see the long clean neck of a new young boy and call to him. He goes to where they are. Inside, it is dark and warm. They give him lemonade in a Mason jar. As he drinks, their eyes float up to him through the bottom of the jar, through the slick sweet water. They give him back his manhood, which he takes aimlessly.

The pieces of Cholly's life could become coherent only in the head of a musician. Only those who talk their talk through the gold of curved metal, or in the touch of black-and-white rectangles and taut skins and strings echoing from wooden corridors, could give true form to his life. Only they would know how to connect the heart of a red watermelon to the asafetida bag to the muscadine to the flashlight on his behind to the fists of money to the lemonade in a Mason jar to a man called Blue and come up with what all of that meant in joy, in pain, in anger, in love, and give it its final and pervading ache of freedom. Only a musician would sense, know, without even knowing that he knew, that Cholly was free. Dangerously free. Free to feel whatever he felt—fear, guilt, shame, love, grief, pity. Free to be tender or violent, to whistle or weep. Free to sleep in doorways or between the white sheets of a singing woman. Free to take a job, free to leave it. He could go to jail and not feel imprisoned, for he had already seen the furtiveness in the eyes of his jailer, free to say, "No, suh," and smile, for he had already killed three white men. Free to take a woman's insults, for his body had already conquered hers. Free even to knock her in the head, for he had already cradled that head in his arms. Free to be gentle when she was sick, or mop her floor, for she knew what and where his maleness was. He was free to drink himself into a silly helplessness, for he had already been a gandy dancer,[4] done thirty days on a chain gang, and picked a woman's bullet out of the calf of his leg. He was free to live his fantasies, and free even to die, the how and the when of which held no interest for him. In those days, Cholly was truly free. Abandoned in a junk heap by his mother, rejected for a crap game by his father, there was nothing more to lose. He was alone with his own perceptions and appetites, and they alone interested him.

It was in this godlike state that he met Pauline Williams. And it was Pauline, or rather marrying her, that did for him what the flashlight did not do. The constantness, varietylessness, the sheer weight of sameness drove him to despair and froze his imagination. To be required to sleep with the same woman forever was a curious and unnatural idea to him; to be expected to dredge up enthusiasms for old acts, and routine ploys; he wondered at the arrogance of the female. When he had met Pauline in Kentucky, she was hanging over a fence scratching herself with a broken foot. The neatness, the charm, the joy he awakened in her made him want to nest with her. He had yet to discover what destroyed that desire. But he did not dwell on it. He thought rather of whatever had happened to the curiosity he used to feel. Nothing, nothing, interested him now. Not himself, not other people. Only in drink was there some break, some floodlight, and when that closed, there was oblivion.

---

4. Slang: a railroad worker.

But the aspect of married life that dumbfounded him and rendered him totally disfunctional was the appearance of children. Having no idea of how to raise children, and having never watched any parent raise himself, he could not even comprehend what such a relationship should be. Had he been interested in the accumulation of things, he could have thought of them as his material heirs; had he needed to prove himself to some nameless "others," he could have wanted them to excel in his own image and for his own sake. Had he not been alone in the world since he was thirteen, knowing only a dying old woman who felt responsible for him, but whose age, sex, and interests were so remote from his own, he might have felt a stable connection between himself and the children. As it was, he reacted to them, and his reactions were based on what he felt at the moment.

So it was on a Saturday afternoon, in the thin light of spring, he staggered home reeling drunk and saw his daughter in the kitchen.

She was washing dishes. Her small back hunched over the sink. Cholly saw her dimly and could not tell what he saw or what he felt. Then he became aware that he was uncomfortable; next he felt the discomfort dissolve into pleasure. The sequence of his emotions was revulsion, guilt, pity, then love. His revulsion was a reaction to her young, helpless, hopeless presence. Her back hunched that way; her head to one side as though crouching from a permanent and unrelieved blow. Why did she have to look so whipped? She was a child—unburdened —why wasn't she happy? The clear statement of her misery was an accusation. He wanted to break her neck—but tenderly. Guilt and impotence rose in a bilious duet. What could he do for her—ever? What give her? What say to her? What could a burned-out black man say to the hunched back of his eleven-year-old daughter? If he looked into her face, he would see those haunted, loving eyes. The hauntedness would irritate him—the love would move him to fury. How dare she love him? Hadn't she any sense at all? What was he supposed to do about that? Return it? How? What could his calloused hands produce to make her smile? What of his knowledge of the world and of life could be useful to her? What could his heavy arms and befuddled brain accomplish that would earn him his own respect, that would in turn allow him to accept her love? His hatred of her slimed in his stomach and threatened to become vomit. But just before the puke moved from anticipation to sensation, she shifted her weight and stood on one foot scratching the back of her calf with her toe. It was a quiet and pitiful gesture. Her hands were going around and around a frying pan, scraping flecks of black into cold, greasy dishwater. The timid, tucked-in look of the scratching toe—that was what Pauline was doing the first time he saw her in Kentucky. Leaning over a fence staring at nothing in particular. The creamy toe of her bare foot scratching a velvet leg. It was such a small and simple gesture, but it filled him then with a wondering softness. Not the usual lust to part tight legs with his own, but a tenderness, a protectiveness. A desire to cover her foot with his hand and gently nibble away the itch from the calf with his teeth. He did it then, and started Pauline into laughter. He did it now.

The tenderness welled up in him, and he sank to his knees, his eyes on the foot of his daughter. Crawling on all fours toward her, he raised his hand and caught the foot in an upward stroke. Pecola lost her balance and was about to careen to the floor. Cholly raised his other hand to her hips to save her from falling. He put his head down and nibbled at the back of her leg. His mouth trembled at the firm sweetness of the flesh. He closed his eyes, letting his fingers dig into her waist. The rigidity of her shocked body, the silence of her stunned throat, was better than Pauline's easy laughter had been. The confused mixture of his memories of Pauline and the doing of a wild and forbidden thing excited him, and a bolt of desire ran down his genitals, giving it length, and softening the lips of his anus. Surrounding all of this lust was a border of politeness. He wanted to fuck her—tenderly. But the tenderness would not hold. The tightness of her vagina was more than he could bear. His soul seemed to slip down to his guts and fly out into her, and the gigantic thrust he made into her then provoked the only sound she made—a hollow suck of air in the back of her throat. Like the rapid loss of air from a circus balloon.

Following the disintegration—the falling away—of sexual desire, he was conscious of her wet, soapy hands on his wrists, the fingers clenching, but whether her grip was from a hopeless but stubborn struggle to be free, or from some other emotion, he could not tell.

Removing himself from her was so painful to him he cut it short and snatched his genitals out of the dry harbor of her vagina. She appeared to have fainted. Cholly stood up and could see only her grayish panties, so sad and limp around her ankles. Again the hatred mixed with tenderness. The hatred would not let him pick her up, the tenderness forced him to cover her.

So when the child regained consciousness, she was lying on the kitchen floor under a heavy quilt, trying to connect the pain between her legs with the face of her mother looming over her.

SEETHEDOGBOWBOWGOESTHEDOG
DOYOUWANTTOPLAYDOYOUWANT
TOPLAYWITHJANESEETHEDOGRUNR

Once there was an old man who loved things, for the slightest contact with people produced in him a faint but persistent nausea. He could not remember when this distaste began nor could he remember ever being free of it. As a young boy he had been greatly disturbed by this revulsion which others did not seem to share, but having got a fine education, he learned, among other things, the word "misanthrope." Knowing his label provided him with both comfort and courage, he believed that to name an evil was to neutralize if not annihilate it. Then, too, he had read several books and made the acquaintance of several great misanthropes of the ages, whose spiritual company soothed him and provided him with yardsticks for measuring his whims, his yearnings, and his antipathies. Moreover, he found misanthropy an excellent means of developing character: when he subdued his revulsion and occasionally touched, helped, counseled, or befriended somebody, he was able to think of his behavior as generous and his intentions as noble. When he was enraged by some human effort or flaw, he was able to regard himself as discriminating, fastidious, and full of nice scruples.

As in the case of many misanthropes, his disdain for people led him into a profession designed to serve them. He was engaged in a line of work that was dependent solely on his ability to win the trust of others, and one in which the most intimate relationships were necessary. Having dallied with the priesthood in the Anglican Church, he abandoned it to become a caseworker. Time and misfortune, however, conspired against him, and he settled finally on a profession that brought him both freedom and satisfaction. He became a "Reader, Adviser, and Interpreter of Dreams." It was a profession that suited him well. His hours were his own, the competition was slight, the clientele was already persuaded and therefore manageable, and he had numerous opportunities to witness human stupidity without sharing it or being compromised by it, and to nurture his fastidiousness by viewing physical decay. Although his income was small, he had no taste for luxury—his experience in the monastery had solidified his natural asceticism while it developed his preference for solitude. Celibacy was a haven, silence a shield.

All his life he had a fondness for things—not the acquisition of wealth or beautiful objects, but a genuine love of worn objects: a coffee pot that had been his mother's, a welcome mat from the door of a rooming house he once lived in, a quilt from a Salvation Army store counter. It was as though his disdain of human contact had converted itself into a craving for things humans had touched. The residue of the human spirit smeared on inanimate objects was all he could withstand of humanity. To contemplate, for example, evidence of human footsteps on the mat—absorb the smell of the quilt and wallow in the sweet certainty that many bodies had sweated, slept, dreamed, made love, been ill, and even died under it. Wherever he went, he took along his things, and was always searching for others. This thirst for worn things led to casual but habitual examinations of trash barrels in alleys and wastebaskets in public places. . . .

All in all, his personality was an arabesque: intricate, symmetrical, balanced, and tightly constructed—except for one flaw. The careful design was marred occasionally by rare but keen sexual cravings.

He could have been an active homosexual but lacked the courage. Bestiality did not occur to him, and sodomy was quite out of the question, for he did not experience sustained erections and could not endure the thought of somebody else's. And besides, the one thing that disgusted him more than entering and caressing a woman was caressing and being caressed by a man. In any case, his cravings, although intense, never relished physical contact. He abhorred flesh on flesh. Body odor, breath odor, overwhelmed him. The sight of dried matter in the corner of the eye, decayed or missing teeth, ear wax, blackheads, moles, blisters, skin crusts—all the natural excretions and protections the body was capable of—disquieted him. His attentions therefore gradually settled on those humans whose bodies were least offensive—children. And since he was too diffident to confront homosexuality, and since little boys were insulting, scary, and stubborn, he further limited his interests to little girls. They were usually manageable and frequently seductive. His sexuality was anything but lewd; his patronage of little girls smacked of innocence and was associated in his mind with cleanliness. He was what one might call a very clean old man.

A cinnamon-eyed West Indian with lightly browned skin.

Although his given name was printed on the sign in his kitchen window, and on the business cards he circulated, he was called by the townspeople Soaphead Church. No one knew where the "Church" part came from—perhaps somebody's recollection of his days as a guest preacher—those reverends who had been called but who had no flock or coop, and were constantly visiting other churches, sitting on the altar with the host preacher. But everybody knew what "Soaphead" meant —the tight, curly hair that took on and held a sheen and wave when pomaded with soap lather. A sort of primitive process.

He had been reared in a family proud of its academic accomplishments and its mixed blood—in fact, they believed the former was based on the latter. A Sir Whitcomb, some decaying British nobleman, who chose to disintegrate under a sun more easeful than England's, had introduced the white strain into the family in the early 1800's. Being a gentleman by order of the King, he had done the civilized thing for his mulatto bastard—provided it with three hundred pounds sterling, to the great satisfaction of the bastard's mother, who felt that fortune had smiled on her. The bastard too was grateful, and regarded as his life's goal the hoarding of this white strain. He bestowed his favors on a fifteen-year-old girl of similar parentage. She, like a good Victorian parody, learned from her husband all that was worth learning—to separate herself in body, mind, and spirit from all that suggested Africa; to cultivate the habits, tastes, preferences that her absent father-in-law and foolish mother-in-law would have approved.

They transferred this Anglophilia[5] to their six children and sixteen grandchildren. Except for an occasional and unaccountable insurgent who chose a restive black, they married "up," lightening the family complexion and thinning out the family features.

With the confidence born of a conviction of superiority, they performed well at schools. They were industrious, orderly, and energetic, hoping to prove beyond a doubt De Gobineau's hypothesis that "all civilizations derive from the white race, that none can exist without its help, and that a society is great and brilliant only so far as it preserves the blood of the noble group that created it."[6] Thus, they were seldom overlooked by schoolmasters who recommended promising students for study abroad. The men studied medicine, law, theology, and emerged repeatedly in the powerless government offices available to the native population. That they were corrupt in public and private practice, both lecherous and lascivious, was considered their noble right, and thoroughly enjoyed by most of the less gifted population.

As the years passed, due to the carelessness of some of the Whitcomb brothers, it became difficult to maintain their whiteness, and some distant and some not so distant relatives married each other. No obviously bad effects were noticed from these ill-advised unions, but one or two old maids or gardener boys marked a weakening of faculties and a disposition toward eccentricity in some of the children. Some flaw outside the usual alcoholism and lechery. They blamed the flaw on intermarriage with the family, however, not on the original genes of the decaying lord. In any case, there were flukes. No more than in any other family, to be sure, but more dangerous because more powerful. One of them was a religious fanatic who founded his own secret sect and fathered four sons, one of whom became a schoolmaster known for the precision of his justice and the control in his violence. This schoolmaster married a sweet, indolent half-Chinese girl for whom the fatigue of bearing a son was too much. She died soon after childbirth. Her son, named Elihue Micah Whitcomb, provided the schoolmaster with ample opportunity to work out his theories of education, discipline, and the good life. Little Elihue learned everything he needed to know well, particularly the fine art of self-deception. He read greedily but understood selectively, choosing the bits and pieces of other men's ideas that supported whatever predilection he had at the moment. Thus he chose

5. Love of England and its customs.
6. Joseph Arthur, comte de Gobineau (1816–1882), wrote *The Inequality of Human Races*, which argues for the innate inferiority of the Negro race.

to remember Hamlet's abuse of Ophelia, but not Christ's love of Mary Magdalene; Hamlet's frivolous politics, but not Christ's serious anarchy.[7] He noticed Gibbon's acidity, but not his tolerance, Othello's love for the fair Desdemona, but not Iago's perverted love of Othello. The works he admired most were Dante's; those he despised most were Dostoyevsky's. For all his exposure to the best minds of the Western world, he allowed only the narrowest interpretation to touch him. He responded to his father's controlled violence by developing hard habits and a soft imagination. A hatred of, and fascination with, any hint of disorder or decay.

At seventeen, however, he met his Beatrice, who was three years his senior. A lovely, laughing big-legged girl who worked as a clerk in a Chinese department store. Velma. So strong was her affection and zest for life, she did not eliminate the frail, sickly Elihue from it. She found his fastidiousness and complete lack of humor touching and longed to introduce him to the idea of delight. He resisted the introduction, but she married him anyway, only to discover that he was suffering from and enjoying an invincible melancholy. When she learned two months into the marriage how important his melancholy was to him, that he was very interested in altering her joy to a more academic gloom, that he equated lovemaking with communion and the Holy Grail,[8] she simply left. She had not lived by the sea all those years, listened to the wharfman's songs all that time, to spend her life in the soundless cave of Elihue's mind.

He never got over her desertion. She was to have been the answer to his unstated, unacknowledged question—where was the life to counter the encroaching nonlife? Velma was to rescue him from the nonlife he had learned on the flat side of his father's belt. But he resisted her with such skill that she was finally driven out to escape the inevitable boredom produced by such a dainty life.

Young Elihue was saved from visible shattering by the steady hand of his father, who reminded him of the family's reputation and Velma's questionable one. He then pursued his studies with more vigor than

7. In Shakespeare's tragedy *Hamlet* the title character insults and mocks his former love Ophelia; in the New Testament Christ cures Mary Magdalene, a repentant prostitute, of evil spirits (Luke 8:2). Hamlet has no serious political views, but he conspires to murder his uncle the king in order to revenge his father's death; Christ preaches subservience to God alone. Edward Gibbon (1737–1794) was an English historian and the author of *The Rise and Fall of the Roman Empire*; in Shakespeare's tragedy *Othello* the title character is a general who kills his wife, Desdemona, because he thinks she has been unfaithful. This suspicion has been planted in his mind by his lieutenant, Iago, whose intense hatred of Othello has sometimes been attributed to repressed homosexual love. Dante Alighieri (1265–1321), Italian poet who wrote *The Divine Comedy*, an epic poem in which he journeys through the cosmos from Hell to Paradise in search of his beloved Beatrice. Fyodor Dostoevsky (1821–1881), Russian novelist who depicted the agony and suffering of minds on the edge of sanity.

8. A chalice thought to have once contained the Blood of Christ, the object of many quests by the knights of King Arthur's legendary Round Table in medieval romance.

before and decided at last to enter the ministry. When he was advised that he had no avocation, he left the island, came to America to study the then budding field of psychiatry. But the subject required too much truth, too many confrontations, and offered too little support to a failing ego. He drifted into sociology, then physical therapy. This diverse education continued for six years, when his father refused to support him any longer, until he "found" himself. Elihue, not knowing where to look, was thrown back on his own devices, and "found" himself quite unable to earn money. He began to sink into a rapidly fraying gentility, punctuated with a few of the white-collar occupations available to black people, regardless of their noble bloodlines, in America: desk clerk at a colored hotel in Chicago, insurance agent, traveling salesman for a cosmetics firm catering to blacks. He finally settled in Lorain, Ohio, in 1931, palming himself off as a minister, and inspiring awe with the way he spoke English. The women of the town early discovered his celibacy, and not being able to comprehend his rejection of them, decided that he was supernatural rather than unnatural.

Once he understood their decision, he quickly followed through, accepting the name (Soaphead Church) and the role they had given him. He rented a kind of back-room apartment from a deeply religious old lady named Bertha Reese. She was clean, quiet, and very close to total deafness. The lodgings were ideal in every way but one. Bertha Reese had an old dog, Bob, who, although as deaf and quiet as she, was not as clean. He slept most of his days away on the back porch, which was Elihue's entrance. The dog was too old to be of any use, and Bertha Reese had not the strength or presence of mind to care for him properly. She fed him, and watered him, left him alone. The dog was mangy; his exhausted eyes ran with a seagreen matter around which gnats and flies clustered. Soaphead was revolted by Bob and wished he would hurry up and die. He regarded this wish for the dog's death as humane, for he could not bear, he told himself, to see anything suffer. It did not occur to him that he was really concerned about his own suffering, since the dog had adjusted himself to frailty and old age. Soaphead finally determined to put an end to the animal's misery, and bought some poison with which to do it. Only the horror of having to go near him had prevented Soaphead from completing his mission. He waited for rage or blinding revulsion to spur him.

Living there among his worn things, rising early every morning from dreamless sleeps, he counseled those who sought his advice.

His business was dread. People came to him in dread, whispered in dread, wept and pleaded in dread. And dread was what he counseled.

Singly they found their way to his door, wrapped each in a shroud stitched with anger, yearning, pride, vengeance, loneliness, misery, defeat, and hunger. They asked for the simplest of things: love, health, and money. Make him love me. Tell me what this dream means. Help me get rid of this woman. Make my mother give me back my clothes. Stop my left hand from shaking. Keep my baby's ghost off the stove. Break so-and-so's fix.[9] To all of these requests he addressed himself. His practice was to do what he was bid—not to suggest to a party that perhaps the request was unfair, mean, or hopeless.

With only occasional, and increasingly rare, encounters with the little girls he could persuade to be entertained by him, he lived rather peaceably among his things, admitting to no regrets. He was aware, of course, that something was awry in his life, and all lives, but put the problem where it belonged, at the foot of the Originator of Life. He believed that since decay, vice, filth, and disorder were pervasive, they must be in the Nature of Things. Evil existed because God had created it. He, God, had made a sloven and unforgivable error in judgment: designing an imperfect universe. Theologians justified the presence of corruption as a means by which men strove, were tested, and triumphed. A triumph of cosmic neatness. But this neatness, the neatness of Dante, was in the orderly sectioning and segregating of all levels of evil and decay. In the world it was not so. The most exquisite-looking ladies sat on toilets, and the most dreadful-looking had pure and holy yearnings. God had done a poor job, and Soaphead suspected that he himself could have done better. It was in fact a pity that the Maker had not sought his counsel.

Soaphead was reflecting once again on these thoughts one late hot afternoon when he heard a tap on his door. Opening it, he saw a little girl, quite unknown to him. She was about twelve or so, he thought, and seemed to him pitifully unattractive. When he asked her what she wanted, she did not answer, but held out to him one of his cards advertising his gifts and services: "If you are overcome with trouble and conditions that are not natural, I can remove them; Overcome Spells, Bad Luck, and Evil Influences. Remember, I am a true Spiritualist and Psychic Reader, born with power, and I will help you. Satisfaction in one visit. During many years of practice I have brought together many in marriage and reunited many who were separated. If you are unhappy, discouraged, or in distress, I can help you. Does bad luck seem to follow you? Has the one you love changed? I can tell you why. I will tell you who your enemies and friends are, and if the one you love is true or false. If you are sick, I can show you the way to health. I locate lost and stolen articles. Satisfaction guaranteed."

Soaphead Church told her to come in.

"What can I do for you, my child?"

9. Hex or spell.

She stood there, her hands folded across her stomach, a little protruding pot of tummy. "Maybe. Maybe you can do it for me."

"Do what for you?"

"I can't go to school no more. And I thought maybe you could help me."

"Help you how? Tell me. Don't be frightened."

"My eyes."

"What about your eyes?"

"I want them blue."

Soaphead pursed his lips, and let his tongue stroke a gold inlay. He thought it was at once the most fantastic and the most logical petition he had ever received. Here was an ugly little girl asking for beauty. A surge of love and understanding swept through him, but was quickly replaced by anger. Anger that he was powerless to help her. Of all the wishes people had brought him—money, love, revenge—this seemed to him the most poignant and the one most deserving of fulfillment. A little black girl who wanted to rise up out of the pit of her blackness and see the world with blue eyes. His outrage grew and felt like power. For the first time he honestly wished he could work miracles. Never before had he really wanted the true and holy power—only the power to make others believe he had it. It seemed so sad, so frivolous, that mere mortality, not judgment, kept him from it. Or did it?

With a trembling hand he made the sign of the cross over her. His flesh crawled; in that hot, dim little room of worn things, he was chilled.

"I can do nothing for you, my child. I am not a magician. I work only through the Lord. He sometimes uses me to help people. All I can do is offer myself to Him as the instrument through which he works. If He wants your wish granted, He will do it."

Soaphead walked to the window, his back to the girl. His mind raced, stumbled, and raced again. How to frame the next sentence? How to hang on to the feeling of power. His eye fell on old Bob sleeping on the porch.

"We must make, ah, some offering, that is, some contact with nature. Perhaps some simple creature might be the vehicle through which He will speak. Let us see."

He knelt down at the window, and moved his lips. After what seemed a suitable length of time, he rose and went to the icebox that stood near the other window. From it he removed a small packet wrapped in pinkish butcher paper. From a shelf he took a small brown bottle and sprinkled some of its contents on the substance inside the paper. He put the packet, partly opened, on the table.

"Take this food and give it to the creature sleeping on the porch. Make sure he eats it. And mark well how he behaves. If nothing happens, you will know that God has refused you. If the animal behaves strangely, your wish will be granted on the day following this one."

The girl picked up the packet; the odor of the dark, sticky meat made her want to vomit. She put a hand on her stomach.

"Courage. Courage, my child. These things are not granted to faint hearts."

She nodded and swallowed visibly, holding down the vomit. Soaphead opened the door, and she stepped over the threshold.

"Good-bye, God bless," he said and quickly shut the door. At the window he stood watching her, his eyebrows pulled together into waves of compassion, his tongue fondling the worn gold in his upper jaw. He saw the girl bending down to the sleeping dog, who, at her touch, opened one liquid eye, matted in the corners with what looked like green glue. She reached out and touched the dog's head, stroking him gently. She placed the meat on the floor of the porch, near his nose. The odor roused him; he lifted his head, and got up to smell it better. He ate it in three or four gulps. The girl stroked his head again, and the dog looked up at her with soft triangle eyes. Suddenly he coughed, the cough of a phlegmy old man—and got to his feet. The girl jumped. The dog gagged, his mouth chomping the air, and promptly fell down. He tried to raise himself, could not, tried again and half-fell down the steps. Choking, stumbling, he moved like a broken toy around the yard. The girl's mouth was open, a little petal of tongue showing. She made a wild, pointless gesture with one hand and then covered her mouth with both hands. She was trying not to vomit. The dog fell again, a spasm jerking his body. Then he was quiet. The girl's hands covering her mouth, she backed away a few feet, then turned, ran out of the yard and down the walk.

Soaphead Church went to the table. He sat down, with folded hands balancing his forehead on the balls of his thumbs. Then he rose and went to a tiny night table with a drawer, from which he took paper and a fountain pen. A bottle of ink was on the same shelf that held the poison. With these things he sat again at the table. Slowly, carefully, relishing his penmanship, he wrote the following letter:

Att: TO HE WHO GREATLY ENNOBLED HUMAN NATURE BY CREATING IT.

Dear God:

The Purpose of this letter is to familiarize you with facts which either have escaped your notice, or which you have chosen to ignore.

Once upon a time I lived greenly and youngish on one of your islands. An island of the archipelago in the South Atlantic between North and South America, enclosing the Caribbean Sea and the Gulf of

Mexico: divided into the Greater Antilles, the Lesser Antilles, and the Bahama Islands. Not the Windward or Leeward Island colonies, mark you, but within, of course, the Greater of the two Antilles (while the precision of my prose may be, at times, laborious, it is necessary that I identify myself to you clearly).

Now.

We in this colony took as our own the most dramatic, and the most obvious, of our white masters' characteristics, which were, of course, their worst. In retaining the identity of our race, we held fast to those characteristics most gratifying to sustain and least troublesome to maintain. Consequently we were not royal but snobbish, not aristocratic but class-conscious; we believed authority was cruelty to our inferiors, and education was being at school. We mistook violence for passion, indolence for leisure, and thought recklessness was freedom. We raised our children and reared our crops; we let infants grow, and property develop. Our manhood was defined by acquisitions. Our womanhood by acquiescence. And the smell of your fruit and the labor of your days we abhorred.

This morning, before the little black girl came, I cried—for Velma. Oh, not aloud. There is no wind to carry, bear, or even refuse to bear, a sound so heavy with regret. But in my silent own lone way, I cried—for Velma. You need to know about Velma to understand what I did today.

She (Velma) left me the way people leave a hotel room. A hotel room is a place to be when you are doing something else. Of itself it is of no consequence to one's major scheme. A hotel room is convenient. But its convenience is limited to the time you need it while you are in that particular town on that particular business; you hope it is comfortable, but prefer, rather, that it be anonymous. It is not, after all, where you *live*.

When you no longer need it, you pay a little something for its use; say, "Thank you, sir," and when your business in that town is over, you go away from that room. Does anybody regret leaving a hotel room? Does anybody, who has a home, a real home somewhere, want to stay there? Does anybody look back with affection, or even disgust, at a hotel room when they leave it? You can only love or despise whatever *living* was done in that room. But the room itself? But you take a souvenir. Not, oh, not, to remember the room. To remember, rather, the time and the place of your business, your adventure. What can anyone feel for a hotel room? One doesn't any more feel for a hotel room than one expects a hotel room to feel for its occupant.

That, heavenly, heavenly Father, was how she left me; or rather, she never left me, because she was never ever there.

You remember, do you, how and of what we are made? Let me tell you now about the breasts of little girls. I apologize for the inappropriateness (is that it?), the imbalance of loving them at awkward times of day, and in awkward places, and the tastelessness of loving those which belonged to members of my family. Do I have to apologize for loving strangers?

But you too are amiss here, Lord. How, why, did you allow it to happen? How is it I could lift my eyes from contemplation of Your Body and fall deeply into the contemplation of theirs? The buds. The buds on some of these saplings. They were mean, you know, mean and tender. Mean little buds resisting the touch, springing like rubber. But aggressive. Daring me to touch. Commanding me to touch. Not a bit shy, as you'd suppose. They stuck out at me, oh yes, at me. Slender-chested, finger-chested lassies. Have you ever seen them, Lord? I mean, really seen them? One could not see them and not love them. You who made them must have considered them lovely even as an idea—how much more lovely is the manifestation of that idea. I couldn't, as you must recall, keep my hands, my mouth, off them. Salt-sweet. Like not quite ripe strawberries covered with the light salt sweat of running days and hopping, skipping, jumping hours.

The love of them—the touch, taste, and feel of them—was not just an easy luxurious human vice; they were, for me, A Thing To Do Instead. Instead of papa, instead of the Cloth,[1] instead of Velma, and I *chose* not to do without them. But I didn't go into the church. At least I didn't do that. As to what I did do? I told people I knew all about You. That I had received Your Powers. It was not a complete *lie*; but it was a *complete* lie. I should never have, I admit, I should never have taken their money in exchange for well-phrased, well-placed, well-faced lies. But, mark you, I hated it. Not for a moment did I love the lies or the money.

But consider: The woman who left the hotel room.

Consider: The greentime, the noontime of the archipelago.

Consider: Their hopeful eyes that were outdone only by their hoping breasts.

Consider: How I needed a comfortable evil to prevent my knowing what I could not bear to know.

Consider: How I hated and despised the money.

And now, consider: Not according to my just deserts, but according to *my* mercy, the little black girl that came a-looning at me today. Tell me, Lord, how could you leave a lass so long so lone that she could find her way to me? How could you? I weep for you, Lord. And it is because I weep for You that I had to do your work for You.

Do you know what she came for? Blue eyes. New, blue eyes, she said. Like she was buying shoes. "I'd like a pair of new blue eyes." She

---

1. The priesthood.

must have asked you for them for a very long time, and you hadn't replied. (A habit, I could have told her, a long-ago habit broken for Job[2] —but no more.) She came to *me* for them. She had one of my cards. (Card enclosed.) By the way, I added the Micah—Elihue Micah Whitcomb. But I am called Soaphead Church. I cannot remember how or why I got the name. What makes one name more a person than another? Is the name the real thing, then? And the person only what his name says? Is that why to the simpliest and friendliest of questions: "What is your name?" put to you by Moses, You would not say, and said instead "I am who I am." Like Popeye? I Yam What I Yam?[3] Afraid you were, weren't you, to give out your name? Afraid they would know the name and then know you? Then they wouldn't fear you? It's quite all right. Don't be vexed. I mean no offense. I understand. I have been a bad man too, and an unhappy man too. But someday *I* will die. I was always so kind. Why do I have to die? The little girls. The little girls are the only things I'll miss. Do you know that when I touched their sturdy little tits and bit them—just a little—I felt I was being friendly? I didn't want to kiss their mouths or sleep in the bed with them or take a child bride for my own. Playful, I felt, and friendly. Not like the newspapers said. Not like the people whispered. And they didn't mind at all. Not at all. Remember how so many of them came back? No one would even try to understand that. If I'd been hurting them, would they have come back? Two of them, Doreen and Sugar Babe, they'd come together. I gave them mints, money, and they'd eat ice cream with their legs open while I played with them. It was like a party. And there wasn't nastiness, and there wasn't any filth, and there wasn't any odor, and there wasn't any groaning—just the light white laughter of little girls and me. And there wasn't any look—any long funny look—any long funny Velma look afterward. No look that makes you feel dirty afterward. That makes you want to die. With little girls it is all clean and good and friendly.

You have to understand that, Lord. You said, "Suffer little children to come unto me, and harm them not."[4] Did you forget? Did you forget about the children? Yes. You forgot. You let them go wanting, sit on road shoulders, crying next to their dead mothers. I've seen them charred, lame, halt. You forgot, Lord. You forgot how and when to be God.

That's why I changed the little black girl's eyes for her, and I didn't touch her; not a finger did I lay on her. But I gave her those blue eyes she wanted. Not for pleasure, and not for money. I did what You did

---

2. In the Book of Job, God speaks to Job directly.
3. God tells Moses "I am that I am" (Exodus 3:14); Popeye is a comic-strip and animated car-

toon character whose motto is "I yam what I yam."
4. Mark 10:14 (the wording in the King James Bible is slightly different).

not, could not, would not do: I looked at that ugly little black girl, and I loved her. I played You. And it was a very good show!

I, I have caused a miracle. I gave her the eyes. I gave her the blue, blue, two blue eyes. Cobalt blue. A streak of it right out of your own blue heaven. No one else will see her blue eyes. But *she* will. And she will live happily ever after. I, I have found it meet and right so to do.

Now you are jealous. You are jealous of me.

You see? I, too, have created. Not aboriginally, like you, but creation is a heady wine, more for the taster than the brewer.

Having therefore imbibed, as it were, of the nectar, I am not afraid of You, of Death, not even of Life, and it's all right about Velma; and it's all right about Papa; and it's all right about the Greater and the Lesser Antilles. Quite all right. Quite.

With kindest regards, I remain,

Your,

Elihue Micah Whitcomb

Soaphead Church folded the sheets of paper into three equal parts and slipped them into an envelope. Although he had no seal, he longed for sealing wax. He removed a cigar box from under the bed and rummaged about in it. There were some of his most precious things: a sliver of jade that had dislodged from a cuff link at the Chicago hotel; a gold pendant shaped like a Y with a piece of coral attached to it that had belonged to the mother he never knew; four large hairpins that Velma had left on the rim of the bathrrom sink; a powder blue grosgrain ribbon from the head of a little girl named Precious Jewel; a blackened faucet head from the sink in a jail cell in Cincinnati; two marbles he had found under a bench in Morningside Park on a very fine spring day; an Old Lucky Hart catalog that smelled still of nut-brown and mocha face powder, and lemon vanishing cream. Distracted by his things, he forgot what he had been looking for. The effort to recall was too great; there was a buzzing in his head, and a wash of fatigue overcame him. He closed his box, eased himself out on the bed, and slipped into an ivory sleep from which he could not hear the tiny yelps of an old lady who had come out of her candy store and found the still carcass of an old dog named Bob.

Summer

I have only to break into the tightness of a strawberry, and I see summer—its dust and lowering skies. It remains for me a season of storms. The parched days and sticky nights are undistinguished in my mind, but the storms, the violent sudden storms, both frightened and quenched me. But my memory is uncertain; I recall a summer storm in the town where we lived and imagine a summer my mother knew in 1929. There was a tornado that year, she said, that blew away half of south Lorain. I mix up her summer with my own. Biting the strawberry, thinking of storms, I see her. A slim young girl in a pink crepe dress. One hand is on her hip; the other lolls about her thigh—waiting. The wind swoops her up, high above the houses, but she is still standing, hand on hip. Smiling. The anticipation and promise in her lolling hand are not altered by the holocaust. In the summer tornado of 1929, my mother's hand is unextinguished. She is strong, smiling, and relaxed while the world falls down about her. So much for memory. Public fact becomes private reality, and the seasons of a Midwestern town become the *Moirai*[5] of our small lives.

The summer was already thick when Frieda and I received our seeds. We had waited since April for the magic package containing the packets and packets of seeds we were to sell for five cents each, which would entitle us to a new bicycle. We believed it, and spent a major part of every day trooping about the town selling them. Although Mama had restricted us to the homes of people she knew or the neighborhoods familiar to us, we knocked on all doors, and floated in and out of every house that opened to us: twelve-room houses that sheltered half as many families, smelling of grease and urine; tiny wooden four-room houses tucked into bushes near the railroad tracks; the up-over places—apartments up over fish markets, butcher shops, furniture stores, saloons, restaurants; tidy brick houses with flowered carpets and glass bowls with fluted edges.

During that summer of the seed selling we thought about the money, thought about the seeds, and listened with only half an ear to what people were saying. In the houses of people who knew us we were asked to come in and sit, given cold water or lemonade; and while we sat there being refreshed, the people continued their conversations or went about their chores. Little by little we began to piece a story together, a secret, terrible, awful story. And it was only after two or three such vaguely overheard conversations that we realized that the story was about Pecola. Properly placed, the fragments of talk ran like this:

"Did you hear about that girl?"

"What? Pregnant?"

"Yas. But guess who?"

"Who? I don't know all these little old boys."

"That's just it. Ain't no little old boy. They say it's Cholly."

"Cholly? Her daddy?"

"Uh-huh."

5. Greek: destinies, fates.

"Lord. Have mercy. That dirty nigger."

" 'Member that time he tried to burn them up? I knew he was crazy for sure then."

"What's she gone do? The mama?"

"Keep on like she been, I reckon. He taken off."

"County ain't gone let her keep that baby, is they?"

"Don't know."

"None of them Breedloves seem right anyhow. That boy is off somewhere every minute, and the girl was always foolish."

"Don't nobody know nothing about them anyway. Where they come from or nothing. Don't seem to have no people."

"What you reckon make him do a thing like that?"

"Beats me. Just nasty."

"Well, they ought to take her out of school."

"Ought to. She carry some of the blame."

"Oh, come on. She ain't but twelve or so."

"Yeah. But you never know. How come she didn't fight him?"

"Maybe she did."

"Yeah? You never know."

"Well, it probably won't live. They say the way her mama beat her she lucky to be alive herself."

"She be lucky if it don't live. Bound to be the ugliest thing walking."

"Can't help but be. Ought to be a law: two ugly people doubling up like that to make more ugly. Be better off in the ground."

"Well, I wouldn't worry none. It be a miracle if it live."

Our astonishment was short-lived, for it gave way to a curious kind of defensive shame; we were embarrassed for Pecola, hurt for her, and finally we just felt sorry for her. Our sorrow drove out all thoughts of the new bicycle. And I believe our sorrow was the more intense because nobody else seemed to share it. They were disgusted, amused, shocked, outraged, or even excited by the story. But we listened for the one who would say, "Poor little girl," or, "Poor baby," but there was only head-wagging where those words should have been. We looked for eyes creased with concern, but saw only veils.

I thought about the baby that everybody wanted dead, and saw it very clearly. It was in a dark, wet place, its head covered, with great O's of wool, the black face holding, like nickels, two clean black eyes, the flared nose, kissing-thick lips, and the living, breathing silk of black skin. No synthetic yellow bangs suspended over marble-blue eyes, no pinched nose and bowline mouth. More strongly than my fondness for Pecola, I felt a need for someone to want the black baby to live—just to counteract the universal love of white baby dolls, Shirley Temples, and Maureen Peals. And Frieda must have felt the same thing. We did not think of the fact that Pecola was not married; lots of girls had babies who were not married. And we did not dwell on the fact that the baby's father was Pecola's father too; the process of having a baby by any male was incomprehensible to us—at least she knew her father. We thought only of this overwhelming hatred for the unborn baby. We remembered Mrs. Breedlove knocking Pecola down and soothing the pink tears of the frozen doll baby that sounded like the door of our icebox. We remembered the knuckled eyes of schoolchildren under the gaze of Meringue Pie and the eyes of these same children when they looked at Pecola. Or maybe we didn't remember; we just knew. We had defended ourselves since memory against everything and everybody, considered all speech a code to be broken by us, and all gestures subject to careful analysis; we had become headstrong, devious and arrogant. Nobody paid us any attention, so we paid very good attention to ourselves. Our limitations were not known to us—not then. Our only handicap was our size; people gave us orders because they were bigger and stronger. So it was with confidence, strengthened by pity and pride, that we decided to change the course of events and alter a human life.

"What we gone do, Frieda?"

"What can we do? Miss Johnson said it would be a miracle if it lived."

"So let's make it a miracle."

"Yeah, but how?"

"We could pray."

"That's not enough. Remember last time with the bird?"

"That was different; it was half-dead when we found it."

"I don't care, I still think we have to do something really strong this time."

"Let's ask Him to let Pecola's baby live and promise to be good for a whole month."

"O.K. But we better give up something so He'll know we really mean it this time."

"Give up what? We ain't got nothing. Nothing but the seed money, two dollars."

"We could give that. Or, you know what? We could give up the bicycle. Bury the money and . . . plant the seeds."

"All of the money?"

"Claudia, do you want to do it or not?"

"O.K. I just thought . . . O.K."

"We have to do it *right*, now. We'll bury the money over by her house so we can't go back and dig it up, and we'll plant the seeds out back of our house so we can watch over them. And when they come up, we'll know everything is all right. All right?"

"All right. Only let me sing this time. You say the magic words."

LOOKLOOKHERECOMESAFRIENDTHE
FRIENDWILLPLAYWITHJANETHEYWI
LLPLAYAGOODGAMEPLAYJANEPLAY

How many times a minute are you going to look inside that old thing?
I didn't look in a long time.
You did too—
So what? I can look if I want to.
I didn't say you couldn't. I just don't know why you have to look every minute. They aren't going anywhere.
I know it. I just like to look.
You scared they might go away?
Of course not. How can they go away?
The others went away.
They didn't go away. They changed.
Go away. Change. What's the difference?
A lot. Mr. Soaphead said they would last forever.
Forever and ever Amen?
Yes, if you want to know.
You don't have to be so smarty when you talk to me.
I'm not being smarty. You started it.
I'd just like to do something else besides watch you stare in that mirror.
You're just jealous.
I am not.
You are. You wish you had them.
Ha. What would I look like with blue eyes?
Nothing much.
If you're going to keep this up, I may as well go on off by myself.
No. Don't go. What you want to do?
We could go outside and play, I guess.
But it's too hot.
You can take your old mirror. Put it in your coat pocket, and you can look at yourself up and down the street.
Boy! I never would have thought you'd be so jealous.
Oh, come on!
You are.
Are what?
Jealous.
O.K. So I'm jealous.
See. I told you.
No. I told you.
Are they really nice?
Yes. Very nice.

Just "very nice"?

Really, truly, very nice.

Really, truly, bluely nice?

Oh, God. You are crazy.

I am not!

I didn't mean it that way.

Well, what did you mean?

Come on. It's too hot in here.

Wait a minute. I can't find my shoes.

Here they are.

Oh. Thank you.

Got your mirror?

Yes dearie. . . .

Well, let's go then. . . . Ow!

What's the matter?

The sun is too bright. It hurts my eyes.

Not mine. I don't even blink. Look. I can look right at the sun.

Don't do that.

Why not? It doesn't hurt. I don't even have to blink.

Well, blink anyway. You make me feel funny, staring at the sun like that.

Feel funny how?

I don't know.

Yes, you do. Feel funny how?

I told you, I don't know.

Why don't you look at me when you say that? You're looking drop-eyed like Mrs. Breedlove.

Mrs. Breedlove look drop-eyed at you?

Yes. Now she does. Ever since I got my blue eyes, she look away from me all of the time. Do you suppose she's jealous too?

Could be. They are pretty, you know.

I know. He really did a good job. Everybody's jealous. Every time I look at somebody, they look off.

Is that why nobody has told you how pretty they are?

Sure it is. Can you imagine? Something like that happening to a person, and nobody but nobody saying anything about it? They all try to pretend they don't see them. Isn't that funny? . . . I said, isn't that funny?

Yes.

You are the only one who tells me how pretty they are.

Yes.

You are a real friend. I'm sorry about picking on you before. I mean, saying you were jealous and all.

That's all right.

No. Really. You are my very best friend. Why didn't I know you before?

You didn't need me before.

Didn't need you?

I mean . . . you were so unhappy before. I guess you didn't notice me before.

I guess you're right. And I was so lonely for friends. And you were right here. Right before my eyes.

No, honey. Right after your eyes.

What?

What does Maureen think about your eyes?

She doesn't say anything about them. Has she said anything to you about them?

No. Nothing.

Do you like Maureen?

Oh. She's all right. For a half-white girl, that is.

I know what you mean. But would you like to be her friend? I mean, would you like to go around with her or anything?

No.

Me neither. But she sure is popular.

Who wants to be popular?

Not me.

Me neither.

But you couldn't be popular anyway. You don't even go to school.

You don't either.

I know. But I used to.

What did you stop for?

They made me.

Who made you?

I don't know. After that first day at school when I had my blue eyes. Well, the next day they had Mrs. Breedlove come out. Now I don't go anymore. But I don't care.

You don't?

No, I don't. They're just prejudiced, that's all.

Yes, they sure are prejudiced.

Just because I got blue eyes, bluer than theirs, they're prejudiced.

That's right.

They are bluer, aren't they?

Oh, yes. Much bluer.

Bluer than Joanna's?

Much bluer than Joanna's.

And bluer than Michelena's?

Much bluer than Michelena's

I thought so. Did Michelena say anything to you about my eyes?

No. Nothing.
Did you say anything to her?
No.
How come?
How come what?
How come you don't talk to anybody?
I talk to you.
Besides me.
I don't like anybody besides you.
Where do you live?
I told you once.
What is your mother's name?
Why are you so busy meddling me?
I just wondered. You don't talk to anybody. You don't go to school.
And nobody talks to you.
How do you know nobody talks to me?
They don't. When you're in the house with me, even Mrs. Breed-
love doesn't say anything to you. Ever. Sometimes I wonder if she even
sees you.
Why wouldn't she see me?
I don't know. She almost walks right over you.
Maybe she doesn't feel too good since Cholly's gone.
Oh, yes. You must be right.
She probably misses him.
I don't know why she would. All he did was get drunk and beat her
up.
Well, you know how grown-ups are.
Yes. No. How are they?
Well, she probably loved him anyway.
HIM?
*Sure. Why not? Anyway, if she didn't love him, she sure let him do it
to her a lot.*
That's nothing.
How do you know?
I saw them all the time. She didn't like it.
Then why'd she let him do it to her?
Because he made her.
How could somebody make you do something like that?
Easy.
Oh, yeah? How easy?
They just make you, that's all.
I guess you're right. And Cholly could make anybody do anything.
He could not.
He made you, didn't he?

Shut up!

I was only teasing.

Shut up!

O.K. O.K..

He just tried, see? He didn't do anything. You hear me?

I'm shutting up.

You'd better. I don't like that kind of talk.

I said I'm shutting up.

You always talk so dirty. Who told you about that, anyway?

I forget.

Sammy?

No. You did.

I did not.

You did. You said he tried to do it to you when you were sleeping on the couch.

See there! You don't even know what you're talking about. It was when I was washing dishes.

Oh, yes. Dishes.

By myself. In the kitchen.

Well, I'm glad you didn't let him.

Yes.

Did you?

Did I what?

Let him.

Now who's crazy?

I am, I guess.

You sure are.

Still. . . .

Well. Go ahead. Still what?

I wonder what it would be like.

Horrible.

Really?

Yes. Horrible.

Then why didn't you tell Mrs. Breedlove?

I did tell her!

I don't mean about the first time. I mean about the second time, when you were sleeping on the couch.

I wasn't sleeping! I was reading!

You don't have to shout.

You don't understand anything, do you? She didn't even believe me when I told her.

So that's why you didn't tell her about the second time?

She wouldn't have believed me then either.

You're right. No use telling her when she wouldn't believe you.

That's what I'm trying to get through your thick head.

O.K. I understand now. Just about.

What do you mean, just about?

You sure are mean today.

You keep on saying mean and sneaky things. I thought you were my friend.

I am. I am.

Then leave me alone about Cholly.

O.K.

There's nothing more to say about him, anyway. He's gone, anyway.

Yes. Good riddance.

Yes. Good riddance.

And Sammy's gone too.

And Sammy's gone too.

So there's no use talking about it. I mean them.

No. No use at all.

It's all over now.

Yes.

And you don't have to be afraid of Cholly coming at you anymore.

No.

That was horrible, wasn't it?

Yes.

The second time too?

Yes.

Really? The second time too?

Leave me alone! You better leave me alone.

Can't you take a joke? I was only funning.

I don't like to talk about dirty things.

Me neither. Let's talk about something else.

What? What will we talk about?

Why, your eyes.

Oh, yes. My eyes. My blue eyes. Let me look again.

See how pretty they are.

Yes. They get prettier each time I look at them.

They are the prettiest I've ever seen.

Really?

Oh, yes.

Prettier than the sky?

Oh, yes. Much prettier than the sky.

Prettier than Alice-and-Jerry Storybook eyes?

Oh, yes. Much prettier than Alice-and-Jerry Storybook eyes.

And prettier than Joanna's?

Oh, yes. And bluer too.

Bluer than Michelena's?

Yes.

Are you sure?

Of course I'm sure.

You don't sound sure. . . .

Well, I am sure. Unless. . . .

Unless what?

Oh, nothing. I was just thinking about a lady I saw yesterday. Her eyes sure were blue. But no. Not bluer than yours.

Are you sure?

Yes. I remember them now. Yours are bluer.

I'm glad.

Me too. I'd hate to think there was anybody around with bluer eyes than yours. I'm sure there isn't. Not around here, anyway.

But you don't know, do you? You haven't seen everybody, have you?

No. I haven't.

So there could be, couldn't there?

Not hardly.

But maybe. Maybe. You said "around here." Nobody "around here" probably has bluer eyes. What about someplace else? Even if my eyes are bluer than Joanna's and bluer than Michelena's and bluer than that lady's you saw, suppose there is somebody way off somewhere with bluer eyes than mine?

Don't be silly.

There could be. Couldn't there?

Not hardly.

But suppose. Suppose a long way off. In Cincinnati, say, there is somebody whose eyes are bluer than mine? Suppose there are *two* people with bluer eyes?

So what? You asked for blue eyes. You got blue eyes.

He should have made them bluer.

Who?

Mr. Soaphead.

Did you say what color blue you wanted them?

No. I forgot.

Oh. Well.

Look. Look over there. At that girl. Look at her eyes. Are they bluer than mine?

No, I don't think so.

Did you look real good?

Yes.

Here comes someone. Look at his. See if they're bluer.

You're being silly. I'm not going to look at everybody's eyes.

You have to.

No I don't.

Please. If there is somebody with bluer eyes than mine, then maybe there is somebody with the bluest eyes. The bluest eyes in the whole world.

That's just too bad, isn't it?

Please help me look.

No.

But suppose my eyes aren't blue enough?

Blue enough for what?

Blue enough for . . . I don't know. Blue enough for something. Blue enough . . . for you!

I'm not going to play with you anymore.

Oh. Don't leave me.

Yes. I am.

Why? Are you mad at me?

Yes.

Because my eyes aren't blue enough? Because I don't have the bluest eyes?

No. Because you're acting silly.

Don't go. Don't leave me. Will you come back if I get them?

Get what?

The bluest eyes. Will you come back then?

Of course I will. I'm just going away for a little while.

You promise?

Sure. I'll be back. Right before your very eyes.

So it was.

A little black girl yearns for the blue eyes of a little white girl, and the horror at the heart of her yearning is exceeded only by the evil of fulfillment.

We saw her sometimes, Frieda and I—after the baby came too soon and died. After the gossip and the slow wagging of heads. She was so sad to see. Grown people looked away; children, those who were not frightened by her, laughed outright.

The damage done was total. She spent her days, her tendril, sap-green days, walking up and down, up and down, her head jerking to the beat of a drummer so distant only she could hear. Elbows bent, hands on shoulders, she flailed her arms like a bird in an eternal, grotesquely futile effort to fly. Beating the air, a winged but grounded bird, intent on the blue void it could not reach—could not even see—but which filled the valleys of the mind.

We tried to see her without looking at her, and never, never went near. Not because she was absurd, or repulsive, or because we were frightened, but because we had failed her. Our flowers never grew. I was convinced that Frieda was right, that I had planted them too deeply. How could I have been so sloven? So we avoided Pecola Breedlove—forever.

And the years folded up like pocket handkerchiefs. Sammy left town long ago; Cholly died in the workhouse;[6] Mrs. Breedlove still does housework. And Pecola is somewhere in that little brown house she and her mother moved to on the edge of town, where you can see her even now, once in a while. The birdlike gestures are worn away to a mere picking and plucking her way between the tire rims and the sunflowers, between Coke bottles and milkweed, among all the waste and beauty of the world—which is what she herself was. All of our waste which we dumped on her and which she absorbed. And all of our beauty, which was hers first and which she gave to us. All of us—all who knew her— felt so wholesome after we cleaned ourselves on her. We were so beautiful when we stood astride her ugliness. Her simplicity decorated us, her guilt sanctified us, her pain made us glow with health, her awkwardness made us think we had a sense of humor. Her inarticulateness made us believe we were eloquent. Her poverty kept us generous. Even her waking dreams we used—to silence our own nightmares. And she let us, and thereby deserved our contempt. We honed our egos on her, padded our characters with her frailty, and yawned in the fantasy of our strength.

And fantasy it was, for we were not strong, only aggressive; we were not free, merely licensed; we were not compassionate, we were polite; not good, but well behaved. We courted death in order to call ourselves brave, and hid like thieves from life. We substituted good grammar for intellect; we switched habits to simulate maturity; we rearranged lies and called it truth, seeing in the new pattern of an old idea the Revelation and the Word.

She, however, stepped over into madness, a madness which protected her from us simply because it bored us in the end.

Oh, some of us "loved" her. The Maginot Line. And Cholly loved her. I'm sure he did. He, at any rate, was the one who loved her enough to touch her, envelop her, give something of himself to her. But his touch was fatal, and the something he gave her filled the matrix of her agony with death. Love is never any better than the lover. Wicked people love wickedly, violent people love violently, weak people love weakly, stupid people love stupidly, but the love of a free man is never safe. There is no gift for the beloved. The lover alone possesses his gift of love. The loved one is shorn, neutralized, frozen in the glare of the lover's inward eye.

6. Work camp for prisoners.

And now when I see her searching the garbage—for what? The thing we assassinated? I talk about how I did *not* plant the seeds too deeply, how it was the fault of the earth, the land, of our town. I even think now that the land of the entire country was hostile to marigolds that year. This soil is bad for certain kinds of flowers. Certain seeds it will not nurture, certain fruit it will not bear, and when the land kills of its own volition, we acquiesce and say the victim had no right to live. We are wrong, of course, but it doesn't matter. It's too late. At least on the edge of my town, among the garbage and the sunflowers of my town, it's much, much, much too late.

1970

ALICE MUNRO
1931–

Fashioning an art that, in the words of the novelist-critic Joyce Carol Oates, "works to conceal itself, in order to celebrate its subject," Alice Munro has published several prize-winning volumes of short stories and two story-sequences that have been read as novels, *Lives of Girls and Women* (1971) and *Who Do You Think You Are?* (1978). The latter, issued in the United States as *The Beggar Maid: Stories of Flo and Rose*, is typical of Munro's work, focusing, as it does, on the relationship of a stepmother (Flo) and a stepdaughter (Rose), who confront their emotionally subtle responses to each other and to the banal people and everyday events that nevertheless continue to surprise them. The subjects Munro celebrates are the small-town Canadians who inhabit the southwestern Ontario of her own childhood. Born in Wingham, Ontario, the daughter of farmers, Alice Laidlaw attended the University of Western Ontario before marrying the bookseller James Munro. Although she brought up her three daughters in Vancouver and Victoria, Munro returned in 1972 to western Ontario. After a divorce in 1976, she married Gerald Fremlin, a geographer. As a reader, Munro has explained, she can "go into [a story], and move back and forth and settle here and there, and stay in it for a while." As a writer, too, she meditates on the enigmatic interrelationships of past and present in a landscape evocative enough to sustain her vision. Whether she writes about piano recitals, high school dances, chance sexual encounters, or fox farming, that vision frequently centers on the lives of girls and women.

Wild Swans

Flo said to watch for White Slavers. She said this was how they operated: an old woman, a motherly or grandmotherly sort, made friends while riding beside you on a bus or train. She offered you candy, which was drugged. Pretty soon you began to droop and mumble, were in no condition to speak for yourself. Oh, help, the woman said, my daughter (granddaughter) is sick, please somebody help me get her off so that she can recover in the fresh air. Up stepped a polite gentleman, pretending to be a stranger, offering assistance. Together, at the next stop, they hustled you off the train or bus, and that was the last the ordinary world ever saw of you. They kept you a prisoner in the White Slave place (to which you had been transported drugged and bound so you wouldn't even know where you were), until such time as you were thoroughly degraded and in despair, your insides torn up by drunken men and invested with vile disease, your mind destroyed by drugs, your hair and teeth fallen out. It took about three years, for you to get to this state. You wouldn't want to go home, then, maybe couldn't remember home, or find your way if you did. So they let you out on the streets.

Flo took ten dollars and put it in a little cloth bag which she sewed to the strap of Rose's slip. Another thing likely to happen was that Rose would get her purse stolen.

Watch out, Flo said as well, for people dressed up as ministers. They were the worst. That disguise was commonly adopted by White Slavers, as well as those after your money.

Rose said she didn't see how she could tell which ones were disguised.

Flo had worked in Toronto once. She had worked as a waitress in a coffee shop in Union Station. That was how she knew all she knew. She never saw sunlight, in those days, except on her days off. But she saw plenty else. She saw a man cut another man's stomach with a knife, just pull out his shirt and do a tidy cut, as if it was a watermelon not a stomach. The stomach's owner just sat looking down surprised, with no time to protest. Flo implied that that was nothing, in Toronto. She saw two bad women (that was what Flo called whores, running the two words together, like badminton) get into a fight, and a man laughed at them, other men stopped and laughed and egged them on, and they had their fists full of each other's hair. At last the police came and took them away, still howling and yelping.

She saw a child die of a fit, too. Its face was black as ink.

"Well I'm not scared," said Rose provokingly. "There's the police, anyway."

"Oh, them! They'd be the first ones to diddle you!"

She did not believe anything Flo said on the subject of sex. Consider the undertaker.

A little bald man, very neatly dressed, would come into the store sometimes and speak to Flo with a placating expression.

"I only wanted a bag of candy. And maybe a few packages of gum.

And one or two chocolate bars. Could you go to the trouble of wrapping them?"

Flo in her mock-deferential tone would assure him that she could. She wrapped them in heavy-duty white paper, so they were something like presents. He took his time with the selection, humming and chatting, then dawdled for a while. He might ask how Flo was feeling. And how Rose was, if she was there.

"You look pale. Young girls need fresh air." To Flo he would say, "You work too hard. You've worked hard all your life."

"No rest for the wicked," Flo would say agreeably.

When he went out she hurried to the window. There it was—the old black hearse with its purple curtains.

"He'll be after them today!" Flo would say as the hearse rolled away at a gentle pace, almost a funeral pace. The little man had been an undertaker, but he was retired now. The hearse was retired too. His sons had taken over the undertaking and bought a new one. He drove the old hearse all over the country, looking for women. So Flo said. Rose could not believe it. Flo said he gave them the gum and the candy. Rose said he probably ate them himself. Flo said he had been seen, he had been heard. In mild weather he drove with the windows down, singing, to himself or to somebody out of sight in the back.

> Her brow is like the snowdrift
> Her throat is like the swan

Flo imitated him singing. Gently overtaking some woman walking on a back road, or resting at a country crossroads. All compliments and courtesy and chocolate bars, offering a ride. Of course every woman who reported being asked said she had turned him down. He never pestered anybody, drove politely on. He called in at houses, and if the husband was home he seemed to like just as well as anything to sit and chat. Wives said that was all he ever did anyway but Flo did not believe it.

"Some women are taken in," she said. "A number." She liked to speculate on what the hearse was like inside. Plush. Plush on the walls and the roof and the floor. Soft purple, the color of the curtains, the color of dark lilacs.

All nonsense, Rose thought. Who could believe it, of a man that age?

Rose was going to Toronto on the train for the first time by herself. She had been once before, but that was with Flo, long before her father died. They took along their own sandwiches and bought milk from the vendor on the train. It was sour. Sour chocolate milk. Rose kept taking tiny sips, unwilling to admit that something so much desired could fail her. Flo sniffed it, then hunted up and down the train until she found the old man in his red jacket, with no teeth and the tray hanging around his neck. She invited him to sample the chocolate milk. She invited people nearby to smell it. He let her have some ginger ale for nothing. It was slightly warm.

"I let him know," Flo said looking around after he had left. "You have to let them know."

A woman agreed with her but most people looked out the window. Rose drank the warm ginger ale. Either that, or the scene with the vendor, or the conversation Flo and the agreeing woman now got into about where they came from, why they were going to Toronto, and Rose's morning constipation which was why she was lacking color, or the small amount of chocolate milk she had got inside her, caused her to throw up in the train toilet. All day long she was afraid people in Toronto could smell vomit on her coat.

This time Flo started the trip off by saying, "Keep an eye on her, she's never been away from home before!" to the conductor, then looking around and laughing, to show that was jokingly meant. Then she had to get off. It seemed the conductor had no more need for jokes than Rose had, and no intention of keeping an eye on anybody. He never spoke to Rose except to ask for her ticket. She had a window seat, and was soon extraordinarily happy. She felt Flo receding, West Hanratty flying away from her, her own wearying self discarded as easily as everything else. She loved the towns less and less known. A woman was standing at her back door in her nightgown, not caring if everybody on the train saw her. They were traveling south, out of the snow belt, into an earlier spring, a tenderer sort of landscape. People could grow peach trees in their backyards.

Rose collected in her mind the things she had to look for in Toronto. First, things for Flo. Special stockings for her varicose veins. A special kind of cement for sticking handles on pots. And a full set of dominoes.

For herself Rose wanted to buy hair-remover to put on her arms and legs, and if possible an arrangement of inflatable cushions, supposed to reduce your hips and thighs. She thought they probably had hair-remover in the drugstore in Hanratty, but the woman in there was a friend of Flo's and told everything. She told Flo who bought hair dye and slimming medicine and French safes. As for the cushion business, you could send away for it but there was sure to be a comment at the Post Office, and Flo knew people there as well. She also planned to buy some bangles, and an angora sweater. She had great hopes of silver bangles and powder-blue angora. She thought they could transform her, make her calm and slender and take the frizz out of her hair, dry her underarms and turn her complexion to pearl.

The money for these things, as well as the money for the trip, came from a prize Rose had won, for writing an essay called "Art and Science in the World of Tomorrow." To her surprise, Flo asked if she could read it, and while she was reading it, she remarked that they must have thought they had to give Rose the prize for swallowing the dictionary. Then she said shyly, "It's very interesting."

She would have to spend the night at Cela McKinney's. Cela McKinney was her father's cousin. She had married a hotel manager and thought she had gone up in the world. But the hotel manager came home one day and sat down on the dining room floor between two chairs and said, "I am never going to leave this house again." Nothing unusual had happened, he had just decided not to go out of the house again, and he didn't, until he died. That had made Cela McKinney odd and nervous. She locked her doors at eight o'clock. She was also very stingy. Supper was usually oatmeal porridge, with raisins. Her house was dark and narrow and smelled like a bank.

The train was filling up. At Brantford a man asked if she would mind if he sat down beside her.

"It's cooler out than you'd think," he said. He offered her part of his newspaper. She said no thanks.

Then lest he think her rude she said it really was cooler. She went on looking out the window at the spring morning. There was no snow left, down here. The trees and bushes seemed to have a paler bark than they did at home. Even the sunlight looked different. It was as different from home, here, as the coast of the Mediterranean would be, or the valleys of California.

"Filthy windows, you'd think they'd take more care," the man said. "Do you travel much by train?"

She said no.

Water was lying in the fields. He nodded at it and said there was a lot this year.

"Heavy snows."

She noticed his saying *snows*, a poetic-sounding word. Anyone at home would have said *snow*.

"I had an unusual experience the other day. I was driving out in the country. In fact I was on my way to see one of my parishioners, a lady with a heart condition—"

She looked quickly at his collar. He was wearing an ordinary shirt and tie and a dark blue suit.

"Oh, yes," he said. "I'm a United Church minister. But I don't always wear my uniform. I wear it for preaching in. I'm off duty today.

"Well as I said I was driving through the country and I saw some Canada geese down on a pond, and I took another look, and there were some swans down with them. A whole great flock of swans. What a lovely sight they were. They would be on their spring migration, I expect, heading up north. What a spectacle. I never saw anything like it."

Rose was unable to think appreciatively of the wild swans because she was afraid he was going to lead the conversation from them to Nature in general and then to God, the way a minister would feel obliged to do. But he did not, he stopped with the swans.

"A very fine sight. You would have enjoyed them."

He was between fifty and sixty years old, Rose thought. He was short, and energetic-looking, with a square ruddy face and bright waves of gray hair combed straight up from his forehead. When she realized he was not going to mention God she felt she ought to show her gratitude.

She said they must have been lovely.

"It wasn't even a regular pond, it was only some water lying in a field. It was just luck the water was lying there and they came down and I came driving by at the right time. Just luck. They come in at the east end of Lake Erie, I think. But I never was lucky enough to see them before."

She turned by degrees to the window, and he returned to his paper. She remained slightly smiling, so as not to seem rude, not to seem to be rejecting conversation altogether. The morning really was cool, and she had taken down her coat off the hook where she put it when she first got on the train, she had spread it over herself, like a lap robe. She had set her purse on the floor when the minister sat down, to give him room. He took the sections of the paper apart, shaking and rustling them in a leisurely, rather showy, way. He seemed to her the sort of person who does everything in a showy way. A ministerial way. He brushed aside the sections he didn't want at the moment. A corner of newspaper touched her leg, just at the edge of her coat.

She thought for some time that it was the paper. Then she said to herself, what if it is a hand? That was the kind of thing she could imagine. She would sometimes look at men's hands, at the fuzz on their forearms, their concentrating profiles. She would think about everything they could do. Even the stupid ones. For instance the driver-salesman who brought the bread to Flo's store. The ripeness and confidence of manner, the settled mixture of ease and alertness with which he handled the bread truck. A fold of mature belly over the belt did not displease her. Another time she had her eye on the French teacher at school. Not a Frenchman at all, really, his name was McLaren, but Rose thought teaching French had rubbed off on him, made him look like one. Quick and sallow; sharp shoulders; hooked nose and sad eyes. She saw him lapping and coiling his way through slow pleasures, a perfect autocrat of indulgences. She had a considerable longing to be somebody's object. Pounded, pleasured, reduced, exhausted.

But what if it was a hand? What if it really was a hand? She shifted slightly, moved as much as she could toward the window. Her imagination seemed to have created this reality, a reality she was not prepared for at all. She found it alarming. She was concentrating on that leg, that bit of skin with the stocking over it. She could not bring herself to look. Was there a pressure, or was there not? She shifted again. Her legs had been, and remained, tightly closed. It was. It was a hand. It was a hand's pressure.

Please don't. That was what she tried to say. She shaped the words in her mind, tried them out, then couldn't get them past her lips. Why was that? The embarrassment, was it, the fear that people might hear? People were all around them, the seats were full.

It was not only that.

She did manage to look at him, not raising her head but turning it cautiously. He had tilted his seat back and closed his eyes. There was his dark blue suit sleeve, disappearing under the newspaper. He had arranged the paper so that it overlapped Rose's coat. His hand was underneath, simply resting, as if flung out in sleep.

Now, Rose could have shifted the newspaper and removed her coat. If he was not asleep, he would have been obliged to draw back his hand. If he was asleep, if he did not draw it back, she could have whispered, *Excuse me*, and set his hand firmly on his own knee. This solution, so obvious and foolproof, did not occur to her. And she would have to wonder, why not? The minister's hand was not, or not yet, at all welcome to her. It made her feel uncomfortable, resentful, slightly disgusted, trapped and wary. But she could not take charge of it, to reject it. She could not insist that it was there, when he seemed to be insisting that it was not. How could she declare him responsible, when he lay there so harmless and trusting, resting himself before his busy day, with such a pleased and healthy face? A man older than her father would be, if he were living, a man used to deference, an appreciator of Nature, delighter in wild swans. If she did say *Please don't* she was sure he would ignore her, as if overlooking some silliness or impoliteness on her part. She knew that as soon as she said it she would hope he had not heard.

But there was more to it than that. Curiosity. More constant, more imperious, than any lust. A lust in itself, that will make you draw back and wait, wait too long, risk almost anything, just to see what will happen. *To see what will happen.*

The hand began, over the next several miles, the most delicate, the most timid, pressures and investigations. Not asleep. Or if he was, his hand wasn't. She did feel disgust. She felt a faint, wandering nausea.

She thought of flesh: lumps of flesh, pink snouts, fat tongues, blunt fingers, all on their way trotting and creeping and lolling and rubbing, looking for their comfort. She thought of cats in heat rubbing themselves along the top of board fences, yowling with their miserable complaint. It was pitiful, infantile, this itching and shoving and squeezing. Spongy tissues, inflamed membranes, tormented nerve-ends, shameful smells; humiliation.

All that was starting. His hand, that she wouldn't ever have wanted to hold, that she wouldn't have squeezed back, his stubborn patient hand was able, after all, to get the ferns to rustle and the streams to flow, to waken a sly luxuriance.

Nevertheless, she would rather not. She would still rather not. Please remove this, she said out the window. Stop it, please, she said to the stumps and barns. The hand moved up her leg past the top of her stocking to her bare skin, had moved higher, under her suspender, reached her underpants and the lower part of her belly. Her legs were still crossed, pinched together. While her legs stayed crossed she could lay claim to innocence, she had not admitted anything. She could still believe that she would stop this in a minute. Nothing was going to happen, nothing more. Her legs were never going to open.

But they were. They were. As the train crossed the Niagra Escarpment above Dundas, as they looked down at the preglacial valley, the silver-wooded rubble of little hills, as they came sliding down to the shores of Lake Ontario, she would make this slow, and silent, and definite, declaration, perhaps disappointing as much as satisfying the hand's owner. He would not lift his eyelids, his face would not alter, his fingers would not hesitate, but would go powerfully and discreetly to work. Invasion, and welcome, and sunlight flashing far and wide on the lake water; miles of bare orchards stirring round Burlington.

This was disgrace, this was beggary. But what harm in that, we say to ourselves at such moments, what harm in anything, the worse the better, as we ride the cold wave of greed, of greedy assent. A stranger's hand, or root vegetables or humble kitchen tools that people tell jokes about; the world is tumbling with innocent-seeming objects ready to declare themselves, slippery and obliging. She was careful of her breathing. She could not believe this. Victim and accomplice she was borne past Glassco's Jams and Marmalades, past the big pulsating pipes of oil refineries. They glided into suburbs where bedsheets, and towels used to wipe up intimate stains, flapped leeringly on the clotheslines, where even the children seemed to be frolicking lewdly in the schoolyards, and the very truckdrivers stopped at the railway crossings must be thrusting their thumbs gleefully into curled hands. Such cunning antics now, such popular visions. The gates and towers of the Exhibition Grounds came into view, the painted domes and pillars floated marvelously against her eyelids' rosy sky. Then flew apart in celebration. You could have had such a flock of birds, wild swans, even, wakened under one big dome together, exploding from it, taking to the sky.

She bit the edge of her tongue. Very soon the conductor passed through the train, to stir the travelers, warn them back to life.

In the darkness under the station the United Church minister, refreshed, opened his eyes and got his paper folded together, then asked if she would like some help with her coat. His gallantry was self-satisfied, dismissive. No, said Rose, with a sore tongue. He hurried out of the train ahead of her. She did not see him in the station. She never saw him again in her life. But he remained on call, so to speak, for years and years, ready to slip into place at a critical moment, without even any regard, later on, for husband or lovers. What recommended him? She could never understand it. His simplicity, his arrogance, his perversely appealing lack of handsomeness, even of ordinary grown-up masculinity? When he stood up she saw that he was shorter even than she had thought, that his face was pink and shiny, that there was something crude and pushy and childish about him.

Was he a minister, really, or was that only what he said? Flo had mentioned people who were not ministers, dressed up as if they were. Not real ministers dressed as if they were not. Or, stranger still, men who were not real ministers pretending to be real but dressed as if they were not. But that she had come as close as she had, to what could happen, was an unwelcome thing. Rose walked through Union Station feeling the little bag with the ten dollars rubbing at her, knew she would feel it all day long, rubbing its reminder against her skin.

She couldn't stop getting Flo's messages, even with that. She remembered, because she was in Union Station, that there was a girl named Mavis working here, in the Gift Shop, when Flo was working in the coffee shop. Mavis had warts on her eyelids that looked like they were going to turn into sties but they didn't, they went away. Maybe she had them removed, Flo didn't ask. She was very good-looking, without them. There was a movie star in those days she looked a lot like. The movie star's name was Frances Farmer.

Frances Farmer. Rose had never heard of her.

That was the name. And Mavis went and bought herself a big hat that dipped over one eye and a dress entirely made of lace. She went off for the weekend to Georgian Bay, to a resort up there. She booked herself in under the name of Florence Farmer. To give everybody the idea she was really the other one, Frances Farmer, but calling herself Florence because she was on holiday and didn't want to be recognized. She had a little cigarette holder that was black and mother-of-pearl. She could have been arrested, Flo said. For the *nerve*.

Rose almost went over to the Gift Shop, to see if Mavis was still there and if she could recognize her. She thought it would be an especially fine thing, to manage a transformation like that. To dare it; to get away with it, to enter on preposterous adventures in your own, but newly named, skin.

1978

SYLVIA PLATH
1932–1963

"I am afraid of getting older," wrote the seventeen-year-old Sylvia Plath in 1949, "I am afraid of getting married. Spare me from cooking three meals a day—spare me from the relentless cage of routine and rote. I want to be free. . . . I want, I think, to be ominiscient . . . . I think I would like to call myself 'The girl who wanted to be God.' " Plath's adolescent anxieties were prophetic, for, fourteen years after she wrote these words, the failure of her marriage and the "relentless cage of routine and rote" in which she felt imprisoned as she struggled alone in London to care for two young children appear to have led directly to her suicide, an event that continues to arouse controversy. Equally controversial, however, is the poetry that she wrote shortly before she died. Published posthumously in *Ariel* (1965), her last verses are fiercely innovative and sometimes ferociously vituperative, exulting in their own aesthetic liberation as if to remind us of the early ambitions of this "girl who wanted to be God." Excoriated by some critics for—in the words of the British psychoanalyst David Holbrook—seducing "us to taste of [their] poisoned chalice," they have also been praised as—in the phrase of the American poet Robert Lowell—the productions of "one of those super-real, hypnotic, great classical heroines."

The girl who was to end her life as the center of both a personal and a public melodrama was born and brought up in comparatively quiet, middle-class circumstances. Her parents, German immigrants, were ambitious, hard-working professionals: Otto Plath, an entomologist, taught at Boston University, where Aurelia Plath was also to become a faculty member, teaching secretarial skills. The older of two children, Sylvia Plath herself exhibited an early precocity, as well as a penchant for hard work. With her mother's encouragement, she began to write stories and poems when she was quite young, and by the time she confided to her diary that she wanted to be "omniscient" she had already published some of this work in *Seventeen* and other periodicals. What might have been simply a prosperous and productive girlhood had been darkened, however, by her father's death (from a gangrenous leg, to which she refers in *Daddy*) when she was eight. In the myth into which she increasingly transformed her life throughout her later work—for example, the sardonic curse-poem *Daddy* (1963) and the comic novel *The Bell Jar* (1963)—this event consistently played a central part, marking a fall from childhood innocence to adult experience, from grace to loss.

In 1950, Plath won a scholarship to Smith College, where for several years she continued her career as a "superachiever," accumulating a steady string of honors and prizes along with high grades and accolades from her teachers. But the distinction that made the greatest difference in her career at the time (as well as in her later life) proved problematic: in 1953, Plath became one of a dozen "Guest Editors" of the New York fashion magazine *Mademoiselle* and traveled to the city to work on the journal's staff for a month. Thinly fictionalized, her feelings and experiences there are recounted in some detail in *The Bell Jar*, where she records the ambivalences that marked her initiation into the Madison Avenue world of female glamour and professional high style. Returning to her mother's home in Wellesley, Massachusetts, she suffered a serious breakdown and she attempted suicide—an attempt that she would later record not only in *The Bell Jar* but also in such poems as *Daddy* and *Lady Lazarus*.

Following her breakdown, Plath was institutionalized for a year and given (among other therapies) electric shock treatments, treatments whose intensity may inform some of her most violent metaphors of physical and spiritual transformation. When she returned to Smith in 1954, however, she seems easily to have resumed her successful academic career. In 1955, she graduated *summa cum laude* and won a Fulbright to Cambridge University, where she studied for a graduate degree in English literature and where, in 1956, she met and married the poet Ted Hughes, an ambitous and energetic artist whose intellectual and emotional support significantly aided her development during their early years together. In the late fifties, the couple traveled to the United States, and Plath taught for a year at Smith, but, passionately committed to her literary vocation, she ultimately rejected academic ambition. Instead, she and Hughes settled first in London, then in a farmhouse in Devon, where Plath devoted herself to writing and to her two children—Frieda and Nicholas—born in the early sixties.

After her marriage broke up in the summer of 1962, Plath moved back to London and struggled to continue her work while caring for her children through the coldest winter England had seen in decades. Her letters to her mother from this period (edited in *Letters Home*, by Aurelia Schober Plath) are characterized by intense bitterness over the collapse of her marriage and mounting anxiety about her future and her children's. At the same time, they are marked by extraordinary exultation, for Plath was now producing—sometimes at the rate of two or three a day—the poems that would later appear in *Ariel*, and she knew their value. "I am a writer . . . I am a genius of a writer . . . I am writing the best poems of my life; they will make my name," she told her mother. Nevertheless, despite her awareness of the nature of her achievement, there is considerable evidence that she was again experiencing a breakdown not unlike the one that had led to her suicide attempt in 1953. Early in the morning of February 11, 1963, she left mugs of milk next to her children's cribs, carefully stuffed towels into the cracks around her kitchen door, and gassed herself in the oven of her stove.

The mythologizing of self and family that energizes Plath's later poems, as well as earlier works like *The Colossus* and *The Disquieting Muses*, has almost certainly led to much of the critical misunderstanding that continues to surround her poetry with controversy. About *Daddy*, for instance, the critic Elizabeth Hardwick has complained that Plath's real father "died of a long illness, but there is no pity for *his* lost life," adding that he "did not kill anyone and 'the fat black heart' [of the poem] is really [Plath's] own," and concluding that to bring "strangers, the town . . . into the punishment of her father . . . is somehow the most biting and ungenerous thought of all." The problem with such remarks, which are representative of a good many attacks that have been mounted against Plath, is that the literary figure of "Daddy" in the poem of that name (like the father figure in *The Colossus*) is not identical with, but rather *generalized* from, Plath's literal father.

Similarly, though late poems like *Ariel*, *Fever 103*, and *Edge* are death-haunted, they cannot be said to "predict" Plath's suicide, despite Robert Lowell's comment that these verses "are playing Russian roulette with six cartridges in the cylinder." Rather, it is important to understand that Plath's demise, far from being the consequence of fearfully unleashed imaginative forces, was the result of a series of personal calamities. Lately some feminists have worried that because this artist was not a "survivor" she does not offer younger women who study her life a "positive role model." Yet, as Plath's own poems show, the works that would "make [her] name" were inspired by yearning to endure and overcome the ice of circumstance. *Wintering*, the poem with which she herself had planned to end *Ariel*, concludes with a question and answer that express just such longing. "Will the hive survive, . . . / To enter another year?" the poet wonders, and replies to her own query with an affirmation of certainty: "The bees are flying. They taste the spring." Sylvia Plath herself may not have lasted out her struggle to "taste" another spring, but her poems record her will to triumph.

The Disquieting Muses[1]

Mother, mother, what illbred aunt
Or what disfigured and unsightly
Cousin did you so unwisely keep
Unasked to my christening,[2] that she
Sent these ladies in her stead   5
With heads like darning-eggs to nod
And nod and nod at foot and head
And at the left side of my crib?

Mother, who made to order stories
Of Mixie Blackshort the heroic bear,   10
Mother, whose witches always, always
Got baked into gingerbread, I wonder

1. Greek goddesses of poetry and inspiration.
2. An allusion to the fairy tale *Sleeping Beauty*, in which a young princess is cast into a deep sleep by a spiteful aunt who was not invited to the girl's christening.

Whether you saw them, whether you said
Words to rid me of those three ladies
Nodding by night around my bed,   15
Mouthless, eyeless, with stitched bald head.

In the hurricane, when father's twelve
Study windows bellied in
Like bubbles about to break, you fed
My brother and me cookies and Ovaltine   20
And helped the two of us to choir:
"Thor [3] is angry: boom boom boom!
Thor is angry: we don't care!"
But those ladies broke the panes.

When on tiptoe the schoolgirls danced,   25
Blinking flashlights like fireflies
And singing the glowworm song, I could
Not lift a foot in the twinkle-dress
But, heavy-footed, stood aside
In the shadow cast by my dismal-headed   30
Godmothers, and you cried and cried:
And the shadows stretched, the lights went out.

Mother, you sent me to piano lessons
And praised my arabesques and trills
Although each teacher found my touch   35
Oddly wooden in spite of scales
And the hours of practicing, my ear
Tone-deaf and yes, unteachable.
I learned, I learned, I learned elsewhere,
From muses unhired by you, dear mother.   40

I woke one day to see you, mother,
Floating above me in bluest air
On a green balloon bright with a million
Flowers and bluebirds that never were
Never, never, found anywhere.   45
But the little planet bobbed away
Like a soap-bubble as you called: Come here!
And I faced my traveling companions.

Day now, night now, at head, side, feet,
They stand their vigil in gowns of stone,   50
Faces blank as the day I was born,
Their shadows long in the setting sun
That never brightens or goes down.

3. The Norse god of war and thunder.

And this is the kingdom you bore me to,
Mother, mother. But no frown of mine   55
Will betray the company I keep.

1957   1960

The Colossus[4]

I shall never get you put together entirely,
Pieced, glued, and properly jointed.
Mule-bray, pig-grunt and bawdy cackles
Proceed from your great lips.
It's worse than a barnyard.   5

Perhaps you consider yourself an oracle,
Mouthpiece of the dead, or of some god or other.
Thirty years now I have labored
To dredge the silt from your throat.
I am none the wiser.   10

Scaling little ladders with gluepots and pails of Lysol
I crawl like an ant in mourning
Over the weedy acres of your brow
To mend the immense skull-plates and clear
The bald, white tumuli of your eyes.   15

A blue sky out of the Oresteia[5]
Arches above us. O father, all by yourself
You are pithy and historical as the Roman Forum.[6]
I open my lunch on a hill of black cypress.
Your fluted bones and acanthine[7] hair are littered   20

In their old anarchy to the horizon-line.
It would take more than a lightning-stroke
To create such a ruin.
Nights, I squat in the cornucopia
Of your left ear, out of the wind,   25

Counting the red stars and those of plum-color.
The sun rises under the pillar of your tongue.
My hours are married to shadow.

4. A gigantic statue that stood at the entrance to the harbor of Rhodes, Greece, in the third century B.C.
5. A cycle of three plays by Aeschylus (525–456 B.C.) which recount the story of the young Greek prince Orestes' efforts to avenge the murder of his father, Agamemnon.
6. The public square in ancient Rome, where legal and political proceedings took place.
7. I.e., sculptured (as in Greek columns) like the leaves of the acanthus plant; "fluted": grooved (again, as in columns).

No longer do I listen for the scrape of a keel
On the blank stones of the landing.   30

1959   1960

Parliament Hill Fields

On this bald hill the new year hones its edge.
Faceless and pale as china
The round sky goes on minding its business.
Your absence is inconspicuous;
Nobody can tell what I lack.   5

Gulls have threaded the river's mud bed back
To this crest of grass. Inland, they argue,
Settling and stirring like blown paper
Or the hands of an invalid. The wan
Sun manages to strike such tin glints   10

From the linked ponds that my eyes wince
And brim; the city melts like sugar.
A crocodile of small girls
Knotting and stopping, ill-assorted, in blue uniforms,
Opens to swallow me. I'm a stone, a stick,   15

One child drops a barrette of pink plastic;
None of them seem to notice.
Their shrill, gravelly gossip's funneled off.
Now silence after silence offers itself.
The wind stops my breath like a bandage.   20

Southward, over Kentish Town, an ashen smudge
Swaddles roof and tree.
It could be a snowfield or a cloudbank.
I suppose it's pointless to think of you at all.
Already your doll grip lets go.   25

The tumulus, even at noon, guards its black shadow:
You know me less constant,
Ghost of a leaf, ghost of a bird.
I circle the writhen trees. I am too happy.
These faithful dark-boughed cypresses   30

Brood, rooted in their heaped losses.
Your cry fades like the cry of a gnat.
I lose sight of you on your blind journey,
While the heath grass glitters and the spindling rivulets
Unspool and spend themselves. My mind runs with them,   35

Pooling in heel-prints, fumbling pebble and stem.
The day empties its images
Like a cup or a room. The moon's crook whitens,
Thin as the skin seaming a scar.
Now, on the nursery wall,   40

The blue night plants, the little pale blue hill
In your sister's birthday picture start to glow.
The orange pompons, the Egyptian papyrus
Light up. Each rabbit-eared
Blue shrub behind the glass   45

Exhales an indigo nimbus,
A sort of cellophane balloon.
The old dregs, the old difficulties take me to wife.
Gulls stiffen to their chill vigil in the drafty half-light;
I enter the lit house.   50

February 11, 1961   1971

The Bee Meeting

Who are these people at the bridge to meet me? They
     are the villagers—
The rector, the midwife, the sexton, the agent for bees.
In my sleeveless summery dress I have no protection,
And they are all gloved and covered, why did nobody tell me?
They are smiling and taking out veils tacked to ancient hats.   5

I am nude as a chicken neck, does nobody love me?
Yes, here is the secretary of bees with her white shop smock,
Buttoning the cuffs at my wrists and the slit from my neck
     to my knees.
Now I am milkweed silk, the bees will not notice.
They will not smell my fear, my fear, my fear.   10

Which is the rector now, is it that man in black?
Which is the midwife, is that her blue coat?
Everybody is nodding a square black head, they are knights in visors,
Breastplates of cheesecloth knotted under the armpits.

Their smiles and their voices are changing. I am led
     through a beanfield.   15

Strips of tinfoil winking like people,
Feather dusters fanning their hands in a sea of bean flowers,

Creamy bean flowers with black eyes and leaves like bored hearts.
Is it blood clots the tendrils are dragging up that string?
No, no, it is scarlet flowers that will one day be edible.   20

Now they are giving me a fashionable white straw Italian hat
And a black veil that molds to my face, they are making
      me one of them.
They are leading me to the shorn grove, the circle of hives.
Is it the hawthorn that smells so sick?
The barren body of hawthorn, etherizing its children.   25

Is it some operation that is taking place?
It is the surgeon my neighbors are waiting for,
This apparition in a green helmet,
Shining gloves and white suit.
Is it the butcher, the grocer, the postman, someone I know?   30

I cannot run, I am rooted, and the gorse hurts me
With its yellow purses, its spiky armory.
I could not run without having to run forever.
The white hive is snug as a virgin,
Sealing off her brood cells, her honey, and quietly
      humming.   35

Smoke rolls and scarves in the grove.
The mind of the hive thinks this is the end of everything.
Here they come, the outriders, on their hysterical elastics.
If I stand very still, they will think I am cow-parsley,
A gullible head untouched by their animosity,   40

Not even nodding, a personage in a hedgerow.
The villagers open the chambers, they are hunting
      the queen.[8]
Is she hiding, is she eating honey? She is very clever.
She is old, old, old, she must live another year, and she
      knows it.
While in their fingerjoint cells the new virgins   45

Dream of a duel they will win inevitably,
A curtain of wax dividing them from the bride flight,
The upflight of the murderess into a heaven that loves her.
The villagers are moving the virgins, there will be no killing.
The old queen does not show herself, is she so ungrateful?   50

I am exhausted, I am exhausted—
Pillar of white in a blackout of knives.

8. I.e., the queen bee.

I am the magician's girl who does not flinch.
The villagers are untying their disguises, they are shaking
    hands.
Whose is that long white box in the grove,
    what have they accomplished, why am I cold.   55

October 3, 1962   1963

The Arrival of the Bee Box

I ordered this, this clean wood box
Square as a chair and almost too heavy to lift.
I would say it was the coffin of a midget
Or a square baby
Were there not such a din in it.   5

The box is locked, it is dangerous.
I have to live with it overnight
And I can't keep away from it.
There are no windows, so I can't see what is in there.
There is only a little grid, no exit.   10

I put my eye to the grid.
It is dark, dark,
With the swarmy feeling of African hands
Minute and shrunk for export,
Black on black, angrily clambering.   15

How can I let them out?
It is the noise that appalls me most of all,
The unintelligible syllables.
It is like a Roman mob,[9]
Small, taken one by one, but my god, together!   20

I lay my ear to furious Latin.
I am not a Caesar.[1]
I have simply ordered a box of maniacs.
They can be sent back.
They can die, I need feed them nothing, I am the owner.   25

I wonder how hungry they are.
I wonder if they would forget me
If I just undid the locks and stood back and turned into a tree.
There is the laburnum, its blond colonnades,
And the petticoats of the cherry.   30

9. Thought of (as in Shakespeare's *Julius Cae-*   1. I.e., ruler, emperor.
sar) as being unruly and unmanageable.

They might ignore me immediately
In my moon suit and funeral veil.
I am no source of honey
So why should they turn on me?
Tomorrow I will be sweet God, I will set them free.   35

The box is only temporary.

October 4, 1962   1963

Stings

Bare-handed, I hand the combs.
The man in white smiles, bare-handed,
Our cheesecloth gauntlets neat and sweet,
The throats of our wrists brave lilies.
He and I   5

Have a thousand clean cells between us,
Eight combs of yellow cups,
And the hive itself a teacup,
White with pink flowers on it,
With excessive love I enameled it   10

Thinking "Sweetness, sweetness."
Brood cells gray as the fossils of shells
Terrify me, they seem so old.
What am I buying, wormy mahogany?
Is there any queen at all in it?   15

If there is, she is old,
Her wings torn shawls, her long body
Rubbed of its plush—
Poor and bare and unqueenly and even shameful.
I stand in a column   20

Of winged, unmiraculous women,
Honey-drudgers.[2]
I am no drudge
Though for years I have eaten dust
And dried plates with my dense hair.   25

And seen my strangeness evaporate,
Blue dew from dangerous skin.
Will they hate me,

2. I.e., the female worker bees who produce the hive's honey.

These women who only scurry,
Whose news is the open cherry, the open clover?   30

It is almost over.
I am in control.
Here is my honey-machine,
It will work without thinking,
Opening, in spring, like an industrious virgin   35

To scour the creaming crests
As the moon, for its ivory powders, scours the sea.
A third person is watching.
He has nothing to do with the bee-seller or with me.
Now he is gone   40

In eight great bounds, a great scapegoat.
Here is his slipper, here is another,
And here the square of white linen
He wore instead of a hat.
He was sweet,   45

The sweat of his efforts a rain
Tugging the world to fruit.
The bees found him out,
Molding onto his lips like lies,
Complicating his features.   50

They thought death was worth it, but I
Have a self to recover, a queen.
Is she dead, is she sleeping?
Where has she been,
With her lion-red body, her wings of glass?   55

Now she is flying
More terrible than she ever was, red
Scar in the sky, red comet
Over the engine that killed her—
The mausoleum, the wax house.   60

October 6, 1962   1965

The Swarm

Somebody is shooting at something in our town—
A dull pom, pom in the Sunday street.
Jealousy can open the blood,

It can make black roses.
Who are they shooting at?   5

It is you the knives are out for
At Waterloo, Waterloo, Napoleon,[3]
The hump of Elba on your short back,
And the snow, marshaling its brilliant cutlery
Mass after mass, saying Shh!   10

Shh! These are chess people you play with,
Still figures of ivory.
The mud squirms with throats,
Stepping stones for French bootsoles.
The gilt and pink domes of Russia melt and float off   15

In the furnace of greed. Clouds, clouds.
So the swarm balls and deserts
Seventy feet up, in a black pine tree.
It must be shot down. Pom! Pom!
So dumb it thinks bullets are thunder.   20

It thinks they are the voice of God
Condoning the beak, the claw, the grin of the dog
Yellow-haunched, a pack-dog,
Grinning over its bone of ivory
Like the pack, the pack, like everybody.   25

The bees have got so far. Seventy feet high!
Russia, Poland and Germany![4]
The mild hills, the same old magenta
Fields shrunk to a penny
Spun into a river, the river crossed.   30

The bees argue, in their black ball,
A flying hedgehog, all prickles.
The man with gray hands stands under the honeycomb
Of their dream, the hived station
Where trains, faithful to their steel arcs,   35

Leave and arrive, and there is no end to the country.
Pom! Pom! They fall
Dismembered, to a tod[5] of ivy.
So much for the charioteers, the outriders, the Grand Army!
A red tatter, Napoleon!   40

---

3. Napoleon Bonaparte (1769–1821) was
France's emperor and military leader until his
defeat by the British at the battle of Waterloo in
1815. He spent his last days on the island of
Elba, off the western coast of Italy.
4. Three countries which Napoleon attempted
to conquer.
5. A clump (British).

The last badge of victory.
The swarm is knocked into a cocked straw hat.
Elba, Elba, bleb[6] on the sea!
The white busts of marshals, admirals, generals
Worming themselves into niches.   45

How instructive this is!
The dumb, banded bodies
Walking the plank draped with Mother France's upholstery
Into a new mausoleum,
An ivory palace, a crotch pine.   50

The man with gray hands smiles—
The smile of a man of business, intensely practical.
They are not hands at all
But asbestos receptacles.
Pom! Pom! "They would have killed *me*."   55

Stings big as drawing pins!
It seems bees have a notion of honor,
A black intractable mind.
Napoleon is pleased, he is pleased with everything.
O Europe! O ton of honey!   60

October 7, 1962   1965

Wintering

This is the easy time, there is nothing doing.
I have whirled the midwife's extractor,[7]
I have my honey,
Six jars of it,
Six cat's eyes in the wine cellar,   5

Wintering in a dark without window
At the heart of the house
Next to the last tenant's rancid jam
And the bottles of empty glitters—
Sir So-and-so's gin.   10

This is the room I have never been in
This is the room I could never breathe in.
The black bunched in there like a bat,

6. A small blister.
7. A device used for extracting honey from beehives.

No light
But the torch and its faint   15

Chinese yellow on appalling objects—
Black asininity. Decay.
Possession.
It is they who own me.
Neither cruel nor indifferent,   20

Only ignorant.
This is the time of hanging on for the bees—the bees
So slow I hardly know them,
Filing like soldiers
To the syrup tin   25

To make up for the honey I've taken.
Tate and Lyle[8] keeps them going,
The refined snow.
It is Tate and Lyle they live on, instead of flowers.
They take it. The cold sets in.   30

Now they ball in a mass,
Black
Mind against all that white.
The smile of the snow is white.
It spreads itself out, a mile-long body of Meissen,[9]   35

Into which, on warm days,
They can only carry their dead.
The bees are all women,
Maids and the long royal lady.
They have got rid of the men,   40

The blunt, clumsy stumblers, the boors.
Winter is for women—
The woman, still at her knitting,
At the cradle of Spanish walnut,
Her body a bulb in the cold and too dumb to think.   45

Will the hive survive, will the gladiolas
Succeed in banking their fires
To enter another year?
What will they taste of, the Christmas roses?
The bees are flying. They taste the spring.   50

October 9, 1962   1965

---

8. A commercial food for bees.   9. A kind of porcelain made in Germany.

Daddy

You do not do, you do not do
Any more, black shoe
In which I have lived like a foot
For thirty years, poor and white,
Barely daring to breathe or Achoo.   5

Daddy, I have had to kill you.
You died before I had time—
Marble-heavy, a bag full of God,
Ghastly statue with one gray toe[1]
Big as a Frisco seal   10

And a head in the freakish Atlantic
Where it pours bean green over blue
In the waters off beautiful Nauset.[2]
I used to pray to recover you.
Ach, du.[3]   15

In the German tongue, in the Polish town[4]
Scraped flat by the roller
Of wars, wars, wars.
But the name of the town is common.
My Polack friend   20

Says there are a dozen or two.
So I never could tell where you
Put your foot, your root,
I never could talk to you.
The tongue stuck in my jaw.   25

It stuck in a barb wire snare.
Ich, ich, ich, ich,[5]
I could hardly speak.
I thought every German was you.
And the language obscene   30

An engine, an engine
Chuffing me off like a Jew.
A Jew to Dachau, Auschwitz, Belsen.[6]
I began to talk like a Jew.
I think I may well be a Jew.   35

---

1. Plath's father's toe turned black from gangrene.
2. Beach north of Boston.
3. Ah, you: the first of a series of references to her father's German origins.
4. Grabow, the birthplace of Otto Plath, the poet's father.
5. I.
6. German concentration camps, where millions of Jews were murdered during World War II.

The snows of the Tyrol,[7] the clear beer of Vienna
Are not very pure or true.
With my gipsy ancestress and my weird luck
And my Taroc pack and my Taroc pack[8]
I may be a bit of a Jew.   40

I have always been scared of *you*,
With your Luftwaffe,[9] your gobbledygoo.
And your neat mustache
And your Aryan eye, bright blue.
Panzer-man, panzer-man,[1] O You—   45

Not God but a swastika
So black no sky could squeak through.
Every woman adores a Fascist,
The boot in the face, the brute
Brute heart of a brute like you.   50

You stand at the blackboard, daddy,
In the picture I have of you,
A cleft in your chin instead of your foot
But no less a devil for that, no not
Any less the black man who   55

Bit my pretty red heart in two.
I was ten when they buried you.
At twenty I tried to die[2]
And get back, back, back to you.
I thought even the bones would do.   60

But they pulled me out of the sack,
And they stuck me together with glue.
And then I knew what to do.
I made a model of you,
A man in black with a Meinkampf[3] look   65

And a love of the rack and the screw.
And I said I do, I do.
So daddy, I'm finally through.
The black telephone's off at the root,
The voices just can't worm through.   70

7. Austrian Alpine region.
8. Variant of Tarot, ancient fortune-telling cards.
9. The German air force.
1. Adolf Hitler, who had a neat moustache, preached the superiority of the Aryan race— persons with blond hair and blue eyes, as opposed to those with darker, Semitic characteristics. "Panzer" means "armor" in German.
2. An allusion to Plath's first suicide attempt.
3. A reference to Hitler's political autobiography, *Mein Kampf* (*My Struggle*), written and published before his rise to power, in which the future dictator outlined his plans for world conquest.

If I've killed one man, I've killed two—
The vampire who said he was you
And drank my blood for a year,
Seven years, if you want to know.
Daddy, you can lie back now.   75

There's a stake in your fat black heart
And the villagers never liked you.
They are dancing and stamping on you.
They always *knew* it was you.
Daddy, daddy, you bastard, I'm through.   80

October 12, 1962   1965

Medusa[4]

Off that landspit of stony mouth-plugs,
Eyes rolled by white sticks,
Ears cupping the sea's incoherences,
You house your unnerving head—God-ball,
Lens of mercies,   5

Your stooges
Plying their wild cells in my keel's shadow,
Pushing by like hearts,
Red stigmata[5] at the very center,
Riding the rip tide to the nearest point of departure,   10

Dragging their Jesus hair.
Did I escape, I wonder?
My mind winds to you
Old barnacled umbilicus, Atlantic cable,[6]
Keeping itself, it seems, in a state of miraculous repair. 15

In any case, you are always there,
Tremulous breath at the end of my line,
Curve of water upleaping
To my water rod, dazzling and grateful,
Touching and sucking.   20

I didn't call you.
I didn't call you at all.
Nevertheless, nevertheless

---

4. A jellyfish; also a mythological woman with snakes for hair, whose look has the power to turn men to stone.
5. Signs on the body resembling Christ's wounds.
6. A telephone cable, laid on the ocean floor, which connects America and Europe.

You steamed to me over the sea,
Fat and red, a placenta   25

Paralysing the kicking lovers.
Cobra light
Squeezing the breath from the blood bells
Of the fuchsia. I could draw no breath,
Dead and moneyless,   30

Overexposed, like an X-ray.
Who do you think you are?
A Communion wafer? Blubbery Mary?[7]
I shall take no bite of your body,
Bottle in which I live,   35

Ghastly Vatican.[8]
I am sick to death of hot salt.
Green as eunuchs, your wishes
Hiss at my sins.
Off, off, eely tentacle!   40

There is nothing between us.

October 16, 1962   1965

Ariel[9]

Stasis in darkness.
Then the substanceless blue
Pour of tor and distances.

God's lioness,
How one we grow,   5
Pivot of heels and knees!—The furrow

Splits and passes, sister to
The brown arc
Of the neck I cannot catch,

Nigger-eye   10
Berries cast dark
Hooks—

7. A pun on "Bloody Mary," the title given to Mary Tudor (1516–1558), the queen of England and Ireland from 1553 to 1558, renowned for her slaughtering of Protestant dissidents. The Communion wafer is part of the Catholic Mass, where it is believed to incarnate the Body of Christ.
8. The residence of the Pope in Rome.
9. The name of the horse Plath frequently rode; also the name of a fairy or spirit in Shakespeare's *The Tempest*.

Black sweet blood mouthfuls,
Shadows.
Something else   15

Hauls me through air—
Thighs, hair;
Flakes from my heels.

White
Godiva,[1] I unpeel—   20
Dead hands, dead stringencies.

And now I
Foam to wheat, a glitter of seas.
The child's cry

Melts in the wall.   25
And I
Am the arrow,

The dew that flies
Suicidal, at one with the drive
Into the red   30

Eye, the cauldron of morning.

October 27, 1962   1965

Nick and the Candlestick[2]

I am a miner. The light burns blue.
Waxy stalactites
Drip and thicken, tears

The earthen womb
Exudes from its dead boredom.   5
Black bat airs

Wrap me, raggy shawls,
Cold homicides.
They weld to me like plums.

1. According to legend, Lady Godiva (1010?–1067) rode naked through the streets of Coventry in order to persuade her husband, the local lord, to lower heavy taxes.
2. Plath's son, Nicholas, was less than a year old when this poem was written.

Old cave of calcium   10
Icicles, old echoer.
Even the newts are white,

Those holy Joes.[3]
And the fish, the fish—
Christ! they are panes of ice,   15

A vice of knives,
A piranha
Religion, drinking

Its first communion out of my live toes.
The candle   20
Gulps and recovers its small altitude,

Its yellows hearten.
O love, how did you get here?
O embryo

Remembering, even in sleep,   25
Your crossed position.
The blood blooms clean

In you, ruby.
The pain
You wake to is not yours.   30

Love, love,
I have hung our cave with roses,
With soft rugs—

The last of Victoriana.[4]
Let the stars   35
Plummet to their dark address,

Let the mercuric
Atoms that cripple drip
Into the terrible well,

You are the one   40
Solid the spaces lean on, envious.
You are the baby in the barn.[5]

October 29, 1962   1965

---

3. A pious person or clergyman (British slang).
4. I.e., the rich furnishings and decor associated
with the Victorian age.

5. An allusion to the infant Jesus, who was
nursed in a manger.

Lady Lazarus[6]

I have done it again.
One year in every ten
I manage it——

A sort of walking miracle, my skin
Bright as a Nazi lampshade,[7]   5
My right foot

A paperweight,
My face a featureless, fine
Jew linen.

Peel off the napkin   10
O my enemy.
Do I terrify?——

The nose, the eye pits, the full set of teeth?
The sour breath
Will vanish in a day.   15

Soon, soon the flesh
The grave cave ate will be
At home on me

And I a smiling woman.
I am only thirty.   20
And like the cat I have nine times to die.

This is Number Three.
What a trash
To annihilate each decade.

What a million filaments.   25
The peanut-crunching crowd
Shoves in to see

Them unwrap me hand and foot——
The big strip tease.
Gentlemen, ladies   30

These are my hands
My knees.
I may be skin and bone,

6. Lazarus, the brother of Mary and Martha, was raised by Jesus from the dead (John 11:1–44).

7. The Nazis made use of the corpses of Jews whom they had killed by turning their skin into lampshades and their bodies into soap.

Nevertheless, I am the same, identical woman.
The first time it happened I was ten.   35
It was an accident.

The second time I meant
To last it out and not come back at all.
I rocked shut

As a seashell.   40
They had to call and call
And pick the worms off me like sticky pearls.

Dying
Is an art, like everything else.
I do it exceptionally well.   45

I do it so it feels like hell.
I do it so it feels real.
I guess you could say I've a call.

It's easy enough to do it in a cell.
It's easy enough to do it and stay put.   50
It's the theatrical

Comeback in broad day
To the same place, the same face, the same brute
Amused shout:

"A miracle!"   55
That knocks me out.
There is a charge

For the eyeing of my scars, there is a charge
For the hearing of my heart—
It really goes.   60

And there is a charge, a very large charge
For a word or a touch
Or a bit of blood

Or a piece of my hair or my clothes.
So, so, Herr Doktor.   65
So, Herr Enemy.

I am your opus,
I am your valuable,
The pure gold baby

That melts to a shriek.   70
I turn and burn.
Do not think I underestimate your great concern.

Ash, ash—
You poke and stir.
Flesh, bone, there is nothing there—   75

A cake of soap,
A wedding ring,
A gold filling.

Herr God, Herr Lucifer[8]
Beware   80
Beware.

Out of the ash
I rise with my red hair
And I eat men like air.

October 23–29, 1962   1965

Words

Axes
After whose stroke the wood rings,
And the echoes!
Echoes traveling
Off from the center like horses.   5

The sap
Wells like tears, like the
Water striving
To re-establish its mirror
Over the rock   10

That drops and turns,
A white skull,
Eaten by weedy greens.
Years later I
Encounter them on the road—   15

Words dry and riderless,
The indefatigable hoof-taps.

---

8. The devil. "Herr" is the German equivalent of "Mister."

While
From the bottom of the pool, fixed stars
Govern a life.   20

February 1, 1963   1965

Edge

The woman is perfected.
Her dead

Body wears the smile of accomplishment,
The illusion of a Greek necessity[9]

Flows in the scrolls of her toga,   5
Her bare

Feet seem to be saying:
We have come so far, it is over.

Each dead child coiled, a white serpent,
One at each little   10

Pitcher of milk, now empty.
She has folded

Them back into her body as petals
Of a rose close when the garden

Stiffens and odors bleed   15
From the sweet, deep throats of the night flower.

The moon has nothing to be sad about,
Staring from her hood of bone.

She is used to this sort of thing.
Her blacks crackle and drag.   20

February 5, 1963   1965

9. The Greek idea of necessity or *ananke*.

EDNA O'BRIEN

1932–

After Edna O'Brien completed a trilogy of novels (composed of *The Country Girls*, *The Lonely Girl*, and *Girls in Their Married Bliss*, 1960–1964), she explained to an interviewer that, while women can become high-court judges, "the high-court judge will still have to come home and make the evening meal." Her skepticism about women's social progress, like her rejection of her own Catholic upbringing, is based on the belief that most human beings feel themselves to be engaged in a struggle to insure their own survival. O'Brien's fiction is characterized, on the one hand, by her robust handling of explicitly sexual themes and, on the other, by her indictment of what she perceives as the poverty and fanaticism of her cultural roots. Born in a small village in the west of Ireland, O'Brien attended Pharmaceutical College in Dublin. At the age of twenty, she married and, after the birth of two sons, she moved to London, where she currently resides. Besides the trilogy, she has composed several novels, a play, some television scripts, and a number of short stories. Like Irish fiction writers from James Joyce to Julia O'Faolain, O'Brien captures the spiritual and social atmosphere of Irish family life. In addition, *A Rose in the Heart* explores the dynamics of mother-daughter bonding that the psychologist Nancy Chodorow has recently associated with the origins of female psychosexual development, a bonding that Chodorow sees as related to the "fluid" boundaries of female identity.

A Rose in the Heart[1]

December night. Jack Frost in scales along the outside of the windows giving to the various rooms a white filtered light. The ice like bits of mirror bevelling the puddles of the potholes. The rooms were cold inside, and for the most part identically furnished. The room with no furniture at all—save for the apples gathered in the autumn—was called The Vacant Room. The apples were all over the floor and in rows along the curb of the tiled fireplace. Their smell was heady, many of them having begun to rot. Rooms into which no-one had stepped for days and yet these rooms and their belongings would become part of the remembered story. A solemn house, set in its own grounds, away from the lazy bustle of the village. A lonesome house it would prove to be, and with a strange lifelikeness as if it was not a house at all but a person observing and breathing, a presence amid a cluster of trees and sturdy wind-shorn hedges.

1. This story has also appeared under the titles *There's a Rose in the Heart of New York* and A *Rose in the Heart of New York*.

The overweight midwife hurried up the drive, her serge cape blowing behind her. She was puffing. She carried her barrel-shaped leather
bag in which were disinfectant, forceps, instruments and a small bottle
of holy water[2] lest the new child should prove to be in danger of death.
More infants died around Christmas time than in any other month of
the year. When she passed the little sycamore tree that was halfway up
she began to hear the roaring and beseeching to God. Poor mother, she
thought, poor poor mother. She was not too early, had come more or
less at the correct time, even though she had been summoned hours
before by Donal the serving boy who worked on the farm. She had
brought most of the children of that parish into the world yet had neither kith nor kin of her own. Coming in the back door she took off her
bonnet and then attached it to the knob by means of its elastic string.

It was a blue room—walls of dark wet morose blue, furniture made
of walnut, including the bed on which the event was taking place.
Fronting the fireplace was a huge lid of a chocolate box with the representation of a saucy-looking lady. The tassel of the blind kept bobbing
against the frosted windowpane. There was a washstand, a basin and
ewer of off-white with big roses splashed throughout the china itself,
and a huge lumbering beast of a wardrobe. The midwife recalled once
going to a house up the mountain, and finding the child smothered by
the time she arrived; the fatherless child had been stuffed in a drawer.
The moans filled that room and went beyond the distempered walls out
into the cold hall outside, where the black felt doggie with the amber
eyes stood sentinel on a tall varnished whatnot. At intervals the woman
apologised to the midwife for the untoward commotion, said sorry in a
gasping whisper, and then was seized again by a pain, that at different
times she described as being a knife, a dagger, a hell on earth. It was her
fourth labour. The previous child had died two days after being born.
An earlier child, also a daughter, had died of whooping cough. Her
womb was sick unto death. Why be a woman. Oh cruel life, oh merciless fate, oh heartless man, she sobbed. Gripping the coverlet and remembering that between those self-same, much-patched sheets, she
had been pried apart, again and again, with not a word to her, not a little
endearment, only rammed through and told to open up.

  When she married she had escaped the life of a serving girl, the possible experience of living in some grim institution but as time went on
and the trousseau drawer[3] was emptied of its gifts, she saw that she was
made to serve in an altogether other way. When she wasn't screaming

---

2. In the Catholic church, water that has been
blessed by a priest and is used in religious ceremonies such as baptism.
3. Drawer in which wedding gifts are kept.

she was grinding her head into the pillow, and praying for it to be all over. She dreaded the bloodshed long before they saw any. The midwife made her ease up as she put an old sheet under her and over that a bit of oilcloth. The midwife said it was no joke and repeated the hypothesis that if men had to give birth there would not be a child born in the whole wide world.

The husband was downstairs getting paralytic. Earlier, when his wife had announced that she would have to go upstairs because of her labour, he said, looking for the slightest pretext for a celebration, that if there was any homemade wine or altar wine[4] stacked away, to get it out, to produce it, and also the cut glasses. She said there was none and well he knew it since they could hardly afford tea and sugar. He started to root and to rummage, to empty cupboards of their contents of rags, garments and provisions, even to put his hand inside the bolster case, to delve into pillows; on he went, rampaging until he found a bottle in the wardrobe, in the very room into which she delivered her moans and exhortations. She begged of him not to, but all he did was to wield the amber-coloured bottle in her direction, and then put it to his head so that the spirit started to go glug-glug. It was intoxicating stuff. By a wicked coincidence a crony of his had come to sell them another stove, most likely another crock, a thing that would have to be coaxed alight with constant attention and puffing, to create a draught. The other child was with a neighbour, the dead ones in a graveyard six or seven miles away, among strangers and distant relatives, without their names being carved on the crooked rain-soaked tomb.

"Oh Jesus," she cried out as he came back to ask for the knitting needle to skewer out the bit of broken cork.

"Blazes," he said to her as she coiled into a knot and felt the big urgent ball—that would be the head—as it pressed on the base of her bowels, and battered at her insides.

Curses and prayers combined to issue out of her mouth, and as time went on, they became most pitiful and were interrupted with screams. The midwife put a facecloth on her forehead and told her to push, in the name of the Lord to push. She said she had no strength left, but the midwife went on enjoining her, and simulating a hefty breath. It took over an hour. The little head showing its tonsure would recoil, would reshow itself, each time a fraction more, although in between it was seeming to shrink from the world that it was hurtling towards. She said to the nurse that she was being burst apart, and that she no longer cared if she died, or if they drank themselves to death. In the kitchen they were sparring over who had the best greyhound, who had the successor

4. Wine used in the Catholic Mass, symbolizing Christ's Blood.

to Mick the Miller. The crucifix that had been in her hand had fallen out, and her hands themselves felt bony and skinned because of the way they wrenched one another.

"In the name of God push, Missus."

She would have pushed everything out of herself, her guts, her womb, her craw, her lights[5] and her liver but the centre of her body was holding on and this centre seemed to be the governor of her. She wished to be nothing, a shell, devoid of everything and everyone and she was announcing that, and roaring and raving when the child came hurtling out, slowly at first as if its neck could not wring its way through, then the shoulder—that was the worst bit—carving a straight course, then the hideous turnabout, and a scream other than her own, and an urgent presage of things, as the great gouts of blood and lymph followed upon the mewling creature itself. Her last bit of easiness was then torn from her, and she was without hope. It had come into the world lopsided and the first announcement from the midwife was a fatality, was that it had clubbed feet. Its little feet she ventured to say, were like two stumps adhering to one another, and the blasted cord was bound around its neck. The result was a mewling piece of screwed-up, inert, dark, purple misery.

The men subsided a little when the announcement was shouted down and they came to say congrats. The father waved a strip of pink flesh on a fork that he was carrying and remarked on its being unappetising. They were cooking a goose downstairs and he said in future he would insist on turkey as goose was only for gobs and goms.[6] The mother felt green and disgusted, asked them to leave her alone. The salesman said was it a boy or a child, although he had just been told that it was a daughter. The mother could feel the blood gushing out of her, like water at a weir.[7] The midwife told them to go down and behave like gentlemen.

Then she got three back numbers of the weekly paper, a shoe box with a lid, and into it she stuffed the mess and the unnecessaries. She hummed as she prepared to do the stitching down the line of torn flesh that was gaping and coated with blood. The mother roared again and said this indeed was her vinegar and gall. She bit into the crucifix, and dented it further. She could feel her mouth and her eyelids being stitched too, she was no longer a lovely body, she was a vehicle for pain and for insult. The child was so quiet it scarcely breathed. The afterbirth was placed on the stove, where the dog Shep sniffed at it through its layers of paper and for his curiosity got a kick in the tail. The stove had quenched and the midwife said to the men that it was a crying

5. Her stomach and her eyes.   7. Dam.
6. Gluttons and fools.

shame to leave a good goose like that, neither cooked nor uncooked. The men had torn off bits of the breast so that the goose looked wounded, like the woman upstairs who was then tightening her heart and soul, tightening inside the array of catgut stitches and regarding her whole life as a vast disappointment. The midwife carried the big bundle up to the cellar, put an oil rag to it, set a match to it and knew that she would have to be off soon to do the same task elsewhere. She would have liked to stay and swaddle the infant, and comfort the woman and drink hot sweet tea but there was not enough time. There was never enough time and she hadn't even cleaned out the ashes or the cinders in her grate that morning.

The child was in a corner of the room in a brown cot with the slats that rattled because of the racket they had received from the previous children. The mother was not proud, far from it. She fed the child its first bottle, looked down at its wizened face and thought where have you come from and why. She had no choice of a name. In fact she said to her first visitor, a lieutenant from the army, not to tell her a pack of lies because this child had the ugliest face that had ever seen the light of day. That Christmas the drinking and sparring went on, the odd neighbour called, the mother got up on the third day and staggered down to do something about the unruly kitchen. Each evening at nightfall she got a bit of a candle to have handy and re-oiled the Sacred Heart lamp for when the child cried. They both contracted bronchitis and the child was impounded in masses of flannel and flannelette.

Things changed. The mother came to idolise the child, because it was so quiet, never bawling, never asking for anything, just covert, in its pram, the dog watching over it, its eyes staring out at whatever happened to loom in. Its very ugliness disappeared. Its feet were all right. It seemed to drink them all in with its huge, contemplating, slightly hazed-over, navy eyes. They shone at whatever they saw. The mother would look in the direction of the pram and say a little prayer for it, or smile, and often at night she held the candle shielded by her hand to see the face, to say pet, or tush, to say nonsenses to it. It ate whatever it was given but as time went on it knew what it liked and had a sweet tooth. The food was what united them, eating off the same plate using the same spoon, watching one another's chews, feeling the food as it went down the other's gullet. The child was slow to crawl and slower still to walk but it knew everything, it perceived everything. When it ate blancmange or junket[8] it was eating part of the lovely substance of its mother.

8. Puddinglike desserts.

They were together, always together. If its mother went to the post office the child stood in the middle of the drive praying until its mother returned safely. The child cut the ridges of four fingers, along the edge of a razor blade that had been wedged upright in the wood of the dresser, and seeing these four deep horizontal identical slits the mother took the poor fingers into her own mouth and sucked them, to lessen the pain, and licked them to abolish the blood, and kept saying soft things until the child was stilled again. Her mother's knuckles were her knuckles, her mother's veins were her veins, her mother's lap was a second heaven, her mother's forehead a copybook onto which she traced A B C D, her mother's body was a recess that she would wander inside for ever and ever, a sepulchre growing deeper and deeper. When she saw other people, especially her pretty sister, she would simply wave from that safe place, she would not budge, would not be lured out.

Her father took a hatchet to her mother and threatened that he would split open the head of her. The child watched through the kitchen window because this assault took place out of doors on a hillock under the three beech trees where the clothes line stretched, then sagged. The mother had been hanging out the four sheets washed that morning, the two off each bed. The child was engaged in twisting her hair, looping it around bits of white rag, to form ringlets, decking herself in the kitchen mirror, and then every other minute running across to the window to reconnoitre, wondering what she ought to do, jumping up and down as if she had a pain, not knowing what to do, running back to the mirror, hoping that the terrible scene would pass, that the ground would open up and swallow her father, that the hatchet would turn into a magic wand, that her mother would come through the kitchen door and say, "Fear Not," that travail would all be over. Later she heard a verbatim account of what had happened. Her father demanded money, her mother refused same on the grounds that she had none, but added that if she had it she would hang sooner than give it to him. That did it. It was then he really got bucking, gritted his teeth and his muscles, said that he would split the head of her and the mother said that if he did so there was a place for him. That place was the lunatic asylum. It was twenty or thirty miles away, a big grey edifice, men and women lumped in together, some in strait jackets, some in padded cells, some blindfolded because of having sacks thrown over their heads, some strapped across the chest to quell and impede them. Those who did not want to go there were dragged by relatives, or by means of rope, some being tied onto the end of a plough or a harrow and brought in on all fours like beasts of the earth. Then when they were not so mad, not so rampaging, they were let home again where they were very peculiar, and given to smiling and to chattering to themselves and in no time they were ripe to go off again or to be dragged off. March was the worst month, when everything went askew, even the wind, even the March hares.[9]

Her father did not go there. He went off on a batter[1] and then went to a monastery, and then was brought home and shook in the bed chair for five days eating bread and milk, and asking who would convey him over the fields, until he saw his yearlings, and when no one volunteered to, it fell to her because she was the youngest. Over in the fields he patted the yearlings and said soppy things that he'd never say indoors, or to a human, and he cried and said he'd never touch a drop again, and there was a dribble on his pewter-brown moustache, that was the remains of the mush that he had been eating, and the bay yearling herself became fidgety and fretful as if she might bolt or stamp the ground to smithereens. The girl and her mother took walks on Sundays—strolls, picked blackberries, consulted them for worms, made preserve, and slept side by side, entwined like twigs of trees or the ends of the sugar tongs.

When she wakened and found that her mother had got up and was already mixing meal for the hens or stirabout for the young pigs she hurried down carrying her clothes under her arm and dressed in whatever spot that she could feast on the sight of her mother, most. Always an egg for breakfast. An egg a day and she would grow strong. Her mother never ate an egg but topped the girl's egg and fed her it off the tarnished eggy spoon and gave her little sups of tea with which to wash it down. She had her own mug, red enamel and with not a chip. The girl kept looking back as she went down the drive for school, and as time went on she mastered the knack of walking backwards to be able to look all the longer, look at the aproned figure waving or holding up a potato pounder or a colander or whatever happened to be in her hand.

The girl came home once and the mother was missing. Her mother had actually fulfilled her promise of going away one day and going to a spot where she would not be found. That threatened spot was the bottom of the lake. But in fact her mother had gone back to her own family because the father had taken a shotgun to her and had shot her but was not a good aim like William Tell, had missed, had instead made a hole in the Blue Room wall. What were they doing upstairs in the middle of the day, an ascent they never made except the mother alone to dress the two beds. She could guess. She slept in a neighbour's house, slept in a bed with two old people who reeked of eucalyptus. She kept most of her clothes on, and shrivelled into herself, not wanting to touch or be

---

9. Hares were thought to go mad in March, during their mating season. 1. A binge.

touched by these two old people buried in their various layers of skin and hair and winceyette.[2] Outside the window was a climbing rose with three or four red flowers along the bow of it, and looking at the flowers and thinking of the wormy clay she would try to shut out what these two old people were saying, in order that she could remember the mother whom she despaired of ever seeing again.

Not far away was their own house with the back door wide open so that any stranger or tinker could come in or out. The dog was probably lonely and bloodied from hunting rabbits, the hens were forgotten about, and were probably in their coops, hysterical, and picking at each other's feathers because of their nerves. Eggs would rot. Her father could be anywhere. If she stood on the low whitewashed wall that fronted the cottage she could see over the high limestone wall that bounded their fields and then look to the driveway that led to the abandoned house itself. To her it was like a kind of castle where strange things had happened and would go on happening. She loved it and she feared it. The sky behind and above gave it mystery, sometimes made it broody[3] and gave it a kind of splendour when the red streaks in the heavens were like torches that betokened the performance of a gory play. All of a sudden standing there, with a bit of grass between her front teeth, looking at her home and imagining this future drama she heard the nearby lich[4] gate open, and then shut with a clang, and saw her father appear, and jumped so clumsily she thought she had broken everything, particularly her ribs. She felt she was in pieces. She would be like Humpty Dumpty, and all the king's horses and all the king's men would not be able to put her together again.

Dismemberment did happen, a long time before, the time when her neck swelled out into a big fleshed balloon. She could only move her neck on one side, because the other side was like a ball and full of fluid that made gluggles when touched with the fingers. They were going to lance it. They placed her on a kitchen chair. Her mother boiled a saucepan of water. Her mother stood on another chair and reached far into the rear of a cupboard and hauled out a new towel. Everything was in that cupboard, sugar and tea, and round biscuits and white flour and linen and must and mice. First one man, then another man, then another man, then a last man who was mending the chimney, and then last of all her father, each took a hold of her—an arm, another arm, a shoulder, a waist and her two flying legs that were doing everything possible not to be there. The lady doctor said nice things and cut into the big football of her neck and it was like a pig's bladder bursting all

---

2. "Wincey": a durable cloth.
3. I.e., brooding, somber.
4. Roofed gateway to a churchyard under which

a corpse is set down to await the arrival of the clergyman.

over, the waters flowing out, and then it was not like that at all, it was like a sword on the bone of her neck sawing, cutting into the flesh, deeper and deeper, the men pressing upon her with all their might saying that she was a demon and the knife went into her swallow or where she thought of forever more as her swallow, and the lady doctor said "drat it," because she had done the wrong thing—had cut too deep and had to start scraping now and her elder sister danced a jig out in the flag,[5] so that neighbours going down the road would not get the impression that someone was being murdered to death. Long afterwards she came back to the world of voices, muffled voices, and their reassurances, and a little something sweet to help her get over it all and the lady doctor putting on her brown fur coat and hurrying to her next important work of mercy.

When she slept with the neighbours the old man asked the old woman were they ever going to be rid of her, were they going to have this dunce off their hands, were they saddled with her for the rest of their blooming lives. She declined the milk they gave her because it was goat's milk and too yellow and there was dust in it. She would answer them in single syllables, just yes or no, mostly no. She was learning to frown so that she too would have ABCs. Her mother's forehead and hers would meet in heaven, salute, and all their lines would coincide. She refused food. She pined. In all it was about a week.

The day her mother returned home—it was still January—the water pipes had burst and when she got to the neighbours, and was told she could go on up home, she ran with all her might and resolution so that her windpipes ached and then stopped aching when she found her mother down on her knees dealing with pools of water that had gushed from the red pipes. The brown rag was wet every other second and had to be wrung out, and squeezed in the big chapped basin, the one she was first bathed in. The lodges[6] of water were everywhere, lapping back and forth, threatening to expand, to discolour the tiles, and it was of this hazard they talked and fretted over rather than the mother's disappearance, or the dire cause of it, or the reason for her return. They went indoors and got the ingredients and the utensils and the sieve so as to make an orange cake with orange filling and orange and lemon icing. She never tasted anything so wonderful in all her life. She ate three big hunks and her mother put her hand around her and said if she ate any more she would have a little corporation.[7]

The father came from the hospital, cried again, said that sure he wouldn't hurt a fly and predicted that he would never break his pledge

5. Flagstones or pavement in front of the house.   7. I.e., a protruding belly.
6. Reservoirs.

or go outside the gate again, only to Mass, never leave his own sweet acres.

As before, the girl slept with her mother, recited the rosary[8] with her, and shared the small cubes of dark raisin-filled chocolate, then trembled while her mother went along to her father's bedroom, for a tick, to stop him bucking.[9] The consequences of those visits were deterred by the bits of tissue paper, a protection between herself and any emission. No other child got conceived and there was no further use for the baggy napkins, the bottle, and the dark-brown mottled teat. The cot itself was sawn up and used to back two chairs, and they constituted something of the furniture in the big upstairs landing, where the felt dog still lorded it, but now had an eye missing because a visiting child had poked wire at it. The chairs were painted ox-blood red and had the sharp end of a nail dragged along the varnish to give a wavering effect. Also on the landing there was a bowl with a bit of wire inside to hold a profusion of artificial tea roses. These tea roses were a two-toned colour, were red and yellow plastic and the point of each petal was seared like the point of a thorn. Cloth flowers were softer. She had seen some once, very pale pink and purple, tumbling roses made of voile, in another house, in a big jug, on a lady's bureau. In the landing at home too was the speared head of Christ that assayed on all the proceedings with endless patience, endless commiseration. Underneath Christ was a pussy cat of black papier mâché which originally had sweets stuffed into its middle, sweets the exact image of strawberries and even with a little leaf at the base, a leaf made of green glazed angelica.[1] They liked the same things—apple sauce and beetroot and tomato sausages and angelica. They cleaned the windows, one the inside, the other the outside, they sang duets, they put newspapers over the newly washed dark-red tiles so as to keep them safe from the muck and trampalations[2] of the men. About everything they agreed, or almost everything.

In the dark nights the wind used to sweep through the window and out on the landing and into the other rooms, and into the Blue Room, by now uninhabited. The wardrobe door would open of its own accord, or the ewer would rattle, or the lovely buxom Our Lady of Limerick[3] picture would fall onto the marble washstand and there was a rumpus followed by prognostications of bad luck for seven years.

When the other child came back from secretarial school the girl was at first excited, prepared lovingly for her, made cakes, and soon after, was plunged into a state of wretchedness. Her mother was being taken away from her, or worse was gladly giving her speech, her attention, her

---

8. A series of Catholic prayers.
9. Complaining. "For a tick": briefly.
1. A candied plant used in baking.

2. Trampling.
3. A picture of the Virgin Mary associated with the cathedral at Limerick, Ireland.

hands, and all of her gaze to this intruder. Her mother and her elder sister would go up-stairs where her mother would have some little treat for her, a hanky or a hanky sachet,[4] and once a remnant that had been got at the mill at reduced price, due to a fire there. Beautiful, a flecked salmon pink.

Downstairs *she* had to stack dishes onto the tray. She banged the cups, she put a butter knife into the two-pound pot of blackcurrant jam and hauled out a big helping, then stuck the greasy plates one on top of the other whereas normally she would have put a fork in between to protect the undersides. She dreamt that her mother and her rival sister were going for a walk and she asked to go too but they sneaked off. She followed on a bicycle, but once outside the main gate could not decide whether to go to the left or the right, and then having decided, made the wrong choice and stumbled on a herd of bullocks, all butting one another and endeavouring to get up into one another's backsides. She turned back and there they were strolling up on the drive, like two sedate ladies linking and laughing, and the salmon-flecked remnant was already a garment, a beautiful swagger coat[5] which her sister wore with a dash.

"I wanted to be with you," she said, and one said to the other, "She wanted to be with us," and then no matter what she said, no matter what the appeal, they repeated it as if she wasn't there. In the end she knew that she would have to turn away from them because she was not wanted, she was in their way. As a result of that dream, or rather the commotion that she made in her sleep, it was decided that she had worms and the following morning they gave her a dose of turpentine and castor oil the same as they gave the horses. When her sister went back to the city happiness was restored again. Her mother consulted her about the design on a leather bag which she was making. Her mother wanted a very old design, something concerning the history of their country. She said there would have to be atrocious battles and then peace and wonderful lace-like scenes from nature. Her mother said that there must be a lot of back history to a land and that education was a very fine thing. Finer than the bog her mother said. She said when she grew up that she would get a very good job and bring her mother to America. Her mother mentioned the street in Brooklyn where she had lodged and said that it had adjoined a park. They would go there one day. Her mother said maybe.

The growing girl began to say the word "backside" to herself and knew that her mother would be appalled. The girl laughed at bullocks and the sport they had. Then she went one further and jumped up and

4. A little bag containing dried herbs or flowers.   5. A coat for going out.

down and said "Jumping Jack" as if some devil were inside her, touching and tickling the lining of her. It was creepy. It was done out of doors, far from the house, out in the fields, in a grove, or under a canopy of rhododendrons. The buds of the rhododendrons were sticky and oozed with life and everything along with herself was soaking wet and she was given to wandering flushes, and then fits of untoward laughter so that she had to scold herself into some state of normality and this she did by slapping both cheeks vehemently. As a dire punishment she took cups of glauber salts[6] three times a day, choosing to drink it when it was lukewarm and at its most nauseating. She would be told by her father to get out, to stop hatching, to get out from under her mother's apron strings, and he would send her for a spin on the woeful brakeless bicycle. She would go to the chapel finding it empty of all but herself and the lady sacristan who spent her life in there, polishing and rearranging the artificial flowers; or she would go down into a bog and make certain unattainable wishes, but always at the end of every day, and at the end of every thought, and at the beginning of sleep, and the precise moment of wakening it was of her mother and for her mother she existed and her prayers and her good deeds and her ringlets and the ire on her legs[7]—created by the serge of her gym frock—were for her mother's intention, and on and on. Only death could part them and not even that because she resolved that she would take her own life if some disease or some calamity snatched her mother away. Her mother's three-quarter length jacket she would don, sink her hands into the deep pockets and say the name "Delia," her mother's, say it in different tones of voice, over and over again, always in a whisper and a note of conspiracy.

A lovely thing happened. Her mother and father went on a journey by hire car to do a transaction whereby they could get some credit on his lands, and her father did not get drunk but ordered a nice pot of tea, and then sat back gripping his braces and gave her mother a few bob,[8] with which her mother procured a most beautiful lipstick in a ridged gold case. It was like fresh fruit so moist was it, and dark red in colour. Her mother and she tried it on over and over again, were comical with it, trying it on, then wiping it off, trying it on again, making cupids[9] so that her mother expostulated and said what scatterbrains they were, and even the father joined in the hilarity and daubed down the mother's cheek and said Fannie Annie and the mother said that was enough, as the lipstick was liable to get broken. With her thumb nail she pressed on the little catch pushing the lipstick down into its case, into its bed. As the years went on it dried out, and developed a peculiar shape and they

6. A medicine used as a laxative.　　　8. Shillings, small British currency.
7. A rash.　　　9. Bow-shaped lips.

read somewhere that a lady's character could be told by that particular shape, and they wished that they could discover whether the mother was the extrovert or the shy violet.

The girl had no friends, she didn't need any. Her cup was full. Her mother was the cup, the cupboard, the press[1] with all the things in it, the tabernacle with God in it, the lake with the legends in it, the bog with the wishing wells in it, the sea with the oyster and the corpses in it, her mother a gigantic sponge, a habitation in which she longed to sink and disappear for ever and ever. Yet she was afraid to sink; caught in that hideous trap between fear of sinking and fear of swimming, she moved like a flounderer through this and that; through school, through inoculation, through a man who put his white handkerchief between naked her and naked him, and against a galvanised boway door came, gruntling and disgruntling like a tethered beast upon her; through a best friend, a girl friend who tried to clip the hairs of her vagina with a shears. The hairs of her vagina were mahogany coloured and her best friend said that that denoted mortal sin. She agonised over it.

Then came a dreadful blow. Two nuns called and her mother and her father said that she was to stay outside in the kitchen and see that the kettle boiled and then lift it off so that the water would not boil over. She went on tiptoe through the hall and listened at the door of the room. She got it in snatches. She was being discussed. She was being sent away to school. A fee was being discussed and her mother was asking if they could make a reduction. She ran out of the house in a dreadful state. She ran to the chicken run and went inside to cry and to go berserk. The floor was full of damp and grey-green mottled droppings. The nests were full of sour sops of hay. She thought she was going out of her mind. When they found her later her father said to cut out the bull but her mother tried to comfort her by saying they had a prospectus[2] and that she would have to get a whole lot of new clothes in navy blue. But where would the money come from?

In the convent to which they sent her she eventually found solace. A nun became her new idol. A nun with a dreadfully pale face, and a Master's Degree in Science. This nun and herself worked out codes with the eyelids, and the flutter of the lashes, so they always knew each other's moods and feelings, so that the slightest hurt imposed by one was spotted by the other and responded to with a cough. The nun gave another girl more marks at the mid-term examination, and did it solely to hurt her, to wound her pride; the nun addressed her briskly in front of the whole class, said her full name and asked her a theological conundrum that was impossible to answer. In turn she let one of the nun's

---

1. An upright closet or case.   2. Description of the school.

holy pictures fall on the chapel floor where of course it was found by the
cleaning nun who gave it back to the nun who gave it to her with a
"This seems to have got mislaid." They exchanged Christmas presents
and notes that contained blissful innuendos. She had given chocolates
with a kingfisher on the cover and she had received a prayer book with
gilt edging and it was as tiny as her middle finger. She could not read
the print but she held it to herself like a talisman, like a secret scroll in
which love was mentioned.

Home on holiday it was a different story. Now *she* did the avoiding,
the shunning. All the little treats and the carrageen soufflé[3] that her
mother had prepared were not gloated over. Then the pink crêpe-de-
chine apron that her mother had made from an old dance dress, did not
receive the acclamation that the mother expected. It was fitted on and
at once taken off, and flung over the back of a chair with no praise except to remark on the braiding which was cleverly done.

'These things are not to be sniffed at,' her mother said, passing the
plate of scones[4] for the third or fourth time. The love of the nun dominated all her thoughts and the nun's pale face got between her and the
visible world that she was supposed to be seeing. At times she could
taste it. It interfered with her studies, her other friendships, it got known
about. She was called to see the Reverend Mother. The nun and herself
never had a tête-à-tête again and never swapped holy pictures. The day
she was leaving for ever they made an illicit date to meet in the sum-
mer-house, out in the grounds, but neither of them turned up. They
each sent a message with an apology and it was in fact the messengers
who met, a junior girl and a postulant[5] carrying the same sentence on
separate lips—"So-and-so is sorry—she wishes to say she can't . . ."
They might have broken down or done anything, they might have
kissed.

Out of school, away from the spell of nuns and gods and flower gardens and acts of contrition, away from the chapel with its incense and its
brimstone sermons, away from surveillance, she met a bakery man who
was also a notable hurley[6] player and they started up that kind of courtship common to their sort—a date at the pillar two evenings a week,
then to a café to have coffee and cream cakes, to hold hands under the
table, to take a bus to her digs, to kiss against a railing and devour each
other's faces, as earlier they had devoured the mock cream and the
sugar-dusted sponge cakes. But these orgies only increased her hunger,
made it into something that could not be appeased. She would recall
her mother from the very long ago, in the three-quarter-length jacket of

---

3. An egg dish made with seaweed.
4. British tea-biscuits.
5. A novice, applicant for admission to a relig-

ious order.
6. Irish version of hockey.

salmon tweed, the brooch on the lapel, the smell of face powder, the lipstick hurriedly put on so that a little of it always smudged on the upper or the lower lip and appeared like some kind of birthmark. Recall that they even had the same mole on the back of the left hand, a mole that did not alter winter or summer and was made to seem paler when the fist was clenched. But she was recalling someone whom she wanted to banish. The bakery man got fed-up, wanted more than a cuddle, hopped it.[7]

Then there was no-one; just a long stretch, doing novenas,[8] working in the library, and her mother's letters arriving, saying the usual things, how life was hard, how inclement the weather, how she'd send a cake that day or the next day as soon as there were enough eggs to make it with. The parcels arrived once a fortnight, bound in layers of newspaper, and then a strong outer layer of brown paper, all held with hideous assortments of twines—binding twine, very white twine, and coloured plastic string from the stools that she had taken to making; then great spatters of sealing wax adorning it. Always a registered parcel, always a cake, a pound of butter, and a chicken that had to be cooked at once, because of its being nearly putrid from the four-day journey. It was not difficult to imagine the kitchen table, the bucket full of feathers, the moled hand picking away at the pin feathers, the other hand plunging in and drawing out all the undesirables, tremulous, making sure not to break a certain little pouch, which if broken its tobacco-coloured contents would taint the flavour of the bird itself. Phow. Always the same implications in each letter, the same cry—"Who knows what life brings. Your father is not hardboiled despite his failings. It makes me sad to think of the little things that I used to be able to do for you." She hated those parcels despite the fact that they were most welcome.

She married. Married in haste. Her mother said from the outset that he was as odd as two left shoes. He worked on an encyclopaedia and was a mine of information on certain subjects. His theme was vegetation in pond life. The family lived to themselves. She learned to do chores, to bottle and preserve, to comply, to be a wife, to undress neatly at night, to fold her clothes, to put them on a cane chair making sure to put her corset and her underthings respectfully under her dress or her skirt. It was like being at school again. The mother did not visit, being at odds with the censuring husband. Mother and daughter would meet in a market town midway between each of their rural homes and when they met they sat in some hotel lounge, ordered tea and discussed things that can easily be discussed—recipes, patterns for knitting, her sister, items of furniture that they envisaged buying.

---

7. Left.
8. A nine-day recitation of prayers.

Her mother was getting older, had developed a slight stoop and held up her hands to show the rheumatism in her joints. Then all of a sudden, as if she had just remembered it, she spoke about the cataracts and her journey to the specialist and how the specialist had asked her if she remembered anything about her eyes and how she had to tell him that she had lost her sight for five or six minutes one morning and that then it came back. He told her how lucky it was because in some instances it does not come back at all. She said yes that the shades of life were closing in on her.

The daughter knew that her marriage would not last but she dared not say so. Things were happening such as that they had separate meals, that he did not speak for weeks on end, and yet she defended him, talked of the open pine dresser he had made and her mother rued the fact that she never had a handyman to do odd things for her. She said the window had broken in a storm and that there was still a bit of cardboard in it. She said she had her eye on two armchairs with a slight rock. The daughter longed to give them to her and thought that she might steal from her husband when he was asleep, steal the deposit that is, and pay for them on hire purchase.[9] But they said none of the things that they should have said.

"You didn't get any new style," the mother said, restating her particular dislike for a tweed coat.

"I don't want it," the girl said tersely.

"You were always a softie," the mother said, and inherent in this was disapproval for a man who allowed his wife to be dowdy. Perhaps she thought that her daughter's marriage might have amended for her own.

When her marriage did end the girl wrote and said that it was all over and the mother wrote post-haste exacting two dire promises—the girl must write back on her oath and promise her that she would never touch an alcoholic drink as long as she lived and she would never again have to do with any man in body or soul. High commands. At the time the girl was walking the streets in a daze and stopping strangers in her plight. One day in a park she met a man who was very sympathetic, a sort of tramp. She told him her story and then all of a sudden he told her this terrible dream. He had wakened up and he was swimming in water and the water kept changing colour, it was blue and red and green and these changing colours terrified him. She saw that he was not all there and invented an excuse to be somewhere.

In time she sold her bicycle and pawned a gold bracelet and a gold watch and chain. She fled to England. She wanted to go somewhere where she knew no one. She was trying to start afresh to wipe out the

9. Renting towards eventual purchase.

previous life. She was staggered by the assaults of memory—a bowl with her mother's menstrual cloth soaking in it and her sacrilegious idea that if lit it could resemble the heart of Christ, the conical wick of the aladdin lamp[1] being lit too high and disappearing into a jet of black, the roses, the five freakish winter roses that were in bloom when the pipes burst, the mice that came out of the shoes, then out of the shoe closet itself, onto the floor where the newspapers had been laid to prevent the muck and manure of the trampling men, the little box of rouge that almost asked to be licked so dry and rosy was it, the black range whose temperature could be tested by just spitting on it and watching the immediate jig and trepidation of the spit, the pancakes on Shrove Tuesday[2] (if there wasn't a row), the flitches of bacon hanging to smoke, the forgotten jam jars with inevitably the bit of mouldy jam in the bottom, and always, like an overseeing spirit, the figure of the mother who was responsible for each and every one of these facets, and always the pending doom in which the mother would perhaps be struck with the rim of a bucket, or a sledgehammer, or some improvised weapon; struck by the near-crazed father. It would be something as slight as that the mother had a splinter under her nail and the girl felt her own nail being lifted up, felt hurt to the quick, or felt her mother's sputum, could taste it like a dish.

She was possessed by these thoughts, in the library where she worked day in and day out, filing and cataloguing and handing over books. They were more than thoughts, they were the presence of this woman whom she resolved to kill. Yes she would have to kill. She would have to take up arms and commit a murder. She thought of choking or drowning. Certainly the method had to do with suffocation, and she foresaw herself holding big suffocating pillows or a bolster, in the secrecy of the Blue Room where it had all began. Her mother turned into the bursting red pipes, into the brown dishcloths, into swamps of black-brown blooded water. Her mother turned into a streetwalker, and paraded. Her mother was taking down her knickers in public, squatting to do awful things, left little piddles, small as puppies' piddles, her mother was drifting down a well in a big bucket, crying for help but no help was forthcoming. The oddest dream came along. Her mother was on her deathbed, having just given birth to her—the little tonsured head jutted above the sheet—and had a neck rash, and was busy trying to catch a little insect, trying to cup it in the palms of her hands and was saying that in the end "all there is, is yourself and this little insect that you're trying to kill." The word kill was everywhere, on the hoardings, in the evening air, on the tip of her thoughts.

---

1. An oil-burning lamp like that from which Aladdin summoned a genie in *The Arabian* *Nights*.
2. The Tuesday preceding Ash Wednesday.

But life goes on. She bought a yellow two-piece, worsted, and wrote home and said, "I must be getting cheerful, I wear less black." Her mother wrote, "I have only one wish now and it is that we will be buried together." The more she tried to kill the more potent the advances became. Her mother was taking out all old souvenirs, the brown scapulars[3] salvaged from the hurtful night in December, a mug, with their similar initials on it, a tablecloth that the girl had sent from her first earnings when she qualified as a librarian. The mother's letters began to show signs of wander. They broke off in mid-sentence, one was written on blotting paper and almost indecipherable, they contained snatches of information such as "So-and-so died, there was a big turn-out at the funeral," "I could do with a copper bracelet for rheumatism," "You know life gets lonelier."

She dreaded the summer holidays but still she went. The geese and the gander would be trailing by the river bank, the cows would gape at her as if an alien had entered their terrain. It was only the horses she avoided—always on the nervy side as if ready to bolt. The fields themselves as beguiling as ever, fields full of herbage and meadowsweet, fields adorned with spangles of gold as the buttercups caught the shafts of intermittent sunshine. If only she could pick them up and carry them away. They sat indoors. The dog had a deep cut in his paw and it was thought that a fox did it, that the dog and the fox had tussled one night. As a result of this he was admitted to the house. The mother and the dog spoke although not a word passed between them. The father asked pointed questions such as would it rain or was it tea-time. For a pastime they then discussed all the dogs that they had had. The mother especially remembered Monkey and said that he was a queer one, that he'd know what you were thinking of. The father and daughter remembered further back to Shep the big collie who guarded the child's pram and drove thoroughbred horses off the drive, causing risk to his own person. Then there were the several pairs of dogs all of whom sparred and quarrelled throughout their lives, yet all of whom died within a week of one another, the surviving dog dying of grief for his pal. No matter how they avoided it, death crept into the conversation. The mother said unconvincingly how lucky they were never to have been crippled, to have enjoyed good health and enough to eat. The curtains behind her chair were a warm red velveteen and gave a glow to her face. A glow that was reminiscent of her lost beauty.

She decided on a celebration. She owed it to her mother. They

---

3. Garments worn by monks and nuns.

would meet somewhere else, away from that house, and its skeletons and its old cunning tug at the heart strings. She planned it a year in advance, a holiday in a hotel, set in beautiful woodland surroundings and on the verge of the Atlantic Ocean. Their first hours were happily and most joyfully passed as they looked at the rooms, the view, the various tapestries, found where things were located, looked at the games room and then at the display cabinets where there was cut glass and marble souvenirs on sale. The mother said that everything was "Poison, dear." They took a walk by the seashore and remarked one to the other on the different stripes of colour on the water, how definite they were, each colour claiming its surface of sea, just like oats or grass or a ploughed land. The brown plaits of seaweed slapped and slathered over rocks, long-legged birds let out their lonesome shrieks and the mountains that loomed beyond seemed to hold the spectre of continents inside them so vast were they, so old. They dined early. Afterwards there was a sing-song and the mother whispered that money wasn't everything. She said, "Look at the hard-boiled faces."

Something snapped inside of the girl and forgetting that this was her errand of mercy, she thought instead how this mother had a whole series of grudges, bitter grudges concerning love, happiness, and her hard inpecunious fate. The angora jumpers,[4] the court shoes, the brown and the fawn garments, the milk complexion, the auburn tresses, the little breathlessnesses, the hands worn by toil, the sore feet, these were but the trimmings and behind them lay the real person who demanded her pound of flesh from life. They sat on a sofa. The mother sipped tea and she her whiskey. They said cheers.

The girl tried to get the conversation back, to before she was born, or before other children were born, to the dances and the annual race-day and the courtship that pre-empted the marriage. The mother refused to speak, baulked, had no story to tell, said that even if she had a story she would not tell it. Said she hated raking up the past. The girl tweezed it out of her in scraps. The mother said yes, that as a young girl she was bold and obstinate and she did have fancy dreams but soon learnt to toe the line. Then she burst out laughing and said she climbed up a ladder once into the chapel, and into the confessional so as to be the first person there to have her confession heard by the missioner. The missioner nearly lost his life because he didn't know how anyone could possibly have got in, since the door was bolted and he had simply come to sit in the confessional to compose himself, when there she was spouting sins. What sins? The mother said, "Oh I forget, love, I forget everything now."

The girl said, "No you don't."

4. Sweaters; "court shoes": tennis shoes.

They said good-night and arranged to meet in the dining room the following morning.

The mother didn't sleep a wink, complained that her eyes and her nose were itchy, and she feared she was catching a cold. She drank tea noisily, slugged it down. They walked by the sea that was now the colour of gun-metal and the mountains were no longer a talking point. They visited a ruined monastery where the nettles, the sorrel, the clover and the seedy dock grew high in a rectangle. Powder shed from walls that were built of solid stone. The mother said that probably it was a chapel or a chancery, a seat of sanctity down through the centuries and she genuflected. To the girl it was just a ruin, unhallowed, full of weeds and buzzing with wasps and insects. Outside there was a flock of noisy starlings. She could feel the trouble brewing. She said that there was a lovely smell, that it was most likely some wild herb and she got down on her knees to locate it. Peering with eyes and fingers among the low grass she came upon a nest of ants that were crawling over a tiny bit of ground with an amazing amount of energy and will. She felt barely in control.

They trailed back in time for coffee. The mother said hotel life was demoralising as she bit into an iced biscuit.[5] The porter fetched the paper. Two strange little puppies lapped at the mother's feet, and the porter said they would have to be drowned if they were not claimed before dusk. The mother said what a shame and recalled her own little pups who didn't eat clothes on the line during the day but when night came got down to work on them.

"You'd be fit to kill them, but of course you couldn't," she said lamely.

She was speaking of puppies from ten or fifteen years back.

He asked if she was enjoying it and the mother said, "I quote the saying 'See Naples and Die,' the same applies to this."

The daughter knew that the mother wanted to go home there and then, but they had booked for four days and it would be an admission of failure to cut it short. She asked the porter to arrange a boat trip to the island inhabited by seabirds, then a car drive to the lakes of Killarney and another to see the home of the liberator, Daniel O'Connell,[6] the man who had asked to have his dead heart sent to Rome, to the Holy See. The porter said certainly and made a great to-do about accepting the tip she gave him. It was he who told them where Daniel O'Connell's heart lay, and the mother said it was the most rending thing she had ever heard, and the most devout. Then she said yes that a holiday was an uplift, but that it came too late as she wasn't used to the spoiling.

---

5. Frosted cookie.   6. Irish Catholic political leader (1775–1847).

The girl did not like that. The girl showed the porter a photograph of a gouged torso, said that was how she felt, that was the state of her mind. The mother said later she didn't think the girl should have said such a thing and wasn't it a bit extreme. Then the mother wrote a six-page letter to her friend Molly and the girl conspired to be the one to post it so that she could read it and find some clue to the chasm that stretched between them. As it happened she could not bring herself to read it, because the mother gave it to her unsealed, as if she had guessed those thoughts and the girl bit her lower lip and said "How's Molly doing?"

The mother became very sentimental and said "Poor creature, blind as a bat," but added that people were kind and how when they saw her with the white cane, they knew. The letter would be read to her by a daughter who was married and overweight and who suffered with her nerves. The girl recalled an autograph book, the mother's, with its confectionery-coloured pages and its likewise rhymes and ditties. The mother recalled ice creams that she had eaten in Brooklyn long before. The mother remembered the embroidery she had done, making the statement in stitches that there was a rose in the heart of New York. The girl said stitches played such an important role in life and said, "A stitch in time saves nine." They tittered. They were getting nearer.

The girl delicately enquired into the name and occupation of the mother's previous lover, in short the father's rival. The mother would not divulge, except to say that he loved his mother, loved his sister, was most thoughtful, and that was that. Another long silence. Then the mother stirred in her chair, coughed, confided, said that in fact she and this thoughtful man, fearing, somehow sensing that they would not be man and wife, had made each other a solemn pact one Sunday afternoon in Coney Island[7] over an ice. They swore that they would get in touch with each other towards the end of their days. Lo and behold after fifty-five years the mother wrote that letter!

The girl's heart quickened, and her blood danced to the news of this tryst, this long sustained clandestine passion. She felt that something momentous was about to get uttered. They could be true at last, they need not hide from one another's gaze. Her mother would own up. Her own life would not be one of curtained shame. She thought of the married man who was waiting for her in London, the one who took her for delicious weekends and she shivered. The mother said that her letter had been returned and probably his sister had refused it, always being jealous. The girl begged to know the contents of the letter. The mother said it was harmless. The girl said go on. She tried to revive the spark but the mother's mind was made up. The mother said that there was no such thing as love between the sexes and that it was all bull. She reaf-

7. Amusement park in Brooklyn, New York.

firmed that there was only one kind of love and that was a mother's love for her child.

There passed between them then such a moment, not a moment of sweetness, not a moment of reaffirmation but a moment dense with hate—one hating and the other receiving it like rays, and then it was glossed over by the mother's remark about the grandeur of the ceiling. The girl gritted her teeth and resolved that they would not be buried in the same grave, and vehemently lit a cigarette although they had hardly tasted the first course.

"I think you're very unsettled," her mother said.

"I didn't get that from the ground," the daughter said.

The mother bridled, stood up to leave, but was impeded by a waiter who was carrying a big chafing dish, over which a bright blue flame riotously spread. She sat down as if pushed down and said that that remark was the essence of cruelty. The girl said sorry. The mother said she had done all she could and that, without maid, or car or cheque book or any of life's luxuries. Life's dainties had not dropped on her path, she had to knit her own sweaters, cut and sew her own skirts, be her own hairdresser. The girl said for God's sake to let them enjoy it. The mother said that at seventy-eight one had time to think.

"And at thirty-eight," the girl said.

She wished then that her mother's life had been happier, and had not exacted so much from her and she felt she was being milked emotionally. With all her heart she pitied this woman, pitied her for having her dreams pulped and for betrothing herself to a life of suffering. But also she blamed her. They were both wild with emotion. They were speaking out of turn and eating carelessly, the very food seemed to taunt them. The mother wished that one of those white-coated waiters would tactfully take her plate of dinner away and replace it with a nice warm pot of tea, or better still that she could be home in her own house by her own fireside, and furthermore she wished that her daughter had never grown into the cruel feelingless hussy that she was.

"What else could I have done?" the mother said.

"A lot," the girl said, and gulped at once.

The mother excused herself. "When I pass on, I won't be sorry," she said.

Up in the room she locked and bolted the door, and lay curled up on the bed, knotted as a foetus, with a clump of paper handkerchiefs in front of her mouth. Downstairs she left behind her a grown girl, remembering a woman she most bottomlessly loved, then unloved, and cut off from herself in the middle of a large dining room while confronting a plate of undercooked lamb strewn with mint.

Death in its way comes just as much of a surprise as birth. We know we will die, just as the mother knows that she is primed to deliver around such and such a time, yet there is a fierce inner exclamation from her at the first onset of labour and when the water breaks she is already a shocked woman. So it was. The reconciliation that she had hoped for, and indeed intended to instigate never came. She was abroad at a conference when her mother died and when she arrived through her own front door the phone was ringing with the news of her mother's death. The message though clear to her ears was incredulous to herself. How had her mother died and why? In a hospital, as a result of a heart attack. Straight away she set back for the airport hoping to get a seat on a late-night flight.

The last plane had gone but she decided to sit there until dawn and thought to herself that she might be sitting up at her mother's wake. The tube lighting[8] drained the colour from all the other waiting faces and though she could not cry she longed to tell someone that something incalculable had happened to her. They seemed as tired and as inert as she did. Coffee, bread, whiskey, all tasted the same, tasted of nothing, or at best of blotting paper. There was no man in her life at the moment, no one to ring up and tell the news to. Even if there was, she thought that lovers never know the full story of one another, only know the bit they meet, never know the iceberg of hurts, that have gone before, and therefore are always strangers, or semi-strangers, even in the folds of love. She could not cry. She asked herself if perhaps her heart had turned to lead. Yet she dreaded that on impulse she might break down, and that an attendant might have to lead her away.

When she arrived at the hospital next day the remains had been removed and was now on its way through the centre of Ireland. Through Joyce's Ireland[9] as she always called it, and thought of the great central plain open to the elements, the teeming rain, the drifting snow, the winds that gave chapped faces to farmers and cattle dealers and sometimes croup to the young calves. She passed the big towns and the lesser towns, recited snatches of recitation that she remembered and hoped that no one could consider her disrespectful because the hire car was a bright ketchup red. When she got to her own part of the world the sign of the mountains moved her as they had always done—solemn, beautiful, unchanging except for different streaks of colour. Solid and timeless. She had bought a sandwich at the airport and now removed the glacé paper[1] with her teeth and bit into it. The two days ahead would be awful. There would be her father's wild grief, there would be her aunt's grief, there would be cousins and friends, and strays and workmen, there would be a grave wide open and as they walked to it they would walk over other graves under hawthorn stamping the nettles as they went. She knew the graveyard very well, since childhood. She knew the

8. Fluorescent lighting.
9. The novelist James Joyce (1882–1941).

1. Waxed paper.

tombs, the headstones and the hidden vaults. She used to play there alone and both challenge and cower from ghosts. The inside of the grave was always a rich broody brown and the gravedigger would probably lace it with a trellis of ivy or convolvulus leaf.

At that very moment she found that she had just caught up with the funeral cortege but she could hardly believe that it would be her mother's. Too much of a coincidence. They drove at a great pace and without too much respect for the dead. She kept up with them. The light was fading, the bushes were like blurs, the air bat-black, the birds had ceased and the mountains were dark bulks. If the file of cars took a right from the main road towards the lake town then it must certainly be her mother's. It did. The thought of catching up with it was what made her cry. She cried with such a delight, cried like a child who has done something good and is being praised for it and yet cannot bear the weight of emotion. She cried the whole way through the lakeside town and sobbed as they crossed the old bridge towards the lovely dark leafy country road that led towards home. She cried like a homing bird. She was therefore seen as a daughter deeply distressed when she walked past the file of mourners outside the chapel gate, and when she shook the hand or touched the sleeves of those who had come forward to meet her. Earlier a friend had left flowers at the car-hire desk and she carried them as if she had specially chosen them. She thought they think it is grief but it is not the grief they think it is. It is emptiness more than grief. It is a grief at not being able to be whole-hearted again. It is not a false grief but it is unyielding, it is blood from a stone.

Inside the chapel she found her father howling, and in the first rows closest to the altar and to the coffin the chief mourners, both men and women, were sobbing, or having just sobbed were drying their eyes. As she shook hands with each one of them she heard the same condolence—"Sorry for your trouble, sorry for your trouble, sorry for your trouble."

That night in her father's house, people supped and ate and reminisced. As if in mourning a huge branch of a nearby tree had fallen down. Its roots were like a hand stuck up in the air. The house already reeked of neglect. She kept seeing her mother's figure coming through the door with a large tray, laden down with dainties. The undertaker called her out. He said since she had not seen the remains he would bring her to the chapel and unscrew the lid. She shrank from it but she went because to say no would have wrought her disgrace. The chapel was cold, the wood creaked and even the flowers at night seemed to have departed from themselves, like ghost flowers. Just as he lifted the lid he asked her to please step away and she thought something fateful has happened, the skin has turned black or a finger moves or, the worst or, she is not dead, she has merely visited the other world. Then he called her and she walked solemnly over and she almost screamed. The mouth was trying to speak. She was sure of it. One eyelid was not fully shut. It was unfinished. She kissed the face and felt a terrible pity.

"Oh soul," she said, "where are you, on your voyaging and oh soul, are you immortal?"

Suddenly she was afraid for her mother's fate and afraid for the fact that one day she too would have to make it. She longed to hold the face and utter consolations to it but she was unable. She thought of the holiday that had been such a fiasco and the love that she had first so cravenly and so rampantly given and the love that she had so callously and so conclusively taken back. She thought why did she have to withdraw, why do people have to withdraw, why?

After the funeral she went around the house tidying and searching —as if for some secret. In the Blue Room damp had seeped through the walls and there were little burrs of fungus that clung like bobbins on a hat veiling.[2] In the drawers she found bits of her mother's life. Wishes. Dreams contained in such things as a gauze rose of the darkest drenchingest red. Perfume bottles, dance shoes, boxes of handkerchiefs and the returned letter. It was from the man called Vincent, the man her mother had intended to marry but whom she had forsaken when she left New York and came back to Ireland, back to her destiny. For the most part it was a practical letter outlining the size of her farm, the crops they grew, asking about mutual friends, his circumstances and so forth. It seems he worked in a meat factory. There was only one little leak—"I think of you, you would not believe how often." The envelope had marked on the outside—"Return to Sender." The words seemed brazen as if he himself had written them.

There were so many hats, hats with flowers, hats with veiling, all of pastel colour, hats conceived for summer outings and meant for rainless climes. Ah the garden parties she must have conceived. Never having had the money for real style her mother had invested in imitation things—an imitation crocodile handbag and an imitation fur bolero.[3] It felt light as if made of hair. There were, too, pink embroidered corsets, long bloomers and three unworn cardigans.

For some reason she put her hand above the mantelpiece to the place where they hid shillings when she was young. There wrapped in cobweb was an envelope addressed to herself in her mother's handwriting. It sent shivers through her and she prayed that it did not bristle with accusations. Inside there were some trinkets, a gold sovereign and some money. The notes were dirty, crumpled and folded many times. How

---

2. I.e., like knots in a veil that hangs from a hat.   3. A short jacket.

long had the envelope lain there? How had her mother managed to save? There was no letter, yet in her mind she concocted little tendernesses that her mother might have written—words such as "Buy yourself a jacket," or "Have a night out," or "Don't spend this on masses." She wanted something, some communiqué. But there was no such thing.

A new wall had arisen, stronger and sturdier than before. Their life together and all those exchanges were like so many split feelings and she looked to see some sign, or hear some murmur. Instead a silence filled the room and there was a vaster silence beyond as if the house itself had died or had been carefully put down to sleep.

1978

ANNE STEVENSON

1933–

The author of more than half a dozen collections of verse, several radio plays, and a critical study of Elizabeth Bishop, Anne Stevenson was born in Cambridge, England, but raised and educated in the United States, where she attended the University of Michigan. Twice married and divorced, she is the mother of three children and has worked at a number of universities, including, in England, the Open University and Lady Margaret Hall, Oxford. In addition, since 1978, she has been co-editor of *Other Poetry* magazine and Mid-Day Publications, both in Oxford. Acknowledging the influence of "Ursula Le Guin, and Angela Carter, among moderns," Stevenson has explained that "fiction . . . taught me to write poetry." At the same time, however, she has observed that "to Emily Dickinson, Robert Frost, Elizabeth Bishop, and the Scots poet G. F. Dutton I owe the beginnings of a vision of life which I hope I have made my own." Many of her poems deal with the suppression and repression of women's lives, but the Bishopesque cadences of *Re-reading Jane* celebrate female achievement, adding another major woman of letters to Stevenson's list of literary models.

The Marriage

They will fit, she thinks,
but only if her backbone
cuts exactly into his rib cage,
and only if his knees
dock exactly under her knees   5
and all four
agree on a common angle.

All would be well
if only
they could face each other.   10

Even as it is
there are compensations
for having to meet
nose to neck
chest to scapula[1]   15
groin to rump
when they sleep.

They look, at least,
as if they were going
in the same direction.   20

                                               1974

Respectable House

Worth keeping your foot in the door.
Worth letting the lamplight stripe your shoe
and escape in the dark behind you.

Worth the candle-width of a velvet floor,
the swell of a stair, a tinkle of glasses,   5
and overheard—rising and flaring—those fortunate voices.

Push open the door. More. And a little more.
You seem to be welcome. You can't help stepping inside.
You see how light and its residents have lied.

You see what the gun on the table has to be used for.   10

                                               1977

Re-reading Jane

The memorial to Jane Austen in Winchester Cathedral reads, in part, as follows: "The benevolence of her heart, the sweetness of her temper, and the extraordinary endowments of her mind obtained the regard of all who knew her and the warmest love of her intimate connections." No mention is made of her novels.

To women in contemporary voice and dislocation
She is closely invisible, almost an annoyance.

1. Shoulder blade.

Why do we turn to her sampler squares for solace?
Nothing she saw was free of snobbery or class.
Yet the needlework of those needle eyes. . . .   5
We are pricked to tears by the justice of her violence:
Emma on Box Hill, rude to poor Miss Bates,
By Mr. Knightley's *Were she your equal in situation—*
But consider how far this is from being the case
Shamed into compassion, and in shame, a grace.[2]   10

Or wicked Wickham and selfish pretty Willoughby,[3]
Their vice, pure avarice which, displacing love,
Defiled the honour marriages should be made of;
She punished them with very silly wives.
Novels of manners? Hymenal theology!   15
Six little circles of hell with attendant humours.[5]
For what do we live but to make sport for our neighbours
And laugh at them in our turn?[6] The philosophy
Paused at the door of Mr. Bennet's century;
The Garden of Eden goes on in the grounds of Pemberley.[7] 20

The amazing epitaph's "benevolence of heart"
Precedes "the extraordinary endowments of her mind"
And would have pleased her, who was not unkind.
Dear votary of order, sense, clear art
And irresistible fun, please pitch our lives   25
Outside self-pity we have wrapped them in,
And show us how absurd we'd seem to you.
You knew the mischief poetry could do.
And when Anne Elliot[8] spoke of its *misfortune*
To be seldom safely enjoyed by those who   30
Enjoyed it completely, she spoke for you.

                                                    1983

2. In Jane Austen's novel *Emma* the heroine, an intelligent heiress, hurts the feelings of the impoverished and somewhat silly though very good-natured Miss Bates by obliquely commenting on her foolishness during an excursion to Box Hill. Mr. Knightley reprimands Emma.
3. The dishonorable Wickham runs off with Lydia Bennet in *Pride and Prejudice* and has to be bribed into marrying her; he also slanders his former benefactor, Mr. Darcy. Willoughby, having squandered his own inheritance, jilts Marianne Dashwood in *Sense and Sensibility* in order to marry an heiress, Miss Grey, whom he does not love and who makes his life miserable.
4. Hymen was the Greek god of marriage.
5. Austen wrote six novels; there are seven circles of hell in Dante's *Inferno*. The "humours" were thought to control a person's psychological makeup.
6. Spoken by Mr. Bennett, the heroine's father, in *Pride and Prejudice*.
7. The estate of Mr. Darcy, the hero of *Pride and Prejudice*.
8. Heroine of *Persuasion*.

FLEUR ADCOCK

1934–

Kareen Fleur Adcock was born in Papakura, New Zealand, and educated at Victoria University in Wellington. Twice briefly married and the mother of two children, she has worked mainly as a librarian, first in New Zealand and then in London, where she joined the Foreign and Commonwealth Office in 1963. One year later, her first volumes of poetry began to appear in print: *The Eye of the Hurricane* (1964) was followed by *Tigers* (1967), *High Tide in the Garden* (1971), *The Scenic Route* (1974), *The Inner Harbour* (1979), and *Selected Poems* (1983). Characterized by a disconcerting juxtaposition of the mundane with the bizarre, her poems have earned her a number of awards in her native New Zealand. While she has been praised for the "suballegory" she makes out of domesticity in elegantly wrought poems, Adcock has also been recognized for dream poems in which "something angry, or nightmarish, or discomfiting leaps out." Perhaps it is what one reviewer called her "well-bred, genteel air" that allows Adcock to write a poem like *Against Coupling* on the previously unmentionable subject of "the solitary act."

Against Coupling

I write in praise of the solitary act:
of not feeling a trespassing tongue
forced into one's mouth, one's breath
smothered, nipples crushed against the
ribcage, and that metallic tingling   5
in the chin set off by a certain odd nerve:

unpleasure. Just to avoid those eyes would help—
such eyes as a young girl draws life from,
listening to the vegetal
rustle within her, as his gaze   10
stirs polypal[1] fronds in the obscure
sea-bed of her body, and her own eyes blur.

There is much to be said for abandoning
this no longer novel exercise—
for not "participating in   15
a total experience"—when
one feels like the lady in Leeds who
had seen *The Sound of Music*[2] eighty-six times;

---

1. Like the tiny organism the polyp, which has a mouth surrounded by tentacles.
2. A very popular sentimental musical film by Rodgers and Hammerstein, starring Julie Andrews (1965).

or more, perhaps, like the school drama mistress
producing *A Midsummer Night's Dream*[3]   20
for the seventh year running, with
yet another cast from 5B.
Pyramus and Thisbe are dead, but
the hole in the wall can still be troublesome.

I advise you, then, to embrace it without   25
encumbrance. No need to set the scene,
dress up (or undress), make speeches.
Five minutes of solitude are
enough—in the bath, or to fill
that gap between the Sunday papers and lunch.   30

                                                  1971

The Ex-Queen among the Astronomers

They serve revolving saucer eyes,
dishes of stars; they wait upon
huge lenses hung aloft to frame
the slow procession of the skies.

They calculate, adjust, record,   5
watch transits, measure distances.
They carry pocket telescopes
to spy through when they walk abroad.

Spectra[4] possess their eyes; they face
upwards, alert for meteorites,   10
cherishing little glassy worlds:
receptacles for outer space.

But she, exile, expelled, ex-queen,
swishes among the men of science
waiting for cloudy skies, for nights   15
when constellations can't be seen.

She wears the rings he let her keep;
she walks as she was taught to walk
for his approval, years ago.
His bitter features taunt her sleep.   20

And so when these have laid aside
their telescopes, when lids are closed

---

3. A comedy by William Shakespeare (1595)
which includes a short burlesque of the story of
Pyramus and Thisbe, two doomed lovers who
had to communicate through a hole in a wall because their families forbade them to meet.
4. Plural of *spectrum*.

between machine and sky, she seeks
terrestrial bodies to bestride.

She plucks this one or that among   25
the astronomers, and is become
his canopy, his occultation;[5]
she sucks at earlobe, penis, tongue

mouthing the tubes of flesh; her hair
crackles, her eyes are comet-sparks.   30
She brings the distant briefly close
above his dreamy abstract stare.

1979

5. In astronomy, the passage of one celestial   in an eclipse.
body between an observer and another body, as

KAMALA DAS

1934–

Kamala Das has traced her love of poetry back to her grand-uncle Nalapat Nar-
ayana Menon, a philosopher, to her mother, Nalapat Balamani Amma, a poet,
and to the matriarchal community of Nayars, with its four-hundred-year-old
ancestral house that contained a number of ancient manuscripts and books of
mantras. She was born in Malabar, South India, and privately educated. At fifteen years of age, she married K. Madhava Das, and the couple had three sons.
Several volumes of verse—*Summer in Calcutta: Fifty Poems* (1965), *The Descendants* (1967), and *The Old Playhouse and Other Poems* (1973)—have established her reputation as a lyricist who defies the traditional taboos placed on
upper-class married Indian women, specifically the taboo against candid sexual
expression. In addition, she has published a novel, *Alphabet of Lust* (1977),
many volumes of short stories, including *Mathilukah (Walls,* 1972) and *A Doll
for the Child Prostitute* (1977), and an autobiography, *My Story* (1978). According to Das, her novel, stories, and autobiography were "tor[n] . . . to
shreds" by critics, who viewed her works as eccentric or naïve. Yet, together
with her verse, they also established her effort "to be real and honest to my
readers." Composed, for the most part, in an English fashioned to retain Indian
cadences and concerns, Das's poetry also reflects the Indo-Anglian inheritance
she analyzes in *An Introduction*.

An Introduction

I don't know politics but I know the names
Of those in power, and can repeat them like
Days of the week, or names of months, beginning with

Nehru.[1] I am Indian, very brown, born in
Malabar, I speak three languages, write in   5
Two, dream in one. Don't write in English, they said,
English is not your mother-tongue. Why not leave
Me alone, critics, friends, visiting cousins,
Every one of you? Why not let me speak in
Any language I like? The language I speak   10
Becomes mine, its distortions, its queernesses
All mine, mine alone. It is half English, half
Indian, funny perhaps, but it is honest,
It is as human as I am human, don't
You see? It voices my joys, my longings, my   15
Hopes, and it is useful to me as cawing
Is to crows or roaring to the lions, it
Is human speech, the speech of the mind that is
Here and not there, a mind that sees and hears and
Is aware. Not the deaf, blind speech   20
Of trees in storm or of monsoon clouds or of rain or the
Incoherent mutterings of the blazing
Funeral pyre. I was child, and later they
Told me I grew, for I became tall, my limbs
Swelled and one or two places sprouted hair. When   25
I asked for love, not knowing what else to ask
For, he drew a youth of sixteen into the
Bedroom and closed the door. He did not beat me
But my sad woman-body felt so beaten.
The weight of my breasts and womb crushed me. I shrank   30
Pitifully. Then . . . I wore a shirt and my
Brother's trousers, cut my hair short and ignored
My womanliness. Dress in saris,[2] be girl,
Be wife, they said. Be embroiderer, be cook,
Be a quarreller with servants. Fit in. Oh,   35
Belong, cried the categorizers. Don't sit
On walls or peep in through our lace-draped windows.
Be Amy, or be Kamala. Or, better
Still, be Madhavikutty.[3] It is time to
Choose a name, a role. Don't play pretending games.
Don't play at schizophrenia or be a
Nympho. Don't cry embarrassingly loud when
Jilted in love . . . I met a man, loved him. Call
Him not by any name, he is every man
Who wants a woman, just as I am every   45
Woman who seeks love. In him . . . the hungry haste
Of rivers, in me . . . the ocean's tireless

---

1. Jawaharlal Nehru (1889–1964), India's first
prime minister after she gained independence.
2. Traditional dress of Indian women.

3. "Madhavikutty is the pseudonym I use
when I write stories in Malayalam, the language
spoken here in Kerala State" [Das's note].

Waiting. Who are you, I ask each and everyone,
The answer is, it is I. Anywhere and
Everywhere, I see the one who calls himself   50
I; in this world, he is tightly packed like the
Sword in its sheath. It is I who drink lonely
Drinks at twelve, midnight, in hotels of strange towns,
It is I who laugh, it is I who make love
And then feel shame, it is I who lie dying   55
With a rattle in my throat. I am sinner,
I am saint. I am the beloved and the
Betrayed. I have no joys which are not yours, no
Aches which are not yours. I too call myself I.

1962   1962, 1965

AUDRE LORDE

1934–

Audre Lorde has described herself as a "black lesbian feminist warrior poet,"
adding that "when I say myself, I mean not only the Audre who inhabits my
body but all those feisty, incorrigible black women who insist on standing up
and saying '*I am* and you cannot wipe me out, no matter how irritating I am,
how much you fear what I might represent.' " Of West Indian descent, Lorde
was born and educated in New York City, receiving a B.A. from Hunter College and an M.L.S. from Columbia University. After some years as a librarian
for the City University of New York, she became a teacher of creative writing,
first at Tougaloo College in Mississippi and later at John Jay College in New
York. At present she is professor of English at Hunter College in New York.
Her more than half a dozen collections of verse include *The First Cities*
(1968), *Cables to Rage* (1970), *Coal* (1976), and *The Black Unicorn* (1978),
along with an account of her struggle with breast cancer, *The Cancer Journals*
(1980), and a fictionalized memoir of her coming of age as a lesbian, *Zami: A
New Spelling of My Name* (1982), which she calls a "biomythography."

Lorde has explained that her work owes much to the "legends of . . . struggle
and survival" embedded in the writings of such Afro-American artists as Toni
Morrison and Ralph Ellison, and to similar legends recounted by African
writers ranging from Chinua Achebe and Amos Tutuola to Flora Nwapa and
Ama Ata Aidoo; in addition, she has long been fascinated by the matriarchal
myths and goddesses of Africa and of the West Indian island Carriacou, where
her mother was born. As the title *Cables to Rage* indicates, however, she has
been conscious of the roots of her own anger at North American racism and
sexism from early in her career, and the poem *Coal* suggests the strength
through which she can transform rage at racism into triumphant self-assertion.
In an essay entitled *The Uses of the Erotic*, Lorde has indicated, moreover, that
for her "love [is] a source of tremendous power," while in a recent interview

she explained that "I speak of the erotic as the deepest life force, a force which moves us toward living in a fundamental way. And when I say living I mean it as that force which moves us toward what will accomplish real positive change."

Coal

I
is the total black, being spoken
from the earth's inside.
There are many kinds of open
how a diamond comes into a knot of flame
how sound comes into a word, colored   5
by who pays what for speaking.

Some words are open like a diamond
on glass windows
singing out within the passing crash of sun
Then there are words like stapled wagers   10
in a perforated book,—buy and sign and tear apart—
and come whatever wills all chances
the stub remains
an ill-pulled tooth with a ragged edge.
Some words live in my throat   15
breeding like adders. Others know sun
seeking like gypsies over my tongue
to explode through my lips
like young sparrows bursting from shell
Some words   20
bedevil me.

Love is a word, another kind of open.
As the diamond comes into a knot of flame
I am Black because I come from the earth's inside
now take my word for jewel in the open light.   25

1976

On a Night of the Full Moon

I

Out of my flesh that hungers
and my mouth that knows
comes the shape I am seeking
for reason.

The curve of your waiting body   5
fits my waiting hand
your breasts warm as sunlight
your lips quick as young birds
between your thighs the sweet
sharp taste of limes.   10

Thus I hold you
frank in my heart's eye
in my skin's knowing
as my fingers conceive your flesh
I feel your stomach   15
moving against me.

Before the moon wanes again
we shall come together.

II

And I would be the moon
spoken over your beckoning flesh   20
breaking against reservations
beaching thought
my hands at your high tide
over and under inside you
and the passing of hungers   25
attended, forgotten.

Darkly risen
the moon speaks
my eyes
judging your roundness   30
delightful.

                                                  1976

Now that I Am Forever with Child

How the days went
while you were blooming within me
I remember each upon each—
the swelling changed planes of my body
and how you first fluttered, then jumped   5
and I thought it was my heart.

How the days wound down
and the turning of winter
I recall, with you growing heavy

against the wind. I thought   10
now her hands
are formed, and her hair
has started to curl
now her teeth are done
now she sneezes.   15
Then the seed opened
I bore you one morning just before spring
My head rang like a fiery piston
my legs were towers between which
A new world was passing.   20

Since then
I can only distinguish
one thread within running hours
You, flowing through selves
toward You.   25

                                              1976

From the House of Yemanjá[1]

My mother had two faces and a frying pot
where she cooked up her daughters
into girls
before she fixed our dinner.
My mother had two faces   5
and a broken pot
where she hid out a perfect daughter
who was not me
I am the sun and moon and forever hungry
for her eyes.   10

I bear two women upon my back
one dark and rich and hidden
in the ivory hungers of the other
mother
pale as a witch   15
yet steady and familiar
brings me bread and terror

1. "Mother of the other *Orisha* [goddesses and gods of the Yoruba people of Western Nigeria], Yemanjá is also the goddess of oceans. Rivers are said to flow from her breasts. One legend has it that a son tried to rape her. She fled until she collapsed, and from her breasts, the rivers flowed. Another legend says that a husband in- sulted Yemanjá's long breasts, and when she fled with her pots he knocked her down. From her breasts flowed the rivers, and from her body then sprang forth all the other *Orisha*. River-smooth stones are Yemanjá's symbol, and the sea is sacred to her followers. Those who please her are blessed with many children" [Lorde's note].

in my sleep
her breasts are huge exciting anchors
in the midnight storm.   20

All this has been
before
in my mother's bed
time has no sense
I have no brothers   25
and my sisters are cruel.

Mother I need
mother I need
mother I need your blackness now
as the august earth needs rain.   30
I am
the sun and moon and forever hungry
the sharpened edge
where day and night shall meet
and not be   35
one.

                                                          1978

Coniagui[2] Women

The Coniagui women
wear their flesh like war
bear children who have eight days
to choose their mothers
it is up to the children   5
who must decide to stay.

Boys burst from the raised loins
twisting and shouting
from the bush secret
they run   10
beating the other women
avoiding the sweet flesh
hidden
near their mother's fire
but they must take her blood as a token   15
the wild trees have warned them
beat her and you will be free

2. "A West African people who occupy the area   coast" [Lorde's note].
which is now part of Guinea and the African

on the third day
they creep up to her cooking pot
bubbling over the evening's fire   20
and she feeds them
yam soup
and silence.

"Let us sleep in your bed" they whisper
"Let us sleep in your bed" they whisper   25
"Let us sleep in your bed"
but she has mothered before them.
She closes her door.

They become men.

                                                                   1978

The Women of Dan[3] Dance with Swords in Their Hands
to Mark the Time When They Were Warriors

I did not fall from the sky
I
nor descend like a plague of locusts
to drink color and strength from the earth
and I do not come like rain   5
as a tribute or symbol for earth's becoming
I come as a woman
dark and open
some times I fall like night
softly   10
and terrible
only when I must die
in order to rise again.

I do not come like a secret warrior
with an unsheathed sword in my mouth   15
hidden behind my tongue
slicing my throat to ribbons
of service with a smile
while the blood runs
down and out   20
through holes in the two sacred mounds
on my chest.

---

3. "An ancient name for the kingdom of Dahomey" [Lorde's note].

I come like a woman
who I am
spreading out through nights   25
laughter and promise
and dark heat
warming whatever I touch
that is living
consuming   30
only
what is already dead.

                                                          1978

LUCILLE CLIFTON
1936–

Lucille Clifton's daring and exuberance as a poet stand in marked contrast to
what in one poem she characterizes as her own mother's anxious reticence:
"She got us almost through the high grass / then seemed like she turned around
and ran / right back in / right back on in." At the same time, however, Clifton's
irreverence echoes what she describes as the feistiness of her father, a man who
changed his name from Sayle to Sayles because he knew that "there will be
more than one of me." Whether she speaks as her parents' daughter or as the
mother of six children, Clifton presents herself as a woman linked to history
through her family, an ordinary woman trying to deal with the fears and joys of
everyday life.

She was born in Depew, New York, and attended Howard University and
Fredonia State Teachers' College. In 1958, she married Fred J. Clifton, an educator and writer. Three volumes of poetry—*Good Times* (1969), *Good News
about the Earth* (1972), and *An Ordinary Woman* (1974)—were followed by a
memoir, *Generations* (1976), in which she recounts the genealogical stories
that animate so much of her writing. The author of numerous books for children, Clifton most recently published a volume of verse entitled *Two-Headed
Woman* (1980). Although she strenuously rejects what she calls "white ways,"
her work is never marked by rancor. In poems that focus on the activist Angela
Davis or on the biblical figure of the Virgin Mary, she extends the invitation explicit in her poem *After Kent State*, an invitation to "come into the / Black / and
live."

Admonitions

boys
i don't promise you nothing
but this

what you pawn
i will redeem   5
what you steal
i will conceal
my private silence to
your public guilt
is all i got   10

girls
first time a white man
opens his fly
like a good thing
we'll just laugh   15
laugh real loud my
black women

children
when they ask you
why is your mama so funny   20
say
she is a poet
she don't have no sense

1969

the astrologer predicts at mary's birth[1]

this one lie down on grass.
this one old men will follow
calling Mother   Mother.
she womb will blossom then die.
this one she hide from evening.   5
at a certain time when she hear something
it will burn her ear.
at a certain place when she see something
it will break her eye.

1980

anna speaks of the childhood of mary her daughter

we rise up early and
we work. work is the medicine

1. This sequence of poems concerns the life of Mary, the mother of Jesus Christ. According to the New Testament, Mary was a virgin, and Christ's father was God. Mary's mother was St. Anne or Anna; her husband was Joseph. When Christ was born he was nursed in a manger, a trough for feeding animals in a barn, filled with straw.

for dreams.
        that dream
i am having again;   5
she washed in light,
whole world bowed to its knees,
she on a hill looking up,
face all long tears.
        and shall i give her up   10
to dreaming then? i fight this thing.
all day we scrubbing scrubbing.

                   1980

mary's dream

winged women was saying
"full of grace" and like.
was light beyond sun and words
of a name and a blessing.
winged women to only i.   5
i joined them, whispering
yes.

                   1980

how is he coming then

like a pot turned on the straw
nuzzled by cows and an old man
dressed like a father. like a loaf
a poor baker sets in the haystack to cool.
like a shepherd who hears in his herding   5
his mother whisper   my son   my son.

                   1980

holy night

joseph, i afraid of stars,
their brilliant seeing.
so many eyes. such light.
joseph, i cannot still these limbs,
i hands keep moving toward i breasts,   5
so many stars. so bright.
joseph, is wind burning from east

joseph, i shine, oh joseph, oh
illuminated night.

1980

a song of mary

somewhere it being yesterday.
i a maiden in my mother's house.
the animals silent outside.
is morning.
princes sitting on thrones in the east   5
studying the incomprehensible heavens.
joseph carving a table somewhere
in another place.
i watching my mother.
i smiling an ordinary smile.   10

1980

island mary

after the all been done and i
one old creature carried on
another creature's back, i wonder
could i have fought these thing?
surrounded by no son of mine save   5
old men calling Mother like in the tale
the astrologer tell, i wonder
could i have walk away when voices
singing in my sleep? i one old woman.
always i seem to worrying now for   10
another young girl asleep
in the plain evening.
what song around her ear?
what star still choosing?

1980

MARGE PIERCY
1936–

Born during the depression to working-class parents, Marge Piercy was the first
member of her family to go to college. She received a B.A. in 1957 from the

University of Michigan and an M.A. in 1958 from Northwestern University. Piercy began publishing her poems in the sixties, when she was participating in the antiwar movement. A frequently anthologized essay, *The Grand Coolee Dam* (1969), describes how the misogyny of many early activists led to her involvement with the growing women's movement. Such volumes as *Breaking Camp* (1968), *Hard Loving* (1969), *To Be of Use* (1972), and *Living in the Open* (1976) contain a number of satiric and lyric meditations that elaborate on Piercy's belief, articulated in the prose poem *Laying Down the Tower*, that "the defeated in history lose their names, their goddesses, their language, their culture." Because "the myths we imagine we are living (old westerns, true romances) shape our choices," Piercy believes that "what we use we must remake," and thus, while living near Wellfleet, Cape Cod, in a communal household, she has produced a number of novels that rewrite traditional plots. From *Going Down Fast* (1969) and *Dance the Eagle to Sleep* (1970) to *Small Changes* (1973), *Woman on the Edge of Time* (1976), and *Vida* (1979), Piercy's realistic and utopian fiction documents the struggle of militants to combat the economic, racial, and sexual inequality she identifies with contemporary American life.

The Friend

We sat across the table.
he said, cut off your hands.
they are always poking at things.
they might touch me.
I said yes.   5

Food grew cold on the table.
he said, burn your body.
it is not clean and smells like sex.
it rubs my mind sore.
I said yes.   10

I love you, I said.
that's very nice, he said
I like to be loved,
that makes me happy.
Have you cut off your hands yet?   15

1969

The Token Woman

The token woman gleams like a gold molar in a toothless
    mouth.

The token woman arrives like a milkbottle on the stoop
coming full and departing emptied.

The token woman carries a bouquet of hothouse celery
and a stenographer's pad: she will take   5
the minutes, perk the coffee, smile
like a plastic daisy and put out
the black cat of her sensuous anger
to howl on the fence all night.

A fertility god serves a season   10
then is ritually dismembered
yet the name, the function live on:
so she finds the shopping lists
of exiled women in her coat pockets.

The token woman stands in the Square of the Immaculate   15
Exception[1] blessing pigeons from a blue pedestal.
The token woman falls like a melon seed
on the cement: why has she no star shaped yellow flowers?
The token woman is placed like a scarecrow
in the longhaired corn: her muscles are wooden.   20
Why does she ride into battle on a clothes horse?
The token woman is a sandbag plugging
the levee: shall the river
call her sister as the flood waters rage?

The token woman is a black Chicana fluent in Chinese   25
who has borne 1.2 babies
(not on the premises, no child care provided)
owns a Ph.D., will teach freshmen English
for a decade and bleach your laundry
with tears, silent as a china egg.   30
Your department orders her from a taxidermist's catalog
and she comes luxuriously stuffed with goosedown
able to double as sleeping
or punching bag.

Another woman can never join her,   35
help her, sister her, tickle her
but only replace her to become her
unless we make common cause,
unless she grows out, one finger of a hand,
the entering wedge, the runner   40
from the bed of rampant peppermint

---

1. A parody of the Catholic phrase "Immacu-   motherhood of Christ; often used in the name of
late Conception" as applied to the Virgin Mary's   churches, squares, etc.

as it invades the neat clipped turf
of the putting green.

1976

You don't understand me,

you gulp, a frog suddenly on my dinner
plate hopping through the buttered noodles
blinking cold eyes of reproach.

I can interpret the language of your hands
warm under calluses. Your body speaks into mine.   5
We are native users of the same jangling American.

A casual remark lets ants loose in your ears.
The wrong tone drips ice water on your nape.
Waiting I finger the bruise-colored why.

Look, I can't study you like the engine   10
of an old car coughing into silence on wet mornings.
Can't read the convolutions of your brain through the skull.

You want hieroglyphs at the corners of your squint decoded
in perfect silence that folds into your ribbed side,
a woman of soft accordion-pleated wool with healer's hands.   15

I don't understand you: you are not a book,
an argument, a theory. Speak to me.
I listen, and I speak back.

1983

JOANNA RUSS

1937–

Explaining that female concerns are not considered central in our culture, Joanna Russ has written that "when I became aware [in college] of my 'wrong' experience, I chose fantasy. Convinced that I had no real experience of life, since my own obviously wasn't part of Great Literature, I decided consciously that I'd write of things nobody knew anything about, dammit. So I wrote realism disguised as fantasy, that is, science fiction." Now the author of a number of important science-fiction novels—including, most notably, *The Female Man* (1975) and *The Two of Them* (1978)—as well as several volumes of short stories and a book of feminist criticism (*How to Suppress Women's Writing*, 1983), Russ was born and raised in New York City. A precociously intellectual child who won a Westinghouse Science Prize in 1953, she graduated from Cornell University and the Yale School of Drama, and she has written plays and essays as well as novels and short stories. Since the middle sixties, she has taught English and women's studies at a range of universities and colleges, including Cornell, the University of Colorado, and, most recently, the University of Washington. Throughout her career, however, she has consistently struggled—as she does in *When It Changed*—to illuminate "things nobody knew anything about," particularly the adventurous energy of female heroes, in increasingly complex fantasies about an alternative reality.

When It Changed

Katy drives like a maniac; we must have been doing over 120 kilometers per hour on those turns. She's good, though, extremely good, and I've seen her take the whole car apart and put it together again in a day. My birthplace on Whileaway was largely given to farm machinery and I refuse to wrestle with a five-gear shift at unholy speeds, not having been brought up to it, but even on those turns in the middle of the night, on a country road as bad as only our district can make them, Katy's driving didn't scare me. The funny thing about my wife, though: she will not handle guns. She has even gone hiking in the forests above the forty-eight parallel without firearms, for days at a time. And that *does* scare me.

Katy and I have three children between us, one of hers and two of mine. Yuriko, my eldest, was asleep in the back seat, dreaming twelve-year-old dreams of love and war: running away to sea, hunting in the North, dreams of strangely beautiful people in strangely beautiful places, all the wonderful guff you think up when you're turning twelve and the glands start going. Some day soon, like all of them, she will disappear for weeks on end to come back grimy and proud, having knifed her first cougar or shot her first bear, dragging some abominably dangerous dead beastie behind her, which I will never forgive for what it might have done to my daughter. Yuriko says Katy's driving puts her to sleep.

For someone who has fought three duels, I am afraid of far, far too much. I'm getting old. I told this to my wife.

"You're thirty-four," she said. Laconic to the point of silence, that one. She flipped the lights on, on the dash—three kilometers to go and the road getting worse all the time. Far out in the country. Electric-green trees rushed into our headlights and around the car. I reached down next to me where we bolt the carrier panel to the door and eased my rifle into my lap. Yuriko stirred in the back. My height but Katy's eyes, Katy's face. The car engine is so quiet, Katy says, that you can hear breathing in the back seat. Yuki had been alone in the car when the message came, enthusiastically decoding her dot-dashes (silly to mount a wide-frequency transceiver near an I.C. engine, but most of Whileaway is on steam). She had thrown herself out of the car, my gangly and gaudy offspring, shouting at the top of her lungs, so of course she had had to come along. We've been intellectually prepared for this ever since the Colony was founded, ever since it was abandoned, but this is different. This is awful.

"Men!" Yuki had screamed, leaping over the car door. "They've come back! Real Earth men!"

We met them in the kitchen of the farmhouse near the place where they had landed; the windows were open, the night air very mild. We had passed all sorts of transportation when we parked outside—steam tractors, trucks, an I.C. flatbed, even a bicycle. Lydia, the district biologist, had come out of her Northern taciturnity long enough to take blood and urine samples and was sitting in a corner of the kitchen shaking her head in astonishment over the results; she even forced herself (very big, very fair, very shy, always painfully blushing) to dig up the old language manuals—though I can talk the old tongues in my sleep. And do. Lydia is uneasy with us; we're Southerners and too flamboyant. I counted twenty people in that kitchen, all the brains of North Continent. Phyllis Spet, I think, had come in by glider. Yuki was the only child there.

Then I saw the four of them.

They are bigger than we are. They are bigger and broader. Two were taller than I, and I am extremely tall, one meter eighty centimeters in my bare feet. They are obviously of our species but *off*, indescribably off, and as my eyes could not and still cannot quite comprehend the lines of those alien bodies, I could not, then, bring myself to touch them, though the one who spoke Russian—what voices they have— wanted to "shake hands," a custom from the past, I imagine. I can only say they were apes with human faces. He seemed to mean well, but I found myself shuddering back almost the length of the kitchen—and then I laughed apologetically—and then to set a good example (*interstellar amity*, I thought) did "shake hands" finally. A hard, hard hand. They are heavy as draft horses. Blurred, deep voices. Yuriko had sneaked in between the adults and was gazing at *the men* with her mouth open.

He turned *his* head—those words have not been in our language for six hundred years—and said, in bad Russian:

"Who's that?"

"My daughter," I said, and added (with that irrational attention to good manners we sometimes employ in moments of insanity), "My daughter, Yuriko Janetson. We use the patronymic. You would say matronymic."

He laughed, involuntarily. Yuki exclaimed, "I thought they would be *good-looking!*" greatly disappointed at this reception of herself. Phyllis Helgason Spet, whom someday I shall kill, gave me across the room a cold, level venomous look, as if to say: *Watch what you say. You know what I can do.* It's true that I have little formal status, but Madam President will get herself in serious trouble with both me and her own staff if she continues to consider industrial espionage good clean fun. Wars and rumors of wars, as it says in one of our ancestors' books. I translated Yuki's words into *the man's* dog-Russian, once our *lingua franca,*[1] and *the man* laughed again.

"Where are all your people?" he said conversationally.

I translated again and watched the faces around the room; Lydia embarrassed (as usual), Spet narrowing her eyes with some damned scheme, Katy very pale.

"This is Whileaway," I said.

He continued to look unenlightened.

"Whileaway," I said. "Do you remember? Do you have records? There was a plague on Whileaway."

He looked moderately interested. Heads turned in the back of the room, and I caught a glimpse of the local professions-parliament delegate; by morning every town meeting, every district caucus, would be in full session.

"Plague?" he said. "That's most unfortunate."

"Yes," I said. "Most unfortunate. We lost half our population in one generation."

He looked properly impressed.

"Whileaway was lucky," I said. "We had a big initial gene pool, we had been chosen for extreme intelligence, we had a high technology and a large remaining population in which every adult was two-or-three experts in one. The soil is good. The climate is blessedly easy. There are thirty millions of us now. Things are beginning to snowball in industry—do you understand?—give us seventy years and we'll have more than one real city, more than a few industrial centers, full-time professions, full-time radio operators, full-time machinists, give us seventy years and not everyone will have to spend three-quarters of a lifetime on the farm." And I tried to explain how hard it is when artists can practice full-time only in old age, when there are so few, so very few who can be free, like Katy and myself. I tried also to outline our government, the two houses, the one by professions and the geographic one; I

---

1. Any hybrid language used to communicate   Frankish tongue).
between people of different languages (Italian:

told him the district caucuses handled problems too big for the individual towns. And that population control was not a political issue, not yet, though give us time and it would be. This was a delicate point in our history; give us time. There was no need to sacrifice the quality of life for an insane rush into industrialization. Let us go our own pace. Give us time.

"Where are all the people?" said that monomaniac.

I realized then that he did not mean people, he meant *men*, and he was giving the word the meaning it had not had on Whileaway for six centuries.

"They died," I said. "Thirty generations ago."

I thought we had poleaxed him. He caught his breath. He made as if to get out of the chair he was sitting in; he put his hand to his chest; he looked around at us with the strangest blend of awe and sentimental tenderness. Then he said, solemnly and earnestly:

"A great tragedy."

I waited, not quite understanding.

"Yes," he said, catching his breath again with that queer smile, that adult-to-child smile that tells you something is being hidden and will be presently produced with cries of encouragement and joy, "a great tragedy. But it's over." And again he looked around at all of us with the strangest deference. As if we were invalids.

"You've adapted amazingly," he said.

"To what?" I said. He looked embarrassed. He looked inane. Finally he said, "Where I come from, the women don't dress so plainly."

"Like you?" I said. "Like a bride?" for the men were wearing silver from head to foot. I had never seen anything so gaudy. He made as if to answer and then apparently thought better of it; he laughed at me again. With an odd exhilaration—as if we were something childish and something wonderful, as if he were doing us an enormous favor—he took one shaky breath and said, "Well, we're here."

I looked at Spet, Spet looked at Lydia, Lydia looked at Amalia, who is the head of the local town meeting, Amalia looked at I don't know whom. My throat was raw. I cannot stand local beer, which the farmers swill as if their stomachs had iridium linings but I took it anyway, from Amalia (it was her bicycle we had seen outside as we parked), and swallowed it all. This was going to take a long time. I said, "Yes, here you are," and smiled (feeling like a fool), and wondered seriously if male-Earth-people's minds worked so very differently from female-Earth-people's minds, but that couldn't be so or the race would have died out long ago. The radio network had got the news around planet by now and we had another Russian speaker, flown in from Varna; I decided to cut out when *the man* passed around pictures of his wife, who looked like the priestess of some arcane cult. He proposed to question Yuki, so

I barreled her into a back room in spite of her furious protests, and went out on the front porch. As I left, Lydia was explaining the difference between parthenogenesis[2] (which is so easy that anyone can practice it) and what we do, which is the merging of ova. That is why Katy's baby looks like me. Lydia went on to the Ansky Process and Katy Ansky, our one full-polymath genius and the great-great-I don't know how many times great-grandmother of my own Katharina.

A dot-dash transmitter in one of the outbuildings chattered faintly to itself: operators flirting and passing jokes down the line.

There was a man on the porch. The other tall man. I watched him for a few minutes—I can move very quietly when I want to—and when I allowed him to see me, he stopped talking into the little machine hung around his neck. Then he said calmly, in excellent Russian, "Did you know that sexual equality has been reestablished on Earth?"

"You're the real one," I said, "aren't you? The other one's for show." It was a great relief to get things cleared up. He nodded affably.

"As a people, we are not very bright," he said. "There's been too much genetic damage in the last few centuries. Radiation. Drugs. We can use Whileaway's genes, Janet." Strangers do not call strangers by the first name.

"You can have cells enough to drown in," I said. "Breed your own."

He smiled. "That's not the way we want to do it." Behind him I saw Katy come into the square of light that was the screened-in door. He went on, low and urbane, not mocking me, I think, but with the self-confidence of someone who has always had money and strength to spare, who doesn't know what it is to be second-class or provincial. Which is very odd, because the day before, I would have said that was an exact description of me.

"I'm talking to you, Janet," he said, "because I suspect you have more popular influence than anyone else here. You know as well as I do that parthenogenetic culture has all sorts of inherent defects, and we do not—if we can help it—mean to use you for anything of the sort. Pardon me; I should not have said 'use.' But surely you can see that this kind of society is unnatural."

"Humanity is unnatural," said Katy. She had my rifle under her left arm. The top of that silky head does not quite come up to my collarbone, but she is as tough as steel; he began to move, again with that queer smiling deference (which his fellow had showed to me but he had not), and the gun slid into Katy's grip as if she had shot with it all her life.

"I agree," said the man. "Humanity is unnatural. I should know. I

---

2. The reproduction of organisms without   Such a process produces offspring from a single
bringing together two sets of chromosomes.   parent.

have metal in my teeth and metal pins here." He touched his shoulder. "Seals are harem animals," he added, "and so are men; apes are promiscuous and so are men; doves are monogamous and so are men; there are even celibate men and homosexual men. There are homosexual cows, I believe. But Whileaway is still missing something." He gave a dry chuckle. I will give him the credit of believing that it had something to do with nerves.

"I miss nothing," said Katy, "except that life isn't endless."

"You are—?" said the man, nodding from me to her.

"Wives," said Katy. "We're married." Again the dry chuckle.

"A good economic arrangement," he said, "for working and taking care of the children. And as good an arrangement as any for randomizing heredity, if your reproduction is made to follow the same pattern. But think, Katharina Michaelason, if there isn't something better that you might secure for your daughters. I believe in instincts, even in Man, and I can't think that the two of you—a machinist, are you? and I gather you are some sort of chief of police—don't feel somehow what even you must miss. You know it intellectually, of course. There is only half a species here. Men must come back to Whileaway."

Katy said nothing.

"I should think, Katharina Michaelason," said the man gently "that you, of all people, would benefit most from such a change," and he walked past Katy's rifle into the square of light coming from the door. I think it was then that he noticed my scar, which really does not show unless the light is from the side: a fine line that runs from temple to chin. Most people don't even know about it.

"Where did you get that?" he said, and I answered with an involuntary grin. "In my last duel." We stood there bristling at each other for several seconds (this is absurd but true) until he went inside and shut the screen door behind him. Katy said in a brittle voice, "You damned fool, don't you know when we've been insulted?" and swung up the rifle to shoot him through the screen, but I got to her before she could fire and knocked the rifle out of aim; it burned a hole through the porch floor. Katy was shaking. She kept whispering over and over, "That's why I never touched it, because I knew I'd kill someone. I knew I'd kill someone." The first man—the one I'd spoken with first—was still talking inside the house, something about the grand movement to recolonize and rediscover all that Earth had lost. He stressed the advantages to Whileaway: trade, exchange of ideas, education. He, too, said that sexual equality had been reestablished on Earth.

Katy was right, of course; we should have burned them down where they stood. Men are coming to Whileaway. When one culture has the big guns and the other has none, there is a certain predictability about the outcome. Maybe men would have come eventually in any case, I like to think that a hundred years from now my great-grandchildren could have stood them off or fought them to a standstill, but even that's no odds; I will remember all my life those four people I first met who were muscled like bulls and who made me—if only for a moment—feel small. A neurotic reaction, Katy says. I remember everything that happened that night; I remember Yuki's excitement in the car, I remember Katy's sobbing when we got home as if her heart would break, I remember her lovemaking, a little peremptory as always, but wonderfully soothing and comforting. I remember prowling restlessly around the house after Katy fell asleep with one bare arm flung into a patch of light from the hall. The muscles of her forearms are like metal bars from all that driving and testing of her machines. Sometimes I dream about Katy's arms. I remember wandering into the nursery and picking up my wife's baby, dozing for a while with the poignant, amazing warmth of an infant in my lap, and finally returning to the kitchen to find Yuriko fixing herself a late snack. My daughter eats like a Great Dane.

"Yuki," I said, "do you think you could fall in love with a man?" and she whooped derisively. "With a ten-foot toad!" said my tactful child.

But men are coming to Whileaway. Lately I sit up nights and worry about the men who will come to this planet, about my two daughters and Betta Katharinason, about what will happen to Katy, to me, to my life. Our ancestors' journals are one long cry of pain and I suppose I ought to be glad now, but one can't throw away six centuries, or even (as I have lately discovered) thirty-four years. Sometimes I laugh at the question those four men hedged about all evening and never quite dared to ask, looking at the lot of us, hicks in overalls, farmers in canvas pants and plain shirts: *Which of you plays the role of the man?* As if we had to produce a carbon copy of their mistakes! I doubt very much that sexual equality has been reestablished on Earth. I do not like to think of myself mocked, of Katy deferred to as if she were weak, of Yuki made to feel unimportant or silly, of my other children cheated of their full humanity or turned into strangers. And I'm afraid that my own achievements will dwindle from what they were—or what I thought they were—to the not-very-interesting curiosa of the human race, the oddities you read about in the back of the book, things to laugh at sometimes because they are so exotic, quaint but not impressive, charming but not useful. I find this more painful than I can say. You will agree that for a woman who has fought three duels, all of them kills, indulging in such fears is ludicrous. But what's around the corner now is a duel so big that I don't think I have the guts for it; in Faust's words: *Verweile doch, du bist so schoen!*[3] Keep it as it is. Don't change.

---

3. German: linger a while, you are so fair. From the dramatic poem *Faust*, by Johann Wolfgang von Goethe (1749–1832). Faust uses these words in his pact with Mephistopheles; if he ever finds himself so happy that he bids the moment to stay, the devil will have won his wager.

Sometimes at night I remember the original name of this planet, changed by the first generation of our ancestors, those curious women for whom, I suppose, the real name was too painful a reminder after the men died. I find it amusing, in a grim way, to see it all so completely turned around. This, too, shall pass. All good things must come to an end.

Take my life but don't take away the meaning of my life.

For-A-While.

1972

DIANE WAKOSKI

1937–

"I write in the first person because I have always wanted to make my life more interesting than it was," explained the poet Diane Wakoski in 1974, adding that in her work "I created a Diane whose real experiences were dramatized and exaggerated" as a way of "inventing myself into a new life." In more than twenty volumes of poetry, Wakoski has succeeded in accomplishing exactly the self-transformation she describes in this statement. Born in Whittier, California, she has deliberately allowed her "real" origins to remain obscure, refusing to include biographical statements in her books and implying in her poems a personal history that cannot be definitively verified. (According to the critic Estella Lauter, her "poems indicate that she and one sister were born to poor Polish-American parents and were deserted by their father in early childhood." In addition, she "may have borne two children and given them up for adoption before 1971, and she has experienced at least two cycles of marriage and divorce.")

Educated at the University of California, Berkeley, Wakoski settled in New York City in the early sixties, where she worked in a bookstore and taught junior high school English until 1969, while writing and publishing such volumes as *Coins and Coffins* (1962), *The George Washington Poems* (1967), and *Inside the Blood Factory* (1968). More recently, she has supported herself with university teaching and by giving poetry readings and conducting verse-writing workshops; her publications from this period include *Waiting for the King of Spain* (1976) and *The Man Who Shook Hands* (1978). As the fantastic leaps and surrealistic images of *Blue Monday* indicate, however, her life as an "invented" person has continually taken precedence over ordinary existence. Whether disguised as an acolyte of George Washington, of Beethoven, of the "motorcycle betrayer," or of "the King of Spain"—all figures who play prominent parts in the poems that constitute her imaginary autobiography—Wakoski has devoted herself to the construction of what the modernist American poet Wallace Stevens once called "a Supreme Fiction."

Belly Dancer

Can these movements which move themselves
be the substance of my attraction?
Where does this thin green silk come from that covers
    my body?
Surely any woman wearing such fabrics
would move her body just to feel them touching every
    part of her.   5

Yet most of the women frown, or look away, or laugh stiffly.
They are afraid of these materials and these movements
    in some way.
The psychologists would say they are afraid of
    themselves, somehow.
Perhaps awakening too much desire—   10
that their men could never satisfy?

So they keep themselves laced and buttoned and made up
in hopes that the framework will keep them stiff enough
    not to feel
the whole register.
In hopes that they will not have to experience that
    unquenchable desire for rhythm and contact.   15

If a snake glided across this floor
most of them would faint or shrink away.
Yet that movement could be their own.
That smooth movement frightens them—
awakening ancestors and relatives to the tips of the
    arms and toes.   20

So my bare feet
and my thin green silks
my bells and finger cymbals
offend them—frighten their old-young bodies.
While the men simper and leer—   25
glad for the vicarious experience and exercise.
They do not realize how I scorn them:
or how I dance for their frightened,
unawakened, sweet
women.   30

1966

Blue Monday

Blue of the heaps of beads poured into her breasts
and clacking together in her elbows;

blue of the silk
that covers lily-town at night;
blue of her teeth   5
that bite cold toast
and shatter on the streets;
blue of the dyed flower petals with gold stamens
hanging like tongues
over the fence of her dress   10
at the opera/ opals clasped under her lips
and the moon breaking over her head a
gush of blood-red lizards.

Blue Monday. Monday at 3:00 and
Monday at 5. Monday at 7:30 and   15
Monday at 10:00. Monday passed under the rippling
California fountain. Monday alone
a shark in the cold blue waters.

    You are dead: wound round like a paisley shawl.
    I cannot shake you out of the sheets. Your name   20
    is still wedged in every corner of the sofa.

    Monday is the first of the week,
    and I think of you all week.
    I beg Monday not to come
    so that I will not think of you   25
    all week.

You paint my body blue. On the balcony
in the soft muddy night, you paint me
with bat wings and the crystal
the crystal   30
the crystal
the crystal in your arm cuts away
the night, folds back ebony whale skin
and my face, the blue of new rifles,
and my neck, the blue of Egypt,   35
and my breast, the blue of sand,
and my arms, bass-blue,
and my stomach, arsenic;

there is electricity dripping from me like cream;
there is love dripping from me I cannot use—like acacia or   40
jacaranda[1]—fallen blue and gold flowers, crushed into the street.

    Love passed me in a blue business suit
    and fedora.

_____

1. A tree with pale purple flowers; "acacia": a tree with small yellow or white flowers.

His glass cane, hollow and filled with
sharks and whales . . .   45
He wore black
patent leather shoes
and had a mustache. His hair was so black
it was almost blue.

"Love," I said.   50
"I beg your pardon," he said.
"Mr. Love," I said.
"I beg your pardon," he said.

So I saw there was no use bothering him on the street.

Love passed me on the street in a blue   55
business suit. He was a banker
I could tell.

So blue trains rush by in my sleep.
Blue herons fly overhead.
Blue paint cracks in my   60
arteries and sends titanium[2]
floating into my bones.
Blue liquid pours down
my poisoned throat and blue veins
rip open my breast. Blue daggers tip   65
and are juggled on my palms.
Blue death lives in my fingernails.

If I could sing one last song
with water bubbling through my lips
I would sing with my throat torn open,   70
the blue jugular spouting that black shadow pulse,
and on my lips
I would balance volcanic rock
emptied out of my veins. At last
my children strained out   75
of my body. At last my blood
solidified and tumbling into the ocean.
It is blue.
It is blue.
It is blue.   80

1968

2. A strong white metal sometimes used as a paint pigment.

Ringless

I cannot stand the man who wears
a ring
on his little finger/ a white peacock walking on the moon
and splinters of silver dust his body;
but the great man, George, cracked in half in my living room   5
one day and I saw he was made of marble
with black veins. It does not justify the ring to say
someone gave it to you and the little finger is the only one
it will fit;
it does not justify to say Cocteau wore one   10
and still made the man burst silently through the mirror[3]—
many beautiful
poems have been made with rings worn on the little finger.
That
isn't the point.   15
Flaubert had jasper; Lorca had jade; Dante had
amber; and Browning had carnelian;[4]
George Washington had solid gold—even Kelly once
    wore a scarab there;
but I am telling you I cannot stand the man
who wears a ring   20
on his little finger. He may indeed
run the world;
that does not make him any better in
my needlepoint eyes.
Why   25
is a story.

          There were heaps of fish lying, shimmering in the sun
          with red gashes still heaving
          and the mouths of medieval lovers.
          There were gold and green glass balls bobbing in their   30
          nets on the waves.
          There were black-eyed men with hair all over their bodies
          There were black-skirted ladies baking bread
          and there were gallons and gallons of red wine.
          A girl spilled one drop of hot wax on her lover's neck   35
          as she glanced at his white teeth and thick arms.
          There were red and silver snakes coiling around the legs
          of the dancers.
          There was hot sun and there was no talk.

3. A reference, perhaps, to scenes in the film *Orphée* (1950), by the French director Jean Cocteau (1889–1963), in which the poet Orphée returns from the underworld through a mirror.
4. Gustave Flaubert (1821–1880), French novelist; Federico García Lorca (1899–1938), Spanish poet; Dante (1265–1321), author of *The Divine Comedy*; Robert Browning (1812–1889), English poet. "Kelly" is Robert Kelly, a poet and friend of Wakoski's.

How do I reconcile these images with our cool president, 40
George Washington, walking the streets? Every bone
in my body is ivory and has the word, "America"
carved on it, but
my head takes me away from furniture and pewter
to the sun tugging at my nipples and trying to squeeze   45
under my toes.
The sun appeared in the shape of a man and he had
a ring made of sun around his little finger.
"It will burn up your hand," I said.
But he made motions in the air and passed by.   50
The moon appeared in the shape of a young negro boy,
and he had a ring made of dew around his little finger.
"You'll lose it," I said,
but he touched my face,
not losing a drop and passed away. Then I saw   55
Alexander Hamilton,[5] whom I loved,
and he had a ring on his little finger,
but he wouldn't touch me.
And Lorca had rings around both little fingers,
and suddenly everyone I knew appeared,   60
and they all had rings on their little fingers,
and I was the only one in the world left without any
rings
on any
of my fingers whatsoever.   65
And worst of all,
there was George Washington
walking down the senate aisles
with a ring on his little finger—managing
the world,   70
managing *my* world.
This is what I mean—you wear a ring on your
        little finger
        and you manage the world,
        and I am ringless   75
        ringless . . .
I cannot stand the man who wears
a ring
on his little finger;

not even if it is you.   80

                                                      1968

---

5. Alexander Hamilton (1755–1804), American statesman.

6. Toklas (1877–1967) was companion to the
expatriate American writer Stein (1874–1946).

My Trouble

my trouble
is that I have the spirit of Gertrude Stein
but the personality of Alice B. Toklas;[6]
craggy, grand
stony ideas   5
but
all I can do
is embroider Picasso's drawings
and bake hashish fudge.[7]
I am poor   10
and don't have very much to say
am usually taken for
somebody's
secretary.

1972

The Mirror of a Day Chiming Marigold

Astronomer,
I strike my gong for you.
It is gold.
Ancient.
Engraved with a calendar   5
of my heart.
And I strike it.
It rings
loud and melodious,
the sound of seashells,   10
the shouting of marigolds,
the angry book of dragonflies,
thunder,
an erupting volcano,
my heart pounding in exhaustion.   15

I strike it,
and it sounds for you.
As all of us are instruments
recording the heart,
playing its jealous and beautiful sounds,   20
the mirror breaking and shattering

7. Allegedly a party delicacy served by Toklas;   was championed early by Stein.
the Spanish painter Pablo Picasso (1881–1973)

past our tongues
when the fire burns our skins.

The astronomer looks at the sky and sees
all the phenomena of light.   25
This one gives himself a solar corona
while I stand in the shade of the moon.

There is
an ancient priestess
whose tears make the spiderlilies grow.   30
She knows my name is darkness.
We are sisters.
As my tears are the blue lilies of the nile themselves,
my tongue,
a stamen waiting to be touched by the breath of insects   35
my life, a rock;
I look for a poet,
an astronomer,
one who studies
     my moon.   40

         1973

JOYCE CAROL OATES
1938–

Whether her characters are situated in contemporary urban centers or, as recently, in the towns of a Victorian past, Joyce Carol Oates has established her reputation as a psychologist of what she has called "the human soul caught in the stampede of time." In a remarkably prolific career, Oates has produced many novels, short stories, books of essays, and volumes of poems. The violence associated with some of her fiction is a result of her sense that ordinary people cannot always articulate or even understand the ways in which they are trapped in the convulsions of history.

Oates was born to Irish-Catholic, working-class parents in Lockport, New York. After graduating Phi Beta Kappa from Syracuse University and receiving an M.A. in English from the University of Wisconsin, she began an academic career that moved her from the University of Detroit and the University of Windsor, Ontario, to Princeton, New Jersey, where she currently resides with her husband, the scholar Raymond Smith. Whether, as in *Expensive People* (1968), she focuses on a murderous child, or, as in *them* (1969), on prostitution and male aggression, Oates documents the sometimes grotesque violence of contemporary family life. While in *Wonderland* (1971) and *Do with Me What You Will* (1973), she deals with the psychological tactics individuals use to avoid reality, in works like *Bellefleur* (1980) and *The Bloodsmoor Romance* (1983) she has begun to focus her attention on the situation of women in social history and on the aesthetic dimensions of the novel form. However, Oates's most successful volumes of stories—from *By the North Gate* (1963) to *The Goddess and Other Women* (1974)—characteristically dramatize unsettling, unpleasant, even macabre subjects. Defending herself against critics who fault her analyses of pain, Oates has explained that "the more violent the murders in *Macbeth*, the more relief one can feel at *not* having to perform them. Great art," she continued, "is cathartic; it is always moral."

Where Are You Going, Where Have You Been?

For Bob Dylan[1]

Her name was Connie. She was fifteen and she had a quick, nervous giggling habit of craning her neck to glance into mirrors or checking other people's faces to make sure her own was all right. Her mother, who noticed everything and knew everything and who hadn't much reason any longer to look at her own face, always scolded Connie about it. "Stop gawking at yourself. Who are you? You think you're so pretty?" she would say. Connie would raise her eyebrows at these familiar old complaints and look right through her mother, into a shadowy vision of herself as she was right at that moment: she knew she was pretty and that was everything. Her mother had been pretty once too, if you could believe those old snapshots in the album, but now her looks were gone and that was why she was always after Connie.

"Why don't you keep your room clean like your sister? How've you got your hair fixed—what the hell stinks? Hair spray? You don't see your sister using that junk."

Her sister June was twenty-four and still lived at home. She was a secretary in the high school Connie attended, and if that wasn't bad enough—with her in the same building—she was so plain and chunky and steady that Connie had to hear her praised all the time by her mother and her mother's sisters. June did this, June did that, she saved money and helped clean the house and cooked and Connie couldn't do a thing, her mind was all filled with trashy daydreams. Their father was away at work most of the time and when he came home he wanted supper and he read the newspaper at supper and after supper he went to bed. He didn't bother talking much to them, but around his bent head Connie's mother kept picking at her until Connie wished her mother was dead and she herself was dead and it was all over. "She makes me want to throw up sometimes," she complained to her friends. She had a

1. Popular American folk and rock singer, a symbol of youth protest during the sixties.

high, breathless, amused voice that made everything she said sound a little forced, whether it was sincere or not.

There was one good thing: June went places with girl friends of hers, girls who were just as plain and steady as she, and so when Connie wanted to do that her mother had no objections. The father of Connie's best girl friend drove the girls the three miles to town and left them at a shopping plaza so they could walk through the stores or go to a movie, and when he came to pick them up again at eleven he never bothered to ask what they had done.

They must have been familiar sights, walking around the shopping plaza in their shorts and flat ballerina slippers that always scuffed on the sidewalk, with charm bracelets jingling on their thin wrists; they would lean together to whisper and laugh secretly if someone passed who amused or interested them. Connie had long dark blond hair that drew anyone's eye to it, and she wore part of it pulled up on her head and puffed out and the rest of it she let fall down her back. She wore a pull-over jersey blouse that looked one way when she was at home and another way when she was away from home. Everything about her had two sides to it, one for home and one for anywhere that was not home: her walk, which could be childlike and bobbing, or languid enough to make anyone think she was hearing music in her head; her mouth, which was pale and smirking most of the time, but bright and pink on these evenings out; her laugh, which was cynical and drawling at home —"Ha, ha, very funny,"—but high-pitched and nervous anywhere else, like the jingling of the charms on her bracelet.

Sometimes they did go shopping or to a movie, but sometimes they went across the highway, ducking fast across the busy road, to a drive-in restaurant where older kids hung out. The restaurant was shaped like a big bottle, though squatter than a real bottle, and on its cap was a revolving figure of a grinning boy holding a hamburger aloft. One night in midsummer they ran across, breathless with daring, and right away someone leaned out a car window and invited them over, but it was just a boy from high school they didn't like. It made them feel good to be able to ignore him. They went up through the maze of parked and cruising cars to the bright-lit, fly-infested restaurant, their faces pleased and expectant as if they were entering a sacred building that loomed up out of the night to give them what haven and blessing they yearned for. They sat at the counter and crossed their legs at the ankles, their thin shoulders rigid with excitement, and listened to the music that made everything so good: the music was always in the background, like music at a church service; it was something to depend upon.

A boy named Eddie came in to talk with them. He sat backwards on his stool, turning himself jerkily around in semicircles and then stopping and turning back again, and after a while he asked Connie if she would like something to eat. She said she would so she tapped her friend's arm on her way out—her friend pulled her face up into a brave, droll look—and Connie said she would meet her at eleven across the way. "I just hate to leave her like that," Connie said earnestly, but the boy said that she wouldn't be alone for long. So they went out to his car, and on the way Connie couldn't help but let her eyes wander over the windshields and faces all around her, her face gleaming with a joy that had nothing to do with Eddie or even this place; it might have been the music. She drew her shoulders up and sucked in her breath with the pure pleasure of being alive, and just at that moment she happened to glance at a face just a few feet away from hers. It was a boy with shaggy black hair, in a convertible jalopy painted gold. He stared at her and then his lips widened into a grin. Connie slit her eyes at him and turned away, but she couldn't help glancing back and there he was, still watching her. He wagged a finger and laughed and said, "Gonna get you, baby," and Connie turned away again without Eddie noticing anything.

She spent three hours with him, at the restaurant where they ate hamburgers and drank Cokes in wax cups that were always sweating, and then down an alley a mile or so away, and when he left her off at five to eleven only the movie house was still open at the plaza. Her girl friend was there, talking with a boy. When Connie came up, the two girls smiled at each other and Connie said, "How was the movie?" and the girl said, "*you* should know." They rode off with the girl's father, sleepy and pleased, and Connie couldn't help but look back at the darkened shopping plaza with its big empty parking lot and its signs that were faded and ghostly now, and over at the drive-in restaurant where cars were still circling tirelessly. She couldn't hear the music at this distance.

Next morning June asked her how the movie was and Connie said, "So-so."

She and that girl and occasionally another girl went out several times a week, and the rest of the time Connie spent around the house—it was summer vacation—getting in her mother's way and thinking, dreaming about the boys she met. But all the boys fell back and dissolved into a single face that was not even a face but an idea, a feeling, mixed up with the urgent insistent pounding of the music and the humid night air of July. Connie's mother kept dragging her back to the daylight by finding things for her to do or saying suddenly, "What's this about the Pettinger girl?"

And Connie would say nervously, "Oh, her. That dope." She always drew thick clear lines between herself and such girls, and her mother was simple and kind enough to believe it. Her mother was so simple, Connie thought, that it was maybe cruel to fool her so much. Her mother went scuffling around the house in old bedroom slippers and complained over the telephone to one sister about the other, then the other called up and the two of them complained about the third one. If June's name was mentioned her mother's tone was approving, and if Connie's name was mentioned it was disapproving. This did not really mean she disliked Connie, and actually Connie thought that her mother preferred her to June just because she was prettier, but the two of them kept up a pretense of exasperation, a sense that they were tugging and struggling over something of little value to either of them. Sometimes, over coffee, they were almost friends, but something would come up—some vexation that was like a fly buzzing suddenly around their heads—and their faces went hard with contempt.

One Sunday Connie got up at eleven—none of them bothered with church—and washed her hair so that it could dry all day long in the sun. Her parents and sister were going to a barbecue at an aunt's house and Connie said no, she wasn't interested, rolling her eyes to let her mother know just what she thought of it. "Stay home alone then," her mother said sharply. Connie sat out back in a lawn chair and watched them drive away, her father quiet and bald, hunched around so that he could back the car out, her mother with a look that was still angry and not at all softened through the windshield, and in the back seat poor old June, all dressed up as if she didn't know what a barbecue was, with all the running yelling kids and the flies. Connie sat with her eyes closed in the sun, dreaming and dazed with the warmth about her as if this were a kind of love, the caresses of love, and her mind slipped over onto thoughts of the boy she had been with the night before and how nice he had been, how sweet it always was, not the way someone like June would suppose but sweet, gently, the way it was in movies and promised in songs; and when she opened her eyes she hardly knew where she was, the back yard ran off into weeds and a fence-like line of trees and behind it the sky was perfectly blue and still. The asbestos "ranch house" that was now three years old startled her—it looked small. She shook her head as if to get awake.

It was too hot. She went inside the house and turned on the radio to drown out the quiet. She sat on the edge of her bed, barefoot, and listened for an hour and a half, to a program called XYZ Sunday Jamboree, record after record of hard, fast, shrieking songs she sang along with, interspersed by exclamations from "Bobby King": "An' look here, you girls at Napoleon's—Son and Charley want you to pay real close attention to this song coming up!"

And Connie paid close attention herself, bathed in a glow of slow-pulsed joy that seemed to rise mysteriously out of the music itself and lay languidly about the airless little room, breathed in and breathed out with each gentle rise and fall of her chest.

After a while she heard a car coming up the drive. She sat up at once, startled, because it couldn't be her father so soon. The gravel kept crunching all the way in from the road—the driveway was long—and Connie ran to the window. It was a car she didn't know. It was an open jalopy, painted a bright gold that caught the sunlight opaquely. Her heart began to pound and her fingers snatched at her hair, checking it, and she whispered, "Christ, Christ," wondering how she looked. The car came to a stop at the side door and the horn sounded four short taps, as if this were a signal Connie knew.

She went into the kitchen and approached the door slowly, then hung out the screen door, her bare toes curling down off the step. There were two boys in the car and now she recognized the driver: he had shaggy black hair that looked crazy as a wig and he was grinning at her.

"I ain't late, am I?" he said.

"Who the hell do you think you are?" Connie said.

"Toldja I'd be out, didn't I?"

"I don't even know who you are."

She spoke sullenly, careful to show no interest or pleasure, and he spoke in a fast, bright monotone. Connie looked past him to the other boy, taking her time. He had fair brown hair, with a lock that fell onto his forehead. His sideburns gave him a fierce, embarrassed look, but so far he hadn't even bothered to glance at her. Both boys wore sunglasses. The driver's glasses were metallic and mirrored everything in miniature.

"You wanta come for a ride?" he said.

Connie smirked and let her hair fall loose over one shoulder.

"Don'tcha like my car? New paint job," he said. "Hey."

"What?"

"You're cute."

She pretended to fidget, chasing flies away from the door.

"Don'tcha believe me, or what?" he said.

"Look, I don't even know who you are," Connie said in disgust.

"Hey, Ellie's got a radio, see. Mine broke down." He lifted his friend's arm and showed her the little transistor radio the boy was holding, and now Connie began to hear the music. It was the same program that was playing inside the house.

"Bobby King?" she said.

"I listen to him all the time. I think he's great."

"He's kind of great," Connie said reluctantly.

"Listen, that guy's *great*. He knows where the action is."

Connie blushed a little, because the glasses made it impossible for her to see just what this boy was looking at. She couldn't decide if she liked him or if he was a jerk, and so she dawdled in the doorway and wouldn't come down or go back inside. She said, "What's all that stuff painted on your car?"

"Can'tcha read it?" He opened the door very carefully, as if he were afraid it might fall off. He slid out just as carefully, planting his feet firmly on the ground, the tiny metallic world in his glasses slowing down like gelatine hardening, and in the midst of it Connie's bright green blouse. "This here is my name, to begin with," he said. ARNOLD FRIEND was written in tarlike black letters on the side, with a drawing of a round, grinning face that reminded Connie of a pumpkin, except it wore sunglasses. "I wanta introduce myself. I'm Arnold Friend and that's my real name and I'm gonna be your friend, honey, and inside the car's Ellie Oscar, he's kinda shy." Ellie brought his transistor radio up to his shoulder and balanced it there. "Now, these numbers are a secret code, honey," Arnold Friend explained. He read off the numbers 33, 19, 17 and raised his eyebrows at her to see what she thought of that, but she didn't think much of it. The left rear fender had been smashed and around it was written, on the gleaming gold background: DONE BY CRAZY WOMAN DRIVER. Connie had to laugh at that. Arnold Friend was pleased at her laughter and looked up at her. "Around the other side's a lot more—you wanta come and see them?"

"No."

"Why not?"

"Why should I?"

"Don'tcha wanta see what's on the car? Don'tcha wanta go for a ride?"

"I don't know."

"Why not?"

"I got things to do."

"Like what?"

"Things."

He laughed as if she had said something funny. He slapped his thighs. He was standing in a strange way, leaning back against the car as if he were balancing himself. He wasn't tall, only an inch or so taller than she would be if she came down to him. Connie liked the way he was dressed, which was the way all of them dressed: tight faded jeans stuffed into black, scuffed boots, a belt that pulled his waist in and showed how lean he was, and a white pull-over shirt that was a little soiled and showed the hard small muscles of his arms and shoulders. He looked as if he probably did hard work, lifting and carrying things. Even his neck looked muscular. And his face was a familiar face, somehow; the jaw and chin and cheeks slightly darkened because he hadn't shaved for a day or two, and the nose long and hawlike, sniffing as if she were a treat he was going to gobble up and it was all a joke.

"Connie, you ain't telling the truth. This is your day set aside for a ride with me and you know it," he said, still laughing. The way he straightened and recovered from his fit of laughing showed that it had been all fake.

"How do you know what my name is?" she said suspiciously.

"It's Connie."

"Maybe and maybe not."

"I know my Connie," he said, wagging his finger. Now she remembered him even better, back at the restaurant, and her cheeks warmed at the thought of how she had sucked in her breath just at the moment she passed him—how she must have looked to him. And he had remembered her. "Ellie and I come out here especially for you," he said. "Ellie can sit in back. How about it?"

"Where?"

"Where what?"

"Where're we going?"

He looked at her. He took off the sunglasses and she saw how pale the skin around his eyes was, like holes that were not in shadow but instead in light. His eyes were like chips of broken glass that catch the light in an amiable way. He smiled. It was as if the idea of going for a ride somewhere, to someplace, was a new idea to him.

"Just for a ride, Connie sweetheart."

"I never said my name was Connie," she said.

"But I know what it is. I know your name and all about you, lots of things," Arnold Friend said. He had not moved yet but stood still leaning back against the side of his jalopy. "I took a special interest in you, such a pretty girl, and found out all about you—like I know your parents and sister are gone somewheres and I know where and how long they're going to be gone, and I know who you were with last night, and your best girl friend's name is Betty. Right?"

He spoke in a simple lilting voice, exactly as if he were reciting the words to a song. His smile assured her that everything was fine. In the car Ellie turned up the volume on his radio and did not bother to look around at them.

"Ellie can sit in the back seat," Arnold Friend said. He indicated his friend with a casual jerk of his chin, as if Ellie did not count and she should not bother with him.

"How'd you find out all that stuff?" Connie said.

"Listen: Betty Schultz and Tony Fitch and Jimmy Pettinger and Nancy Pettinger," he said in a chant. "Raymond Stanley and Bob Hutter—"

"Do you know all those kids?"

"I know everybody."

"Look, you're kidding. You're not from around here."

"Sure."

"But—how come we never saw you before?"

"Sure you saw me before," he said. He looked down at his boots, as if he were a little offended. "You just don't remember."

"I guess I'd remember you," Connie said.

"Yeah?" He looked up at this, beaming. He was pleased. He began to mark time with the music from Ellie's radio, tapping his fists lightly together. Connie looked away from his smile to the car, which was painted so bright it almost hurt her eyes to look at it. She looked at that name, ARNOLD FRIEND. And up at the front fender was an expression that was familiar—MAN THE FLYING SAUCERS. It was an expression kids had used the year before but didn't use this year. She looked at it for a while as if the words meant something to her that she did not yet know.

"What're you thinking about? Huh?" Arnold Friend demanded. "Not worried about your hair blowing around in the car, are you?"

"No."

"Think I maybe can't drive good?"

"How do I know?"

"You're a hard girl to handle. How come?" he said. "Don't you know I'm your friend? Didn't you see me put my sign in the air when you walked by?"

"What sign?"

"My sign." And he drew an X in the air, leaning out toward her. They were maybe ten feet apart. After his hand fell back to his side the X was still in the air, almost visible. Connie let the screen door close and stood perfectly still inside it, listening to the music from her radio and the boy's blend together. She stared at Arnold Friend. He stood there so stiffly relaxed, pretending to be relaxed, with one hand idly on the door handle as if he were keeping himself up that way and had no intention of ever moving again. She recognized most things about him, the tight jeans that showed his thighs and buttocks and the greasy leather boots and tight shirt, and even that slippery friendly smile of his, that sleepy dreamy smile that all the boys used to get across ideas they didn't want to put into words. She recognized all this and also the sing-song way he talked, slightly mocking, kidding, but serious and a little melancholy, and she recognized the way he tapped one fist against the other in homage to the perpetual music behind him. But all these things did not come together.

She said suddenly, "Hey, how old are you?"

His smile faded. She could see then that he wasn't a kid, he was much older—thirty, maybe more. At this knowledge her heart began to pound faster.

"That's a crazy thing to ask. Can'tcha see I'm your own age?"

"Like hell you are."

"Or maybe a couple years older. I'm eighteen."

"Eighteen?" she said doubtfully.

He grinned to reassure her and lines appeared at the corners of his mouth. His teeth were big and white. He grinned so broadly his eyes became slits and she saw how thick the lashes were, thick and black as if painted with a black tarlike material. Then, abruptly, he seemed to become embarrassed and looked over his shoulder at Ellie. "*Him,* he's crazy," he said. "Ain't he a riot? He's a nut, a real character." Ellie was still listening to the music. His sunglasses told nothing about what he was thinking. He wore a bright orange shirt unbuttoned halfway to show his chest, which was a pale, bluish chest and not muscular like Arnold Friend's. His shirt collar was turned up all around and the very tips of the collar pointed out past his chin as if they were protecting him. He was pressing the transistor radio up against his ear and sat there in a kind of daze, right in the sun.

"He's kinda strange," Connie said.

"Hey, she says you're kinda strange! Kinda strange!" Arnold Friend cried. He pounded on the car to get Ellie's attention. Ellie turned for the first time and Connie saw with shock that he wasn't a kid either—he had a fair, hairless face, cheeks reddened slightly as if the veins grew too close to the surface of his skin, the face of a forty-year-old baby. Connie felt a wave of dizziness rise in her at this sight and she stared at him as if waiting for something to change the shock of the moment, make it all right again. Ellie's lips kept shaping words, mumbling along with the words blasting in his ear.

"Maybe you two better go away," Connie said faintly.

"What? How come?" Arnold Friend cried. "We come out here to take you for a ride. It's Sunday." He had the voice of the man on the radio now. It was the same voice, Connie thought. "Don'tcha know it's Sunday all day? And honey, no matter who you were with last night, today you're with Arnold Friend and don't you forget it! Maybe you better step out here," he said, and this last was in a different voice. It was a little flatter, as if the heat was finally getting to him.

"No. I got things to do."

"Hey."

"You two better leave."

"We ain't leaving until you come with us."

"Like hell I am—"

"Connie, don't fool around with me. I mean—I mean, don't fool *around,*" he said, shaking his head. He laughed incredulously. He placed his sunglasses on top of his head, carefully, as if he were indeed wearing a wig, and brought the stems down behind his ears. Connie stared at him, another wave of dizziness and fear rising in her so that for a moment he wasn't even in focus but was just a blur standing there against his gold car, and she had the idea that he had driven up the driveway all right but had come from nowhere before that and belonged nowhere and that everything about him and even about the music that was so familiar to her was only half real.

"If my father comes and sees you—"

"He ain't coming. He's at a barbecue."

"How do you know that?"

"Aunt Tillie's. Right now they're—uh—they're drinking. Sitting around," he said vaguely, squinting as if he were staring all the way to town and over to Aunt Tillie's back yard. Then the vision seemed to get clear and he nodded energetically. "Yeah. Sitting around. There's your sister in a blue dress, huh? And high heels, the poor sad bitch—nothing like you, sweetheart! And your mother's helping some fat woman with the corn, they're cleaning the corn—husking the corn—"

"What fat woman?" Connie cried.

"How do I know what fat woman, I don't know every goddamn fat woman in the world!" Arnold Friend laughed.

"Oh, that's Mrs. Hornsby. . . . Who invited her?" Connie said. She felt a little lightheaded. Her breath was coming quickly.

"She's too fat. I don't like them fat. I like them the way you are, honey," he said, smiling sleepily at her. They stared at each other for a while through the screen door. He said softly, "Now, what you're going to do is this: you're going to come out that door. You're going to sit up front with me and Ellie's going to sit in the back, the hell with Ellie, right? This isn't Ellie's date. You're my date. I'm your lover, honey."

"What? You're crazy—"

"Yes. I'm your lover. You don't know what that is but you will," he said. "I know that too. I know all about you. But look: it's real nice and you couldn't ask for nobody better than me, or more polite. I always keep my word. I'll tell you how it is, I'm always nice at first, the first time. I'll hold you so tight you won't think you have to try to get away or pretend anything because you'll know you can't. And I'll come inside you where it's all secret and you'll give in to me and you'll love me—"

"Shut up! You're crazy!" Connie said. She backed away from the door. She put her hands up against her ears as if she'd heard something terrible, something not meant for her. "People don't talk like that, you're crazy," she muttered. Her heart was almost too big now for her chest and its pumping made sweat break out all over her. She looked out to see Arnold Friend pause and then take a step toward the porch, lurching. He almost fell. But, like a clever drunken man, he managed to catch his balance. He wobbled in his high boots and grabbed hold of one of the porch posts.

"Honey?" he said. "You still listening?"

"Get the hell out of here!"

"Be nice, honey. Listen."

"I'm going to call the police—"

He wobbled again and out of the side of his mouth came a fast spat curse, an aside not meant for her to hear. But even this "Christ!" sounded forced. Then he began to smile again. She watched this smile come, awkward as if he were smiling from inside a mask. His whole face was a mask, she thought wildly, tanned down to his throat but then running out as if he had plastered makeup on his face but had forgotten about his throat.

"Honey—? Listen, here's how it is. I always tell the truth and I promise you this: I ain't coming in that house after you."

"You better not! I'm going to call the police if you—if you don't—"

"Honey," he said, talking right through her voice, "honey. I'm not coming in there but you are coming out here. You know why?"

She was panting. The kitchen looked like a place she had never seen before, some room she had run inside but that wasn't good enough, wasn't going to help her. The kitchen window had never had a curtain, after three years, and there were dishes in the sink for her to do—probably—and if you ran your hand across the table you'd probably feel something sticky there.

"You listening, honey? Hey?"

"—going to call the police—"

"Soon as you touch the phone I don't need to keep my promise and can come inside. You won't want that."

She rushed forward and tried to lock the door. Her fingers were shaking. "But why lock it," Arnold Friend said gently, talking right into her face. "It's just a screen door. It's just nothing." One of his boots was at a strange angle, as if his foot wasn't in it. It pointed out to the left, bent at the ankle. "I mean, anybody can break through a screen door and glass and wood and iron or anything else if he needs to, anybody at all, and specially Arnold Friend. If the place got lit up with a fire, honey, you'd come runnin' out into my arms, right into my arms an' safe at home—like you knew I was your lover and'd stopped fooling around. I don't mind a nice shy girl but I don't like no fooling around." Part of those words were spoken with a slight rhythmic lilt, and Connie somehow recognized them—the echo of a song from last year, about a girl rushing into her boy friend's arms and coming home again—

Connie stood barefoot on the linoleum floor, staring at him. "What do you want?" she whispered.

"I want you," he said.

"What?"

"Seen you that night and thought, that's the one, yes sir. I never needed to look anymore."

"But my father's coming back. He's coming to get me. I had to wash my hair first—" She spoke in a dry, rapid voice, hardly raising it for him to hear.

"No, your daddy is not coming and yes, you had to wash your hair and you washed it for me. It's nice and shining and all for me. I thank you sweetheart," he said with a mock bow, but again he almost lost his balance. He had to bend and adjust his boots. Evidently his feet did not go all the way down; the boots must have been stuffed with something so that he would seem taller. Connie stared out at him and behind him at Ellie in the car, who seemed to be looking off toward Connie's right, into nothing. Then Ellie said, pulling the words out of the air one after another as if he were just discovering them, "You want me to pull out the phone?"

"Shut your mouth and keep it shut," Arnold Friend said, his face red from bending over or maybe from embarrassment because Connie had seen his boots. "This ain't none of your business."

"What—what are you doing? What do you want?" Connie said. "If I call the police they'll get you, they'll arrest you—"

"Promise was not to come in unless you touch that phone, and I'll keep that promise," he said. He resumed his erect position and tried to force his shoulders back. He sounded like a hero in a movie, declaring something important. But he spoke too loudly and it was as if he were speaking to someone behind Connie. "I ain't made plans for coming in that house where I don't belong but just for you to come out to me, the way you should. Don't you know who I am?"

"You're crazy," she whispered. She backed away from the door but did not want to go into another part of the house, as if this would give him permission to come through the door. "What do you . . . you're crazy, you. . . ."

"Huh? What're you saying, honey?"

Her eyes darted everywhere in the kitchen. She could not remember what it was, this room.

"This is how it is, honey: you come out and we'll drive away, have a nice ride. But if you don't come out we're gonna wait till your people come home and then they're all going to get it."

"You want that telephone pulled out?" Ellie said. He held the radio away from his ear and grimaced, as if without the radio the air was too much for him.

"I toldja shut up, Ellie," Arnold Friend said, "you're deaf, get a hearing aid, right? Fix yourself up. This little girl's no trouble and's gonna be nice to me, so Ellie keep to yourself, this ain't your date— right? Don't hem in on me, don't hog, don't crush, don't bird dog, don't trail me," he said in a rapid, meaningless voice, as if he were running through all the expressions he'd learned but was no longer sure which of them was in style, then rushing on to new ones, making them up with his eyes closed. "Don't crawl under my fence, don't squeeze in my chipmunk hole, don't sniff my glue, suck my popsicle, keep your own greasy fingers on yourself!" He shaded his eyes and peered in at Connie, who was backed against the kitchen table. "Don't mind him, honey, he's just a creep. He's a dope. Right? I'm the boy for you and like I said, you come out here nice like a lady and give me your hand, and nobody else gets hurt, I mean, your nice old bald-headed daddy and your mummy and your sister in her high heels. Because listen: why bring them in this?"

"Leave me alone," Connie whispered.

"Hey, you know that old woman down the road, the one with the chickens and stuff—you know her?"

"She's dead!"

"Dead? What? You know her?" Arnold Friend said.

"She's dead—"

"Don't you like her?"

"She's dead—she's—she isn't here any more—"

"But don't you like her, I mean, you got something against her? Some grudge or something?" Then his voice dipped as if he were conscious of a rudeness. He touched the sunglasses perched up on top of his head as if to make sure they were still there. "Now, you be a good girl."

"What are you going to do?"

"Just two things, or maybe three," Arnold Friend said. "But I promise it won't last long and you'll like me the way you get to like people you're close to. You will. It's all over for you here, so come on out. You don't want your people in any trouble, do you?"

She turned and bumped against a chair or something, hurting her leg, but she ran into the back room and picked up the telephone. Something roared in her ear, a tiny roaring, and she was so sick with fear that she could do nothing but listen to it—the telephone was clammy and very heavy and her fingers groped down to the dial but were too weak to touch it. She began to scream into the phone, into the roaring. She cried out, she cried for her mother, she felt her breath start jerking back and forth in her lungs as if it were something Arnold Friend was stabbing her with again and again with no tenderness. A noisy sorrowful wailing rose all about her and she was locked inside it the way she was locked inside this house.

After a while she could hear again. She was sitting on the floor with her wet back against the wall.

Arnold Friend was saying from the door, "That's a good girl. Put the phone back."

She kicked the phone away from her.

"No, honey. Pick it up. Put it back right."

She picked it up and put it back. The dial tone stopped.

"That's a good girl. Now, you come outside."

She was hollow with what had been fear but what was now just an emptiness. All that screaming had blasted it out of her. She sat, one leg cramped under her, and deep inside her brain was something like a pinpoint of light that kept going and would not let her relax. She thought, I'm not going to see my mother again. She thought, I'm not going to sleep in my bed again. Her bright green blouse was all wet.

Arnold Friend said, in a gentle-loud voice that was like a stage voice, "The place where you come from ain't there any more, and where you had in mind to go is cancelled out. This place you are now—inside your daddy's house—is nothing but a cardboard box I can knock down any time. You know that and always did know it. You hear me?"

She thought, I have got to think. I have got to know what to do.

"We'll go out to a nice field, out in the country here where it smells so nice and it's sunny," Arnold Friend said. "I'll have my arms tight around you so you won't need to try to get away and I'll show you what love is like, what it does. The hell with this house! It looks solid all right," he said. He ran his fingernail down the screen and the noise did not make Connie shiver, as it would have the day before. "Now, put your hand on your heart, honey. Feel that? That feels solid too but we know better. Be nice to me, be sweet like you can because what else is there for a girl like you but to be sweet and pretty and give in?—and get away before her people get back?"

She felt her pounding heart. Her hand seemed to enclose it. She thought for the first time in her life that it was nothing that was hers, that belonged to her, but just a pounding, living thing inside this body that wasn't really hers either.

"You don't want them to get hurt," Arnold Friend went on. "Now, get up, honey. Get up all by yourself."

She stood.

"Now, turn this way. That's right. Come over here to me.—Ellie, put that away, didn't I tell you? You dope. You miserable creepy dope," Arnold Friend said. His words were not angry but only part of an incantation. The incantation was kindly. "Now, come out through the kitchen to me, honey, and let's see a smile, try it, you're a brave, sweet little girl and now they're eating corn and hot dogs cooked to bursting over an outdoor fire, and they don't know one thing about you and never did and honey, you're better than them because not a one of them would have done this for you."

Connie felt the linoleum under her feet; it was cool. She brushed her hair back out of her eyes. Arnold Friend let go of the post tentatively and opened his arms for her, his elbows pointing in toward each other and his wrists limp, to show that this was an embarrassed embrace and a little mocking, he didn't want to make her self-conscious.

She put out her hand against the screen. She watched herself push the door slowly open as if she were back safe somewhere in the other doorway, watching this body and his head of long hair moving out into the sunlight where Arnold Friend waited.

"My sweet little blue-eyed girl," he said in a half-sung sigh that had nothing to do with her brown eyes but was taken up just the same by the vast sunlit reaches of the land behind him and on all sides of him—so much land that Connie had never seen before and did not recognize except to know that she was going to it.

1970

MARGARET ATWOOD

1939–

Although Margaret Atwood has explained that she grew up singing *Rule, Britannia*, drawing the Union Jack, and reading stacks of Captain Marvel and Batman comic books, she has helped disengage Canada's cultural identity from both English and American influences. Most directly, she did this by working as an editor for the House of Anansi Press, by writing what she called "a map" for the uncharted territory of Canadian literature, *Survival* (1972), and by compiling *The Oxford Book of Canadian Verse* (1982). Just as important, as if to elaborate on the significance of her thesis that the central image for Canadians is survival, Atwood has produced a number of influential volumes of poems, stories, and novels that meditate on the impediments Canadians, and often Canadian women, encounter in their efforts to stay alive.

Atwood was born and raised in Ottawa, Ontario, but her formal schooling there was frequently interrupted by extensive family trips in the northern Ontario and Quebec bush, where her father did entomological research. In the year that she graduated from the University of Toronto, she published her first book of poems, *Double Persephone* (1962). After receiving a master's degree from Radcliffe College and studying Victorian fantasy at Harvard, she took a series of positions in the English departments of several Canadian universities. Six volumes of verse appeared between 1966 and 1974, as well as two novels, both of them hailed by critics for their sometimes comic, sometimes grim analyses of the mysteries of the self when, in isolation, it confronts a fractured or distorted image of itself.

In many of her poems, Atwood is similarly concerned with the splitting up of the self as it does "tricks with mirrors," or with the "power politics" between lovers, or with the need to revise mythic stories, like those of Homer's Ulysses, in order to retell them from the silenced perspective of the female who has been seduced and abandoned. In such novels as *The Edible Woman* (1969), *Surfacing* (1972), *Lady Oracle* (1976), and *Life before Man* (1979), moreover, she presents individuals questing for personal integrity and for a more harmonious relationship with the natural world. Atwood's poetry and fiction often attempt to provide what she calls, in one book title, *Procedures for Underground* (1970), where the underground is understood as the unconscious or the other side of what has been defined as normal by a given culture. Frequently this journey into the interior offers a visionary solution to the psychosexual problems Atwood associates with modern technological society. Whether her central character is a pioneer woman or an author of Gothic romances, she seeks some form of control over an environment that is seen as alien or alienating.

A number of Atwood's characters are moving toward the conclusion of the heroine of *Surfacing*: "This above all, to refuse to be a victim." Because, in Atwood's view, Canadians have viewed themselves as victims of either English or American imperialism, and because women have perceived themselves as victims of masculine privilege, Atwood implies that cultural colonization and sexual subordination are parallel, if not identical, situations. Both the humor and the tenderness of her most recently published work indicate how writing continues to empower Atwood herself to defy colonization.

This Is a Photograph of Me

It was taken some time ago.
At first it seems to be
a smeared
print: blurred lines and grey flecks
blended with the paper;   5

then, as you scan
it, you see in the left-hand corner
a thing that is like a branch: part of a tree
(balsam or spruce) emerging
and, to the right, halfway up   10
what ought to be a gentle
slope, a small frame house.

In the background there is a lake,
and beyond that, some low hills.

(The photograph was taken   15
the day after I drowned.

I am in the lake, in the center
of the picture, just under the surface.

It is difficult to say where
precisely, or to say   20
how large or small I am:
the effect of water
on light is a distortion

but if you look long enough,
eventually   25
you will be able to see me.)

                                                                1966

The Animals in That Country

In that country the animals
have the faces of people:

the ceremonial
cats possessing the streets

the fox run   5
politely to earth, the huntsmen
standing around him, fixed
in their tapestry of manners

the bull, embroidered
with blood and given   10
an elegant death, trumpets, his name
stamped on him, heraldic brand
because

(when he rolled
on the sand, sword in his heart, the teeth   15
in his blue mouth were human)

he is really a man

even the wolves, holding resonant
conversations in their
forests thickened with legend.   20

          In this country the animals
          have the faces of
          animals.

          Their eyes
          flash once in car headlights   25
          and are gone.

Their deaths are not elegant.

They have the faces of
no-one.

                                                            1968

The Landlady

This is the lair of the landlady.

She is
a raw voice
loose in the rooms beneath me,

the continuous henyard   5
squabble going on below
thought in this house like
the bicker of blood through the head.

She is everywhere, intrusive as the smells
that bulge in under my doorsill;   10
she presides over my
meagre eating, generates
the light for eyestrain.

From her I rent my time:
she slams   15
my days like doors.
Nothing is mine

and when I dream images
of daring escapes through the snow
I find myself walking   20
always over a vast face
which is the land-
lady's, and wake up shouting.

She is a bulk, a knot
swollen in space. Though I have tried   25
to find some way around
her, my senses
are cluttered by perception
and can't see through her.

She stands there, a raucous fact   30
blocking my way:

immutable, a slab
of what is real,

solid as bacon.

1968

Procedures for Underground

(Northwest Coast)

The country beneath
the earth has a green sun
and the rivers flow backwards;

the trees and rocks are the same
as they are here, but shifted.   5
Those who live there are always hungry;

from them you can learn
wisdom and great power,
if you can descend and return safely.

You must look for tunnels, animal   10
burrows or the cave in the sea
guraded by the stone man;

when you are down you will find
those who were once your friends
but they will be changed and dangerous.   15

Resist them, be careful
never to eat their food.
Afterwards, if you live, you will be able

to see them when they prowl as winds,
as thin sounds in our village. You will   20
tell us their names, what they want, who

has made them angry by forgetting them.
For this gift, as for all gifts, you must
suffer: those from the underland

will be always with you, whispering their   25
complaints, beckoning you
back down; while among us here

you will walk wrapped in an invisible
cloak. Few will seek your help
with love, none without fear.   30

1970

[You fit into me]

you fit into me
like a hook into an eye

a fish hook
an open eye

1971

From Circle/Mud Poems[1]

People come from all over to consult me, bringing their limbs
which have unaccountably fallen off, they don't know why,
my front porch is waist deep in hands, bringing their blood
hoarded in pickle jars, bringing their fears about their hearts,
which they either can or can't hear at night. They offer me   5
their pain, hoping in return for a word, a word, any word
from those they have assaulted daily, with shovels, axes,
electric saws, the silent ones, the ones they accused of being
silent because they would not speak in the received language.

I spend my days with my head pressed to the earth, to stones,   10
to shrubs, collecting the few muted syllables left over; in the
evenings I dispense them, a letter at a time, trying to be fair,
to the clamouring suppliants, who have built elaborate staircases across the level ground so they can approach me on
their knees. Around me everything is worn down, the grass,   15
the roots, the soil, nothing is left but the bared rock.

Come away with me, he said, we will live on a desert island.
I said, I am a desert island. It was not what he had in mind.

———————

I made no choice
I decided nothing   20

1. In Homer's *Odyssey*, the wandering hero
Odysseus and his men put ashore at an island inhabited by the sorceress Circe. Using her magic
potions, she turns his men into pigs; however,
Odysseus has a substance called *moly* which re-
stores his men, and they escape. This speaker is
Circe.

One day you simply appeared in your stupid boat,
your killer's hands, your disjointed body, jagged as a shipwreck,
skinny-ribbed, blue-eyed, scorched, thirsty, the usual,
pretending to be—what? a survivor?

Those who say they want nothing   25
want everything.
It was not this greed
that offended me, it was the lies.

Nevertheless I gave you
the food you demanded for the journey   30
you said you planned; but you planned no journey
and we both knew it.

You've forgotten that,
you made the right decision.
The trees bend in the wind, you eat, you rest,   35
you think of nothing,
your mind, you say,
is like your hands, vacant:

vacant is not innocent.

_____

This story was told to me by another traveller, just passing   40
through. It took place in a foreign country, as everything
does.

When he was young he and another boy constructed a woman
out of mud. She began at the neck and ended at the knees
and elbows: they stuck to the essentials. Every sunny day   45
they would row across to the island where she lived, in the
afternoon when the sun had warmed her, and make love to
her, sinking with ecstacy into her soft moist belly, her brown
wormy flesh where small weeds had already rooted. They
would take turns, they were not jealous, she preferred them   50
both. Afterwards they would repair her, making her hips
more spacious, enlarging her breasts with their shining stone
nipples.

His love for her was perfect, he could say anything to her, into
her he spilled his entire life. She was swept away in a sudden   55
flood. He said no woman since then has equalled her.

Is this what you would like me to be, this mud woman? Is
this what I would like to be? It would be so simple.

It's the story that counts. No use telling me this isn't a story,
or not the same story. I know you've fulfilled everything   60
you promised, you love me, we sleep till noon and we spend
the rest of the day eating, the food is superb, I don't deny
that. But I worry about the future. In the story the boat
disappears one day over the horizon, just disappears, and it
doesn't say what happens then. On the island that is. It's   65
the animals I'm afraid of, they weren't part of the bargain,
in fact you didn't mention them, they may transform themselves back into men. Am I really immortal, does the sun
care, when you leave will you give me back the words? Don't
evade, don't pretend you won't leave after all: you leave in   70
the story and the story is ruthless.

1974

Spelling

My daughter plays on the floor
with plastic letters,
red, blue & hard yellow,
learning how to spell,
spelling,   5
how to make spells

and I wonder how many women
denied themselves daughters,
closed themselves in rooms,
drew the curtains   10
so they could mainline words.

A child is not a poem,
a poem is not a child.
There is no either/or.
However.   15

I return to the story
of the woman caught in the war
& in labor, her thighs tied
together by the enemy
so she could not give birth.   20

Ancestress: the burning witch,
her mouth covered by leather
to strangle words.

A word after a word
after a word is power.   25

At the point where language falls away
from the hot bones, at the point
where the rock breaks open and darkness
flows out of it like blood, at
the melting point of granite   30
when the bones know
they are hollow & the word
splits & doubles & speaks
the truth & the body
itself becomes a mouth.   35

This is a metaphor.

How do you learn to spell?
Blood, sky & the sun,
your own name first,
your first naming, your first name,   40
your first word.

1981

Rape Fantasies

The way they're going on about it in the magazines you'd think it
was just invented, and not only that but it's something terrific, like a
vaccine for cancer. They put it in capital letters on the front cover, and
inside they have these questionnaires like the ones they used to have
about whether you were a good enough wife or an endomorph or an
ectomorph,[2] remember that? with the scoring upside down on page 73,
and then these numbered do-it-yourself dealies, you know? RAPE, TEN
THINGS TO DO ABOUT IT, like it was ten new hairdos or something. I
mean, what's so new about it?

So at work they all have to talk about it because no matter what magazine you open, there it is, staring you right between the eyes, and

---

2. I.e., possessing a short and wide body structure or a tall and narrow one.

they're beginning to have it on the television, too. Personally I'd prefer a June Allyson movie[3] anytime but they don't make them any more and they don't even have them that much on the Late Show. For instance, day before yesterday, that would be Wednesday, thank god it's Friday as they say, we were sitting around in the women's lunch room—the *lunch* room, I mean you'd think you could get some peace and quiet in there—and Chrissy closes up the magazine she's been reading and says, "How about it, girls, do you have rape fantasies?"

The four of us were having our game of bridge the way we always do, and I had a bare twelve points counting the singleton with not that much of a bid in anything. So I said one club, hoping Sondra would remember about the one club convention, because the time before when I used that she thought I really meant clubs and she bid us up to three, and all I had was four little ones with nothing higher than a six, and we went down two and on top of that we were vulnerable. She is not the world's best bridge player. I mean, neither am I but there's a limit.

Darlene passed but the damage was done, Sondra's head went round like it was on ball bearings and she said, "*What* fantasies?"

"Rape fantasies," Chrissy said. She's a receptionist and she looks like one; she's pretty but cool as a cucumber, like she's been painted all over with nail polish, if you know what I mean. Varnished. "It says here all women have rape fantasies."

"For Chrissake, I'm eating an egg sandwich," I said, "and I bid one club and Darlene passed."

"You mean, like some guy jumping you in an alley or something," Sondra said. She was eating her lunch, we all eat our lunches during the game, and she bit into a piece of that celery she always brings and started to chew away on it with this thoughtful expression in her eyes and I knew we might as well pack it in as far as the game was concerned.

"Yeah, sort of like that," Chrissy said. She was blushing a little, you could see it even under her makeup.

"I don't think you should go out alone at night," Darlene said, "you put yourself in a position," and I may have been mistaken but she was looking at me. She's the oldest, she's forty-one though you wouldn't know it and neither does she, but I looked it up in the employees' file. I like to guess a person's age and then look it up to see if I'm right. I let myself have an extra pack of cigarettes if I am, though I'm trying to cut down. I figure it's harmless as long as you don't tell. I mean, not everyone has access to that file, it's more or less confidential. But it's all right if I tell you, I don't expect you'll ever meet her, though you never know, it's a small world. Anyway.

3. June Allyson portrayed smiling small-town girls in many musical-comedy films of the forties and fifties.

"For *heaven's* sake, it's only *Toronto*," Greta said. She worked in Detroit for three years and she never lets you forget it, it's like she thinks she's a war hero or something, we should all admire her just for the fact that she's still walking this earth, though she was really living in Windsor the whole time, she just worked in Detroit. Which for me doesn't really count. It's where you sleep, right?

"Well, do you?" Chrissy said. She was obviously trying to tell us about hers but she wasn't about to go first, she's cautious, that one.

"I certainly don't," Darlene said, and she wrinkled up her nose, like this, and I had to laugh. "I think it's disgusting." She's divorced, I read that in the file too, she never talks about it. It must've been years ago anyway. She got up and went over to the coffee machine and turned her back on us as though she wasn't going to have anything more to do with it.

"Well," Greta said. I could see it was going to be between her and Chrissy. They're both blondes, I don't mean that in a bitchy way but they do try to outdress each other. Greta would like to get out of Filing, she'd like to be a receptionist too so she could meet more people. You don't meet much of anyone in Filing except other people in Filing. Me, I don't mind it so much, I have outside interests.

"Well," Greta said, "I sometimes think about, you know my apartment? It's got this little balcony, I like to sit out there in the summer and I have a few plants out there. I never bother that much about locking the door to the balcony, it's one of those sliding glass ones, I'm on the eighteenth floor for heaven's sake, I've got a good view of the lake and the CN Tower and all. But I'm sitting around one night in my housecoat, watching TV with my shoes off, you know how you do, and I see this guy's feet, coming down past the window, and the next thing you know he's standing on the balcony, he's let himself down by a rope with a hook on the end of it from the floor above, that's the nineteenth, and before I can even get up off the chesterfield he's inside the apartment. He's all dressed in black with black gloves on"—I knew right away what show she got the black gloves off because I saw the same one—"and then he, well, you know."

"You know what?" Chrissy said, but Greta said, "And afterwards he tells me that he goes all over the outside of the apartment building like that, from one floor to another, with his rope and his hook . . . and then he goes out to the balcony and tosses his rope, and he climbs up it and disappears."

"Just like Tarzan," I said, but nobody laughed.

"Is that all?" Chrissy said. "Don't you ever think about, well, I think about being in the bathtub, with no clothes on . . ."

"So who takes a bath in their clothes?" I said, you have to admit it's stupid when you come to think of it, but she just went on, " . . . with lots

of bubbles, what I use is Vitabath, it's more expensive but it's so relaxing, and my hair pinned up, and the door opens and this fellow's standing there. . . ."

"How'd he get in?" Greta said.

"Oh, I don't know, through a window or something. Well, I can't
very well get out of the bathtub, the bathroom's too small and besides
he's blocking the doorway, so I just *lie* there, and he starts to very slowly
take his own clothes off, and then he gets into the bathtub with me."

"Don't you scream or anything?" said Darlene. She'd come back
with her cup of coffee, she was getting really interested. "I'd scream like
bloody murder."

"Who'd hear me?" Chrissy said. "Besides, all the articles say it's
better not to resist, that way you don't get hurt."

"Anyway you might get bubbles up your nose," I said, "from the
deep breathing," and I swear all four of them looked at me like I was in
bad taste, like I'd insulted the Virgin Mary or something. I mean, I
don't see what's wrong with a little joke now and then. Life's too short,
right?

"Listen," I said, "those aren't *rape* fantasies. I mean, you aren't getting *raped*, it's just some guy you haven't met formally who happens to
be more attractive than Derek Cummins"—he's the Assistant Manager, he wears elevator shoes or at any rate they have these thick soles
and he has this funny way of talking, we call him Derek Duck—"and
you have a good time. Rape is when they've got a knife or something
and you don't want to."

"So what about you, Estelle," Chrissy said, she was miffed because I
laughed at her fantasy, she thought I was putting her down. Sondra was
miffed too, by this time she'd finished her celery and she wanted to tell
about hers, but she hadn't got in fast enough.

"All right, let me tell you one," I said. "I'm walking down this dark
street at night and this fellow comes up and grabs my arm. Now it so
happens that I have a plastic lemon in my purse, you know how it
always says you should carry a plastic lemon in your purse? I don't really
do it, I tried it once but the darn thing leaked all over my chequebook,
but in this fantasy I have one, and I say to him, "You're intending to
rape me, right?" and he nods, so I open my purse to get the plastic
lemon, and I can't find it! My purse is full of all this junk, Kleenex and
cigarettes and my change purse and my lipstick and my driver's licence,
you know the kind of stuff; so I ask him to hold out his hands, like this,
and I pile all this junk into them and down at the bottom there's the
plastic lemon, and I can't get the top off. So I hand it to him and he's
very obliging, he twists the top off and hands it back to me, and I squirt
him in the eye."

I hope you don't think that's too vicious. Come to think of it, it is a bit mean, especially when he was so polite and all.

"*That's* your rape fantasy?" Chrissy says. "I don't believe it."

"She's a card," Darlene says, she and I are the ones that've been here the longest and she never will forget the time I got drunk at the office party and insisted I was going to dance under the table instead of on top of it, I did a sort of Cossack number[4] but then I hit my head on the bottom of the table—actually it was a desk—when I went to get up, and I knocked myself out cold. She's decided that's the mark of an original mind and she tells everyone new about it and I'm not sure that's fair. Though I did do it.

"I'm being totally honest," I say. I always am and they know it. There's no point in being anything else, is the way I look at it, and sooner or later the truth will out so you might as well not waste the time, right? "You should hear the one about the Easy-Off Oven Cleaner."

But that was the end of the lunch hour, with one bridge game shot to hell, and the next day we spent most of the time arguing over whether to start a new game or play out the hands we had left over from the day before, so Sondra never did get a chance to tell about her rape fantasy.

It started me thinking though, about my own rape fantasies. Maybe I'm abnormal or something, I mean I have fantasies about handsome strangers coming in through the window too, like Mr. Clean,[5] I wish one would, please god somebody without flat feet and big sweat marks on his shirt, and over five feet five, believe me being tall is a handicap though it's getting better, tall guys are starting to like someone whose nose reaches higher than their belly button. But if you're being totally honest you can't count those as rape fantasies. In a real rape fantasy, what you should feel is this anxiety, like when you think about your apartment building catching on fire and whether you should use the elevator or the stairs or maybe just stick your head under a wet towel, and you try to remember everything you've read about what to do but you can't decide.

For instance, I'm walking along this dark street at night and this short, ugly fellow comes up and grabs my arm, and not only is he ugly, you know, with a sort of puffy nothing face, like those fellows you have to talk to in the bank when your account's overdrawn—of course I don't mean they're all like that—but he's absolutely covered in pimples. So he gets me pinned against the wall, he's short but he's heavy, and he starts to undo himself and the zipper gets stuck. I mean, one of the most

---

4. I.e., a folk dance called the *kazatzka*, performed in a squatting position by Cossacks, a people of southern Russia.

5. A muscular bald genie featured in advertisements for Mr. Clean detergent.

significant moments in a girl's life, it's almost like getting married or having a baby or something, and he sticks the zipper.

So I say, kind of disgusted, "Oh for Chrissake," and he starts to cry. He tells me he's never been able to get anything right in his entire life, and this is the last straw, he's going to go jump off a bridge.

"Look," I say, I feel so sorry for him, in my rape fantasies I always end up feeling sorry for the guy, I mean there has to be something *wrong* with them, if it was Clint Eastwood[6] it'd be different but worse luck it never is. I was the kind of little girl who buried dead robins, know what I mean? It used to drive my mother nuts, she didn't like me touching them, because of the germs I guess. So I say, "Listen, I know how you feel. You really should do something about those pimples, if you got rid of them you'd be quite good looking, honest; then you wouldn't have to go around doing stuff like this. I had them myself once," I say, to comfort him, but in fact I did, and it ends up I give him the name of my old dermatologist, the one I had in high school, that was back in Leamington, except I used to go to St. Catharine's for the dermatologist. I'm telling you, I was really lonely when I first came here; I thought it was going to be such a big adventure and all, but it's a lot harder to meet people in a city. But I guess it's different for a guy.

Or I'm lying in bed with this terrible cold, my face is all swollen up, my eyes are red and my nose is dripping like a leaky tap, and this fellow comes in through the window and *he* has a terrible cold too, it's a new kind of flu that's been going around. So he says, "I'b goig do rabe you" —I hope you don't mind me holding my nose like this but that's the way I imagine it—and he lets out this terrific sneeze, which slows him down a bit, also I'm no object of beauty myself, you'd have to be some kind of pervert to want to rape someone with a cold like mine, it'd be like raping a bottle of LePages mucilage the way my nose is running. He's looking wildly around the room, and I realize it's because he doesn't have a piece of Kleenex! "Id's ride here," I say, and I pass him the Kleenex, god knows why he even bothered to get out of bed, you'd think if you were going to go around climbing in windows you'd wait till you were healthier, right? I mean, that takes a certain amount of energy. So I ask him why doesn't he let me fix him a NeoCitran[7] and scotch, that's what I always take, you still have the cold but you don't feel it, so I do and we end up watching the Late Show together. I mean, they aren't all sex maniacs, the rest of the time they must lead a normal life. I figure they enjoy watching the Late Show just like anybody else.

I do have a scarier one though . . . where the fellow says he's hearing angel voices that're telling him he's got to kill me, you know, you read

6. Macho star of western and crime films of the sixties, seventies, and eighties.

7. Citrus-flavored cold medicine.

about things like that all the time in the papers. In this one I'm not in the apartment where I live now, I'm back in my mother's house in Leamington and the fellow's been hiding in the cellar, he grabs my arm when I go downstairs to get a jar of jam and he's got hold of the axe too, out of the garage, that one is really scary. I mean, what do you say to a nut like that?

So I start to shake but after a minute I get control of myself and I say, is he sure the angel voices have got the right person, because I hear the same angel voices and they've been telling me for some time that I'm going to give birth to the reincarnation of St. Anne[8] who in turn has the Virgin Mary and right after that comes Jesus Christ and the end of the world, and he wouldn't want to interfere with that, would he? So he gets confused and listens some more, and then he asks for a sign and I show him my vaccination mark, you can see it's sort of an odd-shaped one, it got infected because I scratched the top off, and that does it, he apologizes and climbs out the coal chute again, which is how he got in in the first place, and I say to myself there's some advantage in having been brought up a Catholic even though I haven't been to church since they changed the service into English, it just isn't the same, you might as well be a Protestant. I must write to Mother and tell her to nail up that coal chute, it always has bothered me. Funny, I couldn't tell you at all what this man looks like but I know exactly what kind of shoes he's wearing, because that's the last I see of him, his shoes going up the coal chute, and they're the old-fashioned kind that lace up the ankles, even though he's a young fellow. That's strange, isn't it?

Let me tell you though I really sweat until I see him safely out of there and I go upstairs right away and make myself a cup of tea. I don't think about that one much. My mother always said you shouldn't dwell on unpleasant things and I generally agree with that, I mean, dwelling on them doesn't make them go away. Though not dwelling on them doesn't make them go away either, when you come to think of it.

Sometimes I have these short ones where the fellow grabs my arm but I'm really a Kung-Fu expert, can you believe it, in real life I'm sure it would just be a conk on the head and that's that, like getting your tonsils out, you'd wake up and it would be all over except for the sore places, and you'd be lucky if your neck wasn't broken or something, I could never even hit the volleyball in gym and a volleyball is fairly large, you know?—and I just go *zap* with my fingers into his eyes and that's it, he falls over, or I flip him against a wall or something. But I could never really stick my fingers in anyone's eyes, could you? It would feel like hot jello and I don't even like cold jello, just thinking about it gives me the creeps. I feel a bit guilty about that one, I mean how would you like

8. Mother of Mary, the mother of Jesus Christ.

walking around knowing someone's been blinded for life because of you?

But maybe it's different for a guy.

The most touching one I have is when the fellow grabs my arm and I say, sad and kind of dignified, "You'd be raping a corpse." That pulls him up short and I explain that I've just found out I have leukaemia and the doctors have only given me a few months to live. That's why I'm out pacing the streets alone at night, I need to think, you know, come to terms with myself. I don't really have leukaemia but in the fantasy I do, I guess I chose that particular disease because a girl in my grade four class died of it, the whole class sent her flowers when she was in the hospital. I didn't understand then that she was going to die and I wanted to have leukaemia too so I could get flowers. Kids are funny, aren't they? Well, it turns out that he has leukaemia himself, and *he* only has a few months to live, that's why he's going around raping people, he's very bitter because he's so young and his life is being taken from him before he's really lived it. So we walk along gently under the street lights, it's spring and sort of misty, and we end up going for coffee, we're happy we've found the only other person in the world who can understand what we're going through, it's almost like fate, and after a while we just sort of look at each other and our hands touch, and he comes back with me and moves into my apartment and we spend our last months together before we die, we just sort of don't wake up in the morning, though I've never decided which one of us gets to die first. If it's him I have to go on and fantasize about the funeral, if it's me I don't have to worry about that, so it just about depends on how tired I am at the time. You may not believe this but sometimes I even start crying. I cry at the ends of movies, even the ones that aren't all that sad, so I guess it's the same thing. My mother's like that too.

The funny thing about these fantasies is that the man is always someone I don't know, and the statistics in the magazines, well, most of them anyway, they say it's often someone you do know, at least a little bit, like your boss or something—I mean, it wouldn't be *my* boss, he's over sixty and I'm sure he couldn't rape his way out of a paper bag, poor old thing, but it might be someone like Derek Duck, in his elevator shoes, perish the thought—or someone you just met, who invites you up for a drink, it's getting so you can hardly be sociable any more, and how are you supposed to meet people if you can't trust them even that basic amount? You can't spend your whole life in the Filing Department or cooped up in your own apartment with all the doors and windows locked and the shades down. I'm not what you would call a drinker but I like to go out now and then for a drink or two in a nice place, even if I am by myself, I'm with Women's Lib on that even though I can't agree with a lot of the other things they say. Like here for instance, the waiters all know me and if anyone, you know, bothers me . . . I don't know why I'm telling you all this, except I think it helps you get to know a person, especially at first, hearing some of the things they think about. At work they call me the office worry wart, but it isn't so much like worrying, it's more like figuring out what you should do in an emergency, like I said before.

Anyway, another thing about it is that there's a lot of conversation, in fact I spend most of my time, in the fantasy that is, wondering what I'm going to say and what he's going to say, I think it would be better if you could get a conversation going. Like, how could a fellow do that to a person he's just had a long conversation with, once you let them know you're human, you have a life too, I don't see how they could go ahead with it, right? I mean, I know it happens but I just don't understand it, that's the part I really don't understand.

1977

TONI CADE BAMBARA

1939–

As if to explain why she later took the name Bambara from a signature on a sketchbook she found in her great-grandmother's trunk, Toni Cade dedicated her anthology *The Black Woman* (1970) "to the uptown mammas who nudged me to just set it down in print so it gets to be a habit to write letters to each other, so maybe that way we don't keep treadmilling the same ole ground." In an essay within that volume, moreover, Bambara identified the "old ground" as racism and sexism, urging black women to reject ready-made definitions of manhood and womanhood "until realistic definitions emerge through a commitment to Blackhood."

Toni Cade grew up in the impoverished districts of Harlem and Bedford-Stuyvestant, New York. After receiving a B.A. from Queens College in 1959 and an M.A. from what she called Harlem University (the City College of New York) in 1963, she worked as a social investigator with the New York State Department of Welfare and as a youth counselor, community organizer, and free-lance writer. *Tales and Stories for Black Folks* (1971), *Gorilla, My Love* (1972), and *The Sea Birds Are Still Alive* (1977) contain a number of stories that have recently received critical acclaim for their implicit critique of stereotypes about black women and for their explicit analysis of the generational struggle between black parents and their children.

My Man Bovanne

Blind people got a hummin jones[1] if you notice. Which is under-standable completely once you been around one and notice what no eyes will force you into to see people, and you get past the first time, which seems to come out of nowhere, and it's like you in church again with fat-chest ladies and old gents gruntin a hum low in the throat to whatever the preacher be saying. Shakey Bee bottom lip all swole up with Sweet Peach[2] and me explainin how come the sweet-potato bread was a dollar-quarter this time stead of dollar regular and he say uh hunh he understand, then he break into this *thizzin* kind of hum which is quiet, but fiercesome just the same, if you ain't ready for it. Which I wasn't. But I got used to it and the onliest time I had to say somethin bout it was when he was playin checkers on the stoop one time and he commemt to hummin quite churchy seem to me. So I says, "Look here Shakey Bee, I can't beat you and Jesus too." He stop.

So that's how come I asked My Man Bovanne to dance. He ain't my man mind you, just a nice ole gent from the block that we all know cause he fixes things and the kids like him. Or used to fore Black Power got hold their minds and mess em around till they can't be civil to ole folks. So we at this benefit for my niece's cousin who's runnin for somethin with this Black party somethin or other behind her. And I press up close to dance with Bovanne who blind and I'm hummin and he hum-min, chest to chest like talkin. Not jammin my breasts into the man. Wasn't bout tits. Was bout vibrations. And he dug it and asked me what color dress I had on and how my hair was fixed and how I was doin without a man, not nosy but nice-like, and who was at this affair and was the canapés dainty-stingy or healthy enough to get hold of proper. Comfy and cheery is what I'm tryin to get across. Touch talkin like the heel of the hand on the tambourine or on a drum.

But right away Joe Lee come up on us and frown for dancin so close to the man. My own son who knows what kind of warm I am about; and don't grown men all call me long distance and in the middle of the night for a little Mama comfort? But he frown. Which ain't right since Bo-vanne can't see and defend himself. Just a nice old who fixes toasters and busted irons and bicycles and things and changes the lock on my door when my men friends get messy. Nice man. Which is not why they invited him. Grass roots you see. Me and Sister Taylor and the woman who does heads at Mamies and the man from the barber shop, we all there on account of we grass roots. And I ain't never been souther than Brooklyn Battery and no more country than the window box on my fire escape. And just yesterday my kids tellin me to take them

---

1. A compelling need.   2. A brand of dipping snuff.

countrified rags off my head and be cool. And now can't get Black enough to suit 'em. So everybody passin sayin My Man Bovanne. Big deal, keep steppin and don't even stop a minute to get the man a drink or one of them cute sandwiches or tell him what's goin on. And him standin there with a smile ready case someone do speak he want to be ready. So that's how come I pull him on the dance floor and we dance squeezin past the tables and chairs and all them coats and people standin round up in each other face talkin bout this and that but got no use for this blind man who mostly fixed skates and skooters for all these folks when they were just kids. So I'm pressed up close and we touch talkin with the hum. And here come my daughter cuttin her eye[3] at me like she do when she tell me about my "apolitical" self like I got hoof and mouf disease and there ain't no hope at all. And I don't pay her no mind and just look up in Bovanne shadow face and tell him his stomach like a drum and he laugh. Laugh real loud. And here come my youngest, Task, with a tap on my elbow like he the third grade monitor and I'm cuttin up on the line to assembly.

"I was just talkin on the drums," I explained when they hauled me into the kitchen. I figured drums was my best defense. They can get ready for drums what with all this heritage business. And Bovanne stomach just like that drum Task give me when he come back from Africa. You just touch it and it hum thizzm, thizzm. So I stuck to the drum story. "Just drummin that's all."

"Mama, what are you talkin about?"

"She had too much to drink," say Elo to Task cause she don't hardly say nuthin to me direct no more since that ugly argument about my wigs.

"Look here Mama," say Task, the gentle one. "We just trying to pull your coat. You were makin a spectacle of yourself out there dancing like that."

"Dancin like what?"

Task run a hand over his left ear like his father for the world and his father before that.

"Like a bitch in heat," say Elo.

"Well uhh, I was goin to say like one of them sex-starved ladies gettin on in years and not too discriminating. Know what I mean?"

I don't answer cause I'll cry. Terrible thing when your own children talk to you like that. Pullin me out the party and hustlin me into some stranger's kitchen in the back of a bar just like the damn police. And ain't like I'm old old. I can still wear me some sleeveless dresses without the meat hangin off my arm. And I keep up with some thangs through

3. Giving a sharp look.

my kids. Who ain't kids no more. To hear them tell it. So I don't say
nuthin.

"Dancin with that tom," say Elo to Joe Lee, who leanin on the folks'
freezer. "His feet can smell a cracker a mile away and go into their
shuffle number post haste. And them eyes. He could be a little considerate and put on some shades. Who wants to look into them blown-out
fuses that—"

"Is this what they call the generation gap?" I say.

"Generation gap," spits Elo, like I suggested castor oil and fricassee
possum in the milk-shakes or somethin. "That's a white concept for a
white phenomenon. There's no generation gap among Black people.
We are a col—"

"Yeh, well never mind," says Joe Lee. "The point is Mama . . .
well, it's pride. You embarrass yourself and us too dancin like that."

"I wasn't shame." Then nobody say nuthin. Them standin there in
they pretty clothes with drinks in they hands and gangin up on me, and
me in the third-degree chair and nary a olive to my name. Felt just like
the police got hold to me.

"First of all," Task say, holdin up his hand and tickin off the offenses,
"the dress. Now that dress is too short, Mama, and too low-cut for a
woman your age. And Tamu's going to make a speech tonight to kick
off the campaign and will be introducin you and expecting you to organize the council of elders—"

"Me? Didn nobody ask me nuthin. You mean Nisi? She change her
name?"

"Well, Norton was supposed to tell you about it. Nisi wants to introduce you and then encourage the older folks to form a Council of the
Elders to act as an advisory—"

"And you going to be standing there with your boobs out and that
wig on your head and that hem up to your ass. And people'll say, 'Ain't
that the horny bitch that was grindin with the blind dude?' "

"Elo, be cool a minute," say Task, gettin to the next finger. "And
then there's the drinkin. Mama, you know you can't drink cause next
thing you know you be laughin loud and carryin on," and he grab another finger for the loudness. "And then there's the dancin. You been
tattooed on the man for four records straight and slow draggin even on
the fast numbers. How you think that look for a woman your age?"

"What's my age?"

"What?"

"I'm axin you all a simple question. You keep talkin bout what's
proper for a woman my age. How old am I anyhow?" And Joe Lee
slams his eyes shut and squinches up his face to figure. And Task run a
hand over his ear and stare into his glass like the ice cubes goin calculate

for him. And Elo just starin at the top of my head like she goin rip the wig off any minute now.

"Is your hair braided up under that thing? If so, why don't you take it off? You always did do a neat cornroll."[4]

"Uh huh," cause I'm thinkin how she couldn't undo her hair fast enough talking bout cornroll so countrified. None of which was the subject. "How old, I say?"

"Sixtee-one or—"

"You a damn lie Joe Lee Peoples."

"And that's another thing," say Task on the fingers.

"You know what you all can kiss," I say, gettin up and brushin the wrinkles out my lap.

"Oh, Mama," Elo say, puttin a hand on my shoulder like she hasn't done since she left home and the hand landin light and not sure it supposed to be there. Which hurt me to my heart. Cause this was the child in our happiness fore Mr. Peoples die. And I carried that child strapped to my chest till she was nearly two. We was close is what I'm tryin to tell you. Cause it was more me in the child than the others. And even after Task it was the girlchild I covered in the night and wept over for no reason at all less it was she was a chub-chub like me and not very pretty, but a warm child. And how did things get to this, that she can't put a sure hand on me and say Mama we love you and care about you and you entitled to enjoy yourself cause you a good woman?

"And then there's Reverend Trent," say Task, glancin from left to right like they hatchin a plot and just now lettin me in on it. "You were suppose to be talking with him tonight, Mama, about giving us his basement for campaign headquarters and—"

"Didn nobody tell me nuthin. If grass roots mean you kept in the dark I can't use it. I really can't. And Reven Trent a fool anyway the way he tore into the widow man up there on Edgecomb cause he wouldn't take in three of them foster children and the woman not even comfy in the ground yet and the man's mind messed up and—"

"Look here," say Task. "What we need is a family conference so we can get all this stuff cleared up and laid out on the table. In the meantime I think we better get back into the other room and tend to business. And in the meantime, Mama, see if you can't get to Reverend Trent and—"

"You want me to belly rub with the Reven, that it?"

"Oh damn," Elo say and go through the swingin door.

"We'll talk about all this at dinner. How's tomorrow night, Joe Lee?" While Joe Lee being self-important I'm wonderin who's doin

---

4. Cornrow, a hairstyle in which all the hair is interwoven from the scalp into small braids.

the cookin and how come no body ax me if I'm free and do I get a corsage and things like that. Then Joe nod that it's O.K. and he go through
the swingin door and just a little hubbub come through from the other
room. Then Task smile his smile, lookin just like his daddy, and he
leave. And it just me and this stranger's kitchen, which was a mess I
wouldn't never let my kitchen look like. Poison you just to look at the
pots. Then the door swing the other way and it's My Man Bovanne
standin there sayin Miss Hazel but lookin at the deep fry and then at the
steam table, and most surprised when I come up on him from the other
direction and take him on out of there. Pass the folks pushin up towards
the stage where Nisi and some other people settin and ready to talk, and
folks gettin to the last of the sandwiches and the booze fore they settle
down in one spot and listen serious. And I'm thinkin bout tellin Bovanne what a lovely long dress Nisi got on and the earrings and her hair
piled up in a cone and the people bout to hear how we all gettin
screwed and gotta form our own party and everybody there listenin and
lookin. But instead I just haul the man on out of there, and Joe Lee and
his wife look at me like I'm terrible, but they ain't said boo to the man
yet. Cause he blind and old and don't nobody there need him since they
grown up and don't need they skates fixed no more.

"Where we goin, Miss Hazel?" Him knowin all the time.

"First we gonna buy you some dark sunglasses. Then you comin
with me to the supermarket so I can pick up tomorrow's dinner, which
is goin to be a grand thing proper and you invited. Then we goin to my
house."

"That be fine. I surely would like to rest my feet." Bein cute, but you
got to let men play out they little show, blind or not. So he chat on bout
how tired he is and how he appreciate me takin him in hand this way.
And I'm thinkin I'll have him change the lock on my door first thing.
Then I'll give the man a nice warm bath with jasmine leaves in the
water and a little Epsom salt on the sponge to do his back. And then a
good rubdown with rose water and olive oil. Then a cup of lemon tea
with a taste in it. And a little talcum, some of that fancy stuff Nisi
mother sent over last Christmas. And then a massage, a good face massage round the forehead which is the worryin part. Cause you gots to
take care of the older folks. And let them know they still needed to run
the mimeo machine and keep the spark plugs clean and fix the mail-
boxes for folks who might help us get the breakfast program goin, and
the school for the little kids and the campaign and all. Cause old folks in
the nation. That what Nisi was sayin and I mean to do my part.

"I imagine you are a very pretty woman, Miss Hazel."

"I surely am," I say just like the hussy my daughter always say I was.

MARGARET DRABBLE

1939–

Explaining that her work is mainly concerned with "privilege, justice, and salvation," Margaret Drabble has added that none of her books is about feminism "because my belief in the necessity for justice for women . . . is so basic that I never think of using it as a subject. It is part of a whole." From her first novel, *A Summer Bird-Cage* (1962), to her more recent *The Middle Ground* (1980), Drabble has analyzed both the privileges and the privations of intelligent and well-educated women who seek justice or salvation in their work, in their domestic lives, or, most difficult of all to obtain, in the integration of these two.

The second of four children, Drabble was born into a well-educated family: her mother was a schoolteacher, her father a judge, and her sister, A. S. Byatt, became a novelist and a scholar. Educated at the Mount School, York, and at Newnham College, Cambridge, where she graduated with honors in 1960, Drabble initially pursued an acting career. After joining the Royal Shakespeare Company with her husband, the actor Clive Swift, she began composing fiction when she was pregnant and sitting backstage as an understudy. Early novels, which were best sellers in England, won her a wide audience, and soon she received a number of prestigious awards, including the Rhys Memorial Prize (1966), the Black Memorial Prize (1968), and the E. M. Forster Award (1973). The mother of two sons and a daughter, Drabble has also pursued her scholarly interest in English literature by writing critical works on William Wordsworth, on Arnold Bennett, and on Virginia Woolf; in addition, she has edited an anthology of criticism on Thomas Hardy as well as a collection of Jane Austen's unfinished works. Her literary criticism illuminates her fiction, for her novels seek to extend the great tradition of nineteenth-century English fiction.

"I'd rather be at the end of a dying tradition, which I admire, than at the beginning of a tradition I deplore," Drabble has declared, thereby explaining her refusal to write experimental fiction and her commitment to realism. Yet, as a writer who is also a mother, Drabble has approached realistic conventions from a new perspective by dealing explicitly with the ways in which women come to terms with the demands of a career, their desire for erotic attachments, and their involvement with their children. Her heroines are literary scholars (as in *The Millstone*, 1965), poets (*The Waterfall*, 1969), archeologists (*The Realms of Gold*, 1975), and journalists (*The Middle Ground*), all of whom try to integrate the detachment their professions often require with the passion and compassion they experience as lovers, wives, and mothers. Frequently, Drabble looks back on her literary matrilineage to explain why her female characters deal fatalistically with the limits of traditional roles. The heroine of *The Waterfall*, for example, feels haunted by the ghosts of Jane Austen, Charlotte Brontë, and George Eliot. Brooding over "the sexual doom of womanhood, its sad inheritance," she—like the main character in *A Voyage to Cythera* and like Drabble herself—realizes that she cannot reject but must instead revise conventional fictions of femininity in order to begin the process that the critic Carolyn Heilbrun has called "reinventing womanhood."

A Voyage to Cythera[1]

> Beloved,
> lost to begin with, never greeted,
> I do not know what tones most please you.
> No more when the future's wave hangs poised is it you
> I try to discern there. All the greatest
> images in me, far-off experienced landscape,
> towers and towns and bridges and un-suspected
> turns of the way,
> and the power of those lands once intertwined
> with the life of the gods:
> mount up within me to mean
> you, who forever elude.
>
> Oh, you are the garden. . . .
> —Rainer Maria Rilke[2]

There are some people who cannot get onto a train without imagining that they are about to voyage into the significant unknown; as though the notion of movement were inseparably connected with the notion of discovery, as though each displacement of the body were a displacement of the soul. Helen was so much this way, and with so little lasting justification, that she was continually surprising herself by the intensity of her expectation; she could get excited by the prospect of any journey longer than 30 miles, and the thought of travel to the Continent was enough to reduce her to a state of feverish anticipation. The mere mention of the names of certain places would make her tremble, and she was addicted to railway stations, air terminals, ports, motorways, travel brochures, and all other points and emblems of departure. A phrase in a novel could make her feel weak with desire, and when once at the Gare de l'Est in Paris she saw a train with Budapest written on it, she felt her skin tighten and her hair stand on end. Her most erotic dreams were not of men but of places; she would dream of piazzas and marble fountains, of mountains and terraces with great lumps of baroque statuary, of great buildings abandoned in green fields, and she would wake from these dreams cold with the sweat of fading passion. There was a certain angle of road that never failed to affect her, whenever she approached it: a rising angle, with a bare empty curve breasting

1. Island home of Aphrodite, Greek goddess of love.

2. From an untitled poem by the German poet (1875–1926).

infinity, the blue-sky space of infinity. She always felt that the sea might lie beyond such rising nothingness, and sometimes it was the sea, but more often it was the Caledonian Market or a row of Hampstead houses; though whatever it was was somehow irrelevant, for it was that tense moment of expectation before revelation that she so much cherished.

Once she talked of this preoccupation of hers to a much-traveled old man, and he said that she felt this way because whenever she went to a new place she hoped to fall in love. He had been the same, he said; restless, expectant; and she knew that he was telling the truth, for his life illustrated his explanation. "When I was young," he said, "I thought there was a woman waiting for me in every railway compartment, on every airplane, in every hotel. How can one not think this? One thinks the plane will crash, and that one will die, and that one must die in the arms of the woman in the next seat. Isn't that so?"

And she had, in a way, thought that it was so, though the truth was that she herself would never fall in love in any of these temporary places, for she could not speak to strangers. Though that in itself proved nothing, for she supposed that nevertheless she might one day do so, and that it might be for this one moment of sudden communication that she so persistently sought. People spoke to her, from time to time, but always the wrong people, always the motherly women and the fatherly men and the dull irrepressible youths. Her own kind did not speak to her, nor she to them. She traveled once overnight from Milan, alone in a compartment with a girl who was reading the same book she herself was reading; a book both of them might have been proud to acknowledge and not a word did they exchange. Another time, in a crowded train from Edinburgh, she sat opposite a woman who started to weep as the train left the station; she wept silently and effortlessly for hours, great tears rolling down her white cheeks into the neck of her emerald-green sweater, and at York Helen offered her a cigarette, and she declined it, and ceased weeping. On another occasion a man kissed her in a corridor as they drew into Oxford; she liked him, he was a lovely man, but he was drunk and she turned away her face and turned up the collar of her coat.

And yet despite these wasted opportunities she continued to expect. Truly, she thought to herself, as she got onto the London train at Reading Station late one cold night, truly, it is a proof of madness that the prospect of this journey should not appall. It is cold, the train is half an hour late, I am hungry; this is the kind of situation about which I hear my friends most tirelessly and tiresomely complain. And yet I am looking forward to it. I shall sit here in the dark and the cold, with nothing to watch but the reflection of my own face in the cold pane, and I shall not care. As soon as the train moves, I shall sit back, and feel it move with me, and feel that I am moving, although I know quite well that all I am doing is going back home again to an empty flat. There will be rain and steam on the glass of this window by my face, and I shall look at it, and that will be all. What a hardened case I am, that such dull mileage should recall those other landscapes, those snowy precipices, those sunny plains, those fields of corn, those gritty swaying breakfasts in the pale light of transient Switzerland or angel-watched Marseilles. I am a child, I like to rock and dream, I dream as if I were in a cradle.

And she shut her eyes, waiting for the whistle and the metallic connections of machinery; so with her eyes shut she did not see the man come into the compartment, and could never know for certain whether he had seen her, whether he had joined her because he had wanted to join her. All she knew was that when she opened her eyes, aware of the intrusion, aware of the draft from the opened door, he was already there, putting his overcoat up on the rack, arranging his books and papers on the seat next to him, settling himself in the empty compartment as far away from her as he could, on the corridor side, diagonally opposite, where she could not fail to watch him. She turned her fur collar up defensively against her face, and arranged her legs more tidily together, and opened her book upon her knee, disclaiming all threat of human contact, coldly repelling any acknowledgment of her presence, and all the time she watched him discreetly through her half-shut eyes. Because the truth was that not since she was 17, more years ago than she cared to think, had she sat on a train so near to such a man. When she was 17 she had sat in a compartment with an actor, on the late night train to Brighton, and he had talked to her all the way, and amused her by imitating Laurence Olivier[3] for her and other famous men whom she did not recognize and when they had parted on the station he had kissed her soft and girlish and impressionable cheek, and murmured, "Bless you, bless you," as though he had a right to bless. She had subsequently followed his unremarkable career, catching sight of his name in the *Radio Times*, admiring him once on the television, glimpsing him as he passed on the cinema screen; she felt quietly possessive about him, quietly amused by her sense of intimacy with one who must so long ago have forgotten her, and who would hardly now recognize her from what she then had been. Sometimes she wondered idly whether her preoccupation with journeys might not date from this experience; but chronologically this was not so, for her preoccupation had long preceded it. She had been this way since childhood, when she had shrunk and trembled at the sight of the huge pistons, when she had

---

3. Famous British actor.

stopped her ears in delighted terror as she heard the roar of the approaching seaside train.

This man, this night, did not look as though he wished to amuse her with imitations of Laurence Olivier. He looked preoccupied. In fact, the more she watched him, the more she realized that he was almost grotesquely preoccupied. He was restless; he could not sit still: he kept picking up one book from his pile, then another, then turning over the pages of his *New Statesman*, then staring out into the corridor and onto the dark platform. At first she thought that he might be waiting for someone to come, half-expecting somebody to join him, but she decided that this was not so, for she could perceive no augmenting of his anxiety as the time drew on, no sudden start when the loud-speaker apologized for the delay and said that the train would leave in two minutes; nor did his nervousness seem to be directed toward the door and the platform, as it would have been had he been waiting. She recalled that she herself had once developed a dreadful pain in the neck from sitting with her neck to the window through which she knew that she might glimpse the first sign of a long-awaited arrival. But this man's nervousness was as it were diffused, rather than directed; it attached itself to nothing and to everything. She could not take her eyes off him, and not only because of the nakedness of his condition, which in another might have appeared merely ludicrous; indeed, embarrassment would have turned away her eyes, had it not been for the extreme elegance of his gestures, and the lovely angles into which each struggle against immobility brought him. There was the way he had of clutching his eyebrows with one wide-spanned long nicotine-fingered hand that filled her with an intense delight; the hand covered the eyes, bringing to him no doubt an illusion of concealment, but she could see beneath it the anxious movement of the lips, trembling with some expression that she could not catch, with speech or smiling or perhaps with a sigh. And as he made this gesture, each time, he tossed his head slightly backward, and then again forward, so that his long hair fell tenderly over his fingers. It was the color that she had always liked, but she had never before seen it adorning such vexed, haggard, and experienced features: for it was a dark gold, the color of health and innocence. It was a dark golden yellow, and it was streaked with gray. It was soft hair, and it fell gently.

When the train moved off, he flung himself back into his corner, and shut his eyes, with an appearance of resolution, as though his own restlessness had finally begun to irritate him: as though he had decided to sit still. Helen looked out of the window by her face, into the lights and darkness of the disappearing town. In one piece of glass she could see the reflection of his face, and she watched it, quite confidently aware that he would not be able to keep his eyes shut, and after a few minutes he was leaning forward in his seat once more, his elbows on his knees, staring at the ground. Then, even as she watched, she saw a thought strike him: she saw the conception of the idea, she saw him reach into his pocket and take out a pack of cigarettes and a box of matches, and abstract a cigarette, and light it, all with the dreamy movements of a habitual smoker, and yet with a kind of surprise, for the truth was, as she could so clearly see, that he had even in his abstraction forgotten the possibility of such a trivial solace. As he drew on the cigarette she could see his relief, his gratitude toward his own recollection. The smoke consoled him, and she could feel in her the nature of the consolation: for she herself, when tormented by love, had found comfort in the repetition of small and necessary acts, in washing cups and emptying bins and fastening her stockings and remembering that it was time to have a meal. It seemed clear to her that it was love that was tormenting him: she knew those painful symptoms of disease.

And indeed, ten minutes later, when the ash of his last activity lay scattered all over the floor and all over his trousers, he stood up and got a packet of letters out of his overcoat pocket, and began to read them. He could not more clearly have indicated his malady if he had turned to her and told her what was in his mind. She watched the reflection of his face as he read, ashamed now to watch him directly, though she knew that he could not know that she so keenly watched him, that she was so expert in the intimate language of his state. She felt that she could tell everything from the way he handled those letters: he was still rapt in the first five minutes of love, that brief and indefinite breathless pause before familiarity, affection, disillusion, rot, decay. The number of letters in his hands supported her divination, as well as the quality of his attention; there were five of them, only five, and the paper of them was new, although they were crumbling wearily at the folds from overuse. She felt such pangs, in his presence, of she knew not what: of envy, of regret, of desire. At his age, with those graying strands and those profound wrinkles, he must surely know the folly of his obsession, and the inevitable tragic close before him; and she found such a willful confrontation of pain almost unbearably moving. She herself, enduring daily the painful death of such an attitude, the chilly destination of such deliberately romantic embarkations, could hardly prevent the tears from rising to her eyes; and in fact, they rose, warm in the cold skin of her lids, making her nose prick and her eyes ache, yet warm, coming from within her, and chilling only at the touch of the outside air. Absurd, she said to herself, absurd: absurd to weep. His image turned into a blur, and it was like the image of time itself, human, lovely, perishing, intent.

When he had read and reread his letters, he stood up again, and got a pen out of his coat pocket, and tore a piece of paper off a block of typing paper, and started to write. He wrote slowly, after the first three words, hesitantly, as though what he was saying was of no interest, as though all the interest lay in the way of saying it. She wondered what he was, who he was, what his woman was, and jealously whether she were worth such care. He took a quarter of an hour to write his letter, and when he had finished it he had covered only half a page. She wondered whether he would have an envelope, and saw that he had; it was a brown business envelope. He folded his letter up and put it in the envelope, and then sealed it up. She waited for him to write the address, but he did not write the address: he sat there looking down at the small brown oblong, and as he looked at it she became in some indefinable way aware that he had become aware of her own presence, that he was at last considering her, in some significant way. Later, she wondered how this shadowy and delicate intimation could ever have reached her—for reach her it did, and she was one of those who believe that no intimations are too delicate to exist—and she concluded that it could only have been a sudden stillness on his part, a sudden fading of restlessness, as he returned from whatever other place he had been in to contemplate her in her proximity. She felt his attention: she endured it, for five minutes at least, before he spoke.

She was pretending to read when he spoke to her. He said to her, "I wonder, I wonder if you would do something for me?" and she looked up and met his eyes, and found that he was smiling at her with a most peculiar mixture of diffidence and vanity: he was truly nervous at the prospect of speaking to her, and those five silent minutes were a measure of his nervousness, and yet at the same time he had taken the measure of her curiosity and helpless attraction: she knew that he knew that she would like to be addressed. And his tone enchanted her, for it was her own tone: a tone of cool, anxious, irresistible appeal. She knew that he too did not speak often to strangers.

"It depends what it is," she said, smiling back at him with his own smile.

"It's a very simple thing," he said, "not at all incriminating. Or at least, not for you."

"It would be, then, for you?" she said.

"Of course it would," he said. "That's why I'm making the effort of asking you to do it."

"What is it?" she said.

"I wondered if you would address this envelope for me," he said.

"Well, yes," she said. "I don't see any harm in that. I'd do that for you."

"I thought you would do it," he said. "If I hadn't thought that you would, I wouldn't have asked you. I wouldn't have liked it if you had said no."

"I might ask you what it was about me that made you think I would say yes," she said, "but such a question might embarrass you."

"Oh," he said, "oh, no," rising to his feet and crossing to her with the envelope, "oh, no, I don't mind answering, it was because of that book you're reading, and the kind of shoes you're wearing, and the way your hair is. I liked that book when I read it."

And then he sat down by her, and handed her the envelope, and said, "Look, I'll write it down for you and you can copy it. It's hard to hear when people dictate things, isn't it?"

And he wrote the name and address on another piece of his block of paper. He wrote:

> Mrs. H. Smithson,
> 24 Victoria Place,
> London N.W. 1.

And Helen dutifully copied it out, on the brown envelope, then handed it back to him.

"I hope," she said, "that my handwriting is sufficiently unlike yours."

"I was just thinking," he said, "that after all it's rather similar. But dissimilar enough."

Then he said no more, but he remained sitting by her. She would in a way have preferred him to move, because where he now was she could not really see him, either overtly or covertly. And she had nothing to say to him: for she could hardly have said, I was right about you, I guessed right. He said nothing to her, for a while: he got a wallet from his pocket, and took out a sheet of fourpenny stamps, and tore one off, licked it, and stuck it on. She liked watching his hands, and the way they moved. Then, still holding the letter, he said to her, "Where do you live?"

She must have recoiled slightly from the question, because immediately he followed it up with, "Only, I was meaning, from the point of view of postmarks."

"Oh," she said. "I see. Yes. I live in S.W.7. You want me to post it, do you?"

"Would you mind posting it?" he asked.

"No, I would post it for you," she said.

"You take my point very quickly," he said, then, with some difficulty, looking downward and away from her, hardly able to bring himself to thank her more formally.

"I've had to make such points before myself," she said.

"I thought, somehow, that you would not mind about such things," he said.

"You wouldn't have asked me if you'd thought I minded. Tell me, do you really trust me to remember to post it?"

"Of course I do," he said. "One wouldn't not post a stranger's letter."

And this was so exactly the truth that it silenced her, and they said no more to each other until the train drew into Paddington: and as they walked together off the platform, he said, "Thank you, and good-bye."

And she said, "Goodbye," and she carried the letter in her hand all the way home, and dropped it into the letterbox on her block. Then she went down the basement steps to her dark flat, and she knew that the name and the address, written there in her own writing, so strangely, were imprinted upon her memory forever.

And indeed, over the next month, she sometimes fancied that she thought of little else. She knew that this was not the truth, that it was merely a fancy, because of course she did think of other things; of her job, of her friends, of her mother, of what to buy for supper, of whether she wanted to go to the cinema on Wednesday night. But she did not think of these other things in the mad, romantic, obsessive way that she thought of Mrs. H. Smithson, and the nameless man, and the whole curious, affecting incident: in a sense she resented the incident, because it did so much to vindicate her own crazy expectancy, her foolish faith in revelation. She knew, in her better, saner self, that such faith was foolish, and she suspected that such partial hints of its validity were a delusion, a temptation, and that if she heeded them she would be disabled forever, and disqualified from real life, as Odysseus would have been by the Sirens.[4] And yet at the same time she knew, in her other self, that it was that man she was thinking about, however unreasonably. She looked for him as she walked along the streets of London, and she could not convince herself that it was not for him that she was looking. She speculated about the identity and appearance of Mrs. Smithson, and supplied her endlessly with Christian names, until she remembered that the H. might well have stood for her husband's name, not hers. She speculated about the deceived husband. Although most of her own friends were married and had children, she still found it hard to acknowledge that Mrs. Smithson might well be a woman of her own generation, for the prefix *Mrs.* invariably supplied her with a material image, the image of her own mother: and she would realize from time to time, with a start, that the women that she thought of as mothers were in fact grandmothers, and that the young girls she saw pushing prams on Saturday mornings and quarreling with vigorous toddlers on buses were not in fact elder sisters but mothers. Mrs. Smithson, Mrs. Smithson. She could not give form to Mrs. Smithson.

---

4. On his voyage in the *Odyssey*, the Greek hero Odysseus stops the ears of his crew with wax, and has himself tied to the mast, so that they will not be tempted to destruction by the enchantment of the Sirens' singing.

It was in the week before Christmas that she decided to go and have a look at Mrs. Smithson. The idea occurred to her at lunchtime one day, in the middle of a lunchtime business Christmas party. She stood there, drinking too much and not getting enough to eat, defeated as ever by the problems of buffet technique, and as she listened to a very nice man whom she had known and liked for several years describe to her the felicities of his new central heating, she suddenly decided to go and look at Mrs. Smithson. After all, she said to herself, what could be more harmless, what more undetectable? All I need to do is to knock on her door and ask, say, for Alice. And then I would know. I don't know what I would know, but I would know it. And she smiled at the man, and allowed her glass to be once more filled, and then told him politely all about some other friends of hers whose central heating had entirely ruined all their antique furniture, and split all the antique paneling of their rather priceless house. And as she talked, she was already in her heart on her way to Mrs. Smithson's, already surrendering to the lure of that fraught, romantic, painful world, which seemed to call her, to call her continually from the endurable sorrows of daily existence to some possible other country of the passions, a country where she felt she would recognize, though strange to it, the scenery and landmarks. She thought often of this place, as of some place perpetually existing, and yet concealed: and she could describe it to herself only in terms of myth or allegory, unsatisfactory terms, she felt, and perniciously implanted in her by her classical education. It was a place other than the real world, or what she felt to be the real world, and it was both more beautiful and more valid, though valid in itself only: and it could be entered not at will, but intermittently, by accident, and yet always with some sense of temptation and surrender. Some people, she could see, passed most of their lives in its confines, and governed by its laws only, like that old man, himself a poet, who had first defined for her the nature of her expectations. There were enough of such people in the world to keep alive before her the possibility of a permanent, irreversible entry through those mysteriously inscribed and classic gates: a poet, a drunken Frenchman, a girl she had known who said one day: "I will go to Bagdad," and went. They crossed her path, these people, or their names came to her, garlanded with wreaths of that unfamiliar foliage: Yves was seen in Marseilles carrying a lobster, Esther was seen in a bookshop in New York wearing a fur coat and with diamonds in her hair, Esther was in Marrakesh, living in one room with an Arab. Yves had gone to Ireland and started a lobster farm. Oh, messages from a foreign country, oh, disquieting glimpses of brightness. Helen gulped down the remains of her fourth glass of wine, and looked at her watch, which said that it was five past three; and said to the central-heating man that she must go.

She walked to Victoria Place, pausing dazed at traffic lights, stumbling at each irregularity of the pavement, running her hand idly along grimy railings. It was cold, but she could not feel the cold: her face was burning. She knew her way because she had looked Victoria Place up a month ago, the day after she had posted the letter, in her A to Z Guide to London: she remembered the moment when she had done so, because she had pretended to herself that she was doing no such thing, and her mind had not known what her hands and eyes were doing. But her mind now remembered what it had then refused to acknowledge, and she took herself there as though entranced, the trance persisting long after the effects of walking had dispelled the effects of so much drink on so empty a stomach. I must be mad, she said to herself more than once: I must be mad. And at the very end of the journey she began, very slightly, to lose her nerve: she thought that she would not dare to knock upon the door, she thought that perhaps after all only insignificant disaffection could await her, that she could do no more than dispel what had already in its own way been perfection.

But there was no need to knock at the door. Victoria Place, when she reached it, was a short main street of tall terraced houses, either newly recovered or so smart that they had never lapsed: the number 24 was brightly illuminated, shining brightly forth into the gathering darkness. She walked slowly toward it, realizing that she would be able to see whatever there was to see without knocking: realizing that fate had connived with her curiosity by providing a bus stop directly outside the house, so that she could stand there and wait without fear of detection. She took her place at the bus stop, and stood there for a moment before she gathered her courage to turn around, and then she turned. The lights were on in the two lower floors, and she could see straight into the basement, a room which most closely resembled in shape the one where she herself lived. The room seemed at first sight to be full of people, and there was so much activity that it took some time to sort them out. There were two women, and four children; no, five children, for there was a baby sitting in a corner on a blue rug. The larger children were putting up a Christmas tree, and one of the women was laying the table for tea, while the other, her back to the window, one elbow on the mantelpiece, appeared to be reading aloud a passage from a book. It was a large, bright room, with a green carpet, and white walls, and red painted wooden furniture; even the table was painted red. A children's room. It shone, it glittered. A mobile of golden fishes hung from the ceiling, and the carpet was strewn with colored glass and tinsel decorations for the tree. The plates on the table were blue and white, and the silver knives caught the light; on the mantelpiece stood two many-faceted cut glasses and an open bottle of wine. Two of the children had fair hair, and the other three were dark: and the woman laying the table had red hair, a huge coil of dark red hair from which whole heavy locks escaped, dragging down the back of her neck, falling against her face at each movement, and she moved endlessly, restlessly, vigorously, taking buns out of a bag, slicing bread, pouring black currant juice into beakers, turning to listen to the other woman, and suddenly laughing, throwing back her head with a kind of violence and laughing: and the other woman at the mantelpiece laughed too, her thin shoulders shaking, and the children, irritated by their mother's laughter, flung themselves at her, clinging angrily onto her knees, shouting, until the red-haired woman tried to silence them with slices of bread and butter, which were rejected and flung around the floor: so she followed them up with the iced buns, tossing them round and yet talking, all the time talking, to the other woman and not to the children, intent upon some point, some anecdote too precious to lose, and the children chewed at the buns while she scooped up the torn pieces of bread and bestowed them all, with a smile of such lovely passing affection, upon the baby, a smile so tender and amused and solicitous that Helen, overseeing it, felt her heart stand still.

And as she stood there, out there in the cold, and watched, she felt herself stiffen slowly into the breathlessness of attention: because it seemed to her that she had been given, freely, a vision of something so beautiful that its relevance could not be measured. The hints and arrows that had led her here took on the mysterious significance of fate itself: she felt that everything was joined and drawn together, that all things were part of some pattern of which she caught by sheer chance a sudden hopeful sense: and that those two women, and their children, and the man on the train, and the bright and radiant uncurtained room, an island in the surrounding darkness, were symbols to her of things too vague to name, of happiness, of hope, of brightness, warmth, and celebration. She gazed into that room, where emotion lay, like water unimaginably profound. The red-haired woman was kneeling now, on the green carpet, rubbing with a corner of the tea towel at a buttery mark on the carpet, and at the same time looking up and listening, with an expression upon her face in which vexation with the children, carelessness of her own vexation, and a kind of soft rapt delight in the other woman's company were inextricably confused; and the other woman had turned slightly, so that Helen from the window could see her face, and she was twisting in her hands a length of red-and-silver tinsel, idly pulling shreds from it as she spoke. And Helen thought of all the other dark cold rooms of London and the world, of loneliness, of the blue chilly flickerings of television sets, of sad children, silenced mothers, and unmarried girls; and she wondered if so much delight were truly gathered up and concentrated into one place, or whether these windows were not windows through which she viewed the real huge spacious anterior lovely world. And it seemed possible to see them so, because she did not know that house, nor those women, nor their names, nor the name of the man who had led her there: the poetry of inspiration being to a certain extent, as she knew, the poetry of ignorance, and the connections between symbols a destructive folly to draw. She did not even know which of these women was Mrs. Smithson, whom she had come to see, for if one woman had laid the table, the other cleared it, equally at home. She knew nothing, and could therefore believe everything, drawing faith from such a vision, as she had drawn faith from unfamiliar cities: drawing faith from the passionate vision of intimacy, where intimacy itself failed her; as Wordsworth turned from his life to his keener recollections, and Yeats to lions and towers and hawks.[5]

By the time that one of the children was sent to draw the curtains, she was stiff and white with cold. She turned away, as the child, a small girl with straight dark hair and a face suddenly grave with the weight of her task, began to struggle with the heavy floor-length hangings, shutting inch by inch away from her the colored angles of refracted light, the Christmas tree, the airy fishes, the verdant green, the small angelic innocent faces, the shining spheres of glass, and those two young worn women: and as she turned she felt the first snowflakes of the year settle softly on her skin, and looking up, she saw the dim blue sky full of snow. She glanced back, to see if the child had seen it, but the curtains were already drawn, and she saw nothing but her own image, pale in the glass. So she started to walk down the street, away from the house, away from the bus stop, but before she had taken ten steps a car drew up, just by her side, a slow yard from her, and there was the man from the train, sitting there and looking at her. She paused, and he opened the door, and sitting there still he said to her, "I don't know what to say to you, you look so fragile that a word might hurt you." And she smiled at him, a slow dazed smile, knowing that as he for her, so she for him was some mysterious apparition, some faintly gleaming memorable image: and she turned away, and walked down the street away from him into the snowy darkness, and he got out of his car and went into the house.

She walked carefully, because her ankles were so brittle from the cold that she feared that if she stumbled, they would snap.

1967

5. William Wordsworth (1770–1850), British poet who wrote of "spots of time" in his child-hood; William Butler Yeats (1865–1939), Irish poet who developed his own mythology.

ANGELA CARTER

1940–

Angela Carter claims "witch blood on her father's side; solid radical trade-unionists on mother's." In the essays she has published in many British magazines and in book form, she has written with fierce irreverence about such diverse subjects as the eighteenth-century French pornographer the Marquis de Sade and contemporary movie stars. A self-proclaimed leftist in politics, she was born Angela Stalker in London and attended the University of Bristol, from which she graduated in 1965. Married for twelve years, Carter published her first novel at the age of twenty-six. It was quickly followed by such children's books as *The Magic Toyshop* (1967), *The Dark Young Lady* (1970), and *The Donkey Prince* (1970), and by a number of adult novels, including *Love* (1971), *The Infernal Desire Machines of Doctor Hoffman* (1972), and *The Passion of New Eve* (1977). In *The Bloody Chamber* (1979), a book whose title refers to the Bluebeard story, Carter has brought together her fascination with the dynamics of female desire and her work on children's literature, for in this collection the grim quality of many fairy tales is fully explored in surrealistic meditations on such traditional fantasies.

The Company of Wolves[1]

One beast and only one howls in the woods by night.

The wolf is carnivore incarnate and he's as cunning as he is ferocious; once he's had a taste of flesh, then nothing else will do.

At night, the eyes of wolves shine like candle flames, yellowish, reddish, but that is because the pupils of their eyes fatten on darkness and catch the light from your lantern to flash it back to you—red for danger; if a wolf's eyes reflect only moonlight, then they gleam a cold and unnatural green, a mineral, a piercing color. If the benighted traveler spies those luminous, terrible sequins stitched suddenly on the black thickets, then he knows he must run, if fear has not struck him stock-still.

But those eyes are all you will be able to glimpse of the forest assassins as they cluster invisibly round your smell of meat as you go through the wood unwisely late. They will be like shadows, they will be like wraiths, gray members of a congregation of nightmare. Hark! his long, wavering howl . . . an aria of fear made audible.

---

1. The story is based on the children's folk tale *Little Red Riding Hood*, in which a young girl goes through the woods to visit her grandmother and meets a wolf, who rushes ahead and eats the grandmother, then tries to pass himself off as the old woman so as to eat Little Red Riding Hood. A passing woodsman rescues the girl.

The wolfsong is the sound of the rending you will suffer, in itself a murdering.

It is winter and cold weather. In this region of mountain and forest, there is now nothing for the wolves to eat. Goats and sheep are locked up in the byre,[2] the deer departed for the remaining pasturage on the southern slopes—wolves grow lean and famished. There is so little flesh on them that you could count the starveling ribs through their pelts, if they gave you time before they pounced. Those slavering jaws; the lolling tongue; the rime[3] of saliva on the grizzled chops—of all the teeming perils of the night and the forest, ghosts, hobgoblins, ogres that grill babies upon gridirons, witches that fatten their captives in cages for cannibal tables, the wolf is worst, for he cannot listen to reason.

You are always in danger in the forest, where no people are. Step between the portals of the great pines where the shaggy branches tangle about you, trapping the unwary traveler in nets as if the vegetation itself were in a plot with the wolves who live there, as though the wicked trees go fishing on behalf of their friends—step between the gateposts of the forest with the greatest trepidation and infinite precautions, for if you stray from the path for one instant, the wolves will eat you. They are gray as famine, they are as unkind as plague.

The grave-eyed children of the sparse villages always carry knives with them when they go out to tend the little flocks of goats that provide the homesteads with acrid milk and rank, maggoty cheeses. Their knives are half as big as they are; the blades are sharpened daily.

But the wolves have ways of arriving at your own hearthside. We try and try but sometimes we cannot keep them out. There is no winter's night the cottager does not fear to see a lean, gray, famished snout questing under the door, and there was a woman once bitten in her own kitchen as she was straining the macaroni.

Fear and flee the wolf; for worst of all, the wolf may be more than he seems.

There was a hunter once, near here, that trapped a wolf in a pit. This wolf had massacred the sheep and goats; eaten up a mad old man who used to live by himself in a hut halfway up the mountain and sing to Jesus all day; pounced on a girl looking after the sheep, but she made such a commotion that men came with rifles and scared him away and tried to track him into the forest but he was cunning and easily gave them the slip. So this hunter dug a pit and put a duck in it, for bait, all alive-oh; and he covered the pit with straw smeared with wolf dung. Quack, quack! went the duck, and a wolf came slinking out of the forest, a big one, a heavy one, he weighed as much as a grown man and the

---

2. Barn.   3. Coating of frost.

straw gave way beneath him—into the pit he tumbled. The hunter jumped down after him, slit his throat, cut off all his paws for a trophy.

And then no wolf at all lay in front of the hunter but the bloody trunk of a man, headless, footless, dying, dead.

A witch from up the valley once turned an entire wedding party into wolves because the groom had settled on another girl. She used to order them to visit her, at night, from spite, and they would sit and howl around her cottage for her, serenading her with their misery.

Not so very long ago, a young woman in our village married a man who vanished clean away on her wedding night. The bed was made with new sheets and the bride lay down in it; the groom said he was going out to relieve himself, insisted on it, for the sake of decency, and she drew the coverlet up to her chin and she lay there. And she waited and she waited and then she waited again—surely he's been gone a long time? Until she jumps up in bed and shrieks to hear a howling, coming on the wind from the forest.

That long-drawn, wavering howl has, for all its fearful resonance, some inherent sadness in it, as if the beasts would love to be less beastly if only they knew how and never cease to mourn their own condition. There is a vast melancholy in the canticles[4] of the wolves, melancholy infinite as the forest, endless as these long nights of winter, and yet that ghastly sadness, that mourning for their own, irremediable appetites, can never move the heart, for not one phrase in it hints at the possibility of redemption; grace could not come to the wolf from its own despair, only through some external mediator, so that, sometimes, the beast will look as if he half welcomes the knife that dispatches him.

The young woman's brothers searched the outhouses and the hays-tacks but never found any remains, so the sensible girl dried her eyes and found herself another husband, not too shy to piss into a pot, who spent the nights indoors. She gave him a pair of bonny babies and all went right as a trivet until, one freezing night, the night of the solstice, the hinge of the year when things do not fit together as well as they should, the longest night, her first good man came home again.

A great thump on the door announced him as she was stirring the soup for the father of her children and she knew him the moment she lifted the latch to him although it was years since she'd worn black for him and now he was in rags and his hair hung down his back and never saw a comb, alive with lice.

"Here I am again, missis," he said. "Get me my bowl of cabbage and be quick about it."

Then her second husband came in with wood for the fire and when

4. Hymns.

the first one saw she'd slept with another man and, worse, clapped his red eyes on her little children, who'd crept into the kitchen to see what all the din was about, he shouted: "I wish I were a wolf again, to teach this whore a lesson!" So a wolf he instantly became and tore off the eldest boy's left foot before he was chopped up with the hatchet they used for chopping logs. But when the wolf lay bleeding and gasping its last, the pelt peeled off again and he was just as he had been, years ago, when he ran away from his marriage bed, so that she wept and her second husband beat her.

They say there's an ointment the Devil gives you that turns you into a wolf the minute you rub it on. Or that he was born feet first and had a wolf for his father and his torso is a man's but his legs and genitals are a wolf's. And he has a wolf's heart.

Seven years is a werewolf's natural span, but if you burn his human clothing you condemn him to wolfishness for the rest of his life, so old wives hereabouts think it some protection to throw a hat or an apron at the werewolf, as if clothes made the man. Yet by the eyes, those phosphorescent eyes, you know him in all his shapes; the eyes alone unchanged by metamorphosis.

Before he can become a wolf, the lycanthrope[5] strips stark naked. If you spy a naked man among the pines, you must run as if the Devil were after you.

It is midwinter and the robin, the friend of man, sits on the handle of the gardener's spade and sings. It is the worst time in all the year for wolves, but this strong-minded child insists she will go off through the wood. She is quite sure the wild beasts cannot harm her although, well-warned, she lays a carving knife in the basket her mother has packed with cheeses. There is a bottle of harsh liquor distilled from brambles; a batch of flat oat cakes baked on the hearthstone; a pot or two of jam. The flaxen-haired girl will take these delicious gifts to a reclusive grandmother so old the burden of her years is crushing her to death. Granny lives two hours' trudge through the winter woods; the child wraps herself up in her thick shawl, draws it over her head. She steps into her stout wooden shoes; she is dressed and ready and it is Christmas Eve. The malign door of the solstice still swings upon its hinges, but she has been too much loved ever to feel scared.

Children do not stay young for long in this savage country. There are no toys for them to play with, so they work hard and grow wise, but this one, so pretty and the youngest of her family, a little latecomer, had been indulged by her mother and the grandmother who'd knitted her

5. Werewolf.

the red shawl that, today, has the ominous if brilliant look of blood on snow. Her breasts have just begun to swell; her hair is like lint, so fair it hardly makes a shadow on her pale forehead; her cheeks are an emblematic scarlet and white and she has just started her woman's bleeding, the clock inside her that will strike, henceforward, once a month.

She stands and moves within the invisible pentacle[6] of her own virginity. She is an unbroken egg; she is a sealed vessel; she has inside her a magic space the entrance to which is shut tight with a plug of membrane; she is a closed system; she does not know how to shiver. She has her knife and she is afraid of nothing.

Her father might forbid her, if he were home, but he is away in the forest, gathering wood, and her mother cannot deny her.

The forest closed upon her like a pair of jaws.

There is always something to look at in the forest, even in the middle of winter—the huddled mounds of birds, succumbed to the lethargy of the season, heaped on the creaking boughs and too forlorn to sing; the bright frills of the winter fungi on the blotched trunks of the trees; the cuneiform[7] slots of rabbits and deer, the herringbone tracks of the birds, a hare as lean as a rasher of bacon streaking across the path where the thin sunlight dapples the russet brakes of last year's bracken.

When she heard the freezing howl of a distant wolf, her practiced hand sprang to the handle of her knife, but she saw no sign of a wolf at all, nor of a naked man, neither, but then she heard a clattering among the brushwood and there sprang onto the path a fully clothed one, a very handsome young one, in the green coat and wide-awake hat of a hunter, laden with carcasses of game birds. She had her hand on her knife at the first rustle of twigs, but he laughed with a flash of white teeth when he saw her and made her a comic yet flattering little bow; she'd never seen such a fine fellow before, not among the rustic clowns[8] of her native village. So on they went together, through the thickening light of the afternoon.

Soon they were laughing and joking like old friends. When he offered to carry her basket, she gave it to him although her knife was in it because he told her his rifle would protect them. As the day darkened, it began to snow again; she felt the first flakes settle on her eyelashes, but now there was only half a mile to go and there would be a fire, and hot tea, and a welcome, a warm one, surely, for the dashing huntsman as well as for herself.

This young man had a remarkable object in his pocket. It was a compass. She looked at the little round glass face in the palm of his hand and watched the wavering needle with a vague wonder. He assured her

---

6. Five-pointed star, an occult symbol.
7. Ancient Babylonian writing, made up of lines and wedge-shaped symbols.
8. Here, country folk.

this compass had taken him safely through the wood on his hunting trip because the needle always told him with perfect accuracy where the north was. She did not believe it; she knew she should never leave the path on the way through the wood or else she would be lost instantly. He laughed at her again; gleaming trails of spittle clung to his teeth. He said if he plunged off the path into the forest that surrounded them, he could guarantee to arrive at her grandmother's house a good quarter of an hour before she did, plotting his way through the undergrowth with his compass, while she trudged the long way, along the winding path.

I don't believe you. Besides, aren't you afraid of the wolves?

He only tapped the gleaming butt of his rifle and grinned.

Is it a bet? he asked her. Shall we make a game of it? What will you give me if I get to your grandmother's house before you?

What would you like? she asked disingenuously.

A kiss.

Commonplaces of a rustic seduction; she lowered her eyes and blushed.

He went through the undergrowth and took her basket with him, but she forgot to be afraid of the beasts, although now the moon was rising, for she wanted to dawdle on her way to make sure the handsome gentleman would win his wager.

Grandmother's house stood by itself a little way out of the village. The freshly falling snow blew in eddies about the kitchen garden and the young man stepped delicately up the snowy path to the door as if he were reluctant to get his feet wet, swinging his bundle of game and the girl's basket and humming a little tune to himself.

There is a faint trace of blood on his chin; he has been snacking on his catch.

He rapped upon the panels with his knuckles.

Aged and frail, granny is three-quarters succumbed to the mortality the ache in her bones promises her and almost ready to give in entirely. A boy came out from the village to build up her hearth for the night an hour ago and the kitchen crackles with busy firelight. She has her Bible for company; she is a pious old woman. She is propped up on several pillows in the bed set into the wall peasant fashion, wrapped up in the patchwork quilt she made before she was married, more years ago than she cares to remember. Two china spaniels with liver-colored blotches on their coats and black noses sit on either side of the fireplace. There is a bright rug of woven rags on the pantiles. The grandfather clock ticks away her eroding time.

We keep the wolves outside by living well.

He rapped upon the panels with his hairy knuckles.

It is your granddaughter, he mimicked in a high soprano.

Lift up the latch and walk in, my darling.

You can tell them by their eyes, eyes of a beast of prey, nocturnal, devastating eyes as red as a wound; you can hurl your Bible at him and your apron after, granny; you thought that was a sure prophylactic against these infernal vermin. . . . Now call on Christ and his mother and all the angels in heaven to protect you, but it won't do you any good.

His feral muzzle is sharp as a knife; he drops his golden burden of gnawed pheasant on the table and puts down your dear girl's basket, too. Oh, my God, what have you done with her?

Off with his disguise, that coat of forest-colored cloth, the hat with the feather tucked into the ribbon; his matted hair streams down his white shirt and she can see the lice moving in it. The sticks in the hearth shift and hiss; night and the forest has come into the kitchen with darkness tangled in its hair.

He strips off his shirt. His skin is the color and texture of vellum. A crisp stripe of hair runs down his belly, his nipples are ripe and dark as poison fruit, but he's so thin you could count the ribs under his skin if only he gave you the time. He strip off his trousers and she can see how hairy his legs are. His genitals, huge. Ah! huge.

The last thing the old lady saw in all this world was a young man, eyes like cinders, naked as a stone, approaching her bed.

The wolf is carnivore incarnate.

When he had finished with her, he licked his chops and quickly dressed himself again, until he was just as he had been when he came through her door. He burned the inedible hair in the fireplace and wrapped the bones up in a napkin that he hid away under the bed in the wooden chest in which he found a clean pair of sheets. These he carefully put on the bed instead of the telltale stained ones he stowed away in the laundry basket. He plumped up the pillows and shook out the patchwork quilt, he picked up the Bible from the floor, closed it and laid it on the table. All was as it had been before except that grandmother was gone. The sticks twitched in the grate, the clock ticked and the young man sat patiently, deceitfully beside the bed in granny's nightcap.

Rat-a-tap-tap.

Who's there, he quavers in granny's antique falsetto.

Only your granddaughter.

So she came in, bringing with her a flurry of snow that melted in tears on the tiles, and perhaps she was a little disappointed to see only her grandmother sitting beside the fire. But then he flung off the blanket and sprang to the door, pressing his back against it so that she could not get out again.

The girl looked round the room and saw there was not even the indentation of a head on the smooth cheek of the pillow and how, for the first time she'd seen it so, the Bible lay closed on the table. The tick of the clock cracked like a whip. She wanted her knife from her basket but she did not dare reach for it because his eyes were fixed upon her— huge eyes that now seemed to shine with a unique, interior light, eyes the size of saucers, saucers full of Greek fire,[9] diabolic phosphorescence.

What big eyes you have.

All the better to see you with.

No trace at all of the old woman except for a tuft of white hair that had caught in the bark of an unburned log. When the girl saw that, she knew she was in danger of death.

Where is my grandmother?

There's nobody here but we two, my darling.

Now a great howling rose up all around them, near, very near, as close as the kitchen garden, the howling of a multitude of wolves; she knew the worst wolves are hairy on the inside and she shivered, in spite of the scarlet shawl she pulled more closely round herself as if it could protect her, although it was as red as the blood she must spill.

Who has come to sing us carols? she said.

Those are the voices of my brothers, darling; I love the company of wolves. Look out of the window and you'll see them.

Snow half-caked the lattice and she opened it to look into the garden. It was a white night of moon and snow; the blizzard whirled round the gaunt, gray beasts who squatted on their haunches among the rows of winter cabbage, pointing their sharp snouts to the moon and howling as if their hearts would break. Ten wolves; twenty wolves—so many wolves she could not count them, howling in concert as if demented or deranged. Their eyes reflected the light from the kitchen and shone like a hundred candles.

It is very cold, poor things, she said; no wonder they howl so.

She closed the window on the wolves' threnody and took off her scarlet shawl, the color of poppies, the color of sacrifices, the color of her menses, and since her fear did her no good, she ceased to be afraid.

What shall I do with my shawl?

Throw it on the fire, dear one. You won't need it again.

She bundled up her shawl and threw it on the blaze, which instantly consumed it. Then she drew her blouse over her head; her small breasts gleamed as if the snow had invaded the room.

What shall I do with my blouse?

Into the fire with it, too, my pet.

The thin muslin went flaring up the chimney like a magic bird and now off came her skirt, her woolen stockings, her shoes, and onto the

9. Flammable mixture that burns on wetting.

fire they went, too, and were gone for good. The firelight shone through the edges of her skin; now she was clothed only in her untouched integument of flesh. Thus dazzling, naked, she combed out her hair with her fingers; her hair looked white as the snow outside. Then went directly to the man with red eyes in whose unkempt mane the lice moved; she stood up on tiptoe and unbottoned the collar of his shirt.

What big arms you have.

All the better to hug you with.

Every wolf in the world now howled a prothalamion[1] outside the window as she freely gave the kiss she owed him.

What big teeth you have!

She saw how his jaw began to slaver and the room was full of the clamor of the forest's *Liebestod*,[2] but the wise child never flinched, even when he answered:

All the better to eat you with.

The girl burst out laughing; she knew she was nobody's meat. She laughed at him full in the face, she ripped off his shirt for him and flung it into the fire, in the fiery wake of her own discarded clothing. The flames danced like dead souls on Walpurgisnacht[3] and the old bones under the bed set up a terrible clattering, but she did not pay them any heed.

Carnivore incarnate, only immaculate flesh appeases him.

She will lay his fearful head on her lap and she will pick out the lice from his pelt and perhaps she will put the lice into her mouth and eat them, as he will bid her, as she would do in a savage marriage ceremony.

The blizzard will die down.

The blizzard died down, leaving the mountains as randomly covered with snow as if a blind woman had thrown a sheet over them, the upper branches of the forest pines limed, creaking, swollen with the fall.

Snowlight, moonlight, a confusion of pawprints.

All silent, all still.

Midnight; and the clock strikes. It is Christmas Day, the werewolves' birthday; the door of the solstice stands wide open; let them all sink through.

See! Sweet and sound she sleeps in granny's bed, between the paws of the tender wolf.

1979

---

1. Song before marriage.
2. German: love-death; applied to the closing scene of Richard Wagner's opera *Tristan and* *Isolde* (1865), in which Isolde joyfully dies to join her lover, Tristan.
3. Witches' celebration.

JUDY GRAHN

1940–

Judy Grahn was raised in New Mexico and currently resides in Oakland, California. Hers is a defiantly irreverent poetry which addresses the political, social, and sexual issues facing working-class and lesbian women. Published predominantly by independent women's presses, her five chapbooks—*Edward the Dyke and Other Poems, The Common Woman, She Who, A Woman Is Talking to Death,* and *Confrontations with the Devil in the Form of Love*—have been collected in *The Work of a Common Woman* (1978). This title is a clue to the use Grahn has made of her own work as a waitress, meat wrapper, maid, and secretary. It also points toward her effort to rename and reclaim the ordinary experiences of working-class women, whose "lives are chock full of actions . . . and stories which haven't been printed, made into novels, dictionaries, philosophies." Like Pat Parker, Alta, and Ntozake Shange, poets she reads and quotes, Grahn experiments with innovative forms like satiric prose dialogues interspersed with poems and repetitive chants based on American Indian songs. Her poetry has evolved from an articulation of rage against male mistreatment of women to a celebration of women's survival skills.

[in the place where]

in the place where
her breasts come together
two thumbs' width of
channel ride my
eyes to anchor   5
hands to angle
in the place where
her legs come together
I said "you smell like the
ocean" and lay down my tongue   10
beside the dark tooth edge
of sleeping
"swim" she told me and I
did, I did

1978

From The Common Women

II. *Ella, in a square apron, along Highway 80*

She's a copperheaded[1] waitress,
tired and sharp-worded, she hides
her bad brown tooth behind a wicked
smile, and flicks her ass
out of habit, to fend off the pass   5
that passes for affection.
She keeps her mind the way men
keep a knife—keen to strip the game
down to her size. She has a thin spine,
swallows her eggs cold, and tells lies.   10
She slaps a wet rag at the truck drivers
if they should complain. She understands
the necessity for pain, turns away
the smaller tips, out of pride, and
keeps a flask under the counter. Once,   15
she shot a lover who misused her child.
Before she got out of jail, the courts had pounced
and given the child away. Like some isolated lake,
her flat blue eyes take care of their own stark
bottoms. Her hands are nervous, curled, ready   20
to scrape.
The common woman is as common
as a rattlesnake.

III. *Nadine, resting on her neighbor's stoop*

She holds things together, collects bail,
makes the landlord patch the largest holes.   25
At the Sunday social she would spike
every drink, and offer you half of what she knows,
which is plenty. She pokes at the ruins of the city
like an armored tank; but she thinks
of herself as a ripsaw cutting through   30
knots in wood. Her sentences come out
like thick pine shanks
and her big hands fill the air like smoke.
She's a mud-chinked cabin in the slums,
sitting on the doorstep counting   35
rats and raising 15 children,
half of them her own. The neighborhood
would burn itself out without her;
one of these days she'll strike the spark herself.

---

1. A kind of rattlesnake.

She's made of grease   40
and metal, with a hard head
that makes the men around her seem frail.
The common woman is as common as a nail.

1978

MAXINE HONG KINGSTON
1940–

The daughter of Chinese immigrants who operated a laundry in Stockton, California, Maxine Hong Kingston recorded the mysteries and marvels of "a girlhood among ghosts" in *The Woman Warrior* (1976), a book which combines autobiography and fiction to counterpoint memories of a Chinese-American childhood with fantasies about Chinese history and culture. Educated at the University of California, Berkeley, Kingston married the actor Earll Kingston in 1962, and in 1967 she settled in Honolulu with him and their son, Joseph. There she has taught English at the Mid-Pacific Institute, a private high school, and at the University of Hawaii, while continuing to explore the dynamics of Chinese-American society, most recently in *China Men* (1980), a reconstruction of her grandfather's and her father's pilgrimages to America, the "Gold Mountain" of Chinese legend.

The "ghosts" who haunted Kingston's girlhood are both the alien Caucasian-Americans with whom she went to school and the mystifying Asian ancestors whose stories her mother told her—often, in particular, damned or glamorous female characters like "No Name Woman" and the "Woman Warrior." No doubt because this artist has so brilliantly illuminated the intricate processes by which "femininity" is constructed in a culture different from our own, the novelist Kay Boyle has written with delight that *The Woman Warrior* is "a woman's book that has the vitality to take one far, . . . from the domestic grievances of American suburbia, . . . into the wit, and the love, and grief, of another place entirely."

No Name Woman

"You must not tell anyone," my mother said, "what I am about to tell you. In China your father had a sister who killed herself. She jumped into the family well. We say that your father has all brothers because it is as if she had never been born.

"In 1924 just a few days after our village celebrated seventeen hurry-up weddings—to make sure that every young man who went 'out on the road' would responsibly come home—your father and his brothers and your grandfather and his brothers and your aunt's new husband sailed for America, the Gold Mountain. It was your grandfather's last trip. Those lucky enough to get contracts waved good-bye from the decks. They fed and guarded the stowaways and helped them off in Cuba, New York, Bali, Hawaii. 'We'll meet in California next year,' they said. All of them sent money home.

"I remember looking at your aunt one day when she and I were dressing; I had not noticed before that she had such a protruding melon of a stomach. But I did not think, 'She's pregnant,' until she began to look like other pregnant women, her shirt pulling and the white tops of her black pants showing. She could not have been pregnant, you see, because her husband had been gone for years. No one said anything. We did not discuss it. In early summer she was ready to have the child, long after the time when it could have been possible.

"The village had also been counting. On the night the baby was to be born the villagers raided our house. Some were crying. Like a great saw, teeth strung with lights, files of people walked zigzag across our land, tearing the rice. Their lanterns doubled in the disturbed black water, which drained away through the broken bunds.[1] As the villagers closed in, we could see that some of them, probably men and women we knew well, wore white masks. The people with long hair hung it over their faces. Women with short hair made it stand up on end. Some had tied white bands around their foreheads, arms, and legs.

"At first they threw mud and rocks at the house. Then they threw eggs and began slaughtering our stock. We could hear the animals scream their deaths—the roosters, the pigs, a last great roar from the ox. Familiar wild heads flared in our night windows; the villagers encircled us. Some of the faces stopped to peer at us, their eyes rushing like searchlights. The hands flattened against the panes, framed heads, and left red prints.

"The villagers broke in the front and the back doors at the same time, even though we had not locked the doors against them. Their knives dripped with the blood of our animals. They smeared blood on the doors and walls. One woman swung a chicken, whose throat she had slit, splattering blood in red arcs about her. We stood together in the middle of our house, in the family hall with the pictures and tables of the ancestors around us, and looked straight ahead.

"At that time the house had only two wings. When the men came back, we would build two more to enclose our courtyard and a third one to begin a second courtyard. The villagers pushed through both wings, even your grandparents' rooms, to find your aunt's, which was also mine until the men returned. From this room a new wing for one of the

1. Embankments.

younger families would grow. They ripped up her clothes and shoes and broke her combs, grinding them underfoot. They tore her work from the loom. They scattered the cooking fire and rolled the new weaving in it. We could hear them in the kitchen breaking our bowls and banging the pots. They overturned the great waist-high earthenware jugs; duck eggs, pickled fruits, vegetables burst out and mixed in acrid torrents. The old woman from the next field swept a broom through the air and loosed the spirits-of-the-broom over our heads. 'Pig.' 'Ghost.' 'Pig,' they sobbed and scolded while they ruined our house.

"When they left, they took sugar and oranges to bless themselves. They cut pieces from the dead animals. Some of them took bowls that were not broken and clothes that were not torn. Afterward we swept up the rice and sewed it back up into sacks. But the smells from the spilled preserves lasted. Your aunt gave birth in the pigsty that night. The next morning when I went for the water, I found her and the baby plugging up the family well.

"Don't let your father know that I told you. He denies her. Now that you have started to menstruate, what happened to her could happen to you. Don't humiliate us. You wouldn't like to be forgotten as if you had never been born. The villagers are watchful."

Whenever she had to warn us about life, my mother told stories that ran like this one, a story to grow up on. She tested our strength to establish realities. Those in the emigrant generations who could not reassert brute survival died young and far from home. Those of us in the first American generations have had to figure out how the invisible world the emigrants built around our childhoods fit in solid America.

The emigrants confused the gods by diverting their curses, misleading them with crooked streets and false names. They must try to confuse their offspring as well, who, I suppose, threaten them in similar ways—always trying to get things straight, always trying to name the unspeakable. The Chinese I know hide their names; sojourners take new names when their lives change and guard their real names with silence.

Chinese-Americans, when you try to understand what things in you are Chinese, how do you separate what is peculiar to childhood, to poverty, insanities, one family, your mother who marked your growing with stories, from what is Chinese? What is Chinese tradition and what is the movies?

If I want to learn what clothes my aunt wore, whether flashy or ordinary, I would have to begin, "Remember Father's drowned-in-the-well sister?" I cannot ask that. My mother has told me once and for all the useful parts. She will add nothing unless powered by Necessity, a riverbank that guides her life. She plants vegetable gardens rather than lawns; she carries the odd-shaped tomatoes home from the fields and eats food left for the gods.

Whenever we did frivolous things, we used up energy; we flew high kites. We children came up off the ground over the melting cones our parents brought home from work and the American movie on New Year's Day—*Oh, You Beautiful Doll* with Betty Grable one year, and *She Wore a Yellow Ribbon* with John Wayne another year. After the one carnival ride each, we paid in guilt; our tired father counted his change on the dark walk home.

Adultery is extravagance. Could people who hatch their own chicks and eat the embryos and the heads for delicacies and boil the feet in vinegar for party food, leaving only the gravel, eating even the gizzard lining—could such people engender a prodigal aunt? To be a woman, to have a daughter in starvation time was a waste enough. My aunt could not have been the lone romantic who gave up everything for sex. Women in the old China did not choose. Some man had commanded her to lie with him and be his secret evil. I wonder whether he masked himself when he joined the raid of her family.

Perhaps she encountered him in the fields or on the mountain where the daughters-in-law collected fuel. Or perhaps he first noticed her in the marketplace. He was not a stranger because the village housed no strangers. She had to have dealings with him other than sex. Perhaps he worked an adjoining field, or he sold her the cloth for the dress she sewed and wore. His demand must have surprised, then terrified her. She obeyed him; she always did as she was told.

When the family found a young man in the next village to be her husband, she stood tractably beside the best rooster, his proxy, and promised before they met that she would be his forever. She was lucky that he was her age and she would be the first wife, an advantage secure now. The night she first saw him, he had sex with her. Then he left for America. She had almost forgotten what he looked like. When she tried to envision him, she only saw the black and white face in the group photograph the men had had taken before leaving.

The other man was not, after all, much different from her husband. They both gave orders: she followed. "If you tell your family, I'll beat you. I'll kill you. Be here again next week." No one talked sex, ever. And she might have separated the rapes from the rest of living if only she did not have to buy her oil from him or gather wood in the same forest. I want her fear to have lasted just as long as rape lasted so that the fear could have been contained. No drawn-out fear. But women at sex hazarded birth and hence lifetimes. The fear did not stop but permeated everywhere. She told the man, "I think I'm pregnant." He organized the raid against her.

On nights when my mother and father talked about their life back home, sometimes they mentioned an "outcast table" whose business they still seemed to be settling, their voices tight. In a commensal[2] tradition, where food is precious, the powerful older people made wrongdoers eat alone. Instead of letting them start separate new lives like the Japanese, who could become samurais and geishas, the Chinese family, faces averted but eyes glowering sideways, hung on to the offenders and fed them leftovers. My aunt must have lived in the same house as my parents and eaten at an outcast table. My mother spoke about the raid as if she had seen it, when she and my aunt, a daughter-in-law to a different household, should not have been living together at all. Daughters-in-law lived with their husbands' parents, not their own; a synonym for marriage in Chinese is "taking a daughter-in-law." Her husband's parents could have sold her, mortgaged her, stoned her. But they had sent her back to her own mother and father, a mysterious act hinting at disgraces not told me. Perhaps they had thrown her out to deflect the avengers.

She was the only daughter; her four brothers went with her father, husband, and uncles "out on the road" and for some years became western men. When the goods were divided among the family, three of the brothers took land, and the youngest, my father, chose an education. After my grandparents gave their daughter away to her husband's family, they had dispensed all the adventure and all the property. They expected her alone to keep the traditional ways, which her brothers, now among the barbarians, could fumble without detection. The heavy, deep-rooted women were to maintain the past against the flood, safe for returning. But the rare urge west had fixed upon our family, and so my aunt crossed boundaries not delineated in space.

The work of preservation demands that the feelings playing about in one's guts not be turned into action. Just watch their passing like cherry blossoms. But perhaps my aunt, my forerunner, caught in a slow life, let dreams grow and fade and after some months or years went toward what persisted. Fear at the enormities of the forbidden kept her desires delicate, wire and bone. She looked at a man because she liked the way the hair was tucked behind his ears, or she liked the question-mark line of a long torso curving at the shoulder and straight at the hip. For warm eyes or a soft voice or a slow walk—that's all—a few hairs, a line, a brightness, a sound, a pace, she gave up family. She offered us up for a charm that vanished with tiredness, a pigtail that didn't toss when the wind died. Why, the wrong lighting could erase the dearest thing about him.

2. Eating together, at the same table.

It could very well have been, however, that my aunt did not take subtle enjoyment of her friend, but, a wild woman, kept rollicking company. Imagining her free with sex doesn't fit, though. I don't know any women like that, or men either. Unless I see her life branching into mine, she gives me no ancestral help.

To sustain her being in love, she often worked at herself in the mirror, guessing at the colors and shapes that would interest him, changing them frequently in order to hit on the right combination. She wanted him to look back.

On a farm near the sea, a woman who tended her appearance reaped a reputation for eccentricity. All the married women blunt-cut their hair in flaps about their ears or pulled it back in tight buns. No nonsense. Neither style blew easily into heart-catching tangles. And at their weddings they displayed themselves in their long hair for the last time. "It brushed the backs of my knees," my mother tells me. "It was braided, and even so, it brushed the backs of my knees."

At the mirror my aunt combed individuality into her bob. A bun could have been contrived to escape into black streamers blowing in the wind or in quiet wisps about her face, but only the older women in our picture album wear buns. She brushed her hair back from her forehead, tucking the flaps behind her ears. She looped a piece of thread, knotted into a circle between her index fingers and thumbs, and ran the double strand across her forehead. When she closed her fingers as if she were making a pair of shadow geese bite, the string twisted together catching the little hairs. Then she pulled the thread away from her skin, ripping the hairs out neatly, her eyes watering from the needles of pain. Opening her fingers, she cleaned the thread, then rolled it along her hairline and the tops of her eyebrows. My mother did the same to me and my sisters and herself. I used to believe that the expression "caught by the short hairs" meant a captive held with a depilatory string. It especially hurt at the temples, but my mother said we were lucky we didn't have to have our feet bound when we were seven. Sisters used to sit on their beds and cry together, she said, as their mothers or their slaves removed the bandages for a few minutes each night and let the blood gush back into their veins. I hope that the man my aunt loved appreciated a smooth brow, that he wasn't just a tits-and-ass man.

Once my aunt found a freckle on her chin, at a spot that the almanac said predestined her for unhappiness. She dug it out with a hot needle and washed the wound with peroxide.

More attention to her looks than these pullings of hairs and pickings at spots would have caused gossip among the villagers. They owned work clothes and good clothes, and they wore good clothes for feasting the new seasons. But since a woman combing her hair hexes beginnings, my aunt rarely found an occasion to look her best. Women looked like great sea snails—the corded wood, babies, and laundry they carried were the whorls on their backs. The Chinese did not admire a bent back; goddesses and warriors stood straight. Still there must have been a marvelous freeing of beauty when a worker laid down her burden and stretched and arched.

Such commonplace loveliness, however, was not enough for my aunt. She dreamed of a lover for the fifteen days of New Year's, the time for families to exchange visits, money, and food. She plied her secret comb. And sure enough she cursed the year, the family, the village, and herself.

Even as her hair lured her imminent lover, many other men looked at her. Uncles, cousins, nephews, brothers would have looked, too, had they been home between journeys. Perhaps they had already been restraining their curiosity, and they left, fearful that their glances, like a field of nesting birds, might be startled and caught. Poverty hurt, and that was their first reason for leaving. But another, final reason for leaving the crowded house was the never-said.

She may have been unusually beloved, the precious only daughter, spoiled and mirror gazing because of the affection the family lavished on her. When her husband left, they welcomed the chance to take her back from the in-laws; she could live like the little daughter for just a while longer. There are stories that my grandfather was different from other people, "crazy ever since the little Jap bayoneted him in the head." He used to put his naked penis on the dinner table, laughing. And one day he brought home a baby girl, wrapped up inside his brown western-style greatcoat. He had traded one of his sons, probably my father, the youngest, for her. My grandmother made him trade back. When he finally got a daughter of his own, he doted on her. They must have all loved her, except perhaps my father, the only brother who never went back to China, having once been traded for a girl.

Brothers and sisters, newly men and women, had to efface their sexual color and present plain miens. Disturbing hair and eyes, a smile like no other threatened the ideal of five generations living under one roof. To focus blurs, people shouted face to face and yelled from room to room. The immigrants I know have loud voices, unmodulated to American tones even after years away from the village where they called their friendships out across the fields. I have not been able to stop my mother's screams in public libraries or over telephones. Walking erect (knees straight, toes pointed forward, not pigeon-toed, which is Chinese-feminine) and speaking in an inaudible voice, I have tried to turn myself American-feminine. Chinese communication was loud, public. Only sick people had to whisper. But at the dinner table, where the family members came nearest one another, no one could talk, not the outcasts nor any eaters. Every word that falls from the mouth is a coin lost. Silently they gave and accepted food with both hands. A preoccupied child who took his bowl with one hand got a sideways glare. A complete moment of total attention is due everyone alike. Children and lovers have no singularity here, but my aunt used a secret voice, a separate attentiveness.

She kept the man's name to herself throughout her labor and dying; she did not accuse him that he be punished with her. To save her inseminator's name she gave silent birth.

He may have been somebody in her own household, but intercourse with a man outside the family would have been no less abhorrent. All the village were kinsmen, and the titles shouted in loud country voices never let kinship be forgotten. Any man within visiting distance would have been neutralized as a lover—"brother," "younger brother, "older brother"—one hundred and fifteen relationship titles. Parents researched birth charts probably not so much to assure good fortune as to circumvent incest in a population that has but one hundred surnames. Everybody has eight million relatives. How useless then sexual mannerisms, how dangerous.

As if it came from an atavism deeper than fear, I used to add "brother" silently to boys' names. It hexed the boys who would or would not ask me to dance, and made them less scary and as familiar and deserving of benevolence as girls.

But, of course, I hexed myself also—no dates. I should have stood up, both arms waving, and shouted out across libraries, "Hey, you! Love me back." I had no idea, though, how to make attraction selective, how to control its direction and magnitude. If I made myself American-pretty so that the five or six Chinese boys in the class fell in love with me, everyone else—the Caucasian, Negro, and Japanese boys—would too. Sisterliness, dignified and honorable, made much more sense.

Attraction eludes control so stubbornly that whole societies designed to organize relationships among people cannot keep order, not even when they bind people to one another from childhood and raise them together. Among the very poor and the wealthy, brothers married their adopted sisters, like doves. Our family allowed some romance, paying adult brides' prices and providing dowries so that their sons and daughters could marry strangers. Marriage promises to turn strangers into friendly relatives—a nation of siblings.

In the village structure, spirits shimmered among the live creatures, balanced and held in equilibrium by time and land. But one human being flaring up into violence could open up a black hole, a maelstrom that pulled in the sky. The frightened villagers, who depended on one another to maintain the real, went to my aunt to show her a personal, physical representation of the break she had made in the "roundness."

Misallying couples snapped off the future, which was to be embodied in true offspring. The villagers punished her for acting as if she could have a private life, secret and apart from them.

If my aunt had betrayed the family at a time of large grain yields and peace, when many boys were born, and wings were being built on many houses, perhaps she might have escaped such severe punishment. But the men—hungry, greedy, tired of planting in dry soil, cuckolded —had had to leave the village in order to send food-money home. There were ghost plagues, bandit plagues, wars with the Japanese, floods. My Chinese brother and sister had died of an unknown sickness. Adultery, perhaps only a mistake during good times, became a crime when the village needed food.

The round moon cakes and round doorways, the round tables of graduated size that fit one roundness inside another, round windows and rice bowls—these talismen had lost their power to warn this family of the law: a family must be whole, faithfully keeping the descent line by having sons to feed the old and the dead, who in turn look after the family. The villagers came to show my aunt and her lover-in-hiding a broken house. The villagers were speeding up the circling of events because she was too shortsighted to see that her infidelity had already harmed the village, that waves of consequences would return unpredictably, sometimes in disguise, as now, to hurt her. This roundness had to be made coin-sized so that she would see its circumference: punish her at the birth of her baby. Awaken her to the inexorable. People who refused fatalism because they could invent small resources insisted on culpability. Deny accidents and wrest fault from the stars.

After the villagers left, their lanterns now scattering in various directions toward home, the family broke their silence and cursed her. "Aiaa, we're going to die. Death is coming. Death is coming. Look what you've done. You've killed us. Ghost! Dead ghost! Ghost! You've never been born." She ran out into the fields, far enough from the house so that she could no longer hear their voices, and pressed herself against the earth, her own land no more. When she felt the birth coming, she thought that she had been hurt. Her body seized together. "They've hurt me too much," she thought. "This is gall, and it will kill me." Her forehead and knees against the earth, her body convulsed and then released her onto her back. The black well of sky and stars went out and out and out forever; her body and her complexity seemed to disappear. She was one of the stars, a bright dot in blackness, without home, without a companion, in eternal cold and silence. An agoraphobia rose in her, speeding higher and higher, bigger and bigger; she would not be able to contain it; there would be no end to fear.

Flayed, unprotected against space, she felt pain return, focusing her body. This pain chilled her—a cold, steady kind of surface pain. Inside, spasmodically, the other pain, the pain of the child, heated her. For hours she lay on the ground, alternately body and space. Sometimes a vision of nomal comfort obliterated reality: she saw the family in the evening gambling at the dinner table, the young people massaging their elders' backs. She saw them congratulating one another, high joy on the mornings the rice shoots came up. When these pictures burst, the stars drew yet further apart. Black space opened.

She got to her feet to fight better and remembered that old-fashioned women gave birth in their pigsties to fool the jealous, pain-dealing gods, who do not snatch piglets. Before the next spasms could stop her, she ran to the pigsty, each step a rushing out into emptiness. She climbed over the fence and knelt in the dirt. It was good to have a fence enclosing her, a tribal person alone.

Laboring, this woman who had carried her child as a foreign growth that sickened her every day, expelled it at last. She reached down to touch the hot, wet, moving mass, surely smaller than anything human, and could feel that it was human after all—fingers, toes, nails, nose. She pulled it up on to her belly, and it lay curled there, butt in the air, feet precisely tucked one under the other. She opened her loose shirt and buttoned the child inside. After resting, it squirmed and thrashed and she pushed it up to her breast. It turned its head this way and that until it found her nipple. There, it made little snuffling noises. She clenched her teeth at its preciousness, lovely as a young calf, a piglet, a little dog.

She may have gone to the pigsty as a last act of responsibility: she would protect this child as she had protected its father. It would look after her soul, leaving supplies on her grave. But how would this tiny child without family find her grave when there would be no marker for her anywhere, neither in the earth nor the family hall? No one would give her a family hall name. She had taken the child with her into the wastes. At its birth the two of them had felt the same raw pain of separation, a wound that only the family pressing tight could close. A child with no descent line would not soften her life but only trail after her, ghostlike, begging her to give it purpose. At dawn the villagers on their way to the fields would stand around the fence and look.

Full of milk, the little ghost slept. When it awoke, she hardened her breasts against the milk that crying loosens. Toward morning she picked up the baby and walked to the well.

Carrying the baby to the well shows loving. Otherwise abandon it. Turn its face into the mud. Mothers who love their children take them along. It was probably a girl; there is some hope of forgiveness for boys.

"Don't tell anyone you had an aunt. Your father does not want to hear her name. She has never been born." I have believed that sex was unspeakable and words so strong and fathers so frail that "aunt" would do my father mysterious harm. I have thought that my family, having settled among immigrants who had also been their neighbors in the ancestral land, needed to clean their name, and a wrong word would incite the kinspeople even here. But there is more to this silence: they want me to participate in her punishment. And I have.

In the twenty years since I heard this story I have not asked for details nor said my aunt's name; I do not know it. People who can comfort the dead can also chase after them to hurt them further—a reverse ancestor worship. The real punishment was not the raid swiftly inflicted by the villagers, but the family's deliberately forgetting her. Her betrayal so maddened them, they saw to it that she would suffer forever, even after death. Always hungry, always needing, she would have to beg food from other ghosts, snatch and steal it from those whose living descendants give them gifts. She would have to fight the ghosts massed at crossroads for the buns a few thoughtful citizens leave to decoy her away from village and home so that the ancestral spirits could feast unharassed. At peace, they could act like gods, not ghosts, their descent lines providing them with paper suits and dresses, spirit money, paper houses, paper automobiles, chicken, meat, and rice into eternity[3]—essences delivered up in smoke and flames, steam and incense rising from each rice bowl. In an attempt to make the Chinese care for people outside the family, Chairman Mao[4] encourages us now to give our paper replicas to the spirits of outstanding soldiers and workers, no matter whose ancestors they may be. My aunt remains forever hungry. Goods are not distributed evenly among the dead.

My aunt haunts me—her ghost drawn to me because now, after fifty years of neglect, I alone devote pages of paper to her, though not origamied[5] into houses and clothes. I do not think she always means me well. I am telling on her, and she was a spite suicide, drowning herself in the drinking water. The Chinese are always very frightened of the drowned one, whose weeping ghost, wet hair hanging and skin bloated, waits silently by the water to pull down a substitute.

1976

3. According to Chinese custom, these objects are periodically left as offerings at the graves of dead ancestors.
4. Mao Tse-tung (1893–1976), leader of the Chinese Communist party and head of state from 1949 to 1959.
5. Origami is the Asian art of folding paper to produce sculptures of animals and other objects.

AMA ATA AIDOO

1942–

"Things are working out towards their dazzling conclusions," begins Christina Ama Ata Aidoo's characteristically wry yet hopeful epigraph for *Our Sister Killjoy, or Reflections from a Black-Eyed Squint* (1966), her first novel. Born near Dominase, in the center of Ghana, Aidoo has been one of Africa's most productive and talented younger writers: she is the author of two plays (*Dilemma of a Ghost*, 1965, and *Anowa*, 1970), as well as poems and a collection of short stories (*No Sweetness Here*, 1969), work which, the American writer Alice Walker recently remarked, has "reaffirmed my faith in the power of the written word to reach, to teach, to empower and encourage." After graduation from the University of Ghana and a period as a research fellow at that university's Institute of African Studies, Aidoo studied creative writing at Stanford University, in California, and she has subsequently taught English and African literature at the University of Ghana, Cape Coast branch. In much of her fiction, she explores with poignancy, verve, and wit the dissonance between Western culture and the civilization of an Africa just emerging from colonization, even while she seeks to imagine the ways in which, particularly for African women, things might work out toward a surprising and "dazzling" conclusion.

The Message

"Look here my sister, it should not be said but they say they opened her up."

"They opened her up?"

"Yes, opened her up."

"And the baby removed?"

"Yes, the baby removed."

"Yes the baby removed."

"I say. . . ."

"They do not say, my sister."

"Have you heard it?"

"What?"

"This and this and that. . . ."

"A-a-ah! that is it. . . ."

"*Meewuo!*"[1]

"They don't say *meewuo*. . . ."

"And how is she?"

"Am I not here with you? Do I know the highway which leads to Cape Coast?"

"Hmmm. . . ."

"And anyway how can she live? What is it like even giving birth with a stomach which is whole . . . eh? . . . I am asking you. And if you are always standing on the brink of death who go to war with a stomach that is whole, then how would she do whose stomach is open to the winds?"

"Oh, *poo*,[2] pity. . . ."

"I say. . . ."

---

1. "I'm going to die!" We are indebted to Dan Avorgbedor for his invaluable help in translating   Ghanaian words and phrases.
2. An exclamation.

My little bundle, come. You and I are going to Cape Coast today.

I am taking one of her own cloths with me, just in case. These people on the coast do not know how to do a thing and I am not going to have anybody mishandling my child's body. I hope they give it to me. Horrible things I have heard done to people's bodies. Cutting them up and using them for instructions. Whereas even murderers still have decent burials.

I see Mensima coming. . . . And there is Nkama too . . . and Adwoa Meenu. . . . Now they are coming to . . . "*poo* pity" me. Witches, witches, witches . . . they have picked mine up while theirs prosper around them, children, grandchildren and great-grandchildren—theirs shoot up like mushrooms.

"Esi, we have heard of your misfortune. . . ."

"That our little lady's womb has been opened up. . . ."

"And her baby removed. . . ."

Thank you very much.

"Has she lived through it?"

I do not know.

"Esi, bring her here, back home whatever happens."

Yoo,[3] thank you. If the government's people allow it, I shall bring her home.

"And have you got ready your things?"

Yes. . . . No.

I cannot even think well.

It feels so noisy in my head. . . . Oh my little child. . . . I am wasting time. . . . And so I am going. . . .

Yes, to Cape Coast.

No, I do not know anyone there now but do you think no one would show me the way to this big hospital . . . if I asked around?

Hmmm . . . it's me has ended up like this. I was thinking that everything was alright now. . . . Yoo. And thank you too. Shut the door for me when you are leaving. You may stay too long outside if you wait for me, so go home and be about your business. I will let you know when I bring her in.

"Maami Amfoa, where are you going?"

My daughter, I am going to Cape Coast.

"And what is our old mother going to do with such swift steps? Is it serious?"

My daughter, it is very serious.

"Mother, may God go with you."

Yoo, my daughter.

"Eno, and what calls at this hour of the day?"

3. "Yes."

They want me at Cape Coast.

"Does my friend want to go and see how much the city has changed since we went there to meet the new Wesleyan Chairman,[4] twenty years ago?"

My sister, do you think I have knees to go parading on the streets of Cape Coast?

"Is it heavy?"

Yes, very heavy indeed. They have opened up my grandchild at the hospital, *hi, hi, hi.* . . .

"Eno *due, due, due.*[5] . . . I did not know. May God go with you. . . ."

Thank you *Yaa.*

"O, the world!"

"It's her grandchild. The only daughter of her only son. Do you remember Kojo Amisa who went to sodja[6] and fell in the great war, overseas?"

"Yes, it's his daughter. . . ."

. . . O, *poo*, pity.

"Kobina, run to the street, tell Draba Anan to wait for Nana Amfoa."

". . . Draba Anan, Draba, my mother says I must come and tell you to wait for Nana Amfoa."

"And where is she?"

"There she comes."

"Just look at how she hops like a bird . . . does she think we are going to be here all day? And anyway we are full already. . . ."

O, you drivers!

"What have drivers done?"

"And do you think it shows respect when you speak in this way? It is only that things have not gone right; but she could, at least have been your mother. . . ."

"But what have I said? I have not insulted her. I just think that only Youth must be permitted to see Cape Coast, the town of the Dear and Expensive. . . ."

"And do you think she is going on a peaceful journey? The only daughter of her only son has been opened up and her baby removed from her womb."

O . . . God.

O

O

O

Poo, pity.

4. Official in the Wesleyan mission, which was   5. An expression of lamentation.
active in Ghana.   6. I.e., soldier.

"Me . . . *poo*—pity, I am right about our modern wives. I always say they are useless as compared with our mothers."

"You drivers!"

"Now what have your modern wives done?"

"Am I not right what I always say about them?"

"You go and watch them in the big towns. All so thin and dry as sticks—you can literally blow them away with your breath. No decent flesh anywhere. Wooden chairs groan when they meet with their hard exteriors."

"O you drivers. . . ."

"But of course all drivers. . . ."

"What have I done? Don't all my male passengers agree with me? These modern girls. . . . Now here is one who cannot even have a baby in a decent way. But must have the baby removed from her stomach. *Tchiaa!*[7]

"What. . . ."

"Here is the old woman."

"Whose grandchild. . . . ?"

"Yes."

"Nana, I hear you are coming to Cape Coast with us."

Yes my master.

"We nearly left you behind but we heard it was you and that it is a heavy journey you are making."

Yes my master . . . thank you my master.

"Push up please . . . push up. Won't you push up? Why do you all sit looking at me with such eyes as if I was a block of wood?"

"It is not that there is nowhere to push up to. Five fat women should go on that seat, but look at you!

And our own grandmother here is none too plump herself. . . . Nana, if they won't push, come to the front seat with me."

". . . Hei,[8] scholar, go to the back. . . .

. . . And do not scowl on me. I know your sort too well. Something tells me you do not have any job at all. As for that suit you are wearing and looking so grand in, you hired or borrowed it. . . ."

"Oh you drivers!"

Oh you drivers. . . .

The scholar who read this tengram[9] thing, said it was made about three days ago. My lady's husband sent it. . . . Three days. . . . God— that is too long ago. Have they buried her . . . where? Or did they cut her up. . . . I should not think about it . . . or something will happen to

7. Expression of the absurdity of things.
8. "Hey there" or "Keep quiet!"
9. I.e., telegram.

me. Eleven or twelve . . . Efua Panyin, Okuma, Kwame Gyasi and who else? But they should not have left me here. Sometimes . . . ah, I hate this nausea. But it is this smell of petrol. Now I have remembered I never could travel in a lorry.[1] I always was so sick. But now I hope at least that will not happen. These young people will think it is because I am old and they will laugh. At least if I knew the child of my child was alive, it would have been good. And the little things she sent me. . . . Sometimes some people like Mensima and Nkansa make me feel as if I had been a barren woman instead of only one with whom infant-mortality pledged friendship. . . .

I will give her that set of earrings, bracelet and chain which Od-wumfo Ata made for me. It is the most beautiful and the most expensive thing I have. . . . It does not hurt me to think that I am going to die very soon and have them and their children gloating over my things. After all what did they swallow my children for? It does not hurt me at all. If I had been someone else, I would have given them all away before I died. But it does not matter. They can share their own curse. Now, that is the end of me and my roots. . . . Eternal death has worked like a warrior rat, with diabolical sense of duty, to gnaw my bottom. Every-thing is finished now. The vacant lot is swept and the scraps of old sugar-cane pulp, dry sticks and bunches of hair burnt . . . how it reeks, the smoke!

"O, Nana do not weep. . . ."

"Is the old woman weeping?"

"If the only child of your only child died, won't you weep?"

"Why do you ask me? Did I know her grandchild is dead?"

"Where have you been, not in this lorry? Where were your ears when we were discussing it?"

"I do not go putting my mouth in other people's affairs. . . ."

"So what?"

"So go and die."

"*Hei, hei*, it is prohibited to quarrel in my lorry."

"Draba, here is me, sitting quiet and this lady of muscles and bones being cheeky to me."

"Look, I can beat you."

"Beat me . . . beat me . . . let's see."

"*Hei*, you are not civilised, eh?"

"Keep quiet and let us think, both of you, or I will put you down."

"Nana, do not weep. There is God above."

Thank you my master.

"But we are in Cape Coast already."

Meewuo! My God, hold me tight or something will happen to me.

---

1. Truck or bus.

My master, I will come down here.

"O Nana, I thought you said you were going to the hospital. . . . We are not there yet."

I am saying maybe I will get down here and ask my way around.

"Nana, you do not know these people, eh? They are very impudent here. They have no use for old age. So they do not respect it. Sit down, I will take you there."

Are you going there, my master?

"No, but I will take you there."

Ah, my master, your old mother thanks you. Do not shed a tear when you hear of my death . . . my master, your old mother thanks you.

I hear there is somewhere where they keep corpses until their owners claim them . . . if she has been buried, then I must find her husband . . . Esi Amfoa, what did I come to do under this sky? I have buried all my children and now I am going to bury my only grandchild!

"Nana we are there."

Is this the hospital?

"Yes, Nana. What is your child's name?"

Esi Amfoa. His father named her after me.

"Do you know her European name?"

No, my master.

"What shall we do?"

" . . . Ei lady, Lady Nurse, we are looking for somebody."

"You are looking for somebody and can you read? If you cannot, you must ask someone what the rules in the hospital are. You can only come and visit people at three o'clock."

Lady, please. She was my only grandchild. . . .

"Who? And anyway, it is none of our business."

Nana, you must be patient . . . and not cry. . . .

"Old woman, why are you crying, it is not allowed here. No one must make any noise. . . ."

My lady, I am sorry but she was all I had.

"Who? Oh, are you the old woman who is looking for somebody?"

Yes.

"Who is he?"

She was my granddaughter—the only child of my only son.

"I mean, what was her name?"

Esi Amfoa.

"Esi Amfoa . . . Esi Amfoa. I am sorry, we do not have anyone whom they call like that here."

Is that it?

"Nana, I told you they may know only her European name here."

My master, what shall we do then?

"What is she ill with?"

She came here to have a child. . . .

". . . And they say, they opened her stomach and removed the baby. Oh . . . oh, I see."

My Lord, hold me tight so that nothing will happen to me now.

"I see. It is the Caesarean case."

"Nurse, you know her?"

And when I take her back, Anona Ebusuafo will say that I did not wait for them to come with me. . . .

"Yes. Are you her brother?"

"No. I am only the driver who brought the old woman."

"Did she bring all her clan?"

"No. She came alone."

"Strange thing for a villager to do."

I hope they have not cut her up already.

"Did she bring a whole bag full of cassava and plantain and kenkey?"[2]

"No. She has only her little bundle."

"Follow me. But you must not make any noise. This is not the hour for coming here. . . ."

My master, does she know her?

"Yes."

I hear it is very cold where they put them. . . .

It was feeding time for new babies. When old Esi Amfoa saw young Esi Amfoa, the latter was all neat and nice. White sheets and all. She did not see the beautiful stitches under the sheets. "This woman is a tough bundle," Dr. Gyamfi had declared after the identical twins had been removed, the last stitches had been threaded off and Mary Koomson, alias Esi Amfoa, had come to.

The old woman somersaulted into the room and lay groaning, not screaming, by the bed. For was not her last pot broken? So they lay them in state even in hospitals and not always cut them up for instruction?

The Nursing Sister was furious. Young Esi Amfoa spoke. And this time old Esi Amfoa wept loud and hard—wept all her tears.

Scrappy nurse-under-training, Jessy Treeson, second-generation-Cape Coaster-her-grandmother still-remembered-at-Egyaa No. 7[3] said, "As for these villagers," and giggled.

Draba Anan looked hard at Jessy Treeson, looked hard at her, all of her: her starched uniform, apron and cap . . . and then dismissed them

---

2. A staple food made from fermented corn;   3. Cape Coast is a principal city in Ghana.
"cassava": another staple food.

all. . . . "Such a cassava stick . . . but maybe I will break my toe if I kicked at her buttocks," he thought.

And by the bed the old woman was trying hard to rise and look at the only pot which had refused to get broken.

1970

ERICA JONG
1942–

When the heroine of Erica Jong's best-selling novel *Fear of Flying* (1973) wonders where the women are "who were *really* free," she meditates on Emily Dickinson, the Brontës, Virginia Woolf, Carson McCullers, and Sylvia Plath, only to decide in dismay that most women artists were timid in their lives and brave only in their art: "What a group! Severe, suicidal, strange." Moving through a series of comic escapades toward independence, Jong's would-be female Chaucer aspires to become the "one lusty lady who had juice and joy and love and talent too": in this, she resembles her author, whose work dramatizes with exuberant wit the special gratifications and dangers facing women who want to be free.

Jong grew up on Manhattan's Upper West Side in a Jewish family. The second of three daughters born to Seymour and Eda Mirsky Mann, she majored in English at Barnard College and earned an M.A. in eighteenth-century literature at Columbia, where she received several fellowships. After teaching English at a number of colleges, she lived in Europe for several years with her second husband, Allen Jong. More recently, she has settled in Connecticut with the writer Jonathan Fast, the father of her daughter, Molly Miranda. Jong became famous for the ribald sexuality of *Fear of Flying*, of its sequel, *How to Save Your Own Life* (1977), and of her most recent novel, *Fanny, Being the True History of the Adventures of Fanny Hackabout-Jones* (1980), an imitation of such eighteenth-century novels as *Tom Jones* and *Fanny*; however, the five volumes of prize-winning verse she has published are just as wry and wary as her fiction.

Castration of the Pen

The pen is an index finger
which has learned
to give milk
like a breast.

It is curious.   5
It explores
the cunts of girls.
It explores
& tells.

It is nourishing.   10
It can suckle babies
with the bluest,
blackest milk.

It is clever,
has an endless store   15
an anecdotes & fables.

It is logical,
can do research,
can put its tip
against your piglike nose,   20
can even say
FUCK YOU.

But unlike your finger
or your breast
your pen is fickle.   25
It writes speeches
for two rival politicians.
It endorses checks
from almost anyone.
It writes bad lines   30
& writes good ones
without caring
& leaves you
to sort out the mess.

By this time   35
you have gathered
that the pen's a symbol.

Is it breast?
Or is it penis?

Cut it off!   40

1973

Alcestis[1] on the Poetry Circuit

(IN MEMORIAM Marina Tsvetayeva, Anna Wickham, Sylvia Plath,
Shakespeare's sister,[2] etc., etc.)

The best slave
does not need to be beaten.
She beats herself.

Not with a leather whip,
or with sticks or twigs,   5
not with a blackjack
or a billyclub,
but with the fine whip
of her own tongue
& the subtle beating   10
of her mind
against her mind.

For who can hate her half so well
as she hates herself?
& who can match the finesse   15
of her self-abuse?

Years of training
are required for this.
Twenty years
of subtle self-indulgence,   20
self-denial;
until the subject
thinks herself a queen
& yet a beggar—
both at the same time.   25
She must doubt herself
in everything but love.

She must choose passionately
& badly.
She must feel lost as a dog   30
without her master.
She must refer all moral questions
to her mirror.
She must fall in love with a cossack
or a poet.   35

---

1. In Greek myth, a devoted wife who sacrificed
herself to save her husband Admetus's life.
2. Marina Tsvetayeva (1892–1941), Russian
poet; Anna Wickham (1884–1947), English
poet; Sylvia Plath (1932–1963), American poet.
Shakespeare's sister is the subject of a meditation
by Virginia Woolf on the difficulties of female
artists, in A Room of One's Own.

She must never go out of the house
unless veiled in paint.
She must wear tight shoes
so she always remembers her bondage.
She must never forget   40
she is rooted in the ground.

Though she is quick to learn
& admittedly clever,
her natural doubt of herself
should make her so weak   45
that she dabbles brilliantly
in half a dozen talents
& thus embellishes
but does not change
our life.   50

If she's an artist
& comes close to genius,
the very fact of her gift
should cause her such pain
that she will take her own life   55
rather than best us.

& after she dies, we will cry
& make her a saint.

1973

LOUISE GLÜCK

1943–

As the critic Helen Vendler has observed, Louise Glück's "cryptic narratives" are in some ways "far removed from the more circumstantial poetry written by women poets in the last ten years, but they remain poems chiefly about childhood, family life, love, and motherhood." Born in New York City, Louise Glück attended Sarah Lawrence College and Columbia University. The mother of one son, she has been twice married and at present lives in Vermont with her husband John Dranow. Her well-received collections of poetry include *Firstborn* (1968) and *Descending Figure* (1980). She has won Rockefeller and Guggenheim Fellowships, and she has taught verse writing at such institutions as Columbia University, the University of Iowa, and Williams College.

Throughout her career, as both the style and the subject of her *Illuminations* reveal, Glück has been intensely attentive to the sun that "rises / cold and single over the map of language." Whether stripped and chill or ecstatically pure, her beautifully crafted lines evoke essence more than circumstance. Yet, as Vendler argues, in their precise attention to such subjects as anorexia, motherhood, and marriage, Glück's words imply the details as well as the desires of femininity.

Illuminations[1]

1

My son squats in the snow in his blue snowsuit.
All around him stubble, the brown
degraded bushes. In the morning air
they seem to stiffen into words.
And, between, the white steady silence.   5
A wren hops on the airstrip
under the sill, drills
for sustenance, then spreads
its short wings, shadows
dropping from them.   10

2

Last winter he could barely speak.
I moved his crib to face the window:
in the dark mornings
he would stand and grip the bars
until the walls appeared,   15
calling *light, light,*
that one syllable, in
demand or recognition.

3

He sits at the kitchen window
with his cup of apple juice.   20
Each tree forms where he left it,
leafless, trapped in his breath.
How clear their edges are,
no limb obscured by motion,
as the sun rises   25
cold and single over the map of language.

1980

1. The title of a sequence of visionary prose   Rimbaud (1854–1891).
poems by the French symbolist poet Arthur

Dedication to Hunger

1 From the Suburbs

They cross the yard
and at the back door
the mother sees with pleasure
how alike they are, father and daughter—
I know something of that time.   5
The little girl purposefully
swinging her arms, laughing
her stark laugh:

It should be kept secret, that sound.
It means she's realized   10
that he never touches her.
She is a child; he could touch her
if he wanted to.

2 Grandmother

"Often I would stand at the window—
your grandfather   15
was a young man then—
waiting, in the early evening."

That is what marriage is.
I watch the tiny figure
changing to a man   20
as he moves toward her,
the last light rings in his hair.
I do not question
their happiness. And he rushes in
with his young man's hunger,   25
so proud to have taught her that:
his kiss would have been
clearly tender—

Of course, of course. Except
it might as well have been   30
his hand over her mouth.

3 Eros[2]

To be male, always
to go to women

2. Greek god of love.

and be taken back
into the pierced flesh: 35

       I suppose
memory is stirred.
And the girl child
who wills herself
into her father's arms   40
likewise loved him
second. Nor is she told
what need to express.
There is a look one sees,
the mouth somehow desperate—   45

Because the bond
cannot be proven.

4   *The Deviation*[3]

It begins quietly
in certain female children:
the fear of death, taking as its form   50
dedication to hunger,
because a woman's body
is a grave; it will accept
anything. I remember
lying in bed at night   55
touching the soft, digressive breasts,
touching, at fifteen,
the interfering flesh
that I would sacrifice
until the limbs were free   60
of blossom and subterfuge: I felt
what I feel now, aligning these words—
it is the same need to perfect,
of which death is the mere byproduct.

5   *Sacred Objects*

Today in the field I saw   65
the hard, active buds of the dogwood
and wanted, as we say, to capture them,
to make them eternal. That is the premise
of renunciation: the child,
having no self to speak of,   70
comes to life in denial—

---

3. Glück is referring to *anorexia nervosa*, an eating disorder.

I stood apart in that achievement,
in that power to expose
the underlying body, like a god
for whose deed   75
there is no parallel in the natural world.

                                                        1980

Horse[4]

What does the horse give you
that I cannot give you?

I watch you when you are alone,
when you ride into the field behind the dairy,
your hands buried in the mare's   5
dark mane.

Then I know what lies behind your silence:
scorn, hatred of me, of marriage. Still,
you want me to touch you; you cry out
as brides cry, but when I look at you I see   10
there are no children in your body.
Then what is there?

Nothing, I think. Only haste
to die before I die.

In a dream, I watched you ride the horse   15
over the dry fields and then
dismount; you two walked together;
in the dark, you had no shadows.
But I felt them coming toward me
since at night they go anywhere,   20
they are their own masters.

Look at me. You think I don't understand?
What is the animal
if not passage out of this life?

                                                        1983

4. "A man is addressing his young wife" [Glück's note].

SUSAN GRIFFIN

1943–

A native Californian, Susan Griffin has expressed her deep commitment to feminist change in a variety of forms and modes, including a collection of poetry (*Like the Iris of an Eye*, 1976), a radio drama (*Voices*, 1975), and two impressively researched, compellingly written prose examinations of women's situation (*Woman and Nature: The Roaring inside Her*, 1978, and *Pornography and Silence: Culture's Revenge against Nature*, 1981). Graduated from San Francisco State University in 1965, Griffin is divorced and lives in Berkeley, California, with her daughter. While working at a number of jobs—as a waitress, a switchboard operator, a house painter, and a teacher, for instance—she has been consistently productive and persistently feminist in her writing. In such poems as *An Answer to a Man's Question*, "What Can I Do about Women's Liberation?" and *I Like to Think of Harriet Tubman*, she sometimes passionately, sometimes wittily rebukes the "men who practice the law, / who revere the law, / who make the law" and "do not want / to take the women seriously," while in *Woman and Nature* she demonstrates the seriousness of her own engagement with the problem of woman's oppression. At the same time, in all her work, she dreams of a regeneration of female energy, for, as Adrienne Rich has remarked, Griffin's work is not only "about memory and mutilation," it is about "female anger as power, female presence as transforming force."

I Like to Think of Harriet Tubman[1]

I like to think of Harriet Tubman.
Harriet Tubman who carried a revolver,
who had a scar on her head from a rock thrown
by a slave-master (because she
talked back), and who   5
had a ransom on her head
of thousands of dollars and who
was never caught, and who
had no use for the law
when the law was wrong,   10
who defied the law. I like
to think of her.
I like to think of her especially
when I think of the problem of
feeding children.   15

The legal answer
to the problem of feeding children

1. Tubman (1820?–1913) was a fugitive slave and a rescuer of slaves.

is ten free lunches every month,
being equal, in the child's real life,
to eating lunch every other day.   20
Monday but not Tuesday.
I like to think of the President
eating lunch Monday, but not
Tuesday.
And when I think of the President   25
and the law, and the problem of
feeding children, I like to
think of Harriet Tubman
and her revolver.

And then sometimes   30
I think of the President
and other men,
men who practice the law,
who revere the law,
who make the law,   35
who enforce the law,
who live behind
and operate through
and feed themselves
at the expense of   40
starving children
because of the law.

Men who sit in paneled offices
and think about vacations
and tell women   45
whose care it is
to feed children
not to be hysterical
not to be hysterical as in the word
hysterikos, the greek for   50
womb suffering,
not to suffer in their
wombs,
not to care,
not to bother the men   55
because they want to think
of other things
and do not want
to take the women seriously.
I want them   60
to take women seriously.

I want them to think about Harriet Tubman,
and remember,

remember she was beat by a white man
and she lived   65
and she lived to redress her grievances,
and she lived in swamps
and wore the clothes of a man
bringing hundreds of fugitives from
slavery, and was never caught,   70
and led an army,
and won a battle,
and defied the laws
because the laws were wrong, I want men
to take us seriously.   75
I am tired wanting them to think
about right and wrong.
I want them to fear.
I want them to feel fear now
as I have felt suffering in the womb, and   80
I want them
to know
that there is always a time
there is always a time to make right
what is wrong,   85
there is always a time
for retribution
and that time
is beginning.

1976

ALICE WALKER

1944–

Alice Walker's father, Willie Lee Walker, farmed as a sharecropper in Georgia. Her mother, Minnie Grant Walker, "labored beside—not behind" her husband when she was not caring for her eight children. "As I remember it," Alice Walker—her youngest child—has reminisced, "we were really not allowed to be discouraged. Discouragement couldn't hold out against her faith." It is characteristic of Walker to be proud of her origins, for she believes that "the grace with which we embrace life, in spite of the pain, the sorrows, is always a measure of what has gone before." In her short story *Everyday Use* and in her autobiographical essay *In Search of Our Mothers' Gardens*, Walker explores the dynamics of the empowerment she gained through her own matrilineage.

Walker attended Spelman College in Atlanta, Georgia, and Sarah Lawrence in New York before she began publishing poetry that was influenced by her involvement in the voter registration movement in Georgia and the welfare rights movement in Mississippi and New York. Her first volume of verse, *Once*

(1968), appeared when she was teaching at Jackson State University in Mississippi. Sardonic and lyrical by turns, the poems recount not only her experiences in civil rights work but also her travels in Africa. Her next volume of poetry, *Revolutionary Petunias* (1973), describes the rural Georgia of her childhood. While both books were well received, Walker has achieved national prominence through her work as the editor of an anthology of Zora Neale Hurston's writings (*I Love Myself When I Am Laughing*, 1979), as a contributing editor to the magazine *Ms.*, and, even more importantly, through her own fiction.

From *The Third Life of Grange Copeland* (1970) to *In Love and Trouble* (1973), *Meridian* (1976), and *The Color Purple* (1982), Walker analyzes the effect of racism on black men and celebrates the resiliency of black women. *Meridian*, which documents the struggles of several civil rights workers during the sixties, is no less focused on black women's survival skills than *The Color Purple*, which won the National Book Award. *The Color Purple* experiments with epistolary form to present the linguistic strategies of characters who struggle to articulate their feelings about divinity, sexuality, and identity from the complex perspective of Afro-American experience. In this novel, as in her earlier stories, Walker extends the fictional techniques of her two favorite authors: Zora Neale Hurston and Jean Toomer. Not only does Walker portray the impact of racism on the relationships between black men and women and the importance of female networks of support, she also captures the humor and the pathos of her characters' erotic entanglements. Her most recent volume of essays, *In Search of Our Mothers' Gardens* (1983), offers insight into the achievements of such black women as the mystical writer Rebecca Cox Jackson and Coretta Scott King, the widow of the civil rights advocate Martin Luther King, Jr., providing, too, a portrait of the artist herself as she reconciles her commitment to writing with the responsibilities of motherhood.

Everyday Use

for your grandmama

I will wait for her in the yard that Maggie and I made so clean and wavy yesterday afternoon. A yard like this is more comfortable than most people know. It is not just a yard. It is like an extended living room. When the hard clay is swept clean as a floor and the fine sand around the edges lined with tiny, irregular grooves, anyone can come and sit and look up into the elm tree and wait for the breezes that never come inside the house.

Maggie will be nervous until after her sister goes: she will stand hopelessly in corners, homely and ashamed of the burn scars down her arms and legs, eying her sister with a mixture of envy and awe. She thinks her sister has held life always in the palm of one hand, that "no" is a word the world never learned to say to her.

You've no doubt seen those TV shows where the child who has "made it" is confronted, as a surprise, by her own mother and father, tottering in weakly from backstage.[1] (A pleasant surprise, of course: What would they do if parent and child came on the show only to curse out and insult each other?) On TV mother and child embrace and smile into each other's faces. Sometimes the mother and father weep, the child wraps them in her arms and leans across the table to tell how she would not have made it without their help. I have seen these programs.

Sometimes I dream a dream in which Dee and I are suddenly brought together on a TV program of this sort. Out of a dark and soft-seated limousine I am ushered into a bright room filled with many people. There I meet a smiling, gray, sporty man like Johnny Carson who shakes my hand and tells me what a fine girl I have. Then we are on the stage and Dee is embracing me with tears in her eyes. She pins on my dress a large orchid, even though she has told me once that she thinks orchids are tacky flowers.

In real life I am a large, big-boned woman with rough, man-working hands. In the winter I wear flannel nightgowns to bed and overalls during the day. I can kill and clean a hog as mercilessly as a man. My fat keeps me hot in zero weather. I can work outside all day, breaking ice to get water for washing; I can eat pork liver cooked over the open fire minutes after it comes steaming from the hog. One winter I knocked a bull calf straight in the brain between the eyes with a sledge hammer and had the meat hung up to chill before nightfall. But of course all this does not show on television. I am the way my daughter would want me to be: a hundred pounds lighter, my skin like an uncooked barley pancake. My hair glistens in the hot bright lights. Johnny Carson has much to do to keep up with my quick and witty tongue.

But that is a mistake. I know even before I wake up. Who ever knew a Johnson with a quick tongue? Who can even imagine me looking a strange white man in the eye? It seems to me I have talked to them always with one foot raised in flight, with my head turned in whichever way is farthest from them. Dee, though. She would always look anyone in the eye. Hesitation was no part of her nature.

"How do I look, Mama?" Maggie says, showing just enough of her thin body enveloped in pink skirt and red blouse for me to know she's there, almost hidden by the door.

"Come out into the yard," I say.

Have you ever seen a lame animal, perhaps a dog run over by some

---

1. A reference to the popular television program *This Is Your Life*, in which celebrities were taken to a studio and surprised by a gathering of their friends, relatives, and associates.

careless person rich enough to own a car, sidle up to someone who is ignorant enough to be kind to him? That is the way my Maggie walks. She has been like this, chin on chest, eyes on ground, feet in shuffle, ever since the fire that burned the other house to the ground.

Dee is lighter than Maggie, with nicer hair and a fuller figure. She's a woman now, though sometimes I forget. How long ago was it that the other house burned? Ten, twelve years? Sometimes I can still hear the flames and feel Maggie's arms sticking to me, her hair smoking and her dress falling off her in little black papery flakes. Her eyes seemed stretched open, blazed open by the flames reflected in them. And Dee. I see her standing off under the sweet gum tree she used to dig gum out of; a look of concentration on her face as she watched the last dingy gray board of the house fall in toward the red-hot brick chimney. Why don't you do a dance around the ashes? I'd wanted to ask her. She had hated the house that much.

I used to think she hated Maggie, too. But that was before we raised the money, the church and me, to send her to Augusta[2] to school. She used to read to us without pity; forcing words, lies, other folks' habits, whole lives upon us two, sitting trapped and ignorant underneath her voice. She washed us in a river of make-believe, burned us with a lot of knowledge we didn't necessarily need to know. Pressed us to her with the serious way she read, to shove us away at just the moment, like dimwits, we seemed about to understand.

Dee wanted nice things. A yellow organdy dress to wear to her graduation from high school; black pumps to match a green suit she'd made from an old suit somebody gave me. She was determined to stare down any disaster in her efforts. Her eyelids would not flicker for minutes at a time. Often I fought off the temptation to shake her. At sixteen she had a style of her own: and knew what style was.

I never had an education myself. After second grade the school was closed down. Don't ask my why: in 1927 colored asked fewer questions than they do now. Sometimes Maggie reads to me. She stumbles along good-naturedly but can't see well. She knows she is not bright. Like good looks and money, quickness passed her by. She will marry John Thomas (who has mossy teeth in an earnest face) and then I'll be free to sit here and I guess just sing church songs to myself. Although I never was a good singer. Never could carry a tune. I was always better at a man's job. I used to love to milk till I was hooked in the side[3] in '49. Cows are soothing and slow and don't bother you, unless you try to milk them the wrong way.

I have deliberately turned my back on the house. It is three rooms,

---

2. Large city in Georgia, site of Paine College.　　　3. I.e., a cow kicked her.

just like the one that burned, except the roof is tin; they don't make shingle roofs any more. There are no real windows, just some holes cut in the sides, like the portholes in a ship, but not round and not square, with rawhide holding the shutters up on the outside. This house is in a pasture, too, like the other one. No doubt when Dee sees it she will want to tear it down. She wrote me once that no matter where we "choose" to live, she will manage to come see us. But she will never bring her friends. Maggie and I thought about this and Maggie asked me, "Mama, when did Dee ever *have* any friends?"

She had a few. Furtive boys in pink shirts hanging about on washday after school. Nervous girls who never laughed. Impressed with her they worshiped the well-turned phrase, the cute shape, the scalding humor that erupted like bubbles in lye. She read to them.

When she was courting Jimmy T she didn't have much time to pay to us, but turned all her faultfinding power on him. He *flew* to marry a cheap city girl from a family of ignorant flashy people. She hardly had time to recompose herself.

When she comes I will meet—but there they are!

Maggie attempts to make a dash for the house, in her shuffling way, but I stay her with my hand. "Come back here," I say. And she stops and tries to dig a well in the sand with her toe.

It is hard to see them clearly through the strong sun. But even the first glimpse of leg out of the car tells me it is Dee. Her feet were always neat-looking, as if God himself had shaped them with a certain style. From the other side of the car comes a short, stocky man. Hair is all over his head a foot long and hanging from his chin like a kinky mule tail. I hear Maggie suck in her breath. "Uhnnnh," is what it sounds like. Like when you see the wriggling end of a snake just in front of your foot on the road. "Uhnnnh."

Dee next. A dress down to the ground, in this hot weather. A dress so loud it hurts my eyes. There are yellows and oranges enough to throw back the light of the sun. I feel my whole face warming from the heat waves it throws out. Earrings gold, too, and hanging down to her shoulders. Bracelets dangling and making noises when she moves her arm up to shake the folds of the dress out of her armpits. The dress is loose and flows, and as she walks closer, I like it. I hear Maggie go "Uhnnnh" again. It is her sister's hair. It stands straight up like the wool on a sheep. It is black as night and around the edges are two long pigtails that rope about like small lizards disappearing behind her ears.

"Wa-su-zo-Tean-o!"[4] she says, coming on in that gliding way the dress makes her move. The short stocky fellow with the hair to his navel

4. African dialect greeting.

is all grinning and he follows up with "Asalamalakim,[5] my mother and sister!" He moves to hug Maggie but she falls back, right up against the back of my chair. I feel her trembling there and when I look up I see the perspiration falling off her chin.

"Don't get up," says Dee. Since I am stout it takes something of a push. You can see me trying to move a second or two before I make it. She turns, showing white heels through her sandals, and goes back to the car. Out she peeks next with a Polaroid. She stoops down quickly and lines up picture after picture of me sitting there in front of the house with Maggie cowering behind me. She never takes a shot without making sure the house is included. When a cow comes nibbling around the edge of the yard she snaps it and me and Maggie *and* the house. Then she puts the Polaroid in the back seat of the car, and comes up and kisses me on the forehead.

Meanwhile Asalamalakim is going through motions with Maggie's hand. Maggie's hand is as limp as a fish, and probably as cold, despite the sweat, and she keeps trying to pull it back. It looks like Asalamalakim wants to shake hands but wants to do it fancy. Or maybe he don't know how people shake hands. Anyhow, he soon gives up on Maggie.

"Well," I say. "Dee."

"No, Mama," she says. "Not 'Dee,' Wangero Leewanika Kemanjo!"

"What happened to 'Dee'?" I wanted to know.

"She's dead," Wangero said. "I couldn't bear it any longer, being named after the people who oppress me."

"You know as well as me you was named after your aunt Dicie," I said. Dicie is my sister. She named Dee. We called her "Big Dee" after Dee was born.

"But who was *she* named after?" asked Wangero.

"I guess after Grandma Dee," I said.

"And who was she named after?" asked Wangero.

"Her mother," I said, and saw Wangero was getting tired. "That's about as far back as I can trace it," I said. Though, in fact, I probably could have carried it back beyond the Civil War through the branches.

"Well," said Asalamalakim, "there you are."

"Uhnnnh," I heard Maggie say.

"There I was not," I said, "before 'Dicie' cropped up in our family, so why should I try to trace it that far back?"

He just stood there grinning, looking down on me like somebody inspecting a Model A car.[6] Every once in a while he and Wangero sent eye signals over my head.

"How do you pronounce this name?" I asked.

5. Muslim greeting.
6. Very old automobile designed by Henry Ford.

"You don't have to call me by it if you don't want to," said Wangero.

"Why shouldn't I?" I asked. "If that's what you want us to call you, we'll call you."

"I know it might sound awkward at first," said Wangero.

"I'll get used to it," I said. "Ream it out again."

Well, soon we got the name out of the way. Asalamalakim had a name twice as long and three times as hard. After I tripped over it two or three times he told me to just call him Hakim-a-barber. I wanted to ask him was he a barber, but I didn't really think he was, so I didn't ask.

"You must belong to those beef-cattle peoples down the road," I said. They said "Asalamalakim" when they met you, too, but they didn't shake hands. Always too busy: feeding the cattle, fixing the fences, putting up salt-lick shelters,[7] throwing down hay. When the white folks poisoned some of the herd the men stayed up all night with rifles in their hands. I walked a mile and a half just to see the sight.

Hakim-a-barber said, "I accept some of their doctrines, but farming and raising cattle is not my style." (They didn't tell me, and I didn't ask, whether Wangero (Dee) had really gone and married him.)

We sat down to eat and right away he said he didn't eat collards and pork was unclean. Wangero, though, went on through the chitlins and corn bread, the greens and everything else. She talked a blue streak over the sweet potatoes. Everything delighted her. Even the fact that we still used the benches her daddy made for the table when we couldn't afford to buy chairs.

"Oh, Mama!" she cried. Then turned to Hakim-a-barber. "I never knew how lovely these benches are. You can feel the rump prints," she said, running her hands underneath her and along the bench. Then she gave a sigh and her hand closed over Grandma Dee's butter dish. "That's it!" she said. "I knew there was something I wanted to ask you if I could have." She jumped up from the table and went over in the corner where the churn stood, the milk in it clabber[8] by now. She looked at the churn and looked at it.

"This churn top is what I need," she said. "Didn't Uncle Buddy whittle it out of a tree you all used to have?"

"Yes," I said.

"Uh huh," she said happily. "And I want the dasher, too."

"Uncle Buddy whittle that, too?" asked the barber.

Dee (Wangero) looked up at me.

"Aunt Dee's first husband whittled the dash," said Maggie so low you almost couldn't hear her. "His name was Henry, but they called him Stash."

"Maggie's brain is like an elephant's," Wangero said, laughing. "I

7. A shelter where cows are given salt to lick to   8. Curdled milk.
protect them from the heat.

can use the churn top as a centerpiece for the alcove table," she said, sliding a plate over the churn, "and I'll think of something artistic to do with the dasher."

When she finished wrapping the dasher the handle stuck out. I took it for a moment in my hands. You didn't even have to look close to see where hands pushing the dasher up and down to make butter had left a kind of sink in the wood. In fact, there were a lot of small sinks; you could see where thumbs and fingers had sunk into the wood. It was beautiful light yellow wood, from a tree that grew in the yard where Big Dee and Stash had lived.

After dinner Dee (Wangero) went to the trunk at the foot of my bed and started rifling through it. Maggie hung back in the kitchen over the dishpan. Out came Wangero with two quilts. They had been pieced by Grandma Dee and then Big Dee and me had hung them on the quilt frames on the front porch and quilted them. One was in the Lone Star pattern. The other was Walk Around the Mountain. In both of them were scraps of dresses Grandma Dee had worn fifty and more years ago. Bits and pieces of Grandpa Jarrell's Paisley shirts. And one teeny faded blue piece, about the size of a penny matchbox, that was from Great Grandpa Ezra's uniform that he wore in the Civil War.

"Mama," Wangero said sweet as a bird. "Can I have these old quilts?"

I heard something fall in the kitchen, and a minute later the kitchen door slammed.

"Why don't you take one or two of the others?" I asked. "These old things was just done by me and Big Dee from some tops your grandma pieced before she died."

"No," said Wangero. "I don't want those. They are stitched around the borders by machine."

"That'll make them last better," I said.

"That's not the point," said Wangero. "These are all pieces of dresses Grandma used to wear. She did all this stitching by hand. Imagine!" She held the quilts securely in her arms, stroking them.

"Some of the pieces, like those lavender ones, come from old clothes her mother handed down to her," I said, moving up to touch the quilts. Dee (Wangero) moved back just enough so that I couldn't reach the quilts. They already belonged to her.

"Imagine!" she breathed again, clutching them closely to her bosom.

"The truth is," I said, "I promised to give them quilts to Maggie, for when she marries John Thomas."

She gasped like a bee had stung her.

"Maggie can't appreciate these quilts!" she said. "She'd probably be backward enough to put them to everyday use."

"I reckon she would," I said. "God knows I been saving 'em for long enough with nobody using 'em. I hope she will!" I didn't want to bring up how I had offered Dee (Wangero) a quilt when she went away to college. Then she had told me they were old-fashioned, out of style.

"But they're *priceless*!" she was saying now, furiously; for she has a temper. "Maggie would put them on the bed and in five years they'd be in rags. Less than that!"

"She can always make some more," I said. "Maggie knows how to quilt."

Dee (Wangero) looked at me with hatred. "You just will not understand. The point is these quilts, *these* quilts!"

"Well," I said, stumped. "What would *you* do with them?"

"Hang them," she said. As if that was the only thing you *could* do with quilts.

Maggie by now was standing in the door. I could almost hear the sound her feet made as they scraped over each other.

"She can have them, Mama," she said, like somebody used to never winning anything, or having anything reserved for her. "I can 'member Grandma Dee without the quilts."

I looked at her hard. She had filled her bottom lip with checkerberry snuff and it gave her face a kind of dopey, hangdog look. It was Grandma Dee and Big Dee who taught her how to quilt herself. She stood there with her scarred hands hidden in the folds of her skirt. She looked at her sister with something like fear but she wasn't mad at her. This was Maggie's portion. This was the way she knew God to work.

When I looked at her like that something hit me in the top of my head and ran down to the soles of my feet. Just like when I'm in church and the spirit of God touches me and I get happy and shout. I did something I never had done before: hugged Maggie to me, then dragged her on into the room, snatched the quilts out of Miss Wangero's hands and dumped them into Maggie's lap. Maggie just sat there on my bed with her mouth open.

"Take one or two of the others," I said to Dee.

But she turned without a word and went out to Hakim-a-barber.

"You just don't understand," she said, as Maggie and I came out to the car.

"What don't I understand?" I wanted to know.

"Your heritage," she said. And then she turned to Maggie, kissed her, and said, "You ought to try to make something of yourself, too, Maggie. It's really a new day for us. But from the way you and Mama still live you'd never know it."

She put on some sunglasses that hid everything above the tip of her nose and her chin.

Maggie smiled; maybe at the sunglasses. But a real smile, not scared. After we watched the car dust settle I asked Maggie to bring me a dip of snuff. And then the two of us sat there just enjoying, until it was time to go in the house and go to bed.

1973

In Search of Our Mothers' Gardens

> I described her own nature and temperament. Told how they needed a larger life for their expression. . . . I pointed out that in lieu of proper channels, her emotions had overflowed into paths that dissipated them. I talked, beautifully I thought, about an art that would be born, an art that would open the way for women the likes of her. I asked her to hope, and build up an inner life against the coming of that day. . . . I sang, with a strange quiver in my voice, a promise song.
>
> —Jean Toomer, "Avey," *Cane*[9]

The poet speaking to a prostitute who falls asleep while he's talking—

When the poet Jean Toomer walked through the South in the early twenties, he discovered a curious thing: black women whose spirituality was so intense, so deep, so *unconscious*, that they were themselves unaware of the richness they held. They stumbled blindly through their lives: creatures so abused and mutilated in body, so dimmed and confused by pain, that they considered themselves unworthy even of hope. In the selfless abstractions their bodies became to the men who used them, they became more than "sexual objects," more even than mere women: they became "Saints." Instead of being perceived as whole persons, their bodies became shrines: what was thought to be their minds became temples suitable for worship. These crazy Saints stared out at the world, wildly, like lunatics—or quietly, like suicides; and the "God" that was in their gaze was as mute as a great stone.

Who were these Saints? These crazy, loony, pitiful women?

Some of them, without a doubt, were our mothers and grandmothers.

In the still heat of the post-Reconstruction South,[1] this is how they seemed to Jean Toomer: exquisite butterflies trapped in an evil honey, toiling away their lives in an era, a century, that did not acknowledge them, except as "the *mule* of the world." They dreamed dreams that no one knew—not even themselves, in any coherent fashion—and saw visions no one could understand. They wandered or sat about the countryside crooning lullabies to ghosts, and drawing the mother of Christ in charcoal on courthouse walls.

9. The major work of Jean Toomer (1894–1967), one of the writers of the Harlem Renaissance; the book is a mixture of narrative prose and lyric poetry.

1. I.e., the South after the efforts at "Reconstruction" which followed the Civil War, and included the education of newly freed slaves.

They forced their minds to desert their bodies and their striving spirits sought to rise, like frail whirlwinds from the hard red clay. And when those frail whirlwinds fell, in scattered particles, upon the ground, no one mourned. Instead, men lit candles to celebrate the emptiness that remained, as people do who enter a beautiful but vacant space to resurrect a God.

Our mothers and grandmothers, some of them: moving to music not yet written. And they waited.

They waited for a day when the unknown thing that was in them would be made known; but guessed, somehow in their darkness, that on the day of their revelation they would be long dead. Therefore to Toomer they walked, and even ran, in slow motion. For they were going nowhere immediate, and the future was not yet within their grasp. And men took our mothers and grandmothers, "but got no pleasure from it." So complex was their passion and their calm.

To Toomer, they lay vacant and fallow as autumn fields, with harvest time never in sight: and he saw them enter loveless marriages, without joy; and become prostitutes, without resistance; and become mothers of children, without fulfillment.

For these grandmothers and mothers of ours were not Saints, but Artists; driven to a numb and bleeding madness by the springs of creativity in them for which there was no release. They were Creators, who lived lives of spiritual waste, because they were so rich in spirituality—which is the basis of Art—that the strain of enduring their unused and unwanted talent drove them insane. Throwing away this spirituality was their pathetic attempt to lighten the soul to a weight their work-worn, sexually abused bodies could bear.

What did it mean for a black woman to be an artist in our grandmothers' time? In our great-grandmothers' day? It is a question with an answer cruel enough to stop the blood.

Did you have a genius of a great-great-grandmother who died under some ignorant and depraved white overseer's lash? Or was she required to bake biscuits for a lazy backwater tramp, when she cried out in her soul to paint watercolors of sunsets, or the rain falling on the green and peaceful pasturelands? Or was her body broken and forced to bear children (who were more often than not sold away from her)—eight, ten, fifteen, twenty children—when her one joy was the thought of modeling heroic figures of rebellion, in stone or clay?

How was the creativity of the black woman kept alive, year after year and century after century, when for most of the years black people have been in America, it was a punishable crime for a black person to read or write? And the freedom to paint, to sculpt, to expand the mind with action did not exist. Consider, if you can bear to imagine it, what might have been the result if singing, too, had been forbidden by law. Listen

to the voices of Bessie Smith, Billie Holiday, Nina Simone, Roberta
Flack, and Aretha Franklin,[2] among others, and imagine those voices
muzzled for life. Then you may begin to comprehend the lives of our
"crazy," "Sainted" mothers and grandmothers. The agony of the lives
of women who might have been Poets, Novelists, Essayists, and Short-
Story Writers (over a period of centuries), who died with their real gifts
stifled within them.

And, if this were the end of the story, we would have cause to cry out
in my paraphrase of Okot p'Bitek's[3] great poem:

> O, my clanswomen
> Let us all cry together!
> Come,
> Let us mourn the death of our mother,
> The death of a Queen
> The ash that was produced
> By a great fire!
> O, this homestead is utterly dead
> Close the gates
> With *lacari* thorns,
> For our mother
> The creator of the Stool is lost!
> And all the young women
> Have perished in the wilderness!

But this is not the end of the story, for all the young women—our
mothers and grandmothers, *ourselves*—have not perished in the wilderness. And if we ask ourselves why, and search for and find the answer, we will know beyond all efforts to erase it from our minds, just
exactly who, and of what, we black American women are.

One example, perhaps the most pathetic, most misunderstood one,
can provide a backdrop for our mothers' work: Phillis Wheatley,[4] a
slave in the 1700s.

Virginia Woolf,[5] in her book *A Room of One's Own*, wrote that in
order for a woman to write fiction she must have two things, certainly: a
room of her own (with key and lock) and enough money to support
herself.

What then are we to make of Phillis Wheatley, a slave, who owned
not even herself? This sickly, frail black girl who required a servant of
her own at times—her health was so precarious—and who, had she
been white, would have been easily considered the intellectual superior
of all the women and most of the men in the society of her day.

---

2. A series of female black singers from the
twenties to the present.
3. African poet (b. 1931).
4. Phillis Wheatley (1753–1784), highly edu-

cated black slave who wrote formal, neoclassical
poems.
5. British novelist and essayist (1882–1941).

Virginia Woolf wrote further, speaking of course not of our Phillis, that "any woman born with a great gift in the sixteenth century [insert "eighteenth century," insert "black woman," insert "born or made a slave"] would certainly have gone crazed, shot herself, or ended her days in some lonely cottage outside the village, half witch, half wizard [insert "Saint"], feared and mocked at. For it needs little skill and psychology to be sure that a highly gifted girl who had tried to use her gift for poetry would have been so thwarted and hindered by contrary instincts [add "chains, guns, the lash, the ownership of one's body by someone else, submission to an alien religion"], that she must have lost her health and sanity to a certainty."

The key words, as they relate to Phillis, are "contrary instincts." For when we read the poetry of Phillis Wheatley—as when we read the novels of Nella Larsen or the oddly false-sounding autobiography of that freest of all black women writers, Zora Hurston[6]—evidence of "contrary instincts" is everywhere. Her loyalties were completely divided, as was, without question, her mind.

But how could this be otherwise? Captured at seven, a slave of wealthy, doting whites who instilled in her the "savagery" of the Africa they "rescued" her from . . . one wonders if she was even able to remember her homeland as she had known it, or as it really was.

Yes, because she did try to use her gift for poetry in a world that made her a slave, she was "so thwarted and hindered by . . . contrary instincts, that she . . . lost her health. . . ." In the last years of her brief life, burdened not only with the need to express her gift but also with a penniless, friendless "freedom" and several small children for whom she was forced to do strenuous work to feed, she lost her health, certainly. Suffering from malnutrition and neglect and who knows what mental agonies, Phillis Wheatley died.

So torn by "contrary instincts" was black, kidnapped, enslaved Phillis that her description of "the Goddess"—as she poetically called the Liberty she did not have—is ironically, cruelly humorous. And, in fact, has held Phillis up to ridicule for more than a century. It is usually read prior to hanging Phillis's memory as that of a fool. She wrote:

> The Goddess comes, she moves divinely fair,
> Olive and laurel binds her *golden* hair.
> Wherever shines this native of the skies,
> Unnumber'd charms and recent graces rise. [My italics]

It is obvious that Phillis, the slave, combed the "Goddess's" hair every morning; prior, perhaps, to bringing in the milk, or fixing her

6. Zora Neale Hurston (1901–1960), black American novelist.

mistress's lunch. She took her imagery from the one thing she saw elevated above all others.

With the benefit of hindsight we ask, "How could she?"

But at last, Phillis, we understand. No more snickering when your stiff, struggling, ambivalent lines are forced on us. We know now that you were not an idiot or a traitor; only a sickly little black girl, snatched from your home and country and made a slave; a woman who still struggled to sing the song that was your gift, although in a land of barbarians who praised you for your bewildered tongue. It is not so much what you sang, as that you kept alive, in so many of our ancestors, *the notion of song.*

Black women are called, in the folklore that so aptly identifies one's status in society, "the *mule* of the world," because we have been handed the burdens that everyone else—*everyone* else—refused to carry. We have also been called "Matriarchs," "Superwomen," and "Mean and Evil Bitches." Not to mention "Castraters" and "Sapphire's Mama."[7] When we have pleaded for understanding, our character has been distorted; when we have asked for simple caring, we have been handed empty inspirational appellations, then stuck in the farthest corner. When we have asked for love, we have been given children. In short, even our plainer gifts, our labors of fidelity and love, have been knocked down our throats. To be an artist and a black woman, even today, lowers our status in many respects, rather than raises it: and yet, artists we will be.

Therefore we must fearlessly pull out of ourselves and look at and identify with our lives the living creativity some of our great-grandmothers were not allowed to know. I stress *some* of them because it is well known that the majority of our great-grandmothers knew, even without "knowing" it, the reality of their spirituality, even if they didn't recognize it beyond what happened in the singing at church—and they never had any intention of giving it up.

How they did it—those millions of black women who were not Phillis Wheatley, or Lucy Terry or Frances Harper or Zora Hurston or Nella Larsen or Bessie Smith; or Elizabeth Catlett, or Katherine Dunham,[8] either—brings me to the title of this essay, "In Search of Our Mothers' Gardens," which is a personal account that is yet shared, in its theme and its meaning, by all of us. I found, while thinking about the

---

7. Sapphire: wife of "the Kingfish" in *Amos and Andy*, a popular early radio and television show.
8. Lucy Terry (1730–1821), black poet and fictionist; Frances E. W. Harper (1825–1911), black woman poet; Nella Larsen (1893–1964), black woman novelist of the Harlem Renaissance; Bessie Smith (1898–1937), black American blues singer; Elizabeth Catlett (b. 1915?), black educator and sculptor; Katherine Dunham (b. 1910), black American dancer and choreographer.

far-reaching world of the creative black woman, that often the truest answer to a question that really matters can be found very close.

In the late 1920s my mother ran away from home to marry my father. Marriage, if not running away, was expected of seventeen-year-
old girls. By the time she was twenty, she had two children and was
pregnant with a third. Five children later, I was born. And this is how I
came to know my mother: she seemed a large, soft, loving-eyed woman
who was rarely impatient in our home. Her quick, violent temper was
on view only a few times a year, when she battled with the white landlord who had the misfortune to suggest to her that her children did not
need to go to school.

She made all the clothes we wore, even my brothers' overalls. She
made all the towels and sheets we used. She spent the summers canning
vegetables and fruits. She spent the winter evenings making quilts
enough to cover all our beds.

During the "working" day, she labored beside—not behind—my father in the fields. Her day began before sunup, and did not end until
late at night. There was never a moment for her to sit down, undisturbed, to unravel her own private thoughts; never a time free from interruption—by work or the noisy inquiries of her many children. And
yet, it is to my mother—and all our mothers who were not famous—
that I went in search of the secret of what has fed that muzzled and
often mutilated, but vibrant, creative spirit that the black woman has
inherited, and that pops out in wild and unlikely places to this day.

But when, you will ask, did my overworked mother have time to
know or care about feeding the creative spirit?

The answer is so simple that many of us have spent years discovering
it. We have constantly looked high, when we should have looked high
—and low.

For example: in the Smithsonian Institution in Washington, D.C.,
there hangs a quilt unlike any other in the world. In fanciful, inspired,
and yet simple and identifiable figures, it portrays the story of the Crucifixion. It is considered rare, beyond price. Though it follows no
known pattern of quilt-making, and though it is made of bits and pieces
of worthless rags, it is obviously the work of a person of powerful imagination and deep spiritual feeling. Below this quilt I saw a note that says
it was made by "an anonymous Black woman in Alabama, a hundred
years ago."

If we could locate this "anonymous" black woman from Alabama,
she would turn out to be one of our grandmothers—an artist who left
her mark in the only materials she could afford, and in the only medium
her position in society allowed her to use.

As Virginia Woolf wrote further, in *A Room of One's Own*:

Yet genius of a sort must have existed among women as it must have existed among the working class. [Change this to "slaves" and "the wives
and daughters of sharecroppers."] Now and again an Emily Brontë or a
Robert Burns [change this to "a Zora Hurston or a Richard Wright"][9]
blazes out and proves its presence. But certainly it never got itself on to
paper. When, however, one reads of a witch being ducked, of a woman
possessed by devils [or "Sainthood"], of a wise woman selling herbs [our
root workers], or even a very remarkable man who had a mother, then I
think we are on the track of a lost novelist, a suppressed poet, of some mute
and inglorious Jane Austen. . . . Indeed, I would venture to guess that
Anon, who wrote so many poems without signing them, was often a
woman. . . .

And so our mothers and grandmothers have, more often than not
anonymously, handed on the creative spark, the seed of the flower they
themselves never hoped to see: or like a sealed letter they could not
plainly read.

And so it is, certainly, with my own mother. Unlike "Ma" Rainey's[1]
songs, which retained their creator's name even while blasting forth
from Bessie Smith's mouth, no song or poem will bear my mother's
name. Yet so many of the stories that I write, that we all write, are my
mother's stories. Only recently did I fully realize this: that through years
of listening to my mother's stories of her life, I have absorbed not only
the stories themselves, but something of the manner in which she
spoke, something of the urgency that involves the knowledge that her
stories—like her life—must be recorded. It is probably for this reason
that so much of what I have written is about characters whose counterparts in real life are so much older than I am.

But the telling of these stories, which came from my mother's lips as
naturally as breathing, was not the only way my mother showed herself
as an artist. For stories, too, were subject to being distracted, to dying
without conclusion. Dinners must be started, and cotton must be gathered before the big rains. The artist that was and is my mother showed
itself to me only after many years. This is what I finally noticed:

Like Mem, a character in *The Third Life of Grange Copeland*,[2] my
mother adorned with flowers whatever shabby house we were forced to
live in. And not just your typical straggly country stand of zinnias, either. She planted ambitious gardens—and still does—with over fifty
different varieties of plants that bloom profusely from early March until
late November. Before she left home for the fields, she watered her
flowers, chopped up the grass, and laid out new beds. When she returned from the fields she might divide clumps of bulbs, dig a cold pit,

9. Black American novelist (1908–1960);   1. Gertrude Pridgett Rainey (1886–1939),
Emily Brontë (1819–1848), English novelist   black blues singer and songwriter.
and poet; Robert Burns (1759–1796), Scottish   2. Walker's first novel.
poet.

uproot and replant roses, or prune branches from her taller bushes or trees—until night came and it was too dark to see.

Whatever she planted grew as if by magic, and her fame as a grower of flowers spread over three counties. Because of her creativity with her flowers, even my memories of poverty are seen through a screen of blooms—sunflowers, petunias, roses, dahlias, forsythia, spirea, delphiniums, verbena . . . and on and on.

And I remember people coming to my mother's yard to be given cuttings from her flowers; I hear again the praise showered on her because whatever rocky soil she landed on, she turned into a garden. A garden so brilliant with colors, so original in its design, so magnificent with life and creativity, that to this day people drive by our house in Georgia—perfect strangers and imperfect strangers—and ask to stand or walk among my mother's art.

I notice that it is only when my mother is working in her flowers that she is radiant, almost to the point of being invisible—except as Creator: hand and eye. She is involved in work her soul must have. Ordering the universe in the image of her personal conception of Beauty.

Her face, as she prepared the Art that is her gift, is a legacy of respect she leaves to me, for all that illuminates and cherishes life. She has handed down respect for the possibilities—and the will to grasp them.

For her, so hindered and intruded upon in so many ways, being an artist has still been a daily part of her life. This ability to hold on, even in very simple ways, is work black women have done for a very long time.

This poem is not enough, but it is something, for the woman who literally covered the holes in our walls with sunflowers:

> They were women then
> My mama's generation
> Husky of voice—Stout of
> Step
> With fists as well as
> Hands
> How they battered down
> Doors
> And ironed
> Starched white
> Shirts
> How they led
> Armies
> Headragged Generals
> Across mined
> Fields
> Booby-trapped
> Kitchens

> To discover books
> Desks
> A place for us
> How they knew what we
> *Must* know
> Without knowing a page
> Of it
> Themselves.

Guided by my heritage of a love of beauty and a respect for strength —in search of my mother's garden, I found my own.

And perhaps in Africa over two hundred years ago, there was just such a mother; perhaps she painted vivid and daring decorations in oranges and yellows and greens on the walls of her hut; perhaps she sang —in a voice like Roberta Flack's—*sweetly* over the compounds of her village; perhaps she wove the most stunning mats or told the most ingenious stories of all the village storytellers. Perhaps she was herself a poet—though only her daughter's name is signed to the poems that we know.

Perhaps Phillis Wheatley's mother was also an artist.

Perhaps in more than Phillis Wheatley's biological life is her mother's signature made clear.

1974, 1983

LESLIE MARMON SILKO
1948–

"It's stories that make this a community," Leslie Marmon Silko has remarked about the native-American world of Laguna Pueblo, New Mexico, in which she grew up, and in three books—*Laguna Woman* (1974), *Ceremony* (1977), and *Storyteller* (1981)—she has told and retold the tales that, she believes, make her people who they are. Of mixed native-American, Mexican, and Caucasian descent, Leslie Marmon attended Bureau of Indian Affairs schools at Laguna until entering high school, then studied at the University of New Mexico and later matriculated in law school before deciding to do graduate work in English and devote herself to a literary career. Divorced from John Silko, she has taught at Navajo Community College in Arizona and at the University of New Mexico, is the mother of two sons, and is the recipient of a MacArthur Foundation fellowship. Her ceremonial impulse to tell stories that are both self-defining and celebratory of her community has issued in an art that employs many forms: poetry, short stories, legendary tales, a novel, and, most recently, film scripts. The version of a Navajo lullaby that concludes her poignant and perceptive *Lullaby*, for instance, is only one example of the urgent need to recreate origins that impels this talented writer to cross conventional lines of genre in order to reconstitute the trails, trials, and traditions of a lost past.

Lullaby

The sun had gone down but the snow in the wind gave off its own light. It came in thick tufts like new wool—washed before the weaver spins it. Ayah reached out for it like her own babies had, and she smiled when she remembered how she had laughed at them. She was an old woman now, and her life had become memories. She sat down with her back against the wide cottonwood tree, feeling the rough bark on her back bones; she faced east and listened to the wind and snow sing a high-pitched Yeibechei song. Out of the wind she felt warmer, and she could watch the wide fluffy snow fill in her tracks, steadily, until the direction she had come from was gone. By the light of the snow she could see the dark outline of the big arroyo[1] a few feet away. She was sitting on the edge of Cebolleta Creek, where in the springtime the thin cows would graze on grass already chewed flat to the ground. In the wide deep creek bed where only a trickle of water flowed in the summer, the skinny cows would wander, looking for new grass along winding paths splashed with manure.

Ayah pulled the old Army blanket over her head like a shawl. Jimmie's blanket—the one he had sent to her. That was a long time ago and the green wool was faded, and it was unraveling on the edges. She did not want to think about Jimmie. So she thought about the weaving and the way her mother had done it. On the tall wooden loom set into the sand under a tamarack tree for shade. She could see it clearly. She had been only a little girl when her grandma gave her the wooden combs to pull the twigs and burrs from the raw, freshly washed wool. And while she combed the wool, her grandma sat beside her, spinning a silvery strand of yarn around the smooth cedar spindle. Her mother worked at the loom with yarns dyed bright yellow and red and gold. She watched them dye the yarn in boiling black pots full of beeweed petals, juniper berries, and sage. The blankets her mother made were soft and woven so tight that rain rolled off them like birds' feathers. Ayah remembered sleeping warm on cold windy nights, wrapped in her mother's blankets on the hogan's[2] sandy floor.

The snow drifted now, with the northwest wind hurling it in gusts. It drifted up around her black overshoes—old ones with little metal buckles. She smiled at the snow which was trying to cover her little by

1. A gully or ditch.　　　　　　　　　　2. An earth-covered Navajo dwelling.

little. She could remember when they had no black rubber overshoes; only the high buckskin leggings that they wrapped over their elkhide moccasins. If the snow was dry or frozen, a person could walk all day and not get wet; and in the evenings the beams of the ceiling would hang with lengths of pale buckskin leggings, drying out slowly.

She felt peaceful remembering. She didn't feel cold any more. Jimmie's blanket seemed warmer than it had ever been. And she could remember the morning he was born. She could remember whispering to her mother, who was sleeping on the other side of the hogan, to tell her it was time now. She did not want to wake the others. The second time she called to her, her mother stood up and pulled on her shoes; she knew. They walked to the old stone hogan together, Ayah walking a step behind her mother. She waited alone, learning the rhythms of the pains while her mother went to call the old woman to help them. The morning was already warm even before dawn and Ayah smelled the bee flowers blooming and the young willow growing at the springs. She could remember that so clearly, but his birth merged into the births of the other children and to her it became all the same birth. They named him for the summer morning and in English they called him Jimmie.

It wasn't like Jimmie died. He just never came back, and one day a dark blue sedan with white writing on its doors pulled up in front of the boxcar shack where the rancher let the Indians live. A man in a khaki uniform trimmed in gold gave them a yellow piece of paper and told them that Jimmie was dead. He said the Army would try to get the body back and then it would be shipped to them; but it wasn't likely because the helicopter had burned after it crashed. All of this was told to Chato because he could understand English. She stood inside the doorway holding the baby while Chato listened. Chato spoke English like a white man and he spoke Spanish too. He was taller than the white man and he stood straighter too. Chato didn't explain why; he just told the military man they could keep the body if they found it. The white man looked bewildered; he nodded his head and he left. Then Chato looked at her and shook his head, and then he told her, "Jimmie isn't coming home anymore," and when he spoke, he used the words to speak of the dead. She didn't cry then, but she hurt inside with anger. And she mourned him as the years passed, when a horse fell with Chato and broke his leg, and the white rancher told them he wouldn't pay Chato until he could work again. She mourned Jimmie because he would have worked for his father then; he would have saddled the big bag horse and ridden the fence lines each day, with wire cutters and heavy gloves, fixing the breaks in the barbed wire and putting the stray cattle back inside again.

She mourned him after the white doctors came to take Danny and Ella away. She was at the shack alone that day they came. It was back in

the days before they hired Navajo women to go with them as interpreters. She recognized one of the doctors. She had seen him at the
children's clinic at Cañoncito about a month ago. They were wearing
khaki uniforms and they waved papers at her and a black ball-point pen,
trying to make her understand their English words. She was frightened
by the way they looked at the children, like the lizard watches the fly.
Danny was swinging on the tire swing on the elm tree behind the
rancher's house, and Ella was toddling around the front door, dragging
the broomstick horse Chato made for her. Ayah could see they wanted
her to sign the papers, and Chato had taught her to sign her name. It
was something she was proud of. She only wanted them to go, and to
take their eyes away from her children.

She took the pen from the man without looking at his face and she
signed the papers in three different places he pointed to. She stared at
the ground by their feet and waited for them to leave. But they stood
there and began to point and gesture at the children. Danny stopped
swinging. Ayah could see his fear. She moved suddenly and grabbed
Ella into her arms; the child squirmed, trying to get back to her toys.
Ayah ran with the baby toward Danny; she screamed for him to run and
then she grabbed him around his chest and carried him too. She ran
south into the foothills of juniper trees and black lava rock. Behind her
she heard the doctors running, but they had been taken by surprise, and
as the hills became steeper and the cholla cactus were thicker, they
stopped. When she reached the top of the hill, she stopped to listen in
case they were circling around her. But in a few minutes she heard a car
engine start and they drove away. The children had been too surprised
to cry while she ran with them. Danny was shaking and Ella's little
fingers were gripping Ayah's blouse.

She stayed up in the hills for the rest of the day, sitting on a black lava
boulder in the sunshine where she could see for miles all around her.
The sky was light blue and cloudless, and it was warm for late April.
The sun warmth relaxed her and took the fear and anger away. She lay
back on the rock and watched the sky. It seemed to her that she could
walk into the sky, stepping through clouds endlessly. Danny played
with little pebbles and stones, pretending they were birds eggs and then
little rabbits. Ella sat at her feet and dropped fistfuls of dirt into the
breeze, watching the dust and particles of sand intently. Ayah watched
a hawk soar high above them, dark wings gliding; hunting or only
watching, she did not know. The hawk was patient and he circled all
afternoon before he disappeared around the high volcanic peak the
Mexicans called Guadalupe.

Late in the afternoon, Ayah looked down at the gray boxcar shack
with the paint all peeled from the wood; the stove pipe on the roof was
rusted and crooked. The fire she had built that morning in the oil drum

stove had burned out. Ella was asleep in her lap now and Danny sat close to her, complaining that he was hungry; he asked when they would go to the house. "We will stay up here until your father comes," she told him, "because those white men were chasing us." The boy remembered then and he nodded at her silently.

If Jimmie had been there he could have read those papers and explained to her what they said. Ayah would have known then, never to sign them. The doctors came back the next day and they brought a BIA policeman[3] with them. They told Chato they had her signature and that was all they needed. Except for the kids. She listened to Chato sullenly; she hated him when he told her it was the old woman who died in the winter, spitting blood; it was her old grandma who had given the children this disease. "They don't spit blood," she said coldly. "The whites lie." She held Ella and Danny close to her, ready to run to the hills again. "I want a medicine man first," she said to Chato, not looking at him. He shook his head. "It's too late now. The policeman is with them. You signed the paper." His voice was gentle.

It was worse than if they had died: to lose the children and to know that somewhere, in a place called Colorado, in a place full of sick and dying strangers, her children were without her. There had been babies that died soon after they were born, and one that died before he could walk. She had carried them herself, up to the boulders and great pieces of the cliff that long ago crashed down from Long Mesa; she laid them in the crevices of sandstone and buried them in fine brown sand with round quartz pebbles that washed down the hills in the rain. She had endured it because they had been with her. But she could not bear this pain. She did not sleep for a long time after they took her children. She stayed on the hill where they had fled the first time, and she slept rolled up in the blanket Jimmie had sent her. She carried the pain in her belly and it was fed by everything she saw: the blue sky of their last day together and the dust and pebbles they played with; the swing in the elm tree and broomstick horse choked life from her. The pain filled her stomach and there was no room for food or for her lungs to fill with air. The air and the food would have been theirs.

She hated Chato, not because he let the policeman and doctors put the screaming children in the government car, but because he had taught her to sign her name. Because it was like the old ones always told her about learning their language or any of their ways: it endangered you. She slept alone on the hill until the middle of November when the first snows came. Then she made a bed for herself where the children had slept. She did not lie down beside Chato again until many years later, when he was sick and shivering and only her body could keep him

---

3. Bureau of Indian Affairs officer.

warm. The illness came after the white rancher told Chato he was too old to work for him anymore, and Chato and his old woman should be out of the shack by the next afternoon because the rancher had hired new people to work there. That had satisfied her. To see how the white man repaid Chato's years of loyalty and work. All of Chato's fine-sounding English talk didn't change things.

It snowed steadily and the luminous light from the snow gradually diminished into the darkness. Somewhere in Cebolleta a dog barked and other village dogs joined with it. Ayah looked in the direction she had come, from the bar where Chato was buying the wine. Sometimes he told her to go on ahead and wait; and then he never came. And when she finally went back looking for him, she would find him passed out at the bottom of the wooden steps to Azzie's Bar. All the wine would be gone and most of the money too, from the pale blue check that came to them once a month in a government envelope. It was then that she would look at his face and his hands, scarred by ropes and the barbed wire of all those years, and she would think, this man is a stranger; for forty years she had smiled at him and cooked his food, but he remained a stranger. She stood up again, with the snow almost to her knees, and she walked back to find Chato.

It was hard to walk in the deep snow and she felt the air burn in her lungs. She stopped a short distance from the bar to rest and readjust the blanket. But this time he wasn't waiting for her on the bottom step with his old Stetson hat[4] pulled down and his shoulders hunched up in his long wool overcoat.

She was careful not to slip on the wooden steps. When she pushed the door open, warm air and cigarette smoke hit her face. She looked around slowly and deliberately, in every corner, in every dark place that the old man might find to sleep. The bar owner didn't like Indians in there, especially Navajos, but he let Chato come in because he could talk Spanish like he was one of them. The men at the bar stared at her, and the bartender saw that she left the door open wide. Snowflakes were flying inside like moths and melting into a puddle on the oiled wood floor. He motioned to her to close the door, but she did not see him. She held herself straight and walked across the room slowly, searching the room with every step. The snow in her hair melted and she could feel it on her forehead. At the far corner of the room, she saw red flames at the mica window of the old stove door; she looked behind the stove just to make sure. The bar got quiet except for the Spanish polka music playing on the jukebox. She stood by the stove and shook the snow from her blanket and held it near the stove to dry. The wet

4. A high, wide-brimmed "ten-gallon" hat.

wool smell reminded her of new-born goats in early March, brought inside to warm near the fire. She felt calm.

In past years they would have told her to get out. But her hair was white now and her face was wrinkled. They looked at her like she was a spider crawling slowly across the room. They were afraid; she could feel the fear. She looked at their faces steadily. They reminded her of the first time the white people brought her children back to her that winter. Danny had been shy and hid behind the thin white woman who brought them. And the baby had not known her until Ayah took her into her arms, and then Ella had nuzzled close to her as she had when she was nursing. The blonde woman was nervous and kept looking at a dainty gold watch on her wrist. She sat on the bench near the small window and watched the dark snow clouds gather around the mountains; she was worrying about the unpaved road. She was frightened by what she saw inside too: the strips of venison drying on a rope across the ceiling and the children jabbering excitedly in a language she did not know. So they stayed for only a few hours. Ayah watched the government car disappear down the road and she knew they were already being weaned from these lava hills and from this sky. The last time they came was in early June, and Ella stared at her the way the men in the bar were now staring. Ayah did not try to pick her up; she smiled at her instead and spoke cheerfully to Danny. When he tried to answer her, he could not seem to remember and he spoke English words with the Navajo. But he gave her a scrap of paper that he had found somewhere and carried in his pocket; it was folded in half, and he shyly looked up at her and said it was a bird. She asked Chato if they were home for good this time. He spoke to the white woman and she shook her head. "How much longer?" he asked, and she said she didn't know; but Chato saw how she stared at the boxcar shack. Ayah turned away then. She did not say good-bye.

She felt satisfied that the men in the bar feared her. Maybe it was her face and the way she held her mouth with teeth clenched tight, like there was nothing anyone could do to her now. She walked north down the road, searching for the old man. She did this because she had the blanket, and there would be no place for him except with her and the blanket in the old adobe barn near the arroyo. They always slept there when they came to Cebolleta. If the money and the wine were gone, she would be relieved because then they could go home again; back to the old hogan with a dirt roof and rock walls where she herself had been born. And the next day the old man could go back to the few sheep they still had, to follow along behind them, guiding them, into dry sandy arroyos where sparse grass grew. She knew he did not like walking behind old ewes when for so many years he rode big quarter horses and worked with cattle. But she wasn't sorry for him; he should have known all along what would happen.

There had not been enough rain for their garden in five years; and that was when Chato finally hitched a ride into the town and brought back brown boxes of rice and sugar and big tin cans of welfare peaches. After that, at the first of the month they went to Cebolleta to ask the postmaster for the check; and then Chato would go to the bar and cash it. They did this as they planted the garden every May, not because anything would survive the summer dust, but because it was time to do this. The journey passed the days that smelled silent and dry like the caves above the canyon with yellow painted buffaloes on their walls.

He was walking along the pavement when she found him. He did not stop or turn around when he heard her behind him. She walked beside him and she noticed how slowly he moved now. He smelled strong of woodsmoke and urine. Lately he had been forgetting. Sometimes he called her by his sister's name and she had been gone for a long time. Once she had found him wandering on the road to the white man's ranch, and she asked him why he was going that way; he laughed at her and said, "You know they can't run that ranch without me," and he walked on determined, limping on the leg that had been crushed many years before. Now he looked at her curiously, as if for the first time, but he kept shuffling along, moving slowly along the side of the highway. His gray hair had grown long and spread out on the shoulders of the long overcoat. He wore the old felt hat pulled down over his ears. His boots were worn out at the toes and he had stuffed pieces of an old red shirt in the holes. The rags made his feet look like little animals up to their ears in snow. She laughed at his feet; the snow muffled the sound of her laugh. He stopped and looked at her again. The wind had quit blowing and the snow was falling straight down; the southeast sky was beginning to clear and Ayah could see a star.

"Let's rest awhile," she said to him. They walked away from the road and up the slope to the giant boulders that had tumbled down from the red sandrock mesa throughout the centuries of rainstorms and earth tremors. In a place where the boulders shut out the wind, they sat down with their backs against the rock. She offered half of the blanket to him and they sat wrapped together.

The storm passed swiftly. The clouds moved east. They were massive and full, crowding together across the sky. She watched them with the feeling of horses—steely blue-gray horses startled across the sky. The powerful haunches pushed into the distances and the tail hairs streamed white mist behind them. The sky cleared. Ayah saw that there was nothing between her and the stars. The light was crystalline. There was no shimmer, no distortion through earth haze. She breathed the

clarity of the night sky; she smelled the purity of the half moon and the
stars. He was lying on his side with his knees pulled up near his belly for
warmth. His eyes were closed now, and in the light from the stars and
the moon, he looked young again.

She could see it descend out of the night sky: an icy stillness from the
edge of the thin moon. She recognized the freezing. It came gradually,
sinking snowflake by snowflake until the crust was heavy and deep. It
had the strength of the stars in Orion, and its journey was endless. Ayah
knew that with the wine he would sleep. He would not feel it. She
tucked the blanket around him, remembering how it was when Ella had
been with her; and she felt the rush so big inside her heart for the
babies. And she sang the only song she knew to sing for babies. She
could not remember if she had ever sung it to her children, but she
knew that her grandmother had sung it and her mother had sung it:

> *The earth is your mother,*
>   *she holds you.*
> *The sky is your father,*
>   *he protects you.*
> *Sleep,*
> *sleep.*
> *Rainbow is your sister,*
>   *she loves you.*
> *The winds are your brothers,*
>   *they sing to you.*
> *Sleep,*
> *sleep.*
> *We are together always*
> *We are together always*
> *There never was a time*
> *when this*
> *was not so.*

1981

Selected Bibliographies

For ease of reference, all the authors are listed in alphabetical order. Parentheses around dates indicate first publication of primary sources or periodical publication.

Fleur Adcock

Adcock's poetry includes *Tigers* (1967), *High Tide in the Garden* (1971), *The Scenic Route* (1974), *The Inner Harbour* (1979), and *Selected Poems* (1983). She translated *The Virgin and the Nightingale: Medieval Poems* in 1983. She is also the author of several texts and libretti for musical works by the composer Gillian Whitehead.

Ama Ata Aidoo

Aidoo's works include the book of short stories *No Sweetness Here* (1969), the plays *Dilemma of a Ghost* (1965) and *Anowa* (1970), and the novel *Our Sister Kill Joy, or, Reflections from a Black-Eyed Squint* (1979). For critical material, see Dapo Adelugba, "Language and Drama: Ama Ata Aidoo," *African Literature Today* 8 (1976); Marion Kilson, "Women and African Literature," *Journal of African Studies* 4 (1977); Kathleen McCaffrey, "Images of the Mother in the Stories of Ama Ata Aidoo," *Africa Women* 23 (1979); and Karen C. Chapman " 'Introduction' to Ama Ata Aidoo's *Dilemma of a Ghost*" in *Sturdy Black Bridges: Visions of Black Women in Literature*, ed. Roseann P. Bell, Bettye J. Parker and Beverly Guy-Sheftall, 1979. Alice Walker includes a discussion of Aidoo in *In Search of Our Mothers' Gardens*, 1984.

Louisa May Alcott

Besides Alcott's famous children's novels —*Little Women* (1869), *Little Men* (1871), *Eight Cousins* (1875), *Jo's Boys* (1886), and many others, all currently available in many editions—a number of other Alcott works have recently been republished, including *Hospital Sketches* (1863), ed. Bessie Z. Jones, 1960; *Behind a Mask: The Unknown Thrillers of Louisa May Alcott*, ed. and with an introduction by Madeline Stern, 1975; *Plots and Counterplots: More Unknown Thrillers of Louisa May Alcott* (1976), also edited by Stern; and *Work: A Story of Experience* (1873), with an introduction by Elizabeth Hardwick, 1977.

Valuable background information is included in *Louisa May Alcott, Her Life, Letters, and Journals*, ed. Ednah D. Cheney, 1889. The many biographies of Alcott include Cornelia Lynde Meigs, *The Story of the Author of Little Women: Invincible Louisa*, 1933; Katharine Susan Anthony, *Louisa May Alcott*, 1939; Marjorie Worthington, *Miss Alcott of Concord, a Biography*, 1958; and Martha Sexton, *Louisa May: A Modern Biography of Louisa May Alcott*, 1977.

Critical studies include Cornelia Lynde Meigs, *Louisa May Alcott and the American Family Story*, 1970, and Ruth K. McDonald, *Louisa May Alcott*, 1983. Important short analyses are Carolyn Heilbrun, "Louisa May Alcott: The Influence of *Little Women*" in *Women, the Arts, and the 1920's in Paris and New York*, ed. Kenneth Wheeler and Virginia Lee Dussier, 1982, and Nina Auerbach's discussion of *Little Women* in *Communities of Women*, 1979. Two recent bibliographies are very helpful: Alma J. Payne, *Louisa May Alcott, a Reference Guide*, 1980, and Ruth K. McDonald, "Recent

Alcott Criticism," *Children's Literature* 9 (1981).

Maya Angelou

Angelou's works are *I Know Why the Caged Bird Sings* (1970), *Just Give Me a Cool Drink of Water 'Fore I Diiie* (1971), *Georgia, Georgia* (1972), *Gather Together in My Name* (1974), *Oh Pray My Wings Are Gonna Fit Me Well* (1975), *Singin' and Swingin' and Gettin' Merry Like Christmas* (1976), *And Still I Rise* (1978), and *The Heart of a Woman* (1981). Useful interviews appear in "The Black Scholar Interviews Maya Angelou," *Black Scholar* 8, iv (1977), and in *Black Women Writers at Work*, ed. Claudia Tate, 1984. Critical essays on her achievement include Sidonie A. Smith, "The Song of a Caged Bird: Maya Angelou's Quest After Self-Acceptance," *Southern Humanities Review* 7 (1973); George E. Kent, "Maya Angelou's *I Know Why the Caged Bird Sings* and Black Autobiographical Tradition," *Kansas Quarterly* 7 (1975); Myra K. McMurry, "Role-Playing as Art in Maya Angelou's *Caged Bird*," *South Atlantic Bulletin* 41 (1976); and R. B. Stepto, "The Phenomenal Woman and the Severed Daughter," *Parnassus* (1980). Two useful essays—Selwyn R. Cudjoe, "Maya Angelou and the Autobiographical Statement," and Sandra O'Neale, "Reconstruction of the Composite Self"—appear in *Black Women Writers (1950–1980)*, ed. Mari Evans, 1984.

Mary Astell

Besides *A Serious Proposal to the Ladies* (1694), Astell's works include *Letters Concerning the Love of God* (1695), *Some Reflections on Marriage* (1700), *Moderation Truly Stated* (1704), and *The Christian Religion as Professed by a Daughter of the Church of England* (1705). The early *Mary Astell*, 1916, by Florence M. Smith is the only full-length study. Ruth Perry has two valuable articles on Astell: "Two Forgotten Wits" in *The Antioch Review* (Fall 1981), and "The Veil of Chastity: Mary Astell's Feminism" in Paul-Gabriel Bouce, ed., *Sexuality in Eighteenth Century Britain*, 1982. Astell is discussed in Hilda Smith, *Reason's Disciples*, 1982, and Joan Kinnaird writes

about Astell in *Feminist Theorists*, ed. Dale Spender, 1984.

Margaret Atwood

The best introduction to Atwood's poetry is *Selected Poems* (1976). Her novels are *The Edible Woman* (1969), *Surfacing* (1972), *Lady Oracle* (1976), *Life before Man* (1979), and *Bodily Harm* (1982). She has also written short stories, plays, books for children, and literary criticism. There are many published interviews with Atwood, one by Joyce Carol Oates in *The New York Times Book Review* (21 May 1978). A full-length study is *Violent Duality: A Study of Margaret Atwood* by Sherrill Grace, 1980. Three useful collections of critical essays on Atwood are *Margaret Atwood: A Symposium*, ed. Linda Sandler, *The Malahat Review* (Jan. 1977); *The Art of Margaret Atwood: Essays in Criticism*, ed. Arnold E. Davidson and Cathy N. Davidson, 1981; and *Margaret Atwood: Language, Text, and System*, ed. Sherrill E. Grace and Lorraine Weir, 1983. Other useful critical material is included in Barbara Hill Rigney, *Madness and Sexual Politics in the Feminist Novel*, 1978.

Jane Austen

The standard edition of Austen's work—including *Sense and Sensibility* (1811), *Pride and Prejudice* (1813), *Mansfield Park* (1814), *Emma* (1816), *Persuasion* (1818), and *Northanger Abbey* (1818)—is *The Works of Jane Austen*, edited by R. W. Chapman, first published in the twenties and reprinted in the seventies with revisions by Mary Lascelles. Chapman also collected and edited *Jane Austen's Letters*, 1952, reprinted 1979. Norton Critical Editions of *Emma*, ed. Stephen M. Parrish, and *Pride and Prejudice*, ed. Donald J. Gray, contain valuable secondary material. Useful biographical information can be found in William and Richard Austen-Leigh, *Jane Austen: Her Life and Letters*, 1913; Mary A. Austen-Leigh, *Personal Aspects of Jane Austen*, 1920; and James Edward Austen-Leigh, *Memoir of Jane Austen*, 1926. More recent biographies include *Jane Austen, Facts and Problems* by R. W. Chapman, 1948; *Jane Austen* by Margaret Kennedy, 1950; *Jane Austen and Her World* by Marghanita Laski,

1969; *Jane Austen: A Character Study* by Margaret Llewelyn, 1977; *A Goodly Heritage: A History of Jane Austen's Family* by George H. Tucker, 1983; and *The Life of Jane Austen* by John Halperin, 1984.

Full-length critical studies of Austen's novels are numerous. Among the more influential are Mary Lascelles, *Jane Austen and Her Art*, 1938; Marvin Mudrick, *Jane Austen: Irony as Defense and Discovery*, 1952; Andrew H. Wright, *Jane Austen's Novels*, 1957; A. Walton Litz, *Jane Austen*, 1965; Joseph Wiesenfarth, *The Errand of Form*, 1967; Alistair M. Duckworth, *The Improvement of the Estate*, 1971, and Stuart M. Tave, *Some Words of Jane Austen*, 1973. More recent are *Jane Austen's Novels: Social Change and Literary Form* by Julia P. Brown, 1979; *In the Meantime: Character and Perception in Jane Austen's Fiction* by Susan Morgan, 1980; *An Understanding of Jane Austen's Novels: Character, Value and Ironic Perspective* by John Odmark, 1981; and *Jane Austen, a Reassessment* by P. J. M. Scott, 1982. Collections of essays include *Jane Austen: Bicentenary Essays*, ed. John Halperin, 1975; *Jane Austen Today*, ed. Joel Weinscheimer, 1975; and the latest, feminist, collection, *Jane Austen: New Perspectives*, ed. Janet Todd, 1983. B. C. Southam has edited both a collection of essays, *Critical Essays on Jane Austen*, 1968, and a selection of historically important critical material, *Jane Austen: The Critical Heritage*, 1968. Feminist approaches to Austen's work can be found in *Victims of Convention* by Jean Kennard, 1977; *The Madwoman in the Attic* by Sandra M. Gilbert and Susan Gubar, 1979; *Becoming a Heroine* by Rachel Brownstein, 1982; and *The Proper Lady and the Woman Writer* by Mary Poovey, 1984. For further references, see David Gibson, *A Bibliography of Jane Austen*, 1982.

Toni Cade Bambara

Bambara's works include *Gorilla, My Love* (1972), *The Sea Birds Are Still Alive: Collected Stories* (1977), and *The Salt Eaters* (1980), as well as two anthologies: *The Black Woman* (1970) and *Tales and Stories* (1971). Two useful pieces appeared in *First World* 2, iv (1980): Kalamu ya Salaam, "An Interview: Searching for the Mother Tongue," and Eleanor Traylor, "The Salt Eaters: My Soul Looks Back in Wonder." Also helpful are "Commitment: Toni Cade Bambara Speaks," in *Sturdy Black Bridges: Visions of Black Women in Literature*, ed. Roseann Bell, Bettye Parker, and Beverly Guy-Sheftall, 1979; an interview included in *Black Women Writers at Work*, ed. Claudia Tate, 1984; and two essays— Ruth Elizabeth Burks, "From Baptism to Resurrection," and Eleanor W. Traylor, "Music as Theme"—in *Black Women Writers (1950–1980)*, ed. Mari Evans, 1984.

Djuna Barnes

Known primarily for her novel *Nightwood* (1937), Barnes wrote many other works, which are just beginning to receive critical attention. They include *The Book of Repulsive Women, Eight Rhythms and Five Drawings* (1915), *Ladies' Almanack* (1928, rpt. 1972), *Ryder* (1928), *The Antiphon* (1958), *Spillway* (1962), and *Creatures in an Alphabet* (1982). There is a 1962 edition of *The Selected Works of Djuna Barnes. Smoke and Other Early Stories*, edited and with an introduction by Douglas Messerli, was published in 1982.

Full-length biographies and critical studies include *Djuna Barnes* by James B. Scott, 1976; *The Art of Djuna Barnes: Duality and Damnation* by Louis F. Kannestine, 1977; and *Djuna: The Life and Times of Djuna Barnes* by Andrew Field, 1983. Critical essays include Carolyn Allen, " 'Dressing the Unknowable in the Garments of the Known': The Style of Djuna Barnes in *Nightwood*," in *Women's Language and Style*, ed. Douglas Butturff and Edmund L. Epstein, *Studies in Contemporary Language* (1978); Susan Sniader Lanser, "Speaking in Tongues: *Ladies' Almanack* and the Language of Celebration," *Frontiers* 4, 3 (Fall 1979); and Lynn DeVore, "The Background of *Nightwood*: Robin, Felix, and Nora," *Journal of Modern Literature* 10 (March 1983). Douglas Messerli compiled *Djuna Barnes: A Bibliography*, 1975.

Aphra Behn

Behn's many plays—which include *The Forced Marriage* (1671), *The Rover* (1677, 1681), and *The Lucky Chance*

(1687)—are collected in the multivolume *Works of Aphra Behn*, ed. Montague Summers, 1915. Her nondramatic works include A *Discovery of New Worlds* (1688), *The Fair Jilt* (1688), *Oroonoko* (1688), and *The Adventure of the Black Lady* (1696). Good introductions are Vita Sackville-West, *Aphra Behn, the Incomparable Astrea*, 1927; W. J. Cameron, *New Light on Aphra Behn*, 1961; and Frederick M. Link, *Aphra Behn*, 1968; also worth consulting is George Woodcock, *The Incomparable Aphra*, 1948. In addition, two biographies have appeared in the last decade: *The Passionate Shepherdess: Aphra Behn 1640–1689* by Maureen Duffy, 1977, and *Reconstructing Aphra: A Social Biography of Aphra Behn* by Angeline Goreau, 1980. Recent articles of interest are "Aphra Behn: Sexuality and Self-Respect" by Judith Kegan Gardiner, *Women's Studies* 7, i–ii (1980), and in the same journal, 7, iii, "Muses in the Mud: The Female Wits Anthropologically Considered" by Robert Adams Day. Behn is also discussed by Fidelis Morgan in *The Female Wits*, 1981, and by Angeline Goreau in *Feminist Theorists*, ed. Dale Spender, 1984.

Elizabeth Bishop

The Complete Poems of Elizabeth Bishop, 1927–1979, was published in 1983 and *The Collected Prose* in 1984. Anne Stevenson's biographical and critical study, *Elizabeth Bishop*, appeared in 1966. Useful critical essays on Bishop's poetry appear in the issue of *World Literature Today* (1976) devoted to her and in David Kalstone, *Five Temperaments* (1977). More recent is Richard Mullen, "Elizabeth Bishop's Surrealist Inheritance," *American Literature* 54, i (1982). A valuable collection of essays, *Elizabeth Bishop and Her Art*, ed. Lloyd Schwartz and Sybil P. Estess, was published in 1983. Also helpful are *Elizabeth Bishop: A Bibliography, 1927–1979*, comp. Candace W. McMahon, 1980, and *Elizabeth Bishop and Howard Nemerov: A Reference Guide* by Diana E. Wyllie, 1983.

Louise Bogan

Among the collections of Bogan's poetry are *Collected Poems, 1923–1953* (1954) and *The Blue Estuaries: Poems, 1923–* 1968 (1968). Her *Selected Criticism* was published in 1955. William Jay Smith edited a lecture delivered at the Library of Congress, *Louise Bogan: A Woman's Words*, 1971, and Ruth Limmer edited the selected letters of 1920–1970, *What the Woman Lived*, 1973, as well as a series of passages from her work put together to constitute a memoir, *Journey Around My Room: The Autobiography of Louise Bogan: A Mosaic*, 1980. A useful critical essay is Patrick Moore, "Symbol, Mask, and Meter in the Poetry of Louise Bogan," *Women and Literature* 1 (1980).

Elizabeth Bowen

Bowen's *Collected Stories* were published in 1981. Among her best known novels are *The Hotel* (1927), *The House in Paris* (1935), *The Death of the Heart* (1938), *The Heat of the Day* (1949), *The Little Girls* (1964), and *Eva Trout or Changing Scenes* (1968), all of which are available in paperback editions. She also wrote many nonfiction works, including *Collected Impressions* (1950) and *Pictures and Conversations* (1975), a posthumous collection. A useful biography is Victoria Glendinning, *Elizabeth Bowen: Portrait of a Writer*, 1977. Full-length critical studies include William W. Heath, *Elizabeth Bowen: An Introduction to Her Novels*, 1961; Allen E. Austin, *Elizabeth Bowen*, 1971; Harriet Blodgett, *Patterns of Reality: Elizabeth Bowen's Novels*, 1975; and Hermione Lee, *Elizabeth Bowen: An Estimation*, 1981. J'nan Sellery and William O. Harris compiled the valuable *Elizabeth Bowen: A Bibliography*, 1981.

Kay Boyle

Fifty Stories appeared in 1980, and *Collected Poems* in 1962. Among her numerous novels are *Plagued by the Nightingale* (1931), *Death of a Man* (1936), *Monday Night* (1938), *1939* (1948), *Generation without Farewell* (1960), and *The Underground Woman* (1974). A book of essays, *The Long Walk at San Francisco State*, appeared in 1970. A memoir written with Robert McAlmon, *Being Geniuses Together*, appeared in 1968 and was reissued in 1984. Other sources of biographical material are Kathy Drew, "Jails Don't Daunt Protesting Grandmother: Kay Boyle Dedicates Self to Human Dignity,"

Lost Generation Journal 4, i (1976), and Patricia Holt's interview with Boyle, *Publisher's Weekly* 17 (Oct. 1980). A helpful critical essay is Richard C. Carpenter, "Kay Boyle: The Figure in the Carpet," *Critique* VII, ii (1964–1965). Roberta Sharp, "A Bibliography of Works by and about Kay Boyle," *Bulletin of Bibliography* 35 (1978), is also useful.

Anne Bradstreet

Jeannine Hensley's edition, *The Works of Anne Bradstreet*, 1967, has an introduction by Adrienne Rich; this essay also appears, with a later preface, in Rich's *On Lies, Secrets, and Silence*, 1979. *The Complete Works of Anne Bradstreet*, ed. Joseph McElrath and Allan Robb, came out in 1981. Useful critical discussions may be found in Josephine Piercy, *Anne Bradstreet*, 1965; Elizabeth W. White, *Anne Bradstreet: The Tenth Muse*, 1971, and Ann Stanford, *Anne Bradstreet: The Worldly Puritan*, 1977. Recent feminist work appears in Wendy Martin, "Anne Bradstreet's Poetry: A Study of Subversive Piety" in *Shakespeare's Sisters*, ed. Sandra M. Gilbert and Susan Gubar, 1979; and, also by Martin, *An American Triptych*, 1984. Other helpful articles include Emily Stipes Watts, " 'The Posy Unity': Anne Bradstreet's Search for Order" in *Puritan Influences in American Literature*, ed. Emory Elliott, 1979; Ellen B. Brandt, "Anne Bradstreet: The Erotic Component in Puritan Poetry," *Women's Studies* 7, i–ii (1980); and Eileen Margerum, "Anne Bradstreet's Public Poetry and the Tradition of Humility," *Early American Literature* (Fall 1982).

Anna Hempstead Branch

Besides *Sonnets from a Lock Box* (1929), Branch's verse collections include *The Shoes That Danced, and Other Poems* (1905), *Rose of the Wind, and Other Poems* (1910), and *Last Poems of Anna Hempstead Branch*, ed. and with a foreword by Ridgely Torrence, 1944.

Linda Brent

A reprint of Brent's *Incidents in the Life of a Slave Girl* (1861) was edited by Walter Teller in 1973.

Charlotte Brontë

The standard edition of Brontë's work—including *Jane Eyre* (1847), *Shirley* (1849), *Villette* (1853), and *The Professor* (1857)—is *The Shakespeare Head Brontë*, ed. Thomas James Wise and John Alexander Symington, 1931–1938. The same editors also produced *The Brontës: Their Lives, Friendships, and Correspondence*, 4 vols., 1932. Brontë's juvenilia is included in *Legends of Angria*, ed. Fannie E. Ratchford, with the collaboration of William Clyde DeVane, 1933. In addition, numerous editions of Brontë's individual novels exist, including a Penguin series with valuable introductions and a Norton Critical Edition of *Jane Eyre*, with a number of critical articles and a bibliography, ed. Richard J. Dunn, 1971. *Five Novelettes* was edited by Winifred Gérin, 1971, and *The Secret and Lily Hart: Two Tales*, by William Holtz, 1979. *Poems by the Brontë Sisters*, reprinted in 1948, has an introduction by M. R. D. Seaward, and Christine Alexander edited *Something about Arthur*, 1981.

The best biographies are Elizabeth Gaskell's justly famous *The Life of Charlotte Brontë* (1857) and Winifred Gérin's *Charlotte Brontë: The Evolution of Genius*, 1967, but Helene Moglen's critical biography, *Charlotte Brontë: The Self Conceived*, 1976, also offers useful psychological insights. Critical works include Robert Bernard Martin, *The Accents of Persuasion*, 1966; Earl A. Knies, *The Art of Charlotte Brontë*, 1969; Margot Peters, *Charlotte Brontë: Style in the Novel*, 1973; Lawrence Jay Dessner, *The Homely Web of Truth: A Study of Charlotte Brontë's Novels*, 1973; Charles Burkhart, *Charlotte Brontë: A Psychosexual Study of Her Novels*, 1973; Patricia Beer, *Reader, I Married Him*, 1974; Terence Eagleton, *Myths of Power: A Marxist Study of the Brontës*, 1975; and Christine Alexander, *The Early Writings of Charlotte Brontë*, 1983. Feminist approaches can be found in Elaine Showalter, *A Literature of Their Own*, 1977; in Barbara Hill Rigney, *Madness and Sexual Politics in the Feminist Novel*, 1978; in Sandra M. Gilbert and Susan Gubar, *The Madwoman in the Attic*, 1979; in Judith Lowder Newton, *Women, Power, and Subversion*, 1981; and in Dianne F. Sadoff, *Monsters of Affection: Dickens, Eliot and Brontë on Fatherhood*, 1982. Essay collections include *The Brontës, The Critical Heritage*, ed. Miriam Allot, 1974, and *The Brontës: A Collection of Critical Essays*, ed. Ian Gregor, 1970. Also useful is Rebecca Crump, *Charlotte and Emily Brontë: A Reference Guide*, 1982.

Emily Brontë

A definitive edition of Brontë's *The Complete Poems* was produced by C. W. Hatfield in 1941, while her Gondal narrative was reconstructed in Fannie E. Ratchford, *The Brontës' Web of Childhood*, 1941, and in Ratchford, *Gondal's Queen: A Novel in Verse*, 1955. The best biography is Winifred Gérin, *Emily Brontë*, 1971, and a useful recent edition of *Wuthering Heights* (1847) is the Norton Critical Edition, ed. William M. Sale, Jr.

Full-length critical studies include *The Drug-like Brontë Dream* by Margaret Lane, 1980; *The Genesis of Wuthering Heights* by Mary Visick, 1980; and *Emily Brontë: The Artist as a Free Man* by Stevie Davies, 1983, while feminist analyses appear in Sandra M. Gilbert and Susan Gubar, *The Madwoman in the Attic*, 1979; in Nina Auerbach, "This Changeful Life: Emily Brontë's Anti-Romance," in *Shakespeare's Sisters*, ed. Sandra M. Gilbert and Susan Gubar, 1979; in Margaret Homans, *Women Writers and Poetic Identity*, 1980; and in Christine Gallant, "The Archetypal Feminine in Emily Brontë's Poetry," *Women's Studies* 7, i–ii (1980). A useful collection of essays is *The Art of Emily Brontë*, ed. Anne Smith, 1977. Also helpful is Janet M. Barclay, *Emily Brontë Criticism, 1900–1980: An Annotated Checklist*, 1984.

Gwendolyn Brooks

Gwendolyn Brooks's volumes include *A Street in Bronzeville* (1945), *Annie Allen* (1949), *Bronzeville Boys and Girls* (1956), *The Bean Eaters* (1960), *Selected Poems* (1963), *In the Mecca* (1968), *Riot* (1969), *Family Pictures* (1970), *The World of Gwendolyn Brooks* (1971), *Aloneness* (1972), *Beckonings* (1975), and *To Disembark* (1981). She has also written novels, including *Maud Martha* (1953), and an autobiographical work,

Report from Part One (1972). Other sources of biographical information are George E. Kent, "Gwendolyn Brooks: Portrait, in Part, of the Artist as a Young Girl and Apprentice Writer," *Callaloo* 2 (1979), and Martha H. Brown's interview with Brooks in *Great Lakes Review* 6 (1979).

A critical study is *Gwendolyn Brooks* by Harry B. Shaw, 1980. Essays on Brooks include a chapter in Eugene B. Redmond, *Drumvoices*, 1976, as well as two useful articles—Addison Gayle, Jr., "Gwendolyn Brooks: Poet of the Whirlwind" and George Kent, "Gwendolyn Brooks' Poetic Realism"—in *Black Women Writers (1950–1980)*, ed. Mari Evans, 1984. For a feminist approach, see Suzanne Juhasz's chapter on Brooks and Nikki Giovanni in *Naked and Fiery Forms: Modern American Poetry by Women—A New Tradition*, 1976. R. Baxter Miller compiled *Langston Hughes and Gwendolyn Brooks: A Reference Guide* in 1978.

Elizabeth Barrett Browning

Barrett Browning's works—including *An Essay on Mind, with Other Poems* (1826), *The Seraphim, and Other Poems* (1838), *Poems* (1844), *Sonnets from the Portuguese* (1850), *Casa Guidi Windows* (1851), *Aurora Leigh* (1857), *Poems before Congress* (1860), and *Last Poems* (1862)—have been collected in the standard *Complete Works of Elizabeth Barrett Browning*, ed. Charlotte Porter and Helen Clarke, 6 vols., 1900. In addition, Julia Markus's edition of *Casa Guidi Windows*, 1977, and Cora Kaplan's edition of *Aurora Leigh and Other Poems*, 1978, are useful recent texts. Volumes of letters include *The Letters of Elizabeth Barrett Browning*, ed. Frederic G. Kenyon, 1899; *Elizabeth Barrett to Mr. Boyd*, ed. Barbara McCarthy, 1955; *The Letters of Robert Browning and Elizabeth Barrett 1845–1846*, 2 vols., 1964; and *The Letters of Elizabeth Barrett Browning to Mary Russell Mitford, 1836–1854*, ed. Meredith Raymond and Mary Rose Sullivan, 1983.

Among biographies and biographical studies, the most helpful are Gardner B. Taplin, *The Life of Elizabeth Barrett Browning*, 1957; Alethea Hayter, *Elizabeth Barrett Browning*, 1965; Edward C. McAlzer, *The Brownings at Casa Guidi*,

1979; Rosalie Mander, *Mrs. Browning: The Story of Elizabeth Barrett*, 1980; and Roy E. Gridley, *The Brownings and France: A Chronicle with Commentary*, 1982. Virginia Woolf's appreciative essay, "Aurora Leigh," appeared in 1932 in the *Second Common Reader*, but much of the critical work on this poet is very recent. Ellen Moers discusses her in *Literary Women*, 1976; Helen Cooper's valuable essay, "Working into Light: Elizabeth Barrett Browning," appears in *Shakespeare's Sisters*, ed. Sandra M. Gilbert and Susan Gubar, 1979, and Barrett Browning is also discussed in Gilbert and Gubar's *The Madwoman in the Attic*, 1979. In addition, a number of essays have lately appeared in journals: "The Ring, the Rescue and the Risorgimento: Reunifying the Brownings' Italy" by Flavia Alaya, *Browning Institute Studies* 6 (1978); "Beyond the Sun: Patriarchal Images in *Aurora Leigh*" by Virginia Steinmetz, *Studies in Browning and His Circle*, 9, 2 (1981); "*Aurora Leigh*: The Vocation of the Woman Poet" by Barbara Gelpi, *Victorian Poetry* 19, 1 (1981); "The Female Poet and the Embarrassed Reader: Elizabeth Barrett Browning's *Sonnets from the Portuguese*" by Dorothy Mermin, *ELH* (Summer 1981); "Face to Face: Elizabeth Barrett Browning's *Aurora Leigh* and 19th-Century Poetry" by Dolores Rosenblum, *Victorian Studies* 26, 3 (1983); and "From Patria to Matria: Elizabeth Barrett Browning's Risorgimento" by Sandra M. Gilbert, *PMLA* (March 1984).

Fanny Burney
Fanny Burney's works include *Evelina* (1778), *Cecilia* (1782), *Camilla* (1796), *The Wanderer; or, Female Difficulties* (1814), and *The Memoirs of Dr. Burney* (1832). Eight volumes of her *Journals and Letters* have been edited by Joyce Hemlow, 1972–1980. Biographies include *Be Loved No More; The Life and Environment of Fanny Burney* by Arthur B. Tourtellot, 1938; *A Degree of Prudery* by Emily Hahn, 1950; *The Young Fanny Burney* by Winifred Gérin, 1961; and *Fanny Burney* by Michael E. Adelstein, 1968. Among more recent studies are *Fanny Burney* by Sarah Kilpatrick, 1980, and a chapter in Judith Lowder Newton, *Women, Power, and Subversion*, 1981.

Also useful is Joseph A. Grau, *Fanny Burney: An Annotated Bibliography*, 1981.

Angela Carter
Carter's fiction includes *Shadow Dance* (1965), *The Magic Toyshop* (1967), *Several Perceptions* (1968), *Heroes and Villains* (1969), *Love* (1971), *The Infernal Desire Machine of Doctor Hoffman* (1972), and *The Passion of New Eve* (1977). She has translated Charles Perrault's fairy tales and has published two collections of short stories, *Fireworks* (1974) and *The Bloody Chamber* (1979). *The Sadeian Woman: An Exercise in Cultural History* appeared in 1979, and *Nothing Sacred: Selected Writings* appeared in 1982.

Willa Cather
Cather's collection of poems, *April Twilights* (1903, rev. 1923), and her book of essays, *Not under Forty* (1936), supplement the standard edition of her fiction, *The Novels and Stories of Willa Cather*, 1937–1941, which includes such works as *O Pioneers!* (1913), *The Song of the Lark* (1915), *My Ántonia* (1918), *Youth and the Bright Medusa* (1920), *A Lost Lady* (1923), *The Professor's House* (1925), *Death Comes for the Archbishop* (1927), and *Shadows on the Rock* (1931). Other texts include *The Old Beauty and Others*, posthumously collected short stories (1948); *Willa Cather on Writing*, 1949; *Writings from Willa Cather's Campus Years*, ed. James Shively, 1950; *Collected Short Fiction, 1892–1912*, ed. Virginia Faulkner, 1965; and *The Kingdom of Art: Willa Cather's First Principles and Critical Statements*, ed. Bernice Slote, 1967.

Personal memoirs include Edith Lewis, *Willa Cather Living*, 1953, and Elizabeth Sergeant, *Willa Cather: A Memoir*, 1953. Among biographies and critical studies are David Daiches, *Willa Cather*, 1951; E. K. Brown, *Willa Cather*, 1953; Dorothy Van Ghent, *Willa Cather*, 1964; James Woodress, *Willa Cather*, 1970; Philip Gerber, *Willa Cather*, 1975; David Stouck, *Willa Cather's Imagination*, 1975; and Phyllis C. Robinson, *Willa: The Life of Willa Cather*, 1983. Commentaries on Cather are gathered in *Willa Cather and Her Critics*, ed. James Schroeter, 1967; in *The Art of Willa*

Cather, ed. Bernice Slote and Virginia Faulkner, 1974; and in Blanche Gelfant, *Women Writing in America*, 1985. Joan Crane compiled the valuable *Willa Cather: A Bibliography*, 1982.

Margaret Cavendish, Duchess of Newcastle

There is no modern edition of Cavendish's work, but some of her writings are *Poems and Fancies* (1653), *Nature's Pictures* (1656), *The Description of a New World* (1666), *Grounds of Natural Philosophy* (1668), and *Letters* (1676). She is discussed in Reverend J. Granger, *Biographical History of England*, 1824, and Louisa Costello, *Memoirs of Eminent Englishwomen*, 1844. Douglas Grant, *Margaret the First*, 1957, is the only full length study of her life and work. A more recent feminist approach can be found in three important articles: Dolores Palomo, "Margaret Cavendish: Defining the Female Self," *Women's Studies* 7, i–ii (1980); Patricia A. Sullivan, "Female Writing Beside the Rhetorical Tradition," *International Journal of Women's Studies* 3 (1981); and Natalie Zemon Davis, "Gender and Genre: Women as Historical Writers 1400–1820," in *Beyond Their Sex: Learned Women of the European Past*, ed. Patricia H. Labalme, 1980.

Kate Chopin

Chopin's works include *At Fault* (1890), *Bayou Folk* (1894), *A Night in Acadie* (1897), and *The Awakening* (1899). A definitive *Complete Works of Kate Chopin*, 1969, appeared in two volumes edited by Per Seyersted, who is also the author of *Kate Chopin: A Critical Biography*, 1969; in addition, with Emily Toth, Seyersted edited *A Kate Chopin Miscellany*, 1979. An early critical biography is Daniel Rankin, *Kate Chopin and Her Creole Stories*, 1932.

Among important recent articles are Robert Cantwell, "The Awakening by Kate Chopin," *Georgia Review* 10 (1956); Larzer Ziff, "An Abyss of Inequality: Sarah Orne Jewett, Mary Wilkins Freeman, Kate Chopin," in *The American 1890s*, 1966; George Spangler, "Kate Chopin's *The Awakening*: A Partial

Dissent," *Novel* 3 (1970); Cynthia Griffin Wolff, "Thanatos and Eros: Kate Chopin's *The Awakening*," *American Quarterly* 25 (1973); Ruth Sullivan and Stewart Smith, "Narrative Stance in Kate Chopin's *The Awakening*," *Studies in American Fiction* 1 (1973); Otis B. Wheeler, "The Five Awakenings of Edna Pontellier," *The Southern Review* 11 (1975); Jane P. Tompkins, "*The Awakening*: An Evaluation," *Feminist Studies* 3 (1976); Margaret Culley, "Edna Pontellier: 'A Solitary Soul,'" in *The Awakening*: A *Norton Critical Edition*, ed. Margaret Culley, 1976; Emily Toth, "Kate Chopin's *The Awakening* as Feminist Criticism," *Louisiana Studies* 15 (1976); Priscilla Allen, "Old Critics and New: The Treatment of Chopin's *The Awakening*," in *The Authority of Experience*, ed. Arlyn Diamond and Lee R. Edwards, 1977; Lawrence Thornton, "*The Awakening*: A Political Romance," *American Literature* 52 (1980); Anne Goodwyn Jones, "Kate Chopin: The Life Behind the Mask," in *Tomorrow Is Another Day* by Jones, 1981; and Sandra M. Gilbert, "The Second Coming of Aphrodite: Kate Chopin's Fantasy of Desire," *Kenyon Review* 5 (1983). Valuable, though somewhat outdated, is Marlene Springer, *Edith Wharton and Kate Chopin: A Reference Guide*, 1976.

Lady Mary Chudleigh

Chudleigh's works include *The Female Advocate; or, A Plea for the Just Liberty of the Tender Sex and Particularly of Married Women* (1701), *The Ladies Defence; or, "The Bride-Woman's Counseller" Answer'd* (1701), and *Poems on Several Occasions* (1703).

Lucille Clifton

Besides numerous books for children, Clifton's works include *Good Times* (1969), *Good News about the Earth* (1972), *An Ordinary Woman* (1974), *Generations: A Memoir* (1976), *Two-Headed Woman* (1980), and *Sonora Beautiful* (1981). Audrey McCluskey, "Tell the Good News: A View of the Works of Lucille Clifton," and Haki Madhubuti, "Lucille Clifton: Warm Water, Greased Legs, and Dangerous Poetry," appear in *Black Women Writers (1950–1980)*, ed. Mari Evans, 1984.

Mary Elizabeth Coleridge

Theresa Whistler edited and introduced Coleridge's *Collected Poems*, 1954, which includes verse from *Poems* (1908) and additional, previously unpublished material. Edith Sichel wrote a memoir which is included in *Gathered Leaves from the Prose of Mary E. Coleridge*, 1910. Among Coleridge's other works are a novel, *The Seven Sleepers of Ephesus* (1893), and a biographical study, *Holman Hunt* (1908).

Kamala Das

Among Das's works are a novel, *Alphabet of Lust* (1977), several books of short stories including *A Doll for the Child Prostitute* (1977), and a number of collections of poetry, including *Summer in Calcutta* (1965) and *The Descendants* (1967). She has also published an autobiography, *My Story* (1976). Full-length studies of her career include *Virgin Whiteness, the Poetry of Kamala Das*, by Devendra Kohl, 1968; *Kamala Das*, also by Kohl, 1975, and *Expressive Form in the Poetry of Kamala Das*, by Anisur Rahman, 1981. Two useful essays are Anne Brewster, " 'The Freedom to Decompose': The Poetry of Kamala Das," *Journal of Indian Writing in English* 8 (Jan.–July 1980), and Eunice de Souza, "Kamala Das," in *Indian Poetry in English: A Critical Assessment*, ed. Vasant A. Shahane, 1981.

Rebecca Harding Davis

Davis's most famous story, *Life in the Iron-Mills; or, The Korl Woman* (1861), was reissued by the Feminist Press in 1972, with a biographical interpretation by Tillie Olsen. Other works by Davis include *Margaret Howth* (1862, rpt. 1970), *Waiting for the Verdict* (1868, rpt. 1968), *Pro Aris et Focis—A Plea for Our Altars and Hearths* (1870), *John Andross* (1874), *Doctor Warrick's Daughters* (1896), and *Frances Waldeaux* (1896).

Little has been written on Davis, but see Walter Hesford, "The Literary Context of *Life in the Iron-Mills*," *American Literature*, 49, 1 (1977), and Jean Pfaelzer, "Rebecca Harding Davis: Domesticity, Social Order, and the Industrial

Novel," *International Journal of Women's Studies* 4, 3 (1981).

Emily Dickinson

The Poems of Emily Dickinson, 1955, was edited by Thomas H. Johnson, and he and Theodora Ward edited three companion volumes of *The Letters of Emily Dickinson*, 1958. More recently, Ralph W. Franklin has edited *The Manuscript Books of Emily Dickinson*, 1981. In addition, Jay Leyda's compendious *The Years and Hours of Emily Dickinson*, 1960, provides documents about the poet's life and time. Richard B. Sewall, *The Life of Emily Dickinson*, 1974, is probably the most definitive biography, but Thomas H. Johnson, *Emily Dickinson: An Interpretive Biography*, 1955, is also an important one. John Cody, *After Great Pain: The Inner Life of Emily Dickinson*, 1971, is an interesting but controversial psychoanalytic study.

Full-length critical works include George Whicher, *This Was a Poet: A Critical Biography of Emily Dickinson*, 1939; Richard Chase, *Emily Dickinson*, 1951; Charles R. Anderson, *Emily Dickinson's Poetry*, 1960; Clark Griffith, *The Long Shadow: Emily Dickinson's Tragic Poetry*, 1964; Albert J. Gelpi, *Emily Dickinson: The Mind of the Poet*, 1965; Brita Lindberg-Seyersted, *The Voice of the Poet: Aspects of Style in the Poetry of Emily Dickinson*, 1968; Ruth Miller, *The Poetry of Emily Dickinson*, 1968; Rebecca Patterson, *Emily Dickinson's Imagery*, 1974; and Robert Weisbuch, *Emily Dickinson's Poetry*, 1975. More recent studies include Paul J. Ferlazzo, *Emily Dickinson*, 1976; Sharon Cameron, *Lyric Time*, 1979; Karl Keller, *The Only Kangaroo among the Beauty: Emily Dickinson and America*, 1979; and David Porter, *Dickinson: The Modern Idiom*, 1981.

Feminist analyses of Dickinson's work are represented by Joanne Feit Diehl, *Dickinson and the Romantic Imagination*, 1981; Barbara Clarke Mossberg, *Emily Dickinson: When a Writer Is a Daughter*, 1982; Suzanne Juhasz, *The Undiscovered Continent: Emily Dickinson and the Space of the Mind*, 1983; and Vivian R. Pollak, *Dickinson: The Anxiety of Gender*, 1984. In addition, Juhasz has edited a collection of essays, *Feminist Critics Read Emily Dickinson*, 1983, while Dickinson is also analyzed in significant portions of Sandra M. Gilbert and Susan Gubar, *The Madwoman in the Attic*, 1979; Margaret Homans, *Women Writers and Poetic Identity*, 1980; Cheryl Walker, *The Nightingale's Burden*, 1982; and Wendy Martin, *An American Tryptich*, 1984. There are three useful essays on the poet in *Shakespeare's Sisters*, ed. Gilbert and Gubar, 1979. S. P. Rosenbaum has produced A *Concordance to the Poems of Emily Dickinson*, 1964, and Joseph Duchac has compiled *The Poems of Emily Dickinson: An Annotated Guide to Commentary*, 1979.

Isak Dinesen
Dinesen's books in English include *Seven Gothic Tales* (1934), *Out of Africa* (1937), *Winter's Tales* (1942), *Last Tales* (1957), *Anecdotes of Destiny* (1958), *Shadows on the Grass* (1961), and *Ehrengard* (1963).

Her *Letters from Africa, 1914–1931*, were edited by Frans Lasson and translated by Anne Born, 1981. Biographies and memoirs include Clara Svendesen, *Isak Dinesen: A Memorial*, 1965; Migel Parmenia, *Titania: The Biography of Isak Dinesen*, 1967; Lasson, *The Life and Destiny of Isak Dinesen*, 1970; Thomas Dinesen, *My Sister, Isak Dinesen* (trans. Joan Tate), 1975; and Judith Thurman, *Isak Dinesen: The Life of a Storyteller*, 1982.

Among full-length critical studies are *The Gayety of Vision: A Study of Isak Dinesen's Art* by Robert W. Langbaum, 1965; *'Isak Dinesen' and Karen Blixen: The Mask and the Reality* by Donald Hannah, 1971; and *Isak Dinesen's Aesthetics* by Thomas R. Whissen, 1973. A feminist perspective is represented by Susan Gubar, " 'The Blank Page' and the Issues of Female Creativity," in *Writing and Sexual Difference*, ed. Elizabeth Abel, 1982.

H. D. (Hilda Doolittle)
Louis Martz has recently edited *H. D.: Collected Poems, 1912–1944*, 1983, which includes her major published (and some previously unpublished) work in verse except for the late volumes *Helen in Egypt* (1961) and *Hermetic Definition* (1972), both of which are available in paperback. Her prose fiction includes *Palimpsest* (1926), *Hedylus* (1928), and *Bid Me to Live* (1960). *By Avon River* (1949) celebrates Shakespeare in prose and verse. The autobiographical *HERmione*, with a forward by Perdita Schaffner, was published in 1981 and *The Gift* in 1982. *Tribute to Freud* (1944, 1956), her account of her psychoanalysis by Freud, and *End to Torment* (1979), a memoir of Ezra Pound, are available in paperback.

H. D. figures in *The Heart to Artemis: A Writer's Memoirs*, 1962, the autobiography of her closest friend and traveling companion, Bryher (Winifred Ellerman). Early critical studies include a chapter entitled "The Perfect Imagist" in Glenn Hughes, *Imagism and the Imagists*, 1931, and Harold H. Watts, "H. D. and the Age of Myth," *The Sewanee Review* LVI (1948), as well as Thomas Burnett Swann, *The Classical World of H. D.*, 1962, and Vincent Quinn, *Hilda Doolittle*, 1967. The autumn 1969 issue of *Contemporary Literature* was devoted exclusively to·H. D. and contains useful background information.

Recent feminist interest in H. D.'s work has followed Susan Stanford Friedman's landmark essay, "Who Buried H. D.?," *College English* 36, 7 (March 1975). There are two biographies, of which *H. D.: The Life and Work of an American Poet* by Janice Robinson, 1982, is somewhat controversial, while *Herself Defined: The Poet H. D. and Her World* by Barbara Guest, 1984, is useful. The most valuable full-length critical study is *Psyche Reborn: The Emergence of H. D.* by Susan Stanford Friedman, 1981. Important essay-length feminist studies are Susan Gubar, "The Echoing Spell of H. D.'s Trilogy," in *Shakespeare's Sisters*, ed. Sandra M. Gilbert and Susan Gubar, 1979; Rachel Blau DuPlessis, "Romantic Thralldom in H. D.," *Contemporary Literature* 20, 2 (Summer 1979); Friedman and DuPlessis, "Woman is Perfect: H. D.'s Debate with Freud," *Feminist Studies* 7, 3 (Fall 1981); Albert Gelpi, "Hilda in Egypt," *The Southern Review* (Summer 1982); Susan Friedman, " 'I go where I love': An Intertextual Study of H. D. and Adrienne Rich," *Signs* 9, 2

(Winter 1983); and a chapter in Alicia Ostriker, *Writing Like a Woman*, 1983.

Mourning Dove (Hum-Ishu-Ma)

Mourning Dove's collection of *Tales of the Okanogans*, based on her *Coyote Stories* (1933), was edited by Donald M. Hines and published in 1976. Issued in 1927 and reprinted in 1981 with a helpful introduction by Dexter Fisher is Mourning Dove, *Cogewea, the Half Blood: A Depiction of the Great Montana Cattle Range*, "given through Sho-pow-tan" with notes and biographical sketch by Lucullus Virgil McWhorter.

Margaret Drabble

Drabble's novels include *A Summer Bird-Cage* (1962), *The Garrick Year* (1964), *The Millstone* (1965), *Jerusalem the Golden* (1967), *The Waterfall* (1969), *The Needle's Eye* (1972), *The Realms of Gold* (1975), *The Ice Age* (1977), and *The Middle Ground* (1980). Most are available in paperback. Her volumes of nonfiction are *Wordsworth* (1966), *Arnold Bennett* (1974), *For Queen and Country: Britain in the Victorian Age* (1979), and *A Writer's Britain: Landscape in Literature* (1979). She has also edited *Lady Susan, The Watsons, Sanditon* by Jane Austen (1974) and *The Genius of Thomas Hardy* (1976). There are several published interviews with Drabble: useful are those with Nancy S. Hardin in *Contemporary Literature* 14, 2 (Summer 1973), with Barbara Milton in *The Paris Review* 74 (Fall-Winter 1978), and with Diana Cooper-Clark in *Atlantic Monthly* (November 1980). Full-length studies of her writing include Valerie Grosvenor Myer, *Margaret Drabble: Puritanism and Permissiveness*, 1974; Ellen Cronan Rose, *The Novels of Margaret Drabble: Equivocal Figures*, 1980; and Mary Hurley Moran, *Margaret Drabble: Existing within Structures*, 1983. Feminist essays include Marion Vlastos Libby, "Fate and Feminism in the Novels of Margaret Drabble," *Contemporary Literature* 16 (1975); Virginia K. Beards, "Margaret Drabble: Novels of a Cautious Feminist," in *Contemporary Women Novelists*, ed. Patricia Meyer Spacks, 1977; and the concluding chapter in Elaine Showalter, *A Literature of Their Own*, 1977.

Alice Dunbar-Nelson

Ruby Ora Williams edited *An Alice Dunbar-Nelson Reader*, 1978, with critical comments by Agnes Moreland. Also available are *The Goodness of St. Rocque, and Other Stories* (1899, rpt. 1969) and *Give Us Each Day: The Diary of Alice Dunbar-Nelson*, ed. Gloria T. Hull, 1985. Articles about Dunbar-Nelson include Gloria T. Hull, "Alice Dunbar-Nelson: Delaware Writer and Woman of Affairs," *Delaware History* (Fall-Winter 1976); Hull, "Researching Alice Dunbar-Nelson: A Personal and Literary Perspective," *Feminist Studies* 6 (1980); and Roger Whitlow, "Alice Dunbar-Nelson: New Orleans Writer," *RFI* 4, i (1978). Ruby Ora Williams has also compiled a valuable bibliography in *College Language Association Journal* 19 (1976).

Maria Edgeworth

Ten volumes of Edgeworth's *Tales and Novels*, 1893—including *Castle Rackrent* (1800), *Belinda* (1801), *Leonora* (1806), *Tales of Fashionable Life* (1809, 1812), and *The Absentee* (1812)—were reprinted in 1967. Editions of her nonfiction and letters include *Letters from England, 1813–1844*, ed. Christina Colvin, 1971; *Letters for Literary Ladies*, with an introduction by Gina Luria, 1974; and *The Education of the Heart: The Correspondence of Rachel Mordecai Lazarus and Maria Edgeworth*, ed. Edgar E. MacDonald, 1977.

Among older biographical works are Honorable Emily Lawless, *Maria Edgeworth*, 1904; Constance Hill, *Maria Edgeworth and Her Circle in the Days of Bonaparte and Bourbon*, 1910; and Isabel Constance Clarke, *Maria Edgeworth, Her Family and Friends*, 1950. More recently, a valuable biography is Marilyn Butler, *Maria Edgeworth*, 1971. In addition, James Newcomer has two full-length studies—*Maria Edgeworth, the Novelist, 1767–1849*, 1967, and *Maria Edgeworth*, 1973—while other studies include *Doubt and Dogma in Maria Edgeworth* by Mark D. Hawthorne, 1967; *Maria Edgeworth and the Public Scene* by Michael Hurst, 1969; and *Maria Edgeworth's Art of Prose Fiction* by Oleta Elizabeth McWhorter Harden, 1971. Edgeworth is also discussed by Vineta Colby in *Yesterday's*

Women, 1974, and by Patricia Voss-Clesly in *Tendencies of Character Depiction in the Domestic Novels of Burney, Edgeworth, and Austen*, 1979.

George Eliot

Eliot's publications include *Scenes of Clerical Life* (1858), *Adam Bede* (1859), *The Mill on the Floss* (1860), *Silas Marner* (1861), *Romola* (1863), *Felix Holt the Radical* (1866), *The Spanish Gypsy* (1868), *Armgart* (1871), *Middlemarch* (1872), *Daniel Deronda* (1876), and *Impressions of Theophrastus Such* (1876). Ten volumes of her works were published by Blackwood in the 1890s. Gordon S. Haight edited *The George Eliot Letters*, 1954–1978, and Joseph Wiesenfarth edited *A Writer's Notebook, 1854–1879, and Uncollected Writings*, 1981. Also useful is the three volume *George Eliot's Life as Related in Her Letters and Journals*, arranged and edited by her husband, J. W. Cross, 1885. There are, of course, numerous editions of the novels, some of which, like the Penguins, contain valuable introductions and notes. *Middlemarch* appears in a Norton Critical Edition, ed. Bert G. Hornback.

There have been many biographies; the best of them is Gordon S. Haight, *George Eliot*, 1968. Haight also wrote *George Eliot and John Chapman*, 1969, and edited *A Century of George Eliot Critics*, 1965. In addition, with Rosemary T. VanArsdel, he edited *George Eliot, A Centenary Tribute*, 1982. Also useful is Ruby V. Redinger's biography, *George Eliot: The Emergent Self*, 1975, while valuable full-length studies include Barbara Hardy, *The Novels of George Eliot: A Study in Form*, 1959; U. C. Knoepflmacher, *George Eliot's Early Novels: The Limits of Realism* 1968; Felicia Bonaparte, *Will and Destiny: Morality and Tragedy in George Eliot's Novels*, 1975; Joseph Wiesenfarth, *George Eliot's Mythmaking*, 1977; Mary Ellen Doyle, *The Sympathetic Response: George Eliot's Fictional Rhetoric*, 1981; Karen S. Mann, *The Language That Makes George Eliot's Fiction*, 1983; and Suzanne Graver, *George Eliot and Community: A Study in Social Theory and Fictional Form*, 1984. Among feminist treatments are chapters in *The Female Imagination*, by Patricia

Meyer Spacks, 1975; in *A Literature of Their Own* by Elaine Showalter, 1977; in *The Madwoman in the Attic* by Sandra M. Gilbert and Susan Gubar, 1979; in *Monsters of Affection* by Dianne F. Sadoff, 1982; and in *Parallel Lives: Five Victorian Marriages* by Phyllis Rose, 1983. Collections of critical essays include *George Eliot and Her Readers: A Selection of Contemporary Reviews*, ed. John Holmstrom and Laurence Lerner, 1966; *Critical Essays on George Eliot*, ed. Barbara Hardy, 1970; *George Eliot: A Collection of Critical Essays*, ed. George R. Creeger, 1970; and *George Eliot: The Critical Heritage*, ed. David Carroll, 1971. There are also numerous collections on individual Eliot novels, such as the helpful *This Particular Web: Essays on Middlemarch*, ed. Ian Adams, 1975.

Queen Elizabeth I

The standard edition of Elizabeth's poems is Leicester Bradner, *The Poems of Queen Elizabeth I*, 1964. There are many collections of her letters; the most inclusive is *The Letters of Queen Elizabeth*, 1935, ed. G. B. Harrison, but forty previously unprinted letters were recently edited by E. I. Kouri and titled *Elizabethan England and Europe*, 1982. George P. Rice, Jr. published selected official addresses in *The Public Speaking of Queen Elizabeth*, 1951. Several literary figures have written about Elizabeth, including Thomas Heywood, *England's Elizabeth*, 1631; Lytton Strachey, *Elizabeth and Essex, a Tragic History*, 1928; and Edith Sitwell, *Fanfare for Elizabeth*, 1946. Elizabeth Jenkins, *Elizabeth the Great*, 1959, and *Elizabeth and Leicester*, 1962, are valuable studies, as is Paul Johnson, *Elizabeth I: A Study in Power and Intellect*, 1974. More recent is Alison Plowden, *Elizabeth Regina: The Age of Triumph, 1588–1603*, 1980.

Anne Finch

Myra Reynolds's *The Poems of Anne Countess of Winchilsea*, 1903, is out of print, but Katharine M. Rogers edited *Selected Poems of Anne Finch* in 1979. Rogers also wrote an essay on Finch, "An Augustan Woman Poet," for *Shakespeare's Sisters*, 1979, ed. Sandra M. Gilbert and Susan Gubar. In addition, Finch's work appears in Rogers's own anthology, *Before Their Time: Six Women Writers of the Eighteenth Century*, 1979. Elizabeth Hampsten has an introduction to "Poems by Anne Finch" in *Women's Studies* 7, i–ii (1980). Other recent articles include Lucy Brashear, "Finch's 'The Bird and the Arras,' " *Explicator* (Spring 1981), and Ann Messenger, "Publishing without Perishing: Lady Winchilsea's Miscellany Poems of 1713," *Restoration* (Spring 1981). Finch is also discussed in Hilda Smith, *Reason's Disciples*, 1982.

Mary E. Wilkins Freeman

Of the six volumes of short stories Freeman published, the two best known are *A Humble Romance* (1887) and *A New England Nun* (1891). Two collections of Freeman's work are *The Best Stories of Mary E. Wilkins*, 1927, ed. Henry W. Lanier, and the *Selected Stories of Mary E. Wilkins Freeman*, 1983, ed. Marjorie Pryse. Freeman also wrote a number of novels, including *Pembroke* (1894), *By the Light of the Soul* (1906), *The Portion of Labor* (1901), and *The Shoulders of Atlas* (1908). *Pembroke* has recently been reprinted.

Full-length critical/biographical studies include Edward Foster, *Mary E. Wilkins Freeman*, 1956; Abigail Ann Hamblen, *The New England Art of Mary E. Wilkins Freeman*, 1966; and Perry D. Westbrook, *Mary Wilkins Freeman*, 1967. Among articles, especially useful are Ann Douglas Wood, "The Literature of Impoverishment: The Women Local Colorists in America 1865–1914," *Women's Studies* 1, 1 (1972); Alice G. Brand, "Mary Wilkins Freeman: Misanthropy as Propaganda," *New England Quarterly* 50 (1977); Joseph E. McElrath, Jr., "The Artistry of Mary E. Wilkins Freeman's 'The Revolt,' " and Sarah W. Sherman, "The Great Goddess in New England: Mary Wilkins Freeman's 'Christmas Jenny,' " both in *Studies in Short Fiction* 17 (1980).

Margaret Fuller

Fuller's works include *Summer on the Lakes* (1844), *Woman in the Nineteenth Century* (1845), *Papers on Literature and Art* (1846), and numerous magazine essays and newspaper articles, some of which appear in the posthumous collections *At Home and Abroad* (1856) and

Life Without and Life Within (1859), both edited by her brother, Arthur B. Fuller. The somewhat bowdlerized *Memoirs of Margaret Fuller Ossoli*, 1852, was prepared by W. H. Channing, James Freeman Clarke, and Ralph Waldo Emerson, but two accurate and substantial recent collections of Fuller's writings are Bell Gale Chevigny, *The Woman and the Myth: Margaret Fuller's Life and Writings*, 1976, and Joel Myerson, *Margaret Fuller: Essays on American Life and Letters*, 1978.

Biographies include Mason Wade, *Margaret Fuller*, 1940; Madeleine B. Stern, *The Life of Margaret Fuller*, 1942; Arthur W. Brown, *Margaret Fuller*, 1964; and Joseph J. Deiss, *The Roman Years of Margaret Fuller*, 1969. Full-length critical studies include Paula Blanchard, *Margaret Fuller, From Transcendentalism to Revolution*, 1978; Margaret Allen, *The Achievement of Margaret Fuller*, 1979; and Marie Urbanski, *Margaret Fuller's "Woman in the 19th Century": A Literary Study of Form and Content, of Sources and Influence*, 1980. Joel Myerson has published annotated bibliographies of secondary material, 1977, and of Fuller's own work, 1978, as well as a recent collection of *Critical Essays on Margaret Fuller*, 1980.

Elizabeth Gaskell

The standard edition of Gaskell's novels —including *Mary Barton* (1848), *Cranford* (1853), *Ruth* (1853), *North and South* (1955), *Sylvia's Lovers* (1863), and *Wives and Daughters* (1866)—is *The Works of Mrs. Gaskell*, 1906–1920, with an introduction by A. W. Ward. In addition, much of this fiction, along with Gaskell's *The Life of Charlotte Brontë* (1857), has been published in modern editions, most notably a Penguin series with good critical introductions. The author's letters appear in *The Letters of Mrs. Gaskell*, ed. J. A. V. Chapple and Arthur Pollard, 1966; *Letters of Mrs. Gaskell and Charles Eliot Norton, 1855–1865*, ed. with an introduction by Jane Whitehill, 1973; and *Elizabeth Gaskell: A Portrait in Letters*, ed. J. A. V. Chapple, 1980. There are many biographies, the best of which is Winifred Gérin, *Elizabeth Gaskell*, 1976. Full-length critical studies include Aina

Rubenius, *The Woman Question in Mrs. Gaskell's Life and Works*, 1950; A. B. Hopkins, *Elizabeth Gaskell: Her Life and Work*, 1952; Edgar Wright, *Mrs. Gaskell: The Basis for Reassessment*, 1965; Margaret Ganz, *Elizabeth Gaskell: The Artist in Conflict*, 1969; J. G. Sharps, *Mrs. Gaskell's Observation and Invention*, 1970; Angus Easson, *Elizabeth Gaskell*, 1979; and Enid Lowry Duthie, *The Themes of Elizabeth Gaskell*, 1980. Nina Auerbach takes a feminist approach to *Cranford* in *Communities of Women: An Idea in Fiction*, 1978. Useful reference works are Robert L. Selig, *Elizabeth Gaskell: A Reference Guide*, 1977, and Jeffrey Welch, *Elizabeth Gaskell: An Annotated Bibliography, 1929–1975*, 1977.

Charlotte Perkins Gilman

A recent collection of Gilman's fiction is *The Charlotte Perkins Gilman Reader: The Yellow Wallpaper, and Other Fiction*, 1980, ed. and with an introduction by Ann J. Lane, who also wrote the introduction for the 1979 Pantheon edition of *Herland* (1915). Other reprinted works include the Feminist Press edition of *The Yellow Wallpaper* (1892, rpt. 1973), with an afterward by Elaine R. Hedges; *Women and Economics: A Study of the Economic Relation between Men and Women as a Factor in Social Evolution* (1898, rpt. 1975); *The Home, Its Work and Influence* (1903, rpt. 1970); and *The Man-Made World; or, Our Androcentric Culture* (1911, rpt. 1970). Of great interest is the writer's autobiography, *The Living of Charlotte Perkins Gilman* (1935).

Three important feminist studies are Carl N. Degler, "Charlotte Perkins Gilman on the Theory and Practice of Feminism," *American Quarterly* (Spring 1956); Mary A. Hill, "Charlotte Perkins Gilman: A Feminist Struggle with Womanhood," *Massachusetts Review* 23, 3 (Fall 1980); and Hill, *Charlotte Perkins Gilman: The Making of a Radical Feminist 1860–1896*, 1980.

Ellen Glasgow

Glasgow's novels include *The Descendant* (1897), *The Voice of the People* (1900), *Barren Ground* (1925), *The Romantic Comedians* (1926), *They Stooped to Folly* (1929), *The Sheltered Life* (1932), and *Vein of Iron* (1935). Her *Works*, including twelve titles, were published in 1938. Richard K. Mecker edited *Collected Stories*, 1973; and Blair Rouse edited and introduced her *Letters*, 1958. Her autobiography, *The Woman Within*, was published in 1954. Several of her novels have been reprinted, including *The Descendant* and *The Romantic Comedians*, both with introductions by Elizabeth Hardwick, both 1977, and *The Sheltered Life*, with an introduction by Paul Binding, 1981.

James Branch Cabell's memoir, *Of Ellen Glasgow*, 1938, is of interest, and there are a number of biographies, including *Ellen Glasgow* by Blair Rouse, 1962, and the recent *Ellen Glasgow* by Marcelle Thiebaux, 1982.

Full-length critical studies of the author include *Ellen Glasgow and the Ironic Art of Fiction* by Frederick P. W. McDowell, 1960; *Ellen Glasgow's American Dream* by Joan Foster Santas, 1965; *Ellen Glasgow's Development as a Novelist* by Marion K. Richards, 1971; *From the Sunken Garden: The Fiction of Ellen Glasgow 1916–1945* by Julius Raper, 1980; and *Ellen Glasgow: Beyond Convention* by Linda W. Wagner, 1982. M. Thomas Inge edited *Centennial Essays*, 1976.

Susan Glaspell

A collection of Glaspell's short dramas, *Plays*, was published in 1920. Her three-act plays include *The Verge* (1921), *The Comic Artist* (1927), and *Alison's House* (1930); among her novels are *The Visioning* (1911), *Fidelity* (1915), *Ambrose Holt and Family* (1931), and *The Morning Is Near Us* (1939). Glaspell's biography of George Cram Cook, *A Road to the Temple* (1927), includes useful background information on the Provincetown Players.

Susan Glaspell by Arthur E. Waterman, 1966, is a helpful introduction to her life and work; also by Waterman is "Susan Glaspell's *The Verge*: An Experiment in Feminism," *Great Lakes Review* 6, i (1979). Of interest are Marcia Noe, "Susan Glaspell's Analysis of the Midwestern Character," *Books at Iowa* 27 (1977), and Cynthia Sutherland, "American Women Playwrights as Mediators of the 'Woman Problem,'" *Modern Drama* 21 (1978). *Books at Iowa* 27 also contains a Susan Glaspell checklist. Another bibliographical source is Gerhard Bach, "Susan Glaspell (1876–1938): A Bibliography of Dramatic Criticism," *Great Lakes Review* 8, ii (1977).

Louise Glück

Glück's volumes of poetry are *Firstborn* (1969), *The House on Marshland* (1976), *The Garden* (1976), and *Descending Figure* (1980). Critical essays include Calvin Bedient, "Birth, Not Death, Is the Hard Loss," *Parnassus* 9, 1 (1981); and Robert Miklitsch, "Assembling a Landscape: The Poetry of Louise Glück," *The Hollins Critic* 19, 4 (1982). See also the chapter on Glück in Alan Williamson, *Introspection and Contemporary Poetry*, 1984.

Nadine Gordimer

A volume of Gordimer's *Selected Stories* appeared in 1976. Among her best-known novels are *The Late Bourgeois World* (1966), *A Guest of Honor* (1970), *The Conservationist* (1974), *Burger's Daughter* (1979), and *July's People* (1981). She has also published a book of criticism, *The Black Interpreters* (1973). Critical studies include *Nadine Gordimer* by Robert F. Haugh, 1974; *Nadine Gordimer* by Michael Wade, 1978; and "Hand in Glove: Nadine Gordimer, South African Writer," by Rose Moss, *Pacific Quarterly* 6 (1981).

Judy Grahn

Grahn's poems from 1964–1977 were collected in *The Work of a Common Woman* (1978), with an introduction by Adrienne Rich. Among subsequent volumes are *The Queen of Wands* (1982), and *Another Mother Tongue: Gay Words, Gay Worlds* (1984).

Lady Augusta Gregory

Gregory's plays—including *Spreading the News* (1909), *The Full Moon* (1913), *The Image* (1922), *The Dragon* (1923), *Aristotle's Bellows* (1923), and *Dave* (1928) —were edited in the four-volume *Collected Plays*, 1970, by Ann Saddlemyer. The Coole Edition, under the general editorship of T. R. Henn and Colin Smythe, also includes *Poets and Dreamers: Studies and Translations from the Irish* (1903, rpt. 1974), *Gods and*

Fighting Men: The Story of the Tuatha de Danaan and of the Fianna of Ireland (1904, rpt. 1970), *Our Irish Theatre: A Chapter of Autobiography* (1913, rpt. 1972), *Lady Gregory's Journals* (1946, rpt. 1978), and *Seventy Years: Being the Autobiography of Lady Gregory*, ed. Colin Smythe, 1974.

Memoirs include Anne Gregory, *Me and Nu: Childhood at Coole*, 1970, and E. H. Mikhail, *Lady Gregory: Interviews and Recollections*, 1977. Full-length critical studies are Elizabeth Coxhead, *J. M. Synge and Lady Gregory*, 1962, and her *Lady Gregory: A Literary Portrait*, 1966; Ann Saddlemyer, *In Defense of Lady Gregory, Playwright*, 1966; Hazard Adams, *Lady Gregory*, 1973; and Edward A. Kopper, *Lady Isabella Persse Gregory*, 1976. Useful chapters on Lady Gregory appear in Herbert Howarth, *The Irish Writers, 1880–1940*, 1958; Elizabeth Coxhead, *Daughters of Erin: Five Women of the Irish Renaissance*, 1965; Sean McCann, ed., *The Story of the Abbey Theatre*, 1967; Arra Garab, *Beyond Byzantium: The Last Phase of Yeats's Career*, 1969; Daniel Arthur Harris, *Yeats: Coole Park and Ballylee*, 1974; and Elizabeth Hale Winkler, *The Clown in Modern Anglo-Irish Drama*, 1977. Useful, too, is E. H. Mikhail, *Lady Gregory: An Annotated Bibliography of Criticism*, 1982.

Susan Griffin

Griffin's works include *Dear Sky* (1971), *Let Them be Said* (1973), *The Sink* (1974), *Voices* (1975), *Like the Iris of an Eye* (1976), *Woman and Nature: The Roaring Inside Her* (1978), *Rape: The Power of Consciousness* (1979), *Pornography and Silence: Culture's Revenge against Nature* (1981), and *Made from This Earth: An Anthology of Writings* (1982). Griffin's "Thoughts on Writing: A Diary" appears in *The Writer on Her Work*, ed. Janet Sternburg, 1980. Her poetry is discussed briefly in Barbara Charlesworth Gelpi, "A Common Language: The American Woman Poet" in *Shakespeare's Sisters*, ed. Sandra M. Gilbert and Susan Gubar, 1979.

Radclyffe Hall

Hall's novels and short story collections include *The Unlit Lamp* (1924), *The*

Forge (1924), *A Saturday Life* (1925), *Adam's Breed* (1929), *The Master of the House* (1932), *The Sixth Beatitude* (1933), *Miss Ogilvy Finds Herself* (1934), as well as the famous *The Well of Loneliness* (1928), which has been reissued in a number of editions since its first printing; in addition, *The Unlit Lamp* has been reissued in a Virago Press edition, 1981. Hall also published several volumes of poetry, including *The Forgotten Island* (1915).

Vera M. Brittain discusses Hall's life as well as the *Well of Loneliness* trial in *Radclyffe Hall: A Case of Obscenity*, 1969. Fuller biographies include Lady Una Troubridge's memoir, *The Life and Death of Radclyffe Hall*, 1961, and Lovat Dickson, *Radclyffe Hall at the Well of Loneliness: A Sapphic Chronicle*, 1975. A helpful full-length study of Hall's work is Claudia S. Franks, *Beyond the Well of Loneliness: The Fiction of Radclyffe Hall*, 1982, but Hall is also discussed in Lillian Faderman, *Surpassing the Love of Men: Romantic Friendship and Love between Women from the Renaissance to the Present*, 1981, and in a useful essay, Catharine R. Stimpson, "Zero Degree Deviancy: The Lesbian Novel in English," *Critical Inquiry* 8, 2 (1981).

Lorraine Hansberry

The two plays by Hansberry that were produced during her lifetime—*A Raisin in the Sun* (1959) and *The Sign in Sidney Brustein's Window* (1965)—are available in a paperback edited by Robert Nemiroff. *Lorraine Hansberry: The Collected Last Plays*, 1983, also edited by Nemiroff, contains *Les Blancs*, *The Drinking Gourd*, and *What Use Are Flowers?*. Hansberry composed the text of a photohistory, *The Movement: Documentary of a Struggle for Equality* (1964), as well as a number of essays, including "The Negro Writer and His Roots," which appears in *Black Scholar* (March-April 1981). Biographical material is provided by *To Be Young, Gifted and Black: An Informal Autobiography of Lorraine Hansberry*, 1969, edited by Robert Nemiroff, who also produced a play with this title. Elizabeth C. Phillips, *The Works of Lorraine Hansberry*, appeared in 1973. Critical discussions are included in C. W. E. Bigsby,

Confrontation and Commitment: A Study of Contemporary American Drama 1959–1966, 1969; Lloyd W. Brown, "Lorraine Hansberry as Ironist," *Journal of Black Studies* IV, 3 (March 1974); and Jeanne-Marie A. Miller, "Images of Black Women in Plays by Black Playwrights," *CLA Journal* 20, 4 (1977). Important critical essays by James Baldwin, Nikki Giovanni, Alex Haley, Adrienne Rich, and Margaret B. Wilkerson appear in *Lorraine Hansberry: Art of Thunder, Vision of Light*, a special issue of *Freedomways*, ed. Jean Carey Bond (Fourth Quarter 1979).

Frances E. W. Harper

Harper's published works include *Poems on Miscellaneous Subjects* (1854), *Poems* (1871), *Sketches of Southern Life* (1872), *Iola Leroy; or, Shadows Uplifted* (1892), and *The Martyr of Alabama and Other Poems* (c. 1894). She is discussed in three broad studies: William H. Robinson, Jr., *Early Black American Poets*, 1971; Joan Sherman, *Invisible Poets: Afro-American Women of the Nineteenth Century*, 1974; and Gloria Hull, "Afro-American Women Poets: A Bio-Critical Survey," in *Shakespeare's Sisters*, ed. Sandra M. Gilbert and Susan Gubar, 1979. A valuable recent essay is Patricia L. Hill, "Let Me Make the Songs for the People: A Study of Frances W. Harper's Poetry," *Black American Literature Forum* 15, 2 (Summer 1981).

Lillian Hellman

Hellman's plays—including *The Children's Hour* (1934), *The Little Foxes* (1939), *Watch on the Rhine* (1941), *The Searching Wind* (1944), *Another Part of the Forest* (1946), and *Toys in the Attic* (1960)—were reissued in her *Collected Plays* (1972). She also wrote seven screenplays. Three books of memoirs—*An Unfinished Woman* (1969), *Pentimento* (1973), and *Scoundrel Time* (1976)—have been reprinted with Hellman's recent commentaries in *Three* (1979).

Two interviews provide useful background information: John Phillips and Anne Hollander, "The Art of the Theater," *Paris Review* 33 (1965); and Christine Doudna, an interview in *Rolling Stone* 233 (February 1977). Among book-length studies of Hellman are Jacob H. Adler, *Lillian Hellman*, 1969; Richard Moody, *Lillian Hellman, Playwright*, 1972; Doris V. Falk, *Lillian Hellman*, 1978; Katherine Lederer, *Lillian Hellman*, 1979; and Bernard F. Dick, *Hellman in Hollywood*, 1982. A recent feminist approach to Hellman's work is "Lillian Hellman and the Strategy of the Other" by Marcus K. Billson and Sidonie A. Smith in *Women's Autobiographies*, ed. Estelle C. Jelinek, 1980. Also helpful are Mark W. Estrin, *Lillian Hellman: A Reference Guide*, 1980, and Mary Marguerite Riordan, *Lillian Hellman: A Bibliography*, 1980.

Mary Sidney Herbert, Countess of Pembroke

Herbert's published works include *The Psalms of Sir Philip Sidney and the Countess of Pembroke*, ed. J. C. A. Rathmell, 1963; *Two Poems by the Countess of Pembroke*, ed. Bent Juel-Jensen, 1962; *The Triumph of Death, and Other Unpublished and Uncollected Poems*, ed. G. F. Waller, 1977; *The Countess of Pembroke's Antonie*, ed. Alice Luce, 1897; and *The Countess of Pembroke's Emanuell*, ed. A. B. Grosart, in *Miscellanies*, 1871. Herbert is included in *Memoirs of Several Ladies of Great Britain* by George Ballard, 1752, and in *Memoirs of Eminent Englishwomen* by Louisa Costello, 1844. Biographical materials include M. M. Bulloch, *Mary Sidney, Countess of Pembroke, an Elizabethan Historiette*, 1895, and the useful *Mary Sidney, Countess of Pembroke* by Frances B. Young, 1912. G. F. Waller has written the useful *Mary Sidney, Countess of Pembroke, A Critical Study of Her Writings and Literary Milieu* (1979). More recently, her work is discussed in Coburn Freer, "The Countess of Pembroke in a World of Words," *Style* 5 (1980).

Zora Neale Hurston

Hurston's volumes include *Jonah's Gourd Vine* (1934), *Mules and Men* (1935), *Their Eyes Were Watching God* (1937), *Tell My Horse* (1938), *Moses, Man of the Mountain* (1939), *Dust Tracks on a Road* (1942), and *Seraph on the Suwanee* (1948). An excellent anthology of Hurston's work, ed. and with useful introductions by Alice Walker and Mary Helen Washington, is *I Love Myself When I Am Laughing . . . And Then Again When I Am Looking Mean and Impressive: A Zora Neale Hurston Reader*, 1979.

A good biography, *Zora Neale Hurston* by Robert E. Hemenway, appeared in 1977, and Lillie P. Howard wrote *Zora Neale Hurston*, 1980. Articles include Erlene Stetson, "*Their Eyes Were Watching God*," *Regionalism and the Female Imagination* 4, i (1978); Florence E. Borders, "Zora Neale Hurston: Hidden Woman," *Callaloo* 2 (May 1979); Mary Jane Lupton, "Zora Neale Hurston and the Survival of the Female," *Southern Literary Journal* 15, 1 (Fall 1982); and Cheryl A. Wall, "Zora Neale Hurston: Changing Her Own Words," in *American Novelists Revisited: Essays in Feminist Criticism*, ed. Fritz Fleischmann, 1982.

Rebecca Cox Jackson

Jackson's work has recently been collected in *Gifts of Power: The Writings of Rebecca Jackson, Black Visionary, Shaker Eldress*, ed. and with an introduction by Jean McMahon Humez, 1981. Richard E. Williams's biography, *Called and Chosen: The Story of Mother Rebecca Jackson and the Philadelphia Shakers*, has been edited by Cheryl Dorschner and republished in 1981. A valuable essay, occasioned by the publication of *Gifts of Power*, appears in Alice Walker's recent volume, *In Search of Our Mothers' Gardens*, 1983.

Shirley Jackson

Two collections of Jackson's stories and essays are *The Magic of Shirley Jackson* (1966) and *Come Along with Me* (1968), both edited by her husband, Stanley Edgar Hyman. Her novels include *Hangsaman* (1951) and *We Have Always Lived in the Castle* (1962). *Shirley Jackson*, a short introduction to her life and work, was written by Lenemaja Friedman, 1975. Two useful essays on her fiction are Steven K. Hoffman, "Individuation and Character Development in the Fiction of Shirley Jackson," *Hartford Studies in Literature* 8 (1976), and John G. Parks, " 'The Possibility of Evil': A Key to Shirley Jackson's Fiction," in *Studies in Science Fiction* 15 (1978). Further analyses are represented in J. W. Aldridge, *After the Lost Generation: A Critical Study of the Writers of*

Two Wars, 1958, and J. O. Lyons, *The College Novel in America*, 1962.

Alice James

James's work can be found in *Alice James, Her Brothers—Her Journal*, ed. and with an introduction by Anna Robeson Burr, 1934; *The Diary of Alice James*, ed. and with an introduction by Leon Edel, 1964; and *The Death and Letters of Alice James*, ed. and with a biographical essay by Ruth Bernard Yeazell, 1981.

Secondary material includes Francis Otto Matthiessen, *The James Family*, 1947, and Jean Strouse, *Alice James: A Biography*, 1980.

Sarah Orne Jewett

Jewett's work includes *Deephaven* (1877), *A Country Doctor* (1884), *A White Heron and Other Stories* (1886), and *The Country of the Pointed Firs* (1896). Her *Stories and Tales* were published in seven volumes in 1910, but a more readily available collection, *The Best Stories of Sarah Orne Jewett*, 1925, was edited in two volumes with a foreword by Willa Cather. *The Country of the Pointed Firs, and Other Stories* was edited by Mary Ellen Chase in 1968 and reissued, with an introduction by Marjorie Pryse, in 1981. Richard Cary edited *The Uncollected Short Stories of Sarah Orne Jewett*, 1971, as well as the *Sarah Orne Jewett Letters*, revised and enlarged in 1967.

Critical biographies include F. O. Matthiessen, *Sarah Orne Jewett*, 1929; Richard Cary, *Sarah Orne Jewett*, 1962; and Margaret Thorp, *Sarah Orne Jewett*, 1966. Cary also edited a collection of essays, *Appreciation of Sarah Orne Jewett*, 1973. More recent studies include Josephine Donovan, *Sarah Orne Jewett*, 1980, and Perry Westbrook, *Acres of Flint: Sarah Orne Jewett and Her Contemporaries*, 1981. A valuable reference guide is *Sarah Orne Jewett* by Gwen L. Nagel, 1978.

Erica Jong

Jong's volumes of poetry—*Fruits and Vegetables* (1971), *Half-Lives* (1973), and *Loveroot* (1975)—were collected with several critical essays in *Here Comes, and Other Poems* (1975). Later volumes of poetry include *At the Edge of the Body* (1979) and *Ordinary Miracles: New Poems* (1983). Works of fiction include *Fear of Flying* (1973), *How to Save Your Own Life* (1977), and *Fanny* (1980). *Witches* (1981) and *Molly's Book of Divorce* (1984) represent Jong's recent work in criticism and in children's literature. Useful critical articles are Arlyn Diamond, "Flying from Work," *Frontiers* 2, iii (1977); Jane C. Nitzsche, " 'Isadora Icarus': The Mythic Unity of Erica Jong's *Fear of Flying*," *Rice University Studies* 64 (1978); Joan Reardon, "*Fear of Flying*: Developing the Feminist Novel," *International Journal of Women's Studies* 1 (1978); and Evelyn G. Avery, "Tradition and Independence in Jewish Feminist Novels," *MELUS* 7, iv (1980).

Julian of Norwich

Marion Glasscoe has edited a reliable edition of the Middle English text of Julian's *A Revelation of Divine Love*, 1976, but a more readable modern version is *A Book of Showings*, edited and translated by Edmund Colledge, O.S.A. and James Walsh, S.J., 1978. P. Franklin Chambers, *Juliana of Norwich*, 1955, and Paul Molinari, S.J., *Julian of Norwich*, 1958, are general introductions to her work; Robert Stone, *Middle English Prose Style*, 1970, treats both Julian and Margery Kempe. More recent works are Brant Pelphrey, *Love Was His Meaning: The Theology and Mysticism of Julian of Norwich*, 1982, and Jennifer P. Hummel, *"God Is Our Mother": Julian of Norwich, and the Medieval Image of Feminine Divinity*, 1982. Mary Mason's useful article, "The Other Voice: Autobiography of Women Writers," in *Autobiography*, ed. James Olney, 1980, puts Julian's work in the context of women's autobiography.

Margery Kempe

Colonel W. E. I. Butler-Bowdon edited and modernized *The Book of Margery Kempe*, 1936. In 1940, Sanford Brown Meech edited a transcription of the Butler-Bowdon manuscript which includes a prefatory note by Hope Emily Allen. Valuable introductions are Katharine Cholmeley, *Margery Kempe, Genius and Mystic*, 1947; Martin Thornton, *Margery Kempe, an Example in the English Pastoral Tradition*, 1960; and Louise

Collis, *Memoirs of a Medieval Woman: The Life and Times of Margery Kempe,* 1964. A recent, readable book is *Mystic and Pilgrim: The Book and the World of Margery Kempe* by Clarissa W. Atkinson, 1983. Robert Stone discusses her in his *Middle English Prose Style,* 1970, as do Mary Mason in "The Other Voice: Autobiography of Women's Writers," in *Autobiography,* ed. James Olney, 1980, and Hope Phyllis Weissman in "Margery Kempe in Jerusalem: *Hysterica Compassio* in the Late Middle Ages," in *Acts of Interpretation,* ed. Mary J. Carruthers and Elizabeth D. Kirk, 1982.

Anne Killigrew
Killigrew's work is collected in *Poems* (1686). A facsimile reproduction, with an introduction by Richard Morton, was published in 1967.

Maxine Hong Kingston
Kingston's works are *The Woman Warrior* (1976) and *China Men* (1980). She also has an important article, "Cultural Misreading by American Reviewers," in *Asian and Western Writers in Dialogue: New Cultural Identities,* 1982. Critical essays on Kingston include Patricia Lin Blinde, "The Icicle in the Desert: Perspective and Form in the Works of Two Chinese-American Women Writers," *MELUS* 6, iii (1979); Deborah Homsher, "*The Woman Warrior,* by Maxine Hong Kingston: A Bridging of Autobiography and Fiction," *Iowa Review* 10, iv (1979); Linda Ching Sledge, "Maxine Hong Kingston's *China Men:* The Family Historian as Epic Poet," *MELUS* 7, iv (1980); and Robert Rolf, "On Maxine Hong Kingston and *The Woman Warrior,*" *Kyushu American Literature* 23 (1982).

Carolyn Kizer
Kizer's books of poetry include *The Ungrateful Garden* (1961), *Knock upon Silence: Poems* (1965), *Midnight Was My Cry: New and Selected Poems* (1971), *Yin* (1984), and *Mermaids in the Basement: Poems for Women* (1984). An interesting essay on her work is Dominic Cheung, "Carolyn Kizer and her Chinese Imitations," in *China and the West: Comparative Literature Studies* (1980), ed.

William Tay, Chou Ying-hsiung, and Yuan Heh-hsiang.

Maxine Kumin
Kumin's works include children's books, novels, and verse collections; some of the most notable are *Through Dooms of Love* (1965), *Up Country* (1972), *The Designated Heir* (1974), *House, Bridge, Fountain, Gate* (1975), *The Retrieval System* (1978), and *Our Ground Time Here Will Be Brief* (1982). *To Make a Prairie* (1979) is a book of essays.

Two interesting interviews are Karla Hammond, "An Interview with Maxine Kumin," *Western Humanities Review* 33 (1979), and Shelley Armitage, "An Interview with Maxine Kumin," *Paintbrush* 7–8 (1980–1981). Critical pieces include Philip Booth, "Maxine Kumin's Survival," *American Poetry Review* (1978) and Sybil P. Estess, "Past Halfway: *The Retrieval System* by Maxine Kumin," *Iowa Review* 10, iv (1979).

Amelia Lanier
Lanier's long poem, *Salve Deus Rex Judaeorum* (1611), appears as *The Poems of Shakespeare's Dark Lady,* 1979, ed. and with an introduction by A. L. Rowse. She is discussed in George Ballard, *Memoirs of Several Ladies of Great Britain,* 1752; H. T. C. de la Fontaine, *The King's Musick,* 1909; and Eric Blom, *Grove's Dictionary of Music and Musicians,* 1954, supplement 1961. More recently, some of her work is included in *The Female Spectator,* ed. Mary R. Mahl and Helene Koon, 1977.

Margaret Laurence
Laurence's novels include *This Side Jordan* (1960), *The Stone Angel* (1964), *A Jest of God* (1966), *The Fire-Dwellers* (1969), and *The Diviners* (1974). She has several books of short stories; a recent one is *The Olden-Days Coat* (1979). Other works include literary studies, children's books, and a collection of essays, *Heart of a Stranger* (1976). A full-length critical study is *Margaret Laurence* by Patricia Morley, 1981, and a good collection of critical essays is *Margaret Laurence,* 1977. Two useful essays are Judy Kearns, "Rachel and Social Determinism: A Feminist Reading of *A Jest of God,*" *Journal of Ca-*

nadian Fiction 27 (1980) and Harriet Blodgett, "The Real Lives of Margaret Laurence's Women," *Critique* 23, 1 (1981). There is an annotated bibliography of Laurence, by Susan J. Warwick, in *The Annotated Bibliography of Canada's Major Authors I*, ed. Robert Lecker and Jack David, 1979.

Jane Lead

Lead's published works include *A Fountain of Gardens Watered by the River of Divine Pleasure and Springing Up in All Variety of Spiritual Plants* (1677–1701) and *Wars of David* (1700). Most of the recent studies are by Catherine F. Smith and include "A Note on Jane Lead with Selections from Her Writings," *Studia Mystica* 3, IV; "Mysticism and Feminism: Jacob Boehme and Jane Lead," in *Women and Men: The Consequences of Power*, 1977, ed. Dana V. Hiller and Robin Ann Sheets; "Jane Lead: The Feminist Mind and Art of a 17th-Century Protestant Mystic," in *Women of Spirit*, ed. Rosemary Ruether and Eleanor McLaughlin, 1979; and "Jane Lead: Mysticism and the Woman Clothed with the Sun," in *Shakespeare's Sisters*, ed. Sandra M. Gilbert and Susan Gubar, 1979.

Ursula Le Guin

Le Guin's works include *Rocannon's World* (1966), *A Wizard of Earthsea* (1968), *The Left Hand of Darkness* (1969), *The Dispossessed* (1974), *The Wind's Twelve Quarters* (1975), *Orsinian Tales* (1976), *Malafrena* (1979), *The Beginning Place* (1980), and *The Compass Rose* (1982). She has also written numerous essays as well as *Hard Works, and Other Poems* (1981). Full-length studies include George E. Slusser, *The Farthest Shores of Ursula K. Le Guin*, 1976, and Barbara J. Bucknall, *Ursula K. Le Guin*, 1981. Two collections of critical essays about her work are *Ursula K. Le Guin*, ed. Joseph Olender and Martin Greenberg, 1979, and *Ursula K. Le Guin: Voyager to Inner Lands and to Outer Space*, ed. Joe DeBolt, 1979. Two interesting articles appeared in *Extrapolation* 21 (1980): Rosemarie Arbur, "Le Guin's 'Song' of Innermost Feminism" and Dena C. Bain, "The *Tao Te Ching* as Background to the Novels of Ursula K. Le Guin." Extremely useful is *Ursula K. Le Guin: A Primary and Secondary Bibliography* by Elizabeth Cummins Cogell, 1983.

Doris Lessing

Most of Lessing's collections of short stories and her novels—including the five-volume *Children of Violence* (1952–1969), *The Golden Notebook* (1962), *A Man and Two Women* (1963), *African Stories* (1969), *Briefing for a Descent into Hell* (1971), and *Summer before the Dark* (1973)—are available in paperback. Her most recent work includes a series of science-fiction novels beginning with *Shikasta* (1979). *A Small Personal Voice*, ed. Paul Schlueter, 1974, is a selection of Lessing's essays on her life and writings, on other writers, and on Africa. *Notebooks, Memoirs, Archives: Reading and Re-Reading Doris Lessing*, ed. Jenny Taylor, came out in 1982.

Critical and biographical full-length studies include *Doris Lessing* by Dorothy Brewster, 1965; *The Novels of Doris Lessing* by Paul Schleuter, 1973; *The City and the Veld* by Mary Ann Singleton, 1977; *The Novelistic Vision of Doris Lessing* by Roberta Rubenstein, 1979; *Doris Lessing* by Lorna Sage, 1983; *Substance under Pressure: Artistic Coherence and Evolving Form in the Novels of Doris Lessing* by Betsy Draine, 1983; and *Doris Lessing* by Mona Kapp, 1984. A useful collection is *Doris Lessing: Critical Essays*, ed. Annis Pratt and L. S. Dembo, 1974. Dee Seligman compiled an annotated bibliography in 1981.

Meridel Le Sueur

Le Sueur's works include *Annunciation* (1935), *Salute to Spring* (1940), *North Star Country* (1945), *Sparrow Hawk* (1950), *Crusaders* (1955), *Corn Village* (1970), and *Women on the Bread Lines* (1978). *Harvest: Collected Stories* appeared in 1977. Elaine Hedges includes important biographical background in her edition of and introduction to *Ripening: Selected Work of Meridel Le Sueur*, *1927–1980*, 1982. Interesting critical essays are Neala J. Y. Scheuning, "Meridel Le Sueur: Toward a New Regionalism," *Books at Iowa* 33 (1980); Erika Duncan, "Writing and Surviving: A Portrait of Meridel Le Sueur," *Book Forum* 6,

1 (1982); and Blanche H. Gelfant's chapter on Le Sueur in *Women Writing in America*, 1985.

Denise Levertov

Levertov's books of poems include *The Double Image* (1946), *Here and Now* (1957), *Overland to the Islands* (1958), *With Eyes at the Back of Our Heads* (1960), *The Jacob's Ladder* (1961), *O Taste and See* (1964), *The Sorrow Dance* (1967), *Relearning the Alphabet* (1970), *To Stay Alive* (1971), *Footprints* (1972), *The Freeing of the Dust* (1975), *Life in the Forest* (1978), and *Candles in Babylon* (1982). She also has two recent collections: *Collected Earlier Poems 1940–1960* (1979) and *Poems, 1960–1967* (1983). *The Poet in the World* (1973) and *Light Up the Cave* (1981) are collections of her essays and reviews, as is *Denise Levertov: In Her Own Province*, ed. Linda W. Wagner, 1979.

Two interviews with Levertov were published in 1979: Kenneth J. Atchity's in *The San Francisco Review of Books*, and Fay Zwicky's in *Westerly* ii. Valuable analyses of her work include Rachel Blau DuPlessis, "The Critique of Consciousness and Myth in Levertov, Rich, and Rukeyser," in *Shakespeare's Sisters*, ed. Sandra M. Gilbert and Susan Gubar, 1979; Linda W. Wagner, "Levertov and Rich: The Later Poems," *South Carolina Review* 11, ii (1979); Diana Surman, "Inside and Outside in the Poetry of Denise Levertov," *Critical Quarterly* 22 (1980); and Bonnie Costello, " 'Flooded with Otherness,' " *Parnassus* 8, 1 (1980).

Dorothy Livesay

Volumes of Livesay's poetry include *Selected Poems 1926–1956* (1957), *The Documentaries: Selected Longer Poems* (1968), and *Collected Poems: The Two Seasons* (1972). Subsequent collections include *Nine Poems of Farewell 1972–1973* (1973), *Ice Age* (1975), and *The Woman I Am* (1977), as well as a volume of short stories, *A Winnipeg Childhood* (1973). For biographical information, see two interviews: Doug Beardsley and Rosemary Sullivan's piece in *Canadian Poetry* 3 (1978) and Jorn Carlsen's in *Kunapipi* 1, i (1979). Critical essays include Peter Stevens, "Out of Silence and Across the Distance: The Poetry of Dorothy Livesay," *Queen's Quarterly* 4 (Winter 1969) and his "Dorothy Livesay: The Love Poetry," *Canadian Literature* (Winter 1971); Debbie Foulks, "Livesay's Two Seasons of Love," *Canadian Literature* 74 (1977); and Lee B. Thompson, "A Coat of Many Cultures: The Poetry of Dorothy Livesay," *Journal of Popular Culture* 15, 3 (Winter 1981).

Audre Lorde

The most nearly complete collection of Lorde's poetry is *Chosen Poems, Old and New* (1982). Other volumes include *First Cities* (1968), *Cables to Rage* (1970), *New York Headshop and Museum* (1974), *Coal* (1976), *The Black Unicorn* (1978), *The Cancer Journal* (1980), and *Zami: A New Spelling of My Name* (1982). She has also written a pamphlet, *Uses of the Erotic: The Erotic as Power* (n.d.). Karla Hammond has a useful interview with Lorde in *Denver Quarterly* 16, 1 (Spring 1981), and there is another interview in *Black Women Writers at Work*, ed. Claudia Tate, 1984. An interesting critical essay on Lorde and Maya Angelou is R. G. Stepto, "The Phenomenal Woman and the Severed Daughter," *Parnassus* 8, i (1980). Jerome Brooks, "In the Name of the Father: The Poetry of Audre Lorde," and Joan Martins, "The Unicorn Is Black: Audre Lorde in Retrospect," appear in *Black Women Writers (1950–1980)*, ed. Mari Evans, 1894.

Amy Lowell

Lowell's *The Complete Poetical Works* was published in 1955. Harley F. MacNair edited *Florence Ayscough and Amy Lowell: Correspondence of a Friendship*, 1945. Valuable background can be found in Clemens David Heymann, *American Aristocracy: The Lives and Times of James Russell, Amy, and Robert Lowell*, 1980. Full-length studies and biographies include *Amy Lowell* by Damon S. Foster, 1935; *Amy Lowell* by F. Cudworth Flint, 1969; *The Thorn of a Rose: Amy Lowell Reconsidered* by Glenn R. Ruihley, 1975; and *Amy: The World of Amy Lowell and the Imagist Movement* by Jean Gould, 1975. An analysis of Lowell's relationship to the lesbian tradition is offered in Lillian Faderman, "Warding off the Watch and

Ward Society: Amy Lowell's Treatment of the Lesbian Theme," *Gay Books Bulletin* (1979).

Katherine Mansfield

Mansfield's stories appear in a complete one-volume edition, *The Short Stories of Katherine Mansfield*, 1937. Her *Journal* was edited by J. Middleton Murry, revised ed., 1954, and *Letters and Journals of Katherine Mansfield: A Selection*, by C. K. Stead, 1977. The first volume of *The Collected Letters of Katherine Mansfield, 1888–1917*, ed. Vincent O'Sullivan and Margaret Scott, was published in 1984.

Biographies, memoirs, and critical studies include *Katherine Mansfield, a Critical Study* by S. Berkman, 1951; *Katherine Mansfield* by Leslie Moore, 1971; *Lives and Letters* by John Carswell, 1978; *Katherine Mansfield: A Biography* by Jeffrey Meyers, 1978; *The Life of Katherine Mansfield* by Anthony Alpers, 1980; *Gurdjieff and Mansfield* by James Moore, 1980; *Writers in Exile: The Identity of Home in Modern Literature* by Andrew Gurr, 1981; and *Katherine Mansfield* by Clare Hanson and Andrew Gurr, 1981. Mary Burgan, "Childbirth Trauma in Katherine Mansfield's Early Stories," *Modern Fiction Studies* 24, 3 (Autumn 1978), is useful, as are a number of the other articles in this special issue devoted to Katherine Mansfield.

Mary McCarthy

Mary McCarthy has published two collections of stories: *The Company She Keeps* (1942) and *Cast a Cold Eye* (1950). Her novels are *The Oasis* (1948), *The Groves of Academe* (1952), *A Charmed Life* (1955), *The Group* (1963), *Birds of America* (1971), and *Cannibals and Missionaries* (1979). Her autobiographical *Memories of a Catholic Girlhood* appeared in 1957. *On the Contrary* (1961) and *The Writings on the Wall* (1970) are collections of essays on literary and cultural topics. Travel books are *Venice Observed* (1956) and *The Stones of Florence* (1959). Her essays on Vietnam and the Watergate hearings are collected in *The Seventeenth Degree* (1974). *Sights and Spectacles* (1956) has been republished and enlarged as *Mary McCarthy's Theater Chronicles 1937–1962* (1963).

Critical and biographical writings about her include *The Company She Kept* by Doris Grumbach, 1967; *Mary McCarthy* by Irwin Stock, 1967; and *Mary McCarthy* by Willena S. Hardy, 1981. Useful essays include Elizabeth Hardwick's chapter in *A View of My Own*, 1963; and Rosalie Hewitt, "A 'Home Address for the Self': Mary McCarthy's Autobiographical Journey," *Journal of Narrative Technique* 12, 2 (1982). Sherli Goldman, *Mary McCarthy: A Bibliography* was published in 1968.

Carson McCullers

McCullers's works are *The Heart Is a Lonely Hunter* (1940), *Reflections in a Golden Eye* (1941), *The Member of the Wedding* (1946), *The Ballad of the Sad Cafe* (1951), *The Square Root of Wonderful* (1958), *Clock without Hands* (1961), *Sweet as a Pickle and Clean as a Pig: Poems* (1964), and *The Mortgaged Heart*, ed. M. G. Smith, 1971. There are two biographies: Virginia S. Carr, *The Lonely Hunter: A Biography of Carson McCullers*, 1975, and Richard Cook, *Carson McCullers*, 1975.

Critical studies include Oliver Evans, *The Ballad of Carson McCullers*, 1966; and Margaret McDowell, *Carson McCullers*, 1980. Among critical essays are "Androgyny and the Musical Vision: A Study of Two Novels by Carson McCullers" by Patricia S. Box, *Southern Quarterly* 16 (1978); "Imperfect Androgyny and Imperfect Love in the Works of Carson McCullers" by Mary Roberts, *University of Hartford Studies in Literature* 12 (1980); "The Patterns of Love in Carson McCuller's Fiction" by Marzenna Raczkowska, *Studia Anglica Posnaniensia* 12 (1980), and "Carson McCullers's Amazon Nightmare" by Louise Westling, *Modern Fiction Studies* 28, 3 (1982). A valuable annotated bibliography, *Carson McCullers*, comp. Adrian Shapiro, Jackson Bryer, and Kathleen Field, appeared in 1980.

Charlotte Mew

Two volumes of Mew's collected work have been produced since her death: *Collected Poems of Charlotte Mew*, with a memoir by Alida Monro, 1953; and *Col-*

lected Poems and Prose, 1981, ed., with an introduction and helpful critical bibliography, by Val Warner. Val Warner also wrote one of the few critical pieces on Mew, "Mary Magdalene and the Bride: The Work of Charlotte Mew," *Poetry Nation* 4 (1975).

Alice Meynell

Meynell's collected poems appear in *The Poems of Alice Meynell* (1923). *Alice Meynell, Prose and Poetry* is a centenary volume edited by Frederick Page, with a biographical and critical introduction by Vita Sackville-West, 1947. A centenary collection of her essays, with an introduction by Sir Francis Meynell, was reprinted in 1970. Another selection of her essays, edited and introduced by P. M. Fraser, is *The Wares of Autolycus*, 1965.

For useful biographical information see *Alice Meynell: A Memoir* by Viola Meynell, 1929, and *The Slender Tree: A Life of Alice Meynell* by June Badeni, 1981. A feminist approach is represented by Beverly Ann Schlack, "The 'Poetess of Poets': Alice Meynell Rediscovered," *Women's Studies* 7, i–ii (1980).

Josephine Miles

Miles's volumes of verse include *Lines at Intersection* (1939), *Poems on Several Occasions* (1941), *Local Measures* (1946), *After This Sea* (1947), *Prefabrications* (1955), *Poems, 1930–1960* (1960), *Civil Poems* (1967), *Kinds of Affection* (1967), *Saving the Bay* (1967), *Fields of Learning* (1968), *American Poems* (1970), *To All Appearances* (1975), and *Coming to Terms* (1979). She has also written many volumes of criticism, including *Wordsworth and the Vocabulary of Emotion* (1942), *The Vocabulary of Poetry* (1946), and *Poetry and Change* (1974), and she has edited a number of critical volumes, including *Criticism: The Foundations of Modern Literary Judgment*, with Mark Schorer and Gordon McKenzie (1948, rev. 1958), *The Poem: A Critical Anthology* (1959, rev. 1961), and *Classic Essays in English* (1961). Recent essays on Miles's poetry include Stephen Mooney, "Josephine Miles: Successive Views," *Voyage* 2, 3 (Fall 1968); and Julia Randall, "Dickinson with

a Difference: The Poetry of Josephine Miles," *Hollins Critic* 17.

Edna St. Vincent Millay

Millay's *Collected Sonnets* (1941) and *Collected Lyrics* (1943) were followed by *Collected Poems: Edna St. Vincent Millay*, ed. Norma Millay, 1956. Her prose sketches, *Distressing Dialogues*, published under the pseudonym Nancy Boyd, appeared in 1924. Her three verse plays— *Aria da Capo* (1920), *The Lamp and the Bell* (1921), *Two Slatterns and a King* (1921)—were collected in *Three Plays* (1926).

Allan Ross Macdougall edited *Letters of Edna St. Vincent Millay* in 1952. Recent biographical studies are Joan Dash, *A Life of One's Own: Three Gifted Women and the Men They Married*, 1973, and Anne Cheney, *Millay in Greenwich Village*, 1975. Fuller treatments are Miriam Gurko, *Restless Spirit*, 1957, and Jean Gould, *The Poet and Her Book*, 1969. Useful brief introductions are Norman A. Brittin, *Edna St. Vincent Millay*, 1967; James Gray, *Edna St. Vincent Millay*, 1967; and Norman A. Brittin, *Edna St. Vincent Millay*, 1967, rev. ed. 1982. A feminist approach is represented in Jane Stanbrough, "Edna St. Vincent Millay and the Language of Vulnerability," in *Shakespeare's Sisters*, ed. Sandra Gilbert and Susan Gubar, 1979. Karl Yost, *A Bibliography of the Works of Edna St. Vincent Millay*, appeared in 1937, and Judith Nierman, *Edna St. Vincent Millay: A Reference Guide*, in 1977.

Lady Mary Wortley Montagu

Lord J. S. W. Wharncliffe, Montagu's great grandson, edited *The Letters and Works of Lady Mary Wortley Montagu*, 1837. A modern edition of the *Complete Letters* is edited by Robert Halsband, 1965, who also edited Montagu's *The Nonsense of Common Sense*, 1947, and, with Isobel Grundy, *Essays and Poems of Lady Mary Wortley Montagu*, 1977. Halsband also wrote a definitive biography, *The Life of Lady Mary Wortley Montagu*, 1956, while Grundy has a recent article in *The Book Collector* (Spring 1982) on "The Politics of Female Authorship: Lady Mary Wortley Montagu's Reaction to the Printing of Her Poems." In addition, Montagu's work is represented in *By a Woman Writt*, ed. Joan Goulianos, 1973, and in *Before Their Time*, ed. Katharine M. Rogers, 1979.

Marianne Moore

No collection of Moore's verse is definitive because each excluded some earlier poems while offering extensive revisions of others. Her separate volumes include *Poems* (1921), *Observations* (1924), *The Pangolin, and Other Verse* (1936), *What Are Years?* (1941), *Nevertheless* (1944), *Like a Bulwark* (1956), *O to Be a Dragon* (1959), and *Tell Me, Tell Me* (1966). Collections include *Selected Poems* (1935), *Collected Poems* (1951), and *The Complete Poems of Marianne Moore* (1967), which also offers selections from her translation of *The Fables of La Fontaine* (1954). In addition, she translated Adalbert Stifter's *Rock Crystal: A Christmas Tale* (1945), and a collection of her critical essays, *Predilections*, appeared in 1955.

Four important and perceptive essays on Moore are by poet-critics: T. S. Eliot's introduction to Moore's *Selected Poems*; R. P. Blackmur, "The Method of Marianne Moore," in *The Double Agent*, 1935; Kenneth Burke, "Motives and Motifs in the Poetry of Marianne Moore," reprinted in *A Grammar of Motives*, 1945; and Randall Jarrell, "Thoughts about Marianne Moore," reprinted in *Poetry and the Age*, 1953. Hugh Kenner, "Disliking It," is in *A Homemade World: The American Modernist Writers*, 1975. Book-length studies include Bernard F. Engel, *Marianne Moore*, 1963; Jean Garrigue, *Marianne Moore*, 1965; George W. Nitchie, *Marianne Moore: An Introduction to the Poetry*, 1969; Donald Hall, *Marianne Moore: The Cage and the Animal*, 1970; Pamela W. Hadas, *Marianne Moore, Poet of Affection*, 1977; Laurence Stapleton, *Marianne Moore: The Poet's Advance*, 1978; Marie Borroff, *Language and the Poet: Verbal Artistry in Frost, Stevens, and Moore*, 1979; Bonnie Costello, *Marianne Moore: Imaginary Possessions*, 1981; and Elizabeth Philips, *Marianne Moore*, 1982. Two collections of essays are *Festschrift for Marianne Moore's Seventy-fifth Birthday—by Various Hands*, ed. M. J. Tambimuttu, 1964,

and *Marianne Moore: A Collection of Critical Essays*, ed. Charles Tomlinson, 1969. Helpful, too, are Gary Lane, A *Concordance to the Poems of Marianne Moore*, 1972; Eugene P. Sheehy and Kenneth A. Lohf, *The Achievement of Marianne Moore: A Descriptive Bibliography*, 1977; and Craig S. Abbot, *Marianne Moore: A Reference Guide*, 1978.

Toni Morrison

Morrison's novels are *The Bluest Eye* (1970), *Sula* (1973), *Song of Solomon* (1977), and *Tar Baby* (1981). Three interesting interviews with Morrison are Robert B. Stepto, " 'Intimate Things in Place': A Conversation with Toni Morrison," *Massachusetts Review* 18 (1977); Jane Bakerman, "The Seams Can't Show," *Black American Literature Forum* 12 (1978); and Bettye J. Parker, "Complexity: Toni Morrison's Women: An Interview Essay," in *Sturdy Black Bridges: Visions of Black Women In Literature*, ed. Roseann Bell, Bettye Parker, and Beverly Guy-Sheftall, 1979.

Critical articles include Chikwenye Okonjo Ogunyemi, "Order and Disorder in Toni Morrison's *The Bluest Eye*," *Critique* 19 (1977); Marilyn J. Atlas, "A Woman Both Shiny and Brown: Feminist Strength in Toni Morrison's *Song of Solomon*," *Society for the Study of Midwestern Literature Newsletter* 9 (1979); Phyllis R. Klotman, "Dick and Jane and the Shirley Temple Sensibility in *The Bluest Eye*," *Black American Literature Forum* 13 (1979); Jane Bakerman, "Failures of Love: Female Initiation in the Novels of Toni Morrison," *American Literature* 52, 4 (1981); Cynthia Davis, "Self, Society and Myth in Toni Morrison's Fiction," *Contemporary Literature* 23, 3 (1982); Susan Willis, "Eruptions of Funk: Historicizing Toni Morrison," *Black American Literature Forum* 16, 1 (1982); Elizabeth B. House, "The 'Sweet Life' in Toni Morrison's Fiction," *American Literature* 56, 2 (1984). *Black Women Writers (1950–1980)*, ed. Mari Evans, 1984, contains two interesting essays: Dorothy H. Lee, "The Quest for Self: Triumph and Failure in the Works of Toni Morrison," and Darwin T. Turner, "Theme, Characterization, and Style in the Works of Toni Morrison." A useful bibliography appeared in *Obsidian* 5 (1979), comp. Robert Fikes, Jr.

Alice Munro

Munro's fiction includes both short stories and novels: *Dance of the Happy Shades* (1968), *Lives of Girls and Women* (1971), *Something I've Been Meaning to Tell You* (1974), *The Beggar Maid* (1982), and *The Moons of Jupiter* (1983). Geoffry Hancock has an interesting interview with the author in *Canadian Fiction Magazine* 63 (1982).

Useful critical essays are Rae M. Macdonald, "A Madman Loose in the World: The Vision of Alice Munro," *Modern Fiction Studies* 22 (1976); Hallvard Dahlie, "The Fiction of Alice Munro," *Ploughshares* 4, iii (1978); Eileen Dambrowski, " 'Down to Death': Alice Munro and Transcience," *University of Windsor Review* 14 (1978); Miriam Packer, "*Lives of Girls and Women*: A Creative Search for Completion," in *The Canadian Novel: Here and Now*, ed. John Moss, 1978; Bronwen Wallace, "Women's Lives: Alice Munro," in *The Human Elements: Critical Essays*, ed. David Helwig, 1978; and Nancy J. Bailey, "The Masculine Image in *Lives of Girls and Women*," *Canadian Literature* 80 (1979). Helpful is J. R. Struthers, "Some Highly Subversive Activities: A Brief Polemic and a Checklist of Works on Alice Munro," *Studies in Canadian Literature* 6, i (1981).

Florence Nightingale

The only generally available works by Nightingale are *Florence Nightingale in Rome: Letters Written by Florence Nightingale in Rome in the Winter of 1847–1848*, ed. Mary Keele, 1981; and *Cassandra*, which originally appeared in the appendices of Ray Strachey's *The Cause: A Short History of the Women's Movement in Great Britain*, 1928, and which has been published separately by The Feminist Press, ed. Myra Stark, 1978. Biographies include Sir Edward Tyas Cook, *The Life of Florence Nightingale*, 1913; Cecil Woodham-Smith, *Florence Nightingale, 1820–1910*, 1951; and Elspeth Huxley, *Florence Nightingale*, 1975.

Lytton Strachey wrote a famous essay on Nightingale in *Eminent Victorians*, 1918, and she is discussed in George Pickering, *Creative Malady*, 1974. Two more recent studies are Nancy Boyd, *Josephine Butler, Octavia Hill, Florence Nightingale: Three Victorian Women Who Changed Their World*, 1982; and F. B. Smith, *Florence Nightingale: Reputation and Power*, 1982. A valuable feminist essay is Elaine Showalter, "Florence Nightingale's Feminist Complaint: Women, Religion, and *Suggestions for Thought*," *Signs* 6, 3 (Spring 1981).

Anaïs Nin

Nin's famous *Diary* has been published in several volumes from 1966–1980, ed. and with an introduction by Gunther Stuhlmann. *Linotte*, her early diary, is also available, 1978–1982. The *Anaïs Nin Reader*, ed. Philip K. Jason, appeared in 1973. Her many other works, both fiction and nonfiction, include *The Winter of Artifice* (1939), *Ladders to Fire* (1946), *On Writing* (1947), *The Four-Chambered Heart* (1950), *A Spy in the House of Love* (1954), and *Collages* (1964), as well as *Paris Revisted* (1972).

Several full-length books have been written about Nin, including Oliver Evans, *Anaïs Nin*, 1968; Valerie Harms, ed., *Celebration with Anaïs Nin*, 1973; Evelyn J. Hinz, *The Mirror and the Garden*, 1973, and her *The World of Anaïs Nin*, 1978; Bettina L. Knapp, *Anaïs Nin*, 1978; Benjamin Franklin and Duane Schneider, *Anaïs Nin: An Introduction*, 1979. There is also a quarterly, which began in 1970, called *Under the Sign of Pisces: Anaïs Nin and Her Circle*. The useful *Anaïs Nin: A Reference Guide* by Rose Marie Cutting, 1978, has been updated yearly by Richard R. Centing in *Under the Sign of Pisces* and *Seahorse*. For a summary of criticism see Evelyn J. Hinz, "Recent Nin Criticism: Who's on First," *Canadian Review of American Studies* 13 (Winter 1982).

Joyce Carol Oates

Oates's over fifty published works include the novels *them* (1969), *Do with Me What You Will* (1973), *Unholy Loves* (1979), *Bellefleur* (1980), and *A Bloodsmoor Romance* (1982), as well as such short-story collections as *Upon the Sweeping Flood, and Other Stories* (1966),

Marriages and Infidelities (1972), and *The Goddess and Other Women* (1974). Her volumes of poetry are *Women in Love, and Other Poems* (1968) and *Women Whose Lives are Food, Men Whose Lives Are Money* (1978). Her critical essays include *Contraries* (1981) and *The Profane Art: Essays and Reviews* (1983). Full-length studies include *The Tragic Vision of Joyce Carol Oates* by Mary K. Grant, 1978; *Joyce Carol Oates* by Joanne V. Creighton, 1979; *Joyce Carol Oates* by Ellen G. Friedman, 1980; and *Joyce Carol Oates's Short Stories: Between Tradition and Innovation* by Katherine Bastian, 1983. Linda W. Wagner compiled *Critical Essays on Joyce Carol Oates*, 1979. For a helpful bibliography, see Donald C. Dickson, "Joyce Carol Oates," *American Book Collector* 2, 6 (Nov.–Dec. 1981).

Edna O'Brien

O'Brien's works include the trilogy *The Country Girls* (1960), *The Lonely Girl* (1962), and *Girls in Their Married Bliss* (1964), as well as *A Pagan Place: A Play* (1973), *Mrs. Reinhart and Other Stories* (1980), and *James and Nora: A Portrait of Joyce's Marriage* (1981). She has also written a play about Virginia Woolf, *Virginia* (1981). Critical articles about her work include Raymonde Popot, "Edna O'Brien's Paradise Lost," *Cahiers Irlandais* 4–5 (1976); Lotus Snow, " 'That Trenchant Childhood Route?': Quest in Edna O'Brien's Novels," *Eire* 14, 1 (1979); and Darcy O'Brien, "Edna O'Brien: A Kind of Irish Childhood," in *Twentieth-Century Women Novelists*, ed. Thomas Staley, 1982.

Flannery O'Connor

Flannery O'Connor's novels are *Wise Blood* (1952) and *The Violent Bear It Away* (1960). Two collections of stories —*A Good Man Is Hard to Find* (1955) and *Everything That Rises Must Converge* (1965)—are included with earlier, previously uncollected stories in *Complete Stories*, 1971. Her letters are collected in *The Habit of Being: The Letters of Flannery O'Connor*, 1979. A collection of O'Connor's nonfictional prose is *Mystery and Manners*, ed. Sally and Robert Fitzgerald, 1969, and a collection of her book

reviews, *The Presence of Grace*, was compiled by Leo J. Zuber and ed. with an introduction by Carter W. Martin, 1983.

Robert Fitzgerald's memoir, prefaced to *Everything That Rises Must Converge*, offers a portrait of the artist. Other biographical material can be found in Robert Coles, *Flannery O'Connor's South*, 1980; Barbara McKenzie, *Flannery O'Connor's Georgia*, 1980; Lorine M. Getz, *Flannery O'Connor: Her Life, Library and Book Reviews*, 1980; and Marion Montgomery, *Why Flannery O'Connor Stayed Home*, 1981.

Full-length studies of O'Connor's fiction include Carol Schloss, *Flannery O'Connor's Dark Comedies: The Limits of Inference*, 1980; James M. Grimshaw, Jr., *The Flannery O'Connor Companion*, 1981; Kathleen Feeley, *Flannery O'Connor: Voice of the Peacock*, 1982. (2nd ed.); and Frederick Asals, *Flannery O'Connor, the Imagination of Extremity*, 1982, along with the collection of essays, *The Added Dimension: The Art and Mind of Flannery O'Connor*, ed. M. J. Freedman and L. A. Lawson, 1966. *Flannery O'Connor: A Descriptive Bibliography* by David R. Farmer, 1980, is very helpful.

Tillie Olsen

Olsen's works are *Tell Me a Riddle* (1961), *Yonnondio: From the Thirties* (1974), and *Silences*(1978). Recent critical studies include Deborah Rosenfelt, "From the Thirties: Tillie Olsen and the Radical Tradition," *Feminist Studies* 7, 3 (Fall 1981); Joanne S. Frye, " 'I Stand Here Ironing': Motherhood as Experience and Metaphor," *Studies in Short Fiction* 18, 3 (1981); and Erika Duncan, "Coming of Age in the Thirties: A Portrait of Tillie Olsen," *Book Forum* 6, 2 (1982).

P. K. Page

P. K. Page's volumes of verse include *As Ten as Twenty* (1946), *The Metal and the Flower* (1954), *Cry Ararat: Poems New and Selected* (1967), and *Poems Selected and New* (1974).

Grace Paley

Paley's two short-story collections are *The Little Disturbances of Man* (1959) and *Enormous Changes at the Last Minute* (1974). The May 1982 issue of *Delta*, ed. Kathleen Hulley, is devoted to Grace

Paley and includes Hulley's interview with the writer. Other essays on this writer's work include Blanche Gelfant, "Grace Paley: Fragments for a Portrait in Collage," *New England Review* 3 (1980); John W. Crawford, "Archetypal Patterns in Grace Paley's 'Runner,' " *Notes on Contemporary Literature* 11, 4 (1981); and Marianne DeKoven, "Mrs. Hegel-Shtein's Tears," *Partisan Review* 48, 2 (1981).

Dorothy Parker

The Penguin Dorothy Parker, 1977, contains fiction, poetry, criticism, and journalism. Other collections include *Collected Stories of Dorothy Parker* (1942), *Collected Poetry of Dorothy Parker* (1944), and *The Portable Dorothy Parker* (1944, rpt. 1973). Her *Constant Reader*, a collection of critical pieces, appeared in 1970.

Biographical material is contained in *You Might as Well Live: The Life and Times of Dorothy Parker* by John Keats, 1970. Another full-length study is *Dorothy Parker* by Arthur F. Kinney, 1978. Feminist approaches to her work are taken in Suzanne L. Bunkers, " 'I am outraged womanhood': Dorothy Parker as Feminist and Social Critic," *Regionalism and the Female Imagination* 4, ii (1978); and Paula A. Treichler, "Verbal Subversions in Dorothy Parker: 'Trapped like a trap in a trap,' " *Language and Style* 13, iv (1980).

Katherine Philips

Philips's poems appear in *Poems by the Most Deservedly Admired Mrs. Katherine Philips, the Matchless Orinda* (1669); *Selected Poems*, ed. L. I. Guiney, 1904–1905; and *Minor Poets of the Caroline Period*, vol. I, ed. George Saintsbury, 1905. A full-length study is Philip Webster Sower, *The Matchless Orinda*, 1931, but Philips is also included in Louisa Costello, *Memoirs of Eminent Englishwomen*, 1844. More recent discussions are Lucy Brashear, "The Forgotten Legacy of the 'Matchless Orinda,' " *Anglo-Welsh Review* 65; Catherine Cole Mambretti, " 'Fugitive Papers': A New Orinda Poem and Problems in Her Canon," *Papers of the Bibliographical Society of America* 71; and Fidelis Morgan, *The Female Wits*, 1981.

Marge Piercy

A good selection of Piercy's poetry is *Circles on the Water* (1982). A subsequent volume, *Stone, Paper, Knife*, appeared in 1983. Piercy's novels include *Going Down Fast* (1969), *Dance the Eagle to Sleep* (1970), *Small Changes* (1973), *Woman on the Edge of Time* (1976), *The High Cost of Living* (1979), *Vida* (1979), *Braided Lives* (1982), and *Fly Away Home* (1984). An excellent introduction to Piercy's life and work is *Parti-Colored Blocks for a Quilt* (1982), which offers interviews with Piercy and her own reflections on her writing as well as comments on the writing of many contemporary women.

Critical articles on Piercy include Victor Contoski, "Marge Piercy: A Vision of the Peaceable Kingdom," *Modern Poetry Studies* 8 (1977); Joyce R. Ladeson, "Marge Piercy's Revolutionary Feminism," *Society for the Study of Midwestern Literature Newsletter* 10, ii (1980); and Susan Kress, "In and Out of Time: The Form of Marge Piercy's Novels," in *Future Females: A Critical Anthology*, ed. Marleen S. Barr, 1981.

Ruth Pitter

Poems 1926–1966 (1968) includes selections from *A Mad Lady's Garland* (1935), *A Trophy of Arms* (1936), *The Spirit Watchers* (1940), *The Rude Potato* (1941), *The Bridge* (1945), *Pitter on Cats* (1947), *Urania* (1951), *The Ermine* (1953), and *Still by Choice* (1966). *End of Drought* appeared in 1975. An early critical work which contains material on Pitter is Rudolph Gilbert, *Four Living Poets*, 1944, rpt. 1973. *Ruth Pitter: Homage to a Poet*, ed. Arthur Russell, 1969, offers appreciative short essays and a biographical sketch.

Sylvia Plath

Plath's *The Collected Poems*—including *The Colossus and Other Poems* (1960) and *Ariel* (1965)—was edited by Ted Hughes in 1981. Plath's mother, Aurelia Schober Plath, selected and edited the useful *Letters Home: Correspondence 1950–63*, 1975. Hughes, with Frances McCullough, edited *The Journals of Sylvia Plath*, 1982, and Hughes also edited *Johnny Panic and the Bible of Dreams*, *and Other Prose Writings,* 1978. Plath's novel, *The Bell Jar,* was published in 1963 and has appeared in several paperback editions.

Among full-length studies of Plath are two hostile but useful works: Edward Butscher, *Sylvia Plath: Method and Madness,* 1976, and David Holbrook, *Sylvia Plath: Poetry and Existence,* 1976. More positive are Eileen Aird, *Sylvia Plath: Her Life and Work,* 1975; Judith Kroll, *Chapters in a Mythology: The Poetry of Sylvia Plath,* 1976; Caroline King, *Sylvia Plath,* 1978; Jon Rosenblatt, *Sylvia Plath: The Poetry of Initiation,* 1979; Mary Lynn Broe, *Protean Poetic: The Poetry of Sylvia Plath,* 1980; and Lynda K. Bundtzen, *Plath's Incarnations: Women and the Creative Process,* 1983.

Further biographical and critical material can be found in *Sylvia Plath and Ted Hughes* by Margaret D. Uroff, 1979. In addition, a number of informative essays appear in *The Art of Sylvia Plath,* ed. Charles Newman, 1970; *Sylvia Plath: New Views on the Poetry,* ed. Gary Lane, 1979; and *Critical Essays on Sylvia Plath,* ed. Linda W. Wagner, 1984. A feminist essay is Sandra M. Gilbert, "A Fine, White Flying Myth: The Life/Work of Sylvia Plath," in *Shakespeare's Sisters,* ed. Sandra M. Gilbert and Susan Gubar, 1979. Also useful is the chapter on Plath in Alan Williamson, *Introspection and Contemporary Poetry,* 1984.

Katherine Anne Porter

Katherine Anne Porter's publications include volumes of short stories—*Flowering Judas* (1930), *Noon Wine* (1937), *Pale Horse, Pale Rider* (1939), and *The Leaning Tower, and Other Stories* (1944)—as well as the novel *Ship of Fools* (1962). Her *Collected Stories* appeared in 1965, and her *Collected Essays* in 1970. A useful biography is *Katherine Anne Porter: A Life* by Joan Givner, 1982, but other biographical information can be found in *Conversations with Katherine Anne Porter, Refugee from Indian Creek* by Enrique Hank Lopez, 1981, and an interview with Porter by George Plimpton appeared in the *Paris Review Interviews,* 1963.

For surveys of her career and writings, relevant texts include Harry J. Mooney, *The Fiction and Criticism of Katherine*

Anne Porter, 1962; Ray West, *Katherine Anne Porter,* 1963; William L. Nance, *Katherine Anne Porter and the Art of Rejection,* 1964; George Hendrick, *Katherine Anne Porter,* 1965; W. S. Emmons, *Katherine Anne Porter: The Regional Stories,* 1967; Paul R. Baumgartner, *Katherine Anne Porter,* 1969; and M. M. Liberman, *Katherine Anne Porter's Fiction,* 1971. Important essays on Porter are in Robert Penn Warren, *Selected Essays,* 1958; Glenway Wescott, *Images of Truth,* 1962; *Katherine Anne Porter: A Critical Symposium,* ed. Lodwiej Hartley and George Gore, 1969; and Warren's more recent *Katherine Anne Porter: A Collection of Critical Essays,* 1979. For a feminist approach, see Jane K. Demouy, *Katherine Anne Porter's Women: The Eye of Her Fiction,* 1983. Bibliographies include *A Bibliography of the Works of Katherine Anne Porter,* ed. Louise Waldrip and Shirley Ann Bauer, 1969.

Katharine Susannah Prichard

Prichard's fiction includes *The Pioneers* (1915), *Black Opal* (1921), *Working Bullocks* (1926), *Coonardoo: The Well in the Shadow* (1929), *Kiss on the Lips, and Other Stories* (1932), *Intimate Strangers* (1937), *Potch and Colour* (1944), and *Winged Seeds* (1950). She also published an autobiography, *Child of the Hurricane* (1963). *Coonardoo* was reissued in 1975. Two valuable full-length studies are Henrietta Drake-Brockman, *Katharine Susannah Prichard,* 1967; and Ric Throssel, *Wild Weeds and Wind Flowers: The Life and Letters of Katharine Susannah Prichard,* 1975. A helpful essay is Veronica Brady, "Katharine Susannah Prichard and the Tyranny of History: Intimate Strangers," *Westerly* (Dec. 1981).

Kathleen Raine

Raine's volumes of verse include *Stone and Flower: Poems, 1935–43* (1943), *Living in Time* (1946), *The Pythoness and Other Poems* (1948), *Selected Poems* (1952), *The Year One* (1953), *Collected Poems* (1956), *The Hollow Hill, and Other Poems, 1960–64* (1965), *Defending Ancient Springs* (1967), *On a Deserted Shore* (1973), and *The Oval Portrait and Other Poems* (1977). She has translated a number of books, and she has edited the work of Samuel Taylor Coleridge, William Butler Yeats, and Percy Bysshe Shelley. Her critical books include *Blake and Tradition* (1968), *William Blake* (1971) and *Yeats, the Tarot, and the Golden Dawn* (1972). Autobiographical works include *Faces of Day and Night* (1972), *Farewell Happy Fields* (1973), *The Land Unknown* (1975), and *The Lion's Mouth* (1977). A full-length critical study is Ralph J. Mills, Jr., *Kathleen Raine: A Critical Essay*, 1967. Two recent articles are C. Garnier, "Kathleen Raine et la fleur talisman," and J. Genet and C. Garnier, "Le mythe de l'Eden et la tradition néoplatonicienne dans la poésie de Kathleen Raine," both in J. Genet and R. Gallet, ed., *Poètes anglais contemporains*, 1982.

Jean Rhys

Rhys's published works include *The Left Bank: Sketches and Studies in Present-Day Bohemian Paris* (1927), *After Leaving Mr. MacKenzie* (1930), *Good Morning, Midnight* (1939), *Wide Sargasso Sea* (1966), *Tigers Are Better Looking* (1968), *Quartet* (first printed as *Postures*, 1928, rep. 1957, 1971), *My Day: Three Pieces* (1975), *Sleep It off, Lady* (1976), and *Smile Please: An Unfinished Autobiography* (1979). Most of them are available in paperback editions.

Francis Wyndham and Diana Melly edited *The Letters of Jean Rhys*, 1984, and David Plante, *Difficult Women: A Memoir of Three*, 1983, includes source material. Four useful full-length studies of Rhys's life and work are Louis James, *Jean Rhys*, 1978; Thomas F. Staley, *Jean Rhys: A Critical Study*, 1979; Peter Wolfe, *Jean Rhys*, 1980; and Helen Nebeker, *Jean Rhys, Woman in Passage: A Critical Study of the Novels of Jean Rhys*, 1981. Elgin Mellowin compiled *A Descriptive and Annotated Bibliography of Works and Criticism* in 1984.

Adrienne Rich

Rich's *The Fact of a Doorframe: Poems Selected and New, 1950–84* (1984) draws upon poems from most of the poet's books: *A Change of World* (1951), *The Diamond Cutters* (1955), *Snapshots of a Daughter-in-Law* (1963, 1967), *Necessities of Life* (1966), *Leaflets* (1969), *The Will to Change* (1971), *Diving into the Wreck* (1973), *The Dream of a Common Language* (1978), and *A Wild Patience Has Taken Me This Far* (1981). She has also published *Poems Selected and New, 1950–1974* (1974) and *Sources* (1983). She is the author of the study *Of Woman Born: Motherhood as Experience and Institution* (1976), and she has collected her essays, lectures, and speeches in *On Lies, Secrets, and Silence: Selected Prose 1966–1978* (1979).

There are valuable essays and an interview in the Norton Critical Edition of *Adrienne Rich's Poetry*, ed. Barbara Charlesworth Gelpi and Albert Gelpi, 1975. Other useful essays are Marilyn R. Farwell, "Adrienne Rich and an Organic Feminist Criticism," *College English* 39 (1977); Dacia Maraini, "On *Of Woman Born*," *Signs* 4 (1979); Alicia Ostriker, "Her Cargo: Adrienne Rich and the Common Language," *American Poetry Review* 8, iv (1979); Diane Middlebrook, "Making Visible the Common World: Walt Whitman and Feminist Poetry," *Kenyon Review* 2, iv (1980); Joanne Feit Diehl, "'Cartographies of Silence': Rich's Common Language and the Woman Poet," *Feminist Studies* 6 (1980); Adalaide Morris, "Imitations and Identities: Adrienne Rich's *A Change of World*," *Modern Poetry Studies* 10 (1981); S. H. Karp, "Beginning Here: A Reading of Adrienne Rich's *The Dream of a Common Language* as Feminist Manifesto and Myth," *Proceedings of the 2nd CUNY English Forum*, 1981; and Betty S. Flowers, "The 'I' in Adrienne Rich: Individuation and the Androgyne Archetype," in *Theory and Practice of Feminist Literary Criticism*, ed. Gabriela Mora and Karen S. van Hooft, 1982. In addition, useful critical analyses are included in Suzanne Juhasz, *Naked and Fiery Forms*, 1976; David Kalstone, *Five Temperaments*, 1977; Wendy Martin, *An American Triptych*, 1984; and *Reading Adrienne Rich: Reviews and Re-Visions, 1951–81*, ed. Jane Roberta Cooper, 1984.

Dorothy M. Richardson

The four volumes of Richardson's *Pilgrimage* (1915–1938) have been republished by Virago Press, 1979, with an introduction by Gillian E. Hanscombe. A helpful introduction to Richardson's life and work is *Dorothy Richardson* by Thomas F. Staley, 1976. Two useful biographies are John D. Rosenberg, *Dorothy Richardson: The Genius They Forgot: A Critical Biography*, 1973, and Gloria G. Fromm, *Dorothy Richardson: A Biography*, 1977.

A feminist approach is offered in Gillian E. Hanscombe's recent full-length study, *The Art of Life: Dorothy Richardson and the Development of Feminist Consciousness*, 1982. In addition, Richardson's achievement is analyzed in Sidney Janet Kaplan, *Feminine Consciousness in the Modern British Novel*, 1975.

Henry Handel Richardson

Richardson's novels include *The Getting of Wisdom* (1910), *Maurice Guest* (1908), and *The Fortunes of Richard Mahony* (1930). The last two have been republished recently by Virago Press, with useful introductions. Karl-Johan Rossing edited *Letters of Henry Handel Richardson to Nettie Palmer*, 1953. *Henry Handel Richardson*, by William D. Elliott, 1975, offers a helpful overview of her work. Other biographical and critical studies include Nettie Palmer, *Henry Handel Richardson: A Study*, 1950; Vincent Buckley, *Henry Handel Richardson*, 1961; and J. R. Nichols, *Art and Irony: The Tragic Vision of Henry Handel Richardson*, 1982. Also of interest are two articles: Dorothy Green, "The Tradition of Social Responsibility in the Australian Novel: Richardson and Murphy," *Literary Criticism* 15, 3–4 (1980), and Margaret K. Butcher, "From *Maurice Guest* to *Martha Quest*: The Female *Bildungsroman* in Commonwealth Literature," *World Literature Written in English* (Summer 1982).

Christina Rossetti

Rossetti's volumes—including *Goblin Market, and Other Poems* (1862), *The Prince's Progress* (1866), *Sing-Song* (1972), and *New Poems* (1896)—were collected in *The Poetical Works of Christina Rossetti*, ed. W. M. Rossetti in 1904, and Rebecca Crump has edited Volume I of *The Complete Poems of Christina Rossetti*, 1979. Biographical studies include Mackenzie Bell, *Christina Rossetti: A Bi-ographical and Critical Study*, 1898; Marya Zaturenska, *Christina Rossetti: A Portrait*, 1949; Lona M. Packer, *Christina Rossetti*, 1963; Georgina Battiscombe, *Christina Rossetti*, 1965; Fredegond Shove, *Christina Rossetti: A Study*, 1969; Margaret Sawtell, *Christina Rossetti: Her Life and Religion*, 1974; Ralph A. Bellas, *Christina Rossetti*, 1977; and Georgina Battiscombe, *Christina Rossetti: A Divided Life*, 1981.

Critical essays on her life and work include Virginia Woolf's appreciative " 'I Am Christina Rossetti,' " in *The Second Common Reader*, 1932, as well as two recent pieces by Jerome J. McGann: "Christina Rossetti's Poems: A New Edition and Revaluation," *Victorian Studies* 23 (Winter 1980), and "The Religious Poetry of Christina Rossetti," *Critical Inquiry* 10, 1 (1983). Feminist approaches are represented by a chapter in Ellen Moers, *Literary Women*, 1976; by Dolores Rosenblum, "Christina Rossetti: The Inward Pose," in *Shakespeare's Sisters*, ed. Sandra M. Gilbert and Susan Gubar, 1979; by a chapter in Gilbert and Gubar, *The Madwoman in the Attic*, 1979; and by a section in Nina Auerbach, *Woman and the Demon*, 1982. Two useful reference works are *Christina Rossetti: A Reference Guide* by Rebecca W. Crump, 1976; and *The Bible and the Poetry of Christina Rossetti: A Concordance*, comp. Nilda Jimenez, 1979.

Mary Rowlandson

Rowlandson's major work is *The Narrative of the Captivity and Restoration of Mrs. Mary Rowlandson* (1682). Richard Slotkin, *Regeneration through Violence*, 1973, contains a useful discussion of her captivity. See also *Captives among the Indians*, ed. Horace Kephart, 1915, and R. H. Pearce, "The Significances of the Captivity Narrative," *American Literature* 19 (1947). A recent discussion is David Downing, " 'Streams of Scripture Comfort': Mary Rowlandson's Typological Use of the Bible," *Early American Literature* 15 (1980–1981).

Muriel Rukeyser

The Collected Poems of Muriel Rukeyser appeared in 1978. Besides her own poetry, Rukeyser published several translations, including *Selected Poems of Octavio Paz* (1963). She also wrote biographies, including *Willard Gibbs* (1942), *One Life* (1957), and *The Traces of Thomas Hariot* (1971), as well as children's books. A full-length study is *The Poetic Vision of Muriel Rukeyser* by Louise Kertesz, 1980, while critical essays include Robert Coles, "Muriel Rukeyser's *The Gates*," *American Poetry Review* 7, 3 (May–June 1978); and Rachel Blau DuPlessis, "The Critique of Consciousness and Myth in Levertov, Rich, and Rukeyser," in *Shakespeare's Sisters*, ed. Sandra M. Gilbert and Susan Gubar, 1979.

Joanna Russ

Russ's works include *Picnic on Paradise* (1968), *And Chaos Died* (1970), *The Female Man* (1975), *Alyx* (1976), *The Two of Them* (1978), *The Zanzibar Cat* (1983), and *Extra(ordinary) People* (1984). A book of feminist criticism, *How to Suppress Women's Writing*, appeared in 1983.

Critical articles about her achievement include Samuel R. Delaney, "The Order of Chaos," *Science Fiction Studies* 6 (1979); Douglass Barbour, "Joanna Russ's *The Female Man*: An Appreciation," *Sphinx* 4, (1981); Natalie M. Rosinsky, "A Female Man? The 'Medusan' Humor of Joanna Russ," *Extrapolation* 23, 1 (Spring 1982); and Marilyn J. Holt, "Joanna Russ," in *Science Fiction Writers: Critical Studies of the Major Authors*, ed. Everett F. Bleiler, 1982.

May Sarton

Among Sarton's many novels are *The Single Hound* (1938), *A Shower of Summer Days* (1952), *The Small Room* (1961), *Joanna and Ulysses* (1963), *Mrs. Stevens Hears the Mermaids Singing* (1965), and *Kinds of Love* (1970). Her *Collected Poems (1930–1973)* appeared in 1974. Her journal volumes include *Plant Dreaming Deep* (1968), *Journal of a Solitude* (1973), *The House by the Sea* (1977), *Recovering* (1980), and *At Seventy* (1984). Constance Hunting edited *Writings on Writing*, 1980, and *May Sarton, Woman and Poet*, 1982. Other helpful biographical material appears in Sarton's own *I Knew a Phoenix: Sketches for an Autobiography* (1978), and in Do-

lores Shelley, "A Conversation with May Sarton," *Women and Literature* 7, ii (1979), as well as in *May Sarton* by Agnes Sibley, 1972.

Essays on Sarton's work include Dawn Holt Anderson, "May Sarton's Women," in Susan Koppelman Cornillon, ed., *Images of Women in Fiction*, 1972; Doris L. Eder, "Woman Writer: May Sarton's *Mrs. Stevens Hears the Mermaids Singing*," *International Journal of Women's Studies* 1 (1978); Jane S. Bakerman, " 'Kinds of Love': Love and Friendship in the Novels of May Sarton," *Critique* 20, ii (1978); and Marlene Springer, "As We Shall Be: May Sarton and Aging," *Frontiers* 5, 3 (Fall 1980). Lenora Blouin compiled a bibliography, *May Sarton*, in 1978.

Olive Schreiner

Among the works published in Schreiner's lifetime, most important are *The Story of an African Farm* (1883), *Dreams* (1890), *Trooper Peter Halkett of Mashonoland* (1897), *Dream Life and Real Life* (1893, 1912), and *Woman and Labour* (1911); the last two have recently been reprinted by the Cassandra and Virago Presses, while *The Story of an African Farm* is available in a number of editions. *Stories, Dreams and Allegories* (1924), *From Man to Man* (1926), and *Undine* (1919) were published posthumously and have also been recently reprinted. In addition, there are two collections of Schreiner's writing available: *Olive Schreiner, a Selection*, ed. Uys Krige, 1968, and *A Track to the Water's Edge: The Olive Schreiner Reader*, ed. Howard Thurman, 1973. S. C. Cronwright-Schreiner edited *The Letters of Olive Schreiner*, 1924. Biographical and critical studies include Vera Buchanan-Gould, *Not without Honor: The Life and Writings of Olive Schreiner*, 1948; Daisy Lucie Hofman, *Olive Schreiner, Her Friends and Times*, 1955; Joyce Avrech Berkman, *Olive Schreiner: Feminism on the Frontier*, 1979; and Ruth First and Ann Scott, *Olive Schreiner*, 1980. Additional information can be found in Roslyn Davis, *Olive Schreiner 1920–1971: A Bibliography*, 1972.

Anne Sexton

Sexton's *The Complete Poems*, with a foreword by Maxine Kumin, was published in 1981. Another useful collection is *Words for Dr. Y.: Uncollected Poems with Three Stories*, ed. Linda Sexton, 1978. A *Self-Portrait in Letters*, 1977, gives helpful biographical material. Important interviews and critical essays are to be found in J. D. McClatchy, *Anne Sexton: The Artist and Her Critics*, 1978. Recent critical essays include Suzanne Juhasz, "Seeking the Exit or the Home: Poetry and Salvation in the Career of Anne Sexton," in *Shakespeare's Sisters*, ed. Sandra M. Gilbert and Susan Gubar, 1979; Margaret Houton, "The Double Image and the Division of Parts: A Study of Mother/Daughter Relationships in the Poetry of Anne Sexton," *Journal of Women's Studies in Literature* 1 (1979); Kathleen L. Nicholas, "The Hungry Beast Rowing toward God: Anne Sexton's Later Religious Poetry," *Notes on Modern American Literature* 21 (1979); Jeanne H. Kammer, "The Witches' Life: Confession and Control in the Early Poetry of Anne Sexton," *Language and Style* 13 (1980); Rosemary Johnson, "The Woman of Private (but Published) Hungers," *Parnassus* 8 (1980); and Alicia Ostriker, "That Story: Anne Sexton and Her Transformations," *American Poetry Review* 11, 4 (July–Aug. 1982). Valuable but somewhat dated is *Sylvia Plath and Anne Sexton: A Reference Guide*, C. Northouse and R. P. Walsh, 1974.

Mary Shelley

Although there is no collected edition of Mary Shelley's works, a number of titles have been republished. *Frankenstein* (1818) is available in many modern reprints; especially useful is the scholarly edition by James Rieger, 1974. *The Last Man* (1826) has been reprinted in an edition by Hugh J. Luke, Jr., 1965; *Mathilda*, which the author left in manuscript, was printed for the first time by Elizabeth Nitchie, 1959; and Shelley's short fiction has been edited by Charles E. Robinson in *Mary Shelley: Collected Tales and Stories*, 1976. Her prefaces and notes to her husband's poems appear in *The Complete Poetical Works of Percy Bysshe Shelley*, ed. Thomas Hutchinson and rev. G. M. Matthews, 1970.

Frederick L. Jones has edited *The Letters of Mary W. Shelley*, 1946, and *Mary Shelley's Journal*, 1947. Betty T. Bennett has edited two volumes of *The Letters of Mary Wollstonecraft Shelley*, 1980, 1983. Biographies include R. Glynn Grylls, *Mary Shelley: A Biography*, 1938; Muriel Spark, *Child of Light: A Reassessment of Mary Shelley*, 1951; Elizabeth Nitchie, *Mary Shelley, Author of "Frankenstein,"* 1953; Jane Dunn, *Moon in Eclipse: A Life of Mary Shelley*, 1978; and Bonnie R. Neumann, *The Lonely Muse: A Critical Biography of Mary Shelley*, 1979. In addition, William A. Walling, *Mary Shelley*, 1972, offers a succinct treatment of Shelley's life along with analyses of her major writings.

Most of the critical work on Shelley deals with *Frankenstein*. *The Endurance of Frankenstein*, 1979, a collection of essays, ed. George Levine and U. C. Knoepflmacher, is valuable. Feminist analyses are represented by chapters in *Literary Women* by Ellen Moers, 1976; in *The Madwoman in the Attic* by Sandra M. Gilbert and Susan Gubar, 1979; and in *The Proper Lady and the Woman Writer* by Mary Poovey, 1984. Further references may be found in W. H. Lyles, *Mary Shelley: An Annotated Bibliography*, 1975.

Leslie Marmon Silko

Silko's works include *Laguna Woman* (1974), *Ceremony* (1977), and *Storyteller* (1981). Useful background material is offered in "Two Interviews with Leslie Marmon Silko" by Per Seyersted, *American Studies in Scandinavia* 13 (1981), and in "The Novel and Oral Tradition: An Interview with Leslie Marmon Silko" by Elaine Jahner, *Book Forum* 5, 3 (1981). In addition, Seyersted has written a full-length critical study, *Leslie Marmon Silko*, 1980, and there have been numerous critical essays, including Edith Blicksilver, "Traditionalism vs. Modernity: Leslie Silko on American Indian Women," *Southwest Review* 64, 2 (1979); Ronald E. McFarland, "Leslie Silko's Story of Stories," *A Journal of Contemporary Literature* 4, 2 (1979); A. LaVonne Ruoff, "Ritual and Renewal: Keres Traditions in the Short Fiction of Leslie Silko," *MELUS* 5 (1979); and Jim Ruppert,

"Story Telling: The Fiction of Leslie Silko," *The Journal of Ethnic Studies* 9, 1 (1981).

May Sinclair

Sinclair's works include numerous volumes of poetry, criticism, philosophy, and short stories, as well as twenty-four novels, among them *The Divine Fire* (1904), *The Three Sisters* (1914), *The Tree of Heaven* (1917), *Mary Olivier: A Life* (1919), *Life and Death of Harriett Frean* (1922), and *Anne Severn and the Fieldings* (1924). *The Three Sisters*, *Mary Olivier*, and *Life and Death of Harriet Frean* have been recently republished by Virago Press, with helpful introductions.

Biographical studies include Theophilus Ernest Martin Boll, *Miss May Sinclair, Novelist: A Biographical and Critical Introduction*, 1973; and Hrisey D. Zegger, *May Sinclair*, 1976. In addition, Sinclair's work is extensively discussed in Sidney Janet Kaplan, *Feminine Consciousness in the Modern British Novel*, 1975. Useful articles include Diane F. Gillespie, "May Sinclair and the Stream of Consciousness: Metaphors and Metaphysics," *English Literature in Transition* 21 (1978), and Rebeccah Kinnamon Neff, " 'New Mysticism' in the Writings of May Sinclair and T. S. Eliot," *Twentieth Century Literature* 26 (1979).

Edith Sitwell

In addition to more than thirty volumes of poetry, culminating in *Collected Poems* (1957), and *Selected Poems*, with an introduction by John Lehmann (1965), Edith Sitwell produced a variety of critical and other prose works. These include *Alexander Pope* (1930), *Aspects of Modern Poetry* (1934), *A Poet's Notebook* (1950), and *Taken Care Of: An Autobiography* (1965). John Lehmann and Derek Parker edited *Edith Sitwell: Selected Letters 1919–1964*, and Lehmann has written an informative account of Sitwell's family and background in *A Nest of Tigers: Edith, Osbert and Sacheverell Sitwell in their Times*, 1968. Other biographical and critical works include *Edith Sitwell: The Symbolist Order* by J. D. Brophy, 1968; *A Map of Modern English Verse* by John Press, 1969; "Poets Old and New: Edith

Sitwell," in *Assays* by Kenneth Rexroth, 1961; and *The Last Years of a Rebel: A Memoir of Edith Sitwell* by E. Salter, 1967. Four full-length studies have appeared recently: *Facades: Edith, Osbert, and Sacheverell Sitwell* by John Pearson, 1978; *Edith Sitwell* by Elizabeth Salter, 1979; *Edith Sitwell: A Biography* by Geoffrey Elborn, 1981; and *Edith Sitwell: A Unicorn among Lions* by Victoria Glendinning, 1981.

Charlotte Smith

Among Smith's numerous novels are *Emmeline* (1788), *Ethelinde* (1789), *Celestina* (1791), *Desmond* (1792), *The Old Manor House* (1793), and *The Wanderings of Warwick* (1794). She also published poetry in *Elegiac Sonnets* (1784) and *Beachy Head: With Other Poems* (1807). *Emmeline* and *The Old Manor House* have been reprinted with an introduction by Anne Henry Ehrenpreis, 1969, 1971. The only biography is Florence May Anna Hillbish, *Charlotte Smith, Poet and Novelist*, 1941, but Katharine M. Rogers includes a discussion of Smith in "Inhibitions in Eighteenth-Century Women Novelists," *Eighteenth-Century Studies* (Fall 1977), and in her anthology *Before Their Time*, 1979. In addition, Smith is discussed in Margaret Doody, "English Women Novelists and the French Revolution," in *La Femme en Angleterre et dans les colonies américaines aux XVIIe et XVIIIe siécles*, 1975.

Stevie Smith

Stevie Smith's books of poetry include *A Good Time Was Had by All* (1937), *Harold's Leap* (1950), *Not Waving but Drowning* (1957), and *Scorpion, and Other Poems*, published posthumously with an introduction by Patrick Dickinson in 1972. Both the *Selected Poems*, 1962, and the *Collected Poems*, 1976, ed. James MacGibbon, reproduce many of the drawings she originally printed with her poems. Smith also wrote three novels: *Novel on Yellow Paper, or, Work It Out for Yourself* (1936), *Over the Frontier* (1938), and *The Holiday* (1949). All have been recently reissued in paperbound editions.

There is at present no full-length critical or biographical work on Smith; two interviews, in *The Poet Speaks*, ed. Peter Orr, 1966, and in *Ivy and Stevie* by Kay Dick, 1971, are worth consulting. Useful essays are the chapter in *Eight Contemporary Poets* by Calvin Bedient, 1974; Philip Larkin, "Frivolous and Vulnerable," *New Statesman* (1962); an anonymous review entitled "The Voice of Genteel Decay," *Times Literary Supplement* (1972); Steven Wade, "Stevie Smith and the Untruth of Myth," 15 (1977); Steven Helmling, "Delivered for a Time from Silence," *Parnassus* 6 (1977); Janice Thaddeus, "Stevie Smith and the Gleeful Macabre," *Contemporary Poetry* 3, 14 (1978); and Mark Storey, "Why Stevie Smith Matters," *Critical Quarterly* 21, ii (1979).

Muriel Spark

Spark's numerous works include *Memento Mori* (1959), *The Prime of Miss Jean Brodie* (1961), *Emily Brontë, Her Life and Work* (with Derek Stanford, 1966), *Collected Stories* (1967), *Collected Poems* (1967), *The Abbess of Crewe* (1974), and *The Only Problem* (1984). Full-length studies of her life and work are Karl Malkoff, *Muriel Spark*, 1968; Patricia Stubb, *Muriel Spark*, 1973; Peter Kemp, *Muriel Spark*, 1974; and Ruth Whittaker, *The Faith and Fiction of Muriel Spark*, 1982. Among critical essays are chapters in Judy Little, *Comedy and the Woman Writer: Woolf, Spark, and Feminism*, 1983, and William McBrien, "Muriel Spark: The Novelist as Dandy," in *Twentieth Century Woman Novelists*, ed. Thomas Staley, 1982.

Elizabeth Cady Stanton

Stanton's *History of Woman Suffrage* (1881–1886), ed. with Susan B. Anthony and Matilda Joslyn Gage, was reprinted in 1969; *The Woman's Bible* (1895, 1898) has been republished as *The Original Feminist Attack on the Bible*, with an introduction by Barbara Welter, 1974; *Elizabeth Cady Stanton* (1922), ed. Theodore Stanton and Harriot Stanton Blatch, was reissued in 1969; *Eighty Years and More (1815–1897): Reminiscences of Elizabeth Cady Stanton* (1898) was reprinted in 1970. Also useful is *Elizabeth Cady Stanton, Susan B. Anthony: Correspondence, Writing, Speeches*, ed. with critical commentary by Ellen Carol DuBois, 1981.

Biographies include Alma Lutz, *Created Equal: A Biography of Elizabeth Cady Stanton, 1815–1902*, 1940; Mary Ann B. Oakley, *Elizabeth Cady Stanton*, 1972; and Lois W. Banner, *Elizabeth Cady Stanton: A Radical for Women's Rights*, 1980.

Gertrude Stein

Although there is no complete edition of Gertrude Stein's writings, *The Yale Edition of the Unpublished Writings of Gertrude Stein*, ed. Carl Van Vechten, 1951–1958, contains eight volumes of poetry, prose fiction, portraits, and essays. Among the prose works published during Stein's lifetime are *Three Lives* (1909), *Tender Buttons* (1914), *The Making of Americans* (1925), the children's book *The World Is Round* (1926), *Lucy Church Amiably* (1930), *Ida: A Novel* (1941), and *Brewsie and Willie* (1946). *Geography and Plays* (1922), *Operas and Plays* (1932), and *Last Operas and Plays*, ed. Carl Van Vechten (1949), contain dramatic pieces. Autobiographical material may be found in *The Autobiography of Alice B. Toklas* (1933), *Portraits and Prayers* (1934), *Everybody's Autobiography* (1937), and *Wars I Have Seen* (1945). Other works, including meditations, essays, sketches, and sociolinguistic treatises, are *Useful Knowledge* (1928), *How to Write* (1931), *Lectures in America* (1935), *Narration: Four Lectures by Gertrude Stein* (1935), *What Are Masterpieces* (1940), and *Four in America* (1947). A useful introductory collection of Stein's writings is *Selected Writings of Gertrude Stein*, ed. Carl Van Vechten, 1962.

Donald C. Gallup has edited *Fernhurst, Q. E. D., and Other Early Writings by Gertrude Stein*, 1971, as well as a collection of letters to Gertrude Stein, *The Flowers of Friendship*, 1953. *Dear Sammy: Letters from Gertrude Stein and Alice B. Toklas*, ed. Samuel M. Steward, appeared in 1977. Memoirs of Stein include W. G. Rogers, *When This You See Remember Me: Gertrude Stein in Person*, 1948, and Alice B. Toklas, *What Is Remembered*, 1953. Linda Simon, *The Biog-*

raphy of Alice B. Toklas, 1977, provides useful background information.

Biographical studies of Gertrude Stein are Elizabeth Sprigg, *Gertrude Stein: Her Life and Work*, 1957; John Malcolm Brinnin, *The Third Rose: Gertrude Stein and Her World*, 1959; Howard Greenfield, *Gertrude Stein: A Biography*, 1973; James R. Mellow, *Charmed Circle: Gertrude Stein and Company*, 1974; and Janet Hobhouse, *Everybody Who Was Anybody*, 1975. Critical studies include Donald Sutherland, *Gertrude Stein: A Biography of Her Work*, 1951; Michael Hoffman, *The Development of Abstractionism in the Writings of Gertrude Stein*, 1965; Allegra Stewart, *Gertrude Stein and the Present*, 1967; Norman Weinstein, *Gertrude Stein and the Literature of Modern Consciousness*, 1970; Richard Bridgemen, *Gertrude Stein in Pieces*, 1970; Robert B. Haas, *A Primer for the Gradual Understanding of Gertrude Stein*, 1971; Carolyn F. Copeland, *Language and Time and Gertrude Stein*, 1975; Michael Hoffman, *Gertrude Stein*, 1976; Wendy Steiner, *Exact Resemblance to Exact Resemblance: The Literary Portraiture of Gertrude Stein's Experimental Writing*, 1983; and Marianne DeKoven, *A Different Language: Gertrude Stein's Experimental Writing*, 1983. A number of recent articles on Stein's work are collected in a special issue of *Widening Circle* I, 4 (1973). Two feminist essays are Elizabeth Fifer, "Is Flesh Advisable: The Interior Theater of Gertrude Stein," *Signs* 4, 3 (Spring 1979), and Carolyn Burke, "Gertrude Stein, the Cone Sisters, and the Puzzle of Female Friendship," in *Writing and Sexual Difference*, ed. Elizabeth Abel, 1982. Two valuable bibliographies are *Gertrude Stein* by Maureen R. Liston, 1979, and *Gertrude Stein and Alice B. Toklas: A Reference Guide* by Ray L. White, 1984.

Anne Stevenson

Stevenson's works include *Living in America* (1965), *Reversals* (1969), *Correspondences: A Family History in Letters* (1974), *Traveling behind Glass: Selected Poems 1963–1973* (1974), *A Morden Tower Reading 3* (1977), *Cliff Walk* (1977), *Enough of Green* (1977), *Turkish Rondo* (1981), and *Minute by Glass Min-*

ute (1982). Two helpful autobiographical essays are "Writing as a Woman," in *Women Writing and Writing about Women*, ed. Mary Jacobus, 1979, and "The Music of the House: Scenes from Childhood," *Poetry Review* 72, 3 (1982). More information is offered in Jay Parini, "On Anne Stevenson," *Ploughshares* 4, iii (1978).

Elizabeth Drew Stoddard

Stoddard's most important novel and some of her short fiction have been recently republished in Lawrence Buell and Sandra Zagarell, ed., *The Morgesons, and Other Writings*, 1984. Also of interest is Maurice Kramer, "Alone at Home with Elizabeth Stoddard," *American Transcendental Quarterly* (Summer–Fall 1980).

Ruth Stone

Stone's collections of poetry are *In an Iridescent Time* (1958), *Topography, and Other Poems* (1970), and *Cheap: New Poems and Ballads* (1975). For a series of short, appreciative essays, see "On Ruth Stone," Sandra M. Gilbert, *et al.*, *Iowa Review* 12, 23 (1981).

Harriet Beecher Stowe

Stowe's major works include *Uncle Tom's Cabin* (1851–1852), *Sunny Memories of Foreign Lands* (1854), *Dred* (1856), *The Minister's Wooing* (1859), *The Pearl of Orr's Island* (1862), *Oldtown Folks* (1869), *Oldtown Fireside Stories* (1872), and *Poganuc People* (1878). *The Writings of Harriet Beecher Stowe*, 16 vols., 1896, is still the standard edition. More recently, John M. Moran, Jr. edited *Collected Poems*, 1967, while Margaret G. Mair, Earl A. French, and Diana Royce produced *The Papers of Harriet Beecher Stowe*, 1977. An excellent edition of *Uncle Tom's Cabin*, with an introduction by Ann Douglas, appeared in 1981.

Several memoirs were written during Stowe's lifetime or soon after she died, but Robert Forrest Wilson, *Crusader in Crinoline: The Life of Harriet Beecher Stowe*, 1941, is the standard biography, and Johanna Johnston, *Runaway to Heaven: The Story of Harriet Beecher Stowe*, 1963, is a good popular biography. Others include Edward Wagenknecht, *Harriet Beecher Stowe: The Known and the Unknown*,

1965, and Noel B. Gerson, *Harriet Beecher Stowe: A Biography*, 1976.

Critical studies include Charles H. Foster, *The Rungless Ladder: Harriet Beecher Stowe and New England Puritanism*, 1954; John R. Adams, *Harriet Beecher Stowe*, 1963; Alice C. Crozier, *The Novels of Harriet Beecher Stowe*, 1969; Elizabeth Ammons, ed., *Critical Essays on Harriet Beecher Stowe*, 1980; and Gayle Kimball, *The Religious Ideas of Harriet Beecher Stowe: Her Gospel of Womanhood*, 1982. Two valuable feminist articles have appeared recently: Jane P. Tompkins, "Sentimental Power: *Uncle Tom's Cabin* and the Politics of Literary History," *Glyph* (1981); and Laurie Crumpacker, "Four Novels of Harriet Beecher Stowe: A Study in 19th Century Androgyny," in *American Novelists Revisited: Essays in Feminist Criticism*, ed. Fritz Fleischmann, 1982. Stowe's work is also treated in Ann Douglas, *The Feminization of American Culture*, 1977, and in Leslie Fiedler, *The Inadvertent Epic: From "Uncle Tom's Cabin" to "Roots*," 1980.

May Swenson

Swenson's volumes of poems include *Another Animal* (1954), *A Cage of Spines* (1958), *To Mix with Time: New and Selected Poems* (1963), *Poems to Solve* (1966), *Half Sun Half Sleep* (1967), *Iconographs* (1970), *More Poems to Solve* (1971), *The Guess and Spell Coloring Book* (1976), and *New and Selected Things Taking Place* (1978). Swenson's comments are also included in *Poets on Poetry*, ed. Howard Nemerov, 1966, and Karla Hammond interviewed Swenson for *Parnassus* 7, 1 (1978). Useful critical essays are Ann Stanford, "The Art of Perceiving," *Southern Review* 6 (Winter 1969); Alicia Ostriker, "May Swenson and the Shapes of Speculation," in *Shakespeare's Sisters*, ed. Sandra M. Gilbert and Susan Gubar, 1979; and Ann S. Wicks, "Music, Meaning, and the Adaptation of Literature," *Literature in Performance* 2, i (1981).

Eleanor Ross Taylor

Taylor's volumes of poetry include *Wilderness of Ladies* (1960), *Welcome Eumenides* (1972), and *New and Selected Poems* (1983).

Sojourner Truth

Truth's speeches can be found in Elizabeth Cady Stanton *et al.*, *History of Woman Suffrage*, vols. I–III (1881–1886). Truth's story is told in the *Narrative of Sojourner Truth, a Northern Slave, Emancipated from Bodily Servitude by the State of New York, in 1828*, an account written by Olive Gilbert in 1850 and reprinted with a new introduction in 1968. Also reprinted is Arthur Huff Fauset, *Sojourner Truth: God's Faithful Pilgrim*, 1938, 1971. More recent biographies are Hertha Ernestine Pauli, *Her Name Was Sojourner Truth*, 1962, and Jacqueline Bernard, *Journey toward Freedom: The Story of Sojourner Truth*, 1967.

Diane Wakoski

Wakoski's works include *Trilogy* (1974) —her first three books in one volume—as well as *The Motorcycle Betrayal Poems* (1971), *Waiting for the King of Spain* (1976), *Toward a New Poetry* (1980), *The Lady Who Drove Me to the Airport* (1982), *The Magician's Feastletters* (1982), and *The Complete Greed, Parts 1–13* (1984). For interesting biographical information, see Taffy Martin, "An Interview with Diane Wakoski," *Dalhousie Review* 61, 3 (Autumn 1981). Helpful critical articles include T. Olson ed., "A Symposium on Diane Wakoski," *Margins* (1976); Evan Watkins, "Historical Criticism and Contemporary Poetry," *Contemporary Literature* 22, 4 (1981), and Taffy W. Martin, "Diane Wakoski's Personal Mythology: Dionysian Music, Created Presence," *Boundary* 2 (1982).

Alice Walker

Walker's works are *Once* (1968), *The Third Life of Grange Copeland* (1970), *Revolutionary Petunias* (1973), *Langston Hughes* (1974), *In Love and Trouble* (1973), *Meridian* (1976), *Good Night Willie Lee, I'll See You in the Morning* (1979), *You Can't Keep a Good Woman Down* (1981), *The Color Purple* (1982), and *In Search of Our Mothers' Gardens: Womanist Prose* (1983). An interview appears in *Black Women Writers at Work*, ed. Claudia Tate, 1984.

Critical essays on Walker's work include Trudier Harris, "Folklore in the Fiction of Alice Walker," *Black American Literature Forum* 11 (1977); Chester J. Fantenot, "Alice Walker, 'The Diary of an African Nun' and Du Bois' Double Consciousness," and Mary Helen Washington, "An Essay on Alice Walker," both in *Sturdy Black Bridges: Visions of Black Women in Literature*, ed. Roseann Bell, Bettye Parker, and Beverly Guy-Sheftall, 1979; Peter Erickson, " 'Cast out Alone / To Heal / and Re-create / Ourselves': Family-Based Identity in the Work of Alice Walker," *College Language Association Journal* 23 (1979); Deborah McDowell, "The Self in Bloom: Alice Walker's *Meridian*," *College Language Association Journal* 24 (1981); Klaus Enssler, "Collective Experience and Individual Responsibility: Alice Walker's *The Third Life of Grange Copeland*," in *The Afro-American Novel Since 1960*, ed. Peter Bruck and Wolfgang Karrer, 1982; Trudier Harris, "Tiptoeing through Taboo: Incest in 'The Child Who Favored Daughter,' " *Modern Fiction Studies* 28, 3 (Autumn 1982); along with Barbara Christian, "Alice Walker," and Bettye J. Parker-Smith, "Alice Walker's Women," both in *Black Women Writers (1950–1980)*, ed. Mari Evans, 1984.

Margaret Walker

Walker's works include *For My People* (1942), *Jubilee* (1966), *Prophets for a New Day* (1970), *How I Wrote Jubilee* (1972), *October Journey* (1973), *A Poetic Equation: Conversations with Nikki Giovani* (1974), and *The Daemonic Genius of Richard Wright* (1984). Three helpful interviews are Charles H. Robell, "Poetry, History, and Humanism: An Interview with Margaret Walker," *Blackworld* 25 (1975); Phanuel Egejuru and Robert E. Fox, "An Interview with Margaret Walker," *Callaloo* 2, ii (1979); and an interview in *Black Women Writers at Work*, ed. Claudia Tate, 1984. Critical essays on Walker include Phyllis R. Klotman, " 'Oh Freedom': Women and History in Margaret Walker's *Jubilee*," *Black American Literature Forum* 11 (1977); James E. Spears, "Black Folk Elements in Margaret Walker's *Jubilee*," *Mississippi Folklore Register* 14, 4 (1980); R. Baxter Miller,

"The 'Etched Flame' of Margaret Walker: Biblical and Literary Recreation in Southern History," *Tennessee Studies in Literature* 26 (1981); and two pieces in *Black Women Writers (1950–1980)*, ed. Mari Evans, 1984: Eugenia Colliers, "Fields Watered with Blood: Myth and Ritual in the Poetry of Margaret Walker," and Eleanor Traylor, "Music as Theme: The Blues Mode in the Works of Margaret Walker."

Eudora Welty

Welty's volumes of fiction include *A Curtain of Green, and Other Stories* (1941), *The Robber Bridegroom* (1942), *The Wide Net, and Other Stories* (1943), *The Leaning Tower, and Other Stories* (1944), *Delta Wedding* (1946), *The Golden Apples* (1949), *The Bride of the Innisfallen, and Other Stories* (1955), *The Shoe Bird* (1964), and *The Optimist's Daughter* (1972). *The Selected Stories of Eudora Welty*, 1954, has a valuable introduction by Katherine Anne Porter. *One Time and Place* (1971) is Welty's book of photographs, and *One Writer's Beginnings* (1983) is her literary autobiography. The recent *Conversations with Eudora Welty*, ed. Peggy Prenshaw, 1984, is helpful.

Full-length studies of her writing include Ruth M. Vande Kieft, *Eudora Welty*, 1962; Alfred Appel, *A Season of Dreams: The Fiction of Eudora Welty*, 1965; Joseph A. Bryant, Jr., *Eudora Welty*, 1968; Zelma T. Howard, *The Rhetoric of Eudora Welty's Short Stories*, 1973; Michael Kreyling, *Eudora Welty's Achievement of Order*, 1980; Elizabeth Evans, *Eudora Welty*, 1981; and Albert J. Devlin, *Eudora Welty's Chronicle: A Story of Mississippi Life*, 1983. Three useful collections of critical essays are *A Still Moment: Essays on the Art of Eudora Welty*, ed. John F. Desmond, 1978; *Eudora Welty: Critical Essays*, ed. Peggy Prenshaw, 1979; and *Eudora Welty: A Form of Thanks*, ed. Louis Dollarhide and Ann J. Abadie, 1979. Also valuable is Victor H. Thompson, *Eudora Welty: A Reference Guide*, 1976.

Rebecca West

West's numerous works include novels—notably *The Return of the Soldier* (1918), *The Judge* (1922), and *Harriet Hume*

(1930)—a number of which have recently been reprinted, as well as several volumes of stories and many volumes of nonfictional prose, including books on Henry James and D. H. Lawrence. A valuable anthology of her early journalism is *The Young Rebecca*, ed. Jane Marcus, 1982. Full-length studies of her life and work include *Rebecca West: Artist and Thinker* by Peter Wolfe, 1971; *H. G. Wells and Rebecca West* by Gordon N. Ray, 1974; and *Rebecca West* by Motley F. Deakin, 1980. George E. Hutchinson compiled *A Preliminary List of the Writings of Rebecca West*, 1957, which was followed by Motley F. Deakin, "Rebecca West: A Supplement to Hutchinson's Preliminary List," *Bulletin of Bibliography* (June 1982).

Edith Wharton

Wharton's works include *The Decoration of Houses* (1897), *The House of Mirth* (1905), *Madame de Tréymes* (1907), *Tales of Men and Ghosts* (1910), *Ethan Frome* (1911), *The Custom of the Country* (1913), *Xingu* (1916), *Summer* (1917), *The Age of Innocence* (1920), and *Old New York* (1924), most of which have been reissued in the Scribner Library. In addition, Louis Auchincloss edited *The Edith Wharton Reader*, 1965, and R. W. B. Lewis edited in two volumes *The Collected Short Stories of Edith Wharton*, 1968.

Two major biographies are R. W. B. Lewis, *Edith Wharton: A Biography*, 1975, and Cynthia Griffin Wolff, *A Feast of Words: The Triumph of Edith Wharton*, 1977. Other useful biographical and critical studies include Blake Nevius, *Edith Wharton: A Study of Her Fiction*, 1953; Marilyn J. Lyde, *Edith Wharton: Convention and Morality in the Work of a Novelist*, 1959; Louis Auchincloss, *Edith Wharton*, 1961; Millicent Bell, *Edith Wharton and Henry James: The Story of Their Friendship*, 1965; Geoffrey Walton, *Edith Wharton: A Critical Interpretation*, 1971; Margaret B. McDowell, *Edith Wharton*, 1976; Richard H. Lawson, *Edith Wharton*, 1977; Elizabeth Ammons, *Edith Wharton's Argument with America*, 1980; and Carol Wershaven, *The Female Intruder in the Novels of Edith Wharton*, 1982.

Phillis Wheatley

Wheatley's only book is *Poems on Various Subjects, Religious and Moral* (1773); a good current edition is that edited by Julian D. Mason, 1966. Shirley Graham, *The Story of Phillis Wheatley*, 1969, and William G. Allen, *Wheatley, Banneher and Harton*, 1970, are two useful critical biographies. William Henry Robinson has three recent, important contributions: *Phillis Wheatley in the Black American Beginnings*, 1975; *Phillis Wheatley: A Bio-bibliography*, 1981; and *Critical Essays on Phillis Wheatley*, 1982.

Anna Wickham

Wickham's *Selected Poems*—which appeared in many volumes during her lifetime—were edited with an introduction by David Garnett, 1971. Little critical work has been done, but see Margaret Newlin, "Anna Wickham: 'The Sexless Part Which is My Mind,' " *Southern Review* 14 (1978), and Myra Stark, "Feminist Themes in Anna Wickham's 'The Contemplative Quarry' and 'The Man with a Hammer,' " *Four Decades of Poetry* 2 (1978).

Harriet E. Wilson

Recently discovered by Henry Louis Gates is Wilson's book *Our Nig* (1859), republished by Vintage Books in 1983, with a useful critical and biographical introduction by Gates.

Mary Wollstonecraft

There is still no complete edition of Mary Wollstonecraft's writings, though we now have the *Collected Letters*, ed. Ralph M. Wardle, 1979. Nevertheless, a number of individual works are available in modern reprints. Of these the most important are: *A Vindication of the Rights of Man* (1790), facsimile ed. by Eleanor Louise Nicholes, 1960; *A Vindication of the Rights of Woman* (1792), a Norton Critical Edition, ed. Carol H. Poston, 1975; and a reprint in a single volume (ed. Gary Kelly, 1976) of her two novels, *Mary, a Fiction* (1788), and *Maria; or, The Wrongs of Woman*, 1797, the second of which she left unfinished at her death.

Many biographers have drawn upon

William Godwin's *Memoirs of the Author of "A Vindication of the Rights of Woman,"* 1798. Modern critical biographies include Ralph Wardle, *Mary Wollstonecraft*, 1951; Eleanor Flexner, *Mary Wollstonecraft: A Biography*, 1972; Claire Tomlin, *The Life and Death of Mary Wollstonecraft*, 1975; and Janet M. Todd and Moira Ferguson, *Mary Wollstonecraft*, 1984. Interesting appreciative essays include Virginia Woolf, "Mary Wollstonecraft," in *The Second Common Reader*, 1932 (reprinted in Carol Poston's edition of *A Vindication of the Rights of Woman*), and Ruth Benedict, "Mary Wollstonecraft," in *An Anthropologist at Work*, ed. Margaret Mead, 1959. There is also considerable discussion of Wollstonecraft in Ellen Moers, *Literary Women*, 1976. In addition, Wollstonecraft is treated in an article by Miriam Brody in *Feminist Theorists*, 1984, ed. Dale Spender, and in Mary Poovey, *The Proper Lady and the Woman Writer*, 1984; and Janet M. Todd has compiled an annotated bibliography, *Mary Wollstonecraft*, 1976.

Virginia Woolf

Woolf's novels, which include *The Voyage Out* (1915), *Night and Day* (1919), *Jacob's Room* (1922), *Mrs. Dalloway* (1925), *To the Lighthouse* (1927), *Orlando* (1928), *The Waves* (1931), *The Years* (1937), and *Between the Acts* (1941)—have all been issued in paperback, as have her two major polemical volumes, *A Room of One's Own* (1929) and *Three Guineas* (1938). Her *Collected Essays*, 4 vols., 1966–1967, are supplemented by *Books and Portraits*, ed. Mary Lyon, 1977; by *Virginia Woolf on Women and Writing*, ed. Michèle Barrett, 1979; and by *Contemporary Writers* (with preface by Jean Guiget), 1966, a further collection of her book reviews. Woolf's *Moments of Being*, ed. Jeanne Schulkind, 1976, contains a group of memoirs, as well as a helpful introduction. *The Diary of Virginia Woolf*, ed. Anne Olivier Bell, began appearing in 1977, and *The Letters of Virginia Woolf*, ed. Nigel Nicholson and Joanne Trautmann, 1975–1980, are now available.

Biographies include Quentin Bell, *Virginia Woolf*, 2 vols., 1972; Phyllis Rose, *Woman of Letters: A Life of Virginia Woolf*, 1978; and Roger Poole, *The Unknown Virginia Woolf*, 1978. Among the most useful of the many full-length critical studies of Woolf's work are: Winifred Holtby, *Virginia Woolf*, 1935, rpt. 1978; David Daiches, *Virginia Woolf*, rev. 1963; Joan Bennett, *Virginia Woolf: Her Art as a Novelist*, 2nd ed. 1964; Jean Guiget, *Virginia Woolf and Her Works* (trans. Jean Stewart), 1965; Herbert Marder, *Feminism and Art: A Study of Virginia Woolf*, 1968; Harvena Richter, *Virginia Woolf: The Inward Voyage*, 1970; James Naremore, *The World without a Self*, 1973; Jean O. Love, *Virginia Woolf: Sources of Madness in Art*, 1977; Mark Spilka, *Virginia Woolf's Quarrel with Grieving*, 1980; Perry Meisel, *The Absent Father: Virginia Woolf and Walter Pater*, 1980; and Maria DiBattista, *Virginia Woolf's Major Novels: The Fables of Anon.*, 1980.

Essay collections include *Virginia Woolf: A Collection of Critical Essays*, ed. Thomas Lewis, 1975; *Virginia Woolf: Reevaluation and Continuity*, ed. Ralph Freedman, 1980; and *New Feminist Essays on Virginia Woolf*, 1981, as well as *Virginia Woolf: A Feminist Slant*, 1983, both ed. Jane Marcus. A feminist approach is also represented in a chapter of Carolyn Heilbrun, *Toward a Recognition of Androgyny*, 1973. For other books and articles, see Brownlee Jean Kirkpatrick, *A Bibliography of Virginia Woolf*, 1980.

Dorothy Wordsworth

Mary Moorman edited *Journals: The Alfoxden Journal, 1798*, and *The Grasmere Journals, 1800–1803*, with an introduction by Helen Darbishire, 1971; and Wordworth's letters are collected with those of her brother in *The Letters of William and Dorothy Wordsworth*, 6 vols., 1935–1939, revised C. L. Shaver *et al.*, 1967–1982. The standard biography is Ernest de Selincourt, *Dorothy Wordsworth*, 1933. More recent is Elizabeth Gunn, *A Passion for the Particular: Dorothy Wordsworth, a Portrait*, 1981. Also useful is Sean Manley, *Dorothy and William Wordsworth: The Heart of a Circle of Friends*, 1974, while a feminist approach to this writer's career is represented by a chapter in Margaret Homans, *Women Writers and Poetic Identity*, 1980.

Judith Wright

Wright's *Collected Poems* appeared in 1971. She has also edited *Australian Poetry* (1948) and *New Land, New Language: An Anthology of Australian Verse* (1957). Besides a number of books for children, Wright has written a critical biography, *Charles Harpur* (1963), as well as a critical volume, *Preoccupations in Australian Poetry* (1965). Recent articles on her work include Stephen Tatum, "Tradition of the Exile: Judith Wright's Australian 'West'" in *Women, Women Writers, and the West*, 1979; Leonie Kramer, "Judith Wright, Hope, McAuley," *The Literary Criterion* 15, 3–4 (1980); Anne Godschalk, "The Australianness of Judith Wright: Landscape, Metaphor, and Analogy," *Dutch Quarterly Review of Anglo-American Letters* 12, 4 (1982); Delip Kumar Sen, "The Poetry of Judith Wright: An Attempt at Interpretation," *Journal of the Department of English (Calcutta)* 18, 1 (1982–1983); Syed Anunuddan, "Judith Wright: A Major Australian Poet," *Creative Moment* 13/14; and David Dawling, "Judith Wright's Delicate Balance," *Australian Literary Studies* 9.

Elinor Wylie

Elinor Wylie's books—published in a brief, eight-year period—include four collections of verse: *Nets to Catch the Wind* (1921), *Black Armour* (1923), *Trivial Breath* (1928), and *Angels and Earthly Creatures* (1929). She also published four novels: *Jennifer Lorn* (1923), *The Venetian Glass Nephew* (1925), *The Orphan Angel* (1926), and *Mr. Hodge and Mr. Hazard* (1928). In 1912 her mother had privately printed in London *Incidental Numbers*, containing her youthful verse.

The Collected Poems of Elinor Wylie, ed. William Rose Benét, appeared in 1932, and her *Collected Prose* came out the following year. *Last Poems* (1943) brought together previously uncollected poetry as well as some juvenilia from *Incidental Numbers* and transcriptions from manuscripts, with an appreciation by the English novelist Edith Olivier.

Memoirs and appreciations include Elizabeth S. Sergeant, *Fire under the Andes: A Group of North American Portraits*, 1927; William Rose Benét, *The Prose and Poetry of Elinor Wylie*, 1934; Nancy Hoyt's portrait of her sister, *Elinor Wylie: Portrait of an Unknown Lady*, 1935; Carl Van Doren, *Three Worlds*, 1936; Mary Colum, *Life and the Dream*, 1947; and Edmund Wilson's essays in *Shores of Light*, 1952. A full-length biography is *Elinor Wylie: A Life Apart* by Stanley Olson, 1979. Recent critical studies are Thomas Gray, *Elinor Wylie*, 1969, and Judith Farr, *The Life and Art of Elinor Wylie*, 1983.

Anzia Yezierska

Alice Kessler-Harris edited and wrote an introduction for *The Open Cage: An Anzia Yezierska Collection*, 1979. She also edited and introduced the 1976 reprint of *Bread Givers* (1925). Other volumes by Yezierska include *Hungry Hearts* (1920, rpt. 1975), *Salome of the Tenements* (1922), *Children of Loneliness* (1923), *Arrogant Beggar* (1927), *All I Could Never Be* (1932), and *Red Ribbon on a White Horse* (1950). A good introduction to her life and work is *Anzia Yezierska* by Carol B. Shoen, 1982. Also helpful is Milton Hindus, "The Art of Anzia Yezierska," *Chicago Jewish Forum* (Winter 1966–1967).

Index